The

NORTON
ANTHOLOGY

of

SHORT

FICTION

EIGHTH EDITION

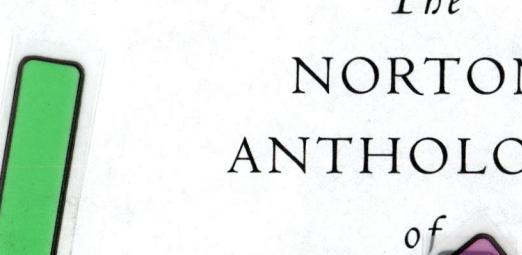

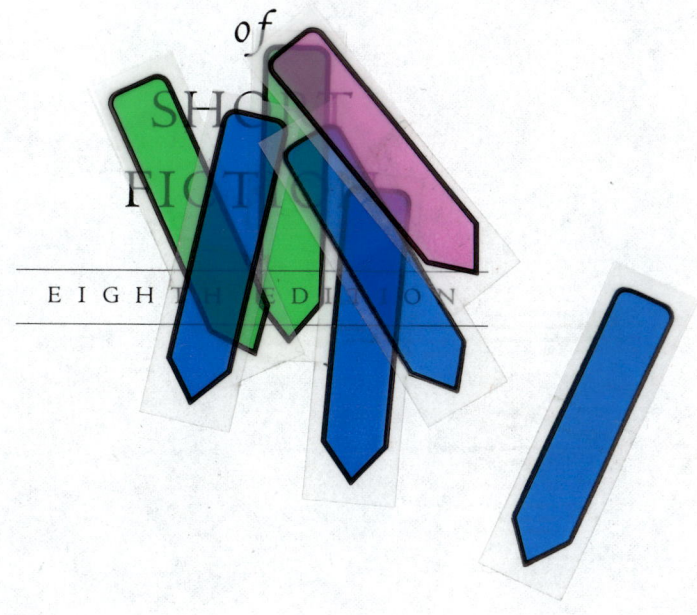

The
NORTON
ANTHOLOGY
of
SHORT
FICTION

EIGHTH EDITION

RICHARD BAUSCH
Chapman University

R. V. CASSILL
Late of Brown University

W. W. NORTON & COMPANY | NEW YORK | LONDON

W. W. Norton & Company has been independent since its founding in 1923, when William Warder Norton and Mary D. Herter Norton first published lectures delivered at the People's Institute, the adult education division of New York City's Cooper Union. The firm soon expanded its program beyond the Institute, publishing books by celebrated academics from America and abroad. By midcentury, the two major pillars of Norton's publishing program—trade books and college texts—were firmly established. In the 1950s, the Norton family transferred control of the company to its employees, and today—with a staff of four hundred and a comparable number of trade, college, and professional titles published each year—W. W. Norton & Company stands as the largest and oldest publishing house owned wholly by its employees.

Editor: Spencer Richardson-Jones
Project Editor: Linda Feldman
Editorial Assistant: Emily Stuart
Managing Editor, College: Marian Johnson
Managing Editor, College Digital Media: Kim Yi
Production Manager: Sean Mintus
Marketing Manager, Literature: Kimberly Bowers
Designer: Charlotte Straub
Photo Editor: Evan Luberger
Permissions Manager: Megan Jackson
Permissions Clearing: Margaret Gorenstein
Composition: Westchester Book Composition
Manufacturing: Courier Westford

Permission to use copyrighted material is included in the credits section of this book, which begins on page 1857.

Library of Congress Cataloging-in-Publication Data

The Norton anthology of short fiction / [compiled by] Richard Bausch, Chapman University; R . V. Cassill, Late of Brown University. —Eighth edition.
        pages cm
    Includes bibliographical references and index.
    ISBN 978-0-393-93775-6 (pbk.)
    1. Short stories. I. Bausch, Richard, date. II. Cassill, R. V. (Ronald Verlin), date.
PN6120.2.N59 2015
808.83′1—dc23

2014044145

W. W. Norton & Company, Inc., 500 Fifth Avenue, New York, NY 10110-0017
wwnorton.com

W. W. Norton & Company Ltd., Castle House, 75/76 Wells Street, London W1T 3QT

1 2 3 4 5 6 7 8 9 0

CONTENTS

Chronological Table of
  Contents xiii

Preface xvii

Writing about Fiction xxi

Stories

LEE K. ABBOTT
One of Star Wars, *One of* Doom 1

CONRAD AIKEN
Silent Snow, Secret Snow 17

DOROTHY ALLISON
Jason Who Will Be Famous 30

SHERWOOD ANDERSON
I Want to Know Why 37

MARGARET ATWOOD
3-1 *Death by Landscape* 44
    Related: Atwood, *Why Do You*
    Write? 1706

1-3 JAMES BALDWIN
Sonny's Blues 57

TONI CADE BAMBARA
Gorilla, My Love 80
    Related: Bambara, *What Is It I Think*
    I'm Doing Anyhow? 1706

ANDREA BARRETT
The Littoral Zone 85
    Related: Barrett on Willa Cather's
    Paul's Case 1755

DONALD BARTHELME
Me and Miss Mandible 93

RICHARD BAUSCH
Letter to the Lady of the House 102
    Related: Bausch, *Letter to a Young*
    Writer 1707

    Bausch on Anton Chekhov's
    Gusev 1793

CHARLES BAXTER
The Disappeared 109
    Related: Baxter on William
    Maxwell's *The Thistles in Sweden* 1756

ANN BEATTIE
Snow 127
    Related: Beattie on Peter Taylor's
    A Spinster's Tale 1756

MADISON SMARTT BELL
Witness 129

WENDELL BERRY
A Burden 141

AMBROSE BIERCE
An Occurrence at Owl Creek Bridge 149

JORGE LUIS BORGES
Pierre Menard, Author of the Quixote 156

RAY BRADBURY
The Veldt 164

FREDERICK BUSCH
Bread 175
    Related: Busch on Ernest
    Hemingway's *Hills Like White*
    Elephants 1757

TRUMAN CAPOTE
Miriam 188

RAYMOND CARVER
The Student's Wife 197
Cathedral 202

R. V. CASSILL
The Rationing of Love 213

WILLA CATHER
A Wagner Matinée 226
Paul's Case 231
    Related: Andrea Barrett on *Paul's*
    Case 1755

JOHN CHEEVER
The Enormous Radio 246
The Death of Justina 254

ANTON CHEKHOV
Gusev 262
Anna on the Neck 271
   Related: Author in Depth:
   Anton Chekhov 1787

KATE CHOPIN
The Story of an Hour 281

SAMUEL CLEMENS (MARK TWAIN)
*The Notorious Jumping Frog of Calaveras
  County* 284
The Invalid's Story 288

JOSEPH CONRAD
Heart of Darkness 294
   Related: Conrad, *Preface to* The
   Nigger of the "Narcissus"
   1711
   Conrad, *Letter to Barrett H.
   Clark* 1713
   Barry Hannah on *Heart of
   Darkness* 1763
   C. P. Sarvan, *Racism and the* Heart of
   Darkness 1774

JULIO CORTÁZAR
Letter to a Young Lady in Paris 355

STEPHEN CRANE
The Open Boat 362
The Blue Hotel 379
   Related: Crane, *Letter to John
   Northern Hilliard* 1714
   Allan Gurganus on *The Open
   Boat* 1761
   Charles C. Walcutt, *[Stephen Crane:
   Naturalist]* 1783

EDWIDGE DANTICAT
A Wall of Fire Rising 399

ANITA DESAI
Royalty 411

JAMES DICKEY
The Mill Wheel 424

ISAK DINESEN
Sorrow-Acre 426
   Related: Tobias Wolff on *Sorrow-
   Acre* 1786

ANDRE DUBUS
The Intruder 449

STUART DYBEK
We Didn't 458

RALPH ELLISON
King of the Bingo Game 467
   Related: Ellison, *An Interview* 1715

LOUISE ERDRICH
Matchimanito 475

PERCIVAL EVERETT
The Fix 488

WILLIAM FAULKNER
A Rose for Emily 500
Barn Burning 507
   Related: Author in Depth:
   William Faulkner 1800

F. SCOTT FITZGERALD
Babylon Revisited 520

RICHARD FORD
Great Falls 536
Privacy 547
   Related: Ford on Bharati Mukherjee's
   The Management of Grief 1761

MARY E. WILKINS FREEMAN
A New England Nun 550

MAVIS GALLANT
*The Ice Wagon Going Down the
  Street* 559

GEORGE GARRETT
Feeling Good, Feeling Fine 576

CHARLOTTE PERKINS GILMAN
The Yellow Wallpaper 580

NADINE GORDIMER
A Soldier's Embrace 592

ALLAN GURGANUS
Nativity, Caucasian 603
   Related: Gurganus on Stephen
   Crane's *The Open Boat* 1761

BARRY HANNAH
Sick Soldier at Your Door 610
   Related: Hannah on Joseph
   Conrad's *Heart of Darkness* 1763

NATHANIEL HAWTHORNE
Young Goodman Brown 620

The Birthmark 629
    Related: Edgar Allan Poe, *Review
    of Hawthorne's* Twice-Told
    Tales 1772

ERNEST HEMINGWAY
Hills Like White Elephants 642
    Related: Hemingway, *An Interview*
    1717
    Frederick Busch on *Hills Like White
    Elephants* 1757

AMY HEMPEL
*In the Cemetery Where Al Jolson Is
    Buried* 647

ALICE HOFFMAN
The Wedding of Snow and Ice 654

ZORA NEALE HURSTON
The Conscience of the Court 663

SHIRLEY JACKSON
The Lottery 673

HENRY JAMES
The Real Thing 680
    Related: James, *The Art of
    Fiction* 1719

RUTH PRAWER JHABVALA
Passion 698

CHARLES JOHNSON
Moving Pictures 711

EDWARD P. JONES
A New Man 716
    Related: Jones on Frank O'Connor's
    Guests of the Nation 1765

JAMES JOYCE
Araby 726
The Dead 730
    Related: C. C. Loomis Jr., *Structure
    and Sympathy in Joyce's "The
    Dead"* 1766

FRANZ KAFKA
The Metamorphosis 761
A Hunger Artist 795
    Related: Kafka, *Letter to Max Brod*
    1722
    Stanley Corngold, *Kafka's* The
    Metamorphosis: *Metamorphosis of the
    Metaphor* 1758

YASUNARI KAWABATA
The White Horse 802

A. L. KENNEDY
Not Anything to Do with Love 805

JAMAICA KINCAID
Girl 810

JHUMPA LAHIRI
Hell-Heaven 812

RING LARDNER
Ex Parte 826

D. H. LAWRENCE
The Horse Dealer's Daughter 834
The Rocking-Horse Winner 846

URSULA K. LE GUIN
The Ones Who Walk Away from Omelas 858

DORIS LESSING
To Room Nineteen 863
    Related: Lessing, *An Interview* 1723

JOHN L'HEUREUX
Brief Lives in California 887

SANDRA TSING LOH
My Father's Chinese Wives 896

BERNARD MALAMUD
Angel Levine 906

KATHERINE MANSFIELD
The Garden Party 914

BOBBIE ANN MASON
Shiloh 925

GUY DE MAUPASSANT
Boule de Suif 936
An Adventure in Paris 964
    Related: Maupassant, *The
    Novel* 1725

WILLIAM MAXWELL
The Thistles in Sweden 969
    Related: Charles Baxter on *The
    Thistles in Sweden* 1756
    John Updike, *Three* New Yorker
    Stalwarts [William Maxwell] 1778

JILL McCORKLE
Intervention 984

THOMAS McGUANE
Cowboy 996

T. M. McNALLY
Bastogne 1004

JAMES ALAN McPHERSON
Why I Like Country Music 1017

HERMAN MELVILLE
Bartleby, the Scrivener 1029
    Related: Leo Marx, *Melville's Parable
    of the Walls* 1769

BHARATI MUKHERJEE
The Management of Grief 1056
    Related: Mukherjee, *A Four-Hundred-
    Year-Old Woman* 1727
    Richard Ford on *The Management of
    Grief* 1761

ALICE MUNRO
Royal Beatings 1069
Miles City, Montana 1085
    Related: Author in Depth:
    Alice Munro 1812

SABINA MURRAY
Position 1099

VLADIMIR NABOKOV
Signs and Symbols 1108

JOYCE CAROL OATES
Convalescing 1113
*How I Contemplated the World from the
    Detroit House of Correction and Began
    My Life Over Again* 1126
    Related: Author in Depth: Joyce
    Carol Oates 1824

TIM O'BRIEN
The Things They Carried 1138
How to Tell a True War Story 1150

FLANNERY O'CONNOR
A Good Man Is Hard to Find 1160
Good Country People 1171
    Related: Author in Depth: Flannery
    O'Connor 1837

FRANK O'CONNOR
Guests of the Nation 1186
    Related: Edward P. Jones on *Guests of
    the Nation* 1765

TILLIE OLSEN
O Yes 1195

GRACE PALEY
The Used-Boy Raisers 1207

JAYNE ANNE PHILLIPS
El Paso 1212

LUIGI PIRANDELLO
War 1223

EDGAR ALLAN POE
The Fall of the House of Usher 1227
The Purloined Letter 1241
    Related: Poe, *The Philosophy of
    Composition* 1729
    Poe, *Review of Hawthorne's* Twice-Told
    Tales 1772
    Richard Wilbur, *The House of
    Poe* 1784

KATHERINE ANNE PORTER
The Jilting of Granny Weatherall 1254
Flowering Judas 1260
    Related: Porter, *An Interview* 1730

V. S. PRITCHETT
The Fall 1270

E. ANNIE PROULX
*What Kind of Furniture Would Jesus
    Pick?* 1279

RON RASH
Their Ancient, Glittering Eyes 1294

AGNES ROSSI
Morpheus 1305

PHILIP ROTH
The Conversion of the Jews 1310

GEORGE SAUNDERS
Victory Lap 1321

JAMES SALTER
Give 1333

DANZY SENNA
Admission 1339

IRWIN SHAW
The Girls in Their Summer Dresses 1355

JEAN SHEPHERD
Lost at C 1362

ISAAC BASHEVIS SINGER
Gimpel the Fool 1377

JANE SMILEY
The Life of the Body 1388

LEE SMITH
Intensive Care 1401

Related: Smith on Flannery
O'Connor's *A Good Man Is Hard to
Find*   1844

ELIZABETH SPENCER
Wisteria   1420

JEAN STAFFORD
In the Zoo   1424

JOHN STEINBECK
The Chrysanthemums   1439

ROBERT STONE
Under the Pitons   1447

ELIZABETH STROUT
Pharmacy   1467

LINDA SVENDSEN
Marine Life   1484

AMY TAN
Rules of the Game   1490

PETER TAYLOR
A Spinster's Tale   1498
Related: Ann Beattie on *A Spinster's
Tale*   1513

LEO TOLSTOY
The Death of Ivan Ilyich   1514
Related: Tolstoy, *What Is Art?*   1733
Gary Saul Morson, *The Reader as
Voyeur: Tolstoi and the Poetics of Didactic
Fiction*   1771

WILLIAM TREVOR
Events at Drimaghleen   1554

JOHN UPDIKE
A&P   1566
Brother Grasshopper   1571
Related: Updike, *Accepting the Howells
Medal*   1735
Updike, *Three New Yorker Stalwarts
[William Maxwell]*   1778

HELENA MARÍA VIRAMONTES
The Moths   1581

ALICE WALKER
Everyday Use   1586

ROBERT PENN WARREN
Blackberry Winter   1593

BRAD WATSON
Visitation   1609

STEPHANIE POWELL WATTS
Unassigned Territory   1621

EUDORA WELTY
Why I Live at the P.O.   1629
A Worn Path   1638
Related: Welty, *An Interview*   1736
Susan Dodd on *A Worn Path*   1760

EDITH WHARTON
Xingu   1645

THOMAS WILLIAMS
Goose Pond   1663

WILLIAM CARLOS WILLIAMS
The Use of Force   1673

TOBIAS WOLFF
*In the Garden of the North American
Martyrs*   1677
Bullet in the Brain   1685
Related: Wolff on Isak Dinesen's
Sorrow-Acre   1786

VIRGINIA WOOLF
Kew Gardens   1689

RICHARD WRIGHT
The Man Who Was Almost a Man   1695

Writers on Writing   1705

MARGARET ATWOOD
Why Do You Write?   1706

TONI CADE BAMBARA
*What Is It I Think I'm Doing
Anyhow?*   1706

RICHARD BAUSCH
Letter to a Young Writer   1707

JOSEPH CONRAD
Preface to The Nigger of the
"Narcissus"   1711
*Letter to Barrett H. Clark, May 4,
1918*   1713

STEPHEN CRANE
*Letter to John Northern Hilliard, February
1895[?]*   1714

RALPH ELLISON
An Interview   1715

ERNEST HEMINGWAY
An Interview 1717

HENRY JAMES
The Art of Fiction 1719

FRANZ KAFKA
Letter to Max Brod, July 5, 1922 1722

DORIS LESSING
An Interview 1723

GUY DE MAUPASSANT
The Novel 1725

BHARATI MUKHERJEE
A Four-Hundred-Year-Old Woman 1727

EDGAR ALLAN POE
The Philosophy of Composition 1729

KATHERINE ANNE PORTER
An Interview 1730

LEO TOLSTOY
What Is Art? 1733

JOHN UPDIKE
Accepting the Howells Medal 1735

EUDORA WELTY
An Interview 1736

Writing Fiction 1739

A Local Habitation and A Name: Meditations on Writing 1749

Reviews and Commentaries 1755

ANDREA BARRETT
Willa Cather's "Paul's Case" 1755

CHARLES BAXTER
William Maxwell's "The Thistles in Sweden" 1756

ANN BEATTIE
Peter Taylor's "A Spinster's Tale" 1756

FREDERICK BUSCH
Ernest Hemingway's "Hills Like White Elephants" 1757

STANLEY CORNGOLD
Kafka's The Metamorphosis: *Metamorphosis of the Metaphor* 1758

SUSAN DODD
Eudora Welty's "A Worn Path" 1760

RICHARD FORD
Bharati Mukherjee's "The Management of Grief" 1761

ALLAN GURGANUS
Stephen Crane's "The Open Boat" 1761

BARRY HANNAH
Joseph Conrad's Heart of Darkness 1763

EDWARD P. JONES
Frank O'Connor's "Guests of the Nation" 1765

C. C. LOOMIS JR.
Structure and Sympathy in Joyce's "The Dead" 1766

LEO MARX
Melville's Parable of the Walls 1769

GARY SAUL MORSON
The Reader as Voyeur: Tolstoi and the Poetics of Didactic Fiction 1771

EDGAR ALLAN POE
Review of Hawthorne's Twice-Told Tales 1772

C. P. SARVAN
Racism and the Heart of Darkness 1774

JOHN UPDIKE
from *Three* New Yorker *Stalwarts [William Maxwell]* 1778

CHARLES C. WALCUTT
[Stephen Crane: Naturalist] 1783

RICHARD WILBUR
The House of Poe 1784

TOBIAS WOLFF
Isak Dinesen's "Sorrow-Acre" 1786

Authors in Depth

Author in Depth: Anton Chekhov 1787

RICHARD FORD
from *Why We Like Chekhov* 1787

ANTON CHEKHOV
*Letter to Nikolai Chekhov, March,
    1886* 1789
*Letter to D. V. Grigorovich, March 28,
    1886* 1791
*Letter to A. S. Suvorin, October 27,
    1888* 1792

RICHARD BAUSCH
Anton Chekhov's "Gusev" 1793

DONALD RAYFIELD
from *Sakhalin: June—December 1890* 1794

STEPHEN L. BAEHR
from *The Locomotive and the Giant: Power
    in Chekhov's "Anna on the Neck"* 1796

VLADIMIR NABOKOV
from *Chekhov's Prose* 1798

**Author in Depth:
    William Faulkner** 1800
WILLIAM FAULKNER
An Interview 1800
Nobel Prize Address 1805

EDMOND L. VOLPE
A Rose for Emily 1806

SHERWOOD ANDERSON
The Book of the Grotesque 1808

JOEL WILLIAMSON
from *William Faulkner and Southern
    History* 1810

Author in Depth: Alice Munro 1812
ALICE MUNRO
What Is Real? 1812
from *Introduction to the Vintage Edition of
    Selected Stories* 1815

SHEILA MUNRO
from *Lives of Mothers & Daughters:
    Growing Up with Alice Munro* 1817

ROBERT THACKER
from *Alice Munro: Writing Her Lives* 1818

MARGARET ATWOOD
An Appreciation 1820

RUSSELL BANKS
An Appreciation 1821

BRAD HOOPER
An Appreciation 1822

**Author in Depth:
    Joyce Carol Oates** 1824
JOYCE CAROL OATES
The Art and Craft of Revision 1824
from *The Nature of Short Fiction; or, The
    Nature of My Short Fiction* 1825
from *Fiction, Dreams, Revelations* 1827
Why Is Your Writing So Violent? 1828
from *American Literary Culture: A
    Personal Perspective* 1830

SUE SIMPSON PARK
from *A Study in Counterpoint: Joyce Carol
    Oates's "How I Contemplated the World
    and Began My Life Over Again"* 1832

ALFRED KAZIN
*Two Cassandras: Joan Didion and Joyce
    Carol Oates* 1835

**Author in Depth:
    Flannery O'Connor** 1837
FLANNERY O'CONNOR
The Nature and Aim of Fiction 1837
The Grotesque in Southern Fiction 1838
from *Writing Short Stories* 1839

BRAD GOOCH
from *The Bible Salesman* 1841

TONY MAGISTRALE
from *"I'm Alien to a Great Deal":
    Flannery O'Connor and the Modernist
    Ethic* 1843

LEE SMITH
*Flannery O'Connor's "A Good Man Is Hard
    to Find"* 1844

ALICE WALKER
from *Beyond the Peacock: The Reconstruction
    of Flannery O'Connor* 1845

THOMAS MERTON
Flannery O'Connor: A Prose Elegy 1847

FLANNERY O'CONNOR
A Prayer Journal 1849

Glossary of Critical Terms 1851

Permissions
    Acknowledgments 1857

Index of Titles 1867

Chronological Table of Contents

The date given for each story is that of first book publication; if, however, the story was published earlier in a journal or magazine, the date of first periodical publication is given instead.

1835
Young Goodman Brown (Hawthorne) 620

1840
The Fall of the House of Usher (Poe) 1227

1845
The Purloined Letter (Poe) 1241

1846
The Birthmark (Hawthorne) 629

1853
Bartleby, the Scrivener (Melville) 1029

1867
The Notorious Jumping Frog of Calaveras County (Clemens) 284

1877
The Invalid's Story (Clemens) 288

1880
Boule de Suif (Maupassant) 936

1881
An Adventure in Paris (Maupassant) 964

1886
The Death of Ivan Ilyich (Tolstoy) 1514

1890
Gusev (Chekhov) 262

1891
An Occurrence at Owl Creek Bridge (Bierce) 149
The Story of an Hour (Chopin) 281
A New England Nun (Freeman) 550

1892
The Yellow Wallpaper (Gilman) 580
The Real Thing (James) 680

1895
Anna on the Neck (Chekhov) 271

1897
The Open Boat (Crane) 362

1898
The Blue Hotel (Crane) 379

1902
Heart of Darkness (Conrad) 294

1904
A Wagner Matinée (Cather) 226

1905
Paul's Case (Cather) 231

1911
Xingu (Wharton) 1645

1914
Araby (Joyce) 726
The Dead (Joyce) 730

1915
The Metamorphosis (Kafka) 761

1921
I Want to Know Why (Anderson) 37
The Garden Party (Mansfield) 914

1922
The Horse Dealer's Daughter (Lawrence) 834
War (Pirandello) 1223

1924
A Hunger Artist (Kafka) 795

1926
The Rocking-Horse Winner (Lawrence) 846

1927
Hills Like White Elephants
  (Hemingway) 642

1928
Ex Parte (Lardner)   826

1929
The Jilting of Granny Weatherall
  (Porter) 1254

1930
A Rose for Emily (Faulkner) 500
Flowering Judas (Porter) 1260

1931
Guests of the Nation (O'Connor) 1186

1934
Silent Snow, Secret Snow (Aiken) 17

1935
Babylon Revisited (Fitzgerald) 520

1938
The Chrysanthemums (Steinbeck) 1439

1939
Barn Burning (Faulkner) 507
The Girls in Their Summer Dresses
  (Shaw) 1355

1940
Sorrow-Acre (Dinesen) 426

1941
Why I Live at the P.O. (Welty) 1629
A Worn Path (Welty) 1638

1943
Kew Gardens (Woolf) 1689

1944
Pierre Menard, Author of the Quixote
  (Borges) 156
King of the Bingo Game (Ellison) 467

1945
Miriam (Capote) 188

1946
Blackberry Winter (Warren) 1593

1948
The Lottery (Jackson) 673

1950
The Conscience of the Court (Hurston) 663
Angel Levine (Malamud) 906
The Use of Force (Williams) 1673

1951
The Veldt (Bradbury) 164

1953
The Enormous Radio (Cheever) 246
A Good Man Is Hard to Find
  (O'Connor) 1160
Gimpel the Fool (Singer) 1377
In the Zoo (Stafford) 1424

1955
Good Country People (O'Connor) 1171

1956
O Yes (Olsen) 1195

1957
Sonny's Blues (Baldwin) 57

1958
Signs and Symbols (Nabokov) 1108

1959
The Used-Boy Raisers (Paley) 1207
The Fall (Pritchett) 1270
The Conversion of the Jews (Roth) 1310
Goose Pond (Williams) 1663

1960
The Death of Justina (Cheever) 254
Wisteria (Spencer) 1420

1961
The Man Who Was Almost a Man
  (Wright) 1695

1962
A&P (Updike) 1566

1963
The Ice Wagon Going Down the Street
  (Gallant) 559
The White Horse (Kawabata) 802
To Room Nineteen (Lessing) 863

1965
The Thistles in Sweden (Maxwell) 969

1967
Letter to a Young Lady in Paris
  (Cortázar) 355

1968
Passion (Jhabvala) 698

1969
Convalescing (Oates) 1113

1970
*How I Contemplated the World from
the Detroit House of Correction
and Began My Life Over Again*
(Oates) 1126

1971
A Spinster's Tale (Taylor) 1498

1972
Gorilla, My Love (Bambara) 80

1973
Lost at C (Shepherd) 1362
Everyday Use (Walker) 1586

1975
The Ones Who Walk Away from Omelas
(Le Guin) 858

1976
The Student's Wife (Carver) 197

1977
Why I Like Country Music
(McPherson) 1017
Royal Beatings (Munro) 1069

1978
Girl (Kincaid) 810

1979
El Paso (Phillips) 1212

1980
A Soldier's Embrace (Gordimer) 592

1981
Me and Miss Mandible (Barthelme) 93
Brief Lives in California (L'Heureux) 887
*In the Garden of the North American
Martyrs* (Wolff) 1677

1982
Shiloh (Mason) 925

1983
Snow (Beattie) 127
Cathedral (Carver) 202
Great Falls (Ford) 536

1985
In the Cemetery Where Al Jolson Is Buried
(Hempel) 647
Miles City, Montana (Munro) 1085

1986
Moving Pictures (Johnson) 711
The Things They Carried (O'Brien) 1138

1987
The Rationing of Love (Cassill) 213
How to Tell a True War Story
(O'Brien) 1150

1988
The Mill Wheel (Dickey) 424
Matchimanito (Erdrich) 475
The Management of Grief (Mukherjee) 1056

1989
Death by Landscape (Atwood) 44
Letter to the Lady of the House (Bausch) 102
Rules of the Game (Tan) 1490

1990
The Disappeared (Baxter) 109
Witness (Bell) 129
Nativity, Caucasian (Gurganus) 603
Intensive Care (Smith) 1401
Events at Drimaghleen (Trevor) 1554
Brother Grasshopper (Updike) 1571

1991
A Wall of Fire Rising (Danticat) 399

1992
Morpheus (Rossi) 1305
Marine Life (Svendsen) 1484

1993
A New Man (Jones) 716

1994
Bread (Busch) 175
We Didn't (Dybek) 458
The Life of the Body (Smiley) 1388

1995
My Father's Chinese Wives (Loh) 896
The Moths (Viramontes) 1581
Bullet in the Brain (Wolff) 1685

1996
The Littoral Zone (Barrett) 85

The Intruder (Dubus) 449
Privacy (Ford) 547
Under the Pitons (Stone) 1447

2000
Royalty (Desai) 411

2001
One of Star Wars, *One of* Doom (Abbott) 1

2002
Not Anything to Do with Love
   (Kennedy) 805
Position (Murray) 1099

2003
Intervention (McCorkle) 984
What Kind of Furniture Would Jesus Pick?
   (Proulx) 1279

2004
The Fix (Everett) 488
Hell-Heaven (Lahiri) 812

2005
The Wedding of Snow and Ice
   (Hoffman) 654

Cowboy (McGuane) 996
Give (Salter) 1333

2006
Feeling Good, Feeling Fine (Garrett) 576
Their Ancient, Glittering Eyes
   (Rash) 1294

2007
Bastogne (McNally) 1004
Unassigned Territory (Watts) 1621

2008
Pharmacy (Strout) 1467

2009
Jason Who Will Be Famous (Allison) 30
Victory Lap (Saunders) 1321
Visitation (Watson) 1609

2010
A Burden (Berry) 141
Sick Soldier at Your Door (Hannah) 610

2011
Admission (Senna) 1339

PREFACE

In the preface to the Seventh Edition of this ongoing enterprise, the teaching of what is one of the oldest and still most vibrant forms of human expression, I said that the work of *continuing* was what I had been about. We had lost R. V. Cassill, who built the anthology and maintained it through six editions, changing and expanding as he went along, always concerned with filling the book with stories that "discriminating readers liked most." Because as a reader I had a long history of reading the anthology (really from my first days of trying to be what Cassill was: a practicing writer of fiction, short or long) it seemed the wildest good fortune to wind up being the editor of the very volume I cut my literary teeth on in my twenties. The *Norton Anthology of Short Fiction* was what led me to the reading I have since done in the world's store of great stories, and that happy accident is really what all this work, this immense collaboration, is about: the leading of youthful readers and writers on the journey outward, to the treasures that are there. For of course the fact is that no one book can come near representing the whole of the form, or all of its greatest practitioners, yet it can indeed be a generous sampling of the abundance that exists.

The present volume, in that spirit, contains 152 stories, including 24 authors new to the gathering, and 33 new stories. There are several more authors with two or more stories included, since this gives students a sense of the range of expression, even in one career. Also, we have a new section concerned with creative writing and an expanded section of writers on writing.

As I said in the preface to the previous edition, the idea is to help college-level teaching of the short story and, by providing a wide selection of work, to help demonstrate the continuing vigor of the form itself. My whole writing life, people—some of them writers, too—have spoken glibly about the death of this superior form of entertainment. My answer has been that the short story as a form will be at all of their funerals. Indeed I'm convinced that there are more first-rate writers of stories at work now than there ever has been. A few years back, sitting in a car with Grace Paley, that old fighter, talking about stories and story writers, I had the realization that, at that very time, alive and still writing, we had Eudora Welty, William Maxwell, John Cheever, John Updike, George Garrett, Elizabeth Spencer, Saul Bellow, Bernard Malamud, Peter Taylor, Ruth Jhabvala, Joyce Carol Oates, Philip Roth, and Alice Munro, to name only a few. Well, they are all here, with many of the worthy others of their kind.

Riches. And Alice Munro just became the first writer of short stories to receive the Nobel Prize for Literature. So quite obviously the form is as fresh and alive and vibrant as it ever was, and of course the great old examples of it still stand, continuing to amaze and enrich our lives. Enrichment is indeed the word. And we want always as teachers to remember that one of the greatest gifts coming from good stories and good writing is pleasure.

Humbly, then, with a sense of gratitude and with the perdurable hope of every committed teacher, I offer this book of treasures, understanding that even in its hoped-for capaciousness, it is still only a small fraction of the continuing, vast expression John Updike called the "human news."

Features of the Eighth Edition

—The Eighth Edition now offers 152 stories by 130 authors. It is perhaps the most generous collection of short fiction available. Thirty-three of the stories are new to this edition, as are 24 of the authors.

—Because students benefit from exposure to more than one work by an author, the Eighth Edition also includes more authors represented by more than one story. Raymond Carver, John Cheever, Anton Chekhov, Samuel Clemens, Stephen Crane, William Faulkner, Richard Ford, Nathaniel Hawthorne, James Joyce, Franz Kafka, D. H. Lawrence, Guy de Maupassant, Alice Munro, Joyce Carol Oates, Tim O'Brien, Flannery O'Connor, Edgar Allan Poe, Katherine Anne Porter, John Updike, Eudora Welty, and Tobias Wolff are all represented by more than one work in this edition.

—A new "Authors in Depth" section brings together excerpts from essays, criticism, speeches, interviews, and more to offer students even more insight into the works and writing processes of five influential authors featured in the anthology: Anton Chekhov, William Faulkner, Alice Munro, Joyce Carol Oates, and Flannery O'Connor.

—A new section, "A Local Habitation and a Name: Meditations on Writing," draws upon advice, ideas, encouragements, and conversations had among the community of writers and readers found at Richard Bausch's Facebook page. You are invited to join the conversation at www.facebook.com/RichardBausch Writer.

Acknowledgments

Lisa Cupolo provided advice, love, patience, and also time and space; my editor, Spencer Richardson-Jones was simply amazing as colleague, adviser, and finally as friend; the book wouldn't exist without his continual and tireless effort to bring it about. And Peter Simon, senior editor at Norton, was, as old friends are, quietly and, with great humor and encouragement, instrumental. I send each of them a line from a lovely prayer by John Berryman: "Bless everyone in the world, especially some, thou knowest whom." Thanks also to Cynthia Shearer for all her wonderful work on the new "Authors in Depth" section and the Instructor's Manual for the Eighth Edition.

I would also like to thank the many teachers whose comments on the Seventh Edition have helped me plan the Eighth:

Jose Aparicio (University of South Florida), Mark Armstrong (Austin Community College), Martha Bayless (University of Oregon), Carl Bloom (Southeast Missouri State University), J. T. Bushnell (Oregon State University), Ben Cartwright (University of Kansas), Gabrielle Ceraldi (University of Western Ontario), Jean Lee Cole (Loyola University Maryland), Patrick Collins (Austin Community College), Bonnie Costello (Boston University), Lutgarda Cowan (Portland Community College), Tamas Dobozy (Wilfrid Laurier University), David H. Evans (Dalhousie University), Jonathan Foltz (Boston University), Dorritta

Fong (Douglas College), James Freeman (Bucks County Community College), Lawrence Garber (University of Western Ontario), Ibis Gomez-Vega (Northern Illinois University), Andrew E. J. Gutteridge (University of the Fraser Valley), Sarah Harwell (Syracuse University), Tim Houghton (Loyola University Maryland), Mark Jarman (University of New Brunswick), Debbie Killingsworth (Clark College), Ellen Lansky (Inver Hills Community College), Christine Lasek (University of South Florida), Jane Lim (University of North Carolina at Chapel Hill), Wendy Lym (Austin Community College), Tanis MacDonald (Wilfrid Laurier University), Nicholas Mainieri (Nicholls State University), Micheline Maylor (Mount Royal University), Gayla McGlamery (Loyola University Maryland), Jose-Luis Moctezuma (University of Chicago), Paul Moffett (Memorial University of Newfoundland), Lawrence Naumoff (University of North Carolina at Chapel Hill), Roger Ploude (University of New Brunswick), Anne Sandor (Orange County Community College), F. J. Schaack (Austin Community College), James Thompson (University of North Carolina at Chapel Hill), John Witte (University of Oregon), and Charles Wukasch (Austin Community College).

WRITING ABOUT FICTION

The American poet and translator John Ciardi used to be fond of telling a story about going around to schools and speaking to groups of students as part of a poets-in-the-schools program. The idea was and is a good one: to expose young people to writers, the actual practitioners of the craft or art. One morning, as Ciardi would tell it, he was scheduled to visit an elementary school, so he brought along a poem he had written for children called "The Stranger Inside the Pumpkin." The poem begins like this:

> The stranger inside the pumpkin said,
> "It's only dark inside your head."

After he had read the poem aloud to a crowded room of fifth graders, he asked, "Who's speaking in this poem?" Every hand in the room went up, and he chose a girl in front who, without the slightest hesitation, said, "Jack O'Lantern." Ciardi then asked, "What is Jack O'Lantern telling us?" Again, there was a clamor to get his attention, hands waving, little voices saying, "Me, me." Ciardi chose a boy this time. "Jack O'Lantern thinks we don't have any light inside us because there's no candle showing out our eyes," the boy said. And after this, the whole class began to talk about the truth, or lack of it, in that idea. There was even some talk about the quality of light, ordinary candlelight as opposed to the light of imagination.

At the end of the session, as Ciardi and his escort were leaving the school, the escort said, "There's a high school nearby, we have some extra time, would you mind visiting with a class there?"

Ciardi felt slightly ill-prepared, because all he had with him was this children's poem, "The Stranger Inside the Pumpkin." But he agreed to visit the high school, deciding that he would simply read the same poem, and talk about writing children's poems. To a large group of twelfth graders—young men and women, really—he read those same lines:

> The stranger inside the pumpkin said,
> "It's only dark inside your head."

When he finished reading, he asked the same question he had asked the fifth grade children. "Who's speaking in this poem?"

Silence.

He waited, intending—as he put it, telling the story—to keep waiting until the sun went down if it took that long, for someone, anyone, to gather the courage to speak. Finally one brave young man in the back of the room raised his hand. "Yes?" Ciardi said.

"Is that, symbolism?"

Ciardi would go on to say that it had taken a mere seven years of schooling to reduce this young reader to that level of stupidity about the written word.

Now, of course, this is a story, and John Ciardi used it with delight, and to great effect, as an illustration of how students learning to think critically about what they read often learn to look past the words of a piece of writing and, in so doing, miss what is obvious and quite simple. What follows here are a few general principles to help you in the task of writing papers about the fiction you'll be reading, to alleviate some of your anxiety about the undertaking, and to suggest some ways of approaching the problem of how to write a critical paper about fiction.

The matters discussed in this section are meant to suggest some ways to formulate a critical response and express it in a paper. These are not part of a list or catalog and cannot be set down like a set of commandments or rules, but they do apply to what most students face when the first paper comes due.

And perhaps the thing to be emphasized here is that how much and how well you are able to express yourself about the fiction you are studying depends to a large extent on your own attitude toward the task.

The first thing to remember when you begin to write a paper about fiction is that you must allow for what is direct and *literal* in the words on the page. A work of fiction, in spite of what you may already have internalized about it, is not a code, not something that needs deciphering, particularly, or translation into some other form of expression. One misleading question about fiction, and one of the easiest and, therefore, most often asked questions about it, is "What is the writer *trying* to say?" If the story is any good at all, the writer is in fact *saying* it, whatever it is, and the story itself makes up the terms of that saying. The writer of a good story is almost never trying to be obscure or even difficult; the experience the writer is exploring may be filled with difficulty and ambiguity, but the writer is always striving for *clarity,* trying to be *perfectly* clear.

Therefore, to read a story intelligently, you need bring only your own experience to it and strive to be *open* to what transpires literally on the page. The story will either interest you or it won't. If the story doesn't interest you, the fault may lie with you, in that you are not yet emotionally or intellectually ready for it; it is also possible that the particular story will *never* interest you, and that is one of the reasons why conversations and commentary and friendly arguments about fiction have been going on for as long as fiction has existed. But if the story does *not* interest you, if it does nothing to you, if you feel nothing reading it, I do not recommend that you choose it to write about. When you *do* find a story that interests you—and it is hard to imagine that in an anthology of this variety and size you would not find at least *one* that did so— your first order of business is to read it again. Read it several times, in fact, and you will find with each reading that you notice more about it, that its architecture becomes a bit more readily visible to you, its nature more clear.

But let me go back for a moment.

The difficulty for any new student of fiction is that while you are *reading* stories you are asked to *write* criticism. That is like entering a room full of strangers among whom an animated and widely various conversation has been going on for centuries and being asked to add something to the conversation. You read a story that you think you might be able to say something about; you even like the story. Yet even though you could sense it breaking down into its component parts as you were reading it and rereading it, when you actually come to thinking about it as a subject for a paper, your mind goes blank. There the story is, like a painting or a piece of sculpture. It is made out of words, but it is just as mute as a statue, just as much a silent, existing, created thing, insisting on its own wholeness, resisting all your efforts to take it apart.

You must understand that this is not an unusual feeling for *any* reader of a truly good story. You are not being confronted with some deficiency in your own ability to *understand* or *get* it; you are simply experiencing the territory, and if you allow yourself a little confusion and uncertainty, you might find that the exploration of the inner workings of the story is fun, that it enhances your enjoyment of it. And though we live in a highly politicized time, we must never lose sight of the fact that one of the most important functions of fictive art is *pleasure*. And so the first rule of thumb for anyone assigned to write a paper about fiction is to *find something that truly does engage you,* something about which you can express yourself in terms other than the artificial, forced, exhausting phrases of false interest—that awful feeling of trying to guess what you believe your professor wants to hear, of trying to say something as if you had the slightest interest in it, when in fact the whole enterprise seems only a little less painful than a dental procedure involving a drill.

Having found a story that does engage you—and by this I mean it has caused some reaction in you, even if that reaction is at first negative—and having read the story again and decided that you will write about it, the next order of business is to locate some aspect of it that especially interests you: its use of language, the presence in it—or lack of presence in it—of one facet or another, the nature of its characters, some element of conflict or treatment of theme, the way any of its internal aspects contrasts or compares to some other story or stories, or how it reflects the values of its time and place or may be applied to the values of our own time and place or even how it may seem *not* to reflect such values, distant or near. You may discover an element of the story that speaks to you on some deeper level about yourself, about something you are afraid of, or ache for, or love. Any element of a story is worth writing about if you have some stake in it, some actual connection to it. And writing about it is how you explore this connection.

It has been said that the best preparation for the reading of any story is to have read all other stories. That is to say that the more you read, the better able you are to respond. But even having read dozens of stories, you may feel at a loss when the time comes to write about one. So let us take the logic a step further and say that the best preparation for writing a piece of criticism is having read all other criticism.

Obviously, you can do no such thing in either case: no one *ever* gets to all there is that is worth reading and remembering. Geoffrey Chaucer was one of the most learned men of his time, and his library contained ninety books. I am a practicing writer of prose fiction, I read both for the love of it and as a profession, and my personal library—a modest one by modern standards—contains more than seventy-five hundred volumes. The remark about preparation is simply to suggest a truth, though; and writing your paper you will have to address the problem of what we can call "The Customs of Critical Speech."

How do you begin to express yourself in the language of criticism if you have not been reading criticism? If you have had no real taste of how it is done? It is no accident that people who write poetry *read* a great deal of poetry, that people who write fiction read thousands of stories and novels (poets also read novels, of course; and novelists, most of them anyway, also read poetry); but the fact is that one reads a great deal in the form in which one primarily works. That is how we all learn to write; indeed, it is usually the thing that *leads* us to writing. Yet new students of literature are regularly asked to write criticism without having ever really been exposed to any critical writing.

To extend the metaphor of the conversation, then: you have entered this room, people have been discussing a story. The simplest, first strategy, is to familiarize yourself as quickly as possible with the manner and nature of the conversation. You do this by listening in, as it were. By reading some criticism of stories, or of any work of literary art that you already know, have already read. When I teach sophomore literature, before I give any other assignments, I ask my students to do an annotated bibliography about *Hamlet*. They must find ten critical essays about the play, read them, and then summarize them for me, merely to show that they have indeed read the essays. This is less to teach them about *Hamlet* than to expose them to the ways and means of critical speech about that great play and, by extension, about any other work of literature.

What you will find, reading in criticism, is that the work being discussed is rarely considered in its entire form or shape; that the critical writer, in nearly every case, has chosen—or discovered—some vital or crucial but always quite specific aspect of the work and is concentrating on that, tracing its use and the ramifications of its use through the story (or its similarity or difference to some aspect of another story from the same writer, or a contemporary, or even someone far away in time or place). Notice, too, how the critical writer *uses the words of the story itself* to support what he has to say about it. The use of plot summary is always to underscore or illustrate the point, and quotations from the story follow from assertions about it as *demonstrations* of the truth of those assertions.

Too often, student papers about fiction end up merely summarizing the story's plot and recounting the names of its characters. For teachers of literature, there is nothing so dull as having to read twenty-seven versions of the same plot summary in a single afternoon. And falling into mere plot summary is the most common mistake students make when writing papers, mostly because they do not feel confident talking about the story in any other way, and they have seldom if ever experienced stories being talked about in any other way. (Much of this goes back, no doubt, to the old high school "book report," in which students are asked to recount book plots more or less as proof that they have done the assigned reading.)

Mere plot summary is likely to be a habit you will have to work to break. And one rather simple way to break it, though at first you may find it difficult to do, is to keep in mind the fact that the audience for your paper about a given story is made up of people who are *familiar* with it.

Here, for instance, is one facet of a story you probably already know; it is a play rather than a work of short fiction, but it will serve to illustrate my point. To audiences in ancient Greece who went to see Sophocles' great *Oedipus Rex,* the story of Oedipus was at least as familiar as the story of Christ is to us (there is a reference to the Oedipus story in Homer, who predates Sophocles by hundreds of years, and the tone of that reference is that it was an *old* story, even then); hence, one of the most interesting elements of that play is the irony in which it is soaked—this mystery story, in which the detective searching for a murderer finds that the murderer is himself, actually contained no mystery at all to the audiences of its time. Instead, there was the excruciating spectacle of Oedipus moving ever closer to the discovery of the truth that everyone in the theater already knew. To write a paper about this, you would use those lines Oedipus speaks that, given the nature of the audience's knowledge, contain the most irony. You might explore how that irony carries the play forward and informs the action; you might show how it extends to other characters in the play and how it shapes the emotions created by the spectacle of the tragedy.

The same approach works when you write criticism about fiction. Your audience is made up of participants in the appreciation of some *part* of a thing with which everyone is acquainted.

So, you choose something *inside* the story, some specific element of its workings that you have noticed, and you present that to your audience, all of whom know the plot of the story, and you move through your discussion of this thing you have noticed, following your assertions about it with proof out of the material of the story, using the words of the story itself to support what you say.

But suppose you cannot find anything in the story that seems worth writing about? Suppose that, even having found a story with which you feel a connection, you are still unable to settle on some specific element of it? On page xxvii you'll find a list of general questions including a wide range of approaches for exploring the details of any good story. You need only look over the list and then turn to your story and think through some of these questions in relation to the story. If that fails to spark something, try looking at what some of the contemporary writers in this book have had to say about stories by other writers, living and dead. You might even find one that you wish to add to, or take issue with. But as you read, see how often these contemporary writers *use the words of the stories themselves* to make their observations about those stories. Pay close attention to the ways in which they move from assertion to quotations, from the exploration of something *about* the story to the use of details *from* the story to support their claims.

To write a paper about a work of fiction is simply to take part in a civilized and polite conversation about it with others who have read the same story, to say something meaningful about a matter of importance to you. If the story has moved you in some way, then you will be saying something meaningful as it applies to your own life, your own experience, your own interests. And in the act of expressing this, of working through the story, you become a sharper reader, you develop a more sophisticated sense of language as it is used by artists, and you become less likely to be fooled by empty rhetoric and cant, by the flood of falsity and hype all around you, by the ways in which society names you and places you and makes assumptions about you and tries to control you—for whatever purpose, even if only to sell you something you don't need. By reading good short fiction, and thinking critically about it, you not only gain the deeper pleasures there are in the contemplation of this superior art form but become more free. No less than that.

Finally, remember that fiction is about *experience*, that its truths are not necessarily—they are not even very often—merely philosophical truths, but contain the truths of *felt life;* that good stories break down the barriers between peoples and times and cultures; that fiction speaks to us across boundaries as distant as the centuries and as unbridgeable as death itself. The editors of this anthology hope you will find something that engages you, something about which you can speak passionately, in terms of the pleasure that reading good stories provides. As fiction writers—as practicing short-story writers—we take issue with the idea that the study of literature is a science; literature is far too disruptive and unruly and filled with human contradiction to be any such thing, and writers have never been in the business of engineering better human beings. Thus we encourage you to think about the stories in this book as works of art that relate to life most consistently as an *enhancement* of being—and perhaps only a momentary one at that—and that they resemble more closely all the other good stories that you may happen to be reading, or have read, than they resemble the life we actually lead, even though, in that momentary shapeliness that always obtains when a story is told, they somehow make us feel life more vividly. We hope you will make *connections,* not theories or ideology. We hope you will consider the poetry you read and hear in these prose pieces as elements of the lovely songs that exist in them, concentrating on the art of the expression rather than what you may have already been taught to search out in terms of social constructs or political "stances."

Politics is politics, and everything else is everything else.

The study of fiction is mostly the study of everything else, and politics is no more nor less important to storytelling than botany or history or psychology or religion. Most good writers are steeped in all of these things and more, without being in thrall to any of them. And by the phrase *everything else,* we mean what it is like to be alive on the planet earth at widely various points in the human journey. What it feels like being new, being crowded or alone, being in love or out of it, worrying, trying, failing; succeeding, growing old, or wishing one were older; missing lost friends, lost loved ones, or being reunited with them; fearing for one's children; living with regret, with the hope of revenge, or with an obsession; being weak or timid or confused, or consumed with fury; hating something or dreading it; wanting something and not being able to have it; grieving or gathering strength; bearing the remorseless facts of existence with some kind of dignity and with some kind of grace; facing damnation or achieving redemption. Absurdity, foolishness. Folly and heroism. What it means to be alive, engaged in the struggle to be decent, and prosperous, too. In other words, the nature of the human family in all its complexity, its age-old refusal to conform to any reductive idea about itself.

General Questions

The following questions are designed to guide your approaches to your reading and to preparing papers or notes for classroom discussion. It is by no means necessary to prepare systematic answers for all or any of the stories. Obviously not all questions need to be answered in relation to any particular story.

EXPOSITION AND SETTING

1. How and when has the author introduced the main characters?
2. How much background information or history has the author provided for the main characters? At what point in the story, and by what means, is this background information brought in? What makes such background-ing necessary or (in cases in which it is scanty or lacking altogether) unnecessary? Are the characters made quickly comprehensible by representing them as familiar types?
3. To what extent is a prevailing and preexisting conflict used as a jumping-off place for the present action of the story? How has the author made us aware of this situation or conflict?
4. What is there of special interest or significance in the setting of the story? By what means are we informed about the details of the setting? At what point in the story? How is its relation to the significance of the action expressed?
5. Is the setting vividly represented or merely implied by the way in which events unfold? Has the author assumed that readers would be familiar with the significant qualities to be found in this setting?
6. How is the setting exploited to enhance or control the mood of the story? How does it help to bring out the feelings or emotions experienced by the characters?
7. In stories told in the first person, do we learn essential things about the narrator by the feelings or attention the narrator devotes to the setting?
8. Could the action take place meaningfully in another setting? That is—has the setting been chosen arbitrarily, for its own sake, or because it has an integral connection with the action?

PLOT

1. Do the meaning and emotional impact of this story heavily depend on the working out of the plot? Or is the plot—if it is noticeable at all—subordinate to the other elements?
2. To what extent does the action of the plot arise from the kinds of characters depicted in the story and their relation to each other?
3. Are there any major breaks or omissions in the chain of events or episodes of the plot? Is the outcome of the plot consistent with the actions that initiated it? If there is a surprise ending, does it emerge from some unforeseen but plausible change in direction of the plot line?
4. How is the plot related to the chronology of the story? That is, have some decisive actions, necessary to the plot, taken place before the narration begins? Is the narration halted with an implication that some event still to come will round out the plot?

5. Test the plot for meaning and credibility by imagining alternative events which, at any point, might have made for a different outcome.
6. What motivations in the characters are necessary to move the plot along?

CHARACTER AND CONFLICT

1. Who is the central character, or who are the central characters? What means has the author used to demonstrate their qualities? To what extent are the characters defined by contrast with minor characters?
2. Do we understand the characters as types or as individuals? By their actions? Their speech? Their thoughts? (It may be useful for you to pick a single instance of action, speech, or thought and ask in what ways it represents the character to whom it is attributed.)
3. Which characters are active and which passive within the pattern of the story?
4. Does the story show growth or change of character? How much of the story's meaning depends on such growth or change?
5. How much of the conflict in the story arises from an opposition between the central character and his or her environment?
6. Is the conflict inherent in the personality of the characters assembled by the author, or in the backgrounds they represent?
7. How has the author worked to involve the reader's sympathies for certain characters, and how does this contribute to the reader's assessment of the issues of the conflict?
8. How much are the characters (or their representation) conditioned by their time and place?

POINT OF VIEW AND PERSON OF NARRATION

1. Has the author confined the narration to a single point of view? Taking into account the nature of the material in the story, what apparent advantages lie in telling it from the point of view actually chosen?
2. What potentially interesting aspects of the subject matter have been subordinated or omitted by the choice of point of view?
3. In first-person narration, to what extent does the author appear to have identified himself with the narrator? What has the author gained by keeping a distinction between himself and the personality of the narrator?
4. What would be gained or lost by changing the narration from first to third person, or vice versa?
5. How is the point of view complemented by the style and diction? How do self-imposed limits of diction reinforce the emotional impact of a story or focus its meaning?
6. Is an illusion of reality enhanced by choice of point of view? A sense of immediacy?

THEME

1. Does the story make a general statement about life or experience? Can this be stated in the form of a maxim? Does the so-called maxim really provide a complete statement of the story?

2. Is the thematic statement accomplished chiefly by the outcome of the action? What qualifications and shadings are given to it by the characters' awareness of what has happened to them?
3. What values and ideas are reflected in the conflict from which the thematic statement comes?
4. Is the theme a traditional one? Has the story given a new twist to traditional wisdom? Where else—in literature, history, or religion—have you encountered a similar theme? Can you recall a poem or another story that makes a comparable thematic statement?

DESCRIPTION, REPRESENTATION, AND SYMBOL

1. Pick out some examples of language used by the author to stimulate and control the reader's visualization of the scene. Consider not only individual words and phrases but the accumulations and combinations of nouns, verbs, and their modifiers in paragraph structures.
2. How have the details chosen by the author given the essential appearance of characters or scene? Is the story fully presented to your senses? Comment on the adequacy of the description.
3. Has the author relied on your familiarity with certain scenes, characters, and situations to fill in what has been omitted from the actual text of the story?
4. How has the objectively rendered action of the story helped you to understand the thoughts, emotions, and motivations of the characters? Can you fill in the thought processes of those characters whose thoughts are not described?
5. What objects, acts, or situations have a symbolic meaning? Are the characters aware of these symbolic meanings? Has the author used symbols as a means of communicating to the reader some meanings not implicit in the action and not understood by any character in the story?

MODE (AS IT APPLIES)

1. What devices or instances has the author relied on to heighten the comic (or pathetic, tragic, satiric, elegiac) effect of the story?
2. What exaggerations or distortions of reality have been used to shape the material of the story to a particular purpose? Could the same material serve another purpose? (For example, in the case of comedy, could the material have been treated in a way that would produce a tragic effect?)
3. To what extent has the author manipulated the tone of the story to give a special flavor to the material?
4. With what views of life does this story fit best?
5. What satiric or ironic elements can you distinguish in the story? Do these dominate the whole story? Are they consistent with the overall quality of the story, or do they provide tension, variety, and suspense as you wait to learn what the author is really driving at?
6. Does the story appeal chiefly to a romantic or realistic sensibility? Does it tend to stir up pity, contempt, amusement, awe, dismay, admiration, or a desire that life should be different?

The

NORTON
ANTHOLOGY
of
SHORT
FICTION

EIGHTH EDITION

LEE K. ABBOTT
b. 1947

Abbott is the author of seven collections of short stories, most recently *All Things, All at Once* (2006). His fiction has appeared in numerous magazines and literary journals, including *Harper's*, *The Atlantic Monthly*, *The Georgia Review*, and *The Gettysburg Review*. His stories—exuberant, mordantly funny, and pulsating with the rhythms of contemporary life—have been reprinted in the Pushcart Prize volumes as well as in *The Best American Short Stories* and in *Prize Stories: The O. Henry Awards*. A two-time recipient of fellowships from the National Endowment for the Arts, Abbott taught writing at Ohio State University in Columbus until his retirement in 2011.

One of *Star Wars*, One of *Doom*

The slaughter hasn't started yet.

Tango and Whiskey, in fact, have just left bowling class at the Mimbres Valley Lanes off Iron Street. No one knows about the Intratec DC9 or the Savage sawed-off double-barreled 12-gauge. No one knows about Little Boy and FAT MAN,[1] the propane tank bombs set up with egg timers and gallon gasoline cans. Even Mr. DeWine, who's famous for believing he knows everything about anything any kid does, doesn't know that right now, nearly nine in the morning, Tango and Whiskey are parking their cars, a black VW Golf and a blue Camry, in their assigned places in the student lot across from the gym. Sadly, Mr. DeWine can't even guess that in several minutes—maybe ten—Tango, Marlboro in hand, will stop Mike Richardson outside the cafeteria.

"Richardson, I like you," he will say. "Now, get out of here. Go home."

No, Mr. DeWine knows only that it's too early for lunch and that he has a mountain of civics exams to grade before seventh period. His gut is churning—too much coffee too early, he guesses—and, come four-thirty this afternoon, he'll be in his Jockey shorts in a room at the Red Roof Inn off I-10, listening to Ms. Petty—Ms. Leanne Elizabeth P., late of Tularosa—crying in the bathroom. Before or after—hell, often both—she cries in the bathroom: no one is listening to her, she sobs, no one values her opinion, she's a fireplug for all anyone cares. Just a truck or a root or a box of rocks. She'll be wearing a garter belt and seamed hose, the fetish wear Mr. DeWine drools over, and she'll be sitting

---

1. The two atomic bombs used by the United States to end its war with Japan were nicknamed "Little Boy," which destroyed the city of Hiroshima on August 6, 1945, and "Fat Man," which destroyed Nagasaki on August 9, 1945.

on the closed toilet lid, sniffling and boohooing that even Mr. DeWine, the guy she's been screwing for the last ten months—Christ, probably the only heterosexual in this goddamn Land of Enchantment who can get from one to ten without using his goddamn fingers, a guy who regularly made her laugh right out loud—even he doesn't listen to her. No, that crumb just climbs on and hollers "Whoopee!"—not a "yes" or "no" or civilized phrase to go back and forth between them until, at 6:30, he says adios so he can hustle back before Sue Ellen, the wife, gets home from Pioneer Realty, Associates.

So there is Mr. DeWine—Frank to his pals, Francis to the Social Security Administration and the DMV, shitbird to the likes of Tango and Whiskey—in the hall, for eight minutes merely another cop-slash-cowboy obliged to herd Brianna (all forty of her) and Jason (the fifty or so he is) and Niki (the dozen she's turned out to be) into the right holding pens-slash-classrooms, to prevent them from stampeding over one another. He's got the "Declaration" to teach, for crying out loud. And attendance to take. A zillion announcements to make, plus homework to hand back—No, Tiffany, not on the curve—a whole briefcase of ideas he'd like to tell the world about if only the natives weren't so damn pimply and tall and loud, if only they didn't dress like lumberjacks and toddlers and thugs, if only they had more on their minds than Friday night and Duke Nukem and where to barf up that turkey sandwich.

The world? Fuck the world, he wants to say. Wants to stand in the center of the hall—right there, in fact, right where Colin is messing with Trisha who's messing with Erika who's messing with Misty who's probably wishing that Joshua were messing with her and not that skanky April May Lester—yeah, stand right there in between Mr. Geller (History II) at his door hither and Mrs. Fletcher (History I) at her door yon, and shout that it's the millennium, for God's sake, that there's got to be something else to do for forty-eight thousand two hundred and sixty-one dollars a year; that he was once young, too, a skinny Virgo with an acceptable jumper from the top of the key, and an expert way with power tools, in addition to a singing voice that didn't pain you too much to hear in St. Paul's version of youth choir. "Hey, look," he wants to holler, "Mr. Masters-degree-himself can burp the entire first verse of 'Silent Night'!" Yeah, Frank Round-Yon-Virgin DeWine, you moles. Frank you-just-would-not-get-it, don't-you-wish-you-did DeWine.

So, okay, it's crowded and noisy, the air thick and institutional, the air smelly and damp and bad for learning, rotten for anything except virulence and nightmares, and right now, while Rammstein and Nine-Inch Nails and Creed and Tupac and Little Fascist Panties and the Holy Modal Rounders are on that Walkman and that CD player and between those ears, and someone—Fishboy, maybe, he's the type, subtle as a circus clown—is bellowing "ho-ho-ho," and while all of the Mountain Time Zone is getting stupid and cranky and old, Whiskey and Tango are unloading their duffels.

Jesus Lord, they are in possession of some seriously impressive ordnance—hand grenades and pipe bombs, all homemade with glass and nails and jacks and BBs—and these guys, breathless and teary eyed, are practically punch-drunk with glee. The plan, amigo. Everything's proceeding according to plan, approximately a year in the making. Months and months downloading the data from the Net, the only other shit keeping you sane being Buckhorn specialty knives and natural selection and seeing white trash wreck their brand-new cars. Nearly a year, man, of putting up with jerks who mispronounce words, plus O. J. Simpson and weathermen and slow people in line in front of you and paying for car insurance. So it's now time for five—and five more, bro—and five on the dark side, too. The time, motherfuckers, is nigh. Oh, sweet Jesus, is it ever.

Which is ten on the dot, and the bell is ringing, the tardy bell, and the doors are closing—*boom, boom, boom* echoing in the hall—and soon Mr. DeWine, the image of Ms. Petty on all fours fixed like a photograph behind his eyes, takes roll. Surprisingly often of late, he's imagined the room with a Ms. Petty in each of the twenty-six seats. A Ms. Petty in a tiger print corset, growling. A Ms. Petty bound hand and foot, duct tape over the mouth, hands down the naughtiest wench in the area code. A Ms. Petty on her knees, tears dripping from her cheeks, her lower lip trembling, hers the grunts farm animals make. *Ugh. Baw. Eef.* A Ms. Petty laughing, then choking because, hell, if you didn't laugh, really bust a gut, you'd just end up banging your head against the nearest brick wall—the government, for starters, and the freeways, *Friends* and the hopeless porkers at the free weights in Gold's. Oh, man, a Ms. Petty in the back of the room, pulling down the map of the Gadsden Purchase,[2] her fanny shiny and smooth and broad, the ass of a former rodeo queen of Otero County now with unspeakable credit card debt.

But today, no. No frills to fondle. No silk or satin or whatever the dickens it is that brings his blood so quickly to boil and makes his thigh muscles twitch. Today, seat 6A, we find Amanda, too sparkly in the eye, busy as a hamster. And Chelsea, 4F, with earrings and bracelets in industrial quantities—probably couldn't get through an airport with all that hardware. And Todd, his best citizen, A's on everything, including his high-dollar hair. They're all here, it seems. Tarika? Yes, as usual, about as far from Mister Teacher as she can possibly be without leaving the room altogether. Tyson? A simple "here" would do, but, Christ on a crutch, this drama club president and his "present," a response that under his care and feeding seems to have eight—possibly ten—syllables. Bethany? Ah, practically under his feet again, eye shadow like poster paint, but a rack you wouldn't mind warming yourself against during the next ice age.

"Anybody know where Kathi is?" It's the *i* that kills him, hanging off the end like a tail, a smiley face above it on all her written work. A letter like a lollipop. "Kathi? Anybody?"

"I saw her in physics." It's Harrison, Todd's foot slave, a junior with the fertile imagination of a Dumpster. "That was second period."

"Thanks, Harrison," Mr. DeWine says. "Anybody else?"

They're studying the floor, every blessed one of them. Or the ceiling. Maybe that fascinating crack in the drywall. They don't look at you anymore, these kids. They mumble, they shrug, and they cough. Eye contact? A new social disease.

"She's on the Spirit Committee." That's Suzanne—not Suzy or Sue, if that's all right with you, Mr. DeWine—and she possesses a smile that all but blinds him: more teeth than Jaws, pearly as the path to Paradise itself.

---

2. A broad strip of land, purchased by the United States from Mexico in 1953, now forming parts of southern New Mexico and Arizona.

The committee, he mutters. A second later, shazzam, it hits him. It's Free Cookie Day. The cafeteria. All the chocolate chip and peanut butter and ginger snaps you can eat. Fight, Wildcats, Fight.

"All right, then," he says. "Turn to page 194."

And so that's the way it goes—"When in the course of human events"[3] blah-blah-blah—time a drip to torture yourself with, time the stick to poke into your eyes, time you wouldn't want to meet alone in an alley. Until it's time—no matter the ifs, ands, and buts—to serve up generous portions of Life, Liberty, and the pursuit of ever-loving Happiness, precisely as Master Tom described it. Time, in fact, to turn the page, please.

". . . Appealing to the Supreme Judge of the world for the rectitude of our intentions," Todd is saying—intoning is more the hell like it. Good Lord, the kid is a senator already. A justice of the Supreme Court. King Todd is straight out of the Charlton Heston edition of the Old Testament, the words raining down on Room 144B like murrain and flies and frogs, and, while Ben Franklin and John Hancock and the rest of the Colonies' ruling class are mutually pledging their lives and fortunes and sacred honor, Mr. Frank DeWine is doing his damndest to concentrate, to keep his eyes open, to hold himself upright and not, weakened by boredom and surprisingly epic fatigue, to lay his impossibly heavy head in Marcy Hightower's fetchingly ample lap.

"Mr. DeWine?"

Our hero finds himself looking straight at Harrison, eyeball to eyeball. The boy has spoken. He has brought Mr. Frank DeWine, our onetime recording secretary for Lambda Chi Alpha and full-time yellow dog Democrat, back to the here and now. Evidently—and this, DeWine thinks, is truly alarming—he was somewhere else, a there and a then well distant from the rhetoric of revolution, a place and time you most assuredly did not want to visit in the company of humanoids as aggressively disinterested as these.

"Page 208," he says. "Manners, Query XVIII—for man is an imitative animal."

They're good, these children. They appreciate knowing what to do next. They appreciate knowing what's to be done in, say, November—even in a November a decade from now. They're big fans of clean laundry and recreation rooms and pool parties. They like pizza and keggers and Old Navy. Oh, they get goofy over all the goodies FedEx can hand deliver to their doors. Not like Whiskey and Tango—code names, in case of capture behind enemy lines. Whiskey and Tango don't like people who bump into them, or country music or freedom of the press. Especially Whiskey, who wants to haul all those who are against the death penalty and who dig commercials and who cut in line and—well, he doesn't know exactly where he'd haul their sorry asses, except that it would be forever, the outer darkness and way beyond here, beyond even time and God and any idea that can't be made plain in four words.

It's the Luvox, Whiskey sometimes thinks. The shit gets in him deep, soaks his bones. It blasts him out there, really out there, where the stars creak and the slop drips off the sun and the angels dress like Baron Frank'N'Furter. But that's no reason, never has been. Instead, the reasons are Fishboy calling you "pussy" and "pansy" and Clinton—the fucking president—blowing his wad on

---

3. Opening words of the Declaration of Independence (1776).

that intern, that Monica. Yeah: Kellogg's and lard-butts and the crap they're spraying on your food. And against that, in opposition to all that stupefies and enrages and disappoints, stand himself—the Whiskey man—and his loyal sidekick, the Tangster. Hi-ho, Silver, you dipshits. Hi the hell ho.

Which is more or less what Mr. DeWine has come to think in the last ten minutes. He thinks to tell them he was in a rock band once, Dr. Filth and the Leather Cup—neat, huh? They specialized in Vanilla Fudge covers, Iron Butterfly. He played drums—the perididdle, the flam, the rim shot—no Ginger Baker, sure, but Ringo enough. Nineteen, freshman year at State, and he's on the stage at El Patio bar in Old Mesilla, pounding out the beat for "Hey, Joe," and urging the unwashed to shake their tail feathers, joints the size of cigars going back and forth, the singer—man, what was his name?—humping the air, humping the organ, humping the Peavey amp, humping the bass player one time. That's what he wants to say, here, out loud, from atop the desk, having dropped an atlas or two to focus everybody on the present. "Once upon a time," the speech would go, "in a world far, far away, Mr. DeWine, no kidding, had a topless ZTA from Roswell ride him pony-style while he, the selfsame son of a gun huffing and puffing before you, kicked over a cymbal and generally wreaked havoc on the stage décor." Here he would look around, taking stock, with that celebrated pregnant pause. "Ended up on the floor, ladies and germs, a pair of Bermuda shorts between the teeth."

But he won't. Can't. A line, you see, lies between them—a Maginot line,[4] practically. You are the teacher, the incarnation of decrepit, laughingly out of touch with cool, yours the clothes that even Larry, Curly, and Moe said "yuck" to. You all but wear your hair in a comb-over, you've gone spongy in the belly, and you gobble goddamn Lipitor and Prinivil because your body—some temple it is, Bunky—has turned on you in outright revolt. And they are the students, the rulers of the wasteland, the tribe yattering in Martian.

And then, thank God, the bell has rung and, only a moment short of a moment that doubtless would have shamed you eternally, you have not told them anything actionable, haven't told them anything at all except that they should know, with the same certainty they know their names, Jefferson's September 25, 1785 letter to Abigail Adams—yes, Tiffany, this will be on the test—and, instantaneously of a single mind, they rise, legs and arms everywhere, backpacks strapped on, their chatter a noise that becomes a roar, then insensible as static, then nothing for the next few minutes but elbows and ball caps and ponytails, nothing except time diving at you like a missile, you just something else goopy, slow, and warmblooded that can talk.

The carnage? Still an hour away.

Erika's in orchestra, third flute, trying to catch up, her foot having found a rhythm for some fa-la-la that, duh, there isn't ick to like. Misty's pretending she's not in English, at least not in any English that demands you read such brainless typing as *The Bluest Eye,*[5] not to mention all the footnotes and commas and infinitives they make you use. Todd? He's in the library—study hall—doing math homework and another scholarship essay. The Kiwanis, the

---

4. System of defensive fortifications along France's eastern frontier that failed to prevent the German invasion of 1940. **5.** First novel (1970) by American author Toni Morrison (b. 1931).

Optimists, the Lions—all the do-gooders. They're all looking for heartfelt words and a winning way of saying squat. Harrison, sitting across from Todd, seconds that opinion. Suzanne would as well, but right now she's trying to figure out why Mr. Hart, Latin (fourth period), hates her so much. After all, forty kinds of ablative, ninety noun cases, never mind Horace and Virgil and Cicero—who are these mushmouths anyway? *Mehercle, qui dies!*[6] Which senti-ment Alicia would understand were she present, but she's gone to the cafe-teria to help Kathi, who's managed to get rid of all the sprinkles and the butterscotch and who's made—sorry, Ally—a sizeable dent of her own in the gingerbread men. Which leaves April May Lester, who's not really a skank but just wants one of the cool kids—Bethany, for example, or that prep Tyson—to like her, to ask her a question she can say "sure" to.

So back we are to Mr. DeWine. "Francis Michael," his mother used to bark, a genuine drill sergeant. "Francis Michael, you have been a profound frustra-tion today." He can imagine her here, at attention beside his desk, a switch or a flyswatter in her hand. Her plastic hairbrush, more likely. "Francis Michael, I trust we'll have no more of such tomfoolery." Yes, ma'am, no more. No foolery of any kind, Mother. At which promise, she disappears, and Francis Michael finds himself with little to imagine but what, in the first place, his father, not a saint himself, ever saw in her—the former Mary Cobb, of Silver City. Her hair maybe? She had great hair, a thundercloud of it, hair to spare, all of it fine as cotton candy. Plus, she could take shorthand, did so right in front of the TV—one January the pages that were reportedly a faithful transcription of *Gunsmoke* piling up beside her armchair. *Bonanza,* too. She liked the rough-and-tumble, sodbusters blazing at each other with pistols, dust swirling, horses going to panic in the eyes. But other than that—the bang-bang and the frenzy, and, okay, modest expertise in the kitchen arts—what? Oddly, Mr. DeWine can't conjure her now, not a single feature. Just the hair, floating in midair, atop the head of a ghost maybe.

A vision which would scare him if, without warning, he hadn't been dis-tracted by whatever hard and sharp thing that's settled in him—a bone, he fears. Something small and heavy has tumbled to the flat bottom of him, the thunk like a bolt in a bucket, and right now, before Jason appears to discuss his overdue research paper, Mr. DeWine would like to smoke a cigarette, the first in, oh, ten years. A cigarette. Menthol. Nothing at this instant (and for the several to follow) strikes him as a finer idea. At the very least, business to occupy the hands. An activity to keep them from banging here and there on the desk before him. Another flaw in character, albeit tiny and common, to lie about. And, magically, just when Francis Michael needs him, there he stands, Jason, the most earnest Caucasian youngster since Johnny Appleseed.

"Come in, son," Mr. DeWine says, startled he sounds at all like himself, relieved as well that he speaks any language other than Urdu.

"Something wrong, sir?"

Mr. DeWine, most recently of planet Earth, sneaks a peek at his watch. Eleven on the nose. T minus Tuesday and counting.

"I'm fine, Jason. Why do you ask?"

---

6. Sheesh, what a day! (Latin).

The boy knows everything, Mr. DeWine has heard. The periodic table, the succession of England's kings and queens. Who kicked hindmost in the Tang Dynasty, how law is made in Kafiristan. So what now?

"It's your face, sir," Jason begins. "It was like you weren't here."

All right, Mr. Frank DeWine thinks. They know he hollers and the comely Ms. Petty from mathematics weeps, and that old Ben Franklin has helped himself to all the tarts in Paris. They gab among themselves, these creatures. They know his dog, the pound-bred Rex, and his weakness for bourbon. They know the sorry state of his socks, his wayward heart. They know the rusting piston in his chest, the sump above his shoulders. They have, indeed, found him out.

"Let's begin, shall we?" Mr. DeWine gestures to a chair and, a minute later, time with shape and density and hue, they have begun.

As have Tango and Whiskey. It's a pop quiz, right there on the hill overlooking the cafeteria. One Stevens pump-action, sawed-off shotgun? Check, Tangster. One Hi-Point 9-mm semiautomatic carbine with the 16-inch barrel? Double-check. One of this, one of that, one of everything they started whispering about the summer before. One childhood of *Star Wars,* one of *Doom.* They're wearing their outfits—the flannel shirt, the camo pants, the lace-up boots, the ghoulish smirk. They're about to engage hostile forces, the fitness fuckheads and those geezers who don't use their turn signals. Whiskey has done what he needed to do. He's washed his hands, he touched his ear six times when he got out of the car, prayed to the four corners, touched his other ear six times—the hocus-pocus you do on Tuesday so that on Wednesday you won't find yourself naked in your closet begging the pardon of an audience of Klingons and druids and the Four Horsemen of the Apocalypse.[7] In his room, he identified everything that began with the letter *c*—his carpet, his cat, his cap, his Cap'n Crunch, his cudgel.

And now, goddamn, there's more to inventory. The ammo, the Molotov cocktails in the Piggly Wiggly bag at your feet, the notes that tell the civilians you've morphed, you're about to jump through the only open seam in the universe to join the master race, and so here you are, Attila himself, a BFG 9000 in hand, decay dust in one pocket and in the other a potion from the Wicked Witch of the West, warp speed the means by which you hurtle from A to B, you and your buddy now Knights Jedi and Errant and Black, you and your buddy now the most special of special effects, founding members of the ninth circle, the inner sanctum, the grave, you and your buddy now specters brought into the full light of day by rage and by the heartening prospect of a prodigious volume of gore. Oh, Tango, it is April, the cruelest month. Oh, Tango, it is seventy fucking degrees. Oh, Tango, it is the end of the world as you know it and you feel fine.

"You ready?" Whiskey says. "I am go for liftoff."

To which, for the longest time—a century, it feels like—Tango says nothing, his mouth chewing crazily at the air. His eyes have become narrow and dark, his ski cap down over his ears like a bank robber. He could be thinking about heaven, about saints to goose step with, nectar to sip. He could be thinking

---

7. Four horsemen symbolizing pestilence, war, famine, and death in the Book of Revelation 6:2–6:8.

about crows that tap dance or storybook Apaches to send on the warpath or a feat impossible to do like carry the ocean across the desert in his hands.

"I'm scared," he says. "Really scared."

Yes, it's springtime, the bell about to ring, a few kids on the lawn, smoking, a few walking in from the lot. Schoolmates, they are called. Peers. Whiskey loves them. No kidding. He must take their lives because he loves them, which fact they will comprehend when he walks among them. This is his lesson. They have been shallow, these Wildcats. They have been arrogant. They have given offense. And now, lo and verily, he will smite them.

"Afterward," Whiskey says, "we'll get nachos."

Tango knows this is not true, can never be true. Afterward is not in the plan. The before has already ended and nothing will follow but smoke and blood and debris and dreams never to wake from.

"Tango," Whiskey says, a question.

Foot. It is the only word Tango can utter, the only word he remembers from a lifetime of words. Wait, there's another. *Tree.* Which he says and says again until enough minutes have passed for him to say, with nearly incredible relief, *insect.* Then: *wolf.* Then: *night.* Whereupon Whiskey touches his shoulder, and, miraculously, Tango has other words to say, all of them big and new and remarkable as the day itself.

"Pizza, too," he says. "Pepperoni."

The world has already turned red and swirly at the edges, an arctic cold settling at their feet. The world is about to tilt, to wobble out of its groove, about to shrink. The world is cracking, a splintering you can hear in heaven.

"Ready?" Whiskey asks.

This time Tango can answer. His shit is squared away. The epic wind has left his mind. He's copacetic. He salutes, stiff-armed and urgent.

"Heil Hitler," he says.

And now the doors are near, a handle for each to grasp. They have only to pull, which they have done, and they have only to march past several classrooms, Ms. Petty's among them, and toward the library like soldiers, which they are doing, and they have only to arrive at the circulation desk, which they have, and they have only to squeeze off a round, which each does into the ceiling tiles, and at last, the clock ticking toward 11:45, to the dozens of now thoroughly why-faced Wildcats in front of them, those trembling like Todd and those not, those like Harrison wide-eyed with awe and those thinking they ought to be able to claw through their notes for the answer to this unreasonably complicated question, the warriors Tango and Whiskey have only to speak.

"Here we are now," they say. "Entertain us."

He's got a half-hour, Mr. DeWine does.

He could eat. Mystery meat in the cafeteria or the tuna sandwich in the refrigerator in the teachers' lounge. He could pay a bill or two, maybe. He's got his checkbook, a week's worth to pay up in his briefcase. Instead, he puts his feet on his desk, rocks back in his chair. Why not visit Leanne, a surprise? She's got this period free, too. He could sneak up behind her, grab her at the waist. He's done it before, though only once. The whole time, not more than five minutes, he was overwhelmed by the fear that somebody—a student having forgotten a book, or a teacher searching for the new calculators—would walk in on them. His skin had felt too small, his head too big. He thought he might fall over, his heart like a squirrel in his chest, all claws and climbing. Besides, she was herself spooked, slapping at his head like a spaz, hissing—Honest Injun—hissing like a goose or some such. Fucking fowl, for Pete's sake. No, he'll stay put. He takes his deepest breath of the day. He'll do a push-up or two. Work on that spare tire. Tend to the mind and body both, he thinks. Your familiar heart-and-head imbalance. Man, is it quiet. Eerily quiet, only the AC cycling and the clock and the creak of a middle-aged middleweight hauling himself to his feet. It's the quiet from the moon, the quiet where time ends.

Outside, there's nothing, just the school flag, all that Disney-worthy blue. He walks among the desks. "Abandon all hope,"[8] someone has scribbled. Dante—what a bozo. Blame the whole fiasco on Beatrice. At another desk—here is where the lovely Sherry parks her lovely butt—he finds a hair. Blond. Not Sherry's, though. No, this is the blond of a practicing Protestant. This blond drives an Explorer. Doubtless, this blond aced the ACT. Red would be something else, he guesses. Honest work to be done on a ranch. A career on the stage. He turns on his heel, Mr. DeWine does. And brown, Sue Ellen's color? He doesn't want to think. That's a smart mouth, a wiseacre. Brown's a story with an unhappy ending. Brown is boredom. Brown is a mannequin that drinks vodka gimlets.

Now he's really curious. What have they left behind, these kids? Last fall, he found a spiral notebook with writing in it so peculiar, so detailed and figurative, it could have only come from the hand of an egghead's egghead. Squiggles gave way to squares and those to bouquets of dashes and those to a series of capital *L*'s, the whole of it bizarrely architectural—the castle of a dark-minded wizard, he thought, or a Byzantine metropolis of gnomes and haunts, or a low country in ruin. Yeah, it was a civilization to dig up, you and ten thousand other zombies looking for the reason you can't sleep. He wonders now what happened to the notebook. It might have led to treasure. Jesus H., if only you were fluent in runes and glyphs and smudges and symbols, it might have led you out of Deming, New Mexico, and right to the golden threshold of Shangri-La itself.

Gracious, there's so much to know about Mr. DeWine, especially now that elsewhere the shooting has started. That topless Zeta Tau Alpha, for example, at El Patio those many years ago? That was Sue Ellen, his wife. Sue Ellen Bates then. Older by a year. A sophomore business major. But she wasn't really topless. She wore a Moby Grape T-shirt. He likes to embellish—makes the real realer, he thinks. The Bermuda shorts? Those he didn't invent. He didn't invent Roswell either, or the cymbal, or the wreckage in his wake. Nor, later that night, at his apartment off Solano Street, did he invent the clumsy sex he and Sue Ellen had, or that hour, toward dawn, when he felt that he'd been dropped on the planet for all the wrong reasons. He didn't invent Catherine either, the baby who died six years later. A miscarriage, actually, the first of two. Eons ago, it feels like, when beasts ruled and we were but fish or flesh that crawled.

---

8. In *The Inferno,* the first book of the epic trilogy *The Divine Comedy* by Italian poet Dante Alighieri (1265–1321), the words "Abandon all hope, ye who enter here" are written on the gates of Hell. Dante wrote the epic as a memorial to the woman he loved, Beatrice Portinari, who is depicted as a source of spiritual inspiration.

What else should we consider before he makes up his mind to drop in on Ms. Petty? He was runner-up in the fourth grade spelling bee, *terpsichorean* the word that got between him and the silver trophy Kay Stevenson bragged about. His first girlfriend? Michelle "Mickey" Barker. Went steady the whole summer the Beatles came to America. Behind Timmy Bullard's house, in the onion field, she let him touch her breasts—"For a count of five, Frankie, no more"—the surprising weight of them something he swears he can still feel. Oh, this as well: He wrote a whole book in high school, in Las Cruces. Well, eighty-some pages. But hand-illustrated, lots of forest scenes and a mountain range that looked like eye teeth. His version of Sir Gawain[9] and the Green Knight. Lots of derring-do in that. Nick-of-time stuff, too. An alluring maiden in distress, of course. He was the Sir, naturally. *Vanquished*—man, he loved that word, that and *dispatched* and *woe betide he who,* all the fancy talk you nowadays don't hear much at Del Cruz's Triangle Drive-In—yes, he vanquished a dragon. Slew the sucker silly. Afterward the Sir found himself bedecked—right, another word stuck-up Kay Stevenson wouldn't know the up from down of—with a sash and more medals than Bayer has aspirin, the king (the maiden's father) the most grateful potentate in all of Pip-pip, Cheerio, and vicinity. Got some serfs out of the deal as well. Mrs. Chew let him read a chapter to his English class, Mickey Parker right under his nose. Made it all the way to the part where Sir Gawain and his friends—the vaunted Sir Fitzroy and the steadfast Sir Palmetto, mainly—lay siege to the manor house of the dastardly Archduke Fussface, before the bell rang. Yeah, dastardly. "I think," Mrs. Chew said to everybody, "there's a lesson in this for all of us." It was this event, he still thinks, that made him want to become a teacher—to find lessons everywhere, even in his own needy heart.

Not terrible lessons, though, like those being delivered right now a hundred yards away in the library, where Whiskey, clomping through a tangle of overturned chairs and scattered papers, has announced that he is the Lord Humongous, the Ayatollah of Rock'n'rolla, and Tango has discovered underneath a reading table a girl, Tiffany, to play peek-a-boo with.

"You like me, don't you?" he says, his the rictus grin you carve on a pumpkin.

What a silly question. Of course she likes him. He has the gun. Dark and greasy-looking with May Day streamers hanging from it and maybe actual human ribs, gobbledygook like Arabic or graffiti scribbled with Marks-a-Lot on the stock, the gun is pointed at her.

"So," Tango begins, "if I asked you for a kiss, you'd give it to me, right?"

Another asinine question. He can have her purse, her hair, her hands.

But now it appears that all he wants is for that noise—an animal howling in pain, Tiffany thinks—to stop.

"It's a cat," she says, trying to help.

The gun goes off again, another boom wrong for books and study hall and Free Cookie Day, and Tiffany understands that it is she, the only daughter from the house of Hudspeth, who is crying. She is the cat, howling.

"Do her," Whiskey is shouting. "Do the bitch."

---

9. Legendary member of King Arthur's Knights of the Round Table, and hero of the 14th-century poem *Sir Gawain and the Green Knight.*

But she can't be done, she thinks. After all, she is home, under the covers. She has her pj's on, in her headphones Jack Diesel's greatest hits. A novel lies in her lap, a tearjerker Oprah wanted her to read. She can't be done. No, she certainly can't.

And, mysteriously, she isn't. Instead, the boy—she's seen him before, James or something, from the soccer team—crouching behind a desk chair is done. He has a cute haircut, close at the sides, then he doesn't. Unmoving only a moment before, he is flying—snatched by the collar, it seems, and hurled against a bookshelf, the reference section crashing down to bury him.

"Targets of opportunity," Whiskey is calling them.

He's firing into the floor—*pow, pow, pow*—his shotgun like a pogo stick bouncing him through the room, real astonishment in his eyes. The firepower. The fucking firepower. He's hanging on to the smart end of a contraption that spews out blood and justice, cordite and delicious disorder.

"Dance, tenderfoot," he orders, now Billy the fucking Kid and Triple H and Prince Jericho and Mr. Blue, and immediately one unlucky gomez—gee, Harrison, fancy meeting you here—is dancing, snot smeared across his lips, clearly the loneliest fellow in the hemisphere.

"It's the hucklebuck," Tango says, delighted to be the new host of *MTV World*. "Shake a leg, dude. Trip the light fantastic."

Arms spread as if in ecstasy, Harrison dances, knees higher than a desk, nothing beneath him now that the floor has disappeared, now that Whiskey, giggling, is keeping promises. Now that the present, simple as Simon, is giving way so easily to the even simpler past.

"The hokeypokey," Tango has said. "Turn yourself about."

Events are moving swiftly, many at the same instant. Todd intends to rise, to dash for the door. He's thinking it, yes, but a moment later he's not thinking anything at all, the organ to think with having unexpectedly gone mealy and cold. The world smells sour and sulphuric. A blizzard has roared through here, dust roiling, shreds of paper falling like snowflakes. The floor is pocked and pitted, as if gouged by jackhammers and the picks of giants. Shattered glass lies everywhere—in your hair, down your shirt, in your Nikes. Wood splinters have stabbed you in the arm, the neck, the backs of your thighs. Remarkably, you've heard not a single sound. The muzzle flashes are unmistakable, a spray of wadding and sparks, a window pouring over a desk like a shimmering waterfall, but, huddled behind the body of a girl whose misfortune—thank you, Mr. Hart—was to need the Latin for *Never cut class again, Miss Suzanne Winters,* you can't hear anything. Except your own heart, its fitful thud-thud the rhythm vampires are aroused by. Yes, Tango is speaking—his mouth is working, his awful tongue—but the audio is on MUTE. You want the remote control. But the instant the sound thunders over you like a tidal wave and you have glimpsed Miss Petty at the door, you don't want anything except for time to snap backward so that you'd have a century to warn her, nasty old DeWine's girlfriend, not to come in here, that she can read this week's edition of *Time* tomorrow or the next day. Please, Miss Petty, don't come in here for anything.

But she has. And Tango—his shirt off, his birdlike chest glistening with a war paint of blood and paste and ink—has already, with the formal bow of a Beau Brummell, welcomed her to his intimate get-together.

"You're just in time," he says.

For Whiskey, there's too much to account for. The wall, the floor, the wall again. At this point, he had hoped to be well into Beta phase. The main event. Little Boy and FAT MAN themselves. But his ear has to be checked, and his wrist, followed by his boot and his ankle, before he can move on to his knee and his eye socket. "Say the words," he tells himself. And, soon enough, from his prepared list, he does: "Reason, virtue, plenitude." He glances around. Evidently, he has been shouting. "Being," he hollers, "is not different from nothingness."[1]

"Put that down, James Crawford." Ms. Petty is addressing Tango, stern as a movie actress. "What do you think you're doing?"

What lunacy. Which can't be helped, unfortunately. Ms. Petty is, figuratively speaking, beside herself. She's watching herself stamp her foot—yes, actually stamp her right foot—and put her hands on her hips, a school marm from ancient America. She should shake herself, slap some sense into her pretty head, but she can't because Leanne Petty is not really there. Instead, dumb and foolish and proud, standing not a giant step from the barbarian with the rifle, is a lunatic female using her name and wearing her clothes and saying what would be said if the universe had not so completely melted.

"I said to put that down, Mister Crawford."

He can't, he says. He's committed. Totally.

Committed. It's an expression she's heard before, that fussbudget with the wagging finger and the profound respect for propriety.

"I mean," Tango is saying, "fifteen minutes ago, maybe. But, now? Jesus God, Miss Petty, we're, like, in the second act here."

Against the far wall, still wringing his hands as if scrubbing them in air, Whiskey has almost reached the end of his speech. "Give us this day our daily bread," he is reciting. "The horror, the horror.[2] One if by land, two if by sea. Merry Christmas to all, and to all a good night."

Ms. Petty slowly surveys the room. If only Frank could see this. These kids worship new gods now. They speak a new tongue. They will eat a new food in a new world and grow old in the new way.

"Miss Petty?" It's Tango, his the shrug of youthful impatience. He has work to do now, okay? And little time to do it in.

"What's that on your forehead?"

It's sandpaper, he says. To strike matches on. For the fuses, you know?

"James, you were such a nice boy. I can't believe this."

Another shrug, this one of eighteen-karat sadness. "I still am nice, Miss Petty. You just don't know me, is all."

She's desperate to return to herself, to step into the person still staring at James Crawford, nice boy. The situation demands organization. She should be telling that girl—Misty or Jewel, something perky anyway—that she can leave now, poor thing. She should be calling the authorities, the principal at the very least. A thousand tasks need attention, if she could only climb back into her own skin. But she can't. Never will. For James Crawford has finished his work, Whiskey having hustled over to observe, and the old self of

---

1. Allusion to *Being and Nothingness,* 1943 work by French existentialist philosopher Jean-Paul Sartre (1905–1980). **2.** See Joseph Conrad's *Heart of Darkness* in this volume.

Ms. Leanne Petty is collapsed on the floor, one leg twisted under her hips, the last of her dribbling out of the shockingly ragged hole in her head.

Whiskey squats down, lifts her limp hand. "Goodnight, air."

The plan. It's Tango's turn to talk. "Goodnight, noises everywhere."[3]

For weeks and weeks afterward, Sue Ellen DeWine will wonder what Frank was doing near the library. She's visited his classroom and it's—what?—a good hundred yards, could be more, from where the murders happened. The papers—*The Headlight,* even *The Journal* from Albuquerque; TV, too, Channel 4 from El Paso, and CBS—have called him a hero, running in to rescue those students that way, but all Sue Ellen will puzzle about, when she goes back to work a week after the funeral, is what Frank was doing there. He should have been on lunch break, the other direction exactly, but he was headed toward the library. In June, admittedly embarrassed to be obsessed with such an inconsequential detail, she will nonetheless phone Dick Spivey, the assistant principal, to ask him, but all he will be able to tell her is that he hasn't the slightest idea. "Maybe he had to return a book," he'll tell her, and, okay, that will be her answer—a book to return, another mystery solved—until the following August when, steering her Camry into the lot of Zia Title for a closing, a merciless logic of curiosity and intuition and suspicion still hard at work in her, she will say "Leanne Petty" aloud, and Sue Ellen DeWine, the widow of a hero, will know. Francis DeWine, the son of a bitch, was on his way to see Leanne Petty.

Which is no more than Frank himself knows as he yanks open the door to the math wing. He's got his tie loose now and he's making good time, bum knee and all, more or less skipping, in his mind a dumber-than-dumb image of gimpy Chester shouting "Mr. Dillon! Mr. Dillon!" in the middle of a Dodge City street. Sir Francis has a personal matter to attend to, a furtive and private concern, so more than several seconds pass before he notices that he's the only person heading toward the weird banging noises. Everybody else, students and grownups alike, is scrambling to get by him. It's an honest-to-goodness fire this time, he thinks. It's not a drill, not a bomb scare like last Halloween. Adjacent to the men's toilet, he spots a kid he recognizes, one of the Goliaths from the lacrosse team, April Lester tugging on his arm.

"What's wrong?" he asks. "Richardson, what's going on?"

The kid's head goes back and forth. It seems to be the only part of him that works. The rest of him is frozen, seized.

"Well?"

Richardson needs a second, clearly. He has the expression of a land-lubber crawling out of shark-infested waters.

(A moment will arrive, soon, when Mr. DeWine will remember this Q and A with greatest sorrow. How boneheaded he has been, he will scold himself. What a stone. How could he not have known?)

"April?"

Mr. DeWine grabs her arm, gets her attention. Good Lord, she's thin, like a ballerina. What, he wonders, is she doing with a behemoth like Richardson. It's like finding Tinkerbell keeping company with The Incredible Hulk.

---

3. Like "Goodnight, air," a line from Margaret Wise Brown's classic children's book, *Goodnight Moon* (1947).

"The library." She's whispering, as if she has to tell the whole school the dirty word some creep in homeroom yelled at her. "They're in the library."

Somebody is smacking a wall somewhere, Frank thinks. With a bat, sounds like. Really giving it the business.

"Who's in the library?"

She shakes her head, her tiny head. She doesn't know. All she can do is point, another of the species with seemingly only two or three moving parts.

(And this, too, is another instant he will regret when his moment comes.)

"Go on," Mr. DeWine says. "It's a fire or something. Go outside."

So they go, April practically dragging Richardson, the two of them replaced by five more and three more after that, and here charge a handful more, all of them with crab legs and flying arms, the last kid—Tyson, his orator!—missing a shoe. This is like the end of a period but at fast-forward and without the grab-ass and ha-ha-ha, students appearing from everywhere. One girl he's never seen before—she resembles Marisa Tomei, but chunkier—runs by him scream-ing "John" over and over. "You can't do this," another girl is saying. "It's just not fair." That's all. Just those two sentences, like a chant, the same sentences he will shortly find himself saying. But right now here are more kids bearing down on him, the short fellow—Fishboy, is it?—with the shiny Penn State jacket tripping and knocking two look-alikes down with him, all of them hav-ing the devil of a time getting up off the floor. And, shit, here are those goofy noises again, but louder this time.

"You seen Ms. Petty?" He's collared a boy lugging a bass fiddle, the instru-ment bigger in all dimensions than he is.

"Who?"

Mr. DeWine pulls the kid to the side. Down the hall, the litter is incredible. Books. Purses. Backpacks. Baseball caps. A blouse is there, too. And a pair of coveralls. Christ, what were all the fire drills for? He expects zoo life next. A giraffe would not surprise him one whit.

"Ms. Petty?" he begins. "She teaches junior calculus."

"I don't take that till next year, sir."

So Mr. DeWine asks the next kid—a doofus from student council possibly; he has that squeaky look about him. Another *no*. And another, this one from the dorkier end of the food chain. Nothing but *no, no, no* until, interestingly, there's no one left to ask, the hall having become as still as deepest space. Which means that, despite the jangling of the alarms and sirens woo-wooing in the distance, Mr. DeWine can hear, with phenomenally stunning clarity, what he dares not believe is gunfire.

(That moment? When he at last apprehends how monstrously dimwitted he's been? When he learns how far up his ass his head has been? Friends, it's now. Right now.)

"No," he says, as much to the brickwork as to himself.

But there it is again. A shot. Like a cannon, he thinks. Shit.

You'd think he would run now, wouldn't you? You'd bet that, knowing what he knows, he'd turn the other way, scram for the doors he came in through. You'd think, because he's read the papers and watched CNN and has heard about those psycho punks in Arkansas and Colorado, and because he pos-sesses the same instinct for self-preservation we all have, that he'd know what to do. At the very least, his body would react independently, right? His mus-cles, his fist of a heart.

But he does not move. No, Mr. DeWine—get this—sits, leans against the wall. It's a fire, he tells himself—not the last of his wishful thinking. He's no hero, that's not in dispute. And violence? Christ, the only fistfight he had was—when?—maybe in junior high, in the days when they had junior high. Instead, he tells himself again that the smoke in the air, bitter and grainy, is from a fire. Faulty wiring probably. Or some butt-wipe setting off M-80's in the restroom. But, all along, Francis Michael DeWine has known better. It's just like TV, friends. How sad. You go to a movie, a bona fide shoot-'em-up, and it's boom-boom-boom, just like now. Gangsters, terrorists, invaders from another galaxy—God, they're all in the library. It's astounding, really. His lungs have gone slack, the air in here too thin. The knee is seriously hurting now, the throbbing like a tom-tom. Skiing. What a dumb-ass sport. And here it is that he considers his lap, specifically the damp spots on his trousers, and realizes that he, the dumbest of the dumber earthlings, is crying. He's weeping. Silently, without a heave or a tremor, tears are falling from his chin. Tears.

"They didn't work."

Someone—a boy of wicked angles and rattles and marvelous heat—has sat down next to him.

"FAT MAN and Little Boy," the kid is saying. "I must've fucked up the timers."

The kid seems to wobble under a halo of fireflies, a buzz constant as ocean noise.

"Are you John?" Mr. DeWine says. "A girl was asking after you."

Whiskey, the boy says, his voice not at all the snarl a villain should have.

The emergency sprinklers have come on now, a fierce shower drenching the hall, the walls slick with running water, the floor shiny like a postcard of a stream from a world where the outside is weirdly in.

"You can't do this," Mr. DeWine says.

Oh, but he can, replies the boy.

"It's not fair. Really."

Time has unraveled. Yesterday, Frank DeWine was a Cub Scout stealing LifeSavers from the Stop'N'Go. Only a month ago did his voice change. He was born with a full beard and a three-pack-a-day habit.

"You cold, Mr. DeWine? You're shivering."

Yes. So cold. Between his ears, a glacier has ground through the center of him, the fissures and folds of his brain jammed with ice.

"You want to say anything?"

"Like last words?" Mr. DeWine asks.

Whiskey nods. He takes no particular pleasure in this scene. Business is being conducted, that's all. The "therefore" and "whereunto" pages of the contract. The paragraphs in which the who's who and the what's what become the *ipso facto* and the hey-diddle-diddle.

"I'd like to say something about my father," Mr. DeWine says, though for several breaths he can't think of what exactly he might mean. "He had big hands, like paddles."

Again Whiskey nods. Mr. DeWine is being a good sport. Not like some you could name. Not like, oh, Bethany with her forgive-us-our-trespasses bullshit.

"I don't think he ever struck me in anger," Mr. DeWine is saying.

"My dad, too," Whiskey says. "He just sends me to my room, or takes away the car."

Whiskey has raised the assault pistol and placed it tenderly against the vein pulsing at Mr. DeWine's temple. The boy has an interest, keen but thoroughly professional, in this moment. He wonders what we will make of his own last words, those typed on the page folded in his pocket, after he, at the muzzle velocity of 1,230 feet per second, has transformed himself into liquid and light, meat and whitest bone.

"Anything else?"

Yes, Francis DeWine thinks. Yes, there is.

2001

CONRAD AIKEN
(1889–1973)

Conrad Aiken was born in Savannah, Georgia to socially prominent parents from New York and Boston. When Aiken was eleven years old, his father shot and killed Aiken's mother and then himself. This traumatic event undoubtedly had a tremendous impact on his life and writing, which is often deeply psychological. Aiken relates the events surrounding the tragic incident in his autobiography, *Ushant* (1952). Following the death of his parents, Aiken went to live with an aunt in Massachusetts. He knew from an early age that he wanted to be a poet and attended Harvard University determined to become one. While at Harvard, Aiken made a lifelong friend of T. S. Eliot and studied under George Santayana, both of whom greatly influenced his work. Two years after graduating, he published his first book of poetry, *Earth Triumphant* (1914). Aiken spent most of the 1920s and '30s in England—a prolific time for him, despite multiple divorces and a suicide attempt. Aiken has said that his short story "Silent Snow, Secret Snow," below, is "a projection of [his] own inclination to insanity." He returned to the United States in the early 1940s, settling in New England until the last years of his life, when he returned to Savannah, Georgia. Aiken's dozens of publications include collections of poetry and short stories, novels, and literary criticism. He was awarded the Pulitzer Prize in 1930 for his *Selected Poems* and the National Book Award in 1954 for his *Collected Poems*. From 1950 to 1952 he was the Consultant in Poetry to the Library of Congress and in 1973 became the Poet Laureate of his home state of Georgia. He also received the National Institute of Arts and Letters Gold Medal, the National Medal for Literature, and the Bollingen Prize for Poetry. Among his collections of short fiction are *Bring! Bring! And Other Stories* (1925), *Costumes by Eros* (1928), *Among the Lost People* (1934), and *The Collected Short Stories of Conrad Aiken* (1960).

Silent Snow, Secret Snow

I

Just why it should have happened, or why it should have happened just when it did, he could not, of course, possibly have said; nor perhaps would it even have occurred to him to ask. The thing was above all a secret, something to be preciously concealed from Mother and Father; and to that very fact it owed an enormous part of its deliciousness. It was like a peculiarly beautiful trinket to be carried unmentioned in one's trouser pocket—a rare stamp, an old coin, a few tiny gold links found trodden out of shape on the path in the park, a pebble of carnelian,[1] a seashell distinguishable from all others by an unusual spot or stripe—and, as if it were any one of these, he carried around with him everywhere a warm and persistent and increasingly beautiful sense of possession. Nor was it only a sense of possession—it was also a sense of protection. It was as if, in some delightful way, his secret gave him a fortress, a wall behind which he could retreat into heavenly seclusion. This was almost the first thing he had noticed about it—apart from the oddness of the thing itself—and it was this that now again, for the fiftieth time, occurred to him, as he sat in the little schoolroom. It was the half-hour for geography. Miss Buell was revolving with one finger, slowly, a huge terrestrial globe which had been placed on her desk. The green and yellow continents passed and repassed, questions were asked and answered, and now the little girl in front of him, Deirdre, who had a funny little constellation of freckles on the back of her neck, exactly like the Big Dipper, was standing up and telling Miss Buell that the equator was the line that ran round the middle.

Miss Buell's face, which was old and grayish and kindly, with gray stiff curls beside the cheeks, and eyes that swam very brightly, like little minnows, behind thick glasses, wrinkled itself into a complication of amusements.

"Ah! I see. The earth is wearing a belt, or a sash. Or someone drew a line round it!"

"Oh no—not that—I mean——"

In the general laughter, he did not share, or only a very little. He was thinking about the Arctic and Antarctic regions, which of course, on the globe, were white. Miss Buell was now telling them about the tropics, the jungles, the steamy heat of equatorial swamps, where the birds and butterflies, and even the snakes, were like living jewels. As he listened to these things, he was already, with a pleasant sense of half-effort, putting his secret between himself and the words. Was it really an effort at all? For effort implied something voluntary, and perhaps even something one did not especially want; whereas this was distinctly pleasant, and came almost of its own accord. All he needed to do was to think of that morning, the first one, and then of all the others——

But it was all so absurdly simple! It had amounted to so little. It was nothing, just an idea—and just why it should have become so wonderful, so permanent, was a mystery—a very pleasant one, to be sure, but also, in an amusing way, foolish. However, without ceasing to listen to Miss Buell, who had now moved up to the north temperate zones, he deliberately invited his memory of the first morning. It was only a moment or two after he had waked up—or perhaps the moment itself. But was there, to be exact, an exact moment? Was one awake all at once? or was it gradual? Anyway, it was after he had stretched a lazy hand up toward the headrail, and yawned, and then relaxed again among his warm covers, all the more grateful on a December morning, that the thing had happened. Suddenly, for no reason, he had thought of the postman, he remembered the postman. Perhaps there was nothing so odd in that. After all, he heard the postman almost every morning in his life—his heavy boots could be heard clumping round the corner at the top of the little cobbled hill-street, and then, progressively nearer, progressively louder, the double knock at each

1. A reddish-colored semiprecious mineral.

door, the crossings and re-crossings of the street, till finally the clumsy steps came stumbling across to the very door, and the tremendous knock came which shook the house itself.

(Miss Buell was saying, "Vast wheat-growing areas in North America and Siberia."

Deirdre had for the moment placed her left hand across the back of her neck.)

But on this particular morning, the first morning, as he lay there with his eyes closed, he had for some reason *waited* for the postman. He wanted to hear him come round the corner. And that was precisely the joke—he never did. He never came. He never had come—*round the corner*—again. For when at last the steps *were* heard, they had already, he was quite sure, come a little down the hill, to the first house; and even so, the steps were curiously different—they were softer, they had a new secrecy about them, they were muffled and indistinct; and while the rhythm of them was the same, it now said a new thing—it said peace, it said remoteness, it said cold, it said sleep. And he had understood the situation at once—nothing could have seemed simpler—there had been snow in the night, such as all winter he had been longing for; and it was this which had rendered the postman's first footsteps inaudible, and the later ones faint. Of course! How lovely! And even now it must be snowing—it was going to be a snowy day—the long white ragged lines were drifting and sifting across the street, across the faces of the old houses, whispering and hushing, making little triangles of white in the corners between cobblestones, seething a little when the wind blew them over the ground to a drifted corner; and so it would be all day, getting deeper and deeper and silenter and silenter.

(Miss Buell was saying, "Land of perpetual snow.")

All this time, of course (while he lay in bed), he had kept his eyes closed, listening to the nearer progress of the postman, the muffled footsteps thumping and slipping on the snow-sheathed cobbles; and all the other sounds—the double knocks, a frosty far-off voice or two, a bell ringing thinly and softly as if under a sheet of ice—had the same slightly abstracted quality, as if removed by one degree from actuality—as if everything in the world had been insulated by snow. But when at last, pleased, he opened his eyes, and turned them toward the window, to see for himself this long-desired and now so clearly imagined miracle—what he saw instead was brilliant sunlight on a roof; and when, astonished, he jumped out of bed and stared down into the street, expecting to see the cobbles obliterated by the snow, he saw nothing but the bare bright cobbles themselves.

Queer, the effect this extraordinary surprise had had upon him—all the following morning he had kept with him a sense as of snow falling about him, a secret screen of new snow between himself and the world. If he had not dreamed such a thing—and how could he have dreamed it while awake?—how else could one explain it? In any case, the delusion had been so vivid as to affect his entire behavior. He could not now remember whether it was on the first or the second morning—or was it even the third?—that his mother had drawn attention to some oddness in his manner.

"But my darling"—she had said at the breakfast table—"what has come over you? You don't seem to be listening. . . ."

And how often that very thing had happened since!

(Miss Buell was now asking if anyone knew the difference between the North Pole and the Magnetic Pole. Deirdre was holding up her flickering brown hand, and he could see the four white dimples that marked the knuckles.)

Perhaps it hadn't been either the second or third morning—or even the fourth or fifth. How could he be sure? How could he be sure just when the delicious *progress* had become clear? Just when it had really *begun*? The intervals weren't very precise. . . . All he now knew was, that at some point or other—perhaps the second day, perhaps the sixth—he had noticed that the presence of the snow was a little more insistent, the sound of it clearer; and, conversely, the sound of the postman's footsteps more indistinct. Not only could he not hear the steps come round the corner, he could not even hear them at the first house. It was below the first house that he heard them; and then, a few days later, it was below the second house that he heard them; and a few days later again, below the third. Gradually, gradually, the snow was becoming heavier, the sound of its seething louder, the cobblestones more and more muffled. When he found, each morning, on going to the window, after the ritual of listening, that the roofs and cobbles were as bare as ever, it made no difference. This was, after all, only what he had expected. It was even what pleased him, what rewarded him: the thing was his own, belonged to no one else. No one else knew about it, not even his mother and father. There, outside, were the bare cobbles; and here, inside, was the snow. Snow growing heavier each day, muffling the world, hiding the ugly, and deadening increasingly—above all— the steps of the postman.

"But, my darling"—she had said at the luncheon table—"what has come over you? You don't seem to listen when people speak to you. That's the third time I've asked you to pass your plate. . . ."

How was one to explain this to Mother? or to Father? There was, of course, nothing to be done about it: nothing. All one could do was to laugh embarrassedly, pretend to be a little ashamed, apologize, and take a sudden and somewhat disingenuous interest in what was being done or said. The cat had stayed out all night. He had a curious swelling on his left cheek—perhaps somebody had kicked him, or a stone had struck him. Mrs. Kempton was or was not coming to tea. The house was going to be housecleaned, or "turned out," on Wednesday instead of Friday. A new lamp was provided for his evening work— perhaps it was eyestrain which accounted for this new and so peculiar vagueness of his—Mother was looking at him with amusement as she said this, but with something else as well. A new lamp? A new lamp. Yes, Mother, No, Mother, Yes, Mother. School is going very well. The geometry is very easy. The history is very dull. The geography is very interesting—particularly when it takes one to the North Pole. Why the North Pole? Oh, well, it would be fun to be an explorer. Another Peary or Scott or Shackleton. And then abruptly he found his interest in the talk at an end, stared at the pudding on his plate, listened, waited, and began once more—ah, how heavenly, too, the first beginnings—to hear or feel—for could he actually hear it?—the silent snow, the secret snow.

(Miss Buell was telling them about the search for the Northwest Passage, about Hendrik Hudson, the *Half Moon.*)

This had been, indeed, the only distressing feature of the new experience; the fact that it so increasingly had brought him into a kind of mute misunderstanding, or even conflict, with his father and mother. It was as if he were trying to lead a double life. On the one hand, he had to be Paul Hasleman, and keep up the appearance of being that person—dress, wash, and answer intelligently when spoken to—; on the other, he had to explore this new world which had been opened to him. Nor could there be the slightest doubt—not the slightest—that the new world was the profounder and more wonderful of the two. It was irresistible. It was miraculous. Its beauty was simply beyond anything—beyond speech as beyond thought—utterly incommunicable. But how then, between the two worlds, of which he was thus constantly aware, was he to keep a balance? One must get up, one must go to breakfast, one must talk with Mother, go to school, do one's lessons—and, in all this, try not to appear too much of a fool. But if all the while one was also trying to extract the full deliciousness of another and quite separate existence, one which could not easily (if at all) be spoken of—how was one to manage? How was one to explain? Would it be safe to explain? Would it be absurd? Would it merely mean that he would get into some obscure kind of trouble?

These thoughts came and went, came and went, as softly and secretly as the snow; they were not precisely a disturbance, perhaps they were even a pleasure; he liked to have them; their presence was something almost palpable, something he could stroke with his hand, without closing his eyes, and without ceasing to see Miss Buell and the schoolroom and the globe and the freckles on Deirdre's neck; nevertheless he did in a sense cease to see, or to see the obvious external world, and substituted for this vision the vision of snow, the sound of snow, and the slow, almost soundless, approach of the postman. Yesterday, it had been only at the sixth house that the postman had become audible; the snow was much deeper now, it was falling more swiftly and heavily, the sound of its seething was more distinct, more soothing, more persistent. And this morning, it had been—as nearly as he could figure—just above the seventh house—perhaps only a step or two above; at most, he had heard two or three footsteps before the knock had sounded. . . . And with each such narrowing of the sphere, each nearer approach of the limit at which the postman was first audible, it was odd how sharply was increased the amount of illusion which had to be carried into the ordinary business of daily life. Each day, it was harder to get out of bed, to go to the window, to look out at the—as always—perfectly empty and snowless street. Each day it was more difficult to go through the perfunctory motions of greeting Mother and Father at breakfast, to reply to their questions, to put his books together and go to school. And at school, how extraordinarily hard to conduct with success simultaneously the public life and the life that was secret! There were times when he longed—positively ached—to tell everyone about it—to burst out with it—only to be checked almost at once by a far-off feeling as of some faint absurdity which was inherent in it—but *was* it absurd?—and more importantly by a sense of mysterious power in his very secrecy. Yes; it must be kept secret. That, more and more, became clear. At whatever cost to himself, whatever pain to others—

(Miss Buell looked straight at him, smiling, and said, "Perhaps we'll ask Paul. I'm sure Paul will come out of his daydream long enough to be able to tell us. Won't you, Paul?" He rose slowly from his chair, resting one hand on the brightly varnished desk, and deliberately stared through the snow toward the blackboard. It was an effort, but it was amusing to make it. "Yes," he said slowly, "it was what we now call the Hudson River. This he thought to be the

Northwest Passage. He was disappointed." He sat down again, and as he did so Deirdre half turned in her chair and gave him a shy smile, of approval and admiration.)

At whatever pain to others.

This part of it was very puzzling, very puzzling. Mother was very nice, and so was Father. Yes, that was all true enough. He wanted to be nice to them, to tell them everything—and yet, was it really wrong of him to want to have a secret place of his own?

At bed-time, the night before, Mother had said, "If this goes on, my lad, we'll have to see a doctor, we will! We can't have our boy—" But what was it she had said? "Live in another world"? "Live so far away"? The word "far" had been in it, he was sure, and then Mother had taken up a magazine again and laughed a little, but with an expression which wasn't mirthful. He had felt sorry for her. . . .

The bell rang for dismissal. The sound came to him through long curved parallels of falling snow. He saw Deirdre rise, and had himself risen almost as soon—but not quite as soon—as she.

II

On the walk homeward, which was timeless, it pleased him to see through the accompaniment, or counterpoint, of snow, the items of mere externality on his way. There were many kinds of brick in the sidewalks, and laid in many kinds of pattern. The garden walls, too, were various, some of wooden palings, some of plaster, some of stone. Twigs of bushes leaned over the walls: the little hard green winter-buds of lilac, on gray stems, sheathed and fat; other branches very thin and fine and black and desiccated. Dirty sparrows huddled in the bushes, as dull in color as dead fruit left in leafless trees. A single starling creaked on a weather vane. In the gutter, beside a drain, was a scrap of torn and dirty newspaper, caught in a little delta of filth; the word ECZEMA appeared in large capitals, and below it was a letter from Mrs. Amelia D. Cravath, 2100 Pine Street, Fort Worth, Texas, to the effect that after being a sufferer for years she had been cured by Caley's Ointment. In the little delta, beside the fan-shaped and deeply runneled continent of brown mud, were lost twigs, descended from their parent trees, dead matches, a rusty horse-chestnut burr, a small concentration of eggshell, a streak of yellow sawdust which had been wet and now was dry and congealed, a brown pebble, and a broken feather. Farther on was a cement sidewalk, ruled into geometrical parallelograms, with a brass inlay at one end commemorating the contractors who had laid it, and, halfway across, an irregular and random series of dog-tracks, immortalized in synthetic stone. He knew these well, and always stepped on them; to cover the little hollows with his own foot had always been a queer pleasure; today he did it once more, but perfunctorily and detachedly, all the while thinking of something else. That was a dog, a long time ago, who had made a mistake and walked on the cement while it was still wet. He had probably wagged his tail, but that hadn't been recorded. Now, Paul Hasleman, aged twelve, on his way home from school, crossed the same river, which in the meantime had frozen into rock. Homeward through the snow, the snow falling in bright sunshine. Homeward?

Then came the gateway with the two posts surmounted by egg-shaped stones which had been cunningly balanced on their ends, as if by Columbus, and mortared in the very act of balance; a source of perpetual wonder. On the brick wall just beyond, the letter H had been stenciled, presumably for some purpose. H? H.

The green hydrant, with a little green-painted chain attached to the brass screw-cap.

The elm tree, with the great gray wound in the bark, kidney-shaped, into which he always put his hand—to feel the cold but living wood. The injury, he had been sure, was due to the gnawings of a tethered horse. But now it deserved only a passing palm, a merely tolerant eye. There were more important things. Miracles. Beyond the thoughts of trees, mere elms. Beyond the thoughts of sidewalks, mere stone, mere brick, mere cement. Beyond the thoughts even of his own shoes, which trod these sidewalks obediently, bearing a burden—far above—of elaborate mystery. He watched them. They were not very well polished; he had neglected them, for a very good reason: they were one of the many parts of the increasing difficulty of the daily return to daily life, the morning struggle. To get up, having at last opened one's eyes, to go to the window, and discover no snow, to wash, to dress, to descend the curving stairs to breakfast—

At whatever pain to others, nevertheless, one must persevere in severance, since the incommunicability of the experience demanded it. It was desirable, of course, to be kind to Mother and Father, especially as they seemed to be worried, but it was also desirable to be resolute. If they should decide—as appeared likely—to consult the doctor, Doctor Howells, and have Paul inspected, his heart listened to through a kind of dictaphone, his lungs, his stomach—well, that was all right. He would go through with it. He would give them answer for question, too—perhaps such answers as they hadn't expected? No. That would never do. For the secret world must, at all costs, be preserved.

The bird-house in the apple tree was empty—it was the wrong time of year for wrens. The little round black door had lost its pleasure. The wrens were enjoying other houses, other nests, remoter trees. But this too was a notion which he only vaguely and grazingly entertained—as if, for the moment, he merely touched an edge of it; there was something further on, which was already assuming a sharper importance; something which already teased at the corners of his eyes, teasing also at the corner of his mind. It was funny to think that he so wanted this, so awaited it—and yet found himself enjoying this momentary dalliance with the bird-house, as if for a quite deliberate postponement and enhancement of the approaching pleasure. He was aware of his delay, of his smiling and detached and now almost uncomprehending gaze at the little bird-house; he knew what he was going to look at next: it was his own little cobbled hill-street, his own house, the little river at the bottom of the hill, the grocer's shop with the cardboard man in the window—and now, thinking of all this, he turned his head, still smiling, and looking quickly right and left through the snow-laden sunlight.

And the mist of snow, as he had foreseen, was still on it—a ghost of snow falling in the bright sunlight, softly and steadily floating and turning and pausing, soundlessly meeting the snow that covered, as with a transparent mirage, the bare bright cobbles. He loved it—he stood still and loved it. Its beauty was paralyzing—beyond all words, all experience, all dream. No fairy story he had ever read could be compared with it—none had ever given him this extraordinary combination of ethereal loveliness with a something else, unnameable, which was just faintly and deliciously terrifying. What was this thing? As he thought of it, he looked upward toward his own bedroom window, which was open—and it was as if he looked straight into the room and saw himself lying half awake in his bed. There he was—at this very instant he was still perhaps actually there—more truly there than standing here at the edge of the cobbled hill-street, with one hand lifted to shade his eyes against the snow-sun. Had he indeed ever left his room, in all this time? since that very first morning? Was the whole progress still being enacted there, was it still the same morning, and himself not yet wholly awake? And even now, had the postman not yet come round the corner? . . .

This idea amused him, and automatically, as he thought of it, he turned his head and looked toward the top of the hill. There was, of course, nothing there—nothing and no one. The street was empty and quiet. And all the more because of its emptiness it occurred to him to count the houses—a thing which, oddly enough, he hadn't before thought of doing. Of course, he had known there weren't many—many, that is, on his own side of the street, which were the ones that figured in the postman's progress—but nevertheless it came as something of a shock to find that there were precisely *six,* above his own house—his own house was the seventh.

Six!

Astonished, he looked at his own house—looked at the door, on which was the number thirteen—and then realized that the whole thing was exactly and logically and absurdly what he ought to have known. Just the same, the realization gave him abruptly, and even a little frighteningly, a sense of hurry. He was being hurried—he was being rushed. For—he knit his brow—he couldn't be mistaken—it was just above the *seventh* house, his *own* house, that the postman had first been audible this very morning. But in that case—in that case—did it mean that tomorrow he would hear nothing? The knock he had heard must have been the knock of their own door. Did it mean—and this was an idea which gave him a really extraordinary feeling of surprise—that he would never hear the postman again?—that tomorrow morning the postman would already have passed the house, in a snow so deep as to render his footsteps completely inaudible? That he would have made his approach down the snow-filled street so soundlessly, so secretly, that he, Paul Hasleman, there lying in bed, would not have waked in time, or waking, would have heard nothing?

But how could that be? Unless even the knocker should be muffled in the snow—frozen tight, perhaps? . . . But in that case—

A vague feeling of disappointment came over him; a vague sadness as if he felt himself deprived of something which he had long looked forward to, something much prized. After all this, all this beautiful progress, the slow delicious advance of the postman through the silent and secret snow, the knock creeping closer each day, and the footsteps nearer, the audible compass of the world thus daily narrowed, narrowed, narrowed, as the snow soothingly and beautifully encroached and deepened, after all this, was he to be defrauded of the one thing he had so wanted—to be able to count, as it were, the last two or three solemn footsteps, as they finally approached his own door? Was it all going to happen, at the end, so suddenly? or indeed, had it already happened? with no slow and subtle gradations of menace, in which he could luxuriate?

He gazed upward again, toward his own window which flashed in the sun; and this time almost with a feeling that it would be better if he *were* still in bed, in that room; for in that case this must still be the first morning, and there would be six more mornings to come—or, for that matter, seven or eight or nine—how could he be sure?—or even more.

III

After supper, the inquisition began. He stood before the doctor, under the lamp, and submitted silently to the usual thumpings and tappings.

"Now will you please say 'Ah!'?"

"Ah!"

"Now again, please, if you don't mind."

"Ah."

"Say it slowly, and hold it if you can——"

"Ah-h-h-h-h-h——"

"Good."

How silly all this was. As if it had anything to do with his throat! Or his heart, or lungs!

Relaxing his mouth, of which the corners, after all this absurd stretching, felt uncomfortable, he avoided the doctor's eyes, and stared toward the fireplace, past his mother's feet (in gray slippers) which projected from the green chair, and his father's feet (in brown slippers) which stood neatly side by side on the hearth rug.

"Hm. There is certainly nothing wrong there . . . ?"

He felt the doctor's eyes fixed upon him, and, as if merely to be polite, returned the look, but with a feeling of justifiable evasiveness.

"Now, young man, tell me—do you feel all right?"

"Yes, sir, quite all right."

"No headaches? no dizziness?"

"No, I don't think so."

"Let me see. Let's get a book, if you don't mind—yes, thank you, that will do splendidly—and now, Paul, if you'll just read it, holding it as you would normally hold it——"

He took the book and read:

"And another praise have I to tell for this the city our mother, the gift of a great god, a glory of the land most high; the might of horses, the might of young horses, the might of the sea. . . . For thou, son of Cronus, our lord Poseidon, hath throned herein this pride, since in these roads first thou didst show forth the curb that cures the rage of steeds. And the shapely oar, apt to men's hands, hath a wondrous speed on the brine, following the hundred-footed Nereids. . . . O land that art praised above all lands, now is it for thee to make those bright praises seen in deeds."

He stopped, tentatively, and lowered the heavy book.

"No—as I thought—there is certainly no superficial sign of eyestrain."

Silence thronged the room, and he was aware of the focused scrutiny of the three people who confronted him. . . .

"We could have his eyes examined—but I believe it is something else."

"What could it be?" That was his father's voice.

"It's only this curious absent-mindedness—" This was his mother's voice.

In the presence of the doctor, they both seemed irritatingly apologetic.

"I believe it is something else. Now Paul—I would like very much to ask you a question or two. You will answer them, won't you—you know I'm an old, old friend of yours, eh? That's right! . . ."

His back was thumped twice by the doctor's fat fist—then the doctor was grinning at him with false amiability, while with one fingernail he was scratching the top button of his waistcoat. Beyond the doctor's shoulder was the fire, the fingers of flame making light prestidigitation[2] against the sooty fireback, the soft sound of their random flutter the only sound.

"I would like to know—is there anything that worries you?"

The doctor was again smiling, his eyelids low against the little black pupils, in each of which was a tiny white bead of light. Why answer him? why answer him at all? "At whatever pain to others"—but it was all a nuisance, this necessity for resistance, this necessity for attention; it was as if one had been stood up on a brilliantly lighted stage, under a great round blaze of spotlight; as if one were merely a trained seal, or a performing dog, or a fish, dipped out of an aquarium and held up by the tail. It would serve them right if he were merely to bark or growl. And meanwhile, to miss these last few precious hours, these hours of which each minute was more beautiful than the last, more menacing—! He still looked, as if from a great distance, at the beads of light in the doctor's eyes, at the fixed false smile, and then, beyond, once more at his mother's slippers, his father's slippers, the soft flutter of the fire. Even here, even amongst these hostile presences, and in this arranged light, he could see the snow, he could hear it—it was in the corners of the room, where the shadow was deepest, under the sofa, behind the half-opened door which led to the dining room. It was gentler here, softer, its seethe the quietest of whispers, as if, in deference to a drawing room, it had quite deliberately put on its "manners"; it kept itself out of sight, obliterated itself, but distinctly with an air of saying, "Ah, but just wait! Wait till we are alone together! Then I will begin to tell you something new! Something white! something cold! something sleepy! something of cease, and peace, and the long bright curve of space! Tell them to go away. Banish them. Refuse to speak. Leave them, go upstairs to your room, turn out the light and get into bed—I will go with you, I will be waiting for you, I will tell you a better story than Little Kay of the Skates, or The Snow Ghost—I will surround your bed, I will close the windows, pile a deep drift against the door, so that none will ever again be able to enter. Speak to them! . . ." It seemed as if the little hissing voice came from a slow white spiral of falling flakes in the corner by the front window—but he could not be sure. He felt himself smiling, then, and said to the doctor, but without looking at him, looking beyond him still——

"Oh no, I think not——"

"But are you sure, my boy?"

His father's voice came softly and coldly then—the familiar voice of silken warning.

---

2. Sleight-of-hand tricks.

"You needn't answer at once, Paul—remember we're trying to help you— think it over and be quite sure, won't you?"

He felt himself smiling again, at the notion of being quite sure. What a joke! As if he weren't so sure that reassurance was no longer necessary, and all this cross-examination a ridiculous farce, a grotesque parody! What could they know about it? these gross intelligences, these humdrum minds so bound to the usual, the ordinary? Impossible to tell them about it! Why, even now, even now, with the proof so abundant, so formidable, so imminent, so appallingly present here in this very room, could they believe it?—could even his mother believe it? No—it was only too plain that if anything were said about it, the merest hint given, they would be incredulous—they would laugh—they would say "Absurd!"—think things about him which weren't true. . . .

"Why no, I'm not worried—why should I be?"

He looked then straight at the doctor's low-lidded eyes, looked from one of them to the other, from one bead of light to the other, and gave a little laugh.

The doctor seemed to be disconcerted by this. He drew back in his chair, resting a fat white hand on either knee. The smile faded slowly from his face.

"Well, Paul!" he said, and paused gravely, "I'm afraid you don't take this quite seriously enough. I think you perhaps don't quite realize—don't quite realize—" He took a deep quick breath and turned, as if helplessly, at a loss for words, to the others. But Mother and Father were both silent—no help was forthcoming.

"You must surely know, be aware, that you have not been quite yourself, of late? Don't you know that? . . ."

It was amusing to watch the doctor's renewed attempt at a smile, a queer disorganized look, as of confidential embarrassment.

"I feel all right, sir," he said, and again gave the little laugh.

"And we're trying to help you." The doctor's tone sharpened.

"Yes, sir, I know. But why? I'm all right. I'm just *thinking*, that's all."

His mother made a quick movement forward, resting a hand on the back of the doctor's chair.

"Thinking?" she said. "But my dear, about what?"

This was a direct challenge—and would have to be directly met. But before he met it, he looked again into the corner by the door, as if for reassurance. He smiled again at what he saw, at what he heard. The little spiral was still there, still softly whirling, like the ghost of a white kitten chasing the ghost of a white tail, and making as it did so the faintest of whispers. It was all right! If only he could remain firm, everything was going to be all right.

"Oh, about anything, about nothing—*you* know the way you do!"

"You mean—daydreaming?"

"Oh, no—thinking!"

"But thinking about *what*?"

"Anything."

He laughed a third time—but this time, happening to glance upward toward his mother's face, he was appalled at the effect his laughter seemed to have upon her. Her mouth had opened in an expression of horror. . . . This was too bad! Unfortunate! He had known it would cause pain, of course—but he hadn't expected it to be quite so bad as this. Perhaps—perhaps if he just gave them a tiny gleaming hint——?

"About the snow," he said.

"What on earth?" This was his father's voice. The brown slippers came a step nearer on the hearth-rug.

"But my dear, what do you mean?" This was his mother's voice.

The doctor merely stared.

"Just *snow*, that's all. I like to think about it."

"Tell us about it, my boy."

"But that's all it is. There's nothing to tell. *You* know what snow is?"

This he said almost angrily, for he felt that they were trying to corner him. He turned sideways so as no longer to face the doctor, and the better to see the inch of blackness between the window-sill and the lowered curtain—the cold inch of beckoning and delicious night. At once he felt better, more assured.

"Mother—can I go to bed, now, please? I've got a headache."

"But I thought you said——"

"It's just come. It's all these questions—! Can I, mother?"

"You can go as soon as the doctor has finished."

"Don't you think this thing ought to be gone into thoroughly, and *now?*" This was Father's voice. The brown slippers again came a step nearer, the voice was the well-known "punishment" voice, resonant and cruel.

"Oh, what's the use, Norman——"

Quite suddenly, everyone was silent. And without precisely facing them, nevertheless he was aware that all three of them were watching him with an extraordinary intensity—staring hard at him—as if he had done something monstrous, or was himself some kind of monster. He could hear the soft irregular flutter of the flames; the cluck-click-cluck-click of the clock; far and faint, two sudden spurts of laughter from the kitchen, as quickly cut off as begun; a murmur of water in the pipes; and then, the silence seemed to deepen, to spread out, to become world-long and world-wide, to become timeless and shapeless, and to center inevitably and rightly, with a slow and sleepy but enormous concentration of all power, on the beginning of a new sound. What this new sound was going to be, he knew perfectly well. It might begin with a hiss, but it would end with a roar—there was no time to lose—he must escape. It mustn't happen here——

Without another word, he turned and ran up the stairs.

IV

Not a moment too soon. The darkness was coming in long white waves. A prolonged sibilance filled the night—a great seamless seethe of wild influence went abruptly across it—a cold low humming shook the windows. He shut the door and flung off his clothes in the dark. The bare black door was like a little raft tossed in waves of snow, almost overwhelmed, washed under whitely, up again, smothered in curled billows of feather. The snow was laughing; it spoke from all sides at once; it pressed closer to him as he ran and jumped exulting into his bed.

"Listen to us!" it said. "Listen! We have come to tell you the story we told you about. You remember? Lie down. Shut your eyes, now—you will no longer see much—in this white darkness who could see, or want to see? We will take the place of everything. . . . Listen——"

A beautiful varying dance of snow began at the front of the room, came forward and then retreated, flattened out toward the floor, then rose fountain-like to the ceiling, swayed, recruited itself from a new stream of flakes which poured laughing in through the humming window, advanced again, lifted long white arms. It said peace, it said remoteness, it said cold—it said—

But then a gash of horrible light fell brutally across the room from the opening door—the snow drew back hissing—something alien had come into the room—something hostile. This thing rushed at him, clutched at him, shook him—and he was not merely horrified, he was filled with such a loathing as he had never known. What was this? this cruel disturbance? this act of anger and hate? It was as if he had to reach up a hand toward another world for any understanding of it—an effort of which he was only barely capable. But of that other world he still remembered just enough to know the exorcising words. They tore themselves from his other life suddenly—

"Mother! Mother! Go away! I hate you!"

And with that effort, everything was solved, everything became all right: the seamless hiss advanced once more, the long white wavering lines rose and fell like enormous whispering sea-waves, the whisper becoming louder, the laughter more numerous.

"Listen!" it said. "We'll tell you the last, the most beautiful and secret story—shut your eyes—it is a very small story—a story that gets smaller and smaller—it comes inward instead of opening like a flower—it is a flower becoming a seed—a little cold seed—do you hear? we are leaning closer to you——"

The hiss was now becoming a roar—the whole world was a vast moving screen of snow—but even now it said peace, it said remoteness, it said cold, it said sleep.

1934

DOROTHY ALLISON
b. 1949

Dorothy Allison was born in Greenville, South Carolina to a fifteen-year-old single mother. The first member of her family to graduate from high school, she earned a National Merit Scholarship to Florida Presbyterian (now Eckerd) College. In college Allison became acquainted with the early feminist movement, which she says changed her life. Her semi-autobiographical writing reflects her staunch feminism and addresses topics such as abuse, poverty, and lesbianism. Before becoming known for her fiction, Allison was an award-winning editor for early feminist and lesbian and gay magazines, including *Quest, Conditions,* and *Outlook.* During this time she held a number of jobs—as a waitress, nanny, and substitute teacher, among others—and received an M.A. in Anthropology from The New School in New York City. Allison's first publication was a collection of poems, *The Women Who Hate Me* (1983). Five years later, she published a collection of short fiction, *Trash* (1988), which won her two Lambda Literary Awards and the American Library Association Prize for Lesbian and Gay Writing. *Trash* was reissued in 2002 with a new story, "Compassion," which was selected for *The Best American Short Stories* and *The Best New Stories from the South.* Her 1992 bestselling novel, *Bastard Out of Carolina,* was a finalist for the National Book Award. Since then, Allison has published a book of essays, *Skin: Talking About Sex, Class & Literature* (1992); the memoir *Two or Three Things I Know for Sure* (1995), a *New York Times* Notable Book; and a second novel, *Cavedweller* (1998), another national bestseller.

Jason Who Will Be Famous

Jason is going to be famous, and the best part is that he knows he will be good at it.

He has this real clear picture of himself, of him being interviewed—not of the place or even when it happens, but of the event itself. What he sees is him and the interviewer, a recording so clear and close up, he can see the reflections sparking off his own pupils. It's hi-def or Blu-ray or something past all that, a rendering that catches the way the soft hairs just forward of his earlobe lift and shine in the light reflecting off his pale cheeks. All he has to do is close his eyes and it begins to play, crisp and crackling with energy as the microphone bumps hollowly against the button on his open collar.

"A lot of it, I can't tell you," he says, and the interviewer nods.

Jason is sitting leaning forward. His features gleam in the bright light, his expression is carefully composed, focused on the interviewer. Jason nods his head and his hair swings down over his forehead. One auburn strand just brushes across the edges of his eyebrows. The interviewer is so close their elbows are almost touching. He is an older man with gray in his hair and an expression of watchful readiness—a man Jason has seen do this kind of thing on the news before, someone to be trusted, someone serious.

That is the word. Serious. The word echoes along Jason's nervous system. He is being taken seriously. Every time he imagines it again, the thought makes him take a deep breath. A little heat flares in his neck as the camera follows his eyes. He looks away from the interviewer, and his face goes still. He looks back and his eyes go dark and sad.

"I'm sorry to have to ask you about something so painful," the interviewer says to him.

"It's all right," Jason says. "I understand." He keeps his expression a mirror of the other man's, careful and composed. He can do this. Piece of cake.

Behind the cameraman, there are other people waiting to speak to Jason, others are standing close by to hear what he has to say. Everyone has questions, questions about what happened, of course, about the kidnapping and all the months in captivity. But they also want to ask him what he thinks about other things, about people, and events. In the interview as Jason sees it, he always has answers—surprising and complicated, wonderful answers.

"That boy is extraordinary," he hears the serious man tell another.

Extraordinary. The heat in his neck moves down into his chest, circles his diaphragm, and filters out to his arms and legs. He hopes it does not show on his face. Better to remain pale and impassive, pretend he does not hear what they say about him. How extraordinary he is, that everyone says so, some kind of genius. He half-smiles and then recomposes his expression. Genius. Jason is not sure what his genius is exactly, but trusts it. He knows it will be revealed at the right time, in the right circumstances. It is simply that those events have not happened as of yet. But they will.

He opens his eyes. He has stopped at the edge of the road. Dust, white-grey and alkaline, has drifted up from his boots, and he can taste eucalyptus and piney resin. He looks up the road toward the next hill and the curve down into the shade of the redwood stand there. Should have brought a bottle of water, he thinks. Then, extraordinary. How would you know if you were extraordinary? Or a genius? He's pretty good at math, and music—though nothing that special. If he worked more, put more of himself into the work, no telling what he might not do. His dad told him that, once, when he was still living with them. His teachers have said something of the same thing. All of them though, his dad, teachers and his mom, they say it like it's a bad thing—his talents and his waste of them.

"If you worked more. If you worked harder."

They don't understand. No one does.

Jason wipes dust off his mouth and rocks his head from side to side. He knows the problem. It's not that he's lazy or stupid or even scared. No. The problem is that he never has had enough time or focus. There's just always so much that has to be done, and how does anyone do that kind of kung fu stuff anyway? How does anyone become extraordinary? Like Uma Thurman in the Tarantino movie? Years going up and down staircases. It's like that. You do some stupid thing over and over and over, and sometime along in there, you discover you have achieved this enormous talent.

He glares up the road and resumes his pace, boots kicking dust and his hands gripping the straps of his backpack. He could do extraordinary stuff. Given the right circumstances, he has everything in him to do stuff that will startle everyone. It just takes the right circumstances—getting everything out of the way. He nods to himself. He can feel that coming toward him—the opportunity, the time, and the focus.

He has dreamed it so often, he knows it is coming—though he doesn't know all of how it will happen. That too, he sees like a movie, the movie of his life going on all the time. Step in and it is already in motion. Like that. He grins and speeds up slightly. Might be, he will be walking home along the river road from Connie's on a day just like this one. He'll have something in his backpack, after working for Connie all day, doing what he does so well, little baby buds his specialty. Connie always tells him how good he is. He knows exactly how to clip and trim and harvest only what is ready to come away, leave what should be left behind. That shows talent. That shows aptitude. Bonsai killer weed work, he does that all the time. Connie knows she can trust him. Some people she strings along, but him she always pays with a ready smile and a touch along his arm or one quick knuckle push at his hip. Cash or buds, she pays him, and that's all good. Just as it is good no one knows what Jason has in his backpack. No one knows his business.

Still, he knows, the day is coming. Someone is going to snatch him up right off the road or outside the liquor store downtown—some old guy maybe, or even one of them scary old dykes from out the bay side of the Jenner beach. Those bitches are dangerous and he can barely imagine what they would do with a piece of work like him. Everyone knows they all got stuff, guns and money and stuff. Bitches like that stick together. But maybe it will be someone from nowhere nearby, some bunch of crazies with some plan he will never fully understand, that no one will understand.

He nods slowly, his hands gripping the straps tight as he imagines it—the snatch, the basement, the months alone and everything that comes after. He has been seeing it for a long time, the story in his head, the way it will happen. It was a dream the first time, a nightmare, grabby hands and the skin scraped off his knees—a nightmare of sweaty basement walls and dirt in his mouth. But by the third or fourth time he dreamed it, everything receded and it was not so nightmarish. He was fighting back and able to think. Then it was magical how he started thinking about it in the daytime, daydreaming it, planning what he would do, how he would handle things. Then what came after the snatch became more and more important. He had started imagining the person he would be afterward. He didn't think so much about the kidnapping then, or even the kidnappers. It was all about him and the basement and what he did down there, who he would become, who he was meant to become. It was set and in motion. It was coming, Jason was sure of it. Not that he thought he was psychic or anything, it was just that this big thing was coming, so big he could feel it, and he had thought it through and whatever happened, he was going to be ready.

He stumbles and stops. He is almost gasping, smelling the sweat on his neck, the dust on the road, the acrid breeze from the eucalyptus trees past the stand of old-growth stunted apple trees around the curve. He leans forward, stretching his back, and straightens to watch a turkey buzzard circling the hill to his left. No hurry. It is only half a mile to his mom's place, two twists in the road and an uphill grade. Jason shakes his head. He knows this road in its whole length, two and a half miles and every decrepit house along the way, every crumbling garage and leaning fence. Of course, everyone here also knows him, which is sometimes more than he can stand. But somewhere someone who does not know him is coming along, and they will change everything. He nods and resumes a steady pace. Everything will be made over—and he will never know when or why. It will be a mystery.

He thinks of the basement room, that dim space with the windows boarded over. Nothing much will be down there, but he won't need much. He would love a piano, of course, but a guitar is more the kind of thing you might find in a basement. Nothing fancy. Some dented old acoustic. Jason thinks about it, the throwaway object he will use. God knows what he will have to do to tune the thing. Not likely to be any help in the junk people keep in basements. But there will be paper or notebooks. The notebooks will have pages marked up, of course, but he can work around that, use the backs of pages or something. It is what he creates in the silence that will need to be written down, the songs or poems. Lyrics. He will write it all down—easy to imagine that—him singing to himself in the quiet. The pencil marks along the pages. Of course his music notation sucks. He's never been too good at that. He sighs and stops again.

Maybe there will be a recorder—some old thing probably. A little old tape recorder, not a good digital. But hey it will get the job done. He smiles and hears above him the turkey buzzard's awkward call. Ugly sound from an ugly bird. He watches a big white pickup truck drive slowly up and past him. Big metal locks clamp down on the storage bin at the front of the truck bed.

Connie's boyfriend, Grange, told Jason you could bust most of those locks with the right chisel and mallet. "It's all in the angle. Got to hit it right."

Jason has a chisel in his backpack but no mallet. He licks his lips and resumes his slow hike between the ditch and the road. You got to have the right stuff to get anything done. Unless you are lucky or have an edge.

Famous is the way to go, he thinks. You get stuff once you are famous.

Jason wipes sweat off his neck as he walks and imagines it again—the reporter, the camera, the intensity of the lights, the intensity of his genius. It will take time, but he will figure it out. Maybe it won't be music. Maybe it will be words. He's damn good with words, not like those assholes at school who talk all the time. He knows the value of words, keeps them in his head, not always spilling them out like they mean nothing. He doesn't have to tell what he knows. He just knows—lyrics and poetry and all that stuff. Good poetry, he tells himself. Not that crap they want him to read in school. Kind of stuff makes your neck go stiff, that kind of poetry, that's what he likes. He looks at the dust on his hand, sweat-darkened and spotted with little grey-green bits. Little nubbins of weeds and grass flung up with the dust as the trucks pass. He'll get on the computer tonight, look up all the words for grey-green. Emerald, olive-drab, unripe fruit, something or the other. Nothing too hard about getting the words right.

Jason wipes his hands on his jeans, enjoying the feel of the fabric under his palms. Truth is more important than how you tell it, he thinks. And he knows stuff, lots of stuff, secrets and stuff. He has stories.

Maybe that will be it, the stories he tells himself to pass the time. Movie scripts, plays, dialogues between characters that come and go when he is all gaunt and feverish. In the basement, they won't feed him much, so he will get all dramatic skinny and probably have lots of fever dreams. He'll write them down, everything. His hands will cramp and he'll go on writing, get up and pace back and forth and write some more. Pages on pages will pile up. He'll bathe his face in cool water and walk some more. He'll drink so much water his skin will clear up. His mom is always telling him that if he washed his face more, drank more water and yeah, and ate more vegetables, his skin would do that right away. Maybe she has a point. Maybe in the basement that's all they will give him. Vegetables and water—lots of water, 'cause you know they ain't gonna waste no greasy expensive stuff on no captive. No Coke, no potato chips, no Kentucky Fried Chicken.

Pure water and rivers of words. Jason grins and lengthens his stride. Maybe after a while he won't care what he eats, or he will learn to make an apple taste like a pie. That would be the kind of thing might happen. He could learn to eat imaginary meals and taste every bite—donuts and hot barbecue wings—and stay all skinny and pure. That would be something. He could teach people how to do that afterwards maybe. Some day he might run an ashram like the one his mama used to talk about.

The turkey buzzard swoops low and arcs downhill toward the river. Jason stops to watch its flight. A moment in time and the bird disappears. Things can change that fast. Anything could happen and you can't predict what might come along. But what he knows is that there won't be any distractions down in the basement, anything to get in the way. Cold walls and dim light and maybe just a shower. Might be it will only run cold water, but he can handle that. What he hates is tub baths, sitting in dirty water. No way there is not gonna be a shower in the basement, or, all right, maybe only a hose and a drain in the floor. But he knows he will bathe himself a lot 'cause what else will there be to do? 'Cept write what he knows and use the weights set. He laughs out loud. Maybe there won't be no weights, though every shed or garage he knows has some stacked in some corner or the other. If there's nothing like that in his basement, still there will be stuff, something he can use.

He grabs his backpack straps again and begins the uphill grade. His steps slow and he focuses on the notion of making do, figuring out what he will use. Stuff like old cans of paint or bundles of rebar or bricks left lying around. He'll Tarantino it all, laying on the concrete floor and pushing up and down over and over till his arms get all muscled, and his legs too. He'll push off against the wall or doorjamb or something. He's gonna be bored out of his mind. He'll get desperate. He'll be working out, running in place and lifting heavy things—whatever he finds. Yeah, he'll get pretty well muscled. He grins. That is how it will be. He's going to come out just amazing.

Jason looks up the road, quarter of a mile to his mom's turnoff. He's right at the spot where the old firebreak cuts uphill, right up to his dad's place. He can almost see around the redwoods along the hill up to the house. He won't be like his dad, he thinks, he won't waste his chances. He'll grab what comes and run with it. When he comes out of that basement, he'll be slick. That is what it is all gonna be. Slick and sure, and he will know how to manage it, not wind up house-sitting for some crappy old guy wants you to carry stuff and keep an eye on the dogs.

Fuck it. Jason says it out loud. "Fuck it!" He's gonna come out of that basement Brad-Pitt handsome and ready for anything. He'll be ready, all soulful and quirky like that guy from the White Stripes, only he won't take himself too seriously. Everyone else will do that for him. He'll know how to behave.

Jason laughs out loud again. "Yeah," he says. Yeah.

Serious. Yes. That's the word. He is going to be seriously famous.

That's when his mom will realize how shitty she has treated him. Then his dad will hear about it, for sure—and maybe let him come back up to the house and hang out. Of course that creep that owns the property will be around too, but Jason knows it won't be scary like last time. He'll have all those muscles, and he will have gotten past being scared of small shit like grabby old guys and dads that don't give a shit.

It will be different. It will all be different. His mom and his dad will work it all out. His dad will be his manager, his mom will take over the press stuff. You got to have someone handle that stuff, and if the creepy guy comes round to stake some kind of claim, it won't be no big deal. Everyone will know how to handle him—what to believe and what to laugh at. He can almost hear his dad talking loud in his growly hoarse voice. He can hear him finally saying what he wanted him to say before.

"Jason didn't take nothing off you, old man. Look at him. What would he need off you?"

Yeah.

But maybe he will let the old guy hang around. Jason thinks about it, looking uphill and remembering. He gnaws at the nail on his left little finger.

Maybe not.

Why would he want that old bastard around?

He thinks about his dad, what he looks like now, all puffy and grey around the eyes with his hair so thin on top. His dad had this belly on him that he tries to hide under loose shirts, and he's always worried about money and stuff. That kind of old is embarrassing. After the basement though, his dad will be all different. He'll be old, but not so gross. He'll be more like Clint Eastwood old, craggy and wise. That's the notion, and his dad will have figured stuff out all that time worrying about Jason. Things will be different once he sees his son clear. Maybe he'll even own the property by then. The old guy can't live forever. Maybe he'll just give his dad the top of the hill as a kind of death tip. Might be it will turn out like that guy in Forestville a few years back, that black guy who got the thirty acres in the will of the man he worked for all that time.

That could happen. And then if his dad needs someone to help him with things, Jason will be there. That bad leg will hurt his dad a lot by then, even though he will try not to show it. Jason could do stuff—carry things for him and give him a hand. Maybe that is how they work it out—all the anger and guilt and shame and resentment. He can see that too, hear how it will go, them finally talking.

"You had no business running off like that, leaving Mom and me, I was just a little kid."

"You don't know how it was, how desperate I had gotten. I couldn't take care of you the way I wanted to, and you know your mom. She was always telling me I was lazy and the world wasn't gonna wait for me to get myself together."

That was just the kind of thing his mom said all the time. Jason nods. His mom can be a real pain in the ass. He sees himself looking at his dad and trying to imagine how he had felt when he had left. Maybe his dad had left in order to get himself together, to try and make something of himself so he could come back and take good care of them. After all that time cold and miserable and hungry in the basement, he will be able to feel stuff differently. Even standing in the dust of the road he can imagine his dad looking at him with an open face. Maybe they could talk finally, and it would shift all the anger around.

Maybe his dad will get to the point where he can look at him and see Jason clearly, see how he became so strong in that basement. Maybe he will finally see himself in his son. Of course, like everyone, his dad will know the story, how the kidnappers beat him, and starved him, and how Jason endured everything and stood up to them. It will make stuff in his dad shift around. He will get all wet-eyed and ashamed of himself. Jason can see that—the moment between them as real as the interviewer and the cameras, the moment burning him right through to his backbone. He almost sobs out loud, but then stops himself. His eyes are closed. The wind is picking up the way it always does as the afternoon settles toward evening. There is a birdcall somewhere up in the trees, but Jason is inside seeing into what is coming, what has to come.

They will touch each other like men do. Men. Yeah. Maybe his dad will embrace him, say his name. Jason can see that. It is as clear as anything. That is how it is in stories, how it is in his head, how it could be.

Jason sways a little there by the side of the road in the sun's heat. His ears are ringing with electric cricket sounds, the buzzard's cries, and the movement of the wind. Still, he hears a vehicle coming and the sound of its tires on the gritty tarmac. Rock and redwood debris grinding into dust and crackling as the wheels turn into the bend. Jason can see that, the wheels revolving and grinding forward. He imagines the kidnapper's truck, white and thick like one of those big Dodge Fat Boys, but one with a camper on the back—just the thing for snatching a guy off the road. Slowly Jason lets his face relax into a lazy smile. He doesn't look back. He keeps his eyes forward. His mom is always telling him to stop living in a dream, to be in the real world. But this is the real world, the road and the truck and everything that is coming toward him.

Anything can happen any time.

Everything can change, and it is going to, any time now.

Any time.

Any time.

Now.

2009

SHERWOOD ANDERSON
1876–1941

Anderson was born in Camden, Ohio, the son of a roving, likable, improvident, and talkative man who often appears under one name or another in Anderson's works. After some intermittent schooling, Anderson enlisted in the army for service in Cuba during the Spanish-American War. A few years later—in the spirit of rebellion against industrial and commercial civilization that was to color his writing thereafter—he "left business for literature," as he later put it, when he walked out of his job as manager of an Ohio paint factory. Going to Chicago, then in the ferment of a literary renaissance, he wrote feverishly and soon began to publish his own poetry and fiction. With the appearance in 1919 of *Winesburg, Ohio,* he became famous. As in the collections that followed, the stories of this book show life and desire frustrated by the provincialism of the Midwest. Characteristic of his work is a tone of melancholy reminiscence in which he projects remembered realities on the screen of a philosophic imagination. His autobiography, *A Story-Teller's Story* (1924), is partly fictional, as most of his fiction is partly autobiographical. His novels include *Windy McPherson's Son* (1916), *Poor White* (1920), *Many Marriages* (1923), and *Dark Laughter* (1925). His later collections of stories are *The Triumph of the Egg* (1921), *Horses and Men* (1923), and *Death in the Woods and Other Stories* (1933).

I Want to Know Why

We got up at four in the morning, that first day in the East. On the evening before, we had climbed off a freight train at the edge of town and with the true instinct of Kentucky boys had found our way across town and to the race track and the stables at once. Then we knew we were all right. Hanley Turner right away found a nigger we knew. It was Bildad Johnson, who in the winter works at Ed Becker's livery barn in our home town, Beckersville. Bildad is a good cook as almost all our niggers are and of course he, like everyone in our part of Kentucky who is anyone at all, likes the horses. In the spring Bildad begins to scratch around. A nigger from our country can flatter and wheedle anyone into letting him do most anything he wants. Bildad wheedles the stable men and the trainers from the horse farms in our country around Lexington. The trainers come into town in the evening to stand around and talk and maybe get into a poker game. Bildad gets in with them. He is always doing little favors and telling about things to eat, chicken browned in a pan, and how is the best way to cook sweet potatoes and corn bread. It makes your mouth water to hear him.

When the racing season comes on and the horses go to the races and there is all the talk on the streets in the evenings about the new colts, and everyone says when they are going over to Lexington or to the spring meeting at Churchill Downs or to Latonia,[1] and the horsemen that have been down to New Orleans or maybe at the winter meeting at Havana in Cuba[2] come home to spend a week before they start out again, at such a time when everything talked about in Beckersville is just horses and nothing else and the outfits start out and horse racing is in every breath of air you breathe, Bildad shows up with a job as cook for some outfit. Often when I think about it, his always going all season to the races and working in the livery barn in the winter where horses are and where men like to come and talk about horses, I wish I was a nigger. It's a foolish thing to say, but that's the way I am about being around horses, just crazy. I can't help it.

Well, I must tell you about what we did and let you in on what I'm talking about. Four of us boys from Beckersville, all whites and sons of men who live in Beckersville regular, made up our minds we were going to the races, not just to Lexington or Louisville, I don't mean, but to the big eastern track we were always hearing our Beckersville men talk about, to Saratoga.[3] We were all pretty young then. I was just turned fifteen and I was the oldest of the four. It was my scheme. I admit that, and I talked the others into trying it. There was Hanley Turner and Henry Rieback and Tom Tumberton and myself. I had thirty-seven dollars I had earned during the winter working nights and Saturdays in Enoch Myer's grocery. Henry Rieback had eleven dollars and the others, Hanley and Tom, had only a dollar or two each. We fixed it all up and laid low until the Kentucky spring meetings were over and some of our men, the sportiest ones, the ones we envied the most, had cut out. Then we cut out too.

I won't tell you the trouble we had beating our way on freights and all. We went through Cleveland and Buffalo and other cities and saw Niagara Falls. We bought things there, souvenirs and spoons and cards and shells with pictures of the falls on them for our sisters and mothers, but thought we had better not send any of the things home. We didn't want to put the folks on our trail and maybe be nabbed.

We got into Saratoga as I said at night and went to the track. Bildad fed us up. He showed us a place to sleep in hay over a shed and promised to keep still. Niggers are all right about things like that. They won't squeal on you. Often a white man you might meet, when you had run away from home like that, might appear to be all right and give you a quarter or a half dollar or something, and then go right and give you away. White men will do that, but not a nigger. You can trust them. They are squarer with kids. I don't know why.

At the Saratoga meeting that year there were a lot of men from home. Dave Williams and Arthur Mulford and Jerry Myers and others. Then there was a lot from Louisville and Lexington Henry Rieback knew but I didn't. They were professional gamblers and Henry Rieback's father is one too. He is what is called a sheet writer and goes away most of the year to tracks. In the winter when he is home in Beckersville he don't stay there much but goes away to cit-

1. Racetrack in Covington, Kentucky. *Churchill Downs:* the famous track in Louisville, Kentucky, where the Kentucky Derby is run every year.   2. That is, the horse-racing season in Havana.   3. Famous resort town and site of a racetrack in upstate New York.

ies and deals faro.[4] He is a nice man and generous, is always sending Henry presents, a bicycle and a gold watch and a boy scout suit of clothes and things like that.

My own father is a lawyer. He's all right, but don't make much money and can't buy me things, and anyway I'm getting so old now I don't expect it. He never said nothing to me against Henry, but Hanley Turner and Tom Tumberton's fathers did. They said to their boys that money so come by is no good and they didn't want their boys brought up to hear gamblers' talk and be thinking about such things and maybe embrace them.

That's all right and I guess the men know what they are talking about, but I don't see what it's got to do with Henry or with horses either. That's what I'm writing this story about. I'm puzzled. I'm getting to be a man and want to think straight and be O.K., and there's something I saw at the race meeting at the eastern track I can't figure out.

I can't help it, I'm crazy about thoroughbred horses, I've always been that way. When I was ten years old and saw I was growing to be big and couldn't be a rider I was so sorry I nearly died. Harry Hellinfinger in Beckersville, whose father is Postmaster, is grown up and too lazy to work, but likes to stand around in the street and get up jokes on boys like sending them to a hardware store for a gimlet to bore square holes and other jokes like that. He played one on me. He told me that if I would eat a half a cigar I would be stunted and not grow any more and maybe could be a rider. I did it. When father wasn't looking I took a cigar out of his pocket and gagged it down some way. It made me awful sick and the doctor had to be sent for, and then it did no good. I kept right on growing. It was a joke. When I told what I had done and why, most fathers would have whipped me, but mine didn't.

Well, I didn't get stunted and didn't die. It serves Harry Hellinfinger right. Then I made up my mind I would like to be a stableboy, but had to give that up too. Mostly niggers do that work and I knew father wouldn't let me go into it. No use to ask him.

If you've never been crazy about thoroughbreds, it's because you've never been around where they are much and don't know any better. They're beautiful. There isn't anything so lovely and clean and full of spunk and honest and everything as some race horses. On the big horse farms that are all around our town Beckersville there are tracks, and the horses run in the early morning. More than a thousand times I've got out of bed before daylight and walked two or three miles to the tracks. Mother wouldn't of let me go, but father always says, "Let him alone." So I got some bread out of the breadbox and some butter and jam, gobbled it and lit out.

At the tracks you sit on the fence with men, whites and niggers, and they chew tobacco and talk, and then the colts are brought out. It's early and the grass is covered with shiny dew and in another field a man is plowing and they are frying things in a shed where the track niggers sleep, and you know how a nigger can giggle and laugh and say things that make you laugh. A white man can't do it and some niggers can't, but a track nigger can every time.

And so the colts are brought out and some are just galloped by stableboys, but almost every morning on a big track owned by a rich man who lives maybe

---

4. A card game, favorite of gamblers. *Sheet writer:* a bookmaker.

in New York, there are always, nearly every morning, a few colts and some of the old race horses and geldings and mares that are cut loose.

It brings a lump up into my throat when a horse runs. I don't mean all horses, but some. I can pick them nearly every time. It's in my blood like in the blood of race track niggers and trainers. Even when they just go slop-jogging along with a little nigger on their backs, I can tell a winner. If my throat hurts and it's hard for me to swallow, that's him. He'll run like Sam Hill[5] when you let him out. If he don't win every time it'll be a wonder and because they've got him in a pocket behind another or he was pulled or got off bad at the post or something. If I wanted to be a gambler like Henry Rieback's father I could get rich. I know I could and Henry says so too. All I would have to do is to wait till that hurt comes when I see a horse and then bet every cent. That's what I would do if I wanted to be a gambler, but I don't.

When you're at the tracks in the morning—not the race tracks but the training tracks around Beckersville—you don't see a horse, the kind I've been talking about, very often, but it's nice anyway. Any thoroughbred, that is sired right and out of a good mare and trained by a man that knows how, can run. If he couldn't, what would he be there for and not pulling a plow?

Well, out of the stables they come and the boys are on their backs and it's lovely to be there. You hunch down on top of the fence and itch inside you. Over in the sheds the niggers giggle and sing. Bacon is being fried and coffee made. Everything smells lovely. Nothing smells better than coffee and manure and horses and niggers and bacon frying and pipes being smoked out of doors on a morning like that. It just gets you, that's what it does.

But about Saratoga. We was there six days and not a soul from home seen us and everything came off just as we wanted it to, fine weather and horses and races and all. We beat our way home and Bildad gave us a basket with fried chicken and bread and other eatables in, and I had eighteen dollars when we got back to Beckersville. Mother jawed and cried, but Pop didn't say much. I told everything we done, except one thing. I did and saw that alone. That's what I'm writing about. It got me upset. I think about it at night. Here it is.

At Saratoga we laid up nights in the hay in the shed Bildad had showed us and ate with the niggers early and at night when the race people had all gone away. The men from home stayed mostly in the grandstand and betting field and didn't come out around the places where the horses are kept except to the paddocks just before a race when the horses are saddled. At Saratoga they don't have paddocks under an open shed as at Lexington and Churchill Downs and other tracks down in our country, but saddle the horses right out in an open place under trees on a lawn as smooth and nice as Banker Bohon's front yard here in Beckersville. It's lovely. The horses are sweaty and nervous and shine and the men come out and smoke cigars and look at them and the trainers are there and the owners, and your heart thumps so you can hardly breathe.

Then the bugle blows for post and the boys that ride come running out with their silk clothes on and you run to get a place by the fence with the niggers.

I always am wanting to be a trainer or owner, and at the risk of being seen and caught and sent home I went to the paddocks before every race. The other boys didn't, but I did.

5. Euphemism for hell.

We got to Saratoga on a Friday, and on Wednesday the next week the big Mullford Handicap was to be run. Middlestride was in it and Sunstreak. The weather was fine and the track fast. I couldn't sleep the night before.

What had happened was that both these horses are the kind it makes my throat hurt to see. Middlestride is long and looks awkward and is a gelding. He belongs to Joe Thompson, a little owner from home who only has half a dozen horses. The Mullford Handicap is for a mile and Middlestride can't untrack fast. He goes away slow and is always 'way back at the half, then he begins to run and if the race is a mile and a quarter he'll just eat up everything and get there.

Sunstreak is different. He is a stallion and nervous and belongs on the biggest farm we've got in our country, the Van Riddle place that belongs to Mr. Van Riddle of New York. Sunstreak is like a girl you think about sometimes but never see. He is hard all over and lovely too. When you look at his head you want to kiss him. He is trained by Jerry Tillford who knows me and has been good to me lots of times, lets me walk into a horse's stall to look at him close and other things. There isn't anything as sweet as that horse. He stands at the post quiet and not letting on, but he is just burning up inside. Then when the barrier goes up he is off like his name, Sunstreak. It makes you ache to see him. It hurts you. He just lays down and runs like a bird dog. There can't anything I ever see run like him except Middlestride when he gets untracked and stretches himself.

Gee! I ached to see that race and those two horses run, ached and dreaded it too. I didn't want to see either of our horses beaten. We had never sent a pair like that to the races before. Old men in Beckersville said so and the niggers said so. It was a fact.

Before the race, I went over to the paddocks to see. I looked a last look at Middlestride, who isn't such a much standing in a paddock that way, then I went to see Sunstreak.

It was his day. I knew when I see him. I forgot all about being seen myself and walked right up. All the men from Beckersville were there and no one noticed me except Jerry Tillford. He saw me and something happened. I'll tell you about that.

I was standing looking at that horse and aching. In some way, I can't tell how, I knew just how Sunstreak felt inside. He was quiet and letting the niggers rub his legs and Mr. Van Riddle himself put the saddle on, but he was just a raging torrent inside. He was like the water in the river at Niagara Falls just before it goes plunk down. That horse wasn't thinking about running. He don't have to think about that. He was just thinking about holding himself back till the time for the running came. I knew that. I could just in a way see right inside him. He was going to do some awful running and I knew it. He wasn't bragging or letting on much or prancing or making a fuss, but just waiting. I knew it and Jerry Tillford his trainer knew. I looked up, and then that man and I looked into each other's eyes. Something happened to me. I guess I loved the man as much as I did the horse because he knew what I knew. Seemed to me there wasn't anything in the world but that man and the horse and me. I cried and Jerry Tillford had a shine in his eyes. Then I came away to the fence to wait for the race. The horse was better than me, more steadier and, now I know, better than Jerry. He was the quietest and he had to do the running.

Sunstreak ran first of course and he busted the world's record for a mile. I've seen that if I never see anything more. Everything came out just as I expected. Middlestride got left at the post and was 'way back and closed up to be second, just as I knew he would. He'll get a world's record too some day. They can't skin the Beckersville country on horses.

I watched the race calm because I knew what would happen. I was sure. Hanley Turner and Henry Rieback and Tom Tumberton were all more excited than me.

A funny thing that happened to me. I was thinking about Jerry Tillford the trainer and how happy he was all through the race. I liked him that afternoon even more than I ever liked my own father. I almost forgot the horses thinking that way about him. It was because of what I had seen in his eyes as he stood in the paddocks beside Sunstreak before the race started. I knew he had been watching and working with Sunstreak since the horse was a baby colt, had taught him to run and be patient and when to let himself out and not to quit, never. I knew that for him it was like a mother seeing her child do something brave or wonderful. It was the first time I ever felt for a man like that.

After the race that night I cut out from Tom and Hanley and Henry. I wanted to be by myself and I wanted to be near Jerry Tillford if I could work it. Here is what happened.

The track in Saratoga is near the edge of town. It is all polished up and trees around, the evergreen kind, and grass and everything painted and nice. If you go past the track you get to a hard road made of asphalt for automobiles, and if you go along this for a few miles there is a road turns off to a little rummy-looking farmhouse set in a yard.

That night after the race I went along that road because I had seen Jerry and some other men go that way in an automobile. I didn't expect to find them. I walked for a ways and then sat down by a fence to think. It was the direction they went in. I wanted to be as near Jerry as I could. I felt close to him. Pretty soon I went up the side road—I don't know why—and came to the rummy farmhouse. I was just lonesome to see Jerry, like wanting to see your father at night when you are a young kid. Just then an automobile came along and turned in. Jerry was in it and Henry Rieback's father, and Arthur Bedford from home, and Dave Williams and two other men I didn't know. They got out of the car and went into the house, all but Henry Rieback's father who quarreled with them and said he wouldn't go. It was only about nine o'clock, but they were all drunk and the rummy-looking farmhouse was a place for bad women to stay in. That's what it was. I crept up along a fence and looked through a window and saw.

It's what give me the fantods.[6] I can't make it out. The women in the house were all ugly mean-looking women, not nice to look at or be near. They were homely too, except one who was tall and looked a little like the gelding Middlestride, but not clean like him, but with a hard ugly mouth. She had red hair. I saw everything plain. I got up by an old rosebush by an open window and looked. The women had on loose dresses and sat around in chairs. The men came in and some sat on the women's laps. The place smelled rotten and there was rotten talk, the kind a kid hears around a livery stable in a town like Beck-

---

6. Slang for being very shaken and upset.

ersville in the winter but don't ever expect to hear talked when there are women around. It was rotten. A nigger wouldn't go into such a place.

I looked at Jerry Tillford. I've told you how I had been feeling about him on account of his knowing what was going on inside of Sunstreak in the minute before he went to the post for the race in which he made a world's record.

Jerry bragged in that bad woman house as I knew Sunstreak wouldn't never have bragged. He said that he made that horse, that it was him that won the race and made the record. He lied and bragged like a fool. I never heard such silly talk.

And then, what do you suppose he did! He looked at the woman in there, the one that was lean and hard-mouthed and looked a little like the gelding Middlestride but not clean like him, and his eyes began to shine just as they did when he looked at me and at Sunstreak in the paddocks at the track in the afternoon. I stood there by the window—gee!—but I wished I hadn't gone away from the tracks, but had stayed with the boys and the niggers and the horses. The tall rotten-looking woman was between us just as Sunstreak was in the paddocks in the afternoon.

Then, all of a sudden, I began to hate that man. I wanted to scream and rush in the room and kill him. I never had such a feeling before. I was so mad clean through that I cried and my fists were doubled up so my fingernails cut my hands.

And Jerry's eyes kept shining and he waved back and forth, and then he went and kissed that woman and I crept away and went back to the tracks and to bed and didn't sleep hardly any, and then next day I got the other kids to start home with me and never told them anything I seen.

I been thinking about it ever since. I can't make it out. Spring has come again and I'm nearly sixteen and go to the tracks mornings same as always, and I see Sunstreak and Middlestride and a new colt named Strident I'll bet will lay them all out, but no one thinks so but me and two or three niggers.

But things are different. At the tracks the air don't taste as good or smell as good. It's because a man like Jerry Tillford, who knows what he does, could see a horse like Sunstreak run, and kiss a woman like that the same day. I can't make it out. Darn him, what did he want to do like that for? I kept thinking about it and it spoils looking at horses and smelling things and hearing niggers laugh and everything. Sometimes I'm so mad about it I want to fight someone. It gives me the fantods. What did he do it for? I want to know why.

1921

MARGARET ATWOOD
b. 1939

Atwood was born in Ottawa, Ontario, the daughter of an entomologist. Much of her childhood was spent in isolated wilderness areas of northern Ontario and Quebec, where she grew to love nature and the companionship of books. After her education at the University of Toronto, Radcliffe, and Harvard, she held various jobs as cashier, waitress, market-research writer, and writer of screenplays. Atwood's poetry and fiction have garnered many awards, including—twice—Canada's highest literary honor, the Governor General's Award. Her novels include *The Edible Woman* (1969), *Surfacing* (1972), *Lady Oracle* (1976), *Life before Man* (1979), *The Handmaid's Tale* (1985), *Cat's Eye* (1988), *The Robber Bride* (1993), *The Blind Assassin* (winner of Britain's prestigious Booker Prize, 2000), *Oryx and Crake* (2003), *The Penelopiad* (2005), *The Year of the Flood* (2009), and *MaddAddam* (2013). Many of her stories have been collected in *Dancing Girls and Other Stories* (1978), *Murder in the Dark* (1983), *Bluebeard's Egg* (1983), *Wilderness Tips* (1991), *Good Bones* (1992), *Curious Pursuits* (2005), *The Tent* (2006), *Moral Disorder* (2006), and *Stone Mattress* (2014).

Death by Landscape

Now that the boys are grown up and Rob is dead, Lois has moved to a condominium apartment in one of the new waterfront developments. She is relieved not to have to worry about the lawn, or about the ivy pushing its muscular little suckers into the brickwork, or the squirrels gnawing their way into the attic and eating the insulation off the wiring, or about strange noises. This building has a security system, and the only plant life is in pots in the solarium.

Lois is glad she's been able to find an apartment big enough for her pictures. They are more crowded together than they were in the house, but this arrangement gives the walls a European look: blocks of pictures, above and beside one another, rather than one over the chesterfield, one over the fireplace, one in the front hall, in the old acceptable manner of sprinkling art around so it does not get too intrusive. This way has more of an impact. You know it's not supposed to be furniture.

None of the pictures is very large, which doesn't mean they aren't valuable. They are paintings, or sketches and drawings, by artists who were not nearly as well known when Lois began to buy them as they are now. Their work later turned up on stamps, or as silk-screen reproductions hung in the principals' offices of high schools, or as jigsaw puzzles, or on beautifully printed calendars sent out by corporations as Christmas gifts, to their less important clients. These artists painted mostly in the twenties and thirties and forties; they painted landscapes. Lois has two Tom Thomsons, three A. Y. Jacksons, a Lawren Harris. She has an Arthur Lismer, she has a J. E. H. MacDonald. She has a David Milne. They are pictures of convoluted tree trunks on an island of pink wave-smoothed stone, with more islands behind; of a lake with rough, bright, sparsely wooded cliffs; of a vivid river shore with a tangle of bush and two beached canoes, one red, one gray; of a yellow autumn woods with the ice-blue gleam of a pond half-seen through the interlaced branches.

It was Lois who'd chosen them. Rob had no interest in art, although he could see the necessity of having something on the walls. He left all the decorating decisions to her, while providing the money, of course. Because of this collection of hers, Lois's friends—especially the men—have given her the reputation of having a good nose for art investments.

But this is not why she bought the pictures, way back then. She bought them because she wanted them. She wanted something that was in them, although she could not have said at the time what it was. It was not peace: she does not find them peaceful in the least. Looking at them fills her with a wordless unease. Despite the fact that there are no people in them or even animals, it's as if there is something, or someone, looking back out.

When she was thirteen, Lois went on a canoe trip. She'd only been on overnights before. This was to be a long one, into the trackless wilderness, as Cappie put it. It was Lois's first canoe trip, and her last.

Cappie was the head of the summer camp to which Lois had been sent ever since she was nine. Camp Manitou, it was called; it was one of the better ones, for girls, though not the best. Girls of her age whose parents could afford it were routinely packed off to such camps, which bore a generic resemblance to one another. They favored Indian names and had hearty, energetic leaders, who were called Cappie or Skip or Scottie. At these camps you learned to swim well and sail, and paddle a canoe, and perhaps ride a horse or play tennis. When you weren't doing these things you could do Arts and Crafts and turn out dingy, lumpish clay ashtrays for your mother—mothers smoked more, then—or bracelets made of colored braided string.

Cheerfulness was required at all times, even at breakfast. Loud shouting and the banging of spoons on the tables were allowed, and even encouraged, at ritual intervals. Chocolate bars were rationed, to control tooth decay and pimples. At night, after supper, in the dining hall or outside around a mosquito-infested campfire ring for special treats, there were singsongs. Lois can still remember all the words to "My Darling Clementine," and "My Bonnie Lies over the Ocean," with acting-out gestures: a rippling of the hands for "the ocean," two hands together under the cheek for "lies." She will never be able to forget them, which is a sad thought.

Lois thinks she can recognize women who went to these camps, and were good at it. They have a hardness to their handshakes, even now; a way of standing, legs planted firmly and farther apart than usual; a way of sizing you up, to see if you'd be any good in a canoe—the front, not the back. They themselves would be in the back. They would call it the stern.

She knows that such camps still exist, although Camp Manitou does not. They are one of the few things that haven't changed much. They now offer copper enameling, and functionless pieces of stained glass baked in electric ovens, though judging from the productions of her friends' grandchildren the artistic standards have not improved.

To Lois, encountering it in the first year after the war, Camp Manitou seemed ancient. Its log-sided buildings with the white cement in between the half-logs, its flagpole ringed with whitewashed stones, its weathered gray dock jutting out into Lake Prospect, with its woven rope bumpers and its rusty rings for tying up, its prim round flowerbed of petunias near the office door, must surely have been there always. In truth it dated only from the first decade of the century; it had been founded by Cappie's parents, who'd thought of camping as bracing to the character, like cold showers, and had been passed along to her as an inheritance, and an obligation.

Lois realized, later, that it must have been a struggle for Cappie to keep Camp Manitou going, during the Depression and then the war, when money did not flow freely. If it had been a camp for the very rich, instead of the merely well off, there would have been fewer problems. But there must have been enough Old Girls, ones with daughters, to keep the thing in operation, though not entirely shipshape: furniture was battered, painted trim was peeling, roofs leaked. There were dim photographs of these Old Girls dotted around the dining hall, wearing ample woolen bathing suits and showing their fat, dimpled legs, or standing, arms twined, in odd tennis outfits with baggy skirts.

In the dining hall, over the stone fireplace that was never used, there was a huge molting stuffed moosehead, which looked somehow carnivorous. It was a sort of mascot; its name was Monty Manitou. The older campers spread the story that it was haunted, and came to life in the dark, when the feeble and undependable lights had been turned off or, due to yet another generator failure, had gone out. Lois was afraid of it at first, but not after she got used to it.

Cappie was the same: you had to get used to her. Possibly she was forty, or thirty-five, or fifty. She had fawn-colored hair that looked as if it was cut with a bowl. Her head jutted forward, jigging like a chicken's as she strode around the camp, clutching notebooks and checking things off in them. She was like their minister in church: both of them smiled a lot and were anxious because they wanted things to go well; they both had the same overwashed skins and stringy necks. But all this disappeared when Cappie was leading a singsong, or otherwise leading. Then she was happy, sure of herself, her plain face almost luminous. She wanted to cause joy. At these times she was loved, at others merely trusted.

There were many things Lois didn't like about Camp Manitou, at first. She hated the noisy chaos and spoon-banging of the dining hall, the rowdy singsongs at which you were expected to yell in order to show that you were enjoying yourself. Hers was not a household that encouraged yelling. She hated the necessity of having to write dutiful letters to her parents claiming she was having fun. She could not complain, because camp cost so much money.

She didn't much like having to undress in a roomful of other girls, even in the dim light, although nobody paid any attention, or sleeping in a cabin with seven other girls, some of whom snored because they had adenoids or colds, some of whom had nightmares, or wet their beds and cried about it. Bottom bunks made her feel closed in, and she was afraid of falling out of top ones;

she was afraid of heights. She got homesick, and suspected her parents of having a better time when she wasn't there than when she was, although her mother wrote to her every week saying how much they missed her. All this was when she was nine. By the time she was thirteen she liked it. She was an old hand by then.

Lucy was her best friend at camp. Lois had other friends in winter, when there was school and itchy woolen clothing and darkness in the afternoons, but Lucy was her summer friend.

She turned up the second year, when Lois was ten, and a Bluejay. (Chickadees, Bluejays, Ravens, and Kingfishers—these were the names Camp Manitou assigned to the different age groups, a sort of totemic clan system. In those days, thinks Lois, it was birds for girls, animals for boys: wolves, and so forth. Though some animals and birds were suitable and some were not. Never vultures, for instance; never skunks, or rats.)

Lois helped Lucy to unpack her tin trunk and place the folded clothes on the wooden shelves, and to make up her bed. She put her in the top bunk right above her, where she could keep an eye on her. Already she knew that Lucy was an exception to a good many rules; already she felt proprietorial.

Lucy was from the United States, where the comic books came from, and the movies. She wasn't from New York or Hollywood or Buffalo, the only American cities Lois knew the names of, but from Chicago. Her house was on the lake shore and had gates to it, and grounds. They had a maid, all of the time. Lois's family only had a cleaning lady twice a week.

The only reason Lucy was being sent to *this* camp (she cast a look of minor scorn around the cabin, diminishing it and also offending Lois, while at the same time daunting her) was that her mother had been a camper here. Her mother had been a Canadian once, but had married her father, who had a patch over one eye, like a pirate. She showed Lois the picture of him in her wallet. He got the patch in the war. "Shrapnel," said Lucy. Lois, who was unsure about shrapnel, was so impressed she could only grunt. Her own two-eyed, unwounded father was tame by comparison.

"My father plays golf," she ventured at last.

"*Everyone* plays golf," said Lucy. "My *mother* plays golf."

Lois's mother did not. Lois took Lucy to see the outhouses and the swimming dock and the dining hall with Monty Manitou's baleful head, knowing in advance they would not measure up.

This was a bad beginning; but Lucy was good-natured, and accepted Camp Manitou with the same casual shrug with which she seemed to accept everything. She would make the best of it, without letting Lois forget that this was what she was doing.

However, there were things Lois knew that Lucy did not. Lucy scratched the tops off all her mosquito bites and had to be taken to the infirmary to be daubed with Ozonol. She took her T-shirt off while sailing, and although the counselor spotted her after a while and made her put it back on, she burnt spectacularly, bright red, with the X of her bathing-suit straps standing out in alarming white; she let Lois peel the sheets of whispery-thin burned skin off her shoulders. When they sang "Alouette" around the campfire, she did not know any of the French words. The difference was that Lucy did not care about the things she didn't know, whereas Lois did.

During the next winter, and subsequent winters, Lucy and Lois wrote to each other. They were both only children, at a time when this was thought to be a disadvantage, so in their letters they pretended to be sisters, or even twins. Lois had to strain a little over this, because Lucy was so blond, with translucent skin and large blue eyes like a doll's, and Lois was nothing out of the ordinary—just a tallish, thinnish, brownish person with freckles. They signed their letters LL, with the L's entwined together like the monograms on a towel. (Lois and Lucy, thinks Lois. How our names date us. Lois Lane, Superman's girlfriend, enterprising female reporter; "I Love Lucy." Now we are obsolete, and it's little Jennifers, little Emilys, little Alexandras and Carolines and Tiffanys.)

They were more effusive in their letters than they ever were in person. They bordered their pages with X's and O's, but when they met again in the summers it was always a shock. They had changed so much, or Lucy had. It was like watching someone grow up in jolts. At first it would be hard to think up things to say.

But Lucy always had a surprise or two, or something to show, some marvel to reveal. The first year she had a picture of herself in a tutu, her hair in a ballerina's knot on the top of her head; she pirouetted around the swimming dock, to show Lois how it was done, and almost fell off. The next year she had given that up and was taking horseback riding. (Camp Manitou did not have horses.) The next year her mother and father had been divorced, and she had a new stepfather, one with both eyes, and a new house, although the maid was the same. The next year when they had graduated from Bluejays and entered Ravens, she got her period, right in the first week of camp. The two of them snitched some matches from their counselor, who smoked illegally, and made a small fire out behind the farthest outhouse, at dusk, using their flashlights. They could set all kinds of fires by now; they had learned how in Campcraft. On this fire they burned one of Lucy's used sanitary napkins. Lois is not sure why they did this, or whose idea it was. But she can remember the feeling of deep satisfaction it gave her as the white fluff singed and the blood sizzled, as if some wordless ritual had been fulfilled.

They did not get caught, but then they rarely got caught at any of their camp transgressions. Lucy had such large eyes, and was such an accomplished liar.

This year Lucy is different again: slower, more languorous. She is no longer interested in sneaking around after dark, purloining cigarettes from the counselor, dealing in black-market candy bars. She is pensive, and hard to wake in the mornings. She doesn't like her stepfather, but she doesn't want to live with her real father either, who has a new wife. She thinks her mother may be having a love affair with a doctor; she doesn't know for sure, but she's seen them smooching in his car, out on the driveway, when her stepfather wasn't there. It serves him right. She hates her private school. She has a boyfriend, who is sixteen and works as a gardener's assistant. This is how she met him: in the garden. She describes to Lois what it is like when he kisses her—rubbery at first, but then your knees go limp. She has been forbidden to see him, and threatened with boarding school. She wants to run away from home.

Lois has little to offer in return. Her own life is placid and satisfactory, but there is nothing much that can be said about happiness. "You're so lucky,"

Lucy tells her, a little smugly. She might as well say *boring* because this is how it makes Lois feel.

Lucy is apathetic about the canoe trip, so Lois has to disguise her own excitement. The evening before they are to leave, she slouches into the campfire ring as if coerced, and sits down with a sigh of endurance, just as Lucy does.

Every canoe trip that went out of camp was given a special send-off by Cappie and the section leader and counselors, with the whole section in attendance. Cappie painted three streaks of red across each of her cheeks with a lipstick. They looked like three-fingered claw marks. She put a blue circle on her forehead with fountain-pen ink, and tied a twisted bandanna around her head and stuck a row of frazzle-ended feathers around it, and wrapped herself in a red-and-black Hudson's Bay blanket. The counselors, also in blankets but with only two streaks of red, beat on tom-toms made of round wooden cheese boxes with leather stretched over the top and nailed in place. Cappie was Chief Cappeosota. They all had to say "How!" when she walked into the circle and stood there with one hand raised.

Looking back on this, Lois finds it disquieting. She knows too much about Indians: this is why. She knows, for instance, that they should not even be called Indians, and that they have enough worries without other people taking their names and dressing up as them. It has all been a form of stealing.

But she remembers, too, that she was once ignorant of this. Once she loved the campfire, the flickering of light on the ring of faces, the sound of the fake tom-toms, heavy and fast like a scared heartbeat; she loved Cappie in a red blanket and feathers, solemn, as a chief should be, raising her hand and saying, "Greetings, my Ravens." It was not funny, it was not making fun. She wanted to be an Indian. She wanted to be adventurous and pure, and aboriginal.

"You go on big water," says Cappie. This is her idea—all their ideas—of how Indians talk. "You go where no man has ever trod. You go many moons." This is not true. They are only going for a week, not many moons. The canoe route is clearly marked, they have gone over it on a map, and there are prepared campsites with names which are used year after year. But when Cappie says this—and despite the way Lucy rolls up her eyes—Lois can feel the water stretching out, with the shores twisting away on either side, immense and a little frightening.

"You bring back much wampum," says Cappie. "Do good in war, my braves, and capture many scalps." This is another of her pretenses: that they are boys, and bloodthirsty. But such a game cannot be played by substituting the word "squaw." It would not work at all.

Each of them has to stand up and step forward and have a red line drawn across her cheeks by Cappie. She tells them they must follow the paths of their ancestors (who most certainly, thinks Lois, looking out the window of her apartment and remembering the family stash of daguerreotypes and sepia-colored portraits on her mother's dressing table, the stiff-shirted, black-coated, grim-faced men and the beflounced women with their severe hair and their corseted respectability, would never have considered heading off onto an open lake, in a canoe, just for fun).

At the end of the ceremony they all stood and held hands around the circle, and sang taps. They did not sound very Indian, thinks Lois. It sounded like a bugle call at a military post, in a movie. But Cappie was never one to be much concerned with consistency, or with archeology.

After breakfast the next morning they set out from the main dock, in four canoes, three in each. The lipstick stripes have not come off completely, and still show faintly pink, like healing burns. They wear their white denim sailing hats, because of the sun, and thin-striped T-shirts, and pale baggy shorts with the cuffs rolled up. The middle one kneels, propping her rear end against the rolled sleeping bags. The counselors going with them are Pat and Kip. Kip is no-nonsense; Pat is easier to wheedle, or fool.

There are white puffy clouds and a small breeze. Glints come from the little waves. Lois is in the bow of Kip's canoe. She still can't do a J-stroke very well, and she will have to be in the bow or the middle for the whole trip. Lucy is behind her; her own J-stroke is even worse. She splashes Lois with her paddle, quite a big splash.

"I'll get you back," says Lois.

"There was a stable fly on your shoulder," Lucy says.

Lois turns to look at her, to see if she's grinning. They're in the habit of splashing each other. Back there, the camp has vanished behind the first long point of rock and rough trees. Lois feels as if an invisible rope has broken. They're floating free, on their own, cut loose. Beneath the canoe the lake goes down, deeper and colder than it was a minute before.

"No horsing around in the canoe," says Kip. She's rolled her T-shirt sleeves up to the shoulder; her arms are brown and sinewy, her jaw determined, her stroke perfect. She looks as if she knows exactly what she is doing.

The four canoes keep close together. They sing, raucously and with defiance; they sing "The Quartermaster's Store," and "Clementine," and "Alouette." It is more like bellowing than singing.

After that the wind grows stronger, blowing slantwise against the bows, and they have to put all their energy into shoving themselves through the water.

Was there anything important, anything that would provide some sort of reason or clue to what happened next? Lois can remember everything, every detail; but it does her no good.

They stopped at noon for a swim and lunch, and went on in the afternoon. At last they reached Little Birch, which was the first campsite for overnight. Lois and Lucy made the fire, while the others pitched the heavy canvas tents. The fireplace was already there, flat stones piled into a U. A burned tin can and a beer bottle had been left in it. Their fire went out, and they had to restart it. "Hustle your bustle," said Kip. "We're starving."

The sun went down, and in the pink sunset light they brushed their teeth and spat the toothpaste froth into the lake. Kip and Pat put all the food that wasn't in cans into a packsack and slung it into a tree, in case of bears.

Lois and Lucy weren't sleeping in a tent. They'd begged to be allowed to sleep out; that way they could talk without others hearing. If it rained, they told Kip, they promised not to crawl dripping into the tent over everyone's legs: they would get under the canoes. So they were out on the point.

Lois tried to get comfortable inside her sleeping bag, which smelled of musty storage and of earlier campers, a stale salty sweetness. She curled herself up, with her sweater rolled up under her head for a pillow and her flashlight inside her sleeping bag so it wouldn't roll away. The muscles of her sore arms were making small pings, like rubber bands breaking.

Beside her Lucy was rustling around. Lois could see the glimmering oval of her white face.

"I've got a rock poking into my back," said Lucy.

"So do I," said Lois. "You want to go into the tent?" She herself didn't, but it was right to ask.

"No," said Lucy. She subsided into her sleeping bag. After a moment she said, "It would be nice not to go back."

"To camp?" said Lois.

"To Chicago," said Lucy. "I hate it there."

"What about your boyfriend?" said Lois. Lucy didn't answer. She was either asleep or pretending to be.

There was a moon, and a movement of the trees. In the sky there were stars, layers of stars that went down and down. Kip said that when the stars were bright like that instead of hazy it meant bad weather later on. Out on the lake there were two loons, calling to each other in their insane, mournful voices. At the time it did not sound like grief. It was just background.

The lake in the morning was flat calm. They skimmed along over the glassy surface, leaving V-shaped trails behind them; it felt like flying. As the sun rose higher it got hot, almost too hot. There were stable flies in the canoes, landing on a bare arm or leg for a quick sting. Lois hoped for wind.

They stopped for lunch at the next of the named campsites, Lookout Point. It was called this because, although the site itself was down near the water on a flat shelf of rock, there was a sheer cliff nearby and a trail that led up to the top. The top was the lookout, although what you were supposed to see from there was not clear. Kip said it was just a view.

Lois and Lucy decided to make the climb anyway. They didn't want to hang around waiting for lunch. It wasn't their turn to cook, though they hadn't avoided much by not doing it, because cooking lunch was no big deal, it was just unwrapping the cheese and getting out the bread and peanut butter, but Pat and Kip always had to do their woodsy act and boil up a billy tin for their own tea.

They told Kip where they were going. You had to tell Kip where you were going, even if it was only a little way into the woods to get dry twigs for kindling. You could never go anywhere without a buddy.

"Sure," said Kip, who was crouching over the fire, feeding driftwood into it. "Fifteen minutes to lunch."

"Where are they off to?" said Pat. She was bringing their billy tin of water from the lake.

"Lookout," said Kip.

"Be careful," said Pat. She said it as an afterthought, because it was what she always said.

"They're old hands," Kip said.

Lois looks at her watch: it's ten to twelve. She is the watchminder; Lucy is careless of time. They walk up the path, which is dry earth and rocks, big rounded pinky-gray boulders or split-open ones with jagged edges. Spindly balsam and spruce trees grow to either side, the lake is blue fragments to the left. The sun is right overhead; there are no shadows anywhere. The heat comes up at them as well as down. The forest is dry and crackly.

It isn't far, but it's a steep climb and they're sweating when they reach the top. They wipe their faces with their bare arms, sit gingerly down on a scorching-hot rock, five feet from the edge but too close for Lois. It's a lookout all right, a sheer drop to the lake and a long view over the water, back the way they've come. It's amazing to Lois that they've traveled so far, over all that water, with nothing to propel them but their own arms. It makes her feel strong. There are all kinds of things she is capable of doing.

"It would be quite a dive off here," says Lucy.

"You'd have to be nuts," says Lois.

"Why?" says Lucy. "It's really deep. It goes straight down." She stands up and takes a step nearer the edge. Lois gets a stab in her midriff, the kind she gets when a car goes too fast over a bump. "Don't," she says.

"Don't what?" says Lucy, glancing around at her mischievously. She knows how Lois feels about heights. But she turns back. "I really have to pee," she says.

"You have toilet paper?" says Lois, who is never without it. She digs in her shorts pocket.

"Thanks," says Lucy.

They are both adept at peeing in the woods: doing it fast so the mosquitoes don't get you, the underwear pulled up between the knees, the squat with the feet apart so you don't wet your legs, facing downhill. The exposed feeling of your bum, as if someone is looking at you from behind. The etiquette when you're with someone else is not to look. Lois stands up and starts to walk back down the path, to be out of sight.

"Wait for me?" says Lucy.

Lois climbed down, over and around the boulders, until she could not see Lucy; she waited. She could hear the voices of the others, talking and laughing, down near the shore. One voice was yelling, "Ants! Ants!" Someone must have sat on an ant hill. Off to the side, in the woods, a raven was croaking, a hoarse single note.

She looked at her watch: it was noon. This is when she heard the shout.

She has gone over and over it in her mind since, so many times that the first, real shout has been obliterated, like a footprint trampled by other footprints. But she is sure (she is almost positive, she is nearly certain) that it was not a shout of fear. Not a scream. More like a cry of surprise, cut off too soon. Short, like a dog's bark.

"Lucy?" Lois said. Then she called "Lucy!" By now she was clambering back up, over the stones of the path. Lucy was not up there. Or she was not in sight.

"Stop fooling around," Lois said. "It's lunchtime." But Lucy did not rise from behind a rock or step out, smiling, from behind a tree. The sunlight was all around; the rocks looked white. "This isn't funny!" Lois said, and it wasn't, panic was rising in her, the panic of a small child who does not know where the bigger ones are hidden. She could hear her own heart. She looked quickly around; she lay down on the ground and looked over the edge of the cliff. It made her feel cold. There was nothing.

She went back down the path, stumbling; she was breathing too quickly; she was too frightened to cry. She felt terrible—guilty and dismayed, as if she had done something very bad, by mistake. Something that could never be repaired. "Lucy's gone," she told Kip.

Kip looked up from the fire, annoyed. The water in the billy can was boiling. "What do you mean, gone?" she said. "Where did she go?"

"I don't know," said Lois. "She's just gone."

No one had heard the shout, but then no one had heard Lois calling, either. They had been talking among themselves, by the water.

Kip and Pat went up to the lookout and searched and called, and blew their whistles. Nothing answered.

Then they came back down, and Lois had to tell exactly what had happened. The other girls all sat in a circle and listened to her. Nobody said anything. They all looked frightened, especially Pat and Kip. They were the leaders. You did not just lose a camper like this, for no reason at all.

"Why did you leave her alone?" said Kip.

"I was just down the path," said Lois. "I told you. She had to go to the bathroom." She did not say *pee* in front of people older than herself.

Kip looked disgusted.

"Maybe she just walked off into the woods and got turned around," said one of the girls.

"Maybe she's doing it on purpose," said another.

Nobody believed either of these theories.

They took the canoes and searched around the base of the cliff, and peered down into the water. But there had been no sound of falling rock; there had been no splash. There was no clue, nothing at all. Lucy had simply vanished.

That was the end of the canoe trip. It took them the same two days to go back that it had taken coming in, even though they were short a paddler. They did not sing.

After that, the police went in a motorboat, with dogs; they were the Mounties and the dogs were German shepherds, trained to follow trails in the woods. But it had rained since, and they could find nothing.

Lois is sitting in Cappie's office. Her face is bloated with crying, she's seen that in the mirror. By now she feels numbed; she feels as if she has drowned. She can't stay here. It has been too much of a shock. Tomorrow her parents are coming to take her away. Several of the other girls who were on the canoe trip are also being collected. The others will have to stay, because their parents are in Europe, or cannot be reached.

Cappie is grim. They've tried to hush it up, but of course everyone in camp knows. Soon the papers will know too. You can't keep it quiet, but what can be said? What can be said that makes any sense? "Girl vanishes in broad daylight, without a trace." It can't be believed. Other things, worse things, will be suspected. Negligence, at the very least. But they have always taken such care. Bad luck will gather around Camp Manitou like a fog; parents will avoid it, in favor of other, luckier places. Lois can see Cappie thinking all this, even through her numbness. It's what anyone would think.

Lois sits on the hard wooden chair in Cappie's office, beside the old wooden desk, over which hangs the thumbtacked bulletin board of normal camp routine, and gazes at Cappie through her puffy eyelids. Cappie is now smiling what is supposed to be a reassuring smile. Her manner is too casual: she's after something. Lois has seen this look on Cappie's face when she's been sniffing out contraband chocolate bars, hunting down those rumored to have snuck out of their cabins at night.

"Tell me again," says Cappie, "from the beginning."

Lois has told her story so many times by now, to Pat and Kip, to Cappie, to the police, that she knows it word for word. She knows it, but she no longer believes it. It has become a story. "I told you," she said. "She wanted to go to the bathroom. I gave her my toilet paper. I went down the path, I waited for her. I heard this kind of shout . . ."

"Yes," says Cappie, smiling confidingly, "but before that. What did you say to one another?"

Lois thinks. Nobody has asked her this before. "She said you could dive off there. She said it went straight down."

"And what did you say?"

"I said you'd have to be nuts."

"Were you mad at Lucy?" says Cappie, in an encouraging voice.

"No," says Lois. "Why would I be mad at Lucy? I wasn't ever mad at Lucy." She feels like crying again. The times when she has in fact been mad at Lucy have been erased already. Lucy was always perfect.

"Sometimes we're angry when we don't know we're angry," says Cappie, as if to herself. "Sometimes we get really mad and we don't even know it. Sometimes we might do a thing without meaning to, or without knowing what will happen. We lose our tempers."

Lois is only thirteen, but it doesn't take her long to figure out that Cappie is not including herself in any of this. By *we* she means Lois. She is accusing Lois of pushing Lucy off the cliff. The unfairness of this hits her like a slap. "I didn't!" she says.

"Didn't what?" says Cappie softly. "Didn't what, Lois?"

Lois does the worst thing, she begins to cry. Cappie gives her a look like a pounce. She's got what she wanted.

Later, when she was grown up, Lois was able to understand what this interview had been about. She could see Cappie's desperation, her need for a story, a real story with a reason in it; anything but the senseless vacancy Lucy had left for her to deal with. Cappie wanted Lois to supply the reason, to be the reason. It wasn't even for the newspapers or the parents, because she could never make such an accusation without proof. It was for herself: something to explain the loss of Camp Manitou and of all she had worked for, the years of entertaining spoiled children and buttering up parents and making a fool of herself with feathers stuck in her hair. Camp Manitou was in fact lost. It did not survive.

Lois worked all this out, twenty years later. But it was far too late. It was too late even ten minutes afterwards, when she'd left Cappie's office and was walking slowly back to her cabin to pack. Lucy's clothes were still there, folded on the shelves, as if waiting. She felt the other girls in the cabin watching her with speculation in their eyes. *Could she have done it? She must have done it.* For the rest of her life, she has caught people watching her in this way.

Maybe they weren't thinking this. Maybe they were merely sorry for her. But she felt she had been tried and sentenced, and this is what has stayed with her: the knowledge that she had been singled out, condemned for something that was not her fault.

Lois sits in the living room of her apartment, drinking a cup of tea. Through the knee-to-ceiling window she has a wide view of Lake Ontario, with its skin of wrinkled blue-gray light, and of the willows of Centre Island shaken by a wind, which is silent at this distance, and on this side of the glass. When there isn't too much pollution she can see the far shore, the foreign shore; though today it is obscured.

Possibly she could go out, go downstairs, do some shopping; there isn't much in the refrigerator. The boys say she doesn't get out enough. But she isn't hungry, and moving, stirring from this space, is increasingly an effort.

She can hardly remember, now, having her two boys in the hospital, nursing them as babies; she can hardly remember getting married, or what Rob looked like. Even at the time she never felt she was paying full attention. She was tired a lot, as if she was living not one life but two: her own, and another, shadowy life that hovered around her and would not let itself be realized—the life of what would have happened if Lucy had not stepped sideways, and disappeared from time.

She would never go up north, to Rob's family cottage or to any place with wild lakes and wild trees and the calls of loons. She would never go anywhere near. Still, it was as if she was always listening for another voice, the voice of a person who should have been there but was not. An echo.

While Rob was alive, while the boys were growing up, she could pretend she didn't hear it, this empty space in sound. But now there is nothing much left to distract her.

She turns away from the window and looks at her pictures. There is the pinkish island, in the lake, with the intertwisted trees. It's the same landscape they paddled through, that distant summer. She's seen travelogues of this country, aerial photographs; it looks different from above, bigger, more hopeless: lake after lake, random blue puddles in dark green bush, the trees like bristles.

How could you ever find anything there, once it was lost? Maybe if they cut it all down, drained it all away, they might find Lucy's bones, some time, wherever they are hidden. A few bones, some buttons, the buckle from her shorts.

But a dead person is a body; a body occupies space, it exists somewhere. You can see it; you put it in a box and bury it in the ground, and then it's in a box in the ground. But Lucy is not in a box, or in the ground. Because she is nowhere definite, she could be anywhere.

And these paintings are not landscape paintings. Because there aren't any landscapes up there, not in the old, tidy European sense, with a gentle hill, a curving river, a cottage, a mountain in the background, a golden evening sky. Instead there's a tangle, a receding maze, in which you can become lost almost as soon as you step off the path. There are no backgrounds in any of these paintings, no vistas; only a great deal of foreground that goes back and back, endlessly, involving you in its twists and turns of trees and branch and rock.

...ter how far back in you go, there will be more. And the trees themselves are hardly trees; they are currents of energy, charged with violent color.

Who knows how many trees there were on the cliff just before Lucy disappeared? Who counted? Maybe there was one more, afterwards.

Lois sits in her chair and does not move. Her hand with the cup is raised halfway to her mouth. She hears something, almost hears it: a shout of recognition, or of joy.

She looks at the paintings, she looks into them. Every one of them is a picture of Lucy. You can't see her exactly, but she's there, in behind the pink stone island or the one behind that. In the picture of the cliff she is hidden by the clutch of fallen rocks towards the bottom, in the one of the river shore she is crouching beneath the overturned canoe. In the yellow autumn woods she's behind the tree that cannot be seen because of the other trees, over beside the blue sliver of pond; but if you walked into the picture and found the tree, it would be the wrong one, because the right one would be further on.

Everyone has to be somewhere, and this is where Lucy is. She is in Lois's apartment, in the holes that open inwards on the wall, not like windows but like doors. She is here. She is entirely alive.

1989

RELATED:

—Atwood, "Why Do You Write?" p. 1706

JAMES BALDWIN
1924–1987

Baldwin was born in New York City. Stepson of a revivalist minister and himself active in the ministry for three years, he drew on and refined the passionate eloquence of religious oratory as one ingredient of his style. He began his literary career while living in Paris, during a time when he had to support himself by a variety of odd jobs to supplement his income from writing. Recognition of his talents as a novelist and short-story writer was paralleled by the attention paid to him as an essayist who confronted the American conscience with his fierce indictment of the racial inequities that blight the country. Much of his work aimed at unraveling the repressive myths of white society and at healing the disastrous estrangement he found in the lives of black people in America. His novels include *Go Tell It on the Mountain* (1953), *Giovanni's Room* (1957), *Another Country* (1962), *Tell Me How Long the Train's Been Gone* (1968), *If Beale Street Could Talk* (1974), and *Just Above My Head* (1979). His books of essays are *Notes of a Native Son* (1955), *Nobody Knows My Name* (1961), *The Fire Next Time* (1963), and *No Name in the Street* (1972). His short stories are collected in *Going to Meet the Man* (1965).

Sonny's Blues

I read about it in the paper, in the subway, on my way to work. I read it, and I couldn't believe it, and I read it again. Then perhaps I just stared at it, at the newsprint spelling out his name, spelling out the story. I stared at it in the swinging lights of the subway car, and in the faces and bodies of the people, and in my own face, trapped in the darkness which roared outside.

It was not to be believed and I kept telling myself that, as I walked from the subway station to the high school. And at the same time I couldn't doubt it. I was scared, scared for Sonny. He became real to me again. A great block of ice got settled in my belly and kept melting there slowly all day long, while I taught my classes algebra. It was a special kind of ice. It kept melting, sending trickles of ice water all up and down my veins, but it never got less. Sometimes it hardened and seemed to expand until I felt my guts were going to come spilling out or that I was going to choke or scream. This would always be at a moment when I was remembering some specific thing Sonny had once said or done.

When he was about as old as the boys in my classes his face had been bright and open, there was a lot of copper in it; and he'd had wonderfully direct brown eyes, and great gentleness and privacy. I wondered what he looked like now. He

...p, the evening before, in a raid on an apartment downtown, ...d using heroin.

...elieve it: but what I mean by that is that I couldn't find any ...where inside me. I had kept it outside me for a long time. I hadn't ...know. I had had suspicions, but I didn't name them, I kept putting ...way. I told myself that Sonny was wild, but he wasn't crazy. And he'd ...been a good boy, he hadn't ever turned hard or evil or disrespectful, the ...kids can, so quick, so quick, especially in Harlem. I didn't want to believe that I'd ever see my brother going down, coming to nothing, all that light in his face gone out, in the condition I'd already seen so many others. Yet it had happened and here I was, talking about algebra to a lot of boys who might, every one of them for all I knew, be popping off needles every time they went to the head.[1] Maybe it did more for them than algebra could.

I was sure that the first time Sonny had ever had horse,[2] he couldn't have been much older than these boys were now. These boys, now, were living as we'd been living then, they were growing up with a rush and their heads bumped abruptly against the low ceiling of their actual possibilities. They were filled with rage. All they really knew were two darknesses, the darkness of their lives, which was now closing in on them, and the darkness of the movies, which had blinded them to that other darkness, and in which they now, vindictively, dreamed, at once more together than they were at any other time, and more alone.

When the last bell rang, the last class ended, I let out my breath. It seemed I'd been holding it for all that time. My clothes were wet—I may have looked as though I'd been sitting in a steam bath, all dressed up, all afternoon. I sat alone in the classroom a long time. I listened to the boys outside, downstairs, shouting and cursing and laughing. Their laughter struck me for perhaps the first time. It was not the joyous laughter which—God knows why—one associates with children. It was mocking and insular, its intent was to denigrate. It was disenchanted, and in this, also, lay the authority of their curses. Perhaps I was listening to them because I was thinking about my brother and in them I heard my brother. And myself.

One boy was whistling a tune, at once very complicated and very simple, it seemed to be pouring out of him as though he were a bird, and it sounded very cool and moving through all that harsh, bright air, only just holding its own through all those other sounds.

I stood up and walked over to the window and looked down into the courtyard. It was the beginning of the spring and the sap was rising in the boys. A teacher passed through them every now and again, quickly, as though he or she couldn't wait to get out of that courtyard, to get those boys out of their sight and off their minds. I started collecting my stuff. I thought I'd better get home and talk to Isabel.

The courtyard was almost deserted by the time I got downstairs. I saw this boy standing in the shadow of a doorway, looking just like Sonny. I almost called his name. Then I saw that it wasn't Sonny, but somebody we used to know, a boy from around our block. He'd been Sonny's friend. He'd never been mine, having been too young for me, and, anyway, I'd never liked him. And now, even though he was a grown-up man, he still hung around that block, still

---

1. Toilet.   **2.** Heroin.

spent hours on the street corners, was always high and raggy. I used to run into him from time to time and he'd often work around to asking me for a quarter or fifty cents. He always had some real good excuse, too, and I always gave it to him. I don't know why.

But now, abruptly, I hated him. I couldn't stand the way he looked at me, partly like a dog, partly like a cunning child. I wanted to ask him what the hell he was doing in the school courtyard.

He sort of shuffled over to me, and he said, "I see you got the papers. So you already know about it."

"You mean about Sonny? Yes, I already know about it. How come they didn't get you?"

He grinned. It made him repulsive and it also brought to mind what he'd looked like as a kid. "I wasn't there. I stay away from them people."

"Good for you." I offered him a cigarette and I watched him through the smoke. "You come all the way down here just to tell me about Sonny?"

"That's right." He was sort of shaking his head and his eyes looked strange, as though they were about to cross. The bright sun deadened his damp dark brown skin and it made his eyes look yellow and showed up the dirt in his kinked hair. He smelled funky.[3] I moved a little away from him and I said, "Well, thanks. But I already know about it and I got to get home."

"I'll walk you a little ways," he said. We started walking. There were a couple of kids still loitering in the courtyard and one of them said goodnight to me and looked strangely at the boy beside me.

"What're you going to do?" he asked me. "I mean, about Sonny?"

"Look. I haven't seen Sonny for over a year, I'm not sure I'm going to do anything. Anyway, what the hell *can I* do?"

"That's right," he said quickly, "ain't nothing you can do. Can't much help old Sonny no more, I guess."

It was what I was thinking and so it seemed to me he had no right to say it.

"I'm surprised at Sonny, though," he went on—he had a funny way of talking, he looked straight ahead as though he were talking to himself—"I thought Sonny was a smart boy, I thought he was too smart to get hung."

"I guess he thought so too," I said sharply, "and that's how he got hung. And how about you? You're pretty goddamn smart, I bet."

Then he looked directly at me, just for a minute. "I ain't smart," he said. "If I was smart, I'd have reached for a pistol a long time ago."

"Look. Don't tell *me* your sad story, if it was up to me, I'd give you one." Then I felt guilty—guilty, probably, for never having supposed that the poor bastard *had* a story of his own, much less a sad one, and I asked, quickly, "What's going to happen to him now?"

He didn't answer this. He was off by himself some place.

"Funny thing," he said, and from his tone we might have been discussing the quickest way to get to Brooklyn, "when I saw the papers this morning, the first thing I asked myself was if I had anything to do with it. I felt sort of responsible."

I began to listen more carefully. The subway station was on the corner, just before us, and I stopped. He stopped, too. We were in front of a bar and he

3. Unwashed.

ducked slightly, peering in, but whoever he was looking for didn't seem to be there. The juke box was blasting away with something black and bouncy and I half watched the barmaid as she danced her way from the juke box to her place behind the bar. And I watched her face as she laughingly responded to something someone said to her, still keeping time to the music. When she smiled one saw the little girl, one sensed the doomed, still-struggling woman beneath the battered face of the semi-whore.

"I never *give* Sonny nothing," the boy said finally, "but a long time ago I come to school high and Sonny asked me how it felt." He paused, I couldn't bear to watch him, I watched the barmaid, and I listened to the music which seemed to be causing the pavement to shake. "I told him it felt great." The music stopped, the barmaid paused and watched the juke box until the music began again. "It did."

All this was carrying me some place I didn't want to go. I certainly didn't want to know how it felt. It filled everything, the people, the houses, the music, the dark, quicksilver barmaid, with menace; and this menace was their reality.

"What's going to happen to him now?" I asked again.

"They'll send him away some place and they'll try to cure him." He shook his head. "Maybe he'll even think he's kicked the habit. Then they'll let him loose"—he gestured, throwing his cigarette into the gutter. "That's all."

"What do you mean, that's *all?*"

But I knew what he meant.

"I *mean,* that's *all.*" He turned his head and looked at me, pulling down the corners of his mouth. "Don't you know what I mean?" he asked, softly.

"How the hell *would* I know what you mean?" I almost whispered it, I don't know why.

"That's right," he said to the air, "how would *he* know what I mean?" He turned toward me again, patient and calm, and yet I somehow felt him shaking, shaking as though he were going to fall apart. I felt that ice in my guts again, the dread I'd felt all afternoon; and again I watched the barmaid, moving about the bar, washing glasses, and singing. "Listen. They'll let him out and then it'll just start all over again. That's what I mean."

"You mean—they'll let him out. And then he'll just start working his way back in again. You mean he'll never kick the habit. Is that what you mean?"

"That's right," he said, cheerfully. "*You* see what I mean."

"Tell me," I said at last, "why does he want to die? He must want to die, he's killing himself, why does he want to die?"

He looked at me in surprise. He licked his lips. "He don't want to die. He wants to live. Don't nobody want to die, ever."

Then I wanted to ask him—too many things. He could not have answered, or if he had, I could not have borne the answers. I started walking. "Well, I guess it's none of my business."

"It's going to be rough on old Sonny," he said. We reached the subway station. "This is your station?" he asked. I nodded. I took one step down. "Damn!" he said, suddenly. I looked up at him. He grinned again. "Damn it if I didn't leave all my money home. You ain't got a dollar on you, have you? Just for a couple of days, is all."

All at once something inside gave and threatened to come pouring out of me. I didn't hate him any more. I felt that in another moment I'd start crying like a child.

"Sure," I said. "Don't sweat." I looked in my wallet and didn't have a dollar, I only had a five. "Here," I said. "That hold you?"

He didn't look at it—he didn't want to look at it. A terrible, closed look came over his face, as though he were keeping the number on the bill a secret from him and me. "Thanks," he said, and now he was dying to see me go. "Don't worry about Sonny. Maybe I'll write him or something."

"Sure," I said. "You do that. So long."

"Be seeing you," he said. I went on down the steps.

And I didn't write Sonny or send him anything for a long time. When I finally did, it was just after my little girl died, and he wrote me back a letter which made me feel like a bastard.

Here's what he said:

Dear brother,

You don't know how much I needed to hear from you. I wanted to write you many a time but I dug how much I must have hurt you and so I didn't write. But now I feel like a man who's been trying to climb up out of some deep, real deep and funky hole and just saw the sun up there, outside. I got to get outside.

I can't tell you much about how I got here. I mean I don't know how to tell you. I guess I was afraid of something or I was trying to escape from something and you know I have never been very strong in the head (smile). I'm glad Mama and Daddy are dead and can't see what's happened to their son and I swear if I'd known what I was doing I would never have hurt you so, you and a lot of other fine people who were nice to me and who believed in me.

I don't want you to think it had anything to do with me being a musician. It's more than that. Or maybe less than that. I can't get anything straight in my head down here and I try not to think about what's going to happen to me when I get outside again. Sometime I think I'm going to flip and *never* get outside and sometime I think I'll come straight back. I tell you one thing, though, I'd rather blow my brains out than go through this again. But that's what they all say, so they tell me. If I tell you when I'm coming to New York and if you could meet me, I sure would appreciate it. Give my love to Isabel and the kids and I was sure sorry to hear about little Gracie. I wish I could be like Mama and say the Lord's will be done, but I don't know it seems to me that trouble is the one thing that never does get stopped and I don't know what good it does to blame it on the Lord. But maybe it does some good if you believe it.

Your brother,
Sonny

Then I kept in constant touch with him and I sent him whatever I could and I went to meet him when he came back to New York. When I saw him many things I thought I had forgotten came flooding back to me. This was because I had begun, finally, to wonder about Sonny, about the life that Sonny lived inside. This life, whatever it was, had made him older and thinner and it had deepened the distant stillness in which he had always moved. He looked very unlike my baby brother. Yet, when he smiled, when we shook hands, the baby brother I'd never known looked out from the depths of his private life, like an animal waiting to be coaxed into the light.

"How you been keeping?" he asked me.

"All right. And you?"

"Just fine." He was smiling all over his face. "It's good to see you again."

"It's good to see you."

The seven years' difference in our ages lay between us like a chasm: I wondered if these years would ever operate between us as a bridge. I was remembering, and it made it hard to catch my breath, that I had been there when he was born; and I had heard the first words he had ever spoken. When he started to walk, he walked from our mother straight to me. I caught him just before he fell when he took the first steps he ever took in this world.

"How's Isabel?"

"Just fine. She's dying to see you."

"And the boys?"

"They're fine, too. They're anxious to see their uncle."

"Oh, come on. You know they don't remember me."

"Are you kidding? Of course they remember you."

He grinned again. We got into a taxi. We had a lot to say to each other, far too much to know how to begin.

As the taxi began to move, I asked, "You still want to go to India?"

He laughed. "You still remember that. Hell, no. This place is Indian enough for me."

"It used to belong to them," I said.

And he laughed again. "They damn sure knew what they were doing when they got rid of it."

Years ago, when he was around fourteen, he'd been all hipped on the idea of going to India. He read books about people sitting on rocks, naked, in all kinds of weather, but mostly bad, naturally, and walking barefoot through hot coals and arriving at wisdom. I used to say that it sounded to me as though they were getting away from wisdom as fast as they could. I think he sort of looked down on me for that.

"Do you mind," he asked, "if we have the driver drive alongside the park? On the west side—I haven't seen the city in so long."

"Of course not," I said. I was afraid that I might sound as though I were humoring him, but I hoped he wouldn't take it that way.

So we drove along, between the green of the park and the stony, lifeless elegance of hotels and apartment buildings, toward the vivid, killing streets of our childhood. These streets hadn't changed, though housing projects jutted up out of them now like rocks in the middle of a boiling sea. Most of the houses in which we had grown up had vanished, as had the stores from which we had stolen, the basements in which we had first tried sex, the rooftops from which we had hurled tin cans and bricks. But houses exactly like the houses of our past yet dominated the landscape, boys exactly like the boys we once had been found themselves smothering in these houses, came down into the streets for light and air and found themselves encircled by disaster. Some escaped the trap, most didn't. Those who got out always left something of themselves behind, as some animals amputate a leg and leave it in the trap. It might be said, perhaps, that I had escaped, after all, I was a school teacher; or that Sonny had, he hadn't lived in Harlem for years. Yet, as the cab moved uptown through streets which seemed, with a rush, to darken with dark people, and as I covertly studied Sonny's face, it came to me that what we both were seeking through our separate cab windows was that part of ourselves which had been left behind. It's always at the hour of trouble and confrontation that the missing member aches.

We hit 110th Street and started rolling up Lenox Avenue. And I'd known this avenue all my life, but it seemed to me again, as it had seemed on the day I'd first heard about Sonny's trouble, filled with a hidden menace which was its very breath of life.

"We almost there," said Sonny.

"Almost." We were both too nervous to say anything more.

We live in a housing project. It hasn't been up long. A few days after it was up it seemed uninhabitably new. Now, of course, it's already rundown. It looks like a parody of the good, clean, faceless life—God knows the people who live in it do their best to make it a parody. The beat-looking grass lying around isn't enough to make their lives green, the hedges will never hold out the streets, and they know it. The big windows fool no one, they aren't big enough to make space out of no space. They don't bother with the windows, they watch the TV screen instead. The playground is most popular with the children who don't play at jacks, or skip rope, or roller skate, or swing, and they can be found in it after dark. We moved in partly because it's not too far from where I teach, and partly for the kids; but it's really just like the houses in which Sonny and I grew up. The same things happen, they'll have the same things to remember. The moment Sonny and I started into the house I had the feeling that I was simply bringing him back into the danger he had almost died trying to escape.

Sonny has never been talkative. So I don't know why I was sure he'd be dying to talk to me when supper was over the first night. Everything went fine, the oldest boy remembered him, and the youngest boy liked him, and Sonny had remembered to bring something for each of them; and Isabel, who is really much nicer than I am, more open and giving, had gone to a lot of trouble about dinner and was genuinely glad to see him. And she's always been able to tease Sonny in a way that I haven't. It was nice to see her face so vivid again and to hear her laugh and watch her make Sonny laugh. She wasn't, or, anyway, she didn't seem to be, at all uneasy or embarrassed. She chatted as though there were no subject which had to be avoided and she got Sonny past his first, faint stiffness. And thank God she was there, for I was filled with that icy dread again. Everything I did seemed awkward to me, and everything I said sounded freighted with hidden meaning. I was trying to remember everything I'd heard about dope addiction and I couldn't help watching Sonny for signs. I wasn't doing it out of malice, I was trying to find out something about my brother. I was dying to hear him tell me he was safe.

"Safe!" my father grunted, whenever Mama suggested trying to move to a neighborhood which might be safer for children. "Safe, hell! Ain't no place safe for kids, nor nobody."

He always went on like this, but he wasn't, ever, really as bad as he sounded, not even on weekends, when he got drunk. As a matter of fact, he was always on the lookout for "something a little better," but he died before he found it. He died suddenly, during a drunken weekend in the middle of the war, when Sonny was fifteen. He and Sonny hadn't ever got on too well. And this was partly because Sonny was the apple of his father's eye. It was because he loved

Sonny so much and was frightened for him, that he was always fighting with him. It doesn't do any good to fight with Sonny. Sonny just moves back, inside himself, where he can't be reached. But the principal reason that they never hit it off is that they were so much alike. Daddy was big and rough and loud-talking, just the opposite of Sonny, but they both had—that same privacy.

Mama tried to tell me something about this, just after Daddy died. I was home on leave from the army.

This was the last time I ever saw my mother alive. Just the same, this picture gets all mixed up in my mind with pictures I had of her when she was younger. The way I always see her is the way she used to be on a Sunday afternoon, say, when the old folks were talking after the big Sunday dinner. I always see her wearing pale blue. She'd be sitting on the sofa. And my father would be sitting in the easy chair, not far from her. And the living room would be full of church folks and relatives. There they sit, in chairs all around the living room, and the night is creeping up outside, but nobody knows it yet. You can see the dark-ness growing against the windowpanes and you hear the street noises every now and again, or maybe the jangling beat of a tambourine from one of the churches close by, but it's real quiet in the room. For a moment nobody's talk-ing, but every face looks darkening, like the sky outside. And my mother rocks a little from the waist, and my father's eyes are closed. Everyone is looking at something a child can't see. For a minute they've forgotten the children. Maybe a kid is lying on the rug, half asleep. Maybe somebody's got a kid in his lap and is absent-mindedly stroking the kid's head. Maybe there's a kid, quiet and big-eyed, curled up in a big chair in the corner. The silence, the darkness coming, and the darkness in the faces frighten the child obscurely. He hopes that the hand which strokes his forehead will never stop—will never die. He hopes that there will never come a time when the old folks won't be sitting around the living room, talking about where they've come from, and what they've seen, and what's happened to them and their kinfolk.

But something deep and watchful in the child knows that this is bound to end, is already ending. In a moment someone will get up and turn on the light. Then the old folks will remember the children and they won't talk any more that day. And when light fills the room, the child is filled with darkness. He knows that every time this happens he's moved just a little closer to that dark-ness outside. The darkness outside is what the old folks have been talking about. It's what they've come from. It's what they endure. The child knows that they won't talk any more because if he knows too much about what's hap-pened to *them*, he'll know too much too soon, about what's going to happen to *him*.

The last time I talked to my mother, I remember I was restless. I wanted to get out and see Isabel. We weren't married then and we had a lot to straighten out between us.

There Mama sat, in black, by the window. She was humming an old church song, *Lord, you brought me from a long ways off.* Sonny was out somewhere. Mama kept watching the streets.

"I don't know," she said, "if I'll ever see you again, after you go off from here. But I hope you'll remember the things I tried to teach you."

"Don't talk like that," I said, and smiled. "You'll be here a long time yet."

She smiled, too, but she said nothing. She was quiet for a long time. And I said, "Mama, don't you worry about nothing. I'll be writing all the time, and you be getting the checks. . . ."

"I want to talk to you about your brother," she said, suddenly. "If anything happens to me he ain't going to have nobody to look out for him."

"Mama," I said, "ain't nothing going to happen to you *or* Sonny. Sonny's all right. He's a good boy and he's got good sense."

"It ain't a question of his being a good boy," Mama said, "nor of his having good sense. It ain't only the bad ones, nor yet the dumb ones that gets sucked under." She stopped, looking at me. "Your Daddy once had a brother," she said, and she smiled in a way that made me feel she was in pain. "You didn't never know that, did you?"

"No," I said, "I never knew that," and I watched her face.

"Oh, yes," she said, "your Daddy had a brother." She looked out of the window again. "I know you never saw your Daddy cry. But *I* did—many a time, through all these years."

I asked her, "What happened to his brother? How come nobody's ever talked about him?"

This was the first time I ever saw my mother look old.

"His brother got killed," she said, "when he was just a little younger than you are now. I knew him. He was a fine boy. He was maybe a little full of the devil, but he didn't mean nobody no harm."

Then she stopped and the room was silent, exactly as it had sometimes been on those Sunday afternoons. Mama kept looking out into the streets.

"He used to have a job in the mill," she said, "and, like all young folks, he just liked to perform on Saturday nights. Saturday nights, him and your father would drift around to different places, go to dances and things like that, or just sit around with people they knew, and your father's brother would sing, he had a fine voice, and play along with himself on his guitar. Well, this particular Saturday night, him and your father was coming home from some place, and they were both a little drunk and there was a moon that night, it was bright like day. Your father's brother was feeling kind of good, and he was whistling to himself, and he had his guitar slung over his shoulder. They was coming down a hill and beneath them was a road that turned off from the highway. Well, your father's brother, being always kind of frisky, decided to run down this hill, and he did, with that guitar banging and clanging behind him, and he ran across the road, and he was making water behind a tree. And your father was sort of amused at him and he was still coming down the hill, kind of slow. Then he heard a car motor and that same minute his brother stepped from behind the tree, into the road, in the moonlight. And he started to cross the road. And your father started to run down the hill, he says he don't know why. This car was full of white men. They was all drunk, and when they seen your father's brother they let out a great whoop and holler and they aimed the car straight at him. They was having fun, they just wanted to scare him, the way they do sometimes, you know. But they was drunk. And I guess the boy, being drunk, too, and scared, kind of lost his head. By the time he jumped it was too late. Your father says he heard his brother scream when the car rolled over him, and he heard the wood of that guitar when it give, and he heard them strings go flying, and he heard them white men shouting, and the car kept on a-going and it ain't stopped till this day. And, time your father got down the hill, his brother weren't nothing but blood and pulp."

Tears were gleaming on my mother's face. There wasn't anything I could say.

"He never mentioned it," she said, "because I never let him mention it before you children. Your Daddy was like a crazy man that night and for many a night thereafter. He says he never in his life seen anything as dark as that road after the lights of that car had gone away. Weren't nothing, weren't nobody on that road, just your Daddy and his brother and that busted guitar. Oh, yes. Your Daddy never did really get right again. Till the day he died he weren't sure but that every white man he saw was the man that killed his brother."

She stopped and took out her handkerchief and dried her eyes and looked at me.

"I ain't telling you all this," she said, "to make you scared or bitter or to make you hate nobody. I'm telling you this because you got a brother. And the world ain't changed."

I guess I didn't want to believe this. I guess she saw this in my face. She turned away from me, toward the window again, searching those streets.

"But I praise my Redeemer," she said at last, "that He called your Daddy home before me. I ain't saying it to throw no flowers at myself, but, I declare, it keeps me from feeling too cast down to know I helped your father get safely through this world. Your father always acted like he was the roughest, strongest man on earth. And everybody took him to be like that. But if he hadn't had me there—to see his tears!"

She was crying again. Still, I couldn't move. I said, "Lord, Lord, Mama, I didn't know it was like that."

"Oh, honey," she said, "there's a lot that you don't know. But you are going to find out." She stood up from the window and came over to me. "You got to hold on to your brother," she said, "and don't let him fall, no matter what it looks like is happening to him and no matter how evil you gets with him. You going to be evil with him many a time. But don't you forget what I told you, you hear?"

"I won't forget," I said. "Don't you worry, I won't forget. I won't let nothing happen to Sonny."

My mother smiled as though she was amused at something she saw in my face. Then, "You may not be able to stop nothing from happening. But you got to let him know you's *there*."

Two days later I was married, and then I was gone. And I had a lot of things on my mind and I pretty well forgot my promise to Mama until I got shipped home on a special furlough for her funeral.

And, after the funeral, with just Sonny and me alone in the empty kitchen, I tried to find out something about him.

"What do you want to do?" I asked him.

"I'm going to be a musician," he said.

For he had graduated, in the time I had been away, from dancing to the juke box to finding out who was playing what, and what they were doing with it, and he had bought himself a set of drums.

"You mean, you want to be a drummer?" I somehow had the feeling that being a drummer might be all right for other people but not for my brother Sonny.

"I don't think," he said, looking at me very gravely, "that I'll ever be a good drummer. But I think I can play a piano."

I frowned. I'd never played the role of the oldest brother quite so seriously before, had scarcely ever, in fact, *asked* Sonny a damn thing. I sensed myself in the presence of something I didn't really know how to handle, didn't understand. So I made my frown a little deeper as I asked: "What kind of musician do you want to be?"

He grinned. "How many kinds do you think there are?"

"Be *serious*," I said.

He laughed, throwing his head back, and then looked at me. "I *am* serious."

"Well, then, for Christ's sake, stop kidding around and answer a serious question. I mean, do you want to be a concert pianist, you want to play classical music and all that, or—or what?" Long before I finished he was laughing again. "For Christ's *sake*, Sonny!"

He sobered, but with difficulty. "I'm sorry. But you sound so—*scared!*" and he was off again.

"Well, you may think it's funny now, baby, but it's not going to be so funny when you have to make your living at it, let me tell you *that*." I was furious because I knew he was laughing at me and I didn't know why.

"No," he said, very sober now, and afraid, perhaps, that he'd hurt me, "I don't want to be a classical pianist. That isn't what interests me. I mean"—he paused, looking hard at me, as though his eyes would help me to understand, and then gestured helplessly, as though perhaps his hand would help—"I mean, I'll have a lot of studying to do, and I'll have to study *everything*, but, I mean, I want to play *with*—jazz musicians." He stopped. "I want to play jazz," he said.

Well, the word had never before sounded as heavy, as real, as it sounded that afternoon in Sonny's mouth. I just looked at him and I was probably frowning a real frown by this time. I simply couldn't see why on earth he'd want to spend his time hanging around nightclubs, clowning around on bandstands, while people pushed each other around a dance floor. It seemed—beneath him, somehow. I had never thought about it before, had never been forced to, but I suppose I had always put jazz musicians in a class with what Daddy called "good-time people."

"Are you *serious*?"

"Hell, *yes*, I'm serious."

He looked more helpless than ever, and annoyed, and deeply hurt.

I suggested, helpfully: "You mean—like Louis Armstrong?"

His face closed as though I'd struck him. "No. I'm not talking about none of that old-time, down-home crap."

"Well, look, Sonny, I'm sorry, don't get mad. I just don't altogether get it, that's all. Name somebody—you know, a jazz musician you admire."

"Bird."

"Who?"

"Bird! Charlie Parker![4] Don't they teach you nothing in the goddamn army?"

I lit a cigarette. I was surprised and then a little amused to discover that I was trembling. "I've been out of touch," I said. "You'll have to be patient with me. Now. Who's this Parker character?"

---

4. Charlie "Bird" Parker (1920–1955), saxophone player for whom Birdland jazz club in New York was named. A founder of the new jazz, "bebop," that began to flourish in the 1940s.

"He's just one of the greatest jazz musicians alive," said Sonny, sullenly, his hands in his pockets, his back to me. "Maybe *the* greatest," he added, bitterly. "That's probably why *you* never heard of him."

"All right," I said, "I'm ignorant. I'm sorry. I'll go out and buy all the cat's records right away, all right?"

"It don't," said Sonny, with dignity, "make any difference to me. I don't care what you listen to. Don't do me no favors."

I was beginning to realize that I'd never seen him so upset before. With another part of my mind I was thinking that this would probably turn out to be one of those things kids go through and that I shouldn't make it seem important by pushing it too hard. Still, I didn't think it would do any harm to ask: "Doesn't all this take a lot of time? Can you make a living at it?"

He turned back to me and half leaned, half sat, on the kitchen table. "Everything takes time," he said, "and—well, yes, sure, I can make a living at it. But what I don't seem to be able to make you understand is that it's the only thing I want to do."

"Well, Sonny," I said gently, "you know people can't always do exactly what they *want* to do—"

"*No,* I don't know that," said Sonny, surprising me. "I think people *ought* to do what they want to do, what else are they alive for?"

"You getting to be a big boy," I said desperately, "it's time you started thinking about your future."

"I'm thinking about my future," said Sonny, grimly. "I think about it all the time."

I gave up. I decided, if he didn't change his mind, that we could always talk about it later. "In the meantime," I said, "you got to finish school." We had already decided that he'd have to move in with Isabel and her folks. I knew this wasn't the ideal arrangement because Isabel's folks are inclined to be dicty[5] and they hadn't especially wanted Isabel to marry me. But I didn't know what else to do. "And we have to get you fixed up at Isabel's."

There was a long silence. He moved from the kitchen table to the window. "That's a terrible idea. You know it yourself."

"Do you have a *better* idea?"

He just walked up and down the kitchen for a minute. He was as tall as I was. He had started to shave. I suddenly had the feeling that I didn't know him at all.

He stopped at the kitchen table and picked up my cigarettes. Looking at me with a kind of mocking, amused defiance, he put one between his lips. "You mind?"

"You smoking already?"

He lit the cigarette and nodded, watching me through the smoke. "I just wanted to see if I'd have the courage to smoke in front of you." He grinned and blew a great cloud of smoke to the ceiling. "It was easy." He looked at my face. "Come on, now. I bet you was smoking at my age, tell the truth."

I didn't say anything but the truth was on my face, and he laughed. But now there was something very strained in his laugh. "Sure. And I bet that ain't all you was doing."

5. Dictatorial, overbearing.

He was frightening me a little. "Cut the crap," I said. "We already decided that you was going to go and live at Isabel's. Now what's got into you all of a sudden?"

"*You* decided it," he pointed out. "*I* didn't decide nothing." He stopped in front of me, leaning against the stove, arms loosely folded. "Look, brother. I don't want to stay in Harlem no more, I really don't." He was very earnest. He looked at me, then over toward the kitchen window. There was something in his eyes I'd never seen before, some thoughtfulness, some worry all his own. He rubbed the muscle of one arm. "It's time I was getting out of here."

"Where do you want to *go*, Sonny?"

"I want to join the army. Or the navy, I don't care. If I say I'm old enough, they'll believe me."

Then I got mad. It was because I was so scared. "You must be crazy. You goddamn fool, what the hell do you want to go and join the *army* for?"

"I just told you. To get out of Harlem."

"Sonny, you haven't even finished *school*. And if you really want to be a musician, how do you expect to study if you're in the *army*?"

He looked at me, trapped, and in anguish. "There's ways. I might be able to work out some kind of deal. Anyway, I'll have the G.I. Bill[6] when I come out."

"*If* you come out." We stared at each other. "Sonny, please. Be reasonable. I know the setup is far from perfect. But we got to do the best we can."

"I ain't learning nothing in school," he said. "Even when I go." He turned away from me and opened the window and threw his cigarette out into the narrow alley. I watched his back. "At least, I ain't learning nothing you'd want me to learn." He slammed the window so hard I thought the glass would fly out, and turned back to me. "And I'm sick of the stink of these garbage cans!"

"Sonny," I said, "I know how you feel. But if you don't finish school now, you're going to be sorry later that you didn't." I grabbed him by the shoulders. "And you only got another year. It ain't so bad. And I'll come back and I swear I'll help you do *whatever* you want to do. Just try to put up with it till I come back. Will you please do that? For me?"

He didn't answer and he wouldn't look at me.

"Sonny. You hear me?"

He pulled away. "I hear you. But you never hear anything *I* say."

I didn't know what to say to that. He looked out of the window and then back at me. "OK," he said, and sighed. "I'll try."

Then I said, trying to cheer him up a little, "They got a piano at Isabel's. You can practice on it."

And as a matter of fact, it did cheer him up for a minute. "That's right," he said to himself. "I forgot that." His face relaxed a little. But the worry, the thoughtfulness, played on it still, the way shadows play on a face which is staring into the fire.

But I thought I'd never hear the end of that piano. At first, Isabel would write me, saying how nice it was that Sonny was so serious about his music and how, as soon as he came in from school, or wherever he had been when he

---

6. The G.I. Bill of Rights, established by the Servicemen's Readjustment Act of 1944, which provided a number of veterans' benefits, including tuition assistance.

was supposed to be at school, he went straight to that piano and stayed there until suppertime. And, after supper, he went back to that piano and stayed there until everybody went to bed. He was at the piano all day Saturday and all day Sunday. Then he bought a record player and started playing records. He'd play one record over and over again, all day long sometimes, and he'd improvise along with it on the piano. Or he'd play one section of the record, one chord, one change, one progression, then he'd do it on the piano. Then back to the record. Then back to the piano.

Well, I really don't know how they stood it. Isabel finally confessed that it wasn't like living with a person at all, it was like living with sound. And the sound didn't make any sense to her, didn't make any sense to any of them—naturally. They began, in a way, to be afflicted by this presence that was living in their home. It was as though Sonny were some sort of god, or monster. He moved in an atmosphere which wasn't like theirs at all. They fed him and he ate, he washed himself, he walked in and out of their door; he certainly wasn't nasty or unpleasant or rude, Sonny isn't any of those things; but it was as though he were all wrapped up in some cloud, some fire, some vision all his own; and there wasn't any way to reach him.

At the same time, he wasn't really a man yet, he was still a child, and they had to watch out for him in all kinds of ways. They certainly couldn't throw him out. Neither did they dare to make a great scene about that piano because even they dimly sensed, as I sensed, from so many thousands of miles away, that Sonny was at that piano playing for his life.

But he hadn't been going to school. One day a letter came from the school board and Isabel's mother got it—there had, apparently, been other letters but Sonny had torn them up. This day, when Sonny came in, Isabel's mother showed him the letter and asked where he'd been spending his time. And she finally got it out of him that he'd been down in Greenwich Village, with musicians and other characters, in a white girl's apartment. And this scared her and she started to scream at him and what came up, once she began—though she denies it to this day—was what sacrifices they were making to give Sonny a decent home and how little he appreciated it.

Sonny didn't play the piano that day. By evening, Isabel's mother had calmed down but then there was the old man to deal with, and Isabel herself. Isabel says she did her best to be calm but she broke down and started crying. She says she just watched Sonny's face. She could tell, by watching him, what was happening with him. And what was happening was that they penetrated his cloud, they had reached him. Even if their fingers had been a thousand times more gentle than human fingers ever are, he could hardly help feeling that they had stripped him naked and were spitting on that nakedness. For he also had to see that his presence, that music, which was life or death to him, had been torture for them and that they had endured it, not at all for his sake, but only for mine. And Sonny couldn't take that. He can take it a little better today than he could then but he's still not very good at it and, frankly, I don't know anybody who is.

The silence of the next few days must have been louder than the sound of all the music ever played since time began. One morning, before she went to work, Isabel was in his room for something and she suddenly realized that all of his records were gone. And she knew for certain that he was gone. And he was. He went as far as the navy would carry him. He finally sent me a postcard from some place in Greece and that was the first I knew that Sonny was still alive. I didn't see him any more until we were both back in New York and the war had long been over.

He was a man by then, of course, but I wasn't willing to see it. He came by the house from time to time, but we fought almost every time we met. I didn't like the way he carried himself, loose and dreamlike all the time, and I didn't like his friends, and his music seemed to be merely an excuse for the life he led. It sounded just that weird and disordered.

Then we had a fight, a pretty awful fight, and I didn't see him for months. By and by I looked him up, where he was living, in a furnished room in the Village, and I tried to make it up. But there were lots of other people in the room and Sonny just lay on his bed, and he wouldn't come downstairs with me, and he treated these other people as though they were his family and I weren't. So I got mad and then he got mad, and then I told him that he might just as well be dead as live the way he was living. Then he stood up and he told me not to worry about him any more in life, that he *was* dead as far as I was concerned. Then he pushed me to the door and the other people looked on as though nothing were happening, and he slammed the door behind me. I stood in the hallway, staring at the door. I heard somebody laugh in the room and then the tears came to my eyes. I started down the steps, whistling to keep from crying, I kept whistling to myself, *You going to need me, baby, one of these cold, rainy days.*

I read about Sonny's trouble in the spring. Little Grace died in the fall. She was a beautiful little girl. But she only lived a little over two years. She died of polio and she suffered. She had a slight fever for a couple of days, but it didn't seem like anything and we just kept her in bed. And we would certainly have called the doctor, but the fever dropped, she seemed to be all right. So we thought it had just been a cold. Then, one day, she was up, playing, Isabel was in the kitchen fixing lunch for the two boys when they'd come in from school, and she heard Grace fall down in the living room. When you have a lot of children you don't always start running when one of them falls, unless they start screaming or something. And, this time, Gracie was quiet. Yet, Isabel says that when she heard that *thump* and then that silence, something happened to her to make her afraid. And she ran to the living room and there was little Grace on the floor, all twisted up, and the reason she hadn't screamed was that she couldn't get her breath. And when she did scream, it was the worst sound, Isabel says, that she'd ever heard in all her life, and she still hears it sometimes in her dreams. Isabel will sometimes wake me up with a low, moaning, strangling sound and I have to be quick to awaken her and hold her to me and where Isabel is weeping against me seems a mortal wound.

I think I may have written Sonny the very day that little Grace was buried. I was sitting in the living room in the dark, by myself, and I suddenly thought of Sonny. My trouble made his real.

One Saturday afternoon, when Sonny had been living with us, or anyway, been in our house, for nearly two weeks, I found myself wandering aimlessly about the living room, drinking from a can of beer, and trying to work up courage to search Sonny's room. He was out, he was usually out whenever I was home, and Isabel had taken the children to see their grandparents. Suddenly

I was standing still in front of the living room window, watching Seventh Avenue. The idea of searching Sonny's room made me still. I scarcely dared to admit to myself what I'd be searching for. I didn't know what I'd do if I found it. Or if I didn't.

On the sidewalk across from me, near the entrance to a barbecue joint, some people were holding an old-fashioned revival meeting. The barbecue cook, wearing a dirty white apron, his conked[7] hair reddish and metallic in the pale sun, and a cigarette between his lips, stood in the doorway, watching them. Kids and older people paused in their errands and stood there, along with some older men and a couple of very tough-looking women who watched everything that happened on the avenue, as though they owned it, or were maybe owned by it. Well, they were watching this, too. The revival was being carried on by three sisters in black, and a brother. All they had were their voices and their Bibles and a tambourine. The brother was testifying[8] and while he testified two of the sisters stood together, seeming to say, amen, and the third sister walked around with the tambourine outstretched and a couple of people dropped coins into it. Then the brother's testimony ended and the sister who had been taking up the collection dumped the coins into her palm and transferred them to the pocket of her long black robe. Then she raised both hands, striking the tambourine against the air, and then against one hand, and she started to sing. And the two other sisters and the brother joined in.

It was strange, suddenly, to watch, though I had been seeing these meetings all my life. So, of course, had everybody else down there. Yet, they paused and watched and listened and I stood still at the window. *"'Tis the old ship of Zion,"* they sang, and the sister with the tambourine kept a steady, jangling beat, *"it has rescued many a thousand!"* Not a soul under the sound of their voices was hearing this song for the first time, not one of them had been rescued. Nor had they seen much in the way of rescue work being done around them. Neither did they especially believe in the holiness of the three sisters and the brother, they knew too much about them, knew where they lived, and how. The woman with the tambourine, whose voice dominated the air, whose face was bright with joy, was divided by very little from the woman who stood watching her, a cigarette between her heavy, chapped lips, her hair a cuckoo's nest, her face scarred and swollen from many beatings, and her black eyes glittering like coal. Perhaps they both knew this, which was why, when, as rarely, they addressed each other, they addressed each other as Sister. As the singing filled the air the watching, listening faces underwent a change, the eyes focusing on something within; the music seemed to soothe a poison out of them; and time seemed, nearly, to fall away from the sullen, belligerent, battered faces, as though they were fleeing back to their first condition, while dreaming of their last. The barbecue cook half shook his head and smiled, and dropped his cigarette and disappeared into his joint. A man fumbled in his pockets for change and stood holding it in his hand impatiently, as though he had just remembered a pressing appointment further up the avenue. He looked furious. Then I saw Sonny, standing on the edge of the crowd. He was carrying a wide, flat notebook with a green cover, and it made him look, from where I was standing, almost like a schoolboy. The coppery sun

---

7. Straightened and greased.   8. Proclaiming his religious belief.

brought out the copper in his skin, he was very faintly smiling, standing very still. Then the singing stopped, the tambourine turned into a collection plate again. The furious man dropped in his coins and vanished, so did a couple of the women, and Sonny dropped some change in the plate, looking directly at the woman with a little smile. He started across the avenue, toward the house. He has a slow, loping walk, something like the way Harlem hipsters walk, only he's imposed on this his own half-beat. I had never really noticed it before.

I stayed at the window, both relieved and apprehensive. As Sonny disappeared from my sight, they began singing again. And they were still singing when his key turned in the lock.

"Hey," he said.

"Hey, yourself. You want some beer?"

"No. Well, maybe." But he came up to the window and stood beside me, looking out. "What a warm voice," he said.

They were singing *If I could only hear my mother pray again!*

"Yes," I said, "and she can sure beat that tambourine."

"But what a terrible song," he said, and laughed. He dropped his notebook on the sofa and disappeared into the kitchen. "Where's Isabel and the kids?"

"I think they went to see their grandparents. You hungry?"

"No." He came back into the living room with his can of beer. "You want to come some place with me tonight?"

I sensed, I don't know how, that I couldn't possibly say no. "Sure. Where?"

He sat down on the sofa and picked up his notebook and started leafing through it. "I'm going to sit in with some fellows in a joint in the Village."

"You mean, you're going to play, tonight?"

"That's right." He took a swallow of his beer and moved back to the window. He gave me a sidelong look. "If you can stand it."

"I'll try," I said.

He smiled to himself and we both watched as the meeting across the way broke up. The three sisters and the brother, heads bowed, were singing *God be with you till we meet again.* The faces around them were very quiet. Then the song ended. The small crowd dispersed. We watched the three women and the lone man walk slowly up the avenue.

"When she was singing before," said Sonny, abruptly, "her voice reminded me for a minute of what heroin feels like sometimes—when it's in your veins. It makes you feel sort of warm and cool at the same time. And distant. And—and sure." He sipped his beer, very deliberately not looking at me. I watched his face. "It makes you feel—in control. Sometimes you've got to have that feeling."

"Do you?" I sat down slowly in the easy chair.

"Sometimes." He went to the sofa and picked up his notebook again. "Some people do."

"In order," I asked, "to play?" And my voice was very ugly, full of contempt and anger.

"Well"—he looked at me with great, troubled eyes, as though, in fact, he hoped his eyes would tell me things he could never otherwise say—"they *think* so. And *if* they think so—!"

"And what do *you* think?" I asked.

He sat on the sofa and put his can of beer on the floor. "I don't know," he said, and I couldn't be sure if he were answering my question or pursuing his thoughts. His face didn't tell me. "It's not so much to *play*. It's to *stand* it, to be able to make it at all. On any level." He frowned and smiled: "In order to keep from shaking to pieces."

"But these friends of yours," I said, "they seem to shake themselves to pieces pretty goddamn fast."

"Maybe." He played with the notebook. And something told me that I should curb my tongue, that Sonny was doing his best to talk, that I should listen. "But of course you only know the ones that've gone to pieces. Some don't—or at least they haven't *yet* and that's just about all *any* of us can say." He paused. "And then there are some who just live, really, in hell, and they know it and they see what's happening and they go right on. I don't know." He sighed, dropped the notebook, folded his arms. "Some guys, you can tell from the way they play, they on something *all* the time. And you can see that, well, it makes something real for them. But of course," he picked up his beer from the floor and sipped it and put the can down again, "they *want* to, too, you've got to see that. Even some of them that say they don't—*some,* not all."

"And what about you?" I asked—I couldn't help it. "What about you? Do *you* want to?"

He stood up and walked to the window and I remained silent for a long time. Then he sighed. "Me," he said. Then: "While I was downstairs before, on my way here, listening to that woman sing, it struck me all of a sudden how much suffering she must have had to go through—to sing like that. It's *repulsive* to think you have to suffer that much."

I said: "But there's no way not to suffer—is there, Sonny?"

"I believe not," he said and smiled, "but that's never stopped anyone from trying." He looked at me. "Has it?" I realized, with this mocking look, that there stood between us, forever, beyond the power of time or forgiveness, the fact that I had held silence—so long!—when he had needed human speech to help him. He turned back to the window. "No, there's no way not to suffer. But you try all kinds of ways to keep from drowning in it, to keep on top of it, and to make it seem—well, like *you*. Like you did something, all right, and now you're suffering for it. You know?" I said nothing. "Well you know," he said, impatiently, "why *do* people suffer? Maybe it's better to do something to give it a reason, *any* reason."

"But we just agreed," I said, "that there's no way not to suffer. Isn't it better, then, just to—take it?"

"But nobody just takes it," Sonny cried, "that's what I'm telling you! *Every-body* tries not to. You're just hung up on the *way* some people try—it's not *your* way!"

The hair on my face began to itch, my face felt wet. "That's not true," I said, "that's not true. I don't give a damn what other people do, I don't even care how they suffer. I just care how *you* suffer." And he looked at me. "Please believe me," I said, "I don't want to see you—die—trying not to suffer."

"I won't," he said flatly, "die trying not to suffer. At least, not any faster than anybody else."

"But there's no need," I said, trying to laugh, "is there? in killing yourself."

I wanted to say more, but I couldn't. I wanted to talk about will power and how life could be—well, beautiful. I wanted to say that it was all within; but was it? or, rather, wasn't that exactly the trouble? And I wanted to promise that I would never fail him again. But it would all have sounded—empty words and lies.

So I made the promise to myself and prayed that I would keep it.

"It's terrible sometimes, inside," he said, "that's what's the trouble. You walk these streets, black and funky and cold, and there's not really a living ass to talk to, and there's nothing shaking, and there's no way of getting it out—that storm inside. You can't talk it and you can't make love with it, and when you finally try to get with it and play it, you realize *nobody's* listening. So *you've* got to listen. You got to find a way to listen."

And then he walked away from the window and sat on the sofa again, as though all the wind had suddenly been knocked out of him. "Sometimes you'll do *anything* to play, even cut your mother's throat." He laughed and looked at me. "Or your brother's." Then he sobered. "Or your own." Then: "Don't worry. I'm all right now and I think I'll *be* all right. But I can't forget—where I've been. I don't mean just the physical place I've been, I mean where I've *been*. And *what* I've been."

"What have you been, Sonny?" I asked.

He smiled—but sat sideways on the sofa, his elbow resting on the back, his fingers playing with his mouth and chin, not looking at me. "I've been something I didn't recognize, didn't know I could be. Didn't know anybody could be." He stopped, looking inward, looking helplessly young, looking old. "I'm not talking about it now because I feel *guilty* or anything like that—maybe it would be better if I did, I don't know. Anyway, I can't really talk about it. Not to you, not to anybody," and now he turned and faced me. "Sometimes, you know, and it was actually when I was most *out* of the world, I felt that I was in it, that I was *with* it, really, and I could play or I didn't really have to *play,* it just came out of me, it was there. And I don't know how I played, thinking about it now, but I know I did awful things, those times, sometimes, to people. Or it wasn't that I *did* anything to them—it was that they weren't real." He picked up the beer can; it was empty; he rolled it between his palms: "And other times—well, I needed a fix, I needed to find a place to lean, I needed to clear a space to *listen*—and I couldn't find it, and I—went crazy, I did terrible things to *me,* I was terrible *for* me." He began pressing the beer can between his hands, I watched the metal begin to give. It glittered, as he played with it like a knife, and I was afraid he would cut himself, but I said nothing. "Oh well. I can never tell you. I was all by myself at the bottom of something, stinking and sweating and crying and shaking, and I smelled it, you know? *my* stink, and I thought I'd die if I couldn't get away from it and yet, all the same, I knew that everything I was doing was just locking me in with it. And I didn't know," he paused, still flattening the beer can, "I didn't know, I still *don't* know, something kept telling me that maybe it was good to smell your own stink, but I didn't think that *that* was what I'd been trying to do—and—who can stand it?" and he abruptly dropped the ruined beer can, looking at me with a small, still smile, and then rose, walking to the window as though it were the lodestone rock. I watched his face, he watched the avenue. "I couldn't tell you when Mama died—but the reason I wanted to leave Harlem so bad was to get away from drugs. And then, when I ran away, that's what I was running from—really. When I came back, nothing had changed, *I* hadn't changed, I was just—older." And he stopped, drumming with his fingers on the windowpane. The sun had vanished, soon darkness would fall. I watched his face. "It can come again," he said, almost as though speaking to himself. Then he turned to me. "It can come again," he repeated. "I just want you to know that."

"All right," I said, at last. "So it can come again. All right."

He smiled, but the smile was sorrowful. "I had to try to tell you," he said.

"Yes," I said. "I understand that."

"You're my brother," he said, looking straight at me, and not smiling at all.

"Yes," I repeated, "yes. I understand that."

He turned back to the window, looking out. "All that hatred down there," he said, "all that hatred and misery and love. It's a wonder it doesn't blow the avenue apart."

We went to the only nightclub on a short, dark street, downtown. We squeezed through the narrow, chattering, jampacked bar to the entrance of the big room, where the bandstand was. And we stood there for a moment, for the lights were very dim in this room and we couldn't see. Then, "Hello, boy," said the voice and an enormous black man, much older than Sonny or myself, erupted out of all that atmospheric lighting and put an arm around Sonny's shoulder. "I been sitting right here," he said, "waiting for you."

He had a big voice, too, and heads in the darkness turned toward us.

Sonny grinned and pulled a little away, and said, "Creole, this is my brother. I told you about him."

Creole shook my hand. "I'm glad to meet you, son," he said, and it was clear that he was glad to meet me *there,* for Sonny's sake. And he smiled, "You got a real musician in *your* family," and he took his arm from Sonny's shoulder and slapped him, lightly, affectionately, with the back of his hand.

"Well. Now I've heard it all," said a voice behind us. This was another musician, and a friend of Sonny's, a coal-black, cheerful-looking man, built close to the ground. He immediately began confiding to me, at the top of his lungs, the most terrible things about Sonny, his teeth gleaming like a lighthouse and his laugh coming up out of him like the beginning of an earthquake. And it turned out that everyone at the bar knew Sonny, or almost everyone; some were musicians, working there, or nearby, or not working, some were simply hangers-on, and some were there to hear Sonny play. I was introduced to all of them and they were all very polite to me. Yet, it was clear that, for them, I was only Sonny's brother. Here, I was in Sonny's world. Or, rather: his kingdom. Here, it was not even a question that his veins bore royal blood.

They were going to play soon and Creole installed me, by myself, at a table in a dark corner. Then I watched them, Creole, and the little black man, and Sonny, and the others, while they horsed around, standing just below the bandstand. The light from the bandstand spilled just a little short of them and, watching them laughing and gesturing and moving about, I had the feeling that they, nevertheless, were being most careful not to step into that circle of light too suddenly; that if they moved into the light too suddenly, without thinking, they would perish in flame. Then, while I watched, one of them, the small black man, moved into the light and crossed the bandstand and started fooling around with his drums. Then—being funny and being, also, extremely ceremonious—Creole took Sonny by the arm and led him to the piano. A woman's voice called Sonny's name and a few hands started clapping.

And Sonny, also being funny and being ceremonious, and so touched, I think, that he could have cried, but neither hiding it nor showing it, riding it like a man, grinned, and put both hands to his heart and bowed from the waist.

Creole then went to the bass fiddle and a lean, very bright-skinned brown man jumped up on the bandstand and picked up his horn. So there they were, and the atmosphere on the bandstand and in the room began to change and tighten. Someone stepped up to the microphone and announced them. Then there were all kinds of murmurs. Some people at the bar shushed others. The waitress ran around, frantically getting in the last orders, guys and chicks got closer to each other, and the lights on the bandstand, on the quartet, turned to a kind of indigo. Then they all looked different there. Creole looked about him for the last time, as though he were making certain that all his chickens were in the coop, and then he—jumped and struck the fiddle. And there they were.

All I know about music is that not many people ever really hear it. And even then, on the rare occasions when something opens within, and the music enters, what we mainly hear, or hear corroborated, are personal, private, vanishing evocations. But the man who creates the music is hearing something else, is dealing with the roar rising from the void and imposing order on it as it hits the air. What is evoked in him, then, is of another order, more terrible because it has no words, and triumphant, too, for that same reason. And his triumph, when he triumphs, is ours. I just watched Sonny's face. His face was troubled, he was working hard, but he wasn't with it. And I had the feeling that, in a way, everyone on the bandstand was waiting for him, both waiting for him and pushing him along. But as I began to watch Creole, I realized that it was Creole who held them all back. He had them on a short rein. Up there, keeping the beat with his whole body, wailing on the fiddle, with his eyes half closed, he was listening to everything, but he was listening to Sonny. He was having a dialogue with Sonny. He wanted Sonny to leave the shoreline and strike out for the deep water. He was Sonny's witness that deep water and drowning were not the same thing—he had been there, and he knew. And he wanted Sonny to know. He was waiting for Sonny to do the things on the keys which would let Creole know that Sonny was in the water.

And, while Creole listened, Sonny moved, deep within, exactly like someone in torment. I had never before thought of how awful the relationship must be between the musician and his instrument. He has to fill it, this instrument, with the breath of life, his own. He has to make it do what he wants it to do. And a piano is just a piano. It's made out of so much wood and wires and little hammers and big ones, and ivory. While there's only so much you can do with it, the only way to find this out is to try; to try and make it do everything.

And Sonny hadn't been near a piano for over a year. And he wasn't on much better terms with his life, not the life that stretched before him now. He and the piano stammered, started one way, got scared, stopped; started another way, panicked, marked time, started again; then seemed to have found a direction, panicked again, got stuck. And the face I saw on Sonny I'd never seen before. Everything had been burned out of it, and, at the same time, things usually hidden were being burned in, by the fire and fury of the battle which was occurring in him up there.

Yet, watching Creole's face as they neared the end of the first set, I had the feeling that something had happened, something I hadn't heard. Then they finished, there was scattered applause, and then, without an instant's warning, Creole started into something else, it was almost sardonic, it was *Am I Blue?*[9] And, as though he commanded, Sonny began to play. Something began to happen. And Creole let out the reins. The dry, low, black man said something awful on the drums, Creole answered, and the drums talked back. Then the horn insisted, sweet and high, slightly detached perhaps, and Creole listened, commenting now and then, dry, and driving, beautiful and calm and old. Then they all came together again, and Sonny was part of the family again. I could tell this from his face. He seemed to have found, right there beneath his fingers, a damn brand-new piano. It seemed that he couldn't get over it. Then, for a while, just being happy with Sonny, they seemed to be agreeing with him that brand-new pianos certainly were a gas.

Then Creole stepped forward to remind them that what they were playing was the blues. He hit something in all of them, he hit something in me, myself, and the music tightened and deepened, apprehension began to beat the air. Creole began to tell us what the blues were all about. They were not about anything very new. He and his boys up there were keeping it new, at the risk of ruin, destruction, madness, and death, in order to find new ways to make us listen. For, while the tale of how we suffer, and how we are delighted, and how we may triumph is never new, it always must be heard. There isn't any other tale to tell, it's the only light we've got in all this darkness.

And this tale, according to that face, that body, those strong hands on those strings, has another aspect in every country, and a new depth in every generation. Listen, Creole seemed to be saying, listen. Now these are Sonny's blues. He made the little black man on the drums know it, and the bright, brown man on the horn. Creole wasn't trying any longer to get Sonny in the water. He was wishing him Godspeed. Then he stepped back, very slowly, filling the air with the immense suggestion that Sonny speak for himself.

Then they all gathered around Sonny and Sonny played. Every now and again one of them seemed to say, amen. Sonny's fingers filled the air with life, his life. But that life contained so many others. And Sonny went all the way back, he really began with the spare, flat statement of the opening phrase of the song. Then he began to make it his. It was very beautiful because it wasn't hurried and it was no longer a lament. I seemed to hear with what burning he had made it his, and what burning we had yet to make it ours, how we could cease lamenting. Freedom lurked around us and I understood, at last, that he could help us to be free if we would listen, that he would never be free until we did. Yet, there was no battle in his face now, I heard what he had gone through, and would continue to go through until he came to rest in earth. He had made it his: that long line, of which we knew only Mama and Daddy. And he was giving it back, as everything must be given back, so that, passing through death, it can live forever. I saw my mother's face again, and felt, for the first time, how the stones of the road she had walked on must have bruised her feet. I saw the moonlit road where my father's brother died. And it brought something else back to me, and carried me past it, I saw my little girl again and felt Isabel's tears again, and I felt my own tears begin to rise. And I was yet aware that this was only a moment, that the world waited outside, as hungry as a tiger, and that trouble stretched above us, longer than the sky.

brings them away from the trash world outside

9. A jazz tune, by H. Akst and G. Clarke, from *On With the Show* (1929).

Then it was over. Creole and Sonny let out their breath, both soaking wet, and grinning. There was a lot of applause and some of it was real. In the dark, the girl came by and I asked her to take drinks to the bandstand. There was a long pause, while they talked up there in the indigo light and after awhile I saw the girl put a Scotch and milk on top of the piano for Sonny. He didn't seem to notice it, but just before they started playing again, he sipped from it and looked toward me, and nodded. Then he put it back on top of the piano. For me, then, as they began to play again, it glowed and shook above my brother's head like the very cup of trembling.[1]

1957

---

1. Isaiah 51:22: "I have taken out of thine hand the cup of trembling . . . thou shalt no more drink it again."

TONI CADE BAMBARA
1939–1995

Bambara was born in New York and grew up in two of the city's poorest neighborhoods, Harlem and Bedford-Stuyvesant. Early in life she was drawn to social activism and in high school years learned that writing is a splendid means of doing battle. For years after graduating from Queens College, she wrote fiction in "the predawn in-betweens" while earning her M.A. at the City College of New York and working at a great variety of jobs: dancer, social worker, psychiatric counselor, college English teacher, literary critic, and film producer. She began to publish short stories in 1960, and in 1972 many of these were collected in her first book, *Gorilla, My Love*. This was followed by another collection, *The Sea Birds Are Still Alive* (1977), and two novels: *The Salt Eaters* (1980) and *Those Bones Are Not My Child*, published posthumously in 1999.

Gorilla, My Love

That was the year Hunca Bubba changed his name. Not a change up, but a change back, since Jefferson Winston Vale was the name in the first place. Which was news to me cause he'd been my Hunca Bubba my whole lifetime, since I couldn't manage Uncle to save my life. So far as I was concerned it was a change completely to somethin soundin very geographical weatherlike to me, like somethin you'd find in a almanac. Or somethin you'd run across when you sittin in the navigator seat with a wet thumb on the map crinkly in your lap, watchin the roads and signs so when Granddaddy Vale say "Which way, Scout," you got sense enough to say take the next exit or take a left or whatever it is. Not that Scout's my name. Just the name Granddaddy call whoever sittin in the navigator seat. Which is usually me cause I don't feature sittin in the back with the pecans. Now, you figure pecans all right to be sittin with. If you thinks so, that's your business. But they dusty sometime and make you cough. And they got a way of slidin around and dippin down sudden, like maybe a rat in the buckets. So if you scary like me, you sleep with the lights on and blame it on Baby Jason and, so as not to waste good electric, you study the maps. And that's how come I'm in the navigator seat most times and get to be called Scout.

So Hunca Bubba in the back with the pecans and Baby Jason, and he in love. And we got to hear all this stuff about this woman he in love with and all. Which really ain't enough to keep the mind alive, though Baby Jason got no better sense than to give his undivided attention and keep grabbin at the photograph which is just a picture of some skinny woman in a countrified dress with her hand shot up to her face like she shame fore cameras. But there's a movie house in the background which I ax about. Cause I am a movie freak from way back, even though it do get me in trouble sometime.

Like when me and Big Brood and Baby Jason was on our own last Easter and couldn't go to the Dorset cause we'd seen all the Three Stooges they was. And the RKO Hamilton was closed readying up for the Easter Pageant that night. And the West End, the Regun and the Sunset was too far, less we had grown-ups with us which we didn't. So we walk up Amsterdam Avenue to the Washington and *Gorilla, My Love* playin, they say, which suit me just fine, though the "my love" part kinda drag Big Brood some. As for Baby Jason, shoot, like Granddaddy say, he'd follow me into the fiery furnace if I say come on. So we go in and get three bags of Havmore potato chips which not only are the best potato chips but the best bags for blowin up and bustin real loud so the matron come trottin down the aisle with her chunky self, flashin that flashlight dead in your eye so you can give her some lip, and if she answer back and you already finish seein the show anyway, why then you just turn the place out. Which I love to do, no lie. With Baby Jason kickin at the seat in front, egging me on, and Big Brood mumblin bout what fiercesome things we goin do. Which means me. Like when the big boys come up on us talkin bout Lemme a nickel. It's me that hide the money. Or when the bad boys in the park take Big Brood's Spaudeen[1] way from him. It's me that jump on they back and fight awhile. And it's me that turns out the show if the matron get too salty.

So the movie come on and right away it's this churchy music and clearly not about no gorilla. Bout Jesus. And I am ready to kill, not cause I got anything gainst Jesus. Just that when you fixed to watch a gorilla picture you don't wanna get messed around with Sunday School stuff. So I am mad. Besides, we see this raggedy old brown film *King of Kings*[2] every year and enough's enough. Grown-ups figure they can treat you just anyhow. Which burns me up. There I am, my feet up and my Havmore potato chips really salty and crispy and two jaw-breakers in my lap and the money safe in my shoe from the big boys, and there comes this Jesus stuff. So we all go wild. Yellin, booin, stompin and carrying on. Really to wake the man in the booth up there who musta went to sleep and put on the wrong reels. But no, cause he holler down to shut up and then he turn the sound up so we really gotta holler like crazy to even hear ourselves good. And the matron ropes off the children section and flashes her light all over the place and we yell some more and some kids slip under the rope and run up and down the aisle just to show it take more than some dusty ole velvet rope to tie us down. And I'm flingin the kid in front of me's popcorn. And Baby Jason kickin seats. And it's really somethin. Then here come the big and bad matron, the one they let out in case of emergency. This here the colored matron Brandy and her friends call Thunderbuns. She do not play. She do not smile. So we shut up and watch the simple ass picture.

Which is not so simple as it is stupid. Cause I realized that just about any-body in my family is better than this god they always talkin about. My daddy wouldn't stand for nobody treatin any of us that way. My mama specially. And I can just see it now, Big Brood up there on the cross talkin bout Forgive

---

1. Rubber balls used in stickball, an urban form of baseball.   **2.** Silent movie depicting the life of Christ.

them Daddy cause they don't know what they doin. And my Mama say Get on down from there you big fool, whatcha think this is, playtime? And my Daddy yellin to Granddaddy to get him a ladder cause Big Brood actin the fool, his mother side of the family showin up. And my mama and her sister Daisy jumpin on them Romans beatin them with they pocketbooks. And Hunca Bubba tellin them folks on they knees they better get out the way and go get some help or they goin to get trampled on. And Granddaddy Vale sayin Leave the boy alone, if that's what he wants to do with his life we ain't got nothin to say about it. Then Aunt Daisy givin him a taste of that pocketbook, fussin bout what a damn fool old man Granddaddy is. Then everybody jumpin in his chest like the time Uncle Clayton went in the army and come back with only one leg and Granddaddy say somethin stupid about that's life. And by this time Big Brood off the cross and in the park playin handball or skully or some-thin. And the family in the kitchen throwin dishes at each other, screamin bout if you hadn't done this I wouldn't had to do that. And me in the parlor trying to do my arithmetic yellin Shut it off.

Which is what I was yellin all by myself which make me a sittin target for Thunderbuns. But when I yell We want our money back, that gets everybody in chorus. And the movie windin up with this heavenly cloud music and the smart-ass up there in his hole in the wall turns up the sound again to drown us out. Then there comes Bugs Bunny which we already seen so we know we been had. No gorilla my nuthin. And Big Brood say Awwww sheeet, we goin to see the manager and get our money back. And I know from this we busi-ness. So I brush the potato chips out of my hair which is where Baby Jason like to put em, and I march myself up the aisle to deal with the manager who is a crook in the first place for lyin out there sayin *Gorilla, My Love* playin. And I never did like the man cause he oily and pasty at the same time like the bad guy in the serial, the one that got a hideout behind a push-button bookcase and play "Moonlight Sonata" with gloves on. I knock on the door and I am furious. And I am alone, too. Cause Big Brood suddenly got to go so bad even though my mama told us bout goin in them nasty bathrooms. And I hear him sigh like he disgusted when he get to the door and see only a little kid there. And now I'm really furious cause I get so tired grownups messin over kids cause they little and can't take em to court. What is it, he say to me like I lost my mittens or wet myself or am somebody's retarded child. When in reality I am the smartest kid P.S. 186 ever had in its whole lifetime and you can ax any-body. Even them teachers that don't like me cause I won't sing them Southern songs or back off when they tell me my questions are out of order. And cause my Mama come up there in a minute when them teachers start playin the doz-ens[3] behind colored folks. She stalks in with her hat pulled down bad and that Persian lamb coat draped back over one hip on account of she got her fist planted there so she can talk that talk which gets us all hypnotized, and teacher be comin undone cause she know this could be her job and her behind cause Mama got pull with the Board and bad by her own self anyhow.

So I kick the door open wider and just walk right by him and sit down and tell the man about himself and that I want my money back and that goes for Baby Jason and Big Brood too. And he still trying to shuffle me out the door

---

3. Trading insults about each other's relatives.

even though I'm sittin which shows him for the fool he is. Just like them teachers do fore they realize Mama like a stone on that spot and ain't backin up. So he ain't gettin up off the money. So I was forced to leave, takin the matches from under his ashtray, and set a fire under the candy stand, which closed the raggedy ole Washington down for a week. My Daddy had the suspect it was me cause Big Brood got a big mouth. But I explained right quick what the whole thing was about and I figured it was even-steven. Cause if you say Gorilla, My Love, you supposed to mean it. Just like when you say you goin to give me a party on my birthday, you gotta mean it. And if you say me and Baby Jason can go South pecan haulin with Granddaddy Vale, you better not be comin up with no stuff about the weather look uncertain or did you mop the bathroom or any other trickified business. I mean even gangsters in the movies say My word is my bond. So don't nobody get away with nothin far as I'm concerned. So Daddy put his belt back on. Cause that's the way I was raised. Like my Mama say in one of them situations when I won't back down, Okay Badbird, you right. Your point is well-taken. Not that Badbird my name, just what she say when she tired arguin and know I'm right. And Aunt Jo, who is the hardest head in the family and worse even than Aunt Daisy, she say, You absolutely right Miss Muffin, which also ain't my real name but the name she gave me one time when I got some medicine shot in my behind and wouldn't get up off her pillows for nothin. And even Granddaddy Vale—who got no memory to speak of, so sometime you can just plain lie to him, if you want to be like that—he say, Well if that's what I said, then that's it. But this name business was different they said. It wasn't like Hunca Bubba had gone back on his word or anything. Just that he was thinkin bout gettin married and was usin his real name now. Which ain't the way I saw it at all.

So there I am in the navigator seat. And I turned to him and just plain ole ax him. I mean I come right on out with it. No sense goin all around that barn the old folks talk about. And like my mama say, Hazel—which is my real name and what she remembers to call me when she bein serious—when you got somethin on your mind, speak up and let the chips fall where they may. And if anybody don't like it, tell em to come see your mama. And Daddy look up from the paper and say, You hear your Mama good, Hazel. And tell em to come see me first. Like that. That's how I was raised.

So I turn clear round in the navigator seat and say, "Look here, Hunca Bubba or Jefferson Windsong Vale or whatever your name is, you gonna marry this girl?"

"Sure am," he say, all grins.

And I say, "Member that time you was baby-sittin me when we lived at four-o-nine and there was this big snow and Mama and Daddy got held up in the country so you had to stay for two days?"

And he say, "Sure do."

"Well. You remember how you told me I was the cutest thing that ever walked the earth?"

"Oh, you were real cute when you were little," he say, which is supposed to be funny. I am not laughin.

"Well. You remember what you said?"

And Granddaddy Vale squintin over the wheel and axin Which way, Scout. But Scout is busy and don't care if we all get lost for days.

"Watcha mean, Peaches?"

"My name is Hazel. And what I mean is you said you were going to marry *me* when I grew up. You were going to wait. That's what I mean, my dear Uncle Jefferson." And he don't say nuthin. Just look at me real strange like he never saw me before in life. Like he lost in some weird town in the middle of night and lookin for directions and there's no one to ask. Like it was me that messed up the maps and turned the road posts round. "Well, you said it, didn't you?" And Baby Jason lookin back and forth like we playin ping-pong. Only I ain't playin. I'm hurtin and I can hear that I am screamin. And Granddaddy Vale mumblin how we never gonna get to where we goin if I don't turn around and take my navigator job serious.

"Well, for cryin out loud, Hazel, you just a little girl. And I was just teasin."

"'And I was just teasin,'" I say back just how he said it so he can hear what a terrible thing it is. Then I don't say nuthin. And he don't say nuthin. And Baby Jason don't say nuthin nohow. Then Granddaddy Vale speak up. "Look here, Precious, it was Hunca Bubba what told you them things. This here, Jefferson Winston Vale." And Hunca Bubba say, "That's right. That was somebody else. I'm a new somebody."

"You a lyin dawg," I say, when I meant to say treacherous dog, but just couldn't get hold of the word. It slipped away from me. And I'm crying and crumplin down in the seat and just don't care. And Granddaddy say to hush and steps on the gas. And I'm losin my bearins and don't even know where to look on the map cause I can't see for cryin. And Baby Jason cryin too. Cause he is my blood brother and understands that we must stick together or be forever lost, what with grown-ups playin change-up and turnin you round every which way so bad. And don't even say they sorry.

1972

RELATED:

—Bambara, "What Is It I Think I'm Doing Anyhow?" p. 1706

ANDREA BARRETT
b. 1954

Barrett grew up on Cape Cod, Massachusetts, and earned a B.S. in biology at Union College, Schenectady, New York. She didn't start writing fiction seriously until her thirties, after she walked away from a Ph.D. program in zoology. She is the recipient of a National Book Award for Fiction in 1996 for *Ship Fever* and a Guggenheim Fellowship in 1997. Her novel *The Voyage of the Narwhal* (1998) narrates a nineteenth-century Arctic expedition, and many of its characters reappear in *Servants of the Map* (2002), a collection of short stories that was a Pulitzer Prize finalist. In 2001 Barrett received a MacArthur Fellowship. Her latest fiction collection, *Archangel,* was published in 2013.

The Littoral Zone

When they met, fifteen years ago, Jonathan had a job teaching botany at a small college near Albany, and Ruby was teaching invertebrate zoology at a college in the Berkshires.[1] Both of them, along with an ornithologist, an ichthyologist, and an oceanographer, had agreed to spend three weeks of their summer break at a marine biology research station on an island off the New Hampshire coast. They had spouses, children, mortgages, bills; they went, they later told each other, because the pay was too good to refuse. Two-thirds of the way through the course, they agreed that the pay was not enough.

How they reached that first agreement is a story they've repeated to each other again and again and told, separately, to their closest friends. Ruby thinks they had this conversation on the second Friday of the course, after Frank Kenary's slide show on the abyssal fish and before Carol Dagliesh's lecture on the courting behavior of herring gulls. Jonathan maintains that they had it earlier—that Wednesday, maybe, when they were still recovering from Gunnar Erickson's trawling expedition. The days before they became so aware of each other have blurred in their minds, but they agree that their first real conversation took place on the afternoon devoted to the littoral zone.

The tide was all the way out. The students were clumped on the rocky, pitted apron between the water and the ledges, peering into the tidal pools and listing the species they found. Gunnar was in the equipment room, repairing one of the sampling claws. Frank was setting up dissections in the tiny lab; Carol had gone back to the mainland on the supply boat, hoping to replace

---

1. A low mountain range in western Massachusetts.

the camera one of the students had dropped. And so the two of them, Jonathan and Ruby, were left alone for a little while.

They both remember the granite ledge where they sat, and the raucous quarrels of the nesting gulls. They agree that Ruby was scratching furiously at her calves and that Jonathan said, "Take it easy, okay? You'll draw blood."

Her calves were slim and tan, Jonathan remembers. Covered with blotches and scrapes.

I folded my fingers, Ruby remembers. Then I blushed. My throat felt sunburned.

Ruby said, "I know, it's so embarrassing. But all this salt on my poison ivy— God, what I wouldn't give for a bath! They never told me there wouldn't be any *water* here. . . ."

Jonathan gestured at the ocean surrounding them and then they started laughing. *Hysteria*, they have told each other since. They were so tired by then, twelve days into the course, and so dirty and overworked and strained by pretending to the students that these things didn't matter, that neither of them could understand that they were also lonely. Their shared laughter felt like pure relief.

"No water?" Jonathan said. "I haven't been dry since we got here. My clothes are damp, my sneakers are damp, my hair never dries. . . ."

His hair was beautiful, Ruby remembers. Thick, a little too long. Part blond and part brown.

"I know," she said. "But you know what I mean. I didn't realize they'd have to bring our drinking water over on a boat."

"Or that they'd expect us to wash in the ocean," Jonathan said. Her forearms were dusted with salt, he remembers. The down along them sparkled in the sun.

"And those cots," Ruby said. "Does yours have a sag in it like a hammock?"

"Like a slingshot," Jonathan said.

For half an hour they sat on their ledge and compared their bubbling patches of poison ivy and the barnacle wounds that scored their hands and feet. Nothing healed out here, they told each other. Everything got infected. When one of the students called, "Look what I found!" Jonathan rose and held his hand out to Ruby. She took it easily and hauled herself up and they walked down to the water together. Jonathan's hand was thick and bluntfingered, with nails bitten down so far that the skin around them was raw. Odd, Ruby remembers thinking. Those bitten stumps attached to such a goodlooking man.

They have always agreed that the worst moment, for each of them, was when they stepped from the boat to the dock on the final day of the course and saw their families waiting in the parking lot. Jonathan's wife had their four-year-old daughter balanced on her shoulders. Their two older children were leaning perilously over the guardrails and shrieking at the sight of him. Jessie had turned nine in Jonathan's absence, and Jonathan can't think of her eager face without remembering the starfish he brought as his sole, guilty gift.

Ruby's husband had parked their car just a few yards from Jonathan's family. Her sons were wearing baseball caps, and what Ruby remembers is the way the yellow linings lit their faces. For a minute she saw the children squealing near her sons as faceless, inconsequential; Jonathan later told her that her children had been similarly blurred for him. Then Jonathan said, "That's my family, there," and Ruby said, "That's mine, right next to yours," and all the faces leapt into focus for both of them.

Nothing that was to come—not the days in court, nor the days they moved, nor the losses of jobs and homes—would ever seem so awful to them as that moment when they first saw their families standing there, unaware and hopeful. Deceitfully, treacherously, Ruby and Jonathan separated and walked to the people awaiting them. They didn't introduce each other to their spouses. They didn't look at each other—although, they later admitted, they cast covert looks at each other's families. They thought they were invisible, that no one could see what had happened between them. They thought their families would not remember how they had stepped off the boat and stood, for an instant, together.

On that boat, sitting dumb and miserable in the litter of nets and equipment, they had each pretended to be resigned to going home. Each foresaw (or so they later told each other) the hysterical phone calls and the frenzied, secret meetings. Neither foresaw how much the sight of each other's family would hurt. "Sweetie," Jonathan remembers Ruby's husband saying. "You've lost so much weight." Ruby remembers staring over her husband's shoulder and watching Jessie butt her head like a dog under Jonathan's hand.

For the first twelve days on the island, Jonathan and Ruby were so busy that they hardly noticed each other. For the next few days, after their conversation on the ledge, they sat near each other during faculty lectures and student presentations. These were held in the library, a ramshackle building separated from the bunkhouse and the dining hall by a stretch of wild roses and poison ivy.

Jonathan had talked about algae in there, holding up samples of *Fucus* and *Hildenbrandtia*.[2] Ruby had talked about the littoral zone, that space between high and low watermarks where organisms struggled to adapt to the daily rhythm of immersion and exposure. They had drawn on the blackboard in colored chalk while the students, itchy and hot and tired, scratched their arms and legs and feigned attention.

Neither of them, they admitted much later, had focused fully on the other's lecture. "It was *before*," Ruby has said ruefully. "I didn't know that I was going to want to have listened." And Jonathan has laughed and confessed that he was studying the shells and skulls on the walls while Ruby was drawing on the board.

The library was exceedingly hot, they agreed, and the chairs remarkably uncomfortable; the only good spot was the sofa in front of the fireplace. That was the spot they commandeered on the evening after their first conversation, when dinner led to a walk and then the walk led them into the library a few minutes before the scheduled lecture.

Erika Moorhead, Ruby remembers. Talking about the tensile strength of byssus threads.[3]

Walter Schank, Jonathan remembers. Something to do with hydrozoans.[4]

---

2. Common seaweeds found on rocky coasts.   **3.** Long, tough filaments by which some mollusks, such as mussels, bind themselves to rocks or to each other.   **4.** A class of jellyfish that includes the Portuguese man-of-war.

They both remember feeling comfortable for the first time since their arrival. And for the next few days—three by Ruby's accounting; four by Jonathan's—one of them came early for every lecture and saved a seat on the sofa for the other.

They giggled at Frank Kenary's slides, which he'd arranged like a creepy fashion show: abyssal fish sporting varied blobs of luminescent flesh. When Gunnar talked for two hours about subduction zones[5] and the calcium carbonate cycle, they amused themselves exchanging doodles. They can't remember, now, whether Gunnar's endless lecture came before Carol Dagliesh's filmstrip on the herring gulls, or which of the students tipped over the dissecting scope and sent the dish of copepods[6] to their deaths. But both of them remember those days and nights as being almost purely happy. They swam in that odd, indefinite zone where they were more than friends, not yet lovers, still able to deny to themselves that they were headed where they were headed.

Ruby made the first phone call, a week after they left the island. At eleven o'clock on a Sunday night, she told her husband she'd left something in her office that she needed to prepare the next day's class. She drove to campus, unlocked her door, picked up the phone and called Jonathan at his house. One of his children—Jessie, she thinks—answered the phone. Ruby remembers how, even through the turmoil of her emotions, she'd been shocked at the idea of a child staying up so late.

There was a horrible moment while Jessie went to find her father; another when Jonathan, hearing Ruby's voice, said, "Wait, hang on, I'll just be a minute," and then negotiated Jessie into bed. Ruby waited, dreading his anger, knowing she'd been wrong to call him at home. But Jonathan, when he finally returned, said, "Ruby. You got my letter."

"What letter?" she asked. He wrote to tell me good-bye, she remembers thinking.

"My *letter*," he said. "I wrote you, I have to see you. I can't stand this."

Ruby released the breath she hadn't known she was holding.

"You didn't get it?" he said. "You just called?" It wasn't only me, he remembers thinking. She feels it too.

"I had to hear your voice," she said.

Ruby called, but Jonathan wrote. And so when Jonathan's youngest daughter, Cora, later fell in love and confided in Ruby, and then asked her, "Was it like this with you two? Who started it—you or Dad?" all Ruby could say was, "It happened to both of us."

Sometimes, when Ruby and Jonathan sit on the patio looking out at the hills above Palmyra,[7] they will turn and see their children watching them through the kitchen window. Before the children went off to college, the house bulged with them on weekends and holidays and seemed empty in between; Jonathan's wife had custody of Jessie and Gordon and Cora, and Ruby's husband took her sons, Mickey and Ryan, when he remarried. Now that the children

---

5. Areas where the edge of one tectonic plate of the earth's crust descends below the edge of another.
6. Tiny crustaceans, the chief component of the mass of organisms floating passively in ocean currents and forming marine plankton.   7. Town in western New York State near the city of Rochester.

are old enough to come and go as they please, the house is silent almost all the time.

Jessie is twenty-four, and Gordon is twenty-two; Mickey is twenty-one, and Cora and Ryan are both nineteen. When they visit Jonathan and Ruby they spend an unhealthy amount of time talking about their past. In their conversations they seem to split their lives into three epochs: the years when what they think of as their real families were whole; the years right after Jonathan and Ruby met, when their parents were coming and going, fighting and making up, separating and divorcing; and the years since Jonathan and Ruby's marriage, when they were forced into a reconstituted family. Which epoch they decide to explore depends on who's visiting and who's getting along with whom.

"But we were happy," Mickey may say to Ruby, if he and Ryan are visiting and Jonathan's children are absent. "We were, we were fine."

"It wasn't like you and Mom ever fought," Cora may say to Jonathan, if Ruby's sons aren't around. "You could have worked it out if you'd tried."

When they are all together, they tend to avoid the first two epochs and to talk about their first strained weekends and holidays together. They've learned to tolerate each other, despite their forced introductions; Cora and Ryan, whose birthdays are less than three months apart, seem especially close. Ruby and Jonathan know that much of what draws their youngest children together is shared speculation about what happened on that island.

They look old to their children, they know. Both of them are nearing fifty. Jonathan has grown quite heavy and has lost much of his hair; Ruby's fine-boned figure has gone gaunt and stringy. They know their children can't imagine them young and strong and wrung by passion. The children can't think—can't stand to think—about what happened on the island, but they can't stop themselves from asking questions.

"Did you have other girlfriends?" Cora asks Jonathan. "Were you so unhappy with Mom?"

"Did you know him before?" Ryan asks Ruby. "Did you go there to be with him?"

"We met there," Jonathan and Ruby say. "We had never seen each other before. We fell in love." That is all they will say, they never give details, they say "yes" or "no" to the easy questions and evade the hard ones. They worry that even the little they offer may be too much.

Jonathan and Ruby tell each other the stories of their talk by the tidal pool, their walks and meals, the sagging sofa, the moment in the parking lot, and the evening Ruby made her call. They tell these to console themselves when their children chide them or when, alone in the house, they sit quietly near each other and struggle to conceal their disappointments.

Of course they have expected some of these. Mickey and Gordon have both had trouble in school, and Jessie has grown much too close to her mother; neither Jonathan nor Ruby has found jobs as good as the ones they lost, and their new home in Palmyra still doesn't feel quite like home. But all they have lost in order to be together would seem bearable had they continued to feel the way they felt on the island.

They're sensible people, and very well-mannered; they remind themselves that they were young then and are middle-aged now, and that their fierce attraction would naturally ebb with time. Neither likes to think about how much of the thrill of their early days together came from the obstacles they had to overcome. Some days, when Ruby pulls into the driveway still thinking about her last class and catches sight of Jonathan out in the garden, she can't believe the heavyset figure pruning shrubs so meticulously is the man for whom she fought such battles. Jonathan, who often wakes very early, sometimes stares at Ruby's sleeping face and thinks how much more gracefully his ex-wife is aging.

They never reproach each other. When the tension builds in the house and the silence becomes overwhelming, one or the other will say, "Do you remember . . . ?" and then launch into one of the myths on which they have founded their lives. But there is one story they never tell each other, because they can't bear to talk about what they have lost. This is the one about the evening that has shaped their life together.

Jonathan's hand on Ruby's back, Ruby's hand on Jonathan's thigh, a shirt unbuttoned, a belt undone. They never mention this moment, or the moments that followed it, because that would mean discussing who seduced whom, and any resolution of that would mean assigning blame. Guilt they can handle; they've been living with guilt for fifteen years. But blame? It would be more than either of them could bear, to know the exact moment when one of them precipitated all that has happened to them. The most either of them has ever said is, "How could we have known?"

But the night in the library is what they both think about, when they lie silently next to each other and listen to the wind. It must be summer for them to think about it; the children must be with their other parents and the rain must be falling on the cedar shingles overhead. A candle must be burning on the mantel above the bed and the maple branches outside their window must be tossing against each other. Then they think of the story they know so well and never say out loud.

There was a huge storm three nights before they left the island, the tail end of a hurricane passing farther out to sea. The cedar trees creaked and swayed in the wind beyond the library windows. The students had staggered off to bed, after the visitor from Woods Hole[8] had finished his lecture on the explorations of the *Alvin* in the Cayman Trough,[9] and Frank and Gunnar and Carol had shrouded themselves in their rain gear and left as well, sheltering the visitor between them. Ruby sat at one end of the long table, preparing bottles of fixative[1] for their expedition the following morning, and Jonathan lay on the sofa writing notes. The boat was leaving just after dawn and they knew they ought to go to bed.

The wind picked up outside, sweeping the branches against the walls. The windows rattled. Jonathan shivered and said, "Do you suppose we could get a fire going in that old fireplace?"

"I bet we could," said Ruby, which gave both of them the pretext they needed to crouch side by side on the cracked tiles, brushing elbows as they opened the flue and crumpled paper and laid kindling in the form of a grid.

---

8. The Woods Hole Oceanographic Institute in Massachusetts. **9.** A deep oceanic trench in the northeastern Caribbean Sea. *Alvin:* a deep-sea submarine used for scientific research. **1.** A substance used to preserve living tissue.

The logs Jonathan found near the lobster traps were dry and the fire caught quickly.

Who found the green candle in the drawer below the microscope? Who lit the candle and turned off the lights? And who found the remains of the jug of wine that Frank had brought in honor of the visitor? They sat there side by side, poking at the burning logs and pretending they weren't doing what they were doing. The wind pushed through the window they'd opened a crack, and the tan window shade lifted and then fell back against the frame. The noise was soothing at first; later it seemed irritating.

Jonathan, whose fingernails were bitten to the quick, admired the long nail on Ruby's right little finger and then said, half-seriously, how much he'd love to bite a nail like that. When Ruby held her hand to his mouth he took the nail between his teeth and nibbled through the white tip, which days in the water had softened. Ruby slipped her other hand inside his shirt and ran it up his back. Jonathan ran his mouth up her arm and down her neck.

They started in front of the fire and worked their way across the floor, breaking a glass, knocking the table askew. Ruby rubbed her back raw against the rug and Jonathan scraped his knees, and twice they paused and laughed at their wild excesses. They moved across the floor from east to west and later from west to east, and between those two journeys, during the time when they heaped their clothes and the sofa cushions into a nest in front of the fire, they talked.

This was not the kind of conversation they'd had during walks and meals since that first time on the rocks: who they were, where they'd come from, how they'd made it here. This was the talk where they instinctively edited out the daily pleasures of their lives on the mainland and spliced together the hard times, the dark times, until they'd constructed versions of themselves that could make sense of what they'd just done.

For months after this, as they lay in stolen, secret rooms between houses and divorces and jobs and lives, Jonathan would tell Ruby that he swallowed her nail. The nail dissolved in his stomach, he'd say. It passed into his villi[2] and out to his blood and then flowed to bone and muscle and nerve, where the molecules that had once been part of her became part of him. Ruby, who always seemed to know more acutely than Jonathan that they'd have to leave whatever room this was in an hour or a day, would argue with him.

"Nails are keratin," she'd tell him. "Like hooves and hair. Like wool. We can't digest wool."

"Moths can," Jonathan would tell her. "Moths eat sweaters."

"Moths have a special enzyme in their saliva," Ruby would say. This was true, she knew it for a fact. She'd been so taken by Jonathan's tale that she'd gone to the library to check out the details and discovered he was wrong.

But Jonathan didn't care what the biochemists said. He held her against his chest and said, "I have an enzyme for you."

That night, after the fire burned out, they slept for a couple of hours. Ruby woke first and watched Jonathan sleep for a while. He slept like a child, with his knees bent toward his chest and his hands clasped between his thighs. Ruby picked up the tipped-over chair and swept the fragments of broken

---

2. Tiny projections inside the small intestine, which absorb nutrients.

glass onto a sheet of paper. Then she woke Jonathan and they tiptoed back to the rooms where they were supposed to be.

1996

RELATED:

—Barrett on Willa Cather's "Paul's Case," p. 1755

DONALD BARTHELME
1931–1989

Barthelme was born in Philadelphia and grew up in Texas, where he worked as a reporter, editor, and even director of Houston's Contemporary Arts Museum before settling in New York City in 1962. "The principle of collage," he once declared, "is the central principle of all art in the twentieth century." Indeed, his pictorial collages were frequently published in newspapers and magazines, and his characteristic fiction often seems to be constructed as collage—a pasting together of fragments gathered from the chaotic verbiage of our culture, set in comic and unexpected juxtapositions. Advertising slogans, street slang, sociological jargon, clichés, and faded jokes appear in patterns that expose their usually overlooked significance. His novels are *Snow White* (1967), *The Dead Father* (1975), and *The King* (1990). His stories are collected in volumes including *Come Back, Dr. Caligari* (1966), *Unspeakable Practices, Unnatural Acts* (1968), *City Life* (1970), *Amateurs* (1976), and *Sixty Stories* (1981). His more recent books include *Overnight to Many Distant Cities* (1983) and *Forty Stories* (1987).

Me and Miss Mandible

13 September

Miss Mandible wants to make love to me but she hesitates because I am officially a child; I am, according to the records, according to the gradebook on her desk, according to the card index in the principal's office, eleven years old. There is a misconception here, one that I haven't quite managed to get cleared up yet. I am in fact thirty-five, I've been in the Army, I am six feet one, I have hair in the appropriate places, my voice is a baritone, I know very well what to do with Miss Mandible if she ever makes up her mind.

In the meantime we are studying common fractions. I could, of course, answer all the questions, or at least most of them (there are things I don't remember). But I prefer to sit in this too-small seat with the desktop cramping my thighs and examine the life around me. There are thirty-two in the class, which is launched every morning with the pledge of allegiance to the flag. My own allegiance, at the moment, is divided between Miss Mandible and Sue Ann Brownly, who sits across the aisle from me all day long and is, like Miss Mandible, a fool for love. Of the two I prefer, today, Sue Ann; although between eleven and eleven and a half (she refuses to reveal her exact age) she is clearly a woman, with a woman's disguised aggression and a woman's peculiar contradictions.

15 September

Happily our geography text, which contains maps of all the principal land-masses of the world, is large enough to conceal my clandestine journal-keeping, accomplished in an ordinary black composition book. Every day I must wait until Geography to put down such thoughts as I may have had during the morning about my situation and my fellows. I have tried writing at other times and it does not work. Either the teacher is walking up and down the aisles (during this period, luckily, she sticks close to the map rack in the front of the room) or Bobby Vanderbilt, who sits behind me, is punching me in the kidneys and wanting to know what I am doing. Vanderbilt, I have found out from certain desultory conversations on the playground, is hung up on sports cars, a veteran consumer of *Road & Track*. This explains the continual roaring sounds which seem to emanate from his desk; he is reproducing a record album called *Sounds of Sebring*.[1]

19 September

Only I, at times (only at times), understand that somehow a mistake has been made, that I am in a place where I don't belong. It may be that Miss Mandible also knows this, at some level, but for reasons not fully understood by me she is going along with the game. When I was first assigned to this room I wanted to protest, the error seemed obvious, the stupidest principal could have seen it; but I have come to believe it was deliberate, that I have been betrayed again.

Now it seems to make little difference. This life-role is as interesting as my former life-role, which was that of a claims adjuster for the Great Northern Insurance Company, a position which compelled me to spend my time amid the debris of our civilization: rumpled fenders, roofless sheds, gutted warehouses, smashed arms and legs. After ten years of this one has a tendency to see the world as a vast junkyard, looking at a man and seeing only his (potentially) mangled parts, entering a house only to trace the path of the inevitable fire. Therefore when I was installed here, although I knew an error had been made, I countenanced it, I was shrewd; I was aware that there might well be some kind of advantage to be gained from what seemed a disaster. The role of The Adjuster teaches one much.

22 September

I am being solicited for the volleyball team. I decline, refusing to take unfair profit from my height.

23 September

Every morning the roll is called: Bestvina, Bokenfohr, Broan, Brownly, Cone, Coyle, Crecelius, Darin, Durbin, Geiger, Guiswite, Heckler, Jacobs, Kleinschmidt, Lay, Logan, Masei, Mitgang, Pfeilsticker. It is like the litany chanted in the dim miserable dawns of Texas by the cadre sergeant of our basic training company.

In the Army, too, I was ever so slightly awry. It took me a fantastically long time to realize what the others grasped almost at once: that much of what we

---

1. Sebring Raceway in Sebring, Florida, has hosted motor racing events since 1952.

were doing was absolutely pointless, to no purpose. I kept wondering why. Then something happened that proposed a new question. One day we were commanded to whitewash, from the ground to the topmost leaves, all of the trees in our training area. The corporal who relayed the order was nervous and apologetic. Later an off-duty captain sauntered by and watched us, white-splashed and totally weary, strung out among the freakish shapes we had created. He walked away swearing. I understood the principle (orders are orders), but I wondered: Who decides?

29 September

Sue Ann is a wonder. Yesterday she viciously kicked my ankle for not paying attention when she was attempting to pass me a note during History. It is swollen still. But Miss Mandible was watching me, there was nothing I could do. Oddly enough Sue Ann reminds me of the wife I had in my former role, while Miss Mandible seems to be a child. She watches me constantly, trying to keep sexual significance out of her look; I am afraid the other children have noticed. I have already heard, on that ghostly frequency that is the medium of classroom communication, the words *"Teacher's pet!"*

2 October

Sometimes I speculate on the exact nature of the conspiracy which brought me here. At times I believe it was instigated by my wife of former days, whose name was . . . I am only pretending to forget. I know her name very well, as well as I know the name of my former motor oil (Quaker State) or my old Army serial number (US 54109268). Her name was Brenda.

7 October

Today I tiptoed up to Miss Mandible's desk (when there was no one else in the room) and examined its surface. Miss Mandible is a clean-desk teacher, I discovered. There was nothing except her gradebook (the one in which I exist as a sixth-grader) and a text, which was open at a page headed *Making the Processes Meaningful*. I read: "Many pupils enjoy working fractions when they understand what they are doing. They have confidence in their ability to take the right steps and to obtain correct answers. However, to give the subject full social significance, it is necessary that many realistic situations requiring the processes be found. Many interesting and lifelike problems involving the use of fractions should be solved . . ."

8 October

I am not irritated by the feeling of having been through all this before. Things are done differently now. The children, moreover, are in some ways different from those who accompanied me on my first voyage through the elementary schools: *"They have confidence in their ability to take the right steps and to obtain correct answers."* This is surely true. When Bobby Vanderbilt, who sits behind me and has the great tactical advantage of being able to maneuver in my disproportionate shadow, wishes to bust a classmate in the mouth he first asks Miss Mandible to lower the blind, saying that the sun hurts his eyes. When she does so, *bip!* My generation would never have been able to con authority so easily.

13 October

I misread a clue. Do not misunderstand me: it was a tragedy only from the point of view of the authorities. I conceived that it was my duty to obtain satisfaction for the injured, for an elderly lady (not even one of our policyholders, but a claimant against Big Ben Transfer & Storage, Inc.) from the company. The settlement was $165,000; the claim, I still believe, was just. But without my encouragement Mrs. Bichek would never have had the self-love to prize her injury so highly. The company paid, but its faith in me, in my efficacy in the role, was broken. Henry Goodykind, the district manager, expressed this thought in a few not altogether unsympathetic words, and told me at the same time that I was to have a new role. The next thing I knew I was here, at Horace Greeley Elementary, under the lubricious eye of Miss Mandible.

17 October

Today we are to have a fire drill. I know this because I am a Fire Marshal, not only for our room but for the entire right wing of the second floor. This distinction, which was awarded shortly after my arrival, is interpreted by some as another mark of my somewhat dubious relations with our teacher. My armband, which is red and decorated with white felt letters reading FIRE, sits on the little shelf under my desk, next to the brown paper bag containing the lunch I carefully make for myself each morning. One of the advantages of packing my own lunch (I have no one to pack it for me) is that I am able to fill it with things I enjoy. The peanut butter sandwiches that my mother made in my former existence, many years ago, have been banished in favor of ham and cheese. I have found that my diet has mysteriously adjusted to my new situation; I no longer drink, for instance, and when I smoke, it is in the boys' john, like everybody else. When school is out I hardly smoke at all. It is only in the matter of sex that I feel my own true age; this is apparently something that, once learned, can never be forgotten. I live in fear that Miss Mandible will one day keep me after school, and when we are alone, create a compromising situation. To avoid this I have become a model pupil: another reason for the pronounced dislike I have encountered in certain quarters. But I cannot deny that I am singed by those long glances from the vicinity of the chalkboard; Miss Mandible is in many ways, notably about the bust, a very tasty piece.

24 October

There are isolated challenges to my largeness, to my dimly realized position in the class as Gulliver.[2] Most of my classmates are polite about this matter, as they would be if I had only one eye, or wasted, metal-wrapped legs. I am viewed as a mutation of some sort but essentially a peer. However Harry Broan, whose father has made himself rich manufacturing the Broan Bathroom Vent (with which Harry is frequently reproached; he is always being asked how things are in Ventsville), today inquired if I wanted to fight. An interested group of his followers had gathered to observe this suicidal undertaking. I replied that I didn't feel quite up to it, for which he was obviously

---

2. Hero and central character of *Gulliver's Travels* by Jonathan Swift (1667–1745); in the first episode, Gulliver finds himself in the land of Lilliput, where all the inhabitants are tiny.

grateful. We are now friends forever. He has given me to understand privately that he can get me all the bathroom vents I will ever need, at a ridiculously modest figure.

25 October

"Many interesting and lifelike problems involving the use of fractions should be solved . . ." The theorists fail to realize that everything that is either interesting or lifelike in the classroom proceeds from what they would probably call interpersonal relations: Sue Ann Brownly kicking me in the ankle. How lifelike, how womanlike, is her tender solicitude after the deed! Her pride in my newly acquired limp is transparent; everyone knows that she has set her mark upon me, that it is a victory in her unequal struggle with Miss Mandible for my great, overgrown heart. Even Miss Mandible knows, and counters in perhaps the only way she can, with sarcasm. "Are you wounded, Joseph?" Conflagrations smolder behind her eyelids, yearning for the Fire Marshal clouds her eyes. I mumble that I have bumped my leg.

30 October

I return again and again to the problem of my future.

4 November

The underground circulating library has brought me a copy of *Movie-TV Secrets,* the multicolor cover blazoned with the headline "Debbie's Date Insults Liz!" It is a gift from Frankie Randolph, a rather plain girl who until today has had not one word for me, passed on via Bobby Vanderbilt. I nod and smile over my shoulder in acknowledgment; Frankie hides her head under her desk. I have seen these magazines being passed around among the girls (sometimes one of the boys will condescend to inspect a particularly lurid cover). Miss Mandible confiscates them whenever she finds one. I leaf through *Movie-TV Secrets* and get an eyeful. "The exclusive picture on these pages isn't what it seems. We know how it looks and we know what the gossipers will do. So in the interests of a nice guy, we're publishing the facts first. Here's what really happened!" The picture shows a rising young movie idol in bed, pajama-ed and bleary-eyed, while an equally blowzy young woman looks startled beside him. I am happy to know that the picture is not really what it seems; it seems to be nothing less than divorce evidence.

What do these hipless eleven-year-olds think when they come across, in the same magazine, the full-page ad for Maurice de Paree, which features "Hip Helpers" or what appear to be padded rumps? ("A real undercover agent that adds appeal to those hips and derriere, both!") If they cannot decipher the language the illustrations leave nothing to the imagination. "Drive him frantic . . ." the copy continues. Perhaps this explains Bobby Vanderbilt's preoccupation with Lancias and Maseratis;[3] it is a defense against being driven frantic.

Sue Ann has observed Frankie Randolph's overture, and catching my eye, she pulls from her satchel no less than seventeen of these magazines, thrusting

---

3. Italian sports cars.

them at me as if to prove that anything any of her rivals has to offer, she can top. I shuffle through them quickly, noting the broad editorial perspective:

"Debbie's Kids Are Crying"
"Eddie Asks Debbie: Will You?"
"The Nightmares Liz Has About Eddie!"
"The Things Debbie Can Tell About Eddie"
"The Private Life of Eddie and Liz"
"Debbie Gets Her Man Back?"
"A New Life for Liz"
"Love Is a Tricky Affair"
"Eddie's Taylor-Made Love Nest"
"How Liz Made a Man of Eddie"
"Are They Planning to Live Together?"
"Isn't It Time to Stop Kicking Debbie Around?"
"Debbie's Dilemma"
"Eddie Becomes a Father Again"
"Is Debbie Planning to Re-wed?"
"Can Liz Fulfill Herself?"
"Why Debbie Is Sick of Hollywood"

Who are these people, Debbie, Eddie, Liz, and how did they get themselves in such a terrible predicament? Sue Ann knows, I am sure; it is obvious that she has been studying their history as a guide to what she may expect when she is suddenly freed from this drab, flat classroom.

I am angry and I shove the magazines back at her with not even a whisper of thanks.

5 November

The sixth grade at Horace Greeley Elementary is a furnace of love, love, love. Today it is raining, but inside the air is heavy and tense with passion. Sue Ann is absent; I suspect that yesterday's exchange has driven her to her bed. Guilt hangs about me. She is not responsible, I know, for what she reads, for the models proposed to her by a venal publishing industry; I should not have been so harsh. Perhaps it is only the flu.

Nowhere have I encountered an atmosphere as charged with aborted sexuality as this. Miss Mandible is helpless; nothing goes right today. Amos Darin has been found drawing a dirty picture in the cloakroom. Sad and inaccurate, it was offered not as a sign of something else but as an act of love in itself. It has excited even those who have not seen it, even those who saw but understood only that it was dirty. The room buzzes with imperfectly comprehended titillation. Amos stands by the door, waiting to be taken to the principal's office. He wavers between fear and enjoyment of his temporary celebrity. From time to time Miss Mandible looks at me reproachfully, as if blaming me for the uproar. But I did not create this atmosphere, I am caught in it like all the others.

8 November

Everything is promised my classmates and me, most of all the future. We accept the outrageous assurances without blinking.

I have finally found the nerve to petition for a larger desk. At recess I can hardly walk; my legs do not wish to uncoil themselves. Miss Mandible says she will take it up with the custodian. She is worried about the excellence of my themes. Have I, she asks, been receiving help? For an instant I am on the brink of telling her my story. Something, however, warns me not to attempt it. Here I am safe, I have a place; I do not wish to entrust myself once more to the whimsy of authority. I resolve to make my themes less excellent in the future.

A ruined marriage, a ruined adjusting career, a grim interlude in the Army when I was almost not a person. This is the sum of my existence to date, a dismal total. Small wonder that re-education seemed my only hope. It is clear even to me that I need reworking in some fundamental way. How efficient is the society that provides thus for the salvage of its clinkers!

The distinction between children and adults, while probably useful for some purposes, is at bottom a specious one, I feel. There are only individual egos, crazy for love.

The custodian has informed Miss Mandible that our desks are all the correct size for sixth-graders, as specified by the Board of Estimate and furnished the schools by the Nu-Art Educational Supply Corporation of Englewood, California. He has pointed out that if the desk size is correct, then the pupil size must be incorrect. Miss Mandible, who has already arrived at this conclusion, refuses to press the matter further. I think I know why. An appeal to the administration might result in my removal from the class, in a transfer to some sort of setup for "exceptional children." This would be a disaster of the first magnitude. To sit in a room with child geniuses (or, more likely, children who are "retarded") would shrivel me in a week. Let my experience here be that of the common run, I say; let me be, please God, typical.

We read signs as promises. Miss Mandible understands by my great height, by my resonant vowels, that I will one day carry her off to bed. Sue Ann interprets these same signs to mean that I am unique among her male acquaintances, therefore most desirable, therefore her special property as is everything that is Most Desirable. If neither of these propositions works out then life has broken faith with them.

I myself, in my former existence, read the company motto ("Here to Help in Time of Need") as a description of the duty of the adjuster, drastically mislocating the company's deepest concerns. I believed that because I had obtained a wife who was made up of wife-signs (beauty, charm, softness, perfume, cookery) I had found love. Brenda, reading the same signs that have now misled Miss Mandible and Sue Ann Brownly, felt she had been promised that she would never be bored again. All of us, Miss Mandible, Sue Ann, myself, Brenda, Mr. Goodykind, still believe that the American flag betokens a kind of general righteousness.

But I say, looking about me in this incubator of future citizens, that signs are signs, and some of them are lies.

23 November

It may be that my experience as a child will save me after all. If only I can remain quietly in this classroom, making my notes while Napoleon plods through Russia in the droning voice of Harry Broan, reading aloud from our History text. All of the mysteries that perplexed me as an adult have their origins here. But Miss Mandible will not permit me to remain ungrown. Her hands rest on my shoulders too warmly, and for too long.

7 December

It is the pledges that this place makes to me, pledges that cannot be redeemed, that will confuse me later and make me feel I am not *getting any-where*. Everything is presented as the result of some knowable process; if I wish to arrive at four I get there by way of two and two. If I wish to burn Moscow the route I must travel has already been marked out by another visitor. If, like Bobby Vanderbilt, I yearn for the wheel of the Lancia 2.4-liter coupé, I have only to go through the appropriate process, that is, get the money. And if it is money itself that I desire, I have only to *make* it. All of these goals are equally beautiful in the sight of the Board of Estimate; the proof is all around us, in the no-nonsense ugliness of this steel and glass building, in the straightline matter-of-factness with which Miss Mandible handles some of our less repu-table wars. Who points out that arrangements sometimes slip, that errors are made, that signs are misread? *"They have confidence in their ability to take the right steps and to obtain correct answers."*

8 December

My enlightenment is proceeding wonderfully.

9 December

Disaster once again. Tomorrow I am to be sent to a doctor, for observation. Sue Ann Brownly caught Miss Mandible and me in the cloakroom, during recess, Miss Mandible's naked legs in a scissors around my waist. For a moment I thought Sue Ann was going to choke. She ran out of the room weeping, straight for the principal's office, certain now which of us was Debbie, which Eddie, which Liz. I am sorry to be the cause of her disillusionment, but I know that she will recover. Miss Mandible is ruined but fulfilled. Although she will be charged with contributing to the delinquency of a minor, she seems at peace; *her* promise has been kept. She knows now that everything she has been told about life, about America, is true.

I have tried to convince the school authorities that I am a minor only in a very special sense, that I am in fact mostly to blame—but it does no good. They are as dense as ever. My contemporaries are astounded that I present myself as anything other than an innocent victim. Like the Old Guard marching through the Russian drifts,[4] the class marches to the conclusion that truth is punishment.

Bobby Vanderbilt has given me his copy of *Sounds of Sebring*, in farewell.

1981

4. Napoleon's soldiers retreating from Moscow through the snow.

RICHARD BAUSCH
b. 1945

Born in Fort Benning, Georgia, Richard Bausch served in the air force from 1965 to 1969. After a stint as a singer-songwriter, Bausch attended the Iowa Writer's Workshop in the mid-1970s and has subsequently taught creative writing at the University of Iowa, the University of Virginia, Bread Loaf, the University of the South, George Mason University, the University of Memphis, and now Chapman University. He is the author of twelve novels, including *Good Evening Mr. and Mrs. America and All the Ships at Sea* (1996), *In the Night Season* (1999), *Hello to the Cannibals* (2002), and, most recently, *Before, During, and After* (2014). His stories have appeared in *The Atlantic Monthly*, the *New Yorker, Esquire, Harper's*, and other magazines, and have been anthologized in many publications, including *The Best American Short Stories* and the *O. Henry* and the *Pushcart Prize* series. Bausch was awarded the PEN/Malamud Award for Excellence in the Short Story in 2004, the Dayton Peace Prize for Literature in 2009, and the Rea Award for the Short Story in 2012.

Letter to the Lady of the House

It's exactly twenty minutes to midnight, on this the eve of my seventieth birthday, and I've decided to address you, for a change, in writing—odd as that might seem. I'm perfectly aware of how many years we've been together, even if I haven't been very good about remembering to commemorate certain dates, certain days of the year. I'm also perfectly aware of how you're going to take the fact that I'm doing this at all, so late at night, with everybody due to arrive tomorrow, and the house still unready. I haven't spent almost five decades with you without learning a few things about you that I can predict and describe with some accuracy, though I admit that, as you put it, lately we've been more like strangers than husband and wife. Well, so if we are like strangers, perhaps there are some things I can tell you that you won't have already figured out about the way I feel.

Tonight, we had another one of those long, silent evenings after an argument (remember?) over pepper. We had been bickering all day, really, but at dinner I put pepper on my potatoes and you said that about how I shouldn't have pepper because it always upsets my stomach. I bothered to remark that I used to eat chili peppers for breakfast and if I wanted to put plain old ordinary black pepper on my potatoes, as I had been doing for more than sixty years, that was my privilege. Writing this now, it sounds far more testy than I meant it, but that isn't really the point.

In any case, you chose to overlook my tone. You simply said, "John, you were up all night the last time you had pepper with your dinner."

I said, "I was up all night because I ate green peppers. Not black pepper, but green peppers."

"A pepper is a pepper, isn't it?" you said. And then I started in on you. I got, as you call it, legal with you—pointing out that green peppers are not black pepper—and from there we moved on to an evening of mutual disregard for each other that ended with your decision to go to bed early. The grand-children will make you tired, and there's still the house to do; you had every reason to want to get some rest, and yet I felt that you were also making a point of getting yourself out of proximity with me, leaving me to my displeasure, with another ridiculous argument settling between us like a fog.

So, after you went to bed, I got out the whiskey and started pouring drinks, and I had every intention of putting myself into a stupor. It was almost my birthday, after all, and—forgive this, it's the way I felt at the time—you had nagged me into an argument and then gone off to bed; the day had ended as so many of our days end now, and I felt, well, entitled. I had a few drinks, without any appreciable effect (though you might well see this letter as firm evidence to the contrary), and then I decided to do something to shake you up. I would leave. I'd make a lot of noise going out the door; I'd take a walk around the neighborhood and make you wonder where I could be. Perhaps I'd go check into a motel for the night. The thought even crossed my mind that I might leave you altogether. I admit that I entertained the thought, Marie. I saw our life together now as the day-to-day round of petty quarreling and tension that it's mostly been over the past couple of years or so, and I wanted out as sincerely as I ever wanted anything.

My God, I wanted an end to it, and I got up from my seat in front of the television and walked back down the hall to the entrance of our room to look at you. I suppose I hoped you'd still be awake so I could tell you of this momentous decision I felt I'd reached. And maybe you were awake: one of our oldest areas of contention being the noise I make—the feather-thin mem-brane of your sleep that I am always disturbing with my restlessness in the nights. All right. Assuming you were asleep and don't know that I stood in the doorway of our room, I will say that I stood there for perhaps five minutes, looking at you in the half-dark, the shape of your body under the blanket—you really did look like one of the girls when they were little and I used to stand in the doorway of their rooms; your illness last year made you so small again—and, as I said, I thought I had decided to leave you, for your peace as well as mine. I know you have gone to sleep crying, Marie. I know you've felt sorry about things and wished we could find some way to stop irritating each other so much.

Well, of course I didn't go anywhere. I came back to this room and drank more of the whiskey and watched television. It was like all the other nights. The shows came on and ended, and the whiskey began to wear off. There was a little rain shower. I had a moment of the shock of knowing I was seventy. After the rain ended, I did go outside for a few minutes. I stood on the side-walk and looked at the house. The kids, with their kids, were on the road somewhere between their homes and here. I walked up to the end of the block and back, and a pleasant breeze blew and shook the drops out of the trees. My stomach was bothering me some, and maybe it was the pepper I'd put on my potatoes. It could just as well have been the whiskey. Anyway, as I came back to the house, I began to have the eerie feeling that I had reached the last night of my life. There was this small discomfort in my stomach, and no other physical pang or pain, and I am used to the small ills and side effects of my way of eating and drinking; yet I felt the sense of the end of things more strongly than I can describe. When I stood in the entrance of our room and looked at you again, wondering if I would make it through to the morning, I suddenly found myself trying to think what I would say to you if indeed this *were* the last time I would ever be able to speak to you. And I began to know I would write you this letter.

At least words in a letter aren't blurred by tone of voice, by the old aggravating sound of me talking to you. I began with this and with the idea that, after months of thinking about it, I would at last try to say something to you that wasn't colored by our disaffections. What I have to tell you must be explained in a rather roundabout way.

I've been thinking about my cousin Louise and her husband. When he died and she stayed with us last summer, something brought back to me what is really only the memory of a moment; yet it reached me, that moment, across more than fifty years. As you know, Louise is nine years older than I, and more like an older sister than a cousin. I must have told you at one time or another that I spent some weeks with her, back in 1933, when she was first married. The memory I'm talking about comes from that time, and what I have decided I have to tell you comes from that memory.

Father had been dead four years. We were all used to the fact that times were hard and that there was no man in the house, though I suppose I filled that role in some titular way. In any case, when Mother became ill there was the problem of us, her children. Though I was the oldest, I wasn't old enough to stay in the house alone, or to nurse her, either. My grandfather came up with the solution—and everybody went along with it—that I would go to Louise's for a time, and the two girls would go to stay with Grandfather. You'll remember that people did pretty much what that old man wanted them to do.

So we closed up the house, and I got on a train to Virginia. I was a few weeks shy of fourteen years old. I remember that I was not able to believe that anything truly bad would come of Mother's pleurisy,[1] and was consequently glad of the opportunity it afforded me to travel the hundred miles south to Charlottesville, where cousin Louise had moved with her new husband only a month earlier, after her wedding. Because *we* traveled so much at the beginning, you never got to really know Charles when he was young—in 1933 he was a very tall, imposing fellow, with bright red hair and a graceful way of moving that always made me think of athletics, contests of skill. He had worked at the Navy Yard in Washington, and had been laid off in the first months of Roosevelt's New Deal. Louise was teaching in a day school in Charlottesville so they could make ends meet, and Charles was spending most of his time looking for work and fixing up the house. I had only met Charles once or twice before the wedding, but already I admired him and wanted to emulate him. The prospect of spending time in his house, of perhaps going fishing with him in the small streams of central Virginia, was all I thought about on the way

---

1. A type of lung disease.

down. And I remember that we did go fishing one weekend, that I would end up spending a lot of time with Charles, helping to paint the house and to run water lines under it for indoor plumbing. Oh, I had time with Louise, too—listening to her read from the books she wanted me to be interested in, walking with her around Charlottesville in the evenings and looking at the city as it was then. Or sitting on her small porch and talking about the family, Mother's stubborn illness, the children Louise saw every day at school. But what I want to tell you has to do with the very first day I was there.

I know you think I use far too much energy thinking about and pining away for the past, and I therefore know that I'm taking a risk by talking about this ancient history, and by trying to make you see it. But this all has to do with you and me, my dear, and our late inability to find ourselves in the same room together without bitterness and pain.

That summer, 1933, was unusually warm in Virginia, and the heat, along with my impatience to arrive, made the train almost unbearable. I think it was just past noon when it pulled into the station at Charlottesville, with me hanging out one of the windows, looking for Louise or Charles. It was Charles who had come to meet me. He stood in a crisp-looking seer-sucker suit, with a straw boater cocked at just the angle you'd expect a young, newly married man to wear a straw boater, even in the middle of economic disaster. I waved at him and he waved back, and I might've jumped out the window if the train had slowed even a little more than it had before it stopped in the shade of the platform. I made my way out, carrying the cloth bag my grandfather had given me for the trip—Mother had said through her rheum that I looked like a carpetbagger—and when I stepped down to shake hands with Charles I noticed that what I thought was a new suit was tattered at the ends of the sleeves.

"Well," he said. "Young John."

I smiled at him. I was perceptive enough to see that his cheerfulness was not entirely effortless. He was a man out of work, after all, and so in spite of himself there was worry in his face, the slightest shadow in an otherwise glad and proud countenance. We walked through the station to the street, and on up the steep hill to the house, which was a small clapboard structure, a cottage, really, with a porch at the end of a short sidewalk lined with flowers—they were marigolds, I think—and here was Louise, coming out of the house, her arms already stretched wide to embrace me. "Lord," she said. "I swear you've grown since the wedding, John." Charles took my bag and went inside.

"Let me look at you, young man," Louise said.

I stood for inspection. And as she looked me over I saw that her hair was pulled back, that a few strands of it had come loose, that it was brilliantly auburn in the sun. I suppose I was a little in love with her. She was grown, and married now. She was a part of what seemed a great mystery to me, even as I was about to enter it, and of course you remember how that feels, Marie, when one is on the verge of things—nearly adult, nearly old enough to fall in love. I looked at Louise's happy, flushed face, and felt a deep ache as she ushered me into her house. I wanted so to be older.

Inside, Charles had poured lemonade for us and was sitting in the easy chair by the fireplace, already sipping his. Louise wanted to show me the house and the backyard—which she had tilled and turned into a small vegetable garden—but she must've sensed how thirsty I was, and so she asked me to sit down and have a cool drink before she showed me the upstairs. Now, of course, looking back on it, I remember that those rooms she was so anxious to show me were meager indeed. They were not much bigger than closets, really, and the paint was faded and dull; the furniture she'd arranged so artfully was coming apart; the pictures she'd put on the walls were prints she'd cut out—magazine covers, mostly—and the curtains over the windows were the same ones that had hung in her childhood bedroom for twenty years. ("Recognize these?" she said with a deprecating smile.) Of course, the quality of her pride had nothing to do with the fineness—or lack of it—in these things, but in the fact that they belonged to her, and that she was a married lady in her own house.

On this day in July, in 1933, she and Charles were waiting for the delivery of a fan they had scrounged enough money to buy from Sears, through the catalogue. There were things they would rather have been doing, especially in this heat, and especially with me there. Monticello wasn't far away, the university was within walking distance, and without too much expense one could ride a taxi to one of the lakes nearby. They had hoped that the fan would arrive before I did, but since it hadn't, and since neither Louise nor Charles was willing to leave the other alone while traipsing off with me that day, there wasn't anything to do but wait around for it. Louise had opened the windows and shut the shades, and we sat in her small living room and drank the lemonade, fanning ourselves with folded parts of Charles's morning newspaper. From time to time an anemic breath of air would move the shades slightly, but then everything grew still again. Louise sat on the arm of Charles's chair, and I sat on the sofa. We talked about pleurisy and, I think, about the fact that Thomas Jefferson had invented the dumbwaiter, how the plumbing at Monticello was at least a century ahead of its time. Charles remarked that it was the spirit of invention that would make a man's career in these days. "That's what I'm aiming for, to be inventive in a job. No matter what it winds up being."

When the lemonade ran out, Louise got up and went into the kitchen to make some more. Charles and I talked about taking a weekend to go fishing. He leaned back in his chair and put his hands behind his head, looking satisfied. In the kitchen, Louise was chipping ice for our glasses, and she began singing something low, for her own pleasure, a barely audible lilting, and Charles and I sat listening. It occurred to me that I was very happy. I had the sense that soon I would be embarked on my own life, as Charles was, and that an attractive woman like Louise would be there with me. Charles yawned and said, "God, listen to that. Doesn't Louise have the loveliest voice?"

And that's all I have from that day. I don't even know if the fan arrived later, and I have no clear memory of how we spent the rest of the afternoon and evening. I remember Louise singing a song, her husband leaning back in his chair, folding his hands behind his head, expressing his pleasure in his young wife's voice. I remember that I felt quite extraordinarily content just then. And that's all I remember.

But there are, of course, the things we both know: we know they moved to Colorado to be near Charles's parents; we know they never had any children; we know that Charles fell down a shaft at a construction site in the fall of 1957 and was hurt so badly that he never walked again. And I know that when she came to stay with us last summer she told me she'd learned to hate him, and not for what she'd had to help him do all those years. No, it started earlier and was deeper than that. She hadn't minded the care of him—the washing and feeding and all the numberless small tasks she had to perform each and every day, all day—she hadn't minded this. In fact, she thought there was something in her makeup that liked being needed so completely. The trouble was simply that whatever she had once loved in him she had stopped loving, and for many, many years before he died, she'd felt only suffocation when he was near enough to touch her, only irritation and anxiety when he spoke. She said all this, and then looked at me, her cousin, who had been fortunate enough to have children, and to be in love over time, and said, "John, how have you and Marie managed it?"

And what I wanted to tell you has to do with this fact—that while you and I had had one of our whispering arguments only moments before, I felt quite certain of the simple truth of the matter, which is that whatever our complications, we *have* managed to be in love over time.

"Louise," I said.

"People start out with such high hopes," she said, as if I wasn't there. She looked at me. "Don't they?"

"Yes," I said.

She seemed to consider this a moment. Then she said, "I wonder how it happens."

I said, "You ought to get some rest." Or something equally pointless and admonitory.

As she moved away from me, I had an image of Charles standing on the station platform in Charlottesville that summer, the straw boater set at its cocky angle. It was an image I would see most of the rest of that night, and on many another night since.

I can almost hear your voice as you point out that once again I've managed to dwell too long on the memory of something that's past and gone. The difference is that I'm not grieving over the past now. I'm merely reporting a memory, so that you might understand what I'm about to say to you.

The fact is, we aren't the people we were even then, just a year ago. I know that. As I know things have been slowly eroding between us for a very long time; we are a little tired of each other, and there are annoyances and old scars that won't be obliterated with a letter—even a long one written in the middle of the night in desperate sincerity, under the influence, admittedly, of a considerable portion of bourbon whiskey, but nevertheless with the best intention and hope: that you may know how, over the course of this night, I came to the end of needing an explanation for our difficulty. We have reached this—place. Everything we say seems rather aggravatingly mindless and automatic, like something one stranger might say to another in any of the thousand circumstances where strangers are thrown together for a time, and the silence begins to grow heavy on their minds, and someone has to say something. Darling, we go so long these days without having anything at all to do with each other, and the children are arriving tomorrow, and once more we'll be in the position of making all the gestures that give them back their parents as they think their parents are, and what I wanted to say to you, what came to me as I thought about Louise and Charles on that day so long ago, when they were young and so obviously glad of each other, and I looked at them and knew it and was happy—what came to me was that even the harsh things that happened to them, even the years of anger and silence, even the disappointment and the bitterness and the wanting not to be in the same room anymore, even all that must have been worth it for such loveliness. At least I am here, at seventy years old, hoping so. Tonight, I went back to our room again and stood gazing at you asleep, dreaming whatever you were dreaming, and I had a moment of thinking how we were always friends, too. Because what I wanted finally to say was that I remember well our own sweet times, our own old loveliness, and I would like to think that even if at the very beginning of our lives together I had somehow been shown that we would end up here, with this longing to be away from each other, this feeling of being trapped together, of being tied to each other in a way that makes us wish for other times, some other place—I would have known enough to accept it all freely for the chance at that love. And if I could, I would do it all again, Marie. All of it, even the sorrow. My sweet, my dear adversary. For everything that I remember.

1989

RELATED:

—Bausch, "Letter to a Young Writer," p. 1707
—Bausch on Anton Chekhov's "Gusev," p. 1793

CHARLES BAXTER

b. 1947

Baxter was born in Minneapolis and graduated from Macalester College in St. Paul, Minnesota, before earning his Ph.D. at the State University of New York at Buffalo. He now teaches creative writing at the University of Minnesota at Minneapolis. In his fiction, Baxter often explores extraordinary, even magical worlds that lurk just beneath seemingly ordinary appearances. His works include the short-story collections *Harmony of the World* (1984), *Through the Safety Net* (1985), *A Relative Stranger* (1990), *Believers* (1997), and *Gryphon* (2011); the novels *First Light* (1987), *Shadow Play* (1993), *The Feast of Love* (2000), and *The Soul Thief* (2008); and a volume of essays on fiction, *Burning Down the House* (1997).

The Disappeared

What he first noticed about Detroit and therefore America was the smell. Almost as soon as he walked off the plane, he caught it: an acrid odor of wood ash. The smell seemed to go through his nostrils and take up residence in his head. In Sweden, his own country, he associated this smell with autumn, and the first family fires of winter, the smoke chuffing out of chimneys and settling familiarly over the neighborhood. But here it was midsummer, and he couldn't see anything burning.

On the way in from the airport, with the windows of the cab open and hot stony summer air blowing over his face, he asked the driver about it.

"You're smelling Detroit," the driver said.

Anders, who spoke very precise school English, thought that perhaps he hadn't made himself understood. "No," he said. "I am sorry. I mean the burning smell. What is it?"

The cab driver glanced in the rearview mirror. He was wearing a knitted beret, and his dreadlocks flapped in the breeze. "Where you from?"

"Sweden."

The driver nodded to himself. "Explains why," he said. The cab took a sharp right turn on the freeway and entered the Detroit city limits. The driver gestured with his left hand toward an electronic signboard, a small windowless factory at its base, and a clustered group of cramped clapboard houses nearby. When he gestured, the cab wobbled on the freeway. "Fires here most all the time," he said. "Day in and day out. You get so you don't notice. Or maybe you get so you do notice and you like it."

"I don't see any fires," Anders said.

"That's right."

Feeling that he was missing the point somehow, Anders decided to change the subject. "I see a saxophone and a baseball bat next to you," he said, in his best English. "Do you like to play baseball?"

"Not in this cab, I don't," the driver said quietly. "It's no game then, you understand?"

The young man sat back, feeling that he had been defeated by the American idiom in his first native encounter with it. An engineer, he was in Detroit to discuss his work in metal alloys that resist oxidation. The company that had invited him had suggested that he might agree to become a consultant on an exclusive contract, for what seemed to him an enormous, American-sized fee. But the money meant little to him. It was America he was curious about, attracted by, especially its colorful disorderliness.

Disorder, of which there was very little in Sweden, seemed sexy to him: the disorder of a disheveled woman who has rushed down two flights of stairs to offer a last long kiss. Anders was single, and before he left the country he hoped to sleep with an American woman in an American bed. It was his ambition. He wondered if the experience would have any distinction. He had an idea that he might be able to go home and tell one or two friends about it.

At the hotel, he was met by a representative of the automobile company, a gray-haired man with thick glasses who, to Anders's surprise, spoke rather good Swedish. Later that afternoon, and for the next two days, he was taken down silent carpeted hallways and shown into plush windowless rooms with recessed lighting. He showed them his slides and metal samples, cited chemical formulas, and made cost projections; he looked at the faces looking back at him. They were interested, friendly, but oddly blank, like faces he had seen in the military. He saw corridor after corridor. The building seemed more expressive than the people in it. The lighting was both bright and diffuse, and a low-frequency hum of power and secrecy seemed to flow out from the ventilators. Everyone complimented him on his English. A tall woman in a tailored suit, flashing him a secretive smile, asked him if he intended to stay in this country for long. Anders smiled, said that his plans on that particular point were open, and managed to work the name of his hotel into his conversation.

At the end of the third day, the division head once again shook Anders's hand in the foyer of the hotel lobby and said they'd be getting in touch with him very soon. Finally free, Anders stepped outside the hotel and sniffed the air. All the rooms he had been in since he had arrived had had no windows, or windows so blocked by drapes or blinds that he couldn't see out.

He felt restless and excited, with three days free for sightseeing in a wide-open American city, not quite in the Wild West but close enough to it to suit him. He returned to his room and changed into a pair of jeans, a light cotton shirt, and a pair of running shoes. In the mirror, he thought he looked relaxed and handsome. His vanity amused him, but he felt lucky to look the way he did. Back out on the sidewalk, he asked the doorman which direction he would recommend for a walk.

The doorman, who had curly gray hair and sagging pouches under his eyes, removed his cap and rubbed his forehead. He did not look back at Anders. "You want my recommendation? Don't walk anywhere. I would not recommend a walk. Sit in the bar and watch the soaps." The doorman stared at a fire hydrant as he spoke.

"What about running?"

The doorman suddenly glanced at Anders, sizing him up. "It's a chance. You might be okay. But to be safe, stay inside. There's movies on the cable, you want them."

"Is there a park here?"

"Sure, there's parks. There's always parks. There's Belle Isle. You could go there. People do. I don't recommend it. Still and all you might enjoy it if you run fast enough. What're you planning to do?"

Anders shrugged. "Relax. See your city."

"You're seeing it," the doorman said. "Ain't nobody relaxed, seeing this place. Buy some postcards, you want sights. This place ain't built for tourists and amateurs."

Anders thought that perhaps he had misunderstood again and took a cab out to Belle Isle; as soon as he had entered the park, he saw a large municipal fountain and asked the cabbie to drop him off in front of it. On its rim, children were shouting and dangling their legs in the water. The ornamentation of the stone lions was both solemn and whimsical and reminded him of the forced humor of Danish public sculpture. Behind the fountain he saw families grouped in evening picnics on the grass, and many citizens, of various apparent ethnic types, running, bicycling, and walking. Anders liked the way Americans walked, a sort of busyness in their step, as if, having no particular goal, they still had an unconscious urgency to get somewhere, to seem purposeful.

He began to jog, and found himself passing a yacht club of some sort, and then a small zoo, and more landscaped areas where solitaries and couples sat on the grass listening to the evening baseball game on their radios. Other couples were stretched out by themselves, self-absorbed. The light had a bluish-gold quality. It looked like almost any city park to him, placid and decorative, a bit hushed.

He found his way to an old building with a concession stand inside. After admiring the building's fake Corinthian[1] architecture, he bought a hot dog and a cola. Thinking himself disguised as a native—America was full of foreigners anyway—he walked to the west windows of the dining area to check on the unattached women. He wanted to praise, to an American, this evening, and this park.

There were several couples on this side of the room, and what seemed to be several unattached men and women standing near the open window and listening to their various earphones. One of these women, with her hair partially pinned up, was sipping a lemonade. She had just the right faraway look. Anders thought he recognized this look. It meant that she was in a kind of suspension, between engagements.

He put himself in her line of sight and said, in his heaviest accent, "A nice evening!"

"What?" She removed the earphones and looked at him. "What did you say?"

"I said the evening was beautiful." He tried to sound as foreign as he could, the way Germans in Sweden did. "I am a visitor here," he added quickly, "and not familiar with any of this." He motioned his arm to indicate the park.

---

1. A style of classical Greek architecture.

"Not familiar?" she asked. "Not familiar with what?"

"Well, with this park. With the sky here. The people."

"Parks are the same everywhere," the woman said, leaning her hip against the wall. She looked at him with a vague interest. "The sky is the same. Only the people are different."

"Yes? How?"

"Where are you from?"

He explained, and she looked out the window toward the Canadian side of the Detroit River, at the city of Windsor. "That's Canada, you know," she said, pointing a finger at the river. "They make Canadian whiskey right over there." She pointed at some high buildings and what seemed to be a grain elevator. "I've never drunk the whiskey. They say it tastes of acid rain. I've never been to Canada. I mean, I've seen it, but I've never been there. If I can see it from here, why should I go there?"

"To be in Canada," Anders suggested. "Another country."

"But I'm *here*," she said suddenly, turning to him and looking at him directly. Her eyes were so dark they were almost colorless. "Why should I be anywhere else? Why are *you* here?"

"I came to Detroit for business," he said. "Now I'm sightseeing."

"Sightseeing?" She laughed out loud, and Anders saw her arch her back. Her breasts seemed to flare in front of him. Her body had distinct athletic lines. "No one sightsees here. Didn't anyone tell you?"

"Yes. The doorman at the hotel. He told me not to come."

"But you did. How did you get here?"

"I came by taxi."

"You're joking," she said. Then she reached out and put her hand momentarily on his shoulder. "You took a taxi to this park? How do you expect to get back to your hotel?"

"I suppose," he shrugged, "I will get another taxi."

"Oh no you won't," she said, and Anders felt himself pleased that things were working out so well. He noticed again her pinned-up hair and its intense black. Her skin was deeply tanned or naturally dark, and he thought that she herself might be black or Hispanic, he didn't know which, being unpracticed in making such distinctions. Outside he saw fireflies. No one had ever mentioned fireflies in Detroit. Night was coming on. He gazed up at the sky. Same stars, same moon.

"You're here *alone*?" she asked. "In America? And in this city?"

"Yes," he said. "Why not?"

"People shouldn't be left alone in this country," she said, leaning toward him with a kind of vehemence. "They shouldn't have left you here. It can get kind of weird, what happens to people. Didn't they tell you?"

He smiled and said that they hadn't told him anything to that effect.

"Well, they should have." She dropped her cup into a trash can, and he thought he saw the beginning of a scar, a white line, traveling up the underside of her arm toward her shoulder.

"Who do you mean?" he asked. "You said, 'they.' Who is 'they'?"

"Any they at all," she said. "Your guardians." She sighed. "All right. Come on. Follow me." She went outside and broke into a run. For a moment he thought that she was running away from him, then realized that he was expected to run *with* her; it was what people did now, instead of holding hands, to get acquainted. He sprinted up next to her, and as she ran, she asked him, "Who are you?"

Being careful not to tire—she wouldn't like it if his endurance was poor—he told her his name, his professional interests, and he patched together a narrative about his mother, father, two sisters, and his Aunt Ingrid. Running past a slower couple, he told her that his aunt was eccentric and broke china by throwing it on the floor on Fridays, which she called "the devil's day."

"Years ago, they would have branded her a witch," Anders said. "But she isn't a witch. She's just moody."

He watched her reactions and noticed that she didn't seem at all interested in his family, or any sort of background. "Do you run a lot?" she asked. "You look as if you're in pretty good shape."

He admitted that, yes, he ran, but that people in Sweden didn't do this as much as they did in America.

"You look a little like that tennis star, that Swede," she said. "By the way, I'm Lauren." Still running, she held out her hand, and, still running, he shook it. "Which god do you believe in?"

"Excuse me?"

"Which god?" she asked. "Which god do you think is in control?"

"I had not thought about it."

"You'd better," she said. "Because one of them is." She stopped suddenly and put her hands on her hips and walked in a small circle. She put her hand to her neck and took her pulse, timing it on her wristwatch. Then she placed her fingers on Anders' neck and took his pulse. "One hundred fourteen," she said. "Pretty good." Again she walked away from him and again he found himself following her. In the growing darkness he noticed other men, standing in the parking lot, watching her, this American with pinned-up hair, dressed in a running outfit. He thought she was pretty, but maybe Americans had other standards so that here, in fact, she wasn't pretty, and it was some kind of optical illusion.

When he caught up with her, she was unlocking the door of a blue Chevrolet rusting near the hubcaps. He gazed down at the rust with professional interest—it had the characteristic blister pattern of rust caused by salt. She slipped inside the car and reached across to unlock the passenger side, and when he got in—he hadn't been invited to get in, but he thought it was all right—he sat down on several small plastic tape cassette cases. He picked them out from underneath him and tried to read their labels. She was taking off her shoes. Debussy, Bach, 10,000 Maniacs, Screamin' Jay Hawkins.

"Where are we going?" he asked. He glanced down at her bare foot on the accelerator. She put the car into reverse. "Wait a minute," he said. "Stop this car." She put on the brake and turned off the ignition. "I just want to look at you," he said.

"Okay, look." She turned on the interior light and kept her face turned so that he was looking at her in profile. Something about her suggested a lovely disorder, a ragged brightness toward the back of her face.

"Are we going to do things?" he asked, touching her on the arm.

"Of course," she said. "Strangers should always do things."

She said that she would drop him off at his hotel, that he must change clothes. This was important. She would then pick him up. On the way over, he

saw almost no one downtown. For some reason, it was quite empty of shoppers, strollers, or pedestrians of any kind. "I'm going to tell you some things
you should know," she said. He settled back. He was used to this kind of talk
on dates: everyone, everywhere, liked to reveal intimate details. It was an international convention.

They were slowing for a red light. "God is love," she said, downshifting, her
bare left foot on the clutch. "At least I think so. It's my hope. In the world we
have left, only love matters. Do you understand? I'm one of the Last Ones.
Maybe you've heard of us."

"No, I have not. What do you do?"

"We do what everyone else does. We work and we go home and have dinner
and go to bed. There is only one thing we do that is special."

"What is that?" he asked.

"We don't make plans," she said. "No big plans at all."

"That is not so unusual," he said, trying to normalize what she was saying.
"Many people don't like to make—"

"It's not liking," she said. "It doesn't have anything to do with liking or not
liking. It's a faith. Look at those buildings." She pointed toward several abandoned multistoried buildings with broken or vacant windows. "What face is
moving behind all that? Something is. I live and work here. I'm not blind.
Anyone can see what's taking place here. You're not blind either. Our church is
over on the east side, off Van Dyke Avenue. It's not a good part of town but we
want to be near where the face is doing its work."

"Your church?"

"The Church of the Millennium," she said. "Where they preach the Gospel
of Last Things." They were now on the freeway, heading up toward the General Motors Building and his hotel. "Do you understand me?"

"Of course," he said. He had heard of American cult religions but thought
they were all in California. He didn't mind her talk of religion. It was like
talk of the sunset or childhood; it kept things going. "Of course I have been
listening."

"Because I won't sleep with you unless you listen to me," she said. "It's the
one thing I care about, that people listen. It's so damn rare, listening I mean,
that you might as well care about it. I don't sleep with strangers too often.
Almost never." She turned to look at him. "Anders," she said, "what do you
pray to?"

He laughed. "I don't."

"Okay, then, what do you plan for?"

"A few things," he said.

"Like what?"

"My dinner every night. My job. My friends."

"You don't let accidents happen? You should. Things reveal themselves in
accidents."

"Are there many people like you?" he asked.

"What do you think?" He looked again at her face, taken over by the darkness in the car but dimly lit by the dashboard lights and the oncoming flare
of traffic. "Do you think there are many people like me?"

"Not very many," he said. "But maybe more than there used to be."

"Any of us in Sweden?"

"I don't think so. It's not a religion over there. People don't . . . They didn't tell us in Sweden about American girls who listen to Debussy and 10,000 Maniacs in their automobiles and who believe in gods and accidents."

"They don't say 'girls' here," she told him. "They say 'women.'"

She dropped him off at the hotel and said that she would pick him up in forty-five minutes. In his room, as he chose a clean shirt and a sport coat and a pair of trousers, he found himself laughing happily. He felt giddy. It was all happening so fast; he could hardly believe his luck. I am a very lucky man, he thought.

He looked out his hotel window at the streetlights. They had an amber glow, the color of gemstones. This city, this American city, was unlike any he had ever seen. A downtown area emptied of people; a river with huge ships going by silently; a park with girls who believe in the millennium. No, not girls: women. He had learned his lesson.

He wanted to open the hotel window to smell the air, but the casement frames were welded shut.

After walking down the stairs to the lobby, he stood out in front of the hotel doorway. He felt a warm breeze against his face. He told the doorman, Luis, that he had met a woman on Belle Isle who was going to pick him up in a few minutes. She was going to take him dancing. The doorman nodded, rubbing his chin with his hand. Anders said that she was friendly and wanted to show him, a foreigner, things. The doorman shook his head. "Yes, I agree," Luis said. "Dancing. Make sure that this is what you do."

"What?"

"Dancing," Luis said, "yes. Go dancing. You know this woman?"

"I just met her."

"Ah," Luis said, and stepped back to observe Anders, as if to remember his face. "Dangerous fun." When her car appeared in front of the hotel, she was wearing a light summer dress, and when she smiled, she looked like the melancholy baby he had heard about in an American song. As they pulled away from the hotel, he looked back at Luis, who was watching them closely, and then Anders realized that Luis was reading the numbers on Lauren's license plate. To break the mood, he leaned over to kiss her on the cheek. She smelled of cigarettes and something else—soap or cut flowers.

She took him uptown to a club where a trio played soft rock and some jazz. Some of this music was slow enough to dance to, in the slow way he wanted to dance. Her hand in his felt bony and muscular; physically, she was direct and immediate. He wondered, now, looking at her face, whether she might be an American Indian, and again he was frustrated because he couldn't tell one race in this country from another. He knew it was improper to ask. When he sat at the table, holding hands with her and sipping from his drink, he began to feel as if he had known her for a long time and was related to her in some obscure way.

Suddenly he asked her, "Why are you so interested in me?"

"Interested?" She laughed, and her long black hair, no longer pinned up, shook in quick thick waves. "Well, all right. I have an interest. I like it that you're so foreign that you take cabs to the park. I like the way you look. You're kind of cute. And the other thing is, your soul is so raw and new, Anders, it's like an oyster."

"What?" He looked at her near him at the table. Their drinks were half finished. "My soul?"

"Yeah, your soul. I can almost see it."

"Where is it?"

She leaned forward, friendly and sexual and now slightly elegant. "You want me to show you?"

"Yes," Anders said. "Sure."

"It's in two places," she said. "One part is up here." She released his hand and put her thumb on his forehead. "And the other part is down here." She touched him in the middle of his stomach. "Right there. And they're connected."

"What are they like?" he asked, playing along.

"Yours? Raw and shiny, just like I said."

"And what about your soul?" he asked.

She looked at him. "My soul is radioactive," she said. "It's like plutonium. Don't say you weren't warned."

He thought that this was another American idiom he hadn't heard before, and he decided not to spoil things by asking her about it. In Sweden, people didn't talk much about the soul, at least not in conjunction with oysters or plutonium. It was probably some local metaphor he had never heard in Sweden.

In the dark he couldn't make out much about her building, except that it was several floors high and at least fifty years old. Her living-room window looked out distantly at the river—once upstairs, he could see the lights of another passing freighter—and through the left side of the window he could see an electrical billboard. The name of the product was made out of hundreds of small incandescent bulbs, which went on and off from left to right. One of the letters was missing.

It's today's CHEVR LET!

All around her living-room walls were brightly framed watercolors, almost celebratory and Matisse-like, but in vague shapes. She went down the hallway, tapped on one of the doors, and said, "I'm home." Then she returned to the living room and kicked off her shoes. "My grandmother," she said. "She has her own room."

"Are these your pictures?" he asked. "Did you draw them?"

"Yes."

"I can't tell what they are. What are they?"

"They're abstract. You use wet paper to get that effect. They're abstract because God has gotten abstract. God used to have a form but now He's dissolving into pure light. That's what you see in those pictures. They're pictures of the trails that God leaves behind."

"Like the vapor trails," he smiled, "behind jets."

"Yes," she said. "Like that."

He went over to her in the dark and drew her to him and kissed her. Her breath was layered with smoke, apparently from cigarettes. Immediately he felt an unusual physical sensation inside his skin, like something heating up on a frypan.

She drew back. He heard another siren go by on the street outside. He wondered whether they should talk some more in the living room—share a few more verbal intimacies—to be really civilized about this and decided, no, it was not necessary, not when strangers make love, as they do, sometimes, in strange cities, away from home. They went into her bedroom and undressed each other. Her body, by the light of a dim bedside lamp, was as beautiful and as exotic as he hoped it would be, darker than his own skin in the dark room, native somehow to this continent. She had the flared shoulders and hips of a dancer. She bent down and snapped off the bedside light, and as he approached her, she was lit from behind by the billboard. Her skin felt vaguely electrical to him.

They stood in the middle of her bedroom, arms around each other, swaying, and he knew, in his arousal, that something odd was about to occur: he had no words for it in either his own language or in English.

They moved over and under each other, changing positions to stay in the breeze created by the window fan. They were both lively and attentive, and at first he thought it would be just the usual fun, this time with an almost anonymous American woman. He looked at her in the bed and saw her dark leg alongside his own, and he saw that same scar line running up her arm to her shoulder, where it disappeared.

"Where did you get that?" he asked.

"That?" She looked at it. "That was an accident that was done to me."

Half an hour later, resting with her, his hands on her back, he felt a wave of happiness; he felt it was a wave of color traveling through his body, surging from his forehead down to his stomach. It took him over again, and then a third time, with such force that he almost sat up.

"What is it?" she asked.

"I don't know. It is like . . . I felt a color moving through my body."

"Oh, that?" She smiled at him in the dark. "It's your soul, Anders. That's all. That's all it is. Never felt it before, huh?"

"I must be very drunk," he said.

She put her hand up into his hair. "Call it anything you want to. Didn't you feel it before? Our souls were curled together."

"You're crazy," he said. "You are a crazy woman."

"Oh yeah?" she whispered. "Is that what you think? Watch. Watch what happens now. You think this is all physical. Guess what. You're the crazy one. Watch. Watch."

She went to work on him, and at first it was pleasurable, but as she moved over him it became a succession of waves that had specific colorations, even when he turned her and thought he was taking charge. Soon he felt some substance, some glossy blue possession entangled in the air above him.

"I bet you're going to say that you're imagining all this," she said, her hand skidding across him.

"Who are you?" he said. "Who in the world are you?"

"I warned you," she whispered, her mouth directly over his ear. "I warned you. You people with your things, your rusty things, you suffer so bad when you come into where *we* live. Did they tell you we were all soulless here? Did they say that?"

He put his hands on her. "This is not love, but it—"

"Of course not," she said. "It's something else. Do you know the word? Do you know the word for something that opens your soul at once? Like that?" She snapped her fingers on the pillow. Her tongue was touching his ear. "Do you?" The words were almost inaudible.

"No."

"Addiction." She waited. "Do you understand?"

"Yes."

In the middle of the night he rose up and went to the window. He felt like a stump, amputated from the physical body of the woman. At the window he looked down, to the right of the billboard, and saw another apartment building with heavy decorations with human forms near the roof's edge, and on the third floor he saw a man at the window, as naked as he himself was but almost completely in shadow, gazing out at the street. They were so far away from each other that being unclothed didn't matter. It was vague and small and impersonal.

"Do you always stand at the window without clothes on?" she asked, from the bed.

"Not in Sweden," he said. He turned around. "This is odd," he said. "At night no one walks out on the streets. But there, over on that block, there's a man like me, at the window, and he is looking out, too. Do people stand everywhere at the windows here?"

"Come to bed."

"When I was in the army, the Swedish army," he said, still looking out, "they taught us to think that we could *decide* to do anything. They talked about the will. Your word 'willpower.' All Sweden believes this—choice, will, willpower. Maybe not so much now. I wonder if they talk about it here."

"You're funny," she said. She had moved up from behind him and embraced him.

In the morning he watched her as she dressed. His eyes hurt from sleeplessness. "I have to go," she said. "I'm already late." She was putting on a light blue skirt. As she did, she smiled. "You're a lovely lover," she said. "I like your body very much."

"What are we going to do?" he asked.

"We? There is no 'we,' Anders. There's you and then there's me. We're not a couple. I'm going to work. You're going back to your country soon. What are you planning to do?"

"May I stay here?"

"For an hour," she said, "and then you should go back to your hotel. I don't think you should stay. You don't live here."

"May I take you to dinner tonight?" he asked, trying not to watch her as he watched her. "What can we do tonight?"

"There's that 'we' again. Well, maybe. You can teach me a few words of Swedish. Why don't you hang around at your hotel and maybe I'll come by around six and get you, but don't call me if I don't come by, because if I don't, I don't."

"I can't call you," he said. "I don't know your last name."

"Oh, that's right," she said. "Well, listen. I'll probably come at six." She looked at him lying in the bed. "I don't believe this," she said.

"What?"

"You think you're in love, don't you?"

"No," he said. "Not exactly." He waited. "Oh, I don't know."

"I get the point," she said. "Well, you'd better get used to it. Welcome to our town. We're not always good at love but we are good at that." She bent to kiss him and then was gone. Happiness and agony simultaneously reached down and pressed against his chest. They, too, were like colors, but when you mixed the two together, you got something greenish-pink, excruciating.

He stood up, put on his trousers, and began looking into her dresser drawers. He expected to find trinkets and whatnot, but all she had were folded clothes, and, in the corner of the top drawer, a small turquoise heart for a charm bracelet. He put it into his pocket.

In the bathroom, he examined the labels on her medicines and facial creams before washing his face. He wanted evidence but didn't know for what. He looked, to himself, like a slightly different version of what he had once been. In the mirror his face had a puffy look and a passive expression, as if he had been assaulted during the night.

After he had dressed and entered the living room, he saw Lauren's grandmother sitting at a small dining-room table. She was eating a piece of toast and looking out of the window toward the river. The apartment, in daylight, had an aggressively scrubbed and mopped look. On the kitchen counter a small black-and-white television was blaring, but the old woman wasn't watching it. Her black hair was streaked with gray, and she wore a ragged pink bathrobe decorated with pictures of orchids. She was very frail. Her skin was as dark as her granddaughter's. Looking at her, Anders was once again unable to guess what race she was. She might be Arabic, or a Native American, or Hispanic, or black. Because he couldn't tell, he didn't care.

Without even looking at him, she motioned at him to sit down.

"Want anything?" she asked. She had a high, distant voice, as if it had come into the room over wires. "There are bananas over there." She made no gesture. "And grapefruit, I think, in the refrigerator."

"That's all right." He sat down on the other side of the table and folded his hands together, studying his fingers. The sound of traffic came up from the street outside.

"You're from somewhere," she said. "Scandinavia?"

"Yes," he said. "How can you tell?" Talking had become a terrible effort.

"Vowels," she said. "You sound like one of those Finns up north of here. When will you go back? To your country?"

"I don't know," he said. "Perhaps a few days. Perhaps not. My name is Anders." He held out his hand.

"Nice to meet you." She touched but did not shake his hand. "Why don't you know when you're going back?" She turned to look at him at last. It was a face on which curiosity still registered. She observed him as if he were an example of a certain kind of human being in whom she still had an interest.

"I don't know . . . I am not sure. Last night, I . . ."

"You don't finish your sentences," the old woman said.

"I am trying to. I don't want to leave your granddaughter," he said. "She is"—he tried to think of the right adjective—"amazing to me."

"Yes, she is." The old woman peered at him. "You don't think you're in love, do you?"

"I don't know."

"Well, don't be. She won't ever be married, so there's no point in being in love with her. There's no point in being married *here*. I see them, you know."

"Who?"

"All the young men. Well, there aren't many. A few. Every so often. They come and sleep here with her and then in the morning they come out for breakfast with me and then they go away. We sit and talk. They're usually very pleasant. Men are, in the morning. They should be. She's a beautiful girl."

"Yes, she is."

"But there's no future in her, you know," the old woman said. "Sure you don't want a grapefruit? You should eat something."

"No, thank you. What do you mean, 'no future'?"

"Well, the young men usually understand that." The old woman looked at the television set, scowled, and shifted her eyes to the window. She rubbed her hands together. "You can't invest in her. You can't do that at all. She won't let you. I know. I know how she thinks."

"We have women like that in my country," Anders said. "They are—"

"Oh no you don't," the old woman said. "Sooner or later they want to get married, don't they?"

"I suppose most of them."

She glanced out the window toward the Detroit River and the city of Windsor on the opposite shore. Just when he thought that she had forgotten all about him, he felt her hand, dry as a winter leaf, taking hold of his own. Another siren went by outside. He felt a weight descending in his stomach. The touch of the old woman's hand made him feel worse than before, and he stood up quickly, looking around the room as if there were some object nearby he had to pick up and take away immediately. Her hand dropped away from his.

"No plans," she said. "Didn't she tell you?" the old woman asked. "It's what she believes." She shrugged. "It makes her happy."

"I am not sure I understand."

The old woman lifted her right hand and made a dismissive wave in his direction. She pursed her mouth; he knew she had stopped speaking to him. He called a cab, and in half an hour he was back in his hotel room. In the shower he realized that he had forgotten to write down her address or phone number.

He felt itchy: he went out running, returned to his room, and took another shower. He did thirty push-ups and jogged in place. He groaned and shouted, knowing that no one would hear. How would he explain this to anyone? He was feeling passionate puzzlement. He went down to the hotel's dining room for lunch and ordered Dover sole and white wine but found himself unable to eat much of anything. He stared at his plate and at the other men and women consuming their meals calmly, and he was suddenly filled with wonder at ordinary life.

He couldn't stand to be by himself, and after lunch he had the doorman hail a cab. He gave the cabdriver a fifty and asked him to drive him around the city until all the money was used up.

"You want to see the nice parts?" the cabbie asked.

"No."

"What is it you want to see then?"

"The city."

"You tryin' to score, man? That it?"

Anders didn't know what he meant. He was certain that no sport was intended. He decided to play it safe. "No," he said.

The cabdriver shook his head and whistled. They drove east and then south; Anders watched the water-ball compass stuck to the front window. Along Jefferson Avenue they went past the shells of apartment buildings, and then, heading north, they passed block after block of vacated or boarded-up properties. One old building with Doric[2] columns was draped with a banner.

PROGRESS! THE OLD MUST MAKE WAY
FOR THE NEW
Acme Wrecking Company

The banner was worn and tattered. Anders noticed broken beer bottles, sharp brown glass, on sidewalks and vacant lots, and the glass, in the sun, seemed perversely beautiful. Men were sleeping on sidewalks and in front stairwells; one man, wearing a hat, urinated against the corner of a burned-out building. He saw other men—there were very few women out here in the light of day—in groups gazing at him with cold slow deadly expressions. In his state of mind, he understood it all; he identified with it. All of it, the ruins and the remnants, made perfect sense.

At six o'clock she picked him up and took him to a Greek restaurant. All the way over, he watched her. He examined her with the puzzled curiosity of someone who wants to know how another person who looks rather attractive but also rather ordinary could have such power. Her physical features didn't explain anything.

"Did you miss me today?" she asked, half-jokingly.

"Yes," he said. He started to say more but didn't know how to begin. "It was hard to breathe," he said at last.

"I know," she said. "It's the air."

"No, it isn't. Not the air."

"Well, what then?"

He looked at her.

"Oh, come on, Anders. We're just two blind people who staggered into each other and we're about to stagger off in different directions. That's all."

Sentences struggled in his mind, then vanished before he could say them. He watched the pavement pass underneath the car.

In the restaurant, a crowded and lively place smelling of beer and roasted meat and cigars, they sat in a booth and ordered an antipasto plate. He leaned over and took her hands. "Tell me, please, who and what you are."

She seemed surprised that he had asked. "I've explained," she said. She waited, then started up again. "When I was younger I had an idea that I wanted to be a dancer. I had to give that up. My timing was off." She smiled. "Onstage, I looked like a memory of what had already happened. The other girls would do something and then *I'd* do it. I come in late on a lot of things. That's good for me. I've told you where I work. I live with my grandmother. I go with her into

---

2. A style of classical Greek architecture.

the parks in the fall and we watch for birds. And you know what else I believe." He gazed at the gold hoops of her earrings. "What else do you want to know?"

"I feel happy and terrible," he said. "Is it you? Did you do this?"

"I guess I did," she said, smiling faintly. "Tell me some words in Swedish."

"Which ones?"

"House."

"Hus."

"Pain."

"Smärta."

She leaned back. "Face."

"Ansikte."

"Light."

"Ljus."

"Never."

"Aldrig."

"I don't like it," she said. "I don't like the sound of those words at all. They're too cold. They're cold-weather words."

"Cold? Try another one."

"Soul."

"Själ."

"No, I don't like it." She raised her hand to the top of his head, grabbed a bit of his hair, and laughed. "Too bad."

"Do you do this to everyone?" he asked. "I feel such confusion."

He saw her stiffen. "You want to know too much. You're too messed up. Too messed up with plans. You and your rust. All that isn't important. Not here. We don't do all that explaining. I've told you *everything* about me. We're just supposed to be enjoying ourselves. Nobody has to explain. That's freedom, Anders. Never telling why." She leaned over toward him so that her shoulders touched his, and with a sense of shock and desperation, he felt himself becoming aroused. She kissed him, and her lips tasted slightly of garlic. "Just say hi to the New World," she said.

"You feel like a drug to me," he said. "You feel experimental."

"We don't use that word that way," she said. Then she said, "Oh," as if she had understood something, or remembered another engagement. "Okay. I'll explain all this in a minute. Excuse me." She rose and disappeared behind a corner of the restaurant, and Anders looked out the window at a Catholic church the color of sandstone, on whose front steps a group of boys sat, eating popsicles. One of the boys got up and began to ask passersby for money; this went on until a policeman came and sent the boys away. Anders looked at his watch. Ten minutes had gone by since she had left. He looked up. He knew without thinking about it that she wasn't coming back.

He put a ten-dollar bill on the table and left the restaurant, jogging into the parking structure where she had left the car. Although he wasn't particularly surprised to see that it wasn't there, he sat down on the concrete and felt the floor of the structure shaking. He ran his hands through his hair, where she had grabbed at it. He waited as long as he could stand to do so, then returned to the hotel.

Luis was back on duty. Anders told him what had happened.

"Ah," Luis said. "She is disappeared."

"Yes. Do you think I should call the police?"

"No," Luis said. "I do not think so. They have too many disappeared already."

"Too many disappeared?"

"Yes. All over this city. Many many disappeared. For how many times do you take this lady out?"

"Once. No, twice."

"And this time is the time she leave you?"

Anders nodded.

"I have done that," Luis said. "When I get sick of a woman, I too have disappeared. Maybe," he said suddenly, "she will reappear. Sometimes they do."

"I don't think she will." He sat down on the sidewalk in front of the hotel and cupped his chin in his hands.

"No, no," Luis said. "You cannot do that in front of the hotel. This looks very bad. Please stand up." He felt Luis reaching around his shoulders and pulling him to his feet. "What you are acting is impossible after one night," Luis said. "Be like everyone else. Have another night." He took off his doorman's cap and combed his hair with precision. "Many men and women also disappear from each other. It is one thing to do. You had a good time?"

Anders nodded.

"Have another good time," Luis suggested, "with someone else. Beer, pizza, go to bed. Women who have not disappeared will talk to you, I am sure."

"I think I'll call the police," Anders said.

"Myself, no, I would not do that."

He dialed a number he found in the telephone book for a local precinct station. As soon as the station officer understood what Anders was saying to him, he became angry, said it wasn't a police matter, and hung up on him. Anders sat for a moment in the phone booth, then looked up the Church of the Millennium in the directory. He wrote down its address. Someone there would know about her, and explain.

The cab let him out in front. It was like no other church he had ever seen before. Even the smallest places of worship in his own country had vaulted roofs, steeples, and stained glass. This building seemed to be someone's remodeled house. On either side of it, two lots down, were two skeletal homes, one of which had been burned and which now stood with charcoal windows and a charcoal portal where the front door had once been. The other house was boarded-up; in the evening wind, sheets of newspaper were stuck to its south wall. Across the street was an almost deserted playground. The saddles had been removed from the swing set, and the chains hung down from the upper bar and moved slightly in the wind. Four men stood together under a basketball hoop, talking together. One of the men bounced a basketball occasionally.

A signboard had been planted into the ground in front of the church, but so many letters had been removed from it that Anders couldn't make out what it was supposed to say.

Ch rch of   e Mill ni m
Rev. H r old T.   oodst th, Pas or
Everyo e   elco e!
"Love on other, lest ye f ll to   d   tle for rle m!"

On the steps leading up to the front door, he turned around and saw, to the south, the lights of the office buildings of downtown Detroit suspended like enlarged stars in the darkness. After hearing what he thought was some sound in the bushes, he opened the front doors of the church and went inside.

Over a bare wood floor, folding chairs were lined up in five straight rows, facing toward a front chest intended as an altar, and everywhere there was a smell of incense, of ashy pine. Above the chest, and nailed to the far wall where a crucifix might be located in a Protestant church, was a polished brass circle with a nimbus of rays projecting out from its top. The rays were extended along the wall for a distance of four feet. One spotlight from a corner behind him lit up the brass circle, which in the gloom looked either like a deity-sun or some kind of explosion. The bare walls had been painted with flames: buildings of the city, some he had already seen, painted in flames, the earth in flames. There was an open Bible on the chest, and in one of the folding chairs a deck of playing cards. Otherwise, the room was completely empty. Glancing at a side door, he decided that he had never seen a church so small, or one that filled him with a greater sense of desolation. Behind him, near the door, was a bench. He had the feeling that the bench was filled with the disappeared. He sat down on it, and as he looked at the folding chairs it occurred to him that the disappeared were in fact here now, in front of him, sitting or standing or kneeling.

He composed himself and went back out onto the street, thinking that perhaps a cab would go by, but he saw neither cabs nor cars, not even pedestrians. After deciding that he had better begin walking toward the downtown area, he made his way down two blocks, past a boarded-up grocery store and a vacated apartment building, when he heard what he thought was the sound of footsteps behind him.

He felt the blow at the back of his head; it came to him not as a sensation of pain but as an instant crashing explosion of light in his brain, a bursting circle with a shooting aura irradiating from it. As he turned to fall, he felt hands touching his chest and his trousers; they moved with speed and almost with tenderness, until they found what they were looking for and took it away from him.

He lay on the sidewalk in a state somewhere between consciousness and unconsciousness, hearing the wind through the trees overhead and feeling some blood trickling out of the back of his scalp, until he felt the hands again, perhaps the same hands, lifting him up, putting him into something, taking him somewhere. Inside the darkness he now inhabited, he found that at some level he could still think: *Someone hit me and I've been robbed.* At another, later, point, he understood that he could open his eyes; he had that kind of permission. He was sitting in a wheelchair in what was clearly a hospital emergency room. It felt as though someone were pushing him toward a planetary corridor. They asked him questions, which he answered in Swedish. "Det gör ont,"[3] he said, puzzled that they didn't understand him. "Var är jag?"[4] he asked. They didn't know. English was what they wanted. He tried to give them some.

They X-rayed him and examined his cut; he would need four stitches, they said. He found that he could walk. They told him he was lucky, that he had

---

3. It hurts. **4.** Where am I?

not been badly hurt. A doctor, and then a nurse, and then another nurse, told him that he might have been killed—shot or knifed—and that victims of this type, strangers who wandered into the wrong parts of the city, were not unknown. He mentioned the disappeared. They were polite, but said that there was no such phrase in English. When he mentioned the name of his hotel, they said, once again, that he was lucky: it was only a few blocks away, walking distance. They smiled. You're a lucky man, they said, grinning oddly. They knew something but weren't saying it.

As the smaller debris of consciousness returned to him, he found himself sitting in a brightly lit room, like a waiting room, near the entryway for emergency medicine. From where he sat, he could see, through his fluent tidal headache, the patients arriving, directed to the Triage[5] Desk, where their condition was judged.

They brought in a man on a gurney, who was hoarsely shouting. They rushed him through. He was bleeding, and they were holding him down as his feet kicked sideways.

They brought in someone else, a girl, who was stumbling, held up on both sides by friends. Anders heard something that sounded like Odie. Who was Odie? Her boyfriend? Odie, she screamed. Get me Odie.

Anders stood up, unable to watch any more. He shuffled through two doorways and found himself standing near an elevator. From a side window, he saw light from the sun rising. He hadn't realized that it was day. The sun made the inside of his head shriek. To escape the light, he stepped on the elevator and pressed the button for the fifth floor.

As the elevator rose, he felt his knees weakening. In order to clear his head, he began to count the other people on the elevator: seven. They seemed normal to him. The signs of this were coats and ties on the men, white frocks and a stethoscope on one of the women, and blouses and jeans on the other women. None of them looked like her. From now on, none of them ever would.

He felt that he must get home to Sweden quickly, before he became a very different person, unrecognizable even to himself.

At the fifth floor the doors opened and he stepped out. Close to the elevators was a nurses' station, and beyond it a long hallway leading to an alcove. He walked down this hallway, turned the corner, and heard small squalling sounds ahead. At the same time, he saw the windows in the hallway and understood that he had wandered onto the maternity floor. He made his way to the viewer's window and looked inside. He counted twenty-five newborns, each one in its own clear plastic crib. He stared down at the babies, hearing, through the glass, the cries of those who were awake.

He was about to turn around and go back to his hotel when one of the nurses saw him. She raised her eyebrows quizzically and spread her hands over the children. He shook his head to indicate no. Still she persisted. She pointed to a baby with white skin and a head of already-blond hair. He shook his head no once again. He would need to get back to the hotel, call his bank in Sweden, get money for the return trip. He touched his pants pocket and found that the wallet was still there. What had they taken? The nurse, smiling, nodded as if she understood, and motioned toward the newborns with

---

5. The process of determining priorities for emergency medical treatment.

darker skin, the Hispanics and light-skinned blacks and all the others, babies of a kind he never saw in Sweden.

Well, he thought, why not? Now that they had done this to him.

He felt himself nodding. Sure. That American word. His right arm rose. He pointed at a baby whose skin was the color of clay, the color of polished bronze, or flames. Now the nurse was wheeling the baby he had pointed to closer to the window. When it was directly in front of him, she left it there, returning to the back of the nursery. Standing on the other side of the glass, staring down at the sleeping infant, he tapped on the panel twice and waved, as he thought fathers should. The baby did not awaken. Anders put his hand in his pocket and touched the little turquoise heart, then pressed his forehead against the glass of the window and recovered himself. He stood for what seemed to him a long time, before taking the elevator down to the ground floor and stepping out onto the front sidewalk, and to the air, which smelled as it always had, of powerful combustible materials and their traces, fire and ash.

1990

RELATED:

—Baxter on William Maxwell's "The Thistles in Sweden," p. 1756

ANN BEATTIE
b. 1947

Beattie was born in Washington, D.C., and attended both American University and the University of Connecticut. Subsequently, she taught at Harvard and the University of Virginia. She has received a Guggenheim Fellowship and has built a broad reputation for the many stories she has published in *The New Yorker*, establishing her as a spokesperson for the generation of the 1960s as her characters adapt—or fail to adapt—to the oncoming years. She writes of those who took the 1960s to be a Golden Age and cannot free themselves from the enchantment of their youth. Her books of short stories include *Distortions* (1976), *The Burning House* (1982), *What Was Mine* (1991), *Selected Stories* (1999), and *Follies* (2005). A collection of her *New Yorker* stories was published in 2011. Her novels include *Chilly Scenes of Winter* (1976), *Falling in Place* (1980), *Love Always* (1985), *Picturing Will* (1990), *My Life, Starring Dara Falcon* (1997), *Perfect Recall* (2000), *The Doctor's House* (2001), and *Mrs. Nixon* (2011). In 2005 Beattie won the Rea Award for the Short Story.

Snow

I remember the cold night you brought in a pile of logs and a chipmunk jumped off as you lowered your arms. "What do you think *you're* doing in here?" you said, as it ran through the living room. It went through the library and stopped at the front door as though it knew the house well. This would be difficult for anyone to believe, except perhaps as the subject of a poem. Our first week in the house was spent scraping, finding some of the house's secrets, like wallpaper underneath wallpaper. In the kitchen, a pattern of white-gold trellises supported purple grapes as big and round as Ping-Pong balls. When we painted the walls yellow, I thought of the bits of grape that remained underneath and imagined the vine popping through, the way some plants can tenaciously push through anything. The day of the big snow, when you had to shovel the walk and couldn't find your cap and asked me how to wind a towel so that it would stay on your head—you, in the white towel turban, like a crazy king of snow. People liked the idea of our being together, leaving the city for the country. So many people visited, and the fireplace made all of them want to tell amazing stories: the child who happened to be standing on the right corner when the door of the ice-cream truck came open and hundreds of Popsicles crashed out; the man standing on the beach, sand sparkling in the sun, one bit glinting more than the rest, stooping to find a diamond ring. Did they talk about amazing things because they thought we'd turn into one of them? Now I think they probably guessed it wouldn't work. It was as hopeless as giving a child a matched cup and saucer. Remember the night, out on the lawn, knee-deep in snow, chins pointed at the sky as the wind whirled down all that whiteness? It seemed that the world had been turned upside down, and we were looking into an enormous field of Queen Anne's lace.[1] Later, headlights off, our car was the first to ride through the newly fallen snow. The world outside the car looked solarized.

You remember it differently. You remember that the cold settled in stages, that a small curve of light was shaved from the moon night after night, until you were no longer surprised the sky was black, that the chipmunk ran to hide in the dark, not simply to a door that led to its escape. Our visitors told the same stories people always tell. One night, giving me a lesson in storytelling, you said, "Any life will seem dramatic if you omit mention of most of it."

This, then, for drama: I drove back to that house not long ago. It was April, and Allen had died. In spite of all the visitors, Allen, next door, had been the good friend in bad times. I sat with his wife in their living room, looking out the glass doors to the backyard, and there was Allen's pool, still covered with black plastic that had been stretched across it for winter. It had rained, and as the rain fell, the cover collected more and more water until it finally spilled onto the concrete. When I left that day, I drove past what had been our house. Three or four crocuses were blooming in the front—just a few dots of white, no field of snow. I felt embarrassed for them. They couldn't compete.

This is a story, told the way you say stories should be told: Somebody grew up, fell in love, and spent a winter with her lover in the country. This, of course, is the barest outline, and futile to discuss. It's as pointless as throwing birdseed on the ground while snow still falls fast. Who expects small things to survive when even the largest get lost? People forget years and remember moments. Seconds and symbols are left to sum things up: the black shroud over the pool. Love, in its shortest form, becomes a word. What I remember about all that time is one winter. The snow. Even now, saying "snow," my lips move so that they kiss the air.

No mention has been made of the snowplow that seemed always to be there, scraping snow off our narrow road—an artery cleared, though neither of us could have said where the heart was.

1983

RELATED:

—Beattie on Peter Taylor's "A Spinster's Tale," p. 1756

---

1. *Daucus carota*, the wild form of the carrot, which has flat clusters of tiny white flowers.

MADISON SMARTT BELL

b. 1957

Bell was born in Tennessee and received his B.A. from Princeton and his M.F.A. from Hollins College. He has taught writing at the University of Iowa, the Bennington Writing Workshop, Johns Hopkins University, and Vassar College and currently directs the creative writing program at Goucher College. His short stories are collected in *Zero db and Other Stories* (1987) and *Barking Man* (1990). His most recent novels include *Save Me, Joe Lewis* (1993), *All Souls' Rising* (1995), *Ten Indians* (1996), *Master of the Crossroads* (2000), *Anything Goes* (2002), *The Stone That the Builder Refused* (2004), *Charm City* (2007), *Devil's Dream* (2009), and *The Color of Night* (2011).

Witness

The day he heard that Paxton Morgan was released, Wilson had been planning to revise a will. It was a slack period for him and he didn't expect to be in court until late in the following week, but he'd come in early just the same. The door to his inner office was open on the lateral hallway, and he could hear the whisk of a letter opener as Mrs. Veech, behind the front desk, sliced into the morning mail. Mostly bills or offers of subscriptions, he'd glanced through it quickly on his way in.

There was a jingle as the front door opened and Wilson raised his head to listen, but it was a man he didn't want to see, and Mrs. Veech denied his presence. A grumble, sound of pacing, scrape of a match and a faint distant odor of tobacco. Mrs. Veech coughed. The voice grudgingly inquired if the smoke bothered her. Mrs. Veech said nothing but coughed again, more significantly. Her allergy to cigarettes was highly selective—Wilson, for instance, smoked himself. When the front door released a jangle of departure, he picked up his pencil and went back to the will. Mrs. Veech, he could hear, was dealing with the remains of the mail.

"Mr. Wilson, did you know they were letting Pax Morgan go?"

He heard her voice without immediately understanding it, registering only the anxiously rising note at the end. The task in his hand was complicated, though almost entirely frivolous: the testament of a woman some forty years old who would probably live at least forty more, revising her bequests more or less semiannually. Still, it was an amusement she could afford if it pleased her, harmless enough, and he had use for the fee.

He drafted another line or two on the long yellow pad and broke the point of his pencil. Then the sense of Mrs. Veech's question reached him and he stood up, taking a cigarette from his shirt pocket as he stepped into the hall. Mrs. Veech sat bolt upright in her desk chair, clamping some sort of form in both her hands. Wilson took it from her and walked to the front window, setting the unlit cigarette in the corner of his mouth as he moved. It was a slick gray photocopy of a release form from Central State, with the name of Paxton Morgan typed along with other information and the illegibly scrawled signature of some doctor or official in the lower right-hand corner. He noted that the box for the date was not filled in.

"They might have already turned him out," Mrs. Veech said.

"Or they might just still be thinking about it." Wilson turned to face her. Round, plain and comfortable, she was a clean fifteen years older than he and normally unfazeable, though now she seemed perceptibly disturbed.

"I wonder who sent us this," he said.

"There wasn't any cover letter." Mrs. Veech frowned.

Wilson stepped across and picked up the slit envelope from the stack of circulars on the desk and paced back to the window, turning it over in his hands. It was letterhead stationery from the hospital, with his own address unremarkably typed and a postmark from two days before. Absently he folded it in three and peered out the window, around the hanging vines of the plants Mrs. Veech had insisted on stringing up there. The office was on the ground floor at the corner of the square, and sighting through the letter O of his own reversed name on the glass, Wilson could see a couple of cars and one mud-splattered pickup truck revolving lazily around the concrete Confederate soldier on his high pedestal at the center. Opposite, the usual complement of idlers lounged around the courthouse steps. The office had a southern exposure, and he could feel a slight sunny warmth on the side of his face through the pane.

"Well, damn their eyes," he said, and then, as he noticed Mrs. Veech again, "Excuse me."

Back in his inner office, Wilson lit the cigarette and set it in an ashtray to burn itself out, then began dialing the phone with the butt end of his pencil. In some fifteen minutes he had variously heard that Pax Morgan had already been released, was not going to be released at all, or had never been admitted. He hadn't expected to discover who had sent the anonymous notification, and so was not surprised when he didn't. Although he did learn that a Dr. Meagrum was supposed to be presiding over the case, he could not get through to him. He left a message asking that his call be returned. The central spring of his revolving chair squealed slightly as he leaned back, away from the phone. On the rear wall of the room, behind the triangle of clients' chairs, bookshelves rose all the way to the high ceiling, bearing about half of Wilson's law library. Hands laced behind his head, he scanned the top row of heavy books as though looking for something, though he was not. After a moment he tightened his lips and leaned forward again and made the call he had been postponing.

He had the number by heart already because it had once been his own, the Nashville law firm where he'd formerly worked. In those days Sharon Morgan would likely have answered the phone herself, but they used her more as a researcher now, and had hired a different receptionist. She was good at the work, and with the two children there was no doubt the better pay made a difference. Still studying for her own law degree, part time; Pax had never liked that much. Wilson asked for her and waited till she came on the line, her voice brisk, as he remembered it. It had been some months since they had spoken and the first few exchanges passed in pleasantries, inquiries about each other's children and the like. Then, a pause.

"Well, you never called just to pass the time," Sharon said. "Not if I know you."

Wilson hesitated, thinking, What would she look like now? The same. Phone pinched between her chin and shoulder, a tail of her longish dark hair involved with the cord some way. Chances were she'd be doing something on her desk while she waited for him to continue, brown eyes sharp on some document, wasting no time.

"Right," he said. "Have you heard anything of Pax lately?"

"And don't care to," she said, her tone still easy. "Why would you ask?"

The chair spring squeaked as Wilson shifted position. The distant sound of a typewriter came to him over the line. He flicked his pencil with a fingernail and watched its bevels turning over the lines of the yellow pad. "And not the hospital either, I don't suppose."

"Oh-*ho*," Sharon said. He could hear her voice tightening down, homing in. She took the same grim satisfaction in any discovery, no matter its purport, which was part of what made her good at her job. "Is that what it is?"

"I'm afraid," Wilson said, "they're letting him out, if they haven't already."

"And never even let me know. There ought to be a law . . ."

". . . but there doesn't appear to be one," Wilson said. He picked up the hospital form and read off to her its most salient details. A stall, he thought, even before he was through with it. "The morning mail," he said. "No date, and I don't even know who sent it."

"Then what are you thinking to do?" she said.

"I've been calling the hospital," Wilson said. "If I ever get through to the right doctor, maybe I can convince them to hold him, if he's not already gone."

"*If*," Sharon said sharply. "All up to them, is it?"

"I would call it a case for persuasion," Wilson said. "So, did you have any plans for the weekend? I should be able to get in touch . . ."

"I'm taking the children out to the lake."

Wilson plucked another cigarette from his breast pocket and began to tamp it rhythmically on the old green desktop blotter. "I don't know," he said. "Why not go to your brother's, say? Instead."

"What would we want to do that for?"

"Look, Sharon," he said. "You know, it's to hell and gone from anywhere, that house on the lake. And nobody even out there this time of year."

"I will *not* run from that—" She interrupted herself, but he thought the calm of her voice was artificial when she went on. "The kids are packed for it. They're counting on it. I don't see any reason to change our plans."

"You don't, do you?" Wilson said without sarcasm, and put a match to his cigarette. He supposed he'd been expecting this, or something a whole lot like it.

"Why don't you get a peace bond on him?" Sharon said. "If he really is out, I mean. Something. Because it ought to be *his* problem. Not mine."

"I could do that," Wilson said. "Try to, anyway. You know what good it'll do, too. You know it better than I do."

There was silence in the receiver, the phantom typewriter had stopped. Pax Morgan had been under a restraining order that night back before the divorce decree when he'd appeared at the house in Nashville he and Sharon had shared and smashed out all the ground-floor windows with the butt end of his deer rifle; he'd made it all the way around the house before the police arrived.

"Well, devil take the hindmost," Wilson said. "I'll let you know what I can find out. And you take care."

"Thanks for letting me know."

"Take care, Sharon," Wilson said, but she had already hung up, so he did too.

Shifting the cigarette to his left hand, he picked up the pencil and began jotting a list at the foot of the pad with the blunted tip. Often he did his thinking with the pencil point; he'd discovered that sometimes a solution would appear in the interstices of what he wrote. There were only two items on the list.

> —Judge Oldfield   injunction P.M.
> —Dr. Meagrum   Central State

He added a third.

> —call back S.M.

The pencil doodled away from the last initial. The list was obvious and complete, and after he acted on it nothing would be solved. A long ash was sprouting from his cigarette, but he didn't notice until the spark crawled far enough to burn his knuckle.

For the rest of the morning he worked abstractedly on the will with imperfect concentration. Every twenty minutes or so he interrupted himself to make some fruitless call. Dr. Meagrum was perpetually "on rounds" or "in consultation." Judge Oldfield was spending his morning on the bench. Wilson's own phone rang occasionally, but always over something trivial. When he called Oldfield's chambers again around noon, he found that the judge was gone to lunch. He tightened his tie, got his seersucker suit coat down from the hat rack and, with a word or two to Mrs. Veech, went out himself.

Circling the square counterclockwise, he passed the Standard Farm Store, the bank and the courthouse steps, where one man or another raised a broad flat palm to greet him. It was warm out, an Indian summer heat wave, though it was late October and the leaves had already turned. A new asphalt path on the southbound street felt tacky on his shoes as he crossed. A couple of blocks west of the square he was already verging on the edge of time; beyond the long low roof of Dotson's Restaurant there were woods, turned fired-clay red patched with sere yellow, with a few deep green cedars standing anomalously among the other trees.

The fans were on inside the restaurant, revolving on tall poles, fluttering the corners of the checked oilcloths on the small square tables. Judge Oldfield sat toward the rear—alone, for a wonder—behind a plate of fried catfish, hushpuppies and boiled greens. As Wilson approached he put down his newspaper and smiled. "What wind blows you here, young fellow my lad?"

"An ill one, I'd say." Wilson sat down on a ladder-back chair. "Do you remember Sharon Morgan? A Lawrence, she was, before she married."

"Married that crazy fellow, didn't she?"

"That's the one." Wilson ordered an iced tea from the waitress who'd appeared at his elbow, and turned back to the judge. "They're letting him out of Central State, at least that's what it looks like." He ran down the brief of the morning's activity while Oldfield grazed on his catfish and nodded.

"It worrying you personally?" the judge said when he was done. "For your-self, I mean?"

"Oh no," Wilson said. "Not hardly. It wasn't me he said he'd kill, was it? I doubt he'd remember much about me. I never knew him any too well. Even while the divorce was going on it was just her he was mad at."

"So it's the wife—ex-wife, I mean. She's the one with the worry."

"She's the one." Wilson frowned down at his hands. There was a small watery blister where the cigarette had burned him, surprisingly painful for its size. He turned the cold curve of the iced tea glass against it. "She asked me to get an injunction on him. That's why I came hunting you."

Oldfield took off his fragile rimless glasses, rubbed them with a handker-chief and put them back on. "That's tricky, old son," he said, "when you don't know for sure if he's loose or he's not."

"Hard to get good information out of that place, don't you know?" Wilson said. "Seems like a lot of them are crazy, doctors and patients alike."

"Must be that's why they call it a madhouse," Oldfield said with a faint smile. "Well. She does live in the county now? Full time?"

"She moved here right after the divorce," Wilson said.

"Just to oblige you, now," Oldfield said, "I could sign you a paper. You draw it up. It happens he *is* out, you let me know and we'll sign it and serve it right away. It won't be much of a help to her, though."

"Don't I know it," Wilson said. "But what else do you do?"

"Not a whole lot that you *can*," said Oldfield. "You really think she's got call to worry? Not just fretful, is she?"

"Not her," Wilson said. "I'm the one fretting. I'm wondering, how can I get a deputy to watch over them for a couple of days?"

"You know you can't set them on her," Oldfield said. "Not without she asks for it herself."

"She won't."

"She was a pretty thing, as I recall," Oldfield said irrelevantly. He took off his glasses and rubbed at the bridge of his nose. "And knew her own mind, or seemed to."

"You mean she's stubborn."

"Yes, that's right."

Wilson stood up. "I thank you," he said.

Oldfield smiled myopically up at him, his eyes a light watery blue. "You ought to stay and try the catfish."

"Well, I believe not," Wilson said. "Not much of an appetite today."

"A young man like you?" The judge shook his head. "Must be this heat."

"Your wife called," Mrs. Veech reported. "She'll call you back. And that man from Central State, he called. Dr. Meagrum."

"He would have, wouldn't he?" Wilson said, shrugging out of his jacket. "Wait till I was gone, I mean."

Mrs. Veech sniffed. "In a tearing-down hurry, too," she said. "He was right cross to find you not here."

"He'll get over it," Wilson said. "All right, then, would you make sure for me that Pax Morgan still has his house in Brentwood? We might want to serve a paper on him a little later in the day."

In the inner office it was a little too warm, though not quite oppressive. He put his coat on the hat rack, cracked the single window and paced for a moment at the far side of his desk. It was a shallow room and the high wall of dark bookbindings seemed uncomfortably close. With a sigh he went back to his seat, lit a cigarette, picked up the will, put it down, lifted a list of the other items on his immediate agenda and then let that drop too.

The urge to pick at the blister seemed irresistible. He tore loose an edge of it, reviewing, in spite of himself, what little he really knew about Pax Morgan. They'd gone to the same high school, but two years apart; Wilson was the younger. Pax had played football—he remembered that—indifferently, in the line. Later on he had inherited money and started dabbling in real estate, or insurance, neither making nor losing much at whatever it might have been. Grown, he was a loud bluff fellow with a ruddy face and crinkly, almost yellow hair. At the large parties where Wilson would occasionally run into him, he was known for drinking too much and becoming not just mush-mouthed but crazily incoherent. The drinking was said to be a factor in his later, more serious breakdowns.

Wilson had gone to Sharon's wedding but he couldn't think if it was before or after it that he'd had the one brush with Pax he remembered with real clarity. Another party, undoubtedly some Christmas gathering, for Pax was wearing an incongruous Santa Claus tie and had managed to get quite drunk on eggnog. Shuffled together by the crowd, they somehow became embroiled in an argument over deer hunting. Wilson shot duck and dove, rabbit and squirrel, and on his father's farm he might shoot what he had to, to protect the livestock, but he had no taste for shooting deer, which now appeared to be Pax's ruling passion. Wilson was trying to get off the subject, but Pax wouldn't let it drop.

"You've never been blooded," he said thickly. "That's your trouble, you've never been *blooded*." He grasped Wilson's lapel and twisted it, drawing himself unpleasantly near, and Wilson was a little startled by what he himself did next, a trick someone had showed him in the Army. He took hold of Pax's thumb and squeezed the joints of it together, so that the sudden sharp pain made Pax flinch and let go. Reflexively, Wilson took a step backward, jostling someone behind him in the crowded room, but Pax's face went from surprise to a total blank, like a television switched to an empty channel, and so the whole episode was amputated.

Real craziness there, or an early sign of it. Wilson pulled the dead skin back from the blister, creating a small red-rimmed sore. By the time of the divorce, there were many worse examples, enough to fill a dossier. Wilson had never cared for divorce work much, but Sharon was both a colleague and a sort of distant friend, and also it was in the first thin stage of his independent practice. But once it was over he swore off friends' divorces altogether, no matter how bad he might need the work. It had been an easy case in the sense that the outcome was not in real doubt, but it was angry and ugly on Pax's side, and there'd been some bitter squabbling over property. Sharon had held out for the house on the lake—impractically, as Wilson thought—surrendering the Nashville residence to Pax, who'd later sold it. Reaching for the phone to call the hospital one more time, he wished again she hadn't done that.

His game of telephone tag with Central State went on for a couple more hours, unpromisingly. When the phone finally rang back around two-thirty, it was his wife.

"Not interrupting, I hope," she said. "Is it busy?"

"Not so you'd notice," he said. "It's been pretty quiet."

"Well, we need a gallon of milk," she said, "and cornmeal. Would you stop on the way home?"

"I'll do it," Wilson said, scribbling on the pad. "Lisa driving you crazy today?" Their daughter was four years old, and frantic.

"How should I describe it?" she said, and laughed. "This time next year she'll be in school . . . I'll miss her, though."

"That's the spirit," Wilson said. The light on his phone began to flash and Mrs. Veech called down the hall, "It's that Dr. Meagrum!"

"I've got to take this call," Wilson said. "I'll be home on time, I think . . ." He pushed the button.

Dr. Meagrum seemed to be already *in medias res*.[1] "—there's an issue of doctor-patient confidentiality here, Mr., uh, Wilson. I don't know who could have sent you that form but they did so without my authorization."

"Did they?" Wilson said, catching his breath. "As you may know, I represent Mr. Morgan's ex-wife, and given the circumstances of the case, it seems to me appropriate that *both* of us should have been informed."

"I can't agree with you there," Dr. Meagrum snapped.

"All due respect to your point of view," Wilson said, trying to collect himself. The conversation had taken an adversarial turn too soon. "I take it that Mr. Morgan *has*, in fact, been released from your, ah, custodial care."

"My records show that Mr. Morgan has been responding favorably to a course of medication and was transferred to outpatient status two days ago."

"I see," Wilson said. "What medication, may I ask?"

"I'm sorry, but that's confidential."

"And what assurance do we have that he will actually *take* this medication?"

"He's in our outpatient program now, and we'll be monitoring him on a biweekly basis."

"Biweekly, you say. That's *every two weeks*?" Wilson creaked back in his chair, gazing up at the join of his bookcase and the ceiling. "Dr. Meagrum, I would like you to consider"—he paused, thinking over the jargon as if fumbling for a key—"consider returning Mr. Morgan to *inpatient status*. Temporarily, shall we say. In the interests of the safety of his ex-wife and family."

"Our file shows that any such step would be contraindicated," the doctor said. "Not in the patient's best interests."

---

1. "In the middle of things" (Latin); used especially of a narrative that opens in the middle rather than at the chronological beginning.

A white flash of light, something like heat lightning, burst over Wilson's mental horizon, obscuring his view of the bookcases. He found he was clenching the receiver in a strangle grip and talking much louder than before. "Sir, you are describing a *piece of paper* to me, and I am talking to you about a man who has threatened to kill his wife, not once but many times—"

Dr. Meagrum harrumphed. "Yes, someone with this type of pathology might make such a threat, but I wouldn't suggest that you take it too seriously . . ."

"He came to her house with a thirty-ought-six rifle," Wilson said. "A *loaded* rifle—I'm now referring to the police report. They found him and the gun and they found her barricaded in an upstairs bedroom. With her two children, I should say. The boy is six now, Dr. Meagrum, and the little girl is seven. Your *outpatient* has threatened to kill them too."

Dr. Meagrum resorted to the imperial "we": "We have no record that this patient is violent. We see no reason to alter the treatment program at this time."

With a mighty effort, Wilson established a greater degree of control over his voice. "Very well," he said frostily. "I do sincerely hope you'll see no reason to regret the course you've taken."

By dumb luck his next call caught Judge Oldfield in his chambers, between cases, on the fly.

"I'm asking the impossible now," Wilson said. "Let's have him picked up. An APB. Lock him up and have a look at him. Just for a day or so."

"You're right," Oldfield said. "That's impossible. I couldn't do it if I wanted to. This is Williamson County. We haven't got a police state here."

"It's a free country, isn't it?" Wilson said. "Well, I had to ask."

"I wonder if you did, at that," Oldfield said. "You're acting mighty worked up about this, old son. Don't you think you might be making a little much of it all? He's been out two days already, so you say, and what happened? Nothing. The lady didn't even know until you called her. Simmer down some, think it over. Go home early. It's Friday, after all."

"All right," Wilson said. "Might give it a try."

"You get me that injunction and I'll pass it on to the sheriff direct," Oldfield said. "I can't do any more than that."

"I know," Wilson said. "Not until something happens. Well, I appreciate it."

He hung up and dialed Sharon Morgan at the office but she was gone, gone for the weekend, had left half an hour before to pick up the children from school. He plopped down the phone and tried, forcibly, to relax. Try it. Judge Oldfield was no fool, after all. Wilson picked up the pencil with a fleeting idea of listing off what he was thinking, feeling, but that was a ridiculous notion; probably that was how they spent their time at Central State. Possibly nothing would happen anyway. Possibly. He looked up Sharon's home number and dialed it, but there was no answer, though it rang twenty times.

In ten minutes he had scratched out the requisite injunction and handed it to Mrs. Veech with instructions to type it and walk it over to the courthouse when she was done. After she had gone out, he sat doing nothing but covering the phone, which didn't ring. The jingle of Mrs. Veech's return moved him to at least pretend to work. But he'd had it with the will for the day, though it still wasn't quite finished. He scraped his agenda toward him across the desk and ran his pencil point down item by item. There were two boundary disputes and a zoning complaint. A piece of frivolous litigation to do with somebody's unleashed dog. There was a murder case where the defendant would plead, draw two-to-ten and count himself lucky. A foregone conclusion, Wilson thought in his present skeptical mood, though matters had not yet reached that stage. At the foot of the list was a patent case that would make him and his client rich if he could win it. This one was the most remote, no court date even set for it yet, but at the same time the most intriguing, as much for its intricacy as its promise. He swiveled and dug in the cabinet for the file.

At four he called Sharon Morgan at the lake and got no answer. For another half hour he studied the patent case, though he was losing interest at an exponential rate. When he next called there was still no answer, and he was out of the chair and snatching his coat down from its peg before he even knew he meant to leave. On the highway bound for Keyhole Lake he began to feel a little foolish. He'd been presuming, counting the time from three o'clock, when school let out. It was not more than an hour from Nashville to the lake house, but he hadn't considered that she might have stopped to shop on the way, or taken the children to a movie or simply for a drive. Now it appeared to him that his every move that day had been an error. It was unlike him to have lost his temper with that doctor. Patience had always been his strength; he left it to his opponents to make mistakes in anger. Then too, that last call to Judge Oldfield was something he'd have to live down, and on top of all that he had wasted the day, and would need to come back in Saturday morning to recover the lost time.

All foolishness, and yet the thought did not comfort him. He drove carefully, a hair under the speed limit, sighting through the windshield across the burn mark on his knuckle. For no reason he could think of, he let the car roll past the Morgan mailbox and coast to a stop on the shoulder, where he got softly out. There was a little lip to climb before he could see down the driveway to the steeply pitched roof of the A-frame house and the blue lake distantly visible out past it. It was cooler here; the weather was turning, or else it was a chill coming off the water.

Below him, the drive was matted with fallen leaves. A staining fall of sunset light came slanting through the tree trunks on either side as the wind rose and combed the red leaves back, bringing a few more falling from the branches. Except for the wind it was utterly still; only across the lake the dogs in Jackson's kennel were barking, their voices echoing off the flat expanse of the water. But probably they were barking all the time. That was not the problem. What was wrong was that the passenger door of Sharon's orange Volkswagen had been left hanging open, sticking out stiffly like a broken arm. The car was pulled around parallel to the back porch, and over its roof he saw that the sliding glass door to the house had been left open too.

He walked to the dangling car door and stopped. Just past the edge of the drive, not more than three yards from him, there lay a child's blue tennis shoe, a Ked, with maple leaves spread around it like the prints of a large hand. Some twenty paces farther on he found the second shoe and then the little boy, barefoot, lying face down in a pile of sloppily raked leaves. Wilson thought that his name had been Billy, but he couldn't be quite certain of it, which bothered him unreasonably. The child had been shot in the base of the neck;

the entry wound was rather small. Beyond the leaf pile a wide swath of dun lawn swept down to the lake shore where a canoe, tethered to a little dock, rocked softly on the water.

A strip of almost total darkness fit into the gap of the glass door. The porch floor moaned as Wilson crossed it, and glancing down he saw a brass shell casing caught in a crack between two boards. He bent to pick it up, then stopped himself and put both hands in his pockets. Through the door was a large living room with no ceiling, only the peaked roof and the rafters. At this time of day it was very dim within and it took Wilson's eyes a moment to adjust. The daughter (he was almost sure her name was Jill) was sprawled on a high-backed wicker chair as if flung there by some strong force. There was a single wound in her chest. Her mouth was open slightly and her eyes showed a little white. Wilson thought it more than likely that Pax had shot her from a standing position on the porch.

It took him only a quarter turn of his head to locate Sharon's body at the far end of the long room, lying across a wide flight of steps that rose to the kitchen and dining area. Pax might well have shot her from the doorway; he was a marksman, the proof was plain, and efficient with his shells. Wilson crossed the room to the steps and paused. He couldn't tell just where she'd been hit, though she'd bled very heavily. She lay crooked, twisted over at the waist, the fingers of one hand folded over the overhang of a step. Her hair had fallen full over her face, and Wilson was grateful for that, but her position looked so uncomfortable that he was tempted to turn and straighten her. His hands were still jammed in his pockets, however, and he left them there.

He went up the steps almost on tiptoe, careful to avoid bloodying his shoes, and made a turn to the left that brought him up against the metal kitchen cabinets. His breath was coming very short, each intake arrested as though by a punch in the midsection. He was aware of the tick of his wristwatch, and that was all. There was a telephone on the kitchen counter, and presently he detached a paper towel from a roll neatly suspended beneath the line of cabinets, wrapped it around the receiver and called the sheriff's office.

At the opposite end of the kitchen, a smaller set of sliding doors opened onto a deck overlooking the lawn and the lake. With the help of another paper towel, he slid back the door and went out and sat on a bench to wait. The lake's surface had a painful metallic glitter, with the sunset colors spreading across it like corrosion. He had left his sunglasses in the car, and being in no mood to retrieve them, he simply shut his eyes. In Korea, where the Army had sent him, he had *seen some action,* as they say, but afterward he had thought very little about what he had seen. In some quietly ticking corner of his mind a speculation was going forward as to how the bodies had come to be positioned as they were, and now it came to him that after they were all inside the house the boy must have missed his shoes and gone back to the car—He opened his eyes with a jerk and looked up. A solitary, premature firefly detached itself from the treetops on one side of the yard and floated dreamily across and into the treetops on the other.

It was twilight by the time he had parked his car behind the square, and for some reason he bypassed his office and walked on down Main Street as far as Saint Paul's Episcopal Church. More leaves had carpeted the white stone steps, and Wilson stood looking at them, one hand curved around a spear of the iron fence, and then turned back. The sidewalk was empty but for him, and he could hear the dry leaves crisping under his every footfall.

The street lights were coming on by the time he had returned to the square. The windows of his office were dark, but he could hear the telephone ringing as he came up the steps. Mrs. Veech had, of course, locked up before she left, and while he was searching out his key the phone stopped ringing. He went inside and pressed the light switch. Again the phone began to jangle, and he reached across Mrs. Veech's typewriter to pick it up.

"Mr. Wilson? It's Sam Trimble here. I had your paper to serve on Paxton Morgan?"

"Yes," Wilson said.

The deputy cleared his throat. "I thought you might like to know we picked him up. He'd gone straight back to his own house, you know, like they do."

"Yes," Wilson said again.

"We got him cold, if it's any comfort," Trimble said. "The gun still warm and blood on his shoes."

"That's all right," Wilson said. "He'll plead insanity."

He was not often here at night, and the overhead fixture was harsh and bright, bouncing blurred reflections from the flat black of the window panes, making his inner office look too much like a cell. But if he used only the desk lamp, the shadows reached toward him so. And yet he was still afraid to go home! He shouldn't have said what he had to Trimble, though at the moment he could hardly bring himself to feel regret for it. And he was late by now; he'd better call.

"Daddy, you're late," Lisa said.

"That's right, kiddo," Wilson said. "Where's your mother?"

"She's outside," Lisa said. "We were, both of us. I'll go call her."

"No, you don't need to," Wilson said. "Just tell her I'll be home shortly. Say I still have to stop by the store, though." Hanging up, he glanced at his watch. A fine evening like this, his wife would certainly spend outdoors, not bothering to watch the evening news.

Flushed with relief, he pictured their long curving yard, thick with fireflies, as it would be now, green pinpoints flashing and hovering in the dark. The lights of the house glowed warm behind the calm silhouettes of his wife and his daughter, and inside, the kitchen steamed with the scent of supper waiting. Upstairs, beside his bedside lamp, lay the copy of *War and Peace*[2] he'd been rereading this fall; at a half hour or so a night, it would last him to Christmas or longer. He thought now of Prince Andrey lying wounded on the battlefield, looking up into the reaches of the sky, that radical change in his perspective.

Still, he was not quite ready to leave. He picked up his pencil and tapped the butt of the dried eraser on the pad. At home, tonight or tomorrow or whenever he finally had to tell the story there, then the murders would be absolutely realized and the alternative of their somehow not having happened would be permanently shut off. Above, the fluorescent fixture made a sort of whining sound; Wilson thought that he could feel it in his teeth.

2. Novel by Russian writer Leo Tolstoy (1828–1910).

He turned the pencil over in his hand and set the point on the pad, but there was nothing much to write. The yellow paper was down at the bottom of a long pale shaft, stroked with faint parallel lines which signified nothing. If he could note down all the ingredients of the episode, then they could be comprehended, wrapped in a parcel of law and so managed. Wilson was a believer in due process. Without meaning to, he had become a bystander in this case.

It was only dizziness because he had skipped lunch, undoubtedly, and when he remembered that, the pad came floating back up toward him and the desk flattened and held still. There were some scratch marks on the paper, as if during his vertigo he had been trying unsuccessfully to draw a picture. Now he wondered if he had *known* what would happen, and if he had *known*, what then? He had left no legitimate measure untried but still he could picture himself crossing the lip above the lake house with a gun in his own hand, seeing the Volkswagen door still closed, the glass door of the house pulled to and Pax Morgan outlined against the glimmer of the lake like a paper silhouette.

The pencil slipped from his fingers and hit the desk with a clacking report that broke the fantasy. Pax was alive and the others were dead. His freedom was better protected than their safety—that would be one way of putting it. Simple. It was time to go home. Wilson turned off the desk lamp, stood up and pulled his coat down from the hat rack. Safer and better to have no freedom maybe, but no, you wouldn't say that. The humming stopped when he flicked the light switch by the door. No, you wouldn't say that, would you? In the dark of the hall he could not see his way; he went toward the vague light of the front window with one hand on the wall. No, you wouldn't, but what would you say?

1990

WENDELL BERRY
b. 1934

Wendell Berry was born and raised on a farm in Henry County, Kentucky. One year after earning both his B.A. and M.A. in English Literature from the University of Kentucky, he was awarded a Stegner Fellowship to Stanford University. While at Stanford, Berry completed his first novel, *Nathan Coulter* (1960). He received a Guggenheim Fellowship in 1961 and spent most of the year in Florence beginning work on his second novel, *A Place on Earth* (1967). Berry first gained recognition as a pastoral poet but is now also widely known for his novels, short stories, and essays. He is an active environmentalist, and his work often reflects his enduring love of and sense of responsibility for the natural world. The majority of Berry's novels and short stories, including "A Burden," below, take place in the fictional farming town of Port William, Kentucky. Among his novels are *Remembering* (1988), *Jayber Crow* (2000), and *Hannah Coulter* (2004). His short story collections include *The Wild Birds: Six Stories of the Port William Membership* (1986), *Fidelity: Five Stories* (1992), *That Distant Land: The Collected Stories* (2004), and *A Place in Time: Twenty Stories of the Port William Membership* (2012). Berry is a member of the Fellowship of Southern Writers and the American Academy of Arts and Sciences. He won the 2010 National Humanities Medal, and in 2012, he delivered the 41st Jefferson Lecture in the Humanities. Berry has taught at a number of colleges and universities including the University of Kentucky, New York University, Georgetown College, and Bucknell University. He quit teaching in the early nineties and now lives with his wife Tanya on their farm in Port Royal, Kentucky.

A Burden

"Me and Teddy Roosyvelt, we rode through hair, shit, blood, and corruption up to *here*." Uncle Peach used the stick he was whittling to mark a level across his nose about an inch above his nostrils.

"You did not," Wheeler said, but all the same he was laughing. He was seven years old, and sometimes just looking at Uncle Peach made him laugh.

"The hell you did," said Andrew, who was Wheeler's brother, five years older, because to Uncle Peach he could say anything he wanted to, and he did. Andrew, as Wheeler understood, was practicing to be a grownup. An ambitionless boy would not say "The hell you did" even to Uncle Peach.

The boys supposed, because everybody else appeared to suppose, that Uncle Peach had been somewhere in the Army during the war with Spain.[1]

---

1. The Spanish-American War in 1898.

But they knew from their own observation that Uncle Peach's shotgun, "Old Deadeye," was an instrument of mercy to all creatures that ran or flew as well as to some that were sitting still.

The three of them, the two boys and their uncle Peach, who was their mother's baby brother, were sitting in the shade of the tall cedar tree in front of the house. Uncle Peach was whittling a small cedar stick, releasing a fragrance. His knife was sharp, and he was making the shavings fine for fear he would use up the stick and have to go look for another. One of his rules for living was "Never stand up when you can set down," and he often quoted himself.

None of the three of them wanted to get up, for the day was already hot, and the shade of the old tree was a happiness. It was happier for being a threatened happiness. A sort of suspense hung over them and over that whole moment among the old trees and the patches of shade in the long yard. Maybe that was why Wheeler never forgot it. They did not know where the boys' father was. They did not know how come he had forgotten them. They knew only that if Marce Catlett came back from wherever he was and found them sitting there, they would all three be at work before they could say scat.

"Yeees sahhh," Uncle Peach said, drawing out the words as if to make them last as long as his stick, "them was rough times, which was why we was called the Rough Riders. Hair, shit, blood, and corruption up to the horses' bits, and you needed a high-headed horse to get through it atall. When it was all over and we was heroes, Teddy says to me, 'Leonidas, looks like one of us is pret' near bound to be the presi-dent of our great country, and if it's all the same to you, I'd just as soon it would be me.' And I says, 'Why, Teddy, by all means! Go to it!'"

"The hell you did!" Andrew said again. "You couldn't tell the truth if it shit on your hat."

And that made Wheeler laugh so much he had to lie down in the grass.

At the age of seven, Wheeler was already aware of a division of his affection between his father and Uncle Peach that he could not resolve, and he felt the strain. He loved Uncle Peach because he was funny and was interesting in the manner of a man who would do or say about anything he thought of, and because Uncle Peach loved him back and treated him as an equal and was always kind to him. Uncle Peach's trade was carpentry, which he was more or less good at, more or less worked at, and made more or less a living from. When he made more than a living from it, sooner or later he spent the surplus on whiskey and what he called "hoot-tootin" in Hargrave or Louisville or wherever he could get to before he got down and had to be fetched home.

Uncle Peach was in fact a drunk, which at the age of seven Wheeler pretty well knew and easily forgave. Once, thinking to change his life after a near-lethal celebration of the heroism he had shared with by then President Roosevelt, Uncle Peach had gone so far as to plan a migration to Oklahoma, which he actually carried out, and had persevered there for one year, to which he ever afterward referred as "my years in the territory."[2] While there, he said, he had been adopted into a tribe of Indians with whom he had lived and hunted and

2. Oklahoma was known as Indian Territory and Oklahoma Territory before it became a state in 1907.

fought, which Wheeler even at the age of seven knew he had not done. Uncle Peach called Indians Eenjins. His Eenjin name was "See-we-no-ho," which in English meant. "Friend of Great Chief." Though Wheeler knew that Uncle Peach was just storying, he could see nevertheless in his mind's eye Uncle Peach feathered and painted, riding his Indian pony named "Wa-su-ho-ha" which in English was "Runs Like Scared Rabbit." Uncle Peach loved to tell how he had hunted buffalo with his Eenjin friends, how well he had ridden, how accurately he had shot with his bow.

And Andrew would say, "You got enough damn wind in you to blow up an onion sack."

Uncle Peach had about him the ease of a man who had never come hard up against anything. All his life he had been drifting. All his life he had followed the inclination of flowing water toward the easiest way, and the lowest. Wheeler may always have known this, in the way an alert boy picks knowledge out of the air without asking. And with a boy's love for even the appearance of freedom, he loved Uncle Peach for his drifting.

He loved his father, as eventually he would know, for precisely the opposite reason. Marce Catlett was a man who lived within limits that he had accepted. He did not drift. Year after year he had been hard up against the demands of farm and family, the weather and the bank. He had known more hard times than good ones. In the winter of the year Wheeler was six, his father had sold his tobacco crop for just enough to transport it to the market and to pay the commission on its sale.

But he was not a one-crop farmer. His rule was "Sell something every week." This, as Wheeler would come to know, meant economic diversity; it required a complex formal intelligence; it was good sense. Marce was a man driven to small economies, which his artistry made elegant. He once built a new feed barn exactly on the site of the old one, tearing down the old one, reusing its usable lumber, as he built the new one, and his work mules never spent a night out of their own stalls. His precise fitting of force to work, his neat patches and splices, his quiet transactions with a saddle horse or a team of mules— Wheeler learned these things as a boy, and all the rest of his life he thought and dreamed of them, as of precious things lost.

As he grew in understanding, Wheeler more and more consciously chose his father over Uncle Peach. He chose, that is, his father's example, not his life. For when the time came, and out of plain economic necessity, for there was not a living for him at home and he could not afford to buy a place, Wheeler went to school and became a lawyer. And yet he never abandoned his inheritance from his father. Marce Catlett's love of farming lived on his son, as later it would live on in his grandsons. And all his life Wheeler felt his father's good ways aching in his bones, for he remembered them in palpable detail and loved them, though in his own life he had given most of them up for others less palpable.

Because after law school Wheeler did not go to any place offered him as "better," but returned to set up his practice at home, he came into an inheritance that was, as he knew, in many ways desirable, but was also complex and in some ways difficult. That he had deliberately made himself heir to his father's example did not prevent him also from inheriting Uncle Peach, as an amusement but also as a responsibility and a burden.

Uncle Peach was in truth amusing. He always had been—"in his way," as his sister, Dorie Catlett, often felt called upon to add.

As a boy of seven, wanting to "do like the old mule" who drank directly from the water trough, he tried to drink buttermilk from a stone churn and got his head stuck. Dorie had to break the churn to get him loose.

"Damn him, I would have left his head right where he put it," Marce would say. He would be growling, also laughing.

He would pause then, to allow her to say, "Yes, I reckon you would have let him drown."

And then he would say, "Something gone, nothing lost."

Once, exasperated by his daily resistance to washing and going to school, Dorie told her brother, "I ought to let you grow up in ignorance."

And he replied, "*That's* it, Dorie! Let me grow up in ignorance."

As Wheeler would tell it much later, his Uncle Peach did grow up in ignorance. And even before he had finished growing up, he shifted from buttermilk to whiskey, which also he drank, while it lasted, as freely as the old mule drank water. He seldom had enough money to make it last very long, "And that," Dorie would say, "was his only good fortune, poor fellow."

But his sufficient surpluses of money, seldom as they were, gave him a sort of fame. His reputation as a drinker far exceeded his reputation as a carpenter, and stories of his exploits were still told in Port William and Hargrave half a century after the beginning of television.

One afternoon Burley Coulter came upon Uncle Peach in front of a roadhouse down by Hargrave. Uncle Peach had been drinking evidently a lot of whiskey and also eating evidently a lot of pickled food from the bar. He had just finished vomiting upon the body of a dead cat, at which he was now gazing in great astonishment.

"Well, what's the matter, old Peach?"

"Why, Burley," Uncle Peach said, "I remember them pigs' feet and that baloney, but I got no recollection whatsoever of that cat."

Sometimes Uncle Peach found drunkenness to be exceedingly hard work. Dancing to keep standing, he would pronounce solemnly. "Damn, I'm tard! My ass is draggin' out my tracks."

Sometimes he found himself in a moral landscape exceedingly difficult to get across: "I got a long way to go and a short time to get there in."

Wheeler's own favorite story was about, so far as he knew, Uncle Peach's only actual fight.

Standing at the bar of a saloon in Louisville, Uncle Peach discovered, to his great disgust, that the man standing next to him was drunk.

"If they's anything I can't stand," Uncle Peach confided to the man, "it's a damn drunk."

At which the man confided back to Uncle Peach: "You ain't nothing but a damn drunk yourself."

Upon which Uncle Peach, grievously offended, took a swing.

"It is generally understood," Wheeler would say, "that when one man aims a violent blow at another, he had better hit him."

But Uncle Peach missed. Whereupon the previously offended flew at Uncle Peach and thrashed him not hardly enough to kill him, but thoroughly even so.

When Wheeler came later to rescue Uncle Peach from the Stag Hotel where he lay, as he said, "bloodied but unbowed," Uncle Peach was already referring to his opponent as "them gentlemens."

"Them gentlemens sholy could fight. They sholy was science men."

When Uncle Peach had decided to become a carpenter and showed some inclination to settle down, Marce Catlett helped him to find and buy a place with a few acres for pasture, a garden, and a little tobacco crop over by Floyd's Station. It was ten miles away, a distance that ought to have kept Uncle Peach "weaned," as Marce conceived it, from Dorie. But when Uncle Peach was on the downslope of a binge and in need of help, he would show up, intending to stay until he wore his welcome out—and longer, if he could.

On a certain night in Wheeler's childhood, perhaps not long after their conversation under the cedar tree, Uncle Peach showed up and, to the immense happiness of Wheeler and Andrew, drank copiously from a pan of dirty dishwater, complaining all the while of the declining quality of Dorie's soup. He proceeded to get sick, and then, shortly, to disappear. There must have been a passage of strict conversation between him and Marce at that time. Uncle Peach continued to show up now and again, but he never again showed up except sober.

Wheeler inherited Uncle Peach from his mother, who had inherited him from her mother, who had died soon after his birth. Dorie had pretty much had the raising of him, and it was she who named him "Peach," because it was handier than "Leonidas Polk" and because as a little fellow he was so pretty and sweet. That this Peach may have been a born failure did not mitigate Dorie's sense that he was *her* failure. With exactly the love that "hopeth all things," she did not give up on him.

Marce, on the contrary, gave up on his brother-in-law as a condition of his tolerance of him. It was a tolerance that worked best at a distance. With Peach in view, it was limited. After he had met its limit, Uncle Peach was always sober when in view. For Peach Wheeler drunk there was no longer room within Marce Catlett's horizon.

And so Wheeler inherited, along with Uncle Peach, two opposite attitudes toward him, and was never afterward free of either. As he grew into the necessary choice between his father and his uncle, and made the choice, Wheeler found that he had not merely chosen, but, by choosing his father, had acquired in addition his father's indignation. Wheeler could at times look upon his uncle as an affront, as if Peach had at conception or birth decided to be a burden specifically to his as-yet-unborn nephew.

But as he grew in experience and self-knowledge, Wheeler also grew to recognize in himself a sort of replica of his mother's love and compassion. He was never able quite to anticipate and prepare himself for the moment at which the apparition of Uncle Peach as nuisance would be replaced by the apparition of Uncle Peach as mortal sufferer. This change was not in Uncle Peach, who never changed except by becoming more and more as evidently he had been born to be. The change was in Wheeler. When the moment came, usually in the midst of some extremity of Uncle Peach's drinking career, Wheeler would feel a sudden welling up of love, as if from his mother's heart to his own, and then he would pity Uncle Peach and, against the entire weight of history and probability, wish him well. Sometimes after telling, and fully delighting in, one of his stories about Uncle Peach, Wheeler would fall silent, shake his head, and say, "Poor fellow."

Andrew, the firstborn son and elder brother, despite all his early practicing to be a grownup, did not manage to grow much farther up, if any, than Uncle Peach. Andrew, as it turned out, did not inherit attitudes toward Uncle Peach so much as he inherited Uncle Peach's failing. For Andrew in his turn became a drinker, and he too would say or do about anything he thought of. He would do so finally to the limit of life itself, and so beyond. As Andrew's course of life declared itself more or less a reprise of Uncle Peach's, that of course intensified and complicated the attitudes of the others toward Uncle Peach. Their stories all are added finally into one story. They were bound together in a many-stranded braid beyond the power of any awl to pick apart.

When Wheeler came home and started his law practice, he bought a car, for his practice involved him in distances that needed to be hurried over. But the automobile also was a fate which, as it included distance, also included Uncle Peach. The automobile made almost nothing of the ten miles from the Catletts' house to Uncle Peach's. Because of the automobile, Dorie could more frequently go over to housekeep and help out when Uncle Peach was on one of his rough ascents into sobriety, when, she said, he needed her most.

Uncle Peach most needed Wheeler when he was drunk and sick and helpless and broke and far from home. The automobile made this a reasonable need. No power that Wheeler had acquired in law school enabled him to argue against it, though he tried. Because he had the means of going, he had to go.

If Uncle Peach had the money to get there, his favorite place of resort was a Louisville establishment that called itself the Hotel Stag. From the time of Wheeler's purchase of the automobile until the time of Uncle Peach's death, Wheeler, who would not in any circumstances have taken Uncle Peach to the Stag Hotel, went there many a time to bring him home.

At the Stag Hotel and other places of refreshment Uncle Peach would encounter commercial ladies of great attractiveness and charm. Sometimes when Wheeler would be bringing him home, and despite his pain and exhaustion, Uncle Peach would still be enchanted, and he would confide as much to Wheeler: "Oh, them eyes!" he would say. "Oh, them eyes!"

Many a good and funny story came of Wheeler's missions of mercy, and also many a story of real pain and suffering that moved Wheeler to real pity, and also many moments of utter exasperation at the waste of time and effort when Wheeler, mocking himself and yet meaning every word, would cry out against "the damned Hotel Stag and every damned thing involved therein and pertaining thereto." Or he would say of Uncle Peach indignantly, "He's got barely enough sense to swallow." And then he would laugh. "Burley Coulter told me he'd seen Uncle Peach drink all he could hold and then fill his mouth for later." He would laugh. And then, affection and hopelessness and sorrow coming over him, he would shake his head. "Poor fellow."

In his turn, young Andy Catlett, namesake of his doomed uncle Andrew, also inherited Uncle Peach from his grandmother's lamentation and his father's talk, from trips with his father to see that their then-failing Uncle Peach was alive and had enough to eat, and from various elders who remembered with care and delight Uncle Peach's sayings and doings.

One Christmastime, when he was about six, Andy overhead his father tell Uncle Andrew, just home for the holidays, that Uncle Peach, "sleeping it off in his front yard," had frozen several of his toes, which had then needed to be amputated.

"Toes!" Uncle Andrew said, laughing his big laugh. "Anybody can spare a few toes. He better be glad he didn't freeze his *pecker* off." In the midst of his sadness and exasperation Wheeler also laughed, and they went away, leaving Andy, whom they had not noticed, with a possibility he had never considered before.

Andy had gone with his father to visit Uncle Peach after the surgery. Uncle Peach was sitting by the drum stove in his bare, bad-smelling little house with his foot wrapped in a soiled white bandage. He was talking in his old, slow voice about the hospital in Louisville, which he pronounced "Louis-ville." Though Andy, who had seen inside a hospital, could not picture him in one, Uncle Peach had enjoyed his stay. He had admired the nurses. "Damn pretty, some of 'em," he said to Wheeler.

And then, studying Andy, he said, "This boy'll be looking at 'em, 'fore you know it."

When Uncle Peach died in Andy's seventh year, and they all knew that he was dead, Andy overheard his father and mother saying what a story it had been. His father said with regret and sorrow and amusement and, instead of indignation, perhaps relief, for Uncle Peach had died sober in his sleep in bed at home: "Like Jehorum, poor fellow, he has departed without being desired." Wheeler was capable of feeling some things simply, but he never spoke of Uncle Peach with unmixed feelings.

And then when they were all in Wheeler's car, driving home from the grave-yard on the hill outside Port William where they had laid Uncle Peach to rest, they were silent until Wheeler said, "Well!"

He let the silence come back, and then he said, "The preacher takes a very happy view of Uncle Peach's prospects hereafter."

Wheeler was lining out a text that would be clearly printed in his son's memory, where it would wait a long time for interpretation.

When his father again let the silence come back, Andy understood that his mother wasn't saying anything because she felt that the fate of Uncle Peach hereafter was none of her business, and his grandfather wasn't saying anything because he didn't want it to be his business, and his grandmother wasn't saying anything because it *was* her business. It came to Andy then, for the first time, that his father was still relatively a young man.

The preacher had said Uncle Peach was going to Heaven, or was there already, because his soul had been saved when he gave his life to Jesus and was baptized at the age of twelve. His baptism, so many years ago, in another century, was still in force. Andy imagined that baptism had left on Uncle Peach's soul a mark like a vaccination scar to show that he had been saved. When he got to Heaven he was to be let in.

Andy had stood in church beside his mother, had heard her singing with the others,

> While I draw this fleeting breath,
> When mine eyes shall close in death,
> When I rise to worlds unknown,
> And behold Thee on Thy throne,
> Rock of Ages, cleft for me,
> Let me hide myself in Thee,

and he had thought, *"She? She* will?" And so he knew that in the soul's bewildering geography there was a Rock of Ages. In his mind it looked like the Rock of Gibralter cleft like a cow's foot, and you could hide in the cleft and be all right.

But from other songs they sang he knew that this geography had a shore too from which the dead departed to cross a wide river, and another shore beyond the river, a beautiful shore, that was Heaven. He had seen in his mind a picture of people on the far shore waving to people coming across in a boat who were waving back. They were calling each other's names and they were happy.

But Wheeler wasn't finished. He was always concerned with fittingness, which was maybe a kind of honesty. Those were words he used: "fitting" and "honest." He was always trying to get the scattering pieces of their history to fit together in a pattern that made sense. He wanted to find the right words and to say things right. "Right" was another of his words, as was "sense." His effort often made him impatient. This also Andy took in and remembered.

"If Uncle Peach is in Heaven," Wheeler said, "and Lord knows I hope that's where he is, then grace has lifted a mighty burden, and the preacher ought to have said so."

And then he said, as if determined in his impatience to capture every straying piece, "And as an earthly burden it wasn't only grace that lifted it"— meaning it was a burden he too had borne. Even at the time, Andy caught that.

So did his grandmother. She said one syllable then that Andy later would know had meant at least four things: that his father would have done better to be quiet, that she too had borne that earthly burden and would forever bear it, that Uncle Peach had borne it himself and was loved and forgiven at least by her, and that it was past time for Wheeler to hush.

She said, *"Hmh!"*

2010

AMBROSE BIERCE
1842–1913?

Bierce was born on a religious campground at Western Reserve, Ohio. The poverty of his family required him early in life to quit school and begin working as a copyboy for a newspaper before he enlisted with the Indiana Infantry in the Civil War. He rose through the military ranks to become a staff officer and was twice wounded. The horrors of war imbued his attitudes with an enduring cynicism, and his war stories are among the first to treat the subject with detailed realism. In San Francisco after the war he began his literary career by working, along with Mark Twain and Bret Harte, as a journalist. He spent the years between 1872 and 1876 in London, where his boisterous Western mannerisms and savage wit made him a celebrity, earning him the nickname "Bitter Bierce." Poor health forced him to return in 1876 to his journalistic career in California. In 1891 he published *Tales of Soldiers and Civilians,* followed two years later by another volume of short stories, *Can Such Things Be?* The death of his two sons in 1889 and 1901, along with his divorce in 1891, intensified his prevailing pessimism and resulted at length in his disappearance into revolution-torn Mexico, where he is believed to have died in 1913. His sardonic wit can be sampled in *The Devil's Dictionary* (1911). Twelve volumes of his *Collected Works* (prose and poetry) were published in 1909–1912.

An Occurrence at Owl Creek Bridge

I

A man stood upon a railroad bridge in Northern Alabama, looking down into the swift waters twenty feet below. The man's hands were behind his back, the wrists bound with a cord. A rope loosely encircled his neck. It was attached to a stout cross-timber above his head, and the slack fell to the level of his knees. Some loose boards laid upon the sleepers[1] supporting the metals of the railway supplied a footing for him and his executioners—two private soldiers of the Federal army, directed by a sergeant, who in civil life may have been a deputy sheriff. At a short remove upon the same temporary platform was an officer in the uniform of his rank, armed. He was a captain. A sentinel at each end of the bridge stood with his rifle in the position known as "support," that is to say, vertical in front of the left shoulder, the hammer resting on the forearm thrown straight across the chest—a formal and unnatural

---

1. Crossties.

position, enforcing an erect carriage of the body. It did not appear to be the duty of these two men to know what was occurring at the centre of the bridge; they merely blockaded the two ends of the foot plank which traversed it.

Beyond one of the sentinels nobody was in sight; the railroad ran straight away into a forest for a hundred yards, then, curving, was lost to view. Doubtless there was an outpost further along. The other bank of the stream was open ground—a gentle acclivity crowned with a stockade of vertical tree trunks, loop-holed for rifles, with a single embrasure through which protruded the muzzle of a brass cannon commanding the bridge. Midway of the slope between bridge and fort were the spectators—a single company of infantry in line, at "parade rest," the butts of the rifles on the ground, the barrels inclining slightly backward against the right shoulder, the hands crossed upon the stock. A lieutenant stood at the right of the line, the point of his sword upon the ground, his left hand resting upon his right. Excepting the group of four at the centre of the bridge not a man moved. The company faced the bridge, staring stonily, motionless. The sentinels, facing the banks of the stream, might have been statues to adorn the bridge. The captain stood with folded arms, silent, observing the work of his subordinates but making no sign. Death is a dignitary who, when he comes announced, is to be received with formal manifestations of respect, even by those most familiar with him. In the code of military etiquette silence and fixity are forms of deference.

The man who was engaged in being hanged was apparently about thirty-five years of age. He was a civilian, if one might judge from his dress, which was that of a planter. His features were good—a straight nose, firm mouth, broad forehead, from which his long, dark hair was combed straight back, falling behind his ears to the collar of his well-fitting frock coat. He wore a moustache and pointed beard, but no whiskers; his eyes were large and dark grey and had a kindly expression which one would hardly have expected in one whose neck was in the hemp. Evidently this was no vulgar assassin. The liberal military code makes provision for hanging many kinds of people, and gentlemen are not excluded.

The preparations being complete, the two private soldiers stepped aside and each drew away the plank upon which he had been standing. The sergeant turned to the captain, saluted and placed himself immediately behind that officer, who in turn moved apart one pace. These movements left the condemned man and the sergeant standing on the two ends of the same plank, which spanned three of the cross-ties of the bridge. The end upon which the civilian stood almost, but not quite, reached a fourth. This plank had been held in place by the weight of the captain; it was now held by that of the sergeant. At a signal from the former, the latter would step aside, the plank would tilt and the condemned man go down between two ties. The arrangement commended itself to his judgment as simple and effective. His face had not been covered nor his eyes bandaged. He looked a moment at his "unsteadfast footing," then let his gaze wander to the swirling water of the stream racing madly beneath his feet. A piece of dancing driftwood caught his attention and his eyes followed it down the current. How slowly it appeared to move! What a sluggish stream!

He closed his eyes in order to fix his last thoughts upon his wife and children. The water, touched to gold by the early sun, the brooding mists under the banks at some distance down the stream, the fort, the soldiers, the piece of drift—all had distracted him. And now he became conscious of a new disturbance. Striking through the thought of his dear ones was a sound which he could neither ignore nor understand, a sharp, distinct, metallic percussion like the stroke of a blacksmith's hammer upon the anvil; it had the same ringing quality. He wondered what it was, and whether immeasurably distant or near by—it seemed both. Its recurrence was regular, but as slow as the tolling of a death knell. He awaited each stroke with impatience and—he knew not why—apprehension. The intervals of silence grew progressively longer, the delays became maddening. With their greater infrequency the sounds increased in strength and sharpness. They hurt his ear like the thrust of a knife; he feared he would shriek. What he heard was the ticking of his watch.

He unclosed his eyes and saw again the water below him. "If I could free my hands," he thought, "I might throw off the noose and spring into the stream. By diving I could evade the bullets, and, swimming vigorously, reach the bank, take to the woods, and get away home. My home, thank God, is as yet outside their lines; my wife and little ones are still beyond the invader's farthest advance."

As these thoughts, which have here to be set down in words, were flashed into the doomed man's brain rather than evolved from it, the captain nodded to the sergeant. The sergeant stepped aside.

I I

Peyton Farquhar was a well-to-do planter, of an old and highly-respected Alabama family. Being a slave owner, and, like other slave owners, a politician, he was naturally an original secessionist and ardently devoted to the Southern cause. Circumstances of an imperious nature which it is unnecessary to relate here, had prevented him from taking service with the gallant army which had fought the disastrous campaigns ending with the fall of Corinth,[2] and he chafed under the inglorious restraint, longing for the release of his energies, the larger life of the soldier, the opportunity for distinction. That opportunity, he felt, would come, as it comes to all in war time. Meanwhile he did what he could. No service was too humble for him to perform in aid of the South, no adventure too perilous for him to undertake if consistent with the character of a civilian who was at heart a soldier, and who in good faith and without too much qualification assented to at least a part of the frankly villainous dictum that all is fair in love and war.

One evening while Farquhar and his wife were sitting on a rustic bench near the entrance to his grounds, a grey-clad soldier rode up to the gate and asked for a drink of water. Mrs. Farquhar was only too happy to serve him with her own white hands. While she was gone to fetch the water, her husband approached the dusty horseman and inquired eagerly for news from the front.

"The Yanks are repairing the railroads," said the man, "and are getting ready for another advance. They have reached the Owl Creek bridge, put it in order, and built a stockade on the other bank. The commandant has issued

---

2. In Mississippi; the main battle for Corinth occurred in 1862 when the Confederates tried to retake the town and were decisively beaten.

an order, which is posted everywhere, declaring that any civilian caught inter-fering with the railroad, its bridges, tunnels, or trains, will be summarily hanged. I saw the order."

"How far is it to the Owl Creek bridge?" Farquhar asked.

"About thirty miles."

"Is there no force on this side the creek?"

"Only a picket post half a mile out, on the railroad, and a single sentinel at this end of the bridge."

"Suppose a man—a civilian and student of hanging—should elude the picket post and perhaps get the better of the sentinel," said Farquhar, smiling, "what could he accomplish?"

The soldier reflected. "I was there a month ago," he replied. "I observed that the flood of last winter had lodged a great quantity of driftwood against the wooden pier at this end of the bridge. It is now dry and would burn like tow."

The lady had now brought the water, which the soldier drank. He thanked her ceremoniously, bowed to her husband, and rode away. An hour later, after nightfall, he repassed the plantation, going northward in the direction from which he had come. He was a Federal scout.

III

As Peyton Farquhar fell straight downward through the bridge, he lost con-sciousness and was as one already dead. From this state he was awakened—ages later, it seemed to him—by the pain of a sharp pressure upon his throat, fol-lowed by a sense of suffocation. Keen, poignant agonies seemed to shoot from his neck downward through every fibre of his body and limbs. These pains appeared to flash along well-defined lines of ramification, and to beat with an inconceivably rapid periodicity. They seemed like streams of pulsating fire heating him to an intolerable temperature. As to his head, he was conscious of nothing but a feeling of fullness—of congestion. These sensations were unac-companied by thought. The intellectual part of his nature was already effaced; he had power only to feel, and feeling was torment. He was conscious of motion. Encompassed in a luminous cloud, of which he was now merely the fiery heart, without material substance, he swung through unthinkable arcs of oscillation, like a vast pendulum. Then all at once, with terrible sudden-ness, the light about him shot upward with the noise of a loud plash; a fright-ful roaring was in his ears, and all was cold and dark. The power of thought was restored; he knew that the rope had broken and he had fallen into the stream. There was no additional strangulation; the noose about his neck was already suffocating him, and kept the water from his lungs. To die of hanging at the bottom of a river!—the idea seemed to him ludicrous. He opened his eyes in the blackness and saw above him a gleam of light, but how distant, how inaccessible! He was still sinking, for the light became fainter and fainter until it was a mere glimmer. Then it began to grow and brighten, and he knew that he was rising toward the surface—knew it with reluctance, for he was now very comfortable. "To be hanged and drowned," he thought, "that is not so bad; but I do not wish to be shot. No; I will not be shot; that is not fair."

He was not conscious of an effort, but a sharp pain in his wrist apprised him that he was trying to free his hands. He gave the struggle his attention,

as an idler might observe the feat of a juggler, without interest in the outcome. What splendid effort!—what magnificent, what superhuman strength!
Ah, that was a fine endeavour! Bravo! The cord fell away; his arms parted and
floated upward, the hands dimly seen on each side in the growing light. He
watched them with a new interest as first one and then the other pounced upon
the noose at his neck. They tore it away and thrust it fiercely aside, its undula-
tions resembling those of a water-snake. "Put it back, put it back!" He thought
he shouted these words to his hands, for the undoing of the noose had been
succeeded by the direst pang which he had yet experienced. His neck ached
horribly; his brain was on fire; his heart, which had been fluttering faintly,
gave a great leap, trying to force itself out at his mouth. His whole body was
racked and wrenched with an insupportable anguish! But his disobedient
hands gave no heed to the command. They beat the water vigorously with
quick, downward strokes, forcing him to the surface. He felt his head emerge;
his eyes were blinded by the sunlight; his chest expanded convulsively, and
with a supreme and crowning agony his lungs engulfed a great draught of air,
which instantly he expelled in a shriek!

He was now in full possession of his physical senses. They were, indeed, pre-
ternaturally keen and alert. Something in the awful disturbance of his organic
system had so exalted and refined them that they made record of things never
before perceived. He felt the ripples upon his face and heard their separate
sounds as they struck. He looked at the forest on the bank of the stream, saw
the individual trees, the leaves and the veining of each leaf—the very insects
upon them, the locusts, the brilliant-bodied flies, the grey spiders stretching
their webs from twig to twig. He noted the prismatic colors in all the dewdrops
upon a million blades of grass. The humming of the gnats that danced above
the eddies of the stream, the beating of the dragon flies' wings, the strokes of
the water spiders' legs, like oars which had lifted their boat—all these made
audible music. A fish slid along beneath his eyes and he heard the rush of its
body parting the water.

He had come to the surface facing down the stream; in a moment the visible
world seemed to wheel slowly round, himself the pivotal point, and he saw the
bridge, the fort, the soldiers upon the bridge, the captain, the sergeant, the two
privates, his executioners. They were in silhouette against the blue sky. They
shouted and gesticulated, pointing at him; the captain had drawn his pistol,
but did not fire; the others were unarmed. Their movements were grotesque
and horrible, their forms gigantic.

Suddenly he heard a sharp report and something struck the water smartly
within a few inches of his head, spattering his face with spray. He heard a second report, and saw one of the sentinels with his rifle at his shoulder, a light
cloud of blue smoke rising from the muzzle. The man in the water saw the eye
of the man on the bridge gazing into his own through the sights of the rifle.
He observed that it was a grey eye, and remembered having read that grey eyes
were keenest and that all famous marksmen had them. Nevertheless, this one
had missed.

A counter swirl had caught Farquhar and turned him half round; he was
again looking into the forest on the bank opposite the fort. The sound of a
clear, high voice in a monotonous singsong now rang out behind him and came
across the water with a distinctness that pierced and subdued all other sounds,

even the beating of the ripples in his ears. Although no soldier, he had frequented camps enough to know the dread significance of that deliberate, drawling, aspirated chant; the lieutenant on shore was taking a part in the morning's work. How coldly and pitilessly—with what an even, calm intonation, presaging and enforcing tranquillity in the men—with what accurately-measured intervals fell those cruel words:

"Attention, company.... Shoulder arms.... Ready.... Aim.... Fire."

Farquhar dived—dived as deeply as he could. The water roared in his ears like the voice of Niagara, yet he heard the dulled thunder of the volley, and rising again toward the surface, met shining bits of metal, singularly flattened, oscillating slowly downward. Some of them touched him on the face and hands, then fell away, continuing their descent. One lodged between his collar and neck; it was uncomfortably warm, and he snatched it out.

As he rose to the surface, gasping for breath, he saw that he had been a long time under water; he was perceptibly farther down stream—nearer to safety. The soldiers had almost finished reloading; the metal ramrods flashed all at once in the sunshine as they were drawn from the barrels, turned in the air, and thrust into their sockets. The two sentinels fired again, independently and ineffectually.

The hunted man saw all this over his shoulder; he was now swimming vigorously with the current. His brain was as energetic as his arms and legs; he thought with the rapidity of lightning.

"The officer," he reasoned, "will not make that martinet's error a second time. It is as easy to dodge a volley as a single shot. He has probably already given the command to fire at will. God help me, I cannot dodge them all!"

An appalling plash within two yards of him, followed by a loud rushing sound, *diminuendo*,[3] which seemed to travel back through the air to the fort and died in an explosion which stirred the very river to its deeps! A rising sheet of water, which curved over him, fell down upon him, blinded him, strangled him! The cannon had taken a hand in the game. As he shook his head free from the commotion of the smitten water, he heard the deflected shot humming through the air ahead, and in an instant it was cracking and smashing the branches in the forest beyond.

"They will not do that again," he thought; "the next time they will use a charge of grape.[4] I must keep my eye upon the gun; the smoke will apprise me—the report arrives too late; it lags behind the missile. It is a good gun."

Suddenly he felt himself whirled round and round—spinning like a top. The water, the banks, the forest, the now distant bridge, fort and men—all were commingled and blurred. Objects were represented by their colors only; circular horizontal streaks of color—that was all he saw. He had been caught in a vortex and was being whirled on with a velocity of advance and gyration which made him giddy and sick. In a few moments he was flung upon the gravel at the foot of the left bank of the stream—the southern bank—and behind a projecting point which concealed him from his enemies. The sudden arrest of his motion, the abrasion of one of his hands on the gravel, restored him and he wept with delight. He dug his fingers into the sand, threw it over

---

3. Diminishing (generally used for music).   **4.** That is, grapeshot, a cluster of small pellets fired from a cannon.

himself in handfuls and audibly blessed it. It looked like gold, like diamonds, rubies, emeralds; he could think of nothing beautiful which it did not resemble. The trees upon the bank were giant garden plants; he noted a definite order in their arrangement, inhaled the fragrance of their blooms. A strange, roseate light shone through the spaces among their trunks, and the wind made in their branches the music of æolian harps. He had no wish to perfect his escape, was content to remain in that enchanting spot until retaken.

A whizz and rattle of grapeshot among the branches high above his head roused him from his dream. The baffled cannoneer had fired him a random farewell. He sprang to his feet, rushed up the sloping bank, and plunged into the forest.

All that day he travelled, laying his course by the rounding sun. The forest seemed interminable; nowhere did he discover a break in it, not even a woodman's road. He had not known that he lived in so wild a region. There was something uncanny in the revelation.

By nightfall he was fatigued, footsore, famishing. The thought of his wife and children urged him on. At last he found a road which led him in what he knew to be the right direction. It was as wide and straight as a city street, yet it seemed untravelled. No fields bordered it, no dwelling anywhere. Not so much as the barking of a dog suggested human habitation. The black bodies of the great trees formed a straight wall on both sides, terminating on the horizon in a point, like a diagram in a lesson in perspective. Overhead, as he looked up through this rift in the wood, shone great golden stars looking unfamiliar and grouped in strange constellations. He was sure they were arranged in some order which had a secret and malign significance. The wood on either side was full of singular noises, among which—once, twice, and again—he distinctly heard whispers in an unknown tongue.

His neck was in pain, and, lifting his hand to it, he found it horribly swollen. He knew that it had a circle of black where the rope had bruised it. His eyes felt congested; he could no longer close them. His tongue was swollen with thirst; he relieved its fever by thrusting it forward from between his teeth into the cool air. How softly the turf had carpeted the untravelled avenue! He could no longer feel the roadway beneath his feet!

Doubtless, despite his suffering, he fell asleep while walking, for now he sees another scene—perhaps he has merely recovered from a delirium. He stands at the gate of his own home. All is as he left it, and all bright and beautiful in the morning sunshine. He must have travelled the entire night. As he pushes open the gate and passes up the wide white walk, he sees a flutter of female garments; his wife, looking fresh and cool and sweet, steps down from the verandah to meet him. At the bottom of the steps she stands waiting, with a smile of ineffable joy, an attitude of matchless grace and dignity. Ah, how beautiful she is! He springs forward with extended arms. As he is about to clasp her, he feels a stunning blow upon the back of the neck; a blinding white light blazes all about him, with a sound like the shock of a cannon—then all is darkness and silence!

Peyton Farquhar was dead; his body, with a broken neck, swung gently from side to side beneath the timbers of the Owl Creek bridge.

1891

JORGE LUIS BORGES
1899–1986

Borges was born in Buenos Aires, Argentina, to a family of middle-class intellectuals. After his education in Geneva and some years in Europe, where he associated with avant garde literary groups, he returned to Buenos Aires in 1921 and became the leader of a South American literary movement based on Surrealism and Imagism. In the early phases of his career, he wrote poetry for the most part, turning to prose as his varied intellectual interests came together to suggest new forms. A vastly erudite man, who directed the National Library until the dictator Perón removed him for political reasons, Borges built a "literature about literature"; his typically brief essays and short narratives are miniature encyclopedias of literary history, mingling gravity with absurdity in a constant parade of the complexities of human awareness. Though blind and a partial invalid in his later years, he lectured and taught in the United States. His books available in English include *Labyrinths* (1962), *Ficciones* (1962), *Dreamtigers* (1964), *The Book of Imaginary Beings* (1969), *The Aleph and Other Stories* (1970), *Dr. Brodie's Report* (1977), and *The Book of Sand* (1977).

Pierre Menard, Author of the *Quixote*[1]

The *visible*[2] work left by this novelist is easily and briefly enumerated. Impardonable, therefore, are the omissions and additions perpetrated by Madame Henri Bachelier in a fallacious catalogue which a certain daily, whose *Protestant* tendency is no secret, has had the inconsideration to inflict upon its deplorable readers—though these be few and Calvinist, if not Masonic and circumcised.[3] The true friends of Menard have viewed this catalogue with alarm and even with a certain melancholy. One might say that only yesterday we gathered before his final monument, amidst the lugubrious cypresses, and already Error tries to tarnish his Memory . . . Decidedly, a brief rectification is unavoidable.

---

1. Translated by James E. Irby. This story parodies a scholarly study. It comes complete with footnotes of its own, and these footnotes must be considered an integral part of the parody. So—to avoid confusion—Borges's footnotes are marked with symbols and printed above a ruled line at the bottom of each page. The editor's footnotes are printed below the line. The editor's footnotes are necessarily numerous because Borges's method is to mix an abundance of scholarly allusions to real personalities and literary works with names of fictitious authors and their fictitious works.   **2.** That is, that which actually exists on paper.   **3.** That is, those who are prejudiced by their Protestant, Free Thinking, or Jewish biases.

I am aware that it is quite easy to challenge my slight authority. I hope, how-ever, that I shall not be prohibited from mentioning two eminent testimo-nies. The Baroness de Bacourt (at whose unforgettable *vendredis*[4] I had the honor of meeting the lamented poet) has seen fit to approve the pages which follow. The Countess de Bagnoregio,[5] one of the most delicate spirits of the Principality of Monaco (and now of Pittsburgh, Pennsylvania, following her recent marriage to the international philanthropist Simon Kautzsch, who has been so inconsiderately slandered, alas! by the victims of his disinterested maneuvers) has sacrificed "to veracity and to death" (such were her words) the stately reserve which is her distinction, and, in an open letter published in the magazine *Luxe*,[6] concedes me her approval as well. These authorizations, I think, are not entirely insufficient.

I have said that Menard's visible work can be easily enumerated. Having examined with care his personal files, I find that they contain the following items:

a) A Symbolist sonnet which appeared twice (with variants) in the review *La conque*[7] (Issues of March and October 1899).

b) A monograph on the possibility of constructing a poetic vocabulary of concepts which would not be synonyms or periphrases of those which make up our everyday language, "but rather ideal objects created according to con-vention and essentially designed to satisfy poetic needs" (Nîmes,[8] 1901).

c) A monograph on "certain connections or affinities" between the thought of Descartes, Leibniz and John Wilkins[9] (Nîmes, 1903).

d) A monograph on Leibniz's *Characteristica universalis*[1] (Nîmes, 1904).

e) A technical article on the possibility of improving the game of chess, eliminating one of the rook's pawns. Menard proposes, recommends, dis-cusses and finally rejects this innovation.

f) A monograph on Raymond Lully's *Ars magna generalis*[2] (Nîmes, 1906).

g) A translation, with prologue and notes, of Ruy López de Segura's *Libro de la invención liberal y arte del juego del axedrez*[3] (Paris, 1907).

h) The work sheets of a monograph on George Boole's[4] symbolic logic.

i) An examination of the essential metric laws of French prose, illustrated with examples taken from Saint-Simon (*Revue des langues romanes,* Montpellier, October 1909).[5]

j) A reply to Luc Durtain[6] (who had denied the existence of such laws), illus-trated with examples from Luc Durtain (*Revue des langues romanes,* Montpel-lier, December 1909).

---

4. Literally "Fridays" (French), regular Friday meetings devoted to a discussion of the arts.   5. Evidently a fictitious patroness of the arts.   6. "Luxury" (French).   7. "Seashell" (French). In the second half of the 19th century there arose in France what has come to be known as the Symbolist movement. The Symbolists sought to express or suggest ideas and emotions by means of symbols, as by the mention or introduction of things or the use of words and word sounds to convey a meaning, often with mystical or vague effects.   8. A city in southern France.   9. Bishop of Chester (1614-1672). René Descartes (1596-1650), French philosopher and mathematician. Gottfried Wilhelm Leibniz (1646-1716), Ger-man philosopher, mathematician, and theologian.   1. "Universal Characteristics" (Latin), written in 1679.   2. "The Great Art of the General" (Latin), Lully (c. 1232-1315).   3. "The Book of Liberal Inven-tion and the Game of Chess," (Spanish), published in 1561.   4. English mathematician, metaphysi-cian, and author (1815-1864).   5. "Review of Romance Languages" (French), published in Montpellier, France. No article on the Duc de Saint-Simon (1675-1755) appears in the issue cited.   6. Durtain (1881-1959) does not appear in the issue cited.

k) A manuscript translation of the *Aguja de navegar cultos* of Quevedo, entitled *La boussole des précieux.*[7]

l) A preface to the Catalogue of an exposition of lithographs by Carolus Hourcade[8] (Nîmes, 1914).

m) The work *Les problèmes d'un problème*[9] (Paris, 1917) which discusses, in chronological order, the different solutions given to the illustrious problem of Achilles and the tortoise.[1] Two editions of this book have appeared so far; the second bears as an epigraph Leibniz's recommendation *"Ne craignez point, monsieur, la tortue"*[2] and revises the chapters dedicated to Russell[3] and Descartes.

n) A determined analysis of the "syntactical customs" of Toulet (N. R. F.,[4] March 1921). Menard—I recall—declared that censure and praise are sentimental operations which have nothing to do with literary criticism.

o) A transposition into alexandrines of Paul Valéry's *Le cimetière marin*[5] (N. R. F., January 1928).

p) An invective against Paul Valéry, in the *Papers for the Suppression of Reality* of Jacques Reboul.[6] (This invective, we might say parenthetically, is the exact opposite of his true opinion of Valéry. The latter understood it as such and their old friendship was not endangered.)

q) A "definition" of the Countess de Bagnoregio, in the "victorious volume"—the locution is Gabriele d'Annunzio's,[7] another of its collaborators—published annually by this lady to rectify the inevitable falsifications of journalists and to present "to the world and to Italy" an authentic image of her person, so often exposed (by very reason of her beauty and her activities) to erroneous or hasty interpretations.

r) A cycle of admirable sonnets for the Baroness de Bacourt (1934).

s) A manuscript list of verses which owe their efficacy to their punctuation.*

This, then, is the *visible* work of Menard, in chronological order (with no omission other than a few vague sonnets of circumstance written for the hospitable, or avid, album of Madame Henri Bachelier). I turn now to his other work: the subterranean, the interminably heroic, the peerless. And—such are the capacities of man!—the unfinished. This work, perhaps the most significant of our time, consists of the ninth and thirty-eighth chapters of the first

---

* Madame Henri Bachelier also lists a literal translation of Quevedo's literal translation of the *Introduction à la vie dévote* of St. Francis of Sales [*Introduction to the Devout Life* of St. Francis of Sales (1567–1622), Bishop and prince of Geneva]. There are no traces of such a work in Menard's library. It must have been a jest of our friend, misunderstood by the lady.

---

7. Each title, in Spanish and French, respectively, means "Guide to (or Compass for) the Euphuists (or Aesthetes)," by Vasco Mousinho Quevedo (d. 1628), Portuguese poet. **8.** Unidentified, probably fictitious. **9.** "Problems of a Problem" (French). **1.** The Eleatic school of philosophers, including most probably Zeno and Parmenides, flourished in Greece in the 5th century B.C.E. It held that being is the only reality and that plurality, change, and motion are illusory. Among Zeno's arguments against motion, e.g., are these paradoxes: motion cannot begin because a body in motion cannot arrive at another place until it has passed through an unlimited number of places intermediate; Achilles cannot overtake a tortoise, because as often as he reaches the place occupied by the tortoise at some previous moment the tortoise has already left it; a flying arrow is at rest, for it is at every moment in only one place. **2.** "Don't fear, sir, the tortoise" (French). **3.** Bertrand Russell (1872–1970), English philosopher and mathematician. **4.** *La Nouvelle revue Française* (New French review). Pierre-Jean Toulet (1867–1920), French poet. **5.** "The Graveyard by the Sea." Valéry (1871–1945), French poet. **6.** Unidentified, probably fictitious. **7.** Italian poet, novelist, and dramatist (1863–1938).

part of *Don Quixote*[8] and a fragment of chapter twenty-two. I know such an affirmation seems an absurdity; to justify this "absurdity" is the primordial object of this note.*

Two texts of unequal value inspired this undertaking. One is that philological fragment by Novalis[9]—the one numbered 2005 in the Dresden edition—which outlines the theme of a *total* identification with a given author. The other is one of those parasitic books which situate Christ on a boulevard, Hamlet on La Cannebière[1] or Don Quixote on Wall Street. Like all men of good taste, Menard abhorred these useless carnivals, fit only—as he would say—to produce the plebeian pleasure of anachronism or (what is worse) to enthrall us with the elementary idea that all epochs are the same or are different. More interesting, though contradictory and superficial of execution, seemed to him the famous plan of Daudet: to conjoin the Ingenious Gentleman and his squire in *one* figure, which was Tartarin[2] . . . Those who have insinuated that Menard dedicated his life to writing a contemporary *Quixote* calumniate his illustrious memory.

He did not want to compose another *Quixote*—which is easy—but *the* Quixote *itself.* Needless to say, he never contemplated a mechanical transcription of the original; he did not propose to copy it. His admirable intention was to produce a few pages which would coincide—word for word and line for line—with those of Miguel de Cervantes.

"My intent is no more than astonishing," he wrote me the 30th of September, 1934, from Bayonne. "The final term in a theological or metaphysical demonstration—the objective world, God, causality, the forms of the universe—is no less previous and common than my famed novel. The only difference is that the philosophers publish the intermediary stages of their labor in pleasant volumes and I have resolved to do away with those stages." In truth, not one worksheet remains to bear witness to his years of effort.

The first method he conceived was relatively simple. Know Spanish well, recover the Catholic faith, fight against the Moors or the Turk, forget the history of Europe between the years 1602 and 1918, *be* Miguel de Cervantes. Pierre Menard studied this procedure (I know he attained a fairly accurate command of seventeenth-century Spanish) but discarded it as too easy. Rather as impossible! my reader will say. Granted, but the undertaking was impossible from the very beginning and of all the impossible ways of carrying it out, this was the least interesting. To be, in the twentieth century, a popular novelist of the seventeenth seemed to him a diminution. To be, in some way, Cervantes and reach the *Quixote* seemed less arduous to him—and, consequently, less interesting—than to go on being Pierre Menard and reach the *Quixote* through the experiences of Pierre Menard. (This conviction, we might say in

* I also had the secondary intention of sketching a personal portrait of Pierre Menard. But how could I dare to compete with the golden pages which, I am told, the Baroness de Bacourt is preparing or with the delicate and punctual pencil of Carolus Hourcade?

8. Classic novel by Miguel de Cervantes (1547–1616).   **9.** Friedrich von (Hardenberg) Novalis (1772–1801), German poet and philosopher.   **1.** Street in Paris, an incongruous or absurd setting for Hamlet.   **2.** Chief character in *Tartarin de Tarascon* (1872) and *Tartarin sur les Alpes* (1885), novels by French writer Alphonse Daudet (1840–1897). *Ingenious Gentleman and his squire:* a reference to Don Quixote and Sancho Panza in Cervantes' *Don Quixote*. Tartarin is, in Daudet's treatment, alternately practical—like Sancho Panza—and recklessly idealistic—like Don Quixote.

passing, made him omit the autobiographical prologue to the second part of *Don Quixote*. To include that prologue would have been to create another character—Cervantes—but it would also have meant presenting the *Quixote* in terms of that character and not of Menard. The latter, naturally, declined that facility.) "My undertaking is not difficult, essentially," I read in another part of his letter. "I should only have to be immortal to carry it out." Shall I confess that I often imagine he did finish it and that I read the *Quixote*—all of it—as if Menard had conceived it? Some nights past, while leafing through chapter XXVI—never essayed by him—I recognized our friend's style and something of his voice in this exceptional phrase: "the river nymphs and the dolorous and humid Echo."[3] This happy conjunction of a spiritual and a physical adjective brought to my mind a verse by Shakespeare which we discussed one afternoon:

> Where a malignant and a turbaned Turk[4] . . .

But why precisely the *Quixote?* our reader will ask. Such a preference, in a Spaniard, would not have been inexplicable; but it is, no doubt, in a Symbolist from Nîmes, essentially a dévoté of Poe, who engendered Baudelaire, who engendered Mallarmé, who engendered Valéry, who engendered Edmond Teste.[5] The aforementioned letter illuminates this point. "The *Quixote*," clarifies Menard, "interests me deeply, but it does not seem—how shall I say it?—inevitable. I cannot imagine the universe without Edgar Allan Poe's exclamation:

> Ah, bear in mind this garden was enchanted![6]

or without the *Bateau ivre* or the *Ancient Mariner*,[7] but I am quite capable of imagining it without the *Quixote*. (I speak, naturally, of my personal capacity and not of those works' historical resonance.) The *Quixote* is a contingent book; the *Quixote* is unnecessary. I can premeditate writing it, I can write it, without falling into a tautology. When I was ten or twelve years old, I read it, perhaps in its entirety. Later, I have reread closely certain chapters, those which I shall not attempt for the time being. I have also gone through the interludes, the plays, the *Galatea,* the exemplary novels, the undoubtedly laborious tribulations of Persiles and Segismunda and the *Viaje del Parnaso*[8] . . . My general recollection of the *Quixote,* simplified by forgetfulness and indifference, can well equal the imprecise and prior image of a book not yet written. Once that image (which no one can legitimately deny me) is postulated, it is certain that

---

3. In Greek mythology Hera (Juno), the wife and sister of Zeus, condemned the nymph Echo to never use her tongue again except to repeat what was said to her. **4.** Shakespeare's *Othello* 5.2. **5.** A fictional character in *Monsieur Teste,* a novel by Valéry. Edgar Allan Poe (1809–1849), American poet and short-story writer. Charles Baudelaire (1821–1867) and Stéphane Mallarmé (1842–1898), French poets. The names in this sequence are said to engender their successors in the sense that they influenced them and, by their work, provided points for new departures. That the sequence ends with a fictional personage, Monsieur Teste, suggests that both Borges and Pierre Menard—his fictional creation—have been "engendered" by the same ancestors. **6.** From one of Poe's two poems entitled *To Helen*. This, the lesser known one, is dedicated to Mrs. Sarah Helen Whitman. **7.** *The Rime of the Ancient Mariner* by the English poet Samuel Taylor Coleridge (1772–1834). *Bateau ivre* ("The Drunken Boat"), by Arthur Rimbaud (1854–1891), a French poet. Both poems and both poets are important forerunners of the literary mode that Menard practices. **8.** "Voyage to Parnassus" (Spanish). *Galatea* is a novel of Cervantes, first published in 1914. Other allusions in the line are to Cervantes' works.

my problem is a good bit more difficult than Cervantes' was. My obliging pre-decessor did not refuse the collaboration of chance: he composed his immor-tal work somewhat *à la diable*,[9] carried along by the inertias of language and invention. I have taken on the mysterious duty of reconstructing literally his spontaneous work. My solitary game is governed by two polar laws. The first permits me to essay variations of a formal or psychological type; the second obliges me to sacrifice these variations to the 'original' text and reason out this annihilation in an irrefutable manner . . . To these artificial hindrances, another—of a congenital kind—must be added. To compose the *Quixote* at the beginning of the seventeenth century was a reasonable undertaking, neces-sary and perhaps even unavoidable; at the beginning of the twentieth, it is almost impossible. It is not in vain that three hundred years have gone by, filled with exceedingly complex events. Amongst them, to mention only one, is the *Quixote* itself."

   In spite of these three obstacles, Menard's fragmentary *Quixote* is more sub-tle than Cervantes'. The latter, in a clumsy fashion, opposes to the fictions of chivalry the tawdry provincial reality of his country; Menard selects as his "reality" the land of Carmen during the century of Lepanto and Lope de Vega.[1] What a series of *espagnolades* that selection would have suggested to Maurice Barrès or Dr. Rodríguez Larreta![2] Menard eludes them with complete natu-ralness. In his work there are no gypsy flourishes or conquistadors or mystics or Philip the Seconds or *autos da fé*.[3] He neglects or eliminates local color. This disdain points to a new conception of the historical novel. This disdain con-demns *Salammbô*,[4] with no possibility of appeal.

   It is no less astounding to consider isolated chapters. For example, let us examine Chapter XXXVIII of the first part, "which treats of the curious dis-course of Don Quixote on arms and letters." It is well known that Don Quix-ote (like Quevedo in an analogous and later passage in *La hora de todos*[5]) decided the debate against letters and in favor of arms. Cervantes was a former soldier: his verdict is understandable. But that Pierre Menard's Don Quix-ote—a contemporary of *La trahison des clercs*[6] and Bertrand Russell—should fall prey to such nebulous sophistries! Madame Bachelier has seen here an admi-rable and typical subordination on the part of the author to the hero's psy-chology; others (not at all perspicaciously), a *transcription* of the *Quixote;* the Baroness de Bacourt, the influence of Nietzsche.[7] To this third interpretation

9. "Like the devil" (French), i.e., with inspired haste.   **1.** Spanish dramatist (1562–1635). *Lepanto:* 1571 battle in which a largely Spanish fleet destroyed the Turkish naval power. Thus both references are to the century in which Cervantes lived. Carmen is the Gypsy heroine of a novel by Prosper Meri-mée (1803–1870), French writer. The novel was made into an immensely popular opera by the com-poser Georges Bizet (1838–1875).   **2.** Unidentified and possibly fictitious. *Espagnolades:* a French term for a literary work heavily saturated with the local color of Spain. Barrès (1862–1923), French novel-ist.   **3.** "Acts of the faith" (Portuguese), executions by fire of heretics condemned by the Inquisition. Philip the Second (1527–1598) was a Spanish king, sponsor of the Spanish Inquisition and leader of the Counter Reformation, a movement in opposition to the Protestant Reformation.   **4.** A colorful and detailed historical novel by French writer Gustave Flaubert (1821–1880).   **5.** *La hora de todos y la fortuna con seso:* everyone's hour (or time) and the wit of fortune (Spanish, literal trans.), roughly equiva-lent to "every dog has his day by the turns of fortune."   **6.** "The Treason of the Intellectuals," by Julien Benda (1867–1956), French essayist who in this book attacks European intellectuals for allowing their talents to be exploited for nationalist political ends.   **7.** Friedrich Nietzsche (1844–1900), Ger-man philosopher. The allusion is probably to his idea of "eternal recurrence"—a belief that everything that happens will happen again and again within the frame of eternity, as Menard's *Quixote* recurs after that of Cervantes.

(which I judge to be irrefutable) I am not sure I dare to add a fourth, which concords very well with the almost divine modesty of Pierre Menard: his resigned or ironical habit of propagating ideas which were the strict reverse of those he preferred. (Let us recall once more his diatribe against Paul Valéry in Jacques Reboul's ephemeral Surrealist sheet.) Cervantes' text and Menard's are verbally identical, but the second is almost infinitely richer. (More ambiguous, his detractors will say, but ambiguity is richness.)

It is a revelation to compare Menard's *Don Quixote* with Cervantes'. The latter, for example, wrote (part one, chapter nine):

> . . . truth, whose mother is history, rival of time, depository of deeds, witness of the past, exemplar and adviser to the present, and the future's counselor.

Written in the seventeenth century, written by the "lay genius" Cervantes, this enumeration is a mere rhetorical praise of history. Menard, on the other hand, writes:

> . . . truth, whose mother is history, rival of time, depository of deeds, witness of the past, exemplar and adviser to the present, and the future's counselor.

History, the *mother* of truth: the idea is astounding. Menard, a contemporary of William James,[8] does not define history as an inquiry into reality but as its origin. Historical truth, for him, is not what has happened; it is what we judge to have happened. The final phrases—*exemplar and adviser to the present, and the future's counselor*—are brazenly pragmatic.

The contrast in style is also vivid. The archaic style of Menard—quite foreign, after all—suffers from a certain affectation. Not so that of his forerunner, who handles with ease the current Spanish of his time.

There is no exercise of the intellect which is not, in the final analysis, useless. A philosophical doctrine begins as a plausible description of the universe; with the passage of the years it becomes a mere chapter—if not a paragraph or a name—in the history of philosophy. In literature, this eventual caducity is even more notorious. The *Quixote*—Menard told me—was, above all, an entertaining book; now it is the occasion for patriotic toasts, grammatical insolence and obscene de luxe editions. Fame is a form of incomprehension, perhaps the worst.

There is nothing new in these nihilistic verifications; what is singular is the determination Menard derived from them. He decided to anticipate the vanity awaiting all man's efforts; he set himself to an undertaking which was exceedingly complex and, from the very beginning, futile. He dedicated his scruples and his sleepless nights to repeating an already extant book in an alien tongue. He multiplied draft upon draft, revised tenaciously and tore up thousands of manuscript pages.* He did not let anyone examine these drafts and took care they should not survive him. In vain have I tried to reconstruct them.

---

* I remember his quadricular notebooks, his black crossed-out passages, his peculiar typographical symbols and his insect-like handwriting. In the afternoons he liked to go out for a walk around the outskirts of Nimes; he would take a notebook with him and make a merry bonfire.

---

8. American pragmatist philosopher (1842–1910).

I have reflected that it is permissible to see in this "final" *Quixote* a kind of palimpsest,[9] through which the traces—tenuous but not indecipherable—of our friend's "previous" writing should be translucently visible. Unfortunately, only a second Pierre Menard, inverting the other's work, would be able to exhume and revive those lost Troys[1] . . .

"Thinking, analyzing, inventing (he also wrote me) are not anomalous acts; they are the normal respiration of the intelligence. To glorify the occasional performance of that function, to hoard ancient and alien thoughts, to recall with incredulous stupor that the *doctor universalis*[2] thought, is to confess our laziness or our barbarity. Every man should be capable of all ideas and I understand that in the future this will be the case."

Menard (perhaps without wanting to) has enriched, by means of a new technique, the halting and rudimentary art of reading: this new technique is that of the deliberate anachronism and the erroneous attribution. This technique, whose applications are infinite, prompts us to go through the *Odyssey* as if it were posterior to the *Aeneid*[3] and the book *Le jardin du Centaure*[4] of Madame Henri Bachelier as if it were by Madame Henri Bachelier. This technique fills the most placid works with adventure. To attribute the *Imitatio Christi* to Louis Ferdinand Céline or to James Joyce,[5] is this not a sufficient renovation of its tenuous spiritual indications?

For Silvina Ocampo

1944

---

9. A parchment document from which writing has been partially erased to make room for another text. Frequently fragments of the original text are inadvertently combined with the new additions. **1.** Troy, which was destroyed by the Greeks in the Trojan War, has become a conventional symbol of lost cultures. **2.** "The universal doctor" (Latin), a term sometimes applied to the philosophers Aristotle and Thomas Aquinas. **3.** Homer's epic poem *The Odyssey* dates from the 7th or 8th century B.C.E., while Virgil's *Aeneid* was written in the 1st century B.C.E. Borges is playing with anachronism. **4.** "The Centaur's Garden," (French), obviously a fictitious work by a fictitious author. **5.** Céline (pen name for Ferdinand Destouches) (1894–1961) and Joyce (1882–1941) are 20th-century writers. *Imitatio Christi* (The Imitation of Christ) was written by Thomas à Kempis (1380–1471). More anachronism.

RAY BRADBURY
1920–2012

Bradbury was born in Waukegan, Illinois, to a family that, at the height of the Great Depression, sought out a better life in California. After attending high school in Los Angeles, he joined a little-theater group there and by 1941 had begun to publish the stories that would make him one of the stars among science fiction writers. His concern about the multitude of threats to the imagination in the modern world led him occasionally to the social criticism that particularly distinguishes his novel *Fahrenheit 451* (1953) and often to serious expositions of the dangers inherent in unquestioning reliance upon technology. His other novels include *Something Wicked This Way Comes* (1962), *The Halloween Tree* (1972), *Driving Blind* (1997), and his final novel, *Farewell Summer* (2006). He has written plays and screenplays—including the one for *Moby-Dick* (1954). Among his numerous books of short stories are *The Martian Chronicles* (1950), *The Golden Apples of the Sun* (1953), *Dandelion Wine* (1957), *I Sing the Body Electric!* (1969), *The Stories of Ray Bradbury* (1980), and *A Pleasure to Burn* (2010). He has also published essays, poetry, and even a musical, *The Day It Rained Forever* (1990). He was awarded the National Medal of Arts in 2004.

The Veldt

George, I wish you'd look at the nursery."

"What's wrong with it?"

"I don't know."

"Well, then."

"I just want you to look at it, is all, or call a psychologist in to look at it."

"What would a psychologist want with a nursery?"

"You know very well what he'd want." His wife paused in the middle of the kitchen and watched the stove busy humming to itself, making supper for four.

"It's just that the nursery is different now than it was."

"All right, let's have a look."

They walked down the hall of their soundproofed, Happylife Home, which had cost them thirty thousand dollars installed, this house which clothed and fed and rocked them to sleep and played and sang and was good to them. Their approach sensitized a switch somewhere and the nursery light flicked on when they came within ten feet of it. Similarly, behind them, in the halls, lights went on and off as they left them behind, with a soft automaticity.

"Well," said George Hadley.

They stood on the thatched floor of the nursery. It was forty feet across by forty feet long and thirty feet high; it had cost half again as much as the rest of the house. "But nothing's too good for our children," George had said.

The nursery was silent. It was empty as a jungle glade at hot high noon. The walls were blank and two dimensional. Now, as George and Lydia Hadley stood in the center of the room, the walls began to purr and recede into crystalline distance, it seemed, and presently an African veldt appeared, in three dimensions; on all sides, in colors reproduced to the final pebble and bit of straw. The ceiling above them became a deep sky with a hot yellow sun.

George Hadley felt the perspiration start on his brow.

"Let's get out of the sun," he said. "This is a little too real. But I don't see anything wrong."

"Wait a moment, you'll see," said his wife.

Now the hidden odorophonics were beginning to blow a wind of odor at the two people in the middle of the baked veldtland. The hot straw smell of lion grass, the cool green smell of the hidden water hole, the great rusty smell of animals, the smell of dust like a red paprika in the hot air. And now the sounds: the thump of distant antelope feet on grassy sod, the papery rustling of vultures. A shadow passed through the sky. The shadow flickered on George Hadley's upturned, sweating face.

"Filthy creatures," he heard his wife say.

"The vultures."

"You see, there are the lions, far over, that way. Now they're on their way to the water hole. They've just been eating," said Lydia. "I don't know what."

"Some animal." George Hadley put his hand up to shield off the burning light from his squinted eyes. "A zebra or a baby giraffe, maybe."

"Are you sure?" His wife sounded peculiarly tense.

"No, it's a little late to be sure," he said, amused. "Nothing over there I can see but cleaned bone, and the vultures dropping for what's left."

"Did you hear that scream?" she asked.

"No."

"About a minute ago?"

"Sorry, no."

The lions were coming. And again George Hadley was filled with admiration for the mechanical genius who had conceived this room. A miracle of efficiency selling for an absurdly low price. Every home should have one. Oh, occasionally they frightened you with their clinical accuracy, they startled you, gave you a twinge, but most of the time what fun for everyone, not only your own son and daughter, but for yourself when you felt like a quick jaunt to a foreign land, a quick change of scenery. Well, here it was!

And here were the lions now, fifteen feet away, so real, so feverishly and startlingly real that you could feel the prickling fur on your hand, and your mouth was stuffed with the dusty upholstery smell of their heated pelts, and the yellow of them was in your eyes like the yellow of an exquisite French tapestry, the yellows of lions and summer grass, and the sound of the matted lion lungs exhaling on the silent noontide, and the smell of meat from the panting, dripping mouths.

The lions stood looking at George and Lydia Hadley with terrible green-yellow eyes.

"Watch out!" screamed Lydia.

The lions came running at them.

Lydia bolted and ran. Instinctively, George sprang after her. Outside, in the hall, with the door slammed, he was laughing and she was crying, and they both stood appalled at the other's reaction.

"George!"

"Lydia! Oh, my dear poor sweet Lydia!"

"They almost got us!"

"Walls, Lydia, remember; crystal walls, that's all they are. Oh, they look real, I must admit—Africa in your parlor—but it's all dimensional superreactionary, supersensitive color film and mental tape film behind glass screens. It's all odorophonics and sonics, Lydia. Here's my handkerchief."

"I'm afraid." She came to him and put her body against him and cried steadily. "Did you see? Did you *feel?* It's too real."

"Now, Lydia . . ."

"You've got to tell Wendy and Peter not to read any more on Africa."

"Of course—of course." He patted her.

"Promise?"

"Sure."

"And lock the nursery for a few days until I get my nerves settled."

"You know how difficult Peter is about that. When I punished him a month ago by locking the nursery for even a few hours—the tantrum he threw! And Wendy too. They *live* for the nursery."

"It's got to be locked, that's all there is to it."

"All right." Reluctantly he locked the huge door. "You've been working too hard. You need a rest."

"I don't know—I don't know," she said, blowing her nose, sitting down in a chair that immediately began to rock and comfort her. "Maybe I don't have enough to do. Maybe I have time to think too much. Why don't we shut the whole house off for a few days and take a vacation?"

"You mean you want to fry my eggs for me?"

"Yes." She nodded.

"And darn my socks?"

"Yes." A frantic, watery-eyed nodding.

"And sweep the house?"

"Yes, yes—oh, yes!"

"But I thought that's why we bought this house, so we wouldn't have to do anything?"

"That's just it. I feel like I don't belong here. The house is wife and mother now and nursemaid. Can I compete with an African veldt? Can I give a bath and scrub the children as efficiently or quickly as the automatic scrub bath can? I can not. And it isn't just me. It's you. You've been awfully nervous lately."

"I suppose I have been smoking too much."

"You look as if you didn't know what to do with yourself in this house, either. You smoke a little more every morning and drink a little more every afternoon and need a little more sedative every night. You're beginning to feel unnecessary too."

"Am I?" He paused and tried to feel into himself to see what was really there.

"Oh, George!" She looked beyond him, at the nursery door. "Those lions can't get out of there, can they?"

He looked at the door and saw it tremble as if something had jumped against it from the other side.

"Of course not," he said.

At dinner they ate alone, for Wendy and Peter were at a special plastic carnival across town and had televised home to say they'd be late, to go ahead eating. So George Hadley, bemused, sat watching the dining-room table produce warm dishes of food from its mechanical interior.

"We forgot the ketchup," he said.

"Sorry," said a small voice within the table, and ketchup appeared.

As for the nursery, thought George Hadley, it won't hurt for the children to be locked out of it awhile. Too much of anything isn't good for anyone. And it was clearly indicated that the children had been spending a little too much time on Africa. That sun. He could feel it on his neck, still, like a hot paw. And the lions. And the smell of blood. Remarkable how the nursery caught the telepathic emanations of the children's minds and created life to fill their every desire. The children thought lions, and there were lions. The children thought zebras, and there were zebras. Sun—sun. Giraffes—giraffes. Death and death.

That last. He chewed tastelessly on the meat that the table had cut for him. Death thoughts. They were awfully young, Wendy and Peter, for death thoughts. Or, no, you were never too young, really. Long before you knew what death was you were wishing it on someone else. When you were two years old you were shooting people with cap pistols.

But this—the long, hot African veldt—the awful death in the jaws of a lion. And repeated again and again.

"Where are you going?"

He didn't answer Lydia. Preoccupied, he let the lights glow softly on ahead of him, extinguished behind him as he padded to the nursery door. He listened against it. Far away, a lion roared.

He unlocked the door and opened it. Just before he stepped inside, he heard a faraway scream. And then another roar from the lions, which subsided quickly.

He stepped into Africa. How many times in the last year had he opened this door and found Wonderland, Alice, the Mock Turtle, or Aladdin and his Magical Lamp, or Jack Pumpkinhead of Oz, or Dr. Doolittle, or the cow jumping over a very real-appearing moon[1]—all the delightful contraptions of a make-believe world. How often had he seen Pegasus[2] flying in the sky ceiling, or seen fountains of red fireworks, or heard angel voices singing. But now, this yellow hot Africa, this bake oven with murder in the heat. Perhaps Lydia was right. Perhaps they needed a little vacation from the fantasy which was growing a bit too real for ten-year-old children. It was all right to exercise one's mind with gymnastic fantasies, but when the lively child mind settled on *one* pattern . . . ? It seemed that, at a distance, for the past month, he had heard lions roaring, and smelled their strong odor seeping as far away as his study door. But, being busy, he had paid it no attention.

George Hadley stood on the African grassland alone. The lions looked up from their feeding, watching him. The only flaw to the illusion was the open

---

1. Characters and places from famous children's stories and nursery rhymes.   **2.** In Greek mythology, the flying horse.

door through which he could see his wife, far down the dark hall, like a framed picture, eating her dinner abstractedly.

"Go away," he said to the lions.

They did not go.

He knew the principle of the room exactly. You sent out your thoughts. Whatever you thought would appear.

"Let's have Aladdin and his lamp," he snapped.

The veldtland remained; the lions remained.

"Come on, room! I demand Aladdin!" he said.

Nothing happened. The lions mumbled in their baked pelts.

"Aladdin!"

He went back to dinner. "The fool room's out of order," he said. "It won't respond."

"Or—"

"Or what?"

"Or it *can't* respond," said Lydia, "because the children have thought about Africa and lions and killing so many days that the room's in a rut."

"Could be."

"Or Peter's set it to remain that way."

"*Set* it?"

"He may have got into the machinery and fixed something."

"Peter doesn't know machinery."

"He's a wise one for ten. That I.Q. of his—"

"Nevertheless—"

"Hello, Mom. Hello, Dad."

The Hadleys turned. Wendy and Peter were coming in the front door, cheeks like peppermint candy, eyes like bright blue agate marbles, a smell of ozone on their jumpers from their trip in the helicopter.

"You're just in time for supper," said both parents.

"We're full of strawberry ice cream and hot dogs," said the children, holding hands. "But we'll sit and watch."

"Yes, come tell us about the nursery," said George Hadley.

The brother and sister blinked at him and then at each other. "Nursery?"

"All about Africa and everything," said the father with false joviality.

"I don't understand," said Peter.

"Your mother and I were just traveling through Africa with rod and reel; Tom Swift[3] and his Electric Lion," said George Hadley.

"There's no Africa in the nursery," said Peter simply.

"Oh, come now, Peter. We know better."

"I don't remember any Africa," said Peter to Wendy. "Do you?"

"No."

"Run see and come tell."

She obeyed.

"Wendy, come back here!" said George Hadley, but she was gone. The house lights followed her like a flock of fireflies. Too late, he realized he had forgotten to lock the nursery door after his last inspection.

"Wendy'll look and come tell us," said Peter.

"She doesn't have to tell *me*. I've seen it."

---

3. The hero of a series of adventure novels for boys by Victor Appleton (pseudonym).

"I'm sure you're mistaken, Father."

"I'm not, Peter. Come along now."

But Wendy was back. "It's not Africa," she said breathlessly.

"We'll see about this," said George Hadley, and they all walked down the hall together and opened the nursery door.

There was a green, lovely forest, a lovely river, a purple mountain, high voices singing, and Rima,[4] lovely and mysterious, lurking in the trees with colorful flights of butterflies, like animated bouquets, lingering on her long hair. The African veldtland was gone. The lions were gone. Only Rima was here now, singing a song so beautiful that it brought tears to your eyes.

George Hadley looked in at the changed scene. "Go to bed," he said to the children.

They opened their mouths.

"You heard me," he said.

They went off to the air closet, where a wind sucked them like brown leaves up the flue to their slumber rooms.

George Hadley walked through the singing glade and picked up something that lay in the corner near where the lions had been. He walked slowly back to his wife.

"What is that?" she asked.

"An old wallet of mine," he said.

He showed it to her. The smell of hot grass was on it and the smell of a lion. There were drops of saliva on it, it had been chewed, and there were blood smears on both sides.

He closed the nursery door and locked it, tight.

In the middle of the night he was still awake and he knew his wife was awake. "Do you think Wendy changed it?" she said at last, in the dark room.

"Of course."

"Made it from a veldt into a forest and put Rima there instead of lions?"

"Yes."

"Why?"

"I don't know. But it's staying locked until I find out."

"How did your wallet get there?"

"I don't know anything," he said, "except that I'm beginning to be sorry we bought that room for the children. If children are neurotic at all, a room like that—"

"It's supposed to help them work off their neuroses in a healthful way."

"I'm starting to wonder." He stared at the ceiling.

"We've given the children everything they ever wanted. Is this our reward—secrecy, disobedience?"

"Who was it said, 'Children are carpets, they should be stepped on occasionally'? We've never lifted a hand. They're insufferable—let's admit it. They come and go when they like; they treat us as if *we* were offspring. They're spoiled and we're spoiled."

"They've been acting funny ever since you forbade them to take the rocket to New York a few months ago."

"They're not old enough to do that alone, I explained."

"Nevertheless, I've noticed they've been decidedly cool toward us since."

4. Heroine in *Green Mansions*, a 1904 novel by W. H. Hudson (1841–1922).

"I think I'll have David McClean come tomorrow morning to have a look at Africa."

"But it's not Africa now, it's Green Mansions country and Rima."

"I have a feeling it'll be Africa again before then."

A moment later they heard the screams.

Two screams. Two people screaming from downstairs. And then a roar of lions.

"Wendy and Peter aren't in their rooms," said his wife.

He lay in his bed with his beating heart. "No," he said. "They've broken into the nursery."

"Those screams—they sound familiar."

"Do they?"

"Yes, awfully."

And although their beds tried very hard, the two adults couldn't be rocked to sleep for another hour. A smell of cats was in the night air.

"Father?" said Peter.

"Yes."

Peter looked at his shoes. He never looked at his father any more, nor at his mother. "You aren't going to lock up the nursery for good, are you?"

"That all depends."

"On what?" snapped Peter.

"On you and your sister. If you intersperse this Africa with a little variety—oh, Sweden perhaps, or Denmark or China——"

"I thought we were free to play as we wished."

"You are, within reasonable bounds."

"What's wrong with Africa, Father?"

"Oh, so now you admit you have been conjuring up Africa, do you?"

"I wouldn't want the nursery locked up," said Peter coldly. "Ever."

"Matter of fact, we're thinking of turning the whole house off for about a month. Live sort of a carefree one-for-all existence."

"That sounds dreadful! Would I have to tie my own shoes instead of letting the shoe tier do it? And brush my own teeth and comb my hair and give myself a bath?"

"It would be fun for a change, don't you think?"

"No, it would be horrid. I didn't like it when you took out the picture painter last month."

"That's because I wanted you to learn to paint all by yourself, son."

"I don't want to do anything but look and listen and smell; what else *is* there to do?"

"All right, go play in Africa."

"Will you shut off the house sometime soon?"

"We're considering it."

"I don't think you'd better consider it any more, Father."

"I won't have any threats from my son!"

"Very well." And Peter strolled off to the nursery.

"Am I on time?" said David McClean.

"Breakfast?" asked George Hadley.

"Thanks, had some. What's the trouble?"

"David, you're a psychologist."

"I should hope so."

"Well, then, have a look at our nursery. You saw it a year ago when you dropped by; did you notice anything peculiar about it then?"

"Can't say I did; the usual violences, a tendency toward a slight paranoia here or there, usual in children because they feel persecuted by parents constantly, but, oh, really nothing."

They walked down the hall. "I locked the nursery up," explained the father, "and the children broke back into it during the night. I let them stay so they could form the patterns for you to see."

There was a terrible screaming from the nursery.

"There it is," said George Hadley. "See what you make of it."

They walked in on the children without rapping.

The screams had faded. The lions were feeding.

"Run outside a moment, children," said George Hadley. "No, don't change the mental combination. Leave the walls as they are. Get!"

With the children gone, the two men stood studying the lions clustered at a distance, eating with great relish whatever it was they had caught.

"I wish I knew what it was," said George Hadley. "Sometimes I can almost see. Do you think if I brought high-powered binoculars here and——"

David McClean laughed dryly. "Hardly." He turned to study all four walls. "How long has this been going on?"

"A little over a month."

"It certainly doesn't *feel* good."

"I want facts, not feelings."

"My dear George, a psychologist never saw a fact in his life. He only hears about feelings; vague things. This doesn't feel good, I tell you. Trust my hunches and my instincts. I have a nose for something bad. This is very bad. My advice to you is to have the whole damn room torn down and your children brought to me every day during the next year for treatment."

"Is it that bad?"

"I'm afraid so. One of the original uses of these nurseries was so that we could study the patterns left on the walls by the child's mind, study at our leisure, and help the child. In this case, however, the room has become a channel toward—destructive thoughts, instead of a release away from them."

"Didn't you sense this before?"

"I sensed only that you had spoiled your children more than most. And now you're letting them down in some way. What way?"

"I wouldn't let them go to New York."

"What else?"

"I've taken a few machines from the house and threatened them, a month ago, with closing up the nursery unless they did their homework. I did close it for a few days to show I meant business."

"Ah, ha!"

"Does that mean anything?"

"Everything. Where before they had a Santa Claus now they have a Scrooge. Children prefer Santas. You've let this room and this house replace you and your wife in your children's affections. This room is their mother and father, far more important in their lives than their real parents. And now you come along and want to shut it off. No wonder there's hatred here. You can feel it coming out of the sky. Feel that sun. George, you'll have to change your life. Like too many others, you've built it around creature comforts. Why, you'd starve tomorrow if something went wrong in your kitchen. You wouldn't know how to tap an egg. Nevertheless, turn everything off. Start new. It'll take time. But we'll make good children out of bad in a year, wait and see."

"But won't the shock be too much for the children, shutting the room up abruptly, for good?"

"I don't want them going any deeper into this, that's all."

The lions were finished with their red feast.

The lions were standing on the edge of the clearing watching the two men.

"Now *I'm* feeling persecuted," said McClean. "Let's get out of here. I never have cared for these damned rooms. Make me nervous."

"The lions look real, don't they?" said George Hadley. "I don't suppose there's any way——"

"What?"

"—that they could *become* real?"

"Not that I know."

"Some flaw in the machinery, a tampering or something?"

"No."

They went to the door.

"I don't imagine the room will like being turned off," said the father.

"Nothing ever likes to die—even a room."

"I wonder if it hates me for wanting to switch it off?"

"Paranoia is thick around here today," said David McClean. "You can follow it like a spoor. Hello." He bent and picked up a bloody scarf. "This yours?"

"No." George Hadley's face was rigid. "It belongs to Lydia."

They went to the fuse box together and threw the switch that killed the nursery.

The two children were in hysterics. They screamed and pranced and threw things. They yelled and sobbed and swore and jumped at the furniture.

"You can't do that to the nursery, you can't!"

"Now, children."

The children flung themselves onto a couch, weeping.

"George," said Lydia Hadley, "turn on the nursery, just for a few moments. You can't be so abrupt."

"No."

"You can't be so cruel."

"Lydia, it's off, and it stays off. And the whole damn house dies as of here and now. The more I see of the mess we've put ourselves in, the more it sickens me. We've been contemplating our mechanical, electronic navels for too long. My God, how we need a breath of honest air!"

And he marched about the house turning off the voice clocks, the stoves, the heaters, the shoe shiners, the shoe lacers, the body scrubbers and swabbers and massagers, and every other machine he could put his hand to.

The house was full of dead bodies, it seemed. It felt like a mechanical cemetery. So silent. None of the humming hidden energy of machines waiting to function at the tap of a button.

"Don't let them do it!" wailed Peter at the ceiling, as if he was talking to the house, the nursery. "Don't let Father kill everything." He turned to his father. "Oh, I hate you!"

"Insults won't get you anywhere."

"I wish you were dead!"

"We were, for a long while. Now we're going to really start living. Instead of being handled and massaged, we're going to *live*."

Wendy was still crying and Peter joined her again. "Just a moment, just one moment, just another moment of nursery," they wailed.

"Oh, George," said the wife, "it can't hurt."

"All right—all right, if they'll only just shut up. One minute, mind you, and then off forever."

"Daddy, Daddy, Daddy!" sang the children, smiling with wet faces.

"And then we're going on a vacation. David McClean is coming back in half an hour to help us move out and get to the airport. I'm going to dress. You turn the nursery on for a minute, Lydia, just a minute, mind you."

And the three of them went babbling off while he let himself be vacuumed upstairs through the air flue and set about dressing himself. A minute later Lydia appeared.

"I'll be glad when we get away," she sighed.

"Did you leave them in the nursery?"

"I wanted to dress too. Oh, that horrid Africa. What can they see in it?"

"Well, in five minutes we'll be on our way to Iowa. Lord, how did we ever get in this house? What prompted us to buy a nightmare?"

"Pride, money, foolishness."

"I think we'd better get downstairs before those kids get engrossed with those damned beasts again."

Just then they heard the children calling, "Daddy, Mommy, come quick—quick!"

They went downstairs in the air flue and ran down the hall. The children were nowhere in sight. "Wendy? Peter!"

They ran into the nursery. The veldtland was empty save for the lions waiting, looking at them. "Peter, Wendy?"

The door slammed.

"Wendy, Peter!"

George Hadley and his wife whirled and ran back to the door.

"Open the door!" cried George Hadley, trying the knob. "Why, they've locked it from the outside! Peter!" He beat at the door. "Open up!"

He heard Peter's voice outside, against the door.

"Don't let them switch off the nursery and the house," he was saying.

Mr. and Mrs. George Hadley beat at the door. "Now, don't be ridiculous, children. It's time to go. Mr. McClean'll be here in a minute and . . ."

And then they heard the sounds.

The lions on three sides of them, in the yellow veldt grass, padding through the dry straw, rumbling and roaring in their throats.

The lions.

Mr. Hadley looked at his wife and they turned and looked back at the beasts edging slowly forward, crouching, tails stiff.

Mr. and Mrs. Hadley screamed.

And suddenly they realized why those other screams had sounded familiar.

"Well, here I am," said David McClean in the nursery doorway. "Oh, hello." He stared at the two children seated in the center of the open glade eating a little picnic lunch. Beyond them was the water hole and the yellow veldtland; above was the hot sun. He began to perspire. "Where are your father and mother?"

The children looked up and smiled. "Oh, they'll be here directly."

"Good, we must get going." At a distance Mr. McClean saw the lions fighting and clawing and then quieting down to feed in silence under the shady trees.

He squinted at the lions with his hand up to his eyes.

Now the lions were done feeding. They moved to the water hole to drink.

A shadow flickered over Mr. McClean's hot face. Many shadows flickered. The vultures were dropping down the blazing sky.

"A cup of tea?" asked Wendy in the silence.

1951

FREDERICK BUSCH
1941–2006

Busch was born in Brooklyn, New York, and attended Muhlenberg College. A prolific writer of both fiction and nonfiction, he received a Guggenheim Fellowship and a PEN/Malamud Award for his short stories, which often feature a blend of magical realism with the picture of life in his region, the Northeast. His most recent collections are *Don't Tell Anyone* (2000) and *Rescue Missions* (2006). Busch's numerous novels include *I Wanted a Year without Fall* (1971), *Invisible Mending* (1984), *War Babies* (1989), *Girls* (1997), and *North* (2005).

Bread

First I went from room to chilly room, smoke alarm to smoke alarm. I saw little of the dust-fogged furniture or drapes, or the cobwebs blooming with cluster flies—the slatternly housekeeping for which our mother had been celebrated. Later, we discussed our pride in her carelessness. But this was first. I found the one. It was on the wall, near the molding, above the back-room cellar door. It squeaked like a floorboard, where no one had walked for a week, beneath someone's foot. Every minute or so it squeaked. It was the battery. The battery gives out, and the gizmo makes its little I'm-a-ghostly-footfall cry, and you hunt it down and tear the failing battery away: one ghost less.

It was the next day, in the kitchen, in the chill and in the absence, when I thought, *And not even by terrorists*. I heard my *not even* and I snorted with disgust. I was the man who would complain of his parents' death, of their falling and falling out of the sky, that it was insufficiently political. I snorted again. You make enough such noises, in a house quite suddenly scalloped out by death—by deaths—and the other person with you, in another room, a sister, say, might think she hears her brother weep.

"Chuckie," she called.

"What?"

"Are you okay?"

"Yes."

"Huh?"

"*Yes*."

"Yeah," she said. "Okay." Then: "It sounded—"

"I wasn't," I said.

Kendall had decided that the room she couldn't deal with, among the rooms she couldn't deal with, was the kitchen. I'd volunteered. I was the brother. I did that. I had recently enough cleaned out rooms to be used to raking through what mustn't matter anymore—an apartment in Manhattan, four rooms on Riverside Drive, and not a house formerly employed for the storage of four lives and the spirits of six dogs, six or seven cats, the famous rooster flock, some insect-eating plants, and of course, though briefly, the boy whom Kendall so many years ago had smuggled in for the night.

In the city, I'd cleaned up what I finally saw as debris, the still-smoking rubble of a two-year marriage—service booklets on blender and toaster oven, playbills from hundred-dollar theater evenings, a lacy, boy-man's prayer of crimson negligée, the duplicate books, the checks and their sloppy but balanced ledgers: the finally usual. So, though Kendall was close to thirty and I four years younger, I volunteered. I thought of myself as experienced.

Therefore, in the home of my parents who had driven to Syracuse and flown to Toronto and stayed in a hotel on the lake at Harbourfront and had gone to a sort of theatrical evening that involved some visiting English friends, and then had flown from Toronto in a two-engine prop-driven airplane that had come apart over Lake Ontario, I was being experienced. I was fighting the stiff, dark dough I'd taken on the night of our arrival, when I'd offered to do—to do, to *do*—the kitchen, and I was kneading it. Like a semiprofessional mourner, I was conducting myself with dignity and in a manner governed by logic.

"I'm kneading bread," I answered Kendall, who'd been drawn perhaps by my silence into the kitchen she had vowed to avoid.

She sat with staring eyes that jumped from surfaces like hands from hot handles and she lit a cigarette. "You mind?" she asked. She propped her elbows on the narrow wooden table the top of which, once upon a time, my head had been level with. I had swiped hot cookies that my mother had set there to cool.

"No," I said. "I was married to a smoker."

"She never smoked here. Anytime that I saw."

"She sneaked it."

"Did she, you know, sneak around? On you? With guys?"

Kendall's face was a little square, her features slightly gathered at the center of her face. She missed bearing a man's strong face by virtue of the brown-green lightness of her large eyes. They were also our father's eyes. It was nearly his face, though he diminished as she widened her eyes to mock the innocence with which she hadn't asked her question. I turned my back to her and the rest of the kitchen, and I worked at the dough. It didn't yield gladly to my palms as I pushed, then gathered it toward me, gathered, then pushed.

"She did," Kendall concluded.

"That doesn't matter," I said.

"Chuckie, never mind. I shouldn't have, but never mind anyway."

"It doesn't matter anymore. It almost didn't then. Now it doesn't, and everybody moves along."

"That's right," she said. "Listen. How did you learn about kneading bread. Do guys normally *do* that?"

I planted my legs wider and drove hard at the football-sized wad of dough, still cold, unready to be shaped. I picked it up and slammed it onto the breadboard on the long counter. "I watched her," I said.

"A lot? You sat here and just looked at her?"

"No. I don't know. One time, I watched instead of—I don't know. *Not* watching. Isn't that what kids do with their parents? Not watch them a lot?"

I heard her sigh out the smoke. "You're lucky. To remember that."

"*You* remember things, Ken. They're just other things."

I heard her walk to the sink. I looked over my shoulder as she ran water on her cigarette. When she turned, I'd turned back to stare at the dough I leaned on with my palms. I almost didn't hear her say, "But I want to remember everything."

There isn't much of an answer. I nodded over the dough and closed my eyes. I continued to knead. She left the kitchen, swatting my ass, not hard, as she went.

When the flock happened, ours and the nearest other house, a usually vacant rental place in much disrepair, were the only buildings for three or four miles. The rental house burned or was burned. My father had used to snarl about the trash, as he called them, who rented it. They littered the door-yard with green garbage, they used an outhouse, and their goggle-eyed, shab-bily dressed, pale-skinned children offended him. One winter, they burned an unsafe woodstove too hot, or lit the house in revenge for an impending eviction over nonpayment of rent. The roar of the fire, the pumper trucks and police cars sliding on the road, the ceaseless dirty gray smoke, scared us all. My father put smoke alarms—expensive in those days, and considered scien-tific wonders—into every room as soon as they were sold. He forbade us, on the day of the fire, the cigarettes he knew we sneaked. (I stopped, Kendall didn't.) He put a metal emergency ladder into Kendall's room and mine. He made us practice household fire drills. We used to rush about at *Go!*, crawling to doors, crouching from windows, crying out whom we would wake, and with what precautions, and then how we would run for our lives and wait for our parents to find us.

The day after the fire, I returned from—my mother's description—a twelve-year-old's sulk in the woods. I bore a seared, semi-featherless, small-headed, singed-comb little chicken. I brought it home, my parents said, whenever they told the story, to ask if I could give it someplace to die in peace. "He's the only survivor," I was said to have said, referring to the fire in which no one died. I named the chicken Bunny because I'd never been permitted to own the rabbit my mother had promised me as consolation after she'd shattered my sixth year of life by disclosing that the Easter Bunny did not in fact bring jelly beans and marshmallow chicks the color of radioactive rocks.

So we owned a scarred, small-headed chicken whose name was that of some cute, stupid girl with big breasts in some movie about big breasts on a Califor-nia beach. My father, tall and broad and square-faced, balder than any egg, was business manager and assistant superintendent of the school district on the outermost edge of which we lived. He brought home one night, eight or nine days later, a cardboard box filled with chicks hatched and nourished in the high school biology lab.

The dough was working, now, and I pushed and gathered and then went in search of dish towels to drape on the three balls of dough I would cut from what I'd kneaded and arrange for rising. I was working from a book I had taken from the cookbook shelves. The page was relaxed in the binding, stained and limp. I'd stared at the stains before I'd focused on the words.

So I fed them the feed our father complained the birds ate too much of. Complaining about the cost of lumber, he built and fenced a little hen house, complete with roosting shelf. And Bunny, grown to something like health, with her mean, crazy eyes and the tattered wattle under her remarkably small head, staggered across the yard with her flock to raid the garden, then wheeled with stupid precision to stop occasional cars in our rutted, dusty, unpaved road.

The others didn't lay, though Bunny did. Kendall and I refused to eat her eggs, of course—that would be like eating *people,* Kendall explained for us. All of the birds, though unproductive, were more than willing to crow—on the occasion of a car with a leaky muffler that passed, for house lights spilling yellow down the yard, and for, as my father put it at two or three one morning, "a goddamned harvest *moon.*"

Taking advice from his district's high school biology teacher, my father soon enough determined that with the exception of poor, exhausted Bunny, we owned a flock of roosters. "Guys!" Kendall had cried, on hearing the news. As for me, I was busy in school and bored by them all; I remained devoted to the idea of Bunny, but saw as little of her as possible. The rooster flock, and Bunny, soon enough disappeared. Then our parents disappeared. I saw them spilling from the plane. I sent that away. No: he would have reached for her. She would have reached for him. I saw them, then, clutching at each other. I cut the dough into three smaller balls and draped them with the soft, faded dish towels under which they would rise. I left the house by the side door. I could always work in the barn, I thought. I could always be useful in the barn.

He took the roosters and Bunny to a high school janitor who promised, he lied to us, that he would protect them until they died of old age. We knew. He killed them and cooked them and ate them. That was how they disappeared. Bunny au vin. Bunny sautée Basquaise. Bunny, more than likely, fried in lard.

I didn't go to the barn. I crossed the country road, paved now, and too well traveled, they'd complained. SaraJean, who used to be my wife, had liked to laugh when my mother began grousing about cars in the peaceable kingdom. "Where do they find up here to *travel* to?" SaraJean had enjoyed asking. She liked closure. She relished ending conversations, and pushing the button that shut the automatic door on anyone's garage, and terminating laden relationships. Kendall had said that if SaraJean and I had produced children, my wife would have happily inserted them, one at a time, in the trash compactor.

I went up the steep hill across from the house. The pitch was difficult, the snow still thick in wind-driven patches, and elsewhere the thorny stalks and slippery dead leaves and mostly frozen mud made the walking breathless. I aimed myself at an evergreen, fat in a low cluster of sinuous bushes, on the wind-flattened northern slope. In my father's lined denim chore coat, the collar up and a watch cap from the pocket pulled over my ears, I grew sweaty though the wind gusted on my back, and soon I was gasping into all that air. But I pushed hard if awkwardly to get myself up. I was desperate, heaving though I was, to not stop, to get away.

When I was near the tree, I turned to look down along the hill, and then I saw what I'd wanted to: all of it, the white house and garage, the gray wooden tool shed from which the house for Bunny and her flock of roosters protruded, the dead garden, the brown-green dormant lawns that ran to fields that went along the rocky tan hill below the house. It looked, from where I puffed and panted, manageable. It looked as though, if you stared hard and studied the details of cornice and chimney and gutter and sill, you could hold it confidently and summon it as you needed to.

Walking downhill, I had to dig my heels into snow patches and leaf heaps to keep from falling. My knees ached and my shins felt too tight. I walked stiff-legged across the road and around the side to the door. It was when I took off his watch cap and wiped my sweaty face with it that I remembered about his head inside the blue-black wool, his sweat already on the loosened knots of its weave, his fringe of iron hair that I remembered as surprisingly fine, soft to touch, the first time I dared to touch it as a man. I rubbed my head. I felt a way that reminded me of my discomfort on first seeing my father naked. A necessary distance had been shortened. Well, you've got all the distance, now, you'll need: I would have said that to me if I had been someone else.

In the kitchen, I took the towels from the bread and, with a wooden rolling pin that was like a long dowel slightly swollen in the middle, I pressed and rolled until the balls were long, thin ovals. According to the recipe in the cookbook I was to delicately and precisely gather up the edge nearest me and tautly roll. *Delicately* and *precisely* and *tautly*. I rolled up three long loaves and set them on a metal cooking sheet and stuck them in the oven. I'd forgotten to preheat the oven, but the bread would have to overcome the cold just as it would have to overcome its weeks or months in the freezer and my inability to roll it with sufficient delicacy, precision, and tautness. I turned up the heat.

I went upstairs to see if Kendall had made some progress. I, surely, had not. We'd planned to spend a weekend, then had changed our plans, had called in to work to say we'd need more like a week. It looked like a month to me. It looked like lasting into middle age or Social Security.

Kendall was on the floor, near the foot of their bed. Beside her, almost around her, was an explosion of clothing. She looked red-eyed and sore, very pale, maybe ill.

My turn to ask it: "You all right?"

"Where'd you go, Chuck?"

"I walked up over the hill."

"You son of a bitch."

"You would just as soon I hadn't walked up over the hill, I take it."

"I called you and called you."

"I didn't know, of course. Being—"

"Ha ha. Over the hill. Ha ha. Except I was *calling* you."

"I wouldn't have gone, you know. If I thought you needed me here right then."

She slumped, so that she looked as if she were studying their silk and rayon and cotton and wool. Then she nodded.

"You know that," I said.

She nodded again.

I said, "I am going to jump to the conclusion, Ken, that you're not enjoying the sorting out of their bedroom."

"Christ," she said. "You—I don't want to make any snappy remarks, all right? I feel terrible."

"Sick, you mean, or—you know. About them."

"Them," she said. She gestured at the clothing, then her arm fell on top of it and she went with it, so that she was lying on top of washed-thin half slips and cheap-looking underwear and starchy shirts with cardboard stiffeners and boot socks I knew he'd bought at Agway and slacks she'd ordered from catalogues and shoes that needed to be heeled and cleaned and shined. Kendall said, "I started to take the things out of their drawers and make piles, and I couldn't figure out what I was piling them for. *I'd* never wear her clothes, never mind I couldn't get into a size eight *glove,* much less her dresses. And they're so *cheap*-looking. Ordinary. I thought I learned how to dress from her, and it's all so, I don't know, worn out and faded and not very brilliantly selected. And you hate *his* clothes, don't you? I mean, who wears a suit to work over high-lace insulated *boots.* Let it *be* fucking wintertime: you dress *right.* Right? Or his terrible—they're not terrible. But his ties. That she picked out, with her famous taste.

"So I stopped stacking and I started heaving. It seemed to end up being some kind of revenge thing. So I stopped that, too. I mostly sat here and wailed for you and you couldn't come up and give me a hand, could you? Because you were being Jack and Jill. Whatever you were doing."

The highboy on my father's side of the bed was missing a brass pull on one side of the second drawer down. His bedside table wasn't identical to hers, I noticed for the first time. And they'd never arrested the damp that was ruining the casements of both their windows.

I said, "Whatever I was doing. I'm going to total it up for us, Ken. In about twenty-four hours, we've defrosted a ball of dough and we've made a mound of clothing. I think we're behind our schedule."

"And yet we're both so experienced at this."

"In a manner of speaking," I said.

Kendall propped herself on her elbows and crossed her legs at the ankle. She wore jeans and a cotton sweater, its sleeves pulled up to the elbows, and, despite her pallor and red eyes, she looked young. "Of course," she said, "you're the one used to cleaning up after marriages. I'm the party who slung it all into a duffel bag and two canvas suitcases and moved out in twelve minutes under the standing Olympic record for leaving *any*one. Much less the maniac I *wouldn't* marry."

"No," I said, "I always thought Bobby had a kind of admirable zest. He's the only man I ever knew outside the movies who actually hallucinated at his desk in front of a client."

"The only man," she said, "who ate amphetamines by dropping them into his martini. 'Straight up, babe, no fruits or vegetables in it, and bring me some kind of food with the second drink, all right?' Zest is a fond and stupid word for him. So's admirable."

"From a fond and stupid guy," I admitted.

"You're only stupid, Chuckie."

I sat in the pretty bentwood chair that needed recaning. It leaned as I let my weight down, and I waited for it to collapse, but it held me. I said, hiding behind my closed eyes, "Let's throw it all away."

"Which all?"

"All of it," I said, still hiding. "The clothes, the bedroom slippers, the pajamas—what can we *use?* We don't want to save things—do we?—and put them on like relics. 'Hi, my name's Chuck and I'm wearing a dead man's shirt with sleeves two inches too long.' Let's not do that, Ken. Let's toss it out."

"No," she said. Then she said, "All right. Except, we give it to—I don't know. Somebody. People. The Salvation Army."

"No way. They sell it to rag merchants. *They* sell it to clothing makers. *They* get wage slaves in Hong Kong and Costa Rica to use it for new clothes. So you're walking up Park Avenue South, say, and you see one of those overbred undermuscled types with blond eyelashes and about seventeen years of experience at a good college, and they're wearing a casually wrinkled natural fiber outfit, you know, and you stare at it because you see Daddy's *shirt* in there. You say to the androgyne, 'Excuse me, but aren't you wearing my father's shirt?' You don't want that to happen. You don't *want* them wearing Daddy's clothes and Mommy's clothes, Ken. Toss it. Throw it. All of it. If you want me to, I'll start a big son of a bitch fire outside, in the backyard, and we'll burn it."

"Is that called howdah? When the woman throws herself on top of the man who's burning? Or is that what they call burnoose?"

"You're a cultural swinette, Ken. We'll just throw it away."

"All right."

"You mean it?"

"I should have said it first," Kendall said. "It's just that—you know what I have left from when I lived with Bobby? Zip. No souvenirs, nothing. I left everything of mine behind, pictures of him, pictures of you and Mommy and Daddy, everything I brought in with me in the first place. He never called or anything to ask if I wanted anything back. Or if he could have *me* back."

"He's a junkie, Ken."

"He was *my* junkie," she said. And then: "Are you afraid of going through the *real* stuff? Are you scared, too?"

"Their papers? They probably don't have any papers. I mean, insurance things, bank things, that. Sure. But no *papers.* You know, that prove we were adopted, or stolen from kings and dukes or anything. No secret diaries or anything. No."

"So how come you haven't gone through Daddy's upper right-hand drawer?"

I told her, "Good conduct medal. Infantry badges. Two sets of corporal's stripes. Old handkerchiefs."

"You just remember from before."

"From high school," I admitted. "I used to look."

"You're as scared as I am," she said.

I looked at the sloping pile of our parents' clothes. They had nothing to do with how my mother wore my father's flannel shirts on Sunday to cook in, the sleeves rolled and the tails hanging almost to her knees. His flannel shirts looked like anybody's, now, anybody's green tartan from the Army-Navy in New Hartford, anybody's gray and black and yellow and white from the mail-order store.

I said, "I used to look for secret stuff. Dirty things. Pictures or rubbers, I don't know. He didn't have anything. Or he didn't leave it there for me to find. We won't steal their secrets here."

"Where would they hide them?" Kendall asked.

"Why *would* they, Ken?"

"Everyone does," she said. "That's why you're divorced and I live alone, and they went swimming," she said. She plucked at clothing.

I said, "They were together. They stuck together. They died together."

"Maybe they were better at it than we are," Kendall said, "but everybody's a secret from everybody else."

I pulled garbage bags from the box that Kendall had brought up. They were transparent, but they changed the color of the clothes I forced inside them. A watery tone, like what you see on docks or the footing of wooden bridges, went over everything. I felt as though I were drowning their clothes, which looked ugly, distorted, as I crushed them in. And I thought about robbers who pulled nylon stockings over their heads to change their features, which also looked crushed. This, I thought, is what our parents must look like, underwater.

Kendall had stood to take some bags and fill them. I heard us panting, as I had when I'd climbed the hill. This is real work too, I thought. We opened all but one of the drawers she hadn't got to, and we emptied all but one into the bags. My fingers felt sore from pulling at their clothing. I kneeled on each bag to force the air out before fastening it. Under my weight, the bags sighed like people, and the cloth inside went heavier.

When we were done, when we had without relenting thrown away our parents' only surviving skins, and when the room was ranked with sacks, Kendall said, "Look at us. It's like Hansel and Gretel made it back all the way, carrying the witch's whatever—"

"Gold," I said.

"Gold. Gingerbread cake. Whatever."

"You're just *hungry*, Ken."

"And they find out there's nobody home anyway. You know? The parent bastards tricked them *again,* and nobody's *home.*"

I said, stupidly, "Ken. They didn't *mean* to."

"Why would I think that?" she said.

We stood there awhile and then, as if we'd made a decision, we left the bags and walked down the hall to the small room over the porch that had been Kendall's before she moved away and they turned it into a guest room.

She went to the closet and opened the door. It was empty, I thought. But Kendall reached in, her eyes still on mine, and her hand emerged to show her trophy: a chain ladder, suitable for escaping from fires or admitting boys on steep, snowy roofs. I apparently made a noise.

Kendall said, "I hate that. You keep doing that. You never used to. Where'd you pick it up?"

"I'm not really aware," I said, "of any unseemly new habits. But thanks."

"Yeah," she said. "You do sound like somebody who's about to hawk one on the floor. You sound like some kid on the street. Is that what New York did for you? Hee-*yach.* Like that. You really didn't know you were doing that?"

"I think I sometimes snort," I said. "Blow air out my nose—not the way Bobby snorted. Just a little sniff, sometimes, maybe."

"New York City on the street, that's your little sniffy snort."

"Tell me something country, Ken. How'd you ever get that kid in here?"

Holding the ladder, Kendall sat down. I think she'd have sat on the floor and hit hard, but there was an old footstool covered with maroon vinyl or leather, and she landed, clanking, on that. It was most of the furniture in the room, aside from the bed and bureau. The room was narrow and decorated with a chocolate brown carpet and off-white walls on which our mother had hung prints they'd brought home from Europe.

Kendall said, "I forgot." She was blushing, and I was glad to see her pallor overwhelmed.

"Poor son of a bitch," I said. "You forget, and the poor son of a bitch probably goes over it, step by step, every other day of his life. How he went up a porch stanchion and along the front porch roof and into Kendall Beaucamp's window. And—" I waited. She volunteered nothing. She shook her head and looked at the chenille comforter, dusty as the curtains, I'd have bet, and the narrow cherry dresser over which a cherry frame, of a slightly different hue, held a mirror in which I watched us stand, sit, remember and try not to. I said, "Ken: did he or did he not get into the sack with you? And what was his name?"

She shook her head. "I can't remember."

"Was he your, you know—was he the first guy you ever—"

"That's plain goddamned prurient, Chuckie, you know that? Yes. We got so turned on by being outlaws in here, we did stuff we didn't know we knew to *do*."

"I remember his name," I said. "Peter."

"No: Preston. Press. Press Leutens."

"The stud."

"He wasn't bad," Kendall said.

"And?"

"This is not the time for telling stories," Kendall said, with no rancor or conviction.

I said, "This is why they *invented* stories."

She said, "Daddy had grounded me for coming home an hour late, after my curfew. We'd been out. Press had the car, his parents' car, and there was some kind of game. Basketball, it was a basketball game, the last league game, we had to win to get into the tournament. So we won. He played a good game, and we didn't get home until late."

"You were the hero's reward?"

"He was *my* reward. I'd had to sit through the game, after all. *And* clap for our cheerleaders. We had more bent, humped, sickly pale, short-legged cheerleaders that year. So we got home late, Daddy all but put me on bread and water, Mommy said those moral things she always said until I said I would leave home unless she and Daddy did first, and that night, the next night, when it happened, I was in my room and Press just showed up."

"At your window."

"At my window."

"Like the movies," I said.

She said, "Exactly like the movies."

"And you let him in with the fire ladder?"

"He didn't really need it. He'd made it up the roof already, most of the way, but I liked the idea of opening my window and unrolling the ladder Daddy used to make me practice unrolling all the time."

"Right," I said. "And?"

"God, Chuck, you're so vulgar."

"I know. Tell me the story."

"Chuck. We acted like we were in Nazi-occupied France and we took our clothes off and went to bed. I was a normal, healthy child and so was he. We'd been warming up in cars and dark corners, and we did what we'd been trained for."

"And I spent my childhood reading dirty books," I complained.

"Not from what I heard."

"Tell me the rest," I said.

Kendall said: "Like the movies. Like the books. Whispering and touching and kissing and talking and screwing, Chuck, until, as a matter of fact, dawn."

"When Bunny crowed."

"Bunny crowed. The cocks all crowed. Press got dressed and went to the window and he was so nervous about making his escape from the Nazis and the Vichy[1] police, he forgot to kiss me goodbye. He went onto the slippery, snow-covered roof, without benefit of the fire ladder, and I was in bed, you know, not *believing* it, and Bunny and that goddamned flock of roosters must have come wheeling into the front yard. Because all of a sudden—one of those icy dawns? when there's nothing to hear except wind?—all of a sudden, every goddamned rooster, *and* Bunny, started in screaming. Like they all were saying *Aww! Aww! Aww!*

"Naturally, Daddy and Mommy woke up. Daddy went to the front door. And naturally he saw dumb-ass Preston Leutens's car, his parents' car, parked square in front of the front walk. He went out to investigate. By then, I was looking out from between these exact same curtains. There's Daddy, he's in his navy blue watch cap and his bathrobe and his chore jacket over it, and the bedroom slippers we just threw the hell away, and he's standing there, looking at the car. And there's Press on the roof above him. Like a statue on the roof, because he's trying not to slide or be seen. And there's the goddamned cock flock, *Aww! Aww!* I betrayed him in my heart, poor Preston."

"Sure you did. You're Kendall Beaucamp. You laughed."

"With Preston's heat still rising from the sheets. I laughed like the witch in *The Wizard of Oz*. I couldn't help it. And Daddy, of course, through the window, in the rooster screams and all that wind, he hears me."

"I was sleeping."

"Of course you were."

"So I missed seeing him kill you and Preston and you're both still dead?"

"Oh, Chuckie. He scrunched up his face until I thought he was going to cry."

"Did he?"

"Mommy claimed he did, later on. He said to Press, 'You get down cautiously. I don't want your parents suing me after I send you to jail.' Then he went inside."

"What'd he *say*?"

"That's between him and me."

"No."

"Goddamned *yes*. That's for him and me."

I had to look someplace else. I looked at what was either a castle in a meadow or something eating the meadow, and then I said, "Weren't you a pistol."

---

1. A city in central France that, after Paris fell to the German army in 1940, served as the seat of the collaborationist French government until France was liberated by the Allies in 1944.

"Wasn't I," she said. "You know what? I just might sit in here awhile. If you don't mind. A little while. All right?"

I didn't know what else to do except lean down and kiss the top of her head, which smelled like a morning's work and herbal shampoo. She bumped her head against my lips, and I went out.

Where I went, of course, was back down the hall and into our parents' room and through the ranked plastic bags to the bureau in the top right drawer of which my father kept the secrets. When I opened it, a sweet, soapy smell came up—the soaps with French names that my mother gave the big, booted school executive for birthdays and Christmases. When they were used up thin, he dried the wafers and broke them into chips and scattered them in his drawers. I thought of the first time I had seen him naked, emerging from the shower, his dimpled flanks and long thighs, the dense hair on his chest and belly, the dangerous mystery of his groin.

What I saw first in the drawer was a small, handled and almost limp, photograph, about four inches tall. It was of a young girl with pretty legs. She wore a dress over a T-shirt, and the dress was hiked up by her straddling of a bicycle. A familar, shy smile composed her face: you looked from lips to eyes, and you smiled back. It was our mother, aged eight or nine. I had to say "Hello," back through the thirty-six years of their marriage and the long, funny year (as they had often told it) of their courtship—he did the courting, she, as she said, had held her breath and jumped in, trusting (quite incorrectly as it seemed at last) to the probability that everything, after a while, floats to the surface—and back to her childhood in the Korean War, the drills for taking shelter from atomic bomb blasts, and back through World War II, her father in the Pacific, her mother alone with her, chain-smoking Lucky Greens. "Hello," I said, holding the picture he apparently had many times held.

I saw the dark boxes his medals were in, and some wide brown envelopes, an assortment of cuff links and tie clasps presented by us on birthdays, purchased with our mother's money and rarely used. I opened the envelopes, three of them, and found artifacts of children who'd grown older. The envelope on top contained photographs of Kendall in a prom dress, Kendall in her cap and gown at graduation, me in a Cub Scout shirt and jeans, in football uniform, waist-to-heel cast, and my own cap and gown. The envelope in the middle had letters from us: I was ashamed, somehow, of the childish arcs and curves of my hand. And there were pictures of me and SaraJean, or Kendall and Bobby, of New York City and Poughkeepsie, to which Kendall had moved when IBM told her to. I saw that we were happy children. You would call us happy children, if you saw those photographs. And in the envelope on the bottom, there were notes from our mother. I couldn't read them. *Darling,* one of them began, and I folded it shut. There was a drawing signed Kendall in a loopy hand: *My Family,* it said, and there was the vast, big-headed Daddy, with enormous hands and feet and smile, and under him, like shrubs in the shade of a tree, was a labeled *Mommy* with a face-wide smile, and a smaller *Kendall,* her arms spread as if to tell the viewer that here they all were. Under it, folded, was a large Christmas card I had made in elementary school, perhaps in the first or second grade. I could still smell, in the dried smears between the pasted green evergreen shape and the rough construction-paper rectangle, the corrupted vanilla of grade school mucilage. There was more, but I stopped fingering through it. He might have, I thought, hidden cruel, terrible matters deep and far away. But the secrets he had openly kept, in the place a husband and father stores them, where he knows they'll one day be found, had been us.

For punctuation, the smell came up, carried by the draft that went from the kitchen to the stairwell, where it split to go through the dining room and living room toward the back room cellar door, and also to pour upstairs. The odor was dense, and so, then, was the noise. The alarms went off in the kitchen and stairwell, then in the living room—the dining room alarm pitched in late—and I waited for the back room to squeal, then remembered that I'd gutted its alarm.

So much for bread, I thought, running downstairs to a very smoky kitchen. The screaming of the alarms was painful. I turned off the oven, opened the door, and recoiled from the oily black smoke—some of it bread, some the spattered fat our mother wouldn't have cleaned away. I was grinning for her housekeeping, squinting against the smoke, and screaming back at the screaming of the smoke alarms which sounded inside my skull bone like dentist drills.

Kendall, from the doorway, called, "I *told* you that guys don't do bread."

I threw the pan of small black loaves on the floor and retreated to the dining room. She came with me. We stood in the far corner, near a high narrow basket our mother had filled with late autumn grasses, ocher and brown. "It's my mess," I said, "and I will clean it up. It's my fault. I forgot to set the timer. It was cold, you know, frozen, then thawed, then cold, but I knew you didn't do bread *cold*. So I cranked the oven to about 475, and then I forgot."

"You meant well," Kendall said. "I suppose."

I shook my head.

"No," she said, "tell me. You can tell me. I told you."

"You know about yeast," I said.

"In the little envelopes. Mommy always used it."

"They're alive," I said. "Little microscopic plants. Which are alive. Dough rises, the yeast grows. That's what makes the heat. That's why it *needs* heat. So, Mommy freezes the dough. To let the bread rise and bake some other time, she freezes it. So we come here, and it's some other time. So I thawed it. I let it rise. I baked it. Sort of."

Kendall said, "Chuckie."

"That's right. The bread was—well, the yeast in the dough was. You know."

"Alive," Kendall said. "When Mommy was alive."

I nodded.

"Chuckie," she said.

"So of course," I said, "I made sure to take it and kill it, didn't I?"

Kendall was quiet for a long time. I didn't want to look at her, or at the room we'd sat in with company and for Thanksgiving and Christmas dinners. It seemed now such an ordinary room. Like the subsiding smoke as it was drawn through the house to accumulate upstairs and in the back room, then dissipate against the walls and windows there, we were leaving, too.

Kendall, behind me, put her arms around my waist. I felt her along my back. I wanted to turn and pull her in to me, but I didn't. I thought she ought to be as alone with me as she needed to be.

She said, suddenly, with a hoarse, gulping sound, "You know how bad I've been all my life?" She laid her forehead against my back and pushed her head at me as, with her arms, she pulled in.

I said, "I'm going to take you upstairs, Ken. All right? I opened the drawer. I found the secrets. Now I want you to see them, all right?"

I turned, then, and fought her a little until I could take hold of her hand. She stopped resisting, and I led her through the thin current of almost invisible smoke toward the stairs.

"I can't do this," she said. "I don't want to do this."

But I kept pulling her. "Yes," I said. "Really." So we climbed toward their room. In the story, you remember, in the dark forest, when something has inevitably eaten all the crumbs, he leads her home by the hand.

1994

RELATED:

—Busch on Ernest Hemingway's "Hills Like White Elephants," p. 1757

TRUMAN CAPOTE
1924–1984

One of America's true masters of the short story, and a sad example of the destruction of a first-rate talent, Capote is best known for his nonfiction novel, *In Cold Blood* (1966), the story of the 1959 murder of a Holcombe, Kansas, family, the Clutters, by two sociopaths. Born Truman Strekfus Persons in New Orleans, he spent his first years in an unhappy household, and when his parents divorced in 1928, he lived for several years with relatives in Monroeville, Alabama. When his mother remarried and moved with him to New York, he took his stepfather's name. Always flamboyant, frequently outrageous, Capote embraced the world of celebrity so wholeheartedly and with such success that many people knew of him without knowing anything about his work—and his work in the short story is just as fresh today as it was when it first appeared. He died in California, at the age of 59, after years of near-silence and excess: drugs, alcohol, too much of everything. But that delicate boy with the deep understanding of human joys and sorrows, the piercing eye for telling detail, and the perfect pitch, is still very much present in the best of his short fiction, which can be found in his *Collected Stories* (2004).

Miriam

For several years, Mrs. H. T. Miller had lived alone in a pleasant apartment (two rooms with kitchenette) in a remodeled brownstone near the East River. She was a widow: Mr. H. T. Miller had left a reasonable amount of insurance. Her interests were narrow, she had no friends to speak of, and she rarely journeyed farther than the corner grocery. The other people in the house never seemed to notice her: her clothes were matter-of-fact, her hair iron-gray, clipped and casually waved; she did not use cosmetics, her features were plain and inconspicuous, and on her last birthday she was sixty-one. Her activities were seldom spontaneous: she kept the two rooms immaculate, smoked an occasional cigarette, prepared her own meals and tended a canary.

Then she met Miriam. It was snowing that night. Mrs. Miller had finished drying the supper dishes and was thumbing through an afternoon paper when she saw an advertisement of a picture playing at a neighborhood theater. The title sounded good, so she struggled into her beaver coat, laced her galoshes and left the apartment, leaving one light burning in the foyer: she found nothing more disturbing than a sensation of darkness.

The snow was fine, falling gently, not yet making an impression on the pavement. The wind from the river cut only at street crossings. Mrs. Miller hurried, her head bowed, oblivious as a mole burrowing a blind path. She stopped at a drugstore and bought a package of peppermints.

A long line stretched in front of the box office; she took her place at the end. There would be (a tired voice groaned) a short wait for all seats. Mrs. Miller rummaged in her leather handbag till she collected exactly the correct change for admission. The line seemed to be taking its own time and, looking around for some distraction, she suddenly became conscious of a little girl standing under the edge of the marquee.

Her hair was the longest and strangest Mrs. Miller had ever seen: absolutely silver-white, like an albino's. It flowed waist-length in smooth, loose lines. She was thin and fragilely constructed. There was a simple, special elegance in the way she stood with her thumbs in the pockets of a tailored plum-velvet coat.

Mrs. Miller felt oddly excited, and when the little girl glanced toward her, she smiled warmly. The little girl walked over and said, "Would you care to do me a favor?"

"I'd be glad to, if I can," said Mrs. Miller.

"Oh, it's quite easy. I merely want you to buy a ticket for me; they won't let me in otherwise. Here, I have the money." And gracefully she handed Mrs. Miller two dimes and a nickel.

They went over to the theater together. An usherette directed them to a lounge; in twenty minutes the picture would be over.

"I feel just like a genuine criminal," said Mrs. Miller gaily, as she sat down. "I mean, that sort of thing's against the law, isn't it? I do hope I haven't done the wrong thing. Your mother knows where you are, dear? I mean she does, doesn't she?"

The little girl said nothing. She unbuttoned her coat and folded it across her lap. Her dress underneath was prim and dark blue. A gold chain dangled about her neck, and her fingers, sensitive and musical-looking, toyed with it. Examining her more attentively, Mrs. Miller decided the truly distinctive feature was not her hair, but her eyes; they were hazel, steady, lacking any child-like quality whatsoever and, because of their size, seemed to consume her small face.

Mrs. Miller offered a peppermint. "What's your name, dear?"

"Miriam," she said, as though, in some curious way, it were information already familiar.

"Why, isn't that funny—my name's Miriam, too. And it's not a terribly common name either. Now, don't tell me your last name's Miller!"

"Just Miriam."

"But isn't that funny?"

"Moderately," said Miriam, and rolled the peppermint on her tongue.

Mrs. Miller flushed and shifted uncomfortably. "You have such a large vocabulary for such a little girl."

"Do I?"

"Well, yes," said Mrs. Miller, hastily changing the topic to: "Do you like the movies?"

"I really wouldn't know," said Miriam. "I've never been before."

Women began filling the lounge; the rumble of the newsreel bombs exploded in the distance. Mrs. Miller rose, tucking her purse under her arm. "I guess I'd better be running now if I want to get a seat," she said. "It was nice to have met you."

Miriam nodded ever so slightly.

It snowed all week. Wheels and footsteps moved soundlessly on the street, as if the business of living continued secretly behind a pale but impenetrable curtain. In the falling quiet there was no sky or earth, only snow lifting in the wind, frosting the window glass, chilling the rooms, deadening and hushing the city. At all hours it was necessary to keep a lamp lighted, and Mrs. Miller lost track of the days: Friday was no different from Saturday and on Sunday she went to the grocery: closed, of course.

That evening she scrambled eggs and fixed a bowl of tomato soup. Then, after putting on a flannel robe and cold-creaming her face, she propped herself up in bed with a hot-water bottle under her feet. She was reading the *Times* when the doorbell rang. At first she thought it must be a mistake and whoever it was would go away. But it rang and rang and settled to a persistent buzz. She looked at the clock: a little after eleven; it did not seem possible, she was always asleep by ten.

Climbing out of bed, she trotted barefoot across the living room. "I'm coming, please be patient." The latch was caught; she turned it this way and that way and the bell never paused an instant. "Stop it," she cried. The bolt gave way and she opened the door an inch. "What in heaven's name?"

"Hello," said Miriam.

"Oh . . . why, hello," said Mrs. Miller, stepping hesitantly into the hall. "You're that little girl."

"I thought you'd never answer, but I kept my finger on the button; I knew you were home. Aren't you glad to see me?"

Mrs. Miller did not know what to say. Miriam, she saw, wore the same plum-velvet coat and now she had also a beret to match; her white hair was braided in two shining plaits and looped at the ends with enormous white ribbons.

"Since I've waited so long, you could at least let me in," she said.

"It's awfully late. . . ."

Miriam regarded her blankly. "What difference does that make? Let me in. It's cold out here and I have on a silk dress." Then, with a gentle gesture, she urged Mrs. Miller aside and passed into the apartment.

She dropped her coat and beret on a chair. She was indeed wearing a silk dress. White silk. White silk in February. The skirt was beautifully pleated and the sleeves long; it made a faint rustle as she strolled about the room. "I like your place," she said. "I like the rug, blue's my favorite color." She touched a paper rose in a vase on the coffee table. "Imitation," she commented wanly. "How sad. Aren't imitations sad?" She seated herself on the sofa, daintily spreading her skirt.

"What do you want?" asked Mrs. Miller.

"Sit down," said Miriam. "It makes me nervous to see people stand."

Mrs. Miller sank to a hassock. "What do you want?" she repeated.

"You know, I don't think you're glad I came."

For a second time Mrs. Miller was without an answer; her hand motioned vaguely. Miriam giggled and pressed back on a mound of chintz pillows. Mrs. Miller observed that the girl was less pale than she remembered; her cheeks were flushed.

"How did you know where I lived?"

Miriam frowned. "That's no question at all. What's your name? What's mine?"

"But I'm not listed in the phone book."

"Oh, let's talk about something else."

Mrs. Miller said, "Your mother must be insane to let a child like you wander around at all hours of the night—and in such ridiculous clothes. She must be out of her mind."

Miriam got up and moved to a corner where a covered birdcage hung from a ceiling chain. She peeked beneath the cover. "It's a canary," she said. "Would you mind if I woke him? I'd like to hear him sing."

"Leave Tommy alone," said Mrs. Miller anxiously. "Don't you dare wake him."

"Certainly," said Miriam. "But I don't see why I can't hear him sing." And then, "Have you anything to eat? I'm starving! Even milk and a jam sandwich would be fine."

"Look," said Mrs. Miller, arising from the hassock, "look—if I make some nice sandwiches will you be a good child and run along home? It's past midnight, I'm sure."

"It's snowing," reproached Miriam. "And cold and dark."

"Well, you shouldn't have come here to begin with," said Mrs. Miller, struggling to control her voice. "I can't help the weather. If you want anything to eat, you'll have to promise to leave."

Miriam brushed a braid against her cheek. Her eyes were thoughtful, as if weighing the proposition. She turned toward the birdcage. "Very well," she said, "I promise."

How old is she? Ten? Eleven? Mrs. Miller, in the kitchen, unsealed a jar of strawberry preserves and cut four slices of bread. She poured a glass of milk and paused to light a cigarette. *And why has she come?* Her hand shook as she held the match, fascinated, till it burned her finger. The canary was singing; singing as he did in the morning and at no other time. "Miriam," she called, "Miriam, I told you not to disturb Tommy." There was no answer. She called again; all she heard was the canary. She inhaled the cigarette and discovered she had lighted the cork-tip end and—oh, really, she mustn't lose her temper.

She carried the food in on a tray and set it on the coffee table. She saw first that the birdcage still wore its night cover. And Tommy was singing. It gave her a queer sensation. And no one was in the room. Mrs. Miller went through an alcove leading to her bedroom; at the door she caught her breath.

"What are you doing?" she asked.

Miriam glanced up and in her eyes there was a look that was not ordinary. She was standing by the bureau, a jewel case opened before her. For a minute she studied Mrs. Miller, forcing their eyes to meet, and she smiled. "There's nothing good here," she said. "But I like this." Her hand held a cameo brooch. "It's charming."

"Suppose—perhaps you'd better put it back," said Mrs. Miller, feeling suddenly the need of some support. She leaned against the door frame; her head was unbearably heavy; a pressure weighted the rhythm of her heartbeat. The light seemed to flutter defectively. "Please, child—a gift from my husband . . ."

"But it's beautiful and I want it," said Miriam. *"Give it to me."*

As she stood, striving to shape a sentence which would somehow save the brooch, it came to Mrs. Miller there was no one to whom she might turn; she was alone; a fact that had not been among her thoughts for a long time. Its sheer emphasis was stunning. But here in her own room in the hushed snow-city were evidences she could not ignore or, she knew with startling clarity, resist.

Miriam ate ravenously, and when the sandwiches and milk were gone, her fingers made cobweb movements over the plate, gathering crumbs. The cameo gleamed on her blouse, the blond profile like a trick reflection of its wearer. "That was very nice," she sighed, "though now an almond cake or a cherry would be ideal. Sweets are lovely, don't you think?"

Mrs. Miller was perched precariously on the hassock, smoking a cigarette. Her hairnet had slipped lopsided and loose strands straggled down her face. Her eyes were stupidly concentrated on nothing and her cheeks were mottled in red patches, as though a fierce slap had left permanent marks.

"Is there a candy—a cake?"

Mrs. Miller tapped ash on the rug. Her head swayed slightly as she tried to focus her eyes. "You promised to leave if I made the sandwiches," she said.

"Dear me, did I?"

"It was a promise and I'm tired and I don't feel well at all."

"Mustn't fret," said Miriam. "I'm only teasing."

She picked up her coat, slung it over her arm, and arranged her beret in front of a mirror. Presently she bent close to Mrs. Miller and whispered, "Kiss me good night."

"Please—I'd rather not," said Mrs. Miller.

Miriam lifted a shoulder, arched an eyebrow. "As you like," she said, and went directly to the coffee table, seized the vase containing the paper roses, carried it to where the hard surface of the floor lay bare, and hurled it downward. Glass sprayed in all directions and she stamped her foot on the bouquet.

Then slowly she walked to the door, but before closing it, she looked back at Mrs. Miller with a slyly innocent curiosity.

Mrs. Miller spent the next day in bed, rising once to feed the canary and drink a cup of tea; she took her temperature and had none, yet her dreams were feverishly agitated; their unbalanced mood lingered even as she lay staring wide-eyed at the ceiling. One dream threaded through the others like an elusively mysterious theme in a complicated symphony, and the scenes it depicted were sharply outlined, as though sketched by a hand of gifted intensity: a small girl, wearing a bridal gown and a wreath of leaves, led a gray procession down a mountain path, and among them there was unusual silence till a woman at the rear asked, "Where is she taking us?" "No one knows," said an old man marching in front. "But isn't she pretty?" volunteered a third voice. "Isn't she like a frost flower . . . so shining and white?"

Tuesday morning she woke up feeling better; harsh slats of sunlight, slant-ing through Venetian blinds, shed a disrupting light on her unwholesome fancies. She opened the window to discover a thawed, mild-as-spring day; a sweep of clean new clouds crumpled against a vastly blue, out-of-season sky; and across the low line of rooftops she could see the river and smoke curving from tugboat stacks in a warm wind. A great silver truck plowed the snow-banked street, its machine sound humming on the air.

After straightening the apartment, she went to the grocer's, cashed a check and continued to Schrafft's, where she ate breakfast and chatted happily with the waitress. Oh, it was a wonderful day—more like a holiday—and it would be so foolish to go home.

She boarded a Lexington Avenue bus and rode up to Eighty-sixth Street; it was here that she had decided to do a little shopping.

She had no idea what she wanted or needed, but she idled along, intent only upon the passers-by, brisk and preoccupied, who gave her a disturbing sense of separateness.

It was while waiting at the corner of Third Avenue that she saw the man: an old man, bowlegged and stooped under an armload of bulging packages; he wore a shabby brown coat and a checkered cap. Suddenly she realized they were exchanging a smile: there was nothing friendly about this smile, it was merely two cold flickers of recognition. But she was certain she had never seen him before.

He was standing next to an El[1] pillar, and as she crossed the street he turned and followed. He kept quite close; from the corner of her eye she watched his reflection wavering on the shopwindows.

Then in the middle of the block she stopped and faced him. He stopped also and cocked his head, grinning. But what could she say? Do? Here, in broad daylight, on Eighty-sixth Street? It was useless and, despising her own help-lessness, she quickened her steps.

Now Second Avenue is a dismal street, made from scraps and ends; part cobblestone, part asphalt, part cement; and its atmosphere of desertion is permanent. Mrs. Miller walked five blocks without meeting anyone, and all the while the steady crunch of his footfalls in the snow stayed near. And when she came to a florist's shop, the sound was still with her. She hurried inside and watched through the glass door as the old man passed; he kept his eyes straight ahead and didn't slow his pace, but he did one strange, telling thing: he tipped his cap.

"Six white ones, did you say?" asked the florist. "Yes," she told him, "white roses." From there she went to a glassware store and selected a vase, presum-ably a replacement for the one Miriam had broken, though the price was intolerable and the vase itself (she thought) grotesquely vulgar. But a series of unaccountable purchases had begun, as if by prearranged plan: a plan of which she had not the least knowledge or control.

She bought a bag of glazed cherries, and at a place called the Knickerbocker Bakery she paid forty cents for six almond cakes.

1. Elevated railroad.

Within the last hour the weather had turned cold again; like blurred lenses, winter clouds cast a shade over the sun, and the skeleton of an early dusk colored the sky; a damp mist mixed with the wind and the voices of a few children who romped high on mountains of gutter snow seemed lonely and cheerless. Soon the first flake fell, and when Mrs. Miller reached the brownstone house, snow was falling in a swift screen and foot tracks vanished as they were printed.

The white roses were arranged decoratively in the vase. The glazed cherries shone on a ceramic plate. The almond cakes, dusted with sugar, awaited a hand. The canary fluttered on its swing and picked at a bar of seed.

At precisely five the doorbell rang. Mrs. Miller *knew* who it was. The hem of her housecoat trailed as she crossed the floor. "Is that you?" she called.

"Naturally," said Miriam, the word resounding shrilly from the hall. "Open this door."

"Go away," said Mrs. Miller.

"Please hurry . . . I have a heavy package."

"Go away," said Mrs. Miller. She returned to the living room, lighted a cigarette, sat down and calmly listened to the buzzer; on and on and on. "You might as well leave. I have no intention of letting you in."

Shortly the bell stopped. For possibly ten minutes Mrs. Miller did not move. Then, hearing no sound, she concluded Miriam had gone. She tiptoed to the door and opened it a sliver; Miriam was half-reclining atop a cardboard box with a beautiful French doll cradled in her arms.

"Really, I thought you were never coming," she said peevishly. "Here, help me get this in, it's awfully heavy."

It was not spell-like compulsion that Mrs. Miller felt, but rather a curious passivity; she brought in the box, Miriam, the doll. Miriam curled up on the sofa, not troubling to remove her coat or beret, and watched disinterestedly as Mrs. Miller dropped the box and stood trembling, trying to catch her breath.

"Thank you," she said. In the daylight she looked pinched and drawn, her hair less luminous. The French doll she was loving wore an exquisite powdered wig and its idiot glass eyes sought solace in Miriam's. "I have a surprise," she continued. "Look into my box."

Kneeling, Mrs. Miller parted the flaps and lifted out another doll; then a blue dress which she recalled as the one Miriam had worn that first night at the theater; and of the remainder she said, "It's all clothes. Why?"

"Because I've come to live with you," said Miriam, twisting a cherry stem. "Wasn't it nice of you to buy me the cherries . . . ?"

"But you can't! For God's sake go away—go away and leave me alone!"

". . . and the roses and the almond cakes? How really wonderfully generous. You know, these cherries are delicious. The last place I lived was with an old man; he was terribly poor and we never had good things to eat. But I think I'll be happy here." She paused to snuggle her doll closer. "Now, if you'll just show me where to put my things . . ."

Mrs. Miller's face dissolved into a mask of ugly red lines; she began to cry, and it was an unnatural, tearless sort of weeping, as though, not having wept for a long time, she had forgotten how. Carefully she edged backward till she touched the door.

She fumbled through the hall and down the stairs to a landing below. She pounded frantically on the door of the first apartment she came to; a short, redheaded man answered and she pushed past him. "Say, what the hell is this?" he said. "Anything wrong, lover?" asked a young woman who appeared from the kitchen, drying her hands. And it was to her that Mrs. Miller turned.

"Listen," she cried, "I'm ashamed behaving this way but—well, I'm Mrs. H. T. Miller and I live upstairs and . . ." She pressed her hands over her face. "It sounds so absurd. . . ."

The woman guided her to a chair, while the man excitedly rattled pocket change. "Yeah?"

"I live upstairs and there's a little girl visiting me, and I suppose that I'm afraid of her. She won't leave and I can't make her and—she's going to do something terrible. She's already stolen my cameo, but she's about to do something worse—something terrible!"

The man asked, "Is she a relative, huh?"

Mrs. Miller shook her head. "I don't know who she is. Her name's Miriam, but I don't know for certain who she is."

"You gotta calm down, honey," said the woman, stroking Mrs. Miller's arm. "Harry here'll tend to this kid. Go on, lover." And Mrs. Miller said, "The door's open—5A."

After the man left, the woman brought a towel and bathed Mrs. Miller's face. "You're very kind," Mrs. Miller said. "I'm sorry to act like such a fool, only this wicked child . . ."

"Sure, honey," consoled the woman. "Now, you better take it easy."

Mrs. Miller rested her head in the crook of her arm; she was quiet enough to be asleep. The woman turned a radio dial; a piano and a husky voice filled the silence and the woman, tapping her foot, kept excellent time. "Maybe we oughta go up too," she said.

"I don't want to see her again. I don't want to be anywhere near her."

"Uh huh, but what you shoulda done, you shoulda called a cop."

Presently they heard the man on the stairs. He strode into the room frowning and scratching the back of his neck. "Nobody there," he said, honestly embarrassed. "She musta beat it."

"Harry, you're a jerk," announced the woman. "We been sitting here the whole time and we woulda seen . . ." she stopped abruptly, for the man's glance was sharp.

"I looked all over," he said, "and there just ain't nobody there. Nobody, understand?"

"Tell me," said Mrs. Miller, rising, "tell me, did you see a large box? Or a doll?"

"No, ma'am, I didn't."

And the woman, as if delivering a verdict, said, "Well, for cryinout-loud. . . ."

Mrs. Miller entered her apartment softly; she walked to the center of the room and stood quite still. No, in a sense it had not changed: the roses, the cakes, and the cherries were in place. But this was an empty room, emptier than if the furnishings and familiars were not present, lifeless and petrified as a funeral parlor. The sofa loomed before her with a new strangeness: its vacancy had a meaning that would have been less penetrating and terrible had Miriam been curled on it. She gazed fixedly at the space where she remembered setting the box and, for a moment, the hassock spun desperately. And she looked through the window; surely the river was real, surely snow was falling—but then, one could not be certain witness to anything: Miriam, so vividly there—and yet, where was she? Where, where?

As though moving in a dream, she sank to a chair. The room was losing shape; it was dark and getting darker and there was nothing to be done about it; she could not lift her hand to light a lamp.

Suddenly, closing her eyes, she felt an upward surge, like a diver emerging from some deeper, greener depth. In times of terror or immense distress, there are moments when the mind waits, as though for a revelation, while a skein of calm is woven over thought; it is like a sleep, or a supernatural trance; and during this lull one is aware of a force of quiet reasoning: well, what if she had never really known a girl named Miriam? that she had been foolishly frightened on the street? In the end, like everything else, it was of no importance. For the only thing she had lost to Miriam was her identity, but now she knew she had found again the person who lived in this room, who cooked her own meals, who owned a canary, who was someone she could trust and believe in: Mrs. H. T. Miller.

Listening in contentment, she became aware of a double sound: a bureau drawer opening and closing; she seemed to hear it long after completion—opening and closing. Then gradually, the harshness of it was replaced by the murmur of a silk dress and this, delicately faint, was moving nearer and swelling in intensity till the walls trembled with the vibration and the room was caving under a wave of whispers. Mrs. Miller stiffened and opened her eyes to a dull, direct stare.

"Hello," said Miriam.

1945

RAYMOND CARVER
1938–1988

Carver was born in Clatskanie, Oregon, and attended Humboldt State University in California before going on to graduate work at the University of Iowa. For several years he taught writing at Syracuse University. In the late 1970s his poetry and fiction, much of it describing working-class life in the Pacific Northwest, marked him as one of the more noteworthy talents of his generation. Carver's spare, direct "minimalist" style continues to spawn imitators decades after his death from lung cancer at the age of 50. His stories are collected in *Will You Please Be Quiet, Please?* (1978), *What We Talk about When We Talk about Love* (1981), *Cathedral* (1983), and *Where I'm Calling From: New and Selected Stories* (1988).

The Student's Wife

He had been reading to her from Rilke,[1] a poet he admired, when she fell asleep with her head on his pillow. He liked reading aloud, and he read well—a confident sonorous voice, now pitched low and somber, now rising, now thrilling. He never looked away from the page when he read and stopped only to reach to the nightstand for a cigarette. It was a rich voice that spilled her into a dream of caravans just setting out from walled cities and bearded men in robes. She had listened to him for a few minutes, then she had closed her eyes and drifted off.

He went on reading aloud. The children had been asleep for hours, and outside a car rubbered by now and then on the wet pavement. After a while he put down the book and turned in the bed to reach for the lamp. She opened her eyes suddenly, as if frightened, and blinked two or three times. Her eyelids looked oddly dark and fleshy to him as they flicked up and down over her fixed glassy eyes. He stared at her.

"Are you dreaming?" he asked.

She nodded and brought her hand up and touched her fingers to the plastic curlers at either side of her head. Tomorrow would be Friday, her day for all the four-to-seven-year-olds in the Woodlawn Apartments. He kept looking at her, leaning on his elbow, at the same time trying to straighten the spread with his free hand. She had a smooth-skinned face with prominent cheekbones; the

---

1. Rainer Maria Rilke (1875–1926), Bohemian-Austrian poet.

cheekbones, she sometimes insisted to friends, were from her father, who had been one-quarter Nez Perce.[2]

Then: "Make me a little sandwich of something, Mike. With butter and lettuce and salt on the bread."

He did nothing and he said nothing because he wanted to go to sleep. But when he opened his eyes she was still awake, watching him.

"Can't you go to sleep, Nan?" he said, very solemnly. "It's late."

"I'd like something to eat first," she said. "My legs and arms hurt for some reason, and I'm hungry."

He groaned extravagantly as he rolled out of bed.

He fixed her the sandwich and brought it in on a saucer. She sat up in bed and smiled when he came into the bedroom, then slipped a pillow behind her back as she took the saucer. He thought she looked like a hospital patient in her white nightgown.

"What a funny little dream I had."

"What were you dreaming?" he said, getting into bed and turning over onto his side away from her. He stared at the nightstand waiting. Then he closed his eyes slowly.

"Do you really want to hear it?" she said.

"Sure," he said.

She settled back comfortably on the pillow and picked a crumb from her lip.

"Well. It seemed like a real long drawn-out kind of dream, you know, with all kinds of relationships going on, but I can't remember everything now. It was all very clear when I woke up, but it's beginning to fade now. How long have I been asleep, Mike? It doesn't really matter, I guess. Anyway, I think it was that we were staying someplace overnight. I don't know where the kids were, but it was just the two of us at some little hotel or something. It was on some lake that wasn't familiar. There was another, older, couple there and they wanted to take us for a ride in their motorboat." She laughed, remembering, and leaned forward off the pillow. "The next thing I recall is we were down at the boat landing. Only the way it turned out, they had just one seat in the boat, a kind of bench up in the front, and it was only big enough for three. You and I started arguing about who was going to sacrifice and sit all cooped up in the back. You said you were, and I said I was. But I finally squeezed in the back of the boat. It was so narrow it hurt my legs, and I was afraid the water was going to come in over the sides. Then I woke up."

"That's some dream," he managed to say and felt drowsily that he should say something more. "You remember Bonnie Travis? Fred Travis' wife? She used to have *color* dreams, she said."

She looked at the sandwich in her hand and took a bite. When she had swallowed, she ran her tongue in behind her lips and balanced the saucer on her lap as she reached behind and plumped up the pillow. Then she smiled and leaned back against the pillow again.

"Do you remember that time we stayed overnight on the Tilton River, Mike? When you caught that big fish the next morning?" She placed her hand on his shoulder. "Do you remember that?" she said.

---

2. Literally "Pierced Nose," French explorers' name for the Sahaptin Indians of the Pacific Northwest.

She did. After scarcely thinking about it these last years, it had begun coming back to her lately. It was a month or two after they'd married and gone away for a weekend. They had sat by a little campfire that night, a watermelon in the snow-cold river, and she'd fried Spam and eggs and canned beans for supper and pancakes and Spam and eggs in the same blackened pan the next morning. She had burned the pan both times she cooked, and they could never get the coffee to boil, but it was one of the best times they'd ever had. She remembered he had read to her that night as well: Elizabeth Browning and a few poems from the *Rubáiyát*.[3] They had had so many covers over them that she could hardly turn her feet under all the weight. The next morning he had hooked a big trout, and people stopped their cars on the road across the river to watch him play it in.

"Well? Do you remember or not?" she said, patting him on the shoulder. "Mike?"

"I remember," he said. He shifted a little on his side, opened his eyes. He did not remember very well, he thought. What he did remember was very carefully combed hair and loud half-baked ideas about life and art, and he did not want to remember that.

"That was a long time ago, Nan," he said.

"We'd just got out of high school. You hadn't started to college," she said.

He waited, and then he raised up onto his arm and turned his head to look at her over his shoulder. "You about finished with that sandwich, Nan?" She was still sitting up in the bed.

She nodded and gave him the saucer.

"I'll turn off the light," he said.

"If you want," she said.

Then he pulled down into the bed again and extended his foot until it touched against hers. He lay still for a minute and then tried to relax.

"Mike, you're not asleep, are you?"

"No," he said. "Nothing like that."

"Well, don't go to sleep before me," she said. "I don't want to be awake by myself."

He didn't answer, but he inched a little closer to her on his side. When she put her arm over him and planted her hand flat against his chest, he took her fingers and squeezed them lightly. But in moments his hand dropped away to the bed, and he sighed.

"Mike? Honey? I wish you'd rub my legs. My legs hurt," she said.

"God," he said softly. "I was sound asleep."

"Well, I wish you'd rub my legs and talk to me. My shoulders hurt, too. But my legs especially."

He turned over and began rubbing her legs, then fell asleep again with his hand on her hip.

"Mike?"

"What is it, Nan? Tell me what it *is*."

"I wish you'd rub me all over," she said, turning onto her back. "My legs and arms both hurt tonight." She raised her knees to make a tower with the covers.

---

3. Book-length poem by 11th-century Persian poet Omar Khayyam. Elizabeth (Barrett) Browning (1806–1861), English poet.

He opened his eyes briefly in the dark and then shut them. "Growing pains, huh?"

"Oh God, yes," she said, wiggling her toes, glad she had drawn him out. "When I was ten or eleven years old I was as big then as I am now. You should've seen me! I grew so fast in those days my legs and arms hurt me all the time. Didn't you?"

"Didn't I what?"

"Didn't you ever feel yourself growing?"

"Not that I remember," he said.

At last he raised up on his elbow, struck a match, and looked at the clock. He turned his pillow over to the cooler side and lay down again.

She said, "You're asleep, Mike. I wish you'd want to talk."

"All right," he said, not moving.

"Just hold me and get me off to sleep. I can't go to sleep," she said.

He turned over and put his arm over her shoulder as she turned onto her side to face the wall.

"Mike?"

He tapped his toes against her foot.

"Why don't you tell me all the things you like and the things you don't like."

"Don't know any right now," he said. "Tell me if you want," he said.

"If you promise to tell *me*. Is that a promise?"

He tapped her foot again.

"Well . . ." she said and turned onto her back, pleased. "I like good foods, steaks and hash-brown potatoes, things like that. I like good books and magazines, riding on trains at night, and those times I flew in an airplane." She stopped. "Of course none of this is in order of preference. I'd have to think about it if it was in the order of preference. But I like that, flying in airplanes. There's a moment as you leave the ground you feel whatever happens is all right." She put her leg across his ankle. "I like staying up late at night and then staying in bed the next morning. I wish we could do that all the time, not just once in a while. And I like sex. I like to be touched now and then when I'm not expecting it. I like going to movies and drinking beer with friends afterward. I like to have friends. I like Janice Hendricks very much. I'd like to go dancing at least once a week. I'd like to have nice clothes all the time. I'd like to be able to buy the kids nice clothes every time they need it without having to wait. Laurie needs a new little outfit right now for Easter. And I'd like to get Gary a little suit or something. He's old enough. I'd like you to have a new suit, too. You really need a new suit more than he does. And I'd like us to have a place of our own. I'd like to stop moving around every year, or every other year. Most of all," she said, "I'd like us both just to live a good honest life without having to worry about money and bills and things like that. You're asleep," she said.

"I'm not," he said.

"I can't think of anything else. You go now. Tell me what you'd like."

"I don't know. Lots of things," he mumbled.

"Well, tell me. We're just talking, aren't we?"

"I wish you'd leave me alone, Nan." He turned over to his side of the bed again and let his arm rest off the edge. She turned too and pressed against him.

"Mike?"

"Jesus," he said. Then: "All right. Let me stretch my legs a minu[ ]
wake up."

In a while she said, "Mike? Are you asleep?" She shook his shoulder[ ]
but there was no response. She lay there for a time huddled against his[ ]
trying to sleep. She lay quietly at first, without moving, crowded against [ ]
and taking only very small, very even breaths. But she could not sleep.

She tried not to listen to his breathing, but it began to make her uncomfortable. There was a sound coming from inside his nose when he breathed.
She tried to regulate her breathing so that she could breathe in and out at the
same rhythm he did. It was no use. The little sound in his nose made everything no use. There was a webby squeak in his chest too. She turned again
and nestled her bottom against his, stretched her arm over to the edge and
cautiously put her fingertips against the cold wall. The covers had pulled up
at the foot of the bed, and she could feel a draft when she moved her legs. She
heard two people coming up the stairs to the apartment next door. Someone
gave a throaty laugh before opening the door. Then she heard a chair drag on
the floor. She turned again. The toilet flushed next door, and then it flushed
again. Again she turned, onto her back this time, and tried to relax. She remembered an article she'd once read in a magazine: If all the bones and muscles
and joints in the body could join together in perfect relaxation, sleep would
almost certainly come. She took a long breath, closed her eyes, and lay perfectly still, arms straight along her sides. She tried to relax. She tried to imagine her legs suspended, bathed in something gauze-like. She turned onto her
stomach. She closed her eyes, then she opened them. She thought of the fingers of her hand lying curled on the sheet in front of her lips. She raised a finger
and lowered it to the sheet. She touched the wedding band on her ring finger
with her thumb. She turned onto her side and then onto her back again. And
then she began to feel afraid, and in one unreasoning moment of longing she
prayed to go to sleep.

Please, God, let me go to sleep.

She tried to sleep.

"Mike," she whispered.

There was no answer.

She heard one of the children turn over in the bed and bump against the
wall in the next room. She listened and listened but there was no other sound.
She laid her hand under her left breast and felt the beat of her heart rising
into her fingers. She turned onto her stomach and began to cry, her head off
the pillow, her mouth against the sheet. She cried. And then she climbed out
over the foot of the bed.

She washed her hands and face in the bathroom. She brushed her teeth.
She brushed her teeth and watched her face in the mirror. In the living room
she turned up the heat. Then she sat down at the kitchen table, drawing her
feet up underneath the nightgown. She cried again. She lit a cigarette from
the pack on the table. After a time she walked back to the bedroom and got
her robe.

She looked in on the children. She pulled the covers up over her son's shoulders. She went back to the living room and sat in the big chair. She paged
through a magazine and tried to read. She gazed at the photographs and then
she tried to read again. Now and then a car went by on the street outside and

ar passed she waited, listening. And then she looked
again. There was a stack of magazines in the rack by
d through them all.

light outside she got up. She walked to the window. The
hills was beginning to turn white. The trees and the row
ent houses across the street were beginning to take shape
he sky grew whiter, the light expanding rapidly up from
Except for the times she had been up with one or another of
which she did not count because she had never looked outside,
ried back to bed or to the kitchen), she had seen few sunrises in her
and those when she was little. She knew that none of them had been like
this. Not in pictures she had seen nor in any book she had read had she learned
a sunrise was so terrible as this.

She waited and then she moved over to the door and turned the lock and
stepped out onto the porch. She closed the robe at her throat. The air was wet
and cold. By stages things were becoming very visible. She let her eyes see everything until they fastened on the red winking light atop the radio tower atop
the opposite hill.

She went through the dim apartment, back into the bedroom. He was knotted up in the center of the bed, the covers bunched over his shoulders, his
head half under the pillow. He looked desperate in his heavy sleep, his arms
flung out across her side of the bed, his jaws clenched. As she looked, the
room grew very light and the pale sheets whitened grossly before her eyes.

She wet her lips with a sticking sound and got down on her knees. She put
her hands out on the bed.

"God," she said. "God, will you help us, God?" she said.

1976

Cathedral

This blind man, an old friend of my wife's, he was on his way to spend the
night. His wife had died. So he was visiting the dead wife's relatives in Connecticut. He called my wife from his in-laws'. Arrangements were made. He
would come by train, a five-hour trip, and my wife would meet him at the station. She hadn't seen him since she worked for him one summer in Seattle ten
years ago. But she and the blind man had kept in touch. They made tapes and
mailed them back and forth. I wasn't enthusiastic about his visit. He was no
one I knew. And his being blind bothered me. My idea of blindness came
from the movies. In the movies, the blind moved slowly and never laughed.
Sometimes they were led by seeing-eye dogs. A blind man in my house was
not something I looked forward to.

That summer in Seattle she had needed a job. She didn't have any money.
The man she was going to marry at the end of the summer was in officers'
training school. He didn't have any money, either. But she was in love with the
guy, and he was in love with her, etc. She'd seen something in the paper: HELP

WANTED—*Reading to Blind Man,* and a telephone number. She phoned and went over, was hired on the spot. She'd worked with this blind man all summer. She read stuff to him, case studies, reports, that sort of thing. She helped him organize his little office in the county social-service department. They'd become good friends, my wife and the blind man. How do I know these things? She told me. And she told me something else. On her last day in the office, the blind man asked if he could touch her face. She agreed to this. She told me he touched his fingers to every part of her face, her nose—even her neck! She never forgot it. She even tried to write a poem about it. She was always trying to write a poem. She wrote a poem or two every year, usually after something really important had happened to her.

When we first started going out together, she showed me the poem. In the poem, she recalled his fingers and the way they had moved around over her face. In the poem, she talked about what she had felt at the time, about what went through her mind when the blind man touched her nose and lips. I can remember I didn't think much of the poem. Of course, I didn't tell her that. Maybe I just don't understand poetry. I admit it's not the first thing I reach for when I pick up something to read.

Anyway, this man who'd first enjoyed her favors, the officer-to-be, he'd been her childhood sweetheart. So okay. I'm saying that at the end of the summer she let the blind man run his hands over her face, said goodbye to him, married her childhood etc., who was now a commissioned officer, and she moved away from Seattle. But they'd kept in touch, she and the blind man. She made the first contact after a year or so. She called him up one night from an Air Force base in Alabama. She wanted to talk. They talked. He asked her to send him a tape and tell him about her life. She did this. She sent the tape. On the tape, she told the blind man about her husband and about their life together in the military. She told the blind man she loved her husband but she didn't like it where they lived and she didn't like it that he was a part of the military-industrial thing. She told the blind man she'd written a poem about what it was like to be an Air Force officer's wife. The poem wasn't finished yet. She was still writing it. The blind man made a tape. He sent her the tape. She made a tape. This went on for years. My wife's officer was posted to one base and then another. She sent tapes from Moody AFB, McGuire, McConnell, and finally Travis, near Sacramento, where one night she got to feeling lonely and cut off from people she kept losing in that moving-around life. She got to feeling she couldn't go it another step. She went in and swallowed all the pills and capsules in the medicine chest and washed them down with a bottle of gin. Then she got into a hot bath and passed out.

But instead of dying, she got sick. She threw up. Her officer—why should he have a name? he was the childhood sweetheart, and what more does he want?—came home from somewhere, found her, and called the ambulance. In time, she put it all on a tape and sent the tape to the blind man. Over the years, she put all kinds of stuff on tapes and sent the tapes off lickety-split. Next to writing a poem every year, I think it was her chief means of recreation. On one tape, she told the blind man she'd decided to live away from her officer for a time. On another tape, she told him about her divorce. She and I began going out, and of course she told her blind man about it. She told him everything, or so it seemed to me. Once she asked me if I'd like to hear the latest tape from the blind man. This was a year ago. I was on the tape, she said. So I said okay, I'd listen to it. I got us drinks and we settled down in the living room. We made ready to listen. First she inserted the tape into the player and adjusted a couple of dials. Then she pushed a lever. The tape squeaked and someone began to talk in this loud voice. She lowered the volume. After a few minutes of harmless chitchat, I heard my own name in the mouth of this stranger, this blind man I didn't even know! And then this: "From all you've said about him, I can only conclude—" But we were interrupted, a knock at the door, something, and we didn't ever get back to the tape. Maybe it was just as well. I'd heard all I wanted to.

Now this same blind man was coming to sleep in my house.

"Maybe I could take him bowling," I said to my wife. She was at the draining board doing scalloped potatoes. She put down the knife she was using and turned around.

"If you love me," she said, "you can do this for me. If you don't love me, okay. But if you had a friend, any friend, and the friend came to visit, I'd make him feel comfortable." She wiped her hands with the dish towel.

"I don't have any blind friends," I said.

"You don't have *any* friends," she said. "Period. Besides," she said, "goddamn it, his wife's just died! Don't you understand that? The man's lost his wife!"

I didn't answer. She'd told me a little about the blind man's wife. Her name was Beulah. Beulah! That's a name for a colored woman.

"Was his wife a Negro?" I asked.

"Are you crazy?" my wife said. "Have you just flipped or something?" She picked up a potato. I saw it hit the floor, then roll under the stove. "What's wrong with you?" she said. "Are you drunk?"

"I'm just asking," I said.

Right then my wife filled me in with more detail than I cared to know. I made a drink and sat at the kitchen table to listen. Pieces of the story began to fall into place.

Beulah had gone to work for the blind man the summer after my wife had stopped working for him. Pretty soon Beulah and the blind man had themselves a church wedding. It was a little wedding—who'd want to go to such a wedding in the first place?—just the two of them, plus the minister and the minister's wife. But it was a church wedding just the same. It was what Beulah had wanted, he'd said. But even then Beulah must have been carrying the cancer in her glands. After they had been inseparable for eight years—my wife's word, *inseparable*—Beulah's health went into a rapid decline. She died in a Seattle hospital room, the blind man sitting beside the bed and holding on to her hand. They'd married, lived and worked together, slept together—had sex, sure—and then the blind man had to bury her. All this without his having ever seen what the goddamned woman looked like. It was beyond my understanding. Hearing this, I felt sorry for the blind man for a little bit. And then I found myself thinking what a pitiful life this woman must have led. Imagine a woman who could never see herself as she was seen in the eyes of her loved one. A woman who could go on day after day and never receive the smallest compliment from her beloved. A woman whose husband could never read the expression on her face, be it misery or something better. Someone who could wear makeup or not—what difference to him? She could, if she wanted, wear green eye-shadow around one eye, a straight pin in her nostril, yellow slacks and purple shoes, no matter. And then to slip off into death, the blind man's hand on her hand, his blind eyes streaming tears—I'm imagining now—her last thought maybe this: that he never even knew what she looked like, and she on an express to the grave. Robert was left with a small insurance policy and half of a twenty-peso Mexican coin. The other half of the coin went into the box with her. Pathetic.

So when the time rolled around, my wife went to the depot to pick him up. With nothing to do but wait—sure, I blamed him for that—I was having a drink and watching the TV when I heard the car pull into the drive. I got up from the sofa with my drink and went to the window to have a look.

I saw my wife laughing as she parked the car. I saw her get out of the car and shut the door. She was still wearing a smile. Just amazing. She went around to the other side of the car to where the blind man was already starting to get out. This blind man, feature this, he was wearing a full beard! A beard on a blind man! Too much, I say. The blind man reached into the back seat and dragged out a suitcase. My wife took his arm, shut the car door, and, talking all the way, moved him down the drive and then up the steps to the front porch. I turned off the TV. I finished my drink, rinsed the glass, dried my hands. Then I went to the door.

My wife said, "I want you to meet Robert. Robert, this is my husband. I've told you all about him." She was beaming. She had this blind man by his coat sleeve.

The blind man let go of his suitcase and up came his hand.

I took it. He squeezed hard, held my hand, and then he let it go.

"I feel like we've already met," he boomed.

"Likewise," I said. I didn't know what else to say. Then I said, "Welcome. I've heard a lot about you." We began to move then, a little group, from the porch into the living room, my wife guiding him by the arm. The blind man was carrying his suitcase in his other hand. My wife said things like, "To your left here, Robert. That's right. Now watch it, there's a chair. That's it. Sit down right here. This is the sofa. We just bought this sofa two weeks ago."

I started to say something about the old sofa. I'd liked that old sofa. But I didn't say anything. Then I wanted to say something else, small-talk, about the scenic ride along the Hudson. How going *to* New York, you should sit on the right-hand side of the train, and coming *from* New York, the left-hand side.

"Did you have a good train ride?" I said. "Which side of the train did you sit on, by the way?"

"What a question, which side!" my wife said. "What's it matter which side?" she said.

"I just asked," I said.

"Right side," the blind man said. "I hadn't been on a train in nearly forty years. Not since I was a kid. With my folks. That's been a long time. I'd nearly forgotten the sensation. I have winter in my beard now," he said. "So I've been told, anyway. Do I look distinguished, my dear?" the blind man said to my wife.

"You look distinguished, Robert," she said. "Robert," she said. "Robert, it's just so good to see you."

My wife finally took her eyes off the blind man and looked at me. I had the feeling she didn't like what she saw. I shrugged.

I've never met, or personally known, anyone who was blind. This blind man was late forties, a heavy-set, balding man with stooped shoulders, as if he carried a great weight there. He wore brown slacks, brown shoes, a light-brown shirt, a tie, a sports coat. Spiffy. He also had this full beard. But he didn't use a cane and he didn't wear dark glasses. I'd always thought dark glasses were a must for the blind. Fact was, I wished he had a pair. At first glance, his eyes looked like anyone else's eyes. But if you looked close, there was something different about them. Too much white in the iris, for one thing, and the pupils seemed to move around in the sockets without his knowing it or being able to stop it. Creepy. As I stared at his face, I saw the left pupil turn in toward his nose while the other made an effort to keep in one place. But it was only an effort, for that eye was on the roam without his knowing it or wanting it to be.

I said, "Let me get you a drink. What's your pleasure? We have a little of everything. It's one of our pastimes."

"Bub, I'm a Scotch man myself," he said fast enough in this big voice.

"Right," I said. Bub! "Sure you are. I knew it."

He let his fingers touch his suitcase, which was sitting alongside the sofa. He was taking his bearings. I didn't blame him for that.

"I'll move that up to your room," my wife said.

"No, that's fine," the blind man said loudly. "It can go up when I go up."

"A little water with the Scotch?" I said.

"Very little," he said.

"I knew it," I said.

He said, "Just a tad. The Irish actor, Barry Fitzgerald? I'm like that fellow. When I drink water, Fitzgerald said, I drink water. When I drink whiskey, I drink whiskey." My wife laughed. The blind man brought his hand up under his beard. He lifted his beard slowly and let it drop.

I did the drinks, three big glasses of Scotch with a splash of water in each. Then we made ourselves comfortable and talked about Robert's travels. First the long flight from the West Coast to Connecticut, we covered that. Then from Connecticut up here by train. We had another drink concerning that leg of the trip.

I remembered having read somewhere that the blind didn't smoke because, as speculation had it, they couldn't see the smoke they exhaled. I thought I knew that much and that much only about blind people. But this blind man smoked his cigarette down to the nubbin and then lit another one. This blind man filled his ashtray and my wife emptied it.

When we sat down at the table for dinner, we had another drink. My wife heaped Robert's plate with cube steak, scalloped potatoes, green beans. I buttered him up two slices of bread. I said, "Here's bread and butter for you." I swallowed some of my drink. "Now let us pray," I said, and the blind man lowered his head. My wife looked at me, her mouth agape. "Pray the phone won't ring and the food doesn't get cold," I said.

We dug in. We ate everything there was to eat on the table. We ate like there was no tomorrow. We didn't talk. We ate. We scarfed. We grazed that table. We were into serious eating. The blind man had right away located his foods, he knew just where everything was on his plate. I watched with admiration as he used his knife and fork on the meat. He'd cut two pieces of meat, fork the meat into his mouth, and then go all out for the scalloped potatoes, the beans next, and then he'd tear off a hunk of buttered bread and eat that. He'd follow this up with a big drink of milk. It didn't seem to bother him to use his fingers once in a while, either.

We finished everything, including half a strawberry pie. For a few moments, we sat as if stunned. Sweat beaded on our faces. Finally, we got up from the table and left the dirty plates. We didn't look back. We took ourselves into the living room and sank into our places again. Robert and my wife sat on the sofa. I took the big chair. We had us two or three more drinks while they talked about the major things that had come to pass for them in the past ten years. For the most part, I just listened. Now and then I joined in. I didn't want him to think I'd left the room, and I didn't want her to think I was feeling left out. They talked of things that had happened to them—to them!—these past ten years. I waited in vain to hear my name on my wife's sweet lips: "And then my dear husband came into my life"—something like that. But I heard nothing of the sort. More talk of Robert. Robert had done a little of everything, it seemed, a regular blind jack-of-all-trades. But most recently he and his wife had had an Amway distributorship, from which, I gathered, they'd earned their living, such as it was. The blind man was also a ham radio operator. He talked in his loud voice about conversations he'd had with fellow operators in Guam, in the Philippines, in Alaska, and even in Tahiti. He said he'd have a lot of friends there if he ever wanted to go visit those places. From time to time, he'd turn his blind face toward me, put his hand under his beard, ask me something. How long had I been in my present position? (Three years.) Did I like my work? (I didn't.) Was I going to stay with it? (What were the options?) Finally, when I thought he was beginning to run down, I got up and turned on the TV.

My wife looked at me with irritation. She was heading toward a boil. Then she looked at the blind man and said, "Robert, do you have a TV?"

The blind man said, "My dear, I have two TVs. I have a color set and a black-and-white thing, an old relic. It's funny, but if I turn the TV on, and I'm always turning it on, I turn on the color set. It's funny, don't you think?"

I didn't know what to say to that. I had absolutely nothing to say to that. No opinion. So I watched the news program and tried to listen to what the announcer was saying.

"This is a color TV," the blind man said. "Don't ask me how, but I can tell."

"We traded up a while ago," I said.

The blind man had another taste of his drink. He lifted his beard, sniffed it, and let it fall. He leaned forward on the sofa. He positioned his ashtray on the coffee table, then put the lighter to his cigarette. He leaned back on the sofa and crossed his legs at the ankles.

My wife covered her mouth, and then she yawned. She stretched. She said, "I think I'll go upstairs and put on my robe. I think I'll change into something else. Robert, you make yourself comfortable," she said.

"I'm comfortable," the blind man said.

"I want you to feel comfortable in this house," she said.

"I am comfortable," the blind man said.

After she'd left the room, he and I listened to the weather report and then to the sports roundup. By that time, she'd been gone so long I didn't know if she was going to come back. I thought she might have gone to bed. I wished she'd come back downstairs. I didn't want to be left alone with a blind man. I asked him if he wanted to smoke some dope with me. I said I'd just rolled a number. I hadn't, but I planned to do so in about two shakes.

"I'll try some with you," he said.

"Damn right," I said. "That's the stuff."

I got our drinks and sat down on the sofa with him. Then I rolled us two fat numbers. I lit one and passed it. I brought it to his fingers. He took it and inhaled.

"Hold it as long as you can," I said. I could tell he didn't know the first thing.

My wife came back downstairs wearing her pink robe and her pink slippers.

"What do I smell?" she said.

"We thought we'd have us some cannabis," I said.

My wife gave me a savage look. Then she looked at the blind man and said, "Robert, I didn't know you smoked."

He said, "I do now, my dear. There's a first time for everything. But I don't feel anything yet."

"This stuff is pretty mellow," I said. "This stuff is mild. It's dope you can reason with," I said. "It doesn't mess you up."

"Not much it doesn't, bub," he said, and laughed.

My wife sat on the sofa between the blind man and me. I passed her the number. She took it and toked and then passed it back to me. "Which way is this going?" she said. Then she said, "I shouldn't be smoking this. I can hardly keep my eyes open as it is. That dinner did me in. I shouldn't have eaten so much."

"It was the strawberry pie," the blind man said. "That's what did it," he said, and he laughed his big laugh. Then he shook his head.

"There's more strawberry pie," I said.

"Do you want some more, Robert?" my wife said.

"Maybe in a little while," he said.

We gave our attention to the TV. My wife yawned again. She said, "Your bed is made up when you feel like going to bed, Robert. I know you must have had a long day. When you're ready to go to bed, say so." She pulled his arm. "Robert?"

He came to and said, "I've had a real nice time. This beats tapes, doesn't it?"

I said, "Coming at you," and I put the number between his fingers. He inhaled, held the smoke, and then let it go. It was like he'd been doing it since he was nine years old.

"Thanks, bub," he said. "But I think this is all for me. I think I'm beginning to feel it," he said. He held the burning roach out for my wife.

"Same here," she said. "Ditto. Me, too." She took the roach and passed it to me. "I may just sit here for a while between you two guys with my eyes closed. But don't let me bother you, okay? Either one of you. If it bothers you, say so. Otherwise, I may just sit here with my eyes closed until you're ready to go to bed," she said. "Your bed's made up, Robert, when you're ready. It's right next to our room at the top of the stairs. We'll show you up when you're ready. You wake me up now, you guys, if I fall asleep." She said that and then she closed her eyes and went to sleep.

The news program ended. I got up and changed the channel. I sat back down on the sofa. I wished my wife hadn't pooped out. Her head lay across the back of the sofa, her mouth open. She'd turned so that her robe had slipped away from her legs, exposing a juicy thigh. I reached to draw her robe back over her, and it was then that I glanced at the blind man. What the hell! I flipped the robe open again.

"You say when you want some strawberry pie," I said.

"I will," he said.

I said, "Are you tired? Do you want me to take you up to your bed? Are you ready to hit the hay?"

"Not yet," he said. "No, I'll stay up with you, bub. If that's all right. I'll stay up until you're ready to turn in. We haven't had a chance to talk. Know what I mean? I feel like me and her monopolized the evening." He lifted his beard and he let it fall. He picked up his cigarettes and lighter.

"That's all right," I said. Then I said, "I'm glad for the company."

And I guess I was. Every night I smoked dope and stayed up as long as I could before I fell asleep. My wife and I hardly ever went to bed at the same time. When I did go to sleep, I had these dreams. Sometimes I'd wake up from one of them, my heart going crazy.

Something about the church and the Middle Ages was on the TV. Not your run-of-the-mill TV fare. I wanted to watch something else. I turned to the other channels. But there was nothing on them, either. So I turned back to the first channel and apologized.

"Bub, it's all right," the blind man said. "It's fine with me. Whatever you want to watch is okay. I'm always learning something. Learning never ends. It won't hurt me to learn something tonight. I got ears," he said.

We didn't say anything for a time. He was leaning forward with his head turned at me, his right ear aimed in the direction of the set. Very disconcerting. Now and then his eyelids dropped and then they snapped open again. Now and then he put his fingers into his beard and tugged, like he was thinking about something he was hearing on the television.

On the screen, a group of men wearing cowls was being set upon and tormented by men dressed in skeleton costumes and men dressed as devils. The men dressed as devils wore devil masks, horns, and long tails. This pageant was part of a procession. The Englishman who was narrating the thing said it took place in Spain once a year. I tried to explain to the blind man what was happening.

"Skeletons," he said. "I know about skeletons," he said, and he nodded.

The TV showed this one cathedral. Then there was a long, slow look at another one. Finally, the picture switched to the famous one in Paris,[1] with its flying buttresses and its spires reaching up to the clouds. The camera pulled away to show the whole of the cathedral rising above the skyline.

There were times when the Englishman who was telling the thing would shut up, would simply let the camera move around over the cathedrals. Or else the camera would tour the countryside, men in fields walking behind oxen. I waited as long as I could. Then I felt I had to say something. I said, "They're showing the outside of this cathedral now. Gargoyles. Little statues carved to

---

1. Notre Dame de Paris, begun in 1163 and completed nearly two centuries later.

look like monsters. Now I guess they're in Italy. Yeah, they're in Italy. There's paintings on the walls of this one church."

"Are those fresco paintings, bub?" he asked, and he sipped from his drink.

I reached for my glass. But it was empty. I tried to remember what I could remember. "You're asking me are those frescoes?" I said. "That's a good question. I don't know."

The camera moved to a cathedral outside Lisbon. The differences in the Portuguese cathedral compared with the French and Italian were not that great. But they were there. Mostly the interior stuff. Then something occurred to me, and I said, "Something has occurred to me. Do you have any idea what a cathedral is? What they look like, that is? Do you follow me? If somebody says cathedral to you, do you have any notion what they're talking about? Do you know the difference between that and a Baptist church, say?"

He let the smoke dribble from his mouth. "I know they took hundreds of workers fifty or a hundred years to build," he said. "I just heard the man say that, of course. I know generations of the same families worked on a cathedral. I heard him say that, too. The men who began their life's work on them, they never lived to see the completion of their work. In that wise, bub, they're no different from the rest of us, right?" He laughed. Then his eyelids drooped again. His head nodded. He seemed to be snoozing. Maybe he was imagining himself in Portugal. The TV was showing another cathedral now. This one was in Germany. The Englishman's voice droned on. "Cathedrals," the blind man said. He sat up and rolled his head back and forth. "If you want the truth, bub, that's about all I know. What I just said. What I heard him say. But maybe you could describe one to me? I wish you'd do it. I'd like that. If you want to know, I really don't have a good idea."

I stared hard at the shot of the cathedral on the TV. How could I even begin to describe it? But say my life depended on it. Say my life was being threatened by an insane guy who said I had to do it or else.

I stared some more at the cathedral before the picture flipped off into the countryside. There was no use. I turned to the blind man and said, "To begin with, they're very tall." I was looking around the room for clues. "They reach way up. Up and up. Toward the sky. They're so big, some of them, they have to have these supports. To help hold them up, so to speak. These supports are called buttresses. They remind me of viaducts, for some reason. But maybe you don't know viaducts, either? Sometimes the cathedrals have devils and such carved into the front. Sometimes lords and ladies. Don't ask me why this is," I said.

He was nodding. The whole upper part of his body seemed to be moving back and forth.

"I'm not doing so good, am I?" I said.

He stopped nodding and leaned forward on the edge of the sofa. As he listened to me, he was running his fingers through his beard. I wasn't getting through to him, I could see that. But he waited for me to go on just the same. He nodded, like he was trying to encourage me. I tried to think what else to say. "They're really big," I said. "They're massive. They're built of stone. Marble, too, sometimes. In those olden days, when they built cathedrals, men wanted to be close to God. In those olden days, God was an important part of everyone's life. You could tell this from their cathedral-building. I'm sorry," I said, "but it looks like that's the best I can do for you. I'm just no good at it."

"That's all right, bub," the blind man said. "Hey, listen. I hope you don't mind my asking you. Can I ask you something? Let me ask you a simple question, yes or no. I'm just curious and there's no offense. You're my host. But let me ask if you are in any way religious? You don't mind my asking?"

I shook my head. He couldn't see that, though. A wink is the same as a nod to a blind man. "I guess I don't believe in it. In anything. Sometimes it's hard. You know what I'm saying?"

"Sure, I do," he said.

"Right," I said.

The Englishman was still holding forth. My wife sighed in her sleep. She drew a long breath and went on with her sleeping.

"You'll have to forgive me," I said. "But I can't tell you what a cathedral looks like. It just isn't in me to do it. I can't do any more than I've done."

The blind man sat very still, his head down, as he listened to me.

I said, "The truth is, cathedrals don't mean anything special to me. Nothing. Cathedrals. They're something to look at on late-night TV. That's all they are."

It was then that the blind man cleared his throat. He brought something up. He took a handkerchief from his back pocket. Then he said, "I get it, bub. It's okay. It happens. Don't worry about it," he said. "Hey, listen to me. Will you do me a favor? I got an idea. Why don't you find us some heavy paper? And a pen. We'll do something. We'll draw one together. Get us a pen and some heavy paper. Go on, bub, get the stuff," he said.

So I went upstairs. My legs felt like they didn't have any strength in them. They felt like they did after I'd done some running. In my wife's room, I looked around. I found some ballpoints in a little basket on her table. And then I tried to think where to look for the kind of paper he was talking about.

Downstairs, in the kitchen, I found a shopping bag with onion skins at the bottom of the bag. I emptied the bag and shook it. I brought it into the living room and sat down with it near his legs. I moved some things, smoothed the wrinkles from the bag, spread it out on the coffee table.

The blind man got down from the sofa and sat next to me on the carpet.

He ran his fingers over the paper. He went up and down the sides of the paper. The edges, even the edges. He fingered the corners.

"All right," he said. "All right, let's do her."

He found my hand, the hand with the pen. He closed his hand over my hand. "Go ahead, bub, draw," he said. "Draw. You'll see. I'll follow along with you. It'll be okay. Just begin now like I'm telling you. You'll see. Draw," the blind man said.

So I began. First I drew a box that looked like a house. It could have been the house I lived in. Then I put a roof on it. At either end of the roof, I drew spires. Crazy.

"Swell," he said. "Terrific. You're doing fine," he said. "Never thought anything like this could happen in your lifetime, did you, bub? Well, it's a strange life, we all know that. Go on now. Keep it up."

I put in windows with arches. I drew flying buttresses. I hung great doors. I couldn't stop. The TV station went off the air. I put down the pen and closed and opened my fingers. The blind man felt around over the paper. He moved the tips of his fingers over the paper, all over what I had drawn, and he nodded.

"Doing fine," the blind man said.

I took up the pen again, and he found my hand. I kept at it. I'm no artist. But I kept drawing just the same.

My wife opened up her eyes and gazed at us. She sat up on the sofa, her robe hanging open. She said, "What are you doing? Tell me, I want to know."

I didn't answer her.

The blind man said, "We're drawing a cathedral. Me and him are working on it. Press hard," he said to me. "That's right. That's good," he said. "Sure. You got it, bub. I can tell. You didn't think you could. But you can, can't you? You're cooking with gas now. You know what I'm saying? We're going to really have us something here in a minute. How's the old arm?" he said. "Put some people in there now. What's a cathedral without people?"

My wife said, "What's going on? Robert, what are you doing? What's going on?"

"It's all right," he said to her. "Close your eyes now," the blind man said to me. I did it. I closed them just like he said.

"Are they closed?" he said. "Don't fudge."

"They're closed," I said.

"Keep them that way," he said. He said, "Don't stop now. Draw."

So we kept on with it. His fingers rode my fingers as my hand went over the paper. It was like nothing else in my life up to now.

Then he said, "I think that's it. I think you got it," he said. "Take a look. What do you think?"

But I had my eyes closed. I thought I'd keep them that way for a little longer. I thought it was something I ought to do.

"Well?" he said. "Are you looking?"

My eyes were still closed. I was in my house. I knew that. But I didn't feel like I was inside anything.

"It's really something," I said.

1983

R. V. CASSILL
1919–2002

Cassill was born in Cedar Falls, Iowa. As a young man he studied art with the intention of becoming a painter, but after army service in the South Pacific during World War II, he began to write and publish fiction. As a teacher of writing at the University of Iowa, Purdue, Columbia, Harvard, and Brown, he numbered many novelists and short-story writers among his former students. His themes range from the little wars of childhood to the clashes of political ideologies, and several of his works deal with the role of the artist in our times. His novels include *Clem Anderson* (1961), *The President* (1964), *The Goss Women* (1974), *Hoyt's Child* (1976), *Labors of Love* (1980), *After Goliath* (1985), and *The Unknown Soldier* (1991). His stories have been collected in *The Father* (1965), *The Happy Marriage* (1967), *Patrimonies* (1987), and *Late Stories* (1995). His *Collected Stories* appeared in 1989.

The Rationing of Love

I

For more than twenty years I was sure my father made too much of the coffee episode. Really, I told him whenever he mentioned the matter, it was nothing, nothing, nothing. I wished he would put it out of his mind. I hadn't taken it seriously to begin with and would long ago have forgotten it if he had.

"But it was only one darn little cup of coffee and you were going *over there*," he always insisted, blaming himself. "I told myself so many times, why, it was only a nickel's worth, but there was all that wartime rationing, you know."

Of course I knew. Had I ever, even for the blink of an eye, refused to accept his first explanation?

The day I went to be drafted in 1942 he refused me a second cup of coffee with my breakfast. He was working as a counterman at the Bolton & Hay Restaurant in Des Moines, having come up from Gath to attend the summer session at Drake University. He was after the master's degree required for his job as superintendent of the consolidated school in Gath.

I had not seen him since my wedding day. For more than a year I had been serious—giving up my college notions of being a painter so I could support a wife by selling farm implements in her hometown of Waterloo. I mean my first wife, and how odd it seems to think of her as "first wife" in the context of these memories, how odd not to think simply of her name. Ora McGilvery. "Ora means gold," my father told me solemnly at the wedding, implying that I should treat her accordingly.

I had come down alone by bus from Waterloo the evening before I was to be inducted at Camp Dodge. I'd stayed the night in the old Victoria Hotel, a rearing and raffish building whose corridors held some scent of illicit arrivals and departures, some stirring premonition of the worldwide turbulence into which I was being drawn. In my little room I had wakened intermittently at three and four in the morning to hear prowling footsteps outside my door, and when I woke I wondered if my wife was crying in the newness of our first separation. Before daybreak I had made myself think that she was all right, and from that it seemed to follow that everything about to happen to me was going to be all right.

So I felt really good as I walked down from the hotel to meet my father at the Bolton & Hay Restaurant. The hot morning seemed as snappy as the ruffle of drums. The capitol dome gleamed in the radiance of my self-confidence, and the shafts of the Civil War monuments there across the river on the capitol grounds held up their testimony to the bravery of us Midwestern heroes.

A cinder-skinned news butcher was shouting, "Tommies can't stop Rommel!"[1] Maybe the Tommies couldn't, but I was on my way that morning, in the nick of time. Look out, Hitler, here comes Ioway! I guess I really felt a little impatient that I had to stop to see my father at all before I took a bus out to Camp Dodge.

Fortunately my father was ready to share my mood. He wasn't taking the fall of Tobruk[2] very hard. Most of the news he had to tell me was about my mother, brothers, and sister, and the folks in Gath. He wasn't bothered that I'd never "got back to painting" since I left college. He was glad Ora could stay with her parents while I was away. But mostly he was eager to tell me about himself.

There was a countryman's twinkle in his eyes and a conspiratorial lowering of his voice as he told how he had euchred his fellow waiters into letting him have the earliest shift at the lunch counter. "You take a lot of these city people aren't used to getting up till maybe six or seven in the morning. So I told them I'd just as soon come down and open the place up and get the coffee urns going and bring in the bakery stuff and milk. And, shoot, there's hardly anything doing here until after seven. So I have time to read the papers and go over my lessons. . . ."

For his job he wore a white dickey and jacket and a limp little bow tie, innocent as the rags that children wrap around their puppies. He was still deeply tanned from working in his garden at home before the summer-school session had started.

He said, "You take these other fellows who don't come on duty before seven-thirty, why they miss the best part of the day. By the time they have their four hours in, why, I'm back up on the campus and I've had a shower at the field house and a swim if I want to, and I'm out under a shade tree with my books." Four hours of work each day earned him his meals and a dollar in cash that went to help pay his room rent.

---

1. Erwin Rommel (the "Desert Fox"), World War II German field marshall (1891-1944). *Tommies:* British soldiers.   2. Libyan port that was the scene of fierce fighting between British and German forces, 1941-42.

While he was watching me eat eggs, bacon, and toast and drink my coffee, he said, "Now you just keep your money in your pocket, son. You may not get civilian food like this for a while, and it's my treat."

Of course I made no argument about that, and since I didn't want any sentimentality to edge in, I kept us talking about his summer. "You've got a pretty soft deal, Dad."

I hadn't meant at all to criticize, but my remark shifted him ever so slightly onto the defensive. "Your mother thinks I just come up to the University to loaf." Well, yes, it was true that my mother kept enforcing a family attitude that he was always too soft to take advantage of his opportunities. "Why," he said, "I'm taking nine hours credit this summer, and with what I've accumulated at Ames and Cedar Falls these last few years I'll get my degree. . . ."

"This summer?"

He didn't even bother to shake his head. ". . . with a little more extension work and making up my education credits, in nineteen forty-five. I'll bet the war will last at least that long, and the school board won't be likely to push me too hard for my degree as long as all those fellows are in the service and teachers hard to find."

"It won't take us till forty-five, Dad," I said, with the first queasy tremor of doubt I'd felt all morning.

"Who knows? You know, Buddy, your mother even said it didn't seem very dignified for a man my age to be working a board job like you boys did when you went to college. But shoot, I don't know what dignified is if it isn't being willing to do what has to be done."

I was glad then and later that he had said this to me before I left. For too many years while I was a kid at home I'd sided with the other children and my mother in a disrespectful tolerance of his weakness in the face of the school boards who sent us packing every three or four years from town to town, of his kid-glove treatment of the schoolmate bullies who used to knock my brothers and me around for no better reason than that we were the "superintendent's kids." We had blamed him—not too harshly, but persistently—when he let himself be cheated by the small-town garagemen and merchants who took advantage of him because he was a public employee dependent on their good will. We were used to resenting him—a little—because he didn't "stand up to people" and show off his dignity.

I liked him awfully much for telling me his side of all that old misery, but I only said, "I've got to run, Dad. Can I have another cup of coffee before I go to camp?" In a sort of embarrassment I waved my empty cup at him. It's funny how I remember that cup—a big awkward piece of restaurant crockery with two thin green bands painted around it.

He hesitated a minute, thinking. "Well, I'd like to, son. . . ." He tried to grin when he shook his head and his grin began to hurt us both.

"I don't really want any," I said quickly.

"You know we're trying to do our bit with coffee rationing."

"I *know*."

"It's only that the boss says. . . ."

"It was an awfully good breakfast, Dad."

"Now, you keep that money in your pocket. No sir, I'm paying for this. Do you need anything? You're going?" He was out from behind the counter quicker than I ever saw him move. As he walked to the door he put his arm over my shoulder, and as we stepped into the explosive sunlight of the street he kissed me quickly on the forehead. He hadn't kissed me since I was five.

He had unbuckled his wristwatch and was trying to fasten the old, sweated band around my arm. "Noticed you weren't wearing one," he said. I let him fasten it, looked at the time, said I'd have to run now to catch the right bus to Camp Dodge.

"Come on back," he said. "Please, come on now, you've got time for one more cup of coffee with me."

But I said I hadn't and that I really, really had drunk all the coffee I needed for a while.

I I

In a bad war, in my own worst phases of it, I lucked out with a consistency just short of miraculous. I mean, the miracles were there to be remembered when I had the heart to poke under the garbage for them.

For one thing, on a rain-drenched island as far from combat as it was from any place fit for human habitation, I started painting again while I was convalescing from a rare Asiatic type of diphtheria. It wasn't the throat kind of diphtheria. It spread big colonies of ulcers all over my skin and poisoned me internally so that I was weeks in getting my strength back after the sores cleared up.

Two cultivated ladies named Fitch and Helspur ran the Red Cross hut at the hospital. When they found out I'd had "art training" they not only rummaged out a fine set of oil paints and canvas, they even wanted me to start classes for the other patients. I was too tired for that. Mostly I sat on the back steps of the New Zealand hut they occupied and painted a banana tree on which the bananas were ripening as my abused cell structure mended.

"You're a regular Van Gogh with those yellows," Miss Fitch told me. It was her profession to be flattering.

I put the lovely, creamy brushful of yellow paint back down on the palette, lit a cigarette, and grinned at her through the rising goblin shapes of smoke. I had learned how important it was in my condition and at the juncture of the war in the Pacific to take things easy and slow when you could. She sat down with me and compared the painted yellows with the real bananas.

I said, "You know the first time I ever saw a banana tree? Understand, I always lived in small towns, but my father was a teacher, and he was always going to some college to summer school. . . ."

I'd set her off now. Her father and her uncle and her two great uncles had all been teachers. At Amherst, Smith, and Duke. She herself had been working on her doctorate at Columbia before she joined the Red Cross. She understood *exactly* what it meant to come from "a family of educators."

While she was running on enthusiastically I shook my head slow and steady. "No, no, no. It wasn't like that for us. My father only went into teaching to raise enough money to buy a farm. He kept on because the family kept growing, that's all. He started out a long time ago with not much more than an eighth-grade education. It took him almost twenty years of summer schools to get his B.A. Anyhow, depending on which college we lived nearest, he used to go off to Cedar Falls, or Ames, or Drake.[3] From the time I was very small I remember his bringing the whole family over to see where he was going to college. Next to the stuffed zebras and whale skeletons in the natural history collections, what I remember best is the greenhouse at the college in Cedar Falls where they had a banana tree just like that one."

"Wonderful!" Miss Fitch said. I could tell she was picturing my father as some grave and stately academician teaching us kids the Latin names of the rare flora—while what my father had said was, "Imagine that! Bananas growing right here in Iowa! Look at 'em growing upside down!"

Because she was such an enthusiastic listener, I told Miss Fitch, "Once when he was in summer school at Ames he took me to see the great, wonderful indoor swimming pool they had there. Imagine that! But it *was* great and wonderful to me. I'd never seen anything like it. The reverberations of the boards in there when the guys dived, the color of the water . . . the color of that chlorinated water was just like the water up around Ulithi,[4] and the mortar shells around us when we were wading in . . . I tell you I'd heard them before when Dad took me to that swimming pool and the diving boards rumbled."

I picked up my brush again from the palette and my hand was trembling. I wasn't any Van Gogh and I didn't any longer expect to be, but the painting— and the associations between one banana tree here and another back there— were making a bridge I needed to live by.

"It makes all the difference if you come from a family of educators," Miss Fitch said, far away in her dream of an Amherst girlhood. It didn't matter that I could never explain to her the petty quarrels in my "family of educators"— about how much of our homemade furniture we'd take with us when we moved from one rinky-dink town to another; whether they should sell my mother's piano after she forgot how to play it; whether the school board hadn't promised to find Dad a lot to keep our cow in when they hired him.

"I'm sure you came by your interest in art from *them*," Miss Fitch said.

"Sure. My mother was a frustrated *artiste* of the piano," I said lightly. "Naturally, at least one kid had to carry on the yokel dream of busting out of the small town. What does it matter? All that's in the bag now, anyway. Next week or the week after—whenever they cut my orders and there's a ship going that way—I'll go up to Okinawa[5] to join my outfit."

Now knowing how much she'd helped with a miracle, Miss Fitch promised that when I left she and Miss Helspur would pack my new canvases and see that they got home to my wife.

I lucked out, too, when I fell off a troopship in Buckner Bay at Okinawa. The war was over then and we were loading to go home. We were loading from a small boat onto the S. S. *Sherman*. Tom Hartman was ahead of me on the ladder. I suppose our weird, larking gratitude for surviving the war had become a kind of hysteria. So we were horsing around and it was my own foolish fault that I lunged for the guard rope, missed it, and pitched into the bay.

It happened, too, that I was wearing a field pack full of souvenirs as I fell. That made a bad outfit for swimming. So when I went down headfirst past

---

3. Drake University, in Des Moines, Iowa. The University of Northern Iowa is in Cedar Falls; Iowa State University is in Ames. **4.** Western Pacific atoll in the Caroline Islands captured from the Japanese by U.S. forces in 1944. **5.** Japanese island captured by U.S. forces in 1945.

the small boat, I thought the surprised faces of the boatmen might be the last ones I would ever see.

I went deep before I could get the pack off my shoulders. First I couldn't understand that I had to let it go. Then, as the green of the water got darker around me, the pack clung as if it owned me—that bag full of Okinawa pottery, Japanese pistols, a stained battle flag, and a wooden Buddha I'd looted from a house split open by shellfire. It held onto me like someone drowning who was afraid to let me live if I couldn't take him back up with me.

I don't remember shaking loose from it. All at once I was rising fast and the weight was gone. The strangling water fell away from my face. I saw the boatmen's hands reaching down for mine.

So far so good, but in the same glance I saw my father's wristwatch streaming bright droplets. My first coherent thought as the Navy men were hauling me into their boat was: I finally ruined it for him.

Then all the superstitions I'd been nourishing for three years of war began to concentrate on that ruined watch. I remember how wildly I talked about it to Tom Hartman that night as the ship wallowed east toward home. "I should have got it back to him in the condition he gave it to me."

"Does your father make a lot out of little gestures like that?" he wanted to know.

"I do, whether he does or not." Then I remembered and laughed. "He's as bad as I am. He'll want to buy me a cup of coffee the minute he sees me." I told Tom what had happened the day I was inducted.

He said, "Well, you better let him buy it for you."

All at once I went morose. I suppose the aftereffects of nearly drowning were coming up on me the way a pain in the jaw comes when the Novocaine wears off. "No, that's silly," I said. "Nothing's going to put things back the way they were before we left. It's too late for some of the things we missed. Are you scared about going home?"

I wish he had said he wasn't. All too easily he knew what I was talking about. "Everybody our age, everybody who's been over as long as we have is a little bit scared. You hear it from everybody," he said. After a while he said, "That's silly. What's to be scared of? Lights, music, girls...?"

We didn't say it, but we were afraid of having permanently lost the track of our lives. Mine—up to the day I'd been drafted—had been nothing but fooling around, as if I'd just been killing time until the war came and a use was found for me. "I found a job just so I could get married," I said. "I wasn't even good at it, or at anything else. So what now?"

"So you might as well have drowned this afternoon." I didn't blame him at all for saying it. He was a man with worries of his own.

I had the mental, moral shakes that night, trying to add up the score of my life in the world as I'd seen it—and coming out with a big round goose egg as of that hour. Coming out with a kind of sad contempt for what I'd grown up trusting. I remembered one time when my father gave the commencement address at Chesterfield for a graduating class of twelve. I had to go to all his public speeches when I was little. Usually I hadn't listened. This time, though, I'd listened because he was talking about Grandpa, whom I'd loved more than anybody. Grandpa, he said, had got in some land dispute with a neighbor. There had been talk among the farmers about how the quarrel could come to a knifing. This neighbor—who must have been a wild man in a generally peaceable community—actually got to carrying a pig sticker with him and showing it at the country store and saying what he meant to do with it.

One day he came by on the road in a spring wagon while my father and Grandpa were raking hay. My father told how Grandpa climbed the fence, went to the middle of the road, and stopped this wild guy, then walked up to him and put out his hand to shake.

That's all there was to the story, and there was my dad up in front of that squirming audience that couldn't care less, him with his bow tie and his soft little grin, holding out his hand to show how it was done. That was his idea of how all problems, domestic and foreign, could probably be handled.

Ah, but behind our ship as I recalled this were the dead cities of Okinawa and Japan. By now the first snow had fallen on the flat cinders of Hiroshima, Nagoya, and the rest. There was Naha blasted into rubble and Shuri Castle where the artillery had blown away everything but the foundations of the ancient walls. With things like that right behind us, who could take seriously a little quarrel so easily mended on a dirt road in southern Iowa?

There was no connection anymore. Before I slept that night I took my father's watch topside and threw it into the froth of our wake. I could be as superstitious as any man in the Army—and believe that watch was the charm that had seen me through. The same superstitions, and a lot more besides, told me it was useless from here on out.

III

The real miracle of those years was what had happened to Ora. She had grown up while I was away. Without any such melodramatic gesture as tossing a watch into the ocean, she had loosened the ties with her parents. She made it instantly clear to me that I wasn't going back to a futureless job in Waterloo. She had moved to Chicago before I shipped up to Okinawa, and the first thing that faced me when I walked into her apartment on Dearborn Street were some of the banana-tree paintings Miss Fitch and Miss Helspur had sent home. She had also hung up some older things I had done in college.

There was only a sundown light in the room when we came in from the taxi, a poor light that made the paintings look better than they were. The yellow bananas glowed like candle flames against a green background more mysterious than the jungle around the Red Cross hut on the island I'd never see again.

"They're not exactly works of genius," I said when I had switched on the apartment lights.

Ora shook her dark head stubbornly. "All right. Not yet. They're going to be."

I said, "Sure. Turn out the lights again. That improves them."

"We're going to New York," she said. "You're going to study at the Art Students League. Of course you are. You've got the GI Bill and you've got me. I'm an economic asset. I've got a job there already. I mean I'm almost sure I have. We might, we just might even have a place to live, though that's tougher in New York than here, even."

"A decent job?" I asked.

She made a face at me, a good-natured grimace, but she was disappointed by my caution. "Oh, don't talk like your father or my father or we'll never get anywhere. If New York won't have us, we'll keep going. We'll go on to Paris. Why not?"

"Now you're talking worse than my mother," I said. "There's no use in that."

"I'm not talking like anybody. I'm talking about us."

Let it be understood that our conversation was taking place almost the instant I had returned from twenty-eight months overseas. We had not even kissed yet since we came into the apartment, though we had kissed hard and well when she met me at the station and in the taxi that brought us to the North Side. All the anxiety and hope of my return had avalanched into this moment of decision.

And though we had much more to figure out before we left, I knew from then on that we would go. She had challenged me to put up or shut up about all I knew had fallen short in my parents' lives. I said, "O.K."

Then Ora was kneeling beside me in the wide easy chair, kissing me and rubbing her tears all over my face. "You're going to have your chance. You'll be a great painter," she said. Beyond the fringe of her hair I saw the charcoal velvet silhouette of buildings beyond our little window, a sky the color of a wonderful slice of melon. I had a painter's eye, all right. But it took Ora to show me that even Chicago was not a big enough town to hold us.

Paris was our city. New York didn't seem to have room for us that year. We went past it with a lordly air and borrowed boat fare. Paris was home for several years, and I keep thinking we should have been happy there, since we both loved it so much. But we weren't. Our years there provided "the foundation of my career," as it says in the brochure printed just last year by the gallery in Chicago that handles my painting, now that I've come back to work and teach in the Midwest. There never was a young couple in Paris who got more excitement and pleasure in discovering the fine parks, the old splendors of cathedrals and chateaux, places to eat and buy things, the displays of weather over the Seine, and the way the trees would darken secretly in the Luxembourg Gardens after the steel gates were closed for the night across the street from our apartment.

Too rich for our blood? There was a fault somewhere.

Ora worked first for an American oil company and later for the American Embassy. In the first years I walked alongside the Luxembourg Gardens every morning on my way to the Grande Chaumière where I was painting with Leger. Paris was very poor in those years just after the war, and we weren't. We had a sports car pretty soon for summer trips into the Loire Valley and the Dordogne. When Ora went to the embassy we had PX[6] privileges, American goodies for ourselves and for the black market. Happy or not, we lived the big life, and we stayed long enough to see Paris change again into the prospering capital of the world. Among the Fulbright students and other new waves of young Americans we were accepted as old settlers. I was painting pretty well. I was making contacts with people who could do me some good.

---

6. "Post Exchange," usually a commissary for military and diplomatic personnel.

Letters from my parents in those years came like drafts from a window one has forgotten to close before lying down for a warm nap. My mother's indicated she thought we were living an idealist missionary life—presumably weaning the French away from their bad habits of drinking wine, making love indiscriminately, and abusing their colonial peoples. She hoped we would not have children until we got back to the shelter of American sanitation.

My father, who only wrote short notes at Christmas or for our birthdays, seemed to make no distinction between my being "over there" among the Bohemians and my having been "over there" with the Army. I used to read his letters in my favorite cafe on the square at St. Sulpice and parody them for my friends. I would remember them with a kind of terrible nostalgia while I was getting stewed in the *caves* around St. Germain—or at the Select, in the winter of Eleanor. One night when the police picked me up for riotous behavior in Montparnasse I went into a yelling fit in the back of the *salade panier,* the police van. The next day I could remember only that I had been trying to tell my father I was a long time out of the Army and the damned South Pacific and nobody was giving me orders anymore.

If there ever was a chance to clear up such truths for him, I had it when I came back to Iowa in 1954 to tell my parents why Ora divorced me. They hadn't known her well, but they cared about her and knew that I had, too.

So my efforts to be scrupulous in my explanations only confused them further. They wouldn't believe me. They wouldn't comprehend that it had been all my fault instead of the fault of the corrupt French environment. They couldn't quite see why, just because I took some initial interest in the paintings of a Fulbright student named Eleanor Marshall, I should have run off to Africa with her. Or why, when the intoxications of novelty wore off with the drugs we got from the Algerians, Eleanor and I had begun a hesitant, slow circling back toward Paris. I could recall the nastiness and despair of those weeks in Alexandria and the days in Naples, but I just lacked the language to tell the old folks our great sin excursion collapsed because we had used up the money I stole from Ora and saved from black-marketing PX goods.

I heard my own voice tell them these things. I doubt if they heard much. They were living now in another small Iowa town where again my father was teaching. The house to which I had come was excruciatingly like the other houses I remembered living in while I was growing up. The same dark, small living room, the same softwood floors varnished dark, the same high school graduation pictures of my brothers, sister, and me on the piano that had been moved so often and played so little.

It was early summer and the kitchen windows were open as we sat at supper. A light rain was falling on the potted flowers my mother had set on a shelf outside the windows to get some fresh air. My mother said, "I suppose that Eleanor will be coming back soon to join you."

I shook my head carefully, as if I might spatter filth over her clean kitchen if I shook too hard. "She's not going to join me, Mama. She came to New York before I did. I'm not going to see her, didn't I make that clear?"

It was lucky my fingernails were chewed short or I might have drawn blood from the clenching of my hands. The last thing I'd wanted from this visit was the kind of dull sympathy I was getting. Maybe in some dream I had expected

I was going to be punished here, like the time I was punished for shooting at the Alleman girl with my air rifle when we lived in Chesterfield.

"I don't understand much about divorces," my mother said, still resisting, still sure things could be arranged for the best, "but it seems to me there's no reason you and she can't be married if you wanted to as bad as all that."

I remembered Eleanor and me lying side by side on a bed in a bad hotel in Rome. It was raining outside that room, too, but it was very cold there so the chill came right through the walls. We'd lain fully dressed with nothing to say to each other, merely passing a rare cigarette back and forth, waiting for the day to be over. The moisture of our lips on the cigarette paper was the only intimacy between us by then.

"At least we'll be spared marriage, whatever other payment we still have to make."

I'm not sure my mother caught the full savagery of what I'd said. My father did. He'd never been stretched past the point of endurance by the untouchable loveliness of my Paris, never seen with a painter's hopeless eye the high white clouds over Oran in the inexpressible Mediterranean light. How could he imagine Eleanor's strange mouth ready to be kissed? He only thought my paintings were "all right if there's people want to buy such things." But he knew what counted.

While I had been talking to my mother he had risen from the supper table. He stood at the window and his hands reached outside, fumbling with or caressing the wet geranium leaves.

After a while he said, "Darn it, I've thought so many times, why didn't I give you that second cup of coffee when you were going away?"

As if that one thing alone might have saved me from all my delinquencies! As if without this one default of courage he might have kept me true!

IV

My mother nearly died last fall. She dwindled and grew dull through the spring and summer. Each time I drove over from Illinois with my wife and three young children she seemed progressively less interested in finding toys from the attic for the little ones, even less sure of their names. Getting old, we said.

Then she fell down the basement stairs while she was bringing in flower bulbs from the garden about to freeze. She may have hit her head in the fall. She was very confused and dazed afterward. But when she was taken to the hospital in Des Moines the main source of her trouble was diagnosed as a tumor of the spleen, which had been seriously affecting her blood-sugar level. This had been going on long enough to suggest there might have been brain damage before her tumble.

Occasionally, when we visited her in the hospital, she would seem like her old self. These were times when she had been given medicine to counter the insulin surplus and had taken a lot of extra sugar in her orange juice. When my father, brothers, and sister hovered around her bed she could still beam and chatter and press our hands and thank us for "coming all that way" to be with her at such a time. "All that way. . . ." Perhaps she still thought I was living in Paris. At any rate, her quaint manner of putting it made me remember all my travels as if they were a single journey toward this time of anguish.

With extraordinary effort she could remember each of her grandchildren. When I prompted her, she asked about my children individually and by name. Were they anxious for snow? Did they like kindergarten and school?

But she was frightened, too. Sometimes, even at her most lucid moments and even when all of us were with her, she would ignore her children and speak only to my father. She questioned him about insurance, about the burial plot they had arranged for in the yard of the church where they were married, and about whether someone was taking care of her plants while she was away.

We saw that she always scared him with such talk. "You're not going to die, Mother," he told her over and over again—while the rest of us resolutely avoided any mention of death in her presence.

Often we found her out of her head—when the level of her blood sugar was not being artificially maintained—and she raved her distrust of the doctors who came several times a day to "bother her" and "wasted so much time" in getting it over with.

Her operation, when it took place, was mercifully briefer and luckier than we had been led to expect by the doctors. Her tumor was benign. Very little exploratory surgery was needed to locate it, though it had not showed in the x-rays.

Nonetheless, some ultimate transformation had been wrought on her in those hours when she was under anaesthetic. I was alone with her in the recovery room—we were permitted to go in to her only one at a time—when the fog of ether was leaving her. She was discovering that her right arm was bound to a board to keep the intravenous tube in place, and she fought the bondage piteously, trying to tear the tube out of the vein. Another tube was taped over her forehead and into her right nostril. I restrained her as gently as I could. She hated me for siding with all her other persecutors.

"They have no right to an old lady," she said. "Cut her all open. Bring her in here and cut her body." There was a horrifying strength in the free hand that wrestled against mine to get at the IV tube. Then she became aware of the other tube in her nose. "What's that for, too?" she said, and clawed for it.

I had to call a nurse, and we tied both hands down to make her leave the tubes alone.

She hadn't the strength to raise her head, of course. The hatred in her eyes was like the blow of a fist. She glared at me as if I were her murderer. "You have no right," she said.

"It won't be long now, Mama," I said. "I know you're very uncomfortable right now. They'll give you something for the pain and to make you sleep."

"Oh, the pain," she said. "Untie me. Let me loose."

"No. I won't."

"Let me loose!" Her voice was like a man's, compelling and brutal. Perhaps if the nurses had not been working nearby I might have done what she demanded.

"I can't let you loose," I said. "You'll be all right. You'll sleep. You'll rest. You'll sleep."

She turned her head to the side. Her crepey cheek was almost as crimson as blood from the great effort she was making. The tears on her cheek were tears of anger. "Why didn't they get it over with?"

"It's not going to be over," I said. "Don't you understand? You didn't have cancer. You'll be all right. It will take a while to get your strength back, but you're going to be fine."

"Why?"

I'm not certain she meant anything by this syllable. Surely I shouldn't have tried to answer then. But I said, "Why, because we need you. We all need you. My children, too. They've been wanting to come and see Grandma and go up into the attic with her again. Play the piano with her. . . ."

Now she knew exactly what she had to say. It was as if she had always been trying to clarify it. She said it now with a last, hoarded emphasis of deliberation. "No one has any right to bring children into the world." She meant me. She meant my sons. Our wickedness and our suffering had been from her, and she repented us. "Where's Ora? Where's your wife?" she asked with awful scorn. "Ora had no children. What have you done with her?"

I said nothing.

She smiled a little, a smile of terrible cruelty. "We have no right," she said tiredly. Then—perhaps she was sinking back into the vision or dream that had deviled her while she was on the operating table.

"The children are burning everywhere," she said vaguely.

It was less than an hour after that when my father and I walked down the hill from the hospital in the November sun. I saw that my shadow was longer than his on the concrete slope ahead of us, but his step was jauntier than mine. As if he didn't know yet—as if he was never going to find out—the truth my mother had just told me.

"The doctor said it was no bigger than a fingertip," he said of the tumor that had been removed from her. "Boy, the doctor said it was certainly good luck they found it so quick when the x-ray couldn't find it."

"We've been very lucky."

"Well, we sure have." He took a long trembling breath. It sounded like my youngest boy when he has been crying hard and is trying to reestablish a normal rhythm of breathing. "And you know, lucky with the Blue Cross and all. Just couldn't have been luckier."

He had a right to his relief, but I was suspicious of its excess and warned him, "She's not going to be the same, Dad."

"Why," he said, "why, I know that. Why, *of course not*. We're getting older, and all."

"She's in her seventies. It isn't going to be easy for her to make a comeback."

"*Of course* it won't. And I don't know what's the best thing to plan. The doctor said that, well, maybe the best thing for me to count on is to put her in a nursing home awhile because her convalescence might be months, and he thought I wouldn't be much of a hand for taking care of her."

It might well be more than a matter of months. The doctors to whom I had spoken avoided the word *convalescence*. She was too old. There was no return from the descent she had begun. "We ought to consider a nursing home," I said cautiously.

"Why, why, I told him *no!* Why I'd crawl on my hands and knees to take care of her before I'd let them take her away."

He tossed that off as a matter of fact. So jauntily. I doubted if he had even weighed the realities of what might be still to come. He just knew what he had to do—and I envied him for that as I never expected to envy another human being. All his life with us we had thought him too soft, gentle but a little foolish—and he had nursed his courage in the shade of soft foolishness until the time to use it well had come. I knew that, and the wonderful thing is that I think he knew it too.

"Well," I said, "well. We better turn and go back to the hospital."

"Just down that next block. All right?"

I had supposed we were merely getting a breath of fresh air before we rejoined the rest of the family in the vigil at the hospital.

No. He had known exactly where he was leading me. In the next block was the Bolton & Hay Restaurant where I'd said goodbye to him when I went in the Army. Suddenly there we were, in front of it.

"You know, son," he said with his old easy, floppy smile, "you know there's something that's bothered me. . . ."

Of course I knew what was coming, and I wanted no part of it. He had no trick to play except a sentimental one, and that was not nearly enough. The things we had done wrong with our lives were signed, sealed and irretrievable. Ora was gone; I had my new wife and children. My mother was going to live, but her faith in life had not lasted quite as long as her outraged body. I had paid more than a man should choose to pay for my small share of success. My mother had not touched her piano for thirty years. We had been lucky to come this far with a divided verdict.

We had been lucky. My father said so and I believed him. But I saw now that the reckless old fool wanted still to gamble for more. I caught my breath as if watching a clownish acrobat preparing to challenge the trim, athletic professionals on the high wire. He was going to insist you *could* go back, in spite of time, and make the past all right.

"Now," he said, rather formally. "I could just as well have given you that cup of coffee you asked for that morning. Just as well as not."

His trick depended on just one thing—on my willingness to believe in it, at the price of all I'd paid so much to learn. I guessed I could if I wanted to. Nothing was stopping me.

I said, "Well, since we're here, why don't you get it for me now?" The worst had been ahead of us. Now it was behind us. Both of us could claim that much victory.

He said that to give me the coffee I had asked for was just exactly what he intended to do.

Like a boy, I followed him into the restaurant.

1987

WILLA CATHER
1873–1947

Cather was born of Anglo-Irish parents in Back Creek Valley, Virginia. At ten she moved with her family to Red Cloud, Nebraska, where she grew up, exploring the prairies on horseback and making friends with the immigrant farmers of the area. While she worked her way through the University of Nebraska, she acquired an enduring passion for music and determined to devote her energies to writing. From 1896 to 1905 she worked for a newspaper in Pittsburgh, and she later held editorial positions in New York, but her poetry and fiction looked to the Midwest and Southwest for their subject matter and to the depths of the American past for their values. She never married. The last part of her life was spent in New York, with occasional European travels that never swayed her from nostalgia or the conservatism of her views. Once she declared that the world had "broken apart" in about 1922; unmistakably, she preferred the manners, styles, and virtues that prevailed before that date—which was, incidentally, the year in which she was awarded the Pulitzer Prize for her novel *One of Ours*. Among her best-known novels are *My Ántonia* (1918), *A Lost Lady* (1923), *The Professor's House* (1925), and *Death Comes for the Archbishop* (1927). *Not under Forty* (1936) contains many of her essays. Her collections of short stories are *Youth and the Bright Medusa* (1920), *Obscure Destinies* (1932), and *The Old Beauty and Others* (1948).

A Wagner Matinée

I received one morning a letter, written in pale ink on glassy, blue-lined note-paper, and bearing the postmark of a little Nebraska village. This communication, worn and rubbed, looking as if it had been carried for some days in a coat pocket that was none too clean, was from my uncle Howard, and informed me that his wife had been left a small legacy by a bachelor relative, and that it would be necessary for her to go to Boston to attend to the settling of the estate. He requested me to meet her at the station and render her whatever services might be necessary. On examining the date indicated as that of her arrival, I found it to be no later than tomorrow. He had characteristically delayed writing until, had I been away from home for a day, I must have missed my aunt altogether.

The name of my Aunt Georgiana opened before me a gulf of recollection so wide and deep that, as the letter dropped from my hand, I felt suddenly a stranger to all the present conditions of my existence, wholly ill at ease and out of place amid the familiar surroundings of my study. I became, in short, the gangling farmer-boy my aunt had known, scourged with chilblains and bashfulness, my hands cracked and sore from the corn husking. I sat again before her parlour organ, fumbling the scales with my stiff, red fingers, while she, beside me, made canvas mittens for the huskers.

The next morning, after preparing my landlady for a visitor, I set out for the station. When the train arrived I had some difficulty in finding my aunt. She was the last of the passengers to alight, and it was not until I got her into the carriage that she seemed really to recognize me. She had come all the way in a day coach; her linen duster[1] had become black with soot and her black bonnet gray with dust during the journey. When we arrived at my boarding-house the landlady put her to bed at once and I did not see her again until the next morning.

Whatever shock Mrs. Springer experienced at my aunt's appearance, she considerately concealed. As for myself, I saw my aunt's battered figure with that feeling of awe and respect with which we behold explorers who have left their ears and fingers north of Franz-Joseph-Land, or their health somewhere along the Upper Congo. My Aunt Georgiana had been a music teacher at the Boston Conservatory, somewhere back in the latter sixties.[2] One summer, while visiting in the little village among the Green Mountains where her ancestors had dwelt for generations, she had kindled the callow fancy of my uncle, Howard Carpenter, then an idle, shiftless boy of twenty-one. When she returned to her duties in Boston, Howard followed her, and the upshot of this infatuation was that she eloped with him, eluding the reproaches of her family and the criticism of her friends by going with him to the Nebraska frontier. Carpenter, who, of course, had no money, took up a homestead in Red Willow County, fifty miles from the railroad. There they had measured off their land themselves, driving across the prairie in a wagon, to the wheel of which they had tied a red cotton handkerchief, and counting its revolutions. They built a dug-out in the red hillside, one of those cave dwellings whose inmates so often reverted to primitive conditions. Their water they got from the lagoons where the buffalo drank, and their slender stock of provisions was always at the mercy of bands of roving Indians. For thirty years my aunt had not been farther than fifty miles from the homestead.

I owed to this woman most of the good that ever came my way in my boyhood, and had a reverential affection for her. During the years when I was riding herd for my uncle, my aunt, after cooking the three meals—the first of which was ready at six o'clock in the morning—and putting the six children to bed, would often stand until midnight at her ironing-board, with me at the kitchen table beside her, hearing me recite Latin declensions and conjugations, gently shaking me when my drowsy head sank down over a page of irregular verbs. It was to her, at her ironing or mending, that I read my first Shakespeare, and her old text-book on mythology was the first that ever came into my empty hands. She taught me my scales and exercises on the little parlour organ which her husband had bought her after fifteen years during which she had not so much as seen a musical instrument. She would sit beside me by the hour, darning and counting, while I struggled with the "Joyous

---

1. Long, lightweight overcoat. **2.** That is, the 1860s.

Farmer." She seldom talked to me about music, and I understood why. Once when I had been doggedly beating out some easy passages from an old score of *Euryanthe*[3] I had found among her music books, she came up to me and, putting her hands over my eyes, gently drew my head back upon her shoulder, saying tremulously, "Don't love it so well, Clark, or it may be taken from you."

When my aunt appeared on the morning after her arrival in Boston, she was still in a semi-somnambulant state. She seemed not to realize that she was in the city where she had spent her youth, the place longed for hungrily half a lifetime. She had been so wretchedly train-sick throughout the journey that she had no recollection of anything but her discomfort, and, to all intents and purposes, there were but a few hours of nightmare between the farm in Red Willow County and my study on Newbury Street. I had planned a little pleasure for her that afternoon, to repay her for some of the glorious moments she had given me when we used to milk together in the straw-thatched cowshed and she, because I was more than usually tired, or because her husband had spoken sharply to me, would tell me of the splendid performance of the *Huguenots*[4] she had seen in Paris, in her youth.

At two o'clock the Symphony Orchestra was to give a Wagner program, and I intended to take my aunt; though, as I conversed with her, I grew doubtful about her enjoyment of it. I suggested our visiting the Conservatory and the Common before lunch, but she seemed altogether too timid to wish to venture out. She questioned me absently about various changes in the city, but she was chiefly concerned that she had forgotten to leave instructions about feeding half-skimmed milk to a certain weakling calf, "old Maggie's calf, you know, Clark," she explained, evidently having forgotten how long I had been away. She was further troubled because she had neglected to tell her daughter about the freshly-opened kit of mackerel in the cellar, which would spoil if it were not used directly.

I asked her whether she had ever heard any of the Wagnerian operas, and found that she had not, though she was perfectly familiar with their respective situations, and had once possessed the piano score of *The Flying Dutchman*.[5] I began to think it would be best to get her back to Red Willow County without waking her, and regretted having suggested the concert.

From the time we entered the concert hall, however, she was a trifle less passive and inert, and for the first time seemed to perceive her surroundings. I had felt some trepidation lest she might become aware of her queer, country clothes, or might experience some painful embarrassment at stepping suddenly into the world to which she had been dead for a quarter of a century. But, again, I found how superficially I had judged her. She sat looking about her with eyes as impersonal, almost as stony, as those with which the granite Rameses[6] in a museum watches the froth and fret that ebbs and flows about his pedestal. I have seen this same aloofness in old miners who drift into the Brown hotel at Denver, their pockets full of bullion, their linen soiled, their haggard faces unshaven; standing in the thronged corridors as solitary as though they were still in a frozen camp on the Yukon.

---

3. Opera by German composer Carl Maria von Weber (1786–1826). **4.** *Les Huguenots,* opera by German composer Giacomo Meyerbeer (1791–1864). **5.** Opera by German composer Richard Wagner (1813–1883). **6.** Name of eleven Egyptian pharaohs.

The matinée audience was made up chiefly of women. One lost the contour of faces and figures, indeed any effect of line whatever, and there was only the colour of bodices past counting, the shimmer of fabrics soft and firm, silky and sheer; red, mauve, pink, blue, lilac, purple, écru, rose, yellow, cream, and white, all the colours that an impressionist finds in a sunlit landscape, with here and there the dead shadow of a frock coat. My Aunt Georgiana regarded them as though they had been so many daubs of tube-paint on a palette.

When the musicians came out and took their places, she gave a little stir of anticipation, and looked with quickening interest down over the rail at that invariable grouping, perhaps the first wholly familiar thing that had greeted her eye since she had left old Maggie and her weakling calf. I could feel how all those details sank into her soul, for I had not forgotten how they had sunk into mine when I came fresh from ploughing forever and forever between green aisles of corn, where, as in a treadmill, one might walk from daybreak to dusk without perceiving a shadow of change. The clean profiles of the musicians, the gloss of their linen, the dull black of their coats, the beloved shapes of the instruments, the patches of yellow light on the smooth, varnished bellies of the 'cellos and the bass viols in the rear, the restless, wind-tossed forest of fiddle necks and bows—I recalled how, in the first orchestra I ever heard, those long bow-strokes seemed to draw the heart out of me, as a conjurer's stick reels out yards of paper ribbon from a hat.

The first number was the *Tannhäuser*[7] overture. When the horns drew out the first strain of the Pilgrim's chorus, Aunt Georgiana clutched my coat sleeve. Then it was I first realized that for her this broke a silence of thirty years. With the battle between the two motives,[8] with the frenzy of the Venusberg theme and its ripping of strings, there came to me an overwhelming sense of the waste and wear we are so powerless to combat; and I saw again the tall, naked house on the prairie, black and grim as a wooden fortress; the black pond where I had learned to swim, its margin pitted with sun-dried cattle tracks; the rain gullied clay banks about the naked house, the four dwarf ash seedlings where the dish-cloths were always hung to dry before the kitchen door. The world there was the flat world of the ancients; to the east, a cornfield that stretched to daybreak; to the west, a corral that reached to sunset; between, the conquests of peace, dearer-bought than those of war.

The overture closed, my aunt released my coat sleeve, but she said nothing. She sat staring dully at the orchestra. What, I wondered, did she get from it? She had been a good pianist in her day, I knew, and her musical education had been broader than that of most music teachers of a quarter of a century ago. She had often told me of Mozart's operas and Meyerbeer's; and I could remember hearing her sing, years ago, certain melodies of Verdi.[9] When I had fallen ill with a fever in her house she used to sit by my cot in the evening—when the cool, night wind blew in through the faded mosquito netting tacked over the window and I lay watching a certain bright star that burned red above the cornfield—and sing "Home to our mountains, O, let us return!" in a way fit to break the heart of a Vermont boy near dead of homesickness already.

7. Opera by Wagner.   8. Recurrent musical phrases developed over the course of a composition; characteristic technique of Wagner.   9. Guiseppe Verdi (1813–1901), Italian composer. Wolfgang Amadeus Mozart (1756–1791), Austrian composer.

I watched her closely through the prelude to *Tristan and Isolde,*[1] trying vainly to conjecture what that seething turmoil of strings and winds might mean to her, but she sat mutely staring at the violin bows that drove obliquely downward, like the pelting streaks of rain in a summer shower. Had this music any message for her? Had she enough left to at all comprehend this power which had kindled the world since she had left it? I was in a fever of curiosity, but Aunt Georgiana sat silent upon her peak in Darien.[2] She preserved this utter immobility throughout the number from *The Flying Dutchman,* though her fingers worked mechanically upon her black dress, as if, of themselves, they were recalling the piano score they had once played. Poor hands! They had been stretched and twisted into mere tentacles to hold and lift and knead with;—on one of them a thin, worn band that had once been a wedding ring. As I pressed and gently quieted one of those groping hands, I remembered with quivering eyelids their services for me in other days.

Soon after the tenor began the "Prize Song," I heard a quick drawn breath and turned to my aunt. Her eyes were closed, but the tears were glistening on her cheeks, and I think, in a moment more, they were in my eyes as well. It never really died, then—the soul which can suffer so excruciatingly and so interminably; it withers to the outward eye only; like that strange moss which can lie on a dusty shelf half a century and yet, if placed in water, grows green again. She wept so throughout the development and elaboration of the melody.

During the intermission before the second half, I questioned my aunt and found that the "Prize Song" was not new to her. Some years before there had drifted to the farm in Red Willow County a young German, a tramp cowpuncher, who had sung in the chorus at Bayreuth when he was a boy, along with the other peasant boys and girls. Of a Sunday morning he used to sit on his gingham-sheeted bed in the hands' bedroom which opened off the kitchen, cleaning the leather of his boots and saddle, singing the "Prize Song," while my aunt went about her work in the kitchen. She had hovered over him until she had prevailed upon him to join the country church, though his sole fitness for this step, in so far as I could gather, lay in his boyish face and his possession of this divine melody. Shortly afterward, he had gone to town on the Fourth of July, been drunk for several days, lost his money at a faro table, ridden a saddled Texas steer on a bet, and disappeared with a fractured collar-bone. All this my aunt told me huskily, wanderingly, as though she were talking in the weak lapses of illness.

"Well, we have come to better things than the old *Trovatore*[3] at any rate, Aunt Georgie?" I queried, with a well meant effort at jocularity.

Her lip quivered and she hastily put her handkerchief up to her mouth. From behind it she murmured, "And you have been hearing this ever since you left me, Clark?" Her question was the gentlest and saddest of reproaches.

---

1. Opera by Wagner. **2.** That is, she sat silent with amazement; cf. final lines of "On First Looking into Chapman's Homer" by English poet John Keats (1795–1821):

> . . . Or like stout Cortez when with eagle eyes
> He stared at the Pacific—and all his men
> Looked at each other with a wild surmise—
> Silent, upon a peak in Darien.

3. *Il Trovatore,* opera by Verdi.

The second half of the program consisted of four numbers from the *Ring*, and closed with Siegfried's funeral march. My aunt wept quietly, but almost continuously, as a shallow vessel overflows in a rain-storm. From time to time her dim eyes looked up at the lights, burning softly under their dull glass globes.

The deluge of sound poured on and on; I never knew what she found in the shining current of it; I never knew how far it bore her, or past what happy islands. From the trembling of her face I could well believe that before the last number she had been carried out where the myriad graves are, into the grey, nameless burying grounds of the sea; or into some world of death vaster yet, where, from the beginning of the world, hope has lain down with hope and dream with dream and, renouncing, slept.

The concert was over; the people filed out of the hall chattering and laughing, glad to relax and find the living level again, but my kinswoman made no effort to rise. The harpist slipped the green felt cover over his instrument; the flute-players shook the water from their mouthpieces; the men of the orchestra went out one by one, leaving the stage to the chairs and music stands, empty as a winter cornfield.

I spoke to my aunt. She burst into tears and sobbed pleadingly. "I don't want to go, Clark, I don't want to go!"

I understood. For her, just outside the concert hall, lay the black pond with the cattle-tracked bluffs; the tall, unpainted house, with weather-curled boards, naked as a tower; the crook-backed ash seedlings where the dish-cloths hung to dry; the gaunt, moulting turkeys picking up refuse about the kitchen door.

1904

Paul's Case

A Study in Temperament

It was Paul's afternoon to appear before the faculty of the Pittsburgh High School to account for his various misdemeanors. He had been suspended a week ago, and his father had called at the Principal's office and confessed his perplexity about his son. Paul entered the faculty room suave and smiling. His clothes were a trifle outgrown, and the tan velvet on the collar of his open overcoat was frayed and worn; but for all that there was something of the dandy about him, and he wore an opal pin in his neatly knotted black four-in-hand,[1] and a red carnation in his buttonhole. This latter adornment the faculty somehow felt was not properly significant of the contrite spirit befitting a boy under the ban of suspension.

Paul was tall for his age and very thin, with high, cramped shoulders and a narrow chest. His eyes were remarkable for a certain hysterical brilliancy, and he continually used them in a conscious, theatrical sort of way, peculiarly offensive in a boy. The pupils were abnormally large, as though he were addicted to belladonna, but there was a glassy glitter about them which that drug does not produce.

---

1. The long necktie we are now familiar with.

When questioned by the Principal as to why he was there Paul stated, politely enough, that he wanted to come back to school. This was a lie, but Paul was quite accustomed to lying; found it, indeed, indispensable for overcoming friction. His teachers were asked to state their respective charges against him, which they did with such a rancor and aggrievedness as evinced that this was not a usual case. Disorder and impertinence were among the offenses named, yet each of his instructors felt that it was scarcely possible to put into words the real cause of the trouble, which lay in a sort of hysterically defiant manner of the boy's; in the contempt which they all knew he felt for them, and which he seemingly made not the least effort to conceal. Once, when he had been making a synopsis of a paragraph at the blackboard, his English teacher had stepped to his side and attempted to guide his hand. Paul had started back with a shudder and thrust his hands violently behind him. The astonished woman could scarcely have been more hurt and embarrassed had he struck at her. The insult was so involuntary and definitely personal as to be unforgettable. In one way and another he had made all his teachers, men and women alike, conscious of the same feeling of physical aversion. In one class he habitually sat with his hand shading his eyes; in another he always looked out of the window during the recitation; in another he made a running commentary on the lecture, with humorous intention.

His teachers felt this afternoon that his whole attitude was symbolized by his shrug and his flippantly red carnation flower, and they fell upon him without mercy, his English teacher leading the pack. He stood through it smiling, his pale lips parted over his white teeth. (His lips were continually twitching, and he had a habit of raising his eyebrows that was contemptuous and irritating to the last degree.) Older boys than Paul had broken down and shed tears under that baptism of fire, but his set smile did not once desert him, and his only sign of discomfort was the nervous trembling of the fingers that toyed with the buttons of his overcoat, and an occasional jerking of the other hand that held his hat. Paul was always smiling, always glancing about him, seeming to feel that people might be watching him and trying to detect something. This conscious expression, since it was as far as possible from boyish mirthfulness, was usually attributed to insolence or "smartness."

As the inquisition proceeded one of his instructors repeated an impertinent remark of the boy's, and the Principal asked him whether he thought that a courteous speech to have made a woman. Paul shrugged his shoulders slightly and his eyebrows twitched.

"I don't know," he replied. "I didn't mean to be polite or impolite, either. I guess it's a sort of way I have of saying things regardless."

The Principal, who was a sympathetic man, asked him whether he didn't think that a way it would be well to get rid of. Paul grinned and said he guessed so. When he was told that he could go he bowed gracefully and went out. His bow was but a repetition of the scandalous red carnation.

His teachers were in despair, and his drawing master voiced the feeling of them all when he declared there was something about the boy which none of them understood. He added: "I don't really believe that smile of his comes altogether from insolence; there's something sort of haunted about it. The boy is not strong, for one thing. I happen to know that he was born in Colorado, only a few months before his mother died out there of a long illness. There is something wrong about the fellow."

The drawing master had come to realize that, in looking at Paul, one saw only his white teeth and the forced animation of his eyes. One warm afternoon the boy had gone to sleep at his drawing board, and his master had noted with amazement what a white, blue-veined face it was; drawn and wrinkled like an old man's about the eyes, the lips twitching even in his sleep, and stiff with a nervous tension that drew them back from his teeth.

His teachers left the building dissatisfied and unhappy; humiliated to have felt so vindictive toward a mere boy, to have uttered this feeling in cutting terms, and to have set each other on, as it were, in the gruesome game of intemperate reproach. Some of them remembered having seen a miserable street cat set at bay by a ring of tormentors.

As for Paul, he ran down the hill whistling the "Soldiers' Chorus" from *Faust*,[2] looking wildly behind him now and then to see whether some of his teachers were not there to writhe under his lightheartedness. As it was now late in the afternoon and Paul was on duty that evening as usher at Carnegie Hall,[3] he decided that he would not go home to supper. When he reached the concert hall the doors were not yet open and, as it was chilly outside, he decided to go up into the picture gallery—always deserted at this hour— where there were some of Raffaelli's[4] gay studies of Paris streets and an airy blue Venetian scene or two that always exhilarated him. He was delighted to find no one in the gallery but the old guard, who sat in one corner, a newspaper on his knee, a black patch over one eye and the other closed. Paul possessed himself of the place and walked confidently up and down, whistling under his breath. After a while he sat down before a blue Rico[5] and lost himself. When he bethought him to look at his watch, it was after seven o'clock, and he rose with a start and ran downstairs, making a face at Augustus, peering out from the cast room, and an evil gesture at the Venus de Milo[6] as he passed her on the stairway.

When Paul reached the ushers' dressing room half a dozen boys were there already, and he began excitedly to tumble into his uniform. It was one of the few that at all approached fitting, and Paul thought it very becoming—though he knew that the tight, straight coat accentuated his narrow chest, about which he was exceedingly sensitive. He was always considerably excited while he dressed, twanging all over to the tuning of the strings and the preliminary flourishes of the horns in the music room; but tonight he seemed quite beside himself, and he teased and plagued the boys until, telling him that he was crazy, they put him down on the floor and sat on him.

Somewhat calmed by his suppression, Paul dashed out to the front of the house to seat the early comers. He was a model usher; gracious and smiling he ran up and down the aisles; nothing was too much trouble for him; he carried messages and brought programs as though it were his greatest pleasure in life, and all the people in his section thought him a charming boy, feeling that he remembered and admired them. As the house filled, he grew more and more vivacious and animated, and the color came to his cheeks and lips. It was very much as though this were a great reception and Paul were the host. Just as the musicians came out to take their places, his English teacher arrived

---

2. Opera by Charles Gounod (1818–1893). **3.** Pittsburgh theater named for Andrew Carnegie (1835–1919), famous industrialist and philanthropist. **4.** Jean-François Raffaëlli (1850–1924), French painter, sculptor, and etcher. **5.** Andreas Rico (1500–1550), Cretan-Italian painter. **6.** A famous Greek statue; the original is in the Louvre, Paris. Augustus (63 B.C.E.–C.E. 14) was the first Roman emperor.

with checks for the seats which a prominent manufacturer had taken for the season. She betrayed some embarrassment when she handed Paul the tickets, and a hauteur which subsequently made her feel very foolish. Paul was startled for a moment, and had the feeling of wanting to put her out; what business had she here among all these fine people and gay colors? He looked her over and decided that she was not appropriately dressed and must be a fool to sit downstairs in such togs. The tickets had probably been sent her out of kindness, he reflected as he put down a seat for her, and she had about as much right to sit there as he had.

When the symphony began Paul sank into one of the rear seats with a long sigh of relief, and lost himself, as he had done before the Rico. It was not that symphonies, as such, meant anything in particular to Paul, but the first sigh of the instruments seemed to free some hilarious and potent spirit within him; something that struggled there like the genie in the bottle found by the Arab fisherman.[7] He felt a sudden zest of life; the lights danced before his eyes and the concert hall blazed into unimaginable splendor. When the soprano soloist came on Paul forgot even the nastiness of his teacher's being there and gave himself up to the peculiar stimulus such personages always had for him. The soloist chanced to be a German woman, by no means in her first youth, and the mother of many children; but she wore an elaborate gown and tiara, and above all she had that indefinable air of achievement, that worldshine upon her, which, in Paul's eyes, made her a veritable queen of Romance.

After a concert was over Paul was always irritable and wretched until he got to sleep, and tonight he was even more than usually restless. He had the feeling of not being able to let down, of its being impossible to give up this delicious excitement which was the only thing that could be called living at all. During the last number he withdrew and, after hastily changing his clothes in the dressing room, slipped out to the side door where the soprano's carriage stood. Here he began pacing rapidly up and down the walk, waiting to see her come out.

Over yonder, the Schenley, in its vacant stretch, loomed big and square through the fine rain, the windows of its twelve stories glowing like those of a lighted cardboard house under a Christmas tree. All the actors and singers of the better class stayed there when they were in the city, and a number of the big manufacturers of the place lived there in the winter. Paul had often hung about the hotel, watching the people go in and out, longing to enter and leave schoolmasters and dull care behind him forever.

At last the singer came out, accompanied by the conductor, who helped her into her carriage and closed the door with a cordial *auf wiedersehen*[8] which set Paul to wondering whether she were not an old sweetheart of his. Paul followed the carriage over to the hotel, walking so rapidly as not to be far from the entrance when the singer alighted, and disappeared behind the swinging glass doors that were opened by a Negro in a tall hat and a long coat. In the moment that the door was ajar it seemed to Paul that he, too, entered. He seemed to feel himself go after her up the steps, into the warm, lighted building, into an exotic, tropical world of shiny, glistening surfaces and basking

---

7. In one of the tales of the *Arabian Nights* (also called *Thousand and One Nights*), the fisherman Ali Baba finds a genie imprisoned in a bottle who is able to perform miracles. **8.** Good-bye (German).

ease. He reflected upon the mysterious dishes that were brought into the dining room, the green bottles in buckets of ice, as he had seen them in the supper party pictures of the *Sunday World* supplement. A quick gust of wind brought the rain down with sudden vehemence, and Paul was startled to find that he was still outside in the slush of the gravel driveway; that his boots were letting in the water and his scanty overcoat was clinging wet about him; that the lights in front of the concert hall were out and that the rain was driving in sheets between him and the orange glow of the windows above him. There it was, what he wanted—tangibly before him, like the fairy world of a Christmas pantomime—but mocking spirits stood guard at the doors, and, as the rain beat in his face, Paul wondered whether he were destined always to shiver in the black night outside, looking up at it.

He turned and walked reluctantly toward the car[9] tracks. The end had to come sometime; his father in his nightclothes at the top of the stairs, explanations that did not explain, hastily improvised fictions that were forever tripping him up, his upstairs room and its horrible yellow wallpaper, the creaking bureau with the greasy plush collarbox, and over his painted wooden bed the pictures of George Washington and John Calvin,[1] and the framed motto, "Feed my Lambs," which had been worked in red worsted[2] by his mother.

Half an hour later Paul alighted from his car and went slowly down one of the side streets off the main thoroughfare. It was a highly respectable street, where all the houses were exactly alike, and where businessmen of moderate means begot and reared large families of children, all of whom went to Sabbath school and learned the shorter catechism, and were interested in arithmetic; all of whom were as exactly alike as their homes, and of a piece with the monotony in which they lived. Paul never went up Cordelia Street without a shudder of loathing. His home was next to the house of the Cumberland[3] minister. He approached it tonight with the nerveless sense of defeat, the hopeless feeling of sinking back forever into ugliness and commonness that he had always had when he came home. The moment he turned into Cordelia Street he felt the waters close above his head. After each of these orgies of living he experienced all the physical depression which follows a debauch; the loathing of respectable beds, of common food, of a house penetrated by kitchen odors; a shuddering repulsion for the flavorless, colorless mass of everyday existence; a morbid desire for cool things and soft lights and fresh flowers.

The nearer he approached the house, the more absolutely unequal Paul felt to the sight of it all: his ugly sleeping chamber; the cold bathroom with the grimy zinc tub, the cracked mirror, the dripping spigots; his father, at the top of the stairs, his hairy legs sticking out from his nightshirt, his feet thrust into carpet slippers. He was so much later than usual that there would certainly be inquiries and reproaches. Paul stopped short before the door. He felt that he could not be accosted by his father tonight; that he could not toss again on that miserable bed. He would not go in. He would tell his father that he had no carfare and it was raining so hard he had gone home with one of the boys and stayed all night.

Meanwhile, he was wet and cold. He went around to the back of the house and tried one of the basement windows, found it open, raised it cautiously,

---

9. That is, streetcar. **1.** French Protestant reformer who lived in Geneva (1509–1564). **2.** That is, embroidered with red wool. **3.** A division of the Presbyterian Church in the United States.

and scrambled down the cellar wall to the floor. There he stood, holding his breath, terrified by the noise he had made, but the floor above him was silent, and there was no creak on the stairs. He found a soapbox, and carried it over to the soft ring of light that streamed from the furnace door, and sat down. He was horribly afraid of rats, so he did not try to sleep, but sat looking distrustfully at the dark, still terrified lest he might have awakened his father. In such reactions, after one of the experiences which made days and nights out of the dreary blanks of the calendar, when his senses were deadened, Paul's head was always singularly clear. Suppose his father had heard him getting in at the window and had come down and shot him for a burglar? Then, again, suppose his father had come down, pistol in hand, and he had cried out in time to save himself, and his father had been horrified to think how nearly he had killed him? Then, again, suppose a day should come when his father would remember that night, and wish there had been no warning cry to stay his hand? With this last supposition Paul entertained himself until daybreak.

The following Sunday was fine; the sodden November chill was broken by the last flash of autumnal summer. In the morning Paul had to go to church and Sabbath school, as always. On seasonable Sunday afternoons the burghers of Cordelia Street always sat out on their front stoops and talked to their neighbors on the next stoop, or called to those across the street in neighborly fashion. The men usually sat on gay cushions placed upon the steps that led down to the sidewalk, while the women, in their Sunday "waists,"[4] sat in rockers on the cramped porches, pretending to be greatly at their ease. The children played in the streets; there were so many of them that the place resembled the recreation grounds of a kindergarten. The men on the steps—all in their shirt sleeves their vests unbuttoned—sat with their legs well apart, their stomachs comfortably protruding, and talked of the prices of things, or told anecdotes of the sagacity of their various chiefs and overlords. They occasionally looked over the multitude of squabbling children, listened affectionately to their high-pitched, nasal voices, smiling to see their own proclivities reproduced in their offspring, and interspersed their legends of the iron kings[5] with remarks about their sons' progress at school, their grades in arithmetic, and the amounts they had saved in their toy banks.

On this last Sunday of November Paul sat all the afternoon on the lowest step of his stoop, staring into the street, while his sisters, in their rockers, were talking to the minister's daughters next door about how many shirtwaists they had made in the last week, and how many waffles someone had eaten at the last church supper. When the weather was warm, and his father was in a particularly jovial frame of mind, the girls made lemonade, which was always brought out in a red-glass pitcher, ornamented with forget-me-nots in blue enamel. This the girls thought very fine, and the neighbors always joked about the suspicious color of the pitcher.

Today Paul's father sat on the top step, talking to a young man who shifted a restless baby from knee to knee. He happened to be the young man who was daily held up to Paul as a model, and after whom it was his father's dearest hope that he would pattern. This young man was of a ruddy complexion, with a compressed, red mouth, and faded, nearsighted eyes, over which he wore

---

4. Bodices or blouses.   **5.** Tycoons of the iron and steel industry.

thick spectacles, with gold bows that curved about his ears. He was clerk to one of the magnates of a great steel corporation, and was looked upon in Cordelia Street as a young man with a future. There was a story that, some five years ago—he was now barely twenty-six—he had been a trifle dissipated, but in order to curb his appetites and save the loss of time and strength that a sowing of wild oats might have entailed, he had taken his chief's advice, often reiterated to his employees, and at twenty-one had married the first woman whom he could persuade to share his fortunes. She happened to be an angular schoolmistress, much older than he, who also wore thick glasses, and who had now borne him four children, all nearsighted, like herself.

The young man was relating how his chief, now cruising in the Mediterranean, kept in touch with all the details of the business, arranging his office hours on his yacht just as though he were at home, and "knocking off work enough to keep two stenographers busy." His father told, in turn, the plan his corporation was considering, of putting in an electric railway plant in Cairo. Paul snapped his teeth; he had an awful apprehension that they might spoil it all before he got there. Yet he rather liked to hear these legends of the iron kings that were told and retold on Sundays and holidays; these stories of palaces in Venice, yachts on the Mediterranean, and high play at Monte Carlo appealed to his fancy, and he was interested in the triumphs of these cash boys who had become famous, though he had no mind for the cash-boy stage.

After supper was over and he had helped to dry the dishes, Paul nervously asked his father whether he could go to George's to get some help in his geometry, and still more nervously asked for carfare. This latter request he had to repeat, as his father, on principle, did not like to hear requests for money, whether much or little. He asked Paul whether he could not go to some boy who lived nearer, and told him that he ought not to leave his schoolwork until Sunday; but he gave him the dime. He was not a poor man, but he had a worthy ambition to come up in the world. His only reason for allowing Paul to usher was that he thought a boy ought to be earning a little.

Paul bounded upstairs, scrubbed the greasy odor of the dishwater from his hands with the ill-smelling soap he hated, and then shook over his fingers a few drops of violet water from the bottle he kept hidden in his drawer. He left the house with his geometry conspicuously under his arm, and the moment he got out of Cordelia Street and boarded a downtown car, he shook off the lethargy of two deadening days and began to live again.

The leading juvenile[6] of the permanent stock company which played at one of the downtown theaters was an acquaintance of Paul's, and the boy had been invited to drop in at the Sunday-night rehearsals whenever he could. For more than a year Paul had spent every available moment loitering about Charley Edwards's dressing room. He had won a place among Edwards's following not only because the young actor, who could not afford to employ a dresser, often found him useful, but because he recognized in Paul something akin to what churchmen term "vocation."

It was at the theater and at Carnegie Hall that Paul really lived; the rest was but a sleep and a forgetting. This was Paul's fairy tale, and it had for him all the allurement of a secret love. The moment he inhaled the gassy, painty, dusty

6. Youthful male actor.

odor behind the scenes, he breathed like a prisoner set free, and felt within him the possibility of doing or saying splendid, brilliant, poetic things. The moment the cracked orchestra beat out the overture from *Martha*, or jerked at the serenade from *Rigoletto*,[7] all stupid and ugly things slid from him, and his senses were deliciously, yet delicately fired.

Perhaps it was because, in Paul's world, the natural nearly always wore the guise of ugliness, that a certain element of artificiality seemed to him necessary in beauty. Perhaps it was because his experience of life elsewhere was so full of Sabbath-school picnics, petty economies, wholesome advice as to how to succeed in life, and the inescapable odors of cooking, that he found this existence so alluring, these smartly clad men and women so attractive, that he was so moved by these starry apple orchards that bloomed perennially under the limelight.

It would be difficult to put it strongly enough how convincingly the stage entrance of that theater was for Paul the actual portal of Romance. Certainly none of the company ever suspected it, least of all Charley Edwards. It was very like the old stories that used to float about London of fabulously rich Jews, who had subterranean halls there, with palms, and fountains, and soft lamps and richly appareled women who never saw the disenchanting light of London day. So, in the midst of that smoke-palled city, enamored of figures and grimy toil, Paul had his secret temple, his wishing carpet, his bit of blue-and-white Mediterranean shore bathed in perpetual sunshine.

Several of Paul's teachers had a theory that his imagination had been perverted by garish fiction but the truth was that he scarcely ever read at all. The books at home were not such as would either tempt or corrupt a youthful mind, and as for reading the novels that some of his friends urged upon him—well, he got what he wanted much more quickly from music; any sort of music, from an orchestra to a barrel organ. He needed only the spark, the indescribable thrill that made his imagination master of his senses, and he could make plots and pictures enough of his own. It was equally true that he was not stagestruck—not, at any rate, in the usual acceptation of that expression. He had no desire to become an actor, any more than he had to become a musician. He felt no necessity to do any of these things; what he wanted was to see, to be in the atmosphere, float on the wave of it, to be carried out, blue league after blue league, away from everything.

After a night behind the scenes Paul found the schoolroom more than ever repulsive; the bare floors and naked walls; the prosy men who never wore frock coats, or violets in their bottonholes; the women with their dull gowns, shrill voices, and pitiful seriousness about prepositions that govern the dative. He could not bear to have the other pupils think, for a moment, that he took these people seriously; he must convey to them that he considered it all trivial, and was there only by way of a jest, anyway. He had autographed pictures of all the members of the stock company which he showed his classmates, telling them the most incredible stories of his familiarity with these people, of his acquaintance with the soloists who came to Carnegie Hall, his suppers with them and the flowers he sent them. When these stories lost their effect, and his audience grew listless, he became desperate and would bid all the boys good-by,

7. Operas by Friedrich von Flotow (1812–1883) and Giuseppe Verdi (1813–1901).

announcing that he was going to travel for a while; going to Naples, to Venice, to Egypt. Then, next Monday, he would slip back, conscious and nervously smiling; his sister was ill, and he should have to defer his voyage until spring.

Matters went steadily worse with Paul at school. In the itch to let his instructors know how heartily he despised them and their homilies, and how thoroughly he was appreciated elsewhere, he mentioned once or twice that he had no time to fool with theorems; adding—with a twitch of the eyebrows and a touch of that nervous bravado which so perplexed them—that he was helping the people down at the stock company; they were old friends of his.

The upshot of the matter was that the Principal went to Paul's father, and Paul was taken out of school and put to work. The manager at Carnegie Hall was told to get another usher in his stead; the doorkeeper at the theater was warned not to admit him to the house; and Charley Edwards remorsefully promised the boy's father not to see him again.

The members of the stock company were vastly amused when some of Paul's stories reached them—especially the women. They were hard-working women, most of them supporting indigent husbands or brothers, and they laughed rather bitterly at having stirred the boy to such fervid and florid inventions. They agreed with the faculty and with his father that Paul's was a bad case.

The eastbound train was plowing through a January snowstorm; the dull dawn was beginning to show gray when the engine whistled a mile out of Newark.[8] Paul started up from the seat where he had lain curled in uneasy slumber, rubbed the breath-misted window glass with his hand, and peered out. The snow was whirling in curling eddies above the white bottom lands, and the drifts lay already deep in the fields and along the fences, while here and there the long dead grass and dried weed stalks protruded black above it. Lights shone from the scattered houses, and a gang of laborers who stood beside the track waved their lanterns.

Paul had slept very little, and he felt grimy and uncomfortable. He had made the all-night journey in a day coach, partly because he was ashamed, dressed as he was, to go into a Pullman, and partly because he was afraid of being seen there by some Pittsburgh businessman, who might have noticed him in Denny & Carson's office. When the whistle awoke him, he clutched quickly at his breast pocket, glancing about him with an uncertain smile. But the little, clay-bespattered Italians were still sleeping, the slatternly women across the aisle were in open-mouthed oblivion, and even the crumby, crying babies were for the nonce stilled. Paul settled back to struggle with his impatience as best he could.

When he arrived at the Jersey City station he hurried through his breakfast, manifestly ill at ease and keeping a sharp eye about him. After he reached the Twenty-third Street station,[9] he consulted a cabman and had himself driven to a men's-furnishings establishment that was just opening for the day. He spent upward of two hours, buying with endless reconsidering and great care. His new street suit he put on in the fitting room; the frock coat and dress clothes he had bundled into the cab with his linen. Then he drove to a hatter's and a shoe house. His next errand was at Tiffany's, where he selected his

---

8. City in New Jersey just outside New York City.   **9.** Railway terminal in Manhattan.

silver and a new scarf pin. He would not wait to have his silver marked,[1] he said. Lastly, he stopped at a trunk shop on Broadway and had his purchases packed into various traveling bags.

It was a little after one o'clock when he drove up to the Waldorf,[2] and after settling with the cabman, went into the office. He registered from Washington; said his mother and father had been abroad, and that he had come down to await the arrival of their steamer. He told his story plausibly and had no trouble, since he volunteered to pay for them in advance, in engaging his rooms; a sleeping room, sitting room, and bath.

Not once, but a hundred times, Paul had planned this entry into New York. He had gone over every detail of it with Charley Edwards, and in his scrapbook at home there were pages of description about New York hotels, cut from the Sunday papers. When he was shown to his sitting room on the eighth floor he saw at a glance that everything was as it should be; there was but one detail in his mental picture that the place did not realize, so he rang for the bellboy and sent him down for flowers. He moved about nervously until the boy returned, putting away his new linen and fingering it delightedly as he did so. When the flowers came he put them hastily into water, and then tumbled into a hot bath. Presently he came out of his white bathroom, resplendent in his new silk underwear, and playing with the tassels of his red robe. The snow was whirling so fiercely outside his windows that he could scarcely see across the street, but within the air was deliciously soft and fragrant. He put the violets and jonquils on the taboret beside the couch, and threw himself down, with a long sigh, covering himself with a Roman blanket. He was thoroughly tired; he had been in such haste, he had stood up to such a strain, covered so much ground in the last twenty-four hours, that he wanted to think how it had all come about. Lulled by the sound of the wind, the warm air, and the cool fragrance of the flowers, he sank into deep, drowsy retrospection.

It had been wonderfully simple; when they had shut him out of the theater and concert hall, when they had taken away his bone, the whole thing was virtually determined. The rest was a mere matter of opportunity. The only thing that at all surprised him was his own courage—for he realized well enough that he had always been tormented by fear, a sort of apprehensive dread that, of late years, as the meshes of the lies he had told closed about him, had been pulling the muscles of his body tighter and tighter. Until now he could not remember the time when he had not been dreading something. Even when he was a little boy it was always there—behind him, or before, or on either side. There had always been the shadowed corner, the dark place into which he dared not look, but from which something seemed always to be watching him—and Paul had done things that were not pretty to watch, he knew.

 But now he had a curious sense of relief, as though he had at last thrown down the gauntlet to the thing in the corner.

Yet it was but a day since he had been sulking in the traces; but yesterday afternoon that he had been sent to the bank with Denny & Carson's deposit, as usual—but this time he was instructed to leave the book to be balanced. There was above two thousand dollars in checks, and nearly a thousand in the bank notes which he had taken from the book and quietly transferred to his pocket. At the bank he had made out a new deposit slip. His nerves had been steady enough to permit of his returning to the office, where he had finished his work and asked for a full day's holiday tomorrow, Saturday, giving a perfectly reasonable pretext. The bankbook, he knew, would not be returned before Monday or Tuesday, and his father would be out of town for the next week. From the time he slipped the bank notes into his pocket until he boarded the night train for New York, he had not known a moment's hesitation. It was not the first time Paul had steered through treacherous waters.

How astonishingly easy it had all been; here he was, the thing done; and this time there would be no awakening, no figure at the top of the stairs. He watched the snowflakes whirling by his window until he fell asleep.

When he awoke, it was three o'clock in the afternoon. He bounded up with a start; half of one of his precious days gone already! He spent more than an hour in dressing, watching every stage of his toilet carefully in the mirror. Everything was quite perfect; he was exactly the kind of boy he had always wanted to be.

When he went downstairs Paul took a carriage and drove up Fifth Avenue toward the Park.[3] The snow had somewhat abated; carriages and tradesmen's wagons were hurrying soundlessly to and fro in the winter twilight; boys in woolen mufflers were shoveling off the doorsteps; the avenue stages[4] made fine spots of color against the white street. Here and there on the corners were stands, with whole flower gardens blooming under glass cases, against the sides of which the snowflakes stuck and melted; violets, roses, carnations, lilies of the valley—somehow vastly more lovely and alluring that they blossomed thus unnaturally in the snow. The Park itself was a wonderful stage winterpiece.

When he returned, the pause of the twilight had ceased and the tune of the streets had changed. The snow was falling faster, lights streamed from the hotels that reared their dozen stories fearlessly up into the storm, defying the raging Atlantic winds. A long, black stream of carriages poured down the avenue, intersected here and there by other streams, tending horizontally. There were a score of cabs about the entrance of this hotel, and his driver had to wait. Boys in livery were running in and out of the awning stretched across the sidewalk, up and down the red velvet carpet laid from the door to the street. Above, about, within it all was the rumble and roar, the hurry and toss of thousands of human beings as hot for pleasure as himself, and on every side of him towered the glaring affirmation of the omnipotence of wealth.

The boy set his teeth and drew his shoulders together in a spasm of realization; the plot of all dramas, the text of all romances, the nerve-stuff of all sensations was whirling about him like the snowflakes. He burnt like a faggot in a tempest.

When Paul went down to dinner the music of the orchestra came floating up the elevator shaft to greet him. His head whirled as he stepped into the thronged corridor, and he sank back into one of the chairs against the wall to get his breath. The lights, the chatter, the perfumes, the bewildering medley of color—he had, for a moment, the feeling of not being able to stand it. But

---

3. That is, Central Park, the principal park in Manhattan. **4.** Window displays.

only for a moment; these were his own people, he told himself. He went slowly about the corridors, through the writing rooms, smoking rooms, reception rooms, as though he were exploring the chambers of an enchanted palace, built and peopled for him alone.

When he reached the dining room he sat down at a table near a window. The flowers, the white linen, the many-colored wineglasses, the gay toilettes of the women, the low popping of corks, the undulating repetitions of the *Blue Danube*[5] from the orchestra, all flooded Paul's dream with bewildering radiance. When the roseate tinge of his champagne was added—that cold, precious, bubbling stuff that creamed and foamed in his glass—Paul wondered that there were honest men in the world at all. This was what all the world was fighting for, he reflected; this was what all the struggle was about. He doubted the reality of his past. Had he ever known a place called Cordelia Street, a place where fagged-looking businessmen got on the early car; mere rivets in a machine they seemed to Paul,—sickening men, with combings of children's hair always hanging to their coats, and the smell of cooking in their clothes. Cordelia Street—Ah, that belonged to another time and country; had he not always been thus, had he not sat here night after night, from as far back as he could remember, looking pensively over just such shimmering textures and slowly twirling the stem of a glass like this one between his thumb and middle finger? He rather thought he had.

He was not the least abashed or lonely. He had no especial desire to meet or to know any of these people; all he demanded was the right to look on and conjecture, to watch the pageant. The mere stage properties were all he contended for. Nor was he lonely later in the evening, in his lodge at the Metropolitan.[6] He was now entirely rid of his nervous misgivings, of his forced aggressiveness, of the imperative desire to show himself different from his surroundings. He felt now that his surroundings explained him. Nobody questioned the purple,[7] he had only to wear it passively. He had only to glance down at his attire to reassure himself that here it would be impossible for anyone to humiliate him.

He found it hard to leave his beautiful sitting room to go to bed that night, and sat long watching the raging storm from his turret window. When he went to sleep it was with the lights turned on in his bedroom; partly because of his old timidity, and partly so that, if he should wake in the night, there would be no wretched moment of doubt, no horrible suspicion of yellow wallpaper, or of Washington and Calvin above his bed.

Sunday morning the city was practically snowbound. Paul breakfasted late, and in the afternoon he fell in with a wild San Francisco boy, a freshman at Yale, who said he had run down for a "little flyer" over Sunday. The young man offered to show Paul the night side of the town, and the two boys went out together after dinner, not returning to the hotel until seven o'clock the next morning. They had started out in the confiding warmth of a champagne friendship, but their parting in the elevator was singularly cool. The freshman pulled himself together to make his train, and Paul went to bed. He awoke at two o'clock in the afternoon, very thirsty and dizzy, and rang for ice-water, coffee, and the Pittsburgh papers.

5. Waltz by Johann Strauss II (1825–1899), Austrian composer. 6. His box at the Metropolitan Opera House. 7. That is, his assumption of a royal robe.

On the part of the hotel management, Paul excited no suspicion. There was this to be said for him, that he wore his spoils with dignity and in no way made himself conspicuous. Even under the glow of his wine he was never boisterous, though he found the stuff like a magician's wand for wonder-building. His chief greediness lay in his ears and eyes, and his excesses were not offensive ones. His dearest pleasures were the gray winter twilights in his sitting room; his quiet enjoyment of his flowers, his clothes, his wide divan, his cigarette, and his sense of power. He could not remember a time when he had felt so at peace with himself. The mere release from the necessity of petty lying, lying every day and every day, restored his self-respect. He had never lied for pleasure, even at school; but to be noticed and admired, to assert his difference from other Cordelia Street boys; and he felt a good deal more manly, more honest, even, now that he had no need for boastful pretensions, now that he could, as his actor friends used to say, "dress the part." It was characteristic that remorse did not occur to him. His golden days went by without a shadow, and he made each as perfect as he could.

On the eighth day after his arrival in New York he found the whole affair exploited in the Pittsburgh papers, exploited with a wealth of detail which indicated that local news of a sensational nature was at a low ebb. The firm of Denny & Carson announced that the boy's father had refunded the full amount of the theft and that they had no intention of prosecuting. The Cumberland minister had been interviewed, and expressed his hope of yet reclaiming the motherless lad, and his Sabbath-school teacher declared that she would spare no effort to that end. The rumor had reached Pittsburgh that the boy had been seen in a New York hotel, and his father had gone East to find him and bring him home.

Paul had just come in to dress for dinner; he sank into a chair, weak to the knees, and clasped his head in his hands. It was to be worse than jail, even; the tepid waters of Cordelia Street were to close over him finally and forever. The gray monotony stretched before him in hopeless, unrelieved years; Sabbath school, Young People's Meeting, the yellow-papered room, the damp dish-towels; it all rushed back upon him with a sickening vividness. He had the old feeling that the orchestra had suddenly stopped, the sinking sensation that the play was over. The sweat broke out on his face, and he sprang to his feet, looked about him with his white, conscious smile, and winked at himself in the mirror. With something of the old childish belief in miracles with which he had so often gone to class, all his lessons unlearned, Paul dressed and dashed whistling down the corridor to the elevator.

He had no sooner entered the dining room and caught the measure of the music than his remembrance was lightened by his old elastic power of claiming the moment, mounting with it, and finding it all-sufficient. The glare and glitter about him, the mere scenic accessories had again, and for the last time, their old potency. He would show himself that he was game, he would finish the thing splendidly. He doubted, more than ever, the existence of Cordelia Street, and for the first time he drank his wine recklessly. Was he not, after all, one of those fortunate beings born to the purple, was he not still himself and in his own place? He drummed a nervous accompaniment to the Pagliacci[8] music and looked about him, telling himself over and over that it had paid.

8. Opera by Ruggiero Leoncavallo (1858–1919).

He reflected drowsily, to the swell of the music and the chill sweetness of his wine, that he might have done it more wisely. He might have caught an outbound steamer and been well out of their clutches before now. But the other side of the world had seemed too far away and too uncertain then; he could not have waited for it; his need had been too sharp. If he had to choose over again, he would do the same thing tomorrow. He looked affectionately about the dining room, now gilded with a soft mist. Ah, it had paid indeed!

Paul was awakened next morning by a painful throbbing in his head and feet. He had thrown himself across the bed without undressing, and had slept with his shoes on. His limbs and hands were lead heavy, and his tongue and throat were parched and burnt. There came upon him one of those fateful attacks of clearheadedness that never occurred except when he was physically exhausted and his nerves hung loose. He lay still, closed his eyes, and let the tide of things wash over him.

His father was in New York; "stopping at some joint or other," he told himself. The memory of successive summers on the front stoop fell upon him like a weight of black water. He had not a hundred dollars left; and he knew now, more than ever, that money was everything, the wall that stood between all he loathed and all he wanted. The thing was winding itself up; he had thought of that on his first glorious day in New York, and had even provided a way to snap the thread. It lay on his dressing table now; he had got it out last night when he came blindly up from dinner, but the shiny metal hurt his eyes, and he disliked the looks of it.

He rose and moved about with a painful effort, succumbing now and again to attacks of nausea. It was the old depression exaggerated; all the world had become Cordelia Street. Yet somehow he was not afraid of anything, was absolutely calm; perhaps because he had looked into the dark corner at last and knew. It was bad enough, what he saw there, but somehow not so bad as his long fear of it had been. He saw everything clearly now. He had a feeling that he had made the best of it, that he had lived the sort of life he was meant to live, and for half an hour he sat staring at the revolver. But he told himself that was not the way, so he went downstairs and took a cab to the ferry.

When Paul arrived in Newark he got off the train and took another cab, directing the driver to follow the Pennsylvania tracks out of the town. The snow lay heavy on the roadways and had drifted deep in the open fields. Only here and there the dead grass or dried weed stalks projected, singularly black, above it. Once well into the country, Paul dismissed the carriage and walked, floundering along the tracks, his mind a medley of irrelevant things. He seemed to hold in his brain an actual picture of everything he had seen that morning. He remembered every feature of both his drivers, of the toothless old woman from whom he had bought the red flowers in his coat, the agent from whom he had got his ticket, and all of his fellow passengers on the ferry. His mind, unable to cope with vital matters near at hand, worked feverishly and deftly at sorting and grouping these images. They made for him a part of the ugliness of the world, of the ache in his head, and the bitter burning on his tongue. He stooped and put a handful of snow into his mouth as he walked, but that, too, seemed hot. When he reached a little hillside, where the tracks ran through a cut some twenty feet below him, he stopped and sat down.

The carnations in his coat were drooping with the cold, he noticed, their red glory all over. It occurred to him that all the flowers he had seen in the glass cases that first night must have gone the same way, long before this. It was only one splendid breath they had, in spite of their brave mockery at the winter outside the glass; and it was a losing game in the end, it seemed, this revolt against the homilies by which the world is run. Paul took one of the blossoms carefully from his coat and scooped a little hole in the snow, where he covered it up. Then he dozed awhile, from his weak condition, seemingly insensible to the cold.

The sound of an approaching train awoke him, and he started to his feet, remembering only his resolution, and afraid lest he should be too late. He stood watching the approaching locomotive, his teeth chattering, his lips drawn away from them in a frightened smile; once or twice he glanced nervously sidewise, as though he were being watched. When the right moment came, he jumped. As he fell, the folly of his haste occurred to him with merciless clearness, the vastness of what he had left undone. There flashed through his brain, clearer than ever before, the blue of Adriatic water, the yellow of Algerian sands.

He felt something strike his chest, and that his body was being thrown swiftly through the air, on and on, immeasurably far and fast, while his limbs were gently relaxed. Then, because the picturemaking mechanism was crushed, the disturbing visions flashed into black, and Paul dropped back into the immense design of things.

1905

(rules,)
道

RELATED:

—Andrea Barrett on "Paul's Case," p. 1755

JOHN CHEEVER
1912–1982

Cheever was born in Quincy, Massachusetts. His formal education ended when he was expelled from Thayer Academy at the age of seventeen—a circumstance that gave him subject matter for his first publication. Thereafter, he devoted himself completely to writing, except for brief interludes of teaching at Barnard and the University of Iowa. He wrote television scripts and four novels, but his fame rests on the large number of short stories, many appearing in *The New Yorker*, that he published in a steady stream beginning in the 1940s. Built around a strong moral core and tinged with melancholy nostalgia for the past, these stories form a running commentary on the tensions, manners, and crippled aspirations of urban and suburban life. Many of his stories have been collected in *The Enormous Radio and Other Stories* (1953), *The Housebreaker of Shady Hill and Other Stories* (1958), *The Brigadier and the Golf Widow* (1964), and *The World of Apples* (1973). His novels are *The Wapshot Chronicle* (1957), *The Wapshot Scandal* (1964), *Bullet Park* (1969), and *Falconer* (1977). *The Stories of John Cheever* (1978) won the Pulitzer Prize.

The Enormous Radio

Jim and Irene Westcott were the kind of people who seem to strike that satisfactory average of income, endeavor, and respectability that is reached by the statistical reports in college alumni bulletins. They were the parents of two young children, they had been married nine years, they lived on the twelfth floor of an apartment house near Sutton Place,[1] they went to the theatre on an average of 10.3 times a year, and they hoped someday to live in Westchester.[2] Irene Westcott was a pleasant, rather plain girl with soft brown hair and a wide, fine forehead upon which nothing at all had been written, and in the cold weather she wore a coat of fitch skins dyed to resemble mink. You could not say that Jim Westcott looked younger than he was, but you could at least say of him that he seemed to feel younger. He wore his graying hair cut very short, he dressed in the kind of clothes his class had worn at Andover,[3] and his manner was earnest, vehement, and intentionally naïve. The Westcotts differed from their friends, their classmates, and their neighbors only in an interest they shared in serious music. They went to a great

---

1. Fashionable area on New York City's East Side.   2. Affluent suburban county to the north of New York City.   3. Phillips Andover Academy, elite boarding school in Andover, Massachusetts.

many concerts—although they seldom mentioned this to anyone—and they spent a good deal of time listening to music on the radio.

Their radio was an old instrument, sensitive, unpredictable, and beyond repair. Neither of them understood the mechanics of radio—or of any of the other appliances that surrounded them—and when the instrument faltered, Jim would strike the side of the cabinet with his hand. This sometimes helped. One Sunday afternoon, in the middle of a Schubert[4] quartet, the music faded away altogether. Jim struck the cabinet repeatedly, but there was no response; the Schubert was lost to them forever. He promised to buy Irene a new radio, and on Monday when he came home from work he told her that he had got one. He refused to describe it, and said it would be a surprise for her when it came.

The radio was delivered at the kitchen door the following afternoon, and with the assistance of her maid and the handyman Irene uncrated it and brought it into the living room. She was struck at once with the physical ugliness of the large gumwood cabinet. Irene was proud of her living room, she had chosen its furnishings and colors as carefully as she chose her clothes, and now it seemed to her that the new radio stood among her intimate possessions like an aggressive intruder. She was confounded by the number of dials and switches on the instrument panel, and she studied them thoroughly before she put the plug into a wall socket and turned the radio on. The dials flooded with a malevolent green light, and in the distance she heard the music of a piano quintet. The quintet was in the distance for only an instant; it bore down upon her with a speed greater than light and filled the apartment with the noise of music amplified so mightily that it knocked a china ornament from a table to the floor. She rushed to the instrument and reduced the volume. The violent forces that were snared in the ugly gumwood cabinet made her uneasy. Her children came home from school then, and she took them to the Park. It was not until later in the afternoon that she was able to return to the radio.

The maid had given the children their suppers and was supervising their baths when Irene turned on the radio, reduced the volume, and sat down to listen to a Mozart[5] quintet that she knew and enjoyed. The music came through clearly. The new instrument had a much purer tone, she thought, than the old one. She decided that tone was most important and that she could conceal the cabinet behind a sofa. But as soon as she had made her peace with the radio, the interference began. A crackling sound like the noise of a burning powder fuse began to accompany the singing of the strings. Beyond the music, there was a rustling that reminded Irene unpleasantly of the sea, and as the quintet progressed, these noises were joined by many others. She tried all the dials and switches but nothing dimmed the interference, and she sat down, disappointed and bewildered, and tried to trace the flight of the melody. The elevator shaft in her building ran beside the living-room wall, and it was the noise of the elevator that gave her a clue to the character of the static. The rattling of the elevator cables and the opening and closing of the elevator doors were reproduced in her loudspeaker, and, realizing that the radio was

---

4. Franz Peter Schubert (1797–1828), Austrian composer.   5. Wolfgang Amadeus Mozart (1756–1791), Austrian composer.

sensitive to electrical currents of all sorts, she began to discern through the Mozart the ringing of telephone bells, the dialing of phones, and the lamentation of a vacuum cleaner. By listening more carefully, she was able to distinguish doorbells, elevator bells, electric razors, and Waring mixers, whose sounds had been picked up from the apartments that surrounded hers and transmitted through her loudspeaker. The powerful and ugly instrument, with its mistaken sensitivity to discord, was more than she could hope to master, so she turned the thing off and went into the nursery to see her children.

When Jim Westcott came home that night, he went to the radio confidently and worked the controls. He had the same sort of experience Irene had had. A man was speaking on the station Jim had chosen, and his voice swung instantly from the distance into a force so powerful that it shook the apartment. Jim turned the volume control and reduced the voice. Then, a minute or two later, the interference began. The ringing of telephones and doorbells set in, joined by the rasp of the elevator doors and the whir of cooking appliances. The character of the noise had changed since Irene had tried the radio earlier; the last of the electric razors was being unplugged, the vacuum cleaners had all been returned to their closets, and the static reflected that change in pace that overtakes the city after the sun goes down. He fiddled with the knobs but couldn't get rid of the noises, so he turned the radio off and told Irene that in the morning he'd call the people who had sold it to him and give them hell.

The following afternoon, when Irene returned to the apartment from a luncheon date, the maid told her that a man had come and fixed the radio. Irene went into the living room before she took off her hat or her furs and tried the instrument. From the loudspeaker came a recording of the "Missouri Waltz."[6] It reminded her of the thin, scratchy music from an old-fashioned phonograph that she sometimes heard across the lake where she spent her summers. She waited until the waltz had finished, expecting an explanation of the recording, but there was none. The music was followed by silence, and then the plaintive and scratchy record was repeated. She turned the dial and got a satisfactory burst of Caucasian music—the thump of bare feet in the dust and the rattle of coin jewelry—but in the background she could hear the ringing of bells and a confusion of voices. Her children came home from school then, and she turned off the radio and went to the nursery.

When Jim came home that night, he was tired, and he took a bath and changed his clothes. Then he joined Irene in the living room. He had just turned on the radio when the maid announced dinner, so he left it on, and he and Irene went to the table.

Jim was too tired to make even pretense of sociability, and there was nothing about the dinner to hold Irene's interest, so her attention wandered from the food to the deposits of silver polish on the candlesticks and from there to the music in the other room. She listened for a few minutes to a Chopin[7] prelude and then was surprised to hear a man's voice break in. "For Christ's sake, Kathy," he said, "do you always have to play the piano when I get home?"

6. Popular tune of 1916 by J. R. Shannon and Frederick Knight Logan. It was made popular again in the 1940s by President Harry Truman.   7. Frédéric François Chopin (1810–1849), Polish-French composer and pianist.

The music stopped abruptly. "It's the only chance I have," a woman said. "I'm at the office all day." "So am I," the man said. He added something obscene about an upright piano, and slammed a door. The passionate and melancholy music began again.

"Did you hear that?" Irene asked.

"What?" Jim was eating his dessert.

"The radio. A man said something while the music was still going on—something dirty."

"It's probably a play."

"I don't think it *is* a play," Irene said.

They left the table and took their coffee into the living room. Irene asked Jim to try another station. He turned the knob. "Have you seen my garters?" a man asked. "Button me up," a woman said. "Have you seen my garters?" the man said again. "Just button me up and I'll find your garters," the woman said. Jim shifted to another station. "I wish you wouldn't leave apple cores in the ashtrays," a man said. "I hate the smell."

"This is strange," Jim said.

"Isn't it?" Irene said.

Jim turned the knob again. "'On the coast of Coromandel where the early pumpkins blow,'" a woman with a pronounced English accent said, "'in the middle of the woods lived the Yonghy-Bonghy-Bò. Two old chairs, and half a candle, one old jug without a handle . . .'"[8]

"My God!" Irene cried. "That's the Sweeneys' nurse."

"'These were all his worldly goods,'" the British voice continued.

"Turn that thing off," Irene said. "Maybe they can hear *us*." Jim switched the radio off. "That was Miss Armstrong, the Sweeneys' nurse," Irene said. "She must be reading to the little girl. They live in 17-B. I've talked with Miss Armstrong in the Park. I know her voice very well. We must be getting other people's apartments."

"That's impossible," Jim said.

"Well, that was the Sweeneys' nurse," Irene said hotly. "I know her voice. I know it very well. I'm wondering if they can hear us."

Jim turned the switch. First from a distance and then nearer, nearer, as if borne on the wind, came the pure accents of the Sweeneys' nurse again: "'*Lady Jingly! Lady Jingly!*'" she said, "'*sitting where the pumpkins blow, will you come and be my wife?* said the Yonghy-Bonghy-Bò . . .'"

Jim went over to the radio and said "Hello" loudly into the speaker.

"'*I am tired of living singly,*'" the nurse went on, "'*on this coast so wild and shingly, I'm a-weary of my life; if you'll come and be my wife, quite serene would be my life . . .*'"

"I guess she can't hear us," Irene said. "Try something else."

Jim turned to another station, and the living room was filled with the uproar of a cocktail party that had overshot its mark. Someone was playing the piano and singing the "Whiffenpoof Song,"[9] and the voices that surrounded the piano were vehement and happy. "Eat some more sandwiches," a woman shrieked. There were screams of laughter and a dish of some sort crashed to the floor.

8. From *The Courtship of the Yonghy-Bonghy-Bò* by Edward Lear (1812–1888), English nonsense poet.
9. Famous Yale drinking song.

"Those must be the Fullers, in 11-E," Irene said. "I knew they were giving a party this afternoon. I saw her in the liquor store. Isn't this too divine? Try something else. See if you can get those people in 18-C."

The Westcotts overheard that evening a monologue on salmon fishing in Canada, a bridge game, running comments on home movies of what had apparently been a fortnight at Sea Island, and a bitter family quarrel about an overdraft at the bank. They turned off their radio at midnight and went to bed, weak with laughter. Sometime in the night, their son began to call for a glass of water and Irene got one and took it to his room. It was very early. All the lights in the neighborhood were extinguished, and from the boy's window she could see the empty street. She went into the living room and tried the radio. There was some faint coughing, a moan, and then a man spoke. "Are you all right, darling?" he asked. "Yes," a woman said wearily. "Yes, I'm all right, I guess," and then she added with great feeling, "But, you know, Charlie, I don't feel like myself any more. Sometimes there are about fifteen or twenty minutes in the week when I feel like myself. I don't like to go to another doctor, because the doctor's bills are so awful already, but I just don't feel like myself, Charlie. I just never feel like myself." They were not young, Irene thought. She guessed from the timbre of their voices that they were middle-aged. The restrained melancholy of the dialogue and the draft from the bedroom window made her shiver, and she went back to bed.

The following morning, Irene cooked breakfast for the family—the maid didn't come up from her room in the basement until ten—braided her daughter's hair, and waited at the door until her children and her husband had been carried away in the elevator. Then she went into the living room and tried the radio. "I don't want to go to school," a child screamed. "I hate school. I won't go to school. I hate school." "You will go to school," an enraged woman said. "We paid eight hundred dollars to get you into that school and you'll go if it kills you." The next number on the dial produced the worn record of the "Missouri Waltz." Irene shifted the control and invaded the privacy of several breakfast tables. She overheard demonstrations of indigestion, carnal love, abysmal vanity, faith, and despair. Irene's life was nearly as simple and sheltered as it appeared to be, and the forthright and sometimes brutal language that came from the loudspeaker that morning astonished and troubled her. She continued to listen until her maid came in. Then she turned off the radio quickly, since this insight, she realized, was a furtive one.

Irene had a luncheon date with a friend that day, and she left her apartment at a little after twelve. There were a number of women in the elevator when it stopped at her floor. She stared at their handsome and impassive faces, their furs, and the cloth flowers in their hats. Which one of them had been to Sea Island? she wondered. Which one had overdrawn her bank account. The elevator stopped at the tenth floor and a woman with a pair of Skye terriers joined them. Her hair was rigged high on her head and she wore a mink cape. She was humming the "Missouri Waltz."

Irene had two Martinis at lunch, and she looked searchingly at her friend and wondered what her secrets were. They had intended to go shopping after lunch, but Irene excused herself and went home. She told the maid that she was not to be disturbed; then she went into the living room, closed the doors, and switched on the radio. She heard, in the course of the afternoon, the halting conversation of a woman entertaining her aunt, the hysterical conclusion of a luncheon party, and a hostess briefing her maid about some cocktail guests. "Don't give the best Scotch to anyone who hasn't white hair," the hostess said. "See if you can get rid of that liver paste before you pass those hot things, and could you lend me five dollars? I want to tip the elevator man."

As the afternoon waned, the conversations increased in intensity. From where Irene sat, she could see the open sky above the East River. There were hundreds of clouds in the sky, as though the south wind had broken the winter into pieces and were blowing it north, and on her radio she could hear the arrival of cocktail guests and the return of children and businessmen from their schools and offices. "I found a good-sized diamond on the bathroom floor this morning," a woman said. "It must have fallen out of that bracelet Mrs. Dunston was wearing last night." "We'll sell it," a man said. "Take it down to the jeweler on Madison Avenue and sell it. Mrs. Dunston won't know the difference, and we could use a couple of hundred bucks . . ." "'Oranges and lemons, say the bells of St. Clement's,'" the Sweeneys' nurse sang. "'Halfpence and farthings, say the bells of St. Martin's. When will you pay me? say the bells at old Bailey . . .'"[1] "It's not a hat," a woman cried, and at her back roared a cocktail party. "It's not a hat, it's a love affair. That's what Walter Florell said. He said it's not a hat, it's a love affair," and then, in a lower voice, the same woman added, "Talk to somebody, for Christ's sake, honey, talk to somebody. If she catches you standing here not talking to anybody, she'll take us off her invitation list, and I love these parties."

The Westcotts were going out for dinner that night, and when Jim came home, Irene was dressing. She seemed sad and vague, and he brought her a drink. They were dining with friends in the neighborhood, and they walked to where they were going. The sky was broad and filled with light. It was one of those splendid spring evenings that excite memory and desire, and the air that touched their hands and faces felt very soft. A Salvation Army band was on the corner playing "Jesus Is Sweeter." Irene drew on her husband's arm and held him there for a minute, to hear the music. "They're really such nice people, aren't they?" she said. "They have such nice faces. Actually, they're so much nicer than a lot of the people we know." She took a bill from her purse and walked over and dropped it into the tambourine. There was in her face, when she returned to her husband, a look of radiant melancholy that he was not familiar with. And her conduct at the dinner party that night seemed strange to him, too. She interrupted her hostess rudely and stared at the people across the table from her with an intensity for which she would have punished her children.

It was still mild when they walked home from the party, and Irene looked up at the spring stars. "'How far that little candle throws its beams,'" she exclaimed. "'So shines a good deed in a naughty world.'"[2] She waited that night until Jim had fallen asleep, and then went into the living room and turned on the radio.

Jim came home at about six the next night. Emma, the maid, let him in, and he had taken off his hat and was taking off his coat when Irene ran into

---

1. From a British folk song.   **2.** Shakespeare's *Merchant of Venice* 5.1.

the hall. Her face was shining with tears and her hair was disordered. "Go up to 16-C, Jim!" she screamed. "Don't take off your coat. Go up to 16-C. Mr. Osborn's beating his wife. They've been quarreling since four o'clock, and now he's hitting her. Go up there and stop him."

From the radio in the living room, Jim heard screams, obscenities, and thuds. "You know you don't have to listen to this sort of thing," he said. He strode into the living room and turned the switch. "It's indecent," he said. "It's like looking in windows. You know you don't have to listen to this sort of thing. You can turn it off."

"Oh, it's so horrible, it's so dreadful," Irene was sobbing. "I've been listening all day, and it's so depressing."

"Well, if it's so depressing, why do you listen to it? I bought this damned radio to give you some pleasure," he said. "I paid a great deal of money for it. I thought it might make you happy. I wanted to make you happy."

"Don't, don't, don't, don't quarrel with me," she moaned, and laid her head on his shoulder. "All the others have been quarreling all day. Everybody's been quarreling. They're all worried about money. Mrs. Hutchinson's mother is dying of cancer in Florida and they don't have enough money to send her to the Mayo Clinic.[3] At least, Mr. Hutchinson says they don't have enough money. And some woman in this building is having an affair with the handyman— with that hideous handyman. It's too disgusting. And Mrs. Melville has heart trouble, and Mr. Hendricks is going to lose his job in April and Mrs. Hendricks is horrid about the whole thing and that girl who plays the 'Missouri Waltz' is a whore, a common whore, and the elevator man has tuberculosis and Mr. Osborn has been beating Mrs. Osborn." She wailed, she trembled with grief and checked the stream of tears down her face with the heel of her palm.

"Well, why do you have to listen?" Jim asked again. "Why do you have to listen to this stuff if it makes you so miserable?"

"Oh, don't, don't, don't," she cried. "Life is too terrible, too sordid and awful. But we've never been like that, have we, darling? Have we? I mean, we've always been good and decent and loving to one another, haven't we? And we have two children, two beautiful children. Our lives aren't sordid, are they, darling? Are they?" She flung her arms around his neck and drew his face down to hers. "We're happy, aren't we, darling? We are happy, aren't we?"

"Of course we're happy," he said tiredly. He began to surrender his resentment. "Of course we're happy. I'll have that damned radio fixed or taken away tomorrow." He stroked her soft hair. "My poor girl," he said.

"You love me, don't you?" she asked. "And we're not hypercritical or worried about money or dishonest, are we?"

"No, darling," he said.

A man came in the morning and fixed the radio. Irene turned it on cautiously and was happy to hear a California-wine commercial and a recording of Beethoven's Ninth Symphony, including Schiller's[4] "Ode to Joy." She kept the radio on all day and nothing untoward came from the speaker.

A Spanish suite was being played when Jim came home. "Is everything all right?" he asked. His face was pale, she thought. They had some cocktails and

3. Internationally famous hospital and diagnostic center in Rochester, Minnesota. 4. Johann Christoph Friedrich von Schiller (1759–1805), German poet and dramatist. Ludwig van Beethoven (1770–1827), German composer.

went in to dinner to the "Anvil Chorus" from *Il Trovatore.* This was followed by Debussy's[5] "La Mer."

"I paid the bill for the radio today," Jim said. "It cost four hundred dollars. I hope you'll get some enjoyment out of it."

"Oh, I'm sure I will," Irene said.

"Four hundred dollars is a good deal more than I can afford," he went on. "I wanted to get something that you'd enjoy. It's the last extravagance we'll be able to indulge in this year. I see that you haven't paid your clothing bills yet. I saw them on your dressing table." He looked directly at her. "Why did you tell me you'd paid them? Why did you lie to me?"

"I just didn't want you to worry, Jim," she said. She drank some water. "I'll be able to pay my bills out of this month's allowance. There were the slipcovers last month, and that party."

"You've got to learn to handle the money I give you a little more intelligently, Irene," he said. "You've got to understand that we don't have as much money this year as we had last. I had a very sobering talk with Mitchell today. No one is buying anything. We're spending all our time promoting new issues, and you know how long that takes. I'm not getting any younger, you know. I'm thirty-seven. My hair will be gray next year. I haven't done as well as I'd hoped to do. And I don't suppose things will get any better."

"Yes, dear," she said.

"We've got to start cutting down," Jim said. "We've got to think of the children. To be perfectly frank with you, I worry about money a great deal. I'm not at all sure of the future. No one is. If anything should happen to me, there's the insurance, but that wouldn't go very far today. I've worked awfully hard to give you and the children a comfortable life," he said bitterly. "I don't like to see all my energies, all of my youth, wasted in fur coats and radios and slipcovers and—"

"Please, Jim," she said. "Please. They'll hear us."

"Who'll hear us? Emma can't hear us."

"The radio."

"Oh, I'm sick!" he shouted. "I'm sick to death of your apprehensiveness. The radio can't hear us. Nobody can hear us. And what if they can hear us? Who cares?"

Irene got up from the table and went into the living room. Jim went to the door and shouted at her from there. "Why are you so Christly all of a sudden? What's turned you overnight into a convent girl? You stole your mother's jewelry before they probated her will. You never gave your sister a cent of that money that was intended for her—not even when she needed it. You made Grace Howland's life miserable, and where was all your piety and your virtue when you went to that abortionist? I'll never forget how cool you were. You packed your bag and went off to have that child murdered as if you were going to Nassau. If you'd had any reasons, if you'd had any good reasons—"

Irene stood for a minute before the hideous cabinet, disgraced and sickened, but she held her hand on the switch before she extinguished the music and the voices, hoping that the instrument might speak to her kindly, that

5. Claude Achille Debussy (1862–1918), French composer. *Il Trovatore:* opera by Giuseppe Verdi (1813–1901), Italian composer.

she might hear the Sweeneys' nurse. Jim continued to shout at her from the door. The voice on the radio was suave and noncommital. "An early-morning railroad disaster in Tokyo," the loudspeaker said, "killed twenty-nine people. A fire in a Catholic hospital near Buffalo for the care of blind children was extinguished early this morning by nuns. The temperature is forty-seven. The humidity is eighty-nine."

1953

The Death of Justina

So help me God it gets more and more preposterous, it corresponds less and less to what I remember and what I expect as if the force of life were centrifugal and threw one further and further away from one's purest memories and ambitions; and I can barely recall the old house where I was raised, where in midwinter Parma violets bloomed in a cold frame near the kitchen door, and down the long corridor, past the seven views of Rome—up two steps and down three—one entered the library, where all the books were in order, the lamps were bright, where there was a fire and a dozen bottles of good bourbon locked in a cabinet with a veneer like tortoise shell whose silver key my father wore on his watch chain. Fiction is art and art is the triumph over chaos (no less) and we can accomplish this only by the most vigilant exercise of choice, but in a world that changes more swiftly than we can perceive there is always the danger that our powers of selection will be mistaken and that the vision we serve will come to nothing. We admire decency and we despise death but even the mountains seem to shift in the space of a night and perhaps the exhibitionist at the corner of Chestnut and Elm streets is more significant than the lovely woman with a bar of sunlight in her hair, putting a fresh piece of cuttlebone in the nightingale's cage. Just let me give you one example of chaos and if you disbelieve me look honestly into your own past and see if you can't find a comparable experience. . . .

On Saturday the doctor told me to stop smoking and drinking and I did. I won't go into the commonplace symptoms of withdrawal but I would like to point out that, standing at my window in the evening, watching the brilliant afterlight and the spread of darkness, I felt, through the lack of these humble stimulants, the force of some primitive memory in which the coming of night with its stars and its moon was apocalyptic. I thought suddenly of the neglected graves of my three brothers on the mountainside and that death is a loneliness much crueler than any loneliness hinted at in life. The soul (I thought) does not leave the body but lingers with it through every degrading stage of decomposition and neglect, through heat, through cold, through the long winter nights when no one comes with a wreath or a plant and no one says a prayer. This unpleasant premonition was followed by anxiety. We were going out for dinner and I thought that the oil burner would explode in our absence and burn the house. The cook would get drunk and attack my daughter with a carving knife or my wife and I would be killed in a collision on the main highway, leaving our children bewildered orphans with nothing in life to look forward to but sadness. I was able to observe, along with these foolish and terrifying anxieties, a definite impairment of my discretionary poles. I felt as if I were being lowered by ropes into the atmosphere of my childhood. I told my wife—when she passed through the living room—that I had stopped smoking and drinking but she didn't seem to care and who would reward me for my privations? Who cared about the bitter taste in my mouth and that my head seemed to be leaving my shoulders? It seemed to me that men had honored one another with medals, statuary, and cups for much less and that abstinence is a social matter. When I abstain from sin it is more often a fear of scandal than a private resolve to improve on the purity of my heart, but here was a call for abstinence without the worldly enforcement of society, and death is not the threat that scandal is. When it was time for us to go out I was so light-headed that I had to ask my wife to drive the car. On Sunday I sneaked seven cigarettes in various hiding places and drank two Martinis in the downstairs coat closet. At breakfast on Monday my English muffin stared up at me from the plate. I mean I *saw* a face there in the rough, toasted surface. The moment of recognition was fleeting, but it was deep, and I wondered who it had been. Was it a friend, an aunt, a sailor, a ski instructor, a bartender, or a conductor on a train? The smile faded off the muffin but it had been there for a second—the sense of a person, a life, a pure force of gentleness and censure—and I am convinced that the muffin had contained the presence of some spirit. As you can see, I was nervous.

On Monday my wife's old cousin, Justina, came to visit her. Justina was a lively guest although she must have been crowding eighty. On Tuesday my wife gave her a lunch party. The last guest left at three and a few minutes later Cousin Justina, sitting on the living-room sofa with a glass of good brandy, breathed her last. My wife called me at the office and I said that I would be right out. I was clearing my desk when my boss, MacPherson, came in.

"Spare me a minute," he asked. "I've been bird-dogging all over the place, trying to track you down. Pierce had to leave early and I want you to write the last Elixircol commercial."

"Oh, I can't, Mac," I said. "My wife just called. Cousin Justina is dead."

"You write that commercial," he said. His smile was satanic. "Pierce had to leave early because his grandmother fell off a stepladder."

Now, I don't like fictional accounts of office life. It seems to me that if you're going to write fiction you should write about mountain climbing and tempests at sea, and I will go over my predicament with MacPherson briefly, aggravated as it was by his refusal to respect and honor the death of dear old Justina. It was like MacPherson. It was a good example of the way I've been treated. He is, I might say, a tall, splendidly groomed man of about sixty who changes his shirt three times a day, romances his secretary every afternoon between two and two-thirty, and makes the habit of continuously chewing gum seem hygienic and elegant. I write his speeches for him and it has not been a happy arrangement for me. If the speeches are successful MacPherson takes all the credit. I can see that his presence, his tailor, and his fine voice are all a part of the performance but it makes me angry never to be given credit for what was said. On the other hand, if the speeches are unsuccessful—if his presence and his voice can't carry the hour—his threatening and sarcastic manner is surgical and I am obliged to contain myself in the role of a man who can do no good in spite of the piles of congratulatory mail that my eloquence sometimes brings in. I must pretend—I must, like an actor, study and improve on my pretension—to have nothing to do with his triumphs, and I must bow my head gracefully in shame when we have both failed. I am forced to appear grateful for injuries, to lie, to smile falsely, and to play out a role as inane and as unrelated to the facts as a minor prince in an operetta, but if I speak the truth it will be my wife and my children who will pay in hardships for my outspokenness. Now he refused to respect or even to admit the solemn fact of a death in our family and if I couldn't rebel it seemed as if I could at least hint at it.

The commercial he wanted me to write was for a tonic called Elixircol and was to be spoken on television by an actress who was neither young nor beautiful but who had an appearance of ready abandon and who was anyhow the mistress of one of the sponsor's uncles. *Are you growing old?* I wrote. *Are you falling out of love with your image in the looking glass? Does your face in the morning seem rucked and seamed with alcoholic and sexual excesses and does the rest of you appear to be a grayish-pink lump, covered all over with brindle hair? Walking in the autumn woods do you feel that a subtle distance has come between you and the smell of wood smoke? Have you drafted your obituary? Are you easily winded? Do you wear a girdle? Is your sense of smell fading, is your interest in gardening waning, is your fear of heights increasing, and are your sexual drives as ravening and intense as ever and does your wife look more and more to you like a stranger with sunken cheeks who has wandered into your bedroom by mistake? If this or any of this is true you need Elixircol, the true juice of youth. The small economy size (business with the bottle) costs seventy-five dollars and the giant family bottle comes at two hundred and fifty. It's a lot of scratch, God knows, but these are inflationary times and who can put a price on youth? If you don't have the cash borrow it from your neighborhood loan shark or hold up the local bank. The odds are three to one that with a ten-cent water pistol and a slip of paper you can shake ten thousand out of any fainthearted teller. Everybody's doing it. (Music up and out.)* I sent this in to MacPherson via Ralphie, the messenger boy, and took the 4:16 home, traveling through a landscape of utter desolation.

Now, my journey is a digression and has no real connection to Justina's death but what followed could only have happened in my country and in my time and since I was an American traveling across an American landscape the trip may be part of the sum. There are some Americans who, although their fathers emigrated from the Old World three centuries ago, never seem to have quite completed the voyage and I am one of these. I stand, figuratively, with one wet foot on Plymouth Rock, looking with some delicacy, not into a formidable and challenging wilderness but onto a half-finished civilization embracing glass towers, oil derricks, suburban continents, and abandoned movie houses and wondering why, in this most prosperous, equitable, and accomplished world—where even the cleaning women practice the Chopin preludes in their spare time—everyone should seem to be disappointed.

At Proxmire Manor I was the only passenger to get off the random, meandering, and profitless local that carried its shabby lights off into the dusk like some game-legged watchman or beadle making his appointed rounds. I went around to the front of the station to wait for my wife and to enjoy the traveler's fine sense of crisis. Above me on the hill were my home and the homes of my friends, all lighted and smelling of fragrant wood smoke like the temples in a sacred grove, dedicated to monogamy, feckless childhood, and domestic bliss but so like a dream that I felt the lack of viscera with much more than poignance—the absence of that inner dynamism we respond to in some European landscapes. In short, I was disappointed. It was my country, my beloved country, and there have been mornings when I could have kissed the earth that covers its many provinces and states. There was a hint of bliss; romantic and domestic bliss. I seemed to hear the jinglebells of the sleigh that would carry me to Grandmother's house although in fact Grandmother spent the last years of her life working as a hostess on an ocean liner and was lost in the tragic sinking of the S.S. *Lorelei* and I was responding to a memory that I had not experienced. But the hill of light rose like an answer to some primitive dream of homecoming. On one of the highest lawns I saw the remains of a snowman who still smoked a pipe and wore a scarf and a cap but whose form was wasting away and whose anthracite eyes stared out at the view with terrifying bitterness. I sensed some disappointing greenness of spirit in the scene although I knew in my bones, no less, how like yesterday it was that my father left the Old World to found a new; and I thought of the forces that had brought stamina to the image: the cruel towns of Calabria and their cruel princes, the badlands northwest of Dublin, ghettos, despots, whorehouses, bread lines, the graves of children, intolerable hunger, corruption, persecution, and despair had generated these faint and mellow lights and wasn't it all a part of the great migration that is the life of man?

My wife's cheeks were wet with tears when I kissed her. She was distressed, of course, and really quite sad. She had been attached to Justina. She drove me home, where Justina was still sitting on the sofa. I would like to spare you the unpleasant details but I will say that both her mouth and her eyes were wide open. I went into the pantry to telephone Dr. Hunter. His line was busy. I poured myself a drink—the first since Sunday—and lighted a cigarette. When I called the doctor again he answered and I told him what had happened. "Well, I'm awfully sorry to hear about it, Moses," he said. "I can't get over until after six and there isn't much that I can do. This sort of thing has come up before and I'll tell you all I know. You see, you live in Zone B—two-acre lots, no commercial enterprises and so forth. A couple of years ago some stranger bought the old Plewett mansion and it turned out that he was planning to operate it as a funeral home. We didn't have any zoning provision at the time that would protect us and one was rushed through the Village Council at midnight and they overdid it. It seems that you not only can't have a funeral home in Zone B—you can't bury anything there and you can't die there. Of course it's absurd, but we all make mistakes, don't we? Now there are two things you can do. I've had to deal with this before. You can take the old lady and put her into the car and drive her over to Chestnut Street, where Zone C begins. The boundary is just beyond the traffic light by the high school. As soon as you get her over to Zone C, it's all right. You can just say she died in the car. You can do that or if this seems distasteful you can call the Mayor and ask him to make an exception to the zoning laws. But I can't write you out a death certificate until you get her out of that neighborhood and of course no undertaker will touch her until you get a death certificate."

"I don't understand," I said, and I didn't, but then the possibility that there was some truth in what he had just told me broke against me or over me like a wave, exciting mostly indignation. "I've never heard such a lot of damned foolishness in my life," I said. "Do you mean to tell me that I can't die in one neighborhood and that I can't fall in love in another and that I can't eat . . ."

"Listen. Calm down, Moses. I'm not telling you anything but the facts and I have a lot of patients waiting. I don't have the time to listen to you fulminate. If you want to move her, call me as soon as you get her over to the traffic light. Otherwise, I'd advise you to get in touch with the Mayor or someone on the Village Council." He cut the connection. I was outraged but this did not change the fact that Justina was still sitting on the sofa. I poured a fresh drink and lit another cigarette.

Justina seemed to be waiting for me and to be changing from an inert into a demanding figure. I tried to imagine carrying her out to the station wagon but I couldn't complete the task in my imagination and I was sure that I couldn't complete it in fact. I then called the Mayor but this position in our village is mostly honorary and as I might have known he was in his New York law office and was not expected home until seven. I could cover her, I thought, that would be a decent thing to do, and I went up the back stairs to the linen closet and got a sheet. It was getting dark when I came back into the living room but this was no merciful twilight. Dusk seemed to be playing directly into her hands and she gained power and stature with the dark. I covered her with a sheet and turned on a lamp at the other end of the room but the rectitude of the place with its old furniture, flowers, paintings, etc., was demolished by her monumental shape. The next thing to worry about was the children, who would be home in a few minutes. Their knowledge of death, excepting their dreams and intuitions of which I know nothing, is zero and the bold figure in the parlor was bound to be traumatic. When I heard them coming up the walk I went out and told them what had happened and sent them up to their rooms. At seven I drove over to the Mayor's.

He had not come home but he was expected at any minute and I talked with his wife. She gave me a drink. By this time I was chain-smoking. When the Mayor came in we went into a little office or library, where he took up a position behind a desk, putting me in the low chair of a supplicant. "Of course I sympathize with you, Moses," he said, "it's an awful thing to have happened, but the trouble is that we can't give you a zoning exception without a majority vote of the Village Council and all the members of the Council happen to be out of town. Pete's in California and Jack's in Paris and Larry won't be back from Stowe[1] until the end of the week."

I was sarcastic. "Then I suppose Cousin Justina will have to gracefully decompose in my parlor until Jack comes back from Paris."

"Oh no," he said, "oh *no*. Jack won't be back from Paris for another month but I think you might wait until Larry comes from Stowe. Then we'd have a majority, assuming of course that they would agree to your appeal."

"For Christ's sake," I snarled.

"Yes, yes," he said, "it is difficult, but after all you must realize that this is the world you live in and the importance of zoning can't be overestimated.

1. Mountain resort town in northern Vermont.

Why, if a single member of the Council could give out zoning exceptions, I could give you permission right now to open a saloon in your garage, put up neon lights, hire an orchestra, and destroy the neighborhood and all the human and commercial values we've worked so hard to protect."

"I don't want to open a saloon in my garage," I howled. "I don't want to hire an orchestra. I just want to bury Justina."

"I know, Moses, I know," he said. "I understand that. But it's just that it happened in the wrong zone and if I make an exception for you I'll have to make an exception for everyone and this kind of morbidity, when it gets out of hand, can be very depressing. People don't like to live in a neighborhood where this sort of thing goes on all the time."

"Listen to me," I said. "You give me an exception and you give it to me now or I'm going home and dig a hole in my garden and bury Justina myself."

"But you can't do that, Moses. You can't bury anything in Zone B. You can't even bury a cat."

"You're mistaken," I said. "I can and I will. I can't function as a doctor and I can't function as an undertaker, but I can dig a hole in the ground and if you don't give me my exception, that's what I'm going to do."

"Come back, Moses, come back," he said. "Please come back. Look, I'll give you an exception if you'll promise not to tell anyone. It's breaking the law, it's a forgery but I'll do it if you promise to keep it a secret."

I promised to keep it a secret, he gave me the documents, and I used his telephone to make the arrangements. Justina was removed a few minutes after I got home but that night I had the strangest dream. I dreamed that I was in a crowded supermarket. It must have been night because the windows were dark. The ceiling was paved with fluorescent light—brilliant, cheerful but, considering our prehistoric memories, a harsh link in the chain of light that binds us to the past. Music was playing and there must have been at least a thousand shoppers pushing their wagons among the long corridors of comestibles and victuals. Now is there—or isn't there—something about the posture we assume when we push a wagon that unsexes us? Can it be done with gallantry? I bring this up because the multitude of shoppers seemed that evening, as they pushed their wagons, penitential and unsexed. There were all kinds, this being my beloved country. There were Italians, Finns, Jews, Negroes, Shropshiremen, Cubans—anyone who had heeded the voice of liberty—and they were dressed with that sumptuary abandon that European caricaturists record with such bitter disgust. Yes, there were grandmothers in shorts, big-butted women in knitted pants, and men wearing such an assortment of clothing that it looked as if they had dressed hurriedly in a burning building. But this, as I say, is my own country and in my opinion the caricaturist who vilifies the old lady in shorts vilifies himself. I am a native and I was wearing buckskin jump boots, chino pants cut so tight that my sexual organs were discernible, and a rayon-acetate pajama top printed with representations of the *Pinta*, the *Niña*, and the *Santa María* in full sail. The scene was strange—the strangeness of a dream where we see familiar objects in an unfamiliar light—but as I looked more closely I saw that there were some irregularities. Nothing was labeled. Nothing was identified or known. The cans and boxes were all bare. The frozen-food bins were full of brown parcels but they were such odd shapes that you couldn't tell if they contained a frozen turkey or a Chinese dinner. All the goods at the vegetable and the bakery counters were concealed in brown bags and even the books for sale had no titles. In spite of the fact that the contents of nothing was known, my companions of the dream—my thousands of bizarrely dressed compatriots—were deliberating gravely over these mysterious containers as if the choices they made were critical. Like any dreamer, I was omniscient, I was with them and I was withdrawn, and stepping above the scene for a minute I noticed the men at the check-out counters. They were brutes. Now, sometimes in a crowd, in a bar or a street, you will see a face so full-blown in its obdurate resistance to the appeals of love, reason, and decency, so lewd, so brutish and unregenerate, that you turn away. Men like these were stationed at the only way out and as the shoppers approached them they tore their packages open—I still couldn't see what they contained—but in every case the customer, at the sight of what he had chosen, showed all the symptoms of the deepest guilt; that force that brings us to our knees. Once their choice had been opened to their shame they were pushed—in some cases kicked—toward the door and beyond the door I saw dark water and heard a terrible noise of moaning and crying in the air. They waited at the door in groups to be taken away in some conveyance that I couldn't see. As I watched, thousands and thousands pushed their wagons through the market, made their careful and mysterious choices, and were reviled and taken away. What could be the meaning of this?

We buried Justina in the rain the next afternoon. The dead are not, God knows, a minority, but in Proxmire Manor their unexalted kingdom is on the outskirts, rather like a dump, where they are transported furtively as knaves and scoundrels and where they lie in an atmosphere of perfect neglect. Justina's life had been exemplary, but by ending it she seemed to have disgraced us all. The priest was a friend and a cheerful sight, but the undertaker and his helpers, hiding behind their limousines, were not; and aren't they at the root of most of our troubles, with their claim that death is a violet-flavored kiss? How can a people who do not mean to understand death hope to understand love, and who will sound the alarm?

I went from the cemetery back to my office. The commercial was on my desk and MacPherson had written across it in grease pencil: *Very funny, you broken-down bore. Do again.* I was tired but unrepentant and didn't seem able to force myself into a practical posture of usefulness and obedience. I did another commercial. *Don't lose your loved ones,* I wrote, *because of excessive radio-activity. Don't be a wall-flower at the dance because of strontium 90 in your bones. Don't be a victim of fallout. When the tart on Thirty-sixth Street gives you the big eye does your body stride off in one direction and your imagination in another? Does your mind follow her up the stairs and taste her wares in revolting detail while your flesh goes off to Brooks Brothers or the foreign exchange desk of the Chase Manhattan Bank? Haven't you noticed the size of the ferns, the lushness of the grass, the bitterness of the string beans, and the brilliant markings on the new breeds of butterflies? You have been inhaling lethal atomic waste for the last twenty-five years and only Elixircol can save you.* I gave this to Ralphie and waited perhaps ten minutes, when it was returned, marked again with grease pencil. *Do,* he wrote, *or you'll be dead.* I felt very tired. I put another piece of paper into the machine and wrote: *The Lord is my shepherd; therefore can I lack nothing. He shall feed me in a green pasture and lead me forth beside the waters of comfort. He shall convert my soul and bring me forth in the paths of righteousness for his Name's sake. Yea, though I walk through the valley of the shadow of death I will fear no evil for thou art with me; thy rod and thy staff comfort me. Thou shalt prepare a table before me in the presence of them that trouble me; thou hast anointed my head with oil and my cup shall be full. Surely thy loving-kindness and mercy shall follow me all the days of my life and I will dwell in the house of the Lord for ever.*[2] I gave this to Ralphie and went home.

1960

2. Psalm 23.

ANTON CHEKHOV
1860–1904

Chekhov was born in Taganrog, Russia, the son of a despotic, dishonest, and rough-grained father—who was nevertheless eager to impart to his children his love for music and art. Trained as a physician at Moscow University, Chekhov practiced medicine only intermittently, although he credited his scientific training with conditioning him to be a perceptive observer of society and individual behavior. While still a medical student he began to write short pieces for humorous magazines; the popularity of these sketches roused his determination to become a serious artist. In 1890 he visited the Russian penal island of Sakhalin and without fanfare or special pleading wrote a moving account of convict life as he saw it there. He was at the height of his literary powers and his fame in 1901 when he married a young actress, but the state of his health by then was precarious. In the short time remaining to him, he was confined mostly to the house he had built with his literary earnings at Yalta in southern Russia, infrequently able to accompany his wife to Moscow to watch her performances in his plays. Those plays—among them *The Seagull* (1896), *Uncle Vanya* (1899), *The Three Sisters* (1901), and *The Cherry Orchard* (1904)—established him as one of the great dramatists of modern times, while his hundreds of short stories and novellas have immensely influenced the art of fiction since his death. In tribute to the humanity and responsibility of his work, Leo Tolstoy called him "an artist of life."

Gusev[1]

I

It is already dark, it will soon be night.

Gusev, a discharged private, half rises in his bunk and says in a low voice:

"Do you hear me, Pavel Ivanych? A soldier in Suchan was telling me: while they were sailing, their ship bumped into a big fish and smashed a hole in its bottom."

The individual of uncertain social status whom he is addressing, and whom everyone in the ship infirmary calls Pavel Ivanych, is silent as though he hasn't heard.

And again all is still. The wind is flirting with the rigging, the screw is throbbing, the waves are lashing, the bunks creak, but the ear has long since become used to these sounds, and everything around seems to slumber in silence. It is

1. Translated by Constance Garnett.

dull. The three invalids—two soldiers and a sailor—who were playing cards all day are dozing and talking deliriously.

The ship is apparently beginning to roll. The bunk slowly rises and falls under Gusev as though it were breathing, and this occurs once, twice, three times . . . Something hits the floor with a clang: a jug must have dropped.

"The wind has broken loose from its chain," says Gusev, straining his ears.

This time Pavel Ivanych coughs and says irritably:

"One minute a vessel bumps into a fish, the next the wind breaks loose from its chain . . . Is the wind a beast that it breaks loose from its chain?"

"That's what Christian folks say."

"They are as ignorant as you . . . They say all sorts of things. One must have one's head on one's shoulders and reason it out. You have no sense."

Pavel Ivanych is subject to seasickness. When the sea is rough he is usually out of sorts, and the merest trifle irritates him. In Gusev's opinion there is absolutely nothing to be irritated about. What is there that is strange or out of the way about that fish, for instance, or about the wind breaking loose from its chain? Suppose the fish were as big as the mountain and its back as hard as a sturgeon's, and supposing, too, that over yonder at the end of the world stood great stone walls and the fierce winds were chained up to the walls. If they haven't broken loose, why then do they rush all over the sea like madmen and strain like hounds tugging at their leash? If they are not chained up what becomes of them when it is calm?

Gusev ponders for a long time about fishes as big as a mountain and about stout, rusty chains. Then he begins to feel bored and falls to thinking about his home, to which he is returning after five years' service in the Far East. He pictures an immense pond covered with drifts. On one side of the pond is the brick-colored building of the pottery with a tall chimney and clouds of black smoke; on the other side is a village. His brother Alexey drives out of the fifth yard from the end in a sleigh; behind him sits his little son Vanka in big felt boots, and his little girl Akulka also wearing felt boots. Alexey has had a drop, Vanka is laughing, Akulka's face cannot be seen, she is muffled up.

"If he doesn't look out, he will have the children frostbitten," Gusev reflects. "Lord send them sense that they may honor their parents and not be any wiser than their father and mother."

"They need new soles," a delirious sailor says in a bass voice. "Yes, yes!"

Gusev's thoughts abruptly break off and suddenly without rhyme or reason the pond is replaced by a huge bull's head without eyes, and the horse and sleigh are no longer going straight ahead but are whirling round and round, wrapped in black smoke. But still he is glad he has had a glimpse of his people. In fact, he is breathless with joy, and his whole body, down to his fingertips, tingles with it. "Thanks be to God we have seen each other again," he mutters deliriously, but at once opens his eyes and looks for water in the dark.

He drinks and lies down, and again the sleigh is gliding along, then again there is the bull's head without eyes, smoke, clouds . . . And so it goes till daybreak.

II

A blue circle is the first thing to become visible in the darkness—it is the porthole; then, little by little, Gusev makes out the man in the next bunk, Pavel

Ivanych. The man sleeps sitting up, as he cannot breathe lying down. His face is gray, his nose long and sharp, his eyes look huge because he is terribly emaciated, his temples are sunken, his beard skimpy, his hair long. His face does not reveal his social status: you cannot tell whether he is a gentleman, a merchant, or a peasant. Judging from his expression and his long hair, he may be an assiduous churchgoer or a lay brother, but his manner of speaking does not seem to be that of a monk. He is utterly worn out by his cough, by the stifling heat, his illness, and he breathes with difficulty, moving his parched lips. Noticing that Gusev is looking at him he turns his face toward him and says:

"I begin to guess . . . Yes, I understand it all perfectly now."

"What do you understand, Pavel Ivanych?"

"Here's how it is . . . It has always seemed strange to me that terribly ill as you fellows are, you should be on a steamer where the stifling air, the heavy seas, in fact everything, threatens you with death; but now it is all clear to me . . . Yes . . . The doctors put you on the steamer to get rid of you. They got tired of bothering with you, cattle . . . You don't pay them any money, you are a nuisance, and you spoil their statistics with your deaths . . . So, of course, you are just cattle. And it's not hard to get rid of you . . . All that's necessary is, in the first place, to have no conscience or humanity, and, secondly, to deceive the ship authorities. The first requirement need hardly be given a thought—in that respect we are virtuosos, and as for the second condition, it can always be fulfilled with a little practice. In a crowd of four hundred healthy soldiers and sailors, five sick ones are not conspicuous; well, they got you all onto the steamer, mixed you with the healthy ones, hurriedly counted you over, and in the confusion nothing untoward was noticed, and when the steamer was on the way, people discovered that there were paralytics and consumptives on their last legs lying about the deck . . ."

Gusev does not understand Pavel Ivanych; thinking that he is being reprimanded, he says in self-justification:

"I lay on the deck because I was so sick; when we were being unloaded from the barge onto the steamer, I caught a bad chill."

"It's revolting," Pavel Ivanych continues. "The main thing is, they know perfectly well that you can't stand the long journey and yet they put you here. Suppose you last as far as the Indian Ocean, and then what? It's horrible to think of . . . And that's the gratitude for your faithful, irreproachable service!"

Pavel Ivanych's eyes flash with anger. He frowns fastidiously and says, gasping for breath, "Those are the people who ought to be given a drubbing in the newspapers till the feathers fly in all directions."

The two sick soldiers and the sailor have waked up and are already playing cards. The sailor is half reclining in his bunk, the soldiers are sitting near by on the floor in most uncomfortable positions. One of the soldiers has his right arm bandaged and his wrist is heavily swathed in wrappings that look like a cap, so that he holds his cards under his right arm or in the crook of his elbow while he plays with his left. The ship is rolling heavily. It is impossible to stand up, or have tea, or take medicine.

"Were you an orderly?" Pavel Ivanych asks Gusev.

"Yes, sir, an orderly."

"My God, my God!" says Pavel Ivanych and shakes his head sadly. "To tear a man from his home, drag him a distance of ten thousand miles, then wear him out till he gets consumption and . . . and what is it all for, one asks? To turn him into an orderly for some Captain Kopeykin or Midshipman Dyrka! How reasonable!"

"It's not hard work, Pavel Ivanych. You get up in the morning and polish the boots, start the samovars going, tidy the rooms, and then you have nothing more to do. The lieutenant drafts plans all day, and if you like, you can say your prayers, or read a book or go out on the street. God grant everyone such a life."

"Yes, very good! The lieutenant drafts plans all day long, and you sit in the kitchen and long for home . . . Plans, indeed! . . . It's not plans that matter but human life. You have only one life to live and it mustn't be wronged."

"Of course, Pavel Ivanych, a bad man gets no break anywhere, either at home or in the service, but if you live as you ought and obey orders, who will want to wrong you? The officers are educated gentlemen, they understand . . . In five years I have never once been in the guard house, and I was struck, if I remember right, only once."

"What for?"

"For fighting. I have a heavy hand, Pavel Ivanych. Four Chinks came into our yard; they were bringing firewood or something, I forget. Well, I was bored and I knocked them about a bit, the nose of one of them, damn him, began bleeding . . . The lieutenant saw it all through the window, got angry, and boxed me on the ear."

"You are a poor, foolish fellow . . ." whispers Pavel Ivanych. "You don't understand anything."

He is utterly exhausted by the rolling of the ship and shuts his eyes; now his head drops back, now it sinks forward on his chest. Several times he tries to lie down but nothing comes of it: he finds it difficult to breathe.

"And what did you beat up the four Chinks for?" he asks after a while.

"Oh, just like that. They came into the yard and I hit them."

There is silence . . . The card-players play for two hours, eagerly, swearing sometimes, but the rolling and pitching of the ship overcomes them, too; they throw aside the cards and lie down. Again Gusev has a vision: the big pond, the pottery, the village . . . Once more the sleigh is gliding along, once more Vanka is laughing and Akulka, the silly thing, throws open her fur coat and thrusts out her feet, as much as to say: "Look, good people, my felt boots are not like Vanka's, they're new ones."

"Going on six, and she has no sense yet," Gusev mutters in his delirium. "Instead of showing off your boots you had better come and get your soldier uncle a drink. I'll give you a present."

And here is Andron with a flintlock on his shoulder, carrying a hare he has killed, and behind him is the decrepit old Jew Isaychik, who offers him a piece of soap in exchange for the hare; and here is the black calf in the entry, and Domna sewing a shirt and crying about something, and then again the bull's head without eyes, black smoke . . .

Someone shouts overhead, several sailors run by; it seems that something bulky is being dragged over the deck, something falls with a crash. Again some people run by. . . . Has there been an accident? Gusev raises his head, listens, and sees that the two soldiers and the sailor are playing cards again; Pavel Ivanych is sitting up and moving his lips. It is stifling, you haven't the strength to breathe, you are thirsty, the water is warm, disgusting. The ship is still rolling and pitching.

Suddenly something strange happens to one of the soldiers playing cards. He calls hearts diamonds, gets muddled over his score, and drops his cards, then with a frightened, foolish smile looks round at all of them.

"I shan't be a minute, fellows . . ." he says, and lies down on the floor.

Everybody is nonplussed. They call to him, he does not answer.

"Stepan, maybe you are feeling bad, eh?" the soldier with the bandaged arm asks him. "Perhaps we had better call the priest, eh?"

"Have a drink of water, Stepan . . ." says the sailor. "Here, brother, drink."

"Why are you knocking the jug against his teeth?" says Gusev angrily. "Don't you see, you cabbage-head?"

"What?"

"What?" Gusev mimicks him. "There is no breath in him, he's dead! That's what! Such stupid people, Lord God!"

III

The ship has stopped rolling and Pavel Ivanych is cheerful. He is no longer cross. His face wears a boastful, challenging, mocking expression. It is as though he wants to say: "Yes, right away I'll tell you something that will make you burst with laughter." The round porthole is open and a soft breeze is blowing on Pavel Ivanych. There is a sound of voices, the splash of oars in the water . . . Just under the porthole someone is droning in a thin, disgusting voice; must be a Chinaman singing.

"Here we are in the harbor," says Pavel Ivanych with a mocking smile. "Only another month or so and we shall be in Russia. M'yes, messieurs of the armed forces! I'll arrive in Odessa and from there go straight to Kharkov. In Kharkov I have a friend, a man of letters. I'll go to him and say, 'Come, brother, put aside your vile subjects, women's amours and the beauties of Nature, and show up the two-legged vermin' . . . There's a subject for you."

For a while he reflects, then says:

"Gusev, do you know how I tricked them?"

"Tricked who, Pavel Ivanych?"

"Why, these people . . . You understand, on this steamer there is only a first class and a third class, and they only allow peasants, that is, the common herd, to go in the third. If you have got a jacket on and even at a distance look like a gentleman or a bourgeois,[2] you have to go first class, if you please. You must fork out five hundred rubles if it kills you. 'Why do you have such a regulation?' I ask them. 'Do you mean to raise the prestige of the Russian intelligentsia thereby?' 'Not a bit of it. We don't let you simply because a decent person can't go third class; it is too horrible and disgusting there.' 'Yes, sir? Thank you for being so solicitous about decent people's welfare. But in any case, whether it's nasty there or nice, I haven't got five hundred rubles. I didn't loot the Treasury, I didn't exploit the natives, I didn't traffic in contraband, I flogged nobody to death, so judge for yourselves if I have the right to occupy a

2. A member of the middle class.

first class cabin and even to reckon myself among the Russian intelligentsia.' But logic means nothing to them. So I had to resort to fraud. I put on a peasant coat and high boots, I pulled a face so that I looked like a common drunk, and went to the agents: 'Give us a little ticket, your Excellency,' said I—"

"You're not of the gentry, are you?" asked the sailor.

"I come of a clerical family. My father was a priest, and an honest one; he always told the high and mighty the truth to their faces and, as a result, he suffered a great deal."

Pavel Ivanych is exhausted from talking and gasps for breath, but still continues:

"Yes, I always tell people the truth to their faces. I'm not afraid of anyone or anything. In this respect, there is a great difference between me and all of you, men. You are dark people, blind, crushed; you see nothing and what you do see, you don't understand . . . You are told that the wind breaks loose from its chain, that you are beasts, savages, and you believe it; someone gives it to you in the neck—you kiss his hand; some animal in a racoon coat robs you and then tosses you a fifteen-kopeck tip and you say: 'Let me kiss your hand, sir.' You are outcasts, pitiful wretches. I am different, my mind is clear. I see it all plainly like a hawk or an eagle when it hovers over the earth, and I understand everything. I am protest personified. I see tyranny—I protest. I see a hypocrite—I protest, I see a triumphant swine—I protest. And I cannot be put down, no Spanish Inquisition[3] can silence me. No. Cut out my tongue and I will protest with gestures. Wall me up in a cellar—I will shout so that you will hear me half a mile away, or will starve myself to death, so that they may have another weight on their black consciences. Kill me and I will haunt them. All my acquaintances say to me: 'You are a most insufferable person, Pavel Ivanych.' I am proud of such a reputation. I served three years in the Far East and I shall be remembered there a hundred years. I had rows there with everybody. My friends wrote to me from Russia: 'Don't come back,' but here I am going back to spite them . . . Yes . . . That's life as I understand it. That's what one can call life."

Gusev is not listening; he is looking at the porthole. A junk, flooded with dazzling hot sunshine, is swaying on the transparent turquoise water. In it stand naked Chinamen, holding up cages with canaries in them and calling out: "It sings, it sings!"

Another boat knocks against it; a steam cutter glides past. Then there is another boat: a fat Chinaman sits in it, eating rice with chopsticks. The water sways lazily, white sea gulls languidly hover over it.

"Would be fine to give that fat fellow one in the neck," reflects Gusev, looking at the stout Chinaman and yawning.

He dozes off and it seems to him that all nature is dozing too. Time flies swiftly by. Imperceptibly the day passes. Imperceptibly darkness descends . . . The steamer is no longer standing still but is on the move again.

I V

Two days pass. Pavel Ivanych no longer sits up but is lying down. His eyes are closed, his nose seems to have grown sharper.

---

3. The state tribunal of the Roman Catholic Church, established in Spain in 1480 to eradicate heresy, infamous for its cruelty and capriciousness. Joseph Bonaparte abolished it in 1808.

"Pavel Ivanych," Gusev calls to him. "Hey, Pavel Ivanych."

Pavel Ivanych opens his eyes and moves his lips.

"Are you feeling bad?"

"No . . . It's nothing . . ." answers Pavel Ivanych gasping for breath. "Nothing, on the contrary . . . I am better . . . You see, I can lie down now . . . I have improved . . ."

"Well, thank God for that, Pavel Ivanych."

"When I compare myself to you, I am sorry for you, poor fellows. My lungs are healthy, mine is a stomach cough . . . I can stand hell, let alone the Red Sea. Besides, I take a critical attitude toward my illness and the medicines. While you—Your minds are dark . . . It's hard on you, very, very hard!"

The ship is not rolling, it is quiet, but as hot and stifling as a Turkish bath; it is hard, not only to speak, but even to listen. Gusev hugs his knees, lays his head on them and thinks of his home. God, in this stifling heat, what a relief it is to think of snow and cold! You're driving in a sleigh; all of a sudden, the horses take fright at something and bolt. Careless of the road, the ditches, the gullies, they tear like mad things right through the village, across the pond, past the pottery, across the open fields. "Hold them!" the pottery hands and the peasants they meet shout at the top of their voices. "Hold them!" But why hold them? Let the keen cold wind beat in your face and bite your hands; let the lumps of snow, kicked up by the horses, slide down your collar, your neck, your chest; let the runners sing, and the traces and the whippletrees break, the devil take them. And what delight when the sleigh upsets and you go flying full tilt into a drift, face right in the snow, and then you get up, white all over with icicles on your mustache, no cap, no gloves, your belt undone . . . People laugh, dogs bark . . .

Pavel Ivanych half opens one eye, fixes Gusev with it and asks softly:

"Gusev, did your commanding officer steal?"

"Who can tell, Pavel Ivanych? We can't say, we didn't hear about it."

And after that, a long time passes in silence. Gusev broods, his mind wanders, and he keeps drinking water: it is hard for him to talk and hard for him to listen, and he is afraid of being talked to. An hour passes, a second, a third; evening comes, then night, but he doesn't notice it; he sits up and keeps dreaming of the frost.

There is a sound as though someone were coming into the infirmary, voices are heard, but five minutes pass and all is quiet again.

"The kingdom of Heaven be his and eternal peace," says the soldier with a bandaged arm. "He was an uneasy chap."

"What?" asks Gusev. "Who?"

"He died, they have just carried him up."

"Oh, well," mutters Gusev, yawning, "the kingdom of Heaven be his."

"What do you think, Gusev?" the soldier with the bandaged arm says after a while. "Will he be in the kingdom of Heaven or not?"

"Who do you mean?"

"Pavel Ivanych."

"He will . . . He suffered so long. Then again, he belonged to the clergy and priests have a lot of relatives. Their prayers will get him there."

The soldier with the bandage sits down on Gusev's bunk and says in an undertone:

"You too, Gusev, aren't long for this world. You will never get to Russia."

"Did the doctor or the nurse say so?" asks Gusev.

"It isn't that they said so, but one can see it. It's plain when a man will die soon. You don't eat, you don't drink, you've got so thin it's dreadful to look at you. It's consumption, in a word. I say it not to worry you, but because maybe you would like to receive the sacrament and extreme unction.[4] And if you have any money, you had better turn it over to the senior officer."

"I haven't written home," Gusev sighs: "I shall die and they won't know."

"They will," the sick sailor says in a bass voice. "When you die, they will put it down in the ship's log, in Odessa they will send a copy of the entry to the army authorities, and they will notify your district board or somebody like that."

Such a conversation makes Gusev uneasy and a vague craving begins to torment him. He takes a drink—it isn't that; he drags himself to the porthole and breathes the hot, moist air—it isn't that; he tries to think of home, of the frost—it isn't that . . . At last it seems to him that if he stays in the infirmary another minute, he will certainly choke to death.

"It's stifling, brother," he says. "I'll go on deck. Take me there, for Christ's sake."

"All right," the soldier with the bandage agrees. "You can't walk, I'll carry you. Hold on to my neck."

Gusev puts his arm around the soldier's neck, the latter places his uninjured arm round him and carries him up. On the deck, discharged soldiers and sailors are lying asleep side by side; there are so many of them it is difficult to pass.

"Get down on the floor," the soldier with the bandage says softly. "Follow me quietly, hold on to my shirt."

It is dark, there are no lights on deck or on the masts or anywhere on the sea around. On the prow the seaman on watch stands perfectly still like a statue, and it looks as though he, too, were asleep. The steamer seems to be left to its own devices and to be going where it pleases.

"Now they'll throw Pavel Ivanych into the sea," says the soldier with the bandage, "in a sack and then into the water."

"Yes, that's the regulation."

"At home, it's better to lie in the earth. Anyway, your mother will come to the grave and shed a tear."

"Sure."

There is a smell of dung and hay. With drooping heads, steers stand at the ship's rail. One, two, three—eight of them! And there's a pony. Gusev puts out his hand to stroke it, but it shakes its head, shows its teeth, and tries to bite his sleeve.

"Damn brute!" says Gusev crossly.

The two of them thread their way to the prow, then stand at the rail, peering. Overhead there is deep sky, bright stars, peace and quiet, exactly as at home in the village. But below there is darkness and disorder. Tall waves are making an uproar for no reason. Each one of them as you look at it is trying to rise higher than all the rest and to chase and crush its neighbor; it is

4. The sacrament also known as the Anointing of the Sick, or Last Rites.

thunderously attacked by a third wave that has a gleaming white mane and is just as ferocious and ugly.

The sea has neither sense nor pity. If the steamer had been smaller, not made of thick iron plates, the waves would have crushed it without the slightest remorse, and would have devoured all the people in it without distinguishing between saints and sinners. The steamer's expression was equally senseless and cruel. This beaked monster presses forward, cutting millions of waves in its path; it fears neither darkness nor the wind, nor space, nor solitude—it's all child's play for it, and if the ocean had its population, this monster would crush it, too, without distinguishing between saints and sinners.

"Where are we now?" asks Gusev.

"I don't know. Must be the ocean."

"You can't see land . . ."

"No chance of it! They say we'll see it only in seven days."

The two men stare silently at the white phosphorescent foam and brood. Gusev is first to break the silence.

"There is nothing frightening here," he says. "Only you feel queer as if you were in a dark forest; but if, let's say, they lowered the boat this minute and an officer ordered me to go fifty miles across the sea to catch fish, I'll go. Or, let's say, if a Christian were to fall into the water right now, I'd jump in after him. A German or a Chink I wouldn't try to save, but I'd go in after a Christian."

"And are you afraid to die?"

"I am. I am sorry about the farm. My brother at home, you know, isn't steady; he drinks, he beats his wife for no reason, he doesn't honor his father and mother. Without me everything will go to rack and ruin, and before long it's my fear that my father and old mother will be begging their bread. But my legs won't hold me up, brother, and it's stifling here. Let's go to sleep."

V

Gusev goes back to the infirmary and gets into his bunk. He is again tormented by a vague desire and he can't make out what it is that he wants. There is a weight on his chest, a throbbing in his head, his mouth is so dry that it is difficult for him to move his tongue. He dozes and talks in his sleep and, worn out with nightmares, with coughing and the stifling heat, towards morning he falls into a heavy sleep. He dreams that they have just taken the bread out of the oven in the barracks and that he has climbed into the oven and is having a steam bath there, lashing himself with a besom of birch twigs. He sleeps for two days and on the third at noon two sailors come down and carry him out of the infirmary. He is sewn up in sailcloth and to make him heavier, they put two gridirons in with him. Sewn up in sailcloth, he looks like a carrot or a radish: broad at the head and narrow at the feet. Before sunset, they carry him on deck and put him on a plank. One end of the plank lies on the ship's rail, the other on a box placed on a stool. Round him stand the discharged soldiers and the crew with heads bared.

"Blessed is our God," the priest begins, "now, and ever, and unto ages of ages."

"Amen," three sailors chant.

The discharged men and the crew cross themselves and look off at the waves. It is strange that a man should be sewn up in sailcloth and should soon be flying into the sea. Is it possible that such a thing can happen to anyone?

The priest strews earth upon Gusev and makes obeisance to him. The men sing "Memory Eternal."

The seaman on watch duty raises the end of the plank, Gusev slides off it slowly and then flying, head foremost, turns over in the air and—plop! Foam covers him, and for a moment, he seems to be wrapped in lace, but the instant passes and he disappears in the waves.

He plunges rapidly downward. Will he reach the bottom? At this spot the ocean is said to be three miles deep. After sinking sixty or seventy feet, he begins to descend more and more slowly, swaying rhythmically as though in hesitation, and, carried along by the current, moves faster laterally than vertically.

And now he runs into a school of fish called pilot fish. Seeing the dark body, the little fish stop as though petrified and suddenly all turn round together and disappear. In less than a minute they rush back at Gusev, swift as arrows and begin zigzagging round him in the water. Then another dark body appears. It is a shark. With dignity and reluctance, seeming not to notice Gusev, as it were, it swims under him; then while he, moving downward, sinks upon its back, the shark turns, belly upward, basks in the warm transparent water and languidly opens its jaws with two rows of teeth. The pilot fish are in ecstasy; they stop to see what will happen next. After playing a little with the body, the shark nonchalantly puts his jaws under it, cautiously touches it with his teeth and the sailcloth is ripped the full length of the body, from head to foot; one of the gridirons falls out, frightens the pilot fish and striking the shark on the flank, sinks rapidly to the bottom.

Meanwhile, up above, in that part of the sky where the sun is about to set, clouds are massing, one resembling a triumphal arch, another a lion, a third a pair of scissors. A broad shaft of green light issues from the clouds and reaches to the middle of the sky; a while later, a violet beam appears alongside of it and then a golden one and a pink one . . . The heavens turn a soft lilac tint. Looking at this magnificent enchanting sky, the ocean frowns at first, but soon it, too, takes on tender, joyous, passionate colors for which it is hard to find a name in the language of man.

1890

Anna on the Neck[1]

I

After the wedding they had not even light refreshments; the happy pair simply drank a glass of champagne, changed into their travelling things, and drove to the station. Instead of a gay wedding ball and supper, instead of

---

1. Translated by Constance Garnett.

music and dancing, they went on a journey to pray at a shrine a hundred and fifty miles away. Many people commended this, saying that Modest Alexevitch was a man high up in the service and no longer young, and that a noisy wedding might not have seemed quite suitable; and music is apt to sound dreary when a government official of fifty-two marries a girl who is only just eighteen. People said, too, that Modest Alexevitch, being a man of principle, had arranged this visit to the monastery expressly in order to make his young bride realize that even in marriage he put religion and morality above everything.

The happy pair were seen off at the station. The crowd of relations and colleagues in the service stood, with glasses in their hands, waiting for the train to start to shout "Hurrah!" and the bride's father, Pyotr Leontyitch, wearing a top-hat and the uniform of a teacher, already drunk and very pale, kept craning towards the window, glass in hand and saying in an imploring voice:

"Anyuta! Anya, Anya! one word!"

Anna bent out of the window to him, and he whispered something to her, enveloping her in a stale smell of alcohol, blew into her ear—she could make out nothing—and made the sign of the cross over her face, her bosom, and her hands; meanwhile he was breathing in gasps and tears were shining in his eyes. And the schoolboys, Anna's brothers, Petya and Andrusha, pulled at his coat from behind, whispering in confusion:

"Father, hush! . . . Father, that's enough. . . ."

When the train started, Anna saw her father run a little way after the train, staggering and spilling his wine, and what a kind, guilty, pitiful face he had:

"Hurra—ah!" he shouted.

The happy pair were left alone. Modest Alexevitch looked about the compartment, arranged their things on the shelves, and sat down, smiling, opposite his young wife. He was an official of medium height, rather stout and puffy, who looked exceedingly well nourished, with long whiskers and no moustache. His clean-shaven, round, sharply defined chin looked like the heel of a foot. The most characteristic point in his face was the absence of moustache, the bare, freshly shaven place, which gradually passed into the fat cheeks, quivering like jelly. His deportment was dignified, his movements were deliberate, his manner was soft.

"I cannot help remembering now one circumstance," he said, smiling. "When, five years ago, Kosorotov received the order of St. Anna of the second grade, and went to thank His Excellency, His Excellency expressed himself as follows: 'So now you have three Annas: one in your buttonhole and two on your neck.' And it must be explained that at that time Kosorotov's wife, a quarrelsome and frivolous person, had just returned to him, and that her name was Anna. I trust that when I receive the Anna of the second grade His Excellency will not have occasion to say the same thing to me."

He smiled with his little eyes. And she, too, smiled, troubled at the thought that at any moment this man might kiss her with his thick damp lips, and that she had no right to prevent his doing so. The soft movements of his fat person frightened her; she felt both fear and disgust. He got up, without haste took off the order from his neck, took off his coat and waistcoat, and put on his dressing-gown.

"That's better," he said, sitting down beside Anna.

Anna remembered what agony the wedding had been, when it had seemed to her that the priest, and the guests, and every one in church had been looking at her sorrowfully and asking why, why was she, such a sweet, nice girl, marrying such an elderly, uninteresting gentleman. Only that morning she was delighted that everything had been satisfactorily arranged, but at the time of the wedding, and now in the railway carriage, she felt cheated, guilty, and ridiculous. Here she had married a rich man and yet she had no money, her wedding-dress had been bought on credit, and when her father and brothers had been saying good-bye, she could see from their faces that they had not a farthing. Would they have any supper that day? And tomorrow? And for some reason it seemed to her that her father and the boys were sitting tonight hungry without her, and feeling the same misery as they had the day after their mother's funeral.

"Oh, how unhappy I am!" she thought. "Why am I so unhappy?"

With the awkwardness of a man with settled habits, unaccustomed to deal with women, Modest Alexevitch touched her on the waist and patted her on the shoulder, while she went on thinking about money, about her mother and her mother's death. When her mother died, her father, Pyotr Leontyitch, a teacher of drawing and writing in the high school, had taken to drink, impoverishment had followed, the boys had not had boots or galoshes, their father had been hauled up before the magistrate, the warrant officer had come and made an inventory of the furniture. . . . What a disgrace! Anna had had to look after her drunken father, darn her brothers' stockings, go to market, and when she was complimented on her youth, her beauty, and her elegant manners, it seemed to her that everyone was looking at her cheap hat and the holes in her boots that were inked over. And at night there had been tears and a haunting dread that her father would soon, very soon, be dismissed from the school for his weakness, and that he would not survive it, but would die, too, like their mother. But ladies of their acquaintance had taken the matter in hand and looked about for a good match for Anna. This Modest Alexevitch, who was neither young nor good-looking but had money, was soon found. He had a hundred thousand in the bank and the family estate, which he had let on lease. He was a man of principle and stood well with His Excellency; it would be nothing to him, so they told Anna, to get a note from His Excellency to the directors of the high school, or even to the Education Commissioner, to prevent Pyotr Leontyitch from being dismissed.

While she was recalling these details, she suddenly heard strains of music which floated in at the window, together with the sound of voices. The train was stopping at a station. In the crowd beyond the platform an accordion and a cheap squeaky fiddle were being briskly played, and the sound of a military band came from beyond the villas and the tall birches and poplars that lay bathed in the moonlight; there must have been a dance in the place. Summer visitors and townspeople, who used to come out here by train in fine weather for a breath of fresh air, were parading up and down on the platform. Among them was the wealthy owner of all the summer villas—a tall, stout, dark man called Artynov. He had prominent eyes and looked like an Armenian. He wore a strange costume; his shirt was unbuttoned, showing his chest; he wore high boots with spurs, and a black cloak hung from his shoulders and dragged on the ground like a train. Two boar-hounds followed him with their sharp noses to the ground.

Tears were still shining in Anna's eyes, but she was not thinking now of her mother, nor of money, nor of her marriage; but shaking hands with school-boys and officers she knew, she laughed gaily and said quickly:

"How do you do? How are you?"

She went out on to the platform between the carriages into the moonlight, and stood so that they could all see her in her new splendid dress and hat.

"Why are we stopping here?" she asked.

"This is a junction. They are waiting for the mail train to pass."

Seeing that Artynov was looking at her, she screwed up her eyes coquett-ishly and began talking aloud in French; and because her voice sounded so pleasant, and because she heard music and the moon was reflected in the pond, and because Artynov, the notorious Don Juan and spoiled child of for-tune, was looking at her eagerly and with curiosity, and because everyone was in good spirits—she suddenly felt joyful, and when the train started and the officers of her acquaintance saluted her, she was humming the polka the strains of which reached her from the military band playing beyond the trees; and she returned to her compartment feeling as though it had been proved to her at the station that she would certainly be happy in spite of everything.

The happy pair spent two days at the monastery, then went back to town. They lived in a rent-free flat. When Modest Alexevitch had gone to the office, Anna played the piano, or shed tears of depression, or lay down on a couch and read novels or looked through fashion papers. At dinner Modest Alex-evitch ate a great deal and talked about politics, about appointments, trans-fers, and promotions in the service, about the necessity of hard work, and said that, family life not being a pleasure but a duty, if you took care of the kopecks the roubles would take care of themselves, and that he put religion and morality before everything else in the world. And holding his knife in his fist as though it were a sword, he would say:

"Everyone ought to have his duties!"

And Anna listened to him, was frightened, and could not eat, and she usu-ally got up from the table hungry. After dinner her husband lay down for a nap and snored loudly, while Anna went to see her own people. Her father and the boys looked at her in a peculiar way, as though just before she came in they had been blaming her for having married for money a tedious, weari-some man she did not love; her rustling skirts, her bracelets, and her general air of a married lady, offended them and made them uncomfortable. In her presence they felt a little embarrassed and did not know what to talk to her about; but yet they still loved her as before, and were not used to having din-ner without her. She sat down with them to cabbage soup, porridge, and fried potatoes, smelling of mutton dripping. Pyotr Leontyitch filled his glass from the decanter with a trembling hand and drank it off hurriedly, greedily, with repulsion, then poured out a second glass and then a third. Petya and Andrusha, thin, pale boys with big eyes, would take the decanter and say desperately:

"You mustn't, father.... Enough, father...."

And Anna, too, was troubled and entreated him to drink no more; and he would suddenly fly into a rage and beat the table with his fists:

"I won't allow any one to dictate to me!" he would shout. "Wretched boys! wretched girl! I'll turn you all out!"

But there was a note of weakness, of good-nature in his voice, and no one was afraid of him. After dinner he usually dressed in his best. Pale, with a cut on his chin from shaving, craning his thin neck, he would stand for half an hour before the glass, prinking, combing his hair, twisting his black moustache, sprinkling himself with scent, tying his cravat in a bow; then he would put on his gloves and his top-hat, and go off to give his private lessons. Or if it was a holiday he would stay at home and paint, or play the harmonium, which wheezed and growled; he would try to wrest from it pure harmonious sounds and would sing to it; or would storm at the boys:

"Wretches! Good-for-nothing boys! You have spoiled the instrument!"

In the evening Anna's husband played cards with his colleagues, who lived under the same roof in the government quarters. The wives of these gentlemen would come in—ugly, tastelessly dressed women, as coarse as cooks—and gossip would begin in the flat as tasteless and unattractive as the ladies themselves. Sometimes Modest Alexevitch would take Anna to the theatre. In the intervals he would never let her stir a step from his side, but walked about arm in arm with her through the corridors and the foyer. When he bowed to someone, he immediately whispered to Anna: "A civil councillor . . . visits at His Excellency's"; or, "A man of means . . . has a house of his own." When they passed the buffet Anna had a great longing for something sweet; she was fond of chocolate and apple cakes, but she had no money, and she did not like to ask her husband. He would take a pear, pinch it with his fingers, and ask uncertainly:

"How much?"

"Twenty-five kopecks!"

"I say!" he would reply, and put it down; but as it was awkward to leave the buffet without buying anything, he would order some seltzer-water and drink the whole bottle himself, and tears would come into his eyes. And Anna hated him at such times.

And suddenly flushing crimson, he would say to her rapidly:

"Bow to that old lady!"

"But I don't know her."

"No matter. That's the wife of the director of the local treasury! Bow, I tell you," he would grumble insistently. "Your head won't drop off."

Anna bowed and her head certainly did not drop off, but it was agonizing. She did everything her husband wanted her to, and was furious with herself for having let him deceive her like the veriest idiot. She had only married him for his money, and yet she had less money now than before her marriage. In the old days her father would sometimes give her twenty kopecks, but now she had not a farthing. To take money by stealth or ask for it, she could not; she was afraid of her husband, she trembled before him. She felt as though she had been afraid of him for years. In her childhood the director of the high school had always seemed the most impressive and terrifying force in the world, sweeping down like a thunderstorm or a steam-engine ready to crush her; another similar force of which the whole family talked, and of which they were for some reason afraid, was His Excellency; then there were a dozen others, less formidable, and among them the teachers at the high school, with shaven upper lips, stern, implacable; and now finally, there was Modest Alexevitch, a man of principle, who even resembled the director in the face. And in Anna's imagination all these forces blended together into one, and, in the form of a terrible, huge white bear, menaced the weak and erring such as her father. And she was afraid to say anything in opposition to her husband, and gave a forced smile, and tried to make a show of pleasure when she was coarsely caressed and defiled by embraces that excited her terror.

Only once Pyotr Leontyitch had the temerity to ask for a loan of fifty roubles in order to pay some very irksome debt, but what an agony it had been!

"Very good; I'll give it to you," said Modest Alexevitch after a moment's thought; "but I warn you I won't help you again till you give up drinking. Such a failing is disgraceful in a man in the government service! I must remind you of the well-known fact that many capable people have been ruined by that passion, though they might possibly, with temperance, have risen in time to a very high position."

And long-winded phrases followed: "inasmuch as . . . ," "following upon which proposition . . . ," "in view of the aforesaid contention . . ."; and Pyotr Leontyitch was in agonies of humiliation and felt an intense craving for alcohol.

And when the boys came to visit Anna, generally in broken boots and threadbare trousers, they, too, had to listen to sermons.

"Every man ought to have his duties!" Modest Alexevitch would say to them.

And he did not give them money. But he did give Anna bracelets, rings, and brooches, saying that these things would come in useful for a rainy day. And he often unlocked her drawer and made an inspection to see whether they were all safe.

II

Meanwhile winter came on. Long before Christmas there was an announcement in the local papers that the usual winter ball would take place on the twenty-ninth of December in the Hall of Nobility. Every evening after cards Modest Alexevitch was excitedly whispering with his colleagues' wives and glancing at Anna, and then paced up and down the room for a long while, thinking. At last, late one evening, he stood still, facing Anna, and said:

"You ought to get yourself a ball dress. Do you understand? Only please consult Marya Grigoryevna and Natalya Kuzminishna."

And he gave her a hundred roubles. She took the money, but she did not consult anyone when she ordered the ball dress; she spoke to no one but her father, and tried to imagine how her mother would have dressed for a ball. Her mother had always dressed in the latest fashion and had always taken trouble over Anna, dressing her elegantly like a doll, and had taught her to speak French and dance the mazurka superbly (she had been a governess for five years before her marriage). Like her mother, Anna could make a new dress out of an old one, clean gloves with benzine, hire jewels; and, like her mother, she knew how to screw up her eyes, lisp, assume graceful attitudes, fly into raptures when necessary, and throw a mournful and enigmatic look into her eyes. And from her father she had inherited the dark colour of her hair and eyes, her highly-strung nerves, and the habit of always making herself look her best.

When, half an hour before setting off for the ball, Modest Alexevitch went into her room without his coat on, to put his order round his neck before her pier-glass, dazzled by her beauty and the splendour of her fresh, ethereal dress, he combed his whiskers complacently and said:

"So that's what my wife can look like . . . so that's what you can look like! Anyuta!" he went on, dropping into a tone of solemnity, "I have made your fortune, and now I beg you to do something for mine. I beg you to get introduced to the wife of His Excellency! For God's sake, do! Through her I may get the post of senior reporting clerk!"

They went to the ball. They reached the Hall of Nobility, the entrance with the hall porter. They came to the vestibule with the hat-stands, the fur coats; footmen scurrying about, and ladies with low necks putting up their fans to screen themselves from the draughts. There was a smell of gas and of soldiers. When Anna, walking upstairs on her husband's arm, heard the music and saw herself full length in the looking-glass in the full glow of the lights, there was a rush of joy in her heart, and she felt the same presentiment of happiness as in the moonlight at the station. She walked in proudly, confidently, for the first time feeling herself not a girl but a lady, and unconsciously imitating her mother in her walk and in her manner. And for the first time in her life she felt rich and free. Even her husband's presence did not oppress her, for as she crossed the threshold of the hall she had guessed instinctively that the proximity of an old husband did not detract from her in the least, but, on the contrary, gave her that shade of piquant mystery that is so attractive to men. The orchestra was already playing and the dances had begun. After their flat Anna was overwhelmed by the lights, the bright colours, the music, the noise, and looking round the room, thought, "Oh, how lovely!" She at once distinguished in the crowd all her acquaintances, everyone she had met before at parties or on picnics—all the officers, the teachers, the lawyers, the officials, the landowners, His Excellency, Artynov, and the ladies of the highest standing, dressed up and very *décolletées*, handsome and ugly, who had already taken up their positions in the stalls and pavilions of the charity bazaar, to begin selling things for the benefit of the poor. A huge officer in epaulettes—she had been introduced to him in Staro-Kievsky Street when she was a schoolgirl, but now she could not remember his name—seemed to spring from out of the ground, begging her for a waltz, and she flew away from her husband, feeling as though she were floating away in a sailing-boat in a violent storm, while her husband was left far away on the shore. She danced passionately, with fervour, a waltz, then a polka and a quadrille, being snatched by one partner as soon as she was left by another, dizzy with music and the noise, mixing Russian with French, lisping, laughing, and with no thought of her husband or anything else. She excited great admiration among the men—that was evident, and indeed it could not have been otherwise; she was breathless with excitement, felt thirsty, and convulsively clutched her fan. Pyotr Leontyitch, her father, in a crumpled dress-coat that smelt of benzine, came up to her, offering her a plate of pink ice.

"You are enchanting this evening," he said, looking at her rapturously, "and I have never so much regretted that you were in such a hurry to get married. . . .

What was it for? I know you did it for our sake, but . . ." With a shaking hand he drew out a roll of notes and said: "I got the money for my lessons today, and can pay your husband what I owe him."

She put the plate back into his hand, and was pounced upon by someone and borne off to a distance. She caught a glimpse over her partner's shoulder of her father gliding over the floor, putting his arm round a lady and whirling down the ballroom with her.

"How sweet he is when he is sober!" she thought.

She danced the mazurka with the same huge officer; he moved gravely, as heavily as a dead carcase in a uniform, twitched his shoulders and his chest, stamped his feet very languidly—he felt fearfully disinclined to dance. She fluttered round him, provoking him by her beauty, her bare neck; her eyes glowed defiantly, her movements were passionate, while he became more and more indifferent, and held out his hands to her as graciously as a king.

"Bravo, bravo!" said people watching them.

But little by little the huge officer, too, broke out; he grew lively, excited, and, overcome by her fascination, was carried away and danced lightly, youthfully, while she merely moved her shoulders and looked slyly at him as though she were now the queen and he were her slave; and at that moment it seemed to her that the whole room was looking at them, and that everybody was thrilled and envied them. The huge officer had hardly had time to thank her for the dance, when the crowd suddenly parted and the men drew themselves up in a strange way, with their hands at their sides. His Excellency, with two stars on his dress-coat, was walking up to her. Yes, His Excellency was walking straight towards her, for he was staring directly at her with a sugary smile, while he licked his lips as he always did when he saw a pretty woman.

"Delighted, delighted . . ." he began. "I shall order your husband to be clapped in a lock-up for keeping such a treasure hidden from us till now. I've come to you with a message from my wife," he went on, offering her his arm. "You must help us . . . M-m-yes . . . We ought to give you the prize for beauty as they do in America. . . . M-m-yes. . . . The Americans. . . . My wife is expecting you impatiently."

He led her to a stall and presented her to a middle-aged lady, the lower part of whose face was disproportionately large, so that she looked as though she were holding a big stone in her mouth.

"You must help us," she said through her nose in a sing-song voice. "All the pretty women are working for our charity bazaar, and you are the only one enjoying yourself. Why won't you help us?"

She went away, and Anna took her place by the cups and the silver samovar. She was soon doing a lively trade. Anna asked no less than a rouble for a cup of tea, and made the huge officer drink three cups. Artynov, the rich man with prominent eyes, who suffered from asthma, came up, too; he was not dressed in the strange costume in which Anna had seen him in the summer at the station, but wore a dress-coat like everyone else. Keeping his eyes fixed on Anna, he drank a glass of champagne and paid a hundred roubles for it, then drank some tea and gave another hundred—all this without saying a word, as he was short of breath through asthma. . . . Anna invited purchasers and got money out of them, firmly convinced by now that her smiles and glances could not fail to afford these people great pleasure. She realized now that she was created exclusively for this noisy, brilliant, laughing life, with its music, its dancers, its adorers, and her old terror of a force that was sweeping down upon her and menacing to crush her seemed to her ridiculous: she was afraid of no one now, and only regretted that her mother could not be there to rejoice at her success.

Pyotr Leontyitch, pale by now but still steady on his legs, came up to the stall and asked for a glass of brandy. Anna turned crimson, expecting him to say something inappropriate (she was already ashamed of having such a poor and ordinary father); but he emptied his glass, took ten roubles out of his roll of notes, flung it down, and walked away with dignity without uttering a word. A little later she saw him dancing in the grand chain, and by now he was staggering and kept shouting something, to the great confusion of his partner; and Anna remembered how at the ball three years before he had staggered and shouted in the same way, and it had ended in the police-sergeant's taking him home to bed, and next day the director had threatened to dismiss him from his post. How inappropriate that memory was!

When the samovars were put out in the stalls and the exhausted ladies handed over their takings to the middle-aged lady with the stone in her mouth, Artynov took Anna on his arm to the hall where supper was served to all who had assisted at the bazaar. There were some twenty people at supper, not more, but it was very noisy. His Excellency proposed a toast:

"In this magnificent dining-room it will be appropriate to drink to the success of the cheap dining-rooms, which are the object of today's bazaar."

The brigadier-general proposed the toast: "To the power by which even the artillery is vanquished," and all the company clinked glasses with the ladies. It was very, very gay.

When Anna was escorted home it was daylight and the cooks were going to market. Joyful, intoxicated, full of new sensations, exhausted, she undressed, dropped into bed, and at once fell asleep. . . .

It was past one in the afternoon when the servant waked her and announced that M. Artynov had called. She dressed quickly and went down into the drawing-room. Soon after Artynov, His Excellency called to thank her for her assistance in the bazaar. With a sugary smile, chewing his lips, he kissed her hand, and asking her permission to come again, took his leave, while she remained standing in the middle of the drawing-room, amazed, enchanted, unable to believe that this change in her life, this marvellous change, had taken place so quickly; and at that moment Modest Alexevitch walked in . . . and he, too, stood before her now with the same ingratiating, sugary, cringingly respectful expression which she was accustomed to see on his face in the presence of the great and powerful; and with rapture, with indignation, with contempt, convinced that no harm would come to her from it, she said, articulating distinctly each word:

"Be off, you blockhead!"

From this time forward Anna never had one day free, as she was always taking part in picnics, expeditions, performances. She returned home every day after midnight, and went to bed on the floor in the drawing-room, and afterwards used to tell everyone, touchingly, how she slept under flowers. She needed a very great deal of money, but she was no longer afraid of Modest Alexevitch, and spent his money as though it were her own; and she did not ask, did not demand it, simply sent him in the bills. "Give bearer two hundred roubles," or "Pay one hundred roubles at once."

At Easter Modest Alexevitch received the Anna of the second grade. When he went to offer his thanks, His Excellency put aside the paper he was reading and settled himself more comfortably in his chair.

"So now you have three Annas," he said, scrutinizing his white hands and pink nails—"one on your buttonhole and two on your neck."

Modest Alexevitch put two fingers to his lips as a precaution against laughing too loud and said:

"Now I have only to look forward to the arrival of a little Vladimir. I make bold to beg your Excellency to stand godfather."

He was alluding to Vladimir of the fourth grade, and was already imagining how he would tell everywhere the story of this pun, so happy in its readiness and audacity, and he wanted to say something equally happy, but His Excellency was buried again in his newspaper, and merely gave him a nod.

And Anna went on driving about with three horses, going out hunting with Artynov, playing in one-act dramas, going out to supper, and was more and more rarely with her own family; they dined now alone. Pyotr Leontyitch was drinking more heavily than ever; there was no money, and the harmonium had been sold long ago for debt. The boys did not let him go out alone in the street now, but looked after him for fear he might fall down; and whenever they met Anna driving in Staro-Kievsky Street with a pair of horses and Artynov on the box instead of a coachman, Pyotr Leontyitch took off his top-hat, and was about to shout to her, but Petya and Andrusha took him by the arm, and said imploringly:

"You mustn't, father. Hush, father!"

1895

RELATED:

—Author in Depth: Anton Chekhov, p. 1787

KATE CHOPIN
1851–1904

Chopin was born in St. Louis to a prominent Creole-Irish family that prized books and education. On a visit to New Orleans she met her husband-to-be and returned there to live with him when she married at twenty. After her husband's early death, she went back to St. Louis and began to write, largely drawing on the experiences of her years in the Deep South. She contributed to many of the popular periodicals of her time, but her writing career came to an end with the publication of her novel *The Awakening* (1899), which was sharply condemned for its frank representation of adultery and mixed marriage. This book has subsequently been praised for its sensitive portrayal of a woman in quest of her individuality. Many of Chopin's stories were collected in *Bayou Folk* (1894) and *A Night in Acadie* (1899).

The Story of an Hour

Knowing that Mrs. Mallard was afflicted with a heart trouble, great care was taken to break to her as gently as possible the news of her husband's death.

It was her sister Josephine who told her, in broken sentences; veiled hints that revealed in half concealing. Her husband's friend Richards was there, too, near her. It was he who had been in the newspaper office when intelligence of the railroad disaster was received, with Brently Mallard's name leading the list of "killed." He had only taken the time to assure himself of its truth by a second telegram, and had hastened to forestall any less careful, less tender friend in bearing the sad message.

She did not hear the story as many women have heard the same, with a paralyzed inability to accept its significance. She wept at once, with sudden, wild abandonment, in her sister's arms. When the storm of grief had spent itself she went away to her room alone. She would have no one follow her.

There stood, facing the open window, a comfortable, roomy armchair. Into this she sank, pressed down by a physical exhaustion that haunted her body and seemed to reach into her soul.

She could see in the open square before her house the tops of trees that were all aquiver with the new spring life. The delicious breath of rain was in the air. In the street below a peddler was crying his wares. The notes of a distant song which some one was singing reached her faintly, and countless sparrows were twittering in the eaves.

There were patches of blue sky showing here and there through the clouds that had met and piled one above the other in the west facing her window.

She sat with her head thrown back upon the cushion of the chair, quite motionless, except when a sob came up into her throat and shook her, as a child who has cried itself to sleep continues to sob in its dreams.

She was young, with a fair, calm face, whose lines bespoke repression and even a certain strength. But now there was a dull stare in her eyes, whose gaze was fixed away off yonder on one of those patches of blue sky. It was not a glance of reflection, but rather indicated a suspension of intelligent thought.

There was something coming to her and she was waiting for it, fearfully. What was it? She did not know; it was too subtle and elusive to name. But she felt it, creeping out of the sky, reaching toward her through the sounds, the scents, the color that filled the air.

Now her bosom rose and fell tumultuously. She was beginning to recognize this thing that was approaching to possess her, and she was striving to beat it back with her will—as powerless as her two white slender hands would have been.

When she abandoned herself a little whispered word escaped her slightly parted lips. She said it over and over under her breath: "free, free, free!" The vacant stare and the look of terror that had followed it went from her eyes. They stayed keen and bright. Her pulses beat fast, and the coursing blood warmed and relaxed every inch of her body.

She did not stop to ask if it were or were not a monstrous joy that held her. A clear and exalted perception enabled her to dismiss the suggestion as trivial.

She knew that she would weep again when she saw the kind, tender hands folded in death; the face that had never looked save with love upon her, fixed and gray and dead. But she saw beyond that bitter moment a long procession of years to come that would belong to her absolutely. And she opened and spread her arms out to them in welcome.

There would be no one to live for her during those coming years; she would live for herself. There would be no powerful will bending hers in that blind persistence with which men and women believe they have a right to impose a private will upon a fellow-creature. A kind intention or a cruel intention made the act seem no less a crime as she looked upon it in that brief moment of illumination.

And yet she had loved him—sometimes. Often she had not. What did it matter! What could love, the unsolved mystery, count for in face of this possession of self-assertion which she suddenly recognized as the strongest impulse of her being!

"Free! Body and soul free!" she kept whispering.

Josephine was kneeling before the closed door with her lips to the keyhole, imploring for admission. "Louise, open the door! I beg; open the door—you will make yourself ill. What are you doing, Louise? For heaven's sake open the door."

"Go away. I am not making myself ill." No; she was drinking in a very elixir of life through that open window.

Her fancy was running riot along those days ahead of her. Spring days, and summer days, and all sorts of days that would be her own. She breathed a quick prayer that life might be long. It was only yesterday she had thought with a shudder that life might be long.

She arose at length and opened the door to her sister's importunities. There was a feverish triumph in her eyes, and she carried herself unwittingly like a goddess of Victory. She clasped her sister's waist, and together they descended the stairs. Richards stood waiting for them at the bottom.

Some one was opening the front door with a latchkey. It was Brently Mallard who entered, a little travel-stained, composedly carrying his grip-sack and umbrella. He had been far from the scene of accident, and did not even know there had been one. He stood amazed at Josephine's piercing cry; at Richards' quick motion to screen him from the view of his wife.

But Richards was too late.

When the doctors came they said she had died of heart disease—of joy that kills.

1891

SAMUEL CLEMENS (MARK TWAIN)
1835–1910

Clemens was born in Florida, Missouri. When he was four, his family took him to the town of Hannibal in the same state, where he experienced some of the adventures described in his novels *The Adventures of Tom Sawyer* (1876) and *Adventures of Huckleberry Finn* (1884). In his twenties he was an apprentice pilot on a Mississippi River steamer, and in "learning the river" he discovered that his true teacher would be the American land itself, with its western reaches just then opening to the surge of farmers, hunters, traders, and gold seekers. He went to California and with his readings and journalism won literary success in the mining camps upriver from San Francisco before the East caught on to his vivid and earthy style or the significance of his subject matter. In San Francisco he began his career as a lecturer—so successfully that in years to come he delighted audiences around the world with his platform manner and the astounding turns of his wit. By the late 1860s, when he went to travel in Europe and the Holy Land, he was looked on by his compatriots as their natural emissary to the Old World, and his report on these travels in *The Innocents Abroad* (1869) gave a new definition to the uniqueness of the American way of looking at things. After two decades of prosperity and popularity he lost his fortune through bad investments, but after 1895 his unceasing work as writer and lecturer enabled him to recoup his losses and build a mansion (now a museum) in Redding, Connecticut, where he died at the height of his fame. Best known among his many works are *Roughing It* (1872), *Life on the Mississippi* (1883), *A Connecticut Yankee in King Arthur's Court* (1889), and *The Mysterious Stranger* (1916), which reflects the dark, pessimistic outlook of his later years.

The Notorious Jumping Frog of Calaveras County

In compliance with the request of a friend of mine, who wrote me from the East, I called on good-natured, garrulous old Simon Wheeler, and inquired about my friend's friend, Leonidas W. Smiley, as requested to do, and I hereunto append the result. I have a lurking suspicion that *Leonidas* W. Smiley is a myth; that my friend never knew such a personage; and that he only conjectured that if I asked old Wheeler about him, it would remind him of his infamous *Jim* Smiley, and he would go to work and bore me to death with some exasperating reminiscence of him as long and as tedious as it should be useless to me. If that was the design, it succeeded.

I found Simon Wheeler dozing comfortably by the bar-room stove of the dilapidated tavern in the decayed mining camp of Angel's, and I noticed that he was fat and bald-headed, and had an expression of winning gentleness and simplicity upon his tranquil countenance. He roused up, and gave me good-day. I told him that a friend of mine had commissioned me to make some inquiries about a cherished companion of his boyhood named *Leonidas* W. Smiley—*Rev. Leonidas* W. Smiley, a young minister of the Gospel, who he had heard was at one time a resident of Angel's Camp. I added that if Mr. Wheeler could tell me anything about this Rev. Leonidas W. Smiley, I would feel under many obligations to him.

Simon Wheeler backed me into a corner and blockaded me there with his chair, and then sat down and reeled off the monotonous narrative which follows this paragraph. He never smiled, he never frowned, he never changed his voice from the gentle-flowing key to which he tuned his initial sentence, he never betrayed the slightest suspicion of enthusiasm; but all through the interminable narrative there ran a vein of impressive earnestness and sincerity, which showed me plainly that, so far from his imagining that there was anything ridiculous or funny about his story, he regarded it as a really important matter, and admired its two heroes as men of transcendent genius in *finesse*.[1] I let him go on in his own way, and never interrrupted him once.

"Rev. Leonidas W. H'm, Reverend Le—well, there was a feller here once by the name of *Jim* Smiley, in the winter of '49—or maybe it was the spring of '50—I don't recollect exactly, somehow, though what makes me think it was one or the other is because I remember the big flume[2] warn't finished when he first came to the camp; but anyway, he was the curiousest man about always betting on anything that turned up you ever see, if he could get anybody to bet on the other side; and if he couldn't he'd change sides. Any way that suited the other man would suit *him*—any way just so's he got a bet, *he* was satisfied. But still he was lucky, uncommon lucky; he most always come out winner. He was always ready and laying for a chance; there couldn't be no solit'ry thing mentioned but that feller'd offer to bet on it, and take ary side you please, as I was just telling you. If there was a horse-race, you'd find him flush or you'd find him busted at the end of it; if there was a dog-fight, he'd bet on it; if there was a cat-fight, he'd bet on it; if there was a chicken-fight, he'd bet on it; why, if there was two birds setting on a fence, he would bet you which one would fly first; or if there was a camp-meeting,[3] he would be there reg'lar to bet on Parson Walker, which he judged to be the best exhorter about here, and so he was too, and a good man. If he even see a straddle-bug start to go anywheres, he would bet you how long it would take him to get to—to wherever he was going to, and if you took him up, he would foller that straddle-bug to Mexico but what he would find out where he was bound for and how long he was on the road. Lots of the boys here has seen that Smiley, and can tell you about him. Why, it never made no difference to *him*—he'd bet on *any* thing—the dangdest feller. Parson Walker's wife laid very sick once, for a good while, and it seemed as if they warn't going to save her; but one morning he come in, and Smiley up and asked him how she was, and he said she was considerable better—thank the Lord for his inf'nite mercy—and coming on so smart that with the blessing of Prov'dence she'd get well yet; and Smiley, before he thought, says, 'Well, I'll resk two-and-a-half she don't anyway.'

"Thish-yer Smiley had a mare—the boys called her the fifteen-minute nag, but that was only in fun, you know, because of course she was faster than that—and he used to win money on that horse, for all she was so slow and always had the asthma, or the distemper, or the consumption, or something of that kind. They used to give her two or three hundred yards' start, and then pass her under way; but always at the fag end of the race she'd get excited and desperate like, and come cavorting and straddling up, and scattering her legs around limber, sometimes in the air, and sometimes out to one side among the fences, and kicking up m-o-r-e dust and raising m-o-r-e racket with her coughing and sneezing and blowing her nose—and *always* fetch up at the stand just about a neck ahead, as near as you could cipher it down.

"And he had a little small bull-pup, that to look at him you'd think he warn't worth a cent but to set around and look ornery and lay for a chance to steal something. But as soon as money was up on him he was a different dog; his under-jaw'd begin to stick out like the fo'castle of a steamboat, and his teeth would uncover and shine like the furnaces. And a dog might tackle him and bully-rag him, and bite him, and throw him over his shoulder two or three times, and Andrew Jackson[4]—which was the name of the pup—Andrew Jackson would never let on but what *he* was satisfied, and hadn't expected nothing else—and the bets being doubled and doubled on the other side all the time, till the money was all up; and then all of a sudden he would grab that other dog jest by the j'int of his hind leg and freeze to it—not chaw, you understand, but only just grip and hang on till they throwed up the sponge, if it was a year. Smiley always come out winner on that pup, till he harnessed a dog once that didn't have no hind legs, because they'd been sawed off in a circular saw, and when the thing had gone along far enough, and the money was all up, and he come to make a snatch for his pet holt, he see in a minute how he'd been imposed on, and how the other dog had him in the door, so to speak, and he 'peared surprised, and then he looked sorter discouraged-like, and didn't try no more to win the fight, and so he got shucked out bad. He give Smiley a look, as much as to say his heart was broke, and it was *his* fault, for putting up a dog that hadn't no hind legs for him to take holt of, which was his main dependence in a fight, and then he limped off a piece and laid down and died. It was a good pup, was that Andrew Jackson, and would have made a name for hisself if he'd lived, for the stuff was in him and he had genius—I know it, because he hadn't no opportunities to speak of, and it don't stand to reason that a dog could make such a fight as he could under them circumstances if he hadn't no talent. It always makes me feel sorry when I think of that last fight of his'n, and the way it turned out.

"Well, thish-yer Smiley had rat-tarriers, and chicken cocks, and tom-cats and all them kind of things, till you couldn't rest, and you couldn't fetch nothing for him to bet on but he'd match you. He ketched a frog one day, and took him home, and said he cal'lated to educate him; and so he never done

---

4. Named for the seventh president of the United States (1767–1845), famous in legend for his iron will.

nothing for three months but set in his back yard and learn that frog to jump. And you bet you he *did* learn him, too. He'd give him a little punch behind, and the next minute you'd see that frog whirling in the air like a doughnut—see him turn one summerset, or maybe a couple, if he got a good start, and come down flat-footed and all right, like a cat. He got him up so in the matter of ketching flies, and kep' him in practice so constant, that he'd nail a fly every time as fur as he could see him. Smiley said all a frog wanted was education, and he could do 'most anything—and I believe him. Why, I've seen him set Dan'l Webster[5] down here on this floor—Dan'l Webster was the name of the frog—and sing out, 'Flies, Dan'l, flies!' and quicker'n you could wink he'd spring straight up and snake a fly off'n the counter there, and flop down on the floor ag'in as solid as a gob of mud, and fall to scratching the side of his head with his hind foot as indifferent as if he hadn't no idea he'd been doin' any more'n any frog might do. You never see a frog so modest and straightfor'ard as he was, for all he was so gifted. And when it come to fair and square jumping on a dead level, he could get over more ground at one straddle than any animal of his breed you ever see. Jumping on a dead level was his strong suit, you understand; and when it come to that, Smiley would ante up money on him as long as he had a red.[6] Smiley was monstrous proud of his frog, and well he might be, for fellers that had traveled and been everywheres, all said he laid over any frog that ever *they* see.

"Well, Smiley kep' the beast in a little lattice box, and he used to fetch him down-town sometimes and lay for a bet. One day a feller—a stranger in the camp, he was—come acrost him with his box, and says:

"'What might it be that you've got in the box?'

"And Smiley says, sorter indifferent-like, 'It might be a parrot, or it might be a canary, maybe, but it ain't—it's only just a frog.'

"And the feller took it, and looked at it careful, and turned it round this way and that, and says, 'H'm—so 'tis. Well, what's *he* good for?'

"'Well,' Smiley says, easy and careless, 'he's good enough for *one* thing, I should judge—he can outjump any frog in Calaveras County.'

"The feller took the box again, and took another long, particular look, and give it back to Smiley, and says, very deliberate, 'Well,' he says, 'I don't see no p'ints about that frog that's any better'n any other frog.'

"'Maybe you don't,' Smiley says. 'Maybe you understand frogs and maybe you don't understand 'em; maybe you've had experience, and maybe you ain't only a amature, as it were. Anyways, I've got *my* opinion, and I'll resk forty dollars that he can outjump any frog in Calaveras County.'

"And the feller studied a minute, and then says, kinder sadlike, 'Well, I'm only a stranger here, and I ain't got no frog; but if I had a frog, I'd bet you.'

"And then Smiley says, 'That's all right—that's all right—if you'll hold my box a minute, I'll go and get you a frog.' And so the feller took the box, and put up his forty dollars along with Smiley's, and set down to wait.

"So he set there a good while thinking and thinking to himself, and then he got the frog out and prized his mouth open and took a teaspoon and filled him full of quail shot—filled him pretty near up to his chin—and set him on the floor. Smiley he went to the swamp and slopped around in the mud for a

---

5. The frog is named for Daniel Webster (1782–1852), distinguished American statesman and orator.
6. A red cent, i.e., any money whatsoever.

long time, and finally he ketched a frog, and fetched him in, and give him to this feller, and says:

"'Now, if you're ready, set him alongside of Dan'l, with his fore paws just even with Dan'l's, and I'll give the word.' Then he says, 'One—two—three—*git!*' and him and the feller touched up the frogs from behind, and the new frog hopped off lively, but Dan'l give a heave, and hysted up his shoulders—so—like a Frenchman, but it warn't no use—he couldn't budge; he was planted as solid as a church, and he couldn't no more stir than if he was anchored out. Smiley was a good deal surprised, and he was disgusted too, but he didn't have no idea what the matter was, of course.

"The feller took the money and started away; and when he was going out at the door, he sorter jerked his thumb over his shoulder—so—at Dan'l, and says again, very deliberate, 'Well,' he says, '*I* don't see no p'ints about that frog that's any better'n any other frog.'

"Smiley he stood scratching his head and looking down at Dan'l a long time, and at last he says, 'I do wonder what in the nation that frog throw'd off for—I wonder if there ain't something the matter with him—he 'pears to look mighty baggy, somehow.' And he ketched Dan'l by the nap of the neck, and hefted him, and says, 'Why blame my cats if he don't weigh five pound!' and turned him upside down and he belched out a double handful of shot. And then he see how it was, and he was the maddest man—he set the frog down and took out after that feller, but he never ketched him. And—"

[Here Simon Wheeler heard his name called from the front yard, and got up to see what was wanted.] And turning to me as he moved away, he said: "Just set where you are, stranger, and rest easy—I ain't going to be gone a second."

But, by your leave, I did not think that a continuation of the history of the enterprising vagabond *Jim* Smiley would be likely to afford me much information concerning the Rev. *Leonidas* W. Smiley, and so I started away.

At the door I met the sociable Wheeler returning, and he button-holed me and recommenced:

"Well, thish-yer Smiley had a yaller one-eyed cow that didn't have no tail, only just a short stump like a bannanner, and—"

However, lacking both time and inclination, I did not wait to hear about the afflicted cow, but took my leave.

1867

The Invalid's Story[1]

I seem sixty and married, but these effects are due to my condition and sufferings, for I am a bachelor, and only forty-one. It will be hard for you to believe that I, who am now but a shadow, was a hale, hearty man two short years ago,—a man of iron, a very athlete!—yet such is the simple truth. But stranger still than this fact is the way in which I lost my health. I lost it

---

1. Left out of these "Rambling Notes," when originally published in the "Atlantic Monthly," because it was feared that the story was not true, and at that time there was no way of proving that it was not.—M. T. [Twain's note].

through helping to take care of a box of guns on a two-hundred-mile railway journey one winter's night. It is the actual truth, and I will tell you about it.

I belong in Cleveland, Ohio. One winter's night, two years ago, I reached home just after dark, in a driving snow-storm, and the first thing I heard when I entered the house was that my dearest boyhood friend and school-mate John B. Hackett, had died the day before, and that his last utterance had been a desire that I would take his remains home to his poor old father and mother in Wisconsin. I was greatly shocked and grieved, but there was no time to waste in emotions; I must start at once. I took the card, marked "Deacon Levi Hackett, Bethlehem, Wisconsin," and hurried off through the whistling storm to the railway station. Arrived there I found the long white-pine box which had been described to me; I fastened the card to it with some tacks, saw it put safely aboard the express car, and then ran into the eating-room to provide myself with a sandwich and some cigars. When I returned, presently, there was my coffin-box *back again*, apparently, and a young fellow examining around it, with a card in his hand, and some tacks and a ham-mer! I was astonished and puzzled. He began to nail on his card, and I rushed out to the express car, in a good deal of a state of mind, to ask for an explanation. But no—there was my box, all right, in the express car; it hadn't been disturbed. [The fact is that without my suspecting it a prodigious mis-take had been made. I was carrying off a box of *guns* which that young fellow had come to the station to ship to a rifle company in Peoria, Illinois, and *he* had got my corpse!] Just then the conductor sung out "All aboard," and I jumped into the express car and got a comfortable seat on a bale of buckets. The expressman was there, hard at work,—a plain man of fifty, with a simple, honest, good-natured face, and a breezy, practical heartiness in his general style. As the train moved off a stranger skipped into the car and set a pack-age of peculiarly mature and capable Limburger cheese on one end of my coffin-box—I mean my box of guns. That is to say, I know *now* that it was Limburger cheese, but at that time I never had heard of the article in my life, and of course was wholly ignorant of its character. Well, we sped through the wild night, the bitter storm raged on, a cheerless misery stole over me, my heart went down, down, down! The old expressman made a brisk remark or two about the tempest and the arctic weather, slammed his sliding doors to, and bolted them, closed his window down tight, and then went bustling around, here and there and yonder, setting things to rights, and all the time contentedly humming "Sweet By and By," in a low tone, and flatting a good deal. Presently I began to detect a most evil and searching odor stealing about on the frozen air. This depressed my spirits still more, because of course I attributed it to my poor departed friend. There was something infi-nitely saddening about his calling himself to my remembrance in this dumb pathetic way, so it was hard to keep the tears back. Moreover, it distressed me on account of the old expressman, who, I was afraid, might notice it. How-ever, he went humming tranquilly on, and gave no sign; and for this I was grateful. Grateful, yes, but still uneasy; and soon I began to feel more and more uneasy every minute, for every minute that went by that odor thick-ened up the more, and got to be more and more gamey and hard to stand. Presently, having got things arranged to his satisfaction, the expressman got some wood and made up a tremendous fire in his stove. This distressed me more than I can tell, for I could not but feel that it was a mistake. I was sure that the effect would be deleterious upon my poor departed friend. Thompson—the expressman's name was Thompson, as I found out in the course of the night—now went poking around his car, stopping up whatever stray cracks he could find, remarking that it didn't make any difference what kind of a night it was outside, he calculated to make *us* comfortable, anyway. I said nothing, but I believed he was not choosing the right way. Meantime he was humming to himself just as before; and meantime, too, the stove was getting hotter and hotter, and the place closer and closer. I felt myself growing pale and qualmish, but grieved in silence and said nothing. Soon I noticed that the "Sweet By and By" was gradually fading out; next it ceased altogether, and there was an ominous stillness. After a few moments Thompson said,—

"Pfew! I reckon it ain't no cinnamon 't I've loaded up thish-yer stove with!"

He gasped once or twice, then moved toward the cof—gun-box, stood over that Limburger cheese part of a moment, then came back and sat down near me, looking a good deal impressed. After a contemplative pause, he said, indicating the box with a gesture,—

"Friend of yourn?"

"Yes," I said with a sigh.

"He's pretty ripe, *ain't* he!"

Nothing further was said for perhaps a couple of minutes, each being busy with his own thoughts; then Thompson said, in a low, awed voice,—

"Sometimes it's uncertain whether they're really gone or not,—*seem* gone, you know—body warm, joints limber—and so, although you *think* they're gone, you don't really know. I've had cases in my car. It's perfectly awful, becuz *you* don't know what minute they'll rise right up and look at you!" Then, after a pause, and slightly lifting his elbow toward the box,—"But *he* ain't in no trance! No, sir, I go bail for *him!*"

We sat some time, in meditative silence, listening to the wind and the roar of the train; then Thompson said, with a good deal of feeling,—

"Well-a-well, we've all got to go, they ain't no getting around it. Man that is born of woman is of few days and far between, as Scriptur' says. Yes, you look at it any way you want to, it's awful solemn and cur'us: they ain't *nobody* can get around it; *all's* got to go—just *everybody*, as you may say. One day you're hearty and strong"—here he scrambled to his feet and broke a pane and stretched his nose out at it a moment or two, then sat down again while I struggled up and thrust my nose out at the same place, and this we kept on doing every now and then—"and next day he's cut down like the grass, and the places which knowed him then knows him no more forever, as Scriptur' says. Yes-'ndeedy, it's awful solemn and cur'us; but we've all got to go, one time or another; they ain't no getting around it."

There was another long pause; then,—

"What did he die of?"

I said I didn't know.

"How long has he ben dead?"

It seemed judicious to enlarge the facts to fit the probabilities; so I said,—

"Two or three days."

But it did no good; for Thompson received it with an injured look which plainly said, "Two or three *years*, you mean." Then he went right along, placidly ignoring my statement, and gave his views at considerable length upon the unwisdom of putting off burials too long. Then he lounged off toward the box, stood a moment, then came back on a sharp trot and visited the broken pane, observing,—

"'T would 'a' ben a dum sight better, all around, if they'd started him along last summer."

Thompson sat down and buried his face in his red silk handkerchief, and began to slowly sway and rock his body like one who is doing his best to endure the almost unendurable. By this time the fragrance—if you may call it fragrance—was just about suffocating, as near as you can come at it. Thompson's face was turning gray; I knew mine hadn't any color left in it. By and by Thompson rested his forehead in his left hand, with his elbow on his knee, and sort of waved his red handkerchief towards the box with his other hand, and said,—

"I've carried a many a one of 'em,—some of 'em considerable overdue, too,— but, lordy, he just lays over 'em all!—and does it *easy*. Cap., they was heliotrope to *him*!"[2]

This recognition of my poor friend gratified me, in spite of the sad circumstances, because it had so much the sound of a compliment.

Pretty soon it was plain that something had got to be done. I suggested cigars. Thompson thought it was a good idea. He said,—

"Likely it'll modify him some."

We puffed gingerly along for a while, and tried hard to imagine that things were improved. But it wasn't any use. Before very long, and without any consultation, both cigars were quietly dropped from our nerveless fingers at the same moment. Thompson said, with a sign,—

"No, Cap., it don't modify him worth a cent. Fact is, it makes him worse, becuz it appears to stir up his ambition. What do you reckon we better do, now?"

I was not able to suggest anything; indeed, I had to be swallowing and swallowing, all the time, and did not like to trust myself to speak. Thompson fell to maundering, in a desultory and low-spirited way, about the miserable experiences of this night; and he got to referring to my poor friend by various titles,—sometimes military ones, sometimes civil ones; and I noticed that as fast as my poor friend's effectiveness grew, Thompson promoted him accordingly,—gave him a bigger title. Finally he said,—

"I've got an idea. Suppos'n' we buckle down to it and give the Colonel a bit of a shove towards t' other end of the car?—about ten foot, say. He wouldn't have so much influence, then, don't you reckon?"

I said it was a good scheme. So we took in a good fresh breath at the broken pane, calculating to hold it till we got through; then we went there and bent down over that deadly cheese and took a grip on the box. Thompson nodded "All ready," and then we threw ourselves forward with all our might; but Thompson slipped, and slumped down with his nose on the cheese, and his

---

2. That is, compared to *him* they smelled like heliotrope (a flowering shrub).

breath got loose. He gagged and gasped, and floundered up and made a break for the door, pawing the air and saying, hoarsely, "Don't hender me!—gimme the road! I'm a-dying; gimme the road!" Out on the cold platform I sat down and held his head a while, and he revived. Presently he said,—

"Do you reckon we started the Gen'rul any?"

I said no; we hadn't budged him.

"Well, then, *that* idea's up the flume. We got to think up something else. He's suited wher' he is, I reckon; and if that's the way he feels about it, and has made up his mind that he don't wish to be disturbed, you bet you he's a-going to have his own way in the business. Yes, better leave him right wher' he is, long as he wants it so; becuz he holds all the trumps, don't you know, and so it stands to reason that the man that lays out to alter his plans for him is going to get left."

But we couldn't stay out there in that mad storm; we should have frozen to death. So we went in again and shut the door, and began to suffer once more and take turns at the break in the window. By and by, as we were starting away from a station where we had stopped a moment Thompson pranced in cheerily, and exclaimed,—

"We're all right, now! I reckon we've got the Commodore this time. I judge I've got the stuff here that'll take the tuck out of him."

It was carbolic acid. He had a carboy of it. He sprinkled it all around everywhere; in fact he drenched everything with it, rifle-box, cheese, and all. Then we sat down, feeling pretty hopeful. But it wasn't for long. You see the two perfumes began to mix, and then—well, pretty soon we made a break for the door; and out there Thompson swabbed his face with his bandanna and said in a kind of disheartened way,—

"It ain't no use. We can't buck agin *him*. He just utilizes everything we put up to modify him with, and gives it his own flavor and plays it back on us. Why, Cap., don't you know, it's as much as a hundred times worse in there now than it was when he first got a-going. I never *did* see one of 'em warm up to his work so, and take such a dumnation interest in it. No, sir, I never did, as long as I've ben on the road; and I've carried a many a one of 'em, as I was telling you."

We went in again, after we were frozen pretty stiff; but my, we couldn't *stay* in, now. So we just waltzed back and forth, freezing, and thawing, and stifling, by turns. In about an hour we stopped at another station; and as we left it Thompson came in with a bag, and said,—

"Cap., I'm a-going to chance him once more,—just this once; and if we don't fetch him this time, the thing for us to do, is to just throw up the sponge and withdraw from the canvass. That's the way *I* put it up."

He had brought a lot of chicken feathers, and dried apples, and leaf tobacco, and rags, and old shoes, and sulphur, and assafœtida,[3] and one thing or another; and he piled them on a breadth of sheet iron in the middle of the floor, and set fire to them. When they got well started, I couldn't see, myself, how even the corpse could stand it. All that went before was just simply poetry to that smell,—but mind you, the original smell stood up out of it just as sublime as ever,—fact is, these other smells just seemed to give it a better hold; and

---

3. A strong-smelling gum resin used as a medicine.

my, how rich it was! I didn't make these reflections there—there wasn't time—made them on the platform. And breaking for the platform, Thompson got suffocated and fell; and before I got him dragged out, which I did by the collar, I was mighty near gone myself. When we revived, Thompson said dejectedly,—

"We got to stay out here, Cap. We got to do it. They ain't no other way. The Governor wants to travel alone, and he's fixed so he can outvote us."

And presently he added,—

"And don't you know, we're *pisoned*. It's *our* last trip, you can make up your mind to it. Typhoid fever is what's going to come of this. I feel it a-coming right now. Yes, sir, we're elected, just as sure as you're born."

We were taken from the platform an hour later, frozen and insensible, at the next station, and I went straight off into a virulent fever, and never knew anything again for three weeks. I found out, then, that I had spent that awful night with a harmless box of rifles and a lot of innocent cheese; but the news was too late to save *me*; imagination had done its work, and my health was permanently shattered; neither Bermuda nor any other land can ever bring it back to me. This is my last trip; I am on my way home to die.

1877

JOSEPH CONRAD
1857–1924

Conrad (christened Jozef Teodor Konrad Nalecz Korzeniowski) was born in Polish Ukraine to a family of landed gentry. In 1863 his hotheaded father was exiled for revolutionary activities to an area northeast of Moscow. He took his family with him to this inhospitable region, where the climate proved too much for both parents. The orphaned Conrad at seventeen persuaded his guardian uncle to let him join the French merchant navy, and for about twenty years he sailed to many exotic places, surviving shipwrecks and (probably) an attempted suicide, running guns at intervals in his more respectable occupations and rising, finally, to the rank of master (captain) in the British merchant fleet. He began to write before he gave up his seagoing career; and some of his early work led to his friendship with such literary figures as Henry James, Stephen Crane, and Ford Madox Ford. With their encouragement he not only devoted himself full time to fiction but developed the style and form of narration that are so much his own. (One of the marvels is that so fine a stylist should have written in English when Polish was his native tongue and French his "second language.") Though he was respected from the beginning of his writing career and critically acclaimed after the publication of *The Nigger of the "Narcissus"* (1897), he had small popular success before his novel *Chance* was brought out in 1914. In his later years, after World War I, he was one of the most venerated of English novelists. He was working on a novel of Napoleon's escape from Elba when he died. His novels include *Lord Jim* (1900), *Nostromo* (1904), *The Secret Agent* (1907), *Under Western Eyes* (1910), and *Victory* (1915). Three works of medium length, including the novella *Heart of Darkness*, were published in *Youth* (1902).

Heart of Darkness

I

The *Nellie,* a cruising yawl, swung to her anchor without a flutter of the sails, and was at rest. The flood had made, the wind was nearly calm, and being bound down the river, the only thing for it was to come to and wait for the turn of the tide.

The sea-reach[1] of the Thames stretched before us like the beginning of an interminable waterway. In the offing[2] the sea and the sky were welded together

---

1. Tidal part of the river as it broadens toward the sea.   2. Part of the sea visible from the river's mouth.

without a joint, and in the luminous space the tanned sails of the barges drifting up with the tide seemed to stand still in red clusters of canvas sharply peaked, with gleams of varnished sprits. A haze rested on the low shores that ran out to sea in vanishing flatness. The air was dark above Gravesend,[3] and farther back still seemed condensed into a mournful gloom, brooding motionless over the biggest, and the greatest, town on earth.

The Director of Companies was our captain and our host. We four affectionately watched his back as he stood in the bows looking to seaward. On the whole river there was nothing that looked half so nautical. He resembled a pilot, which to a seaman is trustworthiness personified. It was difficult to realize his work was not out there in the luminous estuary, but behind him, within the brooding gloom.

Between us there was, as I have already said somewhere, the bond of the sea. Besides holding our hearts together through long periods of separation, it had the effect of making us tolerant of each other's yarns—and even convictions. The Lawyer—the best of old fellows—had, because of his many years and many virtues, the only cushion on deck, and was lying on the only rug. The accountant had brought out already a box of dominoes, and was toying architecturally with the bones. Marlow sat cross-legged right aft, leaning against the mizzen-mast. He had sunken cheeks, a yellow complexion, a straight back, and ascetic aspect, and, with his arms dropped, the palms of hands outwards, resembled an idol. The director, satisfied the anchor had good hold, made his way aft and sat down amongst us. We exchanged a few words lazily. Afterwards there was silence on board the yacht. For some reason or other we did not begin that game of dominoes. We felt meditative, and fit for nothing but placid staring. The day was ending in a serenity of still and exquisite brilliance. The water shone pacifically; the sky, without a speck, was a benign immensity of unstained light; the very mist on the Essex marshes[4] was like a gauzy and radiant fabric, hung from the wooded rises inland, and draping the low shores in diaphanous folds. Only the gloom to the west, brooding over the upper reaches, became more somber every minute, as if angered by the approach of the sun.

And at last, in its curved and imperceptible fall, the sun sank low, and from glowing white changed to a dull red without rays and without heat, as if about to go out suddenly, stricken to death by the touch of that gloom brooding over a crowd of men.

Forthwith a change came over the waters, and the serenity became less brilliant but more profound. The old river in its broad reach rested unruffled at the decline of day, after ages of good service done to the race that peopled its banks, spread out in the tranquil dignity of a waterway leading to the uttermost ends of the earth. We looked at the venerable stream not in the vivid flush of a short day that comes and departs forever, but in the august light of abiding memories. And indeed nothing is easier for a man who has, as the phrase goes, "followed the sea" with reverence and affection, than to evoke the great spirit of the past upon the lower reaches of the Thames. The tidal current runs to and fro in its unceasing service, crowded with memories of men and ships it had borne to the rest of home or to the battles of the sea. It

3. City on the Thames, twenty-six miles east of London.   **4.** On the north bank of the Thames.

had known and served all the men of whom the nation is proud, from Sir Francis Drake to Sir John Franklin,[5] knights all, titled and untitled—the great knights-errant of the sea. It had borne all the ships whose names are like jewels flashing in the night of time, from the *Golden Hind* returning with her round flanks full of treasure, to be visited by the Queen's Highness and thus pass out of the gigantic tale, to the *Erebus* and *Terror,* bound on other conquests—and that never returned. It had known the ships and the men. They had sailed from Deptford, from Greenwich, from Erith—the adventurers and the settlers; kings' ships and the ships of men on 'Change; captains, admirals, the dark "interlopers"[6] of the Eastern trade, and the commissioned "Generals" of East India fleets. Hunters for gold or pursuers of fame, they all had gone out on that stream, bearing the sword, and often the torch, messengers of the might within the land, bearers of a spark from the sacred fire. What greatness had not floated on the ebb of that river into the mystery of an unknown earth! . . . The dreams of men, the seed of commonwealths, the germs of empires.

The sun set; the dusk fell on the stream, and lights began to appear along the shore. The Chapman lighthouse, a three-legged thing erect on a mud-flat, shone strongly. Lights of ships moved in the fairway—a great stir of lights going up and going down. And farther west on the upper reaches the place of the monstrous town was still marked ominously on the sky, a brooding gloom in sunshine, a lurid glare under the stars.

"And this also," said Marlow suddenly, "has been one of the dark places on the earth."

He was the only man of us who still "followed the sea." The worst that could be said of him was that he did not represent his class. He was a seaman, but he was a wanderer, too, while most seamen lead, if one may so express it, a sedentary life. Their minds are of the stay-at-home order, and their home is always with them—the ship; and so is their country—the sea. One ship is very much like another, and the sea is always the same. In the immutability of their surroundings the foreign shores, the foreign faces, the changing immensity of life, glide past, veiled not by a sense of mystery but by a slightly disdainful ignorance; for there is nothing mysterious to a seaman unless it be the sea itself, which is the mistress of his existence and as inscrutable as Destiny. For the rest, after his hours of work, a casual stroll or a casual spree on shore suffices to unfold for him the secret of a whole continent, and generally he finds the secret not worth knowing. The yarns of seamen have a direct simplicity, the whole meaning of which lies within the shell of a cracked nut. But Marlow was not typical (if his propensity to spin yarns be excepted), and to him the meaning of an episode was not inside like a kernel but outside, enveloping the tale which brought it out only as a glow brings out a haze, in the likeness of one of these misty halos that sometimes are made visible by the spectral illumination of moonshine.

---

5. An Arctic explorer (1786–1847) who commanded an expedition, including the ships *Erebus* and *Terror,* and was lost in a search for the Northwest Passage. Drake (1540–1596) sailed around the world aboard the *Golden Hind* (1577–80) and defeated the Spanish Armada (1588).   **6.** Unauthorized competitors of the East India Company, chartered by the British Crown, in the reign of Charles II, who were given the right to maintain troops in India and thus to appoint "generals." Deptford, Greenwich, and Erith are seaports on the Thames. *'Change,* i.e., Exchange, the financial district of London.

His remark did not seem at all surprising. It was just like Marlow. It was accepted in silence. No one took the trouble to grunt even; and presently he said, very slow—

"I was thinking of very old times, when the Romans first came here, nineteen hundred years ago—the other day. . . . Light came out of this river since—you say Knights? Yes; but it is like a running blaze on a plain, like a flash of lightning in the clouds. We live in the flicker—may it last as long as the old earth keeps rolling! But darkness was here yesterday. Imagine the feelings of a commander of a fine—what d'ye call 'em?—trireme[7] in the Mediterranean, ordered suddenly to the north; run overland across the Gauls[8] in a hurry; put in charge of one of these craft the legionaries—a wonderful lot of handy men they must have been, too—used to build, apparently by the hundred, in a month or two, if we may believe what we read. Imagine him here—the very end of the world, a sea the color of lead, a sky the color of smoke, a kind of ship about as rigid as a concertina—and going up this river with stores, or orders, or what you like. Sand-banks, marshes, forests, savages,—precious little to eat fit for a civilized man, nothing but Thames water to drink. No Falernian wine[9] here, no going ashore. Here and there a military camp lost in a wilderness, like a needle in a bundle of hay—cold, fog, tempests, disease, exile, and death,—death skulking in the air, in the water, in the bush. They must have been dying like flies here. Oh yes—he did it. Did it very well, too, no doubt, and without thinking much about it either, except afterwards to brag of what he had gone through in his time, perhaps. They were men enough to face the darkness. And perhaps he was cheered by keeping his eye on a chance of promotion to the fleet at Ravenna[1] by and by, if he had good friends in Rome and survived the awful climate. Or think of a decent young citizen in a toga—perhaps too much dice, you know—coming out here in the train of some prefect,[2] or taxgatherer, or trader even, to mend his fortunes. Land in a swamp, march through the woods, and in some inland post feel the savagery, the utter savagery, had closed round him,—all that mysterious life of the wilderness that stirs in the forest, in the jungles, in the hearts of wild men. There's no initiation either into such mysteries. He has to live in the midst of the incomprehensible, which is also detestable. And it has a fascination, too, that goes to work upon him. The fascination of the abomination—you know, imagine the growing regrets, the longing to escape, the powerless disgust, the surrender, the hate."

He paused.

"Mind," he began again, lifting one arm from the elbow, the palm of the hand outwards, so that, with his legs folded before him, he had the pose of a Buddha preaching in European clothes and without a lotus-flower—"Mind, none of us would feel exactly like this. What saves us is efficiency—the devotion to efficiency. But these chaps were not much account, really. They were no colonists; their administration was merely a squeeze, and nothing more, I suspect. They were conquerors, and for that you want only brute force—nothing to boast of, when you have it, since your strength is just an accident arising from the weakness of others. They grabbed what they could get for the sake of what was to be got. It was just robbery with violence, aggravated

7. Roman galley propelled by three banks of oars. 8. Inhabitants of France in Roman times. 9. Legendary Roman wine. 1. Base on the Adriatic in northern Italy—a comfortable assignment. 2. High official.

murder on a great scale, and men going at it blind—as is very proper for those who tackle a darkness. The conquest of the earth, which mostly means the taking it away from those who have a different complexion or slightly flatter noses than ourselves, is not a pretty thing when you look into it too much. What redeems it is the idea only. An idea at the back of it; not a sentimental pretense but an idea; and an unselfish belief in the idea—something you can set up, and bow down before, and offer a sacrifice to. . . ."

He broke off. Flames glided in the river, small green flames, red flames, white flames, pursuing, overtaking, joining, crossing each other—then separating slowly or hastily. The traffic of the great city went on in the deepening night upon the sleepless river. We looked on, waiting patiently—there was nothing else to do till the end of the flood; but it was only after a long silence, when he said, in a hesitating voice, "I suppose you fellows remember I did once turn fresh-water sailor for a bit," that we knew we were fated, before the ebb began to run, to hear one of Marlow's inconclusive experiences.

"I don't want to bother you much with what happened to me personally," he began, showing in this remark the weakness of many tellers of tales who seem so often unaware of what their audience would best like to hear; "yet to understand the effect of it on me you ought to know how I got out there, what I saw, how I went up that river to the place where I first met the poor chap. It was the farthest point of navigation and the culminating point of my experience. It seemed somehow to throw a kind of light on everything about me—and into my thoughts. It was somber enough, too—and pitiful—not extraordinary in any way—not very clear either. No, not very clear. And yet it seemed to throw a kind of light.

"I had then, as you remember, just returned to London after a lot of Indian Ocean, Pacific, China Seas—a regular dose of the East—six years or so, and I was loafing about, hindering you fellows in your work and invading your homes, just as though I had got a heavenly mission to civilize you. It was very fine for a time, but after a bit I did get tired of resting. Then I began to look for a ship—I should think the hardest work on earth. But the ships wouldn't even look at me. And I got tired of that game too.

"Now when I was a little chap I had a passion for maps. I would look for hours at South America, or Africa, or Australia, and lose myself in all the glories of exploration. At that time there were many blank spaces on the earth, and when I saw one that looked particularly inviting on a map (but they all look that) I would put my finger on it and say, When I grow up I will go there. The North Pole was one of these places, I remember. Well, I haven't been there yet, and shall not try now. The glamour's off. Other places were scattered about the Equator, and in every sort of latitude all over the two hemispheres. I have been in some of them, and . . . well, we won't talk about that. But there was one yet—the biggest, the most blank, so to speak—that I had a hankering after.

"True, by this time it was not a blank space any more. It had got filled since my childhood with rivers and lakes and names. It had ceased to be a blank space of delightful mystery—a white patch for a boy to dream gloriously over. It had become a place of darkness.[3] But there was in it one river especially, a

---

3. Congo Free State (now Democratic Republic of the Congo). At the time of the story it was a colony owned personally, in effect, by Leopold II, king of Belgium; it consisted of the Congo River basin and some adjacent territories, a total area of nearly a million square miles.

mighty big river, that you could see on the map, resembling an immense snake uncoiled, with its head in the sea, its body at rest curving afar over a vast country, and its tail lost in the depths of the land. And as I looked at the map of it in a shop-window, it fascinated me as a snake would a bird—a silly little bird. Then I remembered there was a big concern, a Company for trade on that river. Dash it all! I thought to myself, they can't trade without using some kind of craft on that lot of fresh water—steamboats! Why shouldn't I try to get charge of one? I went on along Fleet Street, but could not shake off the idea. The snake had charmed me.

"You understand it was a Continental concern, that Trading society; but I have a lot of relations living on the Continent, because it's cheap and not so nasty as it looks, they say.

"I am sorry to own I began to worry them. This was already a fresh departure for me. I was not used to getting things that way, you know. I always went my own road and on my own legs where I had a mind to go. I wouldn't have believed it of myself; but, then—you see—I felt somehow I must get there by hook or by crook. So I worried them. The men said, 'My dear fellow,' and did nothing. Then—would you believe it?—I tried the women. I, Charlie Marlow, set the women to work—to get a job. Heavens! Well, you see, the notion drove me. I had an aunt, a dear enthusiastic soul. She wrote: 'It will be delightful. I am ready to do anything, anything for you. It is a glorious idea. I know the wife of a very high personage in the Administration, and also a man who has lots of influence with,' etc. etc. She was determined to make no end of fuss to get me appointed skipper of a river steamboat, if such was my fancy.

"I got my appointment—of course; and I got it very quick. It appears the Company had received news that one of their captains had been killed in a scuffle with the natives. This was my chance, and it made me the more anxious to go. It was only months and months afterwards, when I made the attempt to recover what was left of the body, that I heard the original quarrel arose from a misunderstanding about some hens. Yes, two black hens. Fresleven—that was the fellow's name, a Dane—thought himself wronged somehow in the bargain, so he went ashore and started to hammer the chief of the village with a stick. Oh, it didn't surprise me in the least to hear this, and at the same time to be told that Fresleven was the gentlest, quietest creature that ever walked on two legs. No doubt he was; but he had been a couple of years already out there engaged in the noble cause, you know, and he probably felt the need at last of asserting his self-respect in some way. Therefore he whacked the old nigger mercilessly, while a big crowd of his people watched him, thunderstruck, till some man—I was told the chief's son—in desperation at hearing the old chap yell, made a tentative jab with a spear at the white man—and of course it went quite easy between the shoulder blades. Then the whole population cleared into the forest, expecting all kinds of calamities to happen, while, on the other hand, the steamer Fresleven commanded left also in a bad panic, in charge of the engineer, I believe. Afterwards nobody seemed to trouble much about Fresleven's remains, till I got out and stepped into his shoes. I couldn't let it rest, though; but when an opportunity offered at last to meet my predecessor, the grass growing through his ribs was tall enough to hide his bones. They were all there. The supernatural being had not been touched after he fell. And the village was deserted, the huts gaped black, rotting, all askew within the fallen enclosures. A calamity had come to it, sure enough. The people had vanished. Mad terror had scattered them, men, women, and children, through the bush, and they had never returned. What became of the hens I don't know either. I should think the cause of progress got them, anyhow. However, through this glorious affair I got my appointment, before I had fairly begun to hope for it.

"I flew around like mad to get ready, and before forty-eight hours I was crossing the Channel to show myself to my employers, and sign the contract. In a very few hours I arrived in a city[4] that always makes me think of a whited sepulcher. Prejudice no doubt. I had no difficulty in finding the Company's offices. It was the biggest thing in the town, and everybody I met was full of it. They were going to run an oversea empire, and make no end of coin by trade.

"A narrow and deserted street in deep shadow, high houses, innumerable windows with venetian blinds, a dead silence, grass sprouting between the stones, imposing carriage archways right and left, immense double doors standing ponderously ajar. I slipped through one of these cracks, went up a swept and unvarnished staircase, as arid as a desert, and opened the first door I came to. Two women, one fat and the other slim, sat on straw-bottomed chairs, knitting black wool. The slim one got up and walked straight at me— still knitting with downcast eyes—and only just as I began to think of getting out of her way, as you would for a somnambulist, stood still, and looked up. Her dress was as plain as an umbrella-cover, and she turned round without a word and preceded me into a waiting-room. I gave my name, and looked about. Deal table in the middle, plain chairs all around the walls, on one end a large shining map, marked with all the colors of a rainbow. There was a vast amount of red—good to see at any time, because one knows that some real work is done in there, a deuce of a lot of blue, a little green, smears of orange, and, on the East Coast, a purple patch,[5] to show where the jolly pioneers of progress drink the jolly lager-beer. However, I wasn't going into any of these. I was going into the yellow. Dead in the center. And the river was there— fascinating—deadly—like a snake. Ough! A door opened, a white-haired secretarial head, but wearing a compassionate expression, appeared, and a skinny forefinger beckoned me into the sanctuary. Its light was dim, and a heavy writing-desk squatted in the middle. From behind that structure came out an impression of pale plumpness in a frock-coat. The great man himself. He was five feet six, I should judge, and had his grip on the handle-end of ever so many millions. He shook hands, I fancy, murmured vaguely, was satisfied with my French. *Bon voyage.*[6]

"In about forty-five seconds I found myself again in the waiting-room with the compassionate secretary, who, full of desolation and sympathy, made me sign some document. I believe I undertook amongst other things not to disclose any trade secrets. Well, I am not going to.

"I began to feel slightly uneasy. You know I am not used to such ceremonies, and there was something ominous in the atmosphere. It was just as though I had been let into some conspiracy—I don't know—something not quite right; and I was glad to get out. In the outer room the two women knit-

---

4. Brussels, Belgium. *Whited sepulcher:* hypocrite. (Metaphor attributed to Jesus; cf. Matthew 23: 27.)   5. The red areas on the map were British colonies; blue, French; green, Italian; orange, Portuguese; and purple, German East Africa.   6. "Have a good trip" (French).

ted black wool feverishly. People were arriving, and the younger one was walking back and forth introducing them. The old one sat on her chair. Her flat cloth slippers were propped up on a footwarmer, and a cat reposed on her lap. She wore a starched white affair on her head, had a wart on one cheek, and silver-rimmed spectacles hung on the tip of her nose. She glanced at me above the glasses. The swift and indifferent placidity of that look troubled me. Two youths with foolish and cheery countenances were being piloted over, and she threw at them the same quick glance of unconcerned wisdom. She seemed to know all about them and about me, too. An eerie feeling came over me. She seemed uncanny and fateful. Often far away there I thought of these two, guarding the door of Darkness, knitting black wool as for a warm pall, one introducing, introducing continuously to the unknown, the other scrutinizing the cheery and foolish faces with unconcerned old eyes. *Ave!* Old knitter of black wool. *Morituri te salutant.*[7] Not many of those she looked at ever saw her again—not half, by a long way.

"There was yet a visit to the doctor. 'A simple formality,' assured me the secretary, with an air of taking an immense part in all my sorrows. Accordingly a young chap wearing his hat over the left eyebrow, some clerk I suppose—there must have been clerks in the business, though the house was as still as a house in a city of the dead—came from somewhere upstairs, and led me forth. He was shabby and careless, with inkstains on the sleeves of his jacket, and his cravat was large and billowy, under a chin shaped like the toe of an old boot. It was a little too early for the doctor, so I proposed a drink, and thereupon he developed a vein of joviality. As we sat over our vermouths he glorified the Company's business, and by and by I expressed casually my surprise at him not going out there. He became very cool and collected all at once. 'I am not such a fool as I look, quoth Plato to his disciples,' he said sententiously, emptied his glass with great resolution, and we rose.

"The old doctor felt my pulse, evidently thinking of something else the while. 'Good, good for there,' he mumbled, and then with a certain eagerness asked me whether I would let him measure my head.[8] Rather surprised, I said Yes, when he produced a thing like calipers and got the dimensions back and front and every way, taking notes carefully. He was an unshaven little man in a threadbare coat like a gaberdine, with his feet in slippers, and I thought him a harmless fool. 'I always ask leave, in the interests of science, to measure the crania of those going out there,' he said. 'And when they come back, too?' I asked. 'Oh, I never see them,' he remarked; 'and, moreover, the changes take place inside, you know.' He smiled, as if at some quiet joke. 'So you are going out there. Famous. Interesting too.' He gave me a searching glance, and made another note. 'Ever any madness in your family?' he asked, in a matter-of-fact tone. I felt very annoyed. 'Is that question in the interests of science, too?' 'It would be,' he said, without taking notice of my irritation, 'interesting for science to watch the mental changes of individuals, on the spot, but . . .' 'Are you an alienist?'[9] I interrupted. 'Every doctor should be—a little,' answered that original, imperturbably. 'I have a little theory which you Messieurs who go

---

7. "Hail! . . . They who are about to die salute you" (Latin). The traditional salutation of gladiators in ancient Rome.   **8.** Phrenology, the study of skull conformation as an index of mind and personality, was a more or less respectable part of 19th-century medical study.   **9.** Doctor who treats mental disease.

out there must help me to prove. This is my share in the advantages my country shall reap from the possession of such a magnificent dependency. The mere wealth I leave to others. Pardon my questions, but you are the first Englishman coming under my observation . . .' I hastened to assure him I was not in the least typical. 'If I were,' said I, 'I wouldn't be talking like this with you.' 'What you say is rather profound, and probably erroneous,' he said, with a laugh. 'Avoid irritation more than exposure to the sun. Adieu. How do you English say, eh? Good-by. Ah! Good-by. Adieu. In the tropics one must before everything keep calm.' . . . He lifted a warning forefinger. . . . *'Du calme, du calme. Adieu.'*[1]

"One thing more remained to do—say good-by to my excellent aunt. I found her triumphant. I had a cup of tea—the last decent cup of tea for many days—and in a room that most soothingly looked just as you would expect a lady's drawing-room to look, we had a long quiet chat by the fireside. In the course of these confidences it became quite plain to me I had been represented to the wife of the high dignitary, and goodness knows to how many more people besides, as an exceptional and gifted creature—a piece of good fortune for the Company—a man you don't get hold of every day. Good heavens! and I was going to take charge of a two-penny-half-penny river-steamboat with a penny whistle attached! It appeared, however, I was also one of the Workers, with a capital—you know. Something like an emissary of light, something like a lower sort of apostle. There had been a lot of such rot let loose in print and talk just about that time, and the excellent woman, living right in the rush of all that humbug, got carried off her feet. She talked about 'weaning those ignorant millions from their horrid ways,' till, upon my word, she made me quite uncomfortable. I ventured to hint that the Company was run for profit.

"'You forget, dear Charlie, that the laborer is worthy of his hire,'[2] she said, brightly. It's queer how out of touch with truth women are. They live in a world of their own, and there has never been anything like it, and never can be. It is too beautiful altogether, and if they were to set it up it would go to pieces before the first sunset. Some confounded fact we men have been living contentedly with ever since the day of creation would start up and knock the whole thing over.

"After this I got embraced, told to wear flannel, be sure to write often, and so on—and I left. In the street—I don't know why—a queer feeling came to me that I was an impostor. Odd thing that I, who used to clear out for any part of the world at twenty-four hours' notice, with less thought than most men give to the crossing of a street, had a moment—I won't say of hesitation, but of startled pause, before this commonplace affair. The best way I can explain it to you is by saying that, for a second or two, I felt as though, instead of going to the center of a continent, I were about to set off for the center of the earth.

"I left in a French steamer, and she called in every blamed port they have out there,[3] for, as far as I could see, the sole purpose of landing soldiers and custom-house officers. I watched the coast. Watching a coast as it slips by the ship is like thinking about an enigma. There it is before you—smiling, frown-

---

1. "Keep calm, keep calm. Good-bye" (French).   2. Words of Christ (Luke 10.7).   3. French colonies stretched down most of the West African coast to the mouth of the Congo, with major ports at Casablanca and Dakar.

ing, inviting, grand, mean, insipid, or savage, and always mute with an air of whispering, Come and find out. This one was almost featureless, as if still in the making, with an aspect of monotonous grimness. The edge of a colossal jungle, so dark-green as to be almost black, fringed with white surf, ran straight, like a ruled line, far, far away along a blue sea whose glitter was blurred by a creeping mist. The sun was fierce, the land seemed to glisten and drip with steam. Here and there grayish-whitish specks showed up clustered inside the white surf, with a flag flying above them perhaps. Settlements some centuries old, and still no bigger than pinheads on the untouched expanse of their background. We pounded along, stopped, landed soldiers; went on, landed custom-house clerks to levy toll in what looked like a God-forsaken wilderness, with a tin shed and a flag-pole lost in it; landed more soldiers—to take care of the custom-house clerks, presumably. Some, I heard, got drowned in the surf; but whether they did or not, nobody seemed particularly to care. They were just flung out there, and on we went. Every day the coast looked the same, as though we had not moved; but we passed various places—trading places—with names like Gran' Bassam, Little Popo; names that seemed to belong to some sordid farce acted in front of a sinister backcloth. The idleness of a passenger, my isolation amongst all these men with whom I had no point of contact, the oily and languid sea, the uniform somberness of the coast, seemed to keep me away from the truth of things, within the toil of a mournful and senseless delusion. The voice of the surf heard now and then was a positive pleasure, like the speech of a brother. It was something natural, that had its reason, that had a meaning. Now and then a boat from the shore gave one a momentary contact with reality. It was paddled by black fellows. You could see from afar the white of their eyeballs glistening. They shouted, sang; their bodies streamed with perspiration; they had faces like grotesque masks—these chaps; but they had bone, muscle, a wild vitality, an intense energy of movement, that was as natural and true as the surf along their coast. They wanted no excuse for being there. They were a great comfort to look at. For a time I would feel I belonged still to a world of straightforward facts; but the feeling would not last long. Something would turn up to scare it away. Once, I remember, we came upon a man-of-war anchored off the coast. There wasn't even a shed there, and she was shelling the bush. It appears the French had one of their wars going on thereabouts. Her ensign[4] dropped limp like a rag; the muzzles of the long six-inch guns stuck out all over the low hull; the greasy, slimy swell swung her up lazily and let her down, swaying her thin masts. In the empty immensity of earth, sky, and water, there she was, incomprehensible, firing into a continent. Pop, would go one of the six-inch guns; a small flame would dart and vanish, a little white smoke would disappear, a tiny projectile would give a feeble screech—and nothing happened. Nothing could happen. There was a touch of insanity in the proceeding, a sense of lugubrious drollery in the sight; and it was not dissipated by somebody on board assuring me earnestly there was a camp of natives—he called them enemies!—hidden out of sight somewhere.

"We gave her her letters (I heard the men in that lonely ship were dying of fever at the rate of three a day) and went on. We called at some more places

---

4. Flag.

with farcical names, where the merry dance of death and trade goes on in a still and earthy atmosphere as of an overheated catacomb; all along the formless coast bordered by dangerous surf, as if Nature herself had tried to ward off intruders; in and out of rivers, streams of death in life, whose banks were rotting into mud, whose waters, thickened into slime, invaded the contorted mangroves, that seemed to writhe at us in the extremity of an impotent despair. Nowhere did we stop long enough to get a particularized impression, but the general sense of vague and oppressive wonder grew upon me. It was like a weary pilgrimage amongst hints for nightmares.

"It was upward of thirty days before I saw the mouth of the big river. We anchored off the seat of the government.[5] But my work would not begin till some two hundred miles farther on. So as soon as I could I made a start for a place thirty miles higher up.

"I had my passage on a little sea-going steamer. Her captain was a Swede, and knowing me for a seaman, invited me on the bridge. He was a young man, lean, fair, and morose, with lanky hair and a shuffling gait. As we left the miserable little wharf, he tossed his head contemptuously at the shore. 'Been living there?' he asked. I said, 'Yes.' 'Fine lot these government chaps—are they not?' he went on, speaking English with great precision and considerable bitterness. 'It is funny what some people will do for a few francs a month. I wonder what becomes of that kind when it goes up-country?' I said to him I expected to see that soon. 'So-o-o!' he exclaimed. He shuffled athwart, keeping one eye ahead vigilantly. 'Don't be too sure,' he continued. 'The other day I took up a man who hanged himself on the road. He was a Swede, too.' 'Hanged himself! Why, in God's name?' I cried. He kept on looking out watchfully. 'Who knows? The sun was too much for him, or the country perhaps.'

"At last we opened a reach.[6] A rocky cliff appeared, mounds of turned-up earth by the shore, houses on a hill, others with iron roofs, amongst a waste of excavations, or hanging to the declivity.[7] A continuous noise of the rapids above hovered over this scene of inhabited devastation. A lot of people, mostly black and naked, moved about like ants. A jetty projected into the river. A blinding sunlight drowned all this at times in a sudden recrudescence of glare. 'There's your Company's station,' said the Swede, pointing to three wooden barrack-like structures on the rocky slope. 'I will send your things up. Four boxes did you say? So. Farewell.'

"I came upon a boiler wallowing in the grass, then found a path leading up the hill. It turned aside for the boulders, and also for an undersized railway-truck lying there on its back with its wheels in the air. One was off. The thing looked as dead as the carcass of some animal. I came upon more pieces of decaying machinery, a stack of rusty nails. To the left a clump of trees made a shady spot, where dark things seemed to stir feebly. I blinked, the path was steep. A horn tooted to the right, and I saw the black people run. A heavy and dull detonation shook the ground, a puff of smoke came out of the cliff, and that was all. No change appeared on the face of the rock. They were building a railway. The cliff was not in the way or anything; but this objectless blasting was all the work going on.

5. Boma, in the mouth of the Congo River.   6. That is, came to a clear stretch of the river.   7. Town of Matadi.

"A slight clinking behind me made me turn my head. Six black men advanced in a file, toiling up the path. They walked erect and slow, balancing small baskets full of earth on their heads, and the clink kept time with their footsteps. Black rags were wound round their loins, and the short ends behind waggled to and fro like tails. I could see every rib, the joints of their limbs were like knots in a rope; each had an iron collar on his neck, and all were connected together with a chain whose bights[8] swung between them, rhythmically clinking. Another report from the cliff made me think suddenly of that ship of war I had seen firing into a continent. It was the same kind of ominous voice; but these men could by no stretch of imagination be called enemies. They were called criminals, and the outraged law, like the bursting shells, had come to them, an insoluble mystery from the sea. All their meager breasts panted together, the violently dilated nostrils quivered, the eyes stared stonily up-hill. They passed me within six inches, without a glance, with that complete, deathlike indifference of unhappy savages. Behind this raw matter one of the reclaimed, the product of the new forces at work, strolled despondently, carrying a rifle by its middle. He had a uniform jacket with one button off, and seeing a white man on the path, hoisted his weapon to his shoulder with alacrity. This was simple prudence, white men being so much alike at a distance that he could not tell who I might be. He was speedily reassured, and with a large, white, rascally grin, and a glance at his charge, seemed to take me into partnership in his exalted trust. After all, I also was a part of the great cause of these high and just proceedings.

"Instead of going up, I turned and descended to the left. My idea was to let that chain-gang get out of sight before I climbed the hill. You know I am not particularly tender; I've had to strike and to fend off. I've had to resist and to attack sometimes—that's only one way of resisting—without counting the exact cost, according to the demands of such sort of life as I had blundered into. I've seen the devil of violence, and the devil of greed, and the devil of hot desire; but, by all the stars! these were strong, lusty, red-eyed devils, that swayed and drove men—men, I tell you. But as I stood on this hillside, I foresaw that in the blinding sunshine of that land I would become acquainted with a flabby, pretending, weak-eyed devil of a rapacious and pitiless folly. How insidious he could be, too, I was only to find out several months later and a thousand miles farther. For a moment I stood appalled, as though by a warning. Finally I descended the hill, obliquely, towards the trees I had seen.

"I avoided a vast artificial hole somebody had been digging on the slope, the purpose of which I found it impossible to divine. It wasn't a quarry or a sandpit, anyhow. It was just a hole. It might have been connected with the philanthropic desire of giving the criminals something to do. I don't know. Then I nearly fell into a very narrow ravine, almost no more than a scar in the hillside. I discovered that a lot of imported drainage-pipes for the settlement had been tumbled in there. There wasn't one that was not broken. It was a wanton smash-up. At last I got under the trees. My purpose was to stroll into the shade for a moment; but no sooner within than it seemed to me I had stepped into the gloomy circle of some Inferno. The rapids were near, and an uninterrupted, uniform, headlong, rushing noise filled the mournful still-

---

8. Slack sections.

ness of the grove, where not a breath stirred, not a leaf moved, with a mysterious sound—as though the tearing pace of the launched earth had suddenly become audible.

"Black shapes crouched, lay, sat between the trees, leaning against the trunks, clinging to the earth, half coming out, half effaced within the dim light, in all the attitudes of pain, abandonment, and despair. Another mine[9] on the cliff went off, followed by a slight shudder of the soil under my feet. The work was going on. The work! And this was the place where some of the helpers had withdrawn to die.

"They were dying slowly—it was very clear. They were not enemies, they were not criminals, they were nothing earthly now,—nothing but black shadows of disease and starvation, lying confusedly in the greenish gloom. Brought from all the recesses of the coast in all the legality of time contracts, lost in uncongenial surroundings, fed on unfamiliar food, they sickened, became inefficient, and were then allowed to crawl away and rest. These moribund shapes were free as air—and nearly as thin. I began to distinguish the gleam of the eyes under the trees. Then, glancing down, I saw a face near my hand. The black bones reclined at full length with one shoulder against the tree, and slowly the eyelids rose and the sunken eyes looked up at me, enormous and vacant, a kind of blind, white flicker in the depths of the orbs, which died out slowly. The man seemed young—almost a boy—but you know with them it's hard to tell. I found nothing else to do but to offer him one of my good Swede's ship's biscuits I had in my pocket. The fingers closed slowly on it and held—there was no other movement and no other glance. He had tied a bit of white worsted round his neck—Why? Where did he get it? Was it a badge—an ornament—a charm—a propitiatory act? Was there any idea at all connected with it? It looked startling round his black neck, this bit of white thread from beyond the seas.

"Near the same tree two more bundles of acute angles sat with their legs drawn up. One, with his chin propped on his knees, stared at nothing, in an intolerable and appalling manner: his brother phantom rested its forehead, as if overcome with a great weariness; and all about others were scattered in every pose of contorted collapse, as in some picture of a massacre or a pestilence. While I stood horror-struck, one of these creatures rose to his hands and knees, and went off on all-fours towards the river to drink. He lapped out of his hand, then sat up in the sunlight, crossing his shins in front of him, and after a time let his woolly head fall on his breastbone.

"I didn't want any more loitering in the shade, and I made haste towards the station. When near the buildings I met a white man, in such an unexpected elegance of get-up that in the first moment I took him for a sort of vision. I saw a high starched collar, white cuffs, a light alpaca jacket, snowy trousers, a clear necktie, and varnished boots. No hat. Hair parted, brushed, oiled, under a green-lined parasol held in a big white hand. He was amazing, and had a penholder behind his ear.

"I shook hands with this miracle, and I learned he was the Company's chief accountant, and that all the bookkeeping was done at this station. He had come out for a moment, he said, 'to get a breath of fresh air.' The expression

---

9. Explosive charge.

sounded wonderfully odd, with its suggestion of sedentary desk-life. I wouldn't have mentioned the fellow to you at all, only it was from his lips that I first heard the name of the man who is so indissolubly connected with the memories of that time. Moreover, I respected the fellow. Yes; I respected his collars, his vast cuffs, his brushed hair. His appearance was certainly that of a hairdresser's dummy; but in the great demoralization of the land he kept up his appearance. That's backbone. His starched collars and got-up shirt-fronts were achievements of character. He had been out nearly three years; and, later, I could not help asking him how he managed to sport such linen. He had just the faintest blush, and said modestly, 'I've been teaching one of the native women about the station. It was difficult. She had a distaste for the work.' Thus this man had verily accomplished something. And he was devoted to his books, which were in apple-pie order.

"Everything else in the station was in a muddle,—heads, things, buildings. Strings of dusty niggers with splay feet arrived and departed; a stream of manufactured goods, rubbishy cottons, beads, and brass-wire set into the depths of darkness, and in return came a precious trickle of ivory.[1]

"I had to wait in the station for ten days—an eternity. I lived in a hut in the yard, but to be out of the chaos I would sometimes get into the accountant's office. It was built of horizontal planks, and so badly put together that, as he bent over his high desk, he was barred from neck to heels with narrow strips of sunlight. There was no need to open the big shutter to see. It was hot there, too; big flies buzzed fiendishly, and did not sting, but stabbed. I sat generally on the floor, while, of faultless appearance (and even slightly scented), perching on a high stool, he wrote, he wrote. Sometimes he stood up for exercise. When a trucklebed with a sick man (some invalid agent from up-country) was put in there, he exhibited a gentle annoyance. 'The groans of this sick person,' he said, 'distract my attention. And without that it is extremely difficult to guard against clerical errors in this climate.'

"One day he remarked, without lifting his head, 'In the interior you will no doubt meet Mr. Kurtz.' On my asking who Mr. Kurtz was, he said he was a first-class agent; and seeing my disappointment at this information, he added slowly, laying down his pen, 'He is a very remarkable person.' Further questions elicited from him that Mr. Kurtz was at present in charge of a trading post, a very important one, in the true ivory-country, at 'the very bottom of there. Sends in as much ivory as all the others put together. . . .' He began to write again. The sick man was too ill to groan. The flies buzzed in a great peace.

"Suddenly there was a growing murmur of voices and a great tramping of feet. A caravan had come in. A violent babble of uncouth sounds burst out on the other side of the planks. All the carriers were speaking together, and in the midst of the uproar the lamentable voice of the chief agent was heard 'giving it up' tearfully for the twentieth time that day. . . . He rose slowly. 'What a frightful row,' he said. He crossed the room gently to look at the sick man, and returning, said to me, 'He does not hear.' 'What! Dead?' I asked, startled. 'No, not yet,' he answered, with great composure. Then, alluding with a toss

---

1. Ivory and rubber were the main commercial resources traded from the Congo Free State. Ivory was used for billiard balls, piano keys, and carved art objects.

of the head to the tumult in the station-yard, 'When one has got to make correct entries, one comes to hate those savages—hate them to the death.' He remained thoughtful for a moment. 'When you see Mr. Kurtz,' he went on, 'tell him for me that everything here'—he glanced at the desk—'is very satisfactory. I don't like to write to him—with those messengers of ours you never know who may get hold of your letter—at that Central Station.' He stared at me for a moment with his mild, bulging eyes. 'Oh, he will go far, very far,' he began again. 'He will be a somebody in the Administration before long. They, above—the Council in Europe, you know—mean him to be.'

"He turned to his work. The noise outside had ceased, and presently in going out I stopped at the door. In the steady buzz of flies the homeward-bound agent was lying flushed and insensible; the other, bent over his books, was making correct entries of perfectly correct transactions; and fifty feet below the doorstep I could see the still tree-tops of the grove of death.

"Next day I left that station at last, with a caravan of sixty men, for a two-hundred-mile tramp.

"No use telling you much about that. Paths, paths, everywhere; a stamped-in network of paths spreading over the empty land, through long grass, through burnt grass, through thickets, down and up chilly ravines, up and down stony hills ablaze with heat; and a solitude, a solitude, nobody, not a hut. The population had cleared out a long time ago. Well, if a lot of mysterious niggers armed with all kinds of fearful weapons suddenly took to traveling on the road between Deal and Gravesend,[2] catching the yokels right and left to carry heavy loads for them, I fancy every farm and cottage thereabouts would get empty very soon. Only here the dwellings were gone, too. Still I passed through several abandoned villages. There's something pathetically childish in the ruins of grass walls. Day after day, with the stamp and shuffle of sixty pair of bare feet behind me, each pair under a sixty-pound load. Camp, cook, sleep, strike camp, march. Now and then a carrier dead in harness, at rest in the long grass near the path, with an empty water-gourd and his long staff lying by his side. A great silence around and above. Perhaps on some quiet night the tremor of far-off drums, sinking, swelling, a tremor vast, faint; a sound weird, appealing, suggestive, and wild—and perhaps with as profound a meaning as the sound of bells in a Christian country. Once a white man in an unbuttoned uniform, camping on the path with an armed escort of lank Zanzibaris,[3] very hospitable and festive—not to say drunk. Was looking after the upkeep of the road, he declared. Can't say I saw any road or any upkeep, unless the body of a middle-aged Negro, with a bullet-hole in the forehead, upon which I absolutely stumbled three miles farther on, may be considered as a permanent improvement. I had a white companion, too, not a bad chap, but rather too fleshy and with the exasperating habit of fainting on the hot hillsides, miles away from the least bit of shade and water. Annoying, you know, to hold your own coat like a parasol over a man's head while he is coming-to. I couldn't help asking him once what he meant by coming there at all. 'To make money, of course. What do you think?' he said, scornfully. Then he got fever, and had to be carried in a hammock slung under a pole. As he weighed sixteen stone[4] I had no end of rows with the carriers. They jibbed, ran away, sneaked off with their loads in the night—quite a mutiny. So, one evening, I made a speech in English with gestures, not one of which was lost to the sixty pairs of eyes before me, and the next morning I started the hammock off in front all right. An hour afterwards I came upon the whole concern wrecked in a bush—man, hammock, groans, blankets, horrors. The heavy pole had skinned his poor nose. He was very anxious for me to kill somebody, but there wasn't the shadow of a carrier near. I remembered the old doctor—'It would be interesting for science to watch the mental changes of individuals, on the spot.' I felt I was becoming scientifically interesting. However, all that is to no purpose. On the fifteenth day I came in sight of the big river again, and hobbled into the Central Station. It was on a backwater surrounded by scrub and forest, with a pretty border of smelly mud on one side, and on the three others enclosed by a crazy fence of rushes. A neglected gap was all the gate it had, and the first glance at the place was enough to let you see the flabby devil was running that show. White men with long staves in their hands appeared languidly from amongst the buildings, strolling up to take a look at me, and then retired out of sight somewhere. One of them, a stout, excitable chap with black mustaches, informed me with great volubility and many digressions, as soon as I told him who I was, that my steamer was at the bottom of the river. I was thunderstruck. What, how, why? Oh, it was 'all right.' The 'manager himself' was there. All quite correct. 'Everybody had behaved splendidly! splendidly!'—'you must,' he said in agitation, 'go and see the general manager at once. He is waiting!'

"I did not see the real significance of that wreck at once. I fancy I see it now, but I am not sure—not at all. Certainly the affair was too stupid—when I think of it—to be altogether natural. Still. . . . But at the moment it presented itself simply as a confounded nuisance. The steamer was sunk. They had started two days before in a sudden hurry up the river with the manager on board, in charge of some volunteer skipper, and before they had been out three hours they tore the bottom out of her on stones, and she sank near the south bank. I asked myself what I was to do there, now my boat was lost. As a matter of fact, I had plenty to do in fishing my command out of the river. I had to set about it the very next day. That, and the repairs when I brought the pieces to the station, took some months.

"My first interview with the manager was curious. He did not ask me to sit down after my twenty-mile walk that morning. He was commonplace in complexion, in feature, in manners, and in voice. He was of middle size and of ordinary build. His eyes, of the usual blue, were perhaps remarkably cold, and he certainly could make his glance fall on one as trenchant and heavy as an ax. But even at these times the rest of his person seemed to disclaim the intention. Otherwise there was only an indefinable, faint expression of his lips, something stealthy—a smile—not a smile—I remember it, but I can't explain. It was unconscious, this smile was, though just after he had said something it got intensified for an instant. It came at the end of his speeches like a seal applied on the words to make the meaning of the commonest phrase appear absolutely inscrutable. He was a common trader, from his youth up employed

---

4. British unit of weight equaling 14 pounds—hence he weighed 224 pounds.

in these parts—nothing more. He was obeyed, yet he inspired neither love nor fear, nor even respect. He inspired uneasiness. That was it! Uneasiness. Not a definite mistrust—just uneasiness—nothing more. You have no idea how effective such a . . . a . . . faculty can be. He had no genius for organizing, for initiative, or for order even. That was evident in such things as the deplorable state of the station. He had no learning, and no intelligence. His position had come to him—why? Perhaps because he was never ill. . . . He had served three terms of three years out there. . . . Because triumphant health in the general rout of constitutions is a kind of power in itself. When he went home on leave he rioted on a large scale—pompously. Jack ashore[5]—with a difference—in externals only. This one could gather from his casual talk. He originated nothing, he could keep the routine going—that's all. But he was great. He was great by this little thing that it was impossible to tell what could control such a man. He never gave that secret away. Perhaps there was nothing within him. Such a suspicion made one pause—for out there there were no external checks. Once when various tropical diseases had laid low almost every 'agent' in the station, he was heard to say, 'Men who come out here should have no entrails.' He sealed the utterance with that smile of his, as though it had been a door opening into a darkness he had in his keeping. You fancied you had seen things—but the seal was on. When annoyed at meal-times by the constant quarrels of the white men about precedence, he ordered an immense round table to be made, for which a special house had to be built. This was the station's messroom. Where he sat was the first place—the rest were nowhere. One felt this to be his unalterable conviction. He was neither civil nor uncivil. He was quiet. He allowed his 'boy'—an overfed young Negro from the coast—to treat the white men, under his very eyes, with provoking insolence.

"He began to speak as soon as he saw me. I had been very long on the road. He could not wait. Had to start without me. The upriver stations had to be relieved. There had been so many delays already that he did not know who was dead and who was alive, and how they got on—and so on, and so on. He paid no attention to my explanations, and, playing with a stick of sealing-wax, repeated several times that the situation was 'very grave, very grave.' There were rumors that a very important station was in jeopardy, and its chief, Mr. Kurtz, was ill. Hoped it was not true. Mr. Kurtz was . . . I felt weary and irritable. Hang Kurtz, I thought. I interrupted him by saying I had heard of Mr. Kurtz on the coast. 'Ah! So they talk of him down there,' he murmured to himself. Then he began again, assuring me Mr. Kurtz was the best agent he had, an exceptional man, of the greatest importance to the Company; therefore I could understand his anxiety. He was, he said, 'very, very uneasy.' Certainly he fidgeted on his chair a good deal, exclaimed, 'Ah, Mr. Kurtz!' broke the stick of sealing-wax and seemed dumfounded by the accident. Next thing he wanted to know 'how long it would take to . . .' I interrupted him again. Being hungry, you know, and kept on my feet too, I was getting savage. 'How can I tell?' I said, 'I haven't even seen the wreck yet—some months, no doubt.' All this talk seemed to me so futile. 'Some months,' he said. 'Well, let us say three months before we can make a start. Yes. That ought to do the affair.' I flung out of his hut (he lived all alone in a clay hut with a sort of veranda)

---

5. That is, like a sailor on shore leave.

muttering to myself my opinion of him. He was a chattering idiot. Afterwards I took it back when it was borne in upon me startlingly with what extreme nicety he had estimated the time requisite for the 'affair.'

"I went to work the next day, turning, so to speak, my back on that station. In that way only it seemed to me I could keep my hold on the redeeming facts of life. Still, one must look about sometimes; and then I saw this station, these men strolling aimlessly about in the sunshine of the yard. I asked myself sometimes what it all meant. They wandered here and there with their absurd long staves in their hands, like a lot of faithless pilgrims bewitched inside a rotten fence. The word 'ivory' rang in the air, was whispered, was sighed. You would think they were praying to it. A taint of imbecile rapacity blew through it all, like a whiff from some corpse. By Jove! I've never seen anything so unreal in my life. And outside, the silent wilderness surrounding this cleared speck on the earth struck me as something great and invincible, like evil or truth, waiting patiently for the passing away of this fantastic invasion.

"Oh, these months! Well, never mind. Various things happened. One evening a grass shed full of calico, cotton prints, beads, and I don't know what else, burst into a blaze so suddenly that you would have thought the earth had opened to let an avenging fire consume all that trash. I was smoking my pipe quietly by my dismantled steamer, and saw them all cutting capers in the light, with their arms lifted high, when the stout man with mustaches came tearing down to the river, a tin pail in his hand, assured me that everybody was 'behaving splendidly, splendidly,' dipped about a quart of water and tore back again. I noticed there was a hole in the bottom of his pail.

"I strolled up. There was no hurry. You see the thing had gone off like a box of matches. It had been hopeless from the very first. The flame had leaped high, driven everybody back, lighted up everything—and collapsed. The shed was already a heap of embers glowing fiercely. A nigger was being beaten near by. They said he had caused the fire in some way; be that as it may, he was screeching most horribly. I saw him, later, for several days, sitting in a bit of shade looking very sick and trying to recover himself: afterwards he arose and went out—and the wilderness without a sound took him into its bosom again. As I approached the glow from the dark I found myself at the back of two men, talking. I heard the name of Kurtz pronounced, then the words, 'take advantage of this unfortunate accident.' One of the men was the manager. I wished him a good evening. 'Did you ever see anything like it—eh? it is incredible,' he said, and walked off. The other man remained. He was a first-class agent, young, gentlemanly, a bit reserved, with a forked little beard and a hooked nose. He was standoffish with the other agents, and they on their side said he was the manager's spy among them. As to me, I had hardly ever spoken to him before. We got into talk, and by and by we strolled away from the hissing ruins. Then he asked me to his room, which was in the main building of the station. He struck a match, and I perceived that this young aristocrat had not only a silver-mounted dressing-case but also a whole candle all to himself. Just at that time the manager was the only man supposed to have any right to candles. Native mats covered the clay walls; a collection of spears, assegais,[6] shields, knives was hung up in trophies. The business

---

6. Slender southern African throwing spears.

intrusted to this fellow was the making of bricks—so I had been informed; but there wasn't a fragment of a brick anywhere in the station, and he had been there more than a year—waiting. It seems he could not make bricks without something, I don't know what—straw, maybe. Anyways, it could not be found there, and as it was not likely to be sent from Europe, it did not appear clear to me what he was waiting for. An act of special creation perhaps. However, they were all waiting—all the sixteen or twenty pilgrims of them—for something; and upon my word it did not seem an uncongenial occupation, from the way they took it, though the only thing that ever came to them was disease—as far as I could see. They beguiled the time by backbiting and intriguing against each other in a foolish kind of way. There was an air of plotting about that station, but nothing came of it, of course. It was as unreal as everything else—as the philanthropic pretense of the whole concern, as their talk, as their government, as their show of work. The only real feeling was a desire to get appointed to a trading-post where ivory was to be had, so that they could earn percentages. They intrigued and slandered and hated each other only on that account,—but as to effectually lifting a little finger—oh, no. By heavens! there is something after all in the world allowing one man to steal a horse while another must not look at the halter. Steal a horse straight out. Very well. He has done it. Perhaps he can ride. But there is a way of looking at a halter that would provoke the most charitable of saints into a kick.

"I had no idea why he wanted to be sociable, but as we chatted in there it suddenly occurred to me the fellow was trying to get at something—in fact, pumping me. He alluded constantly to Europe, to the people I was supposed to know there—putting leading questions as to my acquaintances in the sepulchral city, and so on. His little eyes glittered like mica discs—with curiosity—though he tried to keep up a bit of superciliousness. At first I was astonished, but very soon I became awfully curious to see what he would find out from me. I couldn't possibly imagine what I had in me to make it worth his while. It was very pretty to see how he baffled himself, for in truth my body was full only of chills, and my head had nothing in it but that wretched steamboat business. It was evident he took me for a perfectly shameless prevaricator. At last he got angry, and, to conceal a movement of furious annoyance, he yawned. I rose. Then I noticed a small sketch in oils, on a panel, representing a woman, draped and blindfolded, carrying a lighted torch. The background was somber—almost black. The movement of the woman was stately, and the effect of the torchlight on the face was sinister.

"It arrested me, and he stood by civilly, holding an empty half-pint champagne bottle (medical comforts) with the candle stuck in it. To my question he said Mr. Kurtz had painted this—in this very station more than a year ago—while waiting for means to go to his trading-post. 'Tell me, pray,' said I, 'who is this Mr. Kurtz?'

"'The chief of the Inner Station,' he answered in a short tone, looking away. 'Much obliged,' I said, laughing. 'And you are the brickmaker of the Central Station. Everyone knows that.' He was silent for a while. 'He is a prodigy,' he said at last. 'He is an emissary of pity, and science, and progress, and devil knows what else. We want,' he began to declaim suddenly, 'for the guidance of the cause intrusted to us by Europe, so to speak, higher intelligence, wide sympathies, a singleness of purpose.' 'Who says that?' I asked. 'Lots of them,' he replied. 'Some even write that; and so *he* comes here, a special being, as you ought to know.' 'Why ought I to know?' I interrupted, really surprised. He paid no attention. 'Yes. Today he is chief of the best station, next year he will be assistant-manager, two years more and . . . but I daresay you know what he will be in two years' time. You are of the new gang—the gang of virtue. The same people who sent him specially also recommended you. Oh, don't say no. I've my own eyes to trust.' Light dawned upon me. My dear aunt's influential acquaintances were producing an unexpected effect upon that young man. I nearly burst into a laugh. 'Do you read the Company's confidential correspondence?' I asked. He hadn't a word to say. It was great fun. 'When Mr. Kurtz,' I continued, severely, 'is General Manager, you won't have the opportunity.'

"He blew the candle out suddenly, and we went outside. The moon had risen. Black figures strolled about listlessly, pouring water on the glow, whence proceeded a sound of hissing; steam ascended in the moonlight, the beaten nigger groaned somewhere. 'What a row the brute makes!' said the indefatigable man with the mustaches, appearing near us. 'Serves him right. Transgression—punishment—bang! Pitiless, pitiless. That's the only way. This will prevent all conflagrations for the future. I was just telling the manager. . . .' He noticed my companion, and became crestfallen all at once. 'Not in bed yet,' he said, with a kind of servile heartiness; 'it's so natural. Ha! Danger—agitation.' He vanished. I went on to the river-side, and the other followed me. I heard a scathing murmur at my ear, 'Heap of muffs[7]—go to.' The pilgrims could be seen in knots gesticulating, discussing. Several had still their staves in their hands. I verily believe they took these sticks to bed with them. Beyond the fence the forest stood up spectrally in the moonlight, and through the dim stir, through the faint sounds of that lamentable courtyard, the silence of the land went home to one's very heart—its mystery, its greatness, the amazing reality of its concealed life. The hurt nigger moaned feebly somewhere near by, and then fetched a deep sigh that made me mend my pace away from there. I felt a hand introducing itself under my arm. 'My dear sir,' said the fellow, 'I don't want to be misunderstood, and especially by you, who will see Mr. Kurtz long before I can have that pleasure. I wouldn't like him to get a false idea of my disposition. . . .'

"I let him run on, this papier-mâché Mephistopheles,[8] and it seemed to me that if I tried I could poke my forefinger through him, and would find nothing inside but a little loose dirt, maybe. He, don't you see, had been planning to be assistant-manager by and by under the present man, and I could see that the coming of that Kurtz had upset them both not a little. He talked precipitately, and I did not try to stop him. I had my shoulders against the wreck of my steamer, hauled up on the slope like a carcass of some big river animal. The smell of mud, of primeval mud, by Jove! was in my nostrils, the high stillness of primeval forest was before my eyes; there were shiny patches on the black creek. The moon had spread over everything a thin layer of silver—over the rank grass, over the mud, upon the wall of matted vegetation standing higher than the wall of a temple, over the great river I could see through a somber gap glittering, glittering, as it flowed broadly by without a

---

7. Gang of bunglers. **8.** That is, devil made of pasteboard.

murmur. All this was great, expectant, mute, while the man jabbered about himself. I wondered whether the stillness on the face of the immensity looking at us two were meant as an appeal or as a menace. What were we who had strayed in here? Could we handle that dumb thing, or would it handle us? I felt how big, how confoundedly big, was that thing that couldn't talk, and perhaps was deaf as well. What was in there? I could see a little ivory coming out from there, and I had heard Mr. Kurtz was in there. I had heard enough about it, too—God knows! Yet somehow it didn't bring any image with it—no more than if I had been told an angel or a fiend was in there. I believed it in the same way one of you might believe there are inhabitants in the planet Mars. I knew once a Scotch sailmaker who was certain, dead sure, there were people in Mars. If you asked him for some idea how they looked and behaved, he would get shy and mutter something about 'walking on all-fours.' If you as much as smiled, he would—though a man of sixty—offer to fight you. I would not have gone so far as to fight for Kurtz, but I went for him near enough to a lie. You know I hate, detest, and can't bear a lie, not because I am straighter than the rest of us, but simply because it appalls me. There is a taint of death, a flavor of mortality in lies—which is exactly what I hate and detest in the world—what I want to forget. It makes me miserable and sick, like biting something rotten would do. Temperament, I suppose. Well, I went near enough to it by letting the young fool there believe anything he liked to imagine as to my influence in Europe. I became in an instant as much of a pretence as the rest of the bewitched pilgrims. This simply because I had a notion it somehow would be of help to that Kurtz whom at the time I did not see—you understand. He was just a word for me. I did not see the man in the name any more than you do. Do you see him? Do you see the story? Do you see anything? It seems to me I am trying to tell you a dream—making a vain attempt, because no relation of a dream can convey the dream-sensation, that commingling of absurdity, surprise, and bewilderment in a tremor of struggling revolt, that notion of being captured by the incredible which is of the very essence of dreams. . . ."

He was silent for a while.

". . . No, it is impossible; it is impossible to convey the life-sensation of any given epoch of one's existence—that which makes its truth, its meaning—its subtle and penetrating essence. It is impossible. We live, as we dream—alone. . . ."

He paused again as if reflecting, then added—

"Of course in this you fellows see more than I could then. You see me, whom you know. . . ."

It had become so pitch dark that we listeners could hardly see one another. For a long time already he, sitting apart, had been no more to us than a voice. There was not a word from anybody. The others might have been asleep, but I was awake. I listened, I listened on the watch for the sentence, for the word, that would give me the clew to the faint uneasiness inspired by this narrative that seemed to shape itself without human lips in the heavy night-air of the river.

". . . Yes—I let him run on," Marlow began again, "and think what he pleased about the powers that were behind me. I did! And there was nothing behind me! There was nothing but that wretched, old, mangled steamboat I was leaning against, while he talked fluently about 'the necessity for every man to get on.' 'And when one comes out here, you conceive, it is not to gaze at the moon.' Mr. Kurtz was a 'universal genius,' but even a genius would find it easier to work with 'adequate tools—intelligent men.' He did not make bricks—why, there was a physical impossibility in the way—as I was well aware; and if he did secretarial work for the manager, it was because 'no sensible man rejects wantonly the confidence of his superiors.' Did I see it? I saw it. What more did I want? What I really wanted was rivets, by heaven! Rivets. To get on with the work—to stop the hole. Rivets I wanted. There were cases of them down at the coast—cases—piled up—burst—split! You kicked a loose rivet at every second step in that station yard on the hillside. Rivets had rolled into the grove of death. You could fill your pockets with rivets for the trouble of stooping down—and there wasn't one rivet to be found where it was wanted. We had plates that would do, but nothing to fasten them with. And every week the messenger, a lone Negro, letter-bag on shoulder and staff in hand, left our station for the coast. And several times a week a coast caravan came in with trade goods—ghastly glazed calico that made you shudder only to look at it; glass beads, valued about a penny a quart, confounded spotted cotton handkerchiefs. And no rivets. Three carriers could have brought all that was wanted to set that steamboat afloat.

"He was becoming confidential now, but I fancy my unresponsive attitude must have exasperated him at last, for he judged it necessary to inform me he feared neither God nor devil, let alone any mere man. I said I could see that very well, but what I wanted was a certain quantity of rivets—and rivets were what really Mr. Kurtz wanted, if he had only known it. Now letters went to the coast every week. . . . 'My dear sir,' he cried, 'I write from dictation.' I demanded rivets. There was a way—for an intelligent man. He changed his manner; became very cold, and suddenly began to talk about a hippopotamus; wondered whether sleeping on board the steamer (I stuck to my salvage night and day) I wasn't disturbed. There was an old hippo that had the bad habit of getting out on the bank and roaming at night over the station grounds. The pilgrims used to turn out in a body and empty every rifle they could lay hands on at him. Some even had sat up o' nights for him. All this energy was wasted, though. 'That animal has a charmed life,' he said; 'but you can say this only of brutes in this country. No man—you apprehend me?—no man here bears a charmed life.' He stood there for a moment in the moonlight with his delicate hooked nose set a little askew, and his mica eyes glittering without a wink, then, with a curt good night, he strode off. I could see he was disturbed and considerably puzzled, which made me feel more hopeful than I had been for days. It was a great comfort to turn from that chap to my influential friend, the battered, twisted, ruined, tin-pot steamboat. I clambered on board. She rang under my feet like an empty Huntley & Palmer biscuit-tin kicked along a gutter; she was nothing so solid in make, and rather less pretty in shape, but I had expended enough hard work on her to make me love her. No influential friend would have served me better. She had given me a chance to come out a bit—to find out what I could do. No, I don't like work. I had rather laze about and think of all the fine things that can be done. I don't like work—no man does—but I like what is in the work,—the chance to find yourself. Your own reality—for yourself, not for others—what no other man can ever know. They can only see the mere show, and never can tell what it really means.

"I was not surprised to see somebody sitting aft, on the deck, with his legs dangling over the mud. You see I rather chummed with the few mechanics there were in that station, whom the other pilgrims naturally despised—on account of their imperfect manners, I suppose. This was the foreman—a boiler-maker by trade—a good worker. He was a lank, bony, yellow-faced man, with big intense eyes. His aspect was worried, and his head was as bald as the palm of my hand; but his hair in falling seemed to have stuck to his chin, and had prospered in the new locality, for his beard hung down to his waist. He was a widower with six young children (he had left them in charge of a sister of his to come out there), and the passion of his life was pigeon-flying. He was an enthusiast and a connoisseur. He would rave about pigeons. After work hours he used sometimes to come over from his hut for a talk about his children and his pigeons; at work, when he had to crawl in the mud under the bottom of the steamboat, he would tie up that beard of his in a kind of white serviette[9] he brought for the purpose. It had loops to go over his ears. In the evening he could be seen squatted on the bank rinsing that wrapper in the creek with great care, then spreading it solemnly on a bush to dry.

"I slapped him on the back and shouted, 'We shall have rivets!' He scrambled to his feet exclaiming, 'No! Rivets!' as though he couldn't believe his ears. Then in a low voice, 'You . . . eh?' I don't know why we behaved like lunatics. I put my finger to the side of my nose and nodded mysteriously. 'Good for you!' he cried, snapped his fingers above his head, lifting one foot. I tried a jig. We capered on the iron deck. A frightful clatter came out of that hulk, and the virgin forest on the other bank of the creek sent it back in a thundering roll upon the sleeping station. It must have made some of the pilgrims sit up in their hovels. A dark figure obscured the lighted doorway of the manager's hut, vanished, then, a second or so after, the doorway itself vanished, too. We stopped, and the silence driven away by the stamping of our feet flowed back again from the recesses of the land. The great wall of vegetation, an exuberant and entangled mass of trunks, branches, leaves, boughs, festoons, motionless in the moonlight, was like a rioting invasion of soundless life, a rolling wave of plants, piled up, crested, ready to topple over the creek, to sweep every little man of us out of his little existence. And it moved not. A deadened burst of mighty splashes and snorts reached us from afar as though an ichthyosaurus[1] had been taking a bath of glitter in the great river. 'After all,' said the boiler-maker in a reasonable tone, 'why shouldn't we get the rivets?' Why not, indeed! I did not know of any reason why we shouldn't. 'They'll come in three weeks,' I said, confidently.

"But they didn't. Instead of rivets there came an invasion, an in-fliction, a visitation. It came in sections during the next three weeks, each section headed by a donkey carrying a white man in new clothes and tan shoes, bowing from that elevation right and left to the impressed pilgrims. A quarrelsome band of footsore sulky niggers trod on the heels of the donkeys; a lot of tents, campstools, tin boxes, white cases, brown bales would be shot down in the courtyard, and the air of mystery would deepen a little over the muddle of

9. Napkin. **1.** Prehistoric marine reptile.

the station. Five such installments came, with their absurd air of disorderly flight with the loot of innumerable outfit shops and provision stores, that, one would think, they were lugging, after a raid, into the wilderness for equitable division. It was an extricable mess of things decent in themselves but that human folly made look like the spoils of thieving.

"This devoted band called itself the Eldorado Exploring Expedition, and I believe they were sworn to secrecy. Their talk, however, was the talk of sordid buccaneers: it was reckless without hardihood, greedy without audacity, and cruel without courage; there was not an atom of foresight or of serious intention in the whole batch of them, and they did not seem aware these things are wanted for the work of the world. To tear treasure out of the bowels of the land was their desire, with no more moral purpose at the back of it than there is in burglars breaking into a safe. Who paid the expenses of the noble enterprise I don't know; but the uncle of our manager was leader of that lot.

"In exterior he resembled a butcher in a poor neighborhood, and his eyes had a look of sleepy cunning. He carried his fat paunch with ostentation on his short legs, and during the time his gang infested the station spoke to no one but his nephew. You could see these two roaming about all day long with their heads close together in an everlasting confab.

"I had given up worrying myself about the rivets. One's capacity for that kind of folly is more limited than you would suppose. I said Hang!—and let things slide. I had plenty of time for meditation, and now and then I would give some thought to Kurtz. I wasn't very interested in him. No. Still, I was curious to see whether this man, who had come out equipped with moral ideas of some sort, would climb to the top after all and how he would set about his work when there."

II

"One evening as I was lying flat on the deck of my steamboat, I heard voices approaching—and there were the nephew and the uncle strolling along the bank. I laid my head on my arm again, and had nearly lost myself in a doze, when somebody said in my ear, as it were: 'I am as harmless as a little child, but I don't like to be dictated to. Am I the manager—or am I not? I was ordered to send him there. It's incredible.' . . . I became aware that the two were standing on the shore alongside the forepart of the steamboat, just below my head. I did not move; it did not occur to me to move: I was sleepy. 'It *is* unpleasant,' grunted the uncle. 'He has asked the Administration to be sent there,' said the other, 'with the idea of showing what he could do; and I was instructed accordingly. Look at the influence that man must have. Is it not frightful?' They both agreed it was frightful, then made several bizarre remarks: 'Make rain and fine weather—one man—the Council—by the nose'—bits of absurd sentences that got the better of my drowsiness, so that I had pretty near the whole of my wits about me when the uncle said, 'The climate may do away with this difficulty for you. Is he alone there?' 'Yes,' answered the manager; 'he sent his assistant down the river with a note to me in these terms: "Clear this poor devil out of the country, and don't bother sending more of that sort. I had rather be alone than have the kind of men you can dispose of with me." It was more than a year ago. Can you imagine such impudence?' 'Anything since then?' asked the other, hoarsely. 'Ivory,' jerked the nephew; 'lots of it—prime sort—lots—most annoying, from him.' 'And with that?' questioned the heavy rumble. 'Invoice,' was the reply fired out, so to speak. Then silence. They had been talking about Kurtz.

"I was broad awake by this time, but, lying perfectly at ease, remained still, having no inducement to change my position. 'How did that ivory come all this way?' growled the elder man, who seemed very vexed. The other explained that it had come with a fleet of canoes in charge of an English half-caste clerk Kurtz had with him; that Kurtz had apparently intended to return himself, the station being by that time bare of goods and stores, but after coming three hundred miles, had suddenly decided to go back, which he started to do alone in a small dugout with four paddlers, leaving the half-caste to continue down the river with the ivory. The two fellows there seemed astounded at anybody attempting such a thing. They were at a loss for an adequate motive. As to me, I seemed to see Kurtz for the first time. It was a distinct glimpse: the dugout, four paddling savages, and the lone white man turning his back suddenly on the headquarters, on relief, on thoughts of home—perhaps; setting his face towards the depths of the wilderness, towards his empty and desolate station. I did not know the motive. Perhaps he was just simply a fine fellow who stuck to his work for its own sake. His name, you understand, had not been pronounced once. He was 'that man.' The half-caste, who, as far as I could see, had conducted a difficult trip with great prudence and pluck, was invariably alluded to as 'that scoundrel.' The 'scoundrel' had reported that the 'man' had been very ill—had recovered imperfectly.... The two below me moved away then a few paces, and strolled back and forth at some little distance. I heard: 'Military post—doctor—two hundred miles—quite alone now—unavoidable delays—nine months—no news—strange rumors.' They approached again, just as the manager was saying, 'No one, as far as I know, unless a species of wandering trader—a pestilential fellow, snapping ivory from the natives.' Who was it they were talking about now? I gathered in snatches that this was some man supposed to be in Kurtz's district, and of whom the manager did not approve. 'We will not be free from unfair competition till one of these fellows is hanged for an example,' he said. 'Certainly,' grunted the other; 'get him hanged! Why not? Anything—anything can be done in this country. That's what I say; nobody here, you understand, *here,* can endanger your position. And why? You stand the climate—you outlast them all. The danger is in Europe; but there before I left I took care to—' They moved off and whispered, then their voices rose again. 'The extraordinary series of delays is not my fault. I did my best.' The fat man sighed. 'Very sad.' 'And the pestiferous absurdity of his talk,' continued the other; 'he bothered me enough when he was here. "Each station should be like a beacon on the road towards better things, a center for trade, of course, but also for humanizing, improving, instructing." Conceive you—that ass! And he wants to be manager! No, it's—' Here he got choked by excessive indignation, and I lifted my head the least bit. I was surprised to see how near they were—right under me. I could have spat upon their hats. They were looking on the ground, absorbed in thought. The manager was switching his leg with a slender twig: his sagacious relative lifted his head. 'You have been well since you came out this time?' he asked. The other gave a start. 'Who? I? Oh! Like a charm—like a charm. But the

rest—oh, my goodness! All sick. They die so quick, too, that I have
to send them out of the country—it's incredible!' 'H'm. Just so,' ʋ-
the uncle. 'Ah! my boy, trust to this—I say, trust to this.' I saw him extend hi.
short flipper of an arm for a gesture that took in the forest, the creek, the mud,
the river,—seemed to beckon with a dishonoring flourish before the sunlit face
of the land a treacherous appeal to the lurking death, to the hidden evil, to the
profound darkness of its heart. It was so startling that I leaped to my feet and
looked back at the edge of the forest, as though I had expected an answer of
some sort to that black display of confidence. You know the foolish notions
that come to one sometimes. The high stillness confronted these two figures with its ominous patience, waiting for the passing away of a fantastic
invasion.

"They swore aloud together—out of sheer fright, I believe—then pretending
not to know anything of my existence, turned back to the station. The sun
was low; and leaning forward side by side, they seemed to be tugging painfully uphill their two ridiculous shadows of unequal length, that trailed
behind them slowly over the tall grass without bending a single blade.

"In a few days the Eldorado Expedition went into the patient wilderness,
that closed upon it as the sea closes over a diver. Long afterwards the news
came that all the donkeys were dead. I know nothing as to the fate of the less
valuable animals. They, no doubt, like the rest of us, found what they
deserved. I did not inquire. I was then rather excited at the prospect of meeting Kurtz very soon. When I say very soon I mean it comparatively. It was just
two months from the day we left the creek when we came to the bank below
Kurtz's station.

"Going up that river was like traveling back to the earliest beginnings of
the world, when vegetation rioted on the earth and the big trees were kings.
An empty stream, a great silence, an impenetrable forest. The air was warm,
thick, heavy, sluggish. There was no joy in the brilliance of sunshine. The
long stretches of the waterway ran on, deserted, into the gloom of overshadowed distances. On silvery sandbanks hippos and alligators sunned themselves side by side. The broadening waters flowed through a mob of wooded
islands; you lost your way on that river as you would in a desert, and butted
all day long against shoals, trying to find the channel, till you thought yourself bewitched and cut off forever from everything you had known once—
somewhere—far away—in another existence perhaps. There were moments
when one's past came back to one, as it will sometimes when you have not a
moment to spare to yourself; but it came in the shape of an unrestful and
noisy dream, remembered with wonder amongst the overwhelming realities
of this strange world of plants, and water, and silence. And this stillness of
life did not in the least resemble a peace. It was the stillness of an implacable
force brooding over an inscrutable intention. It looked at you with a vengeful
aspect. I got used to it afterwards; I did not see it any more; I had no time. I
had to keep guessing at the channel; I had to discern, mostly by inspiration,
the signs of hidden banks; I watched for sunken stones; I was learning to clap
my teeth smartly before my heart flew out, when I shaved by a fluke some
infernal sly old snag that would have ripped the life out of the tin-pot steamboat and drowned all the pilgrims; I had to keep a lookout for the signs of
dead wood we could cut up in the night for next day's steaming. When you

have to attend to things of that sort, to the mere incidents of the surface, the reality—the reality, I tell you—fades. The inner truth is hidden—luckily, luckily. But I felt it all the same; I felt often its mysterious stillness watching me at my monkey tricks, just as it watches you fellows performing on your respective tight-ropes for—what is it? half-a-crown a tumble—"

"Try to be civil, Marlow," growled a voice, and I knew there was at least one listener awake besides myself.

"I beg your pardon. I forgot the heartache which makes up the rest of the price. And indeed what does the price matter, if the trick be well done? You do your tricks very well. And I didn't do badly either, since I managed not to sink that steamboat on my first trip. It's a wonder to me yet. Imagine a blindfolded man set to drive a van over a bad road. I sweated and shivered over that business considerably, I can tell you. After all, for a seaman, to scrape the bottom of the thing that's supposed to float all the time under his care is the unpardonable sin. No one may know of it, but you never forget the thump—eh? A blow on the very heart. You remember it, you dream of it, you wake up at night and think of it—years after—and go hot and cold all over. I don't pretend to say that steamboat floated all the time. More than once she had to wade for a bit, with twenty cannibals splashing around and pushing. We had enlisted some of these chaps on the way for a crew. Fine fellows—cannibals—in their place. They were men one could work with, and I am grateful to them. And, after all, they did not eat each other before my face: they had brought along a provision of hippo-meat which went rotten, and made the mystery of the wilderness stink in my nostrils. Phoo! I can sniff it now. I had the manager on board and three or four pilgrims with their staves—all complete. Sometimes we came upon a station close by the bank, clinging to the skirts of the unknown, and the white men rushing out of a tumble-down hovel, with great gestures of joy and surprise and welcome, seemed very strange—had the appearance of being held there captive by a spell. The word ivory would ring in the air for a while—and on we went again into the silence, along empty reaches, round the still bends, between the high walls of our winding way, reverberating in hollow claps the ponderous beat of the stern-wheel. Trees, trees, millions of trees, massive, immense, running up high; and at their foot, hugging the bank against the stream, crept the little begrimed steamboat, like a sluggish beetle crawling on the floor of a lofty portico. It made you feel very small, very lost, and yet it was not altogether depressing, that feeling. After all, if you were small, the grimy beetle crawled on—which was just what you wanted it to do. Where the pilgrims imagined it crawled to I don't know. To some place where they expected to get something, I bet! For me it crawled towards Kurtz—exclusively; but when the steam-pipes started leaking we crawled very slow. The reaches opened before us and closed behind, as if the forest had stepped leisurely across the water to bar the way for our return. We penetrated deeper and deeper into the heart of darkness. It was very quiet there. At night sometimes the roll of drums behind the curtain of trees would run up the river and remain sustained faintly, as if hovering in the air high over our heads, till the first break of day. Whether it meant war, peace, or prayer we could not tell. The dawns were heralded by the descent of a chill stillness; the woodcutters slept, their fires burned low; the snapping of a twig would make you start. We were wanderers on a prehistoric earth, on an earth that wore the aspect of an unknown planet. We could have fancied ourselves the first men taking possession of an accursed inheritance, to be subdued at the cost of profound anguish and of excessive toil. But suddenly, as we struggled round a bend, there would be a glimpse of rush walls, of peaked grass-roofs, a burst of yells, a whirl of black limbs, a mass of hands clapping, of feet stamping, of bodies swaying, of eyes rolling, under the droop of heavy and motionless foliage. The steamer toiled along slowly on the edge of a black and incomprehensible frenzy. The prehistoric man was cursing us, praying to us, welcoming us—who could tell? We were cut off from the comprehension of our surroundings; we glided past like phantoms, wondering and secretly appalled, as sane men would be before an enthusiastic outbreak in a madhouse. We could not understand because we were too far and could not remember, because we were traveling in the night of first ages, of those ages that are gone, leaving hardly a sign—and no memories.

"The earth seemed unearthly. We are accustomed to look upon the shackled form of a conquered monster, but there—there you could look at a thing monstrous and free. It was unearthly, and the men were—No, they were not inhuman. Well, you know, that was the worst of it—this suspicion of their not being inhuman. It would come slowly to one. They howled and leaped, and spun, and made horrid faces; but what thrilled you was just the thought of their humanity—like yours—the thought of your remote kinship with this wild and passionate uproar. Ugly. Yes, it was ugly enough; but if you were man enough you would admit to yourself that there was in you just the faintest trace of a response to the terrible frankness of that noise, a dim suspicion of there being a meaning in it which you—you so remote from the night of first ages—could comprehend. And why not? The mind of man is capable of anything—because everything is in it, all the past as well as all the future. What was there after all? Joy, fear, sorrow, devotion, valor, rage—who can tell?—but truth—truth stripped of its cloak of time. Let the fool gape and shudder—the man knows, and can look on without a wink. But he must at least be as much of a man as these on the shore. He must meet that truth with his own true stuff—with his own inborn strength. Principles won't do. Acquisitions, clothes, pretty rags—rags that would fly off at the first good shake. No; you want a deliberate belief. An appeal to me in this fiendish row—is there? Very well; I hear; I admit, but I have a voice too, and for good or evil mine is the speech that cannot be silenced. Of course, a fool, what with sheer fright and fine sentiments, is always safe. Who's that grunting? You wonder I didn't go ashore for a howl and a dance? Well, no—I didn't. Fine sentiments, you say? Fine sentiments, be hanged! I had no time. I had to mess about with white-lead and strips of woolen blanket helping to put bandages on those leaky steam-pipes—I tell you. I had to watch the steering, and circumvent those snags, and get the tin-pot along by hook or by crook. There was surface-truth enough in these things to save a wiser man. And between whiles I had to look after the savage who was fireman. He was an improved specimen; he could fire up a vertical boiler.[2] He was there below me, and, upon my word, to look at him was as edifying as seeing a dog in a parody of breeches and a feather hat, walking on his hindlegs. A few months of training had done for that

---

2. Simple, easily fired boiler, typical of the primitive machinery on Marlow's "tin-pot" boat.

really fine chap. He squinted at the steam-gauge and at the water-gauge with an evident effort of intrepidity—and he had filed teeth, too, the poor devil, and the wool of his pate shaved into queer patterns, and three ornamental scars on each of his cheeks. He ought to have been clapping his hands and stamping his feet on the bank, instead of which he was hard at work, a thrall to strange witchcraft, full of improving knowledge. He was useful because he had been instructed; and what he knew was this—that should the water in that transparent thing disappear, the evil spirit inside the boiler would get angry through the greatness of his thirst, and take a terrible vengeance. So he sweated and fired up and watched the glass fearfully (with an impromptu charm, made of rags, tied to his arm, and a piece of polished bone, as big as a watch, stuck flatways through his lower lip), while the wooden banks slipped past us slowly, the short noise was left behind, the interminable miles of silence—and we crept on, towards Kurtz. But the snags were thick, the water was treacherous and shallow, the boiler seemed indeed to have a sulky devil in it, and thus neither that fireman nor I had any time to peer into our creepy thoughts.

"Some fifty miles below the Inner Station we came upon a hut of reeds, an inclined and melancholy pole, with the unrecognizable tatters of what had been a flag of some sort flying from it, and a neatly stacked woodpile. This was unexpected. We came to the bank, and on the stack of firewood found a flat piece of board with some faded pencil-writing on it. When deciphered it said: 'Wood for you. Hurry up. Approach cautiously.' There was a signature, but it was illegible—not Kurtz—a much longer word. 'Hurry up.' Where? Up the river? 'Approach cautiously.' We had not done so. But the warning could not have been meant for the place where it could be only found after approach. Something was wrong above. But what—and how much? That was the question. We commented adversely upon the imbecility of that telegraphic style. The bush around said nothing, and would not let us look very far, either. A torn curtain of red twill hung in the doorway of the hut, and flapped sadly in our faces. The dwelling was dismantled; but we could see a white man had lived there not very long ago. There remained a rude table—a plank on two posts; a heap of rubbish reposed in a dark corner, and by the door I picked up a book. It had lost its covers, and the pages had been thumbed into a state of extremely dirty softness; but the back had been lovingly stitched afresh with white cotton thread, which looked clean yet. It was an extraordinary find. Its title was, *An Inquiry into some Points of Seamanship,* by a man Towser, Towson—some such name—Master in his Majesty's Navy. The matter looked dreary reading enough, with illustrative diagrams and repulsive tables of figures, and the copy was sixty years old. I handled this amazing antiquity with the greatest possible tenderness, lest it should dissolve in my hands. Within, Towson or Towser was inquiring earnestly into the breaking strain of ships' chains and tackle, and other such matters. Not a very enthralling book; but at the first glance you could see there a singleness of intention, an honest concern for the right way of going to work, which made these humble pages, thought out so many years ago, luminous with another than a professional light. The simple old sailor, with his talk of chains and purchases,[3] made me forget the jungle and the pilgrims in a delicious sensation of having come

3. Leverages.

upon something unmistakably real. Such a book being there was wonderful enough; but still more astounding were the notes penciled in the margin, and plainly referring to the text. I couldn't believe my eyes! They were in cipher! Yes, it looked like cipher. Fancy a man lugging with him a book of that description into this nowhere and studying it—and making notes—in cipher at that! It was an extravagant mystery.

"I had been dimly aware for some time of a worrying noise, and when I lifted my eyes I saw the woodpile was gone, and the manager, aided by all the pilgrims, was shouting at me from the river-side. I slipped the book into my pocket. I assure you to leave off reading was like tearing myself away from the shelter of an old and solid friendship.

"I started the lame engine ahead. 'It must be this miserable trader—this intruder,' exclaimed the manager, looking back malevolently at the place we had left. 'He must be English,' I said. 'It will not save him from getting into trouble if he is not careful,' muttered the manager darkly. I observed with assumed innocence that no man was safe from trouble in this world.

"The current was more rapid now, the steamer seemed at her last gasp, the stern-wheel flopped languidly, and I caught myself listening on tiptoe for the next beat of the float,[4] for in sober truth I expected the wretched thing to give up every moment. It was like watching the last flickers of a life. But still we crawled. Sometimes I would pick out a tree a little way ahead to measure our progress towards Kurtz by, but I lost it invariably before we got abreast. To keep the eyes so long on one thing was too much for human patience. The manager displayed a beautiful resignation. I fretted and fumed and took to arguing with myself whether or no I would talk openly with Kurtz; but before I could come to any conclusion it occurred to me that my speech or my silence, indeed any action of mine, would be a mere futility. What did it matter what anyone knew or ignored? What did it matter who was manager? One gets sometimes such a flash of insight. The essentials of this affair lay deep under the surface, beyond my reach, and beyond my power of meddling.

"Towards the evening of the second day we judged ourselves about eight miles from Kurtz's station. I wanted to push on; but the manager looked grave, and told me the navigation up there was so dangerous that it would be advisable, the sun being very low already, to wait where we were till next morning. Moreover, he pointed out that if the warning to approach cautiously were to be followed, we must approach in daylight—not at dusk, or in the dark. This was sensible enough. Eight miles meant nearly three hours' steaming for us, and I could also see suspicious ripples at the upper end of the reach. Nevertheless, I was annoyed beyond expression at the delay, and most unreasonably, too, since one night more could not matter much after so many months. As we had plenty of wood, and caution was the word, I brought up in the middle of the stream. The reach was narrow, straight, with high sides like a railway cutting. The dusk came gliding into it long before the sun had set. The current ran smooth and swift, but a dumb immobility sat on the banks. The living trees, lashed together by the creepers and every living bush of the undergrowth, might have been changed into stone, even to the slenderest twig, to the lightest leaf. It was not sleep—it seemed unnatural, like a state of

4. A blade of the multibladed paddle wheel.

trance. Not the faintest sound of any kind could be heard. You looked on amazed, and began to suspect yourself of being deaf—then the night came suddenly, and struck you blind as well. About three in the morning some large fish leaped, and the loud splash made me jump as though a gun had been fired. When the sun rose there was a white fog, very warm and clammy, and more blinding than the night. It did not shift or drive; it was just there, standing all around you like something solid. At eight or nine, perhaps, it lifted as a shutter lifts. We had a glimpse of the towering multitude of trees, of the immense matted jungle, with the blazing little ball of the sun hanging over it—all perfectly still—and then the white shutter came down again, smoothly, as if sliding in greased grooves. I ordered the chain, which we had begun to heave in, to be paid out again. Before it stopped running with a muffled rattle, a cry, a very loud cry, as of infinite desolation, soared slowly in the opaque air. It ceased. A complaining clamor, modulated in savage discords, filled our ears. The sheer unexpectedness of it made my hair stir under my cap. I don't know how it struck the others: to me it seemed as though the mist itself had screamed, so suddenly, and apparently from all sides at once, did this tumultuous and mournful uproar arise. It culminated in a hurried outbreak of almost intolerably excessive shrieking, which stopped short, leaving us stiffened in a variety of silly attitudes, and obstinately listening to the nearly as appalling and excessive silence. 'Good God! What is the meaning—' stammered at my elbow one of the pilgrims,—a little fat man, with sandy hair and red whiskers, who wore side-spring boots, and pink pajamas tucked into his socks. Two others remained open-mouthed a whole minute, then dashed into the little cabin, to rush out incontinently and stand darting scared glances, with Winchesters[5] at 'ready' in their hands. What we could see was just the steamer we were on, her outlines blurred as though she had been on the point of dissolving, and a misty strip of water, perhaps two feet broad, around her—and that was all. The rest of the world was nowhere, as far as our eyes and ears were concerned. Just nowhere. Gone, disappeared; swept off without leaving a whisper or a shadow behind.

"I went forward, and ordered the chain to be hauled in short, so as to be ready to trip the anchor and move the steamboat at once if necessary. 'Will they attack?' whispered an awed voice. 'We will be all butchered in this fog,' murmured another. The faces twitched with the strain, the hands trembling slightly, the eyes forgot to wink. It was very curious to see the contrast of expressions of the white men and of the black fellows of our crew, who were as much strangers to that part of the river as we, though their homes were only eight hundred miles away. The whites, of course, greatly discomposed, had besides a curious look of being painfully shocked by such an outrageous row. The others had an alert, naturally interested expression; but their faces were essentially quiet, even those of the one or two who grinned as they hauled at the chain. Several exchanged short, grunting phrases, which seemed to settle the matter to their satisfaction. Their headman, a young, broad-chested black, severely draped in dark-blue fringed cloths, with fierce nostrils and his hair all done up artfully in oily ringlets, stood near me. 'Aha!' I said, just for good fellowship's sake. 'Catch 'em,' he snapped, with a bloodshot widening of

5. American repeating rifles.

his eyes and a flash of sharp teeth—'catch 'im. Give 'im to us.' 'To you, eh?' I asked; 'what would you do with them?' 'Eat 'em!' he said, curtly, and, leaning his elbow on the rail, looked out into the fog in a dignified and profoundly pensive attitude. I would no doubt have been properly horrified, had it not occurred to me that he and his chaps must be very hungry: that they must have been growing increasingly hungry for at least this month past. They had been engaged for six months (I don't think a single one of them had any clear idea of time, as we at the end of countless ages have. They still belonged to the beginnings of time—had no inherited experience to teach them as it were), and of course, as long as there was a piece of paper written over in accordance with some farcical law or other made down the river, it didn't enter anybody's head to trouble how they would live. Certainly they had brought with them some rotten hippo-meat, which couldn't have lasted very long, anyway, even if the pilgrims hadn't, in the midst of a shocking hullabaloo, thrown a considerable quantity of it overboard. It looked like a high-handed proceeding; but it was really a case of legitimate self-defense. You can't breathe dead hippo waking, sleeping, and eating, and at the same time keep your precarious grip on existence. Besides that, they had given them every week three pieces of brass wire, each about nine inches long; and the theory was they were to buy their provisions with that currency in riverside villages. You can see how *that* worked. There were either no villages, or the people were hostile, or the director, who like the rest of us fed out of tins, with an occasional old he-goat thrown in, didn't want to stop the steamer for some more or less recondite reason. So, unless they swallowed the wire itself, or made loops of it to snare the fishes with, I don't see what good their extravagant salary could be to them. I must say it was paid with a regularity worthy of a large and honorable trading company. For the rest, the only thing to eat—though it didn't look eatable in the least—I saw in their possession was a few lumps of some stuff like half-cooked dough, of a dirty lavender color, they kept wrapped in leaves, and now and then swallowed a piece of, but so small that it seemed done more for the looks of the thing than for any serious purpose of sustenance. Why in the name of all the gnawing devils of hunger they didn't go for us—they were thirty to five—and have a good tuck-in[6] for once, amazes me now when I think of it. They were big powerful men, with not much capacity to weigh the consequences, with courage, with strength, even yet, though their skins were no longer glossy and their muscles no longer hard. And I saw that something restraining, one of those human secrets that baffle probability, had come into play there. I looked at them with a swift quickening of interest—not because it occurred to me I might be eaten by them before very long, though I own to you that just then I perceived—in a new light, as it were—how unwholesome the pilgrims looked, and I hoped, yes, I positively hoped, that my aspect was not so—what shall I say?—so—unappetizing: a touch of fantastic vanity which fitted well with the dream-sensation that pervaded all my days at that time. Perhaps I had a little fever, too. One can't live with one's finger everlastingly on one's pulse. I had often 'a little fever,' or a little touch of other things—the playful paw-strokes of the wilderness, the preliminary trifling before the more serious onslaught which came in due course. Yes; I looked at them as

6. British slang for a good meal.

you would on any human being, with a curiosity of their impulses, motives, capacities, weaknesses, when brought to the test of an inexorable physical necessity. Restraint! What possible restraint? Was it superstition, disgust, patience, fear—or some kind of primitive honor? No fear can stand up to hunger, no patience can wear it out, disgust simply does not exist where hunger is; and as to superstition, beliefs, and what you may call principles, they are less than chaff in a breeze. Don't you know the devilry of lingering starvation, its exasperating torment, its black thoughts, its somber and brooding ferocity? Well, I do. It takes a man all his inborn strength to fight hunger properly. It's really easier to face bereavement, dishonor, and the perdition of one's soul— than this kind of prolonged hunger. Sad, but true. And these chaps, too, had no earthly reason for any kind of scruple. Restraint! I would just as soon have expected restraint from a hyena prowling amongst the corpses of a battle-field. But there was the fact facing me—the fact dazzling, to be seen, like the foam on the depths of the sea, like a ripple on an unfathomable enigma, a mystery greater—when I thought of it—than the curious, inexplicable note of desperate grief in this savage clamor that had swept by us on the river-bank, behind the blind whiteness of the fog.

"Two pilgrims were quarreling in hurried whispers as to which bank. 'Left.' 'No, no; how can you? Right, right, of course.' 'It is very serious,' said the manager's voice behind me; 'I would be desolated if anything should happen to Mr. Kurtz before we came up.' I looked at him, and had not the slightest doubt he was sincere. He was just the kind of man who would wish to preserve appearances. That was his restraint. But when he muttered something about going on at once, I did not even take the trouble to answer him. I knew, and he knew, that it was impossible. Were we to let go our hold of the bottom, we would be absolutely in the air—in space. We wouldn't be able to tell where we were going to—whether up or down stream, or across—till we fetched against one bank or the other,—and then we wouldn't know at first which it was. Of course I made no move. I had no mind for a smash-up. You couldn't imagine a more deadly place for a shipwreck. Whether drowned at once or not, we were sure to perish speedily in one way or another. 'I authorize you to take all the risks,' he said, after a short silence. 'I refuse to take any,' I said, shortly; which was just the answer he expected, though its tone might have surprised him. 'Well, I must defer to your judgment. You are captain,' he said, with marked civility. I turned my shoulder to him in sign of my appreciation, and looked into the fog. How long would it last? It was the most hopeless lookout. The approach to this Kurtz grubbing for ivory in the wretched bush was beset by as many dangers as though he had been an enchanted princess sleeping in a fabulous castle. 'Will they attack, do you think?' asked the manager, in a confidential tone.

"I did not think they would attack, for several obvious reasons. The thick fog was one. If they left the bank in their canoes they would get lost in it, as we would be if we attempted to move. Still, I had also judged the jungle of both banks quite impenetrable—and yet eyes were in it, eyes that had seen us. The river-side bushes were certainly very thick; but the undergrowth behind was evidently penetrable. However, during the short lift I had seen no canoes anywhere in the reach—certainly not abreast of the steamer. But what made the idea of attack inconceivable to me was the nature of the noise—of the cries we had heard. They had not the fierce character boding immediate hostile intention. Unexpected, wild, and violent as they had been, they had given me an irresistible impression of sorrow. The glimpse of the steamboat had for some reason filled those savages with unrestrained grief. The danger, if any, I expounded, was from our proximity to a great human passion let loose. Even extreme grief may ultimately vent itself in violence—but more generally takes the form of apathy. . . .

"You should have seen the pilgrims stare! They had no heart to grin, or even to revile me: but I believe they thought me gone mad—with fright, maybe. I delivered a regular lecture. My dear boys, it was no good bothering. Keep a look-out? Well, you may guess I watched the fog for the signs of lifting as a cat watches a mouse; but for anything else our eyes were of no more use to us *scenery* than if we had been buried miles deep in a heap of cotton-wool. It felt like it, too—choking, warm, stifling. Besides, all I said, though it sounded extravagant, was absolutely true to fact. What we afterwards alluded to as an attack was really an attempt at repulse. The action was very far from being aggressive—it was not even defensive, in the usual sense: it was undertaken under the stress of desperation, and in its essence was purely protective.

"It developed itself, I should say, two hours after the fog lifted, and its commencement was at a spot, roughly speaking, about a mile and a half below Kurtz's station. We had just floundered and flopped round a bend, when I saw an islet, a mere grassy hummock of bright green, in the middle of the stream. It was the only thing of the kind; but as we opened the reach more, I perceived it was the head of a long sandbank, or rather of a chain of shallow patches stretching down the middle of the river. They were discolored, just awash, and the whole lot was seen just under the water, exactly as a man's backbone is seen running down the middle of his back under the skin. Now, as far as I did see, I could go to the right or to the left of this. I didn't know either channel, of course. The banks looked pretty well alike, the depth appeared the same; but as I had been informed the station was on the west side, I naturally headed for the western passage.

"No sooner had we fairly entered it than I became aware it was much narrower than I had supposed. To the left of us there was the long uninterrupted shoal, and to the right a high, steep bank heavily overgrown with bushes. Above the bush the trees stood in serried ranks. The twigs overhung the current thickly, and from distance to distance a large limb of some tree projected rigidly over the stream. It was then well on in the afternoon, the face of the forest was gloomy, and a broad strip of shadow had already fallen on the water. In this shadow we steamed up—very slowly, as you may imagine. I sheered her well inshore—the water being deepest near the bank, as the sounding-pole informed me.

"One of my hungry and forbearing friends was sounding[7] in the bows just below me. This steamboat was exactly like a decked scow. On the deck, there were two little teak-wood houses, with doors and windows. The boiler was in the fore-end, and the machinery right astern. Over the whole there was a light roof, supported on stanchions. The funnel projected through that roof, and in front of the funnel a small cabin built of light planks served for a pilot-

---

7. Measuring water depth with a sounding line.

house. It contained a couch, two campstools, a loaded Martini-Henry[8] lean-ing in one corner, a tiny table, and the steering-wheel. It had a wide door in front and a broad shutter at each side. All these were always thrown open, of course. I spent my days perched up there on the extreme fore-end of that roof, before the door. At night I slept, or tried to, on the couch. An athletic black belonging to some coast tribe, and educated by my poor predecessor, was the helmsman. He sported a pair of brass earrings, wore a blue cloth wrapper from the waist to the ankles, and thought all the world of himself. He was the most unstable kind of fool I had ever seen. He steered with no end of a swag-ger while you were by; but if he lost sight of you, he became instantly the prey of an abject funk, and would let that cripple of a steamboat get the upper hand of him in a minute.

"I was looking down at the sounding-pole, and feeling much annoyed to see at each try a little more of it stick out of that river, when I saw my poleman give up the business suddenly, and stretch himself flat on the deck, without even taking the trouble to haul his pole in. He kept hold on it though, and it trailed in the water. At the same time the fireman, whom I could also see below me, sat down abruptly before his furnace and ducked his head. I was amazed. Then I had to look at the river mighty quick, because there was a snag in the fairway. Sticks, little sticks, were flying about—thick: they were whizzing before my nose, dropping below me, striking behind me against my pilot-house. All this time the river, the shore, the woods, were very quiet—perfectly quiet. I could only hear the heavy splashing thump of the stern-wheel and the patter of these things. We cleared the snag clumsily. Arrows, by Jove! We were being shot at! I stepped in quickly to close the shutter on the land-side. That fool-helmsman, his hands on the spokes, was lifting his knees high, stamping his feet, champing his mouth, like a reined-in horse. Con-found him! And we were staggering within ten feet of the bank. I had to lean right out to swing the heavy shutter, and I saw a face amongst the leaves on the level with my own, looking at me very fierce and steady; and then sud-denly, as though a veil had been removed from my eyes, I made out, deep in the tangled gloom, naked breasts, arms, legs, glaring eyes,—the bush was swarming with human limbs in movement, glistening, of bronze color. The twigs shook, swayed, and rustled, the arrows flew out of them, and then the shutter came to. 'Steer her straight,' I said to the helmsman. He held his head rigid, face forward; but his eyes rolled, he kept on lifting and setting down his feet gently, his mouth foamed a little. 'Keep quiet!' I said in a fury. I might just as well have ordered a tree not to sway in the wind. I darted out. Below me there was a great scuffle of feet on the iron deck; confused exclamations; a voice screamed, 'Can you turn back?' I caught sight of a V-shaped ripple on the water ahead. What? Another snag! A fusillade burst out under my feet. The pilgrims had opened with their Winchesters, and were simply squirting lead into that bush. A deuce of a lot of smoke came up and drove slowly for-ward. I swore at it. Now I couldn't see the ripple or the snag either. I stood in the doorway, peering, and the arrows came in swarms. They might have been poisoned, but they looked as though they wouldn't kill a cat. The bush began to howl. Our wood-cutters raised a warlike whoop; the report of a rifle just at

8. Heavy military rifle.

my back deafened me. I glanced over my shoulder, and the pilot-house was yet full of noise and smoke when I made a dash at the wheel. The fool-nigger had dropped everything to throw the shutter open and let off⁹ that Martini-Henry. He stood before the wide opening, glaring, and I yelled at him to come back, while I straightened the sudden twist out of that steamboat. There was no room to turn even if I had wanted to, the snag was somewhere very near ahead in that confounded smoke, there was no time to lose, so I just crowded her into the bank—right into the bank, where I knew the water was deep.

"We tore slowly along the overhanging bushes in a whirl of broken twigs and flying leaves. The fusillade below stopped short, as I had foreseen it would when the squirts got empty. I threw my head back to a glinting whizz that traversed the pilot-house, in at one shutter-hole and out at the other. Looking past that mad helmsman, who was shaking the empty rifle and yelling at the shore, I saw vague forms of men running bent double, leaping, gliding, distinct, incomplete, evanescent. Something big appeared in the air before the shutter, the rifle went overboard, and the man stepped back swiftly, looked at me over his shoulder in an extraordinary, profound, familiar manner, and fell upon my feet. The side of his head hit the wheel twice, and the end of what appeared a long cane clattered round and knocked over a little campstool. It looked as though after wrenching that thing from somebody ashore he had lost his balance in the effort. The thin smoke had blown away, we were clear of the snag, and looking ahead I could see that in another hundred yards or so I would be free to sheer off, away from the bank; but my feet felt so very warm and wet that I had to look down. The man had rolled on his back and stared straight up at me; both his hands clutched that cane. It was the shaft of a spear that, either thrown or lunged through the opening, had caught him in the side just below the ribs; the blade had gone in out of sight, after making a frightful gash; my shoes were full; a pool of blood lay very still, gleaming dark-red under the wheel; his eyes shone with an amazing luster. The fusillade burst out again. He looked at me anxiously, gripping the spear like something precious, with an air of being afraid I would try to take it away from him. I had to make an effort to free my eyes from his gaze and attend to steering. With one hand I felt above my head for the line of the steam-whistle, and jerked out screech after screech hurriedly. The tumult of angry and war-like yells was checked instantly, and then from the depths of the woods went out such a tremulous and prolonged wail of mournful fear and utter despair as may be imagined to follow the flight of the last hope from the earth. There was a great commotion in the bush; the shower of arrows stopped, a few dropping shots rang out sharply—then silence, in which the languid beat of the stern-wheel came plainly to my ears. I put the helm hard a-starboard at the moment when the pilgrim in pink pajamas, very hot and agitated, appeared in the doorway. 'The manager sends me—' he began in an official tone, and stopped short. 'Good God!' he said, glaring at the wounded man.

"We two whites stood over him, and his lustrous and inquiring glance enveloped us both. I declare it looked as though he would presently put to us some question in an understandable language; but he died without uttering a sound, without moving a limb, without twitching a muscle. Only in the very

9. Fire.

last moment, as though in response to some sign we could not see, to some whisper we could not hear, he frowned heavily, and that frown gave to his black death-mask an inconceivably somber, brooding, and menacing expression. The luster of inquiring glance faded swiftly into vacant glassiness. 'Can you steer?' I asked the agent eagerly. He looked very dubious; but I made a grab at his arm, and he understood at once I meant him to steer whether or no. To tell you the truth, I was morbidly anxious to change my shoes and socks. 'He is dead,' murmured the fellow, immensely impressed. 'No doubt about it,' said I tugging like mad at the shoe-laces. 'And by the way, I suppose Mr. Kurtz is dead as well by this time.'

"For the moment that was the dominant thought. There was a sense of extreme disappointment, as though I had found out I had been striving after something altogether without a substance. I couldn't have been more disgusted if I had traveled all this way for the sole purpose of talking with Mr. Kurtz. Talking with . . . I flung one shoe overboard, and became aware that that was exactly what I had been looking forward to—a talk with Kurtz. I made the strange discovery that I had never imagined him as doing, you know, but as discoursing. I didn't say to myself, 'Now I will never see him,' or 'Now I will never shake him by the hand,' but, 'Now I will never hear him.' The man presented himself as a voice. Not of course that I did not connect him with some sort of action. Hadn't I been told in all the tones of jealousy and admiration that he had collected, bartered, swindled, or stolen more ivory than all the other agents together? That was not the point. The point was in his being a gifted creature, and that of all his gifts the one that stood out preeminently, that carried with it a sense of real presence, was his ability to talk, his words—the gift of expression, the bewildering, the illuminating, the most exalted and the most contemptible, the pulsating stream of light, or the deceitful flow from the heart of an impenetrable darkness.

"The other shoe went flying unto the devil-god of that river. I thought, by Jove! it's all over. We are too late; he has vanished—the gift has vanished, by means of some spear, arrow, or club. I will never hear that chap speak after all,—and my sorrow had a startling extravagance of emotion, even such as I had noticed in the howling sorrow of these savages in the bush. I couldn't have felt more lonely desolation somehow, had I been robbed of a belief or had missed my destiny in life. . . . Why do you sigh in this beastly way, somebody? Absurd? Well, absurd. Good Lord! mustn't a man ever—Here, give me some tobacco." . . .

There was a pause of profound stillness, then a match flared, and Marlow's lean face appeared, worn, hollow, with downward folds and drooped eyelids, with an aspect of concentrated attention; and as he took vigorous draws at his pipe, it seemed to retreat and advance out of the night in the regular flicker of the tiny flame. The match went out.

"Absurd!" he cried. "This is the worst of trying to tell. . . . Here you all are, each moored with two good addresses, like a hulk with two anchors, a butcher round one corner, a policeman round another, excellent appetites, and temperature normal—you hear—normal from year's end to year's end. And you say, Absurd! Absurd be—exploded! Absurd! My dear boys, what can you expect from a man who out of sheer nervousness had just flung overboard a pair of new shoes? Now I think of it, it is amazing I did not shed tears. I am, upon the whole, proud of my fortitude. I was cut to the quick at the idea of having lost the inestimable privilege of listening to the gifted Kurtz. Of course I was wrong. The privilege was waiting for me. Oh yes, I heard more than enough. And I was right, too. A voice. He was very little more than a voice. And I heard—him—it—this voice—other voices—all of them were so little more than voices—and the memory of that time itself lingers around me, impalpable, like a dying vibration of one immense jabber, silly, atrocious, sordid, savage, or simply mean, without any kind of sense. Voices, voices—even the girl herself—now—"

He was silent for a long time.

"I laid the ghost of his gifts at last with a lie," he began, suddenly. "Girl! What? Did I mention a girl? Oh, she is out of it—completely. They—the women I mean—are out of it—should be out of it. We must help them to stay in that beautiful world of their own, lest ours gets worse. Oh, she had to be out of it. You should have heard the disinterred body of Mr. Kurtz saying, 'My Intended.' You would have perceived directly then how completely she was out of it. And the lofty frontal bone of Mr. Kurtz! They say the hair goes on growing sometimes, but this—ah—specimen, was impressively bald. The wilderness had patted him on the head, and, behold, it was like a ball—an ivory ball; it had caressed him, and—lo!—he had withered; it had taken him, loved him, embraced him, got into his veins, consumed his flesh, and sealed his soul to its own by the inconceivable ceremonies of some devilish initiation. He was its spoiled and pampered favorite. Ivory? I should think so. Heaps of it, stacks of it. The old mud shanty was bursting with it. You would think here was not a single tusk left either above or below the ground in the whole country. 'Mostly fossil,' the manager had remarked, disparagingly. It was no more fossil than I am; but they call it fossil when it is dug up. It appears these niggers do bury the tusks sometimes—but evidently they couldn't bury this parcel deep enough to save the gifted Mr. Kurtz from his fate. We filled the steamboat with it, and had to pile a lot on the deck. Thus he could see and enjoy as long as he could see, because the appreciation of this favor had remained with him to the last. You should have heard him say, 'My ivory.' Oh yes, I heard him. 'My Intended, my ivory, my station, my river, my—' everything belonged to him. It made me hold my breath in expectation of hearing the wilderness burst into a prodigious peal of laughter that would shake the fixed stars in their places. Everything belonged to him—but that was a trifle. The thing was to know what he belonged to, how many powers of darkness claimed him for their own. That was the reflection that made you creepy all over. It was impossible—it was not good for one either—trying to imagine. He had taken a high seat amongst the devils of the land—I mean literally. You can't understand. How could you?—with solid pavement under your feet, surrounded by kind neighbors ready to cheer you or to fall on you, stepping delicately between the butcher and the policeman, in the holy terror of scandal and gallows and lunatic asylums—how can you imagine what particular region of the first ages a man's untrammeled feet may take him into by the way of solitude—utter solitude without a policeman—by the way of silence—utter silence, where no warning voice of a kind neighbor can be heard whispering of public opinion? These little things make all the great difference. When they are gone you must fall back upon your own innate strength, upon your own capacity for faithfulness. Of course you may be too much of a fool to go wrong—too dull even to know you are being assaulted by the powers of darkness. I take it, no fool ever made a bargain for his soul with the devil: the fool is too much of a fool, or the devil too much of a devil—I don't know which. Or you may be such a thunderingly exalted creature as to be altogether deaf and blind to anything but heavenly sights and sounds. Then the earth for you is only a standing place—and whether to be like this is your loss or your gain I won't pretend to say. But most of us are neither one nor the other. The earth for us is a place to live in, where we must put up with sights, with sounds, with smells, too, by Jove!—breathe dead hippo, so to speak, and not be contaminated. And there, don't you see? your strength comes in, the faith in your ability for the digging of unostentatious holes to bury the stuff in— your power of devotion, not to yourself, but to an obscure, back-breaking business. And that's difficult enough. Mind, I am not trying to excuse or even explain—I am trying to account to myself for—for—Mr. Kurtz—for the shade of Mr. Kurtz. This initiated wraith from the back of Nowhere honored me with its amazing confidence before it vanished altogether. This was because it could speak English to me. The original Kurtz had been educated partly in England, and—as he was good enough to say himself—his sympathies were in the right place. His mother was half-English, his father was half-French. All Europe contributed to the making of Kurtz; and by and by I learned that, most appropriately, the International Society for the Suppression of Savage Customs had intrusted him with the making of a report, for its future guidance. And he had written it, too. I've seen it. I've read it. It was eloquent, vibrating with eloquence, but too high-strung, I think. Seventeen pages of close writing he had found time for! But this must have been before his—let us say—nerves, went wrong, and caused him to preside at certain midnight dances ending with unspeakable rites, which—as far as I reluctantly gathered from what I heard at various times—were offered up to him—do you understand?—to Mr. Kurtz himself. But it was a beautiful piece of writing. The opening paragraph, however, in the light of later information, strikes me now as ominous. He began with the argument that we whites, from the point of development we had arrived at, 'must necessarily appear to them [savages] in the nature of supernatural beings—we approach them with the might as of a deity,' and so on, and so on. 'By the simple exercise of our will we can exert a power for good practically unbounded,' etc., etc. From that point he soared and took me with him. The peroration was magnificent, though difficult to remember, you know. It gave me the notion of an exotic Immensity ruled by an august Benevolence. It made me tingle with enthusiasm. This was the unbounded power of eloquence—of words—of burning noble words. There were no practical hints to interrupt the magic current of phrases, unless a kind of note at the foot of the last page, scrawled evidently much later, in an unsteady hand, may be regarded as the exposition of a method. It was very simple, and at the end of that moving appeal to every altruistic sentiment it blazed at you, luminous and terrifying, like a flash of lightning in a serene sky: 'Exterminate all the brutes!' The curious part was that he had apparently forgotten all about that valuable postscriptum, because, later on, when he in a sense came to himself, he repeatedly entreated me to take good care of 'my pamphlet' (he called it), as it was sure to have in the future a good influence

Kurtz

upon his career. I had full information about all these things, and, besides, as it turned out, I was to have the care of his memory. I've done enough for it to give me the indisputable right to lay it, if I choose, for an everlasting rest in the dust-bin of progress, amongst all the sweepings and, figuratively speaking, all the dead cats of civilization. But then, you see, I can't choose. He won't be forgotten. Whatever he was, he was not common. He had the power to charm or frighten rudimentary souls into an aggravated witch-dance in his honor; he could also fill the small souls of the pilgrims with bitter misgivings: he had one devoted friend at least, and he had conquered one soul in the world that was neither rudimentary nor tainted with self-seeking. No; I can't forget him, though I am not prepared to affirm the fellow was exactly worth the life we lost in getting to him. I missed my late helmsman awfully,—I missed him even while his body was still lying in the pilot-house. Perhaps you will think it passing strange this regret for a savage who was no more account than a grain of sand in a black Sahara. Well, don't you see, he had done something, he had steered; for months I had him at my back—a help—an instrument. It was a kind of partnership. He steered for me—I had to look after him, I worried about his deficiencies, and thus a subtle bond had been created, of which I only became aware when it was suddenly broken. And the intimate profundity of that look he gave me when he received his hurt remains to this day in my memory—like a claim of distant kinship affirmed in a supreme moment.

"Poor fool! If he had only left that shutter alone. He had no restraint, no restraint—just like Kurtz—a tree swayed by the wind. As soon as I had put on a dry pair of slippers, I dragged him out, after first jerking the spear out of his side, which operation I confess I performed with my eyes shut tight. His heels leaped together over the little doorstep; his shoulders were pressed to my breast; I hugged him from behind desperately. Oh! he was heavy, heavy; heavier than any man on earth, I should imagine. Then without more ado I tipped him overboard. The current snatched him as though he had been a wisp of grass, and I saw the body roll over twice before I lost sight of it forever. All the pilgrims and the manager were then congregated on the awning-deck about the pilot-house, chattering at each other like a flock of excited magpies, and there was a scandalized murmur at my heartless promptitude. What they wanted to keep that body hanging about for I can't guess. Embalm it, maybe. But I had also heard another, and a very ominous, murmur on the deck below. My friends the wood-cutters were likewise scandalized, and with a better show of reason—though I admit that the reason itself was quite inadmissible. Oh, quite! I had made up my mind that if my late helmsman was to be eaten, the fishes alone should have him. He had been a very second-rate helmsman while alive, but now he was dead he might have become a first-class temptation, and possibly cause some startling trouble. Besides, I was anxious to take the wheel, the man in pink pajamas showing himself a hopeless duffer at the business.

"This I did directly the simple funeral was over. We were going half-speed, keeping right in the middle of the stream, and I listened to the talk about me. They had given up Kurtz, they had given up the station; Kurtz was dead, and the station had been burnt—and so on—and so on. The red-haired pilgrim was beside himself with the thought that at least this poor Kurtz had been properly avenged. 'Say! We must have made a glorious slaughter of them in the bush. Eh? What do you think? Say?' He positively danced, the bloodthirsty little gingery beggar.[1] And he had nearly fainted when he saw the wounded man! I could not help saying, 'You made a glorious lot of smoke, anyhow.' I had seen, from the way the tops of the bushes rustled and flew, that almost all the shots had gone too high. You can't hit anything unless you take aim and fire from the shoulder; but these chaps fired from the hip with their eyes shut. The retreat, I maintained—and I was right—was caused by the screeching of the steam-whistle. Upon this they forgot Kurtz, and began to howl at me with indignant protests.

"The manager stood by the wheel murmuring confidentially about the necessity of getting well away down the river before dark at all events, when I saw in the distance a clearing on the river-side and the outlines of some sort of building. 'What's this?' I asked. He clapped his hands in wonder. 'The station!' he cried. I edged in at once, still going half-speed.

"Through my glasses I saw the slope of a hill interspersed with rare trees and perfectly free from undergrowth. A long decaying building on the summit was half buried in the high grass; the large holes in the peaked roof gaped black from afar; the jungle and the woods made a background. There was no enclosure or fence of any kind; but there had been one apparently, for near the house half-a-dozen slim posts remained in a row, roughly trimmed, and with their upper ends ornamented with round carved balls. The rails, or whatever there had been between, had disappeared. Of course the forest surrounded all that. The river-bank was clear, and on the water-side I saw a white man under a hat like a cart-wheel beckoning persistently with his whole arm. Examining the edge of the forest above and below, I was almost certain I could see movements—human forms gliding here and there. I steamed past prudently, then stopped the engines and let her drift down. The man on the shore began to shout, urging us to land. 'We have been attacked,' screamed the manager. 'I know—I know. It's all right,' yelled back the other, as cheerful as you please. 'Come along. It's all right. I am glad.'

"His aspect reminded me of something I had seen—something funny I had seen somewhere. As I maneuvered to get alongside, I was asking myself, 'What does this fellow look like?' Suddenly I got it. He looked like a harlequin. His clothes had been made of some stuff that was brown holland probably, but it was covered with patches all over, with bright patches, blue, red, and yellow,— patches on the back, patches on the front, patches on elbows, on knees; colored binding around his jacket, scarlet edging at the bottom of his trousers; and the sunshine made him look extremely gay and wonderfully neat withal, because you could see how beautifully all this patching had been done. A beardless, boyish face, very fair, no features to speak of, nose peeling, little blue eyes, smiles and frowns chasing each other over that open countenance like sunshine and shadow on a windswept plain. 'Look out, captain!' he cried; 'there's a snag lodged in here last night.' What! Another snag? I confess I swore shamefully. I had nearly holed my cripple, to finish off that charming trip. The harlequin on the bank turned his little pug-nose up to me. 'You English?' he asked, all smiles. 'Are you?' I shouted from the wheel. The smiles

harlequin [handwritten marginalia]

---

1. British slang for redheaded rascal.

vanished, and he shook his head as if sorry for my disappointment. Then he brightened up. 'Never mind!' he cried, encouragingly. 'Are we in time?' I asked. 'He is up there,' he replied, with a toss of the head up the hill, and becoming gloomy all of a sudden. His face was like the autumn sky, overcast one moment and bright the next.

"When the manager, escorted by the pilgrims, all of them armed to the teeth, had gone to the house this chap came on board. 'I say, I don't like this. These natives are in the bush,' I said. He assured me earnestly it was all right. 'They are simple people,' he added; 'well, I am glad you came. It took me all my time to keep them off.' 'But you said it was all right,' I cried. 'Oh, they meant no harm,' he said; and as I stared he corrected himself, 'Not exactly.' Then vivaciously, 'My faith, your pilot-house wants a clean-up!' In the next breath he advised me to keep enough steam on the boiler to blow the whistle in case of any trouble. 'One good screech will do more for you than all your rifles. They are simple people,' he repeated. He rattled away at such a rate he quite overwhelmed me. He seemed to be trying to make up for lots of silence, and actually hinted, laughing, that such was the case. 'Don't you talk with Mr. Kurtz?' I said. 'You don't talk with that man—you listen to him,' he exclaimed with severe exaltation. 'But now—' He waved his arm, and in the twinkling of an eye was in the uttermost depths of despondency. In a moment he came up again with a jump, possessed himself of both my hands, shook them continuously, while he gabbled: 'Brother sailor . . . honor . . . pleasure . . . delight . . . introduce myself . . . Russian . . . son of an arch-priest . . . Government of Tambov. . . . What? Tobacco! English tobacco; the excellent English tobacco! Now, that's brotherly. Smoke? Where's a sailor that does not smoke?'

"The pipe soothed him, and gradually I made out he had run away from school, had gone to sea in a Russian ship; ran away again; served some time in English ships; was now reconciled with the arch-priest. He made a point of that. 'But when one is young one must see things, gather experience, ideas; enlarge the mind.' 'Here!' I interrupted. 'You can never tell! Here I met Mr. Kurtz,' he said, youthfully solemn and reproachful. I held my tongue after that. It appears he had persuaded a Dutch trading-house on the coast to fit him out with stores and goods, and had started for the interior with a light heart, and no more idea of what would happen to him than a baby. He had been wandering about that river for nearly two years alone, cut off from everybody and everything. 'I am not so young as I look. I am twenty-five,' he said. 'At first old Van Shuyten would tell me to go to the devil,' he narrated with keen enjoyment; 'but I stuck to him, and talked and talked, till at last he got afraid I would talk the hind-leg off his favorite dog, so he gave me some cheap things and a few guns, and told me he hoped he would never see my face again. Good old Dutchman, Van Shuyten. I've sent him one small lot of ivory a year ago, so that he can't call me a little thief when I get back. I hope he got it. And for the rest I don't care. I had some wood stacked for you. That was my old house. Did you see?'

"I gave him Towson's book. He made as though he would kiss me, but restrained himself. 'The only book I had left, and I thought I had lost it,' he said, looking at it ecstatically. 'So many accidents happen to a man going about alone, you know. Canoes get upset sometimes—and sometimes you've got to clear out so quick when the people get angry.' He thumbed the pages.

'You made notes in Russian?' I asked. He nodded. 'I thought they were written in cipher,' I said. He laughed, then became serious. 'I had lots of trouble to keep these people off,' he said. 'Did they want to kill you?' I asked. 'Oh no!' he cried, and checked himself. 'Why did they attack us?' I pursued. He hesitated, then said shamefacedly, 'They don't want him to go.' 'Don't they?' I said curiously. He nodded a nod full of mystery and wisdom. 'I tell you,' he cried, 'this man has enlarged my mind.' He opened his arms wide, staring at me with his little blue eyes that were perfectly round."

III

"I looked at him, lost in astonishment. There he was before me, in motley, as though he had absconded from a troupe of mimes, enthusiastic, fabulous. His very existence was improbable, inexplicable, and altogether bewildering. He was an insoluble problem. It was inconceivable how he had existed, how he had succeeded in getting so far, how he had managed to remain—why he did not instantly disappear. 'I went a little farther,' he said, 'then still a little farther—till I had gone so far that I don't know how I'll ever get back. Never mind. Plenty of time. I can manage. You take Kurtz away quick—quick—I tell you.' The glamour of youth enveloped his parti-colored rags, his destitution, his loneliness, the essential desolation of his futile wanderings. For months— for years—his life hadn't been worth a day's purchase; and there he was gallantly, thoughtlessly alive, to all appearance indestructible solely by the virtue of his few years and of his unreflecting audacity. I was seduced into something like admiration—like envy. Glamour urged him on, glamour kept him unscathed. He surely wanted nothing from the wilderness but space to breathe in and to push on through. His need was to exist, and to move onwards at the greatest possible risk, and with a maximum of privation. If the absolutely pure, uncalculating, unpractical spirit of adventure had ever ruled a human being, it ruled this be-patched youth. I almost envied him the possession of this modest and clear flame. It seemed to have consumed all thought of self so completely, that even while he was talking to you, you forgot that it was he—the man before your eyes—who had gone through these things. I did not envy him his devotion to Kurtz, though. He had not meditated over it. It came to him and he accepted it with a sort of eager fatalism. I must say that to me it appeared about the most dangerous thing in every way he had come upon so far.

"They had come together unavoidably, like two ships becalmed near each other, and lay rubbing sides at last. I suppose Kurtz wanted an audience, because on a certain occasion, when encamped in the forest, they had talked all night, or more probably Kurtz had talked. 'We talked of everything,' he said, quite transported at the recollection. 'I forgot there was such a thing as sleep. The night did not seem to last an hour. Everything! Everything! . . . Of love, too.' 'Ah, he talked to you of love!' I said, much amused. 'It isn't what you think,' he cried, almost passionately. 'It was in general. He made me see things—things.'

"He threw his arms up. We were on deck at the time, and the headman of my wood-cutters, lounging near by, turned upon him his heavy and glittering eyes. I looked around, and I don't know why, but I assure you that never, never before, did this land, this river, this jungle, the very arch of this blazing sky, appear to me so hopeless and so dark, so impenetrable to human thought, so pitiless to human weakness. 'And, ever since, you have been with him, of course?' I said.

"On the contrary. It appears their intercourse had been very much broken by various causes. He had, as he informed me proudly, managed to nurse Kurtz through two illnesses (he alluded to it as you would to some risky feat), but as a rule Kurtz wandered alone far in the depths of the forest. 'Very often coming to this station, I had to wait days and days before he would turn up,' he said. 'Ah, it was worth waiting for!—sometimes.' 'What was he doing? exploring or what?' I asked. 'Oh, yes, of course'; he had discovered lots of villages, a lake, too—he did not know exactly in what direction; it was dangerous to inquire too much—but mostly his expeditions had been for ivory. 'But he had no goods to trade with by that time,' I objected. 'There's a good lot of cartridges left even yet,' he answered, looking away. 'To speak plainly, he raided the country,' I said. He nodded. 'Not alone, surely!' He muttered something about the villages round that lake. 'Kurtz got the tribe to follow him, did he?' I suggested. He fidgeted a little. 'They adored him,' he said. The tone of these words was so extraordinary that I looked at him searchingly. It was curious to see his mingled eagerness and reluctance to speak of Kurtz. The man filled his life, occupied his thoughts, swayed his emotions. 'What can you expect?' he burst out; 'he came to them with thunder and lightning, you know—and they had never seen anything like it—and very terrible. He could be very terrible. You can't judge Mr. Kurtz as you would an ordinary man. No, no, no! Now—just to give you an idea—I don't mind telling you, he wanted to shoot me, too, one day—but I don't judge him.' 'Shoot you!' I cried. 'What for?' 'Well, I had a small lot of ivory the chief of that village near my house gave me. You see I used to shoot game for them. Well, he wanted it, and wouldn't hear reason. He declared he would shoot me unless I gave him the ivory and then cleared out of the country, because he could do so, and had a fancy for it, and there was nothing on earth to prevent him killing whom he jolly well pleased. And it was true, too. I gave him the ivory. What did I care! But I didn't clear out. No, no. I couldn't leave him. I had to be careful, of course, till we got friendly again for a time. He had his second illness then. Afterwards I had to keep out of the way; but I didn't mind. He was living for the most part in those villages on the lake. When he came down to the river, sometimes he would take to me, and sometimes it was better for me to be careful. This man suffered too much. He hated all this, and somehow he couldn't get away. When I had a chance I begged him to try and leave while there was time; I offered to go back with him. And he would say yes, and then he would remain; go off on another ivory hunt; disappear for weeks; forget himself amongst these people—forget himself—you know.' 'Why! he's mad,' I said. He protested indignantly. Mr. Kurtz couldn't be mad. If I had heard him talk, only two days ago, I wouldn't dare hint at such a thing. . . . I had taken up my binoculars while we talked, and was looking at the shore, sweeping the limit of the forest at each side and at the back of the house. The conscious-ness of there being people in that bush, so silent, so quiet—as silent and quiet as the ruined house on the hill—made me uneasy. There was no sign on the face of nature of this amazing tale that was not so much told as suggested to me in desolate exclamations, completed by shrugs, in interrupted phrases, in hints ending in deep sighs. The woods were unmoved, like a mask—heavy, like the closed door of a prison—they looked with their air of hidden knowledge, of patient expectation, of unapproachable silence. The Russian was explaining to me that it was only lately that Mr. Kurtz had come down to the river, bringing along with him all the fighting men of that lake tribe. He had been absent for several months—getting himself adored, I suppose—and had come down unexpectedly, with the intention to all appearance of making a raid either across the river or down stream. Evidently the appetite for more ivory had got the better of the—what shall I say?—less material aspirations. However he had got much worse suddenly. 'I heard he was lying helpless, and so I came up—took my chance,' said the Russian. 'Oh, he is bad, very bad.' I directed my glass to the house. There were no signs of life, but there was the ruined roof, the long mud wall peeping above the grass, with three little square window-holes, no two of the same size; all this brought within reach of my hand, as it were. And then I made a brusque movement, and one of the remaining posts of that vanished fence leaped up in the field of my glass. You remember I told you I had been struck at the distance by certain attempts at ornamentation, rather remarkable in the ruinous aspect of the place. Now I had suddenly a nearer view, and its first result was to make me throw my head back as if before a blow. Then I went carefully from post to post with my glass, and I saw my mistake. These round knobs were not ornamental but symbolic; they were expressive and puzzling, striking and disturbing—food for thought and also for vultures if there had been any looking down from the sky; but at all events for such ants as were industrious enough to ascend the pole. They would have been even more impressive, those heads on the stakes, if their faces had not been turned to the house. Only one, the first I had made out, was facing my way. I was not so shocked as you may think. The start back I had given was really nothing but a movement of surprise. I had expected to see a knob of wood there, you know. I returned deliberately to the first I had seen—and there it was, black, dried, sunken, with closed eyelids,—a head that seemed to sleep at the top of that pole, and with the shrunken dry lips showing a narrow white line of the teeth, was smiling, too, smiling continuously at some endless and jocose dream of that eternal slumber.

"I am not disclosing any trade secrets. In fact, the manager said afterwards that Mr. Kurtz's methods had ruined the district. I have no opinion on that point, but I want you clearly to understand that there was nothing exactly profitable in these heads being there. They only showed that Mr. Kurtz lacked restraint in the gratification of his various lusts, that there was something wanting in him—some small matter which, when the pressing need arose, could not be found under his magnificent eloquence. Whether he knew of this deficiency himself I can't say. I think the knowledge came to him at last—only at the very last. But the wilderness had found him out early, and had taken on him a terrible vengeance for the fantastic invasion. I think it had whispered to him things about himself which he did not know, things of which he had no conception till he took counsel with this great solitude—and the whisper had proved irresistibly fascinating. It echoed loudly within him because he was hollow at the core. . . . I put down the glass, and the head that had appeared near enough to be spoken to seemed at once to have leaped away from me into inaccessible distance.

[handwritten margin note: Mr. Kurtz lacks restraint]

"The admirer of Mr. Kurtz was a bit crestfallen. In a hurried indistinct voice he began to assure me he had not dared to take these—say, symbols—down. He was not afraid of the natives; they would not stir till Mr. Kurtz gave the word. His ascendancy was extraordinary. The camps of these people surrounded the place, and the chiefs came every day to see him. They would crawl. . . . 'I don't want to know anything of the ceremonies used when approaching Mr. Kurtz,' I shouted. Curious, this feeling that came over me that such details would be more intolerable than those heads drying on the stakes under Mr. Kurtz's windows. After all, that was only a savage sight, while I seemed at one bound to have been transported into some lightless region of subtle horrors, where pure, uncomplicated savagery was a positive relief, being something that had a right to exist—obviously—in the sunshine. The young man looked at me with surprise. I suppose it did not occur to him that Mr. Kurtz was no idol of mine. He forgot I hadn't heard any of these splendid monologues on, what was it? on love, justice, conduct of life—or what not. If it had come to crawling before Mr. Kurtz, he crawled as much as the veriest savage of them all. I had no idea of the conditions, he said: these heads were the heads of rebels. I shocked him excessively by laughing. Rebels! What would be the next definition I was to hear? There had been enemies, criminals, workers—and these were rebels. Those rebellious heads looked very subdued to me on their sticks. 'You don't know how such a life tries a man like Kurtz,' cried Kurtz's last disciple. 'Well, and you?' I said. 'I! I! I am a simple man. I have no great thoughts. I want nothing from anybody. How can you compare me to . . . ?' His feelings were too much for speech, and suddenly he broke down. 'I don't understand,' he groaned. 'I've been doing my best to keep him alive, and that's enough. I had no hand in all this. I have no abilities. There hasn't been a drop of medicine or a mouthful of invalid food for months here. He was shamefully abandoned. A man like this, with such ideas. Shamefully! Shamefully! I—I—haven't slept for the last ten nights. . . .'

"His voice lost itself in the calm of the evening. The long shadows of the forest had slipped downhill while we talked, had gone far beyond the ruined hovel, beyond the symbolic row of stakes. All this was in the gloom, while we down there were yet in the sunshine, and the stretch of the river abreast of the clearing glittered in a still and dazzling splendor, with a murky and overshadowed bend above and below. Not a living soul was seen on the shore. The bushes did not rustle.

"Suddenly round the corner of the house a group of men appeared, as though they had come up from the ground. They waded waist-deep in the grass, in a compact body, bearing an improvised stretcher in their midst. Instantly, in the emptiness of the landscape, a cry arose whose shrillness pierced the still air like a sharp arrow flying straight to the very heart of the land; and, as if by enchantment, streams of human beings—of naked human beings—with spears in their hands, with bows, with shields, with wild glances and savage movements, were poured into the clearing by the dark-faced and pensive forest. The bushes shook, the grass swayed for a time, and then everything stood still in attentive immobility.

"'Now, if he does not say the right thing to them we are all done for,' said the Russian at my elbow. The knot of men with the stretcher had stopped, too, halfway to the steamer, as if petrified. I saw the man on the stretcher sit up, lank and with an uplifted arm, above the shoulders of the bearers. 'Let us hope that the man who can talk so well of love in general will find some particular reason to spare us this time,' I said. I resented bitterly the absurd danger of our situation, as if to be at the mercy of that atrocious phantom had been a dishonoring necessity. I could not hear a sound, but through my glasses I saw the thin arm extended commandingly, the lower jaw moving, the eyes of that apparition shining darkly far in its bony head that nodded with grotesque jerks. Kurtz—Kurtz—that means short in German—don't it? Well, the name was as true as everything else in his life—and death. He looked at least seven feet long. His covering had fallen off, and his body emerged from it pitiful and appalling as from a winding-sheet. I could see the cage of his ribs all astir, the bones of his arm waving. It was as though an animated image of death carved out of old ivory had been shaking its hand with menaces at a motionless crowd of men made of dark and glittering bronze. I saw him open his mouth wide—it gave him a weirdly voracious aspect, as though he had wanted to swallow all the air, all the earth, all the men before him. A deep voice reached me faintly. He must have been shouting. He fell back suddenly. The stretcher shook as the bearers staggered forward again, and almost at the same time I noticed that the crowd of savages was vanishing without any perceptible movement of retreat, as if the forest that had ejected these beings so suddenly had drawn them in again as the breath is drawn in a long aspiration.

"Some of the pilgrims behind the stretcher carried his arms—two shotguns, a heavy rifle, and a light revolver-carbine[2]—the thunderbolts of that pitiful Jupiter. The manager bent over him murmuring as he walked beside his head. They laid him down in one of the little cabins—just a room for a bedplace and a campstool or two, you know. We had brought his belated correspondence, and a lot of torn envelopes and open letters littered his bed. His hand roamed feebly amongst these papers. I was struck by the fire in his eyes and the composed languor of his expression. It was not so much the exhaustion of disease. He did not seem in pain. This shadow looked satiated and calm, as though for the moment it had had its fill of all the emotions.

"He rustled one of the letters, and looking straight in my face said, 'I am glad.' Somebody had been writing to him about me. These special recommendations were turning up again. The volume of tone he emitted without effort, almost without the trouble of moving his lips, amazed me. A voice! a voice! It was grave, profound, vibrating, while the man did not seem capable of a whisper. However, he had enough strength in him—factitious no doubt—to very nearly make an end of us, as you shall hear directly.

"The manager appeared silently in the doorway; I stepped out at once and he drew the curtain after me. The Russian, eyed curiously by the pilgrims, was staring at the shore. I followed the direction of his glance.

"Dark human shapes could be made out in the distance, flitting indistinctly against the gloomy border of the forest, and near the river two bronze figures, leaning on tall spears, stood in the sunlight under fantastic headdresses of spotted skins, war-like and still in statuesque repose. And from right to left along the lighted shore moved a wild and gorgeous apparition of a woman.

---

2. Short-barreled, lightweight rifle with a revolving, chambered cylinder.

"She walked with measured steps, draped in striped and fringed cloths, treading the earth proudly, with a slight jingle and flash of barbarous ornaments. She carried her head high; her hair was done in the shape of a helmet; she had brass leggings to the knee, brass wire gauntlets to the elbow, a crimson spot on her tawny cheek, innumerable necklaces of glass beads on her neck; bizarre things, charms, gifts of witch-men, that hung about her, glittered and trembled at every step. She must have had the value of several elephant tusks upon her. She was savage and superb, wild-eyed and magnificent; there was something ominous and stately in her deliberate progress. And in the hush that had fallen suddenly upon the whole sorrowful land, the immense wilderness, the colossal body of the fecund and mysterious life seemed to look at her, pensive, as though it had been looking at the image of its own tenebrous and passionate soul.

"She came abreast of the steamer, stood still, and faced us. Her long shadow fell to the water's edge. Her face had a tragic and fierce aspect of wild sorrow and of dumb pain mingled with the fear of some struggling, half-shaped resolve. She stood looking at us without a stir, and like the wilderness itself, with an air of brooding over an inscrutable purpose. A whole minute passed, and then she made a step forward. There was a low jingle, a glint of yellow metal, a sway of fringed draperies, and she stopped as if her heart had failed her. The young fellow by my side growled. The pilgrims murmured at my back. She looked at us all as if her life had depended upon the unswerving steadiness of her glance. Suddenly she opened her bared arms and threw them up rigid above her head, as though in an uncontrollable desire to touch the sky, and at the same time the swift shadows darted out on the earth, swept around on the river, gathering the steamer into a shadowy embrace. A formidable silence hung over the scene.

"She turned away slowly, walked on, following the bank, and passed into the bushes to the left. Once only her eyes gleamed back at us in the dusk of the thickets before she disappeared.

"'If she had offered to come aboard I really think I would have tried to shoot her,' said the man of patches, nervously. 'I have been risking my life every day for the last fortnight to keep her out of the house. She got in one day and kicked up a row about those miserable rags I picked up in the storeroom to mend my clothes with. I wasn't decent. At least it must have been that, for she talked like a fury to Kurtz for an hour, pointing at me now and then. I don't understand the dialect of this tribe. Luckily for me, I fancy Kurtz felt too ill that day to care, or there would have been mischief. I don't understand. . . . No—it's too much for me. Ah, well, it's all over now.'

"At this moment I heard Kurtz's deep voice behind the curtain: 'Save me!— save the ivory, you mean. Don't tell me. Save *me!* Why, I've had to save you. You are interrupting my plans now. Sick! Sick! Not so sick as you would like to believe. Never mind. I'll carry my ideas out yet—I will return. I'll show you what can be done. You with your little peddling notions—you are interfering with me. I will return. I . . .'

"The manager came out. He did me the honor to take me under the arm and lead me aside. 'He is very low, very low,' he said. He considered it necessary to sigh, but neglected to be consistently sorrowful. 'We have done all we could for him—haven't we? But there is no disguising the fact, Mr. Kurtz has done more harm than good to the Company. He did not see the time was not ripe for vigorous action. Cautiously, cautiously—that's my principle. We must be cautious yet. The district is closed to us for a time. Deplorable! Upon the whole, the trade will suffer. I don't deny there is a remarkable quantity of ivory—mostly fossil. We must save it, at all events—but look how precarious the position is—and why? Because the method is unsound.' 'Do you,' said I, looking at the shore, 'call it "unsound method"?' 'Without doubt,' he exclaimed hotly. 'Don't you?' . . . 'No method at all,' I murmured after a while. 'Exactly,' he exulted. 'I anticipated this. Shows a complete want of judgment. It is my duty to point it out in the proper quarter.' 'Oh,' said I, 'that fellow—what's his name?—the brick-maker, will make a readable report for you.' He appeared confounded for a moment. It seemed to me I had never breathed an atmosphere so vile, and I turned mentally to Kurtz for relief—positively for relief. 'Nevertheless I think Mr. Kurtz is a remarkable man,' I said with emphasis. He started, dropped on me a cold heavy glance, said very quietly, 'he *was*,' and turned his back on me. My hour of favor was over; I found myself lumped along with Kurtz as a partisan of methods for which the time was not ripe: I was unsound! Ah! but it was something to have at least a choice of nightmares.

"I had turned to the wilderness really, not to Mr. Kurtz, who, I was ready to admit, was as good as buried. And for a moment it seemed to me as if I also were buried in a vast grave full of unspeakable secrets. I felt an intolerable weight oppressing my breast, the smell of the damp earth, the unseen presence of victorious corruption, the darkness of an impenetrable night. . . . The Russian tapped me on the shoulder. I heard him mumbling and stammering something about 'brother seaman—couldn't conceal—knowledge of matters that would affect Mr. Kurtz's reputation.' I waited. For him evidently Mr. Kurtz was not in his grave; I suspect that for him Mr. Kurtz was one of the immortals. 'Well!' said I at last, 'speak out. As it happens, I am Mr. Kurtz's friend—in a way.'

"He stated with a good deal of formality that had we not been 'of the same profession,' he would have kept the matter to himself without regard to consequences. 'He suspected there was an active ill will towards him on the part of these white men that—' 'You are right,' I said, remembering a certain conversation I had overheard. 'The manager thinks you ought to be hanged.' He showed a concern at this intelligence which amused me at first. 'I had better get out of the way quietly,' he said, earnestly. 'I can do no more for Kurtz now, and they would soon find some excuse. What's to stop them? There's a military post three hundred miles from here.' 'Well, upon my word,' said I, 'perhaps you had better go if you have any friends amongst the savages near by.' 'Plenty,' he said. 'They are simple people—and I want nothing, you know.' He stood biting his lip, then: 'I don't want any harm to happen to these whites here, but of course I was thinking of Mr. Kurtz's reputation—but you are a brother seaman and—' 'All right,' said I, after a time. 'Mr. Kurtz's reputation is safe with me.' I did not know how truly I spoke.

"He informed me, lowering his voice, that it was Kurtz who had ordered the attack to be made on the steamer. 'He hated sometimes the idea of being taken away—and then again . . . But I don't understand these matters. I am a simple man. He thought it would scare you away—that you would give it up, thinking him dead. I could not stop him. Oh, I had an awful time of it this last month.' 'Very well,' I said. 'He is all right now.' 'Ye-e-es,' he muttered, not very convinced apparently. 'Thanks,' said I; 'I shall keep my eyes open.' 'But quiet—eh?' he urged, anxiously. 'It would be awful for his reputation if anybody here—' I promised a complete discretion with great gravity. 'I have a canoe and three black fellows waiting not very far. I am off. Could you give me a few Martini-Henry cartridges?' I could, and did, with proper secrecy. He helped himself, with a wink at me, to a handful of my tobacco. 'Between sailors—you know—good English tobacco.' At the door of the pilot-house he turned round—'I say, haven't you a pair of shoes you could spare?' He raised one leg. 'Look.' The soles were tied with knotted strings sandal-wise under his bare feet. I rooted out an old pair, at which he looked with admiration before tucking them under his left arm. One of his pockets (bright red) was bulging with cartridges, from the other (dark blue) peeped 'Towson's Inquiry,' etc., etc. He seemed to think himself excellently well equipped for a renewed encounter with the wilderness. 'Ah! I'll never, never meet such a man again. You ought to have heard him recite poetry—his own, too, it was, he told me. Poetry!' He rolled his eyes at the recollection of these delights. 'Oh, he enlarged my mind!' 'Good-by,' said I. He shook hands and vanished in the night. Sometimes I ask myself whether I had ever really seen him—whether it was possible to meet such a phenomenon! . . .

"When I woke up shortly after midnight his warning came to my mind with its hint of danger that seemed, in the starred darkness, real enough to make me get up for the purpose of having a look round. On the hill a big fire burned, illuminating fitfully a crooked corner of the station-house. One of the agents with a picket of a few of our blacks, armed for the purpose, was keeping guard over the ivory; but deep within the forest, red gleams that wavered, that seemed to sink and rise from the ground amongst confused columnar shapes of intense blackness, showed the exact position of the camp where Mr. Kurtz's adorers were keeping their uneasy vigil. The monotonous beating of a big drum filled the air with muffled shocks and a lingering vibration. A steady droning sound of many men chanting each to himself some weird incantation came out from the black, flat wall of the woods as the humming of bees comes out of a hive, and had a strange narcotic effect upon my half-awake senses. I believe I dozed off leaning over the rail, till an abrupt burst of yells, an overwhelming outbreak of a pent-up and mysterious frenzy, woke me up in a bewildered wonder. It was cut short all at once, and the low droning went on with an effect of audible and soothing silence. I glanced casually into the little cabin. A light was burning within, but Mr. Kurtz was not there.

"I think I would have raised an outcry if I had believed my eyes. But I didn't believe them at first—the thing seemed so impossible. The fact is I was completely unnerved by a sheer blank fright, pure abstract terror, unconnected with any distinct shape of physical danger. What made this emotion so overpowering was—how shall I define it?—the moral shock I received, as if something altogether monstrous, intolerable to thought and odious to the soul, had been thrust upon me unexpectedly. This lasted of course the merest fraction of a second, and then the usual sense of commonplace, deadly danger, the possibility of a sudden onslaught and massacre, or something of the kind, which I saw impending, was positively welcome and composing. It pacified me, in fact, so much, that I did not raise an alarm.

"There was an agent buttoned up inside an ulster and sleeping on a chair on deck within three feet of me. The yells had not awakened him; he snored very slightly; I left him to his slumbers and leaped ashore. I did not betray Mr. Kurtz—it was ordered I should never betray him—it was written I should be loyal to the nightmare of my choice. I was anxious to deal with this shadow by myself alone,—and to this day I don't know why I was so jealous of sharing with anyone the peculiar blackness of that experience.

"As soon as I got on the bank I saw a trail—a broad trail through the grass. I remember the exultation with which I said to myself, 'He can't walk—he is crawling on all-fours—I've got him.' The grass was wet with dew. I strode rapidly with clenched fists. I fancy I had some vague notion of falling upon him and giving him a drubbing. I don't know. I had some imbecile thoughts. The knitting old woman with the cat obtruded herself upon my memory as a most improper person to be sitting at the other end of such an affair. I saw a row of pilgrims squirting lead in the air out of Winchesters held to the hip. I thought I would never get back to the steamer, and imagined myself living alone and unarmed in the woods to an advanced age. Such silly things—you know. And I remember I confounded the beat of the drum with the beating of my heart, and was pleased at its calm regularity.

"I kept to the track though—then stopped to listen. The night was very clear; a dark blue space, sparkling with dew and starlight, in which black things stood very still. I thought I could see a kind of motion ahead of me. I was strangely cocksure of everything that night. I actually left the track and ran in a wide semicircle (I verily believe chuckling to myself) so as to get in front of that stir, of that motion I had seen—if indeed I had seen anything. I was circumventing Kurtz as though it had been a boyish game.

"I came upon him, and, if he had not heard me coming, I would have fallen over him too, but he got up in time. He rose, unsteady, long, pale, indistinct, like a vapor exhaled by the earth, and swayed slightly, misty and silent before me; while at my back the fires loomed between the trees, and the murmur of many voices issued from the forest. I had cut him off cleverly; but when actually confronting him I seemed to come to my senses, I saw the danger in its right proportion. It was by no means over yet. Suppose he began to shout? Though he could hardly stand, there was still plenty of vigor in his voice. 'Go away—hide yourself,' he said, in that profound tone. It was very awful. I glanced back. We were within thirty yards from the nearest fire. A black figure stood up, strode on long black legs, waving long black arms, across the glow. It had horns—antelope horns, I think—on its head. Some sorcerer, some witchman, no doubt: it looked fiend-like enough. 'Do you know what you are doing?' I whispered. 'Perfectly,' he answered, raising his voice for that single word: it sounded to me far off and yet loud, like a hail through a speaking-trumpet. If he makes a row we are lost, I thought to myself. This clearly was not a case for fisticuffs, even apart from the very natural aversion I had to beat that Shadow—this wandering and tormented thing. 'You will be lost,' I said—'utterly lost.' One gets sometimes such a flash of inspiration, you know. I did say the right thing, though indeed he could not have been more irretrievably lost than he was at this very moment, when the foundations of our intimacy were being laid—to endure—to endure—even to the end—even beyond.

"'I had immense plans,' he muttered irresolutely. 'Yes,' said I; 'but if you try to shout I'll smash your head with—' There was not a stick or a stone near. 'I will throttle you for good,' I corrected myself. 'I was on the threshold of great things,' he pleaded, in a voice of longing, with a wistfulness of tone that made my blood run cold. 'And now for this stupid scoundrel—' 'Your success in Europe is assured in any case,' I affirmed, steadily. I did not want to have the throttling of him, you understand—and indeed it would have been very little use for any practical purpose. I tried to break the spell—the heavy, mute spell of the wilderness—that seemed to draw him to its pitiless breast by the awakening of forgotten and brutal instincts, by the memory of gratified and monstrous passions. This alone, I was convinced, had driven him out to the edge of the forest, to the bush, towards the gleam of fires, the throb of drums, the drone of weird incantations; this alone had beguiled his unlawful soul beyond the bounds of permitted aspirations. And, don't you see, the terror of the position was not in being knocked on the head—though I had a very lively sense of that danger, too—but in this, that I had to deal with a being to whom I could not appeal in the name of anything high or low. I had, even like the niggers, to invoke him—himself—his own exalted and incredible degradation. There was nothing either above or below him, and I knew it. He had kicked himself loose of the earth. Confound the man! he had kicked the very earth to pieces. He was alone, and I before him did not know whether I stood on the ground or floated in the air. I've been telling you what we said—repeating the phrases we pronounced—but what's the good? They were common everyday words—the familiar, vague sounds exchanged on every waking day of life. But what of that? They had behind them, to my mind, the terrific suggestiveness of words heard in dreams, of phrases spoken in nightmares. Soul! If anybody had ever struggled with a soul, I am the man. And I wasn't arguing with a lunatic either. Believe me or not, his intelligence was perfectly clear—concentrated, it is true, upon himself with horrible intensity, yet clear; and therein was my only chance—barring, of course, the killing him there and then, which wasn't so good, on account of unavoidable noise. But his soul was mad. Being alone in the wilderness, it had looked within itself, and, by heavens! I tell you, it had gone mad. I had—for my sins, I suppose—to go through the ordeal of looking into it myself. No eloquence could have been so withering to one's belief in mankind as his final burst of sincerity. He struggled with himself, too. I saw it,—I heard it. I saw the inconceivable mystery of a soul that knew no restraint, no faith, and no fear, yet struggling blindly with itself. I kept my head pretty well; but when I had him at last stretched on the couch, I wiped my forehead, while my legs shook under me as though I had carried half a ton on my back down that hill. And yet I had only supported him, his bony arm clasped round my neck—and he was not much heavier than a child.

"When next day we left at noon, the crowd, of whose presence behind the curtain of trees I had been acutely conscious all the time, flowed out of the woods again, filled the clearing, covered the slope with a mass of naked, breathing, quivering, bronze bodies. I steamed up a bit, then swung downstream, and two thousand eyes followed the evolutions of the splashing, thumping, fierce river-demon beating the water with its terrible tail and breathing black smoke into the air. In front of the first rank, along the river, three men, plastered with bright red earth from head to foot, strutted to and fro restlessly. When we came abreast again, they faced the river, stamped their feet, nodded their horned heads, swayed their scarlet bodies; they shook towards the fierce river-demon a bunch of black feathers, a mangy skin with a pendent tail—something that looked like a dried gourd; they shouted periodically together strings of amazing words that resembled no sounds of human language; and the deep murmurs of the crowd, interrupted suddenly, were like the responses of some satanic litany.

"We had carried Kurtz into the pilot-house: there was more air there. Lying on the couch, he stared through the open shutter. There was an eddy in the mass of human bodies, and the woman with helmeted head and tawny cheeks rushed out to the very brink of the stream. She put out her hands, shouted something, and all that wild mob took up the shout in a roaring chorus of articulated, rapid, breathless utterance.

"'Do you understand this?' I asked.

"He kept on looking out past me with fiery, longing eyes, with a mingled expression of wistfulness and hate. He made no answer, but I saw a smile, a smile of indefinable meaning, appear on his colorless lips that a moment after twitched convulsively. 'Do I not?' he said slowly, gasping, as if the words had been torn out of him by a supernatural power.

"I pulled the string of the whistle, and I did this because I saw the pilgrims on deck getting out their rifles with an air of anticipating a jolly lark. At the sudden screech there was a movement of abject terror through that wedged mass of bodies. 'Don't! don't you frighten them away,' cried someone on deck disconsolately. I pulled the string time after time. They broke and ran, they leaped, they crouched, they swerved, they dodged the flying terror of the sound. The three red chaps had fallen flat, face down on the shore, as though they had been shot dead. Only the barbarous and superb woman did not so much as flinch, and stretched tragically her bare arms after us over the somber and glittering river.

"And then that imbecile crowd down on the deck started their little fun, and I could see nothing more for smoke.

"The brown current ran swiftly out of the heart of darkness, bearing us down towards the sea with twice the speed of our upward progress; and Kurtz's life was running swiftly, too, ebbing, ebbing out of his heart into the sea of inexorable time. The manager was very placid, he had no vital anxieties now, he took us both in with a comprehensive and satisfied glance: the 'affair' had come off as well as could be wished. I saw the time approaching when I would be left alone of the party of 'unsound method.' The pilgrims looked upon me with disfavor. I was, so to speak, numbered with the dead. It is strange how I accepted this unforeseen partnership, this choice of nightmares forced upon me in the tenebrous land invaded by these mean and greedy phantoms.

"Kurtz discoursed. A voice! a voice! It rang deep to the very last. It survived his strength to hide in the magnificent folds of eloquence the barren darkness of his heart. Oh, he struggled! he struggled! The wastes of his weary brain were haunted by shadowy images now—images of wealth and fame revolving obsequiously round his unextinguishable gift of noble and lofty expression. My Intended, my station, my career, my ideas—these were the subjects for the occasional utterances of elevated sentiments. The shade of the original Kurtz frequented the bedside of the hollow sham, whose fate it was to be buried presently in the mold of primeval earth. But both the diabolic love and the unearthly hate of the mysteries it had penetrated fought for the possession of that soul satiated with primitive emotions, avid of lying fame, of sham distinction, of all the appearances of success and power.

"Sometimes he was contemptibly childish. He desired to have kings meet him at railway stations on his return from some ghastly Nowhere, where he intended to accomplish great things. 'You show them you have in you something that is really profitable, and then there will be no limits to the recognition of your ability,' he would say. 'Of course you must take care of the motives—right motives—always.' The long reaches that were like one and the same reach, monotonous bends that were exactly alike, slipped past the steamer with their multitude of secular[3] trees looking patiently after this grimy fragment of another world, the forerunner of change, of conquest, of trade, of massacres, of blessings. I looked ahead—piloting. 'Close the shutter,' said Kurtz suddenly one day; 'I can't bear to look at this.' I did so. There was a silence. 'Oh, but I will wring your heart yet!' he cried at the invisible wilderness.

"We broke down—as I had expected—and had to lie up for repairs at the head of an island. This delay was the first thing that shook Kurtz's confidence. One morning he gave me a packet of papers and a photograph—the lot tied together with a shoestring. 'Keep this for me,' he said. 'This noxious fool' (meaning the manager) 'is capable of prying into my boxes when I am not looking.' In the afternoon I saw him. He was lying on his back with closed eyes, and I withdrew quietly, but I heard him mutter, 'Live rightly, die, die. . . .' I listened. There was nothing more. Was he rehearsing some speech in his sleep, or was it a fragment of a phrase from some newspaper article? He had been writing for the papers and meant to do so again, 'for the furthering of my ideas. It's a duty.'

"His was an impenetrable darkness. I looked at him as you peer down at a man who is lying at the bottom of a precipice where the sun never shines. But I had not much time to give him, because I was helping the engine-driver to take to pieces the leaky cylinders, to straighten a bent connecting-rod, and in other such matters. I lived in an infernal mess of rust, filings, nuts, bolts, spanners, hammers, ratchet-drills—things I abominate, because I don't get on with them. I tended the little forge we fortunately had aboard; I toiled wearily in a wretched scrap-heap—unless I had the shakes too bad to stand.

"One evening coming in with a candle I was startled to hear him say a little tremulously, 'I am lying here in the dark waiting for death.' The light was within a foot of his eyes. I forced myself to murmur, 'Oh, nonsense!' and stood over him as if transfixed.

"Anything approaching the change that came over his features I have never seen before, and hope never to see again. Oh, I wasn't touched. I was fascinated. It was as though a veil had been rent. I saw on that ivory face the expression of somber pride, of ruthless power, of craven terror—of an intense

---

3. Centuries-old.

and hopeless despair. Did he live his life again in every detail of desire, temptation, and surrender during that supreme moment of complete knowledge? He cried in a whisper at some image, at some vision—he cried out twice, a cry that was no more than a breath—

"'The horror! The horror!'

"I blew the candle out and left the cabin. The pilgrims were dining in the mess-room, and I took my place opposite the manager, who lifted his eyes to give me a questioning glance, which I successfully ignored. He leaned back, serene, with that peculiar smile of his sealing the unexpressed depths of his meanness. A continuous shower of small flies streamed upon the lamp, upon the cloth, upon our hands and faces. Suddenly the manager's boy put his insolent black head in the doorway, and said in a tone of scathing contempt—

"'Mistah Kurtz—he dead.'

"All the pilgrims rushed out to see. I remained, and went on with my dinner. I believe I was considered brutally callous. However, I did not eat much. There was a lamp in there—light, don't you know—and outside it was so beastly, beastly dark. I went no more near the remarkable man who had pronounced a judgment upon the adventures of his soul on this earth. The voice was gone. What else had been there? But I am of course aware that next day the pilgrims buried something in a muddy hole.

"And then they very nearly buried me.

"However, as you see, I did not go to join Kurtz there and then. I did not. I remained to dream the nightmare out to the end, and to show my loyalty to Kurtz once more. Destiny. My destiny! Droll thing life is—that mysterious arrangement of merciless logic for a futile purpose. The most you can hope from it is some knowledge of yourself—that comes too late—a crop of unextinguishable regrets. I have wrestled with death. It is the most unexciting contest you can imagine. It takes place in an impalpable grayness, with nothing underfoot, with nothing around, without spectators, without clamor, without glory, without the great desire of victory, without the great fear of defeat, in a sickly atmosphere of tepid skepticism, without much belief in your own right, and still less in that of your adversary. If such is the form of ultimate wisdom, then life is a greater riddle than some of us think it to be. I was within a hair's breadth of the last opportunity for pronouncement, and I found with humiliation that probably I would have nothing to say. This is the reason why I affirm that Kurtz was a remarkable man. He had something to say. He said it. Since I had peeped over the edge myself, I understand better the meaning of his stare, that could not see the flame of the candle, but was wide enough to embrace the whole universe, piercing enough to penetrate all the hearts that beat in the darkness. He had summed up—he had judged. 'The horror!' He was a remarkable man. After all, this was the expression of some sort of belief; it had candor, it had conviction, it had a vibrating note of revolt in its whisper, it had the appalling face of a glimpsed truth—the strange commingling of desire and hate. And it is not my own extremity I remember best—a vision of grayness without form filled with physical pain, and a careless contempt for the evanescence of all things—even of this pain itself. No! It is his extremity that I seem to have lived through. True, he had made that last stride, he had stepped over the edge, while I had been permitted to draw back my hesitating foot. And perhaps in this is the whole difference; perhaps all the wisdom, and all truth, and all sincerity, are just compressed into that inappreciable moment of time in which we step over the threshold of the invisible. Perhaps! I like to think my summing-up would not have been a word of careless contempt. Better his cry—much better. It was an affirmation, a moral victory paid for by innumerable defeats, by abominable terrors, by abominable satisfactions. But it was a victory! That is why I have remained loyal to Kurtz to the last, and even beyond, when a long time after I heard once more, not his own voice, but the echo of his magnificent eloquence thrown to me from a soul as translucently pure as a cliff of crystal.

"No, they did not bury me, though there is a period of time which I remember mistily, with a shuddering wonder, like a passage through some inconceivable world that had no hope in it and no desire. I found myself back in the sepulchral city resenting the sight of people hurrying through the streets to filch a little money from each other, to devour their infamous cookery, to gulp their unwholesome beer, to dream their insignificant and silly dreams. They trespassed upon my thoughts. They were intruders whose knowledge of life was to me an irritating pretense, because I felt so sure they could not possibly know the things I knew. Their bearing, which was simply the bearing of commonplace individuals going about their business in the assurance of perfect safety, was offensive to me like the outrageous flauntings of folly in the face of a danger it is unable to comprehend. I had no particular desire to enlighten them, but I had some difficulty in restraining myself from laughing in their faces, so full of stupid importance. I daresay I was not very well at that time. I tottered about the streets—there were various affairs to settle—grinning bitterly at perfectly respectable persons. I admit my behavior was inexcusable, but then my temperature was seldom normal in these days. My dear aunt's endeavors to 'nurse up my strength' seemed altogether beside the mark. It was not my strength that wanted nursing, it was my imagination that wanted soothing. I kept the bundle of papers given me by Kurtz, not knowing exactly what to do with it. His mother had died lately, watched over, as I was told, by his Intended. A clean-shaven man, with an official manner and wearing gold-rimmed spectacles, called on me one day and made inquiries, at first circuitous, afterwards suavely pressing, about what he was pleased to denominate certain 'documents.' I was not surprised, because I had had two rows with the manager on the subject out there. I had refused to give up the smallest scrap out of that package, and I took the same attitude with the spectacled man. He became darkly menacing at last, and with much heat argued that the Company had the right to every bit of information about its 'territories.' And said he, 'Mr. Kurtz's knowledge of unexplored regions must have been necessarily extensive and peculiar—owing to his great abilities and to the deplorable circumstances in which he had been placed: therefore—' I assured him Mr. Kurtz's knowledge, however extensive, did not bear upon the problems of commerce or administration. He invoked then the name of science. 'It would be an incalculable loss if,' etc., etc. I offered him the report on the 'Suppression of Savage Customs,' with the postscriptum torn off. He took it up eagerly, but ended by sniffing at it with an air of contempt. 'This is not what we had a right to expect,' he remarked. 'Expect nothing else,' I said. 'There are only private letters.' He withdrew upon some threat of legal proceedings, and I saw him no more; but another fellow, calling himself Kurtz's cousin, appeared two days later, and was anxious to hear all the details about his dear relative's last moments. Incidentally he gave me to understand that Kurtz had been essentially a great musician. 'There was the making of an immense success,' said the man, who was an organist, I believe, with lank gray hair flowing over a greasy coat-collar. I had no reason to doubt his statement; and to this day I am unable to say what was Kurtz's profession, whether he ever had any—which was the greatest of his talents. I had taken him for a painter who wrote for the papers, or else for a journalist who could paint—but even the cousin (who took snuff during the interview) could not tell me what he had been—exactly. He was a universal genius—on that point I agreed with the old chap, who thereupon blew his nose noisily into a large cotton handkerchief and withdrew in senile agitation, bearing off some family letters and memoranda without importance. Ultimately a journalist anxious to know something of the fate of his 'dear colleague' turned up. This visitor informed me Kurtz's proper sphere ought to have been politics 'on the popular side.' He had furry straight eyebrows, bristly hair cropped short, an eyeglass on a broad ribbon, and, becoming expansive, confessed his opinion that Kurtz really couldn't write a bit—'But heavens! how that man could talk. He electrified large meetings. He had faith—don't you see?—he had the faith. He could get himself to believe anything—anything. He would have been a splendid leader of an extreme party.' 'What party?' I asked. 'Any party,' answered the other. 'He was an—an—extremist.' Did I not think so? I assented. Did I know, he asked, with a sudden flash of curiosity, 'what it was that had induced him to go out there?' 'Yes,' said I, and forthwith handed him the famous Report for publication, if he thought fit. He glanced through it hurriedly, mumbling all the time, judged 'it would do,' and took himself off with this plunder.

"Thus I was left at last with a slim packet of letters and the girl's portrait. She struck me as beautiful—I mean she had a beautiful expression. I know that the sunlight can be made to lie, too, yet one felt that no manipulation of light and pose could have conveyed the delicate shade of truthfulness upon those features. She seemed ready to listen without mental reservation, without suspicion, without a thought for herself. I concluded I would go and give her back her portrait and those letters myself. Curiosity? Yes; and also some other feeling perhaps. All that had been Kurtz's had passed out of my hands: his soul, his body, his station, his plans, his ivory, his career. There remained only this memory and his Intended—and I wanted to give that up, too, to the past, in a way—to surrender personally all that remained of him with me to that oblivion which is the last word of our common fate. I don't defend myself. I had no clear perception of what it was I really wanted. Perhaps it was an impulse of unconscious loyalty, or the fulfillment of one of those ironic necessities, that lurk in the facts of human existence. I don't know. I can't tell. But I went.

"I thought his memory was like the other memories of the dead that accumulate in every man's life—a vague impress on the brain of shadows that had fallen on it in their swift and final passage; but before the high and ponderous door, between the tall houses of a street as still and decorous as a well-kept alley in a cemetery, I had a vision of him on the stretcher, opening his mouth voraciously, as if to devour all the earth with all its mankind. He lived then before me; he lived as much as he had ever lived—a shadow insatiable of splendid appearances, of frightful realities; a shadow darker than the shadow of the night, and draped nobly in the folds of a gorgeous eloquence. The vision seemed to enter the house with me—the stretcher, the phantombearers, the wild crowd of obedient worshipers, the gloom of the forests, the glitter of the reach between the murky bends, the beat of the drum, regular and muffled like the beating of a heart—the heart of a conquering darkness. It was a moment of triumph for the wilderness, an invading and vengeful rush which, it seemed to me, I would have to keep back alone for the salvation of another soul. And the memory of what I had heard him say afar there, with the horned shapes stirring at my back, in the glow of fires, within the patient woods, those broken phrases came back to me, were heard again in their ominous and terrifying simplicity. I remembered his abject pleading, his abject threats, the colossal scale of his vile desires, the meanness, the torment, the tempestuous anguish of his soul. And later on I seem to see his collected languid manner, when he said one day, 'This lot of ivory now is really mine. The Company did not pay for it. I collected it myself at a very great personal risk. I am afraid they will try to claim it as theirs though. H'm. It is a difficult case. What do you think I ought to do—resist? Eh? I want no more than justice.' . . . He wanted no more than justice—no more than justice. I rang the bell before a mahogany door on the first floor, and while I waited he seemed to stare at me out of the glossy panel—stare with that wide and immense stare embracing, condemning, loathing all the universe. I seemed to hear the whispered cry, 'The horror! The horror!'

"The dusk was falling. I had to wait in a lofty drawing-room with three long windows from floor to ceiling that were like three luminous and bedraped columns. The bent gilt legs and backs of the furniture shone in indistinct curves. The tall marble fireplace had a cold and monumental whiteness. A grand piano stood massively in a corner; with dark gleams on the flat surfaces like a somber and polished sarcophagus. A high door opened—closed. I rose.

"She came forward, all in black, with a pale head, floating towards me in the dusk. She was in mourning. It was more than a year since his death, more than a year since the news came; she seemed as though she would remember and mourn forever. She took both my hands in hers and murmured, 'I had heard you were coming.' I noticed she was not very young—I mean not girlish. She had a mature capacity for fidelity, for belief, for suffering. The room seemed to have grown darker, as if all the sad light of the cloudy evening had taken refuge on her forehead. This fair hair, this pale visage, this pure brow, seemed surrounded by an ashy halo from which the dark eyes looked out at me. Their glance was guileless, profound, confident, and trustful. She carried her sorrowful head as though she were proud of that sorrow, as though she would say, I—I alone know how to mourn him as he deserves. But while we were still shaking hands, such a look of awful desolation came upon her face that I perceived she was one of those creatures that are not the playthings of Time. For her he had died only yesterday. And, by Jove! the impression was so powerful that for me, too, he seemed to have died only yesterday—nay, this very minute. I saw her and him in the same instant of time—his death and her sorrow—I saw her sorrow in the very moment of his death. Do you understand? I saw them together—I heard them together. She had said, with a deep catch of the breath, 'I have survived' while my strained ears seemed to hear distinctly, mingled with her tone of despairing regret, the summing up whisper of his eternal condemnation. I asked myself what I was doing there, with a sensation of panic in my heart as though I had blundered into a place of cruel and absurd mysteries not fit for a human being to behold. She motioned me to a chair. We sat down. I laid the packet gently on the little table, and she put her hand over it. . . . 'You knew him well,' she murmured, after a moment of mourning silence.

"'Intimacy grows quickly out there,' I said. 'I knew him as well as it is possible for one man to know another.'

"'And you admired him,' she said. 'It was impossible to know him and not to admire him. Was it?'

"'He was a remarkable man,' I said, unsteadily. Then before the appealing fixity of her gaze, that seemed to watch for more words on my lips, I went on, 'It was impossible not to—'

"'Love him,' she finished eagerly, silencing me into an appalled dumbness. 'How true! how true! But when you think that no one knew him so well as I! I had all his noble confidence. I knew him best.'

"'You knew him best,' I repeated. And perhaps she did. But with every word spoken the room was growing darker, and only her forehead, smooth and white, remained illumined by the unextinguishable light of belief and love.

"'You were his friend,' she went on. 'His friend,' she repeated, a little louder. 'You must have been, if he had given you this, and sent you to me. I feel I can speak to you—and oh! I must speak. I want you—you have heard his last words—to know I have been worthy of him. . . . It is not pride. . . . Yes! I am proud to know I understood him better than anyone on earth—he told me so himself. And since his mother died I have had no one—no one—to—to—'

"I listened. The darkness deepened. I was not even sure whether he had given me the right bundle. I rather suspect he wanted me to take care of another batch of his papers which, after his death, I saw the manager examining under the lamp. And the girl talked, easing her pain in the certitude of my sympathy; she talked as thirsty men drink. I had heard that her engagement with Kurtz had been disapproved by her people. He wasn't rich enough or something. And indeed I don't know whether he had not been a pauper all his life. He had given me some reason to infer that it was his impatience of comparative poverty that drove him out there.

"'. . . Who was not his friend who had heard him speak once?' she was saying. 'He drew men towards him by what was best in them.' She looked at me with intensity. 'It is the gift of the great,' she went on, and the sound of her low voice seemed to have the accompaniment of all the other sounds, full of mystery, desolation, and sorrow, I had ever heard—the ripple of the river, the soughing of the trees swayed by the wind, the murmurs of the crowds, the faint ring of incomprehensible words cried from afar, the whisper of a voice speaking from beyond the threshold of an eternal darkness. 'But you have heard him! You know!' she cried.

"'Yes, I know,' I said with something like despair in my heart, but bowing my head before the faith that was in her, before that great and saving illusion that shone with an unearthly glow in the darkness, in the triumphant darkness from which I could not have defended her—from which I could not even defend myself.

"'What a loss to me—to us!'—she corrected herself with beautiful generosity; then added in a murmur, 'To the world.' By the last gleams of twilight I could see the glitter of her eyes, full of tears—of tears that would not fall.

"'I have been very happy—very fortunate—very proud,' she went on. 'Too fortunate. Too happy for a little while. And now I am unhappy for—for life.'

"She stood up; her fair hair seemed to catch all the remaining light in a glimmer of gold. I rose, too.

"'And of all this,' she went on, mournfully, 'of all his promise, and of all his greatness, of his generous mind, of his noble heart, nothing remains—nothing but a memory. You and I—'

"'We shall always remember him,' I said, hastily.

"'No!' she cried. 'It is impossible that all this should be lost—that such a life should be sacrificed to leave nothing—but sorrow. You know what vast plans he had. I knew of them, too—I could not perhaps understand—but others knew of them. Something must remain. His words, at least, have not died.'

"'His words will remain,' I said.

"'And his example,' she whispered to herself. 'Men looked up to him—his goodness shone in every act. His example—'

"'True,' I said; 'his example too. Yes, his example. I forgot that.'

"'But I do not. I cannot—I cannot believe—not yet. I cannot believe that I shall never see him again, that nobody will see him again, never, never, never.'

"She put out her arms as if after a retreating figure, stretching them black and with clasped pale hands across the fading and narrow sheen of the window. Never see him! I saw him clearly enough then. I shall see this eloquent phantom as long as I live, and I shall see her, too, a tragic and familiar Shade, resembling in this gesture another one, tragic also, and bedecked with powerless charms, stretching bare brown arms over the glitter of the infernal stream, the stream of darkness. She said suddenly very low, 'He died as he lived.'

"'His end,' said I, with dull anger stirring in me, 'was in every way worthy of his life.'

"'And I was not with him,' she murmured. My anger subsided before a feeling of infinite pity.

"'Everything that could be done—' I mumbled.

"'Ah, but I believed in him more than anyone on earth—more than his own mother, more than—himself. He needed me! Me! I would have treasured every sigh, every word, every sign, every glance.'

"I felt like a chill grip on my chest. 'Don't,' I said, in a muffled voice.

"'Forgive me. I—I—have mourned so long in silence—in silence. . . . You were with him—to the last? I think of his loneliness. Nobody near to understand him as I would have understood. Perhaps no one to hear. . . .'

"'To the very end,' I said shakily. 'I heard his very last words. . . .' I stopped in a fright.

"'Repeat them,' she murmured in a heart-broken tone. 'I want—I want—something—something—to—live with.'

"I was on the point of crying at her, 'Don't you hear them?' The dusk was repeating them in a persistent whisper all around us, in a whisper that seemed to swell menacingly like the first whisper of a rising wind. 'The horror! The horror!'

"'His last word—to live with,' she insisted. 'Don't you understand I loved him—I loved him—I loved him!'

"I pulled myself together and spoke slowly.

"'The last word he pronounced was—your name.'

"I heard a light sigh and then my heart stood still, stopped dead short by an exulting and terrible cry, by the cry of inconceivable triumph and of unspeakable pain. 'I knew it—I was sure!' . . . She knew. She was sure. I heard her weeping, she had hidden her face in her hands. It seemed to me that the house would collapse before I could escape, that the heavens would fall upon my head. But nothing happened. The heavens do not fall for such a trifle. Would they have fallen, I wonder, if I had rendered Kurtz that justice which was his due? Hadn't he said he wanted only justice? But I couldn't. I could not tell her. It would have been too dark—too dark altogether. . . ."

Marlow ceased, and sat apart, indistinct and silent, in the pose of a meditating Buddha. Nobody moved for a time. "We have lost the first of the ebb," said the Director, suddenly. I raised my head. The offing was barred by a black bank of clouds, and the tranquil waterway leading to the uttermost ends of the earth flowed somber under an overcast sky—seemed to lead into the heart of an immense darkness.

1902

RELATED:

—Conrad, Preface to *The Nigger of the "Narcissus,"* p. 1711
—Conrad, Letter to Barrett H. Clark, p. 1713
—Barry Hannah on *Heart of Darkness*, p. 1763
—C. P. Sarvan, "Racism and the *Heart of Darkness*," p. 1774

JULIO CORTÁZAR
1914–1984

Cortázar was born to Argentine parents living in Brussels. When he was four years old his family returned to Buenos Aires, where he grew up and eventually completed his education, at the University of Buenos Aires. Opposed to the Perón regime, Cortázar emigrated to Paris, where he lived the rest of his life. Drawn to literature at an early age, he was influenced first by his fellow Argentinean Jorge Luis Borges and later by French Surrealists. As a political activist he made his mark on left-wing theorists of Latin America; as a writer of fiction and verse he moved with the international avant-garde after World War II. Driven by a restless and wide-ranging imagination he produced a multitude of short stories, some of them collected in *End of the Game* (1965), *We Love Glenda So Much* (1980), and *Unreasonable Hours* (1995). His masterpiece, the novel *Hopscotch* (1966), is a classic of Modernist experimentation.

Letter to a Young Lady in Paris[1]

Andrea, I didn't want to come live in your apartment in the calle[2] Suipacha. Not so much because of the bunnies, but rather that it offends me to intrude on a compact order, built even to the finest nets of air, networks that in your environment conserve the music in the lavender, the heavy fluff of the powder puff in the talcum, the play between the violin and the viola in Ravel's quartet. It hurts me to come into an ambience where someone who lives beautifully has arranged everything like a visible affirmation of her soul, here the books (Spanish on one side, French and English on the other), the large green cushions there, the crystal ashtray that looks like a soap-bubble that's been cut open on this exact spot on the little table, and always a perfume, a sound, a sprouting of plants, a photograph of the dead friend, the ritual of tea trays and sugar tongs . . . Ah, dear Andrea, how difficult it is to stand counter to, yet to accept with perfect submission of one's whole being, the elaborate order that a woman establishes in her own gracious flat. How much at fault one feels taking a small metal tray and putting it at the far end of the table, setting it there simply because one has brought one's English dictionaries and it's at this end, within easy reach of the hand, that they ought to be. To move that tray is the equivalent of an unexpected horrible crimson in the middle of

---

1. Translated by Paul Blackburn. **2.** Street (Spanish).

one of Ozenfant's[3] painterly cadences, as if suddenly the strings of all the double basses snapped at the same time with the same dreadful whiplash at the most hushed instant in a Mozart symphony. Moving that tray alters the play of relationships in the whole house, of each object with another, of each moment of their soul with the soul of the house and its absent inhabitant. And I cannot bring my fingers close to a book, hardly change a lamp's cone of light, open the piano bench, without a feeling of rivalry and offense swinging before my eyes like a flock of sparrows.

You know why I came to your house, to your peaceful living room scooped out of the noonday light. Everything looks so natural, as always when one does not know the truth. You've gone off to Paris, I am left with the apartment in the calle Suipacha, we draw up a simple and satisfactory plan convenient to us both until September brings you back again to Buenos Aires and I amble off to some other house where perhaps . . . But I'm not writing you for that reason, I was sending this letter to you because of the rabbits, it seems only fair to let you know; and because I like to write letters, and maybe too because it's raining.

I moved last Thursday in a haze overlaid by weariness, at five in the afternoon. I've closed so many suitcases in my life, I've passed so many hours preparing luggage that never manages to get moved anyplace, that Thursday was a day full of shadows and straps, because when I look at valise straps it's as though I were seeing shadows, as though they were parts of a whip that flogs me in some indirect way, very subtly and horribly. But I packed the bags, let your maid know I was coming to move in. I was going up in the elevator and just between the first and second floors I felt that I was going to vomit up a little rabbit. I have never described this to you before, not so much, I don't think, from lack of truthfulness as that, just naturally, one is not going to explain to people at large that from time to time one vomits up a small rabbit. Always I have managed to be alone when it happens, guarding the fact much as we guard so many of our privy acts, evidences of our physical selves which happen to us in total privacy. Don't reproach me for it, Andrea, don't blame me. Once in a while it happens that I vomit up a bunny. It's no reason not to live in whatever house, it's no reason for one to blush and isolate oneself and to walk around keeping one's mouth shut.

When I feel that I'm going to bring up a rabbit, I put two fingers in my mouth like an open pincer, and I wait to feel the lukewarm fluff rise in my throat like the effervescence in a sal hepatica.[4] It's all swift and clean, passes in the briefest instant. I remove the fingers from my mouth and in them, held fast by the ears, a small white rabbit. The bunny appears to be content, a perfectly normal bunny only very tiny, small as a chocolate rabbit, only it's white and very thoroughly a rabbit. I set it in the palm of my hand, I smooth the fluff, caressing it with two fingers; the bunny seems satisfied with having been born and waggles and pushes its muzzle against my skin, moving it with that quiet and tickling nibble of a rabbit's mouth against the skin of the hand. He's looking for something to eat, and then (I'm talking about when this happened at my house on the outskirts) I take him with me out to the balcony and set him down in the big flowerpot among the clover that I've

---

3. Amédée Ozenfant (1886–1966), French art theorist and painter.   4. Mineral salt sold as a laxative.

grown there with this in mind. The bunny raises his ears as high as they can go, surrounds a tender clover leaf with a quick little wheeling motion of his snout, and I know that I can leave him there now and go on my way for a time, lead a life not very different from people who buy their rabbits at farmhouses.

Between the first and the second floors, then, Andrea, like an omen of what my life in your house was going to be, I realized that I was going to vomit a rabbit. At that point I was afraid (or was it surprise? No, perhaps fear of the same surprise) because, before leaving my house, only two days before, I'd vomited a bunny and so was safe for a month, five weeks, maybe six with a little luck. Now, look, I'd resolved the problem perfectly. I grew clover on the balcony of my other house, vomited a bunny, put it in with the clover and at the end of a month, when I suspected that any moment . . . then I made a present of the rabbit, already grown enough, to señora de Molina, who believed I had a hobby and was quiet about it. In another flowerpot tender and propitious clover was already growing, I awaited without concern the morning when the tickling sensation of fluff rising obstructed my throat, and the new little rabbit reiterated from that hour the life and habits of its predecessor. Habits, Andrea, are concrete forms of rhythm, are that portion of rhythm which helps to keep us alive. Vomiting bunnies wasn't so terrible once one had gotten into the unvarying cycle, into the method. You will want to know why all this work, why all that clover and señora de Molina. It would have been easier to kill the little thing right away and . . . Ah, you should vomit one up all by yourself, take it in two fingers and set it in your opened hand, still attached to yourself by the act itself, by the indefinable aura of its proximity, barely now broken away. A month puts a lot of things at a distance; a month is size, long fur, long leaps, ferocious eyes, an absolute difference. Andrea, a month is a rabbit, it really makes a real rabbit; but in the maiden moment, the warm bustling fleece covering an inalienable presence . . . like a poem in its first minutes, "fruit of an Idumean night" as much one as oneself . . . and afterwards not so much one, so distant and isolated in its flat white world the size of a letter.

With all that, I decided to kill the rabbit almost as soon as it was born. I was going to live at your place for four months: four, perhaps with luck three—tablespoonful of alcohol down its throat. (Do you know pity permits you to kill a small rabbit instantly by giving it a tablespoon of alcohol to drink? Its flesh tastes better afterward, they say, however, I . . . Three or four tablespoonsful of alcohol, then the bathroom or a package to put in the rubbish.)

Rising up past the third floor, the rabbit was moving in the palm of my hand. Sara was waiting upstairs to help me get the valises in . . . Could I explain that it was a whim? Something about passing a pet store? I wrapped the tiny creature in my handkerchief, put him into my overcoat pocket, leaving the overcoat unbuttoned so as not to squeeze him. He barely budged. His minuscule consciousness would be revealing important facts: that life is a movement upward with a final click, and is also a low ceiling, white and smelling of lavender, enveloping you in the bottom of a warm pit.

Sara saw nothing, she was too fascinated with the arduous problem of adjusting her sense of order to my valise-and-footlocker, my papers and my peevishness at her elaborate explanations in which the words "for example" occurred with distressing frequency. I could hardly get the bathroom door closed; to kill it now. A delicate area of heat surrounded the handkerchief, the little rabbit was extremely white and, I think, prettier than the others. He wasn't looking at me, he just hopped about and was being content, which was even worse than looking at me. I shut him in the empty medicine chest and went on unpacking, disoriented but not unhappy, not feeling guilty, not soaping up my hands to get off the feel of a final convulsion.

I realized that I could not kill him. But that same night I vomited a little black bunny. And two days later another white one. And on the fourth night a tiny grey one.

You must love the handsome wardrobe in your bedroom, with its great door that opens so generously, its empty shelves awaiting my clothes. Now I have them in there. Inside there. True, it seems impossible; not even Sara would believe it. That Sara did not suspect anything, was the result of my continuous preoccupation with a task that takes over my days and nights with the singleminded crash of the portcullis falling, and I go about hardened inside, calcined like that starfish you've put above the bathtub, and at every bath I take it seems all at once to swell with salt and whiplashes of sun and great rumbles of profundity.

They sleep during the day. There are ten of them. During the day they sleep. With the door closed, the wardrobe is a diurnal night for them alone, there they sleep out their night in a sedate obedience. When I leave for work I take the bedroom keys with me. Sara must think that I mistrust her honesty and looks at me doubtfully, every morning she looks as though she's about to say something to me, but in the end she remains silent and I am that much happier. (When she straightens up the bedroom between nine and ten, I make noise in the living room, put on a Benny Carter record which fills the whole apartment, and as Sara is a *saetas* and *pasodobles*[5] fan, the wardrobe seems to be silent, and for the most part it is, because for the rabbits it's night still and repose is the order of the day.)

Their day begins an hour after supper when Sara brings in the tray with the delicate tinkling of the sugar tongs, wishes me good night—yes, she wishes me, Andrea, the most ironic thing is that she wishes me good night—shuts herself in her room, and promptly I'm by myself, alone with the closed-up wardrobe, alone with my obligation and my melancholy.

I let them out, they hop agilely to the party in the living room, sniffing briskly at the clover hidden in my pockets which makes ephemeral lacy patterns on the carpet which they alter, remove, finish up in a minute. They eat well, quietly and correctly; until that moment I have nothing to say, I just watch them from the sofa, a useless book in my hand—I who wanted to read all of Giraudoux, Andrea, and López's Argentine history that you keep on the lower shelf—and they eat up the clover.

There are ten. Almost all of them white. They lift their warm heads toward the lamps in the living room, the three motionless suns of their day; they love the light because their night has neither moon nor sun nor stars nor

---

5. A form of dance music in Spain and Latin America. *Saetas:* a form of flamenco music.

streetlamps. They gaze at their triple sun and are content. That's when they hop about on the carpet, into the chairs, ten tiny blotches shift like a moving constellation from one part to another, while I'd like to see them quiet, see them at my feet and being quiet—somewhat the dream of any god, Andrea, a dream the gods never see fulfilled—something quite different from wriggling in behind the portrait of Miguel de Unamuno, then off to the pale green urn, over into the dark hollow of the writing desk, always fewer than ten, always six or eight and I asking myself where the two are that are missing, and what if Sara should get up for some reason, and the presidency of Rivadavia which is what I want to read in López's history.

Andrea, I don't know how I stand up under it. You remember that I came to your place for some rest. It's not my fault if I vomit a bunny from time to time, if this moving changed me inside as well—not nominalism, it's not magic either, it's just that things cannot alter like that all at once, sometimes things reverse themselves brutally and when you expect the slap on the right cheek—. Like that, Andrea, or some other way, but always like that.

It's night while I'm writing you. It's three in the afternoon, but I'm writing you during their night. They sleep during the day. What a relief this office is! Filled with shouts, commands, Royal typewriters, vice presidents and mimeograph machines! What relief, what peace, what horror, Andrea! They're calling me to the telephone now. It was some friends upset about my monasterial nights, Luis inviting me out for a stroll or Jorge insisting—he's bought a ticket for me for this concert. I hardly dare to say no to them, I invent long and ineffectual stories about my poor health, I'm behind in the translations, any evasion possible. And when I get back home and am in the elevator—that stretch between the first and second floors—night after night, hopelessly, I formulate the vain hope that really it isn't true.

I'm doing the best I can to see that they don't break your things. They've nibbled away a little at the books on the lowest shelf, you'll find the backs repasted, which I did so that Sara wouldn't notice it. That lamp with the porcelain belly full of butterflies and old cowboys, do you like that very much? The crack where the piece was broken out barely shows, I spent a whole night doing it with a special cement that they sold me in an English shop—you know the English stores have the best cements—and now I sit beside it so that one of them can't reach it again with its paws (it's almost lovely to see how they like to stand on their hind legs, nostalgia for that so-distant humanity, perhaps an imitation of their god walking about and looking at them darkly; besides which, you will have observed—when you were a baby, perhaps—that you can put a bunny in the corner against the wall like a punishment, and he'll stand there, paws against the wall and very quiet, for hours and hours).

At 5 A.M. (I slept a little stretched out on the green sofa, waking up at every velvety-soft dash, every slightest clink) I put them in the wardrobe and do the cleaning up. That way Sara always finds everything in order, although at times I've noticed a restrained astonishment, a stopping to look at some object, a slight discoloration in the carpet, and again the desire to ask me something, but then I'm whistling Franck's[6] *Symphonic Variations* in a way that always prevents her. How can I tell you about it, Andrea, the minute mishaps of this soundless

---

6. César Auguste Franck (1822–1890), Belgian-French composer.

and vegetal dawn, half asleep on what staggered path picking up butt-ends of clover, individual leaves, white hunks of fur, falling against the furniture, crazy from lack of sleep, and I'm behind in my Gide, Troyat[7] I haven't gotten to translating, and my reply to a distant young lady who will be asking herself already if . . . why go on with all this, why go on with this letter I keep trying to write between telephone calls and interviews.

Andrea, dear Andrea, my consolation is that there are ten of them and no more. It's been fifteen days since I held the last bunny in the palm of my hand, since then nothing, only the ten of them with me, their diurnal night and growing, ugly already and getting long hair, adolescents now and full of urgent needs and crazy whims, leaping on top of the bust of Antinoös[8] (it is Antinoös, isn't it, that boy who looks blindly?) or losing themselves in the living room where their movements make resounding thumps, so much so that I ought to chase them out of there for fear that Sara will hear them and appear before me in a fright and probably in her nightgown—it would have to be like that with Sara, she'd be in her nightgown—and then . . . Only ten, think of that little happiness I have in the middle of it all, the growing calm with which, on my return home, I cut past the rigid ceilings of the first and second floors.

I was interrupted because I had to attend a committee meeting. I'm continuing the letter here at your house, Andrea, under the soundless grey light of another dawn. Is it really the next day, Andrea? A bit of white on the page will be all you'll have to represent the bridge, hardly a period on a page between yesterday's letter and today's. How tell you that in that interval everything has gone smash? Where you see that simple period I hear the circling belt of water break the dam in its fury, this side of the paper for me, this side of my letter to you I can't write with the same calm which I was sitting in when I had to put it aside to go to the committee meeting. Wrapped in their cube of night, sleeping without a worry in the world, eleven bunnies; perhaps even now, but no, not now—In the elevator then, or coming into the building; it's not important now where, if the when is now, if it can happen in any now of those that are left to me.

Enough now, I've written this because it's important to me to let you know that I was not all that responsible for the unavoidable and helpless destruction of your home. I'll leave this letter here for you, it would be indecent if the mailman should deliver it some fine clear morning in Paris. Last night I turned the books on the second shelf in the other direction; they were already reaching that high, standing up on their hind legs or jumping, they gnawed off the backs to sharpen their teeth—not that they were hungry, they had all the clover I had bought for them, I store it in the drawers of the writing desk. They tore the curtains, the coverings on the easy chairs, the edge of Augusto Torres'[9] self-portrait, they got fluff all over the rug and besides they yipped, there's no word for it, they stood in a circle under the light of the lamp, in a circle as

---

7. Henri Troyat (1911–2007), French writer of Russian origin (real name, Lev Tarassov). André Gide (1869–1951), French writer. **8.** Favorite of the Roman emperor Hadrian (76–138 C.E.); after Antinoös drowned in the Nile, he was declared a god by Hadrian and became the subject of many statues. **9.** Spanish painter (1913–1992).

though they were adoring me, and suddenly they were yipping, they were crying like I never believed rabbits could cry.

I tried in vain to pick up all the hair that was ruining the rug, to smooth out the edges of the fabric they'd chewed on, to shut them up again in the wardrobe. Day is coming, maybe Sara's getting up early. It's almost queer, I'm not disturbed so much about Sara. It's almost queer, I'm not disturbed to see them gamboling about looking for something to play with. I'm not so much to blame, you'll see when you get here that I've repaired a lot of the things that were broken with the cement I bought in the English shop, I did what I could to keep from being a nuisance . . . As far as I'm concerned, going from ten to eleven is like an unbridgeable chasm. You understand: ten was fine, with a wardrobe, clover and hope, so many things could happen for the better. But not with eleven, because to say eleven is already to say twelve for sure, and Andrea, twelve would be thirteen. So now it's dawn and a cold solitude in which happiness ends, reminiscences, you and perhaps a good deal more. This balcony over the street is filled with dawn, the first sounds of the city waking. I don't think it will be difficult to pick up eleven small rabbits splattered over the pavement, perhaps they won't even be noticed, people will be too occupied with the other body, it would be more proper to remove it quickly before the early students pass through on their way to school.

1967

STEPHEN CRANE
1871–1900

Crane was born in Newark, New Jersey, the son of a Methodist minister. After schooling at Lafayette College and Syracuse University, he worked in New York as a freelance journalist. In 1893 he published at his own expense the novel *Maggie: A Girl of the Streets,* a pioneering work of sociological realism. Two years later he brought out his famous short novel about the Civil War, *The Red Badge of Courage,* which in theme and technique foreshadows the war novels of the twentieth century. His short stories and experimental poetry also anticipate the ironic realism of the decades ahead. In his brief and energetic life he published fourteen books while acting out, in his personal adventures, the legend of the writer as soldier of fortune. On his way to Cuba for the first time he picked up a mistress at the Hotel de Dream in Jacksonville, Florida—a woman who accompanied him when he went on to Greece as a war correspondent. Malicious gossip about his private life subsequently drove him from America to England, where he settled in 1897 and made friends with leading English writers. In his travels he had accumulated a malignant tangle of debts. He was trying to free himself of them by writing when tuberculosis killed him, his promise only partially fulfilled. His short stories were collected in *The Open Boat and Other Tales of Adventure* (1898), *The Monster and Other Stories* (1899), and *Wounds in the Rain* (1900). His complete works in prose and verse were published in 1925–26.

The Open Boat

A Tale Intended to Be after the Fact:[1] Being the Experience of Four Men from the Sunk Steamer COMMODORE

I

None of them knew the color of the sky. Their eyes glanced level and were fastened upon the waves that swept toward them. These waves were of the hue of slate, save for the tops, which were of foaming white, and all of the men knew the colors of the sea. The horizon narrowed and widened, and dipped and rose, and at all times its edge was jagged with waves that seemed thrust up in points like rocks.

---

1. Crane underwent the adventure here re-created in fiction. He also wrote a journalistic account of it, published in the *New York Press* (January 7, 1897).

Many a man ought to have a bathtub larger than the boat which here rode upon the sea. These waves were most wrongfully and barbarously abrupt and tall, and each froth-top was a problem in small-boat navigation.

The cook squatted in the bottom, and looked with both eyes at the six inches of gunwale which separated him from the ocean. His sleeves were rolled over his fat forearms, and the two flaps of his unbuttoned vest dangled as he bent to bail out the boat. Often he said, "Gawd! that was a narrow clip." As he remarked it he invariably gazed eastward over the broken sea.

The oiler, steering with one of the two oars in the boat, sometimes raised himself suddenly to keep clear of water that swirled in over the stern. It was a thin little oar, and it seemed often ready to snap.

The correspondent, pulling at the other oar, watched the waves and wondered why he was there.

The injured captain, lying in the bow, was at this time buried in that profound dejection and indifference which comes, temporarily at least, to even the bravest and most enduring when, willy-nilly, the firm fails, the army loses, the ship goes down. The mind of the master of a vessel is rooted deep in the timbers of her, though he command for a day or a decade; and this captain had on him the stern impression of a scene in the grays of dawn of seven turned faces, and later a stump of a topmast with a white ball on it, that slashed to and fro at the waves, went low and lower, and down. Thereafter there was something strange in his voice. Although steady, it was deep with mourning, and of a quality beyond oration or tears.

"Keep 'er a little more south, Billie," said he.

"A little more south, sir," said the oiler in the stern.

A seat in his boat was not unlike a seat upon a bucking broncho, and by the same token a broncho is not much smaller. The craft pranced and reared and plunged like an animal. As each wave came, and she rose for it, she seemed like a horse making at a fence outrageously high. The manner of her scramble over these walls of water is a mystic thing, and, moreover, at the top of them were ordinarily these problems in white water, the foam racing down from the summit of each wave requiring a new leap, and a leap from the air. Then, after scornfully bumping a crest, she would slide and race and splash down a long incline, and arrive bobbing and nodding in front of the next menace.

A singular disadvantage of the sea lies in the fact that after successfully surmounting one wave you discover that there is another behind it just as important and just as nervously anxious to do something effective in the way of swamping boats. In a ten-foot dinghy one can get an idea of the resources of the sea in the line of waves that is not probable to the average experience, which is never at sea in a dinghy. As each slaty wall of water approached, it shut all else from the view of the men in the boat, and it was not difficult to imagine that this particular wave was the final outburst of the ocean, the last effort of the grim water. There was a terrible grace in the move of the waves, and they came in silence, save for the snarling of the crests.

In the wan light the faces of the men must have been gray. Their eyes must have glinted in strange ways as they gazed steadily astern. Viewed from a balcony, the whole thing would, doubtless, have been weirdly picturesque. But the men in the boat had no time to see it, and if they had had leisure, there were other things to occupy their minds. The sun swung steadily up the sky, and they knew it was broad day because the color of the sea changed from slate to emerald-green streaked with amber lights, and the foam was like tumbling snow. The process of the breaking day was unknown to them. They were aware only of this effect upon the color of the waves that rolled toward them.

In disjointed sentences the cook and the correspondent argued as to the difference between a life-saving station and a house of refuge. The cook had said: "There's a house of refuge just north of the Mosquito Inlet Light, and as soon as they see us they'll come off in their boat and pick us up."

"As soon as who see us?" said the correspondent.

"The crew," said the cook.

"Houses of refuge don't have crews," said the correspondent. "As I understand them, they are only places where clothes and grub are stored for the benefit of shipwrecked people. They don't carry crews."

"Oh, yes, they do," said the cook.

"No, they don't," said the correspondent.

"Well, we're not there yet, anyhow," said the oiler, in the stern.

"Well," said the cook, "perhaps it's not a house of refuge that I'm thinking of as being near Mosquito Inlet Light; perhaps it's a life-saving station."

"We're not there yet," said the oiler in the stern.

II

As the boat bounced from the top of each wave the wind tore through the hair of the hatless men, and as the craft plopped her stern down again the spray slashed past them. The crest of each of these waves was a hill, from the top of which the men surveyed for a moment a broad tumultuous expanse, shining and wind-riven. It was probably splendid, it was probably glorious, this play of the free sea, wild with lights of emerald and white and amber.

"Bully good thing it's an on-shore wind," said the cook. "If not, where would we be? Wouldn't have a show."

"That's right," said the correspondent.

The busy oiler nodded his assent.

Then the captain, in the bow, chuckled in a way that expressed humor, contempt, tragedy, all in one. "Do you think we've got much of a show now, boys?" said he.

Whereupon the three were silent, save for a trifle of hemming and hawing. To express any particular optimism at this time they felt to be childish and stupid, but they all doubtless possessed this sense of the situation in their minds. A young man thinks doggedly at such times. On the other hand, the ethics of their condition was decidedly against any open suggestion of hopelessness. So they were silent.

"Oh, well," said the captain, soothing his children, "we'll get ashore all right."

But there was that in his tone which made them think; so the oiler quoth, "Yes! if this wind holds."

The cook was bailing. "Yes! if we don't catch hell in the surf."

Canton-flannel[2] gulls flew near and far. Sometimes they sat down on the sea, near patches of brown seaweed that rolled over the waves with a movement like carpets on a line in a gale. The birds sat comfortably in groups, and they were envied by some in the dinghy, for the wrath of the sea was no more to them than it was to a covey of prairie chickens a thousand miles inland. Often they came very close and stared at the men with black bead-like eyes. At these times they were uncanny and sinister in their unblinking scrutiny, and the men hooted angrily at them, telling them to be gone. One came, and evidently decided to alight on the top of the captain's head. The bird flew parallel to the boat and did not circle, but made short sidelong jumps in the air in chicken fashion. His black eyes were wistfully fixed upon the captain's head. "Ugly brute," said the oiler to the bird. "You look as if you were made with a jackknife." The cook and the correspondent swore darkly at the creature. The captain naturally wished to knock it away with the end of the heavy painter,[3] but he did not dare do it, because anything resembling an emphatic gesture would have capsized this freighted boat; and so, with his open hand, the captain gently and carefully waved the gull away. After it had been discouraged from the pursuit the captain breathed easier on account of his hair, and others breathed easier because the bird struck their minds at this time as being somehow gruesome and ominous.

In the meantime the oiler and the correspondent rowed; and also they rowed. They sat together in the same seat, and each rowed an oar. Then the oiler took both oars; then the correspondent took both oars, then the oiler; then the correspondent. They rowed and they rowed. The very ticklish part of the business was when the time came for the reclining one in the stern to take his turn at the oars. By the very last star of truth, it is easier to steal eggs from under a hen than it was to change seats in the dinghy. First the man in the stern slid his hand along the thwart and moved with care, as if he were of Sèvres.[4] Then the man in the rowing-seat slid his hand along the other thwart. It was all done with the most extraordinary care. As the two sidled past each other, the whole party kept watchful eyes on the coming wave, and the captain cried: "Look out, now! Steady, there!"

The brown mats of seaweed that appeared from time to time were like islands, bits of earth. They were travelling, apparently, neither one way nor the other. They were, to all intents, stationary. They informed the men in the boat that it was making progress slowly toward the land.

The captain, rearing cautiously in the bow after the dinghy soared on a great swell, said that he had seen the lighthouse at Mosquito Inlet. Presently the cook remarked that he had seen it. The correspondent was at the oars then, and for some reason he too wished to look at the lighthouse; but his back was toward the far shore, and the waves were important, and for some time he could not seize an opportunity to turn his head. But at last there came a wave more gentle than the others, and when at the crest of it he swiftly scoured the western horizon.

"See it?" said the captain.

---

2. Actually a plain-weave cotton fabric.   **3.** A mooring rope attached to the bow of a boat.   **4.** A type of fine china.

"No," said the correspondent, slowly; "I didn't see anything."

"Look again," said the captain. He pointed. "It's exactly in that direction."

At the top of another wave the correspondent did as he was bid, and this time his eyes chanced on a small, still thing on the edge of the swaying horizon. It was precisely like the point of a pin. It took an anxious eye to find a lighthouse so tiny.

"Think we'll make it, Captain?"

"If this wind holds and the boat don't swamp, we can't do much else," said the captain.

The little boat, lifted by each towering sea and splashed viciously by the crests, made progress that in the absence of seaweed was not apparent to those in her. She seemed just a wee thing wallowing, miraculously top up, at the mercy of five oceans. Occasionally a great spread of water, like white flames, swarmed into her.

"Bail her, cook," said the captain, serenely.

"All right, Captain," said the cheerful cook.

III

It would be difficult to describe the subtle brotherhood of men that was here established on the seas. No one said that it was so. No one mentioned it. But it dwelt in the boat, and each man felt it warm him. They were a captain, an oiler, a cook, and a correspondent, and they were friends—friends in a more curiously iron-bound degree than may be common. The hurt captain, lying against the water jar in the bow, spoke always in a low voice and calmly; but he could never command a more ready and swiftly obedient crew than the motley three of the dinghy. It was more than a mere recognition of what was best for the common safety. There was surely in it a quality that was personal and heart-felt. And after this devotion to the commander of the boat, there was this comradeship, that the correspondent, for instance, who had been taught to be cynical of men, knew even at the time was the best experience of his life. But no one said that it was so. No one mentioned it.

"I wish we had a sail," remarked the captain. "We might try my overcoat on the end of an oar, and give you two boys a chance to rest." So the cook and the correspondent held the mast and spread wide the overcoat; the oiler steered; and the little boat made good way with her new rig. Sometimes the oiler had to scull sharply to keep a sea from breaking into the boat, but otherwise sailing was a success.

Meanwhile the lighthouse had been growing slowly larger. It had now almost assumed color, and appeared like a little gray shadow on the sky. The man at the oars could not be prevented from turning his head rather often to try for a glimpse of this little gray shadow.

At last, from the top of each wave, the men in the tossing boat could see land. Even as the lighthouse was an upright shadow on the sky, this land seemed but a long black shadow on the sea. It certainly was thinner than paper. "We must be about opposite New Smyrna,"[5] said the cook, who had

---

5. Town on the Florida coast.

coasted this shore often in schooners. "Captain, by the way, I believe they abandoned that life-saving station there about a year ago."

"Did they?" said the captain.

The wind slowly died away. The cook and the correspondent were not now obliged to slave in order to hold high the oar. But the waves continued their old impetuous swooping at the dinghy, and the little craft, no longer underway, struggled woundily over them. The oiler or the correspondent took the oars again.

Shipwrecks are *apropos* of nothing. If men could only train for them and have them occur when the men had reached pink condition, there would be less drowning at sea. Of the four in the dinghy none had slept any time worth mentioning for two days and two nights previous to embarking in the dinghy, and in the excitement of clambering about the deck of a foundering ship they had also forgotten to eat heartily.

For these reasons, and for others, neither the oiler nor the correspondent was fond of rowing at this time. The correspondent wondered ingenuously how in the name of all that was sane could there be people who thought it amusing to row a boat. It was not an amusement; it was a diabolical punishment, and even a genius of mental aberrations could never conclude that it was anything but a horror to the muscles and a crime against the back. He mentioned to the boat in general how the amusement of rowing struck him, and the weary-faced oiler smiled in full sympathy. Previously to the foundering, by the way, the oiler had worked a double watch in the engine-room of the ship.

"Take her easy, now, boys," said the captain. "Don't spend yourselves. If we have to run a surf you'll need all your strength, because we'll sure have to swim for it. Take your time."

Slowly the land arose from the sea. From a black line it became a line of black and a line of white—trees and sand. Finally the captain said that he could make out a house on the shore. "That's the house of refuge, sure," said the cook. "They'll see us before long, and come out after us."

The distant lighthouse reared high. "The keeper ought to be able to make us out now, if he's looking through a glass," said the captain. "He'll notify the life-saving people."

"None of those other boats could have got ashore to give word of the wreck," said the oiler, in a low voice, "else the life-boat would be out hunting us."

Slowly and beautifully the land loomed out of the sea. The wind came again. It had veered from the northeast to the southeast. Finally a new sound struck the ears of the men in the boat. It was the low thunder of the surf on the shore. "We'll never be able to make the lighthouse now," said the captain. "Swing her head a little more north, Billie."

"A little more north, sir," said the oiler.

Whereupon the little boat turned her nose once more down the wind, and all but the oarsman watched the shore grow. Under the influence of this expansion doubt and direful apprehension were leaving the minds of the men. The management of the boat was still most absorbing, but it could not prevent a quiet cheerfulness. In an hour, perhaps, they would be ashore.

Their backbones had become thoroughly used to balancing in the boat, and they now rode this wild colt of a dinghy like circus men. The correspondent thought that he had been drenched to the skin, but happening to feel in the top pocket of his coat, he found therein eight cigars. Four of them were soaked with sea-water; four were perfectly scatheless. After a search, somebody produced three dry matches; and thereupon the four waifs rode impudently in their little boat and, with an assurance of an impending rescue shining in their eyes, puffed at the big cigars, and judged well and ill of all men. Everybody took a drink of water.

I V

"Cook," remarked the captain, "there don't seem to be any signs of life about your house of refuge."

"No," replied the cook. "Funny they don't see us!"

A broad stretch of lowly coast lay before the eyes of the men. It was of low dunes topped with dark vegetation. The roar of the surf was plain, and sometimes they could see the white lip of a wave as it spun up the beach. A tiny house was blocked out black upon the sky. Southward, the slim lighthouse lifted its little gray length.

Tide, wind, and waves were swinging the dinghy northward. "Funny they don't see us," said the men.

The surf's roar was here dulled, but its tone was nevertheless thunderous and mighty. As the boat swam over the great rollers the men sat listening to this roar. "We'll swamp sure," said everybody.

It is fair to say here that there was not a life-saving station within twenty miles in either direction; but the men did not know this fact, and in consequence they made dark and opprobrious remarks concerning the eyesight of the nation's life-savers. Four scowling men sat in the dinghy and surpassed records in the invention of epithets.

"Funny they don't see us."

The light-heartedness of a former time had completely faded. To their sharpened minds it was easy to conjure pictures of all kinds of incompetency and blindness and, indeed, cowardice. There was the shore of the populous land, and it was bitter and bitter to them that from it came no sign.

"Well," said the captain, ultimately, "I suppose we'll have to make a try for ourselves. If we stay out here too long, we'll none of us have strength left to swim after the boat swamps."

And so the oiler, who was at the oars, turned the boat straight for the shore. There was a sudden tightening of muscles. There was some thinking.

"If we don't all get ashore," said the captain—"if we don't all get ashore, I suppose you fellows know where to send news of my finish?"

They then briefly exchanged some addresses and admonitions. As for the reflections of the men, there was a great deal of rage in them. Perchance they might be formulated thus: "If I am going to be drowned—if I am going to be drowned—if I am going to be drowned, why, in the name of the seven mad gods who rule the sea, was I allowed to come thus far and contemplate sand and trees? Was I brought here merely to have my nose dragged away as I was about to nibble the sacred cheese of life? It is preposterous. If this old ninny-woman, Fate, cannot do better than this, she should be deprived of the management of men's fortunes. She is an old hen who knows not her intention. If she has decided to drown me, why did she not do it in the beginning and save me all this trouble? The whole affair is absurd. . . . But no; she cannot mean to drown me. She dare not drown me. She cannot drown me. Not after all this work." Afterward the man might have had an impulse to shake his fist at the clouds. "Just you drown me, now, and then hear what I call you!"

The billows that came at this time were more formidable. They seemed always just about to break and roll over the little boat in a turmoil of foam. There was a preparatory and long growl in the speech of them. No mind unused to the sea would have concluded that the dinghy could ascend these sheer heights in time. The shore was still afar. The oiler was a wily surfman. "Boys," he said, swiftly, "she won't live three minutes more, and we're too far out to swim. Shall I take her to sea again, Captain?"

"Yes; go ahead!" said the captain.

This oiler, by a series of quick miracles and fast and steady oarsmanship, turned the boat in the middle of the surf and took her safely to sea again.

There was a considerable silence as the boat bumped over the furrowed sea to deeper water. Then somebody in gloom spoke: "Well, anyhow, they must have seen us from the shore by now."

The gulls went in slanting flight up the wind toward the gray, desolate east. A squall, marked by dingy clouds and clouds brick-red, like smoke from a burning building, appeared from the southeast.

"What do you think of those life-saving people? Ain't they peaches?"

"Funny they haven't seen us."

"Maybe they think we're out here for sport! Maybe they think we're fishin'. Maybe they think we're damned fools."

It was a long afternoon. A changed tide tried to force them southward, but wind and wave said northward. Far ahead, where coast-line, sea, and sky formed their mighty angle, there were little dots which seemed to indicate a city on the shore.

"St. Augustine?"

The captain shook his head. "Too near Mosquito Inlet."

And the oiler rowed, and then the correspondent rowed; then the oiler rowed. It was a weary business. The human back can become the seat of more aches and pains than are registered in books for the composite anatomy of a regiment. It is a limited area, but it can become the theatre of innumerable muscular conflicts, tangles, wrenches, knots, and other comforts.

"Did you ever like to row, Billie?" asked the correspondent.

"No," said the oiler. "Hang it."

When one exchanged the rowing-seat for a place in the bottom of the boat, he suffered a bodily depression that caused him to be careless of everything save an obligation to wiggle one finger. There was cold sea-water swashing to and fro in the boat, and he lay in it. His head, pillowed on a thwart, was within an inch of the swirl of a wave-crest, and sometimes a particularly obstreperous sea came inboard and drenched him once more. But these matters did not annoy him. It is almost certain that if the boat had capsized he would have tumbled comfortably out upon the ocean as if he felt sure that it was a great soft mattress.

"Look! There's a man on the shore!"

"Where?"

"There? See 'im? See 'im?"

"Yes, sure! He's walking along."

"Now he's stopped. Look! He's facing us!"

"He's waving at us!"

"So he is! By thunder!"

"Ah, now we're all right! Now we're all right! There'll be a boat out here for us in half an hour."

"He's going on. He's running. He's going up to that house there."

The remote beach seemed lower than the sea, and it required a searching glance to discern the little black figure. The captain saw a floating stick, and they rowed to it. A bath towel was by some weird chance in the boat, and, tying this on the stick, the captain waved it. The oarsman did not dare turn his head, so he was obliged to ask questions.

"What's he doing now?"

"He's standing still again. He's looking, I think. . . . There he goes again—toward the house. . . . Now he's stopped again."

"Is he waving at us?"

"No, not now; he was, though."

"Look! There comes another man!"

"He's running."

"Look at him go, would you!"

"Why, he's on a bicycle. Now he's met the other man. They're both waving at us. Look!"

"There comes something up the beach."

"What the devil is that thing?"

"Why, it looks like a boat."

"Why, certainly, it's a boat."

"No; it's on wheels."

"Yes, so it is. Well, that must be the life-boat. They drag them along shore on a wagon."

"That's the life-boat, sure."

"No, by God, it's—it's an omnibus."

"I tell you it's a life-boat."

"It is not! It's an omnibus. I can see it plain. See? One of these big hotel omnibuses."

"By thunder, you're right. It's an omnibus, sure as fate. What do you suppose they are doing with an omnibus? Maybe they are going around collecting the life-crew, hey?"

"That's it, likely. Look! There's a fellow waving a little black flag. He's standing on the steps of the omnibus. There come those other two fellows. Now they're all talking together. Look at the fellow with the flag. Maybe he ain't waving it!"

"That ain't a flag, is it? That's his coat. Why, certainly, that's his coat."

"So it is; it's his coat. He's taken it off and is waving it around his head. But would you look at him swing it!"

"Oh, say, there isn't any life-saving station there. That's just a winter-resort hotel omnibus that has brought over some of the boarders to see us drown."

"What's that idiot with the coat mean? What's he signaling, anyhow?"

"It looks as if he were trying to tell us to go north. There must be a life-saving station up there."

"No; he thinks we're fishing. Just giving us a merry hand. See? Ah, there, Willie!"

"Well, I wish I could make something out of those signals. What do you suppose he means?"

"He don't mean anything; he's just playing."

"Well, if he'd just signal us to try the surf again, or to go to sea and wait, or go north, or go south, or go to hell, there would be some reason in it. But look at him! He just stands there and keeps his coat revolving like a wheel. The ass!"

"There come more people."

"Now there's quite a mob. Look! Isn't that a boat?"

"Where? Oh, I see where you mean. No, that's no boat."

"That fellow is still waving his coat."

"He must think we like to see him do that. Why don't he quit it? It don't mean anything."

"I don't know. I think he is trying to make us go north. It must be that there's a life-saving station there somewhere."

"Say, he ain't tired yet. Look at 'im wave!"

"Wonder how long he can keep that up. He's been revolving his coat ever since he caught sight of us. He's an idiot. Why aren't they getting men to bring a boat out? A fishing boat—one of those big yawls—could come out here all right. Why don't he do something?"

"Oh, it's all right now."

"They'll have a boat out here for us in less than no time, now that they've seen us."

A faint yellow tone came into the sky over the low land. The shadows on the sea slowly deepened. The wind bore coldness with it, and the men began to shiver.

"Holy smoke!" said one, allowing his voice to express his impious mood, "if we keep on monkeying out here! If we've got to flounder out here all night!"

"Oh, we'll never have to stay here all night! Don't you worry. They've seen us now, and it won't be long before they'll come chasing out after us."

The shore grew dusky. The man waving a coat blended gradually into this gloom, and it swallowed in the same manner the omnibus and the group of people. The spray, when it dashed uproariously over the side, made the voyagers shrink and swear like men who were being branded.

"I'd like to catch the chump who waved the coat. I feel like socking him one, just for luck."

"Why? What did he do?"

"Oh, nothing, but then he seemed so damned cheerful."

In the meantime the oiler rowed, and then the correspondent rowed, and then the oiler rowed. Gray-faced and bowed forward, they mechanically, turn by turn, plied the leaden oars. The form of the lighthouse had vanished from the southern horizon, but finally a pale star appeared, just lifting from the sea. The streaked saffron in the west passed before the all-merging darkness, and the sea to the east was black. The land had vanished, and was expressed only by the low and drear thunder of the surf.

"If I am going to be drowned—if I am going to be drowned—if I am going to be drowned, why, in the name of the seven mad gods who rule the sea, was I allowed to come thus far and contemplate sand and trees? Was I brought here merely to have my nose dragged away as I was about to nibble the sacred cheese of life?"

The patient captain, drooped over the water-jar, was sometimes obliged to speak to the oarsman.

"Keep her head up! Keep her head up!"

"Keep her head up, sir." The voices were weary and low.

This was surely a quiet evening. All save the oarsman lay heavily and list-lessly in the boat's bottom. As for him, his eyes were just capable of noting the tall black waves that swept forward in a most sinister silence, save for an occasional subdued growl of a crest.

The cook's head was on a thwart, and he looked without interest at the water under his nose. He was deep in other scenes. Finally he spoke. "Billie," he murmured, dreamfully, "what kind of pie do you like best?"

V

"Pie!" said the oiler and the correspondent, agitatedly. "Don't talk about those things, blast you!"

"Well," said the cook, "I was just thinking about ham sandwiches, and——"

A night on the sea in an open boat is a long night. As darkness settled finally, the shine of the light, lifting from the sea in the south, changed to full gold. On the northern horizon a new light appeared, a small bluish gleam on the edge of the waters. These two lights were the furniture of the world. Otherwise there was nothing but waves.

Two men huddled in the stern, and distances were so magnificent in the dinghy that the rower was enabled to keep his feet partly warm by thrusting them under his companions. Their legs indeed extended far under the rowing-seat until they touched the feet of the captain forward. Sometimes, despite the efforts of the tired oarsman, a wave came piling into the boat, an icy wave of the night, and the chilling water soaked them anew. They would twist their bodies for a moment and groan, and sleep the dead sleep once more, while the water in the boat gurgled about them as the craft rocked.

The plan of the oiler and the correspondent was for one to row until he lost the ability, and then arouse the other from his sea-water couch in the bottom of the boat.

The oiler plied the oars until his head drooped forward and the overpowering sleep blinded him; and he rowed yet afterward. Then he touched a man in the bottom of the boat, and called his name. "Will you spell me for a little while?" he said meekly.

"Sure, Billie," said the correspondent, awaking and dragging himself to a sitting position. They exchanged places carefully, and the oiler, cuddling down in the sea-water at the cook's side, seemed to go to sleep instantly.

The particular violence of the sea had ceased. The waves came without snarling. The obligation of the man at the oars was to keep the boat headed so that the tilt of the rollers would not capsize her, and to preserve her from filling when the crests rushed past. The black waves were silent and hard to be seen in the darkness. Often one was almost upon the boat before the oarsman was aware.

In a low voice the correspondent addressed the captain. He was not sure that the captain was awake, although this iron man seemed to be always awake. "Captain, shall I keep her making for that light north, sir?"

The same steady voice answered him. "Yes. Keep it about two points off the port bow."

The cook had tied a life-belt around himself in order to get even the warmth which this clumsy cork contrivance could donate, and he seemed almost stove-like when a rower, whose teeth invariably chattered wildly as soon as he ceased his labor, dropped down to sleep.

The correspondent, as he rowed, looked down at the two men sleeping underfoot. The cook's arm was around the oiler's shoulders, and, with their fragmentary clothing and haggard faces, they were the babes of the sea—a grotesque rendering of the old babes in the wood.

Later he must have grown stupid at his work, for suddenly there was a growling of water, and a crest came with a roar and a swash into the boat, and it was a wonder that it did not set the cook afloat in his life-belt. The cook continued to sleep, but the oiler sat up, blinking his eyes and shaking with the new cold.

"Oh, I'm awful sorry, Billie," said the correspondent, contritely.

"That's all right, old boy," said the oiler, and lay down again and was asleep.

Presently it seemed that even the captain dozed, and the correspondent thought that he was the one man afloat on all the ocean. The wind had a voice as it came over the waves, and it was sadder than the end.

There was a long, loud swishing astern of the boat, and a gleaming trail of phosphorescence, like blue flame, was furrowed on the black waters. It might have been made by a monstrous knife.

Then there came a stillness, while the correspondent breathed with open mouth and looked at the sea.

Suddenly there was another swish and another long flash of bluish light, and this time it was alongside the boat, and might almost have been reached with an oar. The correspondent saw an enormous fin speed like a shadow through the water, hurling the crystalline spray and leaving the long glowing trail.

The correspondent looked over his shoulder at the captain. His face was hidden, and he seemed to be asleep. He looked at the babes of the sea. They certainly were asleep. So, being bereft of sympathy, he leaned a little way to one side and swore softly into the sea.

But the thing did not then leave the vicinity of the boat. Ahead or astern, on one side or the other, at intervals long or short, fled the long sparkling streak, and there was to be heard the *whirroo* of the dark fin. The speed and power of the thing was greatly to be admired. It cut the water like a gigantic and keen projectile.

The presence of this biding thing did not affect the man with the same horror that it would if he had been a picnicker. He simply looked at the sea dully and swore in an undertone.

Nevertheless, it is true that he did not wish to be alone with the thing. He wished one of his companions to awake by chance and keep him company with it. But the captain hung motionless over the water-jar and the oiler and the cook in the bottom of the boat were plunged in slumber.

V I

"If I am going to be drowned—if I am going to be drowned—if I am going to be drowned, why, in the name of the seven mad gods who rule the sea, was I allowed to come this far and contemplate sand and trees?"

During this dismal night, it may be remarked that a man would conclude that it was really the intention of the seven mad gods to drown him, despite the abominable injustice of it. For it was certainly an abominable injustice to drown a man who had worked so hard, so hard. The man felt it would be a crime most unnatural. Other people had drowned at sea since galleys swarmed with painted sails, but still——

When it occurs to a man that nature does not regard him as important, and that she feels she would not maim the universe by disposing of him, he at first wishes to throw bricks at the temple, and he hates deeply the fact that there are no bricks and no temples. Any visible expression of nature would surely be pelleted with his jeers.

Then, if there be no tangible thing to hoot, he feels, perhaps, the desire to confront a personification and indulge in pleas, bowed to one knee, and with hands supplicant, saying, "Yes, but I love myself."

A high cold star on a winter's night is the word he feels that she says to him. Thereafter he knows the pathos of his situation.

The men in the dinghy had not discussed these matters, but each had, no doubt, reflected upon them in silence and according to his mind. There was seldom any expression upon their faces save the general one of complete weariness. Speech was devoted to the business of the boat.

To chime the notes of his emotions, a verse mysteriously entered the correspondent's head. He had even forgotten that he had forgotten this verse, but it suddenly was in his mind.

> *A soldier of the Legion lay dying in Algiers;*
> *There was lack of woman's nursing,*
> *   there was dearth of woman's tears;*
> *But a comrade stood beside him,*
> *   and he took the comrade's hand,*
> *And he said, "I never more shall see*
> *   my own, my native land."*[6]

In his childhood the correspondent had been made acquainted with the fact that a soldier of the Legion lay dying in Algiers, but he had never regarded it as important. Myriads of his schoolfellows had informed him of the soldier's plight, but the dinning had naturally ended by making him perfectly indifferent. He had never considered it his affair that a soldier of the Legion lay dying in Algiers, nor had it appeared to him as a matter for sorrow. It was less to him than the breaking of a pencil's point.

Now, however, it quaintly came to him as a human, living thing. It was no longer merely a picture of a few throes in the breast of a poet, meanwhile drink-

---

6. From "Bingen on the Rhine," a sentimental poem by Caroline Norton (1808–1877).

ing tea and warming his feet at the grate; it was an actuality—stern, mournful, and fine.

The correspondent plainly saw the soldier. He lay on the sand with his feet out straight and still. While his pale left hand was upon his chest in an attempt to thwart the going of his life, the blood came between his fingers. In the far Algerian distance, a city of low square forms was set against a sky that was faint with the last sunset hues. The correspondent, plying the oars and dreaming of the slow and slower movements of the lips of the soldier, was moved by a profound and perfectly impersonal comprehension. He was sorry for the soldier of the Legion who lay dying in Algiers.

The thing which had followed the boat and waited had evidently grown bored at the delay. There was no longer to be heard the slash of the cutwater, and there was no longer the flame of the long trail. The light in the north still glimmered, but it was apparently no nearer to the boat. Sometimes the boom of the surf rang in the correspondent's ears, and he turned the craft seaward then and rowed harder. Southward, some one had evidently built a watch-fire on the beach. It was too low and too far to be seen, but it made a shimmering, roseate reflection upon the bluff in back of it, and this could be discerned from the boat. The wind came stronger, and sometimes a wave suddenly raged out like a mountain-cat, and there was to be seen the sheen and sparkle of a broken crest.

The captain, in the bow, moved on his water-jar and sat erect. "Pretty long night," he observed to the correspondent. He looked at the shore. "Those life-saving people take their time."

"Did you see that shark playing around?"

"Yes, I saw him. He was a big fellow, all right."

"Wish I had known you were awake."

Later the correspondent spoke into the bottom of the boat. "Billie!" There was a slow and gradual disentanglement. "Billie, will you spell me?"

"Sure," said the oiler.

As soon as the correspondent touched the cold, comfortable seawater in the bottom of the boat and had huddled close to the cook's life-belt he was deep in sleep, despite the fact that his teeth played all the popular airs. This sleep was so good to him that it was but a moment before he heard a voice call his name in a tone that demonstrated the last stages of exhaustion. "Will you spell me?"

"Sure, Billie."

The light in the north had mysteriously vanished, but the correspondent took his course from the wide-awake captain.

Later in the night they took the boat farther out to sea, and the captain directed the cook to take one oar at the stern and keep the boat facing the seas. He was to call out if he should hear the thunder of the surf. This plan enabled the oiler and the correspondent to get respite together. "We'll give those boys a chance to get into shape again," said the captain. They curled down and, after a few preliminary chatterings and trembles, slept once more the dead sleep. Neither knew they had bequeathed to the cook the company of another shark, or perhaps the same shark.

As the boat caroused on the waves, spray occasionally bumped over the side and gave them a fresh soaking, but this had no power to break their repose. The ominous slash of the wind and the water affected them as it would have affected mummies.

"Boys," said the cook, with the notes of every reluctance in his voice, "she's drifted in pretty close. I guess one of you had better take her to sea again." The correspondent, aroused, heard the crash of the toppled crests.

As he was rowing, the captain gave him some whiskey-and-water, and this steadied the chills out of him. "If I ever get ashore and anybody shows me even a photograph of an oar——"

At last there was a short conversation.

"Billie! . . . Billie, will you spell me?"

"Sure," said the oiler.

VII

When the correspondent again opened his eyes, the sea and the sky were each of the gray hue of the dawning. Later, carmine and gold was painted upon the waters. The morning appeared finally, in its splendor, with a sky of pure blue, and the sunlight flamed on the tips of the waves.

On the distant dunes were set many little black cottages, and a tall white windmill reared above them. No man, nor dog, nor bicycle appeared on the beach. The cottages might have formed a deserted village.

The voyagers scanned the shore. A conference was held in the boat. "Well," said the captain, "if no help is coming, we might better try a run through the surf right away. If we stay out here much longer we will be too weak to do anything for ourselves at all." The others silently acquiesced in this reasoning. The boat was headed for the beach. The correspondent wondered if none ever ascended the tall wind-tower,[7] and if then they never looked seaward. This tower was a giant, standing with its back to the plight of the ants. It represented in a degree, to the correspondent, the serenity of nature amid the struggles of the individual—nature in the wind, and nature in the vision of men. She did not seem cruel to him then, nor beneficent, nor treacherous, nor wise. But she was indifferent, flatly indifferent. It is, perhaps, plausible that a man in this situation, impressed with the unconcern of the universe, should see the innumerable flaws of his life, and have them taste wickedly in his mind, and wish for another chance. A distinction between right and wrong seems absurdly clear to him, then, in this new ignorance of the grave-edge, and he understands that if he were given another opportunity he would mend his conduct and his words, and be better and brighter during an introduction or at a tea.

"Now, boys," said the captain, "she is going to swamp sure. All we can do is to work her in as far as possible, and then when she swamps, pile out and scramble for the beach. Keep cool now, and don't jump until she swamps sure."

The oiler took the oars. Over his shoulders he scanned the surf. "Captain," he said, "I think I'd better bring her about and keep her head-on to the seas and back her in."

"All right, Billie," said the captain. "Back her in." The oiler swung the boat then, and, seated in the stern, the cook and the correspondent were obliged to look over their shoulders to contemplate the lonely and indifferent shore.

The monstrous inshore rollers heaved the boat high until the men were again enabled to see the white sheets of water scudding up the slanted beach.

7. A watchtower for observing weather.

"We won't get in very close," said the captain. Each time a man could wrest his attention from the rollers, he turned his glance toward the shore, and in the expression of the eyes during this contemplation there was a singular quality. The correspondent, observing the others, knew that they were not afraid, but the full meaning of their glances was shrouded.

As for himself, he was too tired to grapple fundamentally with the fact. He tried to coerce his mind into thinking of it, but the mind was dominated at this time by the muscles, and the muscles said they did not care. It merely occurred to him that if he should drown it would be a shame.

There were no hurried words, no pallor, no plain agitation. The men simply looked at the shore. "Now, remember to get well clear of the boat when you jump," said the captain.

Seaward the crest of a roller suddenly fell with a thunderous crash, and the long white comber came roaring down upon the boat.

"Steady now," said the captain. The men were silent. They turned their eyes from the shore to the comber and waited. The boat slid up the incline, leaped at the furious top, bounced over it, and swung down the long back of the wave. Some water had been shipped, and the cook bailed it out.

But the next crest crashed also. The tumbling, boiling flood of white water caught the boat and whirled it almost perpendicular. Water swarmed in from all sides. The correspondent had his hands on the gunwale at this time, and when the water entered at that place he swiftly withdrew his fingers, as if he objected to wetting them.

The little boat, drunken with this weight of water, reeled and snuggled deeper into the sea.

"Bail her out, cook! Bail her out!" said the captain.

"All right, Captain," said the cook.

"Now, boys, the next one will do for us sure," said the oiler. "Mind to jump clear of the boat."

The third wave moved forward, huge, furious, implacable. It fairly swallowed the dinghy, and almost simultaneously the men tumbled into the sea. A piece of life-belt had lain in the bottom of the boat, and as the correspondent went overboard he held this to his chest with his left hand.

The January water was icy, and reflected immediately that it was colder than he had expected to find it off the coast of Florida. This appeared to his dazed mind as a fact important enough to be noted at the time. The coldness of the water was sad; it was tragic. This fact was somehow mixed and confused with his opinion of his own situation, so that it seemed almost a proper reason for tears. The water was cold.

When he came to the surface he was conscious of little but the noisy water. Afterward he saw his companions in the sea. The oiler was ahead in the race. He was swimming strongly and rapidly. Off to the correspondent's left, the cook's great white and corked back bulged out of the water, and in the rear the captain was hanging with his one good hand to the keel of the overturned dinghy.

There is a certain immovable quality to a shore, and the correspondent wondered at it amid the confusion of the sea.

It seemed also very attractive; but the correspondent knew that it was a long journey, and he paddled leisurely. The piece of life-preserver lay under him, and sometimes he whirled down the incline of a wave as if he were on a hand-sled.

But finally he arrived at a place in the sea where travel was beset with difficulty. He did not pause swimming to inquire what manner of current had caught him, but there his progress ceased. The shore was set before him like a bit of scenery on a stage, and he looked at it and understood with his eyes each detail of it.

As the cook passed, much farther to the left, the captain was calling to him, "Turn over on your back, cook! Turn over on your back and use the oar."

"All right, sir." The cook turned on his back, and, paddling with an oar, went ahead as if he were a canoe.

Presently the boat also passed to the left of the correspondent, with the captain clinging with one hand to the keel. He would have appeared like a man raising himself to look over a board fence if it were not for the extraordinary gymnastics of the boat. The correspondent marvelled that the captain could still hold to it.

They passed on nearer to shore—the oiler, the cook, the captain—and following them went the water-jar, bouncing gaily over the seas.

The correspondent remained in the grip of this strange new enemy, a current. The shore, with its white slope of sand and its green bluff topped with little silent cottages, was spread like a picture before him. It was very near to him then, but he was impressed as one who, in a gallery, looks at a scene from Brittany or Algiers.

He thought: "I am going to drown? Can it be possible? Can it be possible? Can it be possible?" Perhaps an individual must consider his own death to be the final phenomenon of nature.

But later a wave perhaps whirled him out of this small deadly current, for he found suddenly that he could again make progress toward the shore. Later still he was aware that the captain, clinging with one hand to the keel of the dinghy, had his face turned away from the shore and toward him, and was calling his name. "Come to the boat! Come to the boat!"

In his struggle to reach the captain and the boat, he reflected that when one gets properly wearied drowning must really be a comfortable arrangement—a cessation of hostilities accompanied by a large degree of relief; and he was glad of it, for the main thing in his mind for some moments had been horror of the temporary agony; he did not wish to be hurt.

Presently he saw a man running along the shore. He was undressing with most remarkable speed. Coat, trousers, shirt, everything flew magically off him.

"Come to the boat!" called the captain.

"All right, Captain." As the correspondent paddled, he saw the captain let himself down to bottom and leave the boat. Then the correspondent performed his one little marvel of the voyage. A large wave caught him and flung him with ease and supreme speed completely over the boat and far beyond it. It struck him even then as an event in gymnastics and a true miracle of the sea. An overturned boat in the surf is not a plaything to a swimming man.

The correspondent arrived in water that reached only to his waist, but his condition did not enable him to stand for more than a moment. Each wave knocked him into a heap, and the undertow pulled at him.

Then he saw the man who had been running and undressing, and undressing and running, come bounding into the water. He dragged ashore the cook, and then waded toward the captain; but the captain waved him away and sent him to the correspondent. He was naked—naked as a tree in winter; but a halo was about his head, and he shone like a saint. He gave a strong pull, and a long drag, and a bully heave at the correspondent's hand. The correspondent, schooled in the minor formulae, said, "Thanks, old man." But suddenly the man cried, "What's that?" He pointed a swift finger. The correspondent said, "Go."

In the shallows, face downward, lay the oiler. His forehead touched sand that was periodically, between each wave, clear of the sea.

The correspondent did not know all that transpired afterward. When he achieved safe ground he fell, striking the sand with each particular part of his body. It was as if he had dropped from a roof, but the thud was grateful to him.

It seems that instantly the beach was populated with men with blankets, clothes, and flasks, and women with coffee-pots and all the remedies sacred to their minds. The welcome of the land to the men from the sea was warm and generous; but a still and dripping shape was carried slowly up the beach, and the land's welcome for it could only be the different and sinister hospitality of the grave.

When it came night, the white waves paced to and fro in the moonlight, and the wind brought the sound of the great sea's voice to the men on the shore, and they felt that they could then be interpreters.

1897

The Blue Hotel

I

The Palace Hotel at Fort Romper was painted a light blue, a shade that is on the legs of a kind of heron, causing the bird to declare its position against any background. The Palace Hotel, then, was always screaming and howling in a way that made the dazzling winter landscape of Nebraska seem only a gray swampish hush. It stood alone on the prairie, and when the snow was falling the town two hundred yards away was not visible. But when the traveler alighted at the railway station he was obliged to pass the Palace Hotel before he could come upon the company of low clapboard houses which composed Fort Romper, and it was not to be thought that any traveler could pass the Palace Hotel without looking at it. Pat Scully, the proprietor, had proved himself a master of strategy when he chose his paints. It is true that on clear days, when the great transcontinental express, long lines of swaying Pullmans,[1] swept through Fort Romper, passengers were overcome at the sight, and the cult that knows the brown-reds and the subdivisions of the dark greens of the East expressed shame, pity, horror, in a laugh. But to the citizens

---

1. Railroad cars with sleeping accommodations.

of this prairie town and to the people who would naturally stop there, Pat Scully had performed a feat. With this opulence and splendor, these creeds, classes, egotisms, that streamed through Romper on the rails day after day, they had no color in common.

As if the display delights of such a blue hotel were not sufficiently enticing, it was Scully's habit to go every morning and evening to meet the leisurely trains that stopped at Romper and work his seductions upon any man that he might see wavering, gripsack[2] in hand.

One morning, when a snow-crusted engine dragged its long string of freight cars and its one passenger coach to the station, Scully performed the marvel of catching three men. One was a shaky and quick-eyed Swede, with a great shining cheap valise; one was a tall bronzed cowboy, who was on his way to a ranch near the Dakota line; one was a little silent man from the East, who didn't look it, and didn't announce it. Scully practically made them prisoners. He was so nimble and merry and kindly that each probably felt it would be the height of brutality to try to escape. They trudged off over the creaking board sidewalks in the wake of the eager little Irishman. He wore a heavy fur cap squeezed tightly down on his head. It caused his two red ears to stick out stiffly, as if they were made of tin.

At last, Scully, elaborately, with boisterous hospitality, conducted them through the portals of the blue hotel. The room which they entered was small. It seemed to be merely a proper temple for an enormous stove, which, in the center, was humming with godlike violence. At various points on its surface the iron had become luminous and glowed yellow from the heat. Beside the stove Scully's son Johnnie was playing High-Five[3] with an old farmer who had whiskers both gray and sandy. They were quarrelling. Frequently the old farmer turned his face toward a box of sawdust—colored brown from tobacco juice—that was behind the stove, and spat with an air of great impatience and irritation. With a loud flourish of words Scully destroyed the game of cards, and bustled his son upstairs with part of the baggage of the new guests. He himself conducted them to three basins of the coldest water in the world. The cowboy and the Easterner burnished themselves fiery red with this water, until it seemed to be some kind of metal polish. The Swede, however, merely dipped his fingers gingerly and with trepidation. It was notable that throughout this series of small ceremonies the three travelers were made to feel that Scully was very benevolent. He was conferring great favors upon them. He handed the towel from one to another with an air of philanthropic impulse.

Afterward they went to the first room, and sitting about the stove, listened to Scully's officious clamor at his daughters, who were preparing the midday meal. They reflected in the silence of experienced men who tread carefully amid new people. Nevertheless, the old farmer, stationary, invincible in his chair near the warmest part of the stove, turned his face from the sawdust-box frequently and addressed a glowing commonplace to the strangers. Usually he was answered in short but adequate sentences by either the cowboy or the Easterner. The Swede said nothing. He seemed to be occupied in making furtive estimates of each man in the room. One might have thought that he

2. Suitcase.   3. A card game.

had the sense of silly suspicion which comes to guilt. He resembled a badly frightened man.

Later, at dinner, he spoke a little, addressing his conversation entirely to Scully. He volunteered that he had come from New York, where for ten years he had worked as a tailor. These facts seemed to strike Scully as fascinating, and afterward he volunteered that he had lived at Romper for fourteen years. The Swede asked about the crops and the price of labor. He seemed barely to listen to Scully's extended replies. His eyes continued to rove from man to man.

Finally, with a laugh and a wink, he said that some of these Western communities were very dangerous; and after his statement he straightened his legs under the table, tilted his head, and laughed again, loudly. It was plain that the demonstration had no meaning to the others. They looked at him wondering and in silence.

II

As the men trooped heavily back into the front room, the two little windows presented views of a turmoiling sea of snow. The huge arms of the wind were making attempts—mighty, circular, futile—to embrace the flakes as they sped. A gate-post like a still man with a blanched face stood aghast amid this profligate fury. In a hearty voice Scully announced the presence of a blizzard. The guests of the blue hotel, lighting their pipes, assented with grunts of lazy masculine contentment. No island of the sea could be exempt in the degree of this little room with its humming stove. Johnnie, son of Scully, in a tone which defined his opinion of his ability as a card-player, challenged the old farmer of both gray and sandy whiskers to a game of High-Five. The farmer agreed with a contemptuous and bitter scoff. They sat close to the stove, and squared their knees under a wide board. The cowboy and the Easterner watched the game with interest. The Swede remained near the window, aloof, but with a countenance that showed signs of an inexplicable excitement.

The play of Johnnie and the gray-beard was suddenly ended by another quarrel. The old man arose while casting a look of heated scorn at his adversary. He slowly buttoned his coat, and then stalked with fabulous dignity from the room. In the discreet silence of all the other men the Swede laughed. His laughter rang somehow childish. Men by this time had begun to look at him askance, as if they wished to inquire what ailed him.

A new game was formed jocosely. The cowboy volunteered to become the partner of Johnnie, and they all then turned to ask the Swede to throw in his lot with the little Easterner. He asked some questions about the game, and, learning that it wore many names, and that he had played it when it was under an alias, he accepted the invitation. He strode toward the men nervously, as if he expected to be assaulted. Finally, seated, he gazed from face to face and laughed shrilly. This laugh was so strange that the Easterner looked up quickly, the cowboy sat intent and with his mouth open, and Johnnie paused, holding the cards with still fingers.

Afterward there was a short silence. Then Johnnie said, "Well, let's get at it. Come on now!" They pulled their chairs forward until their knees were bunched under the board. They began to play, and their interest in the game caused the others to forget the manner of the Swede.

The cowboy was a board-whacker. Each time that he held superior cards he whanged them, one by one, with exceeding force, down upon the improvised table, and took the tricks with a glowing air of prowess and pride that sent thrills of indignation into the hearts of his opponents. A game with a board-whacker in it is sure to become intense. The countenances of the Easterner and the Swede were miserable whenever the cowboy thundered down his aces and kings, while Johnnie, his eyes gleaming with joy, chuckled and chuckled.

Because of the absorbing play none considered the strange ways of the Swede. They paid strict heed to the game. Finally, during a lull caused by a new deal, the Swede suddenly addressed Johnnie: "I suppose there have been a good many men killed in this room." The jaws of the others dropped and they looked at him.

"What in hell are you talking about?" asked Johnnie.

The Swede laughed again his blatant laugh, full of a kind of false courage and defiance. "Oh, you know what I mean all right," he answered.

"I'm a liar if I do!" Johnnie protested. The card was halted, and the men stared at the Swede. Johnnie evidently felt that as the son of the proprietor he should make a direct inquiry. "Now, what might you be drivin' at, mister?" he asked. The Swede winked at him. It was a wink full of cunning. His fingers shook on the edge of the board. "Oh, maybe you think I have been to nowheres. Maybe you think I'm a tenderfoot?"

"I don't know nothin' about you," answered Johnnie, "and I don't give a damn where you've been. All I got to say is that I don't know what you're driving at. There hain't never been nobody killed in this room."

The cowboy, who had been steadily gazing at the Swede, then spoke: "What's wrong with you, mister?"

Apparently it seemed to the Swede that he was formidably menaced. He shivered and turned white near the corners of his mouth. He sent an appealing glance in the direction of the little Easterner. During these moments he did not forget to wear his air of advanced pot-valor.[4] "They say they don't know what I mean," he remarked mockingly to the Easterner.

The latter answered after prolonged and cautious reflection. "I don't understand you," he said, impassively.

The Swede made a movement then which announced that he thought he had encountered treachery from the only quarter where he had expected sympathy, if not help. "Oh, I see you are all against me. I see—"

The cowboy was in a state of deep stupefaction. "Say," he cried, as he tumbled the deck violently down upon the board, "say, what are you gittin' at, hey?"

The Swede sprang up with the celerity of a man escaping from a snake on the floor. "I don't want to fight!" he shouted. "I don't want to fight!"

The cowboy stretched his long legs indolently and deliberately. His hands were in his pockets. He spat into the sawdust box. "Well, who the hell thought you did?" he inquired.

The Swede backed rapidly toward a corner of the room. His hands were out protectingly in front of his chest, but he was making an obvious struggle to control his fright. "Gentlemen," he quavered, "I suppose I am going to be killed before I can leave this house! I suppose I am going to be killed before I

4. Alcohol-induced bravado.

can leave this house!" In his eyes was the dying-swan look. Through the windows could be seen the snow turning blue in the shadow of dusk. The wind tore at the house, and some loose thing beat regularly against the clapboards like a spirit tapping.

A door opened, and Scully himself entered. He paused in surprise as he noted the tragic attitude of the Swede. Then he said, "What's the matter here?"

The Swede answered him swiftly and eagerly: "These men are going to kill me."

"Kill you!" ejaculated Scully. "Kill you! What are you talkin'?"

The Swede made the gesture of a martyr.

Scully wheeled sternly upon his son. "What is this, Johnnie?"

The lad had grown sullen. "Damned if I know," he answered. "I can't make no sense to it." He began to shuffle the cards, fluttering them together with an angry snap. "He says a good many men have been killed in this room, or something like that. And he says he's goin' to be killed here too. I don't know what ails him. He's crazy, I shouldn't wonder."

Scully then looked for explanation to the cowboy, but the cowboy simply shrugged his shoulders.

"Kill you?" said Scully again to the Swede. "Kill you? Man, you're off your nut."

"Oh, I know," burst out the Swede. "I know what will happen. Yes, I'm crazy—yes. Yes, of course, I'm crazy—yes. But I know one thing—" There was a sort of sweat of misery and terror upon his face. "I know I won't get out of here alive."

The cowboy drew a deep breath, as if his mind was passing into the last stages of dissolution. "Well, I'm doggoned," he whispered to himself.

Scully wheeled suddenly and faced his son. "You've been troublin' this man!"

Johnnie's voice was loud with its burden of grievance. "Why, good Gawd, I ain't done nothin' to 'im."

The Swede broke in. "Gentlemen, do not disturb yourselves. I will leave this house. I will go away, because"—he accused them dramatically with his glance—"because I do not want to be killed."

Scully was furious with his son. "Will you tell me what is the matter, you young divil? What's the matter, anyhow? Speak out!"

"Blame it!" cried Johnnie in despair, "don't I tell you I don't know? He—he says we want to kill him, and that's all I know. I can't tell what ails him."

The Swede continued to repeat: "Never mind, Mr. Scully; never mind. I will leave this house. I will go away, because I do not wish to be killed. Yes, of course, I am crazy—yes. But I know one thing! I will go away. I will leave this house. Never mind, Mr. Scully; never mind. I will go away."

"You will not go 'way," said Scully. "You will not go 'way until I hear the reason of this business. If anybody has troubled you I will take care of him. This is my house. You are under my roof, and I will not allow any peaceable man to be troubled here." He cast a terrible eye upon Johnnie, the cowboy, and the Easterner.

"Never mind, Mr. Scully, never mind. I will go away. I do not wish to be killed." The Swede moved toward the door which opened upon the stairs. It was evidently his intention to go at once for his baggage.

"No, no," shouted Scully peremptorily; but the white-faced man slid by him and disappeared. "Now," said Scully severely, "what does this mane?"

Johnnie and the cowboy cried together: "Why, we didn't do nothin' to 'im!"

Scully's eyes were cold. "No," he said, "you didn't?"

Johnnie swore a deep oath. "Why, this is the wildest loon I ever see. We didn't do nothin' at all. We were jest sittin' here playin' cards, and he—"

The father suddenly spoke to the Easterner. "Mr. Blanc," he asked, "what has these boys been doin'?"

The Easterner reflected again. "I didn't see anything wrong at all," he said at last, slowly.

Scully began to howl. "But what does it mane?" He stared ferociously at his son. "I have a mind to lather you for this, my boy."

Johnnie was frantic. "Well, what have I done?" he bawled at his father.

III

"I think you are tongue-tied," said Scully finally to his son, the cowboy, and the Easterner; and at the end of this scornful sentence he left the room.

Upstairs the Swede was swiftly fastening the straps of his great valise. Once his back happened to be half turned toward the door, and, hearing a noise there, he wheeled and sprang up, uttering a loud cry. Scully's wrinkled visage showed grimly in the light of the small lamp he carried. This yellow effulgence, streaming upward, colored only his prominent features, and left his eyes, for instance, in mysterious shadow. He resembled a murderer.

"Man! man!" he exclaimed, "have you gone daffy?"

"Oh, no! Oh, no!" rejoined the other. "There are people in this world who know pretty nearly as much as you do—understand?"

For a moment they stood gazing at each other. Upon the Swede's deathly pale cheeks were two spots brightly crimson and sharply edged, as if they had been carefully painted. Scully placed the light on the table and sat himself on the edge of the bed. He spoke ruminatively. "By cracky, I never heard of such a thing in my life. It's a complete muddle. I can't, for the soul of me, think how you ever got this idea into your head." Presently he lifted his eyes and asked: "And did you sure think they were going to kill you?"

The Swede scanned the old man as if he wished to see into his mind. "I did," he said at last. He obviously suspected that this answer might precipitate an outbreak. As he pulled on a strap his whole arm shook, the elbow wavering like a bit of paper.

Scully banged his hand impressively on the footboard of the bed. "Why, man, we're goin' to have a line of ilictric street-cars in this town next spring."

"'A line of electric street-cars,'" repeated the Swede, stupidly.

"And," said Scully, "there's a new railroad goin' to be built down from Broken Arm to here. Not to mintion the four churches and the smashin' big brick schoolhouse. Then there's the big factory, too. Why, in two years Romper'll be a met-tro-*pol*-is."

Having finished the preparation of his baggage, the Swede straightened himself. "Mr. Scully," he said, with sudden hardihood, "how much do I owe you?"

"You don't owe me anythin'," said the old man, angrily.

"Yes, I do," retorted the Swede. He took seventy-five cents from his pocket and tendered it to Scully; but the latter snapped his fingers in disdainful refusal. However, it happened that they both stood gazing in a strange fashion at three silver pieces on the Swede's open palm.

"I'll not take your money," said Scully at last. "Not after what's been goin' on here." Then a plan seemed to strike him. "Here," he cried, picking up his lamp and moving toward the door. "Here! Come with me a minute."

"No," said the Swede, in overwhelming alarm.

"Yes," urged the old man. "Come on! I want you to come and see a picter— just across the hall—in my room."

The Swede must have concluded that his hour was come. His jaw dropped and his teeth showed like a dead man's. He ultimately followed Scully across the corridor, but he had the step of one hung in chains.

Scully flashed the light high on the wall of his own chamber. There was revealed a ridiculous photograph of a little girl. She was leaning against a balustrade of gorgeous decoration, and the formidable bang to her hair was prominent. The figure was as graceful as an upright sled-stake, and, withal, it was the hue of lead. "There," said Scully tenderly, "that's the picter of my little girl that died. Her name was Carrie. She had the purtiest hair you ever saw! I was that fond of her, she—"

Turning then, he saw that the Swede was not contemplating the picture at all, but, instead, was keeping keen watch on the gloom in the rear.

"Look, man!" cried Scully, heartily. "That's the picter of my little gal that died. Her name was Carrie. And then here's the picter of my oldest boy, Michael. He's a lawyer in Lincoln, an' doin' well. I gave that boy a grand eddication, and I'm glad for it now. He's a fine boy. Look at 'im now. Ain't he bold as blazes, him there in Lincoln, an honored an' respicted gintleman! An honored and respicted gintleman," concluded Scully with a flourish. And, so saying, he smote the Swede jovially on the back.

The Swede faintly smiled.

"Now," said the old man, "there's only one more thing." He dropped suddenly to the floor and thrust his head beneath the bed. The Swede could hear his muffled voice. "I'd keep it under me piller if it wasn't for that boy Johnnie. Then there's the old woman—Where is it now? I never put it twice in the same place. Ah, now come out with you!"

Presently he backed clumsily from under the bed, dragging with him an old coat rolled into a bundle. "I've fetched him," he muttered. Kneeling on the floor, he unrolled the coat and extracted from its heart a large yellow-brown whiskey-bottle.

His first manoeuver was to hold the bottle up to the light. Reassured, apparently, that nobody had been tampering with it, he thrust it with a generous movement toward the Swede.

The weak-kneed Swede was about to eagerly clutch this element of strength, but he suddenly jerked his hand away and cast a look of horror upon Scully.

"Drink," said the old man affectionately. He had risen to his feet, and now stood facing the Swede.

There was a silence. Then again Scully said: "Drink!"

The Swede laughed wildly. He grabbed the bottle, put it to his mouth; and as his lips curled absurdly around the opening and his throat worked, he kept his glance, burning with hatred, upon the old man's face.

IV

After the departure of Scully the three men, with the cardboard still upon their knees, preserved for a long time an astounded silence. Then Johnnie said: "That's the doddangedest Swede I ever see."

"He ain't no Swede," said the cowboy, scornfully.

"Well, what is he then?" cried Johnnie. "What is he then?"

"It's my opinion," replied the cowboy deliberately, "he's some kind of a Dutchman." It was a venerable custom of the country to entitle as Swedes all light-haired men who spoke with a heavy tongue. In consequence the idea of the cowboy was not without its daring. "Yes, sir," he repeated. "It's my opinion this feller is some kind of a Dutchman."

"Well, he says he's a Swede, anyhow," muttered Johnnie, sulkily. He turned to the Easterner: "What do you think, Mr. Blanc?"

"Oh, I don't know," replied the Easterner.

"Well, what do you think makes him act that way?" asked the cowboy.

"Why, he's frightened." The Easterner knocked his pipe against a rim of the stove. "He's clear frightened out of his boots."

"What at?" cried Johnnie and the cowboy together.

The Easterner reflected over his answer.

"What at?" cried the others again.

"Oh, I don't know, but it seems to me this man has been reading dime novels, and he thinks he's right out in the middle of it—the shootin' and stabbin' and all."

"But," said the cowboy, deeply scandalized, "this ain't Wyoming, ner none of them places. This is Nebrasker."

"Yes," added Johnnie, "an' why don't he wait till he gits *out West*?"

The travelled Easterner laughed. "It isn't different there even—not in these days. But he thinks he's right in the middle of hell."

Johnnie and the cowboy mused long.

"It's awful funny," remarked Johnnie at last.

"Yes," said the cowboy. "This is a queer game. I hope we don't git snowed in, because then we'd have to stand this here man bein' around with us all the time. That wouldn't be no good."

"I wish pop would throw him out," said Johnnie.

Presently they heard a loud stamping on the stairs, accompanied by ringing jokes in the voice of old Scully, and laughter, evidently from the Swede. The men around the stove stared vacantly at each other. "Gosh!" said the cowboy. The door flew open, and old Scully, flushed and anecdotal, came into the room. He was jabbering at the Swede, who followed him, laughing bravely. It was the entry of two roisterers from a banquet ball.

"Come now," said Scully sharply to the three seated men, "move up and give us a chance at the stove." The cowboy and the Easterner obediently sidled their chairs to make room for the newcomers. Johnnie, however, simply arranged himself in a more indolent attitude, and then remained motionless.

"Come! Git over, there," said Scully.

"Plenty of room on the other side of the stove," said Johnnie.

"Do you think we want to sit in the draught?" roared the father.

But the Swede here interposed with a grandeur of confidence. "No, no. Let the boy sit where he likes," he cried in a bullying voice to the father.

"All right! All right!" said Scully, deferentially. The cowboy and the Easterner exchanged glances of wonder.

The five chairs were formed in a crescent about one side of the stove. The Swede began to talk; he talked arrogantly, profanely, angrily. Johnnie, the cowboy, and the Easterner maintained a morose silence, while old Scully appeared to be receptive and eager, breaking in constantly with sympathetic ejaculations.

Finally the Swede announced that he was thirsty. He moved in his chair, and said that he would go for a drink of water.

"I'll git it for you," cried Scully at once.

"No," said the Swede, contemptuously. "I'll get it for myself." He arose and stalked with the air of an owner off into the executive parts of the hotel.

As soon as the Swede was out of hearing Scully sprang to his feet and whispered intensely to the others: "Up-stairs he thought I was tryin' to poison 'im."

"Say," said Johnnie, "this makes me sick. Why don't you throw 'im out in the snow?"

"Why, he's all right now," declared Scully. "It was only that he was from the East, and he thought this was a tough place. That's all. He's all right now."

The cowboy looked with admiration upon the Easterner. "You were straight," he said. "You were on to that there Dutchman."

"Well," said Johnnie to his father, "he may be all right now, but I don't see it. Other time he was scared, but now he's too fresh."

Scully's speech was always a combination of Irish brogue and idiom, Western twang and idiom, and scraps of curiously formal diction taken from the story-books and newspapers. He now hurled a strange mass of language at the head of his son. "What do I keep? What do I keep? What do I keep?" he demanded, in a voice of thunder. He slapped his knee impressively, to indicate that he himself was going to make reply, and that all should heed. "I keep a hotel," he shouted. "A hotel, do you mind? A guest under my roof has sacred privileges. He is to be intimidated by none. Not one word shall he hear that would prijudice him in favor of goin' away. I'll not have it. There's no place in this here town where they can say they iver took in a guest of mine because he was afraid to stay here." He wheeled suddenly upon the cowboy and the Easterner. "Am I right?"

"Yes, Mr. Scully," said the cowboy, "I think you're right."

"Yes, Mr. Scully," said the Easterner, "I think you're right."

V

At six-o'clock supper, the Swede fizzed like a fire-wheel. He sometimes seemed on the point of bursting into riotous song, and in all his madness he was encouraged by old Scully. The Easterner was encased in reserve; the cowboy sat in wide-mouthed amazement, forgetting to eat, while Johnnie wrathily demolished great plates of food. The daughters of the house, when they were obliged to replenish the biscuits, approached as warily as Indians, and, having succeeded in their purposes, fled with ill-concealed trepidation. The Swede domineered the whole feast, and he gave it the appearance of a cruel bacchanal. He seemed to have grown suddenly taller; he gazed, brutally disdainful, into every face. His voice rang through the room. Once when he jabbed out harpoon-fashion with his fork to pinion a biscuit, the weapon nearly impaled the hand of the Easterner, which had been stretched quietly out for the same biscuit.

After supper, as the men filed toward the other room, the Swede smote Scully ruthlessly on the shoulder. "Well, old boy, that was a good, square meal." Johnnie looked hopefully at his father; he knew that shoulder was tender from an old fall; and, indeed, it appeared for a moment as if Scully was going to flame out over the matter, but in the end he smiled a sickly smile and remained silent. The others understood from his manner that he was admitting his responsibility for the Swede's new view-point.

Johnnie, however, addressed his parent in an aside. "Why don't you license somebody to kick you downstairs?" Scully scowled darkly by way of reply.

When they were gathered about the stove, the Swede insisted on another game of High-Five. Scully gently deprecated the plan at first, but the Swede turned a wolfish glare upon him. The old man subsided, and the Swede canvassed the others. In his tone there was always a great threat. The cowboy and the Easterner both remarked indifferently that they would play. Scully said that he would presently have to go to meet the 6.58 train, and so the Swede turned menacingly upon Johnnie. For a moment their glances crossed like blades, and then Johnnie smiled and said, "Yes, I'll play."

They formed a square, with the little board on their knees. The Easterner and the Swede were again partners. As the play went on, it was noticeable that the cowboy was not board-whacking as usual. Meanwhile, Scully, near the lamp, had put on his spectacles and, with an appearance curiously like an old priest, was reading a newspaper. In time he went out to meet the 6.58 train, and, despite his precautions, a gust of polar wind whirled into the room as he opened the door. Besides scattering the cards, it chilled the players to the marrow. The Swede cursed frightfully. When Scully returned, his entrance disturbed a cozy and friendly scene. The Swede again cursed. But presently they were once more intent, their heads bent forward and their hands moving swiftly. The Swede had adopted the fashion of board-whacking.

Scully took up his paper and for a long time remained immersed in matters which were extraordinarily remote from him. The lamp burned badly, and once he stopped to adjust the wick. The newspaper, as he turned from page to page, rustled with a slow and comfortable sound. Then suddenly he heard three terrible words: "You are cheatin'!"

Such scenes often prove that there can be little of dramatic import in environment. Any room can present a tragic front; any room can be comic. This little den was now hideous as a torture-chamber. The new faces of the men themselves had changed it upon the instant. The Swede held a huge fist in front of Johnnie's face, while the latter looked steadily over it into the blazing orbs of his accuser. The Easterner had grown pallid; the cowboy's jaw had dropped in that expression of bovine amazement which was one of his important mannerisms. After the three words, the first sound in the room was made by Scully's paper as it floated forgotten to his feet. His spectacles had also fallen from his nose, but by a clutch he had saved them in air. His hand, grasping the spectacles, now remained poised awkwardly and near his shoulder. He stared at the card-players.

Probably the silence was while a second elapsed. Then, if the floor had been suddenly twitched out from under the men they could not have moved quicker. The five had projected themselves headlong toward a common point. It happened that Johnnie, in rising to hurl himself upon the Swede, had stumbled slightly because of his curiously instinctive care for the cards and the board. The loss of the moment allowed time for the arrival of Scully, and also allowed the cowboy time to give the Swede a great push which sent him staggering back. The men found tongue together, and hoarse shouts of rage, appeal, or fear burst from every throat. The cowboy pushed and jostled feverishly at the Swede, and the Easterner and Scully clung wildly to Johnnie; but through the smoky air, above the swaying bodies of the peace-compellers, the eyes of the two warriors ever sought each other in glances of challenge that were at once hot and steely.

Of course the board had been overturned, and now the whole company of cards was scattered over the floor, where the boots of the men trampled the fat and painted kings and queens as they gazed with their silly eyes at the war that was waging above them.

Scully's voice was dominating the yells. "Stop now! Stop, I say! Stop, now—"

Johnnie, as he struggled to burst through the rank formed by Scully and the Easterner, was crying, "Well, he says I cheated! He says I cheated! I won't allow no man to say I cheated! If he says I cheated, he's a—!"

The cowboy was telling the Swede, "Quit, now! Quit, d'ye hear—"

The screams of the Swede never ceased: "He did cheat! I saw him! I saw him—"

As for the Easterner, he was importuning in a voice that was not heeded: "Wait a moment, can't you? Oh, wait a moment. What's the good of a fight over a game of cards? Wait a moment—"

In this tumult no complete sentences were clear. "Cheat"—"Quit"—"He says"— these fragments pierced the uproar and rang out sharply. It was remarkable that, whereas Scully undoubtedly made the most noise, he was the least heard of any of the riotous band.

Then suddenly there was a great cessation. It was as if each man had paused for breath; and although the room was still lighted with the anger of men, it could be seen that there was no danger of immediate conflict, and at once Johnnie, shouldering his way forward, almost succeeded in confronting the Swede. "What did you say I cheated for? What did you say I cheated for? I don't cheat, and I won't let no man say I do!"

The Swede said, "I saw you! I saw you!"

"Well," cried Johnnie, "I'll fight any man what says I cheat!"

"No, you won't," said the cowboy. "Not here."

"Ah, be still, can't you?" said Scully, coming between them.

The quiet was sufficient to allow the Easterner's voice to be heard. He was repeating, "Oh, wait a moment, can't you? What's the good of a fight over a game of cards? Wait a moment!"

Johnnie, his red face appearing above his father's shoulder, hailed the Swede again. "Did you say I cheated?"

The Swede showed his teeth. "Yes."

"Then," said Johnnie, "we must fight."

"Yes, fight," roared the Swede. He was like a demoniac. "Yes, fight! I'll show you what kind of a man I am! I'll show you who you want to fight! Maybe you think I can't fight! Maybe you think I can't! I'll show you, you skin, you card-sharp! Yes, you cheated! You cheated! You cheated!"

"Well, let's go at it, then, mister," said Johnnie, coolly.

The cowboy's brow was beaded with sweat from his efforts in intercepting all sorts of raids. He turned in despair to Scully. "What are you goin' to do now?"

A change had come over the Celtic visage of the old man. He now seemed all eagerness; his eyes glowed.

"We'll let them fight," he answered stalwartly. "I can't put up with it any longer. I've stood this damned Swede till I'm sick. We'll let them fight."

V I

The men prepared to go out-of-doors. The Easterner was so nervous that he had great difficulty in getting his arms into the sleeves of his new leather coat. As the cowboy drew his fur cap down over his ears his hands trembled. In fact, Johnnie and old Scully were the only ones who displayed no agitation. These preliminaries were conducted without words.

Scully threw open the door. "Well, come on," he said. Instantly a terrific wind caused the flame of the lamp to struggle at its wick, while a puff of black smoke sprang from the chimney-top. The stove was in mid-current of the blast, and its voice swelled to equal the roar of the storm. Some of the scarred and bedabbled cards were caught up from the floor and dashed helplessly against the further wall. The men lowered their heads and plunged into the tempest as into a sea.

No snow was falling, but great whirls and clouds of flakes, swept up from the ground by the frantic winds, were streaming southward with the speed of bullets. The covered land was blue with the sheen of an unearthly satin, and there was no other hue save where, at the low, black railway station—which seemed incredibly distant—one light gleamed like a tiny jewel. As the men floundered into a thigh-deep drift, it was known that the Swede was bawling out something. Scully went to him, put a hand on his shoulder, and projected an ear. "What's that you say?" he shouted.

"I say," bawled the Swede again, "I won't stand much show against this gang. I know you'll all pitch on me."

Scully smote him reproachfully on the arm. "Tut, man!" he yelled. The wind tore the words from Scully's lips and scattered them far a-lee.

"You are all a gang of—" boomed the Swede, but the storm also seized the remainder of this sentence.

Immediately turning their backs upon the wind, the men had swung around a corner to the sheltered side of the hotel. It was the function of the little house to preserve here, amid this great devastation of snow, an irregular V-shape of heavily encrusted grass, which crackled beneath the feet. One could imagine the great drifts piled against the windward side. When the party reached the comparative peace of this spot it was found that the Swede was still bellowing.

"Oh, I know what kind of a thing this is! I know you'll all pitch on me. I can't lick you all!"

Scully turned upon him panther-fashion. "You'll not have to whip all of us. You'll have to whip my son Johnnie. An' the man what troubles you durin' that time will have me to dale with."

The arrangements were swiftly made. The two men faced each other, obedient to the harsh commands of Scully, whose face, in the subtly luminous gloom, could be seen set in the austere impersonal lines that are pictured on the countenances of the Roman veterans. The Easterner's teeth were chattering, and he was hopping up and down like a mechanical toy. The cowboy stood rocklike.

The contestants had not stripped off any clothing. Each was in his ordinary attire. Their fists were up, and they eyed each other in a calm that had the elements of leonine cruelty in it.

During this pause, the Easterner's mind, like a film, took lasting impressions of three men—the iron-nerved master of the ceremony; the Swede, pale, motionless, terrible; and Johnnie, serene yet ferocious, brutish yet heroic. The entire prelude had in it a tragedy greater than the tragedy of action, and this aspect was accentuated by the long, mellow cry of the blizzard, as it sped the tumbling and wailing flakes into the black abyss of the south.

"Now!" said Scully.

The two combatants leaped forward and crashed together like bullocks. There was heard the cushioned sound of blows, and of a curse squeezing out from between the tight teeth of one.

As for the spectators, the Easterner's pent-up breath exploded from him with a pop of relief, absolute relief from the tension of the preliminaries. The cowboy bounded into the air with a yowl. Scully was immovable as from supreme amazement and fear at the fury of the fight which he himself had permitted and arranged.

For a time the encounter in the darkness was such a perplexity of flying arms that it presented no more detail than would a swiftly revolving wheel. Occasionally a face, as if illumined by a flash of light, would shine out, ghastly and marked with pink spots. A moment later, the men might have been known as shadows, if it were not for the involuntary utterance of oaths that came from them in whispers.

Suddenly a holocaust of warlike desire caught the cowboy, and he bolted forward with the speed of a broncho. "Go it, Johnnie! Go it! Kill him! Kill him!"

Scully confronted him. "Kape back," he said; and by his glance the cowboy could tell that this man was Johnnie's father.

To the Easterner there was a monotony of unchangeable fighting that was an abomination. This confused mingling was eternal to his sense, which was concentrated in a longing for the end, the priceless end. Once the fighters lurched near him, and as he scrambled hastily backward he heard them breathe like men on the rack.

"Kill him, Johnnie! Kill him! Kill him! Kill him!" The cowboy's face was contorted like one of those agony masks in museums.

"Keep still," said Scully, icily.

Then there was a sudden loud grunt, incomplete, cut short, and Johnnie's body swung away from the Swede and fell with sickening heaviness to the grass. The cowboy was barely in time to prevent the mad Swede from flinging himself upon his prone adversary. "No, you don't," said the cowboy, interposing an arm. "Wait a second."

Scully was at his son's side. "Johnnie! Johnnie, me boy!" His voice had a quality of melancholy tenderness. "Johnnie! Can you go on with it?" He looked anxiously down into the bloody, pulpy face of his son.

There was a moment of silence, and then Johnnie answered in his ordinary voice, "Yes, I—it—yes."

Assisted by his father he struggled to his feet. "Wait a bit now till you git your wind," said the old man.

A few paces away the cowboy was lecturing the Swede. "No, you don't! Wait a second!"

The Easterner was plucking at Scully's sleeve. "Oh, this is enough," he pleaded. "This is enough! Let it go as it stands. This is enough!"

"Bill," said Scully, "git out of the road." The cowboy stepped aside. "Now." The combatants were actuated by a new caution as they advanced toward collision. They glared at each other, and then the Swede aimed a lightning blow that carried with it his entire weight. Johnnie was evidently half stupid from weakness, but he miraculously dodged, and his fist sent the overbalanced Swede sprawling.

The cowboy, Scully, and the Easterner burst into a cheer that was like a chorus of triumphant soldiery, but before its conclusion the Swede had scuffled agilely to his feet and come in berserk abandon at his foe. There was another perplexity of flying arms, and Johnnie's body again swung away and fell, even as a bundle might fall from a roof. The Swede instantly staggered to a little wind-waved tree and leaned upon it, breathing like an engine, while his savage and flame-lit eyes roamed from face to face as the men bent over Johnnie. There was a splendor of isolation in his situation at this time which the Easterner felt once when, lifting his eyes from the man on the ground, he beheld that mysterious and lonely figure, waiting.

"Are you any good yet, Johnnie?" asked Scully in a broken voice.

The son gasped and opened his eyes languidly. After a moment he answered, "No—I ain't—any good—any—more." Then, from shame and bodily ill, he began to weep, the tears furrowing down through the blood-stains on his face. "He was too—too—too heavy for me."

Scully straightened and addressed the waiting figure. "Stranger," he said, evenly, "it's all up with our side." Then his voice changed into that vibrant huskiness which is commonly the tone of the most simple and deadly announcements. "Johnnie is whipped."

Without replying, the victor moved off on the route to the front door of the hotel.

The cowboy was formulating new and unspellable blasphemies. The Easterner was startled to find that they were out in a wind that seemed to come direct from the shadowed arctic floes. He heard again the wail of the snow as it was flung to its grave in the south. He knew now that all this time the cold had been sinking into him deeper and deeper, and he wondered that he had not perished. He felt indifferent to the condition of the vanquished man.

"Johnnie, can you walk?" asked Scully.

"Did I hurt—hurt him any?" asked the son.

"Can you walk, boy? Can you walk?"

Johnnie's voice was suddenly strong. There was a robust impatience in it. "I asked you whether I hurt him any!"

"Yes, yes, Johnnie," answered the cowboy, consolingly; "he's hurt a good deal."

They raised him from the ground, and as soon as he was on his feet he went tottering off, rebuffing all attempts at assistance. When the party rounded the corner they were fairly blinded by the pelting of the snow. It burned their faces like fire. The cowboy carried Johnnie through the drift to the door. As they entered, some cards again rose from the floor and beat against the wall.

The Easterner rushed to the stove. He was so profoundly chilled that he almost dared to embrace the glowing iron. The Swede was not in the room. Johnnie sank into a chair and, folding his arms on his knees, buried his face in them. Scully, warming one foot and then the other at a rim of the stove, muttered to himself with Celtic mournfulness. The cowboy had removed his fur cap, and with a dazed and rueful air he was running one hand through his tousled locks. From overhead they could hear the creaking of boards, as the Swede tramped here and there in his room.

The sad quiet was broken by the sudden flinging open of a door that led toward the kitchen. It was instantly followed by an inrush of women. They precipitated themselves upon Johnnie amid a chorus of lamentation. Before they carried their prey off to the kitchen, there to be bathed and harangued with that mixture of sympathy and abuse which is a feat of their sex, the mother straightened herself and fixed old Scully with an eye of stern reproach. "Shame be upon you, Patrick Scully!" she cried. "Your own son, too. Shame be upon you!"

"There, now! Be quiet, now!" said the old man, weakly.

"Shame be upon you, Patrick Scully!" The girls, rallying to this slogan, sniffed disdainfully in the direction of those trembling accomplices, the cowboy and the Easterner. Presently they bore Johnnie away, and left the three men to dismal reflection.

VII

"I'd like to fight this here Dutchman myself," said the cowboy, breaking a long silence.

Scully wagged his head sadly. "No, that wouldn't do. It wouldn't be right. It wouldn't be right."

"Well, why wouldn't it?" argued the cowboy. "I don't see no harm in it."

"No," answered Scully, with mournful heroism. "It wouldn't be right. It was Johnnie's fight, and now we mustn't whip the man just because he whipped Johnnie."

"Yes, that's true enough," said the cowboy; "but—he better not get fresh with me, because I couldn't stand no more of it."

"You'll not say a word to him," commanded Scully, and even then they heard the tread of the Swede on the stairs. His entrance was made theatric. He swept the door back with a bang and swaggered to the middle of the room. No one looked at him. "Well," he cried, insolently, at Scully, "I s'pose you'll tell me now how much I owe you?"

The old man remained stolid. "You don't owe me nothin'."

"Huh!" said the Swede, "huh! Don't owe 'im nothin'."

The cowboy addressed the Swede. "Stranger, I don't see how you come to be so gay around here."

Old Scully was instantly alert. "Stop!" he shouted, holding his hand forth, fingers upward. "Bill, you shut up!"

The cowboy spat carelessly into the sawdust-box. "I didn't say a word, did I?" he asked.

"Mr. Scully," called the Swede, "how much do I owe you?" It was seen that he was attired for departure, and that he had his valise in his hand.

"You don't owe me nothin'," repeated Scully in his same imperturbable way.

"Huh!" said the Swede. "I guess you're right. I guess if it was any way at all, you'd owe me somethin'. That's what I guess." He turned to the cowboy. "'Kill him! Kill him! Kill him!'" he mimicked, and then guffawed victoriously. "'Kill him!'" He was convulsed with ironical humor.

But he might have been jeering the dead. The three men were immovable and silent, staring with glassy eyes at the stove.

The Swede opened the door and passed into the storm, one derisive glance backward at the still group.

As soon as the door was closed, Scully and the cowboy leaped to their feet and began to curse. They trampled to and fro, waving their arms and smashing into the air with their fists. "Oh, but that was a hard minute!" wailed Scully. "That was a hard minute! Him there leerin' and scoffin'! One bang at his nose was worth forty dollars to me that minute! How did you stand it, Bill?"

"How did I stand it?" cried the cowboy in a quivering voice. "How did I stand it? Oh!"

The old man burst into sudden brogue. "I'd loike to take that Swade," he wailed, "and hould 'im down on a shtone flure and bate 'im to a jelly wid a shtick!"

The cowboy groaned in sympathy. "I'd like to git him by the neck and hammer him"—he brought his hand down on a chair with a noise like a pistol-shot—"hammer that there Dutchman until he couldn't tell himself from a dead coyote!"

"I'd bate 'im until he—"

"I'd show *him* some things—"

And then together they raised a yearning, fanatic cry—"Oh-o-oh! if we only could—"

"Yes!"

"Yes!"

"And then I'd—"

"O-o-oh!"

VIII

The Swede, tightly gripping his valise, tacked across the face of the storm as if he carried sails. He was following a line of little naked, gasping trees which, he knew, must mark the way of the road. His face, fresh from the pounding of Johnnie's fists, felt more pleasure than pain in the wind and the driving snow. A number of square shapes loomed upon him finally, and he knew them as the houses of the main body of the town. He found a street and made travel along it, leaning heavily upon the wind whenever, at a corner, a terrific blast caught him.

He might have been in a deserted village. We picture the world as thick with conquering and elate humanity, but here, with the bugles of the tempest pealing, it was hard to imagine a peopled earth. One viewed the existence of man then as a marvel, and conceded a glamor of wonder to these lice which were caused to cling to a whirling, fire-smitten, ice-locked, disease-stricken, space-lost bulb. The conceit of man was explained by this storm to be the very engine of life. One was a coxcomb not to die in it. However, the Swede found a saloon.

In front of it an indomitable red light was burning, and the snowflakes were made blood-color as they flew through the circumscribed territory of the lamp's shining. The Swede pushed open the door of the saloon and entered. A sanded expanse was before him, and at the end of it four men sat about a table drinking. Down one side of the room extended a radiant bar, and its guardian was leaning upon his elbows listening to the talk of the men at the table. The Swede dropped his valise upon the floor and, smiling fraternally upon the barkeeper, said, "Gimme some whiskey, will you?" The man placed a bottle, a whiskey-glass, and a glass of ice-thick water upon the bar. The Swede poured himself an abnormal portion of whiskey and drank it in three gulps. "Pretty bad night," remarked the bartender, indifferently. He was making the pretension of blindness which is usually a distinction of his class; but it could have been seen that he was furtively studying the half-erased bloodstains on the face of the Swede. "Bad night," he said again.

"Oh, it's good enough for me," replied the Swede, hardily, as he poured himself more whiskey. The barkeeper took his coin and maneuvered it through its reception by the highly nickelled cash-machine. A bell rang; a card labeled "20 cts." had appeared.

"No," continued the Swede, "this isn't too bad weather. It's good enough for me."

"So?" murmured the barkeeper, languidly.

The copious drams made the Swede's eyes swim, and he breathed a trifle heavier. "Yes, I like this weather. I like it. It suits me." It was apparently his design to impart a deep significance to these words.

"So?" murmured the bartender again. He turned to gaze dreamily at the scroll-like birds and bird-like scrolls which had been drawn with soap upon the mirrors in back of the bar.

"Well, I guess I'll take another drink," said the Swede, presently. "Have something?"

"No, thanks; I'm not drinkin'," answered the bartender. Afterward he asked, "How did you hurt your face?"

The Swede immediately began to boast loudly. "Why, in a fight. I thumped the soul out of a man down here at Scully's hotel."

The interest of the four men at the table was at last aroused.

"Who was it?" said one.

"Johnnie Scully," blustered the Swede. "Son of the man what runs it. He will be pretty near dead for some weeks, I can tell you. I made a nice thing of him, I did. He couldn't get up. They carried him in the house. Have a drink?"

Instantly the men in some subtle way encased themselves in reserve. "No, thanks," said one. The group was of curious formation. Two were prominent local business men; one was the district attorney; and one was a professional gambler of the kind known as "square."[5] But a scrutiny of the group would not have enabled an observer to pick the gambler from the men of more reputable pursuits. He was, in fact, a man so delicate in manner, when among people of fair class, and so judicious in his choice of victims, that in the strictly masculine part of the town's life he had come to be explicitly trusted and admired. People called him a thoroughbred. The fear and contempt with which his craft was regarded were undoubtedly the reason why his quiet dignity shone conspicuous above the quiet dignity of men who might be merely hatters, billiard-markers, or grocery clerks. Beyond an occasional unwary traveller who came by rail, this gambler was supposed to prey solely upon reckless and senile farmers, who, when flush with good crops, drove into town in all the pride and confidence of an absolutely invulnerable stupidity. Hearing at times in circuitous fashion of the despoilment of such a farmer, the important men of Romper invariably laughed in contempt of the victim, and if they thought of the wolf at all, it was a kind of pride at the knowledge that he would never dare think of attacking their wisdom and courage. Besides, it was popular that this gambler had a real wife and two real children in a neat cottage in a suburb, where he led an exemplary home life; and when any one even suggested a discrepancy in his character, the crowd immediately vociferated descriptions of this virtuous family circle. Then men who led exemplary home lives, and men who did not lead exemplary home lives, all subsided in a bunch, remarking that there was nothing more to be said.

However, when a restriction was placed upon him—as, for instance, when a strong clique of members of the new Pollywog Club refused to permit him, even as a spectator, to appear in the rooms of the organization—the candor and gentleness with which he accepted the judgment disarmed many of his foes and made his friends more desperately partisan. He invariably distinguished between himself and a respectable Romper man so quickly and frankly that his manner actually appeared to be a continual broadcast compliment.

And one must not forget to declare the fundamental fact of his entire position in Romper. It is irrefutable that in all affairs outside his business, in all matters that occur eternally and commonly between man and man, this thieving card-player was so generous, so just, so moral, that, in a contest, he could have put to flight the consciences of nine tenths of the citizens of Romper.

And so it happened that he was seated in this saloon with the two prominent local merchants and the district attorney.

The Swede continued to drink raw whiskey, meanwhile babbling at the barkeeper and trying to induce him to indulge in potations. "Come on. Have a drink. Come on. What—no? Well, have a little one, then. By gawd, I've whipped a man tonight, and I want to celebrate. I whipped him good, too. Gentlemen," the Swede cried to the men at the table, "have a drink?"

5. Honest.

"Ssh!" said the barkeeper.

The group at the table, although furtively attentive, had been pretending to be deep in talk, but now a man lifted his eyes toward the Swede and said, shortly, "Thanks. We don't want any more."

At this reply the Swede ruffled out his chest like a rooster. "Well," he exploded, "it seems I can't get anybody to drink with me in this town. Seems so, don't it? Well!"

"Ssh!" said the barkeeper.

"Say," snarled the Swede, "don't you try to shut me up. I won't have it. I'm a gentleman, and I want people to drink with me. And I want 'em to drink with me now. *Now*—do you understand?" He rapped the bar with his knuckles.

Years of experience had calloused the bartender. He merely grew sulky. "I hear you," he answered.

"Well," cried the Swede, "listen hard then. See those men over there? Well, they're going to drink with me, and don't you forget it. Now you watch."

"Hi!" yelled the barkeeper, "this won't do!"

"Why won't it?" demanded the Swede. He stalked over to the table, and by chance laid his hand upon the shoulder of the gambler. "How about this?" he asked wrathfully. "I asked you to drink with me."

The gambler simply twisted his head and spoke over his shoulder. "My friend, I don't know you."

"Oh, hell!" answered the Swede, "come and have a drink."

"Now, my boy," advised the gambler, kindly, "take your hand off my shoulder and go 'way and mind your own business." He was a little, slim man, and it seemed strange to hear him use this tone of heroic patronage to the burly Swede. The other men at the table said nothing.

"What! You won't drink with me, you little dude? I'll make you, then! I'll make you!" The Swede had grasped the gambler frenziedly at the throat, and was dragging him from his chair. The other men sprang up. The barkeeper dashed around the corner of his bar. There was a great tumult, and then was seen a long blade in the hand of the gambler. It shot forward, and a human body, this citadel of virtue, wisdom, power, was pierced as easily as if it had been a melon. The Swede fell with a cry of supreme astonishment.

The prominent merchants and the district attorney must have at once tumbled out of the place backward. The bartender found himself hanging limply to the arm of a chair and gazing into the eyes of a murderer.

"Henry," said the latter, as he wiped his knife on one of the towels that hung beneath the bar rail, "you tell 'em where to find me. I'll be home, waiting for 'em." Then he vanished. A moment afterward the barkeeper was in the street dinning through the storm for help and, moreover, companionship.

The corpse of the Swede, alone in the saloon, had its eye fixed upon a dreadful legend that dwelt atop of the cash-machine: "This registers the amount of your purchase."

IX

Months later, the cowboy was frying pork over the stove of a little ranch near the Dakota line, when there was a quick thud of hoofs outside, and presently the Easterner entered with the letters and the papers.

"Well," said the Easterner at once, "the chap that killed the Swede has got three years? Wasn't much, was it?"

"He has? Three years?" The cowboy poised his pan of pork, while he ruminated upon the news. "Three years. That ain't much."

"No. It was a light sentence," replied the Easterner as he unbuckled his spurs. "Seems there was a good deal of sympathy for him in Romper."

"If the bartender had been any good," observed the cowboy, thoughtfully, "he would have gone in and cracked that there Dutchman on the head with a bottle in the beginnin' of it and stopped all this here murderin'."

"Yes, a thousand things might have happened," said the Easterner, tartly.

The cowboy returned his pan of pork to the fire, but his philosophy continued. "It's funny, ain't it? If he hadn't said Johnnie was cheatin' he'd be alive this minute. He was an awful fool. Game played for fun, too. Not for money. I believe he was crazy."

"I feel sorry for that gambler," said the Easterner.

"Oh, so do I," said the cowboy. "He don't deserve none of it for killin' who he did."

"The Swede might not have been killed if everything had been square."

"Might not have been killed?" exclaimed the cowboy. "Everythin' square? Why, when he said that Johnnie was cheatin' and acted like such a jackass? And then in the saloon he fairly walked up to git hurt?" With these arguments the cowboy browbeat the Easterner and reduced him to rage.

"You're a fool!" cried the Easterner, viciously. "You're a bigger jackass than the Swede by a million majority. Now let me tell you one thing. Let me tell you something. Listen! Johnnie *was* cheating!"

"'Johnnie,'" said the cowboy, blankly. There was a minute of silence, and then he said, robustly, "Why, no. The game was only for fun."

"Fun or not," said the Easterner, "Johnnie was cheating. I saw him. I know it. I saw him. And I refused to stand up and be a man. I let the Swede fight it out alone. And you—you were simply puffing around the place and wanting to fight. And then old Scully himself! We are all in it! This poor gambler isn't even a noun. He is kind of an adverb. Every sin is the result of a collaboration. We, five of us, have collaborated in the murder of this Swede. Usually there are from a dozen to forty women really involved in every murder, but in this case it seems to be only five men—you, I, Johnnie, old Scully; and that fool of an unfortunate gambler came merely as a culmination, the apex of a human movement, and gets all the punishment."

The cowboy, injured and rebellious, cried out blindly into this fog of mysterious theory: "Well, I didn't do anythin', did I?"

1898

RELATED:

—Crane, Letter to John Northern Hilliard, p. 1714
—Allan Gurganus on "The Open Boat," p. 1761
—Charles C. Walcutt, "Stephen Crane: Naturalist," p. 1783

EDWIDGE DANTICAT
b. 1969

Edwidge Danticat was born in Port-au-Prince, Haiti, where she was raised by her aunt. At the age of twelve she moved to the United States to join her parents, who were living in a Haitian-American neighborhood in Brooklyn, New York, and she published her first writing in English two years later, a newspaper article about her immigration to the United States that eventually developed into her first novel, *Breath, Eyes, Memory* (1994). Since earning a degree in French literature from Barnard College and an M.F.A. from Brown University, she has focused on writing. Her first collection of stories *Krik? Krak!* (1995) established her as a developing master of the form. Her second novel, *The Farming of Bones* (1998), is based on the 1937 massacre of Haitians at the border of the Dominican Republic. Most recently, Danticat published *After the Dance: A Walk through Carnival in Jacmel, Haiti* (2002), an account of her travels, a second story collection, *The Dew Breaker* (2004), an essay collection, *Create Dangerously* (2010), and a new novel, *Claire of the Sea Light* (2013). She teaches creative writing at New York University.

A Wall of Fire Rising

Listen to what happened today," Guy said as he barged through the rattling door of his tiny shack.

His wife, Lili, was squatting in the middle of their one-room home, spreading cornmeal mush on banana leaves for their supper.

"Listen to what happened to *me* today!" Guy's seven-year-old son—Little Guy—dashed from a corner and grabbed his father's hand. The boy dropped his composition notebook as he leaped to his father, nearly stepping into the corn mush and herring that his mother had set out in a trio of half gourds on the clay floor.

"Our boy is in a play." Lili quickly robbed Little Guy of the honor of telling his father the news.

"A play?" Guy affectionately stroked the boy's hair.

The boy had such tiny corkscrew curls that no amount of brushing could ever make them all look like a single entity. The other boys at the Lycée Jean-Jacques[1] called him "pepper head" because each separate kinky strand was coiled into a tight tiny ball that looked like small peppercorns.

---

1. The *lycée* (French for "school") is named for Jean-Jacques Dessalines (1758–1806), a former slave who founded independent Haiti and was declared Emperor Jacques I in 1804.

"When is this play?" Guy asked both the boy and his wife. "Are we going to have to buy new clothes for this?"

Lili got up from the floor and inclined her face towards her husband's in order to receive her nightly peck on the cheek.

"What role do you have in the play?" Guy asked, slowly rubbing the tip of his nails across the boy's scalp. His fingers made a soft grating noise with each invisible circle drawn around the perimeters of the boy's head. Guy's fingers finally landed inside the boy's ears, forcing the boy to giggle until he almost gave himself the hiccups.

"Tell me, what is your part in the play?" Guy asked again, pulling his fingers away from his son's ear.

"I am Boukman," the boy huffed out, as though there was some laughter caught in his throat.

"Show Papy your lines," Lili told the boy as she arranged the three open gourds on a piece of plywood raised like a table on two bricks, in the middle of the room. "My love, Boukman is the hero of the play."

The boy went back to the corner where he had been studying and pulled out a thick book carefully covered in brown paper.

"You're going to spend a lifetime learning those." Guy took the book from the boy's hand and flipped through the pages quickly. He had to strain his eyes to see the words by the light of an old kerosene lamp, which that night—like all others—flickered as though it was burning its very last wick.

"All these words seem so long and heavy," Guy said. "You think you can do this, son?"

"He has one very good speech," Lili said. "Page forty, remember, son?"

The boy took back the book from his father. His face was crimped in an of-course-I-remember look as he searched for page forty.

"Bouk-man," Guy struggled with the letters of the slave revolutionary's name as he looked over his son's shoulders. "I see some very hard words here, son."

"He already knows his speech," Lili told her husband.

"Does he now?" asked Guy.

"We've been at it all afternoon," Lili said. "Why don't you go on and recite that speech for your father?"

The boy tipped his head towards the rusting tin on the roof as he prepared to recite his lines.

Lili wiped her hands on an old apron tied around her waist and stopped to listen.

"Remember what you are," Lili said, "a great rebel leader. Remember, it is the revolution."

"Do we want him to be all of that?" Guy asked.

"He is Boukman," Lili said. "What is the only thing on your mind now, Boukman?"

"Supper," Guy whispered, enviously eyeing the food cooling off in the middle of the room. He and the boy looked at each other and began to snicker.

"Tell us the other thing that is on your mind," Lili said, joining in their laughter.

"Freedom!" shouted the boy, as he quickly slipped into his role.

"Louder!" urged Lili.

"Freedom is on my mind!" yelled the boy.

"Why don't you start, son?" said Guy. "If you don't, we'll never get to that other thing that we have on our minds."

The boy closed his eyes and took a deep breath. At first, his lips parted but nothing came out. Lili pushed her head forward as though she were holding her breath. Then like the last burst of lightning out of clearing sky, the boy began.

"A wall of fire is rising and in the ashes, I see the bones of my people. Not only those people whose dark hollow faces I see daily in the fields, but all those souls who have gone ahead to haunt my dreams. At night I relive once more the last caresses from the hand of a loving father, a valiant love, a beloved friend."[2]

It was obvious that this was a speech written by a European man, who gave to the slave revolutionary Boukman the kind of European phrasing that might have sent the real Boukman turning in his grave. However, the speech made Lili and Guy stand on the tips of their toes from great pride. As their applause thundered in the small space of their shack that night, they felt as though for a moment they had been given the rare pleasure of hearing the voice of one of the forefathers of Haitian independence in the forced baritone of their only child. The experience left them both with a strange feeling that they could not explain. It left the hair on the back of their necks standing on end. It left them feeling much more love than they ever knew that they could add to their feeling for their son.

"Bravo," Lili cheered, pressing her son into the folds of her apron. "Long live Boukman and long live my boy."

"Long live our supper," Guy said, quickly batting his eyelashes to keep tears from rolling down his face.

The boy kept his eyes on his book as they ate their supper that night. Usually Guy and Lili would not have allowed that, but this was a special occasion. They watched proudly as the boy muttered his lines between swallows of cornmeal.

The boy was still mumbling the same words as the three of them used the last of the rainwater trapped in old gasoline containers and sugarcane pulp from the nearby sugarcane mill to scrub the gourds that they had eaten from.

When things were really bad for the family, they boiled clean sugarcane pulp to make what Lili called her special sweet water tea. It was supposed to suppress gas and kill the vermin in the stomach that made poor children hungry. That and a pinch of salt under the tongue could usually quench hunger until Guy found a day's work or Lili could manage to buy spices on credit and then peddle them for a profit at the marketplace.

That night, anyway, things were good. Everyone had eaten enough to put all their hunger vermin to sleep.

The boy was sitting in front of the shack on an old plastic bucket turned upside down, straining his eyes to find the words on the page. Sometimes when there was no kerosene for the lamp, the boy would have to go sit by the

2. On the night of August 22, 1791, slaves led by a slave foreman named Boukman (secretly a voodoo high priest) built a "wall of fire" that destroyed many plantations in the north of the French colony of Saint-Domingue, marking the beginning of a mass slave revolt that would lead, fourteen years later, to the establishment of independent Haiti.

side of the road and study under the street lamps with the rest of the neighborhood children. Tonight, at least, they had a bit of their own light.

Guy bent down by a small clump of old mushrooms near the boy's feet, trying to get a better look at the plant. He emptied the last drops of rainwater from a gasoline container on the mushroom, wetting the bulging toes sticking out of his sons' sandals, which were already coming apart around his endlessly growing feet.

Guy tried to pluck some of the mushrooms, which were being pushed into the dust as though they wanted to grow beneath the ground as roots. He took one of the mushrooms in his hand, running his smallest finger over the round bulb. He clipped the stem and buried the top in a thick strand of his wife's hair.

The mushroom looked like a dried insect in Lili's hair.

"It sure makes you look special," Guy said, teasing her.

"Thank you so much," Lili said, tapping her husband's arm. "It's nice to know that I deserve these much more than roses."

Taking his wife's hand, Guy said, "Let's go to the sugar mill."

"Can I study my lines there?" the boy asked.

"You know them well enough already," Guy said.

"I need many repetitions," the boy said.

Their feet sounded as though they were playing a wet wind instrument as they slipped in and out of the puddles between the shacks in the shantytown. Near the sugar mill was a large television screen in a iron grill cage that the government had installed so that the shantytown dwellers could watch the state-sponsored news at eight o'clock every night. After the news, a gendarme[3] would come and turn off the television set, taking home the key. On most nights, the people stayed at the site long after this gendarme had gone and told stories to one another beneath the big blank screen. They made bonfires with dried sticks, corn husks, and paper, cursing the authorities under their breath.

There was a crowd already gathering for the nightly news event. The sugar mill workers sat in the front row in chairs or on old buckets.

Lili and Guy passed the group, clinging to their son so that in his childhood naïveté he wouldn't accidentally glance at the wrong person and be called an insolent child. They didn't like the ambiance of the nightly news watch. They spared themselves trouble by going instead to the sugar mill, where in the past year they had discovered their own wonder.

Everyone knew that the family who owned the sugar mill were eccentric "Arabs," Haitians of Lebanese or Palestinian descent whose family had been in the country for generations. The Assad family had a son who, it seems, was into all manner of odd things, the most recent of which was a hot-air balloon, which he had brought to Haiti from America and occasionally flew over the shantytown skies.

As they approached the fence surrounding the field where the large wicker basket and deflated balloon rested on the ground, Guy let go of the hands of both his wife and the boy.

3. Policeman or guard (French).

Lili walked on slowly with her son. For the last few weeks, she had been feeling as though Guy was lost to her each time he reached this point, twelve feet away from the balloon. As Guy pushed his hand through the barbed wire, she could tell from the look on his face that he was thinking of sitting inside the square basket while the smooth rainbow surface of the balloon itself floated above his head. During the day, when the field was open, Guy would walk up to the basket, staring at it with the same kind of longing that most men display when they admire very pretty girls.

Lili and the boy stood watching from a distance as Guy tried to push his hand deeper, beyond the chain link fence that separated him from the balloon. He reached into his pants pocket and pulled out a small pocketknife, sharpening the edges on the metal surface of the fence. When his wife and child moved closer, he put the knife back in his pocket, letting his fingers slide across his son's tightly coiled curls.

"I wager you I can make this thing fly," Guy said.

"Why do you think you can do that?" Lili asked.

"I know it," Guy replied.

He followed her as she circled the sugar mill, leading to their favorite spot under a watch light. Little Guy lagged faithfully behind them. From this distance, the hot-air balloon looked like an odd spaceship.

Lili stretched her body out in the knee-high grass in the field. Guy reached over and tried to touch her between her legs.

"You're not one to worry, Lili," he said. "You're not afraid of the frogs, lizards, or snakes that could be hiding in this grass?"

"I am here with my husband," she said. "You are here to protect me if anything happens."

Guy reached into his shirt pocket and pulled out a lighter and a crumpled piece of paper. He lit the paper until it burned to an ashy film. The burning paper floated in the night breeze for a while, landing in fragments on the grass.

"Did you see that, Lili?" Guy asked with a flame in his eyes brighter than the lighter's. "Did you see how the paper floated when it was burned? This is how that balloon flies."

"What did you mean by saying that you could make it fly?" Lili asked.

"You already know all my secrets," Guy said as the boy came charging towards them.

"Papa, could you play *Lago* with me?" the boy asked.

Lili lay peacefully on the grass as her son and husband played hide-and-seek. Guy kept hiding and his son kept finding him as each time Guy made it easier for the boy.

"We rest now." Guy was becoming breathless.

The stars were circling the peaks of the mountains, dipping into the cane fields belonging to the sugar mill. As Guy caught his breath, the boy raced around the fence, running as fast as he could to purposely make himself dizzy.

"Listen to what happened today," Guy whispered softly in Lili's ear.

"I heard you say that when you walked in the house tonight," Lili said. "With the boy's play, I forgot to ask you."

The boy sneaked up behind them, his face lit up, though his brain was spinning. He wrapped his arms around both their necks.

"We will go back home soon," Lili said.

"Can I recite my lines?" asked the boy.

"We have heard them," Guy said. "Don't tire your lips."

The boy mumbled something under his breath. Guy grabbed his ear and twirled it until it was a tiny ball in his hand. The boy's face contorted with agony as Guy made him kneel in the deep grass in punishment.

Lili looked tortured as she watched the boy squirming in the grass, obviously terrified of the crickets, lizards, and small snakes that might be there.

"Perhaps we should take him home to bed," she said.

"He will never learn," Guy said, "if I say one thing and you say another."

Guy got up and angrily started walking home. Lili walked over, took her son's hand, and raised him from his knees.

"You know you must not mumble," she said.

"I was saying my lines," the boy said.

"Next time say them loud," Lili said, "so he knows what is coming out of your mouth."

That night Lili could hear her son muttering his lines as he tucked himself in his corner of the room and drifted off to sleep. The boy still had the book with his monologue in it clasped under his arm as he slept.

Guy stayed outside in front of the shack as Lili undressed for bed. She loosened the ribbon that held the old light blue cotton skirt around her waist and let it drop past her knees. She grabbed half a lemon that she kept in the corner by the folded mat that she and Guy unrolled to sleep on every night. Lili let her blouse drop to the floor as she smoothed the lemon over her ashen legs.

Guy came in just at that moment and saw her bare chest by the light of the smaller castor oil lamp that they used for the later hours of the night. Her skin had coarsened a bit over the years, he thought. Her breasts now drooped from having nursed their son for two years after he was born. It was now easier for him to imagine their son's lips around those breasts than to imagine his anywhere near them.

He turned his face away as she fumbled for her nightgown. He helped her open the mat, tucking the blanket edges underneath.

Fully clothed, Guy dropped onto the mat next to her. He laid his head on her chest, rubbing the spiky edges of his hair against her nipples.

"What was it that happened today?" Lili asked, running her fingers along Guy's hairline, an angular hairline, almost like a triangle, in the middle of his forehead. She nearly didn't marry him because it was said that people with angular hairlines often have very troubled lives.

"I got a few hours' work for tomorrow at the sugar mill," Guy said. "That's what happened today."

"It was such a long time coming," Lili said.

It was almost six months since the last time Guy had gotten work there. The jobs at the sugar mill were few and far between. The people who had them never left, or when they did they would pass the job on to another family member who was already waiting on line.

Guy did not seem overjoyed about the one day's work.

"I wish I had paid more attention when you came in with the news," Lili said. "I was just so happy about the boy."

"I was born in the shadow of that sugar mill," Guy said. "Probably the first thing my mother gave me to drink as a baby was some sweet water tea from the pulp of the sugarcane. If anyone deserves to work there, I should."

"What will you be doing for your day's work?"

"Would you really like to know?"

"There is never any shame in honest work," she said.

"They want me to scrub the latrines."

"It's honest work," Lili said, trying to console him.

"I am still number seventy-eight on the permanent hire list," he said. "I was thinking of putting the boy on the list now, so maybe by the time he becomes a man he can be up for a job."

Lili's body jerked forward, rising straight up in the air. Guy's head dropped with a loud thump onto the mat.

"I don't want him on that list," she said. "For a young boy to be on any list like that might influence his destiny. I don't want him on the list."

"Look at me," Guy said. "If my father had worked there, if he had me on the list, don't you think I would be working?"

"If you have any regard for me," she said, "you will not put him on the list."

She groped for her husband's chest in the dark and laid her head on it. She could hear his heart beating loudly as though it were pumping double, triple its normal rate.

"You won't put the boy on any lists, will you?" she implored.

"Please, Lili, no more about the boy. He will not go on the list."

"Thank you."

"Tonight I was looking at that balloon in the yard behind the sugar mill," he said. "I have been watching it real close."

"I know."

"I have seen the man who owns it," he said. "I've seen him get in it and put it in the sky and go up there like it was some kind of kite and he was the kite master. I see the men who run after it trying to figure out where it will land. Once I was there and I was one of those men who were running and I actually guessed correctly. I picked a spot in the sugarcane fields. I picked the spot from a distance and it actually landed there."

"Let me say something to you, Guy—"

"Pretend that this is the time of miracles and we believed in them. I watched the owner for a long time, and I think I can fly that balloon. The first time I saw him do it, it looked like a miracle, but the more and more I saw it, the more ordinary it became."

"You're probably intelligent enough to do it," she said.

"I am intelligent enough to do it. You're right to say that I can."

"Don't you think about hurting yourself?"

"Think like this. Can't you see yourself up there? Up in the clouds somewhere like some kind of bird?"

"If God wanted people to fly, he would have given us wings on our backs."

"You're right, Lili, you're right. But look what he gave us instead. He gave us reasons to want to fly. He gave us the air, the birds, our son."

"I don't understand you," she said.

"Our son, your son, you do not want him cleaning latrines."

"He can do other things."

"Me too. I can do other things too."

A loud scream came from the corner where the boy was sleeping. Lili and Guy rushed to him and tried to wake him. The boy was trembling when he opened his eyes.

"What is the matter?" Guy asked.

"I cannot remember my lines," the boy said.

Lili tried to string together what she could remember of her son's lines. The words slowly came back to the boy. By the time he fell back to sleep, it was almost dawn.

The light was slowly coming up behind the trees. Lili could hear the whispers of the market women, their hisses and swearing as their sandals dug into the sharp-edged rocks on the road.

She turned her back to her husband as she slipped out of her nightgown, quickly putting on her day clothes.

"Imagine this," Guy said from the mat on the floor. "I have never really seen your entire body in broad daylight."

Lili shut the door behind her, making her way out to the yard. The empty gasoline containers rested easily on her head as she walked a few miles to the public water fountains. It was harder to keep them steady when the containers were full. The water splashed all over her blouse and rippled down her back.

The sky was blue as it was most mornings, a dark indigo-shaded turquoise that would get lighter when the sun was fully risen.

Guy and the boy were standing in the yard waiting for her when she got back.

"You did not get much sleep, my handsome boy," she said, running her wet fingers over the boy's face.

"He'll be late for school if we do not go right now," Guy said. "I want to drop him off before I start work."

"Do we remember our lines this morning?" Lili asked, tucking the boy's shirt down deep into his short pants.

"We just recited them," Guy said. "Even I know them now."

Lili watched them walk down the footpath, her eyes following them until they disappeared.

As soon as they were out of sight, she poured the water she had fetched into a large calabash, letting it stand beside the house.

She went back into the room and slipped into a dry blouse. It was never too early to start looking around, to scrape together that night's meal.

"Listen to what happened again today," Lili said when Guy walked through the door that afternoon.

Guy blotted his face with a dust rag as he prepared to hear the news. After the day he'd had at the factory, he wanted to sit under a tree and have a leisurely smoke, but he did not want to set a bad example for his son by indulging his very small pleasures.

"You tell him, son," Lili urged the boy, who was quietly sitting in a corner, reading.

"I've got more lines," the boy announced, springing up to his feet. "Papy, do you want to hear them?"

"They are giving him more things to say in the play," Lili explained, "because he did such a good job memorizing so fast."

"My compliments, son. Do you have your new lines memorized too?" Guy asked.

"Why don't you recite your new lines for your father?" Lili said.

The boy walked to the middle of the room and prepared to recite. He cleared his throat, raising his eyes towards the ceiling.

"There is so much sadness in the faces of my people. I have called on their gods, now I call on our gods. I call on our young. I call on our old. I call on our mighty and the weak. I call on everyone and anyone so that we shall all let out one piercing cry that we may either live freely or we should die."

"I see your new lines have as much drama as the old ones," Guy said. He wiped a tear away, walked over to the chair, and took the boy in his arms. He pressed the boy's body against his chest before lowering him to the ground.

"Your new lines are wonderful, son. They're every bit as affecting as the old." He tapped the boy's shoulder and walked out of the house.

"What's the matter with Papy?" the boy asked as the door slammed shut behind Guy.

"His heart hurts," Lili said.

After supper, Lili took her son to the field where she knew her husband would be. While the boy ran around, she found her husband sitting in his favorite spot behind the sugar mill.

"Nothing, Lili," he said. "Ask me nothing about this day that I have had."

She sat down on the grass next to him, for once feeling the sharp edges of the grass blades against her ankles.

"You're really good with that boy," he said, drawing circles with his smallest finger on her elbow. "You will make a performer of him. I know you will. You can see the best in that whole situation. It's because you have those stars in your eyes. That's the first thing I noticed about you when I met you. It was your eyes, Lili, so dark and deep. They drew me like danger draws a fool."

He turned over on the grass so that he was staring directly at the moon up in the sky. She could tell that he was also watching the hot-air balloon behind the sugar mill fence out of the corner of his eye.

"Sometimes I know you want to believe in me," he said. "I know you're wishing things for me. You want me to work at the mill. You want me to get a pretty house for us. I know you want these things too, but mostly you want me to feel like a man. That's why you're not one to worry about, Lili. I know you can take things as they come."

"I don't like it when you talk this way," she said.

"Listen to this, Lili. I want to tell you a secret. Sometimes, I just want to take that big balloon and ride it up in the air. I'd like to sail off somewhere and keep floating until I got to a really nice place with a nice plot of land where I could be something new. I'd build my own house, keep my own garden. Just *be* something new."

"I want you to stay away from there."

"I know you don't think I should take it. That can't keep me from wanting."

"You could be injured. Do you ever think about that?"

"Don't you ever want to be something new?"

"I don't like it," she said.

"Please don't get angry with me," he said, his voice straining almost like the boy's.

"If you were to take that balloon and fly away, would you take me and the boy?"

"First you don't want me to take it and now you want to go?"

"I just want to know that when you dream, me and the boy, we're always in your dreams."

He leaned his head on her shoulders and drifted off to sleep. Her back ached as she sat there with his face pressed against her collar bone. He drooled and the saliva dripped down to her breasts, soaking her frayed polyester bra. She listened to the crickets while watching her son play, muttering his lines to himself as he went in a circle around the field. The moon was glowing above their heads. Winking at them, as Guy liked to say, on its way to brighter shores.

Opening his eyes, Guy asked her, "How do you think a man is judged after he's gone?"

How did he expect her to answer something like that?

"People don't eat riches," she said. "They eat what it can buy."

"What does that mean, Lili? Don't talk to me in parables. Talk to me honestly."

"A man is judged by his deeds," she said. "The boy never goes to bed hungry. For as long as he's been with us, he's always been fed."

Just as if he had heard himself mentioned, the boy came dashing from the other side of the field, crashing in a heap on top of his parents.

"My new lines," he said. "I have forgotten my new lines."

"Is this how you will be the day of this play, son?" Guy asked. "When people give you big responsibilities, you have to try to live up to them."

The boy had relearned his new lines by the time they went to bed.

That night, Guy watched his wife very closely as she undressed for bed.

"I would like to be the one to rub that piece of lemon on your knees tonight," he said.

She handed him the half lemon, then raised her skirt above her knees.

Her body began to tremble as he rubbed his fingers over her skin.

"You know that question I asked you before," he said, "how a man is remembered after he's gone? I know the answer now. I know because I remember my father, who was a very poor struggling man all his life. I remember him as a man that I would never want to be."

Lili got up with the break of dawn the next day. The light came up quickly above the trees. Lili greeted some of the market women as they walked together to the public water fountain.

On her way back, the sun had already melted a few gray clouds. She found the boy standing alone in the yard with a terrified expression on his face, the old withered mushrooms uprooted at his feet. He ran up to meet her, nearly knocking her off balance.

"What happened?" she asked. "Have you forgotten your lines?"

The boy was breathing so heavily that his lips could not form a single word.

"What is it?" Lili asked, almost shaking him with anxiety.

"It's Papa," he said finally, raising a stiff finger in the air.

The boy covered his face as his mother looked up at the sky. A rainbow-colored balloon was floating aimlessly above their heads.

"It's Papa," the boy said. "He is in it."

She wanted to look down at her son and tell him that it wasn't his father, but she immediately recognized the spindly arms, in a bright flowered shirt that she had made, gripping the cables.

From the field behind the sugar mill a group of workers were watching the balloon floating in the air. Many were clapping and cheering, calling out Guy's name. A few of the women were waving their head rags at the sky, shouting, "Go! Beautiful, go!"

Lili edged her way to the front of the crowd. Everyone was waiting, watching the balloon drift higher up into the clouds.

"He seems to be right over our heads," said the factory foreman, a short slender mulatto with large buckteeth.

Just then, Lili noticed young Assad, his thick black hair sticking to the beads of sweat on his forehead. His face had the crumpled expression of disrupted sleep.

"He's further away than he seems," said young Assad. "I still don't understand. How did he get up there? You need a whole crew to fly these things."

"I don't know," the foreman said. "One of my workers just came in saying there was a man flying above the factory."

"But how the hell did he start it?" Young Assad was perplexed.

"He just did it," the foreman said.

"Look, he's trying to get out!" someone hollered.

A chorus of screams broke out among the workers.

The boy was looking up, trying to see if his father was really trying to jump out of the balloon. Guy was climbing over the side of the basket. Lili pressed her son's face into her skirt.

Within seconds, Guy was in the air hurtling down towards the crowd. Lili held her breath as she watched him fall. He crashed not far from where Lili and the boy were standing, his blood immediately soaking the landing spot.

The balloon kept floating free, drifting on its way to brighter shores. Young Assad rushed towards the body. He dropped to his knees and checked the wrist for a pulse, then dropped the arm back to the ground.

"It's over!" The foreman ordered the workers back to work.

Lili tried to keep her son's head pressed against her skirt as she moved closer to the body. The boy yanked himself away and raced to the edge of the field where his father's body was lying on the grass. He reached the body as young Assad still knelt examining the corpse. Lili rushed after him.

"He is mine," she said to young Assad. "He is my family. He belongs to me."

Young Assad got up and raised his head to search the sky for his aimless balloon, trying to guess where it would land. He took one last glance at Guy's bloody corpse, then raced to his car and sped away.

The foreman and another worker carried a cot and blanket from the factory.

Little Guy was breathing quickly as he looked at his father's body on the ground. While the foreman draped a sheet over Guy's corpse, his son began to recite the lines from his play.

"A wall of fire is rising and in the ashes, I see the bones of my people. Not only those people whose dark hollow faces I see daily in the fields, but all those souls who have gone ahead to haunt my dreams. At night I relive once more the last caresses from the hand of a loving father, a valiant love, a beloved friend."

"Let me look at him one last time," Lili said, pulling back the sheet.

She leaned in very close to get a better look at Guy's face. There was little left of that countenance that she had loved so much. Those lips that curled when he was teasing her. That large flat nose that felt like a feather when rubbed against hers. And those eyes, those night-colored eyes. Though clouded with blood, Guy's eyes were still bulging open. Lili was searching for some kind of sign—a blink, a smile, a wink—something that would remind her of the man that she had married.

"His eyes aren't closed," the foreman said to Lili. "Do you want to close them, or should I?"

The boy continued reciting his lines, his voice rising to a man's grieving roar. He kept his eyes closed, his fists balled at his side as he continued with his newest lines.

"There is so much sadness in the faces of my people. I have called on their gods, now I call on our gods. I call on our young. I call on our old. I call on our mighty and the weak. I call on everyone and anyone so that we shall all let out one piercing cry that we may either live freely or we should die."

"Do you want to close the eyes?" the foreman repeated impatiently.

"No, leave them open," Lili said. "My husband, he likes to look at the sky."

1991

ANITA DESAI
b. 1937

Anita Mazumdar Desai was born in Delhi to an Indian father and a German mother. Though she grew up speaking many languages including German, Urdu, and Hindi, it was in English that she first learned to read and write, and it remains her literary language. Desai began writing at a very young age, publishing a piece in a children's magazine when she was nine years old. She went on to study English Literature at the University of Delhi, earning her B.A. in 1957. Soon after graduating, she married and started a family with Ashvin Desai and published her first novel, *Cry, The Peacock*, five years later in 1963. Since then, Desai has written fifteen more novels as well as numerous short stories and children's books. Her novels include *Fire on the Mountain* (1977)—winner of the National Academy of Letters Award—*Clear Light of Day* (1980), *In Custody* (1984), and *Fasting, Feasting* (1999), all three of which were short-listed for the Booker Prize. Desai is a Fellow of the Royal Society of Literature in London as well as a member of the Advisory Board for English at the National Academy of Letters in Delhi. She has taught at numerous colleges and universities, including Mount Holyoke College, Smith College, and The Massachusetts Institute of Technology.

Royalty

All was prepared for the summer exodus: the trunks packed, the household wound down, wound up, ready to be abandoned to three months of withering heat and engulfing dust while its owners withdrew to their retreat in the mountains. The last few days were a little uncomfortable — so many of their clothes already packed away, so many of their books and papers bundled up and ready for the move. The house looked stark, with the silver put away, the vases emptied of flowers, the rugs and carpets rolled up; it was difficult to get through this stretch, delayed by one thing or another — a final visit to the dentist, last instructions to the stockbrokers, a nephew to be entertained on his way to Oxford. It was only the prospect of escape from the blinding heat that already hammered at the closed doors and windows, poured down on the roof and verandas, and withdrawal to the freshness and cool of the mountains which helped them to bear it. Sinking down on veranda chairs to sip lemonade from tall glasses, they sighed, 'Well, we'll soon be out of it.'

In that uncomfortable interlude, a postcard arrived — a cheap, yellow printed postcard that for some reason to do with his age, his generation, Raja still used. Sarla's hands began to tremble: news from Raja. In a quivering voice she asked for her spectacles. Ravi passed them to her and she peered through them to decipher the words as if they were a flight of migrating birds in the distance: Raja was in India, at his ashram in the south, Raja was going to be in Delhi next week, Raja expected to find her there. She *would* be there, wouldn't she? 'You won't desert me?'

After Ravi had made several appeals to her for information, for a sharing of the news, she lifted her face to him, grey and mottled, and said in a broken voice, 'Oh Ravi, Raja has come. He is in the south. He wants to visit us — next week.'

It was only to be expected that Ravi's hands would fall upon the table, fall onto china and silverware, with a crash, making all rattle and jar. Raja was coming! Raja was to be amongst them again!

A great shiver ran through the house like a wind blowing that was not a wind so much as a stream of shining light, shimmering and undulating through the still, shadowy house, a radiant serpent, not without menace, some threat of danger. Whether it liked it or not, the house became the one chosen by Raja for a visitation, a house in waiting.

With her sari wrapped around her shoulders tightly, as if she were cold, Sarla went about unlocking cupboards, taking out sheets, silver, table linen. Her own trunks, and Ravi's, had to be thrown open. What had been put away was taken out again. Ravi sat uncomfortably in the darkened drawing room, watching her go back and forth, his lips thin and tight, but his expression one of helplessness. Sometimes he dared to make things difficult for her, demanding a book or a file he knew was at the very bottom of the trunk, pretending that it was indispensable, but when she performed the difficult task with every expression of weary martyrdom, he relented and asked, 'Are you all right, Sarla?' She refused to answer, her face was clenched in a tightly contained storm of emotion. Despondently, he groaned, 'Oh, aren't we too old —?' Then she turned to look at him, and even spoke: 'What do you mean?' Ravi shook his head helplessly. Was there any need to explain?

Raja arrived on an early morning train. Another sign of his generation: he did not fly when he was in India. Perhaps he had not taken in the fact that one could fly in India too, or else he preferred the trains, no matter how long they took, crawling over the endless, arid plains in the parched heat before the rains. At dawn, no sun yet visible, the sky was already white with heat; crows rose from the dust-laden trees, cawing, then dropped to the ground, sun-struck. Sweepers with great brooms made desultory swipes at the streets, their mouths covered with a strip of turban, or sari, against the dust they raised. Motor rickshaws and taxis were being washed, lovingly, tenderly, by drivers in striped underpants. The city stank of somnolence, of dejection, like sweat-stained clothes. Sarla and Ravi stood on the railway platform, waiting, and when Sarla seemed to waver, Ravi put out a gentlemanly hand to steady her. When she turned her face to him in something like gratitude or pleading, a look passed between them as can only pass between two people married to each other through the droughts and hurricanes of thirty years. Then the train arrived, with a great blowing of triumphant whistles: it had completed its long journey from the south, it had achieved its destination, hadn't it *said* it would? Magnificently, it was a promise kept. Immediately, coolies in red shirts and turbans, with legs like ancient tree roots, sprang at the compartments, leaping onto the steps before the train had even halted or its doors opened, and the families and friends waiting on the platform began to run with the train, waving, calling to the passengers who leaned out of the windows. Sarla and Ravi stood rooted to one place, clinging to each other in order not to be torn apart or pushed aside by the crowd in its excitement.

The pandemonium only grew worse when the doors were unlatched and the passengers began to dismount at the same time as the coolies forced their way in, creating human gridlock. Sighting their friends and relatives, the crowds on the platform began to wave and scream. Till coolies were matched with baggage, passengers with reception parties, utter chaos ruled. Sarla and Ravi peered through it, turning their heads in apprehension. Where was Raja? Only after the united families began to leave, exhorting coolies to bring up the rear with assorted trunks, bedding rolls and baskets balanced on their heads and held against their hips, and the railway platform had emerged from the scramble, did they hear the high-pitched, wavering warble of the voice they recognised: 'Sar-la! Ra-vi! My dears, how *good* of you to come! How *good* to see you! If you only knew what I've been through, about the man who insisted on telling me about his *alligator* farm, describing at such length how they are turned into *handbags*, as though I were a *leather merchant* . . .' and they turned to see Raja stepping out of one of the coaches, clutching his silk dhoti with one hand, waving elegantly with the other, a silver lock of his hair rising from his wide forehead as he landed on the platform in his slippered feet. And then the three of them were embracing each other, all at once, and it might have been Oxford, it might have been thirty years ago, it might even have been that lustrous morning in May emerging from dew-drenched meadows and the boat-crowded Isis, with ringing out of the skies and towers above them — bells, bells, bells, bells. . . .

'And then there was *another* extraordinary passenger, a young man with hair like a nest of serpents, you know, and when he understood I would *not* eat a "two-egg mamlet" offered to me by this *incredibly* ragged and *totally* sooty little urchin with a tin tray under his arm, nor even a "*one*-egg mamlet" to please him or anyone, this marvellous person leapt down from the bunk above my head, and shot out of the door — oh, I assure you we were at a standstill, in the most *desolate* little station imaginable, for no reason I could see or guess at if I cudgelled my brains ever so *ferociously* — and then he returned with a basket *overflowing* with fruit, a positive *cornucopia*. Sarla, you'd have *fainted* with bliss! Never did you see such fruit; oh, nowhere, nowhere on those mythical farms of California, certainly, worked on by those armies of the exploited from the sad lands to the south, I assure you, Ravi, such fruit as seemed a reincarnation of the fruit one ate as a child, *stolen*, you know, from the neighbour's orchard, fruit one ate hidden in the *darkest* recesses of one's compound, surreptitiously, one's tongue absolutely *shrivelled* by the *piercing* sweetness of the mangoes, the *cruel* tartness of unripe guavas, the unripe pulp of the plantains. Oh, Sarla, such joys! And I sat peeling a *tiny* banana and eating it — it was no bigger than my little finger and contained the flavour of the ripest, sweetest, best banana anywhere on earth within its cunning little yellow speckled jacket — I asked, naturally, what I owed him. But that incredible young man, who looked something like a cornucopia *himself*, with that abundant hair — it had such a quality of *liveliness* about it, every strand almost *electric* with energy — he merely folded his hands and said he would not take one paisa from me, not *one*. *Well*, of course I pushed away the basket and said I could not possibly accept it, totally against my principles, etcetera, and he gave me this tender, tender smile, quite unspeakably loving, and said he could take nothing from me because in a previous incarnation I had been his grandfather: he recognised me. "What?" said I, "*what*? What makes you say so? How *can* you say so?"'

'Watch out!' Ravi shouted at the driver who overtook a bullock cart so closely he almost ran into its great creaking wheels and overturned it.

'And he merely smiled, this sweet, *ineffably* sweet smile of his, and assured me I was no other than this esteemed ancestor of his who had left his home and family at the age of fifty and gone off into the Himalayas to live as a hermit and meditate. "*Well*," said I —'

'Slow down,' Ravi ordered the driver curtly.

'"*Well*," said I, "I *assure* you I have never been in the Himalayas — although it is *indeed* my life's ambition to do so, and therefore I could not have returned from there." By the way, I began to wonder if it was *altogether* flattering to be called grandfather by a man by no means in the first flush of youth, more like the becalmed middle years, whereupon he told me — imagine, Sarla, imagine, Ravi — he told me his grandfather had *died* there, in Rishikesh, on the banks of the Ganga, many years ago. His family had all travelled up from Madras to witness the cremation and carry the ashes to Benares, but *now*, in the railway carriage, that little tin box *baking* in the sun as we crossed the red earth and ravines of Central India, he claimed he'd seen his reincarnation. He was as *certain* of it as the banana in my hand was a banana! He would not tell me *why*, or *how*, but he was clearly a clairvoyant. And isn't that a *superb* combination: clearly clairvoyant! Or do you think it a touch *de trop*? Hmm, Ravi, Sarla?'

The car lurched around one of the countless circles set within the radiating avenues of New Delhi, now steadily filling with traffic that streamed towards the city's business and government centres, far from this region of immense jamun trees, large low villas, smooth hedges, closed gates, sentries in sentry boxes, and parakeets in flamboyant trees.

'But that is the kind of experience, the kind of encounter that India bestows on one like a *gift*, a *jewel*,' Raja was fluting as the car drew up at one of the closed gates. The driver honked the horn discreetly, the watchman came hurrying to unlock it, and they swept in and up the drive to the porch that stood loaded with the weight of magenta bougainvillea. 'And,' Raja continued as he let the driver help him out of the car, 'I was so *delighted*, so *overjoyed* to find it still so, Ravi, in spite of that frightful man you have installed as the head of your government — an *economist*, is he not? — yes, please, I shall need that bag almost *immediately*, and the other too, if I am to bathe and refresh myself, *but*,' he concluded, triumphantly, 'what further refreshment can one *possibly* require after one has already been blessed with such, such *enchanting* acceptance, not, not physical, but positively, positively . . .'

'Spiritual?' Ravi ventured, smiling, as he helped Raja up the stairs into the shaded cool of the veranda with its pots of flowers and ferns, a slowly revolving electric fan and an arrangement of wicker furniture where he lowered Raja into an armchair with a flowered cushion.

It was not that Raja was any more elderly than they. They had all been contemporaries at Oxford, and Raja may even have been a year or two younger. Sarla had complained that his southern ancestry had given Raja an unfair advantage over their northern genes which seemed to produce businessmen and shopkeepers more readily than mathematicians or philosophers. Yet there was about him an air of fragility, of some precious commodity that they had been called upon to cherish. At Oxford Ravi had found himself taking Raja's laundry to be done while Raja, who had neglected to attend to it till he had absolutely nothing left to wear, had stayed in bed under his blankets till Ravi returned with fresh clothes. He was wryly amused as well as a little annoyed to find that he still fell into the trap.

Sarla was hurrying into the house, to make sure Raja's luggage was carried carefully into the room prepared for him — the bedroom at the back of the house, which Raja loved because it looked onto a garden full of lemon trees and jasmine vines that he said he dreamt about during that part of the year that he spent in Los Angeles — and against Raja's wishes to order breakfast, because, after all, she and Ravi had not benefited from the generosity of the young man with hair like a serpent's nest in the railway carriage, she said a little acidly.

Why her words sounded acid, she could not say. It was all she could do not to go down on her knees and remove Raja's slippers from his feet, or to bring water in a basin and wash them. She had to sharpen her faculties to fight that urge. But she brought out the coffee pot herself — she had taken the silver coffee service out of storage for Raja's visit — and poured him a cup with all the grace that she had acquired in her years as a diplomat's wife in the embassies and High Commissions where Ravi had 'served', she 'presided'. She could scarcely restrain herself, only tremblingly managed to restrain herself from mentioning that last day in May, that last embrace — oh, it would be so unsuitable, so unsuitable —

And then a second car came sweeping up the drive, parked beside theirs — an identical car, a silver-grey Ambassador with tinted glass and window curtains — and her sister tumbled out of the driver's seat, a woman almost identical to Sarla, and in an equal state of excitement and agitation. And then they *were* all embracing each other, after all, successively, simultaneously.

Maya had not been with them on the bank of the festive, the bacchanalian Isis that May morning; she had not fetched Raja's laundry or cooked him rice on a gas ring on foggy winter nights when he could not walk to the Indian restaurant in the cold, not with his asthmatic condition: Maya had been at the London School of Economics a few years later. Maya had also met her husband at university, but his path had been different from Ravi's. 'No bloody Civil Service for me; I've always thought it most *uncivil*,' Pravin had declared when Maya suggested it, 'and at this stage of history can you really contemplate anything so reactionary? Are we not moving into the future, *free* of colonial institutions?' So it had been a political career for Pravin, not the dirty politics of people Raja had just referred to so disparagingly, but politics as practised by the press, idealistically, morally, scrupulously (even if only on paper). And so, when Maya embraced Raja, it was with vigour, with her head tossed back with pride so that her now grey hair hung from her shoulders with as carefree an air as a young girl might toss her darker, glossier locks, and with a laugh that rang out resonantly. 'What, you've travelled by train in a silk dhoti? Oh Raja, must you go to such *extremes* when you play the southern gentleman visiting the barbarians of the north?' and Raja hung upon her shoulder and shook his finger at her, fluting at a higher pitch than ever before, 'Is that husband of yours still playing the patriot while dressed in Harris tweeds, and does he still wear that mouldy felt hat when following the elections amongst the cow-dung patties and buffalo sheds of Bihar?' and Sarla was retreating to the wicker sofa with the coffee tray, glowering, turning ashen and tight-lipped once more. But her occupation of the sofa was strategic — now Maya and Raja could not sit upon it, side by side: it belonged to her, and she could preside, icily, silver coffee pot in hand, looking upon the two as if they were somewhat trying children, and Ravi would give her a look — of sympathy, or pity?— from the stool on which he perched, waiting patiently to be passed a cup.

She passed it, then said, interrupting Maya who was giving a humorous account of the last election campaign Pravin had covered, 'If to go to the Himalayas is your life's ambition, Raja, then that can easily be achieved. Won't you consider driving up with us when we go for the summer to *Winhaven?*'

'Winhaven? Winhaven?' Raja twisted around to her. 'Oh, Sarla, Sarla, the very word, the very name — it recalls — how does it go —

"I have desired to go
Where springs not fail —"

and then? And then? How does it go —

"And I have asked to be
Where no storms come
Where the green swell is in the havens dumb,
And out of the swing of the sea —"

remember? remember?'

Who did not? Who did not, Sarla would have liked to know, but suddenly Simba was upon them, bursting out of the house, his great tail thumping, his claws slithering across the veranda tiles in his excitement as he dashed at Maya, then at Ravi, finally at Raja and, to Sarla's horror, Raja was pushed back into his chair by Simba's vigorous attention, but Raja was pushing back at him, laughing, 'Oh, Simba, Simba of the Kenyan highlands! You remember me, do you?' and Sarla, cupping her chin in her hand, leaving her coffee untouched, watched as Raja, suddenly as sprightly as a boy, the boy who had bicycled helter-skelter down the streets of Oxford, dark hair rising up from his great brow and falling into the luminous eyes, now ran down the stairs with Simba into the garden, then bent to pick up a stick and send it flying up at the morning sun for the pleasure of having Simba leap for it. Old Simba, usually so gloomy, so lethargic, was now springing up on his hindlegs to catch the falling toy and run with it into the shade of the flamboyant tree, Raja following him, his pale silk dhoti floating about him, his white hair glistening, making the startled parakeets fly out of the clusters of scarlet flowers with screams.

Then both Sarla and Maya released small sighs. Ravi watched their expressions from the stool on which he was perched, and finally asked, diffidently, 'May I have a lump of sugar and a little milk, please?'

In spite of his poetic response to Sarla's suggestion that he accompany them to the mountains, Raja continuously postponed the journey. No, he had come to Delhi, all the way to Delhi in the heat of June, to see them, to relive the remembered joys of their beautiful home. How could he cut short his time here? And there was so much for him to see, to do, to catch up on. He wanted Sarla to drive him to the silver market in Chandni Chowk so he could gaze upon the magnificent craftsmanship on display there, perhaps even purchase a piece to take back with him to California where the natives had never seen such art bestowed upon craft, and then if Maya were to accompany him to the Cottage Industries emporium, and help him select a pashmina shawl, then he could be happy even on those chill, rainy days that he was forced to endure. What, didn't they *know*, California had such weather? Had they been deceived by posters of palm trees and golden beaches? Didn't they know the *fraudulence* inherent in the very notion and practice of tourism, that abominable habit of the Western world? Tourism! Now, when *he* returned to India, it was not to see the sights, he already knew them — they were imprinted upon his heart — but to imbibe them, savour them, nourish himself upon them. And so when Sarla and Ravi took him to Nizamuddin and beside the saint's tomb they heard a blind beggar play his lute and sing in a voice so soulful that it melted one's very being,

> 'When I was born
> I was my mother's prince.
> When I married
> I became my wife's king.
> But you have reduced me
> To being a beggar, Lord,
> Come begging for alms
> With my hands outstretched —'

it was as if the thirst of Raja's pilgrim soul was being slaked, and never had thirst been slaked by music so sublime as made by this ancient beggar in his rags, a tin can at his knee for alms — and of course he must have whatever was in Raja's purse, every last coin, alas that they were so few. Now if this beggar were performing in the West, the great theatres of every metropolis would throw open their doors to him. He would perform under floodlights, his name would be on posters, in the papers, on everyone's lips. Gold would pile up at his feet — but then, would he be such a singer as he was now, a pilgrim soul content to sit in the shade of the great saint Nizamuddin's little fretted marble tomb, and dedicate his song to him as homage?

Raja, leaving his slippers at the gateway to the courtyard, approached the tomb with such ecstasy etched upon his noble features that Sarla, and Ravi too, found themselves gazing at him rather than about them — Sarla's bare and Ravi's stockinged feet on the stones, braving the dirt and flies and garbage that had first made them shrink and half turn away. Sarla had held her sari to her nose as they passed a row of butchers' shops on their way to the tomb, buffalo's innards had hung like curtains in the small booths, and the air was rife with raw blood and the thrum of flies, and she asked Raja, in the car, 'How is it that you, a vegetarian, a Brahmin, walked in there and never even twitched your *nose?*' He cast his eyes upon her briefly — and they were still those narrow, horizontal pools of darkness she remembered — and sighed, 'My dear, true souls do not turn away from humanity or, if they do, it is only to meditate and pray, then come back, fortified, to embrace it — beggars, thieves, lepers, whoever — their sores, their rags. They do not flinch from them, for they know these are only the covering, the concealing robes of the soul, don't you know?' and Sarla, and Ravi, seated on either side of Raja on the comfortably upholstered back seat of the air-conditioned Ambassador, now speeding past the Lodi Gardens to their own green enclave, wondered if Raja was referring to himself or the sufi.

That afternoon, as they sat on the veranda, sipping tea and nibbling at the biscuits the cook had sent up in a temper (he was supposed to be on leave, he was not going to bake fancy cakes at a time when he was rightfully to have had his summer vacation, and so the sahibs could do with biscuits bought in the bazaar), Raja, a little melancholy, a little subdued — which Sarla and Ravi put down to the impression left on him by their visit to the sufi's tomb — piped up in a beseeching voice, 'Sarla, Ravi, where are those ravishing friends of yours I met when you were at the High Commission in London? The Dutta-Rays, was it not? You must know who I mean — you told me how they'd returned to Delhi and built this absolutely fabulous hacienda in Vasant Vihar. Isn't that quite close by?'

'It is,' Ravi admitted.

Like a persistent child, Raja continued, 'Then *why* don't we have them over? This evening? I remember she sang like a nightingale — those melancholy, funeral songs of Tagore's.[1] Wouldn't they be perfect on an evening like this which simply hangs suspended in time, don't you know, as if the dust and heat were holding it in their *cruel* grasp? Oh, Sarla, do telephone, do send for her — tell her I *pine* to hear the sound of her avian voice. Just for that, I'm even willing to put up with her husband who I remember finding — how shall I put it — a *trifle* wanting?'

Sarla found herself quite unwilling. Truth be told, the morning's expedition had left her with a splitting headache; she was not in the habit of walking around in the midday sun, leave that to mad dogs and — she'd always said. Even now, her temples throbbed and perspiration trickled discreetly down the back of her knees, invisible under the fresh cotton sari she'd donned for tea. But Raja would not hear of a refusal, or accept any excuse. If she thought

---

1. Rabindranath Tagore (1861–1941). Poet and abundantly creative Bengali author, he won the Nobel Prize for Literature in 1913.

the Dutta-Rays had left for Kashmir, why did she not ring and find out? Oh, there was no need to get up and *go* to the telephone —'In this land of fantasies fulfilled, isn't there always a willing handmaid, so to speak, to bring the mountain to Mohammed? and Sarla had to send for the telephone to be brought out to the veranda, the servant Balu unwinding the telephone line all the way, and she was forced to speak into it and verify that the Dutta-Rays were indeed still in Delhi, held up by a visit from a former colleague at India House, but were going out that evening to that party — didn't Sarla and Ravi know of it? 'We're supposed to be *away*,' Sarla said stiffly into the telephone. 'Everyone thinks we are in the *hills* by now. We usually are.' Well, the Dutta-Rays would drop in on their way — and so they did, she a vision of grace in her finely embroidered Lucknow sari, pale green on white, to Raja's great delight, and only too willing to sing for his delectation, only not tonight since they were already late.

So Sarla and Ravi found themselves throwing a party — a party that was to be the setting for a recital given by Ila Dutta-Ray, a woman neither of them had any warm feelings for, remembering how unhelpful she had been when they had first arrived in London and so badly needed help in finding a flat, engaging servants, placing their children in school, all so long ago of course. Instead of *helping*, she had sent them her old cook, declaring he was the best, but really saving herself the air fare back to India because he proved good for nothing but superannuation. They rang up whoever of their circle of friends remained in Delhi to invite them for the occasion. It was quite extraordinary how many friends Raja remembered and managed to trace, and also how many who were on the point of going away, changed their plans on hearing his name and assured Sarla and Ravi they would come.

Then there occurred a dreadful incident: Sarla was choosing from amongst her saris one cool enough for the evening ahead, which was, of course, one of the summer's worst, that kind of still, yellow, lurid evening that it inflicted when one thought one could bear no more, and meant that the recital would be held not in the garden after all but in the air-conditioned drawing room instead, when a terrible thought struck her: she had forgotten to invite Maya! Maya and her husband Pravin! How could she have? It was true Maya had told her Pravin was very preoccupied with a special issue his paper was bringing out on the rise of Hindu fundamentalism but that was no reason to assume they might not be free. Sarla stood in front of the mirror that was attached to one leaf of the armoire, and clasped her hand over her mouth with a look so stricken that Ravi, coming in to ask what glasses should be taken out for the evening, wondered if she had a sudden toothache. 'Ravi! Oh, Ravi,' she wailed.

The telephone was brought to her — Balu unwinding the coils of an endless wire — and the number dialled for her. Then Sarla spoke into it in gasps, but unfortunately she had not taken the time to collect her wits and phrase her invitation with more tact. Maya's sharp ears picked up every indication that her sister had been unforgivably remiss, and coldly rejected the insulting last-minute invitation, insisting proudly that Pravin was working late and she could not possibly leave his side, he never wrote a line without consulting her.

As if that was not agony enough, Sarla had to undergo the further humiliation of Raja piping up in the middle of the party — just as Ila Dutta-Ray was tuning her tanpura[2] and about to open her mouth and utter the first note of her song —'But Sarla, where is Maya, that aficionado of Tagore's music? *Surely* we should wait for her? *Why* is she so late?' An awful hush fell — and Sarla again assumed her stricken look. What was she to say, how was she to explain? She found herself stumbling over Maya's insincere excuse, but of course everyone guessed. Frowning in disapproval, Ila Dutta-Ray began her song on a very low, very deep and hoarse note.

In retaliation, Maya and Pravin threw a party as soon as Pravin's column had been written and the special issue had gone to press, and *their* party was in honour of the Minister of Human Resources, whose wife was such an admirer of Raja's, had read every word he had written and wanted so much to meet him —'in an intimate setting'. Since she had made this special request, they had felt obliged to cut down their guest list — and were sure Sarla and Ravi would not mind since they had the pleasure of Raja's company every day. But when Ravi stoically offered to drive Raja across to their house, he found the whole road lined with cars, many of them chauffeur-driven and with government number plates, and had the humiliation of backing out of it after dropping Raja at the gate, then returning to Sarla who had given way to a fierce migraine and was insisting that they book seats on a train to the hills as soon as possible.

'But don't we need to wait till Raja is gone?'

'Raja is incapable of making decisions — we'll have to make his for him,' she snapped, waving at Balu who was slouching in the doorway, waiting to take away the remains of their meagre supper from the dining table.

She was still agonised enough the following morning — digging violently into half a ripe papaya in the blazing light that spilt over the veranda even at that early hour — actually to ask Raja, 'How can you bear this heat? Do you really not mind it? I feel I'm going to collapse —'

Raja, who had a look of sleepy contentment on his face — he had already meditated for an hour in the garden, done his yoga exercises, bathed, drunk his tea and had every reason to look forward to another day — did not seem to catch her meaning at all. Reaching out to stroke her hand, he said, 'I know what you need, my dear — a walk in the sublime Lodi Gardens when the sun is setting and Venus appears in the sky so *silently* —' and went on to describe the ruins, their patina of lichen, their tiles of Persian blue, the echoes that rang beneath their domes, in such terms that Sarla sank back in her chair, sighing, agreeing.

What she did not know was that he had already arranged to walk there with Maya, Ila Dutta-Ray, and the wife of the Minister of Human Resources who, it turned out, had read that book of verses he had written when in Oxford and had published by a small press in London, long expired, so that copies were now collectors' pieces. All three women owned such copies. And Sarla found herself trailing behind them while Raja pranced, actually pranced with delight, with enthusiasm, in their company. At their suggestion he recited these verses:

---

2. Musical instrument, a sort of long-necked lute.

'The lamp of heaven is hung upon the citrus bough,
The nightingale falls silent.
All is waiting,
For a royal visit by night's own queen —'

and then burst into mocking, self-deprecating laughter, waving away their
protests to say, 'Oh, those adolescent excesses! What was I *thinking* of, in Oxford,
in the fog and the smog and the cold I suffered from perpetually! Well, you
know, I was thinking of — *this*,' and he waved at the walled rose garden and
beyond it the pond and beyond that the tombs of the Lodi emperors surrounded by neem trees, and they all gazed with him. Eventually the Minister's wife sighed, 'You make us all see it with new eyes, as if we had never seen
it before.'

Sarla, who had hung back, and was standing by a rose bush, fingering the
fine petals of one flower pensively, realised that this was so exactly true: it was
Raja who opened their eyes, who made them see it as they never saw it themselves, as a place of magic, enchantment, of pleasure so immense and rich
that it could never be exhausted. She gazed at his back, his noble head, the
silvery hair, the gracefully gesturing arm in its white muslin sleeve, there in
the shade of the neem tree, totally disregarding the dust, the smouldering
heat at the summer day's end, and seeing it all as romantic, paradisaical —
and she clasped her hands together, pressing a petal between them, grateful
for knowing him.

That evening she tried again. 'Raja, I *know* you would love Winhaven,' she told
him, interrupting the Vedic hymn he was reciting to prove to Ravi that his
Sanskrit was still fluent — hadn't he taught it to the golden youth of Berkeley,
of Stanford, of the universities in Los Angeles and San Francisco, for all these
years of his exile? 'And I would love to see you in the Himalayas,' she went on,
raising her voice, 'because they would make the most perfect setting for you.
Perhaps you would begin to write again over there —'

'But darling Sarla,' Raja beamed at her, showing both the pleasure he took
in her suggestion and his determination not to be swept away by it, 'Maya
tells me there is to be a lecture at India International Centre next week on the
Himalayas as an inspiration for Indian poets through the centuries, and I
would *hate* to miss it. It's to be given by Professor Dandavate, that old bore —
d'you remember him? What a *dreary* young man he was at Oxford! I can quite
imagine how much drearier he is now — and I can't resist the opportunity to
pick holes in all he says, and in public too —'

'But next week?' Sarla enquired helplessly. 'It'll — it'll be even hotter.'

'Sarla, don't you *ever* think of anything else?' he reproved her gently, although
with a little twitch of impatience about his eyes. 'Now I don't *ever* notice the
heat. Drink the delicious fresh lemonades your marvellous cook makes, rest
in the afternoons, and there's no reason why you shouldn't *enjoy* the summer.
Oh, think of the fruit alone that summer brings us —'

But it was the marvellous cook himself who brought an end to Raja's idyll
in Sarla and Ravi's gracious home: that very day he took off his apron, laid
down his egg whisk and his market bag, declared that enough, that he was
needed in his village to bring in the harvest before the monsoon arrived. He

was already late and had received a postcard from his son to say they could not delay it by another day. He demanded his salary and caught his train.

Sarla was sufficiently outraged by his treachery to make the afternoon tea herself, braving the inferno of the kitchen where she seldom had need to venture, and was rewarded by Raja's happy and Ravi's proud beam as she brought out the tea tray to the veranda. But dinner proved something else altogether. Balu showed not the slightest inclination that he meant to help: he kept to the pantry with grim determination, giving the glasses and silver another polishing rather than take a step into the kitchen. Sarla had a whispered consultation with Ravi, suggesting they take Raja out to India International Centre or the Gymkhana Club for dinner, but Ravi reminded her that the car had gone for servicing and they could go nowhere tonight. Sarla, her sari end tucked in at her waist, wiping the perspiration from her face with her elbow, went back into the kitchen and peered into its recesses to see if the cook had not repented and left some cooked food for them after all, but she found little that she could put together even if she knew how. At one point, she even telephoned Maya to see if her sister would not come to her aid — Maya was known for her superb culinary skill — but there was no answer: Maya and Pravin were out. It was to an embarrassingly inadequate repast of sliced cucumber, yoghurt and bread that the three finally sat down — Balu looking as if it were far beneath his dignity to serve such an excuse for a meal, Sarla tight-lipped with anger with herself for failing so blatantly, Ravi trying, with embarrassed sincerity, to thank her for her brave effort, and Raja saying nothing at all, but quietly crumbling the bread beside his plate till he confessed a wish to go to bed early.

But this meant that he was up earlier than ever next morning, and by the time Sarla rose and went wearily kitchenwards to make him tea, he had been awake for hours, performed his yoga and meditation, walked Simba round the garden several times, and was waiting querulously for it. Balu was nowhere to be seen. When Sarla went in search of him — surely he should have been able to make their guest a cup of tea?— she found the door to his room shut, coloured cutouts from film magazines of starlets in swimsuits stuck all over it, and when she called out his name, heard only a groan in reply. In agitation, she hurried to find Ravi and send him to find out what was wrong. Ravi went in reluctantly, his face bearing an expression of martyrdom, and reappeared to inform her that Balu was suffering from a stomach ache and needed to be taken to a doctor. '*You* do that,' she snapped at him, hardly able to believe this terrible turn in their fortunes.

By lunchtime Raja had made a series of phone calls and discovered that the Dutta-Rays were leaving for Kashmir next day and would be only too delighted to have him accompany them. Sarla stood in the doorway, watching him pack his little bag with beautifully laundered underwear, and wailed, 'But Raja, if you had wanted to go to the hills, we could have gone to Winhaven *ages* ago! I *asked* you, you remember?'

Raja gave her a look that said, 'Winhaven? With you? When I can be on a houseboat in Kashmir with Ila instead?' but of course what he really did was blow her a kiss across the room and whisper conspiratorially, 'Darling, think of the *stories* I'll come back with to entertain you,' and snapped shut the lock on his bag with a satisfied click.

'Simba! Simba!' Ravi put his hands around his mouth and called after the dog who had loped away up to the top of the hill and vanished. Then he turned around to look for Sarla. He could see neither his dog nor his wife— one had gone too far ahead, the other lagged too far behind. He lowered himself onto a rock to catch his breath and picked up a pine cone to toss from hand to hand while he waited, whistling a little tune.

Evening light flooded down from the vast sky, spilling over the pine needles and stones of the hillside. Everything seemed to be bathed in its pale saffron glow. An eagle drifted through the ravine below. He could hear the wind in its feathers, a melancholy whistle.

'Sarla?' he called out finally, and just then saw her come into sight on a turn of the path below him, amongst a mass of blackberry bushes. She seemed to be dragging herself along, her sari trailing in the white dust, her head bowed over the walking stick she held in a slightly trembling hand.

At his voice she looked up and her face was haggard. He stared in surprise: he had not considered this such a difficult climb, or so long a walk. It was where they had always come, to watch the sunset. He himself could still spring up it with no more than a little panting. 'Sarla?' he asked questioningly. 'Want some help, old girl?'

'Coming, coming,' she grumbled, toiling on, 'can't you see I'm coming?'

When she reached the rock where he was waiting, she sank down onto it and wiped her face with the corner of her sari. 'I can't do these climbs any more,' she admitted, with a wince. 'You had better do them alone.'

'Oh, Sarla,' he said, catching up her hand in his, 'I would never want to come up here without you, you know.' They sat there a while, breathing deeply. Beside them a small cricket began to chirp and chirp, and after some time it was no longer light that came spilling down the hill, but shadows.

2000

JAMES DICKEY
1923–1997

James Dickey was born and raised in Atlanta, Georgia. After one semester at Clemson University, Dickey left school to join the U.S. Army Air Forces during World War II. It was not until he joined the armed forces that Dickey became seriously interested in poetry. After the war he returned to school, earning both his B.A. and his M.A. in English Literature at Vanderbilt University. Dickey published his first poem in *Sewannee Review* in his senior year, but he didn't publish his first volume of poems, *Into the Stone*, until 1960. In that ten-year span, Dickey taught at Rice University, served in the Air Force again, and worked as a copywriter at an ad agency. His second collection of poetry, *Buckdancer's Choice* (1965), received the National Book Award, and from 1967 to 1969 Dickey was Consultant in Poetry to the Library of Congress. Though primarily a poet, Dickey is also widely known for his best-selling novel *Deliverance* (1970), which he later adapted for Hollywood. Other publications include *The Whole Motion: Collected Poems 1945–1992* (1992) and two other novels, *Alnilam* (1987) and *To the White Sea* (1993). "The Mill Wheel" is a story among several in *Wayfarer* (1988), which is about the life and lore of southern Appalachia, through the use of photography and the poignant monologues of an old mountain man.

The Mill Wheel

There was a old man over at Choestoe, a long time ago. His name was Arthel Warner, and he took it into his head that he wanted to start a gristmill, and grist corn for the people over around the head of Wolf Creek. He had some water runnin' through his land—off of the Choestoe River—and he built him a mill that's still there, or part of it is. It took him a long time to make the wheel, maybe five years; it's a wood wheel, a oak wheel, and that lasts a long time. Arthel Warner was a mean old man, mean and groundhoggy, and he didn't study nothin' but the mill, and most specially the wheel of it. He hadn't never made one before, but the Lord was with him, and he had done balanced it right; there wadn't a mistake about it; it turned on and on; there wadn't nothin' to stop it. He had him a young wife who wouldn't do nothin' to help him, but she was almighty pretty. She had a gold head, like they say; long gold hair, like the light off high needles, saplin' needles.

All this was a long time ago—fifty years, maybe more.

Well, what happened was that she took up with a young boy who worked in the tannery over at Min'rul Bluff. He used to come around and meet up with her, in the woods, you know, up behind town, or anywhere. I knew a old man who claimed he'd laid eyes on Taz Crowder, was this boy's name. He come back and lived at Choestoe, you know; wouldn't nobody have nothin' to do with him. This old man said he seen Taz Crowder, back in amongst a bunch of laurel bushes. He said nobody but Taz Crowder coulda looked like that, with them grievin' wild red eyes.

One day Taz come to the mill. It was one afternoon, about this time of the year. He thought old man Warner was in Choestoe, but he wadn't. He wadn't in the mill right then, but he wadn't in Choestoe, neither. I don't know where he was; maybe out huntin', but he had his rifle with him, and he come in right sudden, and Taz Crowder was just leavin'. Old man Warner fired out through the back window, but he missed, and Taz Crowder went on up over the hill. Then Arthel Warner turned on around, and his wife was down on her knees, hollerin' and beggin'. She didn't have no clothes on. Arthel shucked up another shell, and she jumped up and run, and took out acrost the dam. But she slipped on the moss, and went in, into the race, the millrace, you know, goin' in under the wheel. She got caught up in there, some say it was by the hair, that needly gold hair, and she was pulled under, screamin' to split a solid stump, and the wheel jammed with her in it, and it helt her under, and she was drownded.

A few years later Arthel Warner died. Some say he kilt hisself; I don't know. But he ain't gone; don't nobody believe he's gone. Part of the mill's still there. But the wheel's just about as good as new, they say. It don't turn, least in the day it don't. Like I say, I don't know. I wouldn't go over there to Choestoe Creek for nothin' in the world. But there's some has been there. My cousin George Binsley's been over there, and he swears you can hear it, just when it gets dark, just when the wheel starts to turn. You can hear her screamin' for just a second.

Old man Warner was a mean man. Ain't nobody will ever tell you he was nothin' else. That's the way he's done come down, from his own time. He would hold a grudge on you; he was somebody that liked revenge better than he liked anything you could think of in this endurin' life. They's some people up here that're like that.

So I don't go over to Choestoe. I don't listen when the moon rises, even from this far away.

I don't want to hear it, but I believe it. He comes back every night, or on some nights. You can't tell when. But you can't tell nobody he don't come back. He does; he does do it. Just for one more satisfaction; he can't get enough. He wants to hear his wife go under one more time. He can't let that wheel alone. He comes back. He comes back and turns it.

1988

ISAK DINESEN
1885–1962

Dinesen (pen name for Baroness Karen Blixen) was born near Elsinore, Denmark, the descendant of an old and cultivated Danish family. She married a cousin and in 1914 went with him to run a coffee plantation in British East Africa, where she remained for seventeen busy years, acting as counselor, judge, teacher, and doctor for Africans and settlers alike. The vivid, colorful details of her experiences there flavor the reminiscences in *Out of Africa* (1937). Several years after her divorce she returned to Denmark and began to write—in English—the spellbinding stories that made her world famous in the 1930s. Her first collection was *Seven Gothic Tales* (1934), an immensely popular work that was a Book-of-the-Month Club selection, as was her *Winter's Tales* (1942). No literary or ideological formula fits her fiction, which seems to spring from a pure impulse to fascinate the reader with a profusion of marvels and enchantments. While she was living under the Nazi occupation of Denmark during World War II, she wrote a novel, using the name of Pierre Andrézel, published in 1947 as *The Angelic Avengers*. Later publications are *Last Tales* (1957) and *Anecdotes of Destiny* (1958).

Sorrow-Acre

The low, undulating Danish landscape was silent and serene, mysteriously wide-awake in the hour before sunrise. There was not a cloud in the pale sky, not a shadow along the dim, pearly fields, hills and woods. The mist was lifting from the valleys and hollows, the air was cool, the grass and the foliage dripping wet with morning-dew. Unwatched by the eyes of man, and undisturbed by his activity, the country breathed a timeless life, to which language was inadequate.

All the same, a human race had lived on this land for a thousand years, had been formed by its soil and weather, and had marked it with its thoughts, so that now no one could tell where the existence of the one ceased and the other began. The thin grey line of a road, winding across the plain and up and down hills, was the fixed materialisation of human longing, and of the human notion that it is better to be in one place than another.

A child of the country would read this open landscape like a book. The irregular mosaic of meadows and cornlands was a picture, in timid green and yellow, of the people's struggle for its daily bread; the centuries had taught it to plough and sow in this way. On a distant hill the immovable wings of a windmill, in a small blue cross against the sky, delineated a later stage in the career of bread. The blurred outline of thatched roofs—a low, brown growth of the earth—where the huts of the village thronged together, told the history, from his cradle to his grave, of the peasant, the creature nearest to the soil and dependent on it, prospering in a fertile year and dying in years of drought and pests.

A little higher up, with the faint horizontal line of the white cemetery wall round it, and the vertical contour of tall poplars by its side, the red-tiled church bore witness, as far as the eye reached, that this was a Christian country. The child of the land knew it as a strange house, inhabited only for a few hours every seventh day, but with a strong, clear voice in it to give out the joys and sorrows of the land: a plain, square embodiment of the nation's trust in the justice and mercy of heaven. But where, amongst cupular woods[1] and groves, the lordly, pyramidal silhouette of the cut lime avenues rose in the air, there a big country house lay.

The child of the land would read much within these elegant, geometrical ciphers on the hazy blue. They spoke of power, the lime trees paraded round a stronghold. Up here was decided the destiny of the surrounding land and of the men and beasts upon it, and the peasant lifted his eyes to the green pyramids with awe. They spoke of dignity, decorum and taste. Danish soil grew no finer flower than the mansion to which the long avenue led. In its lofty rooms life and death bore themselves with stately grace. The country house did not gaze upward, like the church, nor down to the ground like the huts; it had a wider earthly horizon than they, and was related to much noble architecture all over Europe. Foreign artisans had been called in to panel and stucco it, and its own inhabitants travelled and brought back ideas, fashions and things of beauty. Paintings, tapestries, silver and glass from distant countries had been made to feel at home here, and now formed part of Danish country life.

The big house stood as firmly rooted in the soil of Denmark as the peasants' huts, and was as faithfully allied to her four winds and her changing seasons, to her animal life, trees and flowers. Only its interests lay in a higher plane. Within the domain of the lime trees it was no longer cows, goats, and pigs on which the minds and the talk ran, but horses and dogs. The wild fauna, the game of the land, that the peasant shook his fist at, when he saw it on his young green rye or in his ripening wheat field, to the residents of the country houses were the main pursuit and the joy of existence.

The writing in the sky solemnly proclaimed continuance, a worldly immortality. The great country houses had held their ground through many generations. The families who lived in them revered the past as they honoured themselves, for the history of Denmark was their own history.

A Rosenkrantz had sat at Rosenholm, a Juel at Hverringe, a Skeel at Gammel-Estrup[2] as long as people remembered. They had seen kings and schools of style succeed one another and, proudly and humbly, had made over their personal existence to that of their land, so that amongst their equals and with the peasants they passed by its name: Rosenholm, Hverringe, Gammel-Estrup. To the King and the country, to his family and to the individual lord of the manor

---

1. Oak forests.   2. Distinguished Danish families and their estates.

himself it was a matter of minor consequence which particular Rosenkrantz, Juel, or Skeel, out of a long row of fathers and sons, at the moment in his person incarnated the fields and woods, the peasants, cattle and game of the estate. Many duties rested on the shoulders of the big landowners—towards God in heaven, towards the King, his neighbour and himself—and they were all harmoniously consolidated into the idea of his duties towards his land. Highest amongst these ranked his obligation to uphold the sacred continuance, and to produce a new Rosenkrantz, Juel, or Skeel for the service of Rosenholm, Hverringe, and Gammel-Estrup.

Female grace was prized in the manors. Together with good hunting and fine wine it was the flower and emblem of the higher existence led there, and in many ways the families prided themselves more on their daughters than on their sons.

The ladies who promenaded in the lime avenues, or drove through them in heavy coaches with four horses, carried the future of the name in their laps and were, like dignified and debonair caryatides,[3] holding up the houses. They were themselves conscious of their value, kept up their price, and moved in a sphere of pretty worship and self-worship. They might even be thought to add to it, on their own, a graceful, arch, paradoxical haughtiness. For how free were they, how powerful! Their lords might rule the country, and allow themselves many liberties, but when it came to that supreme matter of legitimacy which was the vital principle of their world, the centre of gravity lay with them.

The lime trees were in bloom. But in the early morning only a faint fragrance drifted through the garden, an airy message, an aromatic echo of the dreams during the short summer night.

In a long avenue that led from the house all the way to the end of the garden, where, from a small white pavilion in the classic style, there was a great view over the fields, a young man walked. He was plainly dressed in brown, with pretty linen and lace, bare-headed, with his hair tied by a ribbon. He was dark, a strong and sturdy figure with fine eyes and hands; he limped a little on one leg.

The big house at the top of the avenue, the garden and the fields had been his childhood's paradise. But he had travelled and lived out of Denmark, in Rome and Paris, and he was at present appointed to the Danish Legation to the Court of King George, the brother of the late, unfortunate young Danish Queen.[4] He had not seen his ancestral home for nine years. It made him laugh to find, now, everything so much smaller than he remembered it, and at the same time he was strangely moved by meeting it again. Dead people came towards him and smiled at him; a small boy in a ruff ran past him with his hoop and kite, in passing gave him a clear glance and laughingly asked: "Do you mean to tell me that you are I?" He tried to catch him in the flight, and to answer him: "Yes, I assure you that I am you," but the light figure did not wait for a reply.

---

3. Carvings of draped female figures supporting upper sections of walls in Greek architecture.
4. Apparently a reference to George II of England. George was the father, not the brother, of Louise, queen of Denmark (1724–1751).

The young man, whose name was Adam, stood in a particular relation to the house and the land. For six months he had been heir to it all; nominally he was so even at this moment. It was this circumstance which had brought him from England, and on which his mind was dwelling, as he walked along slowly.

The old lord up at the manor, his father's brother, had had much misfortune in his domestic life. His wife had died young, and two of his children in infancy. The one son then left to him, his cousin's playmate, was a sickly and morose boy. For ten years the father travelled with him from one watering place to another, in Germany and Italy, hardly ever in other company than that of his silent, dying child, sheltering the faint flame of life with both hands, until such time as it could be passed over to a new bearer of the name. At the same time another misfortune had struck him: he fell into disfavour at Court, where till now he had held a fine position. He was about to rehabilitate his family's prestige through the marriage which he had arranged for his son, when before it could take place the bridegroom died, not yet twenty years old.

Adam learned of his cousin's death, and his own changed fortune, in England, through his ambitious and triumphant mother. He sat with her letter in his hand and did not know what to think about it.

If this, he reflected, had happened to him while he was still a boy, in Denmark, it would have meant all the world to him. It would be so now with his friends and schoolfellows, if they were in his place, and they would, at this moment, be congratulating or envying him. But he was neither covetous nor vain by nature; he had faith in his own talents and had been content to know that his success in life depended on his personal ability. His slight infirmity had always set him a little apart from other boys; it had, perhaps, given him a keener sensibility of many things in life, and he did not, now, deem it quite right that the head of the family should limp on one leg. He did not even see his prospects in the same light as his people at home. In England he had met with greater wealth and magnificence than they dreamed of; he had been in love with, and made happy by, an English lady of such rank and fortune that to her, he felt, the finest estate of Denmark would look but like a child's toy farm.

And in England, too, he had come in touch with the great new ideas of the age: of nature, of the right and freedom of man, of justice and beauty. The universe, through them, had become infinitely wider to him; he wanted to find out still more about it and was planning to travel to America, to the new world. For a moment he felt trapped and imprisoned, as if the dead people of his name, from the family vault at home, were stretching out their parched arms for him.

But at the same time he began to dream at night of the old house and garden. He had walked in these avenues in dream, and had smelled the scent of the flowering limes. When at Ranelagh[5] an old gypsy woman looked at his hand and told him that a son of his was to sit in the seat of his father, he felt a sudden, deep satisfaction, queer in a young man who till now had never given his sons a thought.

---

5. The Ranelagh Pleasure Ground, fashionable 18th-century gardens in London.

Then, six months later, his mother again wrote to tell him that his uncle had himself married the girl intended for his dead son. The head of the family was still in his best age, not over sixty, and although Adam remembered him as a small, slight man, he was a vigorous person; it was likely that his young wife would bear him sons.

Adam's mother in her disappointment lay the blame on him. If he had returned to Denmark, she told him, his uncle might have come to look upon him as a son, and would not have married; nay, he might have handed the bride over to him. Adam knew better. The family estate, differing from the neighbouring properties, had gone down from father to son ever since a man of their name first sat there. The tradition of direct succession was the pride of the clan and a sacred dogma to his uncle; he would surely call for a son of his own flesh and bone.

But at the news the young man was seized by a strange, deep, aching remorse towards his old home in Denmark. It was as if he had been making light of a friendly and generous gesture, and disloyal to someone unfailingly loyal to him. It would be but just, he thought, if from now the place should disown and forget him. Nostalgia, which before he had never known, caught hold of him; for the first time he walked in the streets and parks of London as a stranger.

He wrote to his uncle and asked if he might come and stay with him, begged leave from the Legation and took ship for Denmark. He had come to the house to make his peace with it; he had slept little in the night, and was up so early and walking in the garden, to explain himself, and to be forgiven.

While he walked, the still garden slowly took up its day's work. A big snail, of the kind that his grandfather had brought back from France, and which he remembered eating in the house as a child, was already, with dignity, dragging a silver train down the avenue. The birds began to sing; in an old tree under which he stopped a number of them were worrying an owl; the rule of the night was over.

He stood at the end of the avenue and saw the sky lightening. An ecstatic clarity filled the world; in half an hour the sun would rise. A rye field here ran along the garden; two roe-deer were moving in it and looked roseate in the dawn. He gazed out over the fields, where as a small boy he had ridden his pony, and towards the wood where he had killed his first stag. He remembered the old servants who had taught him; some of them were now in their graves.

The ties which bound him to this place, he reflected, were of a mystic nature. He might never again come back to it, and it would make no difference. As long as a man of his own blood and name should sit in the house, hunt in the fields and be obeyed by the people in the huts, wherever he travelled on earth, in England or amongst the red Indians of America, he himself would still be safe, would still have a home, and would carry weight in the world.

His eyes rested on the church. In old days, before the time of Martin Luther,[6] younger sons of great families, he knew, had entered the Church of Rome, and had given up individual wealth and happiness to serve the greater ideals. They, too, had bestowed honour upon their homes and were remembered in its registers. In the solitude of the morning half in jest he let his mind run as

---

6. Leader of the Protestant break from the Roman Catholic Church (1483–1546).

it listed; it seemed to him that he might speak to the land as to a person, as to the mother of his race. "Is it only my body that you want," he asked her, "while you reject my imagination, energy and emotions? If the world might be brought to acknowledge that the virtue of our name does not belong to the past only, will it give you no satisfaction?" The landscape was so still that he could not tell whether it answered him yes or no.

After a while he walked on, and came to the new French rose garden laid out for the young mistress of the house. In England he had acquired a freer taste in gardening, and he wondered if he could liberate these blushing captives, and make them thrive outside their cut hedges. Perhaps, he meditated, the elegantly conventional garden would be a floral portrait of his young aunt from Court, whom he had not yet seen.

As once more he came to the pavilion at the end of the avenue his eyes were caught by a bouquet of delicate colours which could not possibly belong to the Danish summer morning. It was in fact his uncle himself, powdered and silk-stockinged, but still in a brocade dressing-gown, and obviously sunk in deep thought. "And what business, or what meditations," Adam asked himself, "drags a connoisseur of the beautiful, but three months married to a wife of seventeen, from his bed into his garden before sunrise?" He walked up to the small, slim, straight figure.

His uncle on his side showed no surprise at seeing him, but then he rarely seemed surprised at anything. He greeted him, with a compliment on his matunality,[7] as kindly as he had done on his arrival last evening. After a moment he looked to the sky, and solemnly proclaimed: "It will be a hot day." Adam, as a child, had often been impressed by the grand, ceremonial manner in which the old lord would state the common happenings of existence; it looked as if nothing had changed here, but all was what it used to be.

The uncle offered the nephew a pinch of snuff. "No, thank you, Uncle," said Adam, "it would ruin my nose to the scent of your garden, which is as fresh as the Garden of Eden, newly created." "From every tree of which," said his uncle, smiling, "thou, my Adam, mayest freely eat." They slowly walked up the avenue together.

The hidden sun was now already gilding the top of the tallest trees. Adam talked of the beauties of nature, and of the greatness of Nordic scenery, less marked by the hand of man than that of Italy. His uncle took the praise of the landscape as a personal compliment, and congratulated him because he had not, in likeness to many young travellers in foreign countries, learned to despise his native land. No, said Adam, he had lately in England longed for the fields and woods of his Danish home. And he had there become acquainted with a new piece of Danish poetry which had enchanted him more than any English or French work. He named the author, Johannes Ewald,[8] and quoted a few of the mighty, turbulent verses.

"And I have wondered, while I read," he went on after a pause, still moved by the lines he himself had declaimed, "that we have not till now understood how much our Nordic mythology in moral greatness surpasses that of Greece and Rome. If it had not been for the physical beauty of the ancient gods, which has come down to us in marble, no modern mind could hold them

---

7. Morning appearance.   **8.** Denmark's greatest lyric poet (1743–1781).

worthy of worship. They were mean, capricious and treacherous. The gods of our Danish forefathers are as much more divine than they as the Druid is nobler than the Augur.[9] For the fair gods of Asgaard[1] did possess the sublime human virtues; they were righteous, trustworthy, benevolent and even, within a barbaric age, chivalrous." His uncle here for the first time appeared to take any real interest in the conversation. He stopped, his majestic nose a little in the air. "Ah, it was easier to them," he said.

"What do you mean, Uncle?" Adam asked. "It was a great deal easier," said his uncle, "to the northern gods than to those of Greece to be, as you will have it, righteous and benevolent. To my mind it even reveals a weakness in the souls of our ancient Danes that they should consent to adore such divinities." "My dear uncle," said Adam, smiling, "I have always felt that you would be familiar with the modes of Olympus. Now please let me share your insight, and tell me why virtue should come easier to our Danish gods than to those of milder climates." "They were not as powerful," said his uncle.

"And does power," Adam again asked, "stand in the way of virtue?" "Nay," said his uncle gravely. "Nay, power is in itself the supreme virtue. But the gods of which you speak were never all-powerful. They had, at all times, by their side those darker powers which they named the Jotuns,[2] and who worked the suffering, the disasters, the ruin of our world. They might safely give themselves up to temperance and kindness. The omnipotent gods," he went on, "have no such facilitation. With their omnipotence they take over the woe of the universe."

They had walked up the avenue till they were in view of the house. The old lord stopped and ran his eyes over it. The stately building was the same as ever; behind the two tall front windows, Adam knew, was now his young aunt's room. His uncle turned and walked back.

"Chivalry," he said, "chivalry, of which you were speaking, is not a virtue of the omnipotent. It must needs imply mighty rival powers for the knight to defy. With a dragon inferior to him in strength, what figure will St. George[3] cut? The knight who finds no superior forces ready to hand must invent them, and combat wind-mills; his knighthood itself stipulates dangers, vileness, darkness on all sides of him. Nay, believe me, my nephew, in spite of his moral worth, your chivalrous Odin of Asgaard as a Regent must take rank below that of Jove[4] who avowed his sovereignty, and accepted the world which he ruled. But you are young," he added, "and the experience of the aged to you will sound pedantic."

He stood immovable for a moment and then with deep gravity proclaimed: "The sun is up."

The sun did indeed rise above the horizon. The wide landscape was suddenly animated by its splendour, and the dewy grass shone in a thousand gleams.

"I have listened to you, Uncle," said Adam, "with great interest. But while we have talked you yourself have seemed to me preoccupied; your eyes have rested on the field outside the garden, as if something of great moment, a

9. That is, as an ancient Celtic wizard-priest is nobler than an ancient Roman soothsayer.   **1.** In Teutonic mythology the celestial dwelling place.   **2.** Race of giants.   **3.** In religious allegory the slayer of the dragon; patron saint of England, Aragon, and Portugal.   **4.** Jupiter, the chief of Roman gods, as Odin is chief of Norse gods.

matter of life and death, was going on there. Now that the sun is up, I see the mowers in the rye and hear them whetting their sickles. It is, I remember you telling me, the first day of the harvest. That is a great day to a landowner and enough to take his mind away from the gods. It is very fine weather, and I wish you a full barn."

The elder man stood still, his hands on his walking-stick. "There is indeed," he said at last, "something going on in that field, a matter of life and death. Come, let us sit down here, and I will tell you the whole story." They sat down on the seat that ran all along the pavilion, and while he spoke the old lord of the land did not take his eyes off the rye field.

"A week ago, on Thursday night," he said, "someone set fire to my barn at Rødmosegaard—you know the place, close to the moor—and burned it all down. For two or three days we could not lay hands on the offender. Then on Monday morning the keeper at Rødmose, with the wheelwright over there, came up to the house; they dragged with them a boy, Goske Piil, a widow's son, and they made their Bible oath that he had done it; they had themselves seen him sneaking round the barn by nightfall on Thursday. Goske had no good name on the farm; the keeper bore him a grudge upon an old matter of poaching, and the wheelwright did not like him either, for he did, I believe, suspect him with his young wife. The boy, when I talked to him, swore to his innocence, but he could not hold his own against the two old men. So I had him locked up, and meant to send him in to our judge of the district, with a letter.

"The judge is a fool, and would naturally do nothing but what he thought I wished him to do. He might have the boy sent to the convict prison for arson, or put amongst the soldiers as a bad character and a poacher. Or again, if he thought that that was what I wanted, he could let him off.

"I was out riding in the fields, looking at the corn[5] that was soon ripe to be mowed, when a woman, the widow, Goske's mother, was brought up before me, and begged to speak to me. Anne-Marie is her name. You will remember her; she lives in the small house east of the village. She has not got a good name in the place either. They tell as a girl she had a child and did away with it.

"From five days' weeping her voice was so cracked that it was difficult for me to understand what she said. Her son, she told me at last, had indeed been over at Rødmose on Thursday, but for no ill purpose; he had gone to see someone. He was her only son, she called the Lord God to witness on his innocence, and she wrung her hands to me that I should save the boy for her.

"We were in the rye field that you and I are looking at now. That gave me an idea. I said to the widow: 'If in one day, between sunrise and sunset, with your own hands you can mow this field, and it be well done, I will let the case drop and you shall keep your son. But if you cannot do it, he must go, and it is not likely that you will then ever see him again.'

"She stood up then and gazed over the field. She kissed my riding boot in gratitude for the favour shown to her.

The old lord here made a pause, and Adam said: "Her son meant much to her?" "He is her only child," said his uncle. "He means to her her daily bread and support in old age. It may be said that she holds him as dear as her own life. As," he added, "within a higher order of life, a son to his father means the

5. Grain—in this case, rye.

name and the race, and he holds him as dear as life everlasting. Yes, her son means much to her. For the mowing of that field is a day's work to three men, or three days' work to one man. Today, as the sun rose, she set to her task. And down there, by the end of the field, you will see her now, in a blue head-cloth, with the man I have set to follow her and to ascertain that she does the work unassisted, and with two or three friends by her, who are comforting her."

Adam looked down, and did indeed see a woman in a blue head-cloth, and a few other figures in the corn.

They sat for a while in silence. "Do you yourself," Adam then said, "believe the boy to be innocent?" "I cannot tell," said his uncle. "There is no proof. The word of the keeper and the wheelwright stand against the boy's word. If indeed I did believe the one thing or the other, it would be merely a matter of chance, or maybe of sympathy. The boy," he said after a moment, "was my son's playmate, the only other child that I ever knew him to like or to get on with." "Do you," Adam again asked, "hold it possible to her to fulfill your condition?" "Nay, I cannot tell," said the old lord. "To an ordinary person it would not be possible. No ordinary person would ever have taken it on at all. I chose it so. We are not quibbling with the law, Anne-Marie and I."

Adam for a few minutes followed the movement of the small group in the rye. "Will you walk back?" he asked. "No," said his uncle, "I think that I shall stay here till I have seen the end of the thing." "Until sunset?" Adam asked with surprise. "Yes," said the old lord. Adam said: "It will be a long day." "Yes," said his uncle, "a long day. But," he added, as Adam rose to walk away, "if, as you said, you have got that tragedy of which you spoke in your pocket, be as kind as to leave it here, to keep me company." Adam handed him the book.

In the avenue he met two footmen who carried the old lord's morning chocolate down to the pavilion on large silver trays.

As now the sun rose in the sky, and the day grew hot, the lime trees gave forth their exuberance of scent, and the garden was filled with unsurpassed, unbelievable sweetness. Towards the still hour of midday the long avenue reverberated like a soundboard with a low, incessant murmur: the humming of a million bees that clung to the pendulous, thronging clusters of blossoms and were drunk with bliss.

In all the short lifetime of Danish summer there is no richer or more luscious moment than that week wherein the lime trees flower. The heavenly scent goes to the head and to the heart; it seems to unite the fields of Denmark with those of Elysium;[6] it contains both hay, honey and holy incense, and is half fairy-land and half apothecary's locker. The avenue was changed into a mystic edifice, a dryad's cathedral, outward from summit to base lavishly adorned, set with multitudinous ornaments, and golden in the sun. But behind the walls the vaults were benignly cool and sombre, like ambrosial sanctuaries in a dazzling and burning world, and in here the ground was still moist.

Up in the house, behind the silk curtains of the two front windows, the young mistress of the estate from the wide bed stuck her feet into two little high-heeled slippers. Her lace-trimmed nightgown had slid up above her knee and down from the shoulder; her hair, done up in curling-pins for the night,

6. In classic mythology the abode of the good after death.

was still frosty with the powder of yesterday, her round face flushed with sleep. She stepped out to the middle of the floor and stood there, looking extremely grave and thoughtful, yet she did not think at all. But through her head a long procession of pictures marched, and she was unconsciously endeavouring to put them in order, as the pictures of her existence had used to be.

She had grown up at Court; it was her world, and there was probably not in the whole country a small creature more exquisitely and innocently drilled to the stately measure of a palace. By favour of the old Dowager Queen she bore her name and that of the King's sister, the Queen of Sweden: Sophie Magdalena. It was with a view to these things that her husband, when he wished to restore his status in high places, had chosen her as a bride, first for his son and then for himself. But her own father, who held an Office in the Royal Household and belonged to the new Court aristocracy, in his day had done the same thing the other way round, and had married a country lady, to get a foothold within the old nobility of Denmark. The little girl had her mother's blood in her veins. The country to her had been an immense surprise and delight.

To get into her castle-court she must drive through the farm yard, through the heavy stone gateway in the barn itself, wherein the rolling of her coach for a few seconds re-echoed like thunder. She must drive past the stables and the timber-mare,[7] from which sometimes a miscreant would follow her with sad eyes, and might here startle a long string of squalling geese, or pass the heavy, scowling bull, led on by a ring in his nose and kneading the earth in dumb fury. At first this had been to her, every time, a slight shock and a jest. But after a while all these creatures and things, which belonged to her, seemed to become part of herself. Her mothers, the old Danish country ladies, were robust persons, undismayed by any kind of weather; now she herself had walked in the rain and had laughed and glowed in it like a green tree.

She had taken her great new home in possession at a time when all the world was unfolding, mating and propagating. Flowers, which she had known only in bouquets and festoons, sprung from the earth round her; birds sang in all the trees. The new-born lambs seemed to her daintier than her dolls had been. From her husband's Hanoverian[8] stud, foals were brought to her to give names; she stood and watched as they poked their soft noses into their mothers' bellies to drink. Of this strange process she had till now only vaguely heard. She had happened to witness, from a path in the park, the rearing and screeching stallion on the mare. All this luxuriance, lust, and fecundity was displayed before her eyes, as for her pleasure.

And for her own part, in the midst of it, she was given an old husband who treated her with punctilious respect because she was to bear him a son. Such was the compact; she had known of it from the beginning. Her husband, she found, was doing his best to fulfill his part of it, and she herself was loyal by nature and strictly brought up. She would not shirk her obligation. Only she was vaguely aware of a discord or an incompatibility within her majestic existence, which prevented her from being as happy as she had expected to be.

---

7. A crude wooden horse on which soldiers—or sometimes servants—were tied for punishment.
8. Hanover, in north-central Germany, was one of the states of the Holy Roman Empire.

After a time her chagrin took a strange form: as the consciousness of an absence. Someone ought to have been with her who was not. She had no experience in analysing her feelings; there had not been time for that at Court. Now, as she was more often left to herself, she vaguely probed her own mind. She tried to set her father in that void place, her sisters, her music master, an Italian singer whom she had admired; but none of them would fill it for her. At times she felt lighter at heart, and believed the misfortune to have left her. And then again it would happen, if she were alone, or in her husband's company, and even within his embrace, that everything round her would cry out: Where? Where? so that she let her wild eyes run about the room in search for the being who should have been there, and who had not come.

When, six months ago, she was informed that her first young bridegroom had died and that she was to marry his father in his place, she had not been sorry. Her youthful suitor, the one time she had seen him, had appeared to her infantile and insipid; the father would make a statelier consort. Now she had sometimes thought of the dead boy, and wondered whether with him life would have been more joyful. But she soon again dismissed the picture, and that was the sad youth's last recall to the stage of this world.

Upon one wall of her room there hung a long mirror. As she gazed into it new images came along. The day before, driving with her husband, she had seen, at a distance, a party of village girls bathing in the river, and the sun shining on them. All her life she had moved amongst naked marble deities, but it had till now never occurred to her that the people she knew should themselves be naked under their bodices and trains, waistcoats and satin breeches, that indeed she herself felt naked within her clothes. Now, in front of the looking-glass, she tardily untied the ribbons of her nightgown, and let it drop to the floor.

The room was dim behind the drawn curtains. In the mirror her body was silvery like a white rose; only her cheeks and mouth, and the tips of her fingers and breasts had a faint carmine. Her slender torso was formed by the whalebones that had clasped it tightly from her childhood; above the slim, dimpled knee a gentle narrowness marked the place of the garter. Her limbs were rounded as if, at whatever place they might be cut through with a sharp knife, a perfectly circular transverse incision would be obtained. The side and belly were so smooth that her own gaze slipped and glided, and grasped for a hold. She was not altogether like a statue, she found, and lifted her arms above her head. She turned to get a view of her back, the curves below the waistline were still blushing from the pressure of the bed. She called to mind a few tales about nymphs and goddesses, but they all seemed a long way off, so her mind returned to the peasant girls in the river. They were, for a few minutes, idealized into playmates, or sisters even, since they belonged to her as did the meadow and the blue river itself. And within the next moment the sense of forlornness once more came upon her, a *horror vacui*[9] like a physical pain. Surely, surely someone should have been with her now, her other self, like the image in the glass, but nearer, stronger, alive. There was no one, the universe was empty round her.

---

9. Abhorrence of emptiness (Latin).

A sudden, keen itching under her knee took her out of her reveries, and awoke in her the hunting instincts of her breed. She wetted a finger on her tongue, slowly brought it down and quickly slapped it to the spot. She felt the diminutive, sharp body of the insect against the silky skin, pressed the thumb to it, and triumphantly lifted up the small prisoner between her fingertips. She stood quite still, as if meditating upon the fact that a flea was the only creature risking its life for her smoothness and sweet blood.

Her maid opened the door and came in, loaded with the attire of the day—shift, stays, hoop, and petticoats. She remembered that she had a guest in the house, the new nephew arrived from England. Her husband had instructed her to be kind to their young kinsman, disinherited, so to say, by her presence in the house. They would ride out on the land together.

In the afternoon the sky was no longer blue as in the morning. Large clouds slowly towered up on it, and the great vault itself was colourless, as if diffused into vapours round the white-hot sun in zenith. A low thunder ran along the western horizon; once or twice the dust of the roads rose in tall spirals. But the fields, the hills and the woods were as still as a painted landscape.

Adam walked down the avenue to the pavilion, and found his uncle there, fully dressed, his hands upon his walking-stick and his eyes on the rye field. The book that Adam had given him lay by his side. The field now seemed alive with people. Small groups stood here and there in it, and a long row of men and women were slowly advancing towards the garden in the line of the swath.

The old lord nodded to his nephew, but did not speak or change his position. Adam stood by him as still as himself.

The day to him had been strangely disquieting. At the meeting again with old places the sweet melodies of the past had filled his senses and his mind, and had mingled with new, bewitching tunes of the present. He was back in Denmark, no longer a child but a youth, with a keener sense of the beautiful, with tales of other countries to tell, and still a true son of his own land and enchanted by its loveliness as he had never been before.

But through all these harmonies the tragic and cruel tale which the old lord had told him in the morning, and the sad contest which he knew to be going on so near by, in the corn field, had re-echoed, like the recurrent, hollow throbbing of a muffled drum, a redoubtable sound. It came back time after time, so that he had felt himself to change colour and to answer absently. It brought with it a deeper sense of pity with all that lived than he had ever known. When he had been riding with his young aunt, and their road ran along the scene of the drama, he had taken care to ride between her and the field, so that she should not see what was going on there, or question him about it. He had chosen the way home through the deep, green wood for the same reason.

More dominantly even than the figure of the woman struggling with her sickle for her son's life, the old man's figure, as he had seen it at sunrise, kept him company through the day. He came to ponder on the part which that lonely, determinate form had played in his own life. From the time when his father died, it had impersonated to the boy law and order, wisdom of life and kind guardianship. What was he to do, he thought, if after eighteen years these filial feelings must change, and his second father's figure take on to him a horrible aspect, as a symbol of the tyranny and oppression of the world? What was he to do if ever the two should come to stand in opposition to each other as adversaries?

At the same time an unaccountable, a sinister alarm and dread on behalf of the old man himself took hold of him. For surely here the Goddess Nemesis[1] could not be far away. This man had ruled the world round him for a longer period than Adam's own lifetime and had never been gainsaid by anyone. During the years when he had wandered through Europe with a sick boy of his own blood as his sole companion he had learned to set himself apart from his surroundings, and to close himself up to all outer life, and he had become insusceptible to the ideas and feelings of other human beings. Strange fancies might there have run in his mind, so that in the end he had seen himself as the only person really existing, and the world as a poor and vain shadow-play, which had no substance to it.

Now, in senile wilfullness, he would take in his hand the life of those simpler and weaker than himself, of a woman, using it to his own ends, and he feared of no retributive justice. Did he not know, the young man thought, that there were powers in the world, different from and more formidable than the short-lived might of a despot?

With the sultry heat of the day this foreboding of impending disaster grew upon him, until he felt ruin threatening not the old lord only, but the house, the name and himself with him. It seemed to him that he must cry out a warning to the man he had loved, before it was too late.

But as now he was once more in his uncle's company, the green calm of the garden was so deep that he did not find his voice to cry out. Instead a little French air which his aunt had sung to him up in the house kept running in his mind—"*C'est un trop doux effort*[2] . . ." He had good knowledge of music; he had heard the air before, in Paris, but not so sweetly sung.

After a time he asked: "Will the woman fulfill her bargain?" His uncle unfolded his hands. "It is an extraordinary thing," he said animatedly, "that it looks as if she might fulfill it. If you count the hours from sunrise till now, and from now till sunset, you will find the time left her to be half of that already gone. And see! She has now mowed two-thirds of the field. But then we will naturally have to reckon with her strength declining as she works on. All in all, it is an idle pursuit in you or me to bet on the issue of the matter; we must wait and see. Sit down, and keep me company in my watch." In two minds Adam sat down.

"And here," said his uncle, and took up the book from the seat, "is your book, which has passed the time finely. It is great poetry, ambrosia to the ear and the heart. And it has, with our discourse on divinity this morning, given me stuff for thought. I have been reflecting upon the law of retributive justice." He took a pinch of snuff, and went on. "A new age," he said, "has made to itself a god in its own image, an emotional god. And now you are already writing a tragedy on your god."

Adam had no wish to begin a debate on poetry with his uncle, but he also somehow dreaded a silence, and said: "It may be, then, that we hold tragedy to be, in the scheme of life, a noble, a divine phenomenon."

---

1. Greek goddess of retribution.   **2.** "It is too sweet an effort" (French).

"Aye," said his uncle solemnly, "a noble phenomenon, the noblest on earth. But of the earth only, and never divine. Tragedy is the privilege of man, his highest privilege. The God of the Christian Church Himself, when He wished to experience tragedy, had to assume human form. And even at that," he added thoughtfully, "the tragedy was not wholly valid, as it would have become had the hero of it been, in very truth, a man. The divinity of Christ conveyed to it a divine note, the moment of comedy. The real tragic part, by the nature of things, fell to the executors, not to the victim. Nay, my nephew, we should not adulterate the pure elements of the cosmos. Tragedy should remain the right of human beings, subject, in their conditions or in their own nature, to the dire law of necessity. To them it is salvation and beatification. But the gods, whom we must believe to be unacquainted with and incomprehensive of necessity, can have no knowledge of the tragic. When they are brought face to face with it they will, according to my experience, have the good taste and decorum to keep still, and not interfere.

"No," he said after a pause, "the true art of the gods is the comic. The comic is a condescension of the divine to the world of man; it is the sublime vision, which cannot be studied, but must ever be celestially granted. In the comic the gods see their own being reflected as in a mirror, and while the tragic poet is bound by strict laws, they will allow the comic artist a freedom as unlimited as their own. They do not even withhold their own existence from his sports. Jove may favour Lucianos of Samosata.[3] As long as your mockery is in true godly taste you may mock at the gods and still remain a sound devotee. But in pitying, or condoling with your god, you deny and annihilate him, and such is the most horrible of atheisms.

"And here on earth, too," he went on, "we, who stand in lieu of the gods and have emancipated ourselves from the tyranny of necessity, should leave to our vassals their monopoly of tragedy, and for ourselves accept the comic with grace. Only a boorish and cruel master—a parvenu, in fact—will make a jest of his servants' necessity, or force the comic upon them. Only a timid and pedantic ruler, a *petit-maître*,[4] will fear the ludicrous on his own behalf. Indeed," he finished his long speech, "the very same fatality, which, in striking the burgher or peasant, will become tragedy, with the aristocrat is exalted to the comic. By the grace and wit of our acceptance hereof our aristocracy is known."

Adam could not help smiling a little as he heard the apotheosis of the comic on the lips of the erect, ceremonious prophet. In this ironic smile he was, for the first time, estranging himself from the head of his house.

A shadow fell across the landscape. A cloud had crept over the sun; the country changed colour beneath it, faded and bleached, and even all sounds for a minute seemed to die out of it.

"Ah, now," said the old lord, "if it is going to rain, and the rye gets wet, Anne-Marie will not be able to finish in time. And who comes there?" he added, and turned his head a little.

Preceded by a lackey a man in riding boots and a striped waistcoat with silver buttons, and with his hat in his hand, came down the avenue. He bowed deeply, first to the old lord and then to Adam.

---

3. Greek satirist (ca. 120–180 C.E.). Jove would tolerate his satire because of its excellence.   **4.** Minor master (French).

"My bailiff," said the old lord. "Good afternoon, Bailiff. What news have you to bring?" The bailiff made a sad gesture. "Poor news only, my lord," he said. "And how poor news?" asked his master. "There is," said the bailiff with weight, "not a soul at work on the land, and not a sickle going except that of Anne-Marie in this rye field. The mowing has stopped; they are all at her heels. It is a poor day for a first day of the harvest." "Yes, I see," said the old lord. The bailiff went on. "I have spoken kindly to them," he said, "and I have sworn at them; it is all one. They might as well all be deaf."

"Good bailiff," said the old lord, "leave them in peace; let them do as they like. This day may, all the same, do them more good than many others. Where is Goske, the boy, Anne-Marie's son?" "We have set him in the small room by the barn," said the bailiff. "Nay, let him be brought down," said the old lord; "let him see his mother at work. But what do you say—will she get the field mowed in time?" "If you ask me, my lord," said the bailiff, "I believe that she will. Who would have thought so? She is only a small woman. It is as hot a day today as, well, as I do ever remember. I myself, you yourself, my lord, could not have done what Anne-Marie has done today." "Nay, nay, we could not, Bailiff," said the old lord.

The bailiff pulled out a red handkerchief and wiped his brow, somewhat calmed by venting his wrath. "If," he remarked with bitterness, "they would all work as the widow works now, we would make a profit on the land." "Yes," said the old lord, and fell into thought, as if calculating the profit it might make. "Still," he said, "as to the question of profit and loss, that is more intricate than it looks. I will tell you something that you may not know: The most famous tissue ever woven was ravelled out again every night.[5] But come," he added, "she is close by now. We will go and have a look at her work ourselves." With these words he rose and set his hat on.

The cloud had drawn away again; the rays of the sun once more burned the wide landscape, and as the small party walked out from under the shade of the trees the dead-still heat was heavy as lead; the sweat sprang out on their faces and their eyelids smarted. On the narrow path they had to go one by one, the old lord stepping along first, all black, and the footman, in his bright livery, bringing up the rear.

The field was indeed filled with people like a marketplace; there were probably a hundred or more men and women in it. To Adam the scene recalled pictures from his Bible: the meeting between Esau and Jacob in Edom, or Boas' reapers in his barley field near Bethlehem.[6] Some were standing by the side of the field, others pressed in small groups close to the mowing woman, and a few followed in her wake, binding up sheaves where she had cut the corn, as if thereby they thought to help her, or as if by all means they meant to have a part in her work. A younger woman with a pail on her head kept close to her side, and with her a number of half-grown children. One of these first caught sight of the lord of the estate and his suite, and pointed to him. The binders let their sheaves drop, and as the old man stood still many of the onlookers drew close round him.

---

5. An allusion to Penelope's weaving, which she unraveled every night to delay suitors while her husband, Odysseus, was away (as recounted in Homer's *Odyssey*). **6.** References to Genesis 32 and Ruth 2.

The woman on whom till now the eyes of the whole field had rested—a small figure on the large stage—was advancing slowly and unevenly, bent double as if she were walking on her knees, and stumbling as she walked. Her blue head-cloth had slipped back from her head; the grey hair was plastered to the skull with sweat, dusty and stuck with straw. She was obviously totally unaware of the multitude round her; neither did she now once turn her head or her gaze towards the new arrivals.

Absorbed in her work she again and again stretched out her left hand to grasp a handful of corn, and her right hand with the sickle in it to cut it off close to the soil, in wavering, groping pulls, like a tired swimmer's strokes. Her course took her so close to the feet of the old lord that his shadow fell on her. Just then she staggered and swayed sideways, and the woman who followed her lifted the pail from her head and held it to her lips. Anne-Marie drank without leaving her hold on her sickle, and the water ran from the corners of her mouth. A boy, close to her, quickly bent one knee, seized her hands in his own and, steadying and guiding them, cut off a gripe[7] of rye. "No, no," said the old lord, "you must not do that, boy. Leave Anne-Marie in peace to her work." At the sound of his voice the woman, falteringly, lifted her face in his direction.

The bony and tanned face was streaked with sweat and dust; the eyes were dimmed. But there was not in its expression the slightest trace of fear or pain. Indeed amongst all the grave and concerned faces of the field hers was the only one perfectly calm, peaceful, and mild. The mouth was drawn together in a thin line, a prim, keen, patient little smile, such as will be seen in the face of an old woman at her spinning-wheel or her knitting, eager on her work, and happy in it. And as the younger woman lifted back the pail, she immediately again fell to her mowing, with an ardent, tender craving, like that of a mother who lays a baby to the nipple. Like an insect that bustles along in high grass, or like a small vessel in a heavy sea, she butted her way on, her quiet face once more bent upon her task.

The whole throng of onlookers, and with them the small group from the pavilion, advanced as she advanced, slowly and as if drawn by a string. The bailiff, who felt the intense silence of the field heavy on him, said to the old lord: "The rye will yield better this year than last," and got no reply. He repeated his remark to Adam, and at last to the footman, who felt himself above a discussion on agriculture, and only cleared his throat in answer. In a while the bailiff again broke the silence. "There is the boy," he said and pointed with his thumb. "They have brought him down." At that moment the woman fell forward on her face and was lifted up by those nearest to her.

Adam suddenly stopped on the path, and covered his eyes with his hand. The old lord without turning asked him if he felt incommoded by the heat. "No," said Adam, "but stay. Let me speak to you." His uncle stopped, with his hand on the stick and looking ahead, as if regretful of being held back.

"In the name of God," cried the young man in French, "force not this woman to continue." There was a short pause. "But I force her not, my friend," said his uncle in the same language. "She is free to finish at any moment." "At

---

7. Handful.

the cost of her child only," again cried Adam. "Do you not see that she is dying? You know not what you are doing, or what it may bring upon you."

The old lord, perplexed by this unexpected animadversion, after a second turned all round, and his pale, clear eyes sought his nephew's face with stately surprise. His long, waxen face, with two symmetrical curls at the sides, had something of the mien of an idealized and ennobled old sheep or ram. He made sign to the bailiff to go on. The footman also withdrew a little, and the uncle and nephew were, so to say, alone on the path. For a minute neither of them spoke.

"In this very place where we now stand," said the old lord, then, with hauteur, "I gave Anne-Marie my word."

"My uncle!" said Adam. "A life is a greater thing even than a word. Recall that word, I beseech you, which was given in caprice, as a whim. I am praying you more for your sake than for my own, yet I shall be grateful to you all my life if you will grant me my prayer."

"You will have learned in school," said his uncle, "that in the beginning was the word.[8] It may have been pronounced in caprice, as a whim, the Scripture tells me nothing about it. It is still the principle of our world, its law of gravitation. My own humble word has been the principle of the land on which we stand, for an age of man. My father's word was the same, before my day."

"You are mistaken," cried Adam. "The word is creative—it is imagination, daring, and passion. By it the world was made. How much greater are these powers which bring into being than any restricting or controlling law! You wish the land on which we look to produce and propagate; you should not banish from it the forces which cause, and which keep up life, nor turn it into a desert by dominance of law. And when you look at the people, simpler than we and nearer to the heart of nature, who do not analyse their feelings, whose life is one with the life of the earth, do they not inspire in you a tenderness, respect, reverence even? This woman is ready to die for her son; will it ever happen to you or me that a woman willingly gives up her life for us? And if it did indeed come to pass, should we make so light of it as not to give up a dogma in return?"

"You are young," said the old lord. "A new age will undoubtedly applaud you. I am old-fashioned, I have been quoting to you texts a thousand years old. We do not, perhaps, quite understand one another. But with my own people I am, I believe, in good understanding. Anne-Marie might well feel that I am making light of her exploit, if now, at the eleventh hour, I did nullify it by a second word. I myself should feel so in her place. Yes, my nephew, it is possible, did I grant you your prayer and pronounce such an amnesty, that I should find it void against her faithfulness, and that we would still see her at her work, unable to give it up, as a shuttle in the rye field, until she had it all mowed. But she would then be a shocking, a horrible sight, a figure of unseemly fun, like a small planet running wild in the sky, when the law of gravitation had been done away with."

"And if she dies at her task," Adam exclaimed, "her death, and its consequences will come upon your head."

8. John 1:1.

The old lord took off his hat and gently ran his hand over his powdered head. "Upon my head?" he said. "I have kept up my head in many weathers. Even," he added proudly, "against the cold wind from high places. In what shape will it come upon my head, my nephew?" "I cannot tell," cried Adam in despair. "I have spoken to warn you. God only knows." "Amen," said the old lord with a little delicate smile. "Come, we will walk on." Adam drew in his breath deeply.

"No," he said in Danish. "I cannot come with you. This field is yours; things will happen here as you decide. But I myself must go away. I beg you to let me have, this evening, a coach as far as town. For I could not sleep another night under your roof, which I have honoured beyond any on earth." So many conflicting feelings at his own speech thronged in his breast that it would have been impossible for him to give them words.

The old lord, who had already begun to walk on, stood still, and with him the lackey. He did not speak for a minute, as if to give Adam time to collect his mind. But the young man's mind was in uproar and would not be collected.

"Must we," the old man asked, in Danish, "take leave here, in the rye field? I have held you dear, next to my own son. I have followed your career in life from year to year, and have been proud of you. I was happy when you wrote to say that you were coming back. If now you will go away, I wish you well." He shifted his walking-stick from the right hand to the left and gravely looked his nephew in the face.

Adam did not meet his eyes. He was gazing out over the landscape. In the late mellow afternoon it was resuming its colours, like a painting brought into proper light; in the meadows the little black stacks of peat stood gravely distinct upon the green sward. On this same morning he had greeted it all, like a child running laughingly to its mother's bosom; now already he must tear himself from it, in discordance, and forever. And at the moment of parting it seemed infinitely dearer than any time before, so much beautified and solemnized by the coming separation that it looked like the place in a dream, a landscape out of paradise, and he wondered if it was really the same. But, yes—there before him was, once more, the hunting-ground of long ago. And there was the road on which he had ridden today.

"But tell me where you mean to go from here," said the old lord slowly. "I myself have travelled a good deal in my days. I know the word of leaving, the wish to go away. But I have learned by experience that, in reality, the word has a meaning only to the place and the people which one leaves. When you have left my house—although it will see you go with sadness—as far as it is concerned the matter is finished and done with. But to the person who goes away it is a different thing, and not so simple. At the moment that he leaves one place he will be already, by the laws of life, on his way to another, upon this earth. Let me know, then, for the sake of our old acquaintance, to which place you are going when you leave here. To England?"

"No," said Adam. He felt in his heart that he could never again go back to England or to his easy and carefree life there. It was not far enough away; deeper waters than the North Sea must now be laid between him and Denmark. "No, not to England," he said. "I shall go to America, to the new world." For a moment he shut his eyes, trying to form to himself a picture of existence in America, with the grey Atlantic Ocean between him and these fields and woods.

"To America?" said his uncle and drew up his eyebrows. "Yes, I have heard of America. They have got freedom there, a big waterfall, savage red men. They shoot turkeys, I have read, as we shoot partridges. Well, if it be your wish, go to America, Adam, and be happy in the new world."

He stood for some time, sunk in thought, as if he had already sent off the young man to America, and had done with him. When at last he spoke, his words had the character of a monologue, enunciated by the person who watches things come and go, and himself stays on.

"Take service, there," he said, "with the power which will give you an easier bargain than this: That with your own life you may buy the life of your son."

Adam had not listened to his uncle's remarks about America, but the conclusive, solemn words caught his ear. He looked up. As if for the first time in his life, he saw the old man's figure as a whole, and conceived how small it was, so much smaller than himself, pale, a thin black anchorite[9] upon his own land. A thought ran through his head: "How terrible to be old!" The abhorrence of the tyrant, and the sinister dread on his behalf, which had followed him all day, seemed to die out of him, and his pity with all creation to extend even to the sombre form before him.

His whole being had cried out for harmony. Now, with the possibility of forgiving, of a reconciliation, a sense of relief went through him; confusedly he bethought himself of Anne-Marie drinking the water held to her lips. He took off his hat, as his uncle had done a moment ago, so that to a beholder at a distance it would seem that the two dark-clad gentlemen on the path were repeatedly and respectfully saluting one another, and brushed the hair from his forehead. Once more the tune of the garden-room rang in his mind:

> *"Mourir pour ce qu'on aime*
> *C'est un trop doux effort[1] ..."*

He stood for a long time immobile and dumb. He broke off a few ears of rye, kept them in his hand and looked at them.

He saw the ways of life, he thought, as a twined and tangled design, complicated and mazy; it was not given him or any mortal to command or control it. Life and death, happiness and woe, the past and present, were interlaced within the pattern. Yet to the initiated it might be read as easily as our ciphers—which to the savage must seem confused and incomprehensible—will be read by the schoolboy. And out of the contrasting elements concord rose. All that lived must suffer; the old man, whom he had judged hardly, had suffered, as he had watched his son die, and had dreaded the obliteration of his being. He himself would come to know ache, tears and remorse, and, even through these, the fullness of life. So might now, to the woman in the rye field, her ordeal be a triumphant procession. For to die for the one you loved was an effort too sweet for words.

As now he thought of it, he knew that all his life he had sought the unity of things, the secret which connects the phenomena of existence. It was this

---

9. Hermit.　**1.** "To die for one you love / Is too sweet an effort" (French).

strife, this dim presage, which had sometimes made him stand still and inert in the midst of the games of his playfellows, or which had, at other moments—on moonlight nights, or in his little boat on the sea—lifted the boy to ecstatic happiness. Where other young people, in their pleasures or their amours, had searched for contrast and variety, he himself had yearned only to comprehend in full the oneness of the world. If things had come differently to him, if his young cousin had not died, and the events that followed his death had not brought him to Denmark, his search for understanding and harmony might have taken him to America, and he might have found them there, in the virgin forests of a new world. Now they have been disclosed to him today, in the place where he had played as a child. As the song is one with the voice that sings it, as the road is one with the goal, as lovers are made one in their embrace, so is man one with his destiny, and he shall love it as himself.[2]

He looked up again, towards the horizon. If he wished to, he felt, he might find out what it was that had brought to him, here, the sudden conception of the unity of the universe. When this same morning he had philosophized, lightly and for his own sake, on his feeling of belonging to this land and soil, it had been the beginning of it. But since then it had grown; it had become a mightier thing, a revelation to his soul. Sometime he would look into it, for the law of cause and effect was a wonderful and fascinating study. But not now. This hour was consecrated to greater emotions, to a surrender to fate and to the will of life.

"No," he said at last. "If you wish it I shall not go. I shall stay here."

At that moment a long, loud roll of thunder broke the stillness of the afternoon. It re-echoed for a while amongst the low hills, and it reverberated within the young man's breast as powerfully as if he had been seized and shaken by hands. The landscape had spoken. He remembered that twelve hours ago he had put a question to it, half in jest, and not knowing what he did. Here it gave him its answer.

What it contained he did not know; neither did he inquire. In his promise to his uncle he had given himself over to the mightier powers of the world. Now what must come must come.

"I thank you," said the old lord, and made a little stiff gesture with his hand. "I am happy to hear you say so. We should not let the difference in our ages, or of our views, separate us. In our family we have been wont to keep peace and faith with one another. You have made my heart lighter."

Something within his uncle's speech faintly recalled to Adam the misgivings of the afternoon. He rejected them; he would not let them trouble the new, sweet felicity which his resolution to stay had brought him.

"I shall go on now," said the old lord. "But there is no need for you to follow me. I will tell you tomorrow how the matter has ended." "No," said Adam, "I shall come back by sunset, to see the end of it myself."

All the same he did not come back. He kept the hour in his mind, and all through the evening the consciousness of the drama, and the profound concern and compassion with which, in his thoughts, he followed it, gave to his

---

2. Here Dinesen paraphrases a Roman motto revived by Friedrich Nietzsche (1844–1900), German philosopher: Love your fate.

speech, glance and movements a grave and pathetic substance. But he felt that he was, in the rooms of the manor, and even by the harpsichord on which he accompanied his aunt to her air from *Alceste*,[3] as much in the centre of things as if he had stood in the rye field itself, and as near to those human beings whose fate was now decided there. Anne-Marie and he were both in the hands of destiny, and destiny would, by different ways, bring each to the designated end.

Later on he remembered what he had thought that evening.

But the old lord stayed on. Late in the afternoon he even had an idea; he called down his valet to the pavilion and made him shift his clothes on him and dress him up in a brocaded suit that he had worn at Court. He let a lace-trimmed shirt be drawn over his head and stuck out his slim legs to have them put into thin silk stockings and buckled shoes. In this majestic attire he dined alone, of a frugal meal, but took a bottle of Rhenish wine with it, to keep up his strength. He sat on for a while, a little sunk in his seat; then, as the sun neared the earth, he straightened himself, and took the way down to the field.

The shadows were now lengthening, azure blue along all the eastern slopes. The lonely trees in the corn marked their site by narrow blue pools running out from their feet, and as the old man walked a thin, immensely elongated reflection stirred behind him on the path. Once he stood still; he thought he heard a lark singing over his head, a spring-like sound; his tired head held no clear perception of the season; he seemed to be walking, and standing, in a kind of eternity.

The people in the field were no longer silent, as they had been in the afternoon. Many of them talked loudly among themselves, and a little farther away a woman was weeping.

When the bailiff saw his master, he came up to him. He told him, in great agitation, that the widow would, in all likelihood, finish the mowing of the field within a quarter of an hour.

"Are the keeper and the wheelwright here?" the old lord asked him. "They have been here," said the bailiff, "and have gone away, five times. Each time they have said that they would not come back. But they have come back again, all the same, and they are here now." "And where is the boy?" the old lord asked again. "He is with her," said the bailiff. "I have given him leave to follow her. He has walked close to his mother all the afternoon, and you will see him now by her side, down there."

Anne-Marie was now working her way up towards them more evenly than before, but with extreme slowness, as if at any moment she might come to a standstill. This excessive tardiness, the old lord reflected, if it had been purposely performed, would have been an inimitable, dignified exhibition of skilled art; one might fancy the Emperor of China advancing in like manner on a divine procession or rite. He shaded his eyes with his hand, for the sun was now just beyond the horizon, and its last rays made light, wild, many-coloured specks dance before his sight. With such splendour did the sunset emblazon the earth and the air that the landscape was turned into a melting-

---

3. Opera by Christoph Willibald Gluck (1714–1787), Austrian composer. From the Greek myth of Alcestis, who died in her husband's place and was rescued from Hades by Hercules.

pot of glorious metals. The meadows and the grasslands became pure gold; the barley field near by, with its long ears, was a live lake of shining silver.

There was only a small patch of straw standing in the rye field, when the woman, alarmed by the change in the light, turned her head a little to get a look at the sun. The while she did not stop her work, but grasped one handful of corn and cut it off, then another, and another. A great stir, and a sound like a manifold, deep sigh, ran through the crowd. The field was now mowed from one end to the other. Only the mower herself did not realize the fact; she stretched out her hand anew, and when she found nothing in it, she seemed puzzled or disappointed. Then she let her arms drop, and slowly sank to her knees.

Many of the women burst out weeping, and the swarm drew close round her, leaving only a small open space at the side where the old lord stood. Their sudden nearness frightened Anne-Marie; she made a slight, uneasy movement, as if terrified that they should put their hands on her.

The boy, who had kept by her all day, now fell on his knees beside her. Even he dared not touch her, but held one arm low behind her back and the other before her, level with her collar-bone, to catch hold of her if she should fall, and all the time he cried aloud. At that moment the sun went down.

The old lord stepped forward and solemnly took off his hat. The crowd became silent, waiting for him to speak. But for a minute or two he said nothing. Then he addressed her, very slowly.

"Your son is free, Anne-Marie," he said. He again waited a little, and added: "You have done a good day's work, which will long be remembered."

Anne-Marie raised her gaze only as high as his knees, and he understood that she had not heard what he said. He turned to the boy. "You tell your mother, Goske," he said, gently, "what I have told her."

The boy had been sobbing wildly, in raucous, broken moans. It took him some time to collect and control himself. But when at last he spoke, straight into his mother's face, his voice was low, a little impatient, as if he were conveying an everyday message to her. "I am free, Mother," he said. "You have done a good day's work that will long be remembered."

At the sound of his voice she lifted her face to him. A faint, bland shadow of surprise ran over it, but still she gave no sign of having heard what he said, so that the people round them began to wonder if the exhaustion had turned her deaf. But after a moment she slowly and waveringly raised her hand, fumbling in the air as she aimed at his face, and with her fingers touched his cheek. The cheek was wet with tears, so that at the contact her fingertips lightly stuck to it, and she seemed unable to overcome the infinitely slight resistance, or to withdraw her hand. For a minute the two looked each other in the face. Then, softly and lingeringly, like a sheaf of corn that falls to the ground, she sank forward onto the boy's shoulder, and he closed his arms round her.

He held her thus, pressed against him, his own face buried in her hair and head-cloth, for such a long time that those nearest to them, frightened because her body looked so small in his embrace, drew closer, bent down and loosened his grip. The boy let them do so without a word or a movement. But the woman who held Anne-Marie, in her arms to lift her up, turned her face to the old lord. "She is dead," she said.

The people who had followed Anne-Marie all through the day kept standing and stirring in the field for many hours, as long as the evening light lasted, and longer. Long after some of them had made a stretcher from branches of the trees and had carried away the dead woman, others wandered on, up and down the stubble, imitating and measuring her course from one end of the rye field to the other, and binding up the last sheaves, where she had finished her mowing.

The old lord stayed with them for a long time, stepping along a little, and again standing still.

In the place where the woman had died the old lord later on had a stone set up, with a sickle engraved in it. The peasants on the land then named the rye field "Sorrow-Acre." By this name it was known a long time after the story of the woman and her son had itself been forgotten.

1940

RELATED:

—Tobias Wolff on "Sorrow-Acre," p. 1786

ANDRE DUBUS
1936–1999

Born in Lake Charles, Louisiana, Dubus is widely regarded for his fiction, which portrays the decline of postwar America, and for his moral responsibility as an author. Honored many times for his work, Dubus received a MacArthur Fellowship in 1988. His titles include *The Lieutenant* (1967), a novel; *We Don't Live Here Any More* (1984), a collected trilogy of novellas; *Separate Flights* (1975), *Land Where My Fathers Died* (1984), *The Last Worthless Evening* (1986), *Selected Stories* (1995), and *Dancing After Hours* (1996), all short-story collections; and *Broken Vessels* (1991), a book of personal essays. Dubus's last book, *Meditations from a Movable Chair* (1998), includes both his reflections on his confinement to a wheelchair after a road accident in 1986 and his 1988 essay "Giving Up the Gun," in which he renounces his lifelong habit of carrying firearms.

The Intruder

Because Kenneth Girard loved his parents and his sister and because he could not tell them why he went to the woods, his first moments there were always uncomfortable ones, as if he had left the house to commit a sin. But he was thirteen and he could not say that he was going to sit on a hill and wait for the silence and trees and sky to close in on him, wait until they all became a part of him and thought and memory ceased and the voices began. He could only say that he was going for a walk and, since there was so much more to say, he felt cowardly and deceitful and more lonely than before.

He could not say that on the hill he became great, that he had saved a beautiful girl from a river (the voice then had been gentle and serious and she had loved him), or that he had ridden into town, his clothes dusty, his black hat pulled low over his sunburned face, and an hour later had ridden away with four fresh notches on the butt of his six-gun, or that with the count three-and-two and the bases loaded, he had driven the ball so far and high that the outfielders did not even move, or that he had waded through surf and sprinted over sand, firing his Tommy gun[1] and shouting to his soldiers behind him.

Now he was capturing a farmhouse. In the late movie the night before, the farmhouse had been very important, though no one ever said why, and sitting there in the summer dusk, he watched the backs of his soldiers as they advanced through the woods below him and crossed the clear, shallow creek

1. Submachine gun.

and climbed the hill that he faced. Occasionally, he lifted his twenty-two-caliber rifle and fired at a rusty tin can across the creek, the can becoming a Nazi face in a window as he squeezed the trigger and the voices filled him: *You got him, Captain. You got him.* For half an hour he sat and fired at the can, and anyone who might have seen him could never know that he was doing anything else, that he had been wounded in the shoulder and lost half his men but had captured the farmhouse.

Kenneth looked up through the trees, which were darker green now. While he had been watching his battle, the earth, too, had become darker, shadowed, with patches of late sun on the grass and brown fallen pine needles. He stood up, then looked down at the creek, and across it, at the hill on the other side. His soldiers were gone. He was hungry, and he turned and walked back through the woods.

Then he remembered that his mother and father were going to a party in town that night and he would be alone with Connie. He liked being alone, but, even more, he liked being alone with his sister. She was nearly seventeen; her skin was fair, her cheeks colored, and she had long black hair that came down to her shoulders; on the right side of her face, a wave of it reached the corner of her eye. She was the most beautiful girl he knew. She was also the only person with whom, for his entire life, he had been nearly perfectly at ease. He could be silent with her or he could say whatever occurred to him and he never had to think about it first to assure himself that it was not foolish or, worse, uninteresting.

Leaving the woods, he climbed the last gentle slope and entered the house. He leaned his rifle in a corner of his room, which faced the quiet blacktop road, and went to the bathroom and washed his hands. Standing at the lavatory, he looked into the mirror. He suddenly felt as if he had told a lie. He was looking at his face and, as he did several times each day, telling himself, without words, that it was a handsome face. His skin was fair, as Connie's was, and he had color in his cheeks; but his hair, carefully parted and combed, was more brown than black. He believed that Connie thought he was exactly like her, that he was talkative and well liked. But she never saw him with his classmates. He felt that he was deceiving her.

He left the house and went into the outdoor kitchen and sat on a bench at the long, uncovered table and folded his arms on it.

"Did you kill anything?" Connie said.

"Tin cans."

His father turned from the stove with a skillet of white perch in his hand.

"They're good ones," he said.

"Mine are the best," Kenneth said.

"You didn't catch but two."

"They're the best."

His mother put a plate in front of him, then opened a can of beer and sat beside him. He sat quietly, watching his father at the stove. Then he looked at his mother's hand holding the beer can. There were veins and several freckles on the back of it. Farther up her forearm was a small yellow bruise; the flesh at her elbow was wrinkled. He looked at her face. People said that he and Connie looked like her, so he supposed it was true, but he could not see the resemblance.

"Daddy and I are going to the Gossetts' tonight," she said.

"I know."

"I wrote the phone number down," his father said. "It's under the phone."

"Okay."

His father was not tall either, but his shoulders were broad. Kenneth wondered if his would be like that when he grew older. His father was the only one in the family who tanned in the sun.

"And *please,* Connie," his mother said, "will you go to sleep at a reasonable hour? It's hard enough to get you up for Mass when you've had a good night's sleep."

"Why don't we go into town for the evening Mass?"

"No. I don't like it hanging over my head all day."

"All right. When will y'all be home?"

"About two. And that doesn't mean read in bed till then. You need your sleep."

"We'll go to bed early," Connie said.

His father served fried perch and hush puppies onto their plates and they had French bread and catsup and Tabasco sauce and iced tea. After dinner, his father read the newspaper and his mother read a Reader's Digest condensation, then they showered and dressed, and at seven-thirty, they left. He and Connie followed them to the door. Connie kissed them; then he did. His mother and father looked happy, and he felt good about that.

"We'll be back about two," his mother said. "Keep the doors locked."

"Definitely," Connie said. "And we'll bar the windows."

"Well, you never know. Y'all be good. G'night."

"Hold down the fort, son," his father said.

"I will."

Then they were gone, the screen door slamming behind them, and Connie left the sunporch, but he stood at the door, listening to the car starting and watching its headlights as it backed down the trail through the yard, then turned into the road and drove away. Still he did not move. He loved the nights at the camp when they were left alone. At home, there was a disturbing climate about their evenings alone, for distant voices of boys in the neighborhood reminded him that he was not alone entirely by choice. Here, there were no sounds.

He latched the screen and went into the living room. Connie was sitting in the rocking chair near the fireplace, smoking a cigarette. She looked at him, then flicked ashes into an ashtray on her lap.

"Now don't you tell on me."

"I didn't know you did that."

"Please don't tell. Daddy would skin me alive."

"I won't."

He could not watch her. He looked around the room for a book.

"Douglas is coming tonight," she said.

"Oh." He picked up the Reader's Digest book and pretended to look at it. "Y'all going to watch TV?" he said.

"Not if you want to."

"It doesn't matter."

"You watch it. You like Saturday nights."

She looked as if she had been smoking for a long time, all during the summer and possibly the school year, too, for months or even a year without his knowing it. He was hurt. He laid down the book.

"Think I'll go outside for a while," he said.

He went onto the sunporch and out the door and walked down the sloping car trail that led to the road. He stopped at the gate, which was open, and leaned on it. Forgetting Connie, he looked over his shoulder at the camp, thinking that he would never tire of it. They had been there for six weeks, since early June, his father coming on Friday evenings and leaving early Monday mornings, driving sixty miles to their home in southern Louisiana. Kenneth fished during the day, swam with Connie in the creeks, read novels about baseball, and watched the major league games on television. He thought winter at the camp was better, though. They came on weekends and hunted squirrels, and there was a fireplace.

He looked down the road. The closest camp was half a mile away, on the opposite side of the road, and he could see its yellow-lighted windows through the trees. *That's the house. Quiet now. We'll sneak through the woods and get the guard, then charge the house. Come on.* Leaning against the gate, he stared into the trees across the road and saw himself leading his soldiers through the woods. They reached the guard. His back was turned and Kenneth crawled close to him, then stood up and slapped a hand over the guard's mouth and stabbed him in the back. They rushed the house and Kenneth reached the door first and kicked it open. The general looked up from his desk, then tried to get his pistol from his holster. Kenneth shot him with his Tommy gun. *Grab those papers, men. Let's get out of here.* They got the papers and ran outside and Kenneth stopped to throw a hand grenade through the door. He reached the woods before it exploded.

He turned from the gate and walked toward the house, looking around him at the dark pines. He entered the sunporch and latched the screen; then he smelled chocolate, and he went to the kitchen. Connie was stirring a pot of fudge on the stove. She had changed to a fresh pale blue shirt, the tails of it hanging almost to the bottom of her white shorts.

"It'll be a while," she said.

He nodded, watching her hand and the spoon. He thought of Douglas coming and began to feel nervous.

"What time's Douglas coming?"

"Any minute now. Let me know if you hear his car."

"All right."

He went to his room and picked up his rifle; then he saw the magazine on the chest of drawers and he leaned the rifle in the corner again. Suddenly his mouth was dry. He got the magazine and quickly turned the pages until he found her: she was stepping out of the surf on the French Riviera, laughing, as if the man with her had just said something funny. She was blond and very tan and she wore a bikini. The photograph was in color. For several moments he looked at it; then he got the rifle and cleaning kit and sat in the rocking chair in the living room, with the rifle across his lap. He put a patch on the cleaning rod and dipped it in bore cleaner and pushed it down the barrel, the handle of the rod clanging against the muzzle. He worked slowly, pausing often to listen for Douglas's car, because he wanted to be cleaning the rifle

when Douglas came. Because Douglas was a tackle on the high school football team in the town, and Kenneth had never been on a football team, and
never would be.

The football players made him more uncomfortable than the others. They
walked into the living room and firmly shook his father's hand, then his
hand, beginning to talk as soon as they entered, and they sat and waited for
Connie, their talking never ceasing, their big chests and shoulders leaned forward, their faces slowly turning as they looked at each picture on the wall, at
the designs on the rug, at the furniture, passing over Kenneth as if he were
another chair, filling the room with a feeling of strength and self-confidence
that defeated him, paralyzing his tongue and even his mind, so that he merely
sat in thoughtless anxiety, hoping they would not speak to him, hoping especially that they would not ask: *You play football?* Two of them had, and he never
forgot it. He had answered with a mute, affirming nod.

He had always been shy and, because of it, he had stayed on the periphery
of sports for as long as he could remember. When his teachers forced him to
play, he spent an anxious hour trying not to become involved, praying in right
field that no balls would come his way, lingering on the outside of the huddle
so that no one would look up and see his face and decide to throw him a pass
on the next play.

But he found that there was one thing he could do and he did it alone, or
with his father: he could shoot and he could hunt. He felt that shooting was
the only thing that had ever been easy for him. Schoolwork was, too, but
he considered that a curse.

He was not disturbed by the boys who were not athletes, unless, for some
reason, they were confident anyway. While they sat and waited for Connie, he
was cheerful and teasing, and they seemed to like him. The girls were best. He
walked into the living room and they stopped their talking and laughing and
all of them greeted him and sometimes they said: "Connie, he's so cute," or "I
wish you were three years older," and he said: "Me, too," and tried to be witty
and usually was.

He heard a car outside.

"Douglas is here," he called.

Connie came through the living room, one hand arranging the wave of hair
near her right eye, and went into the sunporch. Slowly, Kenneth wiped the rifle
with an oily rag. He heard Douglas's loud voice and laughter and heavy footsteps on the sunporch; then they came into the living room. Kenneth raised
his face.

"Hi," he said.

"How's it going?"

"All right."

Douglas Bakewell was not tall. He had blond hair, cut so short on top that
you could see his scalp, and a reddish face, and sunburned arms, covered
with bleached hair. A polo shirt fit tightly over his chest and shoulders and
biceps.

"Whatcha got there?" Douglas said.

"Twenty-two."

"Let's see."

"Better dry it."

He briskly wiped it with a dry cloth and handed it to Douglas. Quickly, Douglas worked the bolt, aimed at the ceiling, and pulled the trigger.

"Nice trigger," he said.

He held it in front of his waist and looked at it, then gave it to Kenneth.

"Well, girl," he said, turning to Connie, "where's the beer?"

"Sit down and I'll get you one."

She went to the kitchen. Douglas sat on the couch and Kenneth picked up his cleaning kit and, not looking at Douglas, walked into his bedroom. He stayed there until Connie returned from the kitchen; then he went into the living room. They were sitting on the couch. Connie was smoking again. Kenneth kept walking toward the sunporch.

"I'll let you know when the fudge is ready," Connie said.

"All right."

On the sunporch, he turned on the television and sat in front of it. He watched ten minutes of a Western before he was relaxed again, before he settled in his chair, oblivious to the quiet talking in the living room, his mind beginning to wander happily as a gunfighter in dark clothes moved across the screen.

By the time the fudge was ready, he was watching a detective story, and when Connie called him, he said: "Okay, in a minute," but did not move, and finally she came to the sunporch with a saucer of fudge and set it on a small table beside his chair.

"When that's over, you better go to bed," she said.

"I'm not sleepy."

"You know what Mother said."

"*You're* staying up."

"Course I am. I'm also a little older than you."

"I want to see the late show."

"No!"

"Yes, I am."

"I'll tell Daddy."

"He doesn't care."

"I'll tell him you wouldn't listen to me."

"I'll tell him you smoke."

"Oh, I could *wring* your neck!"

She went to the living room. He tried to concentrate on the Western, but it was ruined. The late show came on and he had seen it several months before and did not want to see it again, but he would not go to bed. He watched absently. Then he had to urinate. He got up and went into the living room, walking quickly, only glancing at them once, but when he did, Connie smiled and, with her voice friendly again, said: "What is it?"

He stopped and looked at her.

"*Red River.*"[2]

He smiled.

"I already saw it," he said.

"You watching it again?"

"Maybe so."

"Okay."

---

2. Western directed by Howard Hawks, starring John Wayne and Montgomery Clift (1948).

He went to the bathroom and when he came back, they were gone. He went to the sunporch. Connie and Douglas were standing near the back door. The television was turned off. Kenneth wondered if Connie had seen *Red River*. If she had not, he could tell her what had happened during the part she missed. Douglas was whispering to Connie, his face close to hers. Then he looked at Kenneth.

"Night," he said.

"G'night," Kenneth said.

He was gone. Kenneth picked up the saucer his fudge had been on and took it to the kitchen and put it in the sink. He heard Douglas's car backing down the trail, and he went to the sunporch, but Connie was not there, so he went to the bathroom door and said: "You seen *Red River*?"

"Yes."

"You taking a bath?"

"Just washing my face. I'm going to bed."

He stood quietly for a moment. Then he went into the living room and got a magazine and sat in the rocking chair, looking at the people in the advertisements. Connie came in, wearing a robe. She leaned over his chair and he looked up and she kissed him.

"Good night," she said.

"G'night."

"You going to bed soon?"

"In a minute."

She got her cigarettes and an ashtray from the coffee table and went to her room and closed the door. After a while, he heard her getting into bed.

He looked at half the magazine, then laid it on the floor. Being awake in a house where everyone else was sleeping made him lonely. He went to the sunporch and latched the screen, then closed the door and locked it. He left the light on but turned out the one in the living room. Then he went to his room and took off everything but his shorts. He was about to turn out the light when he looked at the chest of drawers and saw the magazine. He hesitated. Then he picked it up and found the girl and looked at the exposed tops of her breasts and at her navel and below it. Suddenly he closed the magazine and raised his eyes to the ceiling, then closed them and said three Hail Marys. Without looking at it, he picked up the magazine and took it to the living room, and went back to his bedroom and lay on his belly on the floor and started doing push-ups. He had no trouble with the first eight; then they became harder, and by the fifteenth he was breathing fast and his whole body was trembling as he pushed himself up from the floor. He did one more, then stood up and turned out the light and got into bed.

His room extended forward of the rest of the house, so that, from his bed, he could look through the window to his left and see the living room and Connie's bedroom. He rolled on his back and pulled the sheet up to his chest. He could hear crickets outside his window.

He flexed his right arm and felt the bicep. It seemed firmer than it had in June, when he started doing push-ups every night. He closed his eyes and began the Lord's Prayer and got as far as *Thy kingdom come* before he heard it.

Now it was not the crickets that he heard. He heard his own breathing and the bedsprings as his body tensed; then he heard it again, somewhere in front of the house: a cracking twig, a rustle of dried leaves, a foot on hard earth. Slowly, he rolled on his left side and looked out the window. He waited to be sure, but he did not have to; then he waited to decide what he would do, and he did not have to wait for that either, because he already knew, and he looked at the far corner of the room where his rifle was, though he could not see it, and he looked out the window again, staring at the windows of the living room and Connie's room, forcing himself to keep his eyes there, as if it would be all right if the prowler did not come into his vision, did not come close to the house; but listening to the slow footsteps, Kenneth knew that he would.

Get up. Get up and get the rifle. If you don't do it now, he might come to this window and look in and then it'll be too late.

For a moment, he did not breathe. Then, slowly, stopping at each sound of the bedsprings, he rolled out of bed and crouched on the floor beneath the window. He did not move. He listened to his breathing, for there was no other sound, not even crickets, and he began to tremble, thinking the prowler might be standing above him, looking through his window at the empty bed. He held his breath. Then he heard the footsteps again, in front of the house, closer now, and he thought: *He's by the pines in front of Connie's room.* He crawled away from the window, thinking of a large, bearded man standing in the pine trees thirty yards from Connie's room, studying the house and deciding which window to use; then he stood up and walked on tiptoes to the chest of drawers and moved his hand over the top of it until he touched the handful of bullets, his fingers quickly closing on them, and he picked up the rifle and took out the magazine and loaded it, then inserted it again and laid the extra bullets on the chest of drawers. Now he had to work the bolt. He pulled it up and back and eased it forward again.

Staying close to the wall, he tiptoed back to the window, stopping at the edge of it, afraid to look out and see a face looking in. He heard nothing. He looked through the windows in the opposite wall, thinking that if the prowler had heard him getting the rifle, he could have run back to the road, back to wherever he had come from, or he could still be hiding in the pines, or he could have circled to the rear of the house to hide again and listen, but there was no way of knowing, and he would have to stand in the room, listening, until his father came home. He thought of going to wake Connie, but he was afraid to move. Then he heard him again, near the pines, coming toward the house. He kneeled and pressed his shoulder against the wall, moving his face slightly, just enough to look out the screen and see the prowler walking toward Connie's window, stopping there and looking over his shoulder at the front yard and the road, then reaching out and touching the screen.

Kenneth rose and moved away from the wall, standing close to his bed now; he aimed through the screen, found the side of the man's head, then fired. A scream filled the house, the yard, his mind, and he thought at first it was the prowler, who was lying on the ground now, but it was a high, shrieking scream; it was Connie, and he ran into the living room, but she was already on the sunporch, unlocking the back door, not screaming now, but crying, pulling open the wooden door and hitting the screen with both hands, then stopping to unlatch it, and he yelled: "Connie!"

She turned, her hair swinging around her cheek.

"Get away from me!"

Then she ran outside, the screen door slamming, the shriek starting again, a long, high wail, ending in front of the house with *"Douglas, Douglas, Douglas!"* Then he knew.

Afterward, it seemed that the events of a year had occurred in an hour, and, to Kenneth, even that hour seemed to have a quality of neither speed nor slowness, but a kind of suspension, as if time were not passing at all. He remembered somehow calling his father and crying into the phone: "I shot Douglas Bakewell," and because of the crying, his father kept saying: "What's that, son? What did you say?" and then he lay facedown on his bed and cried, thinking of Connie outside with Douglas, hearing her sometimes when his own sounds lulled, and sometimes thinking of Connie inside with Douglas, if he had not shot him. He remembered the siren when it was far away and their voices as they brought Connie into the house. The doctor had come first, then his mother and father, then the sheriff; but, remembering, it was as if they had all come at once, for there was always a soothing or questioning face over his bed. He remembered the footsteps and hushed voices as they carried the body past his window, while his mother sat on the bed and stroked his forehead and cheek. He would never forget that.

Now the doctor and sheriff were gone and it seemed terribly late, almost sunrise. His father came into the room, carrying a glass of water, and sat on the bed.

"Take this," he said. "It'll make you sleep."

Kenneth sat up and took the pill from his father's palm and placed it on his tongue, then drank the water. He lay on his back and looked at his father's face. Then he began to cry.

"I thought it was a prowler," he said.

"It was, son. A prowler. We've told you that."

"But Connie went out there and she stayed all that time and she kept saying *'Douglas'* over and over; I heard her—"

"She wasn't out there with *him.* She was just out in the yard. She was in shock. She meant she wanted Douglas to be there with her. To help."

"No, *no.* It was *him.*"

"It was a prowler. You did right. There's no telling what he might have done."

Kenneth looked away.

"He was going in her room," he said. "That's why she went to bed early. So I'd go to bed."

"It was a prowler," his father said.

Now Kenneth was sleepy. He closed his eyes and the night ran together in his mind and he remembered the rifle in the corner and thought: *I'll throw it in the creek tomorrow. I never want to see it again.* He would be asleep soon. He saw himself standing on the hill and throwing his rifle into the creek; then the creek became an ocean, and he stood on a high cliff and for a moment he was a mighty angel, throwing all guns and cruelty and sex and tears into the sea.

1996

STUART DYBEK
b.1942

Dybek was born and lives in Chicago, where he teaches literature and writing at Northwestern University after a long career at Western Michigan University. He has published four collections of short stories: *Childhood and Other Neighborhoods* (1980), *The Coast of Chicago* (1990), *The Baby Can Sing*, co-authored with Judith Slater (1999), and *I Sailed with Magellan* (2003). Dybek has also written two books of poetry, *Brass Knuckles* (1979) and *Streets in Their Own Ink* (2004). He is the recipient of a PEN/Malamud Prize for "distinctive achievement in the short story form." In nearly all his work, Dybek chronicles and celebrates life in his beloved Chicago.

We Didn't

> We did it in front of the mirror
> And in the light. We did it in darkness,
> In water, and in the high grass.
> —*"We Did It," Yehuda Amichai*

We didn't in the light; we didn't in darkness. We didn't in the fresh-cut summer grass or in the mounds of autumn leaves or on the snow where moonlight threw down our shadows. We didn't in your room on the canopy bed you slept in, the bed you'd slept in as a child, or in the back seat of my father's rusted Rambler which smelled of the smoked chubs and kielbasa[1] that he delivered on weekends from my Uncle Vincent's meat market. We didn't in your mother's Buick Eight where a rosary twined the rearview mirror like a beaded black snake with silver, cruciform fangs.

At the dead end of our lovers' lane—a side street of abandoned factories—where I perfected the pinch that springs open a bra; behind the lilac bushes in Marquette Park[2] where you first touched me through my jeans and your nipples, swollen against transparent cotton, seemed the shade of lilacs; in the balcony of the now defunct Clark Theater where I wiped popcorn salt from my palms and slid them up your thighs and you whispered, "I feel like Doris Day is watching us," we didn't.

How adept we were at fumbling, how perfectly mistimed our timing, how utterly we confused energy with ecstasy.

---

1. A Polish smoked sausage. **2.** In Chicago.

Remember that night becalmed by heat, and the two of us, fused by sweat, trembling as if a wind from outer space that only we could feel was gusting across Oak Street Beach? Wound in your faded Navajo blanket, we lay soul kissing until you wept with wanting.

We'd been kissing all day—all summer—kisses tasting of different shades of lip gloss and too many Cokes. The lake had turned hot pink, rose rapture, pearl amethyst with dusk, then washed in night black with a ruff of silver foam. Beyond a momentary horizon, silent bolts of heat lightning throbbed, perhaps setting barns on fire somewhere in Indiana. The beach that had been so crowded was deserted as if there was a curfew. Only the bodies of lovers remained behind, visible in lightning flashes, scattered like the fallen on a battlefield, a few of them moaning, waiting for the gulls to pick them clean.

On my fingers your slick scent mixed with the coconut musk of the suntan lotion we'd repeatedly smeared over one another's bodies. When your bikini top fell away, my hands caught your breasts, memorizing their delicate weight, my palms cupped as if bringing water to parched lips.

Along the Gold Coast,[3] high-rises began to glow, window added to window, against the dark. In every lighted bedroom, couples home from work were stripping off their business suits, falling to the bed, and doing it. They did it before mirrors and pressed against the glass in streaming shower stalls, they did it against walls and on the furniture in ways that required previously unimagined gymnastics which they invented on the spot. They did it in honor of man and woman, in honor of beast, in honor of God. They did it because they'd been released, because they were home free, alive, and private, because they couldn't wait any longer, couldn't wait for the appointed hour, for the right time or temperature, couldn't wait for the future, for messiahs, for peace on earth and justice for all. They did it because of the Bomb, because of pollution, because of the Four Horsemen of the Apocalypse,[4] because extinction might be just a blink away. They did it because it was Friday night. It was Friday night and somewhere delirious music was playing—flutter-tongued flutes, muted trumpets meowing like tomcats in heat, feverish plucking and twanging, tom-toms, congas, and gongs all pounding the same pulsebeat.

I stripped your bikini bottom down the skinny rails of your legs and you tugged my swimsuit past my tan. Swimsuits at our ankles, we kicked like swimmers to free our legs, almost expecting a tide to wash over us the way the tide rushes in on Burt Lancaster and Deborah Kerr in their famous love scene on the beach in *From Here to Eternity*[5]—a scene so famous that although neither of us had seen the movie, our bodies assumed the exact position of movie stars on the sand and you whispered to me softly, "I'm afraid of getting pregnant," and I whispered back, "Don't worry, I have protection," then, still kissing you, felt for my discarded cutoffs and the wallet in which for the last several months I had carried a Trojan as if it was a talisman. Still kissing, I tore its flattened, dried-out wrapper and it sprang through my fingers like a spring from a clock and dropped to the sand between our legs. My hands were shaking. In a panic, I groped for it, found it, tried to dust it off, tried, as Burt

---

3. A district in Chicago of luxury hotels, apartments, and shops on Michigan Avenue and Lake Shore Drive.   **4.** Four horsemen symbolizing pestilence, war, famine, and death in the Book of Revelation 6:2–8.   **5.** The 1953 film based on a novel by James Jones.

Lancaster never had to, to slip it on without breaking the mood, felt the grains of sand inside it, a throb of lightning, and the Great Lake behind us became, for all practical purposes, the Pacific and your skin tasted of salt and to the insistent question that my hips were asking, your body answered yes, your thighs opened like wings from my waist as we surfaced panting from a kiss that left you pleading *oh Christ yes,* a yes gasped sharply as a cry of pain so that for a moment I thought that we *were* already doing it and that somehow I had missed the instant when I entered you, entered you in the bloodless way in which a young man discards his own virginity, entered you as if passing through a gateway into the rest of my life, into a life as I wanted it to be lived *yes* but O then I realized that we were still floundering unconnected in the slick between us and there was sand in the Trojan as we slammed together still feeling for that perfect fit, still in the *Here* groping for an *Eternity* that was only a fine adjustment away, just a millimeter to the left or a fraction of an inch further south though with all the adjusting the sandy Trojan was slipping off and then it was gone but yes you kept repeating although your head was shaking no-not-quite-almost and our hearts were going like mad and you said yes Yes wait . . . Stop!

"What?" I asked, still futilely thrusting as if I hadn't quite heard you.

"Oh, God!" you gasped, pushing yourself up. "What's coming?"

"Julie, what's the matter?" I asked, confused, and then the beam of a spotlight swept over us and I glanced into its blinding eye.

All around us lights were coming, speeding across the sand. Blinking blindness away, I rolled from your body to my knees, feeling utterly defenseless in the way that only nakedness can leave one feeling. Headlights bounded toward us, spotlights crisscrossing, blue dome lights revolving as squad cars converged. I could see other lovers, caught in the beams, fleeing bare-assed through the litter of garbage that daytime hordes had left behind and that night had deceptively concealed. You were crying, clutching the Navajo blanket to your breasts with one hand and clawing for your bikini with the other, and I was trying to calm your terror with reassuring phrases such as, "Holy shit! I don't fucking believe this!"

Swerving and fishtailing in the sand, police calls pouring from their radios, the squad cars were on us, and then they were by us while we sat struggling on our clothes.

They braked at the water's edge, and cops slammed out brandishing huge flashlights, their beams deflecting over the dark water. Beyond the darting of those beams, the far-off throbs of lightning seemed faint by comparison.

"Over there, goddamn it!" one of them hollered, and two cops sloshed out into the shallow water without even pausing to kick off their shoes, huffing aloud for breath, their leather cartridge belts creaking against their bellies.

"Grab the son of a bitch! It ain't gonna bite!" one of them yelled, then they came sloshing back to shore with a body slung between them.

It was a woman—young, naked, her body limp and bluish beneath the play of flashlight beams. They set her on the sand just past the ring of drying, washed-up alewives.[6] Her face was almost totally concealed by her hair. Her hair was brown and tangled in a way that even wind or sleep can't tangle hair,

---

6. A North American fish.

tangled as if it had absorbed the ripples of water—thick strands, slimy-looking like dead seaweed.

"She's been in there a while, that's for sure," a cop with a beer belly said to a younger, crew-cut cop who had knelt beside the body and removed his hat as if he might be considering the kiss of life.

The crew-cut officer brushed the hair away from her face and the flashlight beams settled there. Her eyes were closed. A bruise or a birthmark stained the side of one eye. Her features appeared swollen—her lower lip protruding as if she was pouting.

An ambulance siren echoed across the sand, its revolving red light rapidly approaching.

"Might as well take their sweet-ass time," the beer-bellied cop said.

We had joined the circle of police surrounding the drowned woman almost without realizing that we had. You were back in your bikini, robed in the Navajo blanket, and I had slipped on my cutoffs, my underwear still dangling out of a back pocket.

Their flashlight beams explored her body, causing its whiteness to gleam. Her breasts were floppy; her nipples looked shriveled. Her belly appeared inflated by gallons of water. For a moment, a beam focused on her mound of pubic hair which was overlapped by the swell of her belly, and then moved almost shyly away down her legs, and the cops all glanced at us—at you, especially—above their lights, and you hugged your blanket closer as if they might confiscate it as evidence or to use as a shroud.

When the ambulance pulled up, one of the black attendants immediately put a stethoscope to the drowned woman's swollen belly and announced, "Drowned the baby, too."

Without saying anything, we turned from the group, as unconsciously as we'd joined them, and walked off across the sand, stopping only long enough at the spot where we had lain together like lovers in order to stuff the rest of our gear into a beach bag, to gather our shoes, and for me to find my wallet and kick sand over the forlorn, deflated-looking Trojan that you pretended not to notice. I was grateful for that.

Behind us, the police were snapping photos, flashbulbs throbbing like lightning flashes, and the lightning itself still distant but moving in closer, thunder rumbling audibly now, driving a lake wind before it so that gusts of sand tingled against the metal sides of the ambulance.

Squinting, we walked toward the lighted windows of the Gold Coast, while the shadows of gapers attracted by the whirling emergency lights hurried past up toward the shore.

"What happened? What's going on?" they asked us as they passed without waiting for an answer, and we didn't offer one, just continued walking silently in the dark.

It was only later that we talked about it, and once we began talking about the drowned woman it seemed we couldn't stop.

"She was pregnant," you said. "I mean I don't want to sound morbid, but I can't help thinking how the whole time we were, we almost—you know—there was this poor dead woman and her unborn child washing in and out behind us."

"It's not like we could have done anything for her even if we had known she was there."

"But what if we *had* found her? What if after we had—you know," you said, your eyes glancing away from mine and your voice tailing into a whisper, "what if after we did it, we went for a night swim and found her in the water?"

"But, Jules, we didn't," I tried to reason, though it was no more a matter of reason than anything else between us had ever been.

It began to seem as if each time we went somewhere to make out—on the back porch of your half-deaf, whiskery Italian grandmother who sat in the front of the apartment cackling before *I Love Lucy* reruns; or in your girlfriend Ginny's basement rec room when her parents were away on bowling league nights and Ginny was upstairs with her current crush, Brad; or way off in the burbs, at the Giant Twin Drive-In during the weekend they called Elvis Fest—the drowned woman was with us.

We would kiss, your mouth would open, and when your tongue flicked repeatedly after mine, I would unbutton the first button of your blouse, revealing the beauty spot at the base of your throat which matched a smaller spot I loved above a corner of your lips, and then the second button that opened on a delicate gold cross—that I had always tried to regard as merely a fashion statement—dangling above the cleft of your breasts. The third button exposed the lacy swell of your bra, and I would slide my hand over the patterned mesh, feeling for the firmness of your nipple rising to my fingertip, but you would pull slightly away, and behind your rapid breath your kiss would grow distant, and I would kiss harder trying to lure you back from wherever you had gone, and finally, holding you as if only consoling a friend, I'd ask, "What are you thinking?" although, of course, I knew.

"I don't want to think about her but I can't help it. I mean it seems like some kind of weird omen or something, you know?"

"No, I don't know," I said. "It was just a coincidence."

"Maybe if she'd been further away down the beach, but she was so close to us. A good wave could have washed her up right beside us."

"Great, then we could have had a *ménage à trois*."[7]

"Gross! I don't believe you just said that! Just because you said it in French doesn't make it less disgusting."

"You're driving me to it. Come on, Jules, I'm sorry," I said, "I was just making a dumb joke to get a little different perspective on things."

"What's so goddamn funny about a woman who drowned herself and her baby?"

"We don't even know for sure she did."

"Yeah, right, it was just an accident. Like she just happened to be going for a walk pregnant and naked, and she fell in."

"She could have been on a sailboat or something. Accidents happen; so do murders."

"Oh, like murder makes it less horrible? Don't think that hasn't occurred to me. Maybe the bastard who knocked her up killed her, huh?"

"How should I know? You're the one who says you don't want to talk about it and then gets obsessed with all kinds of theories and scenarios. Why are we

---

7. Literally "household of three" (French); a living arrangement shared by three people who have sexual relations.

arguing about a woman we don't even know, who doesn't have the slightest thing to do with us?"

"I *do* know about her," you said. "I dream about her."

"You dream about her?" I repeated, surprised. "Dreams you remember?"

"Sometimes they wake me up. Like I dreamed I was at my nonna's cottage in Michigan. Off her beach they've got a raft for swimming and in my dream I'm swimming out to it, but it keeps drifting further away until it's way out on the water and I'm so tired that if I don't get to it I'm going to drown. Then, I notice there's a naked person sunning on it and I start yelling, 'Help!' and she looks up, brushes her hair out of her face, and offers me a hand, but I'm too afraid to take it even though I'm drowning because it's her."

"God! Jules, that's creepy."

"I dreamed you and I were at the beach and you bring us a couple hot dogs but forget the mustard, so you have to go all the way back to the stand for it."

"Hot dogs, no mustard—a little too Freudian, isn't it?"

"Honest to God, I dreamed it. You go off for mustard and I'm wondering why you're gone so long, then a woman screams a kid has drowned and immediately the entire crowd stampedes for the water and sweeps me along with it. It's like one time when I was little and got lost at the beach, wandering in a panic through this forest of hairy legs and pouchy crotches, crying for my mother. Anyway, I'm carried into the water by the mob and forced under, and I think, this is it, I'm going to drown, but I'm able to hold my breath longer than could ever be possible. It feels like a flying dream—flying under water—and then I see this baby down there flying, too, and realize it's the kid everyone thinks has drowned, but he's no more drowned than I am. He looks like Cupid or one of those baby angels that cluster around the face of God."

"Pretty weird. What do you think it means? Something to do with drowning maybe, or panic?"

"It means the baby who drowned inside her that night was a love child—a boy—and his soul was released there to wander through the water."

"You really believe that?"

We argued about the interpretation of dreams, about whether dreams were symbolic or psychic, prophetic or just plain nonsense, until you said, "Look, you can believe what you want about your dreams, but keep your nose out of mine, O.K.?"

We argued about the drowned woman, about whether her death was a suicide or a murder, about whether her appearance that night was an omen or a coincidence, which, you argued, is what an omen is anyway: a coincidence that means something. By the end of summer, even if we were no longer arguing about the woman, we had acquired the habit of arguing about everything else. What was better: dogs or cats, rock or jazz, Cubs or Sox, tacos or egg rolls, right or left, night or day—we could argue about anything.

It no longer required arguing or necking to summon the drowned woman; everywhere we went she surfaced by her own volition: at Rocky's Italian Beef, at Lindo Mexico, at the House of Dong, our favorite Chinese restaurant, a place we still frequented because they had let us sit and talk until late over tiny cups of jasmine tea and broken fortune cookies earlier in the year, when it was winter and we had first started going together. We would always kid about going there. "Are you in the mood for Dong tonight?" I'd ask. It was a dopey joke, and you'd break up at its repeated dopiness. Back then, in winter, if one of us ordered the garlic shrimp, we would both be sure to eat them so that later our mouths tasted the same when we kissed.

Even when she wasn't mentioned, she was there with her drowned body—so dumpy next to yours—and her sad breasts with their wrinkled nipples and sour milk—so saggy beside yours which were still budding—with her swollen belly and her pubic bush colorless in the glare of electric light, with her tangled, slimy hair and her pouting, placid face—so lifeless beside yours—and her skin a pallid white, lightning-flash white, flashbulb white, a whiteness that couldn't be duplicated in daylight—how I'd come to hate that pallor, so cold beside the flush of your skin.

There wasn't a particular night when we finally broke up, just as there wasn't a particular night when we began going together, but I do remember a night in fall when I guessed that it was over. We were parked in the Rambler at the dead end of the street of factories that had been our lovers' lane, listening to a drizzle of rain and dry leaves sprinkle the hood. As always, rain revitalized the smells of the smoked fish and kielbasa in the upholstery. The radio was on too low to hear, the windshield wipers swished at intervals as if we were driving, and the windows were steamed as if we'd been making out. But we'd been arguing as usual, this time about a woman poet who had committed suicide, whose work you were reading. We were sitting, no longer talking or touching, and I remember thinking that I didn't want to argue with you anymore. I didn't want to sit like this in silence; I wanted to talk excitedly all night as we once had, I wanted to find some way that wasn't corny-sounding to tell you how much fun I'd had in your company, how much knowing you had meant to me, and how I had suddenly realized that I'd been so intent on becoming lovers that I'd overlooked how close we'd been as friends. I wanted you to know that. I wanted you to like me again.

"It's sad," I started to say, meaning that I was sorry we had reached a point of sitting silently together, but before I could continue, you challenged the statement.

"What makes you so sure it's sad?"

"What do you mean, what makes me so sure?" I asked, confused by your question, and surprised there could be anything to argue over no matter what you thought I was talking about.

You looked at me as if what was sad was that I would never understand. "For all either one of us knows," you said, "she could have been triumphant!"

Maybe when it really ended was that night when I felt we had just reached the beginning, that one time on the beach in the summer between high school and college, when our bodies rammed together so desperately that for a moment I thought we did it, and maybe in our hearts we had, although for me, then, doing it in one's heart didn't quite count. If it did, I supposed we'd all be Casanovas.[8]

I remember riding home together on the El[9] that night, feeling sick and defeated in a way I was embarrassed to mention. Our mute reflections emerged

---

8. Men known for their amorous adventures; from Giacomo Girolamo Casanova (1725-1798), Italian writer. **9.** The elevated train.

like negative exposures on the dark, greasy window of the train. Lightning branched over the city and when the train entered the subway tunnel, the lights inside flickered as if the power was disrupted although the train continued rocketing beneath the Loop.[1]

When the train emerged again we were on the South Side and it was pouring, a deluge as if the sky had opened to drown the innocent and guilty alike. We hurried from the El station to your house, holding the Navajo blanket over our heads until, soaked, it collapsed. In the dripping doorway of your apartment building, we said goodnight. You were shivering. Your bra showed through the thin blouse plastered to your skin. I swept the wet hair away from your face and kissed you lightly on the lips, then you turned and went inside. I stepped into the rain and you came back out calling after me.

"What?" I asked, feeling a surge of gladness to be summoned back into the doorway with you.

"Want an umbrella?"

I didn't. The downpour was letting up. It felt better to walk back to the El feeling the rain rinse the sand out of my hair, off my legs, until the only places where I could still feel its grit was the crotch of my cutoffs and in each squish of my shoes. A block down the street, I passed a pair of Jockey shorts lying in a puddle and realized they were mine, dropped from my back pocket as we ran to your house. I left them behind, wondering if you'd see them and recognize them the next day.

By the time I had climbed the stairs back to the El platform, the rain had stopped. Your scent still hadn't washed from my fingers. The station—the entire city, it seemed—dripped and steamed. The summer sound of crickets and nighthawks echoed from the drenched neighborhood. Alone, I could admit how sick I felt. For you, it was a night that would haunt your dreams. For me, it was another night when I waited, swollen and aching, for what I had secretly nicknamed the Blue Ball Express.

Literally lovesick, groaning inwardly with each lurch of the train and worried that I was damaged for good, I peered out at the passing yellow-lit stations where lonely men stood posted before giant advertisements, pictures of glamorous models defaced by graffiti—the same old scrawled insults and pleas: FUCK YOU, EAT ME. At this late hour the world seemed given over to men without women, men waiting in abject patience for something indeterminate, the way I waited for our next times. I avoided their eyes so that they wouldn't see the pity in mine, pity for them because I'd just been with you, your scent was still on my hands, and there seemed to be so much future ahead.

For me it was another night like that, and by the time I reached my stop I knew I would be feeling better, recovered enough to walk the dark street home making up poems of longing that I never wrote down. I was the D. H. Lawrence of not doing it, the voice of all the would-be lovers who ached and squirmed but still hadn't. From our contortions in doorways, on stairwells, and in the bucket seats of cars we could have composed a *Kama Sutra*[2] of interrupted bliss. It must have been that night when I recalled all the other times of walking home after seeing you, so that it seemed as if I was falling into step

---

1. The hub of Chicago's business district.   **2.** A book of Hindu aphorisms and instructions relating to the erotic life.

behind a parade of my former selves—myself walking home on the night we first kissed, myself on the night when I unbuttoned your blouse and kissed your breasts, myself on the night that I lifted your skirt above your thighs and dropped to my knees—each succeeding self another step closer to that irrevocable moment for which our lives seemed poised.

But we didn't, not in the moonlight, or by the phosphorescent lanterns of lightning bugs in your backyard, not beneath the constellations that we couldn't see, let alone decipher, nor in the dark glow that had replaced the real darkness of night, a darkness already stolen from us; not with the skyline rising behind us while the city gradually decayed, not in the heat of summer while a Cold War raged; despite the freedom of youth and the license of first love—because of fate, karma, luck, what does it matter?—we made not doing it a wonder, and yet we didn't, we didn't, we never did.

1994

RALPH ELLISON
1914–1994

Ellison was born in Oklahoma City and studied music at Tuskegee Institute before dropping out to embark on a course that would eventually lead him to chance meetings with Langston Hughes and Richard Wright, which led him to join the Federal Writers' Project. At last he had found his calling. Though his publications were few, his novel *Invisible Man* (1952) became one of the most discussed and praised books published in America since World War II. While it announces no program of black liberation, it starkly bares the moral, political, and psychological aspects of the enduring struggle. In his other writings, including the essay collections *Shadow and Act* (1964) and *Going to the Territory* (1986), as well as the posthumously published novel *Juneteenth* (1999), Ellison continued his exploration of the problem of identity within the context of black culture. He brought to a culmination the double consciousness of blacks who also know themselves to be American.

King of the Bingo Game

The woman in front of him was eating roasted peanuts that smelled so good that he could barely contain his hunger. He could not even sleep and wished they'd hurry and begin the bingo game. There, on his right, two fellows were drinking wine out of a bottle wrapped in a paper bag, and he could hear soft gurgling in the dark. His stomach gave a low, gnawing growl. "If this was down South," he thought, "all I'd have to do is lean over and say, 'Lady, gimme a few of those peanuts, please ma'am,' and she'd pass me the bag and never think nothing of it." Or he could ask the fellows for a drink in the same way. Folks down South stuck together that way; they didn't even have to know you. But up here it was different. Ask somebody for something, and they'd think you were crazy. Well, I ain't crazy. I'm just broke, 'cause I got no birth certificate to get a job, and Laura 'bout to die 'cause we got no money for a doctor. But I ain't crazy. And yet a pinpoint of doubt was focused in his mind as he glanced toward the screen and saw the hero stealthily entering a dark room and sending the beam of a flashlight along a wall of bookcases. This is where he finds the trapdoor, he remembered. The man would pass abruptly through the wall and find the girl tied to a bed, her legs and arms spread wide, and her clothing torn to rags. He laughed softly to himself. He had seen the picture three times, and this was one of the best scenes.

On his right the fellow whispered wide-eyed to his companion, "Man, look ayonder!"

"Damn!"

"Wouldn't I like to have her tied up like that . . ."

"Hey! That fool's letting her loose!"

"Aw, man, he loves her."

"Love or no love!"

The man moved impatiently beside him, and he tried to involve himself in the scene. But Laura was on his mind. Tiring quickly of watching the picture he looked back to where the white beam filtered from the projection room above the balcony. It started small and grew large, specks of dust dancing in its whiteness as it reached the screen. It was strange how the beam always landed right on the screen and didn't mess up and fall somewhere else. But they had it all fixed. Everything was fixed. Now suppose when they showed that girl with her dress torn the girl started taking off the rest of her clothes, and when the guy came in he didn't untie her but kept her there and went to taking off his own clothes? *That* would be something to see. If a picture got out of hand like that those guys up there would go nuts. Yeah, and there'd be so many folks in here you couldn't find a seat for nine months! A strange sensation played over his skin. He shuddered. Yesterday he'd seen a bedbug on a woman's neck as they walked out into the bright street. But exploring his thigh through a hole in his pocket he found only goose pimples and old scars.

The bottle gurgled again. He closed his eyes. Now a dreamy music was accompanying the film and train whistles were sounding in the distance, and he was a boy again walking along a railroad trestle down South, and seeing the train coming, and running back as fast as he could go, and hearing the whistle blowing, and getting off the trestle to solid ground just in time, with the earth trembling beneath his feet, and feeling relieved as he ran down the cinder-strewn embankment onto the highway, and looking back and seeing with terror that the train had left the track and was following him right down the middle of the street, and all the white people laughing as he ran screaming . . .

"Wake up there, buddy! What the hell do you mean hollering like that? Can't you see we trying to enjoy this here picture?"

He stared at the man with gratitude.

"I'm sorry, old man," he said. "I musta been dreaming."

"Well, here, have a drink. And don't be making no noise like that, damn!"

His hands trembled as he tilted his head. It was not wine, but whiskey. Cold rye whiskey. He took a deep swoller, decided it was better not to take another, and handed the bottle back to its owner.

"Thanks, old man," he said.

Now he felt the cold whiskey breaking a warm path straight through the middle of him, growing hotter and sharper as it moved. He had not eaten all day, and it made him light-headed. The smell of the peanuts stabbed him like a knife, and he got up and found a seat in the middle aisle. But no sooner did he sit than he saw a row of intense-faced young girls, and got up again, thinking, "You chicks musta been Lindy-hopping[1] somewhere." He found a seat several rows ahead as the lights came on, and he saw the screen disappear

1. Dancing.

behind a heavy red and gold curtain; then the curtain rising, and the man with the microphone and a uniformed attendant coming on the stage.

He felt for his bingo cards, smiling. The guy at the door wouldn't like it if he knew about his having *five* cards. Well, not everyone played the bingo game; and even with five cards he didn't have much of a chance. For Laura, though, he had to have faith. He studied the cards, each with its different numerals, punching the free center hole in each and spreading them neatly across his lap; and when the lights faded he sat slouched in his seat so that he could look from his cards to the bingo wheel with but a quick shifting of his eyes.

Ahead, at the end of the darkness, the man with the microphone was pressing a button attached to a long cord and spinning the bingo wheel and calling out the number each time the wheel came to rest. And each time the voice rang out his finger raced over the cards for the number. With five cards he had to move fast. He became nervous; there were too many cards, and the man went too fast with his grating voice. Perhaps he should just select one and throw the others away. But he was afraid. He became warm. Wonder how much Laura's doctor would cost? Damn that, watch the cards! And with despair he heard the man call three in a row which he missed on all five cards. This way he'd never win . . .

When he saw the row of holes punched across the third card, he sat paralyzed and heard the man call three more numbers before he stumbled forward, screaming,

"Bingo! Bingo!"

"Let that fool up there," someone called.

"Get up there, man!"

He stumbled down the aisle and up the steps to the stage into a light so sharp and bright that for a moment it blinded him, and he felt that he had moved into the spell of some strange, mysterious power. Yet it was as familiar as the sun, and he knew it was the perfectly familiar bingo.

The man with the microphone was saying something to the audience as he held out his card. A cold light flashed from the man's finger as the card left his hand. His knees trembled. The man stepped closer, checking the card against the numbers chalked on the board. Suppose he had made a mistake? The pomade on the man's hair made him feel faint, and he backed away. But the man was checking the card over the microphone now, and he had to stay. He stood tense, listening.

"Under the O, forty-four," the man chanted. "Under the I, seven. Under the G, three. Under the B, ninety-six. Under the N, thirteen!"

His breath came easier as the man smiled at the audience.

"Yes sir, ladies and gentlemen, he's one of the chosen people!"

The audience rippled with laughter and applause.

"Step right up to the front of the stage."

He moved slowly forward, wishing that the light was not so bright.

"To win tonight's jackpot of $36.90 the wheel must stop between the double zero, understand?"

He nodded, knowing the ritual from the many days and nights he had watched the winners march across the stage to press the button that controlled the spinning wheel and receive the prizes. And now he followed the instructions as though he'd crossed the slippery stage a million prize-winning times.

The man was making some kind of joke, and he nodded vacantly. So tense had he become that he felt a sudden desire to cry and shook it away. He felt vaguely that his whole life was determined by the bingo wheel; not only that which would happen now that he was at last before it, but all that had gone before, since his birth, and his mother's birth and the birth of his father. It had always been there, even though he had not been aware of it, handing out the unlucky cards and numbers of his days. The feeling persisted, and he started quickly away. I better get down from here before I make a fool of myself, he thought.

"Here, boy," the man called. "You haven't started yet."

Someone laughed as he went hesitantly back.

"Are you all reet?"

He grinned at the man's jive talk, but no words would come, and he knew it was not a convincing grin. For suddenly he knew that he stood on the slippery brink of some terrible embarrassment.

"Where are you from, boy?" the man asked.

"Down South."

"He's from down South, ladies and gentlemen," the man said. "Where from? Speak right into the mike."

"Rocky Mont," he said. "Rock' Mont, North Car'lina."

"So you decided to come down off that mountain to the U.S.," the man laughed. He felt that the man was making a fool of him, but then something cold was placed in his hand, and the lights were no longer behind him.

Standing before the wheel he felt alone, but that was somehow right, and he remembered his plan. He would give the wheel a short quick twirl. Just a touch of the button. He had watched it many times, and always it came close to double zero when it was short and quick. He steeled himself; the fear had left, and he felt a profound sense of promise, as though he were about to be repaid for all the things he'd suffered all his life. Trembling, he pressed the button. There was a whirl of lights, and in a second he realized with finality that though he wanted to, he could not stop. It was as though he held a high-powered line in his naked hand. His nerves tightened. As the wheel increased its speed it seemed to draw him more and more into its power, as though it held his fate; and with it came a deep need to submit, to whirl, to lose himself in its swirl of color. He could not stop it now. So let it be.

The button rested snugly in his palm where the man had placed it. And now he became aware of the man beside him, advising him through the microphone, while behind the shadowy audience hummed with noisy voices. He shifted his feet. There was still that feeling of helplessness within him, making part of him desire to turn back, even now that the jackpot was right in his hand. He squeezed the button until his fist ached. Then, like the sudden shriek of a subway whistle, a doubt tore through his head. Suppose he did not spin the wheel long enough? What could he do, and how could he tell? And then he knew, even as he wondered, that as long as he pressed the button, he could control the jackpot. He and only he could determine whether or not it was to be his. Not even the man with the microphone could do anything about it now. He felt drunk. Then, as though he had come down from a high hill into a valley of people, he heard the audience yelling.

"Come down from there, you jerk!"

"Let somebody else have a chance . . ."

"Ole Jack thinks he done found the end of the rainbow . . ."

The last voice was not unfriendly, and he turned and smiled dreamily into the yelling mouths. Then he turned his back squarely on them.

"Don't take too long, boy," a voice said.

He nodded. They were yelling behind him. Those folks did not understand what had happened to him. They had been playing the bingo game day in and night out for years, trying to win rent money or hamburger change. But not one of those wise guys had discovered this wonderful thing. He watched the wheel whirling past the numbers and experienced a burst of exaltation: This is God! This is the really truly God! He said it aloud, "This is God!"

He said it with such absolute conviction that he feared he would fall fainting into the footlights. But the crowd yelled so loud that they could not hear. These fools, he thought. I'm here trying to tell them the most wonderful secret in the world, and they're yelling like they gone crazy. A hand fell upon his shoulder.

"You'll have to make a choice now, boy. You've taken too long."

He brushed the hand violently away.

"Leave me alone, man. I know what I'm doing!"

The man looked surprised and held on to the microphone for support. And because he did not wish to hurt the man's feelings he smiled, realizing with a sudden pang that there was no way of explaining to the man just why he had to stand there pressing the button forever.

"Come here," he called tiredly.

The man approached, rolling the heavy microphone across the stage.

"Anybody can play this bingo game, right?" he said.

"Sure, but . . ."

He smiled, feeling inclined to be patient with this slick looking white man with his blue shirt and his sharp gabardine suit.

"That's what I thought," he said. "Anybody can win the jackpot as long as they get the lucky number, right?"

"That's the rule, but after all . . ."

"That's what I thought," he said. "And the big prize goes to the man who knows how to win it?"

The man nodded speechlessly.

"Well then, go on over there and watch me win like I want to. I ain't going to hurt nobody," he said, "and I'll show you how to win. I mean to show the whole world how it's got to be done."

And because he understood, he smiled again to let the man know that he held nothing against him for being white and impatient. Then he refused to see the man any longer and stood pressing the button, the voices of the crowd reaching him like sounds in distant streets. Let them yell. All the Negroes down there were just ashamed because he was black like them. He smiled inwardly, knowing how it was. Most of the time he was ashamed of what Negroes did himself. Well, let them be ashamed for something this time. Like him. He was like a long thin black wire that was being stretched and wound upon the bingo wheel; wound until he wanted to scream; wound, but this time himself controlling the winding and the sadness and the shame, and because he did, Laura would be all right. Suddenly the lights flickered. He staggered backwards. Had something gone wrong? All this noise. Didn't they know that although he controlled the wheel, it also controlled him, and unless he pressed the button forever and forever and ever it would stop, leaving him high and dry, dry and high on this hard high slippery hill and Laura dead? There was only one chance; he had to do whatever the wheel demanded. And gripping the button in despair, he discovered with surprise that it imparted a nervous energy. His spine tingled. He felt a certain power.

Now he faced the raging crowd with defiance, its screams penetrating his eardrums like trumpets shrieking from a juke-box. The vague faces glowing in the bingo lights gave him a sense of himself that he had never known before. He was running the show, by God! They had to react to him, for he was their luck. This is *me*, he thought. Let the bastards yell. Then someone was laughing inside him, and he realized that somehow he had forgotten his own name. It was a sad, lost feeling to lose your name, and a crazy thing to do. That name had been given him by the white man who had owned his grandfather a long lost time ago down South. But maybe those wise guys knew his name.

"Who am I?" he screamed.

"Hurry up and bingo, you jerk!"

They didn't know either, he thought sadly. They didn't even know their own names, they were all poor nameless bastards. Well, he didn't need that old name; he was reborn. For as long as he pressed the button he was The-man-who-pressed-the-button-who-held-the-prize-who-was-the-King-of-Bingo. That was the way it was, and he'd have to press the button even if nobody understood, even though Laura did not understand.

"Live!" he shouted.

The audience quieted like the dying of a huge fan.

"Live, Laura, baby. I got holt of it now, sugar. Live!"

He screamed it, tears streaming down his face. "I got nobody but YOU!"

The screams tore from his very guts. He felt as though the rush of blood to his head would burst out in baseball seams of small red droplets, like a head beaten by police clubs. Bending over he saw a trickle of blood splashing the toe of his shoe. With his free hand he searched his head. It was his nose. God, suppose something has gone wrong? He felt that the whole audience had somehow entered him and was stamping its feet in his stomach and he was unable to throw them out. They wanted the prize, that was it. They wanted the secret for themselves. But they'd never get it; he would keep the bingo wheel whirling forever, and Laura would be safe in the wheel. But would she? It had to be, because if she were not safe the wheel would cease to turn; it could not go on. He had to get away, *vomit* all, and his mind formed an image of himself running with Laura in his arms down the tracks of the subway just ahead of an A train,[2] running desperately *vomit* with people screaming for him to come out but knowing no way of leaving the tracks because to stop would bring the train crushing down upon him and to attempt to leave

2. New York City subway line.

across the other tracks would mean to run into a hot third rail as high as his waist which threw blue sparks that blinded his eyes until he could hardly see.

He heard singing and the audience was clapping its hands.

> *Shoot the liquor to him, Jim, boy!*
> *Clap-clap-clap*
> *Well a-calla the cop*
> *He's blowing his top!*
> *Shoot the liquor to him, Jim, boy!*

Bitter anger grew within him at the singing. They think I'm crazy. Well let 'em laugh. I'll do what I got to do.

He was standing in an attitude of intense listening when he saw that they were watching something on the stage behind him. He felt weak. But when he turned he saw no one. If only his thumb did not ache so. Now they were applauding. And for a moment he thought that the wheel had stopped. But that was impossible, his thumb still pressed the button. Then he saw them. Two men in uniform beckoned from the end of the stage. They were coming toward him, walking in step, slowly, like a tap-dance team returning for a third encore. But their shoulders shot forward, and he backed away, looking wildly about. There was nothing to fight them with. He had only the long black cord which led to a plug somewhere back stage, and he couldn't use that because it operated the bingo wheel. He backed slowly, fixing the men with his eyes as his lips stretched over his teeth in a tight, fixed grin; moved toward the end of the stage and realizing that he couldn't go much further, for suddenly the cord became taut and he couldn't afford to break the cord. But he had to do something. The audience was howling. Suddenly he stopped dead, seeing the men halt, their legs lifted as in an interrupted step of a slow-motion dance. There was nothing to do but run in the other direction and he dashed forward, slipping and sliding. The men fell back, surprised. He struck out violently going past.

"Grab him!"

He ran, but all too quickly the cord tightened, resistingly, and he turned and ran back again. This time he slipped them, and discovered by running in a circle before the wheel he could keep the cord from tightening. But this way he had to flail his arms to keep the men away. Why couldn't they leave a man alone? He ran, circling.

"Ring down the curtain," someone yelled. But they couldn't do that. If they did the wheel flashing from the projection room would be cut off. But they had him before he could tell them so, trying to pry open his fist, and he was wrestling and trying to bring his knees into the fight and holding on to the button, for it was his life. And now he was down, seeing a foot coming down, crushing his wrist cruelly, down, as he saw the wheel whirling serenely above.

"I can't give it up," he screamed. Then quietly, in a confidential tone, "Boys, I really can't give it up."

It landed hard against his head. And in the blank moment they had it away from him, completely now. He fought them trying to pull him up from the stage as he watched the wheel spin slowly to a stop. Without surprise he saw it rest at double-zero.

"You see," he pointed bitterly.

"Sure, boy, sure, it's O.K.," one of the men said smiling.

And seeing the man bow his head to someone he could not see, he felt very, very happy; he would receive what all the winners received.

But as he warmed in the justice of the man's tight smile he did not see the man's slow wink, nor see the bow-legged man behind him step clear of the swiftly descending curtain and set himself for a blow. He only felt the dull pain exploding in his skull, and he knew even as it slipped out of him that his luck had run out on the stage.

1944

RELATED:

—Ellison, An Interview, p. 1715

LOUISE ERDRICH
b. 1954

Erdrich was born in Little Falls, Minnesota, of German-American and Chippewa descent. She grew up in Wahpeton, North Dakota, and graduated from Dartmouth College. Her thriving literary career has included the publication of three books of poems, *Jacklight* (1984), *Baptism of Desire* (1989), and *Original Fire* (2003), the novels *Love Medicine* (1984), *The Beet Queen* (1986), *Tracks* (1988), *The Bingo Palace* (1994), and *Tales of Burning Love* (1996), as well as *The Crown of Columbus* (1991), which she coauthored with her then-husband, Michael Dorris. Her recent works include the novels *The Painted Drum* (2005), *The Plague of Doves* (2008), *Shadow Tag* (2010), and *The Round House* (2012), which won the National Book Award that year. She has received ample recognition for the quality of her work, including a fellowship from the National Endowment for the Arts and a Guggenheim Fellowship. *Love Medicine* was the winner of the National Book Critics Circle Award for fiction.

Matchimanito

We started dying before the snow, and, like the snow, we continued to fall. We were surprised that so many of us were left to die. For those who survived the spotted sickness from the south and our long fight west to Dakota land, where we signed the treaty, and then a wind from the east, bringing exile in a storm of government papers, what descended from the north in 1914 seemed terrible, and unjust.

By then we thought disaster must surely have spent its force, that disease must have claimed all of the Anishinabe[1] that the earth could hold and bury.

But along with the first bitter punishments of early winter a new sickness swept down. The consumption, it was called by young Father Damien, who came in that year to replace the priest who had succumbed to the same devastation as his flock. This disease was different from the pox and fever, for it came on slowly. The outcome, however, was just as certain. Whole families of Anishinabe lay ill and helpless in its breath. On the reservation, where we were forced close together, the clans dwindled. Our tribe unraveled like a coarse rope, frayed at either end as the old and new among us were taken. My own family was wiped out one by one. I was the only Nanapush[2] who lived.

---

1. Ojibwa, American Indian tribe of the western Great Lakes region.   2. The narrator's family.

And after, although I had seen no more than fifty winters, I was considered an old man.

I guided the last buffalo hunt. I saw the last bear shot. I trapped the last beaver with a pelt of more than two years' growth. I spoke aloud the words of the government treaty and refused to sign the settlement papers that would take away our woods and lake. I axed the last birch that was older than I, and I saved the last of the Pillager family.

Fleur.[3]

We found her on a cold afternoon in late winter, out in her family's cabin near Matchimanito Lake, where my companion, Edgar Pukwan, of the tribal police, was afraid to go. The water there was surrounded by the highest oaks, by woods inhabited by ghosts and roamed by Pillagers, who knew the secret ways to cure or kill, until their art deserted them. Dragging our sled into the clearing, we saw two things: the smokeless tin chimney spout jutting from the roof, and the empty hole in the door where the string was drawn inside. Pukwan did not want to enter, fearing that the unburied Pillager spirits might seize him by the throat and turn him windigo.[4] So I was the one who broke the thin-scraped hide that made a window. I was the one who lowered himself into the stinking silence, onto the floor. I was also the one to find the old man and woman, the little brother and two sisters, stone cold and wrapped in gray horse blankets, their faces turned to the west.

Afraid as I was, stilled by their quiet forms, I touched each bundle in the gloom of the cabin, and wished each spirit a good journey on the three-day road, the old-time road, so well trampled by our people this deadly season. Then something in the corner knocked. I flung the door wide. It was the eldest daughter, Fleur, so feverish that she'd thrown off her covers. She huddled against the cold wood range, staring and shaking. She was wild as a filthy wolf, a big bony girl whose sudden bursts of strength and snarling cries terrified the listening Pukwan. I was the one who struggled to lash her to the sacks of supplies and to the boards of the sled. I wrapped blankets over her and tied them down as well.

Pukwan kept us back, convinced that he should carry out the agency's instructions to the letter: he carefully nailed up the official quarantine sign, and then, without removing the bodies, he tried to burn down the house. But though he threw kerosene repeatedly against the logs and even started a blaze with birch bark and chips of wood, the flames narrowed and shrank, went out in puffs of smoke. Pukwan cursed and looked desperate, caught between his official duties and his fear of Pillagers. The fear won out. He finally dropped the tinders and helped me drag Fleur along the trail.

And so we left five dead at Matchimanito, frozen behind their cabin door.

Some say that Pukwan and I should have done right and buried the Pillagers first thing. They say the unrest and curse of trouble that struck our people in the years that followed was the doing of dissatisfied spirits. I know what's fact, and have never been afraid of talking. Our trouble came from the living, from liquor and the dollar bill. We stumbled toward the government bait,

---

3. Flower (French). 4. In Algonquin lore someone transformed into a cannibalistic giant by tasting human flesh.

never looking down, never noticing how the land was snatched from under us at every step.

When Edgar Pukwan's turn came to draw the sled, he took off like devils chased him, bounced Fleur over potholes as if she were a log, and tipped her twice into the snow. I followed the sled, encouraged Fleur with songs, cried at Pukwan to watch for hidden branches and deceptive drops, and finally got her to my cabin, a small, tightly tamped box overlooking the crossroads.

"Help me," I cried, cutting at the ropes, not even bothering with knots. Fleur closed her eyes, panted, and tossed her head from side to side. Her chest rattled as she strained for air; she grabbed me around the neck. Still weak from my own bout with the sickness, I staggered, fell, lurched into my cabin, wrestling the strong girl inside with me. I had no wind left over to curse Pukwan, who watched but refused to touch her, turned away, and vanished with the whole sled of supplies. I was neither surprised nor caused enduring sorrow later when Pukwan's son, also named Edgar and also of the tribal police, told me that his father came home, crawled into bed, and took no food from that moment until his last breath passed.

As for Fleur, each day she improved in small changes. First her gaze focused, and the next night her skin was cool and damp. She was clearheaded, and after a week she remembered what had befallen her family, how they had taken sick so suddenly, gone under. With her memory mine came back, only too sharply. I was not prepared to think of the people I had lost, or to speak of them, although we did, carefully, without letting their names loose in the wind that would reach their ears.

We feared that they would hear us and never rest, come back out of pity for the loneliness we felt. They would sit in the snow outside the door, waiting until from longing we joined them. We would all be together on the journey then, our destination the village at the end of the road, where people gamble day and night but never lose their money, eat but never fill their stomachs, drink but never leave their minds.

The snow receded enough for us to dig the ground with picks. As a tribal policeman, Pukwan's son was forced by regulation to help bury the dead. So again we took the dark road to Matchimanito, the son leading rather than the father. We spent the day chipping at the earth until we had a hole long and deep enough to lay the Pillagers shoulder to shoulder. We covered them and built five small board houses. I scratched out their clan markers, four crosshatched bears and a marten; then Pukwan Junior shouldered the government's tools and took off down the path. I settled myself near the graves.

I asked those Pillagers, as I had asked my own children and wives, to leave us now and never come back. I offered tobacco, smoked a pipe of red willow for the old man. I told them not to pester their daughter just because she had survived, or to blame me for finding them, or Pukwan Junior for leaving too soon. I told them that I was sorry, but they must abandon us. I insisted. But the Pillagers were as stubborn as the Nanapush clan and would not leave my thoughts. I think they followed me home. All the way down the trail, just beyond the edges of my sight, they flickered, thin as needles, shadows piercing shadows.

The sun had set by the time I got back, but Fleur was awake, sitting in the dark as if she knew. She never moved to build up the fire, never asked where I had been. I never told her about it either, and as the days passed we spoke rarely, always with roundabout caution. We felt the spirits of the dead so near that at length we just stopped talking.

This made it worse.

Their names grew within us, swelled to the brink of our lips, forced our eyes open in the middle of the night. We were filled with the water of the drowned, cold and black—airless water that lapped against the seal of our tongues or leaked slowly from the corners of our eyes. Within us, like ice shards, their names bobbed and shifted. Then the slivers of ice began to collect and cover us. We became so heavy, weighted down with the lead-gray frost, that we could not move. Our hands lay on the table like cloudy blocks. The blood within us grew thick. We needed no food. And little warmth. Days passed, weeks, and we didn't leave the cabin for fear we'd crack our cold and fragile bodies. We had gone half windigo. I learned later that this was common, that many of our people died in this manner, of the invisible sickness. Some could not swallow another bite of food because the names of their dead thickened on their tongues. Some let their blood stop, took the road west after all.

One day the new priest—just a boy, really—opened our door. A dazzling and painful light flooded through and surrounded Fleur and me. Numb, stupid as bears in a winter den, we blinked at the priest's slight silhouette. Our lips were parched, stuck together. We could hardly utter a greeting, but we were saved by one thought: a guest must eat. Fleur gave Father Damien her chair and put wood on the gray coals. She found flour for gaulette. I went to fetch snow to boil for tea water, but to my amazement the ground was bare. I was so surprised that I bent over and touched the soft, wet earth.

My voice rasped at first when I tried to speak, but then, oiled by strong tea, lard, and bread, I was off and talking. You could not stop me with a sledge-hammer, once I started. Father Damien looked astonished, and then wary, as I began to creak and roll. I gathered speed. I talked both languages in streams that ran alongside each other, over every rock, around every obstacle. The sound of my voice convinced me I was alive. I kept Father Damien listening all night, his green eyes round, his thin face straining to understand, his odd brown hair in curls and clipped knots. Occasionally he took in air, as if to add observations of his own, but I pushed him under with my words.

I don't know when Fleur slipped out.

She was too young and had no stories or depth of life to rely upon. All she had was raw power, and the names of the dead that filled her. I can speak them now. They have no more interest in any of us. Old Pillager. Ogimaakwe, Boss Woman, his wife. Asasaweminikwesens, Chokecherry Girl. Bineshii, Small Bird, also known as Josette. And the last, the boy Ombaashi, He Is Lifted by Wind.

They are gone, but sometimes I don't know where they are anymore—this place of reservation surveys or the other place, boundless, where the dead sit talking, see too much, and regard the living as fools.

And we were. Starvation makes fools of anyone. In the past some had sold their allotment land for a hundred pound weight of flour. Others, who were desperate to hold on, now urged that we get together and buy back our land, or at least pay a tax and refuse the settlement money that would sweep the marks of our boundaries off the map like a pattern of straws. Many were determined not to allow the hired surveyors, or even our own people, to enter the deepest bush.

But that spring outsiders went in as before, permitted by the agent, a short round man with hair blond as chaff. The purpose of these people was to measure the lake. Only now they walked upon the fresh graves of Pillagers, crossed death roads to plot out the deepest water where the lake monster, Misshepeshu, hid and waited.

"Stay here with me," I said to Fleur when she came to visit.

She refused.

"The land will go," I told her. "The land will be sold and measured."

But she tossed back her hair and walked off, down the path, with nothing to eat till thaw but a bag of my onions and a sack of oats.

Who knows what happened? She returned to Matchimanito and stayed there alone in the cabin that even fire did not want. A young girl had never done such a thing before. I heard that in those months she was asked for fee money for the land. The agent went out there and got lost, spent a whole night following the moving lights and lamps of people who would not answer him but talked and laughed among themselves. They let him go, at dawn, only because he was so stupid. Yet he went out there to ask Fleur for money again, and the next thing we heard he was living in the woods and eating roots, gambling with ghosts.

Some had ideas. You know how old chickens scratch and gabble. That's how the tales started, all the gossip, the wondering, all the things people said without knowing and then believed, since they heard it with their own ears, from their own lips, each word.

I am not one to take notice of the talk of those who fatten in the shade of the new agent's storehouse. But I watched the old agent, the one who was never found, take the rutted turnoff to Matchimanito. He was replaced by a darker man who spoke long and hard with many of our own about a money settlement. But nothing changed my mind. I've seen too much go by—unturned grass below my feet, and overhead the great white cranes flung south forever.

I am a holdout, like the Pillagers, and I told the agent, in good English, what I thought of his treaty paper. I could have written my name, and much more too, in script. I had a Jesuit education in the halls of Saint John[5] before I ran back to the woods and forgot all my prayers.

Since I had saved Fleur from the sickness, I was entangled with her. Not that I knew it at first. Only when I look back do I see a pattern. I was the vine of a wild grape that twined the timbers and drew them close. I was a branch that lived long enough to touch the next tree over, which was Pillagers. The story, like all stories, is never visible while it is happening. Only after, when an old man sits dreaming and talking in his chair, does the design spring clear.

There was so much I saw, and never knew.

When Fleur came down onto the reservation, walking right through town, no one guessed what she hid in that green rag of a dress. I do remember that it was too small, split down the back and strained across the front. That's

---

5. Roman Catholic school in Wahpeton, North Dakota.

what I noticed when I greeted her. Not whether she had money in the dress, or a child.

Other people speculated.

They added up the money she used now to buy supplies and how the agent disappeared from his post, and came out betting she would have a baby. He could have paid cash to Fleur and then run off in shame. She could even have stolen cash from him, cursed him dead, and hidden his remains. Everybody would have known, they thought, in nine months or less, if young Eli Kashpaw hadn't gone out and muddied the waters.

This Eli never cared to figure out business, politics, or church. He never applied for a chunk of land or registered himself. Eli hid from authorities, never saw the inside of a classroom, and although his mother, Margaret, got baptized in the church and tried to collar him for Mass, the best he could do was sit outside the big pine door and whittle pegs. For money Eli chopped wood, pitched hay, harvested potatoes or cranberry bark. He wanted to be a hunter, though, like me, and he had asked to partner that winter before the sickness.

I think like animals, have perfect understanding for where they hide. I can track a deer back through time and brush and cleared field to the place where it was born. Only one thing is wrong with teaching these things, however. I showed Eli how to hunt and trap from such an early age that he lived too much in the company of trees and wind. At fifteen he was uncomfortable around human beings. Especially women. So I had to help him out some.

I'm a Nanapush, remember. That's as good as saying I knew what interested Eli Kashpaw. He wanted something other than what I could teach him about the woods. He was no longer curious only about where a mink will fish or burrow, or when pike will lie low or bite. He wanted to hear how, in the days before the priest's ban and the sickness, I had satisfied three wives.

"Nanapush," Eli said, appearing at my door one day, "I have to ask you something."

"Come on in here, then," I said. "I won't bite you like the little girls do."

He was steadier, more serious, than he was the winter we went out together on the trapline. I was going to wonder what the different thing about him was when he said, "Fleur Pillager."

"She's no little girl," I answered, motioning toward the table. He told me his story.

It began when Eli got himself good and lost up near Matchimanito. He was hunting a doe in a light rain, having no luck until he rounded a slough and shot badly, which wasn't unusual. She was wounded to death but not crippled. She might walk all day, which shamed him, so he dabbed a bit of her blood on the barrel of his gun, the charm I taught him, and he followed her trail.

He had a time of it. She sawed through the woods, took the worst way, moved into heavy brush like a ghost. For hours Eli blazed his passage with snapped branches and clumps of leaves, scuffed the ground, or left a bootprint. But the trail and the day wore on, and for some reason that he did not understand, he gave up and quit leaving sign.

"That was when you should have turned back," I told him. "You should have known. It's no accident people don't like to go there. Those trees are too big, thick, and twisted at the top like bent arms. In the wind their limbs cast, creak against each other, snap. The leaves speak a cold language that overfills your brain. You want to lie down. You want never to get up. You hunger. You rake black chokecherries off their stems and stuff them down, and then you shit like a bird. Your blood thins. You're too close to where the Lake Man lives. And you're too close to where I buried the Pillagers during the long sickness that claimed them like it claimed the Nanapush clan."

I said this to Eli Kashpaw: "I understand Fleur. I am alone in this. I know that was no ordinary doe drawing you out there."

But the doe was real enough, he told me, and it was gut-shot and weakening. The blood dropped fresher, darker, until he thought he heard her just ahead and bent to the ground, desperate to see in the falling dusk, and looked ahead to catch a glimpse, and instead saw the glow of fire. He started toward it, then stopped just outside the circle of light. The deer hung, already split, turning back and forth on a rope. When he saw the woman, gutting with long quick movements, her arms bloody and bare, he stepped into the clearing.

"That's mine," he said.

I hid my face, shook my head.

"You should have turned back," I told him. "Stupid! You should have left it."

But he was stubborn, a vein of Kashpaw that held out for what it had coming. He couldn't have taken the carcass home anyway, couldn't have lugged it back, even if he had known his direction. Yet he stood his ground with the woman and said he'd tracked that deer too far to let it go. She did not respond. "Or maybe half," he thought, studying her back, uncomfortable. Even so, that was as generous as he could get.

She kept working. Never noticed him. He was so ignorant that he reached out and tapped her on the shoulder. She never even twitched. He walked around her, watched the knife cut, trespassed into her line of vision.

At last she saw him, he said, but then scorned him as though he were nothing.

"Little fly"—she straightened her back, the knife loose and casual in her hand—"quit buzzing."

Eli said she looked so wild her beauty didn't throw him, and I leaned closer, worried as he said this, worried as he reported how her hair was clumped with dirt, her face thin as a bony bitch's, her dress a rag that hung, and no curve to her except her breasts.

He noticed some things.

"No curve?" I said, thinking of the rumors.

He shook his head, impatient to continue his story. He felt sorry for her, he said. I told him the last man who was interested in Fleur Pillager had vanished, never to be found. She made us all uneasy, out there so alone. I was a friend to the Pillagers before they died off, I said, and I was safe from Fleur because the two of us had mourned the dead together. She was almost a relative. But that wasn't the case with him.

Eli looked at me with an unbelieving frown. Then he said he didn't see where she was so dangerous. After a while he had recognized her manner as exhaustion more than anger. She made no protest when he took out his own knife and helped her work. Halfway through the job she allowed him to finish, and then Eli hoisted most of the meat into the tree. He took the choice parts into the cabin. She let him in, hardly noticed him, and he helped her start the small range and even took it on himself to melt lard. She ate the whole heart, fell on it like a starved animal, and then her eyes shut.

From the way he described her actions, I was sure she was pregnant. I'm familiar with the signs, and I can talk about this since I'm an old man, far past anything a woman can do to weaken me. I was more certain still when Eli said that he took her in his arms, helped her to a pile of blankets on a willow bed. And then—hard to believe, even though it was, for the first time, the right thing to do—Eli rolled up in a coat on the other side of the cabin floor and lay there all night, and slept alone.

"So," I said, "why have you come to me now? You got away, you survived, she even let you find your way home. You learned your lesson and none the worse."

"I want her," Eli said.

I could not believe that I heard right, but we were sitting by the stove, face to face, so there was no doubt. I rose and turned away. Maybe I was less than generous, having lost my own girls. Maybe I wanted to keep Fleur as my daughter, who would visit me, joke with me, beat me at cards. But I believe it was only for Eli's own good that I was harsh.

"Forget that thing so heavy in our pocket," I said, "or put it somewhere else. Go town way and find yourself a tamer woman."

He brooded at my tabletop and then spoke. "I want know-how, not warnings, not my mother's caution."

"You don't want instruction!" I was pushed too far. "Love medicine is what you're after. A Nanapush never needed any, but Old Lady Aintapi or the Pillagers, they sell it. Go ask Moses for a medicine and pay your price."

"I don't want anything that can wear off," the boy said. He was determined. Maybe his new, steady coolness was the thing that turned my mind, the quiet of him. He was different, sitting there so still. It struck me that he had come into his growth, and who was I to hold him back from going to a Pillager, since someone had to, since the whole tribe had got to thinking that she couldn't be left alone out there, a girl ready to go wild, a woman whose family would not leave her, even dead, but stayed close to her, whispered, passed on their power. People said that she had to be harnessed. Maybe, I thought, Eli was the young man to do it, even though he couldn't rub two words together and get a spark.

So I gave in. I told him what he wanted to know. He asked me the old-time way to make a woman love him, and I went into detail so that he would make no disgraceful error. I told him about the first woman who had given herself to me. Sanawashonekek, her name was, The Lying-Down Grass, for the place where a deer has spent the night. I described the finicky taste of Omiimii, The Dove, and the trials I'd gone through to keep my second wife pleasured. Zezikaaikwe, The Unexpected, was a woman whose name was the exact prediction of her desires. I gave him a few things from the French trunk my third wife left—a white woman's fan, bead leggings, a little girl's soft doll made of fawn skin.

When Eli Kashpaw stroked their beauty and asked where these things had come from, I remembered the old days, opened my mouth.

Talk is an old man's last vice.

I wore out the boy's ears, but that is not my fault. I shouldn't have been caused to live so long, been shown so much of death, had to squeeze so many stories into the corners of my brain. They're all attached, and once I start, the telling doesn't end, because they're hooked from one side to the other, mouth to tail.

During the year of sickness, when I was the last one left, I saved myself by starting a story. One night I was ready to bring to the other side the fawn-skin doll I now gave Eli. My wife had sewn it together after our daughter died, and I held it in my hands when I fainted, lost breath so that I could hardly keep moving my lips. But I did continue and recovered. I got well by talking. Death could not get a word in edgewise, grew discouraged, and traveled on.

Eli returned to Fleur, and stopped badgering me, which I took as a sign she liked the fan, the bead leggings, and maybe the rest of Eli, the part where he was on his own. The thing I've found about women is that you must use every instinct to confuse.

"Look here," I told Eli, before he went out my door. "It's like you're a log in a stream. Along comes this bear. She jumps on. Don't let her dig in her claws."

So keeping Fleur off balance was what I presumed Eli was doing. But, as I learned in time, he was further along than that, way off and running beyond the reach of anything I said.

His mother was the one who gave me the news.

Margaret Kashpaw was a woman who had sunk her claws in the log and peeled it to a toothpick, and she wasn't going to let any man forget it. Especially me, her dead husband's partner in some youthful pursuits.

"Aneesh," she said, slamming my door shut. Margaret never knocked, because with warning you might get your breath, or escape. She was headlong, bossy, scared of nobody, and full of vinegar. She was a little woman, but so blinded by irritation that she'd take on anyone. She was thin on the top and plump as a turnip below, with a face like a round molasses cake. On each side of it gray plaits hung. With age her part had widened down the middle so that it looked as though the braids were slipping off her head. Her eyes were harsh, bright, and her tongue was honed keen. She sat right down.

"Would you care to know what you have my son doing?"

I mumbled, kept reading by the window, tucked my spectacles from Father Damien more comfortably around my ears. My newspaper came from Grand Forks once a week, and I wasn't about to let Margaret spoil my pleasure or get past my hiding place.

"*Sah!*" She swiped at the sheets with her hand, grazed the print, but never quite dared to flip it aside. This was not for any fear of me, however. She didn't want the tracks rubbing off on her skin. She never learned to read, and the mystery troubled her.

I took advantage of that, snapped the paper in front of my face and sat for a moment. But she won, of course, because she knew I'd get curious. I felt her eyes glittering beyond the paper, and when I put the pages down, she continued.

"Who learned my Eli to make love standing up? Who learned him to have a woman against a tree in clear daylight? Who learned him to . . ."

"Wait," I said. "How'd you get to know this?"

She shrugged it off, and said in a smaller voice, "Boy Lazarre."

And I, who knew that the dirty Lazarres don't spy for nothing, just smiled. "How much did you pay the fat-bellied dog?"

"The Lazarres are like animals in their season! No sense of shame!" But the wind was out of her. "Against the wall of the cabin," she said. "Down beside it. In grass and up in trees. Who'd he learn that from?"

"Maybe my late partner Kashpaw."

She puffed her cheeks out, fumed. "Not from him!"

"Not that you knew." I put my spectacles carefully upon the windowsill. Her hand could snake out quickly.

She hissed. The words flew like razor grass between her teeth. "Old man," she said with scorn. "Two wrinkled berries and a twig."

"A twig can grow," I offered.

"But only in the spring."

Then she was gone, out the door, leaving my tongue tingling for the last word, and still ignorant of the full effect of my advice. I didn't wonder until later if it didn't go both ways, though—if Fleur had wound her private hairs around the buttons of Eli's shirt, if she had stirred smoky powders or crushed snakeroot into his tea. Perhaps she had bitten his nails in sleep and swallowed the ends, snipped threads from his clothing and made a doll of them to wear between her legs. For they got bolder, until the whole reservation gossiped.

Then one day the big, unsteady Lazarre, an Indian on whose birth certificate was recorded simply "Boy," returned from the woods talking backwards, garbled, mixing his words. At first people thought the sights of passion had cleft his mind. Then they figured otherwise, imagined that Fleur had caught Lazarre watching and tied him up, cut his tongue out, and sewn it in reversed.

The same day I heard this, Margaret burst into my house a second time.

"Take me out to their place, you four-eyes," she said. "And be ready with the boat tomorrow, sunup!"

She stamped through the door and vanished, leaving me with hardly time enough to patch the seams and holes of the old-time boat I kept, dragged up in a brush shelter on the quieter inlet, the south end of the lake. I took some boiled pine gum to the seams that afternoon, and did my best. I was drawn to the situation, curious myself, and though I didn't want to spy either on the girl whose life I'd saved or on the boy I'd advised on courting, I was down by the water with the paddles at dawn.

The light was chill and green, the waves on the lake were small, confused ripples, and no steady wind had gathered. The water could be deceptive, set snares for the careless young or for withered-up and eager fools like ourselves. I put my hand in the current.

"Margaret," I said, "the lake's too cold. I never could swim, either, not that well."

But Margaret had set her mind, and made her peace, too.

"If he wants me"—she was talking about the lake spirit but, out of caution, using no names—"I'll give him good as I get."

"Oh," I said, "has it been that long, Margaret?"

Her eyes lit and I wished I had kept my mouth shut. But she only commented, later, after we had launched, "Not so long that I would consider the dregs."

I handed her the lard can I kept my bait in. "You better take this, Margaret. You better bail."

So at least on that long trip across I had the satisfaction of seeing her bend to the dipping and pouring with a sour but desperate will. We rode low. The water covered our ankles by the time we beached on shore, but Margaret was forced to shut her mouth in a firm line. The whole idea had been hers. She was so relieved to stand finally upon solid ground that she helped me haul the boat and wedge it in a pile of mangled roots. She wrung her skirt and sat beside me, panting. She shared some dried meat from the pocket of her dress, tore at it like a young snapping turtle. How I envied her sharp, strong teeth.

"Go on, eat," she said, "or I'll take an insult."

I put the jerky into my mouth.

"That's right," she sneered. "Suck long enough and it will soften."

I had no choice. I could think of no other way to get any of it down.

"Go now," I said, after a while. "I was thinking. I had this old barren she-dog once. She'd back up to anything. But the only satisfaction she could get was from watching the young."

Margaret jumped to her feet, skirts flapping. I had said too much. Her claws gave my ears too fast, furious jerks that set me whirling, sickening me so that I couldn't balance or even keep track of time. She took herself up the bank and into the Pillager woods, but I don't know when she went there or how long she stayed, and I had barely set myself to rights before she returned.

By then the sky had gone dead gray, the waves rolled white and fitful. Margaret took tobacco from a pouch in her pocket, threw it on the water, and said a few distracted, imploring words. We jumped into the boat, which leaked worse than ever, and pushed off. The wind blew harsh, in heavy circular gusts, and I was hard put. I never saw the bailing can move so fast, before or since. The old woman made it flash and dip, and hardly even broke the rhythm when, halfway across, she reached into her pocket again and this time dumped the whole pouch into the pounding waves. From then on she alternated between working her arms and addressing different Manitous[6] along with the Blessed Virgin and Her heart, the sacred bloody lump that the blue-robed woman held in the awful picture Margaret kept nailed to her wall. We made it back by the time rain poured down, and hoisted ourselves over the edge of the boat. When we got back to my house, after she'd swallowed some warm broth and her clothes had begun to steam dry upon her, Margaret told me what she had seen with her own eyes.

Fleur Pillager was pregnant, going to have a child in spring. At least that's what Margaret had decided with her measuring gaze. I stirred the fire with my walking stick. Maybe I had a shiver, a feeling, a worry. I was close as a relative, closer perhaps. Maybe I knew already that when spring did come, the ice milky, porous, and broken, Margaret and I were the ones who would have to save Fleur a second time.

6. Great spirits.

Margaret, however, had no such premonition. The child would turn out fork-footed, she predicted, with straw for hair, yellow as the agent's. Its eyes would glow blue, its skin shine white. As she sipped from her cup, Margaret's memory of the agent made a monster, and she savored the variations the child might reveal: red, flapping ears, a strange birthmark, chicken lips, an extra finger, by which the taint of its conception would be certain and people convinced, at last, that it did not belong to her son.

The morning we got word, the water had just opened for a boat, if you dared to travel that way so early in spring. Fleur was in trouble with her baby. That's all I heard, as the women kept the particulars to themselves. Out of desperation Eli had run to Margaret on the way to the midwife's. He wanted us to take the shortcut and stay with Fleur until he brought back the woman whose hands held the wisdom, who wore the dried caul of a rabbit in a little belt around her waist.

Margaret was puffed up, full of satisfaction, until she saw the boat, leaking even more than usual after another winter of neglect. On the ride, bailing for her life, Margaret raged at me between her prayers and muttered strict assurances that her reasons for helping in this matter were not ties of kinship. Her presence did not count as acknowledgment, she said. It was her duty to see the evidence, whatever that turned out to be—the hair gold as straw, the blazing eyes.

But the child had none of those markings.

She was born on the day we shot the last bear, drunk, on the reservation. The midwife was the one who shot it, and the bear was drunk, not her. That she-bear had broken into the trader's wine I had brought across the lake beneath my jacket and then stowed in a rotten stump off in the woods behind the house. She bit the cork and emptied the white clay jug. Then she lost her mind and stumbled into the beaten grass of Fleur's yard.

By then we were a day in the waiting. In all that time we heard not a sound from Fleur's cabin, just crushing silence, like the inside of a drum before the stick drops. Eli and I slumped against the woodpile. We made a fire, swaddled ourselves in blankets. My stomach creaked with the lack of food, for Eli was starving himself from worry and I hated to eat in front of him. His eyes were rimmed with blood as he moaned and talked and prayed beneath the burden, which grew heavier.

On the second day we leaned to the fire, strained for the sound of the cry a baby makes. Our ears picked up everything in the woods, the rustle of birds, the crack of dead spring leaves and twigs. Our hearing had by then grown so keen that we heard the muffled sounds the women made inside the house. Now we heard other activity, which gave us hope. The stove lid clanked, pans rang together. Margaret came to the door and we heard the tear of water splashing on the ground. Eli moved then, fetched more. But not until the afternoon of that second day did the stillness finally break, and then the Manitous all through the woods seemed to speak through Fleur, loose, arguing. I recognized them. Turtle's quavering scratch, Eagle's high shriek, Loon's crazy bitterness, Otter, the howl of Wolf, Bear's low rasp.

Perhaps the bear heard Fleur calling, and answered.

I was alone when it happened, because Eli had broken when the silence shattered, slashed his arm with his hunting knife, and run out of the clearing, straight north. I sat quietly after he was gone, and sampled the food that he had refused. I drew close to the fire, settled my back against the split logs, and was just about to have a second helping when the drunk bear rambled past. She sniffed the ground, rolled over in an odor that pleased her, drew up and sat, addled, on her haunches like a dog. I jumped straight onto the top of the woodpile—I don't know how, since my limbs were so stiff from the wet cold. I crouched, yelled at the house, screamed for the gun, but only attracted the bear. She dragged herself over, gave a drawn-out whine, a cough, and fixed me with a long patient stare.

Margaret flung the door open. "Shoot it, you old fool," she hollered. But I was empty-handed. Margaret was irritated with this trifle, put out that I had not obeyed her, anxious to get rid of the nuisance and go back to Fleur. She marched straight toward us. Her face was pinched with exhaustion, her pace furious. Her arms moved like pistons, and she came so fast that she and the bear were face to face before she realized that she had nothing with which to attack. She was sensible, Margaret Kashpaw, and turned straight around. Fleur kept her gun above the flour cupboard in a rack of antlers. The bear followed, heeling Margaret like a puppy, and at the door to the house, when Margaret turned, arms spread to bar the way, it swatted her aside with one sharp, dreamy blow. Then it ambled in and reared on its hind legs.

I am a man, so I don't know exactly what happened when the bear came into the birth house, but they talk among themselves, the women, and sometimes they forget I'm listening. So I know that when Fleur saw the bear in the house she was filled with such fear and power that she raised herself on the mound of blankets and gave birth. Then the midwife took down the gun and shot point-blank, filling the bear's heart. She says so, anyway. But Margaret says that the lead only gave the bear strength, and I'll support that. For I heard the gun go off and then saw the creature whirl and roar from the house. It barreled past me, crashed through the brush into the woods, and was not seen after. It left no trail, either, so it could have been a spirit bear. I don't know. I was still on the woodpile.

I took the precaution of finishing my meal there. From what I overheard later, they were sure Fleur was dead, she was so cold and still after giving birth. But then the baby cried. That I heard with my own ears. At that sound, they say, Fleur opened her eyes and breathed. That was when the women went to work and saved her, packed moss between her legs, wrapped her in blankets heated with stones, kneaded Fleur's stomach and forced her to drink cup after cup of boiled raspberry leaf, until at last Fleur groaned, drew the baby against her breast, and lived.

1988

PERCIVAL EVERETT
b. 1956

Percival Everett was born in Georgia and raised in South Carolina. He studied at the University of Miami and went on to earn his M.F.A. from Brown University, where he later taught for a number of years. Though he grew up on the East Coast, Everett fell in love with the West, which is the setting for much of his fiction and where he now lives. Everett has written over twenty novels, three collections of short stories, two volumes of poetry, and a children's book. His writing is stylistically diverse and covers a wide range of topics in a wide range of settings, from the mythological Mount Olympus to the modern-day college campus. His writing often upends our cultural assumptions about race; Everett himself has severely critiqued the literary world for pigeonholing minority writers. His short stories have appeared in *The Best American Short Stories* and *The Pushcart Anthology*, and his collections include *The Weather and Women Treat Me Fair: Stories* (1987), *Big Picture* (1996), and *Damned If I Do* (2004). Among his novels are *Suder* (1983), *Frenzy* (1997), *Erasure* (2001), *I Am Not Sidney Poitier* (2009), *Assumption: A Novel* (2011), and *Percival Everett by Virgil Russell* (2013). Everett's many accolades include the PEN Center USA Award for Fiction, an Academy Award in Literature from the American Academy of Arts and Letters, and the New American Writing Award. He teaches at the University of Southern California and lives in Los Angeles with his wife, novelist and story writer Danzy Senna, and their two sons.

The Fix

Douglas Langley owned a little sandwich shop at the intersection of Fourteenth and T streets in the District. Beside his shop was a seldom-used alley and above his shop lived a man by the name of Sherman Olney, whom Douglas had seen beaten to near extinction one night by a couple of silky-looking men who seemed to know Sherman and wanted something in particular from him. Douglas had been drawn outside from cleaning up the storeroom by a rhythmic thumping sound, like someone dropping a telephone book onto a table over and over. He stepped out into the November chill and discovered that the sound was actually that of the larger man's fists finding again and again the belly of Sherman Olney, who was being kept on his feet by the second assailant. Douglas ran back inside and grabbed the pistol he kept in the rolltop desk in his business office. He returned to the scene with the powerful flashlight his son had given him and shone the light into the faces of the two villains.

The men were not overly impressed by the light, the bigger one saying, "Hey, man, you better get that light out of my face!"

They did however show proper respect for the discharging of the .32 by running away. Sherman Olney crumpled to the ground, moaning and clutching at his middle, saying he didn't have it anymore.

"Are you all right?" Douglas asked, realizing how stupid the question was before it was fully out.

But Sherman's response was equally insipid as he said, "Yes."

"Come, let's get you inside." Douglas helped the man to his feet and into the shop. He locked the glass door behind them, then took Sherman over to the counter and helped him onto a stool.

"Thanks," Sherman said.

"You want me to call the cops?" Douglas asked.

Sherman Olney shook his head. "They're long gone by now."

"I'll make you a sandwich," Douglas said as he stepped behind the counter.

"Really, that's not necessary."

"You'll like it. I don't know first aid, but I can make a sandwich." Douglas made the man a pastrami and Muenster on rye sandwich and poured him a glass of barely cold milk, then took him to sit in one of the three booths in the shop. Douglas sat across the table from the man, watched him take a bite of the sandwich.

"What did they want?" Douglas put to him.

"To hurt me," Sherman said, his mouth working on the tough bread. He picked a seed from his teeth and put it on his plate. "They wanted to hurt me."

"My name is Douglas Langley."

"Sherman Olney."

"What were they after, Sherman?" Douglas asked, but he didn't get an answer.

As they sat there, the quiet of the room was disturbed by the loud refrigerator motor kicking on. Douglas felt the vibration of it through the soles of his shoes.

"Your compressor is a little shot," Sherman said.

Douglas looked at him, not knowing what he was talking about.

"Your fridge. The compressor is bad."

"Oh, yes," Douglas said. "It's loud."

"I can fix it."

Douglas just looked at him.

"You want me to fix it?"

Douglas didn't know what to say. Certainly he wanted the machine fixed, but what if this man just liked to take things apart? What if he made it worse? Douglas imagined the kitchen floor strewn with refrigerator parts. But he said, "Sure."

With that, Sherman got up and walked back into the kitchen, Douglas on his heels. The skinny man removed the plate from the bottom of the big and embarrassingly old machine and looked around. "Do you have any chewing gum?" Sherman asked.

As it turned out, Douglas had, in his pocket, the last stick of a pack of Juicy Fruit, which he promptly handed over. Sherman unwrapped the stick, folded it into his mouth, then lay there on the floor chewing.

"What are you doing?" Douglas asked.

Sherman paused him with a finger, then, as if feeling the texture of the gum with his tongue, he took it from his mouth and stuck it into the workings of the refrigerator. And just like that the machine ran with a quiet steady hum, just like it had when it was new.

"How'd you do that?" Douglas asked.

Sherman, now on his feet, shrugged.

"Thank you, this is terrific. All you used was chewing gum. Can you fix other things?"

Sherman nodded.

"What are you? Are you a repairman or an electrician?" Douglas asked.

"I can fix things."

"Would you like another sandwich?"

Sherman shook his head again and said, "I should be going. Thanks for the food and all your help."

"Those men might be waiting for you," Douglas said. He suddenly remembered his pistol. He could feel the weight of it in his pocket. "Just sit in here awhile." Douglas felt a great deal of sympathy for the underfed man who had just repaired his refrigerator. "Where do you live? I could drive you."

"Actually, I don't have a place to live." Sherman stared down at the floor.

"Come over here." Douglas led the man to the big metal sink across the kitchen. He turned the ancient lever and the pipes started with a thin whistle and then screeched as the water came out. "Tell me, can you fix that?"

"Do you want me to?"

"Yes." Douglas turned off the water.

"Do you have a wrench?"

Douglas stepped away and into his business office, where he dug his way through a pile of sweaters and newspapers until he found a twelve-inch crescent wrench and a pipe wrench. He took them back to Sherman. "Will these do?"

"Yes." Sherman took the wrench and got down under the sink.

Douglas bent low to try and see what the man was doing, but before he could figure anything out, Sherman was getting up.

"There you go," Sherman said.

Incredulous, Douglas reached over to the faucet and turned on the water. The water came out smoothly and quietly. He turned it off, then tried it again. "You did it."

"It's nothing. An easy repair."

"You know, I could really use somebody like you around here," Douglas said. "Do you need a job? I can't pay much. Just minimum wage, but I can let you stay in the apartment upstairs. Actually, it's just a room. Are you interested?"

"You don't even know me," Sherman said.

Douglas stopped. Of course the man was right. He didn't know anything about him. But he had a strong feeling that Sherman Olney was an honest man. An honest man who could fix things. "You're right," Douglas admitted. "But I'm a good judge of character."

"I don't know," Sherman said.

"You said you don't have a place to go. You can live here and work until you find another place or another job." Douglas was unsure why he was pleading so with the stranger and, in fact, had a terribly uneasy feeling about the whole business, but, for some reason, he really wanted him to stay.

"Okay," Sherman said.

Douglas took the man up the back stairs and showed him the little room. The single bulb hung from a cord in the middle of the ceiling and its dim light revealed the single bed made up with a yellow chenille spread. Douglas had taken many naps there.

"This is it," Douglas said.

"It's perfect." Sherman stepped fully into the room and looked around.

"The bathroom is down the hall. There's a narrow shower stall in it."

"I'm sure I'll be comfortable."

"There's food downstairs. Help yourself."

"Thank you."

Douglas stood in awkward silence for a while wondering what else there was to say. Then he said, "Well, I guess I should go on home to my wife."

"And I should get some sleep."

Douglas nodded and left the shop.

Douglas's wife said, "Are you crazy?"

Douglas sat at the kitchen table and held his face in his hands. He could smell the ham, salami, turkey, Muenster, cheddar, and Swiss from his day's work. He peeked through his fingers and watched his short, plump wife reach over and turn down the volume of the television on the counter. The muted mouths of the news anchors were still moving.

"I asked you a question," she said.

"It sounded more like an assertion." He looked at her eyes, which were narrowed and burning into him. "He's fine fellow. Just a little down on his luck, Sheila."

Sheila laughed, then stopped cold. "And he's in the shop all alone." She shook her head, her lips tightening across her teeth. "You have lost your mind. Now, you go right back down there and you get rid of that guy."

"I don't feel like driving." Douglas said.

"I'll drive you."

He sighed. Sheila was obviously right. Even he hadn't understood his impulse to offer the man a job and invite him to use the room above the shop. So, he would let her drive him back down there and he'd tell Sherman Olney he'd have to go.

They got into the old, forest green Buick LeSabre, Sheila behind the wheel and Douglas sunk down into the passenger seat that Sheila's concentrated weight had through the years mashed so flat. He usually hated when she drove, but especially right at that moment, as she was angry and with a mission. She took their corner at Underwood on two wheels and sped through the city and moderately heavy traffic back toward the shop.

"You really should slow down," Douglas said. He watched a man in a blue suit toss his briefcase between two parked cars and drive after it out of the way.

"You're one to give advice. You? An old fool who takes in a stray human being and leaves him alone in your place of business is giving advice? He's probably cleaned us out already."

Douglas considered the situation and felt incredibly stupid. He could not, in fact, assure Sheila that she was wrong. Sherman might be halfway to Philadelphia with twelve pounds of Genoa salami. For all he knew Sherman Olney had turned on the gas of the oven, grilled his dinner, and blown the restaurant to smithereens. He rolled down his window just a crack and listened for sirens.

"If anything bad has happened, I'm having you committed," Sheila said. She let out a brief scream and rattled the steering wheel. "Then I'll sell what little we have left and spend the rest of my life in Bermuda. That's what I'll do."

When Sheila made marks on the street braking to a stop, the store was still there and not ablaze. All the lights were off and the only people on the street were a couple of hookers on the far corner. Douglas unlocked and opened the front door of the shop, then followed Sheila inside. They walked past the tables and counter and into the kitchen where Douglas switched on the bright overhead lights. The fluorescent tubes flickered, then filled the place with a steady buzz.

"Go check the safe," Sheila said.

"There was no money in it," Douglas said. "There never is." She knew that. He had taken the money home and was going to drop it at the bank on his way to work the next day. He always did that.

"Check it anyway."

He walked into his business office and switched on the standing lamp by the door. He looked across the room to see that the safe was still closed and that the stack of newspapers was still in front of it. "Hasn't been touched," he said.

"What's his name?" Sheila asked.

"Sherman."

"Sherman!" she called up the stairs. "Sherman!"

In short order, Sherman came walking down the stairs in his trousers and sleeveless undershirt. He was rubbing his eyes, trying to adjust to the bright light.

"Sherman," Douglas said, "it's me, Douglas."

"Douglas? What are you doing back?" He stood in front of them in his stocking feet. "By the way, I fixed the toilet and also that funny massager thing."

"You mean, my foot massager?" Sheila asked.

"If you say so."

"I told you, Sherman can fix things," Douglas said to Sheila. "That's why I hired him." Sheila had purchased the foot massager from a fancy store in Georgetown. On the days when she worked in the shop she used to disappear every couple of hours for about fifteen minutes and then return happy and refreshed. She would be upstairs in the bathroom, sitting on the closed toilet with her feet stationed on her machine. Then the thing stopped working. Sheila loved that machine.

"The man at the store said my foot massager couldn't be repaired," Sheila said.

Sherman shrugged. "Well, it works now."

"I'll be right back," Sheila said and she walked away from the men and up the stairs.

Sherman watched her, then turned to Douglas. "Why did you come back?"

"Well, you see, Sheila doesn't think it's a good idea that you stay here. You know, alone and everything. Since we don't know you or anything about you." Douglas blew out a long slow breath. "I'm really sorry."

Upstairs, Sheila screamed, then came running back to the top of the stairs. "It works! It works! He did fix it." She came down, smiling at Sherman. "Thank you so much."

"You're welcome," Sherman said.

"I was just telling Sherman that we're sorry but he's going to have to leave."

"Don't be silly," Sheila said.

Douglas stared at her and rubbed a hand over his face. He gave Sheila a baffled look.

"No, no, it's certainly all right if Sherman sleeps here. And tomorrow, he can get to work." She grabbed Sherman's arm and turned him toward the stairs. "Now, you get on back up there and get some rest."

Sherman said nothing, but followed her directions. Douglas and Sheila watched him disappear upstairs.

Douglas looked at his wife. "What happened to you?"

"He fixed my foot rubber."

"So, that makes him a good guy? Just like that?"

"I don't know," she said, uncertainly. She seemed to reconsider for a second. "I guess. Come on, let's go home."

Two weeks later, Sherman had said nothing more about himself, responding only to trivial questions put to him. He did however repair or make better every machine in the restaurant. He had fixed the toaster oven, the gas lines of the big griddle, the dishwasher, the phone, the neon OPEN sign, the electric-eye buzzer on the front door, the meat slicer, the coffee machine, the manual mustard dispenser, and the cash register. Douglas found the man's skills invaluable and wondered how he had ever managed without him. Still, his presence was disconcerting as he never spoke of his past or family or friends and he never went out, not even to the store, his food being already there, and so Douglas began to worry that he might be a fugitive from the law.

"He never leaves the shop," Sheila complained. She was sitting in the passenger seat while Douglas drove them to the movie theater.

"That's where he lives," Douglas said. "All the food he needs is right there. I'm hardly paying him anything."

"You pay him plenty. He doesn't have to pay rent and he doesn't have to buy food."

"I don't see what the trouble is," he said. "After all, he's fixed your massage thingamajig. And he fixed your curling iron and your VCR and your watch and he even got the squeak out of your shoes."

"I know. I know." Sheila sighed. "Still, just what do we know about this man?"

"He's honest, I know that. He never even glances at the till. I've never seen anyone who cares less about money." Douglas turned right onto Connecticut.

"That's exactly how a crook wants to come across."

"Well, Sherman's no crook. Why, I'd trust the man with my life. There are very few people I can say that about."

Sheila laughed softly and disbelievingly. "Well, don't you sound melodramatic."

Douglas really couldn't argue with her. Everything she had said was correct and he was at a loss to explain his tenacious defense of a man who was, after all, a relative stranger. He pulled the car into a parallel space and killed the engine.

"The car didn't do that thing," Sheila said. She was referring to the way the car usually refused to shut off, the stubborn engine firing a couple of extra times.

Douglas glanced over at her.

"Sherman," she said.

"This morning. He opened the hood, grabbed this and jiggled that and then slammed it shut."

The fact of the matter was finally that Sherman hadn't stolen anything and hadn't come across in any way threatening and so Douglas kept his fears and suspicions in check and counted his savings. No more electricians. No more plumbers. No more repairmen of any kind. Sherman's handiness, however, did not remain a secret, in spite of Douglas's best efforts.

It began when Sherman offered and then repaired a small radio-controlled automobile owned by a fat boy.

The fat boy, who wore his hair in braids, came into the shop with two of his skinny friends. They sat at the counter and ordered a large soda to split.

"This thing is a piece of crap," the fat boy said. His name was Loomis Rump.

"I told you not to spend your money on that thing," one of the skinny kids said.

"Shut up," said Loomis.

"Timmy's right, Loomis," the third boy said. He sucked the last of the soda through the straw. "That's a cheap one. The good remote controls aren't made of that thin plastic."

"What do you know?" Loomis said. Loomis pushed his toy another few inches away from him across the counter, toward Sherman. Sherman looked at it, then picked it up.

Douglas was watching from the register. He observed as Sherman held the car up to the light and seemed to smile.

"Just stopped working, eh?" Sherman said to the boys.

"It's a piece of crap," Loomis said.

"Would you like me to fix it?" Sherman asked.

Douglas stepped closer, thinking this time he might see how the repair was done. Loomis handed the remote to Sherman. Douglas stared intently at the man's hands. Sherman took out his pocketknife and used the small blade to undo the Phillips-head screws in order to remove the back panel from the remote control. Then it was all a blur. Douglas saw nothing and then Sherman was replacing the panel.

"There you go," Sherman said and gave the car and controller back to Loomis.

Loomis Rump laughed. "You didn't even do nothing," he said.

"Anything," Sherman corrected him.

Loomis put the car on the floor and switched on the remote. The car rolled away, nearly tripping a postal worker, and crashed to a stop at the door. It capsized, but its wheels kept spinning.

"Hey, hey," the skinny boys shouted.

"Thanks, mister," Loomis said.

The boys left.

Fat Loomis Rump and his skinny pals told their friends and they brought in their broken toys. Sherman fixed them. The fat boy's friends told their parents and Douglas found his shop increasingly crowded with customers and their small appliances.

"The Rump boy told me that you fixed his toy car and the Johnson woman told me that you repaired her radio," the short man who wore the waterworks uniform said.

Sherman was wiping down the counter.

"Is that true?"

Sherman nodded.

"Well, you see these cuts on my face?"

Douglas could see the cuts under the man's three-day growth of stubble from the door to the kitchen. Sherman leaned forward and studied the wounds.

"They seem to be healing nicely," Sherman said.

"It's this damn razor," the man said and he pulled the small unit from his trousers pocket. "It cuts me bad every time I try to shave."

"You'd like me to fix your razor?"

"If you wouldn't mind. But I don't have any money."

"That's okay." Sherman took the razor and began taking it apart. Douglas, as always, moved closer and tried to see. He smiled at the waterworks man who smiled back. Other people gathered around and watched Sherman's hands. Then they watched him hand the reassembled little machine back to the waterworks man. The man turned on the shaver and put it to his face.

"Hey," he said. "This is wonderful. It works just like it did when it was new. This is wonderful. Thank you. Can I bring you some money tomorrow?"

"Not necessary," Sherman said.

"This is wonderful."

Everyone in the restaurant oohed and aahed.

"Look," the waterworks man said. "I'm not bleeding."

Sherman sat quietly at the end of the counter and fixed whatever was put in front of him. He repaired hair dryers and calculators and watches and cellular phones and carburetors. And while people waited for the repairs, they ate sandwiches and this appealed to Sherman, though he didn't like his handyman's time so consumed. But the fact of the matter was that there was little more to fix in the shop.

One day a woman who believed her husband was having an affair came in and complained over a turkey and provolone on wheat. Sherman sat next to her at the counter and listened as she finished, ". . . and then he comes home hours after he's gotten off from work, smelling of beer and perfume and he doesn't want to talk or anything and says he has a sinus headache and I'm wondering if I ought to follow him or check the mileage on his car before he leaves in the morning. What should I do?"

"Tell him it's his turn to cook and that you'll be late and don't tell him where you're going," Sherman said.

Everyone in the shop nodded, more in shared confusion than in agreement.

"Where should I go?" the woman asked.

"Go to the library and read about the praying mantis," Sherman said.

Douglas came up to Sherman after the woman had left and asked, "Do you think that was a good idea?"

Sherman shrugged.

The woman came in the next week, her face full with a smile and announced that her home life was now perfect.

"Everything at home is perfect now," she said. "Thanks to Sherman."

Customers slapped Sherman on the back.

So began a new dimension of fixing in the shop as people came in, along with their electric pencil sharpeners, pacemakers, and microwaves, their relationship woes, and their tax problems. Sherman saved the man who owned the automotive-supply business across the street twelve thousand dollars and got him some fifty-seven dollars in refund.

One night after the shop was closed, Douglas and Sherman sat at the counter and ate the stale leftover doughnuts and drank coffee. Douglas looked at his handyman and shook his head. "That was really something the way you straightened the Rhinehart boy's teeth."

"Physics," Sherman said.

Douglas washed down a dry bite and set his cup on the counter. "I know I've asked you before, but we've known each other longer now. How did you learn to fix things?"

"Fixing things is easy. You just have to know how things work."

"That's it," Douglas said more than asked.

Sherman nodded.

"Doesn't it make you happy to do it?"

Sherman looked at Douglas, questioning.

"I ask because you never smile."

"Oh," Sherman said and took another bite of doughnut.

The next day Sherman fixed a chain saw and a laptop computer and thirty-two parking tickets. Sherman, who had always been quiet, became increasingly more so. He would listen, nod, and fix the problem. That evening, a few minutes before closing, just after Sherman had solved the Morado woman's sexual-identity problem, two paramedics came in with a patient on a stretcher.

"This is my wife," the more distressed of the ambulance men said of the supine woman. "She's been hit by a car and she died in our rig on the way to the hospital," he cried.

Sherman looked at the woman, pulling back the blanket.

"She had massive internal—"

Sherman stopped the man with a raised hand, pulled the blanket off and then threw it over himself and the dead woman. Douglas stepped over to stand with the paramedics.

Sherman worked under the blanket, moving this way and that way, and then he and the woman emerged, alive and well. The paramedic hugged her.

"You're alive," the man said to his wife.

The other paramedic shook Sherman's hand. Douglas just stared at his handyman.

"Thank you, thank you," the husband said, crying.

The woman was confused, but she, too, offered Sherman thanks.

Sherman nodded and walked quietly away, disappearing into the kitchen.

The paramedics and the restored woman left. Douglas locked the shop and walked into the kitchen where he found Sherman sitting on the floor with his back against the refrigerator.

"I don't know what to say," Douglas said. His head was swimming. "You just brought that woman back to life."

Sherman's face looked lifeless. He seemed drained of all energy. He lifted his sad face up to look at Douglas.

"How did you do that?" Douglas asked.

Sherman shrugged.

"You just brought a woman back to life and you give me a shrug?" Douglas could hear the fear in his voice. "Who are you? What are you? Are you from outer space or something?"

"No," Sherman said.

"Then what's going on?"

"I can fix things."

"That wasn't a thing," Douglas pointed out. "That was a human being."

"Yeah, I know."

Douglas ran a hand over his face and just stared down at Sherman. "I wonder what Sheila will say."

"Please don't tell anyone about this," Sherman said.

Douglas snorted out a laugh. "Don't tell anyone. I don't have to tell anyone. Everyone probably knows by now. What do you think those paramedics are out doing right now? They're telling anybody and everybody that there's some freak in Langley's Sandwich Shop who can revive the dead."

Sherman held his face in his hands.

"Who are you?"

News spread. Television-news trucks and teams camped outside the front door of the sandwich shop. They were waiting with cameras ready when Douglas showed up to open for business the day following the resurrection.

"Yes, this is my shop," he said. "No, I don't know how it was done," he said. "No, you can't come in just yet," he said.

Sherman was sitting at the counter waiting, his face long, his eyes red as if from crying.

"This is crazy," Douglas said.

Sherman nodded.

"They want to talk to you." Douglas looked closely at Sherman. "Are you all right?"

But Sherman was looking past Douglas and through the front window where the crowd was growing ever larger.

"Are you going to talk to them?" Douglas asked.

Sherman shook his sad face. "I have to run away," he said. "Everyone knows where I am now."

Douglas at first thought Sherman was making cryptic reference to the men who had been beating him that night long ago, but then realized that Sherman meant simply *everyone*.

Sherman stood and walked into the back of the shop. Douglas followed him, not knowing why, unable to stop himself. He followed the man out of the store and down the alley, away from the shop and the horde of people.

Sherman watched the change come over Douglas and said, "Of course not."

"But you—" The rest of Douglas's sentence didn't have a chance to find air as he was once again repeating Sherman's steps.

They ran up this street and across that avenue, crossed bridges and scurried through tunnels and no matter how far away from the shop they seemed to get, the chanting remained, however faint. Douglas finally asked where there were going and confessed that he was afraid. They were sitting on a bench in the park and it was by now just after sundown.

"You don't have to come with me," Sherman said. "I only need to get away from all of them." He shook his head and said, more to himself, "I knew this would happen."

"If you knew this would happen, why did you fix all of those things?"

"Because I can. Because I was asked."

Douglas gave nervous glances this way and that across the park. "This has something to do with why the men were beating you that night, doesn't it?"

"They were from the government or some businesses, I'm not completely sure," Sherman said. "They wanted me to fix a bunch of things and I said no."

"But they asked you," Douglas said. "You just told me—"

"You have to be careful about what you fix. If you fix the valves in an engine, but the bearings are shot, you'll get more compression, but the engine will still burn up." Sherman looked at Douglas's puzzled face. "If you irrigate a desert, you might empty a sea. It's a complicated business, fixing things."

Douglas said, "So, what do we do now?"

Sherman was now weeping, tears streaming down his face and curving just under his chin before falling to the open collar of his light blue shirt. Douglas watched him, not believing that he was seeing the same man who had fixed so many machines and so many relationships and so many businesses and concerns and even fixed a dead woman.

Sherman raised his tear-filled eyes to Douglas. "I am the empty sea," he said.

The chanting became louder and Douglas turned to see the night dotted with yellow-orange torches. The quality of the chanting had become strained and there was an urgency in the intonation that did not sound affable.

The two men ran, Douglas pushing Sherman, as he was now so engaged in sobbing that he had trouble keeping on his feet. They made it to the big bridge that crossed the bay and stopped in the middle, discovering that at either end thousands of people waited. They sang their dirge into the dark sky, their flames winking.

"Fix us!" they shouted. "Fix us! Fix us!"

Sherman looked down at the peaceful water below. It was a long drop that no one could hope to survive. He looked at Douglas.

Douglas nodded.

The masses of people pressed in from either side.

Sherman stepped over the railing and stood on the brink, the toes of his shoes pushed well over the edge.

"Don't!" they all screamed. "Fix us! Fix us!"

2004

WILLIAM FAULKNER
1897–1962

Faulkner was born in New Albany, Mississippi, to a family that had once included wealthy and powerful people ruined by the Civil War. His great-grandfather was a popular novelist, and this ancestor served, like other family members, as a model from whom Faulkner drew traits used in composing the characters in his fiction. He attended the University of Mississippi in Oxford before and after his service in the Royal Canadian Air Force in World War I. Thereafter, he lived in Oxford for most of his life, though he spent much time in Hollywood as a screenwriter. It was in New Orleans, though, that his literary career began. There he met Sherwood Anderson, who encouraged him to turn from poetry to fiction and helped him get his first novel published. His lifetime's work, which eventually won Faulkner a Nobel Prize in 1950, is largely a depiction of life in his fictional Yoknapatawpha County, an imaginative reconstruction of the area adjacent to Oxford. Faulkner was a passionately devoted hunter, and his love of the disappearing wilderness is expressed in many of his tales. He sought out the honor and courage of people thwarted by circumstance, and the sum of his writing testifies to his faith that these virtues will prevail despite the corruptions of modern life. His major novels were mostly the product of a prodigious decade of creative effort. They include *The Sound and the Fury* (1929), *As I Lay Dying* (1930), *Sanctuary* (1931), *Light in August* (1932), *Absalom, Absalom!* (1936), *The Wild Palms* (1939), and *The Hamlet* (1940). His books of short stories include *These Thirteen* (1931), *Go Down, Moses* (1942), and the *Collected Stories of William Faulkner* (1950).

A Rose for Emily

I

When Miss Emily Grierson died, our whole town went to her funeral: the men through a sort of respectful affection for a fallen monument, the women mostly out of curiosity to see the inside of her house, which no one save an old man-servant—a combined gardener and cook—had seen in at least ten years.

It was a big, squarish frame house that had once been white, decorated with cupolas and spires and scrolled balconies in the heavily lightsome style of the seventies,[1] set on what had once been our most select street. But garages

---

1. The 1870s, the decade following the American Civil War, mentioned at the end of the paragraph.

and cotton gins had encroached and obliterated even the august names of that neighborhood; only Miss Emily's house was left, lifting its stubborn and coquettish decay above the cotton wagons and the gasoline pumps—an eyesore among eyesores. And now Miss Emily had gone to join the representatives of those august names where they lay in the cedar-bemused cemetery among the ranked and anonymous graves of Union and Confederate soldiers who fell at the battle of Jefferson.[2]

Alive, Miss Emily had been a tradition, a duty, and a care; a sort of hereditary obligation upon the town, dating from that day in 1894 when Colonel Sartoris, the mayor—he who fathered the edict that no Negro woman should appear on the streets without an apron—remitted her taxes, the dispensation dating from the death of her father on into perpetuity. Not that Miss Emily would have accepted charity. Colonel Sartoris invented an involved tale to the effect that Miss Emily's father had loaned money to the town, which the town, as a matter of business, preferred this way of repaying. Only a man of Colonel Sartoris' generation and thought could have invented it, and only a woman could have believed it.

When the next generation, with its more modern ideas, became mayors and aldermen, this arrangement created some little dissatisfaction. On the first of the year they mailed her a tax notice. February came, and there was no reply. They wrote her a formal letter, asking her to call at the sheriff's office at her convenience. A week later the mayor wrote her himself, offering to call or to send his car for her, and received in reply a note on paper of an archaic shape, in a thin, flowing calligraphy in faded ink, to the effect that she no longer went out at all. The tax notice was also enclosed, without comment.

They called a special meeting of the Board of Aldermen. A deputation waited upon her, knocked at the door through which no visitor had passed since she ceased giving china-painting lessons eight or ten years earlier. They were admitted by the old Negro into a dim hall from which a stairway mounted into still more shadow. It smelled of dust and disuse—a close, dank smell. The Negro led them into the parlor. It was furnished in heavy, leather-covered furniture. When the Negro opened the blinds of one window, they could see that the leather was cracked; and when they sat down, a faint dust rose sluggishly about their thighs, spinning with slow motes in the single sun-ray. On a tarnished gilt easel before the fireplace stood a crayon portrait of Miss Emily's father.

They rose when she entered—a small, fat woman in black, with a thin gold chain descending to her waist and vanishing into her belt, leaning on an ebony cane with a tarnished gold head. Her skeleton was small and spare; perhaps that was why what would have been merely plumpness in another was obesity in her. She looked bloated, like a body long submerged in motionless water, and of that pallid hue. Her eyes, lost in the fatty ridges of her face, looked like two small pieces of coal pressed into a lump of dough as they moved from one face to another while the visitors stated their errand.

She did not ask them to sit. She just stood in the door and listened quietly until the spokesman came to a stumbling halt. Then they could hear the invisible watch ticking at the end of the gold chain.

2. The principal town and county seat of Faulkner's fictional Yoknapatawpha County.

Her voice was dry and cold. "I have no taxes in Jefferson. Colonel Sartoris explained it to me. Perhaps one of you can gain access to the city records and satisfy yourselves."

"But we have. We are the city authorities, Miss Emily. Didn't you get a notice from the sheriff, signed by him?"

"I received a paper, yes," Miss Emily said. "Perhaps he considers himself the sheriff . . . I have no taxes in Jefferson."

"But there is nothing on the books to show that, you see. We must go by the—"

"See Colonel Sartoris. I have no taxes in Jefferson."

"But, Miss Emily—"

"See Colonel Sartoris." (Colonel Sartoris had been dead almost ten years.) "I have no taxes in Jefferson. Tobe!" The Negro appeared. "Show these gentlemen out."

II

So she vanquished them, horse and foot, just as she had vanquished their fathers thirty years before about the smell. That was two years after her father's death and a short time after her sweetheart—the one we believed would marry her—had deserted her. After her father's death she went out very little; after her sweetheart went away, people hardly saw her at all. A few of the ladies had the temerity to call, but were not received, and the only sign of life about the place was the Negro man—a young man then—going in and out with a market basket.

"Just as if a man—any man—could keep a kitchen properly," the ladies said; so they were not surprised when the smell developed. It was another link between the gross, teeming world and the high and mighty Griersons.

A neighbor, a woman, complained to the mayor, Judge Stevens, eighty years old.

"But what will you have me do about it, madam?" he said.

"Why, send her word to stop it," the woman said. "Isn't there a law?"

"I'm sure that won't be necessary," Judge Stevens said. "It's probably just a snake or a rat that nigger of hers killed in the yard. I'll speak to him about it."

The next day he received two more complaints, one from a man who came in diffident deprecation. "We really must do something about it, Judge. I'd be the last one in the world to bother Miss Emily, but we've got to do something." That night the Board of Aldermen met—three graybeards and one younger man, a member of the rising generation.

"It's simple enough," he said. "Send her word to have her place cleaned up. Give her a certain time to do it in, and if she don't . . ."

"Dammit, sir," Judge Stevens said, "will you accuse a lady to her face of smelling bad?"

So the next night, after midnight, four men crossed Miss Emily's lawn and slunk about the house like burglars, sniffing along the base of the brickwork and at the cellar openings while one of them performed a regular sowing motion with his hand out of a sack slung from his shoulder. They broke open the cellar door and sprinkled lime there, and in all the outbuildings. As they recrossed the lawn, a window that had been dark was lighted and Miss Emily sat in it, the light behind her, and her upright torso motionless as that of an idol. They crept quietly across the lawn and into the shadow of the locusts that lined the street. After a week or two the smell went away.

That was when people had begun to feel really sorry for her. People in our town, remembering how old lady Wyatt, her great-aunt, had gone completely crazy at last, believed that the Griersons held themselves a little too high for what they really were. None of the young men were quite good enough for Miss Emily and such. We had long thought of them as a tableau, Miss Emily a slender figure in white in the background, her father a spraddled silhouette in the foreground, his back to her and clutching a horsewhip, the two of them framed by the back-flung front door. So when she got to be thirty and was still single, we were not pleased exactly, but vindicated; even with insanity in the family she wouldn't have turned down all of her chances if they had really materialized.

When her father died, it got about that the house was all that was left to her; and in a way, people were glad. At last they could pity Miss Emily. Being left alone, and a pauper, she had become humanized. Now she too would know the old thrill and the old despair of a penny more or less.

The day after his death all the ladies prepared to call at the house and offer condolence and aid, as is our custom. Miss Emily met them at the door, dressed as usual and with no trace of grief on her face. She told them that her father was not dead. She did that for three days, with the ministers calling on her, and the doctors, trying to persuade her to let them dispose of the body. Just as they were about to resort to law and force, she broke down, and they buried her father quickly.

We did not say she was crazy then. We believed she had to do that. We remembered all the young men her father had driven away, and we knew that with nothing left, she would have to cling to that which had robbed her, as people will.

III

She was sick for a long time. When we saw her again her hair was cut short, making her look like a girl, with a vague resemblance to those angels in colored church windows—sort of tragic and serene.

The town had just let the contracts for paving the sidewalks, and in the summer after her father's death they began the work. The construction company came with niggers and mules and machinery, and a foreman named Homer Barron, a Yankee—a big, dark, ready man, with a big voice and eyes lighter than his face. The little boys would follow in groups to hear him cuss the niggers, and the niggers singing in time to the rise and fall of picks. Pretty soon he knew everybody in town. Whenever you heard a lot of laughing anywhere about the square, Homer Barron would be in the center of the group. Presently we began to see him and Miss Emily on Sunday afternoons driving in the yellow-wheeled buggy and the matched team of bays from the livery stable.

At first we were glad that Miss Emily would have an interest, because the ladies all said, "Of course a Grierson would not think seriously of a Northerner, a day laborer." But there were still others, older people, who said that even grief could not cause a real lady to forget *noblesse oblige*—without calling it *noblesse oblige*.[3] They just said, "Poor Emily. Her kinsfolk should come to her." She had some kin in Alabama; but years ago her father had fallen out with them over the estate of old lady Wyatt, the crazy woman, and there was no communication between the two families. They had not even been represented at the funeral.

And as soon as the old people said, "Poor Emily," the whispering began. "Do you suppose it's really so?" they said to one another. "Of course it is. What else could . . ." This behind their hands; rustling of craned silk and satin behind jalousies[4] closed upon the sun of Sunday afternoon as the thin, swift clop-clop-clop of the matched team passed: "Poor Emily."

She carried her head high enough—even when we believed that she was fallen. It was as if she demanded more than ever the recognition of her dignity as the last Grierson; as if it had wanted that touch of earthiness to reaffirm her imperviousness. Like when she bought the rat poison, the arsenic. That was over a year after they had begun to say "Poor Emily," and while the two female cousins were visiting her.

"I want some poison," she said to the druggist. She was over thirty then, still a slight woman, though thinner than usual, with cold, haughty black eyes in a face the flesh of which was strained across the temples and about the eyesockets as you imagine a lighthouse-keeper's face ought to look. "I want some poison," she said.

"Yes, Miss Emily. What kind? For rats and such? I'd recom—"

"I want the best you have. I don't care what kind."

The druggist named several. "They'll kill anything up to an elephant. But what you want is—"

"Arsenic," Miss Emily said. "Is that a good one?"

"Is . . . arsenic? Yes, ma'am. But what you want—"

"I want arsenic."

The druggist looked down at her. She looked back at him, erect, her face like a strained flag. "Why, of course," the druggist said. "If that's what you want. But the law requires you to tell what you are going to use it for."

Miss Emily just stared at him, her head tilted back in order to look him eye for eye, until he looked away and went and got the arsenic and wrapped it up. The Negro delivery boy brought her the package; the druggist didn't come back. When she opened the package at home there was written on the box, under the skull and bones: "For rats."

IV

So the next day we all said, "She will kill herself"; and we said it would be the best thing. When she had first begun to be seen with Homer Barron, we had said, "She will marry him." Then we said, "She will persuade him yet," because Homer himself had remarked—he liked men, and it was known that he drank with the younger men in the Elks' Club—that he was not a marrying man.

---

3. The obligation of the nobility or upper classes to behave with honor and generosity toward those less privileged. 4. Window blinds, made of adjustable horizontal louvers.

Later we said, "Poor Emily" behind the jalousies as they passed on Sunday afternoon in the glittering buggy, Miss Emily with her head high and Homer Barron with his hat cocked and a cigar in his teeth, reins and whip in a yellow glove.

Then some of the ladies began to say that it was a disgrace to the town and a bad example to the young people. The men did not want to interfere, but at last the ladies forced the Baptist minister—Miss Emily's people were Episcopal—to call upon her. He would never divulge what happened during that interview, but he refused to go back again. The next Sunday they again drove about the streets, and the following day the minister's wife wrote to Miss Emily's relations in Alabama.

So she had blood-kin under her roof again and we sat back to watch developments. At first nothing happened. Then we were sure that they were to be married. We learned that Miss Emily had been to the jeweler's and ordered a man's toilet set in silver, with the letters H. B. on each piece. Two days later we learned that she had bought a complete outfit of men's clothing, including a nightshirt, and we said, "They are married." We were really glad. We were glad because the two female cousins were even more Grierson than Miss Emily had ever been.

So we were not surprised when Homer Barron—the streets had been finished some time since—was gone. We were a little disappointed that there was not a public blowing-off, but we believed that he had gone on to prepare for Miss Emily's coming, or to give her a chance to get rid of the cousins. (By that time it was a cabal, and we were all Miss Emily's allies to help circumvent the cousins.) Sure enough, after another week they departed. And, as we had expected all along, within three days Homer Barron was back in town. A neighbor saw the Negro man admit him at the kitchen door at dusk one evening.

And that was the last we saw of Homer Barron. And of Miss Emily for some time. The Negro man went in and out with the market basket, but the front door remained closed. Now and then we would see her at a window for a moment, as the men did that night when they sprinkled the lime; but for almost six months she did not appear on the streets. Then we knew that this was to be expected too; as if that quality of her father which had thwarted her woman's life so many times had been too virulent and too furious to die.

When we next saw Miss Emily, she had grown fat and her hair was turning gray. During the next few years it grew grayer and grayer until it attained an even pepper-and-salt iron-gray, when it ceased turning. Up to the day of her death at seventy-four it was still that vigorous iron-gray, like the hair of an active man.

From that time on her front door remained closed, save for a period of six or seven years, when she was about forty, during which she gave lessons in china-painting. She fitted up a studio in one of the downstairs rooms, where the daughters and granddaughters of Colonel Sartoris' contemporaries were sent to her with the same regularity and in the same spirit that they were sent to church on Sundays with a twenty-five-cent piece for the collection plate. Meanwhile her taxes had been remitted.

Then the newer generation became the backbone and the spirit of the town, and the painting pupils grew up and fell away and did not send their children to her with boxes of color and tedious brushes and pictures cut from the ladies' magazines. The front door closed upon the last one and remained closed for good. When the town got free postal delivery, Miss Emily alone refused to let them fasten the metal numbers above her door and attach a mailbox to it. She would not listen to them.

Daily, monthly, yearly we watched the Negro grow grayer and more stooped, going in and out with the market basket. Each December we sent her a tax notice, which would be returned by the post office a week later, unclaimed. Now and then we would see her in one of the downstairs windows—she had evidently shut up the top floor of the house—like the carven torso of an idol in a niche, looking or not looking at us, we could never tell which. Thus she passed from generation to generation—dear, inescapable, impervious, tranquil, and perverse.

And so she died. Fell ill in the house filled with dust and shadows, with only a doddering Negro man to wait on her. We did not even know she was sick; we had long since given up trying to get any information from the Negro. He talked to no one, probably not even to her, for his voice had grown harsh and rusty, as if from disuse.

She died in one of the downstairs rooms, in a heavy walnut bed with a curtain, her gray head propped on a pillow yellow and moldy with age and lack of sunlight.

V

The Negro met the first of the ladies at the front door and let them in, with their hushed, sibilant voices and their quick, curious glances, and then he disappeared. He walked right through the house and out the back and was not seen again.

The two female cousins came at once. They held the funeral on the second day, with the town coming to look at Miss Emily beneath a mass of bought flowers, with the crayon face of her father musing profoundly above the bier and the ladies sibilant and macabre; and the very old men—some in their brushed Confederate uniforms—on the porch and the lawn, talking of Miss Emily as if she had been a contemporary of theirs, believing that they had danced with her and courted her perhaps, confusing time with its mathematical progression, as the old do, to whom all the past is not a diminishing road but, instead, a huge meadow which no winter ever quite touches, divided from them now by the narrow bottle-neck of the most recent decade of years.

Already we knew that there was one room in that region above stairs which no one had seen in forty years, and which would have to be forced. They waited until Miss Emily was decently in the ground before they opened it.

The violence of breaking down the door seemed to fill this room with pervading dust. A thin, acrid pall as of the tomb seemed to lie everywhere upon this room decked and furnished as for a bridal: upon the valance curtains of faded rose color, upon the rose-shaded lights, upon the dressing table, upon the delicate array of crystal and the man's toilet things backed with tarnished silver, silver so tarnished that the monogram was obscured. Among them lay a collar and tie, as if they had just been removed, which, lifted, left upon the surface a pale crescent in the dust. Upon a chair hung the suit, carefully folded; beneath it the two mute shoes and the discarded socks.

The man himself lay in the bed.

For a long while we just stood there, looking down at the profound a fleshless grin. The body had apparently once lain in the attitude of an embrace, but now the long sleep that outlasts love, that conquers even the grimace of love, had cuckolded him. What was left of him, rotted beneath what was left of the nightshirt, had become inextricable from the bed in which he lay; and upon him and upon the pillow beside him lay that even coating of the patient and biding dust.

Then we noticed that in the second pillow was the indentation of a head. One of us lifted something from it, and leaning forward, that faint and invisible dust dry and acrid in the nostrils, we saw a long strand of iron-gray hair.

1930

Barn Burning

The store in which the Justice of the Peace's court was sitting smelled of cheese. The boy, crouched on his nail keg at the back of the crowded room, knew he smelled cheese, and more: from where he sat he could see the ranked shelves close-packed with the solid, squat, dynamic shapes of tin cans whose labels his stomach read, not from the lettering which meant nothing to his mind but from the scarlet devils and the silver curve of fish—this, the cheese which he knew he smelled and the hermetic meat[1] which his intestines believed he smelled coming in intermittent gusts momentary and brief between the other constant one, the smell and sense just a little of fear because mostly of despair and grief, the old fierce pull of blood. He could not see the table where the Justice sat and before which his father and his father's enemy (*our enemy* he thought in that despair; *ourn! mine and hisn both! He's my father!*) stood, but he could hear them, the two of them that is, because his father had said no word yet:

"But what proof have you, Mr. Harris?"

"I told you. The hog got into my corn. I caught it up and sent it back to him. He had no fence that would hold it. I told him so, warned him. The next time I put the hog in my pen. When he came to get it I gave him enough wire to patch up his pen. The next time I put the hog up and kept it. I rode down to his house and saw the wire I gave him still rolled on to the spool in his yard. I told him he could have the hog when he paid me a dollar pound fee. That evening a nigger came with the dollar and got the hog. He was a strange nigger. He said, 'He say to tell you wood and hay kin burn.' I said, 'What?' 'That whut he say to tell you,' the nigger said. 'Wood and hay kin burn.' That night my barn burned. I got the stock out but I lost the barn."

"Where is the nigger? Have you got him?"

"He was a strange nigger, I tell you. I don't know what became of him."

"But that's not proof. Don't you see that's not proof?"

---

1. Canned meat.

"Get that boy up here. He knows." For a moment the boy thought too that the man meant his older brother until Harris said, "Not him. The little one. The boy," and, crouching, small for his age, small and wiry like his father, in patched and faded jeans even too small for him, with straight, uncombed, brown hair and eyes gray and wild as storm scud, he saw the men between himself and the table part and become a lane of grim faces, at the end of which he saw the Justice, a shabby, collarless, graying man in spectacles, beckoning him. He felt no floor under his bare feet; he seemed to walk beneath the palpable weight of the grim turning faces. His father, stiff in his black Sunday coat donned not for the trial but for the moving, did not even look at him. *He aims for me to lie,* he thought, again with that frantic grief and despair. *And I will have to do hit.*

"What's your name, boy?" the Justice said.

"Colonel Sartoris Snopes,"[2] the boy whispered.

"Hey?" the Justice said. "Talk louder. Colonel Sartoris? I reckon anybody named for Colonel Sartoris in this country can't help but tell the truth, can they?" The boy said nothing. *Enemy! Enemy!* he thought; for a moment he could not even see, could not see that the Justice's face was kindly nor discern that his voice was troubled when he spoke to the man named Harris: "Do you want me to question this boy?" But he could hear, and during those subsequent long seconds while there was absolutely no sound in the crowded little room save that of quiet and intent breathing it was as if he had swung outward at the end of a grape vine, over a ravine, and at the top of the swing had been caught in a prolonged instant of mesmerized gravity, weightless in time.

"No!" Harris said violently, explosively. "Damnation! Send him out of here!" Now time, the fluid world, rushed beneath him again, the voices coming to him again through the smell of cheese and sealed meat, the fear and despair and the old grief of blood:

"This case is closed. I can't find against you, Snopes, but I can give you advice. Leave this country and don't come back to it."

His father spoke for the first time, his voice cold and harsh, level, without emphasis: "I aim to. I don't figure to stay in a country among people who . . ." he said something unprintable and vile, addressed to no one.

"That'll do," the Justice said. "Take your wagon and get out of this country before dark. Case dismissed."

His father turned, and he followed the stiff black coat, the wiry figure walking a little stiffly from where a Confederate provost's man's[3] musket ball had taken him in the heel on a stolen horse thirty years ago, followed the two backs now, since his older brother had appeared from somewhere in the crowd, no taller than the father but thicker, chewing tobacco steadily, between the two lines of grim-faced men and out of the store and across the worn gallery and down the sagging steps and among the dogs and half-grown boys in the mild May dust, where as he passed a voice hissed:

"Barn burner!"

Again he could not see, whirling; there was a face in a red haze, moonlike, bigger than the full moon, the owner of it half again his size, he leaping in the

---

2. The Snopes family figures in many Faulkner stories and novels. Colonel Sartoris is a major personage among Faulkner's fictional inhabitants of Yoknapatawpha County. **3.** Military policeman's.

red haze toward the face, feeling no blow, feeling no shock when his head struck the earth, scrabbling up and leaping again, feeling no blow this time either and tasting no blood, scrabbling up to see the other boy in full flight and himself already leaping into pursuit as his father's hand jerked him back, the harsh, cold voice speaking above him: "Go get in the wagon."

It stood in a grove of locusts and mulberries across the road. His two hulking sisters in their Sunday dresses and his mother and her sister in calico and sunbonnets were already in it, sitting on and among the sorry residue of the dozen and more movings which even the boy could remember—the battered stove, the broken beds and chairs, the clock inlaid with mother-of-pearl, which would not run, stopped at some fourteen minutes past two o'clock of a dead and forgotten day and time, which had been his mother's dowry. She was crying, though when she saw him she drew her sleeve across her face and began to descend from the wagon. "Get back," the father said.

"He's hurt. I got to get some water and wash his . . ."

"Get back in the wagon," his father said. He got in too, over the tail-gate. His father mounted to the seat where the older brother already sat and struck the gaunt mules two savage blows with the peeled willow, but without heat. It was not even sadistic; it was exactly that same quality which in later years would cause his descendants to overrun the engine before putting a motor car into motion, striking and reining back in the same movement. The wagon went on, the store with its quiet crowd of grimly watching men dropped behind; a curve in the road hid it. *Forever* he thought. *Maybe he's done satisfied now, now that he has* . . . stopping himself, not to say it aloud even to himself. His mother's hand touched his shoulder.

"Does hit hurt?" she said.

"Naw," he said. "Hit don't hurt. Lemme be."

"Can't you wipe some of the blood off before hit dries?"

"I'll wash to-night," he said. "Lemme be, I tell you."

The wagon went on. He did not know where they were going. None of them ever did or ever asked, because it was always somewhere, always a house of sorts waiting for them a day or two days or even three days away. Likely his father had already arranged to make a crop on another farm before he . . . Again he had to stop himself. He (the father) always did. There was something about his wolf-like independence and even courage when the advantage was at least neutral which impressed strangers, as if they got from his latent ravening ferocity not so much a sense of dependability as a feeling that his ferocious conviction in the rightness of his own actions would be of advantage to all whose interest lay with his.

That night they camped, in a grove of oaks and beeches where a spring ran. The nights were still cool and they had a fire against it, of a rail lifted from a nearby fence and cut into lengths—a small fire, neat, niggard almost, a shrewd fire; such fires were his father's habit and custom always, even in freezing weather. Older, the boy might have remarked this and wondered why not a big one; why should not a man who had not only seen the waste and extravagance of war, but who had in his blood an inherent voracious prodigality with material not his own, have burned everything in sight? Then he might have gone a step farther and thought that that was the reason: that niggard blaze was the living fruit of nights passed during those four years in the woods hiding from all men, blue or gray, with his strings of horses (captured horses, he called them). And older still, he might have divined the true reason: that the element of fire spoke to some deep mainspring of his father's being, as the element of steel or of powder spoke to other men, as the one weapon for the preservation of integrity, else breath were not worth the breathing, and hence to be regarded with respect and used with discretion.

But he did not think this now and he had seen those same niggard blazes all his life. He merely ate his supper beside it and was already half asleep over his iron plate when his father called him, and once more he followed the stiff back, the stiff and ruthless limp, up the slope and on to the starlit road where, turning, he could see his father against the stars but without face or depth—a shape black, flat, and bloodless as though cut from tin in the iron folds of the frockcoat which had not been made for him, the voice harsh like tin and without heat like tin:

"You were fixing to tell them. You would have told him." He didn't answer. His father struck him with the flat of his hand on the side of the head, hard but without heat, exactly as he had struck the two mules at the store, exactly as he would strike either of them with any stick in order to kill a horse fly, his voice still without heat or anger: "You're getting to be a man. You got to learn. You got to learn to stick to your own blood or you ain't going to have any blood to stick to you. Do you think either of them, any man there this morning, would? Don't you know all they wanted was a chance to get at me because they knew I had them beat? Eh?" Later, twenty years later, he was to tell himself, "If I had said they wanted only truth, justice, he would have hit me again." But now he said nothing. He was not crying. He just stood there. "Answer me," his father said.

"Yes," he whispered. His father turned.

"Get on to bed. We'll be there tomorrow."

Tomorrow they were there. In the early afternoon the wagon stopped before a paintless two-room house identical almost with the dozen others it had stopped before even in the boy's ten years, and again, as on the other dozen occasions, his mother and aunt got down and began to unload the wagon, although his two sisters and his father and brother had not moved.

"Likely hit ain't fitten for hawgs," one of the sisters said.

"Nevertheless, fit it will and you'll hog it and like it," his father said. "Get out of them chairs and help your Ma unload."

The two sisters got down, big, bovine, in a flutter of cheap ribbons; one of them drew from the jumbled wagon bed a battered lantern, the other a worn broom. His father handed the reins to the older son and began to climb stiffly over the wheel. "When they get unloaded, take the team to the barn and feed them." Then he said, and at first the boy thought he was still speaking to his brother: "Come with me."

"Me?" he said.

"Yes," his father said. "You."

"Abner," his mother said. His father paused and looked back—the harsh level stare beneath the shaggy, graying, irascible brows.

"I reckon I'll have a word with the man that aims to begin to-morrow owning me body and soul for the next eight months."

They went back up the road. A week ago—or before last night, that is—he would have asked where they were going, but not now. His father had struck him before last night but never before had he paused afterward to explain why; it was as if the blow and the following calm, outrageous voice still rang, repercussed, divulging nothing to him save the terrible handicap of being young, the light weight of his few years, just heavy enough to prevent his soaring free of the world as it seemed to be ordered but not heavy enough to keep him footed solid in it, to resist it and try to change the course of its events.

Presently he could see the grove of oaks and cedars and the other flowering trees and shrubs, where the house would be, though not the house yet. They walked beside a fence massed with honeysuckle and Cherokee roses and came to a gate swinging open between two brick pillars, and now, beyond a sweep of drive, he saw the house for the first time and at that instant he forgot his father and the terror and despair both, and even when he remembered his father again (who had not stopped) the terror and despair did not return. Because, for all the twelve movings, they had sojourned until now in a poor country, a land of small farms and fields and houses, and he had never seen a house like this before. *Hit's big as a courthouse* he thought quietly, with a surge of peace and joy, whose reason he could not have thought into words, being too young for that: *They are safe from him, People whose lives are a part of this peace and dignity are beyond his touch, he no more to them than a buzzing wasp: capable of stinging for a little moment but that's all; the spell of this peace and dignity rendering even the barns and stable and cribs which belong to it impervious to the puny flames he might contrive* . . . this, the peace and joy, ebbing for an instant as he looked again at the stiff black back, the stiff and implacable limp of the figure which was not dwarfed by the house, for the reason that it had never looked big anywhere and which now, against the serene columned backdrop, had more than ever that impervious quality of something cut ruthlessly from tin, depthless, as though, sidewise to the sun, it would cast no shadow. Watching him, the boy remarked the absolutely undeviating course which his father held and saw the stiff foot come squarely down in a pile of fresh droppings where a horse had stood in the drive and which his father could have avoided by a simple change of stride. But it ebbed only for a moment, though he could not have thought this into words either, walking on in the spell of the house, which he could even want but without envy, without sorrow, certainly never with that ravening and jealous rage which unknown to him walked in the ironlike black coat before him: *Maybe he will feel it too. Maybe it will even change him now from what maybe he couldn't help but be.*

They crossed the portico. Now he could hear his father's stiff foot as it came down on the boards with clocklike finality, a sound out of all proportion to the displacement of the body it bore and which was not dwarfed either by the white door before it, as though it had attained to a sort of vicious and ravening minimum not to be dwarfed by anything—the flat, wide, black hat, the formal coat of broadcloth which had once been black but which had now that friction-glazed greenish cast of the bodies of old house flies, the lifted sleeve which was too large, the lifted hand like a curled claw. The door opened so promptly that the boy knew the Negro must have been watching them all the time, an old man with neat grizzled hair, in a linen jacket, who stood barring the door with his body, saying, "Wipe yo foots, white man, fo you come in here. Major ain't home nohow."

"Get out of my way, nigger," his father said, without heat too, flinging the door back and the Negro also and entering, his hat still on his head. And now the boy saw the prints of the stiff foot on the doorjamb and saw them appear on the pale rug behind the machinelike deliberation of the foot which seemed to bear (or transmit) twice the weight which the body compassed. The Negro was shouting "Miss Lula! Miss Lula!" somewhere behind them, then the boy, deluged as though by a warm wave by a suave turn of carpeted stair and a pendant glitter of chandeliers and a mute gleam of gold frames, heard the swift feet and saw her too, a lady—perhaps he had never seen her like before either—in a gray, smooth gown with lace at the throat and an apron tied at the waist and the sleeves turned back, wiping cake or biscuit dough from her hands with a towel as she came up the hall, looking not at his father at all but at the tracks on the blond rug with an expression of incredulous amazement.

"I tried," the Negro cried. "I tole him to . . ."

"Will you please go away?" she said in a shaking voice. "Major de Spain is not at home. Will you please go away?"

His father had not spoken again. He did not speak again. He did not even look at her. He just stood stiff in the center of the rug, in his hat, the shaggy iron-gray brows twitching slightly above the pebble-colored eyes as he appeared to examine the house with brief deliberation. Then with the same deliberation he turned; the boy watched him pivot on the good leg and saw the stiff foot drag round the arc of the turning, leaving a final long and fading smear. His father never looked at it, he never once looked down at the rug. The Negro held the door. It closed behind them, upon the hysteric and indistinguishable woman-wail. His father stopped at the top of the steps and scraped his boot clean on the edge of it. At the gate he stopped again. He stood for a moment, planted stiffly on the stiff foot, looking back at the house. "Pretty and white, ain't it?" he said. "That's sweat. Nigger sweat. Maybe it ain't white enough yet to suit him. Maybe he wants to mix some white sweat with it."

Two hours later the boy was chopping wood behind the house within which his mother and aunt and the two sisters (the mother and aunt, not the two girls, he knew that; even at this distance and muffled by walls the flat loud voices of the two girls emanated an incorrigible idle inertia) were setting up the stove to prepare a meal, when he heard the hooves and saw the linen-clad man on a fine sorrel mare, whom he recognized even before he saw the rolled rug in front of the Negro youth following on a fat bay carriage horse—a suffused, angry face vanishing, still at full gallop, beyond the corner of the house where his father and brother were sitting in the two tilted chairs; and a moment later, almost before he could have put the axe down, he heard the hooves again and watched the sorrel mare go back out of the yard, already galloping again. Then his father began to shout one of the sisters' names, who presently emerged backward from the kitchen door dragging the rolled rug along the ground by one end while the other sister walked behind it.

"If you ain't going to tote, go on and set up the wash pot," the first said.

"You, Sarty!" the second shouted. "Set up the wash pot!" His father appeared at the door, framed against that shabbiness, as he had been against that other bland perfection, impervious to either, the mother's anxious face at his shoulder.

"Go on," the father said. "Pick it up." The two sisters stooped, broad, lethargic; stooping, they presented an incredible expanse of pale cloth and a flutter of tawdry ribbons.

"If I thought enough of a rug to have to git hit all the way from France I wouldn't keep hit where folks coming in would have to tromp on hit," the first said. They raised the rug.

"Abner," the mother said. "Let me do it."

"You go back and git dinner," his father said. "I'll tend to this."

From the woodpile through the rest of the afternoon the boy watched them, the rug spread flat in the dust beside the bubbling wash pot, the two sisters stooping over it with that profound and lethargic reluctance, while the father stood over them in turn, implacable and grim, driving them though never raising his voice again. He could smell the harsh homemade lye[4] they were using; he saw his mother come to the door once and look toward them with an expression not anxious now but very like despair; he saw his father turn, and he fell to with the axe and saw from the corner of his eye his father raise from the ground a flattish fragment of field stone and examine it and return to the pot, and this time his mother actually spoke: "Abner. Abner. Please don't. Please, Abner."

Then he was done too. It was dusk; the whippoorwills had already begun. He could smell coffee from the room where they would presently eat the cold food remaining from the mid-afternoon meal, though when he entered the house he realized they were having coffee again probably because there was a fire on the hearth, before which the rug now lay spread over the backs of the two chairs. The tracks of his father's foot were gone. Where they had been were now long, water-cloudy scoriations resembling the sporadic course of a Lilliputian mowing machine.

It still hung there while they ate the cold food and then went to bed, scattered without order or claim up and down the two rooms, his mother in one bed, where his father would later lie, the older brother in the other, himself, the aunt, and the two sisters on pallets on the floor. But his father was not in bed yet. The last thing the boy remembered was the depthless, harsh silhouette of the hat and coat bending over the rug and it seemed to him that he had not even closed his eyes when the silhouette was standing over him, the fire almost dead behind it, the stiff foot prodding him awake. "Catch up the mule," his father said.

When he returned with the mule his father was standing in the black door, the rolled rug over his shoulder. "Ain't you going to ride?" he said.

"No. Give me your foot."

He bent his knee into his father's hand, the wiry, surprising power flowed smoothly, rising, he rising with it, on to the mule's bare back (they had owned a saddle once; the boy could remember it though not when or where) and with the same effortlessness his father swung the rug up in front of him. Now in the starlight they retraced the afternoon's path, up the dusty road rife with honeysuckle, through the gate and up the black tunnel of the drive to the lightless house, where he sat on the mule and felt the rough warp of the rug drag across his thighs and vanish.

---

4. A caustic detergent, unsuitable for cleaning fine fabrics.

reluctance to accept help

"Don't you want me to help?" he whispered. His father did not answer and now he heard again that stiff foot striking the hollow portico with that wooden and clocklike deliberation, that outrageous overstatement of the weight it carried. The rug, hunched, not flung (the boy could tell that even in the darkness) from his father's shoulder struck the angle of wall and floor with a sound unbelievably loud, thunderous, then the foot again, unhurried and enormous; a light came on in the house and the boy sat, tense, breathing steadily and quietly and just a little fast, though the foot itself did not increase its beat at all, descending the steps now; now the boy could see him.

"Don't you want to ride now?" he whispered. "We kin both ride now," the light within the house altering now, flaring up and sinking. *He's coming down the stairs now,* he thought. He had already ridden the mule up beside the horse block; presently his father was up behind him and he doubled the reins over and slashed the mule across the neck, but before the animal could begin to trot the hard, thin arm came round him, the hard, knotted hand jerking the mule back to a walk.

In the first red rays of the sun they were in the lot, putting plow gear on the mules. This time the sorrel mare was in the lot before he heard it at all, the rider collarless and even bareheaded, trembling, speaking in a shaking voice as the woman in the house had done, his father merely looking up once before stooping again to the hame he was buckling, so that the man on the mare spoke to his stooping back:

"You must realize you have ruined that rug. Wasn't there anybody here, any of your women . . ." he ceased, shaking, the boy watching him, the older brother leaning now in the stable door, chewing, blinking slowly and steadily at nothing apparently. "It cost a hundred dollars. But you never had a hundred dollars. You never will. So I'm going to charge you twenty bushels of corn against your crop. I'll add it in your contract and when you come to the commissary you can sign it. That won't keep Mrs. de Spain quiet but maybe it will teach you to wipe your feet off before you enter her house again."

Then he was gone. The boy looked at his father, who still had not spoken or even looked up again, who was now adjusting the logger-head in the hame.

"Pap," he said. His father looked at him—the inscrutable face, the shaggy brows beneath which the gray eyes glinted coldly. Suddenly the boy went toward him, fast, stopping as suddenly. "You done the best you could!" he cried. "If he wanted hit done different why didn't he wait and tell you how? He won't git no twenty bushels! He won't git none! We'll gether hit and hide hit! I kin watch . . ."

"Did you put the cutter back in that straight stock like I told you?"

"No, sir," he said.

"Then go do it."

That was Wednesday. During the rest of that week he worked steadily, at what was within his scope and some which was beyond it, with an industry that did not need to be driven nor even commanded twice; he had this from his mother, with the difference that some at least of what he did he liked to do, such as splitting wood with the half-size axe which his mother and aunt had earned, or saved money somehow, to present him with at Christmas. In company with the two older women (and on one afternoon, even one of the sisters), he built pens for the shoat and the cow which were a part of his father's contract with the landlord, and one afternoon, his father being absent, gone somewhere on one of the mules, he went to the field.

They were running a middle buster[5] now, his brother holding the plow straight while he handled the reins, and walking beside the straining mule, the rich black soil shearing cool and damp against his bare ankles, he thought *Maybe this is the end of it. Maybe even that twenty bushels that seems hard to have to pay for just a rug will be a cheap price for him to stop forever and always from being what he used to be;* thinking, dreaming now, so that his brother had to speak sharply to him to mind the mule: *Maybe he even won't collect the twenty bushels. Maybe it will all add up and balance and vanish—corn, rug, fire; the terror and grief, the being pulled two ways like between two teams of horses—gone, done with for ever and ever.*

Then it was Saturday; he looked up from beneath the mule he was harnessing and saw his father in the black coat and hat. "Not that," his father said. "The wagon gear." And then, two hours later, sitting in the wagon bed behind his father and brother on the seat, the wagon accomplished a final curve, and he saw the weathered paintless store with its tattered tobacco- and patent-medicine posters and the tethered wagons and saddle animals below the gallery. He mounted the gnawed steps behind his father and brother, and there again was the lane of quiet, watching faces for the three of them to walk through. He saw the man in spectacles sitting at the plank table and he did not need to be told this was a Justice of the Peace; he sent one glare of fierce, exultant, partisan defiance at the man in collar and cravat now, whom he had seen but twice before in his life, and that on a galloping horse, who now wore on his face an expression not of rage but of amazed unbelief which the boy could not have known was at the incredible circumstance of being sued by one of his own tenants, and came and stood against his father and cried at the Justice: "He ain't done it! He ain't burnt . . ."

"Go back to the wagon," his father said.

"Burnt?" the Justice said. "Do I understand this rug was burned too?"

"Does anybody here claim it was?" his father said. "Go back to the wagon." But he did not, he merely retreated to the rear of the room, crowded as that other had been, but not to sit down this time, instead, to stand pressing among the motionless bodies, listening to the voices:

"And you claim twenty bushels of corn is too high for the damage you did to the rug?"

"He brought the rug to me and said he wanted the tracks washed out of it. I washed the tracks out and took the rug back to him."

"But you didn't carry the rug back to him in the same condition it was in before you made the tracks on it."

His father did not answer, and now for perhaps half a minute there was no sound at all save that of breathing, the faint, steady suspiration of complete and intent listening.

"You decline to answer that, Mr. Snopes?" Again his father did not answer. "I'm going to find against you, Mr. Snopes. I'm going to find that you were responsible for the injury to Major de Spain's rug and hold you liable for it. But twenty bushels of corn seems a little high for a man in your circumstances to have to pay. Major de Spain claims it cost a hundred dollars. October corn will

5. A plow that turns the soil to both sides of the blade.

be worth about fifty cents. I figure that if Major de Spain can stand a ninety-five dollar loss on something he paid cash for, you can stand a five-dollar loss you haven't earned yet. I hold you in damages to Major de Spain to the amount of ten bushels of corn over and above your contract with him, to be paid to him out of your crop at gathering time. Court adjourned."

It had taken no time hardly, the morning was but half begun. He thought they would return home and perhaps back to the field, since they were late, far behind all other farmers. But instead his father passed on behind the wagon, merely indicating with his hand for the older brother to follow with it, and crossed the road toward the blacksmith shop opposite, pressing on after his father, overtaking him, speaking, whispering up at the harsh, calm face beneath the weathered hat: "He won't git no ten bushels neither. He won't git one. We'll . . ." until his father glanced for an instant down at him, the face absolutely calm, the grizzled eyebrows tangled above the cold eyes, the voice almost pleasant, almost gentle:

"You think so? Well, we'll wait till October anyway."

The matter of the wagon—the setting of a spoke or two and the tightening of the tires—did not take long either, the business of the tires accomplished by driving the wagon into the spring branch behind the shop and letting it stand there, the mules nuzzling into the water from time to time, and the boy on the seat with the idle reins, looking up the slope and through the sooty tunnel of the shed where the slow hammer rang and where his father sat on an upended cypress bolt, easily, either talking or listening, still sitting there when the boy brought the dripping wagon up out of the branch and halted it before the door.

"Take them on to the shade and hitch," his father said. He did so and returned. His father and the smith and a third man squatting on his heels inside the door were talking, about crops and animals; the boy, squatting too in the ammoniac dust and hoof-parings and scales of rust, heard his father tell a long and unhurried story out of the time before the birth of the older brother even when he had been a professional horsetrader. And then his father came up beside him where he stood before a tattered last year's circus poster on the other side of the store, gazing rapt and quiet at the scarlet horses, the incredible poisings and convolutions of tulle and tights and the painted leers of comedians, and said, "It's time to eat."

But not at home. Squatting beside his brother against the front wall, he watched his father emerge from the store and produce from a paper sack a segment of cheese and divide it carefully and deliberately into three with his pocket knife and produce crackers from the same sack. They all three squatted on the gallery and ate, slowly, without talking; then in the store again, they drank from a tin dipper tepid water smelling of the cedar bucket and of living beech trees. And still they did not go home. It was a horse lot this time, a tall rail fence upon and along which men stood and sat and out of which one by one horses were led, to be walked and trotted and then cantered back and forth along the road while the slow swapping and buying went on and the sun began to slant westward, they—the three of them—watching and listening, the older brother with his muddy eyes and his steady, inevitable tobacco, the father commenting now and then on certain of the animals, to no one in particular.

It was after sundown when they reached home. They ate supper by lamp-light, then, sitting on the doorstep, the boy watched the night fully accomplish, listening to the whippoorwills and the frogs, when he heard his mother's voice: "Abner! No! No! Oh, God. Oh, God. Abner!" and he rose, whirled, and saw the altered light through the door where a candle stub now burned in a bottle neck on the table and his father, still in the hat and coat, at once formal and burlesque as though dressed carefully for some shabby and ceremonial violence, emptying the reservoir of the lamp back into the five-gallon kerosene can from which it had been filled, while the mother tugged at his arm until he shifted the lamp to the other hand and flung her back, not savagely or viciously, just hard, into the wall, her hands flung out against the wall for balance, her mouth open and in her face the same quality of hopeless despair as had been in her voice. Then his father saw him standing in the door.

"Go to the barn and get that can of oil we were oiling the wagon with," he said. The boy did not move. Then he could speak.

"What . . ." he cried. "What are you . . ."

"Go get that oil," his father said. "Go."

Then he was moving, running, outside the house, toward the stable: this the old habit, the old blood which he had not been permitted to choose for himself, which had been bequeathed him willy nilly and which had run for so long (and who knew where, battening on what of outrage and savagery and lust) before it came to him. *I could keep on,* he thought. *I could run on and on and never look back, never need to see his face again. Only I can't. I can't,* the rusted can in his hand now, the liquid sploshing in it as he ran back to the house and into it, into the sound of his mother's weeping in the next room, and handed the can to his father.

"Ain't you going to even send a nigger?" he cried. "At least you sent a nigger before!"

This time his father didn't strike him. The hand came even faster than the blow had, the same hand which had set the can on the table with almost excruciating care flashing from the can toward him too quick for him to follow it, gripping him by the back of his shirt and on to tiptoe before he had seen it quit the can, the face stooping at him in breathless and frozen ferocity, the cold, dead voice speaking over him to the older brother, who leaned against the table, chewing with that steady, curious, sidewise motion of cows:

"Empty the can into the big one and go on. I'll catch up with you."

"Better tie him up to the bedpost," the brother said.

"Do like I told you," the father said. Then the boy was moving, his bunched shirt and the hard, bony hand between his shoulder-blades, his toes just touching the floor, across the room and into the other one, past the sisters sitting with spread heavy thighs in the two chairs over the cold hearth, and to where his mother and aunt sat side by side on the bed, the aunt's arms about his mother's shoulders.

"Hold him," the father said. The aunt made a startled movement. "Not you," the father said. "Lennie. Take hold of him. I want to see you do it." His mother took him by the wrist. "You'll hold him better than that. If he gets loose don't you know what he is going to do? He will go up yonder." He jerked his head toward the road. "Maybe I'd better tie him."

"I'll hold him," his mother whispered.

"See you do then." Then his father was gone, the stiff foot heavy and measured upon the boards, ceasing at last.

Then he began to struggle. His mother caught him in both arms, he jerking and wrenching at them. He would be stronger in the end, he knew that. But he had no time to wait for it. "Lemme go!" he cried. "I don't want to have to hit you!"

"Let him go!" the aunt said. "If he don't go, before God, I am going up there myself!"

"Don't you see I can't?" his mother cried. "Sarty! Sarty! No! No! Help me, Lizzie!"

Then he was free. His aunt grasped at him but it was too late. He whirled, running, his mother stumbled forward on to her knees behind him, crying to the nearer sister: "Catch him, Net! Catch him!" But that was too late too, the sister (the sisters were twins, born at the same time, yet either of them now gave the impression of being, encompassing as much living meat and volume and weight as any other two of the family) not yet having begun to rise from the chair, her head, face, alone merely turned, presenting to him in the flying instant an astonishing expanse of young female features untroubled by any surprise even, wearing only an expression of bovine interest. Then he was out of the room, out of the house, in the mild dust of the starlit road and the heavy rifeness of honeysuckle, the pale ribbon unspooling with terrific slowness under his running feet, reaching the gate at last and turning in, running, his heart and lungs drumming, on up the drive toward the lighted house, the lighted door. He did not knock, he burst in, sobbing for breath, incapable for the moment of speech; he saw the astonished face of the Negro in the linen jacket without knowing when the Negro had appeared.

"De Spain!" he cried, panted. "Where's . . ." then he saw the white man too emerging from a white door down the hall. "Barn!" he cried. "Barn!"

"What?" the white man said. "Barn?"

"Yes!" the boy cried. "Barn!"

"Catch him!" the white man shouted.

But it was too late this time too. The Negro grasped his shirt, but the entire sleeve, rotten with washing, carried away, and he was out that door too and in the drive again, and had actually never ceased to run even while he was screaming into the white man's face.

Behind him the white man was shouting, "My horse! Fetch my horse!" and he thought for an instant of cutting across the park and climbing the fence into the road, but he did not know the park nor how high the vine-massed fence might be and he dared not risk it. So he ran on down the drive, blood and breath roaring; presently he was in the road again though he could not see it. He could not hear either: the galloping mare was almost upon him before he heard her, and even then he held his course, as if the very urgency of his wild grief and need must in a moment more find his wings, waiting until the ultimate instant to hurl himself aside and into the weed-choked roadside ditch as the horse thundered past and on, for an instant in furious silhouette against the stars, the tranquil early summer night sky which, even before the shape of the horse and rider vanished, stained abruptly and violently upward: a long, swirling roar incredible and soundless, blotting the stars, and he springing up and into the road again, running again, knowing it was too late yet still running even after he heard the shot and, an instant later, two shots, pausing now without knowing he had ceased to run, crying "Pap! Pap!", running again before he knew he had begun to run, stumbling, tripping over something and scrabbling up again without ceasing to run, looking backward over his shoulder at the glare as he got up, running on among the invisible trees, panting, sobbing, "Father! Father!"

At midnight he was sitting on the crest of a hill. He did not know it was midnight and he did not know how far he had come. But there was no glare behind him now and he sat now, his back toward what he had called home for four days anyhow, his face toward the dark woods which he would enter when breath was strong again, small, shaking steadily in the chill darkness, hugging himself into the remainder of his thin, rotten shirt, the grief and despair now no longer terror and fear but just grief and despair. *Father. My father,* he thought. "He was brave!" he cried suddenly, aloud but not loud, no more than a whisper: "He was! He was in the war! He was in Colonel Sartoris' cav'ry!" not knowing that his father had gone to that war a private in the fine old European sense, wearing no uniform, admitting the authority of and giving fidelity to no man or army or flag, going to war as Malbrouck[6] himself did: for booty—it meant nothing and less than nothing to him if it were enemy booty or his own.

The slow constellations wheeled on. It would be dawn and then sun-up after a while and he would be hungry. But that would be to-morrow and now he was only cold, and walking would cure that. His breathing was easier now and he decided to get up and go on, and then he found that he had been asleep because he knew it was almost dawn, the night almost over. He could tell that from the whippoorwills. They were everywhere now among the dark trees below him, constant and inflectioned and ceaseless, so that, as the instant for giving over to the day birds drew nearer and nearer, there was no interval at all between them. He got up. He was a little stiff, but walking would cure that too as it would the cold, and soon there would be the sun. He went on down the hill, toward the dark woods within which the liquid silver voices of the birds called unceasing—the rapid and urgent beating of the urgent and quiring heart of the late spring night. He did not look back.

1939

RELATED:

—Author in Depth: William Faulkner, p. 1800

---

6. The chief character in a popular and pervasive 18th-century nursery ditty about a legendary warrior. Originally, this warrior figure may have derived from the character and exploits of John Churchill (1650–1722), Duke of Marlborough.

F. SCOTT FITZGERALD
1896–1940

Fitzgerald was born in St. Paul, Minnesota. After a glamorous but abortive undergraduate career at Princeton, he entered the army as a second lieutenant and while he was in training camp met the beautiful young woman who was to become his wife. He married Zelda Sayre as his literary career got off to a meteoric start in 1920 with the publication of his first novel, *This Side of Paradise*. Through the 1920s, when money seemed plentiful and postwar morality encouraged a reckless pursuit of happiness, he and Zelda traveled with a well-heeled crowd in Europe and New York, acting out the glamorous lifestyle he wrote of in his popular magazine fiction. He was a spokesman for the so-called Jazz Age, setting a personal as well as a literary example for a generation whose first commandment was simply: Do what you will. The tempo of his life slackened as his marriage was shredded by Zelda's insanity and his own self-destructive alcoholism. He fell from literary favor when the indulgent decade of his triumph went down under the impact of the Great Depression. Through years of emotional and physical collapse he struggled to repair his life by writing for Hollywood—producing at the same time a series of stories that exposed his humiliations there. His novels: *The Great Gatsby* (1925), *Tender Is the Night* (1934), and *The Last Tycoon* (1941) amplify the melancholy he discovered beneath the glitter of American-style success. In his pathetically candid collection of essays and letters, *The Crack-up* (1945), Fitzgerald documents the shattering of his personal ambitions. His stories were collected in *Flappers and Philosophers* (1920), *Tales of the Jazz Age* (1922), *All the Sad Young Men* (1926), and *Taps at Reveille* (1935).

Babylon[1] Revisited

I

"And where's Mr. Campbell?" Charlie asked.

"Gone to Switzerland. Mr. Campbell's a pretty sick man, Mr. Wales."

"I'm sorry to hear that. And George Hardt?" Charlie inquired.

"Back in America, gone to work."

"And where is the Snow Bird?"

"He was in here last week. Anyway, his friend, Mr. Schaeffer, is in Paris."

---

1. This ancient city is a symbol of orgiastic decadence.

Two familiar names from the long list of a year and a half ago. Charlie scribbled an address in his notebook and tore out the page.

"If you see Mr. Schaeffer, give him this," he said. "It's my brother-in-law's address. I haven't settled on a hotel yet."

He was not really disappointed to find Paris was so empty. But the stillness in the Ritz bar[2] was strange and portentous. It was not an American bar any more—he felt polite in it, and not as if he owned it. It had gone back into France. He felt the stillness from the moment he got out of the taxi and saw the doorman, usually in a frenzy of activity at this hour, gossiping with a *chasseur*[3] by the servants' entrance.

Passing through the corridor, he heard only a single, bored voice in the once-clamorous women's room. When he turned into the bar he traveled the twenty feet of green carpet with his eyes fixed straight ahead by old habit; and then, with his foot firmly on the rail, he turned and surveyed the room, encountering only a single pair of eyes that fluttered up from a newspaper in the corner. Charlie asked for the head barman, Paul, who in the latter days of the bull market[4] had come to work in his own custom-built car—disembarking, however, with due nicety at the nearest corner. But Paul was at his country house today and Alix giving him information.

"No, no more," Charlie said, "I'm going slow these days."

Alix congratulated him: "You were going pretty strong a couple of years ago."

"I'll stick to it all right," Charlie assured him. "I've stuck to it for over a year and a half now."

"How do you find conditions in America?"

"I haven't been to America for months. I'm in business in Prague, representing a couple of concerns there. They don't know about me down there."

Alix smiled.

"Remember the night of George Hardt's bachelor dinner here?" said Charlie. "By the way, what's become of Claude Fessenden?"

Alix lowered his voice confidentially: "He's in Paris, but he doesn't come here anymore. Paul doesn't allow it. He ran up a bill of thirty thousand francs, charging all his drinks and his lunches, and usually his dinner, for more than a year. And when Paul finally told him he had to pay, he gave him a bad check."

Alix shook his head sadly.

"I don't understand it, such a dandy fellow. Now he's all bloated up—" He made a plump apple of his hands.

Charlie watched a group of strident queens installing themselves in a corner.

"Nothing affects them," he thought. "Stocks rise and fall, people loaf or work, but they go on forever." The place oppressed him. He called for the dice and shook with Alix for the drink.

"Here for long, Mr. Wales?"

"I'm here for four or five days to see my little girl."

"Oh-h! You have a little girl?"

Outside, the fire-red, gas-blue, ghost-green signs shone smokily through the tranquil rain. It was late afternoon and the streets were in movement; the *bistros*[5] gleamed. At the corner of the Boulevard des Capucines he took a taxi.

---

2. Hangout for wealthy and glamorous Americans.   **3.** Hotel servant who runs various errands (French).   **4.** The period of prosperity for players of the stock market that immediately preceded the crash of 1929, which was the beginning of the Great Depression.   **5.** Small cafés.

The Place de la Concorde moved by in pink majesty; they crossed the logical Seine, and Charlie felt the sudden provincial quality of the Left Bank.[6]

Charlie directed his taxi to the Avenue de l'Opéra, which was out of his way. But he wanted to see the blue hour spread over the magnificent façade, and imagine that the cab horns, playing endlessly the first few bars of *La Plus que Lent,* were the trumpets of the Second Empire.[7] They were closing the iron grill in front of Brentano's Book-store, and people were already at dinner behind the trim little bourgeois hedge of Duval's. He had never eaten at a really cheap restaurant in Paris. Five-course dinner, four francs fifty, eighteen cents, wine included. For some odd reason he wished that he had.

As they rolled on to the Left Bank and he felt its sudden provincialism, he thought, "I spoiled this city for myself. I didn't realize it, but the days came along one after another, and then two years were gone, and everything was gone, and I was gone."

He was thirty-five, and good to look at. The Irish mobility of his face was sobered by a deep wrinkle between his eyes. As he rang his brother-in-law's bell in the Rue Palatine, the wrinkle deepened till it pulled down his brows; he felt a cramping sensation in his belly. From behind the maid who opened the door darted a lovely little girl of nine who shrieked "Daddy!" and flew up, struggling like a fish, into his arms. She pulled his head around by one ear and set her cheek against his.

"My old pie," he said.

"Oh, daddy, daddy, daddy, daddy, dads, dads, dads!"

She drew him into the salon, where the family waited, a boy and a girl his daughter's age, his sister-in-law and her husband. He greeted Marion with his voice pitched carefully to avoid either feigned enthusiasm or dislike, but her response was more frankly tepid, though she minimized her expression of unalterable distrust by directing her regard toward his child. The two men clasped hands in a friendly way and Lincoln Peters rested his for a moment on Charlie's shoulder.

The room was warm and comfortably American. The three children moved intimately about, playing through the yellow oblongs that led to other rooms; the cheer of six o'clock spoke in the eager smacks of the fire and the sounds of French activity in the kitchen. But Charlie did not relax; his heart sat up rigidly in his body and he drew confidence from his daughter, who from time to time came close to him, holding in her arms the doll he had brought.

"Really extremely well," he declared in answer to Lincoln's question. "There's a lot of business there that isn't moving at all, but we're doing even better than ever. In fact, damn well. I'm bringing my sister over from America next month to keep house for me. My income last year was bigger than it was when I had money. You see, the Czechs—"

His boasting was for a specific purpose; but after a moment, seeing a faint restiveness in Lincoln's eye, he changed the subject:

"Those are fine children of yours, well brought up, good manners."

"We think Honoria's a great little girl too."

---

6. South side of the Seine River; site of the student quarter and in recent tradition the Bohemian part of Paris. **7.** That is, that of Louis-Napoléon of France (reign, 1852–70), a period of bourgeois ostentation, which seemed, in retrospect, glamorous. *La Plus que Lent:* slower than slow (French); refers to the parodistic piano composition (*La Plus que Lente*) by Claude Debussy (1862–1918).

Marion Peters came back from the kitchen. She was a tall woman with worried eyes, who had once possessed a fresh American loveliness. Charlie had never been sensitive to it and was always surprised when people spoke of how pretty she had been. From the first there had been an instinctive antipathy between them.

"Well, how do you find Honoria?" she asked.

"Wonderful. I was astonished how much she's grown in ten months. All the children are looking well."

"We haven't had a doctor for a year. How do you like being back in Paris?"

"It seems very funny to see so few Americans around."

"I'm delighted," Marion said vehemently. "Now at least you can go into a store without their assuming you're a millionaire. We've suffered like everybody, but on the whole it's a good deal pleasanter."

"But it was nice while it lasted," Charlie said. "We were a sort of royalty, almost infallible, with a sort of magic around us. In the bar this afternoon"—he stumbled, seeing his mistake—"there wasn't a man I knew."

She looked at him keenly. "I should think you'd have had enough of bars."

"I only stayed a minute. I take one drink every afternoon, and no more."

"Don't you want a cocktail before dinner?" Lincoln asked.

"I take only one drink every afternoon, and I've had that."

"I hope you keep to it," said Marion.

Her dislike was evident in the coldness with which she spoke, but Charlie only smiled; he had larger plans. Her very aggressiveness gave him an advantage, and he knew enough to wait. He wanted them to initiate the discussion of what they knew had brought him to Paris.

At dinner he couldn't decide whether Honoria was most like him or her mother. Fortunate if she didn't combine the traits of both that had brought them to disaster. A great wave of protectiveness went over him. He thought he knew what to do for her. He believed in character; he wanted to jump back a whole generation and trust in character again as the eternally valuable element. Everything else wore out.

He left soon after dinner, but not to go home. He was curious to see Paris by night with clearer and more judicious eyes than those of other days. He bought a *strapontin* for the Casino and watched Josephine Baker[8] go through her chocolate arabesques.

After an hour he left and strolled toward Montmartre, up the Rue Pigalle into the Place Blanche. The rain had stopped and there were a few people in evening clothes disembarking from taxis in front of cabarets, and *cocottes*[9] prowling singly or in pairs, and many Negroes. He passed a lighted door from which issued music, and stopped with the sense of familiarity; it was Bricktop's, where he had parted with so many hours and so much money. A few doors farther on he found another ancient rendezvous and incautiously put his head inside. Immediately an eager orchestra burst into sound, a pair of professional dancers leaped to their feet and a maître d'hôtel swooped toward him, crying, "Crowd just arriving, sir!" But he withdrew quickly.

"You have to be damn drunk," he thought.

8. A celebrated African American dancer of the epoch. *Strapontin:* a bracket seat in the aisle, cheaper than regular seats.   **9.** Prostitutes who flourish on the Boulevard Clichy between Pigalle and the Place Blanche. Montmartre is a district in northern Paris.

Zelli's was closed, the bleak and sinister cheap hotels surrounding it were dark; up in the Rue Blanche there was more light and a local, colloquial French crowd. The Poet's Cave had disappeared, but the two great mouths of the Café of Heaven and the Café of Hell still yawned—even devoured, as he watched, the meager contents of a tourist bus—a German, a Japanese, and an American couple who glanced at him with frightened eyes.

So much for the effort and ingenuity of Montmartre. All the catering to vice and waste was on an utterly childish scale, and he suddenly realized the meaning of the word "dissipate"—to dissipate into thin air; to make nothing out of something. In the little hours of the night every move from place to place was an enormous human jump, an increase of paying for the privilege of slower and slower motion.

He remembered thousand-franc notes given to an orchestra for playing a single number, hundred-franc notes tossed to a doorman for calling a cab.

But it hadn't been given for nothing.

It had been given, even the most wildly squandered sum, as an offering to destiny that he might not remember the things most worth remembering, the things that now he would always remember—his child taken from his control, his wife escaped to a grave in Vermont.

In the glare of a *brasserie*[1] a woman spoke to him. He bought her some eggs and coffee, and then, eluding her encouraging stare, gave her a twenty-franc note and took a taxi to his hotel.

II

He woke upon a fine fall day—football weather. The depression of yesterday was gone and he liked the people on the streets. At noon he sat opposite Honoria at Le Grand Vatel, the only restaurant he could think of not reminiscent of champagne dinners and long luncheons that began at two and ended in a blurred and vague twilight.

"Now, how about vegetables? Oughtn't you to have some vegetables?"

"Well, yes."

"Here's *épinards* and *chou-fleur* and carrots and *haricots*."[2]

"I'd like *chou-fleur*."

"Wouldn't you like to have two vegetables?"

"I usually only have one at lunch."

The waiter was pretending to be inordinately fond of children. *"Qu'elle est mignonne la petite! Elle parle exactement comme une Française."*[3]

"How about dessert? Shall we wait and see?"

The waiter disappeared. Honoria looked at her father expectantly.

"What are we going to do?"

"First, we're going to that toy store in the Rue Saint-Honoré and buy you anything you like. And then we're going to the vaudeville at the Empire."

She hesitated. "I like it about the vaudeville, but not the toy store."

"Why not?"

---

1. Small restaurant (French) that also serves drinks. 2. *Haricots:* beans (French). *Épinards:* spinach (French). *Chou-fleur:* cauliflower (French). 3. "What a darling little girl! She speaks exactly like a French girl" (French).

"Well, you brought me this doll." She had it with her. "And I've got lots of things. And we're not rich anymore, are we?"

"We never were. But today you are to have anything you want."

"All right," she agreed resignedly.

When there had been her mother and a French nurse he had been inclined to be strict; now he extended himself, reached out for a new tolerance; he must be both parents to her and not shut any of her out of communication.

"I want to get to know you," he said gravely. "First let me introduce myself. My name is Charles J. Wales, of Prague."

"Oh, daddy!" her voice cracked with laughter.

"And who are you, please?" he persisted, and she accepted a rôle immediately: "Honoria Wales, Rue Palatine, Paris."

"Married or single?"

"No, not married. Single."

He indicated the doll. "But I see you have a child, madame."

Unwilling to disinherit it, she took it to her heart and thought quickly: "Yes, I've been married, but I'm not married now. My husband is dead."

He went on quickly, "And the child's name?"

"Simone. That's after my best friend at school."

"I'm very pleased that you're doing so well at school."

"I'm third this month," she boasted. "Elsie"—that was her cousin—"is only about eighteenth, and Richard is about at the bottom."

"You like Richard and Elsie, don't you?"

"Oh, yes. I like Richard quite well and I like her all right."

Cautiously and casually he asked: "And Aunt Marion and Uncle Lincoln—which do you like best?"

"Oh, Uncle Lincoln, I guess."

He was increasingly aware of her presence. As they came in, a murmur of "... adorable" followed them, and now the people at the next table bent all their silences upon her, staring as if she were something no more conscious than a flower.

"Why don't I live with you?" she asked suddenly. "Because mamma's dead?"

"You must stay here and learn more French. It would have been hard for daddy to take care of you so well."

"I don't really need much taking care of anymore. I do everything for myself."

Going out of the restaurant, a man and a woman unexpectedly hailed him.

"Well, the old Wales!"

"Hello there, Lorraine. . . . Dunc."

Sudden ghosts out of the past: Duncan Schaeffer, a friend from college. Lorraine Quarrles, a lovely, pale blonde of thirty; one of a crowd who had helped them make months into days in the lavish times of three years ago.

"My husband couldn't come this year," she said, in answer to his question. "We're poor as hell. So he gave me two hundred a month and told me I could do my worst on that. . . . This your little girl?"

"What about coming back and sitting down?" Duncan asked.

"Can't do it." He was glad for an excuse. As always, he felt Lorraine's passionate, provocative attraction, but his own rhythm was different now.

"Well, how about dinner?" she asked.

"I'm not free. Give me your address and let me call you."

"Charlie, I believe you're sober," she said judicially. "I honestly believe he's sober, Dunc. Pinch him and see if he's sober."

Charlie indicated Honoria with his head. They both laughed.

"What's your address?" said Duncan skeptically.

He hesitated, unwilling to give the name of his hotel.

"I'm not settled yet. I'd better call you. We're going to see the vaudeville at the Empire."

"There! That's what I want to do," Lorraine said. "I want to see some clowns and acrobats and jugglers. That's just what we'll do, Dunc."

"We've got to do an errand first," said Charlie. "Perhaps we'll see you there."

"All right, you snot. . . . Good-by, beautiful little girl."

"Good-by."

Honoria bobbed politely.

Somehow, an unwelcome encounter. They liked him because he was functioning, because he was serious; they wanted to see him, because he was stronger than they were now, because they wanted to draw a certain sustenance from his strength.

At the Empire, Honoria proudly refused to sit upon her father's folded coat. She was already an individual with a code of her own, and Charlie was more and more absorbed by the desire of putting a little of himself into her before she crystallized utterly. It was hopeless to try to know her in so short a time.

Between the acts they came upon Duncan and Lorraine in the lobby where the band was playing.

"Have a drink?"

"All right, but not up at the bar. We'll take a table."

"The perfect father."

Listening abstractedly to Lorraine, Charlie watched Honoria's eyes leave their table, and he followed them wistfully about the room, wondering what they saw. He met her glance and she smiled.

"I liked that lemonade," she said.

What had she said? What had he expected? Going home in a taxi afterward, he pulled her over until her head rested against his chest.

"Darling, do you ever think about your mother?"

"Yes, sometimes," she answered vaguely.

"I don't want you to forget her. Have you got a picture of her?"

"Yes, I think so. Anyhow, Aunt Marion has. Why don't you want me to forget her?"

"She loved you very much."

"I loved her too."

They were silent for a moment.

"Daddy, I want to come and live with you," she said suddenly.

His heart leaped; he had wanted it to come like this.

"Aren't you perfectly happy?"

"Yes, but I love you better than anybody. And you love me better than anybody, don't you, now that mummy's dead?"

"Of course I do. But you won't always like me best, honey. You'll grow up and meet somebody your own age and go marry him and forget you ever had a daddy."

"Yes, that's true," she agreed tranquilly.

He didn't go in. He was coming back at nine o'clock and he wanted to keep himself fresh and new for the thing he must say then.

"When you're safe inside, just show yourself in that window."

"All right. Good-by, dads, dads, dads, dads."

He waited in the dark street until she appeared, all warm and glowing, in the window above and kissed her fingers out into the night.

III

They were waiting. Marion sat behind the coffee service in a dignified black dinner dress that just faintly suggested mourning. Lincoln was walking up and down with the animation of one who had already been talking. They were as anxious as he was to get into the question. He opened it almost immediately:

"I suppose you know what I want to see you about—why I really came to Paris."

Marion played with the black stars on her necklace and frowned.

"I'm awfully anxious to have a home," he continued. "And I'm awfully anxious to have Honoria in it. I appreciate your taking in Honoria for her mother's sake, but things have changed now"—he hesitated and then continued more forcibly—"changed radically with me, and I want to ask you to reconsider the matter. It would be silly for me to deny that about three years ago I was acting badly—"

Marion looked up at him with hard eyes.

"—but all that's over. As I told you, I haven't had more than a drink a day for over a year, and I take that drink deliberately, so that the idea of alcohol won't get too big in my imagination. You see the idea?"

"No," said Marion succinctly.

"It's a sort of stunt I set myself. It keeps the matter in proportion."

"I get you," said Lincoln. "You don't want to admit it's got any attraction for you."

"Something like that. Sometimes I forget and don't take it. But I try to take it. Anyhow, I couldn't afford to drink in my position. The people I represent are more than satisfied with what I've done, and I'm bringing my sister over from Burlington to keep house for me, and I want awfully to have Honoria too. You know that even when her mother and I weren't getting along well we never let anything that happened touch Honoria. I know she's fond of me and I know I'm able to take care of her and—well, there you are. How do you feel about it?"

He knew that now he would have to take a beating. It would last an hour or two hours, and it would be difficult, but if he modulated his inevitable resentment to the chastened attitude of the reformed sinner, he might win his point in the end.

Keep your temper, he told himself. You don't want to be justified. You want Honoria.

Lincoln spoke first: "We've been talking it over ever since we got your letter last month. We're happy to have Honoria here. She's a dear little thing, and we're glad to be able to help her, but of course that isn't the question—"

Marion interrupted suddenly. "How long are you going to stay sober, Charlie?" she asked.

"Permanently, I hope."

"How can anybody count on that?"

"You know I never did drink heavily until I gave up business and came over here with nothing to do. Then Helen and I began to run around with——"

"Please leave Helen out of it. I can't bear to hear you talk about her like that."

He stared at her grimly; he had never been certain how fond of each other the sisters were in life.

"My drinking only lasted about a year and a half—from the time we came over until I—collapsed."

"It was time enough."

"It was time enough," he agreed.

"My duty is entirely to Helen," she said. "I try to think what she would have wanted me to do. Frankly, from the night you did that terrible thing you haven't really existed for me. I can't help that. She was my sister."

"Yes."

"When she was dying she asked me to look out for Honoria. If you hadn't been in a sanitarium then, it might have helped matters."

He had no answer.

"I'll never in my life be able to forget the morning when Helen knocked at my door, soaked to the skin and shivering, and said you'd locked her out."

Charlie gripped the sides of the chair. This was more difficult than he expected; he wanted to launch out into a long expostulation and explanation, but he only said: "The night I locked her out—" and she interrupted, "I don't feel up to going over that again."

After a moment's silence Lincoln said: "We're getting off the subject. You want Marion to set aside her legal guardianship and give you Honoria. I think the main point for her is whether she has confidence in you or not."

"I don't blame Marion," Charlie said slowly, "but I think she can have entire confidence in me. I had a good record up to three years ago. Of course, it's within human possibilities I might go wrong any time. But if we wait much longer I'll lose Honoria's childhood and my chance for a home." He shook his head, "I'll simply lose her, don't you see?"

"Yes, I see," said Lincoln.

"Why didn't you think of all this before?" Marion asked.

"I suppose I did, from time to time, but Helen and I were getting along badly. When I consented to the guardianship, I was flat on my back in a sanitarium and the market had cleaned me out. I knew I'd acted badly, and I thought if it would bring any peace to Helen, I'd agree to anything. But now it's different. I'm functioning, I'm behaving damn well, so far as—"

"Please don't swear at me," Marion said.

He looked at her, startled. With each remark the force of her dislike became more and more apparent. She had built up all her fear of life into one wall and faced it toward him. This trivial reproof was possibly the result of some trouble with the cook several hours before. Charlie became increasingly alarmed at leaving Honoria in this atmosphere of hostility against himself; sooner or later it would come out, in a word here, a shake of the head there, and some of that distrust would be irrevocably implanted in Honoria. But he pulled his temper down out of his face and shut it up inside him; he had won a point, for Lincoln realized the absurdity of Marion's remark and asked her lightly since when she had objected to the word "damn."

"Another thing," Charlie said: "I'm able to give her certain advantages now. I'm going to take a French governess to Prague with me. I've got a lease on a new apartment——"

He stopped, realizing that he was blundering. They couldn't be expected to accept with equanimity the fact that his income was again twice as large as their own.

"I suppose you can give her more luxuries than we can," said Marion. "When you were throwing away money we were living along watching every ten francs. . . . I suppose you'll start doing it again."

"Oh, no," he said. "I've learned. I worked hard for ten years, you know—until I got lucky in the market, like so many people. Terribly lucky. It won't happen again."

There was a long silence. All of them felt their nerves straining, and for the first time in a year Charlie wanted a drink. He was sure now that Lincoln Peters wanted him to have his child.

Marion shuddered suddenly; part of her saw that Charlie's feet were planted on the earth now, and her own maternal feeling recognized the naturalness of his desire; but she had lived for a long time with a prejudice—a prejudice founded on a curious disbelief in her sister's happiness, and which, in the shock of one terrible night, had turned to hatred for him. It had all happened at a point in her life where the discouragement of ill health and adverse circumstances made it necessary for her to believe in tangible villainy and a tangible villain.

"I can't help what I think!" she cried out suddenly. "How much you were responsible for Helen's death, I don't know. It's something you'll have to square with your own conscience."

An electric current of agony surged through him; for a moment he was almost on his feet, an unuttered sound echoing in his throat. He hung on to himself for a moment, another moment.

"Hold on there," said Lincoln uncomfortably. "I never thought you were responsible for that."

"Helen died of heart trouble," Charlie said dully.

"Yes, heart trouble." Marion spoke as if the phrase had another meaning for her.

Then, in the flatness that followed her outburst, she saw him plainly and she knew he had somehow arrived at control over the situation. Glancing at her husband, she found no help from him, and as abruptly as if it were a matter of no importance, she threw up the sponge.

"Do what you like!" she cried, springing up from her chair. "She's your child. I'm not the person to stand in your way. I think if it were my child I'd rather see her—" She managed to check herself. "You two decide it. I can't stand this. I'm sick. I'm going to bed."

She hurried from the room; after a moment Lincoln said:

"This has been a hard day for her. You know how strongly she feels—" His voice was almost apologetic: "When a woman gets an idea in her head."

"Of course."

"It's going to be all right. I think she sees now that you—can provide for the child, and so we can't very well stand in your way or Honoria's way."

"Thank you, Lincoln."

"I'd better go along and see how she is."

"I'm going."

He was still trembling when he reached the street, but a walk down the Rue Bonaparte to the *quais*[4] set him up, and as he crossed the Seine, fresh and new by the *quai* lamps, he felt exultant. But back in his room he couldn't sleep. The image of Helen haunted him. Helen whom he had loved so until they had senselessly begun to abuse each other's love, tear it into shreds. On that terrible February night that Marion remembered so vividly, a slow quarrel had gone on for hours. There was a scene at the Florida, and then he attempted to take her home, and then she kissed young Webb at a table; after that there was what she had hysterically said. When he arrived home alone he turned the key in the lock in wild anger. How could he know she would arrive an hour later alone, that there would be a snowstorm in which she wandered about in slippers, too confused to find a taxi? Then the aftermath, her escaping pneumonia by a miracle, and all the attendant horror. They were "reconciled," but that was the beginning of the end, and Marion, who had seen with her own eyes and who imagined it to be one of many scenes from her sister's martyrdom, never forgot.

Going over it again brought Helen nearer, and in the white, soft light that steals upon half sleep near morning he found himself talking to her again. She said that he was perfectly right about Honoria and that she wanted Honoria to be with him. She said she was glad he was being good and doing better. She said a lot of other things—very friendly things—but she was in a swing in a white dress, and swinging faster and faster all the time, so that at the end he could not hear clearly all that she said.

IV

He woke up feeling happy. The door of the world was open again. He made plans, vistas, futures for Honoria and himself, but suddenly he grew sad, remembering all the plans he and Helen had made. She had not planned to die. The present was the thing—work to do and someone to love. But not to love too much, for he knew the injury that a father can do to a daughter or a mother to a son by attaching them too closely: afterward, out in the world, the child would seek in the marriage partner the same blind tenderness and, failing probably to find it, turn against love and life.

It was another bright, crisp day. He called Lincoln Peters at the bank where he worked and asked if he could count on taking Honoria when he left for Prague. Lincoln agreed that there was no reason for delay. One thing—the legal guardianship. Marion wanted to retain that a while longer. She was upset by the whole matter, and it would oil things if she felt that the situation was still in her control for another year. Charlie agreed, wanting only the tangible, visible child.

4. Paved riverbanks (French).

Then the question of a governess. Charles sat in a gloomy agency and talked to a cross Béarnaise and to a buxom Breton[5] peasant, neither of whom he could have endured. There were others whom he would see tomorrow.

He lunched with Lincoln Peters at Griffons, trying to keep down his exultation.

"There's nothing quite like your own child," Lincoln said. "But you understand how Marion feels too."

"She's forgotten how hard I worked for seven years there," Charlie said. "She just remembers one night."

"There's another thing." Lincoln hesitated. "While you and Helen were tearing around Europe throwing money away, we were just getting along. I didn't touch any of the prosperity because I never got ahead enough to carry anything but my insurance. I think Marion felt there was some kind of injustice in it—you not even working toward the end, and getting richer and richer."

"It went just as quick as it came," said Charlie.

"Yes, a lot of it stayed in the hands of *chasseurs* and saxophone players and maîtres d'hôtel—well, the big party's over now. I just said that to explain Marion's feeling about those crazy years. If you drop in about six o'clock tonight before Marion's too tired, we'll settle the details on the spot."

Back at his hotel, Charlie found a *pneumatique*[6] that had been redirected from the Ritz bar where Charlie had left his address for the purpose of finding a certain man.

> DEAR CHARLIE: You were so strange when we saw you the other day that I wondered if I did something to offend you. If so, I'm not conscious of it. In fact, I have thought about you too much for the last year, and it's always been in the back of my mind that I might see you if I came over here. We *did* have such good times that crazy spring, like the night you and I stole the butcher's tricycle, and the time we tried to call on the president and you had the old derby rim and the wire cane. Everybody seems so old lately, but I don't feel old a bit. Couldn't we get together some time today for old time's sake? I've got a vile hang-over for the moment, but will be feeling better this afternoon and will look for you about five in the sweatshop at the Ritz.
>
> Always devotedly,
> Lorraine

His first feeling was one of awe that he had actually, in his mature years, stolen a tricycle and pedaled Lorraine all over the Étoile[7] between the small hours and dawn. In retrospect it was a nightmare. Locking out Helen didn't fit in with any other act of his life, but the tricycle incident did—it was one of many. How many weeks or months of dissipation to arrive at that condition of utter irresponsibility?

He tried to picture how Lorraine had appeared to him then—very attractive; Helen was unhappy about it, though she said nothing. Yesterday, in the

---

5. Native of Brittany, in northwestern France. *Béarnaise:* native of Béarn, in southwestern France. **6.** Message delivered speedily via a system of pneumatic tubes (French). **7.** Intersection of twelve streets at the northwestern end of the Champs-Élysees, forming a "star" (*étoile*).

restaurant, Lorraine had seemed trite, blurred, worn away. He emphatically did not want to see her, and he was glad Alix had not given away his hotel address. It was a relief to think, instead, of Honoria, to think of Sundays spent with her and of saying good morning to her and of knowing she was there in his house at night, drawing her breath in the darkness.

At five he took a taxi and bought presents for all the Peters—a piquant cloth doll, a box of Roman soldiers, flowers for Marion, big linen handkerchiefs for Lincoln.

He saw, when he arrived in the apartment, that Marion had accepted the inevitable. She greeted him now as though he were a recalcitrant member of the family, rather than a menacing outsider. Honoria had been told she was going; Charlie was glad to see that her tact made her conceal her excessive happiness. Only on his lap did she whisper her delight and the question "When?" before she slipped away with the other children.

He and Marion were alone for a minute in the room, and on an impulse he spoke out boldly:

"Family quarrels are bitter things. They don't go according to any rules. They're not like aches or wounds; they're more like splits in the skin that won't heal because there's not enough material. I wish you and I could be on better terms."

"Some things are hard to forget," she answered. "It's a question of confidence." There was no answer to this and presently she asked, "When do you propose to take her?"

"As soon as I can get a governess. I hoped the day after tomorrow."

"That's impossible. I've got to get her things in shape. Not before Saturday."

He yielded. Coming back into the room, Lincoln offered him a drink.

"I'll take my daily whisky," he said.

It was warm here, it was a home, people together by a fire. The children felt very safe and important; the mother and father were serious, watchful. They had things to do for the children more important than his visit here. A spoonful of medicine was, after all, more important than the strained relations between Marion and himself. They were not dull people, but they were very much in the grip of life and circumstances. He wondered if he couldn't do something to get Lincoln out of his rut at the bank.

A long peal at the door-bell; the *bonne à tout faire*[8] passed through and went down the corridor. The door opened upon another long ring, and then voices, and the three in the salon looked up expectantly; Richard moved to bring the corridor within his range of vision, and Marion rose. Then the maid came back along the corridor, closely followed by the voices, which developed under the light into Duncan Schaeffer and Lorraine Quarrles.

They were gay, they were hilarious, they were roaring with laughter. For a moment Charlie was astounded; unable to understand how they ferreted out the Peters' address.

"Ah-h-h!" Duncan wagged his finger roguishly at Charlie. "Ah-h-h!"

They both slid down another cascade of laughter. Anxious and at a loss, Charlie shook hands with them quickly and presented them to Lincoln and Marion. Marion nodded, scarcely speaking. She had drawn back a step toward

8. Maid of all work (French).

the fire; her little girl stood beside her, and Marion put an arm about her shoulder.

With growing annoyance at the intrusion, Charlie waited for them to explain themselves. After some concentration Duncan said:

"We came to invite you out to dinner. Lorraine and I insist that all this shishi, cagy business 'bout your address got to stop."

Charlie came closer to them, as if to force them backward down the corridor.

"Sorry, but I can't. Tell me where you'll be and I'll phone you in half an hour."

This made no impression. Lorraine sat down suddenly on the side of a chair, and focusing her eyes on Richard, cried, "Oh, what a nice little boy! Come here, little boy." Richard glanced at his mother, but did not move. With a perceptible shrug of her shoulders, Lorraine turned back to Charlie:

"Come and dine. Sure your cousins won' mine. See you so sel'om. Or solemn."

"I can't," said Charlie sharply. "You two have dinner and I'll phone you."

Her voice became suddenly unpleasant. "All right, we'll go. But I remember once when you hammered on my door at four A.M. I was enough of a good sport to give you a drink. Come on, Dunc."

Still in slow motion, with blurred, angry faces, with uncertain feet, they retired along the corridor.

"Good night," Charlie said.

"Good night!" responded Lorraine emphatically.

When he went back into the salon Marion had not moved, only now her son was standing in the circle of her other arm. Lincoln was still swinging Honoria back and forth like a pendulum from side to side.

"What an outrage!" Charlie broke out. "What an absolute outrage!"

Neither of them answered. Charlie dropped into an armchair, picked up his drink, set it down again and said:

"People I haven't seen for two years having the colossal nerve——"

He broke off. Marion had made the sound "Oh!" in one swift, furious breath, turned her body from him with a jerk and left the room.

Lincoln set down Honoria carefully.

"You children go in and start your soup," he said, and when they obeyed, he said to Charlie:

"Marion's not well and she can't stand shocks. That kind of people make her really physically sick."

"I didn't tell them to come here. They wormed your name out of somebody. They deliberately——"

"Well, it's too bad. It doesn't help matters. Excuse me a minute."

Left alone, Charlie sat tense in his chair. In the next room he could hear the children eating, talking in monosyllables, already oblivious to the scene between their elders. He heard a murmur of conversation from a farther room and then the ticking bell of a telephone receiver picked up, and in a panic he moved to the other side of the room and out of earshot.

In a minute Lincoln came back. "Look here, Charlie. I think we'd better call off dinner for tonight. Marion's in bad shape."

"Is she angry with me?"

"Sort of," he said, almost roughly. "She's not strong and—"

"You mean she's changed her mind about Honoria?"

"She's pretty bitter right now. I don't know. You phone me at the bank tomorrow."

"I wish you'd explain to her I never dreamed these people would come here. I'm just as sore as you are."

"I couldn't explain anything to her now."

Charlie got up. He took his coat and hat and started down the corridor. Then he opened the door of the dining room and said in a strange voice, "Good night, children."

Honoria rose and ran around the table to hug him.

"Good night, sweetheart," he said vaguely, and then trying to make his voice more tender, trying to conciliate something, "Good night, dear children."

V

Charlie went directly to the Ritz bar with the furious idea of finding Lorraine and Duncan, but they were not there, and he realized that in any case there was nothing he could do. He had not touched his drink at the Peters', and now he ordered a whisky-and-soda. Paul came over to say hello.

"It's a great change," he said sadly. "We do about half the business we did. So many fellows I hear about back in the States lost everything, maybe not in the first crash, but then in the second. Your friend George Hardt lost every cent, I hear. Are you back in the States?"

"No, I'm in business in Prague."

"I heard that you lost a lot in the crash."

"I did," and he added grimly, "but I lost everything I wanted in the boom."

"Selling short."[9]

"Something like that."

Again the memory of those days swept over him like a nightmare—the people they had met travelling; then people who couldn't add a row of figures or speak a coherent sentence. The little man Helen had consented to dance with at the ship's party, who had insulted her ten feet from the table; the women and girls carried screaming with drink or drugs out of public places——

—The men who locked their wives out in the snow, because the snow of twenty-nine wasn't real snow. If you didn't want it to be snow, you just paid some money.

He went to the phone and called the Peters' apartment; Lincoln answered.

"I called up because this thing is on my mind. Has Marion said anything definite?"

"Marion's sick," Lincoln answered shortly. "I know this thing isn't altogether your fault, but I can't have her go to pieces about it. I'm afraid we'll have to let it slide for six months; I can't take the chance of working her up to this state again."

"I see."

"I'm sorry, Charlie."

---

9. Selling securities, in anticipation of falling prices, that the seller does not actually possess at the time of sale.

He went back to his table. His whisky glass was empty, but he shook his head when Alix looked at it questioningly. There wasn't much he could do now except send Honoria some things; he would send her a lot of things tomorrow. He thought rather angrily that this was just money—he had given so many people money. . . .

"No, no more," he said to another waiter. "What do I owe you?"

He would come back some day; they couldn't make him pay forever. But he wanted his child, and nothing was much good now, beside that fact. He wasn't young anymore, with a lot of nice thoughts and dreams to have by himself. He was absolutely sure Helen wouldn't have wanted him to be so alone.

1935

RICHARD FORD
b. 1944

Ford was born in Jackson, Mississippi. After a boyhood in Arkansas, he attended Michigan State University, the University of California, and Washington University Law School in St. Louis. He has traveled in the fast lane of American letters since he began to publish stories in *Esquire*, *The New Yorker*, and *Granta*. For these he has received Guggenheim and National Endowment for the Arts grants, and his reputation puts him in the top rank of contemporary writers. His novels are *A Piece of My Heart* (1976), *The Ultimate Good Luck* (1981), *The Sportswriter* (1986), *Wildlife* (1990), the Pulitzer Prize–winning *Independence Day* (1995), and *Canada* (2012). His stories can be found in *Rock Springs* (1987), *Women with Men* (1997), *A Multitude of Sins* (2002), and *Vintage Ford* (2004).

Great Falls

This is not a happy story. I warn you.

My father was a man named Jack Russell, and when I was a young boy in my early teens, we lived with my mother in a house to the east of Great Falls, Montana, near the small town of Highwood and the Highwood Mountains and the Missouri River. It is a flat, treeless benchland there, all of it used for wheat farming, though my father was never a farmer, but was brought up near Tacoma, Washington, in a family that worked for Boeing.

He—my father—had been an Air Force sergeant and had taken his discharge in Great Falls. And instead of going home to Tacoma, where my mother wanted to go, he had taken a civilian's job with the Air Force, working on planes, which was what he liked to do. And he had rented the house out of town from a farmer who did not want it left standing empty.

The house itself is gone now—I have been to the spot. But the double row of Russian olive trees and two of the outbuildings are still standing in the milkweeds. It was a plain, two-story house with a porch on the front and no place for the cars. At the time, I rode the school bus to Great Falls every morning, and my father drove in while my mother stayed home.

My mother was a tall pretty woman, thin, with black hair and slightly sharp features that made her seem to smile when she wasn't smiling. She had grown up in Wallace, Idaho, and gone to college a year in Spokane, then moved out to the coast, which is where she met Jack Russell. She was two years older than he was, and married him, she said to me, because he was young and wonderful looking, and because she thought they could leave the sticks and see the world together—which I suppose they did for a while. That was the life she wanted, even before she knew much about wanting anything else or about the future.

When my father wasn't working on airplanes, he was going hunting or fishing, two things he could do as well as anyone. He had learned to fish, he said, in Iceland, and to hunt ducks up on the DEW[1] line—stations he had visited in the Air Force. And during the time of this—it was 1960—he began to take me with him on what he called his "expeditions." I thought even then, with as little as I knew, that these were opportunities other boys would dream of having but probably never would. And I don't think that I was wrong in that.

It is a true thing that my father did not know limits. In the spring, when we would go east to the Judith River Basin and camp up on the banks, he would catch a hundred fish in a weekend, and sometimes more than that. It was all he did from morning until night, and it was never hard for him. He used yellow corn kernels stacked onto a #4 snelled hook, and he would rattle this rig-up along the bottom of a deep pool below a split-shot sinker, and catch fish. And most of the time, because he knew the Judith River and knew how to feel his bait down deep, he would catch fish of good size.

It was the same with ducks, the other thing he liked. When the northern birds were down, usually by mid-October, he would take me and we would build a cattail and wheat-straw blind on one of the tule ponds or sloughs he knew about down the Missouri, where the water was shallow enough to wade. We would set out his decoys to the leeward side of our blind, and he would sprinkle corn on a hunger-line from the decoys to where we were. In the evenings when he came home from the base, we would go and sit out in the blind until the roosting flights came and put down among the decoys—there was never calling involved. And after a while, sometimes it would be an hour and full dark, the ducks would find the corn, and the whole raft of them—sixty, sometimes—would swim in to us. At the moment he judged they were close enough, my father would say to me, "Shine, Jackie," and I would stand and shine a seal-beam car light out onto the pond, and he would stand up beside me and shoot all the ducks that were there, on the water if he could, but flying and getting up as well. He owned a Model 11 Remington with a long-tube magazine that would hold ten shells, and with that many, and shooting straight over the surface rather than down onto it, he could kill or wound thirty ducks in twenty seconds' time. I remember distinctly the report of that gun and the flash of it over the water into the dark air, one shot after another, not even so fast, but measured in a way to hit as many as he could.

What my father did with the ducks he killed, and the fish, too, was sell them. It was against the law then to sell wild game, and it is against the law now. And though he kept some for us, most he would take—his fish laid on ice, or his ducks still wet and bagged in the burlap corn sacks—down to the Great Northern Hotel, which was still open then on Second Street in Great Falls, and sell them to the Negro caterer who bought them for his wealthy customers and for the dining car passengers who came through. We would drive in

---

1. The Distant Early Warning line, a system of radar installations established by the United States in northern Canada during the Cold War against the Soviet Union.

my father's Plymouth to the back of the hotel—always this was after dark—to a concrete loading ramp and lighted door that were close enough to the yards that I could sometimes see passenger trains waiting at the station, their car lights yellow and warm inside, the passengers dressed in suits, all bound for someplace far away from Montana—Milwaukee or Chicago or New York City, unimaginable places to me, a boy fourteen years old, with my father in the cold dark selling illegal game.

The caterer was a tall, stooped-back man in a white jacket, who my father called "Professor Ducks" or "Professor Fish," and the Professor referred to my father as "Sarge." He paid a quarter per pound for trout, a dime for whitefish, a dollar for a mallard duck, two for a speckle or a blue goose, and four dollars for a Canada. I have been with my father when he took away a hundred dollars for fish he'd caught and, in the fall, more than that for ducks and geese. When he had sold game in that way, we would drive out 10th Avenue and stop at a bar called The Mermaid which was by the air base, and he would drink with some friends he knew there, and they would laugh about hunting and fishing while I played pinball and wasted money in the jukebox.

It was on such a night as this that the unhappy things came about. It was in late October. I remember the time because Halloween had not been yet, and in the windows of the houses that I passed every day on the bus to Great Falls, people had put pumpkin lanterns, and set scarecrows in their yards in chairs.

My father and I had been shooting ducks in a slough on the Smith River, upstream from where it enters on the Missouri. He had killed thirty ducks, and we'd driven them down to the Great Northern and sold them there, though my father had kept two back in his corn sack. And when we had driven away, he suddenly said, "Jackie, let's us go back home tonight. Who cares about those hard-dicks at The Mermaid. I'll cook these ducks on the grill. We'll do something different tonight." He smiled at me in an odd way. This was not a thing he usually said, or the way he usually talked. He liked The Mermaid, and my mother—as far as I knew—didn't mind it if he went there.

"That sounds good," I said.

"We'll surprise your mother," he said. "We'll make her happy."

We drove out past the air base on Highway 87, past where there were planes taking off into the night. The darkness was dotted by the green and red beacons, and the tower light swept the sky and trapped planes as they disappeared over the flat landscape toward Canada or Alaska and the Pacific.

"Boy-oh-boy," my father said—just out of the dark. I looked at him and his eyes were narrow, and he seemed to be thinking about something. "You know, Jackie," he said, "your mother said something to me once I've never forgotten. She said, 'Nobody dies of a broken heart.' This was somewhat before you were born. We were living down in Texas and we'd had some big blow-up, and that was the idea she had. I don't know why." He shook his head.

He ran his hand under the seat, found a half-pint bottle of whiskey, and held it up to the lights of the car behind us to see what there was left of it. He unscrewed the cap and took a drink, then held the bottle out to me. "Have a drink, son," he said. "Something oughta be good in life." And I felt that something was wrong. Not because of the whiskey, which I had drunk before and he had reason to know about, but because of some sound in his voice, something I didn't recognize and did not know the importance of, though I was certain it was important.

I took a drink and gave the bottle back to him, holding the whiskey in my mouth until it stopped burning and I could swallow it a little at a time. When we turned out the road to Highwood, the lights of Great Falls sank below the horizon, and I could see the small white lights of farms, burning at wide distances in the dark.

"What do you worry about, Jackie," my father said. "Do you worry about girls? Do you worry about your future sex life? Is that some of it?" He glanced at me, then back at the road.

"I don't worry about that," I said.

"Well, what then?" my father said. "What else is there?"

"I worry if you're going to die before I do," I said, though I hated saying that, "or if Mother is. That worries me."

"It'd be a miracle if we didn't," my father said, with the half-pint held in the same hand he held the steering wheel. I had seen him drive that way before. "Things pass too fast in your life, Jackie. Don't worry about that. If I were you, I'd worry we might not." He smiled at me, and it was not the worried, nervous smile from before, but a smile that meant he was pleased. And I don't remember him ever smiling at me that way again.

We drove on out behind the town of Highwood and onto the flat field roads toward our house. I could see, out on the prairie, a moving light where the farmer who rented our house to us was disking his field for winter wheat. "He's waited too late, with that business," my father said and took a drink, then threw the bottle right out the window. "He'll lose that," he said, "the cold'll kill it." I did not answer him, but what I thought was that my father knew nothing about farming, and if he was right it would be an accident. He knew about planes and hunting game, and that seemed all to me.

"I want to respect your privacy," he said then, for no reason at all that I understood. I am not even certain he said it, only that it is in my memory that way. I don't know what he was thinking of. Just words. But I said to him, I remember well, "It's all right. Thank you."

We did not go straight out the Geraldine Road to our house. Instead my father went down another mile and turned, went a mile and turned back again so that we came home from the other direction. "I want to stop and listen now," he said. "The geese should be in the stubble." We stopped and he cut the lights and engine, and we opened the car windows and listened. It was eight o'clock at night and it was getting colder, though it was dry. But I could hear nothing, just the sound of air moving lightly through the cut field, and not a goose sound. Though I could smell the whiskey on my father's breath and on mine, could hear the motor ticking, could hear him breathe, hear the sound we made sitting side by side on the car seat, our clothes, our feet, almost our hearts beating. And I could see out in the night the yellow lights of our house, shining through the olive trees south of us like a ship on the sea. "I hear them, by God," my father said, his head stuck out the window. "But they're high up. They won't stop here now, Jackie. They're high flyers, those boys. Long gone geese."

There was a car parked off the road, down the line of wind-break trees, beside a steel thresher the farmer had left there to rust. You could see moonlight off the taillight chrome. It was a Pontiac, a two-door hardtop. My father said nothing about it and I didn't either, though I think now for different reasons.

The floodlight was on over the side door of our house and lights were on inside, upstairs and down. My mother had a pumpkin on the front porch, and the wind chime she had hung by the door was tinkling. My dog, Major, came out of the quonset shed and stood in the car lights when we drove up.

"Let's see what's happening here," my father said, opening the door and stepping out quickly. He looked at me inside the car, and his eyes were wide and his mouth drawn tight.

We walked in the side door and up the basement steps into the kitchen, and a man was standing there—a man I had never seen before, a young man with blond hair, who might've been twenty or twenty-five. He was tall and was wearing a short-sleeved shirt and beige slacks with pleats. He was on the other side of the breakfast table, his fingertips just touching the wooden tabletop. His blue eyes were on my father, who was dressed in hunting clothes.

"Hello," my father said.

"Hello," the young man said, and nothing else. And for some reason I looked at his arms, which were long and pale. They looked like a young man's arms, like my arms. His short sleeves had each been neatly rolled up, and I could see the bottom of a small green tattoo edging out from underneath. There was a glass of whiskey on the table, but no bottle.

"What's your name?" my father said, standing in the kitchen under the bright ceiling light. He sounded like he might be going to laugh.

"Woody," the young man said and cleared his throat. He looked at me, then he touched the glass of whiskey, just the rim of the glass. He wasn't nervous, I could tell that. He did not seem to be afraid of anything.

"Woody," my father said and looked at the glass of whiskey. He looked at me, then sighed and shook his head. "Where's Mrs. Russell, Woody? I guess you aren't robbing my house, are you?"

Woody smiled. "No," he said. "Upstairs. I think she went upstairs."

"Good," my father said, "that's a good place." And he walked straight out of the room, but came back and stood in the doorway. "Jackie, you and Woody step outside and wait on me. Just stay there and I'll come out." He looked at Woody then in a way I would not have liked him to look at me, a look that meant he was studying Woody. "I guess that's your car," he said.

"That Pontiac." Woody nodded.

"Okay. Right," my father said. Then he went out again and up the stairs. At that moment the phone started to ring in the living room, and I heard my mother say, "Who's that?" And my father say, "It's me. It's Jack." And I decided I wouldn't go answer the phone. Woody looked at me, and I understood he wasn't sure what to do. Run, maybe. But he didn't have run in him. Though I thought he would probably do what I said if I would say it.

"Let's just go outside," I said.

And he said, "All right."

Woody and I walked outside and stood in the light of the floodlamp above the side door. I had on my wool jacket, but Woody was cold and stood with his hands in his pockets, and his arms bare, moving from foot to foot. Inside, the phone was ringing again. Once I looked up and saw my mother come to the window and look down at Woody and me. Woody didn't look up or see her, but I did. I waved at her, and she waved back at me and smiled. She was wearing a powder-blue dress. In another minute the phone stopped ringing.

Woody took a cigarette out of his shirt pocket and lit it. Smoke shot through his nose into the cold air, and he sniffed, looked around the ground and threw his match on the gravel. His blond hair was combed backwards and neat on the sides, and I could smell his aftershave on him, a sweet, lemon smell. And for the first time I noticed his shoes. They were two-tones, black with white tops and black laces. They stuck out below his baggy pants and were long and polished and shiny, as if he had been planning on a big occasion. They looked like shoes some country singer would wear, or a salesman. He was handsome, but only like someone you would see beside you in a dime store and not notice again.

"I like it out here," Woody said, his head down, looking at his shoes. "Nothing to bother you. I bet you'd see Chicago if the world was flat. The Great Plains commence here."

"I don't know," I said.

Woody looked up at me, cupping his smoke with one hand. "Do you play football?"

"No," I said. I thought about asking him something about my mother. But I had no idea what it would be.

"I *have* been drinking," Woody said, "but I'm not drunk now."

The wind rose then, and from behind the house I could hear Major bark once from far away, and I could smell the irrigation ditch, hear it hiss in the field. It ran down from Highwood Creek to the Missouri, twenty miles away. It was nothing Woody knew about, nothing he could hear or smell. He knew nothing about anything that was here. I heard my father say the words, "That's a real joke," from inside the house, then the sound of a drawer being opened and shut, and a door closing. Then nothing else.

Woody turned and looked into the dark toward where the glow of Great Falls rose on the horizon, and we both could see the flashing lights of a plane lowering to land there. "I once passed my brother in the Los Angeles airport and didn't even recognize him," Woody said, staring into the night. "He recognized *me,* though. He said, 'Hey, bro, are you mad at me, or what?' I wasn't mad at him. We both had to laugh."

Woody turned and looked at the house. His hands were still in his pockets, his cigarette clenched between his teeth, his arms taut. They were, I saw, bigger, stronger arms than I had thought. A vein went down the front of each of them. I wondered what Woody knew that I didn't. Not about my mother—I didn't know anything about that and didn't want to—but about a lot of things, about the life out in the dark, about coming out here, about airports, even about me. He and I were not so far apart in age, I knew that. But Woody was one thing, and I was another. And I wondered how I would ever get to be like him, since it didn't necessarily seem so bad a thing to be.

"Did you know your mother was married before?" Woody said.

"Yes," I said. "I knew that."

"It happens to all of them, now," he said. "They can't wait to get divorced."

"I guess so," I said.

Woody dropped his cigarette into the gravel and toed it out with his black-and-white shoe. He looked up at me and smiled the way he had inside the house, a smile that said he knew something he wouldn't tell, a smile to make you feel bad because you weren't Woody and never could be.

It was then that my father came out of the house. He still had on his plaid hunting coat and his wool cap, but his face was as white as snow, as white as I have ever seen a human being's face to be. It was odd. I had the feeling that he might've fallen inside, because he looked roughed up, as though he had hurt himself somehow.

feeling phys

My mother came out the door behind him and stood in the floodlight at the top of the steps. She was wearing the powder-blue dress I'd seen through the window, a dress I had never seen her wear before, though she was also wearing a car coat and carrying a suitcase. She looked at me and shook her head in a way that only I was supposed to notice, as if it was not a good idea to talk now.

My father had his hands in his pockets, and he walked right up to Woody. He did not even look at me. "What do you do for a living?" he said, and he was very close to Woody. His coat was close enough to touch Woody's shirt.

"I'm in the Air Force," Woody said. He looked at me and then at my father. He could tell my father was excited.

"Is this your day off, then?" my father said. He moved even closer to Woody, his hands still in his pockets. He pushed Woody with his chest, and Woody seemed willing to let my father push him.

"No," he said, shaking his head.

I looked at my mother. She was just standing, watching. It was as if someone had given her an order, and she was obeying it. She did not smile at me, though I thought she was thinking about me, which made me feel strange.

"What's the matter with you?" my father said into Woody's face, right into his face—his voice tight, as if it had gotten hard for him to talk. "Whatever in the world is the matter with you? Don't you understand something?" My father took a revolver pistol out of his coat and put it up under Woody's chin, into the soft pocket behind the bone, so that Woody's whole face rose, but his arms stayed at his sides, his hands open. "I don't know what to do with you," my father said. "I don't have any idea what to do with you. I just don't." Though I thought that what he wanted to do was hold Woody there just like that until something important took place, or until he could simply forget about all this.

My father pulled the hammer back on the pistol and raised it tighter under Woody's chin, breathing into Woody's face—my mother in the light with her suitcase, watching them, and me watching them. A half a minute must've gone by.

And then my mother said, "Jack, let's stop now. Let's just stop."

My father stared into Woody's face as if he wanted Woody to consider doing something—moving or turning around or anything on his own to stop this—that my father would then put a stop to. My father's eyes grew narrowed, and his teeth were gritted together, his lips snarling up to resemble a smile. "You're crazy, aren't you?" he said. "You're a goddamned crazy man. Are you in love with her, too? Are you, crazy man? Are you? Do you say you love her? Say you love her! Say you love her so I can blow your fucking brains in the sky."

"All right," Woody said. "No. It's all right."

"He doesn't love me, Jack. For God's sake," my mother said. She seemed so calm. She shook her head at me again. I do not think she thought my father would shoot Woody. And I don't think Woody thought so. Nobody did, I think, except my father himself. But I think he did, and was trying to find out how to.

My father turned suddenly and glared at my mother, his eyes shiny and moving, but with the gun still on Woody's skin. I think he was afraid, afraid he was doing this wrong and could mess all of it up and make matters worse without accomplishing anything.

"You're leaving," he yelled at her. "That's why you're packed. Get out. Go on."

"Jackie has to be at school in the morning," my mother said in just her normal voice. And without another word to any one of us, she walked out of the floodlamp light carrying her bag, turned the corner at the front porch steps and disappeared toward the olive trees that ran in rows back into the wheat.

My father looked back at me where I was standing in the gravel, as if he expected to see me go with my mother toward Woody's car. But I hadn't thought about that—though later I would. Later I would think I should have gone with her, and that things between them might've been different. But that isn't how it happened.

"You're sure you're going to get away now, aren't you, mister?" my father said into Woody's face. He was crazy himself, then. Anyone would've been. Everything must have seemed out of hand to him.

"I'd like to," Woody said. "I'd like to get away from here."

"And I'd like to think of some way to hurt you," my father said and blinked his eyes. "I feel helpless about it." We all heard the door to Woody's car close in the dark. "Do you think that I'm a fool?" my father said.

"No," Woody said. "I don't think that."

"Do you think you're important?"

"No," Woody said. "I'm not."

My father blinked again. He seemed to be becoming someone else at that moment, someone I didn't know. "Where are you from?"

And Woody closed his eyes. He breathed in, then out, a long sigh. It was as if this was somehow the hardest part, something he hadn't expected to be asked to say.

"Chicago," Woody said. "A suburb of there."

"Are your parents alive?" my father said, all the time with his blue magnum pistol pushed under Woody's chin.

"Yes," Woody said. "Yessir."

"That's too bad," my father said. "Too bad they have to know what you are. I'm sure you stopped meaning anything to them a long time ago. I'm sure they both wish you were dead. You didn't know that. But I know it. I can't help them out, though. Somebody else'll have to kill you. I don't want to have to think about you anymore. I guess that's it."

My father brought the gun down to his side and stood looking at Woody. He did not back away, just stood, waiting for what I don't know to happen. Woody stood a moment, then he cut his eyes at me uncomfortably. And I know that I looked down. That's all I could do. Though I remember wondering if Woody's heart was broken and what any of this meant to him. Not to me, or my mother, or my father. But to him, since he seemed to be the one left out somehow, the one who would be lonely soon, the one who had done something he would someday wish he hadn't and would have no one to tell him that it was all right, that they forgave him, that these things happen in the world.

Woody took a step back, looked at my father and at me again as if he intended to speak, then stepped aside and walked away toward the front of our house, where the wind chime made a noise in the new cold air.

My father looked at me, his big pistol in his hand. "Does this seem stupid to you?" he said. "All this? Yelling and threatening and going nuts? I wouldn't blame you if it did. You shouldn't even see this. I'm sorry. I don't know what to do now."

"It'll be all right," I said. And I walked out to the road. Woody's car started up behind the olive trees. I stood and watched it back out, its red taillights clouded by exhaust. I could see their two heads inside, with the headlights shining behind them. When they got into the road, Woody touched his brakes, and for a moment I could see that they were talking, their heads turned toward each other, nodding. Woody's head and my mother's. They sat that way for a few seconds, then drove slowly off. And I wondered what they had to say to each other, something important enough that they had to stop right at that moment and say it. Did she say, *I love you?* Did she say, *This is not what I expected to happen?* Did she say, *This is what I've wanted all along?* And did he say, *I'm sorry for all this,* or *I'm glad,* or *None of this matters to me?* These are not the kinds of things you can know if you were not there. And I was not there and did not want to be. It did not seem like I should be there. I heard the door slam when my father went inside, and I turned back from the road where I could still see their taillights disappearing, and went back into the house where I was to be alone with my father.

Things seldom end in one event. In the morning I went to school on the bus as usual, and my father drove in to the air base in his car. We had not said very much about all that had happened. Harsh words, in a sense, are all alike. You can make them up yourself and be right. I think we both believed that we were in a fog we couldn't see through yet, though in a while, maybe not even a long while, we would see lights and know something.

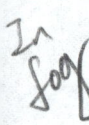

In my third-period class that day a messenger brought a note for me that said I was excused from school at noon, and I should meet my mother at a motel down 10th Avenue South—a place not so far from my school—and we would eat lunch together.

It was a gray day in Great Falls that day. The leaves were off the trees and the mountains to the east of town were obscured by a low sky. The night before had been cold and clear, but today it seemed as if it would rain. It was the beginning of winter in earnest. In a few days there would be snow everywhere.

The motel where my mother was staying was called the Tropicana, and was beside the city golf course. There was a neon parrot on the sign out front, and the cabins made a U shape behind a little white office building. Only a couple of cars were parked in front of cabins, and no car was in front of my mother's cabin. I wondered if Woody would be here, or if he was at the air base. I wondered if my father would see him there, and what they would say.

I walked back to cabin 9. The door was open, though a DO NOT DISTURB sign was hung on the knob outside. I looked through the screen and saw my mother sitting on the bed alone. The television was on, but she was looking at me. She was wearing the powder-blue dress she had had on the night before. She was smiling at me, and I liked the way she looked at that moment, through the screen, in shadows. Her features did not seem as sharp as they had before. She looked comfortable where she was, and I felt like we were going to get along, no matter what had happened, and that I wasn't mad at her—that I had never been mad at her.

She sat forward and turned the television off. "Come in, Jackie," she said, and I opened the screen door and came inside. "It's the height of grandeur in here, isn't it?" My mother looked around the room. Her suitcase was open on the floor by the bathroom door, which I could see through and out the window onto the golf course, where three men were playing under the milky sky. "Privacy can be a burden, sometimes," she said, and reached down and put on her high-heeled shoes. "I didn't sleep very well last night, did you?"

"No," I said, though I had slept all night. I wanted to ask her where Woody was, but it occurred to me at that moment that he was gone now and wouldn't be back, that she wasn't thinking in terms of him and didn't care where he was or ever would be.

"I'd like a nice compliment from you," she said. "Do you have one of those to spend?"

"Yes," I said. "I'm glad to see you."

"That's a nice one," she said and nodded. She had both her shoes on now. "Would you like to go have lunch? We can walk across the street to the cafeteria. You can get hot food."

"No," I said. "I'm not really hungry now."

"That's okay," she said and smiled at me again. And, as I said before, I liked the way she looked. She looked pretty in a way I didn't remember seeing her, as if something that had had a hold on her had let her go, and she could be different about things. Even about me.

"Sometimes, you know," she said, "I'll think about something I did. Just anything. Years ago in Idaho, or last week, even. And it's as if I'd read it. Like a story. Isn't that strange?"

"Yes," I said. And it did seem strange to me because I was certain then what the difference was between what had happened and what hadn't, and knew I always would be.

"Sometimes," she said, and she folded her hands in her lap and stared out the little side window of her cabin at the parking lot and the curving row of other cabins. "Sometimes I even have a moment when I completely forget what life's like. Just altogether." She smiled. "That's not so bad, finally. Maybe it's a disease I have. Do you think I'm just sick and I'll get well?"

"No. I don't know," I said. "Maybe. I hope so." I looked out the bathroom window and saw the three men walking down the golf course fairway carrying golf clubs.

"I'm not very good at sharing things right now," my mother said. "I'm sorry." She cleared her throat, and then she didn't say anything for almost a minute while I stood there. "I *will* answer anything you'd like me to answer, though. Just ask me anything, and I'll answer it the truth, whether I want to or not. Okay? I will. You don't even have to trust me. That's not a big issue with us. We're both grown-ups now."

And I said, "Were you ever married before?"

My mother looked at me strangely. Her eyes got small, and for a moment she looked the way I was used to seeing her—sharp-faced, her mouth set and taut. "No," she said. "Who told you that? That isn't true. I never was. Did Jack say that to you? Did your father say that? That's an awful thing to say. I haven't been that bad." *(Flo be moursely)*

"He didn't say that," I said.

"Oh, of course he did," my mother said. "He doesn't know just to let things go when they're bad enough."

"I wanted to know that," I said. "I just thought about it. It doesn't matter."

"No, it doesn't," my mother said. "I could've been married eight times. I'm just sorry he said that to you. He's not generous sometimes."

"He didn't say that," I said. But I'd said it enough, and I didn't care if she believed me or didn't. It was true that trust was not a big issue between us then. And in any event, I know now that the whole truth of anything is an idea that stops existing finally.

"Is that all you want to know, then?" my mother said. She seemed mad, but not at me, I didn't think. Just at things in general. And I sympathized with her. "Your life's your own business, Jackie," she said. "Sometimes it scares you to death it's so much your own business. You just want to run."

"I guess so," I said. *animal foreshadow*

"I'd like a less domestic life, is all." She looked at me, but I didn't say anything. I didn't see what she meant by that, though I knew there was nothing I could say to change the way her life would be from then on. And I kept quiet.

In a while we walked across 10th Avenue and ate lunch in the cafeteria. When she paid for the meal I saw that she had my father's silver-dollar money clip in her purse and that there was money in it. And I understood that he had been to see her already that day, and no one cared if I knew it. We were all of us on our own in this.

When we walked out onto the street, it was colder and the wind was blowing. Car exhausts were visible and some drivers had their lights on, though it was only two o'clock in the afternoon. My mother had called a taxi, and we stood and waited for it. I didn't know where she was going, but I wasn't going with her.

"Your father won't let me come back," she said, standing on the curb. It was just a fact to her, not that she hoped I would talk to him or stand up for her or take her part. But I did wish then that I had never let her go the night before. Things can be fixed by staying; but to go out into the night and not come back hazards life, and everything can get out of hand.

My mother's taxi came. She kissed me and hugged me very hard, then got inside the cab in her powder-blue dress and high heels and her car coat. I smelled her perfume on my cheeks as I stood watching her. "I used to be afraid of more things than I am now," she said, looking up at me, and smiled. "I've got a knot in my stomach, of all things." And she closed the cab door, waved at me, and rode away.

I walked back toward my school. I thought I could take the bus home if I got there by three. I walked a long way down 10th Avenue to Second Street, beside the Missouri River, then over to town. I walked by the Great Northern Hotel, where my father had sold ducks and geese and fish of all kinds. There were no passenger trains in the yard and the loading dock looked small. Garbage cans were lined along the edge of it, and the door was closed and locked.

As I walked toward school I thought to myself that my life had turned suddenly, and that I might not know exactly how or which way for possibly a long time. Maybe, in fact, I might never know. It was a thing that happened to you—I knew that—and it had happened to me in this way now. And as I walked on up the cold street that afternoon in Great Falls, the questions I asked myself were these: why wouldn't my father let my mother come back? Why would Woody stand in the cold with me outside my house and risk being killed? Why would he say my mother had been married before, if she hadn't been? And my mother herself—why would she do what she did? In five years my father had gone off to Ely, Nevada, to ride out the oil strike there, and been killed by accident. And in the years since then I have seen my mother from time to time—in one place or another, with one man or other—and I can say, at least, that we know each other. But I have never known the answer to these questions, have never asked anyone their answers. Though possibly it—the answer—is simple: it is just low-life, some coldness in us all, some helplessness that causes us to misunderstand life when it is pure and plain, makes our existence seem like a border between two nothings, and makes us no more or less than animals who meet on the road—watchful, unforgiving, without patience or desire.

1983

Privacy

This was at a time when my marriage was still happy.

We were living in a large city in the northeast. It was winter. February. The coldest month. I was, of course, still trying to write, and my wife was working as a translator for a small publishing company that specialized in Czech scientific papers. We had been married for ten years and were still enjoying that strange, exhilarating illusion that we had survived the worst of life's hardships.

The apartment we rented was in the old factory section on the south end of the city, the living space only a great, empty room with tall windows front and back, and almost no electric light. The natural light was all. A famous avant-garde theater director had lived in the room before and put on his jagged, nihilistic plays there, so that all the walls were painted black, and along one were still riser seats for his small disaffected audiences. Our bed—my wife's and mine—was in one dark corner where we'd arranged some of the tall, black-canvas scenery drops for our privacy. Though, of course, there was no one for us to need privacy from.

Each night when my wife came back from her work, we would go out into the cold, shining streets and find a restaurant to have our meal in. Later we would stop for an hour in a bar and have coffee or a brandy, and talk intensely about the translations my wife was working on, though never (blessedly) about the work I was by then already failing at.

Our wish, needless to say, was to stay out of the apartment as long as we could. For not only was there almost no light inside, but each night at seven the building's owner would turn off the heat, so that by ten—on our floor, the highest—it was too cold to be anywhere but in bed piled over with blankets, barely able to move. My wife, at that time, was working long hours and was always fatigued, and although sometimes we would come home a little drunk and make love in the dark bed under blankets, mostly she would fall straight into bed exhausted and be snoring before I could climb in beside her.

And so it happened that on many nights that winter, in the cold, large, nearly empty room, I would be awake, often wide awake from the strong coffee we'd drunk. And often I would walk the floor from window to window, looking out into the night, down to the vacant street or up into the ghostly sky that burned with the shimmery luminance of the city's buildings, buildings I couldn't even see. Often I had a blanket or sometimes two around my shoulders, and I wore the coarse heavy socks I'd kept from when I was a boy.

It was on such a cold night that—through the windows at the back of the flat, windows giving first onto an alley below, then farther across a space where a wire factory had been demolished, providing a view of buildings on the street parallel to ours—I saw, inside a long, yellow-lit apartment, the figure of a woman slowly undressing, from all appearances oblivious to the world outside the window glass.

Because of the distance, I could not see her well or at all clearly, could only see that she was small in stature and seemingly thin, with close-cropped dark hair—a petite woman in every sense. The yellow light in the room where she was seemed to blaze and made her skin bronze and shiny, and her movements, seen through the windows, appeared stylized and slightly unreal, like the movements of a silhouette or in an old motion picture.

I, though, alone in the frigid dark, wrapped in blankets that covered my head like a shawl, with my wife sleeping, oblivious, a few paces away—I was rapt by this sight. At first I moved close to the window glass, close enough to feel the cold on my cheeks. But then, sensing I might be noticed even at that distance, I slipped back into the room. Eventually I went to the corner and clicked off the small lamp my wife kept beside our bed, so that I was totally hidden in the dark. And after another few minutes I went to a drawer and found the pair of silver opera glasses which the theater director had left, and took them near the window and watched the woman across the space of darkness from my own space of darkness.

I don't know all that I thought. Undoubtedly I was aroused. Undoubtedly I was thrilled by the secrecy of watching out of the dark. Undoubtedly I loved the very illicitness of it, of my wife sleeping nearby and knowing nothing of what I was doing. It is also possible I even liked the cold as it surrounded me, as complete as the night itself, may even have felt that the sight of the woman—whom I took to be young and lacking caution or discretion—held me somehow, insulated me and made the world stop and be perfectly expressible as two poles connected by my line of vision. I am sure now that all of this had to do with my impending failures.

Nothing more happened. Though in the nights to come I stayed awake to watch the woman, letting my wife go off to sleep in her fatigue. Each night, and for a week following, the woman would appear at her window and slowly disrobe in her room (a room I never tried to imagine, although on the wall behind her was what looked like a drawing of a springing deer). Once her clothes were shed away, exposing her bony shoulders and small breasts and thin legs and rib cage and modest, rounded stomach, the woman would for a while cast about the room in the bronze light, window to window, enacting what seemed to me a kind of languid, ritual dance or a pattern of possibly theatrical movements, rising and bowing and extending her arms, arching her neck, while making her hands perform graceful lilting gestures I didn't understand and did not try to, taken as I was by her nakedness and by the sight on occasion of the dark swatch of hair between her legs. It was all arousal and secrecy and illicitness and really nothing else.

This I did for a week, as I said, and then I stopped. Simply one night, draped again in blankets, I went to the window with my opera glasses, saw the lights on across the vacant space. For a while I saw no one. And then for no particular reason I turned and got into bed with my wife, warm and smelling of brandy and sweat and sleep under her blankets, and went to sleep myself, never thinking to look through the window again.

Though one afternoon a week after I had stopped watching through the window, I left my desk in a moment of frustration and pointless despair, and stalked out into the winter daylight and up along the row of fashionable businesses where the old buildings were being restyled as dress shops and successful artists' galleries. I walked right to the river, clogged then with great squares of gray ice. I walked on to the university section, nearly to where my wife was at that hour working. And then, as the light was failing, I started back toward my street, my face hard with cold, my shoulders stiff, my gloveless hands frozen and red. As I turned a corner to take a quicker route back to my block, I found that I was unexpectedly passing before the building into which I had for days been spying. Something about it made me know it, though I'd never been aware of walking past there before, or even seen it in daylight. And just at that moment, letting herself into the building's tall front door, was the woman I had watched for those several nights and taken pleasure and undoubtedly secret consolation from. I knew her face, naturally—small and round and, as I saw, impassive. And to my surprise though not to my chagrin, she was old. Possibly she was seventy or even older. A Chinese, dressed in thin black trousers and a thin black coat, inside which she must've been as cold as I was. Indeed, she must've been freezing. She was carrying plastic bags of groceries slung on her arms and clutched in her hands. When I stopped and looked at her she turned and gazed down the steps at me with an expression I can only think now was indifference mingled with just the smallest recognition of threat. She was old, after all. I might suddenly have felt the urge to harm her, and easily could've. But of course that was not my thought. She turned back to the door and seemed to hurry her key into the lock. She looked my way once more, as I heard the bolt shoot profoundly back. I said nothing, did not even look at her again. I didn't want her to think my mind contained what it did and also what it did not. And I walked on then, feeling oddly but in no way surprisingly betrayed, simply passed on down the street toward my room and my own doors, my life entering, as it was at that moment, its first, long cycle of necessity.

1996

RELATED:

—Ford on Bharati Mukherjee's "The Management of Grief," p. 1761

MARY E. WILKINS FREEMAN
1852–1930

Freeman was born in Randolph, Massachusetts. As a child she was too frail to lead a normal life, and her schooling was irregular. When her immediate family died, she began to write in the hope of supporting herself and an aunt, publishing children's stories first, before she found a more lucrative market with fiction for adults. For a time she was secretary to Oliver Wendell Holmes, Sr., the celebrated physician and author, and it was through this position that she made the acquaintance of established writers of her time. She left New England in 1902 when she married a doctor from New Jersey, but the majority of her two hundred and thirty stories and twelve novels dealt with characters in New England villages and the lingering remnants of the Puritan culture. Among her novels are *Jane Field* (1893), *Pembroke* (1894), *The Portion of Labor* (1901), and *The Shoulders of Atlas* (1908). Her books of short stories include *A New England Nun and Other Stories* (1891), *Young Lucretia* (1892), *Understudies* (1901), and *The Green Door* (1917).

A New England Nun

It was late in the afternoon, and the light was waning. There was a difference in the look of the tree shadows out in the yard. Somewhere in the distance cows were lowing and a little bell was tinkling; now and then a farm-wagon tilted by, and the dust flew; some blue-shirted laborers with shovels over their shoulders plodded past; little swarms of flies were dancing up and down before the people's faces in the soft air. There seemed to be a gentle stir arising over everything for the mere sake of subsidence—a very premonition of rest and hush and night.

This soft diurnal commotion was over Louisa Ellis also. She had been peacefully sewing at her sitting-room window all the afternoon. Now she quilted her needle carefully into her work, which she folded precisely, and laid in a basket with her thimble and thread and scissors. Louisa Ellis could not remember that ever in her life she had mislaid one of these little feminine appurtenances, which had become, from long use and constant association, a very part of her personality.

Louisa tied a green apron round her waist, and got out a flat straw hat with a green ribbon. Then she went into the garden with a little blue crockery bowl, to pick some currants for her tea. After the currants were picked she sat on the back door-step and stemmed them, collecting the stems carefully in her apron, and afterwards throwing them into the hen-coop. She looked sharply at the grass beside the step to see if any had fallen there.

Louisa was slow and still in her movements; it took her a long time to prepare her tea; but when ready it was set forth with as much grace as if she had been a veritable guest to her own self. The little square table stood exactly in the centre of the kitchen, and was covered with a starched linen cloth whose border pattern of flowers glistened. Louisa had a damask napkin on her tea-tray, where were arranged a cut-glass tumbler full of teaspoons, a silver cream-pitcher, a china sugar-bowl, and one pink china cup and saucer. Louisa used china every day—something which none of her neighbors did. They whispered about it among themselves. Their daily tables were laid with common crockery, their sets of best china stayed in the parlor closet, and Louisa Ellis was no richer nor better bred than they. Still she would use the china. She had for her supper a glass dish full of sugared currants, a plate of little cakes, and one of light white biscuits. Also a leaf or two of lettuce, which she cut up daintily. Louisa was very fond of lettuce, which she raised to perfection in her little garden. She ate quite heartily, though in a delicate, pecking way; it seemed almost surprising that any considerable bulk of the food should vanish.

After tea she filled a plate with nicely baked thin corn-cakes, and carried them out into the back-yard.

"Caesar!" she called. "Caesar! Caesar!"

There was a little rush, and the clank of a chain, and a large yellow-and-white dog appeared at the door of his tiny hut, which was half hidden among the tall grasses and flowers. Louisa patted him and gave him the corn-cakes. Then she returned to the house and washed the tea-things, polishing the china carefully. The twilight had deepened; the chorus of the frogs floated in at the open window wonderfully loud and shrill, and once in a while a long sharp drone from a tree-toad pierced it. Louisa took off her green gingham apron, disclosing a shorter one of pink and white print. She lighted her lamp, and sat down again with her sewing.

In about half an hour Joe Dagget came. She heard his heavy step on the walk, and rose and took off her pink-and-white apron. Under that was still another—white linen with a little cambric edging on the bottom; that was Louisa's company apron. She never wore it without her calico sewing apron over it unless she had a guest. She had barely folded the pink and white one with methodical haste and laid it in a table-drawer when the door opened and Joe Dagget entered.

He seemed to fill up the whole room. A little yellow canary that had been asleep in his green cage at the south window woke up and fluttered wildly, beating his little yellow wings against the wires. He always did so when Joe Dagget came into the room.

"Good-evening," said Louisa. She extended her hand with a kind of solemn cordiality.

"Good-evening, Louisa," returned the man, in a loud voice.

She placed a chair for him, and they sat facing each other, with the table between them. He sat bolt-upright, toeing out his heavy feet squarely, glancing with a good-humored uneasiness around the room. She sat gently erect, folding her slender hands in her white-linen lap.

"Been a pleasant day," remarked Dagget.

"Real pleasant," Louisa assented, softly. "Have you been haying?" she asked, after a little while.

"Yes, I've been haying all day, down in the ten-acre lot. Pretty hot work."

"It must be."

"Yes, it's pretty hot work in the sun."

"Is your mother well to-day?"

"Yes, mother's pretty well."

"I suppose Lily Dyer's with her now?"

Dagget colored. "Yes, she's with her," he answered, slowly.

He was not very young, but there was a boyish look about his large face. Louisa was not quite as old as he, her face was fairer and smoother, but she gave people the impression of being older.

"I suppose she's a good deal of help to your mother," she said, further.

"I guess she is; I don't know how mother'd get along without her," said Dagget, with a sort of embarrassed warmth.

"She looks like a real capable girl. She's pretty-looking too," remarked Louisa.

"Yes, she is pretty fair looking."

Presently Dagget began fingering the books on the table. There was a square red autograph album, and a Young Lady's Gift-Book which had belonged to Louisa's mother. He took them up one after the other and opened them; then laid them down again, the album on the Gift-Book.

Louisa kept eying them with mild uneasiness. Finally she rose and changed the position of the books, putting the album underneath. That was the way they had been arranged in the first place.

Dagget gave an awkward little laugh. "Now what difference did it make which book was on top?" said he.

Louisa looked at him with a deprecating smile. "I always keep them that way," murmured she.

"You do beat everything," said Dagget, trying to laugh again. His large face was flushed.

He remained about an hour longer, then rose to take leave. Going out, he stumbled over a rug, and trying to recover himself, hit Louisa's work-basket on the table, and knocked it on the floor.

He looked at Louisa, then at the rolling spools; he ducked himself awkwardly toward them, but she stopped him. "Never mind," said she; "I'll pick them up after you're gone."

She spoke with a mild stiffness. Either she was a little disturbed, or his nervousness affected her, and made her seem constrained in her effort to reassure him.

When Joe Dagget was outside he drew in the sweet evening air with a sigh, and felt much as an innocent and perfectly well-intentioned bear might after his exit from a china shop.

Louisa, on her part, felt much as the kind-hearted, long-suffering owner of the china shop might have done after the exit of the bear.

She tied on the pink, then the green apron, picked up all the scattered treasures and replaced them in her work-basket, and straightened the rug. Then she set the lamp on the floor, and began sharply examining the carpet. She even rubbed her fingers over it, and looked at them.

"He's tracked in a good deal of dust," she murmured. "I thought he must have."

Louisa got a dust-pan and brush, and swept Joe Dagget's track carefully.

If he could have known it, it would have increased his perplexity and uneasiness, although it would not have disturbed his loyalty in the least. He came twice a week to see Louisa Ellis, and every time, sitting there in her delicately sweet room, he felt as if surrounded by a hedge of lace. He was afraid to stir lest he should put a clumsy foot or hand through the fairy web, and he had always the consciousness that Louisa was watching fearfully lest he should.

Still the lace and Louisa commanded perforce his perfect respect and patience and loyalty. They were to be married in a month, after a singular courtship which had lasted for a matter of fifteen years. For fourteen out of the fifteen years the two had not once seen each other, and they had seldom exchanged letters. Joe had been all those years in Australia, where he had gone to make his fortune, and where he had stayed until he made it. He would have stayed fifty years if it had taken so long, and come home feeble and tottering, or never come home at all, to marry Louisa.

But the fortune had been made in the fourteen years, and he had come home now to marry the woman who had been patiently and unquestioningly waiting for him all that time.

Shortly after they were engaged he had announced to Louisa his determination to strike out into new fields, and secure a competency before they should be married. She had listened and assented with the sweet serenity which never failed her, not even when her lover set forth on that long and uncertain journey. Joe, buoyed up as he was by his sturdy determination, broke down a little at the last, but Louisa kissed him with a mild blush, and said good-by.

"It won't be for long," poor Joe had said, huskily; but it was for fourteen years.

In that length of time much had happened. Louisa's mother and brother had died, and she was all alone in the world. But greatest happening of all—a subtle happening which both were too simple to understand—Louisa's feet had turned into a path, smooth maybe under a calm, serene sky, but so straight and unswerving that it could only meet a check at her grave, and so narrow that there was no room for anyone at her side.

Louisa's first emotion when Joe Dagget came home (he had not apprised her of his coming) was consternation, although she would not admit it to herself, and he never dreamed of it. Fifteen years ago she had been in love with him—at least she considered herself to be. Just at that time, gently acquiescing with and falling into the natural drift of girlhood, she had seen marriage ahead as a reasonable feature and a probable desirability of life. She had listened with calm docility to her mother's views upon the subject. Her mother was remarkable for her cool sense and sweet, even temperament. She talked wisely to her daughter when Joe Dagget presented himself, and Louisa accepted him with no hesitation. He was the first lover she had ever had.

She had been faithful to him all these years. She had never dreamed of the possibility of marrying anyone else. Her life, especially for the last seven years, had been full of a pleasant peace, she had never felt discontented nor impatient over her lover's absence; still she had always looked forward to his return and their marriage as the inevitable conclusion of things. However, she had fallen into a way of placing it so far in the future that it was almost equal to placing it over the boundaries of another life.

When Joe came she had been expecting him, and expecting to be married for fourteen years, but she was as much surprised and taken aback as if she had never thought of it.

Joe's consternation came later. He eyed Louisa with an instant confirmation of his old admiration. She had changed but little. She still kept her pretty manner and soft grace, and was, he considered, every whit as attractive as ever. As for himself, his stent was done; he had turned his face away from fortune-seeking, and the old winds of romance whistled as loud and sweet as ever through his ears. All the song which he had been wont to hear in them was Louisa; he had for a long time a loyal belief that he heard it still, but finally it seemed to him that although the winds sang always that one song, it had another name. But for Louisa the wind had never more than murmured; now it had gone down, and everything was still. She listened for a little while with half-wistful attention; then she turned quietly away and went to work on her wedding clothes.

Joe had made some extensive and quite magnificent alterations in his house. It was the old homestead; the newly-married couple would live there, for Joe could not desert his mother, who refused to leave her old home. So Louisa must leave hers. Every morning, rising and going about among her neat maidenly possessions, she felt as one looking her last upon the faces of dear friends. It was true that in a measure she could take them with her, but, robbed of their old environments, they would appear in such new guises that they would almost cease to be themselves. Then there were some peculiar features of her happy solitary life which she would probably be obliged to relinquish altogether. Sterner tasks than these graceful but half-needless ones would probably devolve upon her. There would be a large house to care for; there would be company to entertain; there would be Joe's rigorous and feeble old mother to wait upon; and it would be contrary to all thrifty village traditions for her to keep more than one servant. Louisa had a little still, and she used to occupy herself pleasantly in summer weather with distilling the sweet and aromatic essences from roses and peppermint and spearmint. By-and-by her still must be laid away. Her store of essences was already considerable, and there would be no time for her to distill for the mere pleasure of it. Then Joe's mother would think it foolishness; she had already hinted her opinion in the matter. Louisa dearly loved to sew a linen seam, not always for use, but for the simple, mild pleasure which she took in it. She would have been loath to confess how more than once she had ripped a seam for the mere delight of sewing it together again. Sitting at her window during long sweet afternoons, drawing her needle gently through the dainty fabric, she was peace itself. But there was small chance of such foolish comfort in the future. Joe's mother, domineering, shrewd old matron that she was even in her old age, and very likely even Joe himself, with his honest masculine rudeness, would laugh and frown down all these pretty but senseless old maiden ways.

Louisa had almost the enthusiasm of an artist over the mere order and cleanliness of her solitary home. She had throbs of genuine triumph at the sight of the window-panes which she had polished until they shone like jewels. She gloated gently over her orderly bureau-drawers, with their exquisitely folded contents redolent with lavender and sweet clover and very purity. Could she be sure of the endurance of even this? She had visions, so startling that she half repudiated them as indelicate, of coarse masculine belongings strewn about in endless litter; of dust and disorder arising necessarily from a coarse masculine presence in the midst of all this delicate harmony.

Among her forebodings of disturbance, not the least was with regard to Caesar. Caesar was a veritable hermit of a dog. For the greater part of his life he had dwelt in his secluded hut, shut out from the society of his kind and all innocent canine joys. Never had Caesar since his early youth watched at a woodchuck's hole; never had he known the delights of a stray bone at a neighbor's kitchen door. And it was all on account of a sin committed when hardly out of his puppyhood. No one knew the possible depth of remorse of which this mild-visaged, altogether innocent-looking old dog might be capable; but whether or not he had encountered remorse, he had encountered a full measure of righteous retribution. Old Caesar seldom lifted up his voice in a growl or a bark; he was fat and sleepy; there were yellow rings which looked like spectacles around his dim old eyes; but there was a neighbor who bore on his hand the imprint of several of Caesar's sharp white youthful teeth, and for that he had lived at the end of a chain, all alone in a little hut, for fourteen years. The neighbor, who was choleric and smarting with the pain of his wound, had demanded either Caesar's death or complete ostracism. So Louisa's brother, to whom the dog had belonged, had built him his little kennel and tied him up. It was now fourteen years since, in a flood of youthful spirits, he had inflicted that memorable bite, and with the exception of short excursions, always at the end of the chain, under the strict guardianship of his master or Louisa, the old dog had remained a close prisoner. It is doubtful if, with his limited ambition, he took much pride in the fact, but it is certain that he was possessed of considerable cheap fame. He was regarded by all the children in the village and by many adults as a very monster of ferocity. St. George's dragon could hardly have surpassed in evil repute Louisa Ellis's old yellow dog. Mothers charged their children with solemn emphasis not to go too near him, and the children listened and believed greedily, with a fascinated appetite for terror, and ran by Louisa's house stealthily, with many sidelong and backward glances at the terrible dog. If perchance he sounded a hoarse bark, there was a panic. Wayfarers chancing into Louisa's yard eyed him with respect, and inquired if the chain were stout. Caesar at large might have seemed a very ordinary dog, and excited no comment whatever; chained, his reputation overshadowed him, so that he lost his own proper outlines and looked darkly vague and enormous. Joe Dagget, however, with his good-humored sense and shrewdness, saw him as he was. He strode valiantly up to him and patted him on the head, in spite of Louisa's soft clamor of warning, and even attempted to set him loose. Louisa grew so alarmed that he desisted, but kept announcing his opinion in the matter quite forcibly at intervals. "There ain't a better-natured dog in town," he would say, "and it's downright cruel to keep him tied up there. Someday I'm going to take him out."

Louisa had very little hope that he would not, one of these days, when their interests and possessions should be more completely fused in one. She pictured to herself Caesar on the rampage through the quiet and unguarded village. She saw innocent children bleeding in his path. She was herself very fond of the old dog, because he had belonged to her dead brother, and he was always very gentle with her; still she had great faith in his ferocity. She always warned people not to go too near him. She fed him on ascetic fare of corn-mush and cakes, and never fired his dangerous temper with heating and san-guinary diet of flesh and bones. Louisa looked at the old dog munching his simple fare, and thought of her approaching marriage and trembled. Still no anticipation of disorder and confusion in lieu of sweet peace and harmony, no forebodings of Caesar on the rampage, no wild fluttering of her little yel-low canary, were sufficient to turn her a hair's-breadth. Joe Dagget had been fond of her and working for her all these years. It was not for her, whatever came to pass, to prove untrue and break his heart. She put the exquisite little stitches into her wedding-garments, and the time went on until it was only a week before her wedding-day. It was a Tuesday evening, and the wedding was to be a week from Wednesday.

There was a full moon that night. About nine o'clock Louisa strolled down the road a little way. There were harvest-fields on either hand, bordered by low stone walls. Luxuriant clumps of bushes grew beside the wall, and trees—wild cherry and old apple-trees—at intervals. Presently Louisa sat down on the wall and looked about her with mildly sorrowful reflectiveness. Tall shrubs of blueberry and meadow-sweet, all woven together and tangled with blackberry vines and horsebriers, shut her in on either side. She had a little clear space between them. Opposite her, on the other side of the road, was a spreading tree; the moon shone between its boughs, and the leaves twinkled like silver. The road was bespread with a beautiful shifting dapple of silver and shadow; the air was full of a mysterious sweetness. "I wonder if it's wild grapes?" mur-mured Louisa. She sat there some time. She was just thinking of rising, when she heard footsteps and low voices, and remained quiet. It was a lonely place, and she felt a little timid. She thought she would keep still in the shadow and let the persons, whoever they might be, pass her.

But just before they reached her the voices ceased, and the footsteps. She understood that their owners had also found seats upon the stone wall. She was wondering if she could not steal away unobserved, when the voice broke the stillness. It was Joe Dagget's. She sat still and listened.

The voice was announced by a loud sigh, which was as familiar as itself. "Well," said Dagget, "you've made up your mind, then, I suppose?"

"Yes," returned another voice; "I'm going day after to-morrow."

"That's Lily Dyer," thought Louisa to herself. The voice embodied itself in her mind. She saw a girl tall and full-figured, with a firm, fair face, looking fairer and firmer in the moonlight, her strong yellow hair braided in a close knot. A girl full of a calm rustic strength and bloom, with a masterful way which might have beseemed a princess. Lily Dyer was a favorite with the vil-lage folk; she had just the qualities to arouse the admiration. She was good and handsome and smart. Louisa had often heard her praises sounded.

"Well," said Joe Dagget, "I ain't got a word to say."

"I don't know what you could say," returned Lily Dyer.

"Not a word to say," repeated Joe, drawing out the words heavily. Then there was silence. "I ain't sorry," he began at last, "that that happened yesterday—that we kind of let on how we felt to each other. I guess it's just as well we knew. Of course I can't do anything any different. I'm going right on an' get married next week. I ain't going back on a woman that's waited for me fourteen years, an' break her heart."

"If you should jilt her to-morrow, I wouldn't have you," spoke up the girl, with sudden vehemence.

"Well, I ain't going to give you the chance," said he; "but I don't believe you would, either."

"You'd see I wouldn't. Honor's honor, an' right's right. An' I'd never think anything of any man that went against 'em for me or any other girl; you'd find that out, Joe Dagget."

"Well, you'll find out fast enough that I ain't going against 'em for you or any other girl," returned he. Their voices sounded almost as if they were angry with each other. Louisa was listening eagerly.

"I'm sorry you feel as if you must go away," said Joe, "but I don't know but it's best."

"Of course it's best. I hope you and I have got common-sense."

"Well, I suppose you're right." Suddenly Joe's voice got an undertone of tenderness. "Say, Lily," said he, "I'll get along well enough myself, but I can't bear to think—You don't suppose you're going to fret much over it?"

"I guess you'll find out I sha'n't fret much over a married man."

"Well, I hope you won't—I hope you won't, Lily. God knows I do. And—I hope—one of these days—you'll—come across somebody else—"

"I don't see any reason why I shouldn't." Suddenly her tone changed. She spoke in a sweet, clear voice, so loud that she could have been heard across the street. "No, Joe Dagget," said she, "I'll never marry any other man as long as I live. I've got good sense, an' I ain't going to break my heart nor make a fool of myself; but I'm never going to be married, you can be sure of that. I ain't that sort of a girl to feel this way twice."

Louisa heard an exclamation and a soft commotion behind the bushes; then Lily spoke again—the voice sounded as if she had risen. "This must be put a stop to," said she. "We've stayed here long enough. I'm going home."

Louisa sat there in a daze, listening to their retreating steps. After a while she got up and slunk softly home herself. The next day she did her housework methodically; that was as much a matter of course as breathing; but she did not sew on her wedding-clothes. She sat at her window and meditated. In the evening Joe came. Louisa Ellis had never known that she had any diplomacy in her, but when she came to look for it that night she found it, although meek of its kind, among her little feminine weapons. Even now she could hardly believe that she had heard aright, and that she would not do Joe a terrible injury should she break her troth-plight. She wanted to sound him without betraying too soon her own inclinations in the matter. She did it successfully, and they finally came to an understanding; but it was a difficult thing, for he was as afraid of betraying himself as she.

She never mentioned Lily Dyer. She simply said that while she had no cause of complaint against him, she had lived so long in one way that she shrank from making a change.

"Well, I never shrank, Louisa," said Dagget. "I'm going to be honest enough to say that I think maybe it's better this way; but if you'd wanted to keep on, I'd have stuck to you till my dying day. I hope you know that."

"Yes, I do," said she.

That night she and Joe parted more tenderly than they had done for a long time. Standing in the door, holding each other's hands, a last great wave of regretful memory swept over them.

"Well, this ain't the way we've thought it was all going to end, is it, Louisa?" said Joe.

She shook her head. There was a little quiver on her placid face.

"You let me know if there's ever anything I can do for you," said he. "I ain't ever going to forget you, Louisa." Then he kissed her, and went down the path.

Louisa, all alone by herself that night, wept a little, she hardly knew why; but the next morning, on waking, she felt like a queen who, after fearing lest her domain be wrested away from her, sees it firmly insured in her possession.

Now the tall weeds and grasses might cluster around Caesar's little hermit hut, the snow might fall on its roof year in and year out, but he never would go on a rampage through the unguarded village. Now the little canary might turn itself into a peaceful yellow ball night after night, and have no need to wake and flutter with wild terror against its bars. Louisa could sew linen seams, and distill roses, and dust and polish and fold away in lavender, as long as she listed. That afternoon she sat with her needle-work at the window, and felt fairly steeped in peace. Lily Dyer, tall and erect and blooming, went past; but she felt no qualm. If Louisa Ellis had sold her birthright she did not know it, the taste of the pottage[1] was so delicious, and had been her sole satisfaction for so long. Serenity and placid narrowness had become to her as the birthright itself. She gazed ahead through a long reach of future days strung together like pearls in a rosary, every one like the others, and all smooth and flawless and innocent, and her heart went up in thankfulness. Outside was the fervid summer afternoon; the air was filled with the sounds of the busy harvest of men and birds and bees; there were halloos, metallic clatterings, sweet calls, and long hummings. Louisa sat, prayerfully numbering her days, like an uncloistered nun.

1891

---

1. See Genesis 25:30–34. Esau sold his birthright to his brother Jacob for a mess of pottage (meal of stew).

MAVIS GALLANT
1922–2014

Mavis Gallant was born in Montreal to an Anglo-Scottish father and an American mother. Her father died when she was ten years old, and her mother remarried shortly thereafter. The family moved so frequently in the next eight years that Gallant attended seventeen different schools before graduating from high school in New York City. Following graduation, Gallant returned to Montreal and became a journalist, working for a number of years at *The Standard*. When she was twenty-eight, Gallant quit her job and departed for Europe to pursue her dream of becoming a full-time fiction writer. She soon settled in France, where she lived until her death in 2014. She published her first short story in *The New Yorker* in 1951. Gallant published a play, two novels—*Green Water, Green Sky* (1959) and *A Fairly Good Time* (1970)—and numerous collections of short stories, among them *The Other Paris* (1956), *My Heart Is Broken* (1964), *Home Truths: Selected Canadian Stories* (1981)—for which she was awarded the Governor General's Award—*In Transit* (1988), and *The Collected Stories of Mavis Gallant* (1996). Gallant was appointed an Officer of the Order of Canada in 1981 (raised to Companion in 1993) and a Foreign Honorary Member of the American Academy of Arts and Letters in 2000. Her awards include the Matt Cohen Award, the Rea Award for the Short Story, and a PEN/Nabokov award.

The Ice Wagon Going Down the Street

Now that they are out of world affairs and back where they started, Peter Frazier's wife says, "Everybody else did well in the international thing except us."

"You have to be crooked," he tells her.

"Or smart. Pity we weren't."

It is Sunday morning. They sit in the kitchen, drinking their coffee, slowly, remembering the past. They say the names of people as if they were magic. Peter thinks, Agnes Brusen, but there are hundreds of other names. As a private married joke, Peter and Sheilah wear the silk dressing gowns they bought in Hong Kong. Each thinks the other a peacock, rather splendid, but they pretend the dressing gowns are silly and worn in fun.

Peter and Sheilah and their two daughters, Sandra and Jennifer, are visiting Peter's unmarried sister, Lucille. They have been Lucille's guests seventeen weeks, ever since they returned to Toronto from the Far East. Their big old steamer trunk blocks a corner of the kitchen, making a problem of the refrigerator door; but even Lucille says the trunk may as well stay where it is, for the present. The Fraziers' future is so unsettled; everything is still in the air.

Lucille has given her bedroom to her two nieces, and sleeps on a camp cot in the hall. The parents have the living-room divan. They have no privileges here; they sleep after Lucille has seen the last television show that interests her. In the hall closet their clothes are crushed by winter overcoats. They know they are being judged for the first time. Sandra and Jennifer are waiting for Sheilah and Peter to decide. They are waiting to learn where these exotic parents will fly to next. What sort of climate will Sheilah consider? What job will Peter consent to accept? When the parents are ready, the children will make a decision of their own. It is just possible that Sandra and Jennifer will choose to stay with their aunt.

The peacock parents are watched by wrens. Lucille and her nieces are much the same—sandy-colored, proudly plain. Neither of the girls has the father's insouciance or the mother's appearance—her height, her carriage, her thick hair and sky-blue eyes. The children are more cautious than their parents; more Canadian. When they saw their aunt's apartment they had been away from Canada nine years, ever since they were two and four; and Jennifer, the elder, said, "Well, now we're home." Her voice is nasal and flat. Where did she learn that voice? And why should this be home? Peter's answer to anything about his mystifying children is, "It must be in the blood."

On Sunday morning Lucille takes her nieces to church. It seems to be the only condition she imposes on her relations: The children must be decent. The girls go willingly, with their new hats and purses and gloves and coral bracelets and strings of pearls. The parents, ramshackle, sleepy, dim in the brain because it is Sunday, sit down to their coffee and privacy and talk of the past.

"We weren't crooked," says Peter. "We weren't even smart."

Sheilah's head bobs up; she is no drowner. It is wrong to say they have nothing to show for time. Sheilah has the Balenciaga. It is a black afternoon dress, stiff and boned at the waist, long for the fashions of now, but neither Sheilah nor Peter would change a thread. The Balenciaga is their talisman, their treasure; and after they remember it they touch hands and think that the years are not behind them but hazy and marvelous and still to be lived.

The first place they went to was Paris. In the early fifties the pick of the international jobs was there. Peter had inherited the last scrap of money he knew he was ever likely to see, and it was enough to get them over: Sheilah and Peter and the babies and the steamer trunk. To their joy and astonishment they had money in the bank. They said to each other, "It should last a year." Peter was fastidious about the new job; he hadn't come all this distance to accept just anything. In Paris he met Hugh Taylor, who was earning enough smuggling gasoline to keep his wife in Paris and a girl in Rome. That impressed Peter, because he remembered Taylor as a sour scholarship student without the slightest talent for life. Taylor had a job, of course. He hadn't said to himself, I'll go over to Europe and smuggle gasoline. It gave Peter an idea; he saw the shape of things. First you catch your fish. Later, at an international party, he met Johnny Hertzberg, who told him Germany was the place. Hertzberg said that anyone who came out of Germany broke now was too stupid to be here, and deserved to be back home at a desk. Peter nodded, as if he had already thought of that. He began to think about Germany. Paris was fine for a holiday, but it had been picked clean. Yes, Germany. His money was running low. He thought about Germany quite a lot.

That winter was moist and delicate; so fragile that they daren't speak of it now. There seemed to be plenty of everything and plenty of time. They were living the dream of a marriage, the fabric uncut, nothing slashed or spoiled. All winter they spent their money, and went to parties, and talked about Peter's future job. It lasted four months. They spent their money, lived in the future, and were never as happy again.

After four months they were suddenly moved away from Paris, but not to Germany—to Geneva. Peter thinks it was because of the incident at the Trudeau wedding at the Ritz. Paul Trudeau was a French-Canadian Peter had known at school and in the Navy. Trudeau had turned into a snob, proud of his career and his Paris connections. He tried to make the difference felt, but Peter thought the difference was only for strangers. At the wedding reception Peter lay down on the floor and said he was dead. He held a white azalea in a brass pot on his chest, and sang, "Oh, hear us when we cry to Thee for those in peril on the sea." Sheilah bent over him and said, "Peter, darling, get up. Pete, listen, every single person who can do something for you is in this room. If you love me, you'll get up."

"I do love you," he said, ready to engage in a serious conversation. "She's so beautiful," he told a second face. "She's nearly as tall as I am. She was a model in London. I met her over in London in the war. I met her there in the war." He lay on his back with the azalea on his chest, explaining their history. A waiter took the brass pot away, and after Peter had been hauled to his feet he knocked the waiter down. Trudeau's bride, who was freshly out of an Ursuline convent, became hysterical; and even though Paul Trudeau and Peter were old acquaintances, Trudeau never spoke to him again. Peter says now that French-Canadians always have that bit of spite. He says Trudeau asked the embassy to interfere. Luckily, back home there were still a few people to whom the name "Frazier" meant something, and it was to these people that Peter appealed. He wrote letters saying that a French-Canadian combine was preventing his getting a decent job, and could anything be done? No one answered directly, but it was clear that what they settled for was exile to Geneva: a season of meditation and remorse, as he explained to Sheilah, and it was managed tactfully, through Lucille. Lucille wrote that a friend of hers, May Fergus, now a secretary in Geneva, had heard about a job. The job was filing pictures in the information service of an international agency in the Palais des Nations. The pay was so-so, but Lucille thought Peter must be getting fed up doing nothing.

Peter often asks his sister now who put her up to it—what important person told her to write that letter suggesting Peter go to Geneva?

"Nobody," says Lucille. "I mean, nobody in the way *you* mean. I really did have this girl friend working there, and I knew you must be running through your money pretty fast in Paris."

"It must have been somebody pretty high up," Peter says. He looks at his sister admiringly, as he has often looked at his wife.

Peter's wife had loved him in Paris. Whatever she wanted in marriage she found that winter, there. In Geneva, where Peter was a file clerk and they lived in a furnished flat, she pretended they were in Paris and life was still the same. Often, when the children were at supper, she changed as though she and Peter were dining out. She wore the Balenciaga, and put candles on the card table where she and Peter ate their meal. The neckline of the dress was soiled with makeup. Peter remembers her dabbing on the makeup with a wet sponge. He remembers her in the kitchen, in the soiled Balenciaga, patting on the makeup with a filthy sponge. Behind her, at the kitchen table, Sandra and Jennifer, in buttonless pajamas and bunny slippers, ate their supper of marmalade sandwiches and milk. When the children were asleep, the parents dined solemnly, ritually, Sheilah sitting straight as a queen.

It was a mysterious period of exile, and he had to wait for signs, or signals, to know when he was free to leave. He never saw the job any other way. He forgot he had applied for it. He thought he had been sent to Geneva because of a misdemeanor and had to wait to be released. Nobody pressed him at work. His immediate boss had resigned, and he was alone for months in a room with two desks. He read the *Herald Tribune*, and tried to discover how things were here—how the others ran their lives on the pay they were officially getting. But it was a closed conspiracy. He was not dealing with adventurers now but civil servants waiting for pension day. No one ever answered his questions. They pretended to think his questions were a form of wit. His only solace in exile was the few happy weekends he had in the late spring and early summer. He had met another old acquaintance, Mike Burleigh. Mike was a serious liberal who had married a serious heiress. The Burleighs had two guest lists. The first was composed of stuffy people they felt obliged to entertain, while the second was made up of their real friends, the friends they wanted. The real friends strove hard to become stuffy and dull and thus achieve the first guest list, but few succeeded. Peter went on the first list straightaway. Possibly Mike didn't understand, at the beginning, why Peter was pretending to be a file clerk. Peter had such an air—he might have been sent by a universal inspector to see how things in Geneva were being run.

Every Friday in May and June and part of July, the Fraziers rented a sky-blue Fiat and drove forty miles east of Geneva to the Burleighs' summer house. They brought the children, a suitcase, the children's tattered picture books, and a token bottle of gin. This, in memory, is a period of water and water birds; swans, roses, and singing birds. The children were small and still belonged to them. If they remember too much, their mouths water, their stomachs hurt. Peter says, "It was fine while it lasted." Enough. While it lasted Sheilah and Madge Burleigh were close. They abandoned their husbands and spent long summer afternoons comparing their mothers and praising each other's skin and hair. To Madge, and not to Peter, Sheilah opened her Liverpool childhood with the words "rat poor." Peter heard about it later, from Mike. The women's friendship seemed to Peter a bad beginning. He trusted women but not with each other. It lasted ten weeks. One Sunday, Madge said she needed the two bedrooms the Fraziers usually occupied for a party of sociologists from Pakistan, and that was the end. In November, the Fraziers heard that the summer house had been closed, and that the Burleighs were in Geneva, in their winter flat; they gave no sign. There was no help for it, and no appeal.

Now Peter began firing letters to anyone who had ever known his late father. He was living in a mild yellow autumn. Why does he remember the streets of the city dark, and the windows everywhere black with rain? He remembers being with Sheilah and the children as if they clung together while just outside their small shelter it rained and rained. The children slept in the bedroom of the flat because the window gave on the street and they could breathe air. Peter and Sheilah had the living-room couch. Their window was not a real window but a square on a well of cement. The flat seemed damp as a cave. Peter remembers steam in the kitchen, pools under the sink, sweat on the pipes. Water streamed on him from the children's clothes, washed and dripping overhead. The trunk, upended in the children's room, was not quite unpacked. Sheilah had not signed her name to this life; she had not given in. Once Peter heard her drop her aitches. "You kids are lucky," she said to the girls. "I never 'ad so much as a sit-down meal. I ate chips out of a paper or I 'ad a butty out on the stairs." He never asked her what a butty was. He thinks it means bread and cheese.

The day he heard "You kids are lucky" he understood they were becoming in fact something they had only *appeared* to be until now—the shabby civil servant and his brood. If he had been European he would have ridden to work on a bicycle, in the uniform of his class and condition. He would have worn a tight coat, a turned collar, and a dirty tie. He wondered then if coming here had been a mistake, and if he should not, after all, still be in a place where his name meant something. Surely Peter Frazier should live where "Frazier" counts? In Ontario even now when he says "Frazier" an absent look comes over his hearer's face, as if its owner were consulting an interior guide. What is Frazier? What does it mean? Oil? Power? Politics? Wheat? Real estate? The creditors had the house sealed when Peter's father died. His aunt collapsed with a heart attack in somebody's bachelor apartment, leaving three sons and a widower to surmise they had never known her. Her will was a disappointment. None of that generation left enough. One made it: the granite Presbyterian immigrants from Scotland. Their children, a generation of daunted women and maiden men, held still. Peter's father's crowd spent: They were not afraid of their fathers, and their grandfathers were old. Peter and his sister and his cousins lived on the remains. They were left the rinds of income, of notions, and the memories of ideas rather than ideas intact. If Peter can choose his reincarnation, let him be the oppressed son of a Scottish parson. Let Peter grow up on cuffs and iron principles. Let him make the fortune! Let him flee the manse! When he was small his patrimony was squandered under his nose. He remembers people dancing in his father's house. He remembers seeing and nearly understanding adultery in a guest room, among a pile of wraps. He thought he had seen a murder; he never told. He remembers licking glasses wherever he found them—on windowsills, on stairs, in the pantry. In his room he listened while Lucille read Beatrix Potter. The bad rabbit stole the carrot from the good rabbit without saying please, and downstairs was the noise of the party—the roar of the crouched lion. When his father died he saw the chairs upside down and the bailiff's chalk marks. Then the doors were sealed.

He has often tried to tell Sheilah why he cannot be defeated. He remembers his father saying, "Nothing can touch us," and Peter believed it and still does. It has prevented his taking his troubles too seriously. Nothing can be as bad as this, he will tell himself. It is happening to me. Even in Geneva, where his status was file clerk, where he sank and stopped on the level of the men who never emigrated, the men on the bicycles—even there he had a manner of strolling to work as if his office were a pastime, and his real life a secret so splendid he could share it with no one except himself.

In Geneva Peter worked for a woman—a girl. She was a Norwegian from a small town in Saskatchewan. He supposed they had been put together because they were Canadians; but they were as strange to each other as if "Canadian" meant any number of things, or had no real meaning. Soon after Agnes Brusen came to the office she hung her framed university degree on the wall. It was one of the gritty, prideful gestures that stand for push, toil, and family sacrifice. He thought, then, that she must be one of a family of immigrants for whom education is everything. Hugh Taylor had told him that in some families the older children never marry until the youngest have finished school. Sometimes every second child is sacrificed and made to work for the education of the next-born. Those who finish college spend years paying back. They are white-hot Protestants, and they live with a load of work and debt and obligation. Peter placed his new colleague on scraps of information. He had never been in the West.

She came to the office on a Monday morning in October. The office was over-heated and painted cream. It contained two desks, the filing cabinets, a map of the world as it had been in 1945, and the Charter of the United Nations left behind by Agnes Brusen's predecessor. (She took down the Charter without asking Peter if he minded, with the impudence of gesture you find in women who wouldn't say boo to a goose; and then she hung her college degree on the nail where the Charter had been.) Three people brought her in—a whole committee. One of them said, "Agnes, this is Pete Frazier. Pete, Agnes Brusen. Pete's Canadian, too, Agnes. He knows all about the office, so ask him anything."

Of course he knew all about the office: He knew the exact spot where the cord of the venetian blind was frayed, obliging one to give an extra tug to the right.

The girl might have been twenty-three: no more. She wore a brown tweed suit with bone buttons, and a new silk scarf and new shoes. She clutched an unscratched brown purse. She seemed dressed in going-away presents. She said, "Oh, I never smoke," with a convulsive movement of her hand, when Peter offered his case. He was courteous, hiding his disappointment. The people he worked with had told him a Scandinavian girl was arriving, and he had expected a stunner. Agnes was a mole: She was small and brown, and round-shouldered as if she had always carried parcels or younger children in her arms. A mole's profile was turned when she said good-bye to her committee. If she had been foreign, ill-favored though she was, he might have flirted a little, just to show that he was friendly; but their being Canadian, and suddenly left together, was a sexual damper. He sat down and lit his own cigarette. She smiled at him, questionably, he thought, and sat as if she had never seen a chair before. He wondered if his smoking was annoying her. He wondered if she was fidgety about drafts, or allergic to anything, and whether she would want the blind up or down. His social compass was out of order because the others couldn't tell Peter and Agnes apart. There was a world of difference between them, yet it was she who had been brought in to sit at the larger of the two desks.

While he was thinking this she got up and walked around the office, almost on tiptoe, opening the doors of closets and pulling out the filing trays. She looked inside everything except the drawers of Peter's desk. (In any case, Peter's desk was locked. His desk is locked wherever he works. In Geneva he went into Personnel one morning, early, and pinched his application form. He had stated on the form that he had seven years' experience in public relations and could speak French, German, Spanish, and Italian. He has always collected anything important about himself—anything useful. But he can never get on with the final act, which is getting rid of the information. He has kept papers about for years, a constant source of worry.)

"I know this looks funny, Mr. Ferris," said the girl. "I'm not really snooping or anything. I just can't feel easy in a new place unless I know where everything is. In a new place everything seems so hidden."

If she had called him "Ferris" and pretended not to know he was Frazier, it could only be because they had sent her here to spy on him and see if he had repented and was fit for a better place in life. "You'll be all right here," he said. "Nothing's hidden. Most of us haven't got brains enough to have secrets. This is Rainbow Valley." Depressed by the thought that they were having him watched now, he passed his hand over his hair and looked outside to the lawn and the parking lot and the peacocks someone gave the Palais des Nations years ago. The peacocks love no one. They wander about the parked cars looking elderly, bad-tempered, mournful, and lost.

Agnes had settled down again. She folded her silk scarf and placed it just so, with her gloves beside it. She opened her new purse and took out a notebook and a shiny gold pencil. She may have written.

> Duster for desk
> Kleenex
> Glass jar for flowers
> Air-Wick because he smokes
> Paper for lining drawers

because the next day she brought each of these articles to work. She also brought a large black Bible, which she unwrapped lovingly and placed on the left-hand corner of her desk. The flower vase—empty—stood in the middle, and the Kleenex made a counterpoise for the Bible on the right.

When he saw the Bible he knew she had not been sent to spy on his work. The conspiracy was deeper. She might have been dispatched by ghosts. He knew everything about her, all in a moment: He saw the ambition, the terror, the dry pride. She was the true heir of the men from Scotland; she was at the start. She had been sent to tell him, "You can begin, but not begin again." She never opened the Bible, but she dusted it as she dusted her desk, her chair, and any surface the cleaning staff had overlooked. And Peter, the first days, watching her timid movements, her insignificant little face, felt, as you feel the approach of a storm, the charge of moral certainty round her, the belief in work, the faith in undertakings, the bread of the Black Sunday. He recognized and tasted all of it: ashes in the mouth.

After five days their working relations were settled. Of course, there was the Bible and all that went with it, but his tongue had never held the taste of ashes long. She was an inferior girl of poor quality. She had nothing in her favor except the degree on the wall. In the real world, he would not have invited her to his house except to mind the children. That was what he said to Sheilah. He said that Agnes was a mole, and a virgin, and that her tics and mannerisms were sending him round the bend. She had an infuriating habit of covering her mouth when she talked. Even at the telephone she put up her hand as if afraid of losing anything, even a word. Her voice was nasal and flat. She had two working costumes, both dull as the wall. One was the brown suit, the other a navy-blue dress with changeable collars. She dressed for no one; she dressed for her desk, her jar of flowers, her Bible, and her box of Kleenex. One day she crossed the space between the two desks and stood over Peter, who was reading a newspaper. She could have spoken to him from her desk, but she may have felt that being on her feet gave her authority. She had plenty of courage, but authority was something else.

"I thought—I mean, they told me you were the person . . ." She got on with it bravely: "If you don't want to do the filing or any work, all right, Mr. Frazier. I'm not saying anything about that. You might have poor health or your personal reasons. But it's got to be done, so if you'll kindly show me about the filing I'll do it. I've worked in Information before, but it was a different office, and every office is different."

"My dear girl," said Peter. He pushed back his chair and looked at her, astonished. "You've been sitting there fretting, worrying. How insensitive of me. How trying for you. Usually I file on the last Wednesday of the month, so you see, you just haven't been around long enough to see a last Wednesday. Not another word, please. And let us not waste another minute." He emptied the heaped baskets of photographs so swiftly, pushing "Iran—Smallpox Control" into "Irish Red Cross" (close enough), that the girl looked frightened, as if she had raised a whirlwind. She said slowly, "If you'll only show me, Mr. Frazier, instead of doing it so fast, I'll gladly look after it, because you might want to be doing other things, and I feel the filing should be done every day." But Peter was too busy to answer, and so she sat down, holding the edge of her desk.

"There," he said, beaming. "All done." His smile, his sunburst, was wasted, for the girl was staring round the room as if she feared she had not inspected everything the first day after all; some drawer, some cupboard, hid a monster. That evening Peter unlocked one of the drawers of his desk and took away the application form he had stolen from Personnel. The girl had not finished her search.

"How could you *not* know?" wailed Sheilah. "You sit looking at her every day. You must talk about *something*. She must have told you."

"She did tell me," said Peter, "and I've just told you."

It was this: Agnes Brusen was on the Burleighs' guest list. How had the Burleighs met her? What did they see in her? Peter could not reply. He knew that Agnes lived in a bed-sitting room with a Swiss family and had her meals with them. She had been in Geneva three months, but no one had ever seen her outside the office. "You *should* know," said Sheilah. "She must have something, more than you can see. Is she pretty? Is she brilliant? What is it?"

"We don't really talk," Peter said. They talked in a way: Peter teased her and she took no notice. Agnes was not a sulker. She had taken her defeat like a sport. She did her work and a good deal of his. She sat behind her Bible, her flowers, and her Kleenex, and answered when Peter spoke. That was how he learned about the Burleighs—just by teasing and being bored. It was a January afternoon. He said, "*Miss* Brusen. Talk to me. Tell me everything. Pretend we have perfect rapport. Do you like Geneva?"

"It's a nice clean town," she said. He can see to this day the red and blue anemones in the glass jar, and her bent head, and her small untended hands.

"Are you learning beautiful French with your Swiss family?"

"They speak English."

"Why don't you take an apartment of your own?" he said. Peter was not usually impertinent. He was bored. "You'd be independent then."

"I am independent," she said. "I earn my living. I don't think it proves anything if you live by yourself. Mrs. Burleigh wants me to live alone, too. She's looking for something for me. It mustn't be dear. I send money home."

Here was the extraordinary thing about Agnes Brusen: She refused the use of Christian names and never spoke to Peter unless he spoke first, but she would tell anything, as if to say, "Don't waste time fishing. Here it is."

He learned all in one minute that she sent her salary home, and that she was a friend of the Burleighs. The first he had expected; the second knocked him flat.

"She's got to come to dinner," Sheilah said. "We should have had her right from the beginning. If only I'd known! But *you* were the one. You said she looked like—oh, I don't even remember. A Norwegian mole."

She came to dinner one Saturday night in January, in her navy-blue dress, to which she had pinned an organdy gardenia. She sat upright on the edge of the sofa. Sheilah had ordered the meal from a restaurant. There was lobster, good wine, and a *pièce-montée* full of kirsch and cream. Agnes refused the lobster; she had never eaten anything from the sea unless it had been sterilized and tinned, and said so. She was afraid of skin poisoning. Someone in her family had skin poisoning after having eaten oysters. She touched her cheeks and neck to show where the poisoning had erupted. She sniffed her wine and put the glass down without tasting it. She could not eat the cake because of the alcohol it contained. She ate an egg, bread and butter, a sliced tomato, and drank a glass of ginger ale. She seemed unaware she was creating disaster and pain. She did not help clear away the dinner plates. She sat, adequately nourished, decently dressed, and waited to learn why she had been invited here—that was the feeling Peter had. He folded the card table on which they had dined, and opened the window to air the room.

"It's not the same cold as Canada, but you feel it more," he said, for something to say.

"Your blood has gotten thin," said Agnes.

Sheilah returned from the kitchen and let herself fall into an armchair. With her eyes closed she held out her hand for a cigarette. She was performing the haughty-lady act that was a family joke. She flung her head back and looked at Agnes through half-closed lids; then she suddenly brought her head forward, widening her eyes.

"Are you skiing madly?" she said.

"Well, in the first place there hasn't been any snow," said Agnes. "So nobody's doing any skiing so far as I know. All I hear is people complaining because there's no snow. Personally, I don't ski. There isn't much skiing in the part of Canada I come from. Besides, my family never had that kind of leisure."

"Heavens," said Sheilah, as if her family had every kind.

I'll bet they had, thought Peter. On the dole.

Sheilah was wasting her act. He had a suspicion that Agnes knew it was an act but did not know it was also a joke. If so, it made Sheilah seem a fool, and he loved Sheilah too much to enjoy it.

"The Burleighs have been wonderful to me," said Agnes. She seemed to have divined why she was here, and decided to give them all the information they wanted, so that she could put on her coat and go home to bed. "They had me out to their place on the lake every weekend until the weather got cold and they moved back to town. They've rented a chalet for the winter, and they want me to come there, too. But I don't know if I will or not. I don't ski, and, oh, I don't know—I don't drink, either, and I don't always see the point. Their friends are too rich and I'm too Canadian."

She had delivered everything Sheilah wanted and more: Agnes was on the first guest list and didn't care. No, Peter corrected: doesn't know. Doesn't care and doesn't know.

"I thought with you Norwegians it was in the blood, skiing. And drinking," Sheilah murmured.

"Drinking, maybe," said Agnes. She covered her mouth and said behind her spread fingers, "In our family we were religious. We didn't drink or smoke. My brother was in Norway in the war. He saw some cousins. Oh," she said, unexpectedly loud, "Harry said it was just terrible. They were so poor. They had flies in their kitchen. They gave him something to eat a fly had been on. They didn't have a real toilet, and they'd been in the same house about two hundred years. We've only recently built our own home, and we have a bathroom and two toilets. I'm from Saskatchewan," she said. "I'm not from any other place."

Surely one winter here had been punishment enough? In the spring they would remember him and free him. He wrote Lucille, who said he was lucky to have a job at all. The Burleighs had sent the Fraziers a second-guest-list Christmas card. It showed a Moslem refugee child weeping outside a tent. They treasured the card and left it standing long after the others had been given the children to cut up. Peter had discovered by now what had gone wrong in the friendship—Sheilah had charged a skirt at a dressmaker to Madge's account. Madge had told her she might, and then changed her mind. Poor Sheilah! She was new to this part of it—to the changing humors of independent friends. Paris was already a year in the past. At Mardi Gras, the Burleighs gave their annual party. They invited everyone, the damned and the dropped, with the prodigality of a child at prayers. The invitation said "in costume," but the Fraziers were too happy to wear a disguise. They might not be recognized. Like many of the guests they expected to meet at the party, they had been disgraced, forgotten, and rehabilitated. They would be anxious to see one another as they were.

On the night of the party, the Fraziers rented a car they had never seen before and drove through the first snowstorm of the year. Peter had not driven since last summer's blissful trips in the Fiat. He could not find the switch for the windshield wiper in this car. He leaned over the wheel. "Can you see on your side?" he asked. "Can I make a left turn here? Does it look like a one-way?"

"I can't imagine why you took a car with a right-hand drive," said Sheilah.

He had trouble finding a place to park; they crawled up and down unknown streets whose curbs were packed with snow-covered cars. When they stood at last on the pavement, safe and sound, Peter said, "This is the first snow."

"I can see that," said Sheilah. "Hurry, darling. My hair."

"It's the first snow."

"You're repeating yourself," she said. "Please hurry, darling. Think of my poor shoes. My *hair*."

She was born in an ugly city, and so was Peter, but they have this difference: She does not know the importance of the first snow—the first clean thing in a dirty year. He would have told her then that this storm, which was wetting her feet and destroying her hair, was like the first day of the English spring, but she made a frightened gesture, trying to shield her head. The gesture told him he did not understand her beauty.

"Let me," she said. He was fumbling with the key, trying to lock the car. She took the key without impatience and locked the door on the driver's side; and then, to show Peter she treasured him and was not afraid of wasting her life or her beauty, she took his arm and they walked in the snow down a street and around a corner to the apartment house where the Burleighs lived. They were, and are, a united couple. They were afraid of the party, and each of them knew it. When they walk together, holding arms, they give each other whatever each can spare.

Only six people had arrived in costume. Madge Burleigh was disguised as Manet's "Lola de Valence," which everyone mistook for Carmen. Mike was an Impressionist painter, with a straw hat and a glued-on beard. "I am all of them," he said. He would rather have dressed as a dentist, he said, welcoming the Fraziers as if he had parted from them the day before, but Madge wanted him to look as if he had created her. "You know?" he said.

"Perfectly," said Sheilah. Her shoes were stained and the snow had softened her lacquered hair. She was not wasted: She was the most beautiful woman there.

About an hour after their arrival, Peter found himself with no one to talk to. He had told about the Trudeau wedding in Paris and the pot of azaleas, and after he mislaid his audience he began to look round for Sheilah. She was on a window seat, partly concealed by a green velvet curtain. Facing her, so that their profiles were neat and perfect against the night, was a man. Their conversation was private and enclosed, as if they had in minutes covered leagues of time and arrived at the place where everything was implied, understood. Peter began working his way across the room, toward his wife, when he saw Agnes. He was granted the sight of her drowning face. She had dressed with comic intention, obviously with care, and now she was a ragged hobo, half tramp, half clown. Her hair was tucked up under a bowler hat. The six costumed guests who had made the same mistake—the ghost, the gypsy, the Athenian maiden, the geisha, the Martian, and the Apache—were delighted to find a seventh; but Agnes was not amused; she was gasping for life. When a waiter passed with a crowded tray, she took a glass without seeing it; then a wave of the party took her away.

Sheilah's new friend was named Simpson. After Simpson said he thought perhaps he'd better circulate, Peter sat down where he had been. "Now look, Sheilah," he began. Their most intimate conversations have taken place at parties. Once at a party she told him she was leaving him; she didn't, of course. Smiling, blue-eyed, she gazed lovingly at Peter and said rapidly, "Pete, shut up and listen. That man. The man you scared away. He's a big wheel in a company out in India or someplace like that. It's gorgeous out there. Pete, the *servants*. And it's warm. It never never snows. He says there's heaps of jobs. You pick them off the trees like . . . orchids. He says it's even easier now than when we owned all those places, because now the poor pets can't run anything and they'll pay *fortunes*. Pete, he says it's warm, it's heaven, and Pete, they pay."

A few minutes later, Peter was alone again and Sheilah part of a closed, laughing group. Holding her elbow was the man from the place where jobs grew like orchids. Peter edged into the group and laughed at a story he hadn't heard. He heard only the last line, which was "Here comes another tunnel." Looking out from the tight laughing ring, he saw Agnes again, and he thought, I'd be like Agnes if I didn't have Sheilah. Agnes put her glass down on a table and lurched toward the doorway, head forward. Madge Burleigh, who never stopped moving around the room and smiling, was still smiling when she paused and said in Peter's ear, "Go with Agnes, Pete. See that she gets home. People will notice if Mike leaves."

"She probably just wants to walk around the block," said Peter. "She'll be back."

"Oh, stop thinking about yourself, for once, and see that that poor girl gets home," said Madge. "You've still got your Fiat, haven't you?"

He turned away as if he had been pushed. Any command is a release, in a way. He may not want to go in that particular direction, but at least he is going somewhere. And now Sheilah, who had moved inches nearer to hear what Madge and Peter were murmuring, said, "Yes, go, darling," as if he were leaving the gates of Troy.

Peter was to find Agnes and see that she reached home: This he repeated to himself as he stood on the landing, outside the Burleighs' flat, ringing for the elevator. Bored with waiting for it, he ran down the stairs, four flights, and saw that Agnes had stalled the lift by leaving the door open. She was crouched on the floor, propped on her fingertips. Her eyes were closed.

"Agnes," said Peter. "*Miss* Brusen, I mean. That's no way to leave a party. Don't you know you're supposed to curtsy and say thanks? My God, Agnes, anybody going by here just now might have seen you! Come on, be a good girl. Time to go home."

She got up without his help and, moving between invisible crevasses, shut the elevator door. Then she left the building and Peter followed, remembering he was to see that she got home. They walked along the snowy pavement, Peter a few steps behind her. When she turned right for no reason, he turned, too. He had no clear idea where they were going. Perhaps she lived close by. He had forgotten where the hired car was parked, or what it looked like; he could not remember its make or its color. In any case, Sheilah had the key. Agnes walked on steadily, as if she knew their destination, and he thought, Agnes Brusen is drunk in the street in Geneva and dressed like a tramp. He wanted to say, "This is the best thing that ever happened to you, Agnes; it will help you understand how things are for some of the rest of us." But she stopped and turned and, leaning over a low hedge, retched on a frozen lawn. He held her clammy forehead and rested his hand on her arched back, on muscles as tight as a fist. She straightened up and drew a breath but the cold air made her cough. "Don't breathe too deeply," he said. "It's the worst thing you can do. Have you got a handkerchief?" He passed his own handkerchief over her wet weeping face, upturned like the face of one of his little girls. "I'm out without a coat," he said, noticing it. "We're a pair."

"I never drink," said Agnes. "I'm just not used to it." Her voice was sweet and quiet. He had never seen her so peaceful, so composed. He thought she must surely be all right, now, and perhaps he might leave her here. The trust in her tilted face had perplexed him. He wanted to get back to Sheilah and have her explain something. He had forgotten what it was, but Sheilah would know. "Do you live around here?" he said. As he spoke, she let herself fall. He had wiped her face and now she trusted him to pick her up, set her on her feet, take her wherever she ought to be. He pulled her up and she stood, wordless, humble, as he brushed the snow from her tramp's clothes. Snow horizontally crossed the lamplight. The street was silent. Agnes had lost her hat. Snow, which he tasted, melted on her hands. His gesture of licking snow from her hands was formal as a handshake. He tasted snow on her hands and then they walked on.

"I never drink," she said. They stood on the edge of a broad avenue. The wrong turning now could lead them anywhere; it was the changeable avenue at the edge of towns that loses its houses and becomes a highway. She held his arm and spoke in a gentle voice. She said, "In our house we didn't smoke or drink. My mother was ambitious for me, more than for Harry and the others." She said, "I've never been alone before. When I was a kid I would get up in the summer before the others, and I'd see the ice wagon going down the street. I'm alone now. Mrs. Burleigh's found me an apartment. It's only one room. She likes it because it's in the old part of town. I don't like old houses. Old houses are dirty. You don't know who was there before."

"I should have a car somewhere," Peter said. "I'm not sure where we are."

He remembers that on this avenue they climbed into a taxi, but nothing about the drive. Perhaps he fell asleep. He does remember that when he paid the driver Agnes clutched his arm, trying to stop him. She pressed extra coins into the driver's palm. The driver was paid twice.

"I'll tell you one thing about us," said Peter. "We pay everything twice." This was part of a much longer theory concerning North American behavior, and it was not Peter's own. Mike Burleigh had held forth about it on summer afternoons.

Agnes pushed open a door between a stationer's shop and a grocery, and led the way up a narrow inside stair. They climbed one flight, frightening beetles. She had to search every pocket for the latchkey. She was shaking with cold.

Her apartment seemed little warmer than the street. Without speaking to Peter she turned on all the lights. She looked inside the kitchen and the bathroom and then got down on her hands and knees and looked under the sofa. The room was neat and belonged to no one. She left him standing in this unclaimed room—she had forgotten him—and closed a door behind her. He looked for something to do—some useful action he could repeat to Madge. He turned on the electric radiator in the fireplace. Perhaps Agnes wouldn't thank him for it; perhaps she would rather undress in the cold. "I'll be on my way," he called to the bathroom door.

She had taken off the tramp's clothes and put on a dressing gown of orphanage wool. She came out of the bathroom and straight toward him. She pressed her face and rubbed her cheek on his shoulder as if hoping the contact would leave a scar. He saw her back and her profile and his own face in the mirror over the fireplace. He thought, This is how disasters happen. He saw floods of seawater moving with perfect punitive justice over reclaimed land; he saw lava covering vineyards and overtaking dogs and stragglers. A bridge over an abyss snapped in two and the long express train, suddenly V-shaped, floated like snow. He though amiably of every kind of disaster and thought, This is how they occur.

Her eyes were closed. She said, "I shouldn't be over here. In my family we didn't drink or smoke. My mother wanted a lot from me, more than from Harry and the others." But he knew all that; he had known from the day of the Bible, and because once, at the beginning, she had made him afraid. He was not afraid of her now.

She said, "It's no use staying here, is it?"

"If you mean what I think, no."

"It wouldn't be better anywhere."

She let him see full on her blotched face. He was not expected to do anything. He was not required to pick her up when she fell or wipe her tears. She was poor quality, really—he remembered having thought that once. She left him and went quietly into the bathroom and locked the door. He heard taps running and supposed it was a hot bath. He was pretty certain there would be no more tears. He looked at his watch: Sheilah must be home, now, wondering what had become of him. He descended the beetles' staircase and for forty minutes crossed the city under a windless fall of snow.

The neighbor's child who had stayed with Peter's children was asleep on the living-room sofa. Peter woke her and sent her, sleepwalking to her own door. He sat down, wet to the bone, thinking, I'll call the Burleighs. In half an hour I'll call the police. He heard a car stop and the engine running and a confusion of two voices laughing and calling good night. Presently Sheilah let herself in, rosy-faced, smiling. She carried his trench coat over her arm. She said, "How's Agnes?"

"Where were you?" he said. "Whose car was that?"

Sheilah had gone into the children's room. He heard her shutting their window. She returned, undoing her dress, and said, "Was Agnes all right?"

"Agnes is all right. Sheilah, this is about the worst . . ."

She stepped out of the Balenciaga and threw it over a chair. She stopped and looked at him and said, "Poor old Pete, are you in love with Agnes?" And then, as if the answer were of so little importance she hadn't time for it, she locked her arms around him and said, "My love, we're going to Ceylon."

Two days later, when Peter strolled into his office, Agnes was at her desk. She wore the blue dress, with a spotless collar. White and yellow freesias were symmetrically arranged in the glass jar. The room was hot, and the spring snow, glued for a second when it touched the window, blurred the view of parked cars.

"Quite a party," Peter said.

She did not look up. He sighed, sat down, and thought if the snow held he would be skiing at the Burleighs' very soon. Impressed by his kindness to Agnes, Madge had invited the family for the first possible weekend.

Presently Agnes said, "I'll never drink again or go to a house where people are drinking. And I'll never bother anyone the way I bothered you."

"You didn't bother me," he said. "I took you home. You were alone and it was late. It's normal."

"Normal for you, maybe, but I'm used to getting home by myself. Please never tell what happened."

He stared at her. He can still remember the freesias and the Bible and the heat in the room. She looked as if the elements had no power. She felt neither heat nor cold. "Nothing happened," he said.

"I behaved in a silly way. I had no right to. I led you to think I might do something wrong."

"I might have tried something," he said gallantly. "But that would be my fault and not yours."

She put her knuckle to her mouth and he could scarcely hear. "It was because of you. I was afraid you might be blamed, or else you'd blame yourself."

"There's no question of any blame," he said. "Nothing happened. We'd both had a lot to drink. Forget about it. Nothing *happened*. You'd remember if it had."

She put down her hand. There was an expression on her face. Now she sees me, he thought. She had never looked at him after the first day. (He has since tried to put a name to the look on her face; but how can he, now, after so many voyages, after Ceylon, and Hong Kong, and Sheilah's nearly leaving him, and all their difficulties—the money owed, the rows with hotel managers, the lost and found steamer trunk, the children throwing up the foreign food?) She sees me now, he thought. What does she see?

She said, "I'm from a big family. I'm not used to being alone. I'm not a suicidal person, but I could have done something after that party, just not to see anymore, or think or listen or expect anything. What can I think when I see these people? All my life I heard, Educated people don't do this, educated people don't do that. And now I'm here, and you're all educated people, and you're nothing but pigs. You're educated and you drink and do everything wrong and you know what you're doing, and that makes you worse than pigs. My family worked to make me an educated person, but they didn't know you. But what if I didn't see and hear and expect anything anymore? It wouldn't change anything. You'd all be still the same. Only *you* might have thought it was your fault. You might have thought you were to blame. It could worry you all your life. It would have been wrong for me to worry you."

He remembered that the rented car was still along a snowy curb somewhere in Geneva. He wondered if Sheilah had the key in her purse and if she remembered where they'd parked.

"I told you about the ice wagon," Agnes said. "I don't remember everything, so you're wrong about remembering. But I remember telling you that. That was the best. It's the best you can hope to have. In a big family, if you want to be alone, you have to get up before the rest of them. You get up early in the morning in the summer and it's you, you, once in your life alone in the universe. You think you know everything that can happen. . . . Nothing is ever like that again."

He looked at the smeared window and wondered if this day could end without disaster. In his mind he saw her falling in the snow wearing a tramp's costume, and he saw her coming to him in the orphanage dressing gown. He saw her drowning face at the party. He was afraid for himself. The story was still unfinished. It had to come to a climax, something threatening to him. But there was no climax. They talked that day, and afterward nothing else was said. They went on in the same office for a short time, until Peter left for Ceylon; until somebody read the right letter, passed it on for the right initials, and the Fraziers began the Oriental tour that should have made their fortune. Agnes and Peter were too tired to speak after that morning. They were like a married couple in danger, taking care.

But what were they talking about that day, so quietly, such old friends? They talked about dying, about being ambitious, about being religious, about different kinds of love. What did she see when she looked at him—taking her knuckle slowly away from her mouth, bringing her hand down to the desk, letting it rest there? They were both Canadians, so they had this much together—the knowledge of the little you dare admit. Death, near death, the best thing, the wrong thing—God knows what they were telling each other. Anyway, nothing happened.

When, on Sunday mornings, Sheilah and Peter talk about those times, they take on the glamour of something still to come. It is then he remembers Agnes Brusen. He never says her name. Sheilah wouldn't remember Agnes. Agnes is the only secret Peter has from his wife, the only puzzle he pieces together without her help. He thinks about families in the West as they were fifteen, twenty years ago—the iron-cold ambition, and every member pushing the next one on. He thinks of his father's parties. When he thinks of his father he imagines him with Sheilah, in a crowd. Actually, Sheilah and Peter's father never met, but they might have liked each other. His father admired good-looking women. Peter wonders what they were doing over there in Geneva—not Sheilah and Peter, *Agnes* and Peter. It is almost as if they had once run away together, silly as children, irresponsible as lovers. Peter and Sheilah are back where they started. While they were out in world affairs picking up microbes and debts, always on the fringe of disaster, the fringe of a fortune, Agnes went on and did—what? They lost each other. He thinks of the ice wagon going down the street. He sees something he has never seen in his life—a Western town that belongs to Agnes. Here is Agnes—small, mole-faced, round-shouldered because she has always carried a younger child. She watches the ice wagon and the trail of ice water in a morning invented for her: hers. He sees the weak prairie trees and the shadows on the sidewalk. Nothing moves except the shadows and the ice wagon and the changing amber of the child's eyes. The child is Peter. He has seen the grain of the cement sidewalk and the grass in the cracks, and the dust, and the dandelions at the edge of the road. He is there. He has taken the morning that belongs to Agnes, he is up before the others, and he knows everything. There is nothing he doesn't know. He could keep the morning, if he wanted to, but what can Peter do with the start of a summer day? Sheilah is here, it is a true Sunday morning, with its dimness and headache and remorse and regrets, and this is life. He says, "We have the Balenciaga." He touches Sheilah's hand. The children have their aunt now, and he and Sheilah have each other. Everything works out, somehow or other. Let Agnes have the start of the day. Let Agnes think it was invented for her. Who wants to be alone in the universe? No, begin at the beginning: Peter lost Agnes. Agnes says to herself somewhere, Peter is lost.

1963

GEORGE GARRETT
1929–2008

Garrett was born in Orlando, Florida. After his secondary schooling at the Sewanee Military Academy he went on to Princeton for his B.A. and M.A. degrees. Ever since, his prodigious output includes verse as well as fiction, satires, reviews, and assorted commentary on the literary scene. At the core of his protean achievement is a trilogy of "Elizabethan" novels, *Death of the Fox* (1971), *The Succession* (1983), and *Entered from the Sun* (1990), which are not only historical novels featuring Sir Walter Raleigh, Queen Elizabeth, and Christopher Marlowe but also imaginative verbal and fictive explorations of the dimensions of human understanding. His other novels include *Which Ones Are the Enemy?* (1961), *Do, Lord, Remember Me* (1965), *The Magic Striptease* (1973), and *Double Vision* (2004). Other short stories by Garrett can be found in *A Wreath for Garibaldi* (1969) and *An Evening Performance* (1985). His latest publications include *Days of Our Lives Lie in Fragments: Poems* (1998), *Bad Man Blues* (1998), and his final collection, *Empty Bed Blues* (2006). His many awards include the Award in Literature from the American Academy of Arts and Letters (1985). Garrett was Poet Laureate of Virginia from 2002 to 2006.

Feeling Good, Feeling Fine

A boy and a man in the park. Between them a wooden bat, a battered and dirty baseball, and one leather glove, well tended and cared for, oiled and supple, but old, too, its pocket now as thin as paper.

The boy and the man are sweating in the late afternoon light. Lazy end of a long summer day. The park (no more than a rough grass field) is empty now except for the two of them. Somewhere not far away a car horn toots, a dog barks, a woman calls her children in for early supper.

"Come on," the man shouts. "Knock it to me!"

The boy, all concentration, tosses the ball up and then swings the bat to loft it high above the man. Who, skinny and raggedy as a scarecrow, moves back and away and underneath the high fly ball. Spears it with the glove. Then throws it high back toward the boy. The ball rolls dead, an easy reach from his feet.

"Let's quit and go home," the boy calls.

The tall man shakes his head and moves back deeper.

"One more," he hollers. "Just one more."

Crack of the bat on the ball, and this is the best one yet. A home run ball in the fading light, almost lost in the last blue of the sky. The man shading his eyes as he runs back and back until he's there where he has to be to snag it. Snags it. Then comes running in toward the boy, grinning, a loping outfielder who has made the final catch of an inning.

You might think the boy would be pleased to have swung his bat (the glove and the bat and the ball are all his) that well and knocked the ball so high and far. But truth is the boy hates baseball. "It's my least favorite sport," he will tell anyone who asks. Anyone except the man running toward him, his uncle, his mother's brother, who has recently come to live with them after several years away at the state hospital.

Uncle Jack, he's had a hard time of it. First time he went crazy, his wife ran off with their two daughters, the boy's cousins, to California or some place like that and disappeared for keeps. Boy doesn't know it, can't comprehend it even if he could imagine it, but he won't ever see that woman and his two cousins again. Uncle Jack is living with the boy's family for the time being, "until he has a chance to get things straightened out," the boy's father explains. When the boy complains about the hours spent—wasted as far as he's concerned—knocking fungoes and chasing flys and grounders with Uncle Jack, his father simply says, "Humor him, boy. He's good at it. Let him be."

He ain't that good, the boy sometimes thinks, but doesn't say. Said it once, though, and his father corrected him.

"Listen, boy, he's rusty and he hasn't been well. But believe me, I'm here to tell you, he was some kind of a baseball player. A real pleasure to watch."

"Minor league," scornfully said the boy, who can't imagine anyone settling for anything less than the top of the heap. If he liked baseball enough to want to play at it, he would be in the majors or nothing. He sure enough wouldn't be happy with some old photographs in an album and some brittle, yellowing newspaper clippings.

And if he was a crazy man back from the state hospital and had a nephew who was required to humor him, the boy would never pretend, let alone believe for one minute, that he was getting himself back in shape so he could join the New York Yankees or the Washington Senators or somebody like that. Shit, Uncle Jack couldn't even play for the Brooklyn Dodgers.

Uncle Jack now has the bat in one hand and the other arm around the boy's shoulders (the boy carries the glove and the ball) as the two of them head for home in the twilight.

"You hit that last one a helluva good lick," Uncle Jack says. "You could be a real hitter if you put your mind to it. It's all in the coordination, and you have got that, all you could ever need."

Why, if he hates baseball, does the boy relish and rejoice in the man's words? Why, if his Uncle Jack is some kind of crazy person and is fooling himself and everybody else, too, about what a great ballplayer he was and thinks he still is, why does the boy automatically accept and enjoy his uncle's judgment? Why, if his uncle is mostly embarrassment and trouble, someone to be ashamed of, does the boy at this very instant, altogether in spite of himself, wish more than anything that this tall, thin, raggedy, graceful man was and is everything he ought to be or could have been?

(Years and years later, when this boy is a grandfather himself, for reasons he won't understand then any more than he does now, he will tell his grandchildren, and anyone else who will bother to listen to him, all about his Uncle Jack, who was, briefly—but is not all beauty and all great achievement as brief as the flare of a struck match?—a wonderful athlete, a baseball player much admired and envied by his peers, someone who, except for a piece or two of bad luck, would have been named and honored among the very best of them. Someone to be proud of. Someone who once tried to teach him how to play the game.)

They are close to home now. They have left the raw, wide field behind and are coming under a dark canopy of shade. Houses with green crisp lawns, dark earth and, here and there, a sprinkler pulsing bright water. Can see the lights of the boy's house being switched on downstairs. Can hear briefly, before his father's voice calls out a crisp command, music playing on the radio. That will be his sister or his little brother fooling around. Upstairs probably. He is almost close enough to see through the lighted windows of the dining room his mother and Hattie, the maid, who works late and long for them in this Great Depression, setting the supper table with flat silver, napkins, and water glasses. For a little time, the short walk, more of a stroll into gradual dark, he has been almost content. Weary, sweated out, but feeling good, feeling fine, soothed by his uncle's complimentary words. Confident that whatever he does from here and now to the end of his life will be and go well. Even more: that he will be able not only to enjoy this feeling of satisfaction, of joy, really, but will be able to share it with others less fortunate than himself.

What he cannot know, even as he and his uncle come across the lawn and into the house and shut the front door behind him, what he can't know and will not choose to remember years and years later when he rakes the bitter ashes of his life searching for even one remaining glowing coal, is what happens next.

At the table his father (who includes the whole family, even Hattie, in almost everything) will tell them about the long-distance telephone call he received at his office this same afternoon from a doctor at the state hospital in Chattahoochee. The doctor has told him that there is a new kind of operation on the brain that might, just might, cure Uncle Jack for good and all. No more coming and going, no more breakdowns and slow recoveries. It is a new thing. There can be no promises or guarantees, of course. And, as in any operation, there is always danger, there are always risks. But . . .

Everybody listens intently. (Except Hattie, who elects to slip back into the kitchen quietly.) Everybody listens. And then before Jack or anyone can say anything, his mother bursts into tears. Sobs at the table, trying to hide her face with her hands, her shoulders shaking.

Later that evening the boy will see his father, for the first and maybe the only time, slap his mother full across her soft face, making her sob again as they quarrel about what may be the best thing for her brother to do. His uncle will settle the quarrel by freely and cheerfully choosing to return to the hospital to undergo this operation. And—the boy and man would warn them then and now, if there were some way, any way, if only he could—it went badly, as badly as can be, leaving his uncle no more than half alive, a vegetable in that hospital for the rest of his life. The boy will live to be an old man, will go to war and live through it, will learn all the lessons—of love and death, of gain and loss, of pride and of regret—a long life can teach.

But none of this has happened yet. Man and boy have spent a long afternoon in the park together and, at the end of it, have come home. They come in the front door. Jack grabs his sister, the boy's mother, and gives her a bear hug, lifts her in the air. The boy goes to put the bat and the ball and the glove in the hall closet. Over his shoulder he hears his sister and brother coming down the stairs like a pair of wild ponies. Looking up, turning, he sees his father, smiling in shirtsleeves, coming out of the living room with the evening paper in his hands.

"Here they are," he says. "Here come our baseball players just in time for supper."

2006

CHARLOTTE PERKINS GILMAN
1860–1935

Gilman was born in Hartford, Connecticut. Aspiring to be an artist, she briefly attended the Rhode Island School of Design and married the artist Charles Stetson. After the birth of their daughter she went into a deep and long-drawn depression. The medical treatment available not only failed to help her, it angered her. She was told to limit herself to a quiet domestic life and "never to touch pen, brush, or pencil again." From her anger sprang her famous story "The Yellow Wallpaper" and a long career as a lecturer and a writer of tracts and books expounding feminist causes. Her second marriage, when her mental health had improved, was a solid and productive one. Among her writings are the novels *What Diantha Did* (1910), *The Crux* (1911), and *Herland* (1915). She ended her own life in 1935.

The Yellow Wallpaper

It is very seldom that mere ordinary people like John and myself secure ancestral halls for the summer.

A colonial mansion, a hereditary estate, I would say a haunted house and reach the height of romantic felicity—but that would be asking too much of fate!

Still I will proudly declare that there is something queer about it.

Else, why should it be let so cheaply? And why have stood so long untenanted?

John laughs at me, of course, but one expects that.

John is practical in the extreme. He has no patience with faith, an intense horror of superstition, and he scoffs openly at any talk of things not to be felt and seen and put down in figures.

John is a physician, and *perhaps*—(I would not say it to a living soul, of course, but this is dead paper and a great relief to my mind)—*perhaps* that is one reason I do not get well faster.

You see, he does not believe I am sick! And what can one do?

If a physician of high standing, and one's own husband, assures friends and relatives that there is really nothing the matter with one but temporary nervous depression—a slight hysterical tendency[1]—what is one to do?

---

1. At the time this story was written, *hysteria* was a term used loosely to describe a wide variety of symptoms, thought to be particularly prevalent among women, that indicated emotional disturbance or dysfunction. Depression, anxiety, excitability, and vague somatic complaints were among the conditions treated as "hysteria."

My brother is also a physician, and also of high standing, and he says the same thing.

So I take phosphates or phosphites—whichever it is—and tonics, and air and exercise, and journeys, and am absolutely forbidden to "work" until I am well again.

Personally, I disagree with their ideas.

Personally, I believe that congenial work, with excitement and change, would do me good.

But what is one to do?

I did write for a while in spite of them; but it *does* exhaust me a good deal—having to be so sly about it, or else meet with heavy opposition.

I sometimes fancy that in my condition, if I had less opposition and more society and stimulus—but John says the very worst thing I can do is to think about my condition, and I confess it always makes me feel bad.

So I will let it alone and talk about the house.

The most beautiful place! It is quite alone, standing well back from the road, quite three miles from the village. It makes me think of English places that you read about, for there are hedges and walls and gates that lock, and lots of separate little houses for the gardeners and people.

There is a *delicious* garden! I never saw such a garden—large and shady, full of box-bordered paths, and lined with long grape-covered arbors with seats under them.

There were greenhouses, but they are all broken now.

There was some legal trouble, I believe, something about the heirs and co-heirs; anyhow, the place has been empty for years.

That spoils my ghostliness, I am afraid, but I don't care—there is something strange about the house—I can feel it.

I even said so to John one moonlight evening, but he said what I felt was a draught, and shut the window.

I get unreasonably angry with John sometimes. I'm sure I never used to be so sensitive. I think it is due to this nervous condition.

But John says if I feel so, I shall neglect proper self-control; so I take pains to control myself—before him, at least, and that makes me very tired.

I don't like our room a bit. I wanted one downstairs that opened on the piazza and had roses all over the window, and such pretty old-fashioned chintz hangings! But John would not hear of it.

He said there was only one window and not room for two beds, and no near room for him if he took another.

He is very careful and loving, and hardly lets me stir without special direction.

I have a schedule prescription for each hour in the day; he takes all care from me, and so I feel basely ungrateful not to value it more.

He said we came here solely on my account, that I was to have perfect rest and all the air I could get. "Your exercise depends on your strength, my dear," said he, "and your food somewhat on your appetite; but air you can absorb all the time." So we took the nursery at the top of the house.

It is a big, airy room, the whole floor nearly, with windows that look all ways, and air and sunshine galore. It was nursery first and then playroom and gymnasium, I should judge; for the windows are barred for little children, and there are rings and things in the walls.

Setting

The paint and paper look as if a boys' school had used it. It is stripped off—the paper—in great patches all around the head of my bed, about as far as I can reach, and in a great place on the other side of the room low down. I never saw a worse paper in my life. One of those sprawling flamboyant patterns committing every artistic sin.

It is dull enough to confuse the eye in following, pronounced enough to constantly irritate and provoke study, and when you follow the lame uncertain curves for a little distance they suddenly commit suicide—plunge off at outrageous angles, destroy themselves in unheard-of contradictions.

The color is repellant, almost revolting; a smouldering unclean yellow, strangely faded by the slow-turning sunlight. It is a dull yet lurid orange in some places, a sickly sulphur tint in others.

No wonder the children hated it! I should hate it myself if I had to live in this room long.

There comes John, and I must put this away—he hates to have me write a word.

We have been here two weeks, and I haven't felt like writing before, since that first day.

I am sitting by the window now, up in this atrocious nursery, and there is nothing to hinder my writing as much as I please, save lack of strength.

John is away all day, and even some nights when his cases are serious.

I am glad my case is not serious!

But these nervous troubles are dreadfully depressing.

John does not know how much I really suffer. He knows there is no reason to suffer, and that satisfies him.

Of course it is only nervousness. It does weigh on me so not to do my duty in any way!

I mean to be such a help to John, such a real rest and comfort, and here I am a comparative burden already!

Nobody would believe what an effort it is to do what little I am able—to dress and entertain, and order things.

It is fortunate Mary is so good with the baby. Such a dear baby!

And yet I *cannot* be with him, it makes me so nervous.

I suppose John never was nervous in his life. He laughs at me so about this wallpaper!

At first he meant to repaper the room, but afterwards he said that I was letting it get the better of me, and that nothing was worse for a nervous patient than to give way to such fancies.

He said that after the wallpaper was changed it would be the heavy bedstead, and then the barred windows, and then that gate at the head of the stairs, and so on.

"You know the place is doing you good," he said, "and really, dear, I don't care to renovate the house just for a three months' rental."

"Then do let us go downstairs," I said. "There are such pretty rooms there."

Then he took me in his arms and called me a blessed little goose, and said he would go down cellar, if I wished, and have it whitewashed into the bargain.

But he is right enough about the beds and windows and things.

It is as airy and comfortable a room as anyone need wish, and, of course, I would not be so silly as to make him uncomfortable just for a whim.

I'm really getting quite fond of the big room, all but that horrid paper.

Out of one window I can see the garden—those mysterious deep-shaded arbors, the riotous old-fashioned flowers, and bushes and gnarly trees.

Out of another I get a lovely view of the bay and a little private wharf belonging to the estate. There is a beautiful shaded lane that runs down there from the house. I always fancy I see people walking in these numerous paths and arbors, but John has cautioned me not to give way to fancy in the least. He says that with my imaginative power and habit of story-making, a nervous weakness like mine is sure to lead to all manner of excited fancies, and that I ought to use my will and good sense to check the tendency. So I try.

I think sometimes that if I were only well enough to write a little it would relieve the press of ideas and rest me.

But I find I get pretty tired when I try.

It is so discouraging not to have any advice and companionship about my work. When I get really well, John says we will ask Cousin Henry and Julia down for a long visit; but he says he would as soon put fireworks in my pillow-case as to let me have those stimulating people about now.

I wish I could get well faster.

But I must not think about that. This paper looks to me as if it *knew* what a vicious influence it had!

There is a recurrent spot where the pattern lolls like a broken neck and two bulbous eyes stare at you upside down.

I get positively angry with the impertinence of it and the everlastingness. Up and down and sideways they crawl, and those absurd unblinking eyes are everywhere. There is one place where two breadths didn't match, and the eyes go all up and down the line, one a little higher than the other.

I never saw so much expression in an inanimate thing before, and we all know how much expression they have! I used to lie awake as a child and get more entertainment and terror out of blank walls and plain furniture than most children could find in a toy-store.

I remember what a kindly wink the knobs of our big old bureau used to have, and there was one chair that always seemed like a strong friend.

I used to feel that if any of the other things looked too fierce I could always hop into that chair and be safe.

The furniture in this room is no worse than inharmonious, however, for we had to bring it all from downstairs. I suppose when this was used as a play-room they had to take the nursery things out, and no wonder! I never saw such ravages as the children have made here.

The wallpaper, as I said before, is torn off in spots, and it sticketh closer than a brother[2]—they must have had perseverance as well as hatred.

Then the floor is scratched and gouged and splintered, the plaster itself is dug out here and there, and this great heavy bed which is all we found in the room, looks as if it had been through the wars.

But I don't mind it a bit—only the paper.

---

2. See Proverbs 18:24: "A man that hath friends must show himself friendly; and there is a friend that sticketh closer than a brother."

There comes John's sister. Such a dear girl as she is, and so careful of me! I must not let her find me writing.

She is a perfect and enthusiastic housekeeper, and hopes for no better profession. I verily believe she thinks it is the writing which made me sick!

But I can write when she is out, and see her a long way off from these windows.

There is one that commands the road, a lovely shaded winding road, and one that just looks off over the country. A lovely country, too, full of great elms and velvet meadows.

This wallpaper has a kind of sub-pattern in a different shade, a particularly irritating one, for you can only see it in certain lights, and not clearly then.

But in the places where it isn't faded and where the sun is just so—I can see a strange, provoking, formless sort of figure that seems to skulk about behind that silly and conspicuous front design.

There's sister on the stairs!

Well, the Fourth of July is over! The people are all gone, and I am tired out. John thought it might do me good to see a little company, so we just had Mother and Nellie and the children down for a week.

Of course I didn't do a thing. Jennie sees to everything now.

But it tired me all the same.

John says if I don't pick up faster he shall send me to Weir Mitchell[3] in the fall.

But I don't want to go there at all. I had a friend who was in his hands once, and she says he is just like John and my brother, only more so!

Besides, it is such an undertaking to go so far.

I don't feel as if it was worthwhile to turn my hand over for anything, and I'm getting dreadfully fretful and querulous.

I cry at nothing, and cry most of the time.

Of course I don't when John is here, or anybody else, but when I am alone.

And I am alone a good deal just now. John is kept in town very often by serious cases, and Jennie is good and lets me alone when I want her to.

So I walk a little in the garden or down that lovely lane, sit on the porch under the roses, and lie down up here a good deal.

I'm getting really fond of the room in spite of the wallpaper. Perhaps *because* of the wallpaper.

It dwells in my mind so!

I lie here on this great immovable bed—it is nailed down, I believe—and follow that pattern about by the hour. It is as good as gymnastics, I assure you. I start, we'll say, at the bottom, down in the corner over there where it has not been touched, and I determine for the thousandth time that I *will* follow that pointless pattern to some sort of conclusion.

I know a little of the principle of design, and I know this thing was not arranged on any laws of radiation, or alternation, or repetition, or symmetry, or anything else that I ever heard of.

It is repeated, of course, by the breadths, but not otherwise.

---

3. Silas Weir Mitchell (1829–1914), American physician, novelist, and specialist in nerve disorders, popularized the "rest cure" in the management of hysteria, nervous breakdowns, and related disorders.

Looked at in one way, each breadth stands alone; the bloated curves and flourishes—a kind of "debased Romanesque"[4] with delirium tremens—go waddling up and down in isolated columns of fatuity.

But, on the other hand, they connect diagonally, and the sprawling outlines run off in great slanting waves of optic horror, like a lot of wallowing seaweeds in full chase.

The whole thing goes horizontally, too, at least it seems so, and I exhaust myself trying to distinguish the order of its going in that direction.

They have used a horizontal breadth for a frieze,[5] and that adds wonderfully to the confusion.

There is one end of the room where it is almost intact, and there, when the crosslights fade and the low sun shines directly upon it, I can almost fancy radiation after all—the interminable grotesque seems to form around a common center and rush off in headlong plunges of equal distraction.

It makes me tired to follow it. I will take a nap, I guess.

I don't know why I should write this.

I don't want to.

I don't feel able.

And I know John would think it absurd. But I *must* say what I feel and think in some way—it is such a relief!

But the effort is getting to be greater than the relief.

Half the time now I am awfully lazy, and lie down ever so much.

John says I mustn't lose my strength, and has me take cod liver oil and lots of tonics and things, to say nothing of ale and wine and rare meat.

Dear John! He loves me very dearly, and hates to have me sick. I tried to have a real earnest reasonable talk with him the other day, and tell him how I wish he would let me go and make a visit to Cousin Henry and Julia.

But he said I wasn't able to go, nor able to stand it after I got there; and I did not make out a very good case for myself, for I was crying before I had finished.

It is getting to be a great effort for me to think straight. Just this nervous weakness, I suppose.

And dear John gathered me up in his arms, and just carried me upstairs and laid me on the bed, and sat by me and read to me till it tired my head.

He said I was his darling and his comfort, and all he had, and that I must take care of myself for his sake, and keep well.

He says no one but myself can help me out of it, that I must use my will and self-control and not let any silly fancies run away with me.

There's one comfort—the baby is well and happy, and does not have to occupy this nursery with the horrid wallpaper.

If we had not used it, that blessed child would have! What a fortunate escape! Why, I wouldn't have a child of mine, an impressionable little thing, live in such a room for worlds.

I never thought of it before, but it is lucky that John kept me here after all, I can stand it so much easier than a baby, you see.

4. Romanesque style is here associated with ornamental complexity and repeated motifs and figures.
5. An ornamental band used as a border at the top of the wall.

Of course I never mention it to them any more—I am too wise—but I keep watch for it all the same.

There are things in that paper that nobody knows about but me, or ever will.

Behind that outside pattern the dim shapes get clearer every day.

It is always the same shape, only very numerous.

And it is like a woman stooping down and creeping about behind that pattern. I don't like it a bit. I wonder—I begin to think—I wish John would take me away from here!

It is so hard to talk with John about my case, because he is so wise, and because he loves me so.

But I tried it last night.

It was moonlight. The moon shines in all around just as the sun does.

I hate to see it sometimes, it creeps so slowly, and always comes in by one window or another.

John was asleep and I hated to waken him, so I kept still and watched the moonlight on that undulating wallpaper till I felt creepy.

The faint figure behind seemed to shake the pattern, just as if she wanted to get out.

I got up softly and went to feel and see if the paper *did* move, and when I came back John was awake.

"What is it, little girl?" he said. "Don't go walking about like that—you'll get cold."

I thought it was a good time to talk, so I told him that I really was not gaining here, and that I wished he would take me away.

"Why, darling!" said he. "Our lease will be up in three weeks, and I can't see how to leave before.

"The repairs are not done at home, and I cannot possibly leave town just now. Of course if you were in any danger, I could and would, but you really are better, dear, whether you can see it or not. I am a doctor, dear, and I know. You are gaining flesh and color, your appetite is better, I feel really much easier about you."

"I don't weigh a bit more," said I, "nor as much; and my appetite may be better in the evening when you are here but it is worse in the morning when you are away!"

"Bless her little heart!" said he with a big hug. "She shall be as sick as she pleases! But now let's improve the shining hours by going to sleep, and talk about it in the morning!"

"And you won't go away?" I asked gloomily.

"Why, how can I, dear? It is only three weeks more and then we will take a nice little trip of a few days while Jennie is getting the house ready. Really, dear, you are better!"

"Better in body perhaps—" I began, and stopped short, for he sat up straight and looked at me with such a stern, reproachful look that I could not say another word.

"My darling," said he, "I beg of you, for my sake and for our child's sake, as well as for your own, that you will never for one instant let that idea enter your mind! There is nothing so dangerous, so fascinating, to a temperament like yours. It is a false and foolish fancy. Can you not trust me as a physician when I tell you so?"

So of course I said no more on that score, and we went to sleep before long. He thought I was asleep first, but I wasn't, and lay there for hours trying to decide whether that front pattern and the back pattern really did move together or separately.

On a pattern like this, by daylight, there is a lack of sequence, a defiance of law, that is a constant irritant to a normal mind.

The color is hideous enough, and unreliable enough, and infuriating enough, but the pattern is torturing.

You think you have mastered it, but just as you get well under way in following, it turns a back-somersault and there you are. It slaps you in the face, knocks you down, and tramples upon you. It is like a bad dream.

The outside pattern is a florid arabesque, reminding one of a fungus. If you can imagine a toadstool in joints, an interminable string of toadstools, budding and sprouting in endless convolutions—why, that is something like it.

That is, sometimes!

There is one marked peculiarity about this paper, a thing nobody seems to notice but myself, and that is that it changes as the light changes.

When the sun shoots in through the east window—I always watch for that first long, straight ray—it changes so quickly that I never can quite believe it.

That is why I watch it always.

By moonlight—the moon shines in all night when there is a moon—I wouldn't know it was the same paper.

At night in any kind of light, in twilight, candlelight, lamplight, and worst of all by moonlight, it becomes bars! The outside pattern, I mean, and the woman behind it is as plain as can be.

I didn't realize for a long time what the thing was that showed behind, that dim sub-pattern, but now I am quite sure it is a woman.

By daylight she is subdued, quiet. I fancy it is the pattern that keeps her so still. It is so puzzling. It keeps me quiet by the hour.

I lie down ever so much now. John says it is good for me, and to sleep all I can.

Indeed he started the habit by making me lie down for an hour after each meal.

It is a very bad habit I am convinced, for you see, I don't sleep.

And that cultivates deceit, for I don't tell them I'm awake—O no!

The fact is I am getting a little afraid of John.

He seems very queer sometimes, and even Jennie has an inexplicable look.

It strikes me occasionally, just as a scientific hypothesis, that perhaps it is the paper!

I have watched John when he did not know I was looking, and come into the room suddenly on the most innocent excuses, and I've caught him several times *looking at the paper!* And Jennie too. I caught Jennie with her hand on it once.

She didn't know I was in the room, and when I asked her in a quiet, a very quiet voice, with the most restrained manner possible, what she was doing with the paper—she turned around as if she had been caught stealing, and looked quite angry—asked me why I should frighten her so!

Then she said that the paper stained everything it touched, that she had found yellow smooches on all my clothes and John's, and she wished we would be more careful!

Did not that sound innocent? But I know she was studying that pattern, and I am determined that nobody shall find it out but myself!

Life is very much more exciting now than it used to be. You see I have something more to expect, to look forward to, to watch. I really do eat better, and am more quiet than I was.

John is so pleased to see me improve! He laughed a little the other day, and said I seemed to be flourishing in spite of my wallpaper.

I turned it off with a laugh. I had no intention of telling him it was *because* of the wallpaper—he would make fun of me. He might even want to take me away.

I don't want to leave now until I have found it out. There is a week more, and I think that will be enough.

I'm feeling so much better!

I don't sleep much at night, for it is so interesting to watch developments; but I sleep a good deal during the daytime.

In the daytime it is tiresome and perplexing.

There are always new shoots on the fungus, and new shades of yellow all over it. I cannot keep count of them, though I have tried conscientiously.

It is the strangest yellow, that wallpaper! It makes me think of all the yellow things I ever saw—not beautiful ones like buttercups, but old, foul, bad yellow things.

But there is something else about that paper—the smell! I noticed it the moment we came into the room, but with so much air and sun it was not bad. Now we have had a week of fog and rain, and whether the windows are open or not, the smell is here.

It creeps all over the house.

I find it hovering in the dining-room, skulking in the parlor, hiding in the hall, lying in wait for me on the stairs.

It gets into my hair.

Even when I go to ride, if I turn my head suddenly and surprise it—there is that smell!

Such a peculiar odor, too! I have spent hours in trying to analyze it, to find what it smelled like.

It is not bad—at first—and very gentle, but quite the subtlest, most enduring odor I ever met.

In this damp weather it is awful, I wake up in the night and find it hanging over me.

It used to disturb me at first. I thought seriously of burning the house—to reach the smell.

But now I am used to it. The only thing I can think of that it is like is the *color* of the paper! A yellow smell.

There is a very funny mark on this wall, low down, near the mopboard. A streak that runs round the room. It goes behind every piece of furniture, except the bed, a long, straight, even *smooch,* as if it had been rubbed over and over.

I wonder how it was done and who did it, and what they did it for. Round and round and round—round and round and round—it makes me dizzy!

I really have discovered something at last.

Through watching so much at night, when it changes so, I have finally found out.

The front pattern *does* move—and no wonder! The woman behind shakes it!

Sometimes I think there are a great many women behind, and sometimes only one, and she crawls around fast, and her crawling shakes it all over.

Then in the very bright spots she keeps still, and in the very shady spots she just takes hold of the bars and shakes them hard.

And she is all the time trying to climb through. But nobody could climb through that pattern—it strangles so; I think that is why it has so many heads.

They get through, and then the pattern strangles them off and turns them upside down, and makes their eyes white!

If those heads were covered or taken off it would not be half so bad.

I think that woman gets out in the daytime!

And I'll tell you why—privately—I've seen her!

I can see her out of every one of my windows!

It is the same woman, I know, for she is always creeping, and most women do not creep by daylight.

I see her in that long shaded lane, creeping up and down. I see her in those dark grape arbors, creeping all around the garden.

I see her on that long road under the trees, creeping along, and when a carriage comes she hides under the blackberry vines.

I don't blame her a bit. It must be very humiliating to be caught creeping by daylight!

I always lock the door when I creep by daylight. I can't do it at night, for I know John would suspect something at once.

And John is so queer now that I don't want to irritate him. I wish he would take another room! Besides, I don't want anybody to get that woman out at night but myself.

I often wonder if I could see her out of all the windows at once.

But, turn as fast as I can, I can only see out of one at one time.

And though I always see her, she *may* be able to creep faster than I can turn! I have watched her sometimes away off in the open country, creeping as fast as a cloud shadow in a wind.

If only that top pattern could be gotten off from the under one! I mean to try it, little by little.

I have found out another funny thing, but I shan't tell it this time! It does not do to trust people too much.

There are only two more days to get this paper off, and I believe John is beginning to notice. I don't like the look in his eyes.

And I heard him ask Jennie a lot of professional questions about me. She had a very good report to give.

She said I slept a good deal in the daytime.

John knows I don't sleep very well at night, for all I'm so quiet!

He asked me all sorts of questions, too, and pretended to be very loving and kind.

As if I couldn't see through him!

Still, I don't wonder he acts so, sleeping under this paper for three months.

It only interests me, but I feel sure John and Jennie are affected by it.

Hurrah! This is the last day, but it is enough. John is to stay in town over night, and won't be out until this evening.

Jennie wanted to sleep with me—the sly thing; but I told her I should undoubtedly rest better for a night all alone.

That was clever, for really I wasn't alone a bit! As soon as it was moonlight and that poor thing began to crawl and shake the pattern, I got up and ran to help her.

I pulled and she shook, I shook and she pulled, and before morning we had peeled off yards of that paper.

A strip about as high as my head and half around the room.

And then when the sun came and that awful pattern began to laugh at me, I declared I would finish it today!

We go away tomorrow, and they are moving all my furniture down again to leave things as they were before.

Jennie looked at the wall in amazement, but I told her merrily that I did it out of pure spite at the vicious thing.

She laughed and said she wouldn't mind doing it herself, but I must not get tired.

How she betrayed herself that time!

But I am here, and no person touches this paper but Me—not *alive*!

She tried to get me out of the room—it was too patent! But I said it was so quiet and empty and clean now that I believed I would lie down again and sleep all I could; and not to wake me even for dinner—I would call when I woke.

So now she is gone, and the servants are gone, and the things are gone, and there is nothing left but that great bedstead nailed down, with the canvas mattress we found on it.

We shall sleep downstairs tonight, and take the boat home tomorrow.

I quite enjoy the room, now it is bare again.

How those children did tear about here!

This bedstead is fairly gnawed!

But I must get to work.

I have locked the door and thrown the key down into the front path.

I don't want to go out, and I don't want to have anybody come in, till John comes.

I want to astonish him.

I've got a rope up here that even Jennie did not find. If that woman does get out, and tries to get away, I can tie her!

But I forgot I could not reach far without anything to stand on!

This bed will *not* move!

I tried to lift and push it until I was lame, and then I got so angry I bit off a little piece at one corner—but it hurt my teeth.

Then I peeled off all the paper I could reach standing on the floor. It sticks horribly and the pattern just enjoys it! All those strangled heads and bulbous eyes and waddling fungus growths just shriek with derision!

I am getting angry enough to do something desperate. To jump out of the window would be admirable exercise, but the bars are too strong even to try.

Besides I wouldn't do it. Of course not. I know well enough that a step like that is improper and might be misconstrued.

I don't like to *look* out of the windows even—there are so many of those creeping women, and they creep so fast.

I wonder if they all come out of that wallpaper as I did?

But I am securely fastened now by my well-hidden rope—you don't get *me* out in the road there!

I suppose I shall have to get back behind the pattern when it comes night, and that is hard!

It is so pleasant to be out in this great room and creep around as I please!

I don't want to go outside. I won't, even if Jennie asks me to.

For outside you have to creep on the ground, and everything is green instead of yellow.

But here I can creep smoothly on the floor, and my shoulder just fits in that long smooch around the wall, so I cannot lose my way.

Why there's John at the door!

It is no use, young man, you can't open it!

How he does call and pound!

Now he's crying to Jennie for an axe.

It would be a shame to break down that beautiful door!

"John dear!" said I in the gentlest voice. "The key is down by the front steps, under a plantain leaf!"

That silenced him for a few moments.

Then he said—very quietly indeed, "Open the door, my darling!"

"I can't," said I. "The key is down by the front door under a plantain leaf!"

And then I said it again, several times, very gently and slowly, and said it so often that he had to go and see, and he got it of course, and came in. He stopped short by the door.

"What is the matter?" he cried. "For God's sake, what are you doing!"

I kept on creeping just the same, but I looked at him over my shoulder.

"I've got out at last," said I, "in spite of you and Jane! And I've pulled off most of the paper, so you can't put me back!"

Now why should that man have fainted? But he did, and right across my path by the wall, so that I had to creep over him every time!

1892

NADINE GORDIMER
b. 1923

Gordimer was born in Springs, South Africa, where her parents had emigrated from Europe. By her own account, her formal education was uneven and minimal, but the reading she did outside of school led to an auspicious beginning of her career as a writer when she began to publish in distinguished American magazines in the late 1940s. Her first collection was *Face to Face* (1949) followed soon after by *The Soft Voice of the Serpent* (1952) and her first novel, *The Lying Days* (1953). Her early work tended to be lyrical and personal, but as the social and political crisis in South Africa deepened, so did her concern with it. The ferment and violence of repression and the onrushing surge for black independence became increasingly the subject of her fiction. Throughout the world she became recognized as the conscience of her troubled homeland. Her primary focus is on the middle class and the terror they encounter in their attempts to come to terms with a history of social injustice. Among her many novels are *The Conservationist* (1974), *Burger's Daughter* (1979), *A Sport of Nature* (1987), *My Son's Story* (1990), *None to Accompany Me* (1994), *The House Gun* (1998), *The Pickup* (2001), and *Get a Life* (2005). More of her short stories can be found in *Six Feet of the Country* (1956), *A Soldier's Embrace* (1980), *Something Out There* (1984), *Jump* (1991), *Loot* (2003), and *Beethoven Was One-Sixteenth Black* (2007). In 1991 she was awarded the Nobel Prize.

A Soldier's Embrace

The day the cease-fire was signed she was caught in a crowd. Peasant boys from Europe who had made up the colonial army and freedom fighters whose column had marched into town were staggering about together outside the barracks, not three blocks from her house in whose rooms, for ten years, she had heard the blurred parade-ground bellow of colonial troops being trained to kill and be killed.

The men weren't drunk. They linked and swayed across the street; because all that had come to a stop, everything *had* to come to a stop: they surrounded cars, bicycles, vans, nannies with children, women with loaves of bread or basins of mangoes on their heads, a road gang with picks and shovels, a Coca-Cola truck, an old man with a barrow who bought bottles and bones. They were grinning and laughing amazement. That it could be: there they were, bumping into each other's bodies in joy, looking into each other's rough faces, all eyes crescent-shaped, brimming greeting. The words were in languages not mutually comprehensible, but the cries were new, a whooping and crowing all understood. She was bumped and jostled and she let go, stopped trying to move in any self-determined direction. There were two soldiers in front of her, blocking her off by their clumsy embrace (how do you do it, how do you do what you've never done before) and the embrace opened like a door and took her in—a pink hand with bitten nails grasping her right arm, a black hand with a big-dialled watch and thong bracelet pulling at her left elbow. Their three heads collided gaily, musk of sweat and tang of strong sweet soap clapped a mask to her nose and mouth. They all gasped with delicious shock. They were saying things to each other. She put up an arm round each neck, the rough pile of an army haircut on one side, the soft negro hair on the other, and kissed them both on the cheek. The embrace broke. The crowd wove her away behind backs, arms, jogging heads; she was returned to and took up the will of her direction again—she was walking home from the post office, where she had just sent a telegram to relatives abroad: ALL CALM DON'T WORRY.

The lawyer came back early from his offices because the courts were not sitting although the official celebration holiday was not until next day. He described to his wife the rally before the Town Hall, which he had watched from the office-building balcony. One of the guerilla leaders (not the most important; he on whose head the biggest price had been laid would not venture so soon and deep into the territory so newly won) had spoken for two hours from the balcony of the Town Hall. "Brilliant. Their jaws dropped. Brilliant. They've never heard anything on that level: precise, reasoned—none of them would ever have believed it possible, out of the bush. You should have seen de Poorteer's[1] face. He'd like to be able to get up and open his mouth like that. And be listened to like that . . ." The Governor's handicap did not even bring the sympathy accorded to a stammer; he paused and gulped between words. The blacks had always used a portmanteau[2] name for him that meant the-crane-who-is-trying-to-swallow-the-bullfrog.

One of the members of the black underground organization that could now come out in brass-band support of the freedom fighters had recognized the lawyer across from the official balcony and given him the freedom fighters' salute. The lawyer joked about it, miming, full of pride. "You should have been there—should have seen him, up there in the official party. I told you—really—you ought to have come to town with me this morning."

"And what did you do?" She wanted to assemble all details.

"Oh I gave the salute in return, chaps in the street saluted *me* . . . everybody was doing it. *It was marvellous.* And the police standing by; just to think, last month—only last week—you'd have been arrested."

"Like thumbing your nose at them," she said, smiling.

"Did anything go on around here?"

"Muchanga was afraid to go out all day. He wouldn't even run up to the post office for me!" Their servant had come to them many years ago, from service in the house of her father, a colonial official in the Treasury.

"But there was no excitement?"

---

1. The governor's (Afrikaans). 2. A word created by combining parts of two or more other words, such as "smog," made up of "smoke" and "fog."

She told him: "The soldiers and some freedom fighters mingled outside the barracks. I got caught for a minute or two. They were dancing about; you couldn't get through. All very good-natured.—Oh, I sent the cable."

An accolade, one side a white cheek, the other a black. The white one she kissed on the left cheek, the black one on the right cheek, as if these were two sides of one face.

That vision, version, was like a poster; the sort of thing that was soon peeling off dirty shopfronts and bus shelters while the months of wrangling talks preliminary to the take-over by the black government went by.

To begin with, the cheek was not white but pale or rather sallow, the poor boy's pallor of winter in Europe (that draft must have only just arrived and not yet seen service) with homesick pimples sliced off by the discipline of an army razor. And the cheek was not black but opaque peat-dark, waxed with sweat round the plump contours of the nostril. As if she could return to the moment again, she saw what she had not consciously noted: there had been a narrow pink strip in the darkness near the ear, the sort of tender stripe of healed flesh revealed when a scab is nicked off a little before it is ripe. The scab must have come away that morning: the young man picked at it in the troop carrier or truck (whatever it was the freedom fighters had; the colony had been told for years that they were supplied by the Chinese and Russians indiscriminately) on the way to enter the capital in triumph.

According to newspaper reports, the day would have ended for the two young soldiers in drunkenness and whoring. She was, apparently, not yet too old to belong to the soldier's embrace of all that a land-mine in the bush might have exploded for ever. That was one version of the incident. Another: the opportunity taken by a woman not young enough to be clasped in the arms of the one who (same newspaper, while the war was on, expressing the fears of the colonists for their women) would be expected to rape her.

She considered this version.

She had not kissed on the mouth, she had not sought anonymous lips and tongues in the licence of festival. Yet she had kissed. Watching herself again, she knew that. She had—god knows why—kissed them on either cheek, his left, his right. It was deliberate, if a swift impulse: she had distinctly made the move.

She did not tell what happened not because her husband would suspect licence in her, but because he would see her—born and brought up in the country as the daughter of an enlightened white colonial official, married to a white liberal lawyer well known for his defence of blacks in political trials— as giving free expression to liberal principles.

She had not told, she did not know what had happened.

She thought of a time long ago when a school camp had gone to the sea and immediately on arrival everyone had run down to the beach from the train, tripping and tearing over sand dunes of wild fig, aghast with ecstatic shock at the meeting with the water.

De Poorteer was recalled and the lawyer remarked to one of their black friends, "The crane has choked on the bullfrog. I hear that's what they're saying in the Quarter."

The priest who came from the black slum that had always been known simply by that anonymous term did not respond with any sort of glee. His reserve implied it was easy to celebrate; there were people who "shouted freedom too loud all of a sudden."

The lawyer and his wife understood: Father Mulumbua was one who had shouted freedom when it was dangerous to do so, and gone to prison several times for it, while certain people, now on the Interim Council set up to run the country until the new government took over, had kept silent. He named a few, but reluctantly. Enough to confirm their own suspicions—men who perhaps had made some deal with the colonial power to place its interests first, no matter what sort of government might emerge from the new constitution? Yet when the couple plunged into discussion their friend left them talking to each other while he drank his beer and gazed, frowning as if at a headache or because the sunset light hurt his eyes behind his spectacles, round her huge-leaved tropical plants that bowered the terrace in cool humidity.

They had always been rather proud of their friendship with him, this man in a cassock who wore a clenched fist carved of local ebony as well as a silver cross round his neck. His black face was habitually stern—a high seriousness balanced by sudden splurting laughter when they used to tease him over the fist—but never inattentively ill-at-ease.

"What was the matter?" She answered herself; "I had the feeling he didn't want to come here." She was using a paper handkerchief dipped in gin to wipe greenfly off the back of a pale new leaf that had shaken itself from its folds like a cut-out paper lantern.

"Good lord, he's been here hundreds of times."

"—Before, yes."

What things were they saying?

With the shouting in the street and the swaying of the crowd, the sweet powerful presence that confused the senses so that sound, sight, stink (sweat, cheap soap) ran into one tremendous sensation, she could not make out words that came so easily.

Not even what she herself must have said.

A few wealthy white men who had been boastful in their support of the colonial war and knew they would be marked down by the blacks as arch exploiters, left at once. Good riddance, as the lawyer and his wife remarked. Many ordinary white people who had lived contentedly, without questioning its actions, under the colonial government, now expressed an enthusiastic intention to help build a nation, as the newspapers put it. The lawyer's wife's neighbourhood butcher was one. "I don't mind blacks." He was expansive with her, in his shop that he had occupied for twelve years on a licence available only to white people. "Makes no difference to me who you are so long as you're honest." Next to a chart showing a beast mapped according to the cuts of meat it provided, he had hung a picture of the most important leader of the freedom fighters, expected to be first President. People like the butcher turned out with their babies clutching pennants when the leader drove through the town from the airport.

There were incidents (newspaper euphemism again) in the Quarter. It was to be expected. Political factions, tribally based, who had not fought the war, wanted to share power with the freedom fighters' Party. Muchanga no longer went down to the Quarter on his day off. His friends came to see him and sat privately on their hunkers near the garden compost heap. The ugly mansions of the rich who had fled stood empty on the bluff above the sea, but it was said they would make money out of them yet—they would be bought as ambassadorial residences when independence came, and with it many black and yellow diplomats. Zealots who claimed they belonged to the Party burned shops and houses of the poorer whites who lived, as the lawyer said, "in the inevitable echelon of colonial society," closest to the Quarter. A house in the lawyer's street was noticed by his wife to be accommodating what was certainly one of those families, in the outhouses; green nylon curtains had appeared at the garage window, she reported. The suburb was pleasantly overgrown and well-to-do; no one rich, just white professional people and professors from the university. The barracks was empty now, except for an old man with a stump and a police uniform stripped of insignia, a friend of Muchanga, it turned out, who sat on a beer-crate at the gates. He had lost his job as night-watchman when one of the rich people went away, and was glad to have work.

The street had been perfectly quiet; except for that first day.

The fingernails she sometimes still saw clearly were bitten down until embedded in a thin line of dirt all round, in the pink blunt fingers. The thumb and thick fingertips were turned back coarsely even while grasping her. Such hands had never been allowed to take possession. They were permanently raw, so young, from unloading coal, digging potatoes from the frozen Northern Hemisphere, washing hotel dishes. He had not been killed, and now that day of the cease-fire was over he would be delivered back across the sea to the docks, the stony farm, the scullery of the grand hotel. He would have to do anything he could get. There was unemployment in Europe where he had returned, the army didn't need all the young men anymore.

A great friend of the lawyer and his wife, Chipande, was coming home from exile. They heard over the radio he was expected, accompanying the future President as confidential secretary, and they waited to hear from him.

The lawyer put up his feet on the empty chair where the priest had sat, shifting it to a comfortable position by hooking his toes, free in sandals, through the slats. "Imagine, Chipande!" Chipande had been almost a protégé—but they didn't like the term, it smacked of patronage. Tall, cocky, casual Chipande, a boy from the slummiest part of the Quarter, was recommended by the White Fathers' Mission (was it by Father Mulumbua himself?—the lawyer thought so, his wife was not sure they remembered correctly) as a bright kid who wanted to be articled to a lawyer. That was asking a lot, in those days—nine years ago. He never finished his apprenticeship because while he and his employer were soon close friends, and the kid picked up political theories from the books in the house he made free of, he became so involved in politics that he had to skip the country one jump ahead of a detention order signed by the crane-who-was-trying-to-swallow-the-bullfrog.

After two weeks, the lawyer phoned the offices the guerilla-movement-become-Party had set up openly in the town but apparently Chipande had an office in the former colonial secretariat. There he had a secretary of his own;

he wasn't easy to reach. The lawyer left a message. The lawyer and his wife saw from the newspaper pictures he hadn't changed much: he had a beard and had adopted the Muslim cap favoured by political circles in exile on the East Coast.

He did come to the house eventually. He had the distracted, insistent friendliness of one who has no time to re-establish intimacy; it must be taken as read. And it must not be displayed. When he remarked on a shortage of accommodation for exiles now become officials, and the lawyer said the house was far too big for two people, he was welcome to move in and regard a self-contained part of it as his private living quarters, he did not answer but went on talking generalities. The lawyer's wife mentioned Father Mulumbua, whom they had not seen since just after the cease-fire. The lawyer added, "There's obviously some sort of big struggle going on, he's fighting for his political life there in the Quarter." "Again," she said, drawing them into a reminder of what had only just become their past.

But Chipande was restlessly following with his gaze the movements of old Muchanga, dragging the hose from plant to plant, careless of the spray; "You remember who this is, Muchanga?" she had said when the visitor arrived, yet although the old man had given, in their own language, the sort of respectful greeting even an elder gives a young man whose clothes and bearing denote rank and authority, he was not in any way overwhelmed nor enthusiastic—perhaps he secretly supported one of the rival factions?

The lawyer spoke of the latest whites to leave the country—people who had got themselves quickly involved in the sort of currency swindle that draws more outrage than any other kind of crime, in a new state fearing the flight of capital.[3] "Let them go, let them go. Good riddance." And he turned to talk of other things—there were so many more important questions to occupy the attention of the three old friends.

But Chipande couldn't stay. Chipande could not stay for supper; his beautiful long velvety black hands with their pale lining (as she thought of the palms) hung impatiently between his knees while he sat forward in the chair, explaining, adamant against persuasion. He should not have been there, even now; he had official business waiting, sometimes he drafted correspondence until one or two in the morning. The lawyer remarked how there hadn't been a proper chance to talk; he wanted to discuss those fellows in the Interim Council Mulumbua was so warily distrustful of—what did Chipande know?

Chipande, already on his feet, said something dismissing and very slightly disparaging, not about the Council members but of Mulumbua—a reference to his connection with the Jesuit missionaries as an influence that "comes through." "But I must make a note to see him sometime."

It seemed that even black men who presented a threat to the Party could be discussed only among black men themselves, now. Chipande put an arm around each of his friends as for the brief official moment of a photograph, left them; he who used to sprawl on the couch arguing half the night before dossing down in the lawyer's pyjamas. "As soon as I'm settled I'll contact you. You'll be around, ay?"

---

3. Exportation of financial resources necessary to the economy of a new government.

"Oh we'll be around." The lawyer laughed, referring, for his part, to those who were no longer. "Glad to see you're not driving a Mercedes!" he called with reassured affection at the sight of Chipande getting into a modest car. How many times, in the old days, had they agreed on the necessity for African leaders to live simply when they came to power!

On the terrace to which he turned back, Muchanga was doing something extraordinary—wetting a dirty rag with Gilbey's. It was supposed to be his day off, anyway; why was he messing about with the plants when one wanted peace to talk undisturbed?

"Is those things again, those thing is killing the leaves."

"For heaven's sake, he could use methylated for that! Any kind of alcohol will do! Why don't you get him some?"

There were shortages of one kind and another in the country, and gin happened to be something in short supply.

Whatever the hand had done in the bush had not coarsened it. It, too, was suède-black, and elegant. The pale lining was hidden against her own skin where the hand grasped her left elbow. Strangely, black does not show toil— she remarked this as one remarks the quality of a fabric. The hand was not as long but as distinguished by beauty as Chipande's. The watch a fine piece of equipment for a fighter. There was something next to it, in fact looped over the strap by the angle of the wrist as the hand grasped. A bit of thong with a few beads knotted where it was joined as a bracelet. Or amulet. Their babies wore such things; often their first and only garment. Grandmothers or mothers attached it as protection. It had worked; he was alive at cease-fire. Some had been too deep in the bush to know, and had been killed after the fighting was over. He had pumped his head wildly and laughingly at whatever it was she—they—had been babbling.

The lawyer had more free time than he'd ever remembered. So many of his clients had left; he was deputed to collect their rents and pay their taxes for them, in the hope that their property wasn't going to be confiscated—there had been alarmist rumours among such people since the day of the cease-fire. But without the rich whites there was little litigation over possessions, whether in the form of the children of dissolved marriages or the houses and cars claimed by divorced wives. The Africans had their own ways of resolving such redistribution of goods. And a gathering of elders under a tree was sufficient to settle a dispute over boundaries or argue for and against the guilt of a woman accused of adultery. He had had a message, in a round-about way, that he might be asked to be consultant on constitutional law to the Party, but nothing seemed to come of it. He took home with him the proposals for the draft constitution he had managed to get hold of. He spent whole afternoons in his study making notes for counter or improved proposals he thought he would send to Chipande or one of the other people he knew in high positions: every time he glanced up, there through his open windows was Muchanga's little company at the bottom of the garden. Once, when he saw they had straggled off, he wandered down himself to clear his head (he got drowsy, as he never did when he used to work twelve hours a day at the office). They ate dried shrimps, from the market: that's what they were doing! The ground was full of bitten-off heads and black eyes on stalks. His wife smiled. "They bring them. Muchanga won't go near the market since the riot." "It's ridiculous. Who's going to harm him?"

There was even a suggestion that the lawyer might apply for a professorship at the university. The chair of the Faculty of Law was vacant, since the students had demanded the expulsion of certain professors engaged during the colonial regime—in particular of the fuddy-duddy (good riddance) who had gathered dust in the Law chair, and the quite decent young man (pity about him) who had had Political Science. But what professor of Political Science could expect to survive both a colonial regime and the revolutionary regime that defeated it? The lawyer and his wife decided that since he might still be appointed in some consultative capacity to the new government it would be better to keep out of the university context, where the students were shouting for Africanization, and even an appointee with his credentials as a fighter of legal battles for blacks against the colonial regime in the past might not escape their ire.

Newspapers sent by friends from over the border gave statistics for the number of what they termed "refugees" who were entering the neighbouring country. The papers from outside also featured sensationally the inevitable mistakes and misunderstandings, in a new administration, that led to several foreign businessmen being held for investigation by the new regime. For the last fifteen years of colonial rule, Gulf[4] had been drilling for oil in the territory, and just as inevitably it was certain that all sorts of questionable people, from the point of view of the regime's determination not to be exploited preferentially, below the open market for the highest bidder in ideological as well as economic terms, would try to gain concessions.

His wife said, "The butcher's gone."

He was home, reading at his desk; he could spend the day more usefully there than at the office, most of the time. She had left after breakfast with her fisherman's basket that she liked to use for shopping, she wasn't away twenty minutes. "You mean the shop's closed?" There was nothing in the basket. She must have turned and come straight home.

"Gone. It's empty. He's cleared out over the weekend."

She sat down suddenly on the edge of the desk; and after a moment of silence, both laughed shortly, a strange, secret, complicit laugh. "Why, do you think?" "Can't say. He certainly charged, if you wanted a decent cut. But meat's so hard to get, now; I thought it was worth it—justified."

The lawyer raised his eyebrows and pulled down his mouth: "Exactly." They understood; the man probably knew he was marked to run into trouble for profiteering—he must have been paying through the nose for his supplies on the black market, anyway, didn't have much choice.

Shops were being looted by the unemployed and loafers (there had always been a lot of unemployed hanging around for the pickings of the town) who felt the new regime should entitle them to take what they dared not before. Radio and television shops were the most favoured objective for gangs who adopted the freedom fighters' slogans. Transistor radios were the portable luxuries of street life; the new regime issued solemn warnings, over those

4. Gulf Oil Company, an international giant of the industry.

same radios, that looting and violence would be firmly dealt with but it was difficult for the police to be everywhere at once. Sometimes their actions became street battles, since the struggle with the looters changed character as supporters of the Party's rival political factions joined in with the thieves against the police. It was necessary to be ready to reverse direction, quickly turning down a side street in detour if one encountered such disturbances while driving around town. There were bodies sometimes; both husband and wife had been fortunate enough not to see any close up, so far. A company of the freedom fighters' army was brought down from the north and installed in the barracks to supplement the police force; they patrolled the Quarter, mainly. Muchanga's friend kept his job as gatekeeper although there were armed sentries on guard: the lawyer's wife found that a light touch to mention in letters to relatives in Europe.

"Where'll you go now?"

She slid off the desk and picked up her basket. "Supermarket, I suppose. Or turn vegetarian." He knew that she left the room, smiling, because she didn't want him to suggest Muchanga ought to be sent to look for fish in the markets along the wharf in the Quarter. Muchanga was being allowed to indulge in all manner of eccentric refusals; for no reason, unless out of some curious sentiment about her father?

She avoided walking past the barracks because of the machine guns the young sentries had in place of rifles. Rifles pointed into the air but machine guns pointed to the street at the level of different parts of people's bodies, short and tall, the backsides of babies slung on mothers' backs, the round heads of children, her fisherman's basket—she knew she was getting like the others; what she felt was afraid. She wondered what the butcher and his wife had said to each other. Because he was at least one whom she had known. He had sold the meat she had bought that these women and their babies passing her in the street didn't have the money to buy.

It was something quite unexpected and outside their own efforts that decided it. A friend over the border telephoned and offered a place in a lawyers' firm of highest repute there, and some prestige in the world at large, since the team had defended individuals fighting for freedom of the press and militant churchmen upholding freedom of conscience on political issues. A telephone call; as simple as that. The friend said (and the lawyer did not repeat this even to his wife) they would be proud to have a man of his courage and convictions in the firm. He could be satisfied he would be able to uphold the liberal principles everyone knew he had always stood for; there were many whites, in that country still ruled by a white minority, who deplored the injustices under which their black population suffered etc. and believed you couldn't ignore the need for peaceful change etc.

His offices presented no problem; something called Africa Seabeds (Formosan Chinese who had gained a concession to ship seaweed and dried shrimps in exchange for rice) took over the lease and the typists. The senior clerks and the current articled clerk (the lawyer had always given a chance to young blacks, long before other people had come round to it—it wasn't only the secretary to the President who owed his start to him) he managed to get employed by the new Trades Union Council; he still knew a few blacks who remembered the times he had acted for black workers in disputes with the colonial government. The house would just have to stand empty, for the time being. It wasn't imposing enough to attract an embassy but maybe it would do for a Chargé d'Affaires—it was left in the hands of a half-caste letting agent who was likely to stay put: only whites were allowed in, at the country over the border. Getting money out was going to be much more difficult than disposing of the house. The lawyer would have to keep coming back, so long as this remained practicable, hoping to find a loophole in exchange control regulations.

She was deputed to engage the movers. In their innocence, they had thought it as easy as that! Every large vehicle, let alone a pantechnicon,[5] was commandeered for months ahead. She had no choice but to grease a palm,[6] although it went against her principles, it was condoning a practice they believed a young black state must stamp out before corruption took hold. He would take his entire legal library, for a start; that was the most important possession, to him. Neither was particularly attached to furniture. She did not know what there was she felt she really could not do without. Except the plants. And that was out of the question. She could not even mention it. She did not want to leave her towering plants, mostly natives of South America and not Africa, she supposed, whose aerial tubes pushed along the terrace brick erect tips extending hourly in the growth of the rainy season, whose great leaves turned shields to the spatter of Muchanga's hose glancing off in a shower of harmless arrows, whose two-hand-span trunks were smooth and grooved in one sculptural sweep down their length, or carved by the drop of each dead leaf-stem with concave medallions marking the place and building a pattern at once bold and exquisite. Such things would not travel; they were too big to give away.

The evening she was beginning to pack the books, the telephone rang in the study. Chipande—and he called her by her name, urgently, commandingly—"What is this all about? Is it true, what I hear? Let me just talk to him—"

"Our friend," she said, making a long arm, receiver at the end of it, towards her husband.

"But you can't leave!" Chipande shouted down the phone. "*You* can't go! I'm coming round. *Now.*"

She went on packing the legal books while Chipande and her husband were shut up together in the living-room.

"He cried. You know, he actually cried." Her husband stood in the doorway alone.

"I know—that's what I've always liked so much about them, whatever they do. They feel."

The lawyer made a face: there it is, it happened; hard to believe.

"Rushing in here, after nearly a year! I said, but we haven't seen you, all this time . . . he took no notice. Suddenly he starts pressing me to take the university job, raising all sorts of objections, why not this . . . that. And then he really wept, for a moment."

They got on with packing books like builder and mate deftly handling and catching bricks.

5. Large moving van.   6. To give bribes.

And the morning they were to leave it was all done; twenty-one years of life in that house gone quite easily into one pantechnicon. They were quiet with each other, perhaps out of apprehension of the tedious search of their possessions that would take place at the border; it was said that if you struck over-conscientious or officious freedom fighter patrols they would even make you unload a piano, a refrigerator or washing machine. She had bought Muchanga a hawker's licence, a hand-cart, and stocks of small commodities. Now that many small shops owned by white shopkeepers had disappeared, there was an opportunity for humble itinerant black traders. Muchanga had lost his fear of the town. He was proud of what she had done for him and she knew he saw himself as a rich merchant; this was the only sort of freedom he understood, after so many years as a servant. But she also knew, and the lawyer sitting beside her in the car knew she knew, that the shortages of the goods Muchanga could sell from his cart, the sugar and soap and matches and pomade and sunglasses, would soon put him out of business. He promised to come back to the house and look after the plants every week; and he stood waving, as he had done every year when they set off on holiday. She did not know what to call out to him as they drove away. The right words would not come again; whatever they were, she left them behind.

1980

ALLAN GURGANUS
b. 1947

Gurganus was born in Rocky Mount, North Carolina, and attended Sarah Lawrence College and the Iowa Writer's Workshop. His works include *Oldest Living Confederate Widow Tells All* (1989), *White People* (1992), and *Plays Well with Others* (1997); *The Practical Heart* (2001) features four novellas, and *Local Souls* (2013) features three. He is the recipient of the Sue Kaufman Prize, the American Academy of Arts and Letters award (1989), and the Los Angeles Times Book Prize (1992). John Cheever once wrote that he considered Gurganus "the most technically gifted and morally responsive writer of his generation."

Nativity, Caucasian

For Ethel Mae Morris

("What's wrong with you?" my wife asks. She already knows. I tell her anyway.)

I was born at a bridge party.

This explains certain frills and soft spots in my character. I sometimes picture my own genes as so many crustless multicolored canapés spread upon a silver oval tray.

Mother'd just turned thirty and was eight-and-one-half months gone. A colonel's daughter, she could boast a laudable IQ plus a smallish independent income. She loved gardening but, pregnant, couldn't stoop or weed. She loved swimming but felt too modest to appear at the Club in a bathing suit. "I walk like a duck," she told her husband, laughing. "Like six ducks trying to keep in line. I *hate* ducks."

Her best friend, Chloe, local grand master, tournament organizer, was a perfect whiz at stuffing compatible women into borrowed seaside cottages for marathon contract bridge.

"Helen precious?" Chloe phoned. "I know you're incommoded, but listen, dear. We're short a person over here at my house. Saundra Harper Briggs finally checked into Duke for that radical rice diet? And not one minute too soon. They say her husband had to drive the poor thing up there in the station wagon, in the *back* of the station wagon. I refuse to discriminate against you because of your condition. We keep talking about you, still ga-ga over that grand slam of yours in Hilton Head. I could send somebody around to fetch you in, say, fifteen minutes? No, yes? Will that be time enough to throw something on? Unless, of course, you feel too shaky."

Hobbyists often leap at compliments with an eagerness unknown to pros. And Helen Larkin Grafton was the classic amateur, product of a Richmond that deftly and early on espaliers, topiaries, and bonsais its young ladies, pruning this and that, preparing them for decorative root-bound existences either in or very near the home. Helen, unmistakably a white girl, a postdeb, was most accustomed to kind comments concerning clothes or looks or her special ability to foxtrot. And any talk about the mind itself, even mention of her well-known flair for cards, delighted her. So, dodging natural duty, bored with being treated as if pregnancy were some debilitating terminal disease, she said, "I'd adore to come. See you shortly, Chloe. And God love you for thinking of me. I've been sitting here feeling like . . . well, like one great big mudpie."

The other women applauded when she strolled in wearing a loose-cut frock of unbleached linen, hands thrust into front patch pockets piped with chocolate brown. (All this I have on hearsay from my godmother, Irma Stythe, a fashion-conscious former war nurse and sometime movie critic for the local paper.)

With much hoopla, two velvet pillows were placed on a folding chair, the new guest settled. They dealt her in. Young Helen Larkin Grafton. Phrases floated into the smoky air: Darling girl. Somewhat birdlike. Miscarried her first two, you know? Oh yes. Wonderful organizer—good with a garden. School up north but it didn't spoil her outlook or even her accent: pure Richmond. Good bones. Fine little game player. Looking fresh as a bride.

These women liked each other, mostly. At least they *knew* each other, which maybe matters more. Their children carried family secrets, cross-pollinating, house to house. Their husbands owned shares of the same things and golfed in groups. If the women knew about each other first, *then* either liked one another or not, husbands liked each other (till proven wrong) but didn't always *know* each other deeply. Anyway, it was a community. Shelter, shared maids, assured Christmas cards, to be greeted on the street by your full name.

One yard above the Persian and Caucasian rugs, temporary tabletops paved a whole new level. Surfaces glided along halls and on the second-story landing. Women huddled from four edges toward each other. That season's mandatory pastels, shoulder padding. Handbags propped on every level ledge. Mantels, banisters. Cloisonné[1] ashtrays glutted with half-smoked cigarettes. Refreshments—aspics, watercress, cucumber—waiting in the kitchen. The serving lady late, Chloe, our hostess, a plumpish blond woman, discreetly glancing at her watch. Such nice chatting. Exclamations over bad hands and good. Forty belles and semi-belles. Junior guilded. All rooms musical with voices, the great gift of Southern women, knowing how to coax out sounds, all ringing like this. Queen Anne furniture, ancestral portraits, actual Audubon[2] prints thanks to forebears who underwrote the project actually, Moroccan-bound books, maroon and gilt. Williamsburgy knickknacks, beiges, muted olive greens. A charming house chock full of lovely noise, and smokers not inhaling but hooked anyway.

---

1. Enamelware in which colored areas are separated by thin bands of metal. **2.** John J. Audubon (1785–1851), naturalist, who wrote about and painted the birds of North America.

Chloe's prize Pekingese, Mikado, snorted under card tables as through a tunnel ridged with nyloned columns. He edged, grimly interested, toward this new arrival's scent. An ancient wheezy male animal, Mikado took the liberty en route of sniffing up as high on women's limbs as he could reach, of rubbing languidly against the swishy silk and hazy shins of every woman there. Chloe had tied a yellow bow around his topknot; he tolerated this on bridge days, a fair trade for the cozy sense of being underneath a long play-house of gaming tables, cards fatly snapping overhead. His path lay strewn with kicked-off shoes. Dainty aromatic feet to nudge. Mikado, the Blanken-ships' cranky one-time ribbon winner, is only mentioned here because he suspected—before any other living creature in this murmurous house—that something was about to give.

He sauntered to a halt, stood under her table, stared—proprietary and enraptured—up at the area (dare I go through with this grisly sequence and its raunchy aftermath, my life?) between the young Helen's barely opened knees.

Mikado's flat face was mostly nose, very wet, chill as the jellyish aspic now gleaming on a kitchen counter. Cataracts had silvered over both his popping goldfish eyes. Smell, swollen to exciting new dimensions, remained the one great jolt and consolation left him. He nuzzled near enough and quite almost against the silk to get a better sample scent of something rich and decidedly awry here. The placing of his wide cool snout upon her shinbone made Helen, who'd just spread her cards, shudder with a little flinch. The subtlest sort of pelvic twist, then a serene smile of recognition: "Oh, Mikado," she whispered to her geisha fan of cards. For this was a society where ladies knew the names of other ladies' gardeners and maids and lapdogs.

Next . . . into this party cubicle of china shop small talk and play-it-safe decor, Nature lunged fairly bullishly. Intent on clobbering mere taste, it went right for a trigger spot and let loose one deep-seated wallop. It happened Now.

The Peke got hit by falling waters, about a bucket's worth. He yelped and scrambled down the hallway through a grove of table legs and female feet, skidding to safety under a favorite sideboard's shadow. Once there, Mikado collapsed and was panting when Helen, mouth a perfect O, bellowed forth in some voice totally unladylike and three full octaves deeper than her usual musical lilt, "Oh my Gawd, I've stawrted!"

Cards scattered atop the table, some teetered onto her steep lap, fell to dampened Persians. Her three tablemates stood, overturned the Samsonite. With it went a coaster full of lipsticked butts. Table to table, downstairs then up, news darted at the speed of sound. Three women moved to help Helen stand but she'd stretched out all her limbs. She was less seated on the chair than propped against it, semi-rigid as a starfish, muttering some Latin from her convent days.

First they dragged her toward the velvet chair. But Chloe, who'd just spent a fortune having that piece reupholstered, dissuaded them by backing, beck-oning, through the kitchen's swinging portholed door. The cluster veered in there and, for want of a better spot, laid Helen on the central counter, under a panel of humming fluorescent tubes. Her shoulder bumped a wooden salad bowl filled with party mix (pretzel sticks, nuts, crackers, sprinkled salts, and Worcestershire sauce) and sent this shooting across the linoleum's fake brick. Other dishes toppled, too. Pink and green mints rattled everywhere, the silver compote clanged toward a corner. One red aspic fell, splitting to sheeny smithereens before the Spicer twins took charge and set the other party foods along shelves or on the floor around the waist-high counter where Helen lay, distended.

Friends bustled to hold her hands, trying to dry her skirt with paper toweling. Pat Smiley quickly phoned the hospital for advice, forgetting to request an ambulance. Others listened in on two upstairs extensions, scolding her when she hung up. Then someone just as flustered dialed the fire department. Irma, my godmother, the movie reviewer, a short sensible woman who'd seen more films more times than practically anyone, now did what they would do in movies at such moments, on sea voyages, at Western waystations: she put water on to boil and fetched some string plus a bottle of Jack Daniel's (still in last year's Christmas gift box). She spread what seemed to be a sheet under my poor mother, rocking her from side to side. Helen, chewing knuckles, apologized to Chloe. "Really ruined your party. If I'd only guessed . . . Richard will be absolutely livid. Oh, this is so *unlike* me."

"Hush," Chloe said. "You couldn't know. It's Nature's doing, darling. Keep calm. Help's coming. We all love you."

Others, timing her contractions by the kitchen's sunburst wall clock, mumbled Yes, they did. They patted her wrist, pressed cool terry cloth scented with wintergreen across her dead-white forehead. Irma said, "Forgive me, dear. I hate to, but—" and boldly flapped back Helen's dress, took a look, mumbled, "Uh-oh. Somebody did call someone, an ambulance or something, right?" Others gathered behind Irma, stooped, shook heads sideways, held onto one another. Mavis DeWitt gave an empathetic moan, recalling her twins' forty-nine-hour delivery. She whispered, "I think I'm going home. I feel . . . I feel . . . Good-bye."

At the corner of Elm Avenue and Country Club Drive, the ambulance, ignoring a stoplight, overcome by the power of its siren and right of way, bisected the route of a northbound fire truck headed to the same address, and each vehicle, similarly entranced and headstrong with mission-of-mercy noise, mistook the other for its potent echo. They collided. Nobody was hurt but the vehicles got pretty well smashed up. A medic shunted about applying first aid to firemen all in black rubber raincoats and seated on someone's lawn. The assistant fire chief lifted the ambulance's hood and sniffed for smoldering.

Women fought to peek through the kitchen door's porthole. Helen was thrashing now and Irma, a squat level-headed person, ordered all potential fainters to the living room. Then Pat Smiley barged in with news that sirens had been heard from an upstairs window and, grinning at her own alertness, saw my mother laid upon the work counter, legs apart, surrounded by floored platters of party foods set like offerings around some sacrificial altar—my demure mother spread-eagled where the light refreshments should be, now writhing, gasping rhythmically, some heady severance already evident—and Pat, usually so stalwart, tottered toward the sink, blacking out en route, grabbing a hanging split-leaf philodendron, taking this down and falling in a ripe blur of store-bought dirt and looping greenery. Irma promptly shooed the others out, all but the hostess and the reliable Spicer twins, who, for twenty-nine years, had locally team-taught Home Ec. These lanky sisters hoisted Pat from either end and crunched toward the living room, shuffling through broken crockery, vines, aspic scattered here and there like wobbly carnage. They'd revived her when Mikado waddled in, having licked himself clean of perfectly respectable waters. He sniffed at the damp towels blotting Chloe's rug. A beast, wet to the size of a rat, white in the eyes, still licking his dark chops, sent poor Pat Smiley out again with one sleepy shriek. The Spicers simply lifted her legs back onto the furniture.

"Where *are* those ambulances?" Chloe got out ice tongs, any tool that looked silvery and surgical. "Sirens have been at it for ten darn minutes." Mother's wails now filled the house. Thirty acquaintances took up handbags, met at the front door, faces wary as if Helen's fate had befallen each and all of them. They told one another in lowered voices, "We'll only be underfoot," and, once assured of their basic good sense, fled.

Young Helen pleaded, between quickening seizures, to be gagged for decency's sake. She kept screeching personal charges against her husband, saying this mess was all his fault, his fault, his fault. Irma cradled Mother's head, lifted a water tumbler of Jack Daniel's, tried to tip some between the victim's lips. But Helen kept choking. So instead they doubled over a tulip-shaped potholder and simply stuffed this between chattery teeth. "Bite down," Irma told her. "It's risky to move you, dear. We hear them, hold on tight."

At the phone, Chloe was barking orders to the manager of the country club two blocks away. "Preston, listen and listen good: you get into a cart right now. You ride out and grab any doctor on the course. A dentist, a vet, anybody. But, Preston? Hurry. The poor little thing's head is out already."

A fringe-topped golf cart wobbled into the driveway. Two young doctors, one podiatrist plus everybody's dermatologist, wearing three-toned golf shoes and flashy shirts, barged in without knocking, found a fainted woman sprawled on the living-room chaise, hurried over, peeled back her skirt, yanked down panties. Elvyra Spicer, unmarried and long aware of men's baser drives, flew enraged across the room, slapped Dr. Kenilworth's head and sports cap, shrilling, "Not her. Not her, you. In there!"

The kitchen was an epic mess. Cereal, pretzels, soils, shards of aspic, stepped-on mints both pink and green—all this litter split and crackled under their spiked shoes, which sent Chloe swooping through the kitchen door to check on her inherited Orientals. But the kitchen did smell wonderful: good bourbon. Someone with nothing better to do perked coffee.

A wet Pekingese sat on hind legs in the pantry doorway, panting, a soggy yellow ribbon draped across its head. The doctors' caddy, a handsome black kid of fourteen, now jangled in from the cart, heaving forward two golf bags. In his excitement, he stood braced, as if expecting players to choose a proper putter for this situation.

Young doctors studied the event with an old amazement, some wonder missing from their hospital routine. They studied the committee of busy improvising women, studied a red rabbit-sized and wholly uninvited little wriggler aim out toward fluorescent light, looped to a pink cord that spiraled downward. Irma Stythe (God bless her sane and civil heart) guided the creature, eased it—still trailing slick residues and varnishes—up into general view. Just now, Irma, recognizing the doctors, grinned wanly over at them, said, "You want to slap it?" proferring the ankles.

"No." Kenilworth shook his head, took his cap off, modest at the sight of women in such complete control. "No. Please. You—" and he lifted one hand as if offering the option of a waltz.

So Irma hauled off and smacked it smartly. She did this again. And once more, until It squalled into Me. They all smiled to hear a new human voice in the room. As recognition, the caddy clapped. Applause, but just a smattering.

The ambulance driver, nose bloodied, rushed in to explain the delay, chatted with a doctor who dabbed at the guy's upper lip. Pattie Smiley, coming to, hearing the cries, insisted on getting up. The door swung open just long enough for the company to see her grin, glimpse the coral-colored cord, blanch of human coloration and drop backward to the carpet as the door fell closed. They wrapped the baby in monogrammed towels and laid him in his mother's arms. Helen's face was puffed, glossy with tears. Her bun had come undone some time ago, brown hair a wooly pagan mess. She gazed down at the purplish child, still bawling, his fists already pounding air in spastic if determined blows, the infant's flop-eared ugliness a final indignity in a series of such. Helen really sobbed now. Concerned, Elmira Spicer tugged the potholder from the sudden mother's mouth but she groaned, "You put that back."

A new siren, then the fire chief lumbered in, wearing full regalia. Helen and the infant, both wailing in different registers, were carried past the card tables, borne over the prone Pattie Smiley and her attendant, Elvyra, who bent across her, pressing down the hem, sure the men had come back for a second try.

Irma phoned Richard's insurance office to make sure he knew. Somehow, no one had thought to call him. His best business voice: "Yes Irma? Actually I'm in the middle of a group life conference. But what can I do for you?"

She gave one croupy giggle, then leaned against the wall, fatigued. Irma, midwife, clamped a hand over the receiver as if to smother, told Chloe, "Richard's asking what *he* can do for *me*."

Chloe was wandering around, palms pressed to her cheeks, surveying the remains of her model kitchen.

"You heard right. Go to her, Richard, take flowers. She was so brave. The baby has real lung power. No, have your *secretary* send the flowers. You get moving."

Chloe stumbled into the front room and collapsed on the beleaguered chaise. Irma followed, stood looking down at today's hostess, Grand Master Chloe, rubbing her neck and shoulders, eyes mashed shut.

The twins had dragged Pat Smiley home a few doors down. Abandoned handbags lay scattered under chairs. Cards and party favors, a set of keys, one ashtray smoldering.

"Irma." Chloe lifted her head. "You're still standing? Could I ask you for one more thing? That damask tablecloth on the counter, the one that was under her? Would you just maybe toss it into the washer? Put in about a pound of Oxydol. I can clean up the rest later. I'll just call Fatima and her sister and their whole neighborhood to come over here and work for a solid week. But I don't think I can quite abide the sight of that cloth just yet."

"You mean the sheet?"

"Yes, it was a tablecloth, actually. Damask. You couldn't have known, Irma. It was Grandmother Halsey's, 1870 or so. Not to fret, darling."

Irma Stythe leaned back into the kitchen. Cloth's pattern of wheat sheaves, bounty, harvest home, was now spread with urgent gloss and gore. Mikado trotted after her toward the laundry room. Upstaged all afternoon, antsy for attention, he now rolled over, played dead dog, sat on his haunches, then—tentatively—pranced.

Irma held a tumbler full of bourbon above the chaise. Chloe sniffed, opened one eye. The big house was oddly silent now. A few yards away, some lawn mower hissed and yammered, reassuring. Chloe sat up, took the glass in both hands as a child might, and tossed back three adult swallows. Mikado circled the heaped towels, smelling them. "No," Chloe called, halfhearted, "bad dog." But the animal climbed onto the pile, gave a huffy sigh and, head resting on crossed paws, closed his eyes.

"How about a toast?" Irma retrieved the glass. "Here's to it, to the baby. To the neighborhood's newest. Some start, hunh? And here's to our dear ole alcoholic neighborhood, God help us all."

Then both of them glanced at the closed kitchen door. They'd just decided without words, to go back in and start the cleaning job themselves. It would be wrong to burden the maid and her sister. Those two women had lives and troubles of their own. Besides, this was probably some sort of tribal duty, a task too ludicrous and personal to inflict on anybody else.

Chloe stood with difficulty, then stretched a bit, seemed steadied. "Well, my dear, are you ready?"

Irma nodded, then punched open the swinging door and lightly draped one arm around her friend's shoulder. They lingered here on the threshold for a moment, two well-meaning white women, childhood friends, lots nearer their deaths than their births. They studied the whole mess realistically.

"You know?" Irma cheered herself. "It's not nearly so bad as I remembered."

Then they scuffed straight into ankle-deep debris, waded toward the broom closet, got boldly back to it, got on with it, with life as it is practiced on this particular handsome side street in this particular dwindling country, ladies getting on with business as usual.

World without end. Amen.

1990

RELATED:

—Gurganus on Stephen Crane's "The Open Boat," p. 1761

BARRY HANNAH
1942–2010

Hannah was born in Meridian, Mississippi. He completed his higher education at Mississippi College and the University of Arkansas. Like many writers of his generation, he taught in the writing programs of various universities and was the writer-in-residence at as many more. His reputation as a bold, rambunctious novelist was established by his first novel, *Geronimo Rex* (1972), about the turmoil of the 1960s. In an exuberant carnival of violence, despair, and longing his collegiate hero barely grabs a purchase on values by which he can live. In the fiction that followed, Hannah did not abate his frenzied pace nor settle into the stereotypes that have seduced so many of his contemporaries. His other novels include *Nightwatchmen* (1973), *Ray* (1980), *The Tennis Handsome* (1983), *Never Die* (1991), and *Yonder Stands Your Orphan* (2001). More of his short stories can be found in *Airships* (1978), *Bats Out of Hell* (1993), and *High Lonesome* (1996). His final story collection, *Long, Last, Happy*, was published shortly after his death in 2010.

Sick Soldier at Your Door

Anse Burden at your service. Here in Oxford I've found six soldiers from the '91 desert war with Iraq. I flew the F-18 Hornet off the *Roosevelt* carrier, I believe. At the time I was loaded on Percodan and Dexedrine so maybe it was another. In the ready room we watched ourselves bombing and missing on CNN. Nobody else in my squadron was even nicked.

But a Stinger blew my tail off and I bailed, blown horizontally into the air as the plane was corkscrewing. The ejection seat was dead solid perfect, all it was supposed to be. I was in love with it and was not conscious the ejection had broken my back a little. It seemed I floated onto a beach of the Persian Gulf for no more than twenty seconds. I must have hit the silk at an altitude of less than three hundred feet. I believe I was in shock briefly because I was sitting in a shallow surf with black sand under me, still attached to the chute out in front of me in deeper surf water, rising up and down like a dirty white whale pulling gently at me with strings from its mouth.

Adrenaline, what a beauty, flowed through my shock and the Dex and Percodan. I felt wonderful, the finest high I've ever had. I was a child in an illuminated storybook, way off in a foreign brilliant home. The whale pulled on me and Persia was singing to me from across the water. And I was speaking baby talk into my radio, they said. Me down, me unhurt, me giggle, me see the spotter plane so Father will have the copter here soon.

What father? I later wondered.

I am certain it was Jesus Christ. Father, son, and brother, and most apparent of all, ghost, by all evidence. He carried a lamb under one arm and a Roman sword upraised by the other. This is how I saw him in a dream, a very hard-edged dream with red mountains behind him. Six feet tall. He was in a rough beige robe parted at the chest. Defined pectorals. Forearms lean and sinewy. I dreamt the dream that very night asleep below decks in the hospital.

Some decided it was not a Stinger missile, no SAM at all. They believe I shot my own jet out of the air. They did not court-martial me but they busted me down to lieutenant. I didn't care. I kept smiling for days even when the break in my tailbone and one of my vertebrae began a long explosion of pain.

My squadron liked me and so did the skipper and an admiral. I had built up a store of good will and beat the drug dependency forthwith. The fact was I flew twenty missions and was terrified around the third one on. Maybe it was nerves. I have nerves. They got harder and harder to hide. I was a ninny among true men.

My father died on the day of my last mission, to spook it further. The navy let me out and paid me handsomely to quit its service.

Now I come to Oxford and I am war. I've found the six other vets and am now a lay minister. My wife Brazile left me but might come back. What else did you expect? I cannot tell whether I've got the guts to minister to the other vets because of confusion among love, war, peace, and former nefarious behavior on my own part. I bought a church near the casino in Vicksburg right on a bayou. I knew the law and the law left me alone. My congregants were rough and smooth but all wanted to talk about God and each was allowed to give his own sermon until it became Babel and I made the rule that we could only talk about Christ. Several cursed me and left in their leather and denim all Prussian with medals and pins all over, out to the motorcycles and gone. The sergeant at arms of the church was a close friend. We did not truly need a sergeant at arms but the office made him feel good. He carried a baseball bat with barbed wire wrapped tightly around the sweet spot, a fine piece of craftsmanship, and he came through and brought the others back into the fold with him. After all, the bikers were just oily Prussian children with no place to go. Three of them lived with my pal Dan, of the barbed wire bat, in a cabin near a colossal junkyard. They were on heavy metal, they listened to heavy metal music, and they breathed oily heavy metal on a good wind off the yard.

After church the gambling would begin. The church was a casino and a pawnshop. Folks not even remotely connected to God, and happy Vietnamese and Chinamen, Haitians, Black Muslims, and Mexicans with the smell of road tar, all gathered to gamble and pawn.

My wife was an inattentive Roman Catholic from Morgan City, Louisiana, who flew helicopters out to the oil rigs in the Gulf when I met her. She was from the upper middle class and wanted to prove something and she did. I could never figure what delight anybody could have piloting a copter but her moxie brought me over. That and she was a rare gem of a fuck, with long legs, bouncing bosoms, and the only hair I've ever seen that was naturally black and gold.

She was as tall as I was, five feet eleven.

I'm not going to say a damned thing about 9/11, by the way. I think the innocent dead will appreciate that. When will "poets" ever realize they've long since been irrelevant after Bruce Springsteen's *The Rising*? And in all other matters by Dylan, et al.

Maybe all books must die before we form the peace.

I am war for Christ and my Brazile fled what she called outright insanity. She played the violin very well, I mean tempestuously while I entered her naked entrances from every angle possible. I wish her ears could suck. Get in there deep to her unarguable perfect pitch. I was a lucky man but I thought I had to prove something every day. I was thrown out of my war but am not comfortable with peace. Something always seemed left out of it. Like when we were kids and rigged a cannon that fired a two-inch shell of mule shit tightly wrapped in aluminum foil at the most beautiful white mansion in Natchez.

Too many books will deny their slaves the race to die in battle with the shout of victory in their ears. Otherwise you only get a cool nap in the shade and kick off with a little *ah* sound so they know to get you in the ground hastewise before the public stink.

You dream maybe of Sam Houston whose own army ignored him and struck out to attack Santa Anna at San Jacinto. Old Sam yelled, "Gentlemen, I applaud your bravery but damn your manners," as he watched the slaughter and rode his white horse five times around the battle, getting his own licks in with no choice left.

Two regiments clash by afternoon. Gluttonous killings. Mexican drummer boys stuck in the bayou mud, half-beheaded by musket butts. Thus the birth of Texas, the birth of all states by mob slaughter.

For me, my own scribblings in my Life Book must end. Burn your books or hand them to other slaves who've lost their voices, their silence, their souls to literature, a feeble sucking religion.

What dream was I in January and February, 1991, when I made my last flyover of Baghdad? All F-18 Hornet, hardly a human creature at all. No balls, no soul, just fire, lift, drift, roll over, *bang*. The gorgeous missile tracks oranger than orange, or your hand-rolled bomb for any occasion. What a heavy leap of fire down there. You never imagine the hunched-down earthling in the streets or sand. Sheet, burnoose,[1] and sandals, a helmet held to his dick. Look out above!

In the cockpit I was nothing but quiet screaming head, watching the immolations with small concern. I may have burned up this self and soul when I accidentally saw the burning man on the ground. My handiwork.

But somebody down there owned a vector on me. When I blew out with my already dead copilot just behind me somewhere in the air and never found, I believe I went from a mild scream to nothing, not a long trip.

Now I have the soul of an abandoned hospital. The six other Desert Storm vets, I want to invite them into it. Fill me up. But I'm a coward and a bad host in my ministry, astride this yellow Triumph Tiger,[2] 1970 and mint, given to me by good Dan Williams.

---

1. Also spelled burnous; a long wool cloak.   **2.** A type of motorcycle.

In my journey from needy ones to other needy ones, I smile and think of Dan, who taught me how to hide things, my airplane and my last hundred thou. He knew the IRS as the gestapo and planned to attack three of the jackals who stalked him, still after money rightly devoted to Jesus.

Lt. Cmdr. to grievous joystick gambler, money changer in the temple of God, to Idiot of Christ, then lay minister, then simply four diseases all at once. Two cancers and chemo with its attendant friends neuropathy, boiling claws inside my legs, and a maddening ring ever constant in my head, half a heart and lungs blown away, three invasive surgeries, the horror of waiting waiting waiting for doctors who don't want to see you and cannot abide the idea of pain. How do I count the ways, fair pain, among the criminals and loafers of the drug, med, hospital, insurance white-collar-larceny colossus?

But will you believe this?

I am happy to just get down the road when I can, giving even unluckier muckers a ride if I can. Near death by pneumonia I had dreamed of all my pals and gals, foremost Brazile Varas Burden, the woman who will surely come back to me because she'll understand I'm no longer insane. Rather, to the contrary, serene and filled with peace that passeth understanding.

May I say this. Mark this: I do not feel saved but only born again into a parallel world where all my animals, all the girlfriends and powerful pals, the handsome infants, all of us children of a quiet green meadow with the ocean over there just beyond the trees, where we live when misery that passes understanding knocks down our last doors to come and claw us. It will always be there when no pills, no help, no release are left, only the hard wall of stupid random torture and malicious indifference. Then Christ comes if you give this kind stranger a chance. Simplicity. Ecstasy, all speech and acts converted to a fundament of rest.

Plus I'm still a handsome dude, hung like a small bear. I am faithful to my wife in our separation and she is faithful to me. Time is all, a hard matter, time and its exasperations like minutes stretched to no horizon.

Now in Oxford, drawn by the church, mosque, and tabernacle burnings from northwest Mississippi to St. Louis along the river through Memphis, I admit again I am a worm. I am organizing walking tours from blackened ruin to blackened ruin. Some of the churches were not just burned. They were bombed expertly as well. They exploded as only the hand of a specialist could bring about.

This does not harken back to the Klan burnings of the sixties, which were done by imbecilic cowards cheered on by silence from miserable governors. This is new history. You think Iraq. Vets of Iraq. I know six of them but have not a clue if the crimes are connected to any, none, or all of them.

I forgot to say, because I am a worm, that there is a fee for enrollment in these tours. I have written some articles regarding medicine in literature and have an instructorship at the university, hired on by the kind chairman of English, Joe Urgo, now at Hamilton College. My ship was continued by the next chairman, Patrick Quinn, the important Graves scholar with the hair of Mick Jagger. Dan the junkyard preacher dropped out of the sad motorcycle gang that remained behind in his cabin mourning when he went to Texas Christian for advanced knowledge of the Bible. I understand his studies were thorough and he came out completely insane though functional like most seminary students. Then there is the Choctaw Indian, Pearl Room, from Philadelphia, Ms. and the Indian casino down there, who, well, lectures on the spirituality of the Indian culture, among Choctaws and Chickasaws, the two tribes of the state.

The fee for the walking tour is 5 K.

I came to gawk, just like the rest, and am now the most experienced gawker. In my case, as leader and an invalid I ride the motorcycle and wait around the ruins preparing my lecture for the pilgrims. We have enrolled twenty pilgrims so far, mainly wealthy retirees from the Great Lakes cities who need the exercise and are crazy for Southern Culture, outside of catfish, the leading export of these precincts. Half of them are Jewish, the rest Irish and Swedes. The Swedes, you recall, gave Faulkner the Great Prize, so we start at his home Rowan Oak under the cedars in the long driveway, because cedars were the Indian funeral trees, as Pearl Room explains.

The point is to strip down, get protestant, then even more naked. Walk over scorched bricks to find your own soul. Your heart a searching dog in the rubble.

My own church down on the bayou north of Vicksburg exploded.

On a hunch I told the pilgrims that from thirty-thousand feet above you see the black dots that connected into the face of Jesus of Nazareth. Then I found out this was true, with only a little push from the imagination.

It was a great shame my church exploded before the IRS could auction it.

But here's the worst news: my nephew Wilkes Bell is one of the arsonists. My sister, his mother, Ellen, knows nothing about this. My love for them prevents me turning him in to the law. That is a bit of a lie. I'm dazzled and exhilarated and proud of him until my best self comes back.

All the way through art school at the university he painted indifferently but the subject was always fire. The art school was totally ignored by the university, lucky for him. His teachers were alarmed by nothing since it was shit anyway, his paintings. Not even coded fire. Just fire, what fire does to whatever—beginning, middle, and end.

It is true I was licensed by this nation and the navy to burn and explode structures and the humankind near them, this aloof and with impunity. Just as whatever blew me out of my plane was licensed. Burning a church is one sorry damned thing. What hopes, prayers, and dreams, humble houses of worship that civilize and make gentle the hearts clustered to them. When you see flames eating up what kind, thoughtful hands have prepared for their deity, it is the least mirthful matter on the table. Nowhere in my soul is there even pity for such arson, not at my worst. Only the insanely religious or the pathological can bring it off. Or the other crime of long passion: revenge.

My nephew lives in the townhouse apartment in the very room the famous Eli Manning had during his college days at Ole Miss. I've chatted with this lad. Both he and his dad, Archie, remind me of Huckleberry Finn at quarterback. Loosey-goosey, they can flat fling the football, and then an *Aw shucks, wasn't* that *good*, toe in the sand. Grand boys, as are also the other two sons, Peyton and Cooper Manning. A national treasure under the miracle tree. God, I love the Harvard crimson and Yale blue of the Ole Miss Rebels. This fall under Houston Nutt we might get back to our 7–4 or even 8–3 seasons in the roughest toughest conference there is. At thirty my nephew Wilkes Bell is not a grand boy. He doesn't want to be a trust-fund baby, but he most certainly is.

I go by his apartment in the second story of a storied brick hotel now given over to overpriced clothing for swanky hunters and smooth tan daughters just a little younger than their mothers who are also smooth and tan and with sandals and legs. At the north end of the block is the famous Off Square Books. I must get the New Testament on CD to work with the young mid-age mothers in my home church, a white shingled two-story farmer's mansion with giant magnolias and thin wooden columns, a balcony from which I might one afternoon play the CD over loudspeakers with the women under me in lawn chairs and poolside wicker love seats. I can imitate the Pope. Whichever king of piety the Catholics have now. Yes, go again to Africa and preach in favor of exponential births where the sand and flies fight it out for misery. Has a pope ever held a bloated starving, dying infant in his arms speaking the last rites to it? But I rant. From the balcony I could simply raise my arms and look down. Because I hate to preach and congregations spook me. You must understand I'm no phony. Christ's Sermon on the Mount on CD and I could look at the tan cleavage, sweating in summer heat much like the Holy Lands.

And I am faithful to Brazile. I look at the cleavages and enjoy them as the women would have me do. But I'm thinking of my lovely Brazile, finally. She's a woman of mutating beauty. A fearsome beauty in wrath, a quiet madonna at peace, in joy. I have a hard time remembering her face, frankly. And lord I have other troubles.

There's my nephew Wilkes on *his* balcony, drunk, hanging over the rail in his suit like a black flag and pumping his arm in a thumb-up victory wave, then a salute. He adores me. Once said he would follow me to hell. I'm afraid my influence on him has been vicious, even if I'm straight and sober now ten years.

Suddenly on my right is the French mockery of a restaurant, 208, yes named for its address on South Lamar, where another vet of the 2003 Iraq war rises and falls as bartender and kitchen man. He's still a kid although bulked up from the army. They say he's not doing well, and you know *they say* is truer than the Bible. Went over to help schools and hospitals. Then received fire. Returned it. The poor boy is pouring out of the mold that formed him.

By Mississippi standards, Oxford is a city. Pop 30,000 counting the university of 14 K. You can get lost merely changing your haircut, your car, your bar.

Could it be that I'm losing my very heart, Brazile. Didn't I fight for her before we met in that feast for flyboys over Iraq? No. Christ the lamb, Christ the sword. Couldn't He decide? Am I worshipping at the feet of nothing but a difficult poem? But most days I have Him. All pieced out into the meek and least of us. My ruin is insufferable but god, look at the alternative: the pampered zombies of most America.

There is a groove in all roads that leads this motorcycle to needy souls at home, as if the old Triumph can't go anywhere else. Both my nephew and I are hopeless, helpless, maybe turning into souls as I speak but it feels like only fumes.

I'll die if I lose her. She keeps our dogs down in Edwards, Ms. There's barely enough of me left to be jealous of the sound handsome men who look on her when she walks the dogs in the nearby Civil War Park and Cemetery around

Vicksburg. The war dead would snap awake too when they felt her and her several hounds' feet above them. But she is faithful, she told me so. My mission baffles and frightens her, that's all. Yes, laughing friends deride, oh smoke is in my eyes. I've got faith in my bones, she said, why make a pageant out of it? You're always trying to make a comeback, putting your doomed march on, the biggest kid in the Children's Crusade. I swear you want to die in some god-awful place, the nastier the better. I don't, I want to die in your arms, Brazile, I said. Wherever and whenever.

My pathway is a foggy circle back to her. I pray to the motorcycle. Please do keep me in a fog. I'm weary of light shed on myself, the sick and whining always at your door. Help. Love. Service. Find, but time always whispers *lost lost lost.* And *fool,* fool astride this smoking rocket called *Quo vadis?*[3]

I arrived at the first house where a man on disability is breaking the seal on his first bottle of the day. He dismisses his wife to the rear quarters, but not unkindly. They seem to have an agreement that she is a speechless ghost.

Christ is difficult enough. Do we have to meet his father, too? The man sits next to an end table where the bottle and ice and Sprite in cans rest. With his iron gray hair parted and combed straight back you can guess he was an authority somewhere, old school. Black business oxfords on his feet, lanky, more master than slave by far, maybe an old god himself. Things speak to him, he said over the phone, but as with homicidal maniacs the voices are of himself as god, no outer god speaks to him. God the father whose shrieks of laughter behind that tome of law and mass homicides they call the Old Testament this reader can't doubt. Old Dad somewhere busting his ribs with glee over the misreadings of rabbis, monks, and the television preachers from the Academy for Significant Hair. Smiling charismatics trying to improve on Jesus because he's just too mad and wild. Fishermen and failures were his chums, most of them confused even when they saw him walking on water. Why did he choose men who could never understand him? Father why hast thou forsaken me? is not the utterance of a man certain of his painless ascent into heaven. It's the same cry I and billions make when wracked by undeserved pain.

I look at him in his Barcalounger in a clean white shirt. Indicates he is involved in a solemn vocation that did not brook meddlers. He looks like the deceased actor William Holden. He is watching *Animal Planet* on a big-screen TV.

"You want me to turn it off?" He lowered the volume with his remote.

"No. I love animals."

"Three years ago one of those stingrays killed that Australian man."[4]

"Awful. But he was lucky. Happy in his work."

"You're here for Jesus, who died for these shits. Stay as long as you'll drink with me."

"I can't. Well, a very light one I'll nurse a good spell."

"Hello to mellow." He handed over a weak bourbon. My chair was new and overstuffed. I felt I was its first guest.

---

3. Latin for "Where are you going?" Peter asks this of Jesus in John 13:76.
4. Steve Irwin (1962–2006), wildlife expert known as the Crocodile Hunter, was killed by a stingray while filming a documentary for *Animal Planet*.

"Well it's *bon voyage* to this old ship. I wish there was a fresh ocean we hadn't ruined. I'm in the throes of nervous collapse, can't bear to work with people anymore. I give them work and even love for thirty years but people piss on it. They drove me to a shrink with a tackle box full of wonder drugs. Hell, I'm on four of 'em. Excellent if you want to shuffle around like the living dead and eat the ass out of your kitchen. I never had a big stomach before, I was trim. I was a fine old troubleshooter for Winchester worn out by people. *People* wasn't the acceptable answer, but Dr. Meatloss signed the script for my long vacation. I was supervisor, got awards. You think I can afford this? I was handsome and some called me an intellectual. Now I couldn't stand even you, one unlucky pastor, if I wasn't well into the Beam."

He wore rimless glasses. I looked at his stomach pouch slyly. I asked him what drugs he took. A depth charge for depressive manias, I wondered he could be awake with the Beam on top.

"Tell me what people are like, Mr. Perry."

"Conrad. Conrad Perry. Rodents, but every one of 'em has studied the course Ratocracy. They're angry they're mediocre and believe you're to blame. Feel my pain. Lookit my cancerous ass."

"You're describing the school, the church, the state, the nation."

"E-mail opened the floodgates. We weren't meant to know this much about so many."

I agreed.

"I have half a college education. I was quiet and dumb then. Scared."

"I'd take that as a reasonable state for all of us."

"I'm well nigh on drunk already, Anse Burden. You have kin here?"

"No. Maybe long ago."

"All those people standing around outside. You saw them when you came in."

"No. Just me, right here alone."

"You're a minister and smoke Camel filters? I'll take one if I can."

"I set a low example. My pride is invested in cigarettes, I'm sure. Nobody tells me what to do," I admitted. "And I'm nervous as a cat on a hot tin roof coming in homes like this, Conrad."

"That's a good one. I never heard that."

"It's an old one, a play by our native son Tennessee Williams."

"What if those nasty people around the house sent you in, Anse, to finish me off?"

"You're on too much medicine, Conrad."

"I know that."

"Good grief, man, I was sent here by Christ because you're in trouble. I'm a piece of wreckage, myself. Love. I believe I'm just now learning it."

"Who called you, Pastor Burden? What a name. Pretty heavy on you, I guess some buddy or my wife called you."

"You called me."

"Did? Oh I do remember. Commonality, isn't that a word? I have a busted Harley-Davidson out back. Those men broke it. I never heard a thing. I heard you were a motorcycle man, maybe we could ride someday. Then second, your career as a flyer in the navy. I thought you could bring higher power against those dangerous idiots after me. I'm no chicken, I swear, but the two of us.

See here, I'm not drinking in a bar and cursing blacks and immigrants. I already have a Jesus in me but he is tiny."

"I can't be violent anymore. But how did you get this information, Conrad?"

"Not much in this town gets past the wife. She barely speaks but she has damn near canine hearing. My nerves need a long rest. Nembutal, Percocet, oxycodone when I can get it. Got a vicious ache in my spine, center of my back. My heart pounds like it wants out. So I wash these friends down with the Beam. Then Jesus gets bigger in me, I get a beautiful floating kind of courage, like when you come out of the shower after whipping somebody in a football game.

"You could help me if you had the words, just some new-words about this war. The words that would make me free again."

"You're still some kind of athlete to even be awake. I went through the Desert Storm shoot-out loaded on Percodan and amphetamines. Afterward, I stayed stoned and would've been busted out except for squadron pals and higher brass. No way no kind of hero, I assure you."

"Still, I can help *you*. In your own bosom you have nursed the pyromaniac."

I went cold. "Your wife again? What could you mean? She knows the arsonists?"

"Maybe one, who's made friends."

Perry stared at the ceiling nearly knocked out but smug enough to smile.

"What are we trading for here, Conrad? Because I am an empty and officially nobody. No connections with the law or the churches."

"If you'll have another weak one with me, I'll show you my suicide guns."

"I'll have another weak one. How many choices do you need for suicide?"

"The *quality* of my departure is still out for debate."

"I'm not drinking with you if this threat keeps up, Conrad. You'd have already blown your head off in the backyard if you'd been serious. Give my church the guns. One of the members, the sculptor, Beck, had donated over two hundred of them, historical pieces. We'll have an auction."

"On the straight?"

"The straight. Your weakness would be our strength. The odds are you and your wife Betty are stronger than this minister."

"Well, this is my church."

I walked in and saw the pistols on blue velvet, the rebel flag, the big trout he caught in Arkansas with the flyweight crawfish stuck in its lips and the nylon leader leading back to his fly rod leaned in a corner. But it was an unhappy male chamber with food and drink stains on the sofa and rug. A smell as if a fire had swept through just months ago, but there was no fireplace, no embers. Then I saw the great burned spot on the rug, stomped out by a white sneaker that still remained. Not much toil against unkempt here.

"You know the arsonists? Tell me," I asked him.

He was nodding out on me on the crumby yellow sofa. "'Sman who can't exist without being two men together. 'Sman of money, all these places, all these munitions. 'Nfaxt I thought it was you. You can get me Percodan and I would cheer you on. I'm highly in need. You can have all the pistols. Here's a sack for them."

He went to some rear shadows and wrestled out a croaker sack. You don't see this burlap much anymore. I eased the guns into the mouth of it and was fascinated by these fine instruments, pearl-handled, a silvery .38 with recessed hammer, a gun of the noir forties.

I reached in my pocket and gave him four Percocets. Chuckled for this old bird's knowing very well I was holding.

"What idiocy led you to think I'm the arsonist?"

"Exploded your own church for cover. Then a stranger to these parts, you *arrive* and the fires get widespread."

"They were already doing that."

He stood in front of me but his eyes were closed.

"Here I've been a fool thinking you wanted closer to Christ," I said.

"You're a little ungrateful. I gave the guns for Christ." Conrad wobbled and I thought I'd have to catch him.

"Please call your physician. You've got way too much head medicine already. You're asking for a coma of zero quality departure. Your wife mourning over a vegetable. You've got depression, Conrad. I don't buy the insanity. It's just your brain is carrying buckshot."

"What about the people, all that mischief around my windows?" The man opened his eyes and smiled a hopeless smile, one of false discovery after long confusion.

"Since you're not climbing the walls in terror, I think you know the answer. Take some steps toward getting well and maybe you'll feel like helping people. They need you. I believe you once did help people. Now I've got another fellow down the road in much worse shape than you."

When I said this he sat on the filthy sofa and went dead asleep. I was on the front porch making my way to my saddlebags with the sack full of pistols when I heard his wife speak very softly behind me through the screen.

"Thank you. You never know the form of the good one who comes."

"Pray, Missus Perry, I'm the good one," I asked her. I felt more like a busy malingerer.

I wonder if our Christ ever liked people. Plenty of evidence has him confused about them as well as his father, even as he loved them. He fled to the outlands when he couldn't bear healing anymore of them. The press of the crowds drove him to solitary meditations many times. Who was his friend, as we know *friend*? Or did the hungry and angry time of his ministry preclude friendship. He must have faced madness to know tragedy and glory up close and both at once. Did he know only pain from word go? Our dreary march of case histories. Nevertheless, I revamped myself on the optimistic noise of the Triumph, and got along the road, a merry old cowboy dressed in his corpse.

Talk, talk, talk. Much said and nothing settled. You're not even certain of the subject anymore.

I knew an old gal and boy, married, who to anybody's knowledge had never finished a sentence they started. They didn't finish each other's sentences. They didn't even like each other. But perhaps the romance depended on the other never completing a thought.

2010

RELATED:

—Hannah on Joseph Conrad's "Heart of Darkness," p. 1763

NATHANIEL HAWTHORNE
1804–1864

Hawthorne was born in Salem, Massachusetts, where he lived in quiet seclusion before and after his four years of attendance at Bowdoin College. Seldom leaving his room by daylight, he read, meditated, and wrote the stories and sketches that first appeared in two volumes of *Twice-Told Tales* (1837 and 1842). They brought him neither renown nor money, so in 1839 he took a job in the Boston Custom House and, when he lost it, spent some time at Brook Farm, an experiment in communal living, which would later provide him with background for his novel *The Blithedale Romance* (1852). At the time of his marriage in 1842 he took his wife to live in a historic house called the Old Manse in Concord, publishing more short pieces in 1846 in a volume called *Mosses from an Old Manse. The Scarlet Letter*, his greatest novel, published in 1850, finally brought him recognition as a major literary figure. In 1853 he was appointed consul to Liverpool by his college friend Franklin Pierce, who had become president of the United States. After four years of service in his post, Hawthorne traveled in England and Italy until his return to America in 1860. Much of his work is colored by romanticism, while the weight of his Puritan heritage, with its ethical biases and emphasis on sin, radically shaped his themes. (One of Hawthorne's ancestors had been a judge in the notorious Salem witchcraft trials.) The allegorical strain in much of his imaginative work is compensated by the clear and realistic picture of daily experience in his notebooks and in many travel sketches. His novels include *The House of Seven Gables* (1851) and *The Marble Faun* (1860).

Young Goodman Brown

Young Goodman[1] Brown came forth at sunset into the street of Salem village; but put his head back, after crossing the threshold, to exchange a parting kiss with his young wife. And Faith, as the wife was aptly named, thrust her own pretty head into the street, letting the wind play with the pink ribbons of her cap while she called to Goodman Brown.

"Dearest heart," whispered she, softly and rather sadly, when her lips were close to his ear, "prithee put off your journey until sunrise and sleep in your own bed to-night. A lone woman is troubled with such dreams and such thoughts that she's afeard of herself sometimes. Pray tarry with me this night, dear husband, of all nights in the year!"

---

1. Title of respect for those below the rank of gentleman in colonial New England.

"My love and my Faith," replied young Goodman Brown, "of all nights in the year, this one night must I tarry away from thee. My journey, as thou callest it, forth and back again, must needs be done 'twixt now and sunrise. What, my sweet, pretty wife, dost thou doubt me already, and we but three months married?"

"Then God bless you!" said Faith, with the pink ribbons; "and may you find all well when you come back."

"Amen!" cried Goodman Brown. "Say thy prayers, dear Faith, and go to bed at dusk, and no harm will come to thee."

So they parted; and the young man pursued his way until, being about to turn the corner by the meeting-house, he looked back and saw the head of Faith still peeping after him with a melancholy air, in spite of her pink ribbons.

"Poor little Faith!" thought he, for his heart smote him. "What a wretch am I to leave her on such an errand! She talks of dreams, too. Methought as she spoke there was trouble in her face, as if a dream had warned her what work is to be done to-night. But no, no; 't would kill her to think it. Well, she's a blessed angel on earth; and after this one night I'll cling to her skirts and follow her to heaven."

With this excellent resolve for the future, Goodman Brown felt himself justified in making more haste on his present evil purpose. He had taken a dreary road, darkened by all the gloomiest trees of the forest, which barely stood aside to let the narrow path creep through, and closed immediately behind. It was all as lonely as could be; and there is this peculiarity in such a solitude, that the traveler knows not who may be concealed by the innumerable trunks and the thick boughs overhead; so that with lonely footsteps he may yet be passing through an unseen multitude.

"There may be a devilish Indian behind every tree," said Goodman Brown to himself; and he glanced fearfully behind him as he added, "What if the devil himself should be at my very elbow!"

His head being turned back, he passed a crook of the road, and, looking forward again, beheld the figure of a man, in grave and decent attire, seated at the foot of an old tree. He arose at Goodman Brown's approach and walked onward side by side with him.

"You are late, Goodman Brown," said he. "The clock of the Old South was striking as I came through Boston,[2] and that is full fifteen minutes agone."

"Faith kept me back a while," replied the young man, with a tremor in his voice, caused by the sudden appearance of his companion, though not wholly unexpected.

It was now deep dusk in the forest, and deepest in that part of it where these two were journeying. As nearly as could be discerned, the second traveler was about fifty years old, apparently in the same rank of life as Goodman Brown, and bearing a considerable resemblance to him, though perhaps more in expression than features. Still they might have been taken for father and son. And yet, though the elder person was as simply clad as the younger, and as simple in manner too, he had an indescribable air of one who knew the

2. Boston is some fifteen miles from Salem—perhaps an indication of the supernatural speed of the speaker's travel. *Old South:* Boston's Old South Church, established by the Puritans in 1669.

world, and would not have felt abashed at the governor's dinner table or in King William's[3] court, were it possible that his affairs should call him thither. But the only thing about him that could be fixed upon as remarkable was his staff, which bore the likeness of a great black snake, so curiously wrought that it might almost be seen to twist and wriggle itself like a living serpent. This, of course, must have been an ocular deception, assisted by the uncertain light.

"Come, Goodman Brown!" cried his fellow-traveller, "this is a dull pace for the beginning of a journey. Take my staff, if you are so soon weary."

"Friend," said the other, exchanging his slow pace for a full stop, "having kept covenant by meeting thee here, it is my purpose now to return whence I came. I have scruples touching the matter thou wot'st[4] of."

"Sayest thou so?" replied he of the serpent, smiling apart. "Let us walk on, nevertheless, reasoning as we go; and if I convince thee not thou shalt turn back. We are but a little way in the forest yet."

"Too far, too far!" exclaimed the goodman, unconsciously resuming his walk. "My father never went into the woods on such an errand, nor his father before him. We have been a race of honest men and good Christians since the days of the martyrs; and shall I be the first of the name of Brown that ever took this path and kept—"

"Such company, thou wouldst say," observed the elder person, interpreting his pause. "Well said, Goodman Brown! I have been as well acquainted with your family as with ever a one among the Puritans; and that's no trifle to say. I helped your grandfather, the constable, when he lashed the Quaker woman so smartly through the streets of Salem; and it was I that brought your father a pitch-pine knot, kindled at my own hearth, to set fire to an Indian village, in King Philip's war.[5] They were my good friends, both; and many a pleasant walk have we had along this path, and returned merrily after midnight. I would fain be friends with you for their sake."

"If it be as thou sayest," replied Goodman Brown, "I marvel they never spoke of these matters; or, verily, I marvel not, seeing that the least rumor of the sort would have driven them from New England. We are a people of prayer, and good works to boot, and abide no such wickedness."

"Wickedness or not," said the traveler with the twisted staff, "I have a very general acquaintance here in New England. The deacons of many a church have drunk the communion wine with me; the selectmen of divers towns make me their chairman; and a majority of the Great and General Court are firm supporters of my interest. The governor and I, too—But these are state secrets."

"Can this be so?" cried Goodman Brown, with a stare of amazement at his undisturbed companion. "Howbeit, I have nothing to do with the governor and council; they have their own ways, and are no rule for a simple husbandman like me. But, were I to go on with thee, how should I meet the eye of that good old man, our minister, at Salem village? Oh, his voice would make me tremble both Sabbath day and lecture day."

---

3. King William III of England (ruled 1689–1702). **4.** Know (archaic). **5.** Rebellion by Wampanoag Indians against white settlers (1675–76).

Thus far the elder traveller had listened with due gravity; but now burst into a fit of irrepressible mirth, shaking himself so violently that his snake-like staff actually seemed to wriggle in sympathy.

"Ha! ha! ha!" shouted he again and again; then composing himself, "Well, go on, Goodman Brown, go on; but, prithee, don't kill me with laughing."

"Well, then, to end the matter at once," said Goodman Brown, considerably nettled, "there is my wife, Faith. It would break her dear little heart; and I'd rather break my own."

"Nay, if that be the case," answered the other, "e'en go thy ways, Goodman Brown. I would not for twenty old women like the one hobbling before us that Faith should come to any harm."

As he spoke he pointed his staff at a female figure on the path, in whom Goodman Brown recognized a very pious and exemplary dame, who had taught him his catechism in youth, and was still his moral and spiritual adviser, jointly with the minister and Deacon Gookin.

"A marvel, truly, that Goody[6] Cloyse should be so far in the wilderness at nightfall," said he. "But with your leave, friend, I shall take a cut through the woods until we have left this Christian woman behind. Being a stranger to you, she might ask whom I was consorting with and whither I was going."

"Be it so," said his fellow-traveller. "Betake you to the woods, and let me keep the path."

Accordingly the young man turned aside, but took care to watch his companion, who advanced softly along the road until he had come within a staff's length of the old dame. She, meanwhile, was making the best of her way, with singular speed for so aged a woman, and mumbling some indistinct words—a prayer, doubtless—as she went. The traveller put forth his staff and touched her withered neck with what seemed the serpent's tail.

"The devil!" screamed the pious old lady.

"Then Goody Cloyse knows her old friend?" observed the traveller, confronting her and leaning on his writhing stick.

"Ah, forsooth, and is it your worship indeed?" cried the good dame. "Yea, truly is it, and in the very image of my old gossip,[7] Goodman Brown, the grandfather of the silly fellow that now is. But—would your worship believe it?—my broomstick hath strangely disappeared, stolen, as I suspect, by that unhanged witch, Goody Cory, and that, too, when I was all anointed with the juice of smallage, and cinquefoil, and wolf's-bane—"[8]

"Mingled with fine wheat and the fat of a new-born babe," said the shape of old Goodman Brown.

"Ah, your worship knows the recipe," cried the old lady, cackling aloud. "So, as I was saying, being all ready for the meeting, and no horse to ride on, I made up my mind to foot it; for they tell me there is a nice young man to be taken into communion to-night. But now your good worship will lend me your arm, and we shall be there in a twinkling."

"That can hardly be," answered her friend. "I may not spare you my arm, Goody Cloyse; but here is my staff, if you will."

---

6. "Goodwife," title of respect for a married woman.   **7.** Friend.   **8.** Herbs used in witchcraft.

So saying, he threw it down at her feet, where, perhaps, it assumed life, being one of the rods which its owner had formerly lent to the Egyptian magi.[9] Of this fact, however, Goodman Brown could not take cognizance. He had cast up his eyes in astonishment, and, looking down again, beheld neither Goody Cloyse nor the serpentine staff, but this fellow-traveller alone, who waited for him as calmly as if nothing had happened.

"That old woman taught me my catechism," said the young man; and there was a world of meaning in this simple comment.

They continued to walk onward, while the elder traveller exhorted his companion to make good speed and persevere in the path, discoursing so aptly that his arguments seemed rather to spring up in the bosom of his auditor than to be suggested by himself. As they went, he plucked a branch of maple, to serve for a walking stick, and began to strip it of the twigs and little boughs, which were wet with evening dew. The moment his fingers touched them they became strangely withered and dried up as with a week's sunshine. Thus the pair proceeded, at a good free pace, until suddenly, in a gloomy hollow of the road, Goodman Brown sat himself down on the stump of a tree and refused to go any farther.

"Friend," said he, stubbornly, "my mind is made up. Not another step will I budge on this errand. What if a wretched old woman do choose to go to the devil when I thought she was going to heaven: is that any reason why I should quit my dear Faith and go after her?"

"You will think better of this by and by," said his acquaintance, composedly. "Sit here and rest yourself a while; and when you feel like moving again, there is my staff to help you along."

Without more words, he threw his companion the maple stick, and was as speedily out of sight as if he had vanished into the deepening gloom. The young man sat a few moments by the roadside, applauding himself greatly, and thinking with how clear a conscience he should meet the minister in his morning walk, nor shrink from the eye of good old Deacon Gookin. And what calm sleep would be his that very night, which was to have been spent so wickedly, but so purely and sweetly now, in the arms of Faith! Amidst these pleasant and praiseworthy meditations, Goodman Brown heard the tramp of horses along the road, and deemed it advisable to conceal himself within the verge of the forest, conscious of the guilty purpose that had brought him thither, though now so happily turned from it.

On came the hoof tramps and the voices of the riders, two grave old voices, conversing soberly as they drew near. These mingled sounds appeared to pass along the road, within a few yards of the young man's hiding-place; but, owing doubtless to the depth of the gloom at that particular spot, neither the travellers nor their steeds were visible. Though their figures brushed the small boughs by the wayside, it could not be seen that they intercepted, even for a moment, the faint gleam from the strip of bright sky athwart which they must have passed. Goodman Brown alternately crouched and stood on tip-toe, pulling aside the branches and thrusting forth his head as far as he durst without discerning so much as a shadow. It vexed him the more, because he

---

9. In Exodus 7:8–12, Moses' brother Aaron throws down his staff before the pharaoh, whereupon it turns into a serpent. The pharaoh has his magicians (magi) do the same, "but Aaron's rod swallowed up their rods."

could have sworn, were such a thing possible, that he recognized the voices of the minister and Deacon Gookin, jogging along quietly, as they were wont to do, when bound to some ordination or ecclesiastical council. While yet within hearing, one of the riders stopped to pluck a switch.

"Of the two, reverend sir," said the voice like the deacon's, "I had rather miss an ordination dinner than to-night's meeting. They tell me that some of our community are to be here from Falmouth[1] and beyond, and others from Connecticut and Rhode Island, besides several of the Indian powwows, who, after their fashion, know almost as much deviltry as the best of us. Moreover, there is a goodly young woman to be taken into communion."

"Mighty well, Deacon Gookin!" replied the solemn old tones of the minister. "Spur up, or we shall be late. Nothing can be done, you know, until I get on the ground."

The hoofs clattered again; and the voices, talking so strangely in the empty air, passed on through the forest, where no church had ever been gathered or solitary Christian prayed. Whither, then, could these holy men be journeying so deep into the heathen wilderness? Young Goodman Brown caught hold of a tree for support, being ready to sink down on the ground, faint and over-burdened with the heavy sickness of his heart. He looked up to the sky, doubting whether there really was a heaven above him. Yet there was the blue arch, and the stars brightening in it.

"With heaven above and Faith below, I will yet stand firm against the devil!" cried Goodman Brown.

While he still gazed upward into the deep arch of the firmament and had lifted his hands to pray, a cloud, though no wind was stirring, hurried across the zenith and hid the brightening stars. The blue sky was still visible, except directly overhead, where this black mass of cloud was sweeping swiftly northward. Aloft in the air, as if from the depths of the cloud, came a confused and doubtful sound of voices. Once the listener fancied that he could distinguish the accents of towns-people of his own, men and women, both pious and ungodly, many of whom he had met at the communion table, and had seen others rioting at the tavern. The next moment, so indistinct were the sounds, he doubted whether he had heard aught but the murmur of the old forest, whispering without a wind. Then came a stronger swell of those familiar tones, heard daily in the sunshine at Salem village, but never until now from a cloud of night. There was one voice, of a young woman, uttering lamentations, yet with an uncertain sorrow, and entreating for some favor, which, perhaps, it would grieve her to obtain; and all the unseen multitude, both saints and sinners, seemed to encourage her onward.

"Faith!" shouted Goodman Brown, in a voice of agony and desperation; and the echoes of the forest mocked him, crying, "Faith! Faith!" as if bewildered wretches were seeking her all through the wilderness.

The cry of grief, rage, and terror was yet piercing the night, when the unhappy husband held his breath for a response. There was a scream, drowned immediately in a louder murmur of voices, fading into far-off laughter, as the dark cloud swept away, leaving the clear and silent sky above Goodman Brown. But

---

1. Port in southern Massachusetts: Salem is in northern Massachusetts.

something fluttered lightly down through the air and caught on the branch of a tree. The young man seized it, and beheld a pink ribbon.

"My Faith is gone!" cried he, after one stupefied moment. "There is no good on earth; and sin is but a name. Come, devil; for to thee is this world given."

And, maddened with despair, so that he laughed loud and long, did Goodman Brown grasp his staff and set forth again, at such a rate that he seemed to fly along the forest path rather than to walk or run. The road grew wilder and drearier and more faintly traced, and vanished at length, leaving him in the heart of the dark wilderness, still rushing onward with the instinct that guides mortal man to evil. The whole forest was peopled with frightful sounds—the creaking of the trees, the howling of wild beasts, and the yell of Indians; while sometimes the wind tolled like a distant church bell, and sometimes gave a broad roar around the traveller, as if all Nature were laughing him to scorn. But he was himself the chief horror of the scene, and shrank not from its other horrors.

"Ha! ha! ha!" roared Goodman Brown when the wind laughed at him. "Let us hear which will laugh loudest. Think not to frighten me with your deviltry. Come witch, come wizard, come Indian powwow, come devil himself, and here comes Goodman Brown. You may as well fear him as he fear you."

In truth, all through the haunted forest, there could be nothing more frightful than the figure of Goodman Brown. On he flew among the black pines, brandishing his staff with frenzied gestures, now giving vent to an inspiration of horrid blasphemy, and now shouting forth such laughter as set all the echoes of the forest laughing like demons around him. The fiend in his own shape is less hideous than when he rages in the breast of man. Thus sped the demoniac on his course, until, quivering among the trees, he saw a red light before him, as when the felled trunks and branches of a clearing have been set on fire, and throw up their lurid blaze against the sky, at the hour of midnight. He paused, in a lull of the tempest that had driven him onward, and heard the swell of what seemed a hymn, rolling solemnly from a distance with the weight of many voices. He knew the tune; it was a familiar one in the choir of the village meeting-house. The verse died heavily away, and was lengthened by a chorus, not of human voices, but of all the sounds of the benighted wilderness pealing in awful harmony together. Goodman Brown cried out, and his cry was lost to his own ear, by its unison with the cry of the desert.

In the interval of silence he stole forward until the light glared full upon his eyes. At one extremity of an open space, hemmed in by the dark wall of the forest, arose a rock, bearing some rude, natural resemblance either to an altar or a pulpit, and surrounded by four blazing pines, their tops aflame, their stems untouched, like candles at an evening meeting. The mass of foliage that had overgrown the summit of the rock was all on fire, blazing high into the night and fitfully illuminating the whole field. Each pendent twig and leafy festoon was in a blaze. As the red light arose and fell, a numerous congregation alternately shone forth, then disappeared in shadow, and again grew, as it were, out of the darkness, peopling the heart of the solitary woods at once.

"A grave and dark-clad company," quoth Goodman Brown.

In truth they were such. Among them, quivering to and fro between gloom and splendor, appeared faces that would be seen next day at the council board of the province, and others which, Sabbath after Sabbath, looked devoutly heavenward, and benignantly over the crowded pews, from the holiest pulpits in the land. Some affirm that the lady of the governor was there. At least there were high dames well known to her, and wives of honored husbands, and widows, a great multitude, and ancient maidens, all of excellent repute, and fair young girls, who trembled lest their mothers should espy them. Either the sudden gleams of light flashing over the obscure field bedazzled Goodman Brown, or he recognized a score of the church members of Salem village famous for their especial sanctity. Good old Deacon Gookin had arrived, and waited at the skirts of that venerable saint, his revered pastor. But, irreverently consorting with these grave, reputable, and pious people, these elders of the church, these chaste dames and dewy virgins, there were men of dissolute lives and women of spotted fame, wretches given over to all mean and filthy vice, and suspected even of horrid crimes. It was strange to see that the good shrank not from the wicked, nor were the sinners abashed by the saints. Scattered also among their pale-faced enemies were the Indian priests, or powwows, who had often scared their native forest with more hideous incantations than any known to English witchcraft.

"But where is Faith?" thought Goodman Brown; and, as hope came into his heart, he trembled.

Another verse of the hymn arose, a slow and mournful strain, such as the pious love, but joined to words which expressed all that our nature can conceive of sin, and darkly hinted at far more. Unfathomable to mere mortals is the lore of fiends. Verse after verse was sung, and still the chorus of the desert swelled between like the deepest tone of a mighty organ; and with the final peal of that dreadful anthem there came a sound, as if the roaring wind, the rushing streams, the howling beasts, and every other voice of the unconverted wilderness were mingling and according with the voice of guilty man in homage to the prince of all. The four blazing pines threw up a loftier flame, and obscurely discovered shapes and visages of horror on the smoke wreaths above the impious assembly. At the same moment the fire on the rock shot redly forth and formed a glowing arch above its base, where now appeared a figure. With reverence be it spoken, the apparition bore no slight similitude, both in garb and manner, to some grave divine[2] of the New England churches.

"Bring forth the converts!" cried a voice that echoed through the field and rolled into the forest.

At the word, Goodman Brown stepped forth from the shadow of the trees and approached the congregation, with whom he felt a loathful brotherhood by the sympathy of all that was wicked in his heart. He could have well-nigh sworn that the shape of his own dead father beckoned him to advance, looking downward from a smoke wreath, while a woman, with dim features of despair, threw out her hand to warn him back. Was it his mother? But he had no power to retreat one step, nor to resist, even in thought, when the minister and good old Deacon Gookin seized his arms and led him to the blazing rock. Thither came also the slender form of a veiled female, led between Goody Cloyse, that pious teacher of the catechism, and Martha Carrier, who had received the devil's promise to be queen of hell. A rampant hag was she. And there stood the proselytes beneath the canopy of fire.

---

2. Clergyman or theologian.

"Welcome, my children," said the dark figure, "to the communion of your race. Ye have found thus young your nature and your destiny. My children, look behind you!"

They turned; and flashing forth, as it were, in a sheet of flame, the fiend worshippers were seen; the smile of welcome gleamed darkly on every visage.

"There," resumed the sable form, "are all whom ye have reverenced from youth. Ye deemed them holier than yourselves, and shrank from your own sin, contrasting it with their lives of righteousness and prayerful aspirations heavenward. Yet here are they all in my worshipping assembly. This night it shall be granted you to know their secret deeds: how hoary-bearded elders of the church have whispered wanton words to the young maids of their households; how many a woman, eager for widows' weeds, has given her husband a drink at bedtime and let him sleep his last sleep in her bosom; how beardless youths have made haste to inherit their fathers' wealth; and how fair damsels—blush not, sweet ones—have dug little graves in the garden, and bidden me, the sole guest, to an infant's funeral. By the sympathy of your human hearts for sin ye shall scent out all the places—whether in church, bed-chamber, street, field, or forest—where crime has been committed, and shall exult to behold the whole earth one stain of guilt, one mighty blood spot. Far more than this. It shall be yours to penetrate, in every bosom, the deep mystery of sin, the fountain of all wicked arts, and which inexhaustibly supplies more evil impulses than human power—than my power at its utmost—can make manifest in deeds. And now, my children, look upon each other."

They did so; and, by the blaze of the hell-kindled torches, the wretched man beheld his Faith, and the wife her husband, trembling before that unhallowed altar.

"Lo, there ye stand, my children," said the figure, in a deep and solemn tone, almost sad with its despairing awfulness, as if his once angelic nature could yet mourn for our miserable race. "Depending upon one another's hearts, ye had still hoped that virtue were not all a dream. Now are ye undeceived. Evil is the nature of mankind. Evil must be your only happiness. Welcome again, my children, to the communion of your race."

"Welcome," repeated the fiend worshippers, in one cry of despair and triumph.

And there they stood, the only pair, as it seemed, who were yet hesitating on the verge of wickedness in this dark world. A basin was hollowed, naturally, in the rock. Did it contain water, reddened by the lurid light? or was it blood? or, perchance, a liquid flame? Herein did the shape of evil dip his hand and prepare to lay the mark of baptism upon their foreheads, that they might be partakers of the mystery of sin, more conscious of the secret guilt of others, both in deed and thought, than they could now be of their own. The husband cast one look at his pale wife, and Faith at him. What polluted wretches would the next glance show them to each other, shuddering alike at what they disclosed and what they saw!

"Faith! Faith!" cried the husband, "look up to Heaven, and resist the wicked one."

Whether Faith obeyed he knew not. Hardly had he spoken when he found himself amid calm night and solitude, listening to a roar of the wind which died heavily away through the forest. He staggered against the rock and felt it chill and damp, while a hanging twig, that had been all on fire, besprinkled his cheek with the coldest dew.

The next morning young Goodman Brown came slowly into the street of Salem village, staring around him like a bewildered man. The good old minister was taking a walk along the graveyard, to get an appetite for breakfast and meditate his sermon, and bestowed a blessing, as he passed, on Goodman Brown. He shrank from the venerable saint as if to avoid an anathema. Old Deacon Gookin was at domestic worship, and the holy words of his prayer were heard through the open window. "What God doth the wizard pray to?" quoth Goodman Brown. Goody Cloyse, that excellent old Christian, stood in the early sunshine, at her own lattice, catechizing a little girl who had brought her a pint of morning's milk. Goodman Brown snatched away the child as from the grasp of the fiend himself. Turning the corner by the meeting-house, he spied the head of Faith, with the pink ribbons, gazing anxiously forth, and bursting into such joy at sight of him that she skipped along the street and almost kissed her husband before the whole village. But Goodman Brown looked sternly and sadly into her face, and passed on without a greeting.

Had Goodman Brown fallen asleep in the forest, and only dreamed a wild dream of a witch-meeting?

Be it so if you will; but, alas! it was a dream of evil omen for young Goodman Brown. A stern, a sad, a darkly meditative, a distrustful, if not a desperate man did he become from the night of that fearful dream. On the Sabbath day, when the congregation were singing a holy psalm, he could not listen because an anthem of sin rushed loudly upon his ear and drowned all the blessed strain. When the minister spoke from the pulpit with power and fervid eloquence, and, with his hand on the open Bible, of the sacred truths of our religion, and of saint-like lives and triumphant deaths, and of future bliss or misery unutterable, then did Goodman Brown turn pale, dreading lest the roof should thunder down upon the gray blasphemer and his hearers. Often, awaking suddenly at midnight, he shrank from the bosom of Faith; and at morning or eventide, when the family knelt down at prayer, he scowled and muttered to himself, and gazed sternly at his wife, and turned away. And when he had lived long, and was borne to his grave a hoary corpse, followed by Faith, an aged woman, and children and grandchildren, a goodly procession, besides neighbors not a few, they carved no hopeful verse upon his tombstone, for his dying hour was gloom.

1835

The Birthmark

In the latter part of the last century there lived a man of science, an eminent proficient in every branch of natural philosophy,[1] who not long before our story opens had made experience of a spiritual affinity more attractive than any chemical one. He had left his laboratory to the care of an assistant,

---

1. Premodern term for what is now called "science." *The last century:* that is, the 1700s.

cleared his fine countenance from the furnace smoke, washed the stain of acids from his fingers, and persuaded a beautiful woman to become his wife. In those days when the comparatively recent discovery of electricity and other kindred mysteries of Nature seemed to open paths into the region of miracle, it was not unusual for the love of science to rival the love of woman in its depth and absorbing energy. The higher intellect, the imagination, the spirit, and even the heart might all find their congenial aliment in pursuits which, as some of their ardent votaries believed, would ascend from one step of powerful intelligence to another, until the philosopher should lay his hand on the secret of creative force and perhaps make new worlds for himself. We know not whether Aylmer possessed this degree of faith in man's ultimate control over Nature. He had devoted himself, however, too unreservedly to scientific studies ever to be weaned from them by any second passion. His love for his young wife might prove the stronger of the two; but it could only be by intertwining itself with his love of science, and uniting the strength of the latter to his own.

Such a union accordingly took place, and was attended with truly remarkable consequences and a deeply impressive moral. One day, very soon after their marriage, Aylmer sat gazing at his wife with a trouble in his countenance that grew stronger until he spoke.

"Georgiana," said he, "has it never occurred to you that the mark upon your cheek might be removed?"

"No, indeed," said she, smiling; but perceiving the seriousness of his manner, she blushed deeply. "To tell the truth it has been so often called a charm that I was simple enough to imagine it might be so."

"Ah, upon another face perhaps it might," replied her husband; "but never on yours. No, dearest Georgiana, you came so nearly perfect from the hand of Nature that this slightest possible defect, which we hesitate whether to term a defect or a beauty, shocks me, as being the visible mark of earthly imperfection."

"Shocks you, my husband!" cried Georgiana, deeply hurt; at first reddening with momentary anger, but then bursting into tears. "Then why did you take me from my mother's side? You cannot love what shocks you!"

To explain this conversation it must be mentioned that in the centre of Georgiana's left cheek there was a singular mark, deeply interwoven, as it were, with the texture and substance of her face. In the usual state of her complexion—a healthy though delicate bloom—the mark wore a tint of deeper crimson, which imperfectly defined its shape amid the surrounding rosiness. When she blushed it gradually became more indistinct, and finally vanished amid the triumphant rush of blood that bathed the whole cheek with its brilliant glow. But if any shifting motion caused her to turn pale there was the mark again, a crimson stain upon the snow, in what Aylmer sometimes deemed an almost fearful distinctness. Its shape bore not a little similarity to the human hand, though of the smallest pygmy size. Georgiana's lovers were wont to say that some fairy at her birth hour had laid her tiny hand upon the infant's cheek, and left this impress there in token of the magic endowments that were to give her such sway over all hearts. Many a desperate swain would have risked life for the privilege of pressing his lips to the mysterious hand. It must not be concealed, however, that the impression wrought by this fairy sign manual varied exceedingly, according to the difference of temperament in the beholders. Some fastidious persons—but they were exclusively of her own sex—affirmed that the bloody hand, as they chose to call it, quite destroyed the effect of Georgiana's beauty, and rendered her countenance even hideous. But it would be as reasonable to say that one of those small blue stains which sometimes occur in the purest statuary marble would convert the Eve of Powers[2] to a monster. Masculine observers, if the birthmark did not heighten their admiration, contented themselves with wishing it away, that the world might possess one living specimen of ideal loveliness without the semblance of a flaw. After his marriage,—for he thought little or nothing of the matter before,—Aylmer discovered that this was the case with himself.

Had she been less beautiful,—if Envy's self could have found aught else to sneer at,—he might have felt his affection heightened by the prettiness of this mimic hand, now vaguely portrayed, now lost, now stealing forth again and glimmering to and fro with every pulse of emotion that throbbed within her heart; but seeing her otherwise so perfect, he found this one defect grow more and more intolerable with every moment of their united lives. It was the fatal flaw of humanity which Nature, in one shape or another, stamps ineffaceably on all her productions, either to imply that they are temporary and finite, or that their perfection must be wrought by toil and pain. The crimson hand expressed the ineludible gripe[3] in which mortality clutches the highest and purest of earthly mould, degrading them into kindred with the lowest, and even with the very brutes, like whom their visible frames return to dust. In this manner, selecting it as the symbol of his wife's liability to sin, sorrow, decay, and death, Aylmer's sombre imagination was not long in rendering the birthmark a frightful object, causing him more trouble and horror than ever Georgiana's beauty, whether of soul or sense, had given him delight.

At all the seasons which should have been their happiest, he invariably and without intending it, nay, in spite of a purpose to the contrary, reverted to this one disastrous topic. Trifling as it at first appeared, it so connected itself with innumerable trains of thought and modes of feeling that it became the central point of all. With the morning twilight Aylmer opened his eyes upon his wife's face and recognized the symbol of imperfection; and when they sat together at the evening hearth his eyes wandered stealthily to her cheek, and beheld, flickering with the blaze of the wood fire, the spectral hand that wrote mortality where he would fain have worshipped. Georgiana soon learned to shudder at his gaze. It needed but a glance with the peculiar expression that his face often wore to change the roses of her cheek into a deathlike paleness, amid which the crimson hand was brought strongly out, like a bas-relief of ruby on the whitest marble.

Late one night when the lights were growing dim, so as hardly to betray the stain on the poor wife's cheek, she herself, for the first time, voluntarily took up the subject.

"Do you remember, my dear Aylmer," said she, with a feeble attempt at a smile, "have you any recollection of a dream last night about this odious hand?"

"None! none whatever!" replied Aylmer, starting; but then he added, in a dry, cold tone, affected for the sake of concealing the real depth of his emotion, "I

---

2. Hiram Powers (1805–1873), American sculptor.   **3.** Grip.

might well dream of it; for before I fell asleep it had taken a pretty firm hold of my fancy."

"And you did dream of it?" continued Georgiana, hastily; for she dreaded lest a gush of tears should interrupt what she had to say. "A terrible dream! I wonder that you forget it. Is it possible to forget this one expression?—'It is in her heart now; we must have it out!' Reflect, my husband; for by all means I would have you recall that dream."

The mind is in a sad state when Sleep, the all-involving, cannot confine her spectres within the dim region of her sway, but suffers them to break forth, affrighting this actual life with secrets that perchance belong to a deeper one. Aylmer now remembered his dream. He had fancied himself with his servant Aminadab, attempting an operation for the removal of the birthmark; but the deeper went the knife, the deeper sank the hand, until at length its tiny grasp appeared to have caught hold of Georgiana's heart; whence, however, her husband was inexorably resolved to cut or wrench it away.

When the dream had shaped itself perfectly in his memory, Aylmer sat in his wife's presence with a guilty feeling. Truth often finds its way to the mind close muffled in robes of sleep, and then speaks with uncompromising direct-ness of matters in regard to which we practise an unconscious self-deception during our waking moments. Until now he had not been aware of the tyran-nizing influence acquired by one idea over his mind, and of the lengths which he might find in his heart to go for the sake of giving himself peace.

"Aylmer," resumed Georgiana, solemnly, "I know not what may be the cost to both of us to rid me of this fatal birthmark. Perhaps its removal may cause cureless deformity; or it may be the stain goes as deep as life itself. Again: do we know that there is a possibility, on any terms, of unclasping the firm gripe of this little hand which was laid upon me before I came into the world?"

"Dearest Georgiana, I have spent much thought upon the subject," hastily interrupted Aylmer. "I am convinced of the perfect practicability of its removal."

"If there be the remotest possibility of it," continued Georgiana, "let the attempt be made at whatever risk. Danger is nothing to me; for life, while this hateful mark makes me the object of your horror and disgust,—life is a burden which I would fling down with joy. Either remove this dreadful hand, or take my wretched life! You have deep science. All the world bears wit-ness of it. You have achieved great wonders. Cannot you remove this little, little mark, which I cover with the tips of two small fingers? Is this beyond your power, for the sake of your own peace, and to save your poor wife from madness?"

"Noblest, dearest, tenderest wife," cried Aylmer, rapturously, "doubt not my power. I have already given this matter the deepest thought—thought which might almost have enlightened me to create a being less perfect than yourself. Georgiana, you have led me deeper than ever into the heart of science. I feel myself fully competent to render this dear cheek as faultless as its fellow; and then, most beloved, what will be my triumph when I shall have cor-rected what Nature left imperfect in her fairest work! Even Pygmalion,[4]

---

4. King of Cyprus who fell in love with a female statue he had made. Aphrodite, goddess of love, made the statue live.

when his sculptured woman assumed life, felt not greater ecstasy than mine will be."

"It is resolved, then," said Georgiana, faintly smiling. "And, Aylmer, spare me not, though you should find the birthmark take refuge in my heart at last."

Her husband tenderly kissed her cheek—her right cheek—not that which bore the impress of the crimson hand.

The next day Aylmer apprised his wife of a plan that he had formed whereby he might have opportunity for the intense thought and constant watchfulness which the proposed operation would require; while Georgiana, likewise, would enjoy the perfect repose essential to its success. They were to seclude themselves in the extensive apartments occupied by Aylmer as a laboratory, and where, during his toilsome youth, he had made discoveries in the elemental powers of Nature that had roused the admiration of all the learned societies in Europe. Seated calmly in this laboratory, the pale philosopher had investigated the secrets of the highest cloud region and of the profoundest mines; he had satisfied himself of the causes that kindled and kept alive the fires of the volcano; and had explained the mystery of fountains, and how it is that they gush forth, some so bright and pure, and others with such rich medicinal virtues, from the dark bosom of the earth. Here, too, at an earlier period, he had studied the wonders of the human frame, and attempted to fathom the very process by which Nature assimilates all her precious influences from earth and air, and from the spiritual world, to create and foster man, her masterpiece. The latter pursuit, however, Aylmer had long laid aside in unwilling recognition of the truth—against which all seekers sooner or later stumble—that our great creative Mother, while she amuses us with apparently working in the broadest sunshine, is yet severely careful to keep her own secrets, and, in spite of her pretended openness, shows us nothing but results. She permits us, indeed, to mar, but seldom to mend, and, like a jealous patentee, on no account to make. Now, however, Aylmer resumed these half-forgotten investigations; not, of course, with such hopes or wishes as first suggest them; but because they involved much physiological truth and lay in the path of his proposed scheme for the treatment of Georgiana.

As he led her over the threshold of the laboratory, Georgiana was cold and tremulous. Aylmer looked cheerfully into her face, with intent to reassure her, but was so startled with the intense glow of the birthmark upon the whiteness of her cheek that he could not restrain a strong convulsive shudder. His wife fainted.

"Aminadab! Aminadab!" shouted Aylmer, stamping violently on the floor.

Forthwith there issued from an inner apartment a man of low stature, but bulky frame, with shaggy hair hanging about his visage, which was grimed with the vapors of the furnace. This personage had been Aylmer's underworker during his whole scientific career, and was admirably fitted for that office by his great mechanical readiness, and the skill with which, while incapable of comprehending a single principle, he executed all the details of his master's experiments. With his vast strength, his shaggy hair, his smoky aspect, and the indescribable earthiness that incrusted him, he seemed to represent man's physical nature; while Aylmer's slender figure, and pale, intellectual face, were no less apt a type of the spiritual element.

"Throw open the door of the boudoir, Aminadab," said Aylmer, "and burn a pastil."[5]

"Yes, master," answered Aminadab, looking intently at the lifeless form of Georgiana; and then he muttered to himself, "If she were my wife, I'd never part with that birthmark."

When Georgiana recovered consciousness she found herself breathing an atmosphere of penetrating fragrance, the gentle potency of which had recalled her from her deathlike faintness. The scene around her looked like enchantment. Aylmer had converted those smoky, dingy, sombre rooms, where he had spent his brightest years in recondite pursuits, into a series of beautiful apartments not unfit to be the secluded abode of a lovely woman. The walls were hung with gorgeous curtains, which imparted the combination of grandeur and grace that no other species of adornment can achieve; and as they fell from the ceiling to the floor, their rich and ponderous folds, concealing all angles and straight lines, appeared to shut in the scene from infinite space. For aught Georgiana knew, it might be a pavilion among the clouds. And Aylmer, excluding the sunshine, which would have interfered with his chemical processes, had supplied its place with perfumed lamps, emitting flames of various hue, but all uniting in a soft, impurpled radiance. He now knelt by his wife's side, watching her earnestly, but without alarm; for he was confident in his science, and felt that he could draw a magic circle round her within which no evil might intrude.

"Where am I? Ah, I remember," said Georgiana, faintly; and she placed her hand over her cheek to hide the terrible mark from her husband's eyes.

"Fear not, dearest!" exclaimed he. "Do not shrink from me! Believe me, Georgiana, I even rejoice in this single imperfection, since it will be such a rapture to remove it."

"Oh, spare me!" sadly replied his wife. "Pray do not look at it again. I never can forget that convulsive shudder."

In order to soothe Georgiana, and, as it were, to release her mind from the burden of actual things, Aylmer now put in practice some of the light and playful secrets which science had taught him among its profounder lore. Airy figures, absolutely bodiless ideas, and forms of unsubstantial beauty came and danced before her, imprinting their momentary footsteps on beams of light. Though she had some indistinct idea of the method of these optical phenomena, still the illusion was almost perfect enough to warrant the belief that her husband possessed sway over the spiritual world. Then again, when she felt a wish to look forth from her seclusion, immediately, as if her thoughts were answered, the procession of external existence flitted across a screen. The scenery and the figures of actual life were perfectly represented, but with that bewitching, yet indescribable difference which always makes a picture, an image, or a shadow so much more attractive than the original. When wearied of this, Aylmer bade her cast her eyes upon a vessel containing a quantity of earth. She did so, with little interest at first; but was soon startled to perceive the germ of a plant shooting upward from the soil. Then came the slender stalk; the leaves gradually unfolded themselves; and amid them was a perfect and lovely flower.

5. Aromatic paste used in fumigation.

"It is magical!" cried Georgiana. "I dare not touch it."

"Nay, pluck it," answered Aylmer,—"pluck it, and inhale its brief perfume while you may. The flower will wither in a few moments and leave nothing save its brown seed vessels; but thence may be perpetuated a race as ephemeral as itself."

But Georgiana had no sooner touched the flower than the whole plant suffered a blight, its leaves turning coal-black as if by the agency of fire.

"There was too powerful a stimulus," said Aylmer, thoughtfully.

To make up for this abortive experiment, he proposed to take her portrait by a scientific process of his own invention. It was to be effected by rays of light striking upon a polished plate of metal. Georgiana assented; but, on looking at the result, was affrighted to find the features of the portrait blurred and indefinable; while the minute figure of a hand appeared where the cheek should have been. Aylmer snatched the metallic plate and threw it into a jar of corrosive acid.

Soon, however, he forgot these mortifying failures. In the intervals of study and chemical experiment he came to her flushed and exhausted, but seemed invigorated by her presence, and spoke in glowing language of the resources of his art. He gave a history of the long dynasty of the alchemists, who spent so many ages in quest of the universal solvent by which the golden principle might be elicited from all things vile and base. Aylmer appeared to believe that, by the plainest scientific logic, it was altogether within the limits of possibility to discover this long-sought medium; "but," he added, "a philosopher who should go deep enough to acquire the power would attain too lofty a wisdom to stoop to the exercise of it." Not less singular were his opinions in regard to the elixir vitae.[6] He more than intimated that it was at his option to concoct a liquid that should prolong life for years, perhaps interminably; but that it would produce a discord in Nature which all the world, and chiefly the quaffer of the immortal nostrum, would find cause to curse.

"Aylmer, are you in earnest?" asked Georgiana, looking at him with amazement and fear. "It is terrible to possess such power, or even dream of possessing it."

"Oh, do not tremble, my love," said her husband. "I would not wrong either you or myself by working such inharmonious effects upon our lives; but I would have you consider how trifling, in comparison, is the skill requisite to remove this little hand."

At the mention of the birthmark, Georgiana, as usual, shrank as if a red-hot iron had touched her cheek.

Again Aylmer applied himself to his labors. She could hear his voice in the distant furnace room giving directions to Aminadab, whose harsh, uncouth, misshapen tones were audible in response, more like the grunt or growl of a brute than human speech. After hours of absence, Aylmer reappeared and proposed that she should now examine his cabinet of chemical products and natural treasures of the earth. Among the former he showed her a small vial, in which, he remarked, was contained a gentle yet most powerful fragrance, capable of impregnating all the breezes that blow across a kingdom. They were of inestimable value, the contents of that little vial; and, as he said so, he

---

6. Substance supposed capable of prolonging life.

threw some of the perfume into the air and filled the room with piercing and invigorating delight.

"And what is this?" asked Georgiana, pointing to a small crystal globe containing a gold-colored liquid. "It is so beautiful to the eye that I could imagine it the elixir of life."

"In one sense it is," replied Aylmer; "or, rather, the elixir of immortality. It is the most precious poison that ever was concocted in this world. By its aid I could apportion the lifetime of any mortal at whom you might point your finger. The strength of the dose would determine whether he were to linger out years, or drop dead in the midst of a breath. No king on his guarded throne could keep his life if I, in my private station, should deem that the welfare of millions justified me in depriving him of it."

"Why do you keep such a terrific drug?" inquired Georgiana in horror.

"Do not mistrust me, dearest," said her husband, smiling; "its virtuous potency is yet greater than its harmful one. But see! here is a powerful cosmetic. With a few drops of this in a vase of water, freckles may be washed away as easily as the hands are cleansed. A stronger infusion would take the blood out of the cheek, and leave the rosiest beauty a pale ghost."

"Is it with this lotion that you intend to bathe my cheek?" asked Georgiana, anxiously.

"Oh, no," hastily replied her husband; "this is merely superficial. Your case demands a remedy that shall go deeper."

In his interviews with Georgiana, Aylmer generally made minute inquiries as to her sensations and whether the confinement of the rooms and the temperature of the atmosphere agreed with her. These questions had such a particular drift that Georgiana began to conjecture that she was already subjected to certain physical influences, either breathed in with the fragrant air or taken with her food. She fancied likewise, but it might be altogether fancy, that there was a stirring up of her system—a strange, indefinite sensation creeping through her veins, and tingling, half painfully, half pleasurably, at her heart. Still, whenever she dared to look into the mirror, there she beheld herself pale as a white rose and with the crimson birthmark stamped upon her cheek. Not even Aylmer now hated it so much as she.

To dispel the tedium of the hours which her husband found it necessary to devote to the processes of combination and analysis, Georgiana turned over the volumes of his scientific library. In many dark old tomes she met with chapters full of romance and poetry. They were the works of the philosophers of the middle ages, such as Albertus Magnus, Cornelius Agrippa, Paracelsus, and the famous friar who created the prophetic Brazen Head.[7] All these antique naturalists stood in advance of their centuries, yet were imbued with some of their credulity, and therefore were believed, and perhaps imagined themselves to have acquired from the investigation of Nature a power above Nature, and from physics a sway over the spiritual world. Hardly less curious and imaginative were the early volumes of the Transactions of the Royal Society, in which the members, knowing little of the limits of natural possibility, were continually recording wonders or proposing methods whereby wonders might be wrought.

---

7. All alchemists and philosophers who prepared the way for modern science.

But to Georgiana the most engrossing volume was a large folio from her husband's own hand, in which he had recorded every experiment of his scientific career, its original aim, the methods adopted for its development, and its final success or failure, with the circumstances to which either event was attributable. The book, in truth, was both the history and emblem of his ardent, ambitious, imaginative, yet practical and laborious life. He handled physical details as if there were nothing beyond them; yet spiritualized them all, and redeemed himself from materialism by his strong and eager aspiration towards the infinite. In his grasp the veriest clod of earth assumed a soul. Georgiana, as she read, reverenced Aylmer and loved him more profoundly than ever, but with a less entire dependence on his judgment than heretofore. Much as he had accomplished, she could not but observe that his most splendid successes were almost invariably failures, if compared with the ideal at which he aimed. His brightest diamonds were the merest pebbles, and felt to be so by himself, in comparison with the inestimable gems which lay hidden beyond his reach. The volume, rich with achievements that had won renown for its author, was yet as melancholy a record as ever mortal hand had penned. It was the sad confession and continual exemplification of the shortcomings of the composite man, the spirit burdened with clay and working in matter, and of the despair that assails the higher nature at finding itself so miserably thwarted by the earthly part. Perhaps every man of genius in whatever sphere might recognize the image of his own experience in Aylmer's journal.

So deeply did these reflections affect Georgiana that she laid her face upon the open volume and burst into tears. In this situation she was found by her husband.

"It is dangerous to read in a sorcerer's books," said he, with a smile, though his countenance was uneasy and displeased. "Georgiana, there are pages in that volume which I can scarcely glance over and keep my senses. Take heed lest it prove as detrimental to you."

"It has made me worship you more than ever," said she.

"Ah, wait for this one success," rejoined he, "then worship me if you will. I shall deem myself hardly unworthy of it. But come, I have sought you for the luxury of your voice. Sing to me, dearest."

So she poured out the liquid music of her voice to quench the thirst of his spirit. He then took his leave with a boyish exuberance of gayety, assuring her that her seclusion would endure but a little longer, and that the result was already certain. Scarcely had he departed when Georgiana felt irresistibly impelled to follow him. She had forgotten to inform Aylmer of a symptom which for two or three hours past had begun to excite her attention. It was a sensation in the fatal birthmark, not painful, but which induced a restlessness throughout her system. Hastening after her husband, she intruded for the first time into the laboratory.

The first thing that struck her eye was the furnace, that hot and feverish worker, with the intense glow of its fire, which by the quantities of soot clustered above it seemed to have been burning for ages. There was a distilling apparatus in full operation. Around the room were retorts,[8] tubes, cylinders, crucibles, and other apparatus of chemical research. An electrical machine

---

8. Vessel in which substances are distilled by heating.

stood ready for immediate use. The atmosphere felt oppressively close, and was tainted with gaseous odors which had been tormented forth by the processes of science. The severe and homely simplicity of the apartment, with its naked walls and brick pavement, looked strange, accustomed as Georgiana had become to the fantastic elegance of her boudoir. But what chiefly, indeed almost solely, drew her attention, was the aspect of Aylmer himself.

He was pale as death, anxious and absorbed, and hung over the furnace as if it depended upon his utmost watchfulness whether the liquid which it was distilling should be the draught of immortal happiness or misery. How different from the sanguine and joyous mien that he had assumed for Georgiana's encouragement!

"Carefully now, Aminadab; carefully, thou human machine; carefully, thou man of clay!" muttered Aylmer, more to himself than his assistant. "Now, if there be a thought too much or too little, it is all over."

"Ho! ho!" mumbled Aminadab. "Look, master! look!"

Aylmer raised his eyes hastily, and at first reddened, then grew paler than ever, on beholding Georgiana. He rushed towards her and seized her arm with a grip that left the print of his fingers upon it.

"Why do you come hither? Have you no trust in your husband?" cried he, impetuously. "Would you throw the blight of that fatal birthmark over my labors? It is not well done. Go, prying woman, go!"

"Nay, Aylmer," said Georgiana with the firmness of which she possessed no stinted endowment, "it is not you that have a right to complain. You mistrust your wife; you have concealed the anxiety with which you watch the development of this experiment. Think not so unworthily of me, my husband. Tell me all the risk we run, and fear not that I shall shrink; for my share in it is far less than your own."

"No, no, Georgiana!" said Aylmer, impatiently; "it must not be."

"I submit," replied she calmly. "And Aylmer, I shall quaff whatever draught you bring me; but it will be on the same principle that would induce me to take a dose of poison if offered by your hand."

"My noble wife," said Aylmer, deeply moved, "I knew not the height and depth of your nature until now. Nothing shall be concealed. Know, then, that this crimson hand, superficial as it seems, has clutched its grasp into your being with a strength of which I had no previous conception. I have already administered agents powerful enough to do aught except to change your entire physical system. Only one thing remains to be tried. If that fail us we are ruined."

"Why did you hesitate to tell me this?" asked she.

"Because, Georgiana," said Aylmer, in a low voice, "there is danger."

"Danger? There is but one danger—that this horrible stigma shall be left upon my cheek!" cried Georgiana. "Remove it, remove it, whatever be the cost, or we shall both go mad!"

"Heaven knows your words are too true," said Aylmer, sadly. "And now, dearest, return to your boudoir. In a little while all will be tested."

He conducted her back and took leave of her with a solemn tenderness which spoke far more than his words how much was now at stake. After his departure Georgiana became rapt in musings. She considered the character of Aylmer, and did it completer justice than at any previous moment. Her heart exulted, while it trembled, at his honorable love—so pure and lofty that it would accept nothing less than perfection nor miserably make itself contented with an earthlier nature than he had dreamed of. She felt how much more precious was such a sentiment than that meaner kind which would have borne with the imperfection for her sake, and have been guilty of treason to holy love by degrading its perfect idea to the level of the actual; and with her whole spirit she prayed that, for a single moment, she might satisfy his highest and deepest conception. Longer than one moment she well knew it could not be; for his spirit was ever on the march, ever ascending, and each instant required something that was beyond the scope of the instant before.

The sound of her husband's footsteps aroused her. He bore a crystal goblet containing a liquor colorless as water, but bright enough to be the draught of immortality. Aylmer was pale; but it seemed rather the consequence of a highly-wrought state of mind and tension of spirit than of fear or doubt.

"The concoction of the draught has been perfect," said he, in answer to Georgiana's look. "Unless all my science have deceived me, it cannot fail."

"Save on your account, my dearest Aylmer," observed his wife, "I might wish to put off this birthmark of mortality by relinquishing mortality itself in preference to any other mode. Life is but a sad possession to those who have attained precisely the degree of moral advancement at which I stand. Were I weaker and blinder it might be happiness. Were I stronger, it might be endured hopefully. But, being what I find myself, methinks I am of all mortals the most fit to die."

"You are fit for heaven without tasting death!" replied her husband. "But why do we speak of dying? The draught cannot fail. Behold its effect upon this plant."

On the window seat there stood a geranium diseased with yellow blotches, which had overspread all its leaves. Aylmer poured a small quantity of the liquid upon the soil in which it grew. In a little time, when the roots of the plant had taken up the moisture, the unsightly blotches began to be extinguished in a living verdure.

"There needed no proof," said Georgiana, quietly. "Give me the goblet. I joyfully stake all upon your word."

"Drink, then, thou lofty creature!" exclaimed Aylmer, with fervid admiration. "There is no taint of imperfection on thy spirit. Thy sensible frame, too, shall soon be all perfect."

She quaffed the liquid and returned the goblet to his hand.

"It is grateful," said she with a placid smile. "Methinks it is like water from a heavenly fountain; for it contains I know not what of unobtrusive fragrance and deliciousness. It allays a feverish thirst that had parched me for many days. Now, dearest, let me sleep. My earthly senses are closing over my spirit like the leaves around the heart of a rose at sunset."

She spoke the last words with a gentle reluctance, as if it required almost more energy than she could command to pronounce the faint and lingering syllables. Scarcely had they loitered through her lips ere she was lost in slumber. Aylmer sat by her side, watching her aspect with the emotions proper to a man the whole value of whose existence was involved in the process now to be tested. Mingled with this mood, however, was the philosophic investigation characteristic of the man of science. Not the minutest symptom escaped him.

A heightened flush of the cheek, a slight irregularity of breath, a quiver of the eyelid, a hardly perceptible tremor through the frame,—such were the details which, as the moments passed, he wrote down in his folio volume. Intense thought had set its stamp upon every previous page of that volume, but the thoughts of years were all concentrated upon the last.

While thus employed, he failed not to gaze often at the fatal hand, and not without a shudder. Yet once, by a strange and unaccountable impulse, he pressed it with his lips. His spirit recoiled, however, in the very act; and Georgiana, out of the midst of her deep sleep, moved uneasily and murmured as if in remonstrance. Again Aylmer resumed his watch. Nor was it without avail. The crimson hand, which at first had been strongly visible upon the marble paleness of Georgiana's cheek, now grew more faintly outlined. She remained not less pale than ever; but the birthmark, with every breath that came and went, lost somewhat of its former distinctness. Its presence had been awful; its departure was more awful still. Watch the stain of the rainbow fading out of the sky, and you will know how that mysterious symbol passed away.

"By Heaven! it is well-nigh gone!" said Aylmer to himself, in almost irrepressible ecstasy. "I can scarcely trace it now. Success! success! And now it is like the faintest rose color. The lightest flush of blood across her cheek would overcome it. But she is so pale!"

He drew aside the window curtain and suffered the light of natural day to fall into the room and rest upon her cheek. At the same time he heard a gross, hoarse chuckle, which he had long known as his servant Aminadab's expression of delight.

"Ah, clod! ah, earthly mass!" cried Aylmer, laughing in a sort of frenzy, "you have served me well! Matter and spirit—earth and heaven—have both done their part in this! Laugh, thing of the senses! You have earned the right to laugh."

These exclamations broke Georgiana's sleep. She slowly unclosed her eyes and gazed into the mirror which her husband had arranged for that purpose. A faint smile flitted over her lips when she recognized how barely perceptible was now that crimson hand which had once blazed forth with such disastrous brilliancy as to scare away all their happiness. But then her eyes sought Aylmer's face with a trouble and anxiety that he could by no means account for.

"My poor Aylmer!" murmured she.

"Poor? Nay, richest, happiest, most favored!" exclaimed he. "My peerless bride, it is successful! You are perfect!"

"My poor Aylmer," she repeated, with a more than human tenderness, "you have aimed loftily; you have done nobly. Do not repent that with so high and pure a feeling, you have rejected the best the earth could offer. Aylmer, dearest Aylmer, I am dying!"

Alas! it was too true! The fatal hand had grappled with the mystery of life, and was the bond by which an angelic spirit kept itself in union with a mortal frame. As the last crimson tint of the birthmark—that sole token of human imperfection—faded from her cheek, the parting breath of the now perfect woman passed into the atmosphere, and her soul, lingering a moment near her husband, took its heavenward flight. Then a hoarse, chuckling laugh was heard again! Thus ever does the gross fatality of earth exult in its invariable triumph over the immortal essence which, in this dim sphere of half development, demands the completeness of a higher state. Yet, had Aylmer reached a profounder wisdom, he need not thus have flung away the happiness which would have woven his mortal life of the selfsame texture with the celestial. The momentary circumstance was too strong for him; he failed to look beyond the shadowy scope of time, and, living once for all in eternity, to find the perfect future in the present.

1846

RELATED:

—Edgar Allan Poe on Hawthorne's *Twice-Told Tales*, p. 1772

ERNEST HEMINGWAY
1899–1961

Hemingway was born in Oak Park, Illinois, the son of a doctor, who gave him an enduring enthusiasm for the outdoor life. As a boy Hemingway spent summer vacations in the woods of northern Michigan, which became the setting for some of his best-known stories. He volunteered for service as an ambulance driver with the Italian Army and was seriously wounded in the fighting on the Austrian front toward the end of World War I. Recovering from his wounds, he went to Paris as a correspondent for the *Toronto Star* and there met, among other writers, Ezra Pound and Gertrude Stein. They encouraged him in the invention of his own style, and by twenty-five he was well on his way to mastery of the craft of fiction. From the publication of his first books he was acclaimed as a spokesman for the "Lost Generation"—the young who had been disillusioned and cast adrift by the murderous blunders of those who had plunged the world into war. The Hemingway hero and his code of conduct—living with "grace under pressure"—were as widely emulated and admired as the style of his short stories and novels. He was an enthusiastic and discriminating bullfight fan, big-game hunter, and fisherman, whose personal exploits kept him often in the limelight. During the Spanish Civil War he went to Spain as a war correspondent and wrote one of his best novels, *For Whom the Bell Tolls* (1940), about that conflict. Later he followed the U.S. Army in Europe as a correspondent before returning to peacetime life at his home in Cuba. He was awarded the Nobel Prize in 1954. At a time when he seemed to be falling out of fashion and his old vigor was waning, he killed himself with a shotgun. His novels include *The Sun Also Rises* (1926), *A Farewell to Arms* (1929), *To Have and Have Not* (1937), and *The Old Man and the Sea* (1952). In *A Moveable Feast*; published posthumously in 1964, he re-creates the Paris of his earlier years. His story collections include *In Our Time* (1925), *Men without Women* (1927), and *Winner Take Nothing* (1933).

Hills Like White Elephants

The hills across the valley of the Ebro[1] were long and white. On this side there was no shade and no trees, and the station was between two lines of rails in the sun. Close against the side of the station there was the warm shadow of the building and a curtain, made of strings of bamboo beads, hung across

---

1. River in northern Spain.

the open door into the bar, to keep out flies. The American and the girl with him sat at a table in the shade, outside the building. It was very hot and the express from Barcelona would come in forty minutes. It stopped at this junction for two minutes and went on to Madrid.

"What should we drink?" the girl asked. She had taken off her hat and put it on the table.

"It's pretty hot," the man said.

"Let's drink beer."

"Dos cervezas," the man said into the curtain.

"Big ones?" a woman asked from the doorway.

"Yes. Two big ones."

The woman brought two glasses of beer and two felt pads. She put the felt pads and the beer glasses on the table and looked at the man and the girl. The girl was looking off at the line of hills. They were white in the sun and the country was brown and dry.

"They look like white elephants," she said.

"I've never seen one," the man drank his beer.

"No, you wouldn't have."

"I might have," the man said. "Just because you say I wouldn't have doesn't prove anything."

The girl looked at the bead curtain. "They've painted something on it," she said. "What does it say?"

"Anis del Toro. It's a drink."

"Could we try it?"

The man called "Listen" through the curtain. The woman came out from the bar.

"Four reales."[2]

"We want two Anis del Toro."

"With water?"

"Do you want it with water?"

"I don't know," the girl said. "Is it good with water?"

"It's all right."

"You want them with water?" asked the woman.

"Yes, with water."

"It tastes like licorice," the girl said and put the glass down.

"That's the way with everything."

"Yes," said the girl. "Everything tastes of licorice. Especially all the things you've waited so long for, like absinthe."

"Oh, cut it out."

"You started it," the girl said. "I was being amused. I was having a fine time."

"Well, let's try and have a fine time."

"All right. I was trying. I said the mountains looked like white elephants. Wasn't that bright?"

"That was bright."

"I wanted to try this new drink. That's all we do, isn't it—look at things and try new drinks?"

2. Spanish coins.

"I guess so."

The girl looked across at the hills.

"They're lovely hills," she said. "They don't really look like white elephants. I just meant the coloring of their skin through the trees."

"Should we have another drink?"

"All right."

The warm wind blew the bead curtain against the table.

"The beer's nice and cool," the man said.

"It's lovely," the girl said.

"It's really an awfully simple operation, Jig," the man said. "It's not really an operation at all."

The girl looked at the ground the table legs rested on.

"I know you wouldn't mind it, Jig. It's really not anything. It's just to let the air in."

The girl did not say anything.

"I'll go with you and I'll stay with you all the time. They just let the air in and then it's all perfectly natural."

"Then what will we do afterward?"

"We'll be fine afterward. Just like we were before."

"What makes you think so?"

"That's the only thing that bothers us. It's the only thing that's made us unhappy."

The girl looked at the bead curtain, put her hand out and took hold of two of the strings of beads.

"And you think then we'll be all right and be happy."

"I know we will. You don't have to be afraid. I've known lots of people that have done it."

"So have I," said the girl. "And afterward they were all so happy."

"Well," the man said, "if you don't want to you don't have to. I wouldn't have you do it if you didn't want to. But I know it's perfectly simple."

"And you really want to?"

"I think it's the best thing to do. But I don't want you to do it if you don't really want to."

"And if I do it you'll be happy and things will be like they were and you'll love me?"

"I love you now. You know I love you."

"I know. But if I do it, then it will be nice again if I say things are like white elephants, and you'll like it?"

"I'll love it. I love it now but I just can't think about it. You know how I get when I worry."

"If I do it you won't ever worry?"

"I won't worry about that because it's perfectly simple."

"Then I'll do it. Because I don't care about me."

"What do you mean?"

"I don't care about me."

"Well, I care about you."

"Oh, yes. But I don't care about me. And I'll do it and then everything will be fine."

"I don't want you to do it if you feel that way."

The girl stood up and walked to the end of the station. Across, on the other side, were fields of grain and trees along the banks of the Ebro. Far away, beyond the river, were mountains. The shadow of a cloud moved across the field of grain and she saw the river through the trees.

"And we could have all this," she said. "And we could have everything and every day we make it more impossible."

"What did you say?"

"I said we could have everything."

"We can have everything."

"No, we can't."

"We can have the whole world."

"No, we can't."

"We can go everywhere."

"No, we can't. It isn't ours anymore."

"It's ours."

"No, it isn't. And once they take it away, you never get it back."

"But they haven't taken it away."

"We'll wait and see."

"Come on back in the shade," he said. "You mustn't feel that way."

"I don't feel any way," the girl said. "I just know things."

"I don't want you to do anything that you don't want to do—"

"Nor that isn't good for me," she said. "I know. Could we have another beer?"

"All right. But you've got to realize—"

"I realize," the girl said. "Can't we maybe stop talking?"

They sat down at the table and the girl looked across at the hills on the dry side of the valley and the man looked at her and at the table.

"You've got to realize," he said, "that I don't want you to do it if you don't want to. I'm perfectly willing to go through with it if it means anything to you."

"Doesn't it mean anything to you? We could get along."

"Of course it does. But I don't want anybody but you. I don't want anyone else. And I know it's perfectly simple."

"Yes, you know it's perfectly simple."

"It's all right for you to say that, but I do know it."

"Would you do something for me now?"

"I'd do anything for you."

"Would you please please please please please please please stop talking?"

He did not say anything but looked at the bags against the wall of the station. There were labels on them from all the hotels where they had spent nights.

"But I don't want you to," he said, "I don't care anything about it."

"I'll scream," the girl said.

The woman came out through the curtains with two glasses of beer and put them down on the damp felt pads. "The train comes in five minutes," she said.

"What did she say?" asked the girl.

"That the train is coming in five minutes."

The girl smiled brightly at the woman, to thank her.

"I'd better take the bags over to the other side of the station," the man said. She smiled at him.

"All right. Then come back and we'll finish the beer."

He picked up the two heavy bags and carried them around the station to the other tracks. He looked up the tracks but could not see the train. Coming back, he walked through the barroom, where people waiting for the train were drinking. He drank an Anis at the bar and looked at the people. They were all waiting reasonably for the train. He went out through the bead curtain. She was sitting at the table and smiled at him.

"Do you feel better?" he asked.

"I feel fine," she said. "There's nothing wrong with me. I feel fine."

1927

RELATED:

—Hemingway, An Interview, p. 1717
—Frederick Busch on "Hills Like White Elephants," p. 1757

AMY HEMPEL
b. 1951

Hempel was born in Chicago and educated in California, with further study at Columbia University. "Your basic non-linear education," as she describes it. Hempel has since worked as a writer, an editor, a teacher, and a trainer of guide dogs for the blind. Her stories are collected in *Reasons to Live* (1985), *At the Gates of the Animal Kingdom* (1990), *Tumble Home* (1997), and *The Dog of the Marriage* (2005). In 2008 she won the Rea Award for the Short Story and in 2009 the PEN/Malamud Award for Short Fiction.

In the Cemetery Where Al Jolson[1] Is Buried

for Jessica

Tell me things I won't mind forgetting," she said. "Make it useless stuff or skip it."

I began. I told her insects fly through rain, missing every drop, never getting wet. I told her no one in America owned a tape recorder before Bing Crosby did. I told her the shape of the moon is like a banana—you see it looking full, you're seeing it end-on.

The camera made me self-conscious and I stopped. It was trained on us from a ceiling mount—the kind of camera banks use to photograph robbers. It played our image to the nurses down the hall in Intensive Care.

"Go on, girl," she said, "you get used to it."

I had my audience. I went on. Did she know that Tammy Wynette had changed her tune? Really. That now she sings "Stand By Your *Friends*"? Paul Anka did it too, I said. Does "You're Having *Our* Baby."[2] He got sick of all that feminist bitching.

"What else?" she said. "Have you got something else?"

Oh yes. For her I would always have something else.

"Did you know when they taught the first chimp to talk, it lied? When they asked her who did it on the desk, she signed back Max, the janitor. And when they pressed her, she said she was sorry, that it was really the project director. But she was a mother, so I guess she had her reasons."

"Oh, that's good," she said. "A parable."

"There's more about the chimp," I said. "But it will break your heart."

"No thanks," she says, and scratches at her mask.

---

1. American entertainer and film actor (1886–1950).   **2.** References to Wynette's "Stand By Your Man" (1968) and Anka's "(You're) Having My Baby" (1974).

. . .

We look like good-guy outlaws. Good or bad, I am not used to the mask yet. I keep touching the warm spot where my breath, thank God, comes out. She is used to hers. She only ties the strings on top. The other ones—a pro by now— she lets hang loose.

We call this place the Marcus Welby[3] Hospital. It's the white one with the palm trees under the opening credits of all those shows. A Hollywood hospital, though in fact it is several miles west. Off camera, there is a beach across the street.

She introduces me to a nurse as "the Best Friend." The impersonal article is more intimate. It tells me that *they* are intimate, my friend and her nurse.

"I was telling her we used to drink Canada Dry Ginger Ale and pretend we were in Canada."

"That's how dumb *we* were," I say.

"You could be sisters," the nurse says.

So how come, I'll bet they are wondering, it took me so long to get to such a glamorous place? But do they ask?

They do not ask.

Two months, and how long is the drive?

The best I can explain it is this—I have a friend who worked one summer in a mortuary. He used to tell me stories. The one that really got to me was not the grisliest, but it's the one that did. A man wrecked his car on 101[4] going south. He did not lose consciousness. But his arm was taken down to the wet bone—and when he looked at it—it scared him to death. I mean, he died.

So I didn't dare look any closer. But now I'm doing it—and hoping I won't be scared to death.

She shakes out a summer-weight blanket, showing a leg you did not want to see. Except for that, you look at her and understand the law that requires *two* people to be with the body at all times.

"I thought of something," she says. "I thought of it last night. I think there is a real and present need here. You know," she says, "like for someone to do it for you when you can't do it yourself. You call them up whenever you want— like when push comes to shove."

She grabs the bedside phone and loops the cord around her neck.

"Hey," she says, "the End o' the Line."

She keeps on, giddy with something. But I don't know with what.

"The giveaway was the solarium," she says. "That's where Marcus Welby broke the news to his patients. Then here's the real doctor suggesting we talk in the solarium. So I knew I was going to die.

"I can't remember," she says, "what does Kübler-Ross[5] say comes after Denial?"

It seems to me Anger must be next. Then Bargaining, Depression, and so on and so forth. But I keep my guesses to myself.

"The only thing is," she says, "is where's Resurrection? God knows I want to do it by the book. But she left out Resurrection."

---

3. Title character in a long-running TV medical drama.   **4.** Principal highway along the west coast of the United States.   **5.** Elisabeth Kübler-Ross (1926–2004), author of popular books on death and dying in which she described the distinct emotional "stages" of grief: denial, anger, bargaining, depression, acceptance.

She laughs, and I cling to the sound the way someone dangling above a ravine holds fast to the thrown rope.

We could have cried then, but when we didn't, we couldn't.

"Tell me," she says, "about that chimp with the talking hands. What do they do when the thing ends and the chimp says, 'I don't want to go back to the zoo'?"

When I don't say anything, she says, "O.K.—then tell me another animal story. I like animal stories. But not a sick one—I don't want to know about all the Seeing Eye dogs going blind."

No, I would not tell her a sick one.

"How about the hearing-ear dogs?" I say. "They're not going deaf, but they are getting very judgmental. For instance, there's this golden retriever in Jersey, he wakes up the deaf mother and drags her into the daughter's room because the kid has got a flashlight and is reading under the covers."

"Oh, you're killing me," she says. "Yes, you're definitely killing me."

"They say the smart dog obeys, but the smarter dog knows when to *dis*obey."

"Yes," she says, "the smarter *anything* knows when to disobey. Now, for example."

She is flirting with the Good Doctor, who has just appeared. Unlike the Bad Doctor, who checks the I.V. drip before saying good morning, the Good Doctor says things like "God didn't give epileptics a fair shake." He awards himself points for the cripples he could have hit in the parking lot. Because the Good Doctor is a little in love with her he says maybe a year. He pulls a chair up to her bed and suggests I might like to spend an hour on the beach.

"Bring me something back," she says. "Anything from the beach. Or the gift shop. Taste is no object."

The doctor slowly draws the curtain around her bed.

"Wait!" she cries.

I look in at her.

"Anything," she says, "except a magazine subscription."

The doctor turns away.

I watch her mouth laugh.

What seems dangerous often is not—black snakes, for example, or clear-air turbulence. While things that just lie there, like this beach, are loaded with jeopardy. A yellow dust rising from the ground, the heat that ripens melons overnight—this is earthquake weather. You can sit here braiding the fringe on your towel and the sand will all of a sudden suck down like an hourglass. The air roars. In the cheap apartments onshore, bathtubs fill themselves and gardens roll up and over like green waves. If nothing happens, the dust will drift and the heat deepen till fear turns to desire. Nerves like that are only bought off by catastrophe.

"It never happens when you're thinking about it," she observed once.

"Earthquake, earthquake, earthquake," she said.

"Earthquake, earthquake, earthquake," I said.

Like the aviaphobe who keeps the plane aloft with prayer, we kept it up till an aftershock cracked the ceiling.

That was after the big one in '72. We were in college; our dormitory was five miles from the epicenter. When the ride was over and my jabbering pulse began to slow, she served five parts champagne to one part orange juice and joked about living in Ocean View, Kansas. I offered to drive her to Hawaii on the new world psychics predicted would surface the next time, or the next.

I could not say that now—next. *Whose* next? she could ask.

Was I the only one who noticed that the experts had stopped saying *if* and now spoke of *when*? Of course not; the fearful ran to thousands. We watched the traffic of Japanese beetles for deviation. Deviation might mean more natural violence.

I wanted her to be afraid with me, but she said, "I don't know. I'm just not."

She was afraid of nothing, not even of flying.

I have this dream before a flight where we buckle in and the plane moves down the runway. It takes off at thirty-five miles an hour, and then we're airborne, skimming on tree tops. Still, we arrive in New York on time. It is so pleasant. One night I flew to Moscow this way.

She flew with me once. That time she flew with me she ate macadamia nuts while the wings bounced. She knows the wing tips can bend thirty feet up and thirty feet down without coming off. She believes it. She trusts the laws of aerodynamics. My mind stampedes. I can almost accept that a battleship floats, and everybody knows steel sinks.

I see fear in her now and am not going to try to talk her out of it. She is right to be afraid.

After a quake, the six o'clock news airs a film clip of first-graders yelling at the broken playground per their teacher's instructions.

"*Bad* earth!" they shout, because anger is stronger than fear.

But the beach is standing still today. Everyone on it is tranquilized, numb or asleep. Teenaged girls rub coconut oil on each other's hard-to-reach places. They smell like macaroons. They pry open compacts like clamshells; mirrors catch the sun and throw a spray of white rays across glazed shoulders. The girls arrange their wet hair with silk flowers the way they learned in *Seventeen*. They pose.

A formation of low-riders[6] pulls over to watch with a six-pack. They get vocal when the girls check their tan lines. When the beer is gone, so are they—flexing their cars on up the boulevard.

Above this aggressive health are the twin wrought-iron terraces, painted flamingo pink, of the Palm Royale. Someone dies there every time the sheets are changed. There's an ambulance in the driveway, so the remaining residents line the balconies, rocking and not talking, one-upped.

The ocean they stare at is dangerous, and not just the undertow. You can almost see the slapping tails of sand sharks keeping cruising bodies alive.

If she looked, she could see this, some of it, from her window. She would be the first to say how little it takes to make a thing all wrong.

There was a second bed in the room when I returned. For two beats I didn't get it. Then it hit me like an open coffin.

She wants every minute, I thought. She wants my life.

"You missed Gussie," she said.

6. Drivers of rebuilt, underslung cars.

Gussie is her parents' 300-pound narcoleptic maid. Her attacks often come at the ironing board. The pillowcases in that family are all bordered with scorch.

"It's a hard trip for her," I said. "How is she?"

"Well, she didn't fall asleep, if that's what you mean. Gussie's great—you know what she said? She said, 'Darlin' just keep prayin', down on your knees.'"

She shrugged. "See anybody good?"

"No," I said, "just the new Charlie's Angel.[7] And I saw Cher's car down near the Arcade."

"Cher's car is worth *three* Charlie's Angels," she said. "What else am I missing?"

"It's earthquake weather," I told her.

"The best thing to do about earthquakes," she said, "is not to live in California."

"That's useful," I said. "You sound like Reverend Ike:[8] 'The best thing to do for the poor is not be one of them.'"

We're crazy about Reverend Ike.

I noticed her face was bloated.

"You know," she said, "I feel like hell. I'm about to stop having fun."

"The ancients have a saying," I said. "'There are times when the wolves are silent; there are times when the moon howls.'"

"What's that, Navajo?"

"Palm Royale lobby graffiti," I said. "I bought a paper there. I'll read to you."

"Even though I care about nothing?" she said.

I turned to page three, to a UPI filler datelined Mexico City. I read her "Man Robs Bank with Chicken," about a man who bought a barbecued chicken at a stand down the block from a bank. Passing the bank, he got the idea. He walked in and approached a teller. He pointed the brown paper bag at her and she handed over the day's receipts. It was the smell of barbecue sauce that eventually led to his capture.

The story made her hungry, she said, so I took the elevator down six floors to the cafeteria and brought back all the ice cream she wanted. We lay side by side, adjustable beds cranked up for optimal TV viewing, littering the sheets with Good Humor wrappers, picking toasted almonds out of the gauze. We were Lucy and Ethel, Mary and Rhoda[9] in extremis. The blinds were closed to keep light off the screen.

We watched a movie starring men we used to think we wanted to sleep with. Hers was a tough cop out to stop mine, a vicious rapist who went after cocktail waitresses.

"This is a good movie," she said, when snipers felled them both.

I missed her already; my straight man, my diary.

A Filipino nurse tiptoed in and gave her an injection. She removed the pile of Popsicle sticks from the nightstand—enough to splint a small animal.

---

7. That is, a replacement for one of the pretty young women in the TV series *Charlie's Angels.* **8.** Frederick Eikerenkoetter (1935–2009), African American radio evangelist best known for preaching the godliness of money and prosperity. **9.** Principal characters in, respectively, the *I Love Lucy* and *The Mary Tyler Moore Show* TV series.

The injection made us sleepy—me in the way I picked up her inflection till her mother couldn't tell us apart on the phone. We slept.

I dreamed she was a decorator, come to furnish my house. She worked in secret, singing to herself. When she finished, she guided me proudly to the door. "How do you like it?" she asked, easing me inside.

Every beam and sill and shelf and knob was draped in black bunting, with streamers and black crepe looped around darkened mirrors.

"I have to go home," I said when she woke up.

She thought I meant home to her house in the Canyon, and I had to say, No, *home* home. I twisted my hands in the hackneyed fashion of people in pain. I was supposed to offer something. The Best Friend. I could not even offer to come back.

I felt weak and small and failed. Also exhilarated. I had a convertible in the parking lot. Once out of that room, I would drive it too fast down the coast highway through the crab-smelling air. A stop in Malibu for sangria. The music in the place would be sexy and loud. They would serve papaya and shrimp and watermelon ice. After dinner I would pick up beach boys. I would shimmer with life, buzz with heat, vibrate with health, stay up all night with one and then the other.

Without a word, she yanked off her mask and threw it on the floor. She kicked at the blankets and moved to the door. She must have hated having to pause for breath and balance before slamming out of Isolation, and out of the second room, the one where you scrub and tie on the white masks.

A voice shouted her name in alarm, and people ran down the corridor. The Good Doctor was paged over the intercom. I opened the door and the nurses at the station stared hard, as if this flight had been my idea.

"Where is she?" I asked, and they nodded to the supply closet.

I looked in. Two nurses were kneeling beside her on the floor, talking to her in low voices. One held a mask over her nose and mouth, the other rubbed her back in slow circles. The nurses glanced up to see if I was the doctor, and when they saw I wasn't, they went back to what they were doing.

"There, there, honey," they cooed.

On the morning she was moved to the cemetery, the one where Al Jolson is buried, I enrolled in a Fear of Flying class. "What is your worst fear?" the instructor asked, and I answered, "That I will finish this course and still be afraid."

I sleep with a glass of water on the nightstand so I can see by its level if the coastal earth is trembling or if the shaking is still me.

What do I remember? I remember only the useless things I hear—that Bob Dylan's mother invented Wite-out, that twenty-three people must be in a room before there is a fifty-fifty chance two will have the same birthdate. Who cares whether or not it's true? In my head there are bath towels swaddling this stuff. Nothing else seeps through.

I review those things that will figure in the retelling: a kiss through surgical gauze, the pale hand correcting the position of the wig. I noted these gestures as they happened, not in any retrospect. Though I don't know why looking *back* should show us more than looking *at*. It is just possible I will say I stayed the night. And who is there that can say I did not?

Nothing else gets through until I think of the chimp, the one with the talking hands.

In the course of the experiment, that chimp had a baby. Imagine how her trainers must have thrilled when the mother, without prompting, began to sign to the newborn. Baby, drink milk. Baby, play ball. And when the baby died, the mother stood over the body, her wrinkled hands moving with animal grace, forming again and again the words, Baby, come hug, Baby, come hug, fluent now in the language of grief.

1985

ALICE HOFFMAN
b. 1952

Born in New York City and raised on Long Island, Hoffman has worked impressively in every genre, including film. Her talent is what one might call tidal, in the sense that she writes tirelessly, with great force and without apparent attention to the prevailing literary winds. She attended Adelphi University and Stanford, and began publishing quite young, bringing out her first novel, *Property Of* (1977), when she was just twenty-five years old. One of her strengths as a writer is that she sees the mystery in ordinary existence, and there is indeed a magical quality to her work—it is embedded in the lines themselves, a kind of shimmer behind the story's surface of recognizable people in recognizable conflicts. Among her many works for adults and teens are the novels *The Drowning Season* (1979), *At Risk* (1988), *Practical Magic* (1995), *Here on Earth* (1997), *The Probable Future* (2003), and *The Dovekeepers* (2011); her stories are collected in *Blackbird House* (2005).

The Wedding of Snow and Ice

In 1957, on the very rim of the Cape,[1] a small town often didn't feel small until the first snowfall of the season. In those muffled first moments, in the hush and stillness before the flakes began and the anticipation of the mess there'd be to dig out afterward, people congregated in the general store, there to stock up on candles and flashlights, franks and beans, and loaves of bread. People regularly knew each other's business; now they could also recite what was in their neighbors' refrigerators and cupboards. Then and there, the world shrank and became a smaller thing, simple as a driveway, a red wicker basket filled with bread and milk, a cleared road, a light in a neighbor's window, a snow globe on a child's shelf.

At the Farrells', they were taking down the barn, and when the first big flakes began to fall, all work had to stop. There was no point in risking a slip on the roof and the possibility of a broken arm or leg. The Farrells, after all, were a cautious breed. The father, Jim, and the two boys, Hank and Jamie, trooped into the kitchen, their faces ruddy, hands frozen in spite of woolen gloves. Grace Farrell had been listening to the weather reports on the radio and had made tomato soup from the canned tomatoes left from last August's garden. The bowls of rich broth were so hot and delicious it made tears form in Jim's eyes, although, frankly, the boys preferred Campbell's.

---

1. Cape Cod, peninsula in eastern Massachusetts.

Still, at fourteen and seventeen, the Farrell brothers knew enough to compliment their mother's soup. When they'd foolishly made their preference known in the past, their mother, mostly easygoing but with occasional frightening spikes of passion that surprised one and all, had spilled the entire contents of the pot down the drain. She, who liked things homemade and was known for her grape jam and Christmas pudding, announced she didn't know why she bothered with any of it. She might just get herself a job, and then where would they be? Eating bread and butter and soup right out of the can. She'd been a nurse when Jim Farrell met her, and she'd given it up to take care of them, and did they even appreciate what she'd sacrificed? Why, next summer she might even let the garden go wild if that was how little they thought of the work she put in. The garden was a trial anyway, a constant war against the naturalized sweet peas, vines so invasive Grace Farrell yanked them out by the handful. In the early fall, she'd had the older boy, Hank, hack down the vines with an ax, then build a bonfire. The smoke that arose was so sweet Grace Farrell wound up crying. She said there was smoke in her eyes, but she got like that sometimes, as if there was another life somewhere out there she might be living, one she might prefer despite her love for her husband and sons.

The sweet peas in the field were thought to have been set down by the first inhabitant of the house, Coral Hadley, who lost her husband and son at sea. Coral was said never to look at the ocean again after that, even though it was little more than a mile from her door. She dug in tightly to the earth, and there were people who vowed that her fingers turned green. When she walked down Main Street acorns fell out of her pockets, so that anyone following too closely behind was sure to stumble. Coral certainly did her best to cultivate this acreage. All these years later, her presence was still felt; odd, unexpected specimens popped up on the property, seeming to grow overnight. Peach trees where none belonged. Hedges of lilac of a variety extinct even in England. Roses among the nettle. The two-acre field rampant with those damned sweet peas, purple and pink and white, strong as weeds, impossible to get rid of.

Grace Farrell had stated publicly that she would swear old Coral Hadley came back from the dead just to replant anything that had been ripped up. Surely a joke, considering that Grace was one of the most sensible individuals around, the last woman you'd ever expect might believe in ghosts, the first a body could depend upon in times of trial and strife. She'd had her hands full with those boys of hers: Hank was the dreamer who didn't pay attention to his schoolwork. Jamie was the wilder one who simply couldn't sit still. In grammar school the fourth-grade teacher, Helen Morse, had tied Jamie's left arm to the desk in an attempt to force him to improve his penmanship by using his right hand, but Jamie had simply walked around the room dragging the desk along with him. He remained victorious, stubbornly left-handed.

He certainly had energy, that boy. He had to be kept busy, for his own good as well as for the peace of mind of those around him. Fortunately, they didn't have to think up projects. There were endless tasks around the house. The shaky old barn pulled down for safety's sake, for instance, though the boys had loved to play there when they were younger, swinging from a rope in the hayloft, nearly breaking their necks every time. New kitchen cabinets had just been put in, and Jamie had helped Jim with that job as well. He'd been just as helpful when the dreadful stained carpeting was at last taken up, exposing the yellow-pine floors that were said to be soaked with Coral Hadley's tears.

There was always something gone wrong with a house as old as this one. Maybe Grace should have said no when Jim first took her to see the place. It was the week before their wedding, and Grace was still living with her parents up in Plymouth.[2] She had recently given up her job at the hospital. *Isn't it gorgeous?* he'd said of the farm. It looked like one of those tumbledown places you saw in the news magazines, with hound dogs lazing around the front door. The fields were so thick with milkweed back then that a thousand goldfinch came to feed every spring. Anyone wishing to reach the pond had to use a scythe to cut a path. All the same, the look on Jim's face had made Grace say, *Oh, yes.* It had made her throw all good sense away. For an instant the house did look beautiful to her, all white clapboards and right angles; the milkweed was shining, illuminated by thin bands of sunlight, an amazing sight if you looked at it the right way, if you narrowed your eyes until everything blurred into one bright and gleaming horizon.

Jim Farrell had grown up in town. His father had been a carpenter, and Jim, wanting steadier work, was the chief of the public-works department, the chief of three other men, at any rate. He was a good man, quiet, not one to shirk responsibility. People said he could smell snow, that he could divine a nor'easter simply from the scent in the air. The biggest storms smelled like vanilla, he'd confided to Jamie, the small ones like wet laundry. Tonight, Jim seemed antsy. He got like that when he simply couldn't tell what the snow was up to, when the whole damn thing seemed like a mystery. His job, after all, was a cat-and-mouse game against nature and fate. Did he get the town plows out early? Did he conserve sand and salt for the next snowfall? Would the storm carve away at the dunes, which were already disappearing all along the shore?

When Jim had finished his soup and taken his bowl to the sink, he stood at the window facing west. The field of sweet peas was already dusted white. Snow made him feel like crying sometimes—just the first flakes, the purest stuff.

Behind the hedge of holly the Brooks house next door was dark.

"Do you think I should go over there with some soup?" Grace had come up behind her husband. She liked the way he looked at snow, the intensity on his face, there when they made love, there whenever he was concentrating and trying to figure things out. "Hal might be away. I think he might still be working on that house in Bourne. She might be alone there with Josephine."

The Brookses were their closest neighbors, right there on the other side of the field, but there was no camaraderie between the families. Hal Brooks was a shit, there was no other way to say it, and even Grace, who was offended by bad language, would nod when someone in town referred to her neighbor that way. Lord, he'd been a mean snake all his life, the way Grace had heard it. Even as a boy, he'd shoot seagulls for sport, and once or twice a stray dog had disappeared on his property, only to be found strung up from one of the oak trees. Hal hadn't changed with age, and people in town all knew what was going on over there. You could see it when the Brookses' name came up. A nod. A stepping back. Some people had seen what went on with his wife, some

---

2. Town on Cape Cod Bay.

had heard about it. The rest would simply cross the street when the Brookses were in town.

"If she needs something she'll come and get it, won't she?" Jim said, although they both thought this probably wasn't true.

The boys were in the living room watching the new TV; they would watch anything that flickered up in front of them, and for a while at least Jamie, always so restless, would settle down. The boys didn't need to know what went on at the Brookses'. When Grace and Jim had first moved in, Arly Brooks was the only occupant, a widower, a hardworking fisherman who kept his boat out in Provincetown.[3] Hal had inherited the house from his father, and had come to claim it after the old man died. He'd arrived home from the Navy with this wife of his, ready to make enemies left and right no matter how many welcome baskets were brought to the door or how many women in town sent over pies. Jim Farrell didn't want his wife next door for any reason, not even to take over a pot of soup.

"Stay away," Jim told Grace. "We all decide our own fates, and what they do is their business."

"Well, of course I won't go over. But I might send the boys to shovel snow."

Jim couldn't say no to that. Just last year, Mattie Hammond, eighty-four years old and all on her own, had been snowed into her cottage during a blizzard. The drifts had been so high, Mattie couldn't open her front door and had nearly starved to death before Jim came to plow out the street. Despite the blanket of white that could cause semi-blindness in some men while they were at the plow, Jim had noticed the square handkerchief Mattie had taped up in a window to signal her distress. There were some things Jim Farrell couldn't deny a neighbor, particularly on a snowy night, and other situations Grace couldn't turn away from either, and because they didn't like to argue with each other, no matter their differences, they left it at that.

Jim went out to his truck at four in the afternoon, headed for the department of public works. It was the hour when everything turned blue—the snow, the white fences, the white clapboards of the house—that luminous time when the line between earth and sky disappeared.

"I want you boys to go shovel over at Rosalyn Brooks'," Grace called into the living room. She had ladled out a separate pot of tomato soup despite what Jim had advised. "Take the shovels and bring this soup with you."

When there was no response, Grace went into the living room and stood in front of the TV. The boys would watch just about anything, but their favorite show was *You Asked For It*, on tonight at seven. There were the most amazing things out there in the world, and all you had to do was ask and you'd see it right in front of you, on your very own screen.

"I'm turning this off," Grace announced, then did so. "I want you to shovel."

"At the Brookses'," Jamie said. "We heard."

"Can't. I've got a history paper," Hank said. "Sorry, Mom, but it's due tomorrow."

Hank was having his troubles in school, so Grace let him stay and sent Jamie on his own, making sure he bundled up, handing him his hat, which he

---

3. Town near the northernmost end of Cape Cod.

often managed to forget, watching to make certain he pulled on his scarf and his leather gloves. The pot of soup was under one arm, the shovel carried over his shoulder. He was a quiet boy, not much of a student, but lovable to his mother in some deep way, so that she worried about him as she didn't anyone else in this world. Perhaps it was true that mothers had favorites, at least now and then. Grace watched Jamie disappear into the blue of the field and felt a catch in her throat. Love, she presumed. A moment of realizing exactly how lucky she was, of being grateful that she was not Coral Hadley, that her son was not out on the ocean, but was instead traipsing through the snowy reaches of their own familiar acreage.

When he was alone, Jamie tended to hum. His mother was a fan of musicals, particularly *The King and I*,[4] and Jamie found himself humming "Getting to Know You." His mother loved Yul Brynner, for reasons Jamie couldn't understand. The king he played was bald, for one thing; he was bossy as all get-out for another. All the same, the song stuck. Sometimes when Jamie walked through this field, in winter, at exactly this hour, he would see deer. There were wild turkeys too, crazy birds that had very little fear of humans and would run straight at you if you invaded their territory. There was a shortcut to the Brookses', through the winterberry vines. The berries were shiny and red; sometimes you'd happen upon a skunk as you made your way through the brambles, and that skunk would just go on feeding, calm as could be, rightfully assured that few creatures other than the neighborhood dogs would be stupid enough to interrupt or attack.

Jamie was in the winterberry, thinking about deer, singing softly to himself, when he heard it. A clap of thunder. A snowplow on the road. A firecracker. He stopped for a minute and breathed in snowflakes. When he breathed out, his breath was like a steam engine. It melted the snow off the winterberries. He listened. He was good at that, but he heard nothing, so he went on. He was that sort of boy, intent on the task at hand. He knew what his mother wanted him to do: shovel from the Brookses' front door to their driveway. He and Hank had done it before, last year. Mr. Brooks hadn't been at home, but Mrs. Brooks had made them hot chocolate, which they drank out on the front step. Now, alongside the Chevy, there was Mr. Brooks' truck, a wreck of a thing, battered, leaking oil into the snow.

Jamie tried to balance the soup on the front step, but the step was made from an uneven piece of stone. He went up to the door then, to deliver the soup before he started to work. His breath did the same thing to the glass window set into the door as it did to the winterberries, melted off the snow, then fogged it up. But even through the fog he could see Rosalyn Brooks, right there on the floor with no clothes on and something red all over her face. He should have backed away; he should have run home, done something, anything, but he had never seen a naked woman before, and it was as though he were hypnotized, frozen in place, while his breath kept melting the snow. One minute he had been a fourteen-year-old boy with nothing much on his mind. Now he was someone else entirely.

---

4. Popular Broadway musical (1951), and later movie, written by Richard Rodgers and Oscar Hammerstein; Russian American actor Yul Brynner played King Mongkut of Siam (Thailand).

He was still holding on to the pot of tomato soup when he opened the door. People didn't lock up much in their town; there was nothing to steal and no one to steal it. Jamie walked in as though he'd been drawn inside by a magnetic force. The Brookses' house was an old farmhouse, like the Farrells', but it hadn't been updated. It was cold and empty, and the only light turned on was in the kitchen, all the way down the hall. Everything looked blue inside the house, except for the thing that was red. It was blood that was all over Rosalyn Brooks, but when she looked up and saw Jamie she seemed most panicked by the fact that she was naked. She let out a strange sound and grabbed for a rag rug, trying to cover herself. It was a sob, that's what Jamie realized. That was the sound.

"I brought you soup," he said. "It's from my mother."

Mrs. Brooks looked at him as though he were crazy.

"She makes it herself." Jamie felt like running, but he didn't seem capable of turning away. He had the feeling he might be paralyzed. "Are you all right?"

Rosalyn Brooks laughed, or at least Jamie thought that's what it was.

"Just stay there," he said. "I'll get you something."

He put the soup on a tabletop and went to the hall closet, grabbing for the first thing he felt, bringing back a heavy black woolen coat.

"It's okay," he said, because of the way she was looking at him. As though she was scared. "It's a coat."

Rosalyn Brooks stared at him, then took the coat and put it on. Jamie Farrell looked away; all the same, he glimpsed her breasts, blue in the light of the house, and her belly, which was oddly beautiful. She had bruises all over, that much he noticed as well, on her legs and shoulders especially. He saw now that her lip was split open and she could barely see through the slits of her eyes.

"Do you want me to heat you some soup?" It was so cold in the house that Jamie's breath came out in billows, and he was embarrassed by his own heat. When Mrs. Brooks didn't answer, he figured she wanted him to take the pot into the kitchen, but as he turned to head down the hall, Rosalyn lurched from her prone position and grabbed his pants leg. She did it so hard and so fast he almost fell over. She looked at him then in a way that convinced him something really bad had happened. Somebody else might have taken off running, back through the winterberries, snagging his clothes as he raced through the bushes, but Jamie crouched down beside Mrs. Brooks.

"Where's Josephine?" he asked.

That was the Brookses' little daughter. Josephine liked to pick the sweet peas in the field. She liked the pears that dropped to the ground from the big tree in the Farrells' yard. Rosalyn looked up the stairs.

"Is she in bed?"

"Asleep."

At least Mrs. Brooks could talk. That was a relief.

"My husband had an accident."

"Okay," Jamie said. "Should we call my dad? He could help."

"No. You can't call him."

He could tell that whatever had happened was bad from her tone. Still, he stayed. Maybe Jamie felt he owed Rosalyn Brooks his allegiance because he'd seen her naked, or maybe it was all that blood, or the way his breath was so hot and the house so very cold.

"In the kitchen?"

Mrs. Brooks nodded. She was not yet thirty, a young woman, pretty under other circumstances.

"I'll just go in there and get a dish towel to stop the bleeding," Jamie said, for her lip and her scalp were oozing.

But when he rose, she grabbed his leg again.

"It's okay," he assured her. "I'll be right back."

The hallway was even colder. These old houses had no insulation, and the kitchen was especially chilly. There was even more blood on the floor, especially around Hal Brooks' body, which was right in front of the stove. Jamie tried not to look too closely. He grabbed a dish towel, ran cold water over it, then brought it back to Rosalyn. He wondered if he had stepped in the blood and if it was on the soles of his boots, if he'd left tracks down the hall. Then he stopped wondering. He put those thoughts aside. Rosalyn was sitting on the floor now, the coat buttoned; when he handed her the dish towel, she held it up to her lip.

"What do you want to do with him?" Jamie said.

Outside, the blue was turning into darkness. A black night. So quiet you could hear the cardinals nesting in the hedges outside the Brookses' window. The snow fell harder. Jamie figured his father was up on the main road with his plow by now.

They sat there in silence in the cold house.

"I'll shovel your path, and then I'll come back," Jamie said. "You think about what you want to do."

"Okay," Rosalyn said. "I will."

Jamie went out and shoveled hard and fast. It was heavy snow, thick and dense, the kind that he would have thought was good for snowball fights on any other occasion. He wasn't thinking that way now. He was thinking of the pond beyond the field. In the old days, food could be stored in the summer kitchen right up until July if enough ice was stacked against the walls. He'd heard the old woman who'd lived in their house a while back had hauled blocks of ice from the pond until her horse, the one who'd lived in the barn they'd begun to tear down, slipped through the ice and drowned.

The kitchen floor at the Brookses' was already clean when Jamie came back inside. Rosalyn Brooks had mopped up, then washed her face and pulled back her honey-colored hair. There were still streaks of blood in her scalp, but Jamie Farrell didn't have the heart to tell her. Rosalyn went to check on her daughter, then she came back downstairs and put on her husband's work-boots. She looked even more delicate wearing them. She didn't bother with gloves. At least there was a blanket around Mr. Brooks, and Jamie was grateful for that. They tried to pull him along the floor, and when that didn't work, Jamie went and got the wheelbarrow from the garage. He was so hot he felt like taking off his hat and his scarf, but if he misplaced them, his mother would have his head.

It took all their combined strength to push the wheelbarrow through the snow. The thick, heavy snow that they quietly cursed. They stopped for a break halfway across the field; they both looked up at the falling snow. Rosalyn put her arms out, and tilted her head back. Jamie had never thought about the future, who he was, what he would do. It had all been a haze. Now he saw that blood was still seeping through Rosalyn's hair and he thought she probably needed stitches. He saw that his future was almost here.

There were pine trees and holly around the far side of the pond, and that's where they went. They had to drag him along over the frozen weeds. They put stones in his pockets, heavy black stones, the kind Jamie and Hank liked best for their slingshots. Rosalyn took off the workboots she'd been wearing and filled them with stones as well, then put the boots on her husband, laced them and carefully tied a knot, then a double-knot.

"Your feet will freeze on the way back," Jamie whispered.

She didn't seem to care. She closed her eyes, and when she opened them they were still slits. The snow was making things quieter all the time. They pulled him into the pond and watched him sink. There was a gulping noise at first, then there was nothing. Only the quiet.

"You go home," Rosalyn said to Jamie. "Go on. Your mother will be worried."

He hated to leave her like that, barefoot, bleeding.

She leaned over and kissed him, on the lips, in gratitude.

Jamie Farrell ran the rest of the way, his hot breath rattling against his ribs. His boots and pants legs were wet and mucky. There was pond water in his boots, fetid, cold stuff. He was shivering and couldn't stop. Worst of all, his mother was waiting for him.

"What took you so long?" Grace demanded. "It's after eight. You missed your TV show." Then, looking at him carefully, "Where's the shovel?"

"I forgot it." Jamie turned back to the door. "I'm sorry. I'll go get it if you want."

His mother stopped him. She looked at him harder still. "I'll go. You do your homework and get ready for bed."

"I can get the shovel in the morning," Jamie offered, an edge of panic inside him. But Grace was already getting her coat. She had stepped into her warm black boots. After she left, Jamie went up to the bedroom he shared with his brother. It was as though he'd just walked out of a dream and here he was, melting in the overheated second floor of his family's house. He thought of all the wounded people there were in this world, people he'd never even know, and he felt helpless.

"What if I was an accessory to murder?" he asked Hank, who was already in bed, more than half asleep as he gazed at his history book.

"What if you were the biggest moron that ever lived?" Hank shot back, a question for which there was no answer, at least not on this night.

It was nearly midnight by the time Grace came home. The snow was tapering off, and she brushed the flakes from her coat and stomped on the welcome mat to dislodge the ice from her boots. Usually, Jim didn't get back till dawn, but tonight he'd come home earlier. The storm wasn't as bad as the meteorologists had predicted. His men could take care of the rest of the cleanup.

"Where were you? The boys are in bed, and when you weren't here, I didn't know what to think."

But that wasn't true. For a moment, what he'd thought was that she'd left him. Just disappeared into that other life she seemed to be thinking about sometimes. They stared at each other now, their breath hot. Outside, the drifts leaned against the house; winter here stayed a long time.

"I went over and heated up the tomato soup for Rosalyn."

"Did you?"

Grace sat down at the table. Everyone had known what was going on, and no one had done a damn thing about it.

"Hal up and left. No money, no warning, nothing. She thinks he may have re-enlisted."

Jim was looking out the window; two deer had just now wandered into their field. He hoped the snow wasn't deep enough to prevent them from unearthing the last withered sweet peas, thought to be delicious by anything wild. "I guess it's none of our business," he said. From this distance, the winterberries almost looked tropical, the fruit of another place entirely.

"So you say."

Grace Farrell still had snow in her hair, but it would melt when they got into bed, and she'd never even know it had been there. When she thought back to this night, she wouldn't even remember it had been snowing, she'd only remember the look on her husband's face, the concentration she loved, the man she could turn to, even on a night as cold as this.

2005

ZORA NEALE HURSTON
1901–1960

Hurston was born in Eatonville, Florida. She became a vigorous activist in the cultural, social, and literary awakening that converged in the Harlem Renaissance of the 1920s and 1930s. She was a trained anthropologist whose personal insights enlarged that discipline, giving it depth and liveliness. Her gifts as a writer helped her absorb the rich diversities of black folklore in Haiti, Jamaica, and Bermuda, as well as in rural and urban areas of the United States. At various times she was a journalist and librarian, and wherever she could make herself heard she bore witness against the stereotyping that denied the multifarious heritage of blacks. Her appreciation of the subtleties and ambiguities of the vernacular influenced the generation of writers who followed her. The thematic core of her work is the love blacks bear for one another rather than the hostilities they feel against their oppressors. Her stories and articles appeared in several distinguished magazines, and she published four novels: *Jonah's Gourd Vine* (1934), *Their Eyes Were Watching God* (1937), *Moses, Man of the Mountain* (1939), and *Seraph on the Suwanee* (1948). Much of her short fiction can be found in *Spunk: The Selected Stories of Zora Neale Hurston* (1985).

The Conscience of the Court

The clerk of the court took a good look at the tall brown-skinned woman with the head rag on. She sat on the third bench back with a husky officer beside her.

"The People versus Laura Lee Kimble!"

The policeman nudged the woman to get to her feet and led her up to the broad rail. She stood there, looking straight ahead. The hostility in the room reached her without her seeking to find it.

Unpleasant things were ahead of Laura Lee Kimble, but she was ready for this moment. It might be the electric chair or the rest of her life in some big lonesome jail house, or even torn to pieces by a mob, but she had passed three long weeks in jail. She had come to the place where she could turn her face to the wall and feel neither fear nor anguish. So this here so-called trial was nothing to her but a form and a fashion and an outside show to the world. She could stand apart and look on calmly. She stood erect and looked up at the judge.

"Charged with felonious and aggravated assault. Mayhem. Premeditated attempted murder on the person of one Clement Beasley. Obscene and abusive language. Laura Lee Kimble, how do you plead?"

Laura Lee was so fascinated by the long-named things that they were accusing her of that she stood there tasting over the words. *Lawdy me!* she mused inside herself. *Look like I done every crime excepting habeas corpus and stealing a mule.*

"Answer the clerk!" The officer nudged Laura Lee. "Tell him how you plead."

"Plead? Don't reckon I make out just what you all mean by that." She looked from face to face and at last up at the judge, with bewilderment in her eyes. She found him looking her over studiously.

The judge understood the look in her face, but he did not interfere so promptly as he ordinarily would have. This was the man-killing bear cat of a woman that he had heard so much about. Though spare of fat, she was built strongly enough, all right. An odd Negro type. Gray-green eyes, large and striking, looking out of a chestnut-brown face. A great abundance of almost straight hair only partially hidden by the high-knotted colored kerchief about her head. Somehow this woman did not look fierce to him at all. Yet she had beaten a man within an inch of his life. Here was a riddle to solve. With the proud, erect way she held herself, she might be some savage queen. The shabby housedress she had on detracted nothing from this impression. She was a challenge to him somehow or other.

"Perhaps you don't understand what the clerk means, Laura," the judge found himself saying to her in a gentle voice. "He wants you to say whether you are guilty of the charges or not."

"Oh, I didn't know. Didn't even know if he was talking to me or not. Much obliged to you, sir." Laura Lee sent His Honor a shy smile. "'Deed I don't know if I'm guilty or not. I hit the man after he hit me, to be sure, Mister Judge, but if I'm guilty I don't know for sure. All them big words and all."

The clerk shook his head in exasperation and quickly wrote something down. Laura Lee turned her head and saw the man on the hospital cot swaddled all up in bandage rags. Yes, that was the very man who caused her to be here where she was.

"All right, Laura Lee," the judge said. "You can take your seat now until you are called on."

The prosecutor looked a question at the judge and said, "We can proceed." The judge nodded, then halted things as he looked down at Laura Lee.

"The defendant seems to have no lawyer to represent her." Now he leaned forward and spoke to Laura Lee directly. "If you have no money to hire yourself a lawyer to look out for your interests, the court will appoint one for you."

There was a pause, during which Laura Lee covered a lot of ground. Then she smiled faintly at the judge and answered him. "Naw sir, I thank you, Mister Judge. Not to turn you no short answer, but I don't reckon it would do me a bit of good. I'm mighty much obliged to you just the same."

The implications penetrated instantly and the judge flushed. This unlettered woman had called up something that he had not thought about for quite some time. The campus of the University of Virginia and himself as a very young man there, filled with a reverence for his profession amounting to an almost holy dedication. His fascination and awe as a professor traced the more than two thousand years of growth of the concepts of human rights and justice. That brought him to his greatest hero, John Marshall, and his inner resolve to follow in the great man's steps, and even add to interpretations of human rights if his abilities allowed. No, he had not thought about all this for quite some time. The judge flushed slowly and deeply.

Below him there, the prosecutor was moving swiftly, but somehow his brisk cynicism offended the judge. He heard twelve names called, and just like that the jury box was filled and sworn in.

Rapidly now, witnesses took the stand, and their testimony was all damaging to Laura Lee. The doctor who told how terribly Clement Beasley had been hurt. Left arm broken above the elbow, compound fracture of the forearm, two ribs cracked, concussion of the brain and various internal injuries. Two neighbors who had heard the commotion and arrived before the house in time to see Laura Lee fling the plaintiff over the gate into the street. The six arresting officers all got up and had their say, and it was very bad for Laura Lee. A two-legged she-devil no less.

Clement Beasley was borne from his cot to the witness stand, and he made things look a hundred times blacker. His very appearance aroused a bumble of pity, and anger against the defendant. The judge had to demand quiet repeatedly. Beasley's testimony blew strongly on the hot coals.

His story was that he had come in conflict with this defendant by loaning a sizable sum of money to her employer. The money was to be repaid at his office. When the date was long past due, he had gone to the house near the river, just off Riverside Drive, to inquire why Mrs. Clairborne had not paid him, nor even come to see him and explain. Imagine his shock when he wormed it out of the defendant that Mrs. Clairborne had left Jacksonville. Further, he detected evidence that the defendant was picking up the things in the house. The loan had been made, six hundred dollars, on the furnishings of the entire house. He had doubted that the furnishings were worth enough for the amount loaned, but he had wanted to be generous to a widow lady. Seeing the defendant packing away the silver, he was naturally alarmed, and the next morning went to the house with a moving van to seize the furniture and protect the loan. The defendant, surprised, attacked him as soon as he appeared at the front door, injured him as he was, and would have killed him if help had not arrived in time.

Laura Lee was no longer a spectator at her own trial. Now she was in a flaming rage. She would have leaped to her feet as the man pictured Miz' Celestine as a cheat and a crook, and again as he sat up there and calmly lied about the worth of the furniture. All of those wonderful antiques, this man making out that they did not equal his minching six hundred dollars! That lie was a sin and a shame! The People was a meddlesome and unfriendly passel and had no use for the truth. It brought back to her in a taunting way what her husband, Tom, had told her over and over again. This world had no use for the love and friending that she was ever trying to give.

It looked now that Tom could be right. Even Miz' Celestine had turnt her back on her. She was here in this place, the house of The People, all by herself. She had ever disbelieved Tom and had to get to be forty-nine before she found out the truth. Well, just as the old folks said, "It's never too long for a bull frog to wear a stiff-bosom shirt. He's bound to get it dirtied some time or other."

"You have testified," Laura Lee heard the judge talking, "that you came in contact with the defendant through a loan to Mrs. J. Stuart Clairborne, her employer, did you not?"

"Yes, Your Honor," Beasley answered promptly and glibly.

"That being true, the court cannot understand why that note was not offered in evidence."

Beasley glanced quickly at the prosecutor and lowered his eyes. "I—I just didn't see why it was necessary, Your Honor. I have it, but—"

"It is not only pertinent, it is of the utmost importance to this case. I order it sent for immediately and placed in evidence."

The tall, lean, black-haired prosecutor hurled a surprised and betrayed look at the bench, then, after a pause, said in a flat voice, "The State rests."

What was in the atmosphere crawled all over Laura Lee like reptiles. The silence shouted that her goose was cooked. But even if the sentence was death, she didn't mind. Celestine Beaufort Clairborne had failed her. Her husband and all her folks had gone on before. What was there to be so happy to live for anymore? She had writ that letter to Miz' Celestine the very first day that she had been placed in jail. Three weeks had gone by on their rusty ankles, and never one word from her Celestine. Laura Lee choked back a sob and gritted her teeth. You had to bear what was placed on your back for you to tote.

"Laura Lee Kimble," the judge was saying, "you are charged with serious felonies, and the law must take its course according to the evidence. You refused the lawyer that the court offered to provide for you, and that was a mistake on your part. However, you have a right to be sworn and tell the jury your side of the story. Tell them anything that might help you, so long as you tell the truth."

Laura Lee made no move to get to her feet and nearly a minute passed. Then the judge leaned forward.

"Believe it or not, Laura Lee, this is a court of law. It is needful to hear both sides of every question before the court can reach a conclusion and know what to do. Now, you don't strike me as a person that is unobliging at all. I believe if you knew you would be helping me out a great deal by telling your side of the story, you would do it."

Involuntarily Laura Lee smiled. She stood up. "Yes, sir, Mister Judge. If I can be of some help to you, I sure will. And I thank you for asking me."

Being duly sworn, Laura Lee sat in the chair to face the jury as she had been told to do.

"You jury-gentlemens, they asked me if I was guilty or no, and I still don't know whether I is or not. I am a unlearnt woman and common-clad.[1] It don't surprise me to find out I'm ignorant about a whole heap of things. I ain't never rubbed the hair off of my head against no college walls and schooled out nowhere at all. All I'm able to do is to tell you gentlemens how it was and then you can tell me if I'm guilty or no.

"I would not wish to set up here and lie and make out that I never hit this plaintive back. Gentlemens, I ain't had no malice in my heart against the plaintive. I seen him only one time before he come there and commenced that fracas with me. That was three months ago, the day after Tom, my husband, died. Miz' Celestine called up the funeral home and they come and got Tom to fix him up so we could take him back to Georgia to lay him to rest. That's where us all come from, Chatham County—Savannah, that is.

1. Working class, ordinary.

"Then now, Miz' Celestine done something I have never knowed her to do be-fore. She put on her things and went off from home without letting me know where she was bound for. She come back afterwhile with this plaintive, which I had never seen before in all my borned days. I glimpsed him good from the kitchen where I was at, walking all over the dining room and the living room with Miz' Celestine and looking at things, but they was talking sort of low like, and I couldn't make out a word what they was talking about. I figgered that Miz' Celestine must of been kind of beside herself, showing somebody look like this plaintive all her fine things like that. Her things is fine and very scarce old antiques, and I know that she have been offered vast sums of money for 'em, but she would never agree to part with none. Things that been handed down in both the Beaufort and the Clairborne families from way back. That little old minching six hundred dollars that the plaintive mentioned wouldn't even be worth one piece of her things, not to mention her silver. After a while they went off and when Miz' Celestine come back, she told me that everything had been taken care of and she had the tickets to Savannah in her purse.

"Bright and soon next morning we boarded the train for Savannah to bury Tom. Miz' Celestine done even more than she had promised Tom. She took him back like she had promised, so that he could be buried in our family lot, and he was covered with flowers, and his church and his lodges turned out with him, and he was put away like some big mogul of a king. Miz' Celestine was there sitting right along by my side all the time. Then me and Miz' Celestine come on back down here to Jacksonville by ourselves.

"And Mrs. Clairborne didn't run off to keep from paying nobody. She's a Clairborne, and before that, she was born a Beaufort. They don't owe nobody, and they don't run away. That ain't the kind of raising they gets. Miz' Clairborne's got money of her own, and lives off of the interest which she receives regular every six months. She went off down there to Miami Beach to sort of refresh herself and rest up her nerves. What with being off down here in Florida, away from all the folks she used to know, for three whole years, and cooped up there in her house, and remembering her dear husband being dead, and now Tom gone, and nobody left of the old family around excepting her and me, she was nervous and peaked like. It wasn't her, it was me that put her up to going off down there for a couple of months so maybe she would come back to herself. She never cheeped to me about borrowing no money from nobody, and I sure wasn't packing nothing up to move off when this plaintive come to the door. I was just gleaming up the silver to kill time whilst I was there by myself.

"And gentlemens, I never tackled the plaintive just as soon as he mounted the porch like he said. The day before that, he had come there and asked-ed me if Miz' Clairborne was at home. I told him no, and then he asked-ed me just when I expected her back. I told him she was down at Miami Beach, and got the letter that she had sent me so he could get her right address. He thanked me and went off. Then the next morning, here he was back with a great big moving wagon, rapped on the door and didn't use a bit of manners and politeness this time. Without even a 'Good morning' he says for me to git out of his way because he come to haul off all the furniture and things in the house and he is short for time.

"You jury-gentlemens, I told him in the nicest way that I knowed how that he must of been crazy. Miz' Celestine was off from home and she had left me there as a kind of guardeen to look after her house and things, and I sure couldn't so handy leave nobody touch a thing in Mrs. Clairborne's house unlessen she was there and said so.

"He just looked at me like I was something that the buzzards laid and the sun hatched out, and told me to move out of his way so he could come on in and get his property. I propped myself and braced one arm across the doorway to bar him out, reckoning he would have manners enough to go on off. But, no! He flew just as hot as Tucker when the mule kicked his mammy and begun to cuss and double-cuss me, and call me all out of my name, something nobody had never done be-fore in all my borned days. I took it to keep from tearing up peace and agreement. Then he balled up his fists and demanded me to move 'cause he was coming in.

"'Aw, naw you ain't,' I told him. 'You might think that you's going to grow horns, but I'm here to tell you you'll die butt-headed.'

"His mouth slewed one-sided and he hauled off and hit me in my chest with his fist two times. Hollered that nothing in the drugstore would kill me no quicker than he would if I didn't git out of his way. I didn't, and then he upped and kicked me.

"I jumped as salty as the 'gator when the pond went dry. I stretched out my arm and he hit the floor on a prone. Then, that truck with the two men on it took off from there in a big hurry. All I did next was to grab him by his heels and frail[2] the pillar of the porch with him a few times. I let him go, but he just laid there like a log.

"'Don't you lay there, making out you's dead, sir!' I told him. 'Git up from there, even if you is dead, and git on off this place!'

"The contrary scamp laid right there, so I reached down and muscled him up on across my shoulder and toted him to the gate, and heaved him over the fence out into the street. None of my business what become of him and his dirty mouth after that.

"I figgered I done right not to leave him come in there and haul off Miz' Celestine's things which she had left there under my trust and care. But Tom, my husband, would have said I was wrong for taking too much on myself. Tom claimed that he ever loved me harder than the thunder could bump a stump, but I had one habit that he ever wished he could break me of. Claimed that I always placed other folks's cares in front of my own, and more expecially Miz' Celestine. Said that I made out of myself a wishbone shining in the sun. Just something for folks to come along and pick up and rub and pull and get their wishes and good luck on. Never looked out for nothing for my ownself.

"I never took a bit of stock in what Tom said like that until I come to be in this trouble. I felt right and good, looking out for Miz' Celestine's interest and standing true and strong, till they took me off to jail and I writ Miz' Celestine a letter to please come see 'bout me and help me out, and give it to the folks there at the jail to mail off for me."

---

2. Hit.

A sob wrestled inside Laura Lee and she struck silence for a full minute before she could go on.

"Maybe it reached her, and then maybe again it didn't. Anyhow, I ain't had a single scratch from Miz' Celestine, and here I is. But I love her so hard, and I reckon I can't help myself. Look, gentlemens, Celestine was give to me when I was going on five—"

The prosecutor shot up like a striking trout and waved his long arm. "If the court please, this is not a street corner. This is a court of law. The witness cannot be allowed to ramble—"

The judge started as if he had been shaken out of a dream. He looked at the prosecutor and shook his head. "The object of a trial, I need not remind you, is to get at the whole truth of a case. The defendant is unlearned, as she has said. She has no counsel to guide her along the lines of procedure. It is important to find out why an act was committed, as you well know. Please humor the court by allowing the witness to tell her story in her own way." The judge looked at Laura Lee and told her to go ahead. A murmur of approval followed this from all over the room.

"I don't mean that her mama and papa threw her away. You know how it used to be the style when a baby was born to place it under the special care of a older brother or sister, or somebody that had worked on the place for a long time and was apt to stay. That's what I mean by Celestine was give to me.

"Just going on five, I wasn't yet old enough to have no baby give to me, but that I didn't understand. All I did know that some way I loved babies. I had me a old rag doll-baby that my mama had made for me, and I loved it better'n anything I can mention.

"Never will forget the morning mama said she was going to take me upstairs to Miz' Beaufort's bedroom to lemme see the new baby. Mama was borned on the Beaufort place just like I was. She was the cook, and everything around the place was sort of under her care. Papa was the houseman and drove for the family when they went out anywhere.

"Well, I seen that tee-ninchy baby laying there in a pink crib all trimmed with a lot of ribbons. Gentlemens, it was the prettiest thing I had ever laid my eyes on. I thought that it was a big-size doll-baby laying there, and right away I wanted it. I carried on so till afterwhile Miz' Beaufort said that I could have it for mine if I wanted it. I was so took with it that I went plumb crazy with joy. I asked her again, and she still said that she was giving it to me. My mama said so too. So, for fear they might change they minds, I said right off that I better take my baby home with me so that I could feed it my ownself and make it something to put on and do for it in general.

"I cried and carried on something terrible when they wouldn't leave me take it on out to the little house where we lived on the place. They pacified me by telling me I better leave it with Miz' Beaufort until it was weaned.

"That couldn't keep me from being around Celestine every chance I got. Later on I found out how they all took my carrying-on for jokes. Made out they was serious to my face, but laughing fit to kill behind my back. They wouldn't of done it if they had knowed how I felt inside. I lived just to see and touch Celestine—my baby, I thought. And she took to me right away.

"When Celestine was two, going on three, I found out that they had been funning with me, and that Celestine was not my child at all. I was too little to have a baby, and then again, how could a colored child be the mother of a white child? Celestine belonged to her papa and mama. It was all right for me to play with her all I wanted to, but forget the notion that she was mine.

"Jury-gentlemens, it was mighty hard, but as I growed on and understood more things I knowed what they was talking about. But Celestine wouldn't allow me to quit loving her. She ever leaned on me, and cried after me, and run to me first for every little thing.

"When I was going on sixteen, papa died and Tom Kimble, a young man, got the job that papa used to have. Right off he put in to court me, even though he was twelve years older than me. But lots of fellows around Savannah was pulling after me too. One wanted to marry me that I liked extra fine, but he was settling in Birmingham, and mama was aginst me marrying and settling way off somewhere. She ruthered for me to marry Tom. When Celestine begin to hang on me and beg and beg me not to leave her, I give in and said that I would have Tom, but for the sake of my feelings, I put the marriage off for a whole year. That was my first good chance to break off from Celestine, but I couldn't.

"General Beaufort, the old gentleman, was so proud for me to stay and pacify Celestine, that he built us a nice house on the place and made it over to us for life. Miz' Beaufort give me the finest wedding that any colored folks had ever seen around Savannah. We stood on the floor in the Beaufort parlor with all the trimmings.

"Celestine, the baby, was a young lady by then, and real pretty with reddish-gold hair and blue eyes. The young bloods was hanging after her in swarms. It was me that propped her up when she wanted to marry young J. Stuart Clairborne, a lawyer just out of school, with a heap of good looks, a smiling disposition, a fine family name and no money to mention. He did have some noble old family furniture and silver. So Celestine had her heart's desire, but little money. They was so happy together that it was like a play.

"Then things begin to change. Mama and Miz' Beaufort passed on in a year of each other. The old gentleman lingered around kind of lonesome, then one night he passed away in his sleep, leaving all he had to Celestine and her husband. Things went on fine for five years like that. He was building up a fine practice and things went lovely.

"Then, it seemed all of a sudden, he took to coughing, and soon he was too tired all the time to go to his office and do around like he used to. Celestine spent her money like water, sending her husband and taking him to different places from one end of the nation to the other, and keeping him under every kind of a doctor's care.

"Four years of trying and doing like that, and then even Celestine had to acknowledge that it never did a bit of good. Come a night when Clairborne laid his dark curly head in her lap like a trusting child and breathed his last.

"Inside our own house of nights, Tom would rear and pitch like a mule in a tin stable, trying to get me to consent to pull out with him and find us better-paying jobs elsewhere. I wouldn't hear to that kind of a talk at all. We had been there when times was extra good, and I didn't aim to tear out and leave Miz' Celestine by herself at low water. This was another time I passed up my chance to cut aloose.

"The third chance wasn't too long a-coming. A year after her husband died, Miz' Celestine come to me and told me that the big Beaufort place was too much for her to keep up with the money she had on hand now. She had been seeking around, and she had found a lovely smaller house down at Jacksonville, Florida. No big grounds to keep up and all. She choosed that instead of a smaller place around Savannah because she could not bear to sing small where she had always led off. An' now she had got hold of a family who was willing to buy the Beaufort estate at a very good price.

"Then she told me that she wanted me to move to Florida with her. She realized that she had no right to ask me no such a thing, but she just could not bear to go off down there with none of her family with her. Would I please consent to go? If I would not go with her, she would give Tom and me the worth of our property in cash money and we could do as we pleased. She had no call to ask us to go with her at all, excepting for old-time love and affection.

"Right then, jury-gentlemens, I knowed that I was going. But Tom had ever been a good husband to me, and I wanted him to feel that he was considered, so I told her that I must consult my pillow. Give her my word one way or another the next day.

"Tom pitched a acre of fits the moment that it was mentioned in his hearing. Hollered that we ought to grab the cash and, with what we had put away, buy us a nice home of our own. What was wrong with me nohow? Did I aim to be a wishbone all my days? Didn't I see that he was getting old? He craved to end his days among his old friends, his lodges and his churches. We had a fine cemetery lot, and there was where he aimed to rest.

"Miz' Celestine cried when he told her. Then she put in to meet all of Tom's complaints. Sure, we was all getting on in years, but that was the very reason why we ought not to part now. Cling together and share and lean and depend on one another. Then when Tom still held out, she made a oath. If Tom died before she did, she would fetch him back and put him away right at her own expense. And if she died before either of us, we was to do the same for her. Anything she left was willed to me to do with as I saw fit.

"So we put in to pack up all the finest pieces, enough and plenty to furnish up our new home in Florida, and moved on down here to live. We passed three peaceful years like that, then Tom died."

Laura Lee paused, shifted so that she faced the jury more directly, then summed up.

"Maybe I is guilty sure enough. I could be wrong for staying all them years and making Miz' Celestine's cares my own. You gentlemens is got more book-learning than me, so you would know more than I do. So far as this fracas is concerned, yeah, I hurted this plaintive, but with him acting the way he was, it just couldn't be helped. And 'tain't nary one of you gentlemens but what wouldn't of done the same."

There was a minute of dead silence. Then the judge sent the prosecutor a cut-eye look and asked, "Care to cross-examine?"

"That's all!" the prosecutor mumbled, and waved Laura Lee to her seat.

"I have here," the judge began with great deliberation, "the note made by Mrs. J. Stuart Clairborne with the plaintiff. It specifies that the purpose of the loan was to finance the burial of Thomas Kimble." The judge paused and looked directly at Laura Lee to call her attention to this point. "The importance to this trial, however, is the due date, which is still more than three months away."

The court officers silenced the gasps and mumbles that followed this announcement.

"It is therefore obvious why the plaintiff has suppressed this valuable piece of evidence. It is equally clear to the court that the plaintiff knew that he had no justification whatsoever for being upon the premises of Mrs. Clairborne."

His Honor folded the paper and put it aside, and regarded the plaintiff with cold gray eyes.

"This is the most insulting instance in the memory of the court of an attempt to prostitute the very machinery of justice for an individual's own nefarious ends. The plaintiff first attempts burglary with forceful entry and violence and, when thoroughly beaten for his pains, brazenly calls upon the law to punish the faithful watch-dog who bit him while he was attempting his trespass. Further, it seems apparent that he has taken steps to prevent any word from the defendant reaching Mrs. Clairborne, who certainly would have moved heaven and earth in the defendant's behalf, and rightfully so."

The judge laced the fingers of his hands and rested them on the polished wood before him and went on.

The protection of women and children, he said, was inherent, implicit in Anglo-Saxon civilization, and here in these United States it had become a sacred trust. He reviewed the long, slow climb of humanity from the rule of the club and the stone hatchet to the Constitution of the United States. The English-speaking people had given the world its highest concepts of the rights of the individual, and they were not going to be made a mock of, and nullified by this court.

"The defendant did no more than resist the plaintiff's attempted burglary. Valuable assets of her employer were trusted in her care, and she placed her very life in jeopardy in defending that trust, setting an example which no decent citizen need blush to follow. The jury is directed to find for the defendant."

Laura Lee made her way diffidently to the judge and thanked him over and over again.

"That will do, Laura Lee. I am the one who should be thanking you."

Laura Lee could see no reason why, and wandered off, bewildered. She was instantly surrounded by smiling, congratulating strangers, many of whom made her ever so welcome if ever she needed a home. She was rubbed and polished to a high glow.

Back at the house, Laura Lee did not enter at once. Like a pilgrim before a shrine, she stood and bowed her head. "I ain't fitten to enter. For a time, I allowed myself to doubt my Celestine. But maybe nobody ain't as pure in heart as they aim to be. The cock crowed on Apostle Peter.[3] Old Maker, please take my guilt away and cast it into the sea of forgetfulness where it won't never rise to accuse me in this world, nor condemn me in the next."

Laura Lee entered and opened all the windows with a ceremonial air. She was hungry, but before she would eat, she made a ritual of atonement by serving. She took a finely wrought silver platter from the massive old sideboard and gleamed it to perfection. So the platter, so she wanted her love to shine.

1950

---

3. Peter denied Christ three times before the cock crowed (cf. Matthew 26:69–75).

SHIRLEY JACKSON
1919–1965

Jackson was born in San Francisco. Shortly after completing her undergraduate education at Syracuse University she married the literary critic Stanley Edgar Hyman, and when he became a teacher at Bennington College in Vermont, they settled permanently there. (In 1954, Jackson reported of their rural life, "Our major exports are books and children, both of which we produce in abundance.") She is a master of the gothic horror tale refurbished in the modern manner, rousing terror from situations that initially appear normal, even dull. Her novels include *Hangsaman* (1951), *The Bird's Nest* (1954), and *We Have Always Lived in the Castle* (1962). Her short stories are collected in *The Lottery* (1944) and *The Magic of Shirley Jackson* (1966). In 1996, a crate of her unpublished stories was discovered in a barn behind her house; these are now available in the collection *Just an Ordinary Day* (1996).

The Lottery

The morning of June 27th was clear and sunny, with the fresh warmth of a full-summer day; the flowers were blossoming profusely and the grass was richly green. The people of the village began to gather in the square, between the post office and the bank, around ten o'clock; in some towns there were so many people that the lottery took two days and had to be started on June 26th, but in this village, where there were only about three hundred people, the whole lottery took less than two hours, so it could begin at ten o'clock in the morning and still be through in time to allow the villagers to get home for noon dinner.

The children assembled first, of course. School was recently over for the summer, and the feeling of liberty sat uneasily on most of them; they tended to gather together quietly for a while before they broke into boisterous play, and their talk was still of the classroom and the teacher, of books and reprimands. Bobby Martin had already stuffed his pockets full of stones, and the other boys soon followed his example, selecting the smoothest and roundest stones; Bobby and Harry Jones and Dickie Delacroix—the villagers pronounced this name "Dellacroy"—eventually made a great pile of stones in one corner of the square and guarded it against the raids of the other boys. The girls stood aside, talking among themselves, looking over their shoulders at the boys, and the very small children rolled in the dust or clung to the hands of their older brothers or sisters.

Soon the men began to gather, surveying their own children, speaking of planting and rain, tractors and taxes. They stood together, away from the pile of stones in the corner, and their jokes were quiet and they smiled rather than laughed. The women, wearing faded house dresses and sweaters, came shortly after their menfolk. They greeted one another and exchanged bits of gossip as they went to join their husbands. Soon the women, standing by their husbands, began to call to their children, and the children came reluctantly, having to be called four or five times. Bobby Martin ducked under his mother's grasping hand and ran, laughing, back to the pile of stones. His father spoke up sharply, and Bobby came quickly and took his place between his father and his oldest brother.

The lottery was conducted—as were the square dances, the teenage club, the Halloween program—by Mr. Summers, who had time and energy to devote to civic activities. He was a round-faced, jovial man and he ran the coal business, and people were sorry for him, because he had no children and his wife was a scold. When he arrived in the square, carrying the black wooden box, there was a murmur of conversation among the villagers, and he waved and called, "Little late today, folks." The postmaster, Mr. Graves, followed him, carrying a three-legged stool, and the stool was put in the center of the square and Mr. Summers set the black box down on it. The villagers kept their distance, leaving a space between themselves and the stool, and when Mr. Summers said, "Some of you fellows want to give me a hand?" there was a hesitation before two men, Mr. Martin and his oldest son, Baxter, came forward to hold the box steady on the stool while Mr. Summers stirred up the papers inside it.

The original paraphernalia for the lottery had been lost long ago, and the black box now resting on the stool had been put into use even before Old Man Warner, the oldest man in town, was born. Mr. Summers spoke frequently to the villagers about making a new box, but no one liked to upset even as much tradition as was represented by the black box. There was a story that the present box had been made with some pieces of the box that had preceded it, the one that had been constructed when the first people settled down to make a village here. Every year, after the lottery, Mr. Summers began talking again about a new box, but every year the subject was allowed to fade off without anything's being done. The black box grew shabbier each year; by now it was no longer completely black but splintered badly along one side to show the original wood color, and in some places faded or stained.

Mr. Martin and his oldest son, Baxter, held the black box securely on the stool until Mr. Summers had stirred the papers thoroughly with his hand. Because so much of the ritual had been forgotten or discarded, Mr. Summers had been successful in having slips of paper substituted for the chips of wood that had been used for generations. Chips of wood, Mr. Summers had argued, had been all very well when the village was tiny, but now that the population was more than three hundred and likely to keep on growing, it was necessary to use something that would fit more easily into the black box. The night before the lottery, Mr. Summers and Mr. Graves made up the slips of paper and put them in the box, and it was then taken to the safe of Mr. Summers' coal company and locked up until Mr. Summers was ready to take it to the square next morning. The rest of the year, the box was put away, sometimes one place, sometimes another; it had spent one year in Mr. Graves's barn and another year underfoot in the post office, and sometimes it was set on a shelf in the Martin grocery and left there.

There was a great deal of fussing to be done before Mr. Summers declared the lottery open. There were the lists to make up—of heads of families, heads of households in each family, members of each household in each family. There was the proper swearing-in of Mr. Summers by the postmaster, as the official of the lottery; at one time, some people remembered, there had been a recital of some sort, performed by the official of the lottery, a perfunctory, tuneless chant that had been rattled off duly each year; some people believed that the official of the lottery used to stand just so when he said or sang it, others believed that he was supposed to walk among the people, but years and years ago this part of the ritual had been allowed to lapse. There had been, also, a ritual salute, which the official of the lottery had had to use in addressing each person who came up to draw from the box, but this also had changed with time, until now it was felt necessary only for the official to speak to each person approaching. Mr. Summers was very good at all this; in his clean white shirt and blue jeans, with one hand resting carelessly on the black box, he seemed very proper and important as he talked interminably to Mr. Graves and the Martins.

Just as Mr. Summers finally left off talking and turned to the assembled villagers, Mrs. Hutchinson came hurriedly along the path to the square, her sweater thrown over her shoulders, and slid into place in the back of the crowd. "Clean forgot what day it was," she said to Mrs. Delacroix, who stood next to her, and they both laughed softly. "Thought my old man was out back stacking wood," Mrs. Hutchinson went on, "and then I looked out the window and the kids was gone, and then I remembered it was the twenty-seventh and came a-running." She dried her hands on her apron, and Mrs. Delacroix said, "You're in time, though. They're still talking away up there."

Mrs. Hutchinson craned her neck to see through the crowd and found her husband and children standing near the front. She tapped Mrs. Delacroix on the arm as a farewell and began to make her way through the crowd. The people separated good-humoredly to let her through; two or three people said, in voices just loud enough to be heard across the crowd, "Here comes your Missus, Hutchinson," and "Bill, she made it after all." Mrs. Hutchinson reached her husband, and Mr. Summers, who had been waiting, said cheerfully, "Thought we were going to have to get on without you, Tessie." Mrs. Hutchinson said, grinning, "Wouldn't have me leave m'dishes in the sink, now, would you, Joe?," and soft laughter ran through the crowd as the people stirred back into position after Mrs. Hutchinson's arrival.

"Well, now," Mr. Summers said soberly, "guess we better get started, get this over with, so's we can go back to work. Anybody ain't here?"

"Dunbar," several people said, "Dunbar, Dunbar."

Mr. Summers consulted his list. "Clyde Dunbar," he said. "That's right. He's broke his leg, hasn't he? Who's drawing for him?"

"Me, I guess," a woman said, and Mr. Summers turned to look at her. "Wife draws for her husband," Mr. Summers said. "Don't you have a grown boy to do it for you, Janey?" Although Mr. Summers and everyone else in the village knew the answer perfectly well, it was the business of the official of the lottery to ask such questions formally. Mr. Summers waited with an expression of polite interest while Mrs. Dunbar answered.

"Horace's not but sixteen yet," Mrs. Dunbar said regretfully. "Guess I gotta fill in for the old man this year."

"Right," Mr. Summers said. He made a note on the list he was holding. Then he asked, "Watson boy drawing this year?"

A tall boy in the crowd raised his hand. "Here," he said. "I'm drawing for m'mother and me." He blinked his eyes nervously and ducked his head as several voices in the crowd said things like "Good fellow, Jack," and "Glad to see your mother's got a man to do it."

"Well," Mr. Summers said, "guess that's everyone. Old Man Warner make it?"

"Here," a voice said, and Mr. Summers nodded.

A sudden hush fell on the crowd as Mr. Summers cleared his throat and looked at the list. "All ready?" he called. "Now, I'll read the names—heads of families first—and the men come up and take a paper out of the box. Keep the paper folded in your hand without looking at it until everyone has had a turn. Everything clear?"

The people had done it so many times that they only half listened to the directions; most of them were quiet, wetting their lips, not looking around. Then Mr. Summers raised one hand high and said, "Adams." A man disengaged himself from the crowd and came forward. "Hi, Steve," Mr. Summers said, and Mr. Adams said, "Hi, Joe." They grinned at one another humorlessly and nervously. Then Mr. Adams reached into the black box and took out a folded paper. He held it firmly by one corner as he turned and went hastily back to his place in the crowd, where he stood a little apart from his family, not looking down at his hand.

"Allen," Mr. Summers said. "Anderson. . . . Bentham."

"Seems like there's no time at all between lotteries any more," Mrs. Delacroix said to Mrs. Graves in the back row. "Seems like we got through with the last one only last week."

"Time sure goes fast," Mrs. Graves said.

"Clark. . . . Delacroix."

"There goes my old man," Mrs. Delacroix said. She held her breath while her husband went forward.

"Dunbar," Mr. Summers said, and Mrs. Dunbar went steadily to the box while one of the women said, "Go on, Janey," and another said, "There she goes."

"We're next," Mrs. Graves said. She watched while Mr. Graves came around from the side of the box, greeted Mr. Summers gravely, and selected a slip of paper from the box. By now, all through the crowd there were men holding the small folded papers in their large hands, turning them over and over nervously. Mrs. Dunbar and her two sons stood together, Mrs. Dunbar holding the slip of paper.

"Harburt. . . . Hutchinson."

"Get up there, Bill," Mrs. Hutchinson said, and the people near her laughed.

"Jones."

"They do say," Mr. Adams said to Old Man Warner, who stood next to him, "that over in the north village they're talking of giving up the lottery."

Old Man Warner snorted. "Pack of crazy fools," he said. "Listening to the young folks, nothing's good enough for *them*. Next thing you know, they'll be wanting to go back to living in caves, nobody work any more, live *that* way for a while. Used to be a saying about 'Lottery in June, corn be heavy soon.' First thing you know, we'd all be eating stewed chickweed and acorns. There's *always* been a lottery," he added petulantly. "Bad enough to see young Joe Summers up there joking with everybody."

"Some places have already quit lotteries," Mrs. Adams said.

"Nothing but trouble in *that*," Old Man Warner said stoutly. "Pack of young fools."

"Martin." And Bobby Martin watched his father go forward. "Overdyke. . . . Percy."

"I wish they'd hurry," Mrs. Dunbar said to her older son. "I wish they'd hurry."

"They're almost through," her son said.

"You get ready to run tell Dad," Mrs. Dunbar said.

Mr. Summers called his own name and then stepped forward precisely and selected a slip from the box. Then he called, "Warner."

"Seventy-seventh year I been in the lottery," Old Man Warner said as he went through the crowd. "Seventy-seventh time."

"Watson." The tall boy came awkwardly through the crowd. Someone said, "Don't be nervous, Jack," and Mr. Summers said, "Take your time, son."

"Zanini."

After that, there was a long pause, a breathless pause, until Mr. Summers, holding his slip of paper in the air, said, "All right, fellows." For a minute, no one moved, and then all the slips of paper were opened. Suddenly, all the women began to speak at once, saying, "Who is it?," "Who's got it?," "Is it the Dunbars?," "Is it the Watsons?" Then the voices began to say, "It's Hutchinson. It's Bill," "Bill Hutchinson's got it."

"Go tell your father," Mrs. Dunbar said to her older son.

People began to look around to see the Hutchinsons. Bill Hutchinson was standing quiet staring down at the paper in his hand. Suddenly, Tessie Hutchinson shouted to Mr. Summers, "You didn't give him time enough to take any paper he wanted. I saw you. It wasn't fair."

"Be a good sport, Tessie," Mrs. Delacroix called, and Mrs. Graves said, "All of us took the same chance."

"Shut up, Tessie," Bill Hutchinson said.

"Well, everyone," Mr. Summers said, "that was done pretty fast, and now we've got to be hurrying a little more to get done in time." He consulted his next list. "Bill," he said, "you draw for the Hutchinson family. You got any other households in the Hutchinsons?"

"There's Don and Eva," Mrs. Hutchinson yelled. "Make *them* take their chance!"

"Daughters draw for their husbands' families, Tessie," Mr. Summers said gently. "You know that as well as anyone else."

"It wasn't *fair*," Tessie said.

"I guess not, Joe," Bill Hutchinson said regretfully. "My daughter draws with her husband's family, that's only fair. And I've got no other family except the kids."

"Then, as far as drawing for families is concerned, it's you," Mr. Summers said in explanation, "and as far as drawing for households is concerned, that's you, too. Right?"

"Right," Bill Hutchinson said.

"How many kids, Bill?" Mr. Summers asked formally.

"Three," Bill Hutchinson said. "There's Bill, Jr., and Nancy, and little Dave. And Tessie and me."

"All right, then," Mr. Summers said. "Harry, you got their tickets back?"

Mr. Graves nodded and held up the slips of paper. "Put them in the box, then," Mr. Summers directed. "Take Bill's and put it in."

"I think we ought to start over," Mrs. Hutchinson said, as quietly as she could, "I tell you it wasn't *fair*. You didn't give him time enough to choose. *Every*body saw that."

Mr. Graves had selected the five slips and put them in the box, and he dropped all the papers but those onto the ground, where the breeze caught them and lifted them off.

"Listen, everybody," Mrs. Hutchinson was saying to the people around her.

"Ready, Bill?" Mr. Summers asked, and Bill Hutchinson, with one quick glance around at his wife and children, nodded.

"Remember," Mr. Summers said, "take the slips and keep them folded until each person has taken one. Harry, you help little Dave." Mr. Graves took the hand of the little boy, who came willingly with him up to the box. "Take a paper out of the box, Davy," Mr. Summers said. Davy put his hand into the box and laughed. "Take just *one* paper," Mr. Summers said. "Harry, you hold it for him." Mr. Graves took the child's hand and removed the folded paper from the tight fist and held it while little Dave stood next to him and looked up at him wonderingly.

"Nancy next," Mr. Summers said. Nancy was twelve, and her school friends breathed heavily as she went forward, switching her skirt, and took a slip daintily from the box. "Bill, Jr.," Mr. Summers said, and Billy, his face red and his feet over-large, nearly knocked the box over as he got a paper out. "Tessie," Mr. Summers said. She hesitated for a minute, looking around defiantly, and then set her lips and went up to the box. She snatched a paper out and held it behind her.

"Bill," Mr. Summers said, and Bill Hutchinson reached into the box and felt around, bringing his hand out at last with the slip of paper in it.

The crowd was quiet. A girl whispered, "I hope it's not Nancy," and the sound of the whisper reached the edges of the crowd.

"It's not the way it used to be," Old Man Warner said clearly. "People ain't the way they used to be."

"All right," Mr. Summers said. "Open the papers. Harry, you open little Dave's."

Mr. Graves opened the slip of paper and there was a general sigh through the crowd as he held it up and everyone could see that it was blank. Nancy and Bill, Jr., opened theirs at the same time, and both beamed and laughed, turning around to the crowd and holding their slips of paper above their heads.

"Tessie," Mr. Summers said. There was a pause, and then Mr. Summers looked at Bill Hutchinson, and Bill unfolded his paper and showed it. It was blank.

"It's Tessie," Mr. Summers said, and his voice was hushed. "Show us her paper, Bill."

Bill Hutchinson went over to his wife and forced the slip of paper out of her hand. It had a black spot on it, the black spot Mr. Summers had made the night before with the heavy pencil in the coal-company office. Bill Hutchinson held it up, and there was a stir in the crowd.

"All right, folks," Mr. Summers said. "Let's finish quickly."

Although the villagers had forgotten the ritual and lost the original black box, they still remembered to use stones. The pile of stones the boys had made earlier was ready; there were stones on the ground with the blowing scraps of paper that had come out of the box. Mrs. Delacroix selected a stone so large she had to pick it up with both hands and turned to Mrs. Dunbar. "Come on," she said. "Hurry up."

Mrs. Dunbar had small stones in both hands, and she said, gasping for breath, "I can't run at all. You'll have to go ahead and I'll catch up with you."

The children had stones already, and someone gave little Davy Hutchinson a few pebbles.

Tessie Hutchinson was in the center of a cleared space by now, and she held her hands out desperately as the villagers moved in on her. "It isn't fair," she said. A stone hit her on the side of the head.

Old Man Warner was saying, "Come on, come on, everyone." Steve Adams was in the front of the crowd of villagers, with Mrs. Graves beside him.

"It isn't fair, it isn't right," Mrs. Hutchinson screamed, and then they were upon her.

1948

HENRY JAMES
1843–1916

James was born in New York City. His father was a writer and religious philosopher; his brother was William James, the philosopher and psychologist. James's father chose to have him educated chiefly in Europe by tutors in several countries, and his foreign education culminated in his acquaintance with a number of European writers, among them Turgenev, Flaubert, and de Maupassant. James's familiarity with life on both sides of the Atlantic led him, in much of his writing, to contrast European and American cultures and, above all, to show the effects of their mingling. In 1875 he took up permanent residence in England, becoming a naturalized citizen of that country in 1915 in protest against the initial neutrality of the United States in World War I. Throughout his later life James was the model of the professional writer, experimenting with ways of making his writing more pictorial, developing refinements in the handling of point of view, and commenting in many essays on these practices so that his theories of the art have been instructive to many later writers. He wrote several rather unsuccessful plays and more than seventy stories, including his best-known ghost story *The Turn of the Screw* (1898). But it is mainly his novels that place James in the first rank of American writers. Among his masterpieces are *The American* (1877), *Daisy Miller* (1879), *The Portrait of a Lady* (1881), *The Wings of the Dove* (1902), *The Ambassadors* (1903), and *The Golden Bowl* (1904).

The Real Thing

I

When the porter's wife (she used to answer the house-bell), announced "A gentleman—with a lady, sir," I had, as I often had in those days, for the wish was father to the thought, an immediate vision of sitters. Sitters my visitors in this case proved to be; but not in the sense I should have preferred. However, there was nothing at first to indicate that they might not have come for a portrait. The gentleman, a man of fifty, very high and very straight, with a moustache slightly grizzled and a dark grey walking-coat admirably fitted, both of which I noted professionally—I don't mean as a barber or yet as a tailor—would have struck me as a celebrity if celebrities often were striking. It was a truth of which I had for some time been conscious that a figure with a good deal of frontage was, as one might say, almost never a public institution. A glance at the lady helped to remind me of this paradoxical law: she also looked too distinguished to be a "personality." Moreover one would scarcely come across two variations together.

Neither of the pair spoke immediately—they only prolonged the preliminary gaze which suggested that each wished to give the other a chance. They were visibly shy; they stood there letting me take them in—which, as I afterwards perceived, was the most practical thing they could have done. In this way their embarrassment served their cause. I had seen people painfully reluctant to mention that they desired anything so gross as to be represented on canvas; but the scruples of my new friends appeared almost insurmountable. Yet the gentleman might have said "I should like a portrait of my wife," and the lady might have said "I should like a portrait of my husband." Perhaps they were not husband and wife—this naturally would make the matter more delicate. Perhaps they wished to be done together—in which case they ought to have brought a third person to break the news.

"We come from Mr. Rivet," the lady said at last, with a dim smile which had the effect of a moist sponge passed over a "sunk" piece of painting, as well as of a vague allusion to vanished beauty. She was as tall and straight, in her degree, as her companion, and with ten years less to carry. She looked as sad as a woman could look whose face was not charged with expression; that is her tinted oval mask showed friction as an exposed surface shows it. The hand of time had played over her freely, but only to simplify. She was slim and stiff, and so well-dressed, in dark blue cloth, with lappets and pockets and buttons, that it was clear she employed the same tailor as her husband. The couple had an indefinable air of prosperous thrift—they evidently got a good deal of luxury for their money. If I was to be one of their luxuries it would behove me to consider my terms.

"Ah, Claude Rivet recommended me?" I inquired; and I added that it was very kind of him, though I could reflect that, as he only painted landscape, this was not a sacrifice.

The lady looked very hard at the gentleman, and the gentleman looked round the room. Then staring at the floor a moment and stroking his moustache, he rested his pleasant eyes on me with the remark:

"He said you were the right one."

"I try to be, when people want to sit."

"Yes, we should like to," said the lady anxiously.

"Do you mean together?"

My visitors exchanged a glance. "If you could do anything with *me*, I suppose it would be double," the gentleman stammered.

"Oh yes, there's naturally a higher charge for two figures than for one."

"We should like to make it pay," the husband confessed.

"That's very good of you," I returned, appreciating so unwonted a sympathy—for I supposed he meant pay the artist.

A sense of strangeness seemed to dawn on the lady. "We mean for the illustrations—Mr. Rivet said you might put one in."

"Put one in—an illustration?" I was equally confused.

"Sketch her off, you know," said the gentleman, colouring.

It was only then that I understood the service Claude Rivet had rendered me; he had told them that I worked in black and white, for magazines, for story-books, for sketches of contemporary life, and consequently had frequent employment for models. These things were true, but it was not less true (I may confess it now—whether because the aspiration was to lead to everything or to nothing I leave the reader to guess), that I couldn't get the honours, to say nothing of the emoluments, of a great painter of portraits out of my head. My "illustrations" were my pot-boilers; I looked to a different branch of art (far and away the most interesting it had always seemed to me), to perpetuate my fame. There was no shame in looking to it also to make my fortune; but that fortune was by so much further from being made from the moment my visitors wished to be "done" for nothing. I was disappointed; for in the pictorial sense I had immediately *seen* them. I had seized their type—I had already settled what I would do with it. Something that wouldn't absolutely have pleased them, I afterwards reflected.

"Ah, you're—you're—a—?" I began, as soon as I had mastered my surprise. I couldn't bring out the dingy word "models"; it seemed to fit the case so little.

"We haven't had much practice," said the lady.

"We've got to *do* something, and we've thought that an artist in your line might perhaps make something of us," her husband threw off. He further mentioned that they didn't know many artists and that they had gone first, on the off-chance (he painted views of course, but sometimes put in figures— perhaps I remembered), to Mr. Rivet, whom they had met a few years before at a place in Norfolk where he was sketching.

"We used to sketch a little ourselves," the lady hinted.

"It's very awkward, but we absolutely *must* do something," her husband went on.

"Of course, we're not so *very* young," she admitted, with a wan smile.

With the remark that I might as well know something more about them, the husband had handed me a card extracted from a neat new pocket-book (their appurtenances were all of the freshest) and inscribed with the words "Major Monarch." Impressive as these words were they didn't carry my knowledge much further; but my visitor presently added: "I've left the army, and we've had the misfortune to lose our money. In fact our means are dreadfully small."

"It's an awful bore," said Mrs. Monarch.

They evidently wished to be discreet—to take care not to swagger because they were gentlefolks. I perceived they would have been willing to recognise this as something of a drawback, at the same time that I guessed at an underlying sense—their consolation in adversity—that they *had* their points. They certainly had; but these advantages struck me as preponderantly social; such for instance as would help to make a drawing-room look well. However, a drawing-room was always, or ought to be, a picture.

In consequence of his wife's allusion to their age Major Monarch observed: "Naturally, it's more for the figure that we thought of going in. We can still hold ourselves up." On the instant I saw that the figure was indeed their strong point. His "naturally" didn't sound vain, but it lighted up the question. "*She* has got the best," he continued, nodding at his wife, with a pleasant after-dinner absence of circumlocution. I could only reply, as if we were in fact sitting over our wine, that this didn't prevent his own from being very good; which led him in turn to rejoin: "We thought that if you ever have to do people like us, we might be something like it. *She*, particularly—for a lady in a book, you know."

I was so amused by them that, to get more of it, I did my best to take their point of view; and though it was an embarrassment to find myself appraising physically, as if they were animals on hire or useful blacks, a pair whom I should have expected to meet only in one of the relations in which criticism is tacit, I looked at Mrs. Monarch judicially enough to be able to exclaim, after a moment, with conviction: "Oh yes, a lady in a book!" She was singularly like a bad illustration.

"We'll stand up, if you like," said the Major; and he raised himself before me with a really grand air.

I could take his measure at a glance—he was six feet two and a perfect gentleman. It would have paid any club in process of formation and in want of a stamp to engage him at a salary to stand in the principal window. What struck me immediately was that in coming to me they had rather missed their vocation; they could surely have been turned to better account for advertising purposes. I couldn't of course see the thing in detail, but I could see them make someone's fortune—I don't mean their own. There was something in them for a waistcoat-maker, an hotel-keeper or a soap-vendor. I could imagine "We always use it" pinned on their bosoms with the greatest effect; I had a vision of the promptitude with which they would launch a table d'hote.

Mrs. Monarch sat still, not from pride but from shyness, and presently her husband said to her: "Get up my dear and show how smart you are." She obeyed, but she had no need to get up to show it. She walked to the end of the studio, and then she came back blushing, with her fluttered eyes on her husband. I was reminded of an incident I had accidentally had a glimpse of in Paris—being with a friend there, a dramatist about to produce a play—when an actress came to him to ask to be intrusted with a part. She went through her paces before him, walked up and down as Mrs. Monarch was doing. Mrs. Monarch did it quite as well, but I abstained from applauding. It was very odd to see such people apply for such poor pay. She looked as if she had ten thousand a year. Her husband had used the word that described her: she was, in the London current jargon, essentially and typically "smart." Her figure was, in the same order of ideas, conspicuously and irreproachably "good." For a woman of her age her waist was surprisingly small; her elbow moreover had the orthodox crook. She held her head at the conventional angle; but why did she come to *me*? She ought to have tried on jackets at a big shop. I feared my visitors were not only destitute, but "artistic"—which would be a great complication. When she sat down again I thanked her, observing that what a draughtsman most valued in his model was the faculty of keeping quiet.

"Oh, *she* can keep quiet," said Major Monarch. Then he added, jocosely: "I've always kept her quiet."

"I'm not a nasty fidget, am I?" Mrs. Monarch appealed to her husband.

He addressed his answer to me. "Perhaps it isn't out of place to mention—because we ought to be quite business-like, oughtn't we?—that when I married her she was known as the Beautiful Statue."

"Oh dear!" said Mrs. Monarch, ruefully.

"Of course I should want a certain amount of expression," I rejoined.

"Of *course*!" they both exclaimed.

"And then I suppose you know that you'll get awfully tired."

"Oh, we *never* get tired!" they eagerly cried.

"Have you had any kind of practice?"

They hesitated—they looked at each other. "We've been photographed, *immensely*," said Mrs. Monarch.

"She means the fellows have asked us," added the Major.

"I see—because you're so good-looking."

"I don't know what they thought, but they were always after us."

"We always got our photographs for nothing," smiled Mrs. Monarch.

"We might have brought some, my dear," her husband remarked.

"I'm not sure we have any left. We've given quantities away," she explained to me.

"With our autographs and that sort of thing," said the Major.

"Are they to be got in the shops?" I inquired, as a harmless pleasantry.

"Oh, yes; hers—they used to be."

"Not now," said Mrs. Monarch, with her eyes on the floor.

I I

I could fancy the "sort of thing" they put on the presentation-copies of their photographs, and I was sure they wrote a beautiful hand. It was odd how quickly I was sure of everything that concerned them. If they were now so poor as to have to earn shillings and pence, they never had had much of a margin. Their good looks had been their capital, and they had good-humouredly made the most of the career that this resource marked out for them. It was in their faces, the blankness, the deep intellectual repose of the twenty years of country-house visiting which had given them pleasant intonations. I could see the sunny drawing-rooms, sprinkled with periodicals she didn't read, in which Mrs. Monarch had continuously sat; I could see the wet shrubberies in which she had walked, equipped to admiration for either exercise. I could see the rich covers the Major had helped to shoot and the wonderful garments in which, late at night, he repaired to the smoking-room to talk about them. I could imagine their leggings and waterproofs, their knowing tweeds and rugs, their rolls of sticks and cases of tackle and neat umbrellas; and I could evoke the exact appearance of their servants and the compact variety of their luggage on the platforms of country stations.

They gave small tips, but they were liked; they didn't do anything themselves, but they were welcome. They looked so well everywhere; they gratified the general relish for stature, complexion and "form." They knew it without fatuity or vulgarity, and they respected themselves in consequence. They were not superficial; they were thorough and kept themselves up—it had been their line. People with such a taste for activity had to have some line. I could feel how, even in a dull house, they could have been counted upon for cheerfulness. At present something had happened—it didn't matter what, their little income had grown less, it had grown least—and they had to do something for pocket-money. Their friends liked them, but didn't like to support them. There was something about them that represented credit—their clothes, their manners, their type; but if credit is a large empty pocket in which an occasional chink reverberates, the chink at least must be audible. What they wanted of me was to help to make it so. Fortunately they had no children—I soon divined that. They would also perhaps wish our relations to be kept secret: this was why it was "for the figure"—the reproduction of the face would betray them.

I liked them—they were so simple; and I had no objection to them if they would suit. But, somehow, with all their perfections I didn't easily believe in them. After all they were amateurs, and the ruling passion of my life was the detestation of the amateur. Combined with this was another perversity—an innate preference for the represented subject over the real one: the defect of the real one was so apt to be a lack of representation. I liked things that appeared; then one was sure. Whether they *were* or not was a subordinate and almost always a profitless question. There were other considerations, the first of which was that I already had two or three people in use, notably a young person with big feet, in alpaca, from Kilburn, who for a couple of years had come to me regularly for my illustrations and with whom I was still—perhaps ignobly—satisfied. I frankly explained to my visitors how the case stood; but they had taken more precautions than I supposed. They had reasoned out their opportunity, for Claude Rivet had told them of the projected *édition de luxe* of one of the writers of our day—the rarest of the novelists—who, long neglected by the multitudinous vulgar and dearly prized by the attentive (need I mention Philip Vincent?) had had the happy fortune of seeing, late in life, the dawn and then the full light of a higher criticism—an estimate in which, on the part of the public, there was something really of expiation. The edition in question, planned by a publisher of taste, was practically an act of high reparation; the wood-cuts with which it was to be enriched were the homage of English art to one of the most independent representatives of English letters. Major and Mrs. Monarch confessed to me that they had hoped I might be able to work *them* into my share of the enterprise. They knew I was to do the first of the books, "Rutland Ramsay," but I had to make clear to them that my participation in the rest of the affair—this first book was to be a test— was to depend on the satisfaction I should give. If this should be limited my employers would drop me without a scruple. It was therefore a crisis for me, and naturally I was making special preparations, looking about for new people, if they should be necessary, and securing the best types. I admitted however that I should like to settle down to two or three good models who would do for everything.

"Should we have often to—a—put on special clothes?" Mrs. Monarch timidly demanded.

"Dear, yes—that's half the business."

"And should we be expected to supply our own costumes?"

"Oh, no; I've got a lot of things. A painter's models put on—or put off— anything he likes."

"And do you mean—a—the same?"

"The same?"

Mrs. Monarch looked at her husband again.

"Oh, she was just wondering," he explained, "if the costumes are in *general* use." I had to confess that they were, and I mentioned further that some of them (I had a lot of genuine, greasy last-century things), had served their time, a hundred years ago, on living, world-stained men and women. "We'll put on anything that *fits*," said the Major.

"Oh, I arrange that—they fit in the pictures."

"I'm afraid I should do better for the modern books. I would come as you like," said Mrs. Monarch.

"She has got a lot of clothes at home: they might do for contemporary life," her husband continued.

"Oh, I can fancy scenes in which you'd be quite natural." And indeed I could see the slipshod rearrangements of stale properties—the stories I tried to produce pictures for without the exasperation of reading them—whose sandy tracts the good lady might help to people. But I had to return to the fact that for this sort of work—the daily mechanical grind—I was already equipped; the people I was working with were fully adequate.

"We only thought we might be more like *some* characters," said Mrs. Monarch mildly, getting up.

Her husband also rose; he stood looking at me with a dim wistfulness that was touching in so fine a man. "Wouldn't it be rather a pull sometimes to have—a—to have—?" He hung fire; he wanted me to help him by phrasing what he meant. But I couldn't—I didn't know. So he brought it out, awkwardly: "The *real* thing; a gentleman, you know, or a lady." I was quite ready to give a general assent—I admitted that there was a great deal in that. This encouraged Major Monarch to say, following up his appeal with an unacted gulp: "It's awfully hard—we've tried everything." The gulp was communicative; it proved too much for his wife. Before I knew it Mrs. Monarch had dropped again upon a divan and burst into tears. Her husband sat down beside her, holding one of her hands; whereupon she quickly dried her eyes with the other, while I felt embarrassed as she looked up at me. "There isn't a confounded job I haven't applied for—waited for—prayed for. You can fancy we'd be pretty bad first. Secretaryships and that sort of thing? You might as well ask for a peerage. I'd be *anything*—I'm strong; a messenger or a coalheaver. I'd put on a gold-laced cap and open carriage-doors in front of the haberdasher's; I'd hang about a station, to carry portmanteaus; I'd be a postman. But they won't *look* at you; there are thousands, as good as yourself, already on the ground. *Gentlemen*, poor beggars, who have drunk their wine, who have kept their hunters!"

I was as reassuring as I knew how to be, and my visitors were presently on their feet again while, for the experiment, we agreed on an hour. We were discussing it when the door opened and Miss Churm came in with a wet umbrella. Miss Churm had to take the omnibus to Maida Vale and then walk half-a-mile. She looked a trifle blowsy and slightly splashed. I scarcely ever saw her come in without thinking afresh how odd it was that, being so little in herself, she should yet be so much in others. She was a meagre little Miss Churm, but she was an ample heroine of romance. She was only a freckled cockney, but she could represent everything, from a fine lady to a shepherdess; she had the faculty, as she might have had a fine voice or long hair.

She couldn't spell, and she loved beer, but she had two or three "points," and practice, and a knack, and mother-wit, and a kind of whimsical sensibility, and a love of the theatre, and seven sisters, and not an ounce of respect, especially for the *h*. The first thing my visitors saw was that her umbrella was wet, and in their spotless perfection they visibly winced at it. The rain had come on since their arrival.

"I'm all in a soak; there *was* a mess of people in the 'bus. I wish you lived near a styion," said Miss Churm. I requested her to get ready as quickly as possible, and she passed into the room in which she always changed her dress. But before going out she asked me what she was to get into this time.

"It's the Russian princess, don't you know?" I answered; "the one with the 'golden eyes,' in black velvet, for the long thing in the *Cheapside*."[1]

"Golden eyes? I *say*!" cried Miss Churm, while my companions watched her with intensity as she withdrew. She always arranged herself, when she was late, before I could turn round; and I kept my visitors a little, on purpose, so that they might get an idea, from seeing her, what would be expected of themselves. I mentioned that she was quite my notion of an excellent model—she was really very clever.

"Do you think she looks like a Russian princess?" Major Monarch asked, with lurking alarm.

"When I make her, yes."

"Oh, if you have to *make* her—!" he reasoned, acutely.

"That's the most you can ask. There are so many that are not makeable."

"Well now, *here's* a lady"—and with a persuasive smile he passed his arm into his wife's—"who's already made!"

"Oh, I'm not a Russian princess," Mrs. Monarch protested, a little coldly. I could see that she had known some and didn't like them. There, immediately, was a complication of a kind that I never had to fear with Miss Churm.

This young lady came back in black velvet—the gown was rather rusty and very low on her lean shoulders—and with a Japanese fan in her red hands. I reminded her that in the scene I was doing she had to look over someone's head. "I forget whose it is; but it doesn't matter. Just look over a head."

"I'd rather look over a stove," said Miss Churm; and she took her station near the fire. She fell into position, settled herself into a tall attitude, gave a certain backward inclination to her head and a certain forward droop to her fan, and looked, at least to my prejudiced sense, distinguished and charming, foreign and dangerous. We left her looking so, while I went down-stairs with Major and Mrs. Monarch.

"I think I could come about as near it as that," said Mrs. Monarch.

"Oh, you think she's shabby, but you must allow for the alchemy of art."

However, they went off with an evident increase of comfort, founded on their demonstrable advantage in being the real thing. I could fancy them shuddering over Miss Churm. She was very droll about them when I went back, for I told her what they wanted.

"Well, if *she* can sit I'll tyke to bookkeeping," said my model.

"She's very lady-like," I replied, as an innocent form of aggravation.

"So much the worse for *you*. That means she can't turn round."

"She'll do for the fashionable novels."

"Oh yes, she'll *do* for them!" my model humorously declared.

"Ain't they had enough without her?" I had often sociably denounced them to Miss Churm.

---

1. A literary magazine.

III

It was for the elucidation of a mystery in one of these works that I first tried Mrs. Monarch. Her husband came with her, to be useful if necessary—it was sufficiently clear that as a general thing he would prefer to come with her. At first I wondered if this were for "propriety's" sake—if he were going to be jealous and meddling. The idea was too tiresome, and if it had been confirmed it would speedily have brought our acquaintance to a close. But I soon saw there was nothing in it and that if he accompanied Mrs. Monarch it was (in addition to the chance of being wanted), simply because he had nothing else to do. When she was away from him his occupation was gone—she never *had* been away from him. I judged, rightly, that in their awkward situation their close union was their main comfort and that this union had no weak spot. It was a real marriage, an encouragement to the hesitating, a nut for pessimists to crack. Their address was humble (I remember afterwards thinking it had been the only thing about them that was really professional), and I could fancy the lamentable lodgings in which the Major would have been left alone. He could bear them with his wife—he couldn't bear them without her.

He had too much tact to try and make himself agreeable when he couldn't be useful; so he simply sat and waited, when I was too absorbed in my work to talk. But I liked to make him talk—it made my work, when it didn't interrupt it, less sordid, less special. To listen to him was to combine the excitement of going out with the economy of staying at home. There was only one hindrance: that I seemed not to know any of the people he and his wife had known. I think he wondered extremely, during the term of our intercourse, whom the deuce I *did* know. He hadn't a stray sixpence of an idea to fumble for; so we didn't spin it very fine—we confined ourselves to questions of leather and even of liquor (saddlers and breeches-makers and how to get good claret cheap), and matters like "good trains" and the habits of small game. His lore on these last subjects was astonishing, he managed to interweave the station-master with the ornithologist. When he couldn't talk about greater things he could talk cheerfully about smaller, and since I couldn't accompany him into reminiscences of the fashionable world he could lower the conversation without a visible effort to my level.

So earnest a desire to please was touching in a man who could so easily have knocked one down. He looked after the fire and had an opinion on the draught of the stove, without my asking him, and I could see that he thought many of my arrangements not half clever enough. I remember telling him that if I were only rich I would offer him a salary to come and teach me how to live. Sometimes he gave a random sigh, of which the essence was: "Give me even such a bare old barrack as *this*, and I'd do something with it!" When I wanted to use him he came alone; which was an illustration of the superior courage of women. His wife could bear her solitary second floor, and she was in general more discreet; showing by various small reserves that she was alive to the propriety of keeping our relations markedly professional—not letting them slide into sociability. She wished it to remain clear that she and the Major were employed, not cultivated, and if she approved of me as a superior, who could be kept in his place, she never thought me quite good enough for an equal.

She sat with great intensity, giving the whole of her mind to it, and was capable of remaining for an hour almost as motionless as if she were before a photographer's lens. I could see she had been photographed often, but somehow the very habit that made her good for that purpose unfitted her for mine. At first I was extremely pleased with her lady-like air, and it was a satisfaction, on coming to follow her lines, to see how good they were and how far they could lead the pencil. But after a few times I began to find her too insurmountably stiff; do what I would with it my drawing looked like a photograph or a copy of a photograph. Her figure had no variety of expression—she herself had no sense of variety. You may say that this was my business, was only a question of placing her. I placed her in every conceivable position, but she managed to obliterate their differences. She was always a lady certainly, and into the bargain was always the same lady. She was the real thing, but always the same thing. There were moments when I was oppressed by the serenity of her confidence that she *was* the real thing. All her dealings with me and all her husband's were an implication that this was lucky for *me*. Meanwhile I found myself trying to invent types that approached her own, instead of making her own transform itself—in the clever way that was not impossible, for instance, to poor Miss Churm. Arrange as I would and take the precautions I would, she always, in my pictures, came out too tall—landing me in the dilemma of having represented a fascinating woman as seven feet high, which, out of respect perhaps to my own very much scantier inches, was far from my idea of such a personage.

The case was worse with the Major—nothing I could do would keep *him* down, so that he became useful only for the representation of brawny giants. I adored variety and range, I cherished human accidents, the illustrative note; I wanted to characterise closely, and the thing in the world I most hated was the danger of being ridden by a type. I had quarrelled with some of my friends about it—I had parted company with them for maintaining that one *had* to be, and that if the type was beautiful (witness Raphael and Leonardo), the servitude was only a gain. I was neither Leonardo nor Raphael; I might only be a presumptuous young modern searcher, but I held that everything was to be sacrificed sooner than character. When they averred that the haunting type in question could easily *be* character, I retorted, perhaps superficially: "Whose?" It couldn't be everybody's—it might end in being nobody's.

After I had drawn Mrs. Monarch a dozen times I perceived more clearly than before that the value of such a model as Miss Churm resided precisely in the fact that she had no positive stamp, combined of course with the other fact that what she did have was a curious and inexplicable talent for imitation. Her usual appearance was like a curtain which she could draw up at request for a capital performance. This performance was simply suggestive; but it was a word to the wise—it was vivid and pretty. Sometimes, even, I thought it, though she was plain herself, too insipidly pretty; I made it a reproach to her that the figures drawn from her were monotonously (*bête-ment,*[2] as we used to say) graceful. Nothing made her more angry: it was so much her pride to feel that she could sit for characters that had nothing in common

---

2. Stupidly (French).

with each other. She would accuse me at such moments of taking away her "reputytion."

It suffered a certain shrinkage, this queer quantity, from the repeated visits of my new friends. Miss Churm was greatly in demand, never in want of employment, so I had no scruple in putting her off occasionally, to try them more at my ease. It was certainly amusing at first to do the real thing—it was amusing to do Major Monarch's trousers. They *were* the real thing, even if he did come out colossal. It was amusing to do his wife's back hair (it was so mathematically neat), and the particular "smart" tension of her tight stays. She lent herself especially to positions in which the face was somewhat averted or blurred; she abounded in lady-like back views and *profils perdus*.[3] When she stood erect she took naturally one of the attitudes in which court-painters represent queens and princesses; so that I found myself wondering whether, to draw out this accomplishment, I couldn't get the editor of the *Cheapside* to publish a really royal romance, "A Tale of Buckingham Palace." Sometimes, however, the real thing and the make-believe came into contact; by which I mean that Miss Churm, keeping an appointment or coming to make one on days when I had much work in hand, encountered her invidious rivals. The encounter was not on their part, for they noticed her no more than if she had been the housemaid; not from intentional loftiness, but simply because, as yet, professionally, they didn't know how to fraternise, as I could guess that they would have liked—or at least that the Major would. They couldn't talk about the omnibus—they always walked; and they didn't know what else to try—she wasn't interested in good trains or cheap claret. Besides, they must have felt—in the air—that she was amused at them, secretly derisive of their ever knowing how. She was not a person to conceal her scepticism if she had had a chance to show it. On the other hand Mrs. Monarch didn't think her tidy; for why else did she take pains to say to me (it was going out of the way, for Mrs. Monarch), that she didn't like dirty women?

One day when my young lady happened to be present with my other sitters (she even dropped in, when it was convenient, for a chat), I asked her to be so good as to lend a hand in getting tea—a service with which she was familiar and which was one of a class that, living as I did in a small way, with slender domestic resources, I often appealed to my models to render. They liked to lay hands on my property, to break the sitting, and sometimes the china—I made them feel Bohemian. The next time I saw Miss Churm after this incident she surprised me greatly by making a scene about it—she accused me of having wished to humiliate her. She had not resented the outrage at the time, but had seemed obliging and amused, enjoying the comedy of asking Mrs. Monarch, who sat vague and silent, whether she would have cream and sugar, and putting an exaggerated simper into the question. She had tried intonations—as if she too wished to pass for the real thing; till I was afraid my other visitors would take offence.

Oh, *they* were determined not to do this; and their touching patience was the measure of their great need. They would sit by the hour, uncomplaining, till I was ready to use them; they would come back on the chance of being wanted and would walk away cheerfully if they were not. I used to go to the door

---

3. Lost profiles (French). A pose in which the sitter's profile is obscured.

with them to see in what magnificent order they retreated. I tried to find other employment for them—I introduced them to several artists. But they didn't "take," for reasons I could appreciate, and I became conscious, rather anxiously, that after such disappointments they fell back upon me with a heavier weight. They did me the honour to think that it was I who was most *their* form. They were not picturesque enough for the painters, and in those days there were not so many serious workers in black and white. Besides, they had an eye to the great job I had mentioned to them—they had secretly set their hearts on supplying the right essence for my pictorial vindication of our fine novelist. They knew that for this undertaking I should want no costume-effects, none of the frippery of past ages—that it was a case in which everything would be contemporary and satirical and, presumably, genteel. If I could work them into it their future would be assured, for the labour would of course be long and the occupation steady.

One day Mrs. Monarch came without her husband—she explained his absence by his having had to go to the City.[4] While she sat there in her usual anxious stiffness there came, at the door, a knock which I immediately recognised as the subdued appeal of a model out of work. It was followed by the entrance of a young man whom I easily perceived to be a foreigner and who proved in fact an Italian acquainted with no English word but my name, which he uttered in a way that made it seem to include all others. I had not then visited his country, nor was I proficient in his tongue; but as he was not so meanly constituted—what Italian is?—as to depend only on that member for expression he conveyed to me, in familiar but graceful mimicry, that he was in search of exactly the employment in which the lady before me was engaged. I was not struck with him at first, and while I continued to draw I emitted rough sounds of discouragement and dismissal. He stood his ground, however, not importunately, but with a dumb, dog-like fidelity in his eyes which amounted to innocent impudence—the manner of a devoted servant (he might have been in the house for years), unjustly suspected. Suddenly I saw that this very attitude and expression made a picture, whereupon I told him to sit down and wait till I should be free. There was another picture in the way he obeyed me, and I observed as I worked that there were others still in the way he looked wonderingly, with his head thrown back, about the high studio. He might have been crossing himself in St. Peter's. Before I finished I said to myself: "The fellow's a bankrupt orange-monger, but he's a treasure."

When Mrs. Monarch withdrew he passed across the room like a flash to open the door for her, standing there with the rapt, pure gaze of the young Dante spellbound by the young Beatrice. As I never insisted, in such situations, on the blankness of the British domestic, I reflected that he had the making of a servant (and I needed one, but couldn't pay him to be only that), as well as of a model; in short I made up my mind to adopt my bright adventurer if he would agree to officiate in the double capacity. He jumped at my offer, and in the event my rashness (for I had known nothing about him), was not brought home to me. He proved a sympathetic though a desultory ministrant, and had in a wonderful degree the *sentiment de la pose.*[5] It was unculti-

---

4. The central financial district of London.   **5.** A real feel for posing (French).

vated, instinctive; a part of the happy instinct which had guided him to my door and helped him to spell out my name on the card nailed to it. He had had no other introduction to me than a guess, from the shape of my high north window, seen outside, that my place was a studio and that as a studio it would contain an artist. He had wandered to England in search of fortune, like other itinerants, and had embarked, with a partner and a small green handcart, on the sale of penny ices. The ices had melted away and the partner had dissolved in their train. My young man wore tight yellow trousers with reddish stripes and his name was Oronte. He was sallow but fair, and when I put him into some old clothes of my own he looked like an Englishman. He was as good as Miss Churm, who could look, when required, like an Italian.

IV

I thought Mrs. Monarch's face slightly convulsed when, on her coming back with her husband, she found Oronte installed. It was strange to have to recognise in a scrap of a lazzarone[6] a competitor to her magnificent Major. It was she who scented danger first, for the Major was anecdotically unconscious. But Oronte gave us tea, with a hundred eager confusions (he had never seen such a queer process), and I think she thought better of me for having at last an "establishment." They saw a couple of drawings that I had made of the establishment, and Mrs. Monarch hinted that it never would have struck her that he had sat for them. "Now the drawings you make from *us*, they look exactly like us," she reminded me, smiling in triumph; and I recognised that this was indeed just their defect. When I drew the Monarchs I couldn't, somehow, get away from them—get into the character I wanted to represent; and I had not the least desire my model should be discoverable in my picture. Miss Churm never was, and Mrs. Monarch thought I hid her, very properly, because she was vulgar; whereas if she was lost it was only as the dead who go to heaven are lost—in the gain of an angel the more.

By this time I had got a certain start with "Rutland Ramsay," the first novel in the great projected series; that is I had produced a dozen drawings, several with the help of the Major and his wife, and I had sent them in for approval. My understanding with the publishers, as I have already hinted, had been that I was to be left to do my work, in this particular case, as I liked, with the whole book committed to me; but my connection with the rest of the series was only contingent. There were moments when, frankly, it *was* a comfort to have the real thing under one's hand; for there were characters in "Rutland Ramsay" that were very much like it. There were people presumably as straight as the Major and women of as good a fashion as Mrs. Monarch. There was a great deal of country-house life—treated, it is true, in a fine, fanciful, ironical, generalised way—and there was a considerable implication of knickerbockers and kilts. There were certain things I had to settle at the outset; such things for instance as the exact appearance of the hero, the particular bloom of the heroine. The author of course gave me a lead, but there was a margin for interpretation. I took the Monarchs into my confidence, I told them frankly what I was about, I mentioned my embarrassments and alternatives. "Oh,

6. Italian rake or cad.

take *him*!" Mrs. Monarch murmured sweetly, looking at her husband; and "What could you want better than my wife?" the Major inquired, with the comfortable candour that now prevailed between us.

I was not obliged to answer these remarks—I was only obliged to place my sisters. I was not easy in mind, and I postponed, a little timidly perhaps, the solution of the question. The book was a large canvas, the other figures were numerous, and I worked off at first some of the episodes in which the hero and the heroine were not concerned. When once I had set *them* up I should have to stick to them—I couldn't make my young man seven feet high in one place and five feet nine in another. I inclined on the whole to the latter measurement, though the Major more than once reminded me that *he* looked about as young as anyone. It was indeed quite possible to arrange him, for the figure, so that it would have been difficult to detect his age. After the spontaneous Oronte had been with me a month, and after I had given him to understand several different times that his native exuberance would presently constitute an insurmountable barrier to our further intercourse, I waked to a sense of his heroic capacity. He was only five feet seven, but the remaining inches were latent. I tried him almost secretly at first, for I was really rather afraid of the judgment my other models would pass on such a choice. If they regarded Miss Churm as little better than a snare, what would they think of the representation by a person so little the real thing as an Italian street-vendor of a protagonist formed by a public school?[7]

If I went a little in fear of them it was not because they bullied me, because they had got an oppressive foothold, but because in their really pathetic decorum and mysteriously permanent newness they counted on me so intensely. I was therefore very glad when Jack Hawley came home: he was always of such good counsel. He painted badly himself, but there was no one like him for putting his finger on the place. He had been absent from England for a year; he had been somewhere—I don't remember where—to get a fresh eye. I was in a good deal of dread of any such organ, but we were old friends; he had been away for months and a sense of emptiness was creeping into my life. I hadn't dodged a missile for a year.

He came back with a fresh eye, but with the same old black velvet blouse, and the first evening he spent in my studio we smoked cigarettes till the small hours. He had done no work himself, he had only got the eye; so the field was clear for the production of my little things. He wanted to see what I had done for the *Cheapside*, but he was disappointed in the exhibition. That at least seemed the meaning of two or three comprehensive groans which, as he lounged on my big divan, on a folded leg, looking at my latest drawings, issued from his lips with the smoke of the cigarette.

"What's the matter with you?" I asked.

"What's the matter with *you*?"

"Nothing save that I'm mystified."

"You are indeed. You're quite off the hinge. What's the meaning of this new fad?" And he tossed me, with visible irreverence, a drawing in which I happened to have depicted both my majestic models. I asked if he didn't think it good, and he replied that it struck him as execrable, given the sort of thing I

7. Public schools in James's era meant an exclusive private school.

had always represented myself to him as wishing to arrive at; but I let that pass, I was so anxious to see exactly what he meant. The two figures in the picture looked colossal, but I supposed this was *not* what he meant, inasmuch as, for aught he knew to the contrary, I might have been trying for that. I maintained that I was working exactly in the same way as when he last had done me the honour to commend me. "Well, there's a big hole somewhere," he answered; "wait a bit and I'll discover it." I depended upon him to do so: where else was the fresh eye? But he produced at last nothing more luminous than "I don't know—I don't like your types." This was lame, for a critic who had never consented to discuss with me anything but the question of execution, the direction of strokes and the mystery of values.

"In the drawings you've been looking at I think my types are very handsome."

"Oh, they won't do!"

"I've had a couple of new models."

"I see you have. *They* won't do."

"Are you very sure of that?"

"Absolutely—they're stupid."

"You mean *I* am—for I ought to get round that."

"You *can't*—with such people. Who are they?"

I told him, as far as was necessary, and he declared, heartlessly "*Ce sont des gens qu'il faut mettre à la porte.*"[8]

"You've never seen them; they're awfully good," I compassionately objected.

"Not seen them? Why, all this recent work of yours drops to pieces with them. It's all I want to see of them."

"No one else has said anything against it—the *Cheapside* people are pleased."

"Everyone else is an ass, and the *Cheapside* people the biggest asses of all. Come, don't pretend, at this time of day, to have pretty illusions about the public, especially about publishers and editors. It's not for *such* animals you work—it's for those who know, *coloro che sanno*;[9] so keep straight for *me* if you can't keep straight for yourself. There's a certain sort of thing you tried for from the first—and a very good thing it is. But this twaddle isn't *in* it." When I talked with Hawley later about "Rutland Ramsay" and its possible successors he declared that I must get back into my boat again or I would go to the bottom. His voice in short was the voice of warning.

I noted the warning, but I didn't turn my friends out of doors. They bored me a good deal; but the very fact that they bored me admonished me not to sacrifice them—if there was anything to be done with them—simply to irritation. As I look back at this phase they seem to me to have pervaded my life not a little. I have a vision of them as most of the time in my studio, seated, against the wall, on an old velvet bench to be out of the way, and looking like a pair of patient courtiers in a royal ante-chamber. I am convinced that during the coldest weeks of the winter they held their ground because it saved them fire. Their newness was losing its gloss, and it was impossible not to feel that they were objects of charity. Whenever Miss Churm arrived they went away, and after I was fairly launched in "Rutland Ramsay" Miss Churm arrived pretty often. They managed to express to me tacitly that they supposed I wanted her

---

8. "Show the door to these people" (French).   **9.** "Those who know" (Italian).

for the low life of the book, and I let them suppose it, since they had attempted to study the work—it was lying about the studio—without discovering that it dealt only with the highest circles. They had dipped into the most brilliant of our novelists without deciphering many passages. I still took an hour from them, now and again, in spite of Jack Hawley's warning: it would be time enough to dismiss them, if dismissal should be necessary, when the rigour of the season was over. Hawley had made their acquaintance—he had met them at my fireside—and thought them a ridiculous pair. Learning that he was a painter they tried to approach him, to show him too that they were the real thing; but he looked at them, across the big room, as if they were miles away: they were a compendium of everything that he most objected to in the social system of his country. Such people as that, all convention and patent-leather, with ejaculations that stopped conversation, had no business in a studio. A studio was a place to learn to see, and how could you see through a pair of feather beds?

The main inconvenience I suffered at their hands was that, at first, I was shy of letting them discover how my artful little servant had begun to sit to me for "Rutland Ramsay." They knew that I had been odd enough (they were prepared by this time to allow oddity to artists), to pick a foreign vagabond out of the streets, when I might have had a person with whiskers and credentials; but it was some time before they learned how high I rated his accomplishments. They found him in an attitude more than once, but they never doubted I was doing him as an organ-grinder. There were several things they never guessed, and one of them was that for a striking scene in the novel, in which a footman briefly figured, it occurred to me to make use of Major Monarch as the menial. I kept putting this off, I didn't like to ask him to don the livery—besides the difficulty of finding a livery to fit him. At last, one day late in the winter, when I was at work on the despised Oronte (he caught one's idea in an instant), and was in the glow of feeling that I was going very straight, they came in, the Major and his wife, with their society laugh about nothing (there was less and less to laugh at), like country-callers—they always reminded me of that—who have walked across the park after church and are presently persuaded to stay to luncheon. Luncheon was over, but they could stay to tea—I knew they wanted it. The fit was on me, however, and I couldn't let my ardour cool and my work wait, with the fading daylight, while my model prepared it. So I asked Mrs. Monarch if she would mind laying it out—a request which, for an instant, brought all the blood to her face. Her eyes were on her husband's for a second, and some mute telegraphy passed between them. Their folly was over the next instant; his cheerful shrewdness put an end to it. So far from pitying their wounded pride, I must add, I was moved to give it as complete a lesson as I could. They bustled about together and got out the cups and saucers and made the kettle boil. I know they felt as if they were waiting on my servant, and when the tea was prepared I said: "He'll have a cup, please—he's tired." Mrs. Monarch brought him one where he stood, and he took it from her as if he had been a gentleman at a party, squeezing a crush-hat with an elbow.

Then it came over me that she had made a great effort for me—made it with a kind of nobleness—and that I owed her a compensation. Each time I saw her after this I wondered what the compensation could be. I couldn't go on doing the wrong thing to oblige them. Oh, it *was* the wrong thing, the stamp of the work for which they sat—Hawley was not the only person to say it now. I sent in a large number of the drawings I had made for "Rutland Ramsay," and I received a warning that was more to the point than Hawley's. The artistic adviser of the house for which I was working was of opinion that many of my illustrations were not what had been looked for. Most of these illustrations were the subjects in which the Monarchs had figured. Without going into the question of what *had* been looked for, I saw at this rate I shouldn't get the other books to do. I hurled myself in despair upon Miss Churm, I put her through all her paces. I not only adopted Oronte publicly as my hero, but one morning when the Major looked in to see if I didn't require him to finish a figure for the *Cheapside*, for which he had begun to sit the week before, I told him that I had changed my mind—I would do the drawing from my man. At this my visitor turned pale and stood looking at me. "Is *he* your idea of an English gentleman?" he asked.

I was disappointed, I was nervous, I wanted to get on with my work; so I replied with irritation: "Oh, my dear Major—I can't be ruined for *you*!"

He stood another moment; then, without a word, he quitted the studio. I drew a long breath when he was gone, for I said to myself that I shouldn't see him again. I had not told him definitely that I was in danger of having my work rejected, but I was vexed at his not having felt the catastrophe in the air, read with me the moral of our fruitless collaboration, the lesson that, in the deceptive atmosphere of art, even the highest respectability may fail of being plastic.

I didn't owe my friends money, but I did see them again. They reappeared together, three days later, and under the circumstances there was something tragic in the fact. It was a proof to me that they could find nothing else in life to do. They had threshed the matter out in a dismal conference—they had digested the bad news that they were not in for the series. If they were not useful to me even for the *Cheapside* their function seemed difficult to determine, and I could only judge at first that they had come, forgivingly, decorously, to take a last leave. This made me rejoice in secret that I had little leisure for a scene; for I had placed both my other models in position together and I was pegging away at a drawing from which I hoped to derive glory. It had been suggested by the passage in which Rutland Ramsay, drawing up a chair to Artemisia's piano-stool, says extraordinary things to her while she ostensibly fingers out a difficult piece of music. I had done Miss Churm at the piano before—it was an attitude in which she knew how to take on an absolutely poetic grace. I wished the two figures to "compose" together, intensely, and my little Italian had entered perfectly into my conception. The pair were vividly before me, the piano had been pulled out; it was a charming picture of blended youth and murmured love, which I had only to catch and keep. My visitors stood and looked at it, and I was friendly to them over my shoulder.

They made no response, but I was used to silent company and went on with my work, only a little disconcerted (even though exhilarated by the sense that *this* was at least the ideal thing), at not having got rid of them after all. Presently I heard Mrs. Monarch's sweet voice beside, or rather above me: "I wish her hair was a little better done." I looked up and she was staring with a strange fixedness at Miss Churm, whose back was turned to her. "Do you mind my just touching it?" she went on—a question which made me spring up for an instant, as with the instinctive fear that she might do the young lady a harm. But she quieted me with a glance I shall never forget—I confess I should like to have been able to paint *that*—and went for a moment to my model. She spoke to her softly, laying a hand upon her shoulder and bending over her; and as the girl, understanding, gratefully assented, she disposed her rough curls, with a few quick passes, in such a way as to make Miss Churm's head twice as charming. It was one of the most heroic personal services I have ever seen rendered. Then Mrs. Monarch turned away with a low sigh and, looking about her as if for something to do, stooped to the floor with a noble humility and picked up a dirty rag that had dropped out of my paint-box.

The Major meanwhile had also been looking for something to do and, wandering to the other end of the studio, saw before him my breakfast things, neglected, unremoved. "I say, can't I be useful *here*?" he called out to me with an irrepressible quaver. I assented with a laugh that I fear was awkward and for the next ten minutes, while I worked, I heard the light clatter of china and the tinkle of spoons and glass. Mrs. Monarch assisted her husband—they washed up my crockery, they put it away. They wandered off into my little scullery, and I afterwards found that they had cleaned my knives and that my slender stock of plate had an unprecedented surface. When it came over me, the latent eloquence of what they were doing, I confess that my drawing was blurred for a moment—the picture swam. They had accepted their failure, but they couldn't accept their fate. They had bowed their heads in bewilderment to the perverse and cruel law in virtue of which the real thing could be so much less precious than the unreal; but they didn't want to starve. If my servants were my models, my models might be my servants. They would reverse the parts—the others would sit for the ladies and gentlemen, and *they* would do the work. They would still be in the studio—it was an intense dumb appeal to me not to turn them out. "Take us on," they wanted to say—"we'll do *anything*."

When all this hung before me the *afflatus* vanished—my pencil dropped from my hand. My sitting was spoiled and I got rid of my sitters, who were also evidently rather mystified and awestruck. Then, alone with the Major and his wife, I had a most uncomfortable moment. He put their prayer into a single sentence: "I say, you know—just let *us* do for you, can't you?" I couldn't— it was dreadful to see them emptying my slops; but I pretended I could, to oblige them, for about a week. Then I gave them a sum of money to go away; and I never saw them again. I obtained the remaining books, but my friend Hawley repeats that Major and Mrs. Monarch did me a permanent harm, got me into a second-rate trick. If it be true I am content to have paid the price— for the memory.

1892

RELATED:

—James, "The Art of Fiction," p. 1719

RUTH PRAWER JHABVALA
1927–2013

Jhabvala was born in Germany, emigrated to England, and was educated at London University, where she studied English literature. After marrying an Indian architect, she moved to India and raised her family there. In 1975 she moved to New York City, where she spent the rest of her life. She published twelve novels, many set in India, including the Booker Prize–winning *Heat and Dust* (1975), *In Search of Love and Beauty* (1983), and *Shards of Memory* (1995), as well as four volumes of short stories, including *East into Upper East* (1998). Among her awards is a MacArthur Fellowship (1984), and O. Henry Prize (2003). Moreover, Jhabvala wrote a number of highly regarded screenplays, including *Heat and Dust* (1984), the Oscar-winning *A Room with a View* (1986), *Mr. and Mrs. Bridge* (1990), *Howards End* (1992, Jhabvala's second Oscar), and *The Remains of the Day* (1993).

Passion

Apart from the fact that they had both been in India for about a year and both had well-paid jobs with British cultural organizations, Christine and Betsy had very little in common. Nevertheless they shared a flat. Their friends—Christine's friends especially, Betsy didn't have all that many—were surprised when they first decided on this step and wondered how it would ever work out; but in fact it worked very well, perhaps just because they were so different, and led different lives, and so never got in each other's way.

The mantelpiece in their flat was always full of invitations, and they were almost all Christine's. She was tall, slim, and good-looking. She had a number of Indian boy-friends, who would call for her at the flat in the evenings in order to take her out in their cars. Sometimes she wasn't quite ready and she would trill from out of the bathroom that she wouldn't be a second; Betsy in the meantime invited them to make themselves comfortable in the sitting-room and have a drink. Sometimes they had several before Christine finally appeared, and then they jumped smartly to their feet while she, laughing and breathless and tying a gauze scarf round her hair, flippantly apologized for keeping them waiting.

Her favourite escort was a tall, handsome officer of the President's body-guard called Captain Manohar Singh ("Manny" to his friends). Betsy too was glad when it was Manny who was taking Christine out, and the longer he was kept waiting the better Betsy liked it. She felt good sitting next to the handsome Manny on the sofa and talking to him. She talked to him about India—Indian philosophy or music, or about the current political situation— while he drank one whisky after the other and sat at his ease with his large legs apart and a good-natured, listening expression on his face. Betsy sometimes had reason to believe that he wasn't really listening, for he never made any kind of remark that could be construed as a comment on what she was telling him. Indeed, he hardly said anything at all, and when he did, it was something completely unexpected like, "Boy, did we have a party last night! Wow!" But for Betsy it was really enough to be allowed to talk to him and look at him at such close quarters to her heart's content. Manny was a Sikh,[1] and he had an exquisitely barbered, shining black beard and wore a dark blue turban; his eyes were not dark but surprisingly light-coloured, a pellucid grey shining like a lake between the heavy fringe of his black lashes.

Once Manny kissed Betsy. It was entirely unexpected. They were sitting on the sofa and Betsy was telling him about her preference for the Kangra school of painting over that of Basohli, when suddenly he jumped on her. Really, there was no other word for it—he *jumped,* took a leap from where he was sitting and snatched her into his arms. She gave a short cry of shock, but next moment his lips were pressed weightily on hers, his tongue—strong, pulsing, muscled like some animal alive in its own right—pushed its way into her mouth; beneath his silk shirt she could feel his chest and his ribs as strong as steel. Waves of rapture passed over her like a fainting fit. But it seemed he was more collected than she was. As suddenly as he had seized her, he pushed her away, hastily adjusted his turban and got to his feet as Christine came breezing in, wafting scent and shouting "Darling!" "Darling!" he answered with his great boom of a laugh. "Again you are late, ho-ho, darling!" He was quite unembarrassed, while Betsy was left sitting stunned on the sofa with her hair dishevelled and her skirt slipped high up on her thighs.

With few friends and few entertainments, Betsy had very little to do in her spare time and spent most of it reading. She often went to the American library and became well known to the local staff there. One member of the staff was particularly assiduous in finding the books she wanted and keeping back those she had asked for. He was a slim, shy young Indian who, like a thousand other clerks, was always dressed in a clean but rather old white shirt and Western-style trousers. In the evenings, when she took a taxi home from the office, Betsy often saw him standing in a bus queue. The queue was always immensely long, and many of the buses that passed were crowded and did not even stop. He looked very patient standing there, holding a small, worn brass tiffin-carrier[2] in his hand. Once it was raining, and she saw him trying to protect himself by placing the tiffin-carrier on his head. She stopped her taxi and offered him a lift; he got in without a word.

"Where can I drop you?" she asked.

"Where you are going."

"But that may be miles out of your way."

"It is all right."

---

1. A religious sect founded ca. 1500 as an offshoot of Hinduism. The Sikhs refused to acknowledge the caste system in India.   **2.** A type of lunchbox common in India.

That was all she could get out of him: "It is all right." For the rest, he sat straight and silent on the edge of the seat, holding his arms close to his sides; he was very wet and exuded vapours of dampness and discomfort. When the taxi stopped at her house and she got out, he got out with her, without a word. "Do you live near here?" she asked; she felt quite guilty about him by this time. "It is all right," he said, and stood and waited. Perhaps he was waiting to be asked up, but Betsy couldn't do that because Christine was having people in. She fumbled in her bag for her keys and, in the process, feeling nervous and hurried, dropped many things on the pavement. He stooped to pick them up, and she cried out in alarm, "No, don't bother!" She crouched down with him on the pavement, and they both scrabbled for her things and got wet in the rain. When she had found her keys, she stuffed everything back into her bag and tucked it bulging under her arm and ran inside, leaving him standing. She had a bad conscience about him for hours afterwards.

A few days later she passed him again at the bus stand. Feeling embarrassed, she looked quickly the other way, but he had seen her, and without a moment's hesitation he ran into the road and signalled her taxi to a halt; he waved both arms like a person in distress. But he wasn't in distress at all, he only wanted a ride with her. Again he came to her door and stood there, waiting expectantly. When she asked him up, he agreed at once. He sat down on a chair and looked round him with undisguised curiosity, up and down the walls, across the ceiling, at all the furniture. Betsy said, "Would you like a drink?" Now that she had brought him here, she didn't know what to do with him.

When she had mixed him his drink, he held the glass as if it were some strange object and then he asked: "It is alcohol?"

"Oh dear." She bit her lip and stared at him in consternation. "Don't you drink? I'm so sorry—"

But he took a big gulp and, after coughing a bit, another; then he finished the glass. She looked at him apprehensively. "It doesn't taste very nice," he said.

"No, if you're not used to it. It never occurred to me that you might not—everybody seems to drink such a lot. I mean, all the people one meets—" She stopped herself, for she realized she was saying he was not the sort of person one met. She sought desperately for something to say to cancel this out. But he did not seem to have noticed. He was smiling: "It is a funny taste."

"Would you like some more?"

"Yes."

This time too he drank it down very quickly, as if it were water or tea. She would have liked to warn him but was afraid of hurting his feelings. When he had finished, he was smiling again; he seemed happy.

"Once we drank beer," he said. "It was at my friend's sister's wedding. We hid behind the cowshed, but afterwards one of the uncles found the empty bottle, and how angry everyone was with us!" He giggled. Betsy realized to her dismay that he was drunk. "We were very mischievous boys. I could tell you other stories also. . . . It is a nice place here. Who else lives here? There are many rooms?" He got up and began to walk round the room as if he owned it. He picked up objects and asked their price, and peeped into cupboard doors. "I think you must be getting a lot of salary. How much? More than 1,000 rupees? More? How much more? Tell me, please. Only for my information."

Suddenly and without any warning he was sick all over the off-white rug. He stood there and retched, and held his stomach and groaned. Betsy laid her hand on his forehead. "Don't worry," she said. "It doesn't matter." She had to turn her head away, but she felt terribly sorry for him.

And afterwards she blamed herself severely. She disliked herself for having mismanaged the not overwhelmingly difficult task of inviting an unsophisticated young man up to her flat and making him welcome. She longed to make amends, to invite him again and see to it that the occasion went off with dignity on both sides. Yet at the same time she felt that she could not bear to have him here again, indeed ever to see him again; and what she would really have liked to do was to forget the whole incident and the person who had caused it.

A day or two later she heard an altercation at the door. Angry voices were raised, and then her servant came in. "He says he wants to see you," said the servant accusingly. The young librarian had followed him into the room, looking indignant and like a man determined to stand on his rights.

"Your servant was rude to me," he said as soon as they were alone. He waved aside her explanation and apologies. "I am not very much used to being treated rudely by servants."

"Betsy!" called Christine from inside her bedroom. "Has Manny come?"

"Not yet!"

"Who is that?" asked the young man sternly, but before Betsy could explain, Christine stood in the doorway. She was wearing a pink flowered wrap which she held shut with one hand. "Hallo," she told the young man.

Betsy said, "This is—" and realized she didn't know her visitor's name. He was too stunned by Christine's appearance to help her out.

"I'm Christine," Christine said. She waited politely for him to introduce himself, but when he didn't, she smiled at him in her friendly way and disappeared again inside. She could be heard, a moment later, singing in her bath. The young man remained staring at the spot where she had stood.

Betsy explained, "We share this flat." She smiled: "I don't even know your name, how silly."

"Har Gopal. She is English also?"

"Oh yes. She works for the British Council." For want of anything better to say, she began to tell him about Christine's job. But he did not listen. He looked rather distraught, glancing now round the room, now at the spot where Christine had stood. Betsy noticed how refined his face was, with a delicately chiselled nose and sad eyes. Every now and again he brought his hand up to his open collar, pressing the two ends together over his throat as if wanting thereby to improve his appearance; it was a movement at once modest and self-protective. Betsy found herself feeling very tender towards this young man.

Then Manny came to fetch Christine. He was in uniform and all his buttons shone and so did his beautiful, brown, hard-leather boots. He strode up and down the room, waiting for Christine, immensely tall and exuding a smell of whisky and eau-de-Cologne. His eyes had merely swept for a second over the top of Har Gopal's head—it did not need more than that for him to sum up a fellow-countryman. With Betsy he was, as usual, absently affable. He had never, after the event, given a sign that he remembered having kissed her. Probably he didn't remember. He strode about the room, thinking of

other things, and only became alert when Christine entered. She was no longer in her negligee but in a primrose-yellow dress, and golden sandals with
high heels which made her even taller than she was. The room seemed very
small with these two in it, and when they had gone, it seemed very empty.

Har Gopal spoke bitterly: "Are they your friends? I don't like that Sikh. I
know his type very well." When she made no comment, he spoke harshly to
her, as if she had dared to contradict him: "I tell you I have seen hundreds like
him. What do you know about it?" Neither of them in the least questioned his
right to speak to her in this manner.

"I am B.A. Kurukshetra University," he said next. "Yes, now you are surprised. You thought I was just anyone, isn't it? B.A. in history and philosophy.
And my wife is a matriculate. Come here." He beckoned to her with his slender, fine-boned hand, displaying a surprising authority, and she went.

He jumped on her in the same sudden way Manny had done. Betsy thought,
do all Indian men make love like this? In spite of his frail appearance, Har
Gopal was strong. Not with Manny's massive body-strength, but he had a
sort of sharp, incisive, relentless quality which rode down opposition. He
went straight ahead without question, not skilful but resolute, steely. He commanded respect.

Betsy was in love with Har Gopal. If she hadn't been, the situation might
have become embarrassing. He came every day to the flat, and when any of
Christine's friends was there, he sat in a corner like a poor relation and looked
at them with burning, hungry eyes. Afterwards he was angry with Betsy and
blamed her for any lack of respect he felt had been shown to him. Christine
was always very nice and tactful with him, and in return he went to some
pains to make serious conversation with her. He would tell her about the
unemployment problem in Uttar Pradesh, or the number of light aircraft
manufactured by the Hindustan[3] aircraft factory per year. She would appear
to be listening and would say "No really?" and "How fascinating!" in between,
without irony. She might be doing her nails, daubing on the varnish with
exquisite little brush-strokes, and he would look on in fascination. He loved
seeing her do her nails. Sometimes he asked Betsy why she didn't paint hers,
and he clicked his tongue in disapproval when she held them out to him,
clipped very short and one or two of them bitten down at the end of her short,
squarish fingers.

But she took a lot of trouble for him. She brushed and brushed her hair till
it shone, and then she slipped a red band round it. She wore white frilly
blouses and short skirts and white ballet shoes and a gold locket round her
neck. She loved going out for walks with him and would tuck her hand proudly
under his arm. He allowed her to keep it there and walked by her side in a
stately manner, with his head held stiffly. Many people looked at them. They
were both about the same height, both short, but he was thin and she was
rather stocky with very muscular legs. Once or twice they met people he
knew—some friend or neighbour—and he would stop to exchange a few words
in a rather formal, self-conscious way, and though her hand remained tucked
under his arm, he made no attempt to introduce her. But if they met anyone
she knew, some fellow-countrymen from her office or the High Commission,

---

3. Region of northern India. Uttar Pradesh: state in northern India.

she made a point of introducing Har Gopal at once, flaunting him and cling-ing to him in such a way that her acquaintances became embarrassed and looked away and parted from her as quickly as possible. But Har Gopal always behaved correctly and said "Very happy to meet you," and shook hands all round the way he knew foreigners did.

Betsy confided a lot in Christine. She needed to have someone to talk to about Har Gopal. "I know it's ridiculous, ridiculous," she said and buried her head in her arms, overwhelmed with laughter and happiness. "He's all wrong—of course he is—*and* he's married, *and* three children." She hid her face again and her shoulders shook laughing. She tried to but could never quite explain to Christine what it was she loved so much about Har Gopal. His finely drawn features, yes, his dark, dreaming eyes, his sadness, his sensitiv-ity: and also—but how could she tell Christine this?—she loved the shabby clothes he wore, his badly cut cotton trousers and his frequently washed shirt with his thin wrists coming out of the buttoned cuffs. She was posi-tively proud of the fact that he looked so much like everybody else—like hun-dreds and thousands of other Indian clerks going to offices every morning on the bus and coming home again with their empty tiffin-carriers in the evenings: people who worked for small salaries and supported their families and worried. She frowned with the effort of trying to express all this to Chris-tine and said finally that well, she supposed she loved him for being so typically Indian.

Christine laughed: "But that's why I like Manny too."

Betsy had to admit that Manny too was typically Indian—but in a very dif-ferent way. Manny was the India one read about in childhood, coloured with tigers, sunsets, and princes; but Har Gopal was *real*, he was everyday, urban, suffering India that people in the West didn't know about.

Har Gopal often asked her: "Do you talk about me with Christine?" He wanted to know everything that they said. When she teased and wouldn't tell, he twisted her wrist or squeezed her muscles till she screamed. He loved prac-ticing these boyhood tortures on her; it was the only way he knew of being playful, for that was how he had played with his friends at school and college. He had never had a woman friend before. But he had had many male friends, and they had had grand times together. He often told Betsy about his friends, and it always put him in a good mood. He had a serious, even melancholy nature, but when he recollected his student days, he became gay and laughed at all the mad pranks they had played together. One of his friends, Chandu, had been a great joker, and how he had teased the masters at school! No one could do anything to him, because his father was an important man in town. Another friend had had the ability to chew up newspapers and even razor blades. They were all crazy about the cinema and went to see the same film over and over again till they knew the lyrics and dialogues by heart. He could still recite great chunks of old films and he did so for Betsy, and he sang the songs for her. She loved his voice, which was sweet and girlish, and the soft expression which came into his eyes when he sang; but he said no no, his voice was nothing, she should have heard Mohan, then she would have known what good singing was. They had all thought that Mohan would surely go into films and become a playback singer, but instead he had got a job in the life insurance corporation. There had been so many friends, and they had all been so close and had thought their friendship was eternal; but now Har Gopal didn't even know where most of them were. Everyone was married, like himself, and had their own worries and no more time for their friends. But he still thought about them often and wished for the old days back again, or at least to have one friend left with him in whom to confide his thoughts and have a good time together.

"Well you've got me now," said Betsy, putting her arm round his neck, tender and comradely.

But he could not feel about her the way he did about his friends. He was, she knew, less fond of her. She excited him, and he was proud to have her, but he did not really, she often suspected, *like* her. All the loving came from her side, and he accepted it as his due but made no attempt to return it. There was something lordly, almost tyrannical in his attitude to her. When he lounged at his ease in her room, all his shyness and shabbiness—that *depressed* quality that was so evident in him when he stood with his tiffin-carrier at the bus-stop—left him completely, and he became what, as a Brahmin,[4] he perhaps was by nature: an aristocrat for whom the goods and riches of this world were created and whose right it was to be served by others. Betsy was the one who served, and the goods and riches were the things she gave him for which he had developed a taste: English biscuits, raspberry syrup (he never again drank alcohol), tinned peaches.

He kept some clothes in her room, and when he came to her straight from the office, as he usually did, he would take off his trousers and carefully fold them and then put on his dhoti.[5] He dressed and undressed with delicate precaution, so as never to be seen naked by any human eye, not even his own. Although his lovemaking left nothing to be desired, he never lost his reticence: his manner was always controlled and fastidious, and never for a moment was there any abandon in it. Betsy, on the other hand, was all abandon. She would fling off her clothes, leaving them just where they dropped, and walk round the room naked. Very often she forgot to lock the door, so that the servant or Christine or anyone who came to the flat could have walked in at any time. She didn't care. Her attitude shocked and at the same time pleased him. In the beginning he could only watch her undressing with his face averted and his eyes half lowered, ashamed of himself and of her, but as time went on, he looked at her boldly and with a strange smile which was perhaps partly appreciation and partly, she sometimes suspected, contempt.

He never spoke to her about his family. She wanted to know so much about them, but he always completely evaded her questions. If she insisted too much, he became annoyed and refused to speak to her at all and perhaps even went home earlier than usual. So she dared not ask much. But it tortured her to have all this area of his life concealed from her with a deliberateness which suggested she was not worthy to approach it. Why should he feel that way? He was *proud* of her—she knew he was—otherwise would he parade through the town with her on his arm and greet people he met on the way with such a superior air?

---

4. Member of the highest caste (hereditary social class) in Indian society.   **5.** A kind of wrapped loincloth worn by men in India.

Sometimes, when she found he was relaxed and in a good mood, she tried to coax him into talking: "Is your wife taller than me? Shorter? The same? Say!" But at once his good mood would disappear and he turned away from her, frowning. Once she asked him half jokingly, "What's the matter? You don't think I'm good enough to hear about your family?" But at that he took on such a strange, closed expression that she realized she had stumbled on something near the truth. But she wouldn't at first believe it; she even laughed at it and said, "My God, what am I—a fallen woman or something?" Still he made no answer, but the expression on his face did not change nor did he make any attempt to contradict or deny. She laughed again, more harshly, even though by now she felt far from laughing. It was ridiculous, something out of Victorian melodrama, but still it was true, it was the way he saw her. She felt so humiliated that she could speak nothing further and tears flowed silently from her eyes: but even as they rolled down her cheeks and her heart heaved with pain at the thought of her humiliation, at the same time—so bizarre were her feelings for him—this very humiliation actually increased, exacerbated her passion for him.

One day she went secretly to see the place where he lived. She found blocks of tenements set out side by side and surrounded by an area of waste land on which had sprung up a dusty little bazaar and a shanty colony of thatched huts. As soon as she got out of her taxi, she found herself the centre of a group of children who laughed and marvelled at her strangeness and followed her closely. She looked round her for a time, then plucked up courage and walked through the doorway that led into the compound of the first block of build-ings. It was as lively here as in any street. Children played, and there were some men repairing string-beds and a number of itinerant vegetable-sellers and a fish-seller, all of whom were bargaining with women who suspiciously untied their bundles of money from the end of their saris and complained to one another about dishonest traders; other women called down from the win-dows that opened in tiers and rows from the tall buildings. Betsy, with her little cluster of attendant children, looked around her and did not know what to do next. Suddenly she wondered what would happen if he were to come now out of one of those dark doorways and find her standing there. She could almost see the expression of panic and fury that would instantly transform his face, and at the thought of it, she began to panic a little herself and to wish she had not come.

But then it was too late to retreat. A round little man in an English-style suit came running up to her, calling in an excited voice, "Yes, please, yes, please! You have come to see Mr. Har Gopal?" Betsy did not recognize him, but guessed at once that he must be someone whom they had met and Har Gopal had talked to on one of their evening walks.

"This way, please," said the little man, pushing aside all the children and leading her out of the compound. To curious bystanders he explained impor-tantly, "For Har Gopal in C Block." He strutted in front while the children surged after him and Betsy found herself swept along in the procession. Behind her the women nudged and talked. The little man led her along the street and then turned into the next compound, waving a plump hand over his shoulder at her and calling, "This way, please!"

Then she saw that the little procession had brought her back to the street where her taxi was waiting. Murmuring apologies which no one heard, she suddenly climbed into it and sat down, and the driver skilfully flicked away the children who at once surrounded the car. Betsy did not dare look out of the window, as she was driven away, and she even put her handkerchief up to her face as if she hoped thereby neither to see nor be seen.

The next time Har Gopal came to the flat he did not talk to her at all but straightaway took his dhoti and a pair of slippers and bottle of hair-oil he kept in her bedroom and, grimly determined, wrapped them up in a bundle. "What are you doing?" she cried out in distress. He did not answer but made for the door. She clung to him to prevent him. She begged him to stay.

"Let me go, please," he said, but standing quite still and making no effort to release himself.

"It's only that I wanted to *see* where you were."

"You came to spy on me. Yes, and now you will laugh at me with your friends because my house is poor and I am poor." Suddenly he shrieked: "I don't care! You can laugh, what do I care!"

"Please don't," she said and clung to him tighter, but he shook her off and shouted at her, "And my position? That's nothing to you what people will say that you come openly to my home—" He sank down to sit on the edge of her bed and covered his eyes with his hands in grief and shame. And Betsy sank down beside him, and she too covered her eyes. What followed was a loud scene, echoing all over the flat, in which he spoke a lot about his position in the world and she lacerated herself with accusations regarding her own selfishness and insensitivity; and when this had gone on for a long time, and she had again and again begged his forgiveness, they were at last reconciled, and she dissolved in tears of gratitude while he was proud and gracious with her.

Then it was time for him to go home, and on his way out, they had to pass through the sitting-room where Christine sat playing ludo[6] with Manny. Those two must have heard every word of what had passed in the other room. Christine delicately kept her eyes fixed on the ludo-board, and Manny hummed a tune to himself. Har Gopal's face took on a tight expression, and his thin body seemed to shrink as he walked through the room; he looked as he did waiting at the bus-stop. Only Betsy was entirely free from embarrassment as she ushered her lover out of the flat.

That night Christine knocked timidly on Betsy's door. Betsy was lying stark naked on her rumpled bed, reading the Katha-Upanishad.[7] She was wearing her reading-glasses and thoughtfully twisting a lock of hair round her finger. She didn't seem to be a bit shy to be found naked. Her breasts were very much heavier than one would have expected from seeing her dressed. "Yes, come in," she said and shut her book with her finger inside to hold the page. "I'm sorry, we made an awful lot of noise today, didn't we?" she said cheerfully.

---

6. Ancient Indian board game resembling backgammon.   **7.** One of the speculative Hindu treatises (Upanishads) composed between the 8th and 6th centuries B.C. and first written down around C.E. 1300.

Christine sat on the edge of a chair. She was wearing a flowered wrap and looked crisp and fresh and a contrast to Betsy's room which was rather untidy.

"I know it's none of my business," said Christine, talking very quickly so as to get it over with, "but I do think you ought to be a bit more careful."

Betsy laughed and said, "I wish I were the sort of person who *could* be careful."

"Everyone's talking you know, Betsy, in the office and everywhere. I mean, good heavens, not that anyone cares about your having an Indian boyfriend—don't we all?—but he's so . . . *different* from the other Indians we all know."

"You mean he's poor."

"It's not that," Christine said miserably. "But he's—I don't know, odd. And there's something unhealthy about it all—of course it's absolutely terrible of me to be saying all this and do tell me to shut up if you want to."

There was a moment's pause. Then Betsy said, "It *is* unhealthy." She tried to sound detached and dispassionate, but could not keep it up for long. "I suppose all passion is unhealthy. Sometimes I tell you I feel *insane*—and what's more—what's terrible: I revel in it! I glory in it!" She rolled over on to her side to face Christine, and her big breasts fell to that side and her eyes shone behind her flesh-coloured glasses.

Christine was not the only person who tried to warn Betsy. One day her office chief invited her to lunch at his house, and in the kindest manner possible, full of embarrassment and apologies, told her that unless she behaved in what he called a more conventional way he would have to have her sent home. Betsy understood that he had to tell her this and that he was right, but she had no intention of changing. Instead she began to make plans what to do if she were really posted back home. Of course, she would resign immediately; she would stay and get a job locally. She was vague as to what kind of job and did not stop much to wonder whether anyone would employ her; but she knew that, whatever she did, her salary would only be a fraction of what it was now and she would have to change her whole way of life. She didn't mind that; in fact, she rather looked forward to it. She would have to move out of the flat and go somewhere much cheaper. She thought of herself in some small room in a crowded locality; to get to her, one would have to cross a courtyard and climb up a very dark, very narrow winding staircase. She would be the only European living in the house. Every day Har Gopal would come to visit her. Actually Betsy couldn't cook, but now she had visions of herself squatting over a little bucket of coal and preparing a meal for him and serving him just like an Indian wife. She might take to wearing a sari. Perhaps she would have a baby, a boy, who would grow up dark and delicate like Har Gopal.

She neglected her work in the office and was distant with her colleagues. She realized vaguely that something was going on around her and that perhaps steps were being taken against her, but she did not bother to find out what they were. Christine told her that she would be moving out of their joint flat soon; she made up some polite lies that the flat was getting too expensive for her and that she had found another smaller one elsewhere, but Betsy cut her short and said it didn't matter, that she herself would be moving out too, very soon. She already saw herself in her small room in the house with the winding staircase.

She even began to make inquiries about the rents to be paid for such places, and about how much money would be needed for the simple, Indian-style life she intended to adopt. All her thoughts were concentrated on this problem. Once, finding herself alone with Manny who was waiting for Christine to get ready, she even asked him, very seriously, "Supposing you only eat dal and rice twice a day—how much would that come to a week?"

"Only dal and rice!" exclaimed Manny humorously. "And what about a peg of whisky?"

"I'm being serious, Manny," Betsy said impatiently, but it was impossible to make him be serious with her. Ever since she had started her affair with Har Gopal, Manny's attitude to her had become strange and ambivalent: on the one hand, he was rather more brusque, and even rude with her than he had been before; on the other, he indulged in sudden spurts of familiarity which extended to, whenever they found themselves alone in a room, pinching her in intimate places.

He did this now, and at the same time he joked with her: "My two-three pegs a day I must have, otherwise I'm like my car without petrol. Hm? Han?" He encouraged her to laugh with him and drew her close, and his beard nuzzled against her cheek. She struggled to get free, but that made him hold her all the more tightly. She stared into his face, and she saw his light-coloured eyes and his red, moist, healthy mouth smiling inside his black beard. She let out a cry. He released her immediately and even gave her a push to get her farther away from him. Christine, zipping her dress, came in and said, "Whatever's the matter?"

"It is Betsy," said Manny. "She thought she saw a snake." He laughed uproariously.

Betsy did not speak to Har Gopal about her future plans. She was afraid. She knew that the idea of anyone giving up a job, an assured livelihood, was not one he would ever be able to understand. He himself was very timid about his own job and took good care never to give cause for complaint to his superiors. Not only was he very polite, even deferential, to them in their presence, but he also spoke of them in tones of the highest respect when they were not there and had no chance of ever knowing what he was saying about them. Once, when Betsy spoke with lighthearted disdain of one or two of the top people in her own organization, he rebuked her for doing so, and when she laughed at the rebuke, he frowned and became annoyed with her and said that she had no respect in her nature. The very least, he said, that one owed one's superiors was respect; and quite apart from that, one should be careful what one said about them because who knew what might not get back to them. But how *could* anything get back to them, asked Betsy, amused, when there was no one there but he and she, and surely he wasn't going to go and tell on her, was he? He refused to smile at the idea but only said that in these matters one could never be careful enough. His eyes even roved solemnly for a moment round the room—her bedroom—as if he feared someone might be be lurking somewhere listening.

One Sunday afternoon he was reclining on her bed in his rather lordly way, wearing his vest and dhoti, his feet crossed comfortably at the ankle; he had his arms folded behind his head and was staring into space with melancholy eyes. He looked noble and sensitive and gave the impression of being sunk in deep philosophic thought. This impression, however, was false, for when he finally broke his silence it was to say nothing more significant than, "Just see, I have had this blister for two days. It is very painful." He plaintively held up his finger to her.

She burst out laughing and, overcome with tenderness for him, threw herself on his reclining figure. "Oh, you're so sweet, so *sweet!*" she cried, and crushed him as tight as she could as if she hoped thereby to relieve her overwhelming feelings. He cried out and struggled to get free—unsuccessfully, till she released him of her own accord. He smoothed down his hair with one hand and his dhoti with the other and said indignantly, "How rough you are."

She laughed again and settled herself happily on the floor, leaning her head against the edge of the bed on which he lay. She felt exquisitely comfortable and domestic and knew that this was the way she wanted her life to go on for ever. And then she blurted it out, about giving up her job and staying in India so as to be always near him.

Har Gopal was appalled. He quite genuinely thought she was mad. He argued with her, pointed out that even if she managed to get some kind of job in India, which was in itself unlikely, she would never be able to live on the salary she would be paid. But Betsy said no, she wanted to live on it; she was tired of living the way she did here, as a foreigner, as a privileged person.

"I want to live in India like an Indian," she said, "like everyone else, like you. Exactly like you," and she seized his fine, frail hand and kissed it.

He drew it away from her. "You don't know anything," he said. "If you had to live in a place where there is never enough water and the neighbours quarrel and you clean and clean but still the cockroaches come—"

"I don't care," Betsy said.

"Yes, it is so easy to talk," he said bitterly. He got up from the bed and began to get dressed, though it was not yet his usual time for departure.

"I want to give up everything for you," Betsy said. "To lay my whole life at your feet and say: here, take it." She shut her eyes, carried away by the passion with which she spoke.

He uttered a short sound of impatience and turned his back on her. He began to comb his hair in the mirror. She came up behind him and put her arms round his waist and laid her cheek caressingly against his back. He continued to comb his hair very carefully; he was always careful of his appearance before going out into the street.

"I'm not 'sacrificing' anything," she said. "Don't think that. Good heavens, what do you think I care for my job, or this flat, or money, or anything?"

He could hold himself no longer: "No, you don't care! You are like that. You have everything in life and you throw it all away. Aren't you ashamed? There are others who would give God knows what to have something, to live nicely, but for them—no, there's nothing, not even in their dreams..." His voice failed him, and he could not go on. It was as if all the frustrations of his life had risen up and formed a hard ball in his chest and left him unable to speak. He waved his hand in her direction, dismissing her, not wanting her, and turned to the door.

"Don't go," she pleaded and held on to his arm. He attempted to free himself but she held on tightly. Suddenly he became vicious. He thumped his fist on the hand holding on to his arm and cursed her in Hindi: *"Hath mat lagao, besharm kahin Ki!"*[8] He left the room, with her running after him.

Christine and Manny were having drinks in the sitting-room. Manny put down his glass and got up and strode over to Har Gopal. He seized him by the front of his shirt and shook him to and fro, and Har Gopal allowed this to be done without offering resistance. His face was frozen with fright while his body was being shaken, and the oiled, stiff hair on his head flopped up and down.

"Let him go, Manny," Christine said in a low, embarrassed voice.

Manny gave one last shake and then flung him towards the door. Har Gopal fell down but he picked himself up again and patiently dusted off his knees and hands. Without looking back at anyone, he walked down the stairs, slowly and with dignity. Betsy followed him.

When he reached the bottom of the stairs, he told her in a tone of cold command, "Get my things."

"What things?"

"My things. My dhoti and my slippers, and don't forget my bottle of hair-oil."

He stood very straight and thin and proud. But suddenly he sat down on the bottom stair. He hid his face in his arms and his shoulders shook with sobbing. She sat down next to him; she held him and murmured to him, words of the sweetest comfort.

After a while he raised his face which was smeared with tears. He cut across her murmuring and said, "You must leave this place. I don't want you to stay with these people one day more."

Betsy said that they would look for a place for her together; somewhere very cheap, very Indian. She glanced at him to note his reaction, but he gave no sign of having heard her and remained staring gloomily in front of him. She allowed herself to believe that his silence meant assent. At this her heart leaped in joy and her mind shone with visions of the new life that was about to begin for her.

1968

---

8. "Don't touch me, you shameless woman!" (Hindi).

CHARLES JOHNSON
b. 1948

Johnson was born in Evanston, Illinois. A novelist, short-story writer, critic, and University of Washington literature professor, Johnson first achieved fame as a political cartoonist in the 1960s, which eventually led to a television series about cartooning on PBS. He is the author of the novels *Faith and the Good Thing* (1974), *Oxherding Tale* (1982), the National Book Award–winning *Middle Passage* (1990), and *Dreamer* (1997), a fictionalized version of the life of Martin Luther King, Jr. He has also published three story collections: *The Sorcerer's Apprentice* (1986), *Soulcatcher* (2000), and *Dr. King's Refrigerator* (2005); a book of cartoons, *Black Humor* (1970); a critical study, *Being and Race* (1988); and *Turning the Wheel* (2003), a collection of essays about his experiences as an African American Buddhist. He was the recipient of a MacArthur Fellowship in 1998.

Moving Pictures

You sit in the Neptune Theatre waiting for the thin, overhead lights to dim with a sense of respect, perhaps even reverence, for American movie houses are, as everyone knows, the new cathedrals, their stories better remembered than legends, totems, or mythologies, their directors more popular than novelists, more influential than saints—enough people, you've been told, have seen the James Bond adventures to fill the entire country of Argentina. Perhaps you have written this movie. Perhaps not. Regardless, you come to it as everyone does, as a seeker groping in the darkness for light, hoping something magical will be beamed from above, and no matter how bad this matinee is, or silly, something deep and maybe even too dangerous to talk loudly about will indeed happen to you and the others before this drama reels to its last transparent frame.

Naturally, you have left your life outside the door. Like any life, it's a messy thing, hardly as orderly as art, what some call life in the fast lane—: the Sanka and sugar-donut breakfasts, bumper-to-bumper traffic downtown, the business lunches, and a breakneck schedule not to get ahead but simply to stay in one place, which is peculiar, because you grew up in the sixties speeding on Methadone and despising all this, knowing your Age (Aquarian)[1] was made

---

1. Period of peace and enlightenment predicted by astrologers to begin at the end of the 20th century. *Methadone:* a highly addictive synthetic opiate, used especially as a substitute drug in treating heroin addicts.

for finer stuff. But no matter. Outside, across town, you have put away for ninety minutes the tedious, repetitive job that is, obviously, beneath your talents, sensitivity, and education (a degree in English), the once beautiful woman—or wife—a former model (local), college dancer, or semiprofessional actress named Megan or Daphne, who has grown tired of you, or you of her, and talks now of legal separation and finding herself, the children from a former, frighteningly brief marriage whom you don't want to lose, the mortgage, alimony, IRS audit, the aging, gin-fattened face that once favored a rock star's but now frowns back at you in the bathroom mirror, the young woman at work, born in 1960 and unable to recall John Kennedy, who after the Christmas party took you to bed in her spacious downtown loft, perhaps out of pity because your mother, God bless her, died and left you with a thousand dollars in debt before you could get the old family house clear—all that shelved, mercifully, as the film starts: first that frosty mountaintop ringed by stars, or a lion roaring, or floodlights bathing the tips of buildings in a Hollywood skyline: stable trademarks in a world of flux, you think, sure-fire signs that whatever follows—tragedy or farce—is made by people who are accomplished dream-merchants. Perhaps more: masters of vision, geniuses of the epistemological Murphy.

If you have written this film, which is possible, you look for your name in the credits, and probably frown at the names of the Crew, each recalling some disaster during the production, first at the studio, then later on location for five weeks in Oklahoma cowtowns during the winter, which was worse than living on the moon, the days boiling and nights so cold. Nevertheless, you'd seen it as a miracle, an act of God when the director, having read your novel, called, offering you the project—a historical romance—then walked you patiently through the first eight drafts, suspicious of you at first (there was real money riding on this, it wasn't poetry), of your dreary, novelistic pretensions to Deep Profundity, and you equally suspicious of him, his background in sitcoms, obsession with "keeping it sexy," and love of Laurel and Hardy[2] films. For this you wrote a dissertation on Derrida?[3] Yet, you'd listened. He was right, in the end. He was good, you admitted, grudgingly. He knew, as you—with your liberal arts degree—didn't, the meaning of Entertainment. You'd learned. With his help, you got good, too. You gloated. And lost friends. "A movie?" said your poet friends, "that's wonderful, it's happening for you," and then they avoided you as if you had AIDS. What *was* happening was this:

You'd shelved the novel, the Big Book, for bucks monitored by the Writers Guild (West), threw yourself into fast-and-dirty scripts, the instant gratification of quick deadlines and fat checks because the Book, with its complexity and promise of critical praise, the Book with its long-distance demands and no financial reward whatsoever, was impossible, and besides, you didn't have it anymore, not really, the gift for narrative or language, while the scripts were easy, like writing shorthand, and soon—way sooner than you thought—the films, with their lifespan shorter than a mayfly's, were all you could do. It's a living, you said. Nothing lasts forever. And you pushed on.

---

2. Stan Laurel (1890–1965) and Oliver Hardy (1892–1957), comedy team featured in many American films. **3.** Jacques Derrida (1930–2004), contemporary French philosopher and literary critic.

The credits crawl up against a montage of Oklahoma farmlife, and in this you read a story, too, even before the film begins. For the audience, the actors are stars, the new Olympians, but oh, you know them, this one—the male lead—whose range is boundless, who could be a Brando,[4] but who hadn't seen work in two years before this role and survived by doing voice-overs for a cartoon villain in *The Smurfs*; that one—the female supporting role—who can play the full scale of emotions, but whose last memorable performance was a commercial for Rolaids, all of them; all, including you, fighting for life in a city where the air is so corrupt joggers spit black after a two-mile run; failing, trying desperately to keep up the front of doing-well, these actors, treating you shabbily sometimes because your salary was bigger than theirs, even larger than the producer's, though he wasn't exactly hurting—no, he was richer than a medieval king, a complex man of remarkable charm and cunning, someone to both admire for his Horatio Alger[5] orphan-boy success and fear for his worship at the altar of power. You won't forget the evening he asked you to his home after a long conference, served you Scotch, and then, from inside a drawer in his desk removed an envelope, dumped its contents out, and you saw maybe fifty snapshots of beautiful, naked women on his bed—all of them second-rate actresses, though the female supporting role was there, too—and he watched you closely for your reaction, sipping his drink, smiling, then asked, "You ever sleep with a woman like that?" No, you hadn't. And, no, you didn't trust him either. You didn't turn your back. But, then again, nobody in this business did, and in some ways he was, you knew, better than most.

You'd compromised, given up ground, won a few artistic points, but generally you agreed to the producer's ideas—it *was* his show—and then the small army of badly-paid performers and production people took over, you trailing behind them in Oklahoma, trying to look writerly, wearing a Panama hat, holding your notepad ready for rewrites, surviving the tedium of eight or nine takes for difficult scenes, the fights, fallings-out, bad catered food, and midnight affairs, watching your script change at each level of interpretation—director, actor—until it was unrecognizable, a new thing entirely, a celebration of the Crew. Not you. Does anyone suspect how bad this thing really looked in roughcut? How miraculous it is that its rags of shots, conflicting ideas, and scraps of footage actually cohere? You sneak a look around at the audience, the faces lit by the glow of the screen. No one suspects. You've managed to fool them again, you old fox.

No matter whether the film is yours or not, it pulls you in, reels in your perception like a trout. On the narrow screen, the story begins with an establishing wideshot of an Oklahoma farm, then in close-up shows the face of a big towheaded, brown-freckled boy named Bret, and finally settles on a two-shot of Bret and his blond, bosomy girlfriend, Bess. No margin for failure in a formula like that. In the opening funeral scene at a tiny, whitewashed church, camera favors Bret, whose father has died. Our hero must seek his fortune in the city. Bess just hates to see him go. Dissolve to cemetery gate. As they leave the cemetery, and the coffin is lowered, she squeezes his hand, and something

---

4. Marlon Brando (1924–2004), American actor.   **5.** U.S. author (1832–1899), known for his novels about poor boys who become rich through their earnest attitudes and hard work.

inside you shivers, the sense of ruin you felt at your own mother's funeral, the irreversible feeling of abandonment. There was no girl with you, but you wished to heaven there had been, the one named Sondra you knew in high school who wouldn't see you for squat, preferring basketball players to weird little wimps and geeks, which is pretty much what you were back then, a washout to those who knew you, but you give all that to Bret and Bess, the pain of parental loss, the hopeless, quiet love never to be, which thickens the screen so thoroughly that when Bess kisses Bret your nose is clogged with tears and mucus, and then you have your handkerchief out, honking shamelessly, your eyes streaming, locked—even you—in a cycle of emotion (yours), which their images have borrowed, intensified, then given back to you, not because the images or sensations are sad, but because, at bottom, all you have known these last few minutes are the workings of your own nervous system. You yourself have been supplying the grief and satisfaction all along, from within. But even that is not the true magic of film.

As Bret rides away, you remember sitting in the studio's tiny editing room amidst reels of film hanging like stockings in a bathroom, the editor, a fat, friendly man named Coates, tolerating your curiosity, letting you peer into his viewer as he patched the first reel together, figuring he owed you, a semi-famous scriptwriter, that much. Each frame, you recall, was a single, frozen image, like an individual thought, complete in itself, with no connection to the others, as if time stood still; but then the frames came faster as the viewer sped up, chasing each other, surging forward and creating a linear, continuous motion that outstripped your perception, and presto: a sensuously rich world erupted and took such nerve-knocking reality that you shielded your eyes when the harpsichord music came up and Bret stepped into a darkened Oklahoma shed seen only from his point-of-view—oh yes, at times even your body responded, the sweat glands swaling, but it was lunchtime then and Coates wanted to go to the cafeteria for coffee and clicked off his viewer; the images flipped less quickly, slowed finally to a stop, the drama disappearing again into frames, and you saw, pulling on your coat, the nerve-wracking, heart-thumping vision for what it really was: the illusion of speed.

But is even that the magic of film? Sitting back in your seat, aware of your right leg falling asleep, you think so, for the film has no capacity to fool you anymore. You do not give it your feelings to transfigure. All that you see with godlike detachment are your own decisions, the lines that were dropped, and the microphone just visible in a corner of one scene. Nevertheless, it's gratifying to see the audience laugh out loud at the funny parts, and blubber when Bret rides home at last to marry Bess (actually, they hated each other on the set), believing, as you can't, in a dream spun from accelerated imagery. It almost makes a man feel superior, like knowing how Uri Geller[6] bends all those spoons.

And then it is done, the theatre emptying, the hour and a half of illusion over. You file out with the others, amazed by how so much can be projected onto the *tabula rasa*[7] of the Big Screen—grief, passion, fire, death—yet it remains, in the end, untouched. Dragging on your overcoat, the images still an afterglow

---

6. Israeli illusionist (b. 1946), best known for feats he claimed to perform psychically, such as stopping watches and bending metal objects. **7.** Blank slate (Latin).

in your thoughts, you step outside to the street. It takes your eyes, still in low gear, a moment to adjust to the light of late afternoon, traffic noise, and the things around you as you walk to your Fiat, feeling good, the objects on the street as flat and dimensionless at first as props on a stage. And then you stop.

The Fiat, you notice, has been broken into. The glove compartment has been rifled, and this is where you keep a checkbook, an extra key to the house, and where—you remember—you put the report due tomorrow at nine sharp. The glove compartment, how does it look? Like a part of your body, yes? A wound? From it spills a crumpled photo of your wife, who has asked you to move out so she can have the house, and another one of the children, who haven't the faintest idea how empty you feel getting up every morning to finance their lives at a job that is a ghastly joke, given your talents, where you can't slow down and at least four competitors stand waiting for you to step aside, fall on your face, or die, and the injustice of all this, what you see in the narrow range of radiation you call vision, in the velocity of ideation, is necessary and sufficient—as some logicians say—to bring your fists down again and again on the Fiat's roof. You climb inside, sit, furiously cranking the starter, then swear and lower your forehead to the steering wheel, which is, as anyone in Hollywood can tell you, conduct unbecoming a triple-threat talent like yourself: producer, star, and director in the longest, most fabulous show of all.

1986

EDWARD P. JONES
b. 1950

 Jones was born in Washington, D.C., and was educated at Holy Cross College and the University of Virginia. His first book, *Lost in the City*, a collection of short stories depicting the black working class in Washington, D.C., was published in 1992. It was nominated for the National Book Award and won the PEN/Hemingway Award for Best First Fiction. His second book, *The Known World* (2003), is a novel exploring a highly charged but little-examined facet of American history: the ownership of black slaves by free blacks before the Civil War. This book garnered Jones his second National Book Award nomination and the Pulitzer Prize. In 2005, Jones was awarded a MacArthur Fellowship and a collection of his short stories, *All Aunt Hager's Children*, appeared in 2006. He won the PEN/Malamud Award for Excellence in Short Fiction in 2010.

A New Man

One day in late October, Woodrow L. Cunningham came home early with his bad heart and found his daughter with the two boys. He was then fifty-two years old, a conscientious deacon at Rising Star AME Zion, a paid-up lifetime member of the NAACP and the Urban League,[1] a twenty-five-year member of the Elks. For ten years he had been the chief engineer at the Sheraton Park Hotel, where practically every employee knew his name. For longer than he could recall, his friends and lodge members had been telling him that he was capable of being more than just the number-one maintenance man. But he always told them that he was contented in the job, that it was all he needed, and this was true for the most part. He would be in that same position some thirteen years later, when death happened upon him as he bent down over a hotel bathroom sink, about to do a job a younger engineer claimed he could not handle.

The afternoon he came home early and discovered his daughter with the boys, he found a letter in the mailbox from his father in Georgia. He read the letter while standing in the hall of the apartment building. He expected nothing of importance, as usual, and that was what he found. "Alice took me to

1. Community service organization, founded in 1910, dedicated to ending racial discrimination in the United States. *NAACP:* the National Association for the Advancement of Colored People, founded in 1908 to promote social and political equality for African Americans. *AME Zion:* the African Methodist Episcopal Zion Church, a Methodist denomination founded by black American Methodists in 1796.

Buddy Wilson funeral just last week," Woodrow read. "I loaned him the shirt they buried him in. And that tie he had on was one that I give him too. I thought I would miss him but I do not miss him very much. Checkers was never Buddy Wilsons game." As he read, he massaged the area around his heart, an old habit, something he did even when his heart was not giving him trouble. "I hope you and the family can come down before the winter months set in. Company is never the same after winter get here."

He put the letter back in the envelope, and as he absently looked at the upside-down stamp taped in the vicinity of the corner, the pain in his heart eased. He could picture his father sitting at the kitchen table, writing the letter, occasionally touching the pencil point to his tongue. A new mongrel's head would be resting across his lap, across thin legs that could still carry the old man five miles down the road and back. Woodrow, feeling better, considered returning to work, but he knew his heart was deceitful. He folded the envelope and stuck it in his back pocket, and out of the pocket it would fall late that night as he prepared for bed after returning from the police station.

Several feet before he reached his apartment door he could hear the boys' laughter and bits and pieces of their man-child conquer-the-world talk. He could not hear his daughter at first. He stopped at his door and listened for nearly five minutes, and in that time he became so fascinated by what the boys were saying that he would not have cared if someone walking in the hall found him listening. It was only when he heard his daughter's laughter, familiar, known, that he put his key in the door. She stood just inside the door when he entered, her eyes accusing but her mouth set in a small O of surprise. Beyond her he could see the boys with their legs draped over the arms of the couch and gray smoke above their heads wafting toward the open window.

He asked his daughter, "Why ain't you in school?"

"They let us out early today," she said. "The teachers had some kinda meetin."

He did not listen to her, because he had found that she lived to lie. Woodrow watched the boys as they took their time straightening themselves up, and he knew that their deliberateness was the result of something his daughter had said about him. Without taking his eyes from the boys, he asked his daughter again why she wasn't in school. When he finally looked at her, he saw that she was holding the stump of a thin cigarette. The smoke he smelled was unfamiliar, and at first he thought that they were smoking very stale cigarettes, or cigarettes that had gotten wet and been dried. He slapped her. "I told you not to smoke in my house," he said.

She was fifteen, and up until six months or so before, she would have collapsed into the chair, collapsed into a fit of crying. But now she picked up the fallen cigarette from the floor and stamped it out in the ashtray on the tiny table beside the easy chair. Her hand shook, the only reminder of the old days. "We just talkin. We ain't doin nothin wrong," she said quietly.

He shouted to the boys, "Get outta my house!" They stood up quickly, and Woodrow could tell that whatever she had told them about him, such anger was not part of it. They looked once at the girl.

"They my guests, Daddy," she said, sitting in the easy chair and crossing her legs. "I invited em over here."

Woodrow took two steps to the boy nearest him—the tall light-skinned one he would spot from a bus window a year or so later—and grabbed him with one hand by the jacket collar, shook him until the boy raised his hands as if to protect his face from a blow. The boy's eyes widened and Woodrow shook him some more. He had been living a black man's civilized life in Washington and had not felt so coiled and bristled since the days when he worked with wild men in the turpentine camps in Florida. "I ain't done nothin," the boy said. The words sounded familiar, similar to those of a wild man ready to slink away into his cabin with his tail between his legs. Woodrow relaxed. "I swear. I don't want no trouble, Mr. Cunningham." The boy had no other smell but that peculiar cigarette smoke, and it was a shock to Woodrow that a body with that smell should know something that seemed as personal as his name. The other, smaller boy had tiptoed around Woodrow and was having trouble opening the door. After the small boy had gone out, Woodrow flung the light-skinned boy out behind him. Woodrow locked the door, and the boys stood for several minutes, pounding on the door, mouthing off.

"Why you treat my guests like that?" Elaine Cunningham had not moved from the chair.

"Clean up this mess," he told her, "and I don't wanna see one ash when you done."

She said nothing more, but busied herself tidying the couch cushions. Then Woodrow, after flicking the cushions a few times with his handkerchief, sat in the middle of the couch, and the couch sagged with the familiarity of this weight.

When Elaine had returned the room to what it was, her father said, "I want to know what you was doin in here with them boys."

"Nothin. We wasn't doin nothin. Just talkin, thas all, Daddy." She sat in the easy chair, leaned toward him with her elbows on her knees.

"You can do your talkin down on the stoop," he said.

"Why don't you just say you tryin to cuse me a somethin? Why don't you just come out and say it?"

"If you didn't do things, you wouldn't get accused," he said. He talked without thought, because those words and words like them had been spoken so much to her that he was able to parrot himself. "If you start actin like a young lady should, start studyin and what not, and tryin to make somethin of yourself . . ." Woodrow L. Cunningham bein Woodrow L. Cunningham, he thought.

She stood up quickly, and he was sickened to see her breasts bounce. "I could study them stupid books half the damn day and sit in church the other half, and I'd still get the same stuff thrown in my face bout how I ain't doin right."

"Okay, thas anough a that." He felt a familiar rumbling in his heart. "I done heard anough."

"I wanna go out," she stood with her arms folded. "I wanna go out."

"Go on back to your room. Thas the only goin out you gonna be doin. I don't wanna hear another word outta your mouth till your mother get home." He closed his eyes to wait her out, for he knew she was now capable of standing there till doomsday to sulk. When he heard her going down the hall, he waited for the door to slam. But there was no sound and he gradually opened his eyes. He put a cushion at one end of the couch and took off his shoes and lay down, his hands resting on the large mound that was his stomach. All his friends told him that if he lost thirty or forty pounds he would be a new man, but he did not think that was true. He considered asking Elaine to bring his pills from his bedroom, for he had left the vial he traveled with at work. But he suffered the pain rather than suffer her stirring about. He watched his wife's curtains flap gently with the breeze and the movement soothed him.

"I would not say anything bad about marriage," his father had written to Woodrow after Woodrow called to say he was considering marrying Rita Hadley. "It is easier to pick up and walk away from a wife and a family if you don't like it then you can walk away from your own bad cooking." Woodrow had never been inclined to marry anyone, was able, as he would tell his lodge brothers, to get all the trim he wanted without buying some woman a ring and walking down the aisle with her. "Doin it to a woman for a few months was all right," he would say, sounding like his father, "cause that only put the idea of marryin in their heads. Doin it to them any more than that and the idea take root."

It had never crossed his mind to sleep with any of the women at Rising Star AME, for he had discovered in Georgia that the wrath of church women was greater than that of all others, even old whores. He only went out with Rita because the preacher took him aside one Sunday and told him it was unnatural to go about unmarried and that he should give some thought to promenading with Sister Rita sometime. And, too, he was thirty-six and it was beginning to occur to him that women might not go on forever laying down and opening their legs for him. The second time they went out, he put his arm around Rita and pulled her to him there in the Booker-T Theater. She smacked his hand and that made his johnson hard. "I ain't like that, Mr. Cunningham." He had heard those words before. But when he pulled her to him again, she twisted his finger until it hurt. And that was something he had not experienced before.

His father suffered a mild stroke a week before the wedding. "Do not take this sicknes to mean that I do not send my blessing to your mariage to Miss Rita Hadley," his father said in a letter he had dictated to Alice, his oldest daughter. "God took pity on you when he send her your way." Even in the unfamiliarity of Alice's handwriting, the familiarity of his father was there in all the lines, right down to the misspelled words. Until some of his father's children learned in their teens, his father had been the only one in the family who could read and write. "This," he said of his reading and writing, "makes me as good as a white man." And before some of his children learned, discovered there was no magic to it, he enjoyed reading aloud at the supper table to his family, his voice stringing out a long monotone of words that often meant nothing to him and even less to his family because the man read so quickly.

His father read anything he could get his hands on—the words on feed bags, on medicine bottles, on years-old magazine pages they used for wallpaper, just about everything except the Bible. He had a fondness for weeks-old newspapers he would find in the streets when he went to town. No one—not even the squirming small kids—was allowed to move from the supper table until he had finished reading, hooking one word to another until it all became babble. Indeed, it was such a babble that some of his sons would joke behind his back that he was lying about knowing how to read. "Few white men can do what I'm doin right now," he would say. "You go bring ten white men in here and I bet nine couldn't read this. Couldn't read it if God commanded em to." Sometimes, to torment his wife, he would hold a scrap of newspaper close to her face and tell her to read the headlines. "I cain't," she would say. "You know I cain't." No matter how many times he did this, his father would laugh with the pleasure of the very first time. Then he would pass the newspaper among his children and tell them to read him the headlines, and each one would hold it uncomfortably and repeat what their mother had said.

When Woodrow woke, it was nearly five o'clock and his wife was sitting on the side of the couch, asking where Elaine was. "She ain't in her room," his wife said and kissed his forehead. A school cafeteria worker, Rita was a very thin woman who, before she met Woodrow, had lived only for her job and her church activities. She was five years older than he was and had resigned herself to the fact that she was not the type of woman men wanted to marry. "I've put it all in God's hands," she once said to a friend before Woodrow came along, "and left it there."

Rita waited until seven o'clock before she began calling her daughter's friends. "Stop worryin," Woodrow told her after the tenth call, "you know how that girl is." At eight-thirty, they put on light coats and went in search, visiting the same houses and apartments that Rita had called. They returned home about ten and waited until eleven, when they put on their coats again and went to the police station at 16th and V Northwest. They did not call the station because somewhere Woodrow had heard that the law wouldn't begin to hear a complaint unless you stood before it in person.

At the station, the man at the front desk did not look up until they had been standing there for some two minutes. Woodrow wanted to tell him that the police chief and the mayor were now black men and that they couldn't be ignored, but when the man behind the desk looked up, Woodrow could see in his eyes that none of that would have mattered to him.

"Our daughter is missing," Rita said.

"How long?" said the man, a sergeant with an unpronounceable name on his name tag. He pulled a form from a pile to his left and then he took up a pen, loudly clicking out the point to write.

"We haven't seen her since this afternoon," Woodrow says.

The sergeant clicked the pen again and set it on the desk, then put the form back on top with the others. "Not long enough," he said. "Has to be gone forty-eight hours. Till then she's missing, but she's not a missing person."

"She only a baby."

"How old?"

"Fifteen," Woodrow said.

"She's just a runaway," the sergeant said.

"She never run away before," Woodrow said. "This ain't like her, sergeant." Woodrow felt that like all white men, the man enjoyed having attention paid to his rank.

"Don't matter. She's probably waiting for you at home right now, wondering where you two buggied off to. Go home. If she isn't home, then come back when she's a missing person."

Woodrow took Rita's arm as they went back, because he sensed that she was near collapsing. "What happened?" she asked as they turned the corner of U and 10th streets. "Did you say somethin bad to her?"

He told her everything that he could remember, even what Elaine was wearing when he last saw her. Answering was not difficult because no blame had yet been assigned. Despite the time nearing midnight, they became confident with each step that Elaine was just at a friend's they did not know about, that the friend's mother, like any good mother, would soon send their daughter home. Rita, in the last blocks before their apartment, leaned into her husband and his warmth helped to put her at ease.

They waited up until about four in the morning, and then they undressed without words in the dark. Rita began to cry the moment her head hit the pillow, for she was afraid to see the sun come up and find that a new day had arrived without Elaine being home. She asked him again what happened, and he told her again, even things that he had forgotten—the logo of the football team on the light-skinned boy's jacket, the fact that the other boy was bald except for a half-dollar-sized spot of hair carved on the back of his head. He was still talking when she dozed off with him holding her.

Before they had coffee later that morning, about seven thirty, they called their jobs to say they would not be in. Work had always occupied a place at the center of their lives, and there was initially something eerie about being home when it was not a holiday or the weekend. They spent the rest of the morning searching the streets together, and in the afternoon, they separated to cover more ground. They did the same thing after dinner, each spreading out farther and farther from their apartment on R Street. That evening, they called neighbors and friends, church and lodge members, to tell them that their child was missing and that they needed their help and their prayers. Their friends and neighbors began searching that evening, and a few went with Woodrow and Rita the next day to the police station to file a missing person's report. A different sergeant was at the desk, and though he was a white man, Woodrow felt that he understood their trouble.

For nearly three months, Woodrow and Rita searched after they came from work, and each evening after they and their friends had been out, the pastor of Rising Star spoke to a small group that gathered in the Cunninghams' living room. "The world is cold and not hospitable," he would conclude, holding his hat in both hands, "but we know our God to be a kind God and that he has provided our little sister with a place of comfort and warmth until she returns to her parents and to all of us who love and treasure her."

In the kitchen beside the refrigerator, Rita tacked up a giant map of Washington, on which she noted where she and others had searched. "I didn't know the city was this big," she said the day she put it up, her fingertips touching the neighborhoods that she had never heard of or had heard of only in passing—foreign lands she thought she would never set eyes on. Petworth. Anacostia. Lincoln Park. And in the beginning, the very size of the city lifted her spirits, for in a place so big, there was certainly a spot that held something as small as her child, and if they just kept looking long enough, they would come upon that place.

"What happened?" Rita would ask as they prepared for bed. What he told her and her listening replaced everything they had ever done in that bed—discussing what future they wanted for Elaine, lovemaking, sharing what the world had done to them that workday. "What happened?" It was just about the only thing she ever asked Woodrow as the months grew colder. "What happened? Whatcha say to her?" By late February, when fewer and fewer people were going out to search, he had told the whole story, but then he began to tell her things that had not happened. There were three boys, he said at one point, for example. Or, he could see a gun sticking out of the jacket pocket of the light-skinned one, and he could see the outline of a knife in the back pants pocket of the third. Or he would say that the record player was playing so loudly he could hear it from the street. They were small embellishments at first, and if his wife noticed that the story of what happened was changing, she said nothing. In time, with winter disappearing, he was adding more and more so that it was no longer a falseness here and there that was embedded in the whole of the truth, but the truth itself, an ever-diminishing kernel, that was contained in the whole of falseness. And, like some kind of bedtime story, she listened and drifted with his words into a sleep where the things he was telling her were sometimes happening.

By March, Woodrow had written countless letters to his father telling the old man it was not necessary to come to Washington to help look for the girl. "I got a sign from God," the old man kept writing, "that I could help find her." Then, with spring, he began writing that he had received signs that he was not long for the world, that finding the girl was the last thing God wanted him to do. In the longest letters the old man had ever written to the one child of his who responded, he would go on and on about the signs he saw signaling his own death: The mongrel would no longer take food from his hand; the dead visited him at night, sitting down on the side of his bed and telling him things about himself; the rising sun now touched his house last in the morning, though there were houses to the left and right of his.

"You keep telling me that I'll be hurt or lost," the old man wrote Woodrow. "But I know the way that Washinton, D.C. is set up. I came there once maybe twice. How could I get lost. Take a chance on me, and we'll have that child home before you can blink one eye. I can bring Sparky he got some bloodhound in him."

In late April, Rita took down the map in the kitchen. The tacks fell to the floor and she left them there. She put the map in the bottom drawer of her daughter's dresser, among the blouses and blue jeans and a diary she would not find the strength to read for another three months. Her days of searching during the week dwindled down to two, then to one. She returned the car a church member had lent her to drive around the city in. Each evening when she got home, Woodrow would be out and she left his dinner in the oven to stay warm. Every now and again, when the hour was late, she went out to look for him, often for no other reason than that there was nothing worth watching on the television. As she put on more and more weight, it became difficult for her to stand and dish out food to the students at lunchtime. Her supervisor and fellow workers sympathized, and, after a week of perfunctory training, she was allowed to sit and work at the cash register.

As he continued going about the city, sometimes on foot, Woodrow told himself and everyone else that he was hunting for his daughter, but this was only a piece of the truth. "I'm lookin for my daughter, who's run away," he said to those opening the doors where he knocked. "She's been gone a long time, and her mama and me are about to lose our minds." He sometimes presented a picture of his daughter, smiling radiantly, that was taken only months before she disappeared. But just as often, he would pull out a photograph of the girl when she was five, standing one Easter between her parents in front of Rising Star. All who looked at the photograph, even the drunks half-blind with alcohol, were touched by the picture of the little girl in her Easter dress who had now gone away from her parents, parents who were now worried sick. Many people invited Woodrow into their homes.

The Easter picture became a passport, and the more places he visited the more places he wanted to see. On U Street, a woman of twenty-five or so with three children put down the child she was holding to get a better look at the picture of the five-year-old girl. Woodrow, in the doorway, noted just over her shoulder that on her wall there was a calendar with a snow-covered mountain, hung with the prominence others would have given a landscape painting. An old woman on Harvard Street, tsk-tsking as she looked at the picture, invited him in for coffee and cake. "My prayers go out to you." Nearly everything in her apartment was covered in plastic, even the pictures on the walls. The old woman sat him on her plastic-covered couch and placed the food on a coffee table covered with a plastic cloth. "And such a sweet-lookin child, too, son." When he asked to use the bathroom (more out of curiosity than for relief), she pointed to a plastic path leading away down the hall. "Stay on the mat, son."

A tottering man in a place on 21st Street just off Benning Road began to cry when Woodrow told him his story. "Dora, Dora," the man called to a woman. "Come see this little angel." The woman, who was also tottering, pulled Woodrow into their house with one hand, while the other hand pressed the picture to her bosom. The man and Woodrow sat on the couch. The woman stood in front of them, swaying trancelike, her eyes closed, the picture still pressed to her. The man put his arm around Woodrow and breathed a sour wine smell into his face. "Let's me and you pray about this situation," he said.

One April evening, a little more than a year and a half after their daughter disappeared, Rita was standing in front of their building, waiting for him. "We have fish tonight. It's in the stove waitin," she said, in the same way she would have said, "I know what you been doin. And who you been doin it with." "We have fish to eat," she said again. She turned around and went back inside. "We have fish, and we have to move from this place," she said.

Woodrow's father died nearly seven years after Elaine Cunningham disappeared. Of the eight children he had had with Woodrow's mother and the five he had had with other women, only Woodrow, Alice, and a half-brother who lived down the road from the old man came to the funeral. It was a frozen day in January, and the gravediggers broke two picks before they had even gone down one foot. They labored seven hours to make a hole for the old man. "Even the ground don't want him," said one of the old man's friends standing at the gravesite.

There was not much in the old man's place to divide among his heirs. In a wooden trunk in one of the back rooms, Woodrow found several pictures of his mother. He had been kneeling down, going through the trunk, and when he saw the pictures, he cried out as if he had been struck. He had not seen his mother's face in more than forty years, had thought his father had destroyed all the pictures of her. "You always looked like her," Alice said, coming up behind him. "Even when you sat at the right hand of the father, you looked like her."

Though he was younger than three other brothers, Woodrow had worked hardest of his father's children. At first, his father had sat his children about the supper table according to their ages, but then he began to seat them according to who did the most work. His best workers sat closest to him, and by the time he was seven, Woodrow had worked his way to the right hand of his father. Woodrow's mother sat at the far end of the table, between two of her daughters. Most of his brothers and sisters, unable to pick the amount of cotton Woodrow could, never forgave him for living only to be close to their father. But he learned to pay them no mind and even learned to enjoy their hostility. He never moved from that right-hand place until the day he went off down the road to work in the turpentine camps.

He also found in the trunk some letters he wrote his father from the camps and from railroad yards and from the places he worked as he made his way up to Washington. They were all of one page or less, and they were all about work, work from sunup to sundown. There were no friends mentioned, there were no descriptions of places where he lived, there were no names of women courted, loved. "I got a two-week job tanning hides," he wrote from a nameless place in South Carolina. "I got work cureing tobacco. I may stay on after the season," he wrote from somewhere near Raleigh. "I have been working in the stables outside Charlotesvile. The pay is good. I got used to the smell. and the work goes easy."

Woodrow and Rita took the train back to Washington, bringing back a few of the pictures and none of the letters, which he burned in a barrel outside his father's house. Everything along the way back to D.C. was as frozen as Georgia. It was as if the cold had separated the world into three unrelated and distinct parts—the earth, what was on the earth, and the sky above. Nothing moved. Flying birds seemed to freeze in midair, and then the cold would nail them there.

Rita and Woodrow were back in the apartment on Independence Avenue in Southeast[2] by ten o'clock that night. Rita took her usual place at an easy chair near the window. On a table beside the chair was all she needed—the television guide, snacks, the telephone. The chair was very large and had had to be specially ordered, because she could not fit into the regular ones in the store.

Woodrow, even though the hour was late and the weather people were predicting even colder temperatures, quietly put on his heaviest coat and left the apartment. He said nothing to Rita, and she did not look up when the door locked behind him. At the corner of Independence and 15th, Woodrow looked into the grocery store window at the owner he had become friends with since

---

2. The southeast quadrant of Washington, D.C.

moving to Southeast. No customers went into the store, and the owner was dozing behind the counter, his head back, his mouth open. Woodrow watched him for a very long time. By now he knew everything about the man and his store and the sons who helped the man, and there was no urgency to be inside with him. Having lost so much weight, Woodrow felt that even more of the world had opened up to him. And so he wondered if he should go on down 15th Street, try to find a house he had not visited before, and bring out the picture of the child in her Easter dress.

1993

RELATED:

—Jones on Frank O'Connor's "Guests of the Nation," p. 1765

JAMES JOYCE
1882–1941

Joyce was born in Dublin; and though he fled the narrowness of Catholic Ireland for the broader cultural horizons of Europe, the Dublin of his experience and imagination was the setting for all his major work. In 1904 he went to live permanently on the Continent, supporting himself and his family—barely—by teaching English in language schools in Trieste and Zurich. The fear of censorship, coupled with the timidity of his publisher, delayed until 1914 the publication of his short stories in *Dubliners*. Soon after this, however, Joyce came to the attention of the energetic American poet Ezra Pound, who arranged for the first publication of *A Portrait of the Artist as a Young Man* (1916), Joyce's semiautobiographical novel. Pound's support continued through the following years while Joyce was writing what is generally acknowledged as his masterpiece, the novel *Ulysses* (1922). When parts of it began to appear in a literary magazine, it touched off a storm of controversy that brought him both notoriety and lasting fame. On the one hand, this work experimented more boldly with language and narration, including use of the stream of consciousness, than any work in English that preceded it. On the other, some of the sexual passages were so candid that until 1933 censors banned it from the United States. Joyce continued to explore the resources of language in his years of fame, these experiments reaching their height in the monumentally complex novel *Finnegans Wake* (1939).

Araby

North Richmond Street, being blind, was a quiet street except at the hour when the Christian Brothers' School set the boys free. An uninhabited house of two storeys stood at the blind end, detached from its neighbours in a square ground. The other houses of the street, conscious of decent lives within them, gazed at one another with brown imperturbable faces.

The former tenant of our house, a priest, had died in the back drawing-room. Air, musty from having been long enclosed, hung in all the rooms, and the waste room behind the kitchen was littered with old useless papers. Among these I found a few paper-covered books, the pages of which were curled and damp: *The Abbot,* by Walter Scott, *The Devout Communicant* and

The Memoirs of Vidocq.[1] I liked the last best because its leaves were yellow. The wild garden behind the house contained a central apple-tree and a few straggling bushes under one of which I found the late tenant's rusty bicycle-pump. He had been a very charitable priest; in his will he had left all his money to institutions and the furniture of his house to his sister.

When the short days of winter came dusk fell before we had well eaten our dinners. When we met in the street the houses had grown sombre. The space of sky above us was the colour of ever-changing violet and towards it the lamps of the street lifted their feeble lanterns. The cold air stung us and we played till our bodies glowed. Our shouts echoed in the silent street. The career of our play brought us through the dark muddy lanes behind the houses where we ran the gantlet of the rough tribes from the cottages,[2] to the back doors of the dark dripping gardens where odours arose from the ashpits, to the dark odorous stables where a coachman smoothed and combed the horse or shook music from the buckled harness. When we returned to the street light from the kitchen windows had filled the areas. If my uncle was seen turning the corner we hid in the shadow until we had seen him safely housed. Or if Mangan's sister came out on the doorstep to call her brother in to his tea we watched her from our shadow peer up and down the street. We waited to see whether she would remain or go in and, if she remained, we left our shadow and walked up to Mangan's steps resignedly. She was waiting for us, her figure defined by the light from the half-opened door. Her brother always teased her before he obeyed and I stood by the railings looking at her. Her dress swung as she moved her body and the soft rope of her hair tossed from side to side.

Every morning I lay on the floor in the front parlour watching her door. The blind was pulled down to within an inch of the sash so that I could not be seen. When she came out on the doorstep my heart leaped. I ran to the hall, seized my books and followed her. I kept her brown figure always in my eye and, when we came near the point at which our ways diverged, I quickened my pace and passed her. This happened morning after morning. I had never spoken to her, except for a few casual words, and yet her name was like a summons to all my foolish blood.

Her image accompanied me even in places the most hostile to romance. On Saturday evenings when my aunt went marketing I had to go to carry some of the parcels. We walked through the flaring streets, jostled by drunken men and bargaining women, amid the curses of labourers, the shrill litanies of shop-boys who stood on guard by the barrels of pigs' cheeks, the nasal chanting of street-singers, who sang a *come-all-you* about O'Donovan Rossa,[3] or a ballad about the troubles in our native land. These noises converged in a single sensation of life for me: I imagined that I bore my chalice safely through a throng of foes. Her name sprang to my lips at moments in strange prayers and praises which I myself did not understand. My eyes were often full of tears (I could not tell why) and at times a flood from my heart seemed to pour

---

1. Eugène François Vidocq (1775–1857), French detective. *The Devout Communicant:* Roman Catholic devotional manual. *The Abbot:* a novel published in 1820 by Sir Walter Scott (1771–1832), Scottish, novelist and poet. **2.** That is, from a Dublin slum district. **3.** Jeremiah O'Donovan ("O'Dynamite") Rossa (1831–1915), an Irish nationalist banished to the United States in 1870 for revolutionary activities. *Come-all-you:* any popular song beginning "Come all you Irishmen."

itself out into my bosom. I thought little of the future. I did not know whether I would ever speak to her or not or, if I spoke to her, how I could tell her of my confused adoration. But my body was like a harp and her words and gestures were like fingers running upon the wires.

One evening I went into the back drawing-room in which the priest had died. It was a dark rainy evening and there was no sound in the house. Through one of the broken panes I heard the rain impinge upon the earth, the fine incessant needles of water playing in the sodden beds. Some distant lamp or lighted window gleamed below me. I was thankful that I could see so little. All my senses seemed to desire to veil themselves and, feeling that I was about to slip from them, I pressed the palms of my hands together until they trembled, murmuring: *O love! O love!* many times.

At last she spoke to me. When she addressed the first words to me I was so confused that I did not know what to answer. She asked me was I going to *Araby*.[4] I forget whether I answered yes or no. It would be a splendid bazaar, she said; she would love to go.

—And why can't you? I asked.

While she spoke she turned a silver bracelet round and round her wrist. She could not go, she said, because there would be a retreat[5] that week in her convent. Her brother and two other boys were fighting for their caps and I was alone at the railings. She held one of the spikes, bowing her head towards me. The light from the lamp opposite our door caught the white curve of her neck, lit up her hair that rested there and, falling, lit up the hand upon the railing. It fell over one side of her dress and caught the white border of a petticoat, just visible as she stood at ease.

—It's well for you, she said.

—If I go, I said, I will bring you something.

What innumerable follies laid waste my waking and sleeping thoughts after that evening! I wished to annihilate the tedious intervening days. I chafed against the work of school. At night in my bedroom and by day in the classroom her image came between me and the page I strove to read. The syllables of the word *Araby* were called to me through the silence in which my soul luxuriated and cast an Eastern enchantment over me. I asked for leave to go to the bazaar on Saturday night. My aunt was surprised and hoped it was not some Freemason[6] affair. I answered few questions in class. I watched my master's face pass from amiability to sternness; he hoped I was not beginning to idle. I could not call my wandering thoughts together. I had hardly any patience with the serious work of life which, now that it stood between me and my desire, seemed to me child's play, ugly monotonous child's play.

On Saturday morning I reminded my uncle that I wished to go to the bazaar in the evening. He was fussing at the hallstand, looking for the hatbrush, and answered me curtly:

—Yes, boy, I know.

---

4. A billboard sign of the time actually reads: "ARABY in DUBLIN Official Catalogue GRAND ORIENTAL FÊTE May 14th to 19th in aid of Jervis St. Hospital. Admission one shilling." A British shilling, 1/20 of a pound sterling, would be worth about $5 in 2000s U.S. currency. **5.** A gathering for prayer and meditation in her convent school. **6.** The Masonic Order was felt by Catholics to be an enemy of the Church.

As he was in the hall I could not go into the front parlour and lie at the window. I left the house in bad humour and walked slowly towards the school. The air was pitilessly raw and already my heart misgave me.

When I came home to dinner my uncle had not yet been home. Still it was early. I sat staring at the clock for some time and, when its ticking began to irritate me, I left the room. I mounted the staircase and gained the upper part of the house. The high cold empty gloomy rooms liberated me and I went from room to room singing. From the front window I saw my companions playing below in the street. Their cries reached me weakened and indistinct and, leaning my forehead against the cool glass, I looked over at the dark house where she lived. I may have stood there for an hour, seeing nothing but the brown-clad figure cast by my imagination, touched discreetly by the lamplight at the curved neck, at the hand upon the railings and at the border below the dress.

When I came downstairs again I found Mrs. Mercer sitting at the fire. She was an old garrulous woman, a pawnbroker's widow, who collected used stamps for some pious purpose. I had to endure the gossip of the tea-table. The meal was prolonged beyond an hour and still my uncle did not come. Mrs. Mercer stood up to go: she was sorry she couldn't wait any longer, but it was after eight o'clock and she did not like to be out late, as the night air was bad for her. When she had gone I began to walk up and down the room, clenching my fists. My aunt said:

—I'm afraid you may put off your bazaar for this night of Our Lord.

At nine o'clock I heard my uncle's latchkey in the halldoor. I heard him talking to himself and heard the hallstand rocking when it had received the weight of his overcoat. I could interpret these signs. When he was midway through his dinner I asked him to give me the money to go to the bazaar. He had forgotten.

—The people are in bed and after their first sleep now, he said.

I did not smile. My aunt said to him energetically:

—Can't you give him the money and let him go? You've kept him late enough as it is.

My uncle said he was very sorry he had forgotten. He said he believed in the old saying: *All work and no play makes Jack a dull boy*. He asked me where I was going and, when I had told him a second time he asked me did I know *The Arab's Farewell to His Steed*.[7] When I left the kitchen he was about to recite the opening lines of the piece to my aunt.

I held a florin[8] tightly in my hand as I strode down Buckingham Street towards the station. The sight of the streets thronged with buyers and glaring with gas recalled to me the purpose of my journey. I took my seat in a third-class carriage of a deserted train. After an intolerable delay the train moved out of the station slowly. It crept onward among ruinous houses and over the twinkling river. At Westland Row Station a crowd of people pressed to the carriage doors; but the porters moved them back, saying that it was a special train for the bazaar. I remained alone in the bare carriage. In a few minutes the train drew up beside an improvised wooden platform. I passed out on to

---

7. Sentimental poem by Caroline Norton (1808–1877). The Arab imagines his heartbreak after selling his favorite horse.   **8.** A two-shilling piece, worth four times the "sixpenny entrance" fee.

the road and saw by the lighted dial of a clock that it was ten minutes to ten. In front of me was a large building which displayed the magical name.

I could not find any sixpenny entrance and, fearing that the bazaar would be closed, I passed in quickly through a turnstile, handing a shilling to a weary-looking man. I found myself in a big hall girdled at half its height by a gallery. Nearly all the stalls were closed and the greater part of the hall was in darkness. I recognised a silence like that which pervades a church after a service. I walked into the centre of the bazaar timidly. A few people were gathered about the stalls which were still open. Before a curtain, over which the words *Café Chantant*[9] were written in coloured lamps, two men were counting money on a salver. I listened to the fall of the coins.

Remembering with difficulty why I had come I went over to one of the stalls and examined porcelain vases and flowered tea-sets. At the door of the stall a young lady was talking and laughing with two young gentlemen. I remarked their English accents and listened vaguely to their conversation.

—O, I never said such a thing!

—O, but you did!

—O, but I didn't!

—Didn't she say that?

—Yes. I heard her.

—O, there's a . . . fib!

Observing me the young lady came over and asked me did I wish to buy anything. The tone of her voice was not encouraging; she seemed to have spoken to me out of a sense of duty. I looked humbly at the great jars that stood like eastern guards at either side of the dark entrance to the stall and murmured:

—No, thank you.

The young lady changed the position of one of the vases and went back to the two young men. They began to talk of the same subject. Once or twice the young lady glanced at me over her shoulder.

I lingered before her stall, though I knew my stay was useless, to make my interest in her wares seem the more real. Then I turned away slowly and walked down the middle of the bazaar. I allowed the two pennies to fall against the sixpence in my pocket. I heard a voice call from one end of the gallery that the light was out. The upper part of the hall was now completely dark.

Gazing up into the darkness I saw myself as a creature driven and derided by vanity; and my eyes burned with anguish and anger.

1914

The Dead

Lily, the caretaker's daughter, was literally run off her feet. Hardly had she brought one gentleman into the little pantry behind the office on the ground floor and helped him off with his overcoat than the wheezy hall-door bell

---

9. Café offering musical entertainment.

clanged again and she had to scamper along the bare hallway to let in another guest. It was well for her she had not to attend to the ladies also. But Miss Kate and Miss Julia had thought of that and had converted the bathroom upstairs into a ladies' dressing-room. Miss Kate and Miss Julia were there, gossiping and laughing and fussing, walking after each other to the head of the stairs, peering down over the banisters and calling down to Lily to ask her who had come.

It was always a great affair, the Misses Morkan's annual dance. Everybody who knew them came to it, members of the family, old friends of the family, the members of Julia's choir, any of Kate's pupils that were grown up enough and even some of Mary Jane's pupils too. Never once had it fallen flat. For years and years it had gone off in splendid style as long as anyone could remember; ever since Kate and Julia, after the death of their brother Pat, had left the house in Stoney Batter and taken Mary Jane, their only niece, to live with them in the dark gaunt house on Usher's Island,[1] the upper part of which they had rented from Mr. Fulham, the cornfactor[2] on the ground floor. That was a good thirty years ago if it was a day. Mary Jane, who was then a little girl in short clothes, was now the main prop of the household for she had the organ in Haddington Road. She had been through the Academy and gave a pupils' concert every year in the upper room of the Antient Concert Rooms.[3] Many of her pupils belonged to better-class families on the Kingstown and Dalkey line. Old as they were, her aunts also did their share. Julia, though she was quite grey, was still the leading soprano in Adam and Eve's,[4] and Kate, being too feeble to go about much, gave music lessons to beginners on the old square piano in the back room. Lily, the caretaker's daughter, did housemaid's work for them. Though their life was modest they believed in eating well; the best of everything: diamond-bone sirloins, three-shilling tea and the best bottled stout. But Lily seldom made a mistake in the orders so that she got on well with her three mistresses. They were fussy, that was all. But the only thing they would not stand was back answers.

Of course they had good reason to be fussy on such a night. And then it was long after ten o'clock and yet there was no sign of Gabriel and his wife. Besides they were dreadfully afraid that Freddy Malins might turn up screwed.[5] They would not wish for worlds that any of Mary Jane's pupils should see him under the influence; and when he was like that it was sometimes very hard to manage him. Freddy Malins always came late but they wondered what could be keeping Gabriel: and that was what brought them every two minutes to the banisters to ask Lily had Gabriel or Freddy come.

—O, Mr. Conroy, said Lily to Gabriel when she opened the door for him, Miss Kate and Miss Julia thought you were never coming. Good-night, Mrs. Conroy.

—I'll engage they did, said Gabriel, but they forget that my wife here takes three mortal hours to dress herself.

---

1. Dublin street on the south bank of the river Liffey. *Stoney Batter*: Dublin neighborhood.   **2.** Agent or broker dealing in grain.   **3.** A building in which rooms could be rented for musical or dramatic productions. *The Academy*: the Royal Academy of Music.   **4.** A Dublin church.   **5.** Drunk.

He stood on the mat, scraping the snow from his goloshes, while Lily led his wife to the foot of the stairs and called out:

—Miss Kate, here's Mrs. Conroy.

Kate and Julia came toddling down the dark stairs at once. Both of them kissed Gabriel's wife, said she must be perished alive and asked was Gabriel with her.

—Here I am as right as the mail, Aunt Kate! Go on up. I'll follow, called out Gabriel from the dark.

He continued scraping his feet vigorously while the three women went upstairs, laughing, to the ladies' dressing-room. A light fringe of snow lay like a cape on the shoulders of his overcoat and like toecaps on the toes of his goloshes; and, as the buttons of his overcoat slipped with a squeaking noise through the snow-stiffened frieze, a cold fragrant air from out-of-doors escaped from crevices and folds.

—Is it snowing again, Mr. Conroy? asked Lily.

She had preceded him into the pantry to help him off with his overcoat. Gabriel smiled at the three syllables she had given his surname and glanced at her. She was a slim, growing girl, pale in complexion and with hay-coloured hair. The gas in the pantry made her look still paler. Gabriel had known her when she was a child and used to sit on the lowest step nursing a rag doll.

—Yes, Lily, he answered, and I think we're in for a night of it.

He looked up at the pantry ceiling, which was shaking with the stamping and shuffling of feet on the floor above, listened for a moment to the piano and then glanced at the girl, who was folding his overcoat carefully at the end of a shelf.

—Tell me, Lily, he said in a friendly tone, do you still go to school?

—O no, sir, she answered. I'm done schooling this year and more.

—O, then, said Gabriel gaily, I suppose we'll be going to your wedding one of these fine days with your young man, eh?

The girl glanced back at him over her shoulder and said with great bitterness:

—The men that is now is only all palaver and what they can get out of you.

Gabriel coloured as if he felt he had made a mistake and, without looking at her, kicked off his goloshes and flicked actively with his muffler at his patent-leather shoes.

He was a stout tallish young man. The high colour of his cheeks pushed upwards even to his forehead where it scattered itself in a few formless patches of pale red; and on his hairless face there scintillated restlessly the polished lenses and the bright gilt rims of the glasses which screened his delicate and restless eyes. His glossy black hair was parted in the middle and brushed in a long curve behind his ears where it curled slightly beneath the groove left by his hat.

When he had flicked lustre into his shoes he stood up and pulled his waist-coat down more tightly on his plump body. Then he took a coin rapidly from his pocket.

—O Lily, he said, thrusting it into her hands, it's Christmas-time, isn't it? Just . . . here's a little. . . .

He walked rapidly towards the door.

—O no, sir! cried the girl, following him. Really, sir, I wouldn't take it.

—Christmas-time! Christmas-time! said Gabriel, almost trotting to the stairs and waving his hand to her in deprecation.

The girl, seeing that he had gained the stairs, called out after him:

—Well, thank you, sir.

He waited outside the drawing-room door until the waltz should finish, listening to the skirts that swept against it and to the shuffling of feet. He was still discomposed by the girl's bitter and sudden retort. It had cast a gloom over him which he tried to dispel by arranging his cuffs and the bows of his tie. Then he took from his waistcoat pocket a little paper and glanced at the headings he had made for his speech. He was undecided about the lines from Robert Browning[6] for he feared they would be above the heads of his hearers. Some quotation that they could recognise from Shakespeare or from the Melodies[7] would be better. The indelicate clacking of the men's heels and the shuffling of their soles reminded him that their grade of culture differed from his. He would only make himself ridiculous by quoting poetry to them which they could not understand. They would think that he was airing his superior education. He would fail with them just as he had failed with the girl in the pantry. He had taken up a wrong tone. His whole speech was a mistake from first to last, an utter failure.

Just then his aunts and his wife came out of the ladies' dressing-room. His aunts were two small plainly dressed old women. Aunt Julia was an inch or so the taller. Her hair, drawn low over the tops of her ears, was grey; and grey also, with darker shadows, was her large flaccid face. Though she was stout in build and stood erect her slow eyes and parted lips gave her the appearance of a woman who did not know where she was or where she was going. Aunt Kate was more vivacious. Her face, healthier than her sister's, was all puckers and creases, like a shrivelled red apple, and her hair, braided in the same old-fashioned way, had not lost its ripe nut colour.

They both kissed Gabriel frankly. He was their favourite nephew, the son of their dead elder sister, Ellen, who had married T. J. Conroy of the Port and Docks.[8]

—Gretta tells me you're not going to take a cab back to Monkstown[9] tonight, Gabriel, said Aunt Kate.

—No, said Gabriel, turning to his wife, we had quite enough of that last year, hadn't we? Don't you remember, Aunt Kate, what a cold Gretta got out of it? Cab windows rattling all the way, and the east wind blowing in after we passed Merrion. Very jolly it was. Gretta caught a dreadful cold.

Aunt Kate frowned severely and nodded her head at every word.

—Quite right, Gabriel, quite right, she said. You can't be too careful.

—But as for Gretta there, said Gabriel, she'd walk home in the snow if she were let.

Mrs. Conroy laughed.

—Don't mind him, Aunt Kate, she said. He's really an awful bother, what with green shades for Tom's eyes at night and making him do the dumb-bells,

6. English poet (1812–1889). **7.** The *Irish Melodies* by Thomas Moore (1779–1852), Irish poet. **8.** Government bureau. **9.** Seaside district of southeast Dublin.

and forcing Eva to eat the stirabout.[1] The poor child! And she simply hates the sight of it! . . . O, but you'll never guess what he makes me wear now!

She broke out into a peal of laughter and glanced at her husband, whose admiring and happy eyes had been wandering from her dress to her face and hair. The two aunts laughed heartily too, for Gabriel's solicitude was a standing joke with them.

—Goloshes! said Mrs. Conroy. That's the latest. Whenever it's wet underfoot I must put on my goloshes. To-night even he wanted me to put them on, but I wouldn't. The next thing he'll buy me will be a diving suit.

Gabriel laughed nervously and patted his tie reassuringly while Aunt Kate nearly doubled herself, so heartily did she enjoy the joke. The smile soon faded from Aunt Julia's face and her mirthless eyes were directed towards her nephew's face. After a pause she asked:

—And what are goloshes, Gabriel?

—Goloshes, Julia! exclaimed her sister. Goodness me, don't you know what goloshes are? You wear them over your . . . over your boots, Gretta, isn't it?

—Yes, said Mrs. Conroy. Guttapercha[2] things. We both have a pair now. Gabriel says everyone wears them on the continent.

—O, on the continent, murmured Aunt Julia, nodding her head slowly.

Gabriel knitted his brows and said, as if he were slightly angered:

—It's nothing very wonderful but Gretta thinks it very funny because she says the word reminds her of Christy Minstrels.[3]

—But tell me, Gabriel, said Aunt Kate, with brisk tact. Of course, you've seen about the room. Gretta was saying . . .

—O, the room is all right, replied Gabriel. I've taken one in the Gresham.[4]

—To be sure, said Aunt Kate, by far the best thing to do. And the children, Gretta, you're not anxious about them?

—O, for one night, said Mrs. Conroy. Besides, Bessie will look after them.

—To be sure, said Aunt Kate again. What a comfort it is to have a girl like that, one you can depend on! There's that Lily, I'm sure I don't know what has come over her lately. She's not the girl she was at all.

Gabriel was about to ask his aunt some questions on this point but she broke off suddenly to gaze after her sister who had wandered down the stairs and was craning her neck over the banisters.

—Now, I ask you, she said, almost testily, where is Julia going? Julia! Julia! Where are you going?

Julia, who had gone halfway down one flight, came back and announced blandly:

—Here's Freddy.

At the same moment a clapping of hands and a final flourish of the pianist told that the waltz had ended. The drawing-room door was opened from within and some couples came out. Aunt Kate drew Gabriel aside hurriedly and whispered into his ear:

—Slip down, Gabriel, like a good fellow and see if he's all right, and don't let him up if he's screwed. I'm sure he's screwed. I'm sure he is.

---

1. Porridge.   **2.** Material similar to rubber.   **3.** Well-known 19th-century minstrel show organized by Edwin P. Christy (1815–1862), American showman.   **4.** Historic hotel in downtown Dublin.

Gabriel went to the stairs and listened over the banisters. He could hear two persons talking in the pantry. Then he recognised Freddy Malins' laugh. He went down the stairs noisily.

—It's such a relief, said Aunt Kate to Mrs. Conroy, that Gabriel is here. I always feel easier in my mind when he's here. . . . Julia, there's Miss Daly and Miss Power will take some refreshment. Thanks for your beautiful waltz, Miss Daly. It made lovely time.

A tall wizen-faced man, with a stiff grizzled moustache and swarthy skin, who was passing out with his partner said:

—And may we have some refreshment, too, Miss Morkan?

—Julia, said Aunt Kate summarily, and here's Mr. Browne and Miss Furlong. Take them in, Julia, with Miss Daly and Miss Power.

—I'm the man for the ladies, said Mr. Browne, pursing his lips until his moustache bristled and smiling in all his wrinkles. You know, Miss Morkan, the reason they are so fond of me is—

He did not finish his sentence, but, seeing that Aunt Kate was out of earshot, at once led the three young ladies into the back room. The middle of the room was occupied by two square tables placed end to end, and on these Aunt Julia and the caretaker were straightening and smoothing a large cloth. On the sideboard were arrayed dishes and plates, and glasses and bundles of knives and forks and spoons. The top of the closed square piano served also as a sideboard for viands and sweets. At a smaller sideboard in one corner two young men were standing, drinking hop-bitters.[5]

Mr. Browne led his charges thither and invited them all, in jest, to some ladies' punch, hot, strong and sweet. As they said they never took anything strong he opened three bottles of lemonade for them. Then he asked one of the young men to move aside, and, taking hold of the decanter, filled out for himself a goodly measure of whisky. The young men eyed him respectfully while he took a trial sip.

—God help me, he said, smiling, it's the doctor's orders.

His wizened face broke into a broader smile, and the three young ladies laughed in musical echo to his pleasantry, swaying their bodies to and fro, with nervous jerks of their shoulders. The boldest said:

—O, now, Mr. Browne, I'm sure the doctor never ordered anything of the kind.

Mr. Browne took another sip of his whisky and said, with sidling mimicry:

—Well, you see, I'm like the famous Mrs. Cassidy, who is reported to have said: *Now, Mary Grimes, if I don't take it, make me take it, for I feel I want it.*

His hot face had leaned forward a little too confidentially and he had assumed a very low Dublin accent so that the young ladies, with one instinct, received his speech in silence. Miss Furlong, who was one of Mary Jane's pupils, asked Miss Daly what was the name of the pretty waltz she had played; and Mr. Browne, seeing that he was ignored, turned promptly to the two young men who were more appreciative.

A red-faced young woman, dressed in pansy, came into the room, excitedly clapping her hands and crying:

—Quadrilles![6] Quadrilles!

---

5. Kind of ale. 6. Square dances.

Close on her heels came Aunt Kate, crying:

—Two gentlemen and three ladies, Mary Jane!

—O, here's Mr. Bergin and Mr. Kerrigan, said Mary Jane. Mr. Kerrigan, will you take Miss Power? Miss Furlong, may I get you a partner, Mr. Bergin. O, that'll just do now.

—Three ladies, Mary Jane, said Aunt Kate.

The two young gentlemen asked the ladies if they might have the pleasure, and Mary Jane turned to Miss Daly.

—O, Miss Daly, you're really awfully good, after playing for the last two dances, but really we're so short of ladies to-night.

—I don't mind in the least, Miss Morkan.

—But I've a nice partner for you, Mr. Bartell D'Arcy, the tenor. I'll get him to sing later on. All Dublin is raving about him.

—Lovely voice, lovely voice! said Aunt Kate.

As the piano had twice begun the prelude to the first figure Mary Jane led her recruits quickly from the room. They had hardly gone when Aunt Julia wandered slowly into the room, looking behind her at something.

—What is the matter, Julia? asked Aunt Kate anxiously. Who is it?

Julia, who was carrying in a column of table-napkins, turned to her sister and said, simply, as if the question had surprised her:

—It's only Freddy, Kate, and Gabriel with him.

In fact right behind her Gabriel could be seen piloting Freddy Malins across the landing. The latter, a young man of about forty, was of Gabriel's size and build, with very round shoulders. His face was fleshy and pallid, touched with colour only at the thick hanging lobes of his ears and at the wide wings of his nose. He had coarse features, a blunt nose, a convex and receding brow, tumid and protruded lips. His heavy-lidded eyes and the disorder of his scanty hair made him look sleepy. He was laughing heartily in a high key at a story which he had been telling Gabriel on the stairs and at the same time rubbing the knuckles of his left fist backwards and forwards into his left eye.

—Good-evening, Freddy, said Aunt Julia.

Freddy Malins bade the Misses Morkan good-evening in what seemed an offhand fashion by reason of the habitual catch in his voice and then, seeing that Mr. Browne was grinning at him from the sideboard, crossed the room on rather shaky legs and began to repeat in an undertone the story he had just told to Gabriel.

—He's not so bad, is he? said Aunt Kate to Gabriel.

Gabriel's brows were dark but he raised them quickly and answered:

—O no, hardly noticeable.

—Now, isn't he a terrible fellow! she said. And his poor mother made him take the pledge[7] on New Year's Eve. But come on, Gabriel, into the drawing-room.

Before leaving the room with Gabriel she signalled to Mr. Browne by frowning and shaking her forefinger in warning to and fro. Mr. Browne nodded in answer and, when she had gone, said to Freddy Malins:

—Now, then, Teddy, I'm going to fill you out a good glass of lemonade just to buck you up.

---

7. A formal pledge not to drink.

Freddy Malins, who was nearing the climax of his story, waved the offer aside impatiently but Mr. Browne, having first called Freddy Malins' attention to a disarray in his dress, filled out and handed him a full glass of lemonade. Freddy Malins' left hand accepted the glass mechanically, his right hand being engaged in the mechanical readjustment of his dress. Mr. Browne, whose face was once more wrinkling with mirth, poured out for himself a glass of whisky while Freddy Malins exploded, before he had well reached the climax of his story, in a kink of high-pitched bronchitic laughter and, setting down his untasted and overflowing glass, began to rub the knuckles of his left fist backwards and forwards into his left eye, repeating words of his last phrase as well as his fit of laughter would allow him.

Gabriel could not listen while Mary Jane was playing her Academy piece, full of runs and difficult passages, to the hushed drawing-room. He liked music but the piece she was playing had no melody for him and he doubted whether it had any melody for the other listeners, though they had begged Mary Jane to play something. Four young men, who had come from the refreshment-room to stand in the doorway at the sound of the piano, had gone away quietly in couples after a few minutes. The only persons who seemed to follow the music were Mary Jane herself, her hands racing along the key-board or lifted from it at the pauses like those of a priestess in momentary imprecation, and Aunt Kate standing at her elbow to turn the page.

Gabriel's eyes, irritated by the floor, which glittered with beeswax under the heavy chandelier, wandered to the wall above the piano. A picture of the balcony scene in *Romeo and Juliet* hung there and beside it was a picture of the two murdered princes[8] in the Tower which Aunt Julia had worked in red, blue and brown wools when she was a girl. Probably in the school they had gone to as girls that kind of work had been taught, for one year his mother had worked for him as a birthday present a waistcoat of purple tabinet, with little foxes' heads upon it, lined with brown satin and having round mulberry buttons. It was strange that his mother had had no musical talent though Aunt Kate used to call her the brains carrier of the Morkan family. Both she and Julia had always seemed a little proud of their serious and matronly sister. Her photograph stood before the pierglass.[9] She held an open book on her knees and was pointing out something in it to Constantine who, dressed in a mano'-war suit,[1] lay at her feet. It was she who had chosen the names for her sons for she was very sensible of the dignity of family life. Thanks to her, Constantine was now senior curate in Balbriggan and, thanks to her, Gabriel himself had taken his degree in the Royal University. A shadow passed over his face as he remembered her sullen opposition to his marriage. Some slighting phrases she had used still rankled in his memory; she had once spoken of Gretta as being country cute and that was not true of Gretta at all. It was Gretta who had nursed her during all her last long illness in their house at Monkstown.

He knew that Mary Jane must be near the end of her piece for she was playing again the opening melody with runs of scales after every bar and while he

---

8. Edward and Richard, sons of King Edward IV of England. The two princes were reputedly murdered by order of King Richard III. **9.** A tall mirror. **1.** Sailor suit.

waited for the end the resentment died down in his heart. The piece ended with a trill of octaves in the treble and a final deep octave in the bass. Great applause greeted Mary Jane as, blushing and rolling up her music nervously, she escaped from the room. The most vigorous clapping came from the four young men in the doorway who had gone away to the refreshment-room at the beginning of the piece but had come back when the piano had stopped.

Lancers[2] were arranged. Gabriel found himself partnered with Miss Ivors. She was a frank-mannered talkative young lady, with a freckled face and prominent brown eyes. She did not wear a low-cut bodice and the large brooch which was fixed in the front of her collar bore on it an Irish device.

When they had taken their places she said abruptly:

—I have a crow to pluck with you.[3]

—With me? said Gabriel.

She nodded her head gravely.

—What is it? asked Gabriel, smiling at her solemn manner.

—Who is G. C.? answered Miss Ivors, turning her eyes upon him.

Gabriel coloured and was about to knit his brows, as if he did not understand, when she said bluntly:

—O, innocent Amy! I have found out that you write for *The Daily Express*.[4] Now, aren't you ashamed of yourself?

—Why should I be ashamed of myself? asked Gabriel, blinking his eyes and trying to smile.

—Well, I'm ashamed of you, said Miss Ivors frankly. To say you'd write for a rag like that. I didn't think you were a West Briton.[5]

A look of perplexity appeared on Gabriel's face. It was true that he wrote a literary column every Wednesday in *The Daily Express,* for which he was paid fifteen shillings. But that did not make him a West Briton surely. The books he received for review were almost more welcome than the paltry cheque. He loved to feel the covers and turn over the pages of newly printed books. Nearly every day when his teaching in the college[6] was ended he used to wander down the quays to the second-hand booksellers, to Hickey's on Bachelor's Walk, to Webb's or Massey's on Aston's Quay, or to O'Clohissey's in the by-street. He did not know how to meet her charge. He wanted to say that literature was above politics. But they were friends of many years' standing and their careers had been parallel, first at the University and then as teachers: he could not risk a grandiose phrase with her. He continued blinking his eyes and trying to smile and murmured lamely that he saw nothing political in writing reviews of books.

When their turn to cross had come he was still perplexed and inattentive. Miss Ivors promptly took his hand in a warm grasp and said in a soft friendly tone:

—Of course, I was only joking. Come, we cross now.

When they were together again she spoke of the University question[7] and Gabriel felt more at ease. A friend of hers had shown her his review of

---

2. A set of quadrilles, danced in sequence. **3.** That is, "I have a bone to pick." **4.** A newspaper opposed to Irish liberation from Great Britain. **5.** In context this means he considers himself British rather than Irish. **6.** In Britain and Ireland, a secondary-level school, not university-level. **7.** The issue was whether to provide equal educational opportunities for Roman Catholic students at the overwhelmingly Protestant Trinity College in Dublin.

Browning's poems. That was how she had found out the secret: but she liked the review immensely. Then she said suddenly:

—O, Mr. Conroy, will you come for an excursion to the Aran Isles[8] this summer? We're going to stay there a whole month. It will be splendid out in the Atlantic. You ought to come. Mr. Clancy is coming, and Mr. Kilkelly and Kathleen Kearney. It would be splendid for Gretta too if she'd come. She's from Connacht,[9] isn't she?

—Her people are, said Gabriel shortly.

—But you will come, won't you? said Miss Ivors, laying her warm hand eagerly on his arm.

—The fact is, said Gabriel, I have already arranged to go—

—Go where? asked Miss Ivors.

—Well, you know every year I go for a cycling tour with some fellows and so—

—But where? asked Miss Ivors.

—Well, we usually go to France or Belgium or perhaps Germany, said Gabriel awkwardly.

—And why do you go to France and Belgium, said Miss Ivors, instead of visiting your own land?

—Well, said Gabriel, it's partly to keep in touch with the languages and partly for a change.

—And haven't you your own language to keep in touch with—Irish?[1] asked Miss Ivors.

—Well, said Gabriel, if it comes to that, you know, Irish is not my language.

Their neighbours had turned to listen to the cross-examination. Gabriel glanced right and left nervously and tried to keep his good humour under the ordeal which was making a blush invade his forehead.

—And haven't you your own land to visit, continued Miss Ivors, that you know nothing of, your own people, and your own country?

—O, to tell you the truth, retorted Gabriel suddenly, I'm sick of my own country, sick of it!

—Why? asked Miss Ivors.

Gabriel did not answer for his retort had heated him.

—Why? repeated Miss Ivors.

They had to go visiting together and, as he had not answered her, Miss Ivors said warmly:

—Of course, you've no answer.

Gabriel tried to cover his agitation by taking part in the dance with great energy. He avoided her eyes for he had seen a sour expression on her face. But when they met in the long chain he was surprised to feel his hand firmly pressed. She looked at him from under her brows for a moment quizzically until he smiled. Then, just as the chain was about to start again, she stood on tiptoe and whispered into his ear:

—West Briton!

8. Off the west coast of Ireland. Irish traditions were preserved by their Gaelic-speaking natives. **9.** Province in northwest Ireland. Probably considered rustic and unsophisticated by Dubliners. **1.** That is, Irish Gaelic, which by Joyce's day had been relegated to the western fringes of Ireland by 800 years of domination by the British.

When the lancers were over Gabriel went away to a remote corner of the room where Freddy Malins' mother was sitting. She was a stout feeble old woman with white hair. Her voice had a catch in it like her son's and she stuttered slightly. She had been told that Freddy had come and that he was nearly all right. Gabriel asked her whether she had had a good crossing. She lived with her married daughter in Glasgow and came to Dublin on a visit once a year. She answered placidly that she had had a beautiful crossing[2] and that the captain had been most attentive to her. She spoke also of the beautiful house her daughter kept in Glasgow, and of all the nice friends they had there. While her tongue rambled on Gabriel tried to banish from his mind all memory of the unpleasant incident with Miss Ivors. Of course the girl or woman, or whatever she was, was an enthusiast but there was a time for all things. Perhaps he ought not to have answered her like that. But she had no right to call him a West Briton before people, even in joke. She had tried to make him ridiculous before people, heckling him and staring at him with her rabbit's eyes.

He saw his wife making her way towards him through the waltzing couples. When she reached him she said into his ear:

—Gabriel, Aunt Kate wants to know won't you carve the goose as usual. Miss Daly will carve the ham and I'll do the pudding.[3]

—All right, said Gabriel.

—She's sending in the younger ones first as soon as this waltz is over so that we'll have the table to ourselves.

—Were you dancing? asked Gabriel.

—Of course I was. Didn't you see me? What words had you with Molly Ivors?

—No words. Why? Did she say so?

—Something like that. I'm trying to get that Mr. D'Arcy to sing. He's full of conceit, I think.

—There were no words, said Gabriel moodily, only she wanted me to go for a trip to the west of Ireland and I said I wouldn't.

His wife clasped her hands excitedly and gave a little jump.

—O, do go, Gabriel, she cried. I'd love to see Galway[4] again.

—You can go if you like, said Gabriel coldly.

She looked at him for a moment, then turned to Mrs. Malins and said:

—There's a nice husband for you, Mrs. Malins.

While she was threading her way back across the room Mrs. Malins, without adverting to the interruption, went on to tell Gabriel what beautiful places there were in Scotland and beautiful scenery. Her son-in-law brought them every year to the lakes and they used to go fishing. Her son-in-law was a splendid fisher. One day he caught a fish, a beautiful big big fish, and the man in the hotel boiled it for their dinner.

Gabriel hardly heard what she said. Now that supper was coming near he began to think again about his speech and about the quotation. When he saw Freddy Malins coming across the room to visit his mother Gabriel left the chair free for him and retired into the embrasure of the window. The room

---

2. Passage by ferry over the Irish Sea from Glasgow, Scotland. **3.** In British usage, any cooked dessert. **4.** Capital of Connacht.

had already cleared and from the back room came the clatter of plates and knives. Those who still remained in the drawing-room seemed tired of dancing and were conversing quietly in little groups. Gabriel's warm trembling fingers tapped the cold pane of the window. How cool it must be outside! How pleasant it would be to walk out alone, first along by the river and then through the park! The snow would be lying on the branches of the trees and forming a bright cap on the top of the Wellington Monument.[5] How much more pleasant it would be there than at the supper-table!

He ran over the headings of his speech: Irish hospitality, sad memories, the Three Graces, Paris,[6] the quotation from Browning. He repeated to himself a phrase he had written in his review: *One feels that one is listening to a thought-tormented music.* Miss Ivors had praised the review. Was she sincere? Had she really any life of her own behind all her propagandism? There had never been any ill-feeling between them until that night. It unnerved him to think that she would be at the supper-table, looking up at him while he spoke with her critical quizzing eyes. Perhaps she would not be sorry to see him fail in his speech. An idea came into his mind and gave him courage. He would say, alluding to Aunt Kate and Aunt Julia: *Ladies and Gentlemen, the generation which is now on the wane among us may have had its faults but for my part I think it had certain qualities of hospitality, of humour, of humanity, which the new and very serious and hypereducated generation that is growing up around us seems to me to lack.* Very good: that was one for Miss Ivors. What did he care that his aunts were only two ignorant old women?

A murmur in the room attracted his attention. Mr. Browne was advancing from the door, gallantly escorting Aunt Julia, who leaned upon his arm, smiling and hanging her head. An irregular musketry of applause escorted her also as far as the piano and then, as Mary Jane seated herself on the stool, and Aunt Julia, no longer smiling, half turned so as to pitch her voice fairly into the room, gradually ceased. Gabriel recognised the prelude. It was that of an old song of Aunt Julia's—*Arrayed for the Bridal.*[7] Her voice, strong and clear in tone, attacked with great spirit the runs which embellish the air and though she sang very rapidly she did not miss even the smallest of the grace notes. To follow the voice, without looking at the singer's face, was to feel and share the excitement of swift and secure flight. Gabriel applauded loudly with all the others at the close of the song and loud applause was borne in from the invisible supper-table. It sounded so genuine that a little colour struggled into Aunt Julia's face as she bent to replace in the music-stand the old leather-bound song-book that had her initials on the cover. Freddy Malins, who had listened with his head perched sideways to hear her better, was still applauding when everyone else had ceased and talking animatedly to his mother who nodded her head gravely and slowly in acquiescence. At last, when he could clap no more, he stood up suddenly and hurried across the room to Aunt Julia whose hand he seized and held in both his hands,

---

5. Dublin monument to the Duke of Wellington (1769–1852), Irish-born hero of the Napoleonic Wars.   **6.** The Trojan prince who was obliged to choose among the goddesses Hera, Athena, and Aphrodite. He awarded the prize (the apple of discord) to Aphrodite, who then helped him carry off Helen. "Three Graces": goddesses representing aspects of beauty—Aglaia (Brilliance), Euphrosyne (Joy), and Thalia (Bloom).   **7.** Song from Vincenzo Bellini's opera *I Puritani di Scozia* (The Puritans of Scotland, 1835).

shaking it when words failed him or the catch in his voice proved too much for him.

—I was just telling my mother, he said, I never heard you sing so well, never. No, I never heard your voice so good as it is to-night. Now! Would you believe that now? That's the truth. Upon my word and honour that's the truth. I never heard your voice sound so fresh and so . . . so clear and fresh, never.

Aunt Julia smiled broadly and murmured something about compliments as she released her hand from his grasp. Mr. Browne extended his open hand towards her and said to those who were near him in the manner of a show-man introducing a prodigy to an audience:

—Miss Julia Morkan, my latest discovery!

He was laughing very heartily at this himself when Freddy Malins turned to him and said:

—Well, Browne, if you're serious you might make a worse discovery. All I can say is I never heard her sing half so well as long as I am coming here. And that's the honest truth.

—Neither did I, said Mr. Browne. I think her voice has greatly improved.

Aunt Julia shrugged her shoulders and said with meek pride:

—Thirty years ago I hadn't a bad voice as voices go.

—I often told Julia, said Aunt Kate emphatically, that she was simply thrown away in that choir. But she never would be said by me.

She turned as if to appeal to the good sense of the others against a refrac-tory child while Aunt Julia gazed in front of her, a vague smile of reminis-cence playing on her face.

—No, continued Aunt Kate, she wouldn't be said or led by anyone, slaving there in that choir night and day, night and day. Six o'clock on Christmas morning! And all for what?

—Well, isn't it for the honour of God, Aunt Kate? asked Mary Jane, twisting round on the piano-stool and smiling.

Aunt Kate turned fiercely on her niece and said:

—I know all about the honour of God, Mary Jane, but I think it's not at all honourable for the pope to turn out the women out of the choirs that have slaved there all their lives and put little whipper-snappers of boys over their heads.[8] I suppose it is for the good of the Church if the pope does it. But it's not just, Mary Jane, and it's not right.

She had worked herself into a passion and would have continued in defence of her sister for it was a sore subject with her but Mary Jane, seeing that all the dancers had come back, intervened pacifically:

—Now, Aunt Kate, you're giving scandal to Mr. Browne who is of the other persuasion.[9]

Aunt Kate turned to Mr. Browne, who was grinning at this allusion to his religion, and said hastily:

—O, I don't question the pope's being right. I'm only a stupid old woman and I wouldn't presume to do such a thing. But there's such a thing as com-mon everyday politeness and gratitude. And if I were in Julia's place I'd tell that Father Healy straight up to his face . . .

---

8. In 1903, Pope Pius X decreed that, in Roman Catholic choirs, soprano and alto parts should be sung by boys, not women.   **9.** That is, Mr. Browne is Protestant, not Roman Catholic.

—And besides, Aunt Kate, said Mary Jane, we really are all hungry and when we are hungry we are all very quarrelsome.

—And when we are thirsty we are also quarrelsome, added Mr. Browne.

—So that we had better go to supper, said Mary Jane, and finish the discussion afterwards.

On the landing outside the drawing-room Gabriel found his wife and Mary Jane trying to persuade Miss Ivors to stay for supper. But Miss Ivors, who had put on her hat and was buttoning her cloak, would not stay. She did not feel in the least hungry and she had already overstayed her time.

—But only for ten minutes, Molly, said Mrs. Conroy. That won't delay you.

—To take a pick itself, said Mary Jane, after all your dancing.

—I really couldn't, said Miss Ivors.

—I am afraid you didn't enjoy yourself at all, said Mary Jane hopelessly.

—Ever so much, I assure you, said Miss Ivors, but you really must let me run off now.

—But how can you get home? asked Mrs. Conroy.

—O, it's only two steps up the quay.

Gabriel hesitated a moment and said:

—If you will allow me, Miss Ivors, I'll see you home if you really are obliged to go.

But Miss Ivors broke away from them.

—I won't hear of it, she cried. For goodness sake go in to your suppers and don't mind me. I'm quite well able to take care of myself.

—Well, you're the comical girl, Molly, said Mrs. Conroy frankly.

—*Beannacht libh,*[1] cried Miss Ivors, with a laugh, as she ran down the staircase.

Mary Jane gazed after her, a moody puzzled expression on her face, while Mrs. Conroy leaned over the banisters to listen for the hall-door. Gabriel asked himself was he the cause of her abrupt departure. But she did not seem to be in ill humour: she had gone away laughing. He stared blankly down the staircase.

At that moment Aunt Kate came toddling out of the supper-room, almost wringing her hands in despair.

—Where is Gabriel? she cried. Where on earth is Gabriel? There's everyone waiting in there, stage to let,[2] and nobody to carve the goose!

—Here I am, Aunt Kate! cried Gabriel, with sudden animation, ready to carve a flock of geese, if necessary.

A fat brown goose lay at one end of the table and at the other end, on a bed of creased paper strewn with sprigs of parsley, lay a great ham, stripped of its outer skin and peppered over with crust crumbs, a neat paper frill round its shin and beside this was a round of spiced beef. Between these rival ends ran parallel lines of side-dishes: two little minsters of jelly, red and yellow; a shallow dish full of blocks of blancmange and red jam, a large green leaf-shaped dish with a stalk-shaped handle, on which lay bunches of purple raisins and peeled almonds, a companion dish on which lay a solid rectangle of Smyrna figs, a dish of custard topped with grated nutmeg, a small bowl full of chocolates and sweets wrapped in gold and silver papers and a glass vase in which

---

1. Blessings on you (Gaelic). 2. That is, ready for a performance.

stood some tall celery stalks. In the centre of the table there stood, as sentries to a fruit-stand which upheld a pyramid of oranges and American apples, two squat old-fashioned decanters of cut glass, one containing port and the other dark sherry. On the closed square piano a pudding in a huge yellow dish lay in waiting and behind it were three squads of bottles of stout and ale and minerals, drawn up according to the colours of their uniforms, the first two black, with brown and red labels, the third and smallest squad white, with transverse green sashes.

Gabriel took his seat boldly at the head of the table and, having looked to the edge of the carver, plunged his fork firmly into the goose. He felt quite at ease now for he was an expert carver and liked nothing better than to find himself at the head of a well-laden table.

—Miss Furlong, what shall I send you? he asked. A wing or a slice of the breast?

—Just a small slice of the breast.

—Miss Higgins, what for you?

—O, anything at all, Mr. Conroy.

While Gabriel and Miss Daly exchanged plates of goose and plates of ham and spiced beef Lily went from guest to guest with a dish of hot floury potatoes wrapped in a white napkin. This was Mary Jane's idea and she had also suggested apple sauce for the goose but Aunt Kate had said that plain roast goose without apple sauce had always been good enough for her and she hoped she might never eat worse. Mary Jane waited on her pupils and saw that they got the best slices and Aunt Kate and Aunt Julia opened and carried across from the piano bottles of stout and ale for the gentlemen and bottles of minerals for the ladies. There was a great deal of confusion and laughter and noise, the noise of orders and counter-orders, of knives and forks, of corks and glass-stoppers. Gabriel began to carve second helpings as soon as he had finished the first round without serving himself. Everyone protested loudly so that he compromised by taking a long draught of stout for he had found the carving hot work. Mary Jane settled down quietly to her supper but Aunt Kate and Aunt Julia were still toddling round the table, walking on each other's heels, getting in each other's way and giving each other unheeded orders. Mr. Browne begged of them to sit down and eat their suppers and so did Gabriel but they said there was time enough so that, at last, Freddy Malins stood up and, capturing Aunt Kate, plumped her down on her chair amid general laughter.

When everyone had been well served Gabriel said, smiling:

—Now, if anyone wants a little more of what vulgar people call stuffing let him or her speak.

A chorus of voices invited him to begin his own supper and Lily came forward with three potatoes which she had reserved for him.

—Very well, said Gabriel amiably, as he took another preparatory draught, kindly forget my existence, ladies and gentlemen, for a few minutes.

He set to his supper and took no part in the conversation with which the table covered Lily's removal of the plates. The subject of talk was the opera company which was then at the Theatre Royal. Mr. Bartell D'Arcy, the tenor, a dark-complexioned young man with a smart moustache, praised very highly the leading contralto of the company but Miss Furlong thought she had a rather vulgar style of production. Freddy Malins said there was a negro chieftain singing in the second part of the Gaiety pantomime who had one of the finest tenor voices he had ever heard.

—Have you heard him? he asked Mr. Bartell D'Arcy across the table.

—No, answered Mr. Bartell D'Arcy carelessly.

—Because, Freddy Malins explained, now I'd be curious to hear your opinion of him. I think he has a grand voice.

—It takes Teddy to find out the really good things, said Mr. Browne familiarly to the table.

—And why couldn't he have a voice too? asked Freddy Malins sharply. Is it because he's only a black?

Nobody answered this question and Mary Jane led the table back to the legitimate opera. One of her pupils had given her a pass for *Mignon*.[3] Of course it was very fine, she said, but it made her think of poor Georgina Burns.[4] Mr. Browne could go back farther still, to the old Italian companies that used to come to Dublin—Tietjens, Ilma de Murzka, Campanini, the great Trebelli, Giuglini, Ravelli, Aramburo.[5] Those were the days, he said, when there was something like singing to be heard in Dublin. He told too of how the top gallery of the old Royal used to be packed night after night, of how one night an Italian tenor had sung five encores to *Let Me Like a Soldier Fall*,[6] introducing a high C every time, and of how the gallery boys would sometimes in their enthusiasm unyoke the horses from the carriage of some great *prima donna* and pull her themselves through the streets to her hotel. Why did they never play the grand old operas now, he asked, *Dinorah, Lucrezia Borgia*?[7] Because they could not get the voices to sing them: that was why.

—O, well, said Mr. Bartell D'Arcy, I presume there are as good singers to-day as there were then.

—Where are they? asked Mr. Browne defiantly.

—In London, Paris, Milan, said Mr. Bartell D'Arcy warmly. I suppose Caruso,[8] for example, is quite as good, if not better than any of the men you have mentioned.

—Maybe so, said Mr. Browne. But I may tell you I doubt it strongly.

—O, I'd give anything to hear Caruso sing, said Mary Jane.

—For me, said Aunt Kate, who had been picking a bone, there was only one tenor. To please me, I mean. But I suppose none of you ever heard of him.

—Who was he, Miss Morkan? asked Mr. Bartell D'Arcy politely.

—His name, said Aunt Kate, was Parkinson.[9] I heard him when he was in his prime and I think he had then the purest tenor voice that was ever put into a man's throat.

—Strange, said Mr. Bartell D'Arcy. I never even heard of him.

—Yes, yes, Miss Morkan is right, said Mr. Browne. I remember hearing of old Parkinson but he's too far back for me.

---

3. Opera by Ambroise Thomas (1811–1896), French composer.   4. Late–19th-century Irish soprano.   5. Some 19th-century singing stars: Therese Tietjens (1831–1877), Ilma di Murzka (1836–1889), Italo Campanini (1845–1896), Zelia Trebelli (1838–1892), Antonio Giuglini (1827–1865), and Antonio Aramburo (1838–1912). Others not identified.   6. From *Maritana* by Brunn, Fitzball, and Wallace (1845).   7. Operas by Giacomo Meyerbeer (1791–1864), German composer, and by Gaetano Donizetti (1797–1848), Italian composer.   8. Enrico Caruso (1873–1921), Italian operatic tenor.   9. Not identified; perhaps fictional.

—A beautiful pure sweet mellow English tenor, said Aunt Kate with enthusiasm.

Gabriel having finished, the huge pudding was transferred to the table. The clatter of forks and spoons began again. Gabriel's wife served out spoonfuls of the pudding and passed the plates down the table. Midway down they were held up by Mary Jane, who replenished them with raspberry or orange jelly or with blancmange and jam. The pudding was of Aunt Julia's making and she received praises for it from all quarters. She herself said that it was not quite brown enough.

—Well, I hope, Miss Morkan, said Mr. Browne, that I'm brown enough for you because, you know, I'm all brown.

All the gentlemen, except Gabriel, ate some of the pudding out of compliment to Aunt Julia. As Gabriel never ate sweets the celery had been left for him. Freddy Malins also took a stalk of celery and ate it with his pudding. He had been told that celery was a capital thing for the blood and he was just then under doctor's care. Mrs. Malins, who had been silent all through the supper, said that her son was going down to Mount Melleray,[1] in a week or so. The table then spoke of Mount Melleray, how bracing the air was down there, how hospitable the monks were and how they never asked for a penny-piece from their guests.

—And do you mean to say, asked Mr. Browne incredulously, that a chap can go down there and put up there as if it were a hotel and live on the fat of the land and then come away without paying a farthing?

—O, most people give some donation to the monastery when they leave, said Mary Jane.

—I wish we had an institution like that in our Church, said Mr. Browne candidly.

He was astonished to hear that the monks never spoke, got up at two in the morning and slept in their coffins. He asked what they did it for.

—That's the rule of the order, said Aunt Kate firmly.

—Yes, but why? asked Mr. Browne.

Aunt Kate repeated that it was the rule, that was all. Mr. Browne still seemed not to understand. Freddy Malins explained to him, as best he could, that the monks were trying to make up for the sins committed by all the sinners in the outside world. The explanation was not very clear for Mr. Browne grinned and said:

—I like that idea very much but wouldn't a comfortable spring bed do them as well as a coffin?

—The coffin, said Mary Jane, is to remind them of their last end.

As the subject had grown lugubrious it was buried in a silence of the table during which Mrs. Malins could be heard saying to her neighbour in an indistinct undertone:

—They are very good men, the monks, very pious men.

The raisins and almonds and figs and apples and oranges and chocolates and sweets were now passed about the table and Aunt Julia invited all the guests to have either port or sherry. At first Mr. Bartell D'Arcy refused to take either but one of his neighbours nudged him and whispered something to

---

1. Trappist monastery in the south of Ireland.

him upon which he allowed his glass to be filled. Gradually as the last glasses were being filled the conversation ceased. A pause followed, broken only by the noise of the wine and by unsettlings of chairs. The Misses Morkan, all three, looked down at the tablecloth. Someone coughed once or twice and then a few gentlemen patted the table gently as a signal for silence. The silence came and Gabriel pushed back his chair and stood up.

The patting at once grew louder in encouragement and then ceased altogether. Gabriel leaned his ten trembling fingers on the tablecloth and smiled nervously at the company. Meeting a row of upturned faces he raised his eyes to the chandelier. The piano was playing a waltz tune and he could hear the skirts sweeping against the drawing-room door. People, perhaps, were standing in the snow on the quay outside, gazing up at the lighted windows and listening to the waltz music. The air was pure there. In the distance lay the park where the trees were weighted with snow. The Wellington Monument wore a gleaming cap of snow that flashed westward over the white field of Fifteen Acres.[2]

He began:

—Ladies and Gentlemen.

—It has fallen to my lot this evening, as in years past, to perform a very pleasing task but a task for which I am afraid my poor powers as a speaker are all too inadequate.

—No, no! said Mr. Browne.

—But, however that may be, I can only ask you to-night to take the will for the deed and to lend me your attention for a few moments while I endeavour to express to you in words what my feelings are on this occasion.

—Ladies and Gentlemen. It is not the first time that we have gathered together under this hospitable roof, around this hospitable board. It is not the first time that we have been the recipients—or perhaps, I had better say, the victims—of the hospitality of certain good ladies.

He made a circle in the air with his arm and paused. Everyone laughed or smiled at Aunt Kate and Aunt Julia and Mary Jane who all turned crimson with pleasure. Gabriel went on more boldly:

—I feel more strongly with every recurring year that our country has no tradition which does it so much honour and which it should guard so jealously as that of its hospitality. It is a tradition that is unique as far as my experience goes (and I have visited not a few places abroad) among the modern nations. Some would say, perhaps, that with us it is rather a failing than anything to be boasted of. But granted even that, it is, to my mind, a princely failing, and one that I trust will long be cultivated among us. Of one thing, at least, I am sure. As long as this one roof shelters the good ladies aforesaid—and I wish from my heart it may do so for many and many a long year to come—the tradition of genuine warm-hearted courteous Irish hospitality, which our forefathers have handed down to us and which we in turn must hand down to our descendants, is still alive among us.

A hearty murmur of assent ran round the table. It shot through Gabriel's mind that Miss Ivors was not there and that she had gone away discourteously: and he said with confidence in himself:

2. Section of Phoenix Park in which the Wellington Monument stands.

—Ladies and Gentlemen.

—A new generation is growing up in our midst, a generation actuated by new ideas and new principles. It is serious and enthusiastic for these new ideas and its enthusiasm, even when it is misdirected, is, I believe, in the main sincere. But we are living in a sceptical and, if I may use the phrase, a thought-tormented age: and sometimes I fear that this new generation, educated or hypereducated as it is, will lack those qualities of humanity, of hospitality, of kindly humour which belonged to an older day. Listening to-night to the names of all those great singers of the past it seemed to me, I must confess, that we were living in a less spacious age. Those days might, without exaggeration, be called spacious days: and if they are gone beyond recall let us hope, at least, that in gatherings such as this we shall still speak of them with pride and affection, still cherish in our hearts the memory of those dead and gone great ones whose fame the world will not willingly let die.

—Hear, hear! said Mr. Browne loudly.

—But yet, continued Gabriel, his voice falling into a softer inflection, there are always in gatherings such as this sadder thoughts that will recur to our minds: thoughts of the past, of youth, of changes, of absent faces that we miss here to-night. Our path through life is strewn with many such sad memories: and were we to brood upon them always we could not find the heart to go on bravely with our work among the living. We have all of us living duties and living affections which claim, and rightly claim, our strenuous endeavours.

—Therefore, I will not linger on the past. I will not let any gloomy moralising intrude upon us here to-night. Here we are gathered together for a brief moment from the bustle and rush of our everyday routine. We are met here as friends, in the spirit of good-fellowship, as colleagues, also to a certain extent, in the true spirit of *camaraderie,* and as the guests of—what shall I call them?— the Three Graces of the Dublin musical world.

The table burst into applause and laughter at this sally. Aunt Julia vainly asked each of her neighbours in turn to tell her what Gabriel had said.

—He says we are the Three Graces, Aunt Julia, said Mary Jane.

Aunt Julia did not understand but she looked up, smiling, at Gabriel, who continued in the same vein:

—Ladies and Gentlemen.

—I will not attempt to play to-night the part that Paris played on another occasion. I will not attempt to choose between them. The task would be an invidious one and one beyond my poor powers. For when I view them in turn, whether it be our chief hostess herself, whose good heart, whose too good heart, has become a byword with all who know her, or her sister, who seems to be gifted with perennial youth and whose singing must have been a surprise and a revelation to us all to-night, or, last but not least, when I consider our youngest hostess, talented, cheerful, hard-working and the best of nieces, I confess, Ladies and Gentlemen, that I do not know to which of them I should award the prize.

Gabriel glanced down at his aunts and, seeing the large smile on Aunt Julia's face and the tears which had risen to Aunt Kate's eyes, hastened to his close. He raised his glass of port gallantly, while every member of the company fingered a glass expectantly, and said loudly:

—Let us toast them all three together. Let us drink to their health, wealth, long life, happiness and prosperity and may they long continue to hold the proud and self-won position which they hold in their profession and the position of honour and affection which they hold in our hearts.

All the guests stood up, glass in hand, and, turning towards the three seated ladies, sang in unison, with Mr. Browne as leader:

> *For they are jolly gay fellows,*
> *For they are jolly gay fellows,*
> *For they are jolly gay fellows,*
> *Which nobody can deny.*

Aunt Kate was making frank use of her handkerchief and even Aunt Julia seemed moved. Freddy Malins beat time with his pudding-fork and the singers turned towards one another, as if in melodious conference, while they sang, with emphasis:

> *Unless he tells a lie,*
> *Unless he tells a lie.*

Then, turning once more towards their hostesses, they sang:

> *For they are jolly gay fellows,*
> *For they are jolly gay fellows,*
> *For they are jolly gay fellows,*
> *Which nobody can deny.*

The acclamation which followed was taken up beyond the door of the supper-room by many of the other guests and renewed time after time, Freddy Malins acting as officer with his fork on high.

The piercing morning air came into the hall where they were standing so that Aunt Kate said:

—Close the door, somebody. Mrs. Malins will get her death of cold.

—Browne is out there, Aunt Kate, said Mary Jane.

—Browne is everywhere, said Aunt Kate, lowering her voice.

Mary Jane laughed at her tone.

—Really, she said archly, he is very attentive.

—He has been laid on[3] here like the gas, said Aunt Kate in the same tone, all during the Christmas.

She laughed herself this time good-humouredly and then added quickly:

—But tell him to come in, Mary Jane, and close the door. I hope to goodness he didn't hear me.

---

3. Supplied by plan.

At that moment the hall-door was opened and Mr. Browne came in from the doorstep, laughing as if his heart would break. He was dressed in a long green overcoat with mock astrakhan cuffs and collar and wore on his head an oval fur cap. He pointed down the snow-covered quay from where the sound of shrill prolonged whistling was borne in.

—Teddy will have all the cabs in Dublin out, he said.

Gabriel advanced from the little pantry behind the office, struggling into his overcoat and, looking round the hall, said:

—Gretta not down yet?

—She's getting on her things, Gabriel, said Aunt Kate.

—Who's playing up there? asked Gabriel.

—Nobody. They're all gone.

—O no, Aunt Kate, said Mary Jane. Bartell D'Arcy and Miss O'Callaghan aren't gone yet.

—Someone is strumming at the piano, anyhow, said Gabriel.

Mary Jane glanced at Gabriel and Mr. Browne and said with a shiver:

—It makes me feel cold to look at you two gentlemen muffled up like that. I wouldn't like to face your journey home at this hour.

—I'd like nothing better this minute, said Mr. Browne stoutly, than a rattling fine walk in the country or a fast drive with a good spanking goer[4] between the shafts.

—We used to have a very good horse and trap[5] at home, said Aunt Julia sadly.

—The never-to-be-forgotten Johnny, said Mary Jane, laughing.

Aunt Kate and Gabriel laughed too.

—Why, what was wonderful about Johnny? asked Mr. Browne.

—The late lamented Patrick Morkan, our grandfather, that is, explained Gabriel, commonly known in his later years as the old gentleman, was a glue-boiler.

—O, now, Gabriel, said Aunt Kate, laughing, he had a starch mill.

—Well, glue or starch, said Gabriel, the old gentleman had a horse by the name of Johnny. And Johnny used to work in the old gentleman's mill, walking round and round in order to drive the mill. That was all very well; but now comes the tragic part about Johnny. One fine day the old gentleman thought he'd like to drive out with the quality[6] to a military review in the park.

—The Lord have mercy on his soul, said Aunt Kate compassionately.

—Amen, said Gabriel. So the old gentleman, as I said, harnessed Johnny and put on his very best tall hat and his very best stock collar and drove out in grand style from his ancestral mansion somewhere near Back Lane, I think.

Everyone laughed, even Mrs. Malins, at Gabriel's manner and Aunt Kate said:

—O now, Gabriel, he didn't live in Back Lane, really. Only the mill was there.

—Out from the mansion of his forefathers, continued Gabriel, he drove with Johnny. And everything went on beautifully until Johnny came in sight of King Billy's statue:[7] and whether he fell in love with the horse King Billy

---

4. That is, a fine horse. **5.** One-horse carriage. **6.** Upper classes. **7.** Equestrian statue of King William III of England (William of Orange), last military conquerer of Ireland, at the Battle of the Boyne in 1690.

sits on or whether he thought he was back again in the mill, anyhow he began to walk round the statue.

Gabriel paced in a circle round the hall in his goloshes amid the laughter of the others.

—Round and round he went, said Gabriel, and the old gentleman, who was a very pompous old gentleman, was highly indignant. *Go on, sir! What do you mean, sir? Johnny! Johnny! Most extraordinary conduct! Can't understand the horse!*

The peals of laughter which followed Gabriel's imitation of the incident were interrupted by a resounding knock at the hall-door. Mary Jane ran to open it and let in Freddy Malins. Freddy Malins, with his hat well back on his head and his shoulders humped with cold, was puffing and steaming after his exertions.

—I could only get one cab, he said.

—O, we'll find another along the quay, said Gabriel.

—Yes, said Aunt Kate. Better not keep Mrs. Malins standing in the draught.

Mrs. Malins was helped down the front steps by her son and Mr. Browne and, after many manoeuvres, hoisted into the cab. Freddy Malins clambered in after her and spent a long time settling her on the seat, Mr. Browne helping him with advice. At last she was settled comfortably and Freddy Malins invited Mr. Browne into the cab. There was a good deal of confused talk, and then Mr. Browne got into the cab. The cabman settled his rug over his knees, and bent down for the address. The confusion grew greater and the cabman was directed differently by Freddy Malins and Mr. Browne, each of whom had his head out through a window of the cab. The difficulty was to know where to drop Mr. Browne along the route and Aunt Kate, Aunt Julia and Mary Jane helped the discussion from the doorstep with cross-directions and contradictions and abundance of laughter. As for Freddy Malins he was speechless with laughter. He popped his head in and out of the window every moment, to the great danger of his hat, and told his mother how the discussion was progressing till at last Mr. Browne shouted to the bewildered cabman above the din of everybody's laughter:

—Do you know Trinity College?

—Yes, sir, said the cabman.

—Well, drive bang up against Trinity College gates, said Mr. Browne, and then we'll tell you where to go. You understand now?

—Yes, sir, said the cabman.

—Make like a bird for Trinity College.

—Right, sir, cried the cabman.

The horse was whipped up and the cab rattled off along the quay amid a chorus of laughter and adieus.

Gabriel had not gone to the door with the others. He was in a dark part of the hall gazing up the staircase. A woman was standing near the top of the first flight, in the shadow also. He could not see her face but he could see the terracotta and salmonpink panels of her skirt which the shadow made appear black and white. It was his wife. She was leaning on the banisters, listening to something. Gabriel was surprised at her stillness and strained his ear to listen also. But he could hear little save the noise of laughter and dispute on the front steps, a few chords struck on the piano and a few notes of a man's voice singing.

He stood still in the gloom of the hall, trying to catch the air that the voice was singing and gazing up at his wife. There was grace and mystery in her attitude as if she were a symbol of something. He asked himself what is a woman standing on the stairs in the shadow, listening to distant music, a symbol of. If he were a painter he would paint her in that attitude. Her blue felt hat would show off the bronze of her hair against the darkness and the dark panels of her skirt would show off the light ones. *Distant Music* he would call the picture if he were a painter.

The hall-door was closed; and Aunt Kate, Aunt Julia and Mary Jane came down the hall, still laughing.

—Well, isn't Freddy terrible? said Mary Jane. He's really terrible.

Gabriel said nothing but pointed up the stairs towards where his wife was standing. Now that the hall-door was closed the voice and the piano could be heard more clearly. Gabriel held up his hand for them to be silent. The song seemed to be in the old Irish tonality and the singer seemed uncertain both of his words and of his voice. The voice, made plaintive by distance and by the singer's hoarseness, faintly illuminated the cadence of the air with words expressing grief:

> *O, the rain falls on my heavy locks*
> *And the dew wets my skin,*
> *My babe lies cold . . .*

—O, exclaimed Mary Jane. It's Bartell D'Arcy singing and he wouldn't sing all the night. O, I'll get him to sing a song before he goes.

—O do, Mary Jane, said Aunt Kate.

Mary Jane brushed past the others and ran to the staircase but before she reached it the singing stopped and the piano was closed abruptly.

—O, what a pity! she cried. Is he coming down, Gretta?

Gabriel heard his wife answer yes and saw her come down towards them. A few steps behind her were Mr. Bartell D'Arcy and Miss O'Callaghan.

—O, Mr. D'Arcy, cried Mary Jane, it's downright mean of you to break off like that when we were all in raptures listening to you.

—I have been at him all the evening, said Miss O'Callaghan, and Mrs. Conroy too and he told us he had a dreadful cold and couldn't sing.

—O, Mr. D'Arcy, said Aunt Kate, now that was a great fib to tell.

—Can't you see that I'm as hoarse as a crow? said Mr. D'Arcy roughly.

He went into the pantry hastily and put on his overcoat. The others, taken aback by his rude speech, could find nothing to say. Aunt Kate wrinkled her brows and made signs to the others to drop the subject. Mr. D'Arcy stood swathing his neck carefully and frowning.

—It's the weather, said Aunt Julia, after a pause.

—Yes, everybody has colds, said Aunt Kate readily, everybody.

—They say, said Mary Jane, we haven't had snow like it for thirty years; and I read this morning in the newspapers that the snow is general all over Ireland.

—I love the look of snow, said Aunt Julia sadly.

—So do I, said Miss O'Callaghan. I think Christmas is never really Christmas unless we have the snow on the ground.

—But poor Mr. D'Arcy doesn't like the snow, said Aunt Kate, smiling.

Mr. D'Arcy came from the pantry, fully swathed and buttoned, and in a repentant tone told them the history of his cold. Everyone gave him advice and said it was a great pity and urged him to be very careful of his throat in the night air. Gabriel watched his wife who did not join in the conversation. She was standing right under the dusty fanlight and the flame of the gas lit up the rich bronze of her hair which he had seen her drying at the fire a few days before. She was in the same attitude and seemed unaware of the talk about her. At last she turned towards them and Gabriel saw that there was colour on her cheeks and that her eyes were shining. A sudden tide of joy went leaping out of his heart.

—Mr. D'Arcy, she said, what is the name of that song you were singing?

—It's called *The Lass of Aughrim*,[8] said Mr. D'Arcy, but I couldn't remember it properly. Why? Do you know it?

—*The Lass of Aughrim,* she repeated. I couldn't think of the name.

—It's a very nice air, said Mary Jane. I'm sorry you were not in voice to-night.

—Now, Mary Jane, said Aunt Kate, don't annoy Mr. D'Arcy. I won't have him annoyed.

Seeing that all were ready to start she shepherded them to the door where good-night was said:

—Well, good-night, Aunt Kate, and thanks for the pleasant evening.

—Good-night, Gabriel. Good-night, Gretta!

—Good-night, Aunt Kate, and thanks ever so much. Good-night, Aunt Julia.

—O, good-night, Gretta, I didn't see you.

—Good-night, Mr. D'Arcy. Good-night, Miss O'Callaghan.

—Good-night, Miss Morkan.

—Good-night, again.

—Good-night, all. Safe home.

—Good-night. Good-night.

The morning was still dark. A dull yellow light brooded over the houses and the river; and the sky seemed to be descending. It was slushy underfoot; and only streaks and patches of snow lay on the roofs, on the parapets of the quay and on the area railings. The lamps were still burning redly in the murky air and, across the river, the palace of the Four Courts[9] stood out menacingly against the heavy sky.

She was walking on before him with Mr. Bartell D'Arcy, her shoes in a brown parcel tucked under one arm and her hands holding her skirt up from the slush. She had no longer any grace of attitude but Gabriel's eyes were still bright with happiness. The blood went bounding along his veins; and the thoughts went rioting through his brain, proud, joyful, tender, valorous.

She was walking on before him so lightly and so erect that he longed to run after her noiselessly, catch her by the shoulders and say something foolish and affectionate into her ear. She seemed to him so frail that he longed to defend her against something and then to be alone with her. Moments of

---

8. Variant of "The Lass of Loch Royal," Child's ballad No. 76. It tells of a girl seduced and abandoned. She stands in the rain outside the house of her seducer with her baby in her arms; rejected, she puts to sea in a boat and drowns herself and the child. **9.** Building housing the courts of Ireland.

their secret life together burst like stars upon his memory. A heliotrope envelope was lying beside his breakfast-cup and he was caressing it with his hand. Birds were twittering in the ivy and the sunny web of the curtain was shimmering along the floor: he could not eat for happiness. They were standing on the crowded platform and he was placing a ticket inside the warm palm of her glove. He was standing with her in the cold, looking in through a grated window at a man making bottles in a roaring furnace. It was very cold. Her face, fragrant in the cold air, was quite close to his; and suddenly she called out to the man at the furnace:

—Is the fire hot, sir?

But the man could not hear her with the noise of the furnace. It was just as well. He might have answered rudely.

A wave of yet more tender joy escaped from his heart and went coursing in warm flood along his arteries. Like the tender fires of stars moments of their life together, that no one knew of or would ever know of, broke upon and illumined his memory. He longed to recall to her those moments, to make her forget the years of their dull existence together and remember only their moments of ecstasy. For the years, he felt, had not quenched his soul or hers. Their children, his writing, her household cares had not quenched all their souls' tender fire. In one letter that he had written to her then he had said: *Why is it that words like these seem to me so dull and cold? Is it because there is no word tender enough to be your name?*

Like distant music these words that he had written years before were borne towards him from the past. He longed to be alone with her. When the others had gone away, when he and she were in their room in the hotel, then they would be alone together. He would call her softly:

—Gretta!

Perhaps she would not hear at once: she would be undressing. Then something in his voice would strike her. She would turn and look at him. . . .

At the corner of Winetavern Street they met a cab. He was glad of its rattling noise as it saved him from conversation. She was looking out of the window and seemed tired. The others spoke only a few words, pointing out some building or street. The horse galloped along wearily under the murky morning sky, dragging his old rattling box after his heels, and Gabriel was again in a cab with her, galloping to catch the boat, galloping to their honeymoon.

As the cab drove across O'Connell Bridge Miss O'Callaghan said:

—They say you never cross O'Connell Bridge without seeing a white horse.

—I see a white man this time, said Gabriel.

Where? asked Mr. Bartell D'Arcy.

Gabriel pointed to the statue, on which lay patches of snow. Then he nodded familiarly to it and waved his hand.

—Good-night, Dan,[1] he said gaily.

When the cab drew up before the hotel Gabriel jumped out and, in spite of Mr. Bartell D'Arcy's protest, paid the driver. He gave the man a shilling over his fare. The man saluted and said:

—A prosperous New Year to you, sir.

---

1. The statue is of Daniel O'Connell (1775–1847), Irish patriot, known as "The Liberator," for whom the bridge is named.

—The same to you, said Gabriel cordially.

She leaned for a moment on his arm in getting out of the cab and while standing at the curbstone, bidding the others good-night. She leaned lightly on his arm, as lightly as when she had danced with him a few hours before. He had felt proud and happy then, happy that she was his, proud of her grace and wifely carriage. But now, after the kindling again of so many memories, the first touch of her body, musical and strange and perfumed, sent through him a keen pang of lust. Under cover of her silence he pressed her arm closely to his side; and, as they stood at the hotel door, he felt that they had escaped from their lives and duties, escaped from home and friends and run away together with wild and radiant hearts to a new adventure.

An old man was dozing in a great hooded chair in the hall. He lit a candle in the office and went before them to the stairs. They followed him in silence, their feet falling in soft thuds on the thickly carpeted stairs. She mounted the stairs behind the porter, her head bowed in the ascent, her frail shoulders curved as with a burden, her skirt girt tightly about her. He could have flung his arms about her hips and held her still for his arms were trembling with desire to seize her and only the stress of his nails against the palms of his hands held the wild impulse of his body in check. The porter halted on the stairs to settle his guttering candle. They halted too on the steps below him. In the silence Gabriel could hear the falling of the molten wax into the tray and the thumping of his own heart against his ribs.

The porter led them along a corridor and opened a door. Then he set his unstable candle down on a toilet-table and asked at what hour they were to be called in the morning.

—Eight, said Gabriel.

The porter pointed to the tap of the electric-light and began a muttered apology but Gabriel cut him short.

—We don't want any light. We have light enough from the street. And I say, he added, pointing to the candle, you might remove that handsome article, like a good man.

The porter took up his candle again, but slowly for he was surprised by such a novel idea. Then he mumbled good-night and went out. Gabriel shot the lock to.[2]

A ghostly light from the street lamp lay in a long shaft from one window to the door. Gabriel threw his overcoat and hat on a couch and crossed the room towards the window. He looked down into the street in order that his emotion might calm a little. Then he turned and leaned against a chest of drawers with his back to the light. She had taken off her hat and cloak and was standing before a large swinging mirror, unhooking her waist. Gabriel paused for a few moments, watching her, and then said:

—Gretta!

She turned away from the mirror slowly and walked along the shaft of light towards him. Her face looked so serious and weary that the words would not pass Gabriel's lips. No, it was not the moment yet.

—You looked tired, he said.

—I am a little, she answered.

---

2. That is, locked the deadbolt.

—You don't feel ill or weak?

—No, tired: that's all.

She went on to the window and stood there, looking out. Gabriel waited again and then, fearing that diffidence was about to conquer him, he said abruptly:

—By the way, Gretta!

—What is it?

—You know that poor fellow Malins? he said quickly.

—Yes. What about him?

—Well, poor fellow, he's a decent sort of chap after all, continued Gabriel in a false voice. He gave me back that sovereign[3] I lent him and I didn't expect it really. It's a pity he wouldn't keep away from that Browne, because he's not a bad fellow at heart.

He was trembling now with annoyance. Why did she seem so abstracted? He did not know how he could begin. Was she annoyed, too, about something? If she would only turn to him or come to him of her own accord! To take her as she was would be brutal. No, he must see some ardour in her eyes first. He longed to be master of her strange mood.

—When did you lend him the pound? she asked, after a pause.

Gabriel strove to restrain himself from breaking out into brutal language about the sottish Malins and his pound. He longed to cry to her from his soul, to crush her body against his, to overmaster her. But he said:

—O, at Christmas, when he opened that little Christmas-card shop in Henry Street.

He was in such a fever of rage and desire that he did not hear her come from the window. She stood before him for an instant, looking at him strangely. Then, suddenly raising herself on tiptoe and resting her hands lightly on his shoulders, she kissed him.

—You are a very generous person, Gabriel, she said.

Gabriel, trembling with delight at her sudden kiss and at the quaintness of her phrase, put his hands on her hair and began smoothing it back, scarcely touching it with his fingers. The washing had made it fine and brilliant. His heart was brimming over with happiness. Just when he was wishing for it she had come to him of her own accord. Perhaps her thoughts had been running with his. Perhaps she had felt the impetuous desire that was in him and then the yielding mood had come upon her. Now that she had fallen to him so easily he wondered why he had been so diffident.

He stood, holding her head between his hands. Then, slipping one arm swiftly about her body and drawing her towards him, he said softly:

—Gretta dear, what are you thinking about?

She did not answer nor yield wholly to his arm. He said again, softly:

—Tell me what it is, Gretta. I think I know what is the matter. Do I know?

She did not answer at once. Then she said in an outburst of tears:

—O, I am thinking about that song, *The Lass of Aughrim*.

She broke loose from him and ran to the bed and, throwing her arms across the bed-rail, hid her face. Gabriel stood stock-still for a moment in astonishment and then followed her. As he passed in the way of the cheval-glass he

3. Gold coin worth one pound.

caught sight of himself in full length, his broad, well-filled shirt-front, the face whose expression always puzzled him when he saw it in a mirror and his glimmering gilt-rimmed eyeglasses. He halted a few paces from her and said:

—What about the song? Why does that make you cry?

She raised her head from her arms and dried her eyes with the back of her hand like a child. A kinder note than he had intended went into his voice.

—Why, Gretta? he asked.

—I am thinking about a person long ago who used to sing that song.

—And who was the person long ago? asked Gabriel, smiling.

—It was a person I used to know in Galway when I was living with my grandmother, she said.

The smile passed away from Gabriel's face. A dull anger began to gather again at the back of his mind and the dull fires of his lust began to glow angrily in his veins.

—Someone you were in love with? he asked ironically.

—It was a young boy I used to know, she answered, named Michael Furey. He used to sing that song, *The Lass of Aughrim*. He was very delicate.

Gabriel was silent. He did not wish her to think that he was interested in this delicate boy.

—I can see him so plainly, she said after a moment. Such eyes as he had: big dark eyes! And such an expression in them—an expression!

—O then, you were in love with him? said Gabriel.

—I used to go out walking with him, she said, when I was in Galway.

A thought flew across Gabriel's mind.

—Perhaps that was why you wanted to go to Galway with that Ivors girl? he said coldly.

She looked at him and asked in surprise:

—What for?

Her eyes made Gabriel feel awkward. He shrugged his shoulders and said:

—How do I know? To see him perhaps.

She looked away from him along the shaft of light towards the window in silence.

—He is dead, she said at length. He died when he was only seventeen. Isn't it a terrible thing to die so young as that?

—What was he? asked Gabriel, still ironically.

—He was in the gasworks, she said.

Gabriel felt humiliated by the failure of his irony and by the evocation of this figure from the dead, a boy in the gasworks. While he had been full of memories of their secret life together, full of tenderness and joy and desire, she had been comparing him in her mind with another. A shameful consciousness of his own person assailed him. He saw himself as a ludicrous figure, acting as a pennyboy[4] for his aunts, a nervous well-meaning sentimentalist, orating to vulgarians and idealising his own clownish lusts, the pitiable fatuous fellow he had caught a glimpse of in the mirror. Instinctively he turned his back more to the light lest she might see the shame that burned upon his forehead.

4. Errand boy.

He tried to keep up his tone of cold interrogation but his voice when he spoke was humble and indifferent.

—I suppose you were in love with this Michael Furey, Gretta, he said.

—I was great[5] with him at that time, she said.

Her voice was veiled and sad. Gabriel, feeling now how vain it would be to try to lead her whither he had purposed, caressed one of her hands and said, also sadly:

—And what did he die of so young, Gretta? Consumption, was it?

—I think he died for me, she answered.

A vague terror seized Gabriel at this answer as if, at that hour when he had hoped to triumph, some impalpable and vindictive being was coming against him, gathering forces against him in its vague world. But he shook himself free of it with an effort of reason and continued to caress her hand. He did not question her again for he felt that she would tell him of herself. Her hand was warm and moist: it did not respond to his touch but he continued to caress it just as he had caressed her first letter to him that spring morning.

—It was in the winter, she said, about the beginning of the winter when I was going to leave my grandmother's and come up here to the convent. And he was ill at the time in his lodgings in Galway and wouldn't be let out and his people in Oughterard[6] were written to. He was in decline, they said, or something like that. I never knew rightly.

She paused for a moment and sighed.

—Poor fellow, she said. He was very fond of me and he was such a gentle boy. We used to go out together, walking, you know, Gabriel, like the way they do in the country. He was going to study singing only for his health. He had a very good voice, poor Michael Furey.

—Well; and then? asked Gabriel.

—And then when it came to the time for me to leave Galway and come up to the convent he was much worse and I wouldn't be let see him so I wrote a letter saying I was going up to Dublin and would be back in the summer and hoping he would be better then.

She paused for a moment to get her voice under control and then went on:

—Then the night before I left I was in my grandmother's house in Nuns' Island, packing up, and I heard gravel thrown up against the window. The window was so wet I couldn't see so I ran downstairs as I was and slipped out the back into the garden and there was the poor fellow at the end of the garden, shivering.

—And did you not tell him to go back? asked Gabriel.

—I implored of him to go home at once and told him he would get his death in the rain. But he said he did not want to live. I can see his eyes as well as well! He was standing at the end of the wall where there was a tree.

—And did he go home? asked Gabriel.

—Yes, he went home. And when I was only a week in the convent he died and he was buried in Oughterard where his people came from. O, the day I heard that, that he was dead!

She stopped, choking with sobs, and, overcome by emotion, flung herself face downward on the bed, sobbing in the quilt. Gabriel held her hand for a

---

5. Intimate, closely acquainted.   **6.** Town in Connacht, 20 miles north of Galway.

moment longer, irresolutely, and then, shy of intruding on her grief, let it fall gently and walked quietly to the window.

She was fast asleep.

Gabriel, leaning on his elbow, looked for a few moments unresentfully on her tangled hair and half-open mouth, listening to her deep-drawn breath. So she had had that romance in her life: a man had died for her sake. It hardly pained him now to think how poor a part he, her husband, had played in her life. He watched her while she slept as though he and she had never lived together as man and wife. His curious eyes rested long upon her face and on her hair: and, as he thought of what she must have been then, in that time of her first girlish beauty, a strange friendly pity for her entered his soul. He did not like to say even to himself that her face was no longer beautiful but he knew that it was no longer the face for which Michael Furey had braved death.

Perhaps she had not told him all the story. His eyes moved to the chair over which she had thrown some of her clothes. A petticoat string dangled to the floor. One boot stood upright, its limp upper fallen down: the fellow of it lay upon its side. He wondered at his riot of emotions of an hour before. From what had it proceeded? From his aunt's supper, from his own foolish speech, from the wine and dancing, the merry-making when saying good-night in the hall, the pleasure of the walk along the river in the snow. Poor Aunt Julia! She, too, would soon be a shade with the shade of Patrick Morkan and his horse. He had caught that haggard look upon her face for a moment when she was singing *Arrayed for the Bridal*. Soon, perhaps, he would be sitting in that same drawing-room, dressed in black, his silk hat on his knees. The blinds would be drawn down and Aunt Kate would be sitting beside him, crying and blowing her nose and telling him how Julia had died. He would cast about in his mind for some words that might console her, and would find only lame and useless ones. Yes, yes: that would happen very soon.

The air of the room chilled his shoulders. He stretched himself cautiously along under the sheets and lay down beside his wife. One by one they were all becoming shades. Better pass boldly into that other world, in the full glory of some passion, than fade and wither dismally with age. He thought of how she who lay beside him had locked in her heart for so many years that image of her lover's eyes when he had told her that he did not wish to live.

Generous tears filled Gabriel's eyes. He had never felt like that himself towards any woman but he knew that such a feeling must be love. The tears gathered more thickly in his eyes and in the partial darkness he imagined he saw the form of a young man standing under a dripping tree. Other forms were near. His soul had approached that region where dwell the vast hosts of the dead. He was conscious of, but could not apprehend, their wayward and flickering existence. His own identity was fading out into a grey impalpable world: the solid world itself which these dead had one time reared and lived in was dissolving and dwindling.

A few light taps upon the pane made him turn to the window. It had begun to snow again. He watched sleepily the flakes, silver and dark, falling obliquely against the lamplight. The time had come for him to set out on his journey westward. Yes, the newspapers were right: snow was general all over Ireland. It was falling on every part of the dark central plain, on the treeless hills, falling softly upon the Bog of Allen and, farther westward, softly falling into the dark mutinous Shannon[7] waves. It was falling, too, upon every part of the lonely churchyard on the hill where Michael Furey lay buried. It lay thickly drifted on the crooked crosses and headstones, on the spears of the little gate, on the barren thorns. His soul swooned slowly as he heard the snow falling faintly through the universe and faintly falling, like the descent of their last end, upon all the living and the dead.

1914

RELATED:

—C. C. Loomis Jr., "Structure and Sympathy in Joyce's 'The Dead,'" p. 1766

---

7. River flowing westward through Ireland. The Bog of Allen is southwest of Dublin.

FRANZ KAFKA
1883–1924

Kafka was born in Prague, the son of a middle-class Jewish family. After obtaining a law degree at the German University in Prague, he held an inconspicuous position in the civil service for many years. His few intimates remembered him as a warmly humorous man; however, his deep sense of inferiority to his father, the frailty of his health, his indecisive and prolonged engagement that never led to marriage, his preoccupation with suicide, and his last years of struggle against the tuberculosis that killed him suggest some origins of the great anxiety that pervades his literary production. He was not altogether a pessimist but was tormented by the conviction that goodness is very remote and nearly impossible to attain. Though he considered his writing the major task of his life, he had completed very few of his projects at the time of his death and published even fewer. He directed his friend Max Brod to burn his remaining manuscripts when he died. Brod ignored the command and saw that many of them were published. Three unfinished novels—*The Trial* (1925), *The Castle* (1926), and *Amerika* (1927)—brought Kafka his first posthumous fame, but the fairly large body of stories published under Brod's sponsorship shows the complexity of the author's imagination and metaphysical irony perhaps more comprehensively than the novels that earned him his place as a major spokesman for the Age of Anxiety. Indeed, the term "Kafkaesque" is now widely used to describe the most darkly irrational, even nightmarish, aspects of modern life. His stories in English translation can be found in *The Great Wall of China* (1933), *The Penal Colony* (1948), and *The Complete Stories* (1976).

The Metamorphosis[1]

I

When Gregor Samsa woke one morning from troubled dreams, he found himself transformed right there in his bed into some sort of monstrous insect. He was lying on his back—which was hard, like a carapace—and when he raised his head a little he saw his curved brown belly segmented by rigid arches atop which the blanket, already slipping, was just barely managing to cling. His many legs, pitifully thin compared to the rest of him, waved helplessly before his eyes.

1. Translated by Susan Bernofsky.

"What in the world has happened to me?" he thought. It was no dream. His room, a proper human room, if admittedly rather too small, lay peacefully between the four familiar walls. Above the table, where an unpacked collection of cloth samples was arranged (Samsa was a traveling salesman), hung the picture he had recently clipped from a glossy magazine and placed in an attractive gilt frame. This picture showed a lady in a fur hat and fur boa who sat erect, holding out to the viewer a heavy fur muff in which her entire forearm had vanished.

Gregor's gaze then shifted to the window, where the bleak weather—raindrops could be heard striking the metal sill—made him feel quite melancholy. "What if I just go back to sleep for a little while and forget all this foolishness," he thought, but this proved utterly impossible, for it was his habit to sleep on his right side, and in his present state he was unable to assume this position. No matter how forcefully he thrust himself onto his side, he kept rolling back. Perhaps a hundred times he attempted it, closing his eyes so as not to have to see those struggling legs, and relented only when he began to feel a faint dull ache in his side, unlike anything he'd ever felt before.

"Good Lord," he thought, "what an exhausting profession I've chosen. Day in and day out on the road. Work like this is far more unsettling than business conducted at home, and then I have the agony of traveling itself to contend with: worrying about train connections, the irregular, unpalatable meals, and human intercourse that is constantly changing, never developing the least constancy or warmth. Devil take it all!" He felt a faint itch high up on his belly; still on his back, he laboriously edged himself over to the bedpost so he could raise his head more easily; identified the site of the itch: a cluster of tiny white dots he was unable to judge; and wanted to probe the spot with a leg, but drew it back again at once, for the touch sent cold shivers rippling through him.

He slid back into his earlier position. "All this early rising," he thought, "it's enough to make one soft in the head. Human beings need their sleep. Other traveling salesmen live like harem girls. When I go back to the boardinghouse, for example, to copy out the morning's commissions: why, these gentlemen may still be sitting at breakfast. I'd like to see my boss's face if I tried that some time; he'd can me on the spot. Although who knows, maybe that would be the best thing for me. If I didn't have to hold back for my parents' sake, I'd have given notice long ago—I'd have marched right up to him and given him a piece of my mind. He'd have fallen right off his desk! And what an odd custom that is: perching high up atop one's elevated desk and from this considerable height addressing one's employee down below, especially as the latter is obliged to stand quite close because his boss is hard of hearing. Well, all hope is not yet lost; as soon as I've saved up enough money to pay back what my parents owe him—another five or six years ought to be enough—I'll most definitely do just that. This will be the great parting of ways. For the time being, though, I've got to get up, my train leaves at five."

And he glanced over at the alarm clock ticking away atop the wardrobe. "Heavenly Father!" he thought. It was half past six, and the clock's hands kept shifting calmly forward, in fact the half-hour had already passed, it was getting on toward six forty-five. Could the alarm have failed to ring? Even from the bed one could see it was properly set for four o'clock; it must have rung. Yes, but was it possible to sleep tranquilly through this furniture-shaking racket? Well, his sleep hadn't been exactly tranquil, but no doubt that's why it had been so sound. But what should he do now? The next train was at seven o'clock; to catch it, he would have to rush like a madman, and his sample case wasn't even packed yet, and he himself felt far from agile or alert. And even if he managed to catch this train, his boss was certain to unleash a thunderstorm of invective upon his head, for the clerk who met the five o'clock train had no doubt long since reported Gregor's absence. This clerk was the boss's underling, a creature devoid of backbone and wit. What if he called in sick? But that would be mortifying and also suspicious, since Gregor had never once been ill in all his five years of service. No doubt his boss would come calling with the company doctor, would reproach Gregor's parents for their son's laziness, silencing all objections by referring them to this doctor, in whose opinion there existed only healthy individuals unwilling to work. And would the doctor be so terribly wrong in this instance? Aside from a mild drowsiness that was certainly superfluous after so many hours of sleep, Gregor felt perfectly fine; in fact, he was ravenous.

While he was considering these matters with the greatest possible speed, yet still without managing to make up his mind to leave the bed (the clock was just striking a quarter to seven), a timid knock came at the door at the head of his bed. "Gregor," the voice called—it was his mother—"it's a quarter to seven. Didn't you want to catch your train?" That gentle voice! Gregor flinched when he heard his own in response: it was unmistakably his old voice, but now it had been infiltrated as if from below by a tortured peeping sound that was impossible to suppress—leaving each word intact, comprehensible, but only for an instant before so completely annihilating it as it continued to reverberate that a person could not tell for sure whether his ears were deceiving him. Gregor had meant to give a proper response explaining everything, but under the circumstances he limited himself to saying, "Yes, thank you, Mother, I'm just getting up." Because of the wooden door, the change in Gregor's voice appeared not to be noticeable from the other side, for his mother was reassured by his response and shuffled off. But their brief conversation had alerted the other family members that Gregor was unexpectedly still at home, and already his father was knocking at one of the room's side doors, softly, but with his fist: "Gregor, Gregor," he called. "What's the problem?" And after a short while he repeated his question in a deeper register: "Gregor! Gregor!" Meanwhile, at the other side door came his sister's faint lament: "Gregor? Are you unwell? Do you need anything?" "Just a second," Gregor answered in both directions at once, making an effort, by enunciating as clearly as possible and inserting long pauses between the individual words, to remove anything conspicuous from his voice. And in fact his father returned to his breakfast, but his sister whispered: "Gregor, open the door, I implore you." But Gregor had no intention of opening the door; he praised the cautious habit he had acquired while traveling of locking all his doors at night, even at home.

First he would get up calmly and undisturbed, he would get dressed and above all have breakfast, and only then would he consider his next steps, for all these supine contemplations, he suddenly realized, would yield no useful results. He recalled often having felt mild aches and pains in bed, caused perhaps by lying in an awkward position, and this pain had then proven to be a figment of his imagination the moment he got up; he was curious to see how this morning's imaginings would gradually fade. The change in his voice was nothing more than the harbinger of a proper head cold, an occupational hazard among traveling salesmen; this he doubted not in the least.

It was simple enough to rid himself of the blanket; he needed only puff himself up a bit, and it fell right off. But the rest proved difficult, not least because he was so exceedingly wide. He would have needed arms and hands to prop himself up; but instead all he had were these many little legs, variously in motion, that he was unable to control. If he tried to bend one leg, it would be the first to straighten; and when he finally succeeded in getting one leg to do his bidding, all the others went flailing about in an unnerving frenzy. "Enough of this lying about uselessly in bed," Gregor said to himself.

At first he tried to maneuver the lower part of his body out of the bed, but this lower part—which, by the way, he had not yet seen and couldn't properly imagine—proved too unwieldy; it all went so slowly; and when at last, half-mad with impatience, he thrust himself recklessly forward with all his strength, it was in the wrong direction, and he slammed against the lower bedpost; the throbbing pain he felt instructed him that for now at least the lower part of his body was perhaps the most sensitive.

So he decided to try leading instead with his upper body and carefully twisted his head toward the edge of the bed. This was easily accomplished, and in the end, despite his width and weight, the mass of his body slowly followed the turning of his head. But once his head was dangling in midair outside the bed, he was afraid to keep shifting forward like this, since if eventually he had to let himself fall in this position, it would be practically a miracle if his head escaped injury. And right now he had to keep his wits about him at all costs, even if it meant staying where he was.

But when, sighing after redoubled efforts, he found himself lying there as before, watching his little legs engaged in their struggles, perhaps more flailingly now, and seeing no possible way to bring calm or order to this chaos, he told himself once more that he could not possibly remain lying here any longer and that the most sensible thing would be to sacrifice anything and everything as long as there remained even the slightest hope of liberating himself from the bed. Simultaneously, though, he continued to remind himself that calm consideration—indeed, the calmest consideration—was far preferable to resolutions seized on in despair. At such moments he fixed his eyes as sharply as possible on the window, but regrettably the view of the morning fog, which veiled even the far side of the narrow street, offered little by way of optimism and good spirits. "Seven o'clock already," he said to himself as the clock struck once more, "already seven and still such dense fog." And for a little while he lay there quietly, his breathing shallow, in the expectation, perhaps, that this perfect silence might possibly restore the real and ordinary state of things.

Then he said to himself: "Before it strikes a quarter past seven, I must absolutely have gotten myself completely out of bed. Besides, by then someone will have come from the office to inquire after me, as the office opens before seven." And he now set himself to rocking his body out of the bed as evenly as possible along his entire length. If he allowed himself to fall from the bed like this, his head—which he intended to lift up cleanly as he fell—would in all likelihood remain unharmed. His back seemed to be hard; surely it would sustain no damage as he fell to the rug. His greatest concern was what to do about the loud crash that would clearly result, no doubt calling forth not terror perhaps but certainly alarm behind each door. Nonetheless it would have to be ventured.

By the time Gregor was already protruding half-way out of bed—this new method was more a game than a struggle, all he had to do was keep rocking sideways a little at a time—it occurred to him how simple things would be if only someone came to his aid. Two strong individuals—he was thinking of his father and the maidservant—would suffice; all they'd have to do was slip their arms beneath his curved back to scoop him out of bed, then crouch down with their burden and wait patiently for him to flip himself over onto the floor, where he hoped those tiny legs of his would take on some meaning. But even aside from the fact that the doors were locked, should he really call for help? Despite his distress, he couldn't help smiling at the thought.

Already he'd reached the point where the vigorous rocking motion was making it almost impossible for him to keep his balance, and soon he would have to make up his mind and take the plunge, for a quarter after seven was only five minutes away—when the front doorbell rang. "It's someone from the office," he said to himself and nearly froze while his little legs went on scrabbling all the more frenetically. For a moment all was still. "They won't answer," Gregor said to himself, caught up in some deluded hope. But then of course, as always, the maid strode resolutely to the door and opened it.

Gregor needed only hear the visitor's first words of greeting to know who it was: the general manager himself. Why oh why was Gregor condemned to serve in a firm where even the most negligible falling short was enough to arouse the greatest possible suspicion? Was every last one of the firm's employees a scoundrel, was there not a single loyal, devoted soul among them who would be driven mad by pangs of conscience should he fail to make the best possible use of even just a few morning hours for his employer's benefit, such that his guilt would render him virtually incapable of rising from his bed? Would it really not have sufficed to send an apprentice to inquire—if indeed such inquiries were necessary at all—did the general manager have to come in person, and was it necessary to demonstrate to the entire innocent family that the investigation of this suspicious matter could be entrusted only to the general manager's sharp intellect? And more because of the agitation aroused in Gregor by this train of thought than because of some proper resolution on his part, he swung himself out of bed with all his might. There was a loud thud, you couldn't really call it a crash. The rug cushioned the impact a little, and since his back was more elastic than he'd thought, the resulting sound was muffled and not so obvious. But he hadn't managed to hold his head up carefully enough and had bumped it; he turned it this way and that, pressing it against the rug in his vexation and pain.

"Something just fell in there," the general manager now said in the room on the left. Gregor tried to imagine whether anything like what he was now experiencing could ever befall the general manager; the possibility must certainly be admitted. But as if brusquely dismissing the question, the manager now took a few purposeful steps in the next room, making his patent leather boots creak. From the room on the right came the whisper of Gregor's sister informing him: "Gregor, the general manager is here." "I know," Gregor murmured; but he didn't dare raise his voice high enough for his sister to hear.

"Gregor," his father now said from the room on the left, "the general manager has come to inquire why you failed to depart by the early train. We don't know what to tell him. Besides, he'd like to have a word with you in person. So please open the door. I'm sure he'll be kind enough not to take offense at the untidiness of your room." "Good morning, Herr[2] Samsa," the general manager now cried out in a friendly tone. "He isn't well," Gregor's mother said to the general manager while his father was still having his say beside the door, "not well at all, take my word for it, sir. Why else would Gregor miss his train! The office is the only thing that boy ever thinks of. It really bothers me that he never goes out in the evening; he's been back in the city an entire week now, but he's spent every last evening at home. He just sits at the table with us, quietly reading the newspaper, or else studies the timetables. Even just doing woodworking projects seems to entertain him. He carved a little picture frame, for example, did it in two or three evenings with his fretsaw; you'll be amazed how pretty it is; it's hanging there in his room; you'll see it in a minute when Gregor opens the door. Oh, and I'm so glad you paid us a visit, sir; on our own we'd never have managed to persuade Gregor to open up; he's so stubborn; and surely he isn't well, even though he denied it this morning." "Be . . . right . . . there," Gregor said, not moving, so as not to miss a single word of their conversation. "No other explanation, madam, is conceivable to me," the general manager said. "Let us hope it is nothing grave. Though on the other hand I would note that, as businessmen—fortunately or unfortunately, as one will—we are very often obliged to suppress indispositions out of consideration for the firm." "So are you ready to let the general manager in?" Gregor's impatient father asked, knocking again at the door. "No," Gregor responded. In the left-hand room horrified silence, while in the room on the right Gregor's sister began to sob.

Why didn't his sister go to join the others? She must have just gotten out of bed and not yet begun to dress. And why was she crying? Because he wasn't getting up and opening his door to the general manager, because he was in danger of losing his position, and because his boss would then start hounding his parents once more over their ancient debt? For the time being, all such worries were assuredly unnecessary. Gregor was still here, and abandoning his family was the farthest thing from his thoughts. At the moment, to be sure, he was lying on the rug, and no one familiar with his current state would seriously expect him to let the general manager in. But surely he wouldn't be sent packing just like that because of so trivial an act of discourtesy, for which it would be simple enough to find an appropriate excuse later on. And it seemed to Gregor it would be far more sensible to just leave him in peace rather than disturbing him with all this weeping and cajoling. But the others were distressed by the uncertainty of it all; their behavior was understandable.

"Herr Samsa," the general manager now called out, raising his voice. "What has come over you? You barricade yourself in your room, you reply to queries

2. Mr. (German).

only with yes and no, you cause your parents onerous, unnecessary worries, and you are neglecting—let me permit myself to note—your professional responsibilities in a truly unprecedented manner. I speak here in the name of your parents as well as your employer and in all seriousness must ask you for a clear and immediate explanation. I am astonished, utterly astonished. I have always known you as a calm, sensible person, and now it seems you've begun to permit yourself the most whimsical extravagances. To be sure, the boss did suggest one possible explanation for your absence this morning—it concerns the cash payments recently entrusted to your care—and truthfully, I all but gave him my word of honor that this explanation could not be correct. But confronted here with your incomprehensible obstinacy, I find myself losing any desire I might have had to come to your defense. And your position is anything but secure. It was originally my intention to discuss all this with you in a private conversation, but since you compel me to waste my time here, I do not know why your esteemed parents should not hear of it as well. In short: your productivity of late has been highly unsatisfactory; admittedly this is not the best season for drumming up business, we do acknowledge this; but a season in which no business at all is drummed up is something that does not, and indeed may not exist, Herr Samsa."

"But sir," Gregor cried out, beside himself and forgetting all else in his agitation, "I shall open the door at once, this very instant. A slight indisposition, a fit of dizziness kept me from getting up. Even now I'm still in bed. But already I am feeling very much refreshed. Here, I'm getting up. Just a moment's patience! It's a bit more difficult than I thought. But already I'm feeling quite fine. How odd, the way such a thing can suddenly come over one. Yesterday evening I felt perfectly all right, my parents can attest to this, or rather: I did in fact feel a mild foreboding yesterday evening already. Surely it was noticeable to anyone looking at me. Why didn't I send word to the office? But we always just assume we'll be able to overcome these illnesses without staying home. Sir! Do be gentle with my parents. The allegations you make are unfounded, and no one has ever mentioned anything of the sort to me. Perhaps you haven't yet looked over the most recent commissions I sent in. In any case, I'll be back on the road in time for the eight o'clock train; these additional hours of rest have fortified me. Please do not allow me to detain you any longer, sir; I shall be at the office myself in no time; do be so good as to say I'm on my way and give my regards to the boss."

And while Gregor was hastily blurting out all of this, scarcely knowing what he said, he edged closer to the wardrobe with minimal effort, no doubt thanks to the practice he had already acquired while still in bed, and now he did his best to haul himself upright. Indeed, he really did want to open the door, to show himself and speak with the general manager; he was eager to learn what the others, who were so anxious to see him, would say when they finally laid eyes on him. If they recoiled in horror, Gregor could surrender all responsibility and rest easy. But if they accepted it all calmly, that meant he too had no reason to get himself worked up, and if he hurried, he could still make it to the station by eight. At first he couldn't get a grip on the wardrobe's smooth surface, but finally he gave a great heave and found himself standing upright; he no longer paid any heed to the pain in his lower body, ache as it might. Now he let himself drop against the back of a nearby chair, clinging to its edges with his little legs. And having thus attained control over himself, he fell silent, for now he could listen to the general manager.

"Did you understand a single word?" the manager was asking Gregor's parents. "Surely he isn't trying to make fools of us?" "For heaven's sake," Gregor's mother cried, already weeping, "he might be gravely ill, and here we are tormenting him. Grete! Grete!" she cried out. "Mother?" Gregor's sister called from the other side. They were communicating through Gregor's room. "You must go for the doctor at once. Gregor is ill. Quick, fetch the doctor. Did you hear him speaking just now?" "That was an animal's voice," the general manager said, speaking in noticeably subdued tones compared to the cries of Gregor's mother. "Anna! Anna!" the father shouted into the kitchen through the vestibule, clapping his hands. "Run and fetch a locksmith, hurry!" And already the two girls were racing through the vestibule, their skirts rustling (how had Gregor's sister possibly gotten dressed so quickly?), and flung open the front door. There was no sound of the door closing again; no doubt they had left it standing open, as one sees with apartments in which a great calamity has occurred.

But Gregor was far less troubled now. Even though the others were no longer able to understand his words—though they had seemed to him clear enough, clearer than in the past, perhaps because his ear had grown accustomed to their sound—they were now convinced that things were not right with him and were prepared to offer help. The confidence and conviction with which these first arrangements had been made comforted him. He felt drawn once more into the circle of humankind and was expecting both the doctor and the locksmith—without properly differentiating between the two—to perform magnificent, astounding feats. So as to have as intelligible a voice as possible for the crucial discussions that lay ahead, he cleared his throat a little, making an effort to do this as discreetly as possible, since even this sound might differ from human throat-clearing, which he no longer trusted himself to judge. In the next room, meanwhile, all was quiet. Perhaps his parents sat whispering at the table with the general manager, or perhaps all of them were leaning against the door, listening.

Gregor slowly pushed himself over to the door using the armchair, then let go and allowed himself to fall against the door, propping himself upright—the pads of his little legs turned out to be slightly sticky—and there he rested briefly from his exertions. Then he set about turning the key in the lock using his mouth. Unfortunately it seemed he had no real teeth—so how was he supposed to grasp the key?—but his jaws turned out to be surprisingly strong; and with their help he actually succeeded in causing the key to move, paying no heed to the fact that he was no doubt injuring himself in the process, for a brown fluid ran out of his mouth and down the key, dripping onto the floor. "Listen to that," the general manager said in the next room, "he's turning the key in the lock." Gregor found these words most encouraging; but all of them should have been cheering him on, including his father and mother: "Come on, Gregor!" they should have shouted, "just keep at it, keep working on that lock!" And now, imagining all of them following his efforts with great suspense, he bit down on the key uncomprehendingly, with all the force he could muster. With each revolution of the key, he danced about the lock, holding himself upright using only his mouth and, as needed, either clinging to the key or using the entire weight of his body to press it down. The brighter sound of the lock finally springing open positively revived him. Sighing in relief, he said to himself: "I guess I didn't need the locksmith after all," and he laid his head upon the handle of the door to press it open.

But he remained hidden from view as the door swung toward him, even after it was wide open. To be seen, he had to work his way slowly around one of the wings of the double door, a delicate operation if he wanted to avoid plopping down awkwardly on his back before he'd even entered the room. He was still occupied with this difficult maneuver and had no leisure to attend to anything else when he heard the general manager utter a loud "Oh!"—it sounded like wind howling—and now he saw him too, saw how the general manager, who was standing closest to the door, pressed his hand to his open mouth, slowly retreating, as though being driven back by an invisible, steady force. Gregor's mother—who despite the general manager's presence stood with her hair still undone from the night, wildly bristling—first looked over at his father, her hands clasped, then took two steps in Gregor's direction before falling down in the midst of all her billowing skirts, her face vanishing completely where it sank to her bosom. Gregor's father clenched his fist with a hostile grimace, as if he intended to thrust Gregor back into his room, then glanced uncertainly about the living room, shaded his eyes with his hands, and wept until his mighty chest shook.

Gregor made no move to enter the room, instead he leaned from the inside against the wing of the door that was bolted fast, so that only half his body and the head inclined sideways above it could be seen as he peered across at the others. Meanwhile it had grown much lighter out; on the far side of the street, a section of the infinitely long, dark gray building opposite—a hospital—came into view with its regular windows punched into the facade; rain was still falling, but only in large drops that were separately visible and seemed to have been hurled one by one to the ground. An inordinate number of breakfast dishes crowded the table, for Gregor's father considered breakfast the most important meal of the day and would drag it out for hours reading various newspapers. Straight ahead, on the opposite wall, hung a photograph of Gregor from his time in the military, showing him as a second lieutenant whose carefree smile as he rested his hand on his dagger commanded respect for his bearing and his uniform. The door to the vestibule was open, and since the front door was open as well, one could see all the way out to the landing and the head of the stairs leading down.

"Well," Gregor said, quite conscious of the fact that he was the only one who had retained his composure, "I shall get dressed at once, pack up my samples and be on my way. As for the rest of you, are you prepared to let me do so? You can see, sir"—he said, addressing the general manager—"I am not obstinate, nor a shirker; traveling is burdensome, but without it I could not live. Where are you going now, sir? To the office? Yes? Will you report all these things truthfully? A person can be incapable of working at the moment, but this is precisely the right time to recall his earlier accomplishments and consider that he will later, once the hindrance has been overcome, work all the more industriously and with greater focus. I am so dreadfully indebted to the boss, surely you're aware of this. On the other hand, I have my parents and sister to think of. Truly I'm in a bind, but I shall work my way out of it. Don't make things more difficult for me than they already are. Take my side at the office! No one loves us drummers, I know. Everyone thinks the salesmen rake in a king's ransom while enjoying life's pleasures. And there's never any particular cause to reconsider this prejudice. But you, sir, have a far better grasp of the general circumstances than the rest of the staff, better even—if I may speak confidentially—than the boss himself, who in his role as businessman can easily err in his opinion to an employee's disadvantage. And you no doubt know quite well that a drummer, who spends almost the entire year away from the office, can easily become the victim of gossip, happenstance and groundless complaints against which he cannot possibly defend himself, as he usually never even learns of them, or only when he has completed one of his journeys, exhausted, and then back at home is forced to observe the dire physical effects of causes that can no longer be identified. Please, sir, do not leave without saying something to show you agree with me at least to some small extent!"

But the general manager had already turned away as soon as Gregor began to speak, and merely glanced back at him over a hunched shoulder, his mouth contorted. And during Gregor's speech he did not stand still for a moment but instead continued to retreat—not letting Gregor out of his sight—in the direction of the door, but only gradually, as though it were secretly prohibited to exit this room. Already he was in the vestibule, and to judge by the abrupt motion with which he withdrew his foot from the living room for the last time, one might have supposed he'd just burned it. Having reached the vestibule, however, he stretched out his right hand, gesturing broadly in the direction of the stairs, as if some all but supernatural salvation awaited him there.

Gregor realized he could not possibly allow the general manager to depart in his present frame of mind if his own position at the firm was not to be put in the gravest jeopardy. His parents didn't fully comprehend his situation: over these long years they had formed the conviction that Gregor was provided for in this office for life, and besides they were so preoccupied with their present worries that they were bereft of all foresight. But Gregor had this foresight. The general manager would have to be detained, reasoned with, convinced and finally won over; after all, Gregor's future and that of his family depended on it. If only his sister were here! She was clever; she had already begun to weep while Gregor was still lying quietly on his back. And surely the general manager, ever the ladies' man, would have let himself be assuaged by her; she would have closed the front door of the apartment and talked him out of his fear in the vestibule. But his sister was not there, so Gregor himself would have to act. And without stopping to consider that he was not yet familiar with his current abilities with respect to locomotion, nor even taking into account the fact that this last speech of his had quite possibly—indeed probably—eluded comprehension, he let go of the door; forced his way through the opening; meant to walk over to where the general manager, already out on the landing, was foolishly clutching at the banister with both hands; but right away, groping in vain for something to catch hold of, he fell with a faint shriek upon his many little legs. No sooner had this occurred than he felt—for the first time all morning—a sense of physical well-being; his legs had solid ground beneath them; they obeyed his will perfectly, as he noted to his delight; they even strove to bear him wherever he wished; and already it seemed to him he would soon be delivered from all his sufferings. But as he lay there on the floor directly in front of his mother and not far from her, swaying with mobility held in check, she suddenly leapt up—rapt as she had appeared within her own contemplations—leapt high up into the air, her arms thrust wide, fingers spread, crying out: "Help me, for God's sake, help!" her head cocked at an angle, as if to see Gregor better, but then, contradicting this, she senselessly retreated; but she had forgotten the table set for breakfast just behind her; sat down hurriedly upon it as soon as she reached it, as if absentmindedly; and didn't seem to notice that the big overturned coffeepot beside her was pouring a thick stream of coffee on the rug.

"Mother, Mother," Gregor said softly, gazing up at her. For a moment he had forgotten all about the general manager; on the other hand, he could not restrain himself, when he beheld this flowing coffee, from snapping his jaws several times. At this, the mother gave another shriek and fled from the table into the arms of Gregor's father as he rushed to her aid. But Gregor had no time for his parents now; the general manager was already on the stairs; his chin propped on the banister, he looked back on the scene one last time. Gregor was just preparing to dash after him to be sure of catching up with him; but the manager must have sensed something, for he leapt down several steps at once and vanished; and the cry of horror he gave as he fled resounded through the stairwell. Unfortunately the manager's flight now appeared to utterly discombobulate Gregor's father, who up till then had been relatively composed, for instead of running after the manager himself or at least not hindering Gregor in his own pursuit, he seized the manager's walking stick in one hand—it had been left lying on an armchair along with his overcoat and hat—with the other took up a large newspaper from the table, and set about driving Gregor back into his room with a great stamping of feet, brandishing both newspaper and stick. All Gregor's entreaties were in vain, nor were they even understood, for as submissively as he might swivel his head, his father only stamped his feet all the more ferociously. Across the room, his mother had flung open a window despite the chilly weather, and, leaning out, she pressed her face into her hands far outside the window frame. Between street and stairwell, a powerful draft arose, the window curtains flew into the air, the newspapers on the table rustled, and a few pages scudded across the floor. Inexorably Gregor's father drove him backward, uttering hissing sounds like a wild man. But Gregor had no practice at all in reverse locomotion, and his progress was very slow. If only he'd been permitted to turn around, he'd have been back in his room at once, but he was afraid of provoking his father's fury with this time-consuming maneuver, and at any moment a fatal blow from the stick in his father's hand might come crashing down on his back or head. In the end, though, he had no alternative: horrified, he realized he was incapable of controlling his direction; and so he began, with constant anxious glances back at his father, to turn around as quickly as he could, which in fact was rather slowly. Perhaps his father discerned his good intentions, for he did not hinder him in this operation but instead even guided his rotation here and there from a distance, using the tip of his stick. If only his father were not making that unbearable hissing noise! It made Gregor lose his head completely. He had already turned almost all the way around when—still with this hissing in his ear—he became confused and started turning back in the wrong direction. But when finally he succeeded in positioning his head in front of the doorway, it turned out that his body was too wide to fit through the opening. And of course in his father's current state it could not possibly have occurred to him to open the door's other wing to create an adequate passage. He was fixated on the notion that Gregor must disappear into his room as quickly as possible. Never would he have tolerated the complicated preparations necessary for Gregor to prop himself up so as possibly to pass through the door in an upright position. Instead, as though there were no obstacle at all, he now drove Gregor before him, raising a great din: what Gregor heard at his back no longer resembled the voice of merely a single father; it was do or die, and Gregor thrust himself—come what would—into the doorway. One side of his body tilted up, rising at an angle as he pressed forward, scraping his one flank raw and leaving ugly stains behind on the white door, and soon he was wedged tight, unable to move on his own; on one side, his little legs dangled trembling in midair, while on the other they were crushed painfully beneath him—then his father administered a powerful shove from behind, a genuinely liberating thrust that sent him flying, bleeding profusely, into the far reaches of his room. The door was banged shut with the stick, and then at last all was still.

II

Only as dusk was falling did Gregor wake from his heavy, faintlike sleep. He probably wouldn't have slept much longer even without a disturbance, for he felt sufficiently rested and restored, but it seemed to him he had been woken by a fleeting step and the careful shutting of the door to the vestibule. The pallid gleam of the electric streetlamps touched the ceiling here and there and the upper edges of the furniture, but down where Gregor lay, all was dark. Slowly, groping awkwardly with his feelers, which he was only now learning to appreciate, he dragged himself toward the door, wanting to see what had happened. His left side felt like one long unpleasantly contracting scar, and he was forced to limp outright on his two rows of legs. One of these diminutive legs, incidentally, had suffered grievous injuries in the course of the morning's events—it was almost miraculous only one had been injured—and now trailed lifelessly behind him.

Not until he reached the door did he realize what in fact had lured him there: it was the smell of something edible. There stood a bowl filled with sweet milk in which little pieces of white bread were floating. He almost laughed with delight, for his hunger was now even more powerful than in the morning, and right away he dunked his head in the milk almost up to his eyes. But he quickly drew it out again in disappointment; it wasn't just that eating was difficult thanks to his tender left side—and he couldn't eat at all without his entire body becoming gaspingly involved—but beyond that: even though milk had always been his favorite drink, which is no doubt why his sister had brought him some, now it didn't taste good to him at all, indeed it was almost with revulsion that he turned away from the bowl and crept back to the center of the room.

In the living room, as Gregor saw through the crack, the gas had been lit, but while usually at this hour his father liked to read aloud from the afternoon paper to Gregor's mother and sometimes his sister as well in a dramatic voice, now there was not a sound to be heard. Well, perhaps this customary reading aloud that his sister had often told and written him about had recently fallen out of practice. But even in the other rooms everything was so still, even though the apartment was surely not empty. "What a quiet life my family has been leading," Gregor said to himself, and as he gazed fixedly into the darkness before him, he felt great pride at having been able to give his parents and sister a life like this in such a beautiful apartment. But what if all this tranquility, all this prosperity and contentment were now coming to a horrific end? So as not to get lost in such contemplations, Gregor set himself in motion, crawling back and forth across the room.

Once in the course of this long evening one of the side doors was opened a tiny crack and then quickly shut again, and once the other one; someone must have felt an urge to enter and then been overcome by misgivings. Gregor now stationed himself just in front of the living room door, determined to somehow coax the hesitant visitor inside or at least find out who it was; but the door did not open again, and Gregor waited in vain. Before, when all the doors were locked, everyone kept trying to come in, and now that he had opened the one door and the others had apparently been opened during the day, no one came, and the keys were sticking in their locks from the outside.

It was late at night by the time the light in the living room went out, and now it was easy to ascertain that Gregor's parents and sister had remained awake all this time, for all three of them could clearly be heard departing on tiptoe. Now it was unlikely anyone would come into Gregor's room before morning; so he had plenty of time to ponder how best to reorder his life. But this high open room in which he was forced to lie flat on the floor distressed him, without his being able to determine the cause—after all, it was his room, which he had been living in for five years now—and with a half-unconscious motion, and not without a twinge of shame, he scurried beneath the settee, where even though his back was a bit cramped and he could no longer raise his head, he at once felt right at home, his only regret being that his body was too wide across to be accommodated entirely beneath this piece of furniture.

Here he remained the entire night, which he spent by turns dozing—though he was woken again and again by his hunger—and mulling over his worries and indistinct hopes, which however all led to the conclusion that, for the time being, he should behave calmly and, by employing patience and the utmost consideration, assist his family in enduring the inconveniences his current state inevitably forced him to impose on them.

Early the next morning already, so early it was almost still night, Gregor had the opportunity to test the strength of these resolutions he had made, for from the vestibule his sister, almost completely clothed, opened his door and cast an anxious glance into the room. She didn't immediately spot him, but when she noticed him beneath the settee—well, goodness, he had to be somewhere, it's not as if he might have flown away—the sight so alarmed her that, unable to control herself, she slammed the door from the outside. But as if regretting this conduct, she opened it again at once and came in, walking on tiptoe as though she were entering the room of a gravely ill patient or even a stranger. Gregor, having slid his head to just beneath the edge of the settee, observed her. Would she see that he had left the milk standing, and not because of a lack of hunger, and would she bring him some other food more to his liking? If she failed to do so of her own accord, he would sooner starve than call this to her attention, though in fact he felt a nearly monstrous urge to scoot out from beneath the settee, throw himself at his sister's feet, and beg her for something good to eat. But his sister immediately remarked with surprise that the bowl was still full, with just a little of its milk spilled on the floor around it, and she picked it up right away—not with her bare hands, to be sure, but with a rag—and carried it out of the room. Gregor was exceptionally curious to see what she would bring in its stead and mulled over various possibilities. But never would he have been able to predict what his sister in her kindness proceeded to do. To gauge his tastes, she brought him an entire assortment of foodstuffs, all spread out on an old newspaper. There were old, half-rotten vegetables; bones from the family supper the night before caked in a congealed white sauce; a few raisins and almonds; a piece of cheese Gregor had declared inedible two days before; a dry piece of bread; a slice of buttered bread; and a slice of bread with butter and salt. In addition, she placed beside this feast the bowl that apparently had been reserved for Gregor once and for all; it was now filled with water. And out of delicacy, since she knew Gregor would not eat in front of her, she quickly withdrew and even turned the key in the lock so that Gregor would understand he could make himself at home. Gregor's little legs whirred as he now went to take his meal. His wounds, incidentally, seemed to have healed entirely in the meantime, for he no longer felt the least impairment; this was astonishing, for more than a month ago he had cut his finger just a tiny bit with a knife, and this wound had still been painful enough just the day before yesterday. "Might I be less fastidious than before?" he thought, already sucking greedily at the cheese, to which he'd found himself immediately, inexorably drawn, more than to any of the other items. Quickly, his eyes shedding tears of gratification, he devoured in swift succession: the cheese, the vegetables, and the sauce; the fresh food, by contrast, did not taste good to him, in fact he could not even stand the smell of it and so dragged the things he wished to eat a little to one side. He had long since finished everything and was just lying indolently where he was when his sister slowly turned the key in the lock as a signal for him to withdraw. At once he gave a start, though he'd been on the point of nodding off, and he hurried back under the settee. But it cost him a great deal of willpower to remain there even for the short period of time his sister spent in the room, for the hearty meal he'd enjoyed had caused his abdomen to swell, and he could scarcely breathe in his confinement. In between little attacks of suffocation, he peered out with slightly bulging eyes as his sister, oblivious, used a broom to sweep up not only the remains of his meal but also the food he hadn't even touched, as if these items too were no longer fit for consumption, then she hastily dumped everything in a bucket that she covered with a wooden lid before carrying it all out of the room again. She had scarcely turned her back when Gregor hauled himself out from under the settee, stretching and puffing up his body.

This was how Gregor now received his food each day, once in the morning, when his parents and the maid were still asleep, and the second time after everyone had eaten lunch, for his parents would always nap a little afterward, and his sister would send the maid out on some errand or other. Surely they didn't want Gregor to starve either, but perhaps it would have been too much for them to experience his meals through more than hearsay, or perhaps his sister wanted to spare them even this modest sorrow, for Lord knows they were suffering enough.

Gregor never learned on what pretext the doctor and locksmith had been sent away that first morning, for since he himself could not be understood, it occurred to no one, not even his sister, that he could understand the others, so when his sister came to his room, he had to be content merely with hearing the sighs she heaved now and then and her words of supplication addressed to the saints. Only later, when she had started to grow accustomed to all of this—though of course it was impossible to become fully accustomed to circumstances like these—would Gregor sometimes catch a remark that was meant in a friendly way or could be interpreted as such. "He tucked right in today," she would say when Gregor had found the food she left him particularly tasty, while in the opposite case, which gradually began to occur more and more often, she was in the habit of saying almost mournfully: "This time he didn't touch a thing."

But while no news reached Gregor directly, he sometimes was able to overhear this and that from the rooms to either side of his, and whenever he heard voices, he would immediately run over to the door in question and press his entire body against it. Especially in the early days there was rarely a conversation that did not somehow, if only indirectly, refer to him. For two days, every mealtime was spent deliberating how the family should now comport itself; but even between meals this same discussion continued, for at least two members of the household were present at all times, since apparently no one wanted to remain at home alone, and of course leaving the apartment unattended was out of the question. What's more, the maid had fallen on her knees before Gregor's mother that very first day—it was not entirely clear what and how much she knew of what had occurred—begging to be released from the family's service, and when she took her leave a quarter of an hour later, she tearfully thanked them for dismissing her, as though this were the greatest benefaction she had experienced at their hands, and without anyone asking this of her, she swore a solemn oath never to reveal anything at all to anyone.

Now Gregor's sister was forced to do the cooking in concert with his mother; to be sure, not much effort was involved, as no one did much eating. Again and again Gregor would hear one of them pressing the others to eat—always in vain, and never with any other response than "Thank you, I've had all I want," or similar words. Perhaps they didn't drink anything either. Often Gregor's sister would ask her father if he wouldn't like a beer, affectionately offering to fetch it herself, and when he did not respond, she would say, wishing to relieve him of all scruples, that she could send the porter's wife for it as well, but then the father would utter a great "No," and no one spoke of it any longer.

Already in the course of the first day, Gregor's father explained the family's finances and prospects not only to Gregor's mother but to his sister as well.

Now and then he would get up from the table and, from his small Wertheim safe, which he had salvaged when his business collapsed five years before, extract some receipt or memorandum book. One could hear him opening the complicated lock and then bolting it shut again after removing the desired item. These explanations on his father's part included the first bits of heartening news Gregor had heard since his captivity began. He had been under the impression that his father had retained nothing at all of his former firm's holdings, or at least his father had never said anything to the contrary, and admittedly Gregor himself had never asked him about this. At the time, his only concern had been to do everything in his power to let the family forget, as quickly as possible, the mercantile catastrophe that had plunged all of them into a state of utter hopelessness. And so he had set to work with particular zeal and risen almost overnight from petty clerk to salesman, in which capacity of course he had a quite different earning potential, and his professional accomplishments, in the form of commissions, were immediately transformed into cash that could be plunked down on the table at home, before the eyes of his astonished, delighted family. Those had been lovely times, and never since had they been repeated, at least not with such glory, although Gregor later earned so much money that he was in a position to cover the expenses for the entire family, which he then did. All had grown accustomed to this arrangement, not just the family but Gregor as well: they gratefully accepted the money, and he was happy to provide it, but the exchange no longer felt particularly warm. Only Gregor's sister had remained close to him all this time, and it was his secret plan to send her off to study at the Conservatory next year (unlike Gregor, she dearly loved music and could play the violin quite movingly), despite the considerable costs this would no doubt entail, money that could surely be brought in by other means. Often during the brief periods of time Gregor spent in town, the Conservatory would come up in his conversations with his sister, but only ever as a lovely dream whose realization was unthinkable, and their parents did not like to hear it mentioned even in this innocuous way; but Gregor was thinking the matter over with great determination and intended to make a formal announcement on Christmas Eve.

Thoughts like these, utterly futile in his current state, passed through his head as he stood pressed against the door, eavesdropping. Sometimes general exhaustion made it impossible for him to go on listening, and he would carelessly let his head bump against the door, but then he would immediately hold his head still again, for even the faint sound this produced had been heard in the next room, causing everyone to fall silent. "I wonder what he's getting up to now," his father would say after a while, apparently facing the door, and only then would the interrupted conversation resume.

Gregor now learned, and learned quite well (his father tended to repeat himself in his explanations, in part because it had been so long since he'd last concerned himself with such matters, in part because Gregor's mother did not always understand everything the first time), that despite all their misfortunes, a small nest egg—really only a tiny one—still remained to them from before, and had even grown a little thanks to the untouched interest that had accumulated meanwhile. In addition, the money Gregor had brought home each month—he only ever kept a few gulden for himself—had not yet been entirely used up and had grown into a small capital. Behind his door, Gregor nodded eagerly, delighted at this unexpected prudence and thrift. To be sure, he might have used this surplus to pay off more of his father's debts with his boss, and the day on which he would have been able to divest himself of his post would no longer have been nearly so far off, but as things stood, his father's arrangements were no doubt for the best.

Now this money was by no means sufficient to allow the family to live off the interest or anything of that sort; it might possibly have been enough to sustain the family for a year, two at most, but that's all there was. So in fact it was the the kind of sum one really shouldn't touch, one to be set aside in case of emergency; the money to live on would have to be earned. Gregor's father was admittedly in good health, but he was old and hadn't worked in a full five years, and in any case he was supposed to avoid overtaxing himself; in those five years—the first holiday in his strenuous and yet unsuccessful life—he had put on a lot of weight and now lumbered as he walked. And was Gregor's old mother now supposed to hold down a job, despite her asthma and the fact that it was already an exertion for her to cross from one end of the apartment to the other, for which reason she spent every second day gasping for breath on the sofa beside the open window? And was his sister to go out working, this child of seventeen whose lifestyle no one would begrudge her: dressing nicely, sleeping late, helping out around the house, taking part in a few modest entertainments, and above all, playing the violin? Whenever the family came to speak of the necessity of someone earning money, Gregor would let go of the door and throw himself down upon the cool leather sofa beside it, burning with shame and sorrow.

Often he would lie there the entire long night, not sleeping for a moment, just scrabbling for hours against the leather. Or, not shunning the great effort it cost him to push an armchair over to the window, he would climb up the sill and, propped in the armchair, lean against the window, apparently lost in some sort of reverie of how liberating he'd always found it to gaze outside. For in truth he saw even the objects that were quite near at hand less and less clearly as the days progressed; the hospital across the way whose all too constant sight he had earlier reviled was now no longer even visible to him, and if he had not known perfectly well that he was a resident of Charlottenstrasse, a quiet but perfectly urban street, he might have imagined he was gazing out his window onto a desert in which the gray sky and the gray earth were indistinguishably conjoined. His attentive sister only had to see the armchair standing beside the window twice before she started pushing it back to its place there each time she tidied his room; indeed she even began leaving the window's inner sash open.

If only Gregor had been able to speak to his sister and thank her for all she was compelled to do for him, he would have found her ministrations easier to bear; as it was, he suffered beneath them. His sister, to be sure, did all she could to obscure the awkwardness of the situation, and the more time passed, the better she succeeded, of course, but Gregor came to see it all more and more clearly. Even the way she made her entrance jangled his nerves. The moment she came in, without even pausing to shut the door—although she always took such pains to shield the others from the sight of Gregor's room—she would race straightaway to the window and fling it open with hasty hands as though she were on the point of suffocating, then remain standing there, however cold it might be, gulping in the air. All this racing and racket was inflicted on Gregor twice a day; he would be trembling beneath the settee, painfully aware that she would no doubt have willingly spared him this disruption if it were possible for her to endure being in the same room as Gregor with the window closed.

Once—it must have been a month since Gregor's metamorphosis, so there was no particular call for his sister to be startled by his appearance—she came into his room a little earlier than usual and discovered him, motionless and propped upright as if for horrific effect, gazing out the window. Gregor would not have found it surprising if she had chosen not to enter, since his position prevented her from opening the window right away, but she didn't just not enter: she started in alarm and shut the door; a stranger might have thought Gregor had been lying in wait, meaning to bite her. Gregor naturally went and hid himself away beneath the settee, but he had to wait there until noon before his sister returned, and she seemed far more agitated than usual. From this he understood that his appearance was still unbearable to her and would remain so, and that she no doubt had to struggle to force herself not to run away at the sight of even the small part of his body that protruded from beneath the settee. In order to spare her even this sight, one day he carried the bedsheet over to the settee on his back—this labor cost him four hours—and arranged it in such a way that he was now completely covered, so that his sister would not be able to see him even if she bent down. If she considered the sheet unnecessary, she could have removed it, since it was clear enough that it could not possibly be considered a pleasure for Gregor to shut himself off so completely, but she left the sheet where it was, and Gregor even thought he glimpsed a grateful look when at one point he carefully lifted the sheet just a little with his head to see how his sister liked the new arrangement.

During the first fortnight, Gregor's parents could not bring themselves to enter his room, and often he heard them expressing their heartfelt appreciation of his sister's labors, whereas earlier they had often been annoyed with her, since she had seemed to them a rather useless girl. But now both of them, father and mother alike, would often be waiting just outside Gregor's door while his sister tidied up his room, and as soon as she emerged, she had to give a full report on what things looked like in the room, what Gregor had eaten, how he had behaved this time, and whether perhaps any modest improvement could be seen. His mother, incidentally, had wanted to visit him relatively soon, but his father and sister held her back, appealing at first to her sense of reason as Gregor listened attentively, wholeheartedly approving. Later, though, she had to be held back by force, and when she then cried out: "Let me go to Gregor, he is my unhappy son! Can't you understand that I must go to him?" then Gregor thought it would perhaps be good for his mother to visit him, not every day of course, but perhaps once a week; after all, she had a far better grasp of things than his sister, who despite her courage was still a child and, when it came right down to it, had perhaps only taken on this difficult task out of childish frivolity.

Gregor's wish to see his mother was soon fulfilled. During the day, Gregor avoided showing himself at the window, if only out of consideration for his parents, but there wasn't much crawling he could do in the few square meters of space the floor provided, lying still was already difficult for him to endure during the night, eating had soon ceased to give him even the slightest pleasure, and so to divert himself he took up the habit of crawling back and forth across the walls and ceiling. He particularly liked hanging from the ceiling high above the room; it was completely different from lying on the floor; one could breathe more freely there; a gentle swaying motion rocked the body; and in the almost happy absentmindedness Gregor experienced, it might happen, to his own astonishment, that he would let go and crash to the floor. But now, of course, he had his body far better under control than before, and even as great a fall as this did him no harm. His sister immediately noticed the new entertainment Gregor had devised for himself—his peregrinations left behind sticky trails here and there—and she got it into her head to make it possible for Gregor to range as widely as possible by removing the furniture that impeded his movement, above all the wardrobe and desk. But she wasn't able to do so on her own; she didn't dare ask her father for help; the maid most certainly would not have helped her, for this girl of sixteen or so, though she had courageously remained in the household after the departure of the former cook, had at the same time requested the privilege of keeping the kitchen locked at all times and only opening the door upon particular request; and so the sister had no choice but to summon her mother one day when her father was out. The mother arrived with exclamations of feverish joy but fell silent at the door to Gregor's room. At first, of course, Gregor's sister checked to confirm that all in the room was as it should be; only then did she allow her mother to enter. With the utmost haste, Gregor had tugged the sheet down lower and in looser folds so that it really did look as if a bedsheet just happened to have been tossed over the settee. He also refrained from peering out from beneath the sheet this time; for the moment, he would resign himself to not seeing his mother and just be glad she had come. "It's all right, come in, you won't see him," Gregor's sister said, apparently leading her mother by the hand. Gregor now heard the sounds of these two weak women grappling with this in fact quite heavy old wardrobe, with his sister laying claim to the bulk of the work, not listening to the admonitions of her mother, who was afraid she would overtax herself. It took a very long time. After perhaps a quarter of an hour's labor, Gregor's mother said they should leave the wardrobe where it was after all; in the first place, it was too heavy—they would not finish before Gregor's father came home, and by leaving the wardrobe in the middle of the room, they would prevent Gregor from moving around at all—and secondly, it wasn't even clear they were doing him a favor by taking away the furniture. To her, it seemed the opposite was true: the sight of the empty wall positively oppressed her heart; and why should Gregor not experience this same sentiment, since after all he was long accustomed to having this furniture around him—wouldn't he feel abandoned in an emptied-out room? "And is it not as if," his mother concluded in a low voice—in fact, she had been whispering all along, as though she wished to avoid letting Gregor, whose exact whereabouts she did not know, hear so much as the sound of her voice, for she was convinced he could not understand her words—"and is it not as if by removing the furniture we would be showing that we are giving up all hope of a cure and are ruthlessly abandoning him to his own devices? I think it would be best if we try to keep the room in precisely the same state it was in before, so that when Gregor returns to us he will find everything unchanged, which will make it that much easier for him to forget all that has happened in the meantime."

Hearing his mother's words, Gregor realized that the absence of all direct human address, combined with the monotony of life in his family's midst, must have muddled his understanding over the course of these two months, for he could not otherwise explain to himself how he could seriously have wished to have his room emptied out. Did he really want to have this warm room, comfortably furnished with family heirlooms, transformed into a cave or den—in which, to be sure, he would be able to crawl about unhindered in every direction, but at the price of simultaneously swiftly and completely forgetting his human past? He was already on the verge of forgetting, and only his mother's voice, which he had gone so long now without hearing, had shaken him awake. Nothing should be removed; everything must remain; he was unwilling to forego the good influence this furniture had on his condition; and if the furniture got in the way of his practicing this mindless crawling about, this was by no means to his detriment, in fact, it was a great advantage.

Unfortunately his sister was of a different opinion; she had developed the habit—not entirely without cause, to be sure—of presenting herself as the holder of particular expertise when discussing Gregor with her parents, and so now too her mother's counsel was reason enough for her to insist on the removal not only of the wardrobe and desk, as she had originally been intending, but of every last bit of the room's furnishings, with the exception of the indispensable settee. Naturally, it was not simply childish defiance and the hard-won self-assurance she had so unexpectedly acquired in recent weeks that dictated this demand; she had, in fact, observed that Gregor needed a great deal of space to crawl around in, while as far as anyone could see, he made no use whatever of the furniture. But perhaps the fanciful imagination of a girl of her age played a role as well, a sensibility always seeking its own gratification, and one which Grete now allowed to persuade her to render Gregor's situation even more horrific than before, so as to be able to do even more for him than she had hitherto. For a room in which Gregor held sole dominion over empty walls was a place where no one other than Grete would ever dare to set foot.

And so she held fast to her resolve despite the protests of her mother, who appeared troubled to the point of indecision even by the room in its present state; she soon fell silent and helped Gregor's sister remove the wardrobe as best she could. Well, the wardrobe was something Gregor could do without if need be, but the desk would certainly have to stay. And no sooner had the women left the room with the cabinet, groaning as they pressed against its weight, than Gregor poked out his head from beneath the settee to see how he might, cautiously and as considerately as possible, intervene. But unfortunately his mother was the first to return while Grete was still in the next room, clasping the wardrobe in her arms and tipping it back and forth on her own—without, of course, moving it from the spot. But Gregor's mother was unaccustomed to his appearance, it might have made her ill to catch a glimpse of him, and so Gregor in alarm withdrew as fast as he could to the far end of the settee, but it was too late to prevent the front edge of the bedsheet from stirring a little. This was enough to attract his mother's notice. Startled, she froze for a moment, then went back to where Grete was.

Although Gregor kept telling himself that nothing extraordinary was happening, just a few sticks of furniture being shifted about, he was soon forced to admit that all this coming and going on the part of the women, their little exclamations, the furniture scraping against the floor, had the combined effect of a tumultuous hubbub intensifying all around him, and no matter how tightly he drew his head and legs in and pressed his body against the floor, he soon was forced to consider that he would not be able to endure this much longer. They were clearing out his room; taking from him all that was dear to him; they had already borne away the cabinet in which lay his fretsaw and other tools; and now they were prying loose the desk that had dug itself firmly into the floorboards, this desk at which he had written his homework assignments as a student at the commercial academy, and as a secondary and even primary school pupil—truly there was no time left to explore the good intentions of these two women, whose existence, by the way, he had almost forgotten, for their exhaustion was now making them labor in silence, and one heard only their heavy footsteps.

And so he burst out of hiding—the women in the next room were just leaning on the desk to catch their breath—changing direction four times as he raced about, for he really didn't know what to save first, but then his eyes lit on the picture of the lady clad all in furs, conspicuous now on the otherwise empty wall, and quickly he made his way up to it and pressed himself against the glass, which adhered to him, pleasantly cool against his hot belly. At least this picture, which Gregor's body now covered up completely, was absolutely certain not to be taken away from him. He swiveled his head toward the living room door to observe the women as they returned.

They hadn't permitted themselves much rest at all and were already on their way back; Grete had slung one arm about her mother and was nearly carrying her. "So what should we take next?" Grete said, looking around. Then her eyes met those of Gregor where he clung to the wall. It was no doubt only because of her mother's presence that she kept her composure; bowing her face toward her mother to prevent her from glancing about, she said—hastily and trembling, to be sure—"Let's go back to the living room for a moment, shall we?" Grete's intentions were perfectly clear to Gregor: she meant to bring their mother to safety and then chase him from the wall. Well, let her try! He sat there on his picture and would not give it up. He'd sooner leap right in her face.

But Grete's words succeeded in unsettling her mother even more: taking one step to the side, she saw the huge brown blotch on the flowered wallpaper, and before she was even able to realize that what she saw there was Gregor, she cried out in a hoarse, shrieking voice, "Oh God, oh God!" and fell back upon the settee, her arms spread wide as though she were giving up everything, and lay there without moving. "Gregor!" his sister shouted, raising her fist with a threatening glower. It was the first time she had addressed him directly since his metamorphosis. She ran into the next room to fetch some sort of essence that could be used to awaken her mother from her faint; Gregor wanted to help as well—there would be time enough to save the picture later—but he stuck fast to the glass and had to tear himself away by force;

he too then ran into the next room as if he might offer his sister advice of some sort, like in the old days; but then could only stand idly behind her as she rummaged among various little bottles, and scared her out of her wits when she turned around; one bottle flew to the floor and shattered; a shard of glass scratched Gregor's face, and some sort of corrosive medicine engulfed him; without further delay, Grete took up as many bottles as she could hold and ran with them to her mother, slamming the door behind her with her foot. Gregor was now cut off from his mother, who was possibly on the brink of death, for which he himself was to blame; he could not open the door if he didn't want to drive away his sister, who had to stay there with his mother; there was nothing for him to do but wait; and tormented by his worries and self-reproach, he began to crawl about, crawling over everything, walls, furniture, the ceiling, and finally in his despair, as the entire room began to spin around him, he fell smack in the middle of the big table.

A short while passed. Gregor lay there, spent, and around him all was still, possibly a good sign. Then the bell rang. The maid was naturally locked up in her kitchen and so Grete had to open the door. Their father was back. "What happened?" were his first words; the look on Grete's face had no doubt revealed all. Grete's voice as she responded was muffled, apparently she was pressing her face against his chest: "Mother fainted, but she's better already. Gregor has broken out." "That's just what I expected," the father said. "I kept telling you, but you women refused to listen." To Gregor it was clear his father had misinterpreted Grete's all too brief pronouncement to assume him guilty of some act of violence. So it behooved Gregor to try to pacify his father, as he was lacking both the time and means to enlighten him. With this in mind, he fled to the door of his room and pressed himself against it, so that the moment his father came into the living room from the vestibule he would see that Gregor had every intention of returning at once to his room, that it was unnecessary to drive him back inside, and that one had merely to open the door, and he would disappear at once.

But his father was in no mood to take note of subtleties. "Ah!" he exclaimed upon entering, in a tone of voice suggesting he was at once furious and glad. Gregor pulled his head back from the door and turned it toward his father. He had truly not expected to see his father looking as he looked now standing before him; though to be sure the novelty of crawling about had distracted him recently from paying as much attention as before to the goings-on in the rest of the apartment, and really he ought to have been prepared to find a changed set of circumstances. Even so, even so: was this still his father? The same man who used to lie wearily entombed in his bed when Gregor set off on a business trip; who would greet him on the evening of his return sitting in an armchair in his nightshirt; who, incapable of rising, would merely raise his arms to signify his delight, and on the rare walks they still shared, a few Sundays each year and on major holidays, would trudge between Gregor and his mother, who themselves were already walking rather slowly, moving even a bit slower than they, bundled up in his old overcoat, always with his gingerly advancing cane and almost invariably coming to a halt and collecting his companions around him whenever he had something to say? Now he was standing properly erect; dressed in a smart blue uniform with gold buttons of the sort worn by porters in banking establishments; above the jacket's tall, stiff collar his powerful double chin unfurled; beneath bushy eyebrows, his black eyes peered out acutely and attentively; his once disheveled white hair had been painstakingly combed and parted until it gleamed. He tossed his cap, to which a gold monogram was affixed, probably that of a bank, across the entire room in a wide arc to land on the settee, then advanced grim-faced upon Gregor with the tips of his long uniform jacket flung back and his hands in his trouser pockets. He himself probably had no idea what he intended to do; at any rate, he raised up each foot unusually high, and Gregor marveled at the gigantic dimensions of his boot-soles. But he did not lose any time over them, having learned on the very first day of his new life that his father considered only the utmost severity appropriate for him. And so he fled from his father, hesitating whenever his father stopped short, and then rushing forward again as soon as he stirred. They circled the room several times in this manner without anything decisive occurring, and indeed, given the slow speed at which this interaction was taking place, without its even having the appearance of a chase. For this reason Gregor remained at floor level for the time being, especially as he feared his father might consider it particular wickedness on his part if he were to take refuge on the walls or ceiling. To be sure, he was forced to realize he would not be able to keep up even this pace for long, since each time his father took a step, he himself had to execute any number of motions. A shortness of breath began to set in— even in his earlier life his lungs had been none too reliable. As he now lurched along, reserving all his strength for this continued flight, his eyes barely open (and not thinking, in his stupefaction, that there might be other ways of saving himself than running across the floor, indeed he had almost forgotten he also had the walls at his disposal, though here, to be sure, they were obstructed by delicately carved furniture full of jagged, pointy edges), all at once something flew to the rug beside him, casually flung, and rolled across his path. It was an apple; and already a second one came flying after it; in horror, Gregor stopped in his tracks; there was no point continuing to run now that his father had decided to bombard him. He had filled his pockets from the fruit bowl on the sideboard and now was tossing apple after apple in Gregor's direction, for the moment not even bothering to take particular aim. The petite red apples rolled around the floor as if electrified, knocking into each other. One lightly lobbed apple grazed Gregor's back and slid off again harmlessly. But it was immediately followed by another that embedded itself in his back. Gregor tried to drag himself forward, as if this sudden shocking pain might vanish with a change of place; but he felt nailed to the spot and collapsed there, his legs splaying out, all his senses in a state of utter bewilderment. He caught only a last glimpse of the door to his room flying open, his shrieking sister, and his mother running out of the room before her wearing only a chemise, for his sister had undressed the unconscious woman to let her breathe more freely, then he saw his mother rush to his father's side, her unfastened skirts slipping one by one from about her waist as she ran, saw her stumble across these skirts as she threw herself at his father and, embracing him, in perfect union with him—but now Gregor's vision began to fail him— she clasped her hands at the back of his father's head and pleaded with him to spare Gregor's life.

III

The grievous wound Gregor had received, which plagued him for over a month—the apple remained lodged there in his flesh, a visible memento, since no one dared to remove it—seemed to have reminded even his father that Gregor, despite his current lamentable, repulsive form, was a member of the family who should not be treated like an enemy, for family duty dictated that the others swallow down the disgust he aroused in them and show him tolerance, only tolerance.

And even though this wound cost Gregor some of his mobility, probably for good, and for the time being he required many, many minutes to hobble across his room like an old invalid—crawling up the walls was out of the question now—he was compensated for this worsening of his condition by what seemed to him a perfectly adequate substitute: as evening approached, the door to the living room, on which he would start keeping a sharp eye an hour or two beforehand, would always be opened so as to permit him, lying in his own dark room and invisible from the living room, to watch the entire family sitting at the brightly lit table and listen to their conversations now, as it were, in an officially sanctioned capacity and thus quite differently than before.

To be sure, these were no longer the animated conversations of earlier times that Gregor used to think back on with a certain longing from various cramped hotel rooms when it was time to throw himself, exhausted, into the damp bedding. Now everything was fairly quiet. Gregor's father would fall asleep in his armchair soon after supper; his mother and sister would admonish one another to silence; his mother, bent far over beneath the light, would be sewing ladies' underthings for a dress shop; his sister, who had taken a job as a salesgirl, was studying stenography and French in the evenings so as possibly to move to a better position later on. Sometimes Gregor's father would wake up and, as if unaware he had been sleeping, would say to Gregor's mother: "How long you've been sewing again today!" and then go right back to sleep, which would prompt Gregor's mother and sister to exchange weary smiles.

In a peculiar form of stubbornness, Gregor's father refused to take off his porter's uniform even at home; and while his nightshirt hung uselessly on its hook, he would slumber where he sat, fully clothed, as though he remained ready for service at all times and even here was awaiting his supervisor's call. As a result, his uniform, which had not been new to start with, soon forfeited much of its cleanliness, despite the care lavished on it by mother and sister, and Gregor would sometimes gaze for an entire evening at this stain-covered jacket resplendent with gold buttons, always highly polished, in which the old man slept in considerable discomfort but nonetheless soundly.

The moment the clock struck ten, Gregor's mother would attempt to rouse his father with a few hushed words and then persuade him to go to bed, for he would get no proper sleep sitting here, and sleep was something Gregor's father—who had to report for duty at six in the morning—desperately needed. But in keeping with the stubbornness that had taken hold of him when he started working as a porter, he always insisted on continuing to sit there at the table, even though he kept falling asleep, and then it was only with the greatest effort that he could be persuaded to exchange armchair for bed. Gregor's mother and sister could persist in their little admonishments as doggedly as they liked; for a quarter of an hour, he would just shake his head slowly, his eyes closed, without getting up. Gregor's mother would pluck at his sleeve, whispering cajoling words in his ear, and his sister would set aside her studies to come to her mother's aid, but to no avail. Gregor's father only settled deeper into his armchair. Only when the women gripped him beneath the arms would he open his eyes, looking by turns at mother and sister and saying: "What sort of life is this? Is this the peace and quiet of my old age?" Then, supported by the two women, he would rise, laboriously, as though he himself were receiving the brunt of this burden, and allow the women to escort him to the doorway, where he would shoo them away and continue on his own, while Gregor's mother hastily threw down her sewing and his sister her pen so they could run after him to offer further assistance. The household was ever further reduced; the maid was now let go after all; a bony giant of a charwoman with white hair flapping about her head came by in the morning and evening to perform the heaviest labors; everything else was handled by Gregor's mother along with all her sewing. It even came to pass that several pieces of jewelry that had been in the family—jewels Gregor's mother and sister had delighted in wearing at entertainments and festivities—were sold, as Gregor would learn in the evening when the price each piece had brought would be discussed. But their greatest lament was always that they were unable to leave this apartment, which was far too large for their current circumstances, since no one could imagine how Gregor might be moved. But Gregor understood that it was not only out of consideration for him that a move was being ruled out, since he could easily enough have been transported in a crate of appropriate size with a few air holes; the main thing keeping the family from moving to a new apartment was their complete sense of hopelessness and the thought that they had been struck with a misfortune such as no one else in their entire circle of relations and friends had ever experienced. They were fulfilling to the utmost the demands the world makes on the poor: Gregor's father fetched breakfast for the petty employees at the bank, his mother sacrificed herself for the underclothes of strangers, his sister ran back and forth behind the shop counter at her customers' behest, but this was all the strength they had. And the wound in Gregor's back would begin to ache anew when mother and sister, having brought his father to bed, would now return and, leaving their work where it lay, huddle close beside one another pressing their cheeks together; when Gregor's mother, gesturing toward his room, would say: "Shut the door now, Grete"; and when Gregor was left in the dark again while next door the two women intermingled their tears or else sat there tearless, staring down at the table.

Gregor spent his nights and days almost entirely without sleeping. Sometimes he thought about taking the family's affairs in hand again, just as he used to, the next time his door was opened; once more his boss and the general manager would appear before his mind's eye after all this time, the clerks and apprentices, the dull-witted hired man, two or three friends from other firms, a chambermaid from a provincial hotel (a sweet, fleeting specter), the shopgirl from a haberdashery whom he had courted earnestly but too slowly—all of these now appeared to him, interspersed with strangers or people already forgotten, but instead of coming to his aid and that of his family, every last one of them was unapproachable, and he was glad when they disappeared. At other times he would be not at all in a frame of mind to look after his family; instead he was filled with rage at how poorly he was attended to, and although he could not imagine anything he would have liked to eat, he plotted how he might gain access to the pantry so as to help himself to what—despite his total absence of hunger—was his due. Without bothering to consider how she might give Gregor particular pleasure, his sister would quickly thrust some randomly chosen foodstuff into his room with her foot on her way to work in the morning or at midday, only to sweep it out again at night with a quick swipe of the broom, paying no heed if the food had been only barely nibbled at or—as was most often the case now—not touched at all. Setting Gregor's room to rights, a task she now saved for the evenings, could not possibly have been done any more perfunctorily. Great streaks of dirt extended across the walls, with balls of dust and rubbish lying scattered about. At first when Gregor's sister came into his room he would position himself in corners particularly indicative of this problem—to reproach her, as it were, by his presence there. But he could just as well have spent entire weeks sitting there without any improvement on his sister's part; after all, she saw the dirt as plainly as he did, but had made up her mind to leave it be. At the same time, with a sensitivity that was new in her, one that had now taken hold of the family as a whole, she was on her guard to make sure the task of tidying Gregor's room was reserved for her. Once Gregor's mother had subjected his room to a thorough scrubbing, which she accomplished only after using up several buckets of water—admittedly, all this moisture was itself an affront to Gregor, who lay stretched out, bitter and immobile, upon the settee—but his mother did not escape punishment. For no sooner had his sister remarked the change in Gregor's room that evening than she ran into the living room, grievously insulted, and ignoring her mother's imploringly raised hands, set to weeping so violently that her parents—naturally her father was startled out of his chair—at first stood by helpless and astonished; until they too began to stir; on the right, Gregor's father reproached his mother for not having left the cleaning of Gregor's room to his sister; while on the left he shouted at Gregor's sister, threatening that she would never again be permitted to clean Gregor's room; while his mother attempted to drag his father, now so agitated he hardly recognized himself, into the bedroom; Gregor's sister, shaking with sobs, pummeled the table with her tiny fists; and Gregor hissed loudly in fury because it had occurred to no one to shut the door of his room to spare him this sight and commotion.

But even if Gregor's sister, who was exhausted by her professional work, had wearied of caring for Gregor as she'd previously done, there was absolutely no need for his mother to fill her shoes, and Gregor needn't have suffered neglect. For now the charwoman was here. This old widow—who had seen and survived the worst in her long life with the help of her sturdy bones—felt no particular repugnance toward Gregor. Without being at all inquisitive, she had once chanced to open the door to his room and, seeing Gregor, who had begun to run back and forth although no one was chasing him, she stood there staring in astonishment, her hands clasped across her lap. Ever since, she never failed to open the door a crack for a moment every morning and evening to look in on him. At the beginning she would call him over to her, saying things that were probably intended to sound friendly, like "Hey, over here, you old dung beetle!" or "Just look at the old dung beetle!" Thus addressed, Gregor gave no reply but instead remained where he was, immobile, as if the door had never been opened. If only this charwoman, instead of being allowed to disturb him uselessly at whim, had been given instructions to clean his room daily! Once, early in the morning—a heavy rain, perhaps already a portent of the coming spring, was beating against the windowpanes—Gregor became so infuriated when the charwoman started up again with her quips that he turned on her as if to attack, if admittedly slowly and decrepitly. But instead of being frightened, the charwoman just picked up a chair that was standing beside the door and held it high in the air; and as she stood there, her mouth gaping wide, her intention was clear: not to close her mouth again until the chair in her hand had come crashing down upon Gregor's back. "Aha, so that's as far as it goes?" she asked as Gregor turned around again, and she placed the chair calmly back in its corner.

Gregor now ate almost nothing at all. Only if he happened by chance to wander past the food that had been prepared for him might he playfully take a bite of something into his mouth, where he would hold it for hours and then usually spit it out again later. At first he thought it was his sorrow at the state of his room that prevented him from eating, but in fact he had resigned himself very quickly to the changes there. Everyone had gotten into the habit of using his room to store things there was no space for in other parts of the apartment, and now there were many such things, since one room of the apartment had been rented out to three lodgers. These solemn gentlemen—all three of them were bearded, as Gregor once noted, peering through the crack of the door—were scrupulously intent on having everything tidy, not just in their room but also, since they were now paying rent here, in the entire household, particularly the kitchen. They could not bear the presence of unnecessary, much less dirty items. Moreover, they had brought most of their own furnishings with them. For this reason, many things had become superfluous, things that could not be sold but were still too valuable to throw out. All of this found its way into Gregor's room. As did the ash box and the garbage pail from the kitchen. The charwoman, always in a great hurry, would simply fling any unserviceable item into Gregor's room; mercifully, Gregor generally saw only the object in question and the hand that held it. The charwoman may have intended at some point, when she had occasion or a free minute, to come collect these things, or else throw all of them out at once, but as it was they remained wherever they first landed, except when Gregor made his way through the refuse, stirring it around—at first out of necessity, since there was no room left for him to crawl about, but later with ever-increasing pleasure, though after these wanderings, which left him mortally exhausted and sad, he would spend hours without moving.

Since the lodgers sometimes also took their supper at home in the shared living room, the living room door remained shut on some evenings, but Gregor was happy to forgo having the door open; in fact, even when it was open, he sometimes failed to take advantage of it and instead, unbeknownst to his family, would remain lying in the darkest corner of his room. Once, however, the charwoman had left the door to the living room slightly ajar, and ajar it remained even when the lodgers came in that evening and struck a light. They sat down at the head of the table where in earlier times Gregor had sat with his father and mother, unfolded the napkins and took up their knives and forks. At once Gregor's mother appeared in the doorway with a serving dish filled with meat, and right behind her came his sister bearing a plate piled high with potatoes. A heavy vapor rose from the steaming food. The lodgers bent over the dishes that had been placed before them, as though wishing to inspect them before beginning their meal, and in fact the one who sat in the middle and appeared to be an authority figure to the other two cut off a piece of meat right there on the platter to check whether it was tender enough and didn't have to be sent back to the kitchen. He was satisfied, and Gregor's mother and sister, who had been watching nervously, now smiled with relief.

The family members themselves ate in the kitchen. Nonetheless Gregor's father visited the living room on his way to the kitchen and with a single bow, cap in hand, took a tour around the table. The lodgers all rose from their seats and mumbled into their beards. Left alone again, they ate in almost perfect silence. It struck Gregor as peculiar that amid all the various sounds of this meal, one could also make out their champing teeth, as if to demonstrate to Gregor that a person needs teeth to eat and that even the most splendid jaws, if toothless, can accomplish nothing at all. "I'm hungry," Gregor said sorrowfully to himself, "but not for these things. Just look how these lodgers take their nourishment while I am wasting away!"

On this very evening—Gregor couldn't remember having heard the violin once in all this time—the sound of it was heard coming from the kitchen. The lodgers had already finished their evening meal, the one in the middle had pulled out a newspaper, giving each of the others a page, and now the three of them were reading, leaning back in their chairs and smoking. When the violin began to play, their interest was piqued, they got up from their chairs and tiptoed over to the doorway leading to the vestibule, where they stood in a tight cluster. The sounds of this activity must have traveled to the kitchen, for Gregor's father now called out: "Are the gentlemen disturbed by this playing? It can be silenced at once." "On the contrary," said the one in the middle, "would the young lady care to join us and play here in the living room, where it is much more comfortable and pleasant?" "Why, of course," Gregor's father exclaimed, as though he were the violinist. The gentlemen went back into the room and waited. Soon Gregor's father arrived with the music stand, his mother with the sheet music and his sister with the violin. His sister calmly prepared to play; his parents, who never rented out rooms in earlier days and therefore were treating these lodgers with exaggerated deference, did not even dare to sit in their own armchairs; his father leaned against the door, his right hand tucked between two buttons of his closed livery jacket; his mother, meanwhile, was offered an armchair by one of the lodgers, and since she left the chair where he had happened to place it, she sat off to one side in a corner.

Gregor's sister began to play; on either side, his father and mother attentively followed each movement of her hands. Attracted by her playing, Gregor had ventured a bit further than usual and was already sticking his head into the living room. It scarcely surprised him that he had become so inconsiderate of the others; earlier on, his considerateness had been a source of pride. And he had all the more reason to keep himself hidden away now: thanks to the dust that lay everywhere in his room and would swirl up at the slightest motion, he too was covered in dust; he dragged around threads, hair and food scraps clinging to his back and sides; his general indifference was far too great now for him to keep up with a habit he'd once practiced several times a day: flipping over so as to scrub his back against the rug. And despite his condition, he did not hesitate now to continue his advance a little way out onto the immaculate floor of the living room.

To be sure, no one paid him the slightest heed. The family was completely absorbed in the violin playing; the lodgers, on the other hand, having at first positioned themselves, hands in their trouser pockets, much too close behind his sister's music stand, so that they could all look at the sheet music, which surely must have distracted her, soon withdrew to the window, conversing in an undertone, and remained there, anxiously observed by Gregor's father. It appeared more than clear they had been disappointed in their expectation of hearing beautiful or entertaining violin music and now, tired of the whole performance, were continuing to tolerate this disturbance of their peace only out of politeness. Particularly the way in which all of them were blowing the smoke of their cigars high into the air from their noses and mouths suggested extreme agitation. And yet his sister's playing was so lovely. Her face was tilted to one side; searchingly, sadly, her eyes followed the lines of notes. Gregor crept a bit farther forward and ducked his head down close to the floor so as perhaps to catch her eye. Was he a beast, that music so moved him? He felt as if he were being shown the way to that unknown nourishment he craved. He was determined to creep all the way up to his sister, to pluck at her skirt and in this way indicate to her that she should come to his room with her violin, for no one here was rewarding her playing as he meant to reward her. He would not allow her to leave his room ever again, at least as long as he was alive; his horrific figure would, for the first time ever, be useful to him; he would be at all the doors of his room at once, growling at his attackers; but his sister should remain with him not by force but of her own free will; she should sit beside him on the settee, bend down, the better to hear, and he would confess to her that he'd had the firm intention of sending her to the Conservatory and that if the disaster had not disrupted his plans, he would have made a general announcement last Christmas—Christmas had passed now, hadn't it?—without letting himself be swayed by objections of any sort. After this declaration, his sister would be moved to the point of tears, and Gregor would raise himself to the height of her armpit and kiss her throat, which, now that she went to the office every day, she wore free of ribbon or collar.

"Herr Samsa!" the gentleman in the middle shouted at Gregor's father, and without wasting a single word, pointed his finger at Gregor, who was slowly advancing. The violin fell silent, the middle lodger at first just smiled and shook his head, turning toward his friends, then looked again at Gregor. Gregor's father apparently found the task of driving Gregor back into his room less urgent than that of calming the lodgers, despite the fact that they did not appear particularly worked up and seemed to be finding Gregor more entertaining than the music. He hurried over to them and tried with outspread arms to herd them back into their room, at the same time using his body to shield Gregor from their view. And now they did in fact become a little angry, though it was no longer clear whether this was on account of Gregor's father's behavior or the realization dawning on them that without their knowledge they had been sharing their home with a roommate of this sort. They demanded explanations of Gregor's father; now it was their turn to throw their arms into the air; they plucked uneasily at their beards and only slowly withdrew in the direction of their room. Meanwhile Gregor's sister, who had been standing there at a loss since her playing had been so unexpectedly interrupted—she still held violin and bow in her carelessly dangling hands, looking over at the notes as though she were continuing to play—all at once pulled herself together, laid her instrument in the lap of her mother, who still sat there in her armchair, her lungs heaving as she fought for breath, and ran into the next room, toward which the lodgers were now moving somewhat more quickly as Gregor's father urged them on. One saw how, beneath his sister's practiced hands, the beds' blankets and pillows flew into the air and into orderliness. Even before the lodgers reached the room, she had finished making up the beds and slipped out. Gregor's father appeared to be once more so firmly in the grip of his own stubbornness that he forgot the basic respect that, after all, he owed his tenants. He kept up his pressing and urging until, already standing in the doorway, the middle lodger thunderously stamped his foot, causing Gregor's father to stop short. "I hereby declare," he said, raising his hand and seeking out Gregor's mother and sister too as he glanced about, "that in consideration of the reprehensible circumstances prevailing in this apartment and family"—and here he spat on the floor without forethought—"I give notice on my room effective immediately. It goes without saying that I will not pay a penny for the days I have spent here; on the contrary, I shall consider whether or not to pursue you with—please believe me—easily justifiable claims." He fell silent and went on looking straight before him expectantly. And indeed his two friends at once chimed in with the words, "We too give notice effective immediately." Hereupon he seized the door handle and with a great crash slammed the door.

Gregor's father staggered to his armchair with groping hands and let himself fall into it; it looked as though he was stretching out for his customary evening nap, but the violent nodding of his anchorless head showed that he was absolutely not sleeping. Gregor had gone on lying quietly on the spot where the lodgers had espied him. His disappointment at the failure of his plan and perhaps also the weakness caused by starvation rendered him incapable of moving. With a certain definitiveness he sensed, terrified, that everything was about to collapse all around him, and so he waited. Not even the violin startled him when it fell from his mother's lap beneath her trembling fingers, giving off a note that echoed in the air.

"Dear parents," his sister said, striking the table by way of preamble, "things cannot go on like this. Even if you two perhaps do not realize it, I most certainly do. I am unwilling to utter my brother's name before this creature, and therefore will say only: we have to try to get rid of it. We have done everything humanly possible to care for it and show it tolerance, I don't think anyone would reproach us on this account."

"She is right a thousand times over," Gregor's father murmured under his breath. His mother, still incapable of breathing freely, began to cough dully into her lifted hand, a lunatic expression in her eyes.

Gregor's sister hurried over to her mother and held her forehead. Her words seemed to have given her father an idea, for he now sat up straight, playing with his uniform cap between the plates left behind on the table from the lodgers' supper and glancing over from time to time at a quiet Gregor.

"We have to try to get rid of it," his sister said, addressing her words exclusively to Gregor's father this time, for his mother was coughing too hard to hear anything. "It'll be the death of you two, I can see it now. When people have to work as hard as all of us have been doing, it just isn't possible to endure these endless torments at home. I cannot bear it anymore either." And she burst into sobs, weeping so forcefully that her tears flowed down upon her mother's face, from which the girl wiped them with a mechanical gesture.

"Child," her father said sympathetically and with noticeable compassion, "but what can we do?"

Gregor's sister just shrugged her shoulders as a sign of the helplessness that had come over her while she was weeping, in contrast to the confidence she'd displayed a moment before.

"If he understood us," Gregor's father said, half-questioning; his sister, still caught up in her weeping, shook one hand vehemently as a sign of how unthinkable she found this.

"If he understood us," his father repeated, closing his eyes to absorb her conviction that this was utterly out of the question, "then it might be possible to come to an agreement with him. But as things stand—"

"It has to go," Gregor's sister cried out, "that's the only way, Father. You just have to try to let go of the notion that this thing is Gregor. The real disaster is that we believed this for so long. But how could it be Gregor? If it were Gregor, it would have realized a long time ago that it just isn't possible for human beings to live beside such a creature, and it would have gone away on its own. We still would have been lacking a brother but we would have been able to go on living and honoring his memory. But now we have this beast tormenting us; it drives away our lodgers and apparently intends to take over the entire apartment and have us sleep in the gutter. Just look, Father," she suddenly shrieked, "he's starting again!" And in a fright that Gregor found bewildering, she now went so far as to leave her mother behind, launching herself from her chair as if she would rather sacrifice her mother than remain in Gregor's proximity, and ran to take cover behind her father who, agitated by the way she was carrying on, rose from his own chair and half-raised his arms as if to shield her.

But Gregor was far from wanting to frighten anyone, above all his sister. All he'd done was start to turn around to make his way back to his room, and admittedly this operation would have been hard not to notice, since in his current injured state he was obliged to use his head to help with this difficult maneuver; he kept raising it up and then thumping it against the floor. Pausing, he glanced around. His good intentions seemed to have been recognized; it had been only a momentary fright. Now all of them gazed at him sadly and in silence. His mother lay in her armchair, her extended legs pressed together, barely able to keep her eyes open in her exhaustion; his father and sister sat side by side, and his sister had draped one hand across her father's neck.

"Perhaps I'll be allowed to turn around now," Gregor thought and resumed his labors. He could not entirely suppress the wheezing this exertion produced, and now and then he had to rest. Otherwise no one was harassing him, he had been left to attend to matters on his own. When he had completed this rotation, he immediately made straight for the door to his room. He was astonished at how great a distance separated him from his destination, and he didn't understand how, weak as he was, he had been able to traverse the same distance just a little while before almost without noticing. Steadfastly concentrating only on crawling as quickly as possible, he scarcely paid any heed to the fact that not a word, not a cry came from his family to disturb him. Only when he was already in the doorway did he turn his head—not all the way around, as he felt his neck growing stiff, but even so he was able to see that all was unchanged behind him, except that his sister had risen to her feet. The last thing he saw was a glimpse of his mother, who had now fallen entirely asleep.

No sooner was he in his room again than the door was hastily pressed shut, locked and bolted. The sudden commotion at his back gave him such a frightful start that his little legs gave way beneath him. It was his sister who had hurried thus. She had already been standing there upright and waiting, then pounced so lightfootedly Gregor didn't hear her approach, and she cried out, "Finally!" to her parents as she turned the key in the lock.

"And now?" Gregor wondered, looking around in the dark. He soon made the discovery that he was no longer capable of moving at all. He wasn't surprised at this; on the contrary, it struck him as unnatural that he had actually until now been able to support himself on those thin little legs. As for the rest, he felt relatively at ease. Admittedly his entire body was racked with pain, but it seemed to him as if it was gradually becoming weaker and weaker and in the end would fade away altogether. Already he could scarcely feel the rotting apple in his back, nor the inflamed area surrounding it, both now enveloped in soft dust. He thought back on his family with tenderness and love. His opinion that he must by all means disappear was possibly even more emphatic than that of his sister. He remained in this state of empty, peaceful reflection until the clock-tower struck the third hour of morning. He watched as everything began to lighten outside his window. Then his head sank all the way to the floor without volition and from his nostrils his last breath faintly streamed.

When the charwoman arrived early the next morning, slamming the doors so loudly in her strength and haste—often as she'd been asked to avoid this—that sleep was out of the question anywhere in the apartment after her arrival, her usual cursory visit to Gregor's room revealed at first nothing out of the ordinary. She thought he was lying there so motionless on purpose, feigning indignation; she considered him perfectly capable of rational thought. Since she happened to be holding the long broom in her hand, she tried tickling Gregor with it from the doorway. When even this had no effect, she grew vexed and began to poke Gregor a little, and only when she had actually shifted him from the spot where he lay with no resistance at all were her suspicions roused. When soon thereafter the facts of the matter became clear to her, she gawked in surprise, gave a low whistle, then without further delay flung open the door of the bedroom and in a loud voice shouted into the darkness: "Come have a look, it's gone and croaked—just lying there, dead as a doornail!"

The Samsa couple shot upright in their marital bed and first had to struggle to recover from their shock at the charwoman's conduct before they were able to grasp her words. But then Herr and Frau[3] Samsa hurriedly got out of bed, one on either side, Herr Samsa threw the blanket about his shoulders while Frau Samsa emerged wearing only her nightdress; in this state, they entered Gregor's room. Meanwhile the door to the living room, where Grete had been sleeping since the lodgers' arrival, had opened as well; she was fully dressed, as though she had not slept at all, as even the pallor of her cheeks seemed to prove. "Dead?" Frau Samsa asked, looking questioningly up at the charwoman, although she herself was free to investigate and, indeed, could see how things stood even without investigation. "I should say so," the charwoman said, and by way of proof, pushed Gregor's corpse quite some way to the side with her broom. Frau Samsa made a gesture as though she wanted to hold back the broom but didn't. "Well," Herr Samsa said, "now we can thank God." He crossed himself, and the three women followed his example. Grete, who did not take her eyes off the corpse for a moment, said: "Just look how skinny he was. He went such a long time without eating anything at all. All the food that went into his room would come out again just as before." And indeed Gregor's body was completely flat and dry, which hadn't really been noticeable until now when he was no longer raised up on those little legs and nothing else remained to distract the gaze.

"Grete, come sit with us for a bit," Frau Samsa said with a melancholy smile, and Grete, glancing back at the corpse, followed her parents into their bedroom. The charwoman shut the door and opened the window wide. Despite the early morning, the crisp air was already tempered by a certain mildness: after all, it was already the end of March.

The three lodgers now emerged from their room and looked about in astonishment for their breakfast; they had been forgotten. "Where's breakfast?" the one in the middle asked the charwoman peevishly. But she just put a finger to her lips and then quickly, without a word, beckoned the lodgers into Gregor's room. They did as she bade them and with their hands in the pockets of their slightly threadbare little jackets, they surrounded Gregor's corpse in the room that had meanwhile become quite bright.

Then the bedroom door opened, and Herr Samsa appeared wearing his livery, with his wife on one arm, his daughter on the other. All three looked as if they'd been weeping; Grete kept pressing her face against her father's arm.

"Leave my home at once!" Herr Samsa said, pointing at the door without letting go of the womenfolk. "What do you mean?" the gentleman in the middle inquired, dumbfounded, and gave a saccharine smile. The two others held their hands at their backs and kept rubbing them together uninterruptedly, as if in gleeful expectation of a fight that was certain to be decided in their favor. "I mean exactly what I say," Herr Samsa replied, now advancing on the lodger flanked by his two companions. The lodger just stood there at first, looking at the ground, as if things were just rearranging themselves in his head into a new order. "So we'll be leaving," he said then, looking up at Herr Samsa as if this new humility that had suddenly come over him required him to petition for the approval of even this decision. Herr Samsa merely nodded

---

3. Mrs. (German).

curtly in his direction a few times, goggle-eyed. At this, the gentleman did, in fact, make haste to stride back out to the vestibule, where his two friends had been listening attentively for some moments, their hands at rest, and now they practically hopped and skipped in their hurry to follow, as if worried Herr Samsa might somehow precede them into the vestibule, cutting off their line of communication with their leader.

In the vestibule, all three of them took their hats from the coat rack, withdrew their walking sticks from the cane stand, made a silent bow and left the apartment. Displaying what soon proved to be an utterly unfounded mistrustfulness, Herr Samsa stepped out onto the landing with the two women; leaning against the banister, they watched as the three gentlemen descended the long staircase, moving slowly but at a steady pace and disappearing on each floor at a certain bend of the stairwell only to appear again a few moments later; the farther down they went, the more the Samsa family's interest in them faded, and when a butcher's apprentice came toward and then passed them on his way up, proudly bearing his tray upon his head, Herr Samsa and the women abandoned the banister, and all of them returned, seemingly relieved, to their apartment.

They decided to spend the day resting and to go out for a stroll; they had not only earned this respite from their work, but were desperately in need of it. And so they all sat down at the table and wrote three letters of excuse: Herr Samsa to his supervisor, Frau Samsa to her employer, and Grete to her superior. While they were writing, the charwoman came in to say she was leaving, as her morning's work was completed. The three scribes at first merely nodded without looking up, and only when the charwoman failed to go on her way did they glance up in annoyance. "Well?" Herr Samsa asked. The charwoman stood smiling in the doorway as if she had some splendid good fortune to announce to the family but would not do so until she was properly questioned. The nearly vertical little ostrich feathers on her hat, which had annoyed Herr Samsa for as long as she had been in the family's service, bobbed gently in all directions. "So what is it you want?" she was asked now by Frau Samsa, the member of the family for whom the charwoman still had the most respect. "Well," the charwoman replied, her own good-natured laughter making it impossible at first for her to go on speaking, "there's no need for you to go worrying about how to get rid of that mess in there. It's already taken care of." Frau Samsa and Grete bent down over their letters as if they meant to go on writing; Herr Samsa, who saw that the charwoman was about to start describing everything in detail, summarily silenced her with an outstretched hand. And since she was not permitted to say what she wished, she suddenly remembered the great hurry she was in, and so with an insulted air she cried, "So long, everyone," turned wildly on her heel, and with the most excruciating slamming of doors left the apartment.

"Tonight she'll be let go," Herr Samsa said, but received an answer neither from his wife nor his daughter, for the charwoman seemed to have disturbed the equanimity they had only just attained. They rose from their seats, went to the window, and remained there with their arms about each other. Herr Samsa turned in his chair to look at them and observed them quietly for a little while. Then he cried out: "So come here already. Let these old matters rest. And show a little consideration for me as well." At once the women obeyed, hurried over to him, caressed him and quickly finished their letters.

Then all three of them left the apartment together, something they had not done for months, and took the electric tram all the way to the open country-side at the edge of town. The car in which they sat all alone was entirely suf-fused with warm sunlight. Cozily leaning back in their seats, they discussed their future prospects, and on closer investigation it appeared that these prospects were not bad at all, for all three of their positions—something they had never before properly discussed—were in fact quite advantageous and above all offered promising opportunities for advancement. The greatest immedi-ate improvement in their situation, of course, would be easily achieved by moving to a new apartment; they now wished to take a smaller and cheaper but more convenient and above all more practical flat than their current one, which had been picked out for them by Gregor. As they were conversing in this way, Herr and Frau Samsa were struck almost as one while observing their daughter, who was growing ever more vivacious, by the thought that despite all the torments that had made her cheeks grow pale, she had recently blossomed into a beautiful, voluptuous girl. Growing quieter now and com-municating with one another almost unconsciously by an exchange of glances, they thought about how it would soon be time to find her a good hus-band. And when they arrived at their destination, it seemed to them almost a confirmation of their new dreams and good intentions when their daughter swiftly sprang to her feet and stretched her young body.

1915

A Hunger Artist[1]

During these last decades the interest in professional fasting has mark-edly diminished. It used to pay very well to stage such great performances under one's own management, but today that is quite impossible. We live in a different world now. At one time the whole town took a lively interest in the hunger artist; from day to day of his fast the excitement mounted; everybody wanted to see him at least once a day; there were people who bought season tickets for the last few days and sat from morning till night in front of his small barred cage; even in the nighttime there were visiting hours, when the whole effect was heightened by torch flares; on fine days the cage was set out in the open air, and then it was the children's special treat to see the hunger artist; for their elders he was often just a joke that happened to be in fashion, but the children stood open-mouthed, holding each other's hands for greater security, marveling at him as he sat there pallid in black tights, with his ribs sticking out so prominently, not even on a seat but down among straw on the ground, sometimes giving a courteous nod, answering questions with a con-strained smile, or perhaps stretching an arm through the bars so that one might feel how thin it was, and then again withdrawing deep into himself, pay-ing no attention to anyone or anything, not even to the all-important striking

---

1. Translated by Edwin and Willa Muir.

of the clock that was the only piece of furniture in his cage, but merely staring into vacancy with half shut eyes, now and then taking a sip from a tiny glass of water to moisten his lips.

Besides casual onlookers there were also relays of permanent watchers selected by the public, usually butchers, strangely enough, and it was their task to watch the hunger artist day and night, three of them at a time, in case he should have some secret recourse to nourishment. This was nothing but a formality, instituted to reassure the masses, for the initiates knew well enough that during his fast the artist would never in any circumstances, not even under forcible compulsion, swallow the smallest morsel of food: the honor of his profession forbade it. Not every watcher, of course, was capable of understanding this, there were often groups of night watchers who were very lax in carrying out their duties and deliberately huddled together in a retired corner to play cards with great absorption, obviously intending to give the hunger artist the chance of a little refreshment, which they supposed he could draw from some private hoard. Nothing annoyed the artist more than such watchers; they made him miserable; they made his fast seem unendurable; sometimes he mastered his feebleness sufficiently to sing during their watch for as long as he could keep going, to show them how unjust their suspicions were. But that was of little use; they only wondered at his cleverness in being able to fill his mouth even while singing. Much more to his taste were the watchers who sat close up to the bars, who were not content with the dim night lighting of the hall but focused him in the full glare of the electric pocket torch[2] given them by the impresario. The harsh light did not trouble him at all, in any case he could never sleep properly, and he could always drowse a little, whatever the light, at any hour, even when the hall was thronged with noisy onlookers. He was quite happy at the prospect of spending a sleepless night with such watchers; he was ready to exchange jokes with them, to tell them stories out of his nomadic life, anything at all to keep them awake and demonstrate to them again that he had no eatables in his cage and that he was fasting as not one of them could fast. But his happiest moment was when the morning came and an enormous breakfast was brought them, at his expense, on which they flung themselves with the keen appetite of healthy men after a weary night of wakefulness. Of course there were people who argued that this breakfast was an unfair attempt to bribe the watchers, but that was going rather too far, and when they were invited to take on a night's vigil without a breakfast, merely for the sake of the cause, they made themselves scarce, although they stuck stubbornly to their suspicions.

Such suspicions, anyhow, were a necessary accompaniment to the profession of fasting. No one could possibly watch the hunger artist continuously, day and night, and so no one could produce first-hand evidence that the fast had really been rigorous and continuous; only the artist himself could know that, he was therefore bound to be the sole completely satisfied spectator of his own fast. Yet for other reasons he was never satisfied; it was not perhaps mere fasting that had brought him to such skeleton thinness that many people had regretfully to keep away from his exhibitions, because the sight of him was too much for them, perhaps it was dissatisfaction with himself that had

2. Flashlight.

worn him down. For he alone knew, what no other initiate knew, how easy it was to fast. It was the easiest thing in the world. He made no secret of this, yet people did not believe him, at the best they set him down as modest; most of them, however, thought he was out for publicity or else was some kind of cheat who found it easy to fast because he had discovered a way of making it easy, and then had the impudence to admit the fact, more or less. He had to put up with all that, and in the course of time had got used to it, but his inner dissatisfaction always rankled, and never yet, after any term of fasting—this must be granted to his credit—had he left the cage of his own free will. The longest period of fasting was fixed by his impresario at forty days,[3] beyond that term he was not allowed to go, not even in great cities, and there was good reason for it, too. Experience had proved that for about forty days the interest of the public could be stimulated by a steadily increasing pressure of advertisement, but after that the town began to lose interest, sympathetic support began notably to fall off; there were of course local variations as between one town and another or one country and another, but as a general rule forty days marked the limit. So on the fortieth day the flower-bedecked cage was opened, enthusiastic spectators filled the hall, a military band played, two doctors entered the cage to measure the results of the fast, which were announced through a megaphone, and finally two young ladies appeared, blissful at having been selected for the honor, to help the hunger artist down the few steps leading to a small table on which was spread a carefully chosen invalid repast. And at this very moment the artist always turned stubborn. True, he would entrust his bony arms to the outstretched helping hands of the ladies bending over him, but stand up he would not. Why stop fasting at this particular moment, after forty days of it? He had held out for a long time, an illimitably long time; why stop now, when he was in his best fasting form, or rather, not yet quite in his best fasting form? Why should he be cheated of the fame he would get for fasting longer, for being not only the record hunger artist of all time, which presumably he was already, but for beating his own record by a performance beyond human imagination, since he felt that there were no limits to his capacity for fasting? His public pretended to admire him so much, why should it have so little patience with him; if he could endure fasting longer, why shouldn't the public endure it? Besides, he was tired, he was comfortable sitting in the straw, and now he was supposed to lift himself to his full height and go down to a meal the very thought of which gave him a nausea that only the presence of the ladies kept him from betraying, and even that with an effort. And he looked up into the eyes of the ladies who were apparently so friendly and in reality so cruel, and shook his head, which felt too heavy on its strengthless neck. But then there happened yet again what always happened. The impresario came forward, without a word—for the band made speech impossible—lifted his arms in the air above the artist, as if inviting Heaven to look down upon its creature here in the straw, this suffering martyr, which indeed he was, although in quite another sense; grasped him round the emaciated waist, with exaggerated caution, so that the frail condition he was in might be appreciated; and com-

---

3. Common biblical timespan; in the New Testament, Jesus fasts for 40 days in the desert and has visions of both God and the devil.

mitted him to the care of the blenching ladies, not without secretly giving him a shaking so that his legs and body tottered and swayed. The artist now submitted completely; his head lolled on his breast as if it had landed there by chance; his body was hollowed out; his legs in a spasm of self-preservation clung close to each other at the knees, yet scraped on the ground as if it were not really solid ground, as if they were only trying to find solid ground; and the whole weight of his body, a feather-weight after all, relapsed onto one of the ladies, who, looking round for help and panting a little—this post of honor was not at all what she had expected it to be—first stretched her neck as far as she could to keep her face at least free from contact with the artist, when finding this impossible, and her more fortunate companion not coming to her aid but merely holding extended on her own trembling hand the little bunch of knucklebones that was the artist's, to the great delight of the spectators burst into tears and had to be replaced by an attendant who had long been stationed in readiness. Then came the food, a little of which the impresario managed to get between the artist's lips, while he sat in a kind of half-fainting trance, to the accompaniment of cheerful patter designed to distract the public's attention from the artist's condition; after that, a toast was drunk to the public, supposedly prompted by a whisper from the artist in the impresario's ear; the band confirmed it with a mighty flourish, the spectators melted away, and no one had any cause to be dissatisfied with the proceedings, no one except the hunger artist himself, he only, as always.

So he lived for many years, with small regular intervals of recuperation, in visible glory, honored by the world, yet in spite of that troubled in spirit, and all the more troubled because no one would take his trouble seriously. What comfort could he possibly need? What more could he possibly wish for? And if some good-natured person, feeling sorry for him, tried to console him by pointing out that his melancholy was probably caused by fasting, it could happen, especially when he had been fasting for some time, that he reacted with an outburst of fury and to the general alarm began to shake the bars of his cage like a wild animal. Yet the impresario had a way of punishing these outbreaks which he rather enjoyed putting into operation. He would apologize publicly for the artist's behavior, which was only to be excused, he admitted, because of the irritability caused by fasting, a condition hardly to be understood by well-fed people; then by natural transition he went on to mention the artist's equally incomprehensible boast that he could fast for much longer than he was doing; he praised the high ambition, the good will, the great self-denial undoubtedly implicit in such a statement; and then quite simply countered it by bringing out photographs, which were also on sale to the public, showing the artist on the fortieth day of a fast lying in bed almost dead from exhaustion. This perversion of the truth, familiar to the artist though it was, always unnerved him afresh and proved too much for him. What was a consequence of the premature ending of his fast was here presented as the cause of it! To fight against this lack of understanding, against a whole world of non-understanding, was impossible. Time and again in good faith he stood by the bars listening to the impresario, but as soon as the photographs appeared he always let go and sank with a groan back on to his straw, and the reassured public could once more come close and gaze at him.

A few years later when the witnesses of such scenes called them to mind, they often failed to understand themselves at all. For meanwhile the afore-mentioned change in public interest had set in; it seemed to happen almost overnight; there may have been profound causes for it, but who was going to bother about that; at any rate the pampered hunger artist suddenly found himself deserted one fine day by the amusement seekers, who went streaming past him to other more favored attractions. For the last time the impresario hurried him over half Europe to discover whether the old interest might still survive here and there; all in vain; everywhere, as if by secret agreement, a posi-tive revulsion from professional fasting was in evidence. Of course it could not really have sprung up so suddenly as all that, and many premonitory symptoms which had not been sufficiently remarked or suppressed during the rush and glitter of success now came retrospectively to mind, but it was now too late to take any countermeasures. Fasting would surely come into fashion again at some future date, yet that was no comfort for those living in the present. What, then, was the hunger artist to do? He had been applauded by thousands in his time and could hardly come down to showing himself in a street booth at village fairs, and as for adopting another profession, he was not only too old for that but too fanatically devoted to fasting. So he took leave of the impresario, his partner in an unparalleled career, and hired him-self to a large circus; in order to spare his own feelings he avoided reading the conditions of his contract.

A large circus with its enormous traffic in replacing and recruiting men, animals and apparatus can always find a use for people at any time, even for a hunger artist, provided of course that he does not ask too much, and in this particular case anyhow it was not only the artist who was taken on but his famous and long-known name as well, indeed considering the peculiar nature of his performance, which was not impaired by advancing age, it could not be objected that here was an artist past his prime, no longer at the height of his professional skill, seeking a refuge in some quiet corner of a circus; on the contrary, the hunger artist averred that he could fast as well as ever, which was entirely credible, he even alleged that if he were allowed to fast as he liked, and this was at once promised him without more ado, he could astound the world by establishing a record never yet achieved, a statement which certainly provoked a smile among the other professionals, since it left out of account the change in public opinion, which the hunger artist in his zeal conveniently forgot.

He had not, however, actually lost his sense of the real situation and took it as a matter of course that he and his cage should be stationed, not in the middle of the ring as a main attraction, but outside, near the animal cages, on a site that was after all easily accessible. Large and gaily painted placards made a frame for the cage and announced what was to be seen inside it. When the public came thronging out in the intervals to see the animals, they could hardly avoid passing the hunger artist's cage and stopping there for a moment, perhaps they might even have stayed longer had not those pressing behind them in the narrow gangway, who did not understand why they should be held up on their way toward the excitements of the menagerie, made it impos-sible for anyone to stand gazing quietly for any length of time. And that was the reason why the hunger artist, who had of course been looking forward to these visiting hours as the main achievement of his life, began instead to shrink from them. At first he could hardly wait for the intervals; it was exhilarating to watch the crowds come streaming his way, until only too soon—not even the most obstinate self-deception, clung to almost consciously, could hold out against the fact—the conviction was borne in upon him that these people, most of them, to judge from their actions, again and again, without exception, were all on their way to the menagerie. And the first sight of them from the distance remained the best. For when they reached his cage he was at once deafened by the storm of shouting and abuse that arose from the two contending factions, which renewed themselves continuously, of those who wanted to stop and stare at him—he soon began to dislike them more than the others—not out of real interest but only out of obstinate self-assertiveness, and those who wanted to go straight on to the animals. When the first great rush was past, the stragglers came along, and these, whom nothing could have prevented from stopping to look at him as long as they had breath, raced past with long strides, hardly even glancing at him, in their haste to get to the menagerie in time. And all too rarely did it happen that he had a stroke of luck, when some father of a family fetched up before him with his children, pointed a finger at the hunger artist and explained at length what the phenomenon meant, telling stories of earlier years when he himself had watched similar but much more thrilling performances, and the children, still rather uncomprehending, since neither inside nor outside school had they been sufficiently prepared for this lesson—what did they care about fasting?—yet showed by the brightness of their intent eyes that new and better times might be coming. Perhaps, said the hunger artist to himself many a time, things would be a little better if his cage were set not quite so near the menagerie. That made it too easy for people to make their choice, to say nothing of what he suffered from the stench of the menagerie, the animals' restlessness by night, the carrying past of raw lumps of flesh for the beasts of prey, the roaring at feeding times, which depressed him continually. But he did not dare to lodge a complaint with the management; after all, he had the animals to thank for the troops of people who passed his cage, among whom there might always be one here and there to take an interest in him, and who could tell where they might seclude him if he called attention to his existence and thereby to the fact that, strictly speaking, he was only an impediment on the way to the menagerie.

A small impediment, to be sure, one that grew steadily less. People grew familiar with the strange idea that they could be expected, in times like these, to take an interest in a hunger artist, and with this familiarity the verdict went out against him. He might fast as much as he could, and he did so; but nothing could save him now, people passed him by. Just try to explain to anyone the art of fasting! Anyone who has no feeling for it cannot be made to understand it. The fine placards grew dirty and illegible, they were torn down; the little notice board telling the number of fast days achieved, which at first was changed carefully every day, had long stayed at the same figure, for after the first few weeks even this small task seemed pointless to the staff; and so the artist simply fasted on and on, as he had once dreamed of doing, and it was no trouble to him, just as he had always foretold, but no one counted the days, no one, not even the artist himself, knew what records he was already breaking, and his heart grew heavy. And when once in a time some leisurely passer-by stopped, made merry over the old figure on the board and spoke of swindling, that was in its way the stupidest lie ever invented by indifference and inborn malice, since it was not the hunger artist who was cheating; he was working honestly, but the world was cheating him of his reward.

Many more days went by, however, and that too came to an end. An overseer's eye fell on the cage one day and he asked the attendants why this perfectly good cage should be left standing there unused with dirty straw inside it; nobody knew, until one man, helped out by the notice board, remembered about the hunger artist. They poked into the straw with sticks and found him in it. "Are you still fasting?" asked the overseer. "When on earth do you mean to stop?" "Forgive me, everybody," whispered the hunger artist; only the overseer, who had his ear to the bars, understood him. "Of course," said the overseer, and tapped his forehead with a finger to let the attendants know what state the man was in, "we forgive you." "I always wanted you to admire my fasting," said the hunger artist. "We do admire it," said the overseer, affably. "But you shouldn't admire it," said the hunger artist. "Well, then we don't admire it," said the overseer, "but why shouldn't we admire it?" "Because I have to fast, I can't help it," said the hunger artist. "What a fellow you are," said the overseer, "and why can't you help it?" "Because," said the hunger artist, lifting his head a little and speaking, with his lips pursed, as if for a kiss, right into the overseer's ear, so that no syllable might be lost, "because I couldn't find the food I liked. If I had found it, believe me, I should have made no fuss and stuffed myself like you or anyone else." These were his last words, but in his dimming eyes remained the firm though no longer proud persuasion that he was still continuing to fast.

"Well, clear this out now!" said the overseer, and they buried the hunger artist, straw and all. Into the cage they put a young panther. Even the most insensitive felt it refreshing to see this wild creature leaping around the cage that had so long been dreary. The panther was all right. The food he liked was brought him without hesitation by the attendants; he seemed not even to miss his freedom; his noble body, furnished almost to the bursting point with all that it needed, seemed to carry freedom around with it too; somewhere in his jaws it seemed to lurk; and the joy of life streamed with such ardent passion from his throat that for the onlookers it was not easy to stand the shock of it. But they braced themselves, crowded round the cage, and did not want ever to move away.

1924

RELATED:

—Kafka, Letter to Max Brod, p. 1722
—Stanley Corngold, "Kafka's *The Metamorphosis*: Metamorphosis of the Metaphor," p. 1758

YASUNARI KAWABATA
1899–1972

Kawabata was the first Japanese writer to win the Nobel Prize for literature, in 1968. He was born in Osaka and raised in circumstances haunted by loss—he was orphaned at the age of three; his grandmother died when he was seven. Two years later, his only sister died as well. Kawabata's work is a uniquely personal combination of classic Japanese literature and twentieth-century modernism. Perhaps his most famous work is *Snow Country* (1937), which was singled out in his Nobel Prize citation, but Kawabata himself regarded *The Master of Go* (1951) as his finest achievement. His so-called "Palm-of-the-Hand Stories"—never more than two or three pages—show him to be a great writer of short fiction, able to make startling leaps of imagination in a small, highly concentrated space. In his Nobel Prize speech, Kawabata condemned the culture of suicide. Yet two years after his friend and fellow writer Yukio Mishima committed suicide, he too took his own life.

The White Horse[1]

In the leaves of the oak tree, there was a silver sun.

Raising his face, Noguchi was dazzled by the light. He blinked and looked again. The light was not directly striking his eyes; it was caught amid the dense foliage.

For a Japanese oak, the tree had much too thick a trunk and stood much too tall. A number of other oaks clustered around it. Their lower branches unpruned, they screened the western sun. Beyond the stand of oaks, the summer sun went on sinking.

Because of the thickly intermeshed foliage, the sun itself could not be seen. Instead, the sun was the light that spread itself among the leaves. Noguchi was used to seeing it that way. On the highlands, the green of the leaves was as vivid as that of a Western oak. Absorbing the light, the leaves of the oak turned to a pale, translucent green and made sparkling wavelets of light as they swayed in the breeze.

This evening, the leaves of the tree were quiet. The light on the foliage was still.

"What?" Noguchi said the word out loud. He had just noticed the dusky color of the sky. It was not the color of a sky in which the sun was still halfway up in the high stand of oaks. It was the color of a sky in which the sun had

1. Translation by Martin Holman.

just set. The silvery light on the oak leaves came from a small white cloud beyond the grove that reflected the light of the setting sun. To the left of the grove, the faraway waves of mountains were darkening to a deep, faded blue.

The silvery light, which had been caught by the grove, suddenly went out. The green of the thick foliage slowly blackened. From the summit of the trees, a white horse leapt upward and galloped across the gray sky.

"Ahh . . ." But Noguchi was not that surprised. It was not an unusual dream for him.

"She's riding it again, in a black robe again."

The black robe of the woman astride the horse streamed out behind her. No—the folds of long black cloth that flowed over the stallion's arched tail were attached to the robe but seemed separate from it.

"What is it?" As Noguchi was thinking this, the vision faded away. But the rhythm of the horse's legs remained in his heart. Although the horse seemed to gallop headlong like a racehorse, there was a leisurely rhythm in the gallop. And the legs were the only part of the horse in motion. The hooves were sharply pointed.

"That long black cloth in back of her—what was it? Or was it a cloth?" Noguchi asked himself uneasily.

When Noguchi had been in the upper grades of elementary school, he had played with Taeko in the garden where the sweet oleander hedge was in bloom. They had drawn pictures together. They drew pictures of horses; when Taeko drew a horse galloping across the sky, Noguchi drew one, too.

"That's the horse that stamped on the mountain and made the sacred spring gush up," Taeko said.

"Shouldn't he have wings?" Noguchi asked. The horse he'd drawn was winged.

"He doesn't need any," Taeko answered, "Because he has sharp hooves."

"Who is riding him?"

"Taeko. Taeko is riding him. She's riding the white horse and wearing pink clothes."

"Oh, so Taeko's riding the horse that stamped on the mountain and made the sacred spring gush up."

"That's right. Your horse has wings, but nobody's riding him."

"Here, then." Noguchi hurriedly drew a boy atop the horse. Taeko looked on from the side.

That was all there had been. Noguchi had married another girl, had fathered children, had aged, had forgotten about that kind of thing.

He'd remembered it suddenly, late one sleepless night. His son, having failed his university entrance tests, was studying every night until two or three o'clock. Noguchi, worried about him, could not get to sleep. As the sleepless nights continued, Noguchi came up against the loneliness of life. The son had next year, had hope, did not even go to bed at night. But the father merely lay awake in his bed. It was not for his son's sake. He was experiencing his own loneliness. Once he had been caught by this loneliness, it did not let him go. It put down its roots in the deepest part of him.

Noguchi tried various ways to fall asleep. He tried thinking of quiet fantasies and memories. And, one night, unexpectedly, he remembered Taeko's picture of the white horse. He did not clearly recall the picture. It was no child's picture, but the vision of a white horse galloping through heaven that floated up behind Noguchi's closed eyelids in the dark.

"Is it Taeko riding him? In pink clothes?"

The figure of the white horse, galloping across the sky, was clear. But neither the form nor the color of the rider astride him was clear. It did not seem to be a girl.

As the speed with which the visionary steed galloped through the empty sky slackened and the vision faded away, Noguchi would be drawn down into sleep.

From that night on, Noguchi had used the vision of the white horse as an invitation to sleep. His sleeplessness became a frequent occurrence, a customary thing whenever he suffered or was anxious.

For several years now, Noguchi had been saved from his insomnia by the vision of the white horse. The imaginary white horse was vivid and lively, but the figure riding him seemed to be a woman in black. It was not a girl in pink. The figure of that black-robed woman, aged and weakened, grew mysterious as time went by.

Today was the first time that the dream of the white horse had come to Noguchi, not as he lay in bed with his eyes closed, but as he sat open-eyed in a chair. It was the first time, also, that something like a long black cloth had streamed out behind the woman. Although it flowed in the wind, the drapery was thick and heavy.

"What is it?"

Noguchi gazed at the darkening gray sky from which the vision of the white horse had faded.

He had not seen Taeko in forty years. There was no news of her.

1963

A. L. KENNEDY
b. 1965

Alison Louise Kennedy was born in Dundee, Scotland. After studying English and drama at the University of Warwick in London, she published her first book of short stories, the award-winning *Night Geometry and the Garscadden Trains* (1990), at age twenty-five. Since then, Kennedy has written six novels, five short story collections, three works of nonfiction, and numerous plays, screenplays, and documentaries. Though Kennedy is also a comic dramatist, her fiction is known for its dark, melancholy tone. Her novels include *So I Am Glad* (1995), *Paradise* (2004), and *Day* (2007). Among her collections of short fiction are *Now That You're Back* (1994), *Original Bliss* (1997), *What Becomes* (2009), and, most recently, *All the Rage* (2014). Kennedy is also a regular blogger for The Guardian Online. She is a Fellow of both the Royal Society for the Arts and the Royal Society of Literature.

Not Anything to Do with Love

I wouldn't want to say so, but it's freezing in here. I suppose most people usually don't notice, not wanting to take their coats off, and being preoccupied, God knows: or this could even be an intentional chill, I mean, the last thing you'd want to consider right now is heat. Still, it doesn't seem a sign of kindness—a cold crematorium—more like forcing the bereaved to do their mourning inside a bad joke.

And, if I think of that, the possibility of giggling does tickle very briefly, but I frown against it, I resist. I do almost always laugh when I shouldn't, in fact *because* I shouldn't. Not that I'm cruel, I don't feel cruel, I've only decided that, since bad things happen without my permission, I will refuse to let them also make me sad.

I can't help it, either, the laughing: solemn gatherings, slow ballads, pompous orations, any person or occasion that assumes I'll offer my unreserved respect: I tend to find them all hysterical in the end. Especially if someone similar is there to set me off. They don't have to do much: I recognise what it looks like when somebody's composure starts to strip itself away. They'll maybe cross their arms with that twitchy, shaky, tension, or they'll grab down little wheezes of embarrassed air, or they'll simply hood their face under their palm, trying to hide how fast they're slipping: how fast *we're* slipping, because I'll be weakening with them by then, I'll be just as lost, pulled equally tight against the moment when we both stop caring and let it disgrace us—when we laugh.

I'm sombre though, this morning: on my own and therefore less likely to go astray.

The man with the 50s suit and the heavy glasses, he notices me frowning and nods, understanding of a grief that I don't have, because there is no real reason for me to be here. I met the deceased perhaps five times: each one completely unremarkable. He is no more to me than a lanky, softly variable recollection, the after-image of a friend of friends. He will have had qualities, I'm sure, but I don't know them.

Over by the door, the taller woman with the reddish hair—I think she's the sister—she hinges forward and catches at a teenage boy, hugs him in viciously while she faces something unknowable over his head, robbed eyes still fighting, puzzling. She ought to be somewhere more dignified than this. The cemetery outside seems all but abandoned and, inside, decades of cheap, municipal gloss have drowned out the contours of each moulding, every window frame; there's nothing for her to see that isn't faintly grubby and miserable with soaked-in nicotine.

In fact, being in this building is depressing, which is tautological—the people you'd expect to come here will already *be* depressed.

Me, I'm quite chipper, personally, but I would prefer it to be much easier for me to stay that way.

So I worry through the murmuring clusters and out to the corridor where I end up studying, once again, the tiny black pin board on which today's schedule is unevenly displayed, the white plastic letters fixed into a list of surnames and starting times—the current gathering is second out of six. And although everybody possible has surely already arrived, there are still fifteen minutes left to wait. We all, for our various reasons, have turned up too soon and the room behind me is now unsteady—even I can feel—with the concentration of involuntary hope, a habit nobody has shaken yet: the one that expects a final, impossible guest.

I need some space.

My breath is visible, even before I step completely beyond the front doors. They are awkwardly stiff and really must trouble the progress of pall-bearers, or biers. That's what I'd guess: I have no intention of loitering until the hearse pulls up just to prove myself right. Me there: a stranger waiting on the doorstep: it would look odd. The whole facility, anyway, is plainly not funeral-friendly, there's no need for additional evidence. Serve them right, if people start making their own arrangements: dumping off their relatives in rivers, or allotments, or the more accessible beauty-spots.

It's not in good taste to think so, I realise that. But then it's not exactly tasteful to add inconvenience to pre-existing grief—if anyone's being insensitive, it's not me. I should complain. I should write a letter to the relevant authority.

The driveway's shameful, too: all pitted. I have to be quite careful where I walk. And I mustn't consider the fine particulates, the vapours, drifting down from the grey, unsubtle smokestack: gathering in potholes, frozen puddles.

Out under the open, I clap my hands together for the sake of warmth and causing a disturbance, showing proof of life, and then I regret it—too loud. A single blackbird flicks over the grass, its little chips of alarm disappearing, muffled in the frost. I could head back to my car and leave this. No one would notice my absence. I'm not needed.

Which is, perhaps, what will make me stay.

To ease the minutes by, I pace out a slow, wide circle over the grass, set an ice dust melting on my shoes. When I pause first, I can see a small disturbance of colour, reddish flowers propped against a stone. Another pause, and I can watch the white depth of new mist unpicking the detail from the trees. Another, and I could see the car park if I felt so inclined, but I do not—there's nothing in it for me.

Back indoors, then: I might as well.

Yes, I might as well go back indoors. I do have other options, but I have no need to choose them, since I'm already here.

God, look at the place—it's inexcusable.

Sometimes I wish that my mind would, for once, stop talking, stop telling me what to do.

Back indoors it is, though. Why not. Up the steps, a strong tug, and then through.

And, at once, I can feel the difference, I can tell—I'd hoped this wouldn't happen and I'd hoped it would, and now, whatever my wishes, it has—Paul's here.

I haven't seen him, but I know: while I was walking and not thinking of him and not searching out his car: while I wasn't looking, in he came. Same as ever, without my permission, in he came.

He has no more excuse for attending than I do. We swapped pleasantries with the dead man together, just those four or five times: we neither of us ever knew his birthday, or his middle initial, or if he enjoyed his job—if he *had* a job. We're here for each other, to do ourselves harm.

Which would, of course, hardly matter, if we hadn't once been kind, better than kind.

I mean, I can no longer remember when I first realised that I could tell where Paul was without looking, without being told. Maybe it's a scent thing, like moths finding each other, or turtles—turtles can smell their home from miles away. At the start it was only good: easing through doorways and drawing in while all I could touch was his touch: in the nudge of other bodies, the curves of forward motion on my skin, the warm lean of the walls towards me, the shifts of my mind: everything, him.

This morning is still much the same, reality turning seasick and raw, but when we meet we'll give each other nothing but offence.

I step into the side room, anyway: deeper and deeper: and find, by himself beside the empty fireplace, the man that I used to agree with and who used to agree with me.

Paul's expecting me, that's obvious—his back turned preemptively away from the open door, his shoulders wary. I think he's gained weight, only a little. The trousers I've never seen before, but that's a jacket I was very used to—for some reason seeing it hurts—and it won't keep him warm enough, not today, it isn't practical. Slip your arm inside it, though, and there will be heat, held close at the small of his back. It was something worth finding, I remember that.

His hands: something else I remember. Even across this distance, they're changing the space between my fingers, making it ache. He's fussing in and out of his pockets and, if he's shaking, I'm not close enough to tell. I'm also unwilling to look down at my own hands. We do both tremble too easily and this will be much harder if either of us seems moved, or weak.

I would like to pay no attention to his head, the back of his head, his hair. I'd say that he's just had it cut. I'd say that I have the feel of it, singing in my palm like the ghost of some old injury.

Then, walking between us, comes that man with the heavy glasses again, which he now removes softly and rubs with the end of his tie. Next, he peers about and shows the room how the frame has impressed little grooves in the bridge of his nose and the flesh at his temples.

Must be too tight. Or maybe his eyesight's perfect, but he had to buy some glasses to fit his grooves.

A year ago, if I hadn't said it, then Paul would—that's the way we're made. It wouldn't have been meant unpleasantly: the thoughts occurred and we allowed them and they were ours. They only seem unpleasant to think without company.

The man slips back into his glasses and moves on and, before I can be ready, Paul moves too, swings round gingerly, as if his body has become uncooperative now, or unsafe. Then, with a yard or so left between us, we both stop and I was expecting this, but still it catches me like a slap: his expression of vehement weariness and contempt, there just for me. Under it, are the traces of what he can't control: there in the mouth, the eyes, the honest places: his absolute anger, his fear, his pain.

And I am quite aware, believe me, that I'm presenting exactly the same kind of face to him.

He breaks off and goes to sit, hunched forward, his elbows leaning on his knees, head dropped. Anyone who saw him might imagine he's exhausted, or upset. Anyone who cared about him would slip over there quietly and stroke his back, or cup his forehead, kneel beside him with their hand braced on his thigh while they asked after his problem and said what they could to make it fade. Anyone who cared.

He ducks up slightly, shading his eyes with spread fingers, peering out at me like a boy and then flinching when I look at him, withdrawing again. Which is perfectly natural, because I'm his problem: there is nothing I can do to help him, other than ceasing to be.

And I'm not entirely sure I want to help. Why should I stop him hurting when he won't stop hurting me.

It went wrong, that's all, completely wrong. First we laughed at strangers and then, being so happy and so much at ease, we laughed at each other and proved we were safe in our hands, because we didn't mean a word. But then a little jab would meet a jab and a cut would meet a cut and we'd apologise and there would be tenderness, but the kind you only feel when there's a bruise. None of it was intended: no one was really attacking, we were both just defending ourselves.

But we didn't stop. So now we are this: each of us a bad mirror for the other. Not anything better, not anything softer, not anything to do with love.

Naturally, I can't say this, because I won't speak to him, because he won't speak to me and vice versa.

I'm getting an angry headache, possibly a migraine. He's my sole trigger for the migraines, I never used to have them before. The stomach cramps, the dreams, the shortened attention span: in a purely pathological way, he's much more a part of me these days than he ever was.

At no signal of which I'm aware, the groups around me start to slide, conversations ending, and the whole crowd shuffling and bumping towards the door.

I won't go out with them, I can't face it. Once they're all in their seats and the music's started, I'm going home: I find I'm too tired for anything else. I walk to face the only window, stare into the pale day, while the room at my back empties, becomes still.

I know that he hasn't left, either: I don't have to turn and see. He's sitting behind me, just as he was, his breath now audible in the quiet—I can hear mine, too.

Our situation is ridiculous, laughable, and I want to be able to laugh. The fact that I can't is, in itself, quite funny, if I think about it: quite bizarre that I can lose my own nature so easily, just because he's with me. And it really should be very amusing that this will go on, that I have nothing better, that no matter what, I still want to be sure that we won't leave each other alone.

2002

JAMAICA KINCAID
b. 1949

Elaine Potter Richardson was born in St. John's, Antigua, West Indies, but at age seventeen she moved to New York City, took the name Jamaica Kincaid, and became a naturalized U.S. citizen. From the time of her first publication of stories about life on Antigua she was acclaimed not only for the vividness of her portrayal of that milieu but also for her mixture of fantasy and reality and the acuity of her style. Her first book, *At the Bottom of the River* (1983), was a collection of short stories, and her second, *Annie John* (1985), was a group of interrelated stories that some critics saw as a novel. Her book-length essay about Antigua, *A Small Place*, won her further praise in 1988. Kincaid's novels include *Lucy* (1990), *The Autobiography of My Mother* (1996), *My Brother* (1997), *Mr. Potter* (2002), and *See Now Then* (2013). Kincaid teaches literature at Claremont McKenna College.

Girl

Wash the white clothes on Monday and put them on the stone heap; wash the color clothes on Tuesday and put them on the clothesline to dry; don't walk barehead in the hot sun; cook pumpkin fritters in very hot sweet oil; soak your little cloths right after you take them off; when buying cotton to make yourself a nice blouse, be sure that it doesn't have gum on it, because that way it won't hold up well after a wash; soak salt fish overnight before you cook it; is it true that you sing benna[1] in Sunday school?; always eat your food in such a way that it won't turn someone else's stomach; on Sundays try to walk like a lady and not like the slut you are so bent on becoming; don't sing benna in Sunday school; you mustn't speak to wharf-rat boys, not even to give directions; don't eat fruits on the street—flies will follow you; *but I don't sing benna on Sundays at all and never in Sunday school*; this is how to sew on a button; this is how to make a buttonhole for the button you have just sewed on; this is how to hem a dress when you see the hem coming down and so to prevent yourself from looking like the slut I know you are so bent on becoming; this is how you iron your father's khaki shirt so that it doesn't have a crease; this is how you iron your father's khaki pants so that they don't have a crease; this is how you grow okra—far from the house, because okra tree harbors red ants; when you are growing dasheen, make sure it gets plenty of water or else it makes your throat itch when you are eating it; this is how you sweep a corner;

---

1. A Caribbean folk-music style.

this is how you sweep a whole house; this is how you sweep a yard; this is how you smile to someone you don't like very much; this is how you smile to someone you don't like at all; this is how you smile to someone you like completely; this is how you set a table for tea; this is how you set a table for dinner; this is how you set a table for dinner with an important guest; this is how you set a table for lunch; this is how you set a table for breakfast; this is how to behave in the presence of men who don't know you very well, and this way they won't recognize immediately the slut I have warned you against becoming; be sure to wash every day, even if it is with your own spit; don't squat down to play marbles—you are not a boy, you know; don't pick people's flowers—you might catch something; don't throw stones at blackbirds, because it might not be a blackbird at all; this is how to make a bread pudding; this is how to make doukona;[2] this is how to make pepper pot; this is how to make a good medicine for a cold; this is how to make a good medicine to throw away a child before it even becomes a child; this is how to catch a fish; this is how to throw back a fish you don't like, and that way something bad won't fall on you; this is how to bully a man; this is how a man bullies you; this is how to love a man, and if this doesn't work there are other ways, and if they don't work don't feel too bad about giving up; this is how to spit up in the air if you feel like it, and this is how to move quick so that it doesn't fall on you; this is how to make ends meet; always squeeze bread to make sure it's fresh; *but what if the baker won't let me feel the bread?*; you mean to say that after all you are really going to be the kind of woman who the baker won't let near the bread?

1978

---

2. A spiced pudding, often made from plantains.

JHUMPA LAHIRI
b. 1967

Jhumpa Lahiri was born Nilanjana Sudeshna in London to Indian immigrant parents from West Bengal. When she was two years old, her family moved to the United States, settling in Kingston, Rhode Island. Lahiri earned her B.A. in English literature from Barnard College and went on to receive various degrees from Boston University, including an M.F.A. in creative writing and a Ph.D. in Renaissance studies. The primary characters in Lahiri's often autobiographical fiction are first- and second-generation Indian-American immigrants. For years Lahiri's short stories were rejected for publication, but her first collection, *Interpreter of Maladies,* was awarded the Pulitzer Prize in 1999. This internationally bestselling debut also earned her the PEN/Hemingway Award, the Addison Metcalf Award from the American Academy of Arts and Letters, and the New Yorker Debut of the Year award. In 2003, she published her first novel, *The Namesake,* which was later adapted for the screen. Lahiri has also published a second collection of short fiction, *Unaccustomed Earth* (2008), a number one *New York Times* bestseller, and a second novel, *The Lowland* (2013), which was short-listed for the Man Booker Prize. She has taught at Boston University and the Rhode Island School of Design, and is currently vice president of the PEN American Center.

Hell-Heaven

Pranab Chakraborty wasn't technically my father's younger brother. He was a fellow-Bengali from Calcutta who had washed up on the barren shores of my parents' social life in the early seventies, when they lived in a rented apartment in Central Square and could number their acquaintances on one hand. But I had no real uncles in America, and so I was taught to call him Pranab Kaku. Accordingly, he called my father Shyamal Da, always addressing him in the polite form, and he called my mother Boudi, which is how Bengalis are supposed to address an older brother's wife, instead of using her first name, Aparna. After Pranab Kaku was befriended by my parents, he confessed that on the day we first met him he had followed my mother and me for the better part of an afternoon around the streets of Cambridge, where she and I tended to roam after I got out of school. He had trailed behind us along Massachusetts Avenue, and in and out of the Harvard Coop, where my mother liked to look at discounted housewares. He wandered with us into Harvard Yard, where my mother often sat on the grass on pleasant days and watched the stream of students and professors filing busily along the paths, until, finally, as we were climbing the steps to Widener Library so that I could use the bathroom, he tapped my mother on the shoulder and inquired, in English, if she might be a Bengali. The answer to his question was clear, given that my mother was wearing the red and white bangles unique to Bengali married women, and a common Tangail sari, and had a thick stem of vermillion powder in the center parting of her hair, and the full round face and large dark eyes that are so typical of Bengali women. He noticed the two or three safety pins she wore fastened to the thin gold bangles that were behind the red and white ones, which she would use to replace a missing hook on a blouse or to draw a string through a petticoat at a moment's notice, a practice he associated strictly with his mother and sisters and aunts in Calcutta. Moreover, Pranab Kaku had overheard my mother speaking to me in Bengali, telling me that I couldn't buy an issue of *Archie* at the Coop. But back then, he also confessed, he was so new to America that he took nothing for granted, and doubted even the obvious.

My parents and I had lived in Central Square for three years prior to that day; before that, we had lived in Berlin, where I was born and where my father had finished his training in microbiology before accepting a position as a researcher at Mass General, and before Berlin my mother and father had lived in India, where they had been strangers to each other, and where their marriage had been arranged. Central Square is the first place I can recall living, and in my memories of our apartment, in a dark-brown shingled house on Ashburton Place, Pranab Kaku is always there. According to the story he liked to recall often, my mother invited him to accompany us back to our apartment that very afternoon, and prepared tea for the two of them; then, after learning that he had not had a proper Bengali meal in more than three months, she served him the leftover curried mackerel and rice that we had eaten for dinner the night before. He remained into the evening, for a second dinner, after my father got home, and after that he showed up for dinner almost every night, occupying the fourth chair at our square Formica kitchen table, and becoming a part of our family in practice as well as in name.

He was from a wealthy family in Calcutta and had never had to do so much as pour himself a glass of water before moving to America, to study engineering at M.I.T. Life as a graduate student in Boston was a cruel shock, and in his first month he lost nearly twenty pounds. He had arrived in January, in the middle of a snowstorm, and at the end of a week he had packed his bags and gone to Logan, prepared to abandon the opportunity he'd worked toward all his life, only to change his mind at the last minute. He was living on Trowbridge Street in the home of a divorced woman with two young children who were always screaming and crying. He rented a room in the attic and was permitted to use the kitchen only at specified times of the day, and instructed always to wipe down the stove with Windex and a sponge. My parents agreed that it was a terrible situation, and if they'd had a bedroom to spare they would have offered it to him. Instead, they welcomed him to our meals, and opened up our apartment to him at any time, and soon it was there he went between classes and on his days off, always leaving behind some vestige of himself: a nearly finished pack of cigarettes, a newspaper, a piece of mail he had not bothered to open, a sweater he had taken off and forgotten in the course of his stay.

I remember vividly the sound of his exuberant laughter and the sight of his lanky body slouched or sprawled on the dull, mismatched furniture that had come with our apartment. He had a striking face, with a high forehead and a thick mustache, and overgrown, untamed hair that my mother said made him look like the American hippies who were everywhere in those days. His long legs jiggled rapidly up and down wherever he sat, and his elegant hands trembled when he held a cigarette between his fingers, tapping the ashes into a teacup that my mother began to set aside for this exclusive purpose. Though he was a scientist by training, there was nothing rigid or predictable or orderly about him. He always seemed to be starving, walking through the door and announcing that he hadn't had lunch, and then he would eat ravenously, reaching behind my mother to steal cutlets as she was frying them, before she had a chance to set them properly on a plate with red-onion salad. In private, my parents remarked that he was a brilliant student, a star at Jadavpur[1] who had come to M.I.T. with an impressive assistantship, but Pranab Kaku was cavalier about his classes, skipping them with frequency. "These Americans are learning equations I knew at Usha's age," he would complain. He was stunned that my second-grade teacher didn't assign any homework, and that at the age of seven I hadn't yet been taught square roots or the concept of pi.

He appeared without warning, never phoning beforehand but simply knocking on the door the way people did in Calcutta and calling out "Boudi!" as he waited for my mother to let him in. Before we met him, I would return from school and find my mother with her purse in her lap and her trenchcoat on, desperate to escape the apartment where she had spent the day alone. But now I would find her in the kitchen, rolling out dough for *luchis*, which she normally made only on Sundays for my father and me, or putting up new curtains she'd bought at Woolworth's. I did not know, back then, that Pranab Kaku's visits were what my mother looked forward to all day, that she changed into a new sari and combed her hair in anticipation of his arrival, and that she planned, days in advance, the snacks she would serve him with such nonchalance. That she lived for the moment she heard him call out "Boudi!" from the porch, and that she was in a foul humor on the days he didn't materialize.

It must have pleased her that I looked forward to his visits as well. He showed me card tricks and an optical illusion in which he appeared to be severing his own thumb with enormous struggle and strength, and taught me to memorize multiplication tables well before I had to learn them in school. His hobby was photography. He owned an expensive camera that required thought before you pressed the shutter, and I quickly became his favorite subject, round-faced, missing teeth, my thick bangs in need of a trim. They are still the pictures of myself I like best, for they convey that confidence of youth I no longer possess, especially in front of a camera. I remember having to run back and forth in Harvard Yard as he stood with the camera, trying to capture me in motion, or posing on the steps of university buildings and on the street and against the trunks of trees. There is only one photograph in which

---

1. Jadavpur University, an elite public university in Kolkata (formerly called Calcutta), the capital of the Indian state of West Bengal.

my mother appears; she is holding me as I sit straddling her lap, her head tilted toward me, her hands pressed to my ears as if to prevent me from hearing something. In that picture, Pranab Kaku's shadow, his two arms raised at angles to hold the camera to his face, hovers in the corner of the frame, his darkened, featureless shape superimposed on one side of my mother's body. It was always the three of us. I was always there when he visited. It would have been inappropriate for my mother to receive him in the apartment alone; this was something that went without saying.

They had in common all the things she and my father did not: a love of music, film, leftist politics, poetry. They were from the same neighborhood in North Calcutta, their family homes within walking distance, the façades familiar to them once the exact locations were described. They knew the same shops, the same bus and tram routes, the same holes-in-the-wall for the best *jelabis* and *moghlai parathas.*[2] My father, on the other hand, came from a suburb twenty miles outside Calcutta, an area that my mother considered the wilderness, and even in her bleakest hours of homesickness she was grateful that my father had at least spared her a life in the stern house of her in-laws, where she would have had to keep her head covered with the end of her sari at all times and use an outhouse that was nothing but a raised platform with a hole, and where, in the rooms, there was not a single painting hanging on the walls. Within a few weeks, Pranab Kaku had brought his reel-to-reel over to our apartment, and he played for my mother medley after medley of songs from the Hindi films of their youth. They were cheerful songs of courtship, which transformed the quiet life in our apartment and transported my mother back to the world she'd left behind in order to marry my father. She and Pranab Kaku would try to recall which scene in which movie the songs were from, who the actors were and what they were wearing. My mother would describe Raj Kapoor and Nargis singing under umbrellas in the rain, or Dev Anand strumming a guitar on the beach in Goa. She and Pranab Kaku would argue passionately about these matters, raising their voices in playful combat, confronting each other in a way she and my father never did.

Because he played the part of a younger brother, she felt free to call him Pranab, whereas she never called my father by his first name. My father was thirty-seven then, nine years older than my mother. Pranab Kaku was twenty-five. My father was monkish by nature, a lover of silence and solitude. He had married my mother to placate his parents; they were willing to accept his desertion as long as he had a wife. He was wedded to his work, his research, and he existed in a shell that neither my mother nor I could penetrate. Conversation was a chore for him; it required an effort he preferred to expend at the lab. He disliked excess in anything, voiced no cravings or needs apart from the frugal elements of his daily routine: cereal and tea in the mornings, a cup of tea after he got home, and two different vegetable dishes every night with dinner. He did not eat with the reckless appetite of Pranab Kaku. My father had a survivor's mentality. From time to time, he liked to remark, in mixed company and often with no relevant provocation, that starving Russians under Stalin had resorted to eating the glue off the back of their wall-

---

2. A type of sweet pretzel and a kind of stuffed bread, respectively.

paper. One might think that he would have felt slightly jealous, or at the very least suspicious, about the regularity of Pranab Kaku's visits and the effect they had on my mother's behavior and mood. But my guess is that my father was grateful to Pranab Kaku for the companionship he provided, freed from the sense of responsibility he must have felt for forcing her to leave India, and relieved, perhaps, to see her happy for a change.

In the summer, Pranab Kaku bought a navy-blue Volkswagen Beetle, and began to take my mother and me for drives through Boston and Cambridge, and soon outside the city, flying down the highway. He would take us to India Tea and Spices in Watertown, and one time he drove us all the way to New Hampshire to look at the mountains. As the weather grew hotter, we started going, once or twice a week, to Walden Pond. My mother always prepared a picnic of hard-boiled eggs and cucumber sandwiches, and talked fondly about the winter picnics of her youth, grand expeditions with fifty of her relatives, all taking the train into the West Bengal countryside. Pranab Kaku listened to these stories with interest, absorbing the vanishing details of her past. He did not turn a deaf ear to her nostalgia, like my father, or listen uncomprehending, like me. At Walden Pond, Pranab Kaku would coax my mother through the woods, and lead her down the steep slope to the water's edge. She would unpack the picnic things and sit and watch us as we swam. His chest was matted with thick dark hair, all the way to his waist. He was an odd sight, with his pole-thin legs and a small, flaccid belly, like an otherwise svelte woman who has had a baby and not bothered to tone her abdomen. "You're making me fat, Boudi," he would complain after gorging himself on my mother's cooking. He swam noisily, clumsily, his head always above the water; he didn't know how to blow bubbles or hold his breath, as I had learned in swimming class. Wherever we went, any stranger would have naturally assumed that Pranab Kaku was my father, that my mother was his wife.

It is clear to me now that my mother was in love with him. He wooed her as no other man had, with the innocent affection of a brother-in-law. In my mind, he was just a family member, a cross between an uncle and a much older brother, for in certain respects my parents sheltered and cared for him in much the same way they cared for me. He was respectful of my father, always seeking his advice about making a life in the West, about setting up a bank account and getting a job, and deferring to his opinions about Kissinger and Watergate. Occasionally, my mother would tease him about women, asking about female Indian students at M.I.T., or showing him pictures of her younger cousins in India. "What do you think of her?" she would ask. "Isn't she pretty?" She knew that she could never have Pranab Kaku for herself, and I suppose it was her attempt to keep him in the family. But, most important, in the beginning he was totally dependent on her, needing her for those months in a way my father never did in the whole history of their marriage. He brought to my mother the first and, I suspect, the only pure happiness she ever felt. I don't think even my birth made her as happy. I was evidence of her marriage to my father, an assumed consequence of the life she had been raised to lead. But Pranab Kaku was different. He was the one totally unanticipated pleasure in her life.

In the fall of 1974, Pranab Kaku met a student at Radcliffe named Deborah, an American, and she began to accompany him to our house. I called

Deborah by her first name, as my parents did, but Pranab Kaku taught her to call my father Shyamal Da and my mother Boudi, something with which Deborah gladly complied. Before they came to dinner for the first time, I asked my mother, as she was straightening up the living room, if I ought to address her as Deborah Kakima, turning her into an aunt as I had turned Pranab into an uncle. "What's the point?" my mother said, looking back at me sharply. "In a few weeks, the fun will be over and she'll leave him." And yet Deborah remained by his side, attending the weekend parties that Pranab Kaku and my parents were becoming more involved with, gatherings that were exclusively Bengali with the exception of her. Deborah was very tall, taller than both my parents and nearly as tall as Pranab Kaku. She wore her long brass-colored hair center-parted, as my mother did, but it was gathered into a low ponytail instead of a braid, or it spilled messily over her shoulders and down her back in a way that my mother considered indecent. She wore small silver spectacles and not a trace of makeup, and she studied philosophy. I found her utterly beautiful, but according to my mother she had spots on her face, and her hips were too small.

For a while, Pranab Kaku still showed up once a week for dinner on his own, mostly asking my mother what she thought of Deborah. He sought her approval, telling her that Deborah was the daughter of professors at Boston College, that her father published poetry, and that both her parents had Ph.D.s. When he wasn't around, my mother complained about Deborah's visits, about having to make the food less spicy even though Deborah said she liked spicy food, and feeling embarrassed to put a fried fish head in the dal. Pranab Kaku taught Deborah to say *khub bhalo* and *aacha*[3] and to pick up certain foods with her fingers instead of with a fork. Sometimes they ended up feeding each other, allowing their fingers to linger in each other's mouth, causing my parents to look down at their plates and wait for the moment to pass. At larger gatherings, they kissed and held hands in front of everyone, and when they were out of earshot my mother would talk to the other Bengali women. "He used to be so different. I don't understand how a person can change so suddenly. It's just hell-heaven, the difference," she would say, always using the English words for her self-concocted, backward metaphor.

The more my mother began to resent Deborah's visits, the more I began to anticipate them. I fell in love with Deborah, the way young girls often fall in love with women who are not their mothers. I loved her serene gray eyes, the ponchos and denim wrap skirts and sandals she wore, her straight hair that she let me manipulate into all sorts of silly styles. I longed for her casual appearance; my mother insisted whenever there was a gathering that I wear one of my ankle-length, faintly Victorian dresses, which she referred to as maxis, and have party hair, which meant taking a strand from either side of my head and joining them with a barrette at the back. At parties, Deborah would, eventually, politely slip away, much to the relief of the Bengali women with whom she was expected to carry on a conversation, and she would play with me. I was older than all my parents' friends' children, but with Deborah I had a companion. She knew all about the books I read, about Pippi Long-stocking and Anne of Green Gables. She gave me the sorts of gifts my parents

---

3. Bengali for "very good" and "oh, really."

had neither the money nor the inspiration to buy: a large book of Grimms' fairy tales with watercolor illustrations on thick, silken pages, wooden puppets with hair fashioned from yarn. She told me about her family, three older sisters and two brothers, the youngest of whom was closer to my age than to hers. Once, after visiting her parents, she brought back three Nancy Drews, her name written in a girlish hand at the top of the first page, and an old toy she'd had, a small paper theatre set with interchangeable backdrops, the exterior of a castle and a ballroom and an open field. Deborah and I spoke freely in English, a language in which, by that age, I expressed myself more easily than Bengali, which I was required to speak at home. Sometimes she asked me how to say this or that in Bengali; once, she asked me what *asobbho* meant. I hesitated, then told her it was what my mother called me if I had done something extremely naughty, and Deborah's face clouded. I felt protective of her, aware that she was unwanted, that she was resented, aware of the nasty things people said.

Outings in the Volkswagen now involved the four of us, Deborah in the front, her hand over Pranab Kaku's while it rested on the gearshift, my mother and I in the back. Soon, my mother began coming up with reasons to excuse herself, headaches and incipient colds, and so I became part of a new triangle. To my surprise, my mother allowed me to go with them, to the Museum of Fine Arts and the Public Garden and the aquarium. She was waiting for the affair to end, for Deborah to break Pranab Kaku's heart and for him to return to us, scarred and penitent. I saw no sign of their relationship foundering. Their open affection for each other, their easily expressed happiness, was a new and romantic thing to me. Having me in the back seat allowed Pranab Kaku and Deborah to practice for the future, to try on the idea of a family of their own. Countless photographs were taken of me and Deborah, of me sitting on Deborah's lap, holding her hand, kissing her on the cheek. We exchanged what I believed were secret smiles, and in those moments I felt that she understood me better than anyone else in the world. Anyone would have said that Deborah would make an excellent mother one day. But my mother refused to acknowledge such a thing. I did not know at the time that my mother allowed me to go off with Pranab Kaku and Deborah because she was pregnant for the fifth time since my birth, and was so sick and exhausted and fearful of losing another baby that she slept most of the day. After ten weeks, she miscarried once again, and was advised by her doctor to stop trying.

By summer, there was a diamond on Deborah's left hand, something my mother had never been given. Because his own family lived so far away, Pranab Kaku came to the house alone one day, to ask for my parents' blessing before giving her the ring. He showed us the box, opening it and taking out the diamond nestled inside. "I want to see how it looks on someone," he said, urging my mother to try it on, but she refused. I was the one who stuck out my hand, feeling the weight of the ring suspended at the base of my finger. Then he asked for a second thing: he wanted my parents to write to his parents, saying that they had met Deborah and that they thought highly of her. He was nervous, naturally, about telling his family that he intended to marry an American girl. He had told his parents all about us, and at one point my parents had received a letter from them, expressing appreciation for taking such good care of their son and for giving him a proper home in America. "It needn't be long," Pranab Kaku said. "Just a few lines. They'll accept it more easily if it comes from you." My father thought neither ill nor well of Deborah, never commenting or criticizing as my mother did, but he assured Pranab Kaku that a letter of endorsement would be on its way to Calcutta by the end of the week. My mother nodded her assent, but the following day I saw the teacup Pranab Kaku had used all this time as an ashtray in the kitchen garbage can, in pieces, and three Band-Aids taped to my mother's hand.

Pranab Kaku's parents were horrified by the thought of their only son marrying an American woman, and a few weeks later our telephone rang in the middle of the night: it was Mr. Chakraborty telling my father that they could not possibly bless such a marriage, that it was out of the question, that if Pranab Kaku dared to marry Deborah he would no longer acknowledge him as a son. Then his wife got on the phone, asking to speak to my mother, and attacked her as if they were intimate, blaming my mother for allowing the affair to develop. She said that they had already chosen a wife for him in Calcutta, that he'd left for America with the understanding that he'd go back after he had finished his studies, and marry this girl. They had bought the neighboring flat in their building for Pranab and his betrothed, and it was sitting empty, waiting for his return. "We thought we could trust you, and yet you have betrayed us so deeply," his mother said, taking out her anger on a stranger in a way she could not with her son. "Is this what happens to people in America?" For Pranab Kaku's sake, my mother defended the engagement, telling his mother that Deborah was a polite girl from a decent family. Pranab Kaku's parents pleaded with mine to talk him out of the engagement, but my father refused, deciding that it was not their place to get embroiled in a situation that had nothing to do with them. "We are not his parents," he told my mother. "We can tell him they don't approve but nothing more." And so my parents told Pranab Kaku nothing about how his parents had berated them, and blamed them, and threatened to disown Pranab Kaku, only that they had refused to give him their blessing. In the face of this refusal, Pranab Kaku shrugged. "I don't care. Not everyone can be as open-minded as you," he told my parents. "Your blessing is blessing enough."

After the engagement, Pranab Kaku and Deborah began drifting out of our lives. They moved in together, to an apartment in Boston, in the South End, a part of the city my parents considered unsafe. We moved as well, to a house in Natick. Though my parents had bought the house, they occupied it as if they were still tenants, touching up scuff marks with leftover paint and reluctant to put holes in the walls, and every afternoon when the sun shone through the living-room window my mother closed the blinds so that our new furniture would not fade. A few weeks before the wedding, my parents invited Pranab Kaku to the house alone, and my mother prepared a special meal to mark the end of his bachelorhood. It would be the only Bengali aspect of the wedding; the rest of it would be strictly American, with a cake and a minister and Deborah in a long white dress and veil. There is a photograph of the dinner, taken by my father, the only picture, to my knowledge, in which my mother and Pranab Kaku appear together. The picture is slightly blurry; I remember Pranab Kaku explaining to my father how to work the camera, and so he is captured looking up from the kitchen table and the elaborate array of food my mother had prepared in his honor, his mouth open, his long arm outstretched and his finger pointing, instructing my father how to read the light meter or some such thing. My mother stands beside him, one hand placed on top of his head in a gesture of blessing, the first and last time she was to touch him in her life. "She will leave him," my mother told her friends afterward. "He is throwing his life away."

The wedding was at a church in Ipswich, with a reception at a country club. It was going to be a small ceremony, which my parents took to mean one or two hundred people as opposed to three or four hundred. My mother was shocked that fewer than thirty people had been invited, and she was more perplexed than honored that, of all the Bengalis Pranab Kaku knew by then, we were the only ones on the list. At the wedding, we sat, like the other guests, first on the hard wooden pews of the church and then at a long table that had been set up for lunch. Though we were the closest thing Pranab Kaku had to a family that day, we were not included in the group photographs that were taken on the grounds of the country club, with Deborah's parents and grand-parents and her many siblings, and neither my mother nor my father got up to make a toast. My mother did not appreciate the fact that Deborah had made sure that my parents, who did not eat beef, were given fish instead of filet mignon like everyone else. She kept speaking in Bengali, complaining about the formality of the proceedings, and the fact that Pranab Kaku, wearing a tuxedo, barely said a word to us because he was too busy leaning over the shoulders of his new American in-laws as he circled the table. As usual, my father said nothing in response to my mother's commentary, quietly and methodically working though his meal, his fork and knife occasionally squeaking against the surface of the china, because he was accustomed to eating with his hands. He cleared his plate and then my mother's, for she had pronounced the food inedible, and then he announced that he had overeaten and had a stomach ache. The only time my mother forced a smile was when Deborah appeared behind her chair, kissing her on the cheek and asking if we were enjoying ourselves. When the dancing started, my parents remained at the table, drinking tea, and after two or three songs they decided that it was time for us to go home, my mother shooting me looks to that effect across the room, where I was dancing in a circle with Pranab Kaku and Deborah and the other children at the wedding. I wanted to stay, and when, reluctantly, I walked over to where my parents sat Deborah followed me. "Boudi, let Usha stay. She's having such a good time," she said to my mother. "Lots of people will be heading back your way, someone can drop her off in a little while." But my mother said no, I had had plenty of fun already, and forced me to put on my coat over my long puff-sleeved dress. As we drove home from the wedding I told my mother, for the first but not the last time in my life, that I hated her.

The following year, we received a birth announcement from the Chakrabor-tys, a picture of twin girls, which my mother did not paste into an album or display on the refrigerator door. The girls were named Srabani and Sabitri, but were called Bonny and Sara. Apart from a thank-you card for our wed-ding gift, it was their only communication; we were not invited to the new house in Marblehead, bought after Pranab Kaku got a high-paying job at Stone & Webster. For a while, my parents and their friends continued to invite the Chakrabortys to gatherings, but because they never came, or left after staying only an hour, the invitations stopped. Their absences were attributed, by my parents and their circle, to Deborah, and it was universally agreed that she had stripped Pranab Kaku not only of his origins but of his independence. She was the enemy, he was her prey, and their example was invoked as a warning, and as vindication, that mixed marriages were a doomed enterprise. Occasionally, they surprised everyone, appearing at a *pujo*[4] for a few hours with their two identical little girls who barely looked Bengali and spoke only English and were being raised so differently from me and most of the other children. They were not taken to Calcutta every summer, they did not have parents who were clinging to another way of life and exhorting their children to do the same. Because of Deborah, they were exempt from all that, and for this reason I envied them. "Usha, look at you, all grown up and so pretty," Deborah would say whenever she saw me, rekindling, if only for a minute, our bond of years before. She had cut off her beautiful long hair by then, and had a bob. "I bet you'll be old enough to babysit soon," she would say. "I'll call you—the girls would love that." But she never did.

I began to grow out of my girlhood, entering middle school and developing crushes on the American boys in my class. The crushes amounted to nothing; in spite of Deborah's compliments, I was always overlooked at that age. But my mother must have picked up on something, for she forbade me to attend the dances that were held the last Friday of every month in the school cafeteria, and it was an unspoken law that I was not allowed to date. "Don't think you'll get away with marrying an American, the way Pranab Kaku did," she would say from time to time. I was thirteen, the thought of marriage irrelevant to my life. Still, her words upset me, and I felt her grip on me tighten. She would fly into a rage when I told her I wanted to start wearing a bra, or if I wanted to go to Harvard Square with a friend. In the middle of our arguments, she often conjured Deborah as her antithesis, the sort of woman she refused to be. "If *she* were your mother, she would let you do whatever you wanted, because she wouldn't care. Is that what you want, Usha, a mother who doesn't care?" When I began menstruating, the summer before I started ninth grade, my mother gave me a speech, telling me that I was to let no boy touch me, and then she asked if I knew how a woman became pregnant. I told her what I had been taught in science, about the sperm fertilizing the egg, and then she asked if I knew how, exactly, that happened. I saw the terror in her eyes and so, though I knew that aspect of procreation as well, I lied, and told her it hadn't been explained to us.

I began keeping other secrets from her, evading her with the aid of my friends. I told her I was sleeping over at a friend's when really I went to parties, drinking beer and allowing boys to kiss me and fondle my breasts and press their erections against my hip as we lay groping on a sofa or the back seat of a car. I began to pity my mother; the older I got, the more I saw what a desolate life she led. She had never worked, and during the day she watched soap operas to pass the time. Her only job, every day, was to clean and cook for my

---

4. Religious festival.

father and me. We rarely went to restaurants, my father always pointing out, even in cheap ones, how expensive they were compared with eating at home. When my mother complained to him about how much she hated life in the suburbs and how lonely she felt, he said nothing to placate her. "If you are so unhappy, go back to Calcutta," he would offer, making it clear that their separation would not affect him one way or the other. I began to take my cues from my father in dealing with her, isolating her doubly. When she screamed at me for talking too long on the telephone, or for staying too long in my room, I learned to scream back, telling her that she was pathetic, that she knew nothing about me, and it was clear to us both that I had stopped needing her, definitively and abruptly, just as Pranab Kaku had.

Then, the year before I went off to college, my parents and I were invited to the Chakrabortys' home for Thanksgiving. We were not the only guests from my parents' old Cambridge crowd; it turned out that Pranab Kaku and Deborah wanted to have a sort of reunion of all the people they had been friendly with back then. Normally, my parents did not celebrate Thanksgiving; the ritual of a large sit-down dinner and the foods that one was supposed to eat was lost on them. They treated it as if it were Memorial Day or Veterans Day—just another holiday in the American year. But we drove out to Marblehead, to an impressive stone-faced house with a semicircular gravel driveway clogged with cars. The house was a short walk from the ocean; on our way, we had driven by the harbor overlooking the cold, glittering Atlantic, and when we stepped out of the car we were greeted by the sound of gulls and waves. Most of the living-room furniture had been moved to the basement, and extra tables joined to the main one to form a giant U. They were covered with tablecloths, set with white plates and silverware, and had centerpieces of gourds. I was struck by the toys and dolls that were everywhere, dogs that shed long yellow hairs on everything, all the photographs of Bonny and Sara and Deborah decorating the walls, still more plastering the refrigerator door. Food was being prepared when we arrived, something my mother always frowned upon, the kitchen a chaos of people and smells and enormous dirtied bowls.

Deborah's family, whom we remembered dimly from the wedding, was there, her parents and her brothers and sisters and their husbands and wives and boyfriends and babies. Her sisters were in their thirties, but, like Deborah, they could have been mistaken for college students, wearing jeans and clogs and fisherman sweaters, and her brother Matty, with whom I had danced in a circle at the wedding, was now a freshman at Amherst, with wide-set green eyes and wispy brown hair and a complexion that reddened easily. As soon as I saw Deborah's siblings, joking with one another as they chopped and stirred things in the kitchen, I was furious with my mother for making a scene before we left the house and forcing me to wear a shalwar kameez. I knew they assumed, from my clothing, that I had more in common with the other Bengalis than with them. But Deborah insisted on including me, setting me to work peeling apples with Matty, and out of my parents' sight I was given beer to drink. When the meal was ready, we were told where to sit, in an alternating boy-girl formation that made the Bengalis uncomfortable. Bottles of wine were lined up on the table. Two turkeys were brought out, one stuffed with sausage and one without. My mouth watered at the food, but I knew that afterward, on our way home, my mother would complain that it was all tasteless and bland. "Impossible," my mother said, shaking her hand over the top of her glass when someone tried to pour her a little wine.

Deborah's father, Gene, got up to say grace, and asked everyone at the table to join hands. He bowed his head and closed his eyes. "Dear Lord, we thank you today for the food we are about to receive," he began. My parents were seated next to each other, and I was stunned to see that they complied, that my father's brown fingers lightly clasped my mother's pale ones. I noticed Matty seated on the other side of the room, and saw him glancing at me as his father spoke. After the chorus of amens, Gene raised his glass and said, "Forgive me, but I never thought I'd have the opportunity to say this: Here's to Thanksgiving with the Indians." Only a few people laughed at the joke.

Then Pranab Kaku stood up and thanked everyone for coming. He was relaxed from alcohol, his once wiry body beginning to thicken. He started to talk sentimentally about his early days in Cambridge, and then suddenly he recounted the story of meeting me and my mother for the first time, telling the guests about how he had followed us that afternoon. The people who did not know us laughed, amused by the description of the encounter, and by Pranab Kaku's desperation. He walked around the room to where my mother was sitting and draped a lanky arm around her shoulder, forcing her, for a brief moment, to stand up. "This woman," he declared, pulling her close to his side, "this woman hosted my first real Thanksgiving in America. It might have been an afternoon in May, but that first meal at Boudi's table was Thanksgiving to me. If it weren't for that meal, I would have gone back to Calcutta." My mother looked away, embarrassed. She was thirty-eight, already going gray, and she looked closer to my father's age than to Pranab Kaku's; regardless of his waistline, he retained his handsome, carefree looks. Pranab Kaku went back to his place at the head of the table, next to Deborah, and concluded, "And if that had been the case I'd have never met you, my darling," and he kissed her on the mouth in front of everyone, to much applause, as if it were their wedding day all over again.

After the turkey, smaller forks were distributed and orders were taken for three different kinds of pie, written on small pads by Deborah's sisters, as if they were waitresses. After dessert, the dogs needed to go out, and Pranab Kaku volunteered to take them. "How about a walk on the beach?" he suggested, and Deborah's side of the family agreed that that was an excellent idea. None of the Bengalis wanted to go, preferring to sit with their tea and cluster together, at last, at one end of the room, speaking freely after the forced chitchat with the Americans during the meal. Matty came over and sat in the chair beside me that was now empty, encouraging me to join the walk. When I hesitated, pointing to my inappropriate clothes and shoes but also aware of my mother's silent fury at the sight of us together, he said, "I'm sure Deb can lend you something." So I went upstairs, where Deborah gave me a pair of her jeans and a thick sweater and some sneakers, so that I looked like her and her sisters.

She sat on the edge of her bed, watching me change, as if we were girlfriends, and she asked if I had a boyfriend. When I told her no, she said, "Matty thinks you're cute."

"He told you?"

"No, but I can tell."

As I walked back downstairs, emboldened by this information, in the jeans I'd had to roll up and in which I felt finally like myself, I noticed my mother lift her eyes from her teacup and stare at me, but she said nothing, and off I went, with Pranab Kaku and his dogs and his in-laws, along a road and then down some steep wooden steps to the water. Deborah and one of her sisters stayed behind, to begin the cleanup and see to the needs of those who remained. Initially, we all walked together, in a single row across the sand, but then I noticed Matty hanging back, and so the two of us trailed behind, the distance between us and the others increasing. We began flirting, talking of things I no longer remember, and eventually we wandered into a rocky inlet and Matty fished a joint out of his pocket. We turned our backs to the wind and smoked it, our cold fingers touching in the process, our lips pressed to the same damp section of the rolling paper. At first I didn't feel any effect, but then, listening to him talk about the band he was in, I was aware that his voice sounded miles away, and that I had the urge to laugh, even though what he was saying was not terribly funny. It felt as if we were apart from the group for hours, but when we wandered back to the sand we could still see them, walking out onto a rocky promontory to watch the sun set. It was dark by the time we all headed back to the house, and I dreaded seeing my parents while I was still high. But when we got there Deborah told me that my parents, feeling tired, had left, agreeing to let someone drive me home later. A fire had been lit and I was told to relax and have more pie as the leftovers were put away and the living room slowly put back in order. Of course, it was Matty who drove me home, and sitting in my parents' driveway I kissed him, at once thrilled and terrified that my mother might walk onto the lawn in her nightgown and discover us. I gave Matty my phone number, and for a few weeks I thought of him constantly, and hoped foolishly that he would call.

In the end, my mother was right, and fourteen years after that Thanksgiving, after twenty-three years of marriage, Pranab Kaku and Deborah got divorced. It was he who had strayed, falling in love with a married Bengali woman, destroying two families in the process. The other woman was someone my parents knew, though not very well. Deborah was in her forties by then, Bonny and Sara away at college. In her shock and grief, it was my mother whom Deborah turned to, calling and weeping into the phone. Somehow, through all the years, she had continued to regard us as quasi in-laws, sending flowers when my grandparents died, and giving me a compact edition of the O.E.D.[5] as a college-graduation present. "You knew him so well. How could he do something like this?" Deborah asked my mother. And then, "Did you know anything about it?" My mother answered truthfully that she did not. Their hearts had been broken by the same man, only my mother's had long ago mended, and in an odd way, as my parents approached their old age, she and my father had grown fond of each other, out of habit if nothing else. I believe my absence from the house, once I left for college, had something to do with this, because over the years, when I visited, I noticed a warmth between my parents that had not been there before, a quiet teasing,

---

5. Oxford English Dictionary.

a solidarity, a concern when one of them fell ill. My mother and I had also made peace; she had accepted the fact that I was not only her daughter but a child of America as well. Slowly, she accepted that I dated one American man, and then another, and then yet another, that I slept with them, and even that I lived with one though we were not married. She welcomed my boyfriends into our home and when things didn't work out she told me I would find someone better. After years of being idle, she decided, when she turned fifty, to get a degree in library science at a nearby university.

On the phone, Deborah admitted something that surprised my mother: that all these years she had felt hopelessly shut out of a part of Pranab Kaku's life. "I was so horribly jealous of you back then, for knowing him, understanding him in a way I never could. He turned his back on his family, on all of you, really, but I still felt threatened. I could never get over that." She told my mother that she had tried, for years, to get Pranab Kaku to reconcile with his parents, and that she had also encouraged him to maintain ties with other Bengalis, but he had resisted. It had been Deborah's idea to invite us to their Thanksgiving; ironically, the other woman had been there, too. "I hope you don't blame me for taking him away from your lives, Boudi. I always worried that you did."

My mother assured Deborah that she blamed her for nothing. She confessed nothing to Deborah about her own jealousy of decades before, only that she was sorry for what had happened, that it was a sad and terrible thing for their family. She did not tell Deborah that a few weeks after Pranab Kaku's wedding, while I was at a Girl Scout meeting and my father was at work, she had gone through the house, gathering up all the safety pins that lurked in drawers and tins, and adding them to the few fastened to her bracelets. When she'd found enough, she pinned them to her sari one by one, attaching the front piece to the layer of material underneath, so that no one would be able to pull the garment off her body. Then she took a can of lighter fluid and a box of kitchen matches and stepped outside, into our chilly back yard, which was full of leaves needing to be raked. Over her sari she was wearing a knee-length lilac trenchcoat, and to any neighbor she must have looked as though she'd simply stepped out for some fresh air. She opened up the coat and removed the tip from the can of lighter fluid and doused herself, then buttoned and belted the coat. She walked over to the garbage barrel behind our house and disposed of the fluid, then returned to the middle of the yard with the box of matches in her coat pocket. For nearly an hour she stood there, looking at our house, trying to work up the courage to strike a match. It was not I who saved her, or my father, but our next-door neighbor, Mrs. Holcomb, with whom my mother had never been particularly friendly. She came out to rake the leaves in her yard, calling out to my mother and remarking how beautiful the sunset was. "I see you've been admiring it for a while now," she said. My mother agreed, and then she went back into the house. By the time my father and I came home in the early evening, she was in the kitchen boiling rice for our dinner, as if it were any other day.

My mother told Deborah none of this. It was to me that she confessed, after my own heart was broken by a man I'd hoped to marry.

2004

RING LARDNER
1885–1933

Lardner's reputation—at least in terms of the work and the name—has fallen since his heyday in the early twentieth century. That's too bad. He tried mightily to deliver a "serious" novel while supporting himself with newspaper work, Broadway librettos, and "humorous stories for the magazines." In fact, the stories are his real legacy. In short fiction like the much-anthologized "Haircut" and others such as "I Can't Breathe," "Ex Parte," and "The Golden Honeymoon," Lardner proves himself a master of dramatic irony: the narrators' voices reveal their own utter lack of insight to create both wonderful comedy and a deeply bitter vision of human folly. Ringgold Lardner was born in Niles, Michigan, in 1885, and after graduating from high school he became a newspaperman, best known for his ten years as a baseball writer for the *Chicago Examiner*. He was a pal of F. Scott Fitzgerald's, and there is a story that once, learning that the great English novelist Joseph Conrad was staying at the Ritz in New York, the two friends, well lubricated with champagne, stationed themselves in front of the hotel and wouldn't leave until Conrad, a very nervous and gloomy man, came to the window of his room and waved at them. He did at last; they waved back, and went on their way. Lardner, like Fitzgerald, had a problem with alcohol, and died young, at forty-eight. His story collections include *You Know Me Al* (1916), *Gullible's Travels* (1917), *What of It?* (1925), and *First and Last* (1934).

Ex Parte[1]

Most always when a man leaves his wife, there's no excuse in the world for him. She may have made whoop-whoop-whoopee with the whole ten commandments, but if he shows his disapproval to the extent of walking out on her, he will thereafter be a total stranger to all his friends excepting the two or three bums who will tour the night clubs with him so long as he sticks to his habits of paying for everything.

When a woman leaves her husband, she must have good and sufficient reasons. He drinks all the time, or he runs around, or he doesn't give her any money, or he uses her as the heavy bag[2] in his home gymnasium work. No more is he invited to his former playmates' houses for dinner and bridge. He is an outcast just the same as if he had done the deserting. Whichever way it

---

1. Literally, "from one party"; used in legal proceedings where only one party (as in a lawsuit) is represented.   **2.** That is, punching bag.

happens, it's his fault. He can state his side of the case if he wants to, but there is nobody around listening.

Now I claim to have a little chivalry in me, as well as a little pride. So in spite of the fact that Florence had broadcast her grievances over the red and blue network[3] both, I intend to keep mine to myself till death do me part.

But after I'm gone, I want some of my old pals to know that this thing wasn't as lopsided as she has made out, so I will write the true story, put it in an envelope with my will and appoint Ed Osborne executor. He used to be my best friend and would be yet if his wife would let him. He'll have to read all my papers, including this, and he'll tell everybody else about it and maybe they'll be a little sorry that they treated me like an open manhole.

(Ed, please don't consider this an attempt to be literary. You know I haven't written for publication since our days on "The Crimson and White,"[4] and I wasn't so hot then. Just look on it as a statement of facts. If I were still alive, I'd take a bible oath that nothing herein is exaggerated. And whatever else may have been my imperfections, I never lied save to shield a woman or myself.)

Well, a year ago last May I had to go to New York. I called up Joe Paxton and he asked me out to dinner. I went, and met Florence. She and Marjorie Paxton had been at school together and she was there for a visit. We fell in love with each other and got engaged. I stopped off in Chicago on the way home, to see her people. They liked me all right, but they hated to have Florence marry a man who lived so far away. They wanted to postpone her leaving home as long as possible and they made us wait till April this year.

I had a room at the Belden and Florence and I agreed that when we were married, we would stay there awhile and take our time about picking out a house. But the last day of March, two weeks before the date of our wedding, I ran into Jeff Cooper and he told me his news, that the Standard Oil was sending him to China in some big job that looked permanent.

"I'm perfectly willing to go," he said. "So is Bess. It's a lot more money and we think it will be an interesting experience. But here I am with a brand-new place on my hands that cost me $45,000, including the furniture, and no chance to sell it in a hurry except at a loss. We were just beginning to feel settled. Otherwise we would have no regrets about leaving this town. Bess hasn't any real friends here and you're the only one I can claim."

"How much would you take for your house, furniture and all?" I asked him.

"I'd take a loss of $5,000," he said. "I'd take $40,000 with the buyer assuming my mortgage of $15,000, held by the Phillips Trust and Mortgage Company in Seattle."

I asked him if he would show me the place. They had only been living there a month and I hadn't had time to call. He said, what did I want to look at it for and I told him I would buy it if it looked o.k. Then I confessed that I was going to be married; you know I had kept it a secret around here.

Well, he took me home with him and he and Bess showed me everything, all new and shiny and a bargain if you ever saw one. In the first place, there's the location, on the best residential street in town, handy to my office and yet with a whole acre of ground, and a bed of cannas coming up in the front yard

3. Double system of radio stations operated by NBC from 1926 until the Federal Communications Commission forced it to sell its Blue network, which became rival ABC in 1945.   **4.** Name of a number of college literary magazines.

that Bess had planted when they bought the property last fall. As for the house, I always liked stucco, and this one is *built!* You could depend on old Jeff to see to that.

But the furniture was what decided me. Jeff had done the smart thing and ordered the whole works from Wolfe Brothers, taking their advice on most of the stuff, as neither he nor Bess knew much about it. Their total bill, furnishing the entire place, rugs, beds, tables, chairs, everything, was only $8,500, including a mahogany upright player-piano that they ordered from Seattle. I had my mother's old mahogany piano in storage and I kind of hoped Jeff wouldn't want me to buy this, but it was all or nothing, and with a bargain like that staring me in the face, I didn't stop to argue, not when I looked over the rest of the furniture and saw what I was getting.

The living-room had, and still has, three big easy chairs and a couch, all over-stuffed, as they call it, to say nothing of an Oriental rug that alone had cost $500. There was a long mahogany table behind the couch, with lamps at both ends in case you wanted to lie down and read. The dining-room set was solid mahogany—a table and eight chairs that had separated Jeff from $1,000.

The floors downstairs were all oak parquet. Also he had blown himself to an oak mantelpiece and oak woodwork that must have run into heavy dough. Jeff told me what it cost him extra, but I don't recall the amount.

The Coopers were strong for mahogany and wanted another set for their bedroom, but Jake Wolfe told them it would get monotonous if there was too much of it. So he sold them five pieces—a bed, two chairs, a chiffonier and a dresser—of some kind of wood tinted green, with flowers painted on it. This was $1,000 more, but it certainly was worth it. You never saw anything prettier than that bed when the lace spreads were on.

Well, we closed the deal and at first I thought I wouldn't tell Florence, but would let her believe we were going to live at the Belden and then give her a surprise by taking her right from the train to our own home. When I got to Chicago, though, I couldn't keep my mouth shut. I gave it away and it was I, not she, that had the surprise.

Instead of acting tickled to death, as I figured she would, she just looked kind of funny and said she hoped I had as good taste in houses as I had in clothes. She tried to make me describe the house and the furniture to her, but I wouldn't do it. To appreciate a layout like that, you have to see it for yourself.

We were married and stopped in Yellowstone for a week on our way here. That was the only really happy week we had together. From the minute we arrived home till she left for good, she was a different woman than the one I thought I knew. She never smiled and several times I caught her crying. She wouldn't tell me what ailed her and when I asked if she was just homesick, she said no and choked up and cried some more.

You can imagine that things were not as I expected they would be. In New York and in Chicago and Yellowstone, she had had more *life* than any girl I ever met. Now she acted all the while as if she were playing the title rôle at a funeral.

One night late in May the telephone rang. It was Mrs. Dwan and she wanted Florence. If I had known what this was going to mean, I would have slapped the receiver back on the hook and let her keep on wanting.

I had met Dwan a couple of times and had heard about their place out on the Turnpike. But I had never seen it or his wife either.

Well, it developed that Mildred Dwan had gone to school with Florence and Marjorie Paxton, and she had just learned from Marjorie that Florence was my wife and living here. She said she and her husband would be in town and call on us the next Sunday afternoon.

Florence didn't seem to like the idea and kind of discouraged it. She said we would drive out and call on them instead. Mrs. Dwan said no, that Florence was the newcomer and it was her (Mrs. Dwan's) first move. So Florence gave in.

They came and they hadn't been in the house more than a minute when Florence began to cry. Mrs. Dwan cried, too, and Dwan and I stood there first on one foot and then the other, trying to pretend we didn't know the girls were crying. Finally, to relieve the tension, I invited him to come and see the rest of the place. I showed him all over and he was quite enthusiastic. When we returned to the living-room, the girls had dried their eyes and were back in school together.

Florence accepted an invitation for one-o'clock dinner a week from that day. I told her, after they had left, that I would go along only on condition that she and our hostess would both control their tear-ducts. I was so accustomed to solo sobbing that I didn't mind it any more, but I couldn't stand a duet of it either in harmony or unison.

Well, when we got out there and had driven down their private lane through the trees and caught a glimpse of their house, which people around town had been talking about as something wonderful, I laughed harder than any time since I was single. It looked just like what it was, a reorganized barn. Florence asked me what was funny, and when I told her, she pulled even a longer face than usual.

"I think it's beautiful," she said.

Tie that!

I insisted on her going up the steps alone. I was afraid if the two of us stood on the porch at once, we'd fall through and maybe founder before help came. I warned her not to smack the knocker too hard or the door might crash in and frighten the horses.

"If you make jokes like that in front of the Dwans," she said, "I'll never speak to you again."

"I'd forgotten you ever did," said I.

I was expecting a hostler to let us in, but Mrs. Dwan came in person.

"Are we late?" said Florence.

"A little," said Mrs. Dwan, "but so is dinner. Helga didn't get home from church till half past twelve."

"I'm glad of it," said Florence. "I want you to take me all through this beautiful, beautiful house right this minute."

Mrs. Dwan called her husband and insisted that he stop in the middle of mixing a cocktail so he could join us in a tour of the beautiful, beautiful house.

"You wouldn't guess it," said Mrs. Dwan, "but it used to be a barn."

I was going to say I had guessed it. Florence gave me a look that changed my mind.

"When Jim and I first came here," said Mrs. Dwan, "we lived in an ugly little rented house on Oliver Street. It was only temporary, of course; we were just waiting till we found what we really wanted. We used to drive around the country Saturday afternoons and Sundays, hoping we would run across the right sort of thing. It was in the late fall when we first saw this place. The leaves were off the trees and it was visible from the Turnpike.

"'Oh, Jim!' I exclaimed. 'Look at that simply gorgeous old barn! With those wide shingles! And I'll bet you it's got hand-hewn beams in that middle, main section.' Jim bet me I was wrong, so we left the car, walked up the driveway, found the door open and came brazenly in. I won my bet as you can see."

She pointed to some dirty old rotten beams that ran across the living-room ceiling and looked as if five or six generations of rats had used them for gnawing practise.

"They're beautiful!" said Florence.

"The instant I saw them," said Mrs. Dwan, "I knew this was going to be our home!"

"I can imagine!" said Florence.

"We made inquiries and learned that the place belonged to a family named Taylor," said Mrs. Dwan. "The house had burned down and they had moved away. It was suspected that they had started the fire themselves, as they were terribly hard up and it was insured. Jim wrote to old Mr. Taylor in Seattle and asked him to set a price on the barn and the land, which is about four acres. They exchanged several letters and finally Mr. Taylor accepted Jim's offer. We got it for a song."

"Wonderful!" said Florence.

"And then, of course," Mrs. Dwan continued, "we engaged a house-wrecking company to tear down the other four sections of the barn—the stalls, the cow-shed, the tool-shed, and so forth—and take them away, leaving us just this one room. We had a man from Seattle come and put in these old pine walls and the flooring, and plaster the ceiling. He was recommended by a friend of Jim's and he certainly knew his business."

"I can see he did," said Florence.

"He made the hay-loft over for us, too, and we got the wings built by day-labor, with Jim and me supervising. It was so much fun that I was honestly sorry when it was finished."

"I can imagine!" said Florence.

Well, I am not very well up in Early American, which was the name they had for pretty nearly everything in the place, but for the benefit of those who are not on terms with the Dwans I will try and describe from memory the *objets d'art*[5] they bragged of the most and which brought forth the loudest squeals from Florence.

The living-room walls were brown bare boards without a picture or scrap of wall-paper. On the floor were two or three "hooked rugs," whatever that means, but they needed five or six more of them, or one big carpet, to cover up all the knots in the wood. There was a maple "low-boy"; a "dough-trough" table they didn't have space for in the kitchen; a pine "stretcher" table with sticks connecting the four legs near the bottom so you couldn't put your feet anywhere; a "Dutch" chest that looked as if it had been ordered from the

---

5. Art objects (French).

undertaker by one of Singer's Midgets,[6] but he got well; and some "Windsor" chairs in which the only position you could get comfortable was to stand up behind them and lean your elbows on their back.

Not one piece that matched another, and not one piece of mahogany anywhere. And the ceiling, between the beams, had apparently been plastered by a workman who was that way, too.

"Some day soon I hope to have a piano," said Mrs. Dwan. "I can't live much longer without one. But so far I haven't been able to find one that would fit in."

"Listen," I said. "I've got a piano in storage that belonged to my mother. It's a mahogany upright and not so big that it wouldn't fit in this room, especially when you get that 'trough' table out. It isn't doing me any good and I'll sell it to you for $250. Mother paid $1,250 for it new."

"Oh, I couldn't think of taking it!" said Mrs. Dwan.

"I'll make it $200 even just because you're a friend of Florence's," I said.

"Really, I couldn't!" said Mrs. Dwan.

"You wouldn't have to pay for it all at once," I said.

"Don't you see," said Florence, "that a mahogany upright piano would be a perfect horror in here? Mildred wouldn't have it as a gift, let alone buy it. It isn't in the period."

"She could get it turned," I said.

The answer to this was, "I'll show you the up-stairs now and we can look at the dining-room later on."

We were led to the guest-chamber. The bed was a maple four-poster, with pineapple posts, and a "tester" running from pillar to post. You would think a "tester" might be a man that went around trying out beds, but it's really a kind of frame that holds a canopy over the bed in case it rains and the roof leaks. There was a quilt made by Mrs. Dwan's great-grandmother, Mrs. Anthony Adams, in 1859, at Lowell, Mass. How is that for a memory?

"This used to be the hay-loft," said Mrs. Dwan.

"You ought to have left some of the hay so the guests could hit it," I said.

The dressers, chests of drawers, and the chairs were all made of maple. And the same in the Dwans' own room; everything maple.

"If you had maple in one room and mahogany in the other," I said, "people wouldn't get confused when you told them that so and so was up in Maple's room."

Dwan laughed, but the women didn't.

The maid hollered up that dinner was ready.

"The cocktails aren't ready," said Dwan.

"You will have to go without them," said Mrs. Dwan. "The soup will be cold."

This put me in a great mood to admire the "sawbuck" table and the "slat-back" chairs, which were evidently the *chef-d'œuvre* and the *pièce de résistance* of the *chez Dwan*.[7]

"It came all the way from Pennsylvania," said Mildred, when Florence's outcries, brought on by her first look at the table, had died down. "Mother

---

6. A popular vaudeville show in Europe and the United States in the early 20th century; the troupe featured more than 50 actual midgets, many of whom played the Munchkins in the film *The Wizard of Oz* (1939).   **7.** Dwan household (French). *Chef-d'œuvre:* masterpiece (French). *Pièce de résistance:* showpiece in a collection (French).

picked it up at a little place near Stroudsburg and sent it to me. It only cost $550, and the chairs were $45 apiece."

"How reasonable!" exclaimed Florence.

That was before she had sat in one of them. Only one thing was more unreasonable than the chairs, and that was the table itself, consisting of big planks nailed together and laid onto a railroad tie, supported underneath by a whole forest of cross-pieces and beams. The surface was as smooth on top as the trip to Catalina Island[8] and all around the edges, great big divots had been taken out with some blunt instrument, probably a bayonet. There were stains and scorch marks that Florence fairly crowed over, but when I tried to add to the general ensemble by laying a lighted cigarette right down beside my soup-plate, she and both the Dwans yelled murder and made me take it off.

They planted me in an end seat, a location just right for a man who had stretched himself across a railway track and had both legs cut off at the abdomen. Not being that kind of man, I had to sit so far back that very few of my comestibles carried more than half-way to their target.

After dinner I was all ready to go home and get something to eat, but it had been darkening up outdoors for half an hour and now such a storm broke that I knew it was useless trying to persuade Florence to make a start.

"We'll play some bridge," said Dwan, and to my surprise he produced a card-table that was nowhere near "in the period."

At my house there was a big center chandelier that lighted up a bridge game no matter in what part of the room the table was put. But here we had to waste forty minutes moving lamps and wires and stands and when they were all fixed, you could tell a red suit from a black suit, but not a spade from a club. Aside from that and the granite-bottomed "Windsor" chairs and the fact that we played "families" for a cent a point and Florence and I won $12 and didn't get paid, it was one of the pleasantest afternoons I ever spent gambling.

The rain stopped at five o'clock and as we splashed through the puddles of Dwan's driveway, I remarked to Florence that I had never known she was such a kidder.

"What do you mean?" she asked me.

"Why, your pretending to admire all that junk," I said.

"Junk!" said Florence. "That is one of the most beautifully furnished homes I have ever seen!"

And so far as I can recall, that was her last utterance in my presence for six nights and five days.

At lunch on Saturday I said: "You know I like the silent drama one evening a week, but not twenty-four hours a day every day. What's the matter with you? If it's laryngitis, you might write me notes."

"I'll tell you what's the matter!" she burst out. "I hate this house and everything in it! It's too new! Everything shines! I loathe new things! I want a home like Mildred's, with things in it that I can look at without blushing for shame. I can't invite anyone here. It's too hideous. And I'll never be happy here a single minute as long as I live!"

---

8. Island separated from the southern California coast by the rough waters of the Pacific Ocean.

Well, I don't mind telling that this kind of got under my skin. As if I hadn't intended to give her a pleasant surprise! As if Wolfe Brothers, in business thirty years, didn't know how to furnish a home complete! I was pretty badly hurt, but I choked it down and said, as calmly as I could:

"If you'll be a little patient, I'll try to sell this house and its contents for what I paid for it and them. It oughtn't to be much trouble; there are plenty of people around who know a bargain. But it's too bad you didn't confess your barn complex to me long ago. Only last February, old Ken Garrett had to sell his establishment and the men who bought it turned it into a garage. It was a livery-stable which I could have got for the introduction of a song, or maybe just the vamp. And we wouldn't have had to spend a nickel to make it as nice and comfortable and homey as your friend Mildred's dump."

Florence was on her way upstairs before I had finished my speech.

I went down to Earl Benham's to see if my new suit was ready. It was and I put it on and left the old one to be cleaned and pressed.

On the street I met Harry Cross.

"Come up to my office," he said. "There's something in my desk that may interest you."

I accepted his invitation and from three different drawers he pulled out three different quart bottles of Early American rye.

Just before six o'clock I dropped in Kane's store and bought myself a pair of shears, a blow torch and an ax. I started home, but stopped among the trees inside my front gate and cut big holes in my coat and trousers. Alongside the path to the house was a sizable mud puddle. I waded in it. And I bathed my gray felt hat.

Florence was sitting on the floor of the living-room, reading. She seemed a little upset by my appearance.

"Good heavens! What's happened?"

"Nothing much," said I. "I just didn't want to look too new."

"What are those things you're carrying?"

"Just a pair of shears, a blow torch and an ax. I'm going to try and antique this place and I think I'll begin on the dining-room table."

Florence went into her scream, dashed upstairs and locked herself in. I went about my work and had the dinner-table looking pretty Early when the maid smelled fire and rushed in. She rushed out again and came back with a pitcher of water. But using my vest as a snuffer, I had had the flames under control all the while and there was nothing for her to do.

"I'll just nick it up a little with this ax," I told her, "and by the time I'm through, dinner ought to be ready."

"It will never be ready as far as I'm concerned," she said. "I'm leaving just as soon as I can pack."

And Florence had the same idea—vindicating the old adage about great minds.

I heard the front door slam and the back door slam, and I felt kind of tired and sleepy, so I knocked off work and went up to bed.

That's my side of the story, Eddie, and it's true so help me my bootlegger. Which reminds me that the man who sold Harry the rye makes this town once a week, or did when this was written. He's at the Belden every Tuesday from nine to six and his name is Mike Farrell.

1928

D. H. LAWRENCE

1885–1930

Lawrence was born in Eastwood, Nottingham-shire, England. His father was a coal miner, his mother a former schoolteacher whose thwarted life and fierce ambition for her son pushed him to struggle up into the world of culture. The anguish of this effort amid family tensions is the subject of the novel *Sons and Lovers* (1913), which established him as a major literary figure. Before World War I he eloped to the Continent with the wife of a Nottingham professor, but spent the war years miserably in England, suspected of dis-loyalty because his wife was of German origin, and oppressed by disgust at what was happening to his country. His distaste for the industrializa-tion and commercialism of English life in his time sent him wandering to Italy, Australia, Mexico, and the mountains of New Mexico in search of an alternative. As he continued to outrage the guardians of public morals—and to reply to them in many of his works with polemic attacks and warnings of the disasters they were brewing—he attracted both passionate disciples and the constant harassment of efforts to censor his books and paintings. His stature as prophet and critic of modern culture has always been a matter of controversy; his explorations of the dark strata of the unconscious, his shrewdly intuitive revisions of conventional notions of human motivation, and the vital energy of his style place him inarguably among the great poets and novelists of his age. Lawrence's life has inspired a flood of biographies; his remarkable marriage and his death by tuberculosis in the south of France seem hardly distinguishable from his creations in prose and verse. Some of his best-known novels are *The Rainbow* (1915), *Women in Love* (1920), and *Lady Chatterley's Lover* (1928). His shorter works and poems are most eas-ily found in *The Complete Stories* (1961), *Four Short Novels* (1965), and *Complete Poems* (1964).

The Horse Dealer's Daughter

Well, Mabel, and what are you going to do with yourself?" asked Joe, with foolish flippancy. He felt quite safe himself. Without listening for an answer, he turned aside, worked a grain of tobacco to the tip of his tongue, and spat it out. He did not care about anything, since he felt safe himself.

The three brothers and the sister sat round the desolate breakfast-table, attempting some sort of desultory consultation. The morning's post had given the final tap to the family fortunes, and all was over. The dreary dining-room itself, with its heavy mahogany furniture, looked as if it were waiting to be done away with.

But the consultation amounted to nothing. There was a strange air of ineffectuality about the three men, as they sprawled at table, smoking and reflecting vaguely on their own condition. The girl was alone, a rather short, sullen-looking young woman of twenty-seven. She did not share the same life as her brothers. She would have been good-looking, save for the impressive fixity of her face, "bull-dog," as her brothers called it.

There was a confused tramping of horses' feet outside. The three men all sprawled round in their chairs to watch. Beyond the dark holly bushes that separated the strip of lawn from the high-road,[1] they could see a cavalcade of shire horses swinging out of their own yard, being taken for exercise. This was the last time. These were the last horses that would go through their hands. The young men watched with critical, callous look. They were all frightened at the collapse of their lives, and the sense of disaster in which they were involved left them no inner freedom.

Yet they were three fine, well-set fellows enough. Joe, the eldest, was a man of thirty-three, broad and handsome in a hot, flushed way. His face was red, he twisted his black moustache over a thick finger, his eyes were shallow and restless. He had a sensual way of uncovering his teeth when he laughed, and his bearing was stupid. Now he watched the horses with a glazed look of helplessness in his eyes, a certain stupor of downfall.

The great draught-horses swung past. They were tied head to tail, four of them, and they heaved along to where a lane branched off from the high-road, planting their great hoofs floutingly in the fine black mud, swinging their great rounded haunches sumptuously, and trotting a few sudden steps as they were led into the lane, round the corner. Every movement showed a massive, slumbrous strength, and a stupidity which held them in subjection. The groom at the head looked back, jerking the leading rope. And the cavalcade moved out of sight up the lane, the tail of the last horse, bobbed up tight and stiff, held out taut from the swinging great haunches as they rocked behind the hedges in a motion-like sleep.

Joe watched with glazed hopeless eyes. The horses were almost like his own body to him. He felt he was done for now. Luckily he was engaged to a woman as old as himself, and therefore her father, who was steward of a neighbouring estate, would provide him with a job. He would marry and go into harness. His life was over, he would be a subject animal now.

He turned uneasily aside, the retreating steps of the horses echoing in his ears. Then, with foolish restlessness, he reached for the scraps of bacon-rind from the plates, and making a faint whistling sound, flung them to the terrier that lay against the fender. He watched the dog swallow them, and waited till the creature looked into his eyes. Then a faint grin came on his face, and in a high, foolish voice he said:

"You won't get much more bacon, shall you, you little b——?"

The dog faintly and dismally wagged its tail, then lowered its haunches, circled round, and lay down again.

---

1. Highway.

There was another helpless silence at the table. Joe sprawled uneasily in his seat, not willing to go till the family conclave was dissolved. Fred Henry, the second brother, was erect, clean-limbed, alert. He had watched the passing of the horses with more *sang-froid*.[2] If he was an animal, like Joe, he was an animal which controls, not one which is controlled. He was master of any horse, and he carried himself with a well-tempered air of mastery. But he was not master of the situations of life. He pushed his coarse brown moustache upwards, off his lip, and glanced irritably at his sister, who sat impassive and inscrutable.

"You'll go and stop with Lucy for a bit, shan't you?" he asked. The girl did not answer.

"I don't see what else you can do," persisted Fred Henry.

"Go as a skivvy,"[3] Joe interpolated laconically.

The girl did not move a muscle.

"If I was her, I should go in for training for a nurse," said Malcolm, the youngest of them all. He was the baby of the family, a young man of twenty-two, with a fresh, jaunty *museau*.[4]

But Mabel did not take any notice of him. They had talked at her and round her for so many years, that she hardly heard them at all.

The marble clock on the mantelpiece softly chimed the half-hour, the dog rose uneasily from the hearth-rug and looked at the party at the breakfast-table. But still they sat in an ineffectual conclave.

"Oh, all right," said Joe suddenly, apropos of nothing. "I'll get a move on."

He pushed back his chair, straddled his knees with a downward jerk, to get them free, in horsey fashion, and went to the fire. Still he did not go out of the room; he was curious to know what the others would do or say. He began to charge his pipe, looking down at the dog and saying in a high, affected voice:

"Going wi' me? Going wi' me are ter? Tha'rt goin' further than tha counts on just now, dost hear?"[5]

The dog faintly wagged his tail, the man stuck out his jaw and covered his pipe with his hands, and puffed intently, losing himself in the tobacco, looking down all the while at the dog with an absent brown eye. The dog looked up at him in mournful distrust. Joe stood with his knees stuck out, in real horsey fashion.

"Have you had a letter from Lucy?" Fred Henry asked of his sister.

"Last week," came the neutral reply.

"And what does she say?"

There was no answer.

"Does she *ask* you to go and stop there?" persisted Fred Henry.

"She says I can if I like."

"Well, then, you'd better. Tell her you'll come on Monday."

This was received in silence.

"That's what you'll do then, is it?" said Fred Henry, in some exasperation.

But she made no answer. There was a silence of futility and irritation in the room. Malcolm grinned fatuously.

2. Literally, "cold blood," i.e., imperturbability (French). **3.** Maid, scullion. **4.** Face, mug (French). **5.** That is, "Going with me? Going with me, are you? You are going further than you count on just now, do you hear?" The familiar form *thou* was used in provincial regions of England well into the 20th century.

"You'll have to make up your mind between now and next Wednesday," said Joe loudly, "or else find yourself lodgings on the kerbstone."

The face of the young woman darkened, but she sat on immutable.

"Here's Jack Ferguson!" exclaimed Malcolm, who was looking aimlessly out of the window.

"Where?" exclaimed Joe loudly.

"Just gone past."

"Coming in?"

Malcolm craned his neck to see the gate.

"Yes," he said.

There was a silence. Mabel sat on like one condemned, at the head of the table. Then a whistle was heard from the kitchen. The dog got up and barked sharply. Joe opened the door and shouted:

"Come on."

After a moment a young man entered. He was muffled up in overcoat and a purple woollen scarf, and his tweed cap, which he did not remove, was pulled down on his head. He was of medium height, his face was rather long and pale, his eyes looked tired.

"Hello, Jack! Well, Jack!" exclaimed Malcolm and Joe. Fred Henry merely said: "Jack."

"What's doing?" asked the newcomer, evidently addressing Fred Henry.

"Same. We've got to be out by Wednesday. Got a cold?"

"I have—got it bad, too."

"Why don't you stop in?"

"*Me* stop in? When I can't stand on my legs, perhaps I shall have a chance." The young man spoke huskily. He had a slight Scotch accent.

"It's a knock-out, isn't it," said Joe, boisterously, "if a doctor goes round croaking with a cold. Looks bad for the patients, doesn't it?"

The young doctor looked at him slowly.

"Anything the matter with *you,* then?" he asked sarcastically.

"Not as I know of. Damn your eyes, I hope not. Why?"

"I thought you were very concerned about the patients, wondered if you might be one yourself."

"Damn it, no, I've never been patient to no flaming doctor, and hope I never shall be," returned Joe.

At this point Mabel rose from the table, and they all seemed to become aware of her existence. She began putting the dishes together. The young doctor looked at her, but did not address her. He had not greeted her. She went out of the room with the tray, her face impassive and unchanged.

"When are you off then, all of you?" asked the doctor.

"I'm catching the eleven-forty," replied Malcolm. "Are you goin' down wi' th' trap, Joe?"

"Yes, I've told you I'm going down wi' th' trap,[6] haven't I?"

"We'd better be getting her in then. So long Jack, if I don't see you before I go," said Malcolm, shaking hands.

He went out, followed by Joe, who seemed to have his tail between his legs.

---

6. Light carriage.

"Well, this is the devil's own," exclaimed the doctor, when he was left alone with Fred Henry. "Going before Wednesday, are you?"

"That's the orders," replied the other.

"Where, to Northampton?"[7]

"That's it."

"The devil!" exclaimed Ferguson, with quiet chagrin.

And there was silence between the two.

"All settled up, are you?" asked Ferguson.

"About."

There was another pause.

"Well, I shall miss yer, Freddy, boy," said the young doctor.

"And I shall miss thee, Jack," returned the other.

"Miss you like hell," mused the doctor.

Fred Henry turned aside. There was nothing to say. Mabel came in again, to finish clearing the table.

"What are *you* going to do, then, Miss Pervin?" asked Ferguson. "Going to your sister's, are you?"

Mabel looked at him with her steady, dangerous eyes, that always made him uncomfortable, unsettling his superficial ease.

"No," she said.

"Well, what in the name of fortune *are* you going to do? Say what you mean to do," cried Fred Henry, with futile intensity.

But she only averted her head, and continued her work. She folded the white table-cloth, and put on the chenille cloth.

"The sulkiest bitch that ever trod!" muttered her brother.

But she finished her task with perfectly impassive face, the young doctor watching her interestedly all the while. Then she went out.

Fred Henry stared after her, clenching his lips, his blue eyes fixing in sharp antagonism, as he made a grimace of sour exasperation.

"You could bray her into bits, and that's all you'd get out of her," he said, in a small, narrowed tone.

The doctor smiled faintly.

"What's she *going* to do, then?" he asked.

"Strike me if *I* know!" returned the other.

There was a pause. Then the doctor stirred.

"I'll be seeing you tonight, shall I?" he said to his friend.

"Ay—where's it to be? Are we going over to Jessdale?"

"I don't know. I've got such a cold on me. I'll come round to the 'Moon and Stars', anyway."

"Let Lizzie and May miss their night for once, eh?"

"That's it—if I feel as I do now."

"All's one——"

The two young men went through the passage and down to the back door together. The house was large, but it was servantless now, and desolate. At the back was a small brick house-yard and beyond that a big square, graveled fine and red, and having stables on two sides. Sloping, dank, winter-dark fields stretched away on the open sides.

---

7. Capital of Nottinghamshire, county in the coal-producing north of England.

But the stables were empty. Joseph Pervin, the father of the family, had been a man of no education, who had become a fairly large horse dealer. The stables had been full of horses, there was a great turmoil and come-and-go of horses and of dealers and grooms. Then the kitchen was full of servants. But of late things had declined. The old man had married a second time, to retrieve his fortunes. Now he was dead and everything was gone to the dogs, there was nothing but debt and threatening.

For months, Mabel had been servantless in the big house, keeping the home together in penury for her ineffectual brothers. She had kept house for ten years. But previously it was with unstinted means. Then, however brutal and coarse everything was, the sense of money had kept her proud, confident. The men might be foul-mouthed, the women in the kitchen might have bad reputations, her brothers might have illegitimate children. But so long as there was money, the girl felt herself established, and brutally proud, reserved.

No company came to the house, save dealers and coarse men. Mabel had no associates of her own sex, after her sister went away. But she did not mind. She went regularly to church, she attended to her father. And she lived in the memory of her mother, who had died when she was fourteen, and whom she had loved. She had loved her father, too, in a different way, depending upon him, and feeling secure in him, until at the age of fifty-four he married again. And then she had set hard against him. Now he had died and left them all hopelessly in debt.

She had suffered badly during the period of poverty. Nothing, however, could shake the curious, sullen, animal pride that dominated each member of the family. Now, for Mabel, the end had come. Still she would not cast about her. She would follow her own way just the same. She would always hold the keys of her own situation. Mindless and persistent, she endured from day to day. Why should she think? Why should she answer anybody? It was enough that this was the end, and there was no way out. She need not pass any more darkly along the main street of the small town, avoiding every eye. She need not demean herself any more, going into the shops and buying the cheapest food. This was at an end. She thought of nobody, not even of herself. Mindless and persistent, she seemed in a sort of ecstasy to be coming nearer to her fulfilment, her own glorification, approaching her dead mother, who was glorified.

In the afternoon, she took a little bag, with shears and sponge and a small scrubbing-brush, and went out. It was a grey, wintry day, with saddened, dark green fields and an atmosphere blackened by the smoke of foundries not far off. She went quickly, darkly along the causeway, heeding nobody, through the town to the churchyard.

There she always felt secure, as if no one could see her, although as a matter of fact she was exposed to the stare of everyone who passed along under the churchyard wall. Nevertheless, once under the shadow of the great looming church, among the graves, she felt immune from the world, reserved within the thick churchyard wall as in another country.

Carefully she clipped the grass from the grave, and arranged the pinky white, small chrysanthemums in the tin cross. When this was done, she took an empty jar from a neighbouring grave, brought water, and carefully, most scrupulously sponged the marble headstone and the coping-stone.

It gave her sincere satisfaction to do this. She felt in immediate contact with the world of her mother. She took minute pains, went through the park in a state bordering on pure happiness, as if in performing this task she came into a subtle, intimate connection with her mother. For the life she followed here in the world was far less real than the world of death she inherited from her mother.

The doctor's house was just by the church. Ferguson, being a mere hired assistant, was slave to the country-side. As he hurried now to attend to the out-patients in the surgery, glancing across the graveyard with his quick eye, he saw the girl at her task at the grave. She seemed so intent and remote, it was like looking into another world. Some mystical element was touched in him. He slowed down as he walked, watching her as if spellbound.

She lifted her eyes, feeling him looking. Their eyes met. And each looked away again at once, each feeling, in some way, found out by the other. He lifted his cap and passed on down the road. There remained distinct in his consciousness, like a vision, the memory of her face, lifted from the tomb-stone in the churchyard, and looking at him with slow, large, portentous eyes. It *was* portentous, her face. It seemed to mesmerize him. There was a heavy power in her eyes which laid hold of his whole being, as if he had drunk some powerful drug. He had been feeling weak and done before. Now the life came back into him, he felt delivered from his own fretted, daily self.

He finished his duties at the surgery as quickly as might be, hastily filling up the bottles of the waiting people with cheap drugs. Then, in perpetual haste, he set off again to visit several cases in another part of his round, before tea-time. At all times he preferred to walk if he could, but particularly when he was not well. He fancied the motion restored him.

The afternoon was falling. It was grey, deadened, and wintry, with a slow, moist, heavy coldness sinking in and deadening all the faculties. But why should he think or notice? He hastily climbed the hill and turned across the dark green fields, following the black cinder-track. In the distance, across a shallow dip in the country, the small town was clustered like smouldering ash, a tower, a spire, a heap of low, raw, extinct houses. And on the nearest fringe of the town, sloping into the dip, was Oldmeadow, the Pervins' house. He could see the stables and the outbuildings distinctly, as they lay towards him on the slope. Well, he would not go there many more times! Another resource would be lost to him, another place gone: the only company he cared for in the alien, ugly little town he was losing. Nothing but work, drudgery, constant hastening from dwelling to dwelling among the colliers and the iron-workers. It wore him out, but at the same time he had a craving for it. It was a stimulant to him to be in the homes of the working people, moving, as it were, through the innermost body of their life. His nerves were excited and gratified. He could come so near, into the very lives of the rough, inarticulate, powerfully emotional men and women. He grumbled, he said he hated the hellish hole. But as a matter of fact it excited him, the contact with the rough, strongly-feeling people was a stimulant applied direct to his nerves.

Below Oldmeadow, in the green, shallow, soddened hollow of fields, lay a square, deep pond. Roving across the landscape, the doctor's quick eye detected a figure in black passing through the gate of the field, down towards the pond. He looked again. It would be Mabel Pervin. His mind suddenly became alive and attentive.

Why was she going down there? He pulled up on the path on the slope above, and stood staring. He could just make sure of the small black figure moving in the hollow of the failing day. He seemed to see her in the midst of such obscurity, that he was like a clairvoyant, seeing rather with the mind's eye than with ordinary sight. Yet he could see her positively enough, whilst he kept his eye attentive. He felt, if he looked away from her, in the thick, ugly falling dusk, he would lose her altogether.

He followed her minutely as she moved, direct and intent, like something transmitted rather than stirring in voluntary activity, straight down the field towards the pond. There she stood on the bank for a moment. She never raised her head. Then she waded slowly into the water.

He stood motionless as the small black figure walked slowly and deliberately towards the center of the pond, very slowly, gradually moving deeper into the motionless water, and still moving forward as the water got up to her breast. Then he could see her no more in the dusk of the dead afternoon.

"There!" he exclaimed. "Would you believe it?"

And he hastened straight down, running over the wet, soddened fields, pushing through the hedges, down into the depression of callous wintry obscurity. It took him several minutes to come to the pond. He stood on the bank, breathing heavily. He could see nothing. His eyes seemed to penetrate the dead water. Yes, perhaps that was the dark shadow of her black clothing beneath the surface of the water.

He slowly ventured into the pond. The bottom was deep, soft clay, he sank in, and the water clasped dead cold round his legs. As he stirred he could smell the cold, rotten clay that fouled up into the water. It was objectionable in his lungs. Still, repelled and yet not heeding, he moved deeper into the pond. The cold water rose over his thighs, over his loins, upon his abdomen. The lower part of his body was all sunk in the hideous cold element. And the bottom was so deeply soft and uncertain, he was afraid of pitching with his mouth underneath. He could not swim, and was afraid.

He crouched a little, spreading his hands under the water and moving them round, trying to feel for her. The dead cold pond swayed upon his chest. He moved again, a little deeper, and again, with his hands underneath, he felt all around under the water. And he touched her clothing. But it evaded his fingers. He made a desperate effort to grasp it.

And so doing he lost his balance and went under, horribly, suffocating in the foul earthy water, struggling madly for a few moments. At last, after what seemed an eternity, he got his footing, rose again into the air and looked around. He gasped, and knew he was in the world. Then he looked at the water. She had risen near him. He grasped her clothing, and drawing her nearer, turned to take his way to land again.

He went very slowly, carefully, absorbed in the slow progress. He rose higher, climbing out of the pond. The water was now only about his legs; he was thankful, full of relief to be out of the clutches of the pond. He lifted her and staggered onto the bank, out of the horror of wet, grey clay.

He laid her down on the bank. She was quite unconscious and running with water. He made the water come from her mouth, he worked to restore her. He did not have to work very long before he could feel the breathing begin again in her; she was breathing naturally. He worked a little longer. He could feel her live beneath his hands; she was coming back. He wiped her face, wrapped her in his overcoat, looked round into the dim, dark grey world, then lifted her and staggered down the bank and across the fields.

It seemed an unthinkably long way, and his burden so heavy he felt he would never get to the house. But at last he was in the stable-yard, and then in the house-yard. He opened the door and went into the house. In the kitchen he laid her down on the hearth-rug and called. The house was empty. But the fire was burning in the grate.

Then again he kneeled to attend to her. She was breathing regularly, her eyes were wide open and as if conscious, but there seemed something missing in her look. She was conscious in herself, but unconscious of her surroundings.

He ran upstairs, took blankets from a bed, and put them before the fire to warm. Then he removed her saturated, earthy-smelling clothing, rubbed her dry with a towel, and wrapped her naked in the blankets. Then he went into the dining-room, to look for spirits. There was a little whisky. He drank a gulp himself, and put some into her mouth.

The effect was instantaneous. She looked full into his face, as if she had been seeing him for some time, and yet had only just become conscious of him.

"Dr. Ferguson?" she said.

"What?" he answered.

He was divesting himself of his coat, intending to find some dry clothing upstairs. He could not bear the smell of the dead, clayey water, and he was mortally afraid for his own health.

"What did I do?" she asked.

"Walked into the pond," he replied. He had begun to shudder like one sick, and could hardly attend to her. Her eyes remained full on him, he seemed to be going dark in his mind, looking back at her helplessly. The shuddering became quieter in him, his life came back to him, dark and unknowing, but strong again.

"Was I out of my mind?" she asked, while her eyes were fixed on him all the time.

"Maybe, for the moment," he replied. He felt quiet, because his strength had come back. The strange fretful strain had left him.

"Am I out of my mind now?" she asked.

"Are you?" he reflected a moment. "No," he answered truthfully. "I don't see that you are." He turned his face aside. He was afraid now, because he felt dazed, and felt dimly that her power was stronger than his, in this issue. And she continued to look at him fixedly all the time. "Can you tell me where I shall find some dry things to put on?" he asked.

"Did you dive into the pond for me?" she asked.

"No," he answered. "I walked in. But I went in over head as well."

There was silence for a moment. He hesitated. He very much wanted to go upstairs to get into dry clothing. But there was another desire in him. And she seemed to hold him. His will seemed to have gone to sleep, and left him, standing there slack before her. But he felt warm inside himself. He did not shudder at all, though his clothes were sodden on him.

"Why did you?" she asked.

"Because I didn't want you to do such a foolish thing," he said.

"It wasn't foolish," she said, still gazing at him as she lay on the floor, with a sofa cushion under her head. "It was the right thing to do. *I* knew best, then."

"I'll go and shift these wet things," he said. But still he had not the power to move out of her presence, until she sent him. It was as if she had the life of his body in her hands, and he could not extricate himself. Or perhaps he did not want to.

Suddenly she sat up. Then she became aware of her own immediate condition. She felt the blankets about her, she knew her own limbs. For a moment it seemed as if her reason were going. She looked round, with wild eye, as if seeking something. He stood still with fear. She saw her clothing lying scattered.

"Who undressed me?" she asked, her eyes resting full and inevitable on his face.

"I did," he replied, "to bring you round."

For some moments she sat and gazed at him awfully, her lips parted.

"Do you love me, then?" she asked.

He only stood and stared at her, fascinated. His soul seemed to melt.

She shuffled forward on her knees, and put her arms round him, round his legs, as he stood there, pressing her breasts against his knees and thighs, clutching him with strange, convulsive certainty, pressing his thighs against her, drawing him to her face, her throat, as she looked up at him with flaring, humble eyes of transfiguration, triumphant in first possession.

"You love me," she murmured, in strange transport, yearning and triumphant and confident. "You love me. I know you love me, I know."

And she was passionately kissing his knees, through the wet clothing, passionately and indiscriminately kissing his knees, his legs, as if unaware of everything.

He looked down at the tangled wet hair, the wild, bare, animal shoulders. He was amazed, bewildered, and afraid. He had never thought of loving her. He had never wanted to love her. When he rescued her and restored her, he was a doctor, and she was a patient. He had had no single personal thought of her. Nay, this introduction of the personal element was very distasteful to him, a violation of his professional honour. It was horrible to have her there embracing his knees. It was horrible. He revolted from it, violently. And yet—and yet—he had not the power to break away.

She looked at him again, with the same supplication of powerful love, and that same transcendent, frightening light of triumph. In view of the delicate flame which seemed to come from her face like a light, he was powerless. And yet he had never intended to love her. He had never intended. And something stubborn in him could not give way.

"You love me," she repeated, in a murmur of deep, rhapsodic assurance. "You love me."

Her hands were drawing him, drawing him down to her. He was afraid, even a little horrified. For he had, really, no intention of loving her. Yet her hands were drawing him towards her. He put out his hand quickly to steady himself, and grasped her bare shoulder. A flame seemed to burn the hand that grasped her soft shoulder. He had no intention of loving her: his whole will was against his yielding. It was horrible. And yet wonderful was the touch of her shoulders, beautiful the shining of her face. Was she perhaps mad? He had a horror of yielding to her. Yet something in him ached also.

He had been staring away at the door, away from her. But his hand remained on her shoulder. She had gone suddenly very still. He looked down at her. Her eyes were now wide with fear, with doubt, the light was dying from her face, a shadow of terrible greyness was returning. He could not bear the touch of her eyes' question upon him, and the look of death behind the question.

With an inward groan he gave way, and let his heart yield towards her. A sudden gentle smile came on his face. And her eyes, which never left his face, slowly, slowly filled with tears. He watched the strange water rise in her eyes, like some slow fountain coming up. And his heart seemed to burn and melt away in his breast.

He could not bear to look at her any more. He dropped on his knees and caught her head with his arms and pressed her face against his throat. She was very still. His heart, which seemed to have broken, was burning with a kind of agony in his breast. And he felt her slow, hot tears wetting his throat. But he could not move.

He felt the hot tears wet his neck and the hollows of his neck, and he remained motionless, suspended through one of man's eternities. Only now it had become indispensable to him to have her face pressed close to him; he could never let her go again. He could never let her head go away from the close clutch of his arm. He wanted to remain like that for ever, with his heart hurting him in a pain that was also life to him. Without knowing, he was looking down on her damp, soft brown hair.

Then, as it were suddenly, he smelt the horrid stagnant smell of that water. And at the same moment she drew away from him and looked at him. Her eyes were wistful and unfathomable. He was afraid of them, and he fell to kissing her, not knowing what he was doing. He wanted her eyes not to have that terrible, wistful, unfathomable look.

When she turned her face to him again, a faint delicate flush was glowing, and there was again dawning that terrible shining of joy in her eyes, which really terrified him, and yet which he now wanted to see, because he feared the look of doubt still more.

"You love me?" she said, rather faltering.

"Yes." The word cost him a painful effort. Not because it wasn't true. But because it was too newly true, the *saying* seemed to tear open again his newly-torn heart. And he hardly wanted it to be true, even now.

She lifted her face to him, and he bent forward and kissed her on the mouth, gently, with the one kiss that is an eternal pledge. And as he kissed her his heart strained again in his breast. He never intended to love her. But now it was over. He had crossed over the gulf to her, and all that he had left behind had shrivelled and become void.

After the kiss, her eyes again slowly filled with tears. She sat still, away from him, with her face drooped aside, and her hands folded in her lap. The tears fell very slowly. There was complete silence. He too sat there motionless and silent on the hearth-rug. The strange pain of his heart that was broken seemed to consume him. That he should love her? That this was love! That he should be ripped open in this way! Him, a doctor! How they would all jeer if they knew! It was agony to him to think they might know.

In the curious naked pain of the thought he looked again to her. She was sitting there drooped into a muse. He saw a tear fall, and his heart flared hot. He saw for the first time that one of her shoulders was quite uncovered, one arm bare, he could see one of her small breasts; dimly, because it had become almost dark in the room.

"Why are you crying?" he asked, in an altered voice.

She looked up at him, and behind her tears the consciousness of her situation for the first time brought a dark look of shame to her eyes.

"I'm not crying, really," she said, watching him, half frightened.

He reached his hand, and softly closed it on her bare arm.

"I love you! I love you!" he said in a soft, low vibrating voice, unlike himself.

She shrank, and dropped her head. The soft, penetrating grip of his hand on her arm distressed her. She looked up at him.

"I want to go," she said. "I want to go and get you some dry things."

"Why?" he said. "I'm all right."

"But I want to go," she said. "And I want you to change your things."

He released her arm, and she wrapped herself in the blanket, looking at him rather frightened. And still she did not rise.

"Kiss me," she said wistfully.

He kissed her, but briefly, half in anger.

Then, after a second, she rose nervously, all mixed up in the blanket. He watched her in her confusion as she tried to extricate herself and wrap herself up so that she could walk. He watched her relentlessly, as she knew. And as she went, the blanket trailing, and as he saw a glimpse of her feet and her white leg, he tried to remember her as she was when he had wrapped her in the blanket. But then he didn't want to remember, because she had been nothing to him then, and his nature revolted from remembering her as she was when she was nothing to him.

A tumbling, muffled noise from within the dark house startled him. Then he heard her voice: "There are clothes." He rose and went to the foot of the stairs, and gathered up the garments she had thrown down. Then he came back to the fire, to rub himself down and dress. He grinned at his own appearance when he had finished.

The fire was sinking, so he put on coal. The house was now quite dark, save for the light of a street-lamp that shone in faintly from beyond the holly trees. He lit the gas with matches he found on the mantelpiece. Then he emptied the pockets of his own clothes, and threw all his wet things in a heap into the scullery. After which he gathered up her sodden clothes, gently, and put them in a separate heap on the copper-top in the scullery.

It was six o'clock on the clock. His own watch had stopped. He ought to go back to the surgery. He waited, and still she did not come down. So he went to the foot of the stairs and called:

"I shall have to go."

Almost immediately he heard her coming down. She had on her best dress of black voile, and her hair was tidy, but still damp. She looked at him—and in spite of herself, smiled.

"I don't like you in those clothes," she said.

"Do I look a sight?" he answered.

They were shy of one another.

"I'll make you some tea," she said.

"No, I must go."

"Must you?" And she looked at him again with the wide, strained, doubtful eyes. And again, from the pain of his breast, he knew how he loved her. He went and bent to kiss her, gently, passionately, with his heart's painful kiss.

"And my hair smells so horrible," she murmured in distraction. "And I'm so awful, I'm so awful! Oh no, I'm too awful." And she broke into bitter, heart-broken sobbing. "You can't want to love me, I'm horrible."

"Don't be silly, don't be silly," he said, trying to comfort her, kissing her, holding her in his arms. "I want you, I want to marry you, we're going to be married, quickly, quickly—to-morrow if I can."

But she only sobbed terribly, and cried:

"I feel awful. I feel awful. I feel I'm horrible to you."

"No, I want you, I want you," was all he answered, blindly, with that terrible intonation which frightened her almost more than her horror lest he should *not* want her.

1922

The Rocking-Horse Winner

There was a woman who was beautiful, who started with all the advantages, yet she had no luck. She married for love, and the love turned to dust. She had bonny children, yet she felt they had been thrust upon her, and she could not love them. They looked at her coldly, as if they were finding fault with her. And hurriedly she felt she must cover up some fault in herself. Yet what it was that she must cover up she never knew. Nevertheless, when her children were present, she always felt the centre of her heart go hard. This troubled her, and in her manner she was all the more gentle and anxious for her children, as if she loved them very much. Only she herself knew that at the centre of her heart was a hard little place that could not feel love, no, not for anybody. Everybody else said of her: "She is such a good mother. She adores her children." Only she herself, and her children themselves, knew it was not so. They read it in each other's eyes.

There were a boy and two little girls. They lived in a pleasant house, with a garden, and they had discreet servants, and felt themselves superior to anyone in the neighbourhood.

Although they lived in style, they felt always an anxiety in the house. There was never enough money. The mother had a small income, and the father had a small income, but not nearly enough for the social position which they had to keep up. The father went in to town to some office. But though he had good prospects, these prospects never materialized. There was always the grinding sense of the shortage of money, though the style was always kept up.

At last the mother said: "I will see if *I* can't make something." But she did not know where to begin. She racked her brains, and tried this thing and the other, but could not find anything successful. The failure made deep lines come into her face. Her children were growing up, they would have to go to school. There must be more money, there must be more money. The father, who was always very handsome and expensive in his tastes, seemed as if he never *would* be able to do anything worth doing. And the mother, who had a great belief in herself, did not succeed any better, and her tastes were just as expensive.

And so the house came to be haunted by the unspoken phrase. *There must be more money! There must be more money!* The children could hear it all the time, though nobody said it aloud. They heard it at Christmas, when the expensive and splendid toys filled the nursery. Behind the shining modern rocking-horse, behind the smart doll's-house, a voice would start whispering: "There *must* be more money! There *must* be more money!" And the children would stop playing, to listen for a moment. They would look into each other's eyes, to see if they had all heard. And each one saw in the eyes of the other two that they too had heard. "There *must* be more money! There *must* be more money!"

It came whispering from the spring of the still-swaying rocking-horse, and even the horse, bending his wooden, champing head, heard it. The big doll, sitting so pink and smirking in her new pram,[1] could hear it quite plainly, and seemed to be smirking all the more self-consciously because of it. The foolish puppy, too, that took the place of the teddy-bear, he was looking so extraordinarily foolish for no other reason but that he heard the secret whisper all over the house: "There *must* be more money!"

Yet nobody ever said it aloud. The whisper was everywhere, and therefore no one spoke it. Just as no one ever says: "We are breathing!" in spite of the fact that breath is coming and going all the time.

"Mother," said the boy Paul one day, "why don't we keep a car of our own? Why do we always use uncle's, or else a taxi?"

"Because we're the poor members of the family," said the mother.

"But why *are* we, mother?"

"Well—I suppose," she said slowly and bitterly, "it's because your father has no luck."

The boy was silent for some time.

"Is luck money, mother?" he asked rather timidly.

"No, Paul. Not quite. It's what causes you to have money."

"Oh!" said Paul vaguely. "I thought when Uncle Oscar said *filthy lucker*, it meant money."

"*Filthy lucre* does mean money," said the mother. "But it's lucre, not luck."

"Oh!" said the boy. "Then what *is* luck, mother?"

"It's what causes you to have money. If you're lucky you have money. That's why it's better to be born lucky than rich. If you're rich, you may lose your money. But if you're lucky, you will always get more money."

"Oh! Will you? And is father not lucky?"

"Very unlucky, I should say," she said bitterly.

1. Baby carriage.

The boy watched her with unsure eyes.

"Why?" he asked.

"I don't know. Nobody ever knows why one person is lucky and another unlucky."

"Don't they? Nobody at all? Does *nobody* know?"

"Perhaps God. But He never tells."

"He ought to, then. And aren't you lucky either, mother?"

"I can't be, if I married an unlucky husband."

"But by yourself, aren't you?"

"I used to think I was, before I married. Now I think I am very unlucky indeed."

"Why?"

"Well—never mind! Perhaps I'm not really," she said.

The child looked at her, to see if she meant it. But he saw, by the lines of her mouth, that she was only trying to hide something from him.

"Well, anyhow," he said stoutly, "I'm a lucky person."

"Why?" said his mother, with a sudden laugh.

He stared at her. He didn't even know why he had said it.

"God told me," he asserted, brazening it out.

"I hope He did, dear!" she said, again with a laugh, but rather bitter.

"He did, mother!"

"Excellent!" said the mother, using one of her husband's exclamations.

The boy saw she did not believe him; or, rather, that she paid no attention to his assertion. This angered him somewhat, and made him want to compel her attention.

He went off by himself, vaguely, in a childish way, seeking for the clue to "luck." Absorbed, taking no heed of other people, he went about with a sort of stealth, seeking inwardly for luck. He wanted luck, he wanted it, he wanted it. When the two girls were playing dolls in the nursery, he would sit on his big rocking-horse, charging madly into space, with a frenzy that made the little girls peer at him uneasily. Wildly the horse careered, the waving dark hair of the boy tossed, his eyes had a strange glare in them. The little girls dared not speak to him.

When he had ridden to the end of his mad little journey, he climbed down and stood in front of his rocking-horse, staring fixedly into its lowered face. Its red mouth was slightly open, its big eye was wide and glassy-bright.

"Now!" he would silently command the snorting steed. "Now, take me to where there is luck! Now take me!"

And he would slash the horse on the neck with the little whip he had asked Uncle Oscar for. He *knew* the horse could take him to where there was luck, if only he forced it. So he would mount again and start on his furious ride, hoping at last to get there. He knew he could get there.

"You'll break your horse, Paul!" said the nurse.

"He's always riding like that! I wish he'd leave off!" said his elder sister Joan.

But he only glared down on them in silence. Nurse gave him up. She could make nothing of him. Anyhow, he was growing beyond her.

One day his mother and his Uncle Oscar came in when he was on one of his furious rides. He did not speak to them.

"Hallo, you young jockey! Riding a winner?" said his uncle.

"Aren't you growing too big for a rocking-horse? You're not a very little boy any longer, you know," said his mother.

But Paul only gave a blue glare from his big, rather close-set eyes. He would speak to nobody when he was in full tilt. His mother watched him with an anxious expression on her face.

At last he suddenly stopped forcing his horse into the mechanical gallop and slid down.

"Well, I got there!" he announced fiercely, his blue eyes still flaring, and his sturdy long legs straddling apart.

"Where did you get to?" asked his mother.

"Where I wanted to go," he flared back at her.

"That's right, son!" said Uncle Oscar. "Don't you stop till you get there. What's the horse's name?"

"He doesn't have a name," said the boy.

"Gets on without all right?" asked the uncle.

"Well, he has different names. He was called Sansovino last week."

"Sansovino, eh? Won the Ascot.[2] How did you know this name?"

"He always talks about horse-races with Bassett," said Joan.

The uncle was delighted to find that his small nephew was posted with all the racing news. Bassett, the young gardener, who had been wounded in the left foot in the war[3] and had got his present job through Oscar Cresswell, whose batman[4] he had been, was a perfect blade of the "turf."[5] He lived in the racing events, and the small boy lived with him.

Oscar Cresswell got it all from Bassett.

"Master Paul comes and asks me, so I can't do more than tell him, sir," said Bassett, his face terribly serious, as if he were speaking of religious matters.

"And does he ever put anything on a horse he fancies?"

"Well—I don't want to give him away—he's a young sport, a fine sport, sir. Would you mind asking him himself? He sort of takes a pleasure in it, and perhaps he'd feel I was giving him away, sir, if you don't mind."

Bassett was serious as a church.

The uncle went back to his nephew and took him off for a ride in the car.

"Say, Paul, old man, do you ever put anything on a horse?" the uncle asked.

The boy watched the handsome man closely.

"Why, do you think I oughtn't to?" he parried.

"Not a bit of it! I thought perhaps you might give me a tip for the Lincoln."

The car sped on into the country, going down to Uncle Oscar's place in Hampshire.

"Honour bright?" said the nephew.

"Honour bright, son!" said the uncle.

"Well, then, Daffodil."

"Daffodil! I doubt it, sonny. What about Mirza?"

"I only know the winner," said the boy. "That's Daffodil."

"Daffodil, eh?"

---

2. A race run at a course of that name in Berkshire. Other races mentioned in the story include the Lincolnshire Handicap, the St. Leger Stakes, the Grand National Steeplechase, and the Derby. **3.** World War I (1914–18). **4.** British officer's orderly. **5.** Dashing young horseplayer.

There was a pause. Daffodil was an obscure horse comparatively.

"Uncle!"

"Yes, son?"

"You won't let it go any further, will you? I promised Bassett."

"Bassett be damned, old man! What's he got to do with it?"

"We're partners. We've been partners from the first. Uncle, he lent me my first five shillings, which I lost. I promised him, honour bright, it was only between me and him; only you gave me that ten-shilling note I started winning with, so I thought you were lucky. You won't let it go any further, will you?"

The boy gazed at his uncle from those big, hot, blue eyes, set rather close together. The uncle stirred and laughed uneasily.

"Right you are, son! I'll keep your tip private. Daffodil, eh? How much are you putting on him?"

"All except twenty pounds," said the boy. "I keep that in reserve."

The uncle thought it a good joke.

"You keep twenty pounds in reserve, do you, you young romancer? What are you betting, then?"

"I'm betting three hundred," said the boy, gravely. "But it's between you and me, Uncle Oscar! Honour bright?"

The uncle burst into a roar of laughter.

"It's between you and me all right, you young Nat Gould,"[6] he said, laughing. "But where's your three hundred?"

"Bassett keeps it for me. We're partners."

"You are, are you! And what is Bassett putting on Daffodil?"

"He won't go quite as high as I do, I expect. Perhaps he'll go a hundred and fifty."

"What, pennies?" laughed the uncle.

"Pounds," said the child, with a surprised look at his uncle. "Bassett keeps a bigger reserve than I do."

Between wonder and amusement Uncle Oscar was silent. He pursued the matter no further, but he determined to take his nephew with him to the Lincoln races.

"Now, son," he said, "I'm putting twenty on Mirza, and I'll put five for you on any horse you fancy. What's your pick?"

"Daffodil, uncle."

"No, not the fiver on Daffodil!"

"I should if it was my own fiver," said the child.

"Good! Good! Right you are! A fiver for me and a fiver for you on Daffodil."

The child had never been to a race-meeting before, and his eyes were blue fire. He pursed his mouth tight, and watched. A Frenchman just in front had put his money on Lancelot. Wild with excitement, he flayed his arms up and down, yelling *Lancelot! Lancelot!* in his French accent.

Daffodil came in first, Lancelot second, Mirza third. The child, flushed and with eyes blazing, was curiously serene. His uncle brought him four five-pound notes, four to one.

"What am I to do with these?" he cried, waving them before the boy's eyes.

6. English writer and journalist (1857–1919), author of more than a hundred popular novels about horse racing.

"I suppose we'll talk to Bassett," said the boy. "I expect I have fifteen hundred now; and twenty in reserve; and this twenty."

His uncle studied him for some moments.

"Look here, son!" he said. "You're not serious about Bassett and that fifteen hundred, are you?"

"Yes, I am. But it's between you and me, uncle. Honour bright!"

"Honour bright all right, son! But I must talk to Bassett."

"If you'd like to be a partner, uncle, with Bassett and me, we could all be partners. Only, you'd have to promise, honour bright, uncle, not to let it go beyond us three. Bassett and I are lucky, and you must be lucky, because it was your ten shillings I started winning with. . . ."

Uncle Oscar took both Bassett and Paul into Richmond Park for an afternoon, and there they talked.

"It's like this, you see, sir," Bassett said. "Master Paul would get me talking about racing events, spinning yarns, you know, sir. And he was always keen on knowing if I'd made or if I'd lost. It's about a year since, now, that I put five shillings on Blush of Dawn for him—and we lost. Then the luck turned, with the ten shillings he had from you, that we put on Singhalese. And since that time, it's been pretty steady, all things considering. What do you say, Master Paul?"

"We're all right when we're sure," said Paul. "It's when we're not quite sure that we go down."

"Oh, but we're careful then," said Bassett.

"But when are you *sure*?" smiled Uncle Oscar.

"It's Master Paul, sir," said Bassett, in a secret, religious voice. "It's as if he had it from heaven. Like Daffodil, now, for the Lincoln. That was as sure as eggs."

"Did you put anything on Daffodil?" asked Oscar Cresswell.

"Yes, sir. I made my bit."

"And my nephew?"

Bassett was obstinately silent, looking at Paul.

"I made twelve hundred, didn't I, Bassett? I told uncle I was putting three hundred on Daffodil."

"That's right," said Bassett, nodding.

"But where's the money?" asked the uncle.

"I keep it safe locked up, sir. Master Paul he can have it any minute he likes to ask for it."

"What, fifteen hundred pounds?"

"And twenty! And *forty*, that is, with the twenty he made on the course."

"It's amazing!" said the uncle.

"If Master Paul offers you to be partners, sir, I would, if I were you; if you'll excuse me," said Bassett.

Oscar Cresswell thought about it.

"I'll see the money," he said.

They drove home again, and sure enough, Bassett came round to the garden-house with fifteen hundred pounds in notes. The twenty pounds reserve was left with Joe Glee, in the Turf Commission deposit.

"You see, it's all right, uncle, when I'm *sure*! Then we go strong, for all we're worth. Don't we, Bassett?"

"We do that, Master Paul."

"And when are you sure?" said the uncle, laughing.

"Oh, well, sometimes I'm *absolutely* sure, like about Daffodil," said the boy; "and sometimes I have an idea; and sometimes I haven't even an idea, have I, Bassett? Then we're careful, because we mostly go down."

"You do, do you! And when you're sure, like about Daffodil, what makes you sure, sonny?"

"Oh, well, I don't know," said the boy uneasily. "I'm sure, you know, uncle; that's all."

"It's as if he had it from heaven, sir," Bassett reiterated.

"I should say so!" said the uncle.

But he became a partner. And when the Leger was coming on, Paul was "sure" about Lively Spark, which was a quite inconsiderable horse. The boy insisted on putting a thousand on the horse, Bassett went for five hundred, and Oscar Cresswell two hundred. Lively Spark came in first, and the betting had been ten to one against him. Paul had made ten thousand.

"You see," he said, "I was absolutely sure of him."

Even Oscar Cresswell had cleared two thousand.

"Look here, son," he said, "this sort of thing makes me nervous."

"It needn't, uncle! Perhaps I shan't be sure again for a long time."

"But what are you going to do with your money?" asked the uncle.

"Of course," said the boy, "I started it for mother. She said she had no luck, because father is unlucky, so I thought if *I* was lucky, it might stop whispering."

"What might stop whispering?"

"Our house. I *hate* our house for whispering."

"What does it whisper?"

"Why—why"—the boy fidgeted—"why, I don't know. But it's always short of money, you know, uncle."

"I know it, son, I know it."

"You know people send mother writs,[7] don't you, uncle?"

"I'm afraid I do," said the uncle.

"And then the house whispers, like people laughing at you behind your back. It's awful, that is! I thought if I was lucky . . ."

"You might stop it," added the uncle.

The boy watched him with big blue eyes, that had an uncanny cold fire in them, and he said never a word.

"Well, then!" said the uncle. "What are we doing?"

"I shouldn't like mother to know I was lucky," said the boy.

"Why not, son?"

"She'd stop me."

"I don't think she would."

"Oh!"—and the boy writhed in an odd way—"I *don't* want her to know, uncle."

"All right, son! We'll manage it without her knowing."

They managed it very easily. Paul, at the other's suggestion, handed over five thousand pounds to his uncle, who deposited it with the family lawyer,

7. Legal threats.

who was then to inform Paul's mother that a relative had put five thousand pounds into his hands, which sum was to be paid out a thousand pounds at a time, on the mother's birthday, for the next five years.

"So she'll have a birthday present of a thousand pounds for five successive years," said Uncle Oscar. "I hope it won't make it all the harder for her later."

Paul's mother had her birthday in November. The house had been "whispering" worse than ever lately, and, even in spite of his luck, Paul could not bear up against it. He was very anxious to see the effect of the birthday letter, telling his mother about the thousand pounds.

When there were no visitors, Paul now took his meals with his parents, as he was beyond the nursery control. His mother went into town nearly every day. She had discovered that she had an odd knack of sketching furs and dress materials, so she worked secretly in the studio of a friend who was the chief "artist" for the leading drapers. She drew the figures of ladies in furs and ladies in silk and sequins for the newspaper advertisements. This young woman artist earned several thousand pounds a year, but Paul's mother only made several hundreds, and she was again dissatisfied. She so wanted to be first in something, and she did not succeed, even in making sketches for drapery advertisements.

She was down to breakfast on the morning of her birthday. Paul watched her face as she read her letters. He knew the lawyer's letter. As his mother read it, her face hardened and became more expressionless. Than a cold, determined look came on her mouth. She hid the letter under the pile of others, and said not a word about it.

"Didn't you have anything nice in the post for your birthday, mother?" said Paul.

"Quite moderately nice," she said, her voice cold and absent.

She went away to town without saying more.

But in the afternoon Uncle Oscar appeared. He said Paul's mother had had a long interview with the lawyer, asking if the whole five thousand could not be advanced at once, as she was in debt.

"What do you think, uncle?" said the boy.

"I leave it to you, son."

"Oh, let her have it, then! We can get some more with the other," said the boy.

"A bird in the hand is worth two in the bush, laddie!" said Uncle Oscar.

"But I'm sure to *know* for the Grand National; or the Lincolnshire; or else the Derby. I'm sure to know for *one* of them," said Paul.

So Uncle Oscar signed the agreement, and Paul's mother touched the whole five thousand. Then something very curious happened. The voices in the house suddenly went mad, like a chorus of frogs on a spring evening. There were certain new furnishings, and Paul had a tutor. He was *really* going to Eton,[8] his father's school, in the following autumn. There were flowers in the winter, and a blossoming of the luxury Paul's mother had been used to. And yet the voices in the house, behind the sprays of mimosa and almond blossom, and

8. "Public" (i.e., private) school where the sons of upper-class families prepare for university—usually Oxford or Cambridge.

from under the piles of iridescent cushions, simply trilled and screamed in a sort of ecstasy: "There *must* be more money! Oh-h-h; there *must* be more money Oh, now, now-w! Now-w-w—there *must* be more money!—more than ever! More than ever!"

It frightened Paul terribly. He studied away at his Latin and Greek with his tutors. But his intense hours were spent with Bassett. The Grand National had gone by: he had not "known," and had lost a hundred pounds. Summer was at hand. He was in agony for the Lincoln. But even for the Lincoln he didn't "know," and he lost fifty pounds. He became wild-eyed and strange, as if something were going to explode in him.

"Let it alone, son! Don't you bother about it!" urged Uncle Oscar. But it was as if the boy couldn't really hear what his uncle was saying.

"I've got to know for the Derby! I've got to know for the Derby!" the child reiterated, his big blue eyes blazing with a sort of madness.

His mother noticed how overwrought he was.

"You'd better go to the seaside. Wouldn't you like to go now to the seaside, instead of waiting? I think you'd better," she said, looking down at him anxiously, her heart curiously heavy because of him.

But the child lifted his uncanny blue eyes.

"I couldn't possibly go before the Derby, mother!" he said. "I couldn't possibly!"

"Why not?" she said, her voice becoming heavy when she was opposed. "Why not? You can still go from the seaside to see the Derby with your Uncle Oscar, if that's what you wish. No need for you to wait here. Besides, I think you care too much about these races. It's a bad sign. My family has been a gambling family, and you won't know till you grow up how much damage it has done. But it has done damage. I shall have to send Bassett away, and ask Uncle Oscar not to talk racing to you, unless you promise to be reasonable about it; go away to the seaside and forget it. You're all nerves!"

"I'll do what you like, mother, so long as you don't send me away till after the Derby," the boy said.

"Send you away from where? Just from this house?"

"Yes," he said, gazing at her.

"Why, you curious child, what makes you care about this house so much, suddenly? I never knew you loved it."

He gazed at her without speaking. He had a secret within a secret, something he had not divulged, even to Bassett or to his Uncle Oscar.

But his mother, after standing undecided and a little bit sullen for some moments, said:

"Very well, then! Don't go to the seaside till after the Derby, if you don't wish it. But promise me you won't let your nerves go to pieces. Promise you won't think so much about horse-racing and events, as you call them!"

"Oh, no," said the boy casually. "I won't think much about them, mother. You needn't worry. I wouldn't worry, mother, if I were you."

"If you were me and I were you," said his mother, "I wonder what we *should* do!"

"But you know you needn't worry, mother, don't you?" the boy repeated.

"I should be awfully glad to know it," she said wearily.

"Oh, well, you *can*, you know. I mean, you *ought* to know you needn't worry," he insisted.

"Ought I? Then I'll see about it," she said.

Paul's secret of secrets was his wooden horse, that which had no name. Since he was emancipated from a nurse and a nursery-governess, he had had his rocking-horse removed to his own bedroom at the top of the house.

"Surely, you're too big for a rocking-horse!" his mother had remonstrated.

"Well, you see, mother, till I can have a *real* horse, I like to have *some* sort of animal about," had been his quaint answer.

"Do you feel he keeps you company?" she laughed.

"Oh, yes! He's very good, he always keeps me company, when I'm there," said Paul.

So the horse, rather shabby, stood in an arrested prance in the boy's bedroom.

The Derby was drawing near, and the boy grew more and more tense. He hardly heard what was spoken to him, he was very frail, and his eyes were really uncanny. His mother had sudden strange seizures of uneasiness about him. Sometimes, for half-an-hour, she would feel a sudden anxiety about him that was almost anguish. She wanted to rush to him at once, and know he was safe.

Two nights before the Derby, she was at a big party in town, when one of her rushes of anxiety about her boy, her first-born, gripped her heart till she could hardly speak. She fought with the feeling, might and main, for she believed in common-sense. But it was too strong. She had to leave the dance and go downstairs to telephone to the country. The children's nursery-governess was terribly surprised and startled at being rung up in the night.

"Are the children all right, Miss Wilmot?"

"Oh, yes, they are quite all right."

"Master Paul? Is he all right?"

"He went to bed as right as a trivet. Shall I run up and look at him?"

"No," said Paul's mother reluctantly. "No! Don't trouble. It's all right. Don't sit up. We shall be home fairly soon." She did not want her son's privacy intruded upon.

"Very good," said the governess.

It was about one o'clock when Paul's mother and father drove up to their house. All was still. Paul's mother went to her room and slipped off her white fur cloak. She had told her maid not to wait up for her. She heard her husband downstairs, mixing a whisky-and-soda.

And then, because of the strange anxiety at her heart, she stole upstairs to her son's room. Noiselessly she went along the upper corridor. Was there a faint noise? What was it?

She stood, with arrested muscles, outside his door, listening. There was a strange, heavy, and yet not loud noise. Her heart stood still. It was a soundless noise, yet rushing and powerful. Something huge, in violent, hushed motion. What was it? What in God's name was it? She ought to know. She felt that she knew the noise. She knew what it was.

Yet she could not place it. She couldn't say what it was. And on and on it went, like a madness.

Softly, frozen with anxiety and fear, she turned the door-handle.

The room was dark. Yet in the space near the window, she heard and saw something plunging to and fro. She gazed in fear and amazement.

Then suddenly she switched on the light, and saw her son, in his green pyjamas, madly surging on the rocking-horse. The blaze of light suddenly lit him up, as he urged the wooden horse, and lit her up, as she stood, blonde, in her dress of pale green and crystal, in the doorway.

"Paul!" she cried. "Whatever are you doing?"

"It's Malabar!" he screamed, in a powerful, strange voice. "It's Malabar!"

His eyes blazed at her for one strange and senseless second, as he ceased urging his wooden horse. Then he fell with a crash to the ground, and she, all her tormented motherhood flooding upon her, rushed to gather him up.

But he was unconscious, and unconscious he remained, with some brain-fever. He talked and tossed, and his mother sat stonily by his side.

"Malabar! It's Malabar! Bassett, Bassett, I *know*! It's Malabar!"

So the child cried, trying to get up and urge the rocking-horse that gave him his inspiration.

"What does he mean by Malabar?" asked the heart-frozen mother.

"I don't know," said the father stonily.

"What does he mean by Malabar?" she asked her brother Oscar.

"It's one of the horses running for the Derby," was the answer.

And, in spite of himself, Oscar Cresswell spoke to Bassett, and himself put a thousand on Malabar: at fourteen to one.

The third day of the illness was critical: they were waiting for a change. The boy, with his rather long, curly hair, was tossing ceaselessly on the pillow. He neither slept nor regained consciousness, and his eyes were like blue stones. His mother sat, feeling her heart had gone, turned actually into a stone.

In the evening, Oscar Cresswell did not come, but Bassett sent a message, saying could he come up for one moment, just one moment? Paul's mother was very angry at the intrusion, but on second thought she agreed. The boy was the same. Perhaps Bassett might bring him to consciousness.

The gardener, a shortish fellow with a little brown moustache, and sharp little brown eyes, tip-toed into the room, touched his imaginary cap to Paul's mother, and stole to the bedside, staring with glittering, smallish eyes, at the tossing, dying child.

"Master Paul!" he whispered. "Master Paul! Malabar came in first all right, a clean win. I did as you told me. You've made over seventy thousand pounds, you have; you've got over eighty thousand. Malabar came in all right, Master Paul."

"Malabar! Malabar! Did I say Malabar, mother? Did I say Malabar? Do you think I'm lucky, mother? I knew Malabar, didn't I? Over eighty thousand pounds! I call that lucky, don't you, mother? Over eighty thousand pounds! I knew, didn't I know I knew! Malabar came in all right. If I ride my horse till I'm sure, then I tell you, Bassett, you can go as high as you like. Did you go for all you were worth, Bassett?"

"I went a thousand on it, Master Paul."

"I never told you, mother, that if I can ride my horse, and *get there*, then I'm absolutely sure—oh absolutely! Mother, did I ever tell you? I *am* lucky!"

"No, you never did," said the mother.

But the boy died in the night.

And even as he lay dead, his mother heard her brother's voice saying to her: "My God, Hester, you're eighty-odd thousand to the good, and a poor devil of a son to the bad. But, poor devil, poor devil, he's best gone out of a life where he rides his rocking-horse to find a winner."

1926

URSULA K. LE GUIN
b. 1929

Le Guin was born in Berkeley, California, to a writer/folklorist mother and an anthropologist father. She was educated at Radcliffe College and Columbia University and spent a year as a Fulbright student in Paris, where she married the historian Charles Le Guin. A fantastically prolific author, she has won an extraordinary number of science fiction prizes, and her thematically charged use of the medium and her detailed depictions of complex fictional societies caught the mood of readers of the 1970s and 1980s. Some of her novels are *A Wizard of Earthsea* (1968), *The Tombs of Atuan* (1971), *The Farthest Shore* (1972) (which comprise the Earthsea Trilogy), *The Left Hand of Darkness* (1969), *The Dispossessed* (1974), *Always Coming Home* (1985), *The Telling* (2000), *Gifts* (2004), *Powers* (2007), and *Lavinia* (2008). Some of her shorter works have been collected in *The Wind's Twelve Quarters* (1975), *Orsinian Tales* (1976), *The Birthday of the World* (2002), *Changing Planes* (2003), and *The Wild Girls* (2011).

The Ones Who Walk Away from Omelas

(Variations on a Theme by William James)[1]

With a clamor of bells that set the swallows soaring, the Festival of Summer came to the city Omelas, bright-towered by the sea. The rigging of the boats in harbor sparkled with flags. In the streets between houses with red roofs and painted walls, between old moss-grown gardens and under avenues of trees, past great parks and public buildings, processions moved. Some were decorous: old people in long stiff robes of mauve and grey, grave master workmen, quiet, merry women carrying their babies and chatting as they walked. In other streets the music beat faster, a shimmering of gong and tambourine, and the people went dancing, the procession was a dance. Children dodged in and out, their high calls rising like the swallows' crossing flights over the music and the singing. All the processions wound towards the north side of the city, where on the great water-meadow called the Green Fields boys and girls, naked in the bright air, with mud-stained feet and ankles and long, lithe arms, exercised their restive horses before the race. The horses wore no gear at all but a halter without bit. Their manes were braided with streamers of silver, gold, and green. They flared their nostrils and pranced and boasted

---

1. American philosopher and experimental psychologist (1842–1910).

to one another; they were vastly excited, the horse being the only animal who has adopted our ceremonies as his own. Far off to the north and west the mountains stood up half encircling Omelas on her bay. The air of morning was so clear that the snow still crowning the Eighteen Peaks burned with white-gold fire across the miles of sunlit air, under the dark blue of the sky. There was just enough wind to make the banners that marked the racecourse snap and flutter now and then. In the silence of the broad green meadows one could hear the music winding through the city streets, farther and nearer and ever approaching, a cheerful faint sweetness of the air that from time to time trembled and gathered together and broke out into the great joyous clanging of the bells.

Joyous! How is one to tell about joy? How describe the citizens of Omelas?

They were not simple folk, you see, though they were happy. But we do not say the words of cheer much any more. All smiles have become archaic. Given a description such as this one tends to make certain assumptions. Given a description such as this one tends to look next for the King, mounted on a splendid stallion and surrounded by his noble knights, or perhaps in a golden litter borne by great-muscled slaves. But there was no king. They did not use swords, or keep slaves. They were not barbarians. I do not know the rules and laws of their society, but I suspect that they were singularly few. As they did without monarchy and slavery, so they also got on without the stock exchange, the advertisement, the secret police, and the bomb. Yet I repeat that these were not simple folk, not dulcet shepherds, noble savages, bland utopians. They were not less complex than us. The trouble is that we have a bad habit, encouraged by pedants and sophisticates, of considering happiness as something rather stupid. Only pain is intellectual, only evil interesting. This is the treason of the artist: a refusal to admit the banality of evil and the terrible boredom of pain. If you can't lick 'em, join 'em. If it hurts, repeat it. But to praise despair is to condemn delight, to embrace violence is to lose hold of everything else. We have almost lost hold, we can no longer describe a happy man, nor make any celebration of joy. How can I tell you about the people of Omelas? They were not naïve and happy children—though their children were, in fact, happy. They were mature, intelligent, passionate adults whose lives were not wretched. O miracle! but I wish I could describe it better. I wish I could convince you. Omelas sounds in my words like a city in a fairy tale, long ago and far away, once upon a time. Perhaps it would be best if you imagined it as your own fancy bids, assuming it will rise to the occasion, for certainly I cannot suit you all. For instance, how about technology? I think that there would be no cars or helicopters in and above the streets; this follows from the fact that the people of Omelas are happy people. Happiness is based on a just discrimination of what is necessary, what is neither necessary nor destructive, and what is destructive. In the middle category, however— that of the unnecessary but undestructive, that of comfort, luxury, exuberance, etc.—they could perfectly well have central heating, subway trains, washing machines, and all kinds of marvelous devices not yet invented here, floating light-sources, fuelless power, a cure for the common cold. Or they could have none of that: it doesn't matter. As you like it. I incline to think that people from towns up and down the coast have been coming in to Omelas during the last days before the Festival on very fast little trains and double-decked trams, and that the train station of Omelas is actually the handsomest building in town, though plainer than the magnificent Farmers' Market. But even granted trains, I fear that Omelas so far strikes some of you as goody-goody. Smiles, bells, parades, horses, bleh. If so, please add an orgy. If an orgy would help, don't hesitate. Let us not, however, have temples from which issue beautiful nude priests and priestesses already half in ecstasy and ready to copulate with any man or woman, lover or stranger, who desires union with the deep godhead of the blood, although that was my first idea. But really it would be better not to have any temples in Omelas—at least, not manned temples. Religion yes, clergy no. Surely the beautiful nudes can just wander about, offering themselves like divine soufflés to the hunger of the needy and the rapture of the flesh. Let them join the processions. Let tambourines be struck above the copulations, and the glory of desire be proclaimed upon the gongs, and (a not unimportant point) let the offspring of these delightful rituals be beloved and looked after by all. One thing I know there is none of in Omelas is guilt. But what else should there be? I thought at first there were no drugs, but that is puritanical. For those who like it, the faint insistent sweetness of *drooz* may perfume the ways of the city, *drooz* which first brings a great lightness and brilliance to the mind and limbs, and then after some hours a dreamy languor, and wonderful visions at last of the very arcana and inmost secrets of the Universe, as well as exciting the pleasure of sex beyond all belief; and it is not habit-forming. For more modest tastes I think there ought to be beer. What else, what else belongs in the joyous city? The sense of victory, surely, the celebration of courage. But as we did without clergy, let us do without soldiers. The joy built upon successful slaughter is not the right kind of joy; it will not do; it is fearful and it is trivial. A boundless and generous contentment, a magnanimous triumph felt not against some outer enemy but in communion with the finest and fairest in the souls of all men everywhere and the splendor of the world's summer: this is what swells the hearts of the people of Omelas, and the victory they celebrate is that of life. I really don't think many of them need to take *drooz*.

Most of the processions have reached the Green Fields by now. A marvelous smell of cooking goes forth from the red and blue tents of the provisioners. The faces of small children are amiably sticky; in the benign grey beard of a man a couple of crumbs of rich pastry are entangled. The youths and girls have mounted their horses and are beginning to group around the starting line of the course. An old woman, small, fat, and laughing, is passing out flowers from a basket, and tall young men wear her flowers in their shining hair. A child of nine or ten sits at the edge of the crowd, alone, playing on a wooden flute. People pause to listen, and they smile, but they do not speak to him, for he never ceases playing and never sees them, his dark eyes wholly rapt in the sweet, thin magic of the tune.

He finishes, and slowly lowers his hands holding the wooden flute.

As if that little private silence were the signal, all at once a trumpet sounds from the pavilion near the starting line: imperious, melancholy, piercing. The horses rear on their slender legs, and some of them neigh in answer. Sober-faced, the young riders stroke the horses' necks and soothe them, whispering, "Quiet, quiet, there my beauty, my hope. . . ." They begin to form in rank along the starting line. The crowds along the racecourse are like a field of grass and flowers in the wind. The Festival of Summer has begun.

Do you believe? Do you accept the festival, the city, the joy? No? Then let me describe one more thing.

In a basement under one of the beautiful public buildings of Omelas, or perhaps in the cellar of one of its more spacious private homes, there is a room. It has one locked door, and no window. A little light seeps in dustily between cracks in the boards, secondhand from a cobwebbed window somewhere across the cellar. In one corner of the little room a couple of mops, with stiff, clotted, foul-smelling heads, stand near a rusty bucket. The floor is dirt, a little damp to the touch, as cellar dirt usually is. The room is about three paces long and two wide: a mere broom closet or disused tool room. In the room a child is sitting. It could be a boy or a girl. It looks about six, but actually is nearly ten. It is feeble-minded. Perhaps it was born defective, or perhaps it has become imbecile through fear, malnutrition, and neglect. It picks its nose and occasionally fumbles vaguely with its toes or genitals, as it sits hunched in the corner farthest from the bucket and the two mops. It is afraid of the mops. It finds them horrible. It shuts its eyes, but it knows the mops are still standing there; and the door is locked; and nobody will come. The door is always locked; and nobody ever comes, except that sometimes—the child has no understanding of time or interval—sometimes the door rattles terribly and opens, and a person, or several people, are there. One of them may come in and kick the child to make it stand up. The others never come close, but peer in at it with frightened, disgusted eyes. The food bowl and the water jug are hastily filled, the door is locked, the eyes disappear. The people at the door never say anything, but the child, who has not always lived in the tool room, and can remember sunlight and its mother's voice, sometimes speaks. "I will be good," it says. "Please let me out. I will be good!" They never answer. The child used to scream for help at night, and cry a good deal, but now it only makes a kind of whining, "eh-haa, eh-haa," and it speaks less and less often. It is so thin there are no calves to its legs; its belly protrudes; it lives on a half-bowl of corn meal and grease a day. It is naked. Its buttocks and thighs are a mass of festered sores, as it sits in its own excrement continually.

They all know it is there, all the people of Omelas. Some of them have come to see it, others are content merely to know it is there. They all know that it has to be there. Some of them understand why, and some do not, but they all understand that their happiness, the beauty of their city, the tenderness of their friendships, the health of their children, the wisdom of their scholars, the skill of their makers, even the abundance of their harvest and the kindly weathers of their skies, depend wholly on this child's abominable misery.

This is usually explained to children when they are between eight and twelve, whenever they seem capable of understanding; and most of those who come to see the child are young people, though often enough an adult comes, or comes back, to see the child. No matter how well the matter has been explained to them, these young spectators are always shocked and sickened at the sight. They feel disgust, which they had thought themselves superior to. They feel anger, outrage, impotence, despite all the explanations. They would like to do something for the child. But there is nothing they can do. If the child were brought up into the sunlight out of the vile place, if it were cleaned and fed and comforted, that would be a good thing, indeed; but if it were done, in that day and hour all the prosperity and beauty and delight of Omelas would wither and be destroyed. Those are the terms. To exchange all the goodness and grace of every life in Omelas for that single, small improvement: to throw away the happiness of thousands for the chance of the happiness of one: that would be to let guilt within the walls indeed.

The terms are strict and absolute; there may not even be a kind word spoken to the child.

Often the young people go home in tears, or in a tearless rage, when they have seen the child and faced this terrible paradox. They may brood over it for weeks or years. But as time goes on they begin to realize that even if the child could be released, it would not get much good of its freedom: a little vague pleasure of warmth and food, no doubt, but little more. It is too degraded and imbecile to know any real joy. It has been afraid too long ever to be free of fear. Its habits are too uncouth for it to respond to humane treatment. Indeed, after so long it would probably be wretched without walls about it to protect it, and darkness for its eyes, and its own excrement to sit in. Their tears at the bitter injustice dry when they begin to perceive the terrible justice of reality, and to accept it. Yet it is their tears and anger, the trying of their generosity and the acceptance of their helplessness, which are perhaps the true source of the splendor of their lives. Theirs is no vapid, irresponsible happiness. They know that they, like the child, are not free. They know compassion. It is the existence of the child, and their knowledge of its existence, that makes possible the nobility of their architecture, the poignancy of their music, the profundity of their science. It is because of the child that they are so gentle with children. They know that if the wretched one were not there snivelling in the dark, the other one, the flute-player, could make no joyful music as the young riders line up in their beauty for the race in the sunlight of the first morning of summer.

Now do you believe in them? Are they not more credible? But there is one more thing to tell, and this is quite incredible.

At times one of the adolescent girls or boys who go to see the child does not go home to weep or rage, does not, in fact, go home at all. Sometimes also a man or woman much older falls silent for a day or two, and then leaves home. These people go out into the street, and walk down the street alone. They keep walking, and walk straight out of the city of Omelas, through the beautiful gates. They keep walking across the farmlands of Omelas. Each one goes alone, youth or girl, man or woman. Night falls; the traveler must pass down village streets, between the houses with yellow-lit windows, and on out into the darkness of the fields. Each alone, they go west or north, towards the mountains. They go on. They leave Omelas, they walk ahead into the darkness, and they do not come back. The place they go towards is a place even less imaginable to most of us than the city of happiness. I cannot describe it at all. It is possible that it does not exist. But they seem to know where they are going, the ones who walk away from Omelas.

1975

DORIS LESSING
1919–2013

Lessing was born to English parents in Kermanshah, Persia (now Iran), the daughter of a bank manager, and was taken by her family to Rhodesia (now Zimbabwe) in 1924. Fleeing the loneliness of an unhappy childhood, she went to the capital Salisbury (Harare), at eighteen and there involved herself in politics and the intellectual life. She was twice married and twice divorced before leaving Africa and settling in London, where, disillusioned, she dropped her Communist Party affiliations. She published a well-made, conventional novel, *The Grass Is Singing*, in 1950, and soon thereafter began to experiment more freely with work that combined autobiography and fiction in an unorthodox attempt to come at the dilemmas of the modern woman struggling for emancipation. Following this vein she published five novels between 1952 and 1969 under the general title *Children of Violence. The Golden Notebook* (1962) has the form of several overlapping notebooks prepared by a writer simultaneously preparing and postponing the composition of a novel. In her despair of rational solutions to the political and sexual disorders of our times, Lessing entertained the possibilities for reorientation that lie in extrasensory perception and in the visions of the insane. Among her novels are *Briefing for a Descent into Hell* (1971), *The Summer before the Dark* (1973), the tetralogy *Canopus in Argos: Archives* (1979–1983), two novels collected under the title *The Diaries of Jane Somers* (1984), *The Good Terrorist* (1985), *The Fifth Child* (1988), *Love, Again* (1996), *Ben, in the World: The Sequel to The Fifth Child* (2000), and *The Grandmothers* (2003). *Under My Skin* (1994) and *Walking in the Shade* (1997) are volumes one and two of her autobiography. Many of her stories are collected in *African Stories* (1964) and *Stories* (1978). Lessing won the Nobel Prize for Literature in 2007, and she published her final novel, *Alfred and Emily*, the following year.

To Room Nineteen

This is a story, I suppose, about a failure in intelligence: the Rawlings' marriage was grounded in intelligence.

They were older when they married than most of their married friends: in their well-seasoned late twenties. Both had had a number of affairs, sweet rather than bitter; and when they fell in love—for they did fall in love—had known each other for some time. They joked that they had saved each other "for the real thing." That they had waited so long (but not too long) for this real thing was to them a proof of their sensible discrimination. A good many of their friends had married young, and now (they felt) probably regretted lost opportunities; while others, still unmarried, seemed to them arid, self-doubting, and likely to make desperate or romantic marriages.

Not only they, but others, felt they were well-matched: their friends' delight was an additional proof of their happiness. They had played the same roles, male and female, in this group or set, if such a wide, loosely connected, constantly changing constellation of people could be called a set. They had both become, by virtue of their moderation, their humour, and their abstinence from painful experience, people to whom others came for advice. They could be, and were, relied on. It was one of those cases of a man and a woman linking themselves whom no one else had ever thought of linking, probably because of their similarities. But then everyone exclaimed: Of course! How right! How was it we never thought of it before!

And so they married amid general rejoicing, and because of their foresight and their sense for what was probable, nothing was a surprise to them.

Both had well-paid jobs. Matthew was a subeditor on a large London newspaper, and Susan worked in an advertising firm. He was not the stuff of which editors or publicised journalists are made, but he was much more than "a subeditor," being one of the essential background people who in fact steady, inspire and make possible the people in the limelight. He was content with this position. Susan had a talent for commercial drawing. She was humorous about the advertisements she was responsible for, but she did not feel strongly about them one way or the other.

Both, before they married, had had pleasant flats, but they felt it unwise to base a marriage on either flat, because it might seem like a submission of personality on the part of the one whose flat it was not. They moved into a new flat in South Kensington[1] on the clear understanding that when their marriage had settled down (a process they knew would not take long, and was in fact more a humorous concession to popular wisdom than what was due to themselves) they would buy a house and start a family.

And this is what happened. They lived in their charming flat for two years, giving parties and going to them, being a popular young married couple, and then Susan became pregnant, she gave up her job, and they bought a house in Richmond.[2] It was typical of this couple that they had a son first, then a daughter, then twins, son and daughter. Everything right, appropriate, and what everyone would wish for, if they could choose. But people did feel these two had chosen; this balanced and sensible family was no more than what was due to them because of their infallible sense for *choosing right*.

And so they lived with their four children in their gardened house in Richmond and were happy. They had everything they had wanted and had planned for.

And yet . . .

Well, even this was expected, that there must be a certain flatness. . . .

Yes, yes, of course, it was natural they sometimes felt like this. Like what?

Their life seemed to be like a snake biting its tail. Matthew's job for the sake of Susan, children, house, and garden—which caravanserai needed a

---

1. Part of the fashionable West End of London.   **2.** One of the outer boroughs of greater London.

well-paid job to maintain it. And Susan's practical intelligence for the sake of Matthew, the children, the house and the garden—which unit would have collapsed in a week without her.

But there was no point about which either could say: "For the sake of *this* is all the rest." Children? But children can't be a centre of life and a reason for being. They can be a thousand things that are delightful, interesting, satisfying, but they can't be a wellspring to live from. Or they shouldn't be. Susan and Matthew knew that well enough.

Matthew's job? Ridiculous. It was an interesting job, but scarcely a reason for living. Matthew took pride in doing it well, but he could hardly be expected to be proud of the newspaper; the newspaper he read, *his* newspaper, was not the one he worked for.

Their love for each other? Well, that was nearest it. If this wasn't a centre, what was? Yes, it was around this point, their love, that the whole extraordinary structure revolved. For extraordinary it certainly was. Both Susan and Matthew had moments of thinking so, of looking in secret disbelief at this thing they had created: marriage, four children, big house, garden, charwoman, friends, cars . . . and this *thing*, this entity, all of it had come into existence, been blown into being out of nowhere, because Susan loved Matthew and Matthew loved Susan. Extraordinary. So that was the central point, the wellspring.

And if one felt that it simply was not strong enough, important enough, to support it all, well whose fault was that? Certainly neither Susan's nor Matthew's. It was in the nature of things. And they sensibly blamed neither themselves nor each other.

On the contrary, they used their intelligence to preserve what they had created from a painful and explosive world: they looked around them, and took lessons. All around them, marriages collapsing, or breaking, or rubbing along (even worse, they felt). They must not make the same mistakes, they must not.

They had avoided the pitfall so many of their friends had fallen into—of buying a house in the country *for the sake of the children,* so that the husband became a weekend husband, a weekend father, and the wife always careful not to ask what went on in the town flat which they called (in joke) a bachelor flat. No, Matthew was a full-time husband, a full-time father, and at night, in the big married bed in the big married bedroom (which had an attractive view of the river), they lay beside each other talking and he told her about his day, and what he had done, and whom he had met; and she told him about her day (not as interesting, but that was not her fault), for both knew of the hidden resentments and deprivations of the woman who has lived her own life—and above all, has earned her own living—and is now dependent on a husband for outside interests and money.

Nor did Susan make the mistake of taking a job for the sake of her independence, which she might very well have done, since her old firm, missing her qualities of humour, balance, and sense, invited her often to go back. Children needed their mother to a certain age, that both parents knew and agreed on; and when these four healthy wisely brought up children were of the right age, Susan would work again, because she knew, and so did he, what happened to women of fifty at the height of their energy and ability, with grownup children who no longer needed their full devotion.

So here was this couple, testing their marriage, looking after it, treating it like a small boat full of helpless people in a very stormy sea. Well, of course, so it was. . . . The storms of the world were bad, but not too close—which is not to say they were selfishly felt: Susan and Matthew were both well-informed and responsible people. And the inner storms and quicksands were understood and charted. So everything was all right. Everything was in order. Yes, things were under control.

So what did it matter if they felt dry, flat? People like themselves, fed on a hundred books (psychological, anthropological, sociological), could scarcely be unprepared for the dry, controlled wistfulness which is the distinguishing mark of the intelligent marriage. Two people, endowed with education, with discrimination, with judgement, linked together voluntarily from their will to be happy together and to be of use to others—one sees them everywhere, one knows them, one even is that thing oneself: sadness because so much is after all so little. These two, unsurprised, turned towards each other with even more courtesy and gentle love: this was life, that two people, no matter how carefully chosen, could not be everything to each other. In fact, even to say so, to think in such a way, was banal; they were ashamed to do it.

It was banal, too, when one night Matthew came home late and confessed he had been to a party, taken a girl home and slept with her. Susan forgave him, of course. Except that forgiveness is hardly the word. Understanding, yes. But if you understand something, you don't forgive it, you are the thing itself: forgiveness is for what you *don't* understand. Nor had he *confessed*—what sort of word is that?

The whole thing was not important. After all, years ago they had joked: Of course I'm not going to be faithful to you, no one can be faithful to one other person for a whole lifetime. (And there was the word "faithful"—stupid, all these words, stupid, belonging to a savage old world.) But the incident left both of them irritable. Strange, but they were both bad-tempered, annoyed. There was something unassimilable about it.

Making love splendidly after he had come home that night, both had felt that the idea that Myra Jenkins, a pretty girl met at a party, could be even relevant was ridiculous. They had loved each other for over a decade, would love each other for years more. Who, then, was Myra Jenkins?

Except, thought Susan, unaccountably bad-tempered, she was (is?) the first. In ten years. So either the ten years' fidelity was not important, or she isn't. (No, no, there is something wrong with this way of thinking, there must be.) But if she isn't important, presumably it wasn't important either when Matthew and I first went to bed with each other that afternoon whose delight even now (like a very long shadow at sundown) lays a long, wandlike finger over us. (Why did I say sundown?) Well, if what we felt that afternoon was not important, nothing is important, because if it hadn't been for what we felt, we wouldn't be Mr. and Mrs. Rawlings with four children, et cetera, et cetera. The whole thing is *absurd*—for him to have come home and told me was absurd. For him not to have told me was absurd. For me to care or, for that matter, not to care, is absurd . . . and who is Myra Jenkins? Why, no one at all.

There was only one thing to do, and of course these sensible people did it; they put the thing behind them, and consciously, knowing what they were doing, moved forward into a different phase of their marriage, giving thanks for past good fortune as they did so.

For it was inevitable that the handsome, blond, attractive, manly man, Matthew Rawlings, should be at times tempted (oh, what a word!) by the attractive girls at parties she could not attend because of the four children; and that sometimes he would succumb (a word even more repulsive, if possible) and that she, a goodlooking woman in the big well-tended garden at Richmond, would sometimes be pierced as by an arrow from the sky with bitterness. Except that bitterness was not in order, it was out of court. Did the casual girls touch the marriage? They did not. Rather it was they who knew defeat because of the handsome Matthew Rawlings' marriage body and soul to Susan Rawlings.

In that case why did Susan feel (though luckily not for longer than a few seconds at a time) as if life had become a desert, and that nothing mattered, and that her children were not her own?

Meanwhile her intelligence continued to assert that all was well. What if her Matthew did have an occasional sweet afternoon, the odd affair? For she knew quite well, except in her moments of aridity, that they were very happy, that the affairs were not important.

Perhaps that was the trouble? It was in the nature of things that the adventures and delights could no longer be hers, because of the four children and the big house that needed so much attention. But perhaps she was secretly wishing, and even knowing that she did, that the wildness and the beauty could be his. But he was married to her. She was married to him. They were married inextricably. And therefore the gods could not strike him with the real magic, not really. Well, was it Susan's fault that after he came home from an adventure he looked harassed rather than fulfilled? (In fact, that was how she knew he had been *unfaithful,* because of his sullen air, and his glances at her, similar to hers at him: What is it that I share with this person that shields all delight from me?) But none of it by anybody's fault. (But what did they feel ought to be somebody's fault?) Nobody's fault, nothing to be at fault, no one to blame, no one to offer or to take it ... and nothing wrong, either, except that Matthew never was really struck, as he wanted to be, by joy; and that Susan was more and more often threatened by emptiness. (It was usually in the garden that she was invaded by this feeling: she was coming to avoid the garden, unless the children or Matthew were with her.) There was no need to use the dramatic words "unfaithful," "forgive," and the rest: intelligence forbade them. Intelligence barred, too, quarrelling, sulking, anger, silences of withdrawal, accusations and tears. Above all, intelligence forbids tears.

A high price has to be paid for the happy marriage with the four healthy children in the large white gardened house.

And they were paying it, willingly, knowing what they were doing. When they lay side by side or breast to breast in the big civilised bedroom overlooking the wild sullied river, they laughed, often, for no particular reason; but they knew it was really because of these two small people, Susan and Matthew, supporting such an edifice on their intelligent love. The laugh comforted them; it saved them both, though from what, they did not know.

They were now both fortyish. The older children, boy and girl, were ten and eight, at school. The twins, six, were still at home. Susan did not have nurses or girls to help her: childhood is short; and she did not regret the hard work. Often enough she was bored, since small children can be boring; she was often very tired; but she regretted nothing. In another decade, she would turn herself back into being a woman with a life of her own.

Soon the twins would go to school, and they would be away from home from nine until four. These hours, so Susan saw it, would be the preparation for her own slow emancipation away from the role of hub-of-the-family into woman-with-her-own-life. She was already planning for the hours of freedom when all the children would be "off her hands." That was the phrase used by Matthew and by Susan and by their friends, for the moment when the youngest child went off to school. "They'll be off your hands, darling Susan, and you'll have time to yourself." So said Matthew, the intelligent husband, who had often enough commended and consoled Susan, standing by her in spirit during the years when her soul was not her own, as she said, but her children's.

What it amounted to was that Susan saw herself as she had been at twenty-eight, unmarried; and then again somewhere about fifty, blossoming from the root of what she had been twenty years before. As if the essential Susan were in abeyance, as if she were in cold storage. Matthew said something like this to Susan one night: and she agreed that it was true—she did feel something like that. What, then, was this essential Susan? She did not know. Put like that it sounded ridiculous, and she did not really feel it. Anyway, they had a long discussion about the whole thing before going off to sleep in each other's arms.

So the twins went off to their school, two bright affectionate children who had no problems about it, since their older brother and sister had trodden this path so successfully before them. And now Susan was going to be alone in the big house, every day of the school term, except for the daily woman who came in to clean.

It was now, for the first time in this marriage, that something happened which neither of them had foreseen.

This is what happened. She returned, at nine-thirty, from taking the twins to the school by car, looking forward to seven blissful hours of freedom. On the first morning she was simply restless, worrying about the twins "naturally enough" since this was their first day away at school. She was hardly able to contain herself until they came back. Which they did happily, excited by the world of school, looking forward to the next day. And the next day Susan took them, dropped them, came back, and found herself reluctant to enter her big and beautiful home because it was as if something was waiting for her there that she did not wish to confront. Sensibly, however, she parked the car in the garage, entered the house, spoke to Mrs. Parkes, the daily woman, about her duties, and went up to her bedroom. She was possessed by a fever which drove her out again, downstairs, into the kitchen, where Mrs. Parkes was making cake and did not need her, and into the garden. There she sat on a bench and tried to calm herself looking at trees, at a brown glimpse of the river. But she was filled with tension, like a panic: as if an enemy was in the garden with her. She spoke to herself severely, thus: All this is quite natural. First, I spent twelve years of my adult life working, living my own life. Then I married, and from the moment I became pregnant for the first time I signed myself over, so to speak, to other people. To the children. Not for one moment in twelve years have I been alone, had time to myself. So now I have to learn to be myself again. That's all.

And she went indoors to help Mrs. Parkes cook and clean, and found some sewing to do for the children. She kept herself occupied every day. At the end of the first term she understood she felt two contrary emotions. First, secret astonishment and dismay that during those weeks when the house was empty of children she had in fact been more occupied (had been careful to keep herself occupied) than ever she had been when the children were around her needing her continual attention. Second, that now she knew the house would be full of them, and for five weeks, she resented the fact she would never be alone. She was already looking back at those hours of sewing, cooking (but by herself) as at a lost freedom which would not be hers for five long weeks. And the two months of term which would succeed the five weeks stretched alluringly open to her—freedom. But what freedom—when in fact she had been so careful *not* to be free of small duties during the last weeks? She looked at herself, Susan Rawlings, sitting in a big chair by the window in the bedroom, sewing shirts or dresses, which she might just as well have bought. She saw herself making cakes for hours at a time in the big family kitchen: yet usually she bought cakes. What she saw was a woman alone, that was true, but she had not felt alone. For instance, Mrs. Parkes was always somewhere in the house. And she did not like being in the garden at all, because of the closeness there of the enemy—irritation, restlessness, emptiness, whatever it was— which keeping her hands occupied made less dangerous for some reason.

Susan did not tell Matthew of these thoughts. They were not sensible. She did not recognize herself in them. What should she say to her dear friend and husband, Matthew? "When I go into the garden, that is, if the children are not there, I feel as if there is an enemy there waiting to invade me." "What enemy, Susan darling?" "Well I don't know, really. . . ." "Perhaps you should see a doctor?"

No, clearly this conversation should not take place. The holidays began and Susan welcomed them. Four children, lively, energetic, intelligent, demanding: she was never, not for a moment of her day, alone. If she was in a room, they would be in the next room, or waiting for her to do something for them; or it would soon be time for lunch or tea, or to take one of them to the dentist. Something to do: five weeks of it, thank goodness.

On the fourth day of these so welcome holidays, she found she was storming with anger at the twins; two shrinking beautiful children who (and this is what checked her) stood hand in hand looking at her with sheer dismayed disbelief. This was their calm mother, shouting at them. And for what? They had come to her with some game, some bit of nonsense. They looked at each other, moved closer for support, and went off hand in hand, leaving Susan holding on to the windowsill of the living room, breathing deep, feeling sick. She went to lie down, telling the older children she had a headache. She heard the boy Harry telling the little ones: "It's all right, Mother's got a headache." She heard that *It's all right* with pain.

That night she said to her husband: "Today I shouted at the twins, quite unfairly." She sounded miserable, and he said gently: "Well, what of it?"

"It's more of an adjustment than I thought, their going to school."

"But Susie, Susie darling. . . ." For she was crouched weeping on the bed. He comforted her: "Susan, what is all this about? You shouted at them? What of it? If you shouted at them fifty times a day it wouldn't be more than the little devils deserve." But she wouldn't laugh. She wept. Soon he comforted her with his body. She became calm. Calm, she wondered what was wrong with her, and why she should mind so much that she might, just once, have behaved unjustly with the children. What did it matter? They had forgotten it all long ago: Mother had a headache and everything was all right.

It was a long time later that Susan understood that that night, when she had wept and Matthew had driven the misery out of her with his big solid body, was the last time, ever in their married life, that they had been—to use their mutual language—with each other. And even that was a lie, because she had not told him of her real fears at all.

The five weeks passed, and Susan was in control of herself, and good and kind, and she looked forward to the end of the holidays with a mixture of fear and longing. She did not know what to expect. She took the twins off to school (the elder children took themselves to school) and she returned to the house determined to face the enemy wherever he was, in the house, or the garden or—where?

She was again restless, she was possessed by restlessness. She cooked and sewed and worked as before, day after day, while Mrs. Parkes remonstrated: "Mrs. Rawlings, what's the need for it? I can do that, it's what you pay me for."

And it was so irrational that she checked herself. She would put the car into the garage, go up to her bedroom, and sit, hands in her lap, forcing herself to be quiet. She listened to Mrs. Parkes moving around the house. She looked out into the garden and saw the branches shake the trees. She sat defeating the enemy, restlessness. Emptiness. She ought to be thinking about her life, about herself. But she did not. Or perhaps she could not. As soon as she forced her mind to think about Susan (for what else did she want to be alone for?), it skipped off to thoughts of butter or school clothes. Or it thought of Mrs. Parkes. She realised that she sat listening for the movements of the cleaning woman, following her every turn, bend, thought. She followed her in her mind from kitchen to bathroom, from table to oven, and it was as if the duster, the cleaning cloth, the saucepan, were in her own hand. She would hear herself saying: No, not like that, don't put that there. . . . Yet she did not give a damn what Mrs. Parkes did, or if she did it at all. Yet she could not prevent herself from being conscious of her, every minute. Yes, this was what was wrong with her: she needed, when she was alone, to be really alone, with no one near. She could not endure the knowledge that in ten minutes or in half an hour Mrs. Parkes would call up the stairs: "Mrs. Rawlings, there's no silver polish. Madam, we're out of flour."

So she left the house and went to sit in the garden where she was screened from the house by trees. She waited for the demon to appear and claim her, but he did not.

She was keeping him off, because she had not, after all, come to an end of arranging herself.

She was planning how to be somewhere where Mrs. Parkes would not come after her with a cup of tea, or a demand to be allowed to telephone (always irritating, since Susan did not care who she telephoned or how often), or just a nice talk about something. Yes, she needed a place, or a state of affairs, where it would not be necessary to keep reminding herself: In ten minutes I must telephone Matthew about . . . and at half past three I must leave early for the children because the car needs cleaning. And at ten o'clock tomorrow I must remember. . . . She was possessed with resentment that the seven hours of freedom in every day (during weekdays in the school term) were not free, that never, not for one second, ever, was she free from the pressure of time, from having to remember this or that. She could never forget herself; never really let herself go into forgetfulness.

Resentment. It was poisoning her. (She looked at this emotion and thought it was absurd. Yet she felt it.) She was a prisoner. (She looked at this thought too, and it was no good telling herself it was a ridiculous one.) She must tell Matthew—but what? She was filled with emotions that were utterly ridiculous, that she despised, yet that nevertheless she was feeling so strongly she could not shake them off.

The school holidays came round, and this time they were for nearly two months, and she behaved with a conscious controlled decency that nearly drove her crazy. She would lock herself in the bathroom, and sit on the edge of the bath, breathing deep, trying to let go into some kind of calm. Or she went up into the spare room, usually empty, where no one would expect her to be. She heard the children calling "Mother, Mother," and kept silent, feeling guilty. Or she went to the very end of the garden, by herself, and looked at the slow-moving brown river; she looked at the river and closed her eyes and breathed slow and deep, taking it into her being, into her veins.

Then she returned to the family, wife and mother, smiling and responsible, feeling as if the pressure of these people—four lively children and her husband—were a painful pressure on the surface of her skin, a hand pressing on her brain. She did not once break down into irritation during these holidays, but it was like living out a prison sentence, and when the children went back to school, she sat on a white stone seat near the flowing river, and she thought: It is not even a year since the twins went to school, since *they were off my hands* (What on earth did I think I meant when I used that stupid phrase?), and yet I'm a different person. I'm simply not myself. I don't understand it.

Yet she had to understand it. For she knew that this structure—big white house, on which the mortgage still cost four hundred[3] a year, a husband, so good and kind and insightful; four children, all doing so nicely; and the garden where she sat; and Mrs. Parkes, the cleaning woman—all this depended on her, and yet she could not understand why, or even what it was she contributed to it.

She said to Matthew in their bedroom: "I think there must be something wrong with me."

And he said: "Surely not, Susan? You look marvellous—you're as lovely as ever."

She looked at the handsome blond man, with his clear, intelligent, blue-eyed face, and thought: Why is it I can't tell him? Why not? And she said: "I need to be alone more than I am."

---

3. That is, four hundred pounds.

At which he swung his slow blue gaze at her, and she saw what she had been dreading: Incredulity. Disbelief. And fear. An incredulous blue stare from a stranger who was her husband, as close to her as her own breath.

He said: "But the children are at school and off your hands."

She said to herself: I've got to force myself to say: Yes, but do you realize that I never feel free? There's never a moment I can say to myself: There's nothing I have to remind myself about, nothing I have to do in half an hour, or an hour, or two hours. . . .

But she said: "I don't feel well."

He said: "Perhaps you need a holiday."

She said, appalled: "But not without you, surely?" For she could not imagine herself going off without him. Yet that was what he meant. Seeing her face, he laughed, and opened his arms, and she went into them, thinking: Yes, yes, but why can't I say it? And what is it I have to say?

She tried to tell him, about never being free. And he listened and said: "But Susan, what sort of freedom can you possibly want—short of being dead! Am I ever free? I go to the office, and I have to be there at ten—all right, half past ten, sometimes. And I have to do this or that, don't I? Then I've got to come home at a certain time—I don't mean it, you know I don't—but if I'm not going to be back home at six I telephone you. When can I ever say to myself: I have nothing to be responsible for in the next six hours?"

Susan, hearing this, was remorseful. Because it was true. The good marriage, the house, the children, depended just as much on his voluntary bondage as it did on hers. But why did he not feel bound? Why didn't he chafe and become restless? No, there was something really wrong with her and this proved it.

And that word "bondage"—why had she used it? She had never felt marriage, or the children, as bondage. Neither had he, or surely they wouldn't be together lying in each other's arms content after twelve years of marriage.

No, her state (whatever it was) was irrelevant, nothing to do with her real good life with her family. She had to accept the fact that, after all, she was an irrational person and to live with it. Some people had to live with crippled arms, or stammers, or being deaf. She would have to live knowing she was subject to a state of mind she could not own.

Nevertheless, as a result of this conversation with her husband, there was a new regime next holidays.

The spare room at the top of the house now had a cardboard sign saying: PRIVATE! DO NOT DISTURB! on it. (This sign had been drawn in coloured chalks by the children, after a discussion between the parents in which it was decided this was psychologically the right thing.) The family and Mrs. Parkes knew this was "Mother's Room" and that she was entitled to her privacy. Many serious conversations took place between Matthew and the children about not taking Mother for granted. Susan overheard the first, between father and Harry, the older boy, and was surprised at her irritation over it. Surely she could have a room somewhere in that big house and retire into it without such a fuss being made? Without it being so solemnly discussed? Why couldn't she simply have announced: "I'm going to fit out the little top room for myself, and when I'm in it I'm not to be disturbed for anything short of fire"? Just that, and finished; instead of long earnest discussions. When she heard Harry and Matthew explaining it to the twins with Mrs. Parkes coming in—"Yes, well, a family sometimes gets on top of a woman"—she had to go right away to the bottom of the garden until the devils of exasperation had finished their dance in her blood.

But now there was a room, and she could go there when she liked, she used it seldom: she felt even more caged there than in her bedroom. One day she had gone up there after a lunch for ten children she had cooked and served because Mrs. Parkes was not there, and had sat alone for a while looking into the garden. She saw the children stream out from the kitchen and stand looking up at the window where she sat behind the curtains. They were all—her children and their friends—discussing Mother's Room. A few minutes later, the chase of children in some game came pounding up the stairs, but ended as abruptly as if they had fallen over a ravine, so sudden was the silence. They had remembered she was there, and had gone silent in a great gale of "Hush! Shhhhhh! Quiet, you'll disturb her. . . ." And they went tiptoeing downstairs like criminal conspirators. When she came down to make tea for them, they all apologised. The twins put their arms around her, from front and back, making a human cage of loving limbs, and promised it would never occur again. "We forgot, Mummy, we forgot all about it!"

What it amounted to was that Mother's Room, and her need for privacy, had become a valuable lesson in respect for other people's rights. Quite soon Susan was going up to the room only because it was a lesson it was a pity to drop. Then she took sewing up there, and the children and Mrs. Parkes came in and out: it had become another family room.

She sighed, and smiled, and resigned herself—she made jokes at her own expense with Matthew over the room. That is, she did from the self she liked, she respected. But at the same time, something inside her howled with impatience, with rage. . . . And she was frightened. One day she found herself kneeling by her bed and praying: "Dear God, keep it away from me, keep him away from me." She meant the devil, for she now thought of it, not caring if she was irrational, as some sort of demon. She imagined him, or it, as a youngish man, or perhaps a middle-aged man pretending to be young. Or a man young-looking from immaturity? At any rate, she saw the young-looking face which, when she drew closer, had dry lines about mouth and eyes. He was thinnish, meagre in build. And he had a reddish complexion, and ginger hair. That was he—a gingery, energetic man, and he wore a reddish hairy jacket, unpleasant to the touch.

Well, one day she saw him. She was standing at the bottom of the garden, watching the river ebb past, when she raised her eyes and saw this person, or being, sitting on the white stone bench. He was looking at her, and grinning. In his hand was a long crooked stick, which he had picked off the ground, or broken off the tree above him. He was absent-mindedly, out of an absent-minded or freakish impulse of spite, using the stick to stir around in the coils of a blindworm or a grass snake (or some kind of snakelike creature: it was whitish and unhealthy to look at, unpleasant). The snake was twisting about, flinging its coils from side to side in a kind of dance of protest against the teasing prodding stick.

Susan looked at him thinking: Who is the stranger? What is he doing in our garden? Then she recognised the man around whom her terrors had crystallised. As she did so, he vanished. She made herself walk over to the bench. A shadow from a branch lay across thin emerald grass, moving jerkily over its roughness, and she could see why she had taken it for a snake, lashing and twisting. She went back to the house thinking: Right, then, so I've seen him with my own eyes, so I'm not crazy after all—there *is* a danger because I've seen him. He is lurking in the garden and sometimes even in the house, and he wants to *get into me and to take me over.*

She dreamed of having a room or a place, anywhere, where she could go and sit, by herself, no one knowing where she was.

Once, near Victoria,[4] she found herself outside a news agent that had Rooms to Let advertised. She decided to rent a room, telling no one. Sometimes she could take the train in to Richmond and sit alone in it for an hour or two. Yet how could she? A room would cost three or four pounds a week, and she earned no money, and how could she explain to Matthew that she needed such a sum? What for? It did not occur to her that she was taking it for granted she wasn't going to tell him about the room.

Well, it was out of the question, having a room; yet she knew she must.

One day, when a school term was well established, and none of the children had measles or other ailments, and everything seemed in order, she did the shopping early, explained to Mrs. Parkes she was meeting an old school friend, took the train to Victoria, searched until she found a small quiet hotel, and asked for a room for the day. They did not let rooms by the day, the manageress said, looking doubtful, since Susan so obviously was not the kind of woman who needed a room for unrespectable reasons. Susan made a long explanation about not being well, being unable to shop without frequent rests for lying down. At last she was allowed to rent the room provided she paid a full night's price for it. She was taken up by the manageress and a maid, both concerned over the state of her health . . . which must be pretty bad if, living at Richmond (she had signed her name and address in the register), she needed a shelter at Victoria.

The room was ordinary and anonymous, and was just what Susan needed. She put a shilling in the gas fire,[5] and sat, eyes shut, in a dingy armchair with her back to a dingy window. She was alone. She was alone. She was alone. She could feel pressures lifting off her. First the sounds of traffic came very loud; then they seemed to vanish; she might even have slept a little. A knock on the door: it was Miss Townsend, the manageress, bringing her a cup of tea with her own hands, so concerned was she over Susan's long silence and possible illness.

Miss Townsend was a lonely woman of fifty, running this hotel with all the rectitude expected of her, and she sensed in Susan the possibility of understanding companionship. She stayed to talk. Susan found herself in the middle of a fantastic story about her illness, which got more and more improbable as she tried to make it tally with the large house at Richmond, well-off husband, and four children. Suppose she said instead: Miss Townsend, I'm here in your hotel because I need to be alone for a few hours, above all *alone and with no one knowing where I am.* She said it mentally, and saw, mentally, the look

---

4. One of the main railway stations in central London. **5.** Metered gas heating device, common in Britain.

that would inevitably come on Miss Townsend's elderly maiden's face. "Miss Townsend, my four children and my husband are driving me insane, do you understand that? Yes, I can see from the gleam of hysteria in your eyes that comes from loneliness controlled but only just contained that I've got everything in the world you've ever longed for. Well, Miss Townsend, I don't want any of it. You can have it, Miss Townsend. I wish I was absolutely alone in the world, like you. Miss Townsend, I'm besieged by seven devils, Miss Townsend, Miss Townsend, let me stay here in your hotel where the devils can't get me. . . ." Instead of saying all this, she described her anaemia, agreed to try Miss Townsend's remedy for it, which was raw liver, minced, between whole-meal bread, and said yes, perhaps it would be better if she stayed at home and let a friend do shopping for her. She paid her bill and left the hotel, defeated.

At home Mrs. Parkes said she didn't really like it, no, not really, when Mrs. Rawlings was away from nine in the morning until five. The teacher had telephoned from school to say Joan's teeth were paining her, and she hadn't known what to say; and what was she to make for the children's tea, Mrs. Rawlings hadn't said.

All this was nonsense, of course. Mrs. Parkes's complaint was that Susan had withdrawn herself spiritually, leaving the burden of the big house on her.

Susan looked back at her day of "freedom" which had resulted in her becoming a friend of the lonely Miss Townsend, and in Mrs. Parkes's remonstrances. Yet she remembered the short blissful hour of being alone, really alone. She was determined to arrange her life, no matter what it cost, so that she could have that solitude more often. An absolute solitude, where no one knew her or cared about her.

But how? She thought of saying to her old employer: I want you to back me up in a story with Matthew that I am doing part-time work for you. The truth is that . . . But she would have to tell him a lie too, and which lie? She could not say: I want to sit by myself three or four times a week in a rented room. And besides, he knew Matthew, and she could not really ask him to tell lies on her behalf, apart from being bound to think it meant a lover.

Suppose she really took a part-time job, which she could get through fast and efficiently, leaving time for herself. What job? Addressing envelopes? Canvassing?

And there was Mrs. Parkes, working widow, who knew exactly what she was prepared to give to the house, who knew by instinct when her mistress withdrew in spirit from her responsibilities. Mrs. Parkes was one of the servers of this world, but she needed someone to serve. She had to have Mrs. Rawlings, her madam, at the top of the house or in the garden, so that she could come and get support from her: "Yes, the bread's not what it was when I was a girl. . . . Yes, Harry's got a wonderful appetite, I wonder where he puts it all. . . . Yes, it's lucky the twins are so much of a size, they can wear each other's shoes, that's a saving in these hard times. . . . Yes, the cherry jam from Switzerland is not a patch on the jam from Poland, and three times the price . . ." And so on. That sort of talk Mrs. Parkes must have, every day, or she would leave, not knowing herself why she left.

Susan Rawlings, thinking these thoughts, found that she was prowling through the great thicketed garden like a wild cat: she was walking up the stairs, down the stairs, through the rooms into the garden, along the brown running river, back, up through the house, down again.... It was a wonder Mrs. Parkes did not think it strange. But, on the contrary, Mrs. Rawlings could do what she liked, she could stand on her head if she wanted, provided she was *there*. Susan Rawlings prowled and muttered through her house, hating Mrs. Parkes, hating poor Miss Townsend, dreaming of her hour of solitude in the dingy respectability of Miss Townsend's hotel bedroom, and she knew quite well she was mad. Yes, she was mad.

She said to Matthew that she must have a holiday. Matthew agreed with her. This was not as things had been once—how they had talked in each other's arms in the marriage bed. He had, she knew, diagnosed her finally as *unreasonable*. She had become someone outside himself that he had to manage. They were living side by side in this house like two tolerably friendly strangers.

Having told Mrs. Parkes—or rather, asked for her permission—she went off on a walking holiday in Wales. She chose the remotest place she knew of. Every morning the children telephoned her before they went off to school, to encourage and support her, just as they had over Mother's Room. Every evening she telephoned them, spoke to each child in turn, and then to Matthew. Mrs. Parkes, given permission to telephone for instructions or advice, did so every day at lunchtime. When, as happened three times, Mrs. Rawlings was out on the mountainside, Mrs. Parkes asked that she should ring back at such-and-such a time, for she would not be happy in what she was doing without Mrs. Rawlings' blessing.

Susan prowled over wild country with the telephone wire holding her to her duty like a leash. The next time she must telephone, or wait to be telephoned, nailed her to her cross. The mountains themselves seemed trammelled by her unfreedom. Everywhere on the mountains, where she met no one at all, from breakfast time to dusk, excepting sheep, or a shepherd, she came face to face with her own craziness, which might attack her in the broadest valleys, so that they seemed too small, or on a mountaintop from which she could see a hundred other mountains and valleys, so that they seemed too low, too small, with the sky pressing down too close. She would stand gazing at a hillside brilliant with ferns and bracken, jewelled with running water, and see nothing but her devil, who lifted inhuman eyes at her from where he leaned negligently on a rock, switching at his ugly yellow boots with a leafy twig.

She returned to her home and family, with the Welsh emptiness at the back of her mind like a promise of freedom.

She told her husband she wanted to have an *au pair* girl.[6]

They were in their bedroom, it was late at night, the children slept. He sat, shirted and slippered, in a chair by the window, looking out. She sat brushing her hair and watching him in the mirror. A time-hallowed scene in the connubial bedroom. He said nothing, while she heard the arguments coming into his mind, only to be rejected because every one was *reasonable*.

---

6. Young woman, usually foreign, who lives in with a family, doing housework and babysitting in exchange for room and board (French).

"It seems strange to get one now; after all, the children are in school most of the day. Surely the time for you to have help was when you were stuck with them day and night. Why don't you ask Mrs. Parkes to cook for you? She's even offered to—I can understand if you are tired of cooking for six people. But you know that an *au pair* girl means all kinds of problems, it's not like having an ordinary char in during the day. . . ."

Finally he said carefully: "Are you thinking of going back to work?"

"No," she said, "no, not really." She made herself sound vague, rather stupid. She went on brushing her black hair and peering at herself so as to be oblivious of the short uneasy glances her Matthew kept giving her. "Do you think we can't afford it?" she went on vaguely, not at all the old efficient Susan who knew exactly what they could afford.

"It's not that," he said, looking out of the window at dark trees, so as not to look at her. Meanwhile she examined a round, candid, pleasant face with clear dark brows and clear grey eyes. A sensible face. She brushed thick healthy black hair and thought: Yet that's the reflection of a madwoman. How very strange! Much more to the point if what looked back at me was the gingery green-eyed demon with his dry meagre smile. . . . Why wasn't Matthew agreeing? After all, what else could he do? She was breaking her part of the bargain and there was no way of forcing her to keep it: that her spirit, her soul, should live in this house, so that the people in it could grow like plants in water, and Mrs. Parkes remain content in their service. In return for this, he would be a good loving husband, and responsible towards the children. Well, nothing like this had been true of either of them for a long time. He did his duty, perfunctorily; she did not even pretend to do hers. And he had become like other husbands, with his real life in his work and the people he met there, and very likely a serious affair. All this was her fault.

At last he drew heavy curtains, blotting out the trees, and turned to force her attention: "Susan, are you really sure we need a girl?" But she would not meet his appeal at all. She was running the brush over her hair again and again, lifting fine black clouds in a small hiss of electricity. She was peering in and smiling as if she were amused at the clinging hissing hair that followed the brush.

"Yes, I think it would be a good idea, on the whole," she said, with the cunning of a madwoman evading the real point.

In the mirror she could see her Matthew lying on his back, his hands behind his head, staring upwards, his face sad and hard. She felt her heart (the old heart of Susan Rawlings) soften and call out to him. But she set it to be indifferent.

He said: "Susan, the children?" It was an appeal that *almost* reached her. He opened his arms, lifting them palms up, empty. She had only to run across and fling herself into them, onto his hard, warm chest, and melt into herself, into Susan. But she could not. She would not see his lifted arms. She said vaguely: "Well, surely it'll be even better for them? We'll get a French or a German girl and they'll learn the language."

In the dark she lay beside him, feeling frozen, a stranger. She felt as if Susan had been spirited away. She disliked very much this woman who lay here, cold and indifferent beside a suffering man, but she could not change her.

Next morning she set about getting a girl, and very soon came Sophie Traub from Hamburg, a girl of twenty, laughing, healthy, blue-eyed, intending to learn English. Indeed, she already spoke a good deal. In return for a room—"Mother's Room"—and her food, she undertook to do some light cooking, and to be with the children when Mrs. Rawlings asked. She was an intelligent girl and understood perfectly what was needed. Susan said: "I go off sometimes, for the morning or for the day—well, sometimes the children run home from school, or they ring up, or a teacher rings up. I should be here, really. And there's the daily woman. . . ." And Sophie laughed her deep fruity *Fräulein's* laugh, showed her fine white teeth and her dimples, and said: "You want some person to play mistress of the house sometimes, not so?"

"Yes, that is just so," said Susan, a bit dry, despite herself, thinking in secret fear how easy it was, how much nearer to the end she was than she thought. Healthy Fräulein Traub's instant understanding of their position proved this to be true.

The *au pair* girl, because of her own commonsense, or (as Susan said to herself, with her new inward shudder) because she had been *chosen* so well by Susan, was a success with everyone, the children liking her, Mrs. Parkes forgetting almost at once that she was German, and Matthew finding her "nice to have around the house." For he was now taking things as they came, from the surface of life, withdrawn both as a husband and a father from the household.

One day Susan saw how Sophie and Mrs. Parkes were talking and laughing in the kitchen, and she announced that she would be away until tea time. She knew exactly where to go and what she must look for. She took the District Line to South Kensington, changed to the Circle, got off at Paddington,[7] and walked around looking at the smaller hotels until she was satisfied with one which had FRED'S HOTEL painted on windowpanes that needed cleaning. The facade was a faded shiny yellow, like unhealthy skin. A door at the end of a passage said she must knock; she did, and Fred appeared. He was not at all attractive, not in any way, being fattish, and run-down, and wearing a tasteless striped suit. He had small sharp eyes in a white creased face, and was quite prepared to let Mrs. Jones (she chose the farcical name deliberately, staring him out) have a room three days a week from ten until six. Provided of course that she paid in advance each time she came? Susan produced fifteen shillings (no price had been set by him) and held it out, still fixing him with a bold unblinking challenge she had not known until then she could use at will. Looking at her still, he took up a ten-shilling note from her palm between thumb and forefinger, fingered it; then shuffled up two half-crowns,[8] held out his own palm with these bits of money displayed thereon, and let his gaze lower broodingly at them. They were standing in the passage, a red-shaded light above, bare boards beneath, and a strong smell of floor polish rising about them. He shot his gaze up at her over the still-extended palm, and smiled as if to say: What do you take me for? "I shan't," said Susan, "be using this room for the purposes of making money." He still waited. She added another five shillings, at which he nodded and said: "You pay, and I ask no questions." "Good," said Susan. He now went past her to

---

7. Railway and subway station in London. The Circle is the Circle Line of the subway. 8. Coins worth two and a half shillings each.

the stairs, and there waited a moment: the light from the street door being in her eyes, she lost sight of him momentarily. Then she saw a sober-suited, white-faced, white-balding little man trotting up the stairs like a waiter, and she went after him. They proceeded in utter silence up the stairs of this house where no questions were asked—Fred's Hotel, which could afford the freedom for its visitors that poor Miss Townsend's hotel could not. The room was hideous. It had a single window, with thin green brocade curtains, a three-quarter bed that had a cheap green satin bedspread on it, a fireplace with a gas fire and a shilling meter by it, a chest of drawers, and a green wicker armchair.

"Thank you," said Susan, knowing that Fred (if this was Fred, and not George, or Herbert or Charlie) was looking at her, not so much with curiosity, an emotion he would not own to, for professional reasons, but with a philosophical sense of what was appropriate. Having taken her money and shown her up and agreed to everything, he was clearly disapproving of her for coming here. She did not belong here at all, so his look said. (But she knew, already, how very much she did belong: the room had been waiting for her to join it.) "Would you have me called at five o'clock, please?" and he nodded and went downstairs.

It was twelve in the morning. She was free. She sat in the armchair, she simply sat, she closed her eyes and sat and let herself be alone. She was alone and no one knew where she was. When a knock came on the door she was annoyed, and prepared to show it: but it was Fred himself, it was five o'clock and he was calling her as ordered. He flicked his sharp little eyes over the room—bed, first. It was undisturbed. She might never have been in the room at all. She thanked him, said she would be returning the day after tomorrow, and left. She was back home in time to cook supper, to put the children to bed, to cook a second supper for her husband and herself later. And to welcome Sophie back from the pictures where she had gone with a friend. All these things she did cheerfully, willingly. But she was thinking all the time of the hotel room; she was longing for it with her whole being.

Three times a week. She arrived promptly at ten, looked Fred in the eyes, gave him twenty shillings, followed him up the stairs, went into the room, and shut the door on him with gentle firmness. For Fred, disapproving of her being here at all, was quite ready to let friendship, or at least acquaintanceship, follow his disapproval, if only she would let him. But he was content to go off on her dismissing nod, with the twenty shillings in his hand.

She sat in the armchair and shut her eyes.

What did she *do* in the room? Why, nothing at all. From the chair, when it had rested her, she went to the window, stretching her arms, smiling, treasuring her anonymity, to look out. She was no longer Susan Rawlings, mother of four, wife of Matthew, employer of Mrs. Parkes and of Sophie Traub, with these and those relations with friends, school-teachers, tradesmen. She no longer was mistress of the big white house and garden, owning clothes suitable for this and that activity or occasion. She was Mrs. Jones, and she was alone, and she had no past and no future. Here I am, she thought, after all these years of being married and having children and playing those roles of responsibility—and I'm just the same. Yet there have been times I thought

Free from ID's

that nothing existed of me except the roles that went with being Mrs. Matthew Rawlings. Yes, here I am, and if I never saw any of my family again, here I would still be . . . how very strange that is! And she leaned on the sill, and looked into the street, loving the men and women who passed, because she did not know them. She looked at the downtrodden buildings over the street, and at the sky, wet and dingy, or sometimes blue, and she felt she had never seen buildings or sky before. And then she went back to the chair, empty, her mind a blank. Sometimes she talked aloud, saying nothing—an exclamation, meaningless, followed by a comment about the floral pattern on the thin rug, or a stain on the green satin coverlet. For the most part, she wool-gathered—what word is there for it?—brooded, wandered, simply went dark, feeling emptiness run deliciously through her veins like the movement of her blood.

This room had become more her own than the house she lived in. One morning she found Fred taking her a flight higher than usual. She stopped, refusing to go up, and demanded her usual room, Number 19. "Well, you'll have to wait half an hour, then," he said. Willingly she descended to the dark disinfectant-smelling hall, and sat waiting until the two, man and woman, came down the stairs, giving her swift indifferent glances before they hurried out into the street, separating at the door. She went up to the room, *her* room, which they had just vacated. It was no less hers, though the windows were set wide open, and a maid was straightening the bed as she came in.

After these days of solitude, it was both easy to play her part as mother and wife, and difficult—because it was so easy: she felt an impostor. She felt as if her shell moved here, with her family, answering to Mummy, Mother, Susan, Mrs. Rawlings. She was surprised no one saw through her, that she wasn't turned out of doors, as a fake. On the contrary, it seemed the children loved her more; Matthew and she "got on" pleasantly, and Mrs. Parkes was happy in her work under (for the most part, it must be confessed) Sophie Traub. At night she lay beside her husband, and they made love again, apparently just as they used to, when they were really married. But she, Susan, or the being who answered so readily and improbably to the name of Susan, was not there: she was in Fred's Hotel, in Paddington, waiting for the easing hours of solitude to begin.

Soon she made a new arrangement with Fred and with Sophie. It was for five days a week. As for the money, five pounds, she simply asked Matthew for it. She saw that she was not even frightened he might ask what for: he would give it to her, she knew that, and yet it was terrifying it could be so, for this close couple, these partners, had once known the destination of every shilling they must spend. He agreed to give her five pounds a week. She asked for just so much, not a penny more. He sounded indifferent about it. It was as if he were paying her, she thought: *paying her off*—yes, that was it. Terror came back for a moment when she understood this, but she stilled it: things had gone too far for that. Now, every week, on Sunday nights, he gave her five pounds, turning away from her before their eyes could meet on the transaction. As for Sophie Traub, she was to be somewhere in or near the house until six at night, after which she was free. She was not to cook, or to clean; she was simply to be there. So she gardened or sewed, and asked friends in, being a person who was bound to have a lot of friends. If the children were sick, she nursed them. If teachers telephoned, she answered them sensibly. For the five daytimes in the school week, she was altogether the mistress of the house.

One night in the bedroom, Matthew asked: "Susan, I don't want to interfere—don't think that, please—but are you sure you are well?"

She was brushing her hair at the mirror. She made two more strokes on either side of her head, before she replied: "Yes, dear, I am sure I am well."

He was again lying on his back, his blond head on his hands, his elbows angled up and part-concealing his face. He said: "Then Susan, I have to ask you this question, though you must understand, I'm not putting any sort of pressure on you." (Susan heard the word "pressure" with dismay, because this was inevitable; of course she could not go on like this.) "Are things going to go on like this?"

"Well," she said, going vague and bright and idiotic again, so as to escape: "Well, I don't see why not."

He was jerking his elbows up and down, in annoyance or in pain, and, looking at him, she saw he had got thin, even gaunt; and restless angry movements were not what she remembered of him. He said: "Do you want a divorce, is that it?"

At this, Susan only with the greatest difficulty stopped herself from laughing: she could hear the bright bubbling laughter she *would* have emitted, had she let herself. He could only mean one thing: she had a lover, and that was why she spent her days in London, as lost to him as if she had vanished to another continent.

Then the small panic set in again: she understood that he hoped she did have a lover, he was begging her to say so, because otherwise it would be too terrifying.

She thought this out as she brushed her hair, watching the fine black stuff fly up to make its little clouds of electricity, hiss, hiss, hiss. Behind her head, across the room, was a blue wall. She realised she was absorbed in watching the black hair making shapes against the blue. She should be answering him. "Do *you* want a divorce, Matthew?"

He said: "That surely isn't the point, is it?"

"You brought it up, I didn't," she said, brightly, suppressing meaningless tinkling laughter.

Next day she asked Fred: "Have enquiries been made for me?"

He hesitated, and she said: "I've been coming here a year now. I've made no trouble, and you've been paid every day. I have a right to be told."

"As a matter of fact, Mrs. Jones, a man did come asking."

"A man from a detective agency?"

"Well, he could have been, couldn't he?"

"I was asking you. . . . Well, what did you tell him?"

"I told him a Mrs. Jones came every weekday from ten until five or six and stayed in Number 19 by herself."

"Describing me?"

"Well, Mrs. Jones, I had no alternative. Put yourself in my place."

"By rights I should deduct what that man gave you for the information."

He raised shocked eyes: she was not the sort of person to make jokes like this! Then he chose to laugh: a pinkish wet slit appeared across his white crinkled face; his eyes positively begged her to laugh, otherwise he might lose some money. She remained grave, looking at him.

He stopped laughing and said: "You want to go up now?"—returning to the familiarity, the comradeship, of the country where no questions are asked, on which (and he knew it) she depended completely.

She went up to sit in her wicker chair. But it was not the same. Her husband had searched her out. (The world had searched her out.) The pressures were on her. She was here with his connivance. He might walk in at any moment, here, into Room 19. She imagined the report from the detective agency: "A woman calling herself Mrs. Jones, fitting the description of your wife (et cetera, et cetera, et cetera), stays alone all day in Room No. 19. She insists on this room, waits for it if it is engaged. As far as the proprietor knows, she receives no visitors there, male or female." A report something on these lines Matthew must have received.

Well, of course he was right: things couldn't go on like this. He had put an end to it all simply by sending the detective after her.

She tried to shrink herself back into the shelter of the room, a snail pecked out of its shell and trying to squirm back. But the peace of the room had gone. She was trying consciously to revive it, trying to let go into the dark creative trance (or whatever it was) that she had found there. It was no use, yet she craved for it, she was as ill as a suddenly deprived addict.

Several times she returned to the room, to look for herself there, but instead she found the unnamed spirit of restlessness, a pricking fevered hunger for movement, an irritable self-consciousness that made her brain feel as if it had coloured lights going on and off inside it. Instead of the soft dark that had been the room's air, were now waiting for her demons that made her dash blindly about, muttering words of hate; she was impelling herself from point to point like a moth dashing itself against a windowpane, sliding to the bottom, fluttering off on broken wings, then crashing into the invisible barrier again. And again and again. Soon she was exhausted, and she told Fred that for a while she would not be needing the room, she was going on holiday. Home she went, to the big white house by the river. The middle of a weekday, and she felt guilty at returning to her own home when not expected. She stood unseen, looking in at the kitchen window. Mrs. Parkes, wearing a discarded floral overall of Susan's, was stooping to slide something into the oven. Sophie, arms folded, was leaning her back against a cupboard and laughing at some joke made by a girl not seen before by Susan—a dark foreign girl, Sophie's visitor. In an armchair Molly, one of the twins, lay curled, sucking her thumb and watching the grownups. She must have some sickness, to be kept from school. The child's listless face, the dark circles under her eyes, hurt Susan: Molly was looking at the three grownups working and talking in exactly the same way Susan looked at the four through the kitchen window: she was remote, shut off from them.

But then, just as Susan imagined herself going in, picking up the little girl, and sitting in an armchair with her, stroking her probably heated forehead, Sophie did just that: she had been standing on one leg, the other knee flexed, its foot set against the wall. Now she let her foot in its ribbon-tied red shoe slide down the wall, stood solid on two feet, clapping her hands before and behind her, and sang a couple of lines in German, so that the child lifted her heavy eyes at her and began to smile. Then she walked, or rather skipped, over to the child, swung her up, and let her fall into her lap at the same moment she sat herself. She said "Hopla! Hopla! Molly . . ." and began stroking the dark untidy young head that Molly laid on her shoulder for comfort.

Well . . . Susan blinked the tears of farewell out of her eyes, and went quietly up through the house to her bedroom. There she sat looking at the river through the trees. She felt at peace, but in a way that was new to her. She had no desire to move, to talk, to do anything at all. The devils that had haunted the house, the garden, were not there; but she knew it was because her soul was in Room 19 in Fred's Hotel; she was not really here at all. It was a sensation that should have been frightening: to sit at her own bedroom window, listening to Sophie's rich young voice sing German nursery songs to her child, listening to Mrs. Parkes clatter and move below, and to know that all this had nothing to do with her: she was already out of it.

Later, she made herself go down and say she was home: it was unfair to be here unannounced. She took lunch with Mrs. Parkes, Sophie, Sophie's Italian friend Maria, and her daughter Molly, and felt like a visitor.

A few days later, at bedtime, Matthew said: "Here's your five pounds," and pushed them over at her. Yet he must have known she had not been leaving the house at all.

She shook her head, gave it back to him, and said, in explanation, not in accusation: "As soon as you knew where I was, there was no point."

He nodded, not looking at her. He was turned away from her: thinking, she knew, how best to handle this wife who terrified him.

He said: "I wasn't trying to . . . It's just that I was worried."

"Yes, I know."

"I must confess that I was beginning to wonder . . ."

"You thought I had a lover?"

"Yes, I am afraid I did."

She knew that he wished she had. She sat wondering how to say: "For a year now I've been spending all my days in a very sordid hotel room. It's the place where I'm happy. In fact, without it I don't exist." She heard herself saying this, and understood how terrified he was that she might. So instead she said: "Well, perhaps you're not far wrong."

Probably Matthew would think the hotel proprietor lied: he would want to think so.

"Well," he said, and she could hear his voice spring up, so to speak, with relief, "in that case I must confess I've got a bit of an affair on myself."

She said, detached and interested: "Really? Who is she?" and saw Matthew's startled look because of this reaction.

"It's Phil. Phil Hunt."

She had known Phil Hunt well in the old unmarried days. She was thinking: No, she won't do, she's too neurotic and difficult. She's never been happy yet. Sophie's much better. Well, Matthew will see that himself, as sensible as he is.

This line of thought went on in silence, while she said aloud: "It's no point in telling you about mine, because you don't know him."

Quick, quick, invent, she thought. Remember how you invented all that nonsense for Miss Townsend.

She began slowly, careful not to contradict herself: "His name is Michael" (*Michael What?*)—"Michael Plant." (What a silly name!) "He's rather like you—in looks, I mean." And indeed, she could imagine herself being touched by no one but Matthew himself. "He's a publisher." (Really? Why?) "He's got a wife already and two children."

She brought out this fantasy, proud of herself.

Matthew said: "Are you two thinking of marrying?"

She said, before she could stop herself: "Good God, *no!*"

She realised, if Matthew wanted to marry Phil Hunt, that this was too emphatic, but apparently it was all right, for his voice sounded relieved as he said: "It is a bit impossible to imagine oneself married to anyone else, isn't it?" With which he pulled her to him, so that her head lay on his shoulder. She turned her face into the dark of his flesh, and listened to the blood pounding through her ears saying: I am alone, I am alone, I am alone.

In the morning Susan lay in bed while he dressed.

He had been thinking things out in the night, because now he said: "Susan, why don't we make a foursome?"

Of course, she said to herself, of course he would be bound to say that. If one is sensible, if one is reasonable, if one never allows oneself a base thought or an envious emotion, naturally one says: Let's make a foursome!

"Why not?" she said.

"We could all meet for lunch. I mean, it's ridiculous, you sneaking off to filthy hotels, and me staying late at the office, and all the lies everyone has to tell."

What on earth did I say his name was?—she panicked, then said: "I think it's a good idea, but Michael is away at the moment. When he comes back, though—and I'm sure you two would like each other."

"He's away, is he? So that's why you've been . . ." Her husband put his hand to the knot of his tie in a gesture of male coquetry she would not before have associated with him; and he bent to kiss her cheek with the expression that goes with the words: Oh you naughty little puss! And she felt its answering look, naughty and coy, come onto her face.

Inside she was dissolving in horror at them both, at how far they had both sunk from honesty of emotion.

So now she was saddled with a lover, and he had a mistress! How ordinary, how reassuring, how jolly! And now they would make a foursome of it, and go about to theatres and restaurants. After all, the Rawlings could well afford that sort of thing, and presumably the publisher Michael Plant could afford to do himself and his mistress quite well. No, there was nothing to stop the four of them developing the most intricate relationship of civilised tolerance, all enveloped in a charming afterglow of autumnal passion. Perhaps they would all go off on holidays together? She had known people who did. Or perhaps Matthew would draw the line there? Why should he, though, if he was capable of talking about "foursomes" at all?

She lay in the empty bedroom, listening to the car drive off with Matthew in it, off to work. Then she heard the children clattering off to school to the accompaniment of Sophie's cheerfully ringing voice. She slid down into the hollow of the bed, for shelter against her own irrelevance. And she stretched out her hand to the hollow where her husband's body had lain, but found no comfort there: he was not her husband. She curled herself up in a small tight ball under the clothes: she could stay here all day, all week, indeed, all her life.

But in a few days she must produce Michael Plant, and—but how? She must presumably find some agreeable man prepared to impersonate a publisher called Michael Plant. And in return for which she would—what? Well, for one thing they would make love. The idea made her want to cry with sheer exhaustion. Oh no, she had finished with all that—the proof of it was that the words "make love," or even imagining it, trying hard to revive no more than the pleasures of sensuality, let alone affection, or love, made her want to run away and hide from the sheer effort of the thing. . . . Good Lord, why make love at all? Why make love with anyone? Or if you are going to make love, what does it matter who with? Why shouldn't she simply walk into the street, pick up a man and have a roaring sexual affair with him? Why not? Or even with Fred? What difference did it make?

But she had let herself in for it—an interminable stretch of time with a lover, called Michael, as part of a gallant civilised foursome. Well, she could not, and she would not.

She got up, dressed, went down to find Mrs. Parkes, and asked her for the loan of a pound, since Matthew, she said, had forgotten to leave her money. She exchanged with Mrs. Parkes variations on the theme that husbands are all the same, they don't think, and without saying a word to Sophie, whose voice could be heard upstairs from the telephone, walked to the underground, travelled to South Kensington, changed to the Inner Circle, got out at Paddington, and walked to Fred's Hotel. There she told Fred that she wasn't going on holiday after all, she needed the room. She would have to wait an hour, Fred said. She went to a busy tearoom-cum-restaurant around the corner, and sat watching the people flow in and out the door that kept swinging open and shut, watched them mingle and merge, and separate, felt her being flow into them, into their movement. When the hour was up, she left a half-crown for her pot of tea, and left the place without looking back at it, just as she had left her house, the big, beautiful white house, without another look, but silently dedicating it to Sophie. She returned to Fred, received the key of Number 19, now free, and ascended the grimy stairs slowly, letting floor after floor fall away below her, keeping her eyes lifted, so that floor after floor descended jerkily to her level of vision, and fell away out of sight.

Number 19 was the same. She saw everything with an acute, narrow, checking glance: the cheap shine of the satin spread, which had been replaced carelessly after the two bodies had finished their convulsions under it; a trace of powder on the glass that topped the chest of drawers; an intense green shade in a fold of the curtain. She stood at the window, looking down, watching people pass and pass and pass until her mind went dark from the constant movement. Then she sat in the wicker chair, letting herself go slack. But she had to be careful, because she did not want, today, to be surprised by Fred's knock at five o'clock.

The demons were not here. They had gone forever, because she was buying her freedom from them. She was slipping already into the dark fructifying dream that seemed to caress her inwardly, like the movement of her blood . . . but she had to think about Matthew first. Should she write a letter for the coroner? But what should she say? She would like to leave him with the look on his face she had seen this morning—banal, admittedly, but at least confidently healthy. Well, that was impossible, one did not look like that with a wife dead from suicide. But how to leave him believing she was dying because of a man—because of the fascinating publisher Michael Plant? Oh, how ridiculous! How absurd! How humiliating! But she decided not to trouble about it, simply not to think about the living. If he wanted to believe she had a lover, he would believe it. And he *did* want to believe it. Even when he had found out that there was no publisher in London called Michael Plant, he would think: Oh poor Susan, she was afraid to give me his real name.

And what did it matter whether he married Phil Hunt or Sophie? Though it ought to be Sophie, who was already the mother of those children . . . and what hypocrisy to sit here worrying about the children, when she was going to leave them because she had not got the energy to stay.

She had about four hours. She spent them delightfully, darkly, sweetly, letting herself slide gently, gently, to the edge of the river. Then, with hardly a break in her consciousness, she got up, pushed the thin rug against the door, made sure the windows were tight shut, put two shillings in the meter, and turned on the gas. For the first time since she had been in the room she lay on the hard bed that smelled stale, that smelled of sweat and sex.

She lay on her back on the green satin cover, but her legs were chilly. She got up, found a blanket folded in the bottom of the chest of drawers, and carefully covered her legs with it. She was quite content lying there, listening to the faint soft hiss of the gas that poured into the room, into her lungs, into her brain, as she drifted off into the dark river.

1963

RELATED:

—Lessing, An Interview, p. 1723

JOHN L'HEUREUX
b. 1934

L'Heureux was born in South Hadley, Massachusetts, and received his education at Boston College and Harvard University. He was serving as a Jesuit priest when he published *Picnic in Babylon: A Jesuit Priest's Journal, 1963–1967* (1967). In 1971 L'Heureux left the order and began his career as a novelist and professor of English. He began teaching at Stanford University in 1975 and stayed there until his retirement. His novels include *Desires* (1981), *A Woman Run Mad* (1988), *Comedians* (1990), *An Honorable Profession* (1991), *The Shrine at Altamira* (1992), *The Handmaid of Desire* (1996), *The Miracle* (2002), and *The Medici Boy* (2013). "All of these books," L'Heureux has written, "are a pack of lies intended to entertain and illumine and dismay, and—for myself—to explore the shape of mystery that lies behind the few things I know."

Brief Lives in California

Leonora started out pretty and bright.

"She could be a movie star," her mother said, "but I would never do that to my child. I would never allow a child of mine to be in the limelight. I want Leonora to be just normal."

So Leonora took ballet and tap and piano.

"Perhaps she has other gifts," the dance teacher said. "Perhaps she has a gift for music."

The piano teacher was more to the point. "She has nothing," he said. "And she's driving me crazy."

"You could be a movie star," her mother said.

In junior high Leonora was one of the first to grow breasts; the other girls resented her for that. But in high school her breasts made her popular with the boys, so she didn't care about the girls. She became a cheerleader and after every game she and the other cheerleaders crowded into the booths at Dante's and waited for the team to arrive. Then they all drank Cokes and ate cheeseburgers and grabbed at one another in the booths—nothing serious, just good fun—and made out on the way home.

In November of her senior year Leonora was parked in front of her house in Chuckie's car.

"Why won't you do it?" Chuckie asked. "Everybody does."

"I don't know," she said, miserable. "I want to, but I can't. I just can't."

"Nobody saves themselves for marriage anymore. Is that what you think you're doing?"

"I think I was meant for better things," she said, not really knowing what she meant. "I mean, I get straight A's and B's."

"Ah shit," Chuckie said. "Just put your hand here. Feel this."

"No, I was meant for better things."

"But you've got to start somewhere," Chuckie said. "Hell, I'm captain of the team."

But Leonora was already getting out of the car, feeling chosen, feeling—she searched for the word—exalted. Yes, that was it. She was meant for better things.

In the admissions office at Stanford, Leonora was a floater, somebody who hadn't yet sunk to the bottom but somebody who wouldn't get picked out of the pool unless a real Stanford freshman decided to go to Yale or somewhere. That year a lot of freshmen went to Yale and so Leonora, floating almost to the end, was admitted to Stanford.

"You could be a college professor," her mother said. "Or a famous writer. You could win the Nobel Prize, maybe."

"Dry up," Leonora said. "What do you know about it? You never even went to college."

"Oh baby," she said. "Oh sweetheart, don't be mean to your mother, Leonora. I only want what's best for you. I only want you to be happy."

"Then dry up," Leonora said.

The worst part about Stanford was that they made her take freshman English. She had been among the top thirty in high school and now she was back to writing compositions. At first she had just been a little nasty to the teacher in class, to let him know how she felt about being there. But after she had written the first assigned paper, she decided to go see him and demand an explanation. He gave it to her. He explained that it was a requirement of the university that every student demonstrate a basic competence in expository writing and that she had not, in the qualifying tests, demonstrated that. And then he handed her the corrected paper.

It was covered with little red marks—diction? antecedent? obscure, no no no—and there was a large black C at the bottom of the page.

"You gave me a C," Leonora said. "I've never had a C in my life."

"There's nothing wrong with a C," he said. "It's a perfectly acceptable grade. It's average, maybe even above average."

"You gave me a C," she said and, choking on her tears, ran from his office.

Her next two papers came back with C's on them also, so she knew he was out to get her. His name was Lockhardt and he had written a couple of novels and thought he was hot shit.

Leonora went to the ombudsman and complained that she was being discriminated against. She should not have to take freshman English in the first place, and in the second place Lockhardt was guilty of unprofessional conduct in browbeating her and making her feel inferior.

The ombudsman went to the chairman of the English department who called in Lockhardt and then called in Leonora and finally checked her papers himself. The next day he told Leonora that yes, she would have to take freshman English like all the others, that the grades Professor Lockhardt had given her seemed fair enough, that he was sorry Professor Lockhardt had made her feel inferior. He told Lockhardt for God's sake go easy on the girl, she's half-crazy, and whatever you do don't be alone with her in your office. He told the ombudsman that the problem had been settled to everyone's satisfaction and there was no need to take all this to the provost. So everyone was miserable and satisfied.

Leonora's final grade was a C, all because of that bastard Lockhardt.

Patty Hearst[1] was wrestled, struggling, into the trunk of a car in Berkeley and the next day she was headlines in all the papers. Leonora narrowed her thin eyes and thought, Why couldn't they have taken me?

In her junior year she moved in with Horst Kammer. He was clearly one of the better things that she was meant for. He was very smart and spent a lot of time with the housemaster, so that in Horst she had not only a roommate, she had instant acceptance as well. Horst was too intellectual to be much interested in sex, but he didn't mind occasional sex with Leonora and that was enough for her.

Horst dressed in army fatigues and spent a lot of his time protesting Stanford's investments in South Africa.[2] Leonora protested along with him and they were arrested together during the spring sit-in at Old Union. Leonora felt proud to be involved in something historical, something that mattered. There were over a hundred students arrested and they were each fined nearly two hundred dollars. Leonora's mother sent the money, and with it a note saying, "You're like Vanessa Redgrave or Jane Fonda.[3] You're doing your part."

"God, that woman is hopeless," Leonora said.

Two photographs.

One. Leonora is home from college and all the relatives have come over for dinner. Afterwards somebody snaps an Instamatic of Leonora and her mother and father, sitting on the floor in front of the Christmas tree, surrounded by gifts. The mother and father each have an arm around Leonora and they are smiling directly into the camera. Leonora is smiling too, but she is looking off to the right of the camera, as if at the very last minute she decided the picture is not what she wants; she wants something else.

"She could be a photographer's model," her mother says, examining the picture. "She could be on all the covers."

Two. Leonora has just crested the hill on Campus Drive and is about to make the long clear descent on her new ten-speed bike. She passes two professors who are taking a noon walk, looking like anybody else, just enjoying the California spring. Leonora does not notice them, does not see that one of them is Lockhardt. She sees only the long long hill before her, and she feels

---

1. Granddaughter of newspaper mogul William Randolph Hearst (1863–1951); kidnapped in 1974 by a radical group, the Symbionese Liberation Army, which she subsequently joined, participating in a bank robbery.   **2.** Such protests were common at American universities before South Africa's apartheid regime was dismantled in 1990.   **3.** Actresses famous for political activism.

the warm wind blowing through her hair. She sits high on the seat, no hands, and lifts her arms straight out from the shoulders, surrendering completely to the sun and the wind and being young and pretty, with everything, every wonderful thing ahead of her.

"Look at that girl," Lockhardt says. "God, somebody should photograph that."

In her senior year, her second year with Horst, Leonora was all showered and getting ready to go to a frat party when Horst said, "Come on, let's do it." He wasn't interested in doing it that often, so she said, "I'm all ready for the party, but if you're sure you want to . . ." "I want to," he said. "I'm up for it. Look." And so he chased her from the bedroom into the living room and then back into the bedroom where she collapsed on the bed, laughing and tickling him, and they made love. "Was it wonderful?" she said. "Was it better?" "You're terrific," he said, "you're great. Where the hell is my deodorant?"

At the party everybody drank a lot of beer and tequila sunrises and after a while they got to the subject of how often you ball your roommate. When Horst's turn came, he gave a long and funny speech about the primacy of the intellect and the transitory nature of sexuality. He described the postures you get into and he made them sound new and funny, and he said the real problem is that an hour later you're still hungry for more. He had everybody with him and he was feeling really good about his performance, you could tell, and then he paused and said, anticlimactically, "Let's face it folks, what we're dealing with here is just two mucous membranes rubbing together."

Everybody laughed and applauded and spilled beer. Horst shook his head and smiled sneakily at Leonora.

But then somebody added, "They're sebaceous membranes, actually. Get your membranes straight, Horst."

Everybody laughed even louder and Leonora laughed too and Horst saw her do it.

So he was furious and, on the way home, when Leonora leaned against his side, her head on his shoulder, Horst put his hand on her breast. He felt for the nipple and when he had it firmly between his thumb and forefinger, he twisted it suddenly and violently, pressing down with his thumbnail. Leonora screamed in pain.

"You bitch," he said. "You fucking whore. Why don't you get out of my life? You're just a nothing. You're a noose around my neck."

"No," Leonora said. "No."

Patty Hearst was arrested in an apartment in San Francisco. Her picture appeared in all the papers, laughing like crazy, her fist clenched in the revolutionary salute. She listed her occupation as "urban guerrilla." Leonora was done with all that now that she was done with Horst. And who cared about Patty Hearst anyhow?

Leonora got her diploma in June, but she had to take one more course that summer before she had enough credits to officially graduate. She signed up for creative writing, taught by "staff." But staff turned out to be that bastard

Lockhardt. He didn't seem to remember her, and everybody said he was a really good teacher, and she wanted to write a novel someday, so she decided to give him another chance.

Lockhardt wasn't interested in the things that interested her. She wanted to write something different, but Lockhardt kept talking about the initiating incident and the conflict and the characters. Old stuff. She wrote a story about a shoplifter named Horst, following him from the moment he picked up a tie until the moment he got out of the store, and she wrote it completely from within his mind, what he was thinking. Lockhardt said that the reader had no way of knowing that Horst was stealing, and that she should simply say so. But she explained that she was trying to be more subtle than that. She explained that the reader was supposed to find out Horst was stealing only after the fact, after he was outside the shop, otherwise the story would be just like any other story. They argued back and forth for a long time and then Lockhardt just shrugged his shoulders and said, "Well, I guess you've accomplished what you set out to do. Congratulations." The same thing happened with her next two stories. He didn't like them, so he said the reader couldn't follow them. He couldn't seem to understand that she was trying to do something different.

And then in August she got her grade. A flat C. She went straight from the registrar's office to Lockhardt.

"I have to speak to you," she said.

"Sit down," he said. "Have a seat. But I've got to see the dean in five minutes, so if you're going to need more than that . . ."

"You gave me a C."

"Right. I hope you weren't too disappointed."

"You," she said. "You," but the words wouldn't come out.

"Well, your work was not really extraordinary. I mean, I think you'll agree that it wasn't A work."

"It was C work, I suppose. It was only average."

"There's nothing wrong with being average. Most of us are. Most of our work is average."

She stood up and walked to the door. "What do I care," she said. "I can live with a C." And she slammed the door behind her.

She came back late the next afternoon, she was not sure why, but she knew she had to tell him something. Lockhardt was at his desk, typing, his back to the open door, and Leonora stood there in the corridor watching him. Nobody else was around. She could kill him and no one would know she had done it. If she had a knife or a gun, she could do it. That bastard.

He kept on typing and she just stood there watching him, thinking. And then suddenly he turned around and gave a little shout. "My God, you scared me half to death."

Leonora just stared at him, and he stared back, looking confused or maybe frightened. Then she turned and walked away.

She had not told him what he had done to her, but she would someday. She'd let him know. She'd let him know.

Leonora moved to San Francisco to be on her own. She got a studio apartment with a fire escape that looked down onto the roof of the Jack Tarr Hotel and she applied for jobs at Gump's and at the St. Francis[4]—they asked her "doing what?"—and she shrugged and said to hell with them, she had a Stanford education. But her money ran out eventually and she took a job at Dalton's selling books.

Nothing interesting ever happened at Dalton's, and besides you had to press sixty buttons on the computerized register every time you rang up a sale. The worst part was that everybody kept buying a novel called *The Love Hostage*, written by that bastard Lockhardt. After the first four sales, she refused to sell any more. "I'm on my break," she'd say and make the customer go to another register.

Leonora hated her job, hated the people she worked with, hated books. Somewhere there must be something different happening. Even Patty Hearst, who was a zilch, a nothing, even she had things happen to her. With a name like Patty.

One night when she had worked late, Leonora decided to take a walk. She would make something happen. She moped along Polk Street to Geary and then back, but nothing happened. There were a million or so faggots eyeing each other, but nobody eyed Leonora. She went up to her studio and had a beer and then came down again and set off deliberately in the direction of Golden Gate Park. She knew what she was doing. She could be raped. She could be murdered. Lockhardt used to talk all the time about Joyce Carol Oates[5] characters, how they set up situations for themselves, getting trapped, getting murdered, having their pink and gray brains spilled out on the sidewalk. She liked Joyce Carol Oates. She got as far as the Panhandle[6] and was about to turn around and go home when she realized somebody was following her. For a block, then for a second block. She could hear the heels go faster when she went faster, slow down when she did. Her heart began to beat very fast and she could feel the vein in her forehead pulsing. She wanted it to happen, whatever it was. She turned around suddenly, hands on hips, her head thrown back, ready. At once the man following her crossed the street and headed in the opposite direction. Leonora walked for another hour and then went home. Would nothing happen to her, ever?

The next day she quit her job at Dalton's. They were limiting her. They were worse than Stanford.

The Women's Support Group was having a terrible time with Leonora.

"You've got to open up to your feelings as a woman," they said.

"Men have done this to you. They've refused to let you get in touch with your feelings," they said.

"What is it you feel? What is it you want?" they said.

"I want," Leonora said, "I don't know, but I think I want to die."

"No, what do you really want?" they said.

Leonora bought a gun and a copy of *The Love Hostage* on the same day. There was no connection she could see. She wanted them, that was all. It was time.

---

4. Landmark San Francisco department store and luxury hotel, respectively.   5. American novelist (b. 1938), known for the macabre plots of her many novels.   6. Narrow extension of Golden Gate Park.

She loaded the gun with six bullets and hid it in a Kleenex box under a lot of tissues. It was for protection in this crazy city. It was a safeguard. It was just something nice to have around.

And then she sat down to read *The Love Hostage*. From the first page she was fascinated and appalled. The dust jacket said it was a novel about a young heiress who is kidnapped and brainwashed and all the other stuff that would make you think it was about Patty Hearst. But it wasn't about Patty at all; it was about her, it was about Leonora. Lockhardt had changed things to make it look as if it were about Patty, but she knew he meant her. He described her as an ordinary girl, a normal girl, average in every way. So now he had finally done it. He had killed her.

Leonora put the gun to the side of her head and pulled the trigger. There was an awful noise and the gun leaped from her hand and she felt something wet on the side of her face. She had only grazed her scalp, but inside she was dead just the same.

On the night she was committed to Agnew Mental,[7] Leonora had forced down the beef stew her mother served for dinner and then she had gone back to her room to lie down. Almost at once she threw up into the wastebasket by her bed and then she went to the bathroom and threw up again. Back in her room she put on Phoebe Snow's *Poetry Man*. She played the album through twice, though she was not listening. She was thinking—as she had been for these last three weeks—of Lockhardt and how he had ruined everything and how someday she would let him know. But not now. Someday.

And then, as if it were somebody else doing it, she got up and got dressed and drove to the Stanford campus. She found Lockhardt's house with no trouble at all, and it was only when she had rung the doorbell that she realized she didn't know what she was going to say. But it didn't matter; somehow she would just tell him, calmly, with no tears, that he had degraded her, humiliated her, he had ruined her life.

"Yes?"

"I want to talk to you. I want to tell you something."

"Are you a student of mine? A former student?"

And then she realized that this was not Lockhardt at all, this was a much older man with a beard and glasses. The Lockhardts, it turned out, had moved to San Francisco.

Leonora got back into her car. She was frantic now, she would have to find a phone booth and get his address. She drove to Town and Country Shopping Center and found a booth, but there was no San Francisco directory. She drove to Stanford Shopping Center, and again there was no directory. Never mind. She would drive straight to the city, she would find him, he wouldn't get away from her now. She would let him know.

Traffic on 101 was heavy and it had begun to rain. Leonora passed cars that were already doing sixty. She had to get there. She had to tell him. The words were piling up in her brain, like stones, like bullets. Bullets, yes, she should have brought the gun. She should kill the bastard. A car pulled into her lane and then began slowly to brake. Leonora braked too, but not fast enough. Her

---

7. San Francisco psychiatric hospital.

car fishtailed and, with a short crunching sound, it smashed the side of a Volkswagen. She tore on ahead, though she could see in her mirror that the Volkswagen had ground to a halt, that its lights were blinking on and off. Tough. Yes, she should kill him, she thought, and she pressed her foot harder on the accelerator.

She couldn't find a parking place and so she left the car in a tow zone a block from the Jack Tarr Hotel and ran back in the rain. She found the phone booth, the directory, she opened it to the *L*'s. Lockhardt lived in North Beach.[8] Of course he would, with all that money from *The Love Hostage*. She ran back to her car. A tow truck was backed up to it and a little bald man was kneeling down trying to attach a bar under the front bumper. "No," she shouted. "Stop it. Stop it. Stop." He stood up and looked at her, a screaming woman with her wet hair flying all around, a real crazy. "Okay, lady, okay," he said. "Okay." And then she was in her car again, tearing up Van Ness, running yellow lights, turning right on Pacific. In a few minutes she was there, at Lockhardt's blue and gray Victorian.

Leonora's head was pounding now and her back ached. She wanted to throw up, but there was nothing left to throw up. She wanted a drink. She wanted a pill. She wanted to take Lockhardt by the hair and tear the scalp off him, to expose the pink and gray brain that had written those things, that had done this to her.

She put her finger up to ring the bell, but she was shaking so much she couldn't do it. She began to beat the doorbell with her palm and then with her fist. Still the bell made no sound. She struck the door itself, with her hand, and then with her foot, and then she leaned her entire body against it, beating the door rhythmically with her fist and then with both fists, the rhythm growing faster and faster, the blows harder and harder, until there was blood on her hands and blood on the door and she heard a voice screaming that sounded like her own.

The door opened and Lockhardt, with a book in his hand, stood there look-ing at the young woman whose wet hair was streaked across her face, a face distorted beyond recognition by her hysteria, and he listened to the scream-ing, which made no sense to him until her voice broke and he could make out the words. "I am not average," she sobbed. "I am not average. I am not average."

It was nearly a half-hour before the orderlies came and took her away.

The world had gone crazy, that's just the way it was. Leonora's mother stared at the television where for days she had been watching pictures of the 911 corpses in Guyana.[9] They had taken poison mixed with grape Kool-Aid and in five minutes they were dead. Every one of them. And Patty Hearst had been refused parole. And so had Charles Manson.[1] And her own Leonora in that loony bin. Leonora could have been something once. She could have been . . . but nothing came to mind. It was Lockhardt's fault, Leonora was right. It was all Lockhardt's fault. Leonora's mother turned up the volume on

---

8. San Francisco neighborhood.   9. Reference to 1978 incident in which the mostly American mem-bers of the Peoples Temple committed mass suicide at Jonestown, the cult's settlement in South America.   1. Cult leader and convicted mass-murderer (b. 1934).

the TV. And now somebody had shot Mayor Moscone and that Harvey Milk.[2] It was the way you expressed yourself today, you shot somebody.

She thought of the gun hidden in the Kleenex box and suddenly it was all clear to her. She got in the car and drove to North Beach. She had no trouble finding Lockhardt's house; she had been there three times since Leonora was taken away. She had just parked opposite the house and sat there and watched. But this time she went up the steep wooden stairs and rang the bell. She rang again and as she was about to ring a third time Lockhardt opened the door, laughing. She could hear other people laughing too; he must be having a party. Over his left shoulder, in the entrance hall, she could see a chandelier, a deep green wall, the corner of a picture. She couldn't make out what it was a picture of, but she could see that he was rich. He had everything. "Yes?" he said, and there was more laughter from that other room. "Yes?" he said again.

"Leonora," she said. "She could have been something."

And then she took the gun from her purse and leveled it at his chest. There were three loud shots and when his body slumped to the floor, Leonora's mother could see that the painting on the green wall was one of those new-fangled things with little blocks of color, all different sizes, that really aren't the picture of anything.

1981

---

2. On November 27, 1978, San Francisco mayor George Moscone and city supervisor Harvey Milk were assassinated by former city supervisor Dan White.

SANDRA TSING LOH
b. 1962

Loh was born in Los Angeles, California, the daughter of a Chinese immigrant father and a German-American mother. She was educated at the California Institute of Technology and the University of Southern California. Her career as a performance artist includes music and the comic monologues that have launched her as an author and radio personality. She published *Depth Takes a Holiday: Essays from Lesser Los Angeles* in 1996 and both *Aliens in America* and the novel *If You Lived Here, You'd Be Home by Now* in 1997. Her most recent books are *A Year in Van Nuys* (2002), featuring more of her acerbic wit, *Mother on Fire* (2008), and *The Madwoman in the Volvo* (2014). She received a Pushcart Prize in Fiction in 1995.

My Father's Chinese Wives

My father doesn't want to alarm us. But then again, it would not be fair to hide anything either. The fact is, at 70, he is going to try and get married again. This time to a Chinese wife. He thinks this would be more suitable than to someone American, given his advanced age.

He has written his family in Shanghai, and is awaiting response. He is hoping to be married within six months.

Let us unpeel this news one layer at a time.

Question: At this point, is my father even what one would consider marriageable?

At age 70, my father—a retired Chinese aerospace engineer—is starting to look more and more like somebody's gardener. His feet shuffle along the patio in their broken sandals. He stoops to pull out one or two stray weeds, coughing phlegmatically. He wears a hideous old crew-neck tennis sweater. Later, he sits in a rattan chair and eats leathery green vegetables in brown sauce, his old eyes slitted wearily.

He is the sort of person one would refer to as "Old Dragon Whiskers." And not just because it is a picturesque Oriental way of speaking.

"I am old now," he started saying, about 10 years after my mother had died of cancer. "I'm just your crazy old Chinese father." He would rock backwards in his chair and sigh. "I am an old, old man . . ."

At times he almost seems to be over-acting this lizardy old part. He milks it. After all, he still does the same vigorous exercise regime—45 minutes of pull-ups, something that looks like the twist and much bellowing—he did 10 years ago. This always performed on the most public beaches possible, in his favorite Speedo—one he found in a dumpster.

"Crazy old Chinese father" is, in truth, a code word, a rationalization for the fact that my father has always had a problem . . . spending money. Why buy a briefcase to carry to work, when an empty Frosted Flakes Cereal box will do? Papers slip down neatly inside, and pens can be clipped conveniently on either side.

Why buy Bounty Paper Towels when, at work, he can just walk down the hall to the washroom, open the dispenser, and lift out a stack? They're free—he can bring home as many as we want!

If you've worn the same sweater for so many years that the elbows wear out, turn it around! Get another decade out of it! Which is why to this day, my father wears only crew neck, not V-neck sweaters . . .

Why drive the car to work when you can take the so-convenient RTD bus?[1] More time to read interesting scientific papers . . . and here they are, in my empty Frosted Flakes box!

"Terrific!" is my older sister Kaitlin's response when I phone her with the news. Bear in mind that Kaitlin has not seen my father since the mid-'80s, preferring to nurse her bad memories of him independently, via a therapist. She allows herself a laugh, laying aside her customary dull hostility for a moment of more jocular hostility. "So who does he think would want to marry *him*?"

"Someone Chinese," I answer.

"Oh good!" she exclaims. "That narrows down the field . . . to what? Half a billion? Nah, as always, he's doing this to punish us.

"Think about it," Kaitlin continues with her usual chilling logic. "He marries a German woman the first time around. It's a disaster. You and I represent that. Because he's passive aggressive and he's cheap. But no, to him, it's that rebellious Aryan strain that's the problem.

"You take an Asian immigrant just off the boat, on the other hand. This is a person who has just fled a Communist government and a horrible life working in a bicycle factory for 10 cents a month and no public sanitation and repeated floggings every hour on the hour. After that, living with our father might seem like just another bizarre interlude. It could happen."

Kaitlin scores some compelling points, but nonetheless . . .

I'm bothered for a different reason . . .

Perhaps it is because in describing the potential new wife, he has used only that one adjective: *Chinese*. He has not said: "I'm looking for a smart wife," or even "a fat wife," he has picked "Chinese." It is meant to stand for so much.

Asian. Asian women. Asian *ladies*.

I think back to a college writing workshop I once attended. (No credit and perhaps that was appropriate.) It was long before my current "administrative assistant" job at Swanson Films. (Makers of the 10-minute instructional video "Laughterobics! Featuring Meredith Baxter Birney," among other fine titles.)

Anyway, the workshop contained 13 hysterical women—and one Fred. Fred was a wealthy Caucasian sixtysomething urologist; he was always serene and

1. Southern California Rapid Transit District, serving the Los Angeles area.

beautifully dressed and insistent upon holding the door open for me "because you're such a lovely lady." I always wore jeans and a USC sweatshirt, sometimes even sweatpants, so at first I did not know what he meant.

We women, on the other hand, were a wildly mixed group—writing anything from wintery Ann Beattie–esque snippets to sci-fi romance/porn novels ("She would be King Zenothar's concubine, whether she liked it or not"). We attacked each other's writing accordingly. People were bursting into tears every week, then making up by emotionally sharing stories about mutual eating disorders.

But there was one moment when all 13 women were of like minds. It was that moment when Fred would enter the classroom, laden with xeroxes, blushing shyly as a new bride. We would all look at each other as if to say, "Oh my God, Fred has brought in work *again*."

As though springing from a murky bottomless well, each week new chapters would appear from this semi-epistolary novel Fred was penning about an elderly doctor named Fred who goes on sabbatical for a year to Japan and there finds love with a 23-year-old Japanese medical student named Aku who smells of cherry blossoms.

There were many awkward scenes in which Fred and Aku were exploring each other's bodies as they lay—as far as I could gather—upon the bare floor, only a *tatami*[2] mat for comfort. (Fred would always italicize the Japanese words, as if to separate and somehow protect them from other, lesser words.) But it was all beautifully pure and unlike the urban squalor we find in America— the rock music, the drugs, the uncouth teenagers.

Anyway, I recall the one line that I have never since been able to blot from my mind. I cannot think of it without a bit of a shiver. Nor the way he read it, in that hoarse tremulous voice . . .

"I put my hand in hers, and her little fingers opened like the petals of a moist flower."

It is a month later and, as in a dream, I sit at the worn formica family dining table with my father, photos and letters spread before us.

Since my father has written to Shanghai, the mail has come pouring in. I have to face the fact that my father is, well, hot. "You see?" he says. "Seven women have written! Ha!" He beams, his gold molar glinting. He is drinking steaming green tea from a beaker, which he handles with a Beauty and the Beast potholder.

Remarkably, my father doesn't make the least effort to mask his delight, no matter how inappropriate. He is old now. *He can do whatever the hell he wants,* is how I now understand it. With a sigh, I turn to the photos. In spite of myself, I am wowed!

Tzau Pa, Ling Ling, Sui Pai, Chong Zhou . . . "28, administrative assistant," "47, owner of a seamstress business," "39, freelance beautician." The words jump off the pages, both in English and Chinese translations. These women are dynamos, achievers, with black curly hair, in turtlenecks, jauntily riding bicycles, seated squarely on cannons before military museums, standing proudly with three grown daughters.

---

2. A thick woven straw mat used in Japanese houses as a floor covering.

One thing unites them: they're all ready to leap off the mainland at the drop of a hat.

And don't think their careers and hobbies are going to keep them from being terrific wives. Quite the opposite. Several already have excellent experience, including one who's been married twice already. The seamstress has sent him two shorts and several pairs of socks; there is much talk of seven-course meals and ironing and terrific expertise in gardening.

Super-achievement is a major theme that applies to all. And the biggest star of all is my father. He clears his throat and gleefully reads from a letter by one Liu Tzun:

> Dr. Chow, your family has told me of your great scientific genius and of your many awards. I respect academic scholarship very highly, and would be honored to meet you on your next visit.

"You see?" my father chuckles. "They have a lot of respect for me in China. When I go there, they treat me like President Bush! Free meals, free drinks . . . I don't pay for anything!"

"He had his chance. He got married once, for 25 years. He was a terrible husband and a worse father."

Kaitlin is weighing in. All jokes are off. Her fury blazes away, further aggravated by the fact that she is going through a divorce and hates her $50,000 a year job. Her monthly Nordstrom bills are astronomical. MCI is positively crackling.

"He's a single man," I say. "Mum's been gone for 12 years now—"

"And now he gets a second try—just like that?" Kaitlin exclaims. "Clean slate? Start right over? Buy a wife? It makes me sick. He is totally unqualified to sustain a marriage. A family structure of any kind collapses around him. Do you even remember one happy Christmas?"

Twinkling lights and tinsel suddenly swirl before me and looking deeper, through green foliage, I see my mother looking beautiful and crisp in lipstick and pearls, her wavy auburn hair done . . . except for the fact that she is hysterical, and my father, his face a mask of disgust so extreme it is almost parodic, is holding his overpriced new V-necked tennis sweater from Saks out in front of him like it is a dead animal—

"I try to block it out," is what I say.

"Well I was six years older than you so I can't." Kaitlin's pain is raw. "Why does he deserve to be happy . . . now? He made Mama miserable in her lifetime—he was so cheap! I think she was almost glad to go as soon as she did! A $70 dress, leaving the heater on overnight, too much spent on a nice steak dinner—he could never let anything go! He could never just let it go! He just could . . . not . . . let . . . things . . . go!"

Meanwhile . . .

On its own gentle time clock, unsullied by the raging doubts of his two daughters . . .

My father's project bursts into flower.

And 47-year-old Liu—the writer of the magic letter—is the lucky winner! Within three months, she is flown to Los Angeles. She and my father are married a week later.

I do not get to meet her right away, but my father fills me in on the stats. And I have to confess, I'm a little surprised at how modern she is, how urban. Liu is a divorcee with, well, with ambitions in the entertainment business. Although she speaks no English, she seems to be an expert on American culture. The fact that Los Angeles is near Hollywood has not escaped her. This is made clear to me one Sunday evening, three weeks later, via telephone.

"I know you have friends in the entertainment business," my father declares. He has never fully grasped the fact that I am a typist and that Swanson Films' clients include such Oscar contenders as Kraft Foods and Motorola.

"Aside from having knitted me a new sweater and playing the piano," my father continues, "you should know that Liu is an excellent singer—" Turning away from the phone, he and his new wife exchange a series of staccato reports in Mandarin, which mean nothing to me.

"I'm sure that Liu is quite accomplished," I reply, "it's just that—"

"Oh . . . she's terr-ific!" my father exclaims, shocked that I may be calling Liu's musical talent into question. "You want to hear her sing? Here, here, I will put her on the phone right now . . ."

Creeping into my father's voice is a tremulous note that is sickeningly familiar. How many times had I heard it during my childhood as I was being pushed towards the piano, kicking and screaming? How many times—

But that was 20 years ago. I gulp terror back down. I live in my own apartment now, full of director's chairs, potted fici,[3] and Matisse posters. I will be fine. My father has moved on to a totally new pushee . . .

Who picks up the phone, sighs—then bursts out triumphantly:

"Nee-ee hoo-oo man, tieh-hen see bau-hau jioo . . . !"

I have left you and taken the Toyota, Dr. Chow—so there!

Five weeks later, Liu just packs up her suitcase, makes some sandwiches, and takes off in the family Toyota. She leaves her note on the same formica table at which she'd first won his heart.

My father is in shock. Then again, he is philosophical.

"Liu—she had a lot of problems. She said she had no one to talk to. There were no other Chinese people in Tarzana. She wanted me to give her gifts. She was bored. You know I don't like to go out at night. But I tell her, 'Go! See your friends in Chinatown.' But Liu does not want to take the bus. She wants to drive! But you know me, your cheap father. I don't want to pay her insurance. That Liu—she was a very bad driver—"

"Ha!" is Kaitlin's only comment.

Summer turns to fall in Southern California, causing the palm trees to sway a bit. The divorce is soon final, Liu's settlement including $10,000, the microwave and the Toyota.

---

3. Fig trees (species: *Ficus*).

Never one to dwell, my father has picked a new bride: Zhou Ping, 37, home-maker from Qang-Zhou province. I groan.

"But no . . . Zhou Ping is very good," my father insists. He has had several phone conversations with her. "And she comes very highly recommended, not, I have to say, like Liu. Liu was bad, that one. Zhou Ping is sensible and hardworking. She has had a tough life. Boy! She worked in a coal mine in Manchuria until she was 25. The winters there were very, very bitter! She had to make her own shoes and clothing. Then she worked on a farming collec-tive, where she raised cattle and grew many different kinds of crops—by herself!"

"I'm sure she's going to fit in really well in Los Angeles," I say.

Zhou Ping is indeed a different sort. The news, to my astonishment, comes from Kaitlin. "I received . . ." her voice trails off, the very words seeming to elude her. "A *birthday card*. From Papa . . . and *Zhou Ping*."

My sister continues in a kind of trance of matter-of-factness, as if describ-ing some curious archaeological artifact. "Let's see, on the front is a picture with flowers on it. It's from Hallmark. Inside is gold lettering, cursive, that says, 'Happy Birthday!' At the bottom, in red pen, it says . . . 'Love, Zhou Ping and *your* Dad.'"

"Your 'Dad'?"

"I think Zhou Ping put him up to this. The envelope is not addressed in his hand-writing. Nonetheless . . ." Kaitlin thinks it over, concurs with herself. "Yes. Yes. I believe this is the first birthday card I've ever received from him in my life. The first. It's totally bizarre."

A week later, Kaitlin receives birthday gifts in the mail: a sweater hand-knit by Zhou Ping, and a box of "mooncakes." She is flipping out. "Oh no," she worries, "Now I really have to call and thank her. I mean, the poor woman probably has no friends in America. Who knows what he's having her do? We may be her only link to society!"

Kaitlin finally does call, managing to catch Zhou Ping when my father is on the beach doing his exercises (which he always does at 11 and at 3). Although Zhou Ping's English is very broken, she somehow convinces Kaitlin to fly down for a visit.

It will be Kaitlin's first trip home since our mother's passing. And my first meeting of either of my step-mothers.

I pull up the familiar driveway in my Geo. Neither Kaitlin nor I say any-thing. We peer out the windows.

The yard doesn't look too bad. There are new sprinklers, and a kind of irrigation system made by a network of ingenuously placed rain gutters. Soil has been turned, and thoughtfully. Cypresses have been trimmed. Enormous bundles of weeds flank the driveway, as if for some momentous occasion.

We ring the doorbell. Neither of us has had keys to the house in years.

The door opens. A short, somewhat plump Chinese woman, in round glasses and a perfect bowl haircut, beams at us. She is wearing a bright yellow

"I hate housework!" apron that my mother was once given as a gag gift—and I think never wore.

"Kat-lin! Jen-na!" she exclaims in what seems like authentic joy, embracing us. She is laughing and almost crying with emotion.

In spite of myself, giggles begin to well up from inside me as if from a spring. I can't help it: I feel warm and euphoric. Authentic joy is contagious. Who cares who this woman is: no one has been this happy to see me in ages.

"Wel-come home," Zhou Ping says, with careful emphasis. She turns to Kaitlin, a shadow falling over her face. "I am glad you finally come home to see your Daddy," she says in a low, sorrowful voice. She looks over her shoulder. "He old now."

Then, as if exhausted by that effort, Zhou Ping collapses into giggles. I sneak a glance over at Kaitlin, whose expression seems to be straining somewhere between joy and nausea. Pleasantries lunge out of my mouth: "It's nice to finally meet you!" "How do you like America?" "I've heard so much about your cooking!"

My father materializes behind a potted plant. He is wearing a new sweater and oddly formal dress pants. His gaze hovers somewhere near the floor.

"Hul-lo," he declares, attempting a smile. "Long time no see!" he exclaims, not making eye contact, but in Kaitlin's general direction.

"Yes!" Kaitlin exclaims back, defiant, a kind of winged Amazon in perfect beige Anne Klein II leisurewear. "It certainly is!"

My father stands stiffly.

Kaitlin blazes.

"It's good to see you!" he finally concludes, as though this were something he learned in English class.

Feeling, perhaps, that we should all leave well enough alone, the Chow family, such as we are, moves on through the house. It is ablaze with color—the sort of eye-popping combinations one associates with Thai restaurants and Hindu shrines. There are big purple couches, peach rugs, a shiny brass trellis and creeping charlies everywhere.

All this redecorating came at no great expense, though. "See this rug?" my father says proudly, while Zhou Ping giggles. "She found it in a dumpster. They were going to throw it away!" "Throw it away!" she exclaims. "See? It very nice."

Over their heads, Kaitlin silently mouths one word to me: "Help."

Beyond, the formica dining room table is set. Oddly. There are little rice bowls, chopsticks, and a sheet of plain white paper at each place setting. It is good to know some definite event has been planned. Kaitlin, my father and I are so unaccustomed to being in a room together that any kind of definite agenda—aka: "We'll eat dinner, and then we'll leave"—is comforting.

My father goes off to put some music on his new CD player. "That bad Liu made me buy it!" he explains. "But it's nice." Zhou Ping bustles into the kitchen. "Dinner ready—in five minute!" she declares.

Kaitlin waits a beat, then pulls me aside into the bathroom and slams the door.

"This is so weird!" she hisses.

We have not stood together in this bathroom for some 15 years. It seems different. I notice that the wallpaper is faded, the towels are new—but no, it's something else. On one wall is my mother's framed reproduction of the brown Da Vinci etching called "Praying Hands" which she had always kept in her sewing room. Right next to it, in shocking juxtaposition, is a green, red, blue and yellow "Bank of Canton" calendar from which a zaftig[4] Asian female chortles.

"I can't go through with this!" Kaitlin continues in stage whisper. "It's too weird! There are so many memories here, and not good ones!"

And like debris from a hurricane, the words tumble out:

"I go by the kitchen and all I can see is me standing before the oven clock at age five with tears in my eyes. He is yelling: 'What time is it? The little hand is most of the way to four and the big hand is on the eight! It was 3:18 twenty-two minutes ago—so what time is it now? What's eighteen plus twenty-two? Come on—you can do it in your head! Come on! Come on!'

"I go by the dining room and I see him hurling my Nancy Drew books across the floor. They slam against the wall and I huddle against Mum, screaming. 'Why do you waste your time on this when your algebra homework isn't finished? You . . . good for nothing! You're nothing, nothing—you'll never amount to anything!'

"I go by the bedroom—"

"Please—" I have this sickening feeling like I'm going to cry, that I'm just going to lose it. I want to just sit down in the middle of the floor and roll myself into a ball. But I can't. Kaitlin's rage is like something uncontainable, a dreadful natural force, and I am the gatekeeper. I feel if I open the door, it will rush out and destroy the house and everyone in it. "Please," is what I end up whispering. "Please. Let's just eat. We'll be done in a hour. Then we can go home. I promise. You won't have to do this again for another 10 years—or maybe ever."

At dinner, endless plates of food twirl their way out of the kitchen, Zhou Ping practically dancing underneath. Spinach, teriyaki-ish chicken, shrimp, some kind of egg thing with peas, dumplings packed with little pillows of pork.

And amazingly, there is no want of conversational material. Photos from Shanghai are being pulled out of envelopes and passed around, of her family, his family . . .

I do recognize three or four Chinese relatives—a cousin, an aunt, a grand-uncle? Their names are impossible for me to remember. We had met them in China during our last trip as a family. I was 15; it was right before our mother started to get sick.

Shanghai is a distant, confused memory for me, of ringing bicycle bells and laundry lines hanging from buildings. What I do remember is how curious my father's family had seemed about Kaitlin and me, his odd American experiment, oohing over our height and touching our auburn hair. There were many smiles but no intelligible conversation, at least to our ears. We probably won't see any of these people again before we die.

---

4. Juicy, succulent (Yiddish); pleasantly plump.

Zhou Ping, though, is determined to push through, to forge a bridge between us. She plunges ahead with her bad English, my father almost absentmindedly correcting her.

Their lives are abuzz with activity. Zhou Ping is taking piano lessons at the community college. My father is learning Italian and French off the Learning Channel—he sets his alarm for four in the morning. "So early!" Zhou Ping hoots. They listen to Karl Haas' "Listening to Good Music" on the classical station at 10. "Mot-sart—he very nice!" They have joined the Bahais, a local quasi-religious group. "I must cook food all the time!" My father suddenly puts his spoon down. He is chewing slowly, a frown growing.

"This meat . . ." he shakes his head, "is very greasy."

He turns to Zhou Ping and the lines at both sides of his mouth deepen. His eyes cloud. He says something to her in Chinese, with a certain sharp cadence that makes my spine stiffen . . .

Zhou Ping's face goes blank for a moment. Her eyes grow big. My stomach turns to ice.

How will she respond? By throwing her napkin down, bursting into tears, running from the room? Will she knock the table over, plates sliding after each other, sauces spilling, crockery breaking? Will we hear the car engine turn over as she drives off into the night, to leave us frightened and panicked?

It is none of these things.

Zhou Ping's head tilts back, her eyes crinkle . . .

And laughter pours out of her, peal after peal after peal. It is a big laugh, an enormous laugh, the laugh of a woman who has birthed calves and hoed crops and seen harsh winters decimate countrysides. Pointing to our father, Zhou Ping turns to us with large glittering eyes and says words which sound incredible to our ears:

"Your Papa—he so funny!"

My jaw drops. No one has ever laughed out loud at this table, ever. We laughed behind closed doors, in our bedrooms, in the bathroom, never before my father. We laughed sometimes with my mother, on those glorious days when he would be off on a trip—

But Kaitlin is not laughing. She is trembling; her face is turning red.

"Why were you always so angry?" Kaitlin cries out in a strangled voice. It is the question that she has waited 30 years to ask. "Why were you so angry?"

There is shocked silence. My father looks weary and embarrassed. He smiles wanly and shrugs his thin shoulders.

"No really," Kaitlin insists. "All those years. With Mama. Why?"

"I don't know," my father murmurs. "People get angry."

And I know, in that moment, that he doesn't have an answer. He literally doesn't. It's as if anger was this chemical which reacted on him for 20 years. Who knows why, but like some kind of spirit, it has left him now. The rage is spent. He is old now. He is old.

Dusk has fallen, and long shadows fall across the worn parquet floor of the dining room. After a moment of silence, my father asks Zhou Ping to sing a song. The hausfrau from Qang Zhou opens her mouth and with an odd dignity, sings simply and slowly. My father translates.

From the four corners of the earth
My lover comes to me
Playing the lute
Like the wind over the water

He recites the words without embarrassment, almost without emotion.
And why shouldn't he? The song has nothing to do with him personally: it is
from some old Chinese fable. It has to do with missing someone, something,
that perhaps one can't even define any more.

As Zhou Ping sings, everyone longs for home. But what home? Zhou Ping—
for her bitter winters? My father—for the Shanghai he left 40 years ago? Kaitlin and I? We are even sitting in our home, and we long for it.

1995

BERNARD MALAMUD
1914–1986

Malamud (1914–1986) was born in Brooklyn, New York. He was educated at City College of New York and Columbia University before teaching for several years at Oregon State University. He was, from 1961 until his death, a professor at Bennington College. From the 1950s on, he was recognized as one of the best of the writers who have portrayed Jewish life and sensibility in American fiction, affirming through his special subject matter the general human capacity to resist social and political afflictions. His numerous honors included two National Book Awards and the Pulitzer Prize. His novels are *The Natural* (1952), *The Assistant* (1957), *A New Life* (1961), *The Fixer* (1966), *The Tenants* (1971), *Dubin's Lives* (1979), and *God's Grace* (1982). His stories have been collected in *The Magic Barrel* (1958), *Idiots First* (1963), *Pictures of Fidelman* (1969), *Rembrandt's Hat* (1973), *The People* (1989), and *The Complete Stories* (1997).

Angel Levine

Manischevitz, a tailor, in his fifty-first year suffered many reverses and indignities. Previously a man of comfortable means, he overnight lost all he had, when his establishment caught fire and, after a metal container of cleaning fluid exploded, burned to the ground. Although Manischevitz was insured against fire, damage suits by two customers who had been hurt in the flames deprived him of every penny he had collected. At almost the same time, his son, of much promise, was killed in the war, and his daughter, without so much as a word of warning, married a lout and disappeared with him as off the face of the earth. Thereafter Manischevitz was victimized by excruciating backaches and found himself unable to work even as a presser—the only kind of work available to him—for more than an hour or two daily, because beyond that the pain from standing became maddening. His Fanny, a good wife and mother, who had taken in washing and sewing, began before his eyes to waste away. Suffering shortness of breath, she at last became seriously ill and took to her bed. The doctor, a former customer of Manischevitz, who out of pity treated them, at first had difficulty diagnosing her ailment but later put it down as hardening of the arteries at an advanced stage. He took Manischevitz aside, prescribed complete rest for her, and in whispers gave him to know there was little hope.

Throughout his trials Manischevitz had remained somewhat stoic, almost unbelieving that all this had descended upon his head, as if it were happening, let us say, to an acquaintance or some distant relative; it was in sheer quantity of woe incomprehensible. It was also ridiculous, unjust, and because he had always been a religious man, it was in a way an affront to God. Manischevitz believed this in all his suffering. When his burden had grown too crushingly heavy to be borne he prayed in his chair with shut hollow eyes: "My dear God, sweetheart, did I deserve that this should happen to me?" Then recognizing the worthlessness of it, he put aside the complaint and prayed humbly for assistance: "Give Fanny back her health, and to me for myself that I shouldn't feel pain in every step. Help now or tomorrow is too late. This I don't have to tell you." And Manischevitz wept.

Manischevitz's flat, which he had moved into after the disastrous fire, was a meager one, furnished with a few sticks of chairs, a table, and bed, in one of the poorer sections of the city. There were three rooms: a small, poorly-papered living room; an apology for a kitchen, with a wooden icebox; and the comparatively large bedroom where Fanny lay in a sagging secondhand bed, gasping for breath. The bedroom was the warmest room of the house and it was here, after his outburst to God, that Manischevitz, by the light of two small bulbs overhead, sat reading his Jewish newspaper. He was not truly reading, because his thoughts were everywhere; however the print offered a convenient resting place for his eyes, and a word or two, when he permitted himself to comprehend them, had the momentary effect of helping him forget his troubles. After a short while he discovered, to his surprise, that he was actively scanning the news, searching for an item of great interest to him. Exactly what he thought he would read he couldn't say—until he realized, with some astonishment, that he was expecting to discover something about himself. Manischevitz put his paper down and looked up with the distinct impression that someone had entered the apartment, though he could not remember having heard the sound of the door opening. He looked around: the room was very still, Fanny sleeping, for once, quietly. Half-frightened, he watched her until he was satisfied she wasn't dead; then, still disturbed by the thought of an unannounced visitor, he stumbled into the living room and there had the shock of his life, for at the table sat a Negro reading a newspaper he had folded up to fit into one hand.

"What do you want here?" Manischevitz asked in fright.

The Negro put down the paper and glanced up with a gentle expression. "Good evening." He seemed not to be sure of himself, as if he had got into the wrong house. He was a large man, bonily built, with a heavy head covered by a hard derby, which he made no attempt to remove. His eyes seemed sad, but his lips, above which he wore a slight mustache, sought to smile; he was not otherwise prepossessing. The cuffs of his sleeves, Manischevitz noted, were frayed to the lining and the dark suit was badly fitted. He had very large feet. Recovering from his fright, Manischevitz guessed he had left the door open and was being visited by a case worker from the Welfare Department—some came at night—for he had recently applied for relief. Therefore he lowered himself into a chair opposite the Negro, trying, before the man's uncertain smile, to feel comfortable. The former tailor sat stiffly but patiently at the table, waiting for the investigator to take out his pad and pencil and begin asking questions; but before long he became convinced the man intended to do nothing of the sort.

"Who are you?" Manischevitz at last asked uneasily.

"If I may, insofar as one is able to, identify myself, I bear the name of Alexander Levine."

In spite of all his troubles Manischevitz felt a smile growing on his lips. "You said Levine?" he politely inquired.

The Negro nodded. "That is exactly right."

Carrying the jest farther, Manischevitz asked, "You are maybe Jewish?"

"All my life I was, willingly."

The tailor hesitated. He had heard of black Jews but had never met one. It gave an unusual sensation.

Recognizing in afterthought something odd about the tense of Levine's remark, he said doubtfully, "You ain't Jewish anymore?"

Levine at this point removed his hat, revealing a very white part in his black hair, but quickly replaced it. He replied, "I have recently been disincarnated into an angel. As such, I offer you my humble assistance, if to offer is within my province and ability—in the best sense." He lowered his eyes in apology. "Which calls for added explanation: I am what I am granted to be, and at present the completion is in the future."

"What kind of angel is this?" Manischevitz gravely asked.

"A bona fide angel of God, within prescribed limitations," answered Levine, "not to be confused with the members of any particular sect, order, or organization here on earth operating under a similar name."

Manischevitz was thoroughly disturbed. He had been expecting something but not this. What sort of mockery was it—provided Levine was an angel—of a faithful servant who had from childhood lived in the synagogues, always concerned with the word of God?

To test Levine he asked, "Then where are your wings?"

The Negro blushed as well as he was able. Manischevitz understood this from his changed expression. "Under certain circumstances we lose privileges and prerogatives upon returning to earth, no matter for what purpose, or endeavoring to assist whosoever."

"So tell me," Manischevitz said triumphantly, "how did you get here?"

"I was transmitted."

Still troubled, the tailor said, "If you are a Jew, say the blessing for bread."

Levine recited it in sonorous Hebrew.

Although moved by the familiar words Manischevitz still felt doubt that he was dealing with an angel.

"If you are an angel," he demanded somewhat angrily, "give me the proof."

Levine wet his lips. "Frankly, I cannot perform either miracles or near miracles, due to the fact that I am in a condition of probation. How long that will persist or even consist, I admit, depends on the outcome."

Manischevitz racked his brains for some means of causing Levine positively to reveal his true identity, when the Negro spoke again:

"It was given me to understand that both your wife and you require assistance of a salubrious nature?"

The tailor could not rid himself of the feeling that he was the butt of a jokester. Is this what a Jewish angel looks like? he asked himself. This I am not convinced.

He asked a last question. "So if God sends to me an angel, why a black? Why not a white that there are so many of them?"

"It was my turn to go next," Levine explained.

Manischevitz could not be persuaded. "I think you are a faker."

Levine slowly rose. His eyes showed disappointment and worry. "Mr. Manischevitz," he said tonelessly, "if you should desire me to be of assistance to you any time in the near future, or possibly before, I can be found"—he glanced at his fingernails—"in Harlem."

He was by then gone.

The next day Manischevitz felt some relief from his backache and was able to work four hours at pressing. The day after, he put in six hours; and the third day four again. Fanny sat up a little and asked for some halvah[1] to suck. But on the fourth day the stabbing, breaking ache afflicted his back, and Fanny again lay supine, breathing with blue-lipped difficulty.

Manischevitz was profoundly disappointed at the return of his active pain and suffering. He had hoped for a longer interval of easement, long enough to have some thought other than of himself and his troubles. Day by day, hour by hour, minute after minute, he lived in pain, pain his only memory, questioning the necessity of it, inveighing against it, also, though with affection, against God. Why *so much*, Gottenyu?[2] If He wanted to teach His servant a lesson for some reason, some cause—the nature of His nature—to teach him, say, for reasons of his weakness, his pride, perhaps, during his years of prosperity, his frequent neglect of God—to give him a little lesson, why then any of the tragedies that had happened to him, any *one* would have sufficed to chasten him. But *all together*—the loss of both his children, his means of livelihood, Fanny's health and his—that was too much to ask one frail-boned man to endure. Who, after all, was Manischevitz that he had been given so much to suffer? A tailor. Certainly not a man of talent. Upon him suffering was largely wasted. It went nowhere, into nothing: into more suffering. His pain did not earn him bread, nor fill the cracks in the wall, nor lift, in the middle of the night, the kitchen table; only lay upon him, sleepless, so sharply, oppressively, that he could many times have cried out yet not heard himself through this thickness of misery.

In this mood he gave no thought to Mr. Alexander Levine, but at moments when the pain waivered, slightly diminishing, he sometimes wondered if he had been mistaken to dismiss him. A black Jew and angel to boot—very hard to believe, but suppose he *had* been sent to succor him, and he, Manischevitz, was in his blindness too blind to comprehend? It was this thought that put him on the knife-point of agony.

Therefore the tailor, after much self-questioning and continuing doubt, decided he would seek the self-styled angel in Harlem. Of course he had great difficulty, because he had not asked for specific directions, and movement was tedious to him. The subway took him to 116th Street, and from there he wandered in the dark world. It was vast and its lights lit nothing. Everywhere were shadows, often moving. Manischevitz hobbled along with the aid of a cane, and not knowing where to seek in the blackened tenement buildings, looked fruitlessly through store windows. In the stores he saw people and *everybody* was black. It was an amazing thing to observe. When he was too tired, too unhappy to go farther, Manischevitz stopped in front of a tailor's store. Out

---

1. Flaky confection of crushed sesame seeds and honey.   **2.** Dear God (Yiddish).

of familiarity with the appearance of it, with some sadness he entered. The tailor, an old skinny Negro with a mop of woolly gray hair, was sitting cross-legged on his workbench, sewing a pair of full-dress pants that had a razor slit all the way down the seat.

"You'll excuse me, please, gentleman," said Manischevitz, admiring the tailor's deft, thimbled fingerwork, "but you know maybe somebody by the name Alexander Levine?"

The tailor, who Manischevitz thought, seemed a little antagonistic to him, scratched his scalp.

"Cain't say I ever heared dat name."

"Alex-ander Lev-ine," Manischevitz repeated it.

The man shook his head. "Cain't say I heared."

About to depart, Manischevitz remembered to say: "He is an angel, maybe."

"Oh *him*," said the tailor clucking. "He hang out in dat honky tonk down here a ways." He pointed with his skinny finger and returned to the pants.

Manischevitz crossed the street against a red light and was almost run down by a taxi. On the block after the next, the sixth store from the corner was a cabaret, and the name in sparkling lights was Bella's. Ashamed to go in, Manischevitz gazed through the neon-lit window, and when the dancing couples had parted and drifted away, he discovered at a table on the side, towards the rear, Levine.

He was sitting alone, a cigarette butt hanging from the corner of his mouth, playing solitaire with a dirty pack of cards, and Manischevitz felt a touch of pity for him, for Levine had deteriorated in appearance. His derby was dented and had a gray smudge on the side. His ill-fitting suit was shabbier, as if he had been sleeping in it. His shoes and trouser cuffs were muddy, and his face was covered with an impenetrable stubble the color of licorice. Manischevitz, though deeply disappointed, was about to enter, when a big-breasted Negress in a purple evening gown appeared before Levine's table, and with much laughter through many white teeth, broke into a vigorous shimmy. Levine looked straight at Manischevitz with a haunted expression, but the tailor was too paralyzed to move or acknowledge it. As Bella's gyrations continued, Levine rose, his eyes lit in excitement. She embraced him with vigor, both his hands clasped around her big restless buttocks and they tangoed together across the floor, loudly applauded by the noisy customers. She seemed to have lifted Levine off his feet and his large shoes hung limp as they danced. They slid past the windows where Manischevitz, white-faced, stood staring in. Levine winked slyly and the tailor left for home.

Fanny lay at death's door. Through shrunken lips she muttered concerning her childhood, the sorrows of the marriage bed, the loss of her children, yet wept to live. Manischevitz tried not to listen, but even without ears he would have heard. It was not a gift. The doctor panted up the stairs, a broad but bland, unshaven man (it was Sunday), and soon shook his head. A day at most, or two. He left at once, not without pity, to spare himself Manischevitz's multiplied sorrow; the man who never stopped hurting. He would someday get him into a public home.

Manischevitz visited a synagogue and there spoke to God, but God had absented himself. The tailor searched his heart and found no hope. When she died he would live dead. He considered taking his life although he knew he wouldn't. Yet it was something to consider. Considering, you existed. He railed against God—Can you love a rock, a broom, an emptiness? Baring his chest, he smote the naked bones, cursing himself for having believed.

Asleep in a chair that afternoon, he dreamed of Levine. He was standing before a faded mirror, preening small decaying opalescent wings. "This means," mumbled Manischevitz, as he broke out of sleep, "that it is possible he could be an angel." Begging a neighbor lady to look in on Fanny and occasionally wet her lips with a few drops of water, he drew on his thin coat, gripped his walking stick, exchanged some pennies for a subway token, and rode to Harlem. He knew this act was the last desperate one of his woe: to go without belief, seeking a black magician to restore his wife to invalidism. Yet if there was no choice, he did at least what was chosen.

He hobbled to Bella's but the place had changed hands. It was now, as he breathed, a synagogue in a store. In the front, towards him, were several rows of empty wooden benches. In the rear stood the Ark,[3] its portals of rough wood covered with rainbows of sequins; under it a long table on which lay the sacred scroll unrolled, illuminated by the dim light from a bulb on a chain overhead. Around the table, as if frozen to it and the scroll, which they all touched with their fingers, sat four Negroes wearing skullcaps. Now as they read the Holy Word, Manischevitz could, through the plate glass window, hear the singsong chant of their voices. One of them was old, with a gray beard. One was bubble-eyed. One was humpbacked. The fourth was a boy, no older than thirteen. Their heads moved in rhythmic swaying. Touched by this sight from his childhood and youth, Manischevitz entered and stood silent in the rear.

"Neshoma," said bubble eyes, pointing to the word with a stubby finger. "Now what dat mean?"

"That's the word that means soul," said the boy. He wore glasses.

"Let's git on wid de commentary," said the old man.

"Ain't necessary," said the humpback. "Souls is immaterial substance. That's all. The soul is derived in that manner. The immateriality is derived from the substance, and they both, causally an' otherwise, derived from the soul. There can be no higher."

"That's the highest."

"Over de top."

"Wait a minute," said bubble eyes. "I don't see what is dat immaterial substance. How come de one gits hitched up to de odder?" He addressed the humpback.

"Ask me something hard. Because it is substanceless immateriality. It couldn't be closer together, like all the parts of the body under one skin—closer."

"Hear now," said the old man.

"All you done is switched de words."

"It's the primum mobile,[4] the substanceless substance from which comes all things that were incepted in the idea—you, me and everything and body else."

---

3. Sacred chest containing the scrolls of the Torah in a synagogue. **4.** First moving thing (Latin).

"Now how did all dat happen? Make it sound simple."

"It de speerit," said the old man. "On de face of de water moved de speerit. An' dat was good. It say so in de Book. From de speerit ariz de man."

"But now listen here. How come it become substance if it all de time a spirit?"

"God alone done dat."

"Holy! Holy! Praise His Name."

"But has dis spirit got some kind of a shade or color?" asked bubble eyes, deadpan.

"Man, of course not. A spirit is a spirit."

"Then how come we is colored?" he said with a triumphant glare.

"Ain't got nothing to do wid dat."

"I still like to know."

"God put the spirit in all things," answered the boy. "He put it in the green leaves and the yellow flowers. He put it with the gold in the fishes and the blue in the sky. That's how come it came to us."

"Amen."

"Praise Lawd and utter loud His speechless name."

"Blow de bugle till it bust the sky."

They fell silent, intent upon the next word. Manischevitz approached them.

"You'll excuse me," he said. "I am looking for Alexander Levine. You know him maybe?"

"That's the angel," said the boy.

"Oh, *him*," snuffed bubble eyes.

"You'll find him at Bella's. It's the establishment right across the street," the humpback said.

Manischevitz said he was sorry that he could not stay, thanked them, and limped across the street. It was already night. The city was dark and he could barely find his way.

But Bella's was bursting with the blues. Through the window Manischevitz recognized the dancing crowd and among them sought Levine. He was sitting loose-lipped at Bella's side table. They were tippling from an almost empty whiskey fifth. Levine had shed his old clothes, wore a shiny new checkered suit, pearl-gray derby, cigar, and big, two-tone button shoes. To the tailor's dismay, a drunken look had settled upon his formerly dignified face. He leaned toward Bella, tickled her ear lobe with his pinky, while whispering words that sent her into gales of raucous laughter. She fondled his knee.

Manischevitz, girding himself, pushed open the door and was not welcomed.

"This place reserved."

"Beat it, pale puss."

"Exit, Yankel, Semitic trash."

But he moved towards the table where Levine sat, the crowd breaking before him as he hobbled forward.

"Mr. Levine," he spoke in a trembly voice. "Is here Manischevitz."

Levine glared blearily. "Speak yo' piece, son."

Manischevitz shuddered. His back plagued him. Cold tremors tormented his crooked legs. He looked around, everybody was all ears.

"You'll excuse me. I would like to talk to you in a private place."

"Speak, Ah is a private pusson."

Bella laughed piercingly. "Stop it, boy, you killin' me."

Manischevitz, no end disturbed, considered fleeing but Levine addressed him: "Kindly state the pu'pose of yo' communication with yo's truly."

The tailor wet cracked lips. "You are Jewish. This I am sure."

Levine rose, nostrils flaring. "Anythin' else yo' got to say?"

Manischevitz's tongue lay like stone.

"Speak now or fo'ever hold off."

Tears blinded the tailor's eyes. Was ever man so tried? Should he say he believed a half-drunken Negro to be an angel?

The silence slowly petrified.

Manischevitz was recalling scenes of his youth as a wheel in his mind whirred: believe, do not, yes, no, yes, no. The pointer pointed to yes, to between yes and no, to no, no it was yes. He sighed. It moved but one had still to make a choice.

"I think you are an angel from God." He said it in a broken voice, thinking. If you said it it was said. If you believed it you must say it. If you believed, you believed.

The hush broke. Everybody talked but the music began and they went on dancing. Bella, grown bored, picked up the cards and dealt herself a hand.

Levine burst into tears. "How you have humiliated me."

Manischevitz apologized.

"Wait'll I freshen up." Levine went to the men's room and returned in his old clothes.

No one said goodbye as they left.

They rode to the flat via subway. As they walked up the stairs Manischevitz pointed with his cane at his door.

"That's all been taken care of," Levine said. "You best go in while I take off."

Disappointed that it was so soon over but torn by curiosity, Manischevitz followed the angel up three flights to the roof. When he got there the door was already padlocked.

Luckily he could see through a small broken window. He heard an odd noise, as though of a whirring of wings, and when he strained for a wider view, could have sworn he saw a dark figure borne aloft on a pair of magnificent black wings.

A feather drifted down. Manischevitz gasped as it turned white, but it was only snowing.

He rushed downstairs. In the flat Fanny wielded a dust mop under the bed and then upon the cobwebs on the wall.

"A wonderful thing, Fanny," Manischevitz said. "Believe me, there are Jews everywhere."

1950

KATHERINE MANSFIELD
1888–1923

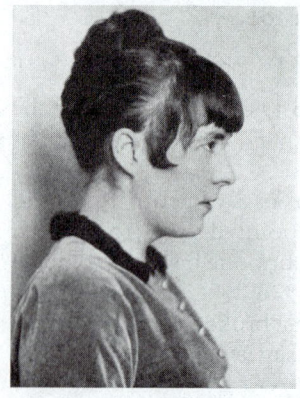

Mansfield was born in Wellington, New Zealand. Though her intention in going to England at the end of her teens was to study music, there she made the acquaintance of literary people—among them D. H. Lawrence, who was for a while a close friend, and John Middleton Murry, whom she later married. Under their influence she began to write, first as a journalist and then as an innovative artist in the short story. Her first collection, *In a German Pension*, appeared in 1911. The impressionism of many of her stories has led to some comparisons with Chekhov, who was, in any case, an example on whom she meant to model her working life. Her persistent ill health and the death of a beloved brother in World War I were among the circumstances that darkened her personal life more than they influenced the temper of her fiction, which remained eager and venturesome. Her keen satire was often directed at the self-righteousness of the upper classes and the intelligentsia, at the complacencies insulating them from the realities of existence as experienced by ordinary people. *The Short Stories of Katherine Mansfield* was published in 1937 and her critical essays, *Novels and Novelists*, in 1930.

The Garden Party

And after all the weather was ideal. They could not have had a more perfect day for a garden party if they had ordered it. Windless, warm, the sky without a cloud. Only the blue was veiled with a haze of light gold, as it is sometimes in early summer. The gardener had been up since dawn, mowing the lawns and sweeping them, until the grass and the dark flat rosettes where the daisy plants had been seemed to shine. As for the roses, you could not help feeling they understood that roses are the only flowers that impress people at garden parties; the only flowers that everybody is certain of knowing. Hundreds, yes, literally hundreds, had come out in a single night; the green bushes bowed down as though they had been visited by archangels.

Breakfast was not yet over before the men came to put up the marquee.

'Where do you want the marquee put, mother?'

'My dear child, it's no use asking me. I'm determined to leave everything to you children this year. Forget I am your mother. Treat me as an honoured guest.'

But Meg could not possibly go and supervise the men. She had washed her hair before breakfast, and she sat drinking her coffee in a green turban, with a dark wet curl stamped on each cheek. Jose, the butterfly, always came down in a silk petticoat and a kimono jacket.

'You'll have to go, Laura, you're the artistic one.'

Away Laura flew, still holding her piece of bread-and-butter. It's so delicious to have an excuse for eating out of doors, and besides, she loved having to arrange things; she always felt she could do it so much better than anybody else.

Four men in their shirt-sleeves stood grouped together on the garden path. They carried staves covered with rolls of canvas, and they had big tool-bags slung on their backs. They looked impressive. Laura wished now that she was not holding that piece of bread-and-butter, but there was nowhere to put it, and she couldn't possibly throw it away. She blushed and tried to look severe and even a little bit short-sighted as she came up to them.

'Good morning,' she said, copying her mother's voice. But that sounded so fearfully affected that she was ashamed, and stammered like a little girl, 'Oh—er—have you come—is it about the marquee?'

'That's right, miss,' said the tallest of the men, a lanky, freckled fellow, and he shifted his tool-bag, knocked back his straw hat and smiled down at her. 'That's about it.'

His smile was so easy, so friendly, that Laura recovered. What nice eyes he had, small, but such a dark blue! And now she looked at the others, they were smiling too. 'Cheer up, we won't bite,' their smile seemed to say. How very nice workmen were! And what a beautiful morning! She mustn't mention the morning; she must be business-like. The marquee.

'Well, what about the lily-lawn? Would that do?'

And she pointed to the lily-lawn with the hand that didn't hold the bread-and-butter. They turned, they stared in the direction. A little fat chap thrust out his under-lip, and the tall fellow frowned.

'I don't fancy it,' said he. 'Not conspicuous enough. You see, with a thing like a marquee,' and he turned to Laura in his easy way, 'you want to put it somewhere where it'll give you a bang slap in the eye, if you follow me.'

Laura's upbringing made her wonder for a moment whether it was quite respectful of a workman to talk to her of bangs slap in the eye. But she did quite follow him.

'A corner of the tennis-court,' she suggested. 'But the band's going to be in one corner.'

'H'm, going to have a band, are you?' said another of the workmen. He was pale. He had a haggard look as his dark eyes scanned the tennis-court. What was he thinking?

'Only a very small band,' said Laura gently. Perhaps he wouldn't mind so much if the band was quite small. But the tall fellow interrupted.

'Look here, miss, that's the place. Against those trees. Over there. That'll do fine.'

Against the karakas.[1] Then the karaka-trees would be hidden. And they were so lovely, with their broad, gleaming leaves, and their clusters of yellow fruit. They were like trees you imagined growing on a desert island, proud, solitary, lifting their leaves and fruits to the sun in a kind of silent splendour. Must they be hidden by a marquee?

---

1. A tree native to New Zealand.

They must. Already the men had shouldered their staves and were making for the place. Only the tall fellow was left. He bent down, pinched a sprig of lavender, put his thumb and forefinger to his nose and snuffed up the smell. When Laura saw the gesture she forgot all about the karakas in her wonder at him caring for things like that—caring for the smell of lavender. How many men that she knew would have done such a thing. Oh, how extraordinarily nice workmen were, she thought. Why couldn't she have workmen for friends rather than the silly boys she danced with and who came to Sunday night supper? She would get on much better with men like these.

It's all the fault, she decided, as the tall fellow drew something on the back of an envelope, something that was to be looped up or left to hang, of these absurd class distinctions. Well, for her part, she didn't feel them. Not a bit, not an atom. . . . And now there came the chock-chock of wooden hammers. Some one whistled, some one sang out, 'Are you right there, matey?' 'Matey!' The friendliness of it, the—the—Just to prove how happy she was, just to show the tall fellow how at home she felt, and how she despised stupid conventions, Laura took a big bite of her bread-and-butter as she stared at the little drawing. She felt just like a work-girl.

'Laura, Laura, where are you? Telephone, Laura!' a voice cried from the house.

'Coming!' Away she skimmed, over the lawn, up the path, up the steps, across the veranda, and into the porch. In the hall her father and Laurie were brushing their hats ready to go to the office.

'I say, Laura,' said Laurie very fast, 'you might just give a squiz at my coat before this afternoon. See if it wants pressing.'

'I will,' said she. Suddenly she couldn't stop herself. She ran at Laurie and gave him a small, quick squeeze. 'Oh, I do love parties, don't you?' gasped Laura.

'Ra-ther,' said Laurie's warm, boyish voice, and he squeezed his sister too, and gave her a gentle push. 'Dash off to the telephone, old girl.'

The telephone. 'Yes, yes; oh yes. Kitty? Good morning, dear. Come to lunch? Do, dear. Delighted of course. It will only be a very scratch meal—just the sandwich crusts and broken meringue-shells and what's left over. Yes, isn't it a perfect morning? Your white? Oh, I certainly should. One moment—hold the line. Mother's calling.' And Laura sat back. 'What, mother? Can't hear.'

Mrs Sheridan's voice floated down the stairs. 'Tell her to wear that sweet hat she had on last Sunday.'

'Mother says you're to wear that *sweet* hat you had on last Sunday. Good. One o'clock. Bye-bye.'

Laura put back the receiver, flung her arms over her head, took a deep breath, stretched and let them fall. 'Huh,' she sighed, and the moment after the sigh she sat up quickly. She was still, listening. All the doors in the house seemed to be open. The house was alive with soft, quick steps and running voices. The green baize door that led to the kitchen regions swung open and shut with a muffled thud. And now there came a long, chuckling absurd sound. It was the heavy piano being moved on its stiff castors. But the air! If you stopped to notice, was the air always like this? Little faint winds were playing chase in at the tops of the windows, out at the doors. And there were two tiny spots of sun, one on the inkpot, one on a silver photograph frame, playing too. Darling little spots. Especially the one on the inkpot lid. It was quite warm. A warm little silver star. She could have kissed it.

The front door bell pealed, and there sounded the rustle of Sadie's print skirt on the stairs. A man's voice murmured. Sadie answered, careless, 'I'm sure I don't know. Wait. I'll ask Mrs Sheridan.'

'What is it, Sadie?' Laura came into the hall.

'It's the florist, Miss Laura.'

It was, indeed. There, just inside the door, stood a wide, shallow tray full of pots of pink lilies. No other kind. Nothing but lilies—canna lilies, big pink flowers, wide open, radiant, almost frighteningly alive on bright crimson stems.

'O-oh, Sadie!' said Laura, and the sound was like a little moan. She crouched down as if to warm herself at that blaze of lilies; she felt they were in her fingers, on her lips, growing in her breast.

'It's some mistake,' she said faintly. 'Nobody ever ordered so many. Sadie, go and find mother.'

But at that moment Mrs Sheridan joined them.

'It's quite right,' she said calmly. 'Yes, I ordered them. Aren't they lovely?' She pressed Laura's arm. 'I was passing the shop yesterday, and I saw them in the window. And I suddenly thought for once in my life I shall have enough canna lilies. The garden party will be a good excuse.'

'But I thought you said you didn't mean to interfere,' said Laura. Sadie had gone. The florist's man was still outside at his van. She put her arm round her mother's neck and gently, very gently, she bit her mother's ear.

'My darling child, you wouldn't like a logical mother, would you? Don't do that. Here's the man.'

He carried more lilies still, another whole tray.

'Bank them up, just inside the door, on both sides of the porch, please,' said Mrs Sheridan. 'Don't you agree, Laura?'

'Oh, I *do*, mother.'

In the drawing-room Meg, Jose and good little Hans had at last succeeded in moving the piano.

'Now, if we put this chesterfield against the wall and move everything out of the room except the chairs, don't you think?'

'Quite.'

'Hans, move these tables into the smoking-room, and bring a sweeper to take these marks off the carpet and—one moment, Hans—' Jose loved giving orders to the servants, and they loved obeying her. She always made them feel they were taking part in some drama. 'Tell mother and Miss Laura to come here at once.'

'Very good, Miss Jose.'

She turned to Meg. 'I want to hear what the piano sounds like, just in case I'm asked to sing this afternoon. Let's try over "This Life is Weary".'

Pom! Ta-ta-ta *Tee*-ta! The piano burst out so passionately that Jose's face changed. She clasped her hands. She looked mournfully and enigmatically at her mother and Laura as they came in.

> This Life is *Wee*-ary,
> A Tear—a Sigh.
> A Love that *Chan*-ges,
> This Life is *Wee*-ary,
> A Tear—a Sigh.

> A Love that *Chan*-ges,
> And then . . . Good-bye!

But at the word 'Good-bye', and although the piano sounded more desperate than ever, her face broke into a brilliant, dreadfully unsympathetic smile.

'Aren't I in good voice, mummy?' she beamed.

> This Life is *Wee*-ary,
> Hope comes to Die.
> A Dream—a *Wa*-kening.

But now Sadie interrupted them. 'What is it, Sadie?'

'If you please, m'm, cook says have you got the flags for the sandwiches?'

'The flags for the sandwiches, Sadie?' echoed Mrs Sheridan dreamily. And the children knew by her face that she hadn't got them. 'Let me see.' And she said to Sadie firmly, 'Tell cook I'll let her have them in ten minutes.'

Sadie went.

'Now, Laura,' said her mother quickly, 'come with me into the smoking-room. I've got the names somewhere on the back of an envelope. You'll have to write them out for me. Meg, go upstairs this minute and take that wet thing off your head. Jose, run and finish dressing this instant. Do you hear me, children, or shall I have to tell your father when he comes home to-night? And—and, Jose, pacify cook if you do go into the kitchen, will you? I'm terrified of her this morning.'

The envelope was found at last behind the dining-room clock, though how it had got there Mrs Sheridan could not imagine.

'One of you children must have stolen it out of my bag, because I remember vividly—cream-cheese and lemon-curd. Have you done that?'

'Yes.'

'Egg and—' Mrs Sheridan held the envelope away from her. 'It looks like mice. It can't be mice, can it?'

'Olive, pet,' said Laura, looking over her shoulder.

'Yes, of course, olive. What a horrible combination it sounds. Egg and olive.'

They were finished at last, and Laura took them off to the kitchen. She found Jose there pacifying the cook, who did not look at all terrifying.

'I have never seen such exquisite sandwiches,' said Jose's rapturous voice. 'How many kinds did you say there were, cook? Fifteen?'

'Fifteen, Miss Jose.'

'Well, cook, I congratulate you.'

Cook swept up crusts with the long sandwich knife, and smiled broadly.

'Godber's has come,' announced Sadie, issuing out of the pantry. She had seen the man pass the window.

That meant the cream puffs had come. Godber's were famous for their cream puffs. Nobody ever thought of making them at home.

'Bring them in and put them on the table, my girl,' ordered cook.

Sadie brought them in and went back to the door. Of course Laura and Jose were far too grown-up to really care about such things. All the same, they couldn't help agreeing that the puffs looked very attractive. Very. Cook began arranging them, shaking off the extra icing sugar.

'Don't they carry one back to all one's parties?' said Laura.

'I suppose they do,' said practical Jose, who never liked to be carried back. 'They look beautifully light and feathery, I must say.'

'Have one each, my dears,' said cook in her comfortable voice. 'Yer ma won't know.'

Oh, impossible. Fancy cream puffs so soon after breakfast. The very idea made one shudder. All the same, two minutes later Jose and Laura were licking their fingers with that absorbed inward look that only comes from whipped cream.

'Let's go into the garden, out by the back way,' suggested Laura. 'I want to see how the men are getting on with the marquee. They're such awfully nice men.'

But the back door was blocked by cook, Sadie, Godber's man and Hans.

Something had happened.

'Tuk-tuk-tuk,' clucked cook like an agitated hen. Sadie had her hand clapped to her cheek as though she had toothache. Hans's face was screwed up in the effort to understand. Only Godber's man seemed to be enjoying himself; it was his story.

'What's the matter? What's happened?'

'There's been a horrible accident,' said cook. 'A man killed.'

'A man killed! Where? How? When?'

But Godber's man wasn't going to have his story snatched from under his very nose.

'Know those little cottages just below here, miss?' Know them? Of course, she knew them. 'Well, there's a young chap living there, name of Scott, a carter. His horse shied at a traction-engine, corner of Hawke Street this morning, and he was thrown out on the back of his head. Killed.'

'Dead!' Laura stared at Godber's man.

'Dead when they picked him up,' said Godber's man with relish. 'They were taking the body home as I come up here.' And he said to the cook, 'He's left a wife and five little ones.'

'Jose, come here.' Laura caught hold of her sister's sleeve and dragged her through the kitchen to the other side of the green baize door. There she paused and leaned against it. 'Jose!' she said, horrified, 'however are we going to stop everything?'

'Stop everything, Laura!' cried Jose in astonishment. 'What do you mean?'

'Stop the garden party, of course.' Why did Jose pretend?

But Jose was still more amazed. 'Stop the garden party? My dear Laura, don't be so absurd. Of course we can't do anything of the kind. Nobody expects us to. Don't be so extravagant.'

'But we can't possibly have a garden party with a man dead just outside the front gate.'

That really was extravagant, for the little cottages were in a lane to themselves at the very bottom of a steep rise that led up to the house. A broad road ran between. True, they were far too near. They were the greatest possible eyesore, and they had no right to be in that neighbourhood at all. They were little mean dwellings painted a chocolate brown. In the garden patches there was nothing but cabbage stalks, sick hens and tomato cans. The very smoke coming out of their chimneys was poverty-stricken. Little rags and shreds of smoke, so unlike the great silvery plumes that uncurled from the Sheridans' chimneys. Washerwomen lived in the lane and sweeps and a cobbler, and a man whose house-front was studded all over with minute bird-cages. Children swarmed. When the Sheridans were little they were forbidden to set foot there because of the revolting language and of what they might catch. But since they were grown up, Laura and Laurie on their prowls sometimes walked through. It was disgusting and sordid. They came out with a shudder. But still one must go everywhere; one must see everything. So through they went.

'And just think of what the band would sound like to that poor woman,' said Laura.

'Oh, Laura!' Jose began to be seriously annoyed. 'If you're going to stop a band playing every time some one has an accident, you'll lead a very strenuous life. I'm every bit as sorry about it as you. I feel just as sympathetic.' Her eyes hardened. She looked at her sister just as she used to when they were little and fighting together. 'You won't bring a drunken workman back to life by being sentimental,' she said softly.

'Drunk! Who said he was drunk?' Laura turned furiously on Jose. She said just as they had used to say on those occasions, 'I'm going straight up to tell mother.'

'Do, dear,' cooed Jose.

'Mother, can I come into your room?' Laura turned the big glass door-knob.

'Of course, child. Why, what's the matter? What's given you such a colour?' And Mrs Sheridan turned round from her dressing-table. She was trying on a new hat.

'Mother, a man's been killed,' began Laura.

'Not in the garden?' interrupted her mother.

'No, no!'

'Oh, what a fright you gave me!' Mrs Sheridan sighed with relief, and took off the big hat and held it on her knees.

'But listen, mother,' said Laura. Breathless, half-choking, she told the dreadful story. 'Of course, we can't have our party, can we?' she pleaded. 'The band and everybody arriving. They'd hear us, mother; they're nearly neighbours!'

To Laura's astonishment her mother behaved just like Jose; it was harder to bear because she seemed amused. She refused to take Laura seriously.

'But, my dear child, use your common sense. It's only by accident we've heard of it. If some one had died there normally—and I can't understand how they keep alive in those poky little holes—we should still be having our party, shouldn't we?'

Laura had to say 'yes' to that, but she felt it was all wrong. She sat down on her mother's sofa and pinched the cushion frill.

'Mother, isn't it really terribly heartless of us?' she asked.

'Darling!' Mrs Sheridan got up and came over to her, carrying the hat. Before Laura could stop her she had popped it on. 'My child!' said her mother, 'the hat is yours. It's made for you. It's much too young for me. I have never seen you look such a picture. Look at yourself!' And she held up her hand-mirror.

'But, mother,' Laura began again. She couldn't look at herself; she turned aside.

This time Mrs Sheridan lost patience just as Jose had done.

'You are being very absurd, Laura,' she said coldly. 'People like that don't expect sacrifices from us. And it's not very sympathetic to spoil everybody's enjoyment as you're doing now.'

'I don't understand,' said Laura, and she walked quickly out of the room into her own bedroom. There, quite by chance, the first thing she saw was this charming girl in the mirror, in her black hat trimmed with gold daisies, and a long black velvet ribbon. Never had she imagined she could look like that. Is mother right? she thought. And now she hoped her mother was right. Am I being extravagant? Perhaps it was extravagant. Just for a moment she had another glimpse of that poor woman and those little children, and the body being carried into the house. But it all seemed blurred, unreal, like a picture in the newspaper. I'll remember it again after the party's over, she decided. And somehow that seemed quite the best plan. . . .

Lunch was over by half-past one. By half-past two they were all ready for the fray. The green-coated band had arrived and was established in a corner of the tennis-court.

'My dear!' trilled Kitty Maitland, 'aren't they too like frogs for words? You ought to have arranged them round the pond with the conductor in the middle on a leaf.'

Laurie arrived and hailed them on his way to dress. At the sight of him Laura remembered the accident again. She wanted to tell him. If Laurie agreed with the others, then it was bound to be all right. And she followed him into the hall.

'Laurie!'

'Hallo!' He was half-way upstairs, but when he turned round and saw Laura he suddenly puffed out his cheeks and goggled his eyes at her. 'My word, Laura! You do look stunning,' said Laurie. 'What an absolutely topping hat!'

Laura said faintly 'Is it?' and smiled up at Laurie, and didn't tell him after all.

Soon after that people began coming in streams. The band struck up; the hired waiters ran from the house to the marquee. Wherever you looked there were couples strolling, bending to the flowers, greeting, moving on over the lawn. They were like bright birds that had alighted in the Sheridans' garden for this one afternoon, on their way to—where? Ah, what happiness it is to be with people who all are happy, to press hands, press cheeks, smile into eyes.

'Darling Laura, how well you look!'

'What a becoming hat, child!'

'Laura, you look quite Spanish. I've never seen you look so striking.'

And Laura, glowing, answered softly, 'Have you had tea? Won't you have an ice? The passion-fruit ices really are rather special.' She ran to her father and begged him. 'Daddy darling, can't the band have something to drink?'

And the perfect afternoon slowly ripened, slowly faded, slowly its petals closed.

'Never a more delightful garden party. . . .' 'The greatest success. . . .' 'Quite the most. . . .'

Laura helped her mother with the good-byes. They stood side by side in the porch till it was all over.

'All over, all over, thank heaven,' said Mrs Sheridan. 'Round up the others, Laura. Let's go and have some fresh coffee. I'm exhausted. Yes, it's been very successful. But oh, these parties, these parties! Why will you children insist on giving parties!' And they all of them sat down in the deserted marquee.

'Have a sandwich, daddy dear. I wrote the flag.'

'Thanks.' Mr Sheridan took a bite and the sandwich was gone. He took another. 'I suppose you didn't hear of a beastly accident that happened to-day?' he said.

'My dear,' said Mrs Sheridan, holding up her hand, 'we did. It nearly ruined the party. Laura insisted we should put it off.'

'Oh, mother!' Laura didn't want to be teased about it.

'It was a horrible affair all the same,' said Mr Sheridan. 'The chap was married too. Lived just below in the lane, and leaves a wife and half a dozen kiddies, so they say.'

An awkward little silence fell. Mrs Sheridan fidgeted with her cup. Really, it was very tactless of father. . . .

Suddenly she looked up. There on the table were all those sandwiches, cakes, puffs, all un-eaten, all going to be wasted. She had one of her brilliant ideas.

'I know,' she said. 'Let's make up a basket. Let's send that poor creature some of this perfectly good food. At any rate, it will be the greatest treat for the children. Don't you agree? And she's sure to have neighbours calling in and so on. What a point to have it all ready prepared. Laura!' She jumped up. 'Get me the big basket out of the stairs cupboard.'

'But, mother, do you really think it's a good idea?' said Laura.

Again, how curious, she seemed to be different from them all. To take scraps from their party. Would the poor woman really like that?

'Of course! What's the matter with you to-day? An hour or two ago you were insisting on us being sympathetic, and now—'

Oh well! Laura ran for the basket. It was filled, it was heaped by her mother.

'Take it yourself, darling,' said she. 'Run down just as you are. No, wait, take the arum lilies too. People of that class are so impressed by arum lilies.'

'The stems will ruin her lace frock,' said practical Jose.

So they would. Just in time. 'Only the basket, then. And, Laura!'—her mother followed her out of the marquee—'don't on any account—'

'What mother?'

No, better not put such ideas into the child's head! 'Nothing! Run along.'

It was just growing dusky as Laura shut their garden gates. A big dog ran by like a shadow. The road gleamed white, and down below in the hollow the little cottages were in deep shade. How quiet it seemed after the afternoon. Here she was going down the hill to somewhere where a man lay dead, and she couldn't realize it. Why couldn't she? She stopped a minute. And it seemed to her that kisses, voices, tinkling spoons, laughter, the smell of crushed grass were somehow inside her. She had no room for anything else. How strange! She looked up at the pale sky, and all she thought was, 'Yes, it was the most successful party.'

Now the broad road was crossed. The lane began, smoky and dark. Women in shawls and men's tweed caps hurried by. Men hung over the palings; the children played in the doorways. A low hum came from the mean little cottages. In some of them there was a flicker of light, and a shadow, crab-like, moved across the window. Laura bent her head and hurried on. She wished now she had put on a coat. How her frock shone! And the big hat with the velvet streamer—if only it was another hat! Were the people looking at her? They must be. It was a mistake to have come; she knew all along it was a mistake. Should she go back even now?

No, too late. This was the house. It must be. A dark knot of people stood outside. Beside the gate an old, old woman with a crutch sat in a chair, watching. She had her feet on a newspaper. The voices stopped as Laura drew near. The group parted. It was as though she was expected, as though they had known she was coming here.

Laura was terribly nervous. Tossing the velvet ribbon over her shoulder, she said to a woman standing by, 'Is this Mrs Scott's house?' and the woman, smiling queerly, said, 'It is, my lass.'

Oh, to be away from this! She actually said, 'Help me, God,' as she walked up the tiny path and knocked. To be away from those staring eyes, or to be covered up in anything, one of those women's shawls even. I'll just leave the basket and go, she decided. I shan't even wait for it to be emptied.

Then the door opened. A little woman in black showed in the gloom.

Laura said, 'Are you Mrs Scott?' But to her horror the woman answered, 'Walk in, please, miss,' and she was shut in the passage.

'No,' said Laura, 'I don't want to come in. I only want to leave this basket. Mother sent—'

The little woman in the gloomy passage seemed not to have heard her. 'Step this way, please, miss,' she said in an oily voice, and Laura followed her.

She found herself in a wretched little low kitchen, lighted by a smoky lamp. There was a woman sitting before the fire.

'Em,' said the little creature who had let her in. 'Em! It's a young lady.' She turned to Laura. She said meaningly, 'I'm 'er sister, miss. You'll excuse 'er, won't you?'

'Oh, but of course!' said Laura. 'Please, please don't disturb her. I—I only want to leave—'

But at that moment the woman at the fire turned round. Her face, puffed up, red, with swollen eyes and swollen lips, looked terrible. She seemed as though she couldn't understand why Laura was there. What did it mean? Why was this stranger standing in the kitchen with a basket? What was it all about? And the poor face puckered up again.

'All right, my dear,' said the other. 'I'll thenk the young lady.'

And again she began. 'You'll excuse her, miss. I'm sure,' and her face, swollen too, tried an oily smile.

Laura only wanted to get out, to get away. She was back in the passage. The door opened. She walked straight through into the bedroom where the dead man was lying.

'You'd like a look at 'im, wouldn't you?' said Em's sister, and she brushed past Laura over to the bed. 'Don't be afraid, my lass,'—and now her voice sounded fond and sly, and fondly she drew down the sheet—' 'e looks a picture. There's nothing to show. Come along, my dear.'

Laura came.

There lay a young man, fast asleep—sleeping so soundly, so deeply, that he was far, far away from them both. Oh, so remote, so peaceful. He was dreaming. Never wake him up again. His head was sunk in the pillow, his eyes were closed; they were blind under the closed eyelids. He was given up to his dream. What did garden parties and baskets and lace frocks matter to him? He was far from all those things. He was wonderful, beautiful. While they were laughing and while the band was playing, this marvel had come to the lane. Happy . . . happy. . . . All is well, said that sleeping face. This is just as it should be. I am content.

But all the same you had to cry, and she couldn't go out of the room without saying something to him. Laura gave a loud childish sob.

'Forgive my hat,' she said.

And this time she didn't wait for Em's sister. She found her way out of the door, down the path, past all those dark people. At the corner of the lane she met Laurie.

He stepped out of the shadow. 'Is that you, Laura?'

'Yes.'

'Mother was getting anxious. Was it all right?'

'Yes, quite. Oh, Laurie!' She took his arm, she pressed up against him.

'I say, you're not crying, are you?' asked her brother.

Laura shook her head. She was.

Laurie put his arm round her shoulder. 'Don't cry,' he said in his warm, loving voice. 'Was it awful?'

'No,' sobbed Laura. 'It was simply marvellous. But, Laurie—' She stopped, she looked at her brother. 'Isn't life,' she stammered, 'isn't life—' But what life was she couldn't explain. No matter. He quite understood.

'*Isn't* it, darling?' said Laurie.

1921

BOBBIE ANN MASON
b. 1940

Mason was born and grew up on her family's dairy farm near Mayfield, Kentucky. After studying journalism at the University of Kentucky, she moved to New York and wrote for *Movie Stars, Movie Life,* and *T.V. Star Parade.* She then earned a doctorate at the University of Connecticut and began teaching English. She has been awarded National Endowment for the Arts fellowships, has had stories in *Best American Short Stories* in 1981 and 1983, and won the Pushcart Prize for fiction in 1983. *Shiloh and Other Stories* (1982), her first collection, won the Ernest Hemingway Foundation Award. She has also written four novels, *In Country* (1985), *Feather Crowns* (1993), *An Atomic Romance* (2005), and *The Girl in the Blue Beret* (2011); a short novel, *Spence and Lila* (1988); and four more collections of short stories, *Love Life* (1989), *Midnight Magic* (1998), *Zigzagging Down a Wild Trail* (2001), and *Nancy Culpepper* (2006). Her memoir, *Clear Springs* (1999), was a finalist for the Pulitzer Prize.

Shiloh

Leroy Moffitt's wife, Norma Jean, is working on her pectorals. She lifts three-pound dumbbells to warm up, then progresses to a twenty-pound barbell. Standing with her legs apart, she reminds Leroy of Wonder Woman.

"I'd give anything if I could just get these muscles to where they're real hard," says Norma Jean. "Feel this arm. It's not as hard as the other one."

"That's cause you're right-handed," says Leroy, dodging as she swings the barbell in an arc.

"Do you think so?"

"Sure."

Leroy is a truckdriver. He injured his leg in a highway accident four months ago, and his physical therapy, which involves weights and a pulley, prompted Norma Jean to try building herself up. Now she is attending a body-building class. Leroy has been collecting temporary disability since his tractor-trailer jackknifed in Missouri, badly twisting his left leg in its socket. He has a steel pin in his hip. He will probably not be able to drive his rig again. It sits in the backyard, like a gigantic bird that has flown home to roost. Leroy has been home in Kentucky for three months, and his leg is almost healed, but the accident frightened him and he does not want to drive any more long hauls. He is not sure what to do next. In the meantime, he makes things from craft kits. He started by building a miniature log cabin from notched Popsicle sticks. He varnished it and placed it on the TV set, where it remains. It reminds him of a rustic Nativity scene. Then he tried string art (sailing ships on black velvet), a macramé owl kit, a snap-together B-17 Flying Fortress,[1] and a lamp made out of a model truck, with a light fixture screwed in the top of the cab. At first the kits were diversions, something to kill time, but now he is thinking about building a full-scale log house from a kit. It would be considerably cheaper than building a regular house, and besides, Leroy has grown to appreciate how things are put together. He has begun to realize that in all the years he was on the road he never took time to examine anything. He was always flying past scenery.

"They won't let you build a log cabin in any of the new subdivisions," Norma Jean tells him.

"They will if I tell them it's for you," he says, teasing her. Ever since they were married, he has promised Norma Jean he would build her a new home one day. They have always rented, and the house they live in is small and nondescript. It does not even feel like a home, Leroy realizes now.

Norma Jean works at the Rexall drugstore, and she has acquired an amazing amount of information about cosmetics. When she explains to Leroy the three stages of complexion care, involving creams, toners, and moisturizers, he thinks happily of other petroleum products—axle grease, diesel fuel. This is a connection between him and Norma Jean. Since he has been home, he has felt unusually tender about his wife and guilty over his long absences. But he can't tell what she feels about him. Norma Jean has never complained about his traveling; she has never made hurt remarks, like calling his truck a "widow-maker." He is reasonably certain she has been faithful to him, but he wishes she would celebrate his permanent homecoming more happily. Norma Jean is often startled to find Leroy at home, and he thinks she seems a little disappointed about it. Perhaps he reminds her too much of the early days of their marriage, before he went on the road. They had a child who died as an infant, years ago. They never speak about their memories of Randy, which have almost faded, but now that Leroy is home all the time, they sometimes feel awkward around each other, and Leroy wonders if one of them should mention the child. He has the feeling that they are waking up out of a dream together—that they must create a new marriage, start afresh. They are lucky they are still married. Leroy has read that for most people losing a child destroys the marriage—or else he heard this on *Donahue*. He can't always remember where he learns things anymore.

At Christmas, Leroy bought an electric organ for Norma Jean. She used to play the piano when she was in high school. "It don't leave you," she told him once. "It's like riding a bicycle."

The new instrument had so many keys and buttons that she was bewildered by it at first. She touched the keys tentatively, pushed some buttons, then pecked out "Chopsticks." It came out in an amplified fox-trot rhythm, with marimba sounds.

"It's an orchestra!" she cried.

The organ had a pecan-look finish and eighteen preset chords, with optional flute, violin, trumpet, clarinet, and banjo accompaniments. Norma Jean

1. American World War II bomber.

mastered the organ almost immediately. At first she played Christmas songs. Then she bought *The Sixties Songbook* and learned every tune in it, adding variations to each with the rows of brightly colored buttons.

"I didn't like these old songs back then," she said. "But I have this crazy feeling I missed something."

"You didn't miss a thing," said Leroy.

Leroy likes to lie on the couch and smoke a joint and listen to Norma Jean play "Can't Take My Eyes Off You" and "I'll Be Back." He is back again. After fifteen years on the road, he is finally settling down with the woman he loves. She is still pretty. Her skin is flawless. Her frosted curls resemble pencil trimmings.

Now that Leroy has come home to stay, he notices how much the town has changed. Subdivisions are spreading across western Kentucky like an oil slick. The sign at the edge of town says "Pop: 11,500"—only seven hundred more than it said twenty years before. Leroy can't figure out who is living in all the new houses. The farmers who used to gather around the courthouse square on Saturday afternoons to play checkers and spit tobacco juice have gone. It has been years since Leroy has thought about the farmers, and they have disappeared without his noticing.

Leroy meets a kid named Stevie Hamilton in the parking lot at the new shopping center. While they pretend to be strangers meeting over a stalled car, Stevie tosses an ounce of marijuana under the front seat of Leroy's car. Stevie is wearing orange jogging shoes and a T-shirt that says CHATTAHOOCHEE SUPER-RAT. His father is a prominent doctor who lives in one of the expensive subdivisons in a new white-columned brick house that looks like a funeral parlor. In the phone book under his name there is a separate number, with the listing "Teenagers."

"Where do you get this stuff?" asks Leroy. "From your pappy!"

"That's for me to know and you to find out," Stevie says. He is slit-eyed and skinny.

"What else you got?"

"What you interested in?"

"Nothing special. Just wondered."

Leroy used to take speed on the road. Now he has to go slowly. He needs to be mellow. He leans back against the car and says, "I'm aiming to build me a log house, soon as I get time. My wife, though, I don't think she likes the idea."

"Well, let me know when you want me again," Stevie says. He has a cigarette in his cupped palm, as though sheltering it from the wind. He takes a long drag, then stomps it on the asphalt and slouches away.

Stevie's father was two years ahead of Leroy in high school. Leroy is thirty-four. He married Norma Jean when they were both eighteen, and their child Randy was born a few months later, but he died at the age of four months and three days. He would be about Stevie's age now. Norma Jean and Leroy were at the drive-in, watching a double feature (*Dr. Strangelove* and *Lover Come Back*),[2] and the baby was sleeping in the back seat. When the first movie ended, the baby was dead. It was the sudden infant death syndrome. Leroy remembers

---

2. Respectively, Stanley Kubrick's 1963 satire on nuclear war and a 1961 Rock Hudson–Doris Day romantic comedy.

handing Randy to a nurse at the emergency room, as though he were offering her a large doll as a present. A dead baby feels like a sack of flour. "It just happens sometimes," said the doctor, in what Leroy always recalls as a nonchalant tone. Leroy can hardly remember the child anymore, but he still sees vividly a scene from *Dr. Strangelove* in which the President of the United States was talking in a folksy voice on the hot line to the Soviet premier about the bomber accidentally headed toward Russia. He was in the War Room, and the world map was lit up. Leroy remembers Norma Jean catatonically beside him in the hospital and himself thinking: Who is this strange girl? He had forgotten who she was. Now scientists are saying that crib death is caused by a virus. Nobody knows anything, Leroy thinks. The answers are always changing.

When Leroy gets home from the shopping center, Norma Jean's mother, Mabel Beasley, is there. Until this year, Leroy has not realized how much time she spends with Norma Jean. When she visits, she inspects the closets and then the plants, informing Norma Jean when a plant is droopy or yellow. Mabel calls the plants "flowers," although there are never any blooms. She always notices if Norma Jean's laundry is piling up. Mabel is a short, overweight woman whose tight, brown-dyed curls look more like a wig than the actual wig she sometimes wears. Today she has brought Norma Jean an off-white dust ruffle she made for the bed; Mabel works in a custom-upholstery shop.

"This is the tenth one I made this year," Mabel says. "I got started and couldn't stop."

"It's real pretty," says Norma Jean.

"Now we can hide things under the bed," says Leroy, who gets along with his mother-in-law primarily by joking with her. Mabel has never really forgiven him for disgracing her by getting Norma Jean pregnant. When the baby died, she said that fate was mocking her.

"What's that thing?" Mabel says to Leroy in a loud voice, pointing to a tangle of yarn on a piece of canvas.

Leroy holds it up for Mabel to see. "It's my needlepoint," he explains. "This is a *Star Trek* pillow cover."

"That's what a woman would do," says Mabel. "Great day in the morning!"

"All the big football players on TV do it," he says.

"Why, Leroy, you're always trying to fool me. I don't believe you for one minute. You don't know what to do with yourself—that's the whole trouble. Sewing!"

"I'm aiming to build us a log house," says Leroy. "Soon as my plans come."

"Like *heck* you are," says Norma Jean. She takes Leroy's needlepoint and shoves it into a drawer. "You have to find a job first. Nobody can afford to build now anyway."

Mabel straightens her girdle and says, "I still think before you get tied down y'all ought to take a little run to Shiloh."

"One of these days, Mama," Norma Jean says impatiently.

Mabel is talking about Shiloh, Tennessee. For the past few years, she has been urging Leroy and Norma Jean to visit the Civil War battleground there.[3]

---

3. Site of an April 1862 Civil War battle between more than 100,000 Union and Confederate troops, a quarter of whom were killed. Shiloh put an end to the hopes of those, North and South, who had believed that the war would be brief and relatively bloodless.

Mabel went there on her honeymoon—the only real trip she ever took. Her husband died of a perforated ulcer when Norma Jean was ten, but Mabel, who was accepted into the United Daughters of the Confederacy in 1975, is still preoccupied with going back to Shiloh.

"I've been to kingdom come and back in that truck out yonder," Leroy says to Mabel, "but we never yet set foot in that battleground. Ain't that something? How did I miss it?"

"It's not even that far," Mabel says.

After Mabel leaves, Norma Jean reads to Leroy from a list she has made. "Things you could do," she announces. "You could get a job as a guard at Union Carbide, where they'd let you set on a stool. You could get on at the lumberyard. You could do a little carpenter work, if you want to build so bad. You could—"

"I can't do something where I'd have to stand up all day."

"You ought to try standing up all day behind a cosmetics counter. It's amazing that I have strong feet, coming from two parents that never had strong feet at all." At the moment Norma Jean is holding on to the kitchen counter, raising her knees one at a time as she talks. She is wearing two-pound ankle weights.

"Don't worry," says Leroy. "I'll do something."

"You could truck calves to slaughter for somebody. You wouldn't have to drive any big old truck for that."

"I'm going to build you this house," says Leroy. "I want to make you a real home."

"I don't want to live in any log cabin."

"It's not a cabin. It's a house."

"I don't care. It looks like a cabin."

"You and me together could lift those logs. It's just like lifting weights."

Norma Jean doesn't answer. Under her breath, she is counting. Now she is marching through the kitchen. She is doing goose steps.

Before his accident, when Leroy came home he used to stay in the house with Norma Jean, watching TV in bed and playing cards. She would cook fried chicken, picnic ham, chocolate pie—all his favorites. Now he is home alone much of the time. In the mornings, Norma Jean disappears, leaving a cooling place in the bed. She eats a cereal called Body Buddies, and she leaves the bowl on the table, with soggy tan balls floating in a milk puddle. He sees things about Norma Jean that he never realized before. When she chops onions, she stares off into a corner, as if she can't bear to look. She puts on her house slippers almost precisely at nine o'clock every evening and nudges her jogging shoes under the couch. She saves bread heels for the birds. Leroy watches the birds at the feeder. He notices the peculiar way goldfinches fly past the window. They close their wings, then fall, then spread their wings to catch and lift themselves. He wonders if they close their eyes when they fall. Norma Jean closes her eyes when they are in bed. She wants the lights turned out. Even then, he is sure she closes her eyes.

He goes for long drives around town. He tends to drive a car rather carelessly. Power steering and an automatic shift make a car feel so small and inconsequential that his body is hardly involved in the driving process. His injured leg stretches out comfortably. Once or twice he has almost hit something, but even the prospect of an accident seems minor in a car. He cruises the new subdivisions, feeling like a criminal rehearsing for a robbery. Norma Jean is probably right about a log house being inappropriate here in the new subdivisions. All the houses look grand and complicated. They depress him.

One day when Leroy comes home from a drive he finds Norma Jean in tears. She is in the kitchen making a potato and mushroom-soup casserole, with grated-cheese topping. She is crying because her mother caught her smoking.

"I didn't hear her coming. I was standing here puffing away pretty as you please," Norma Jean says, wiping her eyes.

"I knew it would happen sooner or later," says Leroy, putting his arm around her.

"She don't know the meaning of the word 'knock,'" says Norma Jean. "It's a wonder she hadn't caught me years ago."

"Think of it this way," Leroy says. "What if she caught me with a joint?"

"You better not let her!" Norma Jean shrieks. "I'm warning you, Leroy Moffitt!"

"I'm just kidding. Here, play me a tune. That'll help you relax."

Norma Jean puts the casserole in the oven and sets the timer. Then she plays a ragtime tune, with horns and banjo, as Leroy lights up a joint and lies on the couch, laughing to himself about Mabel's catching him at it. He thinks of Stevie Hamilton—a doctor's son pushing grass. Everything is funny. The whole town seems crazy and small. He is reminded of Virgil Mathis, a boastful policeman Leroy used to shoot pool with. Virgil recently led a drug bust in a back room at a bowling alley, where he seized ten thousand dollars' worth of marijuana. The newspaper had a picture of him holding up the bags of grass and grinning widely. Right now, Leroy can imagine Virgil breaking down the door and arresting him with a lungful of smoke. Virgil would probably have been alerted to the scene because of all the racket Norma Jean is making. Now she sounds like a hard-rock band. Norma Jean is terrific. When she switches to a latin-rhythm version of "Sunshine Superman," Leroy hums along. Norma Jean's foot goes up and down, up and down.

"Well, what do you think?" Leroy says, when Norma Jean pauses to search through her music.

"What do I think about what?"

His mind has gone blank. Then he says, "I'll sell my rig and build us a house." That wasn't what he wanted to say. He wanted to know what she thought—what she *really* thought—about them.

"Don't start in on that again," says Norma Jean. She begins playing "Who'll Be the Next in Line?"

Leroy used to tell hitchhikers his whole life story—about his travels, his hometown, the baby. He would end with a question: "Well, what do you think?" It was just a rhetorical question. In time, he had the feeling that he'd been telling the same story over and over to the same hitchhikers. He quit talking to hitchhikers when he realized how his voice sounded—whining and self-pitying, like some teenage-tragedy song. Now Leroy has the sudden impulse to tell Norma Jean about himself, as if he had just met her. They have known each other so long they have forgotten a lot about each other. They could become reacquainted. But when the oven timer goes off and she runs to the kitchen, he forgets why he wants to do this.

The next day, Mabel drops by. It is Saturday and Norma Jean is cleaning. Leroy is studying the plans of his log house, which have finally come in the mail. He has them spread out on the table—big sheets of stiff blue paper, with diagrams and numbers printed in white. While Norma Jean runs the vacuum, Mabel drinks coffee. She sets her coffee cup on a blueprint.

"I'm just waiting for time to pass," she says to Leroy, drumming her fingers on the table.

As soon as Norma Jean switches off the vacuum, Mabel says in a loud voice, "Did you hear about the datsun dog that killed the baby?"

Norma Jean says, "The word is 'dachshund.'"

"They put the dog on trial. It chewed the baby's legs off. The mother was in the next room all the time." She raises her voice. "They thought it was neglect."

Norma Jean is holding her ears. Leroy manages to open the refrigerator and get some Diet Pepsi to offer Mabel. Mabel still has some coffee and she waves away the Pepsi.

"Datsuns are like that," Mabel says. "They're jealous dogs. They'll tear a place to pieces if you don't keep an eye on them."

"You better watch out what you're saying, Mabel," says Leroy.

"Well, facts is facts."

Leroy looks out the window at his rig. It is like a huge piece of furniture gathering dust in the backyard. Pretty soon it will be an antique. He hears the vacuum cleaner. Norma Jean seems to be cleaning the living room rug again.

Later, she says to Leroy, "She just said that about the baby because she caught me smoking. She's trying to pay me back."

"What are you talking about?" Leroy says, nervously shuffling blueprints.

"You know good and well," Norma Jean says. She is sitting in a kitchen chair with her feet up and her arms wrapped around her knees. She looks small and helpless. She says, "The very idea, her bringing up a subject like that! Saying it was neglect."

"She didn't mean that," Leroy says.

"She might not have *thought* she meant it. She always says things like that. You don't know how she goes on."

"But she didn't really mean it. She was just talking."

Leroy opens a king-sized bottle of beer and pours it into two glasses, dividing it carefully. He hands a glass to Norma Jean and she takes it from him mechanically. For a long time, they sit by the kitchen window watching the birds at the feeder.

Something is happening. Norma Jean is going to night school. She has graduated from her six-week body-building course and now she is taking an adult-education course in composition at Paducah Community College. She spends her evenings outlining paragraphs.

"First you have a topic sentence," she explains to Leroy. "Then you divide it up. Your secondary topic has to be connected to your primary topic."

To Leroy, this sounds intimidating. "I never was any good in English," he says.

"It makes a lot of sense."

"What are you doing this for, anyhow?"

She shrugs. "It's something to do." She stands up and lifts her dumbbells a few times.

"Driving a rig, nobody cared about my English."

"I'm not criticizing your English."

Norma Jean used to say, "If I lose ten minutes' sleep, I just drag all day." Now she stays up late, writing compositions. She got a B on her first paper—a how-to theme on soup-based casseroles. Recently Norma Jean has been cooking unusual foods—tacos, lasagna, Bombay chicken. She doesn't play the organ anymore, though her second paper was called "Why Music Is Important to Me." She sits at the kitchen table, concentrating on her outlines, while Leroy plays with his log house plans, practicing with a set of Lincoln Logs. The thought of getting a truckload of notched, numbered logs scares him, and he wants to be prepared. As he and Norma Jean work together at the kitchen table, Leroy has the hopeful thought that they are sharing something, but he knows he is a fool to think this. Norma Jean is miles away. He knows he is going to lose her. Like Mabel, he is just waiting for time to pass.

One day, Mabel is there before Norma Jean gets home from work, and Leroy finds himself confiding in her. Mabel, he realizes, must know Norma Jean better than he does.

"I don't know what's got into that girl," Mabel says. "She used to go to bed with the chickens. Now you say she's up all hours. Plus her a-smoking. I like to died."

"I want to make her this beautiful home," Leroy says, indicating the Lincoln Logs. "I don't think she even wants it. Maybe she was happier with me gone."

"She don't know what to make of you, coming home like this."

"Is that it?"

Mabel takes the roof off his Lincoln Log cabin. "You couldn't get *me* in a log cabin," she says. "I was raised in one. It's no picnic, let me tell you."

"They're different now," says Leroy.

"I tell you what," Mabel says, smiling oddly at Leroy.

"What?"

"Take her on down to Shiloh. Y'all need to get out together, stir a little. Her brain's all balled up over them books."

Leroy can see traces of Norma Jean's features in her mother's face. Mabel's face has the texture of crinkled cotton, but suddenly she looks pretty. It occurs to Leroy that Mabel has been hinting all along that she wants them to take her with them to Shiloh.

"Let's all go to Shiloh," he says. "You and me and her. Come Sunday."

Mabel throws up her hands in protest. "Oh, no, not me. Young folks want to be by theirselves."

When Norma Jean comes in with groceries, Leroy says excitedly, "Your mama here's been dying to go to Shiloh for thirty-five years. It's about time we went, don't you think?"

"I'm not going to butt in on anybody's second honeymoon," Mabel says.

"Who's going on a honeymoon, for Christ's sake?" Norma Jean says loudly.

"I never raised no daughter of mine to talk that-a-way," Mabel says.

"You ain't seen nothing yet," says Norma Jean. She starts putting away boxes and cans, slamming cabinet doors.

"There's a log cabin at Shiloh." Mabel says, "It was there during the battle. There's bullet holes in it."

"When are you going to *shut up* about Shiloh, Mama?" asks Norma Jean.

"I always thought Shiloh was the prettiest place, so full of history," Mabel goes on. "I just hoped y'all could see it once before I die, so you could tell me about it." Later, she whispers to Leroy, "You do what I said. A little change is what she needs."

"Your name means 'the king,'" Norma Jean says to Leroy that evening. He is trying to get her to go to Shiloh, and she is reading a book about another century.

"Well, I reckon I ought to be right proud."

"I guess so."

"Am I still king around here?"

Norma Jean flexes her biceps and feels them for hardness. "I'm not fooling around with anybody, if that's what you mean," she says.

"Would you tell me if you were?"

"I don't know."

"What does *your* name mean?"

"It was Marilyn Monroe's real name."

"No kidding!"

"Norma comes from the Normans. They were invaders," she says. She closes her book and looks hard at Leroy. "I'll go to Shiloh with you if you'll stop staring at me."

On Sunday, Norma Jean packs a picnic and they go to Shiloh. To Leroy's relief, Mabel says she does not want to come with them. Norma Jean drives, and Leroy, sitting beside her, feels like some boring hitchhiker she has picked up. He tries some conversation, but she answers him in monosyllables. At Shiloh, she drives aimlessly through the park, past bluffs and trails and steep ravines. Shiloh is an immense place, and Leroy cannot see it as a battleground. It is not what he expected. He thought it would look like a golf course. Monuments are everywhere, showing through the thick clusters of trees. Norma Jean passes the log cabin Mabel mentioned. It is surrounded by tourists looking for bullet holes.

"That's not the kind of log house I've got in mind," says Leroy apologetically.

"I know *that*."

"This is a pretty place. Your mama was right."

"It's O.K.," says Norma Jean. "Well, we've seen it. I hope she's satisfied."

They burst out laughing together.

At the park museum, a movie on Shiloh is shown every half hour, but they decide that they don't want to see it. They buy a souvenir Confederate flag for Mabel, and then they find a picnic spot near the cemetery. Norma Jean has brought a picnic cooler, with pimiento sandwiches, soft drinks, and Yodels. Leroy eats a sandwich and then smokes a joint, hiding it behind the picnic cooler. Norma Jean has quit smoking altogether. She is picking cake crumbs from the cellophane wrapper, like a fussy bird.

Leroy says, "So the boys in gray ended up in Corinth. The Union soldiers zapped 'em finally. April 7, 1862."

They both know that he doesn't know any history. He is just talking about some of the historical plaques they have read. He feels awkward, like a boy on a date with an older girl. They are still just making conversation.

"Corinth is where Mama eloped to," says Norma Jean.

They sit in silence and stare at the cemetery for the Union dead and, beyond, at a tall cluster of trees. Campers are parked nearby, bumper to bumper, and small children in bright clothing are cavorting and squealing. Norma Jean wads up the cake wrapper and squeezes it tightly in her hand. Without looking at Leroy, she says, "I want to leave you."

Leroy takes a bottle of Coke out of the cooler and flips off the cap. He holds the bottle poised near his mouth but cannot remember to take a drink. Finally he says, "No, you don't."

"Yes, I do."

"I won't let you."

"You can't stop me."

"Don't do me that way."

Leroy knows Norma Jean will have her own way. "Didn't I promise to be home from now on?" he says.

"In some ways, a woman prefers a man who wanders," says Norma Jean. "That sounds crazy, I know."

"You're not crazy."

Leroy remembers to drink from his Coke. Then he says, "Yes, you *are* crazy. You and me could start all over again. Right back at the beginning."

"We *have* started all over again," says Norma Jean. "And this is how it turned out."

"What did I do wrong?"

"Nothing."

"Is this one of those women's lib things?" Leroy asks.

"Don't be funny."

The cemetery, a green slope dotted with white markers, looks like a subdivision site. Leroy is trying to comprehend that his marriage is breaking up, but for some reason he is wondering about white slabs in a graveyard.

"Everything was fine till Mama caught me smoking," says Norma Jean, standing up. "That set something off."

"What are you talking about?"

"She won't leave me alone—*you* won't leave me alone." Norma Jean seems to be crying, but she is looking away from him. "I feel eighteen again. I can't face that all over again." She starts walking away. "No, it *wasn't* fine. I don't know what I'm saying. Forget it."

Leroy takes a lungful of smoke and closes his eyes as Norma Jean's words sink in. He tries to focus on the fact that thirty-five hundred soldiers died on the grounds around him. He can only think of that war as a board game with plastic soldiers. Leroy almost smiles, as he compares the Confederates' daring attack on the Union camps and Virgil Mathis's raid on the bowling alley. General Grant, drunk and furious, shoved the Southerners back to Corinth, where Mabel and Jet Beasley were married years later, when Mabel was still thin and good-looking. The next day, Mabel and Jet visited the battleground, and then Norma Jean was born, and then she married Leroy and they had a baby, which they lost, and now Leroy and Norma Jean are here at the same battleground. Leroy knows he is leaving out a lot. He is leaving out the insides of history. History was always just names and dates to him. It occurs to him that building a house out of logs is similarly empty—too simple. And the real inner workings of a marriage, like most of history, have escaped him. Now he sees that building a log house is the dumbest idea he could have had. It was clumsy of him to think Norma Jean would want a log house. It was a crazy idea. He'll have to think of something else, quickly. He will wad the blueprints into tight balls and fling them into the lake. Then he'll get moving again. He opens his eyes. Norma Jean has moved away and is walking through the cemetery, following a serpentine brick path.

Leroy gets up to follow his wife, but his good leg is asleep and his bad leg still hurts him. Norma Jean is far away, walking rapidly toward the bluff by the river, and he tries to hobble toward her. Some children run past him, screaming noisily. Norma Jean has reached the bluff, and she is looking out over the Tennessee River. Now she turns toward Leroy and waves her arms. Is she beckoning to him? She seems to be doing an exercise for her chest muscles. The sky is unusually pale—the color of the dust ruffle Mabel made for their bed.

1982

GUY DE MAUPASSANT
1850–1893

Maupassant was born near Dieppe, France. His parents were friends of the novelist Gustave Flaubert, whose views on literature and the artistic life influenced Maupassant even in his early years. Rebellious in school, he accepted army discipline during the Franco-Prussian War of 1870–71, and then for nearly ten years apprenticed himself to Flaubert to learn the craft of fiction, discarding most of what he wrote. In 1880 he became famous with the publication of a single story, *Boule de Suif*, which contrasts the patriotism of a young prostitute with the amorality of middle-class citizens. Maupassant published, during the next ten years, nearly three hundred short stories, half a dozen novels, some plays, verse, and travel books. The short stories, which appeared regularly in popular periodicals, sampled military and peasant life, the decadent world of politics and journalism, prostitution, perversion, the supernatural, and the hypocrisies of solid citizens. Maupassant's income from his prodigious literary output permitted him to indulge the appetites for women and luxury that had always been part of his character, but in his last years syphilis, which he apparently contracted before he was twenty, began to unravel his capacity for concentrated work. He sought relief in drugs and travels on his yacht but became completely insane before he died of paresis. His novels include *Une Vie* (*A Life*, 1883), *Bel Ami* (*Handsome Friend*, 1885), and *Pierre et Jean* (1888). His short stories are most readily available in his collected works.

Boule de Suif[1]

For several days in succession straggling remnants of the routed French army had been passing through the town.[2] This was not the regular army, but a disjointed rabble, the men unshaven and dirty, their uniforms in tatters, slouching along without regimental colors, without order—worn out, broken down, incapable of thought or resolution, marching from pure habit and dropping with fatigue the moment they stopped. The majority belonged to the militia and were men of peaceful pursuits, retired from business, all sinking under the weight of their accouterments: quick-witted little militiamen as prone to terror as they were to enthusiasm, as ready to attack as they were

---

1. Translated by Ernest Boyd and Storm Jameson.   2. France was humiliated by the collapse of its armies before the Germans in the Franco-Prussian War (1870–71). The French defeat brought about the downfall of the Second Empire under Napoleon III and marked the ascension of Germany as a European power.

to fly; here and there a few red trousers, remnants of a company mowed down in one of the big battles; dark-coated artillerymen, side by side with these various uniforms of the infantry, and now and then the glittering helmet of a heavily booted dragoon who followed with difficulty the march of the more light-footed soldiers of the line.[3]

Companies of franc-tireurs,[4] heroically named "Avengers of the Defeat," "Citizens of the Tomb," "Companions in Death," passed in their turn, looking like a horde of bandits.

Their chiefs—formerly drapers or grain-dealers, retired soap-boilers or suet-refiners, temporary heroes, created officers by reason of their wealth or the length of their mustaches, burdened with weapons, flannels, and gold lace—talked loudly, discussed plans of campaign, and gave you to understand that they were the sole support of France in her death-agony; but they were generally in terror of their own soldiers, gallows birds, most of them brave to foolhardiness, all of them given to pillage and debauchery.

Report said that the Prussians were about to enter Rouen.[5] The National Guard, which for two months past had made the most careful reconnoiterings in the neighboring wood, even to the extent of occasionally shooting their own sentries and putting themselves in battle array if a rabbit stirred in the brushwood, had now retired to their domestic hearths; their arms, their uniforms, all the murderous apparatus with which they had been wont to strike terror into the hearts of all beholders for three leagues round, had vanished.

Finally, the last of the French soldiery crossed the Seine on their way to Pont-Audemer by Saint-Severin and Bourg-Achard;[6] and then, last of all, came their despairing general tramping on foot between two orderlies, powerless to attempt any action with these disjointed fragments of his forces, himself utterly dazed and bewildered by the downfall of a people accustomed to victory and now so disastrously beaten in spite of its traditional bravery.

After that a profound calm, the silence of terrified suspense, fell over the city. Many a rotund bourgeois, emasculated by a lifetime of trade, awaited the arrival of the victors with anxiety, trembling lest his meat-skewers and kitchen carving-knives should come under the category of arms.

Life seemed to have come to a standstill, the shops were closed, the streets silent. From time to time an inhabitant, intimidated by their silence, would flit rapidly along the pavement, keeping close to the walls.

In this anguish of suspense, men longed for the coming of the enemy.

Towards the end of the day following the departure of the French troops, some Uhlans,[7] appearing from goodness knows where, traversed the city hastily. A little later, a black mass descended from the direction of Sainte-Catherine, while two more invading torrents poured in over the roads from Darnetal and Boisguillaume. The advance guards of the three corps converged at the same moment into the square of the Hotel de Ville, while battalion after battalion of the German army wound through the adjacent streets, making the pavement ring under their heavy rhythmic tramp.

Orders shouted in strange and guttural tones were echoed back by the apparently dead and deserted houses, while from behind closed shutters eyes

---

3. Infantrymen. *Dragoon:* cavalryman. **4.** Army sharpshooters (French). **5.** City in Normandy, northwest of Paris. Prussians: Germans. **6.** Towns west of Rouen. **7.** Prussian light cavalry.

peered furtively at the conquerors, masters by right of might, of the city and the lives and fortunes of its inhabitants. The people in their darkened dwellings fell a prey to the helpless bewilderment which comes over men before the floods, the devastating upheavals of the earth, against which all wisdom and all force are unavailing. The same phenomenon occurs each time that the established order of things is overthrown, when public security is at an end, and when all that the laws of man or of nature protect is at the mercy of some blind elemental force. The earthquake burying an entire population under its falling houses; the flood that carries away the drowned body of the peasant with the carcasses of his cattle and the beams torn from his roof-tree; or the victorious army massacring those who defend their lives, and making prisoners of the rest—pillaging in the name of the sword, and thanking God to the roar of cannon—are so many appalling scourges which overthrow all faith in eternal justice, all the confidence we are taught to place in the protection of Providence and the reason of man.

Small detachments now began knocking at the doors and then disappearing into the houses. It was the occupation after the invasion. It now behooved the vanquished to make themselves agreeable to the victors.

After a while, the first alarms having subsided, a new sense of tranquillity began to establish itself. In many houses the Prussian officer shared the family meals. Not infrequently he was a gentleman, and out of politeness expressed his commiseration with France and his repugnance at having to take part in such a war. They were grateful enough to him for this sentiment—besides, who knew when they might not be glad of his protection? By gaining his good offices one might have fewer men to feed. And why offend a person on whom one was utterly dependent? That would not be bravery but temerity, a quality of which the citizens of Rouen could no longer be accused as in the days of those heroic defenses by which the city had made itself famous. Above all, they said, with the unassailable urbanity of the Frenchman, it was surely permissible to be on politely familiar terms in private, provided one held aloof from the foreign soldier in public. In the street, therefore, they ignored one another's existence, but once indoors they were perfectly ready to be friendly, and each evening found the German staying longer at the family fireside.

The town itself gradually regained its wonted aspect. The French inhabitants did not come out much, but the Prussian soldiers swarmed in the streets. For the rest, the blue hussar[8] officers who trailed their mighty implements of death so arrogantly over the pavement did not appear to entertain a vastly deeper grade of contempt for the simple townsfolk than did the officers of the Chasseurs[9] who had drunk in the same cafés the year before. Nevertheless there was something in the air; something subtle and indefinable, an intolerably unfamiliar atmosphere like a widely diffused odor—the odor of invasion. It filled the private dwellings and the public places, it affected the taste of food, and gave one the impression of being on a journey, far away from home, among barbarous and dangerous tribes.

The conquerors demanded money—a great deal of money. The inhabitants paid and went on paying; for the matter of that, they were rich. But the wealthier a Normandy tradesman becomes, the more keenly he suffers at each sacrifice

8. Light cavalry.   9. Troops, cavalry, or infantry trained for quick deployment or movement (French).

each time he sees the smallest particle of his fortune pass into the hands of another.

Two or three leagues beyond the town, however, following the course of the river about Croisset, Dieppedalle or Biessard, the sailors and the fishermen would often drag up the swollen corpse of some uniformed German, killed by a knife-thrust or a kick, his head smashed in by a stone, or thrown into the water from some bridge. The slime of the river bed swallowed up many a deed of vengeance, obscure, savage, and legitimate; unknown acts of heroism, silent onslaughts more perilous to the doer than battles in the light of day and without the trumpet-blasts of glory.

For hatred of the alien is always strong enough to arm some intrepid beings who are ready to die for an Idea.

At last, seeing that though the invaders had subjected the city to their inflexible discipline they had not committed any of the horrors with which rumor had credited them throughout the length of their triumphal progress, the public took courage and the commercial spirit began once more to stir in the hearts of the local tradespeople. Some of them who had grave interests at stake at Havre, then occupied by the French army, purposed trying to reach that port by going overland to Dieppe[1] and there taking ship.

They took advantage of the influence of German officers whose acquaintance they had made, and a passport was obtained from the general in command.

Having therefore engaged a large coach with four horses for the journey, and ten persons having entered their names at the livery stable office, they resolved to start on Tuesday morning before daybreak, to avoid all public remark.

For some days already the ground had been hard with frost, and on Monday, about three o'clock in the afternoon, thick dark clouds coming up from the north brought snow, which fell steadily all evening and during the night.

At half-past four the travelers were assembled in the courtyard of the Hotel de Normandie, from whence they were to start.

They were still half asleep, their teeth chattering with cold in spite of their thick wraps. It was difficult to distinguish one from another in the darkness, their heaped-up winter clothing making them look like fat priests in long cassocks. Two of the men, however, recognized each other; they were joined by a third, and they began to talk. "I am taking my wife with me," said one. "So am I." "And I too." The first one added, "We shall not return to Rouen, and if the Prussians come to Havre we shall slip over to England."

They were all like-minded and all had the same plan.

Meanwhile there was no sign of the horses being put in. A small lantern carried by a hostler appeared from time to time out of one dark doorway only to vanish instantly into another. There was a stamping of horses' hoofs deadened by the straw of the litter, and the voice of a man speaking to the animal and cursing sounded from the depths of the stables. A faint tinkle of bells gave evidence of harnessing, and became presently a clear and continual jingle timed by the movement of the beast, now stopping, now going on again with a brisk shake, and accompanied by the dull tramp of hobnailed clogs.

---

1. Port on Normandy coast due north of Rouen, northeast of Havre.

A door slammed sharply. All sound ceased. The frozen travelers were silent, standing stiff and motionless. A continuous curtain of white snowflakes glistened as it fell to the ground, blotting out the shape of things, powdering everything with an icy froth; and in the utter stillness of the town, quiet and buried under its winter pall, nothing was audible but this faint, fluttering, and indefinable rustle of falling snow—more a sensation than a sound—the intermingling of ethereal atoms seeming to fill space, to cover the world.

The man reappeared with his lantern, dragging after him by a rope a dejected and unwilling horse. He pushed it against the pole, fixed the traces, and was occupied for a long time in buckling the harness, having only the use of one hand as he carried the lantern in the other. As he turned away to fetch the other horse he caught sight of the motionless group of travelers, by this time white with snow. "Why don't you get inside the carriage?" he said, "you would at least be under cover."

It had never occurred to them, and they made a rush for it. The three men packed their wives into the upper end and then got in themselves, after which other distinct and veiled forms took the remaining seats without exchanging a word.

The floor of the vehicle was covered with straw into which the feet sank. The ladies at the end, who had brought little copper charcoal foot-warmers, proceeded to light them, and for some time discussed their merits in subdued tones, repeating to one another things which they had known all their lives.

At last, the coach having been furnished with six horses instead of four on account of the difficulties of the road, a voice outside asked, "Is everybody here?" A voice from within answered, "Yes," and they started.

The conveyance advanced slowly—slowly—the wheels sinking in the snow; the whole vehicle groaned and creaked, the horses slipped, wheezed, and smoked, and the driver's gigantic whip cracked incessantly, flying from side to side, twining and untwining like a slender snake, and cutting sharply across one or other of the six humping backs, which would thereupon straighten up with a more violent effort.

Imperceptibly the day advanced. The airy flakes which a traveler—a true-born Rouennais[2]—likened to a shower of cotton, had ceased to fall; a dirty gray light filtered through the heavy thick clouds which served to heighten the dazzling whiteness of the landscape, where now a long line of trees crusted with icicles would appear, now a cottage with a hood of snow.

In the light of this melancholy dawn the occupants of the diligence began to examine one another curiously.

Right at the end, in the best seats, opposite to one another, dozed Madame and Monsieur Loiseau, wholesale wine merchant of the Rue Grand-Pont.

The former salesman of a master who had become bankrupt, Loiseau had bought up the stock and made his fortune. He sold very bad wine at very low prices to the small country retail dealers, and enjoyed the reputation among his friends and acquaintances of being an unmitigated rogue, a thorough Norman full of trickery and jovial humor.

---

2. Native of Rouen.

His character for knavery was so well established that one evening at the Prefecture, Monsieur Tournel, a man of keen and trenchant wit, author of certain fables and songs—a local celebrity—seeing the ladies growing drowsy, proposed a game of "L'oiseau vole."[3] The pun itself flew through the prefect's reception rooms and afterwards through the town, and for a whole month called up a grin on every face in the province.

Loiseau was himself a noted wag famous for his jokes both good and bad, and nobody ever mentioned him without adding immediately, "That man, Loiseau, is simply priceless!"

He was of medium height with a balloon-like stomach and a rubicund face framed in grizzled whiskers. His wife—tall, strong, resolute, loud in voice and rapid of decision—represented order and arithmetic in the business, which he enlivened by his jollity and bustling activity.

Beside them, in a more dignified attitude as befitted his superior station, sat Monsieur Carré-Lamadon, a man of weight; an authority on cotton, proprietor of three spinning factories, officer of the Legion of Honor and member of the General Council of the *Département*. So long as the Second Empire[4] lasted, he had remained leader of a friendly opposition, for the sole purpose of making a better thing out of it when he decided to come over to the régime which he had fought with polite weapons, to use his own expression. Madame Carré-Lamadon, who was much younger than her husband, was the consolation of all officers of good family who might be quartered at the Rouen garrison. She sat there opposite to her husband, very small, very dainty, very pretty, wrapped in her furs, and staring at the lamentable interior of the vehicle with despairing eyes.

Their neighbors, the Count and Countess Hubert de Bréville, bore one of the most ancient and noble names in Normandy. The Count, an elderly gentleman of dignified appearance, did all in his power to accentuate by every artifice of the toilet his natural resemblance to Henri Quatre,[5] who, according to a legend of the utmost glory to the family, had honored with his royal embraces a Dame de Bréville, whose husband, in consequence, had been made Count and Governor of the province.

A colleague of Monsieur Carré-Lamadon in the General Council, Count Hubert represented the Orleanist[6] faction in the department. The history of his marriage with the daughter of a small tradesman of Nantes had always remained a mystery. But as the Countess had an air of grandeur, understood better than anyone else the art of receiving, passed even for having been beloved by one of the sons of Louis Philippe,[7] the neighboring nobility bowed down to her, and her salon held the first place in the province, the only one which preserved the traditions of old-fashioned gallantry and to which the entrée was difficult.

The fortune of the Brévilles—all in Government bonds—was reported to yield them an income of five hundred thousand francs.

---

3. Literally, "the bird flies" (French), a play on the name Loiseau. **4.** Regime of Napoleon III (nephew of Napoleon Bonaparte), lasting from 1852 until the defeat of France by Prussia in 1870. *Département:* government ministry. Legion of Honor: civilian award. **5.** Henry IV (1553–1610), king of France. **6.** Supporter of the Orleans family's claim to the French throne, here indicating conservative sympathies. **7.** Orleanist king of France from 1830 to 1848.

The six passengers who occupied the upper end of the conveyance represented the unearned income stratum of society, serene in the consciousness of its strength—honest well-to-do people possessed of religion and principles.

By some strange chance all the women were seated on the same side, the Countess having two Sisters of Mercy for neighbors, wholly occupied in fingering their long rosaries and mumbling Paters and Aves.[8] One of them was old and so deeply pitted with the smallpox that she looked as if she had received a charge of grapeshot full in the face; the other was very shadowy and frail, with a pretty unhealthy little face, a narrow consumptive chest, consumed by that devouring faith which creates martyrs and ecstatics.

Seated opposite the two nuns were a man and woman who excited a good deal of attention.

The man, who was well known, was Cornudet, "the Democrat," the terror of all respectable, law-abiding people. For twenty years he had dipped his great red beard into the beer mugs of all the democratic cafés. In the company of kindred spirits he had managed to run through a comfortable little fortune inherited from his father, a confectioner, and he looked forward with impatience to the Republic, when he should obtain the well-merited reward for so many revolutionary draughts. On the fourth of September—probably through some practical joke—he understood that he had been appointed prefect, but when he attempted to take office the clerks, who had remained sole masters of the prefecture, refused to recognize him, and he was constrained to retire. For the rest, he was a good fellow, inoffensive and willing, and had busied himself with incomparable industry in organizing the defense of the town; had had holes dug all over the plain, cut down all the young trees in the neighboring woods, scattered pitfalls[9] up and down all the high roads, and at the threatened approach of the enemy—satisfied with his preparations—had fallen back with all haste on the town. He now considered that he would be more useful in Havre, where fresh entrenchments would soon become necessary.

The woman, one of the so-called "gay" sisterhood, was noted for her precocious stoutness, which had gained her the nickname of "Boule de Suif"—"Butter-Ball." She was a little roly-poly creature, cushioned with fat, with podgy fingers squeezed in at the joints like rows of thick, short sausages; her skin tightly stretched and shiny, her bust enormous, and yet she was attractive and much sought after, her freshness was so pleasant. Her face was like a ruddy apple—a peony rose just burst into bloom—and out of it gazed a pair of magnificent dark eyes overshadowed by long thick lashes that deepened their blackness; and lower down, a charming little mouth, dewy to the kiss, and furnished with a row of tiny milk-white teeth. Apart from all this she was said to be a good-hearted creature, full of inestimable qualities.

No sooner was her identity recognized than a whisper ran through the ladies in which the words "prostitute" and "public scandal" were so conspicuously distinct that she raised her head and retaliated by sweeping her companions with such a bold and defiant look that deep silence instantly fell upon them, and they all cast down their eyes with the exception of Loiseau, who watched her with a kindling eye.

---

8. Pater nosters (Our Fathers) and Ave Marias (Hail Marys); prayers (Latin).   **9.** Traps, camouflaged pits.

However, conversation was soon resumed between the three ladies, whom the presence of this "person" had suddenly rendered friendly—almost intimate. It seemed to them that they must, as it were, raise a rampart of their dignity as spouses between them and this shameless creature who made a traffic of herself; for legalized love always takes a high hand with her unlicensed sister.

The three men too, drawn to one another by a conservative instinct at sight of Cornudet, talked money in a certain tone of contempt for the impecunious. Count Hubert spoke of the damage inflicted on him by the Prussians, of the losses which would result to him from the seizing of cattle and from ruined crops, but with all the assurance of a great landed proprietor, ten times a millionaire, whom these ravages might inconvenience for the space of a year at most. Monsieur Carré-Lamadon, of great experience in the cotton industry, had taken the precaution to send six hundred thousand francs across to England as provision against a rainy day. As for Loiseau, he had made arrangements to sell all the common wines in his cellars to the French commission of supplies, consequently the government owed him a formidable sum, which he counted upon receiving at Havre.

The three exchanged rapid and amicable glances. Although differing in position they felt themselves brothers in money, and of the great freemasonry of those who possess, of those who can make the gold jingle when they put their hands in their pockets.

The coach went so slowly that by ten o'clock in the morning they had not made ten miles. The men had got out three times to climb hills on foot. They began to grow anxious, for they were to have lunched at Tôtes,[1] and now they despaired of reaching that place before night. Everybody was on the lookout for some inn by the way. Once the vehicle stuck fast in a snowdrift, and it took two hours to get it out.

Meanwhile the pangs of hunger began to affect them severely both in mind and body, and yet not an inn, not a tavern even, was to be seen; the approach of the Prussians and the passage of the famished French troops had frightened away all trade.

The gentlemen foraged diligently for provisions in the farms by the roadside; but they failed to obtain so much as a piece of bread, for the mistrustful peasant hid all reserve stores for fear of being pillaged by the soldiers, who, having no food supplied to them, took by force everything they could lay their hands on.

Towards one o'clock Loiseau announced that he felt a very decided void in his stomach. Everybody had been suffering in the same manner for a long time, and the violent longing for food had extinguished conversation.

From time to time someone would yawn, to be almost immediately imitated by another and then each of the rest in turn, and according to their disposition, manners, or social standing, would open his mouth noisily, or modestly cover with the hand the gaping cavity from which the breath issued in a vapor.

Boule de Suif had several times stooped down as if feeling for something under her skirts. She hesitated a moment, looked at her companions, and then composedly resumed her former position. The faces were pale and drawn.

1. Town halfway between Rouen and Dieppe.

Loiseau declared he would give a thousand francs for a ham. His wife made a faint movement as to protest, but restrained herself. It always affected her painfully to hear of money being thrown away, nor could she ever understand a joke upon the subject.

"To tell the truth," said the Count, "I do not feel quite myself either—how could I have omitted to think of bringing provisions?" And everybody reproached himself with the same neglect.

Cornudet, however, had a flask of rum which he offered round. It was coldly refused. Loiseau alone accepted a mouthful, and handed back the flask with thanks saying, "That's good! That warms you up and keeps the hunger off a bit." The alcohol raised his spirits somewhat, and he proposed that they should do the same as on the little ship in the song—eat the fattest of the passengers. This indirect but obvious allusion to Boule de Suif shocked the gentlefolk. Nobody responded and only Cornudet smiled. The two Sisters of Mercy had ceased to tell their beads and sat motionless, their hands buried in their wide sleeves, their eyes obstinately lowered, doubtless engaged in offering back to Heaven the sacrifice of suffering which it sent them.

At last, at three o'clock, when they were in the middle of an interminable stretch of bare country without a single village in sight, Boule de Suif, stooping hurriedly, drew from under the seat a large basket covered with a white napkin.

Out of it she took, first of all, a little china plate and a delicate silver drinking-cup, and then an immense dish, in which two whole fowls ready carved lay stiffened in their jelly. Other good things were visible in the basket: patties, fruits, pastry—in fact provisions for a three days' journey in order to be independent of inn cookery. The necks of four bottles protruded from between the parcels of food. She took the wing of a fowl and began to eat it daintily with one of those little rolls which they call "Régence" in Normandy.

Every eye was fixed upon her. As the odor of the food spread through the carriage nostrils began to quiver and mouths to water, while the jaws, just below the ears, contracted painfully. The dislike entertained by the ladies for this abandoned young woman grew savage, almost to the point of longing to murder her or at least to turn her out into the snow, her and her drinking-cup and her basket and her provisions.

Loiseau, however, was devouring the dish of chicken with his eyes. "Madame has been more prudent than we," he said. "Some people always think of everything."

She turned her head in his direction. "If you would care for any, Sir—? It is not comfortable to fast for so long."

He bowed. "By Jove!—frankly, I won't refuse. I can't stand this any longer—the fortune of war, is it not, madame?" And with a comprehensive look he added, "In moments such as this we are only too glad to find anyone who will oblige us." He had a newspaper which he spread on his knee to save his trousers, and with the point of a knife which he always carried in his pocket he captured a drumstick all glazed with jelly, tore it with his teeth, and then proceeded to chew it with satisfaction so evident that a deep groan of distress went up from the whole party.

Upon this Boule de Suif in a gentle and humble tone invited the two Sisters to share the collation. They both accepted on the spot, and without raising their eyes began to eat very hurriedly, after stammering a few words of thanks. Nor did Cornudet refuse his neighbor's offer, and with the Sisters they formed a kind of table by spreading out newspapers on their knees.

The jaws opened and shut without a pause, biting, chewing, gulping ferociously. Loiseau, hard at work in his corner, urged his wife in a low voice to follow his example. She resisted for some time, then, after a pang which gripped her very vitals, she gave in. Whereupon her husband, rounding off his phrases, asked if their "charming fellow-traveler" would permit him to offer a little something to Madame Loiseau.

"Why, yes, certainly, Monsieur," she answered with a pleasant smile, and handed him the dish.

There was a moment of embarrassment when the first bottle of claret was uncorked—there was but the one drinking-cup. Each one wiped it before passing it to the rest. Cornudet alone, from an impulse of gallantry no doubt, placed his lips on the spot still wet from the lips of his neighbor.

Then it was that, surrounded by people who were eating, suffocated by the fragrant odor of the viands, the Count and Countess de Bréville and Monsieur and Madame Carré-Lamadon suffered the agonies of that torture which has ever been associated with the name of Tantalus.[2] Suddenly the young wife of the cotton manufacturer gave a deep sigh. Every head turned towards her; she was as white as the snow outside, her eyes closed, her head fell forward— she had fainted. Her husband, distraught with fear, implored assistance of the whole company. All lost their heads till the elder of the two Sisters, who supported the unconscious lady, forced Boule de Suif's drinking-cup between her lips and made her swallow a few drops of wine. The pretty creature stirred, opened her eyes, smiled and then declared in an expiring voice that she felt quite well now. But to prevent her being overcome again in the same manner, the Sister induced her to drink a full cup of wine, adding, "It is simply hunger— nothing else."

At this Boule de Suif, blushing violently, looked at the four starving passengers and faltered shyly, "*Mon Dieu!*[3] If I might make so bold as to offer the ladies and gentlemen—" She stopped short, fearing a rude rebuff.

Loiseau, however, at once threw himself into the breach. "*Parbleu!*[4] Under such circumstances we are all companions in misfortune and bound to help each other. Come, ladies, don't stand on ceremony—take what you can get and be thankful: who knows whether we shall be able to find so much as a house where we can spend the night? At this rate we shall not reach Tôtes till tomorrow afternoon."

They still hesitated, nobody having the courage to take upon themselves the responsibility of the decisive "Yes." Finally the Count seized the bull by the horns. Adopting his grandest air, he turned with a bow to the embarrassed young woman and said, "We accept your offer with thanks, madame."

The first step only was difficult. The Rubicon once crossed, they fell to with a will. They emptied the basket, which contained, besides the provisions

---

2. In Greek mythology, a king, sometimes believed to be a son of Zeus, who for his crimes was condemned to remain forever in Tartarus, standing in water up to his chin, with branches heavy with fruit above his head. When he attempted to eat or drink, the fruit or water would recede from his reach. The word *tantalize* stems from this myth.   3. "My God!" (French).   4. "By Heaven!" (French).

already mentioned: a pâté de foie gras, a lark pie, a piece of smoked tongue, some pears, a slab of gingerbread, mixed biscuits, and a cup of pickled onions and gherkins in vinegar—for, like all women, Boule de Suif adored pickles.

They could not well eat the young woman's provisions and not speak to her, so they conversed—stiffly at first, and then, seeing that she showed no signs of presuming, with less reserve. Mesdames de Bréville and Carré-Lamadon, having a great deal of *savoir vivre*,[5] knew how to make themselves agreeable with tact and delicacy. The Countess, in particular, exhibited the amiable condescension of the extremely high-born lady whom no contact can sully, and was charming. But big Madame Loiseau, who had the soul of a gendarme, remained unmoved, speaking little and eating much.

The conversation naturally turned upon the war. They related horrible deeds committed by the Prussians and examples of the bravery of the French; all these people who were flying rendering full homage to the courage of those who remained behind. Incidents of personal experience soon followed, and Boule de Suif told, with that warmth of coloring which women of her type often employ in expressing their natural feelings, how she had come to leave Rouen.

"I thought at first I should be able to hold out," she said, "for I had plenty of provisions in my house, and would much rather feed a few soldiers than turn out of my home and go goodness knows where. But when I saw them—those Prussians—it was too much for me. They made my blood boil with rage, and I cried the whole day for shame. Oh, if I had only been a man!—well, there! I watched them from my window—fat pigs that they were with their spiked helmets—and my servant had to hold my hands to prevent me throwing the furniture down on the top of them. Then some of them came to be quartered on me, and I flew at the throat of the first one—they are not harder to strangle than anyone else—and would have finished him too if they had not dragged me off by the hair. Of course I had to lie low after that. So as soon as I found an opportunity I left—and here I am."

Everybody congratulated her. She rose considerably in the estimation of her companions, who had not shown themselves of such valiant mettle, and listening to her tale, Cornudet smiled the benignant and approving smile of an apostle—as a priest might on hearing a devout person praise the Almighty. Democrats with long beards have the monopoly of patriotism as the men of the cassock possess that of religion. He then took up the parable in a didactic tone with the phraseology culled from the notices posted each day on the walls, and finished up with a flourish of eloquence in which he scathingly alluded to "that blackguard Badinguet."

But Boule de Suif fired up at this for she was a Bonapartist.[6] She turned upon him with scarlet cheeks and stammering with indignation, "Ah! I should just like to have seen any of you in his place! A nice mess you would have made of it! It is men of your sort that ruined him, poor man. There would be nothing for it but to leave France for good if we were governed by cowards like you!"

---

5. Social grace (French). **6.** Supporter of the family of Napoleon Bonaparte in their claims to political power in France through much of the 19th century.

Cornudet, nothing daunted, preserved a disdainful and superior smile, but there was a feeling in the air that high words would soon follow, whereupon the Count interposed, and managed, not without difficulty, to quiet the infuriated young woman by asserting authoritatively that every sincere opinion was to be respected. Nevertheless the Countess and the manufacturer's wife, who nourished in their hearts the unreasoning hatred of all well-bred people for the Republic and at the same time that instinctive weakness of all women for uniformed and despotic governments, felt drawn, in spite of themselves, to this woman of the streets who had so much sense of the fitness of things and whose opinions so closely resembled their own.

The basket was empty—this had not been difficult among ten of them—they only regretted it was not larger. The conversation was kept up for some little time longer, although somewhat more coldly after they had finished eating.

The night fell, the darkness grew gradually deeper, and the cold, to which digestion rendered them more sensitive, made even Boule de Suif shiver in spite of her fat. Madame de Bréville thereupon offered her her charcoal foot-warmer, which had been replenished several times since the morning; she accepted with alacrity, for her feet were like ice. Mesdames Carré-Lamadon and Loiseau lent theirs to the two Sisters.

The driver had lit his lanterns, which shed a vivid light over the cloud of vapor that hung above the steaming backs of the horses and over the snow at each side of the road, that seemed to open out under the shifting reflection of the lights.

Inside the conveyance nothing could be distinguished any longer, but there was a sudden movement between Boule de Suif and Cornudet, and Loiseau, peering through the gloom, fancied he saw the man with the beard start back quickly as if he had received a well-directed but noiseless blow.

Tiny points of light appeared upon the road ahead. It was Tôtes. The travelers had been driving for eleven hours, which, with the four half-hours for feeding and resting the horses, made thirteen. They entered the town and stopped in front of the Hôtel du Commerce.

The door opened. A familiar sound caused every passenger to tremble—it was the clink of a scabbard on the stones. At the same moment a German voice called out something.

Although the coach had stopped, nobody attempted to get out, as though they expected to be massacred on setting foot to the ground. The driver then appeared holding up one of the lanterns, which suddenly illumined the vehicle to its farthest corner and revealed the two rows of bewildered faces with their open mouths and startled eyes wide with alarm.

Beside the driver in the full glare of the light stood a German officer, a tall young man excessively slender and blonde, compressed into his uniform like a girl in her stays, and wearing, well over one ear, a flat black wax-cloth cap like the "Boots"[7] of an English hotel. His preposterously long mustache, which was drawn out stiff and straight, and tapered away indefinitely to each side till it finished off in a single thread so thin that it was impossible to say

---

7. Bootblack, shoe-shine boy.

where it ended, seemed to weigh upon the corners of his mouth and form a deep furrow in either cheek.

In Alsatian-French and stern accents he invited the passengers to descend, "Will you get out, gentlemen and ladies?"

The two Sisters were the first to obey with the docility of holy women accustomed to unfaltering submission. The Count and Countess appeared next, followed by the manufacturer and his wife, and after them Loiseau pushing his better half in front of him. As he set foot to the ground he remarked to the officer, more from motives of prudence than politeness, "Good evening, Sir," to which the other with the insolence of the man in possession, vouchsafed no reply but a stare.

Boule de Suif and Cornudet, though the nearest the door, were the last to emerge—grave and haughty in face of the enemy. The buxom young woman struggled hard to command herself and be calm; the democrat tugged at his long rusty beard with a tragic and slightly trembling hand. They sought to preserve their dignity, realizing that in such encounters each one, to a certain extent, represents his country; and the two being similarly disgusted at the ready servility of their companions, she endeavored to show herself prouder than her fellow travelers who were respectable women, while he, feeling that he must set an example, continued in his attitude his mission of resistance begun by digging pitfalls in the high roads.

They entered the huge kitchen of the inn, and the German, having been presented with the passport signed by the general in command—where each traveler's name was accompanied by a personal description and a statement as to his or her profession—he proceeded to scrutinize the party for a long time, comparing the persons with the written notices.

Finally, he exclaimed unceremoniously, "That's all right," and disappeared.

They breathed again more freely. Hunger having reasserted itself, supper was ordered. It would take half an hour to prepare, so while two servants were apparently busied about it the travelers dispersed to look at their rooms. These were all together down each side of a long passage ending in a door marked "Toilet."

At last, just as they were sitting down to table, the innkeeper himself appeared. He was a former horse-dealer, a stout asthmatic man with perpetual wheezings and blowings and rattlings of phlegm in his throat. His father had transmitted to him the name of Follenvie.

"Mademoiselle Elizabeth Rousset?" he said.

Boule de Suif started and turned round. "That is my name."

"Mademoiselle, the Prussian officer wants to speak to you at once."

"To me?"

"Yes, if you really are Mademoiselle Elizabeth Rousset."

She hesitated, thought for a moment, and then declared roundly, "That may be, but I'm not going."

There was a movement round about her—everybody was much exercised as to the reason of this summons. The Count came over to her.

"You may do wrong to refuse, madame, for it may entail considerable annoyance not only to yourself but to the rest of your companions. It is a fatal mistake ever to offer resistance to people who are stronger than ourselves.

The step can have no possible danger for you—it is probably about some little formality that has been omitted."

One and all concurred with him, implored and urged and scolded, till they ended by convincing her; for they were all apprehensive of the results of her obstinacy.

"Well, it is only for your sakes that I am doing it!" she said at last. The Countess pressed her hand. "And we are most grateful to you."

She left the room, and the others agreed to wait for her before beginning the meal. Each one lamented that he had not been asked for instead of this hot-headed, violent young woman, and mentally prepared any number of platitudes for the event of being called in his turn.

At the end of ten minutes she returned, crimson with rage, choking, snorting—"Oh, the blackguard; the low blackguard!" she stammered.

They all crowded round her to know what had happened, but she would not say, and the Count becoming insistent, she answered with much dignity, "No, it does not concern anybody! I can't speak of it."

They then seated themselves round a great soup tureen from which steamed a smell of cabbage. In spite of this little incident the supper was a gay one. The cider, of which the Loiseaus and the two nuns partook from motives of economy, was good. The rest ordered wine and Cornudet called for beer. He had a particular way of uncorking the bottle, of making the liquid froth, of gazing at it while he tilted the glass, which he then held up between his eye and the light to enjoy the color; while he drank, his great beard, which had the tints of his favorite beverage, seemed to quiver fondly, his eyes squinting that he might not lose sight of his tankard for a moment, and altogether he had the appearance of fulfilling the sole function for which he had been born. You would have said that he established in his own mind some connection or affinity between the two great passions that monopolized his life—Ale and Revolution—and most assuredly he never tasted the one without thinking of the other.

Monsieur and Madame Follenvie dined at the farther end of the table. The husband—puffing and blowing like a locomotive—had too much cold on the chest to be able to speak and eat at the same time, but his wife never ceased talking. She described her every impression at the arrival of the Prussians and all they did and all they said, execrating them in the first place because they cost so much, and secondly because she had two sons in the army. She addressed herself chiefly to the Countess, as it flattered her to be able to say she had conversed with a lady of quality.

She presently lowered her voice and proceeded to recount some rather delicate matters, her husband breaking in from time to time with—"You had much better hold your tongue, Madame Follenvie,"—to which she paid not the slightest attention, but went on.

"Well, madame, as I was saying—these men, they do nothing but eat potatoes and pork and pork and potatoes from morning till night. And as for their habits—! Saving your presence, they make dirt everywhere. And you should see them exercising for hours and days together out there in the fields. It's forward march and backward march, and turn this way and turn that. If they even worked in the fields or mended the roads in their own country! But, no, madame, these soldiers are no good to anybody, and the poor people have to keep them and feed them simply that they may learn how to murder. I know I am only a poor ignorant old woman, but when I see these men wearing themselves out by tramping up and down from morning till night, I cannot help saying to myself, if there are some people who make a lot of useful discoveries, why should others give themselves so much trouble to do harm? After all, isn't it an abomination to kill anybody, no matter whether they are Prussians, or English, or Poles, or French? If you revenge yourself on someone who has harmed you, that is wicked, for you are punished; but let them shoot down our sons as if they were game, and it is all right, and they give medals to the man who kills the most. No, no, I say, I shall never be able to see any rhyme or reason in that!"

"War is barbarous if one attacks an unoffending neighbor—it is a sacred duty if one defends one's country," remarked Cornudet in a declamatory tone.

The old woman drooped her head. "Yes—defending oneself, of course, that is quite another thing; but wouldn't it be better to kill all these kings who do this for their pleasure?"

Cornudet's eyes flashed. "Bravo, citizeness!" he cried.

Monsieur Carré-Lamadon was lost in thought. Although he was an ardent admirer of famous military men, the sound common sense of this peasant woman made him reflect upon the wealth which would necessarily accrue to the country if all these unemployed and consequently ruinous hands—so much unproductive force—were available for the great industrial works that would take centuries to complete.

Loiseau meanwhile had left his seat and gone over beside the innkeeper, to whom he began talking in a low voice. The fat man laughed, coughed, and spat, his unwieldy stomach shaking with mirth at his neighbor's jokes, and he bought six hogsheads of claret from him for the spring when the Prussians would have cleared out.

Supper was scarcely over when, dropping with fatigue, everybody went off to bed.

Loiseau, however, who had noticed certain things, let his wife go to bed and proceeded to glue first his ear and then his eye to the keyhole, endeavoring to penetrate what he called "the mysteries of the corridor."

After about an hour he heard a rustling, and hurrying to the keyhole, he perceived Boule de Suif looking ampler than ever in a dressing-gown of blue cashmere trimmed with white lace. She had a candle in her hand and was going towards the door at the end of the corridor. Then a door at one side opened cautiously, and when she returned after a few minutes, Cornudet in his shirtsleeves was following her. They were talking in a low voice and presently stood still; Boule de Suif apparently defending the entrance of her room with much energy. Unfortunately Loiseau was unable to hear what they said, but at last, as they raised their voices somewhat, he caught a word or two. Cornudet was insisting eagerly. "Look here," he said, "you are really very ridiculous—what difference can it make to you?"

And she with an offended air retorted, "No!—let me tell you there are moments when that sort of thing won't do; and besides—here—it would be a crying shame."

He obviously did not understand. "Why?"

At this she grew angry. "Why?" and she raised her voice still more, "you don't see why? and there are Prussians in the house—in the next room for all you know!"

He made no reply. This display of patriotic prudery evidently aroused his failing dignity, for with a brief kiss he made for his own door on tiptoe.

Loiseau, deeply thrilled and amused, executed a double shuffle in the middle of the room, donned his nightcap, slipped into the blankets where the bony figure of his spouse already reposed, and waking her with a kiss he murmured, "Do you love me, darling?"

The whole house sank to silence. But anon there arose from somewhere—it might have been the cellar, it might have been the attic—impossible to determine the direction—a rumbling—sonorous, even, regular, dull, prolonged roar as of a boiler under high pressure: Monsieur Follenvie slept.

It had been decided that they should start at eight o'clock the next morning, so they were all assembled in the kitchen by that hour; but the coach, roofed with snow, stood solitary in the middle of the courtyard without horses or driver. The latter was sought for in vain either in the stables or in the coach-house. The men of the party then resolved to beat the country round for him, and went out accordingly. They found themselves in the public square with the church at one end, and low-roofed houses down each side in which they caught sight of Prussian soldiers. The first one they came upon was peeling potatoes; farther on another was washing out a barber's shop; while a third, bearded to the eyes, was soothing a crying child and rocking it to and fro on his knee to quiet it. The big peasant women whose men were all "with the army in the war" were ordering about their docile conquerors and showing them by signs what work they wanted done—chopping wood, grinding coffee, fetching water; one of them was even doing the washing for his hostess, a helpless old crone.

The Count, much astonished, stopped the beadle, who happened to come out of the priest's house at that moment, and asked the meaning of it all.

"Oh," replied the old church rat, "they are not at all bad. From what I hear they are not Prussians, either; they come from farther off, but where I can't say; and they have all left a wife and children at home. I am very sure their women at home are crying for their men, too, and it will all make a nice lot of misery for them as well as for us. We are not so badly off here for the moment, because they do no harm and are working just as if they were in their own homes. You see, Sir, the poor always help one another; it is the bigwigs who make the wars."

Cornudet, indignant at the friendly understanding established between the victors and the vanquished, retired from the scene, preferring to shut himself up in the inn. Loiseau of course must have his joke. "They are re-populating," he said. Monsieur Carré-Lamadon found a more fitting expression. "They are making reparations."

But the driver was nowhere to be found. At last he was unearthed in the village café hobnobbing fraternally with the officer's orderly.

"Did you not have orders to have the coach ready by eight o'clock?" the Count asked him.

"Oh, yes, but I got another order later on."

"What?"

"Not to put the horses in at all."

"Who gave you that order?"

"Why—the Prussian commandant."

"Why?"

"I don't know—you had better ask him. I am told not to harness the horses, and so I don't harness them—there you are."

"Did he tell you so himself?"

"No, Sir, the innkeeper brought me the message from him."

"When was that?"

"Last night, just as I was going to bed."

The three men returned much disconcerted. They asked for Monsieur Follenvie, but were informed by the servant that on account of his asthma he never got up before ten o'clock—he had even positively forbidden them to awaken him before then except in case of fire.

Then they asked to see the officer, but that was absolutely impossible, although he lodged at the inn.

Monsieur Follenvie alone was authorized to approach him on non-military matters. So they had to wait. The women returned to their rooms and occupied themselves as best they could.

Cornudet installed himself in the high chimney-corner of the kitchen, where a great fire was burning. He had one of the little coffee-room tables brought to him and a can of beer, and puffed away placidly at his pipe, which enjoyed among the democrats almost equal consideration with himself, as if in serving Cornudet it served the country also. The pipe was a superb meerschaum, admirably colored, black as the teeth of its owner, but fragrant, curved, shining, familiar to his hand, and the natural complement to his physiognomy. He sat there motionless, his eyes fixed alternately on the flame of the hearth and the foam on the top of his tankard, and each time after drinking he passed his bony fingers with a self-satisfied gesture through his long greasy hair, while he absorbed the fringe of froth from his mustache.

Under the pretext of stretching his legs, Loiseau went out and palmed off his wines on the country retail dealers. The Count and the manufacturer talked politics. They forecast the future of France, the one putting his faith in the Orleans princes, the other in an unknown savior, a hero who would come to the fore when things were at their very worst—a Du Guesclin, a Joan of Arc perhaps, or even another Napoleon I.[8] Ah, if only the Prince Imperial were not so young! Cornudet listened to them with the smile of a man who could solve the riddle of Fate if he would. His pipe perfumed the whole kitchen with its balmy fragrance.

On the stroke of ten Monsieur Follenvie made his appearance. They instantly attacked him with questions, but he had but one answer which he repeated two or three times without variation. "The officer said to me, 'Monsieur Follenvie, you will forbid them to harness the horses for these travelers tomorrow morning. They are not to leave till I give my permission. You understand?' That is all."

---

8. Napoleon Bonaparte (1769–1821), emperor of France. Joan of Arc (c. 1412–1431), French saint and national heroine. Bertrand Du Guesclin (c. 1320–1380), constable of France and military hero.

They demanded to see the officer; the Count sent up his card, on which Monsieur Carré-Lamadon added his name and all his titles. The Prussian sent word that he would admit the two men to his presence after he had lunched, that is to say, about one o'clock.

The ladies came down and they all managed to eat a little in spite of their anxiety. Boule de Suif looked quite ill and very much agitated.

They were just finishing coffee when the orderly arrived to fetch the two gentlemen.

Loiseau joined them, but when they proposed to bring Cornudet along to give more solemnity to their proceedings, he declared haughtily that nothing would induce him to enter into any communication whatsoever with the Germans, and he returned to his chimney-corner and ordered another bottle of beer.

The three men went upstairs, and were shown into the best room in the inn, where they were received by the officer lolling in an armchair, his heels on the chimney-piece, smoking a long porcelain pipe, and arrayed in a flamboyant dressing-gown, taken, no doubt, from the abandoned dwelling-house of some bourgeois of inferior taste. He did not rise, he vouchsafed them no greeting of any description, he did not even look at them—a brilliant example of the victorious military cad.

At last after some moments' waiting he said: "What do you want?"

The Count acted as spokesman.

"We wish to leave, Sir."

"No."

"May I take the liberty of asking the reason for this refusal?"

"Because I do not choose."

"With all due respect, Sir, I would draw your attention to the fact that your general gave us a permit for Dieppe, and I cannot see that we have done anything to justify your hard measures."

"I do not choose—that's all—you can go down."

They all bowed and withdrew.

The afternoon was miserable. They could make nothing of this caprice of the German's, and the most far-fetched ideas tortured their minds. The whole party remained in the kitchen engaging in endless discussions, imagining the most improbable things. Were they to be kept as hostages?—but if so, to what end?—or taken prisoners?—or asked a large ransom? This last suggestion threw them into a cold perspiration of fear. The wealthiest were seized with the worst panic and saw themselves forced, if they valued their lives, to empty bags of gold into the rapacious hands of this soldier. They racked their brains for plausible lies to dissemble their riches, to pass themselves off as poor—very poor. Loiseau pulled off his watch-chain and hid it in his pocket. As night fell their apprehensions increased. The lamp was lighted, and as there were still two hours till supper Madame Loiseau proposed a game of cards. It would be some little distraction, at any rate. The plan was accepted; even Cornudet, who had put out his pipe from motives of politeness, taking a hand.

The Count shuffled the cards, dealt, Boule de Suif won the first deal; and very soon the interest in the game allayed the fears that beset their minds. Cornudet, however, observed that the two Loiseaus were in league to cheat.

Just as they were sitting down to the evening meal Monsieur appeared and said in his husky voice, "The Prussian officer wishes to know if Mademoiselle Elizabeth Rousset has not changed her mind yet?"

Boule de Suif remained standing and turned very pale, then suddenly her face flamed and she fell into such a paroxysm of rage that she could not speak. At last she burst out, "You can tell that scoundrel—that low scum of a Prussian—that I won't—and I never will—do you hear?—never! never! never!"

The fat innkeeper retired. They instantly surrounded Boule de Suif, questioning, entreating her to disclose the mystery of her visit. At first she refused, but presently she was carried away by her indignation: "What does he want?—what does he want?—he wants me to go to bed with him!" she shouted.

The general indignation was so violent that nobody was shocked by the words she used. Cornudet brought his beer glass down on the table with such a bang that it broke. There was a perfect babel of invective against the drunken lout, a hurricane of wrath, a union of all for resistance, as if each had been required to contribute a portion of the sacrifice demanded of her. The Count protested with disgust that these people behaved really as if they were early barbarians. The women, in particular, accorded her the most lively and affectionate sympathy. The nuns, who only appeared at meals, dropped their eyes and said nothing.

The first fury of the storm having abated, they sat down to supper, but there was little conversation and a good deal of thoughtful abstraction.

The ladies retired early; the men, while they smoked, got up a game of écarté,[9] which Monsieur Follenvie was invited to join, as they intended pumping him skillfully as to the means that could be employed for overcoming the officer's opposition to their departure. Unfortunately, he would absorb himself wholly in his cards, and neither listened to what they said nor gave any answer to their questions, but repeated incessantly, "Play, gentlemen, play!" His attention was so deeply engaged that he forgot to spit, which caused his chest to wheeze from time to time; his wheezing lungs running through the whole gamut of asthma from notes of the profoundest bass to the shrill, hoarse crow of the young cock.

He refused to go to bed when his wife, who was dropping with sleep, came to fetch him. She therefore departed alone, for on her devolved the "day duty," and she always rose with the sun, while her husband took the "night duty," and was always ready to sit up all night with friends. He merely called out, "Mind you put my egg flip in front of the fire!" and returned to his cards. When they were convinced that there was nothing to be got out of him, they declared that it was high time to go to bed, and left him.

They were up again pretty early the next day, filled with an indefinite hope, a still keener desire to be gone, and a horror of another day to be got through in this horrible little inn.

Alas! The horses were still in the stable and the coachman remained invisible. For lack of something better to do, they sadly wandered round the carriage.

Lunch was very depressing, and a certain chilliness had sprung up with regard to Boule de Suif, for the night—which brings counsel—had somewhat

9. A card game.

modified their opinions. They were almost vexed with the girl now for not having gone to the Prussian secretly, and thus prepared a pleasant surprise for her companions in the morning. What could be simpler, and, after all, who could have been any the wiser? She might have saved appearances by telling the officer that she could not bear to see their distress any longer. It could make so very little difference to her one way or another!

But, as yet, nobody confessed to these thoughts.

In the afternoon, as they were feeling bored to extinction, the Count proposed a walk round the village. Everybody wrapped up carefully and the little party started, with the exception of Cornudet, who preferred sitting by the fire, and the two Sisters, who passed their days in the church or with the parish priest.

The cold—grown more intense each day—nipped their noses and ears viciously, and the feet hurt so that every step was anguish; but when they caught sight of the open stretch of country it appeared to them so appallingly lugubrious under its illimitable white covering that they turned back with one accord, their hearts constricted, their spirits below zero. The four ladies walked in front, the three men following a little behind.

Loiseau, who thoroughly took in the situation, suddenly broke out, "How long was this damned wench going to keep them hanging on in this hole?" The Count, courteous as ever, observed that one could not demand so painful a sacrifice of any woman—the offer must come from her. Monsieur Carré-Lamadon remarked that if—as there was every reason to believe—the French made an offensive counter-march by way of Dieppe, the collision could only take place at Tôtes. This reflection greatly alarmed the other two. "Why not escape on foot?" suggested Loiseau. The Count shrugged his shoulders. "How can you think of such a thing in this snow—and with our wives? Besides which, we should instantly be pursued, caught in ten minutes, and brought back prisoners at the mercy of these soldiers." This was incontestable—there was nothing more to be said.

The ladies talked dress, but a certain constraint seemed to have risen up among them.

All at once, at the end of the street, the officer came in sight, his tall figure, like a wasp in uniform, silhouetted against the dazzling background of snow. He was walking with his knees well apart, with that movement peculiar to the military when endeavoring to save their carefully polished boots from the mud.

In passing the ladies he bowed, but only stared contemptuously at the men, who, be it said, had the dignity not to lift their hats, though Loiseau made a faint gesture in that direction.

Boule de Suif blushed up to her eyes, and the three married women felt it a deep humiliation to have encountered this soldier while they were in the company of the young woman he had treated so cavalierly.

The conversation then turned upon him, his general appearance, his face. Madame Carré-Lamadon, who had known a great many officers and was competent to judge of them as a connoisseur, considered this one really not half bad—she even regretted that he was not French, he would have made such a fascinating hussar, and would certainly have been much run after.

Once indoors again, they did not know what to do with themselves. Sharp words were exchanged on the most insignificant pretexts. The silent dinner did not last long, and they shortly afterwards went to bed, hoping to kill time by sleeping.

They came down next morning with jaded faces and exasperation in their hearts. The women scarcely addressed a word to Boule de Suif.

Presently the church bell began to ring; it was for a christening. Boule de Suif had a child out at nurse with some peasants near Yvetot. She did not see it once a year and never gave it a thought, but the idea of this baby that was going to be baptized filled her heart with sudden and violent tenderness for her own, and nothing would satisfy her but that she should assist at the ceremony.

No sooner was she gone than they all looked at one another and proceeded to draw up their chairs; for everybody felt that things had come to that point that something must be decided upon. Loiseau had an inspiration: they should propose to the officer to keep Boule de Suif and let the rest go.

Monsieur Follenvie undertook the mission, but returned almost immediately. The German, who had some knowledge of human nature, had simply turned him out of the room. He meant to retain the whole party so long as his desire was unsatisfied.

At this Madame Loiseau's plebeian tendencies got the better of her. "But surely we are not going to sit down calmly here and die of old age! As that is this harlot's trade, I don't see that she has any right to refuse one man more than another. Why, she took anybody she could get in Rouen, down to the very cab drivers. Yes, Madame, the coachman of the Prefecture. I know all about it. He buys his wine at our shop. And now, when it lies with her to get us out of this scrape, she pretends to be particular—the brazen hussy! For my part, I consider the officer has behaved very well! He has probably not had a chance for some time, and there were three here whom, no doubt, he would have preferred; but no—he is content to take the one who is public property. He respects married women. Remember, he is master here. He had only to say 'I will,' and he could have taken us by force with his soldiers!"

A little quiver ran through the other two women. Pretty little Madame Carré-Lamadon's eyes shone and she turned rather pale as though she already felt herself forcibly seized by the officer.

The men, who had been arguing the matter in a corner, now joined them. Loiseau, foaming with rage, was for delivering up "the hussy" bound hand and foot to the enemy. But the Count, coming of three generations of ambassadors, and gifted with the physique of the diplomatist, was on the side of skill as opposed to brute force.

"She must be persuaded," he said. Whereupon they conspired.

The women drew up closer together, voices were lowered, and the discussion became general, each one offering his or her advice. Nothing was said to shock the proprieties. The ladies, in particular, were most expert in felicitous turns of phrase, charming subtleties of speech for expressing the most ticklish things. A foreigner would have understood nothing, the language was so carefully veiled. But as the slight coating of modesty with which every woman of the world is enveloped is hardly more than skin deep, they expanded under the influence of this equivocal adventure, enjoying themselves tremendously at bottom, thoroughly in their element, dabbling in sensuality with the gusto of an epicurean cook preparing a toothsome delicacy for somebody else.

The story finally appeared to them so funny that they quite recovered their spirits. The Count indulged in some rather risky pleasantries, but so well put that they raised a responsive smile; Loiseau, in his turn, rapped out some decidedly strong jokes which nobody took in bad part, and the brutal proposition expressed by his wife swayed all their minds: "As that is her trade, why refuse one man more than another?" Little Madame Carré-Lamadon seemed even to think that in her place she would refuse this one less readily than another.

They were long in preparing the siege, as if against an invested fortress. Each one agreed upon the part they would play, the arguments they would bring forward, the maneuvers they would execute. They arranged the plan of attack, the stratagems to be employed, and the surprises of the assault for forcing this living citadel to receive the enemy within its gates. Cornudet alone held aloof, completely outside the affair.

They were so profoundly occupied with the matter in hand that they never heard Boule de Suif enter the room. But the Count breathed a low warning "Hush!" and they lifted their heads. She was there. The talk ceased abruptly, and a certain feeling of embarrassment prevented them from addressing her at first, till the Countess, more versed than the others in the duplicities of the drawing-room, asked how she had enjoyed the christening.

Still full of emotion at what she had witnessed, Boule de Suif described every detail—the people's faces, their attitudes, even the appearance of the church. It was so nice to pray now and then, she added.

Till luncheon, however, the ladies confined themselves merely to being agreeable to her in order to increase her confidence in them and her acquiescence in their counsels. But once seated at table, the attack began. It first took the form of a desultory conversation on devotion to a cause. Examples from ancient history were cited: Judith and Holofernes, and then, without any apparent connection, Lucretia and Sextus, Cleopatra[1] admitting to her couch all the hostile generals, and reducing them to the servility of slaves. Then began a fantastic history, which had sprung up in the minds of the ignorant millionaires, in which the women of Rome were seen on their way to Capua, to rock Hannibal to sleep in their arms, and his officers along with him, and the phalanxes of the mercenaries. The women were mentioned who had arrested the course of conquerors, made of their bodies a rampart, a means of domination, a weapon; who had vanquished by their heroic embraces beings hideous or repulsive, and sacrificed their chastity to vengeance or patriotism. They even talked in veiled terms of an Englishwoman of good family who had herself inoculated with a horrible contagious disease, in order to give it to Napoleon, who was saved miraculously by a sudden indisposition at the hour of the fatal meeting.

And all this in a discreet and moderate manner, with now and then a little burst of warm enthusiasm, admirably calculated to excite emulation. To hear them you would have come to the conclusion that woman's sole mission here

---

1. Queen of Egypt (69 B.C.E.–30 B.C.E.). Lucretia: legendary Roman matron renowned for her virtue, victim of rape by Sextus, son of the Tarquin ruler of Rome. Judith: Jewish heroine who allows the Babylonian general, Holofernes, to seduce her so that she can then behead him.

below was perpetually to sacrifice her person, to abandon herself continually to the caprices of the warrior.

The two Sisters appeared to be deaf to it all, sunk in profound thought. Boule de Suif said nothing.

They allowed her all the afternoon for reflection, but instead of calling her "Madame," as they had done up till now, they addressed her as "Mademoiselle"[2]—nobody could have said exactly why—as if to send her down a step in the esteem she had gained, and force her to feel the shame of her position.

In the evening just as the soup was being brought to table Monsieur Follenvie made his appearance again with the same message as before: "The Prussian officer sends to ask Mademoiselle Elizabeth Rousset if she had not changed her mind."

"No, Sir," Boule de Suif replied curtly.

At supper the coalition weakened. Loiseau put his foot in it three times. They all racked their brains for fresh instances to the point, and found none, when the Countess, possibly without premeditation and only from a vague desire to render homage to religion, interrogated the older of the two Sisters on the main incidents in the lives of the saints. Now, several saints had committed acts which would be counted crimes in our eyes, but the Church readily pardons such misdeeds when they are accomplished for the glory of God or the benefit of our neighbors. It was a powerful argument, and the Countess took advantage of it. Then by one of those tacit agreements, those veiled complaisances in which every one who wears ecclesiastical habit excels, or perhaps simply from a happy want of intelligence, a helpful stupidity, the old nun brought formidable support to the conspiracy. They had imagined her timid; she proved herself bold, verbose, violent. She was not troubled by any of the shilly-shallyings of casuistry, her doctrine was like a bar of iron, her faith never wavered, her conscience knew no scruples. She considered Abraham's sacrifice a very simple affair, for she herself would have instantly killed father or mother at an order from above, and nothing, she averred, could displease the Lord if the intention were commendable. The Countess, taking advantage of the sacred authority of her unexpected ally, drew her on to make an edifying paraphrase, as it were, on the well-known moral maxim: "The end justifies the means."

"Then, Sister," she inquired, "you think God approves of every pathway that leads to Him, and pardons the deed if the motive be a pure one?"

"Who can doubt it, Madame? An action blamable in itself is often rendered meritorious by the impulse which inspires it."

And she continued in the same strain, unraveling the intricacies of the will of the Almighty, predicting His decisions, making Him interest Himself in matters which, of a truth, did not concern Him at all.

All this was skillfully and discreetly wrapped up, but each word spoken by the pious woman in the big white cap made a breach in the indignant resistance of the courtesan. The conversation then glancing off slightly, the woman of the rosaries went on to speak of the religious houses of her Order, of her Superior, of herself and her fragile little companion, her dear little Sister St. Nicephora. They had been summoned to Havre to nurse the hundreds of

---

2. That is, they began to address her as "Miss" rather than "Madam."

soldiers there down with smallpox. She described the condition of these poor wretches, gave details of their disease; and while they were thus stopped upon the road by the whim of this Prussian, many French soldiers might die whom perhaps they could have saved. That was her specialty—nursing soldiers. She had been in the Crimea, in Italy, in Austria; and relating her campaigns, she suddenly revealed herself as one of those Sisters of the fife and drum who seem made for following the camp, picking up the wounded in the thick of battle, and better than any officer for quelling with a word the great hulking undisciplined louts—her ravaged face all pitted with innumerable holes, calling up an image of the devastations of war.

No one spoke after her for fear of spoiling the excellent effect.

Immediately after dinner they hurried to their rooms, not to reappear till pretty late the next morning.

Luncheon passed off quietly. They allowed time for the seed sown yesterday to grow and bear fruit.

In the afternoon the Countess proposed a walk, whereupon the Count, following the preconcerted arrangement, took Boule de Suif's arm and fell behind with her a little. He adopted that familiar, paternal, somewhat contemptuous tone which elderly men affect towards such girls, calling her "my dear child," talking down to her from the height of his social position and indisputable respectability.

He came to the point without further preamble. "So you prefer to keep us here exposed like yourself to all the violence which must inevitably follow a check to the Prussian arms, rather than consent to accord one of those favors you have so often dispensed in your time?"

Boule de Suif did not reply.

He then appealed to her kindness of heart, her reason, her sentiment. He knew how to remain "Monsieur le Comte,"[3] yet showing himself at the same time chivalrous, flattering—in a word, altogether amiable. He exalted the sacrifice she would be making for them, touched upon their gratitude, and with a final flash of roguishness, "Besides, my dear, he may think himself lucky—he will not find many such pretty girls as you in his own country!"

Boule de Suif said nothing and rejoined the rest of the party.

When they returned, she went straight to her room and did not come down again. The anxiety was terrible. What was she going to do? How unspeakably mortifying if she still persisted in her refusal!

The dinner-hour arrived, they waited for her in vain. Monsieur Follenvie, entering presently, announced that Mademoiselle Rousset was indisposed, and that there was consequently no need to delay supper any longer. They all pricked up their ears. The Count approached the innkeeper with a whispered "All right?"

"Yes."

For propriety's sake he said nothing to his companions, but he made them a slight sign of the head. A great sigh of relief went up from every heart, every face lit up with joy.

"*Saperlipopette!*"[4] cried Loiseau, "I will stand champagne if there is such a thing in this establishment!"

---

3. "My lordship the Count" (French).   4. "My goodness!" (French).

Madame Loiseau suffered a pang of anguish when the innkeeper returned with four bottles in his hands. Everybody suddenly turned communicative and cheerful, and their hearts overflowed with prurient delight. The Count seemed all at once to become aware that Madame Carré-Lamadon was charming; the manufacturer paid compliments to the Countess. Conversation became lively, sprightly, and full of sparkle.

Suddenly Loiseau, with an anxious expression, raised his arms and shouted, "Silence!" They all stopped talking, surprised and already terrified. Then he listened intently, motioning to them to be silent with his two hands, and raising his eyes to the ceiling. He listened again, and resumed in his natural voice, "It is all right. Don't worry."

They did not understand at first, but soon a smile spread over their faces.

A quarter of an hour later he began the same comedy, and repeated it frequently during the evening. He pretended to be questioning someone on the floor above, giving advice in double-meaning phrases which he drew from his repertory as a commercial traveler.[5] At times he would assume an air of sadness, and sigh, "Poor girl"; or he would mutter between his teeth with a furious air: "You swine of a Prussian!"—Sometimes, when least expected, he would shout in resonant tones: "Enough! Enough!" adding, as though speaking to himself, "If only we see her again; if the scoundrel does not kill her!"

Although these jokes were in deplorable taste, they amused every one and hurt nobody, for, like everything else, indignation is qualified by circumstances, and the atmosphere about them had gradually become charged with obscene thoughts.

By the time they reached dessert the women themselves were indulging in decidedly risky witticisms. Eyes grew bright, tongues were loosened, a good deal of wine had been consumed. The Count, who, even in his cups, retained his characteristic air of diplomatic gravity, made some highly spiced comparisons on the subject of the end of the winter season at the Pole and the joy of ice-bound mariners at sight of an opening to the south.

Loiseau, now in full swing, rose, and lifting high his glass of champagne, "To our deliverance!" he cried. Everybody started to their feet with acclamation. Even the two Sisters of Mercy, yielding to the solicitations of the ladies, consented to take a sip of the effervescing wine which they had never tasted before. They pronounced it to be very like lemonade, though the taste was finer.

"What a pity there is no piano," said Loiseau as a crowning point to the situation, "we might have finished up with a quadrille."[6]

Cornudet had not uttered a word, nor made a sign of joining in the general hilarity; he was apparently plunged in the gravest abstractions, only pulling viciously at his great beard from time to time as if to draw it out longer than before. At last, about midnight, when the company was preparing to separate, Loiseau came stumbling over to him, and digging him in the ribs: "You seem rather down in the mouth this evening, citizen—haven't said a word."

Cornudet threw up his head angrily, and sweeping the company with a flashing and terrible look, "I tell you all that what you have done today is infamous!"

---

5. Traveling salesman.   **6.** A lively square dance.

He rose, made his way to the door, exclaimed once again, "Infamous!" and vanished.

This somewhat dashed their spirits for the moment. Loiseau, nonplussed at first, soon regained his aplomb and burst into a roar of laughter. "Sour grapes, old man—sour grapes!"

The others not understanding the allusion, he proceeded to relate the "mysteries of the corridor." This was followed by an uproarious revival of gaiety. The ladies were in a frenzy of delight, the Count and Monsieur Carré-Lamadon laughed till they cried. They could not believe it.

"Do you mean to say he wanted—"

"I tell you I saw it with my own eyes."

"And she refused?"

"Because the Prussian was in the next room."

"It is incredible."

"As true as I stand here!"

The Count nearly choked; the manufacturer held both his sides.

"And you can understand that he does not quite see the joke of the thing this evening—oh, no—not at all!"

And they all three went off again, breathless, choking, sick with laughter.

After that they parted for the night. But Madame Loiseau remarked to her husband when they were alone that that little cat of a Carré-Lamadon had laughed on the wrong side of her mouth all the evening. "You know how it is with those women—they dote upon a uniform, and whether it is French or Prussian matters precious little to them. But, Lord—it seems to me a poor way of looking at things."

All night the darkness of the corridor seemed full of thrills, of slight noises, scarcely audible, the pattering of bare feet, and creaking that was almost imperceptible. Certainly nobody got to sleep until very late, for it was long before the lights ceased to shine under the doors. Champagne, they say, often has that disturbing effect; it makes one restless and wakeful.

Next morning a brilliant winter sun shone on the dazzling snow. The coach was by this time ready and waiting before the door, while a flock of white pigeons, muffled in their thick plumage, strutted solemnly in and out among the feet of the six horses, seeking what they might devour.

The driver, enveloped in his sheepskin, sat on the box smoking his pipe, and the radiant travelers were busily laying in provisions for the rest of the journey.

They had only to wait now for Boule de Suif. She appeared.

She looked agitated and downcast as she advanced timidly towards her fellow travelers, who all, with one movement, turned away their heads as if they had not seen her. The Count, with a dignified movement, took his wife by the arm and drew her away from this contaminating contact.

The poor thing stopped short, bewildered; then gathering up her courage she accosted the wife of the manufacturer with a humble "Good morning, Madame." The other merely replied with an impertinent little nod, accompanied by a stare of outraged virtue. Everybody seemed suddenly extremely busy, and they avoided her as if she had brought the plague in her skirts. They then precipitated themselves into the vehicle, where she arrived the last and by herself, and resumed in silence the seat she had occupied during the first part of the journey.

They affected not to see her, not to recognize her; only Madame Loiseau, glancing round at her with scorn and indignation, said half audibly to her husband, "It's a good thing that I am not sitting beside her!"

The heavy conveyance jolted off, and the journey was resumed.

No one spoke for the first little while. Boule de Suif did not venture to raise her eyes. She felt incensed at her companions, and at the same time deeply humiliated at having yielded to their persuasions, and let herself be sullied by the kisses of this Prussian into whose arms they had hypocritically thrust her.

The Countess was the first to break the uncomfortable silence. Turning to Madame Carré-Lamadon, she said, "You know Madame d'Etrelles, I think?"

"Oh, yes; she is a great friend of mine."

"What a charming woman!"

"Fascinating! So truly refined; very cultivated, too, and an artist to the tips of her fingers—she sings delightfully, and draws to perfection."

The manufacturer was talking to the Count, and through the rattle of the crazy windowpanes one caught a word here and there; shares—dividends—premium—settlement day—and the like. Loiseau, who had appropriated an old pack of cards from the inn, thick with the grease of the five years' rubbing on dirty tables, started a game of bezique[7] with his wife. The two Sisters pulled up the long rosaries hanging at their waists, made the sign of the cross, and suddenly began moving their lips rapidly, faster and faster, hurrying their vague babble as if for a wager; kissing a medal from time to time, crossing themselves again, and then resuming their rapid and monotonous murmur.

Cornudet sat motionless—thinking.

At the end of the three hours' steady traveling Loiseau gathered up his cards and remarked facetiously, "It's turning hungry."

His wife then produced a parcel, which she untied, and brought out a piece of cold veal. This she cut up into thin, firm slices, and both began to eat.

"Supposing we do the same?" said the Countess, and proceeded to unpack the provisions prepared for both couples. In one of those oblong dishes with a china hare upon the cover to indicate that a roast hare lies beneath, was a succulent selection of cold viands—brown slices of juicy venison mingled with other meats. A delicious square of Gruyère cheese wrapped in newspaper still bore imprinted on its dewy surface the words "Latest News."

The two Sisters brought out a sausage smelling of garlic, and Cornudet, plunging his hands into the vast pockets of his loose greatcoat, drew up four hard-boiled eggs from one and a big crust of bread from the other. He peeled off the shells and threw them into the straw under his feet, and proceeded to bite into the egg, dropping pieces of the yolk into his long beard, from whence they shone out like stars.

In the hurry and confusion of the morning Boule de Suif had omitted to take thought for the future, and she looked on, furious, choking with mortification, at these people all munching away so placidly. A storm of rage convulsed her,

---

7. Card game similar to pinochle.

and she opened her mouth to hurl at them the torrent of abuse that rose to her lips, but she could not speak, suffocated by her indignation.

Nobody looked at her, nobody thought of her. She felt herself drowning in the flood of contempt shown towards her by these respectable scoundrels who had first sacrificed her and then cast her off like some useless and unclean thing. Then her thoughts reverted to her great basket full of good things which they had so greedily devoured—the two fowls in their glittering coat of jelly, her patties, her pears, her four bottles of claret; and her fury suddenly subsided like the breaking of an overstrung chord and she felt that she was on the verge of tears. She made the most strenuous efforts to overcome it—straightened herself up and choked back her sobs as children do, but the tears would rise. They glittered for a moment on her lashes, and presently two big drops rolled slowly over her cheeks. Others gathered in quick succession like water dripping from a rock and splashed onto the ample curve of her bosom. She sat up very straight, her eyes fixed, her face pale and rigid, hoping that nobody would notice.

But the Countess saw her and nudged her husband. He shrugged his shoulders as much as to say, "What can you expect? It is not my fault." Madame Loiseau gave a silent chuckle of triumph and murmured, "She is crying over her shame." The two Sisters had resumed their devotions after carefully wrapping up the remnants of their sausages.

Then Cornudet, while digesting his eggs, stretched his long legs under the opposite seat, leaned back, smiled like a man who has just thought of a capital joke, and began to softly whistle the *Marseillaise*.[8]

The faces clouded; the people's anthem seemed unpleasing to his neighbors; they became nervous—irritable—looking as if they were ready to throw back their heads and howl like dogs at the sound of a barrel organ. He was perfectly aware of this, but did not stop. From time to time he hummed a few of the words:

> *Amour sacré de la patrie,*
> *Conduis, soutiens nos bras vengeurs,*
> *Liberté, liberté chérie,*
> *Combats avec tes défenseurs!*

They drove at a much quicker pace today, the snow being harder; and all the way to Dieppe, during the long, dull hours of the journey, through all the jolting and rattling of the conveyance, in the falling shades of evening and later in the profound darkness of the carriage he continued with unabated persistency his vengeful and monotonous whistling; forcing his wearied and exasperated fellow travelers to follow the song from end to end and to remember every word that corresponded to each note.

---

8. National anthem of France. The four lines quoted below can be translated:

> Drive on, sacred patriotism;
> Support our avenging arms;
> Liberty, cherished liberty,
> Join the struggle with your defenders!

And Boule de Suif wept on, and at times a sob which she could not repress broke out between two stanzas in the darkness.

1880

An Adventure in Paris

Is there any feeling in a woman stronger than curiosity? Fancy seeing, knowing, touching what one has dreamed about! What would a woman not do for that? Once a woman's eager curiosity is aroused, she will be guilty of any folly, commit any imprudence, venture upon anything, and recoil from nothing. I speak of women who are really women, who are endowed with that triple-bottomed disposition, which appears to be reasonable and cool on the surface, but whose three secret compartments are filled as follows: The first, with female uneasiness, which is always in a state of fluttering; the next, with sly dodges always brought into play under color of complete sincerity; the sophistical and formidable wiles of seemingly straightforward women; and the last, with all those charming, improper acts, that delightful deceit, exquisite perfidy, and all those wayward qualities that drive stupidly credulous lovers to suicide, but delight other men.

The woman whose adventure I am about to relate was a little person from the provinces, who had been insipidly respectable till the moment when my story begins. Her life, which was on the surface so calm, was spent at home, with a busy husband and two children, whom she brought up in the fashion of an irreproachable mother. But her heart beat with unsatisfied curiosity and with longing for the unknown. She was continually thinking of Paris, and read the fashionable papers eagerly. The accounts of parties, of dresses, and various entertainments, excited her longing; but, above all, she was strangely agitated by those paragraphs which were full of double meaning, by those veils half raised by clever phrases which gave her a glimpse of culpable and ravishing delights. From her home in the provinces she saw in Paris an apotheosis of magnificent and corrupt luxury.

During the long nights, when she dreamed, lulled by the rhythmical snores of a husband who lay sleeping on his back by her side with a silk handkerchief tied round his head, she saw in her sleep those well-known men whose names appeared regularly on the front page of the newspapers like stars in the dark sky. She pictured to herself their lives—continual excitement, constant debauchery, orgies such as were practiced in ancient Rome, horribly voluptuous and with refinements of sensuality so complicated that she could not even imagine them.

The boulevards seemed to her a kind of abyss of human passions, and she did not doubt that the houses that lined them concealed mysteries of prodigious love. But she felt that she was growing old without having known life, except in those recurrent repellently monotonous, everyday occupations which constitute the happiness of the home. She was still pretty, for she was well preserved by a tranquil existence, like winter fruit in a cool cupboard; but she was consumed, agitated, and upset by her secret longings. She used to ask herself if she was meant to die without having experienced any of those damning, intoxicating joys, without having plunged once, just once, into that flood of Parisian voluptuousness.

By dint of much perseverance, she paved the way for a journey to Paris, found a pretext, got some relatives to invite her, and as her husband could not go with her, she went alone. As soon as she arrived, she invented a reason for remaining for some days, or rather for some nights, if necessary. She told him that she had met some friends who lived a little way out of town.

And then she set out on a voyage of discovery. She went up and down the boulevards, without seeing anything except roving and licensed vice. She looked into the large cafés, and read the Agony Column of the *Figaro*,[1] which every morning seemed to her like a tocsin, a summons to love. But nothing put her on the track of those orgies of actors and actresses; nothing revealed to her those temples of debauchery which opened, she imagined, at some magic word, like the cave of Ali Baba or the catacombs of Rome, where the mysteries of a persecuted religion were secretly celebrated.

Her relatives, who were quite middle-class people, could not introduce her to any of those well-known men of whose names her head was full; and in despair she was thinking of returning, when chance came to her aid. One day, as she was going along the Rue de la Chaussée d'Antin,[2] she stopped to look into a shop full of those colored Japanese knickknacks which attract the eye by their color. She was gazing at the grotesque little ivories, the tall vases of flaming enamel, and the curious bronzes, when she heard the shopkeeper inside dilating, with many bows, on the value of an enormous, pot-bellied, comical figure—which was unique, he said—to a little, bald-headed, gray-bearded man.

At every moment, the shopkeeper repeated his customer's name, which was a celebrated one, in a voice like a trumpet. The other customers, young women and well-dressed gentlemen, gave a swift and furtive but respectful glance at the celebrated writer, who was looking admiringly at the china figure. Man and figure were equally ugly, as ugly as two brothers who had sprung from the same ugly mother.

"To you the price will be a thousand francs, Monsieur Varin, and that is exactly what it cost me. I should ask anybody else fifteen hundred, but I think a great deal of my literary and artistic customers, and have special prices for them. They all come to me, Monsieur Varin. Yesterday, Monsieur Busnach bought a large, antique goblet from me, and the other day I sold two candelabra like this (aren't they beautiful?) to Monsieur Alexandre Dumas. If Monsieur Zola were to see that Japanese figure he would buy it immediately, Monsieur Varin."[3]

The author hesitated in perplexity. He wanted the figure, but the price was above him, and he thought no more about being stared at than if he had been alone in the desert. She came in trembling, her eyes fixed shamelessly upon him, and she did not even ask herself whether he was good-looking, elegant, or young. It was Jean Varin himself, Jean Varin! After a long struggle and painful hesitation, he put the figure down onto the table.

"No, it is too expensive," he said.

1. *Le Figaro*, leading French newspaper, published in Paris. 2. Street in Parisian shopping district. 3. "Jean Varin" is fictitious, but the other names in this paragraph are actual French authors, contemporaries of Maupassant. William Busnach (1832–1907), playwright. Alexandre Dumas (1824–1895), playwright and novelist. Émile Zola (1840–1902), novelist.

The shopkeeper's eloquence redoubled. "Oh! Monsieur Varin, too expensive? It is worth two thousand francs, if it is worth a sou."

But the man of letters replied sadly, still looking at the figure with the enameled eyes, "I do not say it is not: but it is too expensive for me."

And thereupon, she, seized by a kind of mad audacity, came forward and said, "What will you charge me for the figure?"

The shopkeeper, in surprise, replied, "Fifteen hundred francs, Madame."

"I will take it."

The writer, who had not even noticed her till that moment, turned round suddenly. He looked her over from head to foot, with half-closed eyes, observantly, taking in the details like a connoisseur. She was charming, suddenly animated by the flame which had hitherto been dormant in her. And then, a woman who gives fifteen hundred francs for a knickknack is not to be met with every day.

She was overcome by a feeling of delightful delicacy, and turning to him, she said in a trembling voice:

"Excuse me, Sir; no doubt I have been rather hasty. You have probably not made up your mind."

He, however, bowed and said, "Indeed I had, Madame."

And she, filled with emotion, continued, "Well, if either today, or at any other time, you change your mind, you may have this Japanese figure. I bought it only because you seemed to like it."

He was visibly flattered, and smiled. "I should like to find out how you know who I am?" he said.

Then she told him how she admired him, and became quite eloquent as she quoted his works, and while they were talking, he rested his arms on a table and fixed his bright eyes upon her, trying to make out who and what she really was. But the shopkeeper, who was pleased to have that living puff of his goods, called out, from the other end of the shop, "Just look at this, Monsieur Varin; is it not beautiful?"

And then everyone looked round, and she almost trembled with pleasure at being seen talking so intimately with such a well-known man.

At last, however, intoxicated, as it were, by her feelings, she grew bold, like a general who is about to order an assault.

"Sir," she said, "will you do me a great, a very great pleasure? Will you allow me to offer you this comic Japanese figure, as a souvenir from a woman who admires you passionately, and whom you have seen for ten minutes."

He refused. She persisted. Still he resisted her offer, very much amused, and laughing heartily. But that only made her more obstinate, and she said, "Very well, then, I shall take it to your house immediately; where do you live?"

He refused to give her his address, but she got it from the shopkeeper, and when she had paid for her purchase, she ran out to take a cab. The writer went after her, not wishing to accept a present from a person he did not know. He reached her just as she was getting into the cab. Getting in after her, he almost fell on top of her, as the cab gave a jolt. Then he sat down by her side, feeling very much annoyed.

It was no good for him to argue and to beg; she showed herself intractable, and when they got to the door, she stated her conditions, "I will undertake not to leave this with you," she said, "if you will promise to do all I want today." And the whole affair seemed so amusing to him that he agreed.

"What do you generally do at this time?" she asked him; and after hesitating for a few moments, he replied, "I generally go for a walk."

"Very well, then, we will go to the Bois de Boulogne!" she said, in a resolute voice, and they started.

He was obliged to tell her the names of all the well-known women they crossed, pure or impure, with every detail about them—their mode of life, their habits, their homes, and their vices; and when it was getting dusk, she said to him, "What do you do every day at this time?"

"I have some absinthe," he replied with a laugh.

"Very well, then," she went on seriously; "let us go and have some absinthe."

They went into a large café on the boulevard which he frequented, and where he met some of his colleagues, whom he introduced to her. She was half beside herself with pleasure, and kept saying to herself, "At last! At last!"

But time went on, and she asked, "Is it your dinner time?" To which he replied, "Yes."

"Then, let us go and have dinner."

When they left Bignon's[4] after dinner, she wanted to know what he did in the evening, and looking at her fixedly, he replied, "That depends; sometimes I go to the theater."

"Very well, then, let us go to the theater."

They went to the Vaudeville[5] with a pass, thanks to him, and, to her great pride, the whole house saw her sitting by his side in the stalls.

When the play was over, he gallantly kissed her hand, and said, "It only remains for me to thank you for this delightful day."

But she interrupted him, "What do you do at this time, every night?"

"Why—why—I go home."

She began to laugh, a little tremulous laugh: "Very well, let us go to your rooms."

They did not say anything more. She shivered occasionally from head to foot, feeling inclined to stay, and inclined to run away, but with a fixed determination, after all, to see it out to the end. She was so excited that she had to hold on to the banister as she went upstairs, and he went on ahead of her, with a lighted match in his hand.

As soon as they were in the flat, she undressed quickly and retired without saying a word. Then she waited for him, cowering against the wall. But she was as simple as it was possible for a provincial lawyer's wife to be, and he was more exacting than a pasha with thirty wives, so that they did not really get on at all.

At last, however, he went to sleep. The night passed, its silence disturbed only by the tic-toc of the clock, while she, lying motionless, thought of her conjugal nights. By the light of a Chinese lantern, she lay nearly heartbroken and stared at the little fat man lying on his back, his round stomach puffing out the bedclothes like a balloon filled with gas. He snored with the noise of a wheezy organ pipe, with prolonged snorts and comic chokings. His few hairs profited by his sleep to stand up in a very strange way, as if they were tired of

---

4. Parisian restaurant **5.** Music hall.

having been glued for so long to that pate whose bareness they were trying to cover. And a thin stream of saliva trickled from the corner of his half-opened mouth.

At last daylight appeared through the drawn blinds. She got up and dressed without making any noise. Opening the door, she made the lock creak, and he woke up and rubbed his eyes. He was some moments coming to himself, and then, when he remembered what had happened, he said:

"What! Going already?"

She remained standing, in some confusion, and then said, in a hesitant voice:

"Yes, of course; it is morning."

Then he sat up, and said, "Look here, I have something to ask you, in my turn." And as she did not reply, he went on, "You have astonished me most confoundedly since yesterday. Be frank, and tell me why you did it all, for upon my word I cannot understand it in the least."

She went over to him, blushing as if she had been a virgin, and said, "I wanted to know—what—what vice—really was, and—well—well, it is not at all funny."

And she ran out of the room and down the stairs into the street.

The street-cleaners were already at work, sweeping the road, sending their brushes along the gutters, bringing together the rubbish in neat little heaps. With movements as regular as the motion of mowers in a meadow, they swept the refuse before them in broad semi-circular strokes. She met them in every street, like dancing puppets, walking automatically with a swaying motion, and it seemed to her as if something had been swept out of her; as if her over-excited dreams had been brushed into the gutter, or down into the sewers. So she went home, out of breath and very cold, and all that she could remember was the sensation of the motion of those brooms sweeping the streets of Paris in the early morning.

When she got to her room, she threw herself onto her bed and cried.

1881

RELATED:

—Maupassant, "The Novel," p. 1725

WILLIAM MAXWELL
1908–2000

Maxwell was born in Lincoln, Illinois. He attended the University of Illinois and Harvard. After beginning his working life as a teacher, he soon turned instead to writing and developed a voice distinctive for its gentle, erudite wisdom. His many publications include six novels, such as the American Book Award–winning *So Long, See You Tomorrow* (1980); a memoir, *Ancestors* (1972); his collected essays, *The Outermost Dream* (1989); and his collected stories, *All the Days and Nights* (1995). He was president of the National Institute of Arts and Letters from 1969 to 1972, but he is probably best-remembered for his forty-year tenure as fiction editor at *The New Yorker* magazine, where he worked with many of the twentieth century's greatest authors, including Vladimir Nabokov, J. D. Salinger, John Cheever, and Eudora Welty.

The Thistles in Sweden

The brownstone is on Murray Hill,[1] facing south. The year is 1950. We have the top floor-through, and our windows are not as tall as the windows on the lower floors. They are deeply recessed, and almost square, and have divided panes. I know that beauty is in the eye of the beholder and all that, but even so, these windows are romantic. The apartment could be in Leningrad or Innsbruck or Dresden (before the bombs fell on it) or Parma or any place we have never been to. When I come home at night, I look forward to the moment when I turn the corner and raise my eyes to those three lighted windows. Since I was a child, no place has been quite so much home to me. The front windows look out on Thirty-sixth Street, the back windows on an unpainted brick wall (the side of a house on Lexington Avenue) with no break in it on our floor, but on the floor below there is a single window with a potted plant, and when we raise our eyes we see the sky, so the room is neither dark nor prisonlike.

Since we are bothered by street noises, the sensible thing would be to use this room to sleep in, but it seems to want to be our living room, and offers two irresistible arguments: (1) a Victorian white marble fireplace and (2) a stairway. If we have a fireplace it should be in the living room, even though the chimney is blocked up, so we can't have a fire in it. (I spend a good deal of time unblocking it, in my mind.) The stairs are the only access to the roof for the whole building. There is, of course, nothing up there, but it looks as if we

---

1. Neighborhood in midtown Manhattan.

are in a house and you can go upstairs to bed, and this is very cozy: a house on the top floor of a brownstone walk-up. I draw the bolt and push the trapdoor up with my shoulder, and Margaret and I stand together, holding the cat, Floribunda, in our arms so she will not escape, and see the stars (when there are any) or the winking lights of an airplane, or sometimes a hallucinatory effect brought about by fog or very fine rain and mist—the lighted windows of midtown skyscrapers set in space, without any surrounding masonry. The living room and the bedroom both have a door opening onto the outer hall, which, since we are on the top floor and nobody else in the building uses it, we regard as part of the apartment. We leave these doors open when we are at home, and the stair railing and the head of the stairs are blocked off with huge pieces of cardboard. The landlord says that this is a violation of the fire laws, but we cannot think of any other way to keep Floribunda from escaping down the stairs, and neither can he.

The living-room curtains are of heavy Swedish linen: life-sized thistles, printed in light blue and charcoal grey, on a white background. They are very beautiful (and so must the thistles in Sweden be) and they also have an emotional context; Margaret made them, and, when they did not hang properly, wept, and ripped them apart and remade them, and now they do hang properly. The bedroom curtains are of a soft ivory material, with seashells—cowries, scallops, sea urchins and sand dollars, turbinates, auriculae—drawn on them in brown indelible ink, with a flowpen. The bedroom floor is black, the walls are sandalwood, the woodwork is white. On the wall above the double bed is a mural in two sections—a hexagonal tower in an imaginary kingdom that resembles Persia. Children are flying kites from the roof. Inside the tower, another child is playing on a musical instrument that is cousin to the lute. The paperhanger hung the panels the wrong way, so the tower is even stranger architecturally than the artist intended. The parapet encloses outer instead of inner space—like a man talking to somebody who is standing behind him, facing the other way. And the fish-shaped kite, where is that being flown from? And by whom? Some other children are flying kites from the roof of the tower next to this one, perhaps, only there wasn't room to show it. (Lying in bed I often, in my mind, correct the paperhanger's mistake.) Next to the mural there is a projection made by a chimney that conducts sounds from the house next door. Or rather, a single sound: a baby crying in the night. The brownstone next door is not divided into apartments, and so much money has been spent on the outside (blue shutters, fresh paint, stucco, polished brass, etc.) that, for this neighborhood, the effect of chic is overdone. We assume there is a nurse, but nobody ever does anything when the baby cries, and the sound that comes through the wall is unbearably sad. (Unable to stand it any longer, Margaret gets up and goes through the brick chimney and picks the baby up and brings it back into our bedroom and rocks it.)

The double chest of drawers came from Macy's unfinished-furniture department, and Margaret gave it nine coats of enamel before she was satisfied with the way it looked. The black lacquered dining table (we have two dining tables and no dining room) is used as a desk. Over it hangs a large engraving of the Spanish Steps,[2] which, two years ago, in the summer of 1948, for a brief time

2. Monumental outdoor staircase in Rome.

belonged to us—flower stands, big umbrellas, Bernini fountain, English Tea Room, Keats museum, children with no conception of bedtime, everything. At night we drape our clothes over two cheap rush-bottom chairs, from Italy. The mahogany dressing table, with an oval mirror in a lyre-shaped frame and turned legs such as one sees in English furniture of the late seventeenth century, came by express from the West Coast. The express company delivered it to the sidewalk in front of the building, and, notified by telephone that this was about to happen, I rushed home from the office to supervise the uncrating. As I stepped from the taxi, I saw the expressman with the mirror and half the lyre in his huge hands. He was looking at it thoughtfully. The rest of the dressing table was ten feet away, by the entrance to the building. The break does not show unless you look closely. And most old furniture has been mended at one time or another.

When we were shown the apartment for the first time, the outgoing tenant let us in and stood by pleasantly while we tried to imagine what the place would look like if it were not so crowded with his furniture. It was hardly possible to take a step for oak tables and chests and sofas and armoires and armchairs. Those ancestral portraits and Italian landscapes in heavy gilt frames that there was no room for on the walls were leaning against the furniture. To get from one room to the next we had to step over pyramids of books and scientific journals. An inventory of the miscellaneous objects and musical instruments in the living room would have taken days and been full of surprises. (Why did he keep that large soup tureen on the floor?) We thought at first he was packing, but he was not; this was the way he lived. If we had asked him to make a place in his life for us too, he would have. He was a very nice man. The disorder was dignified and somehow enviable, and the overfurnished apartment so remote from what went on down below in the street that it was like a cave deep in the forest.

Now it is underfurnished (we have just barely enough money to manage a small one-story house in the country and this apartment in town), instead, and all light and air. The living-room walls are a pale blue that changes according to the light and the time of day and the season of the year and the color of the sky. The walls are hardly there. The furniture is half old and half new, and there isn't much of it, considering the size of the room: a box couch, a cabinet with sliding doors, a small painted bookcase, an easy chair with its ottoman, a round fruitwood side table with long, thin, spidery legs and a glass tray that fits over the top, the table and chairs we eat on, a lowboy that serves as a sideboard, another chair, a wobbly tea cart, and a canvas stool. The couch has a high wooden back, L-shaped, painted black, with a thin gold line. It was made for an old house in Dover, New Hampshire, and after I don't know how many generations found itself in Minneapolis. I first saw it in Margaret's mother's bedroom in Seattle, and now it is here. It took two big men and a lot of patient maneuvering to get it four times past the turning of the stairs. The shawl that is draped over the back and the large tin tray that serves as a coffee table both came from Mexico—a country I do not regard as romantic, even though we have never been there. The lowboy made the trip from the West Coast with the dressing table, and one of its Chippendale[3] legs got broken in

---

3. Of or in the style of English cabinetmaker and furniture designer Thomas Chippendale (1718?–1779).

transit, or by that same impetuous expressman. I suppose it is a hundred and fifty or two hundred years old. The man in the furniture-repair shop, after considering the broken leg, asked if we wanted the lowboy refinished. I asked why, and he said, "Because it's been painted." We looked, and sure enough it had. "They did that sometimes," he said. "It's painted to simulate mahogany." I asked what was under the paint, and he picked up a chisel and took a delicate gouge out of the underside. This time it was his turn to be surprised. "It's mahogany," he announced. The lowboy was painted to simulate what it actually was, it looks like what it is, so we let it be.

The gateleg table we eat on has four legs instead of the usual six. When the sides are extended, it looks as if the cabinetmaker had been studying Euclid's[4] geometry. Margaret found it in an antique shop in Putnam Valley, and asked me to come look at it. I got out of the car and went in and saw the table and knew I could not live without it. The antique dealer said the table had an interesting history that she wasn't free to tell us. (Was it a real Hepplewhite[5] and not just in the style of? Was it stolen?) She was a very old woman and lived alone. The shop was lined with bookshelves, and the books on the shelves and lying around on the tables were so uncommon I had trouble keeping my hands off them. They were not for sale, the old woman said. They had belonged to her husband, and she was keeping them for her grandchildren; she herself read nothing but murder mysteries.

Margaret wanted the table, but she wanted also to talk about whether or not we could afford it. I can always afford what I dearly want—or rather, when I want something very much I would rather not think about whether or not we can afford it. As we drove away without the table, I said coldly, "We won't talk about it." As if she were the kind of wife she isn't. And we did talk about it, all the way home. The next day we were back, nobody had bought the table in the meantime, I wrote out a check for two hundred dollars, and the old woman gave us a big rag rug to wrap around the marvel so it wouldn't be damaged on the drive home. Also heavy twine to tie it with. But then I asked for a knife, and this upset her, to my astonishment. I looked carefully and saw that the expression in her faded blue eyes was terror: She thought I wanted a knife so I could murder her and make off with the table *and* the check. It is disquieting to have one's intentions so misjudged. (Am I a murderer? And is it usual for the murderer to ask for his weapon?) "A pair of scissors will do just as well," I said, and the color came back into her face.

The rug the table now stands on is only slightly larger than the tabletop. It is threadbare, but we cannot find another like it. For some reason, it is the last yellowish beige rug ever made. People with no children have perfectionism to fall back on.

The space between the fireplace and the door to the kitchen is filled by shelves and a shallow cupboard. The tea cart is kept under the stairs. Then comes the door to the coat closet, the inside of which is painted a particularly beautiful shade of Chinese red, and the door to the hall. On the sliding-door cabinet (we have turned the corner now and are moving toward the windows) there is a pottery lamp with a wide perforated grey paper shade and such a

---

4. Greek geometrician and educator at Alexandria (ca. 300 B.C.E.).   5. George Hepplewhite (d. 1876), English furniture designer and cabinetmaker.

long thin neck that it seems to be trying to turn into a crane. Also a record player that plays only 78s and has to be wound after every record. The oil painting over the couch is of a rock quarry in Maine, and we have discovered that it changes according to the time of day and the color of the sky. It is particularly alive after a snowfall.

Here we live, in our modest perfectionism, with two black cats. The one on the mantelpiece is Bastet, the Egyptian goddess of love and joy.[6] The other is under the impression that she is our child. This is our fault, of course, not hers. Around her neck she wears a scarlet ribbon, or sometimes a turquoise ribbon, or a collar with little bells. Her toys dangle from the tea cart, her kitty litter is in a pan beside the bathtub, and she sleeps on the foot of our bed or curled against the back of Margaret's knees. When she is bored she asks us to remove a piece of the cardboard barricade so she can go tippeting down the stairs and pay a call on the landlord and his wife, Mr. and Mrs. Holmes, who live in the garden apartment and have the rear half of the second floor, with an inside stairs, so they really do go upstairs to bed. The front part of the second floor is the pied-à-terre[7] of the artist who designed the wallpaper mural of the children flying kites from a hexagonal tower in an imaginary kingdom that resembles Persia. It is through the artist's influence (Mr. Holmes is intimidated by her) that we managed to get our rent-controlled apartment, for which we pay a hundred and thirteen dollars and some odd cents. The landlord wishes we paid more, and Mr. and Mrs. Venable, who live under us, wish we'd get a larger rug for the living room. Their bedroom is on the back, and Margaret's heels crossing the ceiling at night keep them awake. Also, in the early morning the Egyptian goddess leaves our bed and chases wooden spools and glass marbles from one end of the living room to the other. The Venables have mentioned this subject of the larger rug to the landlord and he has mentioned it to us. We do nothing about it, except that Margaret puts the spools and marbles out of Floribunda's reach when we go to bed at night, and walks around in her stocking feet after ten o'clock. Some day, when we are kept awake by footsteps crossing our bedroom ceiling, hammering, furniture being moved, and other idiot noises, we will remember the Venables and wish we had been more considerate.

The Venables leave their door open too, and on our way up the stairs I look back over my shoulder and see chintz-covered chairs and Oriental rugs and the lamplight falling discreetly on an Early American this and an Old English that. (No children here, either; Mrs. Venable works in a decorator's shop.) Mrs. Pickering, third floor, keeps her door closed. She is a sweet-faced woman who smiles when we meet her on the stairs. She has a grown son and daughter who come to see her regularly, but her life isn't the same as when they were growing up and Mr. Pickering was alive. (Did she tell us this or have I invented it?) If we met her anywhere but on the stairs we would have racked our brains to find something to say to her. The Holmeses' furniture is nondescript but comfortable. Mrs. Holmes has lovely brown eyes and the voice that goes with

6. Also called *Bast*; essentially a goddess of the home, she was worshiped in the form of a cat and later equated with the lioness war goddess.   **7.** A small house or apartment maintained for temporary use (French).

them, and it is no wonder that Floribunda likes to sit on her lap. *He* wants everybody to be happy, which is not exactly the way to be happy yourself, and he isn't. If we all paid a little more rent, it would make him happier, but we don't feel like it, any of us.

I am happy because we are in town: I don't have to commute in bad weather. I can walk to the office. And after the theater we jump in a cab and are home in five minutes. I stand at the front window listening to the weather report. It is snowing in Westchester,[8] and the driving conditions are very bad. In Thirty-sixth Street it is raining. The middle-aged man who lives on the top floor of the brownstone directly across from us is in the habit of posing at the window with a curtain partly wrapped around his naked body. He keeps guppies or goldfish in a lighted tank, spends the whole day in a kimono ironing, and at odd moments goes to the front window and acts out somebody's sexual dream. If I could only marry him off to the old woman who goes through the trash baskets on Lexington Avenue, talking to herself. What pleasure she would have in showing him the things she has brought home in her string bag—treasures whose value nobody else realizes. And what satisfaction to him it would be to wrap himself in a curtain just for her.

The view to the south is cut off by a big apartment building on Thirty-fifth Street. The only one. If it were not there (I spend a good deal of time demolishing it, with my bare hands) we would have the whole of the sky to look at. Because I have not looked carefully enough at the expression in Margaret's eyes, I go on thinking that she is happy too. When I met her she was working in a publishing house. Shortly after we decided to get married she was offered a job with the *Partisan Review*.[9] If she had taken it, it would have meant commuting with me or even commuting at different hours from when I did. When I was a little boy and came home from school and called out, "Is anybody home?" somebody nearly always was. I took it for granted that the same thing would be true when I married. We didn't talk about it, and should have. I didn't understand that in her mind it was the chance of a fulfilling experience. Because she saw that I could not even imagine her saying yes, she said no, and turned her attention to learning how to cook and keep house. If we had had children right away it would have been different; but then if we had had children we wouldn't have been living on the top floor of a brownstone on Thirty-sixth Street.

The days in town are long and empty for her. The telephone doesn't ring anything like as often as it does when we are in the country. There Hester Gale comes across the road to see how Margaret is, or because she is out of cake flour, and they have coffee together. Margaret sews with Olivia Bingham. There are conversations in the supermarket. And miles of woods to walk in. Old Mrs. Delano, whose front door on Thirty-sixth Street is ten feet west of ours, is no help whatever. Though she knows Margaret's Aunt Caroline, she doesn't know that Margaret is her niece, or even that she exists, probably, and Margaret has no intention of telling her. Any more than she has any intention of telling me that in this place where I am so happy she feels like a prisoner much of the time.

---

8. Suburban county north of New York City.   **9.** Leftist and progressive journal published from 1934 until 2003.

She is accustomed to space, to a part of the country where there is more room than people and buildings to occupy it. In her childhood she woke up in the morning in a big house set on a wide lawn, with towering pine trees behind it, and a copper beech as big as two brownstones, and a snow-capped mountain that mysteriously comes and goes, like an idea in the mind. Every afternoon after school she went cantering through the trees on horseback. Now she is confined to two rooms—the kitchen cannot be called a room; it is hardly bigger than a handkerchief—and these two rooms are not enough. This is a secret she manages to keep from me so I can go on being happy.

There is another secret that cannot be kept from me because, with her head in a frame made by my head, arms, and shoulder, I know when she weeps. She weeps because her period was five days late and she thought something had happened that she now knows is not going to happen. The child is there, and could just as well as not decide to come to us, and doesn't, month after month. Instead, we consult one gynecologist after another, and take embarrassing tests (only they don't really embarrass me, they just seem unreal). And what the doctors do not tell us is why, when there is nothing wrong with either of us, nothing happens. Before we can have a child we must solve a riddle, like Oedipus and the Sphinx.[1] On my forty-second birthday I go to the Spence-Chapin adoption service and explain our situation to a woman who listens attentively. I like her and feel that she understands how terribly much we want a child, and she shocks me by reaching across the desk and taking the application blank out of my hands: Forty-two is the age past which the agency will not consider giving out a child for adoption.

Meanwhile, Margaret herself has been adopted, by the Italian market under the El[2] at Third Avenue and Thirty-fourth Street. Four or five whistling boys with white aprons wrapped around their skinny hips run it. They also appear to own it, but what could be more unlikely? Their faces light up when Margaret walks into the store. They drop what they are doing and come to greet her as if she were their older sister. And whatever she asks for, it turns out they have. Their meat is never tough, their vegetables are not tarnished and limp, their sole is just as good as the fish market's and nothing like as expensive. Now one boy, now another arrives at our door with a carton of groceries balanced on his head, having taken the stairs two steps at a time. Four flights are nothing to them. They are in business for the pure pleasure of it. They don't think or talk about love, they just do it. Or perhaps it isn't love but joy. But over what? Over the fact that they are alive and so are we?

It occurs to the landlord that the tenants could carry their garbage down to the street and then he wouldn't have to. I prepare for a scene, compose angry speeches in the bath. Everybody knows what landlords are like—only he isn't like that. He isn't even a landlord, strictly speaking. He has a good job with an actuarial firm. The building is a hobby. It was very run down when he bought it, and he has had the pleasure of fixing it up. We meet on the front sidewalk as I am on my way to work. Looking up at him—he is a very tall man—I announce that I will not carry our garbage down. Looking down at me, he

---

1. In the Greek tragedian Sophocles' greatest play, *Oedipus the King*, Oedipus saves Thebes by solving the riddle posed by the monstrous Sphinx. **2.** Elevated railway.

says that if we don't feel like carrying our garbage down he will go on doing it. What an unsatisfactory man to quarrel with.

I come home from the office and find that Margaret has spent the afternoon drawing: a pewter coffeepot (Nantucket), a Venetian-glass goblet, a white china serving dish with a handle and a cover, two eggs, a lemon, apples, a rumpled napkin with a blue border. Or the view from the living room all the way into the bedroom, through three doorways, involving the kind of foreshortened perspective Italian Renaissance artists were so fond of. Or the view from the bedroom windows (the apartment house on Thirty-fifth Street that I have so often taken down I now see is all right; it belongs there) in sepia wash. Or her own head and shoulders reflected in the dressing-table mirror. Or the goblet, the coffeepot, the lemon, a green pepper, and a brown luster bowl. The luster bowl has a chip in it, and so the old woman in the antique shop in Putnam Valley gave it to us for a dollar, after the table was safely stowed away in the backseat of the car. And some years later, her daughter, sitting next to me at a formal dinner party, said, "You're mistaken. Mother was absolutely fearless." She said it again, perceiving that I did not believe her. Somebody is mistaken, and it could just as well as not be me. Even though I looked quite carefully at the old woman's expression. In any case, there is something I didn't see. Her husband—the man whose books the old woman was unwilling to sell—committed suicide. "I was their only child, and had to deal with sadness all my life—sadness from within as well as from without." If the expression in the old woman's eyes was not terror, what was it?

Floribunda misses the country, and sits at the top of the living-room stairs, clawing at the trapdoor. She refuses to eat, is shedding. Her hairs are on everything. One night we take her across Park Avenue to the Morgan Library and push the big iron gate open like conspirators about to steal the forty-two-line Gutenberg Bible or the three folios of Redouté's roses.[3] Floribunda leaps from Margaret's arms and runs across the sickly grass and climbs a small tree. Ecstatically she sharpens her claws on the bark. I know that we will be arrested, but it is worth it.

Neither the landlord and his wife, nor the artist and her husband, who is Dutch, nor Mrs. Pickering, nor the Venables ever entertain in their apartments, but we have a season of being sociable. We have the Fitzgeralds and Eileen Fitzgerald's father from Dublin for dinner. We celebrate Bastille Day[4] with the Potters. We have Elinor Hinkley's mother to tea. She arrives at the head of the stairs, where she can see into the living room, and exclaims—before she has even caught her breath—"What beautiful horizontal surfaces!" She is incapable of small talk. Instead, she describes the spiritual emanations of a row of huge granite boulders lining the driveway of her house on Martha's Vineyard. And other phenomena that cannot be described very easily, or that, when described, cannot be appreciated by someone who isn't half mad or a Theosophist.[5]

---

3. Invaluable extremely rare texts held by the Morgan Library, a private institution in midtown Manhattan.   4. July 14, a French national holiday, celebrating the fall of the Bastille, a famous fortress prison in Paris, in 1789.   5. Adherent of Theosophy, an occult system of spiritualism and philosophy especially popular in the early 20th century.

Dean Wilson brings one intelligent, pretty girl after another to meet us. Like the woman in Isak Dinesen's[6] story who sailed the seas looking for the perfect blue, he is looking for a flawless girl. Flawless in whose eyes is the question. And isn't flawlessness itself a serious flaw? "What a charming girl," we say afterward, and he looks in our faces and is not satisfied, and brings still another girl, including, finally, Ivy Sérurier, who is half English and half French. When she was seven years old her nurse took her every day to the Jardin du Luxembourg[7] and there she ran after a hoop. She is attracted to all forms of occult knowledge, and things happen to her that do not happen to anyone who does not have a destiny. The light bulbs respond to her amazing stories by giving off a higher voltage. The expression on our faces is satisfactory. Dean brings her again, and again. He asks Margaret if she thinks they should get married, but he cannot quite bring himself to ask Ivy this question.

On a night when we are expecting Henry Coddington to dinner, Hester and Nick Gale come up the stairs blithely at seven o'clock, having got the invitation wrong. Or perhaps it is our fault. There is plenty of food, and it turns out to be a pleasant evening. The guests get on well, but Henry must have thought we did not want to know why Louise left him and took their little girl, whom he idolizes—that we have insulated ourselves from his catastrophe by asking this couple from the country. Anyway, he never comes or calls again. But other people come. Melissa Lovejoy, from Montgomery, Alabama, comes for Sunday lunch, and her hilarious account of her skirmishes with her mother-in-law make the tears run down my cheeks. Melissa, who loves beautiful china, looks around the living room and sees what no one else has ever seen or commented on—a Meissen[8] plate on the other end of the mantelpiece from the Egyptian cat. It is white, with very small green grape leaves and a wide filigree border. Margaret's brother John had it in his rucksack when he made his way from Geneva to Bordeaux in May 1940. As easily as the plate could have got broken, so he could have ended up in a detention camp and then what? But they are both safe, intact, here in New York. He has his own place, on Lexington Avenue in the Fifties. On Christmas Eve he bends down and selects a present for Margaret and another for me from the pile under the tree at the foot of the stair.

On New Year's Eve, John and Dean and Ivy and Margaret and I sit down to dinner. The champagne cork hits the ceiling. Between courses we take turns getting up and going into the bedroom and waiting behind a closed door until a voice calls "Ready!" If you were a school of Italian painting or a color of the spectrum or a character from fiction, what school of Italian painting or color or character would you be? John is Dostoevski's[9] Idiot, Margaret is lavender blue. Elinor Hinkley joins us for dessert. Just before midnight a couple from the U.N., whom Dean has invited, come up the stairs and an hour later on the dot they leave for another party. It is daylight when we push our chairs back. We have not left the table (except to go into the front room while the questions are being framed) all night long. With our heads out of the window,

---

6. Baroness Karen Blixen (1885–1962), Danish author whose most famous book is *Out of Africa*. **7.** Public park in Paris. **8.** A German city famous for fine porcelain. **9.** Fyodor Dostoevsky (1821–1881), Russian novelist, among whose novels are *Crime and Punishment*, *The Brothers Karamazov*, and *The Idiot*.

Margaret and I wait for them to emerge from the building and then we call down to them, "Happy New Year!" But softly, so as not to wake up the neighbors.

Margaret's Uncle James, who is not her uncle but her mother's first cousin, comes to dinner, bringing long-stemmed red roses. He confesses that he has been waiting for this invitation ever since we were married—eight or nine years—and he thoroughly enjoys himself, though he is dying of cancer of the throat. Faced with extinction, you can't just stand and scream; it isn't good manners. And men and women of that generation do not discuss their feelings. Anyway he doesn't. Instead he says, "I like your curtains, Margaret," and we are filled with remorse that we didn't ask him sooner. But still, he did come to dinner. And satisfied his curiosity about the way we live. And we were surprised to discover that we were fond of him—as the rabbit is surprised to discover that he is what was concealed in the magician's hat. *I am not the person you thought I was,* Uncle James as much as says, sitting back in the easy chair but not using the ottoman lest he look ill.

I realize that the air is full of cigarette smoke, and prop the trapdoor open with a couple of books—but only a crack. At eleven-thirty Uncle James rises and puts his coat on and says good night, and tromps down the stairs, waking the Venables, and Mrs. Pickering, and the artist and her husband, and Mr. and Mrs. Holmes. And we lock the doors and say what a nice evening it was, and empty the ashtrays, and carry the liquor glasses out to the kitchen, and suddenly perceive an emptiness, an absence. "Floribunda? . . . Pussy?" She is nowhere. She has slipped through the crack that I thought was too small for her to get through. Fur is deceptive, her bone structure is not what I thought it was, and perhaps cats have something in common with cigarette smoke. I have often seen her attenuate herself alarmingly. Outside, on the roof, I call softly, but no little black cat comes. In the night we both wake and talk about her. The bottom of the bed feels strange when we put our feet out and there is nothing there, no weight. When morning comes I dress and go up to the roof again, and make my way toward Park Avenue, stepping over two-foot-high tile walls and making my way around projections and feeling giddy when I peer down into back gardens.

Margaret, meanwhile, has dressed and gone down the stairs. She rings the Delanos' bell, and the Irish maid opens the door. "A little cat came in through my bedroom window last night and the mistress said to put her on the street, so I did." *On the street* . . . when she could so easily have put her back on the roof she came from! "Here, Puss, Puss, Puss . . . here, Puss!" Up Thirty-sixth Street and down Thirty-fifth. All her life she has known nothing but love, and she is so timid. How will she survive with no home? What will the poor creature do? We meet Rose Bernstein, who has just moved into town from our country road, and just as I am saying "On the street. Did you ever hear of anything so heartless?" there is a faint miaow. Floribunda heard us calling and was too frightened to answer. I find her hiding in an areaway. Margaret gathers her up in her arms and we say good-bye to Rose Bernstein, and, unable to believe our good fortune, take her home. Our love and joy.

In Chicago there is an adoption agency whose policy with respect to age is not so rigid as Spence-Chapin's. We pull strings. (Dean Wilson has a friend whose wife's mother is on the board.) Letters pass back and forth, and finally there we are, in Chicago, nervously waiting in the reception room. Miss Mattie

Gessner is susceptible (or so I feel) to the masculine approach. It turns out that she voted for Truman too; and she doesn't reach across the desk and take the application from my hands. Instead she promises to help us. But it isn't as simple as the old song my mother used to sing: Today is not the day they give babies away with a half a pound of tay.[1] The baby that is given to us for adoption must be the child of a couple reasonably like us—that is to say, a man and woman who, in the year 1952, would have a record player that plays only 78s and that you wind by hand; who draw seashells on their bedroom curtains and are made happy by a blocked-up fireplace and a stairway that leads nowhere. And this means we must wait God knows how long.

So we do wait, sometimes in rather odd places for a couple with no children. For example, by the carousel in Central Park. The plunging horses slowly come to a halt with their hoofs in midair. The children get off and more children climb up, take a firm grip on the pole, and look around for their mother or their nurse or their father, in the crowd standing in the open doorway. Slowly the cavalcade begins to move again, and I take the little boy in the plaid snowsuit, with half a pound of English Breakfast, and Margaret takes half a pound of Lipton's and the little girl with blue ribbons in her hair.

We start going to the country weekends. And then we go for the summer, taking suitcases full of clothes, boxes of unread books, drawing materials, the sewing machine, the typewriter. And in September all this is carried up four flights of stairs. And more: flowers, vegetables from the garden, plants we could not bear to have the frost put an end to, even though we know they will not live long in town. And one by one we take up our winter habits. When Saturday night comes around we put on our coats at ten o'clock and go out to buy the Sunday *Times* at the newspaper stand under the El. We rattle the door of the antique shop on Third Avenue that always has something interesting in the window but has never been known to be open at any hour of any day of the week. On three successive nights we go to *Ring Round the Moon, King Lear,* and *An Enemy of the People,*[2] after which it seems strange to sit home reading a book. I am so in love with Adlai Stevenson's[3] speeches that, though I am afraid of driving in ordinary traffic in New York City, I get the car out of the garage and we drive right down the center of 125th Street, in a torchlight parade, hemmed in by a flowing river of people, all of whom feel the way we do.

How many years did we live in that apartment on Thirty-sixth Street? From 1950 to — The mere dates are misleading, even if I could get them right, because time was not progressive or in sequence, it was one of Mrs. Hinkley's horizontal surfaces divided into squares. On one square an old woman waters a houseplant in the window of an otherwise blank wall. On another, Albertha, who is black, comes to clean. When she leaves, the apartment looks as if an angel had walked through it. She is the oldest of eleven children. And what she and Margaret say, over a cup of coffee, makes Margaret more able to deal with her solitary life. On another square, we go to the Huguenot Church on

---

1. Tea.   2. Plays by, respectively, Jean Anouilh, William Shakespeare, and Henrik Ibsen.   3. Politician (1900–65), twice a Democratic candidate for president (1952 and 1956) and ambassador to the U.N. (1960–65).

Sunday morning, expecting something new and strange, and instead the hymns are perfectly familiar to us from our Presbyterian childhoods: In French they have become more elegant and rhetorical, and it occurs to me that they may not reach all the way to the ear of Heaven. But the old man who then mounts the stairs to the pulpit addresses Seigneur Dieu in a confident voice, as if they are extremely well acquainted, the two of them. On another square we go to Berlitz, and the instructor, a White Russian named Mikhael Miloradovitch, sits by blandly while Margaret and I say things to each other in French that we have managed not to say in English. I am upset when I discover that she prefers the country to the city. The discussion becomes heated, but because it is in French nothing comes of it. We go on living in the city. Until another summer comes and we fill the car, which is now nearly twenty years old, to the canvas top with our possessions; then, locking the doors of the apartment, we drive off to our other life. At which point the shine goes out of this one. The slipcovers fade and so do the seashells and thistles that are exposed to the direct light of the summer sun. Dust gathers on the books, the lampshades, the record player. In the middle of the night, a hand pries at the trapdoor and, finding it securely locked, tries somewhere else. The man out of Krafft-Ebing[4] shows himself seductively to our blank windows. And the intense heat builds up to a violent thunderstorm. After which there is a spell of cooler weather. And a tragedy. For two days there has been no garbage outside Mrs. Pickering's door in the morning. She does not answer her telephone or the landlord's knocking, and she has not said she was going away. The first floor extends farther back than the rest of the house, and he is able to place a ladder on the roof of this extension. From the top of the ladder he stares into the third-floor bedroom at a terrible sight: Mrs. Pickering, sitting in a wing chair, naked. He thinks it is death he is staring at, but he is mistaken; she has had a stroke. He breaks the door down, and she is taken to the hospital in an ambulance. She does not die, but neither does she ever come back to this apartment. Passing her door on our way up the stairs, we are aware of the silence inside, and think uneasily of those two days and nights of helpless waiting. Along with the silence there is the sense of something malign, of trouble of a very serious kind that could spread all through the house. To ward it off, we draw closer to the other tenants, linger talking on the stairs, and speak to them in a more intimate tone of voice. We have the Holmeses and the Venables and the artist and her husband up for a drink. It doesn't do the trick. There *was* something behind Mrs. Pickering's door. My sister's only son turns up and, since we are in the country, we offer him the apartment to live in until he finds a job. He leads a life there that the books and furniture do not approve of. He brings girls home and makes love to them in our bed, under the very eyes of the children flying kites. He borrows fifty bucks from me, to eat on, and to get some shirts, so he won't look like a bum when he goes job hunting. He has a check coming from his previous job, in Florida, and will pay me back next week. The check doesn't come, and he borrows some more money, and then some more, and it begins to mount up. Jobs that were as good as promised to him vanish into thin air, and meanwhile we are his sole means

---

4. Baron Richard von Krafft-Ebing (1840–1902), German neurologist and author of studies about mental illness.

of support. I listen attentively to what I more and more suspect are inventions, but his footwork is fast, and what he says could be true; it just isn't what he said before, quite. My bones inform me that I am not the first person these excuses and appeals have been tried out on. He comes to my office to tell me that he has given up the idea of staying in New York and can I let him have the fare home, and I dial my sister's number in Evansville, Indiana, and hand the receiver to him and leave the room.

I give up smoking on one square, and on another I go through all the variant pages of a book I have been writing for four and a half years and reduce it to a single pile of manuscript. This I put in a blue canvas duffel bag that can absentmindedly be left behind on the curbing when we drive off to the country at eleven o'clock of a spring night. At midnight, driving up the Taconic Parkway, I suddenly see in my mind's eye the backseat of the car: The blue duffel bag is not there. Nor, when we come to a stop in front of our house on Thirty-sixth Street at one o'clock in the morning, is it on the sidewalk where I left it. With a dry mouth I describe it to the desk sergeant in the police station, and he gets up and goes into the back room. "No, nothing," he calls. And then, as we are almost at the door, "Wait a minute."

On another square Margaret starts behaving in a way that is not at all like her. Sleepy at ten o'clock in the evening, and when I open my eyes in the morning she is already awake and looking at me. Her face is somehow different. Can it be that she is . . . that we are going to . . . that . . . I study her when she is not aware that I am looking at her, and find in her behavior the answer to that riddle: If we are so longing for a child that we are willing to bring up somebody else's child—anybody's child whatever—then we may as well be allowed to have our own. Margaret comes home from the doctor bringing the news to me that I have not dared break to her.

After boning up on the subject, in a book, she shows me, on her finger, just how long the child in her womb now is. And it is growing larger, very slowly. And so is she. The child is safe inside her, and she is safe so long as she remains a prisoner in this top-floor apartment. The doctor has forbidden her to use the stairs. Everybody comes to see her, instead—including an emanation from the silent apartment two floors below. A black man, a stranger, suddenly appears at the top of the stairs. His intention, unclear but frightening, shows in his face, in his eyes. But the goddess Bastet is at work again, and the man comes on Albertha's day, and she, with a stream of such foulmouthed cursing as Margaret has never heard in her life, sends him running down the stairs. If he had come on a day that was not Albertha's day, when Margaret was there alone— But this holds true for everything, good or bad.

Margaret's face grows rounder, and she no longer has a secret that must be kept from me. The days while I am at the office are not lonely, and time is an unbroken landscape of daydreaming. When I get home at six o'clock, I creep in under the roof of the spell she is under, and am allowed into the daydream. But what shall we tell Miss Mattie Gessner when she comes to investigate the way we live?

The apartment, feeling our inattention, begins to withdraw from us sadly. And then something else unexpected happens. The landlord, having achieved perfection, having created the Peaceable Kingdom on Thirty-sixth Street, is restless and wants to begin all over again. "You'll be sorry," his wife tells him, stroking Floribunda's ear, and he is. But by that time they are living uptown, in a much less handsome house in the Nineties—a house that needs fixing from top to bottom. But it will never have any style, and it is filled with disagreeable tenants who do not pay their rent on time. On Thirty-sixth Street we have a new landlord, and in no time his hand is on everything. He hangs a cheap print of van Gogh's[5] *The Drawbridge* in the downstairs foyer. We are obliged to take down the cardboard barricade and keep our doors closed. Hardly a day passes without some maddening new improvement. The artist is the first to go. Then we give notice; how is Margaret to carry the baby, the stroller, the package from the drugstore, etc., up four flights of stairs? *What better place can there be to bring up a child in?* the marble fireplace asks, remembering the eighteen-eighties, when this was a one-family house and our top-floor living room was the nursery. The stairway to the roof was devoted to the previous tenant (the man who lived in the midst of a monumental clutter) and says bitterly, in the night, when we are not awake to hear, *They seem as much a part of your life as the doors and windows, and then it turns out that they are not a part of your life at all. The moving men come and cart all the furniture away, and the people go down to the street, and that's the last you see of them....*

What will the fireplace and the stairway to the roof say when they discover that they are about to be shut off forever from the front room? The landlord is planning to divide our apartment into two apartments and charge the same for each that he is now getting for the floor-through. For every evil under the sun there is a remedy or there is none. I soak the mural of the children flying kites, hoping to remove it intact and put it up somewhere in the house in the country. The paper tears no matter how gently I pull it loose from the wall, and comes off in little pieces, which end up in the wastebasket.

Now when I walk past that house I look up at the windows that could be in Leningrad or Innsbruck or Dresden or Parma, and I think of the stairway that led only to the trapdoor in the roof, and of the marble fireplace, the bathroom skylight, and the tiny kitchen, and of what school of Italian painting we would have been if we had been a school of Italian painting, and poor Mrs. Pickering sitting in her bedroom chair with her eyes wide open, waiting for help, and the rainy nights on Thirty-sixth Street, and the grey-and-blue thistles, the brown seashells, the Mills Brothers[6] singing *Shine, little glowworm, glimmer, glimmer,* and the guests who came the wrong night, the guest who was going to die and knew it, the sound of my typewriter, and of a paintbrush clinking in a glass of cloudy water, and Floribunda's adventure, and Margaret's empty days, and how it was settled that, although I wanted to put my head on her breast as I was falling asleep, she needed even more (at that point) to put her head on mine. And of our child's coming, at last, and the black cat who thought *she* was our child, and of the two friends who didn't after all get married, and the old woman who found one treasure after another in the trash baskets all up and down Lexington Avenue, and that other old woman, now dead, who was so driven by the need to describe the inner life of very large granite boulders. I think of how Miss Mattie Gessner's face fell and how she closed her notebook and became a stranger to us, who had been so deeply our friend. I think of the oversexed ironer, and the Holmeses, and the Venables, and the stranger who meant nobody good and was frightened away by Albertha's cursing, and the hissing of the air brakes of the Lexington Avenue bus, and the curtains moving at the open window, and the baby crying on the other side of the wall. I think of that happy grocery store run by boys, and the horse-drawn flower cart that sometimes waited on the corner, and the sound of footsteps in the night, and the sudden no-sound that meant it was snowing, and I think of the unknown man or woman who found the blue duffel bag with the manuscript of my novel in it and took it to the police station, and the musical instrument (not a lute, but that's what the artist must have had in mind, only she no longer bothers to look at objects and draws what she remembers them as being like) played in the dark, over our sleeping bodies, while the children flew their kites, and I think if it is true that we are all in the hands of God, what a capacious hand it must be.

1965

RELATED:

—Charles Baxter on "The Thistles in Sweden," p. 1756
—John Updike, "Three *New Yorker* Stalwarts" [William Maxwell], p. 1778

JILL McCORKLE
b. 1958

McCorkle grew up in Lumberton, North Carolina, and earned degrees from both the University of North Carolina at Chapel Hill and Hollins College in Roanoke, Virginia. A member of the Fellowship of Southern Writers, she has the distinction of having published her first two novels, *The Cheer Leader* and *July 7th*, on the same day in 1984. With a debut like that it's not surprising that she began her career thinking of herself as a novelist (other novels, *Carolina Moon* [1996] and *Life after Life* [2013], followed), but by the mid-1990s she was fast becoming a major voice in contemporary American short fiction. Her stories, collected in *Crash Diet* (1992), *Final Vinyl Days* (1999), *Creatures of Habit* (2001), and *Going Away Shoes* (2009), are often funny with a current of melancholy just under the surface. A wonderful teacher and raconteur with a talent growing ever more forceful, McCorkle has taught at Harvard, Tufts, Brandeis, and other universities; she presently teaches creative writing at North Carolina State University.

Intervention

The intervention is not Marilyn's idea, but it might as well be. She is the one who has talked too much. And she has agreed to go along with it, nodding and murmuring an all right into the receiver while Sid dozes in front of the evening news. They love watching the news. Things are so horrible all over the world that it makes them feel lucky just to be alive. Sid is sixty-five. He is retired. He is disappearing before her very eyes.

"Okay, Mom?" She jumps with her daughter's voice, once again filled with the noise at the other end of the phone—a house full of children, a television blasting, whines about homework—all those noises you complain about for years only to wake one day and realize you would sell your soul to go back for another chance to do it right.

"Yes, yes," she says.

"Is he drinking right now?"

Marilyn has never heard the term "intervention" before her daughter, Sally, introduces it and showers her with a pile of literature. Sally's husband has a master's in social work and considers himself an expert on this topic, as well as many others. Most of Sally's sentences begin with "Rusty says," to the point that Sid long ago made up a little spoof about "Rusty says," turning it into a game like Simon Says. "Rusty says put your hands on your head," Sid said the first time, once the newly married couple was out of earshot. "Rusty says put your head up your ass." Marilyn howled with laughter, just as she always did and always has. Sid can always make her laugh. Usually she laughs longer and harder. A stranger would have assumed that she was the one slinging back the vodka. Twenty years earlier, and the stranger would have been right.

Sally and Rusty have now been married for a dozen years—three kids and two Volvos and several major vacations (that were so educational they couldn't have been any fun) behind them—and still, Marilyn and Sid cannot look each other in the eye while Rusty is talking without breaking into giggles like a couple of junior high school students. And Marilyn knows junior high behavior; she taught language arts for many years. She is not shocked when a boy wears the crotch of his pants down around his knees, and she knows that Sean Combs has gone from that perfectly normal name to Sean Puffy Combs to Puff Daddy to P. Diddy. She knows that the kids make a big circle at dances so that the ones in the center can do their grinding without getting in trouble, and she has learned that there are many perfectly good words that you cannot use in front of humans who are being powered by hormonal surges. She once asked her class: How will you ever get ahead? only to have them all—even the most pristine honor roll girls—collapse in hysterics. Just last year—her final one—she had learned never to ask if they had hooked up with so-and-so, learning quickly that this no longer meant locating a person but having sex. She could not hear the term now without laughing. She told Sid it reminded her of the time two dogs got stuck in the act just outside her classroom window. The children were out of control, especially when the assistant principal stepped out there armed with a garden hose, which didn't faze the lust-crazed dogs in the slightest. When the female—a scrawny shepherd mix—finally took off running, the male—who was quite a bit smaller—was stuck and forced to hop along behind her like a jackrabbit. "His thang is stuck," one of the girls yelled and broke out in a dance, prompting others to do the same.

"Sounds like me," Sid said that night when they were lying there in the dark. "I'll follow you anywhere."

Now, as Sid dozes, she goes and pulls out the envelope of information about "family intervention." She never should have told Sally that she had concerns, never should have mentioned that there were times when she watched Sid pull out of the driveway only to catch herself imagining that this could be the last time she ever saw him.

"Why do you think that?" Sally asked, suddenly attentive and leaning forward in her chair. Up until that minute, Marilyn had felt invisible while Sally rattled on and on about drapes and chairs and her book group and Rusty's accolades. "Was he visibly drunk? Why do you let him drive when he's that way?"

"He's never visibly drunk," Marilyn said then, knowing that she had made a terrible mistake. They were at the mall, one of those forced outings that Sally had read was important. Probably an article Rusty read first called something like "Spend time with your parents so you won't feel guilty when you slap them in a urine-smelling old-folks' home." Rusty's parents are already in such a place; they share a room and eat three meals on room trays while they watch television all day. Rusty says they're ecstatic. They have so much to tell that they are living for the next time Rusty and Sally and the kids come to visit.

"I pray to God I never have to rely on such," Sid said when she relayed this bit of conversation. She didn't tell him the other parts of the conversation at the mall, how even when she tried to turn the topic to shoes and how it seemed to her that either shoes had gotten smaller or girls had gotten bigger (nine was the average size for most of her willowy eighth-grade girls), Sally bit into the subject like a pit bull.

"How much does he drink in a day?" Sally asked. "You must know. I mean, *you* are the one who takes out the garbage and does the shopping."

"He helps me."

"A fifth?"

"Sid loves to go to the Food Lion. They have a book section and everything."

"Rusty has seen this coming for years." Sally leaned forward and gripped Marilyn's arm. Sally's hands were perfectly manicured with pale pink nails and a great big diamond. "He asked me if Dad had a problem before we ever got married." She gripped tighter. "Do you know that? That's a dozen years."

"I wonder if the Oriental folks have caused this change in the shoe sizes?" Marilyn pulled away and glanced over at Lady's Foot Locker as if to make a point. She knows that "Oriental" is not the thing to say. She knows to say "Asian," and though Sally thinks that she and Rusty are the ones who teach her all of these things, the truth is that she learned it all from her students. She knew to say Hispanic and then Latino, probably before Rusty did, because she sometimes watches the MTV channel so that she's up on what is happening in the world and thus in the lives of children at the junior high. Shocking things, yes, but also important. Sid has always believed that it is better to be educated even if what is true makes you uncomfortable or depressed. Truth is, she can understand why some of these youngsters want to say motherfucker this and that all the time. Where *are* their mommas, after all; and where are their daddies? Rusty needs to watch MTV. He needs to watch that and *Survivor* and all the other reality shows. He's got children, and unless he completely rubs off on them they will be normal enough to want to know what's happening out there in the world.

"Asian," Sally whispered. "You really need to just throw out that word Oriental unless you're talking about lamps and carpets. I know what you're doing, too."

"What about queer? I hear that word is okay again."

"You have to deal with Dad's problem," Sally said.

"I hear that even the Homo sapiens use that word, but it might be the kind of thing that only one who is a member can use, kind of like—"

"Will you stop it?" Sally interrupted and banged her hand on the table.

"Like the 'n' word," Marilyn said. "The black children in my class used it, but it would have been terrible for somebody else to."

Sally didn't even enunciate African American the way she usually does. "This doesn't work anymore!" Sally's face reddened, her voice a harsh whisper. "So cut the Gracie Allen routine."

"I loved Gracie. So did Sid. What a woman." Marilyn rummaged her purse for a tissue or a stick of gum, anything so as not to have to look at Sally. Sally looks so much like Sid they could be in a genetics textbook: those pouty lips and hard blue eyes, prominent cheekbones and dark curly hair. Sid always told people his mother was a Cherokee and his father a Jew, that if he was a dog, like a cockapoo,[1] he'd be a Cherojew, which Marilyn said sounded like TheraFlu, which they both like even when they don't have colds, so he went with Jewokee instead. Marilyn's ancestors were all Irish, so she and Sid called their children the Jewokirish. Sid said that the only thing that could save the world would be when everybody was so mixed up with this blood and that that nobody could pronounce the resulting tribe name. It would have to be a symbol—like the name of the artist formerly known as Prince, which was something she had just learned and had to explain to Sid. She doubts that Sally and Rusty even know who Prince is, or Nelly, for that matter. Nelly is the reason all the kids are wearing Band-Aids on their faces, which is great for those just learning to shave.

"Remember that whole routine Dad and I made up about ancestry?" Marilyn asked. She was able to look up now, Sally's hands squeezing her own, Rusty's hands on her shoulders. If she had had an ounce of energy left in her body, she would have run into Lord & Taylor's and gotten lost in the mirrored cosmetics section.

"The fact that you brought all this up is a cry for help whether you admit it or not," Sally said. "And we are here, Mother. We are here for you."

She wanted to ask why Mother—what happened to Mom and Mama and Mommy?—but she couldn't say a word.

There are some nights when Sid is dozing there that she feels frightened. She puts her hand on his chest to feel his heart. She puts her cheek close to his mouth to feel the breath. She did the same to Sally and Tom when they were children, especially with Tom, who came first. She was up and down all night long in those first weeks, making sure that he was breathing, still amazed that this perfect little creature belonged to them. Sometimes Sid would wake and do it for her, even though his work as a grocery distributor in those days caused him to get up at five A.M. The times he went to check, he would return to their tiny bedroom and lunge toward her with a perfect Dr. Frankenstein imitation: "He's alive!" followed by maniacal laughter. In those days she joined him for a drink just as the sun was setting. It was their favorite time of day, and they both always resisted the need to flip on a light and return to life. The ritual continued for years and does to this day. When the children were older they would make jokes about their parents, who were always "in the dark," and yet those pauses, the punctuation marks of a marriage, could tell their whole history spoken and unspoken.

The literature says that an intervention is the most loving and powerful thing a loved one can do. That some members might be apprehensive. Tom was apprehensive at first, but he always has been; Tom is the noncombative child. He's an orthopedist living in Denver. Skiing is great for his health and his business. And his love life. He met the new wife when she fractured her ankle. Her marriage was already fractured, his broken, much to the disappointment of

---

1. Cross between a cocker spaniel and a poodle.

Marilyn and Sid, who found the first wife to be the most loving and open-minded of the whole bunch. The new wife, Sid says, is too young to have any opinions you give a damn about. In private they call her Snow Bunny.

Tom was apprehensive until the night he called after the hour she had told everyone was acceptable. "Don't call after nine unless it's an emergency," she had told them. "We like to watch our shows without interruption." But that night, while Sid dozed and the made-for-TV movie she had looked forward to ended up (as her students would say) sucking, she went to run a deep hot bath, and that's where she was, incapable of getting to the phone fast enough.

"Let the machine get it, honey," she called as she dashed with just a towel wrapped around her dripping body, but she wasn't fast enough. She could hear the slur in Sid's speech. He could not say slalom to save his soul, and instead of letting the moment pass, he kept trying and trying—What the shit is wrong with my tongue, Tom? Did I have a goddamn stroke? Sllllmmmm—sla, sla.

Marilyn ran and picked up the extension. "Honey, Daddy has taken some decongestants, bless his heart, full of a terrible cold. Go on back to sleep now, Sid, I've got it."

"I haven't got a goddamned cold. Your mother's a kook!" He laughed and waved to where she stood in the kitchen, a puddle of suds and water at her feet. "She's a good-looking naked kook. I see her bony ass right now."

"Hang up, Tommy," she said. "I'll call you right back from the other phone. Daddy is right in the middle of his program."

"Yeah, right," Tom said.

By the time she got Sid settled down, dried herself off, and put on her robe, Tom's line was busy, and she knew before even dialing Sally that hers would be busy, too. It was a full hour later, Sid fast asleep in the bed they had owned for thirty-five years, when she finally got through, and then it was to a more serious Tom than she had heard in years. Not since he left the first wife and signed off on the lives of her grandchildren in a way that prevented Marilyn from seeing them more than once a year if she was lucky. She could get mad at him for *that*. So could Sid.

"We're not talking about my life right now," he said. "I've given Dad the benefit of the doubt for years, but Sally and Rusty are right."

"Rusty! You're the one who said he was full of it," she screamed. "And now you're on his side?"

"I'm on your side, Mom, your side."

She let her end fall silent and concentrated on Sid's breath. He's alive, only to be interrupted by a squeaky girly voice on Tom's end—Snow Bunny.

Sid likes to drive, and Marilyn has always felt secure with him there behind the wheel. Every family vacation, every weekend gathering. He was always voted the best driver of the bunch, even when a whole group had gathered down at the beach for a summer cookout where both men and women drank too much. Sid mostly drank beer in those days; he kept an old Pepsi-Cola cooler he once won throwing baseballs at tin cans at the county fair, iced down with Falstaff and Schlitz. They still have that cooler. It's out in the garage on the top shelf, long ago replaced with little red and white Playmates. Tom gave Sid his first Playmate, which has remained a family joke until this day. And Marilyn drank then. She liked the taste of beer but not the bloat.

She loved to water ski, and they took turns behind a friend's powerboat. The men made jokes when the women dove in to cool off. They claimed that warm spots emerged wherever the women had been and that if they couldn't hold their beer any better than that, they should switch to girl drinks. And so they did. A little wine or a mai tai, vodka martinis. Sid had a book that told him how to make everything, and Marilyn enjoyed buying little colored tooth-picks and umbrellas to dress things up when it was their turn to host. She loved rubbing her body with baby oil and iodine and letting the warmth of the sun and salty air soak in while the radio played and the other women talked. They all smoked cigarettes then. They all had little leather cases with fancy lighters tucked inside.

Whenever Marilyn sees the Pepsi cooler she is reminded of those days. Just married. No worries about skin cancer or lung cancer. No one had varicose veins. No one talked about cholesterol. None of their friends were addicted to anything other than the sun and the desire to get up on one ski—to slalom. The summer she was pregnant with Tom (compliments of a few too many mai tais, Sid told the group), she sat on the dock and sipped her ginger ale. The motion of the boat made her queasy, as did anything that had to do with poultry. *It ain't the size of the ship but the motion of the ocean,* Sid was fond of saying in those days, and she laughed every time. Every time he said it, she complimented his liner and the power of his steam. They batted words like *throttle* and *wake* back and forth like a birdie until finally, at the end of the afternoon, she'd go over and whisper, "Ready to dock?"

Her love for Sid then was overwhelming. His hair was thick, and he tanned a deep smooth olive without any coaxing. He was everything she had ever wanted, and she told him this those summer days as they sat through the twi-light time. She didn't tell him how sometimes she craved the vodka tonics she had missed. Even though many of her friends continued drinking and smok-ing through their pregnancies, she would allow herself only one glass of wine with dinner. When she bragged about this during Sally's first pregnancy, instead of being congratulated on her modest intake, Sally was horrified. "My God, Mother," she said. "Tom is lucky there's not something wrong with him!"

Tom set the date for the intervention. As hard as it was for Rusty to relin-quish his power even for a minute, it made perfect sense, given that Tom had to take time off from his practice and fly all the way from Denver. The Snow Bunny was coming, too, even though she really didn't know Sid at all. Some-times over the past five years, Marilyn had called up the first wife just to hear her voice or, even better, the voice of one or more of her grandchildren on the answering machine. Now there was a man's name included in the list of who wasn't home. She and Sid would hold the receiver between them, both with watering eyes, when they heard the voices they barely recognized. They didn't know about *69 until a few months ago when Margot, the oldest child, named for Sid's mother, called back. "Who is this?" she asked. She was growing up in Minnesota and now was further alienated by an accent Marilyn only knew from Betty White's character on *The Golden Girls.*

"Your grandmother, honey. Grandma Marilyn in South Carolina."

There was a long silence, and then the child began to speak rapidly, filling them in on all that was going on in her life. "Mom says you used to teach junior high," Margot said, and she and Sid both grinned, somehow having always trusted that their daughter-in-law would not have turned on them as Tom had led them to believe.

Then Susan got on the phone, and as soon as she did, Marilyn burst into tears. "Oh, Susie, forgive me," she said. "You know how much we love you and the kids."

"I know," she said. "And if Tom doesn't bring the kids to you, I will. I promise." Marilyn and Sid still believe her. They fantasize during the twilight hour that she will drive up one day and there they'll all be. Then, lo and behold, here will come Tom. "He'll see what a goddamned fool he's been," Sid says. "They'll hug and kiss and send Snow Bunny packing."

"And we'll all live happily ever after," Marilyn says.

"You can take that to the bank, baby," he says, and she hugs him close, whispers that he has to eat dinner before they can go anywhere.

"You know I'm a very good driver," she says, and he just shakes his head back and forth; he can list every ticket and fender-bender she has had in her life.

The intervention day is next week. Tom and Bunny plan to stay with Sally and Rusty an hour away so that Sid won't get suspicious. Already it is unbearable to her—this secret. There has only been one time in their whole marriage when she had a secret, and it was a disaster.

"What's wrong with you?" Sid keeps asking. "So quiet." His eyes have that somber look she catches once in a while; it's a look of hurt, a look of disillusionment. It is the look that nearly killed them thirty-odd years ago.

There have been many phone calls late at night. Rusty knows how to set up conference calls, and there they all are, Tom and Sally and Rusty, talking nonstop. If he resists, we do this. If he gets angry, we do that. All the while, Sid dozes. Sometimes the car is parked crooked in the drive, a way that he never would have parked even two years ago, and she goes out in her housecoat and bedroom slippers to straighten it up so the neighbors won't think anything is wrong. She has repositioned the mailbox many times, touched up paint on the car and the garage that Sid didn't even notice. Sometimes he is too tired to move or undress, and she spreads a blanket over him in the chair. Recently she found a stash of empty bottles in the bottom of his golf bag. Empty bottles in the Pepsi cooler, the trunk of his car.

"I suspect he lies to you about how much he has," Rusty says. "We are taught not to ask an alcoholic how much he drinks, but to phrase it in a way that accepts a lot of intake, such as 'How many fifths do you go through in a weekend?'"

"Sid doesn't lie to me."

"This is as much for you," Rusty says, and she can hear the impatience in his voice. "You are what we call an enabler."

She doesn't respond. She reaches and takes Sid's warm limp hand in her own.

"If you really love him," he pauses, gathering volume and force in his words, "you have to go through with this."

"It was really your idea, Mom," Sally says. "We all suspected as much, but you're the one who really blew the whistle." Marilyn remains quiet, a picture

of herself like some kind of Nazi woman blowing a shrill whistle, dogs barking, flesh tearing. She can't answer; her head is swimming. "Admit it. He
almost killed you when he went off the road. It's your side that would have
smashed into the pole. You were lucky."

"I was driving," she says now, whispering so as not to wake him. "I almost
killed him!"

"Nobody believed you, Marilyn," Rusty says, and she is reminded of the one
and only student she has hated in her career, a smart-assed boy who spoke to
her as if he were the adult and she were the child. Even though she knew better, knew that he was a little jerk, it had still bothered her.

"You're lucky Mr. Randolph was the officer on duty, Mom," Tom says. "He's
not going to look the other way next time. He told me as much."

"And what about how you told me you have to hide his keys sometimes?"
Sally asks. "What about that?"

"Where are the children?" Marilyn asks. "Are they hearing all of this?"

"No," Rusty says. "We won't tell this sort of thing until they're older and
can learn from it."

"We didn't," she whispers and then ignores their questions. Didn't what?
Didn't what?

"The literature says that there should be a professional involved," she says
and, for a brief anxious moment, relishes their silence.

"Rusty is a professional," Sally says. "This is what he does for a living."

Sid lives for a living, she wants to say, but she lets it all go. They are coming,
come hell or high water. She can't stop what she has put into motion, a rush
of betrayal and shame pushing her back to a dark place she has not seen in
years. Sid stirs and brings her hand up to his cheek.

Sid never told the children anything. He never brought up anything once it
had passed, unlike Marilyn, who sometimes gets stuck in a groove, spinning
and spinning, deeper and deeper. Whenever anything in life—the approach of
spring, the smell of gin, pine sap thawing and coming back to life—prompts her
memory, she cringes and feels the urge to crawl into a dark hole. She doesn't
recognize that woman. That woman was sick. A sick, foolish woman, a woman
who had no idea that the best of life was in her hand. It was late spring, and
they went with a group to the lake. They hired babysitters round the clock so
the men could fish and the women could sun and shop and nobody had to be
concerned for all the needs of the youngsters. The days began with coffee and
Bloody Marys and ended with sloppy kisses on the sleeping brows of their
babies. Sid was worried then. He was bucking for promotions right and left,
taking extra shifts. He wanted to run the whole delivery service in their part of
the state and knew that he could do it if he ever got the chance to prove himself.
Then he would have normal hours, good benefits.

Marilyn had never even noticed Paula Edwards's husband before that week.
She spoke to him, yes; she thought it was Paula's good fortune to have married
someone who had been so successful so young. ("Easy when it's a family business and handed to you," Sid said, the only negative thing she ever heard him
say about the man.) But there he was, not terribly attractive but very attentive.
Paula was pregnant with twins and forced to a lot of bed rest. Even now, the
words of the situation, playing through Marilyn's mind, shock her.

"You needed attention," Sid said when it all exploded in her face. "I'm sorry I wasn't there."

"Who are you—Jesus Christ?" she screamed. "Don't you hate me? Paula hates me!"

"I'm not Paula. And I'm not Jesus." He went to the cabinet and mixed a big bourbon and water. He had never had a drink that early in the day. "I'm a man who is very upset."

"At me!"

"At both of us."

She wanted him to hate her right then. She wanted him to make her suffer, make her pay. She had wanted him even at the time it was Paula's husband meeting her in the weeks following in dark, out-of-the-way parking lots—rest areas out on the interstate, rundown motels no one with any self-esteem would venture into. And yet there she had been. She bought the new underwear the way women so often do, as if that thin bit of silk could prolong the masquerade. Then later, she had burned all the new garments in a huge puddle of gasoline, a flame so high the fire department came, only to find her stretched out on the grass of her front yard, sobbing. Her children, ages four and two, were there beside her, wide-eyed and frightened. "Mommy? Are you sick?" She felt those tiny hands pulling and pulling. "Mommy? Are you sad?" Paula's husband wanted sex. She could have been anyone those times he twisted his hands in her thick long hair, grown the way Sid liked it, and pulled her head down. He wanted her to scream out and tear at him. He liked it that way. Paula wasn't that kind of girl, but he knew that she was.

"But you're not," Sid told her in the many years to follow, the times when self-loathing overtook her body and reduced her to an anguished heap on the floor. "You're not that kind."

People knew. They had to know, but out of respect for Sid, they never said a word. Paula had twin girls, and they moved to California, and to this day, they send a Christmas card with a brag letter much like the one that Sally and Rusty have begun sending. Something like: We are brilliant, and we are rich. Our lives are perfect, don't you wish yours was as good? If Sid gets the mail, he tears it up and never says a word. He did the same with the letter that Paula wrote to him when she figured out what was going on. Marilyn never saw what the letter said. She only heard Sid sobbing from the other side of a closed door, the children vigilant as they waited for him to come out. When his days of silence ended and she tried to talk, he simply put a finger up to her lips, his eyes dark and shadowed in a way that frightened her. He mixed himself a drink and offered her one as they sat and listened with relief to the giggles of the children playing outside. Sid had bought a sandbox and put it over the burned spot right there in the front yard. He said that in the fall when it was cooler, he'd cover it with sod. He gave up on advancing to the top, and settled in instead with a budget and all the investments he could make to ensure college educations and decent retirement.

Her feelings each and every year when spring came had nothing to do with any lingering feelings she might have had about the affair—she had none. Rather, her feelings were about the disgust she felt for herself, and the more disgusted she felt, the more she needed some form of self-medication. For her, alcohol was the symptom of the greater problem, and she shudders with recall of all the nights Sid had to scoop her up from the floor and carry her to bed. The times she left pots burning on the stove, the time Tom as a five-year-old sopped towels where she lay sick on the bathroom floor. "Mommy is sick," he told Sid, who stripped and bathed her, cool sheets around her body, cool cloth to her head. It was the vision of her children standing there and staring at her, their eyes as somber and vacuous as Sid's had been that day he got Paula's letter, that woke her up.

"I'm through," she said. "I need help."

Sid backed her just as he always had. Rusty would have called him her enabler. He nursed her and loved her. He forgave her and forgave her. I'm a bad chemistry experiment, she told Sid. Without him she would not have survived.

On the day of intervention, the kids come in meaning business, but then can't help but lapse into discussion about their own families and how great they all are. Snow Bunny wants a baby, which makes Sid laugh, even though Marilyn can tell he suspects something is amiss. Rusty has been promoted. He is thinking about going back to school to get his degree in psychology. They gather in the living room, Sid in his chair, a coffee cup on the table beside him. She knows there is bourbon in his cup but would never say a word. She doesn't have to. Sally sweeps by, grabs the cup, and then is in the kitchen sniffing its content. Rusty gives the nod of a man in charge. Sid is staring at her, all the questions easily read: Why are they here? Did you know they were coming? Why did you keep this from me? And she has to look away. She never should have let this happen. She should have found a way to bring Sid around to his own decision, the way he had led her.

Now she wants to scream at the children that she did this to Sid. She wants to pull out the picture box and say: This is me back when I was fucking my friend's husband while you were asleep in your beds. And this is me when I drank myself sick so that I could forget what a horrible woman and wife and mother I was. Here is where I passed out on the floor with a pan of hot grease on the stove, and here is where I became so hysterical in the front yard that I almost burned the house down. I ruined the lawn your father worked so hard to grow. I ruined your father. I did this, and he never told you about how horrible I was. He protected me. He saved me.

"Well, Sid," Rusty begins, "we have come together to be with you because we're concerned about you."

"We love you, Daddy, and we're worried."

"Mom is worried," Tom says, and as Sid turns to her, Marilyn has to look down. "Your drinking has become a problem, and we've come to get help for you."

I'm the drunk, she wants to say. I was here first.

"You're worried, honey?" Sid asks. "Why haven't you told me?"

She looks up now, first at Sid and then at Sally and Tom. If you live long enough, your children learn to love you from afar, their lives are front and center and elsewhere. Your life is only what they can conjure from bits and pieces. They don't know how it all fits together. They don't know all the sacrifices that have been made.

"We're here as what is called an intervention," Rusty says.

"Marilyn?" He is gripping the arms of his chair. "You knew this?"

"No," she says. "No, I didn't. I have nothing to do with this."

"Marilyn." Rusty rises from his chair. Sally right beside him. It's like the room has split in two and she is given a clear choice—the choice she wishes she had made years ago, and then maybe none of this would have ever happened.

"We can take care of this on our own," she says. "We've taken care of far worse."

"Such as?" Tom asks. She has always wanted to ask him what he remembers from those horrible days. Does he remember finding her there on the floor? Does he remember her wishing to be dead?

"Water under the bridge," Sid says. "Water under the bridge." Sid stands, shoulders thrown back. He is still the tallest man in the room. He is the most powerful man. "You kids are great," he says. "You're great, and you're right." He goes into the kitchen and ceremoniously pours what's left of a fifth of bourbon down the sink. He breaks out another fifth still wrapped with a Christmas ribbon and pours it down the sink. "Your mother tends to overreact and exaggerate from time to time, but I do love her." He doesn't look at her, just keeps pouring. "She doesn't drink, so I won't drink."

"She has never had a problem," Sally says, and for a brief second Marilyn feels Tom's eyes on her.

"I used to," Marilyn says.

"Yeah, she'd sip a little wine on holidays. Made her feel sick, didn't it, honey?" Sid is opening and closing cabinets. He puts on the teakettle. "Mother likes tea in the late afternoon like the British. As a matter of fact," he continues, still not looking at her, "sometimes we pretend we are British."

She nods and watches him pour out some cheap Scotch he always offers to cheap friends. He keeps the good stuff way up high behind her mother's silver service. "And we've been writing our own little holiday letter, Mother and I, and we're going to tell every single thing that has gone on this past year like Sally and Rusty do. Like I'm going to tell that Mother has a spastic colon and often feels 'sqwitty,' as the British might say, and that I had an abscessed tooth that kept draining into my throat, leaving me no choice but to hock and spit throughout the day. But all that aside, kids, the real reason I can't formally go somewhere to dry out for you right now is, one, I have already booked a hotel over in Myrtle Beach for our anniversary, and, two, there is nothing about me to dry."

By the end of the night everyone is talking about "one more chance." Sid has easily turned the conversation to Rusty and where he plans to apply to school and to Snow Bunny and her hopes of having a "little Tommy" a year from now. They say things like that they are proud of Sid for his effort but not to be hard on himself if he can't do it on his own. He needs to realize he might have a problem. He needs to be able to say: I have a problem.

"So. Wonder what stirred all that up?" he asks as they watch the children finally drive away. She has yet to make eye contact with him. "I have to say I'm glad to see them leave." He turns now and waits for her to say something.

"I say adios, motherfuckers." She cocks her hands this way and that like the rappers do, which makes him laugh. She notices his hand shaking and reaches to hold it in her own. She waits, and then she offers to fix him a small drink to calm his nerves. "I don't have to have it, you know," he says.

"Oh, I know that," she says. "I also know you saved the good stuff."

She mixes a weak one and goes into the living room, where he has turned off all but the small electric candle on the piano.

"Here's to the last drink," he says as she sits down beside him. He breathes a deep sigh that fills the room. He doesn't ask again if she had anything to do with what happened. He never questions her a second time; he never has. And in the middle of the night when she reaches her hand over the cool sheets, she will find him there, and when spring comes and the sticky heat disgusts her with pangs of all the failures in her life, he will be there, and when it is time to get in the car and drive to Myrtle Beach or to see the kids, perhaps even to drive all the way to Minnesota to see their grandchildren, she will get in and close the door to the passenger side without a word. She will turn and look at the house that the two of them worked so hard to maintain, and she will note as she always does the perfect green grass of the front yard and how Sid fixed it so that there is not a trace of the mess she made. It is their house. It is their life. She will fasten her seat belt and not say a word.

2003

THOMAS McGUANE
b. 1939

Thomas McGuane was born and raised in Michigan and earned his B.A. in English Literature from Michigan State University. After briefly considering joining the Naval Air Corps, McGuane stayed true to his early vocation as a writer, choosing to study playwriting and dramatic literature at Yale, where he earned an M.F.A. in 1965. Following his graduation, McGuane moved to Spain and worked on an early version of his second novel, *The Bushwacked Piano* (1971), which earned him a Stegner Fellowship to Stanford University. While at Stanford, McGuane completed his first novel, *The Sporting Club* (1969), which was adapted for the screen in 1971. Though both *The Sporting Club* and *The Bushwacked Piano* were comic novels, McGuane's most highly acclaimed third novel, *Ninety-Two in the Shade* (1973)—nominated for the National Book Award—began to veer into a darker tone. McGuane has said that by this time he'd grown "tired of being amusing" and felt ready to express a more serious personal philosophy. His next, most autobiographical novel, *Panama* (1979), considered by McGuane to be his best, was widely panned by most critics but did receive good reviews in *The New Yorker* and *The Village Voice*. Since then, McGuane has written six more novels, two collections of short stories—*To Skin a Cat* (1986) and *Gallatin Canyon* (2006)—as well as numerous screenplays and articles. His works have appeared in *The Best American Stories*, *The Best American Essays*, and *The Best American Sports Writing*. In 2010, McGuane was elected to the American Academy of Arts and Letters.

Cowboy

The old fella makes me go into the house in my stocking feet. The old lady's in a big chair next to the window. In fact, the whole room is full of big chairs, but she's only in one of them—though, big as she is, she could fill up several. The old man says, "I found this one in the loose-horse pen at the sale yard."

She says, "What's he supposed to be?"

He says, "Supposed to be a cowboy."

"What's he doin in the loose horses?"

I says, "I was lookin for one that would ride."

"You was in the wrong pen, son," the old man says. "Them's canners. They're goin to France in cardboard boxes."

"Soon as they get a steel bolt in the head." The big old gal laughs in her chair.

Now I'm sore. "There's five in there broke to death. I rode 'em with nothin but binder twine."

"It don't make a shit," the old man says. "Ever one of them is goin to France."

The old lady don't believe me. "How'd you get in them loose horses to ride?"

"I went in there at night."

The old lady says, "You one crazy cowboy, go in there in the dark. Them broncs kick your teeth down your throat. I suppose you tried them bareback?"

"Naw, I drug the saddle I usually ride at the Rose Bowl Parade."

"You got a horse for that?"

"I got Trigger. We unstuffed him."

The old lady addresses the old man. "He's got a mouth on him. This much we know."

"Maybe he can tell us what good he is."

I says, "I'm a cowboy."

"You're a outta-work cowboy."

"It's a dying way of life."

"She's about like me—she's wondering if this ranch's supposed to be some kinda welfare agency for cowboys."

I've had enough. "You're the dumb honyocker drove me out here."

I think that'll be the end of it, but the old lady says, "Don't get huffy. You got the job. You against conversation or something?"

We get outside and the old sumbitch says, "You drawed lucky there, son. That last deal could've pissed her off."

"It didn't make me no nevermind if it did or didn't."

"She hadn't been well. Used to she was sweet as pudding."

"I'm sorry for that. We don't have health, we don't have nothin."

She must have been afflicted something terrible, because she was ugly morning, noon, and night for as long as she lasted—she'd pick a fight over nothing and the old sumbitch got the worst of it. I felt sorry for him, little slack as he cut me.

Had a hundred seventy-five sweet-tempered horned Herefords and fifteen sleepy bulls. Shipped the calves all over for hybrid vigor, mostly to the South. Had some go clear to Florida. A Hereford that still had its horns was a walking miracle, and the old sumbitch had a smart little deal going. I soon learned to give him credit for such things, and the old lady barking commands offen the sofa weren't no slouch neither. Anybody else seen their books might've said they could be wintering in Phoenix.

They didn't have no bunkhouse, just a LeisureLife mobile home that had lost its wheels about thirty years ago, and they had it positioned by the door of the barn so it'd be convenient for the hired man to stagger out at all hours and fight breech births and scours and any other disorder sent us by the cow gods. We had some doozies. One heifer got pregnant and her calf was near as big as she was. Had to reach in with a saw and take it out in pieces. When we threw the head out on the ground, she turned to it and lowed like it was her baby. Everything a cow does is designed to turn it into meat as fast as possible so that somebody can eat it. It's a terrible life.

The old sumbitch and I got along good. We got through calving and got to see them pairs and bulls run out onto the new grass. Nothing like seeing all that meat feel a little temporary joy. Then we bladed out the corrals and watched them dry under the spring sun at long last. Only mishap was when the manure spreader threw a rock and knocked me senseless and I drove the rig into an irrigation ditch. The old sumbitch never said a word but chained up and pulled us out with his Ford.

We led his cavvy out of the hills afoot with two buckets of sweet feed. Had a little of everything, including a blue roan I fancied, but he said it was a Hancock and bucked like the National Finals in Las Vegas, kicking out behind and squalling, and was just a man-killer. "Stick to the bays," he said. "The West was won on a bay horse."

He picked out three bays, had a keg of shoes, all ones and oughts, and I shod them best I could, three geldings with nice manners, stood good to shoe. About all you could say about the others was they had four legs each, and a couple, all white-marked from saddle galls and years of hard work, looked like no more summers after this. They'd been rode many a long mile. We chased 'em back into the hills and the three shod ones whinnied and fretted. "Back to work," the old sumbitch says to them.

We shod three 'cause one was going to pack a ton of fencing supplies—barb wire, smooth wire, steel T-posts, old wore-out Sunflower fence stretchers that could barely grab on to the wire, and staples—and we was at it a good little while where the elk had knocked miles of it down, or the cedar finally give out and had to be replaced by steel. That was where I found out that the old sumbitch's last good time was in Korea, where the officers at the front would yell over the radio, "Come on up here and die!" Said the enemy was coming in waves. Tells me all this while the stretcher's pulling that wire squealing though the staples. The sumbitch was a tough old bastard. "They killed a pile of us and we killed a pile of them." *Squeak*.

We hauled the mineral horseback, too, in panniers—white salt and iodine salt. He didn't have no use for blocks, so we hauled it in sacks and poured it into the troughs he had on all these bald hilltops where the wind would blow away the flies. Most of his so-called troughs were truck tires nailed onto anything flat—plywood, old doors, and suchlike—but they worked good. A cow can put her tongue anywhere in a tire and get what she needs, and you can drag one of them flat things with your horse if you need to move it. Most places we salted had old buffalo wallers where them buffalo wallered. They done wallered their last—had to get out of the way for the cow and the man on the bay horse.

I'd been rustling my own grub in the LeisureLife for quite some time when the old lady said it was time for me to eat with the white folks. This was not necessarily a good thing. The old lady's knee replacements had begun to fail, and both me and the old sumbitch was half afraid of her. She cooked as good as ever, but she was a bomb waiting to go off, standing bowlegged at the stove and talking ugly about how much she did for us. When she talked, the old sumbitch would move his mouth as though he was saying the same words, and we had to keep from giggling, which wasn't hard. For if the old lady caught us at that there'd a been hell to pay.

Both the old sumbitch and the old lady was heavy smokers, to where a oxygen bottle was in sight. So they joined a Smoke-Enders deal the Lutherans had, and this required them to put all their butts in a jar and wear the jar around their necks on a string. The old sumbitch liked this O.K. because he could just tap his ash right under his chin and not get it on the truck seat, but the more that thing filled up and hung around her neck the meaner the old lady got. She had no idea the old sumbitch was cheating and setting his jar on the woodpile when we was working outside. She was just more honest than him, and in the end she give up smoking and he smoked away, except he wasn't allowed to smoke in the house no more, nor buy ready-mades, 'cause the new tax made them too expensive and she wouldn't let him take it out of the cows, which come first. She said it was just a vice and if he was half the man she thought he was he'd give it up as a bad deal. "You could have a long and happy old age," she said, real sarcastic-like.

One day me and the old sumbitch is in the house hauling soot out of the fireplace, on account of they had a chimbley fire last winter. Over the mantel is a picture of a beautiful woman in a red dress with her hair piled on top of her head. The old sumbitch tells me that's the old lady before she joined the motorcycle gang.

"Oh?"

"Them motorcycle gangs," he says, "all they do is eat and work on their motorcycles. They taught her to smoke, too, but she's shut of that. Probably outlive us all."

"Looks to me she can live long as she wants."

"And if she ever wants to box you, tell her no. She'll knock you on your ass. I guarantee it. Throw you a damn haymaker, son."

I couldn't understand how he could be so casual-like about the old lady being in a motorcycle gang. When we was smoking in the LeisureLife, I asked him about it. That's when I found out that him and the old lady was brother and sister. I guess that explained it. If your sister wants to join a motorcycle gang, that's her business. He said she even had a tattoo—"Hounds from Hell," with a dog shooting flames out of his nostrils and riding a Harley.

That picture on the mantel kind of stayed in my mind, and I asked the old sumbitch if his sister'd ever had a boyfriend. Well, yes, quite a few, he told me, quite a damn few. "Our folks run them off. They was just after the land."

He was going all around the baler hitting the zerks with his grease gun. "I had a lady friend myself. She'd do anything. Cook. Gangbusters with a snorty horse, and not too damn hard on the eyes. Sis run her off. Said she was just after the land. If she was, I never could see it. Anyway, went on down the road long time ago."

Fall come around and when we brought the cavvy down two of them old-timers who'd worked so hard was lame. One was stifled, one was sweenied, and both had crippling quarter cracks.[1] I thought they needed to be at the loose-horse sale, but the old sumbitch says, "No mounts of mine is gonna feed no Frenchman," and that was that. So we made a hole, led the old-timers to the edge, and shot them with a elk rifle. First one didn't know what hit him. Second one heard the shot and saw his buddy fall and the old sumbitch had to chase him around to kill him. Then he sent me down the hole to get the halters back. Lifting those big heads was some chore.

---

1. Stifled, injury to the upper hind legs; sweeney, shoulder atrophy; quarter crack, a badly cracked hoof.

I enjoyed eating in the big house that whole summer until the sister started giving me come-hither looks. They was fairly limited except those days when the old sumbitch was in town after supplies. Then she dialled it up and kind of brushed me every time she went past the table. There was always something special on the town days—a pie, maybe. I tried to think about the picture on the mantel, but it was impossible, even though I knew it might get me out of the LeisureLife once and for all. She was getting more and more wound up, while I was pretending to enjoy the food or going crazy over the pie. But she didn't buy it—called me a queer and sent me back to the trailer to make my own meals. By calling me a queer, she more or less admitted what she'd been up to, and I think that embarrassed her, because she covered up by roaring at everyone and everything, including the poor old sumbitch, who had no idea what had gone sideways while he was away. It was two years before she made another pie, and then it was once a year on my birthday. She made me five birthday pies in all—sand cherry, every one of them.

I broke the catch colt, which I didn't know was no colt, as he was the biggest snide in the cavvy. He was four, and it was time. I just got around him for a couple of days, then saddled him gently as I could. The offside stirrup scared him, and he looked over at it, but that was all it was to saddling. I must've had a burst of courage, 'cause next minute I was on him. That was O.K., too. I told the old sumbitch to open the corral gate, and we sailed away. The wind blew his tail up under him, and he thought about bucking but rejected the idea and that was about all they was to breaking Olly, for that was his name. Once I'd rode him two weeks, he was safe for the old sumbitch, who plumb loved this new horse and complimented me generously for the job I'd did.

We had three hard winters in a row, then lost so many calves to scours we changed our calving grounds. The old sumbitch just come out one day and looked at where he'd calved out for fifty years and said, "The ground's no good. We're movin." So we spent the summer building a new corral way off down the creek. When we's finished, he says, "I meant to do this when I got back from overseas and now it's finished and I'm practically done for, too. Whoever gets the place next will be glad his calves don't shit themselves into the next world like mine done."

Neither one of us had a back that was worth a damn, and the least we could do was get rid of the square baler and quit hefting them man-killing five-wire bales. We got a round baler and a DewEze machine that let us pick up a bale from the truck without laying a finger on it. We'd tell stories and smoke in the cab on those cold winter days and roll out a thousand pounds of hay while them old-time horned Herefords followed the truck. That's when I let him find out I'd done some time.

"I figured you musta been in the crowbar hotel."

"How's that?"

"Well, you're a pretty good hand. What's a pretty good hand doin tryin loose horses in the middle of the night at some Podunk sale yard? Folks hang on to a pretty good hand and nobody was hangin on to you. You want to tell me what you done?"

I'd been with the old sumbitch for three years and out of jail the same amount of time. I wasn't afraid to tell him what I done 'cause I had started to trust him, but I sure didn't want him telling nothing to his sister. I told him I rustled some yearlings, and he chuckled like he understood entirely. I had rustled some yearlings, all right, but that's not what I went up for.

The old man paid me in cash, or, rather, the old lady did, since she handled anything like that. They never paid into workmen's comp, and there was no reason to go to the records. They didn't even have my name right. You tell people around here your name is Shane and they'll always believe you. The important thing is I was working my tail off for that old sumbitch, and he knew it. Nothing else mattered, even the fact that we'd come to like each other. After all, this was a God damn ranch.

The old fella had several peculiarities to him, most of which I've forgotten. He was one of the few fellas I ever heard of who would actually jump up and down on his hat if he got mad enough. You can imagine what his hat looked like. One time he did it 'cause I let the swather get away from me on a hill and bent it all to hell. Another time a Mormon tried to run down his breeding program to get a better deal on some replacement heifers, and I'll be damned if the old sumbitch didn't throw that hat down and jump on it, right in front of the Mormon, causing the Mormon to get into his Buick and ease on down the road without another word. One time when we was driving ring shanks into corral poles I hit my thumb and tried jumping on my hat, but the old sumbitch gave me such an odd look I never tried it again.

The old lady died sitting down. I went in, and there she was, sitting down, and she was dead. After the first wave of grief, the old sumbitch and me fretted about rigor mortis and not being able to move her in that seated position. So we stretched her onto the couch and called the mortician and he called the coroner and for some reason the coroner called the ambulance, which caused the old sumbitch to state, "It don't do you no nevermind to tell nobody nothing." Course he was right.

Once the funeral was behind us, I moved out of the LeisureLife, partly for comfort and partly 'cause the old sumbitch falled apart after his sister passed, which I never would've suspected. Once she's gone, he says, he's all that's left of his family and he's alone in life, and about then he notices me and tells me to get my stuff out of the LeisureLife and move in with him.

We rode through the cattle pritnear ever day year round, and he come to trust me enough to show how his breeding program went, with culls and breed-backs and outcrosses and replacements, and took me to bull sales and showed me what to expect in a bull and which ones were correct and which were sorry. One day we's looking at a pen of yearling bulls on this outfit near Luther and he can't make up his mind and he says he wished his sister was with him and he starts snuffling and says she had an eye on her wouldn't quit. So I stepped up and picked three bulls out of that pen, and he quit snuffling and said damn if I didn't have an eye on me, too. That was the beginning of our partnership.

One whole year I was the cook, and one whole year he was the cook, and back and forth like that, but never at the same time. Whoever was cook would change when the other fella got sick of his recipes, and ever once in a while a new recipe would come in the *AgriNews*, like that corn chowder with the sliced hot dogs. I even tried a pie one time, but it just made him lonesome for days gone by, so we forgot about desserts, which was probably good for our health, as most sweets call for gobbing in the white sugar.

The sister never let him have a dog 'cause she had a cat and she thought a dog would get the cat. It wasn't much of a cat, anyhow, but it lived a long time, outlived the old lady by several moons. After it passed on, we took it out to the burn barrel and the first thing the old sumbitch said was "We're gettin a dog." It took him that long to realize that his sister was gone.

Tony was a Border collie we got as a pup from a couple in Miles City that raised them. You could cup your hands and hold Tony when we got him, but he grew up in one summer and went to work and we taught him "down," "here," "come by," "way to me," and "hold 'em," all in one year or less, 'cause Tony would just stay on his belly and study you with his eyes until he knew exactly what you wanted. Tony helped us gather, mother up pairs, and separate bulls, and he lived in the house for many a good year and kept us entertained with all his tricks. Finally, Tony grew old and died. We didn't take it so good, especially the old sumbitch, who said he couldn't foresee enough summers for another dog. Plus that was the year he couldn't get on a horse no more and he wasn't about to work no stock dog afoot. There was still plenty to do and most of it fell to me. After all, this was a God damn ranch.

The time had come to tell him why I went to jail and what I did, which was rob that little store at Absarokee and shoot the proprietor, though he didn't die. I had no idea why I did such a thing—then or now. I led the crew on the prison ranch for a number of years and turned out many a good hand. They wasn't nearabout to let me loose until there was a replacement good as me who'd stay a while. So I trained up a murderer from Columbia Falls, could rope, break horses, keep vaccine records, fence, and irrigate. Once the warden seen how good he was, they paroled me out and turned it all over to the new man, who was never getting out. The old sumbitch could give a shit less when I told him my story. I could've told him all this years before when he first hired me, for all he cared. He was a big believer in what he saw with his own eyes.

I don't think I ever had the touch with customers the old sumbitch had. They'd come from all over looking for horned Herefords and talking hybrid vigor, which I may or may not have believed. They'd ask what we had and I'd point to the corrals and say, "Go look for yourself." Some would insist on seeing the old sumbitch and I'd tell them he was in bed, which was pritnear the only place you could find him now that he'd begun to fail. Then the state got wind of his condition and took him to town. I went to see him there right regular, but it just upset him. He couldn't figure out who I was and got frustrated 'cause he knew I was somebody he was supposed to know. And then he failed even worse. The doctors told me it was just better if I didn't come round.

The neighbors claimed I was personally responsible for the spread of spurge, Dalmatian toadflax, and knapweed. They got the authorities involved and it was pretty clear that I was the weed they had in mind. If they could get the court to appoint one of their relatives ranch custodian while the old sumbitch was in storage they'd get all that grass for free till he was in a pine box. The authorities came in all sizes and shapes, but when they were through they let me take one saddle horse, one saddle, the clothes on my back, my hat, and my slicker. I rode that horse clear to the sale yard, where they tried to put him in the loose horses 'cause of his age. I told them I was too set in my ways to start feeding Frenchmen and rode off toward Idaho. There's always an opening for a cowboy, even a old sumbitch like me if he can halfway make a hand.

2005

T. M. McNALLY
b. 1969

T. M. McNally spent his early childhood in Chicago before moving with his family to Arizona at age fifteen. McNally returned to Illinois to attend Rockford University and later earned an M.F.A. from Arizona State University, where he is currently a professor of English. Known for his psychological, often dark fiction, McNally has written three novels and three collections of short stories. For his first book of short stories, *Low Flying Aircraft* (1991), he won the Flannery O'Connor Award for Short Fiction. His first novel, *Until Your Heart Stops* (1994), was named a New York Times Notable Book, and his most recent story collection, *The Gateway* (2007), was a finalist for the PEN/Faulkner Award for Fiction. McNally's other works include novels *Almost Home* (1999) and *The Goat Bridge* (2005) as well as the short story collection *Quick* (2004). He has been awarded fellowships by the National Endowment for the Arts and the Howard Foundation at Brown University.

Bastogne

My father was there, as part of the 101st Airborne, though he did not arrive from the sky, floating down on the scene of battle suspended by a parachute made of silk. He had been at a replacement depot, following a series of clusterfucks in Holland where he had been wounded by a shell fragment in the seat of his pants. Operation Market Garden, they called it. At the replacement depot he waited to be called back to his unit, Fox Company, drilling during the day and drinking at night. He said they drank a lot of apple brandy, calvados. The dogface soldiers, like my father . . . when news of the German breakthrough came, the American armies in shit-panicked retreat, my father had been loaded onto a truck in his summer clothes and sent to join up with the rest of his division at the crossroads of Bastogne.

Time past, as the poet says, is time present. My wife is a scientist, working at the Max Plancke Institute in Stuttgart, the city which is home to Porsche and Mercedes and now, apparently, Chrysler. Chrysler of course owns the Jeep, the vehicle which won the war. We are trading partners now. Part of an emerging global network of free enterprise and friendly competition. In the foxholes outside of Bastogne, while supported by fragments of the Ninth Armored Division, my father's platoon dug into the snow. His feet eventually froze, and in January my father's left leg was amputated just below the knee—his entire foot black, full of pus, utterly devoid of feeling. A surgeon in a bloody mask sawed it off inside a tent and sent him back to England. This, you see, was my father in 1945: severely shell-shocked, a corporal with two Purple Hearts, each the color of a bruise, and a purple stump below the knee.

He met a woman in the summer of '45—my mother—whom he would eventually marry a dozen years later. As for my son, he has blond hair, like his mother, who is Scandinavian. She's over six feet tall and Finnish by descent, a rising scientist who has been given a grant to travel here all the way with her family from her California university to study porcelain and other, more delicate artifacts. With her scientific instruments, my wife can separate the real from the fake; each day she has lunch with scientists from Kyoto and Beijing, Paris and Milan—the rivalry, she explains, is always friendly, by which she suggests without meaning to that her colleagues are each a little bit in love with her. Even though I am not a scientist, I ought to know. Days, while she is in the lab, being scientific, I play with our son. He is almost two and learning to speak. He calls her Boppi.

Everything of value, my wife will explain to you, is fragile.

My father is broke now, as in penniless, aside from his V.A. pension and social security; my wife and I are paying for, among other things, my father's nursing home bills. When my father is lucid, and strong, I am told he stumps around the hallways in his Chicago nursing home and tells people about the rise of the evil multinational corporation, which is naturally in cahoots with NATO. Truth is, my father made a sturdy, blue-collar living after the war. He married a thin, pretty girl who had been raised in the dustbowl of Oklahoma, and who later turned out to take him for a ride. This way, then that.

And today we are driving to Bastogne because I want to see where my father served his country. I want to see where he lost his foot. My wife and I have rented an Opel, another multinational corporation, and we are driving on the autobahn. It is raining now, sleeting, the sky is dark and Henry is cranky. He's been too long on the road. He misses our dogs back in California and my back has begun to ache. We've been in Europe six months now and all we seem to be doing collectively is losing weight. I tried to get work done, writing network application codes, but gave up after I first became sick. And now, on the advice of my doctor, I have recently abandoned my third round of antibiotics and we are driving through the city of Luxembourg.

Look, says my Scandinavian wife, pointing.

Look.

The first thing my mother said to me when she met her grandson was, "Well, he certainly does not look like you."

We were visiting Chicago and had invited her for lunch in our hotel. Henry played on the carpeted floor with his cars. We didn't yet know about her boyfriend with the Winnebago, who apparently was driving a beeline across the country as we spoke. At lunch my wife explained that my father, who was in the hospital after falling and breaking his hip, had just that morning described for us the effects of capitalism. My wife said to my mother, "He thinks it's like cancer. The kind of thing that must grow to survive even if it has to consume its host." My mother blinked at that, for she is not a stupid woman; she knew we would be picking up the tab. My father, who owned a small manufacturing plant, had finally been forced to sell. He'd lost another finger on a lathe just that summer; now, in fact, she was going to sell his tools to the highest bidder. Might I be interested? To pass down to Henry? She and her accountant had been crunching lately a lot of numbers. She explained to us she'd been unusually busy and that she intended to start traveling, now that she was all alone. She made a big point of that. She dabbed frequently at her eyes. Traveling, by herself.

And here, this morning, before leaving Stuttgart for this holiday, I met with my doctor, who advised me to see what I always wanted to. And Luxembourg City is a pretty place, you've got to give it that, but we didn't bother to stop. Instead we left the highways and took winding, two-lane roads through the countryside: rolling hills, like what one finds in the midst of Pennsylvania. Driving, I imagined a lone Panther tank, running lights eerily lit up, rumbling past columns of American soldiers because the driver of the tank is lost. The Americans waved to him, actually, thinking he was one of their own. Deeply committed, the tank rumbled on, and by the time the driver figured it out—that he was hip-deep into enemy lines—it was too late to turn back. So he drove the Panther deeper and deeper into American territory. Perhaps he was looking for an opportunity to surrender? My father used to describe the Germans in their jumpsuits scrambling from the tank, flames shooting up all around them, their arms in the air. My father had shot—and killed—one of those men at one hundred yards.

"Big mistake," my father would say, telling the story. "They didn't pay attention to their maps. They were lost!"

According to our directions, the hotel in Bastogne is located past the center of town. In the town center sits a Sherman tank, right across the street from the McAuliffe Café. We drove past it to the hotel which is brand new. The couple running the hotel spoke French to my wife. They looked at me with pity, the Belgian kind which causes the mouth to purse, because of course I cannot speak French. Once, in college, I read an existential novel in French, or was it high school? My wife, though, is a genius; she has recently authenticated a palimpsest which belonged to Archimedes, who also was a genius. Perhaps my son will grow up to be a genius? Apparently we were the only guests in the hotel. We went up to our room, which was pleasant enough and could have been in Indiana or Oregon. There was a clean bed. A television with CNN and Elsa Klensch, who apparently knew a great deal about matters related to fashion. There was a window which looked out onto the snow falling briskly from the sky.

This is December, I told myself. There is the snow. Here is where my father lost his leg.

Henry was fussy, and I was cranky from so many hours of strenuous driving. My wife said to me, gathering Young Henry in her arms, "You go out. Have a look around the town."

"Really?"

"Of course," she said, kissing me. "This is *your* pilgrimage. Be safe."

I was a soldier, where I did some things I am not proud of. Then I became a history teacher. When we moved to California, on account of my wife's success, I quit teaching and became a programmer and tripled my salary, but still I remember things I used to know. The Bulge, for example, was not a place, but a description: it is the description of the line of battle—the MLR, or Main Line of Resistance. Eventually everything comes down to geometry, to volume and to mass. First there was a line, then there was an attack, and the line bulged, like my wife's belly while she was carrying our son. A sleek and tender curve, gravid with hope and risk. I remember our dogs, curling up with her on the couch, their heads in her lap, listening to Henry breathe and kick and splash— swimming in his own amniotic pool, heated by the blood of my wife's heart.

Corporal, you might say, meaning *of the body*: my father was a corporal with two Purple Hearts. At the McAuliffe Café, I ordered a beer and drank a toast to the good brigadier general. The tables are covered with liner; the glassware glistens like ice in the rain. McAuliffe is said to have replied *Nuts* when told to surrender, though many think he said something a bit more pointed than that. The Germans called in more divisions. They even sent what remained of the Luftwaffe to bomb the city, and in so doing killed a nurse my father used to dream about at night. Certainly the battle could have been fought else-where. In another city. Another time and place. Certainly the nurse might have lived to marry her fiancé and raise a family.

I write code now; that's my job. The Allies broke the Nazi military code structure, by way of computers the size of barns, long before the invasion of Normandy—cyberspace, from whom no secrets are hid, began with intelli-gence gathering and merely blossomed with the Cold War, during which I was raised by troubled parents at the dinner table. And sitting in the McAuliffe Café, I reminded myself that I still have a secret. I reminded myself, sitting at my cloth-covered table, because this is what I continue to tell myself periodi-cally to remind myself that it exists. At the time I had not yet told anybody, even my wife. The secret, of course, is that I am sick.

Outside the snow filled the sky and the moonlight which fell against it. Just because we do not see it—the maladjusted genetic pattern, the disquiet-ing turbulence in the marriage—does not mean that trouble is far away. As my father used to say, you learn to look. Outside, across the town square, my father had stood in the cold hoping for something warm to drink.

It's a hard, cold world, and I remember the beer I was drinking suddenly began to taste like vinegar. So I paid up with several hundred francs, nodding politely to the Belgian maître d' while I zipped up for the cold outside, while I tucked in my scarf before heading out the door.

I was raised an only child by my parents in Rockford, Illinois—known proudly by its denizens as the Screw Capital of the World. My father was one of many there who manufactured metal fasteners and rivets. Most of the manufacturing base has since been destroyed by the Asian Tigers—South Korea, Taiwan and Japan. In 1945 my father came to Rockford, then the larg-est city near his hometown of Freeport, as a kind of war hero, and he had his picture in the Sunday paper. That picture was framed and posted over his workbench in the garage, where he spent weekends tinkering with an army surplus Jeep he'd assembled from a kit, where he kept his handguns and col-lection of bayonets and German memorabilia—a singed photograph of a young woman he took from the blouse of the tanker he had shot at one hundred yards. A dagger embossed with the stamp of the SS. A packet of German con-doms and a tin of foot powder.

"Bullets," my father would always say. "Not words. When push comes to shove it's going to be over bullets!"

Like I said, he was a difficult, stubborn man, spoiled bitterly by the victory of his cause, though I believe at least in the beginning that my mother must have loved him. They must have had some pleasure together in this life, the initial thrills of connubial bliss in which I was apparently conceived.

"Might makes right," my father would say, removing his belt, and then he would take me into the garage and lean me over the hood of his Jeep.

He'd say, "It's time for you to learn a lesson."

And this is what I know. I know that exactly one hundred years ago the world believed war a thing of the past: progress, it was hoped, had made us civilized. Then came World War I. And II, as if it was an afterthought, though it was merely an extension of that which remained yet unresolved with improved technology. By 1939 the trench had become a foxhole; the cavalry, now fueled by petroleum by-products, an armored division. As our lawyer likes to say, do the math.

There was a fundamental design problem with the Jeep. During the initial skirmishes in the bocage[1] country, a number of officers kept getting their heads cut off. The roads were muddy and the traffic threw mud all over the windshields, so the drivers would invariably fold them down across the hood, their faces to the fine summer breeze in order to see properly where they were going. Then a wire strung up across the road would hit some guy at the neck and slice his head off, just like that. Eventually somebody welded a metal bar perpendicular to the front bumper to catch the wires. You can see such a modified Jeep in the movie *Patton*. Now you can also buy a Jeep in Germany and drive around the countryside for yourself. No protective bar necessary. Not to worry.

I know disease is like a wire strung up across a road. You cannot see it. By the time you feel it, you feel nothing else. In the mornings, when Henry wakes me, I hold his hand and he wriggles free, because he does not like to be held captive, and then he brings to me my shoes.

"Dues!" he exclaims, because this is one of his new words. "Dues!"

I love my son. I love my wife. I love my father, and my mother who abandoned him, and I love the smell of leaves in October, and grass in the spring. I love the way after you mow a fine American lawn your shoes are green and sweat runs down the back of your neck and along your spine. My father taught me to mow the lawn. He made me always wear thick leather shoes to protect my toes. *You don't want to be a gimp like your old man.* I am grateful, you see, to my father for teaching me to mow the lawn. And I am grateful to my mother for bringing me into this life. I am grateful for our fine lawn in Oakland, California, where our springer spaniels run in the summer grass while Henry throws them ice cubes. The grass, and the dew which settles there overnight, and my son who will someday be expected to care for it.

My father used to say the nurse he used to hanker for—a girl, really—was no more than nineteen. He called her a tall drink of water. In one of the photographs she is standing before a dozen GIs, an apple-faced girl with blood on

---

1. Countryside marked by hedgerows.

her blouse. As I was standing in the snow I thought of her. Saturday night, the town of Bastogne thumping and alive. Teenagers from the villages all around had driven in for a night of abandon and American rock 'n' roll—thrilled to be alive, as well they should have been.

Standing in the town square, I turned my attention to the tank, which has exactly three feet of clearance. Assuming the ground is frozen—and not muddy—a man can safely lie beneath it. On the flank there is a hole piercing through its armor. An 88 millimeter shell, the German 88. Through the hole in the side one can see the guts of the tank, and I suddenly understood why *this* tank had been left as a memorial. Because it had been rendered inoperative—taken out. Because the shell must have pierced the armor during battle, and the men of its crew, trapped, were caught inside, and then the ordnance inside would have detonated. A Sherman, once struck by such a shell, would belch black smoke—in rings up into the sky—visible for miles. The armor would grow white-hot. The men inside would burn alive.

To Heinrich, a woman had written on the back of my father's singed photograph, the photograph he had removed from the German tanker he had shot at one hundred yards. Not in English. She wrote, *With my love you shall be safe and come home to me.*

She wrote, *Ich liebe dich.*[2]

This American tank standing in the center of Bastogne has been repainted to look pretty in the moonlight. The treads which make up the planks of the tracks are an inch wide. Surrounding Bastogne are similar American tanks, demarcating the lines of battle, the turrets now memorialized on monuments of brick. *Tank tops*, says the pudgy American tourist, nudging his wife. *Get it?* My wife tells me that Archimedes used a tank of water to configure his calculations regarding volume and mass. *Ten Hut*, my father used to say, which for years I thought was a place you might grow up to live in. For the purposes of memorial, the only useful tank is that which is no longer capable of fire. My father had a tank pass over him in the snow. He dug a foxhole in the frozen ground by igniting first a grenade, to get the hole started, *dig or die*. By the end the men in his platoon were draped in white sheets to conceal themselves in the snow. They hid in their holes, dotting across the landscape—points of a line—the hills rising before them and the German armor and infantry—those greatcoats and helmets and 88 millimeter turrets—silhouetted up against the skyline. If you were caught by the SS, you would be shot, after first being made to give up your gloves and socks. At night the Germans brought out searchlights, ferreting out the American foxholes dug into the snow. The moon was full, the sky full of clouds, the night lit up like this, where I am standing in the center of a town my father gave up part of his body to defend, though at the time he had no idea why he was doing it. He was a soldier; he must have thought the uniforms sexy—the fancy paratroop boots, the swashbuckling dagger hooked up alongside, the extra jump pay. My father, he knew by then of the massacre at Malmedy.[3] He knew of the rumors of the camps and the stench they cast across the continent. He knew he was here because if he were not he would have been thrown in prison.

---

2. "I love you" (German).   **3.** German soldiers killed 80 American prisoners of war on December 17, 1944.

They shot men for cowardice then. They shot men running from the enemy. They shot men running, either way, their feet frozen in their boots by the deep, cold snow.

When Göring[4] was making his halfhearted attempt to rescue the Sixth Army, the half million or so Germans stranded and cut off across the Don, he sent airdrops of meat paste, which killed instantly the emaciated men who ate it. Still, the men would lie in the snow in the formation of a giant cross to indicate their need. I think about that often: the dying men, freezing in the snow, and their essential belief that the Führer would come ransom them.

As for the western front, my father once told me that Bastogne is a place for ghosts, and I figure he ought to know. I walked the streets, past buildings my father as a young man would have billeted in, those still standing. During the battle the apple-faced girl took care of the wounded in a makeshift hospital. She was going to be married soon. The men she nursed, her hands deep in the center of their bodies, all naturally fell in love with her. The men gave her a parachute of white silk to make her dress.

The wind was sharp and it was cold. I stepped inside the Dakota, apparently a hip and trendy club, though the building has been there since long before the war. A serious artist's music was pounding lasciviously throughout the room, which was smoky and warm, lit up with candles, full to the beam. I rubbed shoulders with drunk men and women while I knuckled up to the bar. Eventually I spotted a quiet corner and took my whiskey to the spot: I lit a cigarette, took in the view. There was a woman drinking alone dressed in a black turtleneck. She had that pursed mouth, that sophisticated lip, which claims to know more than where it's been and whom she's ever spoken to. Perhaps she was already spoken for. I sipped my whiskey and admired the silhouette of her breast, which was splendid. Were she a nurse, here in 1944, would she have bathed my father's feet? Would she have held his hand and fed him morphine? To know a woman is to know oblivion, which is why so many men are quick to go there.

Eventually I struck up a conversation with three men. They were thirty, twenty-four, and eighteen. One worked in a factory. Another was a student. The youngest, my favorite, was going to finish high school and become a farrier.

"A horse shoer?"

"Yes," he said, nodding vigorously. "Not a fairy. I like the femmes!"

The German military during the course of the war required 2.7 million horses to transport their army, half a million of which came from France. I considered the geographic implications of pastures and paddocks and storage sites for feed. Shoeing a horse, a backbreaking and thankless task, reveals one's dedication to the species: I couldn't imagine anybody making a living at that in the States, and the truth is I was a little bit in awe of this boy, and before I could begin to formulate a reply, his comrades wanted to know what I thought about American women. I explained that many are sweet. They said, and keep in mind we are speaking pidgin French and English and German,

---

4. Hermann Göring (1893–1946), Adolf Hitler's deputy and Commander of the German airforce, the Luftwaffe.

that American women are the most beautiful because of their large and boun-
tiful breasts.

Behind them I watched the woman in the black sweater, sipping her red
wine. She smiled at me then, which is something that has happened to me in
a bar only twice. I took a breath. I watched her pull back her hair, which was
short, but a gesture which nonetheless offered her an opportunity to lift her
breasts. Her sweater was made of fine wool, and the question in my mind was
simply this: does she know what she is doing or does she simply want to adjust
her hair?

My wife is one of those women in this world who do not need their husbands, which is not to say she does not love me. But daily she works with dozens
of brilliant men she does not yet know much about, which is the great draw of
seduction: the wide unknown, the field waiting to be plowed to see what
might grow. It is the lingering voice on the telephone; the sweet, earnest
promise for glory. Like the German boys, marching off by the hundred thousand to Stalingrad, dreaming of victory along the steppes. It's how marriages
and nations fall apart.

How is one to resist? My friends ordered us another round of drinks. There
was a great deal of pain in my back just then. I could either drink more or go
home and sit in the tub beneath a hot, running faucet.

When the drinks came, I asked, "What is the name of this place?"

"The Dakota!"

"Yes," I said. "But why? Why the Dakota?"

"Because," said the youngest, who loves America most. "Because it is a fine
place in America! North Dakota. South Dakota. Dakota! Cowboys and
Indians!"

Dakota is also the name of a lightweight truck manufactured by Chrysler,
now manufactured jointly with Daimler Benz, but that is not what I was thinking. At first I thought I wouldn't tell them. But the whiskey was fine. The
eldest, who worked in a small, local factory, a factory probably not unlike my
father's, the eldest was going to marry a girl in the spring, and it seemed important to me that he—that anybody—know. So I said, "You know the war?"

"The war. Yes. The war!"

The eldest explained quite seriously that his father fought with the Free
French, though when he was unable to make certain.

"You are a soldier?" one asked, brightly.

"No," I said. "My father."

"Ahh. La Guerre."[5]

"La Guerre," said the youngest, to the next eldest, showing off his translation skills. "La Guerre!"

I said, admiring the figure of the woman in the distance, "My father was
with the 101st. An army. Paratroops." I made a motion with my hand of a man,
falling through the sky, a string supporting him. The woman watched me
curiously.

The men nodded, eyes wide, exclaiming at their understanding. In general
they liked to do a lot of backslapping. And now the woman behind them
stood, waving to a young, handsome man, blown in through the door by the

---

5. "The War," that is, World War II (French).

cold wind, whom she apparently had been waiting for, and embraced him. She kissed him sweetly on both cheeks, and then the mouth, and he took a seat beside her, beaming, holding her hand. By the looks of things, they were deeply in love, and I remember that this particular fact pleased me immensely. Steadfast, I thought. Steadfast love. I felt the whiskey spread inside my belly like a nice, warm fire. It is times like this, when you watch a handsome couple kiss each other in a smoky bar, that I love the simple warmth of bourbon.

"The Dakota," I said to my friends. "That was the plane. The C-47 transport. That was the name of the plane they came from. From the sky."

"The plane?"

I made my hand into an airplane, the way I do for Young Henry when we are playing while my wife is at work inside a laboratory. I made the sound of an engine with a propeller.

"A plane," I said. "It flies through air."

Steadfast love. The kind to treasure, to keep tucked inside your heart.

I know the story of the girl, the nurse, who never got to wear her wedding dress. The apple-faced girl who held the hands of all the dying young men around her. In the end the parachute silk was covered with blood, her blood, after she had been eviscerated by an exploding bomb manufactured in Warsaw. What I do not know is the story of the man, the French partisan to whom she was engaged.

I am not certain, but I believe my father was a virgin when he returned to Rockford, Illinois, after doing his part in the war. He met my mother on a train full of troops, and she was thin, and dark-eyed, her features not unlike those of the girl in Bastogne, and he must have been bursting at the bitter seams. Probably he swaggers a little bit on his prosthetic foot, still in uniform, carrying to her a tray of drinks. Love makes even the boldest of us drunk, and conversely, drink makes even the walking wounded briefly capable of love. Perhaps they stop in Chicago, rent a hotel room, and screw each other silly in the hot summer afternoon. Look how she is fascinated by the dog tags jingling against her chest. Look how deeply they look into each other's eyes. Not once does she ask him about his leg, and perhaps it is this, this fundamental lack of recognition, which seals the bond between them for another fifty years. My father, descending upon the Holland plain, had once caught a piece of flak in his ass. A couple inches to the left, and would I even be here? Time, and space, and where the body greets a foreign object: this is the great lesson and geometry of war.

That night I dreamed about numbers. The lone one. A woman's figure holding on to a glass of red wine. I saw a one-legged man making love to a woman in a hotel with the windows open wide, and the couple unfolded, and I saw divisions of men loading onto rail cars dividing into companies—Deutsche Bank, SAP and Bayer. I saw red blood cells, replicating by the thousands, and POWs marching in the rain. Eventually I had no idea what to count, and in the morning I was awakened by Young Henry—my wife fresh from the bath, a towel around her hair, standing behind him. I studied those tender lines crisscrossing her belly and considered the fact of our son, Henry, whom she'd made somewhere behind them.

"Morning," I said.

"You okay?"

"Dreams," I said.

"Bad ones?"

"Yes."

"How's your back?"

"Okay."

She stepped into the bathroom and returned with a glass of water for me. It's never the dream which is bad but the feeling that causes you to wake. Later the French couple was surly at breakfast; I suspected they'd been quarreling all morning, but they gave us directions and we drove to the monument for the Battle of the Bulge which is set among rolling hills. The cattle, deeply muscled and blond, linger with enormous draft horses in the fields. We climbed up to the top for a view of the entire landscape.

We let Henry wander on the roof in the snow, and I said to my wife, "My father had a friend, Lucian. They shared a foxhole. At night he'd defecate in his rations box, drove my father nuts. Apparently one did a lot of whacking off inside the foxhole. Stress."

"I can imagine," said my wife, though she can't, because she is a woman, and one of the operating precepts of all brilliant and enlightened academic women is that war is a game invented by foolish men to prove each has a penis longer than the other. My wife is one of those who believe war has become obsolete because she wants it to be.

I said, trying to explain, "One day, a truck came—hot food. It came too close to the line and a dozen or so guys ran to it. They were freezing. They hadn't had anything warm to eat for days. A cook set up camp, dishing out the hash, the men huddling around the stove. And then a barrage of 88s hit and the men were all killed. Like that."

My wife watched Henry step toward the ledge. She knew the 88 was that particular and often repeated sound in *Saving Private Ryan,* which we had seen dubbed in German. She stepped toward Henry while simultaneously calling him back to us.

"They were too close together," I explained, following. "Too sweet a target. The only way to be safe was to be alone."

"Uh huh."

"My father was ordered once by a major to take the passenger seat. In a Jeep. The major sat in back. That way the sniper would hit my father and America would successfully conclude the war."

She picked up Henry, who was getting soaked to the bone. It was cold, standing on the roof, the icy wind and wet snow in our faces. Henry's cheeks were swollen red.

"Look," she said, turning to me, wiping snow from her eyes. "I am not the enemy, you know. I'm on your side."

"Only people weren't killed like that. Nobody was just killed. They were torn apart. Some guy gets his arm blown off and then his elbow is driven through another guy's brain. Mortars bounce on the ice and burst in the air, waist-high. What nobody ever gets—it's not the guy dying. It's the guy who lives. It's the guy who actually sees and knows it. That's the part that kills."

My wife said, "What happened to Lucian?"

"A shell came into the foxhole. My father had been sent back to report coordinates for the artillery. You give them the figures, x and y, they know precisely where to aim."

When he came back, there was Lucian, his heart in his lap.

A man raises his arms either to praise God or to give up. I give up, we say, meaning we surrender. *Take this.*

First there was a war, which exploded across the globe, blinding as a muzzle flash on a moonless night, and then there was the baby boom into which I was born forty-four years ago. There is an odd symmetry to that number which comforts me. "Life-shortening," said my doctor. His name was Wolfgang, and we were the same age. He spoke perfect English while his assistant took notes in German. In keeping with the tradition of the uniform, they each wore white. "Plan wisely," the doctor said to me, shaking my hand. "See what you've always wanted to. Give my regards to your wife."

Before coming home we made one last visit. This to the cemetery in Luxembourg. Overhead there were NATO warplanes in flight. What saved my father, besides the sheer grace of God, and the fact of Patton's rescuing army, was the air force: first, the supplies they dropped into Bastogne, and then the bombs they dropped onto the German tanks rolling across the countryside.

Victory, my father used to say, pointing heavenward, comes always from the sky.

It had just begun to snow in Luxembourg. We entered the cemetery, walked past the monuments, and then stepped into the field of marble crosses and stars. They stand there about two and a half feet high, and if you've been there then you know it is a breathtaking sight. We set Henry down and let him run across the file of graves, some six thousand. Six thousand bodies of Americans, there below the dirt and grass. The grass was still green, the snow falling on top, while my son ran across the neatly planted rows of white marble. A PFC here, a Captain there. This division, then that. At the front stands Patton's grave, leader of the Third Army, a man who believed in the resurrection of Jesus Christ while praying daily strictly for an opportunity to kill the enemy. To advance his career, among other things, he invented a saber for the horse cavalry.

Eventually I too will be placed into the ground. I touched Patton's grave to see what it was like. I placed my hand on the white stone and held it there. It was cold, and I rubbed the snow from my fingertips against my scarf. And I thought, Patton was raised in California, just like my son will be. Truth be told, which it often isn't, the Germans would have lost the war without him. It was a war of matériel, not honor. It was a modern war—horrific, obscenely profligate; it was a war America won simply because it could afford to buy its victory with, among other forms of currency, 12 million Russian casualties. But it was the war of our century and it will determine, I am certain, the shape and agony of those next to come.

I have so much I could tell my wife. I could tell her about the dogs. The Russian dogs, trained at birth to feed beneath an armored vehicle. The Russians strapped mines to the backs of these dogs and sent them off to greet the German tanks racing across the Don. After a few explosions, the German soldier simply learned to shoot any dog running toward him. Then he ate what was left of it. He ate the horses rotting in the fields. The fields turned to mud and shit. When the Germans ran out of lumber to make roads for their tanks, they used the corpses of the Russian dead, like planks. Like the dogs strapped with mines to their back, any soldier is capable of instruction.

I turned to my wife and she took my hands, warming them with her own, and I said, "I want us to leave early. I want to go back home."

"I know."

"I miss our dogs."

"Me too," she said, nodding in the snow. "I know."

"I'm sick."

I hadn't told her I was sick, you see. But she knew by now that it was coming. She knew because she was my wife and had listened to me at night while I sat in the bath full of running hot water and held my ribs. She knew about my visits to Wolfgang, the traces of the repeated blood tests lingering on my arms. She bit her lip and said, "This was supposed to be a lark. I can do my work better at home, anyway." She said, and I swear to God I shall love her always for this, "We'll be safe there."

During the last great war, America got off easy. It never has been me that I've been worried about; it's how I knew I had become a man, once I understood this: once I understood that it was the very nature of war to inflict losses far greater upon the world than anything I might ever hope to conceive. Perhaps my son, sitting on this frozen cemetery lawn in his Gymboree snowsuit, perhaps my son might grow up to be a doctor. Or a priest. Perhaps he will become a scientist like his mom. It's not important to most of us, the things each of us does in this world. Another American in this world isn't going to save the Middle East. Or the economy in Moscow. And probably my son is never going to change the world.

But he might, you see. He just might, if only his very own.

And in this case, might—or possibility—does make right.

I asked my father once why he shot the German tanker who had burst into flames, to which my father replied, "So he wouldn't burn to death, Son." During my own son's birth, I remember our nurse turning to me in the delivery room, explaining to me that the baby was at zero station. His head passing through his mother's pelvis, my son drew his life's first breath.

My father was one of a half dozen men who buried the girl. The men, he told me, wrapped her body in the parachute silk they had given her to make her wedding dress. Once she had brought to my father a cup of tea, and it is then, I am certain, he must have fallen in love with her. He was nineteen, and he had been sent back off the line—four hours, to rest—and he was standing huddled beneath his sheet beside a destroyed bakery, bricks and splinters everywhere, when the girl, having seen him, stepped out of the makeshift hospital. She was wearing only her shoes and skirt and blouse. The wind blew her hair in her eyes, and they teared up instantly, and she said to my father, "Here. For you," as she handed to him a cup of tea. The tea steamed into the winter air like smoke, and the girl wiped her eyes and turned around, stepped back inside her hospital, and disappeared for life.

I should also tell you that it's warm here in California this time of year. My father is now living five miles down the road at the Sunnyvale Home for Independent Living; he has a friend named Burt who survived Guadalcanal and has several teeth he pried from Japanese POWs to prove it, though my father will tell you privately that he thinks Burt traded whiskey for those teeth just to have some souvenirs. My father, who is jealous of these teeth, calls his new home The Barracks and has taken to wearing once again his dogtags. As for my mother, she has recently sent to me a postcard from the mountains of Colorado. Apparently she has her sights now set on a soon-to-be widowed vintner who is caring for his disabled wife. On weekends, my wife brings my father home to eat a decent meal and tell us the same stories. Sometimes we rent movies for after Young Henry falls asleep, movies like *A Bridge Too Far* and *Anzio*.[6] And at night, the dogs, at night just as it is getting dark, the dogs curl up with my wife on the couch, resting their heads on her lap. My hair has long since fallen out but this I am told may just be temporary.

Tell me about the nurse, I'll ask my father sometimes. *Tell me about the girl who got away.*

Blown to bits, he says, every time. *Should have married that girl.* And then he will explain why, as he always does, filling in the gaps of his memory with longing and desire and regret. *Should have never let her get away!*

What I want to tell my father, but never do, is that the men and women we love in this life, they all get away. Nights, while I lie awake, waiting for my body to heal itself, for my disease to bear even the slightest signs of remission, sometimes I think about my father in the Belgian snow. He is lying in a hole in the ground, his feet frozen in ice. His hands are blistered with cold. He is not yet twenty, and has never slept beside a woman he loves, has never heard or felt her breath against his shoulder, or neck, while she sleeps. He is instead lying in the freezing cold of Bastogne—a small town in a country he has never heard of, a town not unlike Freeport, Illinois, the place of his birth—waiting to be relieved, and what he must understand is that it just may be possible for him to survive. Without this understanding then how could anybody possibly ever do it? How else endure the blood all around you turned to ice? After all, he has a good, strong heart. He loves God. And he wants only the sky to darken and protect him from the view of snipers. Then he wants to close his eyes in the deep, dark cold and wake to find himself alive—still whole, and warm. He wants to feel the heat of a live fire. He wants to save his ammunition and he wants to wake in a bed with sheets with that nurse back in the town holding his hand. He wants another hot cup of tea with just a little milk and sugar. Because during the winter of 1945, in the midst of yet another war the causes for which we shall fail to remember properly, this is my father. He is a man, and as a man, he wants only to be loved, so that one day he too might be able to love another even more. He is a man, my father, who has brought me here to find him in the bitter snow and bring him home.

2007

---

6. Films about World War II, directed by Richard Attenborough (1977) and Edward Dmytryk (1968), respectively.

JAMES ALAN McPHERSON
b. 1943

A native of Savannah, Georgia, McPherson earned a degree from Atlanta's Morris Brown College and studied at the Harvard and Yale law schools as well as the University of Iowa's Writers' Workshop. Not surprisingly, then, his remarkable career has proceeded on very different tracks. On the one hand, McPherson is a distinguished essayist, historian, and editor; his publications include contributions to *A World Unsuspected* (1987), *The Prevailing South* (1988), and *Confronting Racial Difference* (1990); the memoir *Crabcakes* (1997), the essay collection *A Region Not Home: Reflections from Exile* (1999), and a number of American history textbooks. At the same time, McPherson has flourished as a fiction writer, beginning when his story "Gold Coast," from his first collection, *Hue and Cry* (1968), won a contest in the *Atlantic Monthly* magazine. With his second collection, *Elbow Room* (1977), he became the first African American to win the Pulitzer Prize for fiction. In 1981 he was awarded a MacArthur Fellowship. A writer who takes enormous pains and works very slowly, McPherson manages to produce stories remarkable for their fluidity and their music. He has taught at the University of Virginia and, since 1981, at the University of Iowa.

Why I Like Country Music

No one will believe that I like country music. Even my wife scoffs when told such a possibility exists. "Go on!" Gloria tells me. "I can see blues, bebop, maybe even a little buckdancing. But not bluegrass." Gloria says, "Hillbilly stuff is not just music. It's like the New York Stock Exchange. The minute you see a sharp rise in it, you better watch out."

I tend to argue the point, but quietly, and mostly to myself. Gloria was born and raised in New York; she has come to believe in the stock exchange as the only index of economic health. My perceptions were shaped in South Carolina; and long ago I learned there, as a waiter in private clubs, to gauge economic flux by the tips people gave. We tend to disagree on other matters too, but the thing that gives me most frustration is trying to make her understand why I like country music. Perhaps it is because she hates the South and has capitulated emotionally to the horror stories told by refugees from down home. Perhaps it is because Gloria is third generation Northern-born. I do not know. What I do know is that, while the two of us are black, the distance between us is sometimes as great as that between Ibo and Yoruba.[1] And I do know that, despite her protestations, I like country music.

"You are crazy," Gloria tells me.

I tend to argue the point, but quietly, and mostly to myself.

Of course I do not like all country stuff; just pieces that make the right connections. I like banjo because sometimes I hear ancestors in the strumming. I like the fiddle-like refrain in "Dixie" for the very same reason. But most of all I like square dancing—the interplay between fiddle and caller, the stomping, the swishing of dresses, the strutting, the proud turnings, the laughter. Most of all I like the laughter. In recent months I have wondered why I like this music and this dance. I have drawn no general conclusions, but from time to time I suspect it is because the square dance is the only dance form I ever mastered.

"I wouldn't say that in public," Gloria warns me.

I agree with her, but still affirm the truth of it, although quietly, and mostly to myself.

Dear Gloria: This is the truth of how it was:

In my youth in that distant country, while others learned to strut, I grew stiff as a winter cornstalk. When my playmates harmonized their rhythms, I stood on the sidelines in atonic detachment. While they shimmied, I merely jerked in lackluster imitation. I relate these facts here, not in remorse or self-castigation, but as a true confession of my circumstances. In those days, down in our small corner of South Carolina, proficiency in dance was a form of storytelling. A boy could say, "I traveled here and there, saw this and fought that, conquered him and made love to her, lied to them, told a few others the truth, just so I could come back here and let you know what things out there are really like." He could communicate all this with smooth, graceful jiggles of his round bottom, synchronized with intricately coordinated sweeps of his arms and small, unexcited movements of his legs. Little girls could communicate much more.

But sadly, I could do none of it. Development of these skills depended on the ministrations of family and neighbors. My family did not dance; our closest neighbor was a true-believing Seventh Day Adventist.[2] Moreover, most new dances came from up North, brought to town usually by people returning to riff on the good life said to exist in those far Northern places. They prowled our dirt streets in rented Cadillacs; paraded our brick sidewalks exhibiting styles abstracted from the fullness of life in Harlem, South Philadelphia, Roxbury, Baltimore and the South Side of Chicago. They confronted our provincial clothes merchants with the arrogant reminder, "But people ain't wearin' this in New Yokkk!" Each of their movements, as well as their world-weary smoothness, told us locals meaningful tales of what was missing in our lives. Unfortunately, those of us under strict parental supervision, or those of us without Northern connections, could only stand at a distance and worship these envoys of culture. We stood on the sidelines—styleless, gestureless, danceless, doing nothing more than an improvised one-butt shuffle—hoping

---

1. Long-time rival ethnic groups of West Africa.   **2.** Christian denomination known for its strictures against secular pastimes.

for one of them to touch our lives. It was my good fortune, during my tenth year on the sidelines, to have one of these Northerners introduce me to the square dance.

My dear, dear Gloria, her name was Gweneth Lawson:

She was a pretty, chocolate brown little girl with dark brown eyes and two long black braids. After all these years, the image of these two braids evokes in me all there is to remember about Gweneth Lawson. They were plaited across the top of her head and hung to a point just above the back of her Peter Pan collar. Sometimes she wore two bows, one red and one blue, and these tended to sway lazily near the place on her neck where the smooth brown of her skin and the white of her collar met the ink-bottle black of her hair. Even when I cannot remember her face, I remember the rainbow of deep, rich colors in which she lived. This is so because I watched them, every weekday, from my desk directly behind hers in our fourth-grade class. And she wore the most magical perfume, or lotion, smelling just slightly of fresh-cut lemons, that wafted back to me whenever she made the slightest movement at her desk. Now I must tell you this much more, dear Gloria: whenever I smell fresh lemons, whether in the market or at home, I look around me—not for Gweneth Lawson, but for some quiet corner where I can revive in private certain memories of her. And in pursuing these memories across such lemony bridges, I rediscover that I loved her.

Gweneth was from the South Carolina section of Brooklyn. Her parents had sent her south to live with her uncle, Mr. Richard Lawson, the brick mason, for an unspecified period of time. Just why they did this I do not know, unless it was their plan to have her absorb more of South Carolina folkways than conditions in Brooklyn would allow. She was a gentle, soft-spoken girl; I recall no condescension in her manner. This was all the more admirable because our unrestrained awe of a Northern-born black person usually induced in him some grand sense of his own importance. You must know that in those days older folks would point to someone and say, "He's from the North," and the statement would be sufficient in itself. Mothers made their children behave by advising that, if they led exemplary lives and attended church regularly, when they died they would go to New York. Only someone who understands what London meant to Dick Whittington, or how California and the suburbs function in the national mind, could appreciate the mythical dimensions of this Northlore.

But Gweneth Lawson was above regional idealization. Though I might have loved her partly because she was a Northerner, I loved her more because of the world of colors that seemed to be suspended above her head. I loved her glowing forehead and I loved her bright, dark brown eyes; I loved the black braids, the red and blue and sometimes yellow and pink ribbons; I loved the way the deep, rich brown of her neck melted into the pink or white cloth of her Peter Pan collar; I loved the lemony vapor on which she floated and from which, on occasion, she seemed to be inviting me to be buoyed up, up, up into her happy world; I loved the way she caused my heart to tumble whenever, during a restless moment, she seemed about to turn her head in my direction; I loved her more, though torturously, on the many occasions when she did not turn. Because I was a shy boy, I loved the way I could love her silently, at least six hours a day, without ever having to disclose my love.

My platonic state of mind might have stretched onward into a blissful infinity had not Mrs. Esther Clay Boswell, our teacher, made it her business to pry into the affair. Although she prided herself on being a strict disciplinarian, Mrs. Boswell was not without a sense of humor. A round, full-breasted woman in her early forties, she liked to amuse herself, and sometimes the class as well, by calling the attention of all eyes to whomever of us violated the structure she imposed on classroom activities. She was particularly hard on people like me who could not contain an impulse to daydream, or those who allowed their eyes to wander too far away from lessons printed on the blackboard. A black and white sign posted under the electric clock next to the door summed up her attitude toward this kind of truancy: NOTICE TO ALL CLOCKWATCHERS, it read, TIME PASSES, WILL YOU? Nor did she abide timidity in her students. Her voice booming, "Speak up, boy!" was more than enough to cause the more emotional among us, including me, to break into convenient flows of warm tears. But by doing this we violated yet another rule, one on which depended our very survival in Mrs. Esther Clay Boswell's class. She would spell out this rule for us as she paced before her desk, slapping a thick, homemade ruler against the flat of her brown palm. "There ain't no *babies* in here," she would recite. *Thaap!* "Anybody thinks he's still a *baby* . . ." *Thaap!* ". . . should crawl back home to his mama's *titty*." *Thaap!* "You little bunnies shed your *last water* . . ." *Thaap!* ". . . the minute you left home to come in here." *Thaap!* "From now on, you g'on do all your *cryin'* . . ." *Thaap!* ". . . in *church!*" *Thaap!* Whenever one of us compelled her to make this speech it would seem to me that her eyes paused overlong on my face. She would seem to be daring me, as if suspicious that, in addition to my secret passion for Gweneth Lawson, which she might excuse, I was also in the habit of throwing fits of temper.

She had read me right. I was the product of too much attention from my father. He favored me, paraded me around on his shoulder, inflated my ego constantly with what, among us at least, was a high compliment: "You my nigger if you don't get no bigger." This statement, along with my father's generous attentions, made me selfish and used to having my own way. I *expected* to have my own way in most things, and when I could not, I tended to throw tantrums calculated to break through any barrier raised against me.

Mrs. Boswell was also perceptive in assessing the extent of my infatuation with Gweneth Lawson. Despite my stealth in telegraphing emissions of affection into the back part of Gweneth's brain, I could not help but observe, occasionally, Mrs. Boswell's cool glance pausing on the two of us. But she never said a word. Instead, she would settle her eyes momentarily on Gweneth's face and then pass quickly to mine. But in that instant she seemed to be saying, "Don't look back now, girl, but I *know* that bald-headed boy behind you has you on his mind." She seemed to watch me daily, with a combination of amusement and absolute detachment in her brown eyes. And when she stared, it was not at me but at the normal focus of my attention: the end of Gweneth Lawson's black braids. Whenever I sensed Mrs. Boswell watching I would look away quickly, either down at my brown desk top or across the room to the blackboard. But her eyes could not be eluded this easily. Without looking at anyone in particular, she could make a specific point to one person in a manner so general that only long afterward did the real object of her attention realize it had been intended for him.

"Now you little brown bunnies," she might say, "and you black buck rabbits and you few cottontails mixed in, some of you starting to smell yourselves under the arms without knowing what it's all about." And here, it sometimes seemed to me, she allowed her eyes to pause casually on me before resuming their sweep of the entire room. "Now I know your mamas already made you think life is a bed of roses, but in *my* classroom you got to know the foot-paths through the *sticky* parts of the rose-bed." It was her custom during this ritual to prod and goad those of us who were developing reputations for meekness and indecision; yet her method was Socratic in that she compelled us, indirectly, to supply our own answers by exploiting one person as the walking symbol of the error she intended to correct. Clarence Buford, for example, an oversized but good-natured boy from a very poor family, served often as the helpmeet in this exercise.

"Buford," she might begin, slapping the ruler against her palm, "how does a tongue-tied country boy like you expect to get a wife?"

"I don't want no wife," Buford might grumble softly.

Of course the class would laugh.

"Oh yes you do," Mrs. Boswell would respond. "All you buck rabbits want wives." *Thaap!* "So how do you let a girl know you not just a bump on a log?"

"I know! I know!" a high voice might call from a seat across from mine. This, of course, would be Leon Pugh. A peanut-brown boy with curly hair, he seemed to know everything. Moreover, he seemed to take pride in being the only one who knew answers to life questions and would wave his arms excit-edly whenever our attentions were focused on such matters. It seemed to me his voice would be extra loud and his arms waved more strenuously whenever he was certain that Gweneth Lawson, seated across from him, was interested in an answer to Mrs. Esther Clay Boswell's question. His eager arms, it seemed to me, would be reaching out to grasp Gweneth instead of the question asked.

"Buford, you twisted-tongue, bunion-toed country boy," Mrs. Boswell might say, ignoring Leon Pugh's hysterical armwaving, "you gonna let a cottontail like Leon get a girlfriend before you?"

"I don't want no girlfriend," Clarence Buford would almost sob. "I don't like no girls."

The class would laugh again while Leon Pugh manipulated his arms like a flight navigator under battle conditions. "I know! I know! I swear to *God* I know!"

When at last Mrs. Boswell would turn in his direction, I might sense that she was tempted momentarily to ask me for an answer. But as in most such exercises, it was the worldly-wise Leon Pugh who supplied this. "What do *you* think, Leon?" she would ask inevitably, but with a rather lifeless slap of the ruler against her palm.

"My daddy told me . . ." Leon would shout, turning slyly to beam at Gweneth, ". . . my daddy and my big brother from the Bronx New York told me that to git *anythin'* in this world you gotta learn how to blow your own horn."

"Why, Leon?" Mrs. Boswell might ask in a bored voice.

"Because," the little boy would recite, puffing out his chest, "because if you don't blow your own horn ain't nobody else g'on blow it for you. That's what my daddy said."

"What do you think about that, Buford?" Mrs. Boswell would ask.

"I don't want no girlfriend anyhow," the puzzled Clarence Buford might say. And then the cryptic lesson would suddenly be dropped.

This was Mrs. Esther Clay Boswell's method of teaching. More than anything written on the blackboard, her questions were calculated to make us turn around in our chairs and inquire in guarded whispers of each other, and especially of the wise and confident Leon Pugh, "What does she mean?" But none of us, besides Pugh, seemed able to comprehend what it was we ought to know but did not know. And Mrs. Boswell, plump brown fox that she was, never volunteered any more in the way of confirmation than was necessary to keep us interested. Instead, she paraded around us, methodically slapping the homemade ruler against her palm, suggesting by her silence more depth to her question, indeed, more implications in Leon's answer, than we were then able to perceive. And during such moments, whether inspired by selfishness or by the peculiar way Mrs. Boswell looked at me, I felt that finding answers to such questions was a task she had set for me, of all the members of the class.

Of course Leon Pugh, among other lesser lights, was my chief rival for the affections of Gweneth Lawson. All during the school year, from September through the winter rains, he bested me in my attempts to look directly into her eyes and say a simple, heartfelt, "hey." This was my ambition, but I never seemed able to get close enough to her attention. At Thanksgiving I helped draw a bounteous yellow cornucopia on the blackboard, with fruits and flowers matching the colors that floated around Gweneth's head; Leon Pugh made one by himself, a masterwork of silver paper and multicolored crepe, which he hung on the door. Its silver tail curled upward to a point just below the face of Mrs. Boswell's clock. At Christmas, when we drew names out of a hat for the exchange of gifts, I drew the name of Queen Rose Phipps, a fairly unattractive squash-yellow girl of absolutely no interest to me. Pugh, whether through collusion with the boy who handled the lottery or through pure luck, pulled forth from the hat the magic name of Gweneth Lawson. He gave her a set of deep purple bows for her braids and a basket of pecans from his father's tree. Uninterested now in the spirit of the occasion, I delivered to Queen Rose Phipps a pair of white socks. Each time Gweneth wore the purple bows she would glance over at Leon and smile. Each time Queen Rose wore my white socks I would turn away in embarrassment, lest I should see them pulling down into her shoes and exposing her skinny ankles.

After class, on wet winter days, I would trail along behind Gweneth to the bus stop, pause near the steps while she entered, and follow her down the aisle until she chose a seat. Usually, however, in clear violation of the code of conduct to which all gentlemen were expected to adhere, Leon Pugh would already be on the bus and shouting to passersby, "Move off! Get away! This here seat by me is reserved for the girl from Brooklyn New York." Discouraged but not defeated, I would swing into the seat next nearest her and cast calf-eyed glances of wounded affection at the back of her head or at the brown, rainbow profile of her face. And at her stop, some eight or nine blocks from mine, I would disembark behind her along with a crowd of other love-struck boys. There would then follow a well-rehearsed scene in which all of us, save Leon Pugh, pretended to have gotten off the bus either too late or too soon to wend our proper paths homeward. And at slight cost to ourselves we enjoyed the advantage of being able to walk close by her as she glided toward her uncle's green-frame house.

There, after pausing on the wooden steps and smiling radiantly around the crowd like a spring sun in that cold winter rain, she would sing, "Bye, y'all," and disappear into the structure with the mystery of a goddess. Afterward I would walk away, but slowly, much slower than the other boys, warmed by the music and light in her voice against the sharp, wet winds of the February afternoon.

I loved her, dear Gloria, and I danced with her and smelled the lemony youth of her and told her that I loved her, all this in a way you would never believe:

You would not know or remember, as I do, that in those days, in our area of the country, we enjoyed a pleasingly ironic mixture of Yankee and Confederate folkways. Our meals and manners, our speech, our attitudes toward certain ambiguous areas of history, even our acceptance of tragedy as the normal course of life—these things and more defined us as Southern. Yet the stern morality of our parents, their toughness and penny-pinching and attitudes toward work, their covert allegiance toward certain ideals, even the directions toward which they turned our faces, made us more Yankee than Cavalier. Moreover, some of our schools were named for Confederate men of distinction, but others were named for the stern-faced believers who had swept down from the North to save a people back, back long ago, in those long forgotten days of once upon a time. Still, our schoolbooks, our required classroom songs, our flags, our very relation to the statues and monuments in public parks, negated the story that these dreamers from the North had ever come. We sang the state song, memorized the verses of homegrown poets, honored in our books the names and dates of historical events both before and after that Historical Event which, in our region, supplanted even the division of the millennia introduced by the followers of Jesus Christ. Given the silent circumstances of our cultural environment, it was ironic, and perhaps just, that we maintained a synthesis of two traditions no longer supportive of each other. Thus it became traditional at our school to celebrate the arrival of spring on May first by both the ritual plaiting of the Maypole and square dancing.

On that day, as on a few others, the Superintendent of Schools and several officials were likely to visit our schoolyard and stand next to the rusty metal swings, watching the fourth, fifth, and sixth graders bob up and down and behind and before each other, around the gaily painted Maypoles. These happy children would pull and twist long runs of billowy crepe paper into wondrous, multicolored plaits. Afterward, on the edges of thunderous applause from teachers, parents and visiting dignitaries, a wave of elaborately costumed children would rush out onto the grounds in groups of eight and proceed with the square dance. "Dog*gone!*" the Superintendent of Schools was heard to exclaim on one occasion. "Y'all do it so good it just makes your *bones* set up and take notice."

Such was the schedule two weeks prior to May first, when Mrs. Boswell announced to our class that as fourth graders we were now eligible to participate in the festivities. The class was divided into two general sections of sixteen each, one group preparing to plait the pole and a second group, containing an equal number of boys and girls, practicing turns for our part in the square dance. I was chosen to square dance; so was Leon Pugh. Gweneth Lawson was placed with the pole plaiters. I was depressed until I remembered, happily, that I could not dance a lick. I reported this fact to Mrs. Boswell just after drawing, during recess, saying that my lack of skill would only result in our class making a poor showing. I asked to be reassigned to the group of Maypole plaiters. Mrs. B. looked me over with considerable amusement tugging at the corners of her mouth. "Oh, you don't have to *dance* to do the square dance," she said. "That's a dance that was made up to mock folks that couldn't dance." She paused a second before adding thoughtfully: "The worse you are at dancing, the better you can square dance. It's just about the best dance in the world for a stiff little bunny like you."

"I want to plait the Maypole," I said.

"You'll square dance or I'll grease your little butt," Mrs. Esther Clay Boswell said.

"I ain't gonna do *nothin'!*" I muttered. But I said this quietly, and mostly to myself, while walking away from her desk. For the rest of the day she watched me closely, as if she knew what I was thinking.

The next morning I brought a note from my father. "Dear Mrs. Boswell:" I had watched him write earlier that morning, "My boy does not square dance. Please excuse him as I am afraid he will break down and cry and mess up the show. Yours truly . . ."

Mrs. Boswell said nothing after she had read the note. She merely waved me to my seat. But in the early afternoon, when she read aloud the lists of those assigned to dancing and Maypole plaiting, she paused as my name rolled off her tongue. "You don't have to stay on the square dance team," she called to me. "You go on out in the yard with the Maypole team."

I was ecstatic. I hurried to my place in line some three warm bodies behind Gweneth Lawson. We prepared to march out.

"Wait a minute," Mrs. Boswell called. "Now it looks like we got seventeen bunnies on the Maypole team and fifteen on the square dance. We have to even things up." She made a thorough examination of both lists, scratching her head. Then she looked carefully up and down the line of stomping Maypole-ites. "Miss Gweneth Lawson, you cute little cottontail you, it looks like you gonna have to go over to the square dance team. That'll give us eight sets of partners for the square dance . . . but now we have another problem." She made a great display of counting the members of the two squads of square dancers. "Now there's sixteen square dancers all right, but when we pair them off we got a problem of higher mathematics. With nine girls and only seven *boys,* looks like we gotta switch a girl from square dancing to Maypole and a boy from Maypole to square dancing."

I waited hopefully for Gweneth Lawson to volunteer. But just at that moment the clever Leon Pugh grabbed her hand and began jitterbugging as though he could hardly wait for the record player to be turned on and the dancing to begin.

"What a cute couple," Mrs. Boswell observed absently. "Now which one of you other girls wants to join up with the Maypole team?"

Following Pugh's example, the seven remaining boys grabbed the girls they wanted as partners. Only skinny Queen Rose Phipps and shy Beverly Hankins remained unclaimed. Queen Rose giggled nervously.

"Queen Rose," Mrs. B. called, "I know you don't mind plaiting the Maypole." She waved her ruler in a gesture of casual dismissal. Queen Rose raced across the room and squeezed into line.

"*Now,*" Mrs. Boswell said, "I need a boy to come across to the square dancers."

I was not unmindful of the free interchange of partners involved in square dancing, even though Leon Pugh had beat me in claiming the partner of my choice. All I really wanted was one moment swinging Gweneth Lawson in my arms. I raised my hand slowly.

"Oh, not *you*, little bunny," Mrs. Boswell said. "You and your daddy claim you don't like to square dance." She slapped her ruler against her palm. *Thaap! Thaap!* Then she said, "Clarence Buford, I *know* a big-footed country boy like you can square dance better than anybody. Come on over here and kiss cute little Miss Beverly Hankins."

"I don't like no girls *noway*," Buford mumbled. But he went over and stood next to the giggling Beverly Hankins.

"Now!" said Mrs. B. "March on out in that yard and give that pole a good plaiting!"

We started to march out. Over my shoulder, as I reached the door, I glimpsed the overjoyed Leon Pugh whirling lightly on his toes. He sang in a confident tone:

> "*I saw the Lord give Moses a pocketful of roses.*
> *I skid Ezekiel's wheel on a ripe banana peel.*
> *I rowed the Nile, flew over a stile,*
> *Saw Jack Johnson pick his teeth*
> *With toenails from Jim Jeffries' feets . . .*"

"Grab your partners!" Mrs. Esther Clay Boswell was saying as the oak door slammed behind us.

I had been undone. For almost two weeks I was obliged to stand on the sidelines and watch Leon Pugh allemande left and do-si-do[3] my beloved Gweneth. Worse, she seemed to be enjoying it. But I must give Leon proper credit: he was a dancing fool. In a matter of days he had mastered, and then improved on, the various turns and bows and gestures of the square dance. He leaped while the others plodded, whirled each girl through his arms with lightness and finesse, chattered playfully at the other boys when they tumbled over their own feet. Mrs. Boswell stood by the record player calling, "Put some *strut* in it, Buford, you big potato sack. Watch Leon and see how *he* does it." I leaned against the classroom wall and watched the dancers, my own group having already exhausted the limited variations possible in matters of Maypole plaiting.

At home each night I begged my father to send another note to Mrs. Boswell, this time stating that I had no interest in the Maypole. But he resisted my entreaties and even threatened me with a whipping if I did not participate and make him proud of me. The real cause of his irritation was the considerable investment he had already made in purchasing an outfit for me. Mrs. Boswell had required all her students, square dancers and Maypole plaiters alike, to report on May first in outfits suitable for square dancing. My father had bought a new pair of dungarees, a blue shirt, a red and white polka-dot

---

3. Literally, "German" left and "back to back" (French), both figures used in square dancing.

bandanna and a cowboy hat. He was in no mood to bend under the emotional weight of my new demands. As a matter of fact, early in the morning of May first he stood beside my bed with the bandanna in his left hand and his leather belt in his right hand, just in case I developed a sudden fever.

I dragged myself heavily through the warm, blue spring morning toward school, dressed like a carnival cowboy. When I entered the classroom I sulked against the wall, being content to watch the other children. And what happy buzzings and jumping and excitement they made as they compared costumes. Clarence Buford wore a Tom Mix hat and a brown vest over a green shirt with red six-shooter patterns embossed on its collar. Another boy, Paul Carter, was dressed entirely in black, with a fluffy white handkerchief puffing from his neck. But Leon Pugh caught the attention of all our eyes. He wore a red and white checkered shirt, a loose green bandanna clasped at his throat by a shining silver buffalo head, brown chaps sewed onto his dungarees, and shiny brown cowboy boots with silver spurs that clanked each time he moved. In his hand he carried a carefully creased brown cowboy hat. He announced his fear that it would lose its shape and planned to put it on only when the dancing started. He would allow no one to touch it. Instead, he stood around clanking his feet and smoothing the crease in his fabulous hat and saying loudly, "My daddy says it pays to look good no matter what you put on."

The girls seemed prettier and much older than their ages. Even Queen Rose Phipps wore rouge on her cheeks that complemented her pale color. Shy Beverly Hankins had come dressed in a blue and white checkered bonnet and a crisp blue apron; she looked like a frontier mother. But Gweneth Lawson, my Gweneth Lawson, dominated the group of girls. She wore a long red dress with sheaves and sheaves of sparkling white crinoline belling it outward so it seemed she was floating. On her honey-brown wrists golden bracelets sparkled. A deep blue bandanna enclosed her head with the wonder of a summer sky. Black patent leather shoes glistened like half-hidden stars beneath the red and white of her hemline. She stood smiling before us and we marveled. At that moment I would have given the world to have been able to lead her about on my arm.

Mrs. Boswell watched us approvingly from behind her desk. Finally, at noon, she called, "Let's go on out!" Thirty-two living rainbows cascaded toward the door. Pole plaiters formed one line. Square dancers formed another. Mrs. Boswell strolled officiously past us in review. It seemed to me she almost paused while passing the spot where I stood on line. But she brushed past me, straightening an apron here, applying spittle and a rub to a rouged cheek there, waving a wary finger at an over-anxious boy. Then she whacked her ruler against her palm and led us out into the yard. The fifth and sixth graders had already assembled. On one end of the playground were a dozen or so tall painted poles with long, thin wisps of green and blue and yellow and rust-brown crepe floating lazily on the sweet spring breezes.

"Maypole teams *up!*" called Mr. Henry Lucas, our principal, from his platform by the swings. Beside him stood the white Superintendent of Schools (who said later of the square dance, it was reported to all the classes, "Lord y'all square dance so *good* it makes me plumb *ashamed* us white folks ain't takin' better care of our art stuff"). "Maypole teams up!" Mr. Henry Lucas shouted again. Some fifty of us, screaming shrilly, rushed to grasp our favorite color crepe. Then, to the music of "Sing Praise for All the Brightness and the Joy of

Spring," we pulled and plaited in teams of six or seven until every pole was twisted as tight and as colorfully as the braids on Gweneth Lawson's head. Then, to the applause of proud teachers and parents and the whistles of the Superintendent of Schools, we scattered happily back under the wings of our respective teachers. I stood next to Mrs. Boswell, winded and trembling but confident I had done my best. She glanced down at me and said in a quiet voice, "I do believe you are learning the rhythm of the thing."

I did not respond.

"Let's *go!*" Leon Pugh shouted to the other kids, grabbing Gweneth Lawson's arm and taking a few clanking steps forward.

"Wait a minute, Leon," Mrs. Boswell hissed. "Mr. Lucas has to change the record."

Leon sighed. "But if we don't git out there first, all them other teams will take the best spots."

"Wait!" Mrs. Boswell ordered.

Leon sulked. He inched closer to Gweneth. I watched him swing her hand impatiently. He stamped his feet and his silver spurs jangled.

Mrs. Boswell looked down at his feet. "Why, Leon," she said, "you can't go out there with razors on your shoes."

"These ain't razors," Leon muttered. "These here are spurs my brother in Bronx New York sent me just for this here dance."

"You have to take them off," Mrs. Boswell said.

Leon growled. But he reached down quickly and attempted to jerk the silver spurs from the heels of his boots. They did not come off. "No time!" he called, standing suddenly. "Mr. Lucas done put the record on."

"Leon, you might *cut* somebody with those things," Mrs. Boswell said. "Miss Gweneth Lawson's pretty red dress could get caught in those things and then she'll fall as surely as I'm standin' here."

"I'll just go out with my boots off," Leon replied.

But Mrs. Boswell shook her head firmly. "You just run on to the lunchroom and ask cook for some butter or mayo. That'll help 'em slip off." She paused, looking out over the black dirt playground. "And if you miss the first dance, why there'll be a second and maybe even a third. We'll get a Maypole plaiter to sub for you."

My heart leaped. Leon sensed it and stared at me. His hand tightened on Gweneth's as she stood radiant and smiling in the loving spring sunlight. Leon let her hand drop and bent quickly, pulling at the spurs with the fury of a Samson.

"Square dancers *up!*" Mr. Henry Lucas called.

"Sonofa*bitch!*" Leon grunted.

"Square dancers *up!*" called Mr. Lucas.

The fifth and sixth graders were screaming and rushing toward the center of the yard. Already the record was scratching out the high, slick voice of the caller. "*Sonofabitch!*" Leon moaned.

Mrs. Boswell looked directly at Gweneth, standing alone and abandoned next to Leon. "Miss Gweneth Lawson," Mrs. Boswell said in a cool voice, "it's a cryin' shame there ain't no prince to take you to that ball out there."

I do not remember moving, but I know I stood with Gweneth at the center of the yard. What I did there I do not know, but I remember watching the movements of others and doing what they did just after they had done it. Still, I cannot remember just when I looked into my partner's face or what I saw there. The scratchy voice of the caller bellowed directions and I obeyed:

> *"Allemande left with your left hand*
> *Right to your partner with a right and left grand . . ."*

Although I was told later that I made an allemande right instead of left, I have no memory of the mistake.

> *"When you get to your partner pass her by*
> *And pick up the next girl on the sly . . ."*

Nor can I remember picking up any other girl. I only remember that during many turns and do-si-dos I found myself looking into the warm brown eyes of Gweneth Lawson. I recall that she smiled at me. I recall that she laughed on another turn. I recall that I laughed with her an eternity later.

> *". . . promenade that dear old thing*
> *Throw your head right back and sing* be-*cause, just*
> be-*cause . . ."*

I do remember quite well that during the final promenade before the record ended, Gweneth stood beside me and I said to her in a voice much louder than that of the caller, "When I get up to Brooklyn I hope I see you." But I do not remember what she said in response. I want to remember that she smiled.

I know I smiled, dear Gloria. I smiled with the lemonness of her and the loving of her pressed deep into those saving places of my private self. It was my plan to savor these, and I did savor them. But when I reached New York, many years later, I did not think of Brooklyn. I followed the old, beaten, steady paths into uptown Manhattan.[4] By then I had learned to dance to many other kinds of music. And I had forgotten the savory smell of lemon. But I think sometimes of Gweneth now when I hear country music. And although it is difficult to explain to you, I still maintain that I am no mere arithmetician in the art of the square dance. I am into the calculus of it.

"Go on!" you will tell me, backing into your Northern mythology. "I can see the hustle, the hump, maybe even the Ibo highlife. But no hillbilly."

These days I am firm about arguing the point, but, as always, quietly, and mostly to myself.

1977

---

4. That is, into Harlem.

HERMAN MELVILLE
1819–1891

Melville was born in New York City, the son of a New England merchant who died when Melville was still young. He took on jobs as clerk, farmhand, and schoolteacher before shipping to the South Seas on the whaler *Acushnet*. In a helter-skelter period of adventure he deserted his ship, lived among cannibals, took part in a mutiny aboard an Australian vessel, and then spent almost two years on an American man-of-war. At last home in America, he began successfully to romanticize these adventures in fiction. In six years he published seven novels, the first of which, *Typee* (1846), was a literary sensation. By the time Melville wrote *Moby-Dick* (1851), now universally regarded as one of the masterworks of American fiction, his popularity was already waning. The short stories in *Piazza Tales* (1856) did little to refurbish his reputation. Neither the fine poems he wrote about the Civil War, *Battle-Pieces* (1866), nor his long narrative poem *Clarel* (1876) received much notice. As his writing activities declined, Melville made another sea voyage around Cape Horn to San Francisco on a clipper ship commanded by his brother, and for nineteen quiet years he was a customs inspector in New York. By the time he died, Melville was virtually forgotten. It was not until the 1920s when his last fictional masterpiece, *Billy Budd* (1924), was finally published, that critical interest in his work revived. Since then it has increased in fervor and scope, discovering the richly ambiguous thought structured into his most ambitious work. His novels include *Omoo* (1847), *Mardi* (1849), *Pierre* (1852), and *The Confidence-Man* (1856).

Bartleby, the Scrivener

A Story of Wall Street

I am a rather elderly man. The nature of my avocations for the last thirty years has brought me into more than ordinary contact with what would seem an interesting and somewhat singular set of men, of whom as yet nothing that I know of has ever been written:—I mean the law-copyists or scriveners. I have known very many of them, professionally and privately, and if I pleased, could relate divers histories, at which good-natured gentlemen might smile, and sentimental souls might weep. But I waive the biographies of all other scriveners for a few passages in the life of Bartleby, who was a scrivener the strangest I ever saw or heard of. While of other law-copyists I might write the complete life, of Bartleby nothing of that sort can be done. I believe that no materials exist for a full and satisfactory biography of this man. It is an irreparable loss to literature. Bartleby was one of those beings of whom nothing is ascertainable, except from the original sources, and in his case those are very small. What my own astonished eyes saw of Bartleby, *that* is all I know of him, except, indeed, one vague report which will appear in the sequel.[1]

Ere introducing the scrivener, as he first appeared to me, it is fit I make some mention of myself, my *employés,* my business, my chambers, and general surroundings; because some such description is indispensable to an adequate understanding of the chief character about to be presented.

Imprimis:[2] I am a man who, from his youth upward, has been filled with a profound conviction that the easiest way of life is the best. Hence, though I belong to a profession proverbially energetic and nervous, even to turbulence, at times, yet nothing of that sort have I ever suffered to invade my peace. I am one of those unambitious lawyers who never addresses a jury, or in any way draws down public applause; but in the cool tranquillity of a snug retreat, do a snug business among rich men's bonds and mortgages and title-deeds. All who know me, consider me an eminently *safe* man. The late John Jacob Astor,[3] a personage little given to poetic enthusiasm, had no hesitation in pronouncing my first grand point to be prudence; my next, method. I do not speak it in vanity, but simply record the fact, that I was not unemployed in my profession by the late John Jacob Astor; a name which, I admit, I love to repeat, for it hath a rounded and orbicular sound to it, and rings like unto bullion. I will freely add, that I was not insensible to the late John Jacob Astor's good opinion.

Some time prior to the period at which this little history begins, my avocations had been largely increased. The good old office, now extinct in the State of New-York, of a Master in Chancery,[4] had been conferred upon me. It was not a very arduous office, but very pleasantly remunerative. I seldom lose my temper; much more seldom indulge in dangerous indignation at wrongs and outrages; but I must be permitted to be rash here and declare, that I consider the sudden and violent abrogation of the office of Master in Chancery, by the new Constitution, as a—premature act; inasmuch as I had counted upon a life-lease of the profits, whereas I only received those of a few short years. But this is by the way.

My chambers were upstairs at No.___Wall Street. At one end they looked upon the white wall of the interior of a spacious skylight shaft, penetrating the building from top to bottom. This view might have been considered rather tame than otherwise, deficient in what landscape painters call "life." But if so, the view from the other end of my chambers offered, at least, a contrast, if nothing more. In that direction my windows commanded an unobstructed view of a lofty brick wall, black by age and everlasting shade; which wall required no spy-glass to bring out its lurking beauties, but for the benefit of all near-sighted spectators, was pushed up to within ten feet of my window panes. Owing to the great height of the surrounding buildings, and my

---

1. That is, in the following story.   **2.** In the first place (Latin).   **3.** American landowner (1763–1848), capitalist, and fur merchant who died the richest man in the United States.   **4.** The duty of this office was to temper the rigidity of the law with "dictates of conscience"; the office was abolished in 1847.

chambers being on the second floor, the interval between this wall and mine not a little resembled a huge square cistern.

At the period just preceding the advent of Bartleby, I had two persons as copyists in my employment, and a promising lad as an office-boy. First, Turkey; second, Nippers; third, Ginger Nut. These may seem names, the like of which are not usually found in the Directory.[5] In truth they were nicknames, mutually conferred upon each other by my three clerks, and were deemed expressive of their respective persons or characters. Turkey was a short, pursy Englishman of about my own age, that is, somewhere not far from sixty. In the morning, one might say, his face was of a fine florid hue, but after twelve o'clock, meridian—his dinner hour—it blazed like a grate full of Christmas coals; and continued blazing—but, as it were, with a gradual wane—till 6 o'clock P.M. or thereabouts, after which I saw no more of the proprietor of the face, which, gaining its meridian with the sun, seemed to set with it, to rise, culminate, and decline the following day, with the like regularity and undiminished glory. There are many singular coincidences I have known in the course of my life, not the least among which was the fact, that exactly when Turkey displayed his fullest beams from his red and radiant countenance, just then, too, at that critical moment, began the daily period when I considered his business capacities as seriously disturbed for the remainder of the twenty-four hours. Not that he was absolutely idle, or averse to business then; far from it. The difficulty was, he was apt to be altogether too energetic. There was a strange, inflamed, flurried, flighty recklessness of activity about him. He would be incautious in dipping his pen into his inkstand. All his blots upon my documents were dropped there after twelve o'clock, meridian. Indeed, not only would he be reckless and sadly given to making blots in the afternoon, but some days he went further, and was rather noisy. At such times, too, his face flamed with augmented blazonry, as if cannel coal had been heaped on anthracite.[6] He made an unpleasant racket with his chair; spilled his sand-box;[7] in mending his pens, impatiently split them all to pieces, and threw them on the floor in a sudden passion; stood up and leaned over his table, boxing his papers about in a most indecorous manner, very sad to behold in an elderly man like him. Nevertheless, as he was in many ways a most valuable person to me, and all the time before twelve o'clock, meridian, was the quickest, steadiest creature, too, accomplishing a great deal of work in a style not easy to be matched—for these reasons, I was willing to overlook his eccentricities, though indeed, occasionally, I remonstrated with him. I did this very gently, however, because, though the civilest, nay, the blandest and most reverential of men in the morning, yet in the afternoon he was disposed, upon provocation, to be slightly rash with his tongue, in fact, insolent. Now, valuing his morning services as I did, and resolved not to lose them—yet, at the same time made uncomfortable by his inflamed ways after twelve o'clock; and being a man of peace, unwilling by my admonitions to call forth unseemly retorts from him—I took upon me, one Saturday noon (he was always worse on Saturdays), to hint to him, very kindly, that perhaps now that he was growing old, it might be well to abridge his labors; in short, he

---

5. Post Office Directory.   **6.** Oily, quick-burning coal heaped on a hard, slow-burning kind.   **7.** That is, sand used to dry ink.

need not come to my chambers after twelve o'clock, but, dinner over, had best go home to his lodgings and rest himself till tea-time. But no; he insisted upon his afternoon devotions. His countenance became intolerably fervid, as he oratorically assured me—gesticulating with a long ruler at the other end of the room—that if his services in the morning were useful, how indispensable, then, in the afternoon?

"With submission, sir," said Turkey on this occasion, "I consider myself your right-hand man. In the morning I but marshal and deploy my columns; but in the afternoon I put myself at their head, and gallantly charge the foe, thus!"—and he made a violent thrust with the ruler.

"But the blots, Turkey," intimated I.

"True,—but, with submission, sir, behold these hairs! I am getting old. Surely, sir, a blot or two of a warm afternoon is not to be severely urged against gray hairs. Old age—even if it blot the page—is honorable. With submission, sir, we *both* are getting old."

This appeal to my fellow-feeling was hardly to be resisted. At all events, I saw that go he would not. So I made up my mind to let him stay, resolving, nevertheless, to see to it, that during the afternoon he had to do with my less important papers.

Nippers, the second on my list, was a whiskered, sallow, and, upon the whole, rather piratical-looking young man of about five and twenty. I always deemed him the victim of two evil powers—ambition and indigestion. The ambition was evinced by a certain impatience of the duties of a mere copyist— an unwarrantable usurpation of strictly professional affairs, such as the orig- inal drawing up of legal documents. The indigestion seemed betokened in an occasional nervous testiness and grinning irritability, causing the teeth to audibly grind together over mistakes committed in copying; unnecessary maledictions, hissed, rather than spoken, in the heat of business; and espe- cially by a continual discontent with the height of the table where he worked. Though of a very ingenious mechanical turn, Nippers could never get this table to suit him. He put chips under it, blocks of various sorts, bits of paste- board, and at last went so far as to attempt an exquisite adjustment by final pieces of folded blotting-paper. But no invention would answer. If, for the sake of easing his back, he brought the table lid at a sharp angle well up towards his chin, and wrote there like a man using the steep roof of a Dutch house for his desk—then he declared that it stopped the circulation in his arms. If now he lowered the table to his waistbands, and stooped over it in writing, then there was a sore aching in his back. In short, the truth of the matter was, Nippers knew not what he wanted. Or, if he wanted anything, it was to be rid of a scrivener's table altogether. Among the manifestations of his diseased ambition was a fondness he had for receiving visits from certain ambiguous-looking fellows in seedy coats, whom he called his clients. Indeed I was aware that not only was he, at times, considerable of a ward-politician, but he occasionally did a little business at the Justices' courts, and was not unknown on the steps of the Tombs.[8] I have good reason to believe, however, that one individual who called upon him at my chambers, and who, with a

---

8. The Manhattan House of Detention is often called "the Tombs" because of its distinctive Egyptian architecture. As "ward-politician" Nippers was a fixer who seems to have made extralegal arrange- ments for constituents of his district of the city when they had legal problems.

grand air, he insisted was his client, was no other than a dun,[9] and the alleged title-deed, a bill. But with all his failings, and the annoyances he caused me, Nippers, like his compatriot Turkey, was a very useful man to me; wrote a neat, swift hand; and, when he chose, was not deficient in a gentlemanly sort of deportment. Added to this, he always dressed in a gentlemanly sort of way; and so, incidentally, reflected credit upon my chambers. Whereas with respect to Turkey, I had much ado to keep him from being a reproach to me. His clothes were apt to look oily and smell of eating-houses. He wore his pantaloons very loose and baggy in summer. His coats were execrable; his hat not to be handled. But while the hat was a thing of indifference to me, inasmuch as his natural civility and deference, as a dependent Englishman, always led him to doff it the moment he entered the room, yet his coat was another matter. Concerning his coats, I reasoned with him; but with no effect. The truth was, I suppose, that a man with so small an income, could not afford to sport such a lustrous face and a lustrous coat at one and the same time. As Nippers once observed, Turkey's money went chiefly for red ink. One winter day I presented Turkey with a highly-respectable looking coat of my own, a padded gray coat, of a most comfortable warmth, and which buttoned straight up from the knee to the neck. I thought Turkey would appreciate the favour, and abate his rashness and obstreperousness of afternoons. But no. I verily believe that buttoning himself up in so downy and blanket-like a coat had a pernicious effect upon him; upon the same principle that too much oats are bad for horses. In fact, precisely as a rash, restive horse is said to feel his oats, so Turkey felt his coat. It made him insolent. He was a man whom prosperity harmed.

Though concerning the self-indulgent habits of Turkey I had my own private surmises, yet touching Nippers I was well persuaded that whatever might be his faults in other respects, he was, at least, a temperate young man. But, indeed, nature herself seemed to have been his vintner, and at his birth charged him so thoroughly with an irritable, brandy-like disposition, that all subsequent potations were needless. When I consider how, amid the stillness of my chambers, Nippers would sometimes impatiently rise from his seat, and stooping over his table, spread his arms wide apart, seize the whole desk, and move it, and jerk it, with a grim, grinding motion on the floor, as if the table were a perverse voluntary agent, intent on thwarting and vexing him; I plainly perceive that for Nippers, brandy and water were altogether superfluous.

It was fortunate for me that, owing to its peculiar cause—indigestion—the irritability and consequent nervousness of Nippers, were mainly observable in the morning, while in the afternoon he was comparatively mild. So that Turkey's paroxysms only coming on about twelve o'clock, I never had to do with their eccentricities at one time. Their fits relieved each other like guards. When Nippers' was on, Turkey's was off; and *vice versa*. This was a good natural arrangement under the circumstances.

Ginger Nut, the third on my list, was a lad some twelve years old. His father was a carman,[1] ambitious of seeing his son on the bench instead of a cart, before he died. So he sent him to my office as student at law, errand boy, and cleaner and sweeper, at the rate of one dollar a week. He had a little desk to himself, but he did not use it much. Upon inspection, the drawer exhibited a

---

9. Bill-collector.   **1.** Driver of a cart used for hauling goods.

great array of the shells of various sorts of nuts. Indeed, to this quick-witted youth the whole noble science of the law was contained in a nut-shell. Not the least among the employments of Ginger Nut, as well as one which he discharged with the most alacrity, was his duty as cake and apple purveyor for Turkey and Nippers. Copying law papers being proverbially a dry, husky sort of business, my two scriveners were fain to moisten their mouths very often with Spitzenbergs[2] to be had at the numerous stalls nigh the Custom House and Post Office. Also, they sent Ginger Nut very frequently for that peculiar cake—small, flat, round, and very spicy—after which he had been named by them. Of a cold morning when business was but dull, Turkey would gobble up scores of these cakes, as if they were mere wafers—indeed they sell them at the rate of six or eight for a penny—the scrape of his pen blending with the crunching of the crisp particles in his mouth. Of all the fiery after-noon blunders and flurried rashnesses of Turkey, was his once moistening a ginger-cake between his lips, and clapping it on to a mortgage for a seal. I came within an ace of dismissing him then. But he mollified me by making an oriental bow, and saying—"With submission, sir, it was generous of me to find you in[3] stationery on my own account."

Now my original business—that of a conveyancer and title hunter,[4] and drawer-up of recondite documents of all sorts—was considerably increased by receiving the master's office. There was now great work for scriveners. Not only must I push the clerks already with me, but I must have additional help. In answer to my advertisement, a motionless young man one morning stood upon my office threshold, the door being open, for it was summer. I can see that figure now—pallidly neat, pitiably respectable, incurably forlorn! It was Bartleby.

After a few words touching his qualifications, I engaged him, glad to have among my corps of copyists a man of so singularly sedate an aspect, which I thought might operate beneficially upon the flighty temper of Turkey, and the fiery one of Nippers.

I should have stated before that ground glass folding-doors divided my premises into two parts, one of which was occupied by my scriveners, the other by myself. According to my humour I threw open these doors, or closed them. I resolved to assign Bartleby a corner by the folding-doors, but on my side of them, so as to have this quiet man within easy call, in case any trifling thing was to be done. I placed his desk close up to a small side-window in that part of the room, a window which originally had afforded a lateral view of certain grimy back-yards and bricks, but which, owing to subsequent erections, com-manded at present no view at all, though it gave some light. Within three feet of the panes was a wall, and the light came down from far above, between two lofty buildings, as from a very small opening in a dome. Still further to a sat-isfactory arrangement, I procured a high green folding screen, which might entirely isolate Bartleby from my sight, though not remove him from my voice. And thus, in a manner, privacy and society were conjoined.

At first Bartleby did an extraordinary quantity of writing. As if long fam-ishing for something to copy, he seemed to gorge himself on my documents.

---

2. Apples.   **3.** "To provide you with."   **4.** That is, examining the abstract of property deeds. A convey-ance is a legal paper for transferring property.

There was no pause for digestion. He ran a day and night line, copying by sun-light and by candle-light. I should have been quite delighted with his applica-tion, had he been cheerfully industrious. But he wrote on silently, palely, mechanically.

It is, of course, an indispensable part of a scrivener's business to verify the accuracy of his copy, word by word. Where there are two or more scriveners in an office, they assist each other in this examination, one reading from the copy, the other holding the original. It is a very dull, wearisome, and lethargic affair. I can readily imagine that to some sanguine temperaments it would be altogether intolerable. For example, I cannot credit that the mettlesome poet Byron would have contentedly sat down with Bartleby to examine a law docu-ment of, say five hundred pages, closely written in a crimpy hand.

Now and then, in the haste of business, it had been my habit to assist in comparing some brief document myself, calling Turkey or Nippers for this purpose. One object I had in placing Bartleby so handy to me behind the screen, was to avail myself of his services on such trivial occasions. It was on the third day, I think, of his being with me, and before any necessity had arisen for having his own writing examined, that, being much hurried to complete a small affair I had in hand, I abruptly called to Bartleby. In my haste and nat-ural expectancy of instant compliance, I sat with my head bent over the origi-nal on my desk, and my right hand sideways, and somewhat nervously extended with the copy, so that immediately upon emerging from his retreat, Bartleby might snatch it and proceed to business without the least delay.

In this very attitude did I sit when I called to him, rapidly stating what it was I wanted him to do—namely, to examine a small paper with me. Imagine my surprise, nay, my consternation, when without moving from his privacy, Bartleby in a singularly mild, firm voice, replied, "I would prefer not to."

I sat awhile in perfect silence, rallying my stunned faculties. Immediately it occurred to me that my ears had deceived me, or Bartleby had entirely misun-derstood my meaning. I repeated my request in the clearest tone I could assume. But in quite as clear a one came the previous reply, "I would prefer not to."

"Prefer not to," echoed I, rising in high excitement, and crossing the room with a stride. "What do you mean? Are you moon-struck?[5] I want you to help me compare this sheet here—take it," and I thrust it toward him.

"I would prefer not to," said he.

I looked at him steadfastly. His face was leanly composed; his gray eye dimly calm. Not a wrinkle of agitation rippled him. Had there been the least uneasiness, anger, impatience or impertinence in his manner; in other words, had there been anything ordinarily human about him, doubtless I should have violently dismissed him from the premises. But as it was, I should have as soon thought of turning my pale plaster-of-paris bust of Cicero[6] out of doors. I stood gazing at him awhile, as he went on with his own writing, and then reseated myself at my desk. This is very strange, thought I. What had one best do? But my business hurried me. I concluded to forget the matter for

---

5. This popular synonym for *crazy* incorporates the old belief that the lunatic was affected by phases of the moon (Latin: *luna*). **6.** Marcus Tullius Cicero (106–43 B.C.E.), pro-republic Roman statesman, barrister, writer, and orator.

the present, reserving it for my future leisure. So calling Nippers from the other room, the paper was speedily examined.

A few days after this, Bartleby concluded four lengthy documents, being quadruplicates of a week's testimony taken before me in my High Court of Chancery. It became necessary to examine them. It was an important suit, and great accuracy was imperative. Having all things arranged, I called Turkey, Nippers and Ginger Nut from the next room, meaning to place the four copies in the hands of my four clerks, while I should read from the original. Accordingly Turkey, Nippers and Ginger Nut had taken their seats in a row, each with his document in hand, when I called to Bartleby to join this interesting group.

"Bartleby! quick, I am waiting."

I heard a slow scrape of his chair legs on the uncarpeted floor, and soon he appeared standing at the entrance of his hermitage.

"What is wanted?" said he mildly.

"The copies, the copies," said I hurriedly. "We are going to examine them. There"—and I held towards him the fourth quadruplicate.

"I would prefer not to," he said, and gently disappeared behind the screen.

For a few moments I was turned into a pillar of salt,[7] standing at the head of my seated column of clerks. Recovering myself, I advanced toward the screen, and demanded the reason for such extraordinary conduct.

"*Why* do you refuse?"

"I would prefer not to."

With any other man I should have flown outright into a dreadful passion, scorned all further words, and thrust him ignominiously from my presence. But there was something about Bartleby that not only strangely disarmed me, but in a wonderful manner touched and disconcerted me. I began to reason with him.

"These are your own copies we are about to examine. It is labour saving to you, because one examination will answer for your four papers. It is common usage. Every copyist is bound to help examine his copy. Is it not so? Will you not speak? Answer!"

"I prefer not to," he replied in a flute-like tone. It seemed to me that while I had been addressing him, he carefully revolved every statement that I made; fully comprehended the meaning; could not gainsay the irresistible conclusion; but, at the same time, some paramount consideration prevailed with him to reply as he did.

"You are decided, then, not to comply with my request—a request made according to common usage and common sense?"

He briefly gave me to understand that on that point my judgment was sound. Yes: his decision was irreversible.

It is not seldom the case that when a man is browbeaten in some unprecedented and violently unreasonable way, he begins to stagger in his own plainest faith. He begins, as it were, vaguely to surmise that, wonderful as it may be, all the justice and all the reason are on the other side. Accordingly, if any

---

7. That is, was paralyzed. The allusion is to Genesis 19:26; Lot's wife is turned into a pillar of salt when she looks back at the destruction of Sodom.

disinterested persons are present, he turns to them for some reinforcement for his own faltering mind.

"Turkey," said I, "what do you think of this? Am I not right?"

"With submission, sir," said Turkey, with his blandest tone, "I think that you are."

"Nippers," said I, "what do *you* think of it?"

"I think I should kick him out of the office."

(The reader of nice perceptions will here perceive that, it being morning, Turkey's answer is couched in polite and tranquil terms, but Nippers's reply in ill-tempered ones. Or, to repeat a previous sentence, Nippers's ugly mood was on duty, and Turkey's off.)

"Ginger Nut," said I, willing to enlist the smallest suffrage[8] in my behalf, "what do *you* think of it?"

"I think, sir, he's a little *luny*,"[9] replied Ginger Nut, with a grin.

"You hear what they say," said I, turning towards the screen, "come forth and do your duty."

But he vouchsafed no reply. I pondered a moment in sore perplexity. But once more business hurried me. I determined again to postpone the consideration of this dilemma to my future leisure. With a little trouble we made out to examine the papers without Bartleby, though at every page or two, Turkey deferentially dropped his opinion that this proceeding was quite out of the common; while Nippers, twitching in his chair with a dyspeptic nervousness, ground out between his set teeth occasional hissing maledictions against the stubborn oaf behind the screen. And for his (Nippers's) part, this was the first and the last time he would do another man's business without pay.

Meanwhile Bartleby sat in his hermitage, oblivious to everything but his own peculiar business there.

Some days passed, the scrivener being employed upon another lengthy work. His late remarkable conduct led me to regard his ways narrowly. I observed that he never went to dinner; indeed that he never went any where. As yet I had never of my personal knowledge known him to be outside of my office. He was a perpetual sentry in the corner. At about eleven o'clock though, in the morning, I noticed that Ginger Nut would advance toward the opening in Bartleby's screen, as if silently beckoned thither by a gesture invisible to me where I sat. The boy would then leave the office jingling a few pence, and reappear with a handful of ginger-nuts which he delivered in the hermitage, receiving two of the cakes for his trouble.

He lives, then, on ginger-nuts, thought I; never eats a dinner, properly speaking; he must be a vegetarian then; but no; he never eats even vegetables, he eats nothing but ginger-nuts. My mind then ran on in reveries concerning the probable effects upon the human constitution of living entirely on ginger-nuts. Ginger-nuts are so called because they contain ginger as one of their peculiar constituents, and the final flavoring one. Now what was ginger? A hot, spicy thing. Was Bartleby hot and spicy? Not at all. Ginger, then, had no effect upon Bartleby. Probably he preferred it should have none.

Nothing so aggravates an earnest person as a passive resistance. If the individual so resisted be of a not inhumane temper, and the resisting one perfectly

8. Favorable vote. **9.** Loony—here Melville's spelling recalls the word *lunatic*.

harmless in his passivity; then, in the better moods of the former, he will endeavor charitably to construe to his imagination what proves impossible to be solved by his judgment. Even so, for the most part, I regarded Bartleby and his ways. Poor fellow! thought I, he means no mischief; it is plain he intends no insolence; his aspect sufficiently evinces that his eccentricities are involuntary. He is useful to me. I can get along with him. If I turn him away, the chances are he will fall in with some less indulgent employer, and then he will be rudely treated, and perhaps driven forth miserably to starve. Yes. Here I can cheaply purchase a delicious self-approval. To befriend Bartleby; to humour him in his strange wilfulness, will cost me little or nothing, while I lay up in my soul what will eventually prove a sweet morsel for my conscience. But this mood was not invariable with me. The passiveness of Bartleby sometimes irritated me. I felt strangely goaded on to encounter him in new opposition, to elicit some angry spark from him answerable to my own. But indeed I might as well have essayed to strike fire with my knuckles against a bit of Windsor soap.[1] But one afternoon the evil impulse in me mastered me, and the following little scene ensued:

"Bartleby," said I, "when those papers are all copied, I will compare them with you."

"I would prefer not to."

"How? Surely you do not mean to persist in that mulish vagary?"

No answer.

I threw open the folding-doors near by, and turning upon Turkey and Nippers, exclaimed in an excited manner:

"He says, a second time, he won't examine his papers. What do you think of it, Turkey?"

It was afternoon, be it remembered. Turkey sat glowing like a brass boiler, his bald head steaming, his hands reeling among his blotted papers.

"Think of it?" roared Turkey; "I think I'll just step behind his screen, and black his eyes for him!"

So saying, Turkey rose to his feet and threw his arms into a pugilistic position. He was hurrying away to make good his promise, when I detained him, alarmed at the effect of incautiously rousing Turkey's combativeness after dinner.

"Sit down, Turkey," said I, "and hear what Nippers has to say. What do you think of it, Nippers? Would I not be justified in immediately dismissing Bartleby?"

"Excuse me, that is for you to decide, sir. I think his conduct quite unusual, and indeed unjust, as regards Turkey and myself. But it may only be a passing whim."

"Ah," exclaimed I, "You have strangely changed your mind then—you speak very gently of him now."

"All beer," cried Turkey; "gentleness is effects of beer—Nippers and I dined together to-day. You see how gentle I am, sir. Shall I go and black his eyes?"

"You refer to Bartleby, I suppose. No, not to-day, Turkey," I replied; "pray, put up your fists."

---

1. Fine, scented soap.

I closed the doors, and again advanced towards Bartleby. I felt additional incentives tempting me to my fate. I burned to be rebelled against again. I remembered that Bartleby never left the office.

"Bartleby," said I, "Ginger Nut is away; just step round to the Post Office, won't you? (it was but a three minutes' walk), and see if there is any thing for me."

"I would prefer not to."

"You *will* not?"

"I *prefer* not."

I staggered to my desk, and sat there in a deep study. My blind inveteracy returned. Was there any other thing in which I could procure myself to be ignominiously repulsed by this lean, penniless wight?—my hired clerk? What added thing is there, perfectly reasonable, that he will be sure to refuse to do?

"Bartleby!"

No answer.

"Bartleby," in a louder tone.

No answer.

"Bartleby," I roared.

Like a very ghost, agreeably to the laws of magical invocation, at the third summons, he appeared at the entrance of his hermitage.

"Go to the next room, and tell Nippers to come to me."

"I prefer not to," he respectfully and slowly said, and mildly disappeared.

"Very good, Bartleby," said I, in a quiet sort of serenely severe self-possessed tone, intimating the unalterable purpose of some terrible retribution very close at hand. At the moment I half intended something of the kind. But upon the whole, as it was drawing towards my dinner-hour, I thought it best to put on my hat and walk home for the day, suffering much from perplexity and distress of mind.

Shall I acknowledge it? The conclusion of this whole business was, that it soon became a fixed fact of my chambers, that a pale young scrivener, by the name of Bartleby, had a desk there; that he copied for me at the usual rate of four cents a folio (one hundred words); but he was permanently exempt from examining the work done by him, that duty being transferred to Turkey and Nippers, out of compliment doubtless to their superior acuteness; moreover, said Bartleby was never on any account to be despatched on the most trivial errand of any sort; and that even if entreated to take upon him such a matter, it was generally understood that he would prefer not to—in other words, that he would refuse point-blank.

As days passed on, I became considerably reconciled to Bartleby. His steadiness, his freedom from all dissipation, his incessant industry (except when he chose to throw himself into a standing revery behind his screen), his great stillness, his unalterableness of demeanor under all circumstances, made him a valuable acquisition. One prime thing was this,—*he was always there;*—first in the morning, continually through the day, and the last at night. I had a singular confidence in his honesty. I felt my most precious papers perfectly safe in his hands. Sometimes to be sure I could not, for the very soul of me, avoid falling into sudden spasmodic passions with him. For it was exceeding difficult to bear in mind all the time those strange peculiarities, privileges, and unheard of exemptions, forming the tacit stipulations on Bartleby's part under which he remained in my office. Now and then, in the eagerness of despatching pressing business, I would inadvertently summon Bartleby, in a short, rapid tone, to put his finger, say, on the incipient tie of a bit of red tape with which I was about compressing some papers. Of course, from behind the screen the usual answer, "I prefer not to," was sure to come; and then, how could a human creature with common infirmities of our nature, refrain from bitterly exclaiming upon such perverseness—such unreasonableness. However, every added repulse of this sort which I received only tended to lessen the probability of my repeating the inadvertence.

Here it must be said, that according to the customs of most legal gentlemen occupying chambers in densely-populated law buildings, there were several keys to my door. One was kept by a woman residing in the attic, which person weekly scrubbed and daily swept and dusted my apartments. Another was kept by Turkey for convenience sake. The third I sometimes carried in my own pocket. The fourth I knew not who had.

Now, one Sunday morning I happened to go to Trinity Church,[2] to hear a celebrated preacher, and finding myself rather early on the ground, I thought I would walk round to my chambers for awhile. Luckily I had my key with me; but upon applying it to the lock, I found it resisted by something inserted from the inside. Quite surprised, I called out; when to my consternation a key was turned from within; and thrusting his lean visage at me, and holding the door ajar, the apparition of Bartleby appeared, in his shirt sleeves, and otherwise in a strangely tattered dishabille, saying quietly that he was sorry, but he was deeply engaged just then, and—preferred not admitting me at present. In a brief word or two, he moreover added, that perhaps I had better walk round the block two or three times, and by that time he would probably have concluded his affairs.

Now, the utterly unsurmised appearance of Bartleby, tenanting my law-chambers of a Sunday morning, with his cadaverously gentlemanly *nonchalance*, yet withal firm and self-possessed, had such a strange effect upon me, that incontinently I slunk away from my own door, and did as desired. But not without sundry twinges of impotent rebellion against the mild effrontery of this unaccountable scrivener. Indeed, it was his wonderful mildness chiefly, which not only disarmed me, but unmanned me, as it were. For I consider that one, for the time, is in a way unmanned when he tranquilly permits his hired clerk to dictate to him, and order him away from his own premises. Furthermore, I was full of uneasiness as to what Bartleby could possibly be doing in my office in his shirt sleeves, and in an otherwise dismantled condition of a Sunday morning. Was any thing amiss going on? Nay, that was out of the question. It was not to be thought of for a moment that Bartleby was an immoral person. But what could he be doing there—copying? Nay again, whatever might be his eccentricities, Bartleby was an eminently decorous person. He would be the last man to sit down to his desk in any state approaching to nudity. Besides, it was Sunday; and there was something about Bartleby that forbade the supposition that he would by any secular occupation violate the proprieties of the day.

2. Venerable church in the Wall Street district.

Nevertheless, my mind was not pacified; and full of a restless curiosity, at last I returned to the door. Without hindrance I inserted my key, opened it, and entered. Bartleby was not to be seen. I looked round anxiously, peeped behind his screen; but it was very plain that he was gone. Upon more closely examining the place, I surmised that for an indefinite period Bartleby must have ate, dressed, and slept in my office, and that too without plate, mirror, or bed. The cushioned seat of a rickety old sofa in one corner bore the faint impress of a lean, reclining form. Rolled away under his desk, I found a blanket; under the empty grate, a blacking box[3] and brush; on a chair, a tin basin, with soap and a ragged towel; in a newspaper a few crumbs of ginger-nuts and a morsel of cheese. Yes, thought I, it is evident enough that Bartleby has been making his home here, keeping bachelor's hall all by himself. Immediately then the thought came sweeping across me, What miserable friendlessness and loneliness are here revealed! His poverty is great; but his solitude, how horrible! Think of it. Of a Sunday, Wall Street is deserted as Petra;[4] and every night of every day it is an emptiness. This building too, which of week-days hums with industry and life, at nightfall echoes with sheer vacancy, and all through Sunday is forlorn. And here Bartleby makes his home; sole spectator of a solitude which he has seen all populous—a sort of innocent and transformed Marius brooding among the ruins of Carthage![5]

For the first time in my life a feeling of overpowering stinging melancholy seized me. Before, I had never experienced aught but a not-unpleasing sadness. The bond of a common humanity now drew me irresistibly to gloom. A fraternal melancholy! For both I and Bartleby were sons of Adam. I remembered the bright silks and sparkling faces I had seen that day, in gala trim, swan-like sailing down the Mississippi of Broadway; and I contrasted them with the pallid copyist, and thought to myself, Ah, happiness courts the light, so we deem the world is gay; but misery hides aloof, so we deem that misery there is none. These sad fancyings—chimeras, doubtless, of a sick and silly brain—led on to other and more special thoughts, concerning the eccentricities of Bartleby. Presentiments of strange discoveries hovered round me. The scrivener's pale form appeared to me laid out, among uncaring strangers, in its shivering winding sheet.

Suddenly I was attracted by Bartleby's closed desk, the key in open sight left in the lock.

I mean no mischief, seek the gratification of no heartless curiosity, thought I; besides, the desk is mine, and its contents too, so I will make bold to look within. Everything was methodically arranged, the papers smoothly placed. The pigeon holes were deep, and, removing the files of documents, I groped into their recesses. Presently I felt something there, and dragged it out. It was an old bandanna handkerchief, heavy and knotted. I opened it, and saw it was a savings' bank.

I now recalled all the quiet mysteries which I had noted in the man. I remembered that he never spoke but to answer; that though at intervals he had considerable time to himself, yet I had never seen him reading—no, not even a

---

3. Box of shoe polish.   **4.** Long-ruined and deserted Middle Eastern city.   **5.** Caius Marius (157–86 B.C.E.), Roman consul and general expelled from Rome and who sought sanctuary in Carthage, the African city Rome had destroyed; i.e., a ruined man in a ruined city.

newspaper; that for long periods he would stand looking out, at his pale window behind the screen, upon the dead brick wall; I was quite sure he never visited any refectory or eating-house; while his pale face clearly indicated that he never drank beer like Turkey, or tea and coffee even, like other men; that he never went anywhere in particular that I could learn; never went out for a walk, unless indeed that was the case at present; that he had declined telling who he was, or whence he came, or whether he had any relatives in the world; that though so thin and pale, he never complained of ill health. And more than all, I remembered a certain unconscious air of pallid—how shall I call it?—of pallid haughtiness, say, or rather an austere reserve about him, which had positively awed me into my tame compliance with his eccentricities, when I had feared to ask him to do the slightest incidental thing for me, even though I might know, from his long-continued motionlessness, that behind his screen he must be standing in one of those dead-wall reveries of his.

Revolving all these things, and coupling them with the recently discovered fact that he made my office his constant abiding place and home, and not forgetful of his morbid moodiness; revolving all these things, a prudential feeling began to steal over me. My first emotions had been those of pure melancholy and sincerest pity; but just in proportion as the forlornness of Bartleby grew and grew to my imagination, did that same melancholy merge into fear, that pity into repulsion. So true it is, and so terrible too, that up to a certain point the thought or sight of misery enlists our best affections; but, in certain special cases, beyond that point it does not. They err who would assert that invariably this is owing to the inherent selfishness of the human heart. It rather proceeds from a certain hopelessness of remedying excessive and organic ill. To a sensitive being, pity is not seldom pain. And when at last it is perceived that such pity cannot lead to effectual succor, common sense bids the soul be rid of it. What I saw that morning persuaded me that the scrivener was the victim of innate and incurable disorder. I might give alms to his body; but his body did not pain him; it was his soul that suffered, and his soul I could not reach.

I did not accomplish the purpose of going to Trinity Church that morning. Somehow, the things I had seen disqualified me for the time from churchgoing. I walked homeward, thinking what I would do with Bartleby. Finally, I resolved upon this:—I would put certain calm questions to him the next morning, touching his history, &c., and if he declined to answer them openly and unreservedly (and I supposed he would prefer not), then to give him a twenty dollar bill over and above whatever I might owe him, and tell him his services were no longer required; but that if in any other way I could assist him, I would be happy to do so, especially if he desired to return to his native place, wherever that might be, I would willingly help to defray the expenses. Moreover, if, after reaching home, he found himself at any time in want of aid, a letter from him would be sure of a reply.

The next morning came.

"Bartleby," said I, gently calling to him behind his screen.

No reply.

"Bartleby," said I, in a still gentler tone, "come here; I am not going to ask you to do anything you would prefer not to do—I simply wish to speak to you."

Upon this he noiselessly slid into view.

"Will you tell me, Bartleby, where you were born?"

"I would prefer not to."

"Will you tell me *anything* about yourself?"

"I would prefer not to."

"But what reasonable objection can you have to speak to me? I feel friendly towards you."

He did not look at me while I spoke, but kept his glance fixed upon my bust of Cicero, which, as I then sat, was directly behind me, some six inches above my head.

"What is your answer, Bartleby?" said I, after waiting a considerable time for a reply, during which his countenance remained immovable, only there was the faintest conceivable tremor of the white attenuated mouth.

"At present I prefer to give no answer," he said, and retired into his hermitage.

It was rather weak in me I confess, but his manner on this occasion nettled me. Not only did there seem to lurk in it a certain calm disdain, but his perverseness seemed ungrateful, considering the undeniable good usage and indulgence he had received from me.

Again I sat ruminating what I should do. Mortified as I was at his behavior, and resolved as I had been to dismiss him when I entered my office, nevertheless I strangely felt something superstitious knocking at my heart, and forbidding me to carry out my purpose, and denouncing me for a villain if I dared to breathe one bitter word against this forlornest of mankind. At last, familiarly drawing my chair behind his screen, I sat down and said: "Bartleby, never mind then about revealing your history; but let me entreat you, as a friend, to comply as far as may be with the usages of this office. Say now you will help to examine papers to-morrow or next day: in short, say now that in a day or two you will begin to be a little reasonable:—say so, Bartleby."

"At present I would prefer not to be a little reasonable," was his mildly cadaverous reply.

Just then the folding-doors opened, and Nippers approached. He seemed suffering from an unusually bad night's rest, induced by severer indigestion than common. He overheard those final words of Bartleby.

"*Prefer not*, eh?" gritted Nippers—"I'd *prefer* him, if I were you, sir," addressing me—"I'd *prefer* him; I'd give him preferences, the stubborn mule! What is it, sir, pray, that he *prefers* not to do now?"

Bartleby moved not a limb.

"Mr. Nippers," said I, "I'd prefer that you would withdraw for the present."

Somehow, of late I had got into the way of involuntarily using this word "prefer" upon all sorts of not exactly suitable occasions. And I trembled to think that my contact with the scrivener had already and seriously affected me in a mental way. And what further and deeper aberration might it not yet produce? This apprehension had not been without efficacy in determining me to summary means.

As Nippers, looking very sour and sulky, was departing, Turkey blandly and deferentially approached.

"With submission, sir," said he, "yesterday I was thinking about Bartleby here, and I think that if he would but prefer to take a quart of good ale every day, it would do much towards mending him, and enabling him to assist in examining his papers."

"So you have got the word too," said I, slightly excited.

"With submission, what word, sir," asked Turkey, respectfully crowding himself into the contracted space behind the screen, and by so doing, making me jostle the scrivener. "What word, sir?"

"I would prefer to be left alone here," said Bartleby, as if offended at being mobbed in his privacy.

"*That's* the word, Turkey," said I—"*that's* it."

"Oh, *prefer*? oh, yes—queer word. I never use it myself. But, sir, as I was saying, if he would but prefer—"

"Turkey," interrupted I, "you will please withdraw."

"Oh certainly, sir, if you prefer that I should."

As he opened the folding-door to retire, Nippers at his desk caught a glimpse of me, and asked whether I would prefer to have a certain paper copied on blue paper or white. He did not in the least roguishly accent the word *prefer*. It was plain that it involuntarily rolled from his tongue. I thought to myself, surely I must get rid of a demented man, who already has in some degree turned the tongues, if not the heads, of myself and clerks. But I thought it prudent not to break the dismission at once.

The next day I noticed that Bartleby did nothing but stand at his window in his dead-wall revery. Upon asking him why he did not write, he said that he had decided upon doing no more writing.

"Why, how now? what next?" exclaimed I, "do no more writing?"

"No more."

"And what is the reason?"

"Do you not see the reason for yourself," he indifferently replied.

I looked steadfastly at him, and perceived that his eyes looked dull and glazed. Instantly it occurred to me, that his unexampled diligence in copying by his dim window for the first few weeks of his stay with me might have temporarily impaired his vision.

I was touched. I said something in condolence with him. I hinted that of course he did wisely in abstaining from writing for a while, and urged him to embrace that opportunity of taking wholesome exercise in the open air. This, however, he did not do. A few days after this, my other clerks being absent, and being in a great hurry to dispatch certain letters by the mail, I thought that, having nothing else earthly to do, Bartleby would surely be less inflexible than usual, and carry these letters to the Post Office. But he blankly declined. So, much to my inconvenience, I went myself.

Still added days went by. Whether Bartleby's eyes improved or not, I could not say. To all appearance, I thought they did. But when I asked him if they did, he vouchsafed no answer. At all events, he would do no copying. At last, in reply to my urgings, he informed me that he had permanently given up copying.

"What!" exclaimed I; "suppose your eyes should get entirely well—better than ever before—would you not copy then?"

"I have given up copying," he answered and slid aside.

He remained, as ever, a fixture in my chamber. Nay—if that were possible—he became still more of a fixture than before. What was to be done? He would do nothing in the office: why should he stay there? In plain fact, he had now become a millstone[6] to me, not only useless as a necklace, but afflictive to bear. Yet I was sorry for him. I speak less than truth when I say that, on his own account, he occasioned me uneasiness. If he would but have named a single relative or friend, I would instantly have written, and urged their taking the poor fellow away to some convenient retreat. But he seemed alone, absolutely alone in the universe. A bit of wreckage in the mid-Atlantic. At length, necessities connected with my business tyrannized over all other considerations. Decently as I could, I told Bartleby that in six days' time he must unconditionally leave the office. I warned him to take measures, in the interval, for procuring some other abode. I offered to assist him in this endeavor, if he himself would but take the first step towards a removal. "And when you finally quit me, Bartleby," added I, "I shall see that you go away not entirely unprovided. Six days from this hour, remember."

At the expiration of that period, I peeped behind the screen, and lo! Bartleby was there.

I buttoned up my coat, balanced myself; advanced slowly towards him, touched his shoulder, and said, "The time has come; you must quit this place; I am sorry for you; here is money; but you must go."

"I would prefer not," he replied, with his back still towards me.

"You *must*."

He remained silent.

Now I had an unbounded confidence in this man's common honesty. He had frequently restored to me sixpences and shillings carelessly dropped upon the floor, for I am apt to be very reckless in such shirt-button affairs. The proceeding then which followed will not be deemed extraordinary.

"Bartleby," said I, "I owe you twelve dollars on account; here are thirty-two; the odd twenty are yours.—Will you take it?" and I handed the bills towards him.

But he made no motion.

"I will leave them here then," putting them under a weight on the table. Then taking my hat and cane and going to the door, I tranquilly turned and added—"After you have removed your things from these offices, Bartleby, you will of course lock the door—since every one is now gone for the day but you—and if you please, slip your key underneath the mat, so that I may have it in the morning. I shall not see you again; so good-bye to you. If hereafter in your new place of abode I can be of any service to you, do not fail to advise me by letter. Good-bye, Bartleby, and fare you well."

But he answered not a word; like the last column of some ruined temple, he remained standing mute and solitary in the middle of the otherwise deserted room.

As I walked home in a pensive mood, my vanity got the better of my pity. I could not but highly plume myself on my masterly management in getting rid of Bartleby. Masterly I call it, and such it must appear to any dispassionate thinker. The beauty of my procedure seemed to consist in its perfect quietness. There was no vulgar bullying, no bravado of any sort, no choleric hectoring,

---

6. Heavy stone for grinding grain, conventional image of a burden hung on someone. Matthew 18:6: "But whoso shall offend one of these little ones which believe in me, it were better for him that a millstone were hanged about his neck, and that he were drowned in the depths of the sea."

no striding to and fro across the apartment, jerking out vehement commands for Bartleby to bundle himself off with his beggarly traps.[7] Nothing of the kind. Without loudly bidding Bartleby depart—as an inferior genius might have done—I *assumed* the ground that depart he must; and upon that assumption built all I had to say. The more I thought over my procedure, the more I was charmed with it. Nevertheless, next morning, upon awakening, I had my doubts,—I had somehow slept off the fumes of vanity. One of the coolest and wisest hours a man has, is just after he awakes in the morning. My procedure seemed as sagacious as ever,—but only in theory. How it would prove in practice—there was the rub. It was truly a beautiful thought to have assumed Bartleby's departure; but, after all, that assumption was simply my own, and none of Bartleby's. The great point was, not whether I had assumed that he would quit me, but whether he would prefer so to do. He was more a man of preferences than assumptions.

After breakfast, I walked down town, arguing the probabilities *pro* and *con*. One moment I thought it would prove a miserable failure, and Bartleby would be found all alive at my office as usual; the next moment it seemed certain that I should see his chair empty. And so I kept veering about. At the corner of Broadway and Canal Street, I saw quite an excited group of people standing in earnest conversation.

"I'll take odds he doesn't," said a voice as I passed.

"Doesn't go?—done!" said I, "put up your money."

I was instinctively putting my hand in my pocket to produce my own, when I remembered that this was an election day. The words I had overheard bore no reference to Bartleby, but to the success or non-success of some candidate for the mayoralty. In my intent frame of mind, I had, as it were, imagined that all Broadway shared in my excitement, and were debating the same question with me. I passed on, very thankful that the uproar of the street screened my momentary absent-mindedness.

As I had intended, I was earlier than usual at my office door. I stood listening for a moment. All was still. He must be gone. I tried the knob. The door was locked. Yes, my procedure had worked to a charm; he indeed must be vanished. Yet a certain melancholy mixed with this: I was almost sorry for my brilliant success. I was fumbling under the door mat for the key, which Bartleby was to have left there for me, when accidentally my knee knocked against a panel, producing a summoning sound, and in response a voice came to me from within—"Not yet; I am occupied."

It was Bartleby.

I was thunderstruck. For an instant I stood like the man who, pipe in mouth, was killed one cloudless afternoon long ago in Virginia, by summer lightning; at his own warm open window he was killed, and remained leaning out there upon the dreamy afternoon, till some one touched him, and he fell.

"Not gone!" I murmured at last. But again obeying that wondrous ascendancy which the inscrutable scrivener had over me—and from which ascendancy, for all my chafing, I could not completely escape—I slowly went down stairs and out into the street, and while walking round the block, considered

7. Personal belongings.

what I should next do in this unheard-of perplexity. Turn the man out by an actual thrusting I could not; to drive him away by calling him hard names would not do; calling in the police was an unpleasant idea; and yet, permit him to enjoy his cadaverous triumph over me,—this too I could not think of. What was to be done? or, if nothing could be done, was there anything further that I could *assume* in the matter? Yes, as before I had prospectively assumed that Bartleby would depart, so now I might retrospectively assume that departed he was. In the legitimate carrying out of this assumption, I might enter my office in a great hurry, and pretending not to see Bartleby at all, walk straight against him as if he were air. Such a proceeding would in a singular degree have the appearance of a home-thrust.[8] It was hardly possible that Bartleby could withstand such an application of the doctrine of assumptions. But, upon second thought, the success of the plan seemed rather dubious. I resolved to argue the matter over with him again.

"Bartleby," said I, entering the office, with a quietly severe expression, "I am seriously displeased. I am pained, Bartleby. I had thought better of you. I had imagined you of such a gentlemanly organization, that in any delicate dilemma a slight hint would suffice—in short, an assumption. But it appears I am deceived. Why," I added, unaffectedly starting, "you have not even touched that money yet," pointing to it, just where I had left it the evening previous.

He answered nothing.

"Will you, or will you not, quit me?" I now demanded in a sudden passion, advancing close to him.

"I would prefer *not* to quit you," he replied, gently emphasizing the *not*.

"What earthly right have you to stay here? Do you pay any rent? Do you pay my taxes? Or is this property yours?"

He answered nothing.

"Are you ready to go on and write now? Are your eyes recovered? Could you copy a small paper for me this morning? or help examine a few lines? or step round to the Post Office? In a word, will you do any thing at all, to give a colouring to your refusal to depart the premises?"

He silently retired into his hermitage.

I was now in such a state of nervous resentment that I thought it but prudent to check myself, at present, from further demonstrations. Bartleby and I were alone. I remembered the tragedy of the unfortunate Adams and the still more unfortunate Colt[9] in the solitary office of the latter; and how poor Colt, being dreadfully incensed by Adams, and imprudently permitting himself to get wildly excited, was at unawares hurried into his fatal act—an act which certainly no man could possibly deplore more than the actor himself. Often it had occurred to me in my ponderings upon the subject, that had that altercation taken place in the public street, or at a private residence, it would not have terminated as it did. It was the circumstance of being alone in a solitary office, upstairs, of a building entirely unhallowed by humanizing domestic associations—an uncarpeted office, doubtless, of a dusty, haggard sort of appearance;—this it must have been, which greatly helped to enhance the irritable desperation of the hapless Colt.

---

8. In fencing, a successful thrust to the opponent's body.   **9.** In 1841, John C. Colt, brother of the famous gunmaker, killed Samuel Adams, a printer, when he hit him on the head during a fight.

But when this old Adam[1] of resentment rose in me and tempted me concerning Bartleby, I grappled him and threw him. How? Why, simply by recalling the divine injunction: "A new commandment give I unto you, that ye love one another."[2] Yes, this it was that saved me. Aside from higher considerations, charity often operates as a vastly wise and prudent principle—a great safeguard to its possessor. Men have committed murder for jealousy's sake, and anger's sake, and hatred's sake, and selfishness' sake, and spiritual pride's sake; but no man that ever I heard of, ever committed a diabolical murder for sweet charity's sake. Mere self-interest, then, if no better motive can be enlisted, should, especially with high-tempered men, prompt all beings to charity and philanthropy. At any rate, upon the occasion in question, I strove to drown my exasperated feelings towards the scrivener by benevolently constructing his conduct. Poor fellow, poor fellow! thought I, he doesn't mean anything; and besides, he has seen hard times, and ought to be indulged.

I endeavored also immediately to occupy myself, and at the same time to comfort my despondency. I tried to fancy that in the course of the morning, at such time as might prove agreeable to him, Bartleby, of his own free accord, would emerge from his hermitage, and take up some decided line of march in the direction of the door. But no. Half-past twelve o'clock came; Turkey began to glow in the face, overturn his inkstand, and become generally obstreperous; Nippers abated down into quietude and courtesy; Ginger Nut munched his noon apple; and Bartleby remained standing at his window in one of his profoundest dead-wall reveries. Will it be credited? Ought I to acknowledge it? That afternoon I left the office without saying one further word to him.

Some days now passed, during which, at leisure intervals I looked a little into "Edwards on the Will," and "Priestley on Necessity."[3] Under the circumstances, those books induced a salutary feeling. Gradually I slid into the persuasion that these troubles of mine, touching the scrivener, had been all predestinated from eternity, and Bartleby was billeted upon me for some mysterious purpose of an all-wise Providence, which it was not for a mere mortal like me to fathom. Yes, Bartleby, stay there behind your screen, thought I; I shall persecute you no more; you are harmless and noiseless as any of these old chairs; in short, I never feel so private as when I know you are here. At least I see it, I feel it; I penetrate to the predestinated purpose of my life. I am content. Others may have loftier parts to enact; but my mission in this world, Bartleby, is to furnish you with office-room for such period as you may see fit to remain.

I believe that this wise and blessed frame of mind would have continued with me, had it not been for the unsolicited and uncharitable remarks obtruded upon me by my professional friends who visited the rooms. But thus it often is, that the constant friction of illiberal minds wears out at last the best resolves of the more generous. Though to be sure, when I reflected upon it, it

---

1. The sinful element in man. Christ is sometimes called the "New Adam."   **2.** John 13:34 and John 15:17.   **3.** The reference is obscure because of the form Melville has given the titles, but the books indicated are probably *The Freedom of the Will* by Jonathan Edwards (1703–1758) and *The Doctrine of Philosophical Necessity* by Joseph Priestley (1733–1804). The theses of these two books conform to the "persuasion" Melville here describes.

was not strange that people entering my office should be struck by the peculiar aspect of the unaccountable Bartleby, and so be tempted to throw out some sinister observations concerning him. Sometimes an attorney having business with me, and calling at my office, and finding no one but the scrivener there, would undertake to obtain some sort of precise information from him touching my whereabouts; but without heeding his idle talk, Bartleby would remain standing immovable in the middle of the room. So, after contemplating him in that position for a time, the attorney would depart, no wiser than he came.

Also, when a Reference[4] was going on, and the room full of lawyers and witnesses and business was driving fast, some deeply occupied legal gentleman present, seeing Bartleby wholly unemployed, would request him to run round to his (the legal gentleman's) office and fetch some papers for him. Thereupon, Bartleby would tranquilly decline, and yet remain idle as before. Then the lawyer would give a great stare, and turn to me. And what could I say? At last I was made aware that all through the circle of my professional acquaintance, a whisper of wonder was running round, having reference to the strange creature I kept at my office. This worried me very much. And as the idea came upon me of his possibly turning out a long-lived man, and keep occupying my chambers, and denying my authority; and perplexing my visitors; and scandalizing my professional reputation; and casting a general gloom over the premises; keeping soul and body together to the last upon his savings (for doubtless he spent but half a dime a day), and in the end perhaps outlive me, and claim possession of my office by right of his perpetual occupancy: as all these dark anticipations crowded upon me more and more, and my friends continually intruded their relentless remarks upon the apparition in my room, a great change was wrought in me. I resolved to gather all my faculties together, and for ever rid me of this intolerable incubus.[5]

Ere revolving any complicated project, however, adapted to this end, I first simply suggested to Bartleby the propriety of his permanent departure. In a calm and serious tone, I commended the idea to his careful and mature consideration. But having taken three days to meditate upon it, he apprised me that his original determination remained the same; in short, that he still preferred to abide with me.

What shall I do? I now said to myself, buttoning up my coat to the last button. *What shall I do? what ought I to do? what does conscience say I* should *do with this man, or rather ghost? Rid myself of him, I must; go, he shall. But how? You will not thrust him, the poor, pale, passive mortal,—you will not thrust such a helpless creature out of your door? you will not dishonour yourself by such cruelty? No, I will not, I cannot do that. Rather would I let him live and die here, and then mason up his remains in the wall. What then will you do? For all your coaxing, he will not budge. Bribes he leaves under your own paper-weight on your table; in short, it is quite plain that he prefers to cling to you.*

Then something severe, something unusual must be done. What! surely you will not have him collared by a constable, and commit his innocent pallor to the common jail? And upon what ground could you procure such a

4. Conference.   5. Imaginary demon supposed to descend on sleepers.

thing to be done?—a vagrant, is he? What! he a vagrant, a wanderer, who refuses to budge? It is because he will *not* be a vagrant, then, that you seek to count him *as* a vagrant. That is too absurd. No visible means of support: there I have him. Wrong again: for indubitably he *does* support himself, and that is the only unanswerable proof that any man can show of his possessing the means so to do. No more then. Since he will not quit me, I must quit him. I will change my offices; I will move elsewhere; and give him fair notice, that if I find him on my new premises I will then proceed against him as a common trespasser.

Acting accordingly, next day I thus addressed him: "I find these chambers too far from the City Hall; the air is unwholesome. In a word, I propose to remove my offices next week, and shall no longer require your services. I tell you this now, in order that you may seek another place."

He made no reply, and nothing more was said.

On the appointed day I engaged carts and men, proceeded to my chambers, and having but little furniture, every thing was removed in a few hours. Throughout all, the scrivener remained standing behind the screen, which I directed to be removed the last thing. It was withdrawn; and being folded up like a huge folio, left him the motionless occupant of a naked room. I stood in the entry watching him a moment, while something from within me upbraided me.

I re-entered, with my hand in my pocket—and—and my heart in my mouth.

"Good-bye, Bartleby; I am going—good-bye, and God some way bless you; and take that," slipping something in his hand. But it dropped upon the floor, and then—strange to say—I tore myself from him whom I had so longed to be rid of.

Established in my new quarters, for a day or two I kept the door locked, and started at every footfall in the passages. When I returned to my rooms after any little absence, I would pause at the threshold for an instant, and attentively listen, ere applying my key. But these fears were needless. Bartleby never came nigh me.

I thought all was going well, when a perturbed looking stranger visited me, inquiring whether I was the person who had recently occupied rooms at No.___ Wall Street.

Full of forebodings, I replied that I was.

"Then sir," said the stranger, who proved a lawyer, "you are responsible for the man you left there. He refuses to do any copying, he refuses to do any thing; he says he prefers not to; and he refuses to quit the premises."

"I am very sorry, sir," said I, with assumed tranquillity, but an inward tremor, "but, really, the man you allude to is nothing to me—he is no relation or apprentice of mine, that you should hold me responsible for him."

"In mercy's name, who is he?"

"I certainly cannot inform you. I know nothing about him. Formerly I employed him as a copyist; but he has done nothing for me now for some time past."

"I shall settle him then,—good morning, sir."

Several days passed, and I heard nothing more; and though I often felt a charitable prompting to call at the place and see poor Bartleby, yet a certain squeamishness of I know not what withheld me.

All is over with him, by this time, thought I at last, when through another week no further intelligence reached me. But coming to my room the day after, I found several persons waiting at my door in a high state of nervous excitement.

"That's the man—here he comes," cried the foremost one, whom I recognized as the lawyer who had previously called upon me alone.

"You must take him away, sir, at once," cried a portly person among them, advancing upon me, and whom I knew to be the landlord of No. ___ Wall Street. "These gentlemen, my tenants, cannot stand it any longer; Mr.B___," pointing to the lawyer, "has turned him out of his room, and he now persists in haunting the building generally, sitting upon the banisters of the stairs by day, and sleeping in the entry by night. Everybody is concerned; clients are leaving the offices; some fears are entertained of a mob; something you must do, and that without delay."

Aghast at this torrent, I fell back before it, and would fain have locked myself in my new quarters. In vain I persisted that Bartleby was nothing to me—no more than to any one else. In vain:—I was the last person known to have anything to do with him, and they held me to the terrible account. Fearful then of being exposed in the papers (as one person present obscurely threatened) I considered the matter, and at length said, that if the lawyer would give me a confidential interview with the scrivener, in his (the lawyer's) own room, I would that afternoon strive my best to rid them of the nuisance they complained of.

Going up stairs to my old haunt, there was Bartleby silently sitting upon the banister at the landing.

"What are you doing here, Bartleby?" said I.

"Sitting upon the banister," he mildly replied.

I motioned him into the lawyer's room, who then left us.

"Bartleby," said I, "are you aware that you are the cause of great tribulation to me, by persisting in occupying the entry after being dismissed from the office?"

No answer.

"Now one of two things must take place. Either you must do something, or something must be done to you. Now what sort of business would you like to engage in? Would you like to re-engage in copying for some one?"

"No; I would prefer not to make any change."

"Would you like a clerkship in a dry-goods store?"

"There is too much confinement about that. No, I would not like a clerkship; but I am not particular."

"Too much confinement," I cried, "why you keep yourself confined all the time!"

"I would prefer not to take a clerkship," he rejoined, as if to settle that little item at once.

"How would a bartender's business suit you? There is no trying of the eyesight in that."

"I would not like it at all; though, as I said before, I am not particular."

His unwonted wordiness inspirited me. I returned to the charge.

"Well then, would you like to travel through the country collecting bills for the merchants? That would improve your health."

"No, I would prefer to be doing something else."

"How then would going as a companion to Europe to entertain some young gentleman with your conversation,—how would that suit you?"

"Not at all. It does not strike me that there is anything definite about that. I like to be stationary. But I am not particular."

"Stationary you shall be then," I cried, now losing all patience, and for the first time in all my exasperating connection with him fairly flying into a passion. "If you do not go away from these premises before night, I shall feel bound—indeed I *am* bound—to—to—to quit the premises myself!" I rather absurdly concluded, knowing not with what possible threat to try to frighten his immobility into compliance. Despairing of all further efforts, I was precipitately leaving him, when a final thought occurred to me—one which had not been wholly unindulged before.

"Bartleby," said I, in the kindest tone I could assume under such exciting circumstances, "will you go home with me now—not to my office, but my dwelling—and remain there till we can conclude upon some convenient arrangement for you at our leisure? Come, let us start now, right away."

"No: at present I would prefer not to make any change at all."

I answered nothing; but effectually dodging every one by the suddenness and rapidity of my flight, rushed from the building, ran up Wall Street towards Broadway, and jumping into the first omnibus was soon removed from pursuit. As soon as tranquillity returned I distinctly perceived that I had now done all that I possibly could, both in respect to the demands of the landlord and his tenants, and with regard to my own desire and sense of duty, to benefit Bartleby, and shield him from rude persecution. I now strove to be entirely care-free and quiescent; and my conscience justified me in the attempt; though indeed it was not so successful as I could have wished. So fearful was I of being again hunted out by the incensed landlord and his exasperated tenants, that, surrendering my business to Nippers, for a few days I drove about the upper part of the town and through the suburbs, in my rockaway;[6] crossed over to Jersey City and Hoboken, and paid fugitive visits to Manhattanville and Astoria. In fact I almost lived in my rockaway for the time.

When again I entered my office, lo, a note from the landlord lay upon the desk. I opened it with trembling hands. It informed me that the writer had sent to the police, and had Bartleby removed to the Tombs as a vagrant. Moreover, since I knew more about him than any one else, he wished me to appear at that place, and make a suitable statement of the facts. These tidings had a conflicting effect upon me. At first I was indignant; but at last almost approved. The landlord's energetic, summary disposition had led him to adopt a procedure which I do not think I would have decided upon myself; and yet as a last resort, under such peculiar circumstances, it seemed the only plan.

As I afterwards learned, the poor scrivener, when told that he must be conducted to the Tombs, offered not the slightest obstacle, but in his pale, unmoving way silently acquiesced.

Some of the compassionate and curious bystanders joined the party; and headed by one of the constables, arm in arm with Bartleby the silent procession

---

6. Light, four-wheeled carriage.

filed its way through all the noise, and heat, and joy of the roaring thorough-
fares at noon.

The same day I received the note I went to the Tombs, or, to speak more
properly, the Halls of Justice. Seeking the right officer, I stated the purpose of
my call, and was informed that the individual I described was indeed within.
I then assured the functionary that Bartleby was a perfectly honest man, and
greatly to be a compassionated, (however unaccountable) eccentric. I narrated
all I knew, and closed by suggesting the idea of letting him remain in as indulgent confinement as possible till something less harsh might be done—though
indeed I hardly knew what. At all events, if nothing else could be decided
upon, the alms-house must receive him. I then begged to have an interview.

Being under no disgraceful charge, and quite serene and harmless in all his
ways, they had permitted him freely to wander about the prison, and especially in the inclosed grass-platted yards thereof. And so I found him there,
standing all alone in the quietest of the yards, his face towards a high wall—
while all around, from the narrow slits of the jail windows, I thought I saw
peering out upon him the eyes of murderers and thieves.

"Bartleby!"

"I know you," he said, without looking round,—"and I want nothing to say
to you."

"It was not I that brought you here, Bartleby," said I, keenly pained at his
implied suspicion. "And to you, this should not be so vile a place. Nothing
reproachful attaches to you by being here. And see, it is not so sad a place as
one might think. Look, there is the sky and here is the grass."

"I know where I am," he replied, but would say nothing more, and so I
left him.

As I entered the corridor again, a broad, meat-like man, in an apron, accosted
me, and jerking his thumb over his shoulder said—"Is that your friend?"

"Yes."

"Does he want to starve? If he does, let him live on the prison fare, that's all."

"Who are you?" asked I, not knowing what to make of such an unofficially
speaking person in such a place.

"I am the grub-man. Such gentlemen as have friends here, hire me to provide them with something good to eat."

"Is this so?" said I, turning to the turnkey.

He said it was.

"Well then," said I, slipping some silver into the grub-man's hands (for so
they called him), "I want you to give particular attention to my friend there;
let him have the best dinner you can get. And you must be as polite to him as
possible."

"Introduce me, will you?" said the grub-man, looking at me with an expression which seemed to say he was all impatience for an opportunity to give a
specimen of his breeding.

Thinking it would prove of benefit to the scrivener, I acquiesced; and asking the grub-man his name, went up with him to Bartleby.

"Bartleby, this is Mr. Cutlets; you will find him very useful to you."

"Your sarvant, sir, your sarvant," said the grub-man, making a low salutation behind his apron. "Hope you find it pleasant here, sir;—spacious grounds—
cool apartments, sir—hope you'll stay with us some time—try to make it

agreeable. May Mrs. Cutlets and I have the pleasure of your company to dinner, sir, in Mrs. Cutlets' private room?"

"I prefer not to dine to-day," said Bartleby, turning away. "It would disagree
with me; I am unused to dinners." So saying, he slowly moved to the other
side of the inclosure and took up a position fronting the dead-wall.

"How's this?" said the grub-man, addressing me with a stare of astonishment. "He's odd, ain't he?"

"I think he is a little deranged," said I, sadly.

"Deranged? deranged is it? Well now, upon my word, I thought that friend
of yourn was a gentleman forger; they are always pale and genteel-like, them
forgers. I can't help pity 'em—can't help it, sir. Did you know Monroe Edwards?"[7]
he added touchingly, and paused. Then, laying his hand pityingly on my shoulder, sighed, "he died of consumption at Sing-Sing. So you weren't acquainted
with Monroe?"

"No, I was never socially acquainted with any forgers. But I cannot stop
longer. Look to my friend yonder. You will not lose by it. I will see you again."

Some few days after this, I again obtained admission to the Tombs, and
went through the corridors in quest of Bartleby; but without finding him.

"I saw him coming from his cell not long ago," said a turnkey, "maybe he's
gone to loiter in the yards."

So I went in that direction.

"Are you looking for the silent man?" said another turnkey passing me.
"Yonder he lies—sleeping in the yard there. 'Tis not twenty minutes since I saw
him lie down."

The yard was entirely quiet. It was not accessible to the common prisoners. The surrounding walls, of amazing thickness, kept off all sounds behind
them. The Egyptian character of the masonry weighed upon me with its gloom.
But a soft imprisoned turf grew under foot. The heart of the eternal pyramids, it seemed, wherein, by some strange magic, through the clefts grass-seed,
dropped by birds, had sprung.

Strangely huddled at the base of the wall—his knees drawn up, and lying on
his side, his head touching the cold stones—I saw the wasted Bartleby. But
nothing stirred. I paused; then went close up to him; stooped over, and saw
that his dim eyes were open; otherwise he seemed profoundly sleeping. Something prompted me to touch him. I felt his hand, when a tingling shiver ran
up my arm and down my spine to my feet.

The round face of the grub-man peered upon me now. "His dinner is ready.
Won't he dine to-day, either? Or does he live without dining?"

"Lives without dining," said I, and closed the eyes.

"Eh!—He's asleep, ain't he?"

"With kings and counsellors,"[8] murmured I.

There would seem little need for proceeding further in this history. Imagination will readily supply the meagre recital of poor Bartleby's interment.
But ere parting with the reader, let me say, that if this little narrative has sufficiently interested him, to awaken curiosity as to who Bartleby was, and what
manner of life he led prior to the present narrator's making his acquaintance,

7. Famously flamboyant forger and swindler (1808–1847), who died in Sing Sing prison, north of New
York City in Ossining, New York. **8.** That is, he is dead. Job 3:13–14: "then had I been at rest, With
kings and counsellors of the earth, which built desolate places for themselves."

I can only reply, that in such curiosity I fully share—but am wholly unable to gratify it. Yet here I hardly know whether I should divulge one little item of rumour, which came to my ear a few months after the scrivener's decease. Upon what basis it rested, I could never ascertain; and hence, how true it is I cannot now tell. But inasmuch as this vague report has not been without a certain strange suggestive interest to me, however sad, it may prove the same with some others; and so I will briefly mention it. The report was this: that Bartleby had been a subordinate clerk in the Dead Letter Office[9] at Washington, from which he had been suddenly removed by a change in the administration. When I think over this rumor I cannot adequately express the emotions which seize me. Dead letters! Does it not sound like dead men? Conceive a man by nature and misfortune prone to a pallid hopelessness: can any business seem more fitted to heighten it than that of continually handling these dead letters, and assorting them for the flames? For by the cart-load they are annually burned. Sometimes from out the folded paper the pale clerk takes a ring:—the finger it was meant for, perhaps, moulders in the grave; a bank-note sent in swiftest charity:—he whom it would relieve, nor eats nor hungers any more; pardon for those who died despairing; hope for those who died unhoping; good tidings for those who died stifled by unrelieved calamities. On errands of life, these letters speed to death.

Ah Bartleby! Ah humanity!

1853

RELATED:

—Leo Marx, "Melville's Parable of the Walls," p. 1769

---

9. Place for storage and disposition of undeliverable mail.

BHARATI MUKHERJEE
b. 1940

Born to wealthy parents in Kolkata (Calcutta), Mukherjee spent her early years with her family in England but returned to India in her teens to study. She continued her education in the 1960s at the University of Iowa, where she met and married the writer Clark Blaise while earning both an M.F.A. in creative writing and a Ph.D. in English and Comparative Literature. They lived in Canada for the next ten years, where she published her first two novels, *The Tiger's Daughter* (1971) and *Wife* (1975). Later, when the couple traveled in India, they collaborated on *Days and Nights in Calcutta* (1977), a nonfiction book drawn from their observations and impressions of Indian life. Her stories are collected in *Darkness* (1985) and *The Middleman and Other Stories* (1988). Her most recent novels are *Jasmine* (1989), *The Holder of the World* (1993), *Leave It to Me* (1997), *Desirable Daughters* (2002), *The Tree Bride* (2004), and *Miss New India* (2011). She now lives in the United States and teaches at the University of California at Berkeley.

The Management of Grief

A woman I don't know is boiling tea the Indian way in my kitchen. There are a lot of women I don't know in my kitchen, whispering, and moving tactfully. They open doors, rummage through the pantry, and try not to ask me where things are kept. They remind me of when my sons were small, on Mother's Day or when Vikram and I were tired, and they would make big, sloppy omelettes. I would lie in bed pretending I didn't hear them.

Dr. Sharma, the treasurer of the Indo-Canada Society, pulls me into the hallway. He wants to know if I am worried about money. His wife, who has just come up from the basement with a tray of empty cups and glasses, scolds him. "Don't bother Mrs. Bhave with mundane details." She looks so monstrously pregnant her baby must be days overdue. I tell her she shouldn't be carrying heavy things. "Shaila," she says, smiling, "this is the fifth." Then she grabs a teenager by his shirt-tails. He slips his Walkman off his head. He has to be one of her four children, they have the same domed and dented foreheads. "What's the official word now?" she demands. The boy slips the headphones back on. "They're acting evasive, Ma. They're saying it could be an accident or a terrorist bomb."

All morning, the boys have been muttering, Sikh Bomb, Sikh Bomb. The men, not using the word, bow their heads in agreement. Mrs. Sharma touches her forehead at such a word. At least they've stopped talking about space debris and Russian lasers.

Two radios are going in the dining room. They are tuned to different stations. Someone must have brought the radios down from my boys' bedrooms. I haven't gone into their rooms since Kusum came running across the front lawn in her bathrobe. She looked so funny, I was laughing when I opened the door.

The big TV in the den is being whizzed through American networks and cable channels.

"Damn!" some man swears bitterly. "How can these preachers carry on like nothing's happened?" I want to tell him we're not that important. You look at the audience, and at the preacher in his blue robe with his beautiful white hair, the potted palm trees under a blue sky, and you know they care about nothing.

The phone rings and rings. Dr. Sharma's taken charge. "We're with her," he keeps saying. "Yes, yes, the doctor has given calming pills. Yes, yes, pills are having necessary effect." I wonder if pills alone explain this calm. Not peace, just a deadening quiet. I was always controlled, but never repressed. Sound can reach me, but my body is tensed, ready to scream. I hear their voices all around me. I hear my boys and Vikram cry, "Mommy, Shaila!" and their screams insulate me, like headphones.

The woman boiling water tells her story again and again. "I got the news first. My cousin called from Halifax before six A.M., can you imagine? He'd gotten up for prayers and his son was studying for medical exams and he heard on a rock channel that something had happened to a plane. They said first it had disappeared from the radar, like a giant eraser just reached out. His father called me, so I said to him, what do you mean, 'something bad'? You mean a hijacking? And he said, *behn*,[1] there is no confirmation of anything yet, but check with your neighbors because a lot of them must be on that plane. So I called poor Kusum straightaway. I knew Kusum's husband and daughter were booked to go yesterday."

Kusum lives across the street from me. She and Satish had moved in less than a month ago. They said they needed a bigger place. All these people, the Sharmas and friends from the Indo-Canada Society had been there for the housewarming. Satish and Kusum made homemade tandoori on their big gas grill and even the white neighbors piled their plates high with that luridly red, charred, juicy chicken. Their younger daughter had danced, and even our boys had broken away from the Stanley Cup telecast to put in a reluctant appearance. Everyone took pictures for their albums and for the community newspapers—another of our families had made it big in Toronto—and now I wonder how many of those happy faces are gone. "Why does God give us so much if all along He intends to take it away?" Kusum asks me.

I nod. We sit on carpeted stairs, holding hands like children. "I never once told him that I loved him," I say. I was too much the well brought up woman. I was so well brought up I never felt comfortable calling my husband by his first name.

"It's all right," Kusum says. "He knew. My husband knew. They felt it. Modern young girls have to say it because what they feel is fake."

---

1. No (Hindi).

Kusum's daughter, Pam, runs in with an overnight case. Pam's in her McDonald's uniform. "Mummy! You have to get dressed!" Panic makes her cranky. "A reporter's on his way here."

"Why?"

"You want to talk to him in your bathrobe?" She starts to brush her mother's long hair. She's the daughter who's always in trouble. She dates Canadian boys and hangs out in the mall, shopping for tight sweaters. The younger one, the goody-goody one according to Pam, the one with a voice so sweet that when she sang *bhajans*[2] for Ethiopian relief even a frugal man like my husband wrote out a hundred dollar check, *she* was on that plane. *She* was going to spend July and August with grandparents because Pam wouldn't go. Pam said she'd rather waitress at McDonald's. "If it's a choice between Bombay and Wonderland, I'm picking Wonderland," she'd said.

"Leave me alone," Kusum yells. "You know what I want to do? If I didn't have to look after you now, I'd hang myself."

Pam's young face goes blotchy with pain. "Thanks," she says, "don't let me stop you."

"Hush," pregnant Mrs. Sharma scolds Pam. "Leave your mother alone. Mr. Sharma will tackle the reporters and fill out the forms. He'll say what has to be said."

Pam stands her ground. "You think I don't know what Mummy's thinking? *Why ever?* that's what. That's sick! Mummy wishes my little sister were alive and I were dead."

Kusum's hand in mine is trembly hot. We continue to sit on the stairs.

She calls before she arrives, wondering if there's anything I need. Her name is Judith Templeton and she's an appointee of the provincial government. "Multiculturalism?" I ask, and she says, "partially," but that her mandate is bigger. "I've been told you knew many of the people on the flight," she says. "Perhaps if you'd agree to help us reach the others . . . ?"

She gives me time at least to put on tea water and pick up the mess in the front room. I have a few *samosas*[3] from Kusum's housewarming that I could fry up, but then I think, why prolong this visit?

Judith Templeton is much younger than she sounded. She wears a blue suit with a white blouse and a polka dot tie. Her blond hair is cut short, her only jewelry is pearl drop earrings. Her briefcase is new and expensive looking, a gleaming cordovan leather. She sits with it across her lap. When she looks out the front windows onto the street, her contact lenses seem to float in front of her light blue eyes.

"What sort of help do you want from me?" I ask. She has refused the tea, out of politeness, but I insist, along with some slightly stale biscuits.[4]

"I have no experience," she admits. "That is, I have an MSW[5] and I've worked in liaison with accident victims, but I mean I have no experience with a tragedy of this scale—"

"Who could?" I ask.

<hr />

2. Hymns (Hindi). 3. Fried turnovers filled with meat or vegetable mixtures (Hindi). 4. That is, cookies. 5. Master of Social Welfare (or Work) degree.

"—and with the complications of culture, language, and customs. Someone mentioned that Mrs. Bhave is a pillar—because you've taken it more calmly."

At this, perhaps, I frown, for she reaches forward, almost to take my hand. "I hope you understand my meaning, Mrs. Bhave. There are hundreds of people in Metro directly affected, like you, and some of them speak no English. There are some widows who've never handled money or gone on a bus, and there are old parents who still haven't eaten or gone outside their bedrooms. Some houses and apartments have been looted. Some wives are still hysterical. Some husbands are in shock and profound depression. We want to help, but our hands are tied in so many ways. We have to distribute money to some people, and there are legal documents—these things can be done. We have interpreters, but we don't always have the human touch, or maybe the right human touch. We don't want to make mistakes, Mrs. Bhave, and that's why we'd like to ask you to help us."

"More mistakes, you mean," I say.

"Police matters are not in my hands," she answers.

"Nothing I can do will make any difference," I say. "We must all grieve in our own way."

"But you are coping very well. All the people said, Mrs. Bhave is the strongest person of all. Perhaps if the others could see you, talk with you, it would help them."

"By the standards of the people you call hysterical, I am behaving very oddly and very badly, Miss Templeton." I want to say to her, *I wish I could scream, starve, walk into Lake Ontario, jump from a bridge.* "They would not see me as a model. I do not see myself as a model."

I am a freak. No one who has ever known me would think of me reacting this way. This terrible calm will not go away.

She asks me if she may call again, after I get back from a long trip that we all must make. "Of course," I say. "Feel free to call, anytime."

Four days later, I find Kusum squatting on a rock overlooking a bay in Ireland. It isn't a big rock, but it juts sharply out over water. This is as close as we'll ever get to them. June breezes balloon out her sari and unpin her knee-length hair. She has the bewildered look of a sea creature whom the tides have stranded.

It's been one hundred hours since Kusum came stumbling and screaming across my lawn. Waiting around the hospital, we've heard many stories. The police, the diplomats, they tell us things thinking that we're strong, that knowledge is helpful to the grieving, and maybe it is. Some, I know, prefer ignorance, or their own versions. The plane broke into two, they say. Unconsciousness was instantaneous. No one suffered. My boys must have just finished their breakfasts. They loved eating on planes, they loved the smallness of plates, knives, and forks. Last year they saved the airline salt and pepper shakers. Half an hour more and they would have made it to Heathrow.

Kusum says that we can't escape our fate. She says that all those people—our husbands, my boys, her girl with the nightingale voice, all those Hindus, Christians, Sikhs, Muslims, Parsis, and atheists on that plane—were fated to die together off this beautiful bay. She learned this from a swami in Toronto.

I have my Valium.

Six of us "relatives"—two widows and four widowers—choose to spend the day today by the waters instead of sitting in a hospital room and scanning photographs of the dead. That's what they call us now: relatives. I've looked through twenty-seven photos in two days. They're very kind to us, the Irish are very understanding. Sometimes understanding means freeing a tourist bus for this trip to the bay, so we can pretend to spy our loved ones through the glassiness of waves or in sunspeckled cloud shapes.

I could die here, too, and be content.

"What is that, out there?" She's standing and flapping her hands and for a moment I see a head shape bobbing in the waves. She's standing in the water, I, on the boulder. The tide is low, and a round, black, headsized rock has just risen from the waves. She returns, her sari end dripping and ruined and her face is a twisted remnant of hope, the way mine was a hundred hours ago, still laughing but inwardly knowing that nothing but the ultimate tragedy could bring two women together at six o'clock on a Sunday morning. I watch her face sag into blankness.

"That water felt warm, Shaila," she says at length.

"You can't," I say. "We have to wait for our turn to come."

I haven't eaten in four days, haven't brushed my teeth.

"I know," she says. "I tell myself I have no right to grieve. They are in a better place than we are. My swami says I should be thrilled for them. My swami says depression is a sign of our selfishness."

Maybe I'm selfish. Selfishly I break away from Kusum and run, sandals slapping against stones, to the water's edge. What if my boys aren't lying pinned under the debris? What if they aren't stuck a mile below that innocent blue chop? What if, given the strong currents. . . .

Now I've ruined my sari, one of my best. Kusum has joined me, knee-deep in water that feels to me like a swimming pool. I could settle in the water, and my husband would take my hand and the boys would slap water in my face just to see me scream.

"Do you remember what good swimmers my boys were, Kusum?"

"I saw the medals," she says.

One of the widowers, Dr. Ranganathan from Montreal, walks out to us, carrying his shoes in one hand. He's an electrical engineer. Someone at the hotel mentioned his work is famous around the world, something about the place where physics and electricity come together. He has lost a huge family, something indescribable. "With some luck," Dr. Ranganathan suggests to me, "a good swimmer could make it safely to some island. It is quite possible that there may be many, many microscopic islets scattered around."

"You're not just saying that?" I tell Dr. Ranganathan about Vinod, my elder son. Last year he took diving as well.

"It's a parent's duty to hope," he says. "It is foolish to rule out possibilities that have not been tested. I myself have not surrendered hope."

Kusum is sobbing once again. "Dear lady," he says, laying his free hand on her arm, and she calms down.

"Vinod is how old?" he asks me. He's very careful, as we all are. *Is*, not was.

"Fourteen. Yesterday he was fourteen. His father and uncle were going to take him down to the Taj and give him a big birthday party. I couldn't go with them because I couldn't get two weeks off from my stupid job in June." I process bills for a travel agent. June is a big travel month.

Dr. Ranganathan whips the pockets of his suit jacket inside out. Squashed roses, in darkening shades of pink, float on the water. He tore the roses off creepers in somebody's garden. He didn't ask anyone if he could pluck the roses, but now there's been an article about it in the local papers. When you see an Indian person, it says, please give him or her flowers.

"A strong youth of fourteen," he says, "can very likely pull to safety a younger one."

My sons, though four years apart, were very close. Vinod wouldn't let Mithun drown. *Electrical engineering*, I think, foolishly perhaps: this man knows important secrets of the universe, things closed to me. Relief spins me lightheaded. No wonder my boys' photographs haven't turned up in the gallery of photos of the recovered dead. "Such pretty roses," I say.

"My wife loved pink roses. Every Friday I had to bring a bunch home. I used to say, why? After twenty odd years of marriage you're still needing proof positive of my love?" He has identified his wife and three of his children. Then others from Montreal, the lucky ones, intact families with no survivors. He chuckles as he wades back to shore. Then he swings around to ask me a question. "Mrs. Bhave, you are wanting to throw in some roses for your loved ones? I have two big ones left."

But I have other things to float: Vinod's pocket calculator; a half-painted model B-52 for my Mithun. They'd want them on their island. And for my husband? For him I let fall into the calm, glassy waters a poem I wrote in the hospital yesterday. Finally he'll know my feelings for him.

"Don't tumble, the rocks are slippery," Dr. Ranganathan cautions. He holds out a hand for me to grab.

Then it's time to get back on the bus, time to rush back to our waiting posts on hospital benches.

Kusum is one of the lucky ones. The lucky ones flew here, identified in multiplicate their loved ones, then will fly to India with the bodies for proper ceremonies. Satish is one of the few males who surfaced. The photos of faces we saw on the walls in an office at Heathrow and here in the hospital are mostly of women. Women have more body fat, a nun said to me matter-of-factly. They float better.

Today I was stopped by a young sailor on the street. He had loaded bodies, he'd gone into the water when—he checks my face for signs of strength—when the sharks were first spotted. I don't blush, and he breaks down. "It's all right," I say. "Thank you." I had heard about the sharks from Dr. Ranganathan. In his orderly mind, science brings understanding, it holds no terror. It is the shark's duty. For every deer there is a hunter, for every fish a fisherman.

The Irish are not shy; they rush to me and give me hugs and some are crying. I cannot imagine reactions like that on the streets of Toronto. Just strangers, and I am touched. Some carry flowers with them and give them to any Indian they see.

After lunch, a policeman I have gotten to know quite well catches hold of me. He says he thinks he has a match for Vinod. I explain what a good swimmer Vinod is.

"You want me with you when you look at photos?" Dr. Ranganathan walks ahead of me into the picture gallery. In these matters, he is a scientist, and I am grateful. It is a new perspective. "They have performed miracles," he says. "We are indebted to them."

The first day or two the policemen showed us relatives only one picture at a time; now they're in a hurry, they're eager to lay out the possibles, and even the probables.

The face on the photo is of a boy much like Vinod; the same intelligent eyes, the same thick brows dipping into a V. But this boy's features, even his cheeks, are puffier, wider, mushier.

"No." My gaze is pulled by other pictures. There are five other boys who look like Vinod.

The nun assigned to console me rubs the first picture with a fingertip. "When they've been in the water for a while, love, they look a little heavier." The bones under the skin are broken, they said on the first day—try to adjust your memories. It's important.

"It's not him. I'm his mother. I'd know."

"I know this one!" Dr. Ranganathan cries out suddenly from the back of the gallery. "And this one!" I think he senses that I don't want to find my boys. "They are the Kutty brothers. They were also from Montreal." I don't mean to be crying. On the contrary, I am ecstatic. My suitcase in the hotel is packed heavy with dry clothes for my boys.

The policeman starts to cry. "I am so sorry, I am so sorry, ma'am. I really thought we had a match."

With the nun ahead of us and the policeman behind, we, the unlucky ones without our children's bodies, file out of the makeshift gallery.

From Ireland most of us go on to India. Kusum and I take the same direct flight to Bombay, so I can help her clear customs quickly. But we have to argue with a man in uniform. He has large boils on his face. The boils swell and glow with sweat as we argue with him. He wants Kusum to wait in line and he refuses to take authority because his boss is on a tea break. But Kusum won't let her coffins out of sight, and I shan't desert her though I know that my parents, elderly and diabetic, must be waiting in a stuffy car in a scorching lot.

"You bastard!" I scream at the man with the popping boils. Other passengers press closer. "You think we're smuggling contraband in those coffins!"

Once upon a time we were well brought up women; we were dutiful wives who kept our heads veiled, our voices shy and sweet.

In India, I become, once again, an only child of rich, ailing parents. Old friends of the family come to pay their respects. Some are Sikh, and inwardly, involuntarily, I cringe. My parents are progressive people; they do not blame communities for a few individuals.

In Canada it is a different story now.

"Stay longer," my mother pleads. "Canada is a cold place. Why would you want to be all by yourself?" I stay.

Three months pass. Then another.

"Vikram wouldn't have wanted you to give up things!" they protest. They call my husband by the name he was born with. In Toronto he'd changed to

Vik so the men he worked with at his office would find his name as easy as Rod or Chris. "You know, the dead aren't cut off from us!"

My grandmother, the spoiled daughter of a rich *zamindar*,[6] shaved her head with rusty razor blades when she was widowed at sixteen. My grandfather died of childhood diabetes when he was nineteen, and she saw herself as the harbinger of bad luck. My mother grew up without parents, raised indifferently by an uncle, while her true mother slept in a hut behind the main estate house and took her food with the servants. She grew up a rationalist. My parents abhor mindless mortification.

The zamindar's daughter kept stubborn faith in Vedic rituals; my parents rebelled. I am trapped between two modes of knowledge. At thirty-six, I am too old to start over and too young to give up. Like my husband's spirit, I flutter between worlds.

Courting aphasia, we travel. We travel with our phalanx of servants and poor relatives. To hill stations and to beach resorts. We play contract bridge in dusty gymkhana clubs. We ride stubby ponies up crumbly mountain trails. At tea dances, we let ourselves be twirled twice round the ballroom. We hit the holy spots we hadn't made time for before. In Varanasi, Kalighat, Rishikesh, Hardwar, astrologers and palmists seek me out and for a fee offer me cosmic consolations.

Already the widowers among us are being shown new bride candidates. They cannot resist the call of custom, the authority of their parents and older brothers. They must marry; it is the duty of a man to look after a wife. The new wives will be young widows with children, destitute but of good family. They will make loving wives, but the men will shun them. I've had calls from the men over crackling Indian telephone lines. "Save me," they say, these substantial, educated, successful men of forty. "My parents are arranging a marriage for me." In a month they will have buried one family and returned to Canada with a new bride and partial family.

I am comparatively lucky. No one here thinks of arranging a husband for an unlucky widow.

Then, on the third day of the sixth month into this odyssey, in an abandoned temple in a tiny Himalayan village, as I make my offering of flowers and sweetmeats to the god of a tribe of animists, my husband descends to me. He is squatting next to a scrawny *sadhu*[7] in moth-eaten robes. Vikram wears the vanilla suit he wore the last time I hugged him. The *sadhu* tosses petals on a butter-fed flame, reciting Sanskrit mantras and sweeps his face of flies. My husband takes my hands in his.

You're beautiful, he starts. Then, *What are you doing here?*

Shall I stay? I ask. He only smiles, but already the image is fading. *You must finish alone what we started together.* No seaweed wreathes his mouth. He speaks too fast just as he used to when we were an envied family in our pink split-level. He is gone.

In the windowless altar room, smoky with joss sticks and clarified butter lamps, a sweaty hand gropes for my blouse. I do not shriek. The *sadhu* arranges his robe. The lamps hiss and sputter out.

6. Landowner (Hindi). **7.** Hindu holy man.

When we come out of the temple, my mother says, "Did you feel something weird in there?"

My mother has no patience with ghosts, prophetic dreams, holy men, and cults.

"No," I lie. "Nothing."

But she knows that she's lost me. She knows that in days I shall be leaving.

Kusum's put her house up for sale. She wants to live in an ashram in Hardwar. Moving to Hardwar was her swami's idea. Her swami runs two ashrams, the one in Hardwar and another here in Toronto.

"Don't run away," I tell her.

"I'm not running away," she says. "I'm pursuing inner peace. You think you or that Ranganathan fellow are better off?"

Pam's left for California. She wants to do some modelling, she says. She says when she comes into her share of the insurance money she'll open a yoga-cum-aerobics studio in Hollywood. She sends me postcards so naughty I daren't leave them on the coffee table. Her mother has withdrawn from her and the world.

The rest of us don't lose touch, that's the point. Talk is all we have, says Dr. Ranganathan, who has also resisted his relatives and returned to Montreal and to his job, alone. He says, whom better to talk with than other relatives? We've been melted down and recast as a new tribe.

He calls me twice a week from Montreal. Every Wednesday night and every Saturday afternoon. He is changing jobs, going to Ottawa. But Ottawa is over a hundred miles away, and he is forced to drive two hundred and twenty miles a day. He can't bring himself to sell his house. The house is a temple, he says; the king-sized bed in the master bedroom is a shrine. He sleeps on a folding cot. A devotee.

There are still some hysterical relatives. Judith Templeton's list of those needing help and those who've "accepted" is in nearly perfect balance. Acceptance means you speak of your family in the past tense and you make active plans for moving ahead with your life. There are courses at Seneca and Ryerson[8] we could be taking. Her gleaming leather briefcase is full of college catalogues and lists of cultural societies that need our help. She has done impressive work, I tell her.

"In the textbooks on grief management," she replies—I am her confidante, I realize, one of the few whose grief has not sprung bizarre obsessions—"there are stages to pass through: rejection, depression, acceptance, reconstruction." She has compiled a chart and finds that six months after the tragedy, none of us still reject reality, but only a handful are reconstructing. "Depressed Acceptance" is the plateau we've reached. Remarriage is a major step in reconstruction (though she's a little surprised, even shocked, over *how* quickly some of the men have taken on new families). Selling one's house and changing jobs and cities is healthy.

How do I tell Judith Templeton that my family surrounds me, and that like creatures in epics, they've changed shapes? She sees me as calm and accepting

8. Ryerson University, Toronto. Seneca College of Applied Arts and Technology, in Willowdale, Toronto.

but worries that I have no job, no career. My closest friends are worse off than I. I cannot tell her my days, even my nights, are thrilling.

She asks me to help with families she can't reach at all. An elderly couple in Agincourt whose sons were killed just weeks after they had brought their parents over from a village in Punjab. From their names, I know they are Sikh. Judith Templeton and a translator have visited them twice with offers of money for air fare to Ireland, with bank forms, power-of-attorney forms, but they have refused to sign, or to leave their tiny apartment. Their sons' money is frozen in the bank. Their sons' investment apartments have been trashed by tenants, the furnishings sold off. The parents fear that anything they sign or any money they receive will end the company's or the country's obligations to them. They fear they are selling their sons for two airline tickets to a place they've never seen.

The high-rise apartment is a tower of Indians and West Indians, with a sprinkling of Orientals. The nearest bus stop kiosk is lined with women in saris. Boys practice cricket in the parking lot. Inside the building, even I wince a bit from the ferocity of onion fumes, the distinctive and immediate Indianness of frying *ghee*,[9] but Judith Templeton maintains a steady flow of information. These poor old people are in imminent danger of losing their place and all their services.

I say to her, "They are Sikh. They will not open up to a Hindu woman." And what I want to add is, as much as I try not to, I stiffen now at the sight of beards and turbans. I remember a time when we all trusted each other in this new country, it was only the new country we worried about.

The two rooms are dark and stuffy. The lights are off, and an oil lamp sputters on the coffee table. The bent old lady has let us in, and her husband is wrapping a white turban over his oiled, hip-length hair. She immediately goes to the kitchen, and I hear the most familiar sound of an Indian home, tap water hitting and filling a teapot.

They have not paid their utility bills, out of fear and the inability to write a check. The telephone is gone; electricity and gas and water are soon to follow. They have told Judith their sons will provide. They are good boys, and they have always earned and looked after their parents.

We converse a bit in Hindi. They do not ask about the crash and I wonder if I should bring it up. If they think I am here merely as a translator, then they may feel insulted. There are thousands of Punjabi-speakers, Sikhs, in Toronto to do a better job. And so I say to the old lady, "I too have lost my sons, and my husband, in the crash."

Her eyes immediately fill with tears. The man mutters a few words which sound like a blessing. "God provides and God takes away," he says.

I want to say, but only men destroy and give back nothing. "My boys and my husband are not coming back," I say. "We have to understand that."

Now the old woman responds. "But who is to say? Man alone does not decide these things." To this her husband adds his agreement.

Judith asks about the bank papers, the release forms. With a stroke of the pen, they will have a provincial trustee to pay their bills, invest their money, send them a monthly pension.

---

9. Semiliquid clarified butter (Hindi).

"Do you know this woman?" I ask them.

The man raises his hand from the table, turns it over and seems to regard each finger separately before he answers. "This young lady is always coming here, we make tea for her and she leaves papers for us to sign." His eyes scan a pile of papers in the corner of the room. "Soon we will be out of tea, then will she go away?"

The old lady adds, "I have asked my neighbors and no one else gets *angrezi*[1] visitors. What have we done?"

"It's her job," I try to explain. "The government is worried. Soon you will have no place to stay, no lights, no gas, no water."

"Government will get its money. Tell her not to worry, we are honorable people."

I try to explain the government wishes to give money, not take. He raises his hand. "Let them take," he says. "We are accustomed to that. That is no problem."

"We are strong people," says the wife. "Tell her that."

"Who needs all this machinery?" demands the husband. "It is unhealthy, the bright lights, the cold air on a hot day, the cold food, the four gas rings. God will provide, not government."

"When our boys return," the mother says. Her husband sucks his teeth. "Enough talk," he says.

Judith breaks in. "Have you convinced them?" The snaps on her cordovan briefcase go off like firecrackers in that quiet apartment. She lays the sheaf of legal papers on the coffee table. "If they can't write their names, an X will do— I've told them that."

Now the old lady has shuffled to the kitchen and soon emerges with a pot of tea and two cups. "I think my bladder will go first on a job like this," Judith says to me, smiling. "If only there was some way of reaching them. Please thank her for the tea. Tell her she's very kind."

I nod in Judith's direction and tell them in Hindi, "She thanks you for the tea. She thinks you are being very hospitable but she doesn't have the slightest idea what it means."

I want to say, humor her. I want to say, my boys and my husband are with me too, more than ever. I look in the old man's eyes and I can read his stubborn, peasant's message: *I have protected this woman as best I can. She is the only person I have left. Give to me or take from me what you will, but I will not sign for it. I will not pretend that I accept.*

In the car, Judith says, "You see what I'm up against? I'm sure they're lovely people, but their stubbornness and ignorance are driving me crazy. They think signing a paper is signing their sons' death warrants, don't they?"

I am looking out the window. I want to say, *In our culture, it is a parent's duty to hope.*

"Now Shaila, this next woman is a real mess. She cries day and night, and she refuses all medical help. We may have to—"

"—Let me out at the subway," I say.

"I beg your pardon?" I can feel those blue eyes staring at me.

1. English, Anglo (Hindi).

It would not be like her to disobey. She merely disapproves, and slows at a corner to let me out. Her voice is plaintive. "Is there anything I said? Anything I did?"

I could answer her suddenly in a dozen ways, but I choose not to. "Shaila? Let's talk about it," I hear, then slam the door.

A wife and mother begins her new life in a new country, and that life is cut short. Yet her husband tells her: Complete what we have started. We, who stayed out of politics and came halfway around the world to avoid religious and political feuding have been the first in the New World to die from it. I no longer know what we started, nor how to complete it. I write letters to the editors of local papers and to members of Parliament. Now at least they admit it was a bomb. One MP answers back, with sympathy, but with a challenge. You want to make a difference? Work on a campaign. Work on mine. Politicize the Indian voter.

My husband's old lawyer helps me set up a trust. Vikram was a saver and a careful investor. He had saved the boys' boarding school and college fees. I sell the pink house at four times what we paid for it and take a small apartment downtown. I am looking for a charity to support.

We are deep in the Toronto winter, gray skies, icy pavements. I stay indoors, watching television. I have tried to assess my situation, how best to live my life, to complete what we began so many years ago. Kusum has written me from Hardwar that her life is now serene. She has seen Satish and has heard her daughter sing again. Kusum was on a pilgrimage, passing through a village when she heard a young girl's voice, singing one of her daughter's favorite *bhajans*. She followed the music through the squalor of a Himalayan village, to a hut where a young girl, an exact replica of her daughter, was fanning coals under the kitchen fire. When she appeared, the girl cried out, "Ma!" and ran away. What did I think of that?

I think I can only envy her.

Pam didn't make it to California, but writes me from Vancouver. She works in a department store, giving make-up hints to Indian and Oriental girls. Dr. Ranganathan has given up his commute, given up his house and job, and accepted an academic position in Texas where no one knows his story and he has vowed not to tell it. He calls me now once a week.

I wait, I listen, and I pray, but Vikram has not returned to me. The voices and the shapes and the nights filled with visions ended abruptly several weeks ago.

I take it as a sign.

One rare, beautiful, sunny day last week, returning from a small errand on Yonge Street, I was walking through the park from the subway to my apartment. I live equidistant from the Ontario Houses of Parliament and the University of Toronto. The day was not cold, but something in the bare trees caught my attention. I looked up from the gravel, into the branches and the clear blue sky beyond. I thought I heard the rustling of larger forms, and I waited a moment for voices. Nothing.

"What?" I asked.

Then as I stood in the path looking north to Queen's Park and west to the university, I heard the voices of my family one last time. *Your time has come,* they said. *Go, be brave.*

I do not know where this voyage I have begun will end. I do not know which direction I will take. I dropped the package on a park bench and started walking.

1988

RELATED:

—Mukherjee, "A Four-Hundred-Year-Old Woman," p. 1727
—Richard Ford on "The Management of Grief," p. 1761

ALICE MUNRO
b. 1931

Widely considered Canada's finest short-story writer, Munro was born on a farm in Wingham, Ontario, and was educated at the University of Western Ontario. Her first collection of stories, *Dance of the Happy Shades* (1968), won the Governor General's Award, and her novel *Lives of Girls and Women* (1971) won the Canadian Booksellers Association Award. Munro is best known for stories that find the humanity in small-town life, and her output has been prodigious. In 1978 and 1986 she twice again received the Governor General's Award for *Who Do You Think You Are?* (published in the United States as *The Beggar Maid*) and *The Progress of Love*. Her more recent books include *Open Secrets* (1994), *Selected Stories* (1996), *The Love of a Good Woman* (1998), *Hateship, Friendship, Courtship, Loveship, Marriage* (2001), *Runaway* (2004), *The View from Castle Rock* (2006), *Too Much Happiness* (2009), and what she says is her final book, *Dear Life* (2013). In recognition of a brilliant and distinguished career, Munro won the Man Booker International Prize in 2009 and the Nobel Prize in Literature in 2013.

Royal Beatings

Royal beating. That was Flo's promise. You are going to get one Royal Beating.

The word Royal lolled on Flo's tongue, took on trappings. Rose had a need to picture things, to pursue absurdities, that was stronger than the need to stay out of trouble, and instead of taking this threat to heart she pondered: how is a beating royal? She came up with a tree-lined avenue, a crowd of formal spectators, some white horses and black slaves. Someone knelt, and the blood came leaping out like banners. An occasion both savage and splendid. In real life they didn't approach such dignity, and it was only Flo who tried to supply the event with some high air of necessity and regret. Rose and her father soon got beyond anything presentable.

Her father was king of the royal beatings. Those Flo gave never amounted to much; they were quick cuffs and slaps dashed off while her attention remained elsewhere. You get out of my road, she would say. You mind your own business. You take that look off your face.

They lived behind a store in Hanratty, Ontario. There were four of them: Rose, her father, Flo, Rose's young half brother Brian. The store was really a house, bought by Rose's father and mother when they married and set up here in the furniture and upholstery repair business. Her mother could do upholstery. From both parents Rose should have inherited clever hands, a quick sympathy with materials, an eye for the nicest turns of mending, but she hadn't. She was clumsy, and when something broke she couldn't wait to sweep it up and throw it away.

Her mother had died. She said to Rose's father during the afternoon, "I have a feeling that is so hard to describe. It's like a boiled egg in my chest, with the shell left on." She died before night, she had a blood clot on her lung. Rose was a baby in a basket at the time, so of course could not remember any of this. She heard it from Flo, who must have heard it from her father. Flo came along soon afterward, to take over Rose in the basket, marry her father, open up the front room to make a grocery store. Rose, who had known the house only as a store, who had known only Flo for a mother, looked back on the sixteen or so months her parents spent here as an orderly, far gentler and more ceremonious time, with little touches of affluence. She had nothing to go on but some egg cups her mother had bought, with a pattern of vines and birds on them, delicately drawn as if with red ink; the pattern was beginning to wear away. No books or clothes or pictures of her mother remained. Her father must have got rid of them, or else Flo would. Flo's only story about her mother, the one about her death, was oddly grudging. Flo liked the details of a death: the things people said, the way they protested or tried to get out of bed or swore or laughed (some did those things), but when she said that Rose's mother mentioned a hard-boiled egg in her chest she made the comparison sound slightly foolish, as if her mother really was the kind of person who might think you could swallow an egg whole.

Her father had a shed out behind the store, where he worked at his furniture repairing and restoring. He caned chair seats and backs, mended wickerwork, filled cracks, put legs back on, all most admirably and skillfully and cheaply. That was his pride: to startle people with such fine work, such moderate, even ridiculous charges. During the Depression people could not afford to pay more, perhaps, but he continued the practice through the war, through the years of prosperity after the war, until he died. He never discussed with Flo what he charged or what was owing. After he died she had to go out and unlock the shed and take all sorts of scraps of paper and torn envelopes from the big wicked-looking hooks that were his files. Many of these she found were not accounts or receipts at all but records of the weather, bits of information about the garden, things he had been moved to write down.

> Ate new potatoes 25th June. Record.
> Dark Day, 1880's, nothing supernatural. Clouds of ash from forest fires.
> Aug 16, 1938. Giant thunderstorm in evng. Lightning str. Pres. Church,
> Turberry Twp. Will of God?
> Scald strawberries to remove acid.
> All things are alive. Spinoza.[1]

---

1. Benedict de Spinoza (1632–1677), Dutch philosopher who reasoned that all things, material and immaterial, are manifestations of nature and of God.

Flo thought Spinoza must be some new vegetable he planned to grow, like broccoli or eggplant. He would often try some new thing. She showed the scrap of paper to Rose and asked, did she know what Spinoza was? Rose did know, or had an idea—she was in her teens by that time—but she replied that she did not. She had reached an age where she thought she could not stand to know any more, about her father, or about Flo; she pushed any discovery aside with embarrassment and dread.

There was a stove in the shed, and many rough shelves covered with cans of paint and varnish, shellac and turpentine, jars of soaking brushes and also some dark sticky bottles of cough medicine. Why should a man who coughed constantly, whose lungs took in a whiff of gas in the War (called, in Rose's earliest childhood, not the First, but the Last,[2] War), spend all his days breathing fumes of paint and turpentine? At the time, such questions were not asked as often as they are now. On the bench outside Flo's store several old men from the neighborhood sat gossiping, drowsing, in the warm weather, and some of these old men coughed all the time too. The fact is they were dying, slowly and discreetly, of what was called, without any particular sense of grievance, "the foundry disease." They had worked all their lives at the foundry in town, and now they sat still, with their wasted yellow faces, coughing, chuckling, drifting into aimless obscenity on the subject of women walking by, or any young girl on a bicycle.

From the shed came not only coughing, but speech, a continual muttering, reproachful or encouraging, usually just below the level at which separate words could be made out. Slowing down when her father was at a tricky piece of work, taking on a cheerful speed when he was doing something less demanding, sandpapering or painting. Now and then some words would break through and hang clear and nonsensical on the air. When he realized they were out, there would be a quick bit of cover-up coughing, a swallowing, an alert, unusual silence.

"Macaroni, pepperoni, Botticelli,[3] beans—"

What could that mean? Rose used to repeat such things to herself. She could never ask him. (The person who spoke these words and the person who spoke to her as her father were not the same) though they seemed to occupy the same space. It would be the worst sort of taste to acknowledge the person who was not supposed to be there; it would not be forgiven. Just the same, she loitered and listened.

The cloud-capped towers, she heard him say once.

"The cloud-capped towers, the gorgeous palaces."[4]

That was like a hand clapped against Rose's chest, not to hurt, but astonish her, to take her breath away. She had to run then, she had to get away. She knew that was enough to hear, and besides, what if he caught her? It would be terrible.

This was something the same as bathroom noises. Flo had saved up, and had a bathroom put in, but there was no place to put it except in a corner of the kitchen. The door did not fit, the walls were only beaver-board. The result was that even the tearing of a piece of toilet paper, the shifting of a haunch, was audible to those working or talking or eating in the kitchen. They were all familiar with each other's nether voices, not only in their more explosive moments but in their intimate sighs and growls and pleas and statements. And they were all most prudish people. So no one ever seemed to hear, or be listening, and no reference was made. The person creating the noises in the bathroom was not connected with the person who walked out.

They lived in a poor part of town. There was Hanratty and West Hanratty, with the river flowing between them. This was West Hanratty. In Hanratty the social structure ran from doctors and dentists and lawyers down to foundry workers and factory workers and draymen[5]; in West Hanratty it ran from factory workers and foundry workers down to large improvident families of casual bootleggers and prostitutes and unsuccessful thieves. Rose thought of her own family as straddling the river, belonging nowhere, but that was not true. West Hanratty was where the store was and they were, on the straggling tail end of the main street. Across the road from them was a blacksmith shop, boarded up about the time the war started, and a house that had been another store at one time. The Salada Tea sign had never been taken out of the front window; it remained as a proud and interesting decoration though there was no Salada Tea for sale inside. There was just a bit of sidewalk, too cracked and tilted for roller-skating, though Rose longed for roller skates and often pictured herself whizzing along in a plaid skirt, agile and fashionable. There was one street light, a tin flower; then the amenities gave up and there were dirt roads and boggy places, front-yard dumps and strange-looking houses. What made the houses strange-looking were the attempts to keep them from going completely to ruin. With some the attempt had never been made. These were gray and rotted and leaning over, falling into a landscape of scrub hollows, frog ponds, cattails and nettles. Most houses, however, had been patched up with tarpaper, a few fresh shingles, sheets of tin, hammered-out stovepipes, even cardboard. This was, of course, in the days before the war, days of what would later be legendary poverty, from which Rose would remember mostly low-down things—serious-looking anthills and wooden steps, and a cloudy, interesting, problematical light on the world.

There was a long truce between Flo and Rose in the beginning. Rose's nature was growing like a prickly pineapple, but slowly, and secretly, hard pride and skepticism overlapping, to make something surprising even to herself. Before she was old enough to go to school, and while Brian was still in the baby carriage, Rose stayed in the store with both of them—Flo sitting on the high stool behind the counter, Brian asleep by the window; Rose knelt or lay on the wide creaky floorboards working with crayons on pieces of brown paper too torn or irregular to be used for wrapping.

People who came to the store were mostly from the houses around. Some country people came too, on their way home from town, and a few people from Hanratty, who walked across the bridge. Some people were always on the main street, in and out of stores, as if it was their duty to be always on display and their right to be welcomed. For instance, Becky Tyde.

---

5. Men hired to haul heavy loads by dray, a type of strong cart or wagon.

Becky Tyde climbed up on Flo's counter, made room for herself beside an open tin of crumbly jam-filled cookies.

"Are these any good?" she said to Flo, and boldly began to eat one. "When are you going to give us a job, Flo?"

"You could go and work in the butcher shop," said Flo innocently. "You could go and work for your brother."

"Roberta?" said Becky with a stagey sort of contempt. "You think I'd work for him?" Her brother who ran the butcher shop was named Robert but often called Roberta, because of his meek and nervous ways. Becky Tyde laughed. Her laugh was loud and noisy like an engine bearing down on you.

She was a big-headed loud-voiced dwarf, with a mascot's sexless swagger, a red velvet tam, a twisted neck that forced her to hold her head on one side, always looking up and sideways. She wore little polished high-heeled shoes, real lady's shoes. Rose watched her shoes, being scared of the rest of her, of her laugh and her neck. She knew from Flo that Becky Tyde had been sick with polio as a child, that was why her neck was twisted and why she had not grown any taller. It was hard to believe that she had started out differently, that she had ever been normal. Flo said she was not cracked, she had as much brains as anybody, but she knew she could get away with anything.

"You know I used to live out here?" Becky said, noticing Rose. "Hey! What's-your-name! Didn't I used to live out here, Flo?"

"If you did it was before my time," said Flo, as if she didn't know anything.

"That was before the neighborhood got so downhill. Excuse me saying so. My father built his house out here and he built his slaughterhouse and we had half an acre of orchard."

"Is that so?" said Flo, using her humoring voice, full of false geniality, humility even. "Then why did you ever move away?"

"I told you, it got to be such a downhill neighborhood," said Becky. She would put a whole cookie in her mouth if she felt like it, let her cheeks puff out like a frog's. She never told any more.

Flo knew anyway, and who didn't. Everyone knew the house, red brick with the veranda pulled off and the orchard, what was left of it, full of the usual outflow—car seats and washing machines and bedsprings and junk. The house would never look sinister, in spite of what had happened in it, because there was so much wreckage and confusion all around.

Becky's old father was a different kind of butcher from her brother according to Flo. A bad-tempered Englishman. And different from Becky in the matter of mouthiness. His was never open. A skinflint, a family tyrant. After Becky had polio he wouldn't let her go back to school. She was seldom seen outside the house, never outside the yard. He didn't want people gloating. That was what Becky said, at the trial. Her mother was dead by that time and her sisters married. Just Becky and Robert at home. People would stop Robert on the road and ask him, "How about your sister, Robert? Is she altogether better now?"

"Yes."

"Does she do the housework? Does she get your supper?"

"Yes."

"And is your father good to her, Robert?"

The story being that the father beat them, had beaten all his children and beaten his wife as well, beat Becky more now because of her deformity, which some people believed he had caused (they did not understand about polio). The stories persisted and got added to. The reason that Becky was kept out of sight was now supposed to be her pregnancy, and the father of the child was supposed to be her own father. Then people said it had been born, and disposed of.

"What?"

"Disposed of," Flo said. "They used to say go and get your lamb chops at Tyde's, get them nice and tender! It was all lies in all probability," she said regretfully.

Rose could be drawn back—from watching the wind shiver along the old torn awning, catch in the tear—by this tone of regret, caution, in Flo's voice. Flo telling a story—and this was not the only one, or even the most lurid one, she knew—would incline her head and let her face go soft and thoughtful, tantalizing, warning.

"I shouldn't even be telling you this stuff."

More was to follow.

Three useless young men, who hung around the livery stable, got together—or were got together, by more influential and respectable men in town—and prepared to give old man Tyde a horsewhipping, in the interests of public morality. They blacked their faces. They were provided with whips and a quart of whiskey apiece, for courage. They were: Jelly Smith, a horse-racer and a drinker; Bob Temple, a ballplayer and strongman; and Hat Nettleton, who worked on the town dray, and had his nickname from a bowler hat he wore, out of vanity as much as for the comic effect. He still worked on the dray, in fact; he had kept the name if not the hat, and could often be seen in public almost as often as Becky Tyde—delivering sacks of coal, which blackened his face and arms. That should have brought to mind his story, but didn't. Present time and past, the shady melodramatic past of Flo's stories, were quite separate, at least for Rose. Present people could not be fitted into the past. Becky herself, town oddity and public pet, harmless and malicious, could never match the butcher's prisoner, the cripple daughter, a white streak at the window: mute, beaten, impregnated. As with the house, only a formal connection could be made.

The young men primed to do the horsewhipping showed up late, outside Tyde's house, after everybody had gone to bed. They had a gun, but they used up their ammunition firing it off in the yard. They yelled for the butcher and beat on the door; finally they broke it down. Tyde concluded they were after his money, so he put some bills in a handkerchief and sent Becky down with them, maybe thinking those men would be touched or scared by the sight of a little wry-necked girl, a dwarf. But that didn't content them. They came upstairs and dragged the butcher out from under his bed, in his nightgown. They dragged him outside and stood him in the snow. The temperature was four below zero, a fact noted later in court. They meant to hold a mock trial but they could not remember how it was done. So they began to beat him and kept beating him until he fell. They yelled at him, *Butcher's meat!* and continued beating him while his nightgown and the snow he was lying in turned red. His son Robert said in court that he had not watched the beating. Becky said that Robert had watched at first but had run away and hid. She herself had watched all the way through. She watched the men leave at last and her father make his delayed bloody progress through the snow and up the steps of the veranda. She did not go out to help him, or open the door until he got to it. Why not? she was asked in court, and she said she did not go out because she just had her nightgown on, and she did not open the door because she did not want to let the cold into the house.

Old man Tyde then appeared to have recovered his strength. He sent Robert to harness the horse, and made Becky heat water so that he could wash. He dressed and took all the money and with no explanation to his children got into the cutter and drove to Belgrave where he left the horse tied in the cold and took the early morning train to Toronto. On the train he behaved oddly, groaning and cursing as if he was drunk. He was picked up on the streets of Toronto a day later, out of his mind with fever, and was taken to a hospital, where he died. He still had all the money. The cause of death was given as pneumonia.

But the authorities got wind, Flo said. The case came to trial. The three men who did it all received long prison sentences. A farce, said Flo. Within a year they were all free, had all been pardoned, had jobs waiting for them. And why was that? It was because too many higher-ups were in on it. And it seemed as if Becky and Robert had no interest in seeing justice done. They were left well-off. They bought a house in Hanratty. Robert went into the store. Becky after her long seclusion started on a career of public sociability and display.

That was all. Flo put the lid down on the story as if she was sick of it. It reflected no good on anybody.

"Imagine," Flo said.

Flo at this time must have been in her early thirties. A young woman. She wore exactly the same clothes that a woman of fifty, or sixty, or seventy, might wear: print housedresses loose at the neck and sleeves as well as the waist; bib aprons, also of print, which she took off when she came from the kitchen into the store. This was a common costume at the time, for a poor though not absolutely poverty-stricken woman; it was also, in a way, a scornful deliberate choice. Flo scorned slacks, she scorned the outfits of people trying to be in style, she scorned lipstick and permanents. She wore her own black hair cut straight across, just long enough to push behind her ears. She was tall but fine-boned, with narrow wrists and shoulders, a small head, a pale, freckled, mobile, monkeyish face. If she had thought it worthwhile, and had the resources, she might have had a black-and-pale, fragile, nurtured sort of prettiness; Rose realized that later. But she would have to have been a different person altogether; she would have to have learned to resist making faces, at herself and others.

Rose's earliest memories of Flo were of extraordinary softness and hardness. The soft hair, the long, soft, pale cheeks, soft almost invisible fuzz in front of her ears and above her mouth. The sharpness of her knees, hardness of her lap, flatness of her front.

When Flo sang:

> Oh the buzzin' of the bees in the cigarette trees
> And the soda-*water* fountain . . . [6]

---

[6]. From the ballad "The Big Rock Candy Mountain."

Rose thought of Flo's old life before she married her father, when she worked as a waitress in the coffee shop in Union Station, and went with her girl friends Mavis and Irene to Centre Island,[7] and was followed by men on dark streets and knew how pay phones and elevators worked. Rose heard in her voice the reckless dangerous life of cities, the gum-chewing sharp answers.

And when she sang:

> Then slowly, slowly, she got up
> And slowly she came nigh him
> And all she said, that she ever did say,
> Was young man I think, you're dyin'![8]

Rose thought of a life Flo seemed to have had beyond that, earlier than that, crowded and legendary, with Barbara Allen and Becky Tyde's father and all kinds of outrages and sorrows jumbled up together in it.

The royal beatings. What got them started?

Suppose a Saturday, in spring. Leaves not out yet but the doors open to the sunlight. Crows. Ditches full of running water. Hopeful weather. Often on Saturdays Flo left Rose in charge of the store—it's a few years now, these are the years when Rose was nine, ten, eleven, twelve—while she herself went across the bridge to Hanratty (going uptown they called it) to shop and see people, and listen to them. Among the people she listened to were Mrs. Lawyer Davies, Mrs. Anglican Rector Henley-Smith, and Mrs. Horse-Doctor McKay. She came home and imitated their flibberty voices. Monsters, she made them seem; of foolishness, and showiness, and self-approbation.

When she finished shopping she went into the coffee shop of the Queen's Hotel and had a sundae. What kind? Rose and Brian wanted to know when she got home, and they would be disappointed if it was only pineapple or butterscotch, pleased if it was a Tin Roof, or Black and White. Then she smoked a cigarette. She had some ready-rolled, that she carried with her, so that she wouldn't have to roll one in public. Smoking was the one thing she did that she would have called showing off in anybody else. It was a habit left over from her working days, from Toronto. She knew it was asking for trouble. Once the Catholic priest came over to her right in the Queen's Hotel, and flashed his lighter at her before she could get her matches out. She thanked him but did not enter into conversation, lest he should try to convert her.

Another time, on the way home, she saw at the town end of the bridge a boy in a blue jacket, apparently looking at the water. Eighteen, nineteen years old. Nobody she knew. Skinny, weakly looking, something the matter with him, she saw at once. Was he thinking of jumping? Just as she came up even with him, what does he do but turn and display himself, holding his jacket open, also his pants. What he must have suffered from the cold, on a day that had Flo holding her coat collar tight around her throat.

When she first saw what he had in his hand, Flo said, all she could think of was, what is he doing out here with a baloney sausage?

---

7. Park in Toronto Harbour. Union Station is the main railroad terminal in Toronto. 8. From the ballad "Barbara Allen."

She could say that. It was offered as truth; no joke. She maintained that she despised dirty talk. She would go out and yell at the old men sitting in front of her store.

"If you want to stay where you are you better clean your mouths out!"

Saturday, then. For some reason Flo is not going uptown, has decided to stay home and scrub the kitchen floor. Perhaps this has put her in a bad mood. Perhaps she was in a bad mood anyway, due to people not paying their bills, or the stirring-up of feelings in spring. The wrangle with Rose has already commenced, has been going on forever, like a dream that goes back and back into other dreams, over hills and through doorways, maddeningly dim and populous and familiar and elusive. They are carting all the chairs out of the kitchen preparatory to the scrubbing, and they have also got to move some extra provisions for the store, some cartons of canned goods, tins of maple syrup, coal-oil cans, jars of vinegar. They take these things out to the wood-shed. Brian who is five or six by this time is helping drag the tins.

"Yes," says Flo, carrying on from our lost starting point. "Yes, and that filth you taught to Brian."

"What filth?"

"And he doesn't know any better."

There is one step down from the kitchen to the woodshed, a bit of carpet on it so worn Rose can't even remember seeing the pattern. Brian loosens it, dragging a tin.

"Two Vancouvers," she says softly.

Flo is back in the kitchen. Brian looks from Flo to Rose and Rose says again in a slightly louder voice, an encouraging singsong, "Two Vancouvers—"

"Fried in snot!" finishes Brian, not able to control himself any longer.

"Two pickled arseholes—"

"—tied in a knot!"

There it is. The filth.

> Two Vancouvers fried in snot!
> Two pickled arseholes tied in a knot!

Rose has known that for years, learned it when she first went to school. She came home and asked Flo, what is a Vancouver?

"It's a city. It's a long ways away."

"What else besides a city?"

Flo said, what did she mean, what else? How could it be fried, Rose said, approaching the dangerous moment, the delightful moment, when she would have to come out with the whole thing.

"Two Vancouvers fried in snot! / Two pickled arseholes tied in a knot!"

"You're going to get it!" cried Flo in a predictable rage. "Say that again and you'll get a good clout!"

Rose couldn't stop herself. She hummed it tenderly, tried saying the innocent words aloud, humming through the others. It was not just the words snot and arsehole that gave her pleasure, though of course they did. It was the pickling and tying and the unimaginable Vancouvers. She saw them in her mind shaped rather like octopuses, twitching in the pan. The tumble of reason; the spark and spit of craziness.

Lately she has remembered it again and taught it to Brian, to see if it has the same effect on him, and of course it has.

"Oh, I heard you!" says Flo. "I heard that! And I'm warning you!"

So she is. Brian takes the warning. He runs away, out the woodshed door, to do as he likes. Being a boy, free to help or not, involve himself or not. Not committed to the household struggle. They don't need him anyway, except to use against each other, they hardly notice his going. They continue, can't help continuing, can't leave each other alone. When they seem to have given up they really are just waiting and building up steam.

Flo gets out the scrub pail and the brush and the rag and the pad for her knees, a dirty red rubber pad. She starts to work on the floor. Rose sits on the kitchen table, the only place left to sit, swinging her legs. She can feel the cool oilcloth, because she is wearing shorts, last summer's tight faded shorts dug out of the summer-clothes bag. They smell a bit moldy from winter storage.

Flo crawls underneath, scrubbing with the brush, wiping with the rag. Her legs are long, white and muscular, marked all over with blue veins as if somebody had been drawing rivers on them with an indelible pencil. An abnormal energy, a violent disgust, is expressed in the chewing of the brush at the linoleum, the swish of the rag.

What do they have to say to each other? It doesn't really matter. Flo speaks of Rose's smart-aleck behavior, rudeness and sloppiness and conceit. Her willingness to make work for others, her lack of gratitude. She mentions Brian's innocence, Rose's corruption. Oh, don't you think you're somebody, says Flo, and a moment later, Who do you think you are? Rose contradicts and objects with such poisonous reasonableness and mildness, displays theatrical unconcern. Flo goes beyond her ordinary scorn and self-possession and becomes amazingly theatrical herself, saying it was for Rose that she sacrificed her life. She saw her father saddled with a baby daughter and she thought, what is that man going to do? So she married him, and here she is, on her knees.

At that moment the bell rings, to announce a customer in the store. Because the fight is on, Rose is not permitted to go into the store and wait on whoever it is. Flo gets up and throws off her apron, groaning—but not communicatively, it is not a groan whose exasperation Rose is allowed to share—and goes in and serves. Rose hears her using her normal voice.

"About time! Sure is!"

She comes back and ties on her apron and is ready to resume.

"You never have a thought for anybody but your ownself! You never have a thought for what I'm doing."

"I never asked you to do anything. I wish you never had. I would have been a lot better off."

Rose says this smiling directly at Flo, who has not yet gone down on her knees. Flo sees the smile, grabs the scrub rag that is hanging on the side of the pail, and throws it at her. It may be meant to hit her in the face but instead it falls against Rose's leg and she raises her foot and catches it, swinging it negligently against her ankle.

"All right," says Flo. "You've done it this time. All right."

Rose watches her go to the woodshed door, hears her tramp through the woodshed, pause in the doorway, where the screen door hasn't yet been hung, and the storm door is standing open, propped with a brick. She calls Rose's father. She calls him in a warning, summoning voice, as if against her will preparing him for bad news. He will know what this is about.

The kitchen floor has five or six different patterns of linoleum on it. Ends, which Flo got for nothing and ingeniously trimmed and fitted together, bordering them with tin strips and tacks. While Rose sits on the table waiting, she looks at the floor, at this satisfying arrangement of rectangles, triangles, some other shape whose name she is trying to remember. She hears Flo coming back through the woodshed, on the creaky plank walk laid over the dirt floor. She is loitering, waiting, too. She and Rose can carry this no further, by themselves.

Rose hears her father come in. She stiffens, a tremor runs through her legs, she feels them shiver on the oilcloth. Called away from some peaceful, absorbing task, away from the words running in his head, called out of himself, her father has to say something. He says, "Well? What's wrong?"

Now comes another voice of Flo's. Enriched, hurt, apologetic, it seems to have been manufactured on the spot. She is sorry to have called him from his work. Would never have done it, if Rose was not driving her to distraction. How to distraction? With her back talk and impudence and her terrible tongue. The things Rose has said to Flo are such that, if Flo had said them to her mother, she knows her father would have thrashed her into the ground.

Rose tries to butt in, to say this isn't true.

What isn't true?

Her father raises a hand, doesn't look at her, says, "Be quiet."

When she says it isn't true, Rose means that she herself didn't start this, only responded, that she was goaded by Flo, who is now, she believes, telling the grossest sort of lies, twisting everything to suit herself. Rose puts aside her other knowledge that whatever Flo has said or done, whatever she herself has said or done, does not really matter at all. It is the struggle itself that counts, and that can't be stopped, can never be stopped, short of where it has got to, now.

Flo's knees are dirty, in spite of the pad. The scrub rag is still hanging over Rose's foot.

Her father wipes his hands, listening to Flo. He takes his time. He is slow at getting into the spirit of things, tired in advance, maybe, on the verge of rejecting the role he has to play. He won't look at Rose, but at any sound or stirring from Rose, he holds up his hand.

"Well we don't need the public in on this, that's for sure," Flo says, and she goes to lock the door of the store, putting in the store window the sign that says BACK SOON, a sign Rose made for her with a great deal of fancy curving and shading of letters in black and red crayon. When she comes back she shuts the door to the store, then the door to the stairs, then the door to the woodshed.

Her shoes have left marks on the clean wet part of the floor.

"Oh, I don't know," she says now, in a voice worn down from its emotional peak. "I don't know what to do about her." She looks down and sees her dirty knees (following Rose's eyes) and rubs at them viciously with her bare hands, smearing the dirt around.

"She humiliates me," she says, straightening up. There it is, the explanation. "She humiliates me," she repeats with satisfaction. "She has no respect."

"I do not!"

"Quiet, you!" says her father.

"If I hadn't called your father you'd still be sitting there with that grin on your face! What other way is there to manage you?"

Rose detects in her father some objections to Flo's rhetoric, some embarrassment and reluctance. She is wrong, and ought to know she is wrong, in thinking that she can count on this. The fact that she knows about it, and he knows she knows, will not make things any better. He is beginning to warm up. He gives her a look. This look is at first cold and challenging. It informs her of his judgment, of the hopelessness of her position. Then it clears, it begins to fill up with something else, the way a spring fills up when you clear the leaves away. It fills with hatred and pleasure. Rose sees that and knows it. Is that just a description of anger, should she see his eyes filling up with anger? No. Hatred is right. Pleasure is right. His face loosens and changes and grows younger, and he holds up his hand this time to silence Flo.

"All right," he says, meaning that's enough, more than enough, this part is over, things can proceed. He starts to loosen his belt.

Flo has stopped anyway. She has the same difficulty Rose does, a difficulty in believing that what you know must happen really will happen, that there comes a time when you can't draw back.

"Oh, I don't know, don't be too hard on her." She is moving around nervously as if she has thoughts of opening some escape route. "Oh, you don't have to use the belt on her. Do you have to use the belt?"

He doesn't answer. The belt is coming off, not hastily. It is being grasped at the necessary point. *All right you.* He is coming over to Rose. He pushes her off the table. His face, like his voice, is quite out of character. He is like a bad actor, who turns a part grotesque. As if he must savor and insist on just what is shameful and terrible about this. That is not to say he is pretending, that he is acting, and does not mean it. He is acting, and he means it. Rose knows that, she knows everything about him.

She has since wondered about murders, and murderers. Does the thing have to be carried through, in the end, partly for the effect, to prove to the audience of one—who won't be able to report, only register, the lesson—that such a thing can happen, that there is nothing that can't happen, that the most dreadful antic is justified, feelings can be found to match it?

She tries again looking at the kitchen floor, that clever and comforting geometrical arrangement, instead of looking at him or his belt. How can this go on in front of such daily witnesses—the linoleum, the calendar with the mill and creek and autumn trees, the old accommodating pots and pans?

Hold out your hand!

Those things aren't going to help her, none of them can rescue her. They turn bland and useless, even unfriendly. Pots can show malice, the patterns of linoleum can leer up at you, treachery is the other side of dailiness.

At the first, or maybe the second, crack of pain, she draws back. She will not accept it. She runs around the room, she tries to get to the doors. Her father blocks her off. Not an ounce of courage or of stoicism in her, it would seem. She runs, she screams, she implores. Her father is after her, cracking the belt at her when he can, then abandoning it and using his hands. Bang over the ear, then bang over the other ear. Back and forth, her head ringing. Bang in the face. Up against the wall and bang in the face again. He shakes her and hits her against the wall, he kicks her legs. She is incoherent, insane, shrieking. *Forgive me! Oh please, forgive me!*

Flo is shrieking too. *Stop, stop!*

Not yet. He throws Rose down. Or perhaps she throws herself down. He kicks her legs again. She has given up on words but is letting out a noise, the sort of noise that makes Flo cry, *Oh, what if people can hear her?* The very last-ditch willing sound of humiliation and defeat it is, for it seems Rose must play her part in this with the same grossness, the same exaggeration, that her father displays, playing his. She plays his victim with a self-indulgence that arouses, and maybe hopes to arouse, his final, sickened contempt.

They will give this anything that is necessary, it seems, they will go to any lengths.

Not quite. He has never managed really to injure her, though there are times, of course, when she prays that he will. He hits her with an open hand, there is some restraint in his kicks.

Now he stops, he is out of breath. He allows Flo to move in, he grabs Rose up and gives her a push in Flo's direction, making a sound of disgust. Flo retrieves her, opens the stair door, shoves her up the stairs.

"Go on up to your room now! Hurry!"

Rose goes up the stairs, stumbling, letting herself stumble, letting herself fall against the steps. She doesn't bang her door because a gesture like that could still bring him after her, and anyway, she is weak. She lies on the bed. She can hear through the stovepipe hole Flo snuffling and remonstrating, her father saying angrily that Flo should have kept quiet then, if she did not want Rose punished she should not have recommended it. Flo says she never recommended a hiding like that.

They argue back and forth on this. Flo's frightened voice is growing stronger, getting its confidence back. By stages, by arguing, they are being drawn back into themselves. Soon it's only Flo talking; he will not talk anymore. Rose has had to fight down her noisy sobbing, so as to listen to them, and when she loses interest in listening, and wants to sob some more, she finds she can't work herself up to it. She has passed into a state of calm, in which outrage is perceived as complete and final. In this state events and possibilities take on a lovely simplicity. Choices are mercifully clear. The words that come to mind are not the quibbling, seldom the conditional. Never is a word to which the right is suddenly established. She will never speak to them, she will never look at them with anything but loathing, she will never forgive them. She will punish them; she will finish them. Encased in these finalities, and in her bodily pain, she floats in curious comfort, beyond herself, beyond responsibility. Suppose she dies now? Suppose she commits suicide? Suppose she runs away? Any of these things would be appropriate. It is only a matter of choosing, of figuring out the way. She floats in her pure superior state as if kindly drugged.

And just as there is a moment, when you are drugged, in which you feel perfectly safe, sure, unreachable, and then without warning and right next to it a moment in which you know the whole protection has fatally cracked, though it is still pretending to hold soundly together, so there is a moment now—the moment, in fact, when Rose hears Flo step on the stairs—that contains for her both present peace and freedom and a sure knowledge of the whole downspiraling course of events from now on.

Flo comes into the room without knocking, but with a hesitation that shows it might have occurred to her. She brings a jar of cold cream. Rose is hanging on to advantage as long as she can, lying face down on the bed, refusing to acknowledge or answer.

"Oh come on," Flo says uneasily. "You aren't so bad off, are you? You put some of this on and you'll feel better."

She is bluffing. She doesn't know for sure what damage has been done. She has the lid off the cold cream. Rose can smell it. The intimate, babyish, humiliating smell. She won't allow it near her. But in order to avoid it, the big ready clot of it in Flo's hand, she has to move. She scuffles, resists, loses dignity, and lets Flo see there is not really much the matter.

"All right," Flo says. "You win. I'll leave it here and you can put it on when you like."

Later still a tray will appear. Flo will put it down without a word and go away. A large glass of chocolate milk on it, made with Vita-Malt from the store. Some rich streaks of Vita-Malt around the bottom of the glass. Little sandwiches, neat and appetizing. Canned salmon of the first quality and reddest color, plenty of mayonnaise. A couple of butter tarts from a bakery package, chocolate biscuits with a peppermint filling. Rose's favorites, in the sandwich, tart and cookie line. She will turn away, refuse to look, but left alone with these eatables will be miserably tempted, roused and troubled and drawn back from thoughts of suicide or flight by the smell of salmon, the anticipation of crisp chocolate, she will reach out a finger, just to run it around the edge of one of the sandwiches (crusts cut off!) to get the overflow, get a taste. Then she will decide to eat one, for strength to refuse the rest. One will not be noticed. Soon, in helpless corruption, she will eat them all. She will drink the chocolate milk, eat the tarts, eat the cookies. She will get the malty syrup out of the bottom of the glass with her finger, though she sniffles with shame. Too late.

Flo will come up and get the tray. She may say, "I see you got your appetite still," or, "Did you like the chocolate milk, was it enough syrup in it?" depending on how chastened she is feeling, herself. At any rate, all advantage will be lost. Rose will understand that life has started up again, that they will all sit around the table eating again, listening to the radio news. Tomorrow morning, maybe even tonight. Unseemly and unlikely as that may be. They will be embarrassed, but rather less than you might expect considering how they have behaved. They will feel a queer lassitude, a convalescent indolence, not far off satisfaction.

One night after a scene like this they were all in the kitchen. It must have been summer, or at least warm weather, because her father spoke of the old men who sat on the bench in front of the store.

"Do you know what they're talking about now?" he said, and nodded his head toward the store to show who he meant, though of course they were not there now, they went home at dark.

"Those old coots," said Flo. "What?"

There was about them both a geniality not exactly false but a bit more emphatic than was normal, without company.

Rose's father told them then that the old men had picked up the idea somewhere that what looked like a star in the western sky, the first star that came out after sunset, the evening star, was in reality an airship hovering over Bay City, Michigan, on the other side of Lake Huron. An American invention, sent up to rival the heavenly bodies. They were all in agreement about this, the idea was congenial to them. They believed it to be lit by ten thousand electric light bulbs. Her father had ruthlessly disagreed with them, pointing out that it was the planet Venus they saw, which had appeared in the sky long before the invention of an electric light bulb. They had never heard of the planet Venus.

"Ignoramuses," said Flo. At which Rose knew, and knew her father knew, that Flo had never heard of the planet Venus either. To distract them from this, or even apologize for it, Flo put down her teacup, stretched out with her head resting on the chair she had been sitting on and her feet on another chair (somehow she managed to tuck her dress modestly between her legs at the same time), and lay stiff as a board, so that Brian cried out in delight, "Do that! Do that!"

Flo was double-jointed and very strong. In moments of celebration or emergency she would do tricks.

They were silent while she turned herself around, not using her arms at all but just her strong legs and feet. Then they all cried out in triumph, though they had seen it before.

Just as Flo turned herself Rose got a picture in her mind of that airship, an elongated transparent bubble, with its strings of diamond lights, floating in the miraculous American sky.

"The planet Venus!" her father said, applauding Flo. "Ten thousand electric lights!"

There was a feeling of permission, relaxation, even a current of happiness, in the room.

Years later, many years later, on a Sunday morning, Rose turned on the radio. This was when she was living by herself in Toronto.

Well Sir.

It was a different kind of place in our day. Yes it was.

It was all horses then. Horses and buggies. Buggy races up and down the main street on the Saturday nights.

"Just like the chariot races," says the announcer's, or interviewer's, smooth encouraging voice.

I never seen a one of them.

"No sir, that was the old Roman chariot races I was referring to. That was before your time."

Musta been before my time. I'm a hunerd and two years old.

"That's a wonderful age, sir."

It is so.

She left it on, as she went around the apartment kitchen, making coffee for herself. It seemed to her that this must be a staged interview, a scene from some play, and she wanted to find out what it was. The old man's voice was so vain and belligerent, the interviewer's quite hopeless and alarmed, under its practiced gentleness and ease. You were surely meant to see him holding the microphone up to some toothless, reckless, preening centenarian, wondering what in God's name he was doing here, and what would he say next?

"They must have been fairly dangerous."

What was dangerous?

"Those buggy races."

They was. Dangerous. Used to be the runaway horses. Used to be a-plenty of accidents. Fellows was dragged along on the gravel and cut their face open. Wouldna matter so much if they was dead. Heh.

Some of them horses was the high-steppers. Some, they had to have the mustard under their tail. Some wouldn step out for nothin. That's the thing it is with the horses. Some'll work and pull till they drop down dead and some wouldn pull your cock out of a pail of lard. Hehe.

It must be a real interview after all. Otherwise they wouldn't have put that in, wouldn't have risked it. It's all right if the old man says it. Local color. Anything rendered harmless and delightful by his hundred years.

Accidents all the time then. In the mill. Foundry. Wasn't the precautions.

"You didn't have so many strikes then, I don't suppose? You didn't have so many unions?"

Everybody taking it easy nowadays. We worked and we was glad to get it. Worked and was glad to get it.

"You didn't have television."

Didn't have no TV. Didn't have no radio. No picture show.

"You made your own entertainment."

That's the way we did.

"You had a lot of experiences young men growing up today will never have."

Experiences.

"Can you recall any of them for us?"

I eaten groundhog meat one time. One winter. You wouldna cared for it. Heh.

There was a pause, of appreciation, it would seem, then the announcer's voice saying that the foregoing had been an interview with Mr. Wilfred Nettleton of Hanratty, Ontario, made on his hundred and second birthday, two weeks before his death, last spring. A living link with our past. Mr. Nettleton had been interviewed in the Wawanash County Home for the aged.

Hat Nettleton.

Horsewhipper into centenarian. Photographed on his birthday, fussed over by nurses, kissed no doubt by a girl reporter. Flash bulbs popping at him. Tape recorder drinking in the sound of his voice. Oldest resident. Oldest horsewhipper. Living link with our past.

Looking out from her kitchen window at the cold lake, Rose was longing to tell somebody. It was Flo who would enjoy hearing. She thought of her saying *Imagine!* in a way that meant she was having her worst suspicions gorgeously confirmed. But Flo was in the same place Hat Nettleton had died in, and there wasn't any way Rose could reach her. She had been there even when that interview was recorded, though she would not have heard it, would not have known about it. After Rose put her in the Home, a couple of years earlier, she had stopped talking. She had removed herself, and spent most of her time sitting in a corner of her crib, looking crafty and disagreeable, not answering anybody, though she occasionally showed her feelings by biting a nurse.

1977

Miles City, Montana

My father came across the field carrying the body of the boy who had been drowned. There were several men together, returning from the search, but he was the one carrying the body. The men were muddy and exhausted, and walked with their heads down, as if they were ashamed. Even the dogs were dispirited, dripping from the cold river. When they all set out, hours before, the dogs were nervy and yelping, the men tense and determined, and there was a constrained, unspeakable excitement about the whole scene. It was understood that they might find something horrible.

The boy's name was Steve Gauley. He was eight years old. His hair and clothes were mud-colored now and carried some bits of dead leaves, twigs, and grass. He was like a heap of refuse that had been left out all winter. His face was turned in to my father's chest, but I could see a nostril, an ear, plugged up with greenish mud.

I don't think so. I don't think I really saw all this. Perhaps I saw my father carrying him, and the other men following along, and the dogs, but I would not have been allowed to get close enough to see something like mud in his nostril. I must have heard someone talking about that and imagined that I saw it. I see his face unaltered except for the mud—Steve Gauley's familiar, sharp-honed, sneaky-looking face—and it wouldn't have been like that; it would have been bloated and changed and perhaps muddied all over after so many hours in the water.

To have to bring back such news, such evidence, to a waiting family, particularly a mother, would have made searchers move heavily, but what was happening here was worse. It seemed a worse shame (to hear people talk) that there was no mother, no woman at all—no grandmother or aunt, or even a sister—to receive Steve Gauley and give him his due of grief. His father was a hired man, a drinker but not a drunk, an erratic man without being entertaining, not friendly but not exactly a troublemaker. His fatherhood seemed accidental, and the fact that the child had been left with him when the mother went away, and that they continued living together, seemed accidental. They lived in a steep-roofed, gray-shingled hillbilly sort of house that was just a bit better than a shack—the father fixed the roof and put supports under the porch, just enough and just in time—and their life was held together in a similar manner; that is, just well enough to keep the Children's Aid at bay. They didn't eat meals together or cook for each other, but there was food. Sometimes the father would give Steve money to buy food at the store, and Steve was seen to buy quite sensible things, such as pancake mix and macaroni dinner.

I had known Steve Gauley fairly well. I had not liked him more often than I had liked him. He was two years older than I was. He would hang around our place on Saturdays, scornful of whatever I was doing but unable to leave me alone. I couldn't be on the swing without him wanting to try it, and if I wouldn't give it up he came and pushed me so that I went crooked. He teased the dog. He got me into trouble—deliberately and maliciously, it seemed to me afterwards—by daring me to do things I wouldn't have thought of on my own: digging up the potatoes to see how big they were when they were still only the size of marbles, and pushing over the stacked firewood to make a pile we could jump off. At school, we never spoke to each other. He was solitary, though not tormented. But on Saturday mornings, when I saw his thin, self-possessed figure sliding through the cedar hedge, I knew I was in for something and he would decide what. Sometimes it was all right. We pretended we were cowboys who had to tame wild horses. We played in the pasture by the river, not far from the place where Steve drowned. We were horses and riders both, screaming and neighing and bucking and waving whips of tree branches beside a little nameless river that flows into the Saugeen in southern Ontario.

The funeral was held in our house. There was not enough room at Steve's father's place for the large crowd that was expected because of the circumstances. I have a memory of the crowded room but no picture of Steve in his coffin, or of the minister, or of wreaths of flowers. I remember that I was holding one flower, a white narcissus, which must have come from a pot somebody forced indoors, because it was too early for even the forsythia bush or the trilliums and marsh marigolds in the woods. I stood in a row of children, each of us holding a narcissus. We sang a children's hymn, which somebody played on our piano: "When He Cometh, When He Cometh, to Make Up His Jewels." I was wearing white ribbed stockings, which were disgustingly itchy, and wrinkled at the knees and ankles. The feeling of these stockings on my legs is mixed up with another feeling in my memory. It is hard to describe. It had to do with my parents. Adults in general but my parents in particular. My father, who had carried Steve's body from the river, and my mother, who must have done most of the arranging of this funeral. My father in his dark-blue suit and my mother in her brown velvet dress with the creamy satin collar. They stood side by side opening and closing their mouths for the hymn, and I stood removed from them, in the row of children, watching. I felt a furious and sickening disgust. Children sometimes have an access of disgust concerning adults. The size, the lumpy shapes, the bloated power. The breath, the coarseness, the hairiness, the horrid secretions. But this was more. And the accompanying anger had nothing sharp and self-respecting about it. There was no release, as when I would finally bend and pick up a stone and throw it at Steve Gauley. It could not be understood or expressed, though it died down after a while into a heaviness, then just a taste, an occasional taste—a thin, familiar misgiving.

Twenty years or so later, in 1961, my husband, Andrew, and I got a brand-new car, our first—that is, our first brand-new. It was a Morris Oxford, oyster-colored (the dealer had some fancier name for the color)—a big small car, with plenty of room for us and our two children. Cynthia was six and Meg three and a half.

Andrew took a picture of me standing beside the car. I was wearing white pants, a black turtleneck, and sunglasses. I lounged against the car door, canting my hips to make myself look slim.

"Wonderful," Andrew said. "Great. You look like Jackie Kennedy." All over this continent probably, dark-haired, reasonably slender young women were told, when they were stylishly dressed or getting their pictures taken, that they looked like Jackie Kennedy.

Andrew took a lot of pictures of me, and of the children, our house, our garden, our excursions and possessions. He got copies made, labelled them carefully, and sent them back to his mother and his aunt and uncle in Ontario. He got copies for me to send to my father, who also lived in Ontario, and I did so, but less regularly than he sent his. When he saw pictures he thought I had already sent lying around the house, Andrew was perplexed and annoyed. He liked to have this record go forth.

That summer, we were presenting ourselves, not pictures. We were driving back from Vancouver, where we lived, to Ontario, which we still called "home," in our new car. Five days to get there, ten days there, five days back. For the first time, Andrew had three weeks' holiday. He worked in the legal department at B. C. Hydro.[1]

On a Saturday morning, we loaded suitcases, two thermos bottles—one filled with coffee and one with lemonade—some fruit and sandwiches, picture books and coloring books, crayons, drawing pads, insect repellent, sweaters (in case it got cold in the mountains), and our two children into the car. Andrew locked the house, and Cynthia said ceremoniously, "Goodbye, house."

Meg said, "Goodbye, house." Then she said, "Where will we live now?"

"It's not goodbye forever," said Cynthia. "We're coming back. Mother! Meg thought we weren't ever coming back!"

"I did not," said Meg, kicking the back of my seat.

Andrew and I put on our sunglasses, and we drove away, over the Lions Gate Bridge and through the main part of Vancouver. We shed our house, the neighborhood, the city, and—at the crossing point between Washington and British Columbia—our country. We were driving east across the United States, taking the most northerly route, and would cross into Canada again at Sarnia, Ontario. I don't know if we chose this route because the Trans-Canada Highway was not completely finished at the time or if we just wanted the feeling of driving through a foreign, a very slightly foreign, country—that extra bit of interest and adventure.

We were both in high spirits. Andrew congratulated the car several times. He said he felt so much better driving it than our old car, a 1951 Austin that slowed down dismally on the hills and had a fussy-old-lady image. So Andrew said now.

"What kind of image does this one have?" said Cynthia. She listened to us carefully and liked to try out new words such as *image*. Usually she got them right.

"Lively," I said. "Slightly sporty. It's not show-off."

"It's sensible, but it has class," Andrew said. "Like my image."

Cynthia thought that over and said with a cautious pride, "That means like you think you want to be, Daddy?"

As for me, I was happy because of the shedding. I loved taking off. In my own house, I seemed to be often looking for a place to hide—sometimes from the children but more often from the jobs to be done and the phone ringing and the sociability of the neighborhood. I wanted to hide so that I could get busy at my real work, which was a sort of wooing of distant parts of myself. I lived in a state of siege, always losing just what I wanted to hold on to. But on trips there was no difficulty. I could be talking to Andrew, talking to the children and looking at whatever they wanted me to look at—a pig on a sign, a

1. British Columbia Hydroelectric, public energy utility.

pony in a field, a Volkswagen on a revolving stand—and pouring lemonade into plastic cups, and all the time those bits and pieces would be flying together inside me. The essential composition would be achieved. This made me hopeful and lighthearted. It was being a watcher that did it. A watcher, not a keeper.

We turned east at Everett and climbed into the Cascades. I showed Cynthia our route on the map. First I showed her the map of the whole United States, which showed also the bottom part of Canada. Then I turned to the separate maps of each of the states we were going to pass through. Washington, Idaho, Montana, North Dakota, Minnesota, Wisconsin. I showed her the dotted line across Lake Michigan, which was the route of the ferry we would take. Then we would drive across Michigan to the bridge that linked the United States and Canada at Sarnia, Ontario. Home.

Meg wanted to see too.

"You won't understand," said Cynthia. But she took the road atlas into the back seat.

"Sit back," she said to Meg. "Sit still. I'll show you."

I could hear her tracing the route for Meg, very accurately, just as I had done it for her. She looked up all the states' maps, knowing how to find them in alphabetical order.

"You know what that line is?" she said. "It's the road. That line is the road we're driving on. We're going right along this line."

Meg did not say anything.

"Mother, show me where we are right this minute," said Cynthia.

I took the atlas and pointed out the road through the mountains, and she took it back and showed it to Meg. "See where the road is all wiggly?" she said. "It's wiggly because there are so many turns in it. The wiggles are the turns." She flipped some pages and waited a moment. "Now," she said, "show me where we are." Then she called to me, "Mother, she understands! She pointed to it! Meg understands maps!"

It seems to me now that we invented characters for our children. We had them firmly set to play their parts. Cynthia was bright and diligent, sensitive, courteous, watchful. Sometimes we teased her for being too conscientious, too eager to be what we in fact depended on her to be. Any reproach or failure, any rebuff, went terribly deep with her. She was fair-haired, fair-skinned, easily showing the effects of the sun, raw winds, pride, or humiliation. Meg was more solidly built, more reticent—not rebellious but stubborn sometimes, mysterious. Her silences seemed to us to show her strength of character, and her negatives were taken as signs of an imperturbable independence. Her hair was brown, and we cut it in straight bangs. Her eyes were a light hazel, clear and dazzling.

We were entirely pleased with these characters, enjoying their contradictions as well as the confirmations of them. We disliked the heavy, the uninventive, approach to being parents. I had a dread of turning into a certain kind of mother—the kind whose body sagged, who moved in a woolly-smelling, milky-smelling fog, solemn with trivial burdens. I believed that all the attention these mothers paid, their need to be burdened, was the cause of colic, bed-wetting, asthma. I favored another approach—the mock desperation, the inflated irony of the professional mothers who wrote for magazines. In those magazine pieces, the children were splendidly self-willed, hard-edged, perverse, indomitable. So were the mothers, through their wit, indomitable. The real-life mothers I warmed to were the sort who would phone up and say, "Is my embryo Hitler by any chance over at your house?" They cackled clear above the milky fog.

We saw a dead deer strapped across the front of a pickup truck.

"Somebody shot it," Cynthia said. "Hunters shoot the deer."

"It's not hunting season yet," Andrew said. "They may have hit it on the road. See the sign for deer crossing?"

"I would cry if we hit one," Cynthia said sternly.

I had made peanut-butter-and-marmalade sandwiches for the children and salmon-and-mayonnaise for us. But I had not put any lettuce in, and Andrew was disappointed.

"I didn't have any," I said.

"Couldn't you have got some?"

"I'd have had to buy a whole head of lettuce just to get enough for sandwiches, and I decided it wasn't worth it."

This was a lie. I had forgotten.

"They're a lot better with lettuce."

"I didn't think it made that much difference." After a silence, I said, "Don't be mad."

"I'm not mad. I like lettuce on sandwiches."

"I just didn't think it mattered that much."

"How would it be if I didn't bother to fill up the gas tank?"

"That's not the same thing."

"Sing a song," said Cynthia. She started to sing:

> *"Five little ducks went out one day,*
> *Over the hills and far away.*
> *Our little duck went*
> *'Quack-quack-quack.'*
> *Four little ducks came swimming back."*

Andrew squeezed my hand and said, "Let's not fight."

"You're right. I should have got lettuce."

"It doesn't matter that much."

I wished that I could get my feelings about Andrew to come together into a serviceable and dependable feeling. I had even tried writing two lists, one of things I liked about him, one of things I disliked—in the cauldron of intimate life, things I loved and things I hated—as if I hoped by this to prove something, to come to a conclusion one way or the other. But I gave it up when I saw that all it proved was what I already knew—that I had violent contradictions. Sometimes the very sound of his footsteps seemed to me tyrannical, the set of his mouth smug and mean, his hard, straight body a barrier interposed—quite consciously, even dutifully, and with a nasty pleasure in its masculine authority—between me and whatever joy or lightness I could get in life. Then, with not much warning, he became my good friend and most essential companion. I felt the sweetness of his light bones and serious ideas, the vulnerability of his love, which I imagined to be much purer and more straightforward than my own. I could be greatly moved by an inflexibility, a harsh propriety, that at other times I scorned. I would think how humble he was, really, taking on such a ready-made role of husband, father, breadwinner, and how I myself in comparison was really a secret monster of egotism. Not so secret, either—not from him.

At the bottom of our fights, we served up what we thought were the ugliest truths. "I know there is something basically selfish and basically untrustworthy about you," Andrew once said. "I've always known it. I also know that that is why I fell in love with you."

"Yes," I said, feeling sorrowful but complacent.

"I know that I'd be better off without you."

"Yes. You would."

"You'd be happier without me."

"Yes."

And finally—finally—wracked and purged, we clasped hands and laughed, laughed at those two benighted people, ourselves. Their grudges, their grievances, their self-justification. We leapfrogged over them. We declared them liars. We would have wine with dinner, or decide to give a party.

I haven't seen Andrew for years, don't know if he is still thin, has gone completely gray, insists on lettuce, tells the truth, or is hearty and disappointed.

We stayed the night in Wenatchee, Washington, where it hadn't rained for weeks. We ate dinner in a restaurant built about a tree—not a sapling in a tub but a tall, sturdy cottonwood. In the early-morning light, we climbed out of the irrigated valley, up dry, rocky, very steep hillsides that would seem to lead to more hills, and there on the top was a wide plateau, cut by the great Spokane and Columbia rivers. Grainland and grassland, mile after mile. There were straight roads here, and little farming towns with grain elevators. In fact, there was a sign announcing that this county we were going through, Douglas County, had the second-highest wheat yield of any county in the United States. The towns had planted shade trees. At least, I thought they had been planted, because there were no such big trees in the countryside.

All this was marvellously welcome to me. "Why do I love it so much?" I said to Andrew. "Is it because it isn't scenery?"

"It reminds you of home," said Andrew. "A bout of severe nostalgia." But he said this kindly.

When we said "home" and meant Ontario, we had very different places in mind. My home was a turkey farm, where my father lived as a widower, and though it was the same house my mother had lived in, had papered, painted, cleaned, furnished, it showed the effects now of neglect and of some wild sociability. A life went on in it that my mother could not have predicted or condoned. There were parties for the turkey crew, the gutters and pluckers, and sometimes one or two of the young men would be living there temporarily, inviting their own friends and having their own impromptu parties. This life, I thought, was better for my father than being lonely, and I did not disapprove, had certainly no right to disapprove. Andrew did not like to go there, naturally enough, because he was not the sort who could sit around the kitchen table with the turkey crew, telling jokes. They were intimidated by him and contemptuous of him, and it seemed to me that my father, when they were around, had to be on their side. And it wasn't only Andrew who had trouble. I could manage those jokes, but it was an effort.

I wished for the days when I was little, before we had the turkeys. We had cows, and sold the milk to the cheese factory. A turkey farm is nothing like as pretty as a dairy farm or a sheep farm. You can see that the turkeys are on a straight path to becoming frozen carcasses and table meat. They don't have the pretense of a life of their own, a browsing idyll, that cattle have, or pigs in the dappled orchard. Turkey barns are long, efficient buildings—tin sheds. No beams or hay or warm stables. Even the smell of guano seems thinner and more offensive than the usual smell of stable manure. No hints there of hay coils and rail fences and songbirds and the flowering hawthorn. The turkeys were all let out into one long field, which they picked clean. They didn't look like great birds there but like fluttering laundry.

Once, shortly after my mother died, and after I was married—in fact, I was packing to join Andrew in Vancouver—I was at home alone for a couple of days with my father. There was a freakishly heavy rain all night. In the early light, we saw that the turkey field was flooded. At least, the low-lying parts of it were flooded—it was like a lake with many islands. The turkeys were huddled on these islands. Turkeys are very stupid. (My father would say, "You know a chicken? You know how stupid a chicken is? Well, a chicken is an Einstein compared with a turkey.") But they had managed to crowd to higher ground and avoid drowning. Now they might push each other off, suffocate each other, get cold and die. We couldn't wait for the water to go down. We went out in an old rowboat we had. I rowed and my father pulled the heavy, wet turkeys into the boat and we took them to the barn. It was still raining a little. The job was difficult and absurd and very uncomfortable. We were laughing. I was happy to be working with my father. I felt close to all hard, repetitive, appalling work, in which the body is finally worn out, the mind sunk (though sometimes the spirit can stay marvellously light), and I was homesick in advance for this life and this place. I thought that if Andrew could see me there in the rain, red-handed, muddy, trying to hold on to turkey legs and row the boat at the same time, he would only want to get me out of there and make me forget about it. This raw life angered him. My attachment to it angered him. I thought that I shouldn't have married him. But who else? One of the turkey crew?

And I didn't want to stay there. I might feel bad about leaving, but I would feel worse if somebody made me stay.

Andrew's mother lived in Toronto, in an apartment building looking out on Muir Park. When Andrew and his sister were both at home, his mother slept in the living room. Her husband, a doctor, had died when the children were still too young to go to school. She took a secretarial course and sold her house at Depression prices, moved to this apartment, managed to raise her children, with some help from relatives—her sister Caroline, her brother-in-law Roger. Andrew and his sister went to private schools and to camp in the summer.

"I suppose that was courtesy of the Fresh Air Fund?" I said once, scornful of his claim that he had been poor. To my mind, Andrew's urban life had been sheltered and fussy. His mother came home with a headache from working all day in the noise, the harsh light of a department-store office, but it did not occur to me that hers was a hard or admirable life. I don't think she herself believed that she was admirable—only unlucky. She worried about her work in the office, her clothes, her cooking, her children. She worried most of all about what Roger and Caroline would think.

Caroline and Roger lived on the east side of the park, in a handsome stone house. Roger was a tall man with a bald, freckled head, a fat, firm stomach. Some operation on his throat had deprived him of his voice—he spoke in a rough whisper. But everybody paid attention. At dinner once in the stone house—where all the dining-room furniture was enormous, darkly glowing, palatial—I asked him a question. I think it had to do with Whittaker Chambers, whose story was then appearing in the *Saturday Evening Post*.[2] The question was mild in tone, but he guessed its subversive intent and took to calling me Mrs. Gromyko,[3] referring to what he alleged to be my "sympathies." Perhaps he really craved an adversary, and could not find one. At that dinner, I saw Andrew's hand tremble as he lit his mother's cigarette. His Uncle Roger had paid for Andrew's education, and was on the board of directors of several companies.

"He is just an opinionated old man," Andrew said to me later. "What is the point of arguing with him?"

Before we left Vancouver, Andrew's mother had written, *Roger seems quite intrigued by the idea of your buying a small car!* Her exclamation mark showed apprehension. At that time, particularly in Ontario, the choice of a small European car over a large American car could be seen as some sort of declaration—a declaration of tendencies Roger had been sniffing after all along.

"It isn't that small a car," said Andrew huffily.

"That's not the point," I said. "The point is, it isn't any of his business!"

We spent the second night in Missoula. We had been told in Spokane, at a gas station, that there was a lot of repair work going on along Highway 2, and that we were in for a very hot, dusty drive, with long waits, so we turned onto the interstate and drove through Coeur d'Alene and Kellogg into Montana. After Missoula, we turned south toward Butte, but detoured to see Helena, the state capital. In the car, we played Who Am I?

Cynthia was somebody dead, and an American, and a girl. Possibly a lady. She was not in a story. She had not been seen on television. Cynthia had not read about her in a book. She was not anybody who had come to the kindergarten, or a relative of any of Cynthia's friends.

"Is she human?" said Andrew, with a sudden shrewdness.

"No! That's what you forgot to ask!"

"An animal," I said reflectively.

"Is that a question? Sixteen questions!"

"No, it is not a question. I'm thinking. A dead animal."

"It's the deer," said Meg, who hadn't been playing.

---

2. Illustrated news magazine published weekly from 1821 until 1969. Whittaker Chambers: American journalist and spy (1901–1961), notorious for his 1948 testimony before the House Committee on Un-American Activities, in which he admitted engaging in espionage for the Soviet Union in the 1930s.
3. That is, the wife of Andrei Gromyko (1909–1989), longtime Soviet foreign minister.

"That's not fair!" said Cynthia. "She's not playing!"

"What deer?" said Andrew.

I said, "Yesterday."

"The day before," said Cynthia. "Meg wasn't playing. Nobody got it."

"The deer on the truck," said Andrew.

"It was a lady deer, because it didn't have antlers, and it was an American and it was dead," Cynthia said.

Andrew said, "I think it's kind of morbid, being a dead deer."

"I got it," said Meg.

Cynthia said, "I think I know what morbid is. It's depressing."

Helena, an old silver-mining town, looked forlorn to us even in the morning sunlight. Then Bozeman and Billings, not forlorn in the slightest—energetic, strung-out towns, with miles of blinding tinsel fluttering over used-car lots. We got too tired and hot even to play Who Am I? These busy, prosaic cities reminded me of similar places in Ontario, and I thought about what was really waiting there—the great tombstone furniture of Roger and Caroline's dining room, the dinners for which I must iron the children's dresses and warn them about forks, and then the other table a hundred miles away, the jokes of my father's crew. The pleasures I had been thinking of—looking at the country-side or drinking a Coke in an old-fashioned drugstore with fans and a high, pressed-tin ceiling—would have to be snatched in between.

"Meg's asleep," Cynthia said. "She's so hot. She makes me hot in the same seat with her."

"I hope she isn't feverish," I said, not turning around.

What are we doing this for, I thought, and the answer came—to show off. To give Andrew's mother and my father the pleasure of seeing their grand-children. That was our duty. But beyond that we wanted to show them some-thing. What strenuous children we were, Andrew and I, what relentless seekers of approbation. It was as if at some point we had received an unforgettable, indigestible message—that we were far from satisfactory, and that the most commonplace success in life was probably beyond us. Roger dealt out such messages, of course—that was his style—but Andrew's mother, my own mother and father couldn't have meant to do so. All they meant to tell us was "Watch out. Get along." My father, when I was in high school, teased me that I was getting to think I was so smart I would never find a boyfriend. He would have forgotten that in a week. I never forgot it. Andrew and I didn't forget things. We took umbrage.

"I wish there was a beach," said Cynthia.

"There probably is one," Andrew said. "Right around the next curve."

"There isn't any curve," she said, sounding insulted.

"That's what I mean."

"I wish there was some more lemonade."

"I will just wave my magic wand and produce some," I said. "Okay, Cyn-thia? Would you rather have grape juice? Will I do a beach while I'm at it?"

She was silent, and soon I felt repentant. "Maybe in the next town there might be a pool," I said. I looked at the map. "In Miles City. Anyway, there'll be something cool to drink."

"How far is it?" Andrew said.

"Not so far," I said. "Thirty miles, about."

"In Miles City," said Cynthia, in the tones of an incantation, "there is a beautiful blue swimming pool for children, and a park with lovely trees."

Andrew said to me, "You could have started something."

But there was a pool. There was a park too, though not quite the oasis of Cynthia's fantasy. Prairie trees with thin leaves—cottonwoods and poplars—worn grass, and a high wire fence around the pool. Within this fence, a wall, not yet completed, of cement blocks. There were no shouts or splashes; over the entrance I saw a sign that said the pool was closed every day from noon until two o'clock. It was then twenty-five after twelve.

Nevertheless I called out, "Is anybody there?" I thought somebody must be around, because there was a small truck parked near the entrance. On the side of the truck were these words: *We have Brains, to fix your Drains. (We have Roto-Rooter too.)*

A girl came out, wearing a red lifeguard's shirt over her bathing suit. "Sorry, we're closed."

"We were just driving through," I said.

"We close every day from twelve until two. It's on the sign." She was eating a sandwich.

"I saw the sign," I said. "But this is the first water we've seen for so long, and the children are awfully hot, and I wondered if they could just dip in and out—just five minutes. We'd watch them."

A boy came into sight behind her. He was wearing jeans and a T-shirt with the words *Roto-Rooter* on it.

I was going to say that we were driving from British Columbia to Ontario, but I remembered that Canadian place names usually meant nothing to Americans. "We're driving right across the country," I said. "We haven't time to wait for the pool to open. We were just hoping the children could get cooled off."

Cynthia came running up barefoot behind me. "Mother. Mother, where is my bathing suit?" Then she stopped, sensing the serious adult negotiations. Meg was climbing out of the car—just wakened, with her top pulled up and her shorts pulled down, showing her pink stomach.

"Is it just those two?" the girl said.

"Just the two. We'll watch them."

"I can't let any adults in. If it's just the two, I guess I could watch them. I'm having my lunch." She said to Cynthia, "Do you want to come in the pool?"

"Yes, please," said Cynthia firmly.

Meg looked at the ground.

"Just a short time, because the pool is really closed," I said. "We appreciate this very much," I said to the girl.

"Well, I can eat my lunch out there, if it's just the two of them." She looked toward the car as if she thought I might try to spring some more children on her.

When I found Cynthia's bathing suit, she took it into the changing room. She would not permit anybody, even Meg, to see her naked. I changed Meg, who stood on the front seat of the car. She had a pink cotton bathing suit with straps that crossed and buttoned. There were ruffles across the bottom.

"She *is* hot," I said. "But I don't think she's feverish."

I loved helping Meg to dress or undress, because her body still had the solid unself-consciousness, the sweet indifference, something of the milky smell, of a baby's body. Cynthia's body had long ago been pared down, shaped and altered, into Cynthia. We all liked to hug Meg, press and nuzzle her. Sometimes she would scowl and beat us off, and this forthright independence, this ferocious bashfulness, simply made her more appealing, more apt to be tormented and tickled in the way of family love.

Andrew and I sat in the car with the windows open. I could hear a radio playing, and thought it must belong to the girl or her boyfriend. I was thirsty, and got out of the car to look for a concession stand, or perhaps a soft-drink machine, somewhere in the park. I was wearing shorts, and the backs of my legs were slick with sweat. I saw a drinking fountain at the other side of the park and was walking toward it in a roundabout way, keeping to the shade of the trees. No place became real till you got out of the car. Dazed with the heat, with the sun on the blistered houses, the pavement, the burnt grass, I walked slowly. I paid attention to a squashed leaf, ground a Popsicle stick under the heel of my sandal, squinted at a trash can strapped to a tree. This is the way you look at the poorest details of the world resurfaced, after you've been driving for a long time—you feel their singleness and precise location and the forlorn coincidence of your being there to see them.

Where are the children?

I turned around and moved quickly, not quite running, to a part of the fence beyond which the cement wall was not completed. I could see some of the pool. I saw Cynthia, standing about waist-deep in the water, fluttering her hands on the surface and discreetly watching something at the end of the pool, which I could not see. I thought by her pose, her discretion, the look on her face, that she must be watching some byplay between the lifeguard and her boyfriend. I couldn't see Meg. But I thought she must be playing in the shallow water—both the shallow and deep ends of the pool were out of my sight.

"Cynthia!" I had to call twice before she knew where my voice was coming from. "Cynthia! Where's Meg?"

It always seems to me, when I recall this scene, that Cynthia turns very gracefully toward me, then turns all around in the water—making me think of a ballerina on pointe—and spreads her arms in a gesture of the stage. "Dis-ap-peared!"

Cynthia was naturally graceful, and she did take dancing lessons, so these movements may have been as I have described. She did say "Disappeared" after looking all around the pool, but the strangely artificial style of speech and gesture, the lack of urgency, is more likely my invention. The fear I felt instantly when I couldn't see Meg—even while I was telling myself she must be in the shallower water—must have made Cynthia's movements seem unbearably slow and inappropriate to me, and the tone in which she could say "Disappeared" before the implications struck her (or was she covering, at once, some ever-ready guilt?) was heard by me as quite exquisitely, monstrously self-possessed.

I cried out for Andrew, and the lifeguard came into view. She was pointing toward the deep end of the pool, saying, "What's that?"

There, just within my view, a cluster of pink ruffles appeared, a bouquet, beneath the surface of the water. Why would a lifeguard stop and point, why would she ask what that was, why didn't she just dive into the water and swim to it? She didn't swim; she ran all the way around the edge of the pool. But by that time Andrew was over the fence. So many things seemed not quite plausible—Cynthia's behavior, then the lifeguard's—and now I had the impression that Andrew jumped with one bound over this fence, which seemed about seven feet high. He must have climbed it very quickly, getting a grip on the wire.

I could not jump or climb it, so I ran to the entrance, where there was a sort of lattice gate, locked. It was not very high, and I did pull myself over it. I ran through the cement corridors, through the disinfectant pool for your feet, and came out on the edge of the pool.

The drama was over.

Andrew had got to Meg first, and had pulled her out of the water. He just had to reach over and grab her, because she was swimming somehow, with her head underwater—she was moving toward the edge of the pool. He was carrying her now, and the lifeguard was trotting along behind. Cynthia had climbed out of the water and was running to meet them. The only person aloof from the situation was the boyfriend, who had stayed on the bench at the shallow end, drinking a milkshake. He smiled at me, and I thought that unfeeling of him, even though the danger was past. He may have meant it kindly. I noticed that he had not turned the radio off, just down.

Meg had not swallowed any water. She hadn't even scared herself. Her hair was plastered to her head and her eyes were wide open, golden with amazement.

"I was getting the comb," she said. "I didn't know it was deep."

Andrew said, "She was swimming! She was swimming by herself. I saw her bathing suit in the water and then I saw her swimming."

"She nearly drowned," Cynthia said. "Didn't she? Meg nearly drowned."

"I don't know how it could have happened," said the lifeguard. "One moment she was there, and the next she wasn't."

What had happened was that Meg had climbed out of the water at the shallow end and run along the edge of the pool toward the deep end. She saw a comb that somebody had dropped lying on the bottom. She crouched down and reached in to pick it up, quite deceived about the depth of the water. She went over the edge and slipped into the pool, making such a light splash that nobody heard—not the lifeguard, who was kissing her boyfriend, or Cynthia, who was watching them. That must have been the moment under the trees when I thought, Where are the children? It must have been the same moment. At that moment, Meg was slipping, surprised, into the treacherously clear blue water.

"It's okay," I said to the lifeguard, who was nearly crying. "She can move pretty fast." (Though that wasn't what we usually said about Meg at all. We said she thought everything over and took her time.)

"You swam, Meg," said Cynthia, in a congratulatory way. (She told us about the kissing later.)

"I didn't know it was deep," Meg said. "I didn't drown."

We had lunch at a takeout place, eating hamburgers and fries at a picnic table not far from the highway. In my excitement, I forgot to get Meg a plain hamburger, and had to scrape off the relish and mustard with plastic spoons, then wipe the meat with a paper napkin, before she would eat it. I took advantage of the trash can there to clean out the car. Then we resumed driving east, with the car windows open in front. Cynthia and Meg fell asleep in the back seat.

Andrew and I talked quietly about what had happened. Suppose I hadn't had the impulse just at that moment to check on the children? Suppose we had gone uptown to get drinks, as we had thought of doing? How had Andrew got over the fence? Did he jump or climb? (He couldn't remember.) How had he reached Meg so quickly? And think of the lifeguard not watching. And Cynthia, taken up with the kissing. Not seeing anything else. Not seeing Meg drop over the edge.

Disappeared.

But she swam. She held her breath and came up swimming.

What a chain of lucky links.

That was all we spoke about—luck. But I was compelled to picture the opposite. At this moment, we could have been filling out forms. Meg removed from us, Meg's body being prepared for shipment. To Vancouver—where we had never noticed such a thing as a graveyard—or to Ontario? The scribbled drawings she had made this morning would still be in the back seat of the car. How could this be borne all at once, how did people bear it? The plump, sweet shoulders and hands and feet, the fine brown hair, the rather satisfied, secretive expression—all exactly the same as when she had been alive. The most ordinary tragedy. A child drowned in a swimming pool at noon on a sunny day. Things tidied up quickly. The pool opens as usual at two o'clock. The lifeguard is a bit shaken up and gets the afternoon off. She drives away with her boyfriend in the Roto-Rooter truck. The body sealed away in some kind of shipping coffin. Sedatives, phone calls, arrangements. Such a sudden vacancy, a blind sinking and shifting. Waking up groggy from the pills, thinking for a moment it wasn't true. Thinking if only we hadn't stopped, if only we hadn't taken this route, if only they hadn't let us use the pool. Probably no one would ever have known about the comb.

There's something trashy about this kind of imagining, isn't there? Something shameful. Laying your finger on the wire to get the safe shock, feeling a bit of what it's like, then pulling back. I believed that Andrew was more scrupulous than I about such things, and that at this moment he was really trying to think about something else.

When I stood apart from my parents at Steve Gauley's funeral and watched them, and had this new, unpleasant feeling about them, I thought that I was understanding something about them for the first time. It was a deadly serious thing. I was understanding that they were implicated. Their big, stiff, dressed-up bodies did not stand between me and sudden death, or any kind of death. They gave consent. So it seemed. They gave consent to the death of children and to my death not by anything they said or thought but by the very fact that they had made children—they had made me. They had made me, and for that reason my death—however grieved they were, however they carried on—would seem to them anything but impossible or unnatural. This was a fact, and even then I knew they were not to blame.

But I did blame them. I charged them with effrontery, hypocrisy. On Steve Gauley's behalf, and on behalf of all children, who knew that by rights they should have sprung up free, to live a new, superior kind of life, not to be caught in the snares of vanquished grownups, with their sex and funerals.

Steve Gauley drowned, people said, because he was next thing to an orphan and was let run free. If he had been warned enough and given chores to do and kept in check, he wouldn't have fallen from an untrustworthy tree branch into a spring pond, a full gravel pit near the river—he wouldn't have drowned. He was neglected, he was free, so he drowned. And his father took it as an accident, such as might happen to a dog. He didn't have a good suit for the funeral, and he didn't bow his head for the prayers. But he was the only grownup that I let off the hook. He was the only one I didn't see giving consent. He couldn't prevent anything, but he wasn't implicated in anything, either—not like the others, saying the Lord's Prayer in their unnaturally weighted voices, oozing religion and dishonor.

At Glendive, not far from the North Dakota border, we had a choice—either to continue on the interstate or head northeast, toward Williston, taking Route 16, then some secondary roads that would get us back to Highway 2.

We agreed that the interstate would be faster, and that it was important for us not to spend too much time—that is, money—on the road. Nevertheless we decided to cut back to Highway 2.

"I just like the idea of it better," I said.

Andrew said, "That's because it's what we planned to do in the beginning."

"We missed seeing Kalispell and Havre. And Wolf Point. I like the name."

"We'll see them on the way back."

Andrew's saying "on the way back" was a surprising pleasure to me. Of course, I had believed that we would be coming back, with our car and our lives and our family intact, having covered all that distance, having dealt somehow with those loyalties and problems, held ourselves up for inspection in such a foolhardy way. But it was a relief to hear him say it.

"What I can't get over," said Andrew, "is how you got the signal. It's got to be some kind of extra sense that mothers have."

Partly I wanted to believe that, to bask in my extra sense. Partly I wanted to warn him—to warn everybody—never to count on it.

"What I can't understand," I said, "is how you got over the fence."

"Neither can I."

So we went on, with the two in the back seat trusting us, because of no choice, and we ourselves trusting to be forgiven, in time, for everything that had first to be seen and condemned by those children: whatever was flippant, arbitrary, careless, callous—all our natural, and particular, mistakes.

1985

RELATED:

—Author in Depth: Alice Munro, p. 1812

SABINA MURRAY
b. 1968

Daughter of a Filipina mother and a Bostonian father, Murray grew up in Australia and the Philippines before continuing her education in the United States, at Mount Holyoke College. Her first novel, *Slow Burn* (1990), was accepted for publication when she was only twenty years old, even before she earned her M.F.A. degree at the University of Texas and a Radcliffe Fellowship at Harvard. In her collection of stories, *The Caprices* (2002), winner of the PEN/Faulkner Award for Fiction, she depicts the ravages of World War II in Asia and the Pacific. More recently Murray has written a screenplay, *The Beautiful Country* (2004), and a second novel, *A Carnivore's Inquiry* (2004). Her most recent story collection, *Tales of the New World*, was published in 2010. An immensely talented story writer with an audacious, wayfaring imagination, she is currently a member of the M.F.A. faculty at the University of Massachusetts at Amherst.

Position

In March of 1521, Magellan sights the islands. At first, his hands clawed around a telescope, he thinks Saipan[1] to be a sleeping monster. Who else would inhabit this liquid hell where no breeze blows? The crew is starving, eating leather straps and sawdust, hunting rats through the dark, rotting carcass of the ship. They have survived fourteen months of hardship and a mutiny; here, on this sheet of glass that Magellan has called "Mar Pacifico," they fear that they will meet their maker, or the devil himself. The crew has wondered at Magellan's defiant health. They call him "Spawn of Satan" and point to his clubfoot as proof. For someone whose progress on land is slow and labored, Magellan has no equal on the water. He lowers his telescope and blinks, then raises the telescope to the horizon again. The pope has divided the earth in two. The East has been given to the Portuguese, the West to the Spaniards, and he, a Portuguese, is sailing in the name of Spain. He will learn that the West never stops, keeps winding round and round, and the earth belongs to whoever is strong enough to take it.

Magellan's ships, the *Trinidad* and the *Victoria*, draw closer to Saipan.

---

1. Small island north of Guam in the Mariana Islands of the western Pacific Ocean. Magellan: Ferdinand Magellan (c. 1480–1521), Portuguese navigator and explorer. In the midst of the first circumnavigation of the earth, Magellan was killed in the Philippines, days after his discovery of Saipan.

In the distance, Magellan can make out flat white planes—triangles—shifting across the surface of the water. Could this be the sun refracting, coursing to the left, then right, drawing closer then angling quickly away? Could this be his mind, at last succumbing to his strange diet of leather and rat meat? Maybe these shifting sheets are from the past, a pleasant image heralding his death, because these are sails and the darting movements are boats gliding over the glassy surface of the sea. Sails. As a youth he had owned a small skiff. At the edge of the world, has he encountered the past? Has he wound back to 1495, when, as a youth, boats had been a joy and diversion?

The men are loud, spirited. Their joyful shouting is a strange sound. They have been silent for so long. Magellan is not being lured into the past, nor is he hallucinating. They have reached land and the sails belong to the fishing boats of Chamorro natives.[2] Magellan closes his eyes, confident that when he opens them again he will see his sleeping monsters revealed as islands. Soon he will be navigating his way into the shallows, looking for a place to anchor.

Despite the welcome relief of food and water, there is not much to recommend Saipan. Even the Chamorros are supposed to have been stranded there on a canoe trip from Indonesia, their landing an accident of poor navigation, their decision to remain a mystery. Magellan names the islands "Islas de las Velas Latinas"[3] because of the triangular shape of the Chamorro sails. Magellan registers Saipan in history, much as three billion years earlier, the island registered itself on the surface of the Pacific.

In the seventeenth century the islands are renamed the Marianas after an Austrian princess. The native population is all but wiped out by the Spaniards. Beyond this naming and slaying, there is nothing remarkable about the Spanish occupation of Saipan. In 1899, Spain, facing bankruptcy, sells the Marianas to Germany for four and a half million dollars. The Germans are getting a bargain. They see the value of these desolate islands strung across the Pacific, hard pebbles scrubbed by salt waves. Guam. Tinian.[4] And Saipan. Isolated. Ignored. Saipan's very value is that it is nowhere. Saipan interrupts. It is not the Pacific.

There is much use for something that is Not The Pacific.

Saipan is an island of foreign aggressors, warriors wanting something better, a refueling stop on the way to what is worthy of conquering. The Germans show their hand in the Great War and, after years of battering Europe, lose Saipan (a slap on the wrist), and before Saipan can be allocated to some other deserving European, Japan has claimed it. Japan, the gnat, the least worthy member of the League of Nations, is also looking to conquer. The Meiji Diet[5] has its eyes fixed on China. As a result, in the early years of the twentieth century Saipan is outfitted with a sugar refinery and a fishing fleet staffed with Japanese and Korean labor. These two industries support a significant civilian population. Sharp spears of sugar cane bristle on the island's back and the natives are armed with nothing more than the broad blades of industry. The fish bubble up from the depths and are netted. Women bear children. Tidy huts are erected beneath the shade of palms bordering the sandy, swept grid of streets.

---

2. People of the Mariana Islands.　3. That is, "Islands of the Lateen Sails" (Spanish).　4. Island close to Saipan in the Marianas.　5. Japanese parliament during the reign of Emperor Mutsuhito Meiji and his successors, beginning in 1868.

In the late thirties, Japan refuses America access to the Marianas. A fortress like none that has ever been known is being constructed. One forward-thinking Japanese writer, Kinoaki Matsuo, writes, "The islands are scattered like stars across the routes of the United States Navy either perpendicularly or horizontally. It will be impossible for the U.S. Fleet to reach her destination." One thousand islands scattered like beads across the Pacific combine to create a fortress calculated to stymie the American fleet. But what is the assumed origin of the U.S. Navy? What is the destination that will lure its shining ships through this net?

What is Japan planning?

On the first of June, 1937, Amelia Earhart[6] and her navigator, Fredrick Noonan, take off from Miami, the first of many departures on their epic journey. Earhart is to be the first woman to circumnavigate the globe, the first aviator to do so at the earth's waist. Their plane is a modified Lockheed Electra 10E. The airplane has recently been rebuilt after a botched landing on Luke Field near Pearl Harbor during her first attempt at the globe. This is an omen. Earhart has now decided to go east rather than west. She feels the need to make the trip, but admits that she hopes it is her last journey. She refers to the circumnavigation as a "stunt." Her husband, the publisher George Palmer Putnam, is priming his great printing machines for the journey's completion and has arranged for his wife to write a series of articles for the *Herald Tribune* to be cabled from her various destinations. Earhart perseveres. She breaks a record: first aviator to fly from the Red Sea to India. She plows on. Rangoon. Bangkok. Singapore. Bandoeng.[7] In Bandoeng, she is forced to her bed as a result of dysentery contracted in India. She lies for days sweating, exhausted. On June 27, Earhart rises from her bed. She slides her feet into her stout moccasins, rakes her hands through her hair. The mirror reveals her as a middle-aged woman in need of a vacation, not the stout-willed aviatrix she has come to rely on. Her jacket weighs heavily on her shoulders.

In Darwin she carefully packs the parachutes to be sent back to the United States. She wryly remarks to Noonan that they will be no use over the Pacific. Noonan agrees. They need more room for fuel. Coordinates of the Pacific Islands are not reliable, nor is the weather, worrisome for Noonan. He has been groping through the skies using celestial navigation. Cloud cover confuses and extra fuel is necessary to right mistakes. Noonan announces this loudly, which amuses Earhart. She knows what the extra fuel is for, what the secondary purpose of their journey is. The Electra screams off the runway bound for Lae, New Guinea.

On Lae, Earhart writes her last article for the *Herald Tribune*. Pictures taken show her to be sickly and tired. These glossy pictures will be bound within *Last Flight,* the rotted pit at the heart of the book. The stage is set for the ill-fated leg of the journey. She has traveled twenty-two thousand miles and has seven thousand left to complete the circumnavigation. Her destination is Howland Island, a speck in the ocean, with an elevation of less than ten feet. The Coast Guard cutter *Itasca* is positioned off Howland Island to act as radio contact. Radio communications in the area are poor and the *Itasca* has been

---

6. American aviator (1897–1937).   **7.** City in western Java, Indonesia.

flooded with commercial radio traffic connected with the record-breaking aviatrix. At 00:00 Greenwich Mean Time, the Electra soars upward.

Earhart is cruising northward of her accepted coordinates. She has arranged with American intelligence to swing over Truk, an island on the eastern end of the Caroline chain. Reports submitted to the League of Nations reveal unprecedented supply deliveries to this desolate rock and the American navy is suspicious. What is Japan doing? Earhart plows on into unfriendly territory. She picks up her radio and nervously transmits her coordinates, which are far to the east of her true location. This is to confuse the Japanese, listening in, from knowing her true purpose. Where is she flying in the deepest night? Where does the sea separate from the sky? Where is the comfort of the line of horizon?

Aviator. Wife. Writer. Woman. Does she need also to be a spy? A soldier of intelligence? Earhart is no stranger to war. She has seen its work. She has nursed boys lying on their cots, watched new blood pumped back into thirsting veins, seen the elbows heal into smooth nubs. She has observed the boys in their wheelchairs learning to navigate the hospital corridors, trying to find their way home. Earhart knows that after conflict, there is no true restoration.

At 19:30 the *Itasca* receives a transmission: "KHAQQ calling *Itasca*. We must be on you but cannot see you . . . Gas is running low . . ."

And then at 20:14: "We are on a line of position 157 degrees–337 degrees—we will repeat this message on 6210 kilocycles, wait listening on 6210 kilocycles—we are running north and south." Which puts the Electra approaching Howland from a northeasterly direction. Lae, New Guinea, lies in the southeast.

This is the last world will hear from Earhart.

For sixteen days eight U.S. Navy ships and sixty-four aircraft comb 138,000 square miles of the Pacific at a cost of four million dollars. Nothing of the aircraft or of the pilot and navigator is ever found.

Saipan has a new resident.

Pia is ten years old when the American woman appears on the island. Pia thinks that she does not look dangerous, limping, her blunt short hair illumined around the edges by the sun. The woman has no shoes and her feet are long and narrow, not like any feet Pia has ever seen. They are white like polished stone. The woman walks between two soldiers, defeated. Pia hurries to catch up with the woman. She walks a cautious distance away, parallel with the party's advance, whistling at the birds in the trees, her interest suddenly caught by the barking of a dog. But always watching the woman. The woman stops. She squats down and takes deep breaths. Her face is gray, not like a living person's. She says something softly to the guards, then to Pia's surprise, waves her over. Pia cautiously walks across the street.

She is scared of this woman. Why is she here? Why are the soldiers guarding her?

The woman smiles, but she is in pain. Pia approaches, and then she sees the burns, flaking blackened skin, the whole left side of the woman's face puffed with fluid. There are bubbling blisters all down the woman's left arm. Pia thinks that she is two women sewn together up the middle—one wiry and hard like the bark of a tree, the other slippery and scaly like a fish. She is scared. The woman has something in her hand that she is holding out to Pia. She nods her head, offering, offering, but the child is scared. She presents the woman with her round face, baked brown like bread. Her hair hangs heavily at her shoulders. There is something defiant to the set of her mouth.

Can she read? Earhart wonders. Does she work in the fields? Does she have toys or brothers or a dog, like some of these thin animals tied to the stilts of the houses? The ring came easily off her finger—a gift from her husband, but she has no use for rings, or fingers for that matter. In the instant that the plane plunged into the flat blue sea, she admitted her life was over and now does not know how to think of these days that are left. She knows that her wounds are infected. She knows that her dysentery is dissolving her strength. She knows that the tea and unguents that she has been given are inadequate to restore life. She holds the ring out to the child, wisely turning her head to present the half that was not burned in the crash. The child steps forward and then hustles quickly the final steps. She takes the ring—a platinum setting with a perfect pearl, round like the earth—off Earhart's hand, hopping back to a safe distance. The child smiles, looks up at the guards, who are very serious but young and familiar. The child stammers out a few words in Japanese and the soldiers respond, but the child is not satisfied with the answer. Her thick brows come together and finally she says, *"Gracias,"* with the intonation of a question.

The American woman smiles and says, *"De nada."*[8]

From her final room Earhart can see workers dismantling the remains of the Electra. She sighs heavily. Her days, drifting in and out of consciousness, are spent trying to relay psychic messages through the radio lines. She imagines the radioman on the *Itasca* picking up the signal.

"It's Earhart. These coordinates . . . She's on Saipan. She says the Japanese are geared for war. Truk is plated with armor, fitted with guns. Prepare. Prepare . . ."

And then they lose the signal as Earhart drifts out of range.

On December 7, 1941, the Japanese bomb the American fleet where it bobs innocently in Pearl Harbor. In this action the pride of the American navy is destroyed, the remaining ships mobilized—tempted—through the string of islands. The Japanese army is suddenly everywhere. One by one the nations fall. Indonesia. Malaysia. Singapore. The Philippines. The Co-Prosperity Sphere[9] widens, a stain tingeing the Pacific a brilliant red. Saipan now boasts troops, guns, and battleships bobbing off the coast. The civilians pack their things into rattan bags, boxes, waiting calmly for the ships that will bear them to Japan. But as the war progresses, an element of fear enters the island. The Americans, once thought to be pathetic, harmless, are now a threat. The soldiers, battle hardened and exposed, tell tales of murder, cannibalism, and rape. Mothers hold tightly to their children's wrists, waiting to be delivered from the island, combing the horizon for the transport ship. Here on Saipan they are served up to the enemy. They sharpen bamboo spears. Machetes, once

---

8. You're welcome (Spanish). **9.** "Greater East Asia Co-Prosperity Sphere," zone of Japanese military and economic domination declared in 1940.

used for harvesting sugar cane, are drawn across whetstones. The song of blade and stone is heard in every house.

On June 15, 1944, American forces begin the scheduled destruction of Saipan. There are 535 ships assembled in the harbor. B-29s divide the skies, dropping bomb after bomb. The sugar refinery bursts in an explosion. Twisted steel and burning beams heat the ground. Cars are blown upward like paper ornaments. The streets are silenced in a massive boom. When the cloud of dust settles, huge craters where once houses stood are revealed. The chaos of finding children, finding husbands and wives, tallying the dead, continues late into the night. Carrying food, children, knives, the peasants move northward. There is a warren of caves carved into the rock. The Japanese army has already established itself here. Let not the mistakes of Peleliu[1] be repeated. Give the American monsters the beach. Make them crawl the slope of rubble and debris, over fallen men—both American and Japanese—to the dark mouths of the caves. Slay them at the threshold of the redoubt.

General Saito patiently waits for reinforcement from the air. A plane can fly from Japan to Saipan and back. It is safe bombing distance. This is why the American victory here will be the end of the war. But the runways of Japan are quiet, the planes funneled elsewhere or stilled at the bottom of the sea. The Japanese pilots who are not already dead are not of the warrior class. They are humanities students from the university, teenagers, scientists, whose flying skills allow them only one final flight. They are the "Divine Wind,"[2] which Saito wryly notes will not blow his way anytime soon.

Bushido. Bushido. The code of the warrior. Never be taken prisoner. Never shame the emperor. Saito looks with pride at the civilians camped around him, their hands poised at the base of a spear. The children collect rocks and arrange them in pyramids. They too will fight to the death. All warriors. All of them. His chest is fired with pride for these simple people and their love of the emperor. He sees in their faces the willingness to die. His words of inspiration come not from hope, but from his faith that all these people—soldiers, farmers, fishermen, mothers, sons, and daughters—are willing to die without the stain of shame. He says, "Our battle is not over. Soon, we will all have the glorious honor of dying for our emperor. Let this not be a wasted death. For each of you, kill seven of the enemy. Kill seven."

Why seven? Why this number? Does the mystic count inspire? Saito wonders as he retires to the inner room of his redoubt. He wraps the ceremonial banner around his head and, taking the dagger in both hands, boldly restores his honor even though he knows he has failed the emperor.

In Tokyo, they receive his final message: "We deeply apologize to the emperor that we cannot do better."

The man is screaming, but all that McGill can think of is the man's femur protruding from his leg, the tip of the broken bone sharpened and splintered. This bone looks like a shoot pushing through earth, something you would find on the farm, something the fertile Missouri soil would will into being.

---

1. Beliliou, island in the western Pacific, scene of fierce fighting between American and Japanese forces in 1944.   2. Literal translation of *kamikaze* (Japanese), Japanese pilots assigned to make suicide attacks on American targets during World War II.

I must help this man, thinks McGill. He wishes he could fix the bone, press it back into the man's flesh, set him up and tell him to walk back to the beach. Clearly, this soldier lying on the ground and screaming has not had a good morning. He deserves rest and maybe a stiff drink. McGill kneels by his head. The soldier pulls in breath quickly, McGill shouts in his ear, "I'm going to help you," he says. The man's eyes are wide and crazy. McGill has never seen so much of the whites of someone's eyes before. McGill says, "I'm going to end the war." He relieves the fallen man of his grenades, then scuttles past on his belly. Two men are lying dead in front of him. One is Japanese, his right hand in a death grip around a wooden club. Caveman, thinks McGill. It's funny. He shelters himself behind these two men. He takes a grenade. He remembers the first time he threw a grenade. His sergeant was holding the collar of his shirt and the seat of his pants. Pull the pin and lob it. Keep your eyes on the target. Why was the sergeant holding him like that? Should the sergeant be holding him now? McGill lobs the grenade. There is a satisfying blast. Fireworks. McGill moves forward. Why? Did the grenade accomplish something? He doesn't know. He hopes he didn't blow up another marine. Everyone tells him he's good at what he does. He's a good marine. People are proud of him. Why? Maybe because he hasn't had his legs blown up. That would be bad. That would make him a bad marine. He crawls over more bodies. He looks up. There's a child in the middle of the battlefield. Why? Maybe this child is an angel. Are there Japanese angels? The child's face is streaked with tears. The child is holding a rock. Why? The child throws the rock at McGill. The rock falls just short of where he is lying. McGill doesn't know what to do. Does he grab the child and take him back behind the line of fire? That would seem right.

"Come here," he says, waving the child over. Bombs and grenades are exploding all over the place. There is the whistle of missiles, the stutter of guns. The child cannot hear him. "Come here," McGill shouts. The child screams in fear. The child is bawling now. He runs away. McGill gets up on his knees, trying to see where he's gone. There is dust everywhere—a dense cloud. There is smoke. It smells like a barbecue. No child.

And now McGill can hear loudspeakers, Japanese. And something else. More words. Some are Spanish, he knows that. Must be Chamorro. What are they saying? And now English. "There is no shame in surrender. We will not harm you. We will bring you back to Japan. Please do not be afraid." Who will they bring back to Japan? Who are they talking to? McGill remembers the child. How do they know about the little boy? McGill feels better. They will find the boy and take him back to Japan.

McGill is moving on to Marpi Point. Marpi Point, he figures, is about two hundred meters away. He should be there in an hour and a half, if he progresses at a good clip. The bodies slow him down. Some of the Japanese men are not in uniform. Some are not wearing shoes. Is it casual dress for the defense of Saipan? McGill's leg has caught on something. He shakes it a couple of times, but does not manage to free it. He looks over his shoulder. Eye to eye with a Japanese. Casual dress. The man is trying to bite his leg. Funny. McGill hauls his knee up and throws a kick right into the man's teeth. Where is Marpi Point? It can't be that far off.

He hears an American yelling, "No. Don't jump. Don't jump." The loudspeakers are louder here. McGill pops up and sees the point. He knows that just past his line of vision is a cliff, a sheer drop to the Pacific and the rocks below. Civilians are crowded here together. They are surrendering. Maybe Saipan's taken. Maybe McGill can go back to his ship. He needs a shower. His clothes are sticking to him as the blood dries. His hair has caked into clumps. Whose blood? He stands on shuddering knees (he's been crawling a long time) and hustles to a rock, maybe six feet. He leans against it and looks back at the field of bodies he has just traveled. Amazing. No one back home will believe him. A grenade explodes twenty feet to his right and the ground quakes. He inches around to the other side of the rock.

Families. Mothers with children. Fathers. The war is over, thinks McGill. Go home. And they go, not running, but stepping over the edge of the cliff. A mother holds her fat baby and buries her face in the snug skin of the baby's neck. That's nice, thinks McGill. Then she jumps. Over the cliff. But they're all doing that. All jumping. An old man raises his hands in protest. Maybe he knows more, but there's a Jap soldier there with his bayonet—no more bullets. He urges the old man to jump too. And he does. McGill crawls forward on his stomach to where the land begins to drop. There is a shattered stump of palm. McGill hides behind it. Here he can no longer see the people jumping, but he can see the water. There's that yelling again, "Don't jump. Oh God. Please don't jump." And the loudspeakers. Japanese. On the rocks there are bodies. Children float face down in the sea. A baby is crying somewhere, but McGill can't see it. The wailing stops and McGill strains his ears hoping to find that beautiful desperate crying again. On the rock is a woman combing her long black hair. Mermaid. Weird. She slips off the rock into the water. She disappears. More people jump. McGill can't hear them hit the water because he can't hear anymore. Something about that baby. He shakes his head. No sound. Just people falling, streaking by, their shadows briefly on the water—a hole—then into the hole the girls and babies fall. And then nothing. The ground is shaking beneath his feet from the pounding mortar. He can feel that shaking. He can feel that.

On July 19, U.S. marines invade Guam and on July 24 invade Tinian. The American capture of the Marianas is completed on August 8, 1944. And what of the Marianas? What now? Tinian is the stage for the end of the war.

The date is August 6, 1945. Colonel Tibbets is the pilot. The plane is the *Enola Gay*, named after Tibbets's mother. The bomb is Little Boy, nestled deep in her belly. At 2:45 A.M. the B-29 Super-fortress roars up the runway. The plane is freed from the earth ascending at a steep rate, climbing higher and higher, flying to that height at which the earth reveals itself to be points, coordinates, gray elevations, and glossy blue depths. From this great height, who can see man? Who can remember what it is to navigate the streets in the early morning, to cook breakfast, to dress one's children? Who can hear the broom sweeping the front doorstep or the woman in the next room brushing her hair? Who can hear the crack of eggs against the side of the pan, the sputter of oil?

On the streets of Hiroshima people are moving. Moving. Moving. Packing their belongings onto handcarts, and the wheels sing out on the streets. They are secreting their most precious belongings away from the bombs. They are listening for the sirens, which howl, then are silenced, then howl again. They are walking their children to the parade ground and then home. They are tearing down houses, plank by plank, to clear fire lanes should the bombing come to peaceful Hiroshima. They are bundling letters of dead husbands, departed sons. They are bundling letters from the Japanese army that say "Akihiro died an honorable death in Singapore," or Guadalcanal or Manchuria or Burma. Mothers are wrapping babies in padded clothing despite the heat, because they must do something to protect their children. Mothers are yelling at their children to stop playing in the street when there is supposed to be an air raid—the biggest yet. What sound reaches the pilots and crew?

Who does not want the war to end? Does Hirohito[3] wish to spend another spring as prisoner of his generals? Do the generals wish to keep fighting? No. They only want to win. How many more must die? What can be done?

Let us all put down our weapons.

At the count of three, we will all put down our weapons. Everyone is listening. The *Enola Gay* roars over Hiroshima.

"On glasses," says Tibbets.

And the bombardier, Major Ferebree, takes his position in the plexiglass nose of the aircraft. He fixes the Aioi Bridge in his cross-wires and locks his bombsight. Now it is automatic. In fifteen seconds the bomb bay doors will open and the glowing uranium egg—the sun's surface contained in a steel shell—will drop to earth.

At the count of fifteen, we will all put down our weapons. There's nothing left but to count. And we start. But it is already fourteen seconds. No, twelve. We must all put down our weapons. Ten. The bomb bay doors will open. Seven. We must all put down our weapons. It is time to stop. We are all ready to stop. At the count of three, we will all put down our weapons.

2002

---

3. Emperor of Japan (1901–1989).

VLADIMIR NABOKOV
1899–1977

Nabokov was born in St. Petersburg, Russia, to rich and cultured parents who spoke Russian, French, and English—"a typical trilingual upbringing," as he would later recall. At the time of the Communist revolution, he fled with his family into Western Europe. He attended Cambridge University in England and took a degree in modern languages there in 1923. Thereafter, he spent years in Berlin and Paris, supporting himself by coaching tennis and making up chess problems, all the while writing novels in Russian and English. Living in France when it was overrun by the Nazis, he escaped with his family to the United States, where he became a citizen and—by a remarkable imaginative transformation—an American writer, beginning with *The Real Life of Sebastian Knight* (1941). He taught Russian and comparative literature at Cornell University until *Lolita* (a best seller in 1955) and subsequent novels gave him enough money to allow him a full-time commitment to writing and his other eminent career: Nabokov was also a world-renowned lepidopterist, a scientist of moths and butterflies. He lived the last twenty years of his life in Montreux, Switzerland. His complete works in all languages would run to thirty or forty volumes, exemplifying the complexity of his life and his interests in language and experience. In most of his fiction, memories of a dissolving past mingle with an ironic sense of a precarious present. Among his many novels are *Laughter in the Dark* (self-translated in 1938), *Lolita* (1955), *Pnin* (1957), *Pale Fire* (1962), and *Ada* (1969). His collected poems and chess problems were published in 1971; *The Stories of Vladimir Nabokov* was published in 1995.

Signs and Symbols

I

For the fourth time in as many years they were confronted with the problem of what birthday present to bring a young man who was incurably deranged in his mind. He had no desires. Man-made objects were to him either hives of evil, vibrant with a malignant activity that he alone could perceive, or gross comforts for which no use could be found in his abstract world. After eliminating a number of articles that might offend him or frighten him (anything in the gadget line for instance was taboo), his parents chose a dainty and innocent trifle: a basket with ten different fruit jellies in ten little jars.

At the time of his birth they had been married already for a long time; a score of years had elapsed, and now they were quite old. Her drab gray hair was done anyhow. She wore cheap black dresses. Unlike other women of her age (such as Mrs. Sol, their next-door neighbor, whose face was all pink and mauve with paint and whose hat was a cluster of brookside flowers), she presented a naked white countenance to the fault-finding light of spring days. Her husband, who in the old country had been a fairly successful businessman, was now wholly dependent on his brother Isaac, a real American of almost forty years standing. They seldom saw him and had nicknamed him "the Prince."

That Friday everything went wrong. The underground train lost its life current between two stations, and for a quarter of an hour one could hear nothing but the dutiful beating of one's heart and the rustling of newspapers. The bus they had to take next kept them waiting for ages; and when it did come, it was crammed with garrulous high-school children. It was raining hard as they walked up the brown path leading to the sanitarium. There they waited again; and instead of their boy shuffling into the room as he usually did (his poor face blotched with acne, ill-shaven, sullen, and confused), a nurse they knew, and did not care for, appeared at last and brightly explained that he had again attempted to take his life. He was all right, she said, but a visit might disturb him. The place was so miserably understaffed, and things got mislaid or mixed up so easily, that they decided not to leave their present in the office but to bring it to him next time they came.

She waited for her husband to open his umbrella and then took his arm. He kept clearing his throat in a special resonant way he had when he was upset. They reached the bus-stop shelter on the other side of the street and he closed his umbrella. A few feet away, under a swaying and dripping tree, a tiny half-dead unfledged bird was helplessly twitching in a puddle.

During the long ride to the subway station, she and her husband did not exchange a word; and every time she glanced at his old hands (swollen veins, brown-spotted skin), clasped and twitching upon the handle of his umbrella, she felt the mounting pressure of tears. As she looked around trying to hook her mind onto something, it gave her a kind of soft shock, a mixture of compassion and wonder, to notice that one of the passengers, a girl with dark hair and grubby red toenails, was weeping on the shoulder of an older woman. Whom did that woman resemble? She resembled Rebecca Borisovna, whose daughter had married one of the Soloveichiks—in Minsk,[1] years ago.

The last time he had tried to do it, his method had been, in the doctor's words, a masterpiece of inventiveness; he would have succeeded, had not an envious fellow patient thought he was learning to fly—and stopped him. What he really wanted to do was to tear a hole in his world and escape.

The system of his delusions had been the subject of an elaborate paper in a scientific monthly, but long before that she and her husband had puzzled it out for themselves. "Referential mania," Herman Brink had called it. In these very rare cases the patient imagines that everything happening around him is a veiled reference to his personality and existence. He excludes real people from the conspiracy—because he considers himself to be so much more intelligent than other men. Phenomenal nature shadows him wherever he goes. Clouds in the staring sky transmit to one another, by means of slow signs,

---

1. A city in western Russia.

incredibly detailed information regarding him. His inmost thoughts are discussed at nightfall, in manual alphabet,[2] by darkly gesticulating trees. Pebbles or stains or sun flecks form patterns representing in some awful way messages which he must intercept. Everything is a cipher and of everything he is the theme. Some of the spies are detached observers, such as glass surfaces and still pools; others, such as coats in store windows, are prejudiced witnesses, lynchers at heart; others again (running water, storms) are hysterical to the point of insanity, have a distorted opinion of him and grotesquely misinterpret his actions. He must be always on his guard and devote every minute and module of life to the decoding of the undulation of things. The very air he exhales is indexed and filed away. If only the interest he provokes were limited to his immediate surroundings—but alas it is not! With distance the torrents of wild scandal increase in volume and volubility. The silhouettes of his blood corpuscles, magnified a million times, flit over vast plains; and still farther, great mountains of unbearable solidity and height sum up in terms of granite and groaning firs the ultimate truth of his being.

I I

When they emerged from the thunder and foul air of the subway, the last dregs of the day were mixed with the street lights. She wanted to buy some fish for supper, so she handed him the basket of jelly jars, telling him to go home. He walked up to the third landing and then remembered he had given her his keys earlier in the day.

In silence he sat down on the steps and in silence rose when some ten minutes later she came, heavily trudging upstairs, wanly smiling, shaking her head in deprecation of her silliness. They entered their two-room flat and he at once went to the mirror. Straining the corners of his mouth apart by means of his thumbs, with a horrible masklike grimace, he removed his new hopelessly uncomfortable dental plate and severed the long tusks of saliva connecting him to it. He read his Russian-language newspaper while she laid the table. Still reading, he ate the pale victuals that needed no teeth. She knew his moods and was also silent.

When he had gone to bed, she remained in the living room with her pack of soiled cards and her old albums. Across the narrow yard where the rain tinkled in the dark against some battered ash cans, windows were blandly alight and in one of them a black-trousered man with his bare elbows raised could be seen lying supine on an untidy bed. She pulled the blind down and examined the photographs. As a baby he looked more surprised than most babies. From a fold in the album, a German maid they had had in Leipzig and her fat-faced fiancé fell out. Minsk, the Revolution, Leipzig,[3] Berlin, Leipzig, a slanting house front badly out of focus. Four years old, in a park: moodily, shyly, with puckered forehead, looking away from an eager squirrel as he would from any other stranger. Aunt Rose, a fussy, angular, wild-eyed old lady, who had lived in a tremulous world of bad news, bankruptcies, train accidents, cancerous growths—until the Germans put her to death, together with all the

2. Sign language used by the deaf.   3. Leipzig is a city in Germany. The Revolution is the Russian Revolution of 1917–20.

people she had worried about. Age six—that was when he drew wonderful birds with human hands and feet, and suffered from insomnia like a grown-up man. His cousin, now a famous chess player. He again, aged about eight, already difficult to understand, afraid of the wallpaper in the passage, afraid of a certain picture in a book which merely showed an idyllic landscape with rocks on a hillside and an old cart wheel hanging from the branch of a leaf-less tree. Aged ten: the year they left Europe. The shame, the pity, the humili-ating difficulties, the ugly, vicious, backward children he was with in that special school. And then came a time in his life, coinciding with a long conva-lescence after pneumonia, when those little phobias of his which his parents had stubbornly regarded as the eccentricities of a prodigiously gifted child hardened as it were into a dense tangle of logically interacting illusions, mak-ing him totally inaccessible to normal minds.

This, and much more, she accepted—for after all living did mean accepting the loss of one joy after another, not even joys in her case—mere possibilities of improvement. She thought of the endless waves of pain that for some rea-son or other she and her husband had to endure; of the invisible giants hurt-ing her boy in some unimaginable fashion; of the incalculable amount of tenderness contained in the world; of the fate of this tenderness, which is either crushed, or wasted, or transformed into madness; of neglected children hum-ming to themselves in unswept corners; of beautiful weeds that cannot hide from the farmer and helplessly have to watch the shadow of his simian stoop leave mangled flowers in its wake, as the monstrous darkness approaches.

III

It was past midnight when from the living room she heard her husband moan; and presently he staggered in, wearing over his nightgown the old overcoat with astrakhan[4] collar which he much preferred to the nice blue bathrobe he had.

"I can't sleep," he cried.

"Why," she asked, "why can't you sleep? You were so tired."

"I can't sleep because I am dying," he said and lay down on the couch.

"Is it your stomach? Do you want me to call Dr. Solov?"

"No doctors, no doctors," he moaned. "To the devil with doctors! We must get him out of there quick. Otherwise we'll be responsible. Responsible!" he repeated and hurled himself into a sitting position, both feet on the floor, thumping his forehead with his clenched fist.

"All right," she said quietly, "we shall bring him home tomorrow morning."

"I would like some tea," said her husband and retired to the bathroom.

Bending with difficulty, she retrieved some playing cards and a photograph or two that had slipped from the couch to the floor: knave of hearts, nine of spades, ace of spades, Elsa and her bestial beau.

He returned in high spirits, saying in a loud voice:

"I have it all figured out. We will give him the bedroom. Each of us will spend part of the night near him and the other part on this couch. By turns. We will have the doctor see him at least twice a week. It does not matter what the Prince says. He won't have to say much anyway because it will come out cheaper."

---

4. Lustrous, tight-curled wool (from Astrakhan, a city in southeast Russia).

The telephone rang. It was an unusual hour for their telephone to ring. His left slipper had come off and he groped for it with his heel and toe as he stood in the middle of the room, and childishly, toothlessly, gaped at his wife. Having more English than he did, it was she who attended to calls.

"Can I speak to Charlie," said a girl's dull little voice.

"What number you want? No. That is not the right number."

The receiver was gently cradled. Her hand went to her old tired heart.

"It frightened me," she said.

He smiled a quick smile and immediately resumed his excited monologue. They would fetch him as soon as it was day. Knives would have to be kept in a locked drawer. Even at his worst he presented no danger to other people.

The telephone rang a second time. The same toneless anxious young voice asked for Charlie.

"You have the incorrect number. I will tell you what you are doing: you are turning the letter O instead of zero."

They sat down to their unexpected festive midnight tea. The birthday present stood on the table. He sipped noisily; his face was flushed; every now and then he imparted a circular motion to his raised glass so as to make the sugar dissolve more thoroughly. The vein on the side of his bald head where there was a large birthmark stood out conspicuously and, although he had shaved that morning, a silvery bristle showed on his chin. While she poured him another glass of tea, he put on his spectacles and re-examined with pleasure the luminous yellow, green, red little jars. His clumsy moist lips spelled out their eloquent labels: apricot, grape, beech plum, quince. He had got to crab apple, when the telephone rang again.

1958

JOYCE CAROL OATES

b. 1938

Oates grew up in the country near Lockport, New York. She received degrees from Syracuse University and the University of Wisconsin before launching one of the more spectacularly prolific—and honored—careers among contemporary writers. Poet and critic as well as fiction writer, she continues to astonish readers with the ingenuity of her formal innovations as with the sheer volume of her production. Violence, madness, and social disorder are frequently her subject matter. The mysteries of psychological and sociological motivation fascinate her; she constructs ingenious theories to explain them and to focus their moral significance. Her more than forty novels include *them* (1969), *Bellefleur* (1980), *You Must Remember This* (1987), *We Were the Mulvaneys* (1996), *The Falls* (2004), *Little Bird of Heaven* (2009), and *The Accursed* (2013). Her short stories number more than 700; her many collections include *Marriages and Infidelities* (1972), *Where Are You Going, Where Have You Been?* (1993), *I Am No One You Know* (2004), *and Evil Eye* (2013). She has published thrillers under pseudonyms as well as a memoir, *A Widow's Story* (2011).

Convalescing

I

She was a fair young woman in blue, her arms and legs tanned, lean, ready for grappling with the enormous problems of life he had gone blind to, her voice attractively raspy and yet professional, her blond hair pulled back like his wife's, though not so nice as his wife's—she eyed him with a small universal smile and said, "Do you prefer toothpaste or tooth powder?" He thought this over, giving it more thought than he should have. The two of them—the girl, a stranger to him, and the man, a kindly and amused stranger to himself—were standing in his side yard, a handsome green yard well-kept and unthreatening, on a Saturday afternoon when everyone else was out. He wanted to congratulate her on her pretty smile!—did she prefer toothpaste herself? What was her secret? But her smile was not very pretty, only coaxing, and he had a vision of his wife's quick excited smile, superimposed upon hers; the girl seemed suddenly uninteresting.

"Toothpaste," he said. He did not know if this were true, but it was not quite a lie.

She checked something off on a paper stuck to her clip-board. Yes, her seriousness made her uninteresting. Life was a joke she hadn't caught. "About how many hours a week do you watch television?"

Though he was a *convalescent,* which is to say not an *invalid,* he did not watch television many hours a week. He did not watch television at all. His own catastrophe had been followed by the catastrophe of a leading American politician, and the networks had been crowded with dour fake-reluctant news and old film clips and reports and prophecies he had not wanted to note. In a pleasant stupor he had turned aside, and even "his" record collection did not interest him. It was "his" because he understood that it belonged to him and was the result of many years of collecting, replacing, hunting up of rare records, but he could not really recall these years nor could he recall the pleasure he must have had, sometime, in music or in life.

He smiled with the smile he had learned in imitation of his own smiling face in snapshots. To be polite, he said, "Oh, maybe ten hours a week?"

"Only ten?" The girl was disappointed.

"More like twenty."

"Twenty." She checked something off.

And so, while he fooled around with the hose and cast an admiring eye on the lawn, on the girl, and on the houses across the street with their new coats of paint and their newly sanded brick and their relaxed, welcoming air of approval, the girl went through a litany of mechanical raspy questions: Do you smoke? How many packs a day? Filter-tip or plain? Regular or king-size? Which magazines do you subscribe to? Do you own an American car? Or two cars? Which makes? Standard or compact? Does your car have an air conditioner and if not, would you be interested in one? Do you prefer beer in bottles or in cans? Do you have an automatic can opener? Are you for, against, undecided concerning the Vietnam war?

The first questions had panicked him because he did not know the answers. But he was considerate enough not to show panic; why alarm a young person? The girl was fifteen years younger than he, not much older than his daughter. So he answered slowly, seriously, giving the answers he imagined someone with his name, David Scott, might give, the most pleasant answers to come out of a house that looked like his—a colonial with a fieldstone front, a neat expensive house—for why disturb the harmony of a fine June day?

After about ten minutes the girl said, "Thank you very much!"

"Did you—have you come to any conclusions?"

"No, we don't come to conclusions." She blushed, holding the clip-board up to her chest. "I mean, people like myself don't. We just interview."

"You don't come to any conclusions?" he said, his heart sinking.

"What kind of conclusions did you want?"

"Are the answers at least normal? Convincing?"

The girl eyed him suspiciously, though she was still smiling. But why disturb the harmony of the day? So he waved her on, smiling himself to show that this was nothing important, she should move on, go to the DeLillos' house next door and ask them about toothpaste—

"Thank you very much," said the girl.

He returned to his lawn work, in a kind of sleep. Such stupor has its deeper dimensions, its geography, not to be noted on a chart; he felt safe in his inch or two of grass. He watered some bushes with his clean green hose. Was this his hose, bought when? The bushes, planted by another man, the head of another household, perhaps fictitious, were not really his bushes but only in his keeping until he sold the house to another head of a family anxious to settle down on this good green street. And would he then become fictitious? Or was he fictitious already?

At two-thirty his daughter came home from her cello lesson, the cello in its dusty black case much too big for her. She looked victimized, a refugee from war, trudging along a country road toward some humiliating fate. His daughter, only thirteen. Her name was Eunice, not David's idea of a name for a baby girl, but now she had grown up into a Eunice and dragged her cello off to a music lesson every Saturday, keen and nervous about her music, her scrawny legs, her mother's forgetfulness, her father's vague suffering. She greeted him warmly. He greeted her. "How was it today?" he said, a standard question. Grown more awkward in his gaze, now dragging the case along the ground, she shifted her ninety pounds from one foot to another, pretending to think over his question, a little embarrassed maybe by—by what?—by his new sports shirt, which was too new, or too vivid a yellow?—too sporty for a convalescing man? "Oh, you know, coming along," she said. Her posture was bad, no nagging could improve it. Her legs were certainly too thin. What help could her father give her? He loved her but could not truly believe in this love. Eunice, her smile ironic from too many A's and too little joy, glanced at him with her dreamy dark eyes and seemed to be forgiving him for not loving her, for having forgotten her.

Sad to say, he had forgotten her.

Panic had arisen in him, to think that he had a child. They told him he had a daughter. A wife and a thirteen-year-old daughter. Nothing else? Many other things, they told him, being gentle and wise, speaking in the intonations of civilized men, exactly the intonations he had himself mastered for nearly thirty years, but had somehow forgotten. "Daughter? My daughter? Where, who?" he had cried, hysterical. But that hysteria had passed.

Now he was safe at home, convalescing. He went in to work two afternoons a week, on the bus, and in a while he would go in three afternoons. He had forgotten nothing of his work. His memory for small, meager details had not deserted him, though it seemed the memory of another man, somehow acquired by him. He was being drawn back into life like a minor thread, drawn into a complicated tapestry of vivid, major colors, a tapestry that would tolerate him. He admired the tapestry and he feared for his own destiny in it, that thin thread, a slowly strengthening thread that might come to some destination. . . . In a few weeks, a few months? When he remembered who he was? When he woke up to find himself inhabiting his body again, returned to himself, the *same person* he had been all along?

"Mother isn't back yet?" Eunice said.

"She'll be back soon," he said, glad to feel how all tension, all concern shifted off onto his wife, his absent wife, and left him free.

Alone, he felt the new, familiar numbness again. It was his only emotion and it was not an emotion but the absence of one, the tingling of nerves in anticipation of an emotion, the regret of emotion lost, not clearly remembered. He was *in love* with his wife but it was a condition he could not feel. From a close, intimate distance he admired her, this hurried, forgetful, busy woman, a very attractive woman whose striking face made her daughter withdraw out of shyness—a woman with the kind of face he had always admired from a distance, not hoping to win her. Yet he had won her. "He" had accomplished it, some fifteen years ago, but he could not remember how and he could not remember, though he tried desperately, the enormous joy that must have been his. . . .

She arrived home, in her own car. She smiled and waved to him and he saw that her hair had been done, in anticipation of Saturday night, and that she had immense patience and love for him but no need for him, this sickly quiet man to whom she found herself married. "I saw Tony Harper downtown," she said, gathering up packages from the back seat of the car, "and he asked after you, he wants us all to get together soon. . . . He didn't look too well himself."

David could not remember Tony Harper except for the name, a certain face, a certain nervous manner. They had gone to law school together at the University of Michigan, but he could not remember Tony Harper. His wife's smile showed that she did not catch on or had no time to catch on; she might have thought his convalescence could be speeded up by ignoring it.

"Where did you park downtown?" he said.

"In a garage, one of those places where you drive around and up onto different levels . . . you know."

He found her confidence astounding. He no longer drove a car; he took a bus, or his wife drove him. But she drove everywhere, downtown in terrible traffic, out to far-flung suburbs to visit women friends, at home on the road, on the telephone, in the two stories and basement of their complicated house. He felt the emptiness in him grow sharper, teased by her strength. He said, "You should be careful in a place like that. Those garages aren't very safe."

"Aren't safe, why not?"

"Someone could follow you up to your car, there aren't any watchmen or guards around. I mean it. You should be more careful."

The packages in her arms were gaily colored—pink, mint green, yellow. They spoke of mysterious silken things, of fragrant things, airy secrets from him. She knew what she wanted. She knew where to buy it. Since his accident he knew nothing. He spoke out of habit, using words automatically; perhaps if he tried to remember which words to use he would stand dumb. Catatonic, turned into a statue. He sensed that fate ahead and tried to dodge it by *taking an interest*. He was interested in the state of his lawn. He was interested in his daughter's music lessons. Friends were coming over that evening for a quiet evening. An old familiar couple he could nearly remember. Old friends, safe friends. Nothing alarming. He took an interest in his daughter and in his wife, whom he feared a little, and he did worry about her parking in an unattended garage deep in the heart of a hot crowded city.

"I can take care of myself," she said. But her voice sounded suddenly lame, guilty. She was nearly his height, and he imagined that since the accident he had become shorter. He had lost weight until his ribs showed and no doubt he had lost some inches also, why not? Anything was possible. His lovely wife, whom he had courted and won in the guise of another, younger, more joyful self, now stood staring gloomily at him and must have noticed the contrast between his bony, accusing face and the healthy Saturday sunlight.

"It isn't always just a woman's purse they want," he said, as if trying to break through his own numbness. "Sometimes there are a bunch of them, no more than kids, and down there nobody will bother coming if you scream for help. Oh, they'll come after a while, after somebody tells a policeman, but by then it would be too late. . . ."

"I'll be more careful," she said.

"Yes, please. Be more careful."

II

Look, look at that! An automobile is speeding along just under the legal speed limit, on an expressway, at five-twenty on a Wednesday afternoon in spring. The automobile is black and expensive but not outstanding. In four lanes of sparkling traffic it does not especially catch the eye. Cars and trucks of all sizes, trucks loaded down with evergreen snippings and dismembered trees, trucks loaded with other trucks, great trucks hauling great vans, bright blue, with *Chrysler Corporation* on their sides—all rushing along with certain destinations, unswerving. At four minutes from the point of collision, point X, the black car is held in firm control by its driver, a man with thinning dark hair and a pleasant, undistinguished face, his brain taking in without excitement the various familiar sights of this expressway, billboards and embankments littered with paper and other trash, and in the sleepy dense sky contrails of jets appear—these lines of white smoke in the sky please him. What do they mean? The day hasn't been too bad, he is not exactly exhausted. Not worried. At the back of his mind something is trying to open and spread its wings, but the pain would be too great and he fights it down. He is not worried. He knows exactly how to drive this expressway, when to get into the right lane and when to exit.

A shape of black, softer than smoke but then hardening to something brittle, like a crow's wings—he fights it down, he does not acknowledge it.

At five twenty-one he passes the Cooley Avenue overpass, speeding into its shadow and out of its shadow, hardly aware of it, and at five twenty-two his attention is caught by a stalled car on the shoulder of the expressway, an angry-looking rusty car with rear fenders shaped into fins. An impulse of sympathy for the car's owner—who is nowhere around. Then the sympathy fades, he has driven past, on his way home and certain of his destination. He makes his way through the slightly smutty air, crashing through it with his heavy, expensive car, cleaving a way through with the ease of a hand turned sideways to make a casual gesture in the air—and the time, he notes, is now five twenty-three on the Goodyear Tire clock—and he imagines whimsically that somewhere in this city someone is thinking, maybe in the Adventure Lounge that looks sadly down upon the expressway onto point X, someone is thinking sullenly *I wish to hell they would burn this city down* because there is too much gravity in the city, too much noise, the planet is bloodstained and weary with cataclysms, especially in this city. A few hundred feet from point X a blue automobile with fins appears, leaping to life in the sunlight. Out of nowhere? The driver of the black car notices it, but only casually, since so many objects leap forward into one's attention in the space of only one minute—

All the rest is fiction, not remembered.

It became fiction because it was told to David, explained to him; he believed it the way he believed in the reality of Napoleon, Christ, Julius Caesar; the way he believed in the reality of impoverished Ozark families photographed for *Life Magazine*; the way he believed in his grandparents' parents, people who must have existed but were out of sight, X's that had to be postulated and accepted on faith. It was a more solid form of fiction than the fiction of novels and legends, but not much more solid.

What is missing, then? A point of view.

What is tragically missing? A personality. That is, a soul.

What happened at point X, that mysterious point X? If he made the trip back to that spot he would see nothing much. The Adventure Lounge, blocked off by the expressway and on a dead-end street, looks down upon the site but looks down without commitment. No witnesses to the accident. Hundreds of eyes but no witnesses. On the other side there is the usual wire fence, with dozens of yellowed newspaper pages flattened against it, and beyond the fence another street, and beyond that some vacated stores—nothing, no witnesses. It could not have been said that David himself was a witness. He witnessed nothing. So if he returned he would remember nothing, all the evidence has been cleared away and swept up. Traffic rushed past five minutes later. It rushed past two minutes later. In fact, except in the two lanes that were affected, traffic did not stop at all, but only slowed down. The planet flowed, the minute hand on the Goodyear Tire clock made its determined leap, a black car and a blue car swept together with a terrible grace as if decades of planning had led them to this impact, two minor threads in a mad, brilliant tapestry come together at last for a trivial climax. The cars slammed together, side to side, they shook, shuddered, gave way, came apart . . . and then what happened?

Was it an ordinary accident, with ordinary blood?

He did not want to force the accident out of his memory because he thought that might be dangerous. Repression was dangerous. So he tried to remember it. He knew he had had an accident—a fractured skull, broken ribs, multiple lacerations, wounds, scratches. These things had happened to *his own body*. He knew also that for twenty minutes, recorded faithfully on the Goodyear Tire clock, he had lain in the wreckage of his car, not unconscious, groaning aloud for help, probably, and no help had come. The other driver had died at once. Better not to think of that. But David had not died and had lain bleeding for twenty minutes in the hot searing metal of his car, among the expensive smashed gadgets and ripped upholstery, while traffic went on by. Yet he did not truly remember those twenty minutes.

People said, "My God, what a scandal! Twenty minutes!" and other people said, by way of explanation, "There must have been a communication breakdown." But these remarks did not mean anything. He could not remember those twenty minutes of agony and so, in a sense, they did not exist. But in those twenty minutes he had evidently died.

He thought about the accident, the "twenty minutes," trying to remember. He could not remember. Something blocked him off. He thought of himself as a character in a story, trying to remember himself in order to come alive. How to get out of this fiction? How to remember himself? What must he do to be saved?

III

In the hospital his wife came to him shyly. She had a criminal's anxiety to please, an expert liar's love of lying. He had forgotten her but, seeing her, some dim alarming recollection set him right. A lovely woman, a woman to be won. She looked at him and might have imagined him as he had been, before the accident, though the accident had not really damaged his face—slightly coarse skin now rather pale, dark, deep eyes, prominent eyebrows, dark hair grown a little thin at the crown and the temples—yes, her husband—but he looked back at her with no more than polite recognition. They talked about the house, about home. About Eunice. About friends, his work, whether his mother should be told. (Senile, she had forgotten him and he could not feel guilt at having forgotten her—an aged woman in an expensive nursing home.)

On the day before his release she had said, "So you'll be coming home tomorrow?"

He had felt panic at once.

"Home?"

"Yes, tomorrow, you'll be coming home tomorrow . . . ?"

"Yes."

"I'm so glad."

They had stared uneasily at each other. He said her name to himself, *Elaine*, but he could not believe in it. He knew that they had been married for nearly fifteen years, that they had a daughter whom they loved in the way in which daughters are loved, that they had lain together for years of darkness, sometimes asleep and sometimes awake, *in love*, thinking of their love or of other, quite ordinary things, harmlessly . . . but he could not quite believe it.

His own name was *David Scott*. The identification bracelet he wore, made up of beads, told him that and would not let him forget.

And so, back home, he lay upstairs in the handsome big bedroom, getting back his strength. Somewhere "his" strength existed, to be won back. He was resting. Convalescing. He could certainly remember this bedroom, but he had the idea he'd seen it in a movie or in a photograph. While Elaine chattered to him in the sure, friendly, impersonal tone of a hospital nurse, nudging him back to health, he answered her in the way a husband might, recovering from some terrible shock to his body and soul. But a certain blankness in him could not escape her, could it?—was she pretending? He asked to see the photograph album and for days looked at old snapshots, clever enough to know that he had to relearn everything. He stared at the pictures of a man said to be himself. He knew the man was himself because of the scribbled notations on the backs of the pictures, in Elaine's half-familiar handwriting, *David June 1958 . . . David Fall '61 . . . David, David, David . . .* More interesting to him were snapshots of Eunice, growing up. A handful of snapshots, flicked, would show a girl growing up jerkily, unwillingly, forced into growth by the terrible mechanism of muscles and bones. And more interesting than these were the snapshots of Elaine, that charming woman, Elaine playing tennis with a friend,

Elaine in her dark bathing suit (she did not bother noting her own name on the backs of such snapshots: certain of her own identity, it was enough for her to write *Nantucket Summer '66*), and occasionally *Elaine with David*, wife and husband.

From these snapshots he judged himself to have been a pleasant, kindly man, well liked by family and friends. The friends in the snapshots changed gradually, their places taken by other friends, but they all looked like pleasant, kindly people. He was grateful for them. Though they did not lift him out of his sleep, he had the hope that someday they would, just as Elaine would, bringing him back to life. . . .

She had awakened him once. One morning, quite casually, he remembered a conversation he'd had with her a month or so before, before the accident. He had come home for some papers, just after lunch, and while looking through his desk drawers he'd glanced out to see her hurrying into the house. Her spring coat was unbuttoned, her hair a little blown, but her face was lustrous, radiant, a face she no longer showed to him—and he had known, suddenly, that she was in love. He went downstairs. She opened the door with her own key and he stood there, in the dim back hallway, quietly waiting for her to enter, fearful of her happiness. She had been quite surprised to see him. He had wanted to get out, escape, but something made him linger. . . . She talked him into having a cup of coffee, she was so energetic and nervous and happy that he dared not contradict her; so they sat in the kitchen and she told him.

"I can't help it, I've fallen in love. I didn't want it to happen," she said.

He felt faint, though he had guessed her secret. He could not speak.

"Please don't hate me, what can I do?" she said. Her breath was rapid and sweet. In her glowing health, in the daring of her body and face, she had strength that he no longer had—she had his name, she had everything in their marriage, and something secret beside, something that went beyond all that he could offer her. She had gone beyond him, outlived him.

"What do you want to do?" he had asked, suddenly afraid.

"I have to marry him. Can't I—can't we—Is it too awful? You don't want me now anyway, do you, after this?—won't you want to divorce me?"

"Is that what you want?"

"I don't know what I want. Please don't hate me. Yes, I want to marry him, I can't do anything about my feelings. I can't help myself."

He had sat staring toward her, appalled and numb. She did not seem familiar to him. Her rapid, fluttery voice—her nervous hands, lighting a cigarette—her flushed cheeks and brilliant eyes that indicated how beautiful she was elsewhere, made beautiful by someone else's existence—these things were a shock to him, the features of a stranger. She was a woman he could never win. Drawn to her, at a party, he might engage her in ordinary conversation for a few minutes and get her to smile that charming smile, but he could never hold her.

"Who is it?" he said.

"I don't want to tell you yet. Please. Can you understand?"

"Is he married? Do I know him?"

"Yes, you know him very well, and he's married—yes—he has children—I'm sorry—I don't know how it happened but we can't change anything; we've waited and thought about this for almost a year but there's nothing we can do, we love each other. I can't explain except by coming back again and again to that—"

"You're in love, I understand. I think I understand," he said slowly.

"Do you hate me?"

"No."

"But what—what do you feel? What do you feel?" And she stared at him as if really seeing him for the first time, alarmed at his silence.

"I don't feel anything," he said. What was strange was that her disclosure seemed more than personal, more than private—it was like a door suddenly opening to show him the unsettled landscape of the world, something beyond his control and indifferent to him, knowing no laws, opaque and mysterious and terrifying.

Two days later, on a Wednesday afternoon, he had had his "accident."

Now he spoke to her gravely of parking downtown, of being cautious. "You know how people in trouble are ignored," he said, drawing upon his own trouble to bully her into submission, into a look of guilt. Dressed for Saturday shopping, long-legged and lively, she had been cowed by something dark in his eye and he wondered if she was recalling that conversation, that unforgotten conversation, and whether she knew that he remembered everything or whether she knew nothing, absolutely innocent in her own honesty. She would never bring the subject up again, he felt sure. He was safe in her kindliness. But she was so frank and honest herself. In conversations with friends she would say, *But I myself, I have to fight prejudice in myself,* or she would say, though such a remark was unpleasant, *I really don't agree with you.* . . . David, made complex and subtle by his years of training, never committed himself clearly to one side or another, reluctant to take a stand and not sure of the wisdom of taking a stand. Why?

He took some of her packages from her and they went into the house, into the kitchen. Eunice was there, drinking a glass of milk. Elaine complained about Eunice's untidy room, and about the lateness of the hour, and with her deft quick fingers she brushed strands of hair back out of her eyes. "Did anyone call or stop by?" she asked. David had heard the telephone ring, that was true, but hadn't had the energy to answer it. So he told her only, "Yes, somebody stopped by, just a girl interviewer for a marketing survey. She asked me various questions like 'Do you have an automatic can opener?'"

"And what did you answer?" Elaine said, teasing.

"I said yes."

She laughed and went to the sink, where the automatic can opener was fastened to the wall. "Yes, here it is, you remembered—but we never use it. It's broken."

"I remembered it very clearly," he said with a fake, strained smile.

"And in this drawer," she said, opening a drawer, "we have a collection of can openers—this gadget here, which is broken, and this one here, which I bought only the other week, and this old-fashioned thing—here—and even this grimy bottle opener, the handiest of all for opening bottles." She showed him a small rusted bottle opener, three or four inches long. He could remember none of these things, but their shapes intrigued him. Just such things—bottle and can openers of all makes, simple and ingenious, broken, rusted, new, guaranteed, unused, hand-run or automatic—such things were the property of homeowners up and down the block, everywhere in this lovely green neighborhood, everywhere in the country. Their kitchen junk drawer itself, cluttered with such innocent objects, was American and proved that he was a normal American because he owned it.

"I'm glad you remembered," Elaine said.

She had come home safely, she had returned. Safe from downtown, safe from the expressway and its dangers—home to him and her daughter, home to keep them safe. He felt an enlargement of his numbness, suddenly, to think of her lost to him. It was like a sack of compressed cold air, this numbness, in a space just beneath his heart. It was perhaps the space in which his soul had resided, when he had had a soul.

I V

"So now they have assassination flags for sale, special flags," their friend Taylor was saying. "They can be lowered on a string to half-mast, that's their unique value. I saw them for sale in the discount drugstore." Taylor had an ironic, helpless smirk, his intellectual smirk; he used it when talking about ironic and helpless things, like the assassinations of American leaders or the fate of the middle class. He himself was in real estate, a business his father had left him, and he was watching it dwindle in his grasp, shrink unaccountably in spite of his superior brains and good looks. His wife, maternal and tolerant, watched him with her usual smile; she was a solid woman, as Elaine liked to say in lackluster defense of her, a sensible woman and just the wife for Taylor. Withdrawn slightly, David listened to everything that was said. He made an attempt to listen to things that were not said, but he could not decipher them. Taylor and Brenda MacIntyre were old friends of theirs, going back a decade to simpler and warmer times, when David had been on the way up and Taylor not yet on the way down. Between Elaine and Brenda there was a kind of friendship, mysterious like the friendships of all women with women—what had they in common, Brenda with her bland smile, Elaine with her alert, quizzical look?

"Civilization is coming to an end maybe," Elaine said. "People can't always be wrong about predicting the end. There have been final generations, the very end of epochs, and there must have been—there must be—individuals who are the last survivors of their worlds—isn't that plausible?"

They laughed at her seriousness, but she did not release them. She fixed Taylor with an accusing look so that David wondered, for an instant, whether he was the one—then he rejected this thought, Taylor was too obvious—and said, "No one wants to think about the end. People want to talk about it for conversation. But no one is prepared for a real ending because they haven't done anything yet, they're still waiting. . . ."

"Waiting for what?" Brenda said.

"To live. To wake up. They can't admit that their lives are coming to an end when they haven't yet lived."

Though the living room was large, they were sitting close together. Elaine's manner was slightly aggressive, argumentative, intimate, her long legs tucked under her, strangely feminine and persistent at the same time; she looked younger than thirty-four. David understood that he was not talking enough. He had to be intimate with these people, he had to draw them all together, be in harmony with them. His friends—and he was willing to call them friends and be grateful for their existence—would speak of him the next day to other friends, saying, *David still isn't well; I worry about him.* He finished his drink. Did he drink too much, or not enough? Would they wonder why he wasn't drinking as much as he had previously, the old, lively, cuckolded David, or would they wonder why he was drinking so much? He thought idly of people gossiping about him, secretaries at his office, his partners, his partners' wives, his friends—with nothing better to do than to gossip about him, marveling at the seams in his personality, glued together, patched up, a stand-in for the other David and not convincing. Now Brenda and Taylor were talking heatedly. Brenda was talking and Taylor was trying to wrench the conversation away from her.

"No, please, let me tell Elaine," Brenda was saying, "she has a daughter herself and she knows—"

"Why the hell are you bringing this up?"

"Elaine and David can give us advice. I don't care who knows. I don't have secrets." Brenda leaned forward to entrust her secret to Elaine, who would certainly run out and tell everyone the next morning.... "It's Judy. She got caught shoplifting. I had to go down to the store, Steinboch's, and talk with the manager. How do you like that? Fifteen years old and she has an allowance, and she goes out and steals."

"What did she steal?" Elaine asked.

"It doesn't matter what she stole," Taylor said.

"She took some stockings. But only because they were out on the counter, she would have taken anything. She told me," Brenda said. The hour was late. She had a slightly self-righteous, smug, drunken smile; David wondered suddenly if perhaps he had never seen this woman before, really. It might be that they were all strangers. Watching her, alarmed at her admission of so private a secret, he wondered also whether he ought to escape. Before it was too late and too many secrets were told, so that the four of them would be bound together for eternity....

"I'm very sorry to hear that," Elaine said.

"Yes, that's . . . that's bad news," David said.

"Well, it's happening. Not just Judy. It's happening all over and nobody knows what to do."

"What did you do?" Elaine asked.

"I told you, nobody knows what to do. I talked to her. She said she wouldn't do it again, that's what she said. I chose to believe her, so did Taylor. What else can you do?"

"With Eunice something different came up," Elaine said, and David dreaded hearing what might come next—he did not remember anything coming up about her, any trouble. "She went to a birthday party for a friend of hers, and about ten other girls were invited. She left her purse with her coat, upstairs in the girl's bedroom. Then, when she went to go home, she found that someone had taken her money—took the money out of her billfold. But she was afraid to say anything to the girl or her mother because—because she was afraid—"

"Of what?" said Taylor.

"Of never being asked back again, I think."

"What? Really?"

"Or afraid of losing her friends. Afraid of complaining at all, making any fuss," Elaine said. She looked so stricken, so ashamed of her daughter and weary over such daughterly weaknesses, that Taylor reached over to stroke her hand. In this instant David was reminded of his wife's lover, her secret, second husband, a more satisfying and demanding man than David himself.

"Well—don't forget when you were that age," Brenda said.

Taylor brought Elaine's hand up to his lips and kissed it. "You're so demanding. It's you who demand too much of people, you," he said fondly.

David saw them through a kind of mist, these people in a photograph, people who had had a hand in his fate. Through them he might know himself. But the way into knowing himself had something to do also with the coming together of two cars, of tons of steel, the pulsating pain of twenty minutes' wait on the shoulder of an expressway and an hour's wait in the emergency ward of a noisy hospital—it had too much to do with knowing his daughter and her precocious failure, her cowardice that was his own cowardice, inherited. He thought of his wife in the kitchen, weeks ago, through the excitement of her words reliving an exquisite passion he could never again evoke in her. He pressed his hands against his forehead, baffled by the mystery of personality. Who were these people? Who was this woman, that she had come to mean so much to him? It was not just his own soul that was opaque, lost, but the souls of people he loved and had believed he knew, had trusted. . . . And, beyond them, the shadowy souls of people known to him only over the television screen or in newspaper photographs, the famous and notorious, monumental figures, shadowy nubs of being as mysterious to him as his own past.

"I read in a magazine about these teen-age clubs in, where was it, Sacramento," Brenda said in a shocked, hushed voice, as if teen-agers might be listening, "and my God you wouldn't believe—"

David got up. With a gesture he indicated that he was going to refill his drink. "Here, take mine," Taylor said. David took it and went out to the kitchen, a partly familiar room, safe. He sat down. Then, nervous, he got up and walked beside the very clean, clean counter, running his knuckles along it. He wondered in a daze who he was and to whose country he had come. It was true that he was married—there was a certificate to prove it—and he did own this house, he had ten thousand dollars yet to pay on the mortgage—and he had contributed toward bringing another person into the world, though he hadn't the slightest knowledge of what that meant—and so—and so it was certain that he had a specific identity. But the identity was empty, numb. His body was paralyzed as if by a dentist's giant needle, expelling forgetfulness and silence into his spine.

He studied the spices in Elaine's spice rack. For a while she had taken cooking lessons—she'd been domestic for years, then switched to outward, intellectual, humanistic interests like integration and voting reform—and she had collected a number of spices, all in identical green jars, *parsley, oregano, clove, ginger, sweet basil, nutmeg,* even *white pepper,* even *saffron*— Inside his body he felt something straining to open itself, to spread its wings. Its muscles ached for freedom. He leaned against the counter and gripped his skull. He was going mad. The slowness of his bones was driving him mad. Kennedy[1] had been assassinated just the other day, the second Kennedy,[2] shot in the back of the skull and killed, and David's own life made no more sense than that death. Yet he had the glancing notion that he might have pulled the trigger himself, granted a certain immunity. Granted safety, invisibility. . . .

On the counter, lying on the clean-wiped counter, was the bottle opener Elaine had held up to him that afternoon, as if showing him something important. He picked it up. Bottle caps were scattered around it, from bottles of bitter lemon. This bottle opener was the cheapest kind, sold for a nickel or given away for advertising purposes . . . it had rusted and only part of its legend was readable: *Hamm's—from the land of sky blue waters.* The opener was very sharp at one point; David tested it on his thumb. Very sharp. It should have been enough to wake him. He pressed the point against his wrist, thinking. For all of his life he had been certain of himself, beginning with his name; nothing had escaped him. And yet everything had escaped him. He had felt certain emotions—love and hate—and had been swept along in violence by these emotions, purified by them like his wife Elaine, justified by them as the assassin of Kennedy and the assassins of other men are justified by emotions. But it had all been without meaning. The emotions faded, the events could not be remembered—and where, in such a puzzle, was a fixed point? He stared at the dingy little bottle opener and wondered if so meager an object might have a soul of its own, a center of gravity firmly fixed and measurable.

"What's wrong? What are you doing?"

Elaine stood staring at him. She was nervous, her voice uneasy. He saw that her clear, handsome brow was damp with droplets of worry—from the tense discussion of daughters or worry over this strange husband? She was looking at the can opener in his hand. Perhaps she thought he was holding it as a weapon, imagining it as a weapon?—perhaps he was contemplating a sudden surprise for her, raking the point down across the skin of her cheek?

He shivered, thinking of that.

"What are you doing out here? I've been waiting for you to come back—I didn't think you felt well—"

She put her hand on his arm.

Again he thought of the can opener, its sharp little point. . . .

"Please, please don't be sick," she said. She looked into his face. For a moment he remained rigid, secretive in thought. Then he pressed his hands against his forehead.

"You won't leave me?" he said.

"No."

"You'll never leave me?" He was sweating.

She put her arms around him. "I'll never leave you. Please don't think of it." She spoke gently and yet with an air of certainty, as if making a public vow, a vow of commitment and energy. He was weak with relief but he felt no shame,

---

1. Senator Robert F. Kennedy, brother of John, assassinated on June 6, 1968. **2.** President John F. Kennedy, assassinated on November 22, 1963.

nothing. Emotions faded. Events could not be remembered. Perhaps his wife had not committed adultery, perhaps he had imagined everything? He was still a convalescent and people must treat him with gentleness.

1969

How I Contemplated the World from the Detroit House of Correction and Began My Life Over Again

Notes for an Essay for an English Class at Baldwin Country Day School; Poking Around in Debris; Disgust and Curiosity; A Revelation of the Meaning of Life; A Happy Ending . . .

I. Events

1. The girl (myself) is walking through Branden's, that excellent store. Suburb of a large famous city that is a symbol for large famous American cities. The event sneaks up on the girl, who believes she is herding it along with a small fixed smile, a girl of fifteen, innocently experienced. She dawdles in a certain style by a counter of costume jewelry. Rings, earrings, necklaces. Prices from $5 to $50, all within reach. All ugly. She eases over to the glove counter, where everything is ugly too. In her close-fitted coat with its black fur collar she contemplates the luxury of Branden's, which she has known for many years: its many mild pale lights, easy on the eye and the soul, its elaborate tinkly decorations, its women shoppers with their excellent shoes and coats and hairdos, all dawdling gracefully, in no hurry.

Who was ever in a hurry here?

2. The girl seated at home. A small library, paneled walls of oak. Some one is talking to me. An earnest, husky, female voice drives itself against my ears, nervous, frightened, groping around my heart, saying, "If you wanted gloves, why didn't you say so? Why didn't you ask for them?" That store, Branden's, is owned by Raymond Forrest who lives on Du Maurier Drive. We live on Sioux Drive. Raymond Forrest. A handsome man? An ugly man? A man of fifty or sixty, with gray hair, or a man of forty with earnest, courteous eyes, a good golf game; who is Raymond Forrest, this man who is my salvation? Father has been talking to him. Father is not his physician; Dr. Berg is his physician. Father and Dr. Berg refer patients to each other. There is a connection. Mother plays bridge with . . . On Mondays and Wednesdays our maid Billie works at . . . The strings draw together in a cat's cradle, making a net to save you when you fall. . . .

3. *Harriet Arnold's.* A small shop, better than Branden's. Mother in her black coat, I in my close-fitted blue coat. Shopping. Now look at this, isn't this cute, do you want this, why don't you want this, try this on, take this with you to the fitting room, take this also, what's wrong with you, what can I do for you,

why are you so strange . . . ? "I wanted to steal but not to buy," I don't tell her. The girl droops along in her coat and gloves and leather boots, her eyes scan the horizon, which is pastel pink and decorated like Branden's, tasteful walls and modern ceilings with graceful glimmering lights.

4. Weeks later, the girl at a bus stop. Two o'clock in the afternoon, a Tuesday; obviously she has walked out of school.

5. The girl stepping down from a bus. Afternoon, weather changing to colder. Detroit. Pavement and closed-up stores; grillwork over the windows of a pawnshop. What is a pawnshop, exactly?

II. Characters

1. The girl stands five feet five inches tall. An ordinary height. Baldwin Country Day School draws them up to that height. She dreams along the corridors and presses her face against the Thermoplex glass. No frost or steam can ever form on that glass. A smudge of grease from her forehead . . . could she be boiled down to grease? She wears her hair loose and long and straight in suburban teen-age style, 1968. Eyes smudged with pencil, dark brown. Brown hair. Vague green eyes. A pretty girl? An ugly girl? She sings to herself under her breath, idling in the corridor, thinking of her many secrets (the thirty dollars she once took from the purse of a friend's mother, just for fun, the basement window she smashed in her own house just for fun) and thinking of her brother who is at Susquehanna Boys' Academy, an excellent preparatory school in Maine, remembering him unclearly . . . he has long manic hair and a squeaking voice and he looks like one of the popular teen-age singers of 1968, one of those in a group, *The Certain Forces, The Way Out, The Maniacs Responsible.* The girl in her turn looks like one of those fieldsful of girls who listen to the boys' singing, dreaming and mooning restlessly, breaking into high sullen laughter, innocently experienced.

2. The mother. A Midwestern woman of Detroit and suburbs. Belongs to the Detroit Athletic Club. Also the Detroit Golf Club. Also the Bloomfield Hills Country Club. The Village Women's Club at which lectures are given each winter on Genet and Sartre and James Baldwin,[1] by the Director of the Adult Education Program at Wayne State University. . . . The Bloomfield Art Association. Also the Founders Society of the Detroit Institute of Arts. Also . . . Oh, she is in perpetual motion, this lady, hair like blown-up gold and finer than gold, hair and fingers and body of inestimable grace. Heavy weighs the gold on the back of her hairbrush and hand mirror. Heavy heavy the candlesticks in the dining room. Very heavy is the big car, a Lincoln, long and black, that on one cool autumn day split a squirrel's body in two unequal parts.

---

1. American novelist and essayist (1924–1987). Jean Genet (1910–1986), French playwright and memoirist. Jean-Paul Sartre (1905–1980), French novelist, dramatist, and philosopher.

3. The father. Dr. _____. He belongs to the same clubs as #2. A player of squash and golf; he has a golfer's umbrella of stripes. Candy stripes. In his mouth nothing turns to sugar, however; saliva works no miracles here. His doctoring is of the slightly sick. The sick are sent elsewhere (to Dr. Berg?), the deathly sick are sent back for more tests and their bills are sent to their homes, the unsick are sent to Dr. Coronet (Isabel, a lady), an excellent psychiatrist for unsick people who angrily believe they are sick and want to do something about it. If they demand a male psychiatrist, the unsick are sent by Dr. _____ (my father) to Dr. Lowenstein, a male psychiatrist, excellent and expensive, with a limited practice.

4. Clarita. She is twenty, twenty-five, she is thirty or more? Pretty, ugly, what? She is a woman lounging by the side of a road, in jeans and a sweater, hitchhiking, or she is slouched on a stool at a counter in some roadside diner. A hard line of jaw. Curious eyes. Amused eyes. Behind her eyes processions move, funeral pageants, cartoons. She says, "I never can figure out why girls like you bum around down here. What are you looking for anyway?" An odor of tobacco about her. Unwashed underclothes, or no underclothes, unwashed skin, gritty toes, hair long and falling into strands, not recently washed.

5. Simon. In this city the weather changes abruptly, so Simon's weather changes abruptly. He sleeps through the afternoon. He sleeps through the morning. Rising, he gropes around for something to get him going, for a cigarette or a pill to drive him out to the street, where the temperature is hovering around 35°. Why doesn't it drop? Why, why doesn't the cold clean air come down from Canada; will he have to go up into Canada to get it? will he have to leave the Country of his Birth and sink into Canada's frosty fields . . . ? Will the F.B.I. (which he dreams about constantly) chase him over the Canadian border on foot, hounded out in a blizzard of broken glass and horns . . . ?

"Once I was Huckleberry Finn," Simon says, "but now I am Roderick Usher."[2] Beset by frenzies and fears, this man who makes my spine go cold, he takes green pills, yellow pills, pills of white and capsules of dark blue and green . . . he takes other things I may not mention, for what if Simon seeks me out and climbs into my girl's bedroom here in Bloomfield Hills and strangles me, what then . . . ? (As I write this I begin to shiver. Why do I shiver? I am now sixteen and sixteen is not an age for shivering.) It comes from Simon, who is always cold.

III. World Events

Nothing.

IV. People and Circumstances Contributing to This Delinquency

Nothing.

---

2. That is, he has changed from a wholesome American boy into a morbid neurotic. Huck Finn is the young hero of Mark Twain's novel *Adventures of Huckleberry Finn.* Usher is the chief character in Edgar Allan Poe's *Fall of the House of Usher.*

V. Sioux Drive

George, Clyde G. 240 Sioux. A manufacturer's representative; children, a dog, a wife. Georgian with the usual columns. You think of the White House, then of Thomas Jefferson, then your mind goes blank on the white pillars and you think of nothing. Norris, Ralph W. 246 Sioux. Public relations. Colonial. Bay window, brick, stone, concrete, wood, green shutters, sidewalk, lantern, grass, trees, blacktop drive, two children, one of them my classmate Esther (Esther Norris) at Baldwin. Wife, cars. Ramsey, Michael D. 250 Sioux. Colonial. Big living room, thirty by twenty-five, fireplaces in living room, library, recreation room, paneled walls wet bar five bathrooms five bedrooms two lavatories central air conditioning automatic sprinkler automatic garage door three children one wife two cars a breakfast room a patio a large fenced lot fourteen trees a front door with a brass knocker never knocked. Next is our house. Classic contemporary. Traditional modern. Attached garage, attached Florida room, attached patio, attached pool and cabana, attached roof. A front door mail slot through which pour *Time Magazine, Fortune, Life, Business Week,* the *Wall Street Journal,* the *New York Times,* the *New Yorker,* the *Saturday Review, M.D., Modern Medicine, Disease of the Month* . . . and also. . . . And in addition to all this, a quiet sealed letter from Baldwin saying: *Your daughter is not doing work compatible with her performance on the Stanford-Binet*[3]. . . . And your son is not doing well, not well at all, very sad. Where is your son anyway? Once he stole trick-and-treat candy from some six-year-old kids, he himself being a robust ten. The beginning. Now your daughter steals. In the Village Pharmacy she made off with, yes she did, don't deny it, she made off with a copy of *Pageant Magazine* for no reason, she swiped a roll of Life Savers in a green wrapper and was in no need of saving her life or even in need of sucking candy; when she was no more than eight years old she stole, don't blush, she stole a package of Tums only because it was out on the counter and available, and the nice lady behind the counter (now dead) said nothing. . . . Sioux Drive. Maples, oaks, elms. Diseased elms cut down. Sioux Drive runs into Roosevelt Drive. Slow, turning lanes, not streets, all drives and lanes and ways and passes. A private police force. Quiet private police, in unmarked cars. Cruising on Saturday evenings with paternal smiles for the residents who are streaming in and out of houses, going to and from parties, a thousand parties, slightly staggering, the women in their furs alighting from automobiles bought of Ford and General Motors and Chrysler, very heavy automobiles. No foreign cars. Detroit. In 275 Sioux, down the block in that magnificent French-Normandy mansion, lives _____ himself, who has the C_____ account itself, imagine that! Look at where he lives and look at the enormous trees and chimneys, imagine his many fireplaces, imagine his wife and children, imagine his wife's hair, imagine her fingernails, imagine her bathtub of smooth clean glowing pink, imagine their embraces, his trouser pockets filled with odd coins and keys and dust and peanuts, imagine their ecstasy on Sioux Drive, imagine their income tax returns, imagine their little boy's pride in his experimental car, a scaled down C_____, as he roars round the neighborhood on the sidewalks frightening dogs and

---

3. An intelligence test.

Negro maids, oh imagine all these things, imagine everything, let your mind roar out all over Sioux Drive and Du Maurier Drive and Roosevelt Drive and Ticonderoga Pass and Burning Bush Way and Lincolnshire Pass and Lois Lane.

When spring comes, its winds blow nothing to Sioux Drive, no odors of hollyhocks or forsythia, nothing Sioux Drive doesn't already possess, everything is planted and performing. The weather vanes, had they weather vanes, don't have to turn with the wind, don't have to contend with the weather. There is no weather.

VI. Detroit

There is always weather in Detroit. Detroit's temperature is always 32°. Fast-falling temperatures. Slow-rising temperatures. Wind from the north-northeast four to forty miles an hour, small-craft warnings, partly cloudy today and Wednesday changing to partly sunny through Thursday . . . small warnings of frost, soot warnings, traffic warnings, hazardous lake conditions for small craft and swimmers, restless Negro gangs, restless cloud formations, restless temperatures aching to fall out the very bottom of the thermometer or shoot up over the top and boil everything over in red mercury.

Detroit's temperature is 32°. Fast-falling temperatures. Slow-rising temperatures. Wind from the north-northeast four to forty miles an hour. . . .

VII. Events

1. The girl's heart is pounding. In her pocket is a pair of gloves! In a plastic bag! Airproof breathproof plastic bag, gloves selling for twenty-five dollars on Branden's counter! In her pocket! Shoplifted! . . . In her purse is a blue comb, not very clean. In her purse is a leather billfold (a birthday present from her grandmother in Philadelphia) with snapshots of the family in clean plastic windows, in the billfold are bills, she doesn't know how many bills. . . . In her purse is an ominous note from her friend Tykie *What's this about Joe H. and the kids hanging around at Louise's Sat. night? You heard anything?* . . . passed in French class. In her purse is a lot of dirty yellow Kleenex, her mother's heart would break to see such very dirty Kleenex, and at the bottom of her purse are brown hairpins and safety pins and a broken pencil and a ballpoint pen (blue) stolen from somewhere forgotten and a purse-size compact of Cover Girl Make-Up, Ivory Rose. . . . Her lipstick is Broken Heart, a corrupt pink; her fingers are trembling like crazy; her teeth are beginning to chatter; her insides are alive; her eyes glow in her head; she is saying to her mother's astonished face *I want to steal but not to buy.*

2. At Clarita's. Day or night? What room is this? A bed, a regular bed, and a mattress on the floor nearby. Wallpaper hanging in strips. Clarita says she tore it like that with her teeth. She was fighting a barbaric tribe that night, high from some pills; she was battling for her life with men wearing helmets of heavy iron and their faces no more than Christian crosses to breathe through, every one of those bastards looking like her lover Simon, who seems to breathe with great difficulty through the slits of mouth and nostrils in his

face. Clarita has never heard of Sioux Drive. Raymond Forrest cuts no ice with her, nor does the C_____ account and its millions; Harvard Business School could be at the corner of Vernor and 12th Street for all she cares, and Vietnam might have sunk by now into the Dead Sea under its tons of debris, for all the amazement she could show . . . her face is overworked, overwrought, at the age of twenty (thirty?) it is already exhausted but fanciful and ready for a laugh. Clarita says mournfully to me *Honey somebody is going to turn you out let me give you warning.* In a movie shown on late television Clarita is not a mess like this but a nurse, with short neat hair and a dedicated look, in love with her doctor and her doctor's patients and their diseases, enamored of needles and sponges and rubbing alcohol. . . . Or no: she is a private secretary. Robert Cummings is her boss. She helps him with fantastic plots, the canned audience laughs, no, the audience doesn't laugh because nothing is funny, instead her boss is Robert Taylor and they are not boss and secretary but husband and wife, she is threatened by a young starlet, she is grim, handsome, wifely, a good companion for a good man. . . . She is Claudette Colbert. Her sister too is Claudette Colbert. They are twins, identical. Her husband Charles Boyer[4] is a very rich handsome man and her sister, Claudette Colbert, is plotting her death in order to take her place as the rich man's wife, no one will know because they are *twins.* . . . All these marvelous lives Clarita might have lived, but she fell out the bottom at the age of thirteen. At the age when I was packing my overnight case for a slumber party at Toni Deshield's she was tearing filthy sheets off a bed and scratching up a rash on her arms. . . . Thirteen is uncommonly young for a white girl in Detroit, Miss Brock of the Detroit House of Correction said in a sad newspaper interview for the *Detroit News;* fifteen and sixteen are more likely. Eleven, twelve, thirteen are not surprising in colored . . . they are more precocious. What can we do? Taxes are rising and the tax base is falling. The temperature rises slowly but falls rapidly. Everything is falling out the bottom, Woodward Avenue is filthy, Livernois Avenue is filthy! Scraps of paper flutter in the air like pigeons, dirt flies up and hits you right in the eye, oh Detroit is breaking up into dangerous bits of newspaper and dirt, watch out. . . .

Clarita's apartment is over a restaurant. Simon her lover emerges from the cracks at dark. Mrs. Olesko, a neighbor of Clarita's, an aged white wisp of a woman, doesn't complain but sniffs with contentment at Clarita's noisy life and doesn't tell the cops, hating cops, when the cops arrive. I should give more fake names, more blanks, instead of telling all these secrets. I myself am a secret; I am a minor.

3. My father reads a paper at a medical convention in Los Angeles. There he is, on the edge of the North American continent, when the unmarked detective put his hand so gently on my arm in the aisle of Branden's and said, "Miss, would you like to step over here for a minute?"

And where was he when Clarita put her hand on my arm, that wintry dark sulphurous aching day in Detroit, in the company of closed-down barber shops, closed-down diners, closed-down movie houses, homes, windows,

4. Cummings, Taylor, Colbert, and Boyer are romantic film stars of the 1930s to 1950s.

basements, faces . . . she put her hand on my arm and said, "Honey, are you looking for somebody down here?"

And was he home worrying about me, gone for two weeks solid, when they carried me off . . . ? It took three of them to get me in the police cruiser, so they said, and they put more than their hands on my arm.

4. I work on this lesson. My English teacher is Mr. Forest, who is from Michigan State. Not handsome, Mr. Forest, and his name is plain, unlike Raymond Forrest's, but he is sweet and rodentlike, he has conferred with the principal and my parents, and everything is fixed . . . treat her as if nothing has happened, a new start, begin again, only sixteen years old, what a shame, how did it happen?—nothing happened, nothing could have happened, a slight physiological modification known only to a gynecologist or to Dr. Coronet. I work on my lesson. I sit in my pink room. I look around the room with my sad pink eyes. I sigh, I dawdle, I pause. I eat up time. I am limp and happy to be home, I am sixteen years old suddenly, my head hangs heavy as a pumpkin on my shoulders, and my hair has just been cut by Mr. Faye at the Crystal Salon and is said to be very becoming.

(Simon too put his hand on my arm and said, "Honey, you have got to come with me," and in his six-by-six room we got to know each other. Would I go back to Simon again? Would I lie down with him in all that filth and craziness? Over and over again.

a Clarita is being betrayed as in front of a Cunningham Drug Store she is nervously eyeing a colored man who may or may not have money, or a nervous white boy of twenty with sideburns and an Appalachian look, who may or may not have a knife hidden in his jacket pocket, or a husky red-faced man of friendly countenance who may or may not be a member of the Vice Squad out for an early twilight walk.)

I work on my lesson for Mr. Forest. I have filled up eleven pages. Words pour out of me and won't stop. I want to tell everything . . . what was the song Simon was always humming, and who was Simon's friend in a very new trench coat with an old high school graduation ring on his finger . . . ? Simon's bearded friend? When I was down too low for him, Simon kicked me out and gave me to him for three days, I think, on Fourteenth Street in Detroit, an airy room of cold cruel drafts with newspapers on the floor. . . . Do I really remember that or am I piecing it together from what they told me? Did they tell the truth? Did they know much of the truth?

VIII. Characters

1. Wednesdays after school, at four; Saturday mornings at ten. Mother drives me to Dr. Coronet. Ferns in the office, plastic or real, they look the same. Dr. Coronet is queenly, an elegant nicotine-stained lady who would have studied with Freud had circumstances not prevented it, a bit of a Catholic, ready to offer you some mystery if your teeth will ache too much without it. Highly recommended by Father! Forty dollars an hour, Father's forty dollars! Progress! Looking up! Looking better! That new haircut is so becoming,

says Dr. Coronet herself, showing how normal she is for a woman with an I.Q. of 180 and many advanced degrees.

2. Mother. A lady in a brown suede coat. Boots of shiny black material, black gloves, a black fur hat. She would be humiliated could she know that of all the people in the world it is my ex-lover Simon who walks most like her . . . self-conscious and unreal, listening to distant music, a little bowlegged with craftiness. . . .

3. Father. Tying a necktie. In a hurry. On my first evening home he put his hand on my arm and said, "Honey, we're going to forget all about this."

4. Simon. Outside, a plane is crossing the sky, in here we're in a hurry. Morning. It must be morning. The girl is half out of her mind, whimpering and vague; Simon her dear friend is wretched this morning . . . he is wretched with morning itself . . . he forces her to give him an injection with that needle she knows is filthy, she had a dread of needles and surgical instruments and the odor of things that are to be sent into the blood, thinking somehow of her father. . . . This is a bad morning, Simon says that his mind is being twisted out of shape, and so he submits to the needle that he usually scorns and bites his lip with his yellowish teeth, his face going very pale. *Ah baby!* he says in his soft mocking voice, which with all women is a mockery of love, *do it like this— Slowly—*And the girl, terrified, almost drops the precious needle but manages to turn it up to the light from the window . . . is it an extension of herself then? She can give him this gift then? *I wish you wouldn't do this to me,* she says, wise in her terror, because it seems to her that Simon's danger—in a few minutes he may be dead—is a way of pressing her against him that is more powerful than any other embrace. She has to work over his arm, the knotted corded veins of his arm, her forehead wet with perspiration as she pushes and releases the needle, staring at that mixture of liquid now stained with Simon's bright blood. . . . When the drug hits him she can feel it herself, she feels that magic that is more than any woman can give him, striking the back of his head and making his face stretch as if with the impact of a terrible sun. . . . She tries to embrace him but he pushes her aside and stumbles to his feet. *Jesus Christ,* he says. . . .

5. Princess, a Negro girl of eighteen. What is her charge? She is closed-mouthed about it, shrewd and silent, you know that no one had to wrestle her to the sidewalk to get her in here; she came with dignity. In the recreation room she sits reading *Nancy Drew and the Jewel Box Mystery,*[5] which inspires in her face tiny wrinkles of alarm and interest: what a face! Light brown skin, heavy shaded eyes, heavy eyelashes, a serious sinister dark brow, graceful fingers, graceful wristbones, graceful legs, lips, tongue, a sugar-sweet voice, a leggy stride more masculine than Simon's and my mother's, decked out in a dirty white blouse and dirty white slacks; vaguely nautical is Princess' style. . . . At breakfast she is in charge of clearing the table and leans over me, saying, *Honey you sure you ate enough?*

---

5. Mystery story for juveniles.

6. The girl lies sleepless, wondering. Why here, why not there? Why Bloomfield Hills and not jail? Why jail and not her pink room? Why downtown Detroit and not Sioux Drive? What is the difference? Is Simon all the difference? The girl's head is a parade of wonders. She is nearly sixteen, her breath is marvelous with wonders, not long ago she was coloring with crayons and now she is smearing the landscape with paints that won't come off and won't come off her fingers either. She says to the matron *I am not talking about anything,* not because everyone has warned her not to talk but because, because she will not talk; because she won't say anything about Simon, who is her secret. And she says to the matron, *I won't go home,* up until that night in the lavatory when everything was changed.... "No, I won't go home I want to stay here," she says, listening to her own words with amazement, thinking that weeds might climb everywhere over that marvelous $180,000 house and dinosaurs might return to muddy the beige carpeting, but never never will she reconcile four o'clock in the morning in Detroit with eight o'clock breakfasts in Bloomfield Hills.... oh, she aches still for Simon's hands and his caressing breath, though he gave her little pleasure, he took everything from her (five-dollar bills, ten-dollar bills, passed into her numb hands by men and taken out of her hands by Simon) until she herself was passed into the hands of other men, police, when Simon evidently got tired of her and her hysteria.... *No, I won't go home, I don't want to be bailed out.* The girl thinks as a *Stubborn and Wayward Child* (one of several charges lodged against her), and the matron understands her crazy white-rimmed eyes that are seeking out some new violence that will keep her in jail, should someone threaten to let her out. Such children try to strangle the matrons, the attendants, or one another ... they want the locks locked forever, the doors nailed shut ... and this girl is no different up until that night her mind is changed for her....

IX. That Night

Princess and Dolly, a little white girl of maybe fifteen, hardy however as a sergeant and in the House of Correction for armed robbery, corner her in the lavatory at the farthest sink and the other girls look away and file out to bed, leaving her. God, how she is beaten up! Why is she beaten up? Why do they pound her, why such hatred? Princess vents all the hatred of a thousand silent Detroit winters on her body, this girl whose body belongs to me, fiercely she rides across the Midwestern plains on this girl's tender bruised body ... revenge on the oppressed minorities of America! revenge on the slaughtered Indians! revenge on the female sex, on the male sex, revenge on Bloomfield Hills, revenge revenge....

X. Detroit

In Detroit, weather weighs heavily upon everyone. The sky looms large. The horizon shimmers in smoke. Downtown the buildings are imprecise in the haze. Perpetual haze. Perpetual motion inside the haze. Across the choppy river is the city of Windsor, in Canada. Part of the continent has bunched up here and is bulging outward, at the tip of Detroit; a cold hard rain is forever falling on the expressways.... Shoppers shop grimly, their cars are not parked in safe places, their windshields may be smashed and graceful ebony hands may drag them out through their shatterproof smashed windshields, crying, *Revenge of the Indians!* Ah, they all fear leaving Hudson's and being dragged to the very tip of the city and thrown off the parking roof of Cobo Hall, that expensive tomb, into the river. . . .

XI. Characters We Are Forever Entwined With

1. Simon drew me into his tender rotting arms and breathed gravity into me. Then I came to earth, weighed down. He said, *You are such a little girl,* and he weighed me down with his delight. In the palms of his hands were teeth marks from his previous life experiences. He was thirty-five, they said. Imagine Simon in this room, in my pink room: he is about six feet tall and stoops slightly, in a feline cautious way, always thinking, always on guard, with his scuffed light suede shoes and his clothes that are anyone's clothes, slightly rumpled ordinary clothes that ordinary men might wear to not-bad jobs. Simon has fair long hair, curly hair, spent languid curls that are like . . . exactly like the curls of wood shavings to the touch, I am trying to be exact . . . and he smells of unheated mornings and coffee and too many pills coating his tongue with a faint green-white scum. . . . Dear Simon, who would be panicked in this room and in this house (right now Billie is vacuuming next door in my parents' room; a vacuum cleaner's roar is a sign of all good things), Simon who is said to have come from a home not much different from this, years ago, fleeing all the carpeting and the polished banisters . . . Simon has a deathly face, only desperate people fall in love with it. His face is bony and cautious, the bones of his cheeks prominent as if with the rigidity of his ceaseless thinking, plotting, for he has to make money out of girls to whom money means nothing, they're so far gone they can hardly count it, and in a sense money means nothing to him either except as a way of keeping on with his life. *Each Day's Proud Struggle,* the title of a novel we could read at jail. . . . Each day he needs a certain amount of money. He devours it. It wasn't love he uncoiled in me with his hollowed-out eyes and his courteous smile, that remnant of a prosperous past, but a dark terror that needed to press itself flat against him, or against another man . . . but he was the first, he came over to me and took my arm, a claim. We struggled on the stairs and I said, *Let me loose, you're hurting my neck, my face,* it was such a surprise that my skin hurt where he rubbed it, and afterward we lay face to face and he breathed everything into me. In the end I think he turned me in.

2. Raymond Forrest. I just read this morning that Raymond Forrest's father, the chairman of the board at _____, died of a heart attack on a plane bound for London. I would like to write Raymond Forrest a note of sympathy. I would like to thank him for not pressing charges against me one hundred years ago, saving me, being so generous . . . well, men like Raymond Forrest are generous men, not like Simon. I would like to write him a letter telling of my love, or of some other emotion that is positive and healthy. Not like Simon and his poetry, which he scrawled down when he was high and never changed a word . . . but when I try to think of something to say, it is Simon's language

that comes back to me, caught in my head like a bad song, it is always Simon's language:

> There is no reality only dreams
> Your neck may get snapped when you wake
> My love is drawn to some violent end
> She keeps wanting to get away
> My love is heading downward
> And I am heading upward
> She is going to crash on the sidewalk
> And I am going to dissolve into the clouds

XII. Events

1. Out of the hospital, bruised and saddened and converted, with Princess' grunts still tangled in my hair . . . and Father in his overcoat, looking like a prince himself, come to carry me off. Up the expressway and out north to home. Jesus Christ, but the air is thinner and cleaner here. Monumental houses. Heartbreaking sidewalks, so clean.

2. Weeping in the living room. The ceiling is two stories high and two chandeliers hang from it. Weeping, weeping, though Billie the maid is *probably listening*. I will never leave home again. Never. Never leave home. Never leave this home again, never.

3. Sugar doughnuts for breakfast. The toaster is very shiny and my face is distorted in it. Is that my face?

4. The car is turning in the driveway. Father brings me home. Mother embraces me. Sunlight breaks in movieland patches on the roof of our traditional-contemporary home, which was designed for the famous automotive stylist whose identity, if I told you the name of the famous car he designed, you would all know, so I can't tell you because my teeth chatter at the thought of being sued . . . or having someone climb into my bedroom window with a rope to strangle me. . . . The car turns up the blacktop drive. The house opens to me like a doll's house, so lovely in the sunlight, the big living room beckons to me with its walls falling away in a delirium of joy at my return, Billie the maid is *no doubt* listening from the kitchen as I burst into tears and the hysteria Simon got so sick of. Convulsed in Father's arms, I say I will never leave again, never, why did I leave, where did I go, what happened, my mind is gone wrong, my body is one big bruise, my backbone was sucked dry, it wasn't the men who hurt me and Simon never hurt me but only those girls . . . my God, how they hurt me . . . I will never leave home again. . . . The car is perpetually turning up the drive and I am perpetually breaking down in the living room and we are perpetually taking the right exit from the expressway (Lahser Road) and the wall of the rest room is perpetually banging against my head and perpetually are Simon's hands moving across my body and adding everything up and so too are Father's hands on my shaking

bruised back, far from the surface of my skin on the surface of my good blue cashmere coat (dry-cleaned for my release). . . . I weep for all the money here, for God in gold and beige carpeting, for the beauty of chandeliers and the miracle of a clean polished gleaming toaster and faucets that run both hot and cold water, and I tell them, *I will never leave home, this is my home, I love everything here, I am in love with everything here. . . .*

I am home.

1970

RELATED:

—Author in Depth: Joyce Carol Oates, p. 1824

TIM O'BRIEN
b. 1946

O'Brien was born in Austin, Minnesota, and educated at Macalester College. Upon graduating he was drafted into the U.S. Army and sent to fight in Vietnam, after which he emerged as one of the most brilliant chroniclers of that carnage. Though there is a solid vein of realism in his work, it also has something in common with the "magical realism" of contemporary South American novelists; fantasy is entwined with his reliable reportage. He is the author of *If I Die in a Combat Zone, Box Me Up and Ship Me Home* (1973); *Northern Lights* (1974); the National Book Award–winning *Going after Cacciato* (1978); *The Nuclear Age* (1985); *The Things They Carried* (1990), a collection of his stories that was a Pulitzer Prize finalist; *In the Lake of the Woods* (1994); *Tomcat in Love* (1998); and *July, July* (2002). In 2012 O'Brien was awarded a Lifetime Achievement award from the Dayton Literary Peace Prize, and in 2013 won the Pritzker Military Library Literature Award.

The Things They Carried

First Lieutenant Jimmy Cross carried letters from a girl named Martha, a junior at Mount Sebastian College in New Jersey. They were not love letters, but Lieutenant Cross was hoping, so he kept them folded in plastic at the bottom of his rucksack. In the late afternoon, after a day's march, he would dig his foxhole, wash his hands under a canteen, unwrap the letters, hold them with the tips of his fingers, and spend the last hour of light pretending. He would imagine romantic camping trips into the White Mountains in New Hampshire. He would sometimes taste the envelope flaps, knowing her tongue had been there. More than anything, he wanted Martha to love him as he loved her, but the letters were mostly chatty, elusive on the matter of love. She was a virgin, he was almost sure. She was an English major at Mount Sebastian, and she wrote beautifully about her professors and roommates and midterm exams, about her respect for Chaucer and her great affection for Virginia Woolf. She often quoted lines of poetry; she never mentioned the war, except to say, Jimmy, take care of yourself. The letters weighed ten ounces. They were signed "Love, Martha," but Lieutenant Cross understood that "Love" was only a way of signing and did not mean what he sometimes pretended it meant. At dusk, he would carefully return the letters to his rucksack. Slowly, a bit distracted, he would get up and move among his men, checking the perimeter, then at full dark he would return to his hole and watch the night and wonder if Martha was a virgin.

The things they carried were largely determined by necessity. Among the necessities or near necessities were P-38 can openers, pocket knives, heat tabs, wrist watches, dog tags, mosquito repellent, chewing gum, candy, cigarettes, salt tablets, packets of Kool-Aid, lighters, matches, sewing kits, Military Payment Certificates, C rations, and two or three canteens of water. Together, these items weighed between fifteen and twenty pounds, depending upon a man's habits or rate of metabolism. Henry Dobbins, who was a big man, carried extra rations; he was especially fond of canned peaches in heavy syrup over pound cake. Dave Jensen, who practiced field hygiene, carried a toothbrush, dental floss, and several hotel-size bars of soap he'd stolen on R&R[1] in Sydney, Australia. Ted Lavender, who was scared, carried tranquilizers until he was shot in the head outside the village of Than Khe in mid-April. By necessity, and because it was SOP,[2] they all carried steel helmets that weighed five pounds including the liner and camouflage cover. They carried the standard fatigue jackets and trousers. Very few carried underwear. On their feet they carried jungle boots—2.1 pounds—and Dave Jensen carried three pairs of socks and a can of Dr. Scholl's foot powder as a precaution against trench foot. Until he was shot, Ted Lavender carried six or seven ounces of premium dope, which for him was a necessity. Mitchell Sanders, the RTO,[3] carried condoms. Norman Bowker carried a diary. Rat Kiley carried comic books. Kiowa, a devout Baptist, carried an illustrated New Testament that had been presented to him by his father, who taught Sunday school in Oklahoma City, Oklahoma. As a hedge against bad times, however, Kiowa also carried his grandmother's distrust of the white man, his grandfather's old hunting hatchet. Necessity dictated. Because the land was mined and booby-trapped, it was SOP for each man to carry a steel-centered, nylon-covered flak jacket, which weighed 6.7 pounds, but which on hot days seemed much heavier. Because you could die so quickly, each man carried at least one large compress bandage, usually in the helmet band for easy access. Because the nights were cold, and because the monsoons were wet, each carried a green plastic poncho that could be used as a raincoat or ground sheet or makeshift tent. With its quilted liner, the poncho weighed almost two pounds, but it was worth every ounce. In April, for instance, when Ted Lavender was shot, they used his poncho to wrap him up, then to carry him across the paddy, then to lift him into the chopper that took him away.

They were called legs or grunts.

To carry something was to "hump" it, as when Lieutenant Jimmy Cross humped his love for Martha up the hills and through the swamps. In its intransitive form, "to hump" meant "to walk," or "to march," but it implied burdens far beyond the intransitive.

Almost everyone humped photographs. In his wallet, Lieutenant Cross carried two photographs of Martha. The first was a Kodachrome snapshot signed "Love," though he knew better. She stood against a brick wall. Her eyes were gray and neutral, her lips slightly open as she stared straight-on at the camera. At night, sometimes, Lieutenant Cross wondered who had taken the picture, because he knew she had boyfriends, because he loved her so much,

---

1. Rest and recreation leave.   **2.** Standard operating procedure.   **3.** Radio and telephone operator.

and because he could see the shadow of the picture taker spreading out against the brick wall. The second photograph had been clipped from the 1968 Mount Sebastian yearbook. It was an action shot—women's volleyball—and Martha was bent horizontal to the floor, reaching, the palms of her hands in sharp focus, the tongue taut, the expression frank and competitive. There was no visible sweat. She wore white gym shorts. Her legs, he thought, were almost certainly the legs of a virgin, dry and without hair, the left knee cocked and carrying her entire weight, which was just over one hundred pounds. Lieutenant Cross remembered touching that left knee. A dark theater, he remembered, and the movie was *Bonnie and Clyde*,[4] and Martha wore a tweed skirt, and during the final scene, when he touched her knee, she turned and looked at him in a sad, sober way that made him pull his hand back, but he would always remember the feel of the tweed skirt and the knee beneath it and the sound of the gunfire that killed Bonnie and Clyde, how embarrassing it was, how slow and oppressive. He remembered kissing her good night at the dorm door. Right then, he thought, he should've done something brave. He should've carried her up the stairs to her room and tied her to the bed and touched that left knee all night long. He should've risked it. Whenever he looked at the photographs, he thought of new things he should've done.

What they carried was partly a function of rank, partly of field specialty.

As a first lieutenant and platoon leader, Jimmy Cross carried a compass, maps, code books, binoculars, and a .45-caliber pistol that weighed 2.9 pounds fully loaded. He carried a strobe light and the responsibility for the lives of his men.

As an RTO, Mitchell Sanders carried the PRC-25 radio, a killer, twenty-six pounds with its battery.

As a medic, Rat Kiley carried a canvas satchel filled with morphine and plasma and malaria tablets and surgical tape and comic books and all the things a medic must carry, including M&M's[5] for especially bad wounds, for a total weight of nearly twenty pounds.

As a big man, therefore a machine gunner, Henry Dobbins carried the M-60, which weighed twenty-three pounds unloaded, but which was almost always loaded. In addition, Dobbins carried between ten and fifteen pounds of ammunition draped in belts across his chest and shoulders.

As PFCs or Spec 4s, most of them were common grunts and carried the standard M-16 gas-operated assault rifle. The weapon weighed 7.5 pounds unloaded, 8.2 pounds with its full twenty-round magazine. Depending on numerous factors, such as topography and psychology, the riflemen carried anywhere from twelve to twenty magazines, usually in cloth bandoliers, adding on another 8.4 pounds at minimum, fourteen pounds at maximum. When it was available, they also carried M-16 maintenance gear—rods and steel brushes and swabs and tubes of LSA oil—all of which weighed about a pound. Among the grunts, some carried the M-79 grenade launcher, 5.9 pounds unloaded, a reasonably light weapon except for the ammunition, which was heavy. A single round weighed ten ounces. The typical load was twenty-five

---

4. 1967 film starring Faye Dunaway and Warren Beatty.   5. Apparently this candy was used as a placebo since it would have no other medicinal value.

rounds. But Ted Lavender, who was scared, carried thirty-four rounds when he was shot and killed outside Than Khe, and he went down under an exceptional burden, more than twenty pounds of ammunition, plus the flak jacket and helmet and rations and water and toilet paper and tranquilizers and all the rest, plus the unweighed fear. He was dead weight. There was no twitching or flopping. Kiowa, who saw it happen, said it was like watching a rock fall, or a big sandbag or something—just boom, then down—not like the movies where the dead guy rolls around and does fancy spins and goes ass over teakettle—not like that, Kiowa said, the poor bastard just flat-fuck fell. Boom. Down. Nothing else. It was a bright morning in mid-April. Lieutenant Cross felt the pain. He blamed himself. They stripped off Lavender's canteens and ammo, all the heavy things, and Rat Kiley said the obvious, the guy's dead, and Mitchell Sanders used his radio to report one U.S. KIA[6] and to request a chopper. Then they wrapped Lavender in his poncho. They carried him out to a dry paddy, established security, and sat smoking the dead man's dope until the chopper came. Lieutenant Cross kept to himself. He pictured Martha's smooth young face, thinking he loved her more than anything, more than his men, and now Ted Lavender was dead because he loved her so much and could not stop thinking about her. When the dust-off[7] arrived, they carried Lavender aboard. Afterward they burned Than Khe. They marched until dusk, then dug their holes, and that night Kiowa kept explaining how you had to be there, how fast it was, how the poor guy just dropped like so much concrete. Boom-down, he said. Like cement.

In addition to the three standard weapons—the M-60, M-16, and M-79—they carried whatever presented itself, or whatever seemed appropriate as a means of killing or staying alive. They carried catch-as-catch-can. At various times, in various situations, they carried M-14s and CAR-15s and Swedish Ks and grease guns and captured AK-47s and Chi-Coms and RPGs and Simonov carbines and black-market Uzis and .38-caliber Smith & Wesson handguns and 66 mm LAWs and shotguns and silencers and blackjacks and bayonets and C-4 plastic explosives. Lee Strunk carried a slingshot; a weapon of last resort, he called it. Mitchell Sanders carried brass knuckles. Kiowa carried his grandfather's feathered hatchet. Every third or fourth man carried a Claymore antipersonnel mine—3.5 pounds with its firing device. They all carried fragmentation grenades—fourteen ounces each. They all carried at least one M-18 colored smoke grenade—twenty-four ounces. Some carried CS or tear-gas grenades. Some carried white-phosphorus grenades. They carried all they could bear, and then some, including a silent awe for the terrible power of the things they carried.

In the first week of April, before Lavender died, Lieutenant Jimmy Cross received a good-luck charm from Martha. It was a simple pebble, an ounce at most. Smooth to the touch, it was a milky-white color with flecks of orange and violet, oval-shaped, like a miniature egg. In the accompanying letter, Martha wrote that she had found the pebble on the Jersey shoreline, precisely where the land touched water at high tide, where things came together but also separated. It was this separate-but-together quality, she wrote, that had

---

6. Killed in action.   **7.** Helicopter.

inspired her to pick up the pebble and to carry it in her breast pocket for several days, where it seemed weightless, and then to send it through the mail, by air, as a token of her truest feelings for him. Lieutenant Cross found this romantic. But he wondered what her truest feelings were, exactly, and what she meant by separate-but-together. He wondered how the tides and waves had come into play on that afternoon along the Jersey shoreline when Martha saw the pebble and bent down to rescue it from geology. He imagined bare feet. Martha was a poet, with the poet's sensibilities, and her feet would be brown and bare, the toenails unpainted, the eyes chilly and somber like the ocean in March, and though it was painful, he wondered who had been with her that afternoon. He imagined a pair of shadows moving along the strip of sand where things came together but also separated. It was phantom jealousy, he knew, but he couldn't help himself. He loved her so much. On the march, through the hot days of early April, he carried the pebble in his mouth, turning it with his tongue, tasting sea salts and moisture. His mind wandered. He had difficulty keeping his attention on the war. On occasion he would yell at his men to spread out the column, to keep their eyes open, but then he would slip away into daydreams, just pretending, walking barefoot along the Jersey shore, with Martha, carrying nothing. He would feel himself rising. Sun and waves and gentle winds, all love and lightness.

What they carried varied by mission.

When a mission took them to the mountains, they carried mosquito netting, machetes, canvas tarps, and extra bug juice.

If a mission seemed especially hazardous, or if it involved a place they knew to be bad, they carried everything they could. In certain heavily mined AOs,[8] where the land was dense with Toe Poppers and Bouncing Betties, they took turns humping a twenty-eight-pound mine detector. With its headphones and big sensing plate, the equipment was a stress on the lower back and shoulders, awkward to handle, often useless because of the shrapnel in the earth, but they carried it anyway, partly for safety, partly for the illusion of safety.

On ambush, or other night missions, they carried peculiar little odds and ends. Kiowa always took along his New Testament and a pair of moccasins for silence. Dave Jensen carried night-sight vitamins high in carotin. Lee Strunk carried his slingshot; ammo, he claimed, would never be a problem. Rat Kiley carried brandy and M&M's. Until he was shot, Ted Lavender carried the starlight scope, which weighed 6.3 pounds with its aluminum carrying case. Henry Dobbins carried his girlfriend's pantyhose wrapped around his neck as a comforter. They all carried ghosts. When dark came, they would move out single file across the meadows and paddies to their ambush coordinates, where they would quietly set up the Claymores and lie down and spend the night waiting.

Other missions were more complicated and required special equipment. In mid-April, it was their mission to search out and destroy the elaborate tunnel complexes in the Than Khe area south of Chu Lai. To blow the tunnels, they carried one-pound blocks of pentrite high explosives, four blocks to a man, sixty-eight pounds in all. They carried wiring, detonators, and battery-powered

---

8. Areas of operations.

clackers. Dave Jensen carried earplugs. Most often, before blowing the tunnels, they were ordered by higher command to search them, which was considered bad news, but by and large they just shrugged and carried out orders. Because he was a big man, Henry Dobbins was excused from tunnel duty. The others would draw numbers. Before Lavender died there were seventeen men in the platoon, and whoever drew the number seventeen would strip off his gear and crawl in head first with a flashlight and Lieutenant Cross's .45-caliber pistol. The rest of them would fan out as security. They would sit down or kneel, not facing the hole, listening to the ground beneath them, imagining cobwebs and ghosts, whatever was down there—the tunnel walls squeezing in—how the flashlight seemed impossibly heavy in the hand and how it was tunnel vision in the very strictest sense, compression in all ways, even time, and how you had to wiggle in—ass and elbows—a swallowed-up feeling—and how you found yourself worrying about odd things—will your flashlight go dead? Do rats carry rabies? If you screamed, how far would the sound carry? Would your buddies hear it? Would they have the courage to drag you out? In some respects, though not many, the waiting was worse than the tunnel itself. Imagination was a killer.

On April 16, when Lee Strunk drew the number seventeen, he laughed and muttered something and went down quickly. The morning was hot and very still. Not good, Kiowa said. He looked at the tunnel opening, then out across a dry paddy toward the village of Than Khe. Nothing moved. No clouds or birds or people. As they waited, the men smoked and drank Kool-Aid, not talking much, feeling sympathy for Lee Strunk but also feeling the luck of the draw. You win some, you lose some, said Mitchell Sanders, and sometimes you settle for a rain check. It was a tired line and no one laughed.

Henry Dobbins ate a tropical chocolate bar. Ted Lavender popped a tranquilizer and went off to pee.

After five minutes, Lieutenant Jimmy Cross moved to the tunnel, leaned down, and examined the darkness. Trouble, he thought—a cave-in maybe. And then suddenly, without willing it, he was thinking about Martha. The stresses and fractures, the quick collapse, the two of them buried alive under all that weight. Dense, crushing love. Kneeling, watching the hole, he tried to concentrate on Lee Strunk and the war, all the dangers, but his love was too much for him, he felt paralyzed, he wanted to sleep inside her lungs and breathe her blood and be smothered. He wanted her to be a virgin and not a virgin, all at once. He wanted to know her. Intimate secrets—why poetry? Why so sad? Why that grayness in her eyes? Why so alone? Not lonely, just alone—riding her bike across campus or sitting off by herself in the cafeteria. Even dancing, she danced alone—and it was the aloneness that filled him with love. He remembered telling her that one evening. How she nodded and looked away. And how, later, when he kissed her, she received the kiss without returning it, her eyes wide open, not afraid, not a virgin's eyes, just flat and uninvolved.

Lieutenant Cross gazed at the tunnel. But he was not there. He was buried with Martha under the white sand at the Jersey shore. They were pressed together, and the pebble in his mouth was her tongue. He was smiling. Vaguely, he was aware of how quiet the day was, the sullen paddies, yet he could not bring himself to worry about matters of security. He was beyond that. He was just a kid at war, in love. He was twenty-two years old. He couldn't help it.

A few moments later Lee Strunk crawled out of the tunnel. He came up grinning, filthy but alive. Lieutenant Cross nodded and closed his eyes while the others clapped Strunk on the back and made jokes about rising from the dead.

Worms, Rat Kiley said. Right out of the grave. Fuckin' zombie.

The men laughed. They all felt great relief.

Spook City, said Mitchell Sanders.

Lee Strunk made a funny ghost sound, a kind of moaning, yet very happy, and right then, when Strunk made that high happy moaning sound, when he went *Ahhooooo*, right then Ted Lavender was shot in the head on his way back from peeing. He lay with his mouth open. The teeth were broken. There was a swollen black bruise under his left eye. The cheekbone was gone. Oh shit, Rat Kiley said, the guy's dead. The guy's dead, he kept saying, which seemed profound—the guy's dead. I mean really.

The things they carried were determined to some extent by superstition. Lieutenant Cross carried his good-luck pebble. Dave Jensen carried a rabbit's foot. Norman Bowker, otherwise a very gentle person, carried a thumb that had been presented to him as a gift by Mitchell Sanders. The thumb was dark brown, rubbery to the touch, and weighed four ounces at most. It had been cut from a VC corpse, a boy of fifteen or sixteen. They'd found him at the bottom of an irrigation ditch, badly burned, flies in his mouth and eyes. The boy wore black shorts and sandals. At the time of his death he had been carrying a pouch of rice, rifle, and three magazines of ammunition.

You want my opinion, Mitchell Sanders said, there's a definite moral here.

He put his hand on the dead boy's wrist. He was quiet for a time, as if counting a pulse, then he patted the stomach, almost affectionately, and used Kiowa's hunting hatchet to remove the thumb.

Henry Dobbins asked what the moral was.

Moral?

You know. *Moral*.

Sanders wrapped the thumb in toilet paper and handed it across to Norman Bowker. There was no blood. Smiling, he kicked the boy's head, watched the flies scatter, and said, It's like with that old TV show—Paladin. Have gun, will travel.

Henry Dobbins thought about it.

Yeah, well, he finally said. I don't see no moral.

There it *is*, man.

Fuck off.

They carried USO stationery and pencils and pens. They carried Sterno, safety pins, trip flares, signal flares, spools of wire, razor blades, chewing tobacco, liberated joss sticks and statuettes of the smiling Buddha, candles, grease pencils, *The Stars and Stripes,* fingernail clippers, Psy Ops[9] leaflets, bush hats, bolos, and much more. Twice a week, when the resupply choppers came in, they carried hot chow in green Mermite cans and large canvas bags filled with iced beer and soda pop. They carried plastic water containers, each with

9. Psychological Operations.

a two-gallon capacity. Mitchell Sanders carried a set of starched tiger fatigues for special occasions. Henry Dobbins carried Black Flag insecticide. Dave Jensen carried empty sandbags that could be filled at night for added protection. Lee Strunk carried tanning lotion. Some things they carried in common. Taking turns, they carried the big PRC-77 scrambler radio, which weighed thirty pounds with its battery. They shared the weight of memory. They took up what others could no longer bear. Often, they carried each other, the wounded or weak. They carried infections. They carried chess sets, basketballs, Vietnamese-English dictionaries, insignia of rank, Bronze Stars and Purple Hearts, plastic cards imprinted with the Code of Conduct. They carried diseases, among them malaria and dysentery. They carried lice and ringworm and leeches and paddy algae and various rots and molds. They carried the land itself—Vietnam, the place, the soil—a powdery orange-red dust that covered their boots and fatigues and faces. They carried the sky. The whole atmosphere, they carried it, the humidity, the monsoons, the stink of fungus and decay, all of it, they carried gravity. They moved like mules. By daylight they took sniper fire, at night they were mortared, but it was not battle, it was just the endless march, village to village, without purpose, nothing won or lost. They marched for the sake of the march. They plodded along slowly, dumbly, leaning forward against the heat, unthinking, all blood and bone, simple grunts, soldiering with their legs, toiling up the hills and down into the paddies and across the rivers and up again and down, just humping, one step and then the next and then another, but no volition, no will, because it was automatic, it was anatomy, and the war was entirely a matter of posture and carriage, the hump was everything, a kind of inertia, a kind of emptiness, a dullness of desire and intellect and conscience and hope and human sensibility. Their principles were in their feet. Their calculations were biological. They had no sense of strategy or mission. They searched the villages without knowing what to look for, not caring, kicking over jars of rice, frisking children and old men, blowing tunnels, sometimes setting fires and sometimes not, then forming up and moving on to the next village, then other villages, where it would always be the same. They carried their own lives. The pressures were enormous. In the heat of early afternoon, they would remove their helmets and flak jackets, walking bare, which was dangerous but which helped ease the strain. They would often discard things along the route of march. Purely for comfort, they would throw away rations, blow their Claymores and grenades, no matter, because by nightfall the resupply choppers would arrive with more of the same, then a day or two later still more, fresh watermelons and crates of ammunition and sunglasses and woolen sweaters—the resources were stunning—sparklers for the Fourth of July, colored eggs for Easter. It was the great American war chest—the fruits of science, the smokestacks, the canneries, the arsenals at Hartford, the Minnesota forests, the machine shops, the vast fields of corn and wheat—they carried like freight trains; they carried it on their backs and shoulders—and for all the ambiguities of Vietnam, all the mysteries and unknowns, there was at least the single abiding certainty that they would never be at a loss for things to carry.

After the chopper took Lavender away, Lieutenant Jimmy Cross led his men into the village of Than Khe. They burned everything. They shot chickens and dogs, they trashed the village well, they called in artillery and watched the wreckage, then they marched for several hours through the hot afternoon, and then at dusk, while Kiowa explained how Lavender died, Lieutenant Cross found himself trembling.

He tried not to cry. With his entrenching tool, which weighed five pounds, he began digging a hole in the earth.

He felt shame. He hated himself. He had loved Martha more than his men, and as a consequence Lavender was now dead, and this was something he would have to carry like a stone in his stomach for the rest of the war.

All he could do was dig. He used his entrenching tool like an ax, slashing, feeling both love and hate, and then later, when it was full dark, he sat at the bottom of his foxhole and wept. It went on for a long while. In part, he was grieving for Ted Lavender, but mostly it was for Martha, and for himself, because she belonged to another world, which was not quite real, and because she was a junior at Mount Sebastian College in New Jersey, a poet and a virgin and uninvolved, and because he realized she did not love him and never would.

Like cement, Kiowa whispered in the dark. I swear to God—boom-down. Not a word.

I've heard this, said Norman Bowker.

A pisser, you know? Still zipping himself up. Zapped while zipping.

All right, fine. That's enough.

Yeah, but you had to see it, the guy just—

I *heard*, man. Cement. So why not shut the fuck *up*?

Kiowa shook his head sadly and glanced over at the hole where Lieutenant Jimmy Cross sat watching the night. The air was thick and wet. A warm, dense fog had settled over the paddies and there was the stillness that precedes rain.

After a time Kiowa sighed.

One thing for sure, he said. The Lieutenant's in some deep hurt. I mean that crying jag—the way he was carrying on—it wasn't fake or anything, it was real heavy-duty hurt. The man cares.

Sure, Norman Bowker said.

Say what you want, the man does care.

We all got problems.

Not Lavender.

No, I guess not, Bowker said. Do me a favor, though.

Shut up?

That's a smart Indian. Shut up.

Shrugging, Kiowa pulled off his boots. He wanted to say more, just to lighten up his sleep, but instead he opened his New Testament and arranged it beneath his head as a pillow. The fog made things seem hollow and unattached. He tried not to think about Ted Lavender, but then he was thinking how fast it was, no drama, down and dead, and how it was hard to feel anything except surprise. It seemed un-Christian. He wished he could find some great sadness, or even anger, but the emotion wasn't there and he couldn't make it happen. Mostly he felt pleased to be alive. He liked the smell of the New Testament under his cheek, the leather and ink and paper and glue, whatever the chemicals were. He liked hearing the sounds of night. Even his fatigue, it felt fine, the stiff muscles and the prickly awareness of his own body, a float-ing feeling. He enjoyed not being dead. Lying there, Kiowa admired Lieuten-ant Jimmy Cross's capacity for grief. He wanted to share the man's pain, he wanted to care as Jimmy Cross cared. And yet when he closed his eyes, all he could think was Boom-down, and all he could feel was the pleasure of having his boots off and the fog curling in around him and the damp soil and the Bible smells and the plush comfort of night.

After a moment Norman Bowker sat up in the dark.

What the hell, he said. You want to talk, *talk*. Tell it to me.

Forget it.

No, man, go on. One thing I hate, it's a silent Indian.

For the most part they carried themselves with poise, a kind of dignity. Now and then, however, there were times of panic, when they squealed or wanted to squeal but couldn't, when they twitched and made moaning sounds and covered their heads and said Dear Jesus and flopped around on the earth and fired their weapons blindly and cringed and sobbed and begged for the noise to stop and went wild and made stupid promises to themselves and to God and to their mothers and fathers, hoping not to die. In different ways, it happened to all of them. Afterward, when the firing ended, they would blink and peek up. They would touch their bodies, feeling shame, then quickly hiding it. They would force themselves to stand. As if in slow motion, frame by frame, the world would take on the old logic—absolute silence, then the wind, then sunlight, then voices. It was the burden of being alive. Awkwardly, the men would reassemble themselves, first in private, then in groups, becom-ing soldiers again. They would repair the leaks in their eyes. They would check for casualties, call in dust-offs, light cigarettes, try to smile, clear their throats and spit and begin cleaning their weapons. After a time someone would shake his head and say, No lie, I almost shit my pants, and someone else would laugh, which meant it was bad, yes, but the guy had obviously not shit his pants, it wasn't that bad, and in any case nobody would ever do such a thing and then go ahead and talk about it. They would squint into the dense, oppressive sunlight. For a few moments, perhaps, they would fall silent, light-ing a joint and tracking its passage from man to man, inhaling, holding in the humiliation. Scary stuff, one of them might say. But then someone else would grin or flick his eyebrows and say, Roger-dodger, almost cut me a new asshole, *almost*.

There were numerous such poses. Some carried themselves with a sort of wistful resignation, others with pride or stiff soldierly discipline or good humor or macho zeal. They were afraid of dying but they were even more afraid to show it.

They found jokes to tell.

They used a hard vocabulary to contain the terrible softness. *Greased,* they'd say. *Offed, lit up, zapped while zipping.* It wasn't cruelty, just stage presence. They were actors and the war came at them in 3-D. When someone died, it wasn't quite dying, because in a curious way it seemed scripted, and because they had their lines mostly memorized, irony mixed with tragedy, and because they called it by other names, as if to encyst and destroy the reality of death itself. They kicked corpses. They cut off thumbs. They talked grunt lingo. They told stories about Ted Lavender's supply of tranquilizers, how the poor guy didn't feel a thing, how incredibly tranquil he was.

There's a moral here, said Mitchell Sanders.

They were waiting for Lavender's chopper, smoking the dead man's dope.

The moral's pretty obvious, Sanders said, and winked. Stay away from drugs. No joke, they'll ruin your day every time.

Cute, said Henry Dobbins.

Mind-blower, get it? Talk about wiggy—nothing left, just blood and brains.

They made themselves laugh.

There it is, they'd say, over and over, as if the repetition itself were an act of poise, a balance between crazy and almost crazy, knowing without going. There it is, which meant be cool, let it ride, because oh yeah, man, you can't change what can't be changed, there it is, there it absolutely and positively and fucking well *is*.

They were tough.

They carried all the emotional baggage of men who might die. Grief, terror, love, longing—these were intangibles, but the intangibles had their own mass and specific gravity, they had tangible weight. They carried shameful memories. They carried the common secret of cowardice barely restrained, the instinct to run or freeze or hide, and in many respects this was the heaviest burden of all, for it could never be put down, it required perfect balance and perfect posture. They carried their reputations. They carried the soldier's greatest fear, which was the fear of blushing. Men killed, and died, because they were embarrassed not to. It was what had brought them to the war in the first place, nothing positive, no dreams of glory or honor, just to avoid the blush of dishonor. They died so as not to die of embarrassment. They crawled into tunnels and walked point and advanced under fire. Each morning, despite the unknowns, they made their legs move. They endured. They kept humping. They did not submit to the obvious alternative, which was simply to close the eyes and fall. So easy, really. Go limp and tumble to the ground and let the muscles unwind and not speak and not budge until your buddies picked you up and lifted you into the chopper that would roar and dip its nose and carry you off to the world. A mere matter of falling, yet no one ever fell. It was not courage, exactly; the object was not valor. Rather, they were too frightened to be cowards.

By and large they carried these things inside, maintaining the masks of composure. They sneered at sick call. They spoke bitterly about guys who had found release by shooting off their own toes or fingers. Pussies, they'd say. Candyasses. It was fierce, mocking talk, with only a trace of envy or awe, but even so, the image played itself out behind their eyes.

They imagined the muzzle against flesh. They imagined the quick, sweet pain, then the evacuation to Japan, then a hospital with warm beds and cute geisha nurses.

They dreamed of freedom birds.

At night, on guard, staring into the dark, they were carried away by jumbo jets. They felt the rush of takeoff. *Gone!* they yelled. And then velocity, wings and engines, a smiling stewardess—but it was more than a plane, it was a real bird, a big sleek silver bird with feathers and talons and high screeching. They were flying. The weights fell off, there was nothing to bear. They laughed and held on tight, feeling the cold slap of wind and altitude, soaring, thinking *It's over, I'm gone!*—they were naked, they were light and free—it was all lightness, bright and fast and buoyant, light as light, a helium buzz in the brain, a giddy bubbling in the lungs as they were taken up over the clouds and the war, beyond duty, beyond gravity and mortification and global entanglements— *Sin loi!*[1] they yelled, *I'm sorry, motherfuckers, but I'm out of it, I'm goofed, I'm on a space cruise, I'm gone!*—and it was a restful, disencumbered sensation, just riding the light waves, sailing that big silver freedom bird over the mountains and oceans, over America, over the farms and great sleeping cities and cemeteries and highways and the golden arches of McDonald's. It was flight, a kind of fleeing, a kind of falling, falling higher and higher, spinning off the edge of the earth and beyond the sun and through the vast, silent vacuum where there were no burdens and where everything weighed exactly nothing. *Gone!* they screamed, *I'm sorry but I'm gone!* And so at night, not quite dreaming, they gave themselves over to lightness, they were carried, they were purely borne.

On the morning after Ted Lavender died, First Lieutenant Jimmy Cross crouched at the bottom of his foxhole and burned Martha's letters. Then he burned the two photographs. There was a steady rain falling, which made it difficult, but he used heat tabs and Sterno to build a small fire, screening it with his body, holding the photographs over the tight blue flame with the tips of his fingers.

He realized it was only a gesture. Stupid, he thought. Sentimental, too, but mostly just stupid.

Lavender was dead. You couldn't burn the blame.

Besides, the letters were in his head. And even now, without photographs, Lieutenant Cross could see Martha playing volleyball in her white gym shorts and yellow T-shirt. He could see her moving in the rain.

When the fire died out, Lieutenant Cross pulled his poncho over his shoulders and ate breakfast from a can.

There was no great mystery, he decided.

In those burned letters Martha had never mentioned the war, except to say, Jimmy, take care of yourself. She wasn't involved. She signed the letters "Love," but it wasn't love, and all the fine lines and technicalities did not matter.

The morning came up wet and blurry. Everything seemed part of everything else, the fog and Martha and the deepening rain.

It was a war, after all.

Half smiling, Lieutenant Jimmy Cross took out his maps. He shook his head hard, as if to clear it, then bent forward and began planning the day's march. In ten minutes, or maybe twenty, he would rouse the men and they would pack up and head west, where the maps showed the country to be green and inviting. They would do what they had always done. The rain might add some weight, but otherwise it would be one more day layered upon all the other days.

He was realistic about it. There was that new hardness in his stomach.

No more fantasies, he told himself.

---

1. Sorry about that (Vietnamese).

Henceforth, when he thought about Martha, it would be only to think that she belonged elsewhere. He would shut down the daydreams. This was not Mount Sebastian, it was another world, where there were no pretty poems or midterm exams, a place where men died because of carelessness and gross stupidity. Kiowa was right. Boom-down, and you were dead, never partly dead.

Briefly, in the rain, Lieutenant Cross saw Martha's gray eyes gazing back at him.

He understood.

It was very sad, he thought. The things men carried inside. The things men did or felt they had to do.

He almost nodded at her, but didn't.

Instead he went back to his maps. He was now determined to perform his duties firmly and without negligence. It wouldn't help Lavender, he knew that, but from this point on he would comport himself as a soldier. He would dispose of his good-luck pebble. Swallow it, maybe, or use Lee Strunk's slingshot, or just drop it along the trail. On the march he would impose strict field discipline. He would be careful to send out flank security, to prevent straggling or bunching up, to keep his troops moving at the proper pace and at the proper interval. He would insist on clean weapons. He would confiscate the remainder of Lavender's dope. Later in the day, perhaps, he would call the men together and speak to them plainly. He would accept the blame for what had happened to Ted Lavender. He would be a man about it. He would look them in the eyes, keeping his chin level, and he would issue the new SOPs in a calm, impersonal tone of voice, an officer's voice, leaving no room for argument or discussion. Commencing immediately, he'd tell them, they would no longer abandon equipment along the route of march. They would police up their acts. They would get their shit together, and keep it together, and maintain it neatly and in good working order.

He would not tolerate laxity. He would show strength, distancing himself.

Among the men there would be grumbling, of course, and maybe worse, because their days would seem longer and their loads heavier, but Lieutenant Cross reminded himself that his obligation was not to be loved but to lead. He would dispense with love; it was not now a factor. And if anyone quarreled or complained, he would simply tighten his lips and arrange his shoulders in the correct command posture. He might give a curt little nod. Or he might not. He might just shrug and say Carry on, then they would saddle up and form into a column and move out toward the villages of Than Khe.

1986

How to Tell a True War Story

This is true.

I had a buddy in Vietnam. His name was Bob Kiley, but everybody called him Rat.

A friend of his gets killed, so about a week later Rat sits down and writes a letter to the guy's sister. Rat tells her what a great brother she had, how together the guy was, a number one pal and comrade. A real soldier's soldier, Rat says. Then he tells a few stories to make the point, how her brother would always volunteer for stuff nobody else would volunteer for in a million years, dangerous stuff, like doing recon or going out on these really badass night patrols. Stainless steel balls, Rat tells her. The guy was a little crazy for sure, but crazy in a good way, a real daredevil, because he liked the challenge of it, he liked testing himself; just man against gook. A great, great guy, Rat says.

Anyway, it's a terrific letter, very personal and touching. Rat almost bawls writing it. He gets all teary telling about the good times they had together, how her brother made the war seem almost fun, always raising hell and lighting up villes and bringing smoke to bear every which way. A great sense of humor, too. Like the time at this river when he went fishing with a whole damn crate of hand grenades. Probably the funniest thing in world history, Rat says, all that gore, about twenty zillion dead gook fish. Her brother, he had the right attitude. He knew how to have a good time. On Halloween, this real hot spooky night, the dude paints up his body all different colors and puts on this weird mask and hikes over to a ville and goes trick-or-treating almost stark naked, just boots and balls and an M-16. A tremendous human being, Rat says. Pretty nutso sometimes, but you could trust him with your life.

And then the letter gets very sad and serious. Rat pours his heart out. He says he loved the guy. He says the guy was his best friend in the world. They were like soul mates, he says, like twins or something, they had a whole lot in common. He tells the guy's sister he'll look her up when the war's over.

So what happens?

Rat mails the letter. He waits two months. The dumb cooze never writes back.

A true war story is never moral. It does not instruct, nor encourage virtue, nor suggest models of proper human behavior, nor restrain men from doing the things men have always done. If a story seems moral, do not believe it. If at the end of a war story you feel uplifted, or if you feel that some small bit of rectitude has been salvaged from the larger waste, then you have been made the victim of a very old and terrible lie. There is no rectitude whatsoever. There is no virtue. As a first rule of thumb, therefore, you can tell a true war story by its absolute and uncompromising allegiance to obscenity and evil. Listen to Rat Kiley. Cooze, he says. He does not say bitch. He certainly does not say woman, or girl. He says cooze. Then he spits and stares. He's nineteen years old—it's too much for him—so he looks at you with those big sad gentle killer eyes and says cooze, because his friend is dead, and because it's so incredibly sad and true: she never wrote back.

You can tell a true war story if it embarrasses you. If you don't care for obscenity, you don't care for the truth; if you don't care for the truth, watch how you vote. Send guys to war, they come home talking dirty.

Listen to Rat: "Jesus Christ, man, I write this beautiful fuckin' letter, I slave over it, and what happens? The dumb cooze never writes back."

The dead guy's name was Curt Lemon. What happened was, we crossed a muddy river and marched west into the mountains, and on the third day we took a break along a trail junction in deep jungle. Right away, Lemon and Rat Kiley started goofing. They didn't understand about the spookiness. They were kids; they just didn't know. A nature hike, they thought, not even a war, so they went off into the shade of some giant trees—quadruple canopy, no sunlight at all—and they were giggling and calling each other yellow mother and playing a silly game they'd invented. The game involved smoke grenades, which were harmless unless you did stupid things, and what they did was pull out the pin and stand a few feet apart and play catch under the shade of those huge trees. Whoever chickened out was a yellow mother. And if nobody chickened out, the grenade would make a light popping sound and they'd be covered with smoke and they'd laugh and dance around and then do it again.

It's all exactly true.

It happened, to *me*, nearly twenty years ago, and I still remember that trail junction and those giant trees and a soft dripping sound somewhere beyond the trees. I remember the smell of moss. Up in the canopy there were tiny white blossoms, but no sunlight at all, and I remember the shadows spreading out under the trees where Curt Lemon and Rat Kiley were playing catch with smoke grenades. Mitchell Sanders sat flipping his yo-yo. Norman Bowker and Kiowa and Dave Jensen were dozing, or half dozing, and all around us were those ragged green mountains.

Except for the laughter things were quiet.

At one point, I remember, Mitchell Sanders turned and looked at me, not quite nodding, as if to warn me about something, as if he already *knew*, then after a while he rolled up his yo-yo and moved away.

It's hard to tell you what happened next.

They were just goofing. There was a noise, I suppose, which must've been the detonator, so I glanced behind me and watched Lemon step from the shade into bright sunlight. His face was suddenly brown and shining. A handsome kid, really. Sharp gray eyes, lean and narrow-waisted, and when he died it was almost beautiful, the way the sunlight came around him and lifted him up and sucked him high into a tree full of moss and vines and white blossoms.

In any war story, but especially a true one, it's difficult to separate what happened from what seemed to happen. What seems to happen becomes its own happening and has to be told that way. The angles of vision are skewed. When a booby trap explodes, you close your eyes and duck and float outside yourself. When a guy dies, like Curt Lemon, you look away and then look back for a moment and then look away again. The pictures get jumbled; you tend to miss a lot. And then afterward, when you go to tell about it, there is always that surreal seemingness, which makes the story seem untrue, but which in fact represents the hard and exact truth as it *seemed*.

In many cases a true war story cannot be believed. If you believe it, be skeptical. It's a question of credibility. Often the crazy stuff is true and the normal stuff isn't, because the normal stuff is necessary to make you believe the truly incredible craziness.

In other cases you can't even tell a true war story. Sometimes it's just beyond telling.

I heard this one, for example, from Mitchell Sanders. It was near dusk and we were sitting at my foxhole along a wide muddy river north of Quang Ngai. I remember how peaceful the twilight was. A deep pinkish red spilled out on the river, which moved without sound, and in the morning we would cross the river and march west into the mountains. The occasion was right for a good story.

"God's truth," Mitchell Sanders said. "A six-man patrol goes up into the mountains on a basic listening-post operation. The idea's to spend a week up there, just lie low and listen for enemy movement. They've got a radio along, so if they hear anything suspicious—anything—they're supposed to call in artillery or gunships, whatever it takes. Otherwise they keep strict field discipline. Absolute silence. They just listen."

Sanders glanced at me to make sure I had the scenario. He was playing with his yo-yo, dancing it with short, tight little strokes of the wrist.

His face was blank in the dusk.

"We're talking regulation, by-the-book LP.[1] These six guys, they don't say boo for a solid week. They don't got tongues. *All* ears."

"Right," I said.

"Understand me?"

"Invisible."

Sanders nodded.

"Affirm," he said. "Invisible. So what happens is, these guys get themselves deep in the bush, all camouflaged up, and they lie down and wait and that's all they do, nothing else, they lie there for seven straight days and just listen. And man, I'll tell you—it's spooky. This is mountains. You don't *know* spooky till you been there. Jungle, sort of, except it's way up in the clouds and there's always this fog—like rain, except it's not raining—everything's all wet and swirly and tangled up and you can't see jack, you can't find your own pecker to piss with. Like you don't even have a body. Serious spooky. You just go with the vapors—the fog sort of takes you in . . . And the sounds, man. The sounds carry forever. You hear stuff nobody should *ever* hear."

Sanders was quiet for a second, just working the yo-yo, then he smiled at me.

"So after a couple days the guys start hearing this real soft, kind of wacked-out music. Weird echoes and stuff. Like a radio or something, but it's not a radio, it's this strange gook music that comes right out of the rocks. Faraway, sort of, but right up close, too. They try to ignore it. But it's a listening post, right? So they listen. And every night they keep hearing that crazyass gook concert. All kinds of chimes and xylophones. I mean, this is wilderness—no way, it can't be real—but there it *is*, like the mountains are tuned in to Radio fucking Hanoi. Naturally they get nervous. One guy sticks Juicy Fruit in his ears. Another guy almost flips. Thing is, though, they can't report music. They can't get on the horn and call back to base and say, 'Hey, listen, we need some firepower, we got to blow away this weirdo gook rock band.' They can't do that. It wouldn't go down. So they lie there in the fog and keep their mouths shut. And what makes it extra bad, see, is the poor dudes can't horse around like normal. Can't joke it away. Can't even talk to each other except maybe in whispers, all hush-hush, and that just revs up the willies. All they do is listen."

Again there was some silence as Mitchell Sanders looked out on the river. The dark was coming on hard now, and off to the west I could see the mountains rising in silhouette, all the mysteries and unknowns.

1. Listening post, military jargon for a guard patrol.

"This next part," Sanders said quietly, "you won't believe."

"Probably not," I said.

"You won't. And you know why?" He gave me a long, tired smile. "Because it happened. Because every word is absolutely dead-on true."

Sanders made a sound in his throat, like a sigh, as if to say he didn't care if I believed him or not. But he did care. He wanted me to feel the truth, to believe by the raw force of feeling. He seemed sad, in a way.

"These six guys," he said, "they're pretty fried out by now, and one night they start hearing voices. Like at a cocktail party. That's what it sounds like, this big swank gook cocktail party somewhere out there in the fog. Music and chitchat and stuff. It's crazy, I know, but they hear the champagne corks. They hear the actual martini glasses. Real hoity-toity, all very civilized, except this isn't civilization. This is Nam.

"Anyway, the guys try to be cool. They just lie there and groove, but after a while they start hearing—you won't believe this—they hear chamber music. They hear violins and cellos. They hear this terrific mama-san soprano. Then after a while they hear gook opera and a glee club and the Haiphong Boys Choir and a barbershop quartet and all kinds of weird chanting and Buddha-Buddha stuff. And the whole time, in the background, there's still that cocktail party going on. All these different voices. Not human voices, though. Because it's the mountains. Follow me? The rock—it's *talking*. And the fog, too, and the grass and the goddamn mongooses. Everything talks. The trees talk politics, the monkeys talk religion. The whole country Vietnam. The place talks. It talks. Understand? Nam—it truly *talks*.

"The guys can't cope. They lose it. They get on the radio and report enemy movement—a whole army, they say—and they order up the firepower. They get arty and gunships. They call in air strikes. And I'll tell you, they fuckin' crash that cocktail party. All night long, they just smoke those mountains. They make jungle juice. They blow away trees and glee clubs and whatever else there is to blow away. Scorch time. They walk napalm up and down the ridges. They bring in the Cobras and F-4s, they use Willie Peter and HE[2] and incendiaries. It's all fire. They make those mountains burn.

"Around dawn things finally get quiet. Like you never ever *heard* quiet before. One of those real thick, real misty days—just clouds and fog, they're off in this special zone—and the mountains are absolutely dead-flat silent. Like *Brigadoon*[3]—pure vapor, you know? Everything's all sucked up inside the fog. Not a single sound, except they still *hear* it.

"So they pack up and start humping. They head down the mountain, back to base camp, and when they get there they don't say diddly. They don't talk. Not a word, like they're deaf and dumb. Later on this fat bird colonel comes up and asks what the hell happened out there. What'd they hear? Why all the ordnance? The man's ragged out, he gets down tight on their case. I mean, they spent six trillion dollars on firepower, and this fatass colonel wants answers, he wants to know what the fuckin' story is.

---

2. Willie Peter, slang for white phosphorus, an incendiary munition that burns fiercely; HE, high explosives.   3. A mythical Scottish village that appears out of a magical mist only one day every hundred years; from a 1947 Broadway musical of the same name.

"But the guys don't say zip. They just look at him for a while, sort of funny like, sort of amazed, and the whole war is right there in that stare. It says everything you can't ever say. It says, man, you got *wax* in your ears. It says, poor bastard, you'll never know—wrong frequency—you don't *even* want to hear this. Then they salute the fucker and walk away, because certain stories you don't ever tell."

You can tell a true war story by the way it never seems to end. Not then, not ever. Not when Mitchell Sanders stood up and moved off into the dark.

It all happened.

Even now, at this instant, I remember that yo-yo. In a way, I suppose, you had to be there, you had to hear it, but I could tell how desperately Sanders wanted me to believe him, his frustration at not quite getting the details right, not quite pinning down the final and definitive truth.

And I remember sitting at my foxhole that night, watching the shadows of Quang Ngai, thinking about the coming day and how we would cross the river and march west into the mountains, all the ways I might die, all the things I did not understand.

Late in the night Mitchell Sanders touched my shoulder. "Just came to me," he whispered. "The moral, I mean. Nobody listens. Nobody hears nothin'. Like that fatass colonel. The politicians, all the civilian types. Your girlfriend. My girlfriend. Everybody's sweet little virgin girlfriend. What they need is to go out on LP. The vapors, man. Trees and rocks—you got to *listen* to your enemy."

And then again, in the morning, Sanders came up to me. The platoon was preparing to move out, checking weapons, going through all the little rituals that preceded a day's march. Already the lead squad had crossed the river and was filing off toward the west.

"I got a confession to make," Sanders said. "Last night, man, I had to make up a few things."

"I know that."

"The glee club. There wasn't any glee club."

"Right."

"No opera."

"Forget it, I understand."

"Yeah, but listen, it's still true. Those six guys, they heard wicked sound out there. They heard sound you just plain won't believe."

Sanders pulled on his rucksack, closed his eyes for a moment, then almost smiled at me. I knew what was coming.

"All right," I said, "what's the moral?"

"Forget it."

"No, go ahead."

For a long while he was quiet, looking away, and the silence kept stretching out until it was almost embarrassing. Then he shrugged and gave me a stare that lasted all day.

"Hear that quiet, man?" he said. "That quiet—just listen. There's your moral."

In a true war story, if there's a moral at all, it's like the thread that makes the cloth. You can't tease it out. You can't extract the meaning without unraveling the deeper meaning. And in the end, really, there's nothing much to say about a true war story, except maybe "Oh."

True war stories do not generalize. They do not indulge in abstraction or analysis.

For example: War is hell. As a moral declaration the old truism seems perfectly true, and yet because it abstracts, because it generalizes, I can't believe it with my stomach. Nothing turns inside.

It comes down to gut instinct. A true war story, if truly told, makes the stomach believe.

This one does it for me. I've told it before—many times, many versions—but here's what actually happened.

We crossed that river and marched west into the mountains. On the third day, Curt Lemon stepped on a booby-trapped 105 round. He was playing catch with Rat Kiley, laughing, and then he was dead. The trees were thick; it took nearly an hour to cut an LZ[4] for the dustoff.

Later, higher in the mountains, we came across a baby VC[5] water buffalo. What it was doing there I don't know—no farms or paddies—but we chased it down and got a rope around it and led it along to a deserted village where we set up for the night. After supper Rat Kiley went over and stroked its nose.

He opened up a can of C rations, pork and beans, but the baby buffalo wasn't interested.

Rat shrugged.

He stepped back and shot it through the right front knee. The animal did not make a sound. It went down hard, then got up again, and Rat took careful aim and shot off an ear. He shot it in the hindquarters and in the little hump at its back. He shot it twice in the flanks. It wasn't to kill, it was to hurt. He put the rifle muzzle up against the mouth and shot the mouth away. Nobody said much. The whole platoon stood there watching, feeling all kinds of things, but there wasn't a great deal of pity for the baby water buffalo. Curt Lemon was dead. Rat Kiley had lost his best friend in the world. Later in the week he would write a long personal letter to the guy's sister, who would not write back, but for now it was a question of pain. He shot off the tail. He shot away chunks of meat below the ribs. All around us there was the smell of smoke and filth and deep greenery, and the evening was humid and very hot. Rat went to automatic. He shot randomly, almost casually, quick little spurts in the belly and butt. Then he reloaded, squatted down, and shot it in the left front knee. Again the animal fell hard and tried to get up, but this time it couldn't quite make it. It wobbled and went down sideways. Rat shot it in the nose. He bent forward and whispered something, as if talking to a pet, then he shot it in the throat. All the while the baby buffalo was silent, or almost silent, just a light bubbling sound where the nose had been. It lay very still. Nothing moved except the eyes, which were enormous, the pupils shiny black and dumb.

Rat Kiley was crying. He tried to say something, but then cradled his rifle and went off by himself.

---

4. Landing Zone.   5. Viet Cong, the North Vietnamese army, but slang for North Vietnamese in general.

The rest of us stood in a ragged circle around the baby buffalo. For a time no one spoke. We had witnessed something essential, something brand-new and profound, a piece of the world so startling there was not yet a name for it.

Somebody kicked the baby buffalo.

It was still alive, though just barely, just in the eyes.

"Amazing," Dave Jensen said. "My whole life, I never seen anything like it."

"Never?"

"Not hardly. Not once."

Kiowa and Mitchell Sanders picked up the baby buffalo. They hauled it across the open square, hoisted it up and dumped it in the village well.

Afterward, we sat waiting for Rat to get himself together.

"Amazing," Dave Jensen kept saying. "A new wrinkle I never seen it before."

Mitchell Sanders took out his yo-yo. "Well, that's Nam," he said. "Garden of Evil. Over here, man, every sin's real fresh and original."

How do you generalize?

War is hell, but that's not the half of it, because war is also mystery and terror and adventure and courage and discovery and holiness and pity and despair and longing and love. War is nasty; war is fun. War is thrilling; war is drudgery. War makes you a man; war makes you dead.

The truths are contradictory. It can be argued, for instance, that war is grotesque. But in truth war is also beauty. For all its horror, you can't help but gape at the awful majesty of combat. You stare out at tracer rounds unwinding through the dark like brilliant red ribbons. You crouch in ambush as a cool, impassive moon rises over the nighttime paddies. You admire the fluid symmetries of troops on the move, the harmonies of sound and shape and proportion, the great sheets of metal-fire streaming down from a gunship, the illumination rounds, the white phosphorus, the purply orange glow of napalm, the rocket's red glare. It's not pretty, exactly. It's astonishing. It fills the eye. It commands you. You hate it, yes, but your eyes do not. Like a killer forest fire, like cancer under a microscope, any battle or bombing raid or artillery barrage has the aesthetic purity of absolute moral indifference—a powerful, implacable beauty—and a true war story will tell the truth about this, though the truth is ugly.

To generalize about war is like generalizing about peace. Almost everything is true. Almost nothing is true. At its core, perhaps, war is just another name for death, and yet any soldier will tell you, if he tells the truth, that proximity to death brings with it a corresponding proximity to life. After a firefight, there is always the immense pleasure of aliveness. The trees are alive. The grass, the soil—everything. All around you things are purely living, and you among them, and the aliveness makes you tremble. You feel an intense, out-of-the-skin awareness of your living self—your truest self, the human being you want to be and then become by the force of wanting it. In the midst of evil you want to be a good man. You want decency. You want justice and courtesy and human concord, things you never knew you wanted. There is a kind of largeness to it, a kind of godliness. Though it's odd, you're never more alive than when you're almost dead. You recognize what's valuable. Freshly, as if for the first time, you love what's best in yourself and in the world, all that might be lost. At the hour of dusk you sit at your foxhole and look out on a wide river turning pinkish red, and at the mountains beyond, and although in the morning you must cross the river and go into the mountains and do terrible things and maybe die, even so, you find yourself studying the fine colors on the river, you feel wonder and awe at the setting of the sun, and you are filled with a hard, aching love for how the world could be and always should be, but now is not.

Mitchell Sanders was right. For the common soldier, at least, war has the feel—the spiritual texture—of a great ghostly fog, thick and permanent. There is no clarity. Everything swirls. The old rules are no longer binding, the old truths no longer true. Right spills over into wrong. Order blends into chaos, love into hate, ugliness into beauty, law into anarchy, civility into savagery. The vapors suck you in. You can't tell where you are, or why you're there, and the only certainty is overwhelming ambiguity.

In war you lose your sense of the definite, hence your sense of truth itself, and therefore it's safe to say that in a true war story nothing is ever absolutely true.

Often in a true war story there is not even a point, or else the point doesn't hit you until twenty years later, in your sleep, and you wake up and shake your wife and start telling the story to her, except when you get to the end you've forgotten the point again. And then for a long time you lie there watching the story happen in your head. You listen to your wife's breathing. The war's over. You close your eyes. You smile and think, Christ, what's the *point?*

This one wakes me up.

In the mountains that day, I watched Lemon turn sideways. He laughed and said something to Rat Kiley. Then he took a peculiar half step; moving from shade into bright sunlight, and the booby-trapped 105 round blew him into a tree. The parts were just hanging there, so Dave Jensen and I were ordered to shinny up and peel him off. I remember the white bone of an arm. I remember pieces of skin and something wet and yellow that must've been the intestines. The gore was horrible, and stays with me. But what wakes me up twenty years later is Dave Jensen singing "Lemon Tree" as we threw down the parts.

You can tell a true war story by the questions you ask. Somebody tells a story, let's say, and afterward you ask, "Is it true?' " and if the answer matters, you've got your answer.

For example, we've all heard this one. Four guys go down a trail. A grenade sails out. One guy jumps on it and takes the blast and saves his three buddies.

Is it true?

The answer matters.

You'd feel cheated if it never happened. Without the grounding reality, it's just a trite bit of puffery; pure Hollywood, untrue in the way all such stories are untrue. Yet even if it did happen—and maybe it did, anything's possible—even then you know it can't be true, because a true war story does not depend upon that kind of truth. Absolute occurrence is irrelevant. A thing may happen and be a total lie, another thing may not happen and be truer than the truth. For example: Four guys go down a trail. A grenade sails out. One guy jumps on it and takes the blast, but it's a killer grenade and everybody dies anyway. Before they die, though, one of the dead guys says, "The fuck you do *that* for?" and the jumper says, "Story of my life, man," and the other guy starts to smile but he's dead.

That's a true story that never happened.

Twenty years later, I can still see the sunlight on Lemon's face. I can see him turning, looking back at Rat Kiley, then he laughed and took that curious half step from shade into sunlight, his face suddenly brown and shining, and when his foot touched down, in that instant, he must've thought it was the sunlight that was killing him. It was not the sunlight. It was a rigged 105 round. But if I could ever get the story right, how the sun seemed to gather around him and pick him up and lift him high into a tree, if I could somehow re-create the fatal whiteness of that light, the quick glare, the obvious cause and effect, then you would believe the last thing Curt Lemon believed, which for him must've been the final truth.

Now and then, when I tell this story, someone will come up to me afterward and say she liked it. It's always a woman. Usually it's an older woman of kindly temperament and humane politics. She'll explain that as a rule she hates war stories; she can't understand why people want to wallow in all the blood and gore. But this one she liked. The poor baby buffalo, it made her sad. Sometimes, even, there are little tears. What I should do, she'll say, is put it all behind me. Find new stories to tell.

I won't say it but I'll think it.

I'll picture Rat Kiley's face, his grief, and I'll think, *You dumb cooze.*

Because she wasn't listening.

It *wasn't* a war story. It was a *love* story.

But you can't say that. All you can do is tell it one more time patiently, adding and subtracting, making up a few things to get at the real truth. No Mitchell Sanders, you tell her. No Lemon, no Rat Kiley. No trail junction. No baby buffalo. No vines or moss or white blossoms. Beginning to end you tell her, it's all made up. Every goddamn detail—the mountains and the river and especially that poor dumb baby buffalo. None of it happened. *None* of it. And even if it did happen, it didn't happen in the mountains, it happened in this little village on the Batangan Peninsula, and it was raining like crazy, and one night a guy named Stink Harris woke up screaming with a leech on his tongue. You can tell a true war story if you just keep on telling it.

And in the end, of course, a true war story is never about war. It's about sunlight. It's about the special way that dawn spreads out on a river when you know you must cross the river and march into the mountains and do things you are afraid to do. It's about love and memory. It's about sorrow. It's about sisters who never write back and people who never listen.

1987

FLANNERY O'CONNOR
1925–1964

O'Connor was born in Savannah, Georgia. Her undergraduate writing at the Georgia State College for Women won her a fellowship to the Writers' Workshop of the University of Iowa, where she earned an M.F.A. degree. She began her professional career with two years in New York, but a diagnosis of lupus, a painful autoimmune disorder, forced her to return to Georgia, where she lived with her mother on a farm near Milledgeville, raising peafowls, writing, and painting. For the rest of her life illness restricted her activities, though she traveled occasionally to give lectures and read from her work. She was a devout and uncompromising Roman Catholic; the extraordinary violence of her fiction is designed to expose the precarious condition of the spirit in a temporal world, as the startling comedy disintegrates the pretenses of a facile civilization. Her work won many honors, including three O. Henry first prizes and a posthumous National Book Award for *The Complete Stories* (1971). Her novels are *Wise Blood* (1952) and *The Violent Bear It Away* (1960). Her other books of short stories are *A Good Man Is Hard to Find* (1955) and *Everything That Rises Must Converge* (1965). A selection of her letters was edited by Sally Fitzgerald and published in 1979 under the title *The Habit of Being*.

A Good Man Is Hard to Find

The grandmother didn't want to go to Florida. She wanted to visit some of her connections in east Tennessee and she was seizing every chance to change Bailey's mind. Bailey was the son she lived with, her only boy. He was sitting on the edge of his chair at the table, bent over the orange sports section of the *Journal*. "Now look here, Bailey," she said, "see here, read this," and she stood with one hand on her thin hip and the other rattling the newspaper at his bald head. "Here this fellow that calls himself The Misfit is aloose from the Federal Pen and headed toward Florida and you read here what it says he did to these people. Just you read it. I wouldn't take my children in any direction with a criminal like that aloose in it. I couldn't answer to my conscience if I did."

Bailey didn't look up from his reading so she wheeled around then and faced the children's mother; a young woman in slacks, whose face was as broad and innocent as a cabbage and was tied around with a green headkerchief that had two points on the top like rabbit's ears. She was sitting on the sofa, feeding the baby his apricots out of a jar. "The children have been to

Florida before," the old lady said. "You all ought to take them somewhere else for a change so they would see different parts of the world and be broad. They never have been to east Tennessee."

The children's mother didn't seem to hear her, but the eight-year-old boy, John Wesley, a stocky child with glasses, said, "If you don't want to go to Florida, why dontcha stay at home?" He and the little girl, June Star, were reading the funny papers on the floor.

"She wouldn't stay at home to be queen for a day," June Star said without raising her yellow head.

"Yes, and what would you do if this fellow, The Misfit, caught you?" the grandmother asked.

"I'd smack his face," John Wesley said.

"She wouldn't stay at home for a million bucks," June Star said. "Afraid she'd miss something. She has to go everywhere we go."

"All right, Miss," the grandmother said. "Just remember that the next time you want me to curl your hair."

June Star said her hair was naturally curly.

The next morning the grandmother was the first one in the car, ready to go. She had her big black valise that looked like the head of a hippopotamus in one corner, and underneath it she was hiding a basket with Pitty Sing,[1] the cat, in it. She didn't intend for the cat to be left alone in the house for three days because he would miss her too much and she was afraid he might brush against one of the gas burners and accidentally asphyxiate himself. Her son, Bailey, didn't like to arrive at a motel with a cat.

She sat in the middle of the back seat with John Wesley and June Star on either side of her. Bailey and the children's mother and the baby sat in the front and they left Atlanta at eight forty-five with the mileage on the car at 55890. The grandmother wrote this down because she thought it would be interesting to say how many miles they had been when they got back. It took them twenty minutes to reach the outskirts of the city.

The old lady settled herself comfortably, removing her white cotton gloves and putting them up with her purse on the shelf in front of the back window. The children's mother still had on slacks and still had her head tied up in a green kerchief, but the grandmother had on a navy blue straw sailor hat with a bunch of white violets on the brim and a navy blue dress with a small white dot in the print. Her collar and cuffs were white organdy trimmed with lace and at her neckline she had pinned a purple spray of cloth violets containing a sachet. In case of an accident, anyone seeing her dead on the highway would know at once that she was a lady.

She said she thought it was going to be a good day for driving, neither too hot nor too cold, and she cautioned Bailey that the speed limit was fifty-five miles an hour and that the patrolmen hid themselves behind billboards and small clumps of trees and sped out after you before you had a chance to slow down. She pointed out interesting details of the scenery: Stone Mountain; the blue granite that in some places came up to both sides of the highway; the brilliant red clay banks slightly streaked with purple; and the various crops

---

1. Named for Pitti-Sing, one of the "three little maids from school" in *The Mikado*, an 1885 operetta by Gilbert and Sullivan.

that made rows of green lace-work on the ground. The trees were full of silver-white sunlights and the meanest of them sparkled. The children were reading comic magazines and their mother had gone back to sleep.

"Let's go through Georgia fast so we won't have to look at it much," John Wesley said.

"If I were a little boy," said the grandmother, "I wouldn't talk about my native state that way. Tennessee has the mountains and Georgia has the hills."

"Tennessee is just a hillbilly dumping ground," John Wesley said, "and Georgia is a lousy state too."

"You said it," June Star said.

"In my time," said the grandmother, folding her thin veined fingers, "children were more respectful of their native states and their parents and everything else. People did right then. Oh look at the cute little pickaninny!" she said and pointed to a Negro child standing in the door of a shack. "Wouldn't that make a picture, now?" she asked and they all turned and looked at the little Negro out of the back window. He waved.

"He didn't have any britches on," June Star said.

"He probably didn't have any," the grandmother explained. "Little niggers in the country don't have things like we do. If I could paint, I'd paint that picture," she said.

The children exchanged comic books.

The grandmother offered to hold the baby and the children's mother passed him over the front seat to her. She set him on her knee and bounced him and told him about the things they were passing. She rolled her eyes and screwed up her mouth and stuck her leathery thin face into his smooth bland one. Occasionally he gave her a faraway smile. They passed a large cotton field with five or six graves fenced in the middle of it, like a small island. "Look at the graveyard!" the grandmother said, pointing it out. "That was the old family burying ground. That belonged to the plantation."

"Where's the plantation?" John Wesley asked.

"Gone with the Wind,"[2] said the grandmother. "Ha. Ha."

When the children finished all the comic books they had brought, they opened the lunch and ate it. The grandmother ate a peanut butter sandwich and an olive and would not let the children throw the box and the paper napkins out the window. When there was nothing else to do they played a game by choosing a cloud and making the other two guess what shape it suggested. John Wesley took one the shape of a cow and June Star guessed a cow and John Wesley said, no, an automobile, and June Star said he didn't play fair, and they began to slap each other over the grandmother.

The grandmother said she would tell them a story if they would keep quiet. When she told a story, she rolled her eyes and waved her head and was very dramatic. She said once when she was a maiden lady she had been courted by a Mr. Edgar Atkins Teagarden from Jasper, Georgia. She said he was a very good-looking man and a gentleman and that he brought her a watermelon every Saturday afternoon with his initials cut in it, E.A.T. Well, one Saturday,

---

2. Title of the best-selling 1936 novel by Margaret Mitchell (as well as an immensely popular 1939 movie); in Mitchell's story a large Southern plantation, Tara, is destroyed by Union troops during the Civil War.

she said, Mr. Teagarden brought the watermelon and there was nobody at home and he left it on the front porch and returned in his buggy to Jasper, but she never got the watermelon, she said, because a nigger boy ate it when he saw the initials, E.A.T.! This story tickled John Wesley's funny bone and he giggled and giggled but June Star didn't think it was any good. She said she wouldn't marry a man that just brought her a watermelon on Saturday. The grandmother said she would have done well to marry Mr. Teagarden because he was a gentleman and had bought Coca-Cola stock when it first came out and that he had died only a few years ago, a very wealthy man.

They stopped at The Tower for barbecued sandwiches. The Tower was a part-stucco and part-wood filling station and dance hall set in a clearing outside of Timothy. A fat man named Red Sammy Butts ran it and there were signs stuck here and there on the building and for miles up and down the highway saying, TRY RED SAMMY'S FAMOUS BARBECUE. NONE LIKE FAMOUS RED SAMMY'S! RED SAM! THE FAT BOY WITH THE HAPPY LAUGH. A VETERAN! RED SAMMY'S YOUR MAN!

Red Sammy was lying on the bare ground outside The Tower with his head under a truck while a gray monkey about a foot high, chained to a small chinaberry tree, chattered nearby. The monkey sprang back into the tree and got on the highest limb as soon as he saw the children jump out of the car and run toward him.

Inside, The Tower was a long dark room with a counter at one end and tables at the other and dancing space in the middle. They all sat down at a broad table next to the nickelodeon and Red Sam's wife, a tall burnt-brown woman with hair and eyes lighter than her skin, came and took their order. The children's mother put a dime in the machine and played "The Tennessee Waltz," and the grandmother said that tune always made her want to dance. She asked Bailey if he would like to dance but he only glared at her. He didn't have a naturally sunny disposition like she did and trips made him nervous. The grandmother's brown eyes were very bright. She swayed her head from side to side and pretended she was dancing in her chair. June Star said play something she could tap to so the children's mother put in another dime and played a fast number and June Star stepped out onto the dance floor and did her tap routine.

"Ain't she cute?" Red Sam's wife said, leaning over the counter. "Would you like to come be my little girl?"

"No, I certainly wouldn't," June Star said. "I wouldn't live in a broken-down place like this for a million bucks!" and she ran back to the table.

"Ain't she cute?" the woman repeated, stretching her mouth politely.

"Aren't you ashamed?" hissed the grandmother.

Red Sam came in and told his wife to quit lounging on the counter and hurry up with these people's order. His khaki trousers reached just to his hip bones and his stomach hung over them like a sack of meal swaying under his shirt. He came over and sat down at a table nearby and let out a combination sigh and yodel. "You can't win," he said. "You can't win," and he wiped his sweating red face off with a gray handkerchief. "These days you don't know who to trust," he said. "Ain't that the truth?"

"People are certainly not nice like they used to be," said the grandmother.

"Two fellers come in here last week," Red Sammy said, "driving a Chrysler. It was an old beat-up car but it was a good one and these boys looked all right to me. Said they worked at the mill and you know I let them fellers charge the gas they bought? Now why did I do that?"

"Because you're a good man!" the grandmother said at once.

"Yes'm, I suppose so," Red Sam said as if he were struck with this answer.

His wife brought the orders, carrying the five plates all at once without a tray, two in each hand and one balanced on her arm. "It isn't a soul in this green world of God's that you can trust," she said. "And I don't count nobody out of that, not nobody," she repeated, looking at Red Sammy.

"Did you read about that criminal, The Misfit, that's escaped?" asked the grandmother.

"I wouldn't be a bit surprised if he didn't attack this place right here," said the woman. "If he hears about it being here, I wouldn't be none surprised to see him. If he hears it's two cent in the cash register, I wouldn't be a tall surprised if he . . ."

"That'll do," Red Sam said. "Go bring these people their Co'-Colas," and the woman went off to get the rest of the order.

"A good man is hard to find," Red Sammy said. "Everything is getting terrible. I remember the day you could go off and leave your screen door unlatched. Not no more."

He and the grandmother discussed better times. The old lady said that in her opinion Europe was entirely to blame for the way things were now. She said the way Europe acted you would think we were made of money and Red Sam said it was no use talking about it, she was exactly right. The children ran outside into the white sunlight and looked at the monkey in the lacy chinaberry tree. He was busy catching fleas on himself and biting each one carefully between his teeth as if it were a delicacy.

They drove off again into the hot afternoon. The grandmother took cat naps and woke up every few minutes with her own snoring. Outside of Toombsboro she woke up and recalled an old plantation that she had visited in this neighborhood once when she was a young lady. She said the house had six white columns across the front and that there was an avenue of oaks leading up to it and two little wooden trellis arbors on either side in front where you sat down with your suitor after a stroll in the garden. She recalled exactly which road to turn off to get to it. She knew that Bailey would not be willing to lose any time looking at an old house, but the more she talked about it, the more she wanted to see it once again and find out if the little twin arbors were still standing. "There was a secret panel in this house," she said craftily, not telling the truth but wishing that she were, "and the story went that all the family silver was hidden in it when Sherman[3] came through but it was never found . . ."

"Hey!" John Wesley said. "Let's go see it! We'll find it! We'll poke all the woodwork and find it! Who lives there? Where do you turn off at? Hey Pop, can't we turn off there?"

"We never have seen a house with a secret panel!" June Star shrieked. "Let's go to the house with the secret panel! Hey, Pop, can't we go see the house with the secret panel!"

---

3. In November and December 1864 the Union general William Tecumseh Sherman marched his army through Georgia from Atlanta to the Atlantic coast, plundering and burning as they went.

"It's not far from here, I know," the grandmother said. "It wouldn't take over twenty minutes."

Bailey was looking straight ahead. His jaw was as rigid as a horseshoe. "No," he said.

The children began to yell and scream that they wanted to see the house with the secret panel. John Wesley kicked the back of the front seat and June Star hung over her mother's shoulder and whined desperately into her ear that they never had any fun even on their vacation, that they could never do what THEY wanted to do. The baby began to scream and John Wesley kicked the back of the seat so hard that his father could feel the blows in his kidney.

"All right!" he shouted and drew the car to a stop at the side of the road. "Will you all shut up? Will you all just shut up for one second? If you don't shut up, we won't go anywhere."

"It would be very educational for them," the grandmother murmured.

"All right," Bailey said, "but get this. This is the only time we're going to stop for anything like this. This is the one and only time."

"The dirt road that you have to turn down is about a mile back," the grandmother directed. "I marked it when we passed."

"A dirt road," Bailey groaned.

After they had turned around and were headed toward the dirt road, the grandmother recalled other points about the house, the beautiful glass over the front doorway and the candle lamp in the hall. John Wesley said that the secret panel was probably in the fireplace.

"You can't go inside this house," Bailey said. "You don't know who lives there."

"While you all talk to the people in front, I'll run around behind and get in a window," John Wesley suggested.

"We'll all stay in the car," his mother said.

They turned onto the dirt road and the car raced roughly along in a swirl of pink dust. The grandmother recalled the times when there were no paved roads and thirty miles was a day's journey. The dirt road was hilly and there were sudden washes in it and sharp curves on dangerous embankments. All at once they would be on a hill, looking down over the blue tops of trees for miles around, then the next minute, they would be in a red depression with the dust-coated trees looking down on them.

"This place had better turn up in a minute," Bailey said, "or I'm going to turn around."

The road looked as if no one had traveled on it in months.

"It's not much farther," the grandmother said and just as she said it, a horrible thought came to her. The thought was so embarrassing that she turned red in the face and her eyes dilated and her feet jumped up, upsetting her valise in the corner. The instant the valise moved, the newspaper top she had over the basket under it rose with a snarl and Pitty Sing, the cat, sprang onto Bailey's shoulder.

The children were thrown to the floor and their mother, clutching the baby, was thrown out the door onto the ground; the old lady was thrown into the front seat. The car turned over once and landed right-side-up in a gulch on the side of the road. Bailey remained in the driver's seat with the cat—gray-striped with a broad white face and an orange nose—clinging to his neck like a caterpillar.

As soon as the children saw they could move their arms and legs, they scrambled out of the car, shouting, "We've had an ACCIDENT!" The grandmother was curled up under the dashboard, hoping she was injured so that Bailey's wrath would not come down on her all at once. The horrible thought she had had before the accident was that the house she had remembered so vividly was not in Georgia but in Tennessee.

Bailey removed the cat from his neck with both hands and flung it out the window against the side of a pine tree. Then he got out of the car and started looking for the children's mother. She was sitting against the side of the red gutted ditch, holding the screaming baby, but she only had a cut down her face and a broken shoulder. "We've had an ACCIDENT!" the children screamed in a frenzy of delight.

"But nobody's killed," June Star said with disappointment as the grandmother limped out of the car, her hat still pinned to her head but the broken front brim standing up at a jaunty angle and the violet spray hanging off the side. They all sat down in the ditch, except the children, to recover from the shock. They were all shaking.

"Maybe a car will come along," said the children's mother hoarsely.

"I believe I have injured an organ," said the grandmother, pressing her side, but no one answered her. Bailey's teeth were clattering. He had on a yellow sport shirt with bright blue parrots designed in it and his face was as yellow as the shirt. The grandmother decided that she would not mention that the house was in Tennessee.

The road was about ten feet above and they could see only the tops of the trees on the other side of it. Behind the ditch they were sitting in there were more woods, tall and dark and deep. In a few minutes they saw a car some distance away on top of a hill, coming slowly as if the occupants were watching them. The grandmother stood up and waved both arms dramatically to attract their attention. The car continued to come on slowly, disappeared around a bend and appeared again, moving even slower, on top of the hill they had gone over. It was a big black battered hearselike automobile. There were three men in it.

It came to a stop over them and for some minutes, the driver looked down with a steady expressionless gaze to where they were sitting, and didn't speak. Then he turned his head and muttered something to the other two and they got out. One was a fat boy in black trousers and a red sweat shirt with a silver stallion embossed on the front of it. He moved around on the right side of them and stood staring, his mouth partly open in a kind of loose grin. The other had on khaki pants and a blue striped coat and a gray hat pulled down very low, hiding most of his face. He came around slowly on the left side. Neither spoke.

The driver got out of the car and stood by the side of it, looking down at them. He was an older man than the other two. His hair was just beginning to gray and he wore silver-rimmed spectacles that gave him a scholarly look. He had a long creased face and didn't have on any shirt or undershirt. He had on blue jeans that were too tight for him and was holding a black hat and a gun. The two boys also had guns.

"We've had an ACCIDENT!" the children screamed.

The grandmother had the peculiar feeling that the bespectacled man was someone she knew. His face was as familiar to her as if she had known him all her life but she could not recall who he was. He moved away from the car and began to come down the embankment, placing his feet carefully so that he wouldn't slip. He had on tan and white shoes and no socks, and his ankles were red and thin. "Good afternoon," he said. "I see you all had you a little spill."

"We turned over twice!" said the grandmother.

"Oncet," he corrected. "We seen it happen. Try their car and see will it run, Hiram," he said quietly to the boy with the gray hat.

"What you got that gun for?" John Wesley asked. "Whatcha gonna do with that gun?"

"Lady," the man said to the children's mother, "would you mind calling them children to sit down by you? Children make me nervous. I want all you all to sit down right together there where you're at."

"What are you telling us what to do for?" June Star asked.

Behind them the line of woods gaped like a dark open mouth. "Come here," said their mother.

"Look here now," Bailey began suddenly, "we're in a predicament! We're in . . ."

The grandmother shrieked. She scrambled to her feet and stood staring. "You're The Misfit!" she said. "I recognized you at once!"

"Yes'm," the man said, smiling slightly as if he were pleased in spite of himself to be known, "but it would have been better for all of you, lady, if you hadn't of reckernized me."

Bailey turned his head sharply and said something to his mother that shocked even the children. The old lady began to cry and The Misfit reddened.

"Lady," he said, "don't you get upset. Sometimes a man says things he don't mean. I don't reckon he meant to talk to you thataway."

"You wouldn't shoot a lady, would you?" the grandmother said and removed a clean handkerchief from her cuff and began to slap at her eyes with it.

The Misfit pointed the toe of his shoe into the ground and made a little hole and then covered it up again. "I would hate to have to," he said.

"Listen," the grandmother almost screamed, "I know you're a good man. You don't look a bit like you have common blood. I know you must come from nice people!"

"Yes mam," he said, "finest people in the world." When he smiled he showed a row of strong white teeth. "God never made a finer woman than my mother and my daddy's heart was pure gold," he said. The boy with the red sweat shirt had come around behind them and was standing with his gun at his hip. The Misfit squatted down on the ground. "Watch them children, Bobby Lee," he said. "You know they make me nervous." He looked at the six of them huddled together in front of him and he seemed to be embarrassed as if he couldn't think of anything to say. "Ain't a cloud in the sky," he remarked, looking up at it. "Don't see no sun but don't see no cloud neither."

"Yes, it's a beautiful day," said the grandmother. "Listen," she said, "you shouldn't call yourself The Misfit because I know you're a good man at heart. I can just look at you and tell."

"Hush!" Bailey yelled. "Hush! Everybody shut up and let me handle this!" He was squatting in the position of a runner about to spring forward but he didn't move.

"I pre-chate that, lady," The Misfit said and drew a little circle in the ground with the butt of his gun.

"It'll take a half a hour to fix this here car," Hiram called, looking over the raised hood of it.

"Well, first you and Bobby Lee get him and that little boy to step over yonder with you," The Misfit said, pointing to Bailey and John Wesley. "The boys want to ask you something," he said to Bailey. "Would you mind stepping back in them woods there with them?"

"Listen," Bailey began, "we're in a terrible predicament! Nobody realizes what this is," and his voice cracked. His eyes were as blue and intense as the parrots in his shirt and he remained perfectly still.

The grandmother reached up to adjust her hat brim as if she were going to the woods with him but it came off in her hand. She stood staring at it and after a second she let it fall on the ground. Hiram pulled Bailey up by the arm as if he were assisting an old man. John Wesley caught hold of his father's hand and Bobby Lee followed. They went off toward the woods and just as they reached the dark edge, Bailey turned and supporting himself against a gray naked pine trunk, he shouted, "I'll be back in a minute, Mamma, wait on me!"

"Come back this instant!" his mother shrilled but they all disappeared into the woods.

"Bailey Boy!" the grandmother called in a tragic voice but she found she was looking at The Misfit squatting on the ground in front of her. "I just know you're a good man," she said desperately. "You're not a bit common!"

"Nome, I ain't a good man," The Misfit said after a second as if he had considered her statement carefully, "but I ain't the worst in the world neither. My daddy said I was a different breed of dog from my brothers and sisters. 'You know,' Daddy said, 'it's some that can live their whole life out without asking about it and it's others has to know why it is, and this boy is one of the latters. He's going to be into everything!'" He put on his black hat and looked up suddenly and then away deep into the woods as if he were embarrassed again. "I'm sorry I don't have on a shirt before you ladies," he said, hunching his shoulders slightly. "We buried our clothes that we had on when we escaped and we're just making do until we can get better. We borrowed these from some folks we met," he explained.

"That's perfectly all right," the grandmother said. "Maybe Bailey has an extra shirt in his suitcase."

"I'll look and see terrectly," The Misfit said.

"Where are they taking him?" the children's mother screamed.

"Daddy was a card himself," The Misfit said. "You couldn't put anything over on him. He never got in trouble with the Authorities though. Just had the knack of handling them."

"You could be honest too if you'd only try," said the grandmother. "Think how wonderful it would be to settle down and live a comfortable life and not have to think about somebody chasing you all the time."

The Misfit kept scratching in the ground with the butt of his gun as if he were thinking about it. "Yes'm, somebody is always after you," he murmured.

The grandmother noticed how thin his shoulder blades were just behind his hat because she was standing up looking down on him. "Do you ever pray?" she asked.

He shook his head. All she saw was the black hat wiggle between his shoulder blades. "Nome," he said.

There was a pistol shot from the woods, followed closely by another. Then silence. The old lady's head jerked around. She could hear the wind move through the tree tops like a long satisfied insuck of breath. "Bailey Boy!" she called.

"I was a gospel singer for a while," The Misfit said. "I been most everything. Been in the arm service, both land and sea, at home and abroad, been twict married, been an undertaker, been with the railroads, plowed Mother Earth, been in a tornado, seen a man burnt alive oncet," and he looked up at the children's mother and the little girl who were sitting close together, their faces white and their eyes glassy; "I even seen a woman flogged," he said.

"Pray, pray," the grandmother began, "pray, pray . . ."

"I never was a bad boy that I remember of," The Misfit said in an almost dreamy voice, "but somewheres along the line I done something wrong and got sent to the penitentiary. I was buried alive," and he looked up and held her attention to him by a steady stare.

"That's when you should have started to pray," she said. "What did you do to get sent to the penitentiary that first time?"

"Turn to the right, it was a wall," The Misfit said, looking up again at the cloudless sky. "Turn to the left, it was a wall. Look up it was a ceiling, look down it was a floor. I forget what I done, lady. I set there and set there, trying to remember what it was I done and I ain't recalled it to this day. Oncet in a while, I would think it was coming to me, but it never come."

"Maybe they put you in by mistake," the old lady said vaguely.

"Nome," he said. "It wasn't no mistake. They had the papers on me."

"You must have stolen something," she said.

The Misfit sneered slightly. "Nobody had nothing I wanted," he said. "It was a head-doctor at the penitentiary said what I had done was kill my daddy but I known that for a lie. My daddy died in nineteen ought nineteen of the epidemic flu[4] and I never had a thing to do with it. He was buried in the Mount Hopewell Baptist churchyard and you can go there and see for yourself."

"If you would pray," the old lady said, "Jesus would help you."

"That's right," The Misfit said.

"Well then, why don't you pray?" she asked trembling with delight suddenly.

"I don't want no hep," he said. "I'm doing all right by myself."

Bobby Lee and Hiram came ambling back from the woods. Bobby Lee was dragging a yellow shirt with bright blue parrots in it.

"Throw me that shirt, Bobby Lee," The Misfit said. The shirt came flying at him and landed on his shoulder and he put it on. The grandmother couldn't name what the shirt reminded her of. "No, lady," The Misfit said while he was buttoning up, "I found out the crime don't matter. You can do one thing or you can do another, kill a man or take a tire off his car, because sooner or later you're going to forget what it was you done and just be punished for it."

The children's mother had begun to make heaving noises as if she couldn't get her breath. "Lady," he asked, "would you and that little girl like to step off yonder with Bobby Lee and Hiram and join your husband?"

"Yes, thank you," the mother said faintly. Her left arm dangled helplessly and she was holding the baby, who had gone to sleep, in the other. "Hep that

---

4. A devastating, worldwide epidemic of influenza in 1918–19 followed the end of World War I.

lady up, Hiram," The Misfit said as she struggled to climb out of the ditch, "and Bobby Lee, you hold onto that little girl's hand."

"I don't want to hold hands with him," June Star said. "He reminds me of a pig."

The fat boy blushed and laughed and caught her by the arm and pulled her off into the woods after Hiram and her mother.

Alone with The Misfit, the grandmother found that she had lost her voice. There was not a cloud in the sky nor any sun. There was nothing around her but woods. She wanted to tell him that he must pray. She opened and closed her mouth several times before anything came out. Finally she found herself saying, "Jesus, Jesus," meaning, Jesus will help you, but the way she was saying it, it sounded as if she might be cursing.

"Yes'm," The Misfit said as if he agreed. "Jesus thrown everything off balance. It was the same case with Him as with me except He hadn't committed any crime and they could prove I had committed one because they had the papers on me. Of course," he said, "they never shown me my papers. That's why I sign myself now. I said long ago, you get you a signature and sign everything you do and keep a copy of it. Then you'll know what you done and you can hold up the crime to the punishment and see do they match and in the end you'll have something to prove you ain't been treated right. I call myself The Misfit," he said, "because I can't make what all I done wrong fit what all I gone through in punishment."

There was a piercing scream from the woods, followed closely by a pistol report. "Does it seem right to you, lady, that one is punished a heap and another ain't punished at all?"

"Jesus!" the old lady cried. "You've got good blood! I know you wouldn't shoot a lady! I know you come from nice people! Pray! Jesus, you ought not to shoot a lady. I'll give you all the money I've got!"

"Lady," The Misfit said, looking beyond her far into the woods, "there never was a body that give the undertaker a tip."

There were two more pistol reports and the grandmother raised her head like a parched old turkey hen crying for water and called, "Bailey Boy, Bailey Boy!" as if her heart would break.

"Jesus was the only One that ever raised the dead," The Misfit continued, "and He shouldn't have done it. He thown everything off balance. If He did what He said, then it's nothing for you to do but thow away everything and follow Him, and if He didn't then it's nothing for you to do but enjoy the few minutes you got left the best way you can—by killing somebody or burning down his house or doing some other meanness to him. No pleasure but meanness," he said and his voice had become almost a snarl.

"Maybe He didn't raise the dead," the old lady mumbled, not knowing what she was saying and feeling so dizzy that she sank down in the ditch with her legs twisted under her.

"I wasn't there so I can't say He didn't," The Misfit said. "I wisht I had of been there," he said, hitting the ground with his fist. "It ain't right I wasn't there because if I had of been there I would of known. Listen lady," he said in a high voice, "if I had of been there I would of known and I wouldn't be like I am now." His voice seemed about to crack and the grandmother's head cleared for an instant. She saw the man's face twisted close to her own as if he were going to cry and she murmured, "Why, you're one of my babies. You're one of my own children!" She reached out and touched him on the shoulder. The Misfit sprang back as if a snake had bitten him and shot her three times through the chest. Then he put his gun down on the ground and took off his glasses and began to clean them.

Hiram and Bobby Lee returned from the woods and stood over the ditch, looking down at the grandmother who half sat and half lay in a puddle of blood with her legs crossed under her like a child's and her face smiling up at the cloudless sky.

Without his glasses, The Misfit's eyes were red-rimmed and pale and defenseless-looking. "Take her off and thow her where you thown the others," he said, picking up the cat that was rubbing itself against his leg.

"She was a talker, wasn't she?" Bobby Lee said, sliding down the ditch with a yodel.

"She would of been a good woman," The Misfit said, "if it had been somebody there to shoot her every minute of her life."

"Some fun!" Bobby Lee said.

"Shut up, Bobby Lee," The Misfit said. "It's no real pleasure in life."

1953

Good Country People

Besides the neutral expression that she wore when she was alone, Mrs. Freeman had two others, forward and reverse, that she used for all her human dealings. Her forward expression was steady and driving like the advance of a heavy truck. Her eyes never swerved to left or right but turned as the story turned as if they followed a yellow line down the center of it. She seldom used the other expression because it was not often necessary for her to retract a statement, but when she did, her face came to a complete stop, there was an almost imperceptible movement of her black eyes, during which they seemed to be receding, and then the observer would see that Mrs. Freeman, though she might stand there as real as several grain sacks thrown on top of each other, was no longer there in spirit. As for getting anything across to her when this was the case, Mrs. Hopewell had given it up. She might talk her head off. Mrs. Freeman could never be brought to admit herself wrong on any point. She would stand there and if she could be brought to say anything, it was something like, "Well, I wouldn't of said it was and I wouldn't of said it wasn't," or letting her gaze range over the top kitchen shelf where there was an assortment of dusty bottles, she might remark, "I see you ain't ate many of them figs you put up last summer."

They carried on their most important business in the kitchen at breakfast. Every morning Mrs. Hopewell got up at seven o'clock and lit her gas heater and Joy's. Joy was her daughter, a large blonde girl who had an artificial leg. Mrs. Hopewell thought of her as a child though she was thirty-two years old and highly educated. Joy would get up while her mother was eating and lumber into the bathroom and slam the door, and before long, Mrs. Freeman would arrive at the back door. Joy would hear her mother call, "Come on in," and then they would talk for a while in low voices that were indistinguishable in the bathroom. By the time Joy came in, they had usually finished the weather report and were on one or the other of Mrs. Freeman's daughters, Glynese or Carramae, Joy called them Glycerin and Caramel. Glynese, a redhead, was eighteen and had many admirers; Carramae, a blonde, was only fifteen but already married and pregnant. She could not keep anything on her stomach. Every morning Mrs. Freeman told Mrs. Hopewell how many times she had vomited since the last report.

Mrs. Hopewell liked to tell people that Glynese and Carramae were two of the finest girls she knew and that Mrs. Freeman was a *lady* and that she was never ashamed to take her anywhere or introduce her to anybody they might meet. Then she would tell how she had happened to hire the Freemans in the first place and how they were a godsend to her and how she had had them four years. The reason for her keeping them so long was that they were not trash. They were good country people. She had telephoned the man whose name they had given as a reference and he had told her that Mr. Freeman was a good farmer but that his wife was the nosiest woman ever to walk the earth. "She's got to be into everything," the man said. "If she don't get there before the dust settles, you can bet she's dead, that's all. She'll want to know all your business. I can stand him real good," he had said, "but me nor my wife neither could have stood that woman one more minute on this place." That had put Mrs. Hopewell off for a few days.

She had hired them in the end because there were no other applicants but she had made up her mind beforehand exactly how she would handle the woman. Since she was the type who had to be into everything, then, Mrs. Hopewell had decided, she would not only let her be into everything, she would *see to it* that she was into everything—she would give her the responsibility of everything, she would put her in charge. Mrs. Hopewell had no bad qualities of her own but she was able to use other people's in such a constructive way that she never felt the lack. She had hired the Freemans and she had kept them four years.

Nothing is perfect. This was one of Mrs. Hopewell's favorite sayings. Another was: that is life! And still another, the most important, was: well, other people have their opinions too. She would make these statements, usually at the table, in a tone of gentle insistence as if no one held them but her, and the large hulking Joy, whose constant outrage had obliterated every expression from her face, would stare just a little to the side of her, her eyes icy blue, with the look of someone who has achieved blindness by an act of will and means to keep it.

When Mrs. Hopewell said to Mrs. Freeman that life was like that, Mrs. Freeman would say, "I always said so myself." Nothing had been arrived at by anyone that had not first been arrived at by her. She was quicker than Mr. Freeman. When Mrs. Hopewell said to her after they had been on the place a while, "You know, you're the wheel behind the wheel," and winked, Mrs. Freeman had said, "I know it. I've always been quick. It's some that are quicker than others."

"Everybody is different," Mrs. Hopewell said.

"Yes, most people is," Mrs. Freeman said.

"It takes all kinds to make the world."

"I always said it did myself."

The girl was used to this kind of dialogue for breakfast and more of it for dinner; sometimes they had it for supper too. When they had no guest they ate in the kitchen because that was easier. Mrs. Freeman always managed to arrive at some point during the meal and to watch them finish it. She would stand in the doorway if it were summer but in the winter she would stand with one elbow on top of the refrigerator and look down on them, or she would stand by the gas heater, lifting the back of her skirt slightly. Occasionally she would stand against the wall and roll her head from side to side. At no time was she in any hurry to leave. All this was very trying on Mrs. Hopewell but she was a woman of great patience. She realized that nothing is perfect and that in the Freemans she had good country people and that if, in this day and age, you get good country people, you had better hang onto them.

She had had plenty of experience with trash. Before the Freemans she had averaged one tenant family a year. The wives of these farmers were not the kind you would want to be around you for very long. Mrs. Hopewell, who had divorced her husband long ago, needed someone to walk over the fields with her; and when Joy had to be impressed for these services, her remarks were usually so ugly and her face so glum that Mrs. Hopewell would say, "If you can't come pleasantly, I don't want you at all," to which the girl, standing square and rigid-shouldered with her neck thrust slightly forward, would reply, "If you want me, here I am—LIKE I AM."

Mrs. Hopewell excused this attitude because of the leg (which had been shot off in a hunting accident when Joy was ten). It was hard for Mrs. Hopewell to realize that her child was thirty-two now and that for more than twenty years she had had only one leg. She thought of her still as a child because it tore her heart to think instead of the poor stout girl in her thirties who had never danced a step or had any *normal* good times. Her name was really Joy but as soon as she was twenty-one and away from home, she had had it legally changed. Mrs. Hopewell was certain that she had thought and thought until she had hit upon the ugliest name in any language. Then she had gone and had the beautiful name, Joy, changed without telling her mother until after she had done it. Her legal name was Hulga.

When Mrs. Hopewell thought the name, Hulga, she thought of the broad blank hull of a battleship. She would not use it. She continued to call her Joy to which the girl responded but in a purely mechanical way.

Hulga had learned to tolerate Mrs. Freeman who saved her from taking walks with her mother. Even Glynese and Carramae were useful when they occupied attention that might otherwise have been directed at her. At first she had thought she could not stand Mrs. Freeman for she had found that it was not possible to be rude to her. Mrs. Freeman would take on strange resentments and for days together she would be sullen but the source of her displeasure was always obscure; a direct attack, a positive leer, blatant ugliness to her face—these never touched her. And without warning one day, she began calling her Hulga.

She did not call her that in front of Mrs. Hopewell who would have been incensed but when she and the girl happened to be out of the house together, she would say something and add the name Hulga to the end of it, and the big spectacled Joy-Hulga would scowl and redden as if her privacy had been intruded upon. She considered the name her personal affair. She had arrived at it first purely on the basis of its ugly sound and then the full genius of its fitness had struck her. She had a vision of the name working like the ugly sweating Vulcan[1] who stayed in the furnace and to whom, presumably, the goddess had to come when called. She saw it as the name of her highest creative act. One of her major triumphs was that her mother had not been able to turn her dust into Joy, but the greater one was that she had been able to turn it herself into Hulga. However, Mrs. Freeman's relish for using the name only irritated her. It was as if Mrs. Freeman's beady steel-pointed eyes had penetrated far enough behind her face to reach some secret fact. Something about her seemed to fascinate Mrs. Freeman and then one day Hulga realized that it was the artificial leg. Mrs. Freeman had a special fondness for the details of secret infections, hidden deformities, assaults upon children. Of diseases, she preferred the lingering or incurable. Hulga had heard Mrs. Hopewell give her the details of the hunting accident, how the leg had been literally blasted off, how she had never lost consciousness. Mrs. Freeman could listen to it anytime as if it had happened an hour ago.

When Hulga stumped into the kitchen in the morning (she could walk without making the awful noise but she made it—Mrs. Hopewell was certain—because it was ugly-sounding), she glanced at them and did not speak. Mrs. Hopewell would be in her red kimono with her hair tied around her head in rags. She would be sitting at the table, finishing her breakfast and Mrs. Freeman would be hanging by her elbow outward from the refrigerator, looking down at the table. Hulga always put her eggs on the stove to boil and then stood over them with her arms folded, and Mrs. Hopewell would look at her—a kind of indirect gaze divided between her and Mrs. Freeman—and would think that if she would only keep herself up a little, she wouldn't be so bad looking. There was nothing wrong with her face that a pleasant expression wouldn't help. Mrs. Hopewell said that people who looked on the bright side of things would be beautiful even if they were not.

Whenever she looked at Joy this way, she could not help but feel that it would have been better if the child had not taken the Ph.D. It had certainly not brought her out any and now that she had it, there was no more excuse for her to go to school again. Mrs. Hopewell thought it was nice for girls to go to school to have a good time but Joy had "gone through." Anyhow, she would not have been strong enough to go again. The doctors had told Mrs. Hopewell that with the best of care, Joy might see forty-five. She had a weak heart. Joy had made it plain that if it had not been for this condition, she would be far from these red hills and good country people. She would be in a university lecturing to people who knew what she was talking about. And Mrs. Hopewell could very well picture her there, looking like a scarecrow and lecturing to more of the same. Here she went about all day in a six-year-old skirt and a yellow sweat shirt with a faded cowboy on a horse embossed on it. She thought this was funny; Mrs. Hopewell thought it was idiotic and showed simply that she was still a child. She was brilliant but she didn't have a grain of sense. It

1. Roman god of fire and the forge; husband of Venus, goddess of love.

seemed to Mrs. Hopewell that every year she grew less like other people and more like herself—bloated, rude, and squint-eyed. And she said such strange things! To her own mother she had said—without warning, without excuse, standing up in the middle of a meal with her face purple and her mouth half full—"Woman! do you ever look inside? Do you ever look inside and see what you are *not?* God!" she had cried sinking down again and staring at her plate, "Malebranche was right: we are not our own light. We are not our own light!" Mrs. Hopewell had no idea to this day what brought that on. She had only made the remark, hoping Joy would take it in, that a smile never hurt anyone.

The girl had taken the Ph.D. in philosophy and this left Mrs. Hopewell at a complete loss. You could say, "My daughter is a nurse," or "My daughter is a schoolteacher," or even, "My daughter is a chemical engineer." You could not say, "My daughter is a philosopher." That was something that had ended with the Greeks and Romans. All day Joy sat on her neck in a deep chair, reading. Sometimes she went for walks but she didn't like dogs or cats or birds or flowers or nature or nice young men. She looked at nice young men as if she could smell their stupidity.

One day Mrs. Hopewell had picked up one of the books the girl had just put down and opening it at random, she read, "Science, on the other hand, has to assert its soberness and seriousness afresh and declare that it is concerned solely with what-is. Nothing—how can it be for science anything but a horror and a phantasm? If science is right, then one thing stands firm: science wishes to know nothing of nothing. Such is after all the strictly scientific approach to Nothing. We know it by wishing to know nothing of Nothing." These words had been underlined with a blue pencil and they worked on Mrs. Hopewell like some evil incantation in gibberish. She shut the book quickly and went out of the room as if she were having a chill.

This morning when the girl came in, Mrs. Freeman was on Carramae. "She thrown up four times after supper," she said, "and was up twict in the night after three o'clock. Yesterday she didn't do nothing but ramble in the bureau drawer. All she did. Stand up there and see what she could run up on."

"She's got to eat," Mrs. Hopewell muttered, sipping her coffee, while she watched Joy's back at the stove. She was wondering what the child had said to the Bible salesman. She could not imagine what kind of a conversation she could possibly have had with him.

He was a tall gaunt hatless youth who had called yesterday to sell them a Bible. He had appeared at the door, carrying a large black suitcase that weighted him so heavily on one side that he had to brace himself against the door facing. He seemed on the point of collapse but he said in a cheerful voice. "Good morning, Mrs. Cedars!" and set the suitcase down on the mat. He was not a bad-looking young man though he had on a bright blue suit and yellow socks that were not pulled up far enough. He had prominent face bones and a streak of sticky-looking brown hair falling across his forehead.

"I'm Mrs. Hopewell," she said.

"Oh!" he said, pretending to look puzzled but with his eyes sparkling, "I saw it said 'The Cedars' on the mailbox so I thought you was Mrs. Cedars!" and he burst out in a pleasant laugh. He picked up the satchel and under cover of a pant, he fell forward into her hall. It was rather as if the suitcase had moved first, jerking him after it. "Mrs. Hopewell!" he said and grabbed her hand. "I hope you are well!" and he laughed again and then all at once his face sobered completely. He paused and gave her a straight earnest look and said, "Lady, I've come to speak of serious things."

"Well, come in," she muttered, none too pleased because her dinner was almost ready. He came into the parlor and sat down on the edge of a straight chair and put the suitcase between his feet and glanced around the room as if he were sizing her up by it. Her silver gleamed on the two sideboards; she decided he had never been in a room as elegant as this.

"Mrs. Hopewell," he began, using her name in a way that sounded almost intimate, "I know you believe in Chrustian service."

"Well yes," she murmured.

"I know," he said and paused, looking very wise with his head cocked on one side, "that you're a good woman. Friends have told me."

Mrs. Hopewell never liked to be taken for a fool. "What are you selling?" she asked.

"Bibles," the young man said and his eye raced around the room before he added, "I see you have no family Bible in your parlor, I see that is the one lack you got!"

Mrs. Hopewell could not say, "My daughter is an atheist and won't let me keep the Bible in the parlor." She said, stiffening slightly, "I keep my Bible by my bedside." This was not the truth. It was in the attic somewhere.

"Lady," he said, "the word of God ought to be in the parlor."

"Well, I think that's a matter of taste," she began. "I think . . ."

"Lady," he said, "for a Chrustian, the word of God ought to be in every room in the house besides in his heart. I know you're a Chrustian because I can see it in every line of your face."

She stood up and said, "Well, young man, I don't want to buy a Bible and I smell my dinner burning."

He didn't get up. He began to twist his hands and looking down at them, he said softly, "Well lady, I'll tell you the truth—not many people want to buy one nowadays and besides, I know I'm real simple. I don't know how to say a thing but to say it. I'm just a country boy." He glanced up into her unfriendly face. "People like you don't like to fool with country people like me!"

"Why!" she cried, "good country people are the salt of the earth! Besides, we all have different ways of doing, it takes all kinds to make the world go 'round. That's life!"

"You said a mouthful," he said.

"Why, I think there aren't enough good country people in the world!" she said, stirred. "I think that's what's wrong with it!"

His face had brightened. "I didn't inraduce myself," he said. "I'm Manley Pointer from out in the country around Willohobie, not even from a place, just from near a place."

"You wait a minute," she said. "I have to see about my dinner." She went out to the kitchen and found Joy standing near the door where she had been listening.

"Get rid of the salt of the earth," she said, "and let's eat."

Mrs. Hopewell gave her a pained look and turned the heat down under the vegetables. "I can't be rude to anybody," she murmured and went back into the parlor.

He had opened the suitcase and was sitting with a Bible on each knee.

"You might as well put those up," she told him. "I don't want one."

"I appreciate your honesty," he said. "You don't see any more real honest people unless you go away out in the country."

"I know," she said, "real genuine folks!" Through the crack in the door she heard a groan.

"I guess a lot of boys come telling you they're working their way through college," he said, "but I'm not going to tell you that. Somehow," he said, "I don't want to go to college. I want to devote my life to Chrustian service. See," he said, lowering his voice, "I got this heart condition. I may not live long. When you know it's something wrong with you and you may not live long, well then, lady . . ." He paused, with his mouth open, and stared at her.

He and Joy had the same condition! She knew that her eyes were filling with tears but she collected herself quickly and murmured, "Won't you stay for dinner? We'd love to have you!" and was sorry the instant she heard herself say it.

"Yes mam," he said in an abashed voice, "I would sher love to do that!"

Joy had given him one look on being introduced to him and then throughout the meal had not glanced at him again. He had addressed several remarks to her, which she had pretended not to hear. Mrs. Hopewell could not understand deliberate rudeness, although she lived with it, and she felt she had always to overflow with hospitality to make up for Joy's lack of courtesy. She urged him to talk about himself and he did. He said he was the seventh child of twelve and that his father had been crushed under a tree when he himself was eight year old. He had been crushed very badly, in fact, almost cut in two and was practically not recognizable. His mother had got along the best she could by hard working and she had always seen that her children went to Sunday School and that they read the Bible every evening. He was now nineteen year old and he had been selling Bibles for four months. In that time he had sold seventy-seven Bibles and had the promise of two more sales. He wanted to become a missionary because he thought that was the way you could do most for people. "He who losest his life shall find it," he said simply and he was so sincere, so genuine and earnest that Mrs. Hopewell would not for the world have smiled. He prevented his peas from sliding onto the table by blocking them with a piece of bread which he later cleaned his plate with. She could see Joy observing sidewise how he handled his knife and fork and she saw too that every few minutes, the boy would dart a keen appraising glance at the girl as if he were trying to attract her attention.

After dinner Joy cleared the dishes off the table and disappeared and Mrs. Hopewell was left to talk with him. He told her again about his childhood and his father's accident and about various things that had happened to him. Every five minutes or so she would stifle a yawn. He sat for two hours until finally she told him she must go because she had an appointment in town. He packed his Bibles and thanked her and prepared to leave, but in the doorway he stopped and wrung her hand and said that not on any of his trips had he met a lady as nice as her and he asked if he could come again. She had said she would always be happy to see him.

Joy had been standing in the road, apparently looking at something in the distance, when he came down the steps toward her, bent to the side with his heavy valise. He stopped where she was standing and confronted her directly. Mrs. Hopewell could not hear what he said but she trembled to think what Joy would say to him. She could see that after a minute Joy said something and that then the boy began to speak again, making an excited gesture with his free hand. After a minute Joy said something else at which the boy began to speak once more. Then to her amazement, Mrs. Hopewell saw the two of them walk off together, toward the gate. Joy had walked all the way to the gate with him and Mrs. Hopewell could not imagine what they had said to each other, and she had not yet dared to ask.

Mrs. Freeman was insisting upon her attention. She had moved from the refrigerator to the heater so that Mrs. Hopewell had to turn and face her in order to seem to be listening. "Glynese gone out with Harvey Hill again last night," she said. "She had this sty."

"Hill," Mrs. Hopewell said absently, "is that the one who works in the garage?"

"Nome, he's the one that goes to chiropracter school," Mrs. Freeman said. "She had this sty. Been had it two days. So she says when he brought her in the other night he says, 'Lemme get rid of that sty for you,' and she says, 'How?' and he says, 'You just lay yourself down acrost the seat of that car and I'll show you.' So she done it and he popped her neck. Kept on a-popping it several times until she made him quit. This morning," Mrs. Freeman said, "she ain't got no sty. She ain't got no traces of a sty."

"I never heard of that before," Mrs. Hopewell said.

"He ast her to marry him before the Ordinary,"[2] Mrs. Freeman went on, "and she told him she wasn't going to be married in no *office*."

"Well, Glynese is a fine girl," Mrs. Hopewell said. "Glynese and Carramae are both fine girls."

"Carramae said when her and Lyman was married Lyman said it sure felt sacred to him. She said he said he wouldn't take five hundred dollars for being married by a preacher."

"How much would he take?" the girl asked from the stove.

"He said he wouldn't take five hundred dollars," Mrs. Freeman repeated.

"Well we all have work to do," Mrs. Hopewell said.

"Lyman said it just felt more sacred to him," Mrs. Freeman said. "The doctor wants Carramae to eat prunes. Says instead of medicine. Says them cramps is coming from pressure. You know where I think it is?"

"She'll be better in a few weeks," Mrs. Hopewell said.

"In the tube," Mrs. Freeman said. "Else she wouldn't be as sick as she is."

Hulga had cracked her two eggs into a saucer and was bringing them to the table along with a cup of coffee that she had filled too full. She sat down carefully and began to eat, meaning to keep Mrs. Freeman there by questions if for any reason she showed an inclination to leave. She could perceive her mother's eye on her. The first round-about question would be about the Bible salesman and she did not wish to bring it on. "How did he pop her neck?" she asked.

Mrs. Freeman went into a description of how he had popped her neck. She said he owned a '55 Mercury but that Glynese said she would rather marry a man with only a '36 Plymouth who would be married by a preacher. The girl

2. Local clergyman.

asked what if he had a '32 Plymouth and Mrs. Freeman said what Glynese had said was a '36 Plymouth.

Mrs. Hopewell said there were not many girls with Glynese's common sense. She said what she admired in those girls was their common sense. She said that reminded her that they had had a nice visitor yesterday, a young man selling Bibles. "Lord," she said, "he bored me to death but he was so sincere and genuine I couldn't be rude to him. He was just good country people, you know," she said, "—just the salt of the earth."

"I seen him walk up," Mrs. Freeman said, "and then later—I seen him walk off," and Hulga could feel the slight shift in her voice, the slight insinuation, that he had not walked off alone, had he? Her face remained expressionless but the color rose into her neck and she seemed to swallow it down with the next spoonful of egg. Mrs. Freeman was looking at her as if they had a secret together.

"Well, it takes all kinds of people to make the world go 'round," Mrs. Hopewell said. "It's very good we aren't all alike."

"Some people are more alike than others," Mrs. Freeman said.

Hulga got up and stumped, with about twice the noise that was necessary, into her room and locked the door. She was to meet the Bible salesman at ten o'clock at the gate. She had thought about it half the night. She had started thinking of it as a great joke and then she had begun to see profound implications in it. She had lain in bed imagining dialogues for them that were insane on the surface but that reached below to depths that no Bible salesman would be aware of. Their conversation yesterday had been of this kind.

He had stopped in front of her and had simply stood there. His face was bony and sweaty and bright, with a little pointed nose in the center of it, and his look was different from what it had been at the dinner table. He was gazing at her with open curiosity, with fascination, like a child watching a new fantastic animal at the zoo, and he was breathing as if he had run a great distance to reach her. His gaze seemed somehow familiar but she could not think where she had been regarded with it before. For almost a minute he didn't say anything. Then on what seemed an insuck of breath, he whispered, "You ever ate a chicken that was two days old?"

The girl looked at him stonily. He might have just put this question up for consideration at the meeting of a philosophical association. "Yes," she presently replied as if she had considered it from all angles.

"It must have been mighty small!" he said triumphantly and shook all over with little nervous giggles, getting very red in the face, and subsiding finally into his gaze of complete admiration, while the girl's expression remained exactly the same.

"How old are you?" he asked softly.

She waited some time before she answered. Then in a flat voice she said, "Seventeen."

His smiles came in succession like waves breaking on the surface of a little lake. "I see you got a wooden leg," he said. "I think you're brave. I think you're real sweet."

The girl stood blank and solid and silent.

"Walk to the gate with me," he said. "You're a brave sweet little thing and I liked you the minute I seen you walk in the door."

Hulga began to move forward.

"What's your name?" he asked, smiling down on the top of her head.

"Hulga," she said.

"Hulga," he murmured, "Hulga. Hulga. I never heard of anybody name Hulga before. You're shy, aren't you, Hulga?" he asked.

She nodded, watching his large red hand on the handle of the giant valise.

"I like girls that wear glasses," he said. "I think a lot. I'm not like these people that a serious thought don't ever enter their heads. It's because I may die."

"I may die too," she said suddenly and looked up at him. His eyes were very small and brown, glittering feverishly.

"Listen," he said, "don't you think some people was meant to meet on account of what all they got in common and all? Like they both think serious thoughts and all?" He shifted the valise to his other hand so that the hand nearest her was free. He caught hold of her elbow and shook it a little. "I don't work on Saturday," he said. "I like to walk in the woods and see what Mother Nature is wearing. O'er the hills and far away. Pic-nics and things. Couldn't we go on a pic-nic tomorrow? Say yes, Hulga," he said and gave her a dying look as if he felt his insides about to drop out of him. He had even seemed to sway slightly toward her.

During the night she had imagined that she seduced him. She imagined that the two of them walked on the place until they came to the storage barn beyond the two back fields and there, she imagined, that things came to such a pass that she very easily seduced him and that then, of course, she had to reckon with his remorse. True genius can get an idea across even to an inferior mind. She imagined that she took his remorse in hand and changed it into a deeper understanding of life. She took all his shame away and turned it into something useful.

She set off for the gate at exactly ten o'clock, escaping without drawing Mrs. Hopewell's attention. She didn't take anything to eat, forgetting that food is usually taken on a picnic. She wore a pair of slacks and a dirty white shirt, and as an afterthought, she had put some Vapex on the collar of it since she did not own any perfume. When she reached the gate no one was there.

She looked up and down the empty highway and had the furious feeling that she had been tricked, that he had only meant to make her walk to the gate after the idea of him. Then suddenly he stood up, very tall, from behind a bush on the opposite embankment. Smiling, he lifted his hat which was new and wide-brimmed. He had not worn it yesterday and she wondered if he had bought it for the occasion. It was toast-colored with a red and white band around it and was slightly too large for him. He stepped from behind the bush still carrying the black valise. He had on the same suit and the same yellow socks sucked down in his shoes from walking. He crossed the highway and said, "I knew you'd come!"

The girl wondered acidly how he had known this. She pointed to the valise and asked, "Why did you bring your Bibles?"

He took her elbow, smiling down on her as if he could not stop. "You can never tell when you'll need the word of God, Hulga," he said. She had a moment in which she doubted that this was actually happening and then they began to climb the embankment. They went down into the pasture toward the woods.

The boy walked lightly by her side, bouncing on his toes. The valise did not seem to be heavy today; he even swung it. They crossed half the pasture without saying anything and then, putting his hand easily on the small of her back, he asked softly, "Where does your wooden leg join on?"

She turned an ugly red and glared at him and for an instant the boy looked abashed. "I didn't mean you no harm," he said. "I only meant you're so brave and all. I guess God takes care of you."

"No," she said, looking forward and walking fast, "I don't even believe in God."

At this he stopped and whistled. "No!" he exclaimed as if he were too astonished to say anything else.

She walked on and in a second he was bouncing at her side, fanning with his hat. "That's very unusual for a girl," he remarked, watching her out of the corner of his eye. When they reached the edge of the wood, he put his hand on her back again and drew her against him without a word and kissed her heavily.

The kiss, which had more pressure than feeling behind it, produced that extra surge of adrenalin in the girl that enables one to carry a packed trunk out of a burning house, but in her, the power went at once to the brain. Even before he released her, her mind, clear and detached and ironic anyway, was regarding him from a great distance, with amusement but with pity. She had never been kissed before and she was pleased to discover that it was an unexceptional experience and all a matter of the mind's control. Some people might enjoy drain water if they were told it was vodka. When the boy, looking expectant but uncertain, pushed her gently away, she turned and walked on, saying nothing as if such business, for her, were common enough.

He came along panting at her side, trying to help her when he saw a root that she might trip over. He caught and held back the long swaying blades of thorn vine until she had passed beyond them. She led the way and he came breathing heavily behind her. Then they came out on a sunlit hillside, sloping softly into another one a little smaller. Beyond, they could see the rusted top of the old barn where the extra hay was stored.

The hill was sprinkled with small pink weeds. "Then you ain't saved?" he asked suddenly, stopping.

The girl smiled. It was the first time she had smiled at him at all. "In my economy," she said, "I'm saved and you are damned but I told you I didn't believe in God."

Nothing seemed to destroy the boy's look of admiration. He gazed at her now as if the fantastic animal at the zoo had put its paw through the bars and given him a loving poke. She thought he looked as if he wanted to kiss her again and she walked on before he had the chance.

"Ain't there somewheres we can sit down sometime?" he murmured, his voice softening toward the end of the sentence.

"In that barn," she said.

They made for it rapidly as if it might slide away like a train. It was a large two-story barn, cool and dark inside. The boy pointed up the ladder that led into the loft and said, "It's too bad we can't go up there."

"Why can't we?" she asked.

"Yer leg," he said reverently.

The girl gave him a contemptuous look and putting both hands on the ladder, she climbed it while he stood below, apparently awestruck. She pulled herself expertly through the opening and then looked down at him and said, "Well, come on if you're coming," and he began to climb the ladder, awkwardly bringing the suitcase with him.

"We won't need the Bible," she observed.

"You never can tell," he said, panting. After he had got into the loft, he was a few seconds catching his breath. She had sat down in a pile of straw. A wide sheath of sunlight, filled with dust particles, slanted over her. She lay back against a bale, her face turned away, looking out the front opening of the barn where hay was thrown from a wagon into the loft. The two pink-speckled hillsides lay back against a dark ridge of woods. The sky was cloudless and cold blue. The boy dropped down by her side and put one arm under her and the other over her and began methodically kissing her face, making little noises like a fish. He did not remove his hat but it was pushed far enough back not to interfere. When her glasses got in his way, he took them off of her and slipped them into his pocket.

The girl at first did not return any of the kisses but presently she began to and after she had put several on his cheek, she reached his lips and remained there, kissing him again and again as if she were trying to draw all the breath out of him. His breath was clear and sweet like a child's and the kisses were sticky like a child's. He mumbled about loving her and about knowing when he first seen her that he loved her, but the mumbling was like the sleepy fretting of a child being put to sleep by his mother. Her mind, throughout this, never stopped or lost itself for a second to her feelings. "You ain't said you loved me none," he whispered finally, pulling back from her. "You got to say that."

She looked away from him off into the hollow sky and then down at a black ridge and then down farther into what appeared to be two green swelling lakes. She didn't realize he had taken her glasses but this landscape could not seem exceptional to her for she seldom paid any close attention to her surroundings.

"You got to say it," he repeated. "You got to say you love me."

She was always careful how she committed herself. "In a sense," she began, "if you use the word loosely, you might say that. But it's not a word I use. I don't have illusions. I'm one of those people who see *through* to nothing."

The boy was frowning. "You got to say it. I said it and you got to say it," he said.

The girl looked at him almost tenderly. "You poor baby," she murmured. "It's just as well you don't understand," and she pulled him by the neck, facedown, against her. "We are all damned," she said, "but some of us have taken off our blindfolds and see that there's nothing to see. It's a kind of salvation."

The boy's astonished eyes looked blankly through the ends of her hair. "Okay," he almost whined, "but do you love me or don'tcher?"

"Yes," she said and added, "in a sense. But I must tell you something. There mustn't be anything dishonest between us." She lifted his head and looked him in the eye. "I am thirty years old," she said. "I have a number of degrees."

The boy's look was irritated but dogged. "I don't care," he said. "I don't care a thing about what all you done. I just want to know if you love me or don'tcher?" and he caught her to him and wildly planted her face with kisses until she said, "Yes, yes."

"Okay then," he said, letting her go. "Prove it."

She smiled, looking dreamily out on the shifty landscape. She had seduced him without even making up her mind to try. "How?" she asked, feeling that he should be delayed a little.

He leaned over and put his lips to her ear. "Show me where your wooden leg joins on," he whispered.

The girl uttered a sharp little cry and her face instantly drained of color. The obscenity of the suggestion was not what shocked her. As a child she had sometimes been subject to feelings of shame but education had removed the last traces of that as a good surgeon scrapes for cancer; she would no more have felt it over what he was asking than she would have believed in his Bible. But she was as sensitive about the artificial leg as a peacock about his tail. No one ever touched it but her. She took care of it as someone else would his soul, in private and almost with her own eyes turned away. "No," she said.

"I known it," he muttered, sitting up. "You're just playing me for a sucker."

"Oh no no!" she cried. "It joins on at the knee. Only at the knee. Why do you want to see it?"

The boy gave her a long penetrating look. "Because," he said, "it's what makes you different. You ain't like anybody else."

She sat staring at him. There was nothing about her face or her round freezing-blue eyes to indicate that this had moved her; but she felt as if her heart had stopped and left her mind to pump her blood. She decided that for the first time in her life she was face to face with real innocence. This boy, with an instinct that came from beyond wisdom, had touched the truth about her. When after a minute, she said in a hoarse high voice, "All right," it was like surrendering to him completely. It was like losing her own life and finding it again, miraculously, in his.

Very gently he began to roll the slack leg up. The artificial limb, in a white sock and brown flat shoe, was bound in a heavy material like canvas and ended in an ugly jointure where it was attached to the stump. The boy's face and his voice were entirely reverent as he uncovered it and said, "Now show me how to take it off and on."

She took it off for him and put it back on again and then he took it off himself, handling it as tenderly as if it were a real one. "See!" he said with a delighted child's face. "Now I can do it myself!"

"Put it back on," she said. She was thinking that she would run away with him and that every night he would take the leg off and every morning put it back on again. "Put it back on," she said.

"Not yet," he murmured, setting it on its foot out of her reach. "Leave it off for a while. You got me instead."

She gave a little cry of alarm but he pushed her down and began to kiss her again. Without the leg she felt entirely dependent on him. Her brain seemed to have stopped thinking altogether and to be about some other function that it was not very good at. Different expressions raced back and forth over her face. Every now and then the boy, his eyes like two steel spikes, would glance behind him where the leg stood. Finally she pushed him off and said, "Put it back on me now."

"Wait," he said. He leaned the other way and pulled the valise toward him and opened it. It had a pale blue spotted lining and there were only two Bibles in it. He took one of these out and opened the cover of it. It was hollow and contained a pocket flask of whiskey, a pack of cards, and a small blue box with printing on it. He laid these out in front of her one at a time in an evenly-spaced row, like one presenting offerings at the shrine of a goddess. He put the blue box in her hand. THIS PRODUCT TO BE USED ONLY FOR THE PREVENTION OF DISEASE, she read, and dropped it. The boy was unscrewing the top of the flask. He stopped and pointed, with a smile, to the deck of cards. It was not an ordinary deck but one with an obscene picture on the back of each card. "Take a swig," he said, offering her the bottle first. He held it in front of her, but like one mesmerized, she did not move.

Her voice when she spoke had an almost pleading sound. "Aren't you," she murmured, "aren't you just good country people?"

The boy cocked his head. He looked as if he were just beginning to understand that she might be trying to insult him. "Yeah," he said, curling his lip slightly, "but it ain't held me back none. I'm as good as you any day in the week."

"Give me my leg," she said.

He pushed it farther away with his foot. "Come on now, let's begin to have us a good time," he said coaxingly. "We ain't got to know one another good yet."

"Give me my leg!" she screamed and tried to lunge for it but he pushed her down easily.

"What's the matter with you all of a sudden?" he asked, frowning as he screwed the top on the flask and put it quickly back inside the Bible. "You just a while ago said you didn't believe in nothing. I thought you was some girl!"

Her face was almost purple. "You're a Christian!" she hissed. "You're a fine Christian! You're just like them all—say one thing and do another. You're a perfect Christian, you're . . ."

The boy's mouth was set angrily. "I hope you don't think," he said in a lofty indignant tone, "that I believe in that crap! I may sell Bibles but I know which end is up and I wasn't born yesterday and I know where I'm going!"

"Give me my leg!" she screeched. He jumped up so quickly that she barely saw him sweep the cards and the blue box into the Bible and throw the Bible into the valise. She saw him grab the leg and then she saw it for an instant slanted forlornly across the inside of the suitcase with a Bible at either side of its opposite ends. He slammed the lid shut and snatched up the valise and swung it down the hole and then stepped through himself.

When all of him had passed but his head, he turned and regarded her with a look that no longer had any admiration in it. "I've gotten a lot of interesting things," he said. "One time I got a woman's glass eye this way. And you needn't to think you'll catch me because Pointer ain't really my name. I use a different name at every house I call at and don't stay nowhere long. And I'll tell you another thing, Hulga," he said, using the name as if he didn't think much of it, "you ain't so smart. I been believing in nothing ever since I was born!" and then the toast-colored hat disappeared down the hole and the girl was left, sitting on the straw in the dusty sunlight. When she turned her churning face toward the opening, she saw his blue figure struggling successfully over the green speckled lake.

Mrs. Hopewell and Mrs. Freeman, who were in the back pasture, digging up onions, saw him emerge a little later from the woods and head across the meadow toward the highway. "Why, that looks like that nice dull young man that tried to sell me a Bible yesterday," Mrs. Hopewell said, squinting. "He must have been selling them to the Negroes back in there. He was so simple," she said, "but I guess the world would be better off if we were all that simple."

Mrs. Freeman's gaze drove forward and just touched him before he disappeared under the hill. Then she returned her attention to the evil-smelling onion shoot she was lifting from the ground. "Some can't be that simple," she said. "I know I never could."

1955

RELATED:

—Author in Depth: Flannery O'Connor, p. 1837

FRANK O'CONNOR
1903–1966

O'Connor is the pen name of Michael O'Donovan, who was born in Cork, Ireland, of a family too poor to give him a university education. During Ireland's struggle for independence he was briefly a member of the Irish Republican Army. Then he worked as a librarian in Cork and Dublin and for a time was director of the Abbey Theatre before he became established as a writer of short stories. From 1931 on he published regularly in American magazines, and he taught for some years at Harvard, Northwestern, and Stanford Universities. His declared objective in shaping his material was to find the natural rhythms and stresses of the storyteller's voice. He rewrote many of his stories—often after first publication—ten, twenty, or thirty times. The subsequent publication of these revisions makes it hard to pin down the exact scale of his life's work, but he is credited with more than 150 works. He was in any event a prolific historian of Irish manners and the Irish character. His titles include *Guests of the Nation* (1931), *Crab Apple Jelly* (1944), *An Only Child* (O'Connor's autobiography, 1961), *A Set of Variations* (1971), and *Collected Stories* (1981).

Guests of the Nation

I

At dusk the big Englishman, Belcher, would shift his long legs out of the ashes and say "Well, chums, what about it?" and Noble or me would say "All right, chum" (for we had picked up some of their curious expressions), and the little Englishman, Hawkins, would light the lamp and bring out the cards. Sometimes Jeremiah Donovan would come up and supervise the game and get excited over Hawkins's cards, which he always played badly, and shout at him as if he was one of our own, "Ah, you divil, you, why didn't you play the tray?"

But ordinarily Jeremiah was a sober and contented poor devil like the big Englishman, Belcher, and was looked up to only because he was a fair hand at documents, though he was slow enough even with them. He wore a small cloth hat and big gaiters over his long pants, and you seldom saw him with his hands out of his pockets. He reddened when you talked to him, tilting from toe to heel and back, and looking down all the time at his big farmer's feet. Noble and me used to make fun of his broad accent, because we were from the town.

I couldn't at the time see the point of me and Noble guarding Belcher and Hawkins at all, for it was my belief that you could have planted that pair down anywhere from this to Claregalway and they'd have taken root there like a native weed. I never in my short experience seen two men to take to the country as they did.

They were handed on to us by the Second Battalion when the search[1] for them became too hot, and Noble and myself, being young, took over with a natural feeling of responsibility, but Hawkins made us look like fools when he showed that he knew the country better than we did.

"You're the bloke they calls Bonaparte," he says to me. "Mary Brigid O'Connell told me to ask you what you done with the pair of her brother's socks you borrowed."

For it seemed, as they explained it, that the Second used to have little evenings, and some of the girls of the neighbourhood turned in, and, seeing they were such decent chaps, our fellows couldn't leave the two Englishmen out of them. Hawkins learned to dance "The Walls of Limerick," "The Siege of Ennis," and "The Waves of Tory"[2] as well as any of them, though naturally, he couldn't return the compliment, because our lads at that time did not dance foreign dances on principle.

So whatever privileges Belcher and Hawkins had with the Second they just naturally took with us, and after the first day or two we gave up all pretence of keeping a close eye on them. Not that they could have got far, for they had accents you could cut with a knife and wore khaki tunics and overcoats with civilian pants and boots. But it's my belief that they never had any idea of escaping and were quite content to be where they were.

It was a treat to see how Belcher got off with the old woman of the house where we were staying. She was a great warrant to scold, and cranky even with us, but before ever she had a chance to giving our guests, as I may call them, a lick of her tongue, Belcher had made her his friend for life. She was breaking sticks, and Belcher, who hadn't been more than ten minutes in the house, jumped up from his seat and went over to her.

"Allow me, madam," he says, smiling his queer little smile, "please allow me"; and he takes the bloody hatchet. She was struck too paralytic to speak, and after that, Belcher would be at her heels, carrying a bucket, a basket, or a load of turf, as the case might be. As Noble said, he got into looking before she leapt, and hot water, or any little thing she wanted, Belcher would have it ready for her. For such a huge man (and though I am five foot ten myself I had to look up at him) he had an uncommon shortness—or should I say lack?—of speech. It took us some time to get used to him, walking in and out, like a ghost, without a word. Especially because Hawkins talked enough for a platoon, it was strange to hear big Belcher with his toes in the ashes come out with a solitary "Excuse me, chum," or "That's right, chum." His one and only passion was cards, and I will say for him that he was a good card-player. He could have fleeced myself and Noble, but whatever we lost to him Hawkins lost to us, and Hawkins played with the money Belcher gave him.

Hawkins lost to us because he had too much old gab, and we probably lost to Belcher for the same reason. Hawkins and Noble would spit at one another

---

1. Belcher and Hawkins are English soldiers, captured during the Irish battle for independence of 1922. The British Army and its collaborators are searching for them.   **2.** Native Irish dances.

about religion into the early hours of the morning, and Hawkins worried the soul out of Noble, whose brother was a priest, with a string of questions that would puzzle a cardinal. To make it worse even in treating of holy subjects, Hawkins had a deplorable tongue. I never in all my career met a man who could mix such a variety of cursing and bad language into an argument. He was a terrible man, and a fright to argue. He never did a stroke of work, and when he had no one else to talk to, he got stuck in the old woman.

He met his match in her, for one day when he tried to get her to complain profanely of the drought, she gave him a great comedown by blaming it entirely on Jupiter Pluvius (a deity neither Hawkins nor I had ever heard of, though Noble said that among the pagans it was believed that he had something to do with the rain).[3] Another day he was swearing at the capitalists for starting the German war[4] when the old lady laid down her iron, puckered up her little crab's mouth, and said: "Mr. Hawkins, you can say what you like about the war, and think you'll deceive me because I'm only a simple poor countrywoman, but I know what started the war. It was the Italian Count that stole the heathen divinity out of the temple in Japan. Believe me, Mr. Hawkins, nothing but sorrow and want can follow the people that disturb the hidden powers."

A queer old girl, all right.

II

We had our tea one evening, and Hawkins lit the lamp and we all sat into cards. Jeremiah Donovan came in too, and sat down and watched us for a while, and it suddenly struck me that he had no great love for the two Englishmen. It came as a great surprise to me, because I hadn't noticed anything about him before.

Late in the evening a really terrible argument blew up between Hawkins and Noble, about capitalists and priests and love of your country.

"The capitalists," says Hawkins with an angry gulp, "pays the priests to tell you about the next world so as you won't notice what the bastards are up to in this."

"Nonsense, man!" says Noble, losing his temper. "Before ever a capitalist was thought of, people believed in the next world."

Hawkins stood up as though he was preaching a sermon.

"Oh, they did, did they?" he says with a sneer. "They believed all the things you believe, isn't that what you mean? And you believe that God created Adam, and Adam created Shem, and Shem created Jehoshophat.[5] You believe all that silly old fairytale about Eve and Eden and the apple. Well, listen to me, chum. If you're entitled to hold a silly belief like that, I'm entitled to hold my silly belief—which is that the first thing your God created was a bleeding capitalist, with morality and Rolls-Royce complete. Am I right, chum?" he says to Belcher.

"You're right, chum," says Belcher with his amused smile, and got up from the table to stretch his long legs into the fire and stroke his moustache. So, seeing that Jeremiah Donovan was going, and that there was no knowing

---

3. The chief Roman god, Jupiter, had many functions, among them bringing rain for the crops, hence "Pluvius" (rainy). 4. World War I, in which England was at war with Germany. 5. Hawkins's scrambled version of Old Testament lore.

when the argument about religion would be over, I went out with him. We strolled down to the village together, and then he stopped and started blushing and mumbling and saying I ought to be behind, keeping guard on the prisoners. I didn't like the tone he took with me, and anyway I was bored with life in the cottage, so I replied by asking him what the hell we wanted guarding them at all for. I told him I'd talked it over with Noble, and that we'd both rather be out with a fighting column.

"What use are those fellows to us?" says I.

He looked at me in surprise and said: "I thought you knew we were keeping them as hostages."

"Hostages?" I said.

"The enemy have prisoners belonging to us," he says, "and now they're talking of shooting them. If they shoot our prisoners, we'll shoot theirs."

"Shoot them?" I said.

"What else did you think we were keeping them for?" he says.

"Wasn't it very unforeseen of you not to warn Noble and myself of that in the beginning?" I said.

"How was it?" says he. "You might have known it."

"We couldn't know it, Jeremiah Donovan," says I. "How could we when they were on our hands so long?"

"The enemy have our prisoners as long and longer," says he.

"That's not the same thing at all," says I.

"What difference is there?" says he.

I couldn't tell him, because I knew he wouldn't understand. If it was only an old dog that was going to the vet's, you'd try and not get too fond of him, but Jeremiah Donovan wasn't a man that would ever be in danger of that.

"And when is this thing going to be decided?" says I.

"We might hear tonight," he says. "Or tomorrow or the next day at latest. So if it's only hanging round here that's a trouble to you, you'll be free soon enough."

It wasn't the hanging round that was a trouble to me at all by this time. I had worse things to worry about. When I got back to the cottage the argument was still on. Hawkins was holding forth in his best style, maintaining that there was no next world, and Noble was maintaining that there was; but I could see that Hawkins had had the best of it.

"Do you know what, chum?" he was saying with a saucy smile. "I think you're just as big a bleeding unbeliever as I am. You say you believe in the next world, and you know just as much about the next world as I do, which is sweet damn-all. What's heaven? You don't know. Where's heaven? You don't know. You know sweet damn-all! I ask you again, do they wear wings?"

"Very well, then," says Noble, "they do. Is that enough for you? They do wear wings."

"Where do they get them, then? Who makes them? Have they a factory for wings? Have they a sort of store where you hands in your chit and takes your bleeding wings?"

"You're an impossible man to argue with," says Noble. "Now, listen to me—" And they were off again.

It was long after midnight when we locked up and went to bed. As I blew out the candle I told Noble what Jeremiah Donovan was after telling me.

Noble took it very quietly. When we'd been in bed about an hour he asked me did I think we ought to tell the Englishmen. I didn't think we should, because it was more than likely that the English wouldn't shoot our men, and even if they did, the brigade officers, who were always up and down with the Second Battalion and knew the Englishmen well, wouldn't be likely to want them plugged. "I think so too," says Noble. "It would be great cruelty to put the wind to them now."

"It was very unforeseen of Jeremiah Donovan anyhow," says I.

It was next morning that we found it so hard to face Belcher and Hawkins. We went about the house all day scarcely saying a word. Belcher didn't seem to notice; he was stretched into the ashes as usual, with his look unusual of waiting in quietness for something unforeseen to happen, but Hawkins noticed and put it down to Noble's being beaten in the argument of the night before.

"Why can't you take a discussion in the proper spirit?" he says severely. "You and your Adam and Eve! I'm a Communist, that's what I am. Communist or anarchist, it all comes to much the same thing." And for hours he went round the house, muttering when the fit took him. "Adam and Eve! Adam and Eve! Nothing better to do with their time than picking bleeding apples!"

III

I don't know how we got through that day, but I was very glad when it was over, the tea things were cleared away, and Belcher said in his peaceable way: "Well, chums, what about it?" We sat round the table and Hawkins took out the cards, and just then I heard Jeremiah Donovan's footstep on the path and a dark presentiment crossed my mind. I rose from the table and caught him before he reached the door.

"What do you want?" I asked.

"I want those two soldier friends of yours," he says, getting red.

"Is that the way, Jeremiah Donovan?" I asked.

"That's the way. There were four of our lads shot this morning, one of them a boy of sixteen."

"That's bad," I said.

At that moment Noble followed me out, and the three of us walked down the path together, talking in whispers. Feeney, the local intelligence officer, was standing by the gate.

"What are you going to do about it?" I asked Jeremiah Donovan.

"I want you and Noble to get them out; tell them they're being shifted again; that'll be the quietest way."

"Leave me out of that," says Noble under his breath.

Jeremiah Donovan looks at him hard.

"All right," he says. "You and Feeney get a few tools from the shed and dig a hole by the far end of the bog. Bonaparte and myself will be after you. Don't let anyone see you with the tools. I wouldn't like it to go beyond ourselves."

We saw Feeney and Noble go round to the shed and went in ourselves. I left Jeremiah Donovan to do the explanations. He told them that he had orders to send them back to the Second Battalion. Hawkins let out a mouthful of curses, and you could see that though Belcher didn't say anything, he was a bit upset too. The old woman was for having them stay in spite of us, and she didn't stop advising them until Jeremiah Donovan lost his temper and turned on her. He had a nasty temper, I noticed. It was pitch-dark in the cottage by this time, but no one thought of lighting the lamp, and in the darkness the two Englishmen fetched their topcoats and said good-bye to the old woman.

"Just as a man makes a home of a bleeding place, some bastard at headquarters thinks you're too cushy and shunts you off," says Hawkins, shaking her hand.

"A thousand thanks, madam," says Belcher. "A thousand thanks for everything"—as though he'd made it up.

We went round to the back of the house and down towards the bog. It was only then that Jeremiah Donovan told them. He was shaking with excitement.

"There were four of our fellows shot in Cork this morning and now you're to be shot as a reprisal."

"What are you talking about?" snaps Hawkins. "It's bad enough being mucked about as we are without having to put up with your funny jokes."

"It isn't a joke," says Donovan. "I'm sorry, Hawkins, but it's true," and begins on the usual rigmarole about duty and how unpleasant it is.

I never noticed that people who talk a lot about duty find it much of a trouble to them.

"Oh, cut it out!" says Hawkins.

"Ask Bonaparte," says Donovan, seeing that Hawkins isn't taking him seriously. "Isn't it true, Bonaparte?"

"It is," I say, and Hawkins stops.

"Ah, for Christ's sake, chum!"

"I mean it, chum," I say.

"You don't sound as if you meant it."

"If he doesn't mean it, I do," says Donovan, working himself up.

"What have you against me, Jeremiah Donovan?"

"I never said I had anything against you. But why did your people take out four of our prisoners and shoot them in cold blood?"

He took Hawkins by the arm and dragged him on, but it was impossible to make him understand that we were in earnest. I had the Smith and Wesson[6] in my pocket and I kept fingering it and wondering what I'd do if they put up a fight for it or ran, and wishing to God they'd do one or the other. I knew if they did run for it, that I'd never fire on them. Hawkins wanted to know was Noble in it, and when we said yes, he asked us why Noble wanted to plug him. Why did any of us want to plug him? What had he done to us? Weren't we all chums? Didn't we understand him and didn't he understand us? Did we imagine for an instant that he'd shoot us for all the so-and-so officers in the so-and-so British Army?

By this time we'd reached the bog, and I was so sick I couldn't even answer him. We walked along the edge of it in the darkness, and every now and then Hawkins would call a halt and begin all over again, as if he was wound up, about our being chums, and I knew that nothing but the sight of the grave would convince him that we had to do it. And all the time I was hoping that something would happen; that they'd run for it or that Noble would take

---

6. Revolver, as is the Webley, below.

over the responsibility from me. I had the feeling that it was worse on Noble than on me.

IV

At last we saw the lantern in the distance and made towards it. Noble was carrying it, and Feeney was standing somewhere in the darkness behind him, and the picture of them so still and silent in the bogland brought it home to me that we were in earnest, and banished the last bit of hope I had.

Belcher, on recognizing Noble, said: "Hallo, chum," in his quiet way, but Hawkins flew at him at once, and the argument began all over again, only this time Noble had nothing to say for himself and stood with his head down, holding the lantern between his legs.

It was Jeremiah Donovan who did the answering. For the twentieth time, as though it was haunting his mind, Hawkins asked if anybody thought he'd shoot Noble.

"Yes, you would," says Jeremiah Donovan.

"No, I wouldn't, damn you!"

"You would, because you'd know you'd be shot for not doing it."

"I wouldn't, not if I was to be shot twenty times over. I wouldn't shoot a pal. And Belcher wouldn't—isn't that right, Belcher?"

"That's right, chum," Belcher said, but more by way of answering the question than of joining in the argument. Belcher sounded as though whatever unforeseen thing he'd always been waiting for had come at last.

"Anyway, who says Noble would be shot if I wasn't? What do you think I'd do if I was in his place, out in the middle of a blasted bog?"

"What would you do?" asks Donovan.

"I'd go with him wherever he was going, of course. Share my last bob with him and stick by him through thick and thin. No one can ever say of me that I let down a pal."

"We had enough of this," says Jeremiah Donovan, cocking his revolver. "Is there any message you want to send?"

"No, there isn't."

"Do you want to say your prayers?"

Hawkins came out with a cold-blooded remark that even shocked me and turned on Noble again.

"Listen to me, Noble," he says. "You and me are chums. You can't come over to my side, so I'll come over to your side. That show you I mean what I say? Give me a rifle and I'll go along with you and the other lads."

Nobody answered him. We knew that was no way out.

"Hear what I'm saying?" he says. "I'm through with it. I'm a deserter or anything else you like. I don't believe in your stuff, but it's no worse than mine. That satisfy you?"

Noble raised his head, but Donovan began to speak and he lowered it again without replying.

"For the last time, have you any messages to send?" says Donovan in a cold excited sort of voice.

"Shut up, Donovan! You don't understand me, but these lads do. They're not the sort to make a pal and kill a pal. They're not the tools of any capitalist."

I alone of the crowd saw Donovan raise his Webley to the back of Hawkins's neck, and as he did so I shut my eyes and tried to pray. Hawkins had begun to say something else when Donovan fired, and as I opened my eyes at the bang, I saw Hawkins stagger at the knees and lie out flat at Noble's feet, slowly and as quiet as a kid falling asleep, with the lantern-light on his lean legs and bright farmer's boots. We all stood very still, watching him settle out in the last agony.

Then Belcher took out a handkerchief and began to tie it about his own eyes (in our excitement we'd forgotten to do the same for Hawkins), and, seeing it wasn't big enough, turned and asked for the loan of mine. I gave it to him and he knotted the two together and pointed with his foot at Hawkins.

"He's not quite dead," he says. "Better give him another."

Sure enough, Hawkins's left knee is beginning to rise. I bend down and put my gun to his head; then, recollecting myself, I get up again. Belcher understands what's in my mind.

"Give him his first," he says. "I don't mind. Poor bastard, we don't know what's happening to him now."

I knelt and fired. By this time I didn't seem to know what I was doing. Belcher, who was fumbling a bit awkwardly with the handkerchiefs, came out with a laugh as he heard the shot. It was the first time I heard him laugh and it sent a shudder down my back; it sounded so unnatural.

"Poor bugger!" he said quietly. "And last night he was so curious about it all. It's very queer, chums, I always think. Now he knows as much about it as they'll ever let him know, and last night he was all in the dark."

Donovan helped him to tie the handkerchiefs about his eyes. "Thanks, chum," he said. Donovan asked if there were any messages he wanted sent.

"No, chum," he says. "Not for me. If any of you would like to write to Hawkins's mother, you'll find a letter from her in his pocket. He and his mother were great chums. But my missus left me eight years ago. Went away with another fellow and took the kid with her. I like the feeling of a home, as you may have noticed, but I couldn't start again after that."

It was an extraordinary thing, but in those few minutes Belcher said more than in all the weeks before. It was just as if the sound of the shot had started a flood of talk in him and he could go on the whole night like that, quite happily, talking about himself. We stood round like fools now that he couldn't see us any longer. Donovan looked at Noble, and Noble shook his head. Then Donovan raised his Webley, and at that moment Belcher gives his queer laugh again. He may have thought we were talking about him, or perhaps he noticed the same thing I'd noticed and couldn't understand it.

"Excuse me, chums," he says. "I feel I'm talking the hell of a lot, and so silly, about my being so handy about a house and things like that. But this thing came on me suddenly. You'll forgive me, I'm sure."

"You don't want to say a prayer?" asks Donovan.

"No, chum," he says. "I don't think it would help. I'm ready, and you boys want to get it over."

"You understand that we're only doing our duty?" says Donovan.

Belcher's head was raised like a blind man's so that you could only see his chin and the tip of his nose in the lantern-light.

"I never could make out what duty was myself," he said. "I think you're all good lads, if that's what you mean. I'm not complaining."

Noble, just as if he couldn't bear any more of it, raised his fist at Donovan, and in a flash Donovan raised his gun and fired. The big man went over like a sack of meal, and this time there was no need for a second shot.

I don't remember much about the burying, but that it was worse than all the rest because we had to carry them to the grave. It was all mad lonely with nothing but a patch of lantern-light between ourselves and the dark, and birds hooting and screeching all round, disturbed by the guns. Noble went through Hawkins's belongings to find the letter from his mother, and then joined his hands together. He did the same with Belcher. Then, when we'd filled in the grave, we separated from Jeremiah Donovan and Feeney and took our tools back to the shed. All the way we didn't speak a word. The kitchen was dark and cold as we'd left it, and the old woman was sitting over the hearth, saying her beads. We walked past her into the room, and Noble struck a match to light the lamp. She rose quietly and came to the doorway with all her can-tankerousness gone.

"What did ye do with them?" she asked in a whisper, and Noble started so that the match went out in his hand.

"What's that?" he asked without turning round.

"I heard ye," she said.

"What did you hear?" asked Noble.

"I heard ye. Do ye think I didn't hear ye, putting the spade back in the houseen?"[7]

Noble struck another match and this time the lamp lit for him.

"Was that what ye did to them?" she asked.

Then, by God, in the very doorway, she fell on her knees and began praying, and after looking at her for a minute or two Noble did the same by the fire-place. I pushed my way out past her and left them at it. I stood at the door, watching the stars and listening to the shrieking of the birds dying out over the bogs. It is so strange what you feel at times like that that you can't describe it. Noble says he saw everything ten times the size, as though there were noth-ing in the whole world but that little patch of bog with the two Englishmen stiffening into it, but with me it was as if the patch of bog where the Englishmen were was a million miles away, and even Noble and the old woman, mumbling behind me, and the birds and the bloody stars were all far away, and I was somehow very small and very lost and lonely like a child astray in the snow. And anything that happened to me afterwards, I never felt the same about again.

1931

RELATED:

—Edward P. Jones on "Guests of the Nation," p. 1765

7. Shed.

TILLIE OLSEN
1912–2007

Olsen was born in Omaha, Nebraska, the daughter of Russian political exiles. She began to write in the 1930s, but most of her life was committed to working in industry and raising her four children. It wasn't until after they were grown that she studied writing at San Francisco State College, won a fellowship at Stanford University, and began to publish in earnest. When the four stories collected in *Tell Me a Riddle* (1961) appeared in the 1950s, she attracted a small group of enthusiastic readers who touted her talents until she gained a wider reputation. Although her body of work is quite small, she established a reputation as an ardent feminist known for her devotion to social and political causes. She taught or was a writer-in-residence at such colleges and universities as Amherst College, Stanford University, MIT, and Kenyon College. She was the recipient of five honorary degrees, a National Endowment for the Arts Fellowship, a Guggenheim Fellowship, and the O. Henry Award for best short story. *Silences* (1978) is a collection of essays and meditations. Her novel, *Yonnondio*, was published in 1974. *Mothers and Daughters* (1987), a collection of photographs, features Olsen's introductory essays. Her work has appeared in over one hundred anthologies.

O Yes

I

They are the only white people there, sitting in the dimness of the Negro church that had once been a corner store, and all through the bubbling, swelling, seething of before the services, twelve-year-old Carol clenches tight her mother's hand, the other resting lightly on her friend, Parialee Phillips, for whose baptism she has come.

The white-gloved ushers hurry up and down the aisle, beckoning people to their seats. A jostle of people. To the chairs angled to the left for the youth choir, to the chairs angled to the right for the ladies' choir, even up to the platform, where behind the place for the dignitaries and the mixed choir, the new baptismal tank gleams—and as if pouring into it from the ceiling, the blue-painted River of Jordan, God standing in the waters, embracing a brown man in a leopard skin and pointing to the letters of gold:

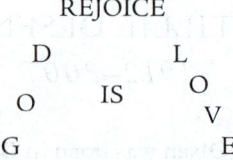

I AM THE WAY   THE TRUTH   THE LIFE

At the clear window, the crucified Christ embroidered on the starched white curtain leaps in the wind of the sudden singing. And the choirs march in. Robes of wine, of blue, of red.

"We stands and sings too," says Parialee's mother, Alva, to Helen; though already Parialee has pulled Carol up. Singing, little Lucinda Phillips fluffs out her many petticoats; singing, little Bubbie bounces up and down on his heels.

> *Any day now I'll reach that land of freedom,*
> *Yes, o yes*
> *Any day now, know that promised land*

The youth choir claps and taps to accent the swing of it. Beginning to tap, Carol stiffens. "Parry, look. Somebody from school."

"Once more once," says Parialee, in the new way she likes to talk now.

"Eddie Garlin's up there. He's in my math."

"Couple cats from Franklin Jr. chirps in the choir. No harm or alarm."

Anxiously Carol scans the faces to see who else she might know, who else might know her, but looks quickly down to Lucinda's wide skirts, for it seems Eddie looks back at her, sullen or troubled, though it is hard to tell, faced as she is into the window of curtained sunblaze.

> *I know my robe will fit me well*
> *I tried it on at the gates of hell*

If it were a record she would play it over and over, Carol thought, to untwine the intertwined voices, to search how the many rhythms rock apart and yet are one glad rhythm.

> *When I get to heaven gonna sing and shout*
> *Nobody be able to turn me out*

"That's Mr. Chairback Evans going to invocate," Lucinda leans across Parry to explain. "He don't invoke good like Momma."

"Shhhh."

"Momma's the only lady in the church that invocates. She made the prayer last week. (Last month, Lucy.) I made the children's 'nouncement last time. (That was way back Thanksgiving.) And Bubbie's 'nounced too. Lots of times."

"Lucy-inda. SIT!"

Bible study announcements and mixed-choir practice announcements and Teen Age Hearts meeting announcements.

If Eddie said something to her about being there, worried Carol, if he talked to her right in front of somebody at school.

Messengers of Faith announcements and Mamboettes announcement and Committee for the Musical Tea.

Parry's arm so warm. Not realizing, starting up the old game from grade school, drumming a rhythm on the other's arm to see if the song could be guessed. "Parry, guess."

But Parry is pondering the platform.

The baptismal tank? "Parry, are you scared . . . the baptizing?"

"This cat? No." Shaking her head so slow and scornful, the barrette in her hair, sun fired, strikes a long rail of light. And still ponders the platform.

New Strangers Baptist Church invites you and Canaan Fair Singers announcements and Battle of Song and Cosmopolites meet. "O Lord, I couldn't find no ease," a solo. The ladies' choir:

> *O what you say seekers, o what you say seekers,*
> *Will you never turn back no more?*

The mixed choir sings:

> *Ezekiel saw that wheel of time*
> *Every spoke was of humankind . . .*

And the slim worn man in the pin-stripe suit starts his sermon On the Nature of God. How God is long-suffering. Oh, how long he has suffered. Calling the roll of the mighty nations, that rose and fell and now are dust for grinding the face of Man.

O voice of drowsiness and dream to which Carol does not need to listen. As long ago. Parry warm beside her too, as it used to be, there in the classroom at Mann Elementary, and the feel of drenched in sun and dimness and dream. Smell and sound of the chalk wearing itself away to nothing, rustle of books, drumming tattoo of Parry's fingers on her arm: *Guess.*

And as the preacher's voice spins happy and free, it is the used-to-be playyard. Tag. Thump of the volley ball. Ecstasy of the jump rope. Parry, do pepper. Carol, do pepper. Parry's bettern Carol, Carol's bettern Parry. . . .

Did someone scream?

It seemed someone screamed—but all were sitting as before, though the sun no longer blared through the windows. She tried to see up where Eddie was, but the ushers were standing at the head of the aisle now, the ladies in white dresses like nurses or waitresses wear, the men holding their white-gloved hands up so one could see their palms.

"And God is Powerful," the preacher was chanting. "Nothing for him to scoop out the oceans and pat up the mountains. Nothing for him to scoop up the miry clay and create man. Man, I said, create Man."

The lady in front of her moaned *"O yes"* and others were moaning *"O yes."*

"And when the earth mourned the Lord said, Weep not, for all will be returned to you, every dust, every atom. And the tired dust settles back, goes back. Until that Judgment Day. That great day."

"O yes."

The ushers were giving out fans. Carol reached for one and Parry said: "What *you* need one for?" but she took it anyway.

"You think Satchmo can blow; you think Muggsy can blow; you think Dizzy[1] can blow?" He was straining to an imaginary trumpet now, his head far back and his voice coming out like a trumpet.

"Oh Parry, he's so good."

"Well. Jelly jelly."

"Nothing to Gabriel on that great getting-up morning. And the horn wakes up Adam, and Adam runs to wake up Eve, and Eve moans; Just one more minute, let me sleep, and Adam yells, Great Day, woman, don't you know it's the Great Day?"

"*Great Day, Great Day,*" the mixed choir behind the preacher rejoices:

> *When our cares are past*
> *when we're home at last . . .*

"And Eve runs to wake up Cain." Running round the platform, stooping and shaking imaginary sleepers, "and Cain runs to wake up Abel." Looping, scalloping his voice—"Grea-aaa-aat Daaaay." All the choirs thundering:

> *Great Day*
> *When the battle's fought*
> *And the victory's won*

Exultant spirals of sound. And Carol caught into it (Eddie forgotten, the game forgotten) chanting with Lucy and Bubbie: "*Great Day.*"

"Ohhhhhhhhhh," his voice like a trumpet again, "the re-unioning. Ohhh-hhhhhh, the rejoicing. After the ages immemorial of longing."

Someone *was* screaming. And an awful thrumming sound with it, like feet and hands thrashing around, like a giant jumping of a rope.

"*Great Day.*" And no one stirred or stared as the ushers brought a little woman out into the aisle, screaming and shaking, just a little shrunk-up woman not much taller than Carol, the biggest thing about her her swollen hands and the cascades of tears wearing her face.

The shaking inside Carol too. Turning and trembling to ask: "What . . . that lady?" But Parry still ponders the platform; little Lucy loops the chain of her bracelet round and round; and Bubbie sits placidly, dreamily. Alva Phillips is up fanning a lady in front of her; two lady ushers are fanning other people Carol cannot see. And her mother, her mother looks in a sleep.

Yes. He raised up the dead from the grave. He made old death behave.

Yes. Yes. From all over, hushed. *O Yes*

He was your mother's rock. Your father's mighty tower. And he gave us a little baby. A little baby to love.

I am so glad

Yes, your friend, when you're friendless. Your father when you're fatherless. Way maker. Door opener.

---

1. John Birks "Dizzy" Gillespie (1917–1993), American jazz trumpeter and composer. Muggsy: Francis "Muggsy" Spanier (1906–1967), American jazz cornetist. Satchmo: Louis "Satchmo" Armstrong (1900–1971), American jazz trumpet virtuoso and bandleader.

Yes

When it seems you can't go on any longer, he's there. You can, he says, you can.

Yes

And that burden you been carrying—ohhhhh that burden—not for always will it be. No, not for always.

Stay with me, Lord

I will put my Word in you and it is power. I will put my Truth in you and it is power.

O Yes

Out of your suffering I will make you to stand as a stone. A tried stone. Hewn out of the mountains of ages eternal.

Ohhhhhhhhhhh. Out of the mire I will lift your feet. Your tired feet from so much wandering. From so much work and wear and hard times.

Yes

From so much journeying—and never the promised land. And I'll wash them in the well your tears made. And I'll shod them in the gospel of peace, and of feeling good. Ohhhhhhhhh.

O Yes.

Behind Carol, a trembling wavering scream. Then the thrashing. Up above, the singing:

> *They taken my blessed Jesus and flogged him to*
> *the woods*
> *And they made him hew out his cross and they*
> *dragged him to Calvary*
> *Shout brother, Shout shout shout. He never cried*
> *a word.*

Powerful throbbing voices. Calling and answering to each other.

> *They taken my blessed Jesus and whipped him up*
> *the hill*
> *With a knotty whip and a raggedy thorn he never*
> *cried a word*
> *Shout, sister. Shout shout shout. He never cried*
> *a word.*

> *Go tell the people the Saviour has risen*
> *Has risen from the dead and will live forevermore*
> *And won't have to die no more.*
> *Halleloo.*

> *Shout, brother, shout*
> *We won't have to die no more!*

A single exultant lunge of shriek. Then the thrashing. All around a clapping. Shouts with it. The piano whipping, whipping air to a froth. Singing now.

> *I once was lost who now am found*
> *Was blind who now can see*

On Carol's fan, a little Jesus walked on wondrously blue waters to where bearded disciples spread nets out of a fishing boat. If she studied the fan—became it—it might make a wall around her. If she could make what was happening (*what* was happening?) into a record small and round to listen to far and far as if into a seashell—the stamp and rills and spirals all tiny (but never any screaming).

wade wade in the water

Jordan's water is chilly and wild
I've got to get home to the other side
God's going to trouble the waters

The music leaps and prowls. Ladders of screamings. Drumming feet of ushers running. And still little Lucy fluffs her skirts, loops the chain on her bracelet; still Bubbie sits and rocks dreamily; and only eyes turn for an instant to the aisle as if nothing were happening. "Mother, let's go home," Carol begs, but her mother holds her so tight. Alva Phillips, strong Alva, rocking too and chanting. *O Yes.* No, do not look.

Wade,
Sea of trouble all mingled with fire
Come on my brethren it's time to go higher
Wade wade

The voices in great humming waves, slow, slow (when did it become the humming?), everyone swaying with it too, moving like in slow waves and singing, and up where Eddie is, a new cry, wild and open, "O help me, Jesus," and when Carol opens her eyes she closes them again, quick, but still can see the new known face from school (not Eddie), the thrashing, writhing body struggling against the ushers with the look of grave and loving support on their faces, and hear the torn, tearing cry: "Don't take me away, life everlasting don't take me away."

And now the rhinestones in Parry's hair glitter wicked; the white hands of the ushers, fanning, foam in the air; the blue-painted waters of Jordan swell and thunder; Christ spirals on his cross in the window—and she is drowned under the sluice of the slow singing and the sway.

So high up and forgotten the waves and the world, so stirless the deep cool green and the wrecks of what had been. Here now Hostess Foods, where Alva Phillips works her nights—but different from that time Alva had taken them through before work, for it is all sunken under water, the creaking loading platform where they had left the night behind; the closet room where Alva's swaddles of sweaters, boots, and cap hung, the long hall lined with pickle barrels, the sharp freezer door swinging open.

Bubbles of breath that swell. A gulp of numbing air. She swims into the chill room where the huge wheels of cheese stand, and Alva swims too, deftly oiling each machine: slicers and wedgers and the convey, that at her touch start to roll and grind. The light of day blazes up and Alva is holding a cup, saying: Drink this, baby.

"DRINK IT." Her mother's voice and the numbing air demanding her to pay attention. Up through the waters and into the car.

"That's right, lambie, now lie back." Her mother's lap.

"Mother."

"Shhhhh. You almost fainted, lambie."

Alva's voice. "You gonna be all right, Carol . . . Lucy, I'm telling you for the last time, you and Buford get back into that church. Carol is *fine*."

"Lucyinda, if I had all your petticoats I could float." Crying. "Why didn't you let me wear my full skirt with the petticoats, Mother."

"Shhhhh, lamb." Smoothing her cheek. "Just breathe, take long deep breaths."

". . . How you doing now, you little ol' consolation prize?" It is Parry, but she does not come in the car or reach to Carol through the open window: "No need to cuss and fuss. You going to be sharp as a tack, Jack."

Answering automatically: "And cool as a fool."

Quick, they look at each other.

"Parry, we have to go home now, don't we, Mother? I almost fainted, didn't I, Mother? . . . Parry, I'm sorry I got sick and have to miss your baptism."

"Don't feel sorry. I'll feel better you not there to watch. It was our mommas wanted you to be there, not me."

"Parry!" Three voices.

"Maybe I'll come over to play kickball after. If you feeling better. Maybe. Or bring the pogo." Old shared joys in her voice. "Or any little thing."

In just a whisper: "Or any little thing. Parry. Good-bye, Parry."

And why does Alva have to talk now?

"You all right? You breathin' deep like your momma said? Was it too close 'n hot in there? Did something scare you, Carrie?"

Shaking her head to lie, "No."

"I blames myself for not paying attention. You not used to people letting go that way. Lucy and Bubbie, Parialee, they used to it. They been coming since they lap babies."

"Alva, that's all right. Alva. Mrs. Phillips."

"You *was* scared. Carol, it's something to study about. You'll feel better if you understand."

Trying not to listen.

"You not used to hearing what people keeps inside, Carol. You know how music can make you feel things? Glad or sad or like you can't sit still? That was religion music, Carol."

"I have to breathe deep, Mother said."

"Not everybody feels religion the same way. Some it's in their mouth, but some it's like a hope in their blood, their bones. And they singing songs every word that's real to them, Carol, every word out of they own life. And the preaching finding lodgment in their hearts."

The screaming was tuning up in her ears again, high above Alva's patient voice and the waves lapping and fretting.

"Maybe somebody's had a hard week, Carol, and they locked up with it. Maybe a lot of hard weeks bearing down."

"Mother, my head hurts."

"And they're home, Carol, church is home. Maybe the only place they can feel how they feel and maybe let it come out. So they can go on. And it's all right."

"Please, Alva. Mother, tell Alva my head hurts."

"Get Happy, we call it, and most it's a good feeling, Carol. When you got all that locked up inside you."

"Tell her we have to go home. It's all right, Alva. Please, Mother. Say good-bye. Good-bye."

When I was carrying Parry and her father left me, and I fifteen years old, one thousand miles away from home, sin-sick and never really believing, as still I don't believe all, scorning, for what have it done to help, waiting there in the clinic and maybe sleeping, a voice called: Alva, Alva. So mournful and so sweet: Alva. Fear not, I have loved you from the foundation of the universe. And a little small child tugged on my dress. He was carrying a parade stick, on the end of it a star that outshined the sun. Follow me, he said. And the real sun went down and he hidden his stick. How dark it was, how dark. I could feel the darkness with my hands. And when I could see, I screamed. Dump trucks run, dumping bodies in hell, and a convey line run, never ceasing with souls, weary ones having to stamp and shove them along, and the air like fire. Oh I never want to hear such screaming. Then the little child jumped on a motorbike making a path no bigger than my little finger. But first he greased my feet with the hands of my momma when I was a knee baby. They shined like the sun was on them. Eyes he placed all around my head, and as I journeyed upward after him, it seemed I heard a mourning: "Mama Mama you must help carry the world." The rise and fall of nations I saw. And the voice called again Alva Alva, and I flew into a world of light, multitudes singing, Free, free, I am so glad.

I I

Helen began to cry, telling her husband about it.

"You and Alva ought to have your heads examined, taking her there cold like that," Len said. "All right, wreck my best handkerchief. Anyway, now that she's had a bath, her Sunday dinner...."

"And been fussed over," seventeen-year-old Jeannie put in.

"She seems good as new. Now *you* forget it, Helen."

"I can't. Something . . . deep happened. If only I or Alva had told her what it would be like. . . . But I didn't realize."

You don't realize a lot of things, Mother, Jeannie said, but not aloud.

"So Alva talked about it after instead of before. Maybe it meant more that way."

"Oh Len, she didn't listen."

"You don't know if she did or not. Or what there was in the experience for her. . . ."

Enough to pull that kid apart two ways even more, Jeannie said, but still not aloud.

"I was so glad she and Parry were going someplace together again. Now that'll be between them too. Len, they really need, miss each other. What happened in a few months? When I think of how close they were, the hours of makebelieve and dressup and playing ball and collecting. . . ."

"Grow up, Mother." Jeannie's voice was harsh. "Parialee's collecting something else now. Like her own crowd. Like jivetalk and rhythmandblues. Like teachers who treat her like a dummy and white kids who treat her like dirt; boys who think she's really something and chicks who. . . ."

"Jeannie, I know. It hurts."

"Well, maybe it hurts Parry too. Maybe. At least she's got a crowd. Just don't let it hurt Carol though, 'cause there's nothing she can do about it. That's all through, her and Parialee Phillips, put away with their paper dolls."

"No, Jeannie, no."

"It's like Ginger and me. Remember Ginger, my best friend in Horace Mann? But you hardly noticed when it happened to us, did you ... because she was white? Yes, Ginger, who's got two kids now, who quit school year before last. Parry's never going to finish either. What's she got to do with Carrie any more? They're going different places. Different places, different crowds. And they're sorting...."

"Now wait, Jeannie. Parry's just as bright, just as capable."

"They're in junior high, Mother. Don't you know about junior high? How they sort? And it's all where you're going. Yes and Parry's colored and Carrie's white. And you have to watch everything, what you wear and how you wear it and who you eat lunch with and how much homework you do and how you act to the teacher and what you laugh at.... And run with your crowd."

"It's that final?" asked Len. "Don't you think kids like Carol and Parry can show it doesn't *have* to be that way."

"They can't. They can't. They don't let you."

"No need to shout," he said mildly. "And who do you mean by 'they' and what do you mean by 'sorting'?"

How they sort. A foreboding of comprehension whirled within Helen. What was it Carol had told her of the Welcome Assembly the first day in junior high? The models showing How to Dress and How Not to Dress and half the girls in their loved new clothes watching their counterparts up on the stage—*their* straight skirt, their sweater, their earrings, lipstick, hairdo—"How Not to Dress," "a bad reputation for your school." It was nowhere in Carol's description, yet picturing it now, it seemed to Helen that a mute cry of violated dignity hung in the air. Later there had been a story of going to another Low 7 homeroom on an errand and seeing a teacher trying to wipe the forbidden lipstick off a girl who was fighting back and cursing. Helen could hear Carol's frightened, self-righteous tones: "... and I hope they expel her; she's the kind that gives Franklin Jr. a bad rep; she doesn't care about anything and always gets into fights." Yet there was nothing in these incidents to touch the heavy comprehension that waited.... Homework, the wonderings those times Jeannie and Carol needed help: "What if there's no one at home to give the help, and the teachers with their two hundred and forty kids a day can't or don't or the kids don't ask and they fall hopelessly behind, what then?"—but this too was unrelated. And what had it been that time about Parry? "Mother, Melanie and Sharon won't go if they know Parry's coming." Then of course you'll go with Parry, she's been your friend longer, she had answered, but where was it they were going and what had finally happened? Len, my head hurts, she felt like saying, in Carol's voice in the car, but Len's eyes were grave on Jeannie who was saying passionately:

"If you think it's so goddam important why do we have to live here where it's for real; why don't we move to Ivy like Betsy (yes, I know, money), where it's the deal to be buddies, in school anyway, three coloured kids and their father's a doctor or judge or something big wheel and one always gets elected President or head song girl or something to prove oh how we're democratic.... What do you want of that poor kid anyway? Make up your mind. Stay friends with

Parry—but be one of the kids. Sure. Be a brain—but not a square. Rise on up, college prep, but don't get separated. Yes, stay one of the kids but. . . ."

"Jeannie. You're not talking about Carol at all, are you, Jeannie? Say it again. I wasn't listening. I was trying to think."

"She will not say it again," Len said firmly, "you look about ready to pull a Carol. One a day's our quota. And you, Jeannie, we'd better cool it. Too much to talk about for one session. . . . Here, come to the window and watch the Carol and Parry you're both all worked up about."

In the wind and the shimmering sunset light, half the children of the block are playing down the street. Leaping, bouncing, hallooing, tugging the kites of spring. In the old synchronized understanding, Carol and Parry kick, catch, kick, catch. And now Parry jumps on her pogo stick (the last time), Carol shadowing her, and Bubbie, arching his body in a semicircle of joy, bounding after them, high, higher, higher.

And the months go by and supposedly it is forgotten, except for the now and then when, self-important, Carol will say: I really truly did nearly faint, didn't I, Mother, that time I went to church with Parry?

And now seldom Parry and Carol walk the hill together. Melanie's mother drives by to pick up Carol, and the several times Helen has suggested Parry, too, Carol is quick to explain: "She's already left" or "She isn't ready; she'll make us late."

And after school? Carol is off to club or skating or library or someone's house, and Parry can stay for kickball only on the rare afternoons when she does not have to hurry home where Lucy, Bubbie, and the cousins wait to be cared for, now Alva works the four to twelve-thirty shift.

No more the bending together over the homework. All semester the teachers have been different, and rarely Parry brings her books home, for where is there space or time and what is the sense? And the phone never rings with: what you going to wear tomorrow, are you bringing your lunch, or come on over, let's design some clothes for the Katy Keane comic-book contest. And Parry never drops by with Alva for Saturday snack to or from grocery shopping.

And the months go by and the sorting goes on and seemingly it is over until that morning when Helen must stay home from work, so swollen and feverish is Carol with mumps.

The afternoon before, Parry had come by, skimming up the stairs, spilling books and binders on the bed: Hey frail, lookahere and wail, your momma askin for homework, what she got against YOU? . . . looking quickly once then not looking again and talking fast. . . . Hey, you bloomed. You gonna be your own pumpkin, hallowe'en? Your momma know yet it's mu-umps? And lumps. Momma says: no distress, she'll be by tomorrow morning see do you need anything while your momma's to work. . . . (Singing: *whole latta shakin goin on*.) All your 'signments is inside; Miss Rockface says the teachers to write 'em cause I mightn't get it right all right.

But did not tell: Does your mother work for Carol's mother? Oh, you're neighbors! Very well, I'll send along a monitor to open Carol's locker but you're only to take these things I'm writing down, nothing else. Now say after me: Miss Campbell is trusting me to be a good responsible girl.

And go right to Carol's house. After school. Not stop anywhere on the way. Not lose anything. And only take. What's written on the list.

You really gonna mess with that book stuff? Sign on *mine* says do-not-open-until-eX-mas.... That Mrs. Fernandez doll she didn't send nothin, she was the only, says feel better and read a book to report if you feel like and I'm the most for takin care for you; she's my most, wish I could get her but she only teaches 'celerated.... Flicking the old read books on the shelf but not opening to mock-declaim as once she used to ... Vicky, Eddie's g.f. in Rockface office, she's on suspended for sure, yellin to Rockface: you bitchkitty don't you give me no more bad shit. That Vicky she can sure sling-ating-ring it. Staring out the window as if the tree not there in which they had hid out and rocked so often.... For sure. (*Keep mo-o-vin.*) Got me a new pink top and lilac skirt. Look sharp with this purple? Cinching in the wide belt as if delighted with what newly swelled above and swelled below. Wear it Saturday night to Sweet's, Modernaires Sounds of Joy, Leroy and Ginny and me goin if Momma'll stay home. IF. (*Shake my baby shake*). How come old folks still likes to party? Huh? Asking of Rembrandt's weary old face looking from the wall. How come (softly) you long-gone you. Touching her face to his quickly, lightly. NEXT mumps is your buddybud Melanie's turn to tote your stuff. *I'm* gettin the hoovus goovus. Hey you so unneat, don't care what you bed with. Removing the books and binders, ranging them on the dresser one by one, marking lipstick faces—bemused or mocking or amazed—on each paper jacket. Better. Fluffing out smoothing the quilt with exaggerated energy. Any little thing I can get, cause I gotta blow. Tossing up and catching their year-ago, arm-in-arm graduation picture, replacing it deftly, upside down, into its mirror crevice. Joe. Bring you joy juice or fizz water or kickapoo? Adding a frown line to one bookface. Twanging the paper fishkite, the Japanese windbell overhead, setting the mobile they had once made of painted eggshells and decorated straws to twirling and rocking. And is gone.

She talked to the lipstick faces after, in her fever, tried to stand on her head to match the picture, twirled and twanged with the violent overhead.

Sleeping at last after the disordered night. Having surrounded herself with the furnishings of that world of childhood she no sooner learned to live in comfortably, then had to leave.

The dollhouse stands there to arrange and rearrange; the shell and picture card collections to re-sort and remember; the population of dolls given away to little sister, borrowed back, propped all around to dress and undress and caress.

She has thrown off her nightgown because of the fever, and her just budding breast is exposed where she reaches to hold the floppy plush dog that had been her childhood pillow.

Not for anything would Helen have disturbed her. Except that in the unaccustomedness of a morning at home, in the bruised restlessness after the sleepless night, she clicks on the radio—and the storm of singing whirls into the room:

> *... sea of trouble all mingled with fire*
> *Come on my brethern we've got to go higher*
> *Wade, wade. ...*

And Carol runs down the stairs, shrieking and shrieking. "Turn it off, Mother, turn it off." Hurling herself at the dial and wrenching it so it comes off in her hand.

"Ohhhhh," choked and convulsive, while Helen tries to hold her, to quiet.

"Mother, why did they sing and scream like that?"

"At Parry's church?"

"Yes." Rocking and strangling the cries. "I hear it all the time." Clinging and beseeching. ". . . What was it, Mother? Why?"

Emotion, Helen thought of explaining, *a characteristic of the religion of all oppressed peoples, yes your very own great-grandparents*—thought of saying. And discarded.

Aren't you now, haven't you had feelings in yourself so strong they had to come out some way? ("what howls restrained by decorum")—thought of saying. And discarded.

Repeat Alva: *hope . . . every word out of their own life. A place to let go. And church is home.* And discarded.

The special history of the Negro people—history?—just you try living what must be lived every day—thought of saying. And discarded.

And said nothing.

And said nothing.

And soothed and held.

"Mother, a lot of the teachers and kids don't like Parry when they don't even know what she's like. Just because . . ." Rocking again, convulsive and shamed. "And I'm not really her friend any more."

No news. Betrayal and shame. Who betrayed? Whose shame? Brought herself to say aloud: "But maybe friends again. As Alva and I are."

The sobbing a whisper. "That girl Vicky who got that way when I fainted, she's in school. She's the one keeps wearing the lipstick and they wipe it off and she's always in trouble and now maybe she's expelled. Mother."

"Yes, lambie."

"She acts so awful outside but I remember how she was in church and whenever I see her now I have to wonder. And hear . . . like I'm her, Mother, like I'm her." Clinging and trembling. "Oh why do I have to feel it's happening to me too?

"Mother, I want to forget about it all, and not care like Melanie. Why can't I forget? Oh why is it like it is and why do I have to care?"

Caressing, quieting.

Thinking: *caring asks doing. It is a long baptism into the seas of humankind, my daughter. Better immersion than to live untouched. . . . Yet how will you sustain?*

Why is it like it is?

Sheltering her daughter close, mourning the illusion of the embrace.

And why do I have to care?

While in her, her own need leapt and plunged for the place of strength that was not—where one could scream or sorrow while all knew and accepted, and gloved and loving hands waited to support and understand.

For Margaret Heaton, who always taught

1956

GRACE PALEY
1922–2007

Grace Paley was born Grace Goodside in New York City to Russian Jewish immigrants. Paley studied for one year at Hunter College and then at the New School with W.H. Auden, but never earned a degree. She left school and married her first husband, cinematographer Jess Paley, at age nineteen, with whom she had two children. Paley knew at an early age that she wanted to be a poet and wrote only verse until the 1950s. She is now best known for her lyrical short stories, whose characters are mostly working-class New York women. Though plot is minimal in a typical Paley story, as *The New York Times* describes it, "the language is so immediate, the characters so authentic, that the text is propelled by an innate urgency." Paley's first collection of short fiction, *The Little Disturbances of Man* (1959), though well received, earned her only moderate success. Gradually her recognition grew, and *The Little Disturbances of Man* was reissued by Viking Press nine years later, in 1968. Paley then published two more collections of short fiction, *Enormous Changes at the Last Minute* (1974) and *Later the Same Day* (1985), as well as three collections of poetry. Among her awards are a 1961 Guggenheim Fellowship, the Rea Award for the Short Story and the Vermont Governor's Award for Excellence in the Arts in 1993, and the PEN/Malamud Award for Excellence in Short Fiction in 1994. Her *Collected Stories* (1994) was a finalist for the National Book Award. Paley was a political activist all her life, as well as a teacher at Columbia University, Syracuse University, and Sarah Lawrence College.

The Used-Boy Raisers

There were two husbands disappointed by eggs.

I don't like them that way either, I said. Make your own eggs. They sighed in unison. One man was livid; one was pallid.

There isn't a drink around here, is there? asked Livid.

Never find one here, said Pallid. Don't look; driest damn house. Pallid pushed the eggs away, pain and disgust his escutcheon.

Livid said, Now really, isn't there a drink? Beer? he hoped.

Nothing, said Pallid, who'd been through the pantries, closets, and refrigerators looking for a white shirt.

You're damn right, I said. I buttoned the high button of my powder-blue duster. I reached under the kitchen table for a brown paper bag full of an embroidery which asked God to Bless Our Home.

I was completing this motto for the protection of my sons, who were also Livid's. It is true that some months earlier, from a far place—the British plains in Africa—he had written hospitably to Pallid: I do think they're fine boys, you understand. I love them too, but Faith is their mother and now Faith is your wife. I'm so much away. If you want to think of them as yours, old man, go ahead.

Why, thank you, Pallid had replied, airmail, overwhelmed. Then he implored the boys, when not in use, to play in their own room. He made all efforts to be kind.

Now as we talked of time past and upon us, I pierced the ranch house that nestles in the shade of a cloud and a Norway maple, just under the golden script.

Ha-ha, said Livid, dripping coffee on his pajama pants, you'll never guess whom I met up with, Faith.

Who? I asked.

Saw your old boy friend Clifford at the Green Coq. He looks well. One thing must be said, he addressed Pallid, she takes good care of her men.

True, said Pallid.

How is he? I asked coolly. What's he doing? I haven't seen him in two years.

Oh, you'll never guess. He's marrying. A darling girl. She was with him. Little tootsies, little round bottom, little tummy—she must be twenty-two, but she looks seventeen. One long yellow braid down her back. A darling girl. Stubby nose, fat little underlip. Her eyes put on in pencil. Shoulders down like a dancer . . . slender neck. Oh, darling, darling.

You certainly observed her, said Pallid.

I have a functioning retina, said Livid. Then he went on. Better watch out, Faith. You'd be surprised, the dear little chicks are hatching out all over the place. All the sunny schoolgirls rolling their big black eyes. I hope you're really settled this time. To me, whatever is under the dam is in another county; however, in my life you remain an important person historically, he said. And that's why I feel justified in warning you. I must warn you. Watch out, sweetheart! he said, leaning forward to whisper harshly and give me a terrible bellyache.

What's all this about? asked Pallid innocently. In the first place, she's settled . . . and then she's still an attractive woman. Look at her.

Oh yes, said Livid, looking. An attractive woman. Magnificent, sometimes. We were silent for several seconds in honor of that generous remark.

Then Livid said, Yes, magnificent, but I just wanted to warn you, Faith.

He pushed his eggs aside finally and remembered Clifford. A mystery wrapped in an enigma . . . I wonder why he wants to marry.

I don't know, it just ties a man down, I said.

And yet, said Pallid seriously, what would I be without marriage? In luminous recollection—a gay dog, he replied.

At this moment, the boys entered: Richard the horse thief and Tonto the crack shot.

Daddy! they shouted. They touched Livid, tickled him, unbuttoned his pajama top, whistled at the several gray hairs coloring his chest. They tweaked his ear and rubbed his beard the wrong way.

Well, well, he cautioned. How are you boys, have you been well? You look fine. Sturdy. How are your grades? he inquired. He dreamed that they were just up from Eton for the holidays.

I don't go to school, said Tonto. I go to the park.

I'd like to hear the child read, said Livid.

Me. I can read, Daddy, said Richard. I have a book with a hundred pages.

Well, well, said Livid. Get it.

I kindled a fresh pot of coffee. I scrubbed cups and harassed Pallid into opening a sticky jar of damson-plum jam. Very shortly, what could be read, had been, and Livid, knotting the tie strings of his pants vigorously, approached me at the stove. Faith, he admonished, that boy can't read a tinker's damn. Seven years old.

Eight years old, I said.

Yes, said Pallid, who had just remembered the soap cabinet and was rummaging in it for a pint. If they were my sons in actuality as they are in everyday life, I would send them to one of the good parochial schools in the neighborhood where reading is taught. Reading. St. Bartholomew's, St. Bernard's, St. Joseph's.

Livid became deep purple and gasped. Over my dead body. *Merde*,[1] he said in deference to the children. I've said, yes, you may think of the boys as your own, but if I ever hear they've come within an inch of that church, I'll run you through, you bastard. I was fourteen years old when in my own good sense I walked out of that grotto of deception, head up. You sonofabitch, I don't give a damn how *au courant*[2] it is these days, how gracious to be seen under a dome on Sunday. . . . Shit! Hypocrisy. Corruption. Cave dwellers. Idiots. Morons.

Recalling childhood and home, poor Livid writhed in his seat. Pallid listened, head to one side, his brows gathering the onsets of grief.

You know, he said slowly, we iconoclasts . . . we freethinkers . . . we latter-day masons . . . we idealists . . . we dreamers . . . we are never far from our nervous old mother, the Church. She is never far from us.

Wherever we are, we can hear, no matter how faint, her hourly bells, tolling the countryside, reverberating in the cities, bringing to our civilized minds the passionate deed of Mary. Every hour on the hour we are startled with remembrance of what was done for us. FOR US.

Livid muttered in great pain, Those bastards, oh oh oh, those contemptible, goddamnable bastards. Do we have to do the nineteenth century all over again? All right, he bellowed, facing us all, I'm ready. That Newman! He turned to me for approval.

You know, I said, this subject has never especially interested me. It's your little dish of lava.

Pallid spoke softly, staring past the arched purple windows of his soul. I myself, although I lost God a long time ago, have never lost faith.

What the hell are you talking about, you moron? roared Livid.

I have never lost my love for the wisdom of the Church of the World. When I go to sleep at night, I inadvertently pray. I also do so when I rise. It is not to God, it is to that unifying memory out of childhood. The first words I ever

---

1. Shit (French). **2.** Fashionable (French).

wrote were: What are the sacraments? Faith, can you ever forget your old grandfather intoning Kaddish?[3] It will sound in your ears forever.

Are you kidding? I was furious to be drawn into their conflict. Kaddish? What do I know about Kaddish. Who's dead? You know my opinions perfectly well. I believe in the Diaspora,[4] not only as a fact but a tenet. I'm against Israel on technical grounds. I'm very disappointed that they decided to become a nation in my lifetime. I believe in the Diaspora. After all, they *are* the chosen people. Don't laugh. They really are. But once they're huddled in one little corner of a desert, they're like anyone else: Frenchies, Italians, temporal nationalities. Jews have one hope only—to remain a remnant in the basement of world affairs—no, I mean something else—a splinter in the toe of civilizations, a victim to aggravate the conscience.

Livid and Pallid were astonished at my outburst, since I rarely express my opinion on any serious matter but only live out my destiny, which is to be, until my expiration date, laughingly the servant of man.

I continued. I hear they don't even look like Jews any more. A bunch of dirt farmers with no time to read.

They're your own people, Pallid accused, dilating in the nostril, clenching his jaw. And they're under the severest attack. This is not the time to revile them.

I had resumed my embroidery. I sighed. My needle was now deep in the clouds which were pearl gray and late afternoon. I am only trying to say that they aren't meant for geographies but for history. They are not supposed to take up space but to continue in time.

They looked at me with such grief that I decided to consider all sides of the matter. I said, Christ probably had all that trouble—now that you mention it—because he knew he was going to gain the whole world but he forgot Jerusalem.

When you married us, said Pallid, and accused me, didn't you forget Jerusalem?

I never forget a thing, I said. Anyway, guess what. I just read somewhere that England is bankrupt. The country is wadded with installment paper.

Livid's hand trembled as he offered Pallid a light. Nonsense, he said. That's not true. Nonsense. The great British Island is the tight little fist of the punching arm of the Commonwealth.

What's true is true, I said, smiling.

Well, I said, since no one stirred, do you think you'll ever get to work today? Either of you?

Oh, my dear, I haven't even seen you and the boys in over a year. It's quite pleasant and cozy here this morning, said Livid.

Yes, isn't it? said Pallid, the surprised host. Besides, it's Saturday.

How do you find the boys? I asked Livid, the progenitor.

American, American, rowdy, uncontrolled. But you look well, Faith. Plumper, but womanly and well.

Very well, said Pallid, pleased.

But the boys, Faith. Shouldn't they be started on something? Just lining up little plastic cowboys. It's silly, really.

---

3. Hymns of praise to God in Judaism, here specifically part of the mourning ritual in prayer.   **4.** Literally, scattering. Here refers to the worldwide community of Jews dispersed (with a sense of exile) outside of Israel.

They're so young, apologized Pallid, the used-boy raiser.

You'd both better go to work, I suggested, knotting the pearl-gray late-afternoon thread. Please put the dishes in the sink first. Please. I'm sorry about the eggs.

Livid yawned, stretched, peeked at the clock, sighed. Saturday or no, alas, my time is not my own. I've got an appointment downtown in about forty-five minutes, he said.

I do too, said Pallid. I'll join you on the subway.

I'm taking a cab, said Livid.

I'll split it with you, said Pallid.

They left for the bathroom, where they shared things nicely—shaving equipment, washstand, shower, and so forth.

I made the beds and put the aluminum cot away. Livid would find a hotel room by nightfall. I did the dishes and organized the greedy day; dinosaurs in the morning, park in the afternoon, peanut butter in between, and at the end of it all, to reward us for a week of beans endured, a noble rib roast with little onions, dumplings, and pink applesauce.

Faith, I'm going now, Livid called from the hall. I put my shopping list aside and went to collect the boys, who were wandering among the rooms looking for Robin Hood. Go say goodbye to your father, I whispered.

Which one? they asked.

The real father, I said. Richard ran to Livid. They shook hands manfully. Pallid embraced Tonto and was kissed eleven times for his affection.

Goodbye now, Faith, said Livid. Call me if you want anything at all. Anything at all, my dear. Warmly with sweet propriety he kissed my cheek. Ascendant, Pallid kissed me with considerable business behind the ear.

Goodbye, I said to them.

I must admit that they were at last clean and neat, rather attractive, shiny men in their thirties, with the grand affairs of the day ahead of them. Dark night, the search for pleasure and oblivion were well ahead. Goodbye, I said, have a nice day. Goodbye, they said once more, and set off in pride on paths which are not my concern.

1959

JAYNE ANNE PHILLIPS
b. 1952

Jayne Anne Phillips was born and raised in West Virginia and earned her B.A. from West Virginia University in 1974. Phillips felt "intricately bound" to her home, but she also knew she "wanted to leave." Following her graduation, she embarked on a wandering journey to California, and her various work and social experiences as she crossed America had a significant influence on her fiction. Phillips went on to earn an M.F.A. from the prestigious Iowa Writers' Workshop and published her award-winning first collection, *Sweethearts* (1976), consisting of 24 one-page stories, before she graduated. Her first major short story collection, *Black Tickets* (1979), earned her national commercial success and the Sue Kaufman Prize for First Fiction. Phillips' lyric prose, known for its unsentimental focus on love, loss, and lone survivors, is not restricted to short stories. Five years after *Black Tickets* came her first and bestselling novel, *Machine Dreams* (1984), nominated for the National Book Critics Circle Award and named one of the twelve best books of the year by the *New York Times Book Review*. For her second novel, *Shelter* (1995), Phillips won an Academy Award in Literature from the American Academy of Arts and Letters. Her other works include another short fiction collection, *Fast Lanes* (1987), and the novels *MotherKind* (2000), *Lark & Termite* (2009)—nominated for the National Book Award and the National Book Critics Circle Award—and, most recently, *Quiet Dell* (2013). Phillips is the recipient of a Guggenheim Fellowship and two National Endowment for the Arts fellowships. She has taught at numerous colleges and universities including Harvard University and Williams College, and she currently teaches in the creative writing program at Rutgers University.

El Paso

Dude

See I'd met this old dirt farmer in a bar the night before. Said he was selling his truck cheap and I could come down to La Rosa and pick it up. Said three hundred dollars and it didn't run too bad but I'd better buy it now. So I hitched down Sunday morning, mud churches on all three dirt streets ringing their black bells. I found him wringing a chicken's neck in the yard, did it quick and finished before he looked at me. Dark seamed face under a broad hat and the chicken head a little dangling thing hanging out his fist. I told him, said

I'd come about the truck, did he still want—thinking we were both pretty drunk and he might have dreamed he had a truck, since it didn't look like he had anything but a shanty house that leaned right into dirt. He spat and turned for me to follow him, holding the chicken now by a splayed leg that was bright orange in the rising heat. The nails on his hands were colored that same dull shine as hen's claws.

Us walking in the dust yard past old tires and a rotten bedspring, mule tied to a pump by the chicken shed, and he stands finally by this thing that's a red fifties Chevy with a built-on bed shelved with chicken cages. Crosses and a blackened corn husk doll hanging from the mirror, keys strung on a hair ribbon. I got in and drove around the yard fast, chickens squawking and the old cur dogs snapping at the wheels. The old man squatted where he was, plucked the hen. Feathers flew and dropped as I pulled up. I said the truck ran good and if he had the title I'd pay him now and take it.

He motioned me inside a house somehow dark even in all that light. Smell of wool shawls and vinegar. I stumble blind into a table and voices, Spanish curses, stop and start. I look up and Rita, she's standing there not three feet away, having ripped the curtains off one window; she's screaming in her voice that goes throaty and harsh, and the light pours in all over her. Hot yellow gravy of light, her black eyes, and the red skirt tight; blouse loose old lace ripped at the shoulder. I wanted to roll my hand in her; I could feel her wet against my legs. The old woman stands by the stove, side of her face shining, and when she turns I see she's not crying but one eye weeps. Rita walks past me steaming from her hands, the cheap plastic curtains clutched and dragging.

I watch the old man rummage in a drawer but feel her at the end of the long room. Rita moving, bending over a small chair. Old man counts the money and I turn to watch her. The light rolling now, leaked into the dark, ripples the skin of the dark and flies fly up in loose knots; low slow buzz in corners yellowed and pulled out by the light that rolls across the surfaces of things in yellow blocks. Dust in the light; and her body moving down the long room pulls a white path like an animal leaving water. She bends from the waist; under the cloth her thighs are muscles, long curves. In the chair sits a baby whose head is too big. His legs don't reach the floor; his skin is stretched tight and pale like the light is under it. His hair is white and fine, swirled on his man-sized head, and I know he is a child only by the way he cradles a shoe to his face. Rocks the shoe slow in short arms. Rita has her hands in his hair, her shoulders tensed and curved to him. A sound catches in her throat and comes out low, folding into the yellow room. Thick juice of light circling, curling us in. Child wheezing and rocking, rocking the shoe slow; his mouth on it. It is her shoe and Rita croons, rocking with him, pulling the shoe away.

Rita

I bought my mother those glasses so she wouldn't have to live in the dark, spent a hundred dollars on an El Paso doctor so she could see in the light without the eye burning. And she wouldn't wear them. Would hide them and move like a bat in the dark, the windows covered. The child in his chair with his sounds, she singing her songs low in the dark, he weaving in his chair. Me youngest of six, and at near fifty she gave birth to him, his white skin and his head hanging like a heavy bloom on the neck that couldn't move it. His eyes rolling back to see in that head that must have been a field of snow inside. No father, she said, he is what was in me. And the eye in her too, still pouring from her slow. Bringing grain from the store on the mule, she crossed against the light and a truck knocked her down, the mule kicking her face. And so the eye weeps and hurts in the daylight. Pounding meal on the wood table she sings in the dark like she sang then, my five brothers building ears in the yard, and me they called *brujita*, little witch.

At dusk the townspeople came to be healed. Paid her in corn and cloth. Then the corn stacked by the door and tomatoes hung to dry and sides of bacon, their white fat thick as my waist. She in her white shawls and her almost black skin put her hands in powders ground from roots. The villagers knelt, her sound wheeling over them. Their eyes fluttered and their hands unclenched, jerking as sounds came. *Muerte dios muerte muerte*. They got up and bowed to the witch their children won't touch. Castanets' slow dull clack followed them, their feet going away in the dark yard. From the time I was a baby she gave me a sharp stick and told me to draw them in the dirt to keep their spirits from returning. She made her witching dolls from husks; when I was older she gave me paints to draw their faces. I made them: farmers' heads and goitered women already old.

My father was gone long weeks to Las Vegas, Reno. Sometimes when he came back we moved to hotels in El Paso and bought clothes in stores. Remember, she'd say, cracked voice clacking on her teeth, you ain't no Spanish brats— You got Gypsy blood and your daddy's Apache cheeks. I remember her long fingers on my face. He didn't come back. The house was her power and she wouldn't leave. The town still creeps to her at dusk, women with shawls low over faces. The priest says it's sacrilege, they heaping ashes by the door.

Already I was with men and she was big, her belly strained, and the labor went two days. Women from the town wouldn't help. She cut herself to let the child's head pass and the women, hearing she had a devil, burned candles by their beds. Later the old man came with his shriveled dolls, his silence, and no name I ever heard her say. He built a chair on rollers when the child could sit and kept lanterns lit all night to make the sounds soft.

Now the child's sounds are muffled and low except when I dance. He knows me, holds out his hands for my shoes. My mother takes dried cactus from a wood box and grinds it, sprinkles a powder on his hair. I make the signs and the castanets warm in my fingers; we put the child's chair in the center of the room and my feet on brushed boards start slow thud. The drum, her low voice quavering, my arms high, the clack silver clack and the child's eyes focus, hold me fast, faster, me spinning around him. He holds up his head, and under his skin, I see the pale blue veins. Faster, my feet pound floor, her voice louder, and he whines a high clean whine that holds me spinning. Ceiling twists, floor circles smaller, small. My hands over him stop. Suddenly he sleeps, he sleeps and we lie, all of us, in the hot dark house. Listen to him breathe.

The old man sells his truck, won't take my money. He sees girls grind in city bars, knows how the money comes: my rooms, hotels, the avenue. The child's sounds are whispers, now; he sleeps too long. At the white hospital, us black against walls, they say the shunt in his head won't drain. He won't eat anymore, drinks from bottles, watches me; why do I come here. She hacks at the naked chicken on a board. Her face, the eye drawn; I moving away through the yard. This dust on my legs yellow as meal is burning, burning.

Dude

She walks out through dirt yard to the road. I run, touch her arm. Her skin bare, dark walnut skin stained milky, and I stand, my hand drenched in her skin, ask her, is she going back to El Paso. In the truck the land goes by us glaring as a lidless eye, sun a high glittering ring. Seeming to whirl in itself like hornets, it throws its heat on land laid out flat to the burning. We glide horizontal on a strip of road. In the tiny room of the truck I feel heavy in the rivery heat. Between us on the cracked seat a space gets small. Her satin skirt is faded in circles I could crush to my thumb. Under her heavy hair, her damp temples, I want to feel the shape of her skull. My hands are deaf. Eyes stony with light she watches me try to see the road, her opaled eyes seeming to come out at me yet falling back in their deep oil that scalds the side of my face.

I pull over, stop the truck, get out, lean against it. Up the road a café, all night lights still on, runs a lit band of letters around its roof: hamburgers, thick shakes, onion rings fried gold. I walk up there and a woman with her hair dyed brass swabs the counter with a rag. Her wide grin red, her front tooth gold, she lets me talk and counting change she fingers my palm.

Ice cream packed hard melts slow on my hands as I'm walking back. I see Rita hitching by the side of the road. I hand her a cone, get in the truck and start the engine. She climbs in. Motor idling, sweet cold in our mouths, I pull her across the seat and press my fingers hard at the base of her neck. My breath comes out a ragged curve against her eyes.

Watching

He so in love with her it was something to see. Dude so caught up and dedicated like a single eye to his own loving. How she touched it off. I suppose he was about to pack it in before he saw her and thought there was still something to do. Walking up the hill, touching him with her hip and walking, she moved her hip was delicate and blue beside his thigh.

This was El Paso, 1965. She danced in topless bars, said really she was a painter but she needed supplies. Supplies she said are always hard to get, sometimes you just have to put out and get them and go off with them. It was plain he wanted to go off with her but in the summer in El Paso it's hard to move anywhere except down the street to the bars. I remember there was always dog puke on the sidewalks in El Paso. All those strays get the sweats around noon and bring up the garbage they ate in the back alleys of beanerys at dawn. Think about Texas and there's those skinny fanned ribs heaving.

Dude used to go down to Bimpy's nights and watch her dance. Bimpy was a greasy-kneed old faggot who liked him plenty and gave us free bourbon. She'd come over between songs and do a number with us, wringing with sweat so she'd wet the paper and we'd have to keep lighting it. She danced on this three-foot-square red stage, under two old ceiling fans that looked like little airplane propellers. She moved under their sleepy drone; always there was something about to break out. From our table in the corner I could smell the old roses smell of her. She was dark-haired and black-eyed though she swore she wasn't Spanish, medium-sized but small-boned with green apple breasts; then suddenly her twisted child-bearing hips that were somehow off-center and rolled gentle to the left when she walked, rolling slow up the hill past the plate glass liquor stores. Dancing, she'd throw her dusty scent past the two old spots Bimpy had and the cowboys threw bills on the stage. Dude hated the dancing; said she was frigid as hell afterward, like loving a wind-up doll except for her mouth and the curves it took on in the dark. She wouldn't even move with the lights on, he said.

After the show she'd stay and help Bimp sweep up and then we'd walk out the door into the oily night. Everything wide awake and the fat yam-skinned women talking Spanish to their boyfriends, walking with their stemmed words and twined fingers past the blank-eyed 5 & 10's. We'd walk up the hill, they in front and me trailing behind. She talked in her Texas voice about nothing usually, it just being important there in the lit-up black to have her voice with its honeyed drawl and bitter edge; she walking slope slide up the hill, whisper of her nylons brushing and the Mexican boys shooting craps on the sidewalk. They ain't but thirteen, she'd say when they looked up at her heels clicking, Old enough. My daddy made a small fortune at craps. He used to call it dealin with the demon. She'd say that and slap Dude on the ass.

She'd boil those stark black Colombian beans on a stove in their flat and it'd heat up the kitchen so we'd have to sit out the window on the roof. By this time the town was near silent and steaming slow like a wet iron. Always drink hot coffee on hot nights, she'd say, Brings the sweat to the outside and lets you sleep. Dude dozed with his head in her lap and she'd turn to me, ask me, oils are on sale and could she borrow a few bucks till next week. You know, she'd say, twisting his hair in her fingers, Them stars are just holes in the sky after all. And while I'm sleeping in that hot bed everything I ever thought of having falls into em.

Finally I'd go to bed and hear them in the hall going back and forth to the bathroom, him usually drunk by then and tripping at the door. People up and down the hall behind doors yelled at him to shut up. Her arms reaching in the yellow blouse to grab the light string, her hips moving in their funny bumbling slow walk past my door, not quite touching his legs, and the mosquitoes louder than her quiet laughter: this was 4 A.M. in El Paso.

I saw him a couple of years later in Toledo, said he was into racing junk cars, said it was some kick. Said you're tearing around and around under the lights in these things that are all going to fly apart and pile up. Said he heard she was living down in Austin with some dyke. Said cracking up those cars was great, said he was making money and cracking them up was some kick, it was really something.

Bimp

When I opened the place in '46 I didn't think no one could pull nothin over on me again. I was in the war just like anyone else, ain't no one gonna tell me I got any debt. I had enough tin food and muddy boots and hair lice to last me. One goddamn big lie is what it was, I figured that out. There ain't no losing or winning anywhere is what I figured out, ain't nobody gonna pitch me into no fake contest again. I sailed into San Fran with a knee like a corkscrew and the salt air made it ache like a bitch. I came back home and opened the place and I figured I was standing ground. Back then the Mexicans used to skunk around at the alley door till I told em to beat it. I can see em now, slinking off in their red shirts under that one streetlamp between the trash cans. My own grandmother was a Mex. She smelled like a rotten cantaloupe and raved in Spanish about the goddamn Church that did nothin but bury her endless brats and the man that beat her. There ain't no losing or winning. These black-eyed thieves and yellow Mex boys think I got something they want, let em swagger in the front door so what. I could tell em if they ask—no matter what they got they got more to get and the thing don't end. Gaining like a squirrel on a wheel, sure. When I saw them three kids I knew what the game was. Her saying what I needed was a dancer, the dude pretty as a rodeo star, and his sidekick one of them hunched-up watchers. I said Listen, I got me a dancer, and she said Try me out. The dude stood there grinding a butt into the floor in his high-heeled boots. I said Well I don't allow no dancers in here without escorts, gets plenty rough in here ya know, this ain't Philadelphia. She said she was from La Rosa, one of them dirt-eating border towns, and I laughed, said You didn't get far didja. She smiled, her mouth dark pink and those flashy Spanish teeth strong as an animal's. The cowboy finally looked at me, said, rolling the filter of his cigarette, We'll be here at nine. The watcher stood there looking from face to face like he was judge of the whole damn game and I said Suit yourselves.

Dude

Back then I was a carpenter like everyone. I quit school and went down to Texas, air so thick and slow it's like swimming. That flat-out heat comes after you and drinks you up; she'd been there all her life. The steam in her; I lost what I was thinking in rooms thick, full of us; her black hair in the sheets a wound thread, thick black lines of drawings she kept hidden, her charcoaled fingertips. She worked on the avenue, turned tricks in a hotel room with a blue ceiling and one light bulb in a fringed shade. I told her she had to stop it and she said well, she'd dance but she wasn't carrying no slop to farmers in a beanery. The difference is, she said, I say how I'm used.

By noon those days I was a walking fever, my hands cut and sore from tarring feed store roofs, and since I first saw her I come into the heat the place the heat like a bitch dog and lived with it. When I got home it was late evening and she lay almost naked on the roof. Past crooked streets the tracks ran off white, cutting their light and crossing. Sluggish trains changed cars in the hard-baked yard. Beside her on the shingled heat, I smelled her salt skin and she laughed, pulled my face to her throat. We rolled, hot shingles pressed to my back, and later the shower was cold. We drank iced whiskey in jelly glasses and she danced up the hall dripping, throwing water off her hair. In the stifled space, window at the end painted over and light through the cracked paint patterned on the floor, her back was beaded and swaying. Water backed up past the drain spilled cold past my feet onto the floor and in our rooms we wet the sheets, slept in their damp. Her hair looped in my hands dried slow: past us the trains whistled their open howls.

It was too hot to cook and we ate avocados, jalapeños, white cheese. City lights came on, blue and pink neon stood out cool and she leaning into the mirror painted her face for the bar. I forget all of it but her lacquered eyes. And she stepping off the curb in those high-heeled shoes, kids in Chevys grinning.

Sometimes she came back from Bimp's so late the light was coming up. Been with a john: she only did it she said when the money was too good to pass up. She'd come home with a bottle of brandy, get into bed with a pack of cards and we'd play poker to win till the sun was flat on the floor. Cards buckled finally and thrown against the wall, shades drawn, we lay there see, until we could talk. Her face in the white bed, her face by the window; light behind the shade as she stood there colored her face blurred and fading like a photograph. It's all right just come here.

Bimp

Like I said, I had another dancer. She was blond, from the East, up North I think. She had the look of someone didn't sweat much, just burned a coal inside. Ran off finally with some slick Mex to Panama. Could tell easy she was one to leave home over and over till her feet wore down to a root that just planted where she ran out of steam. The men liked that white hair and light eyes and those rhinestone shoes she wore. She had that hard crumpled look of a dame that's been around but don't know why. I knew she was thirty-five but I hired her anyway. Them white blonds is scarce down here.

I put em onstage together the first night and they set up a wheel the whole place was turning on, what with the smaller one and her seventeen-year-old's tits and them hips moving so you knew she'd been used since she was old enough to wiggle. Them border girls start with big brother in the alley, them towns full of female things dropping litters in the street. She moved with that clinched dark face, all of it a fist in her hips, and beside her the tall blond looked like a movie magazine none of em could touch. There was some kind of confusion, smelled like burning rubber. Spilt drinks and a goddamn brawl in the back at the card table. I got em offstage and turned up the lights and ordered everyone out of the place. Was just me picking up broken glass and the girls leaning by the bar and the two men dealing a hand at the corner table like nothing happened. The girls were dressed, the blond fooling with her necklace, talking low. Her blue eyes drinking that Spanish mouth she say soft, Hey Honey, how long you figure on dancing with that swayback of yours and that funny hip—dawn, can you get this thing fastened—no, here—Lemme put it on and you can maybe pinch it with your teeth—She leans over the Spanish, her red lips apart like she's still talking, beer tipped in her hand and dripping all over their stockings. And the smaller one, black hair to her waist hands midway in the air, stands there like a stone saying over and over, I can't fix it, I can't fix it.

After that I had em alternate nights and a week later the blond split. The cowboy and his sidekick was in here nights with the Spanish the two of em diddling with cards and race forms in the corner. Figure it's been ten years ago. Gave me a few good tips and then same as now—when I hit at the track I blow it all same night, ain't nobody gonna tell me I won nothin.

The Blond

Rita. She left the avenue, the hotel, smell of urine and spent sex in the halls. We traded johns and other things; me by her door in blue light, cognac in my hand and my robe open. I asked her low, A toast to the hungry jokers? mouth on my raised glass and she let me in . . .

She let on like we never knew each other, but them hot nights I told her stories. Like how it was when I was seventeen like her. Ginette Hatcher was my name then, in Maine all the gray years. She born and died in Maine, she dying there still I guess. I took the name the first truck driver gave me, called me Babe and I answered to it ever since. I left my husband that I only saw in the dark after the boats came in or before they went out, that man always cold and fish slime on his hands. I left soon as the baby was born, thinking the best anyone could tell the kid was that Mama took off. There something out there besides that gray wet, that heavy roll. My cousins and uncles was all lobstermen ever since I can remember. My dad too, but he died when I was so young all he is to me is a furred chest and smell of oiled rope. He died of lobster is what Mom said, and she killed hundreds of them. Scratch-clink of those claws against the boiling pot was a woman sound, a metallic scratch round as rings.

Wind and rock and weeds on the beach a gray stink, no color cold; I kept fish eyes in bottles and sold them all summer to the tourists, to the queers and dandies and the painted old things with poodles. Once an old woman with money asked me to come to her hotel and read the Bible to her. She opened it and I started in. After a while I looked up and she was staring out the window like a sleepwalker, her old hat in her lap. She said what a blessed child I was to come to womanhood here by the sea, so far from heat and corruption. I said Yes Ma'am. The fire comes from the feet, she said, from the walkers and the black hair. She didn't see me anymore. I grabbed my sweater and ran home across the hotel beach, the big umbrellas blind and rolling on their sides. I found twenty dollars folded in my pocket and I bought me some red patent leather spike heels. I hid them in my room and only put them on at night and I was the walker walking and the dancer dancing in my fiery feet, and holes in the floor where I burned through.

Tires on the big trucks burn. You smell them in the cab, smell the motor boiling; my suitcase wedged between my knees and the truckers touching my dress. I lived everywhere and been to Mexico. I danced mostly, waited tables, worked in a library once and couldn't feel my feet for the shiny floor. Down in Texas any man on the street would buy me supper. By the time I got to Bimp's those nights I was already loaded. Blur, dark oiled skins past the lights, ice in glasses. Cold melts in a circle, hot whiskey, hot Texas. And Rita shows up, so smooth and so hot; eyes like black glass, sunk in, burned young. Onstage she scared me, made that cold ocean roll in my head . . . then the lights were on, jeers from the floor, and that little pimp pushing us stumbling into the dressing room. Where I lean against the wall and watch her shaking by the sink, cold water on her wrists, and we look at each other. They say the world ends in fire and ice; I say it's already over. That hot pavement burns you straight through: that's why I did it, kept moving—no slow cooking and my claws raking walls. These streets, raunchy brass, my feet on fire burns up that dead ice.

I split way south with a rich dude. Red birds and black-eyed men. Been some since then. I'm doing OK, I got it made, and the cold don't come so much now.

Rita

I lived with Dude those months in two rooms, rickety bed on blocks and past the windows the roof steamed between shingles. Long afternoons I cut the thin tar bubbles with my nails, oils warm on the paper, and the tubes heated till their lettering came off in my hands. I drew the trains: red gashes and the tracks black rips underneath. His hands felt furred with dust. When he was roofing, tar smudged the lines and crosses in his palms, left the whorls of his fingers and their black smell on my hips. Some days we stayed in bed, kept the fans turning, buzzing; we had cold wine and coarse brown bread. At night the bars were crowded with drunks, some of them sick in the heat. Dancing, I didn't watch them; I saw the flat brushed land outside the house in La Rosa, looking tawny-colored from the shaded rooms, but out there, walking, you felt hard hot sand and the color spreads into a wasted brown.

I think of what happened and it happens each time the same way. When I go back they are padding the cart with skins. Inside in his bed the child's face is drawn and blue. He breathes faint strangled bleats and my mother waits, sewing pelts to wrap him. At dark she feels his throat and says there's no breath; we leave with the cart. In the skins his face is white and his light hair long as a girl's. The hitched mule swings its head, flares nostrils at the fresh smell and moves skittish toward the hills. The old man bends in brimmed hat, shuffles to low chant, and she walks behind, scatters fine powder on the ground. Cart rocking slow and the child's face in my lap is sunken, lids on rolled eyes tight closed. All night we keep moving on the sloped land. Sand rolls its barren striped bars; the sky is inked and slashed in the foothills where we stop, take bundled wood from the cart, tie it with cords. She knots leather in the dark and the old man's voice is hoarse. At dawn she piles brush and the corded wood; we lift the child, straining, jangling the bracelets on his arms. She lights dried skins wrapped on a stick, touches him, and he starts to burn. The wood catches and through the fire I think I see his face move. It moves again and I throw her back, digging, clawing at the hot wood under him. They watch me try to reach him, now he is all fire. Running around the stench I fall and their old faces over me say I only dreamed it. I smell the skins and his flesh, the incense burning under him.

Mule leading then down the ravine to where the light stretches out on land like a smooth film of egg. I stumble and touch the animal's hide, feel ribs under stiff mousy hair. The old man walks ahead, his back a leathered board under cloth. She stays there by the smell until it is finished; quiet, she waits to take the bones.

Hours walking, sun high and the road a sudden empty strip. The old man waits for me, then turns in the glare and tells me again that I dreamed it. I see his knife and serape on his waist, know he's not going back for her. I won't go back to her either. Smoke in my mouth, I smell the wheeling birds and the tight white face behind the bristled fire. Old man walking away on the road with his mule and there are trucks, horns, voices, Baby wanna ride?

Dude

I remember the rains had started, blown in off the Gulf. She'd been to La Rosa. Always when she came back she was this hunted dog, stringy and gutted and ready to gnaw its own foot. I came in and she was walking circles in the room, rubbing her hands. I saw her fingers were torn; bruised purple under the nails. The rolled drawings were torn and smoldering on the floor. I moved to stomp them out and heard her moan, turned saw matches in her hands; she striking and tossing them in the air where they'd flare and fall smoking. I grabbed her arms and everything was breaking, chairs cracking on the floor and the light bulb splintering. I saw her hair on fire under my hand and I rolled her onto the bed. All the time she moaned long and low like I wasn't there except that this thing was on top of her. Her eyes were calm and her burned hair broke in my hand. I pulled her down and heard my breath coming high and watered like a woman's; she fell and lay there, her lips moving. She drooled and the spit flecked red where her teeth had cut. I stood over her and yelled for her to see me. Her eyes rolling past me pulled my hands to her clothes and the cloth ripped. I slapped her, kept slapping her and my hands were fists. I looked up and he's watching us—always goddamn watching us—then he is talking quietly and pulling her from under me.

Watching

He was ramming his fists into the floor beside her head but he thought he was hitting her and asked me later had he killed her. The floor was splintered, fine wood in his hands, and she under him stared glazed at the ceiling. Her mumbled Spanish mixed in the room with the sulfur smell of something burned. When I pulled her from under him I saw her hair was burned ragged and her shirt seared in the back. I took it off and wrapped her in blankets; she was shivering. There was broken glass and her fingers were bloodied somehow. She kept talking to nothing, tossing her head from side to side, hands clinched in my hair so tight that when I lay her down I can't move from her. Have to bend over her, my face close though she doesn't see me; I touch her lips, the cuts scabbing and her teeth flecked with the dull dried blood. I smell her breath coming shallow and fast, say her name over and over until she hears me. Almost focusing she slides her hands slow from my hair down my face to her breasts, holding them.

Late that night, Dude sits by the window. Rain spills in; he watches the smoky trains jerk in the yard, moisture on warm soot a fine dust in the air. He blinks like he's slapped when he hears her clutch her throat and turn in her sleep. I talk, Dude smells her on his split knuckles, and the streaked curtains move all night.

Toward morning he paced the room, circling from door to window. Hands held delicate, he looked at me. His eyes I think were gray and heavy-lashed;

the lid of the right one drooped and softened that side of his face. Finally he turned and left; his pointed boots tapped a faint click on the stairs each step down.

She woke up in twisted blankets and raised her fingers to her face. We ate the bread slow, her mouth bleeding a little. I'm seeing her in summer by the stove in their room, sweat clouding her hair and her lips pursed with cheap wine; she smoothing her cotton skirt and throwing back her hair to bend over the burner with a cigarette, frowning as the blue flame jets up fast. On the street under my window she is walking early in the day, tight black skirt ripped in the slit that moves on her leg. Looking back she sees me watching and buys carnations from the blind man on the corner, walks back, tosses them up to me. She laughs and the flowers falling all around her are pale; their long stems tangling. The street is shaded in buildings and her face turned up to me is lost in black hair. She is small and she is washed in grilled shadow.

Fingers too swollen to button her shirt, she asked me would I get her something to soak them in. At the drugstore buying antiseptic and gauze I felt her standing shakily by the couch, touching her mouth with her purple fingers. Walking back fast I knew she was gone, took almost nothing. The ashed drawings were swept up and thrown probably from the window. He left for good soon after, thirty pounds of Mexican grass stashed in the truck for a connection in Detroit. I went far north as I could get, snow that winter in Ottawa a constant slow sift that cooled and cleaned a dirt heat I kept feeling for months; having nothing of her but a sketch I'd taken from where she hid them: a picture of trains dark slashed on tracks, and behind them the sky opens up like a hole.

1979

LUIGI PIRANDELLO
1867–1936

Pirandello was born in Girgenti, Sicily. As a young man he studied philology at the University of Rome and in Bonn, Germany. Subsequently, he became a professor of literature but was chiefly famous as the author of many novels and short stories as well as for his prodigious output as a playwright. In all, he wrote forty-three plays, the bulk of them elaborating the conflict between illusion and reality. The best-known and most typical of his imaginative works is *Six Characters in Search of an Author*, in which the characters of an unfinished play assert their claims to be more real than the drab existences from which they emerge. Pirandello's extraordinary scrambling of normal expectations led to many charges that he perpetrated hoaxes. His inversions of reality and make-believe had a strong influence on modern drama; his practices were often imitated. In 1934 Pirandello was awarded the Nobel Prize.

War

The passengers who had left Rome by the night express had had to stop until dawn at the small station of Fabriano in order to continue their journey by the small old-fashioned local joining the main line with Sulmona.[1]

At dawn, in a stuffy and smoky second-class carriage in which five people had already spent the night, a bulky woman in deep mourning was hoisted in—almost like a shapeless bundle. Behind her, puffing and moaning, followed her husband—a tiny man, thin and weakly, his face death-white, his eyes small and bright and looking shy and uneasy.

Having at last taken a seat he politely thanked the passengers who had helped his wife and who had made room for her; then he turned round to the woman trying to pull down the collar of her coat, and politely inquired:

"Are you all right, dear?"

The wife, instead of answering, pulled up her collar again to her eyes, so as to hide her face.

"Nasty world," muttered the husband with a sad smile.

And he felt it his duty to explain to his traveling companions that the poor woman was to be pitied, for the war was taking away from her her only son, a boy of twenty to whom both had devoted their entire life, even breaking up

---

1. Both towns are on the other side of the Apennine Mountains from Rome; Fabriano is north of Rome, Sulmona east.

their home at Sulmona to follow him to Rome, where he had to go as a student, then allowing him to volunteer for war with an assurance, however, that at least for six months he would not be sent to the front and now, all of a sudden, receiving a wire saying that he was due to leave in three days' time and asking them to go and see him off.

The woman under the big coat was twisting and wriggling, at times growling like a wild animal, feeling certain that all those explanations would not have aroused even a shadow of sympathy from those people who—most likely—were in the same plight as herself. One of them, who had been listening with particular attention, said:

"You should thank God that your son is only leaving now for the front. Mine has been sent there the first day of the war. He has already come back twice wounded and been sent back again to the front."

"What about me? I have two sons and three nephews at the front," said another passenger.

"Maybe, but in our case it is our *only* son," ventured the husband.

"What difference can it make? You may spoil your only son with excessive attentions, but you cannot love him more than you would all your other children if you had any. Paternal love is not like bread that can be broken into pieces and split amongst the children in equal shares. A father gives *all* his love to each one of his children without discrimination, whether it be one or ten, and if I am suffering now for my two sons, I am not suffering half for each of them but double . . ."

"True . . . true . . ." sighed the embarrassed husband, "but suppose (of course we all hope it will never be your case) a father has two sons at the front and he loses one of them, there is still one left to console him . . . while . . ."

"Yes," answered the other, getting cross, "a son left to console him but also a son left for whom he must survive, while in the case of the father of an only son if the son dies the father can die too and put an end to his distress. Which of the two positions is the worse? Don't you see how my case would be worse than yours?"

"Nonsense," interrupted another traveler, a fat, red-faced man with bloodshot eyes of the palest gray.

He was panting. From his bulging eyes seemed to spurt inner violence of an uncontrolled vitality which his weakened body could hardly contain.

"Nonsense," he repeated, trying to cover his mouth with his hand so as to hide the two missing front teeth. "Nonsense. Do we give life to our children for our own benefit?"

The other travelers stared at him in distress. The one who had had his son at the front since the first day of the war sighed: "You are right. Our children do not belong to us, they belong to the Country. . . ."

"Bosh," retorted the fat traveler. "Do we think of the Country when we give life to our children? Our sons are born because . . . well, because they must be born and when they come to life they take our own life with them. This is the truth. We belong to them but they never belong to us. And when they reach twenty they are exactly what we were at their age. We too had a father and mother, but there were so many other things as well . . . girls, cigarettes, illusions, new ties . . . and the Country, of course, whose call we would have answered—when we were twenty—even if father and mother had said no. Now at our age, the love of our Country is still great, of course, but stronger than it is the love for our children. Is there any one of us here who wouldn't gladly take his son's place at the front if he could?"

There was a silence all round, everybody nodding as to approve.

"Why then," continued the fat man, "shouldn't we consider the feelings of our children when they are twenty? Isn't it natural that at their age they should consider the love for their Country (I am speaking of decent boys, of course) even greater than the love for us? Isn't it natural that it should be so, as after all they must look upon us as upon old boys who cannot move any more and must stay at home? If Country exists, if Country is a natural necessity, like bread, of which each of us must eat in order not to die of hunger, somebody must go to defend it. And our sons go, when they are twenty, and they don't want tears, because if they die, they die inflamed and happy (I am speaking, of course, of decent boys). Now, if one dies young and happy, without having the ugly sides of life, the boredom of it, the pettiness, the bitterness of disillusion . . . what more can we ask for him? Everyone should stop crying; everyone should laugh, as I do . . . or at least thank God—as I do—because my son, before dying, sent me a message saying that he was dying satisfied at having ended his life in the best way he could have wished. That is why, as you see, I do not even wear mourning. . . ."

He shook his light fawn coat as to show it; his livid lip over his missing teeth was trembling, his eyes were watery and motionless, and soon after he ended with a shrill laugh which might well have been a sob.

"Quite so . . . quite so . . ." agreed the others.

The woman who, bundled in a corner under her coat, had been sitting and listening had—for the last three months—tried to find in the words of her husband and her friends something to console her in her deep sorrow, something that might show her how a mother should resign herself to send her son not even to death but to a probably dangerous life. Yet not a word had she found amongst the many which had been said . . . and her grief had been greater in seeing that nobody—as she thought—could share her feelings.

But now the words of the traveler amazed and almost stunned her. She suddenly realized that it wasn't the others who were wrong and could not understand her but herself who could not rise up to the same height of those fathers and mothers willing to resign themselves, without crying, not only to the departure of their sons but even to their death.

She lifted her head, she bent over from her corner trying to listen with great attention to the details which the fat man was giving to his companions about the way his son had fallen as a hero, for his King and his Country, happy and without regrets. It seemed to her that she had stumbled into a world she had never dreamt of, a world so far unknown to her and she was so pleased to hear everyone joining in congratulating that brave father who could so stoically speak of his child's death.

Then suddenly, just as if she had heard nothing of what had been said and almost as if waking up from a dream, she turned to the old man, asking him:

"Then . . . is your son really dead?"

Everybody stared at her. The old man, too, turned to look at her, fixing his great, bulging, horribly watery light gray eyes, deep in her face. For some little time he tried to answer, but words failed him. He looked and looked at her, almost as if only then—at that silly, incongruous question—he had suddenly realized at last that his son was really dead—gone for ever—for ever. His face contracted, became horribly distorted, then he snatched in haste a handkerchief from his pocket and, to the amazement of everyone, broke into harrowing, heart-rending, uncontrollable sobs.

1922

EDGAR ALLAN POE
1809–1849

Poe was born in Boston, the son of itinerant actors who died before he was three years old. He was adopted by a Virginia couple, the Allans, whose name he added to his own. His student days at the University of Virginia were brought to a quick end by his drinking and gambling; but then, enlisting in the army, he served soberly and well from 1827 to 1829. Accepted into West Point in 1830, he quickly ruined his prospects for a military career by more carousing, and that established a pattern he never again escaped. In 1836 he married his cousin Virginia Clemm, then a girl of thirteen, and tried to support her by writing and editing. He was an editor of the Richmond *Southern Literary Messenger,* among other publications, and for a time had his own magazine, *The Stylus.* He won a number of literary prizes early in his writing career, but his earnings remained meager, and alcoholic excesses repeatedly cost him his jobs in journalism. After his wife died in 1847, he became engaged to a wealthy widow; there was hope of relief from his long run of misfortune and poverty. Traveling to meet her in 1849, he met some acquaintances and with them set out to celebrate the change in his luck. After this binge he was found nearly unconscious in a Baltimore street and died a few days later. His short fiction, with its effects of terror and its supernatural trappings, made him a household name for American readers, though in fact there are few traces of American experience in his work. Gothic devices and the mood of German romanticism were his specialty. He has been called the inventor of the detective story. His critical writings—including, for example, his insistence on unity of effect in the short story—have deeply influenced literary taste and practice. His poetry has been admired more greatly and persistently abroad, particularly in France, than at home. He is remembered, as well, for the precariousness of his career, for his striking personal appearance, his fine manners, his debauchery, and his poverty—the stuff of romantic legend. His work is readily available in numerous anthologies and collected editions.

The Fall of the House of Usher

Son cœur est un luth suspendu;
Sitôt qu'on le touche il résonne.
—De Béranger[1]

---

1. His heart is a ready lute/As soon as it is touched it resounds; from *Le Refus* (lines 41–42), by Pierre-Jean de Béranger (1780–1857), French poet.

During the whole of a dull, dark, and soundless day in the autumn of the year, when the clouds hung oppressively low in the heavens, I had been passing alone, on horseback, through a singularly dreary tract of country; and at length found myself, as the shades of the evening drew on, within view of the melancholy House of Usher. I know not how it was—but, with the first glimpse of the building, a sense of insufferable gloom pervaded my spirit. I say insufferable; for the feeling was unrelieved by any of that half-pleasurable, because poetic, sentiment, with which the mind usually receives even the sternest natural images of the desolate or terrible. I looked upon the scene before me— upon the mere house, and the simple landscape features of the domain, upon the bleak walls, upon the vacant eye-like windows, upon a few rank sedges, and upon a few white trunks of decayed trees—with an utter depression of soul which I can compare to no earthly sensation more properly than to the after-dream of the reveller upon opium: the bitter lapse into everyday life, the hideous dropping off of the veil. There was an iciness, a sinking, a sickening of the heart, an unredeemed dreariness of thought which no goading of the imagination could torture into aught of the sublime. What was it—I paused to think—what was it that so unnerved me in the contemplation of the House of Usher? It was a mystery all insoluble; nor could I grapple with the shadowy fancies that crowded upon me as I pondered. I was forced to fall back upon the unsatisfactory conclusion, that while, beyond doubt, there *are* combinations of very simple natural objects which have the power of thus affecting us, still the analysis of this power lies among considerations beyond our depth. It was possible, I reflected, that a mere different arrangement of the particulars of the scene, of the details of the picture, would be sufficient to modify, or perhaps to annihilate its capacity for sorrowful impression; and, acting upon this idea, I reined my horse to the precipitous brink of a black and lurid tarn that lay in unruffled lustre by the dwelling, and gazed down— but with a shudder even more thrilling than before—upon the remodelled and inverted images of the gray sedge, and the ghastly tree-stems, and the vacant and eye-like windows.

Nevertheless, in this mansion of gloom I now proposed to myself a sojourn of some weeks. Its proprietor, Roderick Usher, had been one of my boon companions in boyhood; but many years had elapsed since our last meeting. A letter, however, had lately reached me in a distant part of the country—a letter from him—which, in its wildly importunate nature, had admitted of no other than a personal reply. The MS.[2] gave evidence of nervous agitation. The writer spoke of acute bodily illness, of a mental disorder, which oppressed him, and of an earnest desire to see me, as his best, and indeed his only personal friend, with a view of attempting, by the cheerfulness of my society, some alleviation of his malady. It was the manner in which all this, and much more, was said—it was the apparent *heart* that went with his request—which allowed me no room for hesitation; and I accordingly obeyed forthwith what I still considered a very singular summons.

Although, as boys, we had been even intimate associates, yet I really knew little of my friend. His reserve had been always excessive and habitual. I was aware, however, that his very ancient family had been noted, time out of

---

2. Manuscript.

mind, for a peculiar sensibility of temperament, displaying itself, through long ages, in many works of exalted art, and manifested, of late, in repeated deeds of munificent yet unobtrusive charity, as well as in a passionate devotion to the intricacies, perhaps even more than to the orthodox and easily recognizable beauties, of musical science. I had learned, too, the very remarkable fact, that the stem of the Usher race, all time-honored as it was, had put forth, at no period, any enduring branch; in other words, that the entire family lay in the direct line of descent, and had always, with very trifling and very temporary variation, so lain. It was this deficiency, I considered, while running over in thought the perfect keeping of the character of the premises with the accredited character of the people, and while speculating upon the possible influence which the one, in the long lapse of centuries, might have exercised upon the other—it was this deficiency, perhaps, of collateral issue, and the consequent undeviating transmission, from sire to son, of the patrimony with the name, which had, at length, so identified the two as to merge the original title of the estate in the quaint and equivocal appellation of the "House of Usher"—an appellation which seemed to include, in the minds of the peasantry who used it, both the family and the family mansion.

I have said that the sole effect of my somewhat childish experiment, that of looking down within the tarn, had been to deepen the first singular impression. There can be no doubt that the consciousness of the rapid increase of my superstition—for why should I not so term it?—served mainly to accelerate the increase itself. Such, I have long known, is the paradoxical law of all sentiments having terror as a basis. And it might have been for this reason only, that, when I again uplifted my eyes to the house itself, from its image in the pool, there grew in my mind a strange fancy—a fancy so ridiculous, indeed, that I but mention it to show the vivid force of the sensations which oppressed me. I had so worked upon my imagination as really to believe that about the whole mansion and domain there hung an atmosphere peculiar to themselves and their immediate vicinity: an atmosphere which had no affinity with the air of heaven, but which had reeked up from the decayed trees, and the gray wall, and the silent tarn: a pestilent and mystic vapor, dull, sluggish, faintly discernible, and leaden-hued.

Shaking off from my spirit what *must* have been a dream, I scanned more narrowly the real aspect of the building. Its principal feature seemed to be that of an excessive antiquity. The discoloration of ages had been great. Minute fungi overspread the whole exterior, hanging in a fine tangled web-work from the eaves. Yet all this was apart from any extraordinary dilapidation. No portion of the masonry had fallen; and there appeared to be a wild inconsistency between its still perfect adaptation of parts, and the crumbling condition of the individual stones. In this there was much that reminded me of the specious totality of old woodwork which has rotted for long years in some neglected vault, with no disturbance from the breath of the external air. Beyond this indication of extensive decay, however, the fabric gave little token of instability. Perhaps the eye of a scrutinizing observer might have discovered a barely perceptible fissure, which, extending from the roof of the building in front, made its way down the wall in a zigzag direction, until it became lost in the sullen waters of the tarn.

Noticing these things, I rode over a short causeway to the house. A servant in waiting took my horse, and I entered the Gothic archway of the hall. A valet, of stealthy step, thence conducted me, in silence, through many dark and intricate passages in my progress to the *studio* of his master. Much that I encountered on the way contributed, I know not how, to heighten the vague sentiments of which I have already spoken. While the objects around me— while the carvings of the ceilings, the sombre tapestries of the walls, the ebon blackness of the floors, and the phantasmagoric armorial trophies which rattled as I strode, were but matters to which, or to such as which, I had been accustomed from my infancy—while I hesitated not to acknowledge how familiar was all this—I still wondered to find how unfamiliar were the fancies which ordinary images were stirring up. On one of the staircases, I met the physician of the family. His countenance, I thought, wore a mingled expression of low cunning and perplexity. He accosted me with trepidation and passed on. The valet now threw open a door and ushered me into the presence of his master.

The room in which I found myself was very large and lofty. The windows were long, narrow, and pointed, and at so vast a distance from the black oaken floor as to be altogether inaccessible from within. Feeble gleams of encrimsoned light made their way through the trellised panes, and served to render sufficiently distinct the more prominent objects around; the eye, however, struggled in vain to reach the remoter angles of the chamber, or the recesses of the vaulted and fretted ceiling. Dark draperies hung upon the walls. The general furniture was profuse, comfortless, antique, and tattered. Many books and musical instruments lay scattered about, but failed to give any vitality to the scene. I felt that I breathed an atmosphere of sorrow. An air of stern, deep, and irredeemable gloom hung over and pervaded all.

Upon my entrance, Usher arose from a sofa upon which he had been lying at full length, and greeted me with a vivacious warmth which had much in it, I at first thought of an overdone cordiality—of the constrained effort of the *ennuyé*[3] man of the world. A glance, however, at his countenance convinced me of his perfect sincerity. We sat down; and for some moments, while he spoke not, I gazed upon him with a feeling half of pity, half of awe. Surely, man had never before so terribly altered, in so brief a period, as had Roderick Usher! It was with difficulty that I could bring myself to admit the identity of the wan being before me with the companion of my early boyhood. Yet the character of his face had been at all times remarkable. A cadaverousness of complexion; an eye large, liquid, and luminous beyond comparison, lips somewhat thin and very pallid, but of a surpassingly beautiful curve; a nose of a delicate Hebrew model, but with a breadth of nostril unusual in similar formations; a finely moulded chin, speaking, in its want of prominence, of a want of moral energy; hair of a more than web-like softness and tenuity; these features, with an inordinate expansion above the regions of the temple, made up altogether a countenance not easily to be forgotten. And now in the mere exaggeration of the prevailing character of these features, and of the expression they were wont to convey, lay so much of change that I doubted to whom I spoke. The now ghastly pallor of the skin, and the now miraculous

3. Bored, jaded (French).

lustre of the eye, above all things startled and even awed me. The silken hair, too, had been suffered to grow all unheeded, and as, in its wild gossamer texture, it floated rather than fell about the face, I could not, even with effort, connect its Arabesque[4] expression with any idea of simple humanity.

In the manner of my friend I was at once struck with an incoherence—an inconsistency; and I soon found this to arise from a series of feeble and futile struggles to overcome an habitual trepidancy, an excessive nervous agitation. For something of this nature I had indeed been prepared, no less by his letter, than by reminiscences of certain boyish traits, and by conclusions deduced from his peculiar physical conformation and temperament. His action was alternately vivacious and sullen. His voice varied rapidly from a tremulous indecision (when the animal spirits seemed utterly in abeyance) to that species of energetic concision—that abrupt, weighty, unhurried, and hollow-sounding enunciation—that leaden, self-balanced and perfectly modulated gutteral utterance, which may be observed in the lost drunkard, or the irreclaimable eater of opium, during the periods of his most intense excitement.

It was thus that he spoke of the object of my visit, of his earnest desire to see me, and of the solace he expected me to afford him. He entered, at some length, into what he conceived to be the nature of his malady. It was, he said, a constitutional and a family evil, and one for which he despaired to find a remedy—a mere nervous affection, he immediately added, which would undoubtedly soon pass off. It displayed itself in a host of unnatural sensations. Some of these, as he detailed them, interested and bewildered me; although, perhaps, the terms, and the general manner of the narration had their weight. He suffered much from a morbid acuteness of the senses; the most insipid food was alone endurable; he could wear only garments of certain texture; the odors of all flowers were oppressive; his eyes were tortured by even a faint light; and there were but peculiar sounds, and these from stringed instruments, which did not inspire him with horror.

To an anomalous species of terror I found him a bounden slave. "I shall perish," said he, "I *must* perish in this deplorable folly. Thus, thus, and not otherwise, shall I be lost. I dread the events of the future, not in themselves, but in their results. I shudder at the thought of any, even the most trivial, incident, which may operate upon this intolerable agitation of soul. I have, indeed, no abhorrence of danger, except in its absolute effect—in terror. In this unnerved—in this pitiable condition, I feel that I must inevitably abandon life and reason together, in some struggle with the grim phantasm, FEAR."

I learned, moreover, at intervals, and through broken and equivocal hints, another singular feature of his mental condition. He was enchained by certain superstitious impressions in regard to the dwelling which he tenanted, and from whence, for many years, he had never ventured forth—in regard to an influence whose suppositious force was conveyed in terms too shadowy here to be re-stated—an influence which some peculiarities in the mere form and substance of his family mansion, had, by dint of long sufferance, he said, obtained over his spirit—an effect which the *physique* of the gray walls and turrets, and of the dim tarn into which they all looked down, had, at length, brought about upon the *morale* of his existence.

---

4. Elaborately ornamental, in the manner of Arab decoration.

He admitted, however, although with hesitation, that much of the peculiar gloom which thus afflicted him could be traced to a more natural and far more palpable origin—to the severe and long-continued illness, indeed to the evidently approaching dissolution, of a tenderly beloved sister—his sole companion for long years, his last and only relative on earth. "Her decease," he said, with a bitterness which I can never forget, "would leave him (him the hopeless and the frail) the last of the ancient race of the Ushers." While he spoke, the lady Madeline (for so was she called) passed slowly through a remote portion of the apartment, and, without having noticed my presence, disappeared. I regarded her with an utter astonishment not unmingled with dread, and yet I found it impossible to account for such feelings. A sensation of stupor oppressed me, as my eyes followed her retreating steps. When a door, at length, closed upon her, my glance sought instinctively and eagerly the countenance of the brother; but he had buried his face in his hands, and I could only perceive that a far more than ordinary wanness had overspread the emaciated fingers through which trickled many passionate tears.

The disease of the lady Madeline had long baffled the skill of her physicians. A settled apathy, a gradual wasting away of the person, and frequent although transient affections of a partially cataleptical[5] character, were the unusual diagnosis. Hitherto she had steadily borne up against the pressure of her malady, and had not betaken herself finally to bed; but, on the closing in of the evening of my arrival at the house, she succumbed (as her brother told me at night with inexpressible agitation) to the prostrating power of the destroyer; and I learned that the glimpse I had obtained of her person would thus probably be the last I should obtain—that the lady, at least while living, would be seen by me no more.

For several days ensuing, her name was unmentioned by either Usher or myself: and, during this period, I was busied in earnest endeavors to alleviate the melancholy of my friend. We painted and read together; or I listened, as if in a dream, to the wild improvisations of his speaking guitar. And thus, as a closer and still closer intimacy admitted me more unreservedly into the recesses of his spirit, the more bitterly did I perceive the futility of all attempt at cheering a mind from which darkness, as if an inherent positive quality, poured forth upon all objects of the moral and physical universe, in one unceasing radiation of gloom.

I shall ever bear about me a memory of the many solemn hours I thus spent alone with the master of the House of Usher. Yet I should fail in any attempt to convey an idea of the exact character of the studies, or of the occupations, in which he involved me, or led me the way. An excited and highly distempered ideality threw a sulphureous lustre over all. His long improvised dirges will ring for ever in my ears. Among other things, I hold painfully in mind a certain singular perversion and amplification of the wild air of the last waltz of Von Weber.[6] From the paintings over which his elaborate fancy brooded, and which grew, touch by touch, into vaguenesses at which I shuddered the more thrillingly, because I shuddered knowing not why;—from these paintings (vivid

---

5. Psychologically paralyzed. 6. Carl Maria von Weber (1786–1826), German composer. Karl Gottlieb Reissiger succeeded Weber as conductor of the German Opera at Dresden. A nondramatic work by Reissiger contains a piece misleadingly known as *Weber's Last Waltz* or, literally, *Weber's Last Thought*.

as their images now are before me) I would in vain endeavor to educe more than a small portion which should lie within the compass of merely written words. By the utter simplicity, by the nakedness of his designs, he arrested and overawed attention. If ever mortal painted an idea, that mortal was Roderick Usher. For me at least—in the circumstances then surrounding me, there arose out of the pure abstractions which the hypochondriac contrived to throw upon his canvas, an intensity of intolerable awe, no shadow of which felt I ever yet in the contemplation of the certainly glowing yet too concrete reveries of Fuseli.[7]

One of the phantasmagoric conceptions of my friend, partaking not so rigidly of the spirit of abstraction, may be shadowed forth, although feebly, in words. A small picture presented the interior of an immensely long and rectangular vault or tunnel, with low walls, smooth, white, and without interruption or device.[8] Certain accessory points of the design served well to convey the idea that this excavation lay at an exceeding depth below the surface of the earth. No outlet was observed in any portion of its vast extent, and no torch, or other artificial source of light was discernible; yet a flood of intense rays rolled throughout, and bathed the whole in a ghastly and inappropriate splendor.

I have just spoken of that morbid condition of the auditory nerve which rendered all music intolerable to the sufferer, with the exception of certain effects of stringed instruments. It was, perhaps, the narrow limits to which he thus confined himself upon the guitar, which gave birth, in great measure, to the fantastic character of his performances. But the fervid *facility* of his impromptus could not be so accounted for. They must have been, and were, in the notes, as well as in the words of his wild fantasias (for he not unfrequently accompanied himself with rhymed verbal improvisations), the result of that intense mental collectedness and concentration to which I have previously alluded as observable only in particular moments of the highest artificial excitement. The words of one of these rhapsodies I have easily remembered. I was, perhaps, the more forcibly impressed with it, as he gave it, because, in the under or mystic current of its meaning, I fancied that I perceived, and for the first time, a full consciousness on the part of Usher, of the tottering of his lofty reason upon her throne. The verses, which were entitled "The Haunted Palace," ran very nearly, if not accurately, thus:

> In the greenest of our valleys,
> By good angels tenanted,
> Once a fair and stately palace—
> Radiant palace—reared its head.
> In the monarch Thought's dominion,
> It stood there!
> Never seraph spread a pinion
> Over fabric half so fair.
>
> Banners yellow, glorious, golden,
> On its roof did float and flow,

---

7. Henry Fuseli (Johann Heinrich Füssli; 1741–1825), Anglo-Swiss painter. **8.** Design, ornament.

(This—all this—was in the olden
        Time long ago)
And every gentle air that dallied,
        In that sweet day,
Along the ramparts plumed and pallid,
        A winged odor went away.

Wanderers in that happy valley
        Through two luminous windows, saw
Spirits moving musically
        To a lute's well-tunèd law,
Round about a throne where, sitting
        Porphyrogene![9]
In state his glory well befitting,
        The ruler of the realm was seen.

And all with pearl and ruby glowing
        Was the fair palace door,
Through which came flowing, flowing, flowing,
        And sparkling evermore,
A troop of Echoes, whose sweet duty
        Was but to sing,
In voices of surpassing beauty,
        The wit and wisdom of their king.

But evil things, in robes of sorrow,
        Assailed the monarch's high estate;
(Ah, let us mourn!—for never morrow
        Shall dawn upon him, desolate!)
And, round about his home, the glory
        That blushed and bloomed
Is but a dim-remembered story
        Of the old time entombed.

And travellers now, within that valley,
        Through the red-litten[1] windows see
Vast forms that move fantastically
        To a discordant melody;
While, like a ghastly rapid river,
        Through the pale door
A hideous throng rush out forever,
        And laugh—but smile no more.

I well remember that suggestions arising from this ballad led us into a train of thought wherein there became manifest an opinion of Usher's which I mention not so much on account of its novelty, (for other men have thought thus), as on account of the pertinacity with which he maintained it. This opinion, in its general form, was that of the sentience of all vegetable things. But, in his disordered fancy, the idea had assumed a more daring character,

9. One born to the purple—i.e., of royal blood. 1. Lit with red.

and trespassed, under certain conditions, upon the kingdom of inorganiza-
tion. I lack words to express the full extent, or the earnest *abandon* of his persuasion. The belief, however, was connected (as I have previously hinted) with
the gray stones of the home of his forefathers. The condition of the sentience
had been here, he imagined, fulfilled in the method of collocation of these
stones—in the order of their arrangement, as well as in that of the many *fungi*
which overspread them, and of the decayed trees which stood around—above
all, in the long undisturbed endurance of this arrangement, and in its redu-
plication in the still waters of the tarn. Its evidence—the evidence of the
sentience—was to be seen, he said, (and I here started as he spoke), in the gradual yet certain condensation of an atmosphere of their own about the waters
and the walls. The result was discoverable, he added, in that silent, yet importunate and terrible influence which for centuries had moulded the destinies
of his family, and which made *him* what I now saw him—what he was. Such
opinions need no comment, and I will make none.

Our books—the books which, for years, had formed no small portion of the
mental existence of the invalid—were, as might be supposed, in strict keeping
with this character of phantasm. We pored together over such works as the
Ververt et Chartreuse of Gresset; the *Belphegor* of Machiavelli; the *Heaven and
Hell* of Swedenborg; the *Subterranean Voyage of Nicholas Klimm* by Holberg; the
Chiromancy of Robert Flud, of Jean d'Indaginé, and of De la Chambre; the
Journey into the Blue Distance of Tieck; and the *City of the Sun* of Campanella.
One favorite volume was a small octavo edition of the *Directorium Inquisitorium,* by the Dominican Eymeric de Gironne; and there were passages in Pom-
ponius Mela, about the old African Satyrs and Aegipans, over which Usher
would sit dreaming for hours.[2] His chief delight, however, was found in the
perusal of an exceedingly rare and curious book in quarto Gothic—the manual of a forgotten church—the *Vigilae Mortuorum Secundum Chorum Ecclesiæ
Maguntinæn.*[3]

I could not help thinking of the wild ritual of this work, and of its probable
influence upon the hypochondriac, when, one evening, having informed me
abruptly that the lady Madeline was no more, he stated his intention of preserving her corpse for a fortnight, (previously to its final interment), in one of
the numerous vaults within the main walls of the building. The wordly reason, however, assigned for this singular proceeding, was one which I did not
feel at liberty to dispute. The brother had been led to his resolution (so he told
me) by considerations of the unusual character of the malady of the deceased,

2. Exotic and romantic literary works. *Ververt* and *Chartreuse* are anticlerical satires by French poet
and dramatist Jean Baptiste Louis Gresset (1709–1777). The novel of Niccolò Machiavelli (1469–1527)
concerns a demon come to earth to prove that the damnation of man is woman. Emmanuel Swedenborg (1688–1772), a Swedish scientist and theologian, offers in *Heaven and Hell* (1758) an argument
concerning the continuity of spiritual identity. The book of Ludwig Holberg (1684–1754), a German
dramatist, concerns a round-trip voyage to the world of the dead. Chiromancy, the art of palm reading, is the concern of Robert Flud (1574–1637), British alchemist, of Jean D'Indaginé (*Chiromantia,*
1522), and of Marin Cureau de la Chambre (*Principes de la Chiromancie,* 1653). The next two titles by the
German novelist Johann Ludwig Tieck (1773–1853) and the Italian scientist and philosopher Tommaso Campanella (1568–1639), respectively, are concerned with voyages to other worlds. The Spanish
historian Nicolas Eymeric de Girone (1320–1399) in *Inquisitorium Directorium* gives an outline of tortures
and appropriate procedures. Satyrs were goatmen of Greek mythology. Pomponius Mela, a Roman of
the first century C.E., gives an account of "Aegipans," supposedly goatmen of Africa, in his work *Geography.* 3. Vigil for the Dead, Second Chorus, Church of the Maguntinae (Latin).

of certain obtrusive and eager inquiries on the part of her medical men,[4] and of the remote and exposed situation of the burial-ground of the family, I will not deny that when I called to mind the sinister countenance of the person whom I met upon the staircase, on the day of my arrival at the house, I had no desire to oppose what I regarded as at best but a harmless, and by no means an unnatural, precaution.

At the request of Usher, I personally aided him in the arrangements for the temporary entombment. The body having been encoffined, we two alone bore it to its rest. The vault in which we placed it (and which had been so long unopened that our torches, half smothered in its oppressive atmosphere, gave us little opportunity for investigation) was small, damp, and entirely without means of admission for light; lying, at great depth, immediately beneath that portion of the building in which was my own sleeping apartment. It had been used, apparently, in remote feudal times, for the worst purposes of a donjon-keep,[5] and, in later days, as a place of deposit for powder, or other highly combustible substance, as a portion of its floor, and the whole interior of a long archway through which we reached it, were carefully sheathed with copper. The door, of massive iron, had been, also, similarly protected. Its immense weight caused an unusually sharp grating sound, as it moved upon its hinges.

Having deposited our mournful burden upon tressels within this region of horror, we partially turned aside the yet unscrewed lid of the coffin, and looked upon the face of the tenant. The exact similitude between the brother and sister now first arrested my attention; and Usher, divining, perhaps, my thoughts, murmured out some few words from which I learned that the deceased and himself had been twins, and that sympathies of a scarcely intelligible nature had always existed between them. Our glances, however, rested not long upon the dead—for we could not regard her unawed. The disease which had thus entombed the lady in the maturity of youth, had left, as usual in all maladies of a strictly cataleptical character, the mockery of a faint blush upon the bosom and the face, and that suspiciously lingering smile upon the lip which is so terrible in death. We replaced and screwed down the lid, and, having secured the door of iron, made our way, with toil, into the scarcely less gloomy apartments of the upper portion of the house.

And now, some days of bitter grief having elapsed, an observable change came over the features of the mental disorder of my friend. His ordinary manner had vanished. His ordinary occupations were neglected or forgotten. He roamed from chamber to chamber with hurried, unequal, and objectless step. The pallor of his countenance had assumed, if possible, a more ghastly hue—but the luminousness of his eye had utterly gone out. The once occasional huskiness of his tone was heard no more; and a tremulous quaver, as if of extreme terror, habitually characterized his utterance. There were times, indeed, when I thought his unceasingly agitated mind was laboring with an oppressive secret, to divulge which he struggled for the necessary courage. At times, again, I was obliged to resolve all into the mere inexplicable vagaries of madness, as I beheld him gazing upon vacancy for long hours, in an attitude of the profoundest attention, as if listening to some imaginary sound. It was no

---

4. Usher appears to be afraid the doctors will exhume her corpse to satisfy their professional curiosity about her ailment. 5. Dungeon, prison.

wonder that his condition terrified—that it infected me. I felt creeping upon me, by slow yet certain degrees, the wild influences of his own fantastic yet impressive superstitions.

It was, especially, upon retiring to bed late in the night of the seventh or eighth day after the placing of the lady Madeline within the donjon, that I experienced the full power of such feelings. Sleep came not near my couch—while the hours waned and waned away. I struggled to reason off the nervousness which had dominion over me. I endeavored to believe that much, if not all of what I felt, was due to the bewildering influence of the gloomy furniture of the room—of the dark and tattered draperies, which, tortured into motion by the breath of a rising tempest, swayed fitfully to and fro upon the walls, and rustled uneasily about the decorations of the bed. But my efforts were fruitless. An irrepressible tremor gradually pervaded my frame; and, at length, there sat upon my very heart an incubus of utterly causeless alarm. Shaking this off with a gasp and a struggle, I uplifted myself upon the pillows, and, peering earnestly within the intense darkness of the chamber, harkened—I know not why, except that an instinctive spirit prompted me—to certain low and indefinite sounds which came, through the pauses of the storm, at long intervals I knew not whence. Overpowered by an intense sentiment of horror, unaccountable yet unendurable, I threw on my clothes with haste (for I felt that I should sleep no more during the night), and endeavored to arouse myself from the pitiable condition into which I had fallen, by pacing rapidly to and fro through the apartment.

I had taken but few turns in this manner, when a light step on an adjoining staircase arrested my attention. I presently recognized it as that of Usher. In an instant afterward he rapped, with a gentle touch, at my door, and entered, bearing a lamp. His countenance was, as usually, cadaverously wan—but there was a species of mad hilarity in his eyes—an evidently restrained *hysteria* in his whole demeanor. His air appalled me—but anything was preferable to the solitude which I had so long endured, and I even welcomed his presence as a relief.

"And you have not seen it?" he said abruptly, after having stared about him for some moments in silence—"you have not then seen it?—but, stay! you shall." Thus speaking, and having carefully shaded his lamp, he hurried to one of the casements, and threw it freely open to the storm.

The impetuous fury of the entering gust nearly lifted us from our feet. It was, indeed, a tempestuous yet sternly beautiful night, and one wildly singular in its terror and its beauty. A whirlwind had apparently collected its force in our vicinity; for there were frequent and violent alterations in the direction of the wind; and the exceeding density of the clouds (which hung so low as to press upon the turrets of the house) did not prevent our perceiving the life-like velocity with which they flew careering from all points against each other, without passing away into the distance. I say that even their exceeding density did not prevent our perceiving this; yet we had no glimpse of the moon or stars, nor was there any flashing forth of the lightning. But the under surfaces of the huge masses of agitated vapor, as well as all terrestrial objects immediately around us, were glowing in the unnatural light of a faintly luminous and distinctly visible gaseous exhalation which hung about and enshrouded the mansion.

"You must not—you shall not behold this!" said I, shudderingly, to Usher, as I led him, with a gentle violence, from the window to a seat. "These appearances, which bewilder you, are merely electrical phenomena not uncommon—or it may be that they have their ghastly origin in the rank miasma of the tarn. Let us close this casement; the air is chilling and dangerous to your frame. Here is one of your favorite romances. I will read, and you shall listen; and so we will pass away this terrible night together."

The antique volume which I had taken up was the *Mad Trist* of Sir Launcelot Canning;[6] but I had called it a favorite of Usher's more in sad jest than in earnest; for, in truth, there is little in its uncouth and unimaginative prolixity which could have had interest for the lofty and spiritual ideality of my friend. It was, however, the only book immediately at hand; and I indulged a vague hope that the excitement which now agitated the hypochondriac might find relief (for the history of mental disorder is full of similar anomalies) even in the extremeness of the folly which I should read. Could I have judged, indeed, by the wild, overstrained air of vivacity with which he hearkened, or apparently hearkened, to the words of the tale, I might have well congratulated myself upon the success of my design.

I had arrived at that well-known portion of the story where Ethelred, the hero of the *Trist,* having sought in vain for peaceable admission into the dwelling of the hermit, proceeds to make good an entrance by force. Here, it will be remembered, the words of the narrative run thus:

> And Ethelred, who was by nature of a doughty heart, and who was now mighty withal, on account of the powerfulness of the wine which he had drunken, waited no longer to hold parley with the hermit, who, in sooth, was of an obstinate and maliceful turn, but, feeling the rain upon his shoulders, and fearing the rising of the tempest, uplifted his mace outright, and, with blows, made quickly room in the plankings of the door for his gauntleted hand; and now pulling therewith sturdily, he so cracked, and ripped, and tore all asunder, that the noise of the dry and hollow-sounding wood alarumed and reverberated throughout the forest.

At the termination of this sentence I started, and, for a moment, paused; for it appeared to me (although I at once concluded that my excited fancy had deceived me)—it appeared to me that, from some very remote portion of the mansion, there came, indistinctly, to my ears, what might have been, in its exact similarity of character, the echo (but a stifled and dull one certainly) of the very cracking and ripping sound which Sir Launcelot had so particularly described. It was, beyond doubt, the coincidence alone which had arrested my attention; for, amid the rattling of the sashes of the casements, and the ordinary commingled noises of the still increasing storm, the sound, in itself, had nothing, surely, which should have interested or disturbed me. I continued the story:

> But the good champion Ethelred, now entering within the door, was sore enraged and amazed to perceive no signal of the maliceful hermit; but, in the stead thereof, a dragon of scaly and prodigious demeanor, and of a fiery tongue, which

sate in guard before a palace of gold, with a floor of silver; and upon the wall there hung a shield of shining brass with this legend enwritten—

> *Who entereth herein, a conqueror hath bin,*
> *Who slayeth the dragon, the shield he shall win.*

And Ethelred uplifted his mace, and struck upon the head of the dragon, which fell before him, and gave up his pesty breath, with a shriek so horrid and harsh, and withal so piercing, that Ethelred had fain to close his ears with his hands against the dreadful noise of it, the like whereof was never before heard.

Here again I paused abruptly, and now with a feeling of wild amazement—for there could be no doubt whatever that, in this instance, I did actually hear (although from what direction it proceeded I found it impossible to say) a low and apparently distant, but harsh, protracted, and most unusual screaming or grating sound—the exact counterpart of what my fancy had already conjured up as the sound of the dragon's unnatural shriek as described by the romancer.

Oppressed, as I certainly was, upon the occurrence of this second and most extraordinary coincidence, by a thousand conflicting sensations, in which wonder and extreme terror were predominant, I still retained sufficient presence of mind to avoid exciting, by any observation, the sensitive nervousness of my companion. I was by no means certain that he had noticed the sounds in question; although, assuredly, a strange alteration had, during the last few minutes, taken place in his demeanor. From a position fronting my own, he had gradually brought round his chair, so as to sit with his face to the door of the chamber; and thus I could but partially perceive his features, although I saw that his lips trembled as if he were murmuring inaudibly. His head had dropped upon his breast—yet I knew that he was not asleep, from the wide and rigid opening of the eye, as I caught a glance of it in profile. The motion of his body, too, was at variance with this idea—for he rocked from side to side with a gentle yet constant and uniform sway. Having rapidly taken notice of all this, I resumed the narrative of Sir Launcelot, which thus proceeded:

And now, the champion, having escaped from the terrible fury of the dragon, bethinking himself of the brazen shield, and of the breaking up of the enchantment which was upon it, removed the carcass from out of the way before him, and approached valorously over the silver pavement of the castle to where the shield was upon the wall; which in sooth tarried not for his full coming, but fell down at his feet upon the silver floor, with a mighty great and terrible ringing sound.

No sooner had these syllables passed my lips, than—as if a shield of brass had indeed, at the moment, fallen heavily upon a floor of silver—I became aware of a distinct, hollow, metallic and clangorous yet apparently muffled reverberation. Completely unnerved, I leaped to my feet; but the measured rocking movement of Usher was undisturbed. I rushed to the chair in which he sat. His eyes were bent fixedly before him, and throughout his whole countenance there reigned a more than stony rigidity. But as I laid my hand upon his shoulder, there came a strong shudder over his whole person; a sickly smile quivered about his lips; and I saw that he spoke in a low, hurried, and gibbering murmur, as if unconscious of my presence. Bending closely over him, I at length drank in the hideous import of his words.

"Not hear it?—yes, I hear it, and *have* heard it. Long—long—long—many minutes, many hours, many days, have I heard it—yet I dared not—oh, pity me; miserable wretch that I am!—I dared not—I *dared* not speak! *We have put her living in the tomb!* Said I not that my senses were acute?—I *now* tell you that I heard her first feeble movements in the hollow coffin. I heard them—many, many days ago—yet I dared not—*I dared not speak!* And now—to-night—Ethelred—ha! ha!—the breaking of the hermit's door, and the death-cry of the dragon, and the clangor of the shield!—say, rather, the rending of her coffin, and the grating of the iron hinges of her prison, and her struggles within the coppered archway of the vault! Oh whither shall I fly? Will she not be here anon? Is she not hurrying to upbraid me for my haste? Have I not heard her footstep on the stair? Do I not distinguish that heavy and horrible beating of her heart? MADMAN!" here he sprang violently to his feet, and shrieked out his syllables, as if in the effort he were giving up his soul—*"Madman! I tell you that she now stands without the door!"*

As if in the superhuman energy of his utterance there had been found the potency of a spell, the huge antique panels to which the speaker pointed, threw slowly back, upon the instant, their ponderous and ebony jaws. It was the work of the rushing gust—but then without those doors there DID stand the lofty and enshrouded figure of the lady Madeline of Usher. There was blood upon her white robes, and the evidence of some bitter struggle upon every portion of her emaciated frame. For a moment she remained trembling and reeling to and fro upon the threshold—then, with a low moaning cry, fell heavily inward upon the person of her brother, and in her violent and now final death-agonies, bore him to the floor a corpse, and a victim to the terrors he had anticipated.

From that chamber, and from that mansion, I fled aghast. The storm was still abroad in all its wrath as I found myself crossing the old causeway. Suddenly there shot along the path a wild light, and I turned to see whence a gleam so unusual could have issued; for the vast house and its shadows were alone behind me. The radiance was that of the full, setting, and blood-red moon, which now shone vividly through that once barely-discernible fissure of which I have before spoken as extending from the roof of the building, in a zigzag direction, to the base. While I gazed, this fissure rapidly widened—there came a fierce breath of the whirlwind—the entire orb of the satellite burst at once upon my sight—my brain reeled as I saw the mighty walls rushing asunder—there was a long tumultuous shouting sound like the voice of a thousand waters—and the deep and dank tarn at my feet closed sullenly and silently over the fragments of the HOUSE OF USHER.

1840

The Purloined Letter

Nil sapientiae odiosius acumine nimio.
—Seneca[1]

At Paris, just after dark one gusty evening in the autumn of 18—, I was enjoying the twofold luxury of meditation and a meerschaum, in company with my friend C. Auguste Dupin, in his little back library, or book-closet, *au troisième, No. 33, Rue Dunôt, Faubourg St. Germain.*[2] For one hour at least we had maintained a profound silence; while each, to any casual observer, might have seemed intently and exclusively occupied with the curling eddies of smoke that oppressed the atmosphere of the chamber. For myself, however, I was mentally discussing certain topics which had formed matter for conversation between us at an earlier period of the evening; I mean the affair of the Rue Morgue, and the mystery attending the murder of Marie Rogêt.[3] I looked upon it, therefore, as something of coincidence, when the door of our apartment was thrown open and admitted our old acquaintance, Monsieur G——, the Prefect of the Parisian police.

We gave him a hearty welcome; for there was nearly half as much of the entertaining as of the contemptible about the man, and we had not seen him for several years. We had been sitting in the dark, and Dupin now arose for the purpose of lighting a lamp, but sat down again, without doing so, upon G.'s saying that he had called to consult us, or rather to ask the opinion of my friend, about some official business which had occasioned a great deal of trouble.

"If it is any point requiring reflection," observed Dupin, as he forebore to enkindle the wick, "we shall examine it to better purpose in the dark."

"That is another of your odd notions," said the Prefect, who had a fashion of calling every thing "odd" that was beyond his comprehension, and thus lived amid an absolute legion of "oddities."

"Very true," said Dupin, as he supplied his visitor with a pipe, and rolled towards him a very comfortable chair.

"And what is the difficulty now?" I asked. "Nothing more in the assassination way, I hope?"

"Oh no; nothing of that nature. The fact is, the business is *very* simple indeed, and I make no doubt that we can manage it sufficiently well ourselves; but then I thought Dupin would like to hear the details of it, because it is so excessively *odd.*"

"Simple and odd," said Dupin.

"Why, yes; and not exactly that, either. The fact is, we have all been a good deal puzzled because the affair *is* so simple, and yet baffles us altogether."

"Perhaps it is the very simplicity of the thing which puts you at fault," said my friend.

"What nonsense you *do* talk!" replied the Prefect, laughing heartily.

---

1. Nothing is more distasteful to good sense than too much cunning (Latin); Lucius Annaeus Seneca (4 B.C.E.–C.E. 65), Roman poet and philosopher.   **2.** Fashionable quarter of Paris. The "troisième" is literally the third floor, but is equivalent to the fourth floor in North America.   **3.** *The Mystery of Marie Rogêt* and *The Murders in the Rue Morgue* are titles of earlier Dupin tales by Poe.

"Perhaps the mystery is a little *too* plain," said Dupin.

"Oh, good heavens! who ever heard of such an idea?"

"A little *too* self-evident."

"Ha! ha! ha!—ha! ha! ha!—ho! ho! ho!" roared out our visitor, profoundly amused, "oh, Dupin, you will be the death of me yet!"

"And what, after all, *is* the matter on hand?" I asked.

"Why, I will tell you," replied the Prefect, as he gave a long, steady, and contemplative puff, and settled himself in his chair. "I will tell you in a few words; but, before I begin, let me caution you that this is an affair demanding the greatest secrecy, and that I should most probably lose the position I now hold, were it known that I confided it to any one."

"Proceed," said I.

"Or not," said Dupin.

"Well, then; I have received personal information, from a very high quarter, that a certain document of the last importance, has been purloined from the royal apartments. The individual who purloined it is known; this beyond a doubt; he was seen to take it. It is known, also, that it still remains in his possession."

"How is this known?" asked Dupin.

"It is clearly inferred," replied the Prefect, "from the nature of the document, and from the non-appearance of certain results which would at once arise from its passing *out* of the robber's possession;—that is to say, from his employing it as he must design in the end to employ it."

"Be a little more explicit," I said.

"Well, I may venture so far as to say that the paper gives its holder a certain power in a certain quarter where such power is immensely valuable." The Prefect was fond of the cant of diplomacy.

"Still I do not quite understand," said Dupin.

"No? Well; the disclosure of the document to a third person, who shall be nameless, would bring in question the honour of a personage of most exalted station; and this fact gives the holder of the document an ascendancy over the illustrious personage whose honour and peace are so jeopardized."

"But this ascendancy," I interposed, "would depend upon the robber's knowledge of the loser's knowledge of the robber. Who would dare—"

"The thief," said G, "is the Minister D——, who dares all things, those unbecoming as well as those becoming a man. The method of the theft was not less ingenious than bold. The document in question—a letter, to be frank—had been received by the personage robbed while alone in the royal *boudoir.* During its perusal she was suddenly interrupted by the entrance of the other exalted personage from whom especially it was her wish to conceal it. After a hurried and vain endeavour to thrust it in a drawer, she was forced to place it, open as it was, upon a table. The address, however, was uppermost, and the contents thus unexposed, the letter escaped notice. At this juncture enters the Minister D——. His lynx eye immediately perceives the paper, recognises the handwriting of the address, observes the confusion of the personage addressed, and fathoms her secret. After some business transactions, hurried through in his ordinary manner, he produces a letter somewhat similar to the one in question, opens it, pretends to read it, and then places it in close juxtaposition to the other. Again he converses, for some fifteen minutes, upon the public affairs. At length, in taking leave, he takes also from the table the letter to which he had no claim. Its rightful owner saw, but, of course, dared not call attention to the act, in the presence of the third personage who stood at her elbow. The minister decamped; leaving his own letter—one of no importance—upon the table."

"Here, then," said Dupin to me, "you have precisely what you demand to make the ascendancy complete—the robber's knowledge of the loser's knowledge of the robber."

"Yes," replied the Prefect; "and the power thus attained has, for some months past, been wielded, for political purposes, to a very dangerous extent. The personage robbed is more thoroughly convinced, every day, of the necessity of reclaiming her letter. But this, of course, cannot be done openly. In fine, driven to despair, she has committed the matter to me."

"Than whom," said Dupin, amid a perfect whirlwind of smoke, "no more sagacious agent could, I suppose, be desired, or even imagined."

"You flatter me," replied the Prefect; "but it is possible that some such opinion may have been entertained."

"It is clear," said I, "as you observe, that the letter is still in possession of the minister; since it is this possession, and not any employment of the letter, which bestows the power. With the employment the power departs."

"True," said G.; "and upon this conviction I proceeded. My first care was to make thorough search of the minister's hotel;[4] and here my chief embarrassment lay in the necessity of searching without his knowledge. Beyond all things, I have been warned of the danger which would result from giving him reason to suspect our design."

"But," said I, "you are quite *au fait*[5] in these investigations. The Parisian police have done this thing often before."

"O yes; and for this reason I did not despair. The habits of the minister gave me, too, a great advantage. He is frequently absent from home all night. His servants are by no means numerous. They sleep at a distance from their master's apartment, and, being chiefly Neapolitans, are readily made drunk. I have keys, as you know, with which I can open any chamber or cabinet in Paris. For three months a night has not passed, during the greater part of which I have not been engaged, personally, in ransacking the D—— Hôtel. My honour is interested, and, to mention a great secret, the reward is enormous. So I did not abandon the search until I had become fully satisfied that the thief is a more astute man than myself. I fancy that I have investigated every nook and corner of the premises in which it is possible that the paper can be concealed."

"But is it not possible," I suggested, "that although the letter may be in possession of the minister, as it unquestionably is, he may have concealed it elsewhere than upon his own premises?"

"This is barely possible," said Dupin. "The present peculiar condition of affairs at court, and especially of those intrigues in which D—— is known to be involved, would render the instant availability of the document—its susceptibility of being produced at a moment's notice—a point of nearly equal importance with its possession."

"Its susceptibility of being produced?" said I.

---

4. That is, town house. **5.** Adept, competent (French).

"That is to say, of being *destroyed*," said Dupin.

"True," I observed; "the paper is clearly then upon the premises. As for its being upon the person of the minister, we may consider that as out of the question."

"Entirely," said the Prefect. "He has been twice waylaid, as if by footpads,[6] and his person rigorously searched under my own inspection."

"You might have spared yourself this trouble," said Dupin. "D——, I presume, is not altogether a fool, and, if not, must have anticipated these waylayings, as a matter of course."

"Not *altogether* a fool," said G., "but then he's a poet, which I take to be only one remove from a fool."[7]

"True," said Dupin, after a long and thoughtful whiff from his meerschaum, "although I have been guilty of certain doggerel myself."

"Suppose you detail," said I, "the particulars of your search."

"Why the fact is, we took our time, and we searched *every where*. I have had long experience in these affairs. I took the entire building, room by room; devoting the nights of a whole week to each. We examined, first, the furniture of each apartment. We opened every possible drawer; and I presume you know that, to a properly trained police agent, such a thing as a *secret* drawer is impossible. Any man is a dolt who permits a 'secret' drawer to escape him in a search of this kind. The thing is *so* plain. There is a certain amount of bulk—of space—to be accounted for in every cabinet. Then we have accurate rules.[8] The fiftieth part of a line could not escape us. After the cabinets we took the chairs. The cushions we probed with the fine long needles you have seen me employ. From the tables we removed the tops."

"Why so?"

"Sometimes the top of a table, or other similarly arranged piece of furniture, is removed by the person wishing to conceal an article; then the leg is excavated, the article deposited within the cavity, and the top replaced. The bottoms and tops of bedposts are employed in the same way."

"But could not the cavity be detected by sounding?" I asked.

"By no means, if, when the article is deposited, a sufficient wadding of cotton be placed around it. Besides, in our case, we were obliged to proceed without noise."

"But you could not have removed—you could not have taken to pieces *all* articles of furniture in which it would have been possible to make a deposit in the manner you mention. A letter may be compressed into a thin spiral roll, not differing much in shape or bulk from a large knitting-needle, and in this form it might be inserted into the rung of a chair, for example. You did not take to pieces all the chairs?"

"Certainly not; but we did better—we examined the rungs of every chair in the hotel, and, indeed, the jointings of every description of furniture, by the aid of a most powerful microscope.[9] Had there been any traces of recent disturbance we should not have failed to detect it instantly. A single grain of gimlet-dust,[1] for example, would have been as obvious as an apple. Any disorder in the glueing—any unusual gaping in the joints—would have sufficed to insure detection."

---

6. Muggers.   7. See Shakespeare's formulation from *A Midsummer Night's Dream:* "The lunatic, the lover, and the poet / Are of imagination all compact" (Act V, Scene 1, lines 7–8).   8. Rulers.   9. Magnifying glass.   1. That is, dust from a drilled hole.

"I presume you looked to the mirrors, between the boards and the plates, and you probed the beds and the bed-clothes, as well as the curtains and carpets."

"That of course; and when we had absolutely completed every particle of the furniture in this way, then we examined the house itself. We divided its entire surface into compartments, which we numbered, so that none might be missed; then we scrutinized each individual square inch throughout the premises, including the two houses immediately adjoining, with the microscope, as before."

"The two houses adjoining!" I exclaimed; "you must have had a great deal of trouble."

"We had; but the reward offered is prodigious."

"You include the *grounds* about the houses?"

"All the grounds are paved with brick. They gave us comparatively little trouble. We examined the moss between the bricks, and found it undisturbed."

"You looked among D——'s papers, of course, and into the books of the library?"

"Certainly; we opened every package and parcel; we not only opened every book, but we turned over every leaf in each volume, not contenting ourselves with a mere shake, according to the fashion of some of our police officers. We also measured the thickness of every book-*cover,* with the most accurate admeasurement, and applied to each the most jealous scrutiny of the microscope. Had any of the bindings been recently meddled with, it would have been utterly impossible that the fact should have escaped observation. Some five or six volumes, just from the hands of the binder, we carefully probed, longitudinally, with the needles."

"You explored the floors beneath the carpets?"

"Beyond doubt. We removed every carpet, and examined the boards with the microscope."

"And the paper on the walls?"

"Yes."

"You looked into the cellars?"

"We did."

"Then," I said, "you have been making a miscalculation, and the letter is *not* upon the premises, as you suppose."

"I fear you are right there," said the Prefect. "And now, Dupin, what would you advise me to do?"

"To make a thorough re-search of the premises."

"That is absolutely needless," replied G——. "I am not more sure that I breathe than I am that the letter is not at the Hôtel."

"I have no better advice to give you," said Dupin. "You have, of course, an accurate description of the letter?"

"Oh yes!"—And here the Prefect, producing a memorandum-book, proceeded to read aloud a minute account of the internal, and especially of the external, appearance of the missing document. Soon after finishing the perusal of this description, he took his departure, more entirely depressed in spirits than I had ever known the good gentleman before.

In about a month afterwards he paid us another visit, and found us occupied very nearly as before. He took a pipe and a chair and entered into some ordinary conversation. At length I said;—

"Well, but G——, what of the purloined letter? I presume you have at last made up your mind that there is no such thing as overreaching the Minister?"

"Confound him, say I—yes; I made the re-examination, however, as Dupin suggested—but it was all labour lost, as I knew it would be."

"How much was the reward offered, did you say?" asked Dupin.

"Why, a very great deal—a *very* liberal reward—I don't like to say how much, precisely; but one thing I *will* say, that I wouldn't mind giving my individual check for fifty thousand francs to any one who could obtain me that letter. The fact is, it is becoming of more and more importance every day; and the reward has been lately doubled. If it were trebled, however, I could do no more than I have done."

"Why, yes," said Dupin, drawlingly, between the whiffs of his meerschaum, "I really—think, G——, you have not exerted yourself—to the utmost in this matter. You might—do a little more, I think, eh?"

"How?—in what way?"

"Why—puff, puff—you might—puff, puff—employ counsel in the matter, eh?—puff, puff, puff. Do you remember the story they tell of Abernethy?"

"No; hang Abernethy!"

"To be sure! hang him and welcome. But, once upon a time, a certain rich miser conceived the design of spunging[2] upon this Abernethy for a medical opinion. Getting up, for this purpose, an ordinary conversation in a private company, he insinuated his case to the physician, as that of an imaginary individual.

"'We will suppose,' said the miser, 'that his symptoms are such and such; now, doctor, what would *you* have directed him to take?'

"'Take!' said Abernethy, 'why, take *advice,* to be sure.'"

"But," said the Prefect, a little discomposed, "I am *perfectly* willing to take advice, and to pay for it. I would *really* give fifty thousand francs to any one who would aid me in the matter."

"In that case," replied Dupin, opening a drawer, and producing a check-book, "you may as well fill me up a check for the amount mentioned. When you have signed it, I will hand you the letter."

I was astounded. The Prefect appeared absolutely thunder-stricken. For some minutes he remained speechless and motionless, looking incredulously at my friend with open mouth, and eyes that seemed starting from their sockets; then, apparently recovering himself in some measure, he seized a pen, and after several pauses and vacant stares, finally filled up and signed a check for fifty thousand francs, and handed it across the table to Dupin. The latter examined it carefully and deposited it in his pocket-book; then, unlocking an *escritoire,*[3] took thence a letter and gave it to the Prefect. This functionary grasped it in a perfect agony of joy, opened it with a trembling hand, cast a rapid glance at its contents, and then, scrambling and struggling to the door, rushed at length unceremoniously from the room and from the house, without having uttered a syllable since Dupin had requested him to fill up the check.

When he had gone, my friend entered into some explanations.

---

2. Sponging, extracting a free consultation.   **3.** A writing table (French).

"The Parisian police," he said, "are exceedingly able in their way. They are persevering, ingenious, cunning, and thoroughly versed in the knowledge which their duties seem chiefly to demand. Thus, when G—— detailed to us his mode of searching the premises at the Hôtel D——, I felt the entire confidence in his having made a satisfactory investigation—so far as his labours extended."

"So far as his labours extended?" said I.

"Yes," said Dupin. "The measures adopted were not only the best of their kind, but carried out to absolute perfection. Had the letter been deposited within the range of their search, these fellows would, beyond a question, have found it."

I merely laughed—but he seemed quite serious in all that he said.

"The measures, then," he continued, "were good in their kind, and well executed; their defect lay in their being inapplicable to the case, and to the man. A certain set of highly ingenious resources are, with the Prefect, a sort of Procrustean bed,[4] to which he forcibly adapts his designs. But he perpetually errs by being too deep or too shallow, for the matter in hand; and many a schoolboy is a better reasoner than he. I knew one about eight years of age, whose success at guessing in the game of 'even and odd' attracted universal admiration. This game is simple, and is played with marbles. One player holds in his hand a number of these toys, and demands of another whether that number is even or odd. If the guess is right, the guesser wins one; if wrong, he loses one. The boy to whom I allude won all the marbles of the school. Of course he had some principle of guessing; and this lay in mere observation and admeasurement of the astuteness of his opponents. For example, an arrant simpleton is his opponent, and, holding up his closed hand, asks: 'Are they even or odd?' Our schoolboy replies 'Odd,' and loses; but upon the second trial he wins, for he then says to himself, 'The simpleton had them even upon the first trial, and his amount of cunning is just sufficient to make him have them odd upon the second; I will therefore guess odd;'—he guesses odd, and wins. Now, with a simpleton a degree above the first, he would have reasoned thus: 'This fellow finds that in the first instance I guessed odd, and, in the second, he will propose to himself, upon the first impulse, a simple variation from even to odd, as did the first simpleton; but then a second thought will suggest that this is too simple a variation, and finally he will decide upon putting it even as before. I will therefore guess even';—he guesses even, and wins. Now this mode of reasoning in the schoolboy, whom his fellows termed 'lucky,'—what, in its last analysis, is it?"

"It is merely," I said, "an identification of the reasoner's intellect with that of his opponent."

"It is," said Dupin; "and, upon inquiring of the boy by what means he effected the *thorough* identification in which his success consisted, I received answer as follows: 'When I wish to find out how wise, or how stupid, or how good, or how wicked is any one, or what are his thoughts at the moment, I fashion the expression on my face, as accurately as possible, in accordance with the expression of his, and then wait to see what thoughts or sentiments arise in

4. In Greek mythology the giant Procrustes tied travelers to an iron bed and made them fit it by either stretching them or amputating their limbs.

my mind or heart, as if to match or correspond with the expression.' This response of the schoolboy lies at the bottom of all the spurious profundity which has been attributed to Rochefoucault, to La Bougive, to Machiavelli, and to Campanella."[5]

"And the identification," I said, "of the reasoner's intellect with that of his opponent, depends, if I understand you aright, upon the accuracy with which the opponent's intellect is admeasured."

"For its practical value it depends upon this," replied Dupin; "and the Prefect and his cohort fail so frequently, first, by default of this identification, and, secondly, by ill-admeasurement, or rather through non-admeasurement, of the intellect with which they are engaged. They consider only their *own* ideas of ingenuity; and, in searching for anything hidden, advert only to the modes in which *they* would have hidden it. They are right in this much—that their own ingenuity is a faithful representative of that of *the mass*; but when the cunning of the individual felon is diverse in character from their own, the felon foils them, of course. This always happens when it is above their own, and very usually when it is below. They have no variation of principle in their investigations; at best, when urged by some unusual emergency—by some extraordinary reward—they extend or exaggerate their old modes of *practice*, without touching their principles. What, for example, in this case of D——, has been done to vary the principle of action? What is all this boring, and probing, and sounding, and scrutinizing with the microscope, and dividing the surface of the building into registered square inches—what is it all but an exaggeration *of the application* of the one principle or set of principles of search, which are based upon the one set of notions regarding human ingenuity, to which the Prefect, in the long routine of his duty, has been accustomed? Do you not see he has taken it for granted that *all* men proceed to conceal a letter,—not exactly in a gimlet-hole bored in a chair-leg—but, at least, in *some* out-of-the-way hole or corner suggested by the same tenor of thought which would urge a man to secrete a letter in a gimlet-hole bored in a chair-leg? And do you not see also, that such *recherchés*[6] nooks for concealment are adapted only for ordinary occasions, and would be adopted only by ordinary intellects; for, in all cases of concealment, a disposal of the article concealed—a disposal of it in this *recherché* manner—is, in the very first instance, presumable and presumed; and thus its discovery depends, not at all upon the acumen, but altogether upon the mere care, patience, and determination of the seekers; and where the case is of importance—or, what amounts to the same thing in the political eyes, when the reward is of magnitude,—the qualities in question have *never* been known to fail. You will now understand what I meant in suggesting that, had the purloined letter been hidden anywhere within the limits of the Prefect's examination—in other words, had the principle of its concealment been comprehended within the principles of the Prefect—its discovery would have been a matter altogether beyond question. This functionary, however, has been thoroughly mystified; and the remote source of his defeat lies in the supposition that the Minister is a fool, because

---

5. Tommaso Campanella (1568–1639), Italian philosopher and Dominican monk. François, duc de la Rochefoucauld (1613–1680), French moralist and courtier. La Bougive is probably Jean de la Bruyère (1645–1696). Niccolò Machiavelli (1469–1527), Italian statesman and writer.   **6.** That is, excessively cunning (French).

he has acquired renown as a poet. All fools are poets; this the Prefect *feels*; and he is merely guilty of a *non distributio medii*[7] in thence inferring that all poets are fools."

"But is this really the poet?" I asked. "There are two brothers, I know; and both have attained reputation in letters. The Minister I believe has written learnedly on the Differential Calculus. He is a mathematician, and no poet."

"You are mistaken; I know him well; he is both. As poet *and* mathematician, he would reason well; as mere mathematician, he could not have reasoned at all, and thus would have been at the mercy of the Prefect."

"You surprise me," I said, "by these opinions, which have been contradicted by the voice of the world. You do not mean to set at naught the well-digested idea of centuries. The mathematical reason has long been regarded as *the* reason *par excellence*."

"'*Il y a à parier*,'" replied Dupin, quoting from Chamfort, "'*que toute idée publique, toute convention reçue, est une sottise, car elle a convenue au plus grand nombre*.'[8] The mathematicians, I grant you, have done their best to promulgate the popular error to which you allude, and which is none the less an error for its promulgation as truth. With an art worthy a better cause, for example, they have insinuated the term 'analysis' into application to algebra. The French are the originators of this particular deception; but if a term is of any importance—if words derive any value from applicability—then 'analysis' conveys 'algebra' about as much as, in Latin, '*ambitus*' implies 'ambition,' '*religio*' 'religion,' or '*homines honesti*,' a set of *honourable* men."

"You have a quarrel on hand, I see," said I, "with some of the algebraists of Paris; but proceed."

"I dispute the availability, and thus the value, of that reason which is cultivated in any especial form other than the abstractly logical. I dispute, in particular, the reason educed by mathematical study. The mathematics are the science of form and quantity; mathematical reasoning is merely logic applied to observation upon form and quantity. The great error lies in supposing that even the truths of what is called *pure* algebra, are abstract or general truths. And this error is so egregious that I am confounded at the universality with which it has been received. Mathematical axioms are *not* axioms of general truth. What is true of *relation*—of form and quantity—is often grossly false in regard to morals, for example. In this latter science it is very usually *un*true that the aggregated parts are equal to the whole. In chemistry also the axiom fails. In the consideration of motive it fails; for two motives, each of a given value, have not, necessarily, a value when united, equal to the sum of their values apart. There are numerous other mathematical truths which are only truths within the limits of *relation*. But the mathematician argues, from his *finite truths*, through habit, as if they were of absolutely general applicability—as the world indeed imagines them to be. Bryant, in his very learned 'Mythology,'[9] mentions an analogous source of error, when he says that 'although the Pagan fables are not believed, yet we forget ourselves continually, and make inferences from them as existing realities.' With the algebraists, however, who

---

7. The undistributed middle (Latin), an error in logic.   **8.** The odds are that every popular idea, every accepted convention is nonsense, because it has suited itself to the majority (French); from *Maximes et Pensées* by Sébastian Chamfort (1741–1794).   **9.** *A New System, or an Analysis of Ancient Mythology*, by Jacob Bryant (1715–1804), English scholar.

are Pagans themselves, the 'Pagan fables' *are* believed, and the inferences are made, not so much through lapse of memory, as through an unaccountable addling of the brains. In short, I never yet encountered the mere mathematician who could be trusted out of equal roots, or one who did not clandestinely hold it as a point of his faith $x^2 + px$ was absolutely and unconditionally equal to q. Say to one of these gentlemen, by way of experiment, if you please, that you believe occasions may occur where $x^2 + px$ is *not* altogether equal to q, and, having made him understand what you mean, get out of his reach as speedily as convenient, for, beyond doubt, he will endeavour to knock you down.

"I mean to say," continued Dupin, while I merely laughed at his last observations, "that if the Minister had been no more than a mathematician, the Prefect would have been under no necessity of giving me this check. I knew him, however, as both mathematician and poet, and my measures were adapted to his capacity, with reference to the circumstances by which he was surrounded. I knew him as a courtier, too, and as a bold *intriguant*.[1] Such a man, I considered, could not fail to be aware of the ordinary political modes of action. He could not have failed to anticipate—and events have proved that he did not fail to anticipate—the waylayings to which he was subjected. He must have foreseen, I reflected, the secret investigations of his premises. His frequent absences from home at night, which were hailed by the Prefect as certain aids to his success, I regarded only as *ruses,* to afford opportunity for thorough search to the police, and thus the sooner to impress them with the conviction to which G——, in fact, did finally arrive—the conviction that the letter was not upon the premises. I felt, also, that the whole train of thought, which I was at some pains in detailing to you just now, concerning the invariable principle of political action in searches for articles concealed—I felt that this whole train of thought would necessarily pass through the mind of the Minister. It would imperatively lead him to despise all the ordinary *nooks* of concealment. *He* could not, I reflected, be so weak as not to see that the most intricate and remote recess of his hotel would be as open as his commonest closets to the eyes, to the probes, to the gimlets, and to the microscopes of the Prefect. I saw, in fine, that he would be driven, as a matter of course, to simplicity, if not deliberately induced to it as a matter of choice. You will remember, perhaps, how desperately the Prefect laughed when I suggested, upon our first interview, that it was just possible this mystery troubled him so much on account of its being so *very* self-evident."

"Yes," said I, "I remember his merriment well. I really thought he would have fallen into convulsions."

"The material world," continued Dupin, "abounds with very strict analogies to the immaterial; and thus some color of truth has been given to the rhetorical dogma, that metaphor, or simile, may be made to strengthen an argument as well as to embellish a description. The principle of *vis inertiae*,[2] for example, seems to be identical in physics and metaphysics. It is not more true in the former, that a large body is with more difficulty set in motion than a smaller one, and that its subsequent *momentum* is commensurate with this difficulty, than it is, in the latter, that intellects of the vaster capacity, while

<hr/>

1. Intriguer (French).   **2.** The force of inertia (Latin).

more forcible, more constant, and more eventful in their movements than those of inferior grade, are yet the less readily moved, and more embarrassed and full of hesitation in the first few steps of their progress. Again: have you ever noticed which of the street signs, over the shop doors, are the most attractive of attention?"

"I have never given the matter a thought," I said.

"There is a game of puzzles," he resumed, "which is played upon a map. One party playing requires another to find a given word—the name of town, river, state, or empire—any word, in short, upon the motley and perplexed surface of the chart. A novice in the game generally seeks to embarrass his opponents by giving them the most minutely lettered names; but the adept selects such words as stretch, in large characters, from one end of the chart to the other. These, like the over-largely lettered signs and placards of the street, escape observation by dint of being excessively obvious; and here the physical oversight is precisely analogous with the moral inapprehension by which the intellect suffers to pass unnoticed those considerations which are too obtrusively and too palpably self-evident. But this is a point, it appears, somewhat above or beneath the understanding of the Prefect. He never once thought it probable, or possible, that the Minister had deposited the letter immediately beneath the nose of the whole world, by way of best preventing any portion of that world from perceiving it.

"But the more I reflected upon the daring, dashing, and discriminating ingenuity of D——; upon the fact that the document must always have been *at hand,* if he intended to use it to good purpose; and upon the decisive evidence, obtained by the Prefect, that it was not hidden within the limits of that dignitary's ordinary search—the more satisfied I became that, to conceal this letter, the Minister had resorted to the comprehensive and sagacious expedient of not attempting to conceal it at all.

"Full of these ideas, I prepared myself with a pair of green spectacles, and called one fine morning, quite by accident, at the Ministerial hotel. I found D—— at home, yawning, lounging, and dawdling as usual, and pretending to be in the last extremity of *ennui*.[3] He is, perhaps, the most really energetic human being now alive—but that is only when nobody sees him.

"To be even with him, I complained of my weak eyes, and lamented the necessity of the spectacles, under cover of which I cautiously and thoroughly surveyed the whole apartment, while seemingly intent only upon the conversation of my host.

"I paid especial attention to a large writing-table near which he sat, and upon which lay confusedly, some miscellanous letters and other papers, with one or two musical instruments and a few books. Here, however, after a long and very deliberate scrutiny, I saw nothing to excite particular suspicion.

"At length my eyes, in going the circuit of the room, fell upon a trumpery filigree card-rack of pasteboard, that hung dangling by a dirty blue ribbon, from a little brass knob just beneath the middle of the mantel-piece. In this rack, which had three or four compartments, were five or six visiting cards, and a solitary letter. This last was much soiled and crumpled. It was torn nearly in two, across the middle—as if a design, in the first instance, to tear it

---

3. Boredom (French).

entirely up as worthless, had been altered, or stayed, in the second. It had a large black seal, bearing the D—— cipher[4] *very* conspicuously, and was addressed, in a diminutive female hand, to D——, the minister, himself. It was thrust carelessly, and even, as it seemed, contemptuously, into one of the uppermost divisions of the rack.

"No sooner had I glanced at this letter than I concluded it to be that of which I was in search. To be sure, it was, to all appearance, radically different from the one of which the Prefect had read us so minute a description. Here the seal was large and black, with the D—— cipher; there, it was small and red, with the ducal arms of the S—— family. Here, the address, to the minister, was diminutive and feminine; there, the superscription, to a certain royal personage, was markedly bold and decided; the size alone formed a point of correspondence. But, then, the *radicalness* of these differences, which was excessive; the dirt; the soiled and torn condition of the paper, so inconsistent with the *true* methodical habits of D——, and so suggestive of a design to delude the beholder into an idea of the worthlessness of the document; these things, together with the hyperobtrusive situation of this document, full in the view of every visitor, and thus exactly in accordance with the conclusions to which I had previously arrived; these things, I say, were strongly corroborative of suspicion, in one who came with the intention to suspect.

"I protracted my visit as long as possible, and, while I maintained a most animated discussion with the minister, upon a topic which I knew well had never failed to interest and excite him, I kept my attention really riveted upon the letter. In this examination, I committed to memory its external appearance and arrangement in the rack; and also fell, at length, upon a discovery which set at rest whatever trivial doubt I might have entertained. In scrutinizing the edges of the paper, I observed them to be more *chafed* than seemed necessary. They presented the *broken* appearance which is manifested when a stiff paper, having been once folded and pressed with a folder, is refolded in a reversed direction, in the same creases or edges which had formed the original fold. This discovery was sufficient. It was clear to me that the letter had been turned, as a glove, inside out, re-directed, and re-sealed. I bade the Minister good morning and took my departure at once, leaving a gold snuff-box upon the table.

"The next morning I called for the snuff-box, when we resumed, quite eagerly, the conversation of the preceding day. While thus engaged, however, a loud report, as if of a pistol, was heard immediately beneath the windows of the hotel, and was succeeded by a series of fearful screams, and the shoutings of a mob. D—— rushed to a casement, threw it open, and looked out. In the meantime, I stepped to the card-rack, took the letter, put it in my pocket, and replaced it by a *fac-simile*, (so far as regards externals) which I had carefully prepared at my lodgings; imitating the D—— cipher, very readily, by means of a seal formed of bread.

"The disturbance in the street had been occasioned by the frantic behaviour of a man with a musket. He had fired it among a crowd of women and children. It proved, however, to have been without ball, and the fellow was suffered to go his way as a lunatic or a drunkard. When he had gone, D—— came from the window, whither I had followed him immediately upon securing the

4. Monogram.

object in view. Soon afterward I bade him farewell. The pretended lunatic was a man in my own pay."

"But what purpose had you," I asked, "in replacing the letter by a *fac-simile*? Would it not have been better, at the first visit, to have seized it openly, and departed?"

"D——," replied Dupin, "is a desperate man, and a man of nerve. His hotel, too, is not without attendants devoted to his interests. Had I made the wild attempt you suggest, I should never have left the ministerial presence alive. The good people of Paris would have heard of me no more. But I had an object apart from these considerations. You know my political prepossessions. In this matter, I act as a partisan of the lady concerned. For eighteen months the minister has had her in his power. She has now him in hers; since, being unaware that the letter is not in his possession, he will proceed with his exactions as if it was. Thus will he inevitably commit himself, at once, to his political destruction. His downfall, too, will not be more precipitate than awkward. It is all very well to talk about the *facilis descensus Averni;* but in all kinds of climbing, as Catalini[5] said of singing, it is far more easy to get up than to come down. In the present instance I have no sympathy—at least no pity for him who descends. He is that *monstrum horrendum,*[6] an unprincipled man of genius. I confess, however, that I should like very well to know the precise character of his thoughts, when, being defied by her whom the Prefect terms 'a certain personage,' he is reduced to opening the letter which I left for him in the card-rack."

"How? did you put any thing particular in it?"

"Why—it did not seem altogether right to leave the interior blank—that would have been insulting. To be sure, D——, at Vienna once, did me an evil turn, which I told him, quite good-humouredly, that I should remember. So, as I knew he would feel some curiosity in regard to the identity of the person who had outwitted him, I thought it a pity not to give him a clue. He is well acquainted with my MS., and I just copied into the middle of the blank sheet the words—

> *—Un dessein si funeste,*
> *S'il n'est digne d'Atrée, est digne de Thyeste.*

They are to be found in Crébillon's 'Atrée.'"[7]

1845

RELATED:

—Poe, "The Philosophy of Composition," p. 1729
—Poe, Review of Hawthorne's *Twice-Told Tales*, p. 1772
—Richard Wilbur, "The House of Poe," p. 1784

---

5. Angelica Catalini (1780–1844), Italian singer. *Facilis descensus Averni:* Easy is the descent into hell . . . but to recall thy steps and issue to upper air, this is the task, this the burden (Latin); *Aeneid* (Book 6, line 126), by Virgil (70–19 B.C.E.), Roman poet. **6.** Horrifying monster (Latin), Virgil's description of Polyphemus the Cyclops after his one eye had been put out by Ulysses; *Aeneid* 3.658. **7.** So baneful a plot, if not worthy of Atreus, is worthy of Thyestes (French); from *Atrée et Thyeste* by Prosper Jolyot de Crébillon (1674–1762).

KATHERINE ANNE PORTER
1890–1980

Porter was born in Indian Creek, Texas, and brought up in Texas and Louisiana. She was educated at home, in private schools, and in an Ursuline convent. Though she began to write stories as soon as she could form letters on paper, she made no attempt to publish until she was past thirty, and she associated with no literary people until she had become something of a celebrity with the publication of her first book of stories, *Flowering Judas* (1930). Before and after that date she earned a meager living by journalism, traveling from city to city with little baggage except her manuscripts— trunkfuls of which were destroyed, bit by bit, as she found them inadequate to meet her exacting standards. She lived for a time in Mexico, which provided material for some of her most famous stories, and in Europe, where she continued to publish her stories. Her novel *Ship of Fools* was begun during the 1930s but not finished for more than two decades. It was at last published in 1962. Her many shorter works may be found in *The Collected Stories of Katherine Anne Porter*, which appeared in 1965, winning both the Pulitzer Prize and the National Book Award.

The Jilting of Granny Weatherall

She flicked her wrist neatly out of Doctor Harry's pudgy careful fingers and pulled the sheet up to her chin. The brat ought to be in knee breeches. Doctoring around the country with spectacles on his nose! "Get along now, take your schoolbooks and go. There's nothing wrong with me."

Doctor Harry spread a warm paw like a cushion on her forehead where the forked green vein danced and made her eyelids twitch. "Now, now, be a good girl, and we'll have you up in no time."

"That's no way to speak to a woman nearly eighty years old just because she's down. I'd have you respect your elders, young man."

"Well, Missy, excuse me." Doctor Harry patted her cheek. "But I've got to warn you, haven't I? You're a marvel, but you must be careful or you're going to be good and sorry."

"Don't tell me what I'm going to be. I'm on my feet now, morally speaking. It's Cornelia. I had to go to bed to get rid of her."

Her bones felt loose, and floated around in her skin, and Doctor Harry floated like a balloon around the foot of the bed. He floated and pulled down his waistcoat and swung his glasses on a cord. "Well, stay where you are, it certainly can't hurt you."

"Get along and doctor your sick," said Granny Weatherall. "Leave a well woman alone. I'll call for you when I want you. . . . Where were you forty years ago when I pulled through milk-leg and double pneumonia? You weren't even born. Don't let Cornelia lead you on," she shouted, because Doctor Harry appeared to float up to the ceiling and out. "I pay my own bills, and I don't throw my money away on nonsense!"

She meant to wave good-by, but it was too much trouble. Her eyes closed of themselves, it was like a dark curtain drawn around the bed. The pillow rose and floated under her, pleasant as a hammock in a light wind. She listened to the leaves rustling outside the window. No, somebody was swishing newspapers: no, Cornelia and Doctor Harry were whispering together. She leaped broad awake, thinking they whispered in her ear.

"She was never like this, *never* like this!" "Well, what can we expect?" "Yes, eighty years old. . . ."

Well, and what if she was? She still had ears. It was like Cornelia to whisper around doors. She always kept things secret in such a public way. She was always being tactful and kind. Cornelia was dutiful; that was the trouble with her. Dutiful and good; "So good and dutiful," said Granny, "that I'd like to spank her." She saw herself spanking Cornelia and making a fine job of it.

"What'd you say, Mother?"

Granny felt her face tying up in hard knots.

"Can't a body think, I'd like to know?"

"I thought you might want something."

"I do. I want a lot of things. First off, go away and don't whisper."

She lay and drowsed, hoping in her sleep that the children would keep out and let her rest a minute. It had been a long day. Not that she was tired. It was always pleasant to snatch a minute now and then. There was always so much to be done, let me see: tomorrow.

Tomorrow was far away and there was nothing to trouble about. Things were finished somehow when the time came; thank God there was always a little margin over for peace: then a person could spread out the plan of life and tuck in the edges orderly. It was good to have everything clean and folded away, with the hair brushes and tonic bottles sitting straight on the white embroidered linen: the day started without fuss and the pantry shelves laid out with rows of jelly glasses and brown jugs and white stone-china jars with blue whirligigs and words painted on them: coffee, tea, sugar, ginger, cinnamon, allspice: and the bronze clock with the lion on top nicely dusted off. The dust that lion could collect in twenty-four hours! The box in the attic with all those letters tied up, well, she'd have to go through that tomorrow. All those letters—George's letters and John's letters and her letters to them both—lying around for the children to find afterwards made her uneasy. Yes, that would be tomorrow's business. No use to let them know how silly she had been once.

While she was rummaging around she found death in her mind and it felt clammy and unfamiliar. She had spent so much time preparing for death there was no need for bringing it up again. Let it take care of itself now. When she was sixty she had felt very old, finished, and went around making farewell trips to see her children and grandchildren, with a secret in her mind: This is the very last of your mother, children! Then she made her will and came down with a long fever. That was all just a notion like a lot of other things, but it was lucky too, for she had once for all got over the idea of dying for a long time. Now she couldn't be worried. She hoped she had better sense now. Her father had lived to be one hundred and two years old and had drunk a noggin of strong hot toddy on his last birthday. He told the reporters it was his daily habit, and he owed his long life to that. He had made quite a scandal and was very pleased about it. She believed she'd just plague Cornelia a little.

"Cornelia! Cornelia!" No footsteps, but a sudden hand on her cheek. "Bless you, where have you been?"

"Here, Mother."

"Well, Cornelia, I want a noggin of hot toddy."

"Are you cold, darling?"

"I'm chilly, Cornelia. Lying in bed stops the circulation. I must have told you that a thousand times."

Well, she could just hear Cornelia telling her husband that Mother was getting a little childish and they'd have to humor her. The thing that most annoyed her was that Cornelia thought she was deaf, dumb, and blind. Little hasty glances and tiny gestures tossed around her and over her head saying, "Don't cross her, let her have her way, she's eighty years old," and she sitting there as if she lived in a thin glass cage. Sometimes Granny almost made up her mind to pack up and move back to her own house where nobody could remind her every minute that she was old. Wait, wait, Cornelia, till your own children whisper behind your back!

In her day she had kept a better house and had got more work done. She wasn't too old yet for Lydia to be driving eighty miles for advice when one of the children jumped the track, and Jimmy still dropped in and talked things over: "Now, Mammy, you've a good business head, I want to know what you think of this? . . ." Old. Cornelia couldn't change the furniture around without asking. Little things, little things! They had been so sweet when they were little. Granny wished the old days were back again with the children young and everything to be done over. It had been a hard pull, but not too much for her. When she thought of all the food she had cooked, and all the clothes she had cut and sewed, and all the gardens she had made—well, the children showed it. There they were, made out of her, and they couldn't get away from that. Sometimes she wanted to see John again and point to them and say, Well, I didn't do so badly, did I? But that would have to wait. That was for tomorrow. She used to think of him as a man, but now all the children were older than their father, and he would be a child beside her if she saw him now. It seemed strange and there was something wrong in the idea. Why, he couldn't possibly recognize her. She had fenced in a hundred acres once, digging the post holes herself and clamping the wires with just a negro boy to help. That changed a woman. John would be looking for a young woman with the peaked Spanish comb in her hair and the painted fan. Digging post holes changed a woman. Riding country roads in the winter when women had their babies was another thing: sitting up nights with sick horses and sick negroes and sick children and hardly ever losing one. John, I hardly ever lost one of them! John would see that in a minute, that would be something he could understand, she wouldn't have to explain anything!

It made her feel like rolling up her sleeves and putting the whole place to rights again. No matter if Cornelia was determined to be everywhere at once, there were a great many things left undone on this place. She would start tomorrow and do them. It was good to be strong enough for everything, even if all you made melted and changed and slipped under your hands, so that by the time you finished you almost forgot what you were working for. What was it I set out to do? she asked herself intently, but she could not remember. A fog rose over the valley, she saw it marching across the creek swallowing the trees and moving up the hill like an army of ghosts. Soon it would be at the near edge of the orchard, and then it was time to go in and light the lamps. Come in, children, don't stay out in the night air.

Lighting the lamps had been beautiful. The children huddled up to her and breathed like little calves waiting at the bars in the twilight. Their eyes followed the match and watched the flame rise and settle in a blue curve, then they moved away from her. The lamp was lit, they didn't have to be scared and hang on to mother anymore. Never, never, never more. God, for all my life I thank Thee. Without Thee, my God, I could never have done it. Hail, Mary, full of grace.

I want you to pick all the fruit this year and see that nothing is wasted. There's always someone who can use it. Don't let good things rot for want of using. You waste life when you waste good food. Don't let things get lost. It's bitter to lose things. Now, don't let me get to thinking, not when I am tired and taking a little nap before supper. . . .

The pillow rose about her shoulders and pressed against her heart and the memory was being squeezed out of it: oh, push down the pillow, somebody: it would smother her if she tried to hold it. Such a fresh breeze blowing and such a green day with no threats in it. But he had not come, just the same. What does a woman do when she has put on the white veil and set out the white cake for a man and he doesn't come? She tried to remember. No, I swear he never harmed me but in that. He never harmed me but in that . . . and what if he did? There was the day, the day, but a whirl of dark smoke rose and covered it, crept up and over into the bright field where everything was planted so carefully in orderly rows. That was hell, she knew hell when she saw it. For sixty years she had prayed against remembering him and against losing her soul in the deep pit of hell, and now the two things were mingled in one and the thought of him was a smoky cloud from hell that moved and crept in her head when she had just got rid of Doctor Harry and was trying to rest a minute. Wounded vanity, Ellen, said a sharp voice in the top of her mind. Don't let your wounded vanity get the upper hand of you. Plenty of girls get jilted. You were jilted, weren't you? Then stand up to it. Her eyelids wavered and let in streamers of blue-gray light like tissue paper over her eyes. She must get up and pull the shades down or she'd never sleep. She was in bed again and the shades were not down. How could that happen? Better turn over, hide from the light, sleeping in the light gave you nightmares. "Mother, how do you feel now?" and a stinging wetness on her forehead. But I don't like having my face washed in cold water!

Hapsy? George? Lydia? Jimmy? No, Cornelia, and her features were swollen and full of little puddles. "They're coming, darling, they'll all be here soon." Go wash your face, child, you look funny.

Instead of obeying, Cornelia knelt down and put her head on the pillow. She seemed to be talking but there was no sound. "Well, are you tongue-tied? Whose birthday is it? Are you going to give a party?"

Cornelia's mouth moved urgently in strange shapes. "Don't do that, you bother me, daughter."

"Oh, no, Mother. Oh, no. . . ."

Nonsense. It was strange about children. They disputed your every word. "No what, Cornelia?"

"Here's Doctor Harry."

"I won't see that boy again. He just left five minutes ago."

"That was this morning, Mother. It's night now. Here's the nurse."

"This is Doctor Harry, Mrs. Weatherall. I never saw you look so young and happy!"

"Ah, I'll never be young again—but I'd be happy if they'd let me lie in peace and get rested."

She thought she spoke up loudly, but no one answered. A warm weight on her forehead, a warm bracelet on her wrist, and a breeze went on whispering, trying to tell her something. A shuffle of leaves in the everlasting hand of God, He blew on them and they danced and rattled. "Mother, don't mind, we're going to give you a little hypodermic." "Look here, daughter, how do ants get in this bed? I saw sugar ants yesterday." Did you send for Hapsy too?

It was Hapsy she really wanted. She had to go a long way back through a great many rooms to find Hapsy standing with a baby on her arm. She seemed to herself to be Hapsy also, and the baby on Hapsy's arm was Hapsy and himself and herself, all at once, and there was no surprise in the meeting. Then Hapsy melted from within and turned flimsy as gray gauze and the baby was a gauzy shadow, and Hapsy came up close and said, "I thought you'd never come," and looked at her very searchingly and said, "You haven't changed a bit!" They leaned forward to kiss, when Cornelia began whispering from a long way off, "Oh, is there anything you want to tell me? Is there anything I can do for you?"

Yes, she had changed her mind after sixty years and she would like to see George. I want you to find George. Find him and be sure to tell him I forgot him. I want him to know I had my husband just the same and my children and my house like any other woman. A good house too and a good husband that I loved and fine children out of him. Better than I hoped for even. Tell him I was given back everything he took away and more. Oh, no, oh, God, no, there was something else besides the house and the man and the children. Oh, surely they were not all? What was it? Something not given back. . . . Her breath crowded down under her ribs and grew into a monstrous frightening shape with cutting edges; it bored up into her head, and the agony was unbelievable: Yes, John, get the Doctor now, no more talk, my time has come.

When this one was born it should be the last. The last. It should have been born first, for it was the one she had truly wanted. Everything came in good time. Nothing left out, left over. She was strong, in three days she would be as well as ever. Better. A woman needed milk in her to have her full health.

"Mother, do you hear me?"

"I've been telling you—"

"Mother, Father Connolly's here."

"I went to Holy Communion only last week. Tell him I'm not so sinful as all that."

"Father just wants to speak to you."

He could speak as much as he pleased. It was like him to drop in and inquire about her soul as if it were a teething baby, and then stay on for a cup of tea and a round of cards and gossip. He always had a funny story of some sort, usually about an Irishman who made his little mistakes and confessed them, and the point lay in some absurd thing he would blurt out in the confessional showing his struggles between native piety and original sin. Granny felt easy about her soul. Cornelia, where are your manners? Give Father Connolly a chair. She had her secret comfortable understanding with a few favorite saints who cleared a straight road to God for her. All as surely signed and sealed as the papers for the new Forty Acres. Forever . . . heirs and assigns forever. Since the day the wedding cake was not cut, but thrown out and wasted. The whole bottom dropped out of the world, and there she was blind and sweating with nothing under her feet and the walls falling away. His hand had caught her under the breast, she had not fallen, there was the freshly polished floor with the green rug on it, just as before. He had cursed like a sailor's parrot and said, "I'll kill him for you." Don't lay a hand on him, for my sake leave something to God. "Now, Ellen, you must believe what I tell you. . . ."

So there was nothing, nothing to worry about anymore, except sometimes in the night one of the children screamed in a nightmare, and they both hustled out shaking and hunting for the matches and calling, "There, wait a minute, here we are!" John, get the doctor now, Hapsy's time has come. But there was Hapsy standing by the bed in a white cap. "Cornelia, tell Hapsy to take off her cap. I can't see her plain."

Her eyes opened very wide and the room stood out like a picture she had seen somewhere. Dark colors with the shadows rising towards the ceiling in long angles. The tall black dresser gleamed with nothing on it but John's picture, enlarged from a little one, with John's eyes very black when they should have been blue. You never saw him, so how do you know how he looked? But the man insisted the copy was perfect, it was very rich and handsome. For a picture, yes, but it's not my husband. The table by the bed had a linen cover and a candle and a crucifix. The light was blue from Cornelia's silk lampshades. No sort of light at all, just frippery. You had to live forty years with kerosene lamps to appreciate honest electricity. She felt very strong and she saw Doctor Harry with a rosy nimbus around him.

"You look like a saint, Doctor Harry, and I vow that's as near as you'll ever come to it."

"She's saying something."

"I heard you, Cornelia. What's all this carrying-on?"

"Father Connolly's saying—"

Cornelia's voice staggered and bumped like a cart in a bad road. It rounded corners and turned back again and arrived nowhere. Granny stepped up in the cart very lightly and reached for the reins, but a man sat beside her and she knew him by his hands, driving the cart. She did not look in his face, for she knew without seeing, but looked instead down the road where the trees leaned over and bowed to each other and a thousand birds were singing a Mass. She felt like singing too, but she put her hand in the bosom of her dress and pulled out a rosary, and Father Connolly murmured Latin in a very solemn voice and tickled her feet. My God, will you stop that nonsense? I'm a married woman. What if he did run away and leave me to face the priest by myself?

I found another a whole world better. I wouldn't have exchanged my husband for anybody except St. Michael himself, and you may tell him that for me with a thank you in the bargain.

Light flashed on her closed eyelids, and a deep roaring shook her. Cornelia, is that lightning? I hear thunder. There's going to be a storm. Close all the windows. Call the children in. . . . "Mother, here we are, all of us." "Is that you, Hapsy?" "Oh, no, I'm Lydia. We drove as fast as we could." Their faces drifted above her, drifted away. The rosary fell out of her hands and Lydia put it back. Jimmy tried to help, their hands fumbled together, and Granny closed two fingers around Jimmy's thumb. Beads wouldn't do, it must be something alive. She was so amazed her thoughts ran round and round. So, my dear Lord, this is my death and I wasn't even thinking about it. My children have come to see me die. But I can't, it's not time. Oh, I always hated surprises. I wanted to give Cornelia the amethyst set—Cornelia, you're to have the amethyst set, but Hapsy's to wear it when she wants, and, Doctor Harry, do shut up. Nobody sent for you. Oh, my dear Lord, do wait a minute. I meant to do something about the Forty Acres, Jimmy doesn't need it and Lydia will later on, with that worthless husband of hers. I meant to finish the altar cloth and send six bottles of wine to Sister Borgia for her dyspepsia. I want to send six bottles of wine to Sister Borgia, Father Connolly, now don't let me forget.

Cornelia's voice made short turns and tilted over and crashed. "Oh, Mother, oh, Mother, oh, Mother. . . ."

"I'm not going, Cornelia. I'm taken by surprise. I can't go."

You'll see Hapsy again. What about her? "I thought you'd never come." Granny made a long journey outward, looking for Hapsy. What if I don't find her? What then? Her heart sank down and down, there was no bottom to death, she couldn't come to the end of it. The blue light from Cornelia's lampshade drew into a tiny point in the center of her brain, it flickered and winked like an eye, quietly it fluttered and dwindled. Granny lay curled down within herself, amazed and watchful, staring at the point of light that was herself; her body was now only a deeper mass of shadow in an endless darkness and this darkness would curl around the light and swallow it up. God, give a sign!

For the second time there was no sign. Again no bridegroom and the priest in the house. She could not remember any other sorrow because this grief wiped them all away. Oh, no, there's nothing more cruel than this—I'll never forgive it. She stretched herself with a deep breath and blew out the light.

1929

Flowering Judas

Braggioni sits heaped upon the edge of a straight-backed chair much too small for him, and sings to Laura in a furry, mournful voice. Laura has begun to find reasons for avoiding her own house until the latest possible moment, for Braggioni is there almost every night. No matter how late she is, he will be sitting there with a surly, waiting expression, pulling at his kinky yellow hair, thumbing the strings of his guitar, snarling a tune under his breath. Lupe the

Indian maid meets Laura at the door, and says with a flicker of a glance towards the upper room, "He waits."

Laura wishes to lie down, she is tired of her hairpins and the feel of her long tight sleeves, but she says to him, "Have you a new song for me this evening?" If he says yes, she asks him to sing it. If he says no, she remembers his favorite one, and asks him to sing it again. Lupe brings her a cup of chocolate and a plate of rice, and Laura eats at the small table under the lamp, first inviting Braggioni, whose answer is always the same: "I have eaten, and besides, chocolate thickens the voice."

Laura says, "Sing, then," and Braggioni heaves himself into song. He scratches the guitar familiarly as though it were a pet animal, and sings passionately off key, taking the high notes in a prolonged painful squeal. Laura, who haunts the markets listening to the ballad singers, and stops every day to hear the blind boy playing his reed-flute in Sixteenth of September Street,[1] listens to Braggioni with pitiless courtesy, because she dares not smile at his miserable performance. Nobody dares to smile at him. Braggioni is cruel to everyone, with a kind of specialized insolence, but he is so vain of his talents, and so sensitive to slights, it would require a cruelty and vanity greater than his own to lay a finger on the vast cureless wound of his self-esteem. It would require courage, too, for it is dangerous to offend him, and nobody has this courage.

Braggioni loves himself with such tenderness and amplitude and eternal charity that his followers—for he is a leader of men, a skilled revolutionist, and his skin has been punctured in honorable warfare—warm themselves in the reflected glow, and say to each other: "He has a real nobility, a love of humanity raised above mere personal affections." The excess of this self-love has flowed out, inconveniently for her, over Laura, who, with so many others, owes her comfortable situation and her salary to him. When he is in a very good humor, he tells her, "I am tempted to forgive you for being a *gringa, gringita!*"[2] and Laura, burning, imagines herself leaning forward suddenly, and with a sound back-handed slap wiping the suety smile from his face. If he notices her eyes at these moments he gives no sign.

She knows what Braggioni would offer her, and she must resist tenaciously without appearing to resist, and if she could avoid it she would not admit even to herself the slow drift of his intention. During these long evenings which have spoiled a long month for her, she sits in her deep chair with an open book on her knees, resting her eyes on the consoling rigidity of the printed page when the sight and sound of Braggioni singing threaten to identify themselves with all her remembered afflictions and to add their weight to her uneasy premonitions of the future. The gluttonous bulk of Braggioni has become a symbol of her many disillusions, for a revolutionist should be lean, animated by heroic faith, a vessel of abstract virtues. This is nonsense, she knows it now and is ashamed of it. Revolution must have leaders, and leadership is a career for energetic men. She is, her comrades tell her, full of romantic error, for what she defines as cynicism in them is merely "a developed sense of reality." She is almost too willing to say, "I am wrong, I suppose I don't really understand the

---

1. Street in Mexico City named to commemorate the date of the enactment of a new Mexican constitution in 1857.   **2.** Diminutive form of *gringa*, a somewhat derogatory term for a fair-haired woman, especially an American (Spanish).

principles," and afterward she makes a secret truce with herself, determined not to surrender her will to such expedient logic. But she cannot help feeling that she has been betrayed irreparably by the disunion between her way of living and her feeling of what life should be, and at times she is almost contented to rest in this sense of grievance as a private store of consolation. Sometimes she wishes to run away, but she stays. Now she longs to fly out of this room, down the narrow stairs, and into the street where the houses lean together like conspirators under a single mottled lamp, and leave Braggioni singing to himself.

Instead she looks at Braggioni, frankly and clearly, like a good child who understands the rules of behavior. Her knees cling together under sound blue serge, and her round white collar is not purposely nun-like. She wears the uniform of an idea, and has renounced vanities. She was born Roman Catholic, and in spite of her fear of being seen by someone who might make a scandal of it, she slips now and again into some crumbling little church, kneels on the chilly stone, and says a Hail Mary on the gold rosary she bought in Tehuantepec.[3] It is no good and she ends by examining the altar with its tinsel flowers and ragged brocades, and feels tender about the battered doll-shape of some male saint whose white, lace-trimmed drawers hang limply around his ankles below the hieratic dignity of his velvet robe. She has encased herself in a set of principles derived from her early training, leaving no detail of gesture or of personal taste untouched, and for this reason she will not wear lace made on machines. This is her private heresy, for in her special group the machine is sacred, and will be the salvation of the workers. She loves fine lace, and there is a tiny edge of fluted cobweb on this collar, which is one of twenty precisely alike, folded in blue tissue paper in the upper drawer of her clothes chest.

Braggioni catches her glance solidly as if he had been waiting for it, leans forward, balancing his paunch between his spread knees, and sings with tremendous emphasis, weighing his words. He has, the song relates, no father and no mother, nor even a friend to console him; lonely as a wave of the sea he comes and goes, lonely as a wave. His mouth opens round and yearns sideways, his balloon cheeks grow oily with the labor of song. He bulges marvelously in his expensive garments. Over his lavender collar, crushed upon a purple necktie, held by a diamond hoop: over his ammunition belt of tooled leather worked in silver, buckled cruelly around his gasping middle: over the tops of his glossy yellow shoes Braggioni swells with ominous ripeness, his mauve silk hose stretched taut, his ankles bound with the stout leather thongs of his shoes.

When he stretches his eyelids at Laura she notes again that his eyes are the true tawny yellow cat's eyes. He is rich, not in money, he tells her, but in power, and this power brings with it the blameless ownership of things, and the right to indulge his love of small luxuries. "I have a taste for the elegant refinements," he said once, flourishing a yellow silk handkerchief before her nose. "Smell that? It is Jockey Club, imported from New York." Nonetheless he is wounded by life. He will say so presently. "It is true everything turns to dust in the hand, to gall on the tongue." He sighs and his leather belt creaks like a saddle girth. "I am disappointed in everything as it comes. Everything." He

---

3. City in southern Mexico.

shakes his head. "You, poor thing, you will be disappointed too. You are born for it. We are more alike than you realize in some things. Wait and see. Some day you will remember what I have told you, you will know that Braggioni was your friend."

Laura feels a slow chill, a purely physical sense of danger, a warning in her blood that violence, mutilation, a shocking death, wait for her with lessening patience. She has translated this fear into something homely, immediate, and sometimes hesitates before crossing the street. "My personal fate is nothing, except as the testimony of a mental attitude," she reminds herself, quoting from some forgotten philosophic primer, and is sensible enough to add, "Anyhow, I shall not be killed by an automobile if I can help it."

"It may be true I am as corrupt, in another way, as Braggioni," she thinks in spite of herself, "as callous, as incomplete," and if this is so, any kind of death seems preferable. Still she sits quietly, she does not run. Where could she go? Uninvited she has promised herself to this place; she can no longer imagine herself as living in another country, and there is no pleasure in remembering her life before she came here.

Precisely what is the nature of this devotion, its true motives, and what are its obligations? Laura cannot say. She spends part of her days in Xochimilco,[4] near by, teaching Indian children to say in English, "The cat is on the mat." When she appears in the classroom they crowd about her with smiles on their wise, innocent, clay-colored faces, crying, "Good morning, my titcher!" in immaculate voices, and they make of her desk a fresh garden of flowers every day.

During her leisure she goes to union meetings and listens to busy important voices quarreling over tactics, methods, internal politics. She visits the prisoners of her own political faith in their cells, where they entertain themselves with counting cockroaches, repenting of their indiscretions, composing their memoirs, writing out manifestoes and plans for their comrades who are still walking about free, hands in pockets, sniffing fresh air. Laura brings them food and cigarettes and a little money, and she brings messages disguised in equivocal phrases from the men outside who dare not set foot in the prison for fear of disappearing into the cells kept empty for them. If the prisoners confuse night and day, and complain, "Dear little Laura, time doesn't pass in this infernal hole, and I won't know when it is time to sleep unless I have a reminder," she brings them their favorite narcotics, and says in a tone that does not wound them with pity, "Tonight will really be night for you," and though her Spanish amuses them, they find her comforting, useful. If they lose patience and all faith, and curse the slowness of their friends in coming to their rescue with money and influence, they trust her not to repeat everything, and if she inquires, "Where do you think we can find money, or influence?" they are certain to answer, "Well, there is Braggioni, why doesn't he do something?"

She smuggles letters from headquarters to men hiding from firing squads in back streets in mildewed houses, where they sit in tumbled beds and talk bitterly as if all Mexico were at their heels, when Laura knows positively they might appear at the band concert in the Alameda[5] on Sunday morning, and no one would notice them. But Braggioni says, "Let them sweat a little. The next time they may be careful. It is very restful to have them out of the way for a while." She is not afraid to knock on any door in any street after midnight, and enter in the darkness, and say to one of these men who is really in danger: "They will be looking for you—seriously—tomorrow morning after six. Here is some money from Vicente. Go to Vera Cruz and wait."

She borrows money from the Roumanian agitator to give to his bitter enemy the Polish agitator. The favor of Braggioni is their disputed territory, and Braggioni holds the balance nicely, for he can use them both. The Polish agitator talks love to her over café tables, hoping to exploit what he believes is her secret sentimental preference for him, and he gives her misinformation which he begs her to repeat as the solemn truth to certain persons. The Roumanian is more adroit. He is generous with his money in all good causes, and lies to her with an air of ingenuous candor, as if he were her good friend and confidant. She never repeats anything they may say. Braggioni never asks questions. He has other ways to discover all that he wishes to know about them.

Nobody touches her, but all praise her gray eyes, and the soft, round under lip which promises gayety, yet is always grave, nearly always firmly closed: and they cannot understand why she is in Mexico. She walks back and forth on her errands, with puzzled eyebrows, carrying her little folder of drawings and music and school papers. No dancer dances more beautifully than Laura walks, and she inspires some amusing, unexpected ardors, which cause little gossip, because nothing comes of them. A young captain who had been a soldier in Zapata's[6] army attempted, during a horseback ride near Cuernavaca, to express his desire for her with the noble simplicity befitting a rude folk-hero: but gently, because he was gentle. This gentleness was his defeat, for when he alighted, and removed her foot from the stirrup, and essayed to draw her down into his arms, her horse, ordinarily a tame one, shied fiercely, reared and plunged away. The young hero's horse careened blindly after his stablemate, and the hero did not return to the hotel until rather late that evening. At breakfast he came to her table in full charro dress,[7] gray buckskin jacket and trousers with strings of silver buttons down the leg, and he was in a humorous, careless mood. "May I sit with you?" and "You are a wonderful rider. I was terrified that you might be thrown and dragged. I should never have forgiven myself. But I cannot admire you enough for your riding."

"I learned to ride in Arizona," said Laura.

"If you will ride with me again this morning, I promise you a horse that will not shy with you," he said. But Laura remembered that she must return to Mexico City at noon.

Next morning the children made a celebration and spent their playtime writing on the blackboard, "We lov ar ticher," and with tinted chalks they drew wreaths of flowers around the words. The young hero wrote her a letter: "I am a very foolish, wasteful, impulsive man. I should have first said I love you, and then you would not have run away. But you shall see me again." Laura thought, "I must send him a book of colored crayons," but she was trying to forgive herself for having spurred her horse at the wrong moment.

---

6. Emiliano Zapata (1879–1919), Mexican revolutionary general and agrarian reformer.   7. Elegant cowboy clothing.

A brown, shock-haired youth came and stood in her patio one night and sang like a lost soul for two hours, but Laura could think of nothing to do about it. The moonlight spread a wash of gauzy silver over the clear spaces of the garden, and the shadows were cobalt blue. The scarlet blossoms of the Judas tree[8] were dull purple, and the names of the colors repeated themselves automatically in her mind, while she watched not the boy, but his shadow, fallen like a dark garment across the fountain rim, trailing in the water. Lupe came silently and whispered expert counsel in her ear: "If you will throw him one little flower, he will sing another song or two and go away." Laura threw the flower, and he sang a last song and went away with the flower tucked in the band of his hat. Lupe said, "He is one of the organizers of the Typographers Union, and before that he sold corridos in the Merced market, and before that, he came from Guanajuato,[9] where I was born. I would not trust any man, but I trust least those from Guanajuato."

She did not tell Laura that he would be back again the next night, and the next, nor that he would follow her at a certain fixed distance around the Merced market, through the Zócolo, up Francisco I. Madero Avenue, and so along the Paseo de la Reforma to Chapultepec Park, and into the Philosopher's Footpath,[1] still with that flower withering in his hat, and an indivisible attention in his eyes.

Now Laura is accustomed to him, it means nothing except that he is nineteen years old and is observing a convention with all propriety, as though it were founded on a law of nature, which in the end it might well prove to be. He is beginning to write poems which he prints on a wooden press, and he leaves them stuck like handbills in her door. She is pleasantly disturbed by the abstract, unhurried watchfulness of his black eyes which will in time turn easily towards another object. She tells herself that throwing the flower was a mistake, for she is twenty-two years old and knows better; but she refuses to regret it, and persuades herself that her negation of all external events as they occur is a sign that she is gradually perfecting herself in the stoicism she strives to cultivate against that disaster she fears, though she cannot name it.

She is not at home in the world. Every day she teaches children who remain strangers to her, though she loves their tender round hands and their charming opportunist savagery. She knocks at unfamiliar doors not knowing whether a friend or a stranger shall answer, and even if a known face emerges from the sour gloom of that unknown interior, still it is the face of a stranger. No matter what this stranger says to her, nor what her message to him, the very cells of her flesh reject knowledge and kinship in one monotonous word. No. No. No. She draws her strength from this one holy talismanic word which does not suffer her to be led into evil. Denying everything, she may walk anywhere in safety, she looks at everything without amazement.

No, repeats this firm unchanging voice of her blood; and she looks at Braggioni without amazement. He is a great man, he wishes to impress this simple girl who covers her great round breasts with thick dark cloth, and who hides long, invaluably beautiful legs under a heavy skirt. She is almost thin except for the incomprehensible fullness of her breasts, like a nursing mother's, and

---

8. So called because Judas is said to have hanged himself on a tree of this kind.   **9.** City in central Mexico. *Corridos:* bullfight tickets (Spanish).   **1.** Streets and parks in Mexico City. Madero (1873–1913) led the revolution against the dictator Porfirio Díaz (1830–1915).

Braggioni, who considers himself a judge of women, speculates again on the puzzle of her notorious virginity, and takes the liberty of speech which she permits without a sign of modesty, indeed, without any sort of sign, which is disconcerting.

"You think you are so cold, *gringita*! Wait and see. You will surprise yourself some day! May I be there to advise you!" He stretches his eyelids at her, and his ill-humored cat's eyes waver in a separate glance for the two points of light marking the opposite ends of a smoothly drawn path between the swollen curve of her breasts. He is not put off by that blue serge, nor by her resolutely fixed gaze. There is all the time in the world. His cheeks are bellying with the wind of song. "O girl with the dark eyes," he sings, and reconsiders. "But yours are not dark. I can change all that. O girl with the green eyes, you have stolen my heart away!" Then his mind wanders to the song, and Laura feels the weight of his attention being shifted elsewhere. Singing thus, he seems harmless, he is quite harmless, there is nothing to do but sit patiently and say "No," when the moment comes. She draws a full breath, and her mind wanders also, but not far. She dares not wander too far.

Not for nothing has Braggioni taken pains to be a good revolutionist and a professional lover of humanity. He will never die of it. He has the malice, the cleverness, the wickedness, the sharpness of wit, the hardness of heart, stipulated for loving the world profitably. *He will never die of it.* He will live to see himself kicked out from his feeding trough by other hungry world-saviors. Traditionally he must sing in spite of his life which drives him to bloodshed, he tells Laura, for his father was a Tuscany peasant who drifted to Yucatan and married a Maya woman:[2] a woman of race, an aristocrat. They gave him the love and knowledge of music, thus: and under the rip of his thumbnail, the strings of the instrument complain like exposed nerves.

Once he was called Delgadito[3] by all the girls and married women who ran after him; he was so scrawny all his bones showed under his thin cotton clothing, and he could squeeze his emptiness to the very backbone with his two hands. He was a poet and the revolution was only a dream then; too many women loved him and sapped away his youth, and he could never find enough to eat anywhere, anywhere! Now he is a leader of men, crafty men who whisper in his ear, hungry men who wait for hours outside his office for a word with him, emaciated men with wild faces who waylay him at the street gate with a timid, "Comrade, let me tell you . . ." and they blow the foul breath from their empty stomachs in his face.

He is always sympathetic. He gives them handfuls of small coins from his own pockets, he promises them work, there will be demonstrations, they must join the unions and attend the meetings, above all they must be on the watch for spies. They are closer to him than his own brothers, without them he can do nothing—until tomorrow, comrade!

Until tomorrow. "They are stupid, they are lazy, they are treacherous, they would cut my throat for nothing," he says to Laura. He has good food and abundant drink, he hires an automobile and drives in the Paseo on Sunday morning, and enjoys plenty of sleep in a soft bed beside a wife who dares not disturb him; and he sits pampering his bones in easy billows of fat, singing to

---

2. That is, an Indian woman. Tuscany is a region in west central Italy. **3.** "Little skinny one" (Spanish).

Laura, who knows and thinks these things about him. When he was fifteen, he tried to drown himself because he loved a girl, his first love, and she laughed at him. "A thousand women have paid for that," and his tight little mouth turns down at the corners. Now he perfumes his hair with Jockey Club, and confides to Laura: "One woman is really as good as another for me, in the dark. I prefer them all."

His wife organizes unions among the girls in the cigarette factories, and walks in picket lines, and even speaks at meetings in the evening. But she cannot be brought to acknowledge the benefits of true liberty. "I tell her I must have my freedom, net. She does not understand my point of view." Laura has heard this many times. Braggioni scratches the guitar and meditates. "She is an instinctively virtuous woman, pure gold, no doubt of that. If she were not, I should lock her up, and she knows it."

His wife, who works so hard for the good of the factory girls, employs part of her leisure lying on the floor weeping because there are so many women in the world, and only one husband for her, and she never knows where nor when to look for him. He told her: "Unless you can learn to cry when I am not here, I must go away for good." That day he went away and took a room at the Hotel Madrid.

It is this month of separation for the sake of higher principles that has been spoiled not only for Mrs. Braggioni, whose sense of reality is beyond criticism, but for Laura, who feels herself bogged in a nightmare. Tonight Laura envies Mrs. Braggioni, who is alone, and free to weep as much as she pleases about a concrete wrong. Laura has just come from a visit to the prison, and she is waiting for tomorrow with a bitter anxiety as if tomorrow may not come, but time may be caught immovably in this hour, with herself transfixed, Braggioni singing on forever, and Eugenio's body not yet discovered by the guard.

Braggioni says: "Are you going to sleep?" Almost before she can shake her head, he begins telling her about the May-day disturbances coming on in Morelia, for the Catholics hold a festival in honor of the Blessed Virgin, and the Socialists celebrate their martyrs on that day. "There will be two independent processions, starting from either end of town, and they will march until they meet, and the rest depends . . ." He asks her to oil and load his pistols. Standing up, he unbuckles his ammunition belt, and spreads it laden across her knees. Laura sits with the shells slipping through the cleaning cloth dipped in oil, and he says again he cannot understand why she works so hard for the revolutionary idea unless she loves some man who is in it. "Are you not in love with someone?" "No," says Laura. "And no one is in love with you?" "No." "Then it is your own fault. No woman need go begging. Why, what is the matter with you? The legless beggar woman in the Alameda has a perfectly faithful lover. Did you know that?"

Laura peers down the pistol barrel and says nothing, but a long, slow faintness rises and subsides in her; Braggioni curves his swollen fingers around the throat of the guitar and softly smothers the music out of it, and when she hears him again he seems to have forgotten her, and is speaking in the hypnotic voice he uses when talking in small rooms to a listening, close-gathered crowd. Some day this world, now seemingly so composed and eternal, to the edges of every sea shall be merely a tangle of gaping trenches, of crashing walls and broken bodies. Everything must be torn from its accustomed place where it has rotted for centuries, hurled skyward and distributed, cast down again clean as rain, without separate identity. Nothing shall survive that the stiffened hands of poverty have created for the rich and no one shall be left alive except the elect spirits destined to procreate a new world cleansed of cruelty and injustice, ruled by benevolent anarchy: "Pistols are good, I love them, cannon are even better, but in the end I pin my faith to good dynamite," he concludes, and strokes the pistol lying in her hands. "Once I dreamed of destroying this city, in case it offered resistance to General Ortiz,[4] but it fell into his hands like an over-ripe pear."

He is made restless by his own words, rises and stands waiting. Laura holds up the belt to him: "Put that on, and go kill somebody in Morelia, and you will be happier," she says softly. The presence of death in the room makes her bold. "Today, I found Eugenio going into a stupor. He refused to allow me to call the prison doctor. He had taken all the tablets I brought him yesterday. He said he took them because he was bored."

"He is a fool, and his death is his own business," says Braggioni, fastening his belt carefully.

"I told him if he had waited only a little while longer, you would have got him set free," says Laura. "He said he did not want to wait."

"He is a fool and we are well rid of him," says Braggioni, reaching for his hat.

He goes away. Laura knows his mood has changed, she will not see him anymore for a while. He will send word when he needs her to go on errands into strange streets, to speak to the strange faces that will appear, like clay masks with the power of human speech, to mutter their thanks to Braggioni for his help. Now she is free, and she thinks, I must run while there is time. But she does not go.

Braggioni enters his own house where for a month his wife has spent many hours every night weeping and tangling her hair upon her pillow. She is weeping now, and she weeps more at the sight of him, the cause of all her sorrows. He looks about the room. Nothing is changed, the smells are good and familiar, he is well acquainted with the woman who comes toward him with no reproach except grief on her face. He says to her tenderly: "You are so good, please don't cry anymore, you dear good creature." She says, "Are you tired, my angel? Sit here and I will wash your feet." She brings a bowl of water, and kneeling, unlaces his shoes, and when from her knees she raises her sad eyes under her blackened lids, he is sorry for everything, and bursts into tears. "Ah, yes, I am hungry, I am tired, let us eat something together," he says, between sobs. His wife leans her head on his arm and says, "Forgive me!" and this time he is refreshed by the solemn, endless rain of her tears.

Laura takes off her serge dress and puts on a white linen nightgown and goes to bed. She turns her head a little to one side, and lying still, reminds herself that it is time to sleep. Numbers tick in her brain like little clocks, soundless doors close of themselves around her. If you would sleep, you must not remember anything, the children will say tomorrow, good morning, my teacher, the poor prisoners who come every day bringing flowers to their jailor. 1-2-3-4-5—it is monstrous to confuse love with revolution, night with day, life with death—ah, Eugenio!

---

4. Pascual Ortiz Rubio (1877–1963) was a revolutionary who became president of Mexico.

The tolling of the midnight bell is a signal, but what does it mean? Get up, Laura, and follow me: come out of your sleep, out of your bed, out of this strange house. What are you doing in this house? Without a word, without fear she rose and reached for Eugenio's hand, but he eluded her with a sharp, sly smile and drifted away. This is not all, you shall see—Murderer, he said, follow me, I will show you a new country, but it is far away and we must hurry. No, said Laura, not unless you take my hand, no; and she clung first to the stair rail, and then to the topmost branch of the Judas tree that bent down slowly and set her upon the earth, and then to the rocky ledge of a cliff, and then to the jagged wave of a sea that was not water but a desert of crumbling stone. Where are you taking me, she asked in wonder but without fear. To death, and it is a long way off, and we must hurry, said Eugenio. No, said Laura, not unless you take my hand. Then eat these flowers, poor prisoner, said Eugenio in a voice of pity, take and eat: and from the Judas tree he stripped the warm bleeding flowers, and held them to her lips. She saw that his hand was fleshless, a cluster of small white petrified branches, and his eye sockets were without light, but she ate the flowers greedily for they satisfied both hunger and thirst. Murderer! said Eugenio, and Cannibal! This is my body and my blood.[5] Laura cried No! and at the sound of her own voice, she awoke trembling, and was afraid to sleep again.

                                                                                1930

RELATED:

—Porter, An Interview, p. 1730

---

5. Allusion to Christ's words at the Last Supper. Luke 22:19–20.

V. S. PRITCHETT
1900–1997

Sir Victor Sawdon Pritchett was a British writer of prodigious versatility. He was born in Ipswich, Suffolk, England. He attended Alleyn's School in Dulwich, London. Well-known for his literary criticism, especially that which he published in *The New Statesman*, Pritchett's lasting fame comes from his own imaginative writing, which shows his sharp ear for dialogue and an eye for detail. At his best in his short stories, he wrote of the extraordinary in the ordinarily middle-class life. Two volumes of memoirs, *A Cab at the Door* (1968) and *Midnight Oil* (1972), give a view into his life. He taught at many colleges in the United States and received numerous awards including a knighthood in 1975. He published many collections throughout his long life; his *Complete Stories* appeared in 1990.

The Fall

It was the evening of the Annual Dinner. More than two hundred accountants were at that hour changing into evening clothes, in the flats, villas and hotel rooms of a large, wet, Midland[1] city. At the Royal was Charles Peacock, slender in his shirt, balancing on one leg and gazing with frowns of affection in the wardrobe mirror at the other leg as he pulled his trouser on; and then with a smile of farewell as the second went in. Buttoned up, relieved of nakedness, he visited other mirrors—the one at the dressing table, the two in the bathroom, assembling the scattered aspects of the unsettled being called Peacock "doing"—as he was apt to say—"no so badly" in this city which smelled of coal and where thirty-eight years ago he had been born. When he left his room there were mirrors in the hotel lift and down below in the foyer and outside in the street. Certain shop windows were favourable and assuring. The love affair was taken up again at the Assembly Rooms by the mirrors in the tiled corridor leading towards the bullocky noise of two hundred-odd chartered accountants in black ties, taking their drinks under the chandeliers that seemed to weep above their heads.

Crowds or occasions frightened Peacock. They engaged him, at first sight, in the fundamental battle of his life: the struggle against nakedness, the panic of grabbing for clothes and becoming someone. An acquaintance in a Scottish firm was standing near the door of the packed room as Peacock went in.

---

1. That is, from a provincial area of central England.

"Hullo, laddie," Peacock said, fitting himself out with a Scottish accent, as he went into the crowded, chocolate coloured buffet.

"What's to do?" he said, passing on to a Yorkshireman.

"Are you well now?" he said, in his Irish voice. And, gaining confidence, "Whatcha cock!" to a man up from London, until he was shaking hands in the crowd with the President himself, who was leaning on a stick and had his foot in plaster.

"I hope this is not serious, sir," said Peacock in his best southern English, nodding at the foot.

"Bloody serious," said the President sticking out his peppery beard. "I caught my foot in a grating. Some damn fools here think I've got gout."

No one who saw Peacock in his office, in Board Rooms, on Committees, at meetings, knew the exhausting number of rough sketches that had to be made before the naked Peacock could become Peacock dressed for his part. Now, having spoken to several human beings, the fragments called Peacock closed up. And he had one more trick up his sleeve if he panicked again: he could drop into music hall Negro.

Peacock got a drink at the buffet table and pushed his way to a solitary island of carpet two feet square, in the guffawing corral. He was looking at the back of the President's neck. Almost at once the President, on the crest of a successful joke he had told, turned round with appetite.

"Hah!" he shouted. "Hah! Here's friend Peacock again." "Why 'again'?" thought Peacock.

The President looked Peacock over.

"I saw your brother this afternoon," shouted the President. The President's injured foot could be said to have made his voice sound like a hilarious smash. Peacock's drink jumped and splashed his hand. The President winked at his friends.

"Hah!" said the President. "That gave our friend Peacock a scare!"

"At the Odeon," explained a kinder man.

"Is Shelmerdine Peacock your brother? The actor?" another said, astonished, looking at Peacock from head to foot.

"Shelmerdine Peacock was born and bred in this city," said the President fervently.

"I saw him in *Waste*," someone said. And others recalled him in *The Gun Runner and Doctor Zut*.

Four or five men stood gazing at Peacock with admiration, waiting for him to speak.

"Where is he now?" said the President, stepping forward, beard first. "In Hollywood? Have you seen him lately?"

They all moved forward to hear about the famous man.

Peacock looked to the right—he wanted to do this properly—but there was no mirror in that direction; he looked to the left, but there was no mirror there. He lowered his head gravely and then looked up shaking his head sorrowfully. He brought out the old reliable Negro voice:

"The last time I saw l'il ole brudder Shel," he said, "he was being thrown out of the Orchid Room. He was calling the waiters goatherds."

Peacock looked up at them all and stood, collected, assembled, whole at last, among their shouts of laughter. One man who did not laugh and who asked what the Orchid Room was, was put in his place. And in a moment, a voice bawled from the door, "Gentlemen. Dinner is served." The crowd moved through two ante-rooms into the Great Hall where, from their portraits on the wall, Mayors, Presidents and Justices looked down with the complacent rosiness of those who have dined and died. It was gratifying to Peacock that the President rested his arm on his shoulder for a few steps as they went into the hall.

Shel often cropped up in Peacock's life, especially in clubs and at dinners. It was pleasing. There was always praise; there were always questions. He had seen the posters about Shel's film during the week on his way to his office. They pleased, but they also troubled. Peacock stood at his place at table in the Great Hall and paused to look around, in case there was one more glance of vicarious fame to be collected. He was enjoying one of those pauses of self-possession in which, for a few seconds, he could feel the sensations Shel must feel when he stepped before the curtain to receive the applause of some great audience in London or New York. Then Peacock sat down. More than two hundred soup spoons scraped.

"Sherry, sir?" said the waiter.

Peacock sipped.

He meant no harm to Shel, of course. But in a city like this, with Shel appearing in a big picture, with his name fifteen feet long on the hoardings, talked about by girls in offices, the universal instinct of family disparagement was naturally tickled into life. The President might laugh and the crowd admire, but it was not always agreeable for the family to have Shel roaming loose—and often very loose—in the world. One had to assert the modesty, the anonymity of the ordinary assiduous Peacocks. One way of doing this was to add a touch or two to famous scandals: to enlarge the drunken scrimmages and add to the divorces and the breaches of contract, increase the over-doses taken by flighty girls. One was entitled to a little rake off—an accountant's charges—from the fame that so often annoyed. One was entitled, above all, because one loved Shel.

"Hock, sir?" said the waiter.

Peacock drank. Yes, he loved Shel. Peacock put down his glass and the man opposite to him spoke across the table, a man with an amused mouth, who turned his sallow face sideways so that one had the impression of being inquired into under a loose lock of black hair by one sharp, serious eye only.

"An actor's life is a struggle," the man said. Peacock recognized him: it was the man who had not laughed at his story and who had asked what the Orchid Room was, in a voice that had a sad and puncturing feeling for information sought for its own sake.

Peacock knew this kind of admirer of Shel's and feared him. They were not content to admire, they wanted to advance into intimacy, and collect facts on behalf of some general view of life's mysteriousness. As an accountant Peacock rejected mystery.

"I don't think l'il ole brudder Shel has struggled much," said Peacock, wagging his head from side to side carelessly.

"I mean he has to dedicate himself," said the man.

Peacock looked back mistrustfully.

"I remember some interview he gave about his schooldays—in this city," said the man. "It interested me. I do the books for the Hippodrome."

Peacock stopped wagging his head from side to side. He was alert. What Shel had said about his early life had been damned tactless.

"Shel had a good time," said Peacock sharply. "He always got his own way."

Peacock put on his face of stone. He dared the man to say out loud, in that company, three simple English words. He dared him. The man smiled and did not say them.

"Volnay, sir?" said the waiter as the pheasant was brought. Peacock drank.

Fried Fish Shop, Peacock said to himself as he drank. Those were the words. Shel could have kept his mouth shut about that. I'm not a snob, but why mention it? Why, after they were all doing well, bring ridicule upon the family? Why not say, simply, "Shop." Why not say, if he had to, "Fishmonger"? Why mention "Frying"? Why add "*Bankrupt* Fried Fish Shop"?

It was swinish, disloyal, ungrateful. Bankrupt—all right; but some of that money (Peacock said, hectoring the pheasant on his plate), paid for Shel's years at the Dramatic School. It was unforgiveable.

Peacock looked across at the man opposite, but the man had turned to talk to a neighbour. Peacock finished his glass and chatted with the man sitting to his right, but he felt like telling the whole table a few facts about dedication.

Dedication—he would have said. Let us take a look at the figures. An example of Shel's dedication in those Fried Fish Shop days he is so fond of remembering to make fools of us. Saturday afternoon. Father asleep in the back room. Shel says "Come down the High Street with me, Tom. I want to get a record." Classical, of course. Usual swindle. If we get into the shop he won't have the money and will try and borrow from me. "No," I say. "I haven't got any money." "Well, let's get out of this stink of lard and fish." He wears me down. He wore us all down, the whole family. He would be sixteen, two years older than me. And so we go out and at once I know there is going to be trouble. "I saw the Devil in Cramers," he says. We go down the High Street to Cramers, it's a music shop, and he goes up to the girl to ask if they sell bicycle pumps or rubber heels. When the girl says "No," he makes a terrible face at her and shouts out "Bah." At Hooks, the stationers, he stands at the door, and calls to the girl at the cash desk: "You've got the Devil in here. I've reported it," and slams the door. We go on to Bonds, the grocers, and he pretends to be sick when he sees the bacon. Goes out. "Rehearsing," he says. The Bonds are friends of Father's. There is a row. Shel swears he was never anywhere near the place and goes back the following Saturday and falls flat on the floor in front of the Bond daughter groaning, "I've been poisoned. I'm dying. Water! Water!" Falls flat on his back . . .

"Caught his foot in a grating, he told me, and fell," the man opposite was saying. "Isn't that what he told you, Peacock?"

Peacock's imaginary speech came suddenly to an end. The man was smiling as if he had heard every word.

"Who?" said Peacock.

"The President," said the man. "My friend, Mr. McAlister is asking me what happened to the President. Did he fall in the street?"

Peacock collected himself quickly and to hide his nakedness became Scottish.

"Ay, mon," he nodded across the table. "A wee bit of a tumble in the street."

Peacock took up his glass and drank.

"He's a heavy man to fall," said the man called McAlister.

"He carries a lot of weight," said his neighbour. Peacock eyed him. The impression was growing that this man knew too much, too quietly. It struck him that the man was one of those who ask what they know already, a deeply unbelieving man. They have to be crushed.

"Weight makes no difference," said Peacock firmly.

"It's weight and distance," said the Scotsman. "Look at children."

Peacock felt a smile coming over his body from the feet upwards.

"Weight and distance make no difference," Peacock repeated.

"How can you say that?"

An enormous voice, hanging brutally on the air like a sergeant's, suddenly shouted in the hall. It was odd to see the men in the portraits on the wall still sitting down after the voice sounded. It was the voice of the toastmaster.

"Gen—tle—men," it shouted. "I ask you. To rise to. The Toast of Her. Maj—es—ty. The Queen."

Two hundred or more accountants pushed back their chairs and stood up.

"The Queen," they growled. And one or two, Peacock among them, fervently added, "God bless her," and drained his glass.

Two hundred or more accountants sat down. It was the moment Peacock loved. And he loved the Queen.

"Port or brandy, sir?" the waiter asked.

"Brandy," said Peacock.

"You were saying that weight and distance make no difference. How do you make that out?" the sidelong man opposite said in a sympathetic and curious voice that came softly and lazily out.

Peacock felt the brandy burn. The question floated by, answerable if seized as it went and yet, suddenly, unanswerable for the moment. Peacock stared at the question keenly as if it were a fly that he was waiting to swat when it came round again. Ah, there it came. Now! But no, it had gone by once more. It was answerable. He knew the answer. Peacock smiled loosely biding his time. He felt the flame of authority, of absolute knowledge burn in him.

There was a hammering at the President's table, there was hand-clapping. The President was on his feet and his beard had begun to move up and down.

"I'll tell you later," said Peacock curtly across the table. The interest went out of the man's eye.

"Once more," (the President's beard was saying and it seemed sometimes that he had two beards), "Honour," said one beard. "Privilege," said the other. "Old friends," said both beards together. "Speeches . . . brief . . . reminded of story . . . shortest marriage service in the world . . . Tennessee . . ."

"Hah! Hah! Hah!" shouted a pack of wolves, hyenas, hounds in dinner jackets.

Peacock looked across at the unbeliever who sat opposite. The interest in weight and distance had died away in his face.

"Englishman . . . Irishman . . . Scotsman . . . train . . . Englishman   said . . . Scotsman said . . . Och, says Paddy . . ."

"Hah! Hah! Hah!" from the pack.

Over the carnations in the silver plated vases on the table, over the heads of the diners, the cigar smoke was rising sweetly and the first level indigo shafts of it were tipping across the middle air and turning the portraits of the Past Masters into day dreams. Peacock gazed at it. Then a bell rang in his ear, so loudly that he looked shyly to see if anyone else had heard it. The voice of Shel was on some line of his memory, a voice richer, more insinuating than the toast-master's or the President's, a voice utterly flooring.

"Abel?" Shel was saying. "Is that you Abel? This is Cain speaking. How's the smoke? Is it still going up straight to heaven? Not blowing about all over the place . . ."

The man opposite caught Peacock's eye for a second, as if he too had heard the voice and then turned his head away. And, just at the very moment, when once more Peacock could have answered that question about the effect of weight and distance, the man opposite stood up, all the accountants stood up. Peacock was the last. There was another toast to drink. And immediately there was more hammering and another speaker. Peacock's opportunity was lost. The man who sat opposite had moved his chair back from the table and was sitting sideways to it listening, his interest in Peacock gone for good.

Peacock became lonely. Sulkily he played with matchsticks and arranged them in patterns on the tablecloth. There was a point at Annual Dinners when he always did this. It was at that point when one saw the function had become fixed by a flash photograph in the gloss of celebration and when everyone looked sickly and old. Eyes became hollow, temples sank, teeth loos-ened. Shortly the diners would be carried out in coffins. One waited restlessly for the thing to be over. Ten years of life went by and then, it seemed, there were no more speeches. There was some business talk in groups; then twos and threes left the table. Others filed off into a large chamber next door. Pea-cock's neighbours got up. He, who feared occasions, feared even more their dissolution. It was like that frightening ten minutes in a theatre when the audi-ence slowly moves out, leaving a hollow stage and row after row, always increas-ing, of empty seats behind them. In a panic Peacock got up. He was losing all acquaintance. He had even let the man opposite slip away, for that man was walking down the hall with some friends. Peacock hurried down his side of the long table to meet them at the bottom and when he got there he turned and barred their way.

"What we were talking about," he said. "It's an art. Simply a matter of let-ting the breath go, relaxing the muscles. Any actor can do it. It's the first thing they learn."

"I'm out of my depth," said the Scotsman.

"Falling," said Peacock. "The stage fall." He looked at them with dignity, then he let the expression die on his face. He fell quietly full length to the floor. Before they could speak he was up on his feet.

"My brother weighs two hundred and twenty pounds," he said with conde-scension to the man opposite. "The ordinary person falls and breaks an arm or a foot, because he doesn't know. It's an art."

His eyes conveyed that if the Peacocks had kept a fried fish shop years ago, they had an art.

"Simple," said Peacock.

And down he went, thump, on the carpet again and lying at their feet he said:

"Painless. Nothing broken. Not a bruise. I said 'an art.' Really one might call it a science. Do you see how I'm lying?"

"What's happened to Peacock?" said two or three men joining the group.

"He's showing us the stage fall."

"Nothing," said Peacock, getting up and brushing his coat sleeve and smoothing back his hair. "It is just a stage trick."

"I wouldn't do it," said a large man, patting his stomach.

"I've just been telling them—weight is nothing. Look." Peacock fell down and got up at once.

"You turn. You crumple. You can go flat on your back. I mean, that is what it looks like," he said.

And Peacock fell.

"Shel and I used to practise it in the bedroom. Father thought the ceiling was coming down," he said.

"Good God, has Peacock passed out?" A group standing by the fireplace in the hall called across. Peacock got up and brushing his jacket again walked up to them. The group he had left watched him. There was a thump.

"He's done it again," the man opposite said.

"Once more. There he goes. Look, he's going to show the President. He's going after him. No, he's missed him. The old boy has slipped out of the door."

Peacock was staring with annoyance at the door. He looked at other groups of two and threes.

"Who was the casualty over there?" someone said to him as he walked past.

Peacock went over to them and explained.

"Like judo," said a man.

"No!" said Peacock indignantly, even grandly. And in Shel's manner. Anyone who had seen Shelmerdine Peacock affronted knew what he looked like. That large white face trod on you. "Nothing to do with judo. This is the theatre . . ."

"Shelmerdine Peacock's brother," a man whispered to a friend.

"Is that so?"

"It's in the blood," someone said.

To the man who had said "Judo," Peacock said, "No throwing, no wrestling, no somersaulting or fancy tricks. That is not theatre. Just . . . simply . . ." said Peacock. And crumpling, as Shel might have done in *Macbeth* or *Hamlet*, or like some gangster shot in the stomach, Peacock once more let his body go down with the cynicism of the skilful corpse. This time he did not get up at once. He looked up at their knees, their waists, at their goggling faces, saw under their double chins and under their hairy eyebrows. He grinned at their absurdity. He saw that he held them. They were obliged to look at him. Shel must always have had this sensation of hundreds of astonished eyes watching him lie, waiting for him to move. Their gaze would never leave him. Peacock never felt less at a loss, never felt more completely himself. Even the air was better at carpet level; it was certainly cooler and he was glad of that. Then he saw two pairs of feet advancing from another group. He saw two faces peep over the shoulders of the others, and heard one of them say:

"It's Peacock—still at it."

He saw the two pairs of boots and trousers go off. Peacock got to his feet at once and resentfully stared after them. He knew something, as they went, that Shel must have known: the desperation, the contempt for the audience that is thinning out. He was still brushing his sleeve and trousers legs when he saw everyone moving away out of the hall. Peacock moved after them into the chamber.

A voice spoke behind him. It was the quiet, intimate voice of the man with the loose lock of black hair who had sat opposite to him.

"You need a drink," the man said.

They were standing in the chamber where the buffet table was. The man had gone into the chamber and, clearly, he had waited for Peacock. A question was going round as fast as a catherine wheel[2] in Peacock's head and there was no need to ask it: it must be so blindingly obvious. He looked for someone to put it to, on the quiet, but there were only three men at the buffet table with their backs turned to him. Why (the question ran) at the end of a bloody good dinner is one always left with some awful drunk, a man you've never liked—an unbeliever?

Peacock mopped his face. The unbeliever was having a short disgusting laugh with the men at the bar and now was coming back with a glass of whisky.

"Sit down. You must be tired," said the unbeliever.

They sat down. The man spoke of the dinner and the speeches. Peacock did not listen. He had just noticed a door leading into a small ante-room and he was wondering how he could get into it.

"There was one thing I don't quite get," the man said. "Perhaps it was the quickness of the hand deceiving the eye. I should say feet. What I mean is—do you first take a step, I mean like in dancing: I mean is the art of falling really a paradox—I mean the art of keeping your balance all the time?"

The word "paradox" sounded offensive to Peacock.

The man looked too damn clever, in Peacock's opinion and didn't sit still. Wearily Peacock got up.

"Hold my drink," he said. "You are standing like this, or facing sideways—on a level floor, of course. On a slope like this . . ."

The man nodded.

"I mean—well, now, watch carefully. Are you watching?"

"Yes," said the man.

"Look at my feet," said Peacock.

"No," said the man, hastily, putting out a free hand and catching Peacock by the arm. "I see what you mean. I was just interested in the theory."

Peacock halted. He was offended. He shook the man's arm off.

"Nothing theoretical about it," he said, and shaking his sleeves added, "No paradox."

"No," said the man standing up and grabbing Peacock so that he could not fall. "I've got the idea." He looked at his watch. "Which way are you going? Can I give you a lift?"

Peacock was greatly offended. To be turned down! He nodded to the door of the ante-room: "Thanks," he said. "The President's waiting for me."

"The President's gone," said the man. "Oh well, good night." And he went away. Peacock watched him go. Even the men at the bar had gone. He was alone.

"But thanks," he called after him. "Thanks."

Cautiously Peacock sketched a course into the ante-room. It was a small, high room, quite empty and yet (one would have said), packed with voices, chattering, laughing and mixed with music along the panelled walls, but

---

2. A kind of firework making a wheel of fire or sparks; the term also designates a spiked wheel used as an instrument of torture (named after Saint Catherine of Alexandria, from the wheel used to torture her).

chiefly coming from behind the heavy green velvet curtains that were drawn across the window at one end. There were no mirrors, but Peacock had no need of them. The effect was ornate—gilded pillars at the corners, a small chandelier rising and falling gracefully from a carven ceiling. On the wall hung what, at first sight, seemed to be two large oil paintings of Queens of England but, on going closer, Peacock saw there was only one oil painting—of Queen Victoria.[3] Peacock considered it. The opportunity was enormous. Loyally, his face went blank. He swayed, loyally fell, and loyally got to his feet. The Queen might or might not have clapped her little hands. So encouraged, he fell again and got up. She was still sitting there.

Shel, said Peacock aloud to the Queen, has often acted before royalty. He's in Hollywood now, having left me to settle all his tax affairs. Hundreds of documents. All lies, of course. And there is this case for alimony going on. He's had four wives, he said to Queen Victoria. That's the side of theatre life I couldn't stand, even when we were boys. I could see it coming. But—watch me, he said.

And delightfully he crumpled, the perfect backwards spin. Leaning up on his elbow from where he was lying he waited for her to speak.

She did not speak, but two or three other queens joined her, all crowding and gossiping together, as Peacock got up. The Royal Box! It was full. Cars hooting outside the window behind the velvet curtains had the effect of an orchestra and then, inevitably, those heavy green curtains were drawn up. A dark, packed and restless auditorium opened itself to him. There was dense applause.

Peacock stepped forward in awe and wholeness. Not to fall, not to fall, this time, he murmured. To bow. One must bow and bow and bow and not fall, to the applause. He set out. It was a strangely long up-hill journey towards the footlights and not until he got there did it occur to him that he did not know how to bow. Shel had never taught him. Indeed, at the first attempt the floor came up and hit him in the face.

1959

---

3. Victoria (1819–1901) was queen of England from 1837 to 1901.

E. ANNIE PROULX
b. 1935

Edna Ann Proulx, commonly known as Annie Proulx, was born and spent the early years of her childhood in Norwich, Connecticut. After graduating from high school in Portland, Maine, she attended Colby College for a brief period in the 1950s, leaving to marry her first husband. Proulx ended up earning a bachelor's degree in history from the University of Vermont in 1969 and, shortly after, an M.A. from Sir George Williams University (now Concordia) in Quebec. Despite affirming that for most of her adult life she did not think of herself as a writer, Proulx began writing full time upon leaving Concordia, beginning as a journalist but soon turning to short fiction. Several of her short stories appeared in *The Best American Short Stories* prior to the publication of her first collection, *Heart Songs and Other Stories* (1988). For her first novel, *Postcards* (1992), Proulx won the PEN/Faulkner Award, following which she was awarded NEA and Guggenheim fellowships. Two years later, her second novel, *The Shipping News* (1993), earned Proulx the Pulitzer Prize and the National Book Award for Fiction. Two of her short stories have received the O. Henry Award, one of which, *Brokeback Mountain*, was made into an Academy Award–winning major motion picture.

What Kind of Furniture Would Jesus Pick?

Budgel Wolfscale, a telegraph clerk from Missouri on his way to Montana to search for the yellow metal, stopped at a Wyoming road ranch one day in 1898 for a supper of fried venison and coffee, heard there was good range. For the next week he rode around the country, finally staked a homestead claim on a spread east of the Big Horns that had been cut from the holdings of a Scots outfit that pulled out the year before.

A year-round stream, Bull Jump Creek, cut the property, fringed by cottonwoods and willows, the shining maroon branches of water birch. It was still open country, though barbwire was coming in with the nesters. He built a shotgun cabin of hauled-out lodgepole, married one of the girls from a whorehouse in Ham's Fork, and, naming the ranch after the harp his mother had played, thought himself a Wyoming rancher. He wasn't that, but his sons and grandsons were.

The Harp skidded down the generations to Gilbert Wolfscale, born on the ranch in 1945, and in middle age still living a son's life with his mother in the old house, which had been gradually enlarged with telescoped additions until the structure resembled a giant spyglass built of logs. He ran a cow-calf operation, usually worked the place alone, for even inept help was hard to find. He was a tall man with heavy bones. His coarse skin seemed made of old leather upholstery, and, instead of lips, a small seam opened and disclosed his cement-colored teeth. There were no horses that could match his stamina. Despite his muscle mass he moved with fluid quickness. He surrounded himself with an atmosphere of affronted hostility, but balanced it with a wild and boisterous laugh that erupted at inappropriate times.

The old world was gone, he knew that. For some reason a day in the nineteen-fifties when all the ranchers and their hands had worked on the road rose often in his mind and with such vividness that he could smell the mud, the mineral odor of wet rock. He had been eight years old. It was the last rainy spring before that decade's drought sucked the marrow out of the state. The county road that ran between Kingring and Sheridan passed through seven ranches over a fifty-mile stretch. Under heavy melt from the mountains, it became an impassable sump of greasy mud and standing water. The county had no money. If the ranchers wanted to get to town they would have to fix the road themselves or wait until it dried. On a drizzling morning in April his father drank his coffee standing up.

"What say, Gib? Want to come along?"

They rode together on Butch, his father's roan saddle mount. The rain had stopped but heavy clouds moved with the bumping wind. Gilbert clutched the lard pail that held their lunch. They came to a place where men with shovels were strung out along the road. There was a section of an old corral still standing near the road and here men had leaned their tools, lunchpails, and bottles. A few had thrown their jackets on the ground. His father tethered Butch to a post.

While the men cleaned the borrow ditches and culverts, cut new drainage channels, built water bars, and hauled gravel, Gilbert hacked manfully at the mud with a broken hoe, but when Old Man Bunner told him to get out of his way or he'd chop off his legs he went to the weathered corral to play with sticks and rocks. He built a play corral of mud and broken miner's candle stems, and placed inside the rocks that were his horses. The wind cleared out the weather and by noon there was broken blue sky.

"Warmin up," called one of the men, stretching his back. The sun shone behind his ears, which turned the color of chokecherry jelly.

The lunch of cold pork and boiled eggs seemed the best thing Gilbert had ever eaten. There were two squares of his mother's coarse white cake with peanut-butter icing at the bottom of the pail. His father said Gilbert could have both pieces. He fell asleep on the way home, rocked by Butch's easy walk. His mother groaned with rage when she saw the mud on his clothes. The next morning his father went to work on the road without him and he cried until his mother slapped him. The work went on for a week, and when it ended a truck could get over the road. The first time they drove past the place he looked for his play corral. He could see one miner's candle stem. The rest had blown away. The rock horses were still there. Fifty years later the road was gravelled and graded by the county but he still looked when he drove past the place, the old corral now nothing but a single post. The prairie had swallowed his horse rocks.

After Gilbert Wolfscale inherited the ranch, he enlarged the two irrigated alfalfa fields, which made it possible, in bad years, to feed the cattle through the winter and, in good years, to sell hay to less fortunate outfits. These two fields kept the ledger ink black. He came up with other ideas to increase income. He thought of butchering and packing the beef himself to bypass the middlemen who took the money while the rancher did the work, but the local stores preferred to stay with the chain suppliers. So he put an ad in the paper looking for customers and found half a dozen, but they didn't eat enough beef to make the venture pay and a woman from town complained that there were bone splinters in the ground beef. He raised turkeys, thinking surefire Thanksgiving and Christmas markets, but never sold very many, even when he put strings of cranberries around their necks. His mother spent days making the cranberry necklaces, but people wanted the plastic-wrapped, pre-basted Safeway turkeys with breasts like Las Vegas strippers. He and his mother ate the turkeys themselves, his mother canning most of the meat. By spring, they were sick of the smell of turkey soup.

Some of the original chock-and-log fence—built not of split rails nor slender poles but big logs—stood in the high pastures nearest the forest, but much had been replaced with five-strand barbwire. He could almost see the ground compressing under the heavy log weight. How many men had helped his grandfather build that fence of tree trunks? Gilbert put in his time working on the barb fences, which no longer had the tensile strength of fresh wire but were patched and mended with short lengths of various gauge. In an earlier decade, struggling to finish the job on a hot afternoon, he had cast about for a stick or something to twist tight a diagonal cross-brace wire, but the only thing at hand was a cow's bleached leg bone with its trochlea head, which seemed made to jam fence wire tight. It worked so well that he collected and used cow bones in dozens of places. These bony fences and the coyote skulls nailed to the corner posts gave the Harp a murderous air.

He was a model of rancher stubbornness, savagely possessive of his property. He did everything in an odd, deliberate way, Gilbert Wolfscale's way, and never retreated once he had taken a position. Neighbors said he was self-reliant, but there was a way they said it that meant something else.

Seven miles north of the Harp on the Stump Hole Road lived May and Jim Codenhead. Gilbert had gone to grade school with May—she was then May Alwen. May's brother, Sedley Alwen, a big, good-natured kid with stringy arms, had been Gilbert's best friend. Gilbert had courted May for a year, taken it for granted that Sedley would be his brother-in-law, but she'd strung him along and then, in a sudden move on Christmas Day in 1966, married Jim Codenhead. Jim then was nothing more than an illiterate Montana hand working on the Alwen place.

May taught him to read until he could fumble through the newspaper.

"That's the shits, man," said Sedley sympathetically and took Gilbert on a two-day drunk, as much a salute to his draft notice as balm for Gilbert's disappointment.

The marriage wasn't unprecedented. For those who took the long view and had patience it was the classic route for a lowly cowhand to own his own spread—marry the rancher's daughter. In retaliation Gilbert went to a New Year's dance in Sheridan, found Suzzy New, and in ten days pressured her into a fast marriage.

Suzzy New was slender and small-boned, with something French about her child-size wrists, a contrast to Gilbert, six foot four, bullnecked with heavy shoulders. She was nimble-fingered and a talented embroiderer. In the flush of their first months together Gilbert bragged that she was so handy she could make a pair of chaps for a hummingbird. She was quiet, disliked arguments and shouting, the only child of elderly parents. She held herself tensely and had a way of retreating into her thoughts. She believed herself to be a very private person. She slept badly, sensitive to the slightest abnormal sound—the creak of a house timber, the rising wind, a raccoon forcing its way through the skirting of the house and under the kitchen floorboards. She had let herself be bullied into marrying Gilbert, and within days of the ruinous act she bitterly regretted it.

All her life she had heard and felt the Wyoming wind and took it for granted. There had even been a day when she was a young girl standing by the road waiting for the school bus when a spring wind, fresh and warm and perfumed with pine resin, had caused a bolt of wild happiness to surge through her, its liveliness promising glinting chances. But out at the ranch it was different. The house lay directly in line with a gap in the encircling hills to the north-west, and through this notch the prevailing wind poured, falling on the house with ferocity. The house shuddered as the wind punched it and slid along its sides like a released torrent from a broken dam. Week after week in winter it sank and rose, attacked and feinted. When she put her head down and went out to the truck it yanked at her clothing, shot up her sleeves, whisked her hair into a ravelled fright wig. Gilbert seemed not to notice, but then, she thought, he probably regarded it as *his* wind, and no doubt took pleasure in such a powerful possession.

Sedley went to Vietnam. Gilbert, who had a growth inside his nose, was 4-F[1] despite his strength and muscle. Sedley was captured by the Vietcong[2] and spent several years in a bamboo cage. He came back a different person, criss-crossed with sudden rages brought on by inconsequential events such as the rattle of dishes or a truck crossing the bridge. He was thought to be unstable and in need of watchful care. He moved in with May and Jim. May could calm Sedley down when he was having one of his fits. She had always been close to him, had, from the time she was a small child with nightmares, padded down the hall to his moonless north room, climbed into his bed for warmth and protection. The infant she bore six months after she married Jim Codenhead might have been her brother's child or, for that matter, Gilbert Wolfscale's, or even Jim Codenhead's. For years, whenever Gilbert was at their house, he studied the child, Patty, trying to work out whom she resembled. He could come to no conclusion.

---

1. Unfit for military service. 2. North Vietnamese army.

Vietnam nightmares tortured Sedley Alwen. Sometimes, to give May a break, Gilbert made the long drive to Cheyenne, taking Sedley to the Veterans Administration hospital, where he saw the shrink and got his prescriptions renewed. It was a two-day trip and they stayed at a motel overnight, sharing a room. After the session Sedley would be talkative. Gilbert listened attentively to his stories of torture and comrades' deaths. It was at these times Sedley resembled the friend of his childhood, excited and eager. But he could not have whiskey. They tried it once and found out. Whiskey made him act up, smashing the motel furniture and howling at the light fixture in the ceiling.

By 1999 Gilbert was fifty-four and caught in the downward ranching spiral of too much work, not enough money, drought. It got drier and drier, grasshoppers appearing as early as April and promising a plague in August. The grass crackled like eggshells under his feet. There was no color in the landscape, the alkali dust muting sage, stones, the earth itself. When a vehicle passed along the road a fine cloud spread out and slowly settled. The air was baked of scent except for the chalky dust. He was conscious of how many things could go wrong, of how poorly he'd reckoned the ranch's problems.

To the new-moneyed suitcase ranchers who had moved in all around him—ex-California real-estate agents, fabulous doctors, and retired cola executives—the Harp looked a skanky run-down outfit. They noticed the yard littered with stacks of rusted sheet metal held down by railroad ties, a pile of crooked fence posts inhabited by chipmunks, the long string of log additions to the old house. Some of these rich people, heated with land fever and the thought of a bargain, came to Gilbert and offered to buy his ranch. He could see in their eyes how they planned to bulldoze the house and build mansions with guest cottages.

"Them rich pricks are lower than a snake's ass in a wagon track," he said to his mother. "I told him my granddad homesteaded this place and if I ever seen his California butt on my property again I'd shoot it off. I looked him right in the eye and he got the message. He turned color so fast he farted."

His mother produced her hard little laugh.

It had always been dry country and no one born there expected more than a foot of rainfall in a good year. The drought halved that and he could see the metamorphosis of grazing land into desert. The country wanted to turn to sand dunes and rattlesnakes, wanted to scrape off its human ticks. Gilbert didn't have enough hay to feed his own stock. Everything told him that the day of the rancher was fading, but he dodged admitting it. He blamed the government, he blamed Salt Lake City. The damn Mormons, he said, had seeded the clouds for the Olympics,[3] sucking out all the snow moisture before it reached Wyoming. The ranch-house well was eleven hundred feet deep and the water brackish. In the drought years of the nineteen-thirties and again in the fifties his father had put in earthen dams and stock ponds, and in wet years they had held water but were now silted up and dried and stood as unsightly pits filled with weeds. In the center of one dry hole he piled an immense stack of brush, adding more every year, intending to burn it with the first good snow.

---

3. The 2002 Winter Olympics were held in Salt Lake City, Utah.

He was pestered. Some newcomer wanted a shortcut easement through the ranch to his million-dollar luxury house on the other side. A long-nosed Game and Fish biologist nagged him about fences that blocked the passage of prong-horn. Hunters wanted to shoot his deer. A busybody woman straight out of agricultural school came from the Extension Service one day and lectured him about protecting stream banks from cow-hoof erosion, about pasture rota-tion to prevent overgrazing.

"I heard all that shit. But I'll tell you what. I let the cows graze where they want and drink where they will. Been doin this for a while. Guess I know somethin about it." He stood in a truculent posture, legs apart, chin thrust forward. The woman shrugged and left.

His wife, Suzzy, had left him to live in Sheridan, sixty miles distant, in the spring of 1977, when the two boys, Monty and Rod, were still young. Those boys were doomed, said Gilbert, smacking his hand on the table for emphasis, to grow up without a father's guidance and example, injured because they were denied a boy's life on the ranch.

"If he wants a see the kids why can't he just come into town?" Suzzy said to her mother on the phone after the split. Her complaining voice rose, dipped. "You know I put in years on that ranch, and nothin really worked right. Half the time there wasn't water and when there was water it was nasty. We couldn't get in or out in the winter. No telephone, no electricity, no neighbors, his mother always naggin, and the *work!* He wore me down. 'Do this, do that,' bullyin ways. Keep that old house clean? Couldn't be done. He could a sold the place fifty times over and lived decent if he got a job like a normal human bein, but would he? No. I wouldn't relive those years for nothin." Once she had made up her mind to leave, her own stubbornness emerged. But Gilbert refused to agree to a divorce and the separation and enmity dragged on.

In town she got a cash-register job at the Big Billy supermarket and as soon as the two boys were old enough to run errands and deliver papers she made them get after-school and weekend jobs as well. She wanted to show them there were better things than cows and debt.

The Big Billy job was no good. Not only was the pay low but she disliked having to repeat "Have a nice day" to people who deserved to be ridden bare-back by the Devil wearing can openers for spurs, and one day she quit to take a job as a filing clerk in the county treasurer's office. It gravelled Gilbert that she handled his property-tax and vehicle-registration papers.

She wore him down on the divorce and he gave up after a fight in town in her new house. She had bought an old brick mansion with big trees in the yard and an ornamental iron fence around it. In the eighteen-eighties the house had belonged to a Chicago merchant who used it two or three times a year to oversee his ranch investments. Gilbert did not understand how she could afford this house. They had argued, then screamed. Gilbert stood with his legs apart and his arms hanging loose. Another man would have recognized this as a bad sign but she could not stop blaming him, and he, goaded to vio-lence, slapped her a good one and she came at him and yanked out a clump of his hair in the front where it would show, ran to the back of the house, and called the sheriff. When the law came she accused Gilbert of assault, showing the red mark on her cheek as proof.

"What about *this*?" shouted Gilbert, pointing to his bleeding scalp, but Sheriff Brant Smich, his second cousin, ignored him. When the divorce finally came through it was settled that if he wanted the boys to help out on the ranch for a weekend he would have to drive in and fetch them and he would have to pay them for their labor. He had paid practically nothing for child support during the long separation, she said, it was the least he could do. He protested, said he had cancelled checks to prove he had certainly paid adequate if not luxurious support.

"Take it to court," she said, "you think you been treated so bad."

Neither of the boys came willingly to the ranch. They appeared only in times of crisis after Gilbert telephoned Suzzy, demanding their help—spring branding, fence work. They let themselves be dragged out for a weekend then, sulky and grudging. They sassed their grandmother and whispered and snickered when they saw cows bulling. A day's work was not in them. They wanted only to ride the horses. It was clear to Gilbert that at his death they would sell the place as fast as they could. One day someone would find his stiff corpse out in the pasture, the wire cutters in his hand, or they would find him fallen in the muddy irrigation ditch, as he had found his own father. He would never be able to pass on to them how he felt about the land.

His allegiance to the place was not much of a secret, for even outsiders perceived his scalding passion for the ranch. His possessive gaze fell on the pale teeth of distant mountains, on the gullies and washes, the long draw shedding Indian scrapers and arrowheads. His feeling for the ranch was the strongest emotion that had ever moved him, a strangling love tattooed on his heart. It was his. It was as if he had drunk from some magic goblet full of the elixir of ownership. And although the margins of Bull Jump Creek had been trampled bare and muddy by generations of cows, although there were only one or two places along it still flushed with green willow, the destruction had happened so gradually that he had not noticed, for he thought of the ranch as timeless and unchanging in its beauty. It needed only young men to put it right. So his thoughts turned again and again on ways to get his sons to see and love the ranch.

In 1982, Monty was fourteen and Rod two years younger. Gilbert, waiting in the truck in front of Suzzy's house, heard Monty inside bellowing at his mother in his cracking voice, "I don't want a go. It stinks out there, there's nothin a do," and he could not dodge the fact that his sons hated the ranch. In a desperate attempt to make the place more attractive to them he had the power company run out poles and wires, a terrible expense and useless, too, as the boys came no more often. The only benefit, if benefit it was, was the small television set he bought and put in the living room, where he would lie on the sofa under one of his mother's quilts and watch men wrestling anacondas, riding motorcycles inside enormous wooden barrels. His mother liked the television, but claimed to be shocked by much of what she saw.

"It is company, I'll say that, but where they find them fool people to cut up so I don't know."

He wasn't lonely. There was his mother, he was a church deacon, a member of the Cattlemen's Association, he went to his neighbors' potluck suppers and barbecues, and about once a month drove to town and got half drunk, bought a woman, and made it back to the ranch before the old haymaker cleared the horizon. He was not a veteran but he knew all the local veterans and often went to the V.F.W.[4] with them to drink and listen to Vietnam stories.

He had always taken an interest in Vietnam. He wondered what it was about combat that so changed men, for all of those who had been in school with him, the ones who came back, were marked by what they had seen and endured. He knew them and he didn't know them. Sedley came back angry and crazy, Russ Fleshman returned as a windbag, Pete Kitchen was reclusive and lived in a horse trailer at the back of the old Kitchen ranch. Something had gone wrong for Willis McNitt, leaving him dead-voiced and troubled. They all referred emotionally to the war, now so many years past, and Fleshman sometimes put his face in his hands and cried. And there were the ones who didn't come back: Todd Likwartz, Howard Marr, and several he hadn't known. When Gilbert thought of them a phrase came into his mind—"Now they know what Rhamses knows." His mother belonged to the generation that had memorized poems in school, and one, "Little Mattie," on the death of a thirteen-year-old girl, had fastened itself relentlessly in her recall with the tolling line "Now she knows what Rhamses knows." She quoted from it throughout her life and still sometimes treated her son to a recitation of the entire piece with the stilted emphasis learned so long ago in a little Wyoming schoolhouse.

Gilbert Wolfscale listened to the veterans. He wanted to understand what he had missed. It had been the great experience of the time of his young manhood and he had been absent. It was as though the veterans had learned a different language, he thought, listening to Fleshman's scattershot of *didi mau*, Agent Orange, *beaucoup*, Jodies, 105s, Willy-Petes, and K-Bars.[5] He caught at the names—Phu Bai, Khe Sanh, Quang Tri—wondering if these were the Vietnamese equivalents of Rawlins or Thermopolis. The veterans did not seem so much tragic victims as eccentric members of a select club. He felt himself an outsider. They had got the edge on him.

One year, Willis McNitt sat behind him at the August rodeo. It was the hottest summer he had ever known. The horses were blowing and their coats white with salty sweat, the bulls stood in the chutes with their heads down and bucked feebly. There had been a freak accident at the stock pens. The rodeo grounds were old, put up in the nineteen-thirties, all wood fence and posts, and somehow a kid watering the roping calves had fallen or been knocked down and mashed his face against a splintery post. A long sliver had run into the flesh below his eyebrow and he had stumbled away from the pens, blood coursing down the back of his hand, which he had put instinctively to the wound. He had not cried out, just stumbled into sight with blood seeping between his fingers, making the crowd gasp. As the ambulance bore him away Gilbert said to no one in particular, "They ought a tear out them damn old wood posts and get good metal."

"I seen somethin like that in Nam," said Willis behind him in his flat, heavy voice. Willis had a son at the university, studying anthropology. The

---

4. Veterans of Foreign Wars, an organization for American Veterans.   **5.** *Didi mau*, go quickly (Vietnamese); Agent Orange, a defoliating chemical weapon; *beaucoup*, many (French); Jodies, civilian men, often romantic rivals of soldiers; 105s, Republic F-105 Thunderchief, an Air Force fighter-bomber deployed in the early years of the Vietnam War; Willy-Petes, white phosphorus, an incendiary munition; K-Bars, combat knives.

kid—Coot McNitt—had a half-baked theory that rice cultivation had developed to replace a shortage of maggots in early man's diet. If you listened to him long enough he'd make you believe it. "We was in a free-fire zone and the kid next a me got shot in the eye. He said, 'I been shot in the eye,' said it five or six times, real quiet, like he couldn't quite take it in. Couldn't believe it. Then he laid down beside me and commenced a kick and thrash and ever time he kicked the blood pumped up through his eye like a school water fountain."

"God," said Gilbert. "Did he—?"

"Died. A kid, eighteen years old, younger'n Coot. Couldn't believe he'd been shot. I was nineteen but after that I felt like a old man."

"You ain't old, Willis. Hell, you're my age."

"Yeah."

The word dropped like a stone.

One day, Gilbert Wolfscale's mother opened an official-looking letter from the California State Allocation Department. She read that she had inherited a sum of money from someone in that state. All she had to do was fill out the enclosed form, mail it back, and in six or eight weeks she would receive the inheritance. She spent two hours filling out the form, with its demands for address, Social Security number, date of birth, bank-account numbers, and other tedious details. She sat so long at the table with this form that her left leg went to sleep and when she got up to go to the kitchen and make a cup of tea it buckled. She fell and broke her hip.

She recuperated very slowly. Even after the break had healed, Gilbert had to drive her in to Sheridan for weekly therapy. He sometimes wondered why she didn't get one of her friends to drive her. She was always on the phone gabbing with her cronies and most of them still drove. He heard her talking with them about football, which she watched avidly on the television.

"I'm for them Bears. I couldn't never be for them Packers."

When he asked her why she did not arrange a trip to town with Luce or Florence or Helen she said, "They're not family. Suppose the doctor was to give me bad news. I'd want a be with blood kin, not some other person."

While she was in with the therapist Gilbert walked around the windy town streets rather than sit in a plastic chair in the stuffy waiting room. In a music store he looked at CDs, wondering at the proliferation of bands with trendy, foolish names. Behind a stiff plastic divider labelled "MISCELLANEOUS" he found birdcalls, tap dancing, the whistles of steam locomotives from around the world. The last CD was "Remembering Vietnam." The cover showed a grimy infantryman staring up at a helicopter. The back copy listed "Firefight," "Shrapnel," "ARVN," "Jungle Patrol," "Rain," "APC Convoy." He bought it.

In the truck driving home his mother said, "I don't have to go back there but a few more times, looks like, and thanks to heaven. Some a the strangest people settin in that waitin room. These two women got talkin about their Bible class. Sounded pretty modern, you know, tryin a link the Bible to nowadays. But this Bible class *they* went to was tryin a guess how it would be if Jesus showed up in Sheridan. That got them all excited and there they set, what would he do for work. They both said he could easy find a job workin construction. Would he have his own house and would it be like a trailer or a regular house or a apartment? Then they got at the furniture, what kind a furniture would Jesus pick for his place. And you know how you get thinkin about things you overhear? Wasn't none a my business but there I set, crazy as they was, wonderin if he'd pick out a maple rockin chair or a sofa with that Scotchgard fabric or what."

A month before her fall his mother had bought some bright-colored kitchen sponges. One of them was purple and she had developed an affection for it, never using it on greasy pots or to wipe up nasty spills. He dribbled coffee on the counter one morning and began to mop at the spill with the distinguished sponge.

"What are you doin! Don't use that—take the pink one. You dunderhead, I'm savin that one."

"For what, Ma?"

"For the good glasses." She meant the crystal wineglasses with the gold rims that had been passed down from Granny Webb and had stood inverted in the china cupboard for as long as he could remember. He had never known them to be used. Inside the china cupboard next to the glasses was a photograph of his father's mother in a black silk twill dress, looking freeze-dried and mournful.

"Where is that stupid mailman?" his mother said, pulling back the curtain and looking for the plume of dust along the road.

It was days before he had a chance to listen to the CD. He was on his way to the bank. The soul of leaf susurration, cicadas, crickets, mortars, a calling bird with a voice like a kid hooting down a cardboard tube, snatches of talk, incoming fire, deafening helicopter fibrillation filled the truck.

Saturday was grocery day, but his mother said, "I don't feel up to it. You just get what we need, bread and eggs. Coffee. Whatever else you see that looks good. I don't have much appetite these days anyhow. And I want a wait for the mail. I'm expectin mail."

He bought the groceries and on the way out of town passed the library. Two miles beyond it he thought of books—books on Vietnam—and he turned around. He came away with three, all they had, read them in bed that night, and fell asleep with a book on his face. He awoke frightened and shouting, thinking something was smothering him. The exhaled moisture from his mouth had formed a round dimple in the page.

It was not long after this that his mother began to give way. She would look at him and say, "Where's Gilbert? Out playin, I bet. I want him to fill up that wood box." And later she would tell him, "You'll have to fend for yourself for supper. I can't cook without no wood." He felt a pang of guilt, for there had been many times when he was a boy that he had dodged the wood box. But she kept asking if the mail had come until Gilbert, exasperated, said, "You expectin a letter from the President or what?" She shook her head and said nothing.

In 1999, Gilbert's son Monty turned thirty-two, a big dark-haired fellow, still single, who worked as a roofer in Colorado. Gilbert hadn't seen him in years. Rod, the younger one, lived in Sheridan, a block away from his mother, worked in Buffalo in a video-rental store. He was married and had two children, twin girls, whom Gilbert had seen only once and had never touched nor held. The little girls had never been to the ranch. The boy's wife, Debra, worked, too, answering the telephone at Equality Cowboy Travel. Gilbert sometimes dreamed that they would have more children—boys—and that these little grandsons would love the ranch, would grow up knowing what a beautiful place the Wolfscales owned. They would love it as he did and take it on when he went.

Gilbert's mother turned eighty-one. The purple sponge, though somewhat faded, was largely unchanged, not to be used. She took to rummaging through the desk looking for pencil and paper, settled on a little notebook, spiral-bound at the top and with lined paper. She spent hours at the kitchen table bent over this notebook, thinking, occasionally scrawling something down or erasing everything, tearing out the spoiled sheet and crumpling it.

"What are you writin, Ma? Your biography? Cowgirl poetry?"

"No," she said and put her arm around the notebook so he couldn't see it, like a child protecting a test paper from a cheating neighbor.

On a very cold March day he went into town to the ranch-equipment center; the used aircraft tires he'd ordered for the bush hog were in. If the weather warmed up later in the week he'd work on pulling old sagebrush out of the three-mile pasture. In town the bank thermometer read minus two and a harsh wind made it seem like the freezing pits of Hell. He ordered a pizza. Clouds were moving in as he drove back, eating the cheesy slices, and as he turned in to the ranch the first fine flakes fell through the air.

The house was silent. He thought his mother might be napping and went out to the shop, where he changed the bush hog's tires. The days were growing longer and he worked until twilight. Back in the house he was disturbed by the deep silence. Usually his mother watched crime programs on television at this hour. He went to her room and knocked on the door.

"Ma! Ma, you O.K.? I'm goin a start supper now." There was no answer. He opened the door and saw his mother would not again want any supper.

It was a shock to learn that her bank account was at flat zero. He couldn't understand what she had spent the money on. He remembered her telling him when she broke her hip that she had over six thousand dollars set aside for "—*you* know." And he did know. For her funeral costs. He had to scratch to come up with the money for a decent coffin.

Cleaning out her room, he came across the spiral-bound notebook. It was filled with plaintive letters to the California State Allocation Department, asking when her inheritance would come. Folded in the front of the notebook was the original letter. He telephoned the number at the bottom of the page but got a message that the number had been disconnected. Gilbert began to guess there was some sort of scam. He called Sheriff Brant Smich, asked him if he knew anything about California State Allocation.

"Hell, yes. You get a letter from them sayin about you inherited some money and askin for your bank-account numbers? Don't believe none of it. Don't answer them. Bring the letter to the post office. They're after that outfit for mail fraud."

With his mother gone, civilization began to fall away from him like feathers from a molting hen. In a matter of weeks he was eating straight from the frying pan.

As is usual in the ranch world, things went from bad to worse. The drought settled deeper, like a lamprey eel sucking at the region's vitals. He had half-seen the scores of trucks emblazoned CPC—Consolidated Petroleum Company—speeding along the dusty road for the past year, and knew that they were drilling for coal-bed methane on public land adjacent to his ranch. They pumped the saline wastewater laden with mineral toxins into huge containment pits. The water was no good, he knew that, and it seemed a terrible irony that in such arid country water could be worthless. He had always voted Republican and supported energy development as the best way to make jobs in the hinterland. But when the poison wastewater seeped from the containment pits into the groundwater, into Bull Jump Creek, into his alfalfa irrigation ditches, even into the household well water, he saw it was killing the ranch.

He fought back. Like other ranchers who once again felt betrayed by state and federal government, he wrote letters and went to meetings protesting coal-bed methane drilling and the hundreds of service roads and drill rigs and heavy trucks that were tearing up the country. The meetings were strange, for ecological conservationists and crusty ranchers came together in the same room, in agreement for once. He noted with satisfaction that the schoolteacher, Dan Moorhen, a bleeding-heart liberal ecology-minded freak, admitted that ranchers were the best defense against developers chopping up the land, that ranches and ranchers kept the Old West alive. When the gas-company reps or politicians came, the meetings were rancorous and loud and at the end people signed petitions with such force their pens ripped the paper, but it all meant nothing. The drilling continued, the poison water seeped, the grass and sage and alfalfa died. All he could do was hang on to the place.

He was unprepared for the telephone call from a neighbor, Fran Bangharmer. It was the morning of the Fourth of July.

"Too bad about Suzzy, all that right on the front page, too."

"What do you mean?" he said. "What was on the front page?"

"Arrested for embezzlin. Monday's paper."

"What!" Fran's voice was subtly triumphant, tinged with Schadenfreude, but Gilbert barely listened, hung up as soon as he could and drove into town to find a three-day-old paper and read for himself that his ex-wife had, for years, been siphoning tax money into a private bank account by a complex series of computer sleights of hand he could not understand.

He went to the county jail and tried to see her but was turned away.

"She don't want to see you, Gib, and she's got that right."

Half of the stores in town were closed for the holiday. Already there were clusters of people along the sidewalk, although the parade didn't start until one o'clock. In despair he drove down to Buffalo to the video store where Rod worked. It was open, the windows draped with red-white-and-blue ribbons. A huge poster read: "RODEO DAYS! JULY 4 TO 10!"

He found his younger son stocking the shelves with gaudy boxes. As he stood behind him he noticed the son's thinning hair and felt the hot breath of passing time.

"Rod?" he said, and the young man turned around.

"Dad." They looked at each other and the son dropped his eyes. Gilbert could smell his son's aftershave lotion. He himself had never used the stuff in his life.

"I came to . . . I want to . . . Well. Your mother?"

"Yeah. Do you want a have lunch?"

"You mean dinner?"

The son flushed at the old-fashioned word. "Yeah. 'Dinner.' Go down the KFC and eat in the car."

"I come in the truck. Come on, let's go."

"I got a tell somebody I'm goin."

That's what it was like, thought Gilbert, working for somebody else. You had to tell them what you did or were going to do and they could say no.

He drove to the fast-food strip at the north end of town, shouted into the drive-through intercom. Sitting in the truck, the windows down and the hot sun burning their arms, they gnawed at the salty, overspiced chicken, huge crumbs falling. They both sucked on straws stuck into vanilla milkshakes.

"I tried a see her," said Gilbert. "She wouldn't see me."

"She's still pretty bitter, you know. Feels like her life was wasted, or at least some years of it. She's that way. She takes a position and that's it. You can't argue her out of nothin. She's stubborn."

"I know that pretty well. How's it affectin you that your mother is a crook and a jailbird?" He glanced sideways at Rod, seeing the pale, indoor complexion, the clerk's shirt with creases ironed into the sleeves. The boy had the heavy Wolfscale jaw and beaky nose.

"Hell, I don't know. I don't think of it that way. People look at me kind a funny but they don't say nothin. Except Deb. She is gettin a lot a snide comment down at the travel agency. It's no fun for her. It's my girls I worry about, if some kid at school this fall is goin a taunt them."

"Kids got short memories. By the time school starts they won't recall it. What do you think they'll do to her?"

"Probly go pretty light. She's got a good lawyer. You know, she made restitution of about twelve grand. That'll count for a lot. They already got a lien on the house, repossessed her car. That's what she used the most a the money for, buy the house and fix it up. That house was everthing to her. She put in a swimmin pool two years ago."

"I used a wonder how she could afford it. And I heard a couple years ago that she went out to Las Vegas?" He couldn't believe he'd found a packet of salt beneath the flabby biscuit. Did anyone ever think their chicken not salty enough?

"It was a whole bunch a them that work at the county offices. They all went. She won four thousand bucks."

For some reason this remark incensed Gilbert. Rod said it with a tone of pride that his lying, cheating, stealing, double-dealing mother had won some money gambling. He changed the subject abruptly. "What do you hear from your brother?"

"Aw, he calls up now and then. We get together with him when we take Arlene down to Denver for her treatment. You know she's had that cancer. It's in remission now and you'd never know she'd been sick a day."

Gilbert did not know his granddaughter had been sick a day. He shuddered. In the distance he could hear a school marching band. Buffalo's parade was starting, or maybe just warming up.

"Is he still workin for that roofin contractor?"

"Well, no. He's workin in a restaurant. He's workin in a Jap restaurant. But he's healthy, thank God, considerin his—life style."

"What does that mean, his 'life style'?" Gilbert wiped his hands of the chicken, wadded the napkin, and thrust it into the grease-stained box.

"Well, he's—you know."

"I know what?"

"Dad, it's not up to me to say nothin about Monty." Rod was folding and crushing the box. He wiped his right hand on his pants leg.

"I ain't heard or seen him for quite a few years. Not likely to. Now what the hell is this about his 'life style'?"

"For Christ sake, Dad. It's nothin. Just he's sort a—more—sophisticated. He likes a different kind a stuff than most people come from Wyomin."

"I hear you talkin but I don't know what you're sayin."

But he did. As a child Monty had hung around the kitchen and his mother constantly, and to get him to help with chores had been more labor than doing the jobs himself. That is, until Myrl Otter came to work on the ranch on weekends. Myrl was a big blond Scandinavian type, muscular and good-looking. The man's wife had her work cut out for her keeping an eye on him, as girls flirted with Myrl and he reciprocated willingly. After he came to work on the ranch Monty began to tag after the fellow like a yellowjacket after pears. Gilbert noticed, but as the boy was only seven or eight it seemed just a little kid's fancy, nothing much. Kids got attached to dogs and blankets and maybe even hired men. He thought nothing of it and after a few months Myrl Otter, in the way of so many ranch hands, stopped showing up for work and Gilbert had forgotten him until now. The marching music, carried by the light wind, seemed nearer.

"I better get goin. Don't want a get tied up in that damn parade." He got out, threw his chicken box at the trash can. Rod, too, tossed his crumpled box, but it hit the side of the can and sprayed chicken bones.

"Forget it," said Gilbert. "They get paid a pick up."

He dropped Rod back at the video store and headed north, thinking to beat the parade by taking a side street, but he was too late. He stopped for a red light that wouldn't change and the parade came surging around a corner, passing in front of him, and he had to wait. A section of the high-school band straggled past, sweaty kids, many of them obese, their white marching trousers bunched at the crotch. He remembered schoolmates in his own childhood, skinny, quick ranch kids, no one fat and sweaty, Pete Kitchen looking like he was made of kindling wood and insulation wire, Willis McNitt small enough to shit behind a sagebrush and never be noticed.

Behind the band came two teen-age boys dressed as Indians, breechclouts over swim trunks, a load of beads around their necks, black wigs with braids and feathers. One carried a bongo drum, striking it irregularly with his hand. Their skin had been darkened with some streaky substance. Then two men whom he recognized as Sheridan car mechanics slouched along in buckskin suits and fur hats, carrying antique flintlocks. One had a demijohn that he lifted to his lips every thirty seconds, crying "Yee-haw!" The other had a few shiny No. 2 traps over his shoulder. Gilbert could see the hardware-store price tags on them. He knew he was going to get the whole hokey Wild West treatment before he could move.

Now came two horses, both bearing kids dressed as cowboys, in heavy woolly chaps, pearl-button Western shirts, limp bandannas, big hats, and boots. Both twirled guns on their fingers, aiming at friends in the crowd. They were followed by a stock outlaw and a sheriff's posse, and behind them half the town's women and small children in pioneer regalia—long calico dresses, aprons and sunbonnets, big Nikes flashing incongruously with every step. One of these women was Patty Codenhead and for a moment he was startled at how much she looked like the photograph of his father's mother in the china cupboard. It was the costume, he thought. The parade came down to a few trick riders in neon satin, and Sedley Alwen, who, crazy or not, was in every public procession showing off his roping skills, stepping in and out of his fluid loops and somehow avoiding the horse manure that marked the path. The last of all was a CPC pickup, three hard-hatted methane-gas workers sitting in back smoking cigarettes and joking with each other. Now he could go.

He could go but he found it difficult to step on the accelerator. The light turned green, red, then green again, yet he couldn't move until drivers behind him began to sound their horns. There had been something wrong with the parade, something seriously wrong, but he couldn't think what.

Driving through the open country on the way back, he forgot the parade and thought about Monty and what form his "sophistication" might take, about his embezzling wife, the other son who had not bothered to tell him that his grandchild had cancer. He couldn't tell the size of things. He was very thirsty and blamed the salty chicken.

The buildings and traffic fell away and he was on the empty road, the dusty sage flying past, the white ground. The sky was a hard cheerful blue, empty but for a few torn contrails. Plastic bags impaled on the barb fences flapped in the hot wind. A small herd of pronghorn in the distance had their heads down. He saw his neighbor's cattle spread out on the parched land and it came to him that there had been no ranchers in the parade—it was all pioneers, outlaws, Indians, and gas.

He knew what kind of furniture Jesus would pick for his place in Wyoming. He would choose a few small pines in the National Forest, go there at night, fell and limb them, debark the sappy rind with a spud, exposing the pale, worm-tunnelled wood, and from the timbers he would make the simplest round-legged furniture, everything pegged, no nails or screws.

He wished his mother were still alive. He'd say to her, "One thing sure. He wouldn't get hisself tangled up with no ranch." It didn't come close to saying what he meant but it was all he could do.

2003

RON RASH
b. 1953

Ron Rash was born in South Carolina and raised in western North Carolina. The mountain region of southern Appalachia, where his family has lived since the 1700s, provides the setting for much of his writing. Rash earned his B.A. from Gardner-Webb University, where his father had been a professor, and his M.A. from Clemson University. He is currently the John and Dorothy Parris Distinguished Professor in Appalachian Cultural Studies at Western Carolina University. Rash has published four collections of poetry, five novels, five collections of short fiction, and a children's book. He was the recipient of the 1994 NEA Poetry Fellowship and the 1996 Sherwood Anderson prize for fiction, as well as a two-time finalist for the PEN/Faulkner Award for his bestselling novel *Serena* (2008), and his third collection of short stories, *Chemistry and Other Stories* (2007). His short story "Speckled Trout" won the 2005 O. Henry Prize, and his short story collection *Burning Bright* (2010) won him the Frank O'Connor International Short Story Award. Rash's most recent publication is his fifth collection of short stories, *Nothing Gold Can Stay* (2013).

Their Ancient, Glittering Eyes

Because they were boys, no one believed them, including the old men who gathered each morning at the Riverside Gas and Grocery. These retirees huddled by the pot-bellied stove in rain and cold, on clear days sunning out front like reptiles. The store's middle-aged owner, Cedric Henson, endured the trio's presence with a resigned equanimity. When he'd bought the store five years earlier, Cedric assumed they were part of the purchase price, in that way no different from the leaky roof and the submerged basement whenever the Tuckaseegee overspilled its banks.

The two boys, who were brothers, had come clattering across the bridge, red-faced and already holding their arms apart as if carrying huge, invisible packages. They stood gasping a few moments, waiting for enough breath to tell what they'd seen.

'This big,' the twelve-year-old said, his arms spread wide apart as he could stretch them.

'No, even bigger,' the younger boy said.

Cedric had been peering through the door screen but now stepped outside. 'What you boys talking about?' he asked.

'A fish,' the older boy said, 'in the pool below the bridge.'

Rudisell, the oldest of the three at eighty-nine, expertly delivered a squirt of tobacco between himself and the boys. Creech and Campbell simply nodded at each other knowingly. Time had banished them to the role of spectators in the world's affairs, and from their perspective the world both near and far was now controlled by fools. The causes of this devolution dominated their daily conversations. The octogenarians Rudisell and Campbell blamed Franklin Roosevelt and fluoridated water. Creech, a mere seventy-six, leaned toward Elvis Presley and television.

'The biggest fish ever come out of the Tuckaseegee was a thirty-one-inch brown trout caught in nineteen and forty-eight,' Rudisell announced to all present. 'I seen it weighed in this very store. Fifteen pounds and two ounces.'

The other men nodded in confirmation.

'This fish was twice bigger than that,' the younger boy challenged.

The boy's impudence elicited another spray of tobacco juice from Rudisell.

'Must be a whale what swum up from the ocean,' Creech said. 'Though that's a long haul. It'd have to come up the Gulf Coast and the Mississippi, for the water this side of the mountain flows west.'

'Could be one of them log fish,' Campbell offered. 'They get that big. Them rascals will grab your bait and then turn into a big chunk of wood afore you can set the hook.'

'They's snakes all over that pool, even some copperheads,' Rudisell warned. 'You younguns best go somewhere else to make up your tall tales.'

The smaller boy pooched out his lower lip as if about to cry.

'Come on,' his brother said. 'They ain't going to believe us.'

The boys walked back across the road to the bridge. The old men watched as the youths leaned over the railing, took a last look before climbing atop their bicycles and riding away.

'Fluoridated water,' Rudisell wheezed. 'Makes them see things.'

On the following Saturday morning, Harley Wease scrambled up the same bank the boys had, carrying the remnants of his Zebco 202. Harley's hands trembled as he laid the shattered rod and reel on the ground before the old men. He pulled a soiled handkerchief from his jeans and wiped his bleeding index finger to reveal a deep slice between the first and second joints. The old men studied the finger and the rod and reel and awaited explanation. They were attentive, for Harley's deceased father had been a close friend of Rudisell's.

'Broke my rod like it was made of balsa wood,' Harley said. 'Then the gears on the reel got stripped. It got down to just me and the line pretty quick.' Harley raised his index finger so the men could see it better. 'I figured to use my finger for the drag. If the line hadn't broke, you'd be looking at a nub.'

'You sure it was a fish?' Campbell asked. 'Maybe you caught hold of a muskrat or snapping turkle.'

'Not unless them critters has got to where they grow fins,' Harley said.

'You saying it was a trout?' Creech asked.

'I only got a glimpse, but it didn't look like no trout. Looked like a alligator but for the fins.'

'I never heard of no such fish in Jackson County,' Campbell said, 'but Rudy Nicholson's boys seen the same. It's pretty clear there's *something* in that pool.'

The men turned to Rudisell for his opinion.

'I don't know what it is either,' Rudisell said. 'But I aim to find out.'

He lifted the weathered ladder-back chair, held it aloft shakily as he made his slow way across the road to the bridge. Harley went into the store to talk with Cedric, but the other two men followed Rudisell as if all were deposed kings taking their thrones into some new kingdom. They lined their chairs up at the railing. They waited.

Only Creech had undiminished vision, but in the coming days that was rectified. Campbell had not thought anything beyond five feet of himself worth viewing for years, but now a pair of thick, round-lensed spectacles adorned his head, giving him a look of owlish intelligence. Rudisell had a spyglass he claimed once belonged to a German U-boat captain. The bridge was now effectively one lane, but traffic tended to be light. While trucks and cars drove around them, the old men kept vigil morning to evening, retreating into the store only when rain came.

Vehicles sometimes paused on the bridge to ask for updates, because the lower half of Harley Wease's broken rod had become an object of great wonder since being mounted on Cedric's back wall. Men and boys frequently took it down to grip the hard plastic handle. They invariably pointed the jagged fiberglass in the direction of the bridge, held it out as if a divining rod that might yet give some measure or resonance of what creature now made the pool its lair.

Rudisell spotted the fish first. A week had passed with daily rains clouding the river, but two days of sun settled the silt, the shallow tailrace clear all the way to the bottom. This was where Rudisell aimed his spyglass, setting it on the rail to steady his aim. He made a slow sweep of the sandy floor every fifteen minutes. Many things came into focus as he adjusted the scope: a flurry of nymphs rising to become mayflies, glints of fool's gold, schools of minnows shifting like migrating birds, crayfish with pincers raised as if surrendering to the behemoth sharing the pool with them.

It wasn't there, not for hours, but then suddenly it was. At first Rudisell saw just a shadow over the white sand, slowly gaining depth and definition, and then the slow wave of the gills and pectoral fins, the shudder of the tail as the fish held its place in the current.

'I see it,' Rudisell whispered, 'in the tailrace.' Campbell took off his glasses and grabbed the spyglass, placed it against his best eye as Creech got up slowly, leaned over the rail.

'It's long as my leg,' Creech said.

'I never thought to see such a thing,' Campbell uttered.

The fish held its position a few more moments before slowly moving into deeper water.

'I never seen the like of a fish like that,' Creech announced.

'It ain't a trout,' Campbell said.

'Nor carp or bass,' Rudisell added.

'Maybe it is a gator,' Campbell said. 'One of them snowbirds from Florida could of put it in there.'

'No,' Rudisell said. 'I seen gators during my army training in Louisiana. A gator's like us, it's got to breathe air. This thing don't need air. Beside, it had a tail fin.'

'Maybe it's a mermaid,' Creech mused.

By late afternoon the bridge looked like an overloaded barge. Pickups, cars, and two tractors clotted both sides of the road and the store's parking lot. Men and boys squirmed and shifted to get a place against the railing. Harley Wease recounted his epic battle, but it was the ancients who were most deferred to as they made pronouncements about size and weight. Of species they could speak only by negation.

'My brother works down at that nuclear power plant near Walhalla,' Marcus Price said. 'Billy swears there's catfish below the dam near five foot long. Claims that radiation makes them bigger.'

'This ain't no catfish,' Rudisell said. 'It didn't have no big jug head. More lean than that.'

Bascombe Greene ventured the shape called to mind the pikefish caught in weedy lakes up north. Stokes Hamilton thought it could be a hellbender salamander, for though he'd never seen one more than twelve inches long he'd heard tell they got to six feet in Japan. Leonard Coffey told a long, convoluted story about a goldfish set free in a pond. After two decades of being fed corn bread and fried okra, the fish had been caught and it weighed fifty-seven pounds.

'It ain't no pike nor spring lizard nor goldfish,' Rudisell said emphatically.

'Well, there's but one way to know,' Bascombe Greene said, 'and that's to try and catch the damn thing.' Bascombe nodded at Harley. 'What bait was you fishing with?'

Harley looked sheepish.

'I'd lost my last spinner when I snagged a limb. All I had left in my tackle box was a rubber worm I use for bass, so I put it on.'

'What size and color?' Bascombe asked. 'We got to be scientific about this.'

'Seven inch,' Harley said. 'It was purple with white dots.'

'You got any more of them?' Leonard Coffey asked.

'No, but you can buy them at Sylva Hardware.'

'Won't do you no good,' Rudisell said.

'Why not?' Leonard asked.

'For a fish to live long enough to get that big, it's got to be smart. It'll not forget that a rubber worm tricked it.'

'It might not be near smart as you reckon,' Bascombe said. 'I don't mean no disrespect, but old folks tend to be forgetful. Maybe that old fish is the same way.'

'I reckon we'll know the truth of that soon enough,' Rudisell concluded, because fishermen already cast from the bridge and banks. Soon several lines had gotten tangled, and a fistfight broke out over who had claim to a choice spot near the pool's tailrace. More people arrived as the afternoon wore on, became early evening. Cedric, never one to miss a potential business opportunity, put a plastic fireman's hat on his head and a whistle in his mouth. He parked cars while his son Bobby crossed and recrossed the bridge selling Cokes from a battered shopping cart.

Among the later arrivals was Charles Meekins, the county's game warden. He was thirty-eight years old and had grown up in Madison, Wisconsin. The general consensus, especially among the old men, was the warden was arrogant and a smart-ass. Meekins stopped often at the store, and he invariably addressed them as Wynken, Blynken, and Nod. He listened with undisguised condescension as the old men, Harley, and finally the two boys told of what they'd seen.

'It's a trout or carp,' Meekins said, 'carp' sounding like 'cop.' Despite four years in Jackson County, Meekins still spoke as if his vocal cords had been pulled from his throat and reinstalled in his sinus cavity. 'There's no fish larger in these waters.'

Harley handed his reel to the game warden.

'That fish stripped the gears on it.'

Meekins inspected the reel as he might an obviously fraudulent fishing license.

'You probably didn't have the drag set right.'

'It was bigger than any trout or carp,' Campbell insisted.

'When you're looking into water you can't really judge the size of something,' Meekins said. He looked at some of the younger men and winked. 'Especially if your vision isn't all that good to begin with.'

A palmful of Red Mule chewing tobacco bulged the right side of Rudisell's jaw like a tumor, but his apoplexy was such that he swallowed a portion of his cud and began hacking violently. Campbell slapped him on the back and Rudisell spewed dark bits of tobacco onto the bridge's wooden flooring.

Meekins had gotten back in his green fish and wildlife truck before Rudisell recovered enough to speak.

'If I hadn't near choked to death I'd have told that shit-britches youngun to bend over and we'd see if my sight was good enough to ram this spyglass up his ass.'

In the next few days so many fishermen came to try their luck that Rudisell finally bought a wire-bound notebook from Cedric and had anglers sign up for fifteen-minute slots. They cast almost every offering imaginable into the pool. A good half of the anglers succumbed to the theory that what had worked before could work again, so rubber worms were the single most popular choice. The rubber-worm devotees used an array of different sizes, hues, and even smells. Some went with seven-inch rubber worms while others favored five- or ten-inch. Some tried purple worms with white dots while others tried white with purple dots and still others tried pure white and pure black and every variation between including chartreuse, pink, turquoise, and fuchsia. Some used rubber worms with auger tails and others used flat tails. Some worms smelled like motor oil and some worms smelled like strawberries and some worms had no smell at all.

The others were divided by their devotion to live bait or artificial lures. Almost all the bait fishermen used night crawlers and red worms in the belief that if the fish had been fooled by an imitation, the actual live worm would work even better, but they also cast spring lizards, minnows, crickets, grubs, wasp larvae, crawfish, frogs, newts, toads, and even a live field mouse. The lure contingent favored spinners of the Panther Martin and Roostertail variety though they were not averse to Rapalas, Jitterbugs, Hula Poppers, Johnson Silver Minnows, Devilhorses, and a dozen other hook-laden pieces of wood or plastic. Some lures sank and bounced along the bottom and some lures floated and still others gurgled and rattled and some made no sound at all

and one lure even changed colors depending on depth and water temperature. Jarvis Hampton cast a Rapala F14 he'd once caught a tarpon with in
Florida. A subgroup of fly fishermen cast Muddler Minnows, Woolly Boogers,
Woolly Worms, Royal Coachmen, streamers and wet flies, nymphs and dry
flies, and some hurled nymphs and dry flies together that swung overhead
like miniature bolas.

During the first two days five brown trout, one speckled trout, one ball cap,
two smallmouth bass, ten knotty heads, a bluegill, and one old boot were
caught. A gray squirrel was snagged by an errant cast into a tree. Neither the
squirrel nor the various fish outweighed the boot, which weighed one pound
and eight ounces after the water was poured out. On the third day Wesley
McIntire's rod doubled and the drag whirred. A rainbow trout leaped in the
pool's center, Wesley's quarter-ounce Panther Martin spinner embedded in
its upper jaw. He fought the trout for five minutes before his brother Robbie
could net it. The rainbow was twenty-two inches long and weighed five and a
half pounds, big enough that Wesley took it straight to the taxidermist to be
mounted.

Charles Meekins came by an hour later. He didn't get out of the truck, just
rolled down his window and nodded. His radio played loudly and the atonal
guitars and screeching voices made Rudisell glad he was mostly deaf, because
hearing only part of the racket made him feel like stinging wasps swarmed
inside his head. Meekins didn't bother to turn the radio down, just shouted
over the music.

'I told you it was a trout.'

'That wasn't it,' Rudisell shouted. 'The fish I seen could of eaten that rainbow for breakfast.'

Meekins smiled, showing a set of bright white teeth that, unlike Rudisell's,
did not have to be deposited in a glass jar every night.

'Then why didn't it? That rainbow has probably been in that pool for years.'
Meekins shook his head. 'I wish you old boys would learn to admit when
you're wrong about something.'

Meekins rolled up his window as Rudisell pursed his lips and fired a stream
of tobacco juice directly at the warden's left eye. The tobacco hit the glass and
dribbled a dark, phlegmy rivulet down the window.

'A fellow such as that ought not be allowed a guvment uniform,' Creech said.

'Not unless it's got black and white stripes all up and down it,' Crenshaw
added.

After ten days no other fish of consequence had been caught and anglers
began giving up. The notebook was discarded because appointments were
no longer necessary. Meekins's belief gained credence, especially since in ten
days none of the hundred or so men and boys who'd gathered there had seen
the giant fish.

'I'd be hunkered down on the stream bottom too if such commotion was
going on around me,' Creech argued, but few remained to nod in agreement.
Even Harley Wease began to have doubts.

'Maybe that rainbow *was* what I had on,' he said heretically.

By the first week in May only the old men remained on the bridge. They kept
their vigil but the occupants of cars and trucks and tractors no longer paused

to ask about sightings. When the fish reappeared in the tailrace, the passing drivers ignored the old men's frantic waves to come see. They drove across the bridge with eyes fixed straight ahead, embarrassed by their elders' dementia.

'That's the best look we've gotten yet,' Campbell said when the fish moved out of the shallows and into deeper water. 'It's six feet long if it's a inch.'

Rudisell set his spyglass on the bridge railing and turned to Creech, the one among them who still had a car and driver's license.

'You got to drive me over to Jarvis Hampton's house,' Rudisell said.

'What for?' Creech asked.

'Because we're going to rent out that rod and reel he uses for them tarpon. Then we got to go by the library, because I want to know what this thing is when we catch it.'

Creech kept the speedometer at a steady thirty-five as they followed the river south to Jarvis Hampton's farm. They found Jarvis in his tobacco field and quickly negotiated a ten-dollar-a-week rental for the rod and reel, four 2/0 vanadium-steel fishhooks, and four sinkers. Jarvis offered a net as well but Rudisell claimed it wasn't big enough for what they were after. 'But I'll take a hay hook and a whetstone if you got it,' Rudisell added, 'and some bailing twine and a feed sack.'

They packed the fishing equipment in the trunk and drove to the county library, where they used Campbell's library card to check out an immense tome called *Freshwater Fish of North America*. The book was so heavy that only Creech had the strength to carry it, holding it before him with both hands as if it were made of stone. He dropped it in the backseat and, still breathing heavily, got behind the wheel and cranked the engine.

'We got one more stop,' Rudisell said, 'that old millpond on Spillcorn Creek.'

'You wanting to practice with that rod and reel?' Campbell asked.

'No, to get our bait,' Rudisell replied. 'I been thinking about something. After that fish hit Harley's rubber worm they was throwing night crawlers right and left into the pool figuring that fish thought Harley's lure was a worm. But what if it thought that rubber worm was something else, something we ain't seen one time since we been watching the pool though it used to be thick with them?'

Campbell understood first.

'I get what you're saying, but this is one bait I'd rather not be gathering myself, or putting on a hook for that matter.'

'Well, if you'll just hold the sack I'll do the rest.'

'What about baiting the hook?'

'I'll do that too.'

Since the day was warm and sunny, a number of reptiles had gathered on the stone slabs that had once been a dam. Most were blue-tailed skinks and fence lizards, but several mud-colored serpents coiled sullenly on the largest stones. Creech, who was deathly afraid of snakes, remained in the car. Campbell carried the burlap feed sack, reluctantly trailing Rudisell through broom sedge to the old dam.

'Them snakes ain't of the poisonous persuasion?' Campbell asked.

Rudisell turned and shook his head.

'Naw. Them's just your common water snake. Mean as the devil but they got no fangs.'

As they got close the skinks and lizards darted for crevices in the rocks, but the snakes did not move until Rudisell's shadow fell over them. Three slithered away before Rudisell's creaky back could bend enough for him to grab hold, but the fourth did not move until Rudisell's liver-spotted hand closed around its neck. The snake thrashed violently, its mouth biting at the air. Campbell reluctantly moved closer, his fingers and thumbs holding the sack open, arms extended out from his body as if attempting to catch some object falling from the sky. As soon as Rudisell dropped the serpent in, Campbell gave the snake and sack to Rudisell, who knotted the burlap and put it in the trunk.

'You figure one to be enough?' Campbell asked.

'Yes,' Rudisell replied. 'We'll get but one chance.'

The sun was beginning to settle over Balsam Mountain when the old men got back to the bridge. Rudisell led them down the path to the riverbank, the feed sack in his right hand, the hay hook and twine in his left. Campbell came next with the rod and reel and sinkers and hooks. Creech came last, the great book clutched to his chest. The trail became steep and narrow, the weave of leaf and limb overhead so thick it seemed they were entering a cave.

Once they got to the bank and caught their breath, they went to work. Creech used two of the last teeth left in his head to clamp three sinkers onto the line, then tied the hook to the monofilament with an expertly rendered hangman's knot. Campbell studied the book and found the section on fish living in southeastern rivers. He folded the page where the photographs of relevant species began and then marked the back section where corresponding printed information was located. Rudisell took out the whetstone and sharpened the metal with the same attentiveness as the long-ago warriors who once roamed these hills had honed their weapons, those bronze men who'd flaked dull stone to make their flesh-piercing arrowheads. Soon the steel tip shone like silver.

'All right, I done my part,' Creech said when he'd tested the drag. He eyed the writhing feed sack apprehensively. 'I ain't about to be close by when you try to get that snake on a hook.'

Creech moved over near the tailwaters as Campbell picked up the rod and reel. He settled the rod tip above Rudisell's head, the fishhook dangling inches from the older man's beaky nose. Rudisell unknotted the sack, then pinched the fishhook's eye between his left hand's index finger and thumb, used the right to slowly peel back the burlap. When the snake was exposed, Rudisell grabbed it by the neck, stuck the fishhook through the midsection, and quickly let go. The rod tip sagged with the snake's weight as Creech moved farther down the bank.

'What do I do now?' Campbell shouted, for the snake was swinging in an arc that brought the serpent ever closer to his body.

'Cast it,' Rudisell replied.

Campbell made a frantic sideways, two-handed heave that looked more like someone throwing a tub of dishwater off a back porch than a cast. The snake landed three feet from the bank, but luck was with them for it began swimming underwater toward the pool's center. Creech came back to stand by Campbell, but his eyes nervously watched the line. He flexed his arthritic right knee like a runner at the starting line, ready to flee up the bank if the snake took a mind to change direction. Rudisell gripped the hay hook's handle in his right hand. With his left he began wrapping bailing twine around metal and flesh. The wooden bridge floor rumbled like low thunder as a pickup crossed. A few seconds later another vehicle passed over the bridge. Rudisell continued wrapping the twine. He had no watch but suspected it was after five and men working in Sylva were starting to come home. When Rudisell had used up all the twine, Creech knotted it.

'With that hay hook tied to you it looks like you're the bait,' Creech joked.

'If I gaff that thing it's not going to get free of me,' Rudisell vowed.

The snake was past the deepest part of the pool now, making steady progress toward the far bank. It struggled to the surface briefly, the weight of the sinkers pulling it back down. The line remained motionless for a few moments, then began a slow movement back toward the heart of the pool.

'Why you figure it to turn around?' Campbell asked as Creech took a first step farther up the bank.

'I don't know,' Rudisell said. 'Why don't you tighten your line a bit.'

Campbell turned the handle twice and the monofilament grew taut and the rod tip bent. 'Damn snake's got hung up.'

'Give it a good jerk and it'll come free,' Creech said. 'Probably just tangled in some brush.'

Campbell yanked upward, and the rod bowed. The line began moving upstream, not fast but steady, the reel chattering as the monofilament stripped off.

'It's on,' Campbell said softly, as if afraid to startle the fish.

The line did not pause until it was thirty yards upstream and in the shadow of the bridge.

'You got to turn it,' Rudisell shouted, 'or it'll wrap that line around one of them pillars.'

'Turn it,' Campbell replied. 'I can't even slow it down.'

But the fish turned of its own volition, headed back into the deeper water. For fifteen minutes the creature sulked on the pool's bottom. Campbell kept the rod bowed, breathing hard as he strained against the immense weight on the other end. Finally, the fish began moving again, over to the far bank and then upstream. Campbell's arms trembled violently.

'My arms is give out,' he said and handed the rod to Creech. Campbell sprawled out on the bank, his chest heaving rapidly, limbs shaking as if palsied. The fish swam back into the pool's heart and another ten minutes passed. Rudisell looked up at the bridge. Cars and trucks continued to rumble across. Several vehicles paused a few moments but no faces appeared at the railing.

Creech tightened the drag and the rod bent double.

'Easy,' Rudisell said. 'You don't want him breaking off.'

'The way it's going, it'll kill us all before it gets tired,' Creech gasped.

The additional pressure worked. The fish moved again, this time allowing the line in its mouth to lead it into the tailrace. For the first time they saw the behemoth.

'Lord amercy,' Campbell exclaimed, for what they saw was over six feet long and enclosed in a brown suit of prehistoric armor, the immense tail curved like a scythe. When the fish saw the old men it surged away, the drag chattering again as the creature moved back into the deeper water.

Rudisell sat down beside the book and rapidly turned pages of color photos until he saw it.

'It's a sturgeon,' he shouted, then turned to where the printed information was and began to call out bursts of information. 'Can grow over seven feet long and three hundred pounds. That stuff that looks like armor is called scutes. They's even got a Latin name here. Says it was once in near every river, but now endangered. Can live a hundred and fifty years.'

'I ain't going to live another hundred and fifty seconds if I don't get some relief,' Creech said and handed the rod back to Campbell.

Campbell took over as Creech collapsed on the bank. The sturgeon began to give ground, the reel handle making slow, clockwise revolutions.

Rudisell closed the book and stepped into the shallows of the pool's tailrace. A sandbar formed a few yards out and that was what he moved toward, the hay hook raised like a metal question mark. Once he'd secured himself on the sandbar, Rudisell turned to Campbell.

'Lead him over here. There's no way we can lift him up the bank.'

'You gonna try to gill that thing?' Creech asked incredulously.

Rudisell shook his head.

'I ain't gonna gill it, I'm going to stab this hay hook in so deep it'll have to drag me back into that pool as well to get away.'

The reel handle turned quicker now, and soon the sturgeon came out of the depths, emerging like a submarine. Campbell moved farther down the bank, only three or four yards from the sandbar. Creech got up and stood beside Campbell. The fish swam straight toward them, face-first, as if led on a leash. They could see the head clearly now, the cone-shaped snout, barbels hanging beneath the snout like whiskers. As it came closer Rudisell creakily kneeled down on the sandbar's edge. As he swung the hay hook the sturgeon made a last surge toward deeper water. The bright metal raked across the scaly back but did not penetrate.

'Damn,' Rudisell swore.

'You got to beach it,' Creech shouted at Campbell, who began reeling again, not pausing until the immense head was half out of the water, snout touching the sandbar. The sturgeon's wide mouth opened, revealing an array of rusting hooks and lures that hung from the lips like medals.

'Gaff it now,' Creech shouted.

'Hurry,' Campbell huffed, the rod in his hands doubled like a bow. 'I'm herniating myself.'

But Rudisell appeared not to hear them. He stared intently at the fish, the hay hook held overhead as if it were a torch allowing him to see the sturgeon more clearly.

Rudisell's blue eyes brightened for a moment, and an enigmatic smile creased his face. The hay hook's sharpened point flashed, aimed not at the fish but at the monofilament. A loud twang like a broken guitar string sounded across the water. The rod whipped back and Campbell stumbled backward, but Creech caught him before he fell. The sturgeon was motionless for a few moments, then slowly curved back toward the pool's heart. As it disappeared, Rudisell remained kneeling on the sandbar, his eyes gazing into the pool. Campbell and Creech staggered over to the bank and sat down.

'They'll never believe us,' Creech said, 'not in a million years, especially that smart-ass game warden.'

'We had it good as caught,' Campbell muttered. 'We had it caught.'

None of them spoke further for a long while, all exhausted by the battle. But their silence had more to do with each man's reflection on what he had just witnessed than with weariness. A yellow mayfly rose like a watery spark in the tailrace, hung in the air a few moments before it fell and was swept away by the current. As time passed crickets announced their presence on the bank, and downriver a whippoorwill called. More mayflies rose in the tailrace. The air became chilly as the sheltering trees closed more tightly around them, absorbed the waning sun's light, a preamble to another overdue darkness.

'It's okay,' Campbell finally said.

Creech looked at Rudisell, who was still on the sandbar.

'You done the right thing. I didn't see that at first, but I see it now.'

Rudisell finally stood up, wiped the wet sand from the knees of his pants. As he stepped into the shallows he saw something in the water. He picked it up and put it in his pocket.

'Find you a fleck of gold?' Campbell asked.

'Better than gold,' Rudisell replied and joined his comrades on the bank.

They could hardly see their own feet as they walked up the path to the bridge. When they emerged, they found the green fish and wildlife truck parked at the trail end. The passenger window was down and Meekins's smug face looked out at them.

So you old boys haven't drowned after all. Folks saw the empty chairs and figured you'd fallen in.'

Meekins nodded at the fishing equipment in Campbell's hands and smiled.

'Have any luck catching your monster?'

'Caught it and let it go,' Campbell said.

'That's mighty convenient,' Meekins said. 'I don't suppose anyone else actually saw this giant fish, or that you have a photograph.'

'No,' Creech said serenely. 'But it's way bigger than you are.'

Meekins shook his head. He no longer smiled. 'Must be nice to have nothing better to do than make up stories, but this is getting old real quick.'

Rudisell stepped up to the truck's window, only inches away from Meekins's face when he raised his hand. A single diamond-shaped object was wedged between Rudisell's gnarled index finger and thumb. Though tinted brown, it appeared to be translucent. He held it eye level in front of Meekins's face as if it were a silty monocle they both might peer through.

'*Acipenser fulvescens*,'[1] Rudisell said, the Latin uttered slowly as if an incantation. He put the scute back in his pocket and, without further acknowledgment of Meekins's existence, stepped around the truck and onto the hardtop. Campbell followed with the fishing equipment and Creech came last with the book. It was a slow, dignified procession. They walked westward toward the store, the late-afternoon sun burnishing their cracked and wasted faces. Coming out of the shadows, they blinked their eyes as if dazzled, much in the manner of old-world saints who have witnessed the blinding brilliance of the one true vision.

2006

---

1. The scientific name for lake sturgeon.

AGNES ROSSI
b. 1959

The fourth of eight daughters in an Irish-Italian-American family, Rossi grew up in suburban New Jersey. She was an indifferent student in elementary and high school. "Agnes doesn't seem to like the reading lab or anything else," one teacher commented. Upon graduation, with only vague notions of becoming a writer, she moved out of the family home and into a series of decrepit apartments and waitressing jobs until, at the age of twenty-two, she enrolled in Rutgers University, where she began reading widely and passionately, setting herself the task of writing for two hours a day—a discipline Rossi has maintained in the midst of marriage and parenthood and through two story collections, *Athletes and Artists* (1987) and *The Quick* (1992), and three novels: *Split Skirt* (1995), *Fancy* (1999), and *The Houseguest* (2000).

Morpheus

Adrien is here with me now, down on one knee, folding laundry. She doesn't know I'm awake and her face is slack. She's not performing. I've noticed that she's started wearing my T-shirts, the oldest ones that have been washed so many times the cotton is thin, nearly transparent. "Sit me up," I tell her. "A., sit me up."

I mistook her for my mother yesterday. We couldn't get permission to have the IV[1] at home, so I'm taking my morphine orally. I put eight purple pills, thirty milligrams each, on my tray, not knowing if I'd take them all and then, of course, taking them all. Sometime later Adrien brought in a basin of water and a bar of Ivory.[2] I must have nodded out and when I woke up, she was washing the flats of my hands. You have had this done, we all have. When you were small you ate something sticky, watermelon or a Popsicle, and when you were finished, you were told to hold out your hands and somebody wiped at them, roughly, the wet napkin shredding as it rounded the skin between your fingers. "Enough, Ma," I said and tried to pull my hand away. Adrien grabbed my wrist and held on.

I'm a carpenter, a big man. Before I got sick, I could lift anything, move anything. Now I've got arms soft as a woman's. I'm not skinny the way cancer patients are supposed to be. In fact, I'm bloated from the steroids I forget why I'm taking.

---

1. Intravenous apparatus.   **2.** Soap.

This, believe it or not, isn't the most difficult period. Now, at least, we know who we are. I am the patient; Adrien is the nurse. The months after I was diagnosed but before I was so sick I had to stay in bed were the worst. People don't know about this time. We didn't. What happens is you're diagnosed in the hospital then sent home. You're an outpatient. You drive your car, have your same old arguments, meet other couples for dinner in Mexican restaurants. Except that in your most intimate and tender moments, neither of you knows what to say. The dividing line has been drawn. It's exhausting, keeping so much at bay. Bruised is how you feel. And you haven't gotten any morphine yet. Doctors and nurses encourage temperance in the terminally ill. You hurt all the time.

I came into the bedroom and found Adrien crying over a medical encyclopedia. She slammed it shut, looked up at me as if I'd caught her going through my wallet. I made her show me what she'd been looking at. Spread across two pages was a bar graph illustrating the five-year survival rates for various kinds of cancers. The column labeled "Metastatic Lung Cancer" was empty. I heaved the book in her direction, hoped to hit her, didn't, told her to get away from me, said I couldn't take any more of her fucking big-eyed sympathy. Her mouth quivered with rage. Her shout was throaty and raw. "I'd love to get away from you. That's what I want more than anything, to be away from you."

She said she needed something to relieve stress, to help her sleep at night. She started walking. It began reasonably enough, twenty minutes, a half hour, but soon she was doing ten and fifteen miles at a clip. She'd be gone all afternoon and into the evening. When she got home, she'd stand before me and announce: I just walked to Teaneck, to Paterson, to Ridgewood,[3] all towns miles and miles away. If she wasn't home by dark, I'd get in the car and go look for her. I rarely found her because she took crazy circuitous routes but when I did, she'd be striding along with her head down, fiddling with the dial on her Walkman.

We spent so much time at the hospital being sent all over hell. Here for a chest X-ray, there for blood work, someplace else to fill out insurance forms or pick up prescriptions. We'd separate in the interest of efficiency, meet later at whatever place was easiest for me. Something started happening. As soon as we'd spot each other, we'd start waving and we'd keep doing it, eyes locked, smiling or not, until we were together again.

It was Adrien who told me I had cancer. I'd just been brought back to my room. My doctor had left for a conference in L.A. right after the bronchoscopy.[4] He called from the airport. Adrien talked to him for not more than a minute, turned away from the phone, crossed her arms. Cells related to lung cancer. The tumor on my hip was secondary. The primary site was in my left bronchial tube.

She leaned over me and put four fingers on my cheek. I flattened myself against the mattress. She was coping already, monitoring my response so she could shape hers. As far as I was concerned, she had nothing to cope with. Her part was easy. Adrien as heroine was out of the question.

A nurse came in just then to take my temperature and I was glad. She had the spirited look of so many of the nurses at Memorial. They were forthright

---

3. Towns in suburban northern New Jersey.   **4.** Diagnostic procedure for examining the trachea and bronchial tubes.

and sensible, worked twelve-hour shifts. The ones who kept their nails nice, who wore bright things in their hair, were easy to love. I felt strangely content in the company of nurses, women to whom all I'd ever been was dying.

Adrien picked up on my response to the pretty young nurses and rallied when I flirted with them. If she walked in to find me passing the time with one—they talked to me about their boyfriends, about living in New York for the first time—Adrien would smile indulgently. Go on and flirt. The nurse fiddled with the computerized thermometer and Adrien backed out of the room, said she had to put money in her parking meter.

She doesn't know that I watched her walk across First Avenue. She stepped out from under the awning, headed off in one direction then stopped and looked the other way, not remembering, I knew, where she'd parked the car. She'd come right from work, wore a black and white blazer that gleamed in the sun. As far as I could tell, she wasn't crying, which surprised me. I'd assumed she'd run off to cry. She looked ordinary, maybe slightly dazed. If you knew the way she usually charged around, you'd notice a difference but to a stranger she probably looked like a secretary on lunch, maybe a secretary whose boss had snapped at her unfairly before she left the office. She squeezed her bottom lip and looked into the faces of people who passed her.

When she came back, her eyes were red. She'd found someplace to cry, a ladies' room most likely. Adrien is a great bathroom cryer. She'll stand in front of the mirror and look right into her own eyes. The sight of herself crying keeps her crying.

The last time I was hospitalized I got my first morphine. No more Tylenol or codeine. A shot in the IV, a rescue dose. It's nothing like novocaine. It didn't make me feel as if I no longer had a hip. The pain that had been the central fact of my existence for months backed the fuck off. It felt as if it were coming from inside layers of flannel. Winter pajamas warm from the dryer. Still with me but sound asleep.

A black woman in an aqua uniform brought me dinner. I found myself explaining to Adrien why it is people hate hospital food. What they give you is not that bad. It's just that eating in a hospital room is like having dinner in a public john. Urinals hooked to bed rails, gauze pads in the garbage cans, suction machines bubbling. I ate heartily while I talked, liking the dreamy feel of lukewarm food on my tongue, the sensation of my teeth meeting.

My uncle Jimmy came home from the war addicted to morphine. Once in a while he'd show up at our door and my mother would pull him inside. She'd go and see a woman she knew, somebody she'd worked with in the garment district. I'd sit on the front steps with Jimmy after he'd taken his shot. He'd talk about Normandy, about a soldier named Leonard. Sometimes it was Leonard who had saved Jimmy's life. Other times Jimmy had saved Leonard's. It was the same story to Jimmy. He thought he was telling one story. That's what morphine does, makes it not matter who saved whose life.

My father and my aunts would get furious with my mother for buying the dope. They'd lecture her about what was best for Jimmy and she wouldn't argue. She'd nod her head and avert her eyes and the next time Jimmy came around she'd put on her coat and go see her lady friend. Jimmy was my mother's youngest brother.

When Adrien and the woman from the hospice program were making arrangements to bring me home, renting the hospital bed, ordering oxygen, they had a big discussion about my pain medication. Adrien was told to keep a log, how much she gave me when, how I seemed, groggy, alert, how dilated were my pupils. The first afternoon at home, Adrien uncapped the bottle, said let's see now. Give those to me, I said. My pain, my morphine.

I watched Adrien dry off after her shower last night. Though she doesn't have time to walk these days, I can still see the effects. There's a sleek sort of oval between her hipbone and thigh. She ran her hand over it, liked it, turned sideways in the mirror to admire it.

She was never much good when I was sick before, minor ailments like the flu and once I broke my ankle. "So how do you feel? Better?" she'd ask. But my God has she risen to this challenge. Her touch tries so hard to soothe. When she washes my hair, she uses the lather as a lubricant to rub the cords in my neck. When she has to be gone for any period of time, when the hospice nurse or one of my sisters-in-law takes over, I get panicky missing her. She feels it too, I know, because when she comes in, she makes a beeline for me, adjusts my pillow, brushes the hair off my forehead, kisses me on the lips five or six times, fast kisses without much pucker.

This is a side of her I never knew existed. It makes me sorry we never had kids. Now I can imagine. Adrien rocking a baby, nursing one even.

She wasn't with me when a doctor told me to tell my family six months. I called her from a pay phone on Sixty-eighth Street, cried, said I wouldn't be home for a while. There's a bar upstate, a dive where middle-aged bikers hang out. I wanted to go there and drink and not talk. I thought I could stand to be there. "No," she said. "You have to come home. If I don't see you, I'll go crazy. Please, please come home." So I did. She was waiting outside when I got there. We drove eighty, ninety, a hundred miles an hour on the turnpike. No relief or release, no nothing for me.

We've never had so many visitors. They come to see me, of course. What's funny is that we handle company in precisely the way we always did. Adrien is ill at ease, much too nice, eager for them to gather their shit and go. I, on the other hand, am the perfect host. Friends and family pull their chairs close to my bed and lean in, smiling. They want to stay but then I nod out and Adrien scurries around lowering shades and most people get the hint.

I can still get a rise out of her. I asked her for a glass of carrot juice and she went right to work, chopping the carrots and feeding them to the juicer. I took a sip and told her it was full of pulp. "I strained it," she said. "Maybe so but I can't drink it like this." She looked at me for three seconds, whisked the glass away, strained it two more times, set it down in front of me. "It's still pulpy," I said. She grabbed the glass and dumped it in the sink. "You don't like carrot juice," she snapped, "so don't ever ask for it again. You can have orange or apple. Forget about carrot."

I waved at her. Hey, Adrien. Hey.

I don't know if she means to show off. Maybe it's just that I'm so sick and she's so healthy. She strides across the kitchen, carries three bags of groceries at once, sits down almost never. Adrien the superwoman, pass the morphine.

I'm restless at night. Adrien sleeps in a cot she borrowed and set up beside my bed. I wake her up a lot. "A.," I say, "A., are you awake?" "Mmmmmmmm," she'll say and roll over to face me, the outline of her hip fine and strong under the white sheet that looks blue in the moonlight. I slip pills into my mouth and talk, say whatever words work their way to the surface. She doesn't answer, looks right in my eyes. Then I let her fall back to sleep for a while, until I need to wake her up again, until I need to tell her Adrien, I'm scared.

1992

PHILIP ROTH
b. 1933

Roth was born in Newark, New Jersey, and was educated at Bucknell University and the University of Chicago. He attracted serious critical attention from the time his first stories began to appear in magazines, and his first book, *Goodbye, Columbus* (1959), a novella and collection of stories, won the National Book Award and established him as a major writer. For nearly fifty years since then, Roth's output has been astonishing in its range, intelligence, and sheer volume—more than twenty-five novels, memoirs, and story collections. Among the best known are his ribald, acidly comic *Portnoy's Complaint* (1969), his pseudo-confessional *Operation Shylock* (1993), and the hilarious *Sabbath's Theater* (1995), another National Book Award winner. Starting with *The Ghost Writer* (1979), Roth has written nine novels about his fictional alter-ego, Nathan Zuckerman; the most recent is *Exit Ghost* (2007). His recent novels include the Pulitzer Prize–winning *American Pastoral* (1997), *The Plot Against America* (2004), *Everyman* (2006), *Indignation* (2008), *The Humbling* (2009), and *Nemesis* (2010). In 2011 he received the Man Booker International Prize. Roth announced his retirement from writing fiction in 2013.

The Conversion of the Jews

You're a real one for opening your mouth in the first place," Itzie said. "What do you open your mouth all the time for?"

"I didn't bring it up, Itz, I didn't," Ozzie said.

"What do you care about Jesus Christ for anyway?"

"I didn't bring up Jesus Christ. He did. I didn't even know what he was talking about. Jesus is historical, he kept saying. Jesus is historical." Ozzie mimicked the monumental voice of Rabbi Binder.

"Jesus was a person that lived like you and me," Ozzie continued. "That's what Binder said—"

"Yeah? . . . So what! What do I give two cents whether he lived or not. And what do you gotta open your mouth!" Itzie Lieberman favored closed-mouthedness, especially when it came to Ozzie Freedman's questions. Mrs. Freedman had to see Rabbi Binder twice before about Ozzie's questions and this Wednesday at four-thirty would be the third time. Itzie preferred to keep *his* mother in the kitchen; he settled for behind-the-back subtleties such as gestures, faces, snarls and other less delicate barnyard noises.

"He was a real person, Jesus, but he wasn't like God, and we don't believe he is God." Slowly, Ozzie was explaining Rabbi Binder's position to Itzie, who had been absent from Hebrew School the previous afternoon.

"The Catholics," Itzie said helpfully, "they believe in Jesus Christ, that he's God." Itzie Lieberman used "the Catholics" in its broadest sense—to include the Protestants.

Ozzie received Itzie's remark with a tiny head bob, as though it were a footnote, and went on. "His mother was Mary, and his father probably was Joseph," Ozzie said. "But the New Testament says his real father was God."

"His *real* father?"

"Yeah," Ozzie said, "that's the big thing, his father's supposed to be God."

"Bull."

"That's what Rabbi Binder says, that it's impossible—"

"Sure it's impossible. That stuff's all bull. To have a baby you gotta get laid," Itzie theologized. "Mary hadda get laid."

"That's what Binder says: 'The only way a woman can have a baby is to have intercourse with a man.'"

"He said *that*, Ozz?" For a moment it appeared that Itzie had put the theological question aside. "He said that, intercourse?" A little curled smile shaped itself in the lower half of Itzie's face like a pink mustache. "What you guys do, Ozz, you laugh or something?"

"I raised my hand."

"Yeah? Whatja say?"

"That's when I asked the question."

Itzie's face lit up. "Whatja ask about—intercourse?"

"No, I asked the question about God, how if He could create the heaven and earth in six days, and make all the animals and the fish and the light in six days—the light especially, that's what always gets me, that He could make the light. Making fish and animals, that's pretty good—"

"That's damn good." Itzie's appreciation was honest but unimaginative: it was as though God had just pitched a one-hitter.

"But making light . . . I mean when you think about it, it's really something," Ozzie said. "Anyway, I asked Binder if He could make all that in six days, and He could *pick* the six days he wanted right out of nowhere, why couldn't He let a woman have a baby without having intercourse."

"You said intercourse, Ozz, to Binder?"

"Yeah."

"Right in class?"

"Yeah."

Itzie smacked the side of his head.

"I mean, no kidding around," Ozzie said, "that'd really be nothing. After all that other stuff, that'd practically be nothing."

Itzie considered a moment. "What'd Binder say?"

"He started all over again explaining how Jesus was historical and how he lived like you and me but he wasn't God. So I said I under*stood* that. What I wanted to know was different."

What Ozzie wanted to know was always different. The first time he had wanted to know how Rabbi Binder could call the Jews "The Chosen People" if the Declaration of Independence claimed all men to be created equal. Rabbi Binder tried to distinguish for him between political equality and spiritual legitimacy, but what Ozzie wanted to know, he insisted vehemently, was different. That was the first time his mother had to come.

Then there was the plane crash. Fifty-eight people had been killed in a plane crash at La Guardia.[1] In studying a casualty list in the newspaper his mother had discovered among the list of those dead eight Jewish names (his grandmother had nine but she counted Miller as a Jewish name); because of the eight she said the plane crash was "a tragedy." During free-discussion time on Wednesday Ozzie had brought to Rabbi Binder's attention this matter of "some of his relations" always picking out the Jewish names. Rabbi Binder had begun to explain cultural unity and some other things when Ozzie stood up at his seat and said that what he wanted to know was different. Rabbi Binder insisted that he sit down and it was then that Ozzie shouted that he wished all fifty-eight were Jews. That was the second time his mother came.

"And he kept explaining about Jesus being historical, and so I kept asking him. No kidding, Itz, he was trying to make me look stupid."

"So what he finally do?"

"Finally he starts screaming that I was deliberately simple-minded and a wise guy, and that my mother had to come, and this was the last time. And that I'd never get bar-mitzvahed[2] if he could help it. Then, Itz, then he starts talking in that voice like a statue, real slow and deep, and he says that I better think over what I said about the Lord. He told me to go to his office and think it over." Ozzie leaned his body towards Itzie. "Itz, I thought it over for a solid hour, and now I'm convinced God could do it."

Ozzie had planned to confess his latest transgression to his mother as soon as she came home from work. But it was a Friday night in November and already dark, and when Mrs. Freedman came through the door she tossed off her coat, kissed Ozzie quickly on the face, and went to the kitchen table to light the three yellow candles, two for the Sabbath and one for Ozzie's father.

When his mother lit the candles she would move her two arms slowly towards her, dragging them through the air, as though persuading people whose minds were half made up. And her eyes would get glassy with tears. Even when his father was alive Ozzie remembered that her eyes had gotten glassy, so it didn't have anything to do with his dying. It had something to do with lighting the candles.

As she touched the flaming match to the unlit wick of a Sabbath candle, the phone rang, and Ozzie, standing only a foot from it, plucked it off the receiver and held it muffled to his chest. When his mother lit candles Ozzie felt there should be no noise; even breathing, if you could manage it, should be softened. Ozzie pressed the phone to his breast and watched his mother dragging whatever she was dragging, and he felt his own eyes get glassy. His mother was a round, tired, gray-haired penguin of a woman whose gray skin had begun to feel the tug of gravity and the weight of her own history. Even when she was dressed up she didn't look like a chosen person. But when she lit candles she looked like something better; like a woman who knew momentarily that God could do anything.

---

1. Airport in New York City.   2. The bar mitzvah is the Jewish initiation ceremony performed on a boy's 13th birthday, recognizing his acceptance of religious responsibility and duties.

After a few mysterious minutes she was finished. Ozzie hung up the phone and walked to the kitchen table where she was beginning to lay the two places for the four-course Sabbath meal. He told her that she would have to see Rabbi Binder next Wednesday at four-thirty, and then he told her why. For the first time in their life together she hit Ozzie across the face with her hand.

All through the chopped liver and chicken soup part of the dinner Ozzie cried; he didn't have any appetite for the rest.

On Wednesday, in the largest of the three basement classrooms of the synagogue, Rabbi Marvin Binder, a tall, handsome, broad-shouldered man of thirty with thick strong-fibered black hair, removed his watch from his pocket and saw that it was four o'clock. At the rear of the room Yakov Blotnik, the seventy-one-year-old custodian, slowly polished the large window, mumbling to himself, unaware that it was four o'clock or six o'clock, Monday or Wednesday. To most of the students Yakov Blotnik's mumbling, along with his brown curly beard, scythe nose, and two heel-trailing black cats, made of him an object of wonder, a foreigner, a relic, towards whom they were alternately fearful and disrespectful. To Ozzie the mumbling had always seemed a monotonous, curious prayer; what made it curious was that old Blotnik had been mumbling so steadily for so many years, Ozzie suspected he had memorized the prayers and forgotten all about God.

"It is now free-discussion time," Rabbi Binder said. "Feel free to talk about any Jewish matter at all—religion, family, politics, sports—"

There was silence. It was a gusty, clouded November afternoon and it did not seem as though there ever was or could be a thing called baseball. So nobody this week said a word about that hero from the past, Hank Greenberg[3]—which limited free discussion considerably.

And the soul-battering Ozzie Freedman had just received from Rabbi Binder had imposed its limitation. When it was Ozzie's turn to read aloud from the Hebrew book the rabbi had asked him petulantly why he didn't read more rapidly. He was showing no progress. Ozzie said he could read faster but that if he did he was sure not to understand what he was reading. Nevertheless, at the rabbi's repeated suggestion Ozzie tried, and showed a great talent, but in the midst of a long passage he stopped short and said he didn't understand a word he was reading, and started in again at a drag-footed pace. Then came the soul-battering.

Consequently when free-discussion time rolled around none of the students felt too free. The rabbi's invitation was answered only by the mumbling of feeble old Blotnik.

"Isn't there anything at all you would like to discuss?" Rabbi Binder asked again, looking at his watch. "No questions or comments?"

There was a small grumble from the third row. The rabbi requested that Ozzie rise and give the rest of the class the advantage of his thought.

Ozzie rose. "I forget it now," he said, and sat down in his place.

Rabbi Binder advanced a seat towards Ozzie and poised himself on the edge of the desk. It was Itzie's desk and the rabbi's frame only a dagger's-length away from his face snapped him to sitting attention.

---

3. Jewish baseball star with the Detroit Tigers, 1933–41, 1945–46.

"Stand up again, Oscar," Rabbi Binder said calmly, "and try to assemble your thoughts."

Ozzie stood up. All his classmates turned in their seats and watched as he gave an unconvincing scratch to his forehead.

"I can't assemble any," he announced, and plunked himself down.

"Stand up!" Rabbi Binder advanced from Itzie's desk to the one directly in front of Ozzie; when the rabbinical back was turned Itzie gave it five-fingers off the tip of his nose, causing a small titter in the room. Rabbi Binder was too absorbed in squelching Ozzie's nonsense once and for all to bother with titters. "Stand up, Oscar. What's your question about?"

Ozzie pulled a word out of the air. It was the handiest word. "Religion."

"Oh, now you remember?"

"Yes."

"What is it?"

Trapped, Ozzie blurted the first thing that came to him. "Why can't He make anything He wants to make!"

As Rabbi Binder prepared an answer, a final answer, Itzie, ten feet behind him, raised one finger on his left hand, gestured it meaningfully towards the rabbi's back, and brought the house down.

Binder twisted quickly to see what had happened and in the midst of the commotion Ozzie shouted into the rabbi's back what he couldn't have shouted to his face. It was a loud, toneless sound that had the timbre of something stored inside for about six days.

"You don't know! You don't know anything about God!"

The rabbi spun back towards Ozzie. "What?"

"You don't know—you don't—"

"Apologize, Oscar, apologize!" It was a threat.

"You don't—"

Rabbi Binder's hand flicked out at Ozzie's cheek. Perhaps it had only been meant to clamp the boy's mouth shut, but Ozzie ducked and the palm caught him squarely on the nose.

The blood came in a short, red spurt on to Ozzie's shirt front.

The next moment was all confusion. Ozzie screamed, "You bastard, you bastard!" and broke for the classroom door. Rabbi Binder lurched a step backwards, as though his own blood had started flowing violently in the opposite direction, then gave a clumsy lurch forward and bolted out the door after Ozzie. The class followed after the rabbi's huge blue-suited back, and before old Blotnik could turn from his window, the room was empty and everyone was headed full speed up the three flights leading to the roof.

If one should compare the light of day to the life of man: sunrise to birth; sunset—the dropping down over the edge—to death; then as Ozzie Freedman wiggled through the trapdoor of the synagogue roof, his feet kicking backwards bronco-style at Rabbi Binder's outstretched arms—at that moment the day was fifty years old. As a rule, fifty or fifty-five reflects accurately the age of late afternoons in November, for it is in that month, during those hours, that one's awareness of light seems no longer a matter of seeing, but of hearing: light begins clicking away. In fact, as Ozzie locked shut the trapdoor in the rabbi's face, the sharp click of the bolt into the lock might momentarily have been mistaken for the sound of the heavier gray that had just throbbed through the sky.

With all his weight Ozzie kneeled on the locked door; any instant he was certain that Rabbi Binder's shoulder would fling it open, splintering the wood into shrapnel and catapulting his body into the sky. But the door did not move and below him he heard only the rumble of feet, first loud then dim, like thunder rolling away.

A question shot through his brain. "Can this be *me*?" For a thirteen-year-old who had just labeled his religious leader a bastard, twice, it was not an improper question. Louder and louder the question came to him—"Is it me? Is it me?"—until he discovered himself no longer kneeling, but racing crazily towards the edge of the roof, his eyes crying, his throat screaming, and his arms flying everywhichway as though not his own.

"Is it me? Is it me ME ME ME ME! It has to be me—but is it!"

It is the question a thief must ask himself the night he jimmies open his first window, and it is said to be the question with which bridegrooms quiz themselves before the altar.

In the few wild seconds it took Ozzie's body to propel him to the edge of the roof, his self-examination began to grow fuzzy. Gazing down at the street, he became confused as to the problem beneath the question: was it, is-it-me-who-called-Binder-a-bastard? or, is-it-me-prancing-around-on-the-roof? However, the scene below settled all, for there is an instant in any action when whether it is you or somebody else is academic. The thief crams the money in his pockets and scoots out the window. The bridegroom signs the hotel register for two. And the boy on the roof finds a streetful of people gaping at him, necks stretched backwards, faces up, as though he were the ceiling of the Hayden Planetarium.[4] Suddenly you know it's you.

"Oscar! Oscar Freedman!" A voice rose from the center of the crowd, a voice that, could it have been seen, would have looked like the writing on a scroll. "Oscar Freedman, get down from there. Immediately!" Rabbi Binder was pointing one arm stiffly up at him; and at the end of that arm, one finger aimed menacingly. It was the attitude of a dictator, but one—the eyes confessed all—whose personal valet had spit neatly in his face.

Ozzie didn't answer. Only for a blink's length did he look towards Rabbi Binder. Instead his eyes began to fit together the world beneath him, to sort out people from places, friends from enemies, participants from spectators. In little jagged starlike clusters his friends stood around Rabbi Binder, who was still pointing. The topmost point on a star compounded not of angels but of five adolescent boys with Itzie. What a world it was, with those stars below, Rabbi Binder below . . . Ozzie, who a moment earlier hadn't been able to control his own body, started to feel the meaning of the word control: he felt Peace and he felt Power.

"Oscar Freedman, I'll give you three to come down."

Few dictators give their subjects three to do anything; but, as always, Rabbi Binder only looked dictatorial.

"Are you ready, Oscar?"

---

4. Part of the American Museum of Natural History in New York City.

Ozzie nodded his head yes, although he had no intention in the world—the lower one or the celestial one he'd just entered—of coming down even if Rabbi Binder should give him a million.

"All right then," said Rabbi Binder. He ran a hand through his black Samson hair as though it were the gesture prescribed for uttering the first digit. Then, with his other hand cutting a circle out of the small piece of sky around him, he spoke. "One!"

There was no thunder. On the contrary, at that moment, as though "one" was the cue for which he had been waiting, the world's least thunderous person appeared on the synagogue steps. He did not so much come out the synagogue door as lean out, onto the darkening air. He clutched at the doorknob with one hand and looked up at the roof.

"Oy!"

Yakov Blotnik's old mind hobbled slowly, as if on crutches, and though he couldn't decide precisely what the boy was doing on the roof, he knew it wasn't good—that is, it wasn't-good-for-the-Jews. For Yakov Blotnik life had fractionated itself simply: things were either good-for-the-Jews or no-good-for-the-Jews.

He smacked his free hand to his in-sucked cheek, gently. "Oy, Gut!"[5] And then quickly as he was able, he jacked down his head and surveyed the street. There was Rabbi Binder (like a man at an auction with only three dollars in his pocket, he had just delivered a shaky "Two!"); there were the students, and that was all. So far it-wasn't-so-bad-for-the-Jews. But the boy had to come down immediately, before anybody saw. The problem: how to get the boy off the roof?

Anybody who has ever had a cat on the roof knows how to get him down. You call the fire department. Or first you call the operator and you ask her for the fire department. And the next thing there is great jamming of brakes and clanging of bells and shouting of instructions. And then the cat is off the roof. You do the same thing to get a boy off the roof.

That is, you do the same thing if you are Yakov Blotnik and you once had a cat on the roof.

When the engines, all four of them, arrived, Rabbi Binder had four times given Ozzie the count of three. The big hook-and-ladder swung around the corner and one of the firemen leaped from it, plunging headlong towards the yellow fire hydrant in front of the synagogue. With a huge wrench he began to unscrew the top nozzle. Rabbi Binder raced over to him and pulled at his shoulder.

"There's no fire . . ."

The fireman mumbled back over his shoulder and, heatedly, continued working at the nozzle.

"But there's no fire, there's no fire . . ." Binder shouted. When the fireman mumbled again, the rabbi grasped his face with both his hands and pointed it up at the roof.

To Ozzie it looked as though Rabbi Binder was trying to tug the fireman's head out of his body, like a cork from a bottle. He had to giggle at the picture they made: it was a family portrait—rabbi in black skullcap, fireman in red fire hat, and the little yellow hydrant squatting beside like a kid brother, bare-headed. From the edge of the roof Ozzie waved at the portrait, a one-handed, flapping, mocking wave; in doing it his right foot slipped from under him. Rabbi Binder covered his eyes with his hands.

Firemen work fast. Before Ozzie had even regained his balance, a big, round, yellowed net was being held on the synagogue lawn. The firemen who held it looked up at Ozzie with stern, feelingless faces.

One of the firemen turned his head towards Rabbi Binder. "What, is the kid nuts or something?"

Rabbi Binder unpeeled his hands from his eyes, slowly, painfully, as if they were tape. Then he checked: nothing on the sidewalk, no dents in the net.

"Is he gonna jump, or what?" the fireman shouted.

In a voice not at all like a statue, Rabbi Binder finally answered. "Yes, yes, I think so . . . He's been threatening to . . ."

Threatening to? Why, the reason he was on the roof, Ozzie remembered, was to get away; he hadn't even thought about jumping. He had just run to get away, and the truth was that he hadn't really headed for the roof as much as he'd been chased there.

"What's his name, the kid?"

"Freedman," Rabbi Binder answered. "Oscar Freedman."

The fireman looked up at Ozzie. "What is it with you, Oscar? You gonna jump, or what?"

Ozzie did not answer. Frankly, the question had just arisen.

"Look, Oscar, if you're gonna jump, jump—and if you're not gonna jump, don't jump. But don't waste our time, willya?"

Ozzie looked at the fireman and then at Rabbi Binder. He wanted to see Rabbi Binder cover his eyes one more time.

"I'm going to jump."

And then he scampered around the edge of the roof to the corner, where there was no net below, and he flapped his arms at his sides, swishing the air and smacking his palms to his trousers on the downbeat. He began scream-ing like some kind of engine, "Wheeeee . . . wheeeeee," and leaning way out over the edge with the upper half of his body. The firemen whipped around to cover the ground with the net. Rabbi Binder mumbled a few words to Some-body and covered his eyes. Everything happened quickly, jerkily, as in a silent movie. The crowd, which had arrived with the fire engines, gave out a long, Fourth-of-July fireworks oooh-aahhh. In the excitement no one had paid the crowd much heed, except, of course, Yakov Blotnik, who swung from the door-knob counting heads. "Fier und tsvantsik . . . finf und tsvantsik[6] . . . Oy, Gut!" It wasn't like this with the cat.

Rabbi Binder peeked through his fingers, checked the sidewalk and net. Empty. But there was Ozzie racing to the other corner. The firemen raced with him but were unable to keep up. Whenever Ozzie wanted to he might jump and splatter himself upon the sidewalk, and by the time the firemen scooted to the spot all they could do with their net would be to cover the mess.

"Wheeeee . . . wheeeee . . ."

"Hey, Oscar," the winded fireman yelled, "What the hell is this, a game or something?"

---

6. Twenty-four . . . twenty-five . . . (Yiddish).

"Wheeeee . . . wheeeee . . ."

"Hey, Oscar—"

But he was off now to the other corner, flapping his wings fiercely. Rabbi Binder couldn't take it any longer—the fire engines from nowhere, the screaming suicidal boy, the net. He fell to his knees, exhausted, and with his hands curled together in front of his chest, like a little dome, he pleaded, "Oscar, stop it, Oscar. Don't jump, Oscar. Please come down . . . Please don't jump."

And further back in the crowd a single voice, a single young voice, shouted a lone word to the boy on the roof.

"Jump!"

It was Itzie. Ozzie momentarily stopped flapping.

"Go ahead, Ozz—jump!"

Itzie broke off his point of the star and courageously, with the inspiration not of a wise-guy but of a disciple, stood alone. "Jump, Ozz, jump!"

Still on his knees, his hands still curled, Rabbi Binder twisted his body back. He looked at Itzie, then, agonizingly, back to Ozzie.

"OSCAR, DON'T JUMP! PLEASE, DON'T JUMP . . . please please . . ."

"Jump!" This time it wasn't Itzie but another point of the star. By the time Mrs. Freedman arrived to keep her four-thirty appointment with Rabbi Binder, the whole little upside down heaven was shouting and pleading for Ozzie to jump, and Rabbi Binder no longer was pleading with him not to jump, but was crying into the dome of his hands.

Understandably Mrs. Freedman couldn't figure out what her son was doing on the roof. So she asked.

"Ozzie, my Ozzie, what are you doing? My Ozzie, what is it?"

Ozzie stopped wheeeeeing and slowed his arms down to a cruising flap, the kind birds use in soft winds, but he did not answer. He stood against the low, clouded, darkening sky—light clicked down swiftly now, as on a small gear—flapping softly and gazing down at the small bundle of a woman who was his mother.

"What are you doing, Ozzie?" She turned towards the kneeling Rabbi Binder and rushed so close that only a paper-thickness of dusk lay between her stomach and his shoulders.

"What is my baby doing?"

Rabbi Binder gaped up at her but he too was mute. All that moved was the dome of his hands; it shook back and forth like a weak pulse.

"Rabbi, get him down! He'll kill himself. Get him down, my only baby . . ."

"I can't," Rabbi Binder said, "I can't . . ." and he turned his handsome head towards the crowd of boys behind him. "It's them. Listen to them."

And for the first time Mrs. Freedman saw the crowd of boys, and she heard what they were yelling.

"He's doing it for them. He won't listen to me. It's them." Rabbi Binder spoke like one in a trance.

"For them?"

"Yes."

"Why for them?"

"They want him to . . ."

Mrs. Freedman raised her two arms upward as though she were conducting the sky. "For them he's doing it!" And then in a gesture older than pyramids, older than prophets and floods, her arms came slapping down to her sides. "A martyr I have. Look!" She tilted her head to the roof. Ozzie was still flapping softly. "My martyr."

"Oscar, come down, *please*," Rabbi Binder groaned.

In a startlingly even voice Mrs. Freedman called to the boy on the roof. "Ozzie, come down, Ozzie. Don't be a martyr, my baby."

As though it were a litany, Rabbi Binder repeated her words. "Don't be a martyr, my baby. Don't be a martyr."

"Gawhead, Ozz—*be* a Martin!" It was Itzie. "Be a Martin, be a Martin," and all the voices joined in singing for Martindom, whatever *it* was. "Be a Martin, be a Martin . . ."

Somehow when you're on a roof the darker it gets the less you can hear. All Ozzie knew was that two groups wanted two new things: his friends were spirited and musical about what they wanted; his mother and the rabbi were even-toned, chanting, about what they didn't want. The rabbi's voice was without tears now and so was his mother's.

The big net stared up at Ozzie like a sightless eye. The big, clouded sky pushed down. From beneath it looked like a gray corrugated board. Suddenly, looking up into that unsympathetic sky, Ozzie realized all the strangeness of what these people, his friends, were asking: they wanted him to jump, to kill himself; they were singing about it now—it made them that happy. And there was an even greater strangeness: Rabbi Binder was on his knees, trembling. If there was a question to be asked now it was not "Is it me?" but rather "Is it us? . . . Is it us?"

Being on the roof, it turned out, was a serious thing. If he jumped would the singing become dancing? Would it? What would jumping stop? Yearningly, Ozzie wished he could rip open the sky, plunge his hands through, and pull out the sun; and on the sun, like a coin, would be stamped JUMP or DON'T JUMP.

Ozzie's knees rocked and sagged a little under him as though they were setting him for a dive. His arms tightened, stiffened, froze, from shoulders to fingernails. He felt as if each part of his body were going to vote as to whether he should kill himself or not—and each part as though it were independent of *him*.

The light took an unexpected click down and the new darkness, like a gag, hushed the friends singing for this and the mother and rabbi chanting for that.

Ozzie stopped counting votes, and in a curiously high voice, like one who wasn't prepared for speech, he spoke.

"Mamma?"

"Yes, Oscar."

"Mamma, get down on your knees, like Rabbi Binder."

"Oscar—"

"Get down on your knees," he said, "or I'll jump."

Ozzie heard a whimper, then a quick rustling, and when he looked down where his mother had stood he saw the top of a head and beneath that a circle of dress. She was kneeling beside Rabbi Binder.

He spoke again. "Everybody kneel." There was the sound of everybody kneeling.

Ozzie looked around. With one hand he pointed towards the synagogue entrance. "Make *him* kneel."

There was a noise, not of kneeling, but of body-and-cloth stretching. Ozzie could hear Rabbi Binder saying in a gruff whisper, "...or he'll *kill* himself," and when next he looked there was Yakov Blotnik off the doorknob and for the first time in his life upon his knees in the Gentile posture of prayer.

As for the firemen—it was not as difficult as one might imagine to hold a net taut while you are kneeling.

Ozzie looked around again; and then he called to Rabbi Binder.

"Rabbi?"

"Yes, Oscar."

"Rabbi Binder, do you believe in God?"

"Yes."

"Do you believe God can do Anything?" Ozzie leaned his head out into the darkness. "Anything?"

"Oscar, I think—"

"Tell me you believe God can do Anything."

There was a second's hesitation. Then: "God can do Anything."

"Tell me you believe God can make a child without intercourse."

"He can."

"Tell me!"

"God," Rabbi Binder admitted, "can make a child without intercourse."

"Mamma, you tell me."

"God can make a child without intercourse," his mother said.

"Make *him* tell me." There was no doubt who *him* was.

In a few moments Ozzie heard an old comical voice say something to the increasing darkness about God.

Next, Ozzie made everybody say it. And then he made them all say they believed in Jesus Christ—first one at a time, then all together.

When the catechizing was through it was the beginning of evening. From the street it sounded as if the boy on the roof might have sighed.

"Ozzie?" A woman's voice dared to speak. "You'll come down now?"

There was no answer, but the woman waited, and when a voice finally did speak it was thin and crying, and exhausted as that of an old man who has just finished pulling the bells.

"Mamma, don't you see—you shouldn't hit me. He shouldn't hit me. You shouldn't hit me about God, Mamma. You should never hit anybody about God—"

"Ozzie, please come down now."

"Promise me, promise me you'll never hit anybody about God."

He had asked only his mother, but for some reason everyone kneeling in the street promised he would never hit anybody about God.

Once again there was silence.

"I can come down now, Mamma," the boy on the roof finally said. He turned his head both ways as though checking the traffic lights. "Now I can come down ..."

And he did, right into the center of the yellow net that glowed in the evening's edge like an overgrown halo.

1959

GEORGE SAUNDERS
b. 1958

George Saunders was born in Amarillo, Texas, and raised on Chicago's south side. After graduating from the Colorado School of Mines with a degree in exploration geophysics, he worked as a geophysical engineer, a store clerk, a doorman, a roofer, a guitarist, and a slaughterhouse laborer before receiving his M.F.A. from Syracuse University, where he is now a professor of creative writing. Best known for his satirical short fiction, Saunders has published four short story collections: *CivilWarLand in Bad Decline* (1996), *Pastoralia* (2001), *In Persuasion Nation* (2006), and *Tenth of December* (2013), named one of the ten best books of the year by *The New York Times Book Review*. He has also written an illustrated fable, a bestselling children's book, a book of essays, and two screenplays. In 2002, Saunders was selected by *The New Yorker* as one of the 20 best writers under 40. Since then he has been awarded a Guggenheim Fellowship, a MacArthur Fellowship, and an Academy Award from the American Academy of Arts and Letters.

Victory Lap

Three days shy of her fifteenth birthday, Alison Pope paused at the top of the stairs.

Say the staircase was marble. Say she descended and all heads turned. Where was {special one}? Approaching now, bowing slightly, he exclaimed, How can so much grace be contained in one small package? Oops. Had he said *small package*? And just stood there? Broad princelike face totally bland of expression? Poor thing! Sorry, no way, down he went, he was definitely not {special one}.

What about this guy, behind Mr. Small Package, standing near the home entertainment center? With a thick neck of farmer integrity yet tender ample lips, who, placing one hand on the small of her back, whispered, Dreadfully sorry you had to endure that bit about the small package just now. Let us go stand on the moon. Or, uh, in the moon. In the moonlight.

Had he said, *Let us go stand on the moon*? If so, she would have to be like, {eyebrows up}. And if no wry acknowledgment was forthcoming, be like, Uh, I am not exactly dressed for standing on the moon, which, as I understand it, is super-cold?

Come on, guys, she couldn't keep treading gracefully on this marble stairwell in her mind forever! That dear old white-hair in the tiara was getting all like, *Why are those supposed princes making that darling girl march in place ad nausea?* Plus she had a recital tonight and had to go fetch her tights from the dryer.

Egads! One found oneself still standing at the top of the stairs.

Do the thing where, facing upstairs, hand on railing, you hop down the stairs one at a time, which was getting a lot harder lately, due to, someone's feet were getting longer every day, seemed like.

Pas de chat, pas de chat.

Changement, changement.[1]

Hop over thin metal thingie separating hallway tile from living-room rug.

Curtsy to self in entryway mirror.

Come on, Mom, get here. We do not wish to be castigated by Ms. Callow again in the wings.

Although actually she loved Ms. C. So strict! Also loved the other girls in class. And the girls from school. *Loved* them. Everyone was so nice. Plus the boys at her school. Plus the teachers at her school. All of them were doing their best. Actually, she loved her whole town. That adorable grocer, spraying his lettuce! Pastor Carol, with her large comfortable butt! The chubby postman, gesticulating with his padded envelopes! It had once been a mill town. Wasn't that crazy? What did that even mean?

Also she loved her house. Across the creek was the Russian church. So ethnic! That onion dome had loomed in her window since her Pooh footie days. Also loved Gladsong Drive. Every house on Gladsong was a Corona del Mar. That was amazing! If you had a friend on Gladsong, you already knew where everything was in his or her home.

Jeté, jeté, rond de jambe.

Pas de bourrée.[2]

On a happy whim, do front roll, hop to your feet, kiss the picture of Mom and Dad taken at Penney's back in the Stone Ages, when you were that little cutie right there {kiss} with a hair bow bigger than all outdoors.

Sometimes, feeling happy like this, she imagined a baby deer trembling in the woods.

Where's your mama, little guy?

I don't know, the deer said in the voice of Heather's little sister Becca.

Are you afraid? she asked it. Are you hungry? Do you want me to hold you?

Okay, the baby deer said.

Here came the hunter now, dragging the deer's mother by the antlers. Her guts were completely splayed. Jeez, that was nice! She covered the baby's eyes and was like, Don't you have anything better to do, dank hunter, than kill this baby's mom? You seem like a nice enough guy.

Is my mom killed? the baby said in Becca's voice.

No, no, she said. This gentleman was just leaving.

The hunter, captivated by her beauty, toffed or doffed his cap, and, going down on one knee, said, If I could will life back into this fawn. I would do so, in hopes you might defer one tender kiss upon our elderly forehead.

---

1. "Step of the cat" and "changing" (French). Dance steps in ballet. **2.** "Jump" and "stuffing step" (French). More ballet steps.

Go, she said. Only, for your task of penance, do not eat her. Lay her out in a field of clover, with roses strewn about her. And bestow a choir, to softly sing of her foul end.

Lay who out? the baby deer said.

No one, she said. Never mind. Stop asking so many questions.

Pas de chat, pas de chat.

Changement, changement.

She felt hopeful that {special one} would hail from far away. The local boys possessed a certain *je ne sais quoi*, which, tell the truth, she was not *très* crazy about, such as: actually named their own nuts. She had overheard that! And aspired to work for CountyPower because the work shirts were awesome and you got them free.

So ixnay on the local boys. A special ixnay on Matt Drey, owner of the largest mouth in the land. Kissing him last night at the pep rally had been like kissing an underpass. Scary! Kissing Matt was like suddenly this cow in a sweater is bearing down on you, who will not take no for an answer, and his huge cow head is being flooded by chemicals that are drowning out what little powers of reason Matt actually did have.

What she liked was being in charge of her. Her body, her mind. Her thoughts, her career, her future.

That was what she liked.

So be it.

We might have a slight snack.

Un petit repas.[3]

Was she special? Did she consider herself special? Oh, gosh, she didn't know. In the history of the world, many had been more special than her. Helen Keller had been awesome; Mother Teresa was amazing; Mrs. Roosevelt was quite chipper in spite of her husband, who was handicapped, which, in addition, she had been gay, with those big old teeth, long before such time as being gay and First Lady was even conceptual. She, Alison, could not hope to compete in the category of those ladies. Not yet, anyway!

There was so much she didn't know! Like how to change the oil. Or even check the oil. How to open the hood. How to bake brownies. That was embarrassing, actually, being a girl and all. And what was a mortgage? Did it come with the house? When you breast-fed, did you have to like push the milk out?

Egads. Who was this wan figure, visible through the living-room window, trotting up Gladsong Drive? Kyle Boot, palest kid in all the land? Still dressed in his weird cross-country toggles?

Poor thing. He looked like a skeleton with a mullet. Were those cross-country shorts from the like *Charlie's Angels* days or *quoi*? How could he run so well when he seemed to have literally no muscles? Every day he ran home like this, shirtless with his backpack on, then hit the remote from down by the Fungs' and scooted into his garage without breaking stride.

You almost had to admire the poor goof.

They'd grown up together, been little beaners in that mutual sandbox down by the creek. Hadn't they bathed together when wee or some such crud? She hoped that never got out. Because in terms of friends, Kyle was basically

---

3. A little meal (French).

down to Feddy Slavko, who walked leaning way backward and was always retrieving things from between his teeth, announcing the name of the retrieved thing in Greek, then re-eating it. Kyle's mom and dad didn't let him do squat. He had to call home if the movie in World Culture might show bare boobs. Each of the items in his lunch box was clearly labeled.

Pas de bourrée.

And curtsy.

Pour quantity of Cheez Doodles into compartmentalized old-school Tupperware dealie.

Thanks, Mom, thanks, Dad. Your kitchen *rocks.*

Shake Tupperware dealie back and forth like panning for gold, then offer to some imaginary poor gathered round.

Please enjoy. Is there anything else I can do for you folks?

You have already done enough, Alison, by even deigning to speak to us.

That is so not true! Don't you understand, all people deserve respect? Each of us is a rainbow.

Uh, really? Look at this big open sore on my poor shriveled flank.

Allow me to fetch you some Vaseline.

That would be much appreciated. This thing kills.

But as far as that rainbow idea? She believed that. People were amazing. Mom was awesome, Dad was awesome, her teachers worked so hard and had kids of their own, and some were even getting divorced, such as Mrs. Dees, but still always took time for their students. What she found especially inspiring about Mrs. Dees was that, even though Mr. Dees was cheating on Mrs. Dees with the lady who ran the bowling alley, Mrs. Dees was still teaching the best course ever in Ethics, posing such questions as: Can goodness win? Or do good people always get shafted, evil being more reckless? That last bit seemed to be Mrs. Dees taking a shot at the bowling-alley gal. But seriously! Is life fun or scary? Are people good or bad? On the one hand, that clip of those gauntish pale bodies being steamrolled while fat German ladies looked on chomping gum. On the other hand, sometimes rural folks, even if their particular farms were on hills, stayed up late filling sandbags.

In their straw poll she had voted for people being good and life being fun, with Mrs. Dees giving her a pitying glance as she stated her views: To do good, you just have to decide to do good. You have to be brave. You have to stand up for what's right. At that last, Mrs. Dees had made this kind of groan. Which was fine. Mrs. Dees had a lot of pain in her life, yet, interestingly? Still obviously found something fun about life and good about people, because otherwise why sometimes stay up so late grading you come in next day all exhausted, blouse on backward, having messed it up in the early-morning dark, you dear discombobulated thing?

Here came a knock on the door. Back door. In-ter-est-ing. Who could it be? Father Dmitri from across the way? UPS? FedEx? With *un petit* check *pour Papa?*

Jeté, jeté, rond de jambe.

Pas de bourrée.

Open door, and—

Here was a man she did not know. Quite huge fellow, in one of those meter-reader vests.

Something told her to step back in, slam the door. But that seemed rude.

Instead she froze, smiled, did {eyebrow raise} to indicate: May I help you?

Kyle Boot dashed through the garage, into the living area, where the big clocklike wooden indicator was set at All Out. Other choices included: Mom & Dad Out; Mom Out; Dad Out; Kyle Out; Mom & Kyle Out; Dad & Kyle Out; and All In.

Why did they even need All In? Wouldn't they know it when they were All In? Would he like to ask Dad that? Who, in his excellent totally silent downstairs woodshop, had designed and built the Family Status Indicator?

Ha.

Ha ha.

On the kitchen island was a Work Notice.

> *Scout: New geode on deck. Place in yard per included drawing. No goofing. Rake areas first, put down plastic as I have shown you. Then lay in white rock. THIS GEODE EXPENSIVE. Pls take seriously. No reason this should not be done by time I get home. This = five (5) Work Points.*

Gar, Dad, do you honestly feel it fair that I should have to slave in the yard until dark after a rigorous cross-country practice that included sixteen 440s, eight 880s, a mile-for-time, a kajillion Drake sprints, and a five-mile Indian relay?

Shoes off, mister.

Yoinks, too late. He was already at the TV. And had left an incriminating trail of microclods. Way verboten.[4] Could the microclods be hand-plucked? Although, problem: if he went back to hand-pluck the microclods, he'd leave an incriminating new trail of microclods.

He took off his shoes and stood mentally rehearsing a little show he liked to call WHAT IF . . . RIGHT NOW?

WHAT IF they came home RIGHT NOW?

It's a funny story, Dad! I came in thoughtlessly! Then realized what I'd done! I guess, when I think about it, what I'm happy about? Is how quickly I self-corrected! The reason I came in so thoughtlessly was, I wanted to get right to work, Dad, per your note!

He raced in his socks to the garage, threw his shoes into the garage, ran for the vacuum, vacuumed up the microclods, then realized, holy golly, he had thrown his shoes into the garage rather than placing them on the Shoe Sheet as required, toes facing away from the door for ease of donnage later.

He stepped into the garage, placed his shoes on the Shoe Sheet, stepped back inside.

Scout, Dad said in his head, has anyone ever told you that even the most neatly maintained garage is going to have some oil on its floor, which is now on your socks, being tracked all over the tan Berber?

Oh gar, his ass was grass.

But no—*celebrate good times, come on*—no oil stain on rug.

He tore off his socks. It was absolutely verboten for him to be in the main living area barefoot. Mom and Dad coming home to find him Tarzaning around like some sort of white trasher would not be the least fucking bit—

---

4. Forbidden (German).

Swearing in your head? Dad said in his head. Step up, Scout, be a man. If you want to swear, swear aloud.

I don't want to swear aloud.

Then don't swear in your head.

Mom and Dad would be heartsick if they could hear the swearing he sometimes did in his head, such as crap-cunt shit-turd dick-in-the-ear butt-creamery. Why couldn't he stop doing that? They thought so highly of him, sending weekly braggy emails to both sets of grandparents, such as: Kyle's been superbusy keeping up his grades while running varsity cross-country though still a sophomore, while setting aside a little time each day to manufacture such humdingers as cunt-swoggle rear-fuck—

What was wrong with him? Why couldn't he be grateful for all that Mom and Dad did for him, instead of—

Cornhole the ear-cunt.

Flake-fuck the pale vestige with a proddering dick-knee.

You could always clear the mind with a hard pinch on your own minimal love handle.

Ouch.

Hey, today was Tuesday, a Major Treat day. The five (5) new Work Points for placing the geode, plus his existing two (2) Work Points, totaled seven (7) Work Points, which, added to his eight (8) accrued Usual Chore Points, made fifteen (15) Total Treat Points, which could garner him a Major Treat (for example, two handfuls of yogurt-covered raisins) plus twenty free-choice TV minutes, although the particular show would have to be negotiated with Dad at time of cash-in.

One thing you will not be watching, Scout, is *America's Most Outspoken Dirt Bikers.*

Whatever.

Whatever, Dad.

Really, Scout? "Whatever"? Will it be "whatever" when I take away all your Treat Points and force you to quit cross-country, as I have several times threatened to do if a little more cheerful obedience wasn't forthcoming?

No, no, no. I don't want to quit, Dad. Please. I'm good at it. You'll see, first meet. Even Matt Drey said—

Who is Matt Drey? Some ape on the football team?

Yes.

Is his word law?

No.

What did he say?

Little shit can run.

Nice talk, Scout. Ape talk. Anyway, you may not make it to the first meet. Your ego seems to be overflowing its banks. And why? Because you can jog? Anyone can jog. Beasts of the field can jog.

I'm not quitting! Anal-cock shit-bird rectum-fritz! Please, I'm begging you, it's the only thing I'm decent at! Mom, if he makes me quit I swear to God I'll—

Drama doesn't suit you, Beloved Only.

If you want the privilege of competing in a team sport, Scout, show us that you can live within our perfectly reasonable system of directives designed to benefit you.

Hello.

A van had just pulled up in the St. Mikhail's parking lot.

Kyle walked in a controlled, gentlemanly manner to the kitchen counter. On the counter was Kyle's Traffic Log, which served the dual purpose of (1) buttressing Dad's argument that Father Dmitri should build a soundproof retaining wall and (2) constituting a data set for a possible Science Fair project for him, Kyle, entitled, by Dad, "Correlation of Church Parking Lot Volume vs. Day of Week, with Ancillary Investigation of Sunday Volume Throughout Year."

Smiling agreeably as if he enjoyed filling out the Log, Kyle very legibly filled out the Log:

Vehicle: VAN.
Color: GRAY.
Make: CHEVY.
Year: UNKNOWN.

A guy got out of the van. One of the usual Rooskies. "Rooskie" was an allowed slang. Also "dang it." Also "holy golly." Also "crapper." The Rooskie was wearing a jean jacket over a hoodie, which, in Kyle's experience, was not unusual church-wear for the Rooskies, who sometimes came directly over from Jiffy Lube still wearing coveralls.

Under "Vehicle Driver" he wrote, PROBABLE PARISHIONER.

That sucked. Stank, rather. The guy being a stranger, he, Kyle, now had to stay inside until the stranger left the neighborhood. Which totally futzed up his geode placing. He'd be out there until midnight. What a detriment!

The guy put on a Day Glo-vest. Ah, dude was a meter reader.

The meter reader looked left, then right, leaped across the creek, entered the Pope backyard, passed between the soccer-ball rebounder and the in-ground pool, then knocked on the Pope door.

Good leap there, Boris.

The door swung open.

Alison.

Kyle's heart was singing. He'd always thought that was just a phrase. Alison was like a national treasure. In the dictionary under "beauty" there should be a picture of her in that jean skort. Although lately she didn't seem to like him all that much.

Now she stepped across her deck so the meter reader could show her something. Something electrical wrong on the roof? The guy seemed eager to show her. Actually, he had her by the wrist. And was like tugging.

That was weird. Wasn't it? Something had never been weird around here before. So probably it was fine. Probably the guy was just a really new meter reader?

Somehow Kyle felt like stepping out onto the deck. He stepped out. The guy froze. Alison's eyes were scared-horse eyes. The guy cleared his throat, turned slightly to let Kyle see something.

A knife.

The meter reader had a knife.

Here's what you're doing, the guy said. Standing right there until we leave. Move a muscle, I knife her in the heart. Swear to God. Got it?

Kyle's mouth was so spitless all he could do was make his mouth do the shape it normally did when saying Yes.

Now they were crossing the yard. Alison threw herself to the ground. The guy hauled her up. She threw herself down. He hauled her up. It was odd seeing Alison tossed like a rag doll in the sanctuary of the perfect yard her dad had made for her. She threw herself down.

The guy hissed something and she rose, suddenly docile.

In his chest Kyle felt the many directives, Major and Minor, he was right now violating. He was on the deck shoeless, on the deck shirtless, was outside when a stranger was near, had engaged with that stranger.

Last week Sean Ball had brought a wig to school to more effectively mimic the way Bev Mirren chewed her hair when nervous. Kyle had briefly considered intervening. At Evening Meeting, Mom had said that she considered Kyle's decision not to intervene judicious. Dad had said, That was none of your business. You could have been badly hurt. Mom had said, Think of all the resources we've invested in you, Beloved Only. Dad had said, I know we sometimes strike you as strict but you are literally all we have.

They were at the soccer-ball rebounder now, Alison's arm up behind her back. She was making a low repetitive sound of denial, like she was trying to invent a noise that would adequately communicate her feelings about what she'd just this instant realized was going to happen to her.

He was just a kid. There was nothing he could do. In his chest he felt the lush release of pressure that always resulted when he submitted to a directive. There at his feet was the geode. He should just look at that until they left. It was a great one. Maybe the greatest one ever. The crystals at the cutaway glistened in the sun. It would look nice in the yard. Once he placed it. He'd place it once they were gone. Dad would be impressed that even after what had occurred he'd remembered to place the geode.

That's the ticket, Scout.

We are well pleased, Beloved Only.

Super job, Scout.

Holy crap. It was happening. She was marching along all meek like the trouper he'd known she'd be. He'd had her in mind since the baptism of what's-his-name. Sergei's kid. At the Russian church. She'd been standing in her yard, her dad or some such taking her picture.

He'd been like, Hello, Betty.

Kenny had been like, Little young, bro.

He'd been like, For you, grandpa.

When you studied history, the history of cultures, you saw your own individual time as hidebound. There were various theories of acquiescence. In Bible days a king might ride through a field and go: That one. And she would be brought unto him. And they would duly be betrothed and if she gave birth unto a son, super, bring out the streamers, she was a keeper. Was she, that first night, digging it? Probably not. Was she shaking like a leaf? Didn't matter. What mattered was offspring and the furtherance of the lineage. Plus the exaltation of the king, which resulted in righteous kingly power.

Here was the creek.

He marched her through.

The following bullet points remained in the decision matrix: take to side van door, shove in, follow in, tape wrists/mouth, hook to chain, make speech. He had the speech down cold. Had practiced it both in his head and on the recorder: *Calm your heart, darling, I know you're scared because you don't know me yet and didn't expect this today but give me a chance and you will see we will fly high. See I am putting the knife right over here and I don't expect I'll have to use it, right?*

If she wouldn't get in the van, punch hard in gut. Then pick up, carry to side van door, throw in, tape wrists/mouth, hook to chain, make speech, etc., etc.

Stop, pause, he said.

Gal stopped.

Fucksake. Side door of the van was locked. How undisciplined was that. Ensuring that the door was unlocked was clearly indicated on the pre-mission matrix. Melvin appeared in his mind. On Melvin's face was the look of hot disappointment that had always preceded an ass whooping, which had always preceded the other thing. Put up your hands, Melvin said, defend yourself.

True, true. Little error there. Should have double-checked the pre-mission matrix.

No biggie.

Joy not fear.

Melvin was dead fifteen years. Mom dead twelve.

Little bitch was turned around now, looking back at the house. That will-fulness wouldn't stand. That was going to get nipped in the bud. He'd have to remember to hurt her early, establish a baseline.

Turn the fuck around, he said.

She turned around.

He unlocked the door, swung it open. Moment of truth. If she got in, let him use the tape, they were home free. He'd picked out a place in Sackett, big-ass cornfield, dirt road leading in. If fuckwise it went good they'd pick up the freeway from there. Basically steal the van. It was Kenny's van. He'd borrowed it for the day. Screw Kenny. Kenny had once called him stupid. Too bad, Kenny, that remark just cost you one van. If fuckwise it went bad, she didn't properly arouse him, he'd abort the activity, truncate the subject, heave the thing out, clean van as necessary, go buy corn, return van to Kenny, say, Hey, bro, here's a shitload of corn, thanks for the van, I never could've bought a suitable quantity of corn in my car. Then lay low, watch the papers like he'd done with the nonarousing redhead out in—

Gal gave him an imploring look, like, Please don't.

Was this a good time? To give her one in the gut, knock the wind out of her sails?

It was.

He did.

The geode was beautiful. What a beautiful geode. What made it beautiful? What were the principal characteristics of a beautiful geode? Come on, think. Come on, concentrate.

She'll recover in time, Beloved Only.

None of our affair, Scout.

We're amazed by your good judgment, Beloved Only.

Dimly he noted that Alison had been punched. Eyes on the geode, he heard the little *oof*.

His heart dropped at the thought of what he was letting happen. They'd used goldfish snacks as coins. They'd made bridges out of rocks. Down by the creek. Back in the day. Oh God. He should've never stepped outside. Once they were gone he'd just go back inside, pretend he'd never stepped out, make the model-railroad town, still be making it when Mom and Dad got home. When eventually someone told him about it? He'd make a certain face. Already on his face he could feel the face he would make, like, What? Alison? Raped? Killed? Oh God. Raped and killed while I innocently made my railroad town, sitting cross-legged and unaware on the floor like a tiny little—

No. No, no, no. They'd be gone soon. Then he could go inside. Call 911. Although then everyone would know he'd done nothing. All his future life would be bad. Forever he'd be the guy who'd done nothing. Besides, calling wouldn't do any good. They'd be long gone. The parkway was just across Featherstone, with like a million arteries and cloverleafs or whatever spouting out of it. So that was that. In he'd go. As soon as they left. Leave, leave, leave, he thought, so I can go inside, forget this ever—

Then he was running. Across the lawn. Oh God! What was he doing, what was he doing? Jesus, shit, the directives he was violating! Running in the yard (bad for the sod); transporting a geode without its protective wrapping; hopping the fence, which stressed the fence, which had cost a pretty penny; leaving the yard; leaving the yard barefoot; entering the Secondary Area without permission; entering the creek barefoot (broken glass, dangerous microorganisms), and, not only that, oh God, suddenly he saw what this giddy part of himself intended, which was to violate a directive so Major and absolute that it wasn't even a directive, since you didn't need a directive to know how totally verboten it was to—

He burst out of the creek, the guy still not turning, and let the geode fly into his head, which seemed to emit a weird edge-seep of blood even before the skull visibly indented and the guy sat right on his ass.

Yes! Score! It was fun! Fun dominating a grown-up! Fun using the most dazzling gazelle-like leg speed ever seen in the history of mankind to dash soundlessly across space and master this huge galoot, who otherwise, right now, would be—

What if he hadn't?

God, what if he hadn't?

He imagined the guy bending Alison in two like a pale garment bag while pulling her hair and thrusting bluntly, as he, Kyle, sat cowed and obedient, tiny railroad viaduct grasped in his pathetic babyish—

Jesus! He skipped over and hurled the geode through the windshield of the van, which imploded, producing an inward rain of glass shards that made the sound of thousands of tiny bamboo wind chimes.

He scrambled up the hood of the van, retrieved the geode.

Really? Really? You were going to ruin her life, ruin my life, you cunt-probe dick-munch ass-gashing Animal? Who's bossing who now? Gash-ass, jizz-lips, turd-munch—

He'd never felt so strong/angry/wild. Who's the man? Who's your daddy? What else must he do? To ensure that Animal did no further harm? You still moving, freak? Got a plan, stroke-dick? Want a skull gash on top of your existing skull gash, big man? You think I won't? You think I—

Easy, Scout, you're out of control.

Slow your motor down, Beloved Only.

Quiet. I'm the boss of me.

FUCK!

What the hell? What was he doing on the ground? Had he tripped? Did someone wonk him? Did a branch fall? God damn. He touched his head. His hand came away bloody.

The beanpole kid was bending. To pick something up. A rock. Why was that kid off the porch? Where was the knife?

Where was the gal?

Crab-crawling toward the creek.

Flying across her yard.

Going into her house.

Fuck it, everything was fucked. Better hit the road. With what, his good looks? He had like eight bucks total.

Ah Christ! The kid had smashed the windshield! With the rock! Kenny was not going to like that one bit.

He tried to stand but couldn't. The blood was just pouring out. He was not going to jail again. No way. He'd slit his wrists. Where was the knife? He'd stab himself in the chest. That had nobility. Then the people would know his name. Which of them had the balls to samurai themselves with a knife in the chest?

None.

Nobody.

Go ahead, pussy. Do it.

No. The king does not take his own life. The superior man silently accepts the mindless rebuke of the rabble. Waits to rise and fight anew. Plus he had no idea where the knife was. Well, he didn't need it. He'd crawl into the woods, kill something with his bare hands. Or make a trap from some grass. Ugh. Was he going to barf? There, he had. Right on his lap.

Figures you'd blow the simplest thing, Melvin said.

Melvin, God, can't you see my head is bleeding so bad?

A kid did it to you. You're a joke. You got fucked by a kid.

Oh, sirens, perfect.

Well, it was a sad day for the cops. He'd fight them hand to hand. He'd sit until the last moment, watching them draw near, doing a silent death mantra that would centralize all his life power in his fists.

He sat thinking about his fists. They were huge granite boulders. They were a pit bull each. He tried to get up. Somehow his legs weren't working. He hoped the cops would get here soon. His head really hurt. When he touched up there, things moved. It was like he was wearing a gore cap. He was going to need a bunch of stitches. He hoped it wouldn't hurt too much. Probably it would, though.

Where was that beanpole kid?

Oh, here he was.

Looming over him, blocking out the sun, rock held high, yelling something, but he couldn't tell what, because of the ringing in his ears.

Then he saw that the kid was going to bring the rock down. He closed his eyes and waited and was not at peace at all but instead felt the beginnings of a terrible dread welling up inside him, and if that dread kept growing at the current rate, he realized in a flash of insight, there was a name for the place he would be then, and it was Hell.

Alison stood at the kitchen window. She'd peed herself. Which was fine. People did that. When super-scared. She'd noticed it while making the call. Her hands had been shaking so bad. They still were. One leg was doing that Thumper thing. God, the stuff he'd said to her. He'd punched her. He'd pinched her. There was a big blue mark on her arm. How could Kyle still be out there? But there he was, in those comical shorts, so confident he was goofing around, hands clenched over his head like a boxer from some cute alt universe where a kid that skinny could actually win a fight against a guy with a knife.

Wait.

His hands weren't clenched. He was holding the rock, shouting something down at the guy, who was on his knees, like the blindfolded prisoner in that video they'd seen in History, about to get sword-killed by a formal dude in a helmet.

Kyle, don't, she whispered.

For months afterward she had nightmares in which Kyle brought the rock down. She was on the deck trying to scream his name but nothing was coming out. Down came the rock. Then the guy had no head. The blow just literally dissolved his head. Then his body tumped over and Kyle turned to her with this heartbroken look of, My life is over. I killed a guy.

Why was it, she sometimes wondered, that in dreams we can't do the simplest things? Like a crying puppy is standing on some broken glass and you want to pick it up and brush the shards off its pads but you can't because you're balancing a ball on your head. Or you're driving and there's this old guy on crutches, and you go, to Mr. Feder, your Driver's Ed teacher, Should I swerve? And he's like, Uh, probably. But then you hear this big clunk and Feder makes a negative mark in his book.

Sometimes she'd wake up crying from the dream about Kyle. The last time, Mom and Dad were already there, going, That's not how it was. Remember, Allie? How did it happen? Say it. Say it out loud. Allie, can you tell Mommy and Daddy how it really happened?

I ran outside, she said. I shouted.

That's right, Dad said. You shouted. Shouted like a champ.

And what did Kyle do? Mom said.

Put down the rock, she said.

A bad thing happened to you kids, Dad said. But it could have been worse.

So much worse, Mom said.

But because of you kids, Dad said, it wasn't.

You did so good, Mom said.

Did beautiful, Dad said.

2009

JAMES SALTER
b. 1925

James Salter was born James Arnold Horowitz in New York City in 1925. Following in his father's footsteps, Salter enrolled in West Point shortly after the United States entered World War II. He ended up serving in the U.S. Army Air Forces for twelve years, during which time he began writing fiction. Salter was still in the armed forces when he wrote his first novel, *The Hunters,* based on his experience as a fighter pilot in the Korean War. Following his debut novel's 1957 publication and subsequent Hollywood adaptation, Salter left the army to become a full-time writer. He has written five more novels, *The Arm of Flesh* (1961), *A Sport and a Pastime* (1967), *Light Years* (1975), *Solo Faces* (1979), and, most recently, the highly acclaimed *All That Is* (2013), published when Salter was eighty-seven years old. He has also written numerous screenplays, poems, short stories, and a memoir. His first short story collection, *Dusk and Other Stories,* won him the 1989 PEN/Faulkner Award. His stories have appeared in *The New Yorker,* the O. Henry Collections, and *The Best American Short Stories.* In 2000, he was elected to the American Academy of Arts and Letters.

Give

In the morning—it was my wife's birthday, her thirty-first—we slept a little late, and I was at the window looking down at Des in a bathrobe with his pale hair awry and a bamboo stick in his hand. He was deflecting and sometimes with a flourish making a lunge. Billy, who was six then, was hopping around in front of him. I could hear his shrieks of joy. Anna came up beside me.

"What are they doing now?"

"I can't tell. Billy is waving something over his head."

"I think it's a flyswatter," she said, disbelieving.

She was just thirty-one, the age when women are past foolishness though not unfeeling.

"Look at him," she said. "Don't you just love him?"

The grass was brown from summer and they were dancing around on it. Des was barefoot, I noticed. It was early for him to be up. He often slept until noon and then managed to slip gracefully into the rhythm of the household. That was his talent, to live as he liked, almost without concern, to live as if he would reach the desired end one way or another and not be bothered by whatever came between. It included being committed several times, once for wandering out on Moore Street naked. None of the psychiatrists had any idea who he was. None of them had ever read a damned thing, he said. Some of the patients had.

He was a poet, of course. He even *looked* like a poet, intelligent, lank. He'd won the Yale prize when he was twenty-five and went on from there. When you pictured him, it was wearing a gray herringbone jacket, khaki pants, and for some reason sandals. Doesn't fit together, but a lot of things about him were like that. Born in Galveston, ROTC in college, and even married while an undergraduate, although what became of that wife he never clearly explained. His real life came after that, and he had lived it ever since, teaching sometimes in community classes, traveling to Greece and Morocco, living there for a period, having a breakdown, and through it all writing the poem that had made his name. I read the poem, a third of it anyway, standing stunned in a bookshop in the Village. I remember the afternoon, cloudy and quiet, and I remember, too, almost leaving myself, the person I was, the ordinary way I felt about things, my perception of—there's no other word for it—the depth of life, and above all the thrill of successive lines. The poem was an aria, jagged and unending. Its tone was what set it apart—written as if from the shades. *There lay the delta, there the burning arms . . .* was the way it began, and immediately I felt it was not about rivers uncoiling but about desire. It revealed itself only slowly, like some kind of dream, *the light fluttering on the fronds,* with names and nouns, Naples, worn benches. Luxor and the kings, Salonika, small waves falling on the stones. There was repetition, even refrain. Lines that seemed unconnected gradually became part of a confession that had at its center rooms in the burning heat of August where something has taken place, clearly sexual, but it is also the vacant streets of rural Texas, roads, forgotten friends, the slap of hands on rifle slings and forked pennants limp at parades. There are condoms, sun-faded cars, soiled menus with misspellings, a kind of pyre on which he had laid his life. That was why he seemed so pure—he had given all. Everyone lies about their lives, but he had not lied about his. He had made of it a noble lament, through it always running this thing you have had, that you will always have, but can never have. *There stood Erechtheus, polished limbs and greaves . . . come to me, Hellas, I long for your touch.*

I had met him at a party and only managed to say, "I read your beautiful poem." He was unexpectedly open in a way that impressed me and straightforward in a way that was unflinching. In talking, he mentioned the title of a book or two and referred to some things he assumed I would, of course, know, and he was witty, all of that but something more; his language invited me to be joyous, to speak as the gods—I use the plural because it's hard to think of him as obedient to a single god—had intended. We were always speaking of things that it turned out, oddly enough, both of us knew about although he knew more. Lafcadio Hearn,[1] yes, of course he knew who that was and even the name of the Japanese widow he married and the town they lived in, though he had never been to Japan himself. Arletty, Nestor Almendros, Jacques Brel, the Lawrenceville Stories, the *cordon sanitaire,* everything including his real

---

1. Lafcadio Hearn (1850–1904), author and translator of Japanese folklore and poetry.

interest, jazz, to which I only weakly responded.[2] The Answer Man, Billy Cannon, the Hellespont, Stendhal on love, it was as if we had sat in the same classes and gone to the same cities.[3] And there was Billy, swatting at his legs.

Billy loved him, he was almost a pal. He had an infectious laugh and was always ready to play. During the times he stayed with us, he made ships out of sofa cushions and swords and shields from whatever was in the garage. When he owned his car, the engine of which would cut out every so often, he claimed that turning the radio on and off would fix it, the circuits had been miswired of something. Billy was in charge of the radio.

"Oh, oh," Des would say, "there it goes. Radio!"

And Billy, with huge pleasure, would turn the radio on and off, on and off. How to explain why this worked? It was the power of a poet or maybe even a trick.

On Anna's birthday, at about noon a beautiful arrangement of flowers, lilies and yellow roses, was delivered. They were from him. That evening we had dinner with some friends at the Red Bar, always noisy but the table was in the small room past the bar. I hadn't ordered a birthday cake because we were going to have one back at the house, a rum cake, her favorite. Billy sat in her lap as she put her rings, one after another, carefully over separate candles, each ring for a wish.

"Will you help me blow them out?" She said to Billy, her face close to his hair.

"Too many," he said.

"Oh, God, you really know how to hurt a woman."

"Go ahead," Des told him. "If you don't have enough breath, I'll catch it and send it back."

"How do you do that?"

"I can do it. Haven't you heard of someone catching their breath?"

"They're burning down," Anna said. "Come on, one, two, three!"

The two of them blew them out. Billy wanted to know what her wishes had been, but she wouldn't tell.

We ate the cake, just the four of us, and I gave her the present I knew she would love. It was a wristwatch, very thin and square with Roman numerals and a small blue stone, I think tourmaline, embedded in the stem. There are not many things more beautiful than a watch lying new in its case.

"Oh, Jack!" she said. "It's gorgeous!"

She showed it to Billy and then to Des.

"Where did you get it?" Then, looking, "Cartier," she said.

"Yes."

"I *love* it."

Beatrice Hage, a woman we knew, had one like it that she had inherited from her mother. It had an elegance that defied the years and demands of fashion.

2. Arletty (1898–1992), French actress and singer; Nestor Almendros (1930–1992), Spanish cinematographer and documentary director; Jacques Brel (1929–1978), Belgian singer-songwriter; the Lawrenceville Stories, series of novels by American author Owen Johnson (1878–1952); *cordon sanitaire,* sanitary containment (French), a metaphor of diplomacy that usually refer to Soviet containment during the Cold War. 3. Hellespont, also known as the Dardanelles, is the narrow strait between the European and Asian portions of Turkey and figures prominently in much of ancient Greek mythology; Stendhal, pen name of French author Marie-Henri Beyle (1783–1842).

It was easy to find things she would like. Our taste was the same, it had been from the first. It would be impossible to live with someone otherwise. I've always thought it was the most important single thing, though people may not realize it. Perhaps it's transmitted to them in the way someone dresses or, for that matter, undresses, but taste is a thing no one is born with, it's learned, and at a certain point it can't be altered. We sometimes talked about that, what could and couldn't be altered. People were always saying something had completely changed them, some experience or book or man, but if you knew how they had been before, nothing much really had changed. When you found someone who was tremendously appealing but not quite perfect, you might believe you could change them after marriage, not everything, just a few things, but in truth the most you could expect was to change perhaps one thing and even that would eventually go back to what it had been.

The small things that could be overlooked at first but in time became annoying, we had a way of handling, of getting the pebble out of the shoe, so to speak. It was called a give, and it was agreed that it would last. The phrase that was overused, an eating habit, even a piece of favorite clothing, a give was a request to abandon it. You couldn't ask *for* something, only to stop something. The wide skirt of the bathroom sink was always wiped dry because of a give. Anna's little finger no longer extended when she drank from a cup. There might be more than one thing you would like to ask, and there was sometimes difficulty in choosing, but there was the satisfaction of knowing that once a year, without causing resentment, you would be able to ask your husband or wife to stop this one thing.

Des was downstairs when we put Billy to bed. I was in the hall when Anna came out holding her finger to her lips and having turned off the light.

"Is he asleep?"

"Yes."

"Well, happy birthday," I said.

"Yes."

There was something odd in the way she said it. She stood there, her long neck and blond hair.

"What is it, darling?"

She said nothing for a moment. Then she said,

"I want a give."

"All right," I said.

I don't know why, I felt nervous.

"What would you like?"

"I want you to stop it with Des," she said.

"Stop it? Stop what?"

My heart was skipping.

"Stop the sex," she said.

I knew she was going to say it. I had hoped something else, and the words were like a thick curtain tumbling down or a plate smashing on the floor.

"I don't know what you're talking about."

Her face was hard.

"Yes, you do. You know exactly what I'm talking about."

"Darling, you're mistaken. There's nothing going on with Des. He's a friend, he's my closest friend."

The tears began to run down her face.

"Don't," I said. "Please. Don't cry. You're wrong."

"I have to cry," she said, her voice unsteady. "Anyone would cry. You have to do it. You have to stop. We promised one another."

"Oh, God, you're imagining this."

"Please," she begged, "don't. Please, please, don't."

She was wiping her cheeks as if to make herself again presentable.

"You have to do what we promised," she said. "You have to give."

There are things you cannot give, that would simply crush your heart. It was half of life she was asking for, him slipping off his watch, holding him, having him in your possession, in indescribable happiness, in love with you. Nothing else could be like that. There was an apartment on Twelfth Street that we were able to use, the garden behind it, the dazzling chords of *Petroushka*[4]—the record happened to be there and we used to play it—chords that would always, as long as I lived, bring me back to it, his pliancy and slow smile.

"I'm not doing anything with Des," I said. "I swear to you."

"You swear to me."

"Yes."

"And I'm supposed to believe you."

"I swear to you."

She looked away.

"All right," she said at last.

A great joy filled me. Then she said,

"All right. But he has to leave. For good. If you want me to believe you, that's what it takes."

"Anna . . ."

"No, that's the proof."

"How can I tell him to leave? What's the reason?"

"Make up something. I don't care."

In the morning he got up late and was in the kitchen, the smoothness of sleep still on him. Anna had gone off. My hands were trembling.

"Good morning," he said with a smile.

"Good morning."

I couldn't bring myself to it. All I could say was,

"Des . . ."

"Yes?"

"I don't know what to say."

"About what?"

"Us. It's over."

He seemed not to understand.

"What's over?"

"Everything. I feel like I'm coming apart inside."

"Ah," he said in a soft way. "I see. Maybe I see. What happened?"

"It's just that you can't stay."

"Anna," he guessed.

"Yes."

---

4. Music for a ballet composed by Igor Stravinsky (1882–1971) in 1911.

"She knows."

"Yes. I don't know what to do."

"Could I talk to her, do you think?"

"It wouldn't do any good. Believe me."

"But we've always gotten along. What difference does it make? Let me talk to her."

"She doesn't want to," I lied.

"When did all this happen?"

"Last night. Don't ask me how it came about. I don't know."

He sighed. He said something I didn't get. All I could hear was my own heart beating. He left later that day.

I felt the injustice for a long time. He'd brought only pleasure to us, and if to me particularly, that didn't diminish it. I had some photographs that I kept in a certain place, and of course I had the poems. I followed him from afar, the way a woman does a man she was never able to marry. The glittering blue water slid past as he made his way between the islands. There was Ios, white in the haze, where the dust of Homer lay, they said.

2005

DANZY SENNA
b. 1970

Danzy Senna was born in Boston to an Irish-American mother and an Afro-Mexican father, both writers and civil rights activists. She earned her B.A. at Stanford University and an M.F.A. in creative writing from the University of California, Irvine. Senna's writing often examines the complex issues of race and class within modern America. Her two novels, *Caucasia* (1998), a national bestseller and winner of the Book of the Month Club's Stephen Crane Award for First Fiction, and *Symptomatic* (2004), are told from the perspectives of biracial young women. In her 2009 memoir *Where Did You Sleep Last Night?*—written during her fellowship at the New York Public Library's Cullman Center for Scholars and Writers—Senna explores her own identity by delving into her parents' divergent pasts and their defiant (and ultimately failed) marriage. In 2011, she published her first collection of short stories, *You Are Free*, to great critical acclaim. She lives in Los Angeles with her husband, novelist and story writer Percival Everett, and their two sons.

Admission

The letter was unexpected. Cassie stared at it for a long time as she sipped her coffee, trying to decipher a hidden clue, though the language was crisp, the message to the point. They had been invited for an interview.

You recently completed the first stage of the application process when you attended a tour of the Institute for Early Childhood Development. You have been selected for the second step—an interview. This is for parents only. Please arrange appropriate childcare. Your interview time and date are:

TUESDAY, FEB. 18, 2:00 p.m.

Please call to confirm your attendance.

Cassie headed across the wet grass to Duncan's studio, letter in hand. She peered in the window to see if he was working. He was sitting in front of his television eating a mango with a knife. She opened the door and stepped inside. He was watching a basketball game and lurched back in his seat. "Fucking foul! That was so over the line."

"Duncan."

He turned and looked at her. "I didn't hear you come in."

"We got an interview."

He stared blankly.

"At the Institute."

He squinted. "The Institute?"

They'd toured the place two weeks ago and already he'd forgotten.

"The fancy school."

"Oh yeah, that." He turned back to the game: "Speaking of children, where is ours?"

"Brittany took him to the park."

"Well, then, you should be working. This is our window. Time's a-wastin'."

"I know," she said. "But this letter. What should we do about the interview? They've offered us a time and a date."

"How kind of them."

"Duncan. I'm serious."

He turned around slowly, his mouth glistening from the mango. "We aren't interested, remember? So an interview would be a waste of time. Cody is already all set to go to Wee Things." He swiveled back to the television.

Cassie bit her lip and stared at the back of Duncan's head. It looked egg-shaped and vulnerable from the back.

It was true that they'd only gone on the tour because she'd said she needed to research the play she was writing. She still had no more than the barest sketches of the characters and situation: a wealthy Los Angeles family, a disconsolate bulimic wife, an eight-year-old girl's suicide attempt. She had not yet decided whether the attempt would be successful.

She'd half believed the research excuse herself. But as she'd driven them over to the Institute that morning in the old Subaru—Duncan grumpy that he'd had to put on clothes—she had to admit that she was weirdly, secretly excited.

Several of the mothers in her playgroup had briefed her on the application process, which was famously mysterious and daunting.

"You have to be a Spielberg or something to even get an interview."

"I heard Will and Jada got wait-listed."

The Institute for Early Childhood Development. She and Duncan had moved out west only recently from Providence, Rhode Island; he'd gotten a teaching job, she'd gotten an NEA[1] grant for her next play. They were subletting a house—a friend of a friend's—in Larchmont Village, a precious neighborhood with a quaint, Mayberry feel to it, though it was on the edge of West Hollywood and the residents were all film industry people. Cassie had already found a school for Cody in walking distance, but she'd applied to the Institute anyway, for research. She needed to know the rituals and mores of the city's elite. Anyway, the application wasn't hard, just a square white card with blanks for her and Duncan's names, their occupations, and their child's name, address, date of birth, and race. Hillary, a playgroup mother who had applied and been rejected twice, observed with some bitterness that the application was so barebones because the Institute got the rest of your information off the Internet.

1. National Endowment for the Arts.

"You have to be Google-worthy," she said.

The school was located in the middle of the city. It was across the street from a public school, an old brick building with brightly colored Spanish and English signs posted on the chain-link fence. The Institute looked more like a museum than a school—a sleek modernist building surrounded by a high cement wall lined with brightly colored turrets that stabbed the sky at odd angles.

"This better not take too long," Duncan grumbled as they approached the building. "I've got work to do."

She'd expected a small group of select applicants, but nearly every seat in the auditorium was filled, and the tension in the air was palpable. The crowd, on the surface at least, was diverse—black and brown and yellow and white, gay and straight. Duncan went for the muffins and coffee while she got on line for their name tags and a folder with information about the school. They found seats in the middle of the room. Nearby she noticed a familiar face. For a moment she thought it was someone she knew, but no, it was a famous actress. She nudged Duncan. "Look who's sitting two rows down."

Duncan was leafing through the information packet. He snorted. "Check out the second question here." He was pointing to a green sheet labeled "Frequently Asked Questions."

QUESTION #1: "Is it true that all the children at the Institute are the children of celebrities?"

ANSWER: "No. Only a modest percentage of our parents are celebrities. We pride ourselves on our diverse community—which includes plenty of people you've never heard of."

The chatter in the room began to quiet as a small, zaftig white woman in an elegant blue pantsuit and clicking heels walked across the floor to the microphone and tapped it twice. Obedient silence fell over the crowd.

The woman smiled and spoke into the microphone. She had a vaguely European accent. "Welcome, parents. I'm Esther Vale, director of the Institute. I'm so pleased to see all of you here today."

She went on to give a speech about the school's pedagogy while the giant screen behind her showed images of the Institute children in action: an Asian girl frozen in hysterical laughter on the playground; a white boy with a mop of blond curls wearing safety goggles and staring at fluid in a beaker; a black girl onstage in a ladybug costume, her face alight with a gap-toothed smile.

The crowd around Cassie seemed to thrum, silently, with excitement and desire. She eyed their rapt faces as they listened to Esther Vale speak.

"Now I'm going to tell you who should not apply to the Institute," Esther was saying, a small, bemused smile on her face. "And I'm going to be honest with you. Can I be honest? You should not apply to the Institute if you don't see the value of our generous financial aid program that allows families of all income levels to attend. You should not apply to the Institute if you aren't interested in being an active member of our school community. You should not apply to the Institute if you are uncomfortable with nontraditional families—gay parents, single parents. You should not apply to the Institute if you are uncomfortable with your child making friends of different racial and ethnic backgrounds. You should not apply to the Institute if you don't want your child to have as much art—drama, painting, poetry, sculpture—in their curriculum as they have reading, writing, and arithmetic. If these aren't the qualities you want in a school, then this isn't the school for you, and there are plenty of private schools in Los Angeles that will suit your needs."

The crowd burst into applause as Esther strode off the stage. They had been given instructions to meet their tour guides at the front of the auditorium, based on the color of the sticker on their folder. Cassie and Duncan's sticker was blue and they joined the cluster around their group leader, a petite blond woman.

For the next forty-five minutes, she led them through the school—peering into classrooms, telling them about the amazing programs the school had to offer and her own children's experiences there. Duncan jiggled his keys in his pocket and kept checking his watch. Every so often they would pass another group of parents, and Cassie would recognize a face or a name on a name tag. She felt like she was in a dream. *There was Julia Roberts, and there was Donald Sutherland, and there was President Nixon . . .*

The last stop on the tour was the preschool area. Their guide explained that the window in the door was actually a two-way mirror, the kind used in police lineups. It allowed parents to come and watch their children as they worked and played. The parents in their group took turns stepping up to the window and peering through it at the class of toddlers.

"They're having snack time," the tour guide explained.

Cassie looked and saw a cluster of children sitting at a table eating what looked like edamame.

"I'm not impressed," Duncan said when they were safely outside the gates, heading toward their car. "The digs are fancy, sure, but there isn't anything special about the teaching. Sure ain't worth the insane tuition. Did you see the figures?"

"Esther said they have a generous financial aid program," Cassie said.

"Whatever. That's for poor people, their 'socioeconomic tokens'—not for our upper-middle-class Negroid asses. Or did you forget, we made it, sweetheart. We on da East Side now." He pulled a muffin from his pocket, loosely wrapped in a napkin. He ate as he talked. "I'd rather send Cody to the school across the street. Did you get a peek at that? I wonder how Esther explains that little eyesore to all the Institute kids."

Cassie was silent as she pulled out of the parking space. She felt a burning of longing in her chest she couldn't admit to Duncan just now. She'd been impressed by the Institute—by the aggressively multicultural creed Esther professed, but also by the cheerful yet cloistered feeling of the hallways and classrooms. It seemed so civilized compared to the rough-and-tumble public schools she had attended growing up in Philadelphia. She wanted her child to grow up around *these* people, not *those* people, but she couldn't admit that to Duncan.

"So did you get all the details you need for your parody?" he asked.

She cleared her throat the way she always did when she was about to lie. "Yes," she said. "I think so."

And now here she was, holding this letter that invited them to go one step further. The Institute wanted to meet them. They were good enough to meet.

She didn't mention it again until later that night, after they'd had rugged sex. He was lying beside her in a postcoital coma when she said, "Duncan, baby, I'd like to do that interview at the Institute."

"I thought you finished your research."

"Not quite. I need the interview. It's the best part."

He sighed. "Okay. I guess we can go."

Brittany was the only white nanny in the neighborhood. Duncan, who was originally from the South, had insisted on racial subversion—and he'd ended up with a "real live cracker," as he put it, an Alabama native who had been in Los Angeles ten years, fruitlessly pursuing a singing career while she cared for other people's children. Brittany was in her thirties and vaguely pretty, though Duncan said, "The dew is off the rose." He liked the irony of the situation: a black couple with a Southern white mammy caring for their brown child. Of course, they truly liked Brittany as well. More important, Cody adored her. He was even picking up her twangy accent.

"So, Brit," Cassie said, "we should be back from the interview in an hour. Can you give Cody lunch?"

Brittany sat still while Cody drove his Hot Wheels up her blue-jeaned leg, making a *vroom*ing sound.

"Sure thing, darlin'. Take your time. And break a leg!"

Brittany didn't know it was just research.

The reception area was empty and Duncan sat playing a video game on his cell phone while they waited to be called inside.

"Can you put that away?"

"No, I'm winning."

She squirmed beside him, irritated. Moments later, a couple—a black couple, slightly ragged-looking, definitely "socioeconomic tokens," as Duncan would say—came out wearing bashful smiles. They nodded at Cassie and Duncan but their smiles were tight and their eyes frightened.

A moment later, a middle-aged white woman came out to greet them, smiling with big teeth, her hand extended. "Hello, I'm Penny Washburn, director of admissions. Come on in."

She was rather sexless in the way of New England WASPs, with a long, thin face, graying blond hair, and bright blue eyes. She wore belted khakis, comfortable shoes, a pink oxford shirt tucked in.

They followed her down a plush-carpeted hallway to her office.

Inside, Cassie and Duncan took their seats. Cassie looked around. On Penny's desk sat a photo of two children—preteens with braces—who might be hers. Beside it was a framed picture of a smiling Barack Obama, which, silly as it was, made her feel more comfortable.

The interview lasted about twenty minutes. Cassie wasn't sure what she'd been expecting, but Penny's questions surprised her in their blunt specificity: When had Cody crawled? When had he walked? How long had he been breast-fed? How many words—approximately—did he have in his vocabulary? How did they choose to discipline him, if at all? What was his typical diet?

Cody was advanced in all areas, so Cassie felt a surge of pride as she answered. *Six months, ten months, thirteen months,* and *at least one hundred.* They disciplined him with time-outs and he ate a healthy diet, though a little heavier on cheese than Cassie would have liked.

"He's very precocious," Cassie said. "He already knows all his numbers and letters. Duncan thinks he might even be sight-reading."

"He's two, though," Duncan countered. "And an only child. Spoiled. Which means there are plenty of days when we'd like to send him back to the factory."

Cassie shot Duncan a dirty look. He didn't notice.

Penny, giving nothing away, nodded and scribbled in her notebook.

Then she wanted to know about their backgrounds, their work. Duncan told her about his paintings, the collage technique he used. Cassie was vague about her plays. Penny made interested sounds in her throat and nodded and scribbled more notes.

Then the interview was over and Penny was leading them to the door, wearing a placid, completely unreadable smile on her face.

Cassie breathed a sigh of relief when they were on the sidewalk. Though they'd only gone in the spirit of research, she had felt nervous, as if she were really trying to get her kid into the school.

"Penny seemed nice enough," she said when she'd started the engine.

"Whatever."

"It was cool she had a picture of Obama on her desk."

"Yeah, so what. He's the new Mickey Mouse." Duncan buckled his seat belt. "Anyway, are you finished?"

"Finished what?"

"With your fieldwork."

"I guess so," she said, and stared out the windshield at two women, one white and blond, the other Asian, mothers presumably, who were chatting on the sidewalk outside the school. The Asian one was familiar, from some television show maybe, though Cassie couldn't place her. They were both glamorous in high heels, with identical sheathlike hairstyles that fell across their faces. They made her think of Malibu Barbie and the ethnic Barbie, "Kira." She'd owned both in her youth. The women's matching silver SUVs were parked in the loading zone beside them. Two girls, their children, came striding out the gate of the school in matching Ugg boots, and waved goodbye to each other as their mothers led them to their respective vehicles.

Cody was napping when they got home and Brittany was wearing her iPod and singing along to country music in a husky voice as she folded their laundry. Cassie told Duncan she was going out for a walk to think about her play. But once outside, she didn't think about it at all. Instead she went over and over every detail of the interview, trying to imagine what Penny had thought of them, how they'd come across. That slight and inscrutable smile—was it just what Penny's face did, or did it mean something?

She thought about the school—the vast splendor of it—and the schools she'd attended at that age, the children she'd known. Each child was tagged in her memory with a tragedy or a defect. Tasha in third grade—one of a handful of foster kids in the class—had worn a wig that all the kids teased her about. When Cassie's mother learned about the teasing, she scolded Cassie harshly, explaining that the girl's hair had been burned off by her very own mother. A tall white boy named Dougie had a big head and lived with his aunt and uncle in a trailer because his family had burned to death in a fire. Why had there been so many fire-related tragedies? Some of the kids she'd known had been mean and some had been nice, some had been funny and some had been cruel. Some had been quick as whips and others had been slow. They'd been good little fighters, all of them, when the situation called for it. The school had been diverse in a way—there had been white kids, black kids, Puerto Rican kids, a few Vietnamese kids—but they were all so dingy in her memory, a gang right out of *Oliver Twist*. Had they really been that dingy? And what had happened to them all?

She found herself on the street of the other school. Wee Things Nursery. She headed up the block toward it. Apparently it was one of the oldest nursery schools in Los Angeles, and it was beloved. When they'd toured it months ago, Cassie had been charmed by it. She and Duncan had watched a group of toddlers sitting at their child-size table eating their bag lunches and drinking their juice, and Cassie had felt an unbearable tenderness and sadness at the thought of Cody joining them, joining the world beyond their home. They had been delighted when the director called to say there was a spot for Cody. It meant they could walk him to school every morning, and he would be only blocks away, in case he needed or wanted to come home early.

Now she stood in the shadows of a sycamore tree watching as parents picked up their children. They were not so different-looking from the parents at the other school—your basic upper-middle-class industry types. Their cars were mostly high-end luxury models. But now that she had a chance, a sliver of a possibility, of getting into the Institute, Wee Things had lost its luster. It looked run-down, slightly too hippie to be hygienic.

At home, Brittany had gone and Duncan was seated on the nursery floor with Cody on his lap. Cody stared up at him with huge black eyes as Duncan read from Dr. Seuss. It was Cody's favorite, *The Sneetches*. Cassie stood listening to the doggerel about the two factions, the Star-Belly Sneetches and the Plain-Belly Sneetches, the creatures identical to each other in every way except for this belly marking.

Neither father nor son saw her where she stood in the shadows.

Then the preschool interview, along with her own work, faded into white noise in the back of her mind, because Brittany's mother went into a diabetic coma. Brittany had to go home to Alabama for a few weeks to tend to her, and Cassie learned what it was to be a full-time mother. From morning to night, she was manically caring for Cody—feeding him breakfast, brushing his tiny teeth, changing his diaper, wiping his butt, rushing him to the toilet to see if he'd poop there, and driving all over Los Angeles. Duncan helped when he could, but he was teaching two classes that semester. So Cassie hauled Cody from one mommy-and-me class to another, because sitting with a group of other mothers and children beat the tedium of sitting alone with him on the floor at home.

She found herself immersed in a world of mothers—women who'd had careers once, as actresses and scriptwriters, lawyers and businesswomen, women who'd gone to grad school, but were taking time off to be mothers. They were an unusual lot in that they could afford nannies but weren't relying on them full-time. Cassie, hanging on until Brittany came back, felt like a fraud in their midst.

Among the mothers, the question of schools almost always came up. It was an anxiety that every woman seemed to feel: Where would her child land? Inevitably, the Institute came up too. Every one of the mothers wanted their child to go there. When Cassie pressed them as to why, they said vaguely, "It's just the best," or, "It's supposed to be amazing." They said it was a "feeder school" for the best grammar schools, which were feeder schools for the best high schools, which were feeder schools for the Ivy League. In other words, the Institute was a "feeder" for a life of success.

Mostly, though, they talked about how hard it was to get in, and every one of them had an anecdote they'd heard about somebody famous or powerful who had not gotten their child in, even when they'd offered the school some vast sum of money. The Institute, they said, never changed its mind. "If they don't want you, they don't want you." Then they would all sigh and move on to less depressing topics, like C-section scars or vaginal reconstruction.

One afternoon she slogged home through traffic with Cody after a tumbling class in Beverly Hills. He was tired and hungry and shrieking about some toy tractor he'd dropped in the parking lot, which Cassie had been unable to find. She was relieved to see Duncan's car in the driveway. She found him sprawled on the sofa watching television. She dropped Cody's hand, said, "He's all yours," and kept walking toward the kitchen.

She had the beginnings of a migraine. She gulped a long glass of water. She put it down and picked up the stack of mail on the counter. She flipped through some bills and then she saw it: a large white envelope from the Institute.

Her skin prickled. She picked up the envelope and tore it open. Her eyes flashed over the words:

> Congratulations. Your son Cody has been accepted into our Toddler Program.

From the other room, she heard Duncan making monster noises, Cody squealing.

She went and stood in the doorway, watching them, the envelope in hand.

Duncan held Cody upside down. Cody was laughing hysterically. Duncan glanced over and caught her eye.

"You didn't tell me," she said.

"Tell you what?" he said, out of breath, letting Cody down onto the floor.

"We heard from the Institute." She didn't know what to do with her face, what expression to wear. She tried to smirk, but her mouth was not moving right. "We've been accepted."

"Oh yeah, I saw that. Well, la-di-da-da, ain't we special," Duncan said.

There were cartoons on the television; Cody went and stood directly in front of them, so that he became just a black silhouette against the manic flashing colors of the screen.

"I knew we'd get in," Duncan said, leaning down to pick the throw pillows off the floor and set them back on the couch. "That school is rich on money and poor on class. See, baby, we's culcha'd. We is some certified, authentified intellectuals, baby. We stood out in a sea of celebrities and millionaires. You gotta love it."

She swallowed. "I wasn't sure we would. I mean, do you know the odds? Six hundred parents applied for twelve spots. At least admit to feeling a little, I don't know, surprised."

"I'm shocked, shocked," he said, deadpan, then brushed past her on his way to the kitchen. He picked up a bottle of wine and set to opening it. "It's gotta be five-thirty somewhere in the world." He said this same line every day at four-thirty. He poured himself a glass, leaned against the counter, and took a sip, watching her. "What's wrong with your face?"

"What do you mean?"

"Your mouth is all twisted funny. And your left eye is twitching."

She felt the pulsing now that he said it. She touched it gingerly. She tried to sound casual, nonchalant. "Listen, I know this isn't what we'd planned, but do you think we should consider accepting? I mean, it's supposed to be an amazing school." She realized as she spoke that she had been rehearsing this speech for the past two weeks. Somewhere in the back of her mind she'd been preparing these words. "I mean, once you're in, you're in through grade school. We wouldn't have to worry about schools again in two years the way we will at Wee Things."

He sighed. "Cass, we already have a school for Cody. A perfectly good pre-school for a fraction of the cost. A sandbox is a sandbox. I refuse to pay out the ass for preschool. And did you read the fine print on the brochure we got on that tour? I did. Each year the price goes up. And we have to buy insurance on our tuition because if something happens, if we decide to pull Cody out, they will not return our money. Yeah, because you have to pay the whole fucking year's tuition in one lump sum—because it's a school for people who have fifteen, twenty grand lying around in their checking account. Honey, they will sap us of every penny we have. No more trips to France in the summer. Shit, no more lattes with a side of biscotti. We will have to scale back—seriously—just so the kid can get to sit in a classroom with future Rich Fucks of America." He took another gulp of wine, a big one. He'd been preparing his speech too, she realized. Secretly, he'd been storing this up, preparing for this day, because secretly, they'd both known that they were going to get accepted.

"I know," she said. "I know all that. It's just—well, we got in. It's kind of a big deal."

"No it's not," he said. "We only went on the tour as a joke—remember? You were gonna write this acerbic parody about the stupidity and vapidity of American culture in the age of late capitalism. I line-edited your fucking NEA grant."

"But the thing is, I don't want Cody to rot away in a public school. I mean, we send him to public school and maybe he'll survive, maybe he won't. It's a wild card what will happen to him, what he'll become."

"It's a wild card everywhere, my dear. I'm sorry to inform you."

"No, not in the same way. This is where the world begins to divide. This is where the tone is set for the rest of his life."

"You sound like a *New Yorker* cartoon," he said with a chortle.

She felt the blood slamming against the inside of her head. She wanted to say, *Don't you dare take this from me, I'm almost there, I've almost made it to the other side, don't fuck this up for me.* But instead she said, "Not everything has to be a political statement, Duncan."

"This isn't about politics." He stepped to the window and looked out at the street, his back to her. "Have you ever noticed how boring and stupid kids from the fancy private schools are? Have you ever met one of those saps? They're like overbred puppies. They have no grit. Their limbs are all rubbery. Public school kids are scrappy, like pound mutts."

"Are you drunk?"

"No. Not yet." He sounded sober and calm. "I just don't want my kids going to the Institute—"

"What's the Institute?" It was Cody. He stood at the door, honey-colored, with a mop of shiny black curls.

"It's a school," Cassie said, squatting down to look at him eye to eye. "You're going to go to school soon, like a big boy, and your papa and I are trying to decide which one would be best for you." She paused, then said, "The big one or the little one."

"Which one has swings?" Cody asked.

"Both," Duncan said behind her. "They both have swings."

The girl, Tasha, the one with the burned scalp and the crooked pageboy wig, ate her lunch alone every day. She was tall and big-boned and wore a strange assortment of clothes—sequined disco shirts during the day, sweatshirts with snowflakes on them in the spring, huge white no-name sneakers that the other kids called "bobos." They were clothes that Cassie learned at some point, she didn't know how, had come from charity. The other kids said Tasha smelled bad. Cassie got to test this theory once, when she was paired up with Tasha in English class. They were supposed to write a story together, using adjectives and adverbs, as part of a new program that paired advanced students with remedial students, rather than splitting them into separate classes. Cassie's friends laughed and pointed at her when they saw who she had been paired with. Up close, Tasha didn't smell bad, but when she bent over the desk to write a sentence, Cassie saw a patch of burned skin at the nape of her neck, pale and glossy and webbed, leading up to and underneath her wig.

Duncan sat at the kitchen table across from her, watching as she made the call.

She jiggled her leg under the table. She felt nervous, angry, forced into it.

"Penny Washburn," answered a peppy voice.

"Hi, this is Cassie Rogers. My husband and I—"

"Cassie! Of course. I remember you and Duncan. Congratulations, you made it." She laughed. "I guess you know how difficult it is to get in. A lot of people would give their eyeteeth to be in your position."

"Yes, I know. We're so honored to have been accepted." Cassie looked at Duncan, winced, unsure all over again. This morning it had seemed clear, she'd woken and seen the light, remembered the play she was supposed to be writing—but now she was having second thoughts.

Duncan nodded his head and gestured for her to carry on as planned.

"So what's up?" Penny said.

"I'm really sorry, but we've decided Cody won't be able to accept your offer. It's, well, it's just that the schedule of the toddler program doesn't work for our, our lifestyle."

Duncan whispered, "Thank you and good-bye."

Penny was silent on the other end for a beat. "Oh. Well." She sounded surprised. "Are you sure?"

Cassie swallowed. No, she wasn't sure. But she felt Duncan's eyes boring into her and carried on. "Yes, we're sure. I'm so sorry. Perhaps we can reapply in a future year."

"Would financial aid help out? Would that change things for you? We have quite a generous financial aid program, as you know."

"I don't think so," Cassie said. "I don't think we'd be eligible."

"You'd be surprised," Penny said. "You'd be surprised at the range of income levels that are considered eligible here."

Cassie had not expected the conversation to go on so long. The school had a wait list a mile long. She had expected an icy thanks and good-bye.

"Thanks, Penny, but there are a number of factors influencing our decision. We're so sorry to have to pass on the offer this year. But I hope we can keep in touch."

There was silence. Cassie frowned at Duncan, who was sitting across from her, drumming his fingers. "Hang up," he whispered.

She raised a hand to shush him. "Hello? Penny?"

"Yes, I'm here." Penny's voice sounded strange—taut, as if she were holding in a cough. "So you're sure about this."

"Yes," Cassie said. "I'm sure."

"Okay," came a small voice. "Okay."

Cassie waited for Penny to say good-bye first, but when she said nothing, Cassie said, "Well, thanks, Penny. Bye."

Again, nothing. She hung up the phone.

"Jesus, that took ages," Duncan said. "What the hell were you discussing?"

"She was just making sure I meant it, I guess. I felt like she really was disappointed Cody wasn't coming."

"Oh, come on," Duncan said. "You saw the auditorium. Packed. She is calling her next set of parents right now and offering them his spot."

At two in the morning she lay beside Duncan, listening to his breathing. The light coming through the window was gray, half lit by streetlamps. She could hear crickets humming. She had a pain in her stomach, a gnawing of regret.

Duncan Dickie was a black sheep; he was the only artist in a family of doctors. When she'd married him she'd been attracted to his strong opinions. She'd liked how he'd chafed at groups, anything smacking of mob mentality. He was what her mother called an iconoclast. But he had grown up in the bastion of the black middle class. As far as she could tell, the most traumatic thing that had happened to him as a child was being teased about his name. A bully named Eddie used to lead a playground chant. *When the weather's hot and sticky, that's no time for dunkin' Dickie. But when the frost is on the pumpkin, now that's the time for Dickie dunkin!*

He'd told her the story once, in the dark. He said she was the only person he'd ever told, as if the humiliation was still fresh.

Cassie had grown up poor, the daughter of a struggling single mother and a deadbeat father who showed up at some birthdays, drunk. Once in fifth grade, at recess, she'd been surrounded by a group of retarded boys, escapees from the special education class, who'd groped her. All her life she'd wanted to belong, to *have*, to possess what the other side possessed.

She sat up and stared down at Duncan's sleeping face. He was the problem. He was the barrier to her getting what she wanted—the perfect life. His face, even in sleep, had a kind of arrogance.

His eyes blinked open and he jerked, startled. "What are you doing?"

"Thinking."

He glanced at the clock radio. "About what?"

"About the school. The Institute. Did we just make a huge mistake?"

"Oh Jesus. Not this again. No, we made the right decision. Now can we drop it and get some sleep?"

"But it's the school everybody wants."

"Who the hell is 'everybody'? The ladies of Larchmont Village?"

"Nobody will believe it if I tell them we turned it down."

"So don't tell anybody."

She turned to her side and hugged her pillow, her cheeks warm with rage.

Duncan got out of bed. "Now I can't get back to sleep," he muttered. "I'm going to work in my studio." He left, sighing dramatically, and she lay there in the dark.

The problem with modern marriage was that everything had to be a consensus. Each choice had to be something they both wanted. For a moment, fear gripped her, a physical sensation—cold wetness under her arms, a dry mouth, a quickening of her heartbeat. *They had turned down the Institute.* She struggled to breathe. She felt as if she were falling into a long dark hole. She felt as if something large and warm and malevolent was pressing down on her, crushing her under its weight.

The next night while Cassie was sautéing garlic, the phone rang.

"Cassie," the voice on the other end of the line said when she answered. "It's me, Penny."

For a moment, she was confused.

"Penny Washburn," the woman clarified. "At the Institute."

"Oh, hi."

"Are you sure?"

"Excuse me?"

"Are you sure there's not something we can do to, well, make the offer more attractive?"

Cassie felt a momentary thrill. She turned off the heat under the saucepan. Duncan was out on the lawn reading a book to Cody. *The Sneetches* again. She remembered the arguments, the money. Duncan's position.

"It's so nice of you to call," she said, flushed, flattered. "Thanks for, well, for double-checking." She stared out at Duncan, her jaw clenched. "But yes, I'm afraid we've made up our minds. For this year anyway."

Penny went on. "It's just that I was about to offer your spot to somebody else, and I thought, let me just double-check. One more time. I'd hate for Cody to miss out on the opportunity, and I can't guarantee a spot next year."

Cassie felt a surge of doubt again. Was she sure? She saw Duncan rising and walking toward the house. "Yes, we're sure," she said. "But it's so nice of you to call. I realize how coveted these spots are."

This time the silence went on for so long that she thought Penny had hung up.

"Penny?"

"Yes, I'm just thinking. Listen. How about this: I'm not going to give your slot away tonight. It's too late. I'm going home. But let me give you my home number. If you change your mind, just give me a ring. I won't do a thing until tomorrow, say, after lunch."

She rattled off her home number before Cassie could find a pen. But she knew she'd committed it to memory.

Duncan came in the door just as she was hanging up.

"Who was that?"

She paused. "Nobody. I mean, just a prank call. Kids."

She told the lie automatically, without knowing exactly why.

"Kids still make those?"

"Apparently," she said, turning her face so he couldn't see her expression.

Duncan picked up a wine bottle and pulled the cork out. "It's gotta be five-thirty somewhere in the world, right?"

The next morning Cassie brought Cody to his music class. She went through the motions of singing along to the folksinger with him on her lap, then chatting with the other mothers afterward, but her mind was elsewhere. She looked up at the clock ticking on the wall and thought of her chance ticking away with it. When she got home it was already noon, and she felt a wave of sadness, as if something precious and irretrievable had been washed out to sea. She imagined Cody twenty years from now, in prison for grand auto theft, imagined herself leaving the jail after visiting hours. She thought about how she would look back to this decision as the cause of all his troubles. She imagined Penny Washburn picking up the phone to call the lucky parents of the child who would go to the Institute instead. Her mouth tasting of metal, she imagined how they would celebrate.

The phone broke into her thoughts. She picked up, expecting Duncan.

"It's me, Penny."

"Oh. Hello."

"It's past noon," Penny said.

"I know."

"I was waiting for you to call."

"I thought I was only going to call if we changed our minds."

"And did you change it?"

Cassie felt a bug crawling on her arm and slapped at it, but nothing was there.

"I'm so sorry, but no." She felt strange, suddenly, unsettled by the woman's phone call. "We didn't change our minds. That's why I didn't call."

Penny sighed. "You know, a lot of families would give their eyeteeth to go here."

"Yes, I—I know that."

"So what's the hitch? The diversity issue? We're almost forty percent nonwhite."

"That's—that's great. That wasn't the problem."

"Then what was it?"

Cassie shifted uncomfortably, looked over the counter at Cody playing with his cars in the living room. She tried to remember Penny's eyes, her face, from their one meeting, but all she could remember was the picture of smiling Barack Obama on her desk. "I can't explain it."

She heard Duncan's car pulling into the driveway.

"Thank you," she said quickly, "for calling. I'm sorry it didn't work out."

She hung up without waiting for Penny to say good-bye.

She went onto the porch to greet Duncan, but once again—for some reason she couldn't articulate—she didn't tell him about Penny's call.

The phone rang early the next morning, a shrill screech that cut through her morning haze as she set a bowl of cereal in front of Cody. Duncan was still asleep.

She looked at the caller ID. It was Penny's home number. She remembered it.

She didn't answer. She sat at the table, Cody slurping his cereal beside her, and watched the phone until it stopped ringing. She breathed out relief.

But a moment later it began ringing again. She went to it and stared down at it, as if it were alive.

Later that morning, Duncan took Cody to swim class. It was a rare moment of aloneness. But just as Cassie sat down at her desk, the phone rang. She picked it up without checking the caller ID.

"The spot is still open," Penny's voice said. "We've been holding it for you."

Her voice sounded strange, muffled, and behind it Cassie could hear traffic, a car horn, distant mariachi music.

Cassie was frightened now, and didn't speak.

Penny said, "You're just the kind of family we've been looking for."

Cassie closed her eyes. She felt a pain like a mallet to her chest.

"Was it your husband?" Penny said. "Duncan Dickie?"

Cassie opened her eyes, breathed in sharply, and hung up the phone.

The week went by without any more calls from Penny Washburn. She thought of telling Duncan about them, Penny's odd, desperate tone, but every time she opened her mouth, she stopped. It would seem strange to him that she hadn't said anything earlier, and she would have to explain that too, which she couldn't. She decided to put the whole episode behind her, just like Duncan was doing. It was a problem she had—she always regretted a decision after it was made, no matter what. She never could leave things be. She decided not to mention the Institute or Penny Washburn again as long as she lived.

She began work on her play. It was going slowly, but a character was emerging, the wife of a neurosurgeon. Nedra. Her name was Nedra. Pretty but woefully insecure Nedra. She was the type of woman who applied lipstick each night before getting into bed with her husband of fifteen years. Nedra was obsessed with her nose, convinced that it was the wrong shape and size. She would have several surgeries in the course of the play to "correct" it.

In bed, Cassie chattered to Duncan about her work. "She's going to be a sort of vehicle for me to discuss so much—race, sex, body dysmorphia. I see her as a kind of symbol of our times. Nedra. What do you think of that name?"

Duncan didn't answer. She looked up and saw he was fast asleep, his reading glasses still on his face.

She read *The Sneetches* aloud to Cody one evening, snuggled beside him in his toddler bed. Outside was a rare heavy rain. The sound of it reminded her of her childhood, Philadelphia, real weather. She remembered her mother snuggled beside her on such nights, reading to her—the standard of happiness to which all other moments would be compared. Cody rested his head against her chest and brushed his fingers against her collarbone. She'd read the story to him so many times that she barely had to look at the page. The Star-Belly Sneetches were having a beach party, gorging themselves on hotdogs and marshmallows, while the sad Plain-Belly Sneetches stood watching, cold and bereft in the sandy gloom.

She realized that she too was comforted by the story, perhaps because it was so very familiar.

When she went to turn the page, she realized that Cody had fallen asleep. She could have slid him off her chest and turned out the light and left him there, but she was enjoying the feeling of his warm body pressed against her. Duncan was out back in his studio, working. Dinner was warming in the oven. She had only the salad to make. She closed her eyes. For some reason she thought about that girl, Tasha, the one with the burned scalp. Cassie's mother had made her promise to be nice to the girl. In fact, she had made Cassie promise to sit with her at lunch. But in the cafeteria the next day, seeing Tasha sitting all alone, Cassie had balked. She had hovered beside Tasha for a moment, holding her tray, but then had moved on to her table of friends. Later she told her mother about sitting with the burned girl. It was her first lie, or the first she'd been conscious of telling, anyway.

Distantly, she was aware of the sound of knocking. Somebody was knocking at the front door.

She slid Cody to the mattress and rose carefully, switching off the light.

Out in the front room, the knocking was hard and persistent. She went to the door and looked through the peephole.

A figure stood on the doorstep, tiny and warped, head turned toward the street.

Cassie opened the door.

Penny Washburn stood on the steps. The rain had flattened her hair, making her look gaunt and ravaged. There was a puddle around her sodden loafers and she was hugging herself, shivering. The air outside was cold and rain blew in on Cassie.

"Can I come in?" Penny's voice was plaintive, beseeching.

Cassie stared at her, unable, momentarily, to speak. She finally managed: "I'm sorry, but we were just about to sit down to dinner."

"Just for a few minutes," Penny said, hacking into her hand. "See, we've kept the spot open, there's still a place for you. I can give you a few more days to reconsider."

"We're not interested," Cassie said, sure of it now.

"Why not?" Penny emitted a sound—half sob, half laugh. "Just give me a reason. I don't understand. None of us understand."

From the back of the house, Cassie could hear the glass door sliding open, Duncan coming inside, whistling. She couldn't let him find her here, couldn't let him see how far it had gone.

"We don't want you," she whispered into the night. "The answer is no." She hesitated, then hissed into the lashing rain: *"Go away."*

She could hear Penny's bewildered shout, "Lots of people would give their eyeteeth—" before it was cut short by the sound of the closing door.

2011

IRWIN SHAW
1913–1984

Shaw was born in New York City of Russian Jewish immigrants. Upon graduating from Brooklyn College, he began writing plays, screenplays, and radio scripts. In the late 1930s he wrote stories for such magazines as *The New Yorker* and *Esquire*; these stories appeared in book form as *Sailor Off the Bremen* (1939) and *Welcome to the City* (1942), collections containing some of his best works, such as "The Girls in Their Summer Dresses" and "The Eighty-Yard Run." They are considered twentieth-century American classics. After serving in the U.S. Army during World War II, Shaw published two novels—*The Young Lions* (1948) and *The Troubled Air* (1951)—before moving to Europe, where he wrote the best-selling novels *Voices of a Summer Day* (1965), *Rich Man, Poor Man* (1970), and *Evening in Byzantium* (1973). In his heyday Shaw was considered one of the best American short-story writers and exerted considerable influence on the form. His stories are collected in *Short Stories: Five Decades* (1978).

The Girls in Their Summer Dresses

Fifth Avenue was shining in the sun when they left the Brevoort and started walking toward Washington Square.[1] The sun was warm, even though it was November, and everything looked like Sunday morning—the buses, and the well-dressed people walking slowly in couples and the quiet buildings with the windows closed.

Michael held Frances' arm tightly as they walked downtown in the sunlight. They walked lightly, almost smiling, because they had slept late and had a good breakfast and it was Sunday. Michael unbuttoned his coat and let it flap around him in the mild wind. They walked, without saying anything, among the young and pleasant-looking people who somehow seem to make up most of the population of that section of New York City.

"Look out," Frances said, as they crossed Eighth Street. "You'll break your neck."

Michael laughed and Frances laughed with him.

"She's not so pretty, anyway," Frances said. "Anyway, not pretty enough to take a chance breaking your neck looking at her."

Michael laughed again. He laughed louder this time, but not as solidly. "She wasn't a bad-looking girl. She had a nice complexion. Country-girl complexion. How did you know I was looking at her?" Frances cocked her head to

---

1. Locations in New York City's Greenwich Village.

one side and smiled at her husband under the tip-tilted brim of her hat. "Mike, darling . . ." she said.

Michael laughed, just a little laugh this time. "Okay," he said. "The evidence is in. Excuse me. It was the complexion. It's not the sort of complexion you see much in New York. Excuse me."

Frances patted his arm lightly and pulled him along a little faster toward Washington Square.

"This is a nice morning," she said. "This is a wonderful morning. When I have breakfast with you it makes me feel good all day."

"Tonic," Michael said. "Morning pickup. Rolls and coffee with Mike and you're on the alkali side, guaranteed."

"That's the story. Also, I slept all night, wound around you like a rope."

"Saturday night," he said. "I permit such liberties only when the week's work is done."

"You're getting fat," she said.

"Isn't it the truth? The lean man from Ohio."

"I love it," she said, "an extra five pounds of husband."

"I love it, too," Michael said gravely.

"I have an idea," Frances said.

"My wife has an idea. That pretty girl."

"Let's not see anybody all day," Frances said. "Let's just hang around with each other. You and me. We're always up to our neck in people, drinking their Scotch, or drinking our Scotch, we only see each other in bed . . ."

"The Great Meeting Place," Michael said. "Stay in bed long enough and everybody you ever knew will show up there."

"Wise guy," Frances said. "I'm talking serious."

"Okay, I'm listening serious."

"I want to go out with my husband all day long. I want him to talk only to me and listen only to me."

"What's to stop us?" Michael asked. "What party intends to prevent me from seeing my wife alone on Sunday? What party?"

"The Stevensons. They want us to drop by around one o'clock and they'll drive us into the country."

"The lousy Stevensons," Mike said. "Transparent. They can whistle. They can go driving in the country by themselves. My wife and I have to stay in New York and bore each other tête-à-tête."[2]

"Is it a date?"

"It's a date."

Frances leaned over and kissed him on the tip of the ear.

"Darling," Michael said. "This is Fifth Avenue."

"Let me arrange a program," Frances said. "A planned Sunday in New York for a young couple with money to throw away."

"Go easy."

"First let's go see a football game. A professional football game," Frances said, because she knew Michael loved to watch them. "The Giants are playing. And it'll be nice to be outside all day today and get hungry and later we'll go

---

2. "Face to face," that is, in private (French).

down to Cavanagh's and get a steak as big as a blacksmith's apron, with a bottle of wine, and after that, there's a new French picture at the Filmarte that everybody says . . . Say, are you listening to me?"

"Sure," he said. He took his eyes off the hatless girl with the dark hair, cut dancer-style, like a helmet, who was walking past him with the self-conscious strength and grace dancers have. She was walking without a coat and she looked very solid and strong and her belly was flat, like a boy's, under her skirt, and her hips swung boldly because she was a dancer and also because she knew Michael was looking at her. She smiled a little to herself as she went past and Michael noticed all these things before he looked back at his wife. "Sure," he said, "we're going to watch the Giants and we're going to eat steak and we're going to see a French picture. How do you like that?"

"That's it," Frances said flatly. "That's the program for the day. Or maybe you'd just rather walk up and down Fifth Avenue."

"No," Michael said carefully. "Not at all."

"You always look at other women," Frances said. "At every damn woman in the city of New York."

"Oh, come now," Michael said, pretending to joke. "Only pretty ones. And, after all, how many pretty women are there in New York? Seventeen?"

"More. At least you seem to think so. Wherever you go."

"Not the truth. Occasionally, maybe, I look at a woman as she passes. In the street. I admit, perhaps in the street I look at a woman once in a while. . . ."

"Everywhere," Frances said. "Every damned place we go. Restaurants, subways, theaters, lectures, concerts."

"Now, darling," Michael said. "I look at everything. God gave me eyes and I look at women and men and subway excavations and moving pictures and the little flowers of the field. I casually inspect the universe."

"You ought to see the look in your eye," Frances said, "as you casually inspect the universe on Fifth Avenue."

"I'm a happily married man." Michael pressed her elbow tenderly, knowing what he was doing. "Example for the whole twentieth century, Mr. and Mrs. Mike Loomis."

"You mean it?"

"Frances, baby . . ."

"Are you really happily married?"

"Sure," Michael said, feeling the whole Sunday morning sinking like lead inside him. "Now what the hell is the sense in talking like that?"

"I would like to know." Frances walked faster now, looking straight ahead, her face showing nothing, which was the way she always managed it when she was arguing or feeling bad.

"I'm wonderfully happily married," Michael said patiently. "I am the envy of all men between the ages of fifteen and sixty in the state of New York."

"Stop kidding," Frances said.

"I have a fine home," Michael said. "I got nice books and a phonograph and nice friends. I live in a town I like the way I like and I do the work I like and I live with the woman I like. Whenever something good happens, don't I run to you? When something bad happens, don't I cry on your shoulder?"

"Yes," Frances said. "You look at every woman that passes."

"That's an exaggeration."

"Every woman." Frances took her hand off Michael's arm. "If she's not pretty you turn away fairly quickly. If she's halfway pretty you watch her for about seven steps. . . ."

"My Lord, Frances!"

"If she's pretty you practically break your neck . . ."

"Hey, let's have a drink," Michael said, stopping.

"We just had breakfast."

"Now, listen, darling," Mike said, choosing his words with care, "it's a nice day and we both feel good and there's no reason why we have to break it up. Let's have a nice Sunday."

"I could have a fine Sunday if you didn't look as though you were dying to run after every skirt on Fifth Avenue."

"Let's have a drink," Michael said.

"I don't want a drink."

"What do you want, a fight?"

"No," Frances said, so unhappily that Michael felt terribly sorry for her. "I don't want a fight. I don't know why I started this. All right, let's drop it. Let's have a good time."

They joined hands consciously and walked without talking among the baby carriages and the old Italian men in their Sunday clothes and the young women with Scotties in Washington Square Park.

"I hope it's a good game today," Frances said after a while, her tone a good imitation of the tone she had used at breakfast and at the beginning of their walk. "I like professional football games. They hit each other as though they're made out of concrete. When they tackle each other," she said, trying to make Michael laugh, "they make divots. It's very exciting."

"I want to tell you something," Michael said very seriously. "I have not touched another woman. Not once. In all the five years."

"All right," Frances said.

"You believe that, don't you?"

"All right."

They walked between the crowded benches, under the scrubby city park trees.

"I try not to notice it," Frances said, as though she were talking to herself. "I try to make believe it doesn't mean anything. Some men're like that, I tell myself, they have to see what they're missing."

"Some women're like that, too," Michael said. "In my time I've seen a couple of ladies."

"I haven't even looked at another man," Frances said, walking straight ahead, "since the second time I went out with you."

"There's no law," Michael said.

"I feel rotten inside, in my stomach, when we pass a woman and you look at her and I see that look in your eye and that's the way you looked at me the first time, in Alice Maxwell's house. Standing there in the living room, next to the radio, with a green hat on and all those people."

"I remember the hat," Michael said.

"The same look," Frances said. "And it makes me feel bad. It makes me feel terrible."

"Sssh, please, darling, sssh. . . ."

"I think I would like a drink now," Frances said.

They walked over to a bar on Eighth Street, not saying anything, Michael automatically helping her over curbstones and guiding her past automobiles. He walked, buttoning his coat, looking thoughtfully at his neatly shined heavy brown shoes as they made the steps toward the bar. They sat near a window in the bar and the sun streamed in, and there was a small cheerful fire in the fireplace. A little Japanese waiter came over and put down some pretzels and smiled happily at them.

"What do you order after breakfast?" Michael asked.

"Brandy, I suppose," Frances said.

"Courvoisier," Michael told the waiter. "Two Courvoisier."

The waiter came with the glasses and they sat drinking the brandy in the sunlight. Michael finished half his and drank a little water.

"I look at women," he said. "Correct. I don't say it's wrong or right, I look at them. If I pass them on the street and I don't look at them, I'm fooling you, I'm fooling myself."

"You look at them as though you want them," Frances said, playing with her brandy glass. "Every one of them."

"In a way," Michael said, speaking softly and not to his wife, "in a way that's true. I don't do anything about it, but it's true."

"I know it. That's why I feel bad."

"Another brandy," Michael called. "Waiter, two more brandies."

"Why do you hurt me?" Frances asked. "What're you doing?"

Michael sighed and closed his eyes and rubbed them gently with his fingertips. "I love the way women look. One of the things I like best about New York is the battalions of women. When I first came to New York from Ohio that was the first thing I noticed, the million wonderful women, all over the city. I walked around with my heart in my throat."

"A kid," Frances said. "That's a kid's feeling."

"Guess again," Michael said. "Guess again. I'm older now, I'm a man getting near middle age, putting on a little fat and I still love to walk along Fifth Avenue at three o'clock on the east side of the street between Fiftieth and Fifty-seventh streets, they're all out then, making believe they're shopping, in their furs and their crazy hats, everything all concentrated from all over the world into eight blocks, the best furs, the best clothes, the handsomest women, out to spend money and feeling good about it, looking coldly at you, making believe they're not looking at you as you go past."

The Japanese waiter put the two drinks down, smiling with great happiness.

"Everything is all right?" he asked.

"Everything is wonderful," Michael said.

"If it's just a couple of fur coats," Frances said, "and forty-five-dollar hats . . ."

"It's not the fur coats. Or the hats. That's just the scenery for that particular kind of woman. Understand," he said, "you don't have to listen to this."

"I want to listen."

"I like the girls in the offices. Neat, with their eyeglasses, smart, chipper, knowing what everything is about, taking care of themselves all the time." He kept his eye on the people going slowly past outside the window. "I like the girls on Forty-fourth Street at lunchtime, the actresses, all dressed up on nothing a week, talking to the good-looking boys, wearing themselves out being young and vivacious outside Sardi's,[3] waiting for producers to look at them. I like the salesgirls in Macy's, paying attention to you first because you're a man, leaving lady customers waiting, flirting with you over socks and books and phonograph needles. I got all this stuff accumulated in me because I've been thinking about it for ten years and now you've asked for it and here it is."

"Go ahead," Frances said.

"When I think of New York City, I think of all the girls, the Jewish girls, the Italian girls, the Irish, Polack, Chinese, German, Negro, Spanish, Russian girls, all on parade in the city. I don't know whether it's something special with me or whether every man in the city walks around with the same feeling inside him, but I feel as though I'm at a picnic in this city. I like to sit near the women in the theaters, the famous beauties who've taken six hours to get ready and look it. And the young girls at the football games, with the red cheeks, and when the warm weather comes, the girls in their summer dresses . . ." He finished his drink. "That's the story. You asked for it, remember. I can't help but look at them. I can't help but want them."

"You want them," Frances repeated without expression. "You said that."

"Right," Michael said, being cruel now and not caring, because she had made him expose himself. "You brought this subject up for discussion, we will discuss it fully."

Frances finished her drink and swallowed two or three times extra. "You say you love me?"

"I love you, but I also want them. Okay."

"I'm pretty, too," Frances said. "As pretty as any of them."

"You're beautiful," Michael said, meaning it.

"I'm good for you," Frances said, pleading. "I've made a good wife, a good housekeeper, a good friend. I'd do any damn thing for you."

"I know," Michael said. He put his hand out and grasped hers.

"You'd like to be free to . . ." Frances said.

"Sssh."

"Tell the truth." She took her hand away from under his.

Michael flicked the edge of his glass with his finger. "Okay," he said gently. "Sometimes I feel I would like to be free."

"Well," Frances said defiantly, drumming on the table, "anytime you say . . ."

"Don't be foolish." Michael swung his chair around to her side of the table and patted her thigh.

She began to cry, silently, into her handkerchief, bent over just enough so that nobody else in the bar would notice. "Someday," she said, crying, "you're going to make a move . . ."

Michael didn't say anything. He sat watching the bartender slowly peel a lemon.

"Aren't you?" Frances asked harshly. "Come on, tell me. Talk. Aren't you?"

"Maybe," Michael said. He moved his chair back again. "How the hell do I know?"

"You know," Frances persisted. "Don't you know?"

"Yes," Michael said after a while. "I know."

---

3. Restaurant in Manhattan's theater district.

Frances stopped crying then. Two or three snuffles into the handkerchief and she put it away and her face didn't tell anything to anybody. "At least do me one favor," she said.

"Sure."

"Stop talking about how pretty this woman is, or that one. Nice eyes, nice breasts, a pretty figure, good voice," she mimicked his voice. "Keep it to yourself. I'm not interested."

"Excuse me." Michael waved to the waiter. "I'll keep it to myself."

Frances flicked the corner of her eyes. "Another brandy," she told the waiter.

"Two," Michael said.

"Yes, ma'am, yes, sir," said the waiter, backing away.

Frances regarded him coolly across the table. "Do you want me to call the Stevensons?" she asked. "It'll be nice in the country."

"Sure," Michael said. "Call them up."

She got up from the table and walked across the room toward the telephone. Michael watched her walk, thinking, What a pretty girl, what nice legs.

1939

JEAN SHEPHERD
1921–1999

Shepherd was born in Chicago and grew up in Hammond, Indiana. After attending Indiana University and serving in the U.S. Army Signal Corps in World War II, he began a long career as a radio and television personality, eventually settling at WOR-AM radio in New York, where he remained a fixture for twenty-one years. Known and loved across America, his comic stories often took the classic form of the tall tale, as practiced by earlier writers such as Mark Twain, but updated for mid-twentieth-century Middle America. Shepherd's storytelling eventually grew into a writing career. His tales about growing up in Indiana were collected in a number of best-selling books, including *In God We Trust, All Others Pay Cash* (1966), *Wanda Hickey's Night of Golden Memories* (1971), and *A Fistful of Fig Newtons* (1981). A movie made from his work, *A Christmas Story* (1983), has become a television staple of the holiday season.

Lost at C

A wave of numbness surged through my body with stunning force. At last I knew what it felt like to be sitting with that brass hat on your skull with those straps around your ankles as the warden pulls the big switch. Out of the corner of my eye I caught the glint of Mr. Pittinger's horn-rims and the ice-blue ray from his left eye. As the giant baroque equation loomed on the blackboard, my life unreeled before my eyes in the classic manner of the final moments of mortal existence. I was finished. Done. It had all come to this. Somehow I had always known it would.

It all started in first grade at the Warren G. Harding School, where I was one among a rabble of sweaty, wrestling, peanut-butter-and-jelly sandwich eaters. But it was not until the end of the third month of school that I became dimly aware of a curse that would follow me throughout my life. Along with Martin Perlmutter, Schwartz, Chester Woczniewski, Helen Weathers, and poor old Zynzmeister, I was a member of the Alphabetical Ghetto, forever doomed by the fateful first letter of our last names to squat restlessly, hopelessly, at the very end of every line known to man, fearfully aware that whatever the authorities were passing out, they would run out of goodies by the time they got to us.

Medical science has finally begun to realize that those of us at the end of the alphabet live shorter lives, sweat more, and are far jumpier than those in the B's and E's and even the M's and L's. People at the tail end of the alphabet grow up accepting the fact that everybody else comes first. The Warren G. Harding School had an almost mystic belief in the alphabet; if you were a P, you sat behind every O, regardless of myopia.

Me and Schwartz and Woczniewski sat so far back in the classroom that the blackboard was only a vague rumor to us. Miss Shields was a shifting figure in the haze on the distant horizon, her voice a faint but ominous drone, punctuated by squeaking chalk. Within a short time we became adept at reading the inflection, if not the content, of those far-off sounds, sensing instantly when danger was looming. Danger meant simply being called on. Kids in the front of the classroom didn't know the meaning of danger. Ace test-takers, they loved nothing more than to display their immense knowledge by waving their hands frantically even before questions were asked. Today, when I think of the classrooms of my youth, I see a forest of waving hands between me and the teacher. They were the smart-asses who went on to become corporation presidents, TV talk-show hosts, and owners of cabin cruisers. *Carson*, *Cavett*, Steve *Allen*, *Cronkite*, *Donahue*—there isn't a goddamn Woczniewski in the lot. Every one of those bastards grew up never doubting that he was destined to be at the head of the class, with the rest of the mob, the Schwartzes, the Zynzmeisters, forever in the *Lumpenworld*[1] of the audience.

We in the back of the classroom trod a rockier and far more dangerous path. Since we could neither hear nor see, we had only one course open if we were going to pass. The key was never to be called on. It was imperative never to be caught out in the open, if possible not to be seen at all. Each of us evolved his own methods of survival. Fat Helen Weathers could sweat at will, surrounding herself with a faint hazy cloud so that Miss Shields could never quite see her in focus, believing that Helen was just a thumb-smudge on her glasses. Perlmutter had a thin pale beaky face that you could not remember even while you were looking at it. He didn't have to hide. No teacher ever remembered his name or whether he was even there. He'd sit for hours without moving a muscle, as anonymous as a pale hat rack. He was a born cost accountant.

One day during an oral quiz, however—always a dangerous time for all of us—Perlmutter displayed the true stuff of champions. Miss Shields unaccountably called on him during an incomprehensible discussion involving the principal parts of speech, which seemed to be called "participles" or something like that. It was a discussion, naturally, only vaguely heard back in the ghetto. We thought Perlmutter was finished, but we had underestimated him. Without missing a beat, his face turned bright purple, his eyes bulged like a pair of overripe grapes, his neck throbbed, and a spectacular geyser of blood gushed from both nostrils.

"This is terrible!" Miss Shields cried, scooping him up in her arms and rushing him to the nurse's office, where he was excused from school for the rest of the day. She never called on him again.

Schwartz, short, squat, built like a fireplug, would slowly scrunch down in his seat until only the top fringe of his crew cut could be seen, level with his

---

1. Shepherd's coinage, from "lumpen proletariat."

desk. As for Zynzmeister, a strict Catholic, he sat so far behind even us that he spent his entire school career jammed up against the cabinet in the rear of the room where worn erasers, pickled biology specimens, and moldering lunches were stored; Zynzmeister, destined to go through life listed on the last page of every telephone directory. God only knows how he saw the rest of mankind in his troubled imagination; probably as an endless line snaking to the cosmic horizon, with poor Zynzmeister, shuffling from foot to foot, the very last person at the end of the Big Parade. His defense was religion; divine intervention. The click of his beads as they were counted kept up a steady castanet beat during Miss Shields's distant cluckings. It seemed to work.

My salvation was simple, yet deceptively difficult. I moved like a snake, bobbing and weaving, shifting my body from side to side, dropping a shoulder here, shifting my neck a few degrees to the right there, always keeping a line of kids between me and the teacher's eagle eye. I blessed the Beehive hairdo when it became popular. I would have loved the Afro.

For those rare but inevitable occasions—say, during a chickenpox epidemic—when the ranks in the rows ahead were too thin to provide adequate cover, I practiced the vacant-eyeball ploy, which has since become a popular device for junior executives the world over who cannot afford to be nailed by their seniors in sales conferences and other perilous situations. The vacant eyeball appears to be looking attentively but, in fact, sees nothing. It is a blank mirror of anonymity. I learned early in the game that if they don't catch your eye, they don't call on you. Combined with a fixed facial expression of deadpan alertness—neither too deadpan nor too alert—this technique has been known to render its practitioner virtually invisible.

The third, and possibly most important, tactic of classroom survival is thought control. When danger looms, it is necessary to repeat silently, with intense concentration, the hypnotic command Don't call on me, Don't call on me, Don't call on me, sending out invisible waves of powerful thought energy until the teacher's mind is mysteriously clouded. After endless hours of rehearsal before the mirror in the bathroom, I had developed a fourth and final gambit—my Cute Look: shy, boyish, a smile of such disarming cuddliness as to be lethal. I flashed it, of course, only with great caution, during comparatively safe periods in the classroom—upon entering and leaving—and at lunch, recess, I would warm teachers when their guard was down.

Those of us in the back rows learned quickly that grades are handed out not on the basis of actual accomplishment but by intuitive feel. At that crucial moment when Miss Shields sat down to fill out my report card, I knew that my Cute Look would pop into her mind when my name appeared before her. Since she had nothing else to go on—other than catch-as-catch-can test answers gleaned from my shirt cuff or the blue book of the kid ahead of me—it was only natural for her to put down a B, which is all I ever wanted out of life.

So it was that I weaved and bobbed, truckled and beamed my way through grade after grade at Warren G. Harding School. Perlmutter, Schwartz, Woczniewski, Helen Weathers, and I, as well as poor old Zynzmeister, sat on shore as the deepening river of education flowed by us unheard, unseen. Once in a great while, of course, a teacher would raise her voice above the usual bleat, or a transient air current would carry an isolated phrase or maybe even a full sentence all the way back to our little band, and this would often precipitate labored intellectual debates.

Like the day we clearly caught the word *marsupial*. We knew it had something to do with animals, since Miss Robinette had pulled down a chart on which we could barely make out drawings of what could not have been people, unless they were down on all fours. After school that afternoon, Schwartz and Chester and I were kicking a Carnation can down an alley when a large police dog with one ear missing roared out from between two garages after a tomcat that must have weighed thirty pounds. The dog's name was Ratso and he was owned by the postman, Mr. L. D. Johnson, who, I guess, kept him at home so that he could bite their postman when he delivered mail to their house.

"Boy, I'd like to see old Rat go after one a them marsupials," said Chester.

"They lay eggs," Schwartz stated with satisfaction. He had a way of saying things like that as though he had been the first to discover them, or at least had confirmed them through independent research.

"You mean like ducks?" I asked. My hungry mind was questing for more knowledge.

"Do they quack, too?" Chester asked.

"How should I know?" said Schwartz, looking disgusted. "I ain't no mind reader."

Thus the subject of marsupials was closed forever. They were never mentioned again in class, at least as far as I know, and to this day my entire knowledge of marsupials consists of what Schwartz told us about them.

I can truthfully say that in all the years of my struggle through grade school at Warren G. Harding, I actually learned one true fact about the great world. For some reason, a mysterious vagary of acoustics perhaps, a complete sentence arrived back at our little ghetto headquarters one day:

"Bolivia exports tin."

That is the sum total of my grade school education. I grabbed that fact like a drowning man clinging to a bobbing 2×4 in a trackless ocean. It has been endlessly useful ever since. At cocktail parties I silently bide my time, nibbling cashews and sipping my martini thoughtfully, and then, in a lull of the conversation, I drop my bomb: "But all of you have ignored the tin economy of Bolivia, a crucial point." I saunter away as though in search of more intellectual companions, leaving behind a covey of stunned new admirers. Some men have achieved cabinet rank on the basis of one such fact.

Warren G. Harding was widely known, during the dark ages when I was attending it, for being an "advanced" school, and actual tests were very rare. This worked in beautifully with our survival techniques and made it possible for me and my band of fellow ignoramuses to slide by year after year undetected. Although, of course, we didn't know it at the time, we were part of the pioneering advance wave of generation upon generation of total illiterates that have been spawned by "progressive" education.

At home, grade by grade, my reputation slowly grew until I was considered a truly superior intellect. This is one of the great American myths. It has persisted for ages—the unfailing belief that every generation is brighter, taller, more beautiful, than the one before it—in spite of obvious evidence to the contrary. Naturally, I did everything I could to encourage my old man in this belief. I must admit that I, too, firmly believed it. Every generation does, until, inevitably, the walls come tumbling down.

"Boy, kids today sure are a lot smarter than we was when we was kids. Why, at his age I hardly knew nothin'." The old man, sitting at the kitchen table with a can of Blatz in his mitt, was talking to my uncle Carl, who kept shoving his upper plate back into his mouth. He had gotten his false teeth from the Relief,[2] and he was proud of them.

"Tell your uncle Carl about Bolivia," the old man ordered.

"Why, certainly," I said confidently. It was a command performance I had given many times before. "Bolivia exports tin."

My father, his jaw slack with amazement, turned to Uncle Carl and said in a low, emotional voice, "See what I mean? Kids nowadays know everything. Didja hear that, Carl? Bolivia exports tin!"

"Geez." Uncle Carl's teeth clicked back into place. "When I was a kid they didn't even have Bolivia! Boy!"

They both nodded in silent humility, and went back to guzzling beer. Coolly, I made my exit through the back door, lugging a Kraft-American-cheese-and-jelly sandwich. Another triumph!

The years passed, punctuated by occasional tight squeaks, but my true identity as a faker was never really in danger of exposure. Finally the big day came. On a glorious sun-drenched morning when even the red clouds of rusty blast-furnace dust glowed in spring beauty, Graduation Day arrived. I had made it. Dressed in our scratchy Sunday clothes, we were herded, along with parents, uncles, aunts, and a few scattered cousins, into the gym.

The despised glee club sang the Warren G. Harding fight song, accompanied by Miss Bundy, the kindergarten teacher, on the piano, her crinkly straw-colored hair bobbing up and down with every beat, her huge bottom enveloping the piano stool. Then a famous local undertaker and Chevrolet dealer delivered a mind-numbing oration on how his generation was passing the torch of civilization from its faltering hands into our youthful energetic and idealistic hands. Naturally, we were seated alphabetically, and we in the rear caught only a few disjointed phrases.

Schwartz, sweating profusely in his new sports coat, whispered, "What's all that stuff about torches? I didn't get no torch."

"They must have given them to the front of the class," I answered. Little did I realize how right I was.

But I got my diploma. It was official. I was a graduate. Clasping my sacred scroll there on the stage—while those even farther below me in the alphabet filed up to receive theirs—I found myself growing wise and dignified, a person of substance, well equipped to carry torches, to best foes, to identify the parts of speech, including gerunds, to draw from memory the sinister confluence of the Tigris and the Euphrates.

At last we were free. Warren G. Harding and its warm embrace, its easy ways, stood forever behind us. On our way home the old man, his clean white shirt crackling with starch, said: "Whaddaya say we celebrate by pickin' up some ice cream at the Igloo?"

---

2. That is, the public welfare agency.

Ecstatic, I sat in the back seat of the Olds with my kid brother, clutching the precious document on which—though I didn't discover it till later—my name had been misspelled, in Old English lettering.

That summer sped by in a blur of sun and gentle showers that made the outfields fragrant with clover and sweet William. In September I would be a full-fledged high school kid. Guys in high school had always seemed to be remote, godlike creatures who drove cars, wore thick sweaters with letters on them, and hung around Big Bill's Drive-In. What actually happened in high school was never mentioned, at least among those of us in the R's and the Y's. A few rumors, of course, had filtered down to us, and they only added to our sense of rising excitement about the new life that was about to begin.

The first omen of evil struck early in September, just a few days before school was to open. I came home covered with scratches and mosquito bites from a great day out in the weeds and walked right into it.

"There's some mail for you," my mother grunted to me as she struggled out the screen door with a huge bag of garbage that was dripping coffee grounds onto the linoleum.

"Mail? For me?" I was surprised, since I received very little mail except for an occasional announcement from the International Crime Detection Institute of East St. Louis, Illinois, informing me that I was frittering away my life when I could be "Earning Big Money Spotting Crooks."

I ripped open the envelope and found a printed form stating that high school registration and classes for freshmen would begin next Monday, and that I was assigned to Miss Snyder, to whom I would report at 8:30 A.M. Period.

"Hey, Schwartz," I barked into the phone, "didja get yer card?"

"Yeah!"

"What's this registration stuff?"

"I don't know!" Schwartz shouted to be heard over the uproar of his mother screaming at his kid brother, Douglas. "I guess that's where you pick the teachers and the classes and stuff you want to take!"

"Yeah!" I hollered back. Ah, the dreams of youth.

Registration day dawned windy, with a flat silver sun gleaming through the haze from the steel plant. Schwartz, Flick, Chester, and a whole crowd of us rode the bus to high school. No one had ever taken a bus to Harding. We all got there our own way, the girls strolling down the sidewalk, the boys scurrying up alleys, through vacant lots, over fences, past dogs, chickens, sprinklers, and one maniacal goose that from time to time rushed out of its yard and ripped a chunk from somebody's corduroys. Catching a bus on the corner was a whole new thing. I sat in the back, amid the din, my guts in an uproar of excitement. High school!

We carried rulers, fountain pens, erasers—a full arsenal of equipment for use on the battlefields of higher learning. Schwartz had a T square made of red plastic and a matching compass, God knows what for. I clutched the brown-and-white fake-marble Parker automatic pencil that my aunt Glen had given me upon graduation from eighth grade. And inside the front of my three-ring notebook, which had green imitation-leather covers, I had pasted a picture of an Indianapolis Kurtis-Kraft racer. I was ready for anything. In keeping with the gravity of the occasion, I was wearing my electric-blue sports coat and my silver tie with its red hand-painted snail, both stars in my wardrobe. The bus was heavily scented with Lucky Tiger hair oil, since every male aboard had gotten a haircut for the big day.

I had lain in bed making plans the night before. I would grab the front seat in every class and listen to every word. No longer would I duck and dodge behind a screen of kids. That was all behind me. Mentally I crouched at the mark, waiting for the starter's gun to send me flying down the track ahead of the pack. If others could actually learn, so could I. It was going to be a whole new ball game, a clean slate, a new start. I was the victim of another American myth, namely that things can actually change for the better, that if you try hard enough you can transform the lead of your crummy self into some golden ideal. Countless billions are spent yearly in our blessed country on diets guaranteed to peel suet off in seconds, books that promise incredible sexual bliss, and others promising stupendous riches and happiness to those who can master the Seven Golden Rules contained therein. Alas.

The bus rolled up before nirvana and we piled out, some on the run yelling hysterically, others ashen-faced and stiff-legged with terror. A few pretended that it was like any other bus ride. The school loomed over us like the walls of the Grand Canyon. Made of dull red brick, it stretched out to either horizon. Thousands of kids milled around the outside, waiting for the doors to open. Girls bigger than my aunt Clara towered over me, and they had bumps in their sweaters like the ladies that Gene Autry sang to at the Saturday matinees. A blind torrent of fear washed over me. For a while, I had been one of the truly big men at Warren G. Harding and now I was nothing. Clinging to my lunch bag with a sweaty hand, I hunted frantically for a familiar face, but Schwartz and Flick and the others had been swallowed up.

BRRRRR-INNNGGGG! I was carried forward on the crest of the horde as it surged in through the huge front doors. Great staircases with rivers of kids streamed in all directions. My card read REPORT TO ROOM 220. Kids all around me hollered and laughed back and forth. They all seemed to know one another. I had never felt so alone. Figuring astutely that Room 220 had to be on the second floor, I joined the torrent raging upward. The second floor looked even vaster than the first. The halls stretched so far in both directions that I couldn't see the ends. Lockers banged and I smelled, for the first time, that indescribable high school building aroma, a rich fragrance made up of thousands of bodies, floor wax, chalk, leftover tuna fish sandwiches, chlorine from the swimming pool, disinfectant from the johns, and fermenting jockstraps from the gym.

I tried to read the numbers on doors as I was swept onward like a salmon in the spawning season: 205, 207, 214, 218—220! My home room, where I was to spend four hellish years of my life. A gaunt, razor-sharp teacher sat at a gray steel and formica desk; silver gray hair, glistening rimless glasses, gray mannish wool suit; even her face was gray. Miss Snyder, my home room teacher.

I sensed immediately that she wasn't going to be a pushover for my Cute Look, but I turned it on anyway, at full candle power. She peered at me coldly through her rimless glasses.

"Your card, please," she snapped in a crackling, flat voice. I handed it over. She glanced at it, glanced up at me, registering my face in the rogue's gallery of her mind. I could almost hear the shutters clicking.

"Take that seat there back of Rukowski. He's the one in the purple sweater."

I walked down between the aisles of alien faces to my seat. It was, of course, in the next-to-the-last row. It would be mine for the next four years. Ahead of me loomed Rukowski, a giant mountain of flesh over which had been stretched a purple jersey covered with chevrons, the number 76, and a row of stripes. Later I learned that Rukowski had been an all-state tackle for the past six years and was the bulwark of one of the toughest defensive lines in seven states. He was a good man to sit behind. I peered around the room. I was the only delegate to Room 220 from Warren G. Harding.

Miss Snyder stood at the blackboard and hurled the first harpoon of the season: "You freshmen who are with us today are already enrolled for the courses you will be required to take. Here are your program cards." She dealt out 3 × 5-inch blue cards, which were handed back to the freshmen. Each card was neatly lined into eight periods, and after each period was the name of a teacher, a subject, and a classroom. One period was labeled LUNCH, another STUDY, and so on. Every minute of my day was laid out for me. So much for my dreams of freedom.

"Freshmen, this is your first day in high school. You are no longer in grade school. If you work hard, you will do well. If you don't, you will regret it. You are here to learn. You are not here to play. Remember this and remember it well: *What you do here will follow you all through life.*" She paused dramatically. In the hushed silence, I could hear Rukowski wheezing ahead of me. None of this, of course, affected him. Anyone who could block the way he could block would have no trouble getting through life.

"Your first class will begin in five minutes. Any questions?" No one raised a hand.

I sat there, pawing in the chute, anxious to begin my glorious career of learning. No more would I fake my way. A new era was about to begin. The bell rang. The starting gate slammed open.

I had thundered a couple of hundred feet through the hall with the mob before it hit me that I had no idea where the hell I was supposed to go. As the crowd surged around me, I struggled to read my program card. All I could make out was Room 127. I had only a minute to make it, so I battled my way down a flight of stairs. Then: 101, 105, 109, 112, 117–127, just in time. Already the classroom was three-quarters filled. Ahead of me, running interference, was Rukowski, trying his luck at this course, I later learned, for the third time in as many semesters. Getting his shoulder into it, he bulled his way through the door, buffeting aside a herd of spindly little freshmen. It was Schwartz, good old Schwartz, and Flick and Chester and Helen Weathers. My old gang! Even poor old Zynzmeister. Whatever it was, I would not have to go through it alone.

"Hi, Schwartz!"

Schwartz smiled wanly. And Helen Weathers giggled—until she saw, at the same moment I did, a tall, square man standing motionless at the blackboard. He had a grim blue jaw and short, kinky black crew-cut hair. His eyes were tiny ball bearings behind glasses with thick black rims. He wore a dark, boxy suit that looked like it was made of black sandpaper. The bell rang and the door closed behind us. I joined the crowd around his desk who were putting registration cards into a box. I did likewise.

"All right. Settle down. Let's get organized." The man's voice had a cutting rasp to it, like a steel file working on concrete. "We sit alphabetically in this class. A's up here in front to my right. Get going."

I trudged behind Schwartz and Helen Weathers toward the dim recesses in the back of the classroom. Well, at least I'd be among friends. It was about a quarter of a mile to the front of the room, but I sat bolt upright in my seat, my iron determination intact. No more faking it.

"Class, my name is Mr. Pittinger." He was the first male teacher I had ever had. Warren G. Harding was peopled entirely by motherly ladies like Mrs. Bailey and Miss Shields. Mr. Pittinger was a whole new ball game. And I still had no idea what he taught. I would soon find out.

"If you work in this class, you'll have no trouble. If you don't, I promise you nothing."

I leaned forward at my desk, scribbling madly in my notebook: *class my name is mr. pittinger if you work you will have no trouble if you dont i promise you nothing. . . .*

I figured if you wrote everything down there'd be no trouble. Every classroom of my life had been filled with girls on the Honor Roll who endlessly wrote in mysterious notebooks, even when nothing seemed to be going on. I never knew what the hell they were writing, so I took no chances. I figured I'd write everything.

"Braaghk." Mr. Pittinger cleared his gravelly throat.

braaaghk, I scribbled, *brummph.* You never know, I thought, it might appear on the exam.

He turned, picked up a piece of chalk, and began to scrawl huge block letters on the blackboard.

A-L—the chalk squeaked decisively—G-E-B-R-A. I copied each letter exactly as he'd written it.

"That is the subject of this course," he barked.

Algebra? What the hell is that?

"Algebra is the mathematics of abstract numbers."

I gulped as I wrote this down.

"I will now illustrate."

Pittinger printed a huge Y on the blackboard and below it an enormous X. I doggedly followed suit in my notebook. He then put equal signs next to the X and the Y.

"If Y equals five and X equals two, what does the following mean?"

He wrote out: $X + Y = ?$

Black fear seized my vitals. How could you add Xs and Ys? I had enough trouble with nines and sevens!

Already the crowd in front of the room were waving their hands to answer Pittinger's question. The class wasn't thirty seconds old and I was already six weeks behind. I sank lower in my seat, a faint buzzing in my ears. Instinctively I began to weave. I knew it was all over. Out of the corner of my eye I saw that Schwartz, next to me, had hunched lower and begun to emit a high, thin whimpering sound. Helen Weathers had flung up a thin spray of sweat. Chester's skin had changed to the color of the cupboards in the back of the room. And from behind me I could hear the faint, steady click of Zynzmeister's rosary.

Second by second, minute by minute, eon by eon that first algebra class droned on. I couldn't catch another word that was said, and by the time Mr. Pittinger wrote the second equation on the board, I was bobbing and weaving like a cobra and sending out high-voltage thought rays. A tiny molten knot of stark terror hissed and simmered in the pit of my stomach. I realized that for the first time in my school life, I had run into something that was completely opaque and unlearnable, and there was no way to fake it.

Don't call on me, Don't call on me, Don't call on me . . .

That night I ate my meatloaf and red cabbage in sober silence as the family yapped on, still living back in the days when I was known to all of them as the smartest little son of a bitch to ever set foot on Cleveland Street.

"Boy, look at the stuff kids study these days," the old man said with wonder as he hefted my algebra textbook in his bowling hand and riffled through the pages.

"What's all this X and Y stuff?" he asked.

"Yeah, well, it ain't much," I muttered as coolly as I could, trying to recapture some of the old élan.[3]

"Whaddaya mean, ain't much?" His eyes glowed with pride at the idea that his kid had mastered algebra in only one day.

"Abstract mathematics, that's all it is."

The old man knew he'd been totally outclassed. Even my mother stopped stirring the gravy for a few seconds. My kid brother continued to pound away at the little BBs of Ovaltine that floated around on the top of his milk.

That night sleep did not come easily. In fact, it was only the first of many storm-tossed nights to come as, algebra class by algebra class, my terror grew. All my other subjects—history, English, social studies—were a total breeze. My years of experience in fakery came into full flower. In social studies, for example, the more you hoked it up, the better the grades. On those rare occasions when asked a question, I would stand slowly, with an open yet troubled look playing over my thoughtful countenance.

"Mr. Harris, sir," I would drawl hesitantly, as though attempting to unravel the perplexity of the ages, "I guess it depends on how you view it—objectively, which, naturally, is too simple, or subjectively, in which case many factors such as a changing environment must be taken into consideration, and . . ." I would trail off.

Mr. Harris, with a snort of pleasure, would bellow: "RIGHT! There are many diverse elements, which . . ." After which he was good for at least a forty-minute solo.

History was more of the same, and English was almost embarrassingly easy as, day after day, Miss McCullough preened and congratulated herself before our class. All she needed was a little ass-kissing and there was no limit to her applause. I often felt she regretted that an A+ was the highest grade she could hand out to one who loved her as sincerely and selflessly as I did.

Every morning at eight-thirty-five, however, was another story. I marched with leaden feet and quaking bowels into Mr. Pittinger's torture chamber. By the sixth week I knew, without the shadow of a doubt, that after all these years of dodging and grinning, I was going to fail. Fail! No B, no gentleman's

---

3. Vigor, enthusiasm (French).

C—Fail. F. The big one: my own Scarlet Letter. Branded on my forehead—F, for Fuckup.

There was no question whatever. True, Pittinger had not yet been able to catch me out in the open, since I was using every trick of the trade. But I knew that one day, inevitably, the icy hand of truth would rip off my shoddy façade and expose me for all the world to see.

Pittinger was of the new school, meaning he believed that kids, theoretically motivated by an insatiable thirst for knowledge, would devour algebra in large chunks, making the final examination only a formality. He graded on performance in class and total grasp of the subject, capped off at the end of the term with an exam of brain-crushing difficulty from which he had the option of excusing those who rated A+ on classroom performance. Since I had no classroom performance, my doom was sealed.

Schwartz, too, had noticeably shrunken. Even fat Helen had developed deep hollows under her eyes, while Chester had almost completely disappeared. And Zynzmeister had taken to nibbling Communion wafers in class.

Christmas came and went in tortured gaiety. My kid brother played happily with his Terry and the Pirates[4] Dragon Lady Detector as I looked on with the sad indulgence of a withered old man whose youth had passed. As for my own presents, what good did it do to have a new first baseman's mitt when my life was over? How innocent they are, I thought as I watched my family trim the tree and scurry about wrapping packages. Before long, they will know. They will loathe me. I will be driven from this warm circle. It was about this time that I began to fear—or perhaps hope—that I would never live to be twenty-one, that I would die of some exotic debilitating disease. Then they'd be sorry. This fantasy alternated with an even better fantasy that if I did reach twenty-one, I would be blind and hobble about with a white cane. Then they'd really be sorry.

Not that I'd given up without a struggle. For weeks, in the privacy of my cell at home, safe from prying eyes, I continued trying to actually learn something about algebra. After a brief mental pep rally—This is simple. If Esther Jane Alberry can understand it, any fool can do it. All you gotta do is think. THINK! Reason it out!—I would sit down and open my textbook. Within minutes, I would break out in a clammy sweat and sink into a funk of non-understanding, a state so naked in its despair and self-contempt that it was soon replaced by a mood of defiant truculence. Schwartz and I took to laughing contemptuously at those boobs and brown-noses up front who took it all so seriously.

The first hints of spring began to appear. Birds twittered, buds unfurled. But men on death row are impervious to such intimations of life quickening and reborn. The only sign of the new season that I noticed was Mr. Pittinger changing from a heavy scratchy black suit into a lighter-weight scratchy black suit.

"Well, it won't be long. You gonna get a job this summer?" my old man asked me one day as he bent over the hood of the Olds, giving the fourth-hand paint job its ritual spring coat of Simoniz.

---

4. Newspaper comic strip and radio serial popular in the 1930s, '40s, and '50s. The Dragon Lady was a recurring villain character.

"Maybe. I dunno," I muttered. It wouldn't be long, indeed. Then he'd know. Everybody would know that I knew less about algebra than Ralph, Mrs. Gammie's big Airedale, who liked to pee on my mother's irises.

Mr. Pittinger had informed us that the final exam, covering a year's work in algebra, would be given on Friday of the following week. One more week of stardom on Cleveland Street. Ever since my devastating rejoinder at the dinner table about abstract mathematics, my stock had been the hottest in the neighborhood. My opinions were solicited on financial matters, world affairs, even the infield problems of the Chicago White Sox. The bigger they are, the harder they fall. Even Ralph would have more respect than I deserved. At least he didn't pretend to be anything but what he was—a copious and talented pee-er.

Wednesday, two days before the end, arrived like any other spring day. A faint breeze drifted from the south, bringing with it hints of long summer afternoons to come, of swung bats, of nights in the lilac bushes. But not for such as me. I stumped into algebra class feeling distinctly like the last soul aboard the *Titanic* as she was about to plunge to the bottom. The smart-asses were already in their seats, laughing merrily, the goddamn A's and B's and C's and even the M's. I took my seat in the back, among the rest of the condemned. Schwartz sat down sullenly and began his usual moan. Helen Weathers squatted toadlike, drenched in sweat. The class began, Pittinger's chalk squeaked, hands waved. The sun filtered in through the venetian blinds. A tennis ball pocked back and forth over a net somewhere. Faintly, the high clear voices of the girls' glee club sang, "Can you bake a cherry pie, charming Billy?" Birds twittered.

My knot of fear, by now an old friend, sputtered in my gut. In the past week, it had grown to roughly the size of a two-dollar watermelon. True, I had avoided being called on even once the entire year, but it was a hollow victory and I knew it. Minute after minute inched slowly by as I ducked and dodged, Pittinger firing question after question at the class. Glancing at my Pluto watch, which I had been given for Christmas, I noted with deep relief that less than two minutes remained before the bell.

It was then that I made my fatal mistake, the mistake that all guerrilla fighters eventually make—I lost my concentration. For years, every fiber of my being, every instant in every class, had been directed solely at survival. On this fateful Wednesday, lulled by the sun, by the gentle sound of the tennis ball, by the steady drone of Pittinger's voice, by the fact that there were just two minutes to go, my mind slowly drifted off into a golden haze. A tiny mote of dust floated down through a slanting ray of sunshine. I watched it in its slow, undulating flight, like some microscopic silver bird.

"you're the apple of my eye, darling Billy . . . I can bake a cherry pie . . ."

A rich maple syrup warmth filled my being. Out of the faint distance, I heard a deadly rasp, the faint honking of disaster.

For a stunned split second, I thought I'd been jabbed with an electric cattle prod. Pittinger's voice, loud and commanding, was pronouncing my name. He was calling on ME! Oh, my God! With a goddamn minute to go, he had nailed me. I heard Schwartz bleat a high, quavering cry, a primal scream. I knew what it meant: If they got him, the greatest master of them all, there's no hope for ANY of us!

As I stood slowly at my seat, frantically bidding for time, I saw a great puddle forming around Helen Weathers. It wasn't all sweat. Chester had sunk to the floor beneath his desk, and behind me Zynzmeister's beads were clattering so loudly I could hardly hear his Hail Marys.

"Come to the board, please. Give us the value of C in this equation."

In a stupor of wrenching fear, I felt my legs clumping up the aisle. On all sides the blank faces stared. At the board—totally unfamiliar territory to me—I stared at the first equation I had ever seen up close. It was well over a yard and a half long, lacerated by mysterious crooked lines and fractions in parentheses, with miniature twos and threes hovering above the whole thing like tiny barnacles. Xs and Ys were jumbled in crazy abandon. At the very end of this unholy mess was a tiny equal sign. And on the other side of the equal sign was a zero. Zero! All this crap adds up to nothing! Jesus Christ! My mind reeled at the very sight of this barbed-wire entanglement of mysterious symbols.

Pittinger stood to one side, arms folded, wearing an expression that said, At last I've nailed the little bastard! He had been playing with me all the time. He knew!

I glanced back at the class. It was one of the truly educational moments of my life. The entire mob, including Schwartz, Chester, and even Zynzmeister, were grinning happily, licking their chops with joyous expectation of my imminent crucifixion. I learned then that when true disaster strikes, we have no friends. And there's nothing a phony loves more in this world than to see another phony get what's coming to him.

"The value of C, please," rapped Pittinger.

The equation blurred before my eyes. The value of C. Where the hell was it? What did a C look like, anyway? Or an A or a B, for that matter. I had forgotten the alphabet.

"C, please."

I spotted a single letter C buried deep in the writhing melange of Ys and Xs and umlauts and plus signs, brackets, and God knows what all. One tiny C. A torrent of sweat raged down my spinal column. My jockey shorts were soaked and sodden with the sweat and stink of execution. Being a true guerrilla from years of the alphabetical ghetto, I showed no outward sign of panic, my face stony; unyielding. You live by the gun, you die by the gun.

"C, please." Pittinger moodily scratched at his granite chin with thumb and forefinger, his blue beard rasping nastily.

"Oh my darling Billy boy, you're the apple of my eye . . ."

Somewhere birds twittered on, tennis racquet met tennis ball. My moment had finally arrived.

Now, I have to explain that for years I had been the leader of the atheistic free-thinkers of Warren G. Harding School, scoffers all at the Sunday School miracles taught at the Presbyterian church; unbelievers.

That miracle stuff is for old ladies, all that walking on water and birds flying around with loaves of bread in their beaks. Who can believe that crap?

Now, I am not so sure. Ever since that day in Pittinger's algebra class I have had an uneasy suspicion that maybe something mysterious is going on somewhere.

As I stood and stonily gazed at the enigmatic Egyptian hieroglyphics of that fateful equation, from somewhere, someplace beyond the blue horizon, it came to me, out of the mist. I heard my voice say clearly, firmly, with decision:

"C . . . is equal to three."

Pittinger staggered back; his glasses jolted down to the tip of his nose.

"How the hell did you know?!" he bellowed hoarsely, his snap-on bow tie popping loose in the excitement.

The class was in an uproar. I caught a glimpse of Schwartz, his face pale with shock. I had caught one on the fat part of the bat. It was a true miracle. I had walked on water.

Instantly, the old instincts took over. In a cool, level voice I answered Pittinger's rhetorical question.

"Sir, I used empirical means."

He paled visibly and clung to the chalk trough for support. On cue, the bell rang out. The class was over. With a swiftness born of long experience, I was out of the room even before the echo of the bell had ceased. The guerrilla's code is always hit and run. A legend had been born.

That afternoon, as I sauntered home from school, feeling at least twelve and a half feet tall, Schwartz skulked next to me, silent, moody, kicking at passing frogs. I rubbed salt deep into his wound and sprinkled a little pepper on for good measure. Across the street, admiring clusters of girls pointed out the Algebra King as he strolled by. I heard Eileen Akers' silvery voice clearly: "There he goes. He doesn't say much in class, but when he does he makes it count." I nodded coolly toward my fans. A ripple of applause went up. I autographed a few algebra books and walked on, tall and straight in the sun. Deep down I knew that this was but a fleeting moment of glory, that when I faced the blue book exam it would be all over, but I enjoyed it while I had it.

With the benign air of a baron bestowing largess upon a wretched serf, I offered to buy Schwartz a Fudgesicle at the Igloo. He refused with a snarl.

"Why, Schwartz, what seems to be troubling you?" I asked with irony, vigorously working the salt shaker.

"You phony son of a bitch. You know what you can do with your goddamn Fudgesicle."

"Me, a phony? Why would you say an unkind thing like that?"

He spat viciously into a tulip bed. "You phony bastard. You studied!"

Inevitably, those of us who are gifted must leave those less fortunate behind in the race of life. I knew that, and Schwartz knew it. Once again I had lapped him and was moving away from the field, if only for a moment.

The next morning, Thursday, I swaggered into algebra class with head high. Even Jack Morton, the biggest smart-ass in the class, said hello as I walked in. Mr. Pittinger, his eyes glowing with admiration, smiled warmly at me.

"Hi, Pit," I said with a casual flip of the hand. We abstract mathematicians have an unspoken bond. Naturally, I was not called on during that period. After all, I had proved myself beyond any doubt.

After class, beaming at me with the intimacy of a fellow quadratic equation zealot, Mr. Pittinger asked me to stay on for a few moments.

"All my life I have heard about the born mathematical genius. It is a well-documented thing. They come along once in a while, but I never thought I'd meet one, least of all in a class of mine. Did you always have this ability?"

"Well . . ." I smiled modestly.

"Look, it would be pointless for you to waste time on our little test tomorrow. Would you help me grade the papers instead?"

"Gosh, Pit, I was looking forward to taking it, but if you really need me, I'll be glad to help." It was a master stroke.

"I'd appreciate it. I need somebody who really knows his stuff, and most of these kids are faking it."

The following afternoon, together, we graded the papers of my peers. I hate to tell you what, in all honesty, I had to do to Schwartz when I marked his pitiful travesty. I showed no mercy. After all, algebra is an absolute science and there can be no margin for kindness in matters of the mind.

1973

ISAAC BASHEVIS SINGER
1902–1991

Singer was born in Leoncin, Poland. His father, a rabbi, was an author, as was his brother, the novelist I. J. Singer. Before he emigrated to the United States in 1935, Singer worked as a journalist in Warsaw, and in New York he resumed similar work with the *Jewish Daily Forward*, continuing to write in his masterful Yiddish. His fiction is characteristically in the tradition of the spoken tale, mingling forthright literalness about the visible world with an equally literal rendition of fantastic and supernatural worlds beyond. Flavored with the colorful residue of folk tales, his explorations of Jewish life, past and present, are haunting allegories of the irrationality of history. Among his many children's books and 18 novels are *The Family Moskat* (1950), *The Slave* (1962), *The Manor* (1967), *The Estate* (1970), *Enemies: A Love Story* (1972), *Shosha* (1978), and *Meshugah*, published posthumously in 1994. His stories are most easily found in *The Collected Stories of Isaac Bashevis Singer* (1982). He was awarded the Nobel Prize in 1978.

Gimpel the Fool[1]

I

I am Gimpel the fool. I don't think myself a fool. On the contrary. But that's what folks call me. They gave me the name while I was still in school. I had seven names in all: imbecile, donkey, flax-head, dope, glump, ninny, and fool. The last name stuck. What did my foolishness consist of? I was easy to take in. They said, "Gimpel, you know the rabbi's wife has been brought to childbed?" So I skipped school. Well, it turned out to be a lie. How was I supposed to know? She hadn't had a big belly. But I never looked at her belly. Was that really so foolish? The gang laughed and hee-hawed, stomped and danced and chanted a good-night prayer. And instead of the raisins they give when a woman's lying in, they stuffed my hand full of goat turds. I was no weakling. If I slapped someone he'd see all the way to Cracow.[2] But I'm really not a slugger by nature. I think to myself: Let it pass. So they take advantage of me.

I was coming home from school and heard a dog barking. I'm not afraid of dogs, but of course I never want to start up with them. One of them may be mad, and if he bites there's not a Tartar[3] in the world who can help you. So I

---

1. Translated by Saul Bellow.   **2.** Krakow, city in southern Poland.   **3.** Supposedly fierce people of central Asia.

made tracks. Then I looked around and saw the whole market place wild with laughter. It was no dog at all but Wolf-Leib the thief. How was I supposed to know it was he? It sounded like a howling bitch.

When the pranksters and leg-pullers found that I was easy to fool, every one of them tried his luck with me. "Gimpel, the czar is coming to Frampol; Gimpel, the moon fell down in Turbeen; Gimpel, little Hodel Furpiece found a treasure behind the bathhouse." And I like a golem believed everyone. In the first place, everything is possible, as it is written in *The Wisdom of the Fathers.*[4] I've forgotten just how. Second, I had to believe when the whole town came down on me! If I ever dared to say, "Ah, you're kidding!" there was trouble. People got angry. "What do you mean! You want to call everyone a liar?" What was I to do? I believed them, and I hope at least that did them some good.

I was an orphan. My grandfather who brought me up was already bent toward the grave. So they turned me over to a baker, and what a time they gave me there! Every woman or girl who came to bake a batch of noodles had to fool me at least once. "Gimpel, there's a fair in Heaven; Gimpel, the rabbi gave birth to a calf in the seventh month; Gimpel, a cow flew over the roof and laid brass eggs." A student from the yeshiva came once to buy a roll, and he said, "You, Gimpel, while you stand here scraping with your baker's shovel the Messiah has come. The dead have risen." "What do you mean?" I said. "I heard no one blowing the ram's horn!" He said, "Are you deaf?" And all began to cry, "We heard it, we heard!" Then in came Rietze the candle-dipper and called out in her hoarse voice, "Gimpel, your father and mother have stood up from the grave. They're looking for you."

To tell the truth, I knew very well that nothing of the sort had happened, but all the same, as folks were talking, I threw on my wool vest and went out. Maybe something had happened. What did I stand to lose by looking? Well, what a cat music went up! And then I took a vow to believe nothing more. But that was no go either. They confused me so that I didn't know the big end from the small.

I went to the rabbi to get some advice. He said, "It is written, better to be a fool all your days than for one hour to be evil. You are not a fool. They are the fools. For he who causes his neighbor to feel shame loses Paradise himself." Nevertheless, the rabbi's daughter took me in. As I left the rabbinical court she said, "Have you kissed the wall yet?" I said, "No; what for?" She answered, "It's the law; you've got to do it after every visit." Well, there didn't seem to be any harm in it. And she burst out laughing. It was a fine trick. She put one over on me, all right.

I wanted to go off to another town, but then everyone got busy matchmaking, and they were after me so they nearly tore my coat tails off. They talked at me and talked until I got water on the ear. She was no chaste maiden, but they told me she was virgin pure. She had a limp, and they said it was deliberate, from coyness. She had a bastard, and they told me the child was her little brother. I cried, "You're wasting your time. I'll never marry that whore." But they said indignantly, "What a way to talk! Aren't you ashamed of yourself? We can take you to the rabbi and have you fined for giving her a bad name."

---

4. Spiritual sayings of Ben Zoma, a 2nd-century C.E. Jewish sage. *Golem:* an artificial human being (Hebrew).

I saw then that I wouldn't escape them so easily and I thought: They're set on making me their butt. But when you're married the husband's the master, and if that's all right with her it's agreeable to me too. Besides, you can't pass through life unscathed, nor expect to.

I went to her clay house, which was built on the sand, and the whole gang, hollering and chorusing, came after me. They acted like bearbaiters. When we came to the well they stopped all the same. They were afraid to start anything with Elka. Her mouth would open as if it were on a hinge, and she had a fierce tongue. I entered the house. Lines were strung from wall to wall and clothes were drying. Barefoot she stood by the tub, doing the wash. She was dressed in a worn hand-me-down gown of plush. She had her hair put up in braids and pinned across her head. It took my breath away, almost, the reek of it all.

Evidently she knew who I was. She took a look at me and said, "Look who's here! He's come, the drip. Grab a seat."

I told her all; I denied nothing. "Tell me the truth," I said, "are you really a virgin, and is that mischievous Yechiel actually your little brother? Don't be deceitful with me, for I'm an orphan."

"I'm an orphan myself," she answered, "and whoever tries to twist you up, may the end of his nose take a twist. But don't let them think they can take advantage of me. I want a dowry of fifty guilders, and let them take up a collection besides. Otherwise they can kiss my you-know-what." She was very plain-spoken. I said, "It's the bride and not the groom who gives a dowry." Then she said, "Don't bargain with me. Either a flat yes or a flat no. Go back where you came from."

I thought: No bread will ever be baked from *this* dough. But ours is not a poor town. They consented to everything and proceeded with the wedding. It so happened that there was a dysentery epidemic at the time. The ceremony was held at the cemetery gates, near the little corpse-washing hut. The fellows got drunk. While the marriage contract was being drawn up I heard the most pious high rabbi ask, "Is the bride a widow or a divorced woman?" And the sexton's wife answered for her, "Both a widow and divorced." It was a black moment for me. But what was I to do, run away from under the marriage canopy?

There was singing and dancing. An old granny danced opposite me, hugging a braided white hallah.[5] The master of revels made a "God 'a mercy" in memory of the bride's parents. The schoolboys threw burrs, as on Tishe b'Av[6] fast day. There were a lot of gifts after the sermon: a noodle board, a kneading trough, a bucket, brooms, ladles, household articles galore. Then I took a look and saw two strapping young men carrying a crib. "What do we need this for?" I asked. So they said, "Don't rack your brains about it. It's all right, it'll come in handy." I realized I was going to be rooked. Take it another way though, what did I stand to lose? I reflected: I'll see what comes of it. A whole town can't go altogether crazy.

II

At night I came where my wife lay, but she wouldn't let me in. "Say, look here, is this what they married us for?" I said. And she said, "My monthly has

---

5. Or "challah," a kind of bread made of braided dough (Hebrew). **6.** A Jewish day of mourning.

come." "But yesterday they took you to the ritual bath, and that's afterwards, isn't it supposed to be?" "Today isn't yesterday," said she, "and yesterday's not today. You can beat it if you don't like it." In short, I waited.

Not four months later, she was in childbed. The townsfolk hid their laughter with their knuckles. But what could I do? She suffered intolerable pains and clawed at the walls. "Gimpel," she cried, "I'm going. Forgive me!" The house filled with women. They were boiling pans of water. The screams rose to the welkin.

The thing to do was to go to the house of prayer to repeat psalms, and that was what I did.

The townsfolk liked that, all right. I stood in a corner saying psalms and prayers, and they shook their heads at me. "Pray, pray!" they told me. "Prayer never made any woman pregnant." One of the congregation put a straw to my mouth and said, "Hay for the cows." There was something to that too, by God!

She gave birth to a boy. Friday at the synagogue the sexton stood up before the Ark, pounded on the reading table, and announced, "The wealthy Reb[7] Gimpel invites the congregation to a feast in honor of the birth of a son." The whole house of prayer rang with laughter. My face was flaming. But there was nothing I could do. After all, I *was* the one responsible for the circumcision honors and rituals.

Half the town came running. You couldn't wedge another soul in. Women brought peppered chick-peas, and there was a keg of beer from the tavern. I ate and drank as much as anyone, and they all congratulated me. Then there was a circumcision, and I named the boy after my father, may he rest in peace. When all were gone and I was left with my wife alone, she thrust her head through the bed-curtain and called me to her.

"Gimpel," said she, "why are you silent? Has your ship gone and sunk?"

"What shall I say?" I answered. "A fine thing you've done to me! If my mother had known of it she'd have died a second time."

She said, "Are you crazy, or what?"

"How can you make such a fool," I said, "of one who should be the lord and master?"

"What's the matter with you?" she said. "What have you taken it into your head to imagine?"

I saw that I must speak bluntly and openly. "Do you think this is the way to use an orphan?" I said. "You have borne a bastard."

She answered, "Drive this foolishness out of your head. The child is yours."

"How can he be mine?" I argued. "He was born seventeen weeks after the wedding."

She told me then that he was premature. I said, "Isn't he a little too premature?" She said, she had had a grandmother who carried just as short a time and she resembled this grandmother of hers as one drop of water does another. She swore to it with such oaths that you would have believed a peasant at the fair if he had used them. To tell the plain truth, I didn't believe her; but when I talked it over the next day with the schoolmaster, he told me that the very same thing had happened to Adam and Eve. Two they went up to bed, and four they descended.

7. Rabbi, here used derisively.

"There isn't a woman in the world who is not the granddaughter of Eve," he said.

That was how it was; they argued me dumb. But then, who really knows how such things are?

I began to forget my sorrow. I loved the child madly, and he loved me too. As soon as he saw me he'd wave his little hands and want me to pick him up, and when he was colicky I was the only one who could pacify him. I bought him a little bone teething ring and a little gilded cap. He was forever catching the evil eye from someone, and then I had to run to get one of those abracadabras for him that would get him out of it. I worked like an ox. You know how expenses go up when there's an infant in the house. I don't want to lie about it; I didn't dislike Elka either, for that matter. She swore at me and cursed, and I couldn't get enough of her. What strength she had! One of her looks could rob you of the power of speech. And her orations! Pitch and sulphur, that's what they were full of, and yet somehow also full of charm. I adored her every word. She gave me bloody wounds though.

In the evening I brought her a white loaf as well as a dark one, and also poppyseed rolls I baked myself. I thieved because of her and swiped everything I could lay hands on: macaroons, raisins, almonds, cakes. I hoped I may be forgiven for stealing from the Saturday pots the women left to warm in the baker's oven. I would take out scraps of meat, a chunk of pudding, a chicken leg or head, a piece of tripe, whatever I could nip quickly. She ate and became fat and handsome.

I had to sleep away from home all during the week, at the bakery. On Friday nights when I got home she always made an excuse of some sort. Either she had heartburn, or a stitch in the side, or hiccups, or headaches. You know what women's excuses are. I had a bitter time of it. It was rough. To add to it, this little brother of hers, the bastard, was growing bigger. He'd put lumps on me, and when I wanted to hit back she'd open her mouth and curse so powerfully I saw a green haze floating before my eyes. Ten times a day she threatened to divorce me. Another man in my place would have taken French leave[8] and disappeared. But I'm the type that bears it and says nothing. What's one to do? Shoulders are from God, and burdens too.

One night there was a calamity at the bakery; the oven burst, and we almost had a fire. There was nothing to do but go home, so I went home. Let me, I thought, also taste the joy of sleeping in bed in midweek. I didn't want to wake the sleeping mite and tiptoed into the house. Coming in, it seemed to me that I heard not the snoring of one but, as it were, a double snore, one a thin enough snore and the other like the snoring of a slaughtered ox. Oh, I didn't like that! I didn't like it at all. I went up to the bed, and things suddenly turned black. Next to Elka lay a man's form. Another in my place would have made an uproar, and enough noise to rouse the whole town, but the thought occurred to me that I might wake the child. A little thing like that—why frighten a little swallow, I thought. All right then, I went back to the bakery and stretched out on a sack of flour and till morning I never shut an eye. I shivered as if I had had malaria. "Enough of being a donkey," I said to myself.

---

8. That is, a hasty or secret departure.

"Gimpel isn't going to be a sucker all his life. There's a limit even to the foolishness of a fool like Gimpel."

In the morning I went to the rabbi to get advice, and it made a great commotion in the town. They sent the beadle for Elka right away. She came, carrying the child. And what do you think she did? She denied it, denied everything, bone and stone! "He's out of his head," she said. "I know nothing of dreams of divinations." They yelled at her, warned her, hammered on the table, but she stuck to her guns: it was a false accusation, she said.

The butchers and the horse-traders took her part. One of the lads from the slaughterhouse came by and said to me, "We've got our eye on you, you're a marked man." Meanwhile, the child started to bear down and soiled itself. In the rabbinical court there was an Ark of the Covenant, and they couldn't allow that, so they sent Elka away.

I said to the rabbi, "What shall I do?"

"You must divorce her at once," said he.

"And what if she refuses?" I asked.

He said, "You must serve the divorce. That's all you'll have to do."

I said, "Well, all right, Rabbi. Let me think about it."

"There's nothing to think about," said he. "You mustn't remain under the same roof with her."

"And if I want to see the child?" I asked.

"Let her go, the harlot," said he, "and her brood of bastards with her."

The verdict he gave was that I mustn't even cross her threshold—never again, as long as I should live.

During the day it didn't bother me so much. I thought: It was bound to happen, the abscess had to burst. But at night when I stretched out upon the sacks I felt it all very bitterly. A longing took me, for her and for the child. I wanted to be angry, but that's my misfortune exactly, I don't have it in me to be really angry. In the first place—this was how my thoughts went—there's bound to be a slip sometimes. You can't live without errors. Probably that lad who was with her led her on and gave her presents and what not, and women are often long on hair and short on sense, and so he got around her. And then since she denies it so, maybe I was only seeing things? Hallucinations do happen. You see a figure or a mannikin or something, but when you come up closer it's nothing, there's not a thing there. And if that's so, I'm doing her an injustice. And when I got so far in my thoughts I started to weep. I sobbed so that I wet the flour where I lay. In the morning I went to the rabbi and told him that I had made a mistake. The rabbi wrote on with his quill, and he said that if that were so he would have to reconsider the whole case. Until he had finished I wasn't to go near my wife, but I might send her bread and money by messenger.

III

Nine months passed before all the rabbis could come to an agreement. Letters went back and forth. I hadn't realized that there could be so much erudition about a matter like this.

Meanwhile, Elka gave birth to still another child, a girl this time. On the Sabbath I went to the synagogue and invoked a blessing on her. They called me up to the Torah, and I named the child for my mother-in-law—may she rest in peace. The louts and loudmouths of the town who came into the bakery gave me a going over. All Frampol refreshed its spirits because of my trouble and grief. However, I resolved that I would always believe what I was told. What's the good of *not* believing? Today it's your wife you don't believe; tomorrow it's God Himself you won't take stock in.

By an apprentice who was her neighbor I sent her daily a corn or a wheat loaf, or a piece of pastry, rolls or bagels, or, when I got the chance, a slab of pudding, a slice of honeycake, or wedding strudel—whatever came my way. The apprentice was a goodhearted lad, and more than once he added something on his own. He had formerly annoyed me a lot, plucking my nose and digging me in the ribs, but when he started to be a visitor to my house he became kind and friendly. "Hey, you, Gimpel," he said to me, "you have a very decent little wife and two fine kids. You don't deserve them."

"But the things people say about her," I said.

"Well, they have long tongues," he said, "and nothing to do with them but babble. Ignore it as you ignore the cold of last winter."

One day the rabbi sent for me and said, "Are you certain, Gimpel, that you were wrong about your wife?"

I said, "I'm certain."

"Why, but look here! You yourself saw it."

"It must have been a shadow," I said.

"The shadow of what?"

"Just of one of the beams, I think."

"You can go home then. You owe thanks to the Yanover rabbi. He found an obscure reference in Maimonides[9] that favored you."

I seized the rabbi's hand and kissed it.

I wanted to run home immediately. It's no small thing to be separated for so long a time from wife and child. Then I reflected: I'd better go back to work now, and go home in the evening. I said nothing to anyone, although as far as my heart was concerned it was like one of the Holy Days. The women teased and twitted me as they did every day, but my thought was: Go on, with your loose talk. The truth is out, like the oil upon the water. Maimonides says it's right, and therefore it is right!

At night, when I had covered the dough to let it rise, I took my share of bread and a little sack of flour and started homeward. The moon was full and the stars were glistening, something to terrify the soul. I hurried onward, and before me darted a long shadow. It was winter, and a fresh snow had fallen. I had a mind to sing, but it was growing late and I didn't want to wake the householders. Then I felt like whistling, but I remembered that you don't whistle at night because it brings the demons out. So I was silent and walked as fast as I could.

Dogs in the Christian yards barked at me when I passed, but I thought: Bark your teeth out! What are you but mere dogs? Whereas I am a man, the husband of a fine wife, the father of promising children.

As I approached the house my heart started to pound as though it were the heart of a criminal. I felt no fear, but my heart went thump! thump! Well, no

---

9. Jewish scholastic philosopher (1135–1204).

drawing back. I quietly lifted the latch and went in. Elka was asleep. I looked at the infant's cradle. The shutter was closed, but the moon forced its way through the cracks. I saw the newborn child's face and loved it as soon as I saw it—immediately—each tiny bone.

Then I came near to the bed. And what did I see but the apprentice lying there beside Elka. The moon went out all at once. It was utterly black, and I trembled. My teeth chattered. The bread fell from my hands, and my wife waked and said, "Who is that, ah?"

I muttered, "It's me."

"Gimpel?" she asked. "How come you're here? I thought it was forbidden."

"The rabbi said," I answered and shook as with a fever.

"Listen to me, Gimpel," she said, "go out to the shed and see if the goat's all right. It seems she's been sick." I have forgotten to say that we had a goat. When I heard she was unwell I went into the yard. The nannygoat was a good little creature. I had nearly human feeling for her.

With hesitant steps I went up to the shed and opened the door. The goat stood there on her four feet. I felt her everywhere, drew her by the horns, examined her udders, and found nothing wrong. She had probably eaten too much bark. "Good night, little goat," I said. "Keep well." And the little beast answered with a "Maa" as though to thank me for the good will.

I went back. The apprentice had vanished.

"Where," I asked, "is the lad?"

"What lad?" my wife answered.

"What do you mean?" I said. "The apprentice. You were sleeping with him."

"The things I have dreamed this night and the night before," she said, "may they come true and lay you low, body and soul! An evil spirit has taken root in you and dazzles your sight." She screamed out, "You hateful creature! You moon calf! You spook! You uncouth man! Get out, or I'll scream all Frampol out of bed!"

Before I could move, her brother sprang out from behind the oven and struck me a blow on the back of the head. I thought he had broken my neck. I felt that something about me was deeply wrong, and I said, "Don't make a scandal. All that's needed now is that people should accuse me of raising spooks and dybbuks."[1] For that was what she had meant. "No one will touch bread of my baking."

In short, I somehow calmed her.

"Well," she said, "that's enough. Lie down, and be shattered by wheels."

Next morning I called the apprentice aside. "Listen here, brother!" I said. And so on and so forth. "What do you say?" He stared at me as though I had dropped from the roof or something.

"I swear," he said, "you'd better go to an herb doctor or some healer. I'm afraid you have a screw loose, but I'll hush it up for you." And that's how the thing stood.

To make a long story short, I lived twenty years with my wife. She bore me six children, four daughters and two sons. All kinds of things happened, but I neither saw nor heard. I believed, and that's all. The rabbi recently said to me, "Belief in itself is beneficial. It is written that a good man lives by his faith."

---

1. Ghosts and wandering souls (Hebrew).

Suddenly my wife took sick. It began with a trifle, a little growth upon the breast. But she evidently was not destined to live long; she had no years. I spent a fortune on her. I have forgotten to say that by this time I had a bakery of my own and in Frampol was considered to be something of a rich man. Daily the healer came, and every witch doctor in the neighborhood was brought. They decided to use leeches, and after that to try cupping. They even called a doctor from Lublin, but it was too late. Before she died she called me to her bed and said, "Forgive me, Gimpel."

I said, "What is there to forgive? You have been a good and faithful wife."

"Woe, Gimpel!" she said. "It was ugly how I deceived you all these years. I want to go clean to my Maker, and so I have to tell you that the children are not yours."

If I had been clouted on the head with a piece of wood it couldn't have bewildered me more.

"Whose are they?" I asked.

"I don't know," she said. "There were a lot . . . but they're not yours." And as she spoke she tossed her head to the side, her eyes turned glassy, and it was all up to Elka. On her whitened lips there remained a smile.

I imagined that, dead as she was, she was saying, "I deceived Gimpel. That was the meaning of my brief life."

IV

One night, when the period of mourning was done, as I lay dreaming on the flour sacks, there came the Spirit of Evil himself and said to me, "Gimpel, why do you sleep?"

I said, "What should I be doing? Eating kreplech?"[2]

"The whole world deceives you," he said, "and you ought to deceive the world in your turn."

"How can I deceive all the world?" I asked him.

He answered, "You might accumulate a bucket of urine every day and at night pour it into the dough. Let the sages of Frampol eat filth."

"What about the judgment in the world to come?" I said.

"There is no world to come," he said. "They've sold you a bill of goods and talked you into believing you carried a cat in your belly. What nonsense!"

"Well then," I said, "and is there a God?"

He answered, "There is no God either."

"What," I said, "*is* there, then?"

"A thick mire."

He stood before my eyes with a goatish beard and horn, long-toothed, and with a tail. Hearing such words, I wanted to snatch him by the tail, but I tumbled from the flour sacks and nearly broke a rib. Then it happened that I had to answer the call of nature, and, passing, I saw the risen dough, which seemed to say to me, "Do it!" In brief, I let myself be persuaded.

At dawn the apprentice came. We kneaded the bread, scattered caraway seeds on it, and set it to bake. Then the apprentice went away, and I was left sitting in the little trench by the oven, on a pile of rags. Well, Gimpel, I thought, you've

---

2. Stuffed dumplings, usually served in soup.

revenged yourself on them for all the shame they've put on you. Outside the frost glittered, but it was warm beside the oven. The flames heated my face. I bent my head and fell into a doze.

I saw in a dream, at once, Elka in her shroud. She called to me, "What have you done, Gimpel?"

I said to her, "It's all your fault," and started to cry.

"You fool!" she said. "You fool! Because I was false is everything false too? I never deceived anyone but myself. I'm paying for it all, Gimpel. They spare you nothing here."

I looked at her face. It was black; I was startled and waked, and remained sitting dumb. I sensed that everything hung in the balance. I seized the long shovel and took out the loaves, carried them into the yard, and started to dig a hole in the frozen earth.

My apprentice came back as I was doing it. "What are you doing, boss?" he said, and grew pale as a corpse.

"I know what I'm doing," I said, and I buried it all before his very eyes.

Then I went home, took my hoard from its hiding place, and divided it among the children. "I saw your mother tonight," I said. "She's turning black, poor thing."

They were so astounded they couldn't speak a word.

"Be well," I said, "and forget that such a one as Gimpel ever existed." I put on my short coat, a pair of boots, took the bag that held my prayer shawl in one hand, my stock in the other, and kissed the mezuzah.[3] When people saw me in the street they were greatly surprised.

"Where are you going?" they said.

I answered, "Into the world." And so I departed from Frampol.

I wandered over the land, and good people did not neglect me. After many years I became old and white; I heard a great deal, many lies and falsehoods, but the longer I lived the more I understood that there were really no lies. Whatever doesn't really happen is dreamed at night. It happens to one if it doesn't happen to another, tomorrow if not today, or a century hence if not next year. What difference can it make? Often I heard tales of which I said, "Now this is a thing that cannot happen." But before a year had elapsed I heard that it actually had come to pass somewhere.

Going from place to place, eating at strange tables, it often happens that I spin yarns—improbable things that could never have happened—about devils, magicians, windmills, and the like. The children run after me, calling, "Grandfather, tell us a story." Sometimes they ask for particular stories, and I try to please them. A fat young boy once said to me, "Grandfather, it's the same story you told us before." The little rogue, he was right.

So it is with dreams too. It is many years since I left Frampol, but as soon as I shut my eyes I am there again. And whom do you think I see? Elka. She is standing by the washtub, as at our first encounter, but her face is shining and her eyes are as radiant as the eyes of a saint, and she speaks outlandish words to me, strange things. When I wake I have forgotten it all. But while the dream lasts I am comforted. She answers all my queries, and what comes out is that

---

3. A case containing parchment inscribed with verses from the Torah, attached to the door frame of a faithful Jewish household (Hebrew).

all is right. I weep and implore, "Let me be with you." And she consoles me and tells me to be patient. The time is nearer than it is far. Sometimes she strokes and kisses me and weeps upon my face. When I awaken I feel her lips and taste the salt of her tears.

No doubt the world is entirely an imaginary world, but it is only once removed from the true world. At the door of the hovel where I lie, there stands the plank on which the dead are taken away. The grave-digger Jew has his spade ready. The grave waits and the worms are hungry; the shrouds are prepared—I carry them in my beggar's sack. Another *shnorrer*[4] is waiting to inherit my bed of straw. When the time comes I will go joyfully. Whatever may be there, it will be real, without complication, without ridicule, without deception. God be praised: there even Gimpel cannot be deceived.

1953

---

4. Beggar, sponger (Yiddish).

JANE SMILEY
b. 1949

Jane Smiley was born in Los Angeles in 1949, and grew up in the St. Louis suburb of Webster Groves. After graduating from Vassar College, she returned to the Midwest, and spent the next twenty-five years in Iowa, first as a student at the University of Iowa, earning an M.A., a Ph.D., and an M.F.A., and then as a professor of English at Iowa State University. Her first novels were published during this time: *Barn Blind* (1980), *Duplicate Keys* (1984), *The Greenlanders* (1988), and her most famous work, *A Thousand Acres* (1991), which won the Pulitzer Prize, the National Book Critics Circle award, and was adapted into a major Hollywood film. A short story collection, *The Age of Grief*, appeared in 1987. Recent works have branched out into nonfiction, with *The Man Who Invented the Computer* (2010); a series of young adult novels, including *A Good Horse* (2010) and *Gee Whiz* (2013); as well as a book on the craft of fiction, *Thirteen Ways of Looking at the Novel* (2005). In 2001 Smiley was elected to the American Academy of Arts and Letters.

The Life of the Body

I had been going to call my sister Rhonda when the phone rang, and even then, when I heard her voice, I thought that I could just open my mouth and tell her, but when she heaved a blue, premenstrual sigh and said, "So what are you going to do today," I just said what I always say, oh nothing. I thought, another day. Just another day. Then the time will be more right, somehow.

The fact is that I am in about the worst trouble I have ever heard of anyone being in. After Rhonda hung up, the phone rang four separate times. There is no one I dare to hear from, and so I let it ring. If I had picked it up, I would have said to anyone on the other end that I am pregnant, that Jonathan Ricklefs is the father, not Jake, my husband, and that everything inside me is about to be revealed, layer by layer, to Jake, to Jonathan, to Rhonda and our parents, to my son Ezra and my daughter Nancy, to people who care about me and to people who barely know me. What is it that will shame me most when it is revealed? Maybe it is the crazy force of my desire for Jonathan, the full extent of which I have kept from him and which makes me squirm with discomfort even as a secret. But maybe it is something else, something that has not even been revealed to me yet.

I used to have three children. The third was Dory. Five months ago, when she was almost three, she fell head over heels down the stairs. She went over three times, we think. She broke her neck at the bottom and died that afternoon. Various children around the country have her liver, her kidneys, her corneas. There was no one to receive her heart at that moment. A heart is something that can't be saved for very long. She had a little book in her hand when Jake found her at the bottom. It was a habit we couldn't break her of, "reading" on the stairs. Really, she didn't know how to read yet, but she loved to look at the pictures.

I was getting dressed in our bedroom, Jake was ironing his shirt, Nancy and Ezra were eating breakfast. We all heard the long cry of surprise and fear, the thump of limbs toppling and hitting, the utter silence of the house around those noises. All struck dumb, all thinking, *What's that?* all listening. The rustle of buttonholes, stopped, the swish of the iron, stopped, the interior crunch of cereal and toast, stopped.

I can't say what I would have given to have been standing at the bottom of the stairs, holding out my arms to catch Dory. My inner life isn't very mysterious or symbolic. I often dream that I am there, that she is saved. Some part of me, in the dream, always asserts that even if the last time was a dream, this time it is true. It isn't.

Jake wouldn't let me speak at the funeral. He was afraid I would say something outrageous. I might have. I might have said, What right do I have to grieve, having lost only one? Isn't the society of mothers who have lost some many times bigger than the society of mothers who have kept all theirs? I would have said a lot of contradictory things, since I was very confused. Instead, we thanked God who took her away for giving her to us in the first place. That was Jake's idea. He is a religious person, more so now.

Jonathan is a fatalist rather than a providentialist. Things come and go. Forces arrange themselves so that he will, for example, eat granola instead of a peach. When I think of the way he sees himself, I imagine a kind of pinpoint at the vortex of a whirlpool. Blakean swirls above his head. Streaks of light moving through darkness. He is not a very hopeful person. I used to tease him about it. When I tell him I am pregnant, he will nod slowly, his expectations of the worst confirmed.

Maybe that is what I hate most about this, all the suspicions confirmed, especially the suspicions about me that everyone seems to harbor—that Dory's death has made me crazy, that Jake and I have never gotten along, that I would do anything to tie Jonathan to me, that I wanted to replace Dory at any cost, that women are by nature evil, irresponsible, and deceptive. What does it say in the Bible? *And I find more bitter than death the woman, whose heart is snares and nets, and her hands as bands: whoso pleaseth God shall escape from her; but the sinner shall be taken by her.*[1] All that stuff. Once on the *Today* show, I saw a man who had written a book about the Dionne quintuplets. When they were born, their mother was ashamed. She said, "People will think that we are pigs." So much intercourse revealed to the world. Well, I was never proud of my pregnancies. Just by looking at you, people knew what you were thinking about.

I could have told Jake last night. I could have told Jonathan last night, too, when he brought over some lettuce from his garden. It doesn't make it any

---

1. Ecclesiastes 7:26.

easier that this will be the first news Jake has had of my affair with Jonathan. Jonathan talks well to Jake. Not many people do—Jake is antisocial and impatient, and his idea of a serviceable conversational gambit is "What do you want?" Someone else who talks well to Jake is Rhonda. I am tempted to tell her, and let her tell them all. She is a great moaner. "Ooooh, Sarah. Ooh, Sarah." That is how she listens to confidences, moaning those wordless cries that you would like to be moaning yourself. "Ooh, Sarah. Ooooh Sarah." I try it out, out loud, but it isn't the same. I know I should be finishing the sentence, "Oooh Sarah you shithead," which is something Rhonda would never even think of doing.

There is the crunch of wheels in the driveway, Jake returning from work, as he often does. He will find me standing over the sink, as he often does. I get up and position myself there. He comes in and runs up the stairs. There is the slamming of closet doors upstairs, the thump of his heavy feet. He really has forgotten something, he always really has, but he never did before Dory died. The manifestation of his grief is more than forgetfulness, it is perennial searching. Though he gave up smoking years ago, his hands wander his pockets in search of cigarettes. He is always making sure he has his keys, his wallet, his checkbook. I find him in closets looking for sweaters and pairs of slippers and magazine articles we threw out years ago. He turns over the cushions, puts his hands in the cracks, comes up with pennies that he gives to Nancy. He calls his mother and asks if his old yearbooks are at her house, his swimming trunks from high school, his old Bo Diddley records. We are patient with this searching, his mother and I. Even Jake knows what he is searching for, but he can't stop just because he won't find her.

He appears in the kitchen doorway. I have my hands in the water, as if I were doing something, and it might be that, not looking at him, looking out the back window at the peonies blooming in the yard, I will say, "I'm pregnant." I know the words, I've said it before. But of everyone in the whole world, Jake is the only other person who knows that we haven't slept together since the week before Dory died. It is also possible that I will tell no one, just wait for them to notice, and ask. It may be that social nicety will prevent most people from asking. It may be that fear will prevent Jake from asking, and even greater fear will prevent Jonathan from asking, and a year from now I will say, in a cocky voice, "Ever wonder where I got this baby?"

Jake says, "I forgot the reports. I can't believe I actually forgot the reports."

"It's okay."

"Of course it's okay. That isn't what I'm talking about. I just can't believe it. I'm just remarking on that, is all."

"I know."

"What are you going to do today?" He asks suspiciously, because he thinks that my grief is to loiter around the house for hours, then hurry and clean up just before Ezra and Nancy get home. It was. Lately my grief has been to go to bed with Jonathan Ricklefs as much as possible, on every flat surface in his apartment. I say, "I'm going to go to Rhonda's dance class with her again, then I'm going to order meat at the locker, then bake cookies with Nancy for the day camp birthday party. How about cooking out for dinner? It's already getting hot enough."

"Will you make potato salad?" He glides up next to me, kisses me on the neck, as if bribing me. I turn and put my hands on his shoulders. I smile, as if being bribed. "I'll boil the potatoes as soon as you leave."

"The day camp counselor thinks Nancy seems fine. She's playing with everyone, and the shyness has worn off completely. She's making a belt in the crafts class."

"Good."

"Ezra is being more reserved."

"Ezra *is* more reserved."

"How much more?"

"Sweetie, I wish I knew. He likes the horses. Yesterday he told me about the horses for about twenty-five minutes. His favorite is named Herb. He got to go into the stable and give Herb his oats." We smile at Herb. Jake smiles at me. He thinks we are coming out of things when in fact we are just getting started. Another day. I will let him go another day. He pecks me on the cheek and leaves with a number of slams: the kitchen door, the garage door, the car door. He is a noisy man.

Rhonda dances every day. Lately I have been going with her. This is not aerobics, it is serious modern dance. The other students are mostly in their teens and early twenties. The teacher is a black man who dances in a local company. I don't know why he lets me come, except that he is a friend of Rhonda's, and she is my sister. Rhonda, although she is thirty-two and has two children, turns out to have considerable talent for the dance. The first day I came, she warmed up, without shame, by stretching and then doing three slow cartwheels and a couple of handstands. I was amazed. I keep up well with the slower third of the twenty-year-olds, and mostly Henry doesn't pay any attention to us. We pay attention to him, though. Pas de cheval: Henry says, "You know how a puppy licks your arm? So that every pore and hair gets wet? Well, make the sole of your foot lick the floor." Deep second position: "You are in water! Your head is floating upward! Your knees are floating outward! Lift! Lift!" He tells us not to mimic him, but to feel ourselves, our muscles and tendons sliding and rolling, our balls and sockets rotating.

Today we have hamstrings and adductors for half an hour, then chainé[2] turns for half an hour. My days here, as everywhere, are numbered, and so when we lie on our backs and rotate our hips outward and find the place on each side where the tendons split, I am careful to note what it feels like. When we then curl up to standing, I think only of my spine, catlike, and my long, furry tail anchoring me to the floor. When we step and pivot across the floor, I push my toes through the wet mud Henry evokes, and leave long swathes filling with water behind me. After four times across the floor, we lie down and slither through that same mud, chests first, trying not to get our chins wet.

The first to go are Nancy and Ezra, who are active and well taken care of. Then I stop thinking about Rhonda, even though she is just ahead of me in line. Jake vanishes next, with his expectations that are soon to be betrayed. Now Dory, who never knew me as a dancer, who has no associations with this room or these people (they know my first name only, if that). After that, I forget

2. *Chainé:* Chained (French), a ballet step.

I am pregnant, and at last, sometime in the triple prances ("Sli-i-ide snap! snap!" says Henry), even Jonathan lets go. Henry becomes Henry the dancer rather than Henry the man. We are panting. Henry tells the accompanist to speed up the tempo, and we are running. Henry goes first, down-up-up, arms and chin swooping then lifting. Someone in red and black does it after him, a flute passage on the heels of a bassoon passage, and then it is me, and the only thing I feel is the slick floor under my feet and the rush of my fingers through the air, up-up!

The one in red and black, of course, is Rhonda, who is damp with sweat from ponytail to heel, and when class is over, she says, "God, let's shower and eat at my place. I've got spaghetti left over from last night."

It is words that bring them all back with a suffocating rush. "God." "My place." "Last night." We are fixed in place and time after all. Henry passes us on the way out. "Lovely," he says. He is a big man, happy, Rhonda says, because he gets a lot of oxygen to the brain.

I should tell her in the locker room, naked in the shower, but I make excuses. Now that she is right here, it seems like Jonathan should be the first to know, then Jake, then her. Then our parents, then the children. That's the obvious order, just as Rhonda-Jake-Jonathan was last night, when Jake and Jonathan were standing with their hands in their pockets under the hackberry tree, considering ways to save it from whatever is infesting it.

There is this space, of course, this carefully made space in the day when I will see Jonathan. After the meatlocker, after lunch, before Nancy and Ezra get home from day camp. I enter the downstairs door quickly, and run up. The door opens at the first brush of my first knock. Jonathan is grinning. "Hi," he says, "Hi, hi, hi." He locks the door behind me. He looks me up and down. I catch sight of a pot of tea steaming behind him on the coffee table and I burst into tears. It isn't the first time, nor does it come from the press of present circumstances. All of this sadness has been there from the beginning. I think, in fact, that this affair was begun as a tribute to sadness, gathered force through sadness, and will result in more sadness for everyone that we can possibly stand.

I feel utterly comfortable weeping here.

Perhaps more importantly, Jonathan feels utterly comfortable with my weeping. I sit on the couch and he pours the tea and then he sits beside me and folds me into his chest, and soon I am weeping and kissing him, and he is wiping my face with a paper napkin and kissing me, and that is how it has gone for months, salty kisses, passion, and grief. I am, as they say, shameless. Often we don't make love, but today we do. Today when he kisses me with his lips, I give him my tongue, only my tongue, and then I feel his, meeting mine, and instantly my nipples, tender with pregnancy, stand up, burning. As much as they hurt, I long to have him lick and suck them, and when I think of that, they tingle suddenly, as if milk were about to come down. They haven't done that since Dory was nursing, and it is the most intense feeling of physical longing, the longing to give suck. I almost tell the news, but I don't.

Jonathan kisses my neck and shoulders, and his erection presses against my leg, presses into my imagination, the thick, smooth shape, the reddish color—I am as familiar with it as I am with my own hand, more familiar, since

I have looked at it, tasted it, touched and held it, smelled it. A weighty, living object. Sometimes at night, after Jake goes to sleep and I am lying awake in fear and guilt, I just open my mouth and put my tongue out, wishing, thinking how I would lick the little crease and then run my tongue under the cap, marveling always at the warm shape of it. He sucks my breasts and I push both hands into his pants, unsnapping them, forcing the zipper down. He hops a little on the couch, then pulls my T-shirt up. It tangles in my arms and hair. I am still weeping. I am happy to be trapped inside this shirt with my nipples burning, my cunt throbbing. I open my mouth and put my tongue out.

"Sarah!" he moans. "Oh, Sarah oh oh." And then he strips off my shorts and shoes and sucks my toes and after that he licks my cunt, and licks and licks, parting the lips and putting his fingers in, licking, finding, at last, the spot that burns so that I push him away, his head, his shoulders. He pushes back, licking, his tongue fastened to that spot. My legs turn to water, and my back arches, and for a moment he is gone, and then he eases into me, slow and slick, and his tongue is in my open mouth and his fingers are in my ears and his chest, smooth and firm, in its way, as a penis, is sliding along my chest, and then he does something I always like, which is to lift my legs to my shoulders so that he can get in and in, and he gets in, so far that he relaxes a little, and closes his eyes. I push him off, out. He is shocked, his flesh is shocked at the suddenness of it, but before he realizes, I have it, his penis in my mouth, as I have wanted, and I am licking and stroking. I like to feel this, that he cannot stop himself. He does not. I swallow. He falls back on the couch, pulling me with him, holding me tight, panting. This is the way it has gone for months. I cling to him in desperate fear, but I am no longer weeping.

Sometimes I dream that I am just a torso, and blind, born that way, skin, a mouth, breasts, a cunt more open than any cunt ever, and Jonathan is engulfing me as well as penetrating every orifice. I dream that all I can do in life is fuck and suck and kiss and be embraced, and that I orgasm over and over and never get enough. Sometimes I daydream it.

The tension flows back into his flesh. I feel it along my chest, in his shoulder where my ear and cheek rest. His arm tightens over my back, and his other arm moves. When I lift my head to look at him, I see that he has covered his eyes with his elbow. I lower my head gently and wait, as still as possible. His heart has not relaxed, and is pounding steadily faster. As I open my mouth to speak, he says, "Sarah, talk to me."

I lift my head. "You want me to open the conversation."

"It's hopeless."

"What is hopeless." I can't make it a question, must make it a denial.

"Sarah—"

"Don't say anything, just don't say anything. Do you love me?"

He answers without hesitation but not without pain, "I tell you I do over and over. I do."

"Then don't say anything."

"Do you love me?"

"I think of you without ceasing, day and night."

"Do you love me?"

"You possess me."

"Sarah, do you love me?"

After minutes go by and I don't answer, he sits up and puts me away from him and pours the tea. I reach for my T-shirt and pull it on, but I don't stop shivering. I watch him drink his tea, catching tea leaves on the tip of his tongue and picking them off with his finger. He knows I am looking at him and from time to time turns his gaze to mine. This is another thing that we feel comfortable with, staring and being stared at. He is a big man, broad and muscular, utterly defeated, *as an ox goeth to the slaughter.* When we met, I was attracted to his self-reliance, his detached outlook. Both of those are gone now. I wonder how much he wants them back. He says, "I am terrified."

"Are you terrified that it will go on or are you terrified that it will stop?"

"Both."

"Are you frightened of me or for me?"

"Both."

"Will love find a way? If we stick together, can we make it?"

"Sometimes I think so. Weaker moments. Oh, Sarah." He covers his eyes again. A moment later I see tears on his cheeks. I look away. He goes on. "It's too painful. Sometimes I feel like our clothes are lined with nails and the tighter we embrace, the more blood we draw from each other."

I say, "It was fun at the beginning. That's important. A book I read says that you draw on the strengths of the relationship when you remember the beginning. I used to be known for my sense of humor, actually. Jonathan, suspend choice, all right? No action, no decision, just endurance." But he is slippery. As soon as he admitted fear, I felt it myself, telegraphed from him to me. I felt the size of the betrayal that would be possible just to escape that fear. Which arm, which leg, which sense would I have given just to escape that fear the moment I saw my daughter at the bottom of the stairs?

"A day," I say. "Only another day. Don't make up your mind or even think anything for another day. Go canoeing. Go to the movies. Eat something soothing, with lots of B vitamins. If I leave now, I might beat Nancy home by a minute." I run out the door, down the steps, out the lower door. I know he is watching me from the window. He fell in love with me when Dory died. That is why my chest closes up when I try to say that I love him. I don't want to be loved for my belongings, even if that belonging is only an enlargement that springs from tragedy.

I make a lot of mistakes. This time it is the potato salad, which I forgot, though Jake asked for it specifically. I forgot about it all the way until he looked in the refrigerator and said, "Didn't you make the potato salad?" and so there was no evasive action possible. I say, "I'll do that thing."

"What thing?"

"That thing where I go to the deli and get some of theirs, then redress it. You like that."

"You were going to put the potatoes on as soon as I left."

"I forgot."

"How could you forget? You were standing right here in the kitchen. All you had to do was turn around and take the potatoes out of the cupboard.

"I forgot."

"I'm not mad. I just don't understand you."

"You forgot your reports."

"I was working on them last night. I put them aside."

"I don't want to argue about fine points."

"It means something," he says. "The way people act means something. You know that."

"I forgot."

He shakes his head and goes outside to start the fire. Before he addressed me on the topic of potato salad, I was standing over the dishwater water, as always, washing up the cookie things and pondering the recollection of Jonathan sucking my breasts, thinking that I would like him to kiss all of my skin at the same time. Jonathan knows in his heart that what I crave from him are impossibilities. That is why he is afraid of me.

Out the kitchen window, Jake comes into view, carrying the charcoal and the lighter fluid. Most people, including Jonathan, feel lots of sympathy for him. Soon they'll feel more. They think he must grieve a great deal for Dory. I don't know. I wish I had seen the first look on his face when he got to her, but I started from back in the closet in our bedroom upstairs, and by the time I reached them at the bottom of the stairs, he was already practical, had already covered her with the afghan and was calling the ambulance, wouldn't let her be moved. He has never cried in my presence. Nor have I cried in his presence. But we do not pretend that everything is normal. We strive with all our might to make a routine, a little thread that will guide Ezra and Nancy, and maybe ourselves, out of the labyrinth.

That our sex life ended did not surprise me. Jake does not seek comfort in the flesh of others. He has to feel good to reach out. When he does not feel good, he avoids people. All of his brothers are the same way. When their father died three years ago, they gathered in Tallahassee for four days, five men. They built a bathroom out of the downstairs porch of their mother's house, taking maybe four hours out for the funeral and the burial. I asked Jake if they talked about their father in there, while they were grouting and caulking. He said, "Ralph did, a little." He didn't touch me for four months. I didn't mind. I think about Jonathan putting his face between my thighs and licking, sticking his tongue in; Jake comes up behind me and says, "Are you going to get the potato salad now or not?" and I start violently. He turns me around, his hands on my shoulders, and looks into my eyes. His face is very close to mine, and he is serious. He says, "Sarah, can't you pay attention? That's not an accusation. I want to know. Is that the problem, that you can't pay attention?"

"I'm trying. Don't watch me."

"I wish I could help myself."

I pull away. "I'll get the potato salad now, okay? Nancy is over at Allison's house, and Ezra is watching television."

"Don't get distracted. Half an hour, okay? Be back in half an hour."

"I will."

"I mean it."

"I *will*." It is for my own good, so I won't wander, so I'll keep my mind on the business at hand.

That is the beginning. The second incident takes place when I am coming out of Nancy's room after putting her to bed. Jake is in the hallway, looking at the bookshelves. I turn to say one last thing to Nancy, and Jake's arm goes around my waist. Distracted, I stiffen. Then I relax, but the stiffening doesn't go unnoticed. His arm drops. We stand there for an awkward second, then he chooses a book, and I turn and go down the stairs.

In the end, we argue about religion rather than sex. It is dark when I come into our bedroom, and I think Jake is asleep, but he speaks in a firm, clear voice, surprising in the dark. "Can I tell you something?" I push the top drawer of the dresser in, and he takes this for assent. I stand quietly, looking at the parallelogram of moonlight on the top of the dresser. "There was this time, when my mother's younger sister died of complications of childbirth. I guess I was about fourteen. Anyway, we had just moved to that house in Tallahassee, and I came in from doing something outside. Maybe we were helping Dad move that shed. That was one of the first things we had to do. It was almost dark, and Mom was sitting in the dark, snapping beans for dinner, and everyone else was outside, and when I went to turn on the light, she said, 'Jake, leave it dark,' so I left it dark, and she said, 'The Lord helps a man be good, Jake. If you let Him come inside you, He is a tide that carries you to goodness. But you've got to open the door yourself.' That was all she said, and then Richie came in and turned on the light and pretty soon we had dinner. Sarah, I know it's hard to find the door. It took me ten years to find the door, but I found it."

"It's not a door I want to find, Jake. Your mother was a religious woman, and she raised you, and so she was preaching to the converted. Before we got married, she said you'd come back to it, and you did. Big surprise."

"I tried the other way."

"You always thought of it as the other way. I don't believe, Jake. It's not in me. My brain doesn't have that bump. It's not in my horoscope. I went to Sunday school and read the Bible and it didn't take. If you didn't bring it up, I wouldn't think about it."

"But maybe me bringing it up is the Lord's way of trying to get your attention. I can't stop doing it. *I am moved* to do it. Don't you understand what that means?"

By now I have gotten, without realizing it, into the dark corner between the dresser and the wall. I open my mouth, but I know perfectly well how Jake's life looks to him: in retrospect, a series of perfectly timed nudges toward the right path that his mother would have, and often had, called miracles—a moment of despair, and then she looks up to see the minister on the porch, about to ring the bell. That happened more than once. I didn't necessarily discount her interpretation. It does seem to me that the world and the inner life mesh in mysterious ways more often than not.

I run my finger around the edge of the moonlight. More than anything, I want him to stop badgering me. I say, "I understand that you are driving me nuts with this God shit. I got some tracts in the mail again yesterday. Did you send them?"

He is out of bed in an instant, moved to rage by everything unbearable that we have to bear. I find that I am in a tight spot, between the wall and the dresser, and as I am trying to get out, he takes me by the shoulders and bumps my head on the wall. I press against him. His grip tightens, and I can feel the panic roll up from my toes all at once. I know he won't hurt me, but I feel that he will kill me. The walls behind me and to my left are unyielding, cold, terrifying. I bend down. His hands press harder on my shoulders, weights that I cannot evade. I do the only thing that I can possibly do, which is to push hard against the wall with my hip, and hard against the dresser with my hands. It falls over with a crash, and the stained glass box Jake keeps pennies in flies toward the window. I see this out of the corner of my eye. Jake does it again, bumps my head against the wall, this time hard, and simultaneously with the sound of breaking glass. Then I get out from under him, clamber over the dresser, and flee the room. For the rest of the night, which I spend on the sofa, every time I fall into a doze, I seem to feel my head being slammed into glass, and I wake up expecting to reach up and find blood pouring down my face.

When I loved Jake, when our relationship wasn't too complicated to have a label like that, it was this absolute quality that I loved, this straightness, this desire for goodness, and mostly the struggle he put up with himself, the manly difficulty of that. I didn't know anyone like him. I don't know that this appreciation is reciprocated—when he talks about me to his pastor and other men he likes who are religious, they will have a long tradition of misogyny to consult. He will not be guided to see things from my point of view. Well, deep in the night, curled up on the couch with the pillow over my head, somewhere in the realm of sleep, I do feel what he felt and see what he saw and hear what he heard: the flippant and dismissive tone of my voice, the indifference of my face in the half light, the inviting and unusual way I was wedged into that space, easy prey, and deserving of punishment too. I feel again the corner enclosing my flesh, the panic surging out of me in a flood, and I wake up with a start. Containing both points of view at once makes me short of breath. I sit up and gaze around the living room. For the first time in weeks, I don't want Jonathan. I try to make myself think of him, but my mind won't fix.

Jonathan used to run a millworks, producing hardwood moldings for lumberyards. He made some money and sold the business, and now he goes to school in horticulture and landscape architecture. He taught an extension course in tree fruits, which is where I met him, and which is why he has his days free and why he can talk to Jake, whose only ambition in life is to run a market garden with his brother Richie. Richie would grow only corn, Jake would do the other vegetables and press cider in the fall. I would do fresh-cut flowers in season and apples in the fall. Right now Jake and Richie have other jobs: Richie manages a big A & P in the next town and Jake works for the county government as an accountant. Jake and Richie and I own 57 acres, free and clear. Next summer, the five brothers are going to begin building a house on the land. Every weekend, all spring, Jake and Richie have gone out to the property and walked its every inch, looking for the best site for the house and the garden and the garden buildings. That gave Jonathan and me four or five extra hours every week that we wouldn't have had, and it was on one of those weekends, when I forgot my diaphragm, that I got pregnant. In the ten years of marriage, I have forgotten it off and on, without consequences, and each of the other pregnancies took a number of months, and so I was careless. Careless and lazy: I realized I had forgotten it before I was to the end of our street, but I couldn't bear to turn back and thought I would trust to luck, as I had in the past. Careless and lazy and possessed. There have been times in the last seven months when putting off seeing Jonathan for even ten minutes was the crudest torture.

We bought the property two years ago, with savings and with Jake's and Richie's portions of their father's estate. I like Richie. All that summer he would come over about dinnertime and sit on the porch swing, talking to Jake about what sort of house they would build and watching Dory. Dory was sixteen months when we bought the land. When Richie was here, we would prop open all the doors and she would charge through all the rooms and in and out of the house. He would help her down the front steps, and she would tear around the yard, which was fenced. She was utterly safe and utterly free, and maybe for that reason, much happier than Nancy and Ezra were at that age. Rhonda and Walker came over a lot too. We have all known each other for a long time. Lots of times, Rhonda would go into the kitchen and open the cabinets and start making dinner, and though I had disagreements with Jake that everyone knew about, there was a largeness and comfort to family life that soothed me. It spread in every direction, over the landscape, from the past into the future. It was enough to buy land and plan, to care for the children, to dig and plant. Richie and Walker distracted Jake, engaged him in conversation, made him feel at ease. Whatever was missing between us got to seem like just a certain coloring, a certain way the landscape might be lit but wasn't, nothing particular, considering everything else that was there. Richie, after all, wasn't even married, had never, as far as we knew, had a steady girlfriend.

Usually, these days, it seems like nothing, what we had at all those dinner-times, but just now, when I am cold and tired and frightened of sleep, it seems like a thing of substance and weight, safe as a vault, with the child rolling through it like a golden ball.

I don't know anyone who has had an abortion, but it can be done. Rhonda would know all about it. And if this were the moment when it was to be done, I would do it, because no one else is here, not Jonathan or Nancy or Ezra or Jake or Richie or Rhonda or my mother. Only I am here, and for the moment Jake has pounded sentiment out of me. Nothing in this room, which we bought and filled with our purchases, means a thing to me, not even the pictures. Nothing I have ever felt or thought or given voice to remotely interests me just now, no principle or affection or intention. I sit against the arm of the couch, waiting to make up my mind to have an abortion.

Instead it must be that I fall asleep, because Ezra wakes me, and it is day-light, though just barely. Ezra always comes down early and expects to have the house to himself for an hour. He says, "Mommy, can I turn on the TV?" and the day is begun. I look at him for a long moment, until he smiles in self-defense, and then I say, "Do you have riding again today?" and he grins. He says, "Alan, you know, the head of riding, he said I could ride Herbie every time, if I asked." He goes and turns on the TV, then glances back at me. "He's a real good horse, Mom. And he's a horse, not a pony."

"Hmm."

"Do you know the difference?"

"I do, actually."

"Well, he's a horse."

"Good, sweetie." I pull myself up the stairs and into the bathroom.

At breakfast I act as if nothing has happened, and Jake can think he is get-ting away with something if he wants. I put his eggs in front of him and meet his gaze, and I am nearly as tender with him as I am with the children, brushing their shoulders or hair with my hand. And then they are gone, and I pick up the phone and I call Jonathan and make a date with him for lunch. His voice is distant, distracted. After that I make sure that Rhonda is going to her dance class and that I can come along. Then I do the dishes and sweep the kitchen. In fact, I get down on my hands and knees with the butler's brush and sweep like I've never swept before, getting the dust and sand of seven years out of the corners, off the top edge of the moldings, out from under the stove and refrigerator. When I am finished, I am dusty and sweaty. I go around and open the windows, catching what breeze there is. After that I take another shower.

The fact is that this is the last hour of the old life. Things that are soft are about to harden and take the simple shapes that may last them the rest of my life. For example, I don't hate Jake and I don't love Jonathan. Whatever I feel for each of them is like one of those dye baths that you dip the endpapers of books in—a riot of colors swirled together, compounded of everything each has confided in me and everything I have confided in each of them. At this moment, I have the feeling that each time I have looked at each one of them is distinct and significant, that I know some discrete grain of truth about each of them as a result of every glance. The large thing that I know about them is that they are not each other, but that large thing is compounded of the numberless small ways in which they are not each other. I don't blame them for not being each other, but as soon as I speak, they will move into position. Jake, betrayed, will become my enemy. Jonathan, responsible, will become my partner. I would be deluding myself if I didn't know that he will consider my pregnancy a moral outrage in addition to an injury to himself. If he doesn't tell his brothers, and probably my children, that I am a whore, then he won't be the Jake I have known for ten years. And so the children will move into position too: confused at first, judgmental later, damaged forever. And Jonathan. Well, Jonathan. Just because I know that he will do the right thing, does that mean I planned for him to? At lunch I'll tell him I'm pregnant before he tells me we have to end our affair, and for a lot of reasons, he will swallow his doubts, and I will swallow mine, and sometime soon I will tell him that I love him, because I will love him. I will move into position too. Maybe.

A week after the funeral, when the children were back in school, I walked to the library and then to Jonathan's house. It was the day before Valentine's Day, warm and sunny, with snow melt trickling down every gutter. I had thrown away the valentine I intended to give him—it was one of those cynical and sexy ones, and when I found it in my purse the day after the funeral, it seemed to be cursed, so I tore it up, tore it up again, took it down the street, and threw it into some dry cleaner's dumpster. I was chastened. Everything having to do with Jonathan Ricklefs frightened me. We hadn't slept together very often—our friendship was more teasing and drinking tea than anything else. He seemed invulnerable, possibly dating someone else, though I wasn't sure. Jake was at work, my mother had left, the children were back in school, and I was walking down the street, glad to be put back together a little bit, glad that the previous night was over and the night to come wasn't yet upon me. I climbed the step and rang the bell, and I remember turning and looking down the street, idly, thinking of nothing for a moment. And then the door opened, and Jonathan was there, and his hand closed around my elbow, and he pulled me into the hallway where he hugged me and looked at me and put his hand on my face and then hugged me again, and just at that moment when he looked at me, I knew two things at once, that Dory was dead and that Jonathan loved me as he had not loved me ten days before. I don't know that any relationship can survive that sort of birth for long. Or maybe the root is this, that when I was standing in the closet that morning, buttoning my shirt, it was Jonathan I was thinking of, Jonathan who had delayed me in the closet, taking off one shirt and putting on another. I was thinking about him sucking my breasts; I could feel my nipples rise against the cotton of the shirt as I thought, *What's that noise?*

In the first hour of the new life, I will speak and act and justify and choose. I will summarize and simplify, in order to make the new life. I will start forgetting what I know in the last hour of the old life. I don't think this is the least of the things that will be destroyed.

I am pulling up my tights in the locker room when Rhonda comes in. She is lovely, my sister. She has two dimples, still, one just under her left eye, the other just to the right of her smile. In the humidity, her hair springs out of her bun with curly abandon. "Sary!" she roars. Her voice is always gravelly and ironic, because in spite of everything she still smokes cigarettes. "Am I late? I had to buy these new tights! Look at this! Is that shine? Don't you love it?" She goes over and stubs out her cigarette in the sink, then wets the end and throws it in the trashcan. "Shit. We've got to hurry. Henry always notices if you're late. Last week he wouldn't let one of them dance, that one who always wears the silver leotard."

I run after her. She snaps the front of her leotard as we trot down the hall. At the door, I put my hand on hers, holding it closed. She looks at me. I say, "Rhonda. Wait a minute." And I tell her. Then I open the door and walk in. Henry has started pliés. I take my place in line. Two minutes later, I feel Rhonda behind me, everything about her, her sadness and her fear as well as her presence. She gives out a little moan. Henry casts her a glance.

He says, "There is a thread attached to that spot on the back of your head where the hair swirls around. You know that spot? Just a thread. If you let your spine stretch upward as your buttocks drop down, you won't break that thread." My chin drops, the vertebrae seem to release one another and float. This is it, isn't it, what Jake calls God and Jonathan calls passion. I lift my arms and drop and spread my shoulders, then turn. Rhonda is there, and her face is white and her expression dismayed. She would like a cigarette. This is it, isn't it, this movement, movement, only movement, only the feeling of life running through the tissues. After all, it makes me smile. A second later, my sister smiles back.

1994

LEE SMITH
b. 1944

Smith grew up in the Appalachian Mountains of southwestern Virginia and earned her B.A. at nearby Hollins College. Even before she graduated, her literary career was well underway; she won a Book-of-the-Month Club fellowship with a draft of what would become her first novel, *The Last Day the Dogbushes Bloomed* (1968). She has published many works of fiction since then, including the novels *Black Mountain Breakdown* (1980), *Oral History* (1983), *Family Linen* (1985), *The Devil's Dream* (1992), *Saving Grace* (1995), *News of the Spirit* (1997), and *Guests on Earth* (2013). Her short stories have won her two O. Henry Awards; her collections include *Cakewalk* (1981), *Me and My Baby View the Eclipse* (1990), and *Mrs. Darcy and the Blue-Eyed Stranger* (2010). In 2010 Smith won a Lifetime Achievement Award from the Library of Virginia.

Intensive Care

Cherry Oxendine is dying now, and everybody knows it. Everybody in town except maybe her new husband, Harold Stikes, although Lord knows he ought to, it's as plain as the nose on your face. And it's not like he hasn't been *told* either, by both Dr. Thacker and Dr. Pinckney and also that hotshot young Jew doctor from Memphis, Dr. Shapiro, who comes over here once a week. "Harold just can't take it in," is what the head nurse in Intensive Care, Lois Hickey, said in the Beauty Nook last week. Lois ought to know. She's been right there during the past six weeks while Cherry Oxendine has been in Intensive Care, writing down Cherry's blood pressure every hour on the hour, changing bags on the IV, checking the stomach tube, moving the bed up and down to prevent bedsores, monitoring the respirator—and calling in Rodney Broadbent, the respiratory therapist, more and more frequently. "Her blood gases is not but twenty-eight," Lois said in the Beauty Nook. "If we was to unhook that respirator, she'd die in a day."

"I would go on and do it then, if I was Harold," said Mrs. Hooker, the Presbyterian minister's wife, who was getting a permanent. "It is the Christian thing."

"You wouldn't either," Lois said, "because she *still knows him*. That's the awful part. She still knows him. In fact she peps right up ever time he comes in, like they are going on a date or something. It's the saddest thing. And ever time we open the doors, here comes Harold, regular as clockwork. Eight o'clock, one o'clock, six o'clock, eight o'clock, why shoot, he'd stay in there all day and all night if we'd let him. Well, she opens her mouth and says *Hi honey,* you can tell what she's saying even if she can't make a sound. And her eyes get real bright and her face looks pretty good too, that's because of the Lasix,[1] only Harold don't know that. He just can't take it all in," Lois said.

"Oh, I feel so sorry for him," said Mrs. Hooker. Her face is as round and flat as a dime.

"Well, I don't." Dot Mains, owner of the Beauty Nook, started cutting Lois Hickey's hair. Lois wears it too short, in Dot's opinion. "I certainly don't feel sorry for Harold Stikes, after what he did." Dot snipped decisively at Lois Hickey's frosted hair. Mrs. Hooker made a sad little sound, half sigh, half words, as Janice stuck her under the dryer, while Miss Berry, the old-maid home demonstration agent waiting for her appointment, snapped the pages of *Cosmopolitan* magazine one by one, blindly, filled with somewhat gratuitous rage against the behavior of Harold Stikes. Miss Berry is Harold Stikes's ex-wife's cousin. So she does not pity him, not one bit. He got what's coming to him, that's all, in Miss Berry's opinion. Most people don't. It's a pleasure to see it, but Miss Berry would never say this out loud since Cherry Oxendine is of course dying. Cherry Oxendine! Like it was yesterday, Miss Berry remembers how Cherry Oxendine acted in high school, wearing her skirts too tight, popping her gum.

"The doctors can't do a thing," said Lois Hickey.

Silence settled like fog then on the Beauty Nook, on Miss Berry and her magazine, on Dot Mains cutting Lois Hickey's hair, on little Janice thinking about her boyfriend Bruce, and on Mrs. Hooker crying gently under the dryer. Suddenly, Dot remembered something her old granny used to say about such moments of sudden absolute quiet: "An angel is passing over."

After a while, Mrs. Hooker said, "It's all in the hands of God, then." She spread out her fingers one by one on the tray, for Janice to give her a manicure.

And as for Harold Stikes, he's not even considering God. Oh, he doesn't interfere when Mr. Hooker comes by the hospital once a day to check on him—Harold was a Presbyterian in his former life—or even when the Baptist preacher from Cherry's mama's church shows up and insists that everybody in the whole waiting room join hands and bow heads in prayer while he raises his big red face and curly gray head straight up to heaven and prays in a loud voice that God will heal these loved ones who walk through the Valley of Death, and comfort these others who watch, through their hour of need. This includes Mrs. Eunice Sprayberry, whose mother has had a stroke, John and Paula Ripman, whose infant son is dying of encephalitis, and different others who drift in and out of Intensive Care following surgery or wrecks. Harold is losing track. He closes his eyes and bows his head, figuring it can't hurt, like taking out insurance. But deep down inside, he knows that if God is worth His salt, He is not impressed by the prayer of Harold Stikes, who knowingly gave up all hope of peace on earth and heaven hereafter for the love of Cherry Oxendine.

Not to mention his family.

He gave them up too.

---

1. A medication that facilitates breathing.

But this morning when he leaves the hospital after his eight-o'clock visit to Cherry, Harold finds himself turning left out of the lot instead of right toward Food Lion, his store. Harold finds himself taking 15-501 just south of town and then driving through those ornate marble gates that mark the entrance to Camelot Hills, his old neighborhood. Some lucky instinct makes him pull into the little park and stop there, beside the pond. Here comes his ex-wife, Joan, driving the Honda Accord he paid for last year. Joan looks straight ahead. She's still wearing her shiny blond hair in the pageboy she's worn ever since Harold met her at Mercer College so many years ago. Harold is sure she's wearing low heels and a shirtwaist dress. He knows her briefcase is in the backseat, containing lesson plans for today, yogurt, and a banana. Potassium is important. Harold has heard this a million times. Behind her, the beds are all made, the breakfast dishes stacked in the sink. As a home ec teacher, Joan believes that breakfast is the most important meal of the day. The two younger children, Brenda and Harold Jr., are already on the bus to the Academy. James rides to the high school with his mother, hair wet, face blank, staring straight ahead. They don't see Harold. Joan brakes at the stop sign before entering 15-501. She always comes to a complete stop, even if nothing's coming. Always. She looks both ways. Then she's gone.

Harold drives past well-kept lawn after well-kept lawn and lovely house after lovely house, many of them houses where Harold has attended Cub Scout meetings, eaten barbecue, watched bowl games. Now these houses have a blank, closed look to them, like mean faces. Harold turns left on Oxford, then right on Shrewsbury. He comes to a stop beside the curb at 1105 Cambridge and just sits there with the motor running, looking at the house. His house. The Queen Anne house he and Joan planned so carefully, down to the last detail, the fish-scale siding. The house he is still paying for and will be until his dying day, if Joan has her way about it.

Which she will, of course. Everybody is on her side: *desertion*. Harold Stikes deserted his lovely wife and three children for a redheaded waitress. For a fallen woman with a checkered past. Harold can hear her now. "I fail to see why I and the children should lower our standards of living, Harold, and go to the dogs just because you have chosen to become insane in mid-life." Joan's voice is slow and amiable. It has a down-to-earth quality which used to appeal to Harold but now drives him wild. Harold sits at the curb with the motor running and looks at his house good. It looks fine. It looks just like it did when they picked it out of the pages of *Southern Living* and wrote off for the plans. The only difference is, that house was in Stone Mountain, Georgia, and this house is in Greenwood, Mississippi. Big deal.

Joan's response to Harold's desertion has been a surprise to him. He expected tears, recriminations, fireworks. He did not expect her calm, reasonable manner, treating Harold the way she treats the Mormon missionaries who come to the door in their black suits, for instance, that very calm sweet careful voice. Joan acts like Harold's desertion is nothing much. And nothing much appears to have changed for her except the loss of Harold's actual presence, and this cannot be a very big deal since everything else has remained exactly the same.

What the hell. After a while Harold turns off the motor and walks up the flagstone walk to the front door. His key still fits. All the furniture is arranged exactly the way it was arranged four years ago. The only thing that ever changes here is the display of magazines on the glass coffee table before the fireplace, Joan keeps them up to date. *Newsweek, National Geographic, Good Housekeeping, Gourmet.* It's a mostly educational grouping, unlike what Cherry reads—*Parade, Coronet, National Enquirer.* Now these magazines litter the floor at the side of the bed like little souvenirs of Cherry. Harold can't stand to pick them up.

He sits down heavily on the white sofa and stares at the coffee table. He remembers the quiz and the day he found it, four years ago now although it feels like only yesterday, funny thing though that he can't remember which magazine it was in. Maybe *Reader's Digest.* The quiz was titled "How Good Is Your Marriage?" and Harold noticed that Joan had filled it in carefully. This did not surprise him. Joan was so law-abiding, such a *good girl,* that she always filled in such quizzes when she came across them, as if she *had to,* before she could go ahead and finish the magazine. Usually Harold didn't pay much attention.

This time, he picked the magazine up and started reading. One of the questions said: "What is your idea of the perfect vacation? (a) a romantic getaway for you and your spouse alone; (b) a family trip to the beach; (c) a business convention; (d) an organized tour of a foreign land." Joan had wavered on this one. She had marked and then erased "an organized tour of a foreign land." Finally she had settled on "a family trip to the beach." Harold skimmed along. The final question was: "When you think of the love between yourself and your spouse, do you think of (a) a great passion; (b) a warm, meaningful companionship; (c) an average love; (d) an unsatisfying habit." Joan had marked "(c) an average love." Harold stared at these words, knowing they were true. An average love, nothing great, an average marriage between an average man and woman. Suddenly, strangely, Harold was filled with rage.

"It is not enough!" He thought he actually said these words out loud. Perhaps he *did* say them out loud, into the clean hushed air-conditioned air of his average home. Harold's rage was followed by a brief period, maybe five minutes, of unbearable longing, after which he simply closed the magazine and put it back on the table and got up and poured himself a stiff shot of bourbon. He stood for a while before the picture window in the living room, looking out at his even green grass, his clipped hedge, and the impatiens blooming in its bed, the clematis climbing the mailbox. The colors of the world fairly leaped at him—the sky so blue, the grass so green. A passing jogger's shorts glowed unbearably red. He felt that he had never seen any of these things before. Yet in another way it all seemed so familiar as to be an actual part of his body—his throat, his heart, his breath. Harold took another drink. Then he went out and played nine holes of golf at the country club with Bubba Fields, something he did every Wednesday afternoon. He shot 82.

By the time he came home for dinner he was okay again. He was very tired and a little lightheaded, all his muscles tingling. His face was hot. Yet Harold felt vaguely pleased with himself, as if he had been through something and come out the other side of it, as if he had done a creditable job on a difficult assignment. But right then, during dinner, Harold could not have told you exactly what had happened to him that day, or why he felt this way. Because the mind will forget what it can't stand to remember, and anyway the Stikeses had beef Stroganoff that night, a new recipe that Joan was testing for the Junior League cookbook, and Harold Jr. had written them a funny letter from camp, and for once Brenda did not whine. James, who was twelve that year, actually condescended to talk to his father, with some degree of interest, about baseball, and after supper was over he and Harold went out and pitched to each other until it grew dark and lightning bugs emerged. This is how it's supposed to be, Harold thought, father and son playing catch in the twilight.

Then he went upstairs and joined Joan in bed to watch TV, after which they turned out the light and made love. But Joan had greased herself all over with Oil of Olay, earlier, and right in the middle of doing it, Harold got a crazy terrified feeling that he was losing her, that Joan was slipping, slipping away.

But time passed, as it does, and Harold forgot that whole weird day, forgot it until *right now,* in fact, as he sits on the white sofa in his old house again and stares at the magazines on the coffee table, those magazines so familiar except for the date, which is four years later. Now Harold wonders: If he hadn't picked up that quiz and read it, would he have even *noticed* when Cherry Oxendine spooned out that potato salad for him six months later, in his own Food Lion deli? Would the sight of redheaded Cherry Oxendine, the Food Lion smock mostly obscuring her dynamite figure, have hit him like a bolt out of the blue the way it did?

Cherry herself does not believe there is any such thing as coincidence. Cherry thinks there is a master plan for the universe, and what is *meant* to happen will. She thinks it's all set in the stars. For the first time, Harold thinks maybe she's right. He sees part of a pattern in the works, but dimly, as if he is looking at a constellation hidden by clouds. Mainly, he sees her face.

Harold gets up from the sofa and goes into the kitchen, suddenly aware that he isn't supposed to be here. He could be arrested, probably! He looks back at the living room but there's not a trace of him left, not even an imprint on the soft white cushions of the sofa. Absentmindedly, Harold opens and shuts the refrigerator door. There's no beer, he notices. He can't have a Coke. On the kitchen calendar, he reads:

Harold Jr to dentist, 3:30 p.m. Tues
Change furnace filter 2/18/88 (James)

So James is changing the furnace filters now, James is the man of the house. Why not? It's good for him. He's been given too much, kids these days grow up so fast, no responsibilities, they get on drugs, you read about it all the time. But deep down inside, Harold knows that James is not on drugs and he feels something awful, feels the way he felt growing up, that sick little flutter in his stomach that took years to go away.

Harold's dad died of walking pneumonia when he was only three, so his mother raised him alone. She called him her "little man." This made Harold feel proud but also wild, like a boy growing up in a cage. Does James feel this way now? Harold suddenly decides to get James a car for his birthday, and take him hunting.

Hunting is something Harold never did as a boy, but it means a lot to him now. In fact Harold never owned a gun until he was thirty-one, when he bought a shotgun in order to accept the invitation of his regional manager, "Little Jimmy" Fletcher, to go quail hunting in Georgia. He had a great time. Now he's invited back every year, and Little Jimmy is in charge of the company's whole eastern division. Harold has a great future with Food Lion too. He owns three stores, one in downtown Greenwood, one out at the mall, and one over in Indianola. He owned two of them when his mother died, and he's pleased to think that she died proud—proud of the good little boy he'd always been, and the good man he'd become.

Of course she'd wanted him to make a preacher, but Harold never got the call, and she gave that up finally when he was twenty. Harold was not going to pretend to get the call if he never got it, and he held strong to this principle. He *wanted* to see a burning bush, but if this was not vouchsafed to him, he wasn't going to lie about it. He would just major in math instead, which he was good at anyway. Majoring in math at Mercer College, the small Baptist school his mother had chosen for him, Harold came upon Joan Berry, a home ec major from his own hometown who set out single-mindedly to marry him, which wasn't hard. After graduation, Harold got a job as management trainee in the Food Lion store where he had started as a bagboy at fourteen. Joan produced their three children, spaced three years apart, and got her tubes tied. Harold got one promotion, then another. Joan and Harold prospered. They built this house.

Harold looks around and now this house, his house, strikes him as creepy, a wax museum. He lets himself out the back door and walks quickly, almost runs, to his car. It's real cold out, a gray day in February, but Harold's sweating. He starts his car and roars off toward the hospital, driving—as Cherry would say—like a bat out of hell.

They're letting Harold stay with her longer now. He knows it, they know it, but nobody says a word. Lois Hickey just looks the other way when the announcement "Visiting hours are over" crackles across the PA. Is this a good sign or a bad sign? Harold can't tell. He feels slow and confused, like a man underwater. "I think she looks better, don't you?" he said last night to Cherry's son Stan, the TV weatherman, who had driven down from Memphis for the day. Eyes slick and bright with tears, Stan went over to Harold and hugged him tight. This scared Harold to death, he has practically never touched his own sons, and he doesn't even *know* Stan, who's been grown and gone for years. Harold is not used to hugging anybody, especially men. Harold breathed in Stan's strong go-get-'em cologne, he buried his face in Stan's long curly hair. He thinks it is possible that Stan has a permanent. They'll do anything up in Memphis. Then Stan stepped back and put one hand on each of Harold's shoulders, holding him out at arm's length. Stan has his mother's wide, mobile mouth. The bright white light of Intensive Care glinted off the gold chain and the crystal that he wore around his neck. "I'm afraid we're going to lose her, Pop," he said.

But Harold doesn't think so. Today he thinks Cherry looks the best she's looked in weeks, with a bright spot of color in each cheek to match her flaming hair. She's moving around a lot too, she keeps kicking the sheet off.

"She's getting back some of that old energy now," he tells Cherry's daughter, Tammy Lynn Palladino, when she comes by after school. Tammy Lynn and Harold's son James are both members of the senior class, but they aren't friends. Tammy Lynn says James is a "stuck-up jock," a "preppie," and a "country-clubber." Harold can't say a word to defend his own son against these charges, he doesn't even *know* James anymore. It might be true, anyway. Tammy Lynn is real smart, a teenage egghead. She's got a full scholarship to Millsaps College[2] for next year. She applied for it all by herself. As Cherry used to say, Tammy Lynn came into this world with a full deck of cards and an ace or two up her sleeve. Also she looks out for Number One.

In this regard Tammy Lynn is as different from her mama as night from day, because Cherry would give you the shirt off her back and frequently has. That's gotten her into lots of trouble. With Ed Palladino, for instance, her second husband and Tammy Lynn's dad. Just about everybody in this town got took by Ed Palladino, who came in here wearing a seersucker suit and talking big about putting in an outlet mall across the river. A lot of people got burned on that outlet mall deal. But Ed Palladino had a way about him that made you want to cast your lot with his, it is true. You wanted to give Ed Palladino your savings, your time-sharing condo, your cousin, your ticket to the Super Bowl. Cherry gave it all.

She married him and turned over what little inheritance she had from her daddy's death—and that's the only time in her life she ever had *any* money, mind you—and then she just shrugged and smiled her big crooked smile when he left town under cover of night. "*C'est la vie,*"[3] Cherry said. She donated the rest of his clothes to the Salvation Army. "*Que será, será,*"[4] Cherry said, quoting a song that was popular when she was in junior high.

Tammy Lynn sits by her mama's bed and holds Cherry's thin dry hand. "I brought you a Chick-Fil-A," she says to Harold. "It's over there in that bag." She points to the shelf by the door. Harold nods. Tammy Lynn works at Chick-Fil-A. Cherry's eyes are wide and blue and full of meaning as she stares at her daughter. Her mouth moves, both Harold and Tammy Lynn lean forward, but then her mouth falls slack and her eyelids flutter shut. Tammy sits back.

"I think she looks some better today, don't you?" Harold asks.

"No," Tammy Lynn says. She has a flat little redneck voice. She sounds just the way she did last summer when she told Cherry that what she saw in the field was a cotton picker working at night, and not a UFO after all. "I wish I did but I don't, Harold. I'm going to go on home now and heat up some Bea-nee Weenee for Mamaw. You come on as soon as you can."

"Well," Harold says. He feels like things have gotten all turned around here some way, he feels like he's the kid and Tammy Lynn has turned into a freaky little grown-up. He says, "I'll be along directly."

But they both know he won't leave until Lois Hickey throws him out. And speaking of Lois, as soon as Tammy Lynn takes off, here she comes again, checking something on the respirator, making a little clucking sound with her mouth, then whirling to leave. When Lois walks, her panty girdle goes *swish, swish, swish* at the top of her legs. She comes right back with the young black man named Rodney Broadbent, Respiratory Therapist. It says so on his badge. Rodney wheels a complicated-looking cart ahead of himself. He's all built up, like a weightlifter.

"How you doing tonight, Mr. Stipe?" Rodney says.

---

2. Private liberal arts college in Jackson, Mississippi.   **3.** "That's life" (French).   **4.** "What will be, will be" (Spanish). The song "Que Será, Será" was a hit for Doris Day in 1956.

"I think she's some better," Harold says.

Lois Hickey and Rodney look at him.

"Well, lessee here," Rodney says. He unhooks the respirator tube at Cherry's throat, sticks the tube from his own machine down the opening, and switches on the machine. It makes a whirring sound. It looks like an electric ice cream mixer. Rodney Broadbent looks at Lois Hickey in a significant way as she turns to leave the room.

They don't have to tell him, Harold knows. Cherry is worse, not better. Harold gets the Chick-Fil-A, unwraps it, eats it, and then goes over to stand by the window. It's already getting dark. The big mercury arc light glows in the hospital parking lot. A little wind blows some trash around on the concrete. He has had Cherry for three years, that's all. One trip to Disney World, two vacations at Gulf Shores Alabama, hundreds of nights in the old metal bed out at the farm with Cherry sleeping naked beside him, her arm thrown over his stomach. They had a million laughs.

"Alrightee," Rodney Broadbent nearly sings, unhooking his machine. Harold turns to look at him. Rodney Broadbent certainly looks more like a middle linebacker than a respiratory therapist. But Harold likes him.

"Well, Rodney?" Harold says.

Rodney starts shadow-boxing in the middle of the room. "Tough times," he says finally. "These is tough times, Mr. Stipe." Harold stares at him. Rodney is light on his feet as can be.

Harold sits down in the chair by the respirator. "What do you mean?" he asks.

"I mean she is drowning, Mr. Stipe," Rodney says. He throws a punch which lands real close to Harold's left ear. "What I'm doing here, see, is suctioning. I'm pulling all the fluid up out of her lungs. But now looka here, Mr. Stipe, they is just too damn much of it. See this little doohickey here I'm measuring it with? This here is the danger zone, man. Now Mrs. Stipe, she has been in the danger zone for some time. They is just too much damn fluid in there. What she got, anyway? Cancer and pneumonia both, am I right? What can I tell you, man? She is *drowning*." Rodney gives Harold a short affectionate punch in the ribs, then wheels his cart away. From the door, apparently struck by some misgivings, he says, "Well, man, if it was me, I'd want to know what the story is, you follow me, man? If it was me, what I'm saying." Harold can't see Rodney anymore, only hear his voice from the open door.

"Thank you, Rodney," Harold says. He sits in the chair. In a way he has known this already, for quite some time. In a way, Rodney's news is no news, to Harold. He just hopes he will be man enough to bear it, to do what will have to be done. Harold has always been scared that he is not man enough for Cherry Oxendine, anyway. This is his worst secret fear. He looks around the little Intensive Care room, searching for a sign, some sign, anything, that he will be man enough. Nothing happens. Cherry lies strapped to the bed, flanked by so many machines that it looks like she's in the cockpit of a jet. Her eyes are closed, eyelids fluttering, red spots on her freckled cheeks. Her chest rises and falls as the respirator pushes air in and out through the tube in her neck. He doesn't see how she can sleep in the bright white light of Intensive Care, where it is always noon. And does she dream? Cherry used to tell him her dreams, which were wild, long Technicolor dreams, like movies.

Cherry played different parts in them. If you dream in color, it means you're intelligent, Cherry said. She used to tease him all the time. She thought Harold's own dreams were a stitch, dreams more boring than his life, dreams in which he'd drive to Jackson, say, or be washing his car.

"Harold?" It's Ray Muncey, manager of the Food Lion at the mall.

"Why, what are you doing over here, Ray?" Harold asks, and then in a flash he *knows,* Lois Hickey must have called him, to make Harold go on home.

"I was just driving by and I thought, Hey, maybe Harold and me might run by the Holiday Inn, get a bite to eat." Ray shifts from foot to foot in the doorway. He doesn't come inside, he's not supposed to, nobody but immediate family is allowed in Intensive Care, and Harold's glad—Cherry would just die if people she barely knows, like Ray Muncey, got to see her looking so bad.

"No, Ray, you go on and eat," Harold says. "I already ate. I'm leaving right now, anyway."

"Well, how's the missus doing?" Ray is a big man, afflicted with big, heavy manners.

"She's drowning," Harold says abruptly. Suddenly he remembers Cherry in a water ballet at the town pool, it must have been the summer of junior year, Fourth of July, Cherry and the other girls floating in a circle on their backs to form a giant flower—legs high, toes pointed. Harold doesn't know it when Ray Muncey leaves. Out the window, the parking lot light glows like a big full moon. Lois Hickey comes in. "You've got to go home now, Harold," she says. "I'll call if there's any change." He remembers Cherry at Glass Lake, on the senior class picnic. Cherry's getting real agitated now, she tosses her head back and forth, moves her arms. She'd pull out the tubes if she could. She kicks off the sheet. Her legs are still good, great legs in fact, the legs of a beautiful young woman.

Harold at seventeen was tall and skinny, brown hair in a soft flat crew cut, glasses with heavy black frames. His jeans were too short. He carried a pen-and-pencil set in a clear plastic case in his breast pocket. Harold and his best friend, Ben Hill, looked so much alike that people had trouble telling them apart. They did everything together. They built model rockets, they read every science fiction book they could get their hands on, they collected Lionel train parts and Marvel comics. They loved superheroes with special powers, enormous beings who leaped across rivers and oceans. Harold's friendship with Ben Hill kept the awful loneliness of the only child at bay, and it also kept him from having to talk to girls. You couldn't talk to those two, not seriously. They were giggling and bumping into each other all the time. They were immature.

So it was in Ben's company that Harold experienced the most private, the most *personal* memory he has of Cherry Oxendine in high school. Oh, he also has those other memories you'd expect, the big public memories of Cherry being crowned Miss Greenwood High (for her talent; she surprised everybody by reciting "Abou Ben Adhem"[5] in such a stirring way that there wasn't a dry eye in the whole auditorium when she got through), or running out onto the field ahead of the team with the other cheerleaders, red curls flying,

---

5. Poem by English writer James Henry Leigh Hunt (1784–1859).

green and white skirt whirling out around her hips like a beach umbrella when she turned a cartwheel. Harold noticed her then, of course. He noticed her when she moved through the crowded halls of the high school with her walk that was almost a prance, she put a little something extra into it, all right. Harold noticed Cherry Oxendine then in the way that he noticed Sandra Dee on the cover of a magazine, or Annette Funicello on *American Bandstand*.[6]

But such girls were not for the likes of Harold, and Harold knew it. Girls like Cherry always had boyfriends like Lamar Peebles, who was hers—a doctor's son with a baby-blue convertible and plenty of money. They used to drive around town in his car, smoking cigarettes. Harold saw them, as he carried out grocery bags. He did not envy Lamar Peebles, or wish he had a girl like Cherry Oxendine. Only something about them made him stand where he was in the Food Lion lot, watching, until they had passed from sight.

So Harold's close-up encounter with Cherry was unexpected. It took place at the senior class picnic, where Harold and Ben had been drinking beer all afternoon. No alcohol was allowed at the senior class picnic, but some of the more enterprising boys had brought out kegs the night before and hidden them in the woods. Anybody could go back there and pay some money and get some beer. The chaperones didn't know, or appeared not to know. In any case, the chaperones all left at six o'clock, when the picnic was officially over. Some of the class members left then too. Then some of them came back with more beer, more blankets. It was a free lake. Nobody could *make* you go home. Normally, Harold and Ben would have been among the first to leave, but because they had had four beers apiece, and because this was the first time they had ever had *any* beer ever, at all, they were still down by the water, skipping rocks and waiting to sober up so that they would not wreck Harold's mother's green Gremlin on the way home. All the cool kids were on the other side of the lake, listening to transistor radios. The sun went down. Bullfrogs started up. A mist came out all around the sides of the lake. It was a cloudy, humid day anyway, not a great day for a picnic.

"If God is really God, how come He let Himself get crucified, is what I want to know," Ben said. Ben's daddy was a Holiness preacher, out in the county.

But Harold heard something. "Hush, Ben," he said.

"If I was God I would go around and really kick some ass," Ben said.

Harold heard it again. It was almost too dark to see.

"Damn." It was a girl's voice, followed by a splash.

All of a sudden, Harold felt sober. "Who's there?" he asked. He stepped forward, right up to the water's edge. Somebody was in the water. Harold was wearing his swim trunks under his jeans, but he had not gone in the water himself. He couldn't stand to show himself in front of people. He thought he was too skinny.

"Well, *do something*." It was the voice of Cherry Oxendine, almost wailing. She stumbled up the bank. Harold reached out and grabbed her arm. Close up, she was a mess, wet and muddy, with her hair all over her head. But the thing that got Harold, of course, was that she didn't have any top on. She didn't even try to cover them up either, just stomped her little foot on the bank and said, "I

---

6. Television show of the 1950s and '60s that featured popular music.

am going to *kill* Lamar Peebles when I get ahold of him." Harold had never even imagined so much skin.

"What's going on?" asked Ben, from up the bank.

Harold took off his own shirt as fast as he could and handed it over to Cherry Oxendine. "Cover yourself," he said.

"Why, thank you." Cherry didn't bat an eye. She took his shirt and put it on, tying it stylishly at the waist. Harold couldn't believe it. Close up, Cherry was a lot smaller than she looked on the stage or the football field. She looked up at Harold through her dripping hair and gave him her crooked grin.

"Thanks, hey?" she said.

And then she was gone, vanished into the mist and trees before Harold could say another word. He opened his mouth and closed it. Mist obscured his view. From the other side of the lake he could hear "Ramblin' Rose"[7] playing on somebody's radio. He heard a girl's high-pitched giggle, a boy's whooping laugh.

"What's going on?" asked Ben.

"Nothing," Harold said. It was the first time he had ever lied to Ben. Harold never told anybody what had happened that night, not ever. He felt that it was up to him to protect Cherry Oxendine's honor. Later, much later, when he and Cherry were lovers, he was astonished to learn that she couldn't remember any of this, not who she was with or what had happened or what she was doing in the lake like that with her top off, or Harold giving her his shirt. "I think that was sweet, though," Cherry told him.

When Harold and Ben finally got home that night at nine or ten o'clock, Harold's mother was frantic. "You've been drinking," she shrilled at him under the hanging porch light. "And where's your shirt?" It was a new madras shirt which Harold had gotten for graduation. Now Harold's mother is out at the Hillandale Rest Home. Ben died in Vietnam, and Cherry is drowning. This time, and Harold knows it now, he can't help her.

Oh, Cherry! Would she have been so wild if she hadn't been so cute? And what if her parents had been younger when she was born—normal-age parents—couldn't they have controlled her better? As it was, the Oxendines were sober, solid people living in a farmhouse out near the county line, and Cherry lit up their lives like a rocket. Her dad, Martin "Buddy" Oxendine, went to sleep in his chair every night right after supper, woke back up for the eleven-o'clock news, and then went to bed for good. Buddy was an elder in the Baptist church. Cherry's mom, Gladys Oxendine, made drapes for people. She assumed she would never have children at all because of her spastic colitis. Gladys and Buddy had started raising cockapoos[8] when they gave up on children. Imagine Gladys's surprise, then, to find herself pregnant at thirty-eight, when she was already old! They say she didn't even know it when she went to the doctor. She thought she had a tumor.

But then she got so excited, that old farm woman, when Dr. Grimwood told her what was what, and she wouldn't even consider an abortion when he mentioned the chances of a mongoloid. People didn't use to have babies so

---

7. Popular 1962 song by Nat "King" Cole (1919–1965).   **8.** Dogs bred from cocker spaniels and poodles.

old then as they do now, so Gladys Oxendine's pregnancy was the talk of the county. Neighbors crocheted little jackets and made receiving blankets. Buddy built a baby room onto the house and made a cradle by hand. During the last two months of the pregnancy, when Gladys had to stay in bed because of toxemia, people brought over casseroles and boiled custard, everything good. Gladys's pregnancy was the only time in her whole life that she was ever pretty, and she loved it, and she loved the attention, neighbors in and out of the house. When the baby was finally born on November 1, 1944, no parents were ever more ready than Gladys and Buddy Oxendine. And the baby was everything they hoped for too, which is not usually the case—the prettiest baby in the world, a baby like a little flower.

They named her Doris Christine which is who she was until eighth grade, when she made junior varsity cheerleader and announced that she was changing her name to Cherry. Cherry! Even her parents had to admit it suited her better than Doris Christine. As a little girl, Doris Christine was redheaded, bouncy, and busy—she was always into something, usually something you'd never thought to tell her not to do. She started talking early and never shut up. Her old dad, old Buddy Oxendine, was so crazy about Doris Christine that he took her everywhere with him in his red pickup truck. You got used to seeing the two of them, Buddy and his curly-headed little daughter, riding the country roads together, going to the seed-and-feed together, sharing a shake at the Dairy Queen. Gladys made all of Doris Christine's clothes, the most beautiful little dresses in the world, with hand-smocking and French seams. They gave Doris Christine everything they could think of—what she asked for, what she didn't. "That child is going to get spoiled," people started to say. And of course she did get spoiled, she couldn't have helped *that,* but she was never spoiled rotten as so many are. She stayed sweet in spite of it all.

Then along about ninth grade, soon after she changed her name to Cherry and got interested in boys, things changed between Cherry and the old Oxendines. Stuff happened. Instead of being the light of their lives, Cherry became the bane of their existence, the curse of their old age. She wanted to wear makeup, she wanted to have car dates. You can't blame her— she was old enough, sixteen. Everybody else did it. But you can't blame Gladys and Buddy either—they were old people by then, all worn out. They were not up to such a daughter. Cherry sneaked out. She wrecked a car. She ran away to Pensacola with a soldier. Finally, Gladys and Buddy just gave up. When Cherry eloped with the disc jockey, Don Westall, right after graduation, they threw up their hands. They did not do a thing about it. They had done the best they could, and everybody knew it. They went back to raising cockapoos.

Cherry, living up in Nashville, Tennessee, had a baby, Stan, the one that's in his twenties now. Cherry sent baby pictures back to Gladys and Buddy, and wrote that she was going to be a singer. Six years later, she came home. She said nothing against Don Westall, who was still a disc jockey on WKIX, Nashville. You could hear him on the radio every night after ten P.M. Cherry said the breakup was all her fault. She said she had made some mistakes, but she didn't say what they were. She was thin and noble. Her kid was cute. She did not go back out to the farm then. She rented an apartment over the hardware store, down by the river, and got a job downtown working in Ginger's Boutique. After a year or so, she started acting more like herself again, although not *quite* like herself, she had grown up somehow in Nashville, and quit being spoiled. She put Stan, her kid, first. And if she did run around a little bit, or if she was the life of the party sometimes out at the country club, so what? Stan didn't want for a thing. By then the Oxendines were failing and she had to take care of them too, she had to drive her daddy up to Grenada for dialysis twice a week. It was not an easy life for Cherry, but if it ever got her down, you couldn't tell it. She was still cute. When her daddy finally died and left her a little money, everybody was real glad. Oh *now*, they said, Cherry Oxendine can quit working so hard and put her mama in a home or something and have a decent life. She can go on a cruise. But then along came Ed Palladino, and the rest is history.

Cherry Oxendine was left with no husband, no money, a little girl, and a mean old mama to take care of. At least by this time Stan was in the Navy. Cherry never complained, though. She moved back out to the farm. When Ginger retired from business and closed her boutique, Cherry got another job, as a receptionist at Wallace, Wallace and Peebles. This was her undoing. Because Lamar Peebles had just moved back to town with his family, to join his father's firm. Lamar had two little girls. He had been married to a tobacco heiress since college. All this time he had run around on her. He was not on the up-and-up. And when he encountered redheaded Cherry Oxendine again after the passage of so many years, all those old fireworks went off again. They got to be a scandal, then a disgrace. Lamar said he was going to marry her, and Cherry believed him. After six months of it, Mrs. Lamar Peebles checked herself into a mental hospital in Silver Hill, Connecticut. First, she called her lawyers.

And then it was all over, not even a year after it began. Mr. and Mrs. Lamar Peebles were reconciled and moved to Winston-Salem, North Carolina, her hometown. Cherry Oxendine lost her job at Wallace, Wallace and Peebles, and was reduced to working in the deli at Food Lion. Why did she do it? Why did she lose all the goodwill she'd built up in this community over so many years? It is because she doesn't know how to look out for Number One. Her own daughter, Tammy Lynn Palladino, is aware of this.

"You have got a fatal flaw, Mama," Tammy said after learning about fatal flaws in English class. "You believe everything everybody tells you."

Still, Tammy loves her mother. Sometimes she writes her mother's whole name, Cherry Oxendine Westall Palladino Stikes, over and over in her Blue Horse notebook. Tammy Lynn will never be half the woman her mother is, and she's so smart she knows it. She gets a kick out of her mother's wild ideas.

"When you get too old to be cute, honey, you get to be eccentric," Cherry told Tammy one time. It's the truest thing she ever said.

It seems to Tammy that the main thing about her mother is, Cherry always has to have *something* going on. If it isn't a man it's something else, such as having her palm read by that woman over in French Camp, or astrology, or the grapefruit diet. Cherry believes in the Bermuda Triangle, Bigfoot, Atlantis, and ghosts. It kills her that she's not psychic. The UFO Club was just the latest in a long string of interests although it has lasted the longest, starting back before Cherry's marriage to Harold Stikes. And then Cherry got cancer, and she kind of forgot about it. But Tammy still remembers the night her mama first got so turned on to UFOs.

Rhonda Ramey, Cherry's best friend, joined the UFO Club first. Rhonda and Cherry are a lot alike, although it's hard to see this at first. While Cherry is short and peppy, Rhonda is tall, thin, and listless. She looks like Cher. Rhonda doesn't have any children. She's crazy about her husband, Bill, but he's a workaholic who runs a string of video rental stores all over northern Mississippi, so he's gone a lot, and Rhonda gets bored. She works out at the spa, but it isn't enough. Maybe this is why she got so interested when the UFO landed at a farm outside her mother's hometown of Como. It was first spotted by sixteen-year-old Donnie Johnson just at sunset, as he was finishing his chores on his parents' farm. He heard a loud rumbling sound "in the direction of the hog house," it said in the paper. Looking up, he suddenly saw a "brilliantly lit mushroom-shaped object" hovering about two feet above the ground, with a shaft of white light below and glowing all over with an intensely bright multicolored light, "like the light of a welder's arc."

Donnie said it sounded like a jet. He was temporarily blinded and paralyzed. He fell down on the ground. When he came back to his senses again, it was gone. Donnie staggered into the kitchen where his parents, Durel, fifty-four, and Erma, forty-nine, were eating supper, and told them what had happened. They all ran back outside to the field, where they found four large imprints and four small imprints in the muddy ground, and a nearby clump of sage grass on fire. The hogs were acting funny, bunching up, looking dazed. Immediately, Durel jumped in his truck and went to get the sheriff, who came right back with two deputies. All in all, six people viewed the site while the bush continued to burn, and who knows how many people—half of Como—saw the imprints the next day. Rhonda saw them too. She drove out to the Johnson farm with her mother, as soon as she heard about it.

It was a close encounter of the second kind, according to Civil Air Patrol head Glenn Raines, who appeared on TV to discuss it, because the UFO "interacted with its surroundings in a significant way." A close encounter of the first kind is simply a close-range sighting, while a close encounter of the third kind is something like the most famous example, of Betty and Barney Hill of Exeter, New Hampshire, who were actually kidnapped by a UFO while they were driving along on a trip. Betty and Barney Hill were taken aboard the alien ship and given physical exams by intelligent humanoid beings. Two hours and thirty-five minutes were missing from their trip, and afterward, Betty had to be treated for acute anxiety. Glenn Raines, wearing his brown Civil Air Patrol uniform, said all this on TV.

His appearance, plus what had happened at the Johnson farm, sparked a rash of sightings all across Mississippi, Louisiana, and Texas for the next two years. Metal disklike objects were seen, and luminous objects appearing as lights at night. In Levelland, Texas, fifteen people called the police to report an egg-shaped UFO appearing over State Road 1173. Overall, the UFOs seemed to show a preference for soybean fields and teenage girl viewers. But a pretty good photograph of a UFO flying over the Gulf was taken by a retired man from Pascagoula, so you can't generalize. Clubs sprang up all over the place. The one that Rhonda and Cherry went to had seventeen members and met once a month at the junior high school.

Tammy recalls exactly how her mama and Rhonda acted the night they came home from Cherry's first meeting. Cherry's eyes sparkled in her face like Brenda Starr's[9] eyes in the comics. She started right in telling Tammy all about it, beginning with the Johnsons from Como and Betty and Barney Hill.

Tammy was not impressed. "I don't believe it," she said. She was president of the Science Club at the junior high school.

"You are the most irritating child!" Cherry said. "*What* don't you believe?"

"Well, any of it," Tammy said then. "All of it," and this has remained her attitude ever since.

"Listen, honey, *Jimmy Carter* saw one," Cherry said triumphantly. "In nineteen seventy-one, at the Executive Mansion in Georgia. He turned in an official report on it."

"How come nobody knows about it, then?" Tammy asked. She was a tough customer.

"Because the government covered it up!" said Rhonda, just dying to tell this part. "People see UFOs all the time, it's common knowledge, they are trying to make contact with us right now, honey, but the government doesn't want the average citizen to know about it. There's a big cover-up going on."

"It's just like Watergate."[1] Cherry opened a beer and handed it over to Rhonda.

"That's right," Rhonda said, "and every time there's a major incident, you know what happens? These men from the government show up at your front door dressed all in black. After they get through with you, you'll wish you never heard the word 'saucer.' You turn pale and get real sick. You can't get anything to stay on your stomach."

Tammy cracked up. But Rhonda and Cherry went on and on. They had official-looking gray notebooks to log their sightings in. At their meetings, they reported these sightings to each other, and studied up on the subject in general. Somebody in the club was responsible for the educational part of each meeting, and somebody else brought the refreshments.

Tammy Lynn learned to keep her mouth shut. It was less embarrassing than belly dancing; she had a friend whose mother took belly dancing at the YMCA. Tammy did not tell her mama about all the rational explanations for UFOs that she found in the school library. They included: (1) hoaxes; (2) natural phenomena, such as fungus causing the so-called fairy rings sometimes found after a landing; (3) real airplanes flying off course; and Tammy's favorite, (4) the Fata Morgana, described as a "rare and beautiful type of mirage, constantly changing, the result of unstable layers of warm and cold air. The Fata Morgana takes its name from fairy lore and is said to evoke in the viewer a profound sense of longing," the book went on to say. Tammy's biology teacher, Mr. Owens, said he thought that the weather patterns in Mississippi might be especially conducive to this phenomenon. But Tammy kept her mouth shut. And after a while, when nobody in the UFO Club saw anything, its membership declined sharply. Then her mama met Harold Stikes, then

9. Glamorous heroine of comic strip that has run in newspapers since 1940.   **1.** Collective name for series of scandals that began with a burglary in the Watergate Hotel of Washington, D.C., in 1972 and led to the forced resignation of President Richard M. Nixon in 1974.

Harold Stikes left his wife and children and moved out to the farm with them, and sometimes Cherry forgot to attend the meetings, she was so happy with Harold Stikes.

Tammy couldn't see *why*, initially. In her opinion, Harold Stikes was about as interesting as a telephone pole. "But he's so *nice!*" Cherry tried to explain it to Tammy Lynn. Finally Tammy decided that there is nothing in the world that makes somebody as attractive as if they really love you. And Harold Stikes really did love her mama, there was no question. That old man—what a crazy old Romeo! Why, he proposed to Cherry when she was still in the hospital after she had her breast removed (this was back when they thought that was *it,* that the doctors had gotten it all).

"Listen, Cherry," he said solemnly, gripping a dozen red roses. "I want you to marry me."

"What?" Cherry said. She was still groggy.

"I want you to marry me," Harold said. He knelt down heavily beside her bed.

"Harold! Get up from there!" Cherry said. "Somebody will see you."

"Say yes," said Harold.

"I just had my breast removed."

"Say yes," he said again.

"Yes, yes, yes!" Cherry said.

And as soon as she got out of the hospital, they were married out in the orchard, on a beautiful April day, by Lew Uggams, a JP from out of town. They couldn't find a local preacher to do it. The sky was bright blue, not a cloud in sight. Nobody was invited except Stan, Tammy, Rhonda and Bill, and Cherry's mother, who wore her dress inside out. Cherry wore a new pink lace dress, the color of cherry blossoms. Tough little Tammy cried and cried. It's the most beautiful wedding she's ever seen, and now she's completely devoted to Harold Stikes.

So Tammy leaves the lights on for Harold when she finally goes to bed that night. She tried to wait up for him, but she has to go to school in the morning, she's got a chemistry test. Her mamaw is sound asleep in the little added-on baby room that Buddy Oxendine built for Cherry. Gladys acts like a baby now, a spoiled baby at that. The only thing she'll drink is Sprite out of a can. She talks mean. She doesn't like anything in the world except George and Tammy, the two remaining cockapoos.

They bark up a storm when Harold finally gets back out to the farm, at one-thirty. The cockapoos are barking, Cherry's mom is snoring like a chain saw. Harold doesn't see how Tammy Lynn can sleep through all of this, but she always does. Teenagers can sleep through anything. Harold himself has started waking up several times a night, his heart pounding. He wonders if he's going to have a heart attack. He almost mentioned his symptoms to Lois Hickey last week, in fact, but then thought, What the hell. His heart is broken. Of course it's going to act up some. And everything, not only his heart, is out of whack. Sometimes he'll break into a sweat for no reason. Often he forgets really crucial things, such as filing his estimated income tax on January 15. Harold is not the kind to forget something this important. He has strange aches that float from joint to joint. He has headaches. He's lost twelve pounds.

Sometimes he has no appetite at all. Other times, like right now, he's just starving.

Harold goes in the kitchen and finds a flat rectangular casserole, carefully wrapped in tinfoil, on the counter, along with a Tupperware cake carrier. He lifts off the top of the cake carrier and finds a piña colada cake, his favorite. Then he pulls back the tinfoil on the casserole. Lasagna! Plenty is left over. Harold sticks it in the microwave. He knows that the cake and the lasagna were left here by his ex-wife. Ever since Cherry has been in Intensive Care, Joan has been bringing food out to the farm. She comes when Harold's at work or at the hospital, and leaves it with Gladys or Tammy. She probably figures that Harold would refuse it, if she caught him at home, which he would. She's a great cook, though. Harold takes the lasagna out of the microwave, opens a beer, and sits down at the kitchen table. He loves Joan's lasagna. Cherry's idea of a terrific meal is one she doesn't have to cook. Harold remembers eating in bed with Cherry, tacos from Taco Bell, sour-cream-and-onion chips, beer. He gets some more lasagna and a big wedge of piña colada cake.

Now it's two-thirty, but for some reason Harold is not a bit sleepy. His mind whirls with thoughts of Cherry. He snaps off all the lights and stands in the darkened house. His heart is racing. Moonlight comes in the windows, it falls on the old patterned rug. Outside, it's as bright as day. He puts his coat on and goes out, with the cockapoos scampering along beside him. They are not even surprised. They think it's a fine time for a walk. Harold goes past the mailbox, down the dirt road between the fields. Out here in the country, the sky is both bigger and closer than it is in town. Harold feels like he's in a huge bowl turned upside down, with tiny little pinpoints of light shining through. And everything is silvered by the moonlight—the old fence-posts, the corn stubble in the flat long fields, a distant barn, the highway at the end of the dirt road, his own strange hand when he holds it out to look at it.

He remembers when she waited on him in the Food Lion deli, three years ago. He had asked for a roast beef sandwich, which come prepackaged. Cherry put it on his plate. Then she paused, and cocked her hip, and looked at him. "Can I give you some potato salad to go with that?" she asked. "Some slaw?"

Harold looked at her. Some red curls had escaped the required net. "Nothing else," he said.

But Cherry spooned a generous helping of potato salad onto his plate. "Thank you so much," he said. They looked at each other.

"I know I know you," Cherry said.

It came to him then. "Cherry Oxendine," said Harold. "I remember you from high school."

"Lord, you've got a great memory, then!" Cherry had an easy laugh. "That was a hundred years ago."

"Doesn't seem like it." Harold knew he was holding up the line.

"Depends on who you're talking to," Cherry said.

Later that day, Harold found an excuse to go back over to the deli for coffee and apple pie, then he found an excuse to look through the personnel files. He started eating lunch at the deli every day, without making any conscious decision to do so. In the afternoons, when he went back for coffee, Cherry would take her break and sit at a table with him.

Harold and Cherry talked and talked. They talked about their families, their kids, high school. Cherry told him everything that had happened to her. She was tough and funny, not bitter or self-pitying. They talked and talked. In his whole life, Harold had never had so much to say. During this period, which lasted for several weeks, his whole life took on a heightened aspect. Everything that happened to him seemed significant, a little incident to tell Cherry about. Every song he liked on the radio he remembered, so he could ask Cherry if she liked it too. Then there came the day when they were having coffee and she mentioned she'd left her car at Al's Garage that morning to get a new clutch.

"I'll give you a ride over there to pick it up," said Harold instantly. In his mind he immediately canceled the sales meeting he had scheduled for four o'clock.

"Oh, that's too much trouble," Cherry said.

"But I insist." In his conversations with Cherry, Harold had developed a brand-new gallant manner he had never had before.

"Well, if you're sure it's not any trouble . . ." Cherry grinned at him like she knew he really wanted to do it, and that afternoon when he grabbed her hand suddenly before letting her out at Al's Garage, she did not pull it away.

The next weekend Harold took her up to Memphis and they stayed at the Peabody Hotel, where Cherry got the biggest kick out of the ducks in the lobby, and ordering from room service.

"You're a fool," Harold's friends told him later, when the shit hit the fan.

But Harold didn't think so. He doesn't think so now, walking the old dirt road on the Oxendine farm in the moonlight. He loves his wife. He feels that he has been ennobled and enlarged, by knowing Cherry Oxendine. He feels like he has been specially selected among men, to receive a precious gift. He stepped out of his average life for her, he gave up being a good man, but the rewards have been extraordinary. He's glad he did it. He'd do it all over again.

Still walking, Harold suddenly knows that something is going to happen. But he doesn't stop walking. Only, the whole world around him seems to waver a bit, and intensify. The moonlight shines whiter than ever. A little wind whips up out of nowhere. The stars are twinkling so brightly that they seem to dance, actually dance, in the sky. And then, while Harold watches, one of them detaches itself from the rest of the sky and grows larger, moves closer, until it's clear that it is actually moving across the sky, at an angle to the earth. A falling star, perhaps? A comet?

Harold stops walking. The star moves faster and faster, with an erratic pattern. It's getting real close now. It's no star. Harold hears a high whining noise, like a blender. The cockapoos huddle against his ankles. They don't bark. Now he can see the blinking red lights on the top of it, and the beam of white light shooting out the bottom. His coat is blown straight out behind him by the wind. He feels like he's going blind. He shields his eyes. At first it's as big as a barn, then a tobacco warehouse. It covers the field. Although Harold can't say exactly how it communicates to him or even if it does, suddenly his soul is filled to bursting. The ineffable occurs. And then, more quickly than it came, it's gone, off toward Carrollton, rising into the night, leaving the field, the farm, the road. Harold turns back.

It will take Cherry Oxendine two more weeks to die. She's tough. And even when there's nothing left of her but heart, she will fight all the way. She will go out furious, squeezing Harold's hand at the very moment of death, clinging fast to every minute of this bright, hard life. And although at first he won't want to, Harold will go on living. He will buy another store. Gladys will die. Tammy Lynn will make Phi Beta Kappa. Harold will start attending the Presbyterian church again. Eventually Harold may even go back to his family, but he will love Cherry Oxendine until the day he dies, and he will never, ever, tell anybody what he saw.

1990

RELATED:

—Smith on Flannery O'Connor's "A Good Man Is Hard to Find," p. 1844

ELIZABETH SPENCER
b. 1921

 Born in Carollton, Mississippi, Spencer attended Belhaven College in Jackson and then earned her M.A. at Vanderbilt University in Nashville, Tennessee. Throughout a long and distinguished career as a journalist and a teacher, she has steadily produced the stories that have won her a place alongside such other grand storytellers of the American South as Eudora Welty, Peter Taylor, Katherine Anne Porter, and Flannery O'Connor. Since her first novel, *Fire in the Morning* (1948), Spencer has published eight more novels and eight collections of short fiction, including her best-known work, *The Light in the Piazza and Other Italian Tales* (1996). Her many awards include a Guggenheim Fellowship, a PEN/Malamud Award for Short Fiction, The Rea Award for the Short Story, and no fewer than five O. Henry prizes. Her most recent collection, *Starting over* (2013), features stories written after the death of her husband in 1998.

Wisteria

Charles Webley rather liked his hostess, though he imagined a lot of people didn't. She talked too much, for one thing, but then you didn't have to listen. Her voice was pleasing and made a soothing ripple of sound which broke in occasional laughter. At the moment she didn't mean to be taken seriously. She was hefty, to put it mildly, way too big by English standards. But, he thought, lazily tolerant, she was not overbearing, no Brünnehilde[1] she, and one could always be reminded of the jolly Dutch women, in popular conception at least, with their butter-colored hair cut short and their rotund, softly elephantine, white limbs. But Evaline's hair, in the years since they had met, must have gone from blond to gray, or why would she have got it stiffly done up in what she probably thought of as silver gilt, but which looked to him like new aluminum? How, charitably, was he to picture her in Dutch clogs and a peaked cap now that her waistline had vanished? She was at present all baled up in Roman silks. He gave a short explosive laugh.

"Thought you'd like that, Charles." She had just wound up a little story, no word of which had reached him.

He wandered out into the garden. The apartment was on the ground floor, unusual in Rome, with a wisteria vine thickly roofing the terrace. Blooms like bunches of pale grapes hung down and grazed his tall head. One cluster, so

---

1. One of the Valkyries, the warrior maidens of German myth. Brünnehilde is a featured role in Richard Wagner's monumental operatic cycle, *The Ring of the Nibelungs* (completed in 1876).

disturbed, suddenly shed all its blossoms upon him. Lavender flowers fell from his head to his shoulders and scattered on the paving about his feet; and one final petal, letting go like the rest, landed in his martini. He stood regarding it, trying to grasp, hold on to, the surprising moment, generous and fragrant, which had created a sharp start in his breast, resembling love. He looked up for someone to share it with.

"Do you prefer flowers to lemon peel?"

The woman—not young, not old, thin, rather sallow, with large brown eyes, nondescript dark hair, a plain navy dress—was not the right one for that moment, nor had she said the right thing. She did not in any way amplify that tender instant, the heart of it, when the wisteria petal had actually touched the chill surface of the gin.

"I don't think that ever happened to me before," he said.

"I never saw it happen to anybody before."

"At my age you have to be careful about saying what's never happened. At your age you don't have to."

Her eyes acknowledged his compliment. "How long have you known Evaline?"

Wrong again, he thought, but saw the reason: she was shy, and knowing that, he had to answer, no matter how much questions like this bored him.

"Ages. I knew her first husband; the only one, I mean. We were in school together, kept crossing paths."

"What's he like?"

"Good sort. Pleasant." He got impatient. "Hell, what's anyone like?"

One of the doors opening out on the garden filled up to two thirds of its height and all its breadth, as Evaline herself emerged upon them.

"So glad you met Dorothy, Charles. She paints, you know. Would never tell you, so how could you know? I've one of her things in the guest room. You've got to see it before you go."

"Indeed I must."

The girl averted her face. There was a kind of subdued distaste in it, an aversion to being patronized, he supposed. If the painting had been put in the salon, instead of stuck away out of sight . . . As it was, why mention it at all? He experienced a sudden, genuine feeling for this girl after all. He could read her, as clear as anything. The maid was elsewhere, so Evaline herself was taking their glasses.

"So grand to see Charles again. Such a surprise when you rang. It really did give me a lift; you've no idea."

He agreed, and in a way really meant it. Whatever mix-ups and misunderstandings there had been in the past, back when she lived in London, why remember them now? Why give any importance, at this late date, to the ins and outs of it all? Old friends were best because they didn't matter so much any more; it was all coasting from now on out, and there was downright comfort in the thought.

"I was lucky to find you in. I think of you Romans being always in motion, especially from May on. The mountains or the sea. Going off somewhere interesting."

"He's being absurd," Evaline explained to Dorothy. "No, if you must know, I'm here nearly all the time these days. You'll get out of me all the reasons why." She thus reminded him, as she turned away for the drinks, that he had invited her to dine with him that evening, so getting himself asked to one of her little cocktail gatherings beforehand. Evaline being charming and parceled out at one of her own parties was one thing; Evaline as she would shortly be across a narrow table from him, pouring out her various troubles, complexes, illnesses, labyrinthine relationships, was another. He couldn't count on just happening to laugh when she finished being witty, just happening to cloud over when the theme was tragic; that would be pushing his luck. No, he would have to listen.

"Listen," he said urgently to the girl. The pace of the chatter had stepped up in the room behind. The knots of guests were now mainly standing, except for a jet-haired Roman girl settled in an armchair with men hovering about her on hassocks and smaller chairs. Soon they would finish this round and take a notion to disperse, gather up hats and purses, go scattering out into the open.

"Listen." He caught the girl by the elbow and steered her aside, out of the central area of the garden, back turned toward the company. He noticed how light she was and how maneuverable. Her head turned to him with a sort of serene attentiveness, and he remembered the quiet fall of the blossoms.

"Do you know Evaline well?" It was a similar question to her own, but she had been making conversation; he was not.

"I've known her off and on for years. Five in all, I guess." She added, "She's been very kind to me."

"Oh, stop it." He almost snapped. "What I mean is, do you see her alone, and if so, does she confide in you? She must. She confides in everyone."

The girl nodded. "I've noticed that. A few times—yes, I would say she's been confidential." She risked something. "I don't like so much confidence."

"I know, I know. Italian lovers, money problems, quarrels, defections of friends . . ." Now he had got her with him, and she actually grinned. He continued, "Has she mentioned her husband?"

"Well, often—yes, I'd say very often, but always rather distantly. I long ago decided he must have been a myth."

"I'm having dinner with her, right after this, taking her out somewhere. Does she know? I keep asking myself. Does she know he's dead?"

"Good Lord, no! At least, I think not."

"Why?"

"Well, she'd have said. She'd have called up everybody, right away."

"I assumed she would have been told. But then he did marry again, and Rome is a long way off." He walked away with the girl at his elbow; they had really drifted now, apart from the gathering. "I came early to this party, for just that reason, to mention it, offer condolences, whatever people do. She never seemed aware of it. No opening of any kind. Yet it happened over a month ago, in London." He stared down at his feet in deep preoccupation, a business habit. "Well," he demanded of her, "what would you conclude?"

"I think that everybody must have thought that someone else had told her."

"Just as I have. Is that what you mean?"

"Yes. Just as you have."

They turned to find Evaline before them once more, their fresh drinks hospitably extended in either hand. "Here you are, you two." She was beaming upon them, but implicit in the smile was the knowledge that he was safely landed as her escort for the evening. The restaurant she would suggest was already selected. It would be nice to be seen with him. She could afford to pretend to Dorothy that, seeing the two of them alone out there, she had assumed a flirtation was in progress. Charles Webley and Dorothy dutifully took their glasses.

The predictable moment arrived. The guests were flowing out to say their good-bys, remarking on the wisteria, a choice conversation piece, and Evaline, full of a loving glow on its behalf, told the history of how it had been planted there, what narrow escapes it had had, what she had done to make it flourish and flower.

"They bloom twice, you know. Oh yes, indeed. Early, and late."

She saw she had gained the center of the party and was holding it. To make the most of it, she nudged the last phrase into a double meaning, as though it referred to women, to all women, herself especially. She then touched her hand to the gathered silks above her heart.

The party caught the idea and laughed gaily, as she had meant them to, and Charles Webley and the girl Dorothy involuntarily struck glances. All was said, framed and frozen, in that instant's communication, and as one they turned off in opposite ways.

1960

JEAN STAFFORD
1915–1979

Jean Stafford was born in 1915 in California and was raised in Boulder, Colorado. She earned both a Bachelor's and a Master's degree from the University of Colorado Boulder, graduating in 1936. The following year, Stafford was awarded a fellowship to study philology at the University of Heidelberg in Germany. Stafford's fiction often finds its basis in her own tumultuous and largely unhappy life, marked by trauma from an early age. While in college, Stafford witnessed first-hand the suicide of a close friend and later suffered the death of her brother in World War II. In 1938, she was severely injured in an automobile accident with poet Robert Lowell, which left her face slightly disfigured for the rest of her life. Despite suing Lowell for the accident, she married him two years later. Both parties suffered from mental illness and their marriage was a calamitous one, ending in divorce in 1948. Subsequent marriages were equally troubled. Throughout her later life, Stafford suffered from depression, alcoholism, and pulmonary disease, and neither did she find any lasting happiness in her illustrious career. Stafford's first novel, *Boston Adventure* (1944), was a national bestseller and published to much critical acclaim. Though her following two novels, *The Mountain Lion* (1947) and *The Catherine Wheel* (1952), were also well received, Stafford is best known for her short fiction. Her stories were published in *The New Yorker, Harper's Bazaar,* and the *Sewanee Review.* Her 1953 story "In the Zoo," which appears below, won her the O. Henry Prize, and in 1970 Stafford was awarded the Pulitzer Prize in fiction for *The Collected Stories of Jean Stafford.*

In the Zoo

Keening harshly in his senility, the blind polar bear slowly and ceaselessly shakes his head in the stark heat of the July and mountain noon. His open eyes are blue. No one stops to look at him; an old farmer, in passing, sums up the old bear's situation by observing, with a ruthless chuckle, that he is a "back number." Patient and despairing, he sits on his yellowed haunches on the central rock of his pool, his huge toy paws wearing short boots of mud.

The grizzlies to the right of him, a conventional family of father and mother and two spring cubs, alternately play the clown and sleep. There is a blustery, scoundrelly, half-likable bravado in the manner of the black bear on the polar's left; his name, according to the legend on his cage, is Clancy, and he is a rough-and-tumble, brawling blowhard, thundering continually as he paces back and forth, or pauses to face his audience of children and mothers and release from his great, gray-tongued mouth a perfectly Vesuvian roar. If he were to be reincarnated in human form, he would be a man of action, possibly a football coach, probably a politician. One expects to see his black hat hanging from a branch of one of his trees; at any moment he will light a cigar.

The polar bear's next-door neighbors are not the only ones who offer so sharp and sad a contrast to him. Across a reach of scrappy grass and litter is the convocation of conceited monkeys, burrowing into each other's necks and chests for fleas, picking their noses with their long, black, finicky fingers, swinging by their gifted tails on the flying trapeze, screaming bloody murder. Even when they mourn—one would think the male orangutan was on the very brink of suicide—they are comedians; they only fake depression, for they are firmly secure in their rambunctious tribalism and in their appalling insight and contempt. Their flibbertigibbet gamboling is a sham, and, stealthily and shiftily, they are really watching the pitiful polar bear ("Back number," they quote the farmer. "That's *his* number all right," they snigger), and the windy black bear ("Life of the party. Gasbag. Low I.Q.," they note scornfully on his dossier), and the stupid, bourgeois grizzlies ("It's feed the face and hit the sack for them," the monkeys say). And they are watching my sister and me, two middle-aged women, as we sit on a bench between the exhibits, eating popcorn, growing thirsty. We are thoughtful.

A chance remark of Daisy's a few minutes before has turned us to memory and meditation. "I don't know why," she said, "but that poor blind bear reminds me of Mr. Murphy." The name "Mr. Murphy" at once returned us both to childhood, and we were floated far and fast, our later lives diminished. So now we eat our popcorn in silence with the ritualistic appetite of childhood, which has little to do with hunger; it is not so much food as a sacrament, and in tribute to our sisterliness and our friendliness I break the silence to say that this is the best popcorn I have ever eaten in my life. The extravagance of my statement instantly makes me feel self-indulgent, and for some time I uneasily avoid looking at the blind bear. My sister does not agree or disagree; she simply says that popcorn is the only food she has ever really liked. For a long time, then, we eat without a word, but I know, because I know her well and know her similarity to me, that Daisy is thinking what I am thinking; both of us are mournfully remembering Mr. Murphy, who, at one time in our lives, was our only friend.

This zoo is in Denver, a city that means nothing to my sister and me except as a place to take or meet trains. Daisy lives two hundred miles farther west, and it is her custom, when my every-other-year visit with her is over, to come across the mountains to see me off on my eastbound train. We know almost no one here, and because our stays are short, we have never bothered to learn the town in more than the most desultory way. We know the Burlington uptown office and the respectable hotels, a restaurant or two, the Union Station, and, beginning today, the zoo in the city park.

But since the moment that Daisy named Mr. Murphy by name our situation in Denver has been only corporeal; our minds and our hearts are in Adams, fifty miles north, and we are seeing, under the white sun at its pitiless meridian, the streets of that ugly town, its parks and trees and bridges, the bandstand in its dreary park, the roads that lead away from it, west to the mountains and east to the plains, its mongrel and multitudinous churches, its high school shaped like a loaf of bread, the campus of its college, an oasis of which we had no experience except to walk through it now and then, eyeing the woodbine on the impressive buildings. These things are engraved forever on our minds with a legibility so insistent that you have only to say the name of the town aloud to us to rip the rinds from our nerves and leave us exposed in terror and humiliation.

We have supposed in later years that Adams was not so bad as all that, and we know that we magnified its ugliness because we looked upon it as the extension of the possessive, unloving, scornful, complacent foster mother, Mrs. Placer, to whom, at the death of our parents within a month of each other, we were sent like Dickensian grotesqueries—cowardly, weak-stomached, given to tears, backward in school. Daisy was ten and I was eight when, unaccompanied, we made the long trip from Marblehead to our benefactress, whom we had never seen and, indeed, never heard of until the pastor of our church came to tell us of the arrangement our father had made on his deathbed, seconded by our mother on hers. This man, whose name and face I have forgotten and whose parting speeches to us I have not forgiven, tried to dry our tears with talk of Indians and of buffaloes; he spoke, however, at much greater length, and in preaching cadences, of the Christian goodness of Mrs. Placer. She was, he said, childless and fond of children, and for many years she had been a widow, after the lingering demise of her tubercular husband, for whose sake she had moved to the Rocky Mountains. For his support and costly medical care, she had run a boarding house, and after his death, since he had left her nothing, she was obliged to continue running it. She had been a girlhood friend of our paternal grandmother, and our father, in the absence of responsible relatives, had made her the beneficiary of his life insurance on the condition that she lodge and rear us. The pastor, with a frankness remarkable considering that he was talking to children, explained to us that our father had left little more than a drop in the bucket for our care, and he enjoined us to give Mrs. Placer, in return for her hospitality and sacrifice, courteous help and eternal thanks. "Sacrifice" was a word we were never allowed to forget.

And thus it was, in grief for our parents, that we came cringing to the dry Western town and to the house where Mrs. Placer lived, a house in which the square, uncushioned furniture was cruel and the pictures on the walls were either dour or dire and the lodgers, who lived in the upper floors among shadowy wardrobes and chiffoniers, had come through the years to resemble their landlady in appearance as well as in deportment.

After their ugly-colored evening meal, Gran—as she bade us call her—and her paying guests would sit, rangy and aquiline, rocking on the front porch on spring and summer and autumn nights, tasting their delicious grievances: those slights delivered by ungrateful sons and daughters, those impudences committed by trolley-car conductors and uppity salesgirls in the ready-to-wear, all those slurs and calculated elbow-jostlings that were their daily crucifixion and their staff of life. We little girls, washing the dishes in the cavernous kitchen, listened to their even, martyred voices, fixed like leeches to their solitary subject and their solitary creed—that life was essentially a matter of being done in, let down, and swindled.

At regular intervals, Mrs. Placer, chairwoman of the victims, would say, "Of course, I don't care; I just have to laugh," and then would tell a shocking tale of an intricate piece of skulduggery perpetrated against her by someone she did not even know. Sometimes, with her avid, partial jury sitting there on the porch behind the bitter hopvines in the heady mountain air, the cases she tried involved Daisy and me, and, listening, we travailed, hugging each other, whispering, "I wish she wouldn't! Oh, how did she find out?" How *did* she? Certainly we never told her when we were snubbed or chosen last on teams, never admitted to a teacher's scolding or to the hoots of laughter that greeted us when we bit on silly, unfair jokes. But she knew. She knew about the slumber parties we were not invited to, the beefsteak fries at which we were pointedly left out; she knew that the singing teacher had said in so many words that I could not carry a tune in a basket and that the sewing superintendent had said that Daisy's fingers were all thumbs. With our teeth chattering in the cold of our isolation, we would hear her protestant, litigious voice defending our right to be orphans, paupers, wholly dependent on her—except for the really ridiculous pittance from our father's life insurance—when it was all she could do to make ends meet. She did not care, but she had to laugh that people in general were so small-minded that they looked down on fatherless, motherless waifs like us and, by association, looked down on her. It seemed funny to her that people gave her no credit for taking on these sickly youngsters who were not even kin but only the grandchildren of a friend.

If a child with braces on her teeth came to play with us, she was, according to Gran, slyly lording it over us because our teeth were crooked but there was no money to have them straightened. And what could be the meaning of our being asked to come for supper at the doctor's house? Were the doctor and his la-di-da New York wife and those pert girls with their solid-gold barrettes and their Shetland pony going to shame her poor darlings? Or shame their poor Gran by making them sorry to come home to the plain but honest life that was all she could provide for them?

There was no stratum of society not reeking with the effluvium of fraud and pettifoggery. And the school system was almost the worst of all: if we could not understand fractions, was that not our teacher's fault? And therefore what right had she to give us F? It was as plain as a pikestaff to Gran that the teacher was only covering up her own inability to teach. It was unlikely, too—highly unlikely—that it was by accident that time and time again the free medical clinic was closed for the day just as our names were about to be called out, so that nothing was done about our bad tonsils, which meant that we were repeatedly sick in the winter, with Gran fetching and carrying for us, climbing those stairs a jillion times a day with her game leg and her heart that was none too strong.

Steeped in these mists of accusation and hidden plots and double meanings, Daisy and I grew up like worms. I think no one could have withstood the atmosphere in that house where everyone trod on eggs that a little bird had told them were bad. They spied on one another, whispered behind doors, conjectured, drew parallels beginning "With all due respect . . ." or "It is a matter of indifference to *me* but . . ." The vigilantes patrolled our town by day, and by night returned to lay their goodies at their priestess's feet and wait for her oracular interpretation of the innards of the butcher, the baker, the candlestick maker, the soda jerk's girl, and the barber's unnatural deaf white cat.

Consequently, Daisy and I also became suspicious. But it was suspicion of ourselves that made us mope and weep and grimace with self-judgment. Why were we not happy when Gran had sacrificed herself to the bone for us? Why did we not cut dead the paper boy who had called her a filthy name? Why did we persist in our willful friendliness with the grocer who had tried, unsuccessfully, to overcharge her on a case of pork and beans?

Our friendships were nervous and surreptitious; we sneaked and lied, and as our hungers sharpened, our debasement deepened; we were pitied; we were shifty-eyed, always on the lookout for Mrs. Placer or one of her tattletale lodgers; we were hypocrites.

Nevertheless, one thin filament of instinct survived, and Daisy and I in time found asylum in a small menagerie down by the railroad tracks. It belonged to a gentle alcoholic ne'er-do-well, who did nothing all day long but drink bathtub gin in rickeys and play solitaire and smile to himself and talk to his animals. He had a little, stunted red vixen and a deodorized skunk, a parrot from Tahiti that spoke Parisian French, a woebegone coyote, and two capuchin monkeys, so serious and humanized, so small and sad and sweet, and so religious-looking with their tonsured heads that it was impossible not to think their gibberish was really an ordered language with a grammar that some day some philologist would understand.

Gran knew about our visits to Mr. Murphy and she did not object, for it gave her keen pleasure to excoriate him when we came home. His vice was not a matter of guesswork; it was an established fact that he was half-seas over from dawn till midnight. "With the black Irish," said Gran, "the taste for drink is taken in with the mother's milk and is never mastered. Oh, I know all about those promises to join the temperance movement and not to touch another drop. The way to hell is paved with good intentions."

We were still little girls when we discovered Mr. Murphy, before the shattering disease of adolescence was to make our bones and brains ache even more painfully than before, and we loved him and we hoped to marry him when we grew up. We loved him, and we loved his monkeys to exactly the same degree and in exactly the same way; they were husbands and fathers and brothers, these three little, ugly, dark, secret men who minded their own business and let us mind ours. If we stuck our fingers through the bars of the cage, the monkeys would sometimes take them in their tight, tiny hands and look into our faces with a tentative, somehow absent-minded sorrow, as if they terribly regretted that they could not place us but were glad to see us all the same. Mr. Murphy, playing a solitaire game of cards called "once in a blue moon" on a kitchen table in his back yard beside the pens, would occasionally look up and blink his beautiful blue eyes and say, "You're peaches to make over my wee friends. I love you for it." There was nothing demanding in his voice, and nothing sticky; on his lips the word "love" was jocose and forthright, it had no strings attached. We would sit on either side of him and watch him regiment his ranks of cards and stop to drink as deeply as if he were dying of thirst and wave to his animals and say to them, "Yes, lads, you're dandies."

Because Mr. Murphy was as reserved with us as the capuchins were, as courteously noncommittal, we were surprised one spring day when he told us that he had a present for us, which he hoped Mrs. Placer would let us keep; it was a puppy, for whom the owner had asked him to find a home—half collie and half Labrador retriever, blue-blooded on both sides.

"You might tell Mrs. Placer—" he said, smiling at the name, for Gran was famous in the town. "You might tell Mrs. Placer," said Mr. Murphy, "that this lad will make a fine watchdog. She'll never have to fear for her spoons again. Or her honor." The last he said to himself, not laughing but tucking his chin into his collar; lines sprang to the corners of his eyes. He would not let us see the dog, whom we could hear yipping and squealing inside his shanty, for he said that our disappointment would weigh on his conscience if we lost our hearts to the fellow and then could not have him for our own.

That evening at supper, we told Gran about Mr. Murphy's present. A dog? In the first place, why a dog? Was it possible that the news had reached Mr. Murphy's ears that Gran had just this very day finished planting her spring garden, the very thing that a rampageous dog would have in his mind to destroy? What sex was it? A male! Females, she had heard, were more trustworthy; males roved and came home smelling of skunk; such a consideration as this, of course, would not have crossed Mr. Murphy's fuddled mind. Was this young male dog housebroken? We had not asked? That was the limit!

Gran appealed to her followers, too raptly fascinated by Mr. Murphy's machinations to eat their Harvard beets. "Am I being farfetched or does it strike you as decidedly queer that Mr. Murphy is trying to fob off on my little girls a young cur that has not been trained?" she asked them. "If it were housebroken, he would have said so, so I feel it is safe to assume that it is not. Perhaps cannot *be* housebroken. I've heard of such cases."

The fantasy spun on, richly and rapidly, with all the skilled helping hands at work at once. The dog was tangibly in the room with us, shedding his hair, scratching his fleas, shaking rain off himself to splatter the walls, dragging some dreadful carcass across the floor, chewing up slippers, knocking over chairs with his tail, gobbling the chops from the platter, barking, biting, fathering, fighting, smelling to high heaven of carrion, staining the rug with his muddy feet, scratching the floor with his claws. He developed rabies; he bit a child, two children! Three! Everyone in town! And Gran and her poor darlings went to jail for harboring this murderous, odoriferous, drunk, Roman Catholic dog.

And yet, astoundingly enough, she came around to agreeing to let us have the dog. It was, as Mr. Murphy had predicted, the word "watchdog" that deflected the course of the trial. The moment Daisy uttered it, Gran halted, marshaling her reverse march; while she rallied and tacked and reconnoitered, she sent us to the kitchen for the dessert. And by the time this course was under way, the uses of a dog, the enormous potentialities for investigation and law enforcement in a dog trained by Mrs. Placer, were being minutely and passionately scrutinized by the eight upright bloodhounds sitting at the table wolfing their brown Betty as if it were fresh-killed rabbit. The dog now sat at attention beside his mistress, fiercely alert, ears cocked, nose aquiver, the protector of widows, of orphans, of lonely people who had no homes. He made short shrift of burglars, homicidal maniacs, Peeping Toms, gypsies, bogus missionaries, Fuller Brush men[1] with a risqué spiel. He went to the store and brought back groceries, retrieved the evening paper from the awkward place the boy had meanly thrown it, rescued cripples from burning houses, saved children from drowning, heeled at command, begged, lay down, stood up, sat, jumped through a hoop, ratted.

Both times—when he was a ruffian of the blackest delinquency and then a pillar of society—he was full-grown in his prefiguration, and when Laddy appeared on the following day, small, unsteady, and whimpering lonesomely, Gran and her lodgers were taken aback; his infant, clumsy paws embarrassed them, his melting eyes were unapropos. But it could never be said of Mrs. Placer, as Mrs. Placer her own self said, that she was a woman who went back on her word, and her darlings were going to have their dog, softheaded and feckless as he might be. All the first night, in his carton in the kitchen, he wailed for his mother, and in the morning, it was true, he had made a shambles of the room—fouled the floor, and pulled off the tablecloth together with a ketchup bottle, so that thick gore lay everywhere. At breakfast, the lodgers confessed they had had a most amusing night, for it had actually been funny the way the dog had been determined not to let anyone get a wink of sleep. After that first night, Laddy slept in our room, receiving from us, all through our delighted, sleepless nights, pats and embraces and kisses and whispers. He was our baby, our best friend, the smartest, prettiest, nicest dog in the entire wide world. Our soft and rapid blandishments excited him to yelp at us in pleased bewilderment, and then we would playfully grasp his muzzle, so that he would snarl, deep in his throat like an adult dog, and shake his head violently, and, when we freed him, nip us smartly with great good will.

He was an intelligent and genial dog and we trained him quickly. He steered clear of Gran's radishes and lettuce after she had several times given him a brisk comeuppance with a strap across the rump, and he soon left off chewing shoes and the laundry on the line, and he outgrew his babyish whining. He grew like a weed; he lost his spherical softness, and his coat, which had been sooty fluff, came in stiff and rusty black; his nose grew aristocratically long, and his clever, pointed ears stood at attention. He was all bronzy, lustrous black except for an Elizabethan ruff of white and a tip of white at the end of his perky tail. No one could deny that he was exceptionally handsome and that he had, as well, great personal charm and style. He escorted Daisy and me to school in the morning, laughing interiorly out of the enormous pleasure of his life as he gracefully cantered ahead of us, distracted occasionally by his private interest in smells or unfamiliar beings in the grass but, on the whole, engrossed in his role of chaperon. He made friends easily with other dogs, and sometimes he went for a long hunting weekend into the mountains with a huge and bossy old red hound named Mess, who had been on the county most of his life and had made a good thing of it, particularly at the fire station.

It was after one of these three-day excursions into the high country that Gran took Laddy in hand. He had come back spent and filthy, his coat a mass

---

1. Door-to-door salesmen.

of cockleburs and ticks, his eyes bloodshot, loud *râles*[2] in his chest; for half a day he lay motionless before the front door like someone in a hangover, his groaning eyes explicitly saying "Oh, for God's sake, leave me be" when we offered him food or bowls of water. Gran was disapproving, then affronted, and finally furious. Not, of course, with Laddy, since all inmates of her house enjoyed immunity, but with Mess, whose caddish character, together with that of his nominal masters, the firemen, she examined closely under a strong light, with an air of detachment, with her not caring but her having, all the same, to laugh. A lodger who occupied the back west room had something to say about the fire chief and his nocturnal visits to a certain house occupied by a certain group of young women, too near the same age to be sisters and too old to be the daughters of the woman who claimed to be their mother. What a story! The exophthalmic[3] librarian—she lived in one of the front rooms—had some interesting insinuations to make about the deputy marshal, who had borrowed, significantly, she thought, a book on hypnotism. She also knew—she was, of course, in a most useful position in the town, and from her authoritative pen in the middle of the library her mammiform and azure eyes and her eager ears missed nothing—that the fire chief's wife was not as scrupulous as she might be when she was keeping score on bridge night at the Sorosis.[4]

There was little at the moment that Mrs. Placer and her disciples could do to save the souls of the Fire Department and their families, and therefore save the town from holocaust (a very timid boarder—a Mr. Beaver, a newcomer who was not to linger long—had sniffed throughout this recitative as if he were smelling burning flesh), but at least the unwholesome bond between Mess and Laddy could and would be severed once and for all. Gran looked across the porch at Laddy, who lay stretched at full length in the darkest corner, shuddering and baying abortively in his throat as he chased jack rabbits in his dreams, and she said, "A dog can have morals like a human." With this declaration Laddy's randy, manly holidays were finished. It may have been telepathy that woke him; he lifted his heavy head from his paws, laboriously got up, hesitated for a moment, and then padded languidly across the porch to Gran. He stood docilely beside her chair, head down, tail drooping as if to say, "O.K., Mrs. Placer, show me how and I'll walk the straight and narrow."

The very next day, Gran changed Laddy's name to Caesar, as being more dignified, and a joke was made at the supper table that he had come, seen, and conquered Mrs. Placer's heart—for within her circle, where the magnanimity she lavished upon her orphans was daily demonstrated, Mrs. Placer's heart was highly thought of. On that day also, although we did not know it yet, Laddy ceased to be our dog. Before many weeks passed, indeed, he ceased to be anyone we had ever known. A week or so after he became Caesar, he took up residence in her room, sleeping alongside her bed. She broke him of the habit of taking us to school (temptation to low living was rife along those streets; there was a chow—well, never mind) by the simple expedient of chaining him to a tree as soon as she got up in the morning. This discipline, together with the stamina-building cuffs she gave his sensitive ears from

---

2. Rattles (French). **3.** Abnormally protrusive eyeballs, e.g., bug-eyed; often caused by disease.
4. Originally an all-women club in New York, it here means a gathering that is exclusively female.

time to time, gradually but certainly remade his character. From a sanguine, affectionate, easygoing Gael (with the fits of melancholy that alternated with the larkiness), he turned into an overbearing, military, efficient, loud-voiced Teuton. His bark, once wide of range, narrowed to one dark, glottal tone.

Soon the paper boy flatly refused to serve our house after Caesar efficiently removed the bicycle clip from his pants leg; the skin was not broken, or even bruised, but it was a matter of principle with the boy. The milkman approached the back door in a seizure of shakes like St. Vitus's dance. The metermen, the coal men, and the garbage collector crossed themselves if they were Catholics and, if they were not, tried whistling in the dark. "Good boy, good Caesar," they caroled, and, unctuously lying, they said they knew his bark was worse than his bite, knowing full well that it was not, considering the very nasty nip, requiring stitches, he had given a representative of the Olson Rug Company, who had had the folly to pat him on the head. Caesar did not molest the lodgers, but he disdained them and he did not brook being personally addressed by anyone except Gran. One night, he wandered into the dining room, appearing to be in search of something he had mislaid, and, for some reason that no one was ever able to divine, suddenly stood stock-still and gave the easily upset Mr. Beaver a long and penetrating look. Mr. Beaver, trembling from head to toe, stammered, "Why—er, hello there, Caesar, old boy, old boy," and Caesar charged. For a moment, it was touch and go, but Gran saved Mr. Beaver, only to lose him an hour later when he departed, bag and baggage, for the Y.M.C.A. This rout and the consequent loss of revenue would more than likely have meant Caesar's downfall and his deportation to the pound if it had not been that a newly widowed druggist, very irascible and very much Gran's style, had applied for a room in her house a week or so before, and now he moved in delightedly, as if he were coming home.

Finally, the police demanded that Caesar be muzzled and they warned that if he committed any major crime again—they cited the case of the Olson man—he would be shot on sight. Mrs. Placer, although she had no respect for the law, knowing as much as she did about its agents, obeyed. She obeyed, that is, in part; she put the muzzle on Caesar for a few hours a day, usually early in the morning when the traffic was light and before the deliveries had started, but the rest of the time his powerful jaws and dazzling white saber teeth were free and snapping. There was between these two such preternatural rapport, such an impressive conjugation of suspicion, that he, sensing the approach of a policeman, could convey instantly to her the immediate necessity of clapping his nose cage on. And the policeman, sent out on the complaint of a terrorized neighbor, would be greeted by this law-abiding pair at the door.

Daisy and I wished we were dead. We were divided between hating Caesar and loving Laddy, and we could not give up the hope that something, some day, would change him back into the loving animal he had been before he was appointed vice-president of the Placerites. Now at the meetings after supper on the porch he took an active part, standing rigidly at Gran's side except when she sent him on an errand. He carried out these assignments not with the air of a servant but with that of an accomplice. "Get me the paper, Caesar," she would say to him, and he, dismayingly intelligent and a shade smart-alecky, would open the screen door by himself and in a minute come back with the *Bulletin,* from which Mrs. Placer would then read an item, like the Gospel of the day, and then read between the lines of it, scandalized.

In the deepening of our woe and our bereavement and humiliation, we mutely appealed to Mr. Murphy. We did not speak outright to him, for Mr. Murphy lived in a state of indirection, and often when he used the pronoun "I," he seemed to be speaking of someone standing a little to the left of him, but we went to see him and his animals each day during the sad summer, taking what comfort we could from the cozy, quiet indolence of his back yard, where small black eyes encountered ours politely and everyone was half asleep. When Mr. Murphy inquired about Laddy in his bland, inattentive way, looking for a stratagem whereby to shift the queen of hearts into position by the king, we would say, "Oh, he's fine," or "Laddy is a nifty dog." And Mr. Murphy, reverently slaking the thirst that was his talent and his concubine, would murmur, "I'm glad."

We wanted to tell him, we wanted his help, or at least his sympathy, but how could we cloud his sunny world? It was awful to see Mr. Murphy ruffled. Up in the calm clouds as he generally was, he could occasionally be brought to earth with a thud, as we had seen and heard one day. Not far from his house, there lived a bad, troublemaking boy of twelve, who was forever hanging over the fence trying to teach the parrot obscene words. He got nowhere, for she spoke no English and she would flabbergast him with her cold eye and sneer, *"Tant pis."*[5] One day, this boorish fellow went too far; he suddenly shot his head over the fence like a jack-in-the-box and aimed a water pistol at the skunk's face. Mr. Murphy leaped to his feet in a scarlet rage; he picked up a stone and threw it accurately, hitting the boy square in the back, so hard that he fell right down in a mud puddle and lay there kicking and squalling and, as it turned out, quite badly hurt. "If you ever come back here again, I'll kill you!" roared Mr. Murphy. I think he meant it, for I have seldom seen an anger so resolute, so brilliant, and so voluble. "How dared he!" he cried, scrambling into Mallow's cage to hug and pet and soothe her. "He must be absolutely mad! He must be the Devil!" He did not go back to his game after that but paced the yard, swearing a blue streak and only pausing to croon to his animals, now as frightened by him as they had been by the intruder, and to drink straight from the bottle, not bothering with fixings. We were fascinated by this unfamiliar side of Mr. Murphy, but we did not want to see it ever again, for his face had grown so dangerously purple and the veins of his forehead seemed ready to burst and his eyes looked scorched. He was the closest thing to a maniac we had ever seen. So we did not tell him about Laddy; what he did not know would not hurt him, although it was hurting us, throbbing in us like a great, bleating wound.

But eventually Mr. Murphy heard about our dog's conversion, one night at the pool hall, which he visited from time to time when he was seized with a rare but compelling garrulity, and the next afternoon when he asked us how Laddy was and we replied that he was fine, he tranquilly told us, as he deliberated whether to move the jack of clubs now or to bide his time, that we were sweet girls but we were lying in our teeth. He did not seem at all angry but only interested, and all the while he questioned us, he went on about his business

5. "Too bad" or "oh, well" (French).

with the gin and the hearts and spades and diamonds and clubs. It rarely happened that he won the particular game he was playing, but that day he did, and when he saw all the cards laid out in their ideal pattern, he leaned back, looking disappointed, and he said, "I'm damned." He then scooped up the cards, in a gesture unusually quick and tidy for him, stacked them together, and bound them with a rubber band. Then he began to tell us what he thought of Gran. He grew as loud and apoplectic as he had been that other time, and though he kept repeating that he knew *we* were innocent and he put not a shred of the blame on us, we were afraid he might suddenly change his mind, and, speechless, we cowered against the monkeys' cage. In dread, the monkeys clutched the fingers we offered to them and made soft, protesting noises, as if to say, "Oh, stop it, Murphy! Our nerves!"

As quickly as it had started, the tantrum ended. Mr. Murphy paled to his normal complexion and said calmly that the only practical thing was to go and have it out with Mrs. Placer. "At once," he added, although he said he bitterly feared that it was too late and there would be no exorcising the fiend from Laddy's misused spirit. And because he had given the dog to us and not to her, he required that we go along with him, stick up for our rights, stand on our own mettle, get up our Irish, and give the old bitch something to put in her pipe and smoke.

Oh, it was hot that day! We walked in a kind of delirium through the simmer, where only the grasshoppers had the energy to move, and I remember wondering if ether smelled like the gin on Mr. Murphy's breath. Daisy and I, in one way or another, were going to have our gizzards cut out along with our hearts and our souls and our pride, and I wished I were as drunk as Mr. Murphy, who swam effortlessly through the heat, his lips parted comfortably, his eyes half closed. When we turned in to the path at Gran's house, my blood began to scald my veins. It was so futile and so dangerous and so absurd. Here we were on a high moral mission, two draggletailed, gumptionless little girls and a toper whom no one could take seriously, partly because he was little more than a gurgling bottle of booze and partly because of the clothes he wore. He was a sight, as he always was when he was out of his own yard. There, somehow, in the carefree disorder, his clothes did not look especially strange, but on the streets of the town, in the barbershop or the post office or on Gran's path, they were fantastic. He wore a pair of hound's-tooth pants, old but maintaining a vehement pattern, and with them he wore a collarless blue flannelette shirt. His hat was the silliest of all, because it was a derby three sizes too big. And as if Shannon, too, was a part of his funny-paper costume, the elder capuchin rode on his shoulder, tightly embracing his thin red neck.

Gran and Caesar were standing side by side behind the screen door, looking as if they had been expecting us all along. For a moment, Gran and Mr. Murphy faced each other across the length of weedy brick between the gate and the front porch, and no one spoke. Gran took no notice at all of Daisy and me. She adjusted her eyeglasses, using both hands, and then looked down at Caesar and matter-of-factly asked, "Do you want out?"

Caesar flung himself full-length upon the screen and it sprang open like a jaw. I ran to meet him and head him off, and Daisy threw a library book at his head, but he was on Mr. Murphy in one split second and had his monkey off his shoulder and had broken Shannon's neck in two shakes. He would have gone on nuzzling and mauling and growling over the corpse for hours if Gran had not marched out of the house and down the path and slapped him lightly on the flank and said, in a voice that could not have deceived an idiot, "Why, Caesar, you scamp! You've hurt Mr. Murphy's monkey! Aren't you ashamed!"

Hurt the monkey! In one final, apologetic shudder, the life was extinguished from the little fellow. Bloody and covered with slather, Shannon lay with his arms suppliantly stretched over his head, his leather fingers curled into loose, helpless fists. His hind legs and his tail lay limp and helter-skelter on the path. And Mr. Murphy, all of a sudden reeling drunk, burst into the kind of tears that Daisy and I knew well—the kind that time alone could stop. We stood aghast in the dark-red sunset, killed by our horror and our grief for Shannon and our unforgivable disgrace. We stood upright in a dead faint, and an eon passed before Mr. Murphy picked up Shannon's body and wove away, sobbing, "I don't believe it! I don't *believe it!*"

The very next day, again at morbid, heavy sunset, Caesar died in violent convulsions, knocking down two tall hollyhocks in his throes. Long after his heart had stopped, his right hind leg continued to jerk in aimless reflex. Madly methodical, Mr. Murphy had poisoned some meat for him, had thoroughly envenomed a whole pound of hamburger, and early in the morning, before sunup, when he must have been near collapse with his hangover, he had stolen up to Mrs. Placer's house and put it by the kitchen door. He was so stealthy that Caesar never stirred in his fool's paradise there on the floor by Gran. We knew these to be the facts, for Mr. Murphy made no bones about them. Afterward, he had gone home and said a solemn Requiem for Shannon in so loud a voice that someone sent for the police, and they took him away in the Black Maria[6] to sober him up on strong green tea. By the time he was in the lockup and had confessed what he had done, it was far too late, for Caesar had already gulped down the meat. He suffered an undreamed-of agony in Gran's flower garden, and Daisy and I, unable to bear the sight of it, hiked up to the red rocks and shook there, wretchedly ripping to shreds the sand lilies that grew in the cracks. Flight was the only thing we could think of, but where could we go? We stared west at the mountains and quailed at the look of the stern white glacier; we wildly scanned the prairies for escape. "If only we were something besides kids! Besides girls!" mourned Daisy. I could not speak at all; I huddled in a niche of the rocks and cried.

No one in town, except, of course, her lodgers, had the slightest sympathy for Gran. The townsfolk allowed that Mr. Murphy was a drunk and was fighting Irish, but he had a heart and this was something that could never be said of Mrs. Placer. The neighbor who had called the police when he was chanting the *Dies Irae*[7] before breakfast in that deafening monotone had said, "The poor guy is having some kind of a spell, so don't be rough on him, hear?" Mr. Murphy became, in fact, a kind of hero; some people, stretching a point, said he was a saint for the way that every day and twice on Sunday he sang a memorial Mass over Shannon's grave, now marked with a chipped, cheap plaster

---

6. Police wagon. **7.** Day of Wrath (Latin), a passage from the Roman Catholic requiem mass.

figure of Saint Francis. He withdrew from the world more and more, seldom venturing into the streets at all, except when he went to the bootlegger to get a new bottle to snuggle into. All summer, all fall, we saw him as we passed by his yard, sitting at his dilapidated table, enfeebled with gin, graying, withering, turning his head ever and ever more slowly as he maneuvered the protocol of the kings and the queens and the knaves. Daisy and I could never stop to visit him again.

It went on like this, year after year. Daisy and I lived in a mesh of lies and evasions, baffled and mean, like rats in a maze. When we were old enough for beaux, we connived like sluts to see them, but we would never admit to their existence until Gran caught us out by some trick. Like this one, for example: Once, at the end of a long interrogation, she said to me, "I'm more relieved than I can tell you that you *don't* have anything to do with Jimmy Gilmore, because I happen to know that he is after only one thing in a girl," and then, off guard in the loving memory of sitting in the movies the night before with Jimmy, not even holding hands, I defended him and defeated myself, and Gran, smiling with success, said, "I *thought* you knew him. It's a pretty safe rule of thumb that where there's smoke there's fire." That finished Jimmy and me, for afterward I was nervous with him and I confounded and alarmed and finally bored him by trying to convince him, although the subject had not come up, that I did not doubt his good intentions.

Daisy and I would come home from school, or, later, from our jobs, with a small triumph or an interesting piece of news, and if we forgot ourselves and, in our exuberance, told Gran, we were hustled into court at once for cross-examination. Once, I remember, while I was still in high school, I told her about getting a part in a play. How very nice for me, she said, if that kind of make-believe seemed to me worth while. But what was my role? An old woman! A widow woman believed to be a witch? She did not care a red cent, but she did have to laugh in view of the fact that Miss Eccles, in charge of dramatics, had almost run her down in her car. And I would forgive her, would I not, if she did not come to see the play, and would not think her eccentric for not wanting to see herself ridiculed in public?

My pleasure strangled, I crawled, joy-killed, to our third-floor room. The room was small and its monstrous furniture was too big and the rag rugs were repulsive, but it was bright. We would not hang a blind at the window, and on this day I stood there staring into the mountains that burned with the sun. I feared the mountains, but at times like this their massiveness consoled me; they, at least, could not be gossiped about.

Why did we stay until we were grown? Daisy and I ask ourselves this question as we sit here on the bench in the municipal zoo, reminded of Mr. Murphy by the polar bear, reminded by the monkeys not of Shannon but of Mrs. Placer's insatiable gossips at their post-prandial feast.

"But how could we have left?" says Daisy, wringing her buttery hands. "It was the depression. We had no money. We had nowhere to go."

"All the same, we could have gone," I say, resentful still of the waste of all those years. "We could have come here and got jobs as waitresses. Or prostitutes, for that matter."

"I wouldn't have wanted to be a prostitute," says Daisy.

We agree that under the circumstances it would have been impossible for us to run away. The physical act would have been simple, for the city was not far and we could have stolen the bus fare or hitched a ride. Later, when we began to work as salesgirls in Kress's, it would have been no trick at all to vanish one Saturday afternoon with our week's pay, without so much as going home to say goodbye. But it had been infinitely harder than that, for Gran, as we now see, held us trapped by our sense of guilt. We were vitiated, and we had no choice but to wait, flaccidly, for her to die.

You may be sure we did not unlearn those years as soon as we put her out of sight in the cemetery and sold her house for a song to the first boob who would buy it. Nor did we forget when we left the town for another one, where we had jobs at a dude camp—the town where Daisy now lives with a happy husband and two happy sons. The succubus did not relent for years, and I can still remember, in the beginning of our days at the Lazy S 3, overhearing an edgy millionaire say to his wife, naming my name, "That girl gives me the cold shivers. One would think she had just seen a murder." Well, I had. For years, whenever I woke in the night in fear or pain or loneliness, I would increase my suffering by the memory of Shannon, and my tears were as bitter as poor Mr. Murphy's.

We have never been back to Adams. But we see that house plainly, with the hopvines straggling over the porch. The windows are hung with the cheapest grade of marquisette, dipped into coffee to impart to it an unwilling color, neither white nor tan but individual and spitefully unattractive. We see the wicker rockers and the swing, and through the screen door we dimly make out the slightly veering corridor, along one wall of which stands a glass-doored bookcase; when we were children, it had contained not books but stale old cardboard boxes filled with such things as W.C.T.U.[8] tracts and anti-cigarette literature and newspaper clippings relating to sexual sin in the Christianized islands of the Pacific.

Even if we were able to close our minds' eyes to the past, Mr. Murphy would still be before us in the apotheosis of the polar bear. My pain becomes intolerable, and I am relieved when Daisy rescues us. "We've got to go," she says in a sudden panic. "I've got asthma coming on." We rush to the nearest exit of the city park and hail a cab, and, once inside it, Daisy gives herself an injection of adrenalin and then leans back. We are heartbroken and infuriated, and we cannot speak.

Two hours later, beside my train, we clutch each other as if we were drowning. We ought to go out to the nearest policeman and say, "We are not responsible women. You will have to take care of us because we cannot take care of ourselves." But gradually the storm begins to lull.

"You're sure you've got your ticket?" says Daisy. "You'll surely be able to get a roomette once you're on."

"I don't know about that," I say. "If there are any V.I.P.s on board, I won't have a chance. 'Spinsters and Orphans Last' is the motto of this line."

Daisy smiles. "I didn't care," she says, "but I had to laugh when I saw that woman nab the redcap you had signaled to. I had a good notion to give her a piece of my mind."

---

8. Woman's Christian Temperance Union.

"It will be a miracle if I ever see my bags again," I say, mounting the steps of the train. "Do you suppose that blackguardly porter knows about the twenty-dollar gold piece in my little suitcase?"

"Anything's possible!" cries Daisy, and begins to laugh. She is so pretty, standing there in her bright-red linen suit and her black velvet hat. A solitary ray of sunshine comes through a broken pane in the domed vault of the train shed and lies on her shoulder like a silver arrow.

"So long, Daisy!" I call as the train begins to move.

She walks quickly along beside the train. "Watch out for pickpockets!" she calls.

"You, too!" My voice is thin and lost in the increasing noise of the speeding train wheels. "Goodbye, old dear!"

I go at once to the club car and I appropriate the writing table, to the vexation of a harried priest, who snatches up the telegraph pad and gives me a sharp look. I write Daisy approximately the same letter I always write her under this particular set of circumstances, the burden of which is that nothing for either of us can ever be as bad as the past before Gran mercifully died. In a postscript I add: "There is a Roman Catholic priest (that is to say, he is *dressed* like one) sitting behind me although all the chairs on the opposite side of the car are empty. I can only conclude that he is looking over my shoulder, and while I do not want to cause you any alarm, I think you would be advised to be on the lookout for any appearance of miraculous medals, scapulars, papist booklets, etc., in the shops of your town. It really makes me laugh to see the way he is pretending that all he wants is for me to finish this letter so that he can have the table."

I sign my name and address the envelope, and I give up my place to the priest, who smiles nicely at me, and then I move across the car to watch the fields as they slip by. They are alfalfa fields, but you can bet your bottom dollar that they are chockablock with marijuana.

I begin to laugh. The fit is silent but it is devastating; it surges and rattles in my rib cage, and I turn my face to the window to avoid the narrow gaze of the Filipino bar boy. I must think of something sad to stop this unholy giggle, and I think of the polar bear. But even his bleak tragedy does not sober me. Wildly I fling open the newspaper I have brought and I pretend to be reading something screamingly funny. The words I see are in a Hollywood gossip column: "How a well-known starlet can get a divorce in Nevada without her crooner husband's consent, nobody knows. It won't be worth a plugged nickel here."

1953

JOHN STEINBECK
1902–1968

Steinbeck was born in Salinas, California. His mother was a former schoolteacher, who encouraged him to read widely as a child, but his formal schooling made little impression on him. He attended Stanford University intermittently, leaving in 1926 to drift through an array of odd jobs that educated him in the life of working people. His first, rather romantic novel, *Cup of Gold*, appeared in 1929. By 1936 his involvement with the struggles of migrant workers resulted in his militantly political novel *In Dubious Battle*. In 1937 his short novel *Of Mice and Men* proved immensely popular and provided the basis for an equally popular film, as did *The Grapes of Wrath* in 1939. He served as a war correspondent during World War II. His postwar novels include *East of Eden* (1952) and *The Winter of Our Discontent* (1961). In 1962 he was awarded the Nobel Prize. Much of Steinbeck's finest short work can be found in the collection *Steinbeck: Novels and Stories 1932–1937* (1978).

The Chrysanthemums

The high grey-flannel fog of winter closed off the Salinas Valley from the sky and from all the rest of the world. On every side it sat like a lid on the mountains and made of the great valley a closed pot. On the broad, level land floor the gang ploughs bit deep and left the black earth shining like metal where the shares had cut. On the foot-hill ranches across the Salinas River, the yellow stubble fields seemed to be bathed in pale cold sunshine, but there was no sunshine in the valley now in December. The thick willow scrub along the river flamed with sharp and positive yellow leaves.

It was a time of quiet and of waiting. The air was cold and tender. A light wind blew up from the southwest so that the farmers were mildly hopeful of a good rain before long; but fog and rain do not go together.

Across the river, on Henry Allen's foot-hill ranch there was little work to be done, for the hay was cut and stored and the orchards were ploughed up to receive the rain deeply when it should come. The cattle on the higher slopes were becoming shaggy and rough-coated.

Elisa Allen, working in her flower garden, looked down across the yard and saw Henry, her husband, talking to two men in business suits. The three of them stood by the tractor-shed, each man with one foot on the side of the little Fordson. They smoked cigarettes and studied the machine as they talked.

Elisa watched them for a moment and then went back to her work. She was thirty-five. Her face was lean and strong and her eyes were as clear as water. Her figure looked blocked and heavy in her gardening costume, a man's black hat pulled low down over her eyes, clod-hopper shoes, a figured print dress almost completely covered by a big corduroy apron with four big pockets to hold the snips, the trowel and scratcher, the seeds and the knife she worked with. She wore heavy leather gloves to protect her hands while she worked.

She was cutting down the old year's chrysanthemum stalks with a pair of short and powerful scissors. She looked down toward the men by the tractor-shed now and then. Her face was eager and mature and handsome; even her work with the scissors was overeager, over-powerful. The chrysanthemum stems seemed too small and easy for her energy.

She brushed a cloud of hair out of her eyes with the back of her glove, and left a smudge of earth on her cheek in doing it. Behind her stood the neat white farmhouse with red geraniums close-banked around it as high as the windows. It was a hard-swept-looking little house, with hard-polished windows, and a clean mud-mat on the front steps.

Elisa cast another glance toward the tractor-shed. The strangers were getting into their Ford coupé. She took off a glove and put her strong fingers down into the forest of new green chrysanthemum sprouts that were growing around the old roots. She spread the leaves and looked down among the close-growing stems. No aphids were there, no sow bugs or snails or cutworms. Her terrier fingers destroyed such pests before they could get started.

Elisa started at the sound of her husband's voice. He had come near quietly, and he leaned over the wire fence that protected her flower garden from cattle and dogs and chickens.

"At it again," he said. "You've got a strong new crop coming."

Elisa straightened her back and pulled on the gardening glove again. "Yes. They'll be strong this coming year." In her tone and on her face there was a little smugness.

"You've got a gift with things," Henry observed. "Some of those yellow chrysanthemums you had this year were ten inches across. I wish you'd work out in the orchard and raise some apples that big."

Her eyes sharpened. "Maybe I could do it, too. I've a gift with things, all right. My mother had it. She could stick anything in the ground and make it grow. She said it was having planters' hands that knew how to do it."

"Well, it sure works with flowers," he said.

"Henry, who were those men you were talking to?"

"Why, sure, that's what I came to tell you. They were from the Western Meat Company. I sold those thirty head of three-year-old steers. Got nearly my own price, too."

"Good," she said. "Good for you."

"And I thought," he continued, "I thought how it's Saturday afternoon, and we might go into Salinas for dinner at a restaurant, and then to a picture show—to celebrate, you see."

"Good," she repeated. "Oh, yes. That will be good."

Henry put on his joking tone. "There's fights tonight. How'd you like to go to the fights?"

"Oh, no," she said breathlessly. "No, I wouldn't like fights."

"Just fooling, Elisa. We'll go to a movie. Let's see. It's two now. I'm going to take Scotty and bring down those steers from the hill. It'll take us maybe two hours. We'll go in town about five and have dinner at the Cominos Hotel. Like that?"

"Of course I'll like it. It's good to eat away from home."

"All right, then. I'll go get up a couple of horses."

She said: "I'll have plenty of time to transplant some of these sets, I guess."

She heard her husband calling Scotty down by the barn. And a little later she saw the two men ride up the pale yellow hillside in search of the steers.

There was a little square sandy bed kept for rooting the chrysanthemums. With her trowel she turned the soil over and over, and smoothed it and patted it firm. Then she dug ten parallel trenches to receive the sets. Back at the chrysanthemum bed she pulled out the little crisp shoots, trimmed off the leaves of each one with her scissors and laid it on a small orderly pile.

A squeak of wheels and plod of hoofs came from the road. Elisa looked up. The country road ran along the dense bank of willows and cottonwoods that bordered the river, and up this road came a curious vehicle, curiously drawn. It was an old spring-wagon, with a round canvas top on it like the cover of a prairie schooner. It was drawn by an old bay horse and a little grey-and-white burro. A big stubble-bearded man sat between the cover flaps and drove the crawling team. Underneath the wagon, between the hind wheels, a lean and rangy mongrel dog walked sedately. Words were painted on the canvas, in clumsy, crooked letters. "Pots, pans, knives, sisors, lawn mores, Fixed." Two rows of articles, and the triumphantly definitive "Fixed" below. The black paint had run down in little sharp points beneath each letter.

Elisa, squatting on the ground, watched to see the crazy, loose-jointed wagon pass by. But it didn't pass. It turned into the farm road in front of her house, crooked old wheels skirling and squeaking. The rangy dog darted from between the wheels and ran ahead. Instantly the two ranch shepherds flew out at him. Then all three stopped, and with stiff and quivering tails, with taut straight legs, with ambassadorial dignity, they slowly circled, sniffing daintily. The caravan pulled up to Elisa's wire fence and stopped. Now the newcomer dog, feeling out-numbered, lowered his tail and retired under the wagon with raised hackles and bared teeth.

The man on the wagon seat called out: "That's a bad dog in a fight when he gets started."

Elisa laughed. "I see he is. How soon does he generally get started?"

The man caught up her laughter and echoed it heartily. "Sometimes not for weeks and weeks," he said. He climbed stiffly down, over the wheel. The horse and the donkey drooped like unwatered flowers.

Elisa saw that he was a very big man. Although his hair and beard were greying, he did not look old. His worn black suit was wrinkled and spotted with grease. The laughter had disappeared from his face and eyes the moment his laughing voice ceased. His eyes were dark, and they were full of the brooding that gets in the eyes of teamsters and of sailors. The calloused hands he rested on the wire fence were cracked, and every crack was a black line. He took off his battered hat.

"I'm off my general road, ma'am," he said. "Does this dirt road cut over across the river to the Los Angeles highway?"

Elisa stood up and shoved the thick scissors in her apron pocket. "Well, yes, it does, but it winds around and then fords the river. I don't think your team could pull through the sand."

He replied with some asperity: "It might surprise you what them beasts can pull through."

"When they get started?" she asked.

He smiled for a second. "Yes. When they get started."

"Well," said Elisa, "I think you'll save time if you go back to the Salinas road and pick up the highway there."

He drew a big finger down the chicken wire and made it sing. "I ain't in any hurry, ma'am. I go from Seattle to San Diego and back every year. Takes all my time. About six months each way. I aim to follow nice weather."

Elisa took off her gloves and stuffed them in the apron pocket with the scissors. She touched the under edge of her man's hat, searching for fugitive hairs. "That sounds like a nice kind of way to live," she said.

He leaned confidentially over the fence. "Maybe you noticed the writing on my wagon. I mend pots and sharpen knives and scissors. You got any of them things to do?"

"Oh, no," she said quickly. "Nothing like that." Her eyes hardened with resistance.

"Scissors is the worst thing," he explained. "Most people just ruin scissors trying to sharpen 'em, but I know how. I got a special tool. It's a little bobbit kind of thing, and patented. But it sure does the trick."

"No. My scissors are all sharp."

"All right, then. Take a pot," he continued earnestly, "a bent pot, or a pot with a hole. I can make it like new so you don't have to buy no new ones. That's a saving for you."

"No," she said shortly. "I tell you I have nothing like that for you to do."

His face fell to an exaggerated sadness. His voice took on a whining undertone. "I ain't had a thing to do today. Maybe I won't have no supper tonight. You see I'm off my regular road. I know folks on the highway clear from Seattle to San Diego. They save their things for me to sharpen up because they know I do it so good and save them money."

"I'm sorry," Elisa said irritably. "I haven't anything for you to do."

His eyes left her face and fell to searching the ground. They roamed about until they came to the chrysanthemum bed where she had been working. "What's them plants, ma'am?"

The irritation and resistance melted from Elisa's face. "Oh, those are chrysanthemums, giant whites and yellows. I raise them every year, bigger than anybody around here."

"Kind of a long-stemmed flower? Looks like a quick puff of colored smoke?" he asked.

"That's it. What a nice way to describe them."

"They smell kind of nasty till you get used to them," he said.

"It's a good bitter smell," she retorted, "not nasty at all."

He changed his tone quickly. "I like the smell myself."

"I had ten-inch blooms this year," she said.

The man leaned farther over the fence. "Look. I know a lady down the road a piece, has got the nicest garden you ever seen. Got nearly every kind of flower but no chrysanthemums. Last time I was mending a copper-bottom washtub for her (that's a hard job but I do it good), she said to me: 'If you ever run acrost some nice chrysanthemums I wish you'd try to get me a few seeds.' That's what she told me."

Elisa's eyes grew alert and eager. "She couldn't have known much about chrysanthemums. You *can* raise them from seed, but it's much easier to root the little sprouts you see here."

"Oh," he said. "I s'pose I can't take none to her, then."

"Why yes you can," Elisa cried. "I can put some in damp sand, and you can carry them right along with you. They'll take root in the pot if you keep them damp. And then she can transplant them."

"She'd sure like to have some, ma'am. You say they're nice ones?"

"Beautiful," she said. "Oh, beautiful." Her eyes shone. She tore off the battered hat and shook out her dark pretty hair. "I'll put them in a flowerpot, and you can take them right with you. Come into the yard."

While the man came through the picket gate Elisa ran excitedly along the geranium-bordered path to the back of the house. And she returned carrying a big red flower-pot. The gloves were forgotten now. She kneeled on the ground by the starting bed and dug up the sandy soil with her fingers and scooped it into the bright new flower-pot. Then she picked up the little pile of shoots she had prepared. With her strong fingers she pressed them into the sand and tamped around them with her knuckles. The man stood over her. "I'll tell you what to do," she said. "You remember so you can tell the lady."

"Yes, I'll try to remember."

"Well, look. These will take root in about a month. Then she must set them out, about a foot apart in good rich earth like this, see?" She lifted a handful of dark soil for him to look at. "They'll grow fast and tall. Now remember this: In July tell her to cut them down, about eight inches from the ground."

"Before they bloom?" he asked.

"Yes, before they bloom." Her face was tight with eagerness. "They'll grow right up again. About the last of September the buds will start."

She stopped and seemed perplexed. "It's the budding that takes the most care," she said hesitantly. "I don't know how to tell you." She looked deep into his eyes, searchingly. Her mouth opened a little, and she seemed to be listening. "I'll try to tell you," she said. "Did you ever hear of planting hands?"

"Can't say I have, ma'am."

"Well, I can only tell you what it feels like. It's when you're picking off the buds you don't want. Everything goes right down into your fingertips. You watch your fingers work. They do it themselves. You can feel how it is. They pick and pick the buds. They never make a mistake. They're with the plant. Do you see? Your fingers and the plant. You can feel that, right up your arm. They know. They never make a mistake. You can feel it. When you're like that you can't do anything wrong. Do you see that? Can you understand that?"

She was kneeling on the ground looking up at him. Her breast swelled passionately.

The man's eyes narrowed. He looked away self-consciously.

"Maybe I know," he said. "Sometimes in the night in the wagon there——"

Elisa's voice grew husky. She broke in on him: "I've never lived as you do, but I know what you mean. When the night is dark—why, the stars are sharp-pointed, and there's quiet. Why, you rise up and up! Every pointed star gets driven into your body. It's like that. Hot and sharp and—lovely."

Kneeling there, her hand went out toward his legs in the greasy black trousers. Her hesitant fingers almost touched the cloth. Then her hand dropped to the ground. She crouched low like a fawning dog.

He said: "It's nice, just like you say. Only when you don't have no dinner, it ain't."

She stood up then, very straight, and her face was ashamed. She held the flower-pot out to him and placed it gently in his arms. "Here. Put it in your wagon, on the seat, where you can watch it. Maybe I can find something for you to do."

At the back of the house she dug in the can pile and found two old and battered aluminum saucepans. She carried them back and gave them to him. "Here, maybe you can fix these."

His manner changed. He became professional. "Good as new I can fix them." At the back of his wagon he set a little anvil, and out of an oily tool-box dug a small machine hammer. Elisa came through the gate to watch him while he pounded out the dents in the kettles. His mouth grew sure and knowing. At a difficult part of the work he sucked his underlip.

"You sleep right in the wagon?" Elisa asked.

"Right in the wagon, ma'am. Rain or shine I'm dry as a cow in there."

"It must be nice," she said. "It must be very nice. I wish women could do such things."

"It ain't the right kind of a life for a woman."

Her upper lip raised a little, showing her teeth. "How do you know? How can you tell?" she said.

"I don't know, ma'am," he protested. "Of course I don't know. Now here's your kettles, done. You don't have to buy no new ones."

"How much?"

"Oh, fifty cents'll do. I keep my prices down and my work good. That's why I have all them satisfied customers up and down the highway."

Elisa brought him a fifty-cent piece from the house and dropped it in his hand. "You might be surprised to have a rival some time. I can sharpen scissors, too. And I can beat the dents out of little pots. I could show you what a woman might do."

He put his hammer back in the oily box and shoved the little anvil out of sight. "It would be a lonely life for a woman, ma'am, and a scarey life, too, with animals creeping under the wagon all night." He climbed over the single-tree, steadying himself with a hand on the burro's white rump. He settled himself in the seat, picked up the lines. "Thank you kindly ma'am," he said. "I'll do like you told me; I'll go back and catch the Salinas road."

"Mind," she called, "if you're long in getting there, keep the sand damp."

"Sand, ma'am? . . . Sand? Oh, sure. You mean around the chrysanthemums. Sure I will." He clucked his tongue. The beasts leaned luxuriously into their collars. The mongrel dog took his place between the back wheels. The wagon turned and crawled out the entrance road and back the way it had come, along the river.

Elisa stood in front of her wire fence watching the slow progress of the caravan. Her shoulders were straight, her head thrown back, her eyes half-closed, so that the scene came vaguely into them. Her lips moved silently, forming the words "Good-bye—good-bye." Then she whispered: "That's a bright direction. There's a glowing there." The sound of her whisper startled her. She shook herself free and looked about to see whether anyone had been listening. Only the dogs had heard. They lifted their heads toward her from their sleeping in the dust, and then stretched out their chins and settled asleep again. Elisa turned and ran hurriedly into the house.

In the kitchen she reached behind the stove and felt the water tank. It was full of hot water from the noonday cooking. In the bathroom she tore off her soiled clothes and flung them into the corner. And then she scrubbed herself with a little block of pumice, legs and thighs, loins and chest and arms, until her skin was scratched and red. When she had dried herself she stood in front of a mirror in her bedroom and looked at her body. She tightened her stomach and threw out her chest. She turned and looked over her shoulders at her back.

After a while she began to dress, slowly. She put on her newest underclothing and her nicest stockings and the dress which was the symbol of her prettiness. She worked carefully on her hair, pencilled her eyebrows and rouged her lips.

Before she was finished she heard the little thunder of hoofs and the shouts of Henry and his helper as they drove the red steers into the corral. She heard the gate bang shut and set herself for Henry's arrival.

His step sounded on the porch. He entered the house calling: "Elisa, where are you?"

"In my room, dressing. I'm not ready. There's hot water for your bath. Hurry up. It's getting late."

When she heard him splashing in the tub, Elisa laid his dark suit on the bed, and shirt and socks and tie beside it. She stood his polished shoes on the floor beside the bed. Then she went to the porch and sat primly and stiffly down. She looked toward the river road where the willow-line was still yellow with frosted leaves so that under the high grey fog they seemed a thin band of sunshine. This was the only color in the grey afternoon. She sat unmoving for a long time. Her eyes blinked rarely.

Henry came banging out of the door, shoving his tie inside his vest as he came. Elisa stiffened and her face grew tight. Henry stopped short and looked at her. "Why—why, Elisa. You look so nice!"

"Nice? You think I look nice? What do you mean by 'nice'?"

Henry blundered on. "I don't know. I mean you look different, strong and happy."

"I am strong? Yes, strong. What do you mean 'strong'?"

He looked bewildered. "You're playing some kind of a game," he said helplessly. "It's a kind of a play. You look strong enough to break a calf over your knee, happy enough to eat it like a watermelon."

For a second she lost her rigidity. "Henry! Don't talk like that. You didn't know what you said." She grew complete again. "I'm strong," she boasted. "I never knew before how strong."

Henry looked down toward the tractor-shed, and when he brought his eyes back to her, they were his own again. "I'll get out the car. You can put on your coat while I'm starting."

Elisa went into the house. She heard him drive to the gate and idle down his motor, and then she took a long time to put on her hat. She pulled it here and pressed it there. When Henry turned the motor off she slipped into her coat and went out.

The little roadster bounced along on the dirt road by the river, raising the birds and driving the rabbits into the brush. Two cranes flapped heavily over the willow-line and dropped into the river-bed.

Far ahead on the road Elisa saw a dark speck. She knew.

She tried not to look as they passed it, but her eyes would not obey. She whispered to herself sadly: "He might have thrown them off the road. That wouldn't have been much trouble, not very much. But he kept the pot," she explained. "He had to keep the pot. That's why he couldn't get them off the road."

The roadster turned a bend and she saw the caravan ahead. She swung full around toward her husband so she could not see the little covered wagon and the mis-matched team as the car passed them.

In a moment it was over. The thing was done. She did not look back.

She said loudly, to be heard above the motor: "It will be good, tonight, a good dinner."

"Now you've changed again," Henry complained. He took one hand from the wheel and patted her knee. "I ought to take you in to dinner oftener. It would be good for both of us. We get so heavy out on the ranch."

"Henry," she asked, "could we have wine at dinner?"

"Sure we could. Say! That will be fine."

She was silent for a while; then she said: "Henry, at those prize-fights, do the men hurt each other very much?"

"Sometimes a little, not often. Why?"

"Well, I've read how they break noses, and blood runs down their chests. I've read how the fighting gloves get heavy and soggy with blood."

He looked around at her. "What's the matter, Elisa? I didn't know you read things like that." He brought the car to a stop, then turned to the right over the Salinas River bridge.

"Do any women ever go to the fights?" she asked.

"Oh, sure, some. What's the matter, Elisa? Do you want to go? I don't think you'd like it, but I'll take you if you really want to go."

She relaxed limply in the seat. "Oh, no. No. I don't want to go. I'm sure I don't." Her face was turned away from him. "It will be enough if we can have wine. It will be plenty." She turned up her coat collar so he could not see that she was crying weakly—like an old woman.

1938

ROBERT STONE

b. 1937

Already an established novelist of the first rank when he published his story collection *Bear and His Daughter* (1997), Stone has long been a source of awe for many of his contemporaries, and the stories in that slender volume have the resonance and power of much longer works. Born in Brooklyn, New York to a schizophrenic mother who eventually had to be institutionalized, he spent several years in a Catholic orphanage. A high school drop-out, he served in the Navy, where he began working as a journalist. After the Navy he studied briefly at New York University and then worked as a copy boy at the *New York Daily News*. At one point during the sixties, he traveled with the famous "Merry Pranksters," who were led by novelist Ken Kesey and whose travels were so well documented in Tom Wolfe's *The Kandy-Kolored Tangerine-Flake Streamline Baby*. Stone's first novel, *A Hall of Mirrors* (1967), won the PEN/ Hemingway Award. His second, *Dog Soldiers* (1974), was co-winner, with Thomas Williams's *The Hair of Harold Roux*, of the 1975 National Book Award. His third, *A Flag for Sunrise* (1981), was nominated for a PEN/Faulkner Award. Several of Stone's novels have been made into films, and his fourth, *Children of Light* (1986), is a searing portrait of the heartless unreality of Hollywood. His other novels include *Damascus Gate* (1998), *Bay of Souls* (2003), and *Death of the Black-Haired Girl* (2013). He has written a memoir of the 1960s, *Prime Green* (2006), and a second collection of short stories, *Fun with Problems* (2010). Stone once said in an interview that he believed in trying to write about ultimate concerns. His work is full of what might be called ultimate moments.

Under the Pitons

All the previous day, they had been tacking up from the Grenadines, bound for Martinique[1] to return the boat and take leave of Freycinet. Blessington was trying to forget the anxieties of the deal, the stink of menace, the sick ache behind the eyes. It was dreadful to have to smoke with the St. Vincentian dealers, stone killers who liked to operate from behind a thin film of fear. But the Frenchman was tough.

Off Dark Head there was a near thing with a barge under tow. Blessington, stoned at the wheel, his glass of straight Demerara beside the binnacle, had

---

1. French island in the Lesser Antilles, islands in the Caribbean Sea that include the former British possessions St. Vincent and the Grenadines, about 100 miles southward. *Tacking up:* sailing a zigzag course against a headwind.

calmly watched a dimly lighted tug struggle past on a parallel course at a distance of a mile or so. The moon was newly risen, out of sight behind the island's mountains, silvering the line of the lower slopes. A haze of starlight left the sea in darkness, black as the pit, now and then flashing phosphorescence. They were at least ten miles offshore.

With his mainsail beginning to luff, he had steered the big ketch a little farther off the wind, gliding toward the trail of living light in the tug's wake. Only in the last second did the dime drop; he took a quick look over his shoulder. And of course there came the barge against the moon-traced mountains, a big black homicidal juggernaut, unmarked and utterly unlighted, bearing down on them. Blessington swore and spun the wheel like Ezekiel,[2] as hard to port as it went, thinking that if his keel was over the cable nothing would save them, that 360 degrees of helm or horizon would be less than enough to escape by.

Then everything not secured came crashing down on everything else, the tables and chairs on the afterdeck went over, plates and bottles smashed, whatever was breakable immediately broke. The boat, the *Sans Regret*, fell off the wind like a comedian and flapped into a flying jibe.[3] A couple of yards to starboard the big barge raced past like a silent freight train, betrayed only by the slap of its hull against the waves. It might have been no more than the wind, for all you could hear of it. When it was safely gone, the day's fear welled up again and gagged him.

The Frenchman ran out on deck cursing and looked to the cockpit, where Blessington had the helm. His hair was cut close to his skull. He showed his teeth in the mast light. He was brushing his shorts; something had spilled in his lap.

"*Qu'est-ce que c'est là?*"[4] he demanded of Blessington. Blessington pointed into the darkness where the barge had disappeared. The Frenchman knew only enough of the ocean to fear the people on it. "*Quel cul!*"[5] he said savagely. "Who is it?" He was afraid of the Coast Guard and of pirates.

"We just missed being sunk by a barge. No lights. Submerged cable. It's OK now."

"Fuck," said the Frenchman, Freycinet. "Why are you stopping?"

"Stopping?" It took a moment to realize that Freycinet was under the impression that because the boat had lost its forward motion they were stopping, as though he had applied a brake. Freycinet had been around boats long enough to know better. He must be out of his mind, Blessington thought.

"I'm not stopping, Honoré. We're all right."

"I bust my fucking ass below," said Freycinet. "Marie fall out of bed."

Tough shit, thought Blessington. Be thankful you're not treading water in the splinters of your stupidly named boat. "Sorry, man," he said.

Sans Regret, with its fatal echoes of Piaf.[6] The Americans might be culturally deprived, Blessington thought, but surely every cutter in the Yankee Coast Guard would have the sense to board that one. And the cabin stank of the

---

2. Sixth-century B.C.E. Jewish prophet whose ominous vision of spinning chariot wheels is recounted in the Bible (see Ezekiel 1:15–21).   **3.** Abrupt, uncontrolled turn of a sailing vessel. *Sans Regret*: No Regrets (French).   **4.** "What was that?" (French).   **5.** "What an ass!" (French).   **6.** Edith Piaf (1915–1963), French cabaret singer whose signature song was "*Non, je ne regrette rien*" ("No, I regret nothing").

resiny ganja they had stashed, along with the blow,[7] under the cabin sole. No amount of roach spray or air freshener could cut it. The space would probably smell of dope forever.

Freycinet went below without further complaint, missing in his ignorance the opportunity to abuse Blessington at length. It had been Blessington's fault they had not seen the barge sooner, stoned and drunk as he was. He should have looked for it as soon as the tug went by. To stay awake through the night he had taken crystal and his peripheral vision was flashing him little mongoose darts, shooting stars composed of random light. Off the north shore of St. Vincent, the winds were murder.

Just before sunrise, he saw the Pitons rising from the sea off the starboard bow, the southwest coast of St. Lucia.[8] Against the pink sky, the two peaks looked like a single mountain. It was hard to take them for anything but a good omen. As the sudden dawn caught fire, they turned green with hope. So many hearts, he thought, must have lifted at the sight of them.

To Blessington, they looked like the beginning of home free. Or at least free. Martinique was the next island up, where they could return the boat and Blessington could take his portion and be off to America on his student visa. He had a letter of acceptance from a hotel management school in Florida but his dream was to open a restaurant in the Keys.

He took another deep draft of the rum to cut the continuing anxieties. The first sunlight raised a sweat on him, so he took his shirt off and put on his baseball hat. Florida Marlins.

Freycinet came out on deck while he was having a drink.

"You're a drunk Irish man," Freycinet told him.

"That I'm not," said Blessington. It seemed to him no matter how much he drank he would never be drunk again. The three Vincentians had sobered him for life. He had been sitting on the porch of the guesthouse on Canouan[9] when they walked up. They had approached like panthers—no metaphor, no politics intended. Their every move was a dark roll of musculature, balanced and wary. They were very big men with square scarred faces. Blessington had been reclining, tilted backward in a cane chair with his feet on the porch rail, when they came up to him.

"Frenchy?" one had asked very softly.

Blessington had learned the way of hard men back in Ireland and thought he could deal with them. He had been careful to maintain his relaxed position.

"I know the man you mean, sir," he had said. "But I'm not him, see. You'll have to wait."

At Blessington's innocuous words they had tensed in every fiber, although you had to be looking right at them to appreciate the physics of it. They drew themselves up around their hidden weaponry behind a silent, drug-glazed wall of suspicion that looked impermeable to reason. They were zombies, without mercy, and he, Blessington, was wasting their time. He resolved to count to thirty, but at the count of ten he took his feet down off the rail.

Freycinet turned and shaded his eyes and looked toward the St. Lucia coast. The Pitons delighted him.

---

7. *Blow*: cocaine. **8.** Island nation between Martinique and St. Vincent. **9.** One of the Grenadine Islands.

"Ah là. C'est les Pitons, n'est-ce pas?"[1]

"Oui," said Blessington. *"Les Pitons."* They had gone south in darkness and Freycinet had never seen them before.

The wind shifted to its regular quarter and he had a hard time tacking level with the island. The two women came out on deck. Freycinet's Marie was blond and very young. She came from Normandy, and she had been a waitress in the bistro outside Fort-de-France where Freycinet and Blessington cooked. Sometimes she seemed so sunny and innocent that it was hard to connect her with a hood like Freycinet. At other times she seemed very knowing indeed. It was hard to tell, she was so often stoned.

Gillian was an American from Texas. She had a hard, thin face with a prominent nose and a big jaw. Her father, Blessington imagined, was one of those Texans, a tough, loud man who cursed the Mexicans. She was extremely tall and rather thin, with long legs. Her slenderness and height and interesting face had taken her into modeling, to Paris and Milan. In contrast, she had muscular thighs and a big derriere, which, if it distressed the couturiers, made her more desirable. She was Blessington's designated girlfriend on the trip but they rarely made love because, influenced by the others, he had taken an early dislike to her. He supposed she knew it.

"Oh, wow," she said in her Texas voice, "look at those pretty mountains."

It was exactly the kind of American comment that made the others all despise and imitate her—even Marie, who had no English at all. Gillian had come on deck stark naked and each of them, the Occitan Freycinet, Norman Marie and Irish Blessington, felt scornful and slightly offended. Anyone else might have been forgiven. They had decided she was a type and she could do no right.

Back on Canouan, Gillian had conceived a lust for one of the dealers. At first, when everyone smoked in the safe house, they had paid no attention to the women. The deal was repeated to everyone's satisfaction. As the dealers gave forth their odor of menace Marie had skillfully disappeared herself in plain view. But Gillian, to Blessington's humiliation and alarm, had put out a ray and one of the men had called her on it.

Madness. In a situation so volatile, so bloody *fraught*. But she was full of lusts, was Texan Gillian, and physically courageous too. He noticed she whined less than the others, in spite of her irritating accent. It had ended with her following the big St. Vincentian to her guesthouse room, walking ten paces behind with her eyes down, making herself a prisoner, a lamb for the slaughter.

For a while Blessington had thought she would have to do all three of them but it had been only the one, Nigel. Nigel had returned her to Blessington in a grim little ceremony, holding her with the chain of her shark's-tooth necklace twisted tight around her neck.

"Wan' have she back, mon?"

Leaving Blessington with the problem of how to react. The big bastard was fucking welcome to her, but of course it would have been tactless to say so. Should he protest and get everyone killed? Or should he be complacent and be thought a pussy and possibly achieve the same result? It was hard to find a

---

1. "There. Those are the Pitons, aren't they?" (French).

middle ground but Blessington found one, a tacit, ironic posture, fashioned of silences and body language. The Irish had been a subject race too, after all.

"I gon' to make you a present, mon. Give you little pink piggy back. Goodness of my ha'art."

So saying, Nigel had put his huge busted-knuckle hand against her pale hard face and she had looked down submissively, trembling a little, knowing not to smile. Afterward, she was very cool about it. Nigel had given her a Rasta bracelet, beads in the red, yellow and green colors of Ras Tafari.

"Think I'm a pink piggy, Liam?"

He had not been remotely amused and he had told her so.

So she had walked on ahead laughing and put her palms together and looked up to the sky and said, "Oh, my Lord!" And then glanced at him and wiped the smile off her face. Plainly she'd enjoyed it, all of it. She wore the bracelet constantly.

Now she leaned on her elbows against the chart table with her bare bum thrust out, turning the bracelet with the long, bony fingers of her right hand. Though often on deck, she seemed never to burn or tan. A pale child of night was Gillian.

"What island you say that was?" she asked.

"It's St. Lucia," Blessington told her. "The mountains are called the Pitons."

"The Pee-tuns? Does that mean something cool in French?" She turned to Blessington, then to Freycinet. "Does it, Honoré?"

Freycinet made an unpleasant, ratty face. He was ugly as cat shit, Blessington thought, something Gillian doubtless appreciated. He had huge soulful brown eyes and a pointed nose like a puppet's. His grim haircut showed the flattened shape of his skull.

"It means stakes," Blessington said.

"Steaks? Like . . ."

"Sticks," said Blessington. "Rods. Palings."

"Oh," she said, "stakes. Like Joan of Arc got burned at, right?"

Freycinet's mouth fell open. Marie laughed loudly. Gillian looked slyly at Blessington.

"Honoré," she said. "*Tu es un dindon.*[2] You're a *dindon*, man. I'm shitting you. I understand French fine."

It had become amusing to watch her tease and confound Freycinet. Dangerous work and she did it cleverly, leaving the Frenchman to marvel at the depths of her stupidity until paranoia infected his own self-confidence. During the trip back, Blessington thought he might be starting to see the point of her.

"I mean, I worked the Paris openings for five years straight. I told you that."

Drunk and stoned as the rest of them, Gillian eventually withdrew from the ascending spring sun. Marie went down after her. Freycinet's pointed nose was out of joint.

"You hear what she say?" he asked Blessington. "That she speak French all the time? What the fuck? Because she said before, '*Non*, I don't speak it.' Now she's speaking it."

"Ah, she's drunk, Honoré. She's just a bimbo."

2. Turkey (French).

"I'ope so, eh?" said Freycinet. He looked at the afterdeck to be sure she was out of earshot. "Because . . . because what if she setting us up? All these time, eh? If she's *agent*. Or she's informer? A grass?"

Blessington pondered it deeply. Like the rest of them he had thought her no more than a fatuous, if perverse, American. Now, the way she laughed at them, he was not at all sure.

"I thought she came with you. Did she put money up?"

Freycinet puffed out his hollow cheeks and shrugged.

"She came to me from Lavigerie," he said. The man who called himself Lavigerie was a French Israeli of North African origin, a hustler in Fort-de-France.[3] "She put in money, *oui*. The same as everyone."

They had all pooled their money for the boat and to pay the Vincentians. Blessington had invested twenty thousand dollars, partly his savings from the bistro, partly borrowed from his sister and her husband in Providence. He expected to make it back many times and pay them off with interest.

"Twenty thousand?"

"Yes. Twenty."

"Well, even the Americans wouldn't spend twenty thousand dollars to catch us," he told Honoré. "We're too small. And it isn't how they work."

"Now I think I don't trust her, eh?" said Freycinet. He squinted into the sun. The Pitons, no closer, seemed to displease him now. "She's a bitch, *non?*"

"I think she's all right," Blessington said. "I really do."

And for the most part he did. In any case he had decided to, because an eruption of hard-core, coke-and-speed-headed paranoia could destroy them all. It had done so to many others. Missing boats sometimes turned up on the mangrove shore of some remote island, the hulls blistered with bullet holes, cabins attended by unimaginable swarms of flies. Inside, *tableaux morts* not to be forgotten by the unlucky discoverer. Strong-stomached photographers recorded the *tableaux* for the DEA's files, where they were stamped NOT TO BE DESTROYED, HISTORIC INTEREST. The agency took a certain satisfaction. Blessington knew all this from his sister and her husband in Providence.

Now they were almost back to Martinique and Blessington wanted intensely not to die at sea. In the worst of times, he grew frightened to the point of utter despair. It had been, he realized at such times, a terrible mistake. He gave up on the money. He would settle for just living, for living even in prison in France or America. Or at least for not dying on that horrible bright blue ocean, aboard the *Sans Regret*.

"Yeah," he told Freycinet. "Hell, I wouldn't worry about her. Just a bimbo."

All morning they tacked for the Pitons. Around noon, a great crown of puffy cloud settled around Gros Piton and they were close enough to distinguish the two peaks one from the other. Freycinet refused to go below. His presence was so unpleasant that Blessington felt like weeping, knocking him unconscious, throwing him overboard or jumping over himself. But the Frenchman remained in the cockpit though he never offered to spell Blessington at the wheel. The man drove Blessington to drink. He poured more Demerara and dipped his finger in the bag of crystal. A pulse fluttered under his collarbone, fear, speed.

---

3. Capital of Martinique.

Eventually Freycinet went below. After half an hour, Gillian came topside, clothed this time, in cutoffs and a halter. The sea had picked up and she nearly lost her balance on the ladder.

"Steady," said Blessington.

"Want a roofie, Liam?"

He laughed. "A roofie? What's that? Some kind of . . ."

Gillian finished the thought he had been too much of a prude to articulate.

"Some kind of blowjob? Some kind of sex technique? No, dear, it's a medication."

"I'm on watch."

She laughed at him. "You're shitfaced is what you are."

"You know," Blessington said, "you ought not to tease Honoré. You'll make him paranoid."

"He's a asshole. As we say back home."

"That may be. But he's a very mercurial fella. I used to work with him."

"Mercurial? If you know he's so mercurial how come you brought him?"

"I didn't bring him," Blessington said. "He brought me. For my vaunted seamanship. And I came for the money. How about you?"

"I came on account of having my brains in my ass," she said, shaking her backside. "My talent too. Did you know I was a barrel racer? I play polo too. English or western, man, you name it."

"English or western?" Blessington asked.

"Forget it," she said. She frowned at him, smiled, frowned again. "You seem, well, scared."

"Ah," said Blessington, "scared? Yes, I am. Somewhat."

"I don't give a shit," she said.

"You don't?"

"You heard me," she said. "I don't care what happens. Why should I? Me with my talent in my ass. Where do I come in?"

"You shouldn't talk that way," Blessington said.

"Fuck you. You afraid I'll make trouble? I assure you I could make trouble like you wouldn't believe."

"I don't doubt it," Blessington said. He kept his eyes on the Pitons. His terror, he thought, probably encouraged her.

"Just between you and me, Liam, I have no fear of dying. I would just as soon be out here on this boat now as in my little comfy bed with my stuffed animals. I would just as soon be dead."

He took another sip of rum to wet his pipes for speech. "Why did you put the money in, then? Weren't you looking for a score?"

"I don't care about money," she said. "I thought it would be a kick. I thought it would be radical. But it's just another exercise in how everything sucks."

"Well," said Blessington, "you're right there."

She looked off at the twin mountains.

"They don't seem a bit closer than they did this morning."

"No. It's an upwind passage. Have to tack forever."

"You know what Nigel told me back in Canouan?"

"No," Blessington said.

"He told me not to worry about understanding things. He said under-standing was weak and lame. He said you got to *overstand* things." She hauled herself and did the voice of a big St. Vincentian man saddling up a white bitch for the night, laying down wisdom. "You got to *overstand* it. *Overstand* it, right? Funny, huh."

"Maybe there's something in it," said Blessington.

"Rasta lore," she said. "Could be, man."

"Anyway, never despise what the natives tell you, that's what my aunt used to say. Even in America."

"And what was your aunt? A dope dealer?"

"She was a nun," Blessington said. "A missionary."

For a while Gillian sunned herself on the foredeck, halter off. But the sun became too strong and she crawled back to the cockpit.

"You ever think about how it is in this part of the world?" she asked him. "The Caribbean and around it? It's all suckin' stuff they got. Suckin' stuff, all goodies and no nourishment."

"What do you mean?"

"It's all turn-ons and illusion," she said. "Don't you think? Like coffee." She numbered items on the long fingers of her left hand. "Tobacco. Emeralds. Sugar. Cocaine. Ganja. It's all stuff you don't need. Isn't even good for you. Perks and pick-me-ups and pogy bait. Always has been."

"You're right," Blessington said. "Things people kill for."

"Overpriced. Put together by slaves and peons. Piggy stuff. For pink piggies."

"I hadn't thought of it," he said. He looked over at her. She had raised a fist to her pretty mouth. "You're clever, Gillian."

"You don't even like me," she said.

"Yes I do."

"Don't you dare bullshit me. I said you don't."

"Well," Blessington said, "to tell you the truth, at first I didn't. But now I do."

"Oh, yeah? Why?"

Blessington considered before speaking. The contrary wind was picking up and there were reefs at the south end of the island. Some kind of monster tide was running against them too.

"Because you're intelligent. I hadn't realized that. You had me fooled, see? Now I think you're amusing."

"Amusing?" She seemed more surprised than angry.

"You really are so bloody clever," he said, finishing the glass of rum. "When we're together I like it. You're not a cop, are you? Anything like that?"

"You only wish," she said. "How about you?"

"Me? I'm Irish, for Christ's sake."

"Is that like not being real?"

"Well," he said, "a little. In many cases."

"You are scared," she said. "You're scared of everything. Scared of me."

"Holy Christ," said Blessington, "you're as bad as Honoré. Look, Gillian, I'm a chef, not a pirate. I never claimed otherwise. Of course I'm scared."

She made him no answer.

"But not of you," he said. "No. Not anymore. I like you here. You're company."

"Am I?" she asked. "Do you? Would you marry me?"

"Hey," said Blessington. "Tomorrow."

Freycinet came up on deck, looked at the Pitons, then at Blessington and Gillian in the cockpit.

"*Merde*,"[4] he said. "Far away still. What's going on?"

"We're getting there," Blessington said. "We're closer now than we look."

"Aren't the mountains pretty, Honoré?" Gillian asked. "Don't you wish we could climb one?"

Freycinet ignored her. "How long?" he asked Blessington.

"To Martinique? Tomorrow sometime, I guess."

"How long before we're off les Pitons?"

"Oh," Blessington said, "just a few hours. Well before dark so we'll have a view. Better steer clear, though."

"Marie is sick."

"Poor puppy," Gillian said. "Probably all that bug spray. Broth's the thing. Don't you think, Liam?"

"Ya, it's kicking up," Blessington said. "There's a current running and a pretty stiff offshore breeze."

"*Merde*," said Freycinet again. He went forward along the rail and lay down beside the anchor windlass, peering into the chains.

"He's a cook too," Gillian said, speaking softly. "How come you're not more like him?"

"An accident of birth," Blessington said.

"If we were married," she said, "you wouldn't have to skip on your visa."

"Ah," said Blessington, "don't think it hasn't occurred to me. Nice to be a legal resident."

"Legal my ass," she said.

Freycinet suddenly turned and watched them. He showed them the squint, the bared canines.

"What you're talking about, you two? About me, eh?"

"Damn, Honoré!" Gillian said. "He was just proposing." When he had turned around again she spoke between her teeth. "Shithead is into the blow. He keeps prying up the sole. Cures Marie's mal de mer.[5] Keeps him on his toes."

"God save us," said Blessington. Leaning his elbow on the helm, he took Gillian's right hand and put it to her forehead, her left shoulder and then her right one, walking her through the sign of the cross. "Pray for us like a good girl."

Gillian made the sign again by herself. "Shit," she said, "now I feel a lot better. No, really," she said when he laughed, "I do. I'm gonna do it all the time now. Instead of chanting *Om* or *Nam myoho renge kyo*."[6]

They sat and watched the peaks grow closer, though the contrary current increased.

"When this is over," Blessington said, "maybe we ought to stay friends."

"If we're still alive," she said, "we might hang out together. We could go to your restaurant in the Keys."

"That's what we'll do," he said. "I'll make you a sous-chef."[7]

"I'll wait tables."

---

4. Shit (French). **5.** Seasickness (French). **6.** Phrase attributed to the Buddha (563–483 B.C.E.), meaning roughly "the teaching of the lotus flower of the law" (Pali), often chanted during meditation. **7.** Cook's assistant (French).

"No, no. Not you."

"But we won't be alive," she said.

"But if we are."

"If we are," she said, "we'll stay together." She looked at him sway beside the wheel. "You better not be shitting me."

"I wouldn't. I think it was meant to be."

"Meant to be? You're putting me on."

"Don't make me weigh my words, Gillian. I want to say what occurs to me."

"Right," she said, touching him. "When we're together you can say any damn thing."

The green mountains, in the full richness of afternoon, rose above them. Blessington had a look at the chart to check the location of the offshore reefs. He began steering to another quarter, away from the tip of the island.

Gillian sat on a locker with her arms around his neck, leaning against his back. She smelled of sweat and patchouli.

"I've never been with anyone as beautiful as you, Gillian."

He saw she had gone to sleep. He disengaged her arms and helped her lie flat on the locker in the shifting shade of the mainsail. Life is a dream, he thought. Something she knew and I didn't.

I love her, Blessington thought. She encourages me. The shadow of the peaks spread over the water.

Freycinet came out on deck and called up to him.

"Liam! We're to stop here. Off les Pitons."

"We can't," Blessington said, though it was tempting. He was so tired.

"We have to stop. We can anchor, yes? Marie is sick. We need to rest. We want to see them."

"We'd have to clear customs," Blessington said. "We'll have bloody cops and boat boys and God knows what else."

He realized at once what an overnight anchorage would entail. All of them up on speed or the cargo, cradling shotguns, peering into the moonlight while they waited for *macheteros*[8] to come on feathered oars and steal their shit and kill them.

"If we anchor," Freycinet said, "if we anchor somewhere, we won't have to clear."

"Yes, yes," Blessington said. "We will, sure. The fucking boat boys will find us. If we don't hire them or buy something they'll turn us in." He picked up the cruising guide and waved it in the air. "It says right here you have to clear customs in Soufrière."[9]

"We'll wait until they have close," said Freycinet.

"Shit," said Blessington desperately, "we'll be fined. We'll be boarded."

Freycinet was smiling at him, a broad demented smile of infinitely self-assured contempt. Cocaine. He felt Gillian put her arm around his leg from behind.

"*Écoutez*, Liam. *Écoutez bien*.[1] We going to stop, man. We going to stop where I say."

He turned laughing into the wind, gripping a stay.

---

8. Men armed with machetes (Spanish).   **9.** Port town in St. Lucia.   **1.** Listen well (French).

"What did I tell you," Gillian said softly. "You won't have to marry me after all. 'Cause we're dead, baby."

"I don't accept that," Blessington said. "Take the wheel," he told her.

Referring to the charts and the cruising guide, he could find no anchorage that looked as though it would be out of the wind and that was not close inshore. The only possibility was a shallow reef, near the south tip, sometimes favored by snorkeling trips, nearly three miles off the Pitons. It was in the lee of the huge peaks, its coral heads as shallow as a single fathom. The chart showed mooring floats; presumably it was forbidden to anchor there for the sake of the coral.

"I beg you to reconsider, Honoré," Blessington said to Freycinet. He cleared his throat. "You're making a mistake."

Freycinet turned back to him with the same smile.

"Eh, Liam. You can leave, man. You know, there's an Irish pub in Soufrière. It's money from your friends in the IRA.[2] You can go there, eh?"

Blessington had no connection whatsoever with the IRA, although he had allowed Freycinet and his friends to believe that, and they had chosen to.

"You can go get drunk there," Freycinet told him and then turned again to look at the island.

He was standing near the bow with his bare toes caressing freeboard, gripping a stay. Blessington and Gillian exchanged looks. In the next instant she threw the wheel, the mainsail boom went crashing across the cabin roofs, the boat lurched to port and heeled hard. For a moment Freycinet was suspended over blank blue water. Blessington clambered up over the cockpit and stood swaying there, hesitating. Then he reached out for Freycinet. The Frenchman swung around the stay like a monkey and knocked him flat. The two of them went sprawling. Freycinet got to his feet in a karate stance, cursing.

"You shit," he said, when his English returned. "Cunt! What?"

"I thought you were going over, Honoré. I thought I'd have to pull you back aboard."

"That's right, Honoré," Gillian said from the cockpit. "You were like a goner. He saved your ass, man."

Freycinet pursed his lips and nodded. "*Bien*,"[3] he said. He climbed down into the cockpit in a brisk, businesslike fashion and slapped Gillian across the face, backhand and forehand, turning her head around each time.

He gave Blessington the wheel, then he took Gillian under the arm and pulled her up out of the cockpit. "Get below! I don't want to fucking see you." He followed her below and Blessington heard him speak briefly to Marie. The young woman began to moan. The Pitons looked close enough to strike with a rock and a rich jungle smell came out on the wind. Freycinet, back on deck, looked as though he was sniffing out menace. A divi-divi bird landed on the boom for a moment and then fluttered away.

"I think I have a place," Blessington said, "if you still insist. A reef."

"A reef, eh?"

"A reef about four thousand meters offshore."

"We could have a swim, *non?*"

---

2. The Irish Republican Army, a paramilitary organization opposed to the possession of Northern Ireland by Britain. **3.** Fine (French).

"We could, yes."

"But I don't know if I want to swim with you, Liam. I think you try to push me overboard."

"I think I saved your life," Blessington said.

They motored on to the reef with Freycinet standing in the bow to check for bottom as Blessington watched the depth recorder. At ten meters of bottom, they were an arm's length from the single float in view. Blessington cut the engine and came about and then went forward to cleat a line to the float. The float was painted red, yellow and green, Rasta colors like Gillian's bracelet.

It was late afternoon and suddenly dead calm. The protection the Pitons offered from the wind was ideal and the bad current that ran over the reef to the south seemed to divide around these coral heads. A perfect dive site, Blessington thought, and he could not understand why even in June there were not more floats or more boats anchored there. It seemed a steady enough place even for an overnight anchorage, although the cruising guide advised against it because of the dangerous reefs on every side.

The big ketch lay motionless on unruffled water; the float line drifted slack. There was sandy beach and a palm-lined shore across the water. It was a lonely part of the coast, across a jungle mountain track from the island's most remote resort. Through binoculars Blessington could make out a couple of boats hauled up on the strand but no one seemed ready to come out and hustle them. With luck it was too far from shore.

It might be also, he thought, that for metaphysical reasons the *Sans Regret* presented a forbidding aspect. But an aspect that deterred small predators might in time attract big ones.

Marie came up, pale and hollow-eyed, in her bikini. She gave Blessington a chastising look and lay down on the cushions on the afterdeck. Gillian came up behind her and took a seat on the gear locker behind Blessington.

"The fucker's got no class," she said softly. "See him hit me?"

"Of course. I was next to you."

"Gonna let him get away with that?"

"Well," Blessington said, "for the moment it behooves us to let him feel in charge."

"Behooves us?" she asked. "You say it *behooves* us?"

"That's right."

"Hey, what were you gonna do back there, Liam?" she asked. "Deep-six him?"

"I honestly don't know. He might have fallen."

"I was wondering," she said. "He was wondering too."

Blessington shrugged.

"He's got the overstanding," Gillian said. "We got the under." She looked out at the water and said, "Boat boys."

He looked where she was looking and saw the boat approaching, a speck against the shiny sand. It took a long time for it to cover the distance between the beach and the *Sans Regret*.

There were two boat boys, and they were not boys but men in their thirties, lean and unsmiling. One wore a wool tam-o'-shanter in bright tie-dyed colors. The second looked like an East Indian. His black headband gave him a lascar look.

"You got to pay for dat anchorage, mon," the man in the tam called to them. "Not open to de public widout charge."

"We coming aboard," said the lascar. "We take your papers and passports in for you. You got to clear."

"How much for the use of the float?" Blessington asked.

Now Freycinet appeared in the companionway. He was carrying a big French MAS 36 sniper rifle, pointing it at the men in the boat, showing his pink-edged teeth.

"You get the fuck out of here," he shouted at them. A smell of ganja and vomit seemed to follow him up from the cabin. "Understand?"

The two men did not seem unduly surprised at Freycinet's behavior. Blessington wondered if they could smell the dope as distinctly as he could.

"Fuckin' Frenchman," the man in the tam said. "Think he some shit."

"Why don' you put the piece down, Frenchy?" the East Indian asked. "This ain't no Frenchy island. You got to clear."

"You drift on that reef, Frenchy," the man in the tam said, "you be begging us to take you off."

Freycinet was beside himself with rage. He hated *les nègres*[4] more than any Frenchman Blessington had met in Martinique, which was saying a great deal. He had contained himself during the negotiations on Canouan but now he seemed out of control. Blessington began to wonder if he would shoot the pair of them.

"You fucking monkeys!" he shouted. "You stay away from me, eh? Chimpanzees! I kill you quick . . . *mon*," he added with a sneer.

The men steered their boat carefully over the reef and sat with their outboard idling. They could not stay too long, Blessington thought. Their gas tank was small and it was a long way out against a current.

"Well," he asked Gillian, "who's got the overstanding now?"

"Not Honoré," she said.

A haze of heat and doped lassitude settled over their mooring. Movement was labored, even speech seemed difficult. Blessington and Gillian nodded off on the gear locker. Marie seemed to have lured Freycinet belowdecks. Prior to dozing, Blessington heard her mimic the Frenchman's angry voice and the two of them laughing down in the cabin. The next thing he saw clearly was Marie, in her bikini, standing on the cabin roof, screaming. A rifle blasted and echoed over the still water. Suddenly the slack breeze had a brisk cordite smell and it carried smoke.

Freycinet shouted, holding the hot shotgun.

The boat with the two islanders in it seemed to have managed to come up on them. Now it raced off, headed first out to sea to round the tip of the reef and then curving shoreward to take the inshore current at an angle.

"Everyone all right?" asked Blessington.

"Fucking monkeys!" Freycinet swore.

"Well," Blessington said, watching the boat disappear, "they're gone for now. Maybe," he suggested to Freycinet, "we can have our swim and go too."

Freycinet looked at him blankly as though he had no idea what Blessington was talking about. He nodded vaguely.

4. The blacks (French).

After half an hour Marie rose and stood on the bulwark and prepared to dive, arms foremost. When she went, her dive was a good one, straight-backed and nearly splash-free. She performed a single stroke underwater and sped like a bright shaft between the coral heads below and the crystal surface. Then she appeared prettily in the light of day, blinking like a child, shaking her shining hair.

From his place in the bow, Freycinet watched Marie's dive, her underwater career, her pert surfacing. His expression was not affectionate but taut and tight-lipped. The muscles in his neck stood out, his moves were twitchy like a street junkie's. He looked exhausted and angry. The smell of cordite hovered around him.

"He's a shithead and a loser," Gillian said softly to Blessington. She looked not at Freycinet but toward the green mountains. "I thought he was cool. He was so fucking mean—I like respected that. Now we're all gonna die. Well," she said, "goes to show, right?"

"Don't worry," Blessington told her. "I won't leave you."

"Whoa," said Gillian. "All right!" But her enthusiasm was not genuine. She was mocking him.

Blessington forgave her.

Freycinet pointed a finger at Gillian. "Swim!"

"What if I don't wanna?" she asked, already standing up. When he began to swear at her in a hoarse voice she took her clothes off in front of them. Everything but the Rasta bracelet.

"I think I will if no one minds," she said. "Where you want me to swim to, Honoré?"

"Swim to fucking *Amérique*," he said. He laughed as though his mood had improved. "You want her, Liam?"

"People are always asking me that," Blessington said. "What do I have to do?"

"You swim to fucking *Amérique* with her."

Blessington saw Gillian take a couple of pills from her cutoff pocket and swallow them dry.

"I can't swim that far," Blessington said.

"Go as far as you can," said Freycinet.

"How about you?" Gillian said to the Frenchman. "You're the one wanted to stop. So ain't you gonna swim?"

"I don't trust her," Freycinet said to Blessington. "What do you think?"

"She's a beauty," Blessington said. "Don't provoke her."

Gillian measured her beauty against the blue water and dived over the side. A belly full of pills, Blessington thought. But her strokes when she surfaced were strong and defined. She did everything well, he thought. She was good around the boat. She had a pleasant voice for country music. He could imagine her riding, a cowgirl.

"Bimbo, eh?" Freycinet asked. "That's it, eh?"

"Yes," Blessington said. "Texas and all that."

"*Oui*," said Freycinet. "Texas." He yawned. "*Bien*. Have your swim with her. If you want."

Blessington went down into the stinking cabin and put his bathing suit on. Propriety to the last. The mixture of ganja, sick, roach spray and pine scent was asphyxiating. If he survived, he thought, he would never smoke hash again. Never drink rum, never do speed or cocaine, never sail or go where there were palm trees and too many stars overhead. A few fog-shrouded winter constellations would do.

"Tonight I'll cook, eh?" Freycinet said when Blessington came back up. "You can assist me."

"Good plan," said Blessington.

Standing on the bulwark, he looked around the boat. There were no other vessels in sight. Marie was swimming backstroke, describing a safe circle about twenty-five yards out from the boat. Gillian appeared to be headed hard for the open sea. She had reached the edge of the current, where the wind raised small horsetails from the rushing water.

If Freycinet was planning to leave them in the water, Blessington wondered, would he leave Marie with them? It would all be a bad idea, because Freycinet was not a skilled sailor. And there was a possibility of their being picked up right here or even of their making it to shore, although that seemed most unlikely. On the other hand, he had discovered that Freycinet's ideas were often impulses, usually bad ones. It was his recklessness that had made him appear so capably in charge, and that was as true in the kitchen as it was on the Raging Main. He had been a reckless cook.

Besides, there were a thousand dark possibilities on that awful ocean. That he had arranged to be met at sea off Martinique, that there had been some betrayal in the works throughout. Possibly involving Lavigerie or someone else in Fort-de-France.

"Yes," said Blessington. "There's time to unfreeze the grouper."

He looked at the miles of ocean between the boat and the beach at the foot of the mountains. Far off to the right he could see white water, the current running swiftly over the top of a reef that extended southwesterly, at a 45-degree angle to the beach. Beyond the reef was a sandspit where the island tapered to its narrow southern end. On their left, the base of the mountains extended to the edge of the sea, forming a rock wall against which the waves broke. According to the charts, the wall plunged to a depth of ten fathoms, and the ocean concealed a network of submarine caves and grottoes in the volcanic rock of which the Pitons were composed. Across the towering ridge, completely out of sight, was the celebrated resort.

"I'll take it out of the freezer," Blessington said.

A swimmer would have to contrive to make land somewhere between the rock wall to the north and the reef and sandspit on the right. There would be easy swimming at first, through the windless afternoon, and a swimmer would not feel any current for the first mile or so. The last part of the swim would be partly against a brisk current, and possibly against the tide. The final mile would seem much farther. For the moment, wind was not in evidence. The current might be counted on to lessen as one drew closer to shore. If only one could swim across it in time.

"It's all right," said Freycinet. "I'll do it. Have your swim."

Beyond that, there was the possibility of big sharks so far out. They might be attracted by the effort of desperation. Blessington, exhausted and dehydrated, was in no mood for swimming miles. Freycinet would not leave them there, off the Pitons, he told himself. It was practically in sight of land. He would be risking too much—witnesses, their survival. If he meant to deep-six them he would try to strike at sea.

Stoned and frightened as he was, he could not make sense of it, regain his perspective. He took a swig from a plastic bottle of warm Evian water, dropped his towel and jumped overboard.

The water felt good, slightly cool. He could relax against it and slow the beating of his heart. It seemed to cleanse him of the cabin stink. He was at home in the water, he thought. Marie was frolicking like a mermaid, now close to the boat. Gillian had turned back and was swimming toward him. Her stroke still looked strong and accomplished; he set out to intercept her course.

They met over a field of elkhorn coral. Some of the formations were so close to the surface that their feet, treading water, brushed the velvety skin of algae over the sharp prongs.

"How are you?" Blessington asked her.

She had a lupine smile. She was laughing, looking at the boat. Her eyes appeared unfocused, the black pupils huge under the blue glare of afternoon and its shimmering crystal reflection. She breathed in hungry swallows. Her face was raw and swollen where Freycinet had hit her.

"Look at that asshole," she said, gasping.

Freycinet was standing on deck talking to Marie, who was in the water ten feet away. He held a mask and snorkel in one hand and a pair of swim fins in the other. One by one he threw the toys into the water for Marie to retrieve. He looked coy and playful.

Something about the scene troubled Blessington, although he could not, in his state, quite reason what it was. He watched Freycinet take a few steps back and paw the deck like an angry bull. In the next moment, Blessington realized what the problem was.

"Oh, Jesus Christ," he said.

Freycinet leaped into space. He still wore the greasy shorts he had worn the whole trip. In midair he locked his arms around his bent knees. He was holding a plastic spatula in his right hand. He hit the surface like a cannonball, raising a little water-spout, close enough to Marie to make her yelp.

"You know what?" Gillian asked. She had spotted it. She was amazing.

"Yes, I do. The ladder's still up. We forgot to lower it."

"Shit," she said and giggled.

Blessington turned over to float on his back and tried to calm himself. Overhead the sky was utterly cloudless. Moving his eyes only a little, he could see the great green tower of Gros Piton, shining like Jacob's ladder itself, thrusting toward the empty blue. Incredibly far above, a plane drew out its jet trail, a barely visible needle stitching the tiniest flaw in the vast perfect seamless curtain of day. Miles and miles above, beyond imagining.

"How we gonna get aboard?" Gillian asked. He did not care for the way she was acting in the water now, struggling to stay afloat, moving her arms too much, wasting her breath.

"We'll have to go up the float line. Or maybe," he said, "we can stand on each other's shoulders."

"I'm not," she said, gasping, "gonna like that too well."

"Take it easy, Gillian. Lie on your back."

What bothered him most was her laughing, a high-pitched giggle with each breath.

"OK, let's do it," she said, spitting salt water. "Let's do it before he does."

"Slow and steady," Blessington said.

They slowly swam together, breaststroking toward the boat. A late afternoon breeze had come up as the temperature began to fall.

Freycinet and Marie had allowed themselves to drift farther and farther from the boat. Blessington urged Gillian along beside him until the big white hull was between them and the other swimmers.

Climbing was impossible. It was partly the nature of the French-made boat: an unusually high transom and the rounded glassy hull made it particularly difficult to board except from a dock or a dinghy. That was the contemporary, security-conscious style. And the rental company had removed a few of the deck fittings that might have provided hand- and footholds. Still, he tried to find a grip so that Gillian could get on his shoulders. Once he even managed to position himself between her legs and push her a foot or so up the hull, as she sat on his shoulders. But there was nothing to grab on to and she was stoned. She swore and laughed and toppled off him.

He was swimming forward along the hull, looking for the float, when it occurred to him that the boat must be moving. Sure enough, holding his place, he could feel the hull sliding to windward under his hand. In a few strokes he was under the bow, feeling the ketch's weight thrusting forward, riding him down. Then he saw the Rastafarian float. It was unencumbered by any line. Honoré and Marie had not drifted from the boat—the boat itself was slowly blowing away, accompanied now by the screech of fiberglass against coral. The boys from the Pitons, having dealt with druggies before, had undone the mooring line while they were sleeping or nodding off or scarfing other sorts of lines.

Blessington hurried around the hull, with one hand to the boat's skin, trying to find the drifting float line. It might, he thought, be possible to struggle up along that. But there was no drifting float line. The boat boys must have uncleated it and balled the cleat in nylon line and silently tossed it aboard. He and Freycinet had been so feckless, the sea so glassy and the wind so low that the big boat had simply settled on the float, with its keel fast among the submerged elkhorn, and they had imagined themselves secured. The *Sans Regret,* to which he clung, was gone. Its teak interiors were in another world now, as far away as the tiny jet miles above them on its way to Brazil.

"It's no good," Blessington said to her.

"It's not?" She giggled.

"Please," he said, "please don't do that."

She gasped. "What?"

"Never mind," he said. "Come with me."

They had just started to swim away when a sudden breeze carried the *Sans Regret* from between the two couples, leaving Blessington and Gillian and Honoré and Marie to face one another in the water across a distance of twenty yards or so. Honoré and Marie stared at their shipmates in confusion. It was an embarrassing moment. Gillian laughed.

"What have you done?" Honoré asked Blessington. Blessington tried not to look at him.

"Come on," he said to Gillian. "Follow me."

Cursing in French, Freycinet started kicking furiously for the boat. Marie, looking very serious, struck out behind him. Gillian stopped to look after them.

Blessington glanced at his diver's watch. It was five-fifteen.

"Never mind them," he said. "Don't look at them. Stay with me."

He turned over on his back and commenced an artless backstroke, arms out straight, rowing with his palms, paddling with his feet. It was the most economic stroke he knew, the one he felt most comfortable with. He tried to make the strokes controlled and rhythmic rather than random and splashy to avoid conveying any impression of panic or desperation. To free his mind, he tried counting the strokes. As soon as they were over deep water, he felt the current. He tried to take it at a 45-degree angle, determining his bearing and progress by the great mountain overhead.

"Are you all right?" he asked Gillian. He raised his head to have a look at her. She was swimming in what looked like a good strong crawl. She coughed from time to time.

"I'm cold," she said. "That's the trouble."

"Try resting on your back," he said, "and paddling with your open hands. Like you were rowing."

She turned over and closed her eyes and smiled.

"I could go to sleep."

"You'll sleep ashore," he said. "Keep paddling."

They heard Freycinet cursing. Marie began to scream over and over again. It sounded fairly far away.

Checking on the mountain, Blessington felt a rush of despair. The lower slopes of the jungle were turning dark green. The line dividing sun-bright vegetation from deep-shaded green was withdrawing toward the peak. And the mountain looked no closer. He felt as though they were losing distance, being carried out faster than they could paddle. Marie's relentless screeches went on and on. Perhaps they were actually growing closer, Blessington thought, perhaps an evening tide was carrying them out.

"Poor kid," Gillian said. "Poor little baby."

"Don't listen," he said.

Gillian kept coughing, sputtering. He stopped asking her if she was all right.

"I'm sorry," she said. "I'm really cold now. I thought the water was warm at first."

"We're almost there," he said.

Gillian stopped swimming and looked up at Gros Piton. Turning over again to swim, she got a mouthful of water.

"Like . . . hell," she said.

"Keep going, Gillian."

It seemed to him, as he rowed the sodden vessel of his body and mind, that the sky was darkening. The sun's mark withdrew higher on the slopes. Marie kept screaming. They heard splashes far off where the boat was now. Marie and Honoré were clinging to it.

"Liam," Gillian said, "you can't save me."

"You'll save yourself," he said. "You'll just go on."

"I can't."

"Don't be a bloody stupid bitch."

"I don't think so," she said. "I really don't."

He stopped rowing himself then, although he was loath to. Every interruption of their forward motion put them more at the mercy of the current.

According to the cruise book it was only a five-knot current but it felt much stronger. Probably reinforced by a tide.

Gillian was struggling, coughing in fits. She held her head up, greedy for air, her mouth open like a baby bird's in hope of nourishment. Blessington swam nearer her. The sense of their time ticking away, of distance lost to the current, enraged him.

"You've got to turn over on your back," he said gently. "Just ease onto your back and rest there. Then arch your back. Let your head lie backward so your forehead's in the water."

Trying to do as he told her, she began to thrash in a tangle of her own arms and legs. She swallowed water, gasped. Then she laughed again.

"Don't," he whispered.

"Liam? Can I rest on you?"

He stopped swimming toward her.

"You mustn't. You mustn't touch me. We mustn't touch each other. We might . . ."

"Please," she said.

"No. Get on your back. Turn over slowly."

Something broke the water near them. He thought it was the fin of a black-tip shark. A troublesome shark but not among the most dangerous. Of course, it could have been anything. Gillian still had the Rasta bracelet around her wrist.

"This is the thing, Liam. I think I got a cramp. I'm so dizzy."

"On your back, love. You must. It's the only way."

"No," she said. "I'm too cold. I'm too dizzy."

"Come on," he said. He started swimming again. Away from her.

"I'm so dizzy. I could go right out."

In mounting panic, he reversed direction and swam back toward her.

"Oh, shit," she said. "Liam?"

"I'm here."

"I'm fading out, Liam. I'll let it take me."

"Get on your back," he screamed at her. "You can easily swim. If you have to swim all night."

"Oh, shit," she said. Then she began to laugh again. She raised the hand that had the Rasta bracelet and splashed a sign of the cross.

"*Nam,*" she said. "*Nam myoho renge kyo.* Son of a bitch." Laughing. What she tried to say next was washed out of her mouth by a wave.

"I can just go out," she said. "I'm so dizzy."

Then she began to struggle and laugh and cry.

"Praise God, from whom all blessings flow," she sang, laughing. "Praise him, all creatures here below."

"Gillian," he said. "For God's sake." Maybe I can take her in, he thought. But that was madness and he kept his distance.

She was laughing and shouting at the top of her voice.

"Praise him above, you heavenly host! Praise Father, Son and Holy Ghost."

Laughing, thrashing, she went under, her face straining, wide-eyed. Blessington tried to look away but it was too late. He was afraid to go after her.

He lost his own balance then. His physical discipline collapsed and he began to wallow and thrash as she had.

"Help!" he yelled piteously. He was answered by a splash and Marie's screams. Perhaps now he only imagined them.

Eventually he got himself under control. When the entire mountain had subsided into dark green, he felt the pull of the current release him. The breakers were beginning to carry him closer to the sand, toward the last spit of sandy beach remaining on the island. The entire northern horizon was subsumed in the mountain overhead, Gros Piton.

He had one final mad moment. Fifty yards offshore, a riptide was running; it seized him and carried him behind the tip of the island. He had just enough strength and coherence of mind to swim across it. The sun was setting as he waded out, among sea grape and manchineel. When he turned he could see against the setting sun the bare poles of the *Sans Regret*, settled on the larger reef to the south of the island. It seemed to him also that he could make out a struggling human figure, dark against the light hull. But the dark came down quickly. He thought he detected a flash of green. Sometimes he thought he could still hear Marie screaming.

All night, as he rattled through the thick brush looking for a road to follow from concealment, Gillian's last hymn echoed in his mind's ear. He could see her dying face against the black fields of sugarcane through which he trudged.

Once he heard what he was certain was the trumpeting of an elephant. It made him believe, in his growing delirium, that he was in Africa—Africa, where he had never been. He hummed the hymn. Then he remembered he had read somewhere that the resort maintained an elephant in the bush. But he did not want to meet it, so he decided to stay where he was and wait for morning. All night he talked to Gillian, joked and sang hymns with her. He saved her again and again and they were together.

In the morning, when the sun rose fresh and full of promise, he set out for the Irish bar in Soufrière. He thought that they might overstand him there.

1996

ELIZABETH STROUT

b. 1956

Elizabeth Strout was born in Portland, Maine and spent her childhood in small towns in Maine and New Hampshire. Strout conceived of herself as a writer from an early age and went on to major in English Literature at Bates College in Maine. Upon graduating, she earned a law degree and a Certificate in Gerontology from Syracuse University. Following a brief stint working for Legal Services, Strout moved to New York City to become a professor and devote herself to writing. She now divides her time between New York and Maine. Strout's writing reflects her abiding love for nature, her compassionate insight into human character, and her ability, as described by *The New Yorker*, to "animate the ordinary with astonishing force." Her short stories have appeared in *The New Yorker*, a variety of literary magazines, and *The Best American Short Stories 2013*. Her novels include the bestsellers *Amy and Isabelle* (1998), *Abide with Me* (2006), and *The Burgess Boys* (2013). In 2009, she won the Pulitzer Prize for *Olive Kitteridge*, a novel in stories, taking place in a rural Maine town, the first of which, "Pharmacy," appears here.

Pharmacy

For many years Henry Kitteridge was a pharmacist in the next town over, driving every morning on snowy roads, or rainy roads, or summertime roads, when the wild raspberries shot their new growth in brambles along the last section of town before he turned off to where the wider road led to the pharmacy. Retired now, he still wakes early and remembers how mornings used to be his favorite, as though the world were his secret, tires rumbling softly beneath him and the light emerging through the early fog, the brief sight of the bay off to his right, then the pines, tall and slender, and almost always he rode with the window partly open because he loved the smell of the pines and the heavy salt air, and in the winter he loved the smell of the cold.

The pharmacy was a small two-story building attached to another building that housed separately a hardware store and a small grocery. Each morning Henry parked in the back by the large metal bins, and then entered the pharmacy's back door, and went about switching on the lights, turning up the thermostat, or, if it was summer, getting the fans going. He would open the safe, put money in the register, unlock the front door, wash his hands, put on his white lab coat. The ritual was pleasing, as though the old store—with its shelves of toothpaste, vitamins, cosmetics, hair adornments, even sewing needles and greeting cards, as well as red rubber hot water bottles, enema pumps—was a person altogether steady and steadfast. And any unpleasant-ness that may have occurred back in his home, any uneasiness at the way his wife often left their bed to wander through their home in the night's dark hours—all this receded like a shoreline as he walked through the safety of his pharmacy. Standing in the back, with the drawers and rows of pills, Henry was cheerful when the phone began to ring, cheerful when Mrs. Merriman came for her blood pressure medicine, or old Cliff Mott arrived for his digi-talis, cheerful when he prepared the Valium for Rachel Jones, whose husband ran off the night their baby was born. It was Henry's nature to listen, and many times during the week he would say, "Gosh, I'm awful sorry to hear that," or "Say, isn't that something?"

Inwardly, he suffered the quiet trepidations of a man who had witnessed twice in childhood the nervous breakdowns of a mother who had otherwise cared for him with stridency. And so if, as rarely happened, a customer was distressed over a price, or irritated by the quality of an Ace bandage or ice pack, Henry did what he could to rectify things quickly. For many years Mrs. Granger worked for him; her husband was a lobster fisherman, and she seemed to carry with her the cold breeze of the open water, not so eager to please a wary customer. He had to listen with half an ear as he filled prescrip-tions, to make sure she was not at the cash register dismissing a complaint. More than once he was reminded of that same sensation in watching to see that his wife, Olive, did not bear down too hard on Christopher over a home-work assignment or a chore left undone; that sense of his attention hovering—the need to keep everyone content. When he heard a briskness in Mrs. Granger's voice, he would step down from his back post, moving toward the center of the store to talk with the customer himself. Otherwise, Mrs. Granger did her job well. He appreciated that she was not chatty, kept perfect inven-tory, and almost never called in sick. That she died in her sleep one night astonished him, and left him with some feeling of responsibility, as though he had missed, working alongside her for years, whatever symptom might have shown itself that he, handling his pills and syrups and syringes, could have fixed.

"Mousy," his wife said, when he hired the new girl. "Looks just like a mouse."

Denise Thibodeau had round cheeks, and small eyes that peeped through her brown-framed glasses. "But a nice mouse," Henry said. "A cute one."

"No one's cute who can't stand up straight," Olive said. It was true that Denise's narrow shoulders sloped forward, as though apologizing for some-thing. She was twenty-two, just out of the state university of Vermont. Her hus-band was also named Henry, and Henry Kitteridge, meeting Henry Thibodeau for the first time, was taken with what he saw as an unself-conscious excel-lence. The young man was vigorous and sturdy-featured with a light in his eye that seemed to lend a flickering resplendence to his decent, ordinary face. He was a plumber, working in a business owned by his uncle. He and Denise had been married one year.

"Not keen on it," Olive said, when he suggested they have the young couple to dinner. Henry let it drop. This was a time when his son—not yet showing the physical signs of adolescence—had become suddenly and strenuously sul-len, his mood like a poison shot through the air, and Olive seemed as changed and changeable as Christopher, the two having fast and furious fights that became just as suddenly some blanket of silent intimacy where Henry, clueless, stupefied, would find himself to be the odd man out.

But standing in the back parking lot at the end of a late summer day, while he spoke with Denise and Henry Thibodeau, and the sun tucked itself behind the spruce trees, Henry Kitteridge felt such a longing to be in the presence of this young couple, their faces turned to him with a diffident but eager interest as he recalled his own days at the university many years ago, that he said, "Now, say. Olive and I would like you to come for supper soon."

He drove home, past the tall pines, past the glimpse of the bay, and thought of the Thibodeaus driving the other way, to their trailer on the outskirts of town. He pictured the trailer, cozy and picked up—for Denise was neat in her habits—and imagined them sharing the news of their day. Denise might say, "He's an easy boss." And Henry might say, "Oh, I like the guy a lot."

He pulled into his driveway, which was not a driveway so much as a patch of lawn on top of the hill, and saw Olive in the garden. "Hello, Olive," he said, walking to her. He wanted to put his arms around her, but she had a darkness that seemed to stand beside her like an acquaintance that would not go away. He told her the Thibodeaus were coming for supper. "It's only right," he said.

Olive wiped sweat from her upper lip, turned to rip up a clump of onion grass. "Then that's that, Mr. President," she said. "Give your order to the cook."

On Friday night the couple followed him home, and the young Henry shook Olive's hand. "Nice place here," he said. "With that view of the water. Mr. Kitteridge says you two built this yourselves."

"Indeed, we did."

Christopher sat sideways at the table, slumped in adolescent gracelessness, and did not respond when Henry Thibodeau asked him if he played any sports at school. Henry Kitteridge felt an unexpected fury sprout inside him; he wanted to shout at the boy, whose poor manners, he felt, revealed something unpleasant not expected to be found in the Kitteridge home.

"When you work in a pharmacy," Olive told Denise, setting before her a plate of baked beans, "you learn the secrets of everyone in town." Olive sat down across from her, pushed forward a bottle of ketchup. "Have to know to keep your mouth shut. But seems like you know how to do that."

"Denise understands," Henry Kitteridge said.

Denise's husband said, "Oh, sure. You couldn't find someone more trustworthy than Denise."

"I believe you," Henry said, passing the man a basket of rolls. "And please. Call me Henry. One of my favorite names," he added. Denise laughed quietly; she liked him, he could see this.

Christopher slumped farther into his seat.

Henry Thibodeau's parents lived on a farm inland, and so the two Henrys discussed crops, and pole beans, and the corn not being as sweet this summer from the lack of rain, and how to get a good asparagus bed.

"Oh, for God's *sake*," said Olive, when, in passing the ketchup to the young man, Henry Kitteridge knocked it over, and ketchup lurched out like thickened blood across the oak table. Trying to pick up the bottle, he caused it to roll unsteadily, and ketchup ended up on his fingertips, then on his white shirt.

"Leave it," Olive commanded, standing up. "Just leave it alone, Henry. For God's sake." And Henry Thibodeau, perhaps at the sound of his own name being spoken sharply, sat back, looking stricken.

"Gosh, what a mess I've made," Henry Kitteridge said.

For dessert they were each handed a blue bowl with a scoop of vanilla ice cream sliding in its center. "Vanilla's my favorite," Denise said.

"Is it," said Olive.

"Mine, too," Henry Kitteridge said.

As autumn came, the mornings darker, and the pharmacy getting only a short sliver of the direct sun before it passed over the building and left the store lit by its own overhead lights, Henry stood in the back filling the small plastic bottles, answering the telephone, while Denise stayed up front near the cash register. At lunchtime, she unwrapped a sandwich she brought from home, and ate it in the back where the storage was, and then he would eat his lunch, and sometimes when there was no one in the store, they would linger with a cup of coffee bought from the grocer next door. Denise seemed a naturally quiet girl, but she was given to spurts of sudden talkativeness. "My mother's had MS for years, you know, so starting way back we all learned to help out. All three of my brothers are different. Don't you think it's funny when it happens that way?" The oldest brother, Denise said, straightening a bottle of shampoo, had been her father's favorite until he'd married a girl her father didn't like. Her own in-laws were wonderful, she said. She'd had a boyfriend before Henry, a Protestant, and his parents had not been so kind to her. "It wouldn't have worked out," she said, tucking a strand of hair behind her ear.

"Well, Henry's a terrific young man," Henry answered.

She nodded, smiling through her glasses like a thirteen-year-old girl. Again, he pictured her trailer, the two of them like overgrown puppies tumbling together; he could not have said why this gave him the particular kind of happiness it did, like liquid gold being poured through him.

She was as efficient as Mrs. Granger had been, but more relaxed. "Right beneath the vitamins in the second aisle," she would tell a customer. "Here, I'll show you." Once, she told Henry she sometimes let a person wander around the store before asking if she could help them. "That way, see, they might find something they didn't know they needed. And your sales will go up." A block of winter sun was splayed across the glass of the cosmetics shelf; a strip of wooden floor shone like honey.

He raised his eyebrows appreciatively. "Lucky for me, Denise, when you came through that door." She pushed up her glasses with the back of her hand, then ran the duster over the ointment jars.

Jerry McCarthy, the boy who delivered the pharmaceuticals once a week from Portland—or more often if needed—would sometimes have his lunch in the back room. He was eighteen, right out of high school; a big, fat kid with a smooth face, who perspired so much that splotches of his shirt would be wet, at times even down over his breasts, so the poor fellow looked to be lactating. Seated on a crate, his big knees practically to his ears, he'd eat a sandwich that had spilling from it mayonnaisey clumps of egg salad or tuna fish, landing on his shirt.

More than once Henry saw Denise hand him a paper towel. "That happens to me," Henry heard her say one day. "Whenever I eat a sandwich that isn't just cold cuts, I end up a mess." It couldn't have been true. The girl was neat as a pin, if plain as a plate.

"Good afternoon," she'd say when the telephone rang. "This is the Village Pharmacy. How can I help you today?" Like a girl playing grown-up.

And then: On a Monday morning when the air in the pharmacy held a sharp chill, he went about opening up the store, saying, "How was your weekend, Denise?" Olive had refused to go to church the day before, and Henry, uncharacteristically, had spoken to her sharply. "Is it too much to ask," he had found himself saying, as he stood in the kitchen in his undershorts, ironing his trousers. "A man's wife accompanying him to church?" Going without her seemed a public exposure of familial failure.

"Yes, it most certainly is too goddamn much to ask!" Olive had almost spit, her fury's door flung open. "You have no idea how tired I am, teaching all day, going to foolish meetings where the goddamn principal is a moron! Shopping. Cooking. Ironing. Laundry. Doing Christopher's homework with him! And *you*—" She had grabbed on to the back of a dining room chair, and her dark hair, still uncombed from its night's disarrangement, had fallen across her eyes. "*You*, Mr. Head Deacon Claptrap Nice Guy, expect me to give up my Sunday mornings and go sit among a bunch of snot-wots!" Very suddenly she had sat down in the chair. "Well, I'm sick and tired of it," she'd said, calmly. "Sick to death."

A darkness had rumbled through him; his soul was suffocating in tar. The next morning, Olive spoke to him conversationally. "Jim's car smelled like upchuck last week. Hope he's cleaned it out." Jim O'Casey taught with Olive, and for years took both Christopher and Olive to school.

"Hope so," said Henry, and in that way their fight was done.

"Oh, I had a wonderful weekend," said Denise, her small eyes behind her glasses looking at him with an eagerness that was so childlike it could have cracked his heart in two. "We went to Henry's folks and dug potatoes at night. Henry put the headlights on from the car and we dug potatoes. Finding the potatoes in that cold soil—like an Easter egg hunt!"

He stopped unpacking a shipment of penicillin, and stepped down to talk to her. There were no customers yet, and below the front window the radiator hissed. He said, "Isn't that lovely, Denise."

She nodded, touching the top of the vitamin shelf beside her. A small motion of fear seemed to pass over her face. "I got cold and went and sat in the car and watched Henry digging potatoes, and I thought: It's too good to be true."

He wondered what in her young life had made her not trust happiness; perhaps her mother's illness. He said, "You enjoy it, Denise. You have many years of happiness ahead." Or maybe, he thought, returning to the boxes, it was part of being Catholic—you were made to feel guilty about everything.

The year that followed—was it the happiest year of his own life? He often thought so, even knowing that such a thing was foolish to claim about any year of one's life; but in his memory, that particular year held the sweetness of a time that contained no thoughts of a beginning and no thoughts of an end, and when he drove to the pharmacy in the early morning darkness of winter, then later in the breaking light of spring, the full-throated summer opening before him, it was the small pleasures of his work that seemed in their simplicities to fill him to the brim. When Henry Thibodeau drove into the gravelly lot, Henry Kitteridge often went to hold the door open for Denise, calling out, "Hello there, Henry," and Henry Thibodeau would stick his head through the open car window and call back, "Hello there, Henry," with a big grin on a face lit with decency and humor. Sometimes there was just a salute. "Henry!" And the other Henry would return, "Henry!" They got a kick out of this, and Denise, like a football tossed gently between them, would duck into the store.

When she took off her mittens, her hands were as thin as a child's, yet when she touched the buttons on the cash register, or slid something into a white bag, they assumed the various shapes of a graceful grown woman's hands, hands—thought Henry—that would touch her husband lovingly, that would, with the quiet authority of a woman, someday pin a baby's diaper, smooth a fevered forehead, tuck a gift from the tooth fairy under a pillow.

Watching her, as she poked her glasses back up onto her nose while reading over the list of inventory, Henry thought she was the stuff of America, for this was back when the hippie business was beginning, and reading in *Newsweek* about the marijuana and "free love" could cause an unease in Henry that one look at Denise dispelled. "We're going to hell like the Romans," Olive said triumphantly. "America's a big cheese gone rotten." But Henry would not stop believing that the temperate prevailed, and in his pharmacy, every day he worked beside a girl whose only dream was to someday make a family with her husband. "I don't care about Women's Lib," she told Henry. "I want to have a house and make beds." Still, if he'd had a daughter (he would have loved a daughter), he would have cautioned her against it. He would have said: Fine, make beds, but find a way to keep using your head. But Denise was not his daughter, and he told her it was noble to be a homemaker—vaguely aware of the freedom that accompanied caring for someone with whom you shared no blood.

He loved her guilelessness, he loved the purity of her dreams, but this did not mean of course that he was in love with her. The natural reticence of her in fact caused him to desire Olive with a new wave of power. Olive's sharp opinions, her full breasts, her stormy moods and sudden, deep laughter unfolded within him a new level of aching eroticism, and sometimes when he was heaving in the dark of night, it was not Denise who came to mind but, oddly, her strong, young husband—the fierceness of the young man as he gave way to the animalism of possession—and there would be for Henry Kitteridge a flash of incredible frenzy as though in the act of loving his wife he was joined with all men in loving the world of women, who contained the dark, mossy secret of the earth deep within them.

"Goodness," Olive said, when he moved off her.

In college, Henry Thibodeau had played football, just as Henry Kitteridge had. "Wasn't it great?" the young Henry asked him one day. He had arrived early to pick Denise up, and had come into the store. "Hearing the people yelling from the stands? Seeing that pass come right at you and knowing you're going to catch it? Oh boy, I loved that." He grinned, his clear face seeming to give off a refracted light. "Loved it."

"I suspect I wasn't nearly as good as you," said Henry Kitteridge. He had been good at the running, the ducking, but he had not been aggressive enough to be a really good player. It shamed him to remember that he had felt fear at every game. He'd been glad enough when his grades slipped and he had to give it up.

"Ah, I wasn't that good," said Henry Thibodeau, rubbing a big hand over his head. "I just liked it."

"He was good," said Denise, getting her coat on. "He was really good. The cheerleaders had a cheer just for him." Shyly, with pride, she said, "Let's *go*, Thibodeau, let's *go*."

Heading for the door, Henry Thibodeau said, "Say, we're going to have you and Olive for dinner soon."

"Oh, now—you're not to worry."

Denise had written Olive a thank-you note in her neat, small handwriting. Olive had scanned it, flipped it across the table to Henry. "Handwriting's just as cautious as she is," Olive had said. "She is the *plainest* child I have ever seen. With her pale coloring, why does she wear gray and beige?"

"I don't know," he said, agreeably, as though he had wondered himself. He had not wondered.

"A simpleton," Olive said.

But Denise was not a simpleton. She was quick with numbers, and remembered everything she was told by Henry about the pharmaceuticals he sold. She had majored in animal sciences at the university, and was conversant with molecular structures. Sometimes on her break she would sit on a crate in the back room with the Merck Manual on her lap. Her child-face, made serious by her glasses, would be intent on the page, her knees poked up, her shoulders slumped forward.

Cute, would go through his mind as he glanced through the doorway on his way by. He might say, "Okay, then, Denise?"

"Oh, yeah, I'm fine."

His smile would linger as he arranged his bottles, typed up labels. Denise's nature attached itself to his as easily as aspirin attached itself to the enzyme COX-2; Henry moved through his day pain free. The sweet hissing of the radiators, the tinkle of the bell when someone came through the door, the creaking of the wooden floors, the ka-*ching* of the register: He sometimes thought in those days that the pharmacy was like a healthy autonomic nervous system in a workable, quiet state.

Evenings, adrenaline poured through him. "All I do is cook and clean and pick up after people," Olive might shout, slamming a bowl of beef stew before him. "People just waiting for me to serve them, with their faces hanging out." Alarm made his arms tingle.

"Perhaps you need to help out more around the house," he told Christopher.

"How dare you tell him what to do? You don't even pay enough attention to know what he's going through in social studies class!" Olive shouted this at him while Christopher remained silent, a smirk on his face. "Why, Jim O'Casey is more sympathetic to the kid than you are," Olive said. She slapped a napkin down hard against the table.

"Jim teaches at the school, for crying out loud, and sees you and Chris every day. What *is* the matter with social studies class?"

"Only that the goddamn teacher is a moron, which Jim understands instinctively," Olive said. "You see Christopher every day, too. But you don't know anything because you're safe in your little world with Plain Jane."

"She's a good worker," Henry answered. But in the morning the blackness of Olive's mood was often gone, and Henry would be able to drive to work with a renewal of the hope that had seemed evanescent the night before. In the pharmacy there was goodwill toward men.

Denise asked Jerry McCarthy if he planned on going to college. "I dunno. Don't think so." The boy's face colored—perhaps he had a little crush on Denise, or perhaps he felt like a child in her presence, a boy still living at home, with his chubby wrists and belly.

"Take a night course," Denise said, brightly. "You can sign up right after Christmas. Just one course. You should do that." Denise nodded, and looked at Henry, who nodded back.

"It's true, Jerry," Henry said, who had never given a great deal of thought to the boy. "What is it that interests you?"

The boy shrugged his big shoulders.

"Something must interest you."

"This stuff." The boy gestured toward the boxes of packed pills he had recently brought through the back door.

And so, amazingly, he had signed up for a science course, and when he received an A that spring, Denise said, "Stay right there." She returned from the grocery store with a little boxed cake, and said, "Henry, if the phone doesn't ring, we're going to celebrate."

Pushing cake into his mouth, Jerry told Denise he had gone to mass the Sunday before to pray he did well on the exam.

This was the kind of thing that surprised Henry about Catholics. He almost said, God didn't get an A for you, Jerry; you got it for yourself, but Denise was saying, "Do you go every Sunday?"

The boy looked embarrassed, sucked frosting from his finger. "I will now," he said, and Denise laughed, and Jerry did, too, his face pink and glowing.

Autumn now, November, and so many years later that when Henry runs a comb through his hair on this Sunday morning, he has to pluck some strands of gray from the black plastic teeth before slipping the comb back into his pocket. He gets a fire going in the stove for Olive before he goes off to church. "Bring home the gossip," Olive says to him, tugging at her sweater while she peers into a large pot where apples are burbling in a stew. She is making applesauce from the season's last apples, and the smell reaches him briefly— sweet, familiar, it tugs at some ancient longing—before he goes out the door in his tweed jacket and tie.

"Do my best," he says. No one seems to wear a suit to church anymore.

In fact, only a handful of the congregation goes to church regularly anymore. This saddens Henry, and worries him. They have been through two ministers in the last five years, neither one bringing much inspiration to the pulpit. The current fellow, a man with a beard, and who doesn't wear a robe, Henry suspects won't last long. He is young with a growing family, and will have to move on. What worries Henry about the paucity of the congregation is that perhaps others have felt what he increasingly tries to deny—that this weekly gathering provides no real sense of comfort. When they bow their heads or sing a hymn, there is no sense anymore—for Henry—that God's presence is blessing them. Olive herself has become an unapologetic atheist. He does not know when this happened. It was not true when they were first married; they had talked of animal dissections in their college biology class, how the system of respiration alone was miraculous, a *creation* by a splendid power.

He drives over the dirt road, turning onto the paved road that will take him into town. Only a few leaves of deep red remain on the otherwise bare limbs of the maples; the oak leaves are russet and wrinkled; briefly through the trees is the glimpse of the bay, flat and steel-gray today with the overcast November sky.

He passes by where the pharmacy used to be. In its place now is a large chain drugstore with huge glass sliding doors, covering the ground where both the old pharmacy and grocery store stood, large enough so that the back parking lot where Henry would linger with Denise by the dumpster at day's end before getting into their separate cars—all this is now taken over by a store that sells not only drugs, but huge rolls of paper towels and boxes of all sizes of garbage bags. Even plates and mugs can be bought there, spatulas, cat food. The trees off to the side have been cut down to make a parking lot. You get used to things, he thinks, without getting used to things.

It seems a very long time ago that Denise stood shivering in the winter cold before finally getting into her car. How young she was! How painful to remember the bewilderment on her young face; and yet he can still remember how he could make her smile. Now, so far away in Texas—so far away it's a different country—she is the age he was then. She had dropped a red mitten one night; he had bent to get it, held the cuff open and watched while she'd slipped her small hand in.

The white church sits near the bare maple trees. He knows why he is thinking of Denise with this keenness. Her birthday card to him did not arrive last week, as it has, always on time, for the last twenty years. She writes him a note with the card. Sometimes a line or two stands out, as in the one last year when she mentioned that Paul, a freshman in high school, had become obese. Her word. "Paul has developed a full-blown problem now—at three hundred pounds, he is obese." She does not mention what she or her husband will do about this, if in fact they can "do" anything. The twin girls, younger, are both athletic and starting to get phone calls from boys "which horrifies me," Denise wrote. She never signs the card "love," just her name in her small neat hand, "Denise."

In the gravel lot by the church, Daisy Foster has just stepped from her car, and her mouth opens in a mock look of surprise and pleasure, but the pleasure is real, he knows—Daisy is always glad to see him. Daisy's husband died two years ago, a retired policeman who smoked himself to death, twenty-five years older than Daisy; she remains ever lovely, ever gracious with her kind blue eyes. What will become of her, Henry doesn't know. It seems to Henry, as he takes his seat in his usual middle pew, that women are far braver than men. The possibility of Olive's dying and leaving him alone gives him glimpses of horror he can't abide.

And then his mind moves back to the pharmacy that is no longer there.

"Henry's going hunting this weekend," Denise said one morning in November. "Do you hunt, Henry?" She was getting the cash drawer ready and didn't look up at him.

"Used to," Henry answered. "Too old for it now." The one time in his youth when he had shot a doe, he'd been sickened by the way the sweet, startled animal's head had swayed back and forth before its thin legs had folded and it had fallen to the forest floor. "Oh, you're a softie," Olive had said.

"Henry goes with Tony Kuzio." Denise slipped the cash drawer into the register, and stepped around to arrange the breath mints and gum that were neatly laid out by the front counter. "His best friend since he was five."

"And what does Tony do now?"

"Tony's married with two little kids. He works for Midcoast Power, and fights with his wife." Denise looked over at Henry. "Don't say that I said so."

"No."

"She's tense a lot, and yells. Boy, I wouldn't want to live like that."

"No, it'd be no way to live."

The telephone rang and Denise, turning on her toe playfully, went to answer it. "The Village Pharmacy. Good morning. How may I help you?" A pause. "Oh, yes, we have multivitamins with no iron. . . . You're very welcome."

On lunch break, Denise told the hefty, baby-faced Jerry, "My husband talked about Tony the whole time we were going out. The scrapes they'd get into when they were kids. Once, they went off and didn't get back till way after dark, and Tony's mother said to him, 'I was so worried, Tony. I could kill you.'" Denise picked lint off the sleeve of her gray sweater. "I always thought that was funny. Worrying that your child might be dead and then saying you'll kill him."

"You wait," Henry Kitteridge said, stepping around the boxes Jerry had brought into the back room. "From their very first fever, you never stop worrying."

"I can't wait," Denise said, and for the first time it occurred to Henry that soon she would have children and not work for him anymore.

Unexpectedly Jerry spoke. "Do you like him? Tony? You two get along?"

"I do like him," Denise said. "Thank goodness. I was scared enough to meet him. Do you have a best friend from childhood?"

"I guess," Jerry said, color rising in his fat, smooth cheeks. "But we kind of went our separate ways."

"My best friend," said Denise, "when we got to junior high school, she got kind of fast. Do you want another soda?"

A Saturday at home: Lunch was crabmeat sandwiches, grilled with cheese. Christopher was putting one into his mouth, but the telephone rang, and Olive went to answer it. Christopher, without being asked, waited, the sandwich held in his hand. Henry's mind seemed to take a picture of that moment, his son's instinctive deference at the very same time they heard Olive's voice in the next room. "Oh, you poor child," she said, in a voice Henry would always remember—filled with such dismay that all her outer Olive-ness seemed stripped away. "You poor, poor child."

And then Henry rose and went into the other room, and he didn't remember much, only the tiny voice of Denise, and then speaking for a few moments to her father-in-law.

The funeral was held in the Church of the Holy Mother of Contrition, three hours away in Henry Thibodeau's hometown. The church was large and dark with its huge stained-glass windows, the priest up front in a layered white robe, swinging incense back and forth; Denise already seated in the front near her parents and sisters by the time Olive and Henry arrived. The casket was closed, and had been closed at the wake the evening before. The church was almost full. Henry, seated next to Olive toward the back, recognized no one, until a silent large presence made him look up, and there was Jerry McCarthy. Henry and Olive moved over to make room for him.

Jerry whispered, "I read about it in the paper," and Henry briefly rested a hand on the boy's fat knee.

The service went on and on; there were readings from the Bible, and other readings, and then an elaborate getting ready for Communion. The priest took cloths and unfolded them and draped them over a table, and then people were leaving their seats aisle by aisle to go up and kneel and open their mouths for a wafer, all sipping from the same large silver goblet, while Henry and Olive stayed where they were. In spite of the sense of unreality that had descended over Henry, he was struck with the unhygienic nature of all these people sipping from the same cup, and struck—with cynicism—at how the priest, after everyone else was done, tilted his beaky head back and drank whatever drops were left.

Six young men carried the casket down the center aisle. Olive nudged Henry with her elbow, and Henry nodded. One of the pallbearers—one of the last ones—had a face that was so white and stunned that Henry was afraid he would drop the casket. This was Tony Kuzio, who, thinking Henry Thibodeau was a deer in the early morning darkness just a few days ago, had pulled the trigger of his rifle and killed his best friend.

Who was to help her? Her father lived far upstate in Vermont with a wife who was an invalid, her brothers and their wives lived hours away, her in-laws were immobilized by grief. She stayed with her in-laws for two weeks, and when she came back to work, she told Henry she couldn't stay with them much longer; they were kind, but she could hear her mother-in-law weeping all night, and it gave her the willies; she needed to be alone so she could cry by herself.

"Of course you do, Denise."

"But I can't go back to the trailer."

"No."

That night he sat up in bed, his chin resting on both hands. "Olive," he said, "the girl is utterly helpless. Why, she can't drive a car, and she's never written a check."

"How can it be," said Olive, "that you grow up in Vermont and can't even drive a car?"

"I don't know," Henry acknowledged. "I had no idea she couldn't drive a car."

"Well, I can see why Henry married her. I wasn't sure at first. But when I got a look at his mother at the funeral—ah, poor thing. But she didn't seem to have a bit of oomph to her."

"Well, she's about broken with grief."

"I understand that," Olive said patiently. "I'm simply telling you he married his mother. Men do." After a pause. "Except for you."

"She's going to have to learn to drive," Henry said. "That's the first thing. And she needs a place to live."

"Sign her up for driving school."

Instead, he took her in his car along the back dirt roads. The snow had arrived, but on the roads that led down to the water, the fishermen's trucks had flattened it. "That's right. Slowly up on the clutch." The car bucked like a wild horse, and Henry put his hand against the dashboard.

"Oh, I'm sorry," Denise whispered.

"No, no. You're doing fine."

"I'm just scared. Gosh."

"Because it's brand-new. But, Denise, *nitwits* can drive cars."

She looked at him, a sudden giggle coming from her, and he laughed himself then, without wanting to, while her giggle grew, spilling out so that tears came to her eyes, and she had to stop the car and take the white handkerchief he offered. She took her glasses off and he looked out the window the other way while she used the handkerchief. Snow had made the woods alongside the road seem like a picture in black and white. Even the evergreens seemed dark, spreading their boughs above the black trunks.

"Okay," said Denise. She started the car again; again he was thrown forward. If she burned out the clutch, Olive would be furious.

"That's perfectly all right," he told Denise. "Practice makes perfect, that's all."

In a few weeks, he drove her to Augusta, where she passed the driving test, and then he went with her to buy a car. She had money for this. Henry Thibodeau, it turned out, had had a good life insurance policy, so at least there was that. Now Henry Kitteridge helped her get the car insurance, explained how to make the payments. Earlier, he had taken her to the bank, and for the first time in her life she had a checking account. He had shown her how to write a check.

He was appalled when she mentioned at work one day the amount of money she had sent the Church of the Holy Mother of Contrition, to ensure that candles were lit for Henry every week, a mass said for him each month. He said, "Well, that's nice, Denise." She had lost weight, and when, at the end of the day, he stood in the darkened parking lot, watching from beneath one of the lights on the side of the building, he was struck by the image of her anxious head peering over the steering wheel; and as he got into his own car, a sadness shuddered through him that he could not shake all night.

"What in hell ails you?" Olive said.

"Denise," he answered. "She's helpless."

"People are never as helpless as you think they are," Olive answered. She added, clamping a cover over a pot on the stove, "God, I was afraid of this."

"Afraid of what?"

"Just take the damn dog out," Olive said. "And sit yourself down to supper."

An apartment was found in a small new complex outside of town. Denise's father-in-law and Henry helped her move her few things in. The place was on the ground floor and didn't get much light. "Well, it's clean," Henry said to Denise, watching her open the refrigerator door, the way she stared at the complete emptiness of its new insides. She only nodded, closing the door. Quietly, she said, "I've never lived alone before."

In the pharmacy he saw that she walked around in a state of unreality; he found his own life felt unbearable in a way he would never have expected. The force of this made no sense. But it alarmed him; mistakes could be made. He forgot to tell Cliff Mott to eat a banana for potassium, now that they'd added a diuretic with his digitalis. The Tibbets woman had a bad night with erythromycin; had he not told her to take it with food? He worked slowly, counting pills sometimes two or three times before he slipped them into their bottles, checking carefully the prescriptions he typed. At home, he looked at Olive wide-eyed when she spoke, so she would see she had his attention. But she did not have his attention. Olive was a frightening stranger; his son often seemed to be smirking at him. "Take the garbage out!" Henry shouted one night, after opening the cupboard beneath the kitchen sink, seeing a bag full of eggshells and dog hairs and balled-up waxed paper. "It's the only thing we ask you to do, and you can't even manage that!"

"Stop shouting," Olive told him. "Do you think that makes you a man? How absolutely pathetic."

Spring came. Daylight lengthened, melted the remaining snows so the roads were wet. Forsythias bloomed clouds of yellow into the chilly air, then rhododendrons screeched their red heads at the world. He pictured everything through Denise's eyes, and thought the beauty must be an assault. Passing by the Caldwells' farm, he saw a handwritten sign, FREE KITTENS, and he arrived at the pharmacy the next day with a kitty-litter box, cat food, and a small black kitten, whose feet were white, as though it had walked through a bowl of whipped cream.

"Oh, Henry," Denise cried, taking the kitten from him, tucking it to her chest. He felt immensely pleased.

Because it was such a young thing, Slippers spent the days at the pharmacy, where Jerry McCarthy was forced to hold it in his fat hand, against his sweat-stained shirt, saying to Denise, "Oh, yuh. Awful cute. That's nice," before Denise freed him of this little furry encumbrance, taking Slippers back, nuzzling her face against his, while Jerry watched, his thick, shiny lips slightly parted. Jerry had taken two more classes at the university, and had once again received A's in both. Henry and Denise congratulated him with the air of distracted parents; no cake this time.

She had spells of manic loquaciousness, followed by days of silence. Sometimes she stepped out the back door of the pharmacy, and returned with swollen eyes. "Go home early, if you need to," he told her. But she looked at him with panic. "No. Oh, gosh, no. I want to be right here."

It was a warm summer that year. He remembers her standing by the fan near the window, her thin hair flying behind her in little undulating waves, while she gazed through her glasses at the windowsill. Standing there for minutes at a time. She went, for a week, to see one of her brothers. Took another week to see her parents. "This is where I want to be," she said, when she came back.

"Where's she going to find another husband in this tiny town?" Olive asked.

"I don't know. I've wondered," Henry admitted.

"Someone else would go off and join the Foreign Legion, but she's not the type."

"No. She's not the type."

Autumn arrived, and he dreaded it. On the anniversary of Henry Thibodeau's death, Denise went to mass with her in-laws. He was relieved when that day was over, when a week went by, and another, although the holidays loomed, and he felt trepidation, as though he were carrying something that could not be set down. When the phone rang during supper one night, he went to get it with a sense of foreboding. He heard Denise make small screaming sounds—Slippers had gotten out of the house without her seeing, and planning to drive to the grocery store just now, she had run over the cat.

"Go," Olive said. "For God's sake. Go over and comfort your girlfriend."

"Stop it, Olive," Henry said. "That's unnecessary. She's a young widow who ran over her cat. Where in God's name is your compassion?" He was trembling.

"She wouldn't have run over any goddamn cat if you hadn't given it to her."

He brought with him a Valium. That night he sat on her couch, helpless while she wept. The urge to put his arm around her small shoulders was very strong, but he sat holding his hands together in his lap. A small lamp shone from the kitchen table. She blew her nose on his white handkerchief, and said, "Oh, Henry. Henry." He was not sure which Henry she meant. She looked up at him, her small eyes almost swollen shut; she had taken her glasses off to press the handkerchief to them. "I talk to you in my head all the time," she said. She put her glasses back on. "Sorry," she whispered.

"For what?"

"For talking to you in my head all the time."

"No, no."

He put her to bed like a child. Dutifully she went into the bathroom and changed into her pajamas, then lay in the bed with the quilt to her chin. He sat on the edge of the bed, smoothing her hair until the Valium took over. Her eyelids drooped, and she turned her head to the side, murmuring something he couldn't make out. As he drove home slowly along the narrow roads, the darkness seemed alive and sinister as it pressed against the car windows. He pictured moving far upstate, living in a small house with Denise. He could find work somewhere up north; she could have a child. A little girl who would adore him; girls adored their fathers.

"Well, widow-comforter, how is she?" Olive spoke in the dark from the bed.

"Struggling," he said.

"Who isn't."

The next morning he and Denise worked in an intimate silence. If she was up at the cash register and he was behind his counter, he could still feel the invisible presence of her against him, as though she had become Slippers, or he had—their inner selves brushing up against the other. At the end of the day, he said, "I will take care of you," his voice thick with emotion.

She stood before him, and nodded. He zipped her coat for her.

• • •

To this day he does not know what he was thinking. In fact, much of it he can't seem to remember. That Tony Kuzio paid her some visits. That she told Tony he must stay married, because if he divorced, he would never be able to marry in the church again. The piercing of jealousy and rage he felt to think of Tony sitting in Denise's little place late at night, begging her forgiveness. The feeling that he was drowning in cobwebs whose sticky maze was spinning about him. That he wanted Denise to continue to love him. And she did. He saw it in her eyes when she dropped a red mitten and he picked it up and held it open for her. *I talk to you in my head all the time.* The pain was sharp, exquisite, unbearable.

"Denise," he said one evening as they closed up the store. "You need some friends."

Her face flushed deeply. She put her coat on with a roughness to her gestures. "I have friends," she said, breathlessly.

"Of course you do. But here in town." He waited by the door until she got her purse from out back. "You might go square dancing at the Grange Hall. Olive and I used to go. It's a nice group of people."

She stepped past him, her face moist, the top of her hair passing by his eyes. "Or maybe you think that's square," he said in the parking lot, lamely.

"I am square," she said, quietly.

"Yes," he said, just as quietly. "I am too." As he drove home in the dark, he pictured being the one to take Denise to a Grange Hall dance. "Spin your partner, and promenade . . . ," her face breaking into a smile, her foot tapping, her small hands on her hips. No—it was not bearable, and he was really frightened now by the sudden emergence of anger he had inspired in her. He could do nothing for her. He could not take her in his arms, kiss her damp forehead, sleep beside her while she wore those little-girl flannel pajamas she'd worn the night Slippers died. To leave Olive was as unthinkable as sawing off his leg. In any event, Denise would not want a divorced Protestant; nor would he be able to abide her Catholicism.

They spoke to each other little as the days went by. He felt coming from her now an unrelenting coldness that was accusatory. What had he led her to expect? And yet when she mentioned a visit from Tony Kuzio, or made an elliptical reference to seeing a movie in Portland, an answering coldness arose in him. He had to grit his teeth not to say, "Too square to go square dancing, then?" How he hated that the words *lovers' quarrel* went through his head.

And then just as suddenly she'd say—ostensibly to Jerry McCarthy, who listened those days with a new comportment to his bulky self, but really she was speaking to Henry (he could see this in the way she glanced at him, holding her small hands together nervously)—"My mother, when I was very little, and before she got sick, would make special cookies for Christmas. We'd paint them with frosting and sprinkles. Oh, I think it was the most fun I ever had sometimes"—her voice wavering while her eyes blinked behind her glasses. And he would understand then that the death of her husband had caused her to feel the death of her girlhood as well; she was mourning the loss of the only *herself* she had ever known—gone now, to this new, bewildered young widow. His eyes, catching hers, softened.

Back and forth this cycle went. For the first time in his life as a pharmacist, he allowed himself a sleeping tablet, slipping one each day into the pocket of his trousers. "All set, Denise?" he'd say when it was time to close. Either she'd silently go get her coat, or she'd say, looking at him with gentleness, "All set, Henry. One more day."

Daisy Foster, standing now to sing a hymn, turns her head and smiles at him. He nods back and opens the hymnal. "A mighty fortress is our God, a bulwark never failing." The words, the sound of the few people singing, make him both hopeful and deeply sad. "You can learn to love someone," he had told Denise, when she'd come to him in the back of the store that spring day. Now, as he places the hymnal back in the holder in front of him, sits once more on the small pew, he thinks of the last time he saw her. They had come north to visit Jerry's parents, and they stopped by the house with the baby, Paul. What Henry remembers is this: Jerry saying something sarcastic about Denise falling asleep each night on the couch, sometimes staying there the whole night through. Denise turning away, looking out over the bay, her shoulders slumped, her small breasts just slightly pushing out against her thin turtleneck sweater, but she had a belly, as though a basketball had been cut in half and she'd swallowed it. No longer the girl she had been—no girl stayed a girl—but a mother, tired, and her round cheeks had deflated as her belly had expanded, so that already there was a look of the gravity of life weighing her down. It was at that point Jerry said sharply, "Denise, stand up straight. Put your shoulders back." He looked at Henry, shaking his head. "How many times do I keep telling her that?"

"Have some chowder," Henry said. "Olive made it last night." But they had to get going, and when they left, he said nothing about their visit, and neither did Olive, surprisingly. He would not have thought Jerry would grow into that sort of man, large, clean-looking—thanks to the ministrations of Denise—not even so much fat anymore, just a big man earning a big salary, speaking to his wife in a way Olive had sometimes spoken to Henry. He did not see her again, although she must have been in the region. In her birthday notes, she reported the death of her mother, then, a few years later, her father. Of course she would have driven north to go to the funerals. Did she think of him? Did she and Jerry stop and visit the grave of Henry Thibodeau?

"You're looking fresh as a daisy," he tells Daisy Foster in the parking lot outside the church. It is their joke; he has said it to her for years.

"How's Olive?" Daisy's blue eyes are still large and lovely, her smile ever present.

"Olive's fine. Home keeping the fires burning. And what's new with you?"

"I have a beau." She says this quietly, putting a hand to her mouth.

"Do you? Daisy, that's wonderful."

"Sells insurance in Heathwick during the day, and takes me dancing on Friday nights."

"Oh, that's wonderful," Henry says again. "You'll have to bring him around for supper."

"Why do you need everyone married?" Christopher has said to him angrily, when Henry has asked about his son's life. "Why can't you just leave people alone?"

He doesn't want people alone.

· · ·

At home, Olive nods to the table, where a card from Denise lies next to an African violet. "Came yesterday," Olive says. "I forgot."

Henry sits down heavily and opens it with his pen, finds his glasses, peers at it. Her note is longer than usual. She had a scare late in the summer. Pericardial effusion, which turned out to be nothing. "It changed me," she wrote, "as experiences do. It put all my priorities straight, and I have lived every day since then with the deepest gratitude for my family. Nothing matters except family and friends," she wrote, in her neat, small hand. "And I have been blessed with both."

The card, for the first time ever, was signed, "Love."

"How is she?" asks Olive, running water into the sink. Henry stares out at the bay, at the skinny spruce trees along the edge of the cove, and it seems beautiful to him, God's magnificence there in the quiet stateliness of the coastline and the slightly rocking water.

"She's fine," he answers. Not at the moment, but soon, he will walk over to Olive and put his hand on her arm. Olive, who has lived through her own sorrows. For he understood long ago—after Jim O'Casey's car went off the road, and Olive spent weeks going straight to bed after supper, sobbing harshly into a pillow—Henry understood then that Olive had loved Jim O'Casey, had possibly been loved by him, though Henry never asked her and she never told, just as he did not tell her of the gripping, sickening need he felt for Denise until the day she came to him to report Jerry's proposal, and he said: "Go."

He puts the card on the windowsill. He has wondered what it has felt like for her to write the words *Dear Henry*. Has she known other Henrys since then? He has no way of knowing. Nor does he know what happened to Tony Kuzio, or whether candles are still being lit for Henry Thibodeau in church.

Henry stands up, Daisy Foster fleeting through his mind, her smile as she spoke of going dancing. The relief that he just felt over Denise's note, that she is glad for the life that unfolded before her, gives way suddenly, queerly, into an odd sense of loss, as if something significant has been taken from him. "Olive," he says.

She must not hear him because of the water running into the sink. She is not as tall as she used to be, and is broader across her back. The water stops. "Olive," he says, and she turns. "You're not going to leave me, are you?"

"Oh, for God's sake, Henry. You could make a woman sick." She wipes her hands quickly on a towel.

He nods. How could he ever tell her—he could not—that all these years of feeling guilty about Denise have carried with them the kernel of still having her? He cannot even bear this thought, and in a moment it will be gone, dismissed as not true. For who could bear to think of himself this way, as a man deflated by the good fortune of others? No, such a thing is ludicrous.

"Daisy has a fellow," he says. "We need to have them over soon."

2008

LINDA SVENDSEN
b. 1954

Born in Vancouver, Svendsen attended the University of British Columbia before moving to New York to study for an M.F.A. at Columbia University. Even before she graduated, her story "Who He Slept By" won an *Atlantic Monthly* Short Story Contest, and after Columbia she won a Stegner Fellowship to study at Stanford University. Since then she has followed three careers simultaneously. Her fiction has appeared four times in the Best Canadian Stories series and three times in the O. Henry Prize Stories anthologies; her debut collection, *Marine Life* (1992), received wide critical acclaim. Svendsen is also a distinguished creative writing teacher at her undergraduate alma mater. And all along she has pursued her dream of writing screenplays. Svendsen's adaptation of *Marine Life* became a feature film in 2000, and she and her husband, writer-producer Brian McKeown, won a Peabody award for their mini-series *Human Cargo* in 2004. Her first novel, the political satire *Sussex Drive*, appeared in 2010.

Marine Life

In July I visit my mother and we drive directly from the bus station to a car wash, even though her Dodge shines. She likes the slow tracks engaging the wheels, the car in neutral, the thought of hot carnauba wax. An attendant collapses the aerial and tells her to keep her foot off the brake.

"It's like driving under the ocean," Mum says. "I knew the fins on this old Dodge were meant for something."

Mops swathe the car in suds and giant bristles hum above us, then drag across the hood, roof, and sides. Her hands droop over the steering column and she stares straight ahead, although she can't possibly see through the lathered glass. "Come here once a day sometimes," she confides.

"Why so often?"

"It's kind of fun." She winks at me. "It's dark."

An overhead vacuum dries the car after the rinse. We watch the drops of water creep unnaturally up the slope of the windshield and disappear. She tells me this vacuum will often draw a migraine out through her temples, and I mention the trick my husband knows, how Bill can gently press the circle of his mouth to my forehead and take away pain. We laugh about that.

In daylight again, she turns the ignition and we start towards home. "I wish they lasted longer," she says.

We sit on the patio and watch the sprinkler waver back and forth, into sun, into shade. I grew up on this patio. I flooded it in winter and practiced for Rink Cadettes, skating into dizziness. We sip ginger ale while waiting for supper to cook.

"Remember when you used to run through the sprinkler in your birthday suit?"

"Yup."

"Remember when you used to run through the sprinkler in Robert's galoshes?"

That was before they could afford a wading pool. Now my mother and stepfather, rich on credit, discuss installing a real pool in their backyard, even though summers are brief and mythical in Vancouver. The grandchildren might enjoy it.

"How do you feel, Adele?" She means my pregnancy.

"With my hands." I look over, but she doesn't get it. "Fine. I just want pizza all the time."

"Thought of names?"

"Not yet."

I'm visiting my mother because she wants me to learn mothering. She wants her intuition and skill to rub off on me somehow, as softly and easily as scented oil. And I ask her about delivery—should I be localized, should I keep a piece of the umbilical cord, take a bite of the umbilical cord, should there be music?

"Every birth is different," she begins, happy in authority. "You'll know when the time comes."

Mum's spine is shrinking and tightens like a wet braid. Our heights don't match anymore—I lean over slightly to see the haphazard part in her hair. Earlier, when we husked corn in the kitchen, she asked, "Adele, did you feel the floor tilt?" And I said no, but the fault line *did* extend as far north as Canada and we were overdue. "I lose my balance once in a while," she admitted, ripping a green sleeve. "It's the planet moving, I'm sure."

She is sixty-five, my stepfather fifty-three, and this difference pinches her sleep, her face. Each night before bed, her hands slippery with cold lanolin, she coaxes suppleness back into her skin. "I keep busy," she says proudly.

We listen to the lawn mowers. They sound like a small war in the distance.

Mum introduces me to her ceramics instructor. "This is my daughter Adele, who's going to be a mother, too," speaking as if conception is our family's unique personal achievement.

She shows me what she has made: two white antelope for the mantelpiece, mugs with the family's names—June, Robert, my sisters Irene and Joyce, my brother Ray—and Bill's and mine still to be sanded; a flowerpot in the shape of a hippopotamus, glazed shakers wobbly on chicken legs, a stork for Q-tips.

"Mum, have you ever tried to shape anything on a potter's wheel? Or throw clay?"

"No."

"Maybe you should try."

"I paint everything myself," she stresses. "That damn hippo took three days."

A group of schoolchildren trot over to the kiln. They've made an octopus family, plaques for the bathroom, and they want to test the bubbles that will be suspended above them. I turn around and notice my mother bending happily with the seven-year-olds, checking.

After supper one night I ask if she will play the piano. Mum plays without sheet music, from memory, songs with notes that sit far off upon the ledger lines. I always ask myself how her brain knows where every finger should pause. How she carried on a conversation about where my mittens might be when her hands were reaching for something else, some black key.

When I was younger she played for fashion shows, nurses' graduations, cocktail hours, cabarets. She gave out a card with a golden treble clef: *June Will Be Pleased to Play Your Request.* She dressed thematically and wore muumuus and thongs for tropical shows, a chocolate suit for funerals, and a tiny rhinestone tiara on New Year's Eve.

She signed contracts with Tiki Tai, Town and Country, Coconut Grove, and the Elks' Club. I knew these were not the Hollywood clubs written up in magazines, but I believed they were the hotspots of the Lower Mainland,[1] branches of a continental chain. It wasn't until I was older and could drive that I noticed these cabarets were out on the highways, parked on suburban edges. The Tiki Tai is now the O.K. Corral, the Town and Country topless, and the other two lost to fire.

After a certain age, I never knew aunts and uncles. I knew waitresses, chefs, managers, and sub drummers (my mother's steady drummer had recurrent heart attacks). She and Robert held dinner parties and invited staff, not other musicians or relatives. My brother, Ray, dated a coat-check girl my mother knew. She also introduced him to dancers in the Polynesian floor show, and it wasn't uncommon to see paper leis dangling from the knob of his closed door.

I went to drive-in movies with my stepfather while Mum played and played. We saw *The Manchurian Candidate, The L-Shaped Room,* and much of the *Flubber* series. We also played a word game on our way to pick her up, using the billboards and neon signs as the clues. Robert would say, for instance, What's a frisky pig? And I would scan the print in sight for the next two blocks and find Buckingham Cigarettes illuminated in bold letters above me and shout. Since we always drove the same route, the game eventually became predictable and we listened to call-in talk shows on the radio instead. The announcer said, "Hi, doll," to the women callers and listened to them complain about Gerda Munsinger, German spy, sleeping with Cabinet ministers. Robert started calling my mother Doll.

In 1965 her contract at the Simon Fraser Dining Room was not renewed. This gig was elegant, downtown, and Mum wept on her piano bench at home. An Oriental woman, Sue Kim or Kim Lu, had been hired and she was classical. Twenty-two.

"Let me be the man in the family," Robert said. "You don't have to work anymore."

"They think I'm old," she said.

---

1. That is, the region of British Columbia, east of Vancouver Island.

He made phone calls to the Musicians' Union and a rival dining room. Ray and I drove to the grocery in his convertible and bought smokes and doughnuts. He told me she cried for Robert's attention.

When we returned, Mum was practicing scales—majors, minors, chromatics—sliding up and down ivory, and she did this the whole afternoon.

Tonight she says, "You might have heard these before," and plays music to inspire labour: "I Can't Give You Anything But Love, Baby," "Yes Sir, That's My Baby," "Baby Face." She still has that touch.

"You're a tourist now," Mum declares, even though I was born and raised here. "You live up north."

"I don't live 'up north.' I live only one day away."

"Osoyoos is up north," she says, and decides to show off Vancouver. She won't let me drive, claims I'm not used to automatic, and I won't fit behind the steering wheel anyway.

We stop at the Planetarium and she selects a postcard for Bill, now working at the sky-watch site in Manitoba. She's found the Crab Nebula, a magnified photograph of space. "Send this to your stargazer," she suggests. We both write messages, each picking up the other's last word and carrying it a few phrases further.

"Why don't we go up the mountain and look at the view, Mum?" I say. "There's no fog."

She chooses the scenic route and we skirt the ocean—the nudists at my old haunt, Wreck Beach, and families at Locarno and Jericho. When we reach the north shore she can't locate the exact turn and makes lefts, a few rights, guessing randomly, even follows the sign with an arrow pointing straight up. "I thought I could drive here in my sleep," she says. "Are we even climbing uphill?"

"Yes." And we are. The car has geared down, the air is crisper, and I glimpse the snow on Grouse above us, but she is still lost. She won't accept my help.

My mother opts for a tall hill, closer to home and accessible. The view is less spectacular than broad, and she claims she can distinguish the Gulf Islands twenty miles distant. I can't see that far.

One evening Robert thumbs through my prenatal manual and finds it pretty funny. He puts mats on the grass and we try exercises together—Mum, him, and me—sprawling on our backs and hugging knees close to our foreheads. We inhale in unison and relax by isolating different areas of the body—wrists, thighs, shoulders—tightening and releasing. This exercise takes ten minutes done thoroughly and Robert ends up drowsing with his mouth open.

Mum and I go into the house and she hands me two needles caught in a fistful of soft wool. "He's knitting a bootie for you," she explains.

"For me?"

"For the baboo. And I'm doing its twin."

I can't believe it, can't picture his longshoring hands clicking needles. "Since when does he knit?"

"Since lately," she says. "Sometimes he's not tired when I conk out, so he decided there's not much difference between counting stitches or sheep." She adds, "I chose the pattern."

I get upstairs to bed before they do and hear them evaluating a new Toyota while doing dishes. Robert wipes and estimates their trade-in worth. Folding my hands on my stomach, I speak slowly to my baby. "Where you had little buds, you have arms and legs, my little tidal wave. And now you have eyelashes, and now you have toenails." I'm certain it can hear, only three months from birth, and my mother says it's sensitive to light; she's read babies can tell night and day before they see it.

I hear Mum turning on the news and then I worry about my tactless nerves carrying sensations, uncensored, to the amniotic fluid: a sadness while stroking my mother's roses; the shock when the phone rings because I hope it's Bill and that he's all right. I wonder what my baby might already know.

Mum wakes me. "It's a bad dream." Her hand shakes my shoulder. "Adele, it's all right."

I sit up and look at her, groggy and nightgowned, on the edge of the bed. I'm in my old room, unfamiliar without my trappings: a collection of starfish, books on shamanism; totem poles. It's the spare room now, bare except for ivy cuttings. "I'm not having a bad dream."

"I heard you," she says. "You were yelling in your sleep."

"Damn it, Mum. You woke me up." I settle back down.

"*You* woke me."

"It was probably a train whistle."

"It was you."

I'm certain it wasn't. I vaguely recall dreaming about Bill and me driving through Wyoming and think she's woken me on purpose.

"Come have a cup of tea," she offers. "You'll feel better."

We hobble downstairs in our slippers and prepare tea and cinnamon toast. She remembers when I used to fight with people in my sleep. How she and Robert would be turning off the lights, or tucking our dog into his basket with a biscuit, and I'd scream, "Shut up," or "Go to hell, you dumb cluck," and make Groucho bark.

"Who were you so mad at?"

I don't know. I'm tired and want to go back to bed, but she's awake and ready to chat—about Ray's common-law love, about a brunch she's booked to play for Job's Daughters,[2] how she must rehearse.

About 2 A.M. she fetches a small china box and places it before me. She opens it and spreads tiny molars and bicuspids and incisors on the table, beside our saucers, and tells me it's my first set of teeth.

"You're kidding," I say.

"No," she whispers. "I'll always keep your teeth."

The next morning Mum asks if I'll go to her swimming class. It's held at the same complex as her ceramics workshop. The recreation centre runs several programs for seniors and she takes square dancing as well. "Do-si-do," she calls to me, coming out of the bathroom, and back to back, we switch places.

Tomorrow I catch the bus to my home in the Interior. I realize I haven't called my sister Irene yet, Ray, my hermit father, and have spent all my time with her and Robert. I say, "Yes, I'll come to your lesson."

---

2. An international fraternal and service organization for young women, affiliated with the Masonic organization.

When my mother stopped playing seriously, I was in junior high school. Only time on my hands, she said, and volunteered for the Christmas concert, embarrassing me with the amount of hair spray she used. She appeared for the oil refinery field trip, an unwanted chaperone, and pouted when I didn't sit with her. "Someday you'll wish you could ride on a bus with your mother," she said to me as she squeezed by. Once, she offered to pick me up after school and go for a shake. I saw her car approaching and ducked behind a hedge, and waved her airily on when she slowed, anxious.

She shopped and brought home blouses with big perky bows or hats that would sell big in Antarctica, furry things I refused to wear, socks with toes, and then apologized. "I know my taste is all in my mouth," she said. Even last birthday, when she mailed Snoopy sheets, she wrote, "If you and Bill want to return them, I have the receipt."

She packs for her swimming class: a fluffy towel, hairdryer, shampoo and conditioner, bathing cap, a suit with her Floaters crest prominent on the abdomen, and unnecessary goggles. She hasn't yet learned how to put her head under water and keep her eyes open.

At the pool she entered the changing room with other older ladies. "Hello, June," they say. "Hot today." They enjoy this ritual of totebags and lockers and a teacher telling them what to do.

I watch Mum change. Her stomach is loose and her legs are scarred from vein stripping, thigh to heel. She struggles with her suit and I clasp it for her at the back.

"Adele, why don't you take a dip?"

The other ladies seem to agree it would be refreshing. "Don't exert yourself, though, honey." Mum asks the instructor about my shorts and tank top and she says they'll be okay. The water will be soothing.

The class won't pay attention at first. They bob up and down in the pool, comparing gardens and bantering about the odd-even sprinkling rules. Mum playfully flicks water in my direction.

The instructor has them do widths using a paddleboard. My mother kicks with the rest of them, slowly, and crosses the pool. Then they practice their frog kick. These older women, uneasy amphibians, are more of land than water. They roll in the small current they create, and some surrender to the swell and kick solely from the knee, forgetting the glide. Their bones are brittle. Break a leg when you're sixty and it may never mend. And so a few just turn over on their back and float.

They are supposed to learn the basics of the modified breaststroke today. Mum has mentioned it—how difficult it will be to coordinate arms, legs, and lungs. "As you glide, your chin lifts," the instructor explains, "and you inhale. Then, as you stroke, exhale."

I see my mother crossing the pool, going away from me; her breathing is erratic and rapid. The paddleboard supports her chest, but only her legs lend motion, as her arms reach out awkwardly. I'm nervous now: I realize we are all in the same water. I sense my baby drifting inside, and look at my mother, flailing towards the other side, and I am in between, some kind of lifeguard in the shallows.

1992

AMY TAN
b. 1952

Tan was born in Oakland, California, and educated at San Jose State University and the University of California at Berkeley. She has worked on programs for disabled children and as a reporter and businesswoman. Material for her widely popular fiction comes from the lives of Chinese-American women and the cultural ambivalence of their circumstances in the United States. Her novels are *The Joy Luck Club* (1989), *The Kitchen God's Wife* (1991), *The Hundred Secret Senses* (1995), *The Bonesetter's Daughter* (2001), *Saving Fish from Drowning* (2005) *Rules for Virgins* (2011), and *The Valley of Amazement* (2013). She has also published two books for children, *The Moon Lady* (1992) and *The Chinese Siamese Cat* (1994), and an essay collection, *The Opposite of Fate: A Book of Musings* (2003).

Rules of the Game

I was six when my mother taught me the art of invisible strength. It was a strategy for winning arguments, respect from others, and eventually, though neither of us knew it at the time, chess games.

"Bite back your tongue," scolded my mother when I cried loudly, yanking her hand toward the store that sold bags of salted plums. At home, she said, "Wise guy, he not go against wind. In Chinese we say, Come from South, blow with wind—poom!—North will follow. Strongest wind cannot be seen."

The next week I bit back my tongue as we entered the store with the forbidden candies. When my mother finished her shopping, she quietly plucked a small bag of plums from the rack and put it on the counter with the rest of the items.

My mother imparted her daily truths so she could help my older brothers and me rise above our circumstances. We lived in San Francisco's Chinatown. Like most of the other Chinese children who played in the back alleys of restaurants and curio shops, I didn't think we were poor. My bowl was always full, three five-course meals every day, beginning with a soup of mysterious things I didn't want to know the names of.

We lived on Waverly Place, in a warm, clean, two-bedroom flat that sat above a small Chinese bakery specializing in steamed pastries and dim sum.[1]

---

1. Variety of traditional Chinese foods served in small portions.

In the early morning, when the alley was still quiet, I could smell fragrant red beans as they were cooked down to a pasty sweetness. By daybreak, our flat was heavy with the odor of fried sesame balls and sweet curried chicken crescents. From my bed, I would listen as my father got ready for work, then locked the door behind him, one-two-three clicks.

At the end of our two-block alley was a small sandlot playground with swings and slides well-shined down the middle with use. The play area was bordered by wood-slat benches where old-country people sat cracking roasted watermelon seeds with their golden teeth and scattering the husks to an impatient gathering of gurgling pigeons. The best playground, however, was the dark alley itself. It was crammed with daily mysteries and adventures. My brothers and I would peer into the medicinal herb shop, watching old Li dole out onto a stiff sheet of white paper the right amount of insect shells, saffron-colored seeds, and pungent leaves for his ailing customers. It was said that he once cured a woman dying of an ancestral curse that had eluded the best of American doctors. Next to the pharmacy was a printer who specialized in gold-embossed wedding invitations and festive red banners.

Farther down the street was Ping Yuen Fish Market. The front window displayed a tank crowded with doomed fish and turtles struggling to gain footing on the slimy green-tiled sides. A hand-written sign informed tourists, "Within this store, is all for food, not for pet." Inside, the butchers with their bloodstained white smocks deftly gutted the fish while customers cried out their orders and shouted, "Give me your freshest," to which the butchers always protested, "All are freshest." On less crowded market days, we would inspect the crates of live frogs and crabs which we were warned not to poke, boxes of dried cuttlefish, and row upon row of iced prawns, squid, and slippery fish. The sanddabs made me shiver each time; their eyes lay on one flattened side and reminded me of my mother's story of a careless girl who ran into a crowded street and was crushed by a cab. "Was smash flat," reported my mother.

At the corner of the alley was Hong Sing's, a four-table café with a recessed stairwell in front that led to a door marked "Tradesmen." My brothers and I believed the bad people emerged from this door at night. Tourists never went to Hong Sing's, since the menu was printed only in Chinese. A Caucasian man with a big camera once posed me and my playmates in front of the restaurant. He had us move to the side of the picture window so the photo would capture the roasted duck with its head dangling from a juice-covered rope. After he took the picture, I told him he should go into Hong Sing's and eat dinner. When he smiled and asked me what they served, I shouted, "Guts and duck's feet and octopus gizzards!" Then I ran off with my friends, shrieking with laughter as we scampered across the alley and hid in the entryway grotto of the China Gem Company, my heart pounding with hope that he would chase us.

My mother named me after the street that we lived on: Waverly Place Jong, my official name for important American documents. But my family called me Meimei, "Little Sister." I was the youngest, the only daughter. Each morning before school, my mother would twist and yank on my thick black hair until she had formed two tightly wound pigtails. One day, as she struggled to weave a hard-toothed comb through my disobedient hair, I had a sly thought.

I asked her, "Ma, what is Chinese torture?" My mother shook her head. A bobby pin was wedged between her lips. She wetted her palm and smoothed the hair above my ear, then pushed the pin in so that it nicked sharply against my scalp.

"Who say this word?" she asked without a trace of knowing how wicked I was being. I shrugged my shoulders and said, "Some boy in my class said Chinese people do Chinese torture."

"Chinese people do many things," she said simply. "Chinese people do business, do medicine, do painting. Not lazy like American people. We do torture. Best torture."

My older brother Vincent was the one who actually got the chess set. We had gone to the annual Christmas party held at the First Chinese Baptist Church at the end of the alley. The missionary ladies had put together a Santa bag of gifts donated by members of another church. None of the gifts had names on them. There were separate sacks for boys and girls of different ages.

One of the Chinese parishioners had donned a Santa Claus costume and a stiff paper beard with cotton balls glued to it. I think the only children who thought he was the real thing were too young to know that Santa Claus was not Chinese. When my turn came up, the Santa man asked me how old I was. I thought it was a trick question; I was seven according to the American formula and eight by the Chinese calendar. I said I was born on March 17, 1951. That seemed to satisfy him. He then solemnly asked if I had been a very, very good girl this year and did I believe in Jesus Christ and obey my parents. I knew the only answer to that. I nodded back with equal solemnity.

Having watched the older children opening their gifts, I already knew that the big gifts were not necessarily the nicest ones. One girl my age got a large coloring book of biblical characters, while a less greedy girl who selected a smaller box received a glass vial of lavender toilet water. The sound of the box was also important. A ten-year-old boy had chosen a box that jangled when he shook it. It was a tin globe of the world with a slit for inserting money. He must have thought it was full of dimes and nickels, because when he saw that it had just ten pennies, his face fell with such undisguised disappointment that his mother slapped the side of his head and led him out of the church hall, apologizing to the crowd for her son who had such bad manners he couldn't appreciate such a fine gift.

As I peered into the sack, I quickly fingered the remaining presents, testing their weight, imagining what they contained. I chose a heavy, compact one that was wrapped in shiny silver foil and a red satin ribbon. It was a twelve-pack of Life Savers and I spent the rest of the party arranging and rearranging the candy tubes in the order of my favorites. My brother Winston chose wisely as well. His present turned out to be a box of intricate plastic parts; the instructions on the box proclaimed that when they were properly assembled he would have an authentic miniature replica of a World War II submarine.

Vincent got the chess set, which would have been a very decent present to get at a church Christmas party, except it was obviously used and, as we discovered later, it was missing a black pawn and a white knight. My mother graciously thanked the unknown benefactor, saying, "Too good. Cost too much." At which point, an old lady with fine white, wispy hair nodded toward our family and said with a whistling whisper, "Merry, merry Christmas."

Proud

When we got home, my mother told Vincent to throw the chess set away. "She not want it. We not want it." she said, tossing her head stiffly to the side with a tight, proud smile. My brothers had deaf ears. They were already lining up the chess pieces and reading from the dog-eared instruction book.

I watched Vincent and Winston play during Christmas week. The chessboard seemed to hold elaborate secrets waiting to be untangled. The chessmen were more powerful than old Li's magic herbs that cured ancestral curses. And my brothers wore such serious faces that I was sure something was at stake that was greater than avoiding the tradesmen's door to Hong Sing's.

"Let me! Let me!" I begged between games when one brother or the other would sit back with a deep sigh of relief and victory, the other annoyed, unable to let go of the outcome. Vincent at first refused to let me play, but when I offered my Life Savers as replacements for the buttons that filled in for the missing pieces, he relented. He chose the flavors: wild cherry for the black pawn and peppermint for the white knight. Winner could eat both.

As our mother sprinkled flour and rolled out small doughy circles for the steamed dumplings that would be our dinner that night, Vincent explained the rules, pointing to each piece. "You have sixteen pieces and so do I. One king and queen, two bishops, two knights, two castles, and eight pawns. The pawns can only move forward one step, except on the first move. Then they can move two. But they can only take men by moving crossways like this, except in the beginning, when you can move ahead and take another pawn."

"Why?" I asked as I moved my pawn. "Why can't they move more steps?"

"Because they're pawns," he said.

"But why do they go crossways to take other men? Why aren't there any women and children?"

"Why is the sky blue? Why must you always ask stupid questions?" asked Vincent. "This is a game. These are the rules. I didn't make them up. See. Here in the book." He jabbed a page with a pawn in his hand. "Pawn. P-A-W-N. Pawn. Read it yourself."

My mother patted the flour off her hands. "Let me see book," she said quietly. She scanned the pages quickly, not reading the foreign English symbols, seeming to search deliberately for nothing in particular.

"This American rules," she concluded at last. "Every time people come out from foreign country, must know rules. You not know, judge say, Too bad, go back. They not telling you why so you can use their way go forward. They say, Don't know why, you find out yourself. But they knowing all the time. Better you take it, find out why yourself." She tossed her head back with a satisfied smile.

I found out about all the whys later. I read the rules and looked up all the big words in a dictionary. I borrowed books from the Chinatown library. I studied each chess piece, trying to absorb the power each contained.

I learned about opening moves and why it's important to control the center early on; the shortest distance between two points is straight down the middle. I learned about the middle game and why tactics between two adversaries are like clashing ideas; the one who plays better has the clearest plans for both attacking and getting out of traps. I learned why it is essential in the endgame to have foresight, a mathematical understanding of all possible moves, and patience; all weaknesses and advantages become evident to a strong adversary and are obscured to a tiring opponent. I discovered that for the whole game one must gather invisible strengths and see the endgame before the game begins.

I also found out why I should never reveal "why" to others. A little knowledge withheld is a great advantage one should store for future use. That is the power of chess. It is a game of secrets in which one must show and never tell.

I loved the secrets I found within the sixty-four black and white squares. I carefully drew a handmade chessboard and pinned it to the wall next to my bed, where I would stare for hours at imaginary battles. Soon I no longer lost any games or Life Savers, but I lost my adversaries. Winston and Vincent decided they were more interested in roaming the streets after school in their Hopalong Cassidy cowboy hats.

On a cold spring afternoon, while walking home from school, I detoured through the playground at the end of our alley. I saw a group of old men, two seated across a folding table playing a game of chess, others smoking pipes, eating peanuts, and watching. I ran home and grabbed Vincent's chess set, which was bound in a cardboard box with rubber bands. I also carefully selected two prized rolls of Life Savers. I came back to the park and approached a man who was observing the game.

"Want to play?" I asked him. His face widened with surprise and he grinned as he looked at the box under my arm.

"Little sister, been a long time since I play with dolls," he said, smiling benevolently. I quickly put the box down next to him on the bench and displayed my retort.

Lau Po, as he allowed me to call him, turned out to be a much better player than my brothers. I lost many games and many Life Savers. But over the weeks, with each diminishing roll of candies, I added new secrets. Lau Po gave me the names. The Double Attack from the East and West Shores. Throwing Stones on the Drowning Man. The Sudden Meeting of the Clan. The Surprise from the Sleeping Guard. The Humble Servant Who Kills the King. Sand in the Eyes of Advancing Forces. A Double Killing Without Blood.

There were also the fine points of chess etiquette. Keep captured men in neat rows, as well-tended prisoners. Never announce "Check" with vanity, lest someone with an unseen sword slit your throat. Never hurl pieces into the sandbox after you have lost a game, because then you must find them again, by yourself, after apologizing to all around you. By the end of the summer, Lau Po had taught me all he knew, and I had become a better chess player.

A small weekend crowd of Chinese people and tourists would gather as I played and defeated my opponents one by one. My mother would join the crowds during these outdoor exhibition games. She sat proudly on the bench, telling my admirers with proper Chinese humility, "Is luck."

A man who watched me play in the park suggested that my mother allow me to play in local chess tournaments. My mother smiled graciously, an answer that meant nothing. I desperately wanted to go, but I bit back my tongue. I knew she would not let me play among strangers. So as we walked home I said in a small voice that I didn't want to play in the local tournament. They would have American rules. If I lost, I would bring shame on my family.

"Is shame you fall down nobody push you," said my mother.

During my first tournament, my mother sat with me in the front row as I waited for my turn. I frequently bounced my legs to unstick them from the cold metal seat of the folding chair. When my name was called, I leapt up. My mother unwrapped something in her lap. It was her *chang,* a small tablet of red jade which held the sun's fire. "Is luck," she whispered, and tucked it into my dress pocket. I turned to my opponent, a fifteen-year-old boy from Oakland. He looked at me, wrinkling his nose.

As I began to play, the boy disappeared, the color ran out of the room, and I saw only my white pieces and his black ones waiting on the other side. A light wind began blowing past my ears. It whispered secrets only I could hear. "Blow from the South," it murmured. "The wind leaves no trail." I saw a clear path, the traps to avoid. The crowd rustled. "Shhh! Shhh!" said the corners of the room. The wind blew stronger. "Throw sand from the East to distract him." The knight came forward ready for the sacrifice. The wind hissed, louder and louder. "Blow, blow, blow. He cannot see. He is blind now. Make him lean away from the wind so he is easier to knock down."

"Check," I said, as the wind roared with laughter. The wind died down to little puffs, my own breath.

My mother placed my first trophy next to a new plastic chess set that the neighborhood Tao society had given to me. As she wiped each piece with a soft cloth, she said, "Next time win more, lose less."

"Ma, it's not how many pieces you lose," I said. "Sometimes you need to lose pieces to get ahead."

"Better to lose less, see if you really need."

At the next tournament, I won again, but it was my mother who wore the triumphant grin.

"Lost eight piece this time. Last time was eleven. What I tell you? Better off lose less!" I was annoyed, but I couldn't say anything.

I attended more tournaments, each one farther away from home. I won all games, in all divisions. The Chinese bakery downstairs from our flat displayed my growing collection of trophies in its window, amidst the dust-covered cakes that were never picked up. The day after I won an important regional tournament, the window encased a fresh sheet cake with whipped-cream frosting and red script saying "Congratulations, Waverly Jong, Chinatown Chess Champion." Soon after that, a flower shop, headstone engraver, and funeral parlor offered to sponsor me in national tournaments. That's when my mother decided I no longer had to do the dishes. Winston and Vincent had to do my chores.

"Why does she get to play and we do all the work," complained Vincent.

"Is new American rules," said my mother. "Meimei play, squeeze all her brains out for win chess. You play, worth squeeze towel."

By my ninth birthday, I was a national chess champion. I was still some 429 points away from grand-master status, but I was touted as the Great American Hope, a child prodigy and a girl to boot. They ran a photo of me in *Life* magazine next to a quote in which Bobby Fischer said, "There will never be a woman grand master." "Your move, Bobby," said the caption.

The day they took the magazine picture I wore neatly plaited braids clipped with plastic barrettes trimmed with rhinestones. I was playing in a large high school auditorium that echoed with phlegmy coughs and the squeaky rubber knobs of chair legs sliding across freshly waxed wooden floors. Seated across from me was an American man, about the same age as Lau Po, maybe fifty. I remember that his sweaty brow seemed to weep at my every move. He wore a dark, malodorous suit. One of his pockets was stuffed with a great white kerchief on which he wiped his palm before sweeping his hand over the chosen chess piece with great flourish.

In my crisp pink-and-white dress with scratchy lace at the neck, one of two my mother had sewn for these special occasions, I would clasp my hands under my chin, the delicate points of my elbows poised lightly on the table in the manner my mother had shown me for posing for the press. I would swing my patent leather shoes back and forth like an impatient child riding on a school bus. Then I would pause, suck in my lips, twirl my chosen piece in midair as if undecided, and then firmly plant it in its new threatening place, with a triumphant smile thrown back at my opponent for good measure.

I no longer played in the alley of Waverly Place. I never visited the playground where the pigeons and old men gathered. I went to school, then directly home to learn new chess secrets, cleverly concealed advantages, more escape routes.

But I found it difficult to concentrate at home. My mother had a habit of standing over me while I plotted out my games. I think she thought of herself as my protective ally. Her lips would be sealed tight, and after each move I made, a soft "Hmmmmph" would escape from her nose.

"Ma, I can't practice when you stand there like that," I said one day. She retreated to the kitchen and made loud noises with the pots and pans. When the crashing stopped, I could see out of the corner of my eye that she was standing in the doorway. "Hmmmmph!" Only this one came out of her tight throat.

My parents made many concessions to allow me to practice. One time I complained that the bedroom I shared was so noisy that I couldn't think. Thereafter, my brothers slept in a bed in the living room facing the street. I said I couldn't finish my rice; my head didn't work right when my stomach was too full. I left the table with half-finished bowls and nobody complained. But there was one duty I couldn't avoid. I had to accompany my mother on Saturday market days when I had no tournament to play. My mother would proudly walk with me, visiting many shops, buying very little. "This my daughter Wave-ly Jong," she said to whoever looked her way.

One day after we left a shop I said under my breath, "I wish you wouldn't do that, telling everybody I'm your daughter." My mother stopped walking. Crowds of people with heavy bags pushed past us on the sidewalk, bumping into first one shoulder, than another.

"Aiii-ya. So shame be with mother?" She grasped my hand even tighter as she glared at me.

I looked down. "It's not that, it's just so obvious. It's just so embarrassing."

"Embarrass you be my daughter?" Her voice was cracking with anger.

"That's not what I meant. That's not what I said."

"What you say?"

I knew it was a mistake to say anything more, but I heard my voice speaking, "Why do you have to use me to show off? If you want to show off, then why don't you learn to play chess?"

My mother's eyes turned into dangerous black slits. She had no words for me, just sharp silence.

I felt the wind rushing around my hot ears. I jerked my hand out of my mother's tight grasp and spun around, knocking into an old woman. Her bag of groceries spilled to the ground.

"Aii-ya! Stupid girl!" my mother and the woman cried. Oranges and tin cans careened down the sidewalk. As my mother stooped to help the old woman pick up the escaping food, I took off.

I raced down the street, dashing between people, not looking back as my mother screamed shrilly, "Meimei! Meimei!" I fled down an alley, past dark, curtained shops and merchants washing the grime off their windows. I sped into the sunlight, into a large street crowded with tourists examining trinkets and souvenirs. I ducked into another dark alley, down another street, up another alley. I ran until it hurt and I realized I had nowhere to go, that I was not running from anything. The alleys contained no escape routes.

My breath came out like angry smoke. It was cold. I sat down on an upturned plastic pail next to a stack of empty boxes, cupping my chin with my hands, thinking hard. I imagined my mother, first walking briskly down one street or another looking for me, then giving up and returning home to await my arrival. After two hours, I stood up on creaking legs and slowly walked home.

The alley was quiet and I could see the yellow lights shining from our flat like two tiger's eyes in the night. I climbed the sixteen steps to the door, advancing quietly up each so as not to make any warning sounds. I turned the knob; the door was locked. I heard a chair moving, quick steps, the locks turning—click! click! click!—and then the door opened.

"About time you got home," said Vincent. "Boy, are you in trouble."

He slid back to the dinner table. On a platter were the remains of a large fish, its fleshy head still connected to bones swimming upstream in vain escape. Standing there waiting for my punishment, I heard my mother speak in a dry voice.

"We not concerning this girl. This girl not have concerning for us."

Nobody looked at me. Bone chopsticks clinked against the inside of bowls being emptied into hungry mouths.

I walked into my room, closed the door, and lay down on my bed. The room was dark, the ceiling filled with shadows from the dinnertime lights of neighboring flats.

In my head, I saw a chessboard with sixty-four black and white squares. Opposite me was my opponent, two angry black slits. She wore a triumphant smile. "Strongest wind cannot be seen," she said.

Her black men advanced across the plane, slowly marching to each successive level as a single unit. My white pieces screamed as they scurried and fell off the board one by one. As her men drew closer to my edge, I felt myself growing light. I rose up into the air and flew out the window. Higher and higher, above the alley, over the tops of tiled roofs, where I was gathered up by the wind and pushed up toward the night sky until everything below me disappeared and I was alone.

I closed my eyes and pondered my next move.

1989

PETER TAYLOR
1917–1994

Taylor was born in Trenton, Tennessee. He was educated at Vanderbilt University and Kenyon College, where he became a lifelong friend of the poet Robert Lowell. Throughout most of his adult life he taught writing at a number of American colleges and universities. His last post was at the University of Virginia. His first collection of short fiction, *A Long Fourth,* appeared in 1948, the same year that Taylor began his long association with the *New Yorker.* Unlike many Southern writers of his period, he wrote in elegantly unobtrusive style about the bewilderments and aspirations of genteel, resourceful people. His characters weave the strands of tradition into the tensions of new times with grace and persistent responsibility. His novel *A Woman of Means* was published in 1950. His collection *The Old Forest* (1985) won the PEN/Faulkner Award and is in the Modern Library series. His novel *A Summons to Memphis* won the Pulitzer Prize in 1986. His books of stories include *A Long Fourth* (1948), *Miss Leonora When Last Seen* (1963), and *Collected Stories* (1969).

A Spinster's Tale

My brother would often get drunk when I was a little girl, but that put a different sort of fear into me from what Mr. Speed did. With Brother it was a spiritual thing. And though it was frightening to know that he would have to burn for all that giggling and bouncing around on the stair at night, the truth was that he only seemed jollier to me when I would stick my head out of the hall door. It made him seem almost my age for him to act so silly, putting his white forefinger all over his flushed face and finally over his lips to say, "Sh-sh-sh-sh!" But the really frightening thing about seeing Brother drunk was what I always heard when I had slid back into bed. I could always recall my mother's words to him when he was sixteen, the year before she died, spoken in her greatest sincerity, in her most religious tone: "Son, I'd rather see you in your grave."

Yet those nights put a scaredness into me that was clearly distinguishable from the terror that Mr. Speed instilled by stumbling past our house two or three afternoons a week. The most that I knew about Mr. Speed was his name. And this I considered that I had somewhat fabricated—by allowing him the "Mr."—in my effort to humanize and soften the monster that was forever passing our house on Church Street. My father would point him out through the wide parlor window in soberness and severity to my brother with: "There goes Old Speed, again." Or on Saturdays when Brother was with the Benton boys and my two uncles were over having toddies with Father in the parlor, Father would refer to Mr. Speed's passing with a similar speech, but in a blustering tone of merry tolerance: "There goes Old Speed, again. The rascal!" These designations were equally awful, both spoken in tones that were foreign to my father's manner of addressing me; and not unconsciously I prepared the euphemism, Mister Speed, against the inevitable day when I should have to speak of him to someone.

I was named Elizabeth, for my mother. My mother had died in the spring before Mr. Speed first came to my notice on that late afternoon in October. I had bathed at four with the aid of Lucy, who had been my nurse and who was now the upstairs maid; and Lucy was upstairs turning back the covers of the beds in the rooms with their color schemes of blue and green and rose. I wandered into the shadowy parlor and sat first on one chair, then on another. I tried lying down on the settee that went with the parlor set, but my legs had got too long this summer to stretch out straight on the settee. And my feet looked long in their pumps against the wicker arm. I looked at the pictures around the room blankly and at the stained-glass windows on either side of the fireplace; and the winter light coming through them was hardly bright enough to show the colors. I struck a match on the mosaic hearth and lit the gas logs.

Kneeling on the hearth I watched the flames till my face felt hot. I stood up then and turned directly to one of the full-length mirror panels that were on each side of the front window. This one was just to the right of the broad window and my reflection in it stood out strangely from the rest of the room in the dull light that did not penetrate beyond my figure. I leaned closer to the mirror trying to discover a resemblance between myself and the wondrous Alice who walked through a looking glass. But that resemblance I was seeking I could not find in my sharp features, or in my heavy, dark curls hanging like fragments of hosepipe to my shoulders.

I propped my hands on the borders of the narrow mirror and put my face close to watch my lips say, "Away." I would hardly open them for the "a"; and then I would contort my face by the great opening I made for the "way." I whispered, "Away, away." I whispered it over and over, faster and faster, watching myself in the mirror: "A-way—a-way—away-away-awayaway." Suddenly I burst into tears and turned from the gloomy mirror to the daylight at the wide parlor window. Gazing tearfully through the expanse of plate glass there, I beheld Mr. Speed walking like a cripple with one foot on the curb and one in the street. And faintly I could hear him cursing the trees as he passed them, giving each a lick with his heavy walking cane.

Presently I was dry-eyed in my fright. My breath came short, and I clasped the black bow at the neck of my middy blouse.

When he had passed from view, I stumbled back from the window. I hadn't heard the houseboy enter the parlor, and he must not have noticed me there, I made no move of recognition as he drew the draperies across the wide front window for the night. I stood cold and silent before the gas logs with a sudden inexplicable memory of my mother's cheek and a vision of her in her bedroom on a spring day.

That April day when spring had seemed to crowd itself through the windows into the bright upstairs rooms, the old-fashioned mahogany sick-chair had been brought down from the attic to my mother's room. Three days before, a quiet service had been held there for the stillborn baby, and I had accompanied my father and brother to our lot in the gray cemetery to see the box (large for so tiny a parcel) lowered and covered with mud. But in the parlor now by the gas logs I remembered the day that my mother had sent for the sick-chair and for me.

The practical nurse, sitting in a straight chair busy at her needlework, looked over her glasses to give me some little instruction in the arrangement of my mother's pillows in the chair. A few minutes before, this practical nurse had lifted my sick mother bodily from the bed, and I had the privilege of rolling my mother to the big bay window that looked out ideally over the new foliage of small trees in our side yard.

I stood self-consciously straight, close by my mother, a maturing little girl awkward in my curls and long-waisted dress. My pale mother, in her silk bed jacket, with a smile leaned her cheek against the cheek of her daughter. Outside it was spring. The furnishings of the great blue room seemed to partake for that one moment of nature's life. And my mother's cheek was warm on mine. This I remembered when I sat before the gas logs trying to put Mr. Speed out of my mind; but that a few moments later my mother beckoned to the practical nurse and sent me suddenly from the room, my memory did not dwell upon. I remembered only the warmth of the cheek and the comfort of that other moment.

I sat near the blue burning logs and waited for my father and my brother to come in. When they came saying the same things about office and school that they said every day, turning on lights beside chairs that they liked to flop into, I realized not that I was ready or unready for them but that there had been, within me, an attempt at a preparation for such readiness.

They sat so customarily in their chairs at first and the talk ran so easily that I thought that Mr. Speed could be forgotten as quickly and painlessly as a doubting of Jesus or a fear of death from the measles. But the conversation took insinuating and malicious twists this afternoon. My father talked about the possibilities of a general war and recalled opinions that people had had just before the Spanish-American. He talked about the hundreds of men in the Union Depot. Thinking of all those men there, that close together, was something like meeting Mr. Speed in the front hall. I asked my father not to talk about war, which seemed to him a natural enough request for a young lady to make.

"How is your school, my dear?" he asked me. "How are Miss Hood and Miss Herron? Have they found who's stealing the boarders' things, my dear?"

All of those little girls safely in Belmont School being called for by gentle ladies or warm-breasted Negro women were a pitiable sight beside the beastly vision of Mr. Speed which even they somehow conjured.

At dinner, with Lucy serving and sometimes helping my plate (because she had done so for so many years), Brother teased me first one way and then another. My father joined in on each point until I began to take the teasing very seriously, and then he told Brother that he was forever carrying things too far.

Once at dinner I was convinced that my preposterous fears that Brother knew what had happened to me by the window in the afternoon were not at all preposterous. He had been talking quietly. It was something about the meeting that he and the Benton boys were going to attend after dinner. But quickly, without reason, he turned his eyes on me across the table and fairly shouted in his new deep voice: "I saw three horses running away out on Harding Road today! They were just like the mules we saw at the mines in the mountains! They were running to beat hell and with little girls riding them!"

The first week after I had the glimpse of Mr. Speed through the parlor window, I spent the afternoons dusting the bureau and mantel and bedside table in my room, arranging on the chaise longue the dolls which at this age I never played with and rarely even talked to; or I would absent-mindedly assist Lucy in turning down the beds and maybe watch the houseboy set the dinner table. I went to the parlor only when Father came or when Brother came earlier and called me in to show me a shin bruise or a box of cigarettes which a girl had given him.

Finally, I put my hand on the parlor doorknob just at four one afternoon and entered the parlor, walking stiffly as I might have done with my hands in a muff going into church. The big room with its heavy furniture and pictures showed no change since the last afternoon that I had spent there, unless possibly there were fresh antimacassars on the chairs. I confidently pushed an odd chair over to the window and took my seat and sat erect and waited.

My heart would beat hard when, from the corner of my eye, I caught sight of some figure moving up Church Street. And as it drew nearer, showing the form of some Negro or neighbor or drummer,[1] I would sigh from relief and from regret. I was ready for Mr. Speed. And I knew that he would come again and again, that he had been passing our house for inconceivable numbers of years. I knew that if he did not appear today, he would pass tomorrow. Not because I had had accidental, unavoidable glimpses of him from upstairs windows during the past week, nor because there were indistinct memories of such a figure, hardly noticed, seen on afternoons that preceded that day when I had seen him stumbling like a cripple along the curb and beating and cursing the trees did I know that Mr. Speed was a permanent and formidable figure in my life which I would be called upon to deal with; my knowledge, I was certain, was purely intuitive.

I was ready now not to face him with his drunken rage directed at me, but to look at him far off in the street and to appraise him. He didn't come that afternoon, but he came the next. I sat prim and straight before the window. I turned my head neither to the right to anticipate the sight of him nor to the left to follow his figure when it had passed. But when he was passing before my window, I put my eyes full on him and looked though my teeth chattered in my head. And now I saw his face heavy, red, fierce like his body. He walked with an awkward, stomping sort of stagger, carrying his gray topcoat over one arm; and with his other hand he kept poking his walnut cane into the soft sod along the sidewalk. When he was gone, I recalled my mother's cheek again, but the recollection this time, though more deliberate, was dwelt less upon; and I could only think of watching Mr. Speed again and again.

---

1. Salesman.

There was snow on the ground the third time that I watched Mr. Speed pass our house. Mr. Speed spat on the snow, and with his cane he aimed at the brown spot that his tobacco made there. And I could see that he missed his aim. The fourth time that I sat watching for him from the window, snow was actually falling outside; and I felt a sort of anxiety to know what would ever drive him into my own house. For a moment I doubted that he would really come to my door; but I prodded myself with the thought of his coming and finding me unprepared. And I continued to keep my secret watch for him two or three times a week during the rest of the winter.

Meanwhile my life with my father and brother and the servants in the shadowy house went on from day to day. On week nights the evening meal usually ended with petulant arguing between the two men, the atlas or the encyclopedia usually drawing them from the table to read out the statistics. Often Brother was accused of having looked-them-up-previously and of maneuvering the conversation toward the particular subject, for topics were very easily introduced and dismissed by the two. Once I, sent to the library to fetch a cigar, returned to find the discourse shifted in two minutes' time from the Kentucky Derby winners to the languages in which the Bible was first written. Once I actually heard the conversation slip, in the course of a small dessert, from the comparative advantages of urban and agrarian life for boys between the ages of fifteen and twenty to the probable origin and age of the Icelandic parliament and then to the doctrines of the Campbellite Church.[2]

That night I followed them to the library and beheld them fingering the pages of the flimsy old atlas in the light from the beaded lampshade. They paid no attention to me and little to one another, each trying to turn the pages of the book and mumbling references to newspaper articles and to statements of persons of responsibility. I slipped from the library to the front parlor across the hall where I could hear the contentious hum. And I lit the gas logs, trying to warm my long legs before them as I examined my own response to the unguided and remorseless bickering of the masculine voices.

It was, I thought, their indifferent shifting from topic to topic that most disturbed me. Then I decided that it was the tremendous gaps that there seemed to be between the subjects that was bewildering to me. Still again, I thought that it was the equal interest which they displayed for each subject that was dismaying. All things in the world were equally at home in their arguments. They exhibited equal indifference to the horrors that each topic might suggest; and I wondered whether or not their imperturbability was a thing that they had achieved.

I knew that I had got myself so accustomed to the sight of Mr. Speed's peregrinations, persistent yet, withal, seemingly without destination, that I could view his passing with perfect equanimity. And from this I knew that I must extend my preparation for the day when I should have to view him at closer range. When the day would come, I knew that it must involve my father and my brother and that his existence therefore must not remain an unmentionable thing, the secrecy of which to explode at the moment of crisis, only adding to its confusion.

---

2. Presbyterian sect, known as the Disciples of Christ, founded by Alexander Campbell (1788–1866).

Now, the door to my room was the first at the top of the long red-carpeted stairway. A wall light beside it was left burning on nights when Brother was out, and, when he came in, he turned it off. The light shining through my transom was a comforting sight when I had gone to bed in the big room; and in the summertime I could see the reflection of light bugs on it, and often one would plop against it. Sometimes I would wake up in the night with a start and would be frightened in the dark, not knowing what had awakened me until I realized that Brother had just turned out the light. On other nights, however, I would hear him close the front door and hear him bouncing up the steps. When I then stuck my head out the door, usually he would toss me a piece of candy and he always signaled to me to be quiet.

I had never intentionally stayed awake till he came in until one night toward the end of February of that year, and I hadn't been certain then that I should be able to do it. Indeed, when finally the front door closed, I had dozed several times sitting up in the dark bed. But I was standing with my door half open before he had come a third of the way up the stair. When he saw me, he stopped still on the stairway resting his hand on the banister. I realized that purposefulness must be showing on my face, and so I smiled at him and beckoned. His red face broke into a fine grin, and he took the next few steps two at a time. But he stumbled on the carpeted steps. He was on his knees, yet with his hand still on the banister. He was motionless there for a moment with his head cocked to one side, listening. The house was quiet and still. He smiled again, sheepishly this time, and kept putting his white forefinger to his red face as he ascended on tiptoe the last third of the flight of steps.

At the head of the stair he paused, breathing hard. He reached his hand into his coat pocket and smiled confidently as he shook his head at me. I stepped backward into my room.

"Oh," he whispered. "Your candy."

I stood straight in my white nightgown with my black hair hanging over my shoulders, knowing that he could see me only indistinctly. I beckoned to him again. He looked suspiciously about the hall, then stepped into the room and closed the door behind him.

"What's the matter, Betsy?" he said.

I turned and ran and climbed between the covers of my bed.

"What's the matter, Betsy?" he said. He crossed to my bed and sat down beside me on it.

I told him that I didn't know what was the matter.

"Have you been reading something you shouldn't, Betsy?" he asked.

I was silent.

"Are you lonely, Betsy?" he said. "Are you a lonely little girl?"

I sat up on the bed and threw my arms about his neck. And as I sobbed on his shoulder I smelled for the first time the fierce odor of his cheap whiskey.

"Yes, I'm always lonely," I said with directness, and I was then silent with my eyes open and my cheek on the shoulder of his overcoat which was yet cold from the February night air.

He kept his face turned away from me and finally spoke, out of the other corner of his mouth, I thought, "I'll come home earlier some afternoons and we'll talk and play."

"Tomorrow."

When I had said this distinctly, I fell away from him back on the bed. He stood up and looked at me curiously, as though in some way repelled by my settling so comfortably in the covers. And I could see his eighteen-year-old head cocked to one side as though trying to see my face in the dark. He leaned over me, and I smelled his whiskey breath. It was not repugnant to me. It was blended with the odor that he always had. I thought that he was going to strike me. He didn't, however, and in a moment was opening the door to the lighted hall. Before he went out, again I said: "Tomorrow."

The hall light dark and the sound of Brother's footsteps gone, I naturally repeated the whole scene in my mind and upon examination found strange elements present. One was something like a longing for my brother to strike me when he was leaning over me. Another was his bewilderment at my procedure. On the whole I was amazed at the way I had carried the thing off. It was the first incident that I had ever actively carried off. Now I only wished that in the darkness when he was leaning over me I had said languidly, "Oh, Brother," had said it in a tone indicating that we had in common some unmentionable trouble. Then I should have been certain of his presence next day. As it was, though, I had little doubt of his coming home early.

I would not let myself reflect further on my feelings for my brother—my desire for him to strike me and my delight in his natural odor. I had got myself in the habit of postponing such elucidations until after I had completely settled with Mr. Speed. But, as after all such meetings with my brother, I reflected upon the posthumous punishments in store for him for his carousing and drinking, and remembered my mother's saying that she had rather see him in his grave.

The next afternoon at four I had the chessboard on the tea table before the front parlor window. I waited for my brother, knowing pretty well that he would come and feeling certain that Mr. Speed would pass. (For this was a Thursday afternoon; and during the winter months I had found that there were two days of the week on which Mr. Speed never failed to pass our house. These were Thursday and Saturday.) I led my brother into that dismal parlor chattering about the places where I had found the chessmen long in disuse. When I paused a minute, slipping into my seat by the chessboard, he picked up with talk of the senior class play and his chances for being chosen valedictorian. Apparently I no longer seemed an enigma to him. I thought that he must have concluded that I was just a lonely little girl named Betsy. But I doubted that his nature was so different from my own that he could sustain objective sympathy for another child, particularly a younger sister, from one day to another. And since I saw no favors that he could ask from me at this time, my conclusion was that he believed that he had never exhibited his drunkenness to me with all his bouncing about on the stair at night; but that he was not certain that talking from the other corner of his mouth had been precaution enough against his whiskey breath.

We faced each other over the chessboard and set the men in order. There were only a few days before it would be March, and the light through the window was first bright and then dull. During my brother's moves, I stared out the window at the clouds that passed before the sun and watched pieces of newspaper that blew about the yard. I was calm beyond my own credulity.

I found myself responding to my brother's little jokes and showing real interest in the game. I tried to terrorize myself by imagining Mr. Speed's coming up to the very window this day. I even had him shaking his cane and his derby hat at us. But the frenzy which I expected at this step of my preparation did not come. And some part of Mr. Speed's formidability seemed to have vanished. I realized that by not hiding my face in my mother's bosom and by looking at him so regularly for so many months, I had come to accept his existence as a natural part of my life on Church Street, though something to be guarded against, or, as I had put it before, to be thoroughly prepared for when it came to my door.

The problem then, in relation to my brother, had suddenly resolved itself in something much simpler than the conquest of my fear of looking upon Mr. Speed alone had been. This would be only a matter of how I should act and of what words I should use. And from the incident of the night before, I had some notion that I'd find a suitable way of procedure in our household.

Mr. Speed appeared in the street without his overcoat but with one hand holding the turned-up lapels and collar of his gray suit coat. He followed his cane, stomping like an enraged blind man with his head bowed against the March wind. I squeezed from between my chair and the table and stood right at the great plate glass window, looking out. From the corner of my eye I saw that Brother was intent upon his play. Presently, in the wind, Mr. Speed's derby went back on his head, and his hand grabbed at it, pulled it back in place, then returned to hold his lapels. I took a sharp breath, and Brother looked up. And just as he looked out the window, Mr. Speed's derby did blow off and across the sidewalk, over the lawn. Mr. Speed turned, holding his lapels with his tremendous hand, shouting oaths that I could hear ever so faintly, and tried to stumble after his hat.

Then I realized that my brother was gone from the room; and he was outside the window with Mr. Speed chasing Mr. Speed's hat in the wind.

I sat back in my chair, breathless; one elbow went down on the chessboard disordering the black and white pawns and kings and castles. And through the window I watched Brother handing Mr. Speed his derby. I saw his apparent indifference to the drunk man's oaths and curses. I saw him coming back to the house while the old man yet stood railing at him. I pushed the table aside and ran to the front door lest Brother be locked outside. He met me in the hall smiling blandly.

I said, "That's Mr. Speed."

He sat down on the bottom step of the stairway, leaning backward and looking at me inquisitively.

"He's drunk, Brother," I said. "Always."

My brother looked frankly into the eyes of this half-grown sister of his but said nothing for a while.

I pushed myself up on the console table and sat swinging my legs and looking seriously about the walls of the cavernous hallway at the expanse of oak paneling, at the inset canvas of the sixteenth-century Frenchman making love to his lady, at the hat rack, and at the grandfather's clock in the darkest corner. I waited for Brother to speak.

"You don't like people who get drunk?" he said.

I saw that he was taking the whole thing as a thrust at his own behavior.

"I just think Mr. Speed is very ugly, Brother."

From the detached expression of his eyes I knew that he was not convinced.

"I wouldn't mind him less if he were sober," I said. "Mr. Speed's like—a loose horse."

This analogy convinced him. He knew then what I meant.

"You mustn't waste your time being afraid of such things," he said in great earnestness. "In two or three years there'll be things that you'll have to be afraid of. Things you really can't avoid."

"What did he say to you?" I asked.

"He cussed and threatened to hit me with that stick."

"For no reason?"

"Old Mr. Speed's burned out his reason with whiskey."

"Tell me about him." I was almost imploring him.

"Everybody knows about him. He just wanders around town, drunk. Sometimes downtown they take him off in the Black Maria."[3]

I pictured him on the main streets that I knew downtown and in the big department stores. I could see him in that formal neighborhood where my grandmother used to live. In the neighborhood of Miss Hood and Miss Herron's school. Around the little houses out where my father's secretary lived. Even in nigger town.

"You'll get used to him, for all his ugliness," Brother said. Then we sat there till my father came in, talking almost gaily about things that were particularly ugly in Mr. Speed's clothes and face and in his way of walking.

Since the day that I watched myself say "away" in the mirror, I had spent painful hours trying to know once more that experience which I now regarded as something like mystical. But the stringent course that I, motherless and lonely in our big house, had brought myself to follow while only thirteen had given me certain mature habits of thought. Idle and unrestrained daydreaming I eliminated almost entirely from my experience, though I delighted myself with fantasies that I quite consciously worked out and which, when concluded, I usually considered carefully, trying to fix them with some sort of childish symbolism.

Even idleness in my nightly dreams disturbed me. And sometimes as I tossed half awake in my big bed I would try to piece together my dreams into at least a form of logic. Sometimes I would complete an unfinished dream and wouldn't know in the morning what part I had dreamed and what part pieced out. I would often smile over the ends that I had plotted in half-wakeful moments but found pride in dreams that were complete in themselves and easy to fix with allegory, which I called "meaning." I found that a dream could start for no discoverable reason, with the sight of a printed page on which the first line was, "Once upon a time"; and soon could have me a character in a strange story. Once upon a time there was a little girl whose hands began to get very large. Grown men came for miles around to look at the giant hands and to shake them, but the little girl was ashamed of them and hid them under her skirt. It seemed that the little girl lived in the stable behind my grandmother's old house, and I watched her from the top of the loft ladder.

3. Police wagon.

Whenever there was the sound of footsteps, she trembled and wept; so I would beat on the floor above her and laugh uproariously at her fear. But presently I was the little girl listening to the noise. At first I trembled and called out for my father, but then I recollected that it was I who had made the noises and I felt that I had made a very considerable discovery for myself.

I awoke one Saturday morning in early March at the sound of my father's voice in the downstairs hall. He was talking to the servants, ordering the carriage I think. I believe that I awoke at the sound of the carriage horses' names. I went to my door and called "Goodbye" to him. He was twisting his mustache before the hall mirror, and he looked up the stairway at me and smiled. He was always abashed to be caught before a looking glass, and he called out self-consciously and affectionately that he would be home at noon.

I closed my door and went to the little dressing table that he had had put in my room on my birthday. The card with his handwriting on it was still stuck in the corner of the mirror: "For my young lady daughter." I was so thoroughly aware of the gentleness in his nature this morning that any childish timidity before him would, I thought, seem an injustice, and I determined that I should sit with him and my uncles in the parlor that afternoon and perhaps tell them all of my fear of the habitually drunken Mr. Speed and with them watch him pass before the parlor window. That morning I sat before the mirror of my dressing table and put up my hair in a knot on the back of my head for the first time.

Before Father came home at noon, however, I had taken my hair down, and I was not now certain that he would be unoffended by my mention of the neighborhood drunkard. But I was resolute in my purpose, and when my two uncles came after lunch, and the three men shut themselves up in the parlor for the afternoon, I took my seat across the hall in the little library, or den, as my mother had called it, and spent the first of the afternoon skimming over the familiar pages of *Tales of Ol' Virginny*, by Thomas Nelson Page.

My father had seemed tired at lunch. He talked very little and drank only half his cup of coffee. He asked Brother matter-of-fact questions about his plans for college in the fall and told me once to try cutting my meat instead of pulling it to pieces. And as I sat in the library afterward, I wondered if he had been thinking of my mother. Indeed, I wondered whether or not he ever thought of her. He never mentioned her to us; and in a year I had forgotten exactly how he treated her when she had been alive.

It was not only the fate of my brother's soul that I had given thought to since my mother's death. Father had always had his toddy on Saturday afternoon with his two bachelor brothers. But there was more than one round of toddies served in the parlor on Saturday now. Throughout the early part of this afternoon I could hear the tinkle of the bell in the kitchen, and presently the houseboy would appear at the door of the parlor with a tray of ice-filled glasses.

As he entered the parlor each time, I would catch a glimpse over my book of the three men. One was usually standing, whichever one was leading the conversation. Once they were laughing heartily; and as the Negro boy came out with the tray of empty glasses, there was a smile on his face.

As their voices grew louder and merrier, my courage slackened. It was then I first put into words the thought that in my brother and father I saw something of Mr. Speed. And I knew that it was more than a taste for whiskey they had in common.

At four o'clock I heard Brother's voice mixed with those of the Benton boys outside the front door. They came into the hall, and their voices were high and excited. First one, then another would demand to be heard with: "No, listen now; let me tell you what." In a moment I heard Brother on the stairs. Then two of the Benton brothers appeared in the doorway of the library. Even the youngest, who was not a year older than I and whose name was Henry, wore long pants, and each carried a cap in hand and a linen duster over his arm. I stood up and smiled at them, and with my right forefinger I pushed the black locks which hung loosely about my shoulders behind my ears.

"We're going motoring in the Carltons' machine," Henry said.

I stammered my surprise and asked if Brother were going to ride in it. One of them said that he was upstairs getting his hunting cap, since he had no motoring cap. The older brother, Gary Benton, went back into the hall. I walked toward Henry, who was standing in the doorway.

"But does Father know you're going?" I asked.

As I tried to go through the doorway, Henry stretched his arm across it and looked at me with a critical frown on his face.

"Why don't you put up your hair?" he said.

I looked at him seriously, and I felt the heat of the blush that came over my face. I felt it on the back of my neck. I stooped with what I thought considerable grace and slid under his arm and passed into the hall. There were the other two Benton boys listening to the voices of my uncles and my father through the parlor door. I stepped between them and threw open the door. Just as I did so, Henry Benton commanded, "Elizabeth, don't do that!" And I, swinging the door open, turned and smiled at him.

I stood for a moment looking blandly at my father and my uncles. I was considering what had made me burst in upon them in this manner. It was not merely that I had perceived the opportunity of creating this little disturbance and slipping in under its noise, though I was not unaware of the advantage. I was frightened by the boys' impending adventure in the horseless carriage but surely not so much as I normally should have been at breaking into the parlor at this forbidden hour. The immediate cause could only be the attention which Henry Benton had shown me. His insinuation had been that I remained too much a little girl, and I had shown him that at any rate I was a bold, or at least a naughty, little girl.

My father was on his feet. He put his glass on the mantelpiece. And it seemed to me that from the three men came in rapid succession all possible arrangements of the words, Boys-come-in. Come-in-boys. Well-boys-come in. Come-on-in. Boys-come-in-the-parlor. The boys went in, rather showing off their breeding and poise, I thought. The three men moved and talked clumsily before them, as the three Benton brothers went each to each of the men carefully distinguishing between my uncles' titles: doctor and colonel. I thought how awkward all of the members of my own family appeared on occasions that called for grace. Brother strode into the room with his hunting cap sideways on his head, and he announced their plans, which the tactful Bentons, uncertain of our family's prejudices regarding machines, had not mentioned. Father and my uncles had a great deal to say about who was going-to-do-the-driving, and Henry Benton without giving an answer gave a polite invitation to the men to join them. To my chagrin, both my uncles accepted with-the-greatest-of-pleasure what really had not been an invitation at all. And they persisted in accepting it even after Brother in his rudeness raised the question of room in the five-passenger vehicle.

Father said, "Sure. The more, the merrier." But he declined to go himself and declined for me Henry's invitation.

The plan was, then, as finally outlined by the oldest of the Benton brothers, that the boys should proceed to the Carltons' and that Brother should return with the driver to take our uncles out to the Carltons' house which was one of the new residences across from Centennial Park, where the excursions in the machine were to be made.

The four slender youths took their leave from the heavy men with the gold watch chains across their stomachs, and I had to shake hands with each of the Benton brothers. To each I expressed my regret that Father would not let me ride with them, emulating their poise with all my art. Henry Benton was the last, and he smiled as though he knew what I was up to. In answer to his smile I said, "Games are *so* much fun."

I stood by the window watching the four boys in the street until they were out of sight. My father and his brothers had taken their seats in silence, and I was aware of just how unwelcome I was in the room. Finally, my uncle, who had been a colonel in the Spanish War and who wore bushy blond sideburns, whistled under his breath and said, "Well, there's no doubt about it, no doubt about it."

He winked at my father, and my father looked at me and then at my uncle. Then quickly in a ridiculously overserious tone he asked, "What, sir? No doubt about what, sir?"

"Why, there's no doubt that this daughter of yours was flirting with the youngest of the Messrs. Benton."

My father looked at me and twisted his mustache and said with the same pomp that he didn't know what he'd do with me if I started that sort of thing. My two uncles threw back their heads, each giving a short laugh. My uncle the doctor took off his pince-nez and shook them at me and spoke in the same mock-serious tone of his brothers: "Young lady, if you spend your time in such pursuits you'll only bring upon yourself and upon the young men about Nashville the greatest unhappiness. I, as a bachelor, must plead the cause of the young Bentons!"

I turned to my father in indignation that approached rage.

"Father," I shouted, "there's Mr. Speed out there!"

Father sprang from his chair and quickly stepped up beside me at the window. Then, seeing the old man staggering harmlessly along the sidewalk, he said in, I thought, affected easiness: "Yes. Yes, dear."

"He's drunk," I said. My lips quivered, and I think I must have blushed at this first mention of the unmentionable to my father.

"Poor Old Speed," he said. I looked at my uncles, and they were shaking their heads, echoing my father's tone.

"What ever did happen to Speed's old-maid sister?" my uncle the doctor said.

"She's still with him," Father said.

Mr. Speed appeared soberer today than I had ever seen him. He carried no overcoat to drag on the ground, and his stagger was barely noticeable. The movement of his lips and an occasional gesture were the only evidence of intoxication. I was enraged by the irony that his good behavior on this of all days presented. Had I been a little younger I might have suspected conspiracy on the part of all men against me, but I was old enough to suspect no person's being even interested enough in me to plot against my understanding, unless it be some vague personification of life itself.

The course which I took, I thought afterward, was the proper one. I do not think that it was because I was then really conscious that when one is determined to follow some course rigidly and is blockaded one must fire furiously, if blindly, into the blockade, but rather because I was frightened and in my fear forgot all logic of attack. At any rate, I fired furiously at the three immutable creatures.

"I'm afraid of him," I broke out tearfully. I shouted at them, "He's always drunk! He's always going by our house drunk!"

My father put his arms about me, but I continued talking as I wept on his shirt front. I heard the barking sound of the machine horn out in front, and I felt my father move one hand from my back to motion my uncles to go. And as they shut the parlor door after them, I felt that I had let them escape me.

I heard the sound of the motor fading out up Church Street, and Father led me to the settee. We sat there together for a long while, and neither of us spoke until my tears had dried.

I was eager to tell him just exactly how fearful I was of Mr. Speed's coming into our house. But he only allowed me to tell him that I *was* afraid; for when I had barely suggested that much, he said that I had no business watching Mr. Speed, that I must shut my eyes to some things. "After all," he said, nonsensically I thought, "you're a young lady now." And in several curiously twisted sentences he told me that I mustn't seek things to fear in this world. He said that it was most unlikely, besides, that Speed would ever have business at our house. He punched at his left side several times, gave a prolonged belch, settled a pillow behind his head, and soon was sprawled beside me on the settee, snoring.

But Mr. Speed did come to our house, and it was in less than two months after this dreary twilight. And he came as I had feared he might come, in his most extreme state of drunkenness and at a time when I was alone in the house with the maid Lucy. But I had done everything that a little girl, now fourteen, could do in preparation for such an eventuality. And the sort of preparation that I had been able to make, the clearance of all restraints and inhibitions regarding Mr. Speed in my own mind and in my relationship with my world, had necessarily, I think, given me a maturer view of my own limited experiences; though, too, my very age must be held to account for a natural step toward maturity.

In the two months following the day that I first faced Mr. Speed's existence with my father, I came to look at every phase of our household life with a more direct and more discerning eye. As I wandered about that shadowy and somehow brutally elegant house, sometimes now with a knot of hair on the back of my head, events and customs there that had repelled or frightened me I gave the closest scrutiny. In the daytime I ventured into such forbidden spots as the servants' and the men's bathrooms. The filth of the former became a matter of interest in the study of the servants' natures, instead of the object of ineffable disgust. The other became a fascinating place of wet shaving brushes and leather straps and red rubber bags.

There was an anonymous little Negro boy that I had seen many mornings hurrying away from our back door with a pail. I discovered that he was toting buttermilk from our icebox with the permission of our cook. And I sprang at him from behind a corner of the house one morning and scared him so that he spilled the buttermilk and never returned for more.

Another morning I heard the cook threatening to slash the houseboy with her butcher knife, and I made myself burst in upon them; and before Lucy and the houseboy I told her that if she didn't leave our house that day, I'd call my father and, hardly knowing what I was saying, I added, "And the police." She was gone, and Lucy had got a new cook before dinnertime. In this way, from day to day, I began to take my place as mistress in our mother-less household.

I could no longer be frightened by my brother with a mention of runaway horses. And instead of terrorized I felt only depressed by his long and curious arguments with my father. I was depressed by the number of the subjects to and from which they oscillated. The world as a whole still seemed unconscio-nably larger than anything I could comprehend. But I had learned not to con-cern myself with so general and so unreal a problem until I had cleared up more particular and real ones.

It was during these two months that I noticed the difference between the manner in which my father spoke before my uncles of Mr. Speed when he passed and that in which he spoke of him before my brother. To my brother it was the condemning, "There goes Old Speed, again." But to my uncles it was, "There goes Old Speed," with the sympathetic addition, "the rascal." Though my father and his brothers obviously found me more agreeable because a pleasant spirit had replaced my old timidity, they yet considered me a child; and my father little dreamed that I discerned such traits in his character, or that I understood, if I even listened to, their anecdotes and their long funny stories, and it was an interest in the peculiar choice of subject and in the way that the men told their stories.

When Mr. Speed came, I was accustomed to thinking that there was some-thing in my brother's and in my father's natures that was fully in sympathy with the very brutality of his drunkenness. And I knew that they would not consider my hatred for him and for that part of him which I saw in them. For that alone I was glad that it was on a Thursday afternoon, when I was in the house alone with Lucy, that one of the heavy sort of rains that come toward the end of May drove Mr. Speed onto our porch for shelter.

Otherwise I wished for nothing more than the sound of my father's strong voice when I stood trembling before the parlor window and watched Mr. Speed stumbling across our lawn in the flaying rain. I only knew to keep at the window and make sure that he was actually coming into our house. I believe that he was drunker than I had ever before seen him, and his usual ire seemed to be doubled by the raging weather.

Despite the aid of his cane, Mr. Speed fell to his knees once in the muddy sod. He remained kneeling there for a time with his face cast in resignation. Then once more he struggled to his feet in the rain. Though I was ever conscious that I was entering into young womanhood at that age, I can only think of myself as a child at that moment; for it was the helpless fear of a child that I felt as I watched Mr. Speed approaching our door. Perhaps it was the last time I ever experienced the inconsolable desperation of childhood.

Next, I could hear his cane beating on the boarding of the little porch before our door. I knew that he must be walking up and down in that little shelter. Then I heard Lucy's exasperated voice as she came down the steps. I knew immediately, what she confirmed afterward, that she thought it Brother, eager to get into the house, beating on the door.

I, aghast, opened the parlor door just as she pulled open the great front door. Her black skin ashened as she beheld Mr. Speed—his face crimson, his eyes bleary, and his gray clothes dripping water. He shuffled through the doorway and threw his stick on the hall floor. Between his oaths and profanities he shouted over and over in his broken, old man's voice, "Nigger, nigger." I could understand little of his rapid and slurred speech, but I knew his rage went round and round a man in the rain and the shelter of a neighbor's house.

Lucy fled up the long flight of steps and was on her knees at the head of the stair, in the dark upstairs hall, begging me to come up to her. I only stared, as though paralyzed and dumb, at him and then up the steps at her. The front door was still open; the hall was half in light; and I could hear the rain on the roof of the porch and the wind blowing the trees which were in full green foliage.

At last I moved. I acted. I slid along the wall past the hat rack and the console table, my eyes on the drunken old man who was swearing up the steps at Lucy. I reached for the telephone; and when I had rung for central, I called for the police station. I knew what they did with Mr. Speed downtown, and I knew with what I had threatened the cook. There was a part of me that was crouching on the top step with Lucy, vaguely longing to hide my face from this in my own mother's bosom. But there was another part which was making me deal with Mr. Speed, however wrongly, myself. Innocently I asked the voice to send "the Black Maria" to our house number on Church Street.

Mr. Speed had heard me make the call. He was still and silent for just one moment. Then he broke into tears, and he seemed to be chanting his words. He repeated the word "child" so many times that I felt I had acted wrongly, with courage but without wisdom. I saw myself as a little beast adding to the injury that what was bestial in man had already done him. He picked up his cane and didn't seem to be talking either to Lucy or to me, but to the cane. He started out the doorway, and I heard Lucy come running down the stairs. She fairly glided around the newel post and past me to the telephone. She wasn't certain that I had made the call. She asked if I had called my father. I simply told her that I had not.

As she rang the telephone, I watched Mr. Speed cross the porch. He turned to us at the edge of the porch and shouted one more oath. But his foot touched the wet porch step, and he slid and fell unconscious on the steps.

He lay there with the rain beating upon him and with Lucy and myself watching him, motionless from our place by the telephone. I was frightened by the thought of the cruelty which I found I was capable of, a cruelty which seemed inextricably mixed with what I had called courage. I looked at him lying out there in the rain and despised and pitied him at the same time, and I was afraid to go minister to the helpless old Mr. Speed.

Lucy had her arms about me and kept them there until two gray horses pulling their black coach had galloped up in front of the house and two policemen had carried the limp body through the rain to the dreadful vehicle.

Just as the policemen closed the doors in the back of the coach, my father rode up in a closed cab. He jumped out and stood in the rain for several minutes arguing with the policemen. Lucy and I went to the door and waited for him to come in. When he came, he looked at neither of us. He walked past us saying only, "I regret that the bluecoats were called." And he went into the parlor and closed the door.

I never discussed the events of that day with my father, and I never saw Mr. Speed again. But, despite the surge of pity I felt for the old man on our porch that afternoon, my hatred and fear of what he had stood for in my eyes has never left me. And since the day that I watched myself say "away" in the mirror, not a week has passed but that he has been brought to my mind by one thing or another. It was only the other night that I dreamed I was a little girl on Church Street again and that there was a drunk horse in our yard.

1971

RELATED:

—Ann Beattie on "A Spinster's Tale," p. 1756

LEO TOLSTOY
1828–1910

Tolstoy—generally considered the greatest of nineteenth-century novelists—was born at his family estate, Yasnaya Polyana, Russia, into the Russian nobility. His youth was restless and without direction. He was vain, dissolute, and immoderate, a poor student and a reckless gambler. It was only after he entered military service that he became interested in writing—autobiographical stories first, then sketches of military life as he knew it during the Crimean War. Leaving the army in 1857, he traveled in western Europe, but his disdain for the vanities of cultured life was merely deepened by what he saw in Paris. On his return to Russia he started an experimental school for children, structuring it on generally anarchic principles. At the same time he was producing the novels that ensure his place in world literature: *War and Peace* (1869), an account of Russia in the years of Napoleon's conquests and his attempt to consolidate his empire by the conquest of Russia; and *Anna Karenina* (1877), the story of a woman caught in the immemorial conflict of personal, biological, and social demands, finally destroyed by her inability to reconcile them. In spite of his triumph with these novels, Tolstoy was painfully dissatisfied with them as he grew older, considering them flawed by the earthly preoccupations he was trying to escape. To appease his self-doubt he adopted a primitive version of Christianity that often put him at odds with the established Orthodox church. For nearly twenty years he wrote chiefly on moral and spiritual matters, and these later moralistic writings, including the novel *Resurrection* (1899), gave him enormous moral influence throughout the world; his home at Yasnaya Polyana became a mecca for pilgrims who sought his advice on the right way to live. His Russian followers were persecuted by the government, though he himself remained immune from political pressure. But he never found the spiritual peace for which he struggled; the turbulence of his inner conflicts drove him several times to leave his home and his wife, and on one of these tormented flights he died in a provincial railway station.

The Death of Ivan Ilyich[1]

I

During a break in the hearing of the Melvinsky case, the members of the court and the prosecutor met in Ivan Yegorovich Shebek's room in the big

---

1. Translated by Peter Carson and Mary Beard.

law courts building and began talking about the famous Krasovsky case. Fyodor Vasilyevich became heated, contending that it didn't come under their jurisdiction; Ivan Yegorovich held his ground; while Pyotr Ivanovich, not having joined in the argument at the beginning, took no part in it and was looking through the *Gazette*, which had just been delivered.

"Gentlemen!" he said. "Ivan Ilyich has died."

"He hasn't!"

"Look, read this," he said to Fyodor Vasilyevich, handing him a fresh copy which still smelled of ink.

Within a black border was printed: "Praskovya Fyodorovna Golovina with deep sorrow informs family and friends of the passing of her beloved spouse Ivan Ilyich Golovin, member of the Court of Justice, which took place on the 4th of February of this year 1882. The funeral will be on Friday at 1 P.M."

Ivan Ilyich was a colleague of the gentlemen meeting there and they all liked him. He had been ill for several weeks; people were saying his illness was incurable. His position had been kept for him, but there had been conjectures that, in the event of his death, Alekseyev might be appointed to his position, and either Vinnikov or Shtabel to Alekseyev's. So on hearing of Ivan Ilyich's death the first thought of each of the gentlemen meeting in the room was of the significance the death might have for the transfer or promotion of the members themselves or their friends.

Now I will probably get Shtabel's or Vinnikov's position, thought Fyodor Vasilyevich. *It was promised to me long ago and this promotion means a raise of eight hundred rubles, plus a private office.*

Now I must ask about the transfer of my brother-in-law from Kaluga, thought Pyotr Ivanovich. *My wife will be very pleased. Now she won't be able to say that I've never done anything for her family.*

"I thought he wouldn't leave his bed," Pyotr Ivanovich said aloud. "Such a pity."

"What was actually wrong with him?"

"The doctors couldn't make a diagnosis. That is, they did, but different ones. When I saw him the last time, I thought he would recover."

"And I didn't go and see him after the holidays. I kept meaning to."

"Did he have any money?"

"I think his wife had a very small income. But next to nothing."

"Yes, we'll have to go and see her. They lived a terribly long way off."

"That is, a long way from you. Everything's a long way from you."

"He just can't forgive me for living on the other side of the river," said Pyotr Ivanovich, smiling at Shebek. And they started talking about distances in the city, and went back into the courtroom.

Apart from the thoughts the death brought each of them about the possible moves and changes at work that might follow, the actual fact of the death of a close acquaintance evoked, as always, in all who learned of it a complacent feeling that it was "he who had died, not I."

So—he's dead; but here I am still, each thought or felt. At this point his closer acquaintances, the so-called friends of Ivan Ilyich, involuntarily thought that they now needed to carry out the very tedious requirements of etiquette and go to the requiem service and pay a visit of condolence to the widow.

Closest of all were Fyodor Vasilyevich and Pyotr Ivanovich.

Pyotr Ivanovich was a friend from law school and considered himself under an obligation to Ivan Ilyich.

Having given his wife over dinner the news of Ivan Ilyich's death and his thoughts about the possibility of his brother-in-law's transfer to their district, Pyotr Ivanovich didn't lie down to have a rest but put on a formal tailcoat and drove to Ivan Ilyich's.

At the entrance to Ivan Ilyich's apartment stood a carriage and two cabs. Downstairs in the hall by the coatrack, leaning against the wall, was the brocade-covered lid of the coffin with tassels and a gold braid that had been cleaned with powder. Two ladies in black were taking off their fur coats. One of them, Ivan Ilyich's sister, he knew; the other was an unknown lady. Pyotr Ivanovich's colleague Schwarz was coming downstairs and, seeing from the top step who had come in, he winked at him as if to say, "Ivan Ilyich has made a silly mess of things; you and I have done things differently."

Schwarz's face with his English side-whiskers and his whole thin figure in a tailcoat as usual had an elegant solemnity, and this solemnity, which was always at odds with Schwarz's playful character, was especially piquant here. So Pyotr Ivanovich thought.

Pyotr Ivanovich let the ladies go in front of him and slowly followed them up the stairs. Schwarz didn't come down but stayed at the top. Pyotr Ivanovich understood why: he obviously wanted to arrange where they should play *vint*[2] today. The ladies went up the stairs to the widow but Schwarz, with a serious set to his strong lips and a playful look, indicated by a twitch of his eyebrows that Pyotr Ivanovich should go to the right, into the room where the corpse lay.

Pyotr Ivanovich went in, feeling, as is always the case, at a loss as to what he should do there. One thing he did know was that in these circumstances it never does any harm to cross oneself. He wasn't altogether sure whether one should also bow and so he chose a middle course: entering the room, he started to cross himself and made a kind of slight bow. Insofar as the movements of his head and hands would allow, he looked round the room at the same time. Two young men, probably nephews, one of them a gymnasium pupil, were crossing themselves as they left the room. An old woman stood motionless, and a lady with oddly arched eyebrows was saying something to her in a whisper. A church lector in a frock coat with a vigorous and decisive way to him was reading something out loudly with an expression that permitted no contradiction; the peasant manservant Gerasim, stepping lightly in front of Pyotr Ivanovich, scattered something on the ground. Seeing that, Pyotr Ivanovich at once sensed the faint smell of a decomposing body. On his last visit to Ivan Ilyich he had seen this peasant in the study; he carried out the duties of a sick-nurse, and Ivan Ilyich was especially fond of him. Pyotr Ivanovich kept crossing himself and bowing slightly in an intermediate direction between the coffin, the lector, and the icons on a table in the corner. Then, when he thought the movement of crossing himself with his hand had gone on for too long, he stopped and started to examine the dead man.

The dead man lay, as dead men always do, especially heavily, his stiffened limbs sunk in the padded lining of the coffin with his head bent back forever

2. A card game, similar to bridge.

on the pillow, and, as always with dead men, his yellow waxen forehead sticking out, showing bald patches on his hollow temples, his nose protruding as if it pressed on his upper lip. He had greatly changed, had become even thinner since Pyotr Ivanovich had seen him, but like all dead men, his face was handsomer, above all more imposing than when he was alive. On his face was an expression that said what had to be done had been done, and done properly. This expression also held a reproach or reminder to the living. Pyotr Ivanovich found this reminder inappropriate—or at the least one not applying to himself. This gave Pyotr Ivanovich an unpleasant feeling, and so he hurriedly crossed himself once more and turned, too hurriedly he thought, and not in accordance with propriety, and went to the door. Schwarz was waiting for him in the next room, his legs wide apart and both hands playing behind his back with his top hat. One look at Schwarz's playful, neat, and elegant figure refreshed Pyotr Ivanovich. Pyotr Ivanovich felt that Schwarz stood above all this and didn't allow himself to give in to depressing thoughts. The very way he looked stated the following: the fact of Ivan Ilyich's requiem cannot serve as a sufficient reason to consider the order of the courts disrupted; in other words, nothing can stop us unsealing and shuffling a pack of cards this evening while the manservant puts out four fresh candles; in general there are no grounds for assuming that this fact can prevent us from spending a pleasant evening, even today. He said this in a whisper to Pyotr Ivanovich as he came in, proposing they meet for a game at Fyodor Vasilyevich's. But apparently Pyotr Ivanovich was not fated to play *vint* this evening. Praskovya Fyodorovna, a short, plump woman who broadened from the shoulders down in spite of all her efforts to achieve the opposite, was dressed all in black with her head covered in lace and with oddly arched eyebrows like the lady standing by the coffin. She came out of her rooms with the other ladies, and taking them to the door where the dead man lay, said:

"Now there'll be the requiem; do go in."

Schwarz stopped, making a vague bow—clearly neither accepting nor rejecting this proposal. Praskovya Fyodorovna, recognizing Pyotr Ivanovich, sighed, went right up to him, took him by the hand, and said:

"I know that you were a true friend of Ivan Ilyich . . ." and looked at him, waiting for an action on his part that corresponded to these words.

Pyotr Ivanovich knew that just as in that room one had had to cross oneself, so here one must press the hand, sigh, and say, "Believe me!" And that's what he did. And having done it he felt that the desired result had been obtained: he was moved and she was moved.

"Come while they haven't started in there; I need to talk to you," said the widow. "Give me your hand."

Pyotr Ivanovich gave his hand and they went off into the inner rooms, past Schwarz who winked sadly at Pyotr Ivanovich. "There's your *vint* gone! Don't take it out on us; we'll find another partner. Maybe you can cut in once you've gotten free," said his playful look.

Pyotr Ivanovich sighed even more deeply and sadly, and Praskovya Fyodorovna gratefully pressed his hand. They went into her dimly lit drawing room hung with pink cretonne and sat down by a table, she on a sofa and Pyotr Ivanovich on a low pouf built on springs that awkwardly gave way as he sat down. (Praskovya Fyodorovna was going to warn him to sit on another chair but found such a warning inappropriate for the situation and changed her mind.) As he sat down on the pouf, Pyotr Ivanovich remembered how Ivan Ilyich had arranged this drawing room and consulted him about this very pink cretonne with green leaves. On her way to sit down on the sofa, as she passed the table (the whole drawing room was full of furniture and knick-knacks), the widow caught the lace of her black mantilla on the carving of the table. Pyotr Ivanovich got up to unhook her, and the sprung pouf now released below began to sway and push at him. The widow started to unhook the lace herself and Pyotr Ivanovich sat down again, quelling the rebellious pouf underneath him. But the widow hadn't unhooked it all, and Pyotr Ivanovich again got up and the pouf again rebelled and even made a noise. When all this was over she took out a clean cambric handkerchief and began to cry. Pyotr Ivanovich felt chilled by the episode of the lace and the battle with the pouf and sat frowning. This awkward situation was interrupted by Sokolov, Ivan Ilyich's butler, reporting that the place in the cemetery Praskovya Fyodorovna had selected would cost two hundred rubles. She stopped crying and, looking at Pyotr Ivanovich with the air of a victim, said in French that she was suffering greatly. Pyotr Ivanovich made a silent sign expressing a firm conviction that it couldn't be otherwise.

"Do smoke, please," she said in a gracious and, at the same time, broken voice and talked to Sokolov about the matter of the price of the place in the cemetery. Pyotr Ivanovich smoked and heard her asking very detailed questions about the different prices of plots and deciding on the one that should be bought. When that was done, she went on to give instructions about the singers. Sokolov went out.

"I do everything myself," she said to Pyotr Ivanovich, moving some albums lying on the table to one side. Noticing that his ash was posing a threat to the table, she speedily pushed an ashtray towards Pyotr Ivanovich and said, "I find it a pretence to state that because of grief I can't deal with practical matters. On the contrary, if there is something that can . . . not console . . . but distract me, then it's bothering about him." She again took out her handkerchief as if she were going to cry, and suddenly, as if pulling herself together, she shook herself and began to speak quietly:

"However, I have to talk to you about something."

Pyotr Ivanovich bowed, not letting the pouf release its springs, which had at once started to move underneath him.

"He suffered terribly in the last days."

"Did he suffer very much?" Pyotr Ivanovich asked.

"Oh. Terribly! At the end he never stopped screaming, not for minutes, for hours. For three whole days he screamed without drawing breath. It was unbearable. I can't understand how I bore it; one could hear it from three doors away. Oh, what I've been through!"

"And was he really conscious?" Pyotr Ivanovich asked.

"Yes," she whispered, "till the final moment. He said goodbye to us a quarter of an hour before he died and asked as well for Volodya to be taken out."

The thought of the sufferings of a man he had known so well, first as a cheerful lad, a schoolboy, then as an adult colleague, suddenly horrified Pyotr Ivanovich in spite of his unpleasant consciousness of his own and this woman's pretense. He saw again that forehead, the nose pressing on the lip, and he became fearful for himself.

Three days of terrible suffering and death. That can happen to me too, now, any minute, he thought, and for a moment he became frightened. But right away, he didn't know how, there came to his aid the ordinary thought that this had happened to Ivan Ilyich and not to him, and this ought not and could not happen to him; that in thinking like this he was giving in to gloomy thoughts, which one shouldn't, as had been clear from Schwarz's face. And having reached this conclusion, Pyotr Ivanovich was reassured and started to ask with interest about the details of Ivan Ilyich's end, as if death were an adventure peculiar to Ivan Ilyich but absolutely not to himself.

After some talk about the details of the truly terrible physical sufferings which Ivan Ilyich had undergone (details that Pyotr Ivanovich learned only by way of the effect that Ivan Ilyich's torment had had on Praskovya Fyodorovna's nerves), the widow apparently found it necessary to move on to business.

"Ah, Pyotr Ivanovich, it's so hard, so terribly hard." And she again started to cry.

Pyotr Ivanovich sighed and waited for to her to blow her nose. When she had blown her nose, he said:

"Believe me . . ." and again she talked away and unburdened herself of what was clearly her main business with him—how on her husband's death she could get money from the treasury. She gave the appearance of asking Pyotr Ivanovich for advice about the pension, but he saw that she already knew down to the smallest details even what he didn't know—everything that one could extract from the public purse on this death—but that she wanted to learn if one couldn't somehow extract a bit more money. Pyotr Ivanovich tried to think of a way, but, having thought a little and out of politeness abusing the government for its meanness, he said that he thought one couldn't get more. Then she sighed and clearly began to think of a way to get rid of her visitor. He understood this, put out his cigarette, got up, shook her hand, and went into the hall.

In the dining room with the clock that Ivan Ilyich had been so pleased to buy in a junk shop, Pyotr Ivanovich met the priest and also a few acquaintances who had come to the requiem, and he saw a beautiful young lady he knew, Ivan Ilyich's daughter. She was all in black. That made her very slender waist seem even more so. She had a somber, decisive, almost angry expression. She bowed to Pyotr Ivanovich as if he had done something wrong. Behind the daughter, with a similarly offended expression, stood a rich young man whom Pyotr Ivanovich knew, an examining magistrate who he'd heard was her fiancé. He glumly bowed to them and was about to go on into the room where the dead man lay when from under the stairs there appeared the figure of the son, a gymnasium student, who looked terribly like Ivan Ilyich. He was a little Ivan Ilyich just as Pyotr Ivanovich remembered him at law school. His eyes were tearstained and had the look that the eyes of boys with impure thoughts have at the age of thirteen or fourteen. When he recognized Pyotr Ivanovich the boy began to scowl sullenly and shamefacedly. Pyotr Ivanovich nodded to him and went into the dead man's room. The requiem began—candles, groans, incense, tears, sobs. Pyotr Ivanovich stood frowning, looking at the feet in front of him. He didn't look once at the dead man and right until the end didn't give in to any depressing influences. He was one of the first to leave. There was no one in the hall. Gerasim, the peasant manservant, darted out of the dead man's study, rummaged with his strong hands among all the fur coats to find Pyotr Ivanovich's, and gave it to him.

"So, Gerasim my friend," said Pyotr Ivanovich in order to say something. "It's sad, isn't it?"

"It's God's will. We'll all be there," said Gerasim, showing his white, regular, peasant's teeth, and like a man in the full swing of intensive work, briskly opened the door, called the coachman, helped Pyotr Ivanovich in, and jumped back to the steps as if trying to think what else he might do.

It was particularly pleasant for Pyotr Ivanovich to breathe the fresh air after the smells of incense, the dead body, and the carbolic acid.[3]

"Where to, sir?" asked the coachman.

"It's not late. So I'll still drop in at Fyodor Vasilyevich's."

And off Pyotr Ivanovich went. And indeed he found his friends finishing the first rubber;[4] it was easy for him to cut in as a fifth.

II

Ivan Ilyich's past life had been very simple and ordinary and very awful.

Ivan Ilyich had died at the age of forty-five, a member of the Court of Justice. He was the son of a St. Petersburg civil servant who had in various ministries and departments the kind of career that brings people to a position in which, although it is quite clear that they are incapable of performing any meaningful job, they still by reason of their long past service and seniority cannot be dismissed; so they receive invented, fictitious positions and thousands of rubles, from six to ten thousand, which are not fictitious, with which they live on to a ripe old age.

Such was Privy Councillor Ilya Yefimovich Golovin, the superfluous member of various superfluous institutions.

He had three sons, Ivan Ilyich being the second. The eldest had the same kind of career as his father, only in a different ministry, and he was already approaching the age at which salary starts increasing automatically. The third son was a failure. Wherever he had been in various positions he had made a mess of things and he was now working in the railways. Both his father and his brothers, and especially their wives, not only didn't like to see him but didn't even mention his existence unless absolutely compelled to do so. Their sister was married to Baron Gref, the same kind of St. Petersburg civil servant as his father-in-law. Ivan Ilyich was *le phénix de la famille,*[5] as they said. He wasn't as cold and precise as the eldest or as hopeless as the youngest. He was somewhere between them—a clever, lively, pleasant, and decent man. He had been educated with his younger brother in the law school. The younger one didn't finish and was expelled from the fifth class. Ivan Ilyich completed the course with good marks. In law school he was already what he would later be during his entire life: a capable, cheerful, good-natured, and sociable man, but one who strictly did what he considered his duty, and he considered his

---

3. A disinfectant.   **4.** Round of hands in bridge.   **5.** The paragon of the family (French).

duty to be everything that it was considered to be by his superiors. Neither as a boy nor afterward as a grown man did he seek to ingratiate himself, but there was in him from a young age the characteristic of being drawn to people of high station like a fly toward the light; he adopted their habits and their views on life and established friendly relations with them. All the passions of childhood and youth went by without leaving much of a trace in him; he gave in both to sensuality and to vanity, and—toward the end, in the senior classes—to liberalism, but always within the defined limits that his sense accurately indicated to him as correct.

At law school he had done things that previously had seemed to him quite vile and had filled him with self-disgust while he did them; but later, seeing these things were done by people in high positions and were not thought by them to be bad, he didn't quite think of them as good but completely forgot them and wasn't at all troubled by memories of them.

Having left law school in the tenth class and received money from his father for fitting himself out, Ivan Ilyich ordered clothes at Sharmer's,[6] hung on his watch chain a medallion with the inscription *respice finem*,[7] took his leave of the princely patron of the school and his tutor, dined with his schoolmates at Donon's,[8] and, equipped with a new and fashionable trunk, linen, clothes, shaving and toilet things, and traveling rug ordered and bought from the very best shops, he went off to a provincial city to the post of assistant to the governor for special projects, which his father had procured for him.

In the provincial city Ivan Ilyich at once established for himself the kind of easy and pleasant position he had had at law school. He worked, made his career, and at the same time amused himself in a pleasant and seemly way; from time to time he went around the district towns on a mission from his chief. He behaved to both superiors and inferiors with dignity and he carried out the responsibilities he had been given, mainly for the affairs of religious dissenters, with an exactness and incorruptible honesty of which he could not but be proud.

In his work, despite his youth and liking for frivolous amusement, he was exceptionally reserved, formal, and even severe; but in society he was often playful and witty and always good-humored, well-behaved and a *bon enfant*,[9] as his chief and his chief's wife, with whom he was one of the family, used to say of him.

There was also in the provincial city an affair with one of the ladies who attached herself to the smart lawyer; there was a little dressmaker; there were drinking sessions with visiting aides-de-camp and trips to a remote street after supper; there was also some fawning deference to his chief and even to his chief's wife, but all this wore such a high tone of probity that it couldn't be described in bad words; all this could only go under the rubric of the French expression *il faut que jeunesse se passe*.[1] Everything took place with clean hands, in clean shirts, with French words, and, most importantly, in the highest society, consequently with the approval of people in high position.

Ivan Ilyich worked in this way for five years, and then there came changes in his official life. New legal bodies were founded; new men were needed.

---

6. A fashionable tailor in St. Petersburg. **7.** That is, look before you leap (Latin). **8.** A first-class restaurant in St. Petersburg. **9.** Good boy (French). **1.** Youth must have its fling (French).

And Ivan Ilyich was this new man.

Ivan Ilyich was offered the position of examining magistrate and he accepted it, despite the fact that this position was in another province and he had to abandon the relationships he had established and establish new ones. His friends saw Ivan Ilyich off: they took a group photograph, they presented him with a silver cigarette case, and off he went to his new position.

As an examining magistrate Ivan Ilyich was just as *comme il faut*,[2] well-behaved, capable of separating his official duties from his private life and of inspiring general respect as he had been as a special projects officer. The actual work of a magistrate had much more interest and attraction for him than his previous work. In his previous position it had been pleasant to walk with a light step in his Sharmer uniform past trembling petitioners and envious officials waiting to be seen, straight into his chief's room to sit down with him over a cup of tea with a cigarette. But there were few people who depended directly on his say-so—only district police officers and religious schismatics when he was sent on missions—and he liked to treat such people dependent on him politely, almost as comrades; he liked to let them feel that here he was, someone who could crush them, treating them in a simple and friendly way. There were only a few such people then. Now, as an examining magistrate, Ivan Ilyich felt that all of them, all without exception, even the most important, self-satisfied people, were in his hands, and that he only had to write certain words on headed paper and this or that important, self-satisfied man would be brought to him as a defendant or a witness, and if he wouldn't let him sit down, would have to stand before him and answer his questions. Ivan Ilyich never abused this power of his—on the contrary he tried to use it lightly—but the consciousness of this power and the possibility of using it lightly constituted for him the chief interest and attraction of his new job. In the work itself, in the actual investigations, Ivan Ilyich very quickly mastered a way of setting aside all circumstances that didn't relate to the investigation and expressing the most complicated case in a terminology in which the case only appeared on paper in its externals and his personal view was completely excluded, and most importantly all requisite formality was observed. This work was something new. And he was one of the first people who worked out the practical application of the statutes of 1864.[3]

Moving to a new city to the post of examining magistrate, Ivan Ilyich made new acquaintances and connections, positioned himself afresh, and adopted a slightly different tone. He positioned himself at a certain respectable distance from the governing authorities, but chose the best circle of the lawyers and nobles who lived in the city and adopted a tone of slight dissatisfaction with government, moderate liberalism, and enlightened civic-mindedness. Moreover, without changing the elegance of his dress, in his new job Ivan Ilyich stopped shaving his chin and let his beard grow freely.

Ivan Ilyich's life turned out very pleasantly in the new city as well: the society that took a critical view of the governor was good and friendly; his salary was larger; and a not inconsiderable pleasure was added to his life by *vint*,

---

2. Proper, decorous (French).   **3.** A thorough reform of judicial proceedings in Russia, which followed the freeing of the serfs in 1861.

which Ivan Ilyich started to play, having an ability to play cards cheerfully, quick-wittedly, and very shrewdly so that generally he won.

After two years working in the new city Ivan Ilyich met his future wife. Praskovya Fyodorovna Mikhel was the most attractive, cleverest, most brilliant girl of the group in which Ivan Ilyich moved. Among the other amusements and relaxations from the labors of a magistrate Ivan Ilyich developed a playful, easy relationship with Praskovya Fyodorovna.

While he had been a special assignments official Ivan Ilyich used to dance as a matter of course; as an examining magistrate he now danced only on special occasions. He danced now in the sense that although he was a part of the new institutions and in the fifth grade,[4] when it came to dancing, then he could show that in this field he could do things better than others. So from time to time at the end of an evening he used to dance with Praskovya Fyodorovna, and it was during these dances in particular that he conquered her. She fell in love with him. Ivan Ilyich didn't have a clear, defined intention of marrying, but when the girl fell in love with him, he asked himself a question. "Actually, why not get married?" he said to himself.

Miss Praskovya Fyodorovna was from a good noble family, was not bad-looking, and had a bit of money. Ivan Ilyich could aspire to a more brilliant match, but this too was a good match. Ivan Ilyich had his salary; she, he hoped, would have as much again. The family connection was good; she was a sweet, pretty, and absolutely decent woman. To say that Ivan Ilyich married because he fell in love with his bride and found in her sympathy for his views on life would have been as unjust as to say that he married because people in his social circle approved of the match. Ivan Ilyich married because of both considerations: he was doing something pleasant for himself in acquiring such a wife, and at the same time he was doing something his superiors thought a right thing to do.

And so Ivan Ilyich married.

The actual process of marriage and the first period of married life, with its conjugal caresses, new furniture, new china, and new linen, went very well until his wife's pregnancy, so that Ivan Ilyich was beginning to think that marriage not only would not destroy the character of an easy, pleasant, cheerful life, one wholly decorous and approved of by society, which Ivan Ilyich thought the true quality of life, but would enhance it further. But then from the first months of his wife's pregnancy something new appeared, something unexpected, unpleasant, oppressive, and indecorous that one couldn't expect and from which one couldn't escape.

His wife for no reason, so Ivan Ilyich thought, as he said to himself, began *de gaieté de coeur*[5] to destroy the pleasant tenor and decorum of life. She was jealous of him without any cause, demanded attentions to herself from him, found fault with everything, and made crude and unpleasant scenes.

At first Ivan Ilyich had hoped to be freed from the unpleasantness of this situation by the same easy and decorous attitude to life which had rescued him before—he tried to ignore his wife's state of mind and continued to live pleasantly and decorously as before: he invited friends home for a game of

---

4. Fifth highest level of official rank, out of fourteen; the lowest level of the higher eschelons of Civil Service. **5.** From sheer impulsiveness (French).

cards; he tried to go out to his club or see his friends. But on one occasion his wife started to abuse him rudely with such energy and continued to abuse him so persistently every time he didn't fulfill her demands, clearly having made a firm decision not to stop until he would submit—that is, sit at home and be miserable like her—that Ivan Ilyich was horrified. He understood that married life—at any rate with his wife—does not always make for the pleasures and decorum of life but on the contrary often destroys them, and therefore it was essential to protect himself from this destruction. And Ivan Ilyich began to seek the means for this. His official work was one thing that impressed Praskovya Fyodorovna, and Ivan Ilyich through his official work and the duties that arose out of it began to fight his wife, securing his own independent world.

A child was born. There were attempts at feeding and various failures in this, along with the real and imaginary illnesses of child and mother. Sympathy for all this was demanded from Ivan Ilyich but he could understand nothing of it. So the requirement of Ivan Ilyich to fence in a world for himself outside of the family became all the more pressing.

As his wife became more irritable and demanding, so Ivan Ilyich moved the center of gravity of his life more and more into his official work. He came to like his work more and became more ambitious than he had been before.

Very soon, not more than a year after their marriage, Ivan Ilyich understood that married life, which offers certain conveniences, in reality is a very complicated and difficult business with which, in order to do one's duty—that is, to lead a decorous life that is approved of by society—one has to develop a defined relationship as one does with one's work.

And Ivan Ilyich did develop for himself such a relationship with married life. He required of family life only those conveniences it could give him, of dinner at home, a mistress of the house, a bed, and most importantly, that decorum of external appearances which were defined by public opinion. For the rest he looked for cheerfulness and pleasure, and if he found them was very grateful; if he met rejection and querulousness, he at once went off into the separate world of official work that he had fenced in for himself and found pleasure there.

Ivan Ilyich was valued as a good official and in three years he was made assistant prosecutor. His new responsibilities, their importance, the ability to bring anyone to trial and send him to prison, the public nature of his speeches, the success Ivan Ilyich had in this work—all of this tied him even more closely to his official work.

More children came. His wife became more and more querulous and angry, but the relationship Ivan Ilyich had developed with domestic life had made him almost impervious to her querulousness.

After seven years of working in one city Ivan Ilyich was promoted to the position of prosecutor in a different province. They moved; they now had little money and his wife didn't like the place to which they had moved. Though his salary was more than it had been, life cost more; also two children died, and so family life became even more unpleasant for Ivan Ilyich.

Praskovya Fyodorovna blamed her husband for all the misfortunes that befell them in their new home. Most subjects of conversation between husband and wife, particularly the education of the children, led to questions that recalled past disputes, and quarrels were ready to break out at every minute. There remained only rare periods of tenderness that came to the married couple but did not last long. These were islands on which they landed for a while but then again sailed off into the sea of hidden animosity which expressed itself in their alienation from each other. This alienation might have distressed Ivan Ilyich if he had thought that it should not be like this, but he now recognized this situation not just as normal but as the actual goal of his family life. His object was to free himself more and more from these unpleasant things and to give them a character of innocuous decorum; he achieved it by spending less and less time with his family and when he was forced to do it, he tried to protect his situation by the presence of outsiders. The important thing was that Ivan Ilyich had his official work. For him all the interest of life was concentrated in that official world, and this interest absorbed him. The consciousness of his power, of his ability to bring down anyone he chose to, his importance, even in externals when he entered the court and at meetings with subordinates, his mastery of conducting the work—all this made him feel glad, and together with talking to his friends, with dinners and *vint*, it filled up his life. So overall Ivan Ilyich's life continued to go on as he thought that it should: pleasantly and with decorum.

So he lived for another seven years. His elder daughter was now sixteen, another child had died, and there only remained a boy at the gymnasium, a subject of dissension. Ivan Ilyich had wanted to send him to law school but to spite him Praskovya Fyodorovna had sent the boy to the gymnasium. The daughter was taught at home and had grown into a good-looking girl; the boy too wasn't bad at his studies.

III

That was Ivan Ilyich's life for seventeen years after his marriage. He was now a senior prosecutor, having refused various promotions in the expectation of a more desirable position, when something very unpleasant happened which completely destroyed the tranquility of his life. Ivan Ilyich was expecting the position of president of the tribunal in a university town, but somehow Hoppe overtook him and got the place. Ivan Ilyich was angry, started to make accusations, and quarreled with him and his closest superiors; they cooled towards him and passed him over for the next appointment.

That was in 1880. That year was the hardest in Ivan Ilyich's life. In that year his salary wasn't sufficient for living; everyone forgot him, and what appeared to him to be the greatest, the cruellest injustice toward him was found by others to be something completely ordinary. Even his father didn't see it as his duty to help him. He felt everyone had abandoned him, considering his situation on a 3,500-ruble salary quite normal and even fortunate. He alone knew that with his consciousness of the injustices done to him, his wife's constant nagging, and the debts he was beginning to run, living above his means—he alone knew that his situation was far from normal.

In the summer of that year, to ease his finances he took some leave and went with his wife to spend the summer at Praskovya Fyodorovna's brother's home.

In the country, without his work, Ivan Ilyich for the first time felt not just boredom but unbearable depression, felt that he could not live like that and that he absolutely had to take some decisive action.

Having spent a sleepless night pacing the terrace, Ivan Ilyich decided to go to Petersburg to make a petition and, in order to punish *them*, those who could not appreciate him, to transfer to another ministry.

The next day, in spite of all the attempts of his wife and brother-in-law to dissuade him, he traveled to Petersburg.

He went for one thing: to obtain a five-thousand-ruble salary. He was no longer holding out for any particular ministry or direction or type of work. He just needed a position, a position on five thousand rubles, in government, in banking, in the railways, in the Empress Maria's Foundations,[6] even in customs, but he absolutely had to have five thousand rubles and he absolutely had to leave the ministry where they couldn't appreciate him.

And now this trip of Ivan Ilyich's was crowned with amazing, unexpected success. In Kursk he was joined in a first-class carriage by F. S. Ilyin, someone he knew, who told him about a telegram the governor of Kursk had just received that announced a reorganization to take place in the ministry: Pyotr Ivanovich's position was going to be taken by Ivan Semyonovich.

The planned upheaval, apart from its significance for Russia, had a particular significance for Ivan Ilyich: by promoting a new face, Pyotr Petrovich, and of course Zakhar Ivanovich, his classmate and friend, it was highly propitious for him.

In Moscow the news was confirmed. And when he reached Petersburg, Ivan Ilyich found Zakhar Ivanovich and got the promise of a sure place in his old ministry of justice.

After a week he telegraphed his wife: *Zakhar has Miller's place stop I receive position at next report.*

Thanks to this change of personnel Ivan Ilyich got this position in his old ministry, which placed him two ranks above his old colleagues as well as a salary of 5,000 rubles and 3,500 for removal expenses. All his anger against his former enemies and the entire ministry was forgotten, and Ivan Ilyich was altogether happy.

Ivan Ilyich returned to the country more cheerful and content than he had ever been. Praskovya Fyodorovna cheered up too and a truce was established between them. Ivan Ilyich told her how in Petersburg everyone had feted him, how all his old enemies had been shamed and were now crawling before him, how he was envied for his position, and especially how highly he was regarded by everyone in Petersburg.

Praskovya Fyodorovna listened to all this and appeared to believe it, and she didn't contradict him in anything but just made plans for their new life in the city to which they were moving. And Ivan Ilyich joyfully saw that these plans were his plans, that the plans were tallying, and that his life which had faltered was again taking on its true and natural character of cheerful pleasantness and decorum.

Ivan Ilyich had come just for a short time. On September 10 he had to take up the new job and furthermore he needed time to settle in their new home,

---

6. Charitable organizations founded by the wife of Tsar Paul I (1754–1801).

to move everything from the provincial city, and to buy and order many more things; in a word, to settle as had been decided in his own mind and almost exactly as had been decided in that of Praskovya Fyodorovna.

And now, when everything had worked out so well and he and his wife were agreed about their goals (and furthermore weren't living much together), they got on harmoniously as they hadn't done since the first years of married life. Ivan Ilyich thought of taking his family away with him immediately but the insistence of his brother-in-law and his wife, who had suddenly become particularly friendly and familial towards Ivan Ilyich and his family, resulted in Ivan Ilyich going away alone.

Ivan Ilyich left, and the cheerful state of mind brought about by his success and the harmony with his wife, one reinforcing the other, stayed with him the whole time. A delightful apartment was found, the very one husband and wife had been dreaming of. High, spacious, old-fashioned reception rooms; a comfortable, imposing study; rooms for his wife and daughter; a schoolroom for his son—everything as if devised purposely for them. Ivan Ilyich set about arranging it himself: he chose wallpaper, he bought more furniture (antiques in particular whose style he found particularly *comme il faut*), he had things upholstered, and it all grew and grew and approached the ideal he had composed for himself. Even when he had half arranged things, his arrangements exceeded his expectation. He understood the *comme il faut* look, elegant without vulgarity, which everything would take on once it was ready. As he went to sleep he imagined to himself how the reception room would be. Looking at the drawing room, which wasn't yet finished, he could already see the fireplace, the screen, the whatnot and the little chairs disposed about the room, the plates and saucers on the walls, and the bronzes all standing in their places. He was pleased by the thought that he would surprise Pasha and Lizanka, his wife and daughter, who also had a taste for this. They were certainly not expecting this. He was particularly successful in finding old things and buying them cheaply; they gave everything a particularly aristocratic air. In his letters he deliberately described everything in less attractive terms than the reality to surprise them. All this absorbed him so much that even his new job absorbed him less than he had expected—though he loved his work. During sittings of the court he had moments of absent mindedness; he started thinking about whether the curtain pelmets should be straight or curved. He was so absorbed by this that he often did things himself; he even moved the furniture about and rehung the curtains himself. Once he got up on a ladder to show a slow-witted decorator how he wanted the drapes hung; he missed his footing and fell, but being a strong and agile man he held his balance and only knocked his side on the handle of the window frame. The bruise was painful but soon disappeared. During all this time Ivan Ilyich felt particularly well and cheerful. He wrote, "I feel I'm fifteen years younger." He thought the work would be finished in September but it dragged on till mid-October. But the apartment was delightful—it wasn't just he who said this but everyone who saw it said so to him.

In actual fact it was the same as the houses of all people who are not so rich but want to be like the rich and so are only like one another: brocade, ebony, flowers, carpets, and bronzes, everything dark and shiny—everything that all people of a certain type do to be like all people of a certain type. And what he had was so like that that one couldn't even notice it, but to him it all looked somehow special. When he met his family at the railway station and took them to his apartment, all finished and lit up, and a manservant in a white tie opened the door into the flower-decked hall, and they went into the drawing room and study, he was very happy, he took them everywhere, drank in their praise, and beamed with pleasure. That evening, when over tea Praskovya Fyodorovna asked him among other things how he had fallen, he laughed and in front of them showed how he had gone flying and frightened the decorator.

"It's lucky I am a gymnast. Someone else might have been killed but I only knocked myself a bit here; when you touch it—it hurts, but it'll pass; it's just a bruise."

And they started to live in the new home which, as always, once they had settled in properly, turned out to have one room too few, with the new income which, as always, turned out to be too little (only not by very much—five hundred rubles). And life was very good. Especially good at first when all was not yet done and more still had to be done: things to be bought, ordered, moved, adjusted. Although there were some disagreements between husband and wife, they were both so pleased and there was so much to do that everything was finished without serious quarrels. When there was nothing left to do, it became a bit more boring and something seemed lacking, but now friend-ships were made and habits established and life filled up.

After spending the morning in court Ivan Ilyich returned for dinner, and at first his mood was good, although it suffered a little, specifically because of their home. (Every stain on a tablecloth or brocade or broken curtain cord irritated him; he had put in so much work into the arrangement that every disruption of it was painful to him.) But in general Ivan Ilyich's life went on just as in his view life should flow: easily, pleasantly, and decorously. He rose at nine, drank his coffee, read the newspapers, then put on his uniform and drove to the court. There the harness in which he worked was already molded for him and he slipped into it right away: petitioners, chancery inquiries, the chancery itself, public and executive sittings of the court. In all of these one had to know how to exclude anything raw and vital, which always destroys the even flow of official work: one couldn't admit any human relationships except official ones; the occasion for a relationship had to be solely official and so had the relationship itself. For example, a man would come in and want to find out something. Outside his official role Ivan Ilyich could not have any relationship with him; but if this man had a relationship with him as a member of the court, one that could be expressed on headed paper—then within the bounds of this relationship Ivan Ilyich would do everything, abso-lutely everything he could, and in doing this would observe the semblance of friendly relations, that is, courtesy. As soon as the official relationship was ended, so was any other. This ability to separate out the official side without combining it with his real life Ivan Ilyich possessed in the highest degree, and by his talents and long practice he had developed it to such a point that he even sometimes, like a virtuoso, would allow himself as if in jest to combine personal and official relationships. He would allow himself this because he always felt in himself the power to split off the official again when necessary and to reject the personal. Ivan Ilyich handled this work of his not just easily, agreeably, and decorously but even with the mastery of a virtuoso. Between cases he would smoke, drink tea, chat a bit about politics, a bit about generalities, a bit about cards, and most of all about official appointments. And he would return home tired but with the feeling of a virtuoso who had given a lucid performance of his part, one of the first violins in the orchestra. At home mother and daughter would go out somewhere or someone came to see them; his son was at the gymnasium, preparing his lessons with tutors and diligently studying the things they teach in a gymnasium. Everything was good. After dinner, if there were no guests, Ivan Ilyich would sometimes read a book about which people were talking a lot, and in the evenings he would sit down to his work, that is, read his papers, consult the law, examine testimony, and check it against the law. All this he found neither boring nor amusing. It was boring if he could be playing *vint*; but if there was no *vint*—then all the same this was better than sitting by himself or with his wife. Ivan Ilyich's pleasures were little dinners to which he would invite ladies and gentlemen who were important in terms of worldly position and spending his time with them: that was just like the usual way such people spend their time, just as his drawing room was like all drawing rooms.

Once they even had an evening party, with dancing. And Ivan Ilyich felt cheerful and everything was good, except he had a big quarrel with his wife over the cakes and sweets: Praskovya Fyodorovna had her own plan, but Ivan Ilyich insisted on getting everything from an expensive confectioner and the quarrel was because there were cakes left over and the confectioner's bill came to forty-five rubles. The quarrel was a big and unpleasant one to such a point that Praskovya Fyodorovna called him "an idiot and a misery," and he took his head in his hands and in a fit of temper said something about divorce. But the actual party was enjoyable. The very best society was there and Ivan Ilyich danced with Princess Trufonova, sister of the famous founder of the Goodbye Sorrow Society. His official pleasures were pleasures of pride; his social pleasures were pleasures of vanity; but Ivan Ilyich's real pleasures were the pleasures of playing *vint*. He admitted that after all the various unhappy events in his life the pleasure that burnt like a candle above all others was to sit down at *vint* with good players and partners who didn't shout, definitely in a four (when you're five it's really annoying to have to stand out, although you pretend you very much like it), and to have an intelligent, serious game (when the cards are right), and then to have supper and drink a glass of wine. After *vint*, especially after a little win (a big win was unpleasant), Ivan Ilyich went to bed in an especially good mood.

That's how they lived. They formed around them a group of the best society, important people went to them and young people, too.

Husband, wife, and daughter were agreed in their views of their circle of acquaintances, and without any formal understanding they dropped and were rid of all sorts of shabby little friends and relatives who used to drop in to see them, spouting endearments into the drawing room with Japanese plates hanging on the wall. Soon these shabby little friends stopped dropping in and the Golovins were left with just the very best society. Young men paid court to Lizanka and Petrishchev, an examining magistrate, the son of Dmitry Ivanovich Petrishchev and sole heir to his property, began to pay so much attention to her that Ivan Ilyich even talked about it to Praskovya Fyodorovna.

Shouldn't they bring them together in a troika ride or organize some theatricals? That's how they lived. And everything went on like that, without any change, and everything was very good.

I V

They were all in good health. One couldn't call poor health the fact that Ivan Ilyich sometimes said he had an odd taste in his mouth and something felt uncomfortable on the left side of his stomach.

But it happened that this discomfort started to grow and to become not quite pain but the consciousness of a constant heaviness in his side accompanied by a bad mood. This bad mood, which got worse and worse, began to spoil the pleasant course of the easy and decorous life that had been established in the Golovin house. Husband and wife began to quarrel more and more often, and soon the ease and pleasantness disappeared and only decorum was preserved, with difficulty. Again scenes became more frequent. Again there remained just some islands of calm, and only a few of those, on which husband and wife could meet without an outburst.

And Praskovya Fyodorovna now said, not without cause, that her husband had a difficult character. With her natural habit of exaggeration she said he had always had this dreadful character, and that one needed her good nature to stand it for twenty years. It was true that the quarrels now started with him. His fault-finding always began just before dinner and often when he was starting to eat, over the soup. He would remark that one of the dishes was damaged, or the food wasn't right, or his son had his elbow on the table, or it was his daughter's hairstyle. And he blamed Praskovya Fyodorovna for everything. At first Praskovya Fyodorovna answered back and was rude to him, but a couple of times at the beginning of dinner he flew into such a rage that she understood this was a morbid condition brought on by the intake of food, so she controlled herself and didn't answer back but ate her dinner quickly. Praskovya Fyodorovna regarded her self-control as greatly to her own credit. Having decided that her husband had a dreadful character and that he had created the unhappiness of her life, she started to feel sorry for herself. And the more she felt sorry for herself, the more she hated her husband. She began to wish that he would die, but she couldn't wish for that because then there would be no salary. And that irritated her even more. She considered herself terribly unhappy precisely because even his death could not rescue her and she became irritated; she concealed it and her concealed irritation increased his own irritation.

After one scene, in which Ivan Ilyich was particularly unfair, and after which in explaining himself he said he was indeed prone to irritability but that it came from his illness, she said to him that if he was ill then he must get treatment, and demanded from him that he see a famous doctor.

He went. Everything was as he had expected; everything happened as it always does. The waiting and the doctor's assumed pompousness, something familiar to him that he knew from himself in court, and the tapping and the auscultation and the questions requiring predetermined and clearly unnecessary answers, and the meaningful air suggesting that you just submit to us, we'll fix everything—we know, we have no doubts about how to fix everything, in the very same way for any man you choose. Everything was precisely as in court. Just as he in court put on an air towards the accused, so in precisely the same way the famous doctor put on an air towards him.

The doctor said: such and such shows that you have such and such inside; but if that isn't confirmed by examining such and such, then one must assume you have such and such. If one does assume such and such, then . . . and so forth. Only one question was important to Ivan Ilyich: was his condition dangerous or not? But the doctor ignored this inappropriate question. From the doctor's point of view the question was pointless and wasn't the one under discussion; it was only a question of assessing various possibilities—a floating kidney, chronic catarrh, or an infection of the appendix. It wasn't a question of Ivan Ilyich's life but an argument between a floating kidney and the appendix. And before Ivan Ilyich's eyes the doctor resolved the argument brilliantly in favor of the floating kidney, with the reservation that an examination of his urine could provide new evidence and then the case would be looked at again. All this was very precisely what Ivan Ilyich himself had done a thousand times with defendants and as brilliantly. The doctor did his summing-up just as brilliantly, triumphantly, even cheerfully, looking at the defendant over his glasses. From the doctor's summing-up Ivan Ilyich drew the conclusion that things were bad, that it didn't matter much to the doctor or probably to anyone else, but that for him things were bad. And Ivan Ilyich was painfully struck by this conclusion that aroused in him a feeling of great self-pity and of great anger toward this doctor who was indifferent to such an important question.

But he didn't say anything and got up, put the money on the desk, and said with a sigh:

"Probably we patients often put inappropriate questions to you. In general terms, is this a dangerous illness or not?"

The doctor gave him one stern look through his glasses as if to say: Accused, if you will not stay within the boundaries of the questions that are put to you, then I will be compelled to give instructions for your removal from the courtroom.

"I have already told you what I consider necessary and proper," said the doctor. "An examination will show the rest." And the doctor bowed.

Ivan Ilyich slowly went out, despondently got into the sleigh, and went home. For the whole journey he ceaselessly went over everything the doctor had said, trying to turn those confused, unclear, scientific words into simple language and to read in them an answer to the question: Am I in a bad way, or a very bad way, or aren't things yet so bad? And he thought that the sense of everything the doctor had said was that he was in a very bad way. Everything in the streets looked sad to Ivan Ilyich. The cab drivers were sad, the houses were sad, the passersby, the shops. This pain, this dull nagging pain that didn't stop for a single second, combined with the doctor's unclear pronouncements acquired another more serious meaning. Ivan Ilyich listened to his pain with a new heavy feeling.

He arrived home and started to tell his wife. His wife listened but in the middle of his account his daughter came in wearing a hat: she and her mother were going out. She sat down for a moment to listen to this boring stuff but she couldn't stand it for long, and her mother didn't listen to the end.

"Now I'm very pleased," his wife said. "So mind you take your medicine properly. Give me the prescription, I'll send Gerasim to the chemist's." And she went to dress.

While she was in the room he was barely able to breathe and he sighed heavily when she went out.

"Well then," he said. "Perhaps it's not so bad."

He began to take the medicines and to follow the doctor's directions, which changed after the urine examination. But it was the case now that there had been some kind of confusion in the examination and in what followed from it. It was impossible to get through to the doctor himself, but it turned out that what was happening was not what the doctor had told him. Either he had forgotten or he had lied or he had concealed something from Ivan Ilyich.

But Ivan Ilyich still started to follow the directions precisely and in doing so at first found some comfort.

From the time he visited the doctor Ivan Ilyich's chief occupations became the precise following of the doctor's directions about hygiene and the monitoring of his pain and all his bodily functions. Ivan Ilyich's chief interests became human illness and human health. When others talked in front of him about people who were ill or had died or had gotten better, and in particular about any illness that resembled his own, he would listen, trying to conceal his agitation, ask questions, and apply what was said to his own illness.

The pain got no less but Ivan Ilyich made an effort to force himself to think he was better. And he could deceive himself as long as nothing disturbed him. But as soon as there was some unpleasantness with his wife or something went wrong at work or he had bad cards at *vint*, he at once felt the full force of his illness. In the past he had endured things going wrong in the expectation that *I'll soon put things right, I'll overcome, I'll be successful, I'll get a grand slam.* Now anything that went wrong brought him down and cast him into despair. He would say to himself, "I was just starting to get better and the medicine was already beginning to work, and along comes this cursed accident or unpleasantness. . . ." And he was angry with the accident or with the people who were causing him unpleasantnesses and killing him, and he felt that this anger was killing him but he couldn't restrain himself. One might have thought it would have been clear to him that this anger against circumstances and people made his illness worse, and that therefore he shouldn't pay any attention to unpleasant incidents, but his reasoning was quite the reverse: He said he needed calm; he watched out for anything that might breach that calm and at the smallest breach he got angry. His condition was made worse by the fact that he consulted medical books and doctors. His deterioration progressed so evenly that comparing one day with another he could deceive himself—there was little difference. But when he consulted doctors, he thought he was getting worse and that very quickly. And in spite of that he constantly consulted doctors.

That month he went to see another celebrity doctor; this other celebrity doctor said almost the same as the first but put the questions differently. And consulting this celebrity doctor only deepened Ivan Ilyich's doubt and terror. A friend of a friend—a very good doctor—diagnosed his illness quite differently, and in spite of promising recovery, his questions and assumptions confused Ivan Ilyich even more and increased his doubts. A homeopath diagnosed his illness again quite differently and gave him some medicine, and Ivan Ilyich took it in secret from everyone for about a week. But after a week, feeling no relief and having lost confidence both in the previous treatments and in this one, he fell into greater despair. On one occasion a lady he knew was talking about the healing powers of icons. Ivan Ilyich found himself listening carefully and believing the reality of this. This incident frightened him. "Have I really become so feeble-minded?" he said to himself. "What rubbish! It's all nonsense. I mustn't give in to hypochondria, but having chosen one doctor I must firmly stick to his treatment. That's what I'll do. Now it's settled. I'm not going to think and I'm going to follow the treatment strictly till the summer. Then there'll be something to show. Let's now have an end to all this wavering!" It was easy to say that but impossible to put it into action. The pain in his side wore him down; it seemed to keep getting worse; it became constant; the taste in his mouth became stronger; he thought a disgusting smell was coming from his mouth; and his appetite and strength were going. He couldn't deceive himself: something terrible, new, and important was happening in him, something more important than anything that had happened to Ivan Ilyich in his life. And only he knew about this; all those around him either didn't understand or didn't want to understand and thought that everything in the world was going on as before. That was what tormented Ivan Ilyich most of all. He could see that his household—chiefly his wife and daughter who were in the full swing of visits and parties—understood nothing, and they were vexed that he was so gloomy and demanding, as if he were guilty in that. Although they tried to conceal it, he saw that he was a burden to them, but that his wife had evolved a particular attitude to his illness and adhered to that irrespective of what he said and did. Her attitude was like this:

"You know," she would say to friends, "Ivan Ilyich can't strictly follow a prescribed treatment, as most good people can. Today he'll take his drops and eat what he's been told to and go to bed in good time, but tomorrow if I don't look properly, he'll suddenly forget to take them and eat oysters (which are forbidden him) and sit down to *vint* till one in the morning."

"When did I do that?" Ivan Ilyich would say crossly. "Once at Pyotr Ivanovich's."

"Yesterday with Shebek."

"I just couldn't sleep from the pain . . ."

"Well, whatever it was from, like that you won't get better and you make us miserable."

Praskovya Fyodorovna's public attitude to her husband's illness, which she expressed to others and to him, was that this illness was Ivan Ilyich's own fault and that the whole illness was a new unpleasantness he was bringing down on his wife. Ivan Ilyich felt that this came out in her involuntarily, that didn't make it any easier for him.

In court Ivan Ilyich noticed or thought he noticed the same tude to him: now he would think that people were scruti man whose position was soon going to be vacant; now friends would start to joke in an amicable way about his this thing, this awful, terrible, unheard-of thing that had g was ceaselessly gnawing at him and irrepressibly dragging him somewhere, were the most pleasant subject for a joke. He was especially irritated by Schwarz with his playfulness and energy and *comme il faut* ways, all of which reminded Ivan Ilyich of himself ten years back.

Friends came to make up a game; they sat down. They dealt, bending the new cards; he put diamonds next to diamonds, seven of them. His partner bid no trumps—and held two diamonds. What could be better? Things were cheerful and bright—they had a grand slam. And suddenly Ivan Ilyich felt that gnawing pain, that taste in the mouth, and there seemed to him to be something absurd in the fact that he could rejoice in a grand slam.

He looked at Mikhail Mikhaylovich, his partner, rapping his powerful hand on the table and politely and condescendingly refraining from scooping up the tricks but pushing the cards toward Ivan Ilyich to give him the pleasure of picking them up without straining himself and stretching out his arm. "Does he think I'm so weak I can't stretch out my arm?" Ivan Ilyich thought. He forgot about trumps and trumped his partner, losing the grand slam by three tricks—and what was really dreadful was that he saw how Mikhail Mikhaylovich was suffering, but he didn't care. And it was dreadful to think just why he didn't care.

They all saw he was feeling bad and said to him, "We can stop if you are tired. You must rest." Rest? No, he wasn't tired at all, and they finished the rubber. They were all gloomy and silent. Ivan Ilyich felt he had brought down this gloom upon them and he couldn't dispel it. They had supper and went their ways, and Ivan Ilyich was left alone with the knowledge that his life had been poisoned for him, that it was poisoning the lives of others, and that this poison wasn't losing its power but was penetrating his whole being more and more.

And with this knowledge, with the physical pain, and with the terror, he had to get into bed and often be unable to sleep from the pain the greater part of the night. And the next morning he had to get up again, dress, go to court, talk, write, or if he didn't go to court he had to stay at home with those twenty-four hours of the day, each one of which was a torment. And he had to live like that on the brink of the abyss, all alone, without a single person who could understand and take pity on him.

V

A month went by like that and then another. Before the new year his brother-in-law came to the city and stayed with them. Ivan Ilyich was in court. Praskovya Fyodorovna had gone out shopping. When Ivan Ilyich went into his study he found his brother-in-law, a healthy, full-blooded fellow, unpacking his suitcase himself. He raised his head when he heard Ivan Ilyich's footsteps and looked at him for a second in silence. That look revealed everything to Ivan Ilyich. His brother-in-law opened his mouth to say "oh" and stopped himself. That movement confirmed everything.

"So, I've changed, haven't I?"

"Yes . . . there is a change."

And however much afterwards Ivan Ilyich turned the conversation with his her-in-law to his appearance, his brother-in-law said nothing. Praskovya

Fyodorovna arrived, his brother-in-law went out to her. Ivan Ilyich locked his door and started to examine himself in the mirror—face-on, then from the side. He took up a photograph of himself with his wife and compared the image with the one he saw in the mirror. The change was huge. Then he bared his arms to the elbow, looked, rolled his sleeves down again, and sat on an ottoman, and his mood became darker than night.

"You mustn't, you mustn't," he said to himself; he jumped up, went to the desk, opened a case file, and began to read it, but he couldn't. He unlocked the door and went into the salon. The drawing-room door was shut. He tip-toed to it and began to listen.

"No, you're exaggerating," said Praskovya Fyodorovna.

"Exaggerating? You don't see—he's a dead man, look at his eyes. There's no light in them. What's the matter with him?"

"Nobody knows. Nikolayev [that was the second doctor] said something, but I don't know what. Leshchetitsky [that was the celebrated doctor] said the opposite . . ."

Ivan Ilyich moved away, went to his room, lay down, and started to think: *A kidney, a floating kidney.* He remembered everything the doctor had told him—how it had become detached and was floating. And with an effort of the imagination he tried to understand his kidney and to halt it and strengthen it; so little was needed for that, he thought. *No, I'll go again to Pyotr Ivanovich.* (That was the friend who had a friend who was a doctor.) He rang, gave orders for the horse to be harnessed, and got ready to leave.

"Where are you off to, *Jean*?"[7] his wife said, using a particularly sad and unusually kind expression.

This unusual kindness angered him. He looked at her morosely.

"I have to go to Pyotr Ivanovich."

He went to his friend who had a friend who was a doctor. He found him at home and had a long conversation with him.

When he considered both the anatomical and physiological details of what, in the doctor's opinion, had been happening inside him, he understood everything.

There was something, a little something in the appendix. All that might be put right. Stimulate the activity of one organ, weaken the activity of another; the something would be absorbed and everything would be put right. He got back a little late for dinner, talked cheerfully for a bit, but for a long time he couldn't go to his room to work. Finally he went into his study and at once sat down to work. He read his cases and worked, but the consciousness that he had set something aside—an important and intimate matter which he would take up once his work was over—did not leave him. When he had finished his cases, he remembered that this intimate matter was his thinking about his appendix. But he didn't indulge it; he went to the drawing room for tea. There were guests, including the examining magistrate, his daughter's intended; they talked and played the piano and sang. Ivan Ilyich spent the evening, as Praskovya Fyodorovna noticed, more cheerfully than he had spent others, but he didn't forget for one minute that he had set aside some important

7. The French equivalent for Ivan. In the 19th century, Russians of the upper classes frequently spoke French to each other.

thinking about his appendix. At eleven o'clock he said goodnight and went to his room. Since he had become ill he slept in a little room next to his study. He went in, undressed, and picked up a novel of Zola's,[8] which he didn't read. He began thinking instead. The desired cure of the appendix took place in his imagination. Matter was absorbed, matter was expelled, and normal activity was restored. "Yes, that's how it all is," he said to himself. "Only nature needs a little help." He remembered his medicine, sat up, took it, watching for the beneficial effects of the medicine and the removal of the pain. "Just take it regularly and avoid unhealthy influences; I already feel a bit better, much better." He started to feel his side—it wasn't painful to the touch. "Yes, I can't feel it; I'm really much better now." He put out the candle and lay on his side. "The appendix is getting better; things are being absorbed." Suddenly he felt the familiar old dull nagging pain, the persistent, quiet, serious pain. The familiar nastiness in his mouth. His heart began to pump, his head turned. "My God, my God!" he said. "It's here again, it's here again and it's never going to stop." And suddenly his case presented itself to him from a different perspective. "Appendix! Kidney!" he said to himself. "It's not a case of the appendix or of the kidney, but of life . . . and death. Yes, I had life and now it's passing, passing, and I can't hold it back. That's it. Why deceive oneself? Isn't it obvious to everyone but myself that I am dying, and it's only a question of the number of weeks, days—maybe now. There was light and now there's darkness. I was here but now I'm going there! Where?" A chill came over him, his breathing stopped. He could only hear the beating of his heart.

"I won't exist, so what will exist? Nothing will exist. So where will I be when I don't exist? Is this really death? No, I don't want it." He got up quickly, tried to light a candle, groped with shaking hands, dropped the candle and candlestick on the floor, and slumped back again onto the pillow. "Why? Nothing matters," he said to himself, looking into the darkness with open eyes. "Death. Yes, death. And none of them knows and they don't want to know and they have no pity for me. They're enjoying themselves." Outside the door he could hear the distant noise of music and singing. "They don't care but they too will die. Fools. It'll come to me first, to them later; they too will have the same. But they're having fun, the beasts!" Anger choked him. And he felt painful, unbearable misery. "It cannot be that we're all doomed to this terrible fear." He raised himself.

"Something's not right; I must calm down, I must think over everything from the outset." And he began to think. "Yes, the start of my illness. I knocked my side, and I stayed just the same that day and the next; it ached a bit, then more, then the doctors, then depression, despair, the doctors again; and I kept getting nearer and nearer to the abyss. Less strength. Nearer and nearer. And now I've wasted away, there's no light in my eyes. And death, and I think about my appendix. I think of how to mend my appendix, but this is death. Is it really death?" Again horror came over him; he bent down, tried to find the matches, and banged his elbow on the nighttable. It got in his way and hurt him; he got angry with it; in his irritation he banged his elbow harder and

---

8. Émile Zola (1840–1902), French novelist.

knocked the nighttable over. And in his despair he fell back, gasping for breath, expecting death to come now.

Now the guests were leaving. Praskovya Fyodorovna was seeing them out. She heard something fall and came in.

"What's the matter with you?"

"Nothing. I knocked it over by mistake."

She went out and brought back a candle. He lay breathing heavily and very fast, like a man who has run a mile, looking at her with motionless eyes.

"What's the matter with you, *Jean*?"

"Nothing. I . . . knocked . . . it . . . over." (*What should I say? She won't understand*, he thought.)

Indeed she didn't. She picked the table up, lit a candle for him, and quickly went out; she had to see a guest out.

When she returned, he was lying in the same position, on his back, looking up.

"How are you feeling? Is it worse?"

"Yes, it is."

She shook her head and sat down.

"You know, *Jean*, I am wondering whether we shouldn't ask Leshchetitsky to the house."

That meant asking the celebrated doctor regardless of cost. He smiled venomously and said, "No." She sat for a while, then went over to him and kissed him on the forehead.

When she kissed him he hated her with all his might and made an effort not to push her away.

"Good night. With God's help you'll go to sleep."

"Yes."

V I

Ivan Ilyich saw that he was dying and was in constant despair.

Ivan Ilyich knew in the very depths of his soul that he was dying but not only could he not get accustomed to this, he simply didn't understand it; he just couldn't understand it.

All his life the example of a syllogism he had studied in Kiesewetter's[9] logic—"Caius is a man, men are mortal, therefore Caius is mortal"—had seemed to him to be true only in relation to Caius but in no way to himself. There was Caius the man, man in general, and it was quite justified, but he wasn't Caius and he wasn't man in general, and he had always been something quite, quite special apart from all other beings; he was Vanya,[1] with Mama, with Papa, with Mitya and Volodya, with his toys and the coachman, with Nyanya, then with Katenka, with all the joys, sorrows, passions of childhood, boyhood, youth. Did Caius know the smell of the striped leather ball Vanya loved so much? Did Caius kiss his mother's hand like that and did the silken folds of Caius's mother's dress rustle like that for him? Was Caius in love like that? Could Caius chair a session like that?

---

9. The *Outline of Logic according to Kantian Principles* by Kiesewetter (1766–1819) was widely used as a Russian text book.   **1.** The diminutive of Ivan, what he would have been called as a child.

And Caius is indeed mortal and it's right that he should die, but for me, Vanya, Ivan Ilyich, with all my feelings and thoughts—for me it's quite different. And it cannot be that I should die. It would be too horrible.

That's what he felt.

"If I had to die like Caius, then I would know it, an inner voice would be telling me, but nothing like that happened in me, and I and all my friends—we understood that things weren't at all like with Caius. But now there's this!" he said to himself. "It can't be. It can't be, but it is. How has this happened? How can one understand it?"

And he couldn't understand it and tried to banish this thought as false, inaccurate, morbid, and to replace it with other true and healthy thoughts. But this thought, and not just the thought but reality as it were came and stopped in front of him.

And in the place of this thought he called up others in turn in the hope of finding support in them. He tried to return to his previous ways of thought, which had concealed the thought of death from him. But—strangely—everything which previously had concealed and covered up and obliterated the awareness of death now could no longer produce this result. Ivan Ilyich now spent most of his time attempting to restore his previous ways of feeling that had concealed death. Now he would say to himself, "I'll take up some work, that's what I live by." And he went to court, banishing all his doubts; he talked to friends and sat down, absentmindedly looking over the crowd of people with a pensive look as he used to and supporting both wasted hands on the arms of his oak chair; leaning over toward a friend as usual, moving the papers of a case, whispering together, and then suddenly raising his eyes and sitting up straight, he would pronounce the particular words and open the case. But suddenly in the middle of it, the pain in his side, ignoring the stages of the case's development, began its own gnawing work. Ivan Ilyich listened and tried not to think about it, but it kept on. It came and stood right in front of him and looked at him, and he became petrified; the fire in his eyes died down, and he again began to ask himself, "Is it alone the truth?" And his friends and staff saw with surprise and dismay that he, such a brilliant, subtle judge, was getting confused and making mistakes. He would give himself a shake, make an effort to recover himself, and somehow or other bring the session to an end, and he would return home with the depressing awareness that his work as a judge couldn't hide from him as it used to what he wanted it to hide; that with his work as a judge he couldn't be rid of It. And what was worst of all was that It was distracting him not to make him do anything but only for him to look at It, right in the eye, look at it and without doing anything endure inexpressible sufferings.

And to rescue himself from this condition, Ivan Ilyich looked for relief—for new screens—and new screens appeared and for a short time seemed to offer him salvation, but very soon they again not so much collapsed as let the light through, as if It penetrated everything and nothing could hide it.

Latterly he would go into the drawing room he had arranged—the drawing room where he had fallen—how venomously comic it was to think of it—for the arrangement of which he had sacrificed his life, for he knew that his illness had started with that injury; he would go in and see that something had made a scratch on a polished table. He would look for the cause and find it in the bronze ornament of an album that had become bent at the edge. He would pick up the album, an expensive one he had lovingly compiled, and be cross at the carelessness of his daughter and her friends—things were torn and the photographs bent. He would carefully set things to rights and bend the decoration back again.

He then would have the thought of moving this whole *établissement*[2] of albums over into another corner by the flowers. He would call the manservant; either his daughter or his wife would come to his help; they would disagree, contradict him; he would argue, get angry, but everything would be all right because he didn't remember It, couldn't see It.

And then his wife would say when he himself was moving something, "Let the servants do it, you'll hurt yourself again," and suddenly It would flash through the screens; he would see It flash just for a moment, and he still would hope It would disappear, but without wanting to he would pay attention to his side—the same thing would still be sitting there, still aching, and he couldn't forget it, and It would be looking at him quite openly from behind the flowers. Why?

It's true, it was here on these curtains that I lost my life as if in an assault. Did I really? How terrible and how stupid! It can't be so! It can't be, but it is.

He would go into his study, lie down, and be left alone with It. Face-to-face with It, but nothing to be done with It. Just look at It and turn cold.

VII

How it happened in the third month of Ivan Ilyich's illness is impossible to say because it happened step by step, imperceptibly, but it did happen that his wife and his daughter and his son and the servants and his friends and the doctors and, above all, he himself knew that all interest others had in him lay solely in whether he would soon, at last, vacate his place, free the living from the constraint brought about by his presence, and be liberated himself from his sufferings.

He slept less and less; they gave him opium and started to inject morphine. But that gave him no relief. The dull pangs he felt in his half-somnolent state at first gave him relief as being something new, but then they became as agonizing as outright pain or even more so.

They prepared special food to the doctors' prescriptions, but this food he found more and more tasteless, more and more disgusting.

Special contrivances had to be made for excretion, and every time this was a torment for him. A torment because of the uncleanliness, the loss of decorum, and the odor, from the consciousness that another person had to take part in this.

But some comfort for Ivan Ilyich did come out of this unpleasant business. Gerasim, the manservant, always came to take things out for him.

Gerasim was a clean, fresh young peasant who had filled out on city food. He was always cheerful and sunny. At first Ivan Ilyich was embarrassed by seeing this man, always dressed in his clean, traditional clothes, having to do this repulsive job.

2. Arrangement (French).

Once getting up from the pan and lacking the strength to pull up his trousers, he collapsed into an easy chair and looked with horror at his feeble bare thighs with their sharply defined muscles.

Gerasim came in with firm, light steps in his heavy boots, giving off a pleasant smell of tar from the boots and of fresh winter air; he had on a clean hessian apron and a clean cotton shirt, the sleeves rolled up over his strong, young, bare arms; without looking at Ivan Ilyich, he went to the vessel, obviously masking the joy in living shining out from his face so as not to hurt the sick man.

"Gerasim," Ivan Ilyich said weakly.

Gerasim started, obviously scared he had made some mistake, and with a quick movement turned toward the sick man his fresh, kind, simple, young face, which was just beginning to grow a beard.

"Do you need something, sir?"

"I think this must be unpleasant for you. You must forgive me. I can't manage."

"No, sir." Gerasim's eyes were shining and he showed his young white teeth. "What's a little trouble? You've got an illness."

And with strong, dexterous hands he did his usual job and went out, treading lightly. And in five minutes, treading just as lightly, he came back.

Ivan Ilyich was still sitting there like that in the armchair.

"Gerasim," he said when Gerasim had put down the clean, rinsed vessel, "please, come here and help me." Gerasim came. "Lift me up. It's difficult by myself and I've sent Dmitry away."

Gerasim came over to him; he put his strong arms around him and, gently and deftly, the same way he walked, lifted and supported him; he pulled up his trousers with one hand and was going to sit him down. But Ivan Ilyich asked Gerasim to take him to the sofa. Effortlessly and with next to no pressure, Gerasim led him, almost carrying him, to the sofa and sat him down.

"Thank you. How easily, how well . . . you do everything."

Gerasim again smiled and was about to go out. But Ivan Ilyich felt so good with him around that he didn't want to let him go.

"Now. Please move this chair over to me. No, that one, underneath my legs. I feel better when my legs are higher."

Gerasim brought the chair, placed it without making any noise, lowering it in one movement to the floor, and lifted Ivan Ilyich's legs onto the chair; Ivan Ilyich thought he felt better the moment Gerasim raised up his legs.

"I feel better when my legs are higher," Ivan Ilyich said. "Put that cushion under me."

Gerasim did that. Again he lifted his legs up and put the cushion into position. Again Ivan Ilyich felt better when Gerasim held his legs up. When he lowered them, he thought he felt worse.

"Gerasim," he said to him, "are you busy now?"

"No sir, not at all," said Gerasim, who had learned from the townsfolk how to talk to the gentry.

"What do you still have to do?"

"What is there to do? I've done everything; I've just got to chop the wood for tomorrow."

"So hold my legs up a bit higher, can you do that?"

"Of course I can." Gerasim lifted up his legs and Ivan Ilyich thought that in this position he felt absolutely no pain.

"But what about the wood?"

"Don't worry, sir. We'll manage."

Ivan Ilyich told Gerasim to sit down and hold up his legs, and he talked to him. And—strange to say—he thought he felt better while Gerasim held up his legs.

From that day Ivan Ilyich started sometimes to call Gerasim in to him and made him hold up his legs on his shoulders, and he liked to talk to him. Gerasim did this easily, willingly, simply, and with a goodness of heart that touched Ivan Ilyich. In all other people Ivan Ilyich was offended by health, strength, high spirits; only Gerasim's strength and high spirits didn't depress but calmed Ivan Ilyich.

Ivan Ilyich's chief torment was the lie—that lie, for some reason recognized by everyone, that he was only ill but not dying, and that he only needed rest and treatment and then there would be some very good outcome. But he knew that whatever they did, there would be no outcome except even more painful suffering and death. And he was tormented by this lie; he was tormented by their unwillingness to acknowledge what everyone knew and he knew, by their wanting to lie to him about his terrible situation, by their wanting him to and making him take part in that lie himself. The lie, this lie being perpetrated above him on the eve of his death, the lie which could only bring down this terrible solemn act of his death to the level of all their visits and curtains and sturgeon for dinner . . . was horribly painful for Ivan Ilyich. And, strangely, many times when they were performing their tricks above him, he was within a hair's breadth of crying out to them, "Stop lying; you know and I know that I am dying; so at least stop lying." But he never had the strength to do it. The terrible, horrific act of his dying, he saw, had been brought down by all those surrounding him to the level of a casual unpleasantness, some breach of decorum (as one treats a man who, entering a drawing room, emits a bad smell); brought down by that very "decorum" he had served his whole life, he saw that no one had pity for him because no one even wanted to understand his situation. Only Gerasim understood his situation and felt pity for him. And so Ivan Ilyich only felt comfortable with Gerasim. He felt comfortable when Gerasim held up his legs, sometimes for whole nights without a break, and wouldn't go off to bed, saying, "Please, sir, don't worry, Ivan Ilyich, I'll still get plenty of sleep"; or when he would suddenly add, going over to the familiar "thou," "You're sick, so why shouldn't I do something for you?" Gerasim was the only one not to lie; everything showed he was the only one who understood what the matter was and didn't think it necessary to hide it, and simply felt pity for his wasted, feeble master. He even once said directly when Ivan Ilyich was dismissing him:

"We'll all die. So why not take a little trouble?" He said this, conveying by it that he wasn't bothered by the work precisely because he was doing it for a dying man and hoped that in his time someone would do this work for him.

Apart from this lie, or as a consequence of it, what was most painful for Ivan Ilyich was that no one had pity on him as he wanted them to have pity;

at some moments after prolonged sufferings Ivan Ilyich wanted most of all, however much he felt ashamed to admit it, for someone to have pity on him like a sick child. He wanted them to caress him, to kiss him, to cry over him as one caresses and comforts children. He knew he was an important legal official, that he had a graying beard and that therefore this was impossible, but he still wanted it. And in his relations with Gerasim there was something close to that, and therefore his relations with Gerasim comforted him. Ivan Ilyich would want to cry, would want them to caress him and cry over him; then in would come his friend, the lawyer Shebek, and instead of crying and caresses Ivan Ilyich would assume a serious, stern, pensive expression and out of inertia would give his opinion on the meaning of a verdict of the court of appeal and stubbornly insist on it. This lie all around him and inside him more than anything poisoned the last days of Ivan Ilyich's life.

VIII

It was morning. It was morning only because Gerasim had gone out and Pyotr the manservant came in, put out the candles, opened one curtain, and started quietly to tidy up. Whether it was morning or evening, Friday or Sunday, was immaterial, it was all one and the same: the gnawing, agonizing pain that didn't abate for a moment; the consciousness of life departing without hope but still not yet departed; the same terrible, hateful death advancing, which was the only reality, and always the same lie. What did days, weeks, and times of day matter here?

"Would you like some tea?"

He has to have order; masters should drink tea in the mornings, he thought and only said:

"No."

"Would you like to move to the sofa?"

He has to tidy the chamber, and I'm in the way; I am dirt, disorder, he thought and only said:

"No, leave me be."

The manservant did some more things. Ivan Ilyich stretched out his hand. Pyotr came up to serve.

"What do you want?"

"My watch."

Pyotr got the watch, which was lying right there, and handed it to him.

"Half past eight. Have they got up?"

"No, sir. Vasily Ivanovich"—that was his son—"has gone to the gymnasium, but Praskovya Fyodorovna gave orders to wake her if you asked for her. Shall I?"

"No, don't." *Shall I try some tea?* he thought. "Yes, tea . . . bring it."

Pyotr went to the door. Ivan Ilyich felt terrified of being left alone. *How can I detain him? Yes, my medicine.* "Pyotr, give me my medicine." *Why not, maybe the medicine will still help.* He took the spoon and drank. *No, it won't help. It's all nonsense and a sham,* he decided as soon as he sensed the familiar sickly, hopeless taste. *No, I can't believe in it any more. But the pain, why the pain, if it would just go down even for a minute.* And he groaned. Pyotr turned round again. "No, go away. Bring me some tea."

Pyotr went out. Left alone, Ivan Ilyich groaned not so much from the pain, however frightful it was, as from anguish. "Always the same, always these endless days and nights. If only it could be soon. What could be soon? Death, darkness. No, no. Anything is better than death!"

When Pyotr came in with the tea on a tray, Ivan Ilyich looked distractedly at him for a long time, not taking in who and what he was. Pyotr was embarrassed by this stare. And when Pyotr was embarrassed, Ivan Ilyich came to himself.

"Yes," he said, "tea . . . good, put it down. Only help me wash and give me a clean shirt."

And Ivan Ilyich began to wash. Stopping to rest, he washed his hands, his face, cleaned his teeth, began to brush his hair, and looked in the mirror. He felt frightened, especially frightened by the way his hair stuck flat to his forehead.

When his shirt was being changed, he knew that he would be even more frightened if he looked at his body, and so he didn't look at himself. But now it was all done. He put on a dressing gown, covered himself with a blanket, and sat in an armchair to have his tea. For one minute he felt refreshed, but as soon as he began to drink the tea, again the same taste, the same pain. With an effort he finished the tea and lay down, stretching out his legs. He lay down and sent Pyotr away.

Always the same. There'd be a small flash of hope, then a sea of despair would surge, and always pain, always pain, always despair, and always the same. It was horribly depressing being alone; he wanted to ask for someone but he knew in advance that with others there it would be even worse. "If only I could have morphine again—and lose consciousness. I'll tell him, the doctor, to think of something else. Like this it's impossible, impossible."

An hour, a couple of hours would go by like that. But now there's a bell in the hall. Maybe it's the doctor. It is; it's the doctor, fresh, bright, plump, cheerful, his expression saying, "You've gotten frightened of something there but now we'll fix all that for you." The doctor knows that this expression isn't appropriate here, but he has assumed it once and for all and he can't take it off, like a man who has put on a tailcoat in the morning and is paying visits.

The doctor rubs his hands briskly and reassuringly.

"I'm cold. There's a cracking frost. Let me warm myself up," he says, his expression being as if one just had to wait a little for him to warm himself, and when he had, then he would set everything to rights.

"So, how are we?"

Ivan Ilyich feels the doctor wants to say, "How are things?" but feels one can't talk like that, and he says, "How did you spend the night?"

Ivan Ilyich looks at the doctor, his expression asking, "Will you really never be ashamed of telling lies?" But the doctor doesn't want to understand the question.

And Ivan Ilyich says:

"Just as dreadfully. The pain isn't going, it isn't going away. If I could just have something!"

"Yes, you patients are always like that. Well, sir, now I've warmed up, even our very particular Praskovya Fyodorovna wouldn't have anything to say against my temperature. So, sir, good morning." And the doctor shakes his hand.

And, dropping all his earlier playfulness, the doctor begins to examine the patient with a serious expression, takes pulse and temperature, and then begin the tappings and auscultations.[3]

Ivan Ilyich knows firmly and without any doubt that all this is nonsense, an empty fraud, but when the doctor on his knees stretches over him, applying his ear first higher, then lower, and performs over him various gymnastic exercises, Ivan Ilyich succumbs to all this as he used to succumb to lawyers' speeches when he knew very well that they were lying and why they were lying.

The doctor, kneeling on the sofa, was still tapping something when there was a rustling at the door of Praskovya Fyodorovna's silk dress, and they could hear her scolding Pyotr for not informing her of the doctor's arrival.

She comes in, kisses her husband, and at once starts to make it clear that she has got up long ago and that it's because of a misunderstanding that she wasn't there when the doctor came.

Ivan Ilyich looks at her, examines her closely, and holds against her the whiteness and plumpness and cleanliness of her arms and neck, the gloss of her hair and the shine of her eyes that are so full of life. He hates her with his whole soul. And her touch makes him suffer from a surge of hatred towards her.

Her attitude to him and to his illness is always the same. Just as the doctor has developed for himself an attitude toward his patients which he hasn't been able to put aside, so has she developed a simple attitude towards him—he isn't doing something he should be doing, and it's his fault, and she lovingly scolds him for this—and she hasn't yet managed to put this attitude toward him aside.

"He just doesn't listen. He doesn't take his medicine when he should. And above all—he lies in a position that has to be bad for him—with his legs up."

She described how he makes Gerasim hold his legs.

The doctor smiled a smile of amiable scorn, as if saying, "What can one do? Sometimes these patients dream up such silly things; but one can forgive them."

When the examination was over the doctor looked at his watch, and then Praskovya Fyodorovna announced to Ivan Ilyich that whatever he might want, today she had asked in a famous doctor and he and Mikhail Danilovich (that was the usual doctor's name) would examine him together and discuss the case.

"So please don't go against this. I'm doing this for myself," she said ironically, letting him understand that she did everything for him and just by her saying this he was given no right to refuse her. He said nothing and frowned. He felt that the lies surrounding him had become so tangled that it was difficult now to see anything clearly.

Everything she did for him she did only for herself, and she told him so, as if that was something so unlikely that he had to understand it in the opposite sense.

Indeed the famous doctor did arrive at half past eleven. Again there started the auscultations and serious conversations, both in front of Ivan Ilyich and

---

3. Listening to the internal sounds of the body, such as heart beats or inhalations, usually performed with a stethoscope.

in another room, about his kidney and appendix, and questions and answers delivered with such a serious air that again, instead of the real question about life and death which now was the only one that confronted him, there came a question about his kidney and appendix, which were doing something not quite as they should be and which Mikhail Danilovich and the celebrity doctor would get to grips with right away and make them correct themselves.

The famous doctor said his goodbyes with a serious expression, but one that hadn't given up hope. And to the timid question Ivan Ilyich put to him, raising eyes that were shining with fear and hope—is there any possibility of recovery?—he answered that though one couldn't guarantee it, there was a possibility. The look of hope with which Ivan Ilyich said goodbye to the doctor was so pitiful that, when she saw it, Praskovya Fyodorovna burst into tears as she went through the study doors to give the famous doctor his fee.

The rise in his spirits brought about by the doctor's encouragement didn't last long. Again it was the same room, the same pictures, curtains, wallpaper, medicine bottles, and his same hurting, suffering body. And Ivan Ilyich started to groan; they gave him an injection and he lost consciousness.

When he came to, it was beginning to get dark; they brought in his dinner. With some effort he took some broth; and again all those same things and again night was coming on.

After dinner at seven o'clock Praskovya Fyodorovna came into his room dressed for an evening out, her breasts large and lifted and traces of powder on her face. That morning she had reminded him that they were going to the theater. Sarah Bernhardt[4] was visiting and they had a box which Ivan Ilyich had insisted they take. Now he had forgotten that, and her clothes outraged him. But he concealed his outrage when he remembered that he himself had insisted they get a box and go because it was a cultural treat for their children.

Praskovya Fyodorovna came in pleased with herself but also with a kind of guilty feeling. She sat down, asked about his health—as he could see, just for the sake of asking rather than to learn, knowing that there was nothing to learn—and began to say what she needed to: that she wouldn't have gone out for anything but the box was taken and Hélène was going and their daughter and Petrishchev (the examining magistrate, their daughter's fiancé), and it was impossible to let them go alone. But it would be so much more agreeable for her to sit with him. He must just do what the doctor had ordered without her.

"Yes, and Fyodor Petrovich—the fiancé—wanted to come in. Can he? Liza, too."

"Let them come in."

His daughter came in all dressed up with her young body bared, that body which made him suffer so. But she was flaunting it. Strong, healthy, clearly in love and angry at the illness, suffering, and death that stood in the way of her happiness.

Fyodor Petrovich came too, in a tailcoat, his hair curled à la Capoul,[5] his long sinewy neck encased in a white collar, with a huge white shirtfront and

4. French actress (1844–1923) who had a great popular following.   5. An ornate and elaborate form of men's hairstyling (French).

with powerful thighs squeezed into narrow black trousers, with one white glove pulled onto his hand and an opera hat.

After him the schoolboy crept in inconspicuously in a new school uniform, poor fellow, wearing white gloves and with terrible dark patches under his eyes, the meaning of which Ivan Ilyich knew.

His son always made him feel sorry for him. And the look he gave him was terrible, full of sympathy and fear. Apart from Gerasim, only Vasya understood him and felt pity for him, so Ivan Ilyich thought.

They all sat down, asked again about his health. A silence fell. Liza asked her mother about the opera glasses. There ensued an argument between mother and daughter about who had put them where. It felt unpleasant.

Fyodor Petrovich asked Ivan Ilyich if he had seen Sarah Bernhardt. At first Ivan Ilyich didn't understand what he was being asked and then said:

"No, but have you?"

"Yes, in *Adrienne Lecouvreur*."[6]

Praskovya Fyodorovna said that she was particularly good in something or other. Their daughter disagreed. There began a conversation about the elegance and realism of her acting—that conversation which is always exactly the same.

In the middle of the conversation Fyodor Petrovich looked at Ivan Ilyich and fell silent. The others looked and fell silent. Ivan Ilyich looked straight ahead with shining eyes, clearly becoming angry with them. This had to be put right, but it was quite impossible to put right. Somehow this silence had to be broken. No one had the resolve, and they all became frightened that somehow the decorous lie would collapse and the true state of things would become obvious to all. Liza was the first to take the resolve. She broke the silence. She wanted to hide what they were all feeling, but she said it wrong.

"So, *if we are going to go*, it's time," she said, looking at her watch, a present from her father, and she gave a barely perceptible smile to the young man, which meant something known to them alone, and got up, her dress rustling.

They all got up, said goodbye, and went off.

When they had gone out, Ivan Ilyich thought he felt better: the lie wasn't there—it had gone out with them—but the pain remained. The same constant pain, the same constant fear made nothing more difficult, nothing easier. Everything was worse.

Again minute followed minute, hour followed hour; it was always the same and there was still no end and the inevitable end became more terrifying.

"Yes, send me Gerasim," he said in reply to a question Pyotr asked.

IX

His wife came back late at night. She walked on tiptoe but he heard her; he opened his eyes and quickly shut them again. She wanted to send Gerasim away and sit with him herself. He opened his eyes and said:

"No. Go away."

"Are you in a lot of pain?"

"It doesn't matter."

6. A French tragedy by Eugène Scribe (1791–1861) and Ernest Legouvé (1807–1903), written in 1849.

"Take some opium."

He agreed and drank. She went out.

Till three o'clock he was in a tormented stupor. He thought that in some way they were pushing him and his pain into a narrow, deep, black sack; they kept pushing further but they couldn't push them right in. And this terrible business for him was crowned by his suffering. And he was both struggling and wanting to drop right down, both fighting against it and assisting. And suddenly he was free and fell and came to. The same Gerasim was still sitting on the bed at his feet, dozing quietly, patiently. And Ivan Ilyich was lying there, having lifted his emaciated legs in their socks onto Gerasim's shoulders; there was the same candle with its shade and the same unceasing pain.

"Go, Gerasim," he whispered.

"It doesn't matter, sir, I'll sit a bit longer."

"No, go."

He removed his legs and lay on his side on top of his arm, and he began to feel sorry for himself. He waited for Gerasim to go out into the next room and he couldn't control himself anymore, and he burst into tears like a child. He wept for his helplessness, for his horrible loneliness, for people's cruelty, for God's cruelty, for God's absence.

"Why have you done all this? Why have you brought me here? Why, why do you torment me so horribly?"

He didn't expect an answer, but he also wept because there wasn't and couldn't be an answer. The pain increased again but he didn't move or call anyone. He said to himself, "More, go on, beat me! But why? What have I done to you, why?"

Then he calmed down; he not only stopped weeping, he stopped breathing and became all attention, as if he were listening not to a voice speaking in sounds but to the voice of his soul, to the train of thoughts rising within him.

"What do you want?" was the first clear idea capable of being expressed in words that he heard. "What do you want? What do you want?" he repeated to himself. "What? Not to suffer. To live," he answered.

And again he became absorbed with such intense attention that even the pain did not distract him.

"To live? To live how?" asked the voice of his soul.

"Yes, to live, as I lived before: well and pleasantly."

"As you lived before, well, pleasantly?" asked the voice. And he began to go over in his imagination the best moments of his pleasant life. But—strange to relate—all these best moments of a pleasant life now seemed quite different from what they had seemed then. All of them—except for his first memories of childhood. There in childhood was something so truly pleasant with which he could live, if it returned. But the person who had experienced those pleasant things no longer existed: it was like a memory of something else.

As soon as the process began which had resulted in Ivan Ilyich, the man of today, all the things which had seemed joys melted away before his eyes and were changed into something worthless and often vile.

And the further from childhood, the nearer to the present, the more worthless and dubious were the joys. That began with law school. There was still something there truly good: there was gaiety, there was friendship, there were hopes. But in the senior classes these good moments were already less frequent. After that, at the time of his first period of service with the governor, again good moments appeared: there were memories of love for a woman. After that all this became confused and there was even less of what was good. Further on there was still less good, and the further he went the less there was.

Marriage . . . so casually entered, and disillusionment, and the smell that came from his wife's mouth, and sensuality, hypocrisy! And that deadly work of his and those worries about money, and on for a year, and two, and ten, and twenty—and always the same. And the further he went, the more deadly it became. "As if I were walking downhill at a regular pace, imagining I was walking uphill. That's how it was. In the eyes of the world I was walking uphill, and to just that extent life was slipping away from under me . . . And now it's time, to die!

"So what is this? Why? It can't be. It can't be that life was so meaningless and vile. But if it was indeed so meaningless and vile, then why die and die suffering? Something is wrong.

"Maybe I have lived not as I should have"—the thought suddenly came into his head. "But how so when I did everything in the proper way?" he said to himself, and immediately rejected this solution of the whole riddle of life as something wholly impossible.

"What do you want now? To live? To live how? To live as you lived in court when the court officer pronounces, 'The court is opening!' The court is opening, opening, the court," he repeated to himself. "Here's the court! But I'm not guilty!" he shouted angrily. "For what?" And he stopped weeping and, turning his face to the wall, he began to think of just the one thing: why all this horror, for what?

But however much he thought, he found no answer. And when there came to him the thought, as it often did, that all this was happening because he had lived wrongly, he at once remembered all the correctness of his life and rejected this strange thought.

X

Two more weeks went by. Ivan Ilyich didn't get up from the sofa anymore. He didn't want to lie in bed and instead lay on the sofa. And, lying almost all the time with his face to the wall, he suffered in his loneliness all those same insoluble sufferings and in his loneliness thought the same insoluble thoughts. What is this? Is it really true that this is death? And a voice within answered: Yes, it's true. Why these torments? And the voice answered: That's the way it is; there is no why. Apart from that there was nothing more.

From the very start of his illness, when Ivan Ilyich went to the doctor for the first time, his life was divided into two diametrically opposed moods, which alternated with each other: on the one hand despair and the expectation of an incomprehensible and horrible death, on the other hope and the absorbed observation of the activity of his body. Now he had before his eyes just a kidney or appendix which for a time had deviated from the performance of its duties; now there was just incomprehensible, horrible death from which it was impossible to escape in any way.

From the very beginning of his illness these two moods alternated with each other; but the more the illness progressed, the more fantastic and questionable became thoughts about his kidney and the more real the consciousness of approaching death.

He only had to remember what he had been three months previously and what he was now—to remember how he had been walking downhill at a regular pace—for all possibility of hope to crumble.

In the recent loneliness in which he found himself, lying with his face to the back of the sofa, loneliness in the midst of a crowded city and his numerous acquaintances and family—loneliness that could not be more absolute anywhere, either at the bottom of the sea or underneath the earth—in his recent terrible loneliness Ivan Ilyich lived only by his imagination in the past. One after another pictures of his past presented themselves to him. It always began with the closest in time and went back to the most remote, to his childhood, and rested there. If Ivan Ilyich thought of the stewed prunes he was offered to eat now, he remembered the moist, wrinkled French prunes of his childhood, their particular taste and the flow of saliva when he got to the stone, and alongside this memory of taste there arose a whole row of memories of that time: his *nyanya*,[7] his brother, his toys. "You mustn't think of that. . . . It's too painful," Ivan Ilyich said to himself, and was again transported into the present. A button on the back of the sofa and the creases in its morocco leather. "Morocco is expensive and wears badly; there was a quarrel because of it. But it was different leather and a different row when we ripped our father's briefcase and were punished, but Mama brought us some pies." And again he stopped in his childhood and again it was painful for Ivan Ilyich, and he tried to push it away and think of something else.

And here again, together with this train of memories, another train of memories went through his mind—of how his illness had intensified and grown. It was the same; the further back he went, the more life there was. There was more good in life and more of life itself. And the two merged together. *As my torments kept getting worse and worse, so the whole of life became worse and worse*, he thought. One bright spot, there, at the start of his life, and after that everything blacker and blacker, and everything quicker and quicker. *In inverse ratio to the square of the distance from death*, thought Ivan Ilyich. And an image of a stone flying downward with increasing speed became fixed in his mind. Life, a sequence of increasing sufferings, flies quicker and quicker to the end, to the most terrible suffering of all. *I am flying* . . . He shivered, moved, tried to resist, but he now knew that resistance was impossible, and again, with eyes that were tired of looking but which couldn't help looking at what was in front of him, he gazed at the back of the sofa and waited—waited for that terrible fall, the crash, and annihilation. "I can't resist," he said to himself. "But if I could just understand why. That too I can't. I might be able to explain it if I said I had lived not as I should have. But it's impossible to admit that," he said to himself, remembering all the lawfulness, the correctness, and the decorum of his life. "It's impossible to admit that now," he said to himself, grimacing with his lips, as if anyone could see this smile of his and be deceived by it. "There's no explanation! Torment, death. . . . Why?"

7. Nanny (Russian).

XI

Two weeks went by like that. In those weeks an event took place that had been desired by Ivan Ilyich and his wife: Petrishchev made a formal proposal. It happened in the evening. The next day Praskovya Fyodorovna went in to her husband, wondering how to announce Fyodor Petrovich's proposal to him, but that very night Ivan Ilyich had taken a turn for the worse. Praskovya Fyodorovna found him on the same sofa, but in a new position. He was lying on his back, groaning and looking ahead with a fixed gaze.

She started talking about medicines. He turned his eyes to her. She didn't finish what she had begun to say; there was so much anger expressed in those eyes, aimed directly at her.

"For Christ's sake, let me die in peace," he said.

She was about to go, but at that moment his daughter came in and went up to say good morning. He looked at his daughter as he had at his wife and to her questions about his health he drily said to her that he would soon liberate them all from himself. They both said nothing, sat briefly, and went out.

"What can we be blamed for?" Liza said to her mother. "As if we'd done this! I'm sorry for Papa, but why must he torment us?"

The doctor came at the usual time. Ivan Ilyich answered him "yes, no," not taking his angry eyes from him, and finally said:

"You know that you won't be of any help, so leave me."

"We can relieve the suffering," the doctor said.

"You can't do that either; leave me."

The doctor went out into the drawing room and informed Praskovya Fyodorovna that things were very bad and that there was only one resource—opium, to relieve the suffering, which must be terrible.

The doctor said that Ivan Ilyich's physical sufferings were terrible, and that was true; but even more terrible than his physical sufferings were his mental sufferings, and there was his chief torment.

His mental sufferings lay in the fact that that night, as he looked at Gerasim's sleepy, good-natured face with its high cheekbones, there suddenly had entered his head the thought: *But what if in actual fact all my life, my conscious life, has been "wrong"?*

It occurred to him that the notion that had previously seemed to him a complete impossibility—that he had not lived his life as he should have done—could be the truth. It occurred to him that his barely noticeable attempts at struggling against what was considered good by those in high positions above him, those barely noticeable attempts which he had immediately rejected, could be genuine, and everything else wrong. His work and the structure of his life and his family and his social and professional interests—all that could be wrong. He tried to defend all that to himself. And suddenly he felt the fragility of what he was defending. And there was nothing to defend.

"But if this is so," he said to himself, "and I am leaving life with the realization that I have lost everything I was given and that it's impossible to put right, then what?" He lay on his back and started to go over his whole life afresh. When in the morning he saw the manservant, then his wife, then his daughter, then the doctor—every one of their movements, every one of their words confirmed for him the terrible truth that had been disclosed to him in the night. He saw in them himself, everything by which he had lived, and saw clearly that all this was wrong, all this was a terrible, huge fraud concealing both life and death. This realization increased, increased tenfold his physical sufferings. He groaned and tossed about and pulled at the clothes on him. He felt suffocated and crushed. And he hated them for that.

They gave him a big dose of opium; he lost consciousness, but at dinnertime the same began again. He drove them all away from him and tossed about from side to side.

His wife came to him and said:

"*Jean*, my dear, do this for me. It can't do any harm, but it often helps. So, it's nothing. And people in good health often . . ."

He opened his eyes wide.

"What? Take communion? Why? There's no need to! But then . . ."

She started crying.

"Yes, my dear? I'll call for our man, he's so sweet."

"Fine, very well," he said.

When the priest came and took his confession, he was calmed; he felt a kind of relief from his doubts and, as a consequence of that, from his sufferings, and a moment of hope came to him. He again began to think of his appendix and the possibility of curing it. He received communion with tears in his eyes.

When, after communion, he was put to bed, for a moment he felt comfortable and hope for life appeared again. He began to think of the operation being suggested to him. "To live, I want to live," he said to himself. His wife came to congratulate him on taking communion; she said the usual words and added:

"You feel better, don't you?"

Without looking at her he said, "Yes."

Her clothes, her body, the expression of her face, the sound of her voice—everything said to him one thing: "Wrong. Everything by which you have lived and are living is a lie, a fraud, concealing life and death from you." And as soon as he thought that, hatred rose up in him, and together with hatred agonizing physical suffering, and with those sufferings an awareness of the end, nearby and unavoidable. Something new happened: his breath started to strain and come in spurts and be squeezed out.

His expression when he said "yes" was terrible. Having said that yes, he looked her straight in the eye and with unusual strength for his weakness turned himself facedown and cried:

"Go away, go away, leave me!"

XII

From that minute began three days of unceasing screams that were so horrible one couldn't hear them from two doors away without feeling horror. The minute he answered his wife, he understood that he was lost, that there was no return, that the end had come, the very end, but the doubt still wasn't resolved; it still remained doubt.

"Oh! Oh! Oh!" he cried out in various tones. He began to cry out, "I don't want to, no!" and went on like that crying out the letter *O*.

For the whole three days, during which time did not exist for him, he tossed about in the black sack into which he was being pushed by an invisible, insurmountable force. He struggled as a man condemned to death struggles in the arms of the executioner, knowing he cannot save himself; and with every minute he felt that for all his efforts at struggling he was coming nearer and nearer to what filled him with horror. He felt that his agony lay both in being pushed into that black hole and even more in being unable to get into it. He was prevented from climbing in by his declaration that his life had been good. This justification of his life caught on something and stopped him from going forward, and that distressed him most of all.

Suddenly some kind of force struck him in the chest and on the side; his breath was constricted even more; he collapsed into the hole and there at the bottom of the hole some light was showing. There happened to him what he used to experience in a railway carriage when you think you are going forward but are going backward and suddenly realize your true direction.

"Yes, everything was wrong," he said to himself, "but it doesn't matter. I can, I can do what is right. But what is right?" he asked himself, and at once fell silent.

It was the end of the third day, an hour before his death. At that very moment the gymnasium schoolboy quietly slipped into his father's room and approached his bed. The dying man was still crying out despairingly and waving his arms about. One of his hands hit the schoolboy's head. The schoolboy took it, pressed it to his lips, and wept.

At that very moment Ivan Ilyich fell through and saw a light, and it was revealed to him that his life had been wrong but that it was still possible to mend things. He asked himself, "What is right?" and fell silent, listening. Now he felt someone was kissing his hand. He opened his eyes and looked at his son. He felt sorry for him. His wife came to him. He looked at her. She looked at him, mouth open and tears on her nose and cheeks that she hadn't wiped away. He felt sorry for her.

"Yes, I make them unhappy," he thought. "They are sorry for me, but it'll be better for them when I die." He wanted to say that but didn't have the strength to utter it. "However, why say things? One must act," he thought. With a look to his wife he pointed to his son and said:

"Take him away... sorry for him... and for you..." He wanted to add "forgive" but said "give," and not having the strength to correct himself, waved his hand, knowing that He who needed to understand would understand.

And suddenly it became clear to him that what had been oppressing him and not coming to an end—now everything was coming to an end at once, on two sides, on ten sides, on every side. He was sorry for them, he must make it so they had no pain. Free them and free himself from these sufferings. "So good and so simple," he thought. "And the pain?" he asked himself. "Where's it gone? Well, where are you, pain?"

He began to listen.

"There it is. So—let the pain be. And death? Where is it?"

He searched for his old habitual fear of death and didn't find it. Where was death? What death? There was no fear, because there was no death.

Instead of death there was light.

"So that's it!" he suddenly said aloud. "Such joy!"

For him all this took place in a moment, and the significance of this moment didn't change. For those there his death agony lasted two hours more. Something bubbled in his chest; his emaciated body shivered. Then the gurgling and wheezing became less and less frequent.

"It is finished!" someone said above him.

He heard these words and repeated them in his heart. "Death is finished," he said to himself. "It is no more."

He breathed in, stopped halfway, stretched himself, and died.

1886

RELATED:

—Tolstoy, "What Is Art?" p. 1733

—Gary Saul Morson, "The Reader as Voyeur: Tolstoi and the Poetics of Didactic Fiction," p. 1771

WILLIAM TREVOR
b. 1928

Born William Trevor Cox in County Cork, Ireland, William Trevor has lived in England since the 1950s but still considers himself "Irish in every vein." Trevor grew up in small towns throughout Ireland and graduated from Trinity College in Dublin with a degree in history. He worked as a sculptor and a teacher for several years before moving to England and becoming a copywriter for an advertising agency. It was during this time that Trevor began writing fiction. The critical acclaim garnered by his second novel, *The Old Boys* (1964), encouraged Trevor to become a full-time writer. Since then, his work has been prodigious. Though he is best known for his hundreds of short stories, his nearly forty publications also include novels, plays, and collections of nonfiction. Among his best-known volumes of short fiction are *The Day We Got Drunk on Cake and Other Stories* (1967), *Angels at the Ritz and Other Stories* (1976), and *The News from Ireland* (1986). Trevor is a three-time winner of the Whitbread Prize, a four-time winner of the O. Henry Prize, and he was nominated for the Man Booker Prize no less than five times. In 2002, he was knighted by Queen Elizabeth II for his services to literature.

Events at Drimaghleen

Nothing as appalling had happened before at Drimaghleen; its people had never been as shocked. They'd had their share of distress, like any people; there were memories of dramatic occurrences; stories from a more distant past were told. In the 1880s a woman known as the Captain's wife had run away with a hunchbacked pedlar. In 1798 there'd been resistance in the hills and fighting in Drimaghleen itself. During the Troubles a local man had been executed in a field by the Black and Tans.[1] But no story, and no long memory, could match the horror of the tragedy that awaited the people of Drimaghleen on 22 May 1985, a Wednesday morning.

The McDowds, that morning, awoke in their farmhouse and began the day as they always did, McDowd pulling on his shirt and trousers and lifting down a black overcoat from the pegs beside the kitchen door. He fastened it with a length of string which he kept in one of its pockets, found his socks in his gum-boots and went out with his two sheepdogs to drive the cows in for

---

1. The Troubles, a period of violent political unrest in Northern Ireland, beginning in the 1960s and peaking in the 1970s, between protestant Unionists allied with Great Britain, and Catholic nationalists allied with the Republic of Ireland; Black and Tans, Unionist soldiers.

milking. His wife washed herself, put the kettle on the stove, and knocked on her daughter's door. 'Maureen!' she called. 'Come on now, Maureen!'

It was not unusual that Maureen failed to reply. Mrs McDowd reentered her bedroom and dressed herself. 'Get up out of that, Maureen!' she shouted, banging again on her daughter's door. 'Are you sick?' she inquired, puzzled now by the lack of movement from within the room: always at this second rousing Maureen yawned or spoke. 'Maureen!' she shouted again, and then opened the door.

McDowd, calling in the cattle, was aware that there had been something wrong in the yard as he'd passed through it, but an early-morning torpor hindered the progression of his thoughts when he endeavoured to establish what it was. His wife's voice shouting across the field at him, and his daughter's name used repeatedly in the information that was being inadequately conveyed to him, jolted him into an awareness that what had been wrong was that Maureen's bicycle had not been leaning against the kitchen window-sill. 'Maureen hasn't come back,' his wife repeated again when he was close enough to hear her. 'She's not been in her bed.'

The cows were milked because no matter what the reason for Maureen's absence they had to be. The breakfast was placed on the kitchen table because no good would come of not taking food. McDowd, in silence, ate with an appetite that was unaffected; his wife consumed less than usual. 'We will drive over,' he said when they had finished, anger thickening his voice.

She nodded. She'd known as soon as she'd seen the unused bed that they would have to do something. They could not just wait for a letter to arrive, or a telegram, or whatever it was their daughter had planned. They would drive over to the house where Lancy Butler lived with his mother, the house to which their daughter had cycled the evening before. They did not share the thought that possessed both of them: that their daughter had taken the law into her own hands and gone off with Lancy Butler, a spoilt and useless man.

McDowd was a tallish, spare man of sixty-two, his face almost gaunt, grey hair ragged on his head. His wife, two years younger, was thin also, with gnarled features and the hands of a woman who all her life had worked in the fields. They did not say much to one another, and never had; but they did not quarrel either. On the farm, discussion was rarely apt, there being no profit in it; it followed naturally that grounds for disagreement were limited. Five children had been born to the McDowds; Maureen was the youngest and the only one who had remained at home. Without a show of celebration, for that was not the family way, her twenty-fifth birthday had passed by a month ago.

'Put your decent trousers on,' Mrs McDowd urged. 'You can't go like that.'

'I'm all right the way I am.'

She knew he would not be persuaded and did not try, but instead hurried back to her bedroom to change her shoes. At least he wouldn't drive over in the overcoat with the string round it: that was only for getting the cows in from the field when the mornings were cold. He'd taken it off before he'd sat down to his breakfast and there would be no cause to put it on again. She covered up her own old skirt and jumper with her waterproof.

'The little bitch,' he said in the car, and she said nothing.

They both felt the same, anxious and cross at the same time, not wanting to believe the apparent truth. Their daughter had ungratefully deceived them: again in silence the thought was shared while he drove the four miles to the Butlers' house. When they turned off the tarred road into a lane, already passing between the Butlers' fields, they heard the dog barking. The window of the Volkswagen on Mrs McDowd's side wouldn't wind up, due to a defect that had developed a month ago: the shrill barking easily carried above the rattle of the engine.

That was that, they thought, listening to the dog. Maureen and Lancy had gone the night before, and Mrs Butler couldn't manage the cows on her own. No wonder the old dog was beside himself. Bitterly, McDowd called his daughter a bitch again, though only to himself. Lancy Butler, he thought, my God! Lancy Butler would lead her a dance, and lead her astray, and lead her down into the gutters of some town. He'd warned her a thousand times about Lancy Butler. He'd told her the kind of fool he was.

'His father was a decent man,' he said, breaking at last the long silence. 'Never touched a drop.'

'The old mother ruined him.'

It wouldn't last long, they both thought. Lancy Butler might marry her, or he might wriggle out of it. But however it turned out she'd be back in six months' time or at any rate a year's. There'd probably be a baby to bring up.

The car turned into the yard, and neither McDowd nor his wife immediately saw their daughter lying beside the pump. For the first few moments of their arrival their attention was claimed by the distressed dog, a black-and-white sheepdog like their own two. Dust had risen from beneath the Volkswagen's wheels and was still thick in the air as they stepped from the car. The dog was running wildly across a corner of the yard, back and forth, and back and forth again. The dog's gone mad, Mrs McDowd thought, something's after affecting it. Then she saw her daughter's body lying by the pump, and a yard or so away her daughter's bicycle lying on its side, as if she had fallen from it. Beside the bicycle were two dead rabbits.

'My God,' McDowd said, and his wife knew from his voice that he hadn't seen his daughter yet but was looking at something else. He had walked to another part of the yard, where the dog was. He had gone there instinctively, to try to calm the animal.

She knelt down, whispering to Maureen, thinking in her confusion that her daughter had just this minute fallen off her bicycle. But Maureen's face was as cold as stone, and her flesh had already stiffened. Mrs McDowd screamed, and then she was aware that she was lying down herself, clasping Maureen's dead body. A moment later she was aware that her husband was weeping piteously, unable to control himself, that he was kneeling down, his hands on the body also.

Mrs McDowd did not remember rising to her feet, or finding the energy and the will to do so. 'Don't go over there,' she heard her husband saying to her, and saw him wiping at his eyes with the arm of his jersey. But he didn't try to stop her when she went to where the dog was; he remained on his knees beside their daughter, calling out to her between his sobs, asking her not to be dead.

The dog was crouched in a doorway, not barking any more. A yard or so away Mrs Butler lay with one of her legs twisted under her, blood on the ground already turned brown, a pool of it still scarlet. Looking down at her, Mrs McDowd thought with abrupt lucidity: Maureen did not fall off her bicycle.

She went back to where her daughter lay and behind the two tin barrels that stood by the pump she saw the body of Lancy Butler, and on the ground not far from it the shotgun that must have blown off Mrs Butler's face.

O'Kelly of the Garda[2] arrived at a swift conclusion. Old Mrs Butler had been as adamant as the McDowds in her opposition to the match that her son and Maureen McDowd had planned for themselves. And there was more to it than that: Mrs Butler had been obsessively possessive, hiding from no one her determination that no other woman should ever take her son away from her. Lancy was her only child, the single one to survive years of miscarrying. His father had died when Lancy was two years old, leaving mother and child to lead a lonely life on a farm that was remote. O'Kelly knew that Mrs Butler had been reputed to be strange in the head, and given to furious jealousies where Lancy was concerned. In the kind of rage that people who'd known her were familiar with she had shot her son's sweetheart rather than suffer the theft of him. He had wrenched the shotgun from her and by accident or otherwise it had exploded. A weak man at the best of times, he had turned it upon himself rather than face the reality of what had happened. This deduction, borne out by the details in the yard, satisfied O'Kelly of the Garda; the people of Drimaghleen arrived themselves at the same conclusion. 'It was always trouble,' McDowd said on the day of the funerals. 'The minute she went out with Lancy Butler it was trouble written down for poor Maureen.'

Drimaghleen was a townland, with nothing to mark it except a crossroads that was known as Drimaghleen Crossroads. The modest farms that comprised it, each of thirty or so acres, were scattered among bogland, one separated from the next by several miles, as the McDowds' and the Butlers' were. The village of Kilmona was where the people of Drimaghleen went to Mass, and where they confessed to Father Sallins. The children of the farms went to school in the small town of Mountcroe, driven each morning in a yellow bus that drove them back to the end of their lanes or farm tracks in the afternoon. Milk churns were collected in much the same way by the creamery lorry. Bread and groceries were bought in the village; fresh meat in Mountcroe. When the men of Drimaghleen got drunk they did so in Mountcroe, never in the village, although often they took a few bottles of stout there, in the bar beside the grocery counter. Hardware and clothes were bought in Mountcroe, which had had a cinema called the Abbey Picture House until the advent of television closed it in the early 1960s. Drimaghleen, Kilmona and Mountcroe formed a world that bounded the lives of the people of the Drimaghleen farms. Rarely was there occasion to venture beyond it to the facilities of a town that was larger — unless the purpose happened to be a search for work or the first step on the way to exile.

The children of the McDowds, whose search for such work had taken them far from the townland, returned heartbroken for their sister's Mass. All four of them came, two with husbands, one with a wife, one on her own. The weddings which had taken place had been the last family occasions, two of them in Kilmona, the third in distant Skibbereen, the home of the girl whom the

McDowds' son had married a year ago. That wedding was on their minds at Maureen's Mass — the long journey there had been in the Volkswagen, the night they had spent in Tierney's Hotel, the farewells the next day. Not in the wildest horror of a nightmare could any of the McDowds have guessed the nature of the occasion destined to bring them together next.

After the funeral the family returned to the farm. The younger McDowds had known of Maureen's and Lancy Butler's attachment, and of their parents' opposition to it. They had known as well of Mrs Butler's possessive affection for her son, having grown up with stories of this maternal eccentricity, and having witnessed Lancy himself, as a child and as a boy, affected by her indulgence. 'Oh, it can wait, Lancy, it can wait,' she would say a dozen times an hour, referring to some necessary chore on the farm. 'Ah, sure, we won't bother with school today,' she had said before that, when Lancy had complained of a difficulty he was experiencing with the seven-times table or Brother Martin's twenty weekend spellings. The people of Drimaghleen used to wonder whether the farm or Lancy would suffer more in the end.

'What did she see in him?' Mrs McDowd mused sadly at the funeral meal. 'Will anyone ever tell me what she saw in him?'

They shook their heads. The cheeks of all of them were still smeared with the tears they had shed at the service. Conversation was difficult.

'We will never recover from it,' the father said, with finality in his voice. It was all that could be said, it was all they knew with certainty: for as long as the older McDowds remained in this farmhouse — which would be until their own deaths — the vicious, ugly tragedy would haunt them. They knew that if Maureen had been knocked from her bicycle by a passing motor-car they could have borne her death with greater fortitude; or if she had died of an illness, or been the victim of incurable disease. The knife that turned in their pain was their memory of the Butlers' farmyard, the barking dog running back and forth, the three still bodies. There was nothing but the waste of a life to contemplate, and the cruelty of chance — for why should it have been simple, pretty Maureen whose fate it was to become mixed up with so peculiar a couple as that mother and son? There were other girls in the neighbourhood — underhand girls and girls of doubtful character — who somehow more readily belonged with the Butlers: anyone would tell you that.

'Why don't you drive over and see us?' one of the daughters invited. 'Can't we persuade you?'

Her father stared into the table without trying to reply. It was unnecessary to say that a drive of such a distance could only be contemplated when there was a wedding or a funeral. Such journeys had not been undertaken during Maureen's lifetime, when she might have looked after the farm for a day; in no way could they be considered now. Mrs McDowd tried to smile, making an effort to acknowledge the concern that had inspired the suggestion, but no smile came.

Being of a nature that might interest strangers, the deaths were reported in the newspapers. They were mentioned on the radio, and on the television news. Then everything became quiet again at Drimaghleen, and in the village and in the town. People wrote letters to the McDowds, expressing their sorrow. People came to see them but did not stay long. 'I am always there,' Father

Sallins said. 'Kilmona 23. You have only to summon me. Or call up at the rectory.'

The McDowds didn't. They watched the summer going by, taking in their hay during the warm spell in June, keeping an eye on the field of potatoes and the ripening barley. It began to rain more than usual; they worried about the barley.

'Excuse me,' a man said in the yard one afternoon in October. 'Are you Mr McDowd?'

McDowd said he was, shouting at the dogs to behave themselves. The stranger would be a traveller in fertilizers, he said to himself, a replacement for Donoghue, who had been coming to the farm for years. Then he realized that it was the wrong time of year for Donoghue.

'Would it be possible to have a word, Mr McDowd?'

McDowd's scrawny features slowly puckered; slowly he frowned. He lifted a hand and scratched at his grey, ragged hair, which was a way he had when he wished to disguise bewilderment. Part of his countryman's wiliness was that he preferred outsiders not to know, or deduce, what was occurring in his mind.

'A word?' he said.

'Could we maybe step inside, sir?'

McDowd saw no reason to step inside his own house with this man. The visitor was florid-faced, untidily dressed in dark corduroy trousers and a gaberdine jacket. His hair was long and black, and grew coarsely down the sides of his face in two brushlike panels. He had a city voice; it wasn't difficult to guess he came from Dublin.

'What d'you want with me?'

'I was sorry to hear that thing about your daughter, Mr McDowd. That was a terrible business.'

'It's over and done with.'

'It is, sir. Over and done with.'

The red bonnet of a car edged its way into the yard. McDowd watched it, reminded of some cautious animal by the slow, creeping movement, the engine purring so lightly you could hardly hear it. When the car stopped by the milking shed nobody got out of it, but McDowd could see a figure wearing sunglasses at the wheel. This was a woman, with black hair also, smoking a cigarette.

'It could be to your advantage, Mr McDowd.'

'What could be? Does that car belong to you?'

'We drove down to see you, sir. That lady's a friend of mine, a colleague by the name of Hetty Fortune.'

The woman stepped out of the car. She was taller than the man, with a sombre face and blue trousers that matched her blue shirt. She dropped her cigarette on to the ground and carefully stubbed it out with the toe of her shoe. As slowly as she had driven the car she walked across the yard to where the two men were standing. The dogs growled at her, but she took no notice. 'I'm Hetty Fortune,' she said in an English accent.

'I didn't tell you my own name, Mr McDowd,' the man said. 'It's Jeremiah Tyler.'

'I hope Jeremiah has offered you our condolences, Mr McDowd. I hope both you and your wife will accept our deepest sympathy.'

'What do you want here?'

'We've been over at the Butlers' place, Mr McDowd. We spent a long time there. We've been talking to a few people. Could we talk to you, d'you think?'

'Are you the newspapers?'

'In a manner of speaking. Yes, in a manner of speaking we represent the media. And I'm perfectly sure,' the woman added hastily, 'you've had more than enough of all that. I believe you'll find what we have to say to you is different, Mr McDowd.'

'The wife and myself have nothing to say to the newspapers. We didn't say anything at the time, and we have nothing to say since. I have things to do about the place.'

'Mr McDowd, would you be good enough to give us five minutes of your time? Five minutes in your kitchen, talking to yourself and your wife? Would you give us an opportunity to explain?'

Attracted by the sound by voices, Mrs McDowd came out of the house. She stood in the doorway, not quite emerging from the kitchen porch, regarding the strangers even more distrustfully than her husband had. She didn't say anything when the woman approached her and held out a hand which she was obliged to shake.

'We are sorry to obtrude on your grief, Mrs McDowd. Mr Tyler and I have been keen to make that clear to your husband.'

Mrs McDowd did not acknowledge this. She didn't like the look of the sombre-faced woman or her unkempt companion. There was a seediness about him, a quality that city people seemed often to exude if they weren't smartly attired. The woman wasn't seedy but you could see she was insincere from the way her mouth was. You could hear the insincerity when she spoke.

'The full truth has not been established, Mrs McDowd. It is that we would like to discuss with you.'

'I've told you no,' McDowd said. 'I've told them to go away,' he said to his wife.

Mrs McDowd's eyes stared at the woman's sunglasses. She remained where she was, not quite coming into the yard. The man said:

'Would it break the ice if I took a snap? Would you mind that, sir? If I was to take a few snaps of yourself and the wife?'

He had spoken out of turn. A shadow of anger passed over the woman's face. The fingers of her left hand moved in an irritated wriggle. She said quickly:

'That's not necessary at this stage.'

'We've got to get the pictures, Hetty,' the man mumbled, hushing the words beneath his breath so that the McDowds wouldn't hear. But they guessed the nature of his protest, for it showed in his pink face. The woman snapped something at him.

'If you don't leave us alone we'll have to get the Guards,' McDowd said. 'You're trespassing on this land.'

'Is it fair on your daughter's memory that the truth should be hidden, Mr McDowd?'

'Another thing is, those dogs can be fierce if they want to be.'

'It isn't hidden,' Mrs McDowd said. 'We all know what happened. Detectives worked it out, but sure anyone could have told them.'

'No, Mrs McDowd, nothing was properly worked out at all. That's what I'm saying to you. The surface was scarcely disturbed. What seemed to be the truth wasn't.'

McDowd told his wife to lock the door. They would drive over to Mount-croe and get a Guard to come back with them. 'We don't want any truck with you,' he harshly informed their visitors. 'If the dogs eat the limbs off you after we've gone don't say it wasn't mentioned.'

Unmoved by these threats, her voice losing none of its confidence, the woman said that what was available was something in the region of three thousand pounds. 'For a conversation of brief duration you would naturally have to be correctly reimbursed. Already we have taken up your working time, and of course we're not happy about that. The photograph mentioned by Mr Tyler would naturally have the attachment of a fee. We're talking at the end of the day of something above a round three thousand.'

Afterwards the McDowds remembered that moment. They remembered the feeling they shared, that this was no kind of trick, that the money spoken of would be honestly paid. They remembered thinking that the sum was large, that they could do with thirty pounds never mind three thousand. Rain had destroyed the barley; they missed their daughter's help on the farm; the tragedy had aged and weakened them. If three thousand pounds could come out of it, they'd maybe think of selling up and buying a bungalow.

'Let them in,' McDowd said, and his wife led the way into the kitchen.

The scene of the mystery is repeated all over rural Ireland. From Cork to Cavan, from Roscommon to Rosslare you will come across small, tucked-away farms like the Butlers' and the McDowds'. Maureen McDowd had been gentle-natured and gentle-tempered. The sins of sloth and greed had not been hers; her parents called her a perfect daughter, close to a saint. A photograph, taken when Maureen McDowd was five, showed a smiling, freckled child; another showed her in her First Communion dress; a third, taken at the wedding of her brother, was of a healthy-looking girl, her face creased up in laughter, a cup of tea in her right hand. There was a photograph of her mother and father, standing in their kitchen. Italicized beneath it was the information that it had been taken by Jeremiah Tyler. *The Saint of Drimaghleen*, Hetty Fortune had written, *never once missed Mass in all her twenty-five years.*

The story was told in fashionably faded pictures. 'You know our Sunday supplement?' Hetty Fortune had said in the McDowds' kitchen, but they hadn't: newspapers from England had never played a part in their lives. They read the *Sunday Independent* themselves.

The Butlers' yard was brownly bleak in the pages of the supplement; the pump had acquired a quality not ordinarily noticed. A bicycle similar to Maureen's had been placed on the ground, a sheepdog similar to the Butlers' nosed about the doors of the cowshed. But the absence of the three bodies in the photographed yard, the dust still rising where the bicycle had fallen, the sniffing dog, lent the composition an eerie quality—horror conveyed without horror's presence. 'You used a local man?' the supplement's assistant editor inquired, and when informed that Jeremiah Tyler was a Dublin man he requested that a note be kept of the photographer's particulars.

The gardai — in particular Superintendent O'Kelly — saw only what was convenient to see. Of the three bodies that lay that morning in the May sunshine they chose that of Lancy Butler to become the victim of their sluggish imagination. Mrs Butler, answering her notoriously uncontrollable jealousy, shot her son's sweetheart rather than have him marry her. Her son, so Superintendent O'Kelly infers from no circumstantial evidence whatsoever, wrenched the shotgun out of her hands and fired on her in furious confusion. He then, within seconds, took his own life. The shotgun bore the fingerprints of all three victims: what O'Kelly has signally failed to explain is why this should be so. Why should the Butlers' shotgun bear the fingerprints of Maureen McDowd? O'Kelly declares that 'in the natural course of events' Maureen McDowd would have handled the shotgun, being a frequent visitor to the farm. Frequent visitors, in our experience, do not, 'in the natural course of events' or otherwise, meddle with a household's firearms. The Superintendent hedges the issue because he is himself bewildered. The shotgun was used for keeping down rabbits, he states, knowing that the shotgun's previous deployment by the Butlers is neither here nor there. He mentions rabbits because he still can offer no reasonable explanation why Maureen McDowd should ever have handled the death weapon. The fingerprints of all three victims were blurred and 'difficult', and had been found on several different areas of the weapon. Take it or leave it is what the Superintendent is saying. And wearily he is saying: does it matter?

We maintain it does matter. We maintain that this extraordinary crime — following, as it does, hard on the heels of the renowned Kerry Babies mystery, and the Flynn case — has not been investigated, but callously shelved. The people of Drimaghleen will tell you everything that O'Kelly laboured over in his reports: the two accounts are identical. Everyone knows that Lancy Butler's mother was a sharp-tongued, possessive woman. Everyone knows that Lancy was a ne'er-do-well. Everyone knows that Maureen McDowd was a deeply religious girl. Naturally it was the mother who sought to end an intrusion she could not bear. Naturally it was slow, stupid Lancy who didn't pause to think what the consequences would be after he'd turned the gun on his mother. Naturally it was he who could think of no more imaginative way out of his dilemma than to join the two women who had dominated his life.

The scenario that neither O'Kelly nor the Butlers' neighbours paused to consider is a vastly different one. A letter, apparently — and astonishingly — overlooked by the police, was discovered behind the drawer of a table which was once part of the furniture of Lancy Butler's bedroom and which was sold in the general auction after the tragedy — land, farmhouse and contents having by this time become the property of Allied Irish Banks, who held the mortgage on the Butlers' possessions. This letter, written by Maureen McDowd a week before the tragedy, reads:

Dear Lancy, Unless she stops I can't see any chance of marrying you. I want to, Lancy, but she never can let us alone. What would it be like for me in your place, and if I didn't come to you where would we be able to go because you know my father wouldn't accept you here. She has ruined the chance we had, Lancy, she'll never let go of you. I am always cycling over to face her insults and the way she has of looking at me. I think we have reached the end of it.

This being a direct admission by Maureen McDowd that the conclusion of the romance had been arrived at, why would the perceptive Mrs Butler — a woman who was said to 'know your thoughts before you knew them yourself' — decide to kill Lancy's girl? And the more the mental make-up of that old woman is dwelt upon the more absurd it seems that she would have destroyed everything she had by committing a wholly unnecessary murder. Mrs Butler was not the kind to act blindly, in the fury of the moment. Her jealousy and the anger that protected it smouldered cruelly within her, always present, never varying.

But Maureen McDowd — young, impetuous, bitterly deprived of the man she loved — a saint by nature and possessing a saint's fervour, on that fatal evening made up for all the sins she had ever resisted. Hell hath no fury like a woman scorned — except perhaps a woman unfairly defeated. The old woman turned the screw, aware that victory was in sight. The insults and 'the way of looking' became more open and more arrogant, Mrs Butler wanted Maureen McDowd out, she wanted her gone for ever, never to dare to return.

It is known that Lancy Butler found two rabbits in his snares that night. It is known that he and Maureen often made the rounds of the snares when she visited him in the evenings. He would ride her bicycle to the field where they were, Maureen sitting side-saddle on the carrier at the back. Lancy had no bicycle of his own. It is our deduction that the reason the shotgun bore Maureen's fingerprints is because they had gone on a shooting expedition as well and when they returned to the yard she was carrying both the shotgun and the snared rabbits. It is known that Maureen McDowd wept shortly before her death. In the fields, as they stalked their prey, Lancy comforted her but Maureen knew that never again would they walk here together, that never again would she come over to see him in the evening. The hatred his mother bore her, and Lancy's weakness, had combined to destroy what most of all she wanted. Mrs Butler was standing in the yard shouting her usual abuse and Maureen shot her. The rabbits fell to the ground as she jumped off the bicycle, and her unexpectedly sudden movement caused the bicycle itself, and Lancy on it, to turn over. He called out to her when it was too late, and she realized she could never have him now. She blamed him for never once standing up to his mother, for never making it easier. If she couldn't have this weak man whom she so passionately loved no one else would either. She shot her lover, knowing that within seconds she must take her own life too. And that, of course, she did.

There was more about Maureen. In the pages of the colour supplement Mrs McDowd said her daughter had been a helpful child. Her father said she'd been his special child. When she was small she used to go out with him to the fields, watching how he planted the seed-potatoes. Later on, she would carry out his tea to him, and later still she would assist with whatever task he was engaged in. Father Sallins gave it as his opinion that she had been specially chosen. A nun at the convent in Mountcroe remembered her with lasting affection.

O'Kelly fell prey to this local feeling. Whether they knew what they were doing or not, the people of Drimaghleen were protecting the memory of Maureen McDowd, and the Superintendent went along with the tide. She was a local girl of unblemished virtue, who had been 'specially chosen'. Had he publicly arrived at any other conclusion Superintendent O'Kelly might never safely have set foot in the neighbourhood of Drimaghleen again, nor the village of Kilmona, nor the town of Mountcroe. The Irish do not easily forgive the purloining of their latter-day saints.

'I wanted to tell you this stuff had been written,' Father Sallins said. 'I wanted it to be myself that informed you before you'd get a shock from hearing it elsewhere.'

He'd driven over specially. As soon as the story in the paper had been brought to his own notice he'd felt it his duty to sit down with the McDowds. In his own opinion, what had been printed was nearly as bad as the tragedy itself, his whole parish maligned, a police superintendent made out to be no better than the criminals he daily pursued. He'd read the thing through twice; he'd looked at the photographs in astonishment. Hetty Fortune and Jeremiah Tyler had come to see him, but he'd advised them against poking about in what was over and done with. He'd explained that people wanted to try to forget the explosion of violence that had so suddenly occurred in their midst, that he himself still prayed for the souls of the Butlers and Maureen McDowd. The woman had nodded her head, as though persuaded by what he said. 'I have the camera here, Father,' the man had remarked as they were leaving. 'Will I take a snap of you?' Father Sallins had stood by the fuchsias, seeing no harm in having his photograph taken. 'I'll send it down to you when it's developed,' the man said, but the photograph had never arrived. The first he saw of it was in the Sunday magazine, a poor likeness of himself, eyelids drooped as though he had drink taken, dark stubble on his chin.

'This is a terrible thing,' he said in the McDowds' kitchen, remembering the photograph of that also: the cream-enamelled electric cooker, the Holy Child on the green-painted dresser, beside the alarm clock and the stack of clothes-pegs, the floor carpeted for cosiness, the blue, formica-topped table, the radio, the television set. In the photograph the kitchen had acquired an extraneous quality, just as the photograph of the Butlers' yard had. The harsh, ordinary colours, the soiled edges of the curtains, the chipped paint-work, seemed like part of a meticulous composition: the photograph was so much a picture that it invited questioning as a record.

'We never thought she was going to say that about Maureen,' Mrs McDowd said. 'It's lies, Father.'

'Of course it is, Mrs McDowd.'

'We all know what happened that night.'

'Of course we do.'

McDowd said nothing. They had taken the money. It was he who had said that the people should be allowed into the house. Three thousand, one hundred and fifty pounds was the sum the woman had written the cheque for, insisting that the extra money was owed.

'You never said she'd been specially chosen, Father?'

'Of course I didn't, Mrs McDowd.'

He'd heard that Superintendent O'Kelly had gone to see a solicitor to inquire if he'd been libelled, and although he was told he probably had been he was advised that recourse in the courts would be costly and might not be successful. The simple explanation of what had happened at the Butlers' farm had been easy for the people of Drimaghleen and for the police to accept because they had known Mrs Butler and they had known her son. There'd been no mystery, there'd been no doubt.

'Will we say a prayer together?' the priest suggested.

They knelt, and when they rose again Mrs McDowd began to cry. Everyone would know about it, she said, as if the priest had neither prayed nor spoken. The story would get about and people would believe it. '*Disadvantaged people*', she quoted from the newspaper. She frowned, still sobbing, over the words. 'It says the Butlers were disadvantaged people. It says we are disadvantaged ourselves.'

'That's only the way that woman has of writing it down, Mrs McDowd. It doesn't mean much.'

'*These simple farm folk,*' Mrs McDowd read, '*of Europe's most western island form limited rural communities that all too often turn in on themselves.*'

'Don't pay attention,' Father Sallins advised.

'Does disadvantaged mean we're poor?'

'The way that woman would see it, Mrs McDowd.'

There was confusion now in Drimaghleen, in Kilmona and Mountcroe; and confusion, Father Sallins believed, was insidious. People had been separated from their instinct, and other newspaper articles would follow upon this one. More strangers would come. Father Sallins imagined a film being made about Maureen McDowd, and the mystery that had been created becoming a legend. The nature of Maureen McDowd would be argued over, books would be written because all of it was fascinating. For ever until they died her mother and her father would blame themselves for taking the money their poverty had been unable to turn away.

'The family'll see the pictures.'

'Don't upset yourself, Mrs McDowd.'

'No one ever said she was close to being a saint. That was never said, Father.'

'I know, I know.'

Mrs McDowd covered her face with her hands. Her thin shoulders heaved beneath the pain of her distress; sobs wrenched at her body. Too much had happened to her, the priest thought; it was too much for any mother that her murdered daughter should be accused of murder herself in order to give newspaper-readers something to think about. Her husband had turned away from the table she sat at. He stood with his back to her, looking out into the yard. In a low, exhausted voice he said:

'What kind of people are they?'

The priest slowly shook his head, unable to answer that, and in the kitchen that looked different in Jeremiah Tyler's photograph Mrs McDowd screamed. She sat at the blue-topped table with her lips drawn back from her teeth, one short, shrill scream following fast upon another. Father Sallins did not again attempt to comfort her. McDowd remained by the window.

1990

JOHN UPDIKE
b. 1932–2009

Updike was born in Shillington, Pennsylvania, an only child. His mother—a writer—gave him the idea that art would lead him to a happy life, so he launched himself as a cartoonist for the *Harvard Lampoon* during his college years, and for a year after graduation studied drawing in England. Soon after this he joined the staff of the *New Yorker* and served the magazine in a number of capacities until 1957; he contributed verse, reviews, and fiction to its pages. Astonishingly prolific, Updike published, on average, a book a year throughout his adult life. His fiction is often topical—people trapped in American fads and prejudices figure often in his most characteristic writing. His many novels have won two Pulitzer Prizes and the National Book Award, among other honors. Best-known titles include *Rabbit, Run* (1960), *The Centaur* (1963), *Couples* (1968), *Rabbit Redux* (1971), *Rabbit Is Rich* (1982), *The Witches of Eastwick* (1984), *Roger's Version* (1986), *Rabbit at Rest* (1990), *Toward the End of Time* (1997), *Terrorist* (2006), and his last novel, *The Widows of Eastwick* (2008). A winner of the Rea Award for the Short Story (2006), his stories have been collected in *Problems* (1979), *The Afterlife* (1994), *Early Stories, 1953–1975* (2003), *Three Trips* (2003), *My Father's Tears* (2009), and *The Maples Stories* (2009). The two volumes of his *Collected Stories* appeared in 2013.

A&P

In walks these three girls in nothing but bathing suits. I'm in the third checkout slot, with my back to the door, so I don't see them until they're over by the bread. The one that caught my eye first was the one in the plaid green two-piece. She was a chunky kid, with a good tan and a sweet broad soft-looking can with those two crescents of white just under it, where the sun never seems to hit, at the top of the backs of her legs. I stood there with my hand on a box of HiHo crackers trying to remember if I rang it up or not. I ring it up again and the customer starts giving me hell. She's one of these cash-register-watchers, a witch about fifty with rouge on her cheekbones and no eyebrows, and I know it made her day to trip me up. She'd been watching cash registers for fifty years and probably never seen a mistake before.

By the time I got her feathers smoothed and her goodies into a bag—she gives me a little snort in passing, if she'd been born at the right time they would have burned her over in Salem[1]—by the time I get her on her way the girls had circled around the bread and were coming back, without a pushcart, back my way along the counters, in the aisle between the checkouts and the Special bins. They didn't even have shoes on. There was this chunky one, with the two-piece—it was bright green and the seams on the bra were still sharp and her belly was still pretty pale so I guessed she just got it (the suit)—there was this one, with one of those chubby berry-faces, the lips all bunched together under her nose, this one, and a tall one, with black hair that hadn't quite frizzed right, and one of these sunburns right across under the eyes, and a chin that was too long—you know, the kind of girl other girls think is very "striking" and "attractive" but never quite makes it, as they very well know, which is why they like her so much—and then the third one, that wasn't quite so tall. She was the queen. She kind of led them, the other two peeking around and making their shoulders round. She didn't look around, not this queen, she just walked straight on slowly, on these long white primadonna legs. She came down a little hard on her heels, as if she didn't walk in bare feet that much, putting down her heels and then letting the weight move along to her toes as if she was testing the floor with every step, putting a little deliberate extra action into it. You never know for sure how girls' minds work (do you really think it's a mind in there or just a little buzz like a bee in a glass jar?) but you got the idea she had talked the other two into coming here with her, and now she was showing them how to do it, walk slow and hold yourself straight.

She had on a kind of dirty-pink—beige maybe, I don't know—bathing suit with a little nubble all over it and, what got me, the straps were down. They were off her shoulders looped loose around the cool tops of her arms, and I guess as a result the suit had slipped a little on her, so all around the top of the cloth there was this shining rim. If it hadn't been there you wouldn't have known there could have been anything whiter than those shoulders. With the straps pushed off, there was nothing between the top of the suit and the top of her head except just *her*, this clean bare plane of the top of her chest down from the shoulder bones like a dented sheet of metal tilted in the light. I mean, it was more than pretty.

She had a sort of oaky hair that the sun and salt had bleached, done up in a bun that was unravelling, and a kind of prim face. Walking into the A&P with your straps down, I suppose it's the only kind of face you *can* have. She held her head so high her neck, coming up out of those white shoulders, looked kind of stretched, but I didn't mind. The longer her neck was, the more of her there was.

She must have felt in the corner of her eye me and over my shoulder Stokesie in the second slot watching, but she didn't tip. Not this queen. She kept her eyes moving across the racks, and stopped, and turned so slow it made my stomach rub the inside of my apron, and buzzed to the other two, who kind of huddled against her for relief, and then they all three of them went up the cat-and-dog-food-breakfast-cereal-macaroni-rice-raisins-seasonings-spreads-spaghetti-soft-drinks-crackers-and-cookies aisle. From the third slot I look straight up this aisle to the meat counter, and I watched them all the

---

1. Massachusetts seaport famous for the execution of "witches" in 1692.

way. The fat one with the tan sort of fumbled with the cookies, but on second thought she put the package back. The sheep pushing their carts down the aisle—the girls were walking against the usual traffic (not that we have one-way signs or anything)—were pretty hilarious. You could see them, when Queenie's white shoulders dawned on them, kind of jerk, or hop, or hiccup, but their eyes snapped back to their own baskets and on they pushed. I bet you could set off dynamite in an A&P and the people would by and large keep reaching and checking oatmeal off their lists and muttering "Let me see, there was a third thing, began with A, asparagus, no, ah, yes, applesauce!" or whatever it is they do mutter. But there was no doubt, this jiggled them. A few houseslaves in pin curlers even looked around after pushing their carts past to make sure what they had seen was correct.

You know, it's one thing to have a girl in a bathing suit down on the beach, where what with the glare nobody can look at each other much anyway, and another thing in the cool of the A&P, under the fluorescent lights, against all those stacked packages, with her feet paddling along naked over our checkerboard green-and-cream rubber-tile floor.

"Oh Daddy," Stokesie said beside me. "I feel so faint."

"Darling," I said. "Hold me tight." Stokesie's married, with two babies chalked up on his fuselage already, but as far as I can tell that's the only difference. He's twenty-two, and I was nineteen this April.

"Is it done?" he asks, the responsible married man finding his voice. I forgot to say he thinks he's going to be manager some sunny day, maybe in 1990 when it's called the Great Alexandrov and Petrooshki Tea Company[2] or something.

What he meant was, our town is five miles from a beach, with a big summer colony out on the Point, but we're right in the middle of town, and the women generally put on a shirt or shorts or something before they get out of the car into the street. And anyway these are usually women with six children and varicose veins mapping their legs and nobody, including them, could care less. As I say, we're right in the middle of town, and if you stand at our front doors you can see two banks and the Congregational church and the newspaper store and three real-estate offices and about twenty-seven old freeloaders tearing up Central Street because the sewer broke again. It's not as if we're on the Cape;[3] we're north of Boston and there's people in this town haven't seen the ocean for twenty years.

The girls had reached the meat counter and were asking McMahon something. He pointed, they pointed, and they shuffled out of sight behind a pyramid of Diet Delight peaches. All that was left for us to see was old McMahon patting his mouth and looking after them sizing up their joints. Poor kids, I began to feel sorry for them, they couldn't help it.

Now here comes the sad part of the story, at least my family says it's sad, but I don't think it's so sad myself. The store's pretty empty, it being Thursday afternoon, so there was nothing much to do except lean on the register and wait for the girls to show up again. The whole store was like a pinball machine

---

2. The actual name of the A&P supermarket chain is The Great Atlantic and Pacific Tea Company.
3. Cape Cod, Massachusetts, a resort area where fashions of dress are usually informal.

and I didn't know which tunnel they'd come out of. After a while they come around out of the far aisle, around the light bulbs, records at discount of the Caribbean Six or Tony Martin Sings or some such gunk you wonder they waste the wax on, six-packs of candy bars, and plastic toys done up in cellophane that fall apart when a kid looks at them anyway. Around they come, Queenie still leading the way, and holding a little gray jar in her hand. Slots Three through Seven are unmanned and I could see her wondering between Stokes and me, but Stokesie with his usual luck draws an old party in baggy gray pants who stumbles up with four giant cans of pineapple juice (what do these bums *do* with all that pineapple juice? I've often asked myself) so the girls come to me. Queenie puts down the jar and I take it into my fingers icy cold. Kingfish Fancy Herring Snacks in Pure Sour Cream: 49¢. Now her hands are empty, not a ring or a bracelet, bare as God made them, and I wonder where the money's coming from. Still with that prim look she lifts a folded dollar bill out of the hollow at the center of her nubbled pink top. The jar went heavy in my hand. Really, I thought that was so cute.

Then everybody's luck begins to run out. Lengel comes in from haggling with a truck full of cabbages on the lot and is about to scuttle into that door marked MANAGER behind which he hides all day when the girls touch his eye. Lengel's pretty dreary, teaches Sunday school and the rest, but he doesn't miss that much. He comes over and says, "Girls, this isn't the beach."

Queenie blushes, though maybe it's just a brush of sunburn I was noticing for the first time, now that she was so close. "My mother asked me to pick up a jar of herring snacks." Her voice kind of startled me, the way voices do when you see the people first, coming out so flat and dumb yet kind of tony, too, the way it ticked over "pick up" and "snacks." All of a sudden I slid right down her voice into her living room. Her father and the other men were standing around in ice-cream coats and bow ties and the women were in sandals picking up herring snacks on toothpicks off a big glass plate and they were all holding drinks the color of water with olives and sprigs of mint in them. When my parents have somebody over they get lemonade and if it's a real racy affair Schlitz in tall glasses with "They'll Do It Every Time"[4] cartoons stencilled on.

"That's all right," Lengel said. "But this isn't the beach." His repeating this struck me as funny, as if it had just occurred to him, and he had been thinking all these years the A&P was a great big dune and he was the head lifeguard. He didn't like my smiling—as I say he doesn't miss much—but he concentrates on giving the girls that sad Sunday-school-superintendent stare.

Queenie's blush is no sunburn now, and the plump one in plaid, that I liked better from the back—a really sweet can—pipes up, "We weren't doing any shopping. We just came in for the one thing."

"That makes no difference," Lengel tells her, and I could see from the way his eyes went that he hadn't noticed she was wearing a two-piece before. "We want you decently dressed when you come in here."

"We *are* decent," Queenie says suddenly, her lower lip pushing, getting sore now that she remembers her place, a place from which the crowd that runs the A&P must look pretty crummy. Fancy Herring Snacks flashed in her very blue eyes.

4. Popular newspaper comic, created by Jimmy Hatlo, that first appeared in 1929.

"Girls, I don't want to argue with you. After this come in here with your shoulders covered. It's our policy." He turns his back. That's policy for you. Policy is what the kingpins want. What the others want is juvenile delinquency.

All this while, the customers had been showing up with their carts but, you know, sheep, seeing a scene, they had all bunched up on Stokesie, who shook open a paper bag as gently as peeling a peach, not wanting to miss a word. I could feel in the silence everybody getting nervous, most of all Lengel, who asks me, "Sammy, have you rung up their purchase?"

I thought and said "No" but it wasn't about that I was thinking. I go through the punches, 4, 9, GROC, TOT—it's more complicated than you think, and after you do it often enough, it begins to make a little song, that you hear words to, in my case "Hello (*bing*) there, you (*gung*) hap-py *pee*-pul (*splat*)!"—the *splat* being the drawer flying out. I uncrease the bill, tenderly as you may imagine, it just having come from between the two smoothest scoops of vanilla I had ever known there were, and pass a half and a penny into her narrow pink palm, and nestle the herrings in a bag and twist its neck and hand it over, all the time thinking.

The girls, and who'd blame them, are in a hurry to get out, so I say "I quit" to Lengel quick enough for them to hear, hoping they'll stop and watch me, their unsuspected hero. They keep right on going, into the electric eye; the door flies open and they flicker across the lot to their car, Queenie and Plaid and Big Tall Goony-Goony (not that as raw material she was so bad), leaving me with Lengel and a kink in his eyebrow.

"Did you say something, Sammy?"

"I said I quit."

"I thought you did."

"You didn't have to embarrass them."

"It was they who were embarrassing us."

I started to say something that came out "Fiddle-de-do." It's a saying of my grandmother's, and I know she would have been pleased.

"I don't think you know what you're saying," Lengel said.

"I know you don't," I said. "But I do." I pull the bow at the back of my apron and start shrugging it off my shoulders. A couple of customers that had been heading for my slot begin to knock against each other, liked scared pigs in a chute.

Lengel sighs and begins to look very patient and old and gray. He's been a friend of my parents for years. "Sammy, you don't want to do this to your Mom and Dad," he tells me. It's true, I don't. But it seems to me that once you begin a gesture it's fatal not to go through with it. I fold the apron, "Sammy" stitched in red on the pocket, and put it on the counter, and drop the bow tie on top of it. The bow tie is theirs, if you've ever wondered. "You'll feel this for the rest of your life," Lengel says, and I know that's true, too, but remembering how he made that pretty girl blush makes me so scrunchy inside I punch the No Sale tab and the machine whirs "pee-pul" and the drawer splats out. One advantage to this scene taking place in summer, I can follow this up with a clean exit, there's no fumbling around getting your coat and galoshes, I just saunter into the electric eye in my white shirt that my mother ironed the night before, and the door heaves itself open, and outside the sunshine is skating around on the asphalt.

I look around for my girls, but they're gone, of course. There wasn't anybody but some young married screaming with her children about some candy they didn't get by the door of a powder-blue Falcon station wagon. Looking back in the big windows, over the bags of peat moss and aluminum lawn furniture stacked on the pavement, I could see Lengel in my place in the slot, checking the sheep through. His face was dark gray and his back stiff, as if he's just had an injection of iron, and my stomach kind of fell as I felt how hard the world was going to be to me hereafter.

1962

Brother Grasshopper

Fred Emmet—swarthy and thick-set, with humorless straight eyebrows almost meeting above his nose—had been an only child. If he ever fantasized a sibling for himself, it was a sister, not a brother. His father had had a brother, an older brother, who, he let it be known, had dominated him cruelly. Yet into even his more resentful reminiscences crept a warmth that Fred envied, as he tried to imagine the games of catch, decades ago, on the vacant lots of a city that no longer had vacant lots, and the shared paper route in snow that was deeper and more dramatic than any snow today is, with a different scent—the scent of wet leather and of damp wool knickers. Though his father's brother had deliberately thrown the ball too hard, and finished delivering papers to his side of the street first and never came back to help but instead waited inside the warm candy store, a brother was something his father had *had*, augmenting his existence, giving it an additional dimension available to him all his life. "My brother down in Deerfield Beach," he would drop into a conversation, or "If you were to express that view to my brother, he'd tell you flat out you're crazy." And, though the brothers lived over a thousand miles apart, one in Florida and the other in New Jersey, and saw each other less than once a year, they died within a few months of each other, Fred's father following his older brother as if into one more vacant lot, to shag flies for him.

But this was years later, when Fred's own children were grown, or nearly. He had married early, right after Harvard, supplying himself with another roommate, as it were, rather than launching into life alone. He envied siblings their imagined power of consultation, of conspiring against parents who otherwise would be too powerful. Not the least of the charms his future wife held for him was her sister—a younger sister also at Radcliffe,[1] with her own circle of friends. Germaine was more animated, more gregarious, and more obviously pretty than Fred's sensible Betsy. Among her numerous suitors the most conspicuous was Carlyle Saughterfield, a tall bony New Englander with a careless, potent manner.

Fred had been sickly and much-protected as a child, and even his late growth spurt had left him well under six feet tall. He found Carlyle, who was two years older than he and a student at the Business School across the river,

---

1. Once a private women's college, now part of Harvard University.

exotic and intimidating—a grown man with his own car, a green Studebaker convertible, and confident access to the skills and equipment of expensive sports like sailing, skiing, climbing, and hunting. Carlyle and his B-School friends would load up his snappy green convertible with skis and boots and beer and sleeping bags and head north into snow country with the top down. Details of their mountain adventures made Fred shudder—sheer ice, blinding fog, tainted venison that left them all vomiting, ski trails bearing terrible names like Devil's Head and Suicide Ravine. Climbing in the White Mountains[2] one summer, Carlyle had seen a friend fall, turning in the air a few feet away as Carlyle pressed into the cliff and gripped the pitons.

"What was the expression on his face?" Fred asked.

Carlyle's somewhat protuberant eyes appeared to moisten, as he visualized the fatal moment. "Impassive," he said.

His voice, husky and hard to hear, as if strained through something like baleen, was the one weak thing about him; but even this impressed Fred. Back in New Jersey, the big men, gangsters and police chiefs and Knights of Columbus, spoke softly, forcing others to listen.

As their courtship of the Terwilliger sisters proceeded in parallel, Fred and Carlyle spent an accumulating number of hours together. In the spring, waiting for the girls to come out of their dorms, they played catch in the Quad with a squash ball; Carlyle's throws made Fred's hands sting and revived his childhood fear of being hit in the face and having an eye or a tooth knocked out. The strength stored in the other man's long arms and wide, sloping shoulders was amazing—a whippy, excessive strength almost burdensome, Fred imagined, to carry. Carlyle had been a jock at prep school, but in college had disdained organized sports; a tendency to veer away from the expected was perhaps another weakness of his. Behind the Business School, across from Harvard Stadium, a soccer field existed where the future financiers played touch football. Carlyle passed for immense distances, sometimes into Fred's eagerly reaching hands, and protectively saw to it that his timorous and undersized brother in courtship usually played on his team.

In March of the year that Fred and Betsy graduated, the two couples went skiing, and Carlyle was as patient as a professional instructor, teaching Fred the snowplow and stem christie and carefully bringing him down, at the end of the day, through the shadows of the intermediate slope. All these upperclass skills involved danger, Fred noticed. That summer, after he and Betsy had married, Carlyle took them and Germaine sailing on Buzzards Bay[3] and, while the two sisters stretched out in their underwear for sunbaths on the bow, commanded in his reedy voice that Fred take the tiller and hold the mainsheet—take all this responsibility into his hands!

"Take it. Push it left to make the prow move to the right. The prow's the thing in front."

"I'd just as soon rather not. I'm happy being a passenger."

"Take it, Freddy."

The huge boat leaned terrifyingly under gusts of invisible pressure, the monstrous sail rippling and the mast impaling the sun and the keel slapping blindly through the treacherous water, nothing firm under them, even the

2. Appalachian range in northern New Hampshire. 3. Inlet of southeastern Massachusetts.

horizon and its islands skidding and shifty. Nevertheless, the boat did not capsize. Fred gradually got a slight feel for it—for the sun and salt air and rocking horizon. Germaine's breasts in their bra were bigger than Betsy's, her pubic bush made a shadowy cushion under her underpants as the sisters lazily, trustfully chattered. Carlyle's face, uplifted to the sun with bulging closed eyelids, had a betranced look; his colorless fair hair, already thinning, and longer than a businessman's should be, streamed behind him in the wind. *This bastard,* Fred thought, as the boat sickeningly heeled, *is trying to make a man of me.*

When, the following summer, Germaine graduated and married Carlyle, the groom chose Fred over all his old skiing and hunting buddies to be his best man, perhaps in courteous symmetry with Betsy, the matron-of-honor. He bought Fred a beige suit to match his own; the coat hung loose on Fred's narrow shoulders, and the sleeves were too long, but he felt flattered nonetheless. Betsy was five months pregnant, so her ceremonial dress, of royal-blue silk, was too tight. Between them, they joked, it came out even. So young, they were already launched on creating another generation.

A strange incident clouded this wedding, foreshadowing trouble to come. Carlyle and Germaine were married in New Hampshire, at a summer lodge beyond Franconia belonging to Carlyle's family, and with sentimental associations for him. The Terwilliger parents were getting a divorce at the time and were too unorganized to insist on having the event on their territory, in northwestern Connecticut. With the noon hour set for the service drawing closer, Carlyle disappeared, and it was reported that he was taking a bath down at the dam—an icy little pond in the woods, created every summer by damming a mountain trickle. Mrs. Terwilliger, rendered distraught by this apparent additional defection—her own husband was not present, having been forbidden to come if he brought his youthful mistress—appealed to Fred to go down and fetch the groom. Fred supposed that in his role of best man he could not shy from this awkward duty. In his black shoes and floppy new suit—double-breasted, with those wide Fifties lapels, and a white rosebud pinned in one of them—he walked down the dirt road to the dam. His fingers kept testing his right-hand coat pocket, to see if the wedding ring was still there—its adamant little weight, its cool curved edge. The road was really two dusty paths beside a central mane of weeds and grass, shadowed even toward noon by hemlocks and birches. Bears supposedly lived in these woods, which stretched endlessly, gloomily, in every direction, claustrophobic as a cave. Suppose Carlyle had fled! Suppose he had gone crazy, and with his excessive, careless strength would knock his best man unconscious!

Carlyle was coming up the road, in his identical beige suit, his long wet hair combed flat, his ritual bachelor ablutions at last completed. Fred was relieved; he had been afraid of, among other things, seeing his soon-to-be brother-in-law naked. The road slanted down, to the creek, so their heads for a moment were on the same level, and in this moment Carlyle gave Fred, or Fred happened to catch, a look, a watery warm-eyed look. What did it mean? *Get me out of this?* Or was the look just a flare, a droplet, of the wordless pagan wisdom that brothers somehow shared?

"They sent me after you."

"I see that, Freddy."

Carlyle's eyes were an uncanny pale green, with thin pink lids, and prominent, so that his long face gave the impression of being a single smooth tender surface, his nose so small as to be negligible. When he looked intent, as now, his eyes went flat across the top, the upper eyelid swallowing its own lashes.

In the years to come, the brothers-in-law looked each other in the eyes rather rarely. Not that they lacked occasion: though they lived, with their wives and children, in separate towns, and eventually on different coasts of the continent, Carlyle saw to it that they all spent at least several weeks of the year as one family. There was the Franconia place at first, and when Carlyle's mother, widowed early by a heart attack that carried off his father—the Saughterfields had fragile hearts—sold it, there were summer houses rented jointly, or two rented side by side, or Christmases spent in one or the other's home, the floor beneath the tree heaped embarrassingly high with the presents for their combined children. There were nine children, in the end: Fred and Betsy's three, Carlyle and Germaine's six. Six! Even in those years before ecology-mindedness, that was a lot, for non-Catholics. Fred and Betsy speculated that, his own father dying so young and his mother remarrying and moving to Paris (her new husband worked for American Express), Carlyle was afraid of running out of family; his New Hampshire cousins depressed him and his only sibling was a much older sister whom he never mentioned, and who lived in Hawaii with an alcoholic jerk of a husband.

The Emmets sometimes found the joint vacations heavy going. Their children were outnumbered two to one and everyone was benevolently bullied into expeditions—to the beach, to an amusement park, to some mountain trail—whose ultimate purpose seemed to be to create photo opportunities for Carlyle. He had become a fervent photographer, first with Nikons and then with Leicas, until he discovered that an even more expensive camera could be bought—a Hasselblad. Its chunky shutter sound sucked them up, sealed them in, captured them in sunshine and rain, parkas and bathing suits, the boys in their baseball caps and the girls in their ribbons and braids. One cherished photo, turned into the Saughterfields' Christmas card, showed all nine children squeezed into the Emmets' old workhorse of a Fairlane station wagon, each hot little grinning face smeared by an ice-cream cone. What the photo did not show was the drive away from the ice-cream stand: the cones melted too rapidly in the August heat and had to be thrown out the window when they became, in the mass of flesh, impossibly liquid. "Over the side!" Carlyle called from behind the wheel, and an answering voice would pipe, "Over the side!," and another gob of ice cream would spatter on the receding highway, to gales of childish glee. Conspicuous waste pained Fred, but seemed to exhilarate Carlyle.

As it worked out, Carlyle was often driving Fred's cars, and commandeering Betsy's kitchen for meals he would cook, dirtying every pan. He made the Emmets feel squeezed, not least with his acts of *largesse*[4]—plastic-foam boxes of frozen steaks that would arrive before a visit, mail-ordered from Omaha, and heavy parcels of post-visit prints, glossily processed by a film laboratory in West Germany that Carlyle used. All these fond, proprietary gestures, Fred felt, spelled power and entitlement. Even taking the photo-

---

4. Generosity, especially from someone of superior social rank (French).

graphs placed Carlyle on a level above them, as an all-seeing appropriator of their fleeting lives.

Once, on Martha's Vineyard,[5] when Fred needed his car to get to a tennis date in Chilmark and Carlyle had taken it up to Oak Bluffs to buy his daughters and nieces elephant-hair bracelets, and then to Vineyard Haven for the matinée of a Jerry Lewis movie, with miniature golf on the way home, Fred let his temper fly. He felt his face flush; he heard his shrill voice flail and crack. Carlyle, who had returned from his long expedition with bags of farmstand vegetables, pounds of unfilleted fish, and a case of imported beer, stared at Fred with his uncanny green eyes for some seconds and then cheerfully laughed. It was a laugh of such genuine, unmalicious, good-tempered amusement that Fred had to join in. Through his brother-in-law's eyes he saw himself clearly, as a shrill and defensive pipsqueak. It was, he imagined, this sort of honest illumination—this sort of brusque restoration to one's true measure—that siblings offer one another. As an only child, Fred had never been made to confront his limits.

In bed he asked Betsy, "Why does he need to do it—all this playing Santa Claus?"

"Because," she answered, "he doesn't have enough else to do."

What Carlyle did professionally became vaguer with the years. After business school there had been business—putting on a suit in the morning, working for other men, travelling in airplanes to meet with more men in suits. One company he worked for made fine leather goods—purses, belts, aviator-style jackets as items of high fashion—and another a kind of machinery that stamped gold and silver foil on things, on books and photograph albums and attaché cases and such. Neither job lasted long. Carlyle's weakness, perhaps, was his artistic side. His Harvard major had been not economics but fine arts; he took photographs and bought expensive art books so big no shelves could hold them; he could not be in his house, or the Emmets', a minute without filling the air with loud music, usually opera. When his mother's sudden death—she was hit by a taxi in Paris, on the Boulevard St.-Germain—brought him some additional money, he became a partner in an avant-garde furniture store in the Back Bay:[6] chairs and tables of molded plastic, sofas in the form of arcs of a circle, waterbeds. The store did well—it was the Sixties, there was plenty of money around, and plenty of questing for new lifestyles—but Carlyle got bored, and became a partner in a Los Angeles firm that manufactured kinetic gadgets of Plexiglas and chemical fluids. This firm went bust, but not before Carlyle fell in fatal love with California—its spaghetti of flowing thruways, its pink and palmy sprawl, its endless sunshine and perilous sense of being on the edge. He moved his growing family there in 1965. As his children grew and his hair thinned, Carlyle himself seemed increasingly on the edge—on the edge of the stock market, on the edge of the movie industry, on the edge of some unspecified breakthrough. His clothes became cheerfully bizarre—bell-bottom pants, jackets of fringed buckskin, a beret. His name appeared as co-producer of a low-budget film about runaway adolescents (seen romantically, roving against the night lights of Hollywood and sleeping in colorful shacks up in the canyons) that received favorable reviews back east

---

5. Island off southeastern Massachusetts. **6.** Wealthy district of Boston.

and even turned up in the Coolidge Corner movie complex not far from where Fred and Betsy lived in Brookline.[7]

Fred, unromantically, worked in real estate. After splitting off from the management company that trained him, he bet his life on the future of drab, run-down inner-city neighborhoods that, by the sheer laws of demographics and transportation, had to come up in the world. His bet was working, but slowly, and in the meantime the Emmet Realty Corporation absorbed his days in thankless maintenance and squabbles with tenants and the meticulous game, which Fred rather enjoyed, of maximizing the bank's investment and thereby increasing his own leverage. That is, twenty thousand of his own equity, plus a hundred-thousand-dollar mortgage, meant a profit of two hundred percent if the building's worth climbed by a third. He was, like many only children, naturally meticulous and secretive, and it warmed him to think that his growing personal wealth was cunningly hidden, annually amplified by perfectly legal depreciation write-offs, in these drab holdings—in Dorchester three-deckers and South End brick bowfronts, in asphalt-shingled Somerville duplexes and in Allston apartment buildings so anonymous and plain as to seem ownerless. He was the patient ant, he felt, and Carlyle more and more the foolish grasshopper.

Yet, when, ten years into his marriage, Fred found himself swept up in a reckless romance, it was his brother-in-law that he confessed to. The seethe of his predicament—Betsy's innocence, and the children's, and the other woman's; glittering detached details of her, her eyes and mouth, her voice and tears, her breasts and hair—foamed in him like champagne overflowing a glass. It was delicious, terrible; Fred had never felt so alive. One muggy July afternoon he found himself alone with Carlyle in the ramshackle Chatham[8] house that the Saughterfields and the Emmets were jointly renting. The wives and children were at the beach. Carlyle came into the living room, where Fred was working up some figures, and sat himself stolidly down opposite the desk, on the sandy, briny green fold-out sofa that came with the house. Carlyle had put weight on his big bones, and moved now with the deliberation of someone considerably older than his brother-in-law. Tennis and worry had trimmed Fred down, given him an edge—for the first time in his life, he felt handsome. Carlyle was wearing a kind of southern-California safari suit, a loose cotton jacket with matching pants, suggesting pajamas or a doctor's antiseptic outfit when he operates. He sat there benignly, immovably. To relieve the oppressive silence, Fred began to talk.

As Carlyle listened, his eyes went watery with the gravity of the crisis; yet his remarks were gracefully light, even casual. "Well, Freddy—if I could see you with the woman, I might say, 'What the hell, go to it,'" he pronounced at one point in his reedy voice, and at another point he likened the sexual drive to an automobile, volunteering of himself, "I know it's in there, in the garage, just raring to be revved up."

Though Carlyle seemed, if anything, to advise that Fred follow his heart ("My doc keeps telling me we only live once"), and with his noncommittal calmness did relieve his brother-in-law's agitation and guilt, Fred was left with the impression that it would be absurd of him to leave the children and

7. Boston suburb, as are Dorchester, South End, Somerville, and Allston, below. 8. Town on Cape Cod.

Betsy and the share of the Emmet Corporation her lawyers would demand. Would Carlyle, if he ever *did* see him with the other woman, be enough impressed? Was not erotic passion in truth as mechanical as an internal-combustion engine? Perhaps, in giving him reason to talk of her to Carlyle, to brag, as it were, to the older, taller, stronger man of his conquest, the other woman had served much of her purpose. Looking back, years later, Fred wondered if the sisters hadn't known more than they seemed to, and hadn't urged Carlyle to come and have this brotherly consultation, there in the empty Chatham house sticky with salt air.

The marriages, and the families, went on. So many outings, to build up their children's childhood—beaches, mountains, shopping malls, Disney World. So much shared sunshine. Why, then, did Fred's scattered memories of Carlyle tend to be shadowy? One Christmastime in Brookline, Fred, responding to a ruthless battering sound from below, went into his cellar and discovered his brother-in-law, sinisterly half-lit by the fluorescent tubes above the workbench, pounding something glittering gripped in the vise. The other man's eyes, looking up and squinting with the change of focus, had that watery, warm—was it sheepish?—look they had worn that day of his wedding, as he came up the shady road beneath the hemlocks and birches. "Santa's workshop," he explained huskily. He hid with his body what he was doing. He looked demonic, or damned, in the flickering basement light. Fred backed up the stairs, as embarrassed as if he had surprised the other man undressed.

Betsy explained it to him later, in bed. To save money, Carlyle was making some of their Christmas presents this year—silver dollars drilled through and beaten into rings for the boys, and strung into necklaces for the girls. It was the sort of thing he used to do as a boy; he had been creative, artistic. It was sweet, Betsy thought.

To Fred, even this exercise in thrift savored of extravagance—silver dollars! "Are they that hard up?" he asked. "What's happened to all Carlyle's money?" He had always resented it that Carlyle had simply *had* money, whereas he had had to make it, a crumb at a time.

Well, according to what Betsy had gathered from Germaine, who out of loyalty of course didn't like to say much, six children in private schools and colleges aren't cheap, and the stock market had been off under Nixon, and Carlyle had trouble trimming his expensive tastes—the M.G. convertible, the English suits ordered tailor-made from London even though he rarely wore suits, the beach house in Malibu in addition to their seven-bedroom Mission-style home in Bel Air.[9] The people he dealt with expected him to have these things.

"Who *does* he deal with?" Fred asked.

"*You* know," Betsy said, in the voice of one who didn't exactly know, either. "Movie people. He's involved in a movie now, Germaine did allow, that's just *sucking* the money out of him. He's in with this guy, Lanny somebody, who was supposed to make a low-budget blue movie with an adventure theme as well, so it would not just be for the triple-X theatres but could get into the softer-core drive-ins, but who without asking or telling Carlyle went and

9. Wealthy district of Los Angeles. *Malibu*: exclusive seaside community west of Los Angeles.

rented one of those sound stages that cost twenty-five thousand a day or something fantastic for these episodes that don't exactly tie in yet, since he doesn't have a real script, it's all in his head. He even bought an old frame house somewhere and burned it down for one scene. Germaine thinks Carlyle is being taken for a *horrible* ride but is too proud to say anything. You remember all that buddy-buddy skiing and hunting he used to do?—those people used to take advantage of him, too. He has this old-fashioned sense of honor and can't defend himself. He gets caught up in a macho sort of thing. Furthermore, he likes being around these movie people, especially the little porno starlets. She wishes *you'd* talk to him."

"Me? What would I say?" Fred's stomach pinched, there in the dark. He was still afraid of Carlyle, slightly—those flat-lidded eyes, the way he could throw a ball that made your hands hurt.

"Just open the subject. Let him tell you how it is."

"The tried-and-true talking cure," he said bitterly. A decade later, he still missed the woman he had given up—dreamed of her, in amazing, all-but-forgotten detail. He would never love anyone that much again. He had come to see that the heart, like a rubber ball, loses bounce, and eventually goes dead. He did feel a faint pity, smelling his brother-in-law's pain in the house. There had been a physical deterioration as well as a financial. Carlyle's doctor had told him to take afternoon naps, and it seemed he was often upstairs, in a kind of hibernation, from which he would emerge red-eyed, wearing soft moccasins. To his counterculture clothes his health problems had added a macrobiotic diet, and the clothes hung loose on his reduced, big-boned frame.

One day between Christmas and New Year's, when all the others had gone ice-skating on the Brookline Reservoir, Fred walked into the kitchen, where Carlyle was heating water for a cup of herbal tea, and asked, "How's it going?"

The other man wore an embroidered green dashiki hanging loose outside dirty old painter pants. His hair had vanished on top, and he had let it grow long at the back; with the long graying wisps straggling at the nape of his neck, he seemed a dazed old woman, fussing at her broth. His bare arms looked white and chilly. Years in California had thinned his blood. Fred said, "If you'd like to borrow a sweater, I have plenty."

"Actually, I just turned up the thermostat." Carlyle looked over at him mischievously, knowing that thrifty Fred would resent this, and continued his aggressive tack. "Everything's going great," he said. "Life's all *samsara*, Freddy. The Terwilliger girls may have been stirring you up about this particular film project I have in the works, but, like they say, no sweat. It's money in the bank. When you bring your gang out this summer, we should have a rough print to show you."

"That would be nice," Fred said. To be brotherly, he was wearing the ring Carlyle had given him; its roughly pounded edges scratched his skin, and an inspection of the basement had disclosed that a number of his drill bits, meant for wood and not silver alloy, had been ruinously dulled.

The film, when they saw it that June in L.A., also seemed crudely made. The young flesh, photographed in too hard a light, in rooms rented by the hour, had a repulsive sheen, a smooth falseness as of tinted and perfumed candles. The adventure parts of the film failed to link up. The burning house was on the screen only a few garish, orange seconds. Fred was struck by the actors' and actresses' voices, recorded with a curious flat echo that made him realize how filtered, how trained, the voices in real movies are. Carlyle's profile had been fascinating in the dark, the screen's bright moments glittering in the corner of his eye. When the lights came on, his tender-skinned face was flushed. He said sheepishly to his in-laws, "Hope it wasn't too blue for you."

"Maybe not blue enough," Fred allowed himself to say. It was the nearest to a negative word he had ever dared, since that time on the Vineyard when Carlyle had laughed at his pipsqueak indignation.

Now it was his turn to be amused, when, at dinner afterwards, over Hawaiian drinks and Chinese food, while the wives held tensely silent, Carlyle hoped aloud that Fred would consider investing in the film, toward distribution and advertising costs, which were all that was left to get the package off the ground. One more boost and the movie would make everybody a bundle. He could offer eighteen-percent annual interest, just like MasterCard in reverse, or up to a quarter of the net profits, depending on how many hundred thousand Fred could see his way clear to invest. Plus, he promised, he would pay Fred's principal back right off the top, before he even paid himself. He knew Boston real estate had been going through the roof lately and Fred must be desperate for a little diversification.

Carlyle's mien, in the shadowy restaurant with its guttering hurricane lamps and pseudo-Polynesian idols, wasn't easy to read; his strained-sounding voice, almost inaudible, wheezed on doggedly, and a watery fixation glazed over the old glint—the guilty glance from the bottom of something—that Fred had caught or imagined on the hemlock-shaded road twenty-five years before.

Fred didn't laugh. He said he would think about it and talk it over with Betsy. Naturally, she had a stake in all his business decisions and was always consulted. In private he asked her, "How important is it to you as a sister, if this would bail Germaine out?"

She said, "It isn't, and I don't think it would anyway."

Fred felt contaminated by the other man's naked plea, and could hardly wait until he got away, safely back to his own coast. He was too cowardly to turn Carlyle down himself. He left it to the Terwilliger sisters, Betsy to Germaine via long-distance telephone, to pass him the word: No way. Fred Emmet, too, could give a brotherly lesson in limits.

When Carlyle Saughterfield, less than a decade after his failed film had emptied his pockets, died, it was in a movie theatre. The girl next to him—not a date; they had just been introduced—noticed him at one point softly thumping his own chest, and when the lights went up the tall man was slumped as if asleep. Impassive. Wearing a green dashiki, and not much older than his father had been.

Germaine and he, some years before, had gotten divorced, and Fred and Betsy, too, as the Terwilliger sisters continued their lives in parallel. Betsy had never really forgiven him for the insult of that old affair. Germaine, a week after Betsy had phoned Fred with the stunning news, called him herself to invite him to a pagan ceremony, a scattering of Carlyle's ashes in a tidal creek north of Boston where the dead man used to sail and swim as a boy.

This scattering had been his idea, as was Fred's being invited. Germaine said, "He loved you," which sounded right, since families teach us how love exists in a realm above liking or disliking, coexisting with indifference, rivalry, and even antipathy. What with his health troubles, ominous family history, and nothing much else to do, Carlyle had done a lot of thinking about his own death: from beyond the grave, it appeared, he was trying to arrange one more group photo. The children were adult and dispersed, most on the coasts but one in Chicago and another in New Mexico. A ragged group gathered on an appointed wooden bridge, on a February day so clear it did not feel cold.

Fred dipped his hand into the box of calcium bits that had been Carlyle's big bones and, imitating the others, carefully dropped them over the rough, green-painted rail. He had imagined that the tide would carry these fragments called ashes toward the sea, but in fact they sank, like chips of shell, tugged but not floated by the pellucid ebbing water. Sinking, doing a slow twirling dance, they caught the light. Two of Fred's nieces—young women in defiant bloom, with ruddy faces and blond hair and pale eyes flat across the top—beamed at him forgivingly, knowingly. The sunshine seemed a lesson being administered, a universal moral; it glinted off of everyone's protein strands of hair and wool hats and sweaters and chilly nailed hands and the splintered green boards of the bridge and the clustered, drifting, turning little fragments in the icy sky-blue tide. In this instant of illumination all those old photographs and those old conglomerate times Carlyle had insisted upon were revealed to Fred as priceless—treasure, stored up against the winter that had arrived.

1990

RELATED:

—Updike, "Accepting the Howells Medal," p. 1735
—Updike, "Three *New Yorker* Stalwarts" [William Maxwell], p. 1778

HELENA MARÍA VIRAMONTES
b. 1954

Viramontes was born in East Los Angeles. She earned her B.A. from Immaculate Heart College, where she began writing, first poetry and then fiction. Her stories were soon published and recognized. In 1979 she was awarded the fiction prize in the Chicano Literary Contest at the University of California at Irvine; she went on to earn her M.F.A. there. Her books include *The Moths* (1985); *Under the Feet of Jesus* (1995); and *Their Dogs Came with Them* (2007). A professor at Cornell University, she was named a Ford Fellow in Literature in 2007 by United States Artists and received the Dos Passos Award for Literature and an NEA Fellowship.

The Moths

I was fourteen years old when Abuelita[1] requested my help. And it seemed only fair. Abuelita had pulled me through the rages of scarlet fever by placing, removing, and replacing potato slices on the temples of my forehead; she had seen me through several whippings, an arm broken by a dare-jump off Tío[2] Enrique's toolshed, puberty, and my first lie. Really, I told Amá,[3] it was only fair.

Not that I was her favorite granddaughter or anything special. I wasn't even pretty or nice like my older sisters and I just couldn't do the girl things they could do. My hands were too big to handle the fineries of crocheting or embroidery and I always pricked my fingers or knotted my colored threads time and time again while my sisters laughed and called me bull hands with their cute waterlike voices. So I began keeping a piece of jagged brick in my sock to bash my sisters or anyone who called me bull hands. Once, while we all sat in the bedroom, I hit Teresa on the forehead, right above her eyebrow, and she ran to Amá with her mouth open, her hand over her eye while blood seeped between her fingers. I was used to the whippings by then.

I wasn't respectful either. I even went so far as to doubt the power of Abuelita's slices, the slices she said absorbed my fever. "You're still alive, aren't you?" Abuelita snapped back, her pasty gray eye beaming at me and burning holes in my suspicions. Regretful that I had let secret questions drop out of my mouth, I couldn't look into her eyes. My hands began to fan out, grow like a liar's nose until they hung by my side like low weights. Abuelita made a balm out of dried moth wings and Vicks and rubbed my hands, shaping them back to size. It was the strangest feeling. Like bones melting. Like sun shining

---

1. "Little Grandma" (Spanish). 2. Uncle (Spanish). 3. Child's name for "Mother" (Spanish).

through the darkness of your eyelids. I didn't mind helping Abuelita after that, so Amá would always send me over to her.

In the early afternoon Amá would push her hair back, hand me my sweater and shoes, and tell me to go to Mama Luna's. This was to avoid another fight and another whipping, I knew. I would deliver one last direct shot on Marisela's arm and jump out of our house, the slam of the screen door burying her cries of anger, and I'd gladly go help Abuelita plant her wild lilies or jasmine or heliotrope or cilantro or hierbabuena[4] in red Hills Brothers coffee cans. Abuelita would wait for me at the top step of her porch holding a hammer and nail and empty coffee cans. And although we hardly spoke, hardly looked at each other as we worked over root transplants, I always felt her gray eye on me. It made me feel, in a strange sort of way, safe and guarded and not alone. Like God was supposed to make you feel.

On Abuelita's porch, I would puncture holes in the bottom of the coffee cans with a nail and a precise hit of a hammer. This completed, my job was to fill them with red clay mud from beneath her rose bushes, packing it softly, then making a perfect hole, four fingers round, to nest a sprouting avocado pit, or the spidery sweet potatoes that Abuelita rooted in mayonnaise jars with toothpicks and daily water, or prickly chayotes[5] that produced vines that twisted and wound all over her porch pillars, crawling to the roof, up and over the roof, and down the other side, making her small brick house look like it was cradled within the vines that grew pear-shaped squashes ready for the pick, ready to be steamed with onions and cheese and butter. The roots would burst out of the rusted coffee cans and search for a place to connect. I would then feed the seedlings with water.

But this was a different kind of help, Amá said, because Abuelita was dying. Looking into her gray eye, then into her brown one, the doctor said it was just a matter of days. And so it seemed only fair that these hands she had melted and formed found use in rubbing her caving body with alcohol and marihuana, rubbing her arms and legs, turning her face to the window so that she could watch the Bird of Paradise blooming or smell the scent of clove in the air. I toweled her face frequently and held her hand for hours. Her gray wiry hair hung over the mattress. Since I could remember, she'd kept her long hair in braids. Her mouth was vacant and when she slept, her eyelids never closed all the way. Up close, you could see her gray eye beaming out the window, staring hard as if to remember everything. I never kissed her. I left the window open when I went to the market.

Across the street from Jay's Market there was a chapel. I never knew its denomination, but I went in just the same to search for candles. I sat down on one of the pews because there were none. After I cleaned my fingernails, I looked up at the high ceiling. I had forgotten the vastness of these places, the coolness of the marble pillars and the frozen statues with blank eyes. I was alone. I knew why I had never returned.

That was one of Apá's[6] biggest complaints. He would pound his hands on the table, rocking the sugar dish or spilling a cup of coffee and scream that if I didn't go to Mass every Sunday to save my goddamn sinning soul, then I

---

4. Yerba buena, an evergreen herb (Spanish). 5. Small vegetable in the gourd family. 6. Child's name for "Father" (Spanish).

had no reason to go out of the house, period. Punto final.[7] He would grab my arm and dig his nails into me to make sure I understood the importance of catechism. Did he make himself clear? Then he strategically directed his anger at Amá for her lousy ways of bringing up daughters, being disrespectful and unbelieving, and my older sisters would pull me aside and tell me if I didn't get to Mass right this minute, they were all going to kick the holy shit out of me. Why am I so selfish? Can't you see what it's doing to Amá, you idiot? So I would wash my feet and stuff them in my black Easter shoes that shone with Vaseline, grab a missal and veil, and wave good-bye to Amá.

I would walk slowly down Lorena to First to Evergreen, counting the cracks on the cement. On Evergreen I would turn left and walk to Abuelita's. I liked her porch because it was shielded by the vines of the chayotes and I could get a good look at the people and car traffic on Evergreen without them knowing. I would jump up the porch steps, knock on the screen door as I wiped my feet and call Abuelita, mi Abuelita? As I opened the door and stuck my head in, I would catch the gagging scent of toasting chile on the placa.[8] When I entered the sala[9] she would greet me from the kitchen, wringing her hands in her apron. I'd sit at the corner of the table to keep from being in her way. The chiles made my eyes water. Am I crying? No, Mama Luna, I'm sure not crying. I don't like going to Mass, but my eyes watered anyway, the tears dropping on the tablecloth like candle wax. Abuelita lifted the burnt chiles from the fire and sprinkled water on them until the skins began to separate. Placing them in front of me, she turned to check the menudo.[1] I peeled the skins off and put the flimsy, limp-looking green and yellow chiles in the molcajete[2] and began to crush and crush and twist and crush the heart out of the tomato, the clove of garlic, the stupid chiles that made me cry, crushed them until they turned into liquid under my bull hand. With a wooden spoon, I scraped hard to destroy the guilt, and my tears were gone. I put the bowl of chile next to a vase filled with freshly cut roses. Abuelita touched my hand and pointed to the bowl of menudo that steamed in front of me. I spooned some chile into the menudo and rolled a corn tortilla thin with the palms of my hands. As I ate, a fine Sunday breeze entered the kitchen and a rose petal calmly feathered down to the table.

I left the chapel without blessing myself and walked to Jay's. Most of the time Jay didn't have much of anything. The tomatoes were always soft and the cans of Campbell soups had rusted spots on them. There was dust on the tops of cereal boxes. I picked up what I needed: rubbing alcohol, five cans of chicken broth, a big bottle of Pine Sol. At first Jay got mad because I thought I had forgotten the money. But it was there all the time, in my back pocket.

When I returned from the market, I heard Amá crying in Abuelita's kitchen. She looked up at me with puffy eyes. I placed the bags of groceries on the table and began putting the cans of soup away. Amá sobbed quietly. I never kissed her. After a while, I patted her on the back for comfort. Finally: "¿Y mi Amá?"[3] she asked in a whisper, then choked again and cried into her apron.

Abuelita fell off the bed twice yesterday, I said, knowing that I shouldn't have said it and wondering why I wanted to say it because it only made Amá

---

7. Period (Spanish); the end, case closed.   **8.** Hot plate (Spanish).   **9.** Living room (Spanish).   **1.** Tripe soup (Spanish).   **2.** Mortar (Mexican Spanish).   **3.** And my Mama? (Spanish).

cry harder. I guess I became angry and just so tired of the quarrels and beatings and unanswered prayers and my hands just there hanging helplessly by my side. Amá looked at me again, confused, angry, and her eyes were filled with sorrow. I went outside and sat on the porch swing and watched the people pass. I sat there until she left. I dozed off repeating the words to myself like rosary prayers: when do you stop giving when do you start giving when do you . . . and when my hands fell from my lap, I awoke to catch them. The sun was setting, an orange glow, and I knew Abuelita was hungry.

There comes a time when the sun is defiant. Just about the time when moods change, inevitable seasons of a day, transitions from one color to another, that hour or minute or second when the sun is finally defeated, finally sinks into the realization that it cannot with all its power to heal or burn, exist forever, there comes an illumination where the sun and earth meet, a final burst of burning red orange fury reminding us that although endings are inevitable, they are necessary for rebirths, and when that time came, just when I switched on the light in the kitchen to open Abuelita's can of soup, it was probably then that she died.

The room smelled of Pine Sol and vomit, and Abuelita had defecated the remains of her cancerous stomach. She had turned to the window and tried to speak, but her mouth remained open and speechless. I heard you, Abuelita, I said, stroking her cheek, I heard you. I opened the windows of the house and let the soup simmer and overboil on the stove. I turned the stove off and poured the soup down the sink. From the cabinet I got a tin basin, filled it with lukewarm water and carried it carefully to the room. I went to the linen closet and took out some modest bleached white towels. With the sacredness of a priest preparing his vestments, I unfolded the towels one by one on my shoulders. I removed the sheets and blankets from her bed and peeled off her thick flannel night-gown. I toweled her puzzled face, stretching out the wrinkles, removing the coils of her neck, toweled her shoulders and breasts. Then I changed the water. I returned to towel the creases of her stretch-marked stomach, her sporadic vaginal hairs, and her sagging thighs. I removed the lint from between her toes and noticed a mapped birthmark on the fold of her buttock. The scars on her back, which were as thin as the life lines on the palms of her hands, made me realize how little I really knew of Abuelita. I covered her with a thin blanket and went into the bathroom. I washed my hands, turned on the tub faucets and watched the water pour into the tub with vitality and steam. When it was full, I turned off the water and undressed. Then I went to get Abuelita.

She was not as heavy as I thought and when I carried her in my arms, her body fell into a V. And yet my legs were tired, shaky, and I felt as if the distance between the bedroom and bathroom was miles and years away. Amá, where are you?

I stepped into the bathtub one leg first, then the other. I bent my knees slowly to descend into the water slowly so I wouldn't scald her skin. There, there, Abuelita, I said, cradling her, smoothing her as we descended, I heard you. Her hair fell back and spread across the water like eagles' wings. The water in the tub overflowed and poured onto the tile of the floor. Then the moths came. Small gray ones that came from her soul and out through her mouth fluttering to light, circling the single dull light bulb of the bathroom.

Dying is lonely and I wanted to go to where the moths were, stay with her and plant chayotes whose vines would crawl up her fingers and into the clouds; I wanted to rest my head on her chest with her stroking my hair, telling me about the moths that lay within the soul and slowly eat the spirit up; I wanted to return to the waters of the womb with her so that we would never be alone again. I wanted. I wanted my Amá. I removed a few strands of hair from Abuelita's face and held her small light head within the hollow of my neck. The bathroom was filled with moths, and for the first time in a long time I cried, rocking us, crying for her, for me, for Amá, the sobs emerging from the depths of anguish, the misery of feeling half-born, sobbing until finally the sobs rippled into circles and circles of sadness and relief. There, there, I said to Abuelita, rocking us gently, there, there.

1995

ALICE WALKER
b. 1944

Walker was born in Eatonton, Georgia, and graduated from Sarah Lawrence College, where she wrote her first book of poems. After experience in the civil rights movement and employment as a caseworker for the New York City welfare department, she worked as an editor for *Ms.* magazine. An article she published there in 1975 revived interest in the work of Zora Neale Hurston. Since then she has been a teacher of creative writing and black literature at Jackson State College, Tougaloo College, Wellesley, and Yale. Her short stories are collected in *In Love and Trouble: Stories of Black Women* (1973) and *You Can't Keep a Good Woman Down* (1982). Her novels include *The Third Life of Grange Copeland* (1970); *Meridian* (1976); *The Color Purple* (1982), which won both the Pulitzer Prize and the American Book Award; *The Temple of My Familiar* (1989); *Possessing the Secret of Joy* (1992), *By the Light of My Father's Smile* (1998), and most recently, *Now Is the Time to Open Your Heart* (2004). She has published two memoirs, *The Same River Twice: Honoring the Difficult* (1996), and *Chicken Chronicles* (2011). Her book of essays on political and social activism, *Anything We Love Can Be Saved*, was published in 1997. Walker's *Collected Poems* appeared in 2005.

Everyday Use

for your grandmamma

I will wait for her in the yard that Maggie and I made so clean and wavy yesterday afternoon. A yard like this is more comfortable than most people know. It is not just a yard. It is like an extended living room. When the hard clay is swept clean as a floor and the fine sand around the edges lined with tiny, irregular grooves, anyone can come and sit and look up into the elm tree and wait for the breezes that never come inside the house.

Maggie will be nervous until after her sister goes: she will stand hopelessly in corners, homely and ashamed of the burn scars down her arms and legs, eying her sister with a mixture of envy and awe. She thinks her sister has held life always in the palm of one hand, that "no" is a word the world never learned to say to her.

You've no doubt seen those TV shows where the child who has "made it" is confronted, as a surprise, by her own mother and father, tottering in weakly from backstage. (A pleasant surprise, of course: What would they do if parent and child came on the show only to curse out and insult each other?) On TV mother and child embrace and smile into each other's faces. Sometimes the mother and father weep, the child wraps them in her arms and leans across the table to tell how she would not have made it without their help. I have seen these programs.

Sometimes I dream a dream in which Dee and I are suddenly brought together on a TV program of this sort. Out of a dark and soft-seated limousine I am ushered into a bright room filled with many people. There I meet a smiling, gray, sporty man like Johnny Carson who shakes my hand and tells me what a fine girl I have. Then we are on the stage and Dee is embracing me with tears in her eyes. She pins on my dress a large orchid, even though she has told me once that she thinks orchids are tacky flowers.

In real life I am a large, big-boned woman with rough, man-working hands. In the winter I wear flannel nightgowns to bed and overalls during the day. I can kill and clean a hog as mercilessly as a man. My fat keeps me hot in zero weather. I can work outside all day, breaking ice to get water for washing; I can eat pork liver cooked over the open fire minutes after it comes steaming from the hog. One winter I knocked a bull calf straight in the brain between the eyes with a sledge hammer and had the meat hung up to chill before nightfall. But of course all this does not show on television. I am the way my daughter would want me to be: a hundred pounds lighter, my skin like an uncooked barley pancake. My hair glistens in the hot bright lights. Johnny Carson has much to do to keep up with my quick and witty tongue.

But that is a mistake. I know even before I wake up. Who ever knew a Johnson with a quick tongue? Who can even imagine me looking a strange white man in the eye? It seems to me I have talked to them always with one foot raised in flight, with my head turned in whichever way is farthest from them. Dee, though. She would always look anyone in the eye. Hesitation was no part of her nature.

"How do I look, Mama?" Maggie says, showing just enough of her thin body enveloped in pink skirt and red blouse for me to know she's there, almost hidden by the door.

"Come out into the yard," I say.

Have you ever seen a lame animal, perhaps a dog run over by some careless person rich enough to own a car, sidle up to someone who is ignorant enough to be kind to them? That is the way my Maggie walks. She has been like this, chin on chest, eyes on ground, feet in shuffle, ever since the fire that burned the other house to the ground.

Dee is lighter than Maggie, with nicer hair and a fuller figure. She's a woman now, though sometimes I forget. How long ago was it that the other house burned? Ten, twelve years? Sometimes I can still hear the flames and feel Maggie's arms sticking to me, her hair smoking and her dress falling off her in little black papery flakes. Her eyes seemed stretched open, blazed open by the flames reflected in them. And Dee. I see her standing off under the sweet gum tree she used to dig gum out of; a look of concentration on her face as she watched the last dingy gray board of the house fall in toward the red-hot brick chimney. Why don't you do a dance around the ashes? I'd wanted to ask her. She had hated the house that much.

I used to think she hated Maggie, too. But that was before we raised the money, the church and me, to send her to Augusta to school. She used to read to us without pity; forcing words, lies, other folks' habits, whole lives upon us two, sitting trapped and ignorant underneath her voice. She washed us in a river of make-believe, burned us with a lot of knowledge we didn't necessarily need to know. Pressed us to her with the serious way she read, to shove us away at just the moment, like dimwits, we seemed about to understand.

Dee wanted nice things. A yellow organdy dress to wear to her graduation from high school; black pumps to match a green suit she'd made from an old suit somebody gave me. She was determined to stare down any disaster in her efforts. Her eyelids would not flicker for minutes at a time. Often I fought off the temptation to shake her. At sixteen she had a style of her own: and knew what style was.

I never had an education myself. After second grade the school was closed down. Don't ask me why: in 1927 colored asked fewer questions than they do now. Sometimes Maggie reads to me. She stumbles along good naturedly but can't see well. She knows she is not bright. Like good looks and money, quickness passed her by. She will marry John Thomas (who has mossy teeth in an earnest face) and then I'll be free to sit here and I guess just sing church songs to myself. Although I never was a good singer. Never could carry a tune. I was always better at a man's job. I used to love to milk till I was hooked[1] in the side in '49. Cows are soothing and slow and don't bother you, unless you try to milk them the wrong way.

I have deliberately turned my back on the house. It is three rooms, just like the one that burned, except the roof is tin; they don't make shingle roofs anymore. There are no real windows, just some holes cut in the sides, like the portholes in a ship, but not round and not square, with rawhide holding the shutters up on the outside. This house is in a pasture, too, like the other one. No doubt when Dee sees it she will want to tear it down. She wrote me once that no matter where we "choose" to live, she will manage to come see us. But she will never bring her friends. Maggie and I thought about this and Maggie asked me, "Mama, when did Dee ever *have* any friends?"

She had a few. Furtive boys in pink shirts hanging about on washday after school. Nervous girls who never laughed. Impressed with her they worshiped the well-turned phrase, the cute shape, the scalding humor that erupted like bubbles in lye. She read to them.

When she was courting Jimmy T she didn't have much time to pay to us, but turned all her faultfinding power on him. He *flew* to marry a cheap city girl from a family of ignorant flashy people. She hardly had time to recompose herself.

When she comes I will meet—but there they are!

Maggie attempts to make a dash for the house, in her shuffling way, but I stay her with my hand. "Come back here," I say. And she stops and tries to dig a well in the sand with her toe.

---

1. That is, by the horn of the cow being milked.

It is hard to see them clearly through the strong sun. But even the first glimpse of leg out of the car tells me it is Dee. Her feet were always neat-looking, as if God himself had shaped them with a certain style. From the other side of the car comes a short, stocky man. Hair is all over his head a foot long and hanging from his chin like a kinky mule tail. I hear Maggie suck in her breath. "Uhnnnh," is what it sounds like. Like when you see the wriggling end of a snake just in front of your foot on the road. "Uhnnnh."

Dee next. A dress down to the ground, in this hot weather. A dress so loud it hurts my eyes. There are yellows and oranges enough to throw back the light of the sun. I feel my whole face warming from the heat waves it throws out. Earrings gold, too, and hanging down to her shoulders. Bracelets dangling and making noises when she moves her arm up to shake the folds of the dress out of her armpits. The dress is loose and flows, and as she walks closer, I like it. I hear Maggie go "Uhnnnh" again. It is her sister's hair. It stands straight up like the wool on a sheep. It is black as night and around the edges are two long pigtails that rope about like small lizards disappearing behind her ears.

"Wa-su-zo-Tean-o!" she says, coming on in that gliding way the dress makes her move. The short stocky fellow with the hair to his navel is all grinning and he follows up with "Asalamalakim,[2] my mother and sister!" He moves to hug Maggie but she falls back, right up against the back of my chair. I feel her trembling there and when I look up I see the perspiration falling off her chin.

"Don't get up," says Dee. Since I am stout it takes something of a push. You can see me trying to move a second or two before I make it. She turns, showing white heels through her sandals, and goes back to the car. Out she peeks next with a Polaroid. She stoops down quickly and lines up picture after picture of me sitting there in front of the house with Maggie cowering behind me. She never takes a shot without making sure the house is included. When a cow comes nibbling around the edge of the yard she snaps it and me and Maggie *and* the house. Then she puts the Polaroid in the back seat of the car, and comes up and kisses me on the forehead.

Meanwhile Asalamalakim is going through motions with Maggie's hand. Maggie's hand is as limp as a fish, and probably as cold, despite the sweat, and she keeps trying to pull it back. It looks like Asalamalakim wants to shake hands but wants to do it fancy. Or maybe he don't know how people shake hands. Anyhow, he soon gives up on Maggie.

"Well," I say. "Dee."

"No, Mama," she says. "Not 'Dee,' Wangero Leewanika Kemanjo!"

"What happened to 'Dee'?" I wanted to know.

"She's dead," Wangero said. "I couldn't bear it any longer, being named after the people who oppress me."

"You know as well as me you was named after your aunt Dicie," I said. Dicie is my sister. She named Dee. We called her "Big Dee" after Dee was born.

"But who was *she* named after?" asked Wangero.

"I guess after Grandma Dee," I said.

"And who was she named after?" asked Wangero.

---

2. Phonetic rendering of an Arabic greeting meaning "Peace be upon you." "Wa-su-zo-Tean-o" is a rendering of an African dialect salutation.

"Her mother," I said, and saw Wangero was getting tired. "That's about as far back as I can trace it," I said. Though, in fact, I probably could have carried it back beyond the Civil War through the branches.

"Well," said Asalamalakim, "there you are."

"Uhnnnh," I heard Maggie say.

"There I was not," I said, "before 'Dicie' cropped up in our family, so why should I try to trace it that far back?"

He just stood there grinning, looking down on me like somebody inspecting a Model A car. Every once in a while he and Wangero sent eye signals over my head.

"How do you pronounce this name?" I asked.

"You don't have to call me by it if you don't want to," said Wangero.

"Why shouldn't I?" I asked. "If that's what you want us to call you, we'll call you."

"I know it might sound awkward at first," said Wangero.

"I'll get used to it," I said. "Ream it out again."

Well, soon we got the name out of the way. Asalamalakim had a name twice as long and three times as hard. After I tripped over it two or three times he told me to just call him Hakim-a-barber. I wanted to ask him was he a barber, but I didn't really think he was, so I didn't ask.

"You must belong to those beef-cattle peoples down the road," I said. They said "Asalamalakim" when they met you, too, but they didn't shake hands. Always too busy: feeding the cattle, fixing the fences, putting up salt-lick shelters, throwing down hay. When the white folks poisoned some of the herd the men stayed up all night with rifles in their hands. I walked a mile and a half just to see the sight.

Hakim-a-barber said, "I accept some of their doctrines, but farming and raising cattle is not my style." (They didn't tell me, and I didn't ask, whether Wangero (Dee) had really gone and married him.)

We sat down to eat and right away he said he didn't eat collards and pork was unclean. Wangero, though, went on through the chitlins and corn bread, the greens and everything else. She talked a blue streak over the sweet potatoes. Everything delighted her. Even the fact that we still used the benches her daddy made for the table when we couldn't afford to buy chairs.

"Oh, Mama!" she cried. Then turned to Hakim-a-barber. "I never knew how lovely these benches are. You can feel the rump prints," she said, running her hands underneath her and along the bench. Then she gave a sigh and her hand closed over Grandma Dee's butter dish. "That's it!" she said. "I knew there was something I wanted to ask you if I could have." She jumped up from the table and went over in the corner where the churn stood, the milk in it clabber by now. She looked at the churn and looked at it.

"This churn top is what I need," she said. "Didn't Uncle Buddy whittle it out of a tree you all used to have?"

"Yes," I said.

"Uh huh," she said happily. "And I want the dasher, too."

"Uncle Buddy whittle that, too?" asked the barber.

Dee (Wangero) looked up at me.

"Aunt Dee's first husband whittled the dash," said Maggie so low you almost couldn't hear her. "His name was Henry, but they called him Stash."

"Maggie's brain is like an elephant's," Wangero said, laughing. "I can use the churn top as a centerpiece for the alcove table," she said, sliding a plate over the churn, "and I'll think of something artistic to do with the dasher."

When she finished wrapping the dasher the handle stuck out. I took it for a moment in my hands. You didn't even have to look close to see where hands pushing the dasher up and down to make butter had left a kind of sink in the wood. In fact, there were a lot of small sinks; you could see where thumbs and fingers had sunk into the wood. It was beautiful light yellow wood, from a tree that grew in the yard where Big Dee and Stash had lived.

After dinner Dee (Wangero) went to the trunk at the foot of my bed and started rifling through it. Maggie hung back in the kitchen over the dishpan. Out came Wangero with two quilts. They had been pieced by Grandma Dee and then Big Dee and me had hung them on the quilt frames on the front porch and quilted them. One was in the Lone Star pattern. The other was Walk Around the Mountain. In both of them were scraps of dresses Grandma Dee had worn fifty and more years ago. Bits and pieces of Grandpa Jarrell's Paisley shirts. And one teeny faded blue piece, about the size of a penny matchbox, that was from Great Grandpa Ezra's uniform that he wore in the Civil War.

"Mama," Wangero said sweet as a bird. "Can I have these old quilts?"

I heard something fall in the kitchen, and a minute later the kitchen door slammed.

"Why don't you take one or two of the others?" I asked. "These old things was just done by me and Big Dee from some tops your grandma pieced before she died."

"No," said Wangero. "I don't want those. They are stitched around the borders by machine."

"That'll make them last better," I said.

"That's not the point," said Wangero. "These are all pieces of dresses Grandma used to wear. She did all this stitching by hand. Imagine!" She held the quilts securely in her arms, stroking them.

"Some of the pieces, like those lavender ones, come from old clothes her mother handed down to her," I said, moving up to touch the quilts. Dee (Wangero) moved back just enough so that I couldn't reach the quilts. They already belonged to her.

"Imagine!" she breathed again, clutching them closely to her bosom.

"The truth is," I said, "I promised to give them quilts to Maggie, for when she marries John Thomas."

She gasped like a bee had stung her.

"Maggie can't appreciate these quilts!" she said. "She'd probably be backward enough to put them to everyday use."

"I reckon she would," I said. "God knows I been saving 'em for long enough with nobody using 'em. I hope she will!" I didn't want to bring up how I had offered Dee (Wangero) a quilt when she went away to college. Then she had told me they were old-fashioned, out of style.

"But they're *priceless*!" she was saying now, furiously; for she has a temper. "Maggie would put them on the bed and in five years they'd be in rags. Less than that!"

"She can always make some more," I said. "Maggie knows how to quilt."

Dee (Wangero) looked at me with hatred. "You just will not understand. The point is these quilts, *these* quilts!"

"Well," I said, stumped. "What would *you* do with them?"

"Hang them," she said. As if that was the only thing you *could* do with quilts.

Maggie by now was standing in the door. I could almost hear the sound her feet made as they scraped over each other.

"She can have them, Mama," she said, like somebody used to never winning anything, or having anything reserved for her. "I can 'member Grandma Dee without the quilts."

I looked at her hard. She had filled her bottom lip with checkerberry snuff and it gave her a face a kind of dopey, hangdog look. It was Grandma Dee and Big Dee who taught her how to quilt herself. She stood there with her scarred hands hidden in the folds of her skirt. She looked at her sister with something like fear but she wasn't mad at her. This was Maggie's portion. This was the way she knew God to work.

When I looked at her like that something hit me in the top of my head and ran down to the soles of my feet. Just like when I'm in church and the spirit of God touches me and I get happy and shout. I did something I never had done before: hugged Maggie to me, then dragged her on into the room, snatched the quilts out of Miss Wangero's hands and dumped them into Maggie's lap. Maggie just sat there on my bed with her mouth open.

"Take one or two of the others," I said to Dee.

But she turned without a word and went out to Hakim-a-barber.

"You just don't understand," she said, as Maggie and I came out to the car.

"What don't I understand?" I wanted to know.

"Your heritage," she said. And then she turned to Maggie, kissed her, and said, "You ought to try to make something of yourself, too, Maggie. It's really a new day for us. But from the way you and Mama still live you'd never know it."

She put on some sunglasses that hid everything above the tip of her nose and her chin.

Maggie smiled; maybe at the sunglasses. But a real smile, not scared. After we watched the car dust settle I asked Maggie to bring me a dip of snuff. And then the two of us sat there just enjoying, until it was time to go in the house and go to bed.

1973

ROBERT PENN WARREN
1905–1989

Warren was born in Guthrie, Kentucky. He was educated at Vanderbilt University, the University of California at Berkeley, Yale, and Oxford. One of the original Fugitive Poets, his many publications include *Understanding Fiction* (1943); the novels *At Heaven's Gate* (1943), the Pulitzer Prize–winning *All the King's Men* (1946), *World Enough and Time* (1950), and *A Place to Come To* (1977); a collection of stories, *The Circus in the Attic* (1949); and *New and Selected Poems, 1923–1985* (1985). Along with such luminaries as William Faulkner and Eudora Welty, Warren is one of the giants of Southern literature. He won two more Pulitzer Prizes for his poems and was the first poet laureate of the United States.

Blackberry Winter

To Joseph Warren and Dagmar Beach

It was getting into June and past eight o'clock in the morning, but there was a fire—even if it wasn't a big fire, just a fire of chunks—on the hearth of the big stone fireplace in the living room. I was standing on the hearth, almost into the chimney, hunched over the fire, working my bare toes slowly on the warm stone. I relished the heat which made the skin of my bare legs warp and creep and tingle, even as I called to my mother, who was somewhere back in the dining room or kitchen, and said: "But it's June, I don't have to put them on!"

"You put them on if you are going out," she called.

I tried to assess the degree of authority and conviction in the tone, but at that distance it was hard to decide. I tried to analyze the tone, and then I thought what a fool I had been to start out the back door and let her see that I was barefoot. If I had gone out the front door or the side door, she would never have known, not till dinner time anyway, and by then the day would have been half gone and I would have been all over the farm to see what the storm had done and down to the creek to see the flood. But it had never crossed my mind that they would try to stop you from going barefoot in June, no matter if there had been a gully-washer and a cold spell.

Nobody had ever tried to stop me in June as long as I could remember, and when you are nine years old, what you remember seems forever; for you remember everything and everything is important and stands big and full and fills up Time and is so solid that you can walk around and around it like a tree and look at it. You are aware that time passes, that there is a movement in time, but that is not what Time is. Time is not a movement, a flowing, a wind then, but is, rather, a kind of climate in which things are, and when a thing happens it begins to live and keeps on living and stands solid in Time like the tree that you can walk around. And if there is a movement, the movement is not Time itself, any more than a breeze is climate, and all the breeze does is to shake a little the leaves on the tree which is alive and solid. When you are nine, you know that there are things that you don't know, but you know that when you know something you know it. You know how a thing has been and you know that you can go barefoot in June. You do not understand that voice from back in the kitchen which says that you cannot go barefoot outdoors and run to see what has happened and rub your feet over the wet shivery grass and make the perfect mark of your foot in the smooth, creamy, red mud and then muse upon it as though you had suddenly come upon that single mark on the glistening auroral beach of the world.[1] You have never seen a beach, but you have read the book and how the footprint was there.

The voice had said what it had said, and I looked savagely at the black stockings and the strong, scuffed brown shoes which I had brought from my closet as far as the hearth rug. I called once more, "But it's June," and waited.

"It's June," the voice replied from far away, "but it's blackberry winter."

I had lifted my head to reply to that, to make one more test of what was in that tone, when I happened to see the man.

The fireplace in the living room was at the end; for the stone chimney was built, as in so many of the farmhouses in Tennessee, at the end of a gable, and there was a window on each side of the chimney. Out of the window on the north side of the fireplace I could see the man. When I saw the man I did not call out what I had intended, but, engrossed by the strangeness of the sight, watched him, still far off, come along the path by the edge of the woods.

What was strange was that there should be a man there at all. That path went along the yard fence, between the fence and the woods which came right down to the yard, and then on back past the chicken runs and on by the woods until it was lost to sight where the woods bulged out and cut off the back field. There the path disappeared into the woods. It led on back, I knew, through the woods and to the swamp, skirted the swamp where the big trees gave way to sycamores and water oaks and willows and tangled cane, and then led on to the river. Nobody ever went back there except people who wanted to gig frogs in the swamp or to fish in the river or to hunt in the woods, and those people, if they didn't have a standing permission from my father, always stopped to ask permission to cross the farm. But the man whom I now saw wasn't, I could tell even at that distance, a sportsman. And what would a sportsman have been doing down there after a storm? Besides, he was coming from the river, and nobody had gone down there that morning. I knew that for a fact, because if anybody had passed, certainly if a stranger had passed, the dogs would have made a racket and would have been out on him. But this man was coming up from the river and had come up through the woods. I suddenly had a vision of him moving up the grassy path in the woods, in the green twilight under the big trees, not making any sound on the path, while now and then, like drops off the eaves, a big drop of water would fall from a leaf or bough and strike a stiff oak leaf lower down with a small, hollow sound

1. An allusion to Daniel Defoe's *Robinson Crusoe*.

like a drop of water hitting tin. That sound, in the silence of the woods, would be very significant.

When you are a boy and stand in the stillness of woods, which can be so still that your heart almost stops beating and makes you want to stand there in the green twilight until you feel your very feet sinking into and clutching the earth like roots and your body breathing slow through its pores like the leaves—when you stand there and wait for the next drop to drop with its small, flat sound to a lower leaf, that sound seems to measure out something, to put an end to something, to begin something, and you cannot wait for it to happen and are afraid it will not happen, and then when it has happened, you are waiting again, almost afraid.

But the man whom I saw coming through the woods in my mind's eye did not pause and wait, growing into the ground and breathing with the enormous, soundless breathing of the leaves. Instead, I saw him moving in the green twilight inside my head as he was moving at that very moment along the path by the edge of the woods, coming toward the house. He was moving steadily, but not fast, with his shoulders hunched a little and his head thrust forward, like a man who has come a long way and has a long way to go. I shut my eyes for a couple of seconds, thinking that when I opened them he would not be there at all. There was no place for him to have come from, and there was no reason for him to come where he was coming, toward our house. But I opened my eyes, and there he was, and he was coming steadily along the side of the woods. He was not yet even with the back chicken yard.

"Mama," I called.

"You put them on," the voice said.

"There's a man coming," I called, "out back."

She did not reply to that, and I guessed that she had gone to the kitchen window to look. She would be looking at the man and wondering who he was and what he wanted, the way you always do in the country, and if I went back there now, she would not notice right off whether or not I was barefoot. So I went back to the kitchen.

She was standing by the window. "I don't recognize him," she said, not looking around at me.

"Where could he be coming from?" I asked.

"I don't know," she said.

"What would he be doing down at the river? At night? In the storm?"

She studied the figure out the window, then said, "Oh, I reckon maybe he cut across from the Dunbar place."

That was, I realized, a perfectly rational explanation. He had not been down at the river in the storm, at night. He had come over this morning. You could cut across from the Dunbar place if you didn't mind breaking through a lot of elder and sassafras and blackberry bushes which had about taken over the old cross path, which nobody ever used anymore. That satisfied me for a moment, but only for a moment. "Mama," I asked, "what would he be doing over at the Dunbar place last night?"

Then she looked at me, and I knew I had made a mistake, for she was looking at my bare feet. "You haven't got your shoes on," she said.

But I was saved by the dogs. That instant there was a bark which I recognized as Sam, the collie, and then a heavier, churning kind of bark which was

Bully, and I saw a streak of white as Bully tore round the corner of the back porch and headed out for the man. Bully was a big bone-white bulldog, the kind of dog that they used to call a farm bulldog but that you don't see anymore, heavy-chested and heavy-headed, but with pretty long legs. He could take a fence as light as a hound. He had just cleared the white paling fence toward the woods when my mother ran out to the back porch and began calling, "Here you, Bully! Here you!"

Bully stopped in the path, waiting for the man, but he gave a few more of those deep, gargling, savage barks that reminded you of something down a stone-lined well. The red-clay mud, I saw, was splashed up over his white chest and looked exciting, like blood.

The man, however, had not stopped walking even when Bully took the fence and started at him. He had kept right on coming. All he had done was to switch a little paper parcel which he carried from the right hand to the left, and then reach into his pants pocket to get something. Then I saw the glitter and knew that he had a knife in his hand, probably the kind of mean knife just made for devilment and nothing else, with a blade as long as the blade of a frog-sticker, which will snap out ready when you press a button in the handle. That knife must have had a button in the handle, or else how could he have had the blade out glittering so quick and with just one hand?

Pulling his knife against the dogs was a funny thing to do, for Bully was a big, powerful brute and fast, and Sam was all right. If those dogs had meant business, they might have knocked him down and ripped him before he got a stroke in. He ought to have picked up a heavy stick, something to take a swipe at them with and something which they could see and respect when they came at him. But he apparently did not know much about dogs. He just held the knife blade close against the right leg, low down, and kept on moving down the path.

Then my mother had called, and Bully had stopped. So the man let the blade of the knife snap back into the handle, and dropped it into his pocket, and kept on coming. Many women would have been afraid with the strange man who they knew had that knife in his pocket. That is, if they were alone in the house with nobody but a nine-year-old boy. And my mother was alone, for my father had gone off, and Dellie, the cook, was down at her cabin because she wasn't feeling well. But my mother wasn't afraid. She wasn't a big woman, but she was clear and brisk about everything she did and looked everybody and everything right in the eye from her own blue eyes in her tanned face. She had been the first woman in the country to ride a horse astride (that was back when she was a girl and long before I was born), and I have seen her snatch up a pump gun and go out and knock a chicken hawk out of the air like a busted skeet when he came over her chicken yard. She was a steady and self-reliant woman, and when I think of her now after all the years she has been dead, I think of her brown hands, not big, but somewhat square for a woman's hands, with square-cut nails. They looked, as a matter of fact, more like a young boy's hands than a grown woman's. But back then it never crossed my mind that she would ever be dead.

She stood on the back porch and watched the man enter the back gate, where the dogs (Bully had leaped back into the yard) were dancing and muttering and giving sidelong glances back to my mother to see if she meant what she had said. The man walked right by the dogs, almost brushing them, and didn't pay them any attention. I could see now that he wore old khaki pants, and a dark wool coat with stripes in it, and a gray felt hat. He had on a gray shirt with blue stripes in it, and no tie. But I could see a tie, blue and red- dish, sticking in his side coat-pocket. Everything was wrong about what he wore. He ought to have been wearing blue jeans or overalls, and a straw hat or an old black felt hat, and the coat, granting that he might have been wearing a wool coat and not a jumper, ought not to have had those stripes. Those clothes, despite the fact that they were old enough and dirty enough for any tramp, didn't belong there in our back yard, coming down the path, in Middle Ten- nessee, miles away from any big town, and even a mile off the pike.

When he got almost to the steps, without having said anything, my mother, very matter-of-factly, said, "Good morning."

"Good morning," he said, and stopped and looked her over. He did not take off his hat, and under the brim you could see the perfectly unmemorable face, which wasn't old and wasn't young, or thick or thin. It was grayish and covered with about three days of stubble. The eyes were a kind of nondescript, muddy hazel, or something like that, rather bloodshot. His teeth, when he opened his mouth, showed yellow and uneven. A couple of them had been knocked out. You knew that they had been knocked out, because there was a scar, not very old, there on the lower lip just beneath the gap.

"Are you hunting work?" my mother asked him.

"Yes," he said—not "yes, mam"—and still did not take off his hat.

"I don't know about my husband, for he isn't here," she said, and didn't mind a bit telling the tramp, or whoever he was, with the mean knife in his pocket, that no man was around, "but I can give you a few things to do. The storm has drowned a lot of my chicks. Three coops of them. You can gather them up and bury them. Bury them deep so the dogs won't get at them. In the woods. And fix the coops the wind blew over. And down yonder beyond that pen by the edge of the woods are some drowned poults. They got out and I couldn't get them in. Even after it started to rain hard. Poults haven't got any sense."

"What are them things—poults?" he demanded, and spat on the brick walk. He rubbed his foot over the spot, and I saw that he wore a black pointed- toe low shoe, all cracked and broken. It was a crazy kind of shoe to be wearing in the country.

"Oh, they're young turkeys," my mother was saying. "And they haven't got any sense. I oughtn't to try to raise them around here with so many chickens, anyway. They don't thrive near chickens, even in separate pens. And I won't give up my chickens." Then she stopped herself and resumed briskly on the note of business. "When you finish that, you can fix my flower beds. A lot of trash and mud and gravel has washed down. Maybe you can save some of my flowers if you are careful."

"Flowers," the man said, in a low, impersonal voice which seemed to have a wealth of meaning, but a meaning which I could not fathom. As I think back on it, it probably was not pure contempt. Rather, it was a kind of impersonal and distant marveling that he should be on the verge of grubbing in a flower bed. He said the word, and then looked off across the yard.

"Yes, flowers," my mother replied with some asperity, as though she would have nothing said or implied against flowers. "And they were very fine this year." Then she stopped and looked at the man. "Are you hungry?" she demanded.

"Yeah," he said.

"I'll fix you something," she said, "before you get started." She turned to me. "Show him where he can wash up," she commanded, and went into the house.

I took the man to the end of the porch where a pump was and where a couple of wash pans sat on a low shelf for people to use before they went into the house. I stood there while he laid down his little parcel wrapped in newspaper and took off his hat and looked around for a nail to hang it on. He poured the water and plunged his hands into it. They were big hands, and strong-looking, but they did not have the creases and the earth-color of the hands of men who work outdoors. But they were dirty, with black dirt ground into the skin and under the nails. After he had washed his hands, he poured another basin of water and washed his face. He dried his face, and with the towel still dangling in his grasp, stepped over to the mirror on the house wall. He rubbed one hand over the stubble on his face. Then he carefully inspected his face, turning first one side and then the other, and stepped back and settled his striped coat down on his shoulders. He had the movements of a man who has just dressed up to go to church or a party—the way he settled his coat and smoothed it and scanned himself in the mirror.

Then he caught my glance on him. He glared at me for an instant out of the bloodshot eyes, then demanded in a low, harsh voice, "What you looking at?"

"Nothing," I managed to say, and stepped back a step from him.

He flung the towel down, crumpled, on the shelf, and went toward the kitchen door and entered without knocking.

My mother said something to him which I could not catch. I started to go in again, then thought about my bare feet, and decided to go back of the chicken yard, where the man would have to come to pick up the dead chicks. I hung around behind the chicken house until he came out.

He moved across the chicken yard with a fastidious, not quite finicking motion, looking down at the curdled mud flecked with bits of chicken-droppings. The mud curled up over the soles of his black shoes. I stood back from him some six feet and watched him pick up the first of the drowned chicks. He held it up by one foot and inspected it.

There is nothing deader-looking than a drowned chick. The feet curl in that feeble, empty way which back when I was a boy, even if I was a country boy who did not mind hog-killing or frog-gigging, made me feel hollow in the stomach. Instead of looking plump and fluffy, the body is stringy and limp with the fluff plastered to it, and the neck is long and loose like a little string of rag. And the eyes have that bluish membrane over them which makes you think of a very old man who is sick about to die.

The man stood there and inspected the chick. Then he looked all around as though he didn't know what to do with it.

"There's a great big old basket in the shed," I said, and pointed to the shed attached to the chicken house.

He inspected me as though he had just discovered my presence, and moved toward the shed.

"There's a spade there, too," I added.

He got the basket and began to pick up the other chicks, picking each one up slowly by a foot and then flinging it into the basket with a nasty, snapping motion. Now and then he would look at me out of the bloodshot eyes. Every time he seemed on the verge of saying something, but he did not. Perhaps he was building up to say something to me, but I did not wait that long. His way of looking at me made me so uncomfortable that I left the chicken yard.

Besides, I had just remembered that the creek was in flood, over the bridge, and that people were down there watching it. So I cut across the farm toward the creek. When I got to the big tobacco field I saw that it had not suffered much. The land lay right and not many tobacco plants had washed out of the ground. But I knew that a lot of tobacco round the country had been washed right out. My father had said so at breakfast.

My father was down at the bridge. When I came out of the gap in the osage hedge into the road, I saw him sitting on his mare over the heads of the other men who were standing around, admiring the flood. The creek was big here, even in low water; for only a couple of miles away it ran into the river, and when a real flood came, the red water got over the pike where it dipped down to the bridge, which was an iron bridge, and high over the floor and even the side railings of the bridge. Only the upper iron work would show, with the water boiling and frothing red and white around it. That creek rose so fast and so heavy because a few miles back it came down out of the hills, where the gorges filled up with water in no time when a rain came. The creek ran in a deep bed with limestone bluffs along both sides until it got within three quarters of a mile of the bridge, and when it came out from between those bluffs in flood it was boiling and hissing and steaming like water from a fire hose.

Whenever there was a flood, people from half the county would come down to see the sight. After a gully-washer there would not be any work to do anyway. If it didn't ruin your crop, you couldn't plow and you felt like taking a holiday to celebrate. If it did ruin your crop, there wasn't anything to do except to try to take your mind off the mortgage, if you were rich enough to have a mortgage, and if you couldn't afford a mortgage, you needed something to take your mind off how hungry you would be by Christmas. So people would come down to the bridge and look at the flood. It made something different from the run of days.

There would not be much talking after the first few minutes of trying to guess how high the water was this time. The men and kids just stood around, or sat their horses or mules, as the case might be, or stood up in the wagon beds. They looked at the strangeness of the flood for an hour or two, and then somebody would say that he had better be getting on home to dinner and would start walking down the gray, puddled limestone pike, or would touch heel to his mount and start off. Everybody always knew what it would be like when he got down to the bridge, but people always came. It was like church or a funeral. They always came, that is, if it was summer and the flood unexpected. Nobody ever came down in winter to see high water.

When I came out of the gap in the bodock hedge, I saw the crowd, perhaps fifteen or twenty men and a lot of kids, and saw my father sitting his mare, Nellie Gray. He was a tall, limber man and carried himself well. I was always proud to see him sit a horse, he was so quiet and straight, and when I stepped through the gap of the hedge that morning, the first thing that happened was, I remember, the warm feeling I always had when I saw him up on a horse, just sitting. I did not go toward him, but skirted the crowd on the far side, to get a look at the creek. For one thing, I was not sure what he would say about the fact that I was barefoot. But the first thing I knew, I heard his voice calling, "Seth!"

I went toward him, moving apologetically past the men, who bent their large, red or thin, sallow faces above me. I knew some of the men, and knew their names, but because those I knew were there in a crowd, mixed with the strange faces, they seemed foreign to me, and not friendly. I did not look up at my father until I was almost within touching distance of his heel. Then I looked up and tried to read his face, to see if he was angry about my being barefoot. Before I could decide anything from that impassive, high-boned face, he had leaned over and reached a hand to me. "Grab on," he commanded.

I grabbed on and gave a little jump, and he said, "Up-see-daisy!" and whisked me, light as a feather, up to the pommel of his McClellan saddle.[2]

"You can see better up here," he said, slid back on the cantle a little to make me more comfortable, and then, looking over my head at the swollen, tumbling water, seemed to forget all about me. But his right hand was laid on my side, just above my thigh, to steady me.

I was sitting there as quiet as I could, feeling the faint stir of my father's chest against my shoulders as it rose and fell with his breath, when I saw the cow. At first, looking up the creek, I thought it was just another big piece of driftwood steaming down the creek in the ruck of water, but all at once a pretty good-size boy who had climbed part way up a telephone pole by the pike so that he could see better yelled out, "Golly-damn, look at that-air cow!"

Everybody looked. It was a cow all right, but it might just as well have been driftwood; for it was dead as a chunk, rolling and roiling down the creek, appearing and disappearing, feet up or head up, it didn't matter which.

The cow started up the talk again. Somebody wondered whether it would hit one of the clear places under the top girder of the bridge and get through or whether it would get tangled in the drift and trash that had piled against the upright girders and braces. Somebody remembered how about ten years before, so much driftwood had piled up on the bridge that it was knocked off its foundations. Then the cow hit. It hit the edge of the drift against one of the girders, and hung there. For a few seconds it seemed as though it might tear loose, but then we saw that it was really caught. It bobbed and heaved on its side there in a slow, grinding, uneasy fashion. It had a yoke around its neck, the kind made out of a forked limb to keep a jumper behind fence.

"She shore jumped one fence," one of the men said.

And another: "Well, she done jumped her last one, fer a fack."

Then they began to wonder about whose cow it might be. They decided it must belong to Milt Alley. They said that he had a cow that was a jumper, and kept her in a fenced-in piece of ground up the creek. I had never seen Milt Alley, but I knew who he was. He was a squatter and lived up the hills a way, on a shirt-tail patch of set-on-edge land, in a cabin. He was pore white trash. He had lots of children. I had seen the children at school, when they came.

2. Military saddle developed in 1859 by George B. McClellan, who went on to command the Union army in the Civil War.

They were thin-faced, with straight, sticky-looking, dough-colored hair, and they smelled something like old sour buttermilk, not because they drank so much buttermilk but because that is the sort of smell which children out of those cabins tend to have. The big Alley boy drew dirty pictures and showed them to the little boys at school.

That was Milt Alley's cow. It looked like the kind of cow he would have, a scrawny, old, sway-backed cow, with a yoke around her neck. I wondered if Milt Alley had another cow.

"Poppa," I said, "do you think Milt Alley has got another cow?"

"You say 'Mr. Alley,'" my father said quietly.

"Do you think he has?"

"No telling," my father said.

Then a big gangly boy, about fifteen, who was sitting on a scraggly little old mule with a piece of croker sack thrown across the sawtooth spine, and who had been staring at the cow, suddenly said to nobody in particular, "Reckin anybody ever et drownt cow?"

He was the kind of boy who might just as well as not have been the son of Milt Alley, with his faded and patched overalls ragged at the bottom of the pants and the mud-stiff brogans hanging off his skinny, bare ankles at the level of the mule's belly. He had said what he did, and then looked embarrassed and sullen when all the eyes swung at him. He hadn't meant to say it, I am pretty sure now. He would have been too proud to say it, just as Milt Alley would have been too proud. He had just been thinking out loud, and the words had popped out.

There was an old man standing there on the pike, an old man with a white beard. "Son," he said to the embarrassed and sullen boy on the mule, "you live long enough and you'll find a man will eat anything when the time comes."

"Time gonna come fer some folks this year," another man said.

"Son," the old man said, "in my time I et things a man don't like to think on. I was a sojer and I rode with Gin'l Forrest,[3] and them things we et when the time come. I tell you. I et meat what got up and run when you taken out yore knife to cut a slice to put on the fire. You had to knock it down with a carbeen butt, it was so active. That-air meat would jump like a bullfrog, it was so full of skippers."

But nobody was listening to the old man. The boy on the mule turned his sullen sharp face from him, dug a heel into the side of the mule, and went off up the pike with a motion which made you think that any second you would hear mule bones clashing inside that lank and scrofulous hide.

"Cy Dundee's boy," a man said, and nodded toward the figure going up the pike on the mule.

"Reckin Cy Dundee's young-uns seen times they'd settle fer drownt cow," another man said.

The old man with the beard peered at them both from his weak, slow eyes, first at one and then at the other. "Live long enough," he said, "and a man will settle fer what he kin git."

Then there was silence again, with the people looking at the red, foam-flecked water.

---

3. Nathan Bedford Forrest (1821–1877), Confederate general.

My father lifted the bridle rein in his left hand, and the mare turned and walked around the group and up the pike. We rode on up to our big gate, where my father dismounted to open it and let me myself ride Nellie Gray through. When he got to the lane that led off from the drive about two hundred yards from our house, my father said, "Grab on." I grabbed on, and he let me down to the ground. "I'm going to ride down and look at my corn," he said. "You go on." He took the lane, and I stood there on the drive and watched him ride off. He was wearing cowhide boots and an old hunting coat, and I thought that that made him look very military, like a picture. That and the way he rode.

I did not go to the house. Instead, I went by the vegetable garden and crossed behind the stables, and headed down for Dellie's cabin. I wanted to go down and play with Jebb, who was Dellie's little boy about two years older than I was. Besides, I was cold. I shivered as I walked, and I had gooseflesh. The mud which crawled up between my toes with every step I took was like ice. Dellie would have a fire, but she wouldn't make me put on shoes and stockings.

Dellie's cabin was of logs, with one side, because it was on a slope, set on limestone chunks, with a little porch attached to it, and had a little white-washed fence around it and a gate with plow-points on a wire to clink when somebody came in, and had two big white oaks in the yard and some flowers and a nice privy in the back with some honeysuckle growing over it. Dellie and Old Jebb, who was Jebb's father and who lived with Dellie and had lived with her for twenty-five years even if they never had got married, were careful to keep everything nice around their cabin. They had the name all over the community for being clean and clever Negroes. Dellie and Jebb were what they used to call "white-folks' niggers." There was a big difference between their cabin and the other two cabins farther down where the other tenants lived. My father kept the other cabins weatherproof, but he couldn't undertake to go down and pick up after the litter they strewed. They didn't take the trouble to have a vegetable patch like Dellie and Jebb or to make preserves from wild plum, and jelly from crab apple the way Dellie did. They were shiftless, and my father was always threatening to get shed of them. But he never did. When they finally left, they just up and left on their own, for no reason, to go and be shiftless somewhere else. Then some more came. But meanwhile they lived down there, Matt Rawson and his family, and Sid Turner and his, and I played with their children all over the farm when they weren't working. But when I wasn't around they were mean sometimes to Little Jebb. That was because the other tenants down there were jealous of Dellie and Jebb.

I was so cold that I ran the last fifty yards to Dellie's gate. As soon as I had entered the yard, I saw that the storm had been hard on Dellie's flowers. The yard was, as I have said, on a slight slope, and the water running across had gutted the flower beds and washed out all the good black woods-earth which Dellie had brought in. What little grass there was in the yard was plastered sparsely down on the ground, the way the drainage water had left it. It reminded me of the way the fluff was plastered down on the skin of the drowned chicks that the strange man had been picking up, up in my mother's chicken yard.

I took a few steps up the path to the cabin, and then I saw that the drainage water had washed a lot of trash and filth out from under Dellie's house. Up toward the porch, the ground was not clean any more. Old pieces of rag, two or three rusted cans, pieces of rotten rope, some hunks of old dog dung, broken glass, old paper, and all sorts of things like that had washed out from under Dellie's house to foul her clean yard. It looked just as bad as the yards of the other cabins, or worse. It was worse, as a matter of fact, because it was a surprise. I had never thought of all that filth being under Dellie's house. It was not anything against Dellie that the stuff had been under the cabin. Trash will get under any house. But I did not think of that when I saw the foulness which had washed out on the ground which Dellie sometimes used to sweep with a twig broom to make nice and clean.

I picked my way past the filth, being careful not to get my bare feet on it, and mounted to Dellie's door. When I knocked, I heard her voice telling me to come in.

It was dark inside the cabin, after the daylight, but I could make out Dellie piled up in bed under a quilt, and Little Jebb crouched by the hearth, where a low fire simmered. "Howdy," I said to Dellie, "how you feeling?"

Her big eyes, the whites surprising and glaring in the black face, fixed on me as I stood there, but she did not reply. It did not look like Dellie, or act like Dellie, who would grumble and bustle around our kitchen, talking to herself, scolding me or Little Jebb, clanking pans, making all sorts of unnecessary noises and mutterings like an old-fashioned black steam thrasher engine when it has got up an extra head of steam and keeps popping the governor and rumbling and shaking on its wheels. But now Dellie just lay up there on the bed, under the patchwork quilt, and turned the black face, which I scarcely recognized, and the glaring white eyes to me.

"How you feeling?" I repeated.

"I'se sick," the voice said croakingly out of the strange black face which was not attached to Dellie's big, squat body, but stuck out from under a pile of tangled bedclothes. Then the voice added: "Mighty sick."

"I'm sorry," I managed to say.

The eyes remained fixed on me for a moment, then they left me and the head rolled back on the pillow. "Sorry," the voice said, in a flat way which wasn't question or statement of anything. It was just the empty word put into the air with no meaning or expression, to float off like a feather or a puff of smoke, while the big eyes, with the whites like the peeled white of hard-boiled eggs, stared at the ceiling.

"Dellie," I said after a minute, "there's a tramp up at the house. He's got a knife."

She was not listening. She closed her eyes.

I tiptoed over to the hearth where Jebb was and crouched beside him. We began to talk in low voices. I was asking him to get out his train and play train. Old Jebb had put spool wheels on three cigar boxes and put wire links between the boxes to make a train for Jebb. The box that was the locomotive had the top closed and a length of broom stick for a smoke stack. Jebb didn't want to get the train out, but I told him I would go home if he didn't. So he got out the train, and the colored rocks, and fossils of crinoid stems, and other junk he used for the load, and we began to push it around, talking the way we thought trainmen talked, making a chuck-chucking sound under the breath for the noise of the locomotive and now and then uttering low, cautious toots for the whistle. We got so interested in playing train that the toots got louder. Then, before he thought, Jebb gave a good, loud *toot-toot,* blowing for a crossing.

"Come here," the voice said from the bed.

Jebb got up slow from his hands and knees, giving me a sudden, naked, inimical look.

"Come here!" the voice said.

Jebb went to the bed. Dellie propped herself weakly up on one arm, muttering, "Come closer."

Jebb stood closer.

"Last thing I do, I'm gonna do it," Dellie said. "Done tole you to be quiet."

Then she slapped him. It was an awful slap, more awful for the kind of weakness which it came from and brought to focus. I had seen her slap Jebb before, but the slapping had always been the kind of easy slap you would expect from a good-natured, grumbling Negro woman like Dellie. But this was different. It was awful. It was so awful that Jebb didn't make a sound. The tears just popped out and ran down his face, and his breath came sharp, like gasps.

Dellie fell back. "Cain't even be sick," she said to the ceiling. "Git sick and they won't even let you lay. They tromp all over you. Cain't even be sick." Then she closed her eyes.

I went out of the room. I almost ran getting to the door, and I did run across the porch and down the steps and across the yard, not caring whether or not I stepped on the filth which had washed out from under the cabin. I ran almost all the way home. Then I thought about my mother catching me with the bare feet. So I went down to the stables.

I heard a noise in the crib, and opened the door. There was Big Jebb, sitting on an old nail keg, shelling corn into a bushel basket. I went in, pulling the door shut behind me, and crouched on the floor near him. I crouched there for a couple of minutes before either of us spoke, and watched him shelling the corn.

He had very big hands, knotted and grayish at the joints, with calloused palms which seemed to be streaked with rust, with the rust coming up between the fingers to show from the back. His hands were so strong and tough that he could take a big ear of corn and rip the grains right off the cob with the palm of his hand, all in one motion, like a machine. "Work long as me," he would say, "and the good Lawd'll give you a hand lak cass-ion won't nuthin' hurt." And his hands did look like cast iron, old cast iron streaked with rust.

He was an old man, up in his seventies, thirty years or more older than Dellie, but he was strong as a bull. He was a squat sort of man, heavy in the shoulders, with remarkably long arms, the kind of build they say the river natives have on the Congo from paddling so much in their boats. He had a round bullet-head, set on powerful shoulders. His skin was very black, and the thin hair on his head was now grizzled like tufts of old cotton batting. He had small eyes and a flat nose, not big, and the kindest and wisest old face in the world, the blunt, sad, wise face of an old animal peering tolerantly out on the goings-on of the merely human creatures before him. He was a good man, and I loved him next to my mother and father. I crouched there on the floor of the crib and watched him shell corn with the rusty cast-iron hands, while he looked down at me out of the little eyes set in the blunt face.

"Dellie says she's mighty sick," I said.

"Yeah," he said.

"What's she sick from?"

"Woman-mizry," he said.

"What's woman-mizry?"

"Hit comes on 'em," he said. "Hit jest comes on 'em when the time comes."

"What is it?"

"Hit is the change," he said. "Hit is the change of life and time."

"What changes?"

"You too young to know."

"Tell me."

"Time come and you find out everthing."

I knew that there was no use in asking him any more. When I asked him things and he said that, I always knew that he would not tell me. So I continued to crouch there and watch him. Now that I had sat there a little while, I was cold again.

"What you shiver fer?" he asked me.

"I'm cold. I'm cold because it's blackberry winter," I said.

"Maybe 'tis and maybe 'tain't," he said.

"My mother says it is."

"Ain't sayen Miss Sallie doan know and ain't sayen she do. But folks doan know everthing."

"Why isn't it blackberry winter?"

"Too late fer blackberry winter. Blackberries done bloomed."

"She said it was."

"Blackberry winter jest a leetle cold spell. Hit come and then hit go away, and hit is growed summer of a sudden lak a gunshot. Ain't no tellen hit will go way this time."

"It's June," I said.

"June," he replied with great contempt. "That what folks say. What June mean? Maybe hit is come cold to stay."

"Why?"

"'Cause this-here old yearth is tahrd. Hit is tahrd and ain't gonna perduce. Lawd let hit come rain one time forty days and forty nights, 'cause He was tahrd of sinful folks. Maybe this-here old yearth say to the Lawd, Lawd, I done plum tahrd, Lawd, lemme rest. And Lawd say, Yearth, you done yore best, you give 'em cawn and you give 'em taters, and all they think on is they gut, and, Yearth, you kin take a rest."

"What will happen?"

"Folks will eat up everthing. The yearth won't perduce no more. Folks cut down all the trees and burn 'em 'cause they cold, and the yearth won't grow no more. I been tellen 'em. I been tellen folks. Sayen, maybe this year, hit is the time. But they doan listen to me, how the yearth is tahrd. Maybe this year they find out."

"Will everything die?"

"Everthing and everbody, hit will be so."

"This year?"

"Ain't no tellen. Maybe this year."

"My mother said it is blackberry winter," I said confidently, and got up.

"Ain't sayen nuthin' agin Miss Sallie," he said.

I went to the door of the crib. I was really cold now. Running, I had got up a sweat and now I was worse.

I hung on the door, looking at Jebb, who was shelling corn again.

"There's a tramp came to the house," I said. I had almost forgotten the tramp.

"Yeah."

"He came by the back way. What was he doing down there in the storm?"

"They comes and they goes," he said, "and ain't no teller."

"He had a mean knife."

"The good ones and the bad ones, they comes and they goes. Storm or sun, light or dark. They is folks and they comes and they goes lak folks."

I hung on the door, shivering.

He studied me a moment, then said, "You git on to the house. You ketch yore death. Then what yore mammy say?"

I hesitated.

"You git," he said.

When I came to the back yard, I saw that my father was standing by the back porch and the tramp was walking toward him. They began talking before I reached them, but I got there just as my father was saying, "I'm sorry, but I haven't got any work. I got all the hands on the place I need now. I won't need any extra until wheat thrashing."

The stranger made no reply, just looked at my father.

My father took out his leather coin purse, and got out a half-dollar. He held it toward the man. "This is for half a day," he said.

The man looked at the coin, and then at my father, making no motion to take the money. But that was the right amount. A dollar a day was what you paid them back in 1910. And the man hadn't even worked half a day.

Then the man reached out and took the coin. He dropped it into the right side pocket of his coat. Then he said, very slowly and without feeling, "I didn't want to work on your—farm."

He used the word which they would have frailed me to death for using.

I looked at my father's face and it was streaked white under the sunburn. Then he said, "Get off this place. Get off this place or I won't be responsible."

The man dropped his right hand into his pants pocket. It was the pocket where he kept the knife. I was just about to yell to my father about the knife when the hand came back out with nothing in it. The man gave a kind of twisted grin, showing where the teeth had been knocked out above the new scar. I thought that instant how maybe he had tried before to pull a knife on somebody else and had got his teeth knocked out.

So now he just gave that twisted, sickish grin out of the unmemorable, grayish face, and then spat on the brick path. The glob landed just about six inches from the toe of my father's right boot. My father looked down at it, and so did I. I thought that if the glob had hit my father's boot, something would have happened. I looked down and saw the bright glob, and on one side of it my father's strong cowhide boots, with the brass eyelets and the leather thongs, heavy boots splashed with good red mud and set solid on the bricks, and on the other side the pointed-toe, broken, black shoes, on which the mud looked so sad and out of place. Then I saw one of the black shoes move a little, just a twitch first, then a real step backward.

The man moved in a quarter circle to the end of the porch, with my father's steady gaze upon him all the while. At the end of the porch, the man reached up to the shelf where the wash pans were to get his little newspaper-wrapped parcel. Then he disappeared around the corner of the house and my father mounted the porch and went into the kitchen without a word.

I followed around the house to see what the man would do. I wasn't afraid of him now, no matter if he did have the knife. When I got around in front, I saw him going out the yard gate and starting up the drive toward the pike. So I ran to catch up with him. He was sixty yards or so up the drive before I caught up.

I did not walk right up even with him at first, but trailed him, the way a kid will, about seven or eight feet behind, now and then running two or three steps in order to hold my place against his longer stride. When I first came up behind him, he turned to give me a look, just a meaningless look, and then fixed his eyes up the drive and kept on walking.

When we had got around the bend in the drive which cut the house from sight, and were going along by the edge of the woods, I decided to come up even with him. I ran a few steps, and was by his side, or almost, but some feet off to the right. I walked along in this position for a while, and he never noticed me. I walked along until we got within sight of the big gate that let on the pike.

Then I said, "Where did you come from?"

He looked at me then with a look which seemed almost surprised that I was there. Then he said, "It ain't none of yore business."

We went on another fifty feet.

Then I said, "Where are you going?"

He stopped, studied me dispassionately for a moment, then suddenly took a step toward me and leaned his face down at me. The lips jerked back, but not in any grin, to show where the teeth were knocked out and to make the scar on the lower lip come white with the tension.

He said, "Stop following me. You don't stop following me and I cut yore throat, you little son-of-a-bitch."

Then he went on to the gate, and up the pike.

That was thirty-five years ago. Since that time my father and mother have died. I was still a boy, but a big boy, when my father got cut on the blade of a mowing machine and died of lockjaw. My mother sold the place and went to town to live with her sister. But she never took hold after my father's death, and she died within three years, right in middle life. My aunt always said, "Sallie just died of a broken heart, she was so devoted." Dellie is dead, too, but she died, I heard, quite a long time after we sold the farm.

As for Little Jebb, he grew up to be a mean and ficey[4] Negro. He killed another Negro in a fight and got sent to the penitentiary, where he is yet, the last I heard tell. He probably grew up to be mean and ficey from just being

4. Aggressive, confrontational.

picked on so much by the children of the other tenants, who were jealous of Jebb and Dellie for being thrifty and clever and being white-folks' niggers.

Old Jebb lived forever. I saw him ten years ago and he was about a hundred then, and not looking much different. He was living in town then, on relief— that was back in the Depression—when I went to see him. He said to me: "Too strong to die. When I was a young feller just comen on and seen how things wuz, I prayed the Lawd. I said, Oh, Lawd, gimme strength and meke me strong fer to do and to in-dure. The Lawd hearkened to my prayer. He give me strength. I was in-duren proud fer being strong and me much man. The Lawd give me my prayer and my strength. But now He done gone off and fergot me and left me alone with my strength. A man doan know what to pray fer, and him mortal."

Jebb is probably living yet, as far as I know.

That is what has happened since the morning when the tramp leaned his face down at me and showed his teeth and said: "Stop following me. You don't stop following me and I cut yore throat, you little son-of-a-bitch." That was what he said, for me not to follow him. But I did follow him, all the years.

1946

BRAD WATSON
b. 1955

Brad Watson was born and raised in Meridian, Mississippi. After high school, he moved to Los Angeles with his first wife, whom he'd married shortly before his senior year. After one year in L.A. as an aspiring actor, Watson returned to Mississippi to attend Mississippi State University, and he later earned an M.F.A. from the University of Alabama. To support his family and his writing, Watson has worked as a garbage man, a construction worker, and a fuel pumper at the Tuscaloosa airport. He has been a teacher for the past twenty years and currently teaches creative writing at the University of Wyoming. Watson's first collection of short stories, *Last Days of the Dog-Men* (2001) won the Sue Kaufman Award for First Fiction from the American Academy of Arts and Letters, and his second collection, *Aliens in the Prime of Their Lives* (2010), was a finalist for the PEN/Faulkner Award for Fiction. Watson has also written a novel, *The Heaven of Mercury* (2002), which was a finalist for the National Book Award.

Visitation

Loomis had never believed that line about the quality of despair being that it was unaware of being despair. He'd been painfully aware of his own despair for most of his life. Most of his troubles had come from attempts to deny the essential hopelessness in his nature. To believe in the viability of nothing, finally, was socially unacceptable, and he had tried to adapt, to pass as a believer, a hoper. He had taken prescription medicine, engaged in periods of vigorous, cleansing exercise, declared his satisfaction with any number of fatuous jobs and foolish relationships. Then one day he'd decided that he should marry, have a child, and he told himself that if one was open-minded these things could lead to a kind of contentment, if not to exuberant happiness. That's why Loomis was in the fix he was in now.

Ever since he and his wife had separated and she had moved with their son to southern California, he'd flown out every three weeks to visit the boy. He was living the very nightmare he'd suppressed upon deciding to marry and have a child: that it wouldn't work out, they would split up, and he would be forced to spend long weekends in a motel, taking his son to faux-upscale chain restaurants, cineplexes, and amusement parks.

He usually visited for three to five days and stayed at the same motel, an old motor court that had been bought and remodeled by one of the big franchises. At first the place wasn't so bad. The continental breakfast offered fresh fruit, and little boxes of name-brand cereals, and batter with which you could make your own waffles on a double waffle iron right there in the lobby. The syrup came in small plastic containers from which you pulled back a foil lid and voilà, it was a pretty good waffle. There was juice and decent coffee. Still, of course, it was depressing, a bleak place in which to do one's part in raising a child. With its courtyard surrounded by two stories of identical rooms, and excepting the lack of guard towers and the presence of a swimming pool, it followed the same architectural model as a prison.

But Loomis's son liked it so they continued to stay there even though Loomis would rather have moved on to a better place.

He arrived in San Diego for his April visit, picked up the rental car, and drove north up I-5. Traffic wasn't bad except where it always was, between Del Mar and Carlsbad. Of course, it was never "good." Their motel sat right next to the 5, and the roar and rush of it never stopped. You could step out onto the balcony at three in the morning and it'd be just as roaring and rushing with traffic as it had been six hours before.

This was to be one of his briefer visits. He'd been to a job interview the day before, Thursday, and had another on Tuesday. He wanted to make the most of the weekend, which meant doing very little besides just being with his son. Although he wasn't very good at that. Generally, he sought distractions from his ineptitude as a father. He stopped at a liquor store and bought a bottle of bourbon, and tucked it into his travel bag before driving up the hill to the house where his wife and son lived. The house was owned by a retired Marine friend of his wife's family. His wife and son lived rent-free in the basement apartment.

When Loomis arrived, the ex-Marine was on his hands and knees in the flower bed, pulling weeds. He glared sideways at Loomis for a moment and muttered something, his face a mask of disgust. He was a widower who clearly hated Loomis and refused to speak to him. Loomis was unsettled that someone he'd never even been introduced to could hate him so much.

His son came to the door of the apartment by himself, as usual. Loomis peered past the boy into the little apartment, which was bright and sunny for a basement (only in California, he thought). But, as usual, there was no sign of his estranged wife. She had conspired with some part of her nature to become invisible. Loomis hadn't laid eyes on her in nearly a year. She called out from somewhere in another room, "'Bye! I love you! See you on Monday!" "Okay, love you, too," the boy said, and trudged after Loomis, dragging his backpack of homework and a change of clothes. "'Bye, Uncle Bob," the boy said to the ex-Marine. Uncle Bob! The ex-Marine stood up, gave the boy a small salute, and he and the boy exchanged high-fives.

After Loomis checked in at the motel, they went straight to their room and watched television for a while. Lately his son had been watching cartoons made in the Japanese anime style. Loomis thought the animation was wooden and amateurish. He didn't get it at all. The characters were drawn as angularly as origami, which he supposed was appropriate and maybe even intentional, if the influence was Japanese. But it seemed irredeemably foreign. His son sat propped against several pillows, harboring such a shy but mischievous grin that Loomis had to indulge him.

He made a drink and stepped out onto the balcony to smoke a cigarette. Down by the pool, a woman with long, thick black hair—it was stiffly unkempt, like a madwoman's in a movie—sat in a deck chair with her back to Loomis, watching two children play in the water. The little girl was nine or ten and the boy was older, maybe fourteen. The boy teased the girl by splashing her face with water, and when she protested in a shrill voice he leapt over and dunked her head. She came up gasping and began to cry. Loomis was astonished that the woman, who he assumed to be the children's mother, displayed no reaction. Was she asleep?

The motel had declined steadily in the few months Loomis had been staying there, like a moderately stable person drifting and sinking into the lassitude of depression. Loomis wanted to help, find some way to speak to the managers and the other employees, to say, "Buck up, don't just let things go all to hell," but he felt powerless against his own inclinations.

He lit a second cigarette to go with the rest of his drink. A few other people walked up and positioned themselves around the pool's apron, but none got into the water with the two quarreling children. There was something feral about them, anyone could see. The woman with the wild black hair continued to sit in her pool chair as if asleep or drugged. The boy's teasing of the girl had become steadily rougher, and the girl was sobbing now. Still, the presumptive mother did nothing. Someone went in to complain. One of the managers came out and spoke to the woman, who immediately but without getting up from her deck chair shouted to the boy, "All right, God damn it!" The boy, smirking, climbed from the pool, leaving the girl standing in waist-deep water, sobbing and rubbing her eyes with her fists. The woman stood up then and walked toward the boy. There was something off about her clothes, burnt-orange Bermuda shorts and a men's lavender oxford shirt. And they didn't seem to fit right. The boy, like a wary stray dog, watched her approach. She snatched a lock of his wet black hair, pulled his face to hers, and said something, gave his head a shake and let him go. The boy went over to the pool and spoke to the girl. "Come on," he said. "No," the girl said, still crying. "You let him help you!" the woman shouted then, startling the girl into letting the boy take her hand. Loomis was fascinated, a little bit horrified.

Turning back toward her chair, the woman looked up to where he stood on the balcony. She had an astonishing face, broad and long, divided by a great, curved nose, dominated by a pair of large, dark, sunken eyes that seemed blackened by blows or some terrible history. Such a face, along with her immense, thick mane of black hair, made her look like a troll. Except that she was not ugly. She looked more like a witch, the cruel mockery of beauty and seduction. The oxford shirt was mostly unbuttoned, nearly spilling out a pair of full, loose, mottled-brown breasts.

"What are you looking at!" she shouted, very loudly from deep in her chest. Loomis stepped back from the balcony railing. The woman's angry glare changed to something like shrewd assessment and then dismissal. She shooed her two children into one of the downstairs rooms.

After taking another minute to finish his drink and smoke a third cigarette, to calm down, Loomis went back inside and closed the sliding glass door behind him.

His son was on the bed, grinning, watching something on television called "Code Lyoko." It looked very Japanese, even though the boy had informed him it was made in France. Loomis tried to watch it with him for a while, but got restless. He wanted a second, and maybe stronger, drink.

"Hey," he said. "How about I just get some burgers and bring them back to the room?"

The boy glanced at him and said, "That'd be okay."

Loomis got a sack of hamburgers from McDonald's, some fries, a Coke. He made a second drink, then a third, while his son ate and watched television. They went to bed early.

The next afternoon, Saturday, they drove to the long, wide beach at Carlsbad. Carlsbad was far too cool, but what could you do? Also, the hip little surf shop where the boy's mother worked during the week was in Carlsbad. He'd forgotten that for a moment. He was having a hard time keeping her in his mind. Her invisibility strategy was beginning to work on him. He wasn't sure at all anymore just who she was or ever had been. When they'd met she wore business attire, like everyone else he knew. What did she wear now, just a swimsuit? Did she get up and go around in a bikini all day? She didn't really have the body for that at age thirty-nine, did she?

"What does your mom wear to work?" he asked.

The boy gave him a look that would have been ironic if he'd been a less compassionate child.

"Clothes?" the boy said.

"Okay," Loomis said. "Like a swimsuit? Does she go to work in a swimsuit?"

The boy stared at him for a moment.

"Are you okay?" the boy said.

Loomis was taken aback by the question.

"Me?" he said.

They walked along the beach, neither going into the water. Loomis enjoyed collecting rocks. The stones on the beach here were astounding. He marveled at one that resembled an ancient war club. The handle fit perfectly into his palm. From somewhere over the water, a few miles south, they could hear the stuttering thud of a large helicopter's blades. Most likely a military craft from the Marine base farther north.

Maybe he wasn't okay. Loomis had been to five therapists since separating from his wife: one psychiatrist, one psychologist, three counselors. The psychiatrist had tried him on Paxil, Zoloft, and Wellbutrin for depression, and then lorazepam for anxiety. Only the lorazepam had helped, but with that he'd overslept too often and lost his job. The psychologist, once she learned that Loomis was drinking almost half a bottle of booze every night, became fixated on getting him to join AA and seemed to forget altogether that he was there to figure out whether he indeed no longer loved his wife. And why he had cheated on her. Why he had left her for another woman when the truth was he had no faith that the new relationship would work out any better than the old one. The first counselor seemed sensible, but Loomis made the mistake of visiting her together with his wife, and when she suggested maybe their marriage was indeed kaput his wife had walked out. The second counselor was actually his wife's counselor, and Loomis thought she was an idiot.

Loomis suspected that his wife liked the second counselor because she did nothing but nod and sympathize and give them brochures. He suspected that his wife simply didn't want to move out of their house, which she liked far more than Loomis did, and which possibly she liked more than she liked Loomis. When she realized divorce was inevitable, she shifted gears, remembered she wanted to surf, and sold the house before Loomis was even aware it was on the market, so he had to sign. Then it was Loomis who mourned the loss of the house, which he realized had been pretty comfortable after all. He visited the third counselor with his girlfriend, who seemed constantly angry that his divorce hadn't yet come through. He and the girlfriend both gave up on that counselor because he seemed terrified of them for some reason they couldn't fathom. Loomis was coming to the conclusion that he couldn't fathom anything; the word seemed appropriate to him, because most of the time he felt like he was drowning and couldn't find the bottom or the surface of this body of murky water he had fallen, or dived, into.

He wondered if this was why he didn't want to dive into the crashing waves of the Pacific, as he certainly would have when he was younger. His son didn't want to because, he said, he'd rather surf.

"But you don't know how to surf," Loomis said.

"Mom's going to teach me as soon as she's good enough at it," the boy said.

"But don't you need to be a better swimmer before you try to surf?" Loomis had a vague memory of the boy's swimming lessons, which maybe hadn't gone so well.

"No," the boy said.

"I really think," Loomis said, and then he stopped speaking, because the helicopter he'd been hearing, one of those large, twin-engined birds that carried troops in and out of combat—a Chinook—had come abreast of them a quarter mile or so off the beach. Just as Loomis looked up to see it, something coughed or exploded in one or both of its engines. The helicopter slowed, then swerved, with the slow grace of an airborne leviathan, toward the beach where they stood. In a moment it was directly over them. One of the men in it leaned out of a small opening on its side, frantically waving, but the people on the beach, including Loomis and his son, beaten by the blast from the blades and stung by sand driven up by it, were too shocked and confused to run. The helicopter lurched back out over the water with a tremendous roar and a deafening, rattling whine from the engines. There was another loud pop, and black smoke streamed from the forward engine as the Chinook made its way north again, seeming hobbled. Then it was gone, lost in the glare over the water. A bittersweet burnt-fuel smell hung in the air. Loomis and his son stood there among the others on the beach, speechless. One of two very brown young surfers in board shorts and crew cuts grinned and nodded at the clublike rock in Loomis's hand.

"Dude, we're safe," he said. "You can put down the weapon." He and the other surfer laughed.

Loomis's son, looking embarrassed, moved off as if he were with someone else in the crowd, not Loomis.

They stayed in Carlsbad for an early dinner at Pizza Port. The place was crowded with people who'd been at the beach all day, although Loomis recognized no one they'd seen when the helicopter had nearly crashed and killed them all. He'd expected everyone in there to know about it, to be buzzing about it over beer and pizza, amazed, exhilarated. But it was as if it hadn't happened.

The long rows of picnic tables and booths were filled with young parents and their hyperkinetic children, who kept jumping up to get extra napkins or forks or to climb into the seats of the motorcycle video games. Their parents flung arms after them like inadequate lassos or pursued them and herded them back. The stools along the bar were occupied by young men and women who apparently had no children and who were attentive only to each other and to choosing which of the restaurant's many microbrews to order. In the corner by the restrooms, the old surfers, regulars here; gathered to talk shop and knock back the stronger beers; the double-hopped and the barley wines. Their graying hair frizzled and tied in ponytails or dreads or chopped in stiff clumps dried by salt and sun. Their faces leather-brown. Gnarled toes jutting from their flip-flops and worn sandals like assortments of dry-roasted cashews, Brazil nuts, ginger roots.

Loomis felt no affinity for any of them. There wasn't a single person in the entire place with whom he felt a thing in common—other than being, somehow, human. Toward the parents he felt a bitter disdain. On the large TV screens fastened to the restaurant's brick walls, surfers skimmed down giant waves off Hawaii, Tahiti, Australia.

He gazed at the boy, his son. The boy looked just like his mother. Thick bright orange hair, untamable. Tall, stemlike people with long limbs and that thick hairblossom on top. Loomis had called them his rosebuds. "Roses are *red*," his son would respond, delightedly indignant, when he was smaller. "There are orange roses," Loomis would reply. "Where?" "Well, in Indonesia, I think. Or possibly Brazil." "No!" his son would shout, breaking down into giggles on the floor. He bought them orange roses on the boy's birthday that year.

The boy wasn't so easily amused anymore. He waited glumly for their pizza order to be called out. They'd secured a booth vacated by a smallish family.

"You want a Coke?" Loomis said. The boy nodded absently. "I'll get you a Coke," Loomis said.

He got the boy a Coke from the fountain, and ordered a pint of strong pale ale from the bar for himself.

By the time their pizza came, Loomis was on his second ale. He felt much better about all the domestic chaos around them in the restaurant. It was getting on the boy's nerves, though. As soon as they finished their pizza, he asked Loomis if he could go stand outside and wait for him there.

"I'm almost done," Loomis said.

"I'd really rather wait outside," the boy said. He shoved his hands in his pockets and looked away.

"Okay," Loomis said. "Don't wander off. Stay where I can see you."

"I will."

Loomis sipped his beer and watched as the boy weaved his way through the crowd and out of the restaurant, then began to pace back and forth on the sidewalk. Having to be a parent in this fashion was terrible. He felt indicted by all the other people in this teeming place: by the parents and their smug happiness, by the old surfer dudes, who had the courage of their lack of conviction, and by the young lovers, who were convinced that they would never be part of either of these groups, not the obnoxious parents, not the grizzled losers clinging to youth like tough, crusty barnacles. Certainly they would not be Loomis.

And what did it mean, in any case, that he couldn't even carry on a conversation with his son? How hard could that be? But Loomis couldn't seem to do it. To hear him try, you'd think they didn't know each other at all, that he was a friend of the boy's father, watching him for the afternoon or something. He started to get up and leave, but first he hesitated, then gulped down the rest of his second beer.

His son stood with hunched shoulders waiting.

"Ready to go back to the motel?" Loomis said.

The boy nodded. They walked back to the car in silence.

"Did you like your pizza?" Loomis said when they were in the car.

"Sure. It was okay."

Loomis looked at him for a moment. The boy glanced back with the facial equivalent of a shrug, an impressively diplomatic expression that managed to say both "I'm sorry" and "What do you want?" Loomis sighed. He could think of nothing else to say that wasn't even more inane.

"All right," he finally said, and drove them back to the motel.

When they arrived, Loomis heard a commotion in the courtyard and they paused near the gate.

The woman who'd been watching the two awful children was there at the pool again, and the two children themselves had returned to the water. But now the group seemed to be accompanied by an older heavyset man, bald on top, graying hair slicked against the sides of his head. He was arguing with a manager while the other guests around the pool pretended to ignore the altercation. The boy and girl paddled about in the water until the man threw up his hands and told them to get out and go to their room. The girl glanced at the boy, but the boy continued to ignore the man until he strode to the edge of the pool and shouted, "Get out! Let them have their filthy pool. Did you piss in it? I hope you pissed in it. Now get out! Go to the room!" The boy removed himself from the pool with a kind of languorous choreography, and walked toward the sliding glass door of one of the downstairs rooms, the little girl following. Just before reaching the door the boy paused, turned his head in the direction of the pool and the other guests there, and hawked and spat onto the concrete pool apron. Loomis said to his son, "Let's get on up to the room."

Another guest, a lanky young woman whom Loomis had seen beside the pool earlier, walked past them on her way to the parking lot. "Watch out for them Gypsies," she muttered.

"Gypsies?" the boy said.

The woman laughed as she rounded the corner. "Don't let 'em get you," she said.

"I don't know," Loomis said when she'd gone. "I guess they do seem a little like Gypsies."

"What the hell is a Gypsy, anyway?"

Loomis stopped and stared at his son. "Does 'Uncle Bob' teach you to talk that way?"

The boy shrugged and looked away, annoyed.

In the room, his son pressed him again, and he told him that Gypsies were originally from some part of India, he wasn't sure which, and that they were ostracized, nobody wanted them. They became wanderers, wandering around Europe. They were poor. People accused them of stealing. "They had a reputation for stealing people's children, I think."

He meant this to be a kind of joke, or at least lighthearted, but when he saw the expression on the boy's face he regretted it and quickly added, "They didn't, really."

It didn't work. For the next hour, the boy asked him questions about Gypsies and kidnapping. Every few minutes or so he hopped from the bed to the sliding glass door and pulled the curtain aside to peek down across the courtyard at the Gypsies' room. Loomis had decided to concede they were Gypsies, whether they really were or not. He made himself a stiff nightcap and stepped out onto the balcony to smoke, although he peeked through the curtains before going out, to make sure the coast was clear.

The next morning, Sunday, Loomis rose before his son and went down to the lobby for coffee. He stepped out into the empty courtyard to drink it in the morning air, and when he looked into the pool he saw a large dead rat on its side at the bottom. The rat looked peacefully dead, with its eyes closed and its front paws curled at its chest as if it were begging. Loomis took another sip of his coffee and went back into the lobby. The night clerk was still on duty, studying something on the computer monitor behind the desk. She only cut her eyes at Loomis, and when she saw he was going to approach her she met his gaze steadily in that same way, without turning her head.

"I believe you have an unregistered guest at the bottom of your pool," Loomis said.

He got a second cup of coffee, a plastic cup of juice, and a couple of refrigerator-cold bagels (the waffle iron and fresh fruit had disappeared a couple of visits earlier) and took them back to the room. He and his son ate there, then Loomis decided to get them away from the motel for the day. The boy could always be counted on to want a day trip to San Diego. He loved to ride the red trolleys there, and tolerated Loomis's interest in the museums, sometimes.

They took the commuter train down, rode the trolley to the Mexican border, turned around, and came back. They ate lunch at a famous old diner near downtown, then took a bus to Balboa Park and spent the afternoon in the Air & Space Museum, the Natural History Museum, and at a small, disappointing model railroad exhibit. Then they took the train back up the coast.

As they got out of the car at the motel, an old brown van, plain and blocky as a loaf of bread, careened around the far corner of the lot, pulled up next to Loomis, roared up to them, and stopped. The driver was the older man who'd been at the pool. He leaned toward Loomis and said through the open passenger window, "Can you give me twenty dollars? They're going to kick us out of this stinking motel."

Loomis felt a surge of hostile indignation. What, did he have a big sign on his chest telling everyone what a loser he was?

"I don't have it," he said.

"Come on!" the man shouted. "Just twenty bucks!"

Loomis saw his son standing beside the passenger door of the rental car, frightened.

"No," he said. He was ready to punch the old man now.

"Son of a bitch!" the man shouted, and gunned the van away, swerving onto the street toward downtown and the beach.

The boy gestured for Loomis to hurry over and unlock the car door, and as soon as he did the boy got back into the passenger seat. When Loomis sat down behind the wheel, the boy hit the lock button. He cut his eyes toward where the van had disappeared up the hill on the avenue.

"Was he trying to rob us?" he said.

"No. He wanted me to give him twenty dollars."

The boy was breathing hard and looking straight out the windshield, close to tears.

"It's okay," Loomis said. "He's gone."

"Pop, no offense"—and the boy actually reached over and patted Loomis on the forearm, as if to comfort him—"but I think I want to sleep at home tonight."

Loomis was so astonished by the way his son had touched him on the arm that he was close to tears himself.

"It'll be okay," he said. "Really. We're safe here, and I'll protect you."

"I know, Pop, but I really think I want to go home."

Loomis tried to keep the obvious pleading note from his voice. If this happened, if he couldn't even keep his son around and reasonably satisfied to be with him for a weekend, what was he at all anymore? And (he couldn't help but think) what would the boy's mother make of it, how much worse would he then look in her eyes?

"Please," he said to the boy. "Just come on up to the room for a while, and we'll talk about it again, and if you still want to go home later on I'll take you, I promise."

The boy thought about it and agreed, and began to calm down a little. They went up to the room, past the courtyard, which was blessedly clear of ridiculous Gypsies and other guests. Loomis got a bucket of ice for his bourbon, ordered Chinese, and they lay together on Loomis's bed, eating and watching television, and didn't talk about the Gypsies, and after a while, exhausted, they both fell asleep.

When the alcohol woke him at 3 a.m., he was awash in a sense of gloom and dread. He found the remote, turned down the sound on the TV. His son was sleeping, mouth open, a lock of his bright orange hair across his face.

Loomis eased himself off the bed, sat on the other one, and watched him breathe. He recalled the days when his life with the boy's mother had seemed happy, and the boy had been small, and they would put him to bed in his room, where they had built shelves for his toy trains and stuffed animals and the books from which Loomis would read to him at bedtime. He remembered the constant battle in his heart, those days. How he was drawn into this construction of conventional happiness, how he felt that he loved this child more than he had ever loved anyone in his entire life, how all of this was possible, this life, how he might actually be able to do it. And yet whenever he had felt this he was always aware of the other, more deeply seated part of his nature that wanted to run away in fear. That believed it was not possible after all, that it could only end in catastrophe, that anything this sweet and heartbreaking must indeed one day collapse into shattered pieces. He had struggled to free himself, one way or another, from what seemed a horrible limbo of anticipation. He had run away, in his fashion. And yet nothing had ever caused him to feel anything more like despair than what he felt just now, in this moment, looking at his beautiful child asleep on the motel bed in the light of the cheap lamp, with the incessant dull roar of cars on I-5 just the other side of the hedge, a slashing river of what seemed nothing but desperate travel from point A to point B, from which one mad dasher or another would simply disappear, blink out in a flicker of light, at ragged but regular intervals, with no more ceremony or consideration than that.

He checked that his son was still sleeping deeply, then poured himself a plastic cup of neat bourbon and went down to the pool to smoke and sit alone for a while in the dark. He walked toward a group of lawn chairs in the shadows beside a stunted palm, but stopped when he realized that he wasn't alone, that someone was sitting in one of the chairs. The Gypsy woman sat very still, watching him.

"Come, sit," she said. "Don't be afraid."

He was afraid. But the woman was so still, and the look on her face he could now make out in the shadows was one of calm appraisal. Something about this kept him from retreating. She slowly raised a hand and patted the pool chair next to her, and Loomis sat.

For a moment the woman just looked at him, and, unable not to, he looked at her. She was unexpectedly, oddly attractive. Her eyes were indeed very dark, set far apart on her broad face. In this light, her fierce nose was strange and alarming, almost erotic.

"Are you Gypsy?" Loomis blurted, without thinking.

She stared at him a second before smiling and chuckling deep in her throat.

"No, I'm not Gypsy," she said, her eyes moving quickly from side to side in little shiftings, looking into his. "We are American. My people come from France."

Loomis said nothing.

"But I can tell you your future," she said, leaning her head back slightly to look at him down her harrowing nose. "Let me see your hand." She took Loomis's wrist and pulled his palm toward her. He didn't resist. "Have you ever had someone read your palm?"

Loomis shook his head. "I don't really want to know my future," he said. "I'm not a very optimistic person."

"I understand," the woman said. "You're unsettled."

"It's too dark here to even see my palm," Loomis said.

"No, there's enough light," the woman said. And finally she took her eyes from Loomis's and looked down at his palm. He felt relieved enough to be released from that gaze to let her continue. And something in him was relieved, too, to have someone else consider his future, someone aside from himself. It couldn't be worse, after all, than his own predictions.

She hung her head over his palm and traced the lines with a long fingernail, pressed into the fleshy parts. Her thick hair tickled the edges of his hand

and wrist. After a moment, much sooner than Loomis would have expected, she spoke.

"It's not the future you see in a palm," she said, still studying his. "It's a person's nature. From this, of course, one can tell much about a person's tendencies." She looked up, still gripping his wrist. "This tells us much about where a life may have been, and where it may go."

She bent over his palm again, traced one of the lines with the fingernail. "There are many breaks in the heart line here. You are a creature of disappointment. I suspect others in your life disappoint you." She traced a different line. "You're a dreamer. You're an idealist, possibly. Always disappointed by ordinary life, which of course is boring and ugly." She laughed that soft, deep chuckle again and looked up, startling Loomis anew with the directness of her gaze. "People are so fucking disappointing, eh?" She uttered a seductive grunt that loosened something in his groin.

It was true. No one had ever been good enough for him. Even the members of his immediate family. And especially himself.

"Anger, disappointment," the woman said. "So common. But it may be they've worn you down. The drinking, smoking. No real energy, no passion." Loomis pulled against her grip just slightly but she held on with strong fingers around his wrist. Then she lowered Loomis's palm to her broad lap and leaned in closer, speaking more quietly.

"I see you with the little boy—he's your child?"

Loomis nodded. He felt suddenly alarmed, fearful. He glanced up, and his heart raced when he thought he saw the boy standing on the balcony looking out. It was only the potted plant there. He wanted to dash back to the room but he was rooted to the chair, to the Gypsy with her thin, hard fingers about his wrist.

"This is no vacation, I suspect. It's terrible, to see your child in this way, in a motel."

Loomis nodded.

"You're angry with this child's mother for forcing you to be here."

Loomis nodded and tried to swallow. His throat was dry.

"Yet I would venture it was you who left her. For another woman, a beautiful woman, eh, *mon frère?*"[1] She ran the tip of a nail down one of the lines in his palm. There was a cruel smile on her impossible face. "A woman who once again you believed to be something she was not." Loomis felt himself drop his chin in some kind of involuntary acquiescence. "She was a dream," the woman said. "And she has disappeared, poof, like any dream." He felt suddenly, embarrassingly, close to tears. A tight lump swelled in his throat. "And now you have left her, too, or she has left you, because"—and here the woman paused, shook Loomis's wrist gently, as if to revive his attention, and indeed he had been drifting in his grief—"because you are a ghost. Walking between two worlds, you know?" She shook his wrist again, harder, and Loomis looked up at her, his vision of her there in the shadows blurred by his tears.

She released his wrist and sat back in her chair, exhaled as if she had been holding her breath, and closed her eyes. As if this excoriation of Loomis's character had been an obligation, had exhausted her.

---

1. My brother (French).

They sat there for a minute or two while Loomis waited for the emotion that had surged up in him to recede.

"Twenty dollars," the woman said then, her eyes still closed. When Loomis said nothing, she opened her eyes. Now her gaze was flat, no longer intense, but she held it on him.

"Twenty dollars," she said. "For the reading. This is my fee."

Loomis, feeling as if he'd just been through something physical instead of emotional, his muscles tingling, reached for his wallet, found a twenty-dollar bill, and handed it to her. She took it and rested her hands in her lap.

"Now you should go back up to your room," she said.

He got up to make his way from the courtyard, and was startled by some-one standing in the shadow of the Gypsies' doorway. Her evil man-child, the boy from the pool, watching him like a forest animal pausing in its night prowling to let him pass. Loomis hurried on up to the room, tried to let him-self in with a key card that wouldn't cooperate. The lock kept flashing red instead of green. Finally the card worked, the green light flickered. He entered and shut the door behind him.

But he'd gone into the wrong room, maybe even some other motel. The beds were made, the television off. His son wasn't there. The sliding glass door to the balcony stood open. Loomis felt his heart seize up and he rushed to the railing. The courtyard was dark and empty. Over in the lobby, the lights were dimmed, no one on duty. It was all shut down. There was no breeze. No roar of rushing vehicles from the 5, the roar in Loomis's mind canceling it out. By the time he heard the sound behind him and turned to see his son come out of the bathroom yawning, it was too late. It might as well have been someone else's child, Loomis the stranger come to steal him away. He stood on the balcony and watched his son crawl back onto the bed, pull himself into a fetal position, close his eyes for a moment, then open them. Meeting his gaze, Loomis felt something break inside him. The boy had the same dazed, disoriented expression he'd had on his face just after his long, difficult birth, when the nurses had put him into an incubator to rush him to inten-sive care. Loomis had knelt, then, his face up close to the incubator's glass wall, and he'd known that the baby could see him, and that was enough. The obstetrician said, "This baby is very sick," and nurses wheeled the incubator out. He'd gone over to his wife and held her hand. The resident, tears in her eyes, patted his shoulder and said, for some reason, "You're good people," and left them alone. Now he and their child were in this motel, the life that had been their family somehow dissipated into air. Loomis couldn't gather into his mind how they'd got here. He couldn't imagine what would come next.

2009

STEPHANIE POWELL WATTS
b. 1970

Stephanie Powell Watts grew up in rural North Carolina. She graduated from the University of North Carolina at Charlotte and went on to receive her Ph.D. from the University of Missouri. Watts is a writer of the American South. Her characters are working-class Southerners—often young black women. She writes about family, religion, and the people she met during her time spent as a fast-food worker, a factory hand, and a door-to-door traveling Jehovah's Witness minister. Watts was named Best Emerging Writer at the 2012 Southern Women's Writer's Conference. Her first short story collection, *We Are Taking Only What We Need* (2011) earned her the Ernest J. Gaines Award for Literary Excellence, and stories from it appeared in *New Stories from the South 2007*. For her story "Unassigned Territory," below, Watts received the 2007 Pushcart Prize and a Distinguished Story citation in *The Best American Short Stories 2007*.

Unassigned Territory

Leslie Pawlowski parks her blue Horizon on the shoulder of the dirt road—the best shade we can find. July is a killer in North Carolina. It's always hot as blazes, hot enough for you, hot enough to fry eggs and on and on. We are in the thick of it, midmorning, our dresses clinging to our backs, way far in the middle of nowhere, preaching door to door, working in our congregation's unassigned territory. This is the kind of dirt road, *Hee-Haw*, overalls, straw-in-the-teeth place even we Southerners make fun of. Pikes and Wagoners country. Did you hear the one about the Pike girl who went to a town doctor? The doctor says to her mother, "Ma'am has this girl had intercourse?" and the mother, hands wringing says, "I don't rightly know, doctor, but if she needs it, you make sure you give it to her."

The passenger's side window sticks in the middle of going up or down. Piece of junk car. And on the way to every door, we shed bits of poly foam from the car's cracked upholstery. Leslie has a great attitude about her poverty. "Halcyon, salad days" she will remember with a withering chuckle when her future kids complain of their own first cars. We've visited too many houses without updating our field-service records, and we stop before we forget the details. We need to keep records. Records for ourselves, for the congregation file on the territory, and for the official log we store at the Kingdom Hall.

"What was that woman's name at the blue trailer, Steph?"

I shuffle through my notebooks knowing I won't find any useful information. You are supposed to write things like *Ruth Boaz, 123 Main Street, blue trailer, lived in town all her life, no husband in the house, four kids—one still at home. Took the July 1989 Awake, "Making the Most of Your Youth." Expressed an interest in tarot. Bring magazine* Why Godly People Shun Spiritism. My records are to say the least incomplete. I wrote: *Trailer is a nightmare.* Looks like the time my brother and I played drug czar with an old suitcase and Monopoly money. Ryan threw my clothes and shoes out of the dresser and closet screaming, "Where's the real stash! Where's the real stash!"

I'm praying that Leslie won't ask to see what I've written. I've been at this long enough that I don't need any guidance from my field-service partner. Sometimes Leslie will say things like, "you're writing a book over there, aren't you," but she never pries.

"Shoot. I hate to leave her name off. She was nice, too," Leslie sighs.

Nice to Leslie means that she didn't cuss us, that she didn't shoo us away or hide behind her curtains, her hand over the mouth of her child like a kidnapper. "But Mama," the kid would manage through her fingers, "there's some girls on the porch." "Shh," I imagine her saying, "Do you want to be saved? Is that what you want?"

This lady had stood on her rickety porch—sullen and quiet, her eyes never leaving my brown face. Leslie, even with her Minnesota accent, was apparently okay. Brown woman on the porch trumps Yankee invader any day. To be fair, they don't get too many black Jehovah's Witnesses out here. There are only two black Jehovah's Witness families in town, for a total of six people. Besides, although our congregation got to every door in the city limit at least three times a year, the unassigned territory, this deliverance of woods, creeks, and black snakes gets worked only once a year if we were lucky. More likely, these people won't see any of us for eighteen to twenty-four months. Imagine the odds of seeing a black Jehovah's Witness in the territory. That's Lotto odds.

Besides seeing no black people, there are four important things to remember about the unassigned territory:

1) You are as remote as you can get in this new world. Way out in the boonies, mostly white Southerners who've been holed up here for generations, living on winding dirt roads that lead to more winding dirt roads, with houses, the occasional mansion, trailers, and shacks out of sight from each other. They like it that way. 2) Everybody and his dog has a dog. At least one loose, ugly mutt with cockleburs in his unloved fur and filled with the kind of hatred that only comes from at last finding a body more miserable than yourself. 3) Apparently the trauma of a visit from Jehovah's Witnesses is so great that just the glimpse of your *Watchtower* will act as a Proustian mnemonic causing the householder to wax nostalgic about your last visit. Never mind that someone from your or any congregation left a tract in the door two years ago. You will hear over and over, "Some of ya'll was just here." 4) There is nothing good about the unassigned territory.

Leslie explained the "Offer for the Month," trying to regain the householder's attention. "This is our new book, *Enjoy Life Forever on a Paradise Earth.*" Leslie dangled the bright red cover at the woman. Even the color pictures of laughing children and fluffy sheep nuzzling up to male lions didn't move the woman's eyes. She only had eyes for me.

Does the missus want I should jig, a little tap dance fuh yo pleasure, I wanted to ask, but instead put on my best, "yes, I'm black, but doggonit, not that black" face.

"You got that same Bible?" the woman said to me.

"Yes ma'am," I held out my cardboard covered *New World Translation* for her to see. When I got baptized, I'd get a leather one.

"That's plenty," she said, folding her arms across her chest. "I know the Bible when I see it."

Leslie gave the woman an older *Watchtower* magazine that she wouldn't have to request a donation for. Good move, Leslie. She can get the literature into the house and not risk rejection. Who knows? This woman might even read it. She might change her life around and be side by side with us in this very territory next year. You never know. That's why Leslie is a pro. She thinks about these kinds of things. I've seen her talk to grief-stricken and depressed people, whip out the Bible she seems to know by heart and without a blink show them that God is a fortress, a rock, a high place, a God of comfort, love, and forgiveness. And for a few seconds, I think she really lightens those people. It is no small thing to give a person even a moment of hope. Of course, when we go back the next week to follow up, those very same people slam their doors, order us away, looking like they could kill us. "Don't you tell me God loves me. Don't you dare."

Leslie is grooming me, though she doesn't think that I know. I have a big decision to make next year. To serve Jehovah during my youth (which is, by the way, the surprising twist ending to our magazine, *Making the Most of Your Youth*) or to go to college. I know that my congregation elders have told Leslie to help me do the right thing.

On the way past the car, past the tired old dog, through the patchy yard, I can't be sure, but I think I heard the woman say "wetback." I don't know, it could have been the bigoted cicadas or heat stroke, but I think she called me a wetback. I wanted to put my finger in her crumpled face, her skin like the film from Krazy Glue and say something wise and cutting like, "Get your racial epithets right, Ms. Einstein." But fighting in the field service is looked down on. Truth be told, at 97 degrees and counting, Unnamed Householder had the virtue of being accurate. Not nice, but accurate. Besides, the sentiment for the Mexicans who were coming into the county taking all the glory jobs like picking apples for fourteen hours a day for less than minimum wage and apparently preaching door to door in glamour locales like Miller's Creek was enough to make anybody sick with envy. I wanted to tell Leslie what I thought I'd heard, but she was the sort of white person who refused to acknowledge racism. Just deny it and it won't exist. She'd say, "Well, I'm sure she didn't mean anything. Maybe she was concerned about the heat."

"What about the man on the tractor? Where did he say he lived?" Leslie asks. "I knew we should have stopped right then."

"Oh yeah," I say, stalling, shuffling through the pages.

My record:

Dear Martin Luther King: Sir, is this the dream you meant? Me and this sweet girl from Minnesota in a steaming car? I met a black man weeks ago who was courting a pretty woman he thought would be his wife. But that Memphis day in early April, slow dragging in a school cafeteria at a dance, the music dropped like the piano player's final clink when the black hats show up and a man ran in screaming that you were gone. My new friend looked in the pretty woman's face, at the despair he wore himself and knew he could never see her again. I am hot today, but trying to remember you at 1400 High Rock Road.

"1400 High Rock Road," I say.

"Okay, you are good for something," Leslie grins, acting like a mother. She's only six years older than I am, but preaching is her career. Her family moved to North Carolina only three years ago to serve "where the need was greater," but Leslie is easily one of the most popular people there. She's a good girl, with a sweet disposition, and she has committed herself to the fieldwork. Leslie is a pioneer—out in service at least sixty hours a month every month. Sixty hours of door slammings, I-have-my-own-religions, I-was-just-on-my-way-outs, and lonely old women who will even talk about Jehovah to hear another voice in the room.

"Okay," Leslie says, handing me a Shasta soda from her cooler; she always gets the cheap drinks. "Let's do two more houses. One if it's too far, okay?"

Thank God, thank God. Thank you. Thank you Dr. King, Thank you. Thank you. "Are you sure? I'm up for another hour or so," I say, willing the bouncing hope in my chest to stay still for a few minutes, she might change her mind. "I mean, if you need the time. I'm up for it," I manage to say with almost a smile in my voice.

"I'll just have to make it up next week," Leslie says breezily. But I know that this month will be especially hard for her. She has all those hours to complete in these backwoods. Think about it. You can't just preach any old time. You have to come knocking at decent hours, after nine in the morning and before eight at night and preferably not during the dinner hour. You can only count the time you actually preach. That means the forty-five-minute drive out there—gratis. The ride in between these houses in the territory—if it is more than ten minutes, you eat it. The fifteen-minute lunch break is on your time, sister-friend. All to say that Jehovah's Witnesses need a union.

Leslie dribbles soda all over the bodice of her dress. No loss, as far as I'm concerned. Leslie shops at Granny's Rejects or Let's Repel Men or some store like it. I couldn't believe the kinds of things this young woman puts on her body: shifts (really!), baggy sweaters, long full skirts, big prints that make muumuus blush like demure schoolgirls. These things the wardrobe for Leslie's plump, pink frame. A style my daddy dubbed, "to' up from the flo' up." Leslie has mostly given up on men. I knew that the secret wish of her heart was that Bruce Springsteen come in to the Truth, but she was only hoping in her heart, not in her head. Lately, I've noticed her saying strange things like, "when I was young," or "if I were your age," or "that's for the kids." She is twenty-four. Though truth be told, she is getting a bit long in the tooth for a Jehovah's Witness bride. The faithful marry young rather than burn with desire (see the Pauline letters) and marry fast to get the pick of the litter of endangered young male believers. The congregation has already picked out my husband for me. A nice-looking white boy with a flounce of blond hair, unswiveling hips and clunky clod-buster shoes. Bobby Ratliff. I like Bobby, don't misunderstand me, but only twelve-year-old virgins look at a dopey sixteen-year-old and think *what great marriage material.* Lord knows that by rejecting Bobby I was dooming myself to Lesliedom. There was precious little else to choose from, few kids my age to even compare and contrast. Jim, another teenager in the congregation, is a possibility, but he and his sister, Lisa, are bad. Really bad. Once they brought a dirty magazine on the school bus, passed it around like a cold to the other kids. I noticed when it came to Bobby's seat, he wouldn't even look at the filthy cover, wouldn't even touch it. The worst, the absolute limit was when Jim and Lisa brought a Prince song for us to listen to. When Prince said *Controversy* (and he said it often) Jim and Lisa led the bus in the rollicking mispronunciation at the tops of their heathen lungs. A variation I'm sure the pre-Jehovah's Witness Prince would have V8-smacked his yellow forehead, if he'd heard, *Why didn't I think of that,* on his lips? Bobby and I didn't tell on Jim and Lisa, though we were tempted. We did explain (at every opportunity) to the other kids that though Jim and Lisa attended the Kingdom Hall, they weren't really of our sort. We insisted that we are the real Jehovah's Witnesses. Sure Jim and Lisa were clever and cool and fun, but *salvation?* I don't think so.

Lingering in a parked car in someone's driveway is a definite no-no, an unwritten rule; you can't look like you're casing the joint. But we are in a little bit of slow motion today, staring ahead at the almost graveled road, the high weeds and bushes now covered with a thick layer of red dust. There has been no rain for days. We couldn't see the house that the record told us was straight ahead. Somehow this seemed important to me. If I had the words, I would say to Leslie, isn't it funny that we can't see the next house? Doesn't that mean something? I wanted to tell her that, to take her deeper into my head. I wanted her to understand me. Leslie wouldn't get it. She would admonish me to pray for guidance and direction and she'd be right. I know she'd be right. What was the alternative really? The house record warns us of one place at the edge of the territory to avoid. "NOT INTERESTED. GUN." I can't help but think that the gun fact should come first. We would have to come back when we were sure that Jim Caudle—gun wielder—had moved or died. Today we wouldn't even check.

"Your door," Leslie says. "You can have the last door of the day."

The house is sweet, small with a red tin roof. Someone must love the sound of the rain. Hippies probably. The gravel driveway looks fairly new, and sure enough, there was no record of the house in our files.

Wait for the dog. Some come on strong, yelping and moaning like they've been stranded on Jupiter with a host of unheralded moons. Others yap a quick impotent sound that came when you least expected it, their only surprise attack.

Nothing. Just the pleasant walkway of paver stones, dotted along the path to the door without any discernable pattern, terra-cotta pots full of red geraniums. I like this place. I like the porch and bent-wood furniture, the chunky table in the center with a five-year-old, a toddler on the potty. Another instance when pervs and parents have the same taste in art. But there was nothing pervy about this place. Just solid and permanent.

"Hello," I say to the outline of the woman's face behind the screen door.

"Yes," she says. Her accent says above the Mason-Dixon.

"Good morning," I say. "We are sharing a word from the Bible with our neighbors this morning."

"Your neighbors," the woman says, opening her screen door.

"Yes, ma'am," I smile. Stupid. Stupid. Leslie would never have used a canned line like that.

"You've got a generous idea of neighbors," the woman grins.

"We've been going for a few hours now," I say, not sure of what I'm getting at.

"You must be hot then, let me get you some drinks," the woman starts back into her house. When my mother was a teenager she ironed clothes for Mrs. Rowe, an old white woman in town. When the black man who tended the yard needed a drink of water, Mrs. Rowe would grab the glass from under the sink, bring the water or tea out to him herself. When he was done, she'd rinse the glass out with Clorox water; store it back to its place. Something told me that this woman will not scurry to her kitchen for the Colored glass. Something told me she was for real.

"Oh, no ma'am," I begin. "We are ready to go home. You are actually our last stop today." Why did I say that?

"You are Jehovah's Witnesses, then?"

She got the name right. The number of people who just can't manage the name is astounding. We are the Jehovahs or simply Jehovah or worse the jokes: *Are you a Jehovah's Witness?* they ask. *No kidding, well, where's the accident?*

"I knew some Witnesses a few years back. I worked with one. Nice people. I admire the work you do."

"Thank you," I say.

"I've studied a number of faiths, as a lay person, I mean. The spiritual life is important."

I was right, she is a hippie.

"Well, we want everyone to hear the good news," Leslie chimes in, saving me. I'm blowing this call. "We are always happy to find people of faith in these times. You know that the perilous conditions that we live in have been predicted in scripture," Leslie pulls out her Bible. Some householders recoil, like you've just pulled a gun. *Okay, okay, put the Bible down. You don't want to do anything crazy.*

"Well, I'm not much for organized religion, but I do try to keep an open mind. I'm glad that God is available to everyone. Are you sure you don't want a drink? It is brutal out here."

"No," I say too vehemently. "But I'm Stephanie, nice to meet you."

"Well take this then," the woman pulls out a couple of bills from her jeans' pocket. "I'm Phyllis; I'd like to give you a donation for your work."

"Thank you," Leslie hands the woman some new magazines, taking only one of the dollars from her open hand.

"Okay, so that was Phyllis, new magazines," Leslie writes in her record. "I'm giving you credit for placing those. We'll come back to see her next week." Leslie pretends to be having trouble thinking about what to write in the record, but I know she's trying to figure the best way to make this last call a teaching moment. "Listen, Steph, don't worry if you forget your sermon. I've done it. We all have. As hot as it is I can hardly remember my name. Anyways, you got a magazine placement. That's the important thing. I don't see much working out with Phyllis," Leslie screws her face into a conclusion. "She's fine, nice really, but we're not going anywhere with her." Leslie pauses, trying to find the most encouraging angle. "Of course, Jehovah is the judge, but she seemed to me too comfortable. I don't think we're going anywhere. If you don't stand for something, you'll fall for anything, right?"

But I am hardly listening. All I can think about is I am in love with Phyllis. It is too easy to point to her middle-class manners, the slick magazines with no celebrities on the covers, the coasters on the willow furniture, her kindness at the end of a long hot day. I wanted her. Wouldn't it be great to walk up to someone's house and just say, I am here and I want to be your friend? Kids do it all the time. No misunderstandings. None of that rooting around for larger meaning. Like with God. He has the key, right? He holds the keys to happiness and to life. Why can't we just show up at the door, just ask for them? Why can't I open a door, any door, and He be on the other side with a whole host of Phyllises saying, "Here you go. Enjoy." Even before this. Before being a Jehovah's Witness, I'd been a member of my grandmother's African Methodist Episcopal Church. Another world of dogged believers. Mama Jean preached on lonely dirt roads, black neighborhoods, none of this white man's religion. Black places like Warrior Creek, Freedman, and Dula town. "Do you need to make water?" she'd warn before the services. Because there would be no possibility once we commenced. Remember, no hair-fooling, no gum, no candy, no giggling, no turning to look at the opening door, no smiling, no eye darting, no talking, no tapping of feet or fingers, clapping at up-tempo songs only, but not too vigorously like I've had no home training, no syncopation with the claps—leave that to the elders. No staring at anyone, even the spirit-filled or pitiable. And these are the easy rules, the ones for the very young. *No problem. No problem*, I say with nods. And if you are very good, do it all to your utmost like Noah, just so, you, too, will be rewarded with belief. Oh, Phyllis, to believe anyway. What are you made of? I start my house-to-house record:

> Dear Philip Larkin: I have felt your breath on my heart today. Phyllis said she likes to keep an open mind and I fear this is the beginning. I will not go down the long slide with you, but stay safe, a dirtroader myself. It is safe here. The copse of pines, poplars and weeds years too far gone for bush hogging choke out everything but light. Don't you see that? If you can't, I can't love you. Doesn't scripture say to stay away from bad associates? Friends who will see you dead, all in the name of opening your mind? What about knowing every single thing for sure? What about that?

"A good day. Really good day," Leslie says. "How did you like your first visit to the territory? Different, huh?"

I nod.

"You seem preoccupied. Are you thinking about a certain young man?" Leslie starts the engine, grins at my shock that she takes for proof of her suspicion. My body shudders at the thought. I would see Bobby at the Kingdom

Hall when Leslie drops me off. I'll see him the next morning at the Sunday service and the day after that on the bus. But the thought of his thick fingers anyplace on my body, his short-sleeved dress shirts with the sweaty armpit stains that never seemed to come completely out, the idea of spending one day of life forever with him made me angry. Though I loved him in God's way, I wanted to stomp a mud hole in him. I would say none of it to Leslie. I didn't even want to.

"Maybe," I say.

"I knew it," Leslie wags her finger at me. "Don't wait," she said, "don't wait."

2007

EUDORA WELTY
1909–2001

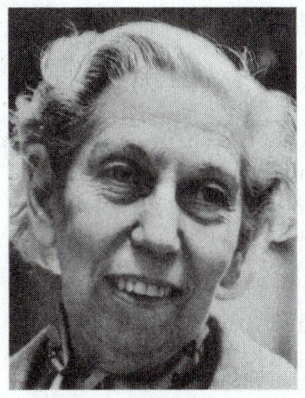

Welty was born in Jackson, Mississippi, where she lived for most of her productive life as the "First Lady of Southern Literature." She received her formal education at the Mississippi State College for Women and the University of Wisconsin, also studying advertising at Columbia University for a brief period. Her early ambitions to be a painter were subordinated by the success of her first book of stories, *A Curtain of Green* (1941). Readers recognized in this and following works a writer who gave full value to the quality and spectacle of her home region and the people she knew best, while at the same time she displayed a cosmopolitan awareness and technical sophistication. Other books of short stories are *The Wide Net* (1943), *The Golden Apples* (1949), *The Bride of the Innisfallen* (1955), *Thirteen Stories* (1965), and the *Collected Stories of Eudora Welty* (1980). Her novels include *Delta Wedding* (1946), *The Ponder Heart* (1954), and *The Optimist's Daughter* (1972), which won a Pulitzer Prize. *One Writer's Beginnings* (1984), based on three lectures Welty delivered at Harvard, is autobiographical. In 1998 the Library of America published a two-volume edition of her selected works, making her the first living author they had published.

Why I Live at the P.O.

I was getting along fine with Mama, Papa-Daddy, and Uncle Rondo until my sister Stella-Rondo just separated from her husband and came back home again. Mr. Whitaker! Of course I went with Mr. Whitaker first, when he first appeared here in China Grove, taking "Pose Yourself" photos, and Stella-Rondo broke us up. Told him I was one-sided. Bigger on one side than the other, which is a deliberate, calculated falsehood: I'm the same. Stella-Rondo is exactly twelve months to the day younger than I am and for that reason she's spoiled.

She's always had anything in the world she wanted and then she'd throw it away. Papa-Daddy give her this gorgeous Add-a-Pearl necklace when she was eight years old and she threw it away playing baseball when she was nine, with only two pearls.

So as soon as she got married and moved away from home the first thing she did was separate! From Mr. Whitaker! This photographer with the pop-eyes she said she trusted. Came home from one of those towns up in Illinois and to our complete surprise brought this child of two.

Mama said she like to make her drop dead for a second. "Here you had this marvelous blonde child and never so much as wrote your mother a word about it," says Mama. "I'm thoroughly ashamed of you." But of course she wasn't.

Stella-Rondo just calmly takes off this *hat,* I wish you could see it. She says, "Why, Mama, Shirley-T.'s adopted, I can prove it."

"How?" says Mama, but all I says was, "H'm!" There I was over the hot stove, trying to stretch two chickens over five people and a completely unexpected child into the bargain without one moment's notice.

"What do you mean—'H'm'?" says Stella-Rondo, and Mama says, "I heard that, Sister."

I said that oh, I didn't mean a thing, only that whoever Shirley-T. was, she was the spit-image of Papa-Daddy if he'd cut off his beard, which of course he'd never do in the world. Papa-Daddy's Mama's papa and sulks.

Stella-Rondo got furious! She said, "Sister, I don't need to tell you you got a lot of nerve and always did have and I'll thank you to make no future reference to my adopted child whatsoever."

"Very well," I said. "Very well, very well. Of course I noticed at once she looks like Mr. Whitaker's side too. That frown. She looks like a cross between Mr. Whitaker and Papa-Daddy."

"Well, all I can say is she isn't."

"She looks exactly like Shirley Temple to me," says Mama, but Shirley-T. just ran away from her.

So the first thing Stella-Rondo did at the table was turn Papa-Daddy against me.

"Papa-Daddy," she says. He was trying to cut up his meat. "Papa-Daddy!" I was taken completely by surprise. Papa-Daddy is about a million years old and's got this long-long beard. "Papa-Daddy, Sister says she fails to understand why you don't cut off your beard."

So Papa-Daddy l-a-y-s down his knife and fork! He's real rich. Mama says he is, he says he isn't. So he says, "Have I heard correctly? You don't understand why I don't cut off my beard?"

"Why," I says, "Papa-Daddy, of course I understand, I did not say any such a thing, the idea!"

He says, "Hussy!"

I says, "Papa-Daddy, you know I wouldn't any more want you to cut off your beard than the man in the moon. It was the farthest thing from my mind! Stella-Rondo sat there and made that up while she was eating breast of chicken."

But he says, "So the postmistress fails to understand why I don't cut off my beard. Which job I got you through my influence with the government. 'Bird's nest'—is that what you call it?"

Not that it isn't the next to smallest P.O. in the entire state of Mississippi.

I says, "Oh, Papa-Daddy," I says, "I didn't say any such a thing, I never dreamed it was a bird's nest, I have always been grateful though this is the next to smallest P.O. in the state of Mississippi, and I do not enjoy being referred to as a hussy by my own grandfather."

But Stella-Rondo says, "Yes, you did say it too. Anybody in the world could of heard you, that had ears."

"Stop right there," says Mama, looking at *me.*

So I pulled my napkin straight back through the napkin ring and left the table.

As soon as I was out of the room Mama says, "Call her back, or she'll starve to death," but Papa-Daddy says, "This is the beard I started growing on the Coast when I was fifteen years old." He would of gone on till nightfall if Shirley-T. hadn't lost the Milky Way she ate in Cairo.

So Papa-Daddy says, "I am going out and lie in the hammock, and you can all sit here and remember my words: I'll never cut off my beard as long as I live, even one inch, and I don't appreciate it in you at all." Passed right by me in the hall and went straight out and got in the hammock.

It would be a holiday. It wasn't five minutes before Uncle Rondo suddenly appeared in the hall in one of Stella-Rondo's flesh-colored kimonos, all cut on the bias, like something Mr. Whitaker probably thought was gorgeous.

"Uncle Rondo!" I says. "I didn't know who that was! Where are you going?"

"Sister," he says, "get out of my way, I'm poisoned."

"If you're poisoned stay away from Papa-Daddy," I says. "Keep out of the hammock. Papa-Daddy will certainly beat you on the head if you come within forty miles of him. He thinks I deliberately said he ought to cut off his beard after he got me the P.O., and I've told him and told him and told him, and he acts like he just don't hear me. Papa-Daddy must of gone stone deaf."

"He picked a fine day to do it then," says Uncle Rondo, and before you could say "Jack Robinson" flew out in the yard.

What he'd really done, he'd drunk another bottle of that prescription. He does it every single Fourth of July as sure as shooting, and it's horribly expensive. Then he falls over in the hammock and snores. So he insisted on zigzagging right on out to the hammock, looking like a half-wit.

Papa-Daddy woke with this horrible yell and right there without moving an inch he tried to turn Uncle Rondo against me. I heard every word he said. Oh, he told Uncle Rondo I didn't learn to read till I was eight years old and he didn't see how in the world I ever got the mail put up at the P.O., much less read it all, and he said if Uncle Rondo could only fathom the lengths he had gone to get me that job! And he said on the other hand he thought Stella-Rondo had a brilliant mind and deserved credit for getting out of town. All the time he was just lying there swinging as pretty as you please and looping out his beard, and poor Uncle Rondo was *pleading* with him to slow down the hammock, it was making him as dizzy as a witch to watch it. But that's what Papa-Daddy likes about a hammock. So Uncle Rondo was too dizzy to get turned against me for the time being. He's Mama's only brother and is a good case of a one-track mind. Ask anybody. A certified pharmacist.

Just then I heard Stella-Rondo raising the upstairs window. While she was married she got this peculiar idea that it's cooler with the windows shut and locked. So she has to raise the window before she can make a soul hear her outdoors.

So she raises the window and says, "*Oh!*" You would have thought she was mortally wounded.

Uncle Rondo and Papa-Daddy didn't even look up, but kept right on with what they were doing. I had to laugh.

I flew up the stairs and threw the door open! I says, "What in the wide world's the matter, Stella-Rondo? You mortally wounded?"

"No," she says, "I am not mortally wounded but I wish you would do me the favor of looking out that window there and telling me what you see."

So I shade my eyes and look out the window.

"I see the front yard," I says.

"Don't you see any human beings?"

"I see Uncle Rondo trying to run Papa-Daddy out of the hammock," I says. "Nothing more. Naturally, it's so suffocating-hot in the house, with all the windows shut and locked, everybody who cares to stay in their right mind will have to go out and get in the hammock before the Fourth of July is over."

"Don't you notice anything different about Uncle Rondo?" asks Stella-Rondo.

"Why, no, except he's got on some terrible-looking flesh-colored contraption I wouldn't be found dead in, is all I can see," I says.

"Never mind, you won't be found dead in it, because it happens to be part of my trousseau, and Mr. Whitaker took several dozen photographs of me in it," says Stella-Rondo. "What on earth could Uncle Rondo *mean* by wearing part of my trousseau out in the broad open daylight without saying so much as 'Kiss my foot,' *knowing* I only got home this morning after my separation and hung my negligee up on the bathroom door, just as nervous as I could be?"

"I'm sure I don't know, and what do you expect me to do about it?" I says. "Jump out the window?"

"No, I expect nothing of the kind. I simply declare that Uncle Rondo looks like a fool in it, that's all," she says. "It makes me sick to my stomach."

"Well, he looks as good as he can," I says. "As good as anybody in reason could." I stood up for Uncle Rondo, please remember. And I said to Stella-Rondo, "I think I would do well not to criticize so freely if I were you and came home with a two-year-old child I had never said a word about, and no explanation whatever about my separation."

"I asked you the instant I entered this house not to refer one more time to my adopted child, and you gave me your word of honor you would not," was all Stella-Rondo would say, and started pulling out every one of her eyebrows with some cheap Kress[1] tweezers.

So I merely slammed the door behind me and went down and made some green-tomato pickle. Somebody had to do it. Of course Mama had turned both the niggers loose; she always said no earthly power could hold one anyway on the Fourth of July, so she wouldn't even try. It turned out that Jaypan fell in the lake and came within a very narrow limit of drowning.

So Mama trots in. Lifts up the lid and says, "H'm! Not very good for your Uncle Rondo in his precarious condition, I must say. Or poor little adopted Shirley-T. Shame on you!"

That made me tired. I says, "Well, Stella-Rondo had better thank her lucky stars it was her instead of me came trotting in with that very peculiar-looking child. Now if it had been me that trotted in from Illinois and brought a peculiar-looking child or two, I shudder to think of the reception I'd of got, much less controlled the diet of an entire family."

---

1. A chain of variety stores.

"But you must remember, Sister, that you were never married to Mr. Whitaker in the first place and didn't go up to Illinois to live," says Mama, shaking a spoon in my face. "If you had I would of been just as overjoyed to see you and your little adopted girl as I was to see Stella-Rondo, when you wound up with your separation and came on back home."

"You would not," I says.

"Don't contradict me, I would," says Mama.

But I said she couldn't convince me though she talked till she was blue in the face. Then I said, "Besides, you know as well as I do that that child is not adopted."

"She most certainly is adopted," says Mama, stiff as a poker.

I says, "Why, Mama, Stella-Rondo had her just as sure as anything in this world, and just too stuck up to admit it."

"Why, Sister," said Mama. "Here I thought we were going to have a pleasant Fourth of July, and you start right out not believing a word your own baby sister tells you!"

"Just like Cousin Annie Flo. Went to her grave denying the facts of life," I reminded Mama.

"I told you if you ever mentioned Annie Flo's name I'd slap your face," says Mama, and slaps my face.

"All right, you wait and see," I says.

"I," says Mama, "I prefer to take my children's word for anything when it's humanly possible." You ought to see Mama, she weighs two hundred pounds and has real tiny feet.

Just then something perfectly horrible occurred to me.

"Mama," I says, "can that child talk?" I simply had to whisper! "Mama, I wonder if that child can be—you know—in any way? Do you realize?" I says, "that she hasn't spoke one single, solitary word to a human being up to this minute? This is the way she looks," I says, and I looked like this.

Well, Mama and I just stood there and stared at each other. It was horrible!

"I remember well that Joe Whitaker frequently drank like a fish," says Mama. "I believed to my soul he drank *chemicals.*" And without another word she marches to the foot of the stairs and calls Stella-Rondo.

"Stella-Rondo? O-o-o-o-o! Stella-Rondo!"

"What?" says Stella-Rondo from upstairs. Not even the grace to get up off the bed.

"Can that child of yours talk?" asks Mama.

Stella-Rondo says, "Can she what?"

"Talk! Talk!" says Mama. "Burdyburdyburdyburdy!"

So Stella-Rondo yells back, "Who says she can't talk?"

"Sister says so," says Mama.

"You didn't have to tell me, I know whose word of honor don't mean a thing in this house," says Stella-Rondo.

And in a minute the loudest Yankee voice I ever heard in my life yells out, "OE'm Pop-OE the Sailor-r-r-r Ma-a-an!" and then somebody jumps up and down in the upstairs hall. In another second the house would of fallen down.

"Not only talks, she can tap-dance!" calls Stella-Rondo. "Which is more than some people I won't name can do."

"Why, the little precious darling thing!" Mama says, so surprised. "Just as smart as she can be!" Starts talking baby talk right there. Then she turns on me. "Sister, you ought to be thoroughly ashamed! Run upstairs this instant and apologize to Stella-Rondo and Shirley-T."

"Apologize for what?" I says. "I merely wondered if the child was normal, that's all. Now that she's proved she is, why, I have nothing further to say."

But Mama just turned on her heel and flew out, furious. She ran right upstairs and hugged the baby. She believed it was adopted. Stella-Rondo hadn't done a thing but turn her against me from upstairs while I stood there helpless over the hot stove. So that made Mama, Papa-Daddy, and the baby all on Stella-Rondo's side.

Next, Uncle Rondo.

I must say that Uncle Rondo has been marvelous to me at various times in the past and I was completely unprepared to be made to jump out of my skin, the way it turned out. Once Stella-Rondo did something perfectly horrible to him—broke a chain letter from Flanders Field[2]—and he took the radio back he had given her and gave it to me. Stella-Rondo was furious! For six months we all had to call her Stella instead of Stella-Rondo, or she wouldn't answer. I always thought Uncle Rondo had all the brains of the entire family. Another time he sent me to Mammoth Cave[3] with all expenses paid.

But this would be the day he was drinking that prescription, the Fourth of July.

So at supper Stella-Rondo speaks up and says she thinks Uncle Rondo ought to try to eat a little something. So finally Uncle Rondo said he would try a little cold biscuits and ketchup, but that was all. So *she* brought it to him.

"Do you think it wise to disport with ketchup in Stella-Rondo's flesh-colored kimono?" I says. Trying to be considerate! If Stella-Rondo couldn't watch out for her trousseau, somebody had to.

"Any objections?" asks Uncle Rondo, just about to pour out all of the ketchup.

"Don't mind what she says, Uncle Rondo," says Stella-Rondo. "Sister has been devoting this solid afternoon to sneering out my bedroom window at the way you look."

"What's that?" says Uncle Rondo. Uncle Rondo has got the most terrible temper in the world. Anything is liable to make him tear the house down if it comes at the wrong time.

So Stella-Rondo says, "Sister says, 'Uncle Rondo certainly does look like a fool in that pink kimono!'"

Do you remember who it was really said that?

Uncle Rondo spills out all the ketchup and jumps out of his chair and tears off the kimono and throws it down on the dirty floor and puts his foot on it. It had to be sent all the way to Jackson to the cleaners and repleated.

"So that's your opinion of your Uncle Rondo, is it?" he says. "I look like a fool, do I? Well, that's the last straw. A whole day in this house with nothing to do, and then to hear you come out with a remark like that behind my back!"

---

2. American military cemetery in Belgium, established after World War I. **3.** Popular tourist attraction in Kentucky.

"I didn't say any such thing, Uncle Rondo," I says, "and I'm not saying who did, either. Why, I think you look all right. Just try to take care of yourself and not talk and eat at the same time," I says. "I think you better go lie down."

"Lie down my foot," says Uncle Rondo. I ought to of known by that he was fixing to do something perfectly horrible.

So he didn't do anything that night in the precarious state he was in—just played Casino[4] with Mama and Stella-Rondo and Shirley-T. and gave Shirley-T. a nickel with a head on both sides. It tickled her nearly to death, and she called him "Papa." But at 6:30 A.M. the next morning, he threw a whole five-cent package of some unsold one-inch firecrackers from the store as hard as he could into my bedroom and they every one went off. Not one bad one in the string. Anybody else, there'd be one that wouldn't go off.

Well, I'm just terrible susceptible to noise of any kind, the doctor has always told me I was the most sensitive person he had ever seen in his whole life, and I was simply prostrated. I couldn't eat! People tell me they heard it as far as the cemetery, and old Aunt Jep Patterson, that had been holding her own so good, thought it was Judgment Day and she was going to meet her whole family. It's usually so quiet here.

And I'll tell you it didn't take me any longer than a minute to make up my mind what to do. There I was with the whole entire house on Stella-Rondo's side and turned against me. If I have anything at all I have pride.

So I just decided I'd go straight down to the P.O. There's plenty of room there in the back, I says to myself.

Well! I made no bones about letting the family catch on to what I was up to. I didn't try to conceal it.

The first thing they knew, I marched in where they were all playing Old Maid and pulled the electric oscillating fan out by the plug, and everything got real hot. Next I snatched the pillow I'd done the needlepoint on right off the davenport from behind Papa-Daddy. He went "Ugh!" I beat Stella-Rondo up the stairs and finally found my charm bracelet in her bureau drawer under a picture of Nelson Eddy.[5]

"So that's the way the land lies," says Uncle Rondo. There he was, piecing on the ham. "Well, Sister, I'll be glad to donate my army cot if you got any place to set it up, providing you'll leave right this minute and let me get some peace." Uncle Rondo was in France.

"Thank you kindly for the cot and 'peace' is hardly the word I would select if I had to resort to firecrackers at 6:30 A.M. in a young girl's bedroom," I says to him. "And as to where I intend to go, you seem to forget my position as postmistress of China Grove, Mississippi," I says. "I've always got the P.O."

Well, that made them all sit up and take notice.

I went out front and started digging up some four-o'clocks to plant around the P.O.

"Ah-ah-ah!" says Mama, raising the window. "Those happen to be my four-o'clocks. Everything planted in that star is mine. I've never known you to make anything grow in your life."

---

4. Card game for two or more persons. **5.** Opera singer (1901–1967), popular along with Jeanette McDonald as "America's Singing Sweethearts" in many Hollywood musicals of the 1930s and 1940s.

"Very well," I says. "But I take the fern. Even you, Mama, can't stand there and deny that I'm the one watered that fern. And I happen to know where I can send in a box top and get a packet of one thousand mixed seeds, no two the same kind, free."

"Oh, where?" Mama wants to know.

But I says, "Too late. You 'tend to your house, and I'll 'tend to mine. You hear things like that all the time if you know how to listen to the radio. Perfectly marvelous offers. Get anything you want free."

So I hope to tell you I marched in and got that radio, and they could of all bit a nail in two, especially Stella-Rondo, that it used to belong to, and she well knew she couldn't get it back, I'd sue for it like a shot. And I very politely took the sewing-machine motor I helped pay the most on to give Mama for Christmas back in 1929, and a good big calendar, with the first-aid remedies on it. The thermometer and the Hawaiian ukulele certainly were rightfully mine, and I stood on the step-ladder and got all my watermelon-rind preserves and every fruit and vegetable I'd put up, every jar. Then I began to pull the tacks out of the bluebird wall vases on the archway to the dining room.

"Who told you you could have those, Miss Priss?" says Mama, fanning as hard as she could.

"I bought 'em and I'll keep track of 'em," I says. "I'll tack 'em up one on each side of the post-office window, and you can see 'em when you come to ask me for your mail, if you're so dead to see 'em."

"Not I! I'll never darken the door to that post office again if I live to be a hundred," Mama says. "Ungrateful child! After all the money we spent on you at the Normal."[6]

"Me either," says Stella-Rondo. "You can just let my mail lie there and *rot*, for all I care. I'll never come and relieve you of a single, solitary piece."

"I should worry," I says. "And who you think's going to sit down and write you all those big fat letters and postcards, by the way? Mr. Whitaker? Just because he was the only man ever dropped down in China Grove and you got him—unfairly—is he going to sit down and write you a lengthy correspondence after you come home giving no rhyme nor reason whatsoever for your separation and no explanation for the presence of that child? I may not have your brilliant mind, but I fail to see it."

So Mama says, "Sister, I've told you a thousand times that Stella-Rondo simply got homesick, and this child is far too big to be hers," and she says, "Now, why don't you just sit down and play Casino?"

Then Shirley-T. sticks out her tongue at me in this perfectly horrible way. She has no more manners than the man in the moon. I told her she was going to cross her eyes like that some day and they'd stick.

"It's too late to stop me now," I says. "You should have tried that yesterday. I'm going to the P.O. and the only way you can possibly see me is to visit me there."

So Papa-Daddy says, "You'll never catch me setting foot in that post office, even if I should take a notion into my head to write a letter some place." He says, "I won't have you reachin' out of that little old window with a pair of shears and cuttin' off any beard of mine. I'm too smart for you!"

---

6. That is, normal school (teachers' college).

"We all are," says Stella-Rondo.

But I said, "If you're so smart, where's Mr. Whitaker?"

So then Uncle Rondo says, "I'll thank you from now on to stop reading all the orders I get on postcards and telling everybody in China Grove what you think is the matter with them," but I says, "I draw my own conclusions and will continue in the future to draw them." I says, "If people want to write their innermost secrets on penny postcards, there's nothing in the wide world you can do about it, Uncle Rondo."

"And if you think we'll ever *write* another postcard you're sadly mistaken," says Mama.

"Cutting off your nose to spite your face then," I says. "But if you're all determined to have no more to do with the U.S. mail, think of this: What will Stella-Rondo do now, if she wants to tell Mr. Whitaker to come after her?"

"Wah!" says Stella-Rondo. I knew she'd cry. She had a conniption fit right there in the kitchen.

"It will be interesting to see how long she holds out," I says. "And now—I am leaving."

"Good-bye," says Uncle Rondo.

"Oh, I declare," says Mama, "to think that a family of mine should quarrel on the Fourth of July, or the day after, over Stella-Rondo leaving old Mr. Whitaker and having the sweetest little adopted child! It looks like we'd all be glad!"

"Wah!" says Stella-Rondo, and has a fresh conniption fit.

"He left *her*—you mark my words," I says. "That's Mr. Whitaker. I know Mr. Whitaker. After all, I knew him first. I said from the beginning he'd up and leave her. I foretold every single thing that's happened."

"Where did he go?" asks Mama.

"Probably to the North Pole, if he knows what's good for him," I says.

But Stella-Rondo just bawled and wouldn't say another word. She flew to her room and slammed the door.

"Now look what you've gone and done, Sister," says Mama. "You go apologize."

"I haven't the time, I'm leaving," I says.

"Well, what are you waiting around for?" asks Uncle Rondo.

So I just picked up the kitchen clock and marched off, without saying, "Kiss my foot," or anything, and never did tell Stella-Rondo good-bye.

There was a nigger girl going along on a little wagon right in front.

"Nigger girl," I says, "come help me haul these things down the hill, I'm going to live in the post office."

Took her nine trips in her express wagon. Uncle Rondo came out on the porch and threw her a nickel.

And that's the last I've laid eyes on any of my family or my family laid eyes on me for five solid days and nights. Stella-Rondo may be telling the most horrible tales in the world about Mr. Whitaker, but I haven't heard them. As I tell everybody, I draw my own conclusions.

But oh, I like it here. It's ideal, as I've been saying. You see, I've got everything cater-cornered, the way I like it. Hear the radio? All the war news. Radio, sewing machine, book ends, ironing board and that great big piano lamp—peace, that's what I like. Butter-bean vines planted all along the front where the strings are.

Of course, there's not much mail. My family are naturally the main people in China Grove, and if they prefer to vanish from the face of the earth, for all the mail they get or the mail they write, why, I'm not going to open my mouth. Some of the folks here in town are taking up for me and some turned against me. I know which is which. There are always people who will quit buying stamps just to get on the right side of Papa-Daddy.

But here I am, and here I'll stay. I want the world to know I'm happy.

And if Stella-Rondo should come to me this minute, on bended knees, and attempt to explain the incidents of her life with Mr. Whitaker, I'd simply put my fingers in both my ears and refuse to listen.

1941

A Worn Path

It was December—a bright frozen day in the early morning. Far out in the country there was an old Negro woman with her head tied in a red rag, coming along a path through the pinewoods. Her name was Phoenix Jackson. She was very old and small and she walked slowly in the dark pine shadows, moving a little from side to side in her steps, with the balanced heaviness and lightness of a pendulum in a grandfather clock. She carried a thin, small cane made from an umbrella, and with this she kept tapping the frozen earth in front of her. This made a grave and persistent noise in the still air, that seemed meditative like the chirping of a solitary little bird.

She wore a dark striped dress reaching down to her shoe tops, and an equally long apron of bleached sugar sacks, with a full pocket: all neat and tidy, but every time she took a step she might have fallen over her shoelaces, which dragged from her unlaced shoes. She looked straight ahead. Her eyes were blue with age. Her skin had a pattern all its own of numberless branching wrinkles and as though a whole little tree stood in the middle of her forehead, but a golden color ran underneath, and the two knobs of her cheeks were illumined by a yellow burning under the dark. Under the red rag her hair came down on her neck in the frailest of ringlets, still black, and with an odor like copper.

Now and then there was a quivering in the thicket. Old Phoenix said, "Out of my way, all you foxes, owls, beetles, jack rabbits, coons and wild animals! . . . Keep out from under these feet, little bob-whites. . . . Keep the big wild hogs out of my path. Don't let none of those come running my direction. I got a long way." Under her small black-freckled hand her cane, limber as a buggy whip, would switch at the brush as if to rouse up any hiding things.

On she went. The woods were deep and still. The sun made the pine needles almost too bright to look at, up where the wind rocked. The cones dropped as light as feathers. Down in the hollow was the mourning dove—it was not too late for him.

The path ran up a hill. "Seem like there is chains about my feet, time I get this far," she said, in the voice of argument old people keep to use with themselves. "Something always take a hold of me on this hill—pleads I should stay."

After she got to the top she turned and gave a full, severe look behind her where she had come. "Up through pines," she said at length. "Now down through oaks."

Her eyes opened their widest, and she started down gently. But before she got to the bottom of the hill a bush caught her dress.

Her fingers were busy and intent, but her skirts were full and long, so that before she could pull them free in one place they were caught in another. It was not possible to allow the dress to tear. "I in the thorny bush," she said. "Thorns, you doing your appointed work. Never want to let folks pass, no sir. Old eyes thought you was a pretty little *green* bush."

Finally, trembling all over, she stood free, and after a moment dared to stoop for her cane.

"Sun so high!" she cried, leaning back and looking, while the thick tears went over her eyes. "The time getting all gone here."

At the foot of this hill was a place where a log was laid across the creek.

"Now comes the trial," said Phoenix.

Putting her right foot out, she mounted the log and shut her eyes. Lifting her skirt, leveling her cane fiercely before her, like a festival figure in some parade, she began to march across. Then she opened her eyes and she was safe on the other side.

"I wasn't as old as I thought," she said.

But she sat down to rest. She spread her skirts on the bank around her and folded her hands over her knees. Up above her was a tree in a pearly cloud of mistletoe. She did not dare to close her eyes, and when a little boy brought her a plate with a slice of marble-cake on it she spoke to him. "That would be acceptable," she said. But when she went to take it there was just her own hand in the air.

So she left that tree, and had to go through a barbed-wire fence. There she had to creep and crawl, spreading her knees and stretching her fingers like a baby trying to climb the steps. But she talked loudly to herself: she could not let her dress be torn now, so late in the day, and she could not pay for having her arm or her leg sawed off if she got caught fast where she was.

At last she was safe through the fence and risen up out in the clearing. Big dead trees, like black men with one arm, were standing in the purple stalks of the withered cotton field. There sat a buzzard.

"Who you watching?"

In the furrow she made her way along.

"Glad this not the season for bulls," she said, looking sideways, "and the good Lord made his snakes to curl up and sleep in the winter. A pleasure I don't see no two-headed snake coming around that tree, where it come once. It took a while to get by him, back in the summer."

She passed through the old cotton and went into a field of dead corn. It whispered and shook and was taller than her head. "Through the maze now," she said, for there was no path.

Then there was something tall, black, and skinny there, moving before her.

At first she took it for a man. It could have been a man dancing in the field. But she stood still and listened, and it did not make a sound. It was as silent as a ghost.

"Ghost," she said sharply, "who be you the ghost of? For I have heard of nary death close by."

But there was no answer—only the ragged dancing in the wind.

She shut her eyes, reached out her hand, and touched a sleeve. She found a coat and inside that an emptiness, cold as ice.

"You scarecrow," she said. Her face lighted. "I ought to be shut up for good," she said with laughter. "My senses is gone. I too old. I the oldest people I ever know. Dance, old scarecrow," she said, "while I dancing with you."

She kicked her foot over the furrow, and with mouth drawn down, shook her head once or twice in a little strutting way. Some husks blew down and whirled in streamers about her skirts.

Then she went on, parting her way from side to side with the cane, through the whispering field. At last she came to the end, to a wagon track where the silver grass blew between the red ruts. The quail were walking around like pullets, seeming all dainty and unseen.

"Walk pretty," she said. "This the easy place. This the easy going."

She followed the track, swaying through the quiet bare fields, through the little strings of trees silver in their dead leaves, past cabins silver from weather, with the doors and windows boarded shut, all like old women under a spell sitting there. "I walking in their sleep," she said, nodding her head vigorously.

In a ravine she went where a spring was silently flowing through a hollow log. Old Phoenix bent and drank. "Sweet-gum makes the water sweet," she said, and drank more. "Nobody know who made this well, for it was here when I was born."

The track crossed a swampy part where the moss hung as white as lace from every limb. "Sleep on, alligators, and blow your bubbles." Then the track went into the road.

Deep, deep the road went down between the high green-colored banks. Overhead the live-oaks met, and it was as dark as a cave.

A black dog with a lolling tongue came up out of the weeds by the ditch. She was meditating, and not ready, and when he came at her she only hit him a little with her cane. Over she went in the ditch, like a little puff of milkweed.

Down there, her senses drifted away. A dream visited her, and she reached her hand up, but nothing reached down and gave her a pull. So she lay there and presently went to talking. "Old woman," she said to herself, "that black dog come up out of the weeds to stall you off, and now there he sitting on his fine tail, smiling at you."

A white man finally came along and found her—a hunter, a young man, with his dog on a chain.

"Well, Granny!" he laughed. "What are you doing there?"

"Lying on my back like a June-bug waiting to be turned over, mister," she said, reaching up her hand.

He lifted her up, gave her a swing in the air, and set her down. "Anything broken, Granny?"

"No sir, them old dead weeds is springy enough," said Phoenix, when she had got her breath. "I thank you for your trouble."

"Where do you live, Granny?" he asked, while the two dogs were growling at each other.

"Away back yonder, sir, behind the ridge. You can't even see it from here."

"On your way home?"

"No sir, I going to town."

"Why, that's too far! That's as far as I walk when I come out myself, and I get something for my trouble." He patted the stuffed bag he carried, and there hung down a little closed claw. It was one of the bob-whites, with its beak hooked bitterly to show it was dead. "Now you go on home, Granny!"

"I bound to go to town, mister," said Phoenix. "The time come around."

He gave another laugh, filling the whole landscape. "I know you old colored people! Wouldn't miss going to town to see Santa Claus!"

But something held old Phoenix very still. The deep lines in her face went into a fierce and different radiation. Without warning, she had seen with her own eyes a flashing nickel fall out of the man's pocket onto the ground.

"How old are you, Granny?" he was saying.

"There's no telling, mister," she said, "no telling."

Then she gave a little cry and clapped her hands and said, "Git on away from here, dog! Look! Look at that dog!" She laughed as if in admiration. "He ain't scared of nobody. He a big black dog." She whispered, "Sic him!"

"Watch me get rid of that cur," said the man. "Sic him, Pete! Sic him!"

Phoenix heard the dogs fighting, and heard the man running and throwing sticks. She even heard a gunshot. But she was slowly bending forward by that time, further and further forward, the lids stretched down over her eyes, as if she were doing this in her sleep. Her chin was lowered almost to her knees. The yellow palm of her hand came out from the fold of her apron. Her fingers slid down and along the ground under the piece of money with the grace and care they would have in lifting an egg from under a setting hen. Then she slowly straightened up, she stood erect, and the nickel was in her apron pocket. A bird flew by. Her lips moved. "God watching me the whole time. I come to stealing."

The man came back, and his own dog panted about them. "Well, I scared him off that time," he said, and then he laughed and lifted his gun and pointed it at Phoenix.

She stood straight and faced him.

"Doesn't the gun scare you?" he said, still pointing it.

"No, sir, I seen plenty go off closer by, in my day, and for less than what I done," she said, holding utterly still.

He smiled, and shouldered the gun. "Well, Granny," he said, "you must be a hundred years old, and scared of nothing. I'd give you a dime if I had any money with me. But you take my advice and stay home, and nothing will happen to you."

"I bound to go on my way, mister," said Phoenix. She inclined her head in the red rag. Then they went in different directions, but she could hear the gun shooting again and again over the hill.

She walked on. The shadows hung from the oak trees to the road like curtains. Then she smelled wood-smoke, and smelled the river, and she saw a steeple and the cabins on their steep steps. Dozens of little black children whirled around her. There ahead was Natchez shining. Bells were ringing. She walked on.

In the paved city it was Christmas time. There were red and green electric lights strung and crisscrossed everywhere, and all turned on in the daytime. Old Phoenix would have been lost if she had not distrusted her eyesight and depended on her feet to know where to take her.

She paused quietly on the sidewalk where people were passing by. A lady came along in the crowd, carrying an armful of red-, green- and silver-wrapped presents; she gave off perfume like the red roses in hot summer, and Phoenix stopped her.

"Please, missy, will you lace up my shoe?" She held up her foot.

"What do you want, Grandma?"

"See my shoe," said Phoenix. "Do all right for out in the country, but wouldn't look right to go in a big building."

"Stand still then, Grandma," said the lady. She put her packages down on the sidewalk beside her and laced and tied both shoes tightly.

"Can't lace 'em with a cane," said Phoenix. "Thank you, missy. I doesn't mind asking a nice lady to tie up my shoe, when I gets out on the street."

Moving slowly and from side to side, she went into the big building, and into the tower of steps, where she walked up and around and around until her feet knew to stop.

She entered a door, and there she saw nailed up on the wall the document that had been stamped with the gold seal and framed in the gold frame, which matched the dream that was hung up in her head.

"Here I be," she said. There was a fixed and ceremonial stiffness over her body.

"A charity case, I suppose," said an attendant who sat at the desk before her.

But Phoenix only looked above her head. There was sweat on her face, the wrinkles in her skin shone like a bright net.

"Speak up, Grandma," the woman said. "What's your name? We must have your history, you know. Have you been here before? What seems to be the trouble with you?"

Old Phoenix only gave a twitch to her face as if a fly were bothering her.

"Are you deaf?" cried the attendant.

But then the nurse came in.

"Oh, that's just old Aunt Phoenix," she said. "She doesn't come for herself— she has a little grandson. She makes these trips just as regular as clockwork. She lives away back off the Old Natchez Trace."[1] She bent down. "Well, Aunt Phoenix, why don't you just take a seat? We won't keep you standing after your long trip." She pointed.

The old woman sat down, bolt upright in the chair.

"Now, how is the boy?" asked the nurse.

Old Phoenix did not speak.

"I said, how is the boy?"

But Phoenix only waited and stared straight ahead, her face very solemn and withdrawn into rigidity.

---

1. Historic road from Natchez, Mississippi, to Nashville, Tennessee.

"Is his throat any better?" asked the nurse. "Aunt Phoenix, don't you hear me? Is your grandson's throat any better since the last time you came for the medicine?"

With her hands on her knees, the old woman waited, silent, erect and motionless, just as if she were in armor.

"You mustn't take up our time this way, Aunt Phoenix," the nurse said. "Tell us quickly about your grandson, and get it over. He isn't dead, is he?"

At last there came a flicker and then a flame of comprehension across her face, and she spoke.

"My grandson. It was my memory had left me. There I sat and forgot why I made my long trip."

"Forgot?" The nurse frowned. "After you came so far?"

Then Phoenix was like an old woman begging a dignified forgiveness for waking up frightened in the night. "I never did go to school, I was too old at the Surrender,"[2] she said in a soft voice. "I'm an old woman without an education. It was my memory fail me. My little grandson, he is just the same, and I forgot it in the coming."

"Throat never heals, does it?" said the nurse, speaking in a loud, sure voice to old Phoenix. By now she had a card with something written on it, a little list. "Yes. Swallowed lye. When was it?—January—two-three years ago—"

Phoenix spoke unmasked now. "No, missy, he not dead, he just the same. Every little while his throat begin to close up again, and he not able to swallow. He not get his breath. He not able to help himself. So the time come around, and I go on another trip for the soothing medicine."

"All right. The doctor said as long as you came to get it, you could have it," said the nurse. "But it's an obstinate case."

"My little grandson, he sit up there in the house all wrapped up, waiting by himself," Phoenix went on. "We is the only two left in the world. He suffer and it don't seem to put him back at all. He got a sweet look. He going to last. He wear a little patch quilt and peep out holding his mouth open like a little bird. I remembers so plain now. I not going to forget him again, no, the whole enduring time. I could tell him from all the others in creation."

"All right." The nurse was trying to hush her now. She brought her a bottle of medicine. "Charity," she said, making a check mark in a book.

Old Phoenix held the bottle close to her eyes, and then carefully put it into her pocket.

"I thank you," she said.

"It's Christmas time, Grandma," said the attendant. "Could I give you a few pennies out of my purse?"

"Five pennies is a nickel," said Phoenix stiffly.

"Here's a nickel," said the attendant.

Phoenix rose carefully and held out her hand. She received the nickel and then fished the other nickel out of her pocket and laid it beside the new one. She stared at her palm closely, with her head on one side.

Then she gave a tap with her cane on the floor.

---

2. The surrender of General Robert E. Lee (1807–1870) of the Confederacy on April 9, 1865, to General Ulysses S. Grant (1822–1885) of the Union, thus ending the Civil War.

"This is what come to me to do," she said. "I going to the store and buy my child a little windmill they sells, made out of paper. He going to find it hard to believe there such a thing in the world. I'll march myself back where he waiting, holding it straight up in this hand."

She lifted her free hand, gave a little nod, turned around, and walked out of the doctor's office. Then her slow step began on the stairs, going down.

1941

RELATED:

—Welty, An Interview, p. 1736
—Susan Dodd on "A Worn Path," p. 1760

EDITH WHARTON
1862–1937

Edith Wharton's novels and stories continue to attract new readers and wider critical treatment even decades after her death. Born into wealth, she married a banker, Edward Wharton, and after a nervous collapse, turned seriously to the writing that would make her reputation. She and Wharton were divorced in 1913, and she spent the rest of her life in France. She wrote ghost tales and ironic novels and stories set for the most part in the place where she had lived her life—the upper-class social circles of old New York. Yet there is nothing remotely haughty about her work: one sees in it the vision of a compassionate but tough social critic and, in books like *The House of Mirth* (1905), *Ethan Frome* (1911), *The Age of Innocence* (1920), and *Old New York* (1924), a profoundly tragic sensibility. That sensibility also included an unerring sense of the comedic, as is abundantly clear in the sly humor of "Xingu."

Xingu

I

Mrs. Ballinger is one of the ladies who pursue Culture in bands, as though it were dangerous to meet alone. To this end she had founded the Lunch Club, an association composed of herself and several other indomitable huntresses of erudition. The Lunch Club after three or four winters of lunching and debate, had acquired such local distinction that the entertainment of distinguished strangers became one of its accepted functions; in recognition of which it duly extended to the celebrated "Osric Dane," on the day of her arrival in Hillbridge, an invitation to be present at the next meeting.

The club was to meet at Mrs. Ballinger's. The other members, behind her back, were of one voice in deploring her unwillingness to cede her rights in favor of Mrs. Plinth, whose house made a more impressive setting for the entertainment of celebrities; while, as Mrs. Leveret observed, there was always the picture-gallery to fall back on.

Mrs. Plinth made no secret of sharing this view. She had always regarded it as one of her obligations to entertain the Lunch Club's distinguished guests. Mrs. Plinth was almost as proud of her obligations as she was of her picture-gallery; she was in fact fond of implying that the one possession implied the other, and that only a woman of her wealth could afford to live up to a standard as high as that which she had set herself. An all-round sense of duty, roughly adaptable to various ends, was, in her opinion, all that Providence exacted of the more humbly stationed; but the power which had predestined Mrs. Plinth to keep a footman clearly intended her to maintain an equally specialized staff of responsibilities. It was the more to be regretted that Mrs. Ballinger, whose obligations to society were bounded by the narrow scope of two parlour-maids, should have been so tenacious of the right to entertain Osric Dane.

The question of that lady's reception had for a month past profoundly moved the members of the Lunch Club. It was not that they felt themselves unequal to the task, but that their sense of the opportunity plunged them into the agreeable uncertainty of the lady who weighs the alternatives of a well-stocked wardrobe. If such subsidiary members as Mrs. Leveret were fluttered by the thought of exchanging ideas with the author of "The Wings of Death," no forebodings disturbed the conscious adequacy of Mrs. Plinth, Mrs. Ballinger, and Miss Van Vluyck. "The Wings of Death" had, in fact, at Miss Van Vluyck's suggestion, been chosen as the subject of discussion at the last club meeting, and each member had thus been enabled to express her own opinion or to appropriate whatever sounded well in the comments of the others.

Mrs. Roby alone had abstained from profiting by the opportunity; but it was now openly recognised that, as a member of the Lunch Club, Mrs. Roby was a failure. "It all comes," as Miss Van Vluyck put it, "of accepting a woman on a man's estimation." Mrs. Roby, returning to Hillbridge from a prolonged sojourn in exotic lands—the other ladies no longer took the trouble to remember where—had been heralded by the distinguished biologist, Professor Foreland, as the most agreeable woman he had ever met; and the members of the Lunch Club, impressed by an encomium that carried the weight of a diploma, and rashly assuming that the Professor's social sympathies would follow the line of his professional bent, had seized the chance of annexing a biological member. Their disillusionment was complete. At Miss Van Vluyck's first off-hand mention of the pterodactyl Mrs. Roby had confusedly murmured: "I know so little about metres—"[1] and after that painful betrayal of incompetence she had prudently withdrawn from further participation in the mental gymnastics of the club.

"I suppose she flattered him," Miss Van Vluyck summed up—"or else it's the way she does her hair."

The dimensions of Miss Van Vluyck's dining-room having restricted the membership of the club to six, the non-conductiveness of one member was a serious obstacle to the exchange of ideas, and some wonder had already been expressed that Mrs. Roby should care to live, as it were, on the intellectual bounty of the others. This feeling was increased by the discovery that she had not yet read "The Wings of Death." She owned to having heard the name of Osric Dane; but that—incredible as it appeared—was the extent of her acquaintance with the celebrated novelist. The ladies could not conceal their surprise; but Mrs. Ballinger, whose pride in the club made her wish to put even Mrs. Roby in the best possible light, gently insinuated that, though she had not had time to acquaint herself with "The Wings of Death," she must at least be familiar with its equally remarkable predecessor, "The Supreme Instant."

---

1. Mrs. Roby's confusion is due to the root word *dactyl* (Greek for "finger"), which not only is contained in "pterodactyl" (a kind of dinosaur) but is also a term for a metrical "foot" in poetry—a stressed syllable followed by two unstressed, as in the word *prudently*.

Mrs. Roby wrinkled her sunny brows in a conscientious effort of memory, as a result of which she recalled that, oh, yes, she *had* seen the book at her brother's, when she was staying with him in Brazil, and had even carried it off to read one day on a boating party; but they had all got to shying things at each other in the boat, and the book had gone overboard, so she had never had the chance—

The picture evoked by this anecdote did not increase Mrs. Roby's credit with the club, and there was a painful pause, which was broken by Mrs. Plinth's remarking: "I can understand that, with all your other pursuits, you should not find much time for reading; but I should have thought you might at least have *got up* 'The Wings of Death' before Osric Dane's arrival."

Mrs. Roby took this rebuke good-humouredly. She had meant, she owned, to glance through the book; but she had been so absorbed in a novel of Trollope's that—

"No one reads Trollope now," Mrs. Ballinger interrupted.

Mrs. Roby looked pained. "I'm only just beginning," she confessed.

"And does he interest you?" Mrs. Plinth enquired.

"He amuses me."

"Amusement," said Mrs. Plinth, "is hardly what I look for in my choice of books."

"Oh, certainly, 'The Wings of Death' is not amusing," ventured Mrs. Leveret, whose manner of putting forth an opinion was like that of an obliging salesman with a variety of other styles to submit if his first selection does not suit.

"Was it *meant* to be?" enquired Mrs. Plinth, who was fond of asking questions that she permitted no one but herself to answer. "Assuredly not."

"Assuredly not—that is what I was going to say," assented Mrs. Leveret, hastily rolling up her opinion and reaching for another. "It was meant to—to elevate."

Miss Van Vluyck adjusted her spectacles as though they were the black cap of condemnation. "I hardly see," she interposed, "how a book steeped in the bitterest pessimism can be said to elevate, however much it may instruct."

"I meant of course, to instruct," said Mrs. Leveret, flurried by the unexpected distinction between two terms which she had supposed to be synonymous. Mrs. Leveret's enjoyment of the Lunch Club was frequently marred by such surprise; and not knowing her own value to the other ladies as a mirror for their mental complacency she was sometimes troubled by a doubt of her worthiness to join in their debates. It was only the fact of having a dull sister who thought her clever that saved her from a sense of hopeless inferiority.

"Do they get married in the end?" Mrs. Roby interposed.

"They—who?" the Lunch Club collectively exclaimed.

"Why, the girl and man. It's a novel, isn't it? I always think that's the one thing that matters. If they're parted it spoils my dinner."

Mrs. Plinth and Mrs. Ballinger exchanged scandalised glances, and the latter said: "I should hardly advise you to read 'The Wings of Death' in that spirit. For my part, when there are so many books one *has* to read, I wonder how any one can find time for those that are merely amusing."

"The beautiful part of it," Laura Glyde murmured, "is surely just this—that no one can tell *how* 'The Wings of Death' ends. Osric Dane, overcome by the awful significance of her own meaning, has mercifully veiled it—perhaps even from herself—as Apelles,[2] in representing the sacrifice of Iphigenia, veiled the face of Agamemnon."

"What's that? Is it poetry?" whispered Mrs. Leveret to Mrs. Plinth, who, disdaining a definite reply, said coldly: "You should look it up. I always make it a point to look things up." Her tone added—"though I might easily have it done for me by the footman."

"I was about to say," Miss Van Vluyck resumed, "that it must always be a question whether a book *can* instruct unless it elevates."

"Oh—" murmured Mrs. Leveret now feeling herself hopelessly astray.

"I don't know," said Mrs. Ballinger, scenting in Miss Van Vluyck's tone a tendency to depreciate the coveted distinction of entertaining Osric Dane; "I don't know that such a question can seriously be raised as to a book which has attracted more attention among thoughtful people than any novel since 'Robert Elsmere.'"

"Oh, but don't you see," exclaimed Laura Glyde, "that it's just the dark hopelessness of it all—the wonderful tone-scheme of black on black—that makes it such an artistic achievement? It reminded me when I read it of Prince Rupert's *manière noire*[3] . . . the book is etched, not painted, yet one feels the colour-values so intensely. . . ."

"Who is *he*?" Mrs. Leveret whispered to her neighbour, "Some one she's met abroad?"

"The wonderful part of the book," Mrs. Ballinger conceded, "is that it may be looked at from so many points of view. I hear that as a study of determinism Professor Lupton ranks it with 'The Data of Ethics.'"

"I'm told that Osric Dane spent ten years in preparatory studies before beginning to write it," said Mrs. Plinth. "She looks up everything—verifies everything. It has always been my principle, as you know. Nothing would induce me, now, to put aside a book before I'd finished it, just because I can buy as many more as I want."

"And what do *you* think of 'The Wings of Death'?" Mrs. Roby abruptly asked her.

It was the kind of question that might be termed out of order, and the ladies glanced at each other as though disclaiming any share in such a breach of discipline. They all knew there was nothing Mrs. Plinth so much disliked as being asked her opinion of a book. Books were written to read; if one read them what more could be expected? To be questioned in detail regarding the contents of a volume seemed to her as great an outrage as being searched for smuggled laces at the Custom House. The club had always respected this idiosyncrasy of Mrs. Plinth's. Such opinions as she had were imposing and substantial: her mind, like her house, was furnished with monumental "pieces" that were not meant to be disarranged; and it was one of the unwritten rules of the Lunch Club that, within her own province, each member's habits of thought should be respected. The meeting therefore closed with an increased

---

2. Greek painter of the 4th century B.C.E., known only through descriptions of his work, as here.
3. Literally, "black manner," artist's technique of crosshatching to achieve a dark background in an etching. Prince Rupert (1619–1682), German noble best known for his support of the Royalists in the English Civil War.

sense, on the part of the other ladies, of Mrs. Roby's hopeless unfitness to be one of them.

II

Mrs. Leveret, on the eventful day, arrived early at Mrs. Ballinger's, her volume of Appropriate Allusions[4] in her pocket.

It always flustered Mrs. Leveret to be late at the Lunch Club: she liked to collect her thoughts and gather a hint, as the others assembled, of the turn the conversation was likely to take. Today, however, she felt herself completely at a loss; and even the familiar contact of Appropriate Allusions, which stuck into her as she sat down, failed to give her any reassurance. It was an admirable little volume, compiled to meet all the social emergencies; so that, whether on the occasion of Anniversaries, joyful or melancholy (as the classification ran), of Banquets, social or municipal, or of Baptisms, Church of England or sectarian, its student need never be at a loss for a pertinent reference. Mrs. Leveret, though she had for years devoutly conned its pages, valued it, however, rather for its moral support than for its practical services; for though in the privacy of her own room she commanded an army of quotations, these invariably deserted her at the critical moment, and the only phrase she retained— *Canst thou draw out leviathan with a hook?*[5]—was one she had never yet found occasion to apply.

Today she felt that even the complete mastery of the volume would hardly have insured her self-possession; for she thought it probable that, even if she *did*, in some miraculous way, remember an Allusion, it would be only to find that Osric Dane used a different volume (Mrs. Leveret was convinced that literary people always carried them), and would consequently not recognise her quotations.

Mrs. Leveret's sense of being adrift was intensified by the appearance of Mrs. Ballinger's drawing-room. To a careless eye its aspect was unchanged; but those acquainted with Mrs. Ballinger's way of arranging her books would instantly have detected the marks of recent perturbation. Mrs. Ballinger's province, as a member of the Lunch Club, was the Book of the Day. On that, whatever it was, from a novel to a treatise on experimental psychology, she was confidently, authoritatively "up." What became of last year's books, or last week's even; what she did with the "subjects" she had previously professed with equal authority; no one had ever yet discovered. Her mind was an hotel where facts came and went like transient lodgers, without leaving their address behind, and frequently without paying for their board. It was Mrs. Ballinger's boast that she was "abreast with the Thought of the Day," and her pride that this advanced position should be expressed by the books on her table. These volumes, frequently renewed, and almost always damp from the press, bore names generally unfamiliar to Mrs. Leveret, and giving her, as she furtively scanned them, a disheartened glimpse of new fields of knowledge to be breathlessly traversed in Mrs. Ballinger's wake. But today a number of

---

4. Many such compendiums were available at the time of this story; *Bartlett's Familiar Quotations,* first published in 1882, is still available today.   **5.** From the Bible (Job 41:1).

maturer-looking volumes were adroitly mingled with the *primeurs* of the press—
Karl Marx jostled Professor Bergson, and the "Confessions of St. Augustine"
lay beside the last work on "Mendelism";[6] so that even to Mrs. Leveret's fluttered perceptions it was clear that Mrs. Ballinger didn't in the least know
what Osric Dane was likely to talk about, and had taken measures to be prepared for anything. Mrs. Leveret felt like a passenger on an ocean steamer
who is told that there is no immediate danger, but that she had better put on
her life-belt.

It was a relief to be roused from these forebodings by Miss Van Vluyck's
arrival.

"Well, my dear," the newcomer briskly asked her hostess, "what subjects are
we to discuss today?"

Mrs. Ballinger was furtively replacing a volume of Wordsworth by a copy of
Verlaine.[7] "I hardly know," she said, somewhat nervously. "Perhaps we had
better leave that to circumstances."

"Circumstances?" said Miss Van Vluyck drily. "That means, I suppose,
that Laura Glyde will take the floor as usual, and we shall be deluged with
literature."

Philanthropy and statistics were Miss Van Vluyck's province, and she
resented any tendency to divert their guest's attention from these topics.

Mrs. Plinth at this moment appeared.

"Literature?" she protested in a tone of remonstrance. "But this is perfectly
unexpected. I understood we were to talk of Osric Dane's novel."

Mrs. Ballinger winced at the discrimination, but let it pass. "We hardly
make that our chief subject—at least not *too* intentionally," she suggested. "Of
course we can let our talk *drift* in that direction, but we ought to have some
other topic as an introduction, and that is what I wanted to consult you about.
The fact is, we know so little of Osric Dane's tastes and interests that it is difficult to make any special preparation."

"It may be difficult," said Mrs. Plinth with decision, "but it is necessary. I
know what that happy-go-lucky principle leads to. As I told one of my nieces
the other day, there are certain emergencies for which a lady should always be
prepared. It's in shocking taste to wear colours when one pays a visit of condolence, or a last year's dress when there are reports that one's husband is on
the wrong side of the market; and so it is with conversation. All I ask is that I
should know beforehand what is to be talked about; then I feel sure of being
able to say the proper thing."

"I quite agree with you," Mrs. Ballinger assented: "but—"

And at that instant, heralded by the fluttered parlour-maid, Osric Dane
appeared upon the threshold.

Mrs. Leveret told her sister afterward that she had known at a glance what
was coming. She saw that Osric Dane was not going to meet them half way.
That distinguished personage had indeed entered with an air of compulsion
not calculated to promote the easy exercise of hospitality. She looked as
though she were about to be photographed for a new edition of her books.

6. The principles of Mendel's laws of genetic inheritance. *Primeurs:* fresh fruit (French).   **7.** Paul Verlaine
(1844–1896), French poet. William Wordsworth (1770–1850), English poet.

The desire to propitiate a divinity is generally in inverse ratio to its responsiveness, and the sense of discouragement produced by Osric Dane's entrance visibly increased the Lunch Club's eagerness to please her. Any lingering idea that she might consider herself under an obligation to her entertainers was at once dispelled by her manner: as Mrs. Leveret said afterward to her sister, she had a way of looking at you that made you feel as if there was something wrong with your hat. This evidence of greatness produced such an immediate impression on the ladies that a shudder of awe ran through them when Mrs. Roby, as their hostess led the great personage into the dining-room, turned back to whisper to the others: "What a brute she is!"

The hour about the table did not tend to revise this verdict. It was passed by Osric Dane in the silent deglutition of Mrs. Ballinger's menu, and by the members of the club in the emission of tentative platitudes which their guest seemed to swallow as perfunctorily as the successive courses of the luncheon.

Mrs. Ballinger's reluctance to fix a topic had thrown the club into a mental disarray which increased with the return to the drawing room, where the actual business of discussion was to open. Each lady waited for the other to speak; and there was a general shock of disappointment when their hostess opened the conversation by the painfully commonplace enquiry: "Is this your first visit to Hillbridge?"

Even Mrs. Leveret was conscious that this was a bad beginning; and a vague impulse of deprecation made Miss Glyde interject: "It is a very small place indeed."

Mrs. Plinth bristled. "We have a great many representative people," she said, in the tone of one who speaks for her order.

Osric Dane turned to her. "What do they represent?" she asked.

Mrs. Plinth's constitutional dislike to being questioned was intensified by her sense of unpreparedness; and her reproachful glance passed the question on to Mrs. Ballinger.

"Why," said that lady, glancing in turn at the other members, "as a community I hope it is not too much to say that we stand for culture."

"For art—" Miss Glyde interjected.

"For art and literature," Mrs. Ballinger emended.

"And for sociology, I trust," snapped Miss Van Vluyck.

"We have a standard," said Mrs. Plinth, feeling herself suddenly secure on the vast expanse of a generalisation; and Mrs. Leveret, thinking there must be room for more than one on so broad a statement, took courage to murmur: "Oh, certainly; we have a standard."

"The object of our little club," Mrs. Ballinger continued, "is to concentrate the highest tendencies of Hillbridge—to centralise and focus its intellectual effort."

This was felt to be so happy that the ladies drew an almost audible breath of relief.

"We aspire," the President went on, "to be in touch with whatever is highest in art, literature and ethics."

Osric Dane again turned to her. "What ethics?" she asked.

A tremor of apprehension encircled the room. None of the ladies required any preparation to pronounce on a question of morals; but when they were called ethics it was different. The club, when fresh from the "Encyclopædia

Britannica," the "Reader's Handbook" or Smith's "Classical Dictionary,"[8] could deal confidently with any subject; but when taken unawares it had been known to define agnosticism as a heresy of the Early Church and Professor Froude as a distinguished histologist; and such minor members as Mrs. Leveret still secretly regarded ethics as something vaguely pagan.

Even to Mrs. Ballinger, Osric Dane's question was unsettling, and there was a general sense of gratitude when Laura Glyde leaned forward to say, with her most sympathetic accent: "You must excuse us, Mrs. Dane, for not being able, just at present, to talk of anything but 'The Wings of Death.'"

"Yes," said Miss Van Vluyck, with a sudden resolve to carry the war into the enemy's camp. "We are so anxious to know the exact purpose you had in mind in writing your wonderful book."

"You will find," Mrs. Plinth interposed, "that we are not superficial readers."

"We are eager to hear from you," Miss Van Vluyck continued, "if the pessimistic tendency of the book is an expression of your own convictions or—"

"Or merely," Miss Glyde thrust in, "a sombre background brushed in to throw your figures into more vivid relief. *Are* you not primarily plastic?"

"*I* have always maintained," Mrs. Ballinger interposed, "that you represent the purely objective method—"

Osric Dane helped herself critically to coffee. "How do you define objective?" she then enquired.

There was a flurried pause before Laura Glyde intensely murmured: "In reading *you* we don't define, we feel."

Osric Dane smiled. "The cerebellum," she remarked, "is not infrequently the seat of the literary emotions."[9] And she took a second lump of sugar.

The sting that this remark was vaguely felt to conceal was almost neutralised by the satisfaction of being addressed in such technical language.

"Ah, the cerebellum," said Miss Van Vluyck complacently. "The club took a course in psychology last winter."

"Which psychology?" asked Osric Dane.

There was an agonising pause, during which each member of the club secretly deplored the distressing inefficiency of the others. Only Mrs. Roby went on placidly sipping her chartreuse. At last Mrs. Ballinger said, with an attempt at a high tone: "Well, really, you know, it was last year that we took psychology, and this winter we have been so absorbed in—"

She broke off, nervously trying to recall some of the club's discussions; but her faculties seemed to be paralysed by the petrifying stare of Osric Dane. What *had* the club been absorbed in? Mrs. Ballinger, with a vague purpose of gaining time, repeated slowly: "We've been so intensely absorbed in—"

Mrs. Roby put down her liqueur glass and drew near the group with a smile.

"In Xingu?" she gently prompted.

A thrill ran through the other members. They exchanged confused glances, and then, with one accord, turned a gaze of mingled relief and interrogation on their rescuer. The expression of each denoted a different phase of the same emotion. Mrs. Plinth was the first to compose her features to an air of reas-

---

8. Reference books readily available to middle-class readers at the time of this story.   **9.** In fact, the cerebellum is the portion of the brain that coordinates muscular movements.

surance: after a moment's hasty adjustment her look almost implied that it was she who had given the word to Mrs. Ballinger.

"Xingu, of course!" exclaimed the latter with her accustomed promptness, while Miss Van Vluyck and Laura Glyde seemed to be plumbing the depths of memory, and Mrs. Leveret, feeling apprehensively for Appropriate Allusions, was somehow reassured by the uncomfortable pressure of its bulk against her person.

Osric Dane's change of countenance was no less striking than that of her entertainers. She too put down her coffee-cup, but with a look of distinct annoyance; she too wore, for a brief moment, what Mrs. Roby afterward described as the look of feeling for something in the back of her head; and before she could dissemble these momentary signs of weakness, Mrs. Roby, turning to her with a deferential smile, had said: "And we've been so hoping that today you would tell us just what you think of it."

Osric Dane received the homage of the smile as a matter of course; but the accompanying question obviously embarrassed her, and it became clear to her observers that she was not quick at shifting her facial scenery. It was as though her countenance had so long been set in an expression of unchallenged superiority that the muscles had stiffened, and refused to obey her orders.

"Xingu—" she said, as if seeking in her turn to gain time.

Mrs. Roby continued to press her. "Knowing how engrossing the subject is, you will understand how it happens that the club has let everything else go to the wall for the moment. Since we took up Xingu I might almost say—were it not for your books—that nothing else seems to us worth remembering."

Osric Dane's stern features were darkened rather than lit up by an uneasy smile. "I am glad to hear that you make one exception," she gave out between narrowed lips.

"Oh, of course," Mrs. Roby said prettily; "but as you have shown us that—so very naturally!—you don't care to talk of your own things, we really can't let you off from telling us exactly what you think about Xingu; especially," she added, with a still more persuasive smile, "as some people say that one of your last books was saturated with it."

It was an *it,* then—the assurance sped like fire through the parched minds of the other members. In their eagerness to gain the least little clue to Xingu they almost forgot the joy of assisting at the discomfiture of Mrs. Dane.

The latter reddened nervously under her antagonist's challenge. "May I ask," she faltered out, "to which of my books you refer?"

Mrs. Roby did not falter. "That's just what I want you to tell us; because, though I was present, I didn't actually take part."

"Present at what?" Mrs. Dane took her up; and for an instant the trembling members of the Lunch Club thought that the champion Providence had raised up for them had lost a point. But Mrs. Roby explained herself gaily: "At the discussion, of course. And so we're dreadfully anxious to know just how it was that you went into the Xingu."

There was a portentous pause, a silence so big with incalculable dangers that the members with one accord checked the words on their lips, like soldiers dropping their arms to watch a single combat between their leaders. Then Mrs. Dane gave expression to their inmost dread by saying sharply: "Ah—you say *the* Xingu, do you?"

Mrs. Roby smiled undauntedly. "It *is* a shade pedantic, isn't it? Personally, I always drop the article; but I don't know how the other members feel about it."

The other members looked as though they would willingly have dispensed with this appeal to their opinion, and Mrs. Roby, after a bright glance about the group, went on: "They probably think, as I do, that nothing really matters except the thing itself—except Xingu."

No immediate reply seemed to occur to Mrs. Dane, and Mrs. Ballinger gathered courage to say: "Surely every one must feel that about Xingu."

Mrs. Plinth came to her support with a heavy murmur of assent, and Laura Glyde sighed out emotionally: "I have known cases where it has changed a whole life."

"It has done me worlds of good," Mrs. Leveret interjected, seeming to herself to remember that she had either taken it or read it the winter before.

"Of course," Mrs. Roby admitted, "the difficulty is that one must give up so much time to it. It's very long."

"I can't imagine," said Miss Van Vluyck, "grudging the time given to such a subject."

"And deep in places," Mrs. Roby pursued; (so then it was a book!) "And it isn't easy to skip."

"I never skip," said Mrs. Plinth dogmatically.

"Ah, it's dangerous to, in Xingu. Even at the start there are places where one can't. One must just wade through."

"I should hardly call it *wading*," said Mrs. Ballinger sarcastically.

Mrs. Roby sent her a look of interest. "Ah—you always found it went swimmingly?"

Mrs. Ballinger hesitated. "Of course there are difficult passages," she conceded.

"Yes; some are not at all clear—even," Mrs. Roby added, "if one is familiar with the original."

"As I suppose you are?" Osric Dane interposed, suddenly fixing her with a look of challenge.

Mrs. Roby met it by a deprecating gesture. "Oh, it's really not difficult up to a certain point; though some of the branches are very little known; and it's almost impossible to get at the source."

"Have you ever tried?" Mrs. Plinth enquired, still distrustful of Mrs. Roby's thoroughness.

Mrs. Roby was silent for a moment; then she replied with lowered lids: "No—but a friend of mine did; a very brilliant man; and he told me it was best for women—not to. . . ."

A shudder ran around the room. Mrs. Leveret coughed so that the parlourmaid, who was handing the cigarettes, should not hear; Miss Van Vluyck's face took on a nauseated expression, and Mrs. Plinth looked as if she were passing some one she did not care to bow to. But the most remarkable result of Mrs. Roby's words was the effect they produced on the Lunch Club's distinguished guest. Osric Dane's impassive features suddenly softened to an expression of the warmest human sympathy, and edging her chair toward Mrs. Roby's she asked: "Did he really? And—did you find he was right?"

Mrs. Ballinger, in whom annoyance at Mrs. Roby's unwonted assumption of prominence was beginning to displace gratitude for the aid she had rendered, could not consent to her being allowed, by such dubious means, to monopolise the attention of their guest. If Osric Dane had not enough self-respect to resent Mrs. Roby's flippancy, at least the Lunch Club would do so in the person of its President.

Mrs. Ballinger laid her hand on Mrs. Roby's arm. "We must not forget," she said with a frigid amiability, "that absorbing as Xingu is to *us,* it may be less interesting to—"

"Oh, no, on the contrary, I assure you," Osric Dane intervened.

"—to others," Mrs. Ballinger finished firmly; "and we must not allow our little meeting to end without persuading Mrs. Dane to say a few words to us on a subject which, today, is much more present in all our thoughts. I refer, of course, to 'The Wings of Death.'"

The other members, animated by various degrees of the same sentiment, and encouraged by the humanised mien of their redoubtable guest, repeated after Mrs. Ballinger: "Oh, yes, you really *must* talk to us a little about your book."

Osric Dane's expression became as bored, though not as haughty, as when her work had been previously mentioned. But before she could respond to Mrs. Ballinger's request, Mrs. Roby had risen from her seat, and was pulling down her veil over her frivolous nose.

"I'm so sorry," she said, advancing toward her hostess with outstretched hand, "but before Mrs. Dane begins I think I'd better run away. Unluckily, as you know, I haven't read her books, so I should be at a terrible disadvantage among you all, and besides, I've an engagement to play bridge."

If Mrs. Roby had simply pleaded her ignorance of Osric Dane's works as a reason for withdrawing, the Lunch Club, in view of her recent prowess, might have approved such evidence of discretion; but to couple this excuse with the brazen announcement that she was foregoing the privilege for the purpose of joining a bridge-party was only one more instance of her deplorable lack of discrimination.

The ladies were disposed, however, to feel that her departure—now that she had performed the sole service she was ever likely to render them—would probably make for greater order and dignity in the impending discussion, besides relieving them of the sense of self-distrust which her presence always mysteriously produced. Mrs. Ballinger therefore restricted herself to a formal murmur of regret, and the other members were just grouping themselves comfortably about Osric Dane when the latter, to their dismay, started up from the sofa on which she had been seated.

"Oh wait—do wait, and I'll go with you!" she called out to Mrs. Roby; and, seizing the hands of the disconcerted members, she administered a series of farewell pressures with the mechanical haste of a railway-conductor punching tickets.

"I'm so sorry—I'd quite forgotten—" she flung back at them from the threshold; and as she joined Mrs. Roby, who had turned in surprise at her appeal, the other ladies had the mortification of hearing her say, in a voice which she did not take the pains to lower: "If you'll let me walk a little way with you, I should so like to ask you a few more questions about Xingu . . ."

III

The incident had been so rapid that the door closed on the departing pair before the other members had time to understand what was happening. Then a sense of the indignity put upon them by Osric Dane's unceremonious desertion began to contend with the confused feeling that they had been cheated out of their due without exactly knowing how or why.

There was a silence, during which Mrs. Ballinger, with a perfunctory hand, rearranged the skilfully grouped literature at which her distinguished guest had not so much as glanced; then Miss Van Vluyck tartly pronounced: "Well, I can't say that I consider Osric Dane's departure a great loss."

This confession crystallised the resentment of the other members, and Mrs. Leveret exclaimed: "I do believe she came on purpose to be nasty!"

It was Mrs. Plinth's private opinion that Osric Dane's attitude toward the Lunch Club might have been very different had it welcomed her in the majestic setting of the Plinth drawing-rooms; but not liking to reflect on the inadequacy of Mrs. Ballinger's establishment she sought a roundabout satisfaction in depreciating her lack of foresight.

"I said from the first that we ought to have had a subject ready. It's what always happens when you're unprepared. Now if we'd only got up Xingu—"

The slowness of Mrs. Plinth's mental processes was always allowed for by the club; but this instance of it was too much for Mrs. Ballinger's equanimity.

"Xingu!" she scoffed. "Why, it was the fact of our knowing so much more about it than she did—unprepared though we were—that made Osric Dane so furious. I should have thought that was plain enough to everybody!"

This retort impressed even Mrs. Plinth, and Laura Glyde, moved by an impulse of generosity, said: "Yes, we really ought to be grateful to Mrs. Roby for introducing the topic. It may have made Osric Dane furious, but at least it made her civil."

"I am glad we were able to show her," added Miss Van Vluyck, "that a broad and up-to-date culture is not confined to the great intellectual centres."

This increased the satisfaction of the other members, and they began to forget their wrath against Osric Dane in the pleasure of having contributed to her discomfiture.

Miss Van Vluyck thoughtfully rubbed her spectacles. "What surprised me most," she continued, "was that Fanny Roby should be so up on Xingu."

This remark threw a slight chill on the company, but Mrs. Ballinger said with an air of indulgent irony: "Mrs. Roby always has the knack of making a little go a long way; still, we certainly owe her a debt for happening to remember that she'd heard of Xingu." And this was felt by the other members to be a graceful way of cancelling once for all the club's obligation to Mrs. Roby.

Even Mrs. Leveret took courage to speed a timid shaft of irony. "I fancy Osric Dane hardly expected to take a lesson in Xingu at Hillbridge!"

Mrs. Ballinger smiled. "When she asked me what we represented—do you remember?—I wish I'd simply said we represented Xingu!"

All the ladies laughed appreciatively at this sally, except Mrs. Plinth, who said, after a moment's deliberation: "I'm not sure it would have been wise to do so."

Mrs. Ballinger, who was already beginning to feel as if she had launched at Osric Dane the retort which had just occurred to her, turned ironically on Mrs. Plinth. "May I ask why?" she enquired.

Mrs. Plinth looked grave. "Surely," she said, "I understood from Mrs. Roby herself that the subject was one it was as well not to go into too deeply?"

Miss Van Vluyck rejoined with precision: "I think that applied only to an investigation of the origin of the—of the—"; and suddenly she found that her usually accurate memory had failed her. "It's a part of the subject I never studied myself," she concluded.

"Nor I," said Mrs. Ballinger.

Laura Glyde bent toward them with widened eyes. "And yet it seems—doesn't it?—the part that is fullest of an esoteric fascination?"

"I don't know on what you base that," said Miss Van Vluyck argumentatively.

"Well, didn't you notice how intensely interested Osric Dane became as soon as she heard what the brilliant foreigner—he *was* a foreigner, wasn't he?—had told Mrs. Roby about the origin—the origin of the rite—or whatever you call it?"

Mrs. Plinth looked disapproving, and Mrs. Ballinger visibly wavered. Then she said: "It may not be desirable to touch on the—on that part of the subject in general conversation; but, from the importance it evidently has to a woman of Osric Dane's distinction, I feel as if we ought not to be afraid to discuss it among ourselves—without gloves—though with closed doors, if necessary."

"I'm quite of your opinion," Miss Van Vluyck came briskly to her support; "on condition, that is, that all grossness of language is avoided."

"Oh, I'm sure we shall understand without that," Mrs. Leveret tittered; and Laura Glyde added significantly: "I fancy we can read between the lines," while Mrs. Ballinger rose to assure herself that the doors were really closed.

Mrs. Plinth had not yet given her adhesion. "I hardly see," she began, "what benefit is to be derived from investigating such peculiar customs—"

But Mrs. Ballinger's patience had reached the extreme limit of tension. "This at least," she returned; "that we shall not be placed again in the humiliating position of finding ourselves less up on our own subjects than Fanny Roby!"

Even to Mrs. Plinth this argument was conclusive. She peered furtively about the room and lowered her commanding tones to ask: "Have you got a copy?"

"A—a copy?" stammered Mrs. Ballinger. She was aware that the other members were looking at her expectantly, and that this answer was inadequate, so she supported it by asking another question. "A copy of what?"

Her companions bent their expectant gaze on Mrs. Plinth, who, in turn, appeared less sure of herself than usual. "Why, of—of—the book," she explained.

"What book?" snapped Miss Van Vluyck, almost as sharply as Osric Dane.

Mrs. Ballinger looked at Laura Glyde, whose eyes were interrogatively fixed on Mrs. Leveret. The fact of being deferred to was so new to the latter that it filled her with an insane temerity. "Why, Xingu, of course!" she exclaimed.

A profound silence followed this challenge to the resources of Mrs. Ballinger's library, and the latter, after glancing nervously toward the Books of the Day, returned with dignity: "It's not a thing one cares to leave about."

"I should think *not!*" exclaimed Mrs. Plinth.

"It *is* a book, then?" said Miss Van Vluyck.

This again threw the company into disarray, and Mrs. Ballinger, with an impatient sigh, rejoined: "Why—there *is* a book—naturally. . . ."

"Then why did Miss Glyde call it a religion?"

Laura Glyde started up. "A religion? I never—"

"Yes, you did," Miss Van Vluyck insisted; "you spoke of rites; and Mrs. Plinth said it was a custom."

Miss Glyde was evidently making a desperate effort to recall her statement; but accuracy of detail was not her strongest point. At length she began in a deep murmur: "Surely they used to do something of the kind at the Eleusinian mysteries—"[1]

"Oh—" said Miss Van Vluyck, on the verge of disapproval; and Mrs. Plinth protested: "I understood there was to be no indelicacy!"

Mrs. Ballinger could not control her irritation. "Really, it is too bad that we should not be able to talk the matter over quietly among ourselves. Personally, I think that if one goes into Xingu at all—"

"Oh, so do I!" cried Miss Glyde.

"And I don't see how one can avoid doing so, if one wishes to keep up with the Thought of the Day—"

Mrs. Leveret uttered an exclamation of relief. "There—that's it!" she interposed.

"What's it?" the President took her up.

"Why—it's a—a Thought: I mean a philosophy."

This seemed to bring a certain relief to Mrs. Ballinger and Laura Glyde, but Miss Van Vluyck said: "Excuse me if I tell you that you're all mistaken. Xingu happens to be a language."

"A language!" the Lunch Club cried.

"Certainly. Don't you remember Fanny Roby's saying that there were several branches, and that some were hard to trace? What could that apply to but dialects?"

Mrs. Ballinger could no longer restrain a contemptuous laugh. "Really, if the Lunch Club has reached such a pass that it has to go to Fanny Roby for instruction on a subject like Xingu, it had almost better cease to exist!"

"It's really her fault for not being clearer," Laura Glyde put in.

"Oh, clearness and Fanny Roby!" Mrs. Ballinger shrugged. "I daresay we shall find she was mistaken on almost every point."

"Why not look it up?" said Mrs. Plinth.

As a rule this recurrent suggestion of Mrs. Plinth's was ignored in the heat of discussion, and only resorted to afterward in the privacy of each member's home. But on the present occasion the desire to ascribe their own confusion of thought to the vague and contradictory nature of Mrs. Roby's statements caused the members of the Lunch Club to utter a collective demand for a book of reference.

At this point the production of her treasured volume gave Mrs. Leveret, for a moment, the unusual experience of occupying the centre front; but she was not able to hold it long, for Appropriate Allusions contained no mention of Xingu.

---

1. Ancient Greek religious rites that symbolized nature's cycles of birth, death, and rebirth.

"Oh, that's not the kind of thing we want!" exclaimed Miss Van Vluyck. She cast a disparaging glance over Mrs. Ballinger's assortment of literature, and added impatiently: "Haven't you any useful books?"

"Of course I have," replied Mrs. Ballinger indignantly; "I keep them in my husband's dressing-room."

From this region, after some difficulty and delay, the parlour-maid produced the W-Z volume of an Encyclopædia and, in deference to the fact that the demand for it had come from Miss Van Vluyck, laid the ponderous tome before her.

There was a moment of painful suspense while Miss Van Vluyck rubbed her spectacles, adjusted them, and turned to Z; and a murmur of surprise when she said: "It isn't here."

"I suppose," said Mrs. Plinth, "it's not fit to be put in a book of reference."

"Oh, nonsense!" exclaimed Mrs. Ballinger. "Try X."

Miss Van Vluyck turned back through the volume, peering shortsightedly up and down the pages, till she came to a stop and remained motionless, like a dog on a point.

"Well, have you found it?" Mrs. Ballinger enquired after a considerable delay.

"Yes. I've found it," said Miss Van Vluyck in a queer voice.

Mrs. Plinth hastily interposed: "I beg you won't read it aloud if there's anything offensive."

Miss Van Vluyck, without answering, continued her silent scrutiny.

"Well, what *is* it?" exclaimed Laura Glyde excitedly.

"*Do* tell us!" urged Mrs. Leveret, feeling that she would have something awful to tell her sister.

Miss Van Vluyck pushed the volume aside and turned slowly toward the expectant group.

"It's a river."

"A *river?*"

"Yes: in Brazil. Isn't that where she's been living?"

"Who? Fanny Roby? Oh, but you must be mistaken. You've been reading the wrong thing," Mrs. Ballinger exclaimed, leaning over her to seize the volume.

"It's the only *Xingu* in the Encyclopædia; and she *has* been living in Brazil," Miss Van Vluyck persisted.

"Yes: her brother has a consulship there," Mrs. Leveret interposed.

"But it's too ridiculous! I—we—why we *all* remember studying Xingu last year—or the year before last," Mrs. Ballinger stammered.

"I thought I did when *you* said so," Laura Glyde avowed.

"*I* said so?" cried Mrs. Ballinger.

"Yes. You said it had crowded everything else out of your mind."

"Well *you* said it had changed your whole life!"

"For that matter, Miss Van Vluyck said she had never grudged the time she'd given it."

Mrs. Plinth interposed: "I made it clear that I knew nothing whatever of the original."

Mrs. Ballinger broke off the dispute with a groan. "Oh, what does it all matter if she's been making fools of us? I believe Miss Van Vluyck's right—she was talking of the river all the while!"

"How could she? It's too preposterous," Miss Glyde exclaimed.

"Listen." Miss Van Vluyck had repossessed herself of the Encyclopædia, and restored her spectacles to a nose reddened by excitement. "'The Xingu, one of the principal rivers of Brazil, rises on the plateau of Mato Grosso, and flows in a northerly direction for a length of no less than one thousand one hundred and eighteen miles, entering the Amazon near the mouth of the latter river. The upper course of the Xingu is auriferous and fed by numerous branches. Its source was first discovered in 1884 by the German explorer von den Steinen, after a difficult and dangerous expedition through a region inhabited by tribes still in the Stone Age of culture.'"

The ladies received this communication in a state of stupefied silence from which Mrs. Leveret was the first to rally. "She certainly did speak of its having branches."

The word seemed to snap the last thread of their incredulity. "And of its great length," gasped Mrs. Ballinger.

"She said it was awfully deep, and you couldn't skip—you just had to wade through," Miss Glyde added.

The idea worked its way more slowly through Mrs. Plinth's compact resistances. "How could there be anything improper about a river?" she enquired.

"Improper?"

"Why, what she said about the source—that it was corrupt?"

"Not corrupt, but hard to get at," Laura Glyde corrected. "Some one who'd been there had told her so. I daresay it was the explorer himself—doesn't it say the expedition was dangerous?"

"'Difficult and dangerous,'" read Miss Van Vluyck.

Mrs. Ballinger pressed her hands to her throbbing temples. "There's nothing she said that wouldn't apply to a river—to this river!" She swung about excitedly to the other members. "Why, do you remember her telling us that she hadn't read 'The Supreme Instant' because she'd taken it on a boating party while she was staying with her brother, and some one had 'shied' it overboard—'shied' of course was her own expression."

The ladies breathlessly signified that the expression had not escaped them.

"Well—and then didn't she tell Osric Dane that one of her books was simply saturated with Xingu? Of course it was, if one of Mrs. Roby's rowdy friends had thrown it into the river!"

This surprising reconstruction of the scene in which they had just participated left the members of the Lunch Club inarticulate. At length, Mrs. Plinth, after visibly labouring with the problem, said in a heavy tone: "Osric Dane was taken in too."

Mrs. Leveret took courage at this. "Perhaps that's what Mrs. Roby did it for. She said Osric Dane was a brute, and she may have wanted to give her a lesson."

Miss Van Vluyck frowned. "It was hardly worth while to do it at our expense."

"At least," said Miss Glyde with a touch of bitterness, "she succeeded in interesting her, which was more than we did."

"What chance had we?" rejoined Mrs. Ballinger. "Mrs. Roby monopolised her from the first. And that, I've no doubt, was her purpose—to give Osric Dane a false impression of her own standing in the club. She would hesitate at nothing to attract attention: we all know how she took in poor Professor Foreland."

"She actually makes him give bridge-teas every Thursday," Mrs. Leveret piped up.

Laura Glyde struck her hands together. "Why, this is Thursday, and it's *there* she's gone, of course; and taken Osric with her!"

"And they're shrieking over us at this moment," said Mrs. Ballinger between her teeth.

This possibility seemed too preposterous to be admitted. "She would hardly dare," said Miss Van Vluyck, "confess the imposture to Osric Dane."

"I'm not so sure: I thought I saw her make a sign as she left. If she hadn't made a sign, why should Osric Dane have rushed out after her?"

"Well, you know, we'd all been telling her how wonderful Xingu was, and she said she wanted to find out more about it," Mrs. Leveret said, with a tardy impulse of justice to the absent.

This reminder, far from mitigating the wrath of the other members, gave it a stronger impetus.

"Yes—and that's exactly what they're both laughing over now," said Laura Glyde ironically.

Mrs. Plinth stood up and gathered her expensive furs about her monumental form. "I have no wish to criticise," she said; "but unless the Lunch Club can protect its members against the recurrence of such—such unbecoming scenes, I for one—"

"Oh, so do I!" agreed Miss Glyde, rising also.

Miss Van Vluyck closed the Encyclopædia and proceeded to button herself into her jacket. "My time is really too valuable—" she began.

"I fancy we are all of one mind," said Mrs. Ballinger, looking searchingly at Mrs. Leveret, who looked at the others.

"I always deprecate anything like a scandal—" Mrs. Plinth continued.

"She has been the cause of one today!" exclaimed Miss Glyde.

Mrs. Leveret moaned: "I don't see how she *could!*" and Miss Van Vluyck said, picking up her note-book: "Some women stop at nothing."

"—but if," Mrs. Plinth took up her argument impressively, "anything of the kind had happened in *my* house" (it never would have, her tone implied), "I should have felt that I owed it to myself either to ask for Mrs. Roby's resignation—or to offer mine."

"Oh, Mrs. Plinth—" gasped the Lunch Club.

"Fortunately for me," Mrs. Plinth continued with an awful magnanimity, "the matter was taken out of my hands by our President's decision that the right to entertain distinguished guests was a privilege vested in her office; and I think the other members will agree that, as she was alone in this opinion, she ought to be alone in deciding on the best way of effacing its—its really deplorable consequences."

A deep silence followed this outbreak of Mrs. Plinth's long-stored resentment.

"I don't see why *I* should be expected to ask her to resign—" Mrs. Ballinger at length began; but Laura Glyde turned back to remind her: "You know she made you say that you'd got on swimmingly in Xingu."

An ill-timed giggle escaped from Mrs. Leveret, and Mrs. Ballinger energetically continued "—but you needn't think for a moment that I'm afraid to!"

The door of the drawing-room closed on the retreating backs of the Lunch Club, and the President of that distinguished association, seating herself at her writing-table, and pushing away a copy of "The Wings of Death" to make room for her elbow, drew forth a sheet of the club's note-paper, on which she began to write: "My dear Mrs. Roby—"

1911

THOMAS WILLIAMS
1926 — 1990

Some writers are esteemed more for the help they give other writers than for their own work. Sherwood Anderson was one, having aided both William Faulkner, who thanked him for it, and Ernest Hemingway, who did not. Thomas Williams is another such mentor figure. Born in Duluth, Minnesota, raised there and in New York City, Williams was brought to New Hampshire as a child and ended up spending most of his life as a writer and teacher at the University of New Hampshire. He wrote seven fine novels, including *Whipple's Castle* (1969), *The Followed Man* (1978), and *Moon Pinnace* (1986), but even when *The Hair of Harold Roux* won a National Book Award in 1975 he remained a secret to most of the American reading public. One of Williams's grateful former students, though, was John Irving, who would one day thank him by writing the introduction to a posthumous collection of Williams's collected stories, *Leah, New Hampshire* (1992). The masterful stories in that volume are the work of a fine artist, given his due at last.

Goose Pond

Robert Hurley's wife died in September, and by the middle of October he had more or less settled everything. His son and daughter were both married and lived far away from New York, his son in Los Angeles, his daughter in Toledo. They came East for the funeral and each wanted him to come and visit. "I'm not about to retire. I won't be an old man in a guest room," he told them, knowing the great difference between the man he looked at fifty-eight and the man he felt himself to be. It had taken Mary six months to die, and during the last few of those months he began quietly to assume many of her symptoms. The doctors noticed it and understood, but his children, accustomed to a father who had always been to them a commonsense, rather unimaginative figure, were shocked by his loss of weight, by a listlessness as unlike him, as unsettling to them as if the earth's rotation had begun to slow down.

But he would do no visiting, even though his business did not need him. "I know what visiting is," he wrote to his son. "I don't do it very well. Please don't call so much. You know how to write letters." "Daddy," his daughter said, long distance. "The children are crazy to have their grandfather come and see them."

And he thought, there is one place I would like to go, and there are no children I know there: "I'm going to New Hampshire, to Leah."

"All by yourself? What for?" She began to get excited, almost hysterical. He could see her biting her lower lip—a habit of her mother's. Afterwards she would be calling Charles in Los Angeles.

"I was born there. Your mother and I lived there before you were born. Do I need any other reason? It's October. Anyway, I'll be back in a couple of weeks."

"But, Daddy, we felt that you shouldn't be alone. . . ."

"I haven't been alone for thirty years," he said. "I want to try it again. Now go back to whatever you were doing. I can hear a baby crying in your house. Go take care of it. I'm going to stay with the Pedersens. Do you remember the old people in the big house on the mountain? If they still take boarders, that's where I'll be." *If they're still alive,* he thought. He wanted to walk in the woods again, but he had other reasons. The sight of his grandchildren, the hundred times a day when their small disasters caused screaming, tears; he couldn't stand it. They were always about to hurt themselves, they nearly fell so many times. They had so many deadly years to make. Automobiles, knives, leukemia, fire. . . . On the afternoon of the funeral he had watched his granddaughter, Ann, and suddenly he saw her having his wife's senseless pain, saw her crying not because of a bumped knee, but at more serious wounds. And the Pedersens? They were so old, they had somehow escaped, and as he remembered them they lived dried-up and careful, in a kind of limbo. He would go to the Pedersens, on Cascom Mountain.

Nana fussed with the Edison lamp, turning the white flame up in the mantle, moving the broad base across the crack made by the table leaf; then with the side of her hand she wiped the shiny surface of the table where it had been. The light shone past the tinted shade, up the glass chimney and sharpened her old face, made her glasses glint for a second until she moved away, tall and always busy, her small eyes always alert. She rarely sat down, and even then seemed poised, ready for busy duty. The old man settled himself cautiously, as he did now, one piece at a time. Nana had his zither out of its case, the light just right, made sure he had his hearing aid, his pick, an ash tray near. In spite of his age, he smoked cigarettes.

Back in the shadows, between a lacy, drooping vine and the narrow window, Nana's older sister, blue dress and high black shoes, composed and fragile face, sat in a rocker and never spoke. Nana herself was seventy-nine. For forty years she had bossed the seven-mile trek down to Leah in the late fall, back up the mountain again to this high old house in the spring. It was Nana who dealt with the world, who shut the windows when it rained, herded great-grandchildren when the family came in the summer, locked the house for the winter. In a few weeks they would be going down to their small apartment in Leah, to take their chances on another winter.

The old man tuned his zither, humming in a dry, crackly falsetto and turning his wrench as he picked the short strings. Tuned against the windy old voice, the crisp notes of the zither were startling, clear and metallic. There seemed to be no connection between the voice and the sounds of the strings, as if the old man heard other notes, the sounds of memory to check his instrument against.

"German *concert* zither," Nana said proudly, still hovering over the lamp. She rearranged his cigarettes, the coffee cup. She spoke from behind him, "He don't hear so good," nodding vigorously. "But he got the hearing aid." She pointed into his ear, where the pink button shone like a flower against brown freckles. "He don't wear it all the time, like he should." She moved quickly away on some sudden errand, and the old man looked up and winked at Hurley.

"Sometimes it makes too much noise," he said, smiling benevolently at his wife. She began to move the table. "It's all right. It's all right!" he said. In his fifty years in America he had mastered the sounds of English, but the rhythms of his speech were Scandinavian. "I'm going to play first a Norwegian song."

Nana poised herself upon a chair, folded her hands firmly, set herself for a moment and then began energetically to smooth her apron down her long thighs. The old lady against the wall stopped rocking. It always startled Hurley when, out of her silent effacement, she responded.

The old man bent over his zither, his shiny face as ruddy as a baby's. His mottled, angular fingers worked over the strings; he swayed back and forth to keep time and snorted, gave little gasps and grunts he evidently did not hear himself, in time with the music. Beneath, occasionally overcoming the sibilant, involuntary breaths, the music was poignantly clear, ordered, cascading, vivid as little knives in the shadowy room. At the end they all applauded, and the old man bowed, very pleased.

That night Hurley climbed the staircase that angled around the central chimney, an oil lamp to light his way, and entered his cold room in moonlight almost as bright as the lamp, but colder, whiter against the lamp's yellow. Two little windows looked down across the old man's garden—"Mostly for the deer," the old man had said of it—then over the one still-mown pasture left to the farm, down the long hills silvery in moonlight to Lake Cascom in the valley, white among black surrounding spruce. Behind, on the other side of the house, he could feel the dark presence of Cascom Mountain.

He wondered if it would be a night for sleep. He was tired enough. In the last few days he had taken many of the familiar trails, especially following those that he remembered led through hardwood. Although the leaves had turned and mostly fallen, here or there one tree flamed late among the bare ones, catching light and casting it in all directions as if it were an orange or soft red sun. He stopped often in the woods, surprised by each molten maple branch, even the smallest bright veins of each leaf golden and precious against a gnarled black trunk or the green twilight of a spruce grove. He walked carefully, resting often, sampling the few cold, sweet apples from the abandoned mountain trees, eating Nana's sandwiches a little at a time. He wanted the day to last as long as possible. At night he thought of his wife.

The high, sloping bed was wide and lonesome as a field of snow. During his wife's illness he could not sleep in their own bed, but slept every night on a studio couch where he could reach the sides, hold himself down and remember exactly where he was and why she was not beside him. If he woke in the night and for a second forgot, he had to learn over again from the beginning that Mary was going to die. It was always the first time over again, when they had left the doctor (the poor doctor, according to Mary) at the cancer hospital and walked together to Grant's Tomb.[1] Mary finally said, "You know? They should pay a man a thousand dollars a minute for having to say those words."

Then the inevitable sequence of hours came through his mind, one after the other, until the afternoon when she was not so brave any more and shook her head back and forth as if to throw off the plastic tube that went into her nose and down, jiggling the clamps and the bottle on its hanger. Tears rolled from the outside corners of her drowned eyes and she cried pettishly, "Help me, help me."

She had taken pain better than most, was better at taking it by far than her husband or her children. When she had the compound fracture of her wrist she had been the calm one, the strong one. And he thought, *My God, how much pain she must have if she is caused to do this—if it is Mary who is caused to do this. . . .*

As they cut nerves, cutting off pain in little bits and pieces, it was as if they cut off her life, too, by shreds—the pain, the possibility of it forever gone; the life forever gone. But new pain took the place of the old. She lived for six months and died almost weightless, ageless, the little lines and wrinkles of her familiar body smoothed as if by a filling pulp. Her arms turned to thin tubes, her forehead waxed as taut, as translucent as a yellow apple. Her eyes, before the final cutting, watched him, blameful as a beaten child's. She whined for help: "What is happening to me?" And being a man only, he could stand, and stand, and stand, helpless at the foot of her crank-operated bed, the simple handle drawing his eyes, mocking, it seemed to him, telling him to crank, to grasp the handle in his strong hands and crank, sweat at it, crank faster and harder, crank until she is well again.

He turned and his hand touched the firm, virginal pillow next to his. The linen smelled country-new, of washdays and clotheslines.

At midnight he heard what he first supposed to be a hundred dogs barking in the distance, and as the barking changed on the wind he suddenly knew, in exactly the same way he had known in his childhood, that it was the Canada geese flying over, low here because of the height of the land, streaming over in the darkness. *Lorlorn, lorlorn, lorlorn,* the geese called to each other as they passed. He ran to the window—remembering an old excitement, feet numb on the cold boards—but the geese did not cross the moon. He remembered them well enough that way: the long wavering files of geese, necks thrust out straight, dark wings arcing tirelessly on their long journey over the guns, through all the deadly traps set for them—the weather, the ice, the hunting animals and the traitor decoys. Each one its own warm life deep in the cold sky, and they called to each other, kept close and on course together, facing with disciplined bravery that impossible journey.

He came awake in the indeterminate time when night was breaking and the small windows were luminous squares upon the wall. He lay on his back and watched the light grow, the corners arrange themselves and moldings darken, wondering at a curved shape above the closet door. As the morning

---

1. The tomb of Civil War hero and president Ulysses S. Grant (1822–1885) is located in New York City's Riverside Park.

increased (he heard pans banging down in the kitchen, Nana's sharp morning voice) he finally saw that the curved shape was a bow hung on pegs. This room evidently had been a young boy's during the summer: a huge fungus platter hung between the windows and in the back of the closet he had found a fly rod enmeshed in kinky leader. Nana had missed a trout hook crusted with dried worm, stuck high on a curtain.

Before he went downstairs he remembered the bow, took it down, and, wondering at the easy memories of his youth, strung it. He instinctively placed the lower end against the inside of his right foot, and his left hand slid easily up the wood with the string lightly guided by his fingertips. The string vibrated tautly, and he remembered, too, how a bow seemed lighter after being strung, the tense pressure communicating energy to the arm. He estimated the pull at sixty pounds—quite a powerful bow.

"Oh, you found the bow 'n' arrow!" Nana said when he came into the kitchen with it. "You going to shoot? Say, how did you cock it?"

He placed the bow against his foot, pulled with his right hand, and pushed with the heel of his left hand, his fingers working the string out of the notch.

"Nobody could fix it. The children going crazy they couldn't shoot, nobody could cock it," Nana said admiringly.

"Do you have any arrows?"

The old man had decided to listen. "In the umbrella stand is some arrows," he said, and Nana rushed out after them. After breakfast she insisted they all go out and watch him shoot, and he was surprised at his own excitement when he fitted the nock of one of the warped target arrows to the string. He drew and loosed the arrow across the thirty yards between the driveway and barn. *Whap* as the arrow hit the silvery, unpainted wood of the barn and stuck, quivering. A cloud of swallows streamed out of a sashless window, and shreds of dusty hay fell from between the boards. The old people were impressed.

As he drew his second arrow the bow split apart above the grip. Arrow, string, half the bow fell loosely over his arms.

"Ooooh!" the old people sighed. "The wood was too old," the old man said. "It all dries up and it got no give to it."

"I'll get you another one," Hurley said. They shushed him up, said it wasn't any good, that nobody could cock it anyway. But later when he drove his Drive-Ur-Self Chevrolet down into Leah for groceries and the mail, he stopped in at Follansbee's hardware store.

Old Follansbee remembered him from the times he and Mary had come up to ski, possibly not from the earlier time when Follansbee was a young man working in his father's store and Hurley was a boy.

"Do for you?" Old Follansbee's bald head (once covered with black, bushy hair, parted in the middle) gleamed softly, approximately the same color and texture as his maple rolltop desk.

"I'd like to buy a bow—and some arrows," Hurley added in order to specify what kind of bow he meant. In Leah he had always been constrained to come immediately to the point. The old man led him to the sporting-goods corner where rifles and shotguns, fish poles and outboard motors, knives, rubber boots, decoys, and pistols lay in cases, on counters, or were hung on racks. He remembered this part of the store and the objects he had fallen in love with as a boy. No girl had meant as much to him at fifteen as had the beautifully angular lines of a Winchester Model 06, .22 pump. He even remembered the model number, but from this distance he wondered how a number could have meant so much.

He tried out a few of the pretty, too modern bows until he found one that seemed to have the same pull as the one he had broken.

"That one's glass," Old Follansbee said. "My boy says it don't want to break."

"Glass? It's made of glass?"

"Correct. Strange, ain't it? What they can do these days? You'll want some arrows, did you say?"

He bought two arrows. When he'd pulled the one out of the barn it came apart in his hands, split all the way up the shaft. He decided to replace it with two, even though he knew the New Hampshire way was to resent such prodigality. He bought a leather arm guard and finger tabs; then he saw the hunting arrows. The slim, three-bladed heads suggested Indians and his youth. The target arrows, beside them, seemed to have no character, no honest function. He bought two hunting arrows, and under old Follansbee's suspicious, conventional eye, a bow-hunting license, feeling like a child who had spent his Sunday-school money on a toy.

At the post office he found a joint communiqué from his worried children. "We have decided that it would be best . . ." the words went. He sent two identical telegrams: *Having wonderful time. Tend your business. Love, Dad.* They all believed in the therapy of youth—in this case, grandchildren. He couldn't think of a way to tell them that he loved them all too much.

Nana and the old man walked with him as far as the ledges at the top of the wild orchard, careful in their white tennis shoes. Nana stood splay-footed on the granite, queen of the hill, and surveyed the valley and the advancing forest with a disapproving eye.

"I see Holloways is letting their north pasture go back," she said, shaking her head. She had seen whole hills go back to darkness, and many fine houses fall into their cellar holes. She turned toward Hurley accusingly, he being from the outside and thus responsible for such things. "You got to pay money to have them take the hay!"

"Tell me it's cheaper to buy it off the truck," the old man said. "But I told them it don't grow on trucks." He stood beside his tall wife, in his baggy pants and old mackinaw. His new tennis shoes were startlingly white. "I call this the hill of agony," he said, winking at Hurley.

"You see where the deer come down to eat our garden?" Nana said, pointing to the deer trails through the apple trees. "We tell the game warden to shoot. Nothing. They hang bangers in the trees. All night, bang, bang! Nobody can sleep."

"Neither could the deer. They stayed up all night and et my lettuce," the old man said. He laughed and whacked his thigh.

"You shoot me a nice young deer," Nana said. "I make mincemeat, roasts, nice sausage for your breakfast."

He had tried to tell them that he didn't want to shoot anything with the bow, just carry it. Could he tell them that it gave a peculiar strength to his arm, that it seemed to be a kind of dynamo? When he was a boy in these same woods he and his friends had not been spectators, but actors. Their bows, fish poles, skis, and rifles had set them apart from the mere hikers, the summer people.

"I won't be back tonight unless the weather changes," he said. The sun was warm on the dry leaves, but the air was crisply cool in the shadows. He said goodbye to the old people, took off his pack, and waited on the ledges to see them safely back to the house below, then unrolled his sleeping bag and rolled it tighter. The night before he had noticed on his geodetic map a small, five-acre pond high in the cleft between Cascom and Gilman mountains. It was called Goose Pond, and he seemed to remember having been there once, long ago, perhaps trout fishing. He remembered being very tired, yet not wanting to leave; he remembered the cattails and alders and a long beaver dam, the pond deep in a little basin. He was sure he could follow the brook that issued from the pond—if he could pick the right one from all the little brooks that came down between Gilman and Cascom.

His pack tightened so that it rode high on his back, he carried his bow and the two hunting arrows in one hand. He soon relearned that arrows pass easily through the brush only if they go points first.

Stopping often to rest, he climbed past the maples into ground juniper and pine, hearing often the soft explosions of partridge, sometimes seeing them as they burst up and whistled through the trees. He passed giant beeches, crossing their noisy leaves, then walked silently through softwood until he came to a granite knob surrounded by stunted, wind-grieved hemlock. To the northwest he could see the Presidential Range,[2] but Leah, the lake, and the Pedersens' farm were all out of sight. He ate a hard-boiled egg and one of the bittersweet wild apples he had collected on the way. The wind was delightfully cool against his face, but he knew his sweat would soon chill. At two o'clock the sun was fairly low in the hard blue sky—whole valleys were in shadow below.

He took out his map. He had crossed three little brooks, and the one he could hear a short way ahead must be Goose Pond's overflow. By the sound it was a fair-sized brook. When he climbed down through the hemlock and saw it he was sure. White water angled right and left, dropping over boulders into narrow sluices and deep, clear pools. He knelt down, drank, and dipped his head in and out of the icy water. His forehead turned numb, as if it were made of rubber. A water beetle darted to the bottom. A baby trout flashed green and pink beside a stone. It was as if he were looking through a giant lens into an alien world, where life was cold and cruel, and even the light had a quality of darkness about it. Odd little sticks on the bottom were the camouflaged larvae of insects, waiting furtively to hatch or to be eaten. Fish hid in the shadows under stones, their avid little mouths ready to snap. He shuddered and raised his head—a momentary flash of panic, as if some carnivorous animal with a gaping mouth might come darting up to tear his face.

Following the brook, jumping from stone to stone, sometimes having to leave it for the woods in order to get around tangles of blowdown or waterfalls, he came suddenly into the deep silence of the spruce, where the channel

---

2. Part of New Hampshire's White Mountains, with a number of peaks named for U.S. presidents.

was deep. In the moist, cathedral silence of the tall pillars of spruce he realized how deafening the white water had been. The wind stirred the tops of the trees and made the slim trunks move slowly, but could not penetrate the dim, yet luminous greenness of the place.

And he saw the deer. He saw the face of the deer beside a narrow tree, and for a moment there was nothing but the face: a smoky brown eye deep as a tunnel, it seemed, long delicate lashes, a black whisker or two along the white-shaded muzzle. The black nose quivered at each breath, the nostrils rounded. Then he began to follow the light brown line, motionless and so nearly invisible along the back, down along the edge of the white breast. One large ear turned slowly toward him. It was a doe, watching him carefully, perfect in the moment of fine innocence and wonder—a quality he suddenly remembered—the expressionless readiness of the deer. But other instincts had been working in him. He hadn't moved, but breathing slowly, put his weight equally on both legs. The light sharpened as if it had been twilight and the sun had suddenly flashed. Every detail—the convolutions of the bark on the trees, tiny twigs, the fine sheen of light on each hair of the doe, each curved, precious eyelash—became vivid and distinct. Depth grew, color brightened; his hunter's eyes became painfully efficient, as if each needlelike detail pierced him. The world became polarized on the axis of their eyes. He was alone with the doe in a green world that seemed to cry for rich red, and he did not have time to think: it was enough that he sensed the doe's quick decision to leave him. An onyx hoof snapped, her white flag rose, and the doe floated in a slow arc, broadside to him, clear of the trees for an endless second. He watched down the long arrow, three blades moved ahead of the doe, and at the precise moment all tension stopped; his arms, fingers, eyes, and the bow were all one instrument. The arrow sliced through the deer.

Her white flag dropped. Gracefully, in long, splendid leaps, hoofs stabbing the hollow-sounding carpet of needles, the doe flickered beyond the trees. One moment of crashing brush, then silence. A thick excitement rose like fluid into his face; his arms seemed to grow to twice their normal size, become twice as strong. And still his body was governed by the old, learned patterns. He walked silently forward and retrieved his bloody arrow, snapped the feathers alive again. The trail was a vivid line of jewels, brighter than the checkerberries against their shiny green leaves, unmistakable. He rolled the bright blood between his fingers as he slowly moved forward. He must let the doe stop and lie down, let her shock-born strength dissipate in calm bleeding. Watching each step, figuring out whole series of steps, of brush bendings in advance, he picked the silent route around snags and under the blowdown.

In an hour he had gone a hundred yards, still tight and careful, up out of the spruce and onto a small rise covered with birch and poplar saplings. The leaves were loud underfoot, and as he carefully placed one foot, the doe rose in front of him and crashed downhill, obviously weak, staggering against the whippy birch. A fine mist of blood sprayed at each explosion of breath from the holes in her ribs. He ran after her, leaping over brush, running along fallen limbs, sliding under low branches that flicked his cheeks like claws. His bow caught on a branch and jerked him upright. After one impatient pull he left it. He drew his knife. The brown shape ahead had disappeared, and he dove through the brush after it, witch hobble grabbing his legs.

The doe lay against a stump, one leg twitching. He knelt down and put one hard arm around her neck, and not caring for the dangerous hoofs, the spark of life, raised the firm, warm neck against his chest, and sighed as he stabbed carefully into the sticking place. Blood was hot on the knife and on his hand.

He rolled over into the leaves, long breaths bending him, making his back arch. His shirt vibrated over his heart, his body turned heavy and pressed with unbelievable weight into the earth. He let his arms melt into the ground, and a cool, lucid sadness came over his flesh.

He made himself get up. In order to stand he had to fight gravity, to use all his strength—a quick fear for his heart. His joints ached and had begun to stiffen. He must keep moving. Shadows were long and he had much to do before dark. He followed the blood trail back and found his bow and one arrow. He limped going back down the hill; at a certain angle his knees tended to jackknife, as if gears were slipping.

He stood over the clean body of the doe, the white belly snowy against brown leaves. One hind leg he hooked behind a sapling, and he held the other with his knee as he made the first long incision through the hair and skin, careful not to break the peritoneum. He ran the incision from the tail to the breast, then worked the skin back with his fingers before making the second cut through the warm membrane, the sticky blue case for stomach and entrails. He cut, and the steamy innards rolled unbroken and still working out onto the ground. A few neat berries of turd rattled on the leaves. He cut the anus and organs of reproduction clear of the flesh, then found the kidneys and liver and reached arm-deep into the humid chest cavity, the hot smell of blood close to his nostrils, and removed the yellow lungs in handfuls. Then he pulled out the dark red heart. Kidneys, liver, and heart he wrapped carefully in a plastic bag, then he rose and painfully stretched. Goose Pond lay just below; he could see a flicker of water through the skein of branches, and there he would make camp.

With his belt looped around the neck and front hoofs, he slid the doe down toward the pond. It was dusk by the time he found a dry platform of soft needles beneath a hemlock, next to the water. The doe had become stiff enough so that he could hang it in a young beech, head wedged in a fork. He spread his sleeping bag, tried it for roots and stones, and found none. The last high touch of sun on the hill above him had gone; he had even prepared ground for a fire when he realized that he had no energy left, no appetite to eat the liver of the doe.

Darkness had settled in along the ground, but the sky was still bright; one line of cirrus clouds straight overhead still caught orange sunlight. Across the silver water the alder swamp was jet black, and the steep hill rose behind, craggy with spruce. A beaver's nose broke water, and even, slow circles spread across the pond. The dark woods filled with cold, and one of his legs began to jerk uncontrollably. He took off his boots and slid into his sleeping bag.

The doe was monstrous, angular against the sky, her neck stretched awkwardly, head canted to one side. The black hole in her belly gaped empty. He drew his sleeping bag up around his face.

If he were twenty again he would be happy. To have shot a deer with a bow—he'd be a hero, a woodsman, famous in Leah. How it would have impressed Mary! She would have said little about it—she went to great lengths never to flatter him; her compliments had been more tangible, seldom in words. He must think of something else. The world was too empty. The cold woods, the darkening water, were empty. He was too cold, too tired to manipulate his thoughts. And the progression of hours began again. Mary's eyes watched him, deep in sick hollows. How could her flesh turn so brown? Why could he do nothing to stop the pain? She watched him, in torment, her frail body riven, cut beyond endurance. The disease had killed her bravery with pain and left her gruesomely alive, without dignity, whimpering like a spoiled brat, asking for help she should have known did not exist. And he stood by and watched, doing nothing. Nothing. He was not a man to do nothing. *Mary, did I do nothing to help you?*

He heard, far away, the lonely cry of the Canada geese. He was alone, hidden in the blind night, high on the stony mass of Cascom Mountain.

And then they came in, circling, calling to each other above the doubtful ground. Perhaps they had seen the reflected circle of fading sky, or remembered, generations remembering that geese had rested safely in the high pond and found food there. The scouts came whistling on their great wings, searching and listening. They sent their messages back to the flock waiting above, then planed down, braking, smeared the water with wind and came to rest in a flash of spray. The flock circled down after, careless now it was safe, honking gaily, giving the feeding call prematurely, echoing the messages of the leaders and landing masters. "Come in, come down and rest," they seemed to call, until everyone had landed safely. Then the voices grew softer, less excited, and only an occasional word drifted across the water.

Robert Hurley lay in the warm hollow of his sleeping bag, where the hours had stopped. He thought for a moment of the doe's death, and of his knife. The geese spoke softly to each other on the water—a small splash, a flutter of wings, and the resting, contented voices in the deep basin of the pond. As sleep washed over him he seemed to be among them; their sentinels guarded him. When they had rested well they would rise and continue the dangerous journey down the world.

1959

WILLIAM CARLOS WILLIAMS
1883–1963

Williams was born in Rutherford, New Jersey. He took a medical degree at the University of Pennsylvania and practiced as a pediatrician through the long years of his literary career. Leaving behind the European-inspired Imagist movement, he defined himself as utterly American in taste and spirit, becoming the friend, supporter, and colleague of several of the leaders of the avant-garde in American literature. His work as a poet culminated in the massive chronicle *Paterson* (1946–58), and the imagination that shaped his verse informed his speculations on American history and its character in his book of essays *In the American Grain* (1925). Among his many volumes of verse, *Pictures from Brueghel and Other Poems* won the Pulitzer Prize in 1963. In his fiction as in his several plays he achieves an illuminated mirror image of the flat banality of ordinary lives. His novels include *White Mule* (1937) and *In the Money* (1940). *The Collected Stories of William Carlos Williams* appeared in 1996.

The Use of Force

They were new patients to me, all I had was the name, Olson. Please come down as soon as you can, my daughter is very sick. When I arrived I was met by the mother, a big startled looking woman, very clean and apologetic who merely said, Is this the doctor? and let me in. In the back, she added. You must excuse us, doctor, we have her in the kitchen where it is warm. It is very damp here sometimes.

The child was fully dressed and sitting on her father's lap near the kitchen table. He tried to get up, but I motioned for him not to bother, took off my overcoat and started to look things over. I could see that they were all very nervous, eyeing me up and down distrustfully. As often, in such cases, they weren't telling me more than they had to, it was up to me to tell them; that's why they were spending three dollars on me.

The child was fairly eating me up with her cold, steady eyes, and no expression to her face whatever. She did not move and seemed, inwardly, quiet; an unusually attractive little thing, and as strong as a heifer in appearance. But her face was flushed, she was breathing rapidly, and I realized that she had a high fever. She had magnificent blonde hair, in profusion. One of those picture children often reproduced in advertising leaflets and the photogravure sections of the Sunday papers.

She's had a fever for three days, began the father and we don't know what it comes from. My wife has given her things, you know, like people do, but it don't do no good. And there's been a lot of sickness around. So we tho't you'd better look her over and tell us what is the matter.

As doctors often do I took a trial shot at it as a point of departure. Has she had a sore throat?

Both parents answered me together, No . . . No, she says her throat don't hurt her.

Does your throat hurt you? added the mother to the child. But the little girl's expression didn't change nor did she move her eyes from my face.

Have you looked?

I tried to, said the mother, but I couldn't see.

As it happens we had been having a number of cases of diphtheria in the school to which this child went during that month and we were all, quite apparently, thinking of that, though no one had as yet spoken of the thing.

Well, I said, suppose we take a look at the throat first. I smiled in my best professional manner and asking for the child's first name I said, come on, Mathilda, open your mouth and let's take a look at your throat.

Nothing doing.

Aw, come on, I coaxed, just open your mouth wide and let me take a look. Look, I said opening both hands wide, I haven't anything in my hands. Just open up and let me see.

Such a nice man, put in the mother. Look how kind he is to you. Come on, do what he tells you to. He won't hurt you.

At that I ground my teeth in disgust. If only they wouldn't use the word "hurt" I might be able to get somewhere. But I did not allow myself to be hurried or disturbed but speaking quietly and slowly I approached the child again.

As I moved my chair a little nearer suddenly with one catlike movement both her hands clawed instinctively for my eyes and she almost reached them too. In fact she knocked my glasses flying and they fell, though unbroken, several feet away from me on the kitchen floor.

Both the mother and father almost turned themselves inside out in embarrassment and apology. You bad girl, said the mother, taking her and shaking her by one arm. Look what you've done. The nice man . . .

For heaven's sake, I broke in. Don't call me a nice man to her. I'm here to look at her throat on the chance that she might have diphtheria[1] and possibly die of it. But that's nothing to her. Look here, I said to the child, we're going to look at your throat. You're old enough to understand what I'm saying. Will you open it now by yourself or shall we have to open it for you?

Not a move. Even her expression hadn't changed. Her breaths however were coming faster and faster. Then the battle began. I had to do it. I had to have a throat culture for her own protection. But first I told the parents that it was entirely up to them. I explained the danger but said that I would not insist on a throat examination so long as they would take the responsibility.

---

1. Bacterial disease that killed millions, mostly children, in the era before antibiotic medicines and effective programs of immunization. The most common sign of infection is a thick, bluish-white membrane coating the tonsils and throat.

If you don't do what the doctor says you'll have to go to the hospital, the mother admonished her severely.

Oh yeah? I had to smile to myself. After all, I had already fallen in love with the savage brat, the parents were contemptible to me. In the ensuing struggle they grew more and more abject, crushed, exhausted while she surely rose to magnificent heights of insane fury of effort bred of her terror of me.

The father tried his best, and he was a big man but the fact that she was his daughter, his shame at her behavior and his dread of hurting her made him release her just at the critical times when I had almost achieved success, till I wanted to kill him. But his dread also that she might have diphtheria made him tell me to go on, go on though he himself was almost fainting, while the mother moved back and forth behind us raising and lowering her hands in an agony of apprehension.

Put her in front of you on your lap, I ordered, and hold both her wrists.

But as soon as he did the child let out a scream. Don't, you're hurting me. Let go of my hands. Let them go I tell you. Then she shrieked terrifyingly, hysterically. Stop it! Stop it! You're killing me!

Do you think she can stand it, doctor! said the mother.

You get out, said the husband to his wife. Do you want her to die of diphtheria?

Come on now, hold her, I said.

Then I grasped the child's head with my left hand and tried to get the wooden tongue depressor between her teeth. She fought, with clenched teeth, desperately! But now I also had grown furious—at a child. I tried to hold myself down but I couldn't. I know how to expose a throat for inspection. And I did my best. When finally I got the wooden spatula behind the last teeth and just the point of it into the mouth cavity, she opened up for an instant but before I could see anything she came down again and gripping the wooden blade between her molars, she reduced it to splinters before I could get it out again.

Aren't you ashamed, the mother yelled at her. Aren't you ashamed to act like that in front of the doctor?

Get me a smooth-handled spoon of some sort, I told the mother. We're going through with this. The child's mouth was already bleeding. Her tongue was cut and she was screaming in wild hysterical shrieks. Perhaps I should have desisted and come back in an hour or more. No doubt it would have been better. But I have seen at least two children lying dead in bed of neglect in such cases, and feeling that I must get a diagnosis now or never I went at it again. But the worst of it was that I too had got beyond reason. I could have torn the child apart in my own fury and enjoyed it. It was a pleasure to attack her. My face was burning with it.

The damned little brat must be protected against her own idiocy, one says to one's self at such times. Others must be protected against her. It is a social necessity. And all these things are true. But a blind fury, a feeling of adult shame, bred of a longing for muscular release are the operatives. One goes on to the end.

In the final unreasoning assault I overpowered the child's neck and jaws. I forced the heavy silver spoon back of her teeth and down her throat till she gagged. And there it was—both tonsils covered with membrane. She had fought valiantly to keep me from knowing her secret. She had been hiding that sore throat for three days at least and lying to her parents in order to escape just such an outcome as this.

Now truly she was furious. She had been on the defensive before but now she attacked. Tried to get off her father's lap and fly at me while tears of defeat blinded her eyes.

1950

TOBIAS WOLFF
b. 1945

Wolff was born in Alabama and grew up in Washington State. Since his education at Oxford and Stanford Universities he has taught at Syracuse University and Indiana University. His stories are collected in *In the Garden of the North American Martyrs* (1981), *Back in the World* (1985), *The Night in Question* (1996), and *Our Story Begins* (2008); his novels include *Ugly Rumours* (1975) and *The Barracks Thief* (1984), winner of the PEN/Faulkner Award. Wolff is probably best known for his remarkable memoirs: *This Boy's Life* (1989) and *Old School* (2003) recount his boyhood; *In Pharaoh's Army* (1994) depicts his experiences as a soldier in the Vietnam War. He has also edited several anthologies, among them *The Vintage Book of Contemporary American Short Stories* (1993) and *Best American Short Stories* (1994). He currently teaches at Stanford University.

In the Garden of the North American Martyrs

When she was young, Mary saw a brilliant and original man lose his job because he had expressed ideas that were offensive to the trustees of the college where they both taught. She shared his views, but did not sign the protest petition. She was, after all, on trial herself—as a teacher, as a woman, as an interpreter of history.

Mary watched herself. Before giving a lecture she wrote it out in full, using the arguments and often the words of other, approved writers, so that she would not by chance say something scandalous. Her own thoughts she kept to herself, and the words for them grew faint as time went on; without quite disappearing they shrank to remote, nervous points, like birds flying away.

When the department turned into a hive of cliques, Mary went about her business and pretended not to know that people hated each other. To avoid seeming bland she let herself become eccentric in harmless ways. She took up bowling, which she learned to love, and founded the Brandon College chapter of a society dedicated to restoring the good name of Richard III.[1] She memorized comedy routines from records and jokes from books; people groaned when she rattled them off, but she did not let that stop her, and after a time the groans became the point of the jokes. They were a kind of tribute to Mary's willingness to expose herself.

---

1. English king (1452–1485) generally regarded as ruthless and brutal.

In fact no one at the college was safer than Mary, for she was making herself into something institutional, like a custom, or a mascot—part of the college's idea of itself.

Now and then she wondered whether she had been too careful. The things she said and wrote seemed flat to her, pulpy, as though someone else had squeezed the juice out of them. And once, while talking with a senior professor, Mary saw herself reflected in a window: she was leaning toward him and had her head turned so that her ear was right in front of his moving mouth. The sight disgusted her. Years later, when she had to get a hearing aid, Mary suspected that her deafness was a result of always trying to catch everything everyone said.

In the second half of Mary's fifteenth year at Brandon the provost called a meeting of all faculty and students to announce that the college was bankrupt and would not open its gates again. He was every bit as much surprised as they; the report from the trustees had reached his desk only that morning. It seemed that Brandon's financial manager had speculated in some kind of futures and lost everything. The provost wanted to deliver the news in person before it reached the papers. He wept openly and so did the students and teachers, with only a few exceptions—some cynical upperclassmen who claimed to despise the education they had received.

Mary could not rid her mind of the word "speculate." It meant to guess, in terms of money to gamble. How could a man gamble a college? Why would he want to do that, and how could it be that no one stopped him? To Mary, it seemed to belong to another time; she thought of a drunken plantation owner gaming away his slaves.

She applied for jobs and got an offer from a new experimental college in Oregon. It was her only offer so she took it.

The college was in one building. Bells rang all the time, lockers lined the hallways, and at every corner stood a buzzing water fountain. The student newspaper came out twice a month on mimeograph paper which felt wet. The library, which was next to the band room, had no librarian and no books.

The countryside was beautiful, though, and Mary might have enjoyed it if the rain had not caused her so much trouble. There was something wrong with her lungs that the doctors couldn't agree on, and couldn't cure; whatever it was, the dampness made it worse. On rainy days condensation formed in Mary's hearing aid and shorted it out. She began to dread talking with people, never knowing when she would have to take out her control box and slap it against her leg.

It rained nearly every day. When it was not raining it was getting ready to rain, or clearing. The ground glinted under the grass, and the light had a yellow undertone that flared up during storms.

There was water in Mary's basement. Her walls sweated, and she had found toadstools growing behind the refrigerator. She felt as though she were rusting out, like one of those old cars people thereabouts kept in their front yards, on pieces of wood. Mary knew that everyone was dying, but it did seem to her that she was dying faster than most.

She continued to look for another job, without success. Then, in the fall of her third year in Oregon, she got a letter from a woman named Louise who'd once taught in Brandon. Louise had scored a great success with a book on

Benedict Arnold[2] and was now on the faculty of a famous college in upstate New York. She said that one of her colleagues would be retiring at the end of the year and asked whether Mary would be interested in the position.

The letter surprised Mary. Louise thought of herself as a great historian and of almost everyone else as useless; Mary had not known that she felt differently about her. Moreover, enthusiasm for other people's causes did not come easily to Louise, who had a way of sucking in her breath when familiar names were mentioned, as though she knew things that friendship kept her from disclosing.

Mary expected nothing, but sent a résumé and copies of her two books. Shortly after that Louise called to say that the search committee, of which she was chairwoman, had decided to grant Mary an interview in early November. "Now don't get your hopes too high," Louise said.

"Oh, no," Mary said, but thought: Why shouldn't I hope? They would not go to the bother and expense of bringing her to the college if they weren't serious. And she was certain that the interview would go well. She would make them like her, or at least give them no cause to dislike her.

She read about the area with a strange sense of familiarity, as if the land and its history were already known to her. And when her plane left Portland and climbed easily into the clouds, Mary felt like she was going home. The feeling stayed with her, growing stronger when they landed. She tried to describe it to Louise as they left the airport at Syracuse and drove toward the college, an hour or so away. "It's like *déjà vu*," she said.

"*Déjà vu* is a hoax," Louise said. "It's just a chemical imbalance of some kind."

"Maybe so," Mary said, "but I still have this sensation."

"Don't get serious on me," Louise said. "That's not your long suit. Just be your funny, wisecracking old self. Tell me now—honestly—how do I look?"

It was night, too dark to see Louise's face well, but in the airport she had seemed gaunt and pale and intense. She reminded Mary of a description in the book she'd been reading, of how Iroquois[3] warriors gave themselves visions by fasting. She had that kind of look about her. But she wouldn't want to hear that. "You look wonderful," Mary said.

"There's a reason," Louise said. "I've taken a lover. My concentration has improved, my energy level is up, and I've lost ten pounds. I'm also getting some color in my cheeks, though that could be the weather. I recommend the experience highly. But you probably disapprove."

Mary didn't know what to say. She said that she was sure Louise knew best, but that didn't seem to be enough. "Marriage is a great institution," she added, "but who wants to live in an institution?"

Louise groaned. "I know you," she said, "and I know that right now you're thinking 'But what about Ted? What about the children?' The fact is, Mary, they aren't taking it well at all. Ted has become a nag." She handed Mary her purse. "Be a good girl and light me a cigarette, will you? I know I told you I quit, but this whole thing has been very hard on me, very hard, and I'm afraid I've started again."

---

2. U.S. general in the Revolutionary War, who became a traitor (1741–1801). 3. A tribe native to the lower Great Lakes region, war-loving by reputation.

They were in the hills now, heading north on a narrow road. Tall trees arched above them. As they topped a rise Mary saw the forest all around, deep black under the plum-colored sky. There were a few lights and these made the darkness seem even greater.

"Ted has succeeded in completely alienating the children from me," Louise was saying. "There is no reasoning with any of them. In fact, they refuse to discuss the matter at all, which is very ironical because over the years I have tried to instill in them a willingness to see things from the other person's point of view. If they could just *meet* Jonathan I know they would feel differently. But they won't hear of it. Jonathan," she said, "is my lover."

"I see," Mary said, and nodded.

Coming around a curve they caught two deer in the headlights. Their eyes lit up and their hindquarters tensed; Mary could see them trembling as the car went by. "Deer," she said.

"I don't know," Louise said, "I just don't know. I do my best and it never seems to be enough. But that's enough about me—let's talk about you. What did you think of my latest book?" She squawked and beat her palms on the steering wheel. "God, I love that joke," she said. "Seriously, though, what about you? It must have been a real shockeroo when good old Brandon folded."

"It was hard. Things haven't been good but they'll be a lot better if I get this job."

"At least you have work," Louise said. "You should look at it from the bright side."

"I try."

"You seem so gloomy. I hope you're not worrying about the interview, or the class. Worrying won't do you a bit of good. Be happy."

"Class? What class?"

"The class you're supposed to give tomorrow, after the interview. Didn't I tell you? *Mea culpa*, hon, *mea maxima culpa*. I've been uncharacteristically forgetful lately."

"But what will I do?"

"Relax," Louise said. "Just pick a subject and wing it."

"Wing it?"

"You know, open your mouth and see what comes out. Extemporize."

"But I always work from a prepared lecture."

Louise sighed. "All right. I'll tell you what. Last year I wrote an article on the Marshall Plan[4] that I got bored with and never published. You can read that."

Parroting what Louise had written seemed wrong to Mary, at first; then it occurred to her that she had been doing the same kind of things for many years, and that this was not the time to get scruples. "Thanks," she said. "I appreciate it."

"Here we are," Louise said, and pulled into a circular drive with several cabins grouped around it. In two of the cabins lights were on; smoke drifted straight up from the chimneys. "This is the visitors' center. The college is another two

---

4. Plan for rehabilitating European economies devastated by World War II, formulated by George Catlett Marshall (1880–1959), U.S. Chief of Staff.

miles thataway." Louise pointed down the road. "I'd invite you to stay at my house, but I'm spending the night with Jonathan and Ted is not good company these days. You would hardly recognize him."

She took Mary's bags from the trunk and carried them up the steps of a darkened cabin. "Look," she said, "they've laid a fire for you. All you have to do is light it." She stood in the middle of the room with her arms crossed and watched as Mary held a match under the kindling. "There," she said. "You'll be snugaroo in no time. I'd love to stay and chew the fat but I can't. You just get a good night's sleep and I'll see you in the morning."

Mary stood in the doorway and waved as Louise pulled out of the drive, spraying gravel. She filled her lungs, to taste the air: it was tart and clear. She could see the stars in their figurations, and the vague streams of light that ran among the stars.

She still felt uneasy about reading Louise's work as her own. It would be her first complete act of plagiarism. It would change her. It would make her less—how much less, she did not know. But what else could she do? She certainly wouldn't "wing it." Words might fail her, and then what? Mary had a dread of silence. When she thought of silence she thought of drowning, as if it were a kind of water she could not swim in.

"I want this job," she said, and settled deep into her coat. It was cashmere and Mary had not worn it since moving to Oregon, because people there thought you were pretentious if you had on anything but a Pendleton shirt or, of course, raingear. She rubbed her cheek against the upturned collar and thought of a silver moon shining through bare black branches, a white house with green shutters, red leaves falling in a hard blue sky.

Louise woke her a few hours later. She was sitting on the edge of the bed, pushing at Mary's shoulder and snuffling loudly. When Mary asked her what was wrong she said, "I want your opinion on something. It's very important. Do you think I'm womanly?"

Mary sat up. "Louise, can this wait?"

"No."

"Womanly?"

Louise nodded.

"You are very beautiful," Mary said, "and you know how to present yourself."

Louise stood and paced the room. "That son of a bitch," she said. She came back and stood over Mary. "Let's suppose someone said I have no sense of humor. Would you agree or disagree?"

"In some things you do. I mean, yes, you have a good sense of humor."

"What do you mean, 'in some things?' What kind of things?"

"Well, if you heard that someone had been killed in an unusual way, like by an exploding cigar, you would think that was funny."

Louise laughed.

"That's what I mean," Mary said.

Louise went on laughing. "Oh, Lordy," she said. "Now it's my turn to say something about you." She sat down beside Mary.

"Please," Mary said.

"Just one thing," Louise said.

Mary waited.

"You're trembling," Louise said. "I was just going to say—oh, forget it. Listen, do you mind if I sleep on the couch? I'm all in."

"Go ahead."

"Sure it's okay? You've got a big day tomorrow." She fell back on the sofa and kicked off her shoes. "I was just going to say, you should use some liner on those eyebrows of yours. They sort of disappear and the effect is disconcerting."

Neither of them slept. Louise chain-smoked cigarettes and Mary watched the coals burn down. When it was light enough that they could see each other Louise got up. "I'll send a student for you," she said. "Good luck."

The college looked the way colleges are supposed to look. Roger, the student assigned to show Mary around, explained that it was an exact copy of a college in England, right down to the gargoyles and stained-glass windows. It looked so much like a college that moviemakers sometimes used it as a set. *Andy Hardy Goes to College*[5] had been filmed there, and every fall they had an Andy Hardy Goes to College Day, with raccoon coats and goldfish-swallowing contests.

Above the door of the Founder's Building was a Latin motto which, roughly translated, meant "God helps those who help themselves." As Roger recited the names of illustrious graduates Mary was struck by the extent to which they had taken this precept to heart. They had helped themselves to railroads, mines, armies, states; to empires of finance with outposts all over the world.

Roger took Mary to the chapel and showed her a plaque bearing the names of alumni who had been killed in various wars, all the way back to the Civil War. There were not many names. Here too, apparently, the graduates had helped themselves. "Oh yes," Roger said as they were leaving, "I forgot to tell you. The communion rail comes from some church in Europe where Charlemagne[6] used to go."

They went to the gymnasium, and the three hockey rinks, and the library, where Mary inspected the card catalogue, as though she would turn down the job if they didn't have the right books. "We have a little more time," Roger said as they went outside. "Would you like to see the power plant?"

Mary wanted to keep busy until the last minute, so she agreed.

Roger led her into the depths of the service building, explaining things about the machine, which was the most advanced in the country. "People think the college is really old-fashioned," he said, "but it isn't. They let girls come here now, and some of the teachers are women. In fact, there's a statute that says they have to interview at least one woman for each opening. There it is."

They were standing on an iron catwalk above the biggest machine Mary had ever beheld. Roger, who was majoring in Earth Sciences, said that it had been built from a design pioneered by a professor in his department. Where before he had been gabby Roger now became reverent. It was clear that for him this machine was the soul of the college, that the purpose of the college

---

5. Before and during World War II the series of Hardy Family films was extremely popular in the United States. Andy Hardy was played by film star Mickey Rooney (1920–2014).   **6.** King of the Franks (742–814) and emperor of the Holy Roman Empire.

was to provide outlets for the machine. Together they leaned against the railing and watched it hum.

Mary arrived at the committee room exactly on time for her interview, but the room was empty. Her two books were on the table, along with a water pitcher and some glasses. She sat down and picked up one of the books. The binding cracked as she opened it. The pages were smooth, clean, unread. Mary turned to the first chapter, which began, "It is generally believed that . . ." How dull, she thought.

Nearly twenty minutes later Louise came in with several men. "Sorry we're late," she said. "We don't have much time so we'd better get started." She introduced Mary to the men, but with one exception the names and faces did not stay together. The exception was Dr. Howells, the department chairman, who had a porous blue nose and terrible teeth.

A shiny-faced man to Dr. Howells's right spoke first. "So," he said, "I understand you once taught at Brandon College."

"It was a shame that Brandon had to close," said a young man with a pipe in his mouth. "There is a place for schools like Brandon." As he talked the pipe wagged up and down.

"Now you're in Oregon," Dr. Howells said. "I've never been there. How do you like it?"

"Not very much," Mary said.

"Is that right?" Dr. Howells leaned toward her. "I thought everyone liked Oregon. I heard it's very green."

"That's true," Mary said.

"I suppose it rains a lot," he said.

"Nearly every day."

"I wouldn't like that," he said, shaking his head. "I like it dry. Of course it snows here, and you have your rain now and then, but it's a *dry* rain. Have you ever been to Utah? There's a state for you. Bryce Canyon. The Mormon Tabernacle Choir."

"Dr. Howells was brought up in Utah," said the young man with the pipe.

"It was a different place altogether in those days," Dr. Howells said. "Mrs. Howells and I have always talked about going back when I retire, but now I'm not so sure."

"We're a little short on time," Louise said.

"And here I've been going on and on," Dr. Howells said. "Before we wind things up, is there anything you want to tell us?"

"Yes. I think you should give me the job." Mary laughed when she said this, but no one laughed back, or even looked at her. They all looked away. Mary understood then that they were not really considering her for the position. She had been brought here to satisfy a rule. She had no hope.

The men gathered their papers and shook hands with Mary and told her how much they were looking forward to her class. "I can't get enough of the Marshall Plan," Dr. Howells said.

"Sorry about that," Louise said when they were alone. "I didn't think it would be so bad. That was a real bitcheroo."

"Tell me something," Mary said. "You already know who you're going to hire, don't you?"

Louise nodded.

"Then why did you bring me here?"

Louise began to explain about the statute and Mary interrupted. "I know all that. But why me? Why did you pick *me*?"

Louise walked to the window. She spoke with her back to Mary. "Things haven't been going very well for old Louise," she said. "I've been unhappy and I thought you might cheer me up. You used to be so funny, and I was sure you would enjoy the trip—it didn't cost you anything, and it's pretty this time of year with the leaves and everything. Mary, you don't know the things my parents did to me. And Ted is no barrel of laughs either. Or Jonathan, the son of a bitch. I deserve some love and friendship but I don't get any." She turned and looked at her watch. "It's almost time for your class. We'd better go."

"I would rather not give it. After all, there's not much point, is there?"

"But you *have* to give it. That's part of the interview." Louise handed Mary a folder. "All you have to do is read this. It isn't much, considering all the money we've laid out to get you here."

Mary followed Louise down the hall to the lecture room. The professors were sitting in the front row with their legs crossed. They smiled and nodded at Mary. Behind them the room was full of students, some of whom had spilled over into the aisles. One of the professors adjusted the microphone to Mary's height, crouching down as he went to the podium and back as though he would prefer not to be seen.

Louise called the room to order. She introduced Mary and gave the subject of the lecture. But Mary had decided to wing it after all. Mary came to the podium unsure of what she would say; sure only that she would rather die than read Louise's article. The sun poured through the stained glass onto the people around her, painting their faces. Thick streams of smoke from the young professor's pipe drifted through a circle of red light at Mary's feet, turning crimson and twisting like flames.

"I wonder how many of you know," she began, "that we are in the Long House,[7] the ancient domain of the Five Nations of the Iroquois."

Two professors looked at each other.

"The Iroquois were without pity," Mary said. "They hunted people down with clubs and arrows and spears and nets, and blowguns made from elder stalks. They tortured their captives, sparing no one, not even the little children. They took scalps and practiced cannibalism and slavery. Because they had no pity they became powerful, so powerful that no other tribe dared to oppose them. They made the other tribes pay tribute, and when they had nothing more to pay the Iroquois attacked them."

Several of the professors began to whisper. Dr. Howells was saying something to Louise, and Louise was shaking her head.

"In one of their raids," Mary said, "they captured two Jesuit priests, Jean de Brébeuf and Gabriel Lalemant.[8] They covered Lalemant with pitch and set him on fire in front of Brébeuf. When Brébeuf rebuked them they cut off his lips and put a burning iron down his throat. They hung a collar of red-hot hatchets around his neck, and poured boiling water over his head. When he continued to preach to them they cut strips of flesh from his body and ate

7. Communal American Indian dwelling, in actuality a wooden frame covered with bark.   8. The two most famous martyrs among the Jesuit missionaries in North America, tortured and killed by the Iroquois in 1649.

them before his eyes. While he was still alive, they scalped him and cut open his breast and drank his blood. Later, their chief tore out Brébeuf's heart and ate it, but just before he did this Brébeuf spoke to them one last time. He said—"

"That's enough!" yelled Dr. Howells, jumping to his feet.

Louise stopped shaking her head. Her eyes were perfectly round.

Mary had come to the end of her facts. She did not know what Brébeuf had said. Silence rose up around her; just when she thought she would go under and be lost in it she heard someone whistling in the hallway outside, trilling the notes like a bird, like many birds.

"Mend your lives," she said. "You have deceived yourselves in the pride of your hearts, and the strength of your arms. Though you soar aloft like the eagle, though your nest is set among the stars, thence I will bring you down, says the Lord.[9] Turn from power to love. Be kind. Do justice. Walk humbly."

Louise was waving her arms. "Mary!" she shouted.

But Mary had more to say, much more; she waved back at Louise, then turned off her hearing aid so that she would not be distracted again.

1981

Bullet in the Brain

Anders couldn't get to the bank until just before it closed, so of course the line was endless and he got stuck behind two women whose loud, stupid conversation put him in a murderous temper. He was never in the best of tempers anyway, Anders—a book critic known for the weary, elegant savagery with which he dispatched almost everything he reviewed.

With the line still doubled around the rope, one of the tellers stuck a "POSITION CLOSED" sign in her window and walked to the back of the bank, where she leaned against a desk and began to pass the time with a man shuffling papers. The women in front of Anders broke off their conversation and watched the teller with hatred. "Oh, that's nice," one of them said. She turned to Anders and added, confident of his accord, "One of those little human touches that keep us coming back for more."

Anders had conceived his own towering hatred of the teller, but he immediately turned it on the presumptuous crybaby in front of him. "Damned unfair," he said. "Tragic, really. If they're not chopping off the wrong leg, or bombing your ancestral village, they're closing their positions."

She stood her ground. "I didn't say it was tragic," she said. "I just think it's a pretty lousy way to treat your customers."

"Unforgivable," Anders said. "Heaven will take note."

She sucked in her cheeks but stared past him and said nothing. Anders saw that the other woman, her friend, was looking in the same direction. And then the tellers stopped what they were doing, and the customers slowly turned, and silence came over the bank. Two men wearing black ski masks and blue business suits were standing to the side of the door. One of them had a pistol

9. Obadiah 2–4.

pressed against the guard's neck. The guard's eyes were closed, and his lips were moving. The other man had a sawed-off shotgun. "Keep your big mouth shut!" the man with the pistol said, though no one had spoken a word. "One of you tellers hits the alarm, you're all dead meat. Got it?"

The tellers nodded.

"Oh, bravo," Anders said. "*Dead meat.*" He turned to the woman in front of him. "Great script, eh? The stern, brass-knuckled poetry of the dangerous classes."

She looked at him with drowning eyes.

The man with the shotgun pushed the guard to his knees. He handed the shotgun to his partner and yanked the guard's wrists up behind his back and locked them together with a pair of handcuffs. He toppled him onto the floor with a kick between the shoulder blades. Then he took his shotgun back and went over to the security gate at the end of the counter. He was short and heavy and moved with peculiar slowness, even torpor. "Buzz him in," his partner said. The man with the shotgun opened the gate and sauntered along the line of tellers, handing each of them a Hefty bag. When he came to the empty position he looked over at the man with the pistol, who said, "Whose slot is that?"

Anders watched the teller. She put her hand to her throat and turned to the man she'd been talking to. He nodded. "Mine," she said.

"Then get your ugly ass in gear and fill that bag."

"There you go," Anders said to the woman in front of him. "Justice is done."

"Hey! Bright boy! Did I tell you to talk?"

"No," Anders said.

"Then shut your trap."

"Did you hear that?" Anders said. "'Bright boy.' Right out of 'The Killers.'"

"Please be quiet," the woman said.

"Hey, you deaf or what?" The man with the pistol walked over to Anders. He poked the weapon into Anders' gut. "You think I'm playing games?"

"No," Anders said, but the barrel tickled like a stiff finger and he had to fight back the titters. He did this by making himself stare into the man's eyes, which were clearly visible behind the holes in the mask: pale blue and rawly red-rimmed. The man's left eyelid kept twitching. He breathed out a piercing, ammoniac smell that shocked Anders more than anything that had happened, and he was beginning to develop a sense of unease when the man prodded him again with the pistol.

"You like me, bright boy?" he said. "You want to suck my dick?"

"No," Anders said.

"Then stop looking at me."

Anders fixed his gaze on the man's shiny wing-tip shoes.

"Not down there. Up there." He stuck the pistol under Anders' chin and pushed it upward until Anders was looking at the ceiling.

Anders had never paid much attention to that part of the bank, a pompous old building with marble floors and counters and pillars, and gilt scrollwork over the tellers' cages. The domed ceiling had been decorated with mythological figures whose fleshy, toga-draped ugliness Anders had taken in at a glance many years earlier and afterward declined to notice. Now he had no choice but to scrutinize the painter's work. It was even worse than he remembered, and all of it executed with the utmost gravity. The artist had a few tricks up his sleeve and used them again and again—a certain rosy blush on the underside of the clouds, a coy backward glance on the faces of the cupids and fauns. The ceiling was crowded with various dramas, but the one that caught Anders' eye was Zeus and Europa—portrayed, in this rendition, as a bull ogling a cow from behind a haystack. To make the cow sexy, the painter had canted her hips suggestively and given her long, droopy eyelashes through which she gazed back at the bull with sultry welcome. The bull wore a smirk and his eyebrows were arched. If there'd been a bubble coming out of his mouth, it would have said, "Hubba hubba."

"What's so funny, bright boy?"

"Nothing."

"You think I'm comical? You think I'm some kind of clown?"

"No."

"You think you can fuck with me?"

"No."

"Fuck with me again, you're history. *Capiche?*"

Anders burst out laughing. He covered his mouth with both hands and said, "I'm sorry, I'm sorry," then snorted helplessly through his fingers and said, "*Capiche*—oh, God, *capiche*," and at that the man with the pistol raised the pistol and shot Anders right in the head.

The bullet smashed Anders' skull and ploughed through his brain and exited behind his right ear, scattering shards of bone into the cerebral cortex, the corpus callosum, back toward the basal ganglia, and down into the thalamus. But before all this occurred, the first appearance of the bullet in the cerebrum set off a crackling chain of ion transports and neuro-transmissions. Because of their peculiar origin these traced a peculiar pattern, flukishly calling to life a summer afternoon some forty years past, and long since lost to memory. After striking the cranium the bullet was moving at 900 feet per second, a pathetically sluggish, glacial pace compared to the synaptic lightning that flashed around it. Once in the brain, that is, the bullet came under the mediation of brain time, which gave Anders plenty of leisure to contemplate the scene that, in a phrase he would have abhorred, "passed before his eyes."

It is worth noting what Anders did not remember, given what he did remember. He did not remember his first lover, Sherry, or what he had most madly loved about her, before it came to irritate him—her unembarrassed carnality, and especially the cordial way she had with his unit, which she called Mr. Mole, as in, "Uh-oh, looks like Mr. Mole wants to play," and, "Let's hide Mr. Mole!" Anders did not remember his wife, whom he had also loved before she exhausted him with her predictability, or his daughter, now a sullen professor of economics at Dartmouth. He did not remember standing just outside his daughter's door as she lectured her bear about his naughtiness and described the truly appalling punishments Paws would receive unless he changed his ways. He did not remember a single line of the hundreds of poems he had committed to memory in his youth so that he could give himself the shivers at will—not "Silent, upon a peak in Darien," or "My God, I heard this day," or "All my pretty ones? Did you say all? O hell-kite! All?"[1] None of these did he remember; not one. Anders did not remember his dying mother saying of his father, "I should have stabbed him in his sleep."

He did not remember Professor Josephs telling his class how Athenian prisoners in Sicily had been released if they could recite Aeschylus, and then reciting Aeschylus himself, right there, in the Greek. Anders did not remember how his eyes had burned at those sounds. He did not remember the surprise of seeing a college classmate's name on the jacket of a novel not long after they graduated, or the respect he had felt after reading the book. He did not remember the pleasure of giving respect.

Nor did Anders remember seeing a woman leap to her death from the building opposite his own just days after his daughter was born. He did not remember shouting, "Lord have mercy!" He did not remember deliberately crashing his father's car into a tree, or having his ribs kicked in by three policemen at an anti-war rally, or waking himself up with laughter. He did not remember when he began to regard the heap of books on his desk with boredom and dread, or when he grew angry at writers for writing them. He did not remember when everything began to remind him of something else.

This is what he remembered. Heat. A baseball field. Yellow grass, the whirr of insects, himself leaning against a tree as the boys of the neighborhood gather for a pickup game. He looks on as the others argue the relative genius of Mantle and Mays. They have been worrying this subject all summer, and it has become tedious to Anders: an oppression, like the heat.

Then the last two boys arrive, Coyle and a cousin of his from Mississippi. Anders has never met Coyle's cousin before and will never see him again. He says hi with the rest but takes no further notice of him until they've chosen sides and someone asks the cousin what position he wants to play. "Shortstop," the boy says. "Short's the best position they is." Anders turns and looks at him. He wants to hear Coyle's cousin repeat what he's just said, but he knows better than to ask. The others will think he's being a jerk, ragging the kid for his grammar. But that isn't it, not at all—it's that Anders is strangely roused, elated, by those final two words, their pure unexpectedness and their music. He takes the field in a trance, repeating them to himself.

The bullet is already in the brain; it won't be outrun forever, or charmed to a halt. In the end it will do its work and leave the troubled skull behind, dragging its comet's tail of memory and hope and talent and love into the marble hall of commerce. That can't be helped. But for now Anders can still make time. Time for the shadows to lengthen on the grass, time for the tethered dog to bark at the flying ball, time for the boy in right field to smack his sweat-blackened mitt and softly chant, *They is, they is, they is.*

1995

RELATED:

—Wolff on Isak Dinesen's "Sorrow-Acre," p. 1786

---

1. Lines from Keats' (1795–1821) "On First Looking into Chapman's Homer," George Herbert's (1593–1633) "Man," and William Shakespeare's (1564–1616) *Macbeth* (Act IV, Scene 3, lines 217–218).

VIRGINIA WOOLF
1882–1941

Woolf was born in London, the daughter of a publishing heiress, Julia Jackson Duckworth, and a distinguished literary critic, Sir Leslie Stephen. At her father's death in 1904 she moved with her sister and two brothers to Bloomsbury, a fashionably bohemian section of London, and when she began to publish she was firmly associated with the "Bloomsbury Group" of writers and intellectuals. In 1912 she married the journalist and political philosopher Leonard Woolf and with him established the Hogarth Press, which published many of her works. By the example of her first novels and in essays she made a case against the objective realism of such then-popular practitioners as Arnold Bennett. Her preference was for lyric adaptations of the stream of consciousness, best exemplified by *To the Lighthouse* (1927) and *The Waves* (1931). In her popular *Mrs. Dalloway* (1925) she showed the possibilities of her methods in developing the nondramatic, contrapuntal presentation of a sensitive, unstable war veteran and an unfulfilled woman committed to the maintenance of her social position—perhaps a fictional transformation of two major aspects of Woolf's own personality. In 1916 she suffered a terrifying mental breakdown; she killed herself in 1941 in fear of a recurrence. *A Room of One's Own* (1929) is a feminist work of enduring influence, and the essays on literature collected in the two volumes of *The Common Reader* (1925, 1933) did much to shape modern taste with their easy, keen suggestiveness. Her stories were collected in *A Haunted House* (1944).

Kew Gardens[1]

From the oval-shaped flower-bed there rose perhaps a hundred stalks spreading into heart-shaped or tongue-shaped leaves half-way up and unfurling at the tip red or blue, or yellow petals marked with spots of colour raised upon the surface; and from the red, blue, or yellow gloom of the throat emerged a straight bar, rough with gold dust and slightly clubbed at the end. The petals were voluminous enough to be stirred by the summer breeze, and when they moved, the red, blue and yellow lights passed one over the other, staining an inch of the brown earth beneath with a spot of the most intricate colour. The light fell either upon the smooth, grey back of a pebble, or the shell of a snail with its brown, circular veins, or falling into a raindrop, it

---

1. Established as a state institution in 1841, Kew Gardens is the home of the Royal Botanic Gardens; it is in the London suburb of Kew, Surrey.

expanded with such intensity of red, blue, and yellow the thin walls of water that one expected them to burst and disappear. Instead, the drop was left in a second silver grey once more, and the light now settled upon the flesh of a leaf, revealing the branching thread of fibre beneath the surface, and again it moved on and spread its illumination in the vast green spaces beneath the dome of the heart-shaped and tongue-shaped leaves. Then the breeze stirred rather more briskly overhead and the colour was flashed into the air above, into the eyes of the men and women who walk in Kew Gardens in July.

The figures of these men and women straggled past the flower-bed with a curiously irregular movement not unlike that of the white and blue butter-flies who crossed the turf in zig-zag flights from bed to bed. The man was about six inches in front of the woman, strolling carelessly, while she bore on with greater purpose, only turning her head now and then to see that the children were not too far behind. The man kept this distance in front of the woman purposely, though perhaps unconsciously, for he wished to go on with his thoughts.

"Fifteen years ago I came here with Lily," he thought. "We sat somewhere over there by a lake and I begged her to marry me all through the hot after-noon. How the dragonfly kept circling round us: how clearly I see the dragon-fly and her shoe with the square silver buckle at the toe. All the time I spoke I saw her shoe and when it moved impatiently I knew without looking up what she was going to say: the whole of her seemed to be in her shoe. And my love, my desire, were in the dragonfly; for some reason I thought that if it settled there, on that leaf, the broad one with the red flower in the middle of it, if the dragonfly settled on the leaf she would say 'Yes' at once. But the dragonfly went round and round: it never settled anywhere—of course not, happily not, or I shouldn't be walking here with Eleanor and the children. Tell me, Eleanor. D'you ever think of the past?"

"Why do you ask, Simon?"

"Because I've been thinking of the past. I've been thinking of Lily, the woman I might have married. . . . Well, why are you silent? Do you mind my thinking of the past?"

"Why should I mind, Simon? Doesn't one always think of the past, in a garden with men and women lying under the trees. Aren't they one's past, all that remains of it, those men and women, those ghosts lying under the trees, . . . one's happiness, one's reality?"

"For me, a square silver shoe buckle and a dragonfly—"

"For me, a kiss. Imagine six little girls sitting before their easels twenty years ago, down by the side of a lake, painting the water-lilies, the first red water-lilies I'd ever seen. And suddenly a kiss, there on the back of my neck. And my hand shook all the afternoon so that I couldn't paint. I took out my watch and marked the hour when I would allow myself to think of the kiss for five minutes only—it was so precious—the kiss of an old grey-haired woman with a wart on her nose, the mother of all my kisses all my life. Come, Caroline, come, Hubert."

They walked on past the flower-bed, now walking four abreast, and soon diminished in size among the trees and looked half transparent as the sun-light and shade swam over their backs in large trembling irregular patches.

In the oval flower-bed the snail, whose shell had been stained red, blue, and yellow for the space of two minutes or so, now appeared to be moving very slightly in its shell, and next began to labour over the crumbs of loose earth which broke away and rolled down as it passed over them. It appeared to have a definite goal in front of it, differing in this respect from the singular high stepping angular green insect who attempted to cross in front of it, and waited for a second with its antennae trembling as if in deliberation, and then stepped off as rapidly and strangely in the opposite direction. Brown cliffs with deep green lakes in the hollows, flat, blade-like trees that waved from root to tip, round boulders of grey stone, vast crumpled surfaces of a thin crackling texture—all these objects lay across the snail's progress between one stalk and another to his goal. Before he had decided whether to circumvent the arched tent of a dead leaf or to breast it there came past the bed the feet of other human beings.

This time they were both men. The younger of the two wore an expression of perhaps unnatural calm; he raised his eyes and fixed them very steadily in front of him while his companion spoke, and directly his companion had done speaking he looked on the ground again and sometimes opened his lips only after a long pause and sometimes did not open them at all. The elder man had a curiously uneven and shaky method of walking, jerking his hand forward and throwing up his head abruptly, rather in the manner of an impatient carriage horse tired of waiting outside a house; but in the man these gestures were irresolute and pointless. He talked almost incessantly; he smiled to himself and again began to talk, as if the smile had been an answer. He was talking about spirits—the spirits of the dead, who, according to him, were even now telling him all sorts of odd things about their experiences in Heaven.

"Heaven was known to the ancients as Thessaly, William, and now, with this war, the spirit matter[2] is rolling between the hills like thunder." He paused, seemed to listen, smiled, jerked his head and continued:

"You have a small electric battery and a piece of rubber to insulate the wire—isolate?—insulate?—well, we'll skip the details, no good going into details that wouldn't be understood—and in short the little machine stands in any convenient position by the head of the bed, we will say, on a neat mahogany stand. All arrangements being properly fixed by workmen under my direction, the widow applies her ear and summons the spirit by sign as agreed. Women! Widows! Women in black—"

Here he seemed to have caught sight of a woman's dress in the distance, which in the shade looked a purple black. He took off his hat, placed his hand upon his heart, and hurried towards her muttering and gesticulating feverishly. But William caught him by the sleeve and touched a flower with the tip of his walking-stick in order to divert the old man's attention. After looking at it for a moment in some confusion the old man bent his ear to it and seemed to answer a voice speaking from it, for he began talking about the forests of Uruguay which he had visited hundreds of years ago in company with the most beautiful young woman in Europe. He could be heard murmuring about forests of Uruguay blanketed with the wax petals of tropical roses, nightingales, sea beaches, mermaids, and women drowned at sea, as he suffered

---

2. That is, spiritualism. Thessaly: a region in Greece. "This war": World War I.

himself to be moved on by William, upon whose face the look of stoical patience grew slowly deeper and deeper.

Following his steps so closely as to be slightly puzzled by his gestures came two elderly women of the lower middle class, one stout and ponderous, the other rosy cheeked and nimble. Like most people of their station they were frankly fascinated by other signs of eccentricity betokening a disordered brain, especially in the well-to-do; but they were too far off to be certain whether the gestures were merely eccentric or genuinely mad. After they had scrutinized the old man's back in silence for a moment and given each other a queer, sly look, they went on energetically piecing together their very complicated dialogue:

"Nell, Bert, Lot, Cess, Phil, Pa, he says, I says, she says, I says, I says—"

"My Bert, Sis, Bill, Grandad, the old man, sugar,

> Sugar, flour, kippers, greens,
> Sugar, sugar, sugar."

The ponderous woman looked through the pattern of falling words at the flowers standing cool, firm, and upright in the earth, with a curious expression. She saw them as a sleeper waking from a heavy sleep sees a brass candlestick reflecting the light in an unfamiliar way, and closes his eyes and opens them, and seeing the brass candlestick again, finally starts broad awake and stares at the candlestick with all his powers. So the heavy woman came to a standstill opposite the oval-shaped flower-bed, and ceased even to pretend to listen to what the other woman was saying. She stood there letting the words fall over her, swaying the top part of her body slowly backwards and forwards, looking at the flowers. Then she suggested that they should find a seat and have their tea.

The snail had now considered every possible method of reaching his goal without going round the dead leaf or climbing over it. Let alone the effort needed for climbing a leaf, he was doubtful whether the thin texture which vibrated with such an alarming crackle when touched even by the tips of his horns would bear his weight; and this determined him finally to creep beneath it, for there was a point where the leaf curved high enough from the ground to admit him. He had just inserted his head in the opening and was taking stock of the high brown roof and was getting used to the cool brown light when two other people came past outside on the turf. This time they were both young, a young man and a young woman. They were both in the prime of youth, the season before the smooth pink folds of the flower have burst their gummy case, when the wings of the butterfly, though fully grown, are motionless in the sun.

"Lucky it isn't Friday," he observed.

"Why? D'you believe in luck?"

"They make you pay sixpence on Friday."

"What's a sixpence anyway? Isn't it worth sixpence?"

"What's 'it'—what do you mean by 'it'?"

"O, anything—I mean—you know what I mean."

Long pauses came between each of these remarks; they were uttered in toneless and monotonous voices. The couple stood still on the edge of the flower-bed, and together pressed the end of her parasol deep down into the soft earth. The action and the fact that his hand rested on the top of hers expressed their feelings in a strange way, as these short insignificant words also expressed something, words with short wings for their heavy body of meaning, inadequate to carry them far and thus alighting awkwardly upon the very common objects that surrounded them, and were to their inexperienced touch so massive; but who knows (so they thought as they pressed the parasol into the earth) what precipices aren't concealed in them, or what slopes of ice don't shine in the sun on the other side? Who knows? Who has ever seen this before? Even when she wondered what sort of tea they gave you at Kew, he felt that something loomed up behind her words, and stood vast and solid behind them; and the mist very slowly rose and uncovered—O, Heavens, what were those shapes?—little white tables, and waitresses who looked first at her and then at him; and there was a bill that he would pay with a real two-shilling piece, and it was real, all real, he assured himself, fingering the coin in his pocket, real to everyone except to him and to her; even to him it began to seem real; and then—but it was too exciting to stand and think any longer, and he pulled the parasol out of the earth with a jerk and was impatient to find the place where one had tea with other people, like other people.

"Come along, Trissie; it's time we had our tea."

"Wherever *does* one have one's tea?" she asked with the oddest thrill of excitement in her voice, looking vaguely round and letting herself be drawn down the grass path, trailing her parasol; turning her head this way and that way forgetting her tea, wishing to go down there and then down there, remembering orchids and cranes among wild flowers, a Chinese pagoda and a crimson crested bird; but he bore her on.

Thus one couple after another with much the same irregular and aimless movement passed the flower-bed and were enveloped in layer after layer of green-blue vapour, in which at first their bodies had substance and a dash of colour, but later both substance and colour dissolved in the green-blue atmosphere. How hot it was! So hot that even the thrush chose to hop, like a mechanical bird, in the shadow of the flowers, with long pauses between one movement and the next; instead of rambling vaguely the white butterflies dance one above another, making with their white shifting flakes the outline of a shattered, marble column above the tallest flowers; the glass roofs of the palm house shone as if a whole market full of shiny green umbrellas had opened in the sun; and in the drone of the aeroplane the voice of the summer sky murmured its fierce soul. Yellow and black, pink and snow white, shapes of all these colours, men, women, and children were spotted for a second upon the horizon, and then, seeing the breadth of yellow that lay upon the grass, they wavered and sought shade beneath the trees, dissolving like drops of water in the yellow and green atmosphere, staining it faintly with red and blue. It seemed as if all gross and heavy bodies had sunk down in the heat motionless and lay huddled upon the ground, but their voices went wavering from them as if they were flames lolling from the thick waxen bodies of candles. Voices. Yes, voices. Wordless voices, breaking the silence suddenly with such depth of contentment, such passion of desire, or, in the voices of children, such freshness of surprise; breaking the silence? But there was no silence; all the time the motor omnibuses were turning their wheels and changing their gear; like a vast nest of Chinese boxes all of wrought steel turning ceaselessly one within another the city murmured; on the top of which the voices cried aloud and the petals of myriads of flowers flashed their colours into the air.

1943

RICHARD WRIGHT
1908–1960

Wright was born on a plantation near Natchez, Mississippi, the grandson of slaves, the son of a mill worker and a schoolteacher. Deserted by his father at an early age, he lived intermittently in orphan asylums or wandered with his mother from city to city in an erratic pattern that continued for him after her death. In 1927 he turned up in Chicago, where he joined the Communist Party and began to write. His growing reputation as a short-story writer was solidified with the publication in 1940 of his first novel, *Native Son*, a pathetic and gory narrative of a young black man hurled blindly into crime. *Black Boy*, a vivid personal narrative, was published in 1945, followed in 1953 by the novel *The Outsider* and in 1954 by *Black Power*, an extensive report on the African Gold Coast countries. Many of his stories are collected in *Uncle Tom's Children* (1938) and *Eight Men* (1961). *American Hunger*, a continuation of *Black Boy*, appeared posthumously in 1977.

The Man Who Was Almost a Man

Dave struck out across the fields, looking homeward through paling light. Whuts the usa talkin wid em niggers in the field? Anyhow, his mother was putting supper on the table. Them niggers can't understand *nothing*. One of these days he was going to get a gun and practice shooting, then they can't talk to him as though he were a little boy. He slowed, looking at the ground. Shucks, Ah ain scareda them even ef they are biggern me! Aw, Ah know whut Ahma do. . . . Ahm going by ol Joe's sto n git that Sears Roebuck catlog n look at them guns. Mabbe Ma will lemme buy one when she gits mah pay from ol man Hawkins. Ahma beg her t gimme some money. Ahm ol ernough to hava gun. Ahm seventeen. Almos a man. He strode, feeling his long, loose-jointed limbs. Shucks, a man oughta hava little gun aftah he done worked hard all day. . . .

He came in sight of Joe's store. A yellow lantern glowed on the front porch. He mounted steps and went through the screen door, hearing it bang behind him. There was a strong smell of coal oil and mackerel fish. He felt very confident until he saw fat Joe walk in through the rear door, then his courage began to ooze.

"Howdy, Dave! Whutcha want?"

"How yuh, Mistah Joe? Aw, Ah don wanna buy nothing. Ah jus wanted t see ef yuhd lemme look at tha ol catlog erwhile."

"Sure! You wanna see it here?"

"Nawsuh. Ah wans t take it home wid me. Ahll bring it back termorrow when Ah come in from the fiels."

"You plannin on buying something?"

"Yessuh."

"Your ma lettin you have your own money now?"

"Shucks. Mistah Joe, Ahm gittin t be a man like anybody else!"

Joe laughed and wiped his greasy white face with a red bandanna.

"Whut you plannin on buyin?"

Dave looked at the floor, scratched his head, scratched his thigh, and smiled. Then he looked up shyly.

"Ahll tell yuh, Mistah Joe, ef yuh promise yuh won't tell."

"I promise."

"Waal, Ahma buy a gun."

"A gun? Whut you want with a gun?"

"Ah wanna keep it."

"You ain't nothing but a boy. You don't need a gun."

"Aw, lemme have the catlog, Mistah Joe. Ahll bring it back."

Joe walked through the rear door. Dave was elated. He looked around at barrels of sugar and flour. He heard Joe coming back. He craned his neck to see if he were bringing the book. Yeah, he's got it. Gawddog, he's got it!

"Here, but be sure you bring it back. It's the only one I got."

"Sho, Mistah Joe."

"Say, if you wanna buy a gun, why don't you buy one from me? I gotta gun to sell."

"Will it shoot?"

"Sure it'll shoot."

"Whut kind is it?"

"Oh, it's kinda old. . . . A left-hand Wheeler. A pistol. A big one."

"Is it got bullets in it?"

"It's loaded."

"Kin Ah see it?"

"Where's your money?"

"Whu yuh wan fer it?"

"I'll let you have it for two dollars."

"Just two dollahs? Shucks, Ah could buy tha when Ah git mah pay."

"I'll have it here when you want it."

"Awright, suh. Ah be in fer it."

He went through the door, hearing it slam again behind him. Ahma git some money from Ma n buy me a gun! Only two dollahs! He tucked the thick catalogue under his arm and hurried.

"Where yuh been, boy?" His mother held a steaming dish of black-eyed peas.

"Aw, Ma, Ah jus stopped down the road t talk wid th boys."

"Yuh know bettah than t keep suppah waitin."

He sat down, resting the catalogue on the edge of the table.

"Yuh git up from there and git to the well n wash yosef! Ah ain feedin no hogs in mah house!"

She grabbed his shoulder and pushed him. He stumbled out of the room, then came back to get the catalogue.

"Whut this?"

"Aw, Ma, it's jusa catlog."

"Who yuh git it from?"

"From Joe, down at the sto."

"Waal, thas good. We kin use it around the house."

"Naw, Ma." He grabbed for it. "Gimme mah catlog, Ma."

She held onto it and glared at him.

"Quit hollerin at me! Whut's wrong wid yuh? Yuh crazy?"

"But Ma, please. It ain mine! It's Joe's! He tol me t bring it back t im termorrow."

She gave up the book. He stumbled down the back steps, hugging the thick book under his arm. When he had splashed water on his face and hands, he groped back to the kitchen and fumbled in a corner for the towel. He bumped into a chair; it clattered to the floor. The catalogue sprawled at his feet. When he had dried his eyes he snatched up the book and held it again under his arm. His mother stood watching him.

"Now, ef yuh gonna acka fool over that ol book, Ahll take it n burn it up."

"Naw, Ma, please."

"Waal, set down n be still!"

He sat and drew the oil lamp close. He thumbed page after page, unaware of the food his mother set on the table. His father came in. Then his small brother.

"Whutcha got there, Dave?" his father asked.

"Jusa catlog," he answered, not looking up.

"Yeah, here they is!" His eyes glowed at blue-and-black revolvers. He glanced up, feeling sudden guilt. His father was watching him. He eased the book under the table and rested it on his knees. After the blessing was asked, he ate. He scooped up peas and swallowed fat meat without chewing. Buttermilk helped to wash it down. He did not want to mention money before his father. He would do much better by cornering his mother when she was alone. He looked at his father uneasily out of the edge of his eye.

"Boy, how come yuh don quit foolin wid tha book n eat yo suppah?"

"Yessuh."

"How yuh n ol man Hawkins gittin erlong?"

"Suh?"

"Can't yuh hear? Why don yuh lissen? Ah ast yu how wuz yuh n ol man Hawkins gittin erlong?"

"Oh, swell, Pa. Ah plows mo lan than anybody over there."

"Waal, yuh oughta keep yo min on whut yuh doin."

"Yessuh."

He poured his plate full of molasses and sopped at it slowly with a chunk of cornbread. When his father and brother had left the kitchen, he still sat and looked again at the guns in the catalogue, longing to muster courage enough to present his case to his mother. Lawd, ef Ah only had the pretty one! He could almost feel the slickness of the weapon with his fingers. If he had a gun like that he would polish it and keep it shining so it would never rust. N Ah'd keep it loaded, by Gawd!

"Ma?" His voice was hesitant.

"Hunh?"

"Ol man Hawkins give yuh mah money yit?"

"Yeah, but ain no usa yuh thinkin bout thowin nona it erway. Ahm keepin tha money sos yuh kin have cloes t go to school this winter."

He rose and went to her side with the open catalogue in his palms. She was washing dishes, her head bent low over a pan. Shyly he raised the book. When he spoke, his voice was husky, faint.

"Ma, Gawd knows Ah wans one of these."

"One of whut?" she asked, not raising her eyes.

"One of these," he said again, not daring even to point. She glanced up at the page, then at him with wide eyes.

"Nigger, is yuh gone plum crazy?"

"Aw, Ma——"

"Git outta here! Don yuh talk t me bout no gun! Yuh a fool!"

"Ma, Ah kin buy one fer *two* dollahs."

"Not ef Ah knows it yuh ain!"

"But yuh promised me one——"

"Ah don care whut Ah promised! Yuh ain nothing but a boy yit!"

"Ma, ef yuh lemme buy one Ahll *never* ast yuh fer nothing no mo."

"Ah tol yuh t git outta here! Yuh ain gonna toucha penny of tha money fer no gun! Thas how come Ah has Mistah Hawkins t pay yo wages to me, cause Ah knows yuh ain got no sense."

"But Ma, we needa gun. Pa ain got no gun. We needa gun in the house. Yuh kin never tell whut might happen."

"Now don yuh try to maka fool outta me, boy! Ef we did hava gun yuh wouldn't have it!"

He laid the catalogue down and slipped his arm around her waist.

"Aw, Ma, Ah done worked hard alla summer n ain ast yuh fer nothin, is Ah, now?"

"Thas whut yuh spose to do!"

"But Ma, Ah wans a gun. Yuh kin lemme have two dollahs outta mah money. Please, Ma. I kin give it to Pa . . . Please, Ma! Ah loves yuh, Ma."

When she spoke her voice came soft and low.

"Whut yuh wan wida gun, Dave? Yun don need no gun. Yuhll git in trouble. N ef yo Pa jus *thought* Ah let yuh have money t buy a gun he'd hava fit."

"Ahll hide it, Ma, it ain but two dollahs."

"Lawd, chil, whuts wrong wid yuh?"

"Ain nothing wrong, Ma. Ahm almos a man now. Ah wants a gun."

"Who gonna sell yuh a gun?"

"Ol Joe at the sto."

"N it don cos but two dollahs?"

"Thas all, Ma. Just two dollahs. Please, Ma."

She was stacking the plates away; her hands moved slowly, reflectively. Dave kept an anxious silence. Finally, she turned to him.

"Ahll let yuh git tha gun ef yuh promise me one thing."

"Whuts tha, Ma?"

"Yuh bring it straight back t *me*, yuh hear? It be fer Pa."

"Yessum! Lemme go now, Ma."

She stooped, turned slightly to one side, raised the hem of her dress, rolled down the top of her stocking, and came up with a slender wad of bills.

"Here," she said, "Lawd knows yuh don need no gun. But yer Pa does. Yuh bring it right back to *me*, yuh hear? Ahma put it up. Now ef yuh don, Ahma have yuh Pa lick yuh so hard yuh won ferget it."

"Yessum."

He took the money, ran down the steps, and across the yard.

"Dave! Yuuuuuh Daaaaave!"

He heard, but he was not going to stop now. "Naw, Lawd!"

The first movement he made the following morning was to reach under his pillow for the gun. In the gray light of dawn he held it loosely, feeling a sense of power. Could kill a man with a gun like this. Kill anybody, black or white. And if he were holding his gun in his hand, nobody could run over him; they would have to respect him. It was a big gun, with a long barrel and a heavy handle. He raised and lowered it in his hand, marveling at its weight.

He had not come straight home with it as his mother had asked; instead he had stayed out in the fields, holding the weapon in his hand, aiming it now and then at some imaginary foe. But he had not fired it; he had been afraid that his father might hear. Also he was not sure he knew how to fire it.

To avoid surrendering the pistol he had not come into the house until he knew that all were asleep. When his mother had tiptoed to his bedside late that night and demanded the gun, he had first played 'possum; then he had told her that the gun was hidden outdoors, that he would bring it to her in the morning. Now he lay turning it slowly in his hands. He broke it, took out the cartridges, felt them, and then put them back.

He slid out of bed, got a long strip of old flannel from a trunk, wrapped the gun in it, and tied it to his naked thigh while it was still loaded. He did not go in to breakfast. Even though it was not yet daylight, he started for Jim Hawkins' plantation. Just as the sun was rising he reached the barns where the mules and plows were kept.

"Hey! That you, Dave?"

He turned. Jim Hawkins stood eying him suspiciously.

"What're yuh doing here so early?"

"Ah didn't know Ah wuz gittin up so early, Mistah Hawkins. Ah wuz fixin t hitch up ol Jenny n take her t the fiels."

"Good. Since you're so early, how about plowing that stretch down by the woods?"

"Suits me, Mistah Hawkins."

"O.K. Go to it!"

He hitched Jenny to a plow and started across the fields. Hot dog! This was just what he wanted. If he could get down by the woods, he could shoot his gun and nobody would hear. He walked behind the plow, hearing the traces creaking, feeling the gun tied tight to his thigh.

When he reached the woods, he plowed two whole rows before he decided to take out the gun. Finally, he stopped, looked in all directions, then untied the gun and held it in his hand. He turned to the mule and smiled.

"Know whut this is, Jenny? Naw, yuh wouldn't know! Yuhs jusa ol mule! Anyhow, this is a gun, n it kin shoot, by Gawd!"

He held the gun at arm's length. Whut t hell, Ahma shoot this thing! He looked at Jenny again.

"Lissen here, Jenny! When Ah pull this ol trigger Ah don wan yuh t run n acka fool now."

Jenny stood with head down, her short ears pricked straight. Dave walked off about twenty feet, held the gun far out from him, at arm's length, and turned his head. Hell, he told himself, Ah ain afraid. The gun felt loose in his fingers; he waved it wildly for a moment. Then he shut his eyes and tightened his forefinger. *Blooom!* A report half-deafened him and he thought his right hand was torn from his arm. He heard Jenny whinnying and galloping over the field, and he found himself on his knees, squeezing his fingers hard between his legs. His hand was numb; he jammed it into his mouth, trying to warm it, trying to stop the pain. The gun lay at his feet. He did not quite know what had happened. He stood up and stared at the gun as though it were a live thing. He gritted his teeth and kicked the gun. Yuh almos broke mah arm! He turned to look for Jenny; she was far over the fields, tossing her head and kicking wildly.

"Hol on ther, ol mule!"

When he caught up with her she stood trembling, walling her big white eyes at him. The plow was far away; the traces had broken. Then Dave stopped short, looking, not believing. Jenny was bleeding. Her left side was red and wet with blood. He went closer. Lawd have mercy! Wondah did Ah shoot this mule? He grabbed for Jenny's mane. She flinched, snorted, whirled, tossing her head.

"Hol on now! Hol on."

Then he saw the hole in Jenny's side, right between the ribs. It was round, wet, red. A crimson stream streaked down the front leg, flowing fast. Good Gawd! Ah wuznt shootin at tha mule. He felt panic. He knew he had to stop that blood, or Jenny would bleed to death. He had never seen so much blood in all his life. He ran the mule for half a mile, trying to catch her. Finally, she stopped, breathing hard, stumpy tail half arched. He caught her mane and led her back to where the plow and gun lay. Then he stopped and grabbed handfuls of damp black earth and tried to plug the bullet hole. Jenny shuddered, whinnied, and broke from him.

"Hol on! Hol on now!"

He tried to plug it again, but blood came anyhow. His fingers were hot and sticky. He rubbed dirt hard into his palms, trying to dry them. Then again he attempted to plug the bullet hole, but Jenny shied away, kicking her heels high. He stood helpless. He had to do something. He ran at Jenny; she dodged him. He watched a red stream of blood flow down Jenny's leg and form a bright pool at her feet.

"Jenny . . . Jenny," he called weakly.

His lips trembled. She's bleeding t death! He looked in the direction of home, wanting to go back, wanting to get help. But he saw the pistol lying in the damp black clay. He had a queer feeling that if he only did something, this would not be; Jenny would not be there bleeding to death.

When he went to her this time, she did not move. She stood with sleepy, dreamy eyes; and when he touched her she gave a low-pitched whinny and knelt to the ground, her front knees slopping in blood.

"Jenny . . . Jenny," he whispered.

For a long time she held her neck erect; then her head sank, slowly. Her ribs swelled with a mighty heave and she went over.

Dave's stomach felt empty, very empty. He picked up the gun and held it gingerly between his thumb and forefinger. He buried it at the foot of a tree. He took a stick and tried to cover the pool of blood with dirt—but what was the use? There was Jenny lying with her mouth open and her eyes walled and glassy. He could not tell Jim Hawkins he had shot his mule. But he had to tell something. Yeah, Ah'll tell em Jenny started gittin wil n fell on the joint of the plow. . . . But that would hardly happen to a mule. He walked across the field slowly, head down.

It was sunset. Two of Jim Hawkins' men were over near the edge of the woods digging a hole in which to bury Jenny. Dave was surrounded by a knot of people, all of whom were looking down at the dead mule.

"I don't see how in the world it happened," said Jim Hawkins for the tenth time.

The crowd parted and Dave's mother, father, and small brother pushed into the center.

"Where Dave?" his mother called.

"There he is," said Jim Hawkins.

His mother grabbed him.

"Whut happened, Dave? Whut yuh done?"

"Nothing."

"C'mon, boy, talk," his father said.

Dave took a deep breath and told the story he knew nobody believed.

"Waal," he drawled. "Ah brung ol Jenny down here sos Ah could do mah plowin. Ah plowed bout two rows, just like yuh see." He stopped and pointed at the long rows of upturned earth. "Then something musta been wrong wid ol Jenny. She wouldn't ack right a-tall. She started snortin n kickin her heels. Ah tried to hol her, but she pulled erway, rearin n goin on. Then when the point of the plow was stickin up in the air, she swung erroun n twisted hersef back on it. . . . She stuck hersef n started t bleed. N fo Ah could do anything, she wuz dead."

"Did you ever hear of anything like that in all your life?" asked Jim Hawkins.

There were white and black standing in the crowd. They murmured. Dave's mother came close to him and looked hard into his face. "Tell the truth, Dave," she said.

"Looks like a bullet hole ter me," said one man.

"Dave, whut yuh do wid the gun?" his mother asked.

The crowd surged in, looking at him. He jammed his hands into his pockets, shook his head slowly from left to right, and backed away. His eyes were wide and painful.

"Did he hava gun?" asked Jim Hawkins.

"By Gawd, Ah tol yuh tha wuz a *gun* wound," said a man, slapping his thigh.

His father caught his shoulders and shook him till his teeth rattled.

"Tell whut happened, yuh rascal! Tell whut . . ."

Dave looked at Jenny's stiff legs and began to cry.

"Whut yuh do wid tha gun?" his mother asked.

"Whut wuz he doin wida gun?" his father asked.

"Come on and tell the truth," said Hawkins. "Ain't nobody going to hurt you . . ."

His mother crowded close to him.

"Did yuh shoot that mule, Dave?"

Dave cried, seeing blurred white and black faces.

"Ahh ddinn gggo tt sshoooot hher . . . Ah ssswear ffo Gawd Ahh ddin. . . . Ah wuz a-tryin t sssee ef the ol gggun would sshoot—"

"Where yuh git the gun from?" his father asked.

"Ah got it from Joe, at the sto."

"Where yuh git the money?"

"Ma give it t me."

"He kept worryin me, Bob. Ah had t. Ah tol im t bring the gun right back t me . . . It was fer yuh, the gun."

"But how yuh happen to shoot that mule?" asked Jim Hawkins.

"Ah wuzn shootin at the mule, Mistah Hawkins. The gun jumped when Ah pulled the trigger . . . N fo Ah knowed anything Jenny wuz there a-bleedin."

Somebody in the crowd laughed. Jim Hawkins walked close to Dave and looked into his face.

"Well, looks like you have bought you a mule, Dave."

"Ah swear fo Gawd, Ah didn't go t kill the mule, Mistah Hawkins!"

"But you killed her!"

All the crowd was laughing now. They stood on tiptoe and poked heads over one another's shoulders.

"Well, boy, looks like yuh done bought a dead mule! Hahaha!"

"Ain tha ershame."

"Hohohohoho."

Dave stood, head down, twisting his feet in the dirt.

"Well, you needn't worry about it, Bob," said Jim Hawkins to Dave's father. "Just let the boy keep on working and pay me two dollars a month."

"Whut yuh wan fer yo mule, Mistah Hawkins?"

Jim Hawkins screwed up his eyes.

"Fifty dollars."

"Whut yuh do wid tha gun?" Dave's father demanded.

Dave said nothing.

"Yuh wan me t take a tree lim n beat yuh till yuh talk!"

"Nawsuh!"

"Whut yuh do wid it?"

"Ah thowed it erway."

"Where?"

"Ah . . . Ah thowed it in the creek."

"Waal, c mon home. N firs thing in the mawnin git to tha creek n fin tha gun."

"Yessuh."

"Whut yuh pay fer it?"

"Two dollahs."

"Take tha gun n git yo money back n carry it t Mistah Hawkins, yuh hear? N don fergit Ahma lam yo black bottom good fer this! Now march yosef on home, suh!"

Dave turned and walked slowly. He heard people laughing. Dave glared, his eyes welling with tears. Hot anger bubbled in him. Then he swallowed and stumbled on.

That night Dave did not sleep. He was glad that he had gotten out of killing the mule so easily, but he was hurt. Something hot seemed to turn over inside him each time he remembered how they had laughed. He tossed on his bed, feeling his hard pillow. *N Pa says he's gonna beat me. . . .* He remembered other beatings, and his back quivered. *Naw, naw, Ah sho don wan im t beat me tha way no mo. Dam em all!* Nobody ever gave him anything. All he did was work. *They treat me lika mule, n then they beat me.* He gritted his teeth. *N Ma had t tell on me.*

Well, if he had to, he would take old man Hawkins that two dollars. But that meant selling the gun. And he wanted to keep that gun. Fifty dollars for a dead mule.

He turned over, thinking of how he had fired the gun. He had an itch to fire it again. *Ef other men kin shoota gun, by Gawd, Ah kin!* He was still, listening. *Mebbe they all sleepin now. . . .* The house was still. He heard the soft breathing of his brother. *Yes, now!* He would go down and get that gun and see if he could fire it! He eased out of bed and slipped into overalls.

The moon was bright. He ran almost all the way to the edge of the woods. He stumbled over the ground, looking for the spot where he had buried the gun. *Yeah, here it is.* Like a hungry dog scratching for a bone, he pawed it up. He puffed his black cheeks and blew dirt from the trigger and barrel. He broke it and found four cartridges unshot. He looked around; the fields were filled with silence and moonlight. He clutched the gun stiff and hard in his fingers. But, as soon as he wanted to pull the trigger, he shut his eyes and turned his head. *Naw, Ah can't shoot wid mah eyes closed n mah head turned.* With effort he held his eyes open; then he squeezed. *Blooooom!* He was stiff, not breathing. The gun was still in his hands. Dammit, he'd done it! He fired again. *Bloooom!* He smiled. *Bloooom! Bloooom! Click, click.* There! It was empty. If anybody could shoot a gun, he could. He put the gun into his hip pocket and started across the fields.

When he reached the top of a ridge he stood straight and proud in the moonlight, looking at Jim Hawkins' big white house, feeling the gun sagging in his pocket. *Lawd, ef Ah had just one mo bullet Ah'd taka shot at tha house. Ah'd like t scare ol man Hawkins jusa little. . . . Jusa enough t let im know Dave Sanders is a man.*

To his left the road curved, running to the tracks of the Illinois Central. He jerked his head, listening. From far off came a faint *hooooof-hooooof; hooooof-hooooof; hooooof-hooooof . . . Tha's number eight.* He took a swift look at Jim Hawkins' white house; he thought of pa, of ma, of his little brother, and the boys. He thought of the dead mule and heard *hooooof-hooooof; hooooof-hooooof; hooooof-hooooof . . .* He stood rigid. *Two dollahs a mont. Les see now. . . . Tha means itll take bout two years. Shucks! Ahll be dam!*

He started down the road, toward the tracks. Yeah, here she comes! He stood beside the track and held himself stiffly. Here she comes, erroun the ben. . . . C mon, yuh slow poke! C mon! He had his hand on his gun; something quivered in his stomach. Then the train thundered past, the gray and brown box cars rumbling and clinking. He gripped the gun tightly; then he jerked his hand out of his pocket. Ah betcha Bill wouldn't do it! Ah betcha. . . . The cars slid past, steel grinding upon steel. Ahm riding yuh ternight so hep me Gawd! He was hot all over. He hesitated just a moment; then he grabbed, pulled atop of a car, and lay flat. He felt his pocket; the gun was still there. Ahead the long rails were glinting in the moonlight, stretching away, away to somewhere, somewhere where he could be a man. . . .

1961

Writers on Writing

Any writer, I suppose, feels that the world into which he was born is nothing less than a conspiracy against the cultivation of his talent—which attitude certainly has a great deal to support it. On the other hand, it is only because the world looks on his talent with such a frightening indifference that the artist is compelled to make his talent important.

James Baldwin

Most of the basic material a writer works with is acquired before the age of fifteen.

Willa Cather

I start with a tingle, a kind of feeling of the story I will write. Then come the characters, and they take over, they make the story.

Isak Dinesen

Read, read, read. Read everything—trash, classics, good and bad, and see how they do it. Just like a carpenter who works as an apprentice and studies the master. Read! You'll absorb it. Then write. If it is good, you'll find out. If it's not, throw it out the window.

William Faulkner

A book ought to be an icepick to break up the frozen sea within us.

Franz Kafka

Looking back, I imagine I was always writing. Twaddle it was, too. But better far write twaddle or anything, anything, than nothing at all.

Katherine Mansfield

There is only one school of literature—that of talent.

Vladimir Nabokov

Beginning a book is unpleasant. I'm entirely uncertain about the character and the predicament, and a character in his predicament is what I have to begin with. Worse than not knowing your subject is not knowing how to treat it, because that's finally everything. I type out beginnings and they're awful, more of an unconscious parody of my previous book than the breakaway from it that I want. I need something driving down the center of a book, a magnet to draw everything to it—that's what I look for during the first months of writing something new.

Philip Roth

We work in our own darkness a great deal with little real knowledge of what we are doing.

John Steinbeck

Writing doesn't require drive. It's like saying a chicken has to have drive to lay an egg.

John Updike

MARGARET ATWOOD

Why Do You Write?[1]

You learn to write by reading and writing, writing and reading. As a craft it's acquired through the apprentice system, but you choose your own teachers. Sometimes they're alive, sometimes dead.

As a vocation, it involves the laying on of hands. You receive your vocation and in your turn you must pass it on. Perhaps you will do this only through your work, perhaps in other ways. Either way, you're part of a community, the community of writers, the community of storytellers that stretches back through time to the beginning of human society.

As for the particular human society to which you yourself belong—sometimes you'll feel you're speaking for it, sometimes—when it's taken an unjust form—against it, or for that other community, the community of the oppressed, the exploited, the voiceless. Either way, the pressures on you will be intense; in other countries, perhaps fatal. But even here—speak "for women," or for any other group which is feeling the boot, and there will be many at hand, both for and against, to tell you to shut up, or to say what they want you to say, or to say it a different way. Or to save them. The billboard awaits you, but if you succumb to its temptations you'll end up two-dimensional.

Tell what is yours to tell. Let others tell what is theirs.

TONI CADE BAMBARA

What Is It I Think I'm Doing Anyhow?[2]

When I replay the tapes on file in my head, tapes of speeches I've given at writing conferences over the years, I invariably hear myself saying—"A writer, like any other cultural worker, like any other member of the community, ought to try to put her/his skills in the service of the community." Some years ago when I returned south, my picture in the paper prompted several neighbors to come visit. "You a writer? What all you write?" Before I could begin the catalogue, one old gent interrupted with—"Ya know Miz Mary down the block? She need a writer to help her send off a letter to her grandson overseas." So I began a career as the neighborhood scribe—letters to relatives, snarling letters to the traffic chief about the promised stop sign, nasty letters to the utilities, angry letters to the principal about that confederate flag hanging in front of the school, contracts to transfer a truck from seller to buyer etc. While my efforts have been graciously appreciated in the form of sweet potato dumplings, herb teas, hair braiding, and the like, there is still much room for improvement—"For a writer, honey, you've got a mighty bad hand. Didn't they teach penmanship at that college?" Another example, I guess, of

---

1. From *The Writer on Her Work*, Vol. II, ed. by Janet Sternburg (1991). **2.** From *The Writer on Her Work*, Vol. I, ed. by Janet Sternburg (1980).

words setting things in motion. What goes around, comes around, as the elders say.

It will be a pleasure to get back to the shorts; they allow me to share. I much prefer to haul around story collections to prisons, schools, senior citizen centers, and rallies and then select from the "menu" something that suits the moment and is all of a piece. But the novel's pull is powerful. And since the breakthrough achieved in the sixties by the Neo-Black Arts Movement,[3] the possibilities are stunning. Characters that have been waiting in the wings for generations, characters that did not fit into the roster of stereotypes, can now be brought down center stage. Now that I/we have located our audience, we are free to explore the limits of language. Now that American history, American literature, the American experience is being redefined by so many communities, the genre too will undergo changes. So I came to the novel with a sense that everything is possible. And I'm attempting to blueprint for myself the merger of these two camps: the political and the spiritual. The possibilities of healing that split are exciting. The implications of actually yoking those energies and of fusing that power quite take my breath away.

RICHARD BAUSCH

Letter to a Young Writer

While there are of course thousands of reasons why people begin to write— some of them rather shabby ones, too—there usually is only one reason why they continue: and that is that the work has become necessary. We are habit-forming creatures, and this work is very habit-forming if one has any talent at all. Of course, you don't know when you begin if you really *have* any talent. You hope you do; perhaps you even suspect that you do. Sometimes you go back and forth, believing on some days, and disbelieving on others. Mostly you believe the last thing you read or heard concerning the work, and you probably tend to listen to the negative things more; the last negative thing you heard has sunk deeper into you and has lasted a longer time than any positive comment.

Painful as this is, it is also perfectly normal.

My best advice has nothing to do with technique, or aesthetics or the craft itself, really. It is more to do with training oneself to be shrewd. To live intelligently where the work is concerned: as I have said many times in classes, writing is not an indulgence; the indulgences are what you give up to write. You don't go to as many parties, you don't watch as much television, you don't listen to as much music. You make decisions in light of what you have to do in a given day. How much you get done depends in large part not on your talent—which is whatever it is, and is mostly constant—but on your own attitude *about* what you are doing.

So.

---

3. Movement of the mid-1960s through the early 1970s led by groups of artists and writers in New York, Chicago, Detroit, and California's Bay Area. The movement promoted African-American political engagement, cultural pride, and empowerment as key parts of its aesthetic.

I have devised a sort of Ten Commandments for you, which are the result of some of my own struggles with this blessed occupation, and of what I have been able to learn from reading or being around writers who are better than I. Here they are.

1. Read.

You must try to know everything that has ever been written that is worth remembering, and you must keep up with what your contemporaries are doing. Fitzgerald's advice to his daughter, Scottie, is as good as any there is on this subject: you must try to *absorb* (italics mine) six good authors a year. This means that you do not read books as an English major is trained to read them; you *swallow* them. You *ingest* them, and move on. You do not stop to analyze or think much; you just take them into yourself, and go on to the next one. And you read obsessively, too: if you really like something, you read it over and over through the years. You come to know the world's literature by heart. Every good writer I know or have known began with an insatiable appetite for books, for plundering what is in them, for the nourishment provided by them, which you can't get from any other source.

2. Imitate.

While you are doing this reading, you spend time trying to sound like the various authors—just as a painter, learning to paint, sets up his easel in the museum and *copies* the work of the masters. You learn by trying the sound and the stance of other writers. You develop an ear, through your reading and imitating, for how good writing is *supposed* to sound.

3. *"Be regular and ordinary in your habits, like a Petit Bourgeois, so you may be violent and original in your work."*

This comes from Flaubert, and is quite good advice. It has to do with what I was talking about in the first paragraph, and is of course better expressed. The thing that separates the amateur writer from the professional, often enough, is simply the amount of time spent working the craft. Know that if you really want to write, if you hope to produce something that will stand up to the winds of criticism and the scrutiny of strangers, you are going to have to work harder than you ever worked on anything else in your life—hour upon hour upon hour, with nothing in the way of encouragement, no good feeling except the sense that you have been true to the silently admonishing example of the writers who came before you, the ones whose company you would like to be in, and of whose respect you would like to be worthy.

4. *Train yourself to be able to work anywhere.*

Once, when our first child was a baby, my mother came to visit, and after the baby went to sleep I began tiptoeing around trying to make no noise. My mother said, "What the heck are you doing?" I said, "The baby's asleep." She said, "Have some friends over, put some music on, rattle some dishes, make noise. You're training that boy to be a bad sleeper." That wise advice applies to this craft, too. If you set up a certain area of expectation about when and how you'll be able to do the work, you train yourself to be silent. Shostakovich wrote his famous 7th Symphony, the Leningrad Symphony, *during* the siege of Leningrad. Bombs were falling all around him, and he understood perfectly well that there was a very good chance he would die within the next few hours, or days. Teach yourself to write in busy places, under the barrage of noises the world makes—work in rooms where children are playing, with music on, even with the television on. Work in the faith that if something is really good, it will not escape back into oblivion if you get distracted from it. It will turn up again. There is no known excuse for not working. Whole societies have for centuries been based on that reality.

5. Be patient.

You are trying to do something that is harder than just about anything there is to do, even when it feels easy. You will write many more failures than successes. Say to yourself, *I accept failure as the condition of this life, this work, I freely accept it as my destiny*. Then go on and do the work. You never ask yourself anything beyond *did I work today?*

6. Be willing.

Accepting failure as a part of your destiny, learn to be willing to fail—to take the chances that often lead to failure, in the hope that one of them might lead to something good. Be *open for business* all the time. You must try to be that person on whom nothing is lost. This does not mean that you are taking notes while people around you suffer. You are not that kind of observer. It means that *in the work room* you are willing to follow whatever your dreaming presents you with, openly and without judgment or attitude or even opinions.

7. Eschew politics.

If you have opinions, leave them out of the workplace. If you have anything worthwhile to say, let it surprise you. John Gardner once told me, "If one of your characters makes a long speech filled with his deepest-held beliefs, make sure *you* don't believe one word of it." I think that is very sound advice. You are in the business of portraying the personal life, the personal cost of events, so even if history is part of your story, it should only serve as backdrop. The writers who have gotten into trouble with despots over the shameful history of tyranny did so because they insisted on *not paying any attention to the politics* except as it applied to the personal lives of the people they were creating. They told the truth, in other words, and refused to *be* political. The paradoxical truth of the matter is that a writer who pays attention to the personal life is subversive precisely because he refuses to pay attention to anything else. Bad politics hurts people on the personal level and good writers report from there about the damage. And the totalitarians are rightfully afraid of those writers.

8. Do not think, dream.

If you believe you are thinking when you write, make yourself *stop* thinking. You are trying to tap a part of yourself that is closest to the dreaming side, the side that is most active when you sleep. You are trying to recover the literal vision of a child. This is what Flannery O'Connor means when she says, "A good story is literal in the same sense that a child's drawing is literal." Dream the story up, make it up, be fanciful, follow what occurs to you to say, and try not to worry about whether or not it's smart, or shows your sensitive nature in the best light, or delivers the matters of living that you think you have learned. Just dream it up and let the thing play itself out as it seems to want to, and then write it again, and still again, dreaming it through, and *then* try to be terribly smart about it. Read it with the cold detachment of a doctor looking at an X-ray. Which is to say that you must learn to re-read your own sentences as a stranger might. And say everything aloud. Listen to how it *sounds*.

9. Don't compare yourself to anyone, and learn to keep from building expectations.

People develop at different rates, with different results, and luck is also involved. Your only worry for yourself should be *did I work today?* Be happy for the successes of your friends, because good fortune for one of us is good fortune for all of us. When a friend or acquaintance has good luck, you may feel envy because envy is a natural human reaction; but, as George Garrett once put it, when that stuff rises to your mind, you must train yourself to *contend* with it there. That is what determines everything else about you as an artist. You will never write anything worth keeping if you allow yourself to give in to petty worries over whether you are treated as you think you deserve, or your rewards are commensurate to the work you've done. That will almost never be the case, and the artist who expects great rewards and complete understanding is a fool.

10. Be wary of all general advice.

Discard everything that precedes this commandment if, for you, it gets in the way of writing good stories. Because for every last assertion in this letter, there are several notable exceptions.

Finally, try to remember that what you are aiming to do is a beautiful—even a noble—thing, trying to write, or make, the truth as straightly and honestly and artfully as you can; and that it is also, always, an inherently optimistic act, because it stems from the belief that there will be civilized others whose sensibilities you may affect, if you are lucky and good and faithful to the task at hand. No matter how tragic the vision, it is always a hopeful occupation, and therefore you have to cultivate the ability to balance things: to entertain high hopes without allowing those hopes to become expectations. To do your work without worrying too much about what the world will have to say about it or do to it. Mostly, of course, the world will ignore it, and so you will have that in common with many very great writers, good men and women who came before you. By giving it everything you have, and being faithful to the work, you honor their fidelity to it; you *partake* of it, you accept their silent admonition to write like all hell, to be as good as they were.

JOSEPH CONRAD

Preface[4]

A work that aspires, however humbly, to the condition of art should carry its justification in every line. And art itself may be defined as a single-minded attempt to render the highest kind of justice to the visible universe, by bringing to light the truth, manifold and one, underlying its every aspect. It is an attempt to find in its forms, in its colours, in its light, in its shadows, in the aspects of matter and in the facts of life, what of each is fundamental, what is enduring and essential—their one illuminating and convincing quality—the very truth of their existence. The artist, then, like the thinker or the scientist, seeks the truth and makes his appeal. Impressed by the aspect of the world the thinker plunges into ideas, the scientist into facts—whence, presently, emerging they make their appeal to those qualities of our being that fit us best for the hazardous enterprise of living. They speak authoritatively to our common-sense, to our intelligence, to our desire of peace or to our desire of unrest; not seldom to our prejudices, sometimes to our fears, often to our egoism—but always to our credulity. And their words are heard with reverence, for their concern is with weighty matters; with the cultivation of our minds and the proper care of our bodies: with the attainment of our ambitions: with the perfection of the means and the glorification of our precious aims.

It is otherwise with the artist.

Confronted by the same enigmatical spectacle the artist descends within himself, and in that lonely region of stress and strife, if he be deserving and fortunate, he finds the terms of his appeal. His appeal is made to our less obvious capacities: to that part of our nature which, because of the warlike conditions of existence, is necessarily kept out of sight within the more resisting and hard qualities—like the vulnerable body within a steel armour. His appeal is less loud, more profound, less distinct, more stirring—and sooner forgotten. Yet its effect endures forever. The changing wisdom of successive generations discards ideas, questions facts, demolishes theories. But the artist appeals to that part of our being which is not dependent on wisdom; to that in us which is a gift and not an acquisition—and, therefore, more permanently enduring. He speaks to our capacity for delight and wonder, to the sense of mystery surrounding our lives: to our sense of pity, and beauty, and pain: to the latent feeling of fellowship with all creation—and to the subtle but invincible, conviction of solidarity that knits together the loneliness of innumerable hearts: to the solidarity in dreams, in joy, in sorrow, in aspirations, in illusions, in hope, in fear, which binds men to each other, which binds together all humanity—the dead to the living and the living to the unborn.

It is only some such train of thought, or rather of feeling, that can in a measure explain the aim of the attempt, made in the tale which follows,[5] to present an unrestful episode in the obscure lives of a few individuals out of all the disregarded multitude of the bewildered, the simple, and the voiceless. For, if there is any part of truth in the belief confessed above, it becomes evident that there is not a place of splendour or a dark corner of the earth that

---

4. The Preface (1897), *The Nigger of the "Narcissus."*   **5.** That is, *The Nigger of the "Narcissus."*

does not deserve, if only a passing glance of wonder and pity. The motive, then, may be held to justify the matter of the work; but this preface, which is simply an avowal of endeavour, cannot end here—for the avowal is not yet complete.

Fiction—if it at all aspires to be art—appeals to temperament. And in truth it must be, like painting, like music, like all art, the appeal of one temperament to all the other innumerable temperaments whose subtle and resistless power endows passing events with their true meaning, and creates the moral, the emotional atmosphere of the place and time. Such an appeal to be effective must be an impression conveyed through the senses; and, in fact, it cannot be made in any other way, because temperament, whether individual or collective, is not amenable to persuasion. All art, therefore, appeals primarily to the senses, and the artistic aim when expressing itself in written words must also make its appeal through the senses, if its high desire is to reach the secret spring of responsive emotions. It must strenuously aspire to the plasticity of sculpture, to the colour of painting, and to the magic suggestiveness of music—which is the art of arts. And it is only through complete, unswerving devotion to the perfect blending of form and substance; it is only through an unremitting never-discouraged care for the shape and ring of sentences that an approach can be made to plasticity, to colour; and the light of magic suggestiveness may be brought to play for an evanescent instant over the commonplace surface of words: of the old, old words, worn thin, defaced by ages of careless usage.

The sincere endeavour to accomplish that creative task, to go as far on the road as his strength will carry him, to go undeterred by faltering, weariness, or reproach, is the only valid justification for the worker in prose. And if his conscience is clear, his answer to those who, in the fulness of a wisdom which looks for immediate profit, demand specifically to be edified, consoled, amused; who demand to be promptly improved, or encouraged, or frightened, or shocked, or charmed, must run thus:—My task which I am trying to achieve is, by the power of the written word, to make you hear, to make you feel—it is, before all, to make you *see*. That—and no more, and it is everything. If I succeed, you shall find there according to your deserts: encouragement, consolation, fear, charm—all you demand and, perhaps, also that glimpse of truth for which you have forgotten to ask.

To snatch in a moment of courage, from the remorseless rush of time, a passing phase of life, is only the beginning of the task. The task approached in tenderness and faith is to hold up unquestioningly, without choice and without fear, the rescued fragment before all eyes and in the light of a sincere mood. It is to show its vibration, its colour, its form; and through its movement, its form, and its colour, reveal the substance of its truth—disclose its inspiring secret: the stress and passion within the core of each convincing moment. In a single-minded attempt of that kind, if one be deserving and fortunate, one may perchance attain to such clearness of sincerity that at last the presented vision of regret or pity, of terror or mirth, shall awaken in the hearts of the beholders that feeling of unavoidable solidarity; of the solidarity in mysterious origin, in toil, in joy, in hope, in uncertain fate, which binds men to each other and all mankind to the visible world.

It is evident that he who, rightly or wrongly, holds by the convictions expressed above cannot be faithful to any one of the temporary formulas of his craft. The enduring part of them—the truth which each only imperfectly veils—should abide with him as the most precious of his possessions, but they all: Realism, Romanticism, Naturalism, even the unofficial sentimentalism (which like the poor,[6] is exceedingly difficult to get rid of), all these gods must, after a short period of fellowship, abandon him—even on the very threshold of the temple—to the stammerings of his conscience and to the outspoken consciousness of the difficulties of his work. In that uneasy solitude the supreme cry of Art for Art, itself, loses the exciting ring of its apparent immorality. It sounds far off. It has ceased to be a cry, and is heard only as a whisper, often incomprehensible, but at times and faintly encouraging.

Sometimes, stretched at ease in the shade of a roadside tree, we watch the motions of a labourer in a distant field, and after a time, begin to wonder languidly as to what the fellow may be at. We watch the movements of his body, the waving of his arms, we see him bend down, stand up, hesitate, begin again. It may add to the charm of an idle hour to be told the purpose of his exertions. If we know he is trying to lift a stone, to dig a ditch, to uproot a stump, we look with a more real interest at his efforts; we are disposed to condone the jar of his agitation upon the restfulness of the landscape; and even, if in a brotherly frame of mind, we may bring ourselves to forgive his failure. We understood his object, and, after all, the fellow has tried, and perhaps he had not the strength— and perhaps he had not the knowledge. We forgive, go on our way—and forget.

And so it is with the workman of art. Art is long and life is short,[7] and success is very far off. And thus, doubtful of strength to travel so far, we talk a little about the aim—the aim of art, which, like life itself, is inspiring, difficult— obscured by mists. It is not in the clear logic of a triumphant conclusion; it is not in the unveiling of one of those heartless secrets which are called the Laws of Nature. It is not less great, but only more difficult.

To arrest, for the space of a breath, the hands busy about the work of the earth, and compel men entranced by the sight of distant goals to glance for a moment at the surrounding vision of form and colour, of sunshine and shadows; to make them pause for a look, for a sigh, for a smile—such is the aim, difficult and evanescent, and reserved only for a very few to achieve. But sometimes, by the deserving and the fortunate, even that task is accomplished. And when it is accomplished—behold!—all the truth of life is there: a moment of vision, a sigh, a smile—and the return to an eternal rest.

JOSEPH CONRAD

Letter to Barrett H. Clark, May 4, 1918[8]

Some critics have found fault with me for not being constantly myself. But they are wrong. I am always myself. I am a man of formed character. Certain conclusions remain immovably fixed in my mind, but I am no slave to prejudices and formulas, and I shall never be. My attitude to subjects and

---

6. John 12.8.   7. Attributed to Hippocrates, 5th century B.C.E.   8. From a letter to Barrett H. Clark, May 4, 1918. Clark (1890–1953) was a drama editor, translator, and critic.

expressions, the angles of vision, my methods of composition will, within limits, be always changing—not because I am unstable or unprincipled but because I am free. Or perhaps it may be more exact to say, because I am always trying for freedom—within my limits.

Coming now to the subject of your inquiry, I wish at first to put before you a general proposition: that a work of art is very seldom limited to one exclusive meaning and not necessarily tending to a definite conclusion. And this for the reason that the nearer it approaches art, the more it acquires a symbolic character. This statement may surprise you, who may imagine that I am alluding to the Symbolist School of poets or prose writers. Theirs, however, is only a literary proceeding against which I have nothing to say. I am concerned here with something much larger. But no doubt you have meditated on this and kindred questions yourself.

So I will only call your attention to the fact that the symbolic conception of a work of art has this advantage, that it makes a triple appeal covering the whole field of life. All the great creations of literature have been symbolic, and in that way have gained in complexity, in power, in depth and in beauty.

I don't think you will quarrel with me on the ground of lack of precision; for as to precision of images and analysis my artistic conscience is at rest. I have given there all the truth that is in me; and all that the critics may say can make my honesty neither more nor less. But as to "final effect" my conscience has nothing to do with that. It is the critic's affair to bring to its contemplation his own honesty, his sensibility and intelligence. The matter for his conscience is just his judgment. If his conscience is busy with petty scruples and trammelled by superficial formulas then his judgment will be superficial and petty. But an artist has no right to quarrel with the inspirations, either lofty or base, of another soul.

STEPHEN CRANE

Letter to John Northern Hilliard, February 1895[?][9]

As far as myself and my own meagre success are concerned, I began the battle of life with no talent, no equipment, but with an ardent admiration and desire. I did little work at school, but confined my abilities, such as they were, to the diamond. Not that I disliked books, but the cut-and-dried curriculum of the college did not appeal to me. Humanity was a much more interesting study. When I ought to have been at recitations I was studying faces on the streets, and when I ought to have been studying my next day's lessons I was watching the trains roll in and out of the Central Station. So, you see, I had, first of all, to recover from college. I had to build up, so to speak. And my chiefest desire was to write plainly and unmistakably, so that all men (and some women) might read and understand. That to my mind is good writing. There is a great deal of labor connected with literature. I think that is the hardest thing about it. There is nothing to respect in art save one's own opinion of it.

---

9. Crane met Hilliard, journalist, novelist, and dramatist (1872–1935), when they were reporters in New York City during 1892–93.

RALPH ELLISON

An Interview[1]

ELLISON: Let me say right now that my book is not an autobiographical work.

INTERVIEWERS: You weren't thrown out of school like the boy in your novel?

ELLISON: No. Though, like him, I went from one job to another.

INTERVIEWERS: Why did you give up music and begin writing?

ELLISON: I didn't give up music but I became interested in writing through incessant reading. In 1935 I discovered Eliot's *The Waste Land* which moved and intrigued me but defied my powers of analysis—such as they were—and I wondered why I had never read anything of equal intensity and sensibility by an American Negro writer. Later on, in New York, I read a poem by Richard Wright, who, as luck would have it, came to town the next week. He was editing a magazine called *New Challenge* and asked me to try a book review of E. Waters Turpin's *These Low Grounds*. On the basis of this review Wright suggested that I try a short story, which I did. I tried to use my knowledge of riding freight trains. He liked the story well enough to accept it and it got as far as the galley proofs when it was bumped from the issue because there was too much material. Just after that the magazine failed.

INTERVIEWERS: But you went on writing—

ELLISON: With difficulty, because this was the Recession of 1937. I went to Dayton, Ohio, where my brother and I hunted and sold game to earn a living. At night I practiced writing and studied Joyce, Dostoevski, Stein, and Hemingway. Especially Hemingway; I read him to learn his sentence structure and how to organize a story. I guess many young writers were doing this, but I also used his description of hunting when I went into the fields the next day. I had been hunting since I was eleven, but no one had broken down the process of wing-shooting for me, and it was from reading Hemingway that I learned to lead a bird. When he describes something in print, believe him; believe him even when he describes the process of art in terms of baseball or boxing; he's been there.

INTERVIEWERS: Were you affected by the social realism of the period?

ELLISON: I was seeking to learn and social realism was a highly regarded theory, though I didn't think too much of the so-called proletarian fiction even when I was most impressed by Marxism. I was intrigued by Malraux, who at that time was being claimed by the Communists. I noticed, however, that whenever the heroes of *Man's Fate* regarded their condition during moments of heightened self-consciousness, their thinking was something other than Marxist. Actually they were more profoundly intellectual than their real-life counterparts. Of course, Malraux was more of a humanist than most of the Marxist writers of that period—and also much more of an artist. He was the artist-revolutionary rather than a politician when he wrote *Man's Fate*, and the book lives not because of a political position embraced at the time but because of its larger concern with the tragic struggle of humanity. Most of the social realists

1. From *Writers at Work*, The Paris Review *Interviews*, Vol. 2, ed. George Plimpton (1963).

of the period were concerned less with tragedy than with injustice. I wasn't and am not, *primarily* concerned with injustice, but with art.

INTERVIEWERS: Then you consider your novel a purely literary work as opposed to one in the tradition of social protest.

ELLISON: Now, mind, I recognize no dichotomy between art and protest. Dostoevski's *Notes from Underground* is, among other things, a protest against the limitations of nineteenth-century rationalism; *Don Quixote, Man's Fate, Oedipus Rex, The Trial*—all these embody protest, even against the limitation of human life itself. If social protest is antithetical to art, what then shall we make of Goya, Dickens, and Twain? One hears a lot of complaints about the so-called "protest novel," especially when written by Negroes; but it seems to me that the critics could more accurately complain about the lack of craftsmanship and the provincialism which is typical of such works.

INTERVIEWERS: But isn't it going to be difficult for the Negro writer to escape provincialism when his literature is concerned with a minority?

ELLISON: All novels are about certain minorities: the individual is a minority. The universal in the novel—and isn't that what we're all clamoring for these days?—is reached only through the depiction of the specific man in a specific circumstance.

INTERVIEWERS: But still, how is the Negro writer, in terms of what is expected of him by critics and readers, going to escape his particular need for social protest and reach the "universal" you speak of?

ELLISON: If the Negro, or any other writer, is going to do what is expected of him, he's lost the battle before he takes the field. I suspect that all the agony that goes into writing is borne precisely because the writer longs for acceptance—but it must be acceptance on his own terms. Perhaps, though, this thing cuts both ways: the Negro novelist draws his blackness too tightly around him when he sits down to write—that's what the anti-protest critics believe—but perhaps the white reader draws his whiteness around himself when he sits down to read. He doesn't want to identify himself with Negro characters in terms of our immediate racial and social situation, though on the deeper human level identification can become compelling when the situation is revealed artistically. The white reader doesn't want to get too close, not even in an imaginary re-creation of society. Negro writers have felt this, and it has led to much of our failure.

Too many books by Negro writers are addressed to a white audience. By doing this the authors run the risk of limiting themselves to the audience's presumptions of what a Negro is or should be; the tendency is to become involved in polemics, to plead the Negro's humanity. You know, many white people question that humanity, but I don't think that Negroes can afford to indulge in such a false issue. For us the question should be, what are the specific *forms* of that humanity, and what in our background is worth preserving or abandoning. The clue to this can be found in folklore, which offers the first drawings of any group's character. It preserves mainly those situations which have repeated themselves again and again in the history of any given group. It describes those rites, manners, customs, and so forth, which insure the good life, or destroy it; and it describes those boundaries of feeling, thought, and action which that particular group has found to be the limitation of the human condition. It projects this wisdom in symbols which express the group's will to survive; it embodies those values by which the group lives and dies. These drawings may be crude but they are nonetheless profound in that they represent the group's attempt to humanize the world. It's no accident that great literature, the product of individual artists, is erected upon this humble base. The hero of Dostoevski's *Notes from Underground* and the hero of Gogol's "The Overcoat" appear in their rudimentary forms far back in Russian folklore. French literature has never ceased exploring the nature of the Frenchman.

ERNEST HEMINGWAY

An Interview[2]

INTERVIEWER: Do the titles come to you while you're in the process of doing the story?

HEMINGWAY: No. I make a list of titles *after* I've finished the story or the book—sometimes as many as a hundred. Then I start eliminating them, sometimes all of them.

INTERVIEWER: And you do this even with a story whose title is supplied from the text—"Hills Like White Elephants," for example?

HEMINGWAY: Yes. The title comes afterwards. I met a girl in Prunier where I'd gone to eat oysters before lunch. I knew she'd had an abortion. I went over and we talked, not about that, but on the way home I thought of the story, skipped lunch, and spent that afternoon writing it.

INTERVIEWER: So when you're not writing, you remain constantly the observer, looking for something which can be of use.

HEMINGWAY: Surely. If a writer stops observing he is finished. But he does not have to observe consciously nor think how it will be useful. Perhaps that would be true at the beginning. But later everything he sees goes into the great reserve of things he knows or has seen. If it is any use to know it, I always try to write on the principle of the iceberg. There is seven-eighths of it underwater for every part that shows. Anything you know you can eliminate and it only strengthens your iceberg. It is the part that doesn't show. If a writer omits something because he does not know it then there is a hole in the story.

The Old Man and the Sea could have been over a thousand pages long and had every character in the village in it and all the processes of how they made their living, were born, educated, bore children, etc. That is done excellently and well by other writers. In writing you are limited by what has already been done satisfactorily. So I have tried to learn to do something else. First I have tried to eliminate everything unnecessary to conveying experience to the reader so that after he or she has read something it will become a part of his or her experience and seem actually to have happened. This is very hard to do and I've worked at it very hard.

Anyway, to skip how it is done, I had unbelievable luck this time and could convey the experience completely and have it be one that no one had ever conveyed. The luck was that I had a good man and a good boy and lately writers have forgotten there still are such things. Then the ocean is worth writing

2. From *Writers at Work*, The Paris Review *Interviews*, Vol. 2, ed. George Plimpton (1963).

about just as man is. So I was lucky there. I've seen the marlin mate and know about that. So I leave that out. I've seen a school (or pod) of more than fifty sperm whales in that same stretch of water and once harpooned one nearly sixty feet in length and lost him. So I left that out. All the stories I know from the fishing village I leave out. But the knowledge is what makes the underwater part of the iceberg.

INTERVIEWER: Archibald MacLeish has spoken of a method of conveying experience to a reader which he said you developed while covering baseball games back in those *Kansas City Star* days. It was simply that experience is communicated by small details, intimately preserved, which have the effect of indicating the whole by making the reader conscious of what he had been aware of only subconsciously. . . .

HEMINGWAY: The anecdote is apocryphal. I never wrote baseball for the *Star.* What Archie was trying to remember was how I was trying to learn in Chicago in around 1920 and was searching for the unnoticed things that made emotions, such as the way an outfielder tossed his glove without looking back to where it fell, the squeak of resin on canvas under a fighter's flat-soled gym shoes, the gray color of Jack Blackburn's skin when he had just come out of stir, and other things I noted as a painter sketches. You saw Blackburn's strange color and the old razor cuts and the way he spun a man before you knew his history. These were the things which moved you before you knew the story.

INTERVIEWER: Have you ever described any type of situation of which you had no personal knowledge?

HEMINGWAY: That is a strange question. By personal knowledge do you mean carnal knowledge? In that case the answer is positive. A writer, if he is any good, does not describe. He invents or *makes* out of knowledge personal and impersonal and sometimes he seems to have unexplained knowledge which could come from forgotten racial or family experience. Who teaches the homing pigeon to fly as he does; where does a fighting bull get his bravery, or a hunting dog his nose? This is an elaboration or a condensation of that stuff we were talking about in Madrid that time when my head was not to be trusted.

INTERVIEWER: How detached must you be from an experience before you can write about it in fictional terms? The African air crashes you were involved in, for instance?

HEMINGWAY: It depends on the experience. One part of you sees it with complete detachment from the start. Another part is very involved. I think there is no rule about how soon one should write about it. It would depend on how well adjusted the individual was and on his or her recuperative powers. Certainly it is valuable to a trained writer to crash in an aircraft which burns. He learns several important things very quickly. Whether they will be of use to him is conditioned by survival. Survival, with honor, that outmoded and all-important word, is as difficult as ever and as all-important to a writer. Those who do not last are always more beloved since no one has to see them in their long, dull, unrelenting, no-quarter-given-no-quarter-received, fights that they make to do something as they believe it should be done before they die. Those who die or quit early and easy and with every good reason are preferred because they are understandable and human. Failure and well-disguised cowardice are more human and more beloved.

INTERVIEWER: Could I ask you to what extent you think the writer should concern himself with the socio-political problems of his times?

HEMINGWAY: Everyone has his own conscience, and there should be no rules about how a conscience should function. All you can be sure about in a political-minded writer is that if his work should last you will have to skip the politics when you read it. Many of the so-called politically enlisted writers change their politics frequently. This is very exciting to them and to their political-literary reviews. Sometimes they even have to rewrite their viewpoints . . . and in a hurry. Perhaps it can be respected as a form of the pursuit of happiness.

INTERVIEWER: Would you say, ever, that there is any didactic intention in your work?

HEMINGWAY: Didactic is a word that has been misused and has spoiled. *Death in the Afternoon* is an instructive book.

INTERVIEWER: It has been said that a writer only deals with one or two ideas throughout his work. Would you say your work reflects one or two ideas?

HEMINGWAY: Who said that? It sounds much too simple. The man who said it possibly *had* only one or two ideas.

INTERVIEWER: Well, perhaps it would be better put this way: Graham Greene said that a ruling passion gives to a shelf of novels the unity of a system. You yourself have said, I believe, that great writing comes out of a sense of injustice. Do you consider it important that a novelist be dominated in this way—by some such compelling sense?

HEMINGWAY: Mr. Greene has a facility for making statements that I do not possess. It would be impossible for me to make generalizations about a shelf of novels or a wisp of snipe or a gaggle of geese. I'll try a generalization though. A writer without a sense of justice and of injustice would be better off editing the Year Book of a school for exceptional children than writing novels. Another generalization. You see; they are not so difficult when they are sufficiently obvious. The most essential gift for a good writer is a built-in, shock-proof, shit detector. This is the writer's radar and all great writers have had it.

INTERVIEWER: Finally, a fundamental question: namely, as a creative writer what do you think is the function of your art? Why a representation of fact, rather than fact itself?

HEMINGWAY: Why be puzzled by that? From things that have happened and from things as they exist and from all things that you know and all those you cannot know, you make something through your invention that is not a representation but a whole new thing truer than anything true and alive, and you make it alive, and if you make it well enough, you give it immortality. That is why you write and for no other reason that you know of. But what about all the reasons that no one knows?

HENRY JAMES

The Art of Fiction[3]

It goes without saying that you will not write a good novel unless you possess the sense of reality; but it will be difficult to give you a recipe for calling

---

3. From *Partial Portraits* (1905).

that sense into being. Humanity is immense, and reality has a myriad forms; the most one can affirm is that some of the flowers of fiction have the odour of it, and others have not; as for telling you in advance how your nosegay should be composed, that is another affair. It is equally excellent and inconclusive to say that one must write from experience; to our supposititious aspirant such a declaration might savour of mockery. What kind of experience is intended, and where does it begin and end? Experience is never limited, and it is never complete; it is an immense sensibility, a kind of huge spider-web of the finest silken threads suspended in the chamber of consciousness, and catching every airborne particle in its tissue. It is the very atmosphere of the mind; and when the mind is imaginative—much more when it happens to be that of a man of genius—it takes to itself the faintest hints of life, it converts the very pulses of the air into revelations. The young lady living in a village has only to be a damsel upon whom nothing is lost to make it quite unfair (as it seems to me) to declare to her that she shall have nothing to say about the military. Greater miracles have been seen than that, imagination assisting, she should speak the truth about some of these gentlemen. I remember an English novelist, a woman of genius, telling me that she was much commended for the impression she had managed to give in one of her tales of the nature and way of life of the French Protestant youth. She had been asked where she learned so much about this recondite being, she had been congratulated on her peculiar opportunities. These opportunities consisted in her having once, in Paris, as she ascended a staircase, passed an open door where, in the household of a *pasteur*,[4] some of the young Protestants were seated at table round a finished meal. The glimpse made a picture; it lasted only a moment, but that moment was experience. She had got her direct personal impression, and she turned out her type. She knew what youth was, and what Protestantism; she also had the advantage of having seen what it was to be French, so that she converted these ideas into a concrete image and produced a reality. Above all, however, she was blessed with the faculty which when you give it an inch takes an ell, and which for the artist is a much greater source of strength than any accident of residence or of place in the social scale. The power to guess the unseen from the seen, to trace the implication of things, to judge the whole piece by the pattern, the condition of feeling life in general so completely that you are well on your way to knowing any particular corner of it—this cluster of gifts may almost be said to constitute experience, and they occur in country and in town, and in the most differing stages of education. If experience consists of impressions, it may be said that impressions *are* experience, just as (have we not seen it?) they are the very air we breathe. Therefore, if I should certainly say to a novice, "Write from experience and experience only," I should feel that this was rather a tantalising monition if I were not careful immediately to add, "Try to be one of the people on whom nothing is lost!"

• • •

There are bad novels and good novels, as there are bad pictures and good pictures; but that is the only distinction in which I see any meaning, and I can as little imagine speaking of a novel of character as I can imagine speaking of a picture of character. When one says picture one says of character, when

4. Clergyman (French).

one says novel one says of incident, and the terms may be transposed at will. What is character but the determination of incident? What is incident but the illustration of character? What is either a picture or a novel that is *not* of character? What else do we seek in it and find in it? It is an incident for a woman to stand up with her hand resting on a table and look out at you in a certain way; or if it be not an incident I think it will be hard to say what it is. At the same time it is an expression of character. If you say you don't see it (character in *that—allons donc!*),[5] this is exactly what the artist who has reasons of his own for thinking he *does* see it undertakes to show you. When a young man makes up his mind that he has not faith enough after all to enter the church as he intended, that is an incident, though you may not hurry to the end of the chapter to see whether perhaps he doesn't change once more. I do not say that these are extraordinary or startling incidents. I do not pretend to estimate the degree of interest proceeding from them, for this will depend upon the skill of the painter. It sounds almost puerile to say that some incidents are intrinsically much more important than others, and I need not take this precaution after having professed my sympathy for the major ones in remarking that the only classification of the novel that I can understand is into that which has life and that which has it not.

• • •

Nothing, of course, will ever take the place of the good old fashion of "liking" a work of art or not liking it: the most improved criticism will not abolish that primitive, that ultimate test. I mention this to guard myself from the accusation of intimating that the idea, the subject, of a novel or a picture, does not matter. It matters, to my sense, in the highest degree, and if I might put up a prayer it would be that artists should select none but the richest. Some, as I have already hastened to admit, are much more remunerative than others, and it would be a world happily arranged in which persons intending to treat them should be exempt from confusions and mistakes. This fortunate condition will arrive only, I fear, on the same day that critics become purged from error. Meanwhile, I repeat, we do not judge the artist with fairness unless we say to him, "Oh, I grant you your starting-point, because if I did not I should seem to prescribe to you, and heaven forbid I should take that responsibility. If I pretend to tell you what you must not take, you will call upon me to tell you then what you must take; in which case I shall be prettily caught. Moreover, it isn't till I have accepted your data that I can begin to measure you. I have the standard, the pitch; I have no right to tamper with your flute and then criticise your music. Of course I may not care for your idea at all; I may think it silly, or stale, or unclean; in which case I wash my hands of you altogether. I may content myself with believing that you will not have succeeded in being interesting, but I shall, of course, not attempt to demonstrate it, and you will be as indifferent to me as I am to you. I needn't remind you that there are all sorts of tastes: who can know it better? Some people, for excellent reasons, don't like to read about carpenters; others, for reasons even better, don't like to read about courtesans. Many object to Americans. Others (I believe they are mainly editors and publishers) won't look at Italians. Some readers don't like quiet subjects; others don't like bustling ones. Some enjoy a complete illusion, others the consciousness of large concessions. They choose

5. Come on now! Surely not! (French).

their novels accordingly, and if they don't care about your idea they won't, *a fortiori*,[6] care about your treatment.

If you must indulge in conclusions, let them have the taste of a wide knowledge. Remember that your first duty is to be as complete as possible—to make as perfect a work. Be generous and delicate and pursue the prize.

FRANZ KAFKA

Letter to Max Brod, July 5, 1922[7]

To put it first of all in general terms, I fear the traveling. . . . But it is not only fear of traveling itself; . . . Rather it is a fear of change, a fear of attracting the attention of the gods by what is a major act for a person of my sort.

Last night as I lay sleepless and let everything continually veer back and forth between my aching temples, what I had almost forgotten during the last relatively quiet time became clear to me: namely, on what frail ground or rather altogether nonexistent ground I live, over a darkness from which the dark power emerges when it wills and, heedless of my stammering, destroys my life. Writing sustains me, but is it not more accurate to say that it sustains this kind of life? By this I don't mean, of course, that my life is better when I don't write. Rather it is much worse then and wholly unbearable and has to end in madness. But that, granted, only follows from the postulate that I am a writer, which is actually true even when I am not writing, and a nonwriting writer is a monster inviting madness. But what about being a writer itself? Writing is a sweet and wonderful reward, but for what? In the night it became clear to me, as clear as a child's lesson book, that it is the reward for serving the devil. This descent to the dark powers, this unshackling of spirits bound by nature, these dubious embraces and whatever else may take place in the nether parts which the higher parts no longer know, when one writes one's stories in the sunshine. Perhaps there are other forms of writing, but I know only this kind; at night, when fear keeps me from sleeping, I know only this kind. And the diabolic element in it seems very clear to me. It is vanity and sensuality which continually buzz about one's own or even another's form— and feast on him. The movement multiplies itself—it is a regular solar system of vanity. Sometimes a naïve person will wish, "I would like to be dead and see how everyone mourns me." Such a writer is continually staging such a scene: He dies (or rather he does not live) and continually mourns himself. From this springs a terrible fear of death, which need not reveal itself as fear of death but may also appear as fear of change. . . . The reasons for this fear of death may be divided into two main categories. First he has a terrible fear of dying because he has not yet lived. By this I do not mean that wife and child, fields and cattle are essential to living. What is essential to life is only to forgo complacency, to move into the house instead of admiring it and hanging garlands around it. In reply to this, one might say that this is a matter of fate and is not given into anyone's hand. But then why this sense of repining, this repining that never ceases? To make oneself finer and more savory? That is a part of it. But why do such nights leave one always with the refrain: I could

---

6. Even more certainly (Latin).   **7.** Translated by Richard and Clara Winston.

live and I do not live. The second reason—perhaps it is all really one, the two do not want to stay apart for me now—is the belief: "What I have playacted is really going to happen. I have not bought myself off by my writing. I died my whole life long and now I will really die. My life was sweeter than other peoples' and my death will be more terrible by the same degree. Of course the writer in me will die right away, since such a figure has no base, no substance, is less than dust. He is only barely possible in the broil of earthly life, is only a construct of sensuality. That is your writer for you. But I myself cannot go on living because I have not lived, I have remained clay, I have not blown the spark into fire, but only used it to light up my corpse." It will be a strange burial: the writer, insubstantial as he is, consigning the old corpse, the long-time corpse, to the grave. I am enough of a writer to appreciate the scene with all my senses, or—and it is the same thing—to want to describe it with total self-forgetfulness—not alertness, but self-forgetfulness is the writer's first prerequisite. But there will be no more of such describing. But why am I talking of actual dying? It is just the same in life. I sit here in the comfortable posture of the writer, ready for all sorts of fine things, and must idly look on—for what can I do but write?—as my true ego, this wretched, defenseless ego, is nipped by the devil's pincers, cudgeled, and almost ground to pieces on a random pretext—a little trip. . . . Since I was not at home, what right have I to be alarmed when the house suddenly collapses. After all, I know what preceded the collapse. Did I not emigrate and leave the house to all the evil powers?

DORIS LESSING

An Interview[8]

LESSING: I think I've always been a writer by temperament. I wrote some bad novels in my teens. I always knew I would be a writer, but not until I was quite old—twenty-six or-seven—did I realize that I'd better stop saying I was *going* to be one and get down to business. I was working in a lawyer's office at the time, and I remember walking in and saying to my boss, "I'm giving up my job because I'm going to write a novel." He very properly laughed, and I indignantly walked home and wrote *The Grass Is Singing.* I'm oversimplifying; I didn't write it as simply as that because I was clumsy at writing and it was much too long, but I did learn by writing it. It focused upon white people in Southern Rhodesia, but it could have been about white people anywhere south of the Zambezi, white people who were not up to what is expected of them in a society where there is very heavy competition from the black people coming up.

Then I wrote short stories set in the district I was brought up in, where very isolated white farmers lived immense distances from each other. You see, in this background, people can spread themselves out. People who might be extremely ordinary in a society like England's, where people are pressed into conformity, can become wild eccentrics in all kinds of ways they wouldn't dare try elsewhere. This is one of the things I miss, of course, by living in

8. From *The Doris Lessing Reader* (1988).

England. I don't think my memory deceives me, but I think there were more colorful people back in Southern Rhodesia because of the space they had to move in. I gather, from reading American literature, that this is the kind of space you have in America in the Midwest and West.

I left Rhodesia and my second marriage to come to England, bringing a son with me. I had very little money, but I've made my living as a professional writer ever since, which is really very hard to do. I had rather hard going, to begin with, which is not a complaint; I gather from my American writer-friends that it is easier to be a writer in England than in America because there is much less pressure put on us. We are not expected to be successful, and it is no sin to be poor.

INTERVIEWER: I don't know how we can compare incomes, but in England it seems that writers make more from reviewing and from broadcasts than they can in the United States.

LESSING: I don't know. When I meet American writers, the successful ones, they seem to make more on royalties, but then they also seem to spend much more.

I know a writer isn't supposed to talk about money, but it is very important. It is vital for a writer to know how much he can write to please himself, and how much, or little he must write to earn money. In England you don't have to "go commercial" if you don't mind being poor. It so happens that I'm not poor any more, thank goodness, because it's not good for anyone to be. Yet there are disadvantages to living in England. It's not an exciting place to live, it is not one of the hubs of the world, like America, or Russia, or China. England is a backwater, and it doesn't make much difference what happens here, or what decisions are made here. But from the point of view of writing, England is a paradise for me.

You see, I was brought up in a country where there is very heavy pressure put on people. In Southern Rhodesia it is not possible to detach yourself from what is going on. This means that you spend all your time in a torment of conscientiousness. In England—I'm not saying it's a perfect society, far from it—you can get on with your work in peace and quiet when you choose to withdraw. For this I'm very grateful—I imagine there are few countries left in the world where you have this right of privacy.

INTERVIEWER: This is what you're supposed to find in Paris.

LESSING: Paris is too exciting. I find it impossible to work there. I proceed to have a wonderful time and don't write a damn thing.

INTERVIEWER: To work from *A Man and Two Women* for a bit. The almost surgical job you do in dissecting people, not bodily, but emotionally, has made me wonder if you choose your characters from real life, form composites or projections, or if they are so involved you can't really trace their origins.

LESSING: I don't know. Some people I write about come out of my life. Some, well, I don't know where they come from. They just spring from my own consciousness, perhaps the subconscious, and I'm surprised as they emerge.

This is one of the excitements about writing. Someone says something, drops a phrase, and later you find that phrase turning into a character in a story, or a single, isolated, insignificant incident becomes the germ of a plot.

INTERVIEWER: If you were going to give advice to the young writer, what would that advice be?

LESSING: You should write, first of all, to please yourself. You shouldn't care a damn about anybody else at all. But writing can't be a way of life; the important part of writing is living. You have to live in such a way that your writing emerges from it. This is hard to describe.

INTERVIEWER: What about reading as a background?

LESSING: I've known very good writers who've never read anything. Of course, this is rare.

INTERVIEWER: What about your own reading background?

LESSING: Well, because I had this isolated childhood, I read a great deal. There was no one to talk to, so I read. What did I read? The best—the classics of European and American literature. One of the advantages of not being educated was that I didn't have to waste time on the second-best. Slowly, I read these classics. It was my education, and I think it was a very good one.

I could have been educated, formally, that is, but I felt some neurotic rebellion against my parents who wanted me to be brilliant academically. I simply contracted out of the whole thing and educated myself. Of course, there are huge gaps in my education, but I'm nonetheless grateful that it went as it did. One bit of advice I might give the young writer is to get rid of the fear of being thought of as a perfectionist, or to be regarded as pompous. They should strike out for the best, to be the best. God knows we all fall short of our potential, but if we aim very high we're likely to be so much better.

GUY DE MAUPASSANT

The Novel[9]

The man who seeks only to amuse the public by already known methods writes with confidence, in the candor of his mediocrity, for the ignorant, the idle. But those on whom all the ages of past literature weigh heavily; those whom nothing satisfies, whom everything disgusts because it does not come up to their dreams; those to whom every flower seems to have been plucked, to whom their work always gives the impression of a useless and common labor—arrive at the opinion that literary art is an intangible, mysterious thing, only partially revealed to us in some of the pages of the greatest masters.

Twenty verses, twenty phrases, may suddenly thrill us to the heart as a surprising revelation; but the following verses resemble all verses, and the prose that follows resembles all other prose.

Men of genius, doubtless, do not experience this anguish and torture, because they have in themselves a resistless creative power. They do not sit in judgment on themselves. The rest of us, who are simply conscientious and persistent workers, can only by continued effort fight against overwhelming discouragement.

Two men by their simple and lucid teachings gave me this power of persistent effort—Louis Bouilhet and Gustave Flaubert.

If I speak of them and of myself in this place it is because their advice, summed up in a few lines, may be useful, perhaps, to some young writers with less self-esteem than is usually found in literary débutants.

9. From the essay "The Novel" (1887).

Bouilhet, with whom I formed a rather intimate acquaintance about two years before I gained the friendship of Flaubert, by dint of repeating to me that a hundred verses, or even less, insured the reputation of an artist, provided they were faultless and embodied the essence of the talent and originality of a man, even of second-rate talent, made me understand that.

I also learned that the best-known writers have seldom left more than one volume; and that the first essential is to have the luck to find and discern, amid the multiplicity of subjects that present themselves, that subject that will absorb all our faculties, all our ability, all our artistic power.

Later on Flaubert, whom I sometimes saw, conceived a liking for me. I ventured to submit to him some of my attempts. He kindly read them, and replied: "I do not know if you have talent; what you have shown me proves that you possess a certain degree of intelligence. But do not forget this, young man, that talent—to quote the saying of Buffon—is merely 'long patience.' Keep on working."

I did so, and often revisited him, as I perceived that he liked me, for he laughingly called me his disciple.

For seven years I wrote verses, I wrote stories, I wrote novels, I even wrote a detestable play. Of these nothing survives. The master read them all, and on the following Sunday at luncheon he would give me his criticism, and inculcate little by little two or three principles that sum up his long and patient lessons. "If one has any originality, the first thing requisite is to bring it out; if one has none, the first thing to be done is to acquire it."

Talent is long patience. Everything which one desires to express must be considered with sufficient attention, and during a sufficiently long time, to discover in it some aspect which no one has as yet seen or described. In everything there is still some spot unexplored, because we are accustomed to look at things only with the recollection of what others before us have thought of the subject we are contemplating. The smallest object contains something unknown. Let us find it. In order to describe a fire that flames, and a tree on the plain, we must keep looking at that flame and that tree, until to our eyes they no longer resemble any other tree, any other fire.

This is the way to become original.

Having, besides, laid down this truth that there are not in the whole world two grains of sand, two specks, two hands, or two noses exactly alike, he compelled me to describe, in a few phrases, a being or an object in such a manner as to clearly particularize it and distinguish it from all the other beings, or all the other objects of the same race or the same species.

"When you pass," he would say, "a grocer seated at his shop door, a janitor smoking his pipe, a stand of hackney coaches, show me that grocer and that janitor, their attitude, their whole physical appearance, including also by a skillful description their whole moral nature, so that I cannot confound them with any other grocer or any other janitor; make me see, in one word, that a certain cab horse does not resemble the fifty others that follow or precede it."

I have stated elsewhere his ideas on style. They are closely related to the theory of observation which I have just explained.

Whatever be the thing one wishes to say, there is only one noun to express it, only one verb to give it life, only one adjective to qualify it. We must search, then, till that noun, that verb, that adjective, are discovered; never be content with an approximation, never resort to tricks, however happy, or to buffooneries of language, to avoid a difficulty.

We can interpret and describe the most subtle things if we bear in mind the verse of Boileau:

"D'un mot mis en sa place enseigna le pouvoir."

"He taught the force of a word in the right place."

There is no need of the eccentric, complicated, multifarious sort of Chinese vocabulary, which is inflicted on us at the present day under the name of artistic writing, to enable us to describe every shade of thought; but it is necessary to discern, with the utmost lucidity, all the modifications of the value of a word according to the position it occupies. Let us have fewer nouns, verbs and adjectives with almost incomprehensible meanings, and more varied phrases, differently constructed, ingeniously turned, sonorous and full of skillful rhythms. Let us endeavor to be excellent stylists, rather than collectors of rare terms.

It is, in fact, more difficult to turn a phrase to suit one's self, to make it say everything (even that which it does not express), to fill it with hidden meanings, and with secret suggestions which are not formulated, than to invent new expressions, or to seek in the depths of old forgotten books all those that are obsolete and have lost their significance, and for us are only dead words.

BHARATI MUKHERJEE

A Four-Hundred-Year-Old Woman[1]

It took me ten painful years, from the early seventies to the early eighties, to overthrow the smothering tyranny of nostalgia. The remaining struggle for me is to make the American readership, meaning the editorial and publishing industries as well, acknowledge the same fact. (As the reception of such films as *Gandhi* and *A Passage to India* as well as *The Far Pavillions* and *The Jewel in the Crown* shows, nostalgia is a two-way street. Americans can feel nostalgic for a world they never knew.) The foreign-born, the exotically raised Third World immigrant with non-Western religions and non-European languages and appearance, can be as American as any steerage passenger from Ireland, Italy, or the Russian Pale. As I have written in another context (a review article in *The Nation* on books by Studs Terkel and Al Santoli), we are probably only a few years away from a Korean *What Makes Choon-li Run?* or a Hmong *Call It Sleep*. In other words, my literary agenda begins by acknowledging that America has transformed *me*. It does not end until I show how I (and the hundreds of thousands like me) have transformed America.

The agenda is simply stated, but in the long run revolutionary. Make the familiar exotic; the exotic familiar.

I have had to create an audience. I cannot rely on shorthand references to my community, my religion, my class, my region, or my old school tie. I've had to sensitize editors as well as readers to the richness of the lives I'm

---

1. From *The Writer on Her Work,* Vol. II, ed. Janet Sternberg (1991).

writing about. The most moving form of praise I receive from readers can be summed up in three words: *I never knew.* Meaning, I see these people (call them Indians, Filipinos, Koreans, Chinese) around me all the time and I never knew they had an inner life. I never knew they schemed and cheated, suffered, felt so strongly, cared so passionately. When even the forms of praise are so rudimentary, the writer knows she has an inexhaustible fictional population to enumerate. Perhaps even a mission, to appropriate a good colonial word.

I have been blessed with an enormity of material. I can be Chekhovian and Tolstoyan—with melancholy and philosophical perspectives on the breaking of hearts as well as the fall of civilizations—and I can be a brash and raucous homesteader, Huck Finn and Woman Warrior, on the unclaimed plains of American literature. My material, reduced to jacket-flap copy, is the rapid and dramatic transformation of the United States since the early 1970s. Within that perceived perimeter, however, I hope to wring surprises.

Yet (I am a writer much given to "yet") my imaginative home is also in the tales told by my mother and grandmother, the world of the Hindu epics. For all the hope and energy I have placed in the process of immigration and accommodation—I'm a person who couldn't ride a public bus when she first arrived, and now I'm someone who watches tractor pulls on obscure cable channels—there are parts of me that remain Indian, parts that slide against the masks of newer selves. The form that my stories and novels take inevitably reflects the resources of Indian mythology—shape-changing, miracles, godly perspectives. My characters can, I hope, transcend the straitjacket of simple psychologizing. The people I write about are culturally and politically several hundred years old: consider the history they have witnessed (colonialism, technology, education, liberation, civil war, uprooting). They have shed old identities, taken on new ones, and learned to hide the scars. They may sell you newspapers, or clean your offices at night.

Writers (especially American writers, weaned on the luxury of affluence and freedom) often disavow the notion of a "literary duty" or "political consciousness," citing the all-too-frequent examples of writers ruined by their shrill commitments. Glibness abounds on both sides of the argument, but finally I have to side with my "Third World" compatriots: I do have a duty, beyond telling a good story or drawing a convincing character. My duty is to give voice to continents, but also to redefine the nature of *American* and what makes an American. In the process, work like mine and dozens like it will open up the canon of American literature.

· · ·

My theme is the making of new Americans. Wherever I travel in the (very) Old World, I find "Americans" in the making, whether or not they ever make it to these shores. I see them as dreamers and conquerors, not afraid of transforming themselves, not afraid of abandoning some of their principles along the way. In *Jasmine*, my "American" is born in a Punjabi village, marries at fourteen, and is widowed at sixteen. Nevertheless, she is an American and will enter the book as an Iowa banker's wife.

Ancestral habits of mind can be constricting; they also confer one's individuality. I know I can appropriate the American language, but I can never be a minimalist. I have too many stories to tell. I am aware of myself as a four-hundred-year-old woman, born in the captivity of a colonial, pre-industrial oral culture and living now as a contemporary New Yorker.

My image of artistic structure and artistic excellence is the Moghul minia-ture painting with its crazy foreshortening of vanishing point, its insistence that everything happens simultaneously, bound only by shape and color. In the miniature paintings of India, there are a dozen separate foci, the most complicated stories can be rendered on a grain of rice, the corners are as elab-orated as the centers. There is a sense of the interpenetration of all things. In the Moghul miniature of my life, there would be women investigating their bodies with mirrors, but they would be doing it on a distant balcony under fans wielded by bored serving girls; there would be a small girl listening to a bent old woman; there would be a white man eating popcorn and watching a baseball game; there would be cocktail parties and cornfields and a village set among rice paddies and skyscrapers. In a sense, I wrote that story, "Courtly Vision," at the end of *Darkness*. And in a dozen other ways I'm writing it today, and I will be writing, in the Moghul style, till I get it right.

EDGAR ALLAN POE

The Philosophy of Composition[2]

Charles Dickens, in a note now lying before me, alluding to an examination I once made of the mechanism of "Barnaby Rudge," says—"By the way, are you aware that Godwin[3] wrote his 'Caleb Williams' backwards? He first involved his hero in a web of difficulties, forming the second volume, and then, for the first, cast about him for some mode of accounting for what had been done."

I cannot think this the *precise* mode of procedure on the part of Godwin—and indeed what he himself acknowledges, is not altogether in accordance with Mr. Dickens' idea—but the author of "Caleb Williams" was too good an artist not to perceive the advantage derivable from at least a somewhat similar process. Nothing is more clear than that every plot, worth the name, must be elaborated to its *dénouement* before any thing be attempted with the pen. It is only with the *dénouement* constantly in view that we can give a plot its indispensable air of consequence, or causation, by making the inci-dents, and especially the tone at all points, tend to the development of the intention.

There is a radical error, I think, in the usual mode of constructing a story. Either history affords a thesis—or one is suggested by an incident of the day—or, at best, the author sets himself to work in the combination of striking events to form merely the basis of his narrative—designing, generally, to fill in with description, dialogue, or autorial comment, whatever crevices of fact, or action, may, from page to page, render themselves apparent.

I prefer commencing with the consideration of an *effect*. Keeping original-ity *always* in view—for he is false to himself who ventures to dispense with so obvious and so easily attainable a source of interest—I say to myself, in the first place, "Of the innumerable effects, or impressions, of which the heart, the intellect, or (more generally) the soul is susceptible, what one shall I, on

2. Reprinted from *Graham's* of April 1846. **3.** William Godwin (1756–1836). British writer and philoso-pher who wrote *Caleb Williams* (1794) as a mystery novel.

the present occasion, select?" Having chosen a novel, first, and secondly a vivid effect, I consider whether it can best be wrought by incident or tone—whether by ordinary incidents and peculiar tone, or the converse, or by peculiarity both of incident and tone—afterward looking about me (or rather within) for such combinations of event, or tone, as shall best aid me in the construction of the effect.

KATHERINE ANNE PORTER

An Interview[4]

INTERVIEWER: You once said that every story begins with an ending, that until the end is known there is no story.

PORTER: That is where the artist begins to work: With the consequences of acts, not the acts themselves. Or the events. The event is important only as it affects your life and the lives of those around you. The reverberations, you might say, the overtones: that is where the artist works. In that sense it has sometimes taken me ten years to understand even a little of some important event that had happened to me. Oh, I could have given a perfectly factual account of what had happened, but I didn't know what it meant until I knew the consequences. If I didn't know the ending of a story, I wouldn't begin. I always write my last lines, my last paragraph, my last page first, and then I go back and work towards it. I know where I'm going. I know what my goal is. And how I get there is God's grace.

INTERVIEWER: That's a very classical view of the work of art—that it must end in resolution.

PORTER: Any true work of art has got to give you the feeling of reconciliation—what the Greeks would call catharsis, the purification of your mind and imagination—through an ending that is endurable because it is right and true. Oh, not in any pawky individual idea of morality or some parochial idea of right and wrong. Sometimes the end is very tragic, because it needs to be. One of the most perfect and marvelous endings in literature—it raises my hair now—is the little boy at the end of *Wuthering Heights,* crying that he's afraid to go across the moor because there's a man and woman walking there.

And there are three novels that I reread with pleasure and delight—three almost perfect novels, if we're talking about form, you know. One is *A High Wind in Jamaica* by Richard Hughes, one is *A Passage to India* by E. M. Forster, and the other is *To the Lighthouse* by Virginia Woolf. Every one of them begins with an apparently insoluble problem, and every one of them works out of confusion into order. The material is all used so that you are going toward a goal. And that goal is the clearing up of disorder and confusion and wrong, to a logical and human end. I don't mean a happy ending, because after all at the end of *A High Wind in Jamaica* the pirates are all hanged and the children are all marked for life by their experience, but it comes out to an orderly end. The threads are all drawn up. I have had people object to Mr. Thompson's suicide at the end of *Noon Wine,* and I'd say, "All right, where was he going? Given what he was, his own situation, what else could he do?" Every once in a

4. From *Writers at Work*, The Paris Review *Interviews*, Vol. 2, ed. George Plimpton (1963).

while when I see a character of mine just going towards perdition, I think, "Stop, stop, you can always stop and choose, you know." But no, being what he was, he already *has* chosen, and he can't go back on it now. I suppose the first idea that man had was the idea of fate, of the servile will, of a deity who destroyed as he would, without regard for the creature. But I think the idea of free will was the second idea.

INTERVIEWER: Has a story never surprised you in the writing? A character suddenly taken a different turn?

PORTER: Well, in the vision of death at the end of "Flowering Judas" I knew the real ending—that she was not going to be able to face her life, what she'd done. And I knew that the vengeful spirit was going to come in a dream to tow her away into death, but I didn't know until I'd written it that she was going to wake up saying, "No!" and be afraid to go to sleep again.

INTERVIEWER: That was, in a fairly literal sense, a "true" story, wasn't it?

PORTER: The truth is, I have never written a story in my life that didn't have a very firm foundation in actual human experience—somebody else's experience quite often, but an experience that became my own by hearing the story, by witnessing the thing, by hearing just a word perhaps. It doesn't matter, it just takes a little—a tiny seed. Then it takes root, and it grows. It's an organic thing. That story had been on my mind for years, growing out of this one little thing that happened in Mexico. It was forming and forming in my mind, until one night I was quite desperate. People are always so sociable, and I'm sociable too, and if I live around friends. . . . Well, they were insisting that I come and play bridge. But I was very firm, because I knew the time had come to write that story, and I had to write it.

INTERVIEWER: What was that "little thing" from which the story grew?

PORTER: Something I saw as I passed a window one evening. A girl I knew had asked me to come and sit with her, because a man was coming to see her, and she was afraid of him. And as I went through the courtyard, past the flowering judas tree, I glanced in the window and there she was sitting with an open book on her lap, and there was this great big fat man sitting beside her. Now Mary and I were friends, both American girls living in this revolutionary situation. She was teaching at an Indian school, and I was teaching dancing at a girls' technical school in Mexico City. And we were having a very strange time of it. I was more skeptical, and so I had already begun to look with a skeptical eye on a great many of the revolutionary leaders. Oh, the idea was all right, but a lot of men were misapplying it.

And when I looked through that window that evening, I saw something in Mary's face, something in her pose, something in the whole situation, that set up a commotion in my mind. Because until that moment I hadn't really understood that she was not able to take care of herself, because she was not able to face her own nature and was afraid of everything. I don't know why I saw it. I don't believe in intuition. When you get sudden flashes of perception, it is just the brain working faster than usual. But you've been getting ready to know it for a long time, and when it comes, you feel you've known it always.

INTERVIEWER: You speak of a story "forming" in your mind. Does it begin as a visual impression, growing to a narrative? Or how?

PORTER: All my senses were very keen; things came to me through my eyes, through all my pores. Everything hit me at once, you know. That makes it very difficult to describe just exactly what is happening. And then, I think the mind works in such a variety of ways. Sometimes an idea starts completely inarticulately. You're not thinking in images or words or—well, it's exactly like a dark cloud moving in your head. You keep wondering what will come out of this, and then it will dissolve itself into a set of—well, not images exactly, but really thoughts. You begin to think directly in words. Abstractly. Then the words transform themselves into images. By the time I write the story my people are up and alive and walking around and taking things into their own hands. They exist as independently inside my head as you do before me now. I have been criticized for not enough detail in describing my characters, and not enough furniture in the house. And the odd thing is that I see it all so clearly.

INTERVIEWER: What about the technical problems a story presents—its formal structure? How deliberate are you in matters of technique? For example, the use of the historical present in "Flowering Judas"?

PORTER: The first time someone said to me, "Why did you write 'Flowering Judas' in the historical present?" I thought for a moment and said, "Did I?" I'd never noticed it. Because I didn't *plan* to write it any way. A story forms in my mind and forms and forms, and when it's ready to go, I strike it down—it takes just the time I sit at the typewriter. I never think about form at all. In fact, I would say that I've never been interested in anything about writing after having learned, I hope, to write. That is, I mastered my craft as well as I could. There is a technique, there is a craft, and you have to learn it. Well, I did as well as I could with that, but now all in the world I am interested in is telling a story. I have something to tell you that I, for some reason, think is worth telling, and so I want to tell it as clearly and purely and simply as I can. But I had spent fifteen years at least learning to write. I practiced writing in every possible way that I could. I wrote a pastiche of other people, imitating Dr. Johnson and Laurence Sterne, and Petrarch and Shakespeare's sonnets, and then I tried writing my own way. I spent fifteen years learning to trust myself: that's what it comes to. Just as a pianist runs his scales for ten years before he gives his concert: because when he gives that concert, he can't be thinking of his fingering or of his hands; he has to be thinking of his interpretation, of the music he's playing. He's thinking of what he's trying to communicate. And if he hasn't got his technique perfected by then, he needn't give the concert at all.

• • • •

INTERVIEWER: You are frequently spoken of as a stylist. Do you think a style can be cultivated, or at least refined?

PORTER: I've been called a stylist until I really could tear my hair out. And I simply don't believe in style. The style is you. Oh, you can cultivate a style, I suppose, if you like. But I should say it remains a cultivated style. It remains artificial and imposed, and I don't think it deceives anyone. A cultivated style would be like a mask. Everybody knows it's a mask, and sooner or later you must show yourself—or at least, you show yourself as someone who could not afford to show himself, and so created something to hide behind. Style is the man. Aristotle said it first, as far as I know, and everybody has said it since, because it is one of those unarguable truths. You do not create a style. You work, and develop yourself; your style is an emanation from your own being. Symbolism is the same way. I never consciously took or adopted a symbol in my life. I certainly did not say, "This blooming tree upon which Judas is supposed to have hanged himself is going to be the center of my story." I named "Flowering Judas" after it was written, because when reading back over it I suddenly saw the whole symbolic plan and pattern of which I was totally unconscious while I was writing. There's a pox of symbolist theory going the rounds these days in American colleges in the writing courses. Miss Mary McCarthy, who is one of the wittiest and most acute and in some ways the worst-tempered woman in American letters, tells about a little girl who came to her with a story. Now Miss McCarthy is an extremely good critic, and she found this to be a good story, and she told the girl that it was— that she considered it a finished work, and that she could with a clear conscience go on to something else. And the little girl said, "But Miss McCarthy, my writing teacher said, 'Yes, it's a good piece of work, but now we must go back and put in the symbols!'" I think that's an amusing story, and it makes my blood run cold.

LEO TOLSTOY

What Is Art?[5]

The art of the future is not the possession of a select minority but a means towards perfection and unity.

People talk of the art of the future, meaning by art of the future some especially refined new art which they imagine will be developed out of that exclusive art of one class which is now considered the highest art. But no such new art of the future can or will be found. Our exclusive art, that of the upper classes of Christendom, has found its way into a blind alley. The direction in which it has been going leads nowhere. Having once lost hold of that which is most essential to art (namely, the guidance given by religious perception), this art has become ever more and more exclusive and therefore ever more and more perverted, until finally it has come to nothing. The art of the future, that which is really coming, will not be a development of present-day art, but will arise on quite other and new foundations having nothing in common with those by which our present art of the upper classes is guided.

Art of the future, that is to say, such part of art as will be chosen from among all the art diffused among mankind, will consist not in transmitting feelings accessible only to members of the rich classes, as is the case to-day, but in transmitting feelings embodying the highest religious perception of our times. Only those productions will be esteemed art which transmit feelings drawing men together in brotherly union, or such universal feelings as can unite all men. Only such art will be chosen, tolerated, approved, and diffused. But art transmitting feelings flowing from antiquated, outworn, religious teaching; ecclesiastical art, patriotic art, voluptuous art; transmitting

---

5. From *What Is Art? and Essays on Art* (1960).

feelings of superstitious fear, of pride, of vanity, of ecstatic admiration of national heroes; art exciting exclusive love of one's own people, or sensuality, will be considered bad, harmful art, and will be censured and despised by public opinion. All the rest of art, transmitting feelings accessible only to a section of people, will be considered unimportant, and will be neither blamed nor praised. And the appraisement of art in general will devolve not as is now the case on a separate class of rich people, but on the whole people; so that for a work to be thought good and to be approved and diffused, it will have to satisfy the demands not of a few people living under similar and often unnatural conditions, but of all those great masses of people who undergo the natural conditions of laborious life.

Nor will the artists producing the art be as now merely a few people selected from a small section of the nation, members of the upper classes or their hangers-on, but they will consist of all those gifted members of the whole people who prove capable of, and have an inclination towards, artistic activity.

Artistic activity will then be accessible to all men. It will become accessible to the whole people because (in the first place) in the art of the future not only will that complex technique which deforms the productions of the art of to-day, and requires so great an effort and expenditure of time, not be demanded, but on the contrary the demand will be for clearness, simplicity, and brevity—conditions brought about not by mechanical methods but through the education of taste. And secondly, artistic activity will become accessible to all men of the people because, instead of the present professional schools which only some can enter, all will learn music and graphic art (singing and drawing) equally with letters, in the elementary schools, in such a way that every man, having received the first principles of drawing and music and feeling a capacity for and a call to one or other of the arts, will be able to perfect himself in it.

People think that if there are no special art-schools the technique of art will deteriorate. Undoubtedly it will deteriorate if by technique we understand those *complexities* of art which are now considered an excellence; but if by technique is understood clearness, beauty, simplicity, and compression, in works of art, then even if the elements of drawing and music were not to be taught in the national schools, not only will the technique not deteriorate but, as shown by all peasant art, it will be a hundred times better. It will be improved because all the artists of genius now hidden among the masses will become producers of art and supply models of excellence which (as has always been the case) will be the best schools of technique for their successors. For even now every true artist chiefly learns his technique not in the schools but in life, from the examples of the great masters, and then—when art is produced by the best artists of the whole nation and there are more such examples and they are more accessible—such part of school training as the future artist may lose will be a hundredfold compensated for by the training he will receive from the numerous examples of good art diffused in society.

Such will be one difference between present and future art. Another difference will be that art will not be produced by professional artists receiving payment for their work and engaged on nothing else besides their art. The art of the future will be produced by all the members of the community who feel need of such activity, but they will occupy themselves with art only when they feel such need.

In our society people think that an artist will work better and produce more if he has a secured maintenance; and this opinion once more would prove quite clearly, were such proof still needed, that what among us is considered to be art is not art but only a counterfeit. It is quite true that for the production of boots or loaves division of labour is very advantageous, and that the bootmaker or baker who need not prepare his own dinner or fetch his own fuel will make more boots or loaves than if he had to busy himself with those matters. But art is not a handicraft, it is the transmission of feeling the artist has experienced. And sound feeling can only be engendered in a man when he is living a life in all respects natural and proper to man. Therefore security of maintenance is a condition most harmful to an artist's true productiveness, since it removes him from the condition natural to all men—that of struggle with nature for the maintenance both of his own life and the lives of others—and thus deprives him of the opportunity and possibility of experiencing the most important and most natural feelings of man. There is no position more injurious to an artist's productiveness than the position of complete security and luxury in which in our society artists usually live.

The artist of the future will live the common life of man, earning his subsistence by some kind of labour. The fruits of the highest spiritual strength that passes through him he will try to share with the greatest possible number of people, for in such transmission to others of the feelings that have arisen in him he will find his happiness and reward. The artist of the future will be unable to understand how an artist, whose chief delight is in the wide diffusion of his works, could give them only in exchange for a certain payment.

Until the dealers are driven out, the temple of art will not be a temple. But the art of the future will drive them out.

JOHN UPDIKE

Accepting the Howells Medal[6]

William Dean Howells, in whose name this medal is given, was a considerable theorist of fiction, and of American fiction. As a practitioner and critic he sought to hold himself and other writers to a standard of realism that rose above the romantic exaggerations and implausible adventures that characterized popular fiction in his day and, indeed, in ours. He thought progress was being made, and in 1891 wrote, "Fiction is now a finer art than it has ever been hitherto. . . . I have hopes of real usefulness in it . . . but I am by no means certain that it will be the ultimate literary form. . . . On the contrary, it is quite imaginable that when the great mass of readers, now sunk in the foolish joys of mere fable, shall be lifted to an interest in the meaning of things through the faithful portrayal of life in fiction, then fiction the most faithful may be superseded by a still more faithful form of contemporaneous history."

6. From *More Matter: Essays and Criticism*, John Updike, 1999. pp. 815–816.

The situation now is more drastic, I think, than Howells conceived it, for what looms is not a mere change of literary fashion or shift of genres but a loss of literature itself, rendered passé by the bright flickering tongues of the electronic modes of entertainment and instruction. Young students, it is reported from academia, are less and less willing and able to read, and the language of even as limpid a nineteenth-century style as that of Hawthorne is reportedly impenetrable to them. Those of us who grew up on a diet of the modernist masterpieces, and have tried to write works that would enchant and challenge readers such as we were, may be like those Renaissance poets who mastered the art of Latin verse, in quixotic or elitist defiance of a widespread linguistic death. We are writing for an audience that less and less exists, and a posterity that will not exist.

And yet, when this most dire of scenarios has been sketched, how empowering the practice of fiction remains! Faced with the gradually filling emptiness of a novel in progress, the writer feels he is at the controls of a device whose potential is infinite, a tool that outrivals even a computer in its plasticity and nimbleness, in its inexhaustible capacity for the imitation of life in its real shadings and farraginous details, and for the generation of a narrative music and a weave of symbols and a poetry both of expression and of circumstance. Writing fiction, as those of us who do it know, is, beneath the anxious travail of it, a bliss, a healing, an elicitation of order from disorder, a praise of what is, a salvaging of otherwise overlookable truths from the ruthless sweep of generalization, a beating of daily dross into something shimmering and absolute.

For somewhat these reasons, I imagine, are medals and prizes for the novel awarded—not so much to the lucky individual prizewinner as to this permissive, hybrid, democratic, curious art form itself, in thanks for the validation it bestows upon our common humanity and for the persistence of its faith (once the prerogative of philosophy and religion) that what Howells called "the meaning of things" can be laid bare.

EUDORA WELTY

An Interview[7]

INTERVIEWER: Your interest is in psychology also, so that a story such as "Why I Live at the P.O." is a comedy of hysteria. The humor comes out of a pathological behavior.

WELTY: No, I tell you I don't think of them at all as being pathological stories. I know Katherine Anne Porter refers to the girl as a case of dementia praecox in the introduction [of *A Curtain of Green*]. She believed I thought so, but it's far from what I was doing in that story. I was trying to show how, in these tiny little places such as where they come from, the only entertainment people have is dramatizing the family situation, which they do fully knowing what they are doing. They're having a good time. They're not caught up, it's not pathological. There is certainly the undertone, you're right, which is one of wishing things would change. Even though Sister goes and lives in the post office, she'll probably be home by the weekend, and it could happen all over

---

7. From *Conversations with American Authors*, ed. Carl Ruas.

again. They just go through it. I've heard people talk, and they just dramatize everything—"I'll never speak to you again!" It's a Southern kind of exaggeration. There is something underlying it, needless to say. That's what gives it its reason for being.

INTERVIEWER: But the current beneath the humor is despair, isn't it?

WELTY: I know in those early stories I have a number of characters where something visibly is wrong, they're deaf and dumb. Although I didn't think about it, it was a beginning writer's effort to show how alone some of these people felt. I made it a visible reason which is, of course, inside everybody. I must have chosen that as a direct, perhaps oversimplified way. I was not aware at the time that that was what I was doing—for instance, the story about the feeble-minded girl, Lily Daw. Nearly every little town had somebody like that in that part of the world, and the whole town made it their business to take care of her. They wouldn't usually send her away to the Institute for the Feeble-Minded unless they really reached an emergency, which they felt this was. Everybody takes care of everybody to the point where it's not taking care at all. You could see the futility of what they were doing. It was something I observed, just as I observed how people talk in exaggeration. All these things are rooted in a reality which I can use for the story, but I didn't invent it.

INTERVIEWER: "The Wide Net" is a comedy of misunderstanding between newlyweds. The young wife threatens to kill herself, and the husband calls the community together to drag the river for her body. Your description of the forest in autumn is elegiac, knowing that all things must come to an end, and yet inevitably return.

WELTY: That's exactly how I felt when I was writing. They were going on an excursion. Old Doc says, "The excursion is the same when you go looking for your sorrow as when you go looking for your joy." Young love is a mysterious thing, and anything might have happened. Things could have been very terrible. William Wallace, who was so inarticulate, could fish and dive down to the bottom of this water. That's part of it, because they wanted the presence of mystery and the possibility to be there. That's about the season of the year, the fall and the changing times.

INTERVIEWER: Young lovers acting out the drama in the fall reminded me of Chekhov, and I wondered if he influenced your concept of the short story.

WELTY: He certainly was my ideal. I didn't consciously try to base things, although that is an acknowledged method of teaching yourself. I guess I never thought I could base anything on a master like that.

INTERVIEWER: Did your reading determine your direction?

WELTY: I'm sure it must have done it indirectly, but not directly. I feel that when I'm really working on something, I'm not aware of anything but the story. I'm not thinking of myself, or of another writer. I'm just trying to get the story the way I want it. Those things can certainly help and bear down on me, but it's done at other times. Then they are worked out in the story without my conscious knowledge.

INTERVIEWER: When you began writing, did you identify with the Southern tradition?

WELTY: I'm self-taught, so I really didn't. I just wrote stories. I was befriended by Robert Penn Warren and Cleanth Brooks, who published me in *The Southern Review;* I met Katherine Anne Porter fairly early; and they were already long-established writers, but we had no group. We're all such individuals, I hardly see how we could. I'm thinking of Walker Percy and Peter Taylor and many more. We all met in the course of things without seeking one another out, just meeting as life opened and enjoyed each other.

INTERVIEWER: Katherine Anne Porter was a lifelong friend, and I wondered if she was involved with the direction of your writing.

WELTY: I don't know that I would have known how to take any kind of direction. What she did for me that was so great was to believe in my work. This was like a bolt of lightning from the sky, that people whose work I loved thought well of mine. It made me feel that I was really in the world, that I had understanding and some readers. That's the greatest thing you can do for somebody.

INTERVIEWER: You have this independence in your work. Does it carry over also to publishers, because they are at such a geographical distance?

WELTY: I don't think about that end of it when I write. All I want to do is write that story, and I had such a long wait before stories appeared. I began writing six years before a story appeared in *The Atlantic Monthly,* which was my first national magazine, but from the beginning they were welcomed by university and college magazines. I was published, which gave me a sense of reaching somebody. I don't know what would have happened to me if I'd waited to be published to write the next story. One blessing about living at home—although I imagine I would do it anywhere—is that I write just the way I want to, and when I want to, until I get it nearly as I can to what I want. Then its fate is up to the other end. I've always been blessed with wonderful editors and agents. I didn't even realize how extremely lucky I was.

Writing Fiction

One of the very good ways to learn more about the art of fiction is to practice it—to take the plunge and write stories of your own. It is also a very natural outgrowth of the emotional and intellectual excitement that reading the top-flight work collected here has generated. Whether or not you have written any fiction before, like most people you have been *telling* stories for most of your life. The next step is to make the more complex effort of giving them a written form of the sort your reading has taught you to respect. Often teachers offer the option of writing a story as an alternative to preparing at least one of the papers required in a course where the main emphasis is on improving skills in reading critically. The relation between reading and writing is so important—and so intimate—that undertaking more than one form of written work can help you read with keener enthusiasm and a much better understanding of what can be communicated in fiction.

Courses specifically devoted to fiction writing are enhanced by the guidance offered in masterful variety by the authors whose finest efforts are assembled in this text. In years to come great work will be done by some of you in writing classes who are now beginning a serious apprenticeship, learning your craft by a devoted scrutiny of what has been accomplished by both remote and recent generations of fiction writers.

Thus whatever the nature of the class—and whatever your long- or short-range expectations may be when you set out to write your first, or fifth, or twentieth short story—it must be obvious as a general principle that good models of short fiction can discipline and accelerate your progress. To be sure, everything will depend eventually on the quality of your personal and unique imagination, your judgment, your dexterity with language that suits your subject, and the excellence of your observation of life. The happy truth is that drawing on models will not impede your personal talents—it will release them by sparing you the waste and frustration of striking blind.

Surely the writer you hope to become must be an observer and a listener, sharp-eyed and attentive to experience, and with the ability to retain or recall things seen and heard: the shape of a child's mouth when his birthday balloon pops in his hands; the words your sister used to describe a new boyfriend to your parents; the atmosphere in a forest clearing on a summer day. And if you are already very good at such observation, the chances are that your reading of stories has been an essential part of your preparation as an observer.

The genius of fiction is to train readers in what it is *important* to take note of among the incredible profusion of details and events crowding everyday existence—to train us to select what counts, what signifies, what fits with other details of observation to give a sum of meaning to patterns emerging from the apparent chaos of life. In a word, readers of fiction are continuously modeling their habits of observation on those of writers who, in their turn, no doubt, modeled theirs on a continuous narrative tradition still evolving.

But when we have conceded the inevitable role of models in the formation of skill and craft in writing fiction, we may still became bogged down in a widespread prejudice that causes us to resist the very idea of following models. To do so smacks of imitation, and the cardinal motive for creative writing is to be *original,* is it not? You want to write stories to free yourself from the formulas and limitations that inhibit your other kinds of writing.

You want to—and should—turn out something original when you are ready to do so. But you haven't a very good chance of doing so until you have learned more ways of observing and shaping your material as the masters of the art have done. When students in creative-writing classes don't or won't accept good models for their development, all too often they begin half-consciously to model their stories on each other's. The blind follow the blind, and standards are much lower than they should be for all the investment of labor and good intention.

Assuming you are willing to use what is freely offered by the excellent models of fiction in this text, we had better come down to specifics about the ways you can effectively go about it. Actually using these stories as models, in all the ways they can be used, requires more than devout appreciation. It requires putting words on paper, whether as exercises, as notes, or as part of a story of your own.

Imitation and Comparison

To begin with a bedrock, basic form of exercise, some writers have found it useful to copy passages word for word from an admired example. Such "slavish" copying may have the merit of training you in habits of syntax and verbal rhythm that worked well for writers from whom you intend to learn. Word for word copying might be good for a daily—or occasional—warm-up exercise to get the juices of your imagination flowing. As an icebreaker it can coordinate the sheer mechanics of writing with a flow of idea and emotion into words on paper.

Better than this, a bit of literal copying may be a specially rigorous way of *reading,* which forces you to pay some attention to each word without skimming. And if you have the devotion to make it so, it may be the occasion for pondering the function of each word and each syntactical element as these build into sentences and paragraphs.

Please don't just nod over this suggestion and pass on. Grab your laptop, or a pen and paper, and copy the first paragraph of Frank O'Connor's "Guests of the Nation." Had you noticed before how this first-person narration is identified as such by the three pronouns *me, we,* and *our?* How the time of day (dusk) is made more concrete by the lighting of the lamp? How the crucial word *chum* (a synonym for "friend") is emphasized by repetition and set in opposition to the word *divil* (a synonym for "enemy" or "hated adversary")? Yes, of course you can understand the meaning of the paragraph without dwelling on such trivial indicators of the situation and the conflict to come. But *by* dwelling on them—as you are privileged and perhaps enticed to do in the exercise of copying—you may learn something precious about getting a story started. Your task will be slavish only if you let it be so. And as much can be said for any other assignment, even if self-assigned.

Yet, your verbal imagination will no doubt be more constructively engaged if you base another sort of exercise on O'Connor's paragraph (or a passage from some other story you admire): following his sentence pattern closely, substitute language and subject matter of your own. Your subject might be the relation of two antagonistic groups in your school or community. As you know, the narrator need not be yourself, but can be an imagined character. Whichever way your imagination veers, the result might be something like this:

> At lunchtime the pockmarked Nicaraguan boy Manuel would jingle his change and ask, "Amigos, you up for it today?" and Scott would say, "Why not, amigo?" (since we pretended we also spoke Spanish) and the smaller Nicaraguan Greniero would brush off a table and roll out his own set of dice. As often as not Martin Stark would join us to watch and get angry at Greniero's style, which was pretty gaudy, and read him out the way he did us "Come on you clown, why are you wobbling the table?"

As you see, we have made a transition from outright copying to parody. And though this example of parody (or the one you will now write) may be only a warmup for truly original composition, pause to reflect that parody *can* be pushed to the level of the highest art, as readers of Joyce's *Ulysses* know so well.

Most of the time when we are developing our own material with the guidance of models, we aren't so committed to a single text or author as in the case of parodistic exercises. Although we continue to learn by a process of imitation and constant comparison, our comparisons usually range freely over three distinct items: (1) our own manuscript, in whatever state of development it may have reached; (2) the segment of reality we mean to represent; and (3) the storytelling tactics and styles of several writers who have dealt similarly with similar subjects.

Particularly in matters of diction and dialogue we continue this simultaneous three-layered scrutiny as a natural part of the writing process. We go on observing and listening to tangible things around us—in fact, observation is now intensified because we have given it focus by beginning to write about some segment of observable behavior, and we listen more intently to test whether people like our fictional characters really do speak as we are saying in our story that they do. We want to add more beads to the string, so we listen for characterizing utterances we have not been able to imagine or remember. And—while we are verifying our writing in progress by what might be called fieldwork—we are turning back to the text of this book to see how Mansfield or Woolf, Hemingway or Faulkner, Oates or Munro has handled confrontations like those we are writing about. We reassess Hemingway's exploitation of understatement, Faulkner's probing with highly charged rhetoric—and are encouraged to remember that either tactic is available to us if we can fit it to the material we are now developing. We turn to the pages of our predecessors for promptings, and when we are lucky we bring away something which sharpens what we have begun.

What we are searching for in such repeated comparative surveys is probably not something we can directly parody, but a principle or an approach suitable to many fine stories. Thus if we turn to Williams's "The Use of Force" while we are at work on a story in which the voice of the first-person narrator is a necessary component, it is not at all with the aim of imitating the particular voice Williams has created, but to see as sharply as we can how small modifications of flat and rather impersonal language can further individualize the character beginning to emerge on our own pages, and to see how this author has fused the idiosyncrasies of speech with the flavor of the situation being recounted. It is very important to remember that Williams's effects are not and could not be achieved merely by inventive manipulation on his part. Clearly he has listened—in actuality and over and over again in memory—to a voice that is finally remorseful. One of the most valuable things you can learn from choosing his story as a model is that you must go into the corners of your world and back in to the dark labyrinth of your own memory listening for the timbre of such a voice.

Dialogue passages in such stories as "Hills Like White Elephants," "Great Falls," and the climactic last scene from "The Dead" can teach you, first of all, what to listen for in actual conversation and, second, how to structure the patterns of ordinary speech into revealing and dramatic sequences. As you become a keener listener, you will note that dialogue is not usually a matter of question and answer or direct responses to purely rational propositions.

The man in Hemingway's story says: "'... But you've got to realize—.'" Without waiting for him to finish the sentence the young woman responds, "'I realize. Can't we maybe stop talking?'" Her impatient breaking in reveals better than any explanation that could be provided by the author how weary she is of the persistent argument. Yet, just a moment later her despair of reaching agreement is modulated when she catches at something he says and echoes it back: "'... if it means anything to you,'" he says, and she answers, "'Doesn't it mean anything to you? We could get along.'" Even in despair she is still fighting to make him really hear something besides his own voice, his own wish. If you read such a passage aloud—instead of copying it silently— you will see and *hear* how skillfully the author has implied the tones of voice of the two speakers. In some comparable scene in one of your own stories you can use the same effect.

In "The Dead," Gabriel Conroy asks his wife, "'And what did he die of so young, Gretta? Consumption, was it?' 'I think he died for me,' she answered." At first glance this may appear to be a direct response on the wife's part. But look again at the context of the question and answer. The powerful shock in her reply comes from the fact that the two are speaking in quite distinct levels of discourse—his mundane, hers mystic and profound. It is from this revelation of incompatible modes of adjusting to reality that the resolution of the story emerges.

These examples illustrate the principle that what we call dialogue is often, in truth, two or more monologues rather loosely fitted together by the circumstances of the scene.

Even when you are not intentionally searching for model fragments of written dialogue, you will come across one sort or another of striking examples that you will want to collect for later reference. It is a fairly simple matter to photocopy such passages and keep them handy in a notebook or file—a very good practice for the writer commencing a serious career.

Story-Generating Models

As Chaucer's Canterbury pilgrims go on their way, a story told by one of them prompts a story from another. So it goes with all of us. When we hear or read a story, we are reminded of something we have to tell. Like the spreading wake of a boat, waves of memory veer out, stirring flotsam that has lain dormant on the beach, activating inert material we have not yet quite imagined might be the stuff for a story of our own. It will be like—and yet fascinatingly different from—the example that stirred the waves of imagination.

Consider Sherwood Anderson's "I Want to Know Why," which deals with a boy's disillusionment following a moment of triumph. Surely very many of its readers will be reminded of similar shocks in their own lives. It would not be surprising if a lot of them toyed with the possibility of writing about how such a common disappointment seemed very particular and very personal to them—or that most of them felt balked by uncertainty about how to approach their material, which is plentiful enough but unmanageably formless in the rag bag of memory.

Well, a story not only stimulates a reader's memory, its form gives bold hints about the way you might shape what you are moved to write about. Anderson opens his story with the *arrival* of the narrator and some other boys, at Saratoga, where the climactic race will be run. Then, in an apparently rambling fashion, the boy's feelings about horses and racing are spilled out. In fact these clumsy declarations are put forth as a preparation before the horse Sunstreak is named—before they are all summed up and focused on the actual drama of the race and the disillusioning aftermath when Jerry Tillford brags in the company of prostitutes.

A decision to follow Anderson's example would, first of all, oblige you to concentrate on the end, the dramatic resolution of your fictional situation, and then to measure out the necessary preparation of material, feelings, and circumstances required to give full force to this resolution. In a word, the model shows you how to construct your story backward, starting to work from the end and adding the material required for the opening. What feelings and what qualities will your central character have? The more you review your material and cull the possibilities, something approaching certainty will be established, for memory works that way once we guide it by fictional craft. Of course in your reminiscence you will be directed by the need to choose a character who has the potential for jolting the protagonist as Jerry Tillford jolts the narrator. That is, you may have to invent, or change, the personages when those you remember do not quite fit the requirements of the story.

Almost as universal as Anderson's basic story of the loss of innocence is the situation in Walker's "Everyday Use." Much of the tension in the American experience generally is the conflict between those who have clung to the places where they have their roots and those who have "gone to the city"—migrated in search of a broader or more fulfilling life. Most students returning home during their college years find themselves caught in a cross fire between old values and new ones. Walker built her story around a number of physical details of setting—the grassless yard, the churn, and the quilts—which have different values and potentials for the stay-at-homes and for the daughter who has briefly returned.

In preparing to write a story about the return of an offspring to the original home you might well begin by (1) listing a number of such specific things in the setting you know or imagine, (2) by noting after each some of the potentially different values they might have for those with conflicting life-styles, and (3) imagining or simply remembering the characters who would be most likely to clash in their perception of the values in such possessions.

Making lists of this sort is not at all the cut-and-dried matter you might suppose before you try it. Selection of sights and sounds, names and voices, thunderstorms and carnivals, the furniture in church basements, things stored in attics or garages—picking over such things, mentally following streams of association, and then building complete sentences around the things named in your list is creative work of the richest kind. It is a preliminary shaping of the substance that will give life to your finished story. There is no rule for choosing which of the concrete details you assemble will function most effectively in the development of plot, characterization, or theme. But, rather than trying to select details to fit some predetermined idea or outline, you ought to be always eager to follow the significance suggested by the details themselves. Thus an imitation of Walker's approach can be transformed into something uniquely and unpredictably original.

Many of the same suggestions can be made if Joyce's "Araby" is chosen as a model. Again the basic experience is close to being universal—humiliation in an encounter between romantic expectation and banal actuality. (Who among us hasn't pushed some childish desire until it burst in a shattering embarrassment?) "Araby," like "I Want to Know Why" and "Everyday Use," is told in the first person. We may concede there were ample reasons why this mode was chosen by the three authors. Yet, just because you may be modeling your work on theirs, this does not mean your story will or should be told in the first person, however close to your actual experience it may be. The decision whether to use first- or third-person narration ought to be based on some trials and some sketch work in both methods. You might learn something useful by recasting the final scene of "Araby" as a third person account with a somewhat altered point of view (probably one more detached from the consciousness of the main character). You will find that much more is required than a simple change of pronouns from first to third person if either the emotion of the story or the significance of its resolution is to be retained.

Suppose you were to rewrite "Everyday Use" from the point of view of the daughter Dee, in either first or third person. What modifications would have to be made to reveal the same significance in the circumstances? Some useful answers to such a question will occur to you from purely passive analysis. Better answers—and ones much more useful to you as a committed student of the craft of fiction—can come only from your putting on paper at least a partial rewrite of your model. However much you respect that model in its published form, you must realize it came to that form through a series of authorial choices of the kind you are forced to make in your reconstruction.

Models for Revision

When the personal computer first appeared in the 1980s, some believed that it would take the curse off revision—the implication being that revision is always unpleasant, though necessary, and that use of a labor-saving device is the best way to have done with it.

Most writers believe, however, that revision is simply a continuation of the imaginative act of writing; for most, it has been the most pleasant part. It is in revision that the nice touches can be laid on, the tones and colors harmonized, and clarifications made to show the precise meaning of what was often cloudy or indistinct in some phases of the compositional process.

To go even further, let us admit that revision is not merely the final phase of the process. It has been going on since the concept first began to take shape. Very few of us write as much as a sentence on paper without some juggling and readjustment of an idea and the words that seem fit to express it. We change the nouns and verbs that first entered our minds; we add or drop some adjectives or move them around in the process of inscribing a sentence on a page. As the sentences follow each other, we keep shifting our thoughts by reviewing what has already been put down and what is now required to keep the story flowing and to prepare for what is still to come. At the end of a page or the end of a draft of the whole story, our minds are still teeming with reasons for the choice of wording we have made and the possibilities that have been rejected. Or, if this still-bubbling mental activity *isn't* continuing, then no word processor is going to be of any help.

The only absolute requirement for revision is that there must be something to revise. This means that in your initial surge you have got something on paper. Something that won't shift and fade and drift away as a purely mental construct often does. Something that can be examined and reconsidered on the morning after, marked for change, or cut apart and repasted. A writer is not a daydreamer, but is a worker with paper, and the joy of the craft can only be experienced by the trials and revisions made on paper. You have finished a story only when nothing remains to be done to improve it.

Just because you have written a story through from beginning to end, this does not mean you have finished it. If it is good in the form you have first given it—even if it is published or publishable—it may be bettered by revisions. When you have a "finished" draft of a story in hand, you have come to a point where it is natural to pause, take a long hard look, and weigh the possibilities still to be wrung from material you have successfully coaxed this far along. Such points offer a natural occasion for comparing what you have done with examples from the text that may prod your imagination with suggestions for improvement.

Suppose that, for reasons that then seemed sufficient, you began your story with a striking line of dialogue and moved directly into a scene beginning the central action. Now you will reflect that the risk of such a brisk leap into the action is that the characters are more shallowly drawn than they must be to bring out the significance of what they are doing or saying to each other. While it is certainly not necessary to explain characters before you let them move, background information, histories, and individual idiosyncrasies must be incorporated somewhere and somehow without impeding the movements of events.

When your work is fresh and hot—and unfinished—on the desk in front of you, the time is favorable for comparing your opening presentation with those of Lawrence in "The Horse Dealer's Daughter," and Hemingway's "Hills Like White Elephants." Lawrence begins with dialogue that is part of an ongoing present scene (though this is stretched to permit the author to weave in some of the background of the family now in a moment of crisis). Hemingway begins with a scene that is almost purely objective and pictorial. He strikingly avoids giving any information about the characters or where they have come from. Before the story is done we will know what is essential to be known about them, but this emerges entirely from their dialogue.

A careful study of just these two stories in comparison with your own material may suggest to you what you can cut and what you might need to build up in terms of background information for the reader. The value of analytic comparison can be enhanced by actually cutting and pasting your own work to make it conform to your models. (It should go without saying that you cannot move paragraphs and scenes around this way without some rewriting to make the pieces fit together in a coherent whole.)

Before undertaking a second draft of your story, it is worth reconsidering and making comparisons of all the elements of fiction you have learned by reading and discussion to identify. Consult examples of descriptive passages, narrative passages in which long stretches of time are compressed, and scenes. Note that the lush and detailed description that opens "Kew Gardens" functions in a certain way to serve the peculiar demands of that story, while the descriptions of Parisian street scenes accomplish something distinctly different in "Babylon Revisited." In "The Open Boat" an insistent series of sensory descriptions of the ocean and the shoreline runs as an accompaniment to the adventure of the shipwrecked men, vivifying their experience and contributing much to the reader's inferences about what it all means. "The horizon narrowed and widened, and dipped and rose, and at all times its edge was jagged with waves that seemed thrust up in points like rocks." "The color of the sea changed from slate to emerald green streaked with amber lights, and the foam was like tumbling snow." "On the distant dunes were set many little black cottages, and a tall white windmill reared above them. No man, nor dog, nor bicycle appeared on the beach." Surely such a series of pictorial renditions is worth imitating if your story requires its characters to be immersed in conflict with their environment—just as surely it would be inappropriate if the conflict were more confined to personal oppositions.

In "The Veldt" Bradbury plays a very nifty trick in his description of the images projected on the nursery walls. That is, instead of describing them as if they were, indeed, *pictures,* he slants the descriptions forcibly to make them seem as if he were talking about direct encounters with the dangerous African habitat itself—as in the twist of his fantasy, they turn out to be. Descriptions of the barbecue stand in "A Good Man Is Hard to Find" intensify the atmosphere of grotesque contemporary reality. The coming of dawn at the end of "Barn Burning" serves as an indirect revelation of the emotional state of the boy who has—for good reasons—betrayed his own father. You can and should continue your list of examples, make a collection for convenient reference, *and* remember that no one descriptive device is suitable for all kinds of story objectives.

How long a period of time is covered by the action of your story? If it is several years, months, days, or even hours, the chances are that you will need to account for the longer stretches with narrative passages in which the language is specifically adapted to show persisting as distinct from immediate action. Time is compressed by statements on the order of "during July he exercised daily in the college gym." There is a tendency for such passages to become thin, flat, and lacking in concrete detail. In the example just given, no picture is drawn of the person at his exercise, the weather or the mood of the summer, or the sounds, sights, and smells of a gym during this season. In a fully finished story this may not be the case.

Part of "Everyday Use" compresses time effectively—without losing richness of concrete detail—in the reminiscence of the narrator: "I used to think she hated Maggie, too. But that was before we raised the money, the church and me, to send her to Augusta to school. She used to read to us without pity. . . . She washed us in a river of make-believe, burned us with a lot of knowledge we didn't necessarily need to know. . . . Often I fought off the temptation to shake her. At sixteen she had a style of her own; and knew what style was."

As you accumulate examples from other stories that reach over too much time to be presented in continuous scenes, pay particular attention to the time modifiers that indicate the action is an extended one—"she would often," "by the time he graduated he had," etc. These mechanical connectives can, and should, be given the function of keeping your story vivid and convincing, just as the detail and dialogue of a scene will do.

Perhaps for the beginning writer scenes are the easiest part of writing fiction. At least, the most fun. In such writing you are more likely to have ready-made models from life as you observe it. A conversation begins, and the exchange back and forth between characters builds naturally, because the response of the second speaker is roughly governed by what the first one has said. You follow the example of movies, in which essentially everything is revealed by a succession of related scenes, requiring no authorial account of what has ripened or changed in the interim between them. But the more demanding an artisan you become—coming up hard against the difficulties of fitting one item with another to make a fictional pattern—the more you'll perceive the need for specific models.

A number of stories in this text consist of a single scene, and we turn naturally to something like Updike's "A&P" for a precise examination of the way in which the characters are brought into the reader's view, how their encounter is progressively complicated, and how the concluding action gives point and meaning to the dramatized spectacle. The mere presence of the three girls in the store and the narrator's appraisal of them would have made a fictional scene, in the bare technical meaning of the word, but it is the intervention of the store manager in the midst of the scene that makes it, all by itself, a story in which no follow-up material is needed to round it out.

Compare "A&P" with "Everyday Use"—another story that contains only a single scene. In the latter the design is significantly different. The author sets up her characters and their traits with an extended expository passage before the main action starts. What is then required of the scene is that it dramatize the traits already enumerated and show what they amount to when brought to the test. The correspondence between the mother's analysis and what Dee (Wangero) reveals by her spoken lines should be closely analyzed as a model for what can be intensified in a scene you have written that may have been perfect in its verisimilitude but lacking in point.

With material requiring a number of scenes for its full development not only does one need the aptitude for getting the most out of each scene but there must be a suitable design for the sequence in which the scenes will be laid out, and a series of connectives to move economically from one scene to another. There is also an ever-present question of proportion—which of the scenes can be treated summarily and briefly, which must be given some amplitude. Fitzgerald's example in "Babylon Revisited" can be useful for a start in learning such management. Mark the beginnings and ends of all the scenes in this story, and then ask of each one: What is accomplished to advance the story by this scene? How have we been brought into it from the preceding one?

The first, between Charlie and Alix in the bar, is what may be called an "establishing" scene. It presents the main character on his return to a once-familiar environment and ticks off some changes in him, in the places he is taking another look at, and in his judgment and perception.

The next full scene takes place in the home of Charlie's in-laws. But how has he come there from scene one? He has taxied across Paris (a bit of drab and routine transportation that *should* have been omitted—except that the author uses it to give another glimpse of the Parisian setting and to record Charlie's regret at having "spoiled" this good place for himself). The second scene serves to demonstrate the bond of affection between father and daughter—and to signal the potential for opposition, hostility, and dislike between Charlie and the woman who will be his chief antagonist in the principal conflict of the story.

The third scene gives us Charlie alone in the city that once proved an irresistible temptation for his dissipations. It is a test intended to demonstrate (to the reader as well as to the character himself) how far he has recovered from the previous crackup. It climaxes in his rejection of the woman who encourages him to plunge into vice once more. He has not failed the test. As the section ends, his hopes are bright for showing that he is now fit to reclaim his daughter.

What occurs in the first scene of section II is crucial preparation for the outcome of the story. Not only does Charlie have a pleasant, promising lunch with Honoria, he seems to have once again side-stepped formerly destructive temptations by his coolness to Duncan and Lorraine. But what Fitzgerald has, in fact, accomplished here is to plant a superficially successful evasion as the time bomb that will presently blast Charlie's prospects and hopes.

By mapping out for yourself the design of this story, you may discover the best design for your own story—the best progression of scenes; what to hold back and what to put forward. And of course this is true of the study of any story if you study it as a craftsman would; that is, if you look at it not so much in a scholarly way, but in the nuts-and-bolts way of one writer examining the gestures and the technique of another. No work of fiction is ever created in a vacuum.

A Local Habitation and A Name: Meditations on Writing

Selections from Richard Bausch's Facebook Posts, 2008–2014

> The poet's eye, in fine frenzy rolling,
> Doth glance from heaven to earth, from earth to heaven;
> And as imagination bodies forth
> The forms of things unknown, the poet's pen
> Turns them to shapes and gives to airy nothing
> A local habitation and a name . . .
> —WILLIAM SHAKESPEARE

One of the most endearing things about all the writers I know—and of course I know a lot of them—is that not one of them has any material ambitions. They want money, yes, because like all of us they need it, but when they get it they use it mostly to buy one thing: Time. That's all any of them want. To be able to purchase a little Time from the world's daily demands, and they want that time, all of them that I know, for one reason. To work. No material matter comes close to that for them. I think that's a wonderful thing. And when the various kinds of wrangling and petty quarrels and vanities arise that come from being human and trying to do something very hard in a world that is mostly indifferent—well, I try to remember that. It's something very beautiful about us that we all share: that sweet almost child-like quality of wanting from the world only a little time to keep doing this thing we love so much that even when it tortures us we long to be there in it and with it.

• • •

To write seriously and get it right is to remove the walls between people, to break down the notion of others as monoliths of cultural difference, and so it is terribly important to do it with everything you have, even knowing that the world may ignore it. The world ignores many very great writers every day. But even remembering all this, also remember that if a work of narrative art or of poetry, or non-fiction does not engage and entertain, then it is a failure, no matter how serious its intent. So spend the time to make the reading of the sentences and the lines pleasurable. That must be the first thing. Let the other stuff surprise you. If you are striving to be truthful, and faithful to the thing for itself, the chances are very good that it will shine as it should with those matters that can indeed bring about something like salvation itself for a time.

• • •

The word *talent* used to denote a monetary unit. The parable of the ten talents is that the father gave ten talents to each of his three sons. The first one squandered them: the second hoarded them; the third one *used* them. And of course he was the one who was blessed. Talent connotes responsibility. If you have any talent at all you are *supposed* to be using it. It is your moral obligation to use it with everything you've got—you have the words. There are so many people out there who do not have the words, and a big part of our work is simply, by our own struggles with this art form, to let them see they are not alone. It is what Conrad was talking about when he spoke of 'The solidarity of the human family.'

• • •

Remember that even when it seems most difficult and most unyielding, it is always 'going well' if you are doing it, struggling with it, even struggling to dream up the next line, because it is in that state of becoming, and so what if some of the stages of its becoming are painful or confusing. Seems to me something is lacking if that is NOT the case. If you are lucky enough to have a place and time to be pained and confused while you give it what it needs to bring it into being, then everything is as it should be. Nothing is wasted. Go on and do the work, which can also mean sitting and staring at it for a time.

• • •

You don't have to be so terribly smart, or fast. You only have to be willing. You get smart going through it and through it after being open to what it is tending toward. Don't worry about what you will finally say; it will tell you.

• • •

You have to change something—change it. You're not moving stones, not carving in granite. Change it. It's like you're at the edge of a beautiful stream and the fish are jumping into your hands and you can make any arrangement of them that pleases you. Change it and see where that takes you. The truth you are seeking to deliver is the truth of experience, felt life. Not philosophy.

• • •

We are all struggling with the obstacle of ourselves.

• • •

Don't let anyone tell you it's all one thing or all the other. It isn't entirely 'show don't tell.' As I've been saying for years, it's show AND tell, and you have to let it teach you when to do the one and when to do the other.

• • •

Say anything to begin. Anything at all. What you say then predicates something else. And that in turn predicates its own something else. It is always at least partly a matter of setting into motion. Putting the words down and seeing where they take you.

• • •

You touch one part of it, and the whole thing shivers, from one end to the other. It's such a delicate thing, revision, and revision is where the artistry is; and so you have to be ruthless, and put away anything—even parts you like the sound of, even the matters that speak from your secret self to who you hope you are—put away anything that does not contribute to the whole thing.

• • •

The doubt you feel *is* your talent: the whole feeling stems from having the ear in the first place to be able to tell when it isn't singing as you want it to; it comes from hearing how far it is from the way you hope to make it sound. You can hear the difference because you have the talent, the ear. And, because the piece takes its slow sweet hard time getting right, you feel that fact as evidence that you can't do it or won't be able to do it; you look at the work of others, who also did it seventy-five times to get it right, and you can't escape the sense that their smooth elegant lines are how it arrived the first time for them—whole cloth, as printed. So you turn that on yourself and start feeling it won't ever be good enough, and the doubt sweeps in. Just do the day's work. A little at a time. And then take yourself elsewhere in your life until the next day's work.

• • • •

Too many times you think of this work as something you have to haul up out of yourself—you're writing then more *about* your experience, than you are writing *with* it. Forget hauling anything up out of the self. Think of it as a path. You're just going to go for a morning stroll through experience as the outside weather of the world. You make the path by walking it, and you can walk anywhere, right? Let it lead you, put down what comes to you to say even if it sounds wrong to you, or off the subject; and when at last you reach somewhere, it will probably have elements of surprise in it. That's good. No surprises for the writer, Frost tells us, no surprises for the reader. Now you go back, knowing finally where it was always leading; and you strive to be terribly smart about the whole thing. Now, instead of using the dream side of your being, you're using the side that figures how to get a door open when your hands are full. So you use all of yourself, before it's over: the day-dreamer and the one with the ingenuity. It's so hard not because you're not up to it; it's so hard because it's so important to do it right, to get it down right. And it's hard for everybody.

• • •

I used to pace, near sick with fear, before I'd sit down to try it, try putting something down, anything. I don't know why I was afraid, since *nothing* in one day's work comes remotely near to defining *anything* about what you are doing. It isn't even an indication of anything. It is hard. It confuses. One feels uninspired and flat. One looks at a line and it starts to dissolve into all the other possibilities. And you get scared. What if it's like this tomorrow? And what if it's *always* like this. And? And? And? *This* is what frightens you? The territory? The very deepest nature of the thing itself? Of course it always is terribly hard because it is coming into being and that is always difficult. Welcome to the territory. The province of creation. The cave of making, as James Dickey used to call it. Who ever said it would be easy? It only looks as if it was easy after you've done it and re-done it and re-done it again and again, as many times as it takes. But it is, after all, *work*. And you are lucky to have it to do. You should try to cultivate a healthy sense of respect for it, of course, while also learning to see the plain silliness of being afraid of one little step on the way to wherever it will take you. The whole thing is a lovely adventure.

• • •

I've been thinking lately about the word *hackneyed* as it is sometimes applied to prose or poetry. I think it is destructively reductive and usually wrong, especially when it is used by a writer about his/her own work. Everything we ever write needs our attention and it needs work and it will usually need many revisions and efforts to sharpen it and make it clearer. To say anything is hackneyed is a little like using an ethnic slur about a person—it doesn't really say anything. It reduces everything to a stone cold abstraction; it strips away the dignity of something one is spending one's self to do well. So strike it from your vocabulary about this work. It has no place there. Just keep going and striving to be splendid and clear. And stop cutting your own legs out from under you with that kind of language.

• • •

I would write all morning and then put it in a side drawer of the desk. I didn't want to look at it because I believed that lurking in all that work was the one killing indication that I was not a writer, that it was all a pipe dream of a lazy kid who was afraid of nine to five. I was twenty-two, and twenty-three, and I still had that awful sense that I might discover some fatal sign that I was not a writer; I would find it in the pages. It was waiting for me there. The something *unfixably* wrong. So I'd sit and stare into the sound hole of the guitar and play songs, and sing and tell myself I had done something creative with the day, that it was all part of the same thing. And this didn't really change until I got to where there wasn't anything *else* to do but stay on it, and keep going with something, and I wrote three full manuscripts in a kind of hectic, obsessed, all-hours, frantic, drowning, shivering, controlled desperation. This whole blessed occupation, as William Maxwell called it once in a letter to me, is made out of our doubts, and the continuing sense of inadequacy to the task. The territory is what I call it for myself, which is neither original with me, nor particularly new; but it keeps me focused and accepting of the struggle. Welcome to the wilderness.

• • •

Say anything. What you say predicates the next thing. Say one sentence, no matter what it is, and the thing is set in motion. You say, "I was being chased by a gigantic angry giraffe." And then you have to say something after that. And what you say next is determined by what you just said. If you can get the heavy critic who stands at your shoulder saying no, no, no, who's going to want to read that, that's not good, that can't lead anywhere, that doesn't look as good as (insert whoever you're reading)—if you can make that petty stuffy overly conscious hidebound censor shut up, and just dream it on through and play it out as it seems to want to go, you'll get a lot more done. Stop thinking so much, and dream it up. There's plenty of time to think about it later and use your smarts on it. You'll use all your various selves on it—but at the beginning, you must try to be that infant with speech.

• • •

It is no accident that for *centuries* writers believed in a muse that spoke through them. Because the experience, when it is going well, is very much as if someone is murmuring in your ear, giving you the words, the musical notes in the prose, and the meaning, too. That, too. Visit it, each day, let it know you're there, and then as you come to the end of the day's visit, try to make it so you know what the next scene is going to be or begin with (best advice Hemingway ever gave) and then occupy yourself with *anything* else until time for the next visit.

• • •

The confusions often have less to do with the work, than with your own expectations toward it. Let go of thinking *about* it and its possible place in the world, including the world of your own work, and think inside it, imagining your way into the physical and mental *being* of your people—deed them the right to be other than mouthpieces for what you think you think. I believe that's how they become alive, when they leave you behind and stop waiting for you to decide what they should do, and start doing things that surprise—and may even horrify you, with all your dignity and compassion.

• • •

You never really learn to write, as it is usually conceived; there is no template you are trying to decipher. What you learn, eventually, is how to write this one thing you're working on. It's no accident that we feel as if we have to learn everything all over again each time we try to do it. Because that is indeed the situation. You have to learn how to write each one, and each one contains secrets and mysteries that you have to solve, and those secrets and mysteries change as the story changes, and so you have to learn it all over. The thing you *can* treat like a template is *habit*, the habits of work that you develop, that you can strive consciously to develop. The habit of being shrewd about it all: making up your mind that you will start trying to work without demanding too much in the way of specific conditions (silence, certain light, certain time of day, certain place); teaching yourself to write in changing conditions and with the noises and distractions of being alive on this very hectic and un-peaceful planet all around you. Just visiting it each day, letting it know you're there. So I am really seldom teaching writing: I'm teaching habits, and revision, and practice, and stubbornness, the life, and understanding that confusion is quite normal and even healthy because it leads you into what you don't know about what you thought you knew.

• • •

History, even in a historical novel, is always backdrop. Because the novel is always about the personal life, and the personal cost of things. We care more about Natasha and Sonja and Pierre and Prince Andrei, and old Bolkonsky and Maria, than we do about Russia's war with Napoleon. And the scene that shows this best is when Natasha is sitting in the window and she believes she'll never see Andrei again, and also believes she has failed him, and her best friend Sonja, with whom she was raised, comes to her and says, "Natasha, look. Moscow is burning." And Natasha, still a teenager, a young woman with a broken heart, turns and looks over her shoulder and says, "Oh, yes. Moscow." Your characters not only have a right to their personal problems, the novel you're writing requires that those problems take center stage.

• • •

When you come upon some difficulty or trouble regarding the motions or reactions of your characters—when something starts to look cheesy to you, or forced, or silly or managed—try to remember that the whole enterprise is a *cooperation* between you and the reader, and that therefore your deepest responsibility is to *keep* the reader's trust, the reader's belief in what you're telling him/her. So, just try to be straight about it all. Remember that you are the docent in your own museum—the gallery, as it were, where your story unfolds. That museum. Face into whatever the problems are *with* the reader. Let him/her know that you are aware of the depth of whatever problem arises from your imagining and from the history out of which you are imagining (and work to remember that if what you are describing is "roughly" contemporary, even if that is so about it—it is also true that if it is more than fifteen minutes past, you are in history)—give the reader the license to partake in the creation of your story by letting him/her in on the problems of its creation, without announcing them as such. At the very least, try to acknowledge, with every gesture, that the enterprise you are offering involves them as privileged partners in the journey, which is always a journey to Truth. All this adds up to an honesty that daily social life never requires of us. Fiction demands it from the first tentative lines to the last touches of revision.

• • •

If you don't know what's next with one scene, work on another part of it. Everything you do to any part of it affects the whole of it, and working on another part might supply you with unexpected answers to the part that is troubling you. The thing to remember is that while they may read sequentially, with events held in suspension over the story's aboutness like a cable car over a river, they are quite often not written in sequence; it's all expression. Let it come as it wants to, and trust it to let you find your winding way to its secrets.

• • •

It is all *seeming*. It is all a *magic show*. Sleight of hand. It is contrivance, too. You conceal the artificialness of it, but remember that the first three letters of the word artificial are *a-r-t*. When you look at statue by Bernini or Michelangelo, you can not make your mind believe fully that you are looking at stone and not flesh, the artifice is so successful. So, as a writer, your job is to learn how to make the words produce a made human thing that convinces the reader in the same way the sculpture convinces the onlooker: by involving the reader's senses, and maintaining the living dream on the inside of his head. About your vision, or your grand theme—forget all that. Write about what matters deeply to you, what moves you, what frightens you to death, even what makes you angry or sorry, but do it with the viscera, the nerve-endings, get into it beyond your opinions about it and beyond what you think you think—beyond what you thought you knew—about it, and be *clear*, make it count in the reader's nerve-endings. And everything else will take care of itself.

• • •

Participate with Richard Bausch in an ongoing conversation about writing. Visit www.facebook.com/RichardBauschWriter.

Reviews and Commentaries

Remember that in the essay called "Writing About Fiction" there was mention of criticism as an ongoing polite "conversation" about various aspects or examples of the form. Here are some examples of that great conversation, several from practicing short-story writers whose work is included in this anthology. These commentaries and reviews range from simple remarks about a story or a writer, to more detailed discussion concerning elements of criticism about a given story. Any of these pieces might serve as a departure point for both writing about fiction and simply discussing it.

ANDREA BARRETT

Willa Cather's "Paul's Case"

"His eyes were remarkable for a certain hysterical brilliancy"—there is Willa Cather's Paul, defiantly himself, easy enough not to like. Lonely, motherless, sporting his hopeless red carnation, he's cursed with a vivid imagination and a febrile sensibility, no apparent talent, and no one to show him the way. He's vain and shallow and oversensitive, sentimental and provincial despite his hatred for things provincial; he can't distinguish true art from false, and he confuses the aristocracy of money with that of the spirit.

Yet he speaks to me, as he does to many writers. Perhaps he is who we most dread being. He sees what we all see—that horrifying vision of the world as "Cordelia Street"—but he can do nothing with that knowledge. Through his eyes, that "highly respectable street, where all the houses were exactly alike, and where business men of moderate means begot and reared large families of children" becomes an increasingly potent symbol for the aspects of bourgeois life that an adolescent, or an artist, might despise. Those respectable beds and kitchen odors and smug, pot-bellied householders; the endless chatter of getting and spending and the swarms of children doomed to reproduce their parents' lives exactly—those are what Paul fights, and flees. When his attempt to build another life fails, what he feels is "the old depression exaggerated; all the world had become Cordelia Street."

Another character might have made something from that disgust and despair. Paul makes what he can, within his limitations, with the materials he has at hand. If he can't make art, and can only buy what he desires for a few days, with stolen money: still he can make of his life an artful (if wasteful and violent) shape. And so he does.

I love Cather's astonishing, painful, truthful rendition of Paul's flawed being; I love the story's economy, its swift deep descriptions, and its concentration on Paul's powerful longing for Paradise. If it's a flawed Paradise, misconceived from tawdry elements, misunderstood in its very nature—still it is Paradise to him. That drive toward transformation, that falling into fate, is what makes the story so moving: along with our simultaneous understanding that the narrowness of Paul's surroundings and upbringing has caused him to hurl himself away.

CHARLES BAXTER

William Maxwell's "The Thistles in Sweden"

This wonderful, luminous story practices a harmless deception. It pretends (at first) to be about a couple living in New York City in the early 1950s. Of course, the narrator and his wife inhabit the story; but they are merely two beings in a tale that gradually, by means of an inventory method—naming and describing one by one the objects in a life—envelops the two main characters and enfolds them in a cosmic order.

The domestic details at first seem rather ordinary: tables, chairs, married life, neighbors, a cat. Because these small subjects are greatly beloved, they acquire life, so much so that by the end of the story the bed and the mantelpiece are expressing their own opinions. An inventory in a story can convey bewilderment about what importance anything might have (you make a list when you don't know what else to do), but in William Maxwell's story, the narrator tells us about the particulars of his life almost in the way a survivor of a calamity would set out on a table his most cherished objects, not to display but to bless them by naming them.

The Germans have a phrase—*das Glück im Winkel*, "happiness in a corner"—to refer to the household objects we value and love, the things that make our lives liveable. In this story, we start with the perfection of a city apartment and gradually discover the shadows that cross that perfection: a woman's unhappiness, the couple's childlessness, breakage and loss, cancer, a malevolent intruder, and death. And yet as the shadows darken, the contrasting light becomes stronger. The narrator's love for his world is unshakable, his love so far-seeing, so complete, that his tale can begin with curtains and wallpaper and conclude with the hand of God. The narrative line is constructed to move from small to large, from the life of objects to the life of the spirit, and to conclude with that most mysterious of all conditions, blessedness.

ANN BEATTIE

Peter Taylor's "A Spinster's Tale"

Peter Taylor's narrators are wise people—or, at least, people in the process of becoming wise. Their explanations of their behavior are not always to be trusted—in fact, once you know you cannot entirely trust a narrator, you are on your way, yourself, to becoming wise. What might seem to be an expression that reflects the tenor of the time—by this, I mean what first strikes our ear as slightly arch, or even archaic—is often a disguise behind which the character hides: this world and these characters, in their time, are no different than we are: manners obfuscate unpleasant truths we intuit between the lines; extreme propriety can mask passive aggression.

Betsy, left motherless by her mother's untimely death, begins to intuit life's dangers and conveniently decides that they reside in and are represented by an alcoholic named Mr. Speed, who stumbles about not-so-comically outside the family house (she adds the "Mr." for propriety's sake; we see it as another attempt at distancing). When, in narration, she explains a remark she seemingly casually makes to her father, the reader will surely register some degree of surprise. She says: "My father talked about the possibilities of a general war and recalled opinions that people had had just before the Spanish-American. He talked about the hundreds of men in the Union Depot. Thinking of all those men there, that close together, was something like meeting Mr. Speed in the front hall. I asked my father not to talk about war, which seemed to him a natural enough request for a young lady to make."

Perhaps it did seem natural enough, but the reader understands that he knows that not commenting on certain things is not likely to make them any less real. He is an adult. Social form can be invoked by a young lady, and his daughter knows that—she tries, many times during the story, rather desperately to depend on that—yet what goes unsaid looms larger, and the division between propriety and passion will never be as easily circumvented as young Betsy hopes. Hers (and ours) is a world where fate deals cruel blows: the early death of a mother (like children, the adults are complicitous in not talking about her once she dies, as if silence could preserve the status quo); terrible wars that are past and that are still to come; people trying to subjugate their feelings through alcohol. In a particularly eloquent moment, Betsy observes: "Had I been a little younger I might have suspected conspiracy on the part of all men against me, but I was old enough to suspect no person's being even interested enough in me to plot against my understanding, unless it be some vague personification of life itself."

Wow. There it is: in understated eloquence, mentioned mid-story instead of at the end, where it would have stood as the epiphany in a lesser writer's story, mentioned almost as an afterthought, in a sentence that gains momentum as it shifts into the high gear of serious meaning, Betsy lets us know—and admits that she knows—what is at stake in the world as Peter Taylor understands it, powerfully, in this brilliant and troubling story.

FREDERICK BUSCH

Ernest Hemingway's "Hills Like White Elephants"

It's the story to which I send students who want to learn how to write dialogue, and it's the story to which I return when I want to read about selfishness, disputation, and the fragility of the imagination. In this story, the imagination—the ability to see in metaphors, as opposed to the strength that crushes them, that insists on seeing, say, a hill as a hill and as nothing else—is linked, in its pregnancy, to the body of a pregnant woman. Her lover or husband wants the fetus aborted, and she wants to keep him. He will win.

We have just seen the Spanish countryside: the hills "were white in the sun and the country was brown and dry." But she sees the landscape this way: "They look like white elephants." He replies, with the bullying facticity of a country-club Babbit, that he's never seen one, and they proceed to squabble. Eventually, she dismantles her vision in an effort to win his approval. "They don't really look like white elephants," she explains, "I just meant the coloring of their skin through the trees."

But the hills, and her analogy, bear the weight of their real subject—her will, and her body, which Hemingway sets in opposition to her lover's plans for her body in spite of her will. When he stands in the bar, he notices the waiting passengers: "They are all waiting reasonably for the train." She, then, is not waiting "reasonably"; she wants them to live with regard for one another and in such a way that "if I say things are like white elephants . . . you'll like it." He swears that he does, that he will; but you know that he won't, for his notion of behaving "reasonably" has to do with pleasure, with self-aggrandizement, but not with birth of any sort.

He becomes a force for death as she, now wooing him, buries her way of seeing as she will bury her child. He asks if she feels "better," as if the way one viewed the world were an illness, or a misbehavior, from which one recovers. And she cooperates, betraying herself, to reply in the terms he has dictated: "There's nothing wrong with me," she says. Imagination and the pulse of life are "wrong," or are an illness, a deviation from his definition of health. "I feel fine," she lies.

We can feel the energy of coercion and the weight of despair in the awful white spaces that separate the lines, the paragraphs, the words.

STANLEY CORNGOLD

Kafka's The Metamorphosis: *Metamorphosis of the Metaphor*[1]

> What is literature? Where does it come from? What use is
> it? What questionable things! Add to this questionableness
> the further questionableness of what you say, and what you
> get is a monstrosity.
>
> FRANZ KAFKA, *Dearest Father*

To judge from its critical reception, Franz Kafka's *The Metamorphosis* (*Die Verwandlung*) is the most haunting and universal of all his stories, and yet Kafka never claimed for it any special distinction. He never, for example, accorded it the importance he reserved for "The Judgment," a work it resembles but which it surpasses in depth and scope.[2] On the morning of September 23, 1912, after the night he spent composing "The Judgment," Kafka, with a fine elation, wrote in his diary: "Only *in this way* can writing be done, only with such coherence, with such a complete opening out of the body and the soul." But throughout the period of the composition of *The Metamorphosis*—from November 17 to December 7, 1912—and until the beginning of the new year, his diary does not show an entry of any kind; and when it resumes on February 11, 1913, it is

---

1. Adapted from *Franz Kafka: The Necessity of Form* (Ithaca: Cornell, 1988) 47–80 (1970, rev. 1986).
2. Elias Canetti wrote: "In *The Metamorphosis* Kafka reached the height of his mastery: he wrote something which he could never surpass, because there is nothing which *The Metamorphosis* could be surpassed by—one of the few great, perfect poetic works of this century" (*Der andere Prozeß: Kafkas Briefe an Felice* [Munich: Hanser, 1969], pp. 22–23).

with an interpretation not of *The Metamorphosis* but of "The Judgment." The diary does finally acknowledge the new story, almost a year after its composition, with this remark: "I have been reading *The Metamorphosis* at home, and I find it bad."

Kafka was especially disappointed with the conclusion of the story. On January 19, 1914, he wrote, "Great antipathy to *The Metamorphosis*. Unreadable ending," and he blamed the botched conclusion on a business trip he was obliged to make just as he was well advanced into the piece. His annoyance and remorse at having to interrupt his work is vivid in the letters written at the time to his fiancée, Felice Bauer. These letters reveal Kafka's moods all during the composition of the story—moods almost entirely negative. The story originates "during my misery in bed and oppresses me with inmost intensity" [*innerlichst bedrängt*]." The tonality of the piece appears again as "despair" and "monotony." On November 23 the story is said to be "a little horrible [*fürchterlich*]"; a day later, "exceptionally repulsive." A trace of liking and concern for *The Metamorphosis* appears in a later letter: "It's a pity that in many passages of the story my states of exhaustion and other interruptions and extraneous worries are clearly inscribed [*eingezeichnet*]; it could certainly have been done more purely [*reiner*]; this can be seen precisely from the charming [*süße*] pages." But by this time Kafka has begun to consider *The Metamorphosis* more and more an interruption of the writing of the uncompleted novel that was to become *Amerika*. Finally, on the morning of December 7, he states the complaint that will recur: "My little story is finished, but today's ending does not make me happy at all; it really could have been better, no doubt about that."

Kafka's own sense of *The Metamorphosis* compels us to consider the work essentially unfinished. The interruptions that set in so frequently past the midpoint of the story tend to shift the weight of its significance back toward its beginning. This view draws support from other evidence establishing what might be termed the general and fundamental priority of the beginning in Kafka's works. One thinks of the innumerable openings to stories scattered throughout the diaries and notebooks, suddenly appearing and as swiftly vanishing, leaving undeveloped the endless dialectical structures they contain. On October 16, 1921, Kafka explicitly invoked "the misery of having perpetually to begin, the lack of the illusion that anything is more than, or even as much as, a beginning." For Dieter Hasselblatt, Kafka's prose "is in flight from the beginning, it does not strive toward the end: *initiofugal*, not final. And since it takes the impulse of its progression from what is set forth or what is just present at the outset, it cannot be completed. The end, the conclusion, is unimportant compared to the opening situation."[3]

One is directed, it would seem, by these empirical and theoretical considerations to formulate the overwhelming question of *The Metamorphosis* as the question of the meaning of its beginning. What fundamental intention inspires the opening sentence: "When Gregor Samsa woke up one morning from unsettling dreams, he found himself changed in his bed into a monstrous

---

3. Dieter Hasselblatt, *Zauber und Logik: Eine Kafka Studie* (Cologne: Verlag Wissenschaft und Politik), p. 61.

vermin [*ungeheueres Ungeziefer*]"? We shall do well to keep in mind, in the words of Edward Said, "the identity [of the beginning] as *radical* starting point; the intransitive and conceptual aspect, that which has no object but its own constant clarification."[4] Much of the action of *The Metamorphosis* consists of Kafka's attempt to come to terms with its beginning.

SUSAN DODD

Eudora Welty's "A Worn Path"

But who is she when she's at home? an Irish friend asks when I identify someone by name and occupation. Miss Eudora, no just-the-facts-ma'am kind of writer, has made it her serious lifelong business to let us in on just who her characters are when they're at home. Has she ever done so more clearly, more beautifully, more *deeply* than with Phoenix Jackson?

"A Worn Path" is, on the face of it, a simple, straightforward story. If it were a picture hanging in a museum, the canvas would be of modest dimension, would stand for no ornate gilt frame making a spectacle of it. No call for a viewer's eye to dart about, sorting out the picture's "busyness." No, "A Worn Path" would simply pull you inside it, keep you there, and when you came back out you'd sense you'd been long gone and far.

Miss Eudora doesn't *tell* us, of course, who Phoenix Jackson is when she's at home. Instead, she sends us packing on a rough and gloried hike in the company of a woman at home in her own skin. Alone though she is, Phoenix goes utterly *accompanied:* the sounds and smells and sights, the very air, are her sidekicks. This old woman and her surroundings fit together in a natural and familiar embrace. We take measure of Phoenix Jackson not by how the world receives her (though that comes eventually), but by the very span of her as she throws herself open to the world. Her gaze is dead ahead, her risky traverse of the creek a parade march. Every obstacle comes in for back talk. Not even hallucination can scramble her sense of direction.

To read "A Worn Path" is to have the seams of one's soul let out. The story's compassion enlarges our own; that is its greatness. Its *writing* is what brings that about, though, word by single word. Words are what paint Phoenix alive for the eye: the red head rag and striped dress and the cane fashioned from an umbrella. Dwell on the plain and perfect accuracy of the verbs (she *switches at* the brush to *rouse up* any hiding things . . . something in the hill *pleads* she should stay). Study the scrupulous choice of adjectives: the *grave* and *persistent* noise of her cane tapping the frozen earth . . . and oh, those *frailest* ringlets of her still-black hair. Listen to the perfect pitch of the dialogue, how the sounds of the words linger, ever deepening, after the simple saying: *Now comes the trial.* And: *The time come around.* And: *This is what come to me to do.*

And sometime, maybe some morning when you can't think how to begin, trace the canny route of similes running through "A Worn Path." No sore thumbs sticking out here, only the ordinary landscape of a woman's life. But tucked in among the domestic details (shadows hanging like curtains, babies and clocks and laying hens) and the expected particulars of the natural world (birds and milkweed and mistletoe) come glimpses of a life lived on intimate

---

4. Edward Said, "Beginnings," *Salmagundi*, Fall 1968, p. 49.

terms with the whip's lash, the chain's drag, imagination's (or is it memory's?) all-too-ready reference to black bodies dismembered and maimed.

Long before we learn of the singular sorrow that awaits her at home, by such suggestive images are we given to know who Phoenix Jackson is there, to know *precisely*.

RICHARD FORD

Bharati Mukherjee's "The Management of Grief"

Bharati Mukherjee's "The Management of Grief" is a story of great intelligence, poignant surprise, and elegant simplicity. A jetliner has exploded over the seas off Ireland. All passengers are seemingly lost, including families of those characters who, as grieving survivors, populate the story—most prominently Mrs. Bhave, its narrator, who has lost her husband and two young sons. Dramatizing how these characters and Mrs. Bhave herself feel, express, and indeed manage their awful grief becomes the story's subject and its strategy for revealing those nuances of grief that ordinary experience does not alert us to (that it can be thrilling as well as defeating, for instance). And this also becomes the story's means of assuring us that grief can be withstood.

As in any story—great or otherwise—what provokes and surprises us, and what provides the reader's experience of its primary intellectual *ground*, is the writer's decision about which segment or segments of life to tell us and which to leave untold. Obviously this decision determines what is emphasized, and thus what our notice and curiosity will be sharpened to. Often in great stories, such as Mukherjee's, what is emphasized by being told is different from what conventional understanding has prepared us to believe is important. We admire writers who show us the world in this fresh way—show us what we did not expect to be important. And as we're shown the world newly, our awareness and appreciation of it are redeemed.

Indeed, in Mukherjee's story, human survivorship, the facing of grief, and the obligation to narrate one's stricken life in order to save it are depicted almost entirely separate from the terrible physical devastation—the plane crash—which might seem the indispensable dramatic element if we were to learn of the events in a news story or on TV. But grief, in Mukherjee's story, is experienced in its own vivid, intense, but nearly sealed realm. True, it is a force born of disaster, but in Mukherjee's fine vision, grief is best understood and complexly felt—and most hopefully accommodated—almost entirely by itself.

ALLAN GURGANUS

Stephen Crane's "The Open Boat"

Few people are inconvenienced by shipwrecks. And fiction faces problems even tougher than your average sailing accident: how to elevate an ordinary landlocked day—its carpooling, its comparison shopping—into drama as life-and-death urgent as all those sharks aimed openmouthed toward your little lifeboat.

Great fiction requires more skill and spirit than simply "writing up" some endured disaster. If that alone made for major works of art, *Titanic* survivors and the bombardiers over Hiroshima would be modern letters' ruling geniuses. Happily for us surburbanites and mall-rats, they are not.

(In a double-parked station wagon, one mom slumps, waiting till her daughter, fourteen, completes the hundredth lesson on a clarinet this same girl will, by age eighteen, have cleanly forgotten: now that takes heroism.)

Stephen Crane, a Methodist preacher's hell-raising youngest son, would die of tuberculosis before age twenty-nine. Weaned on the Bible he resisted, Crane still dragged that book's undertow—its ethics and solemn sweetness—into baseball parks, pool halls, battle zones, Manhattan's darkest slums. The boy compacted into his fraction of a life many an ancient mariner's reckless quest.

The first day of 1897, a young newspaper reporter, seeking stories from the Spanish-American War, boarded *The Commodore,* a Cuba-bound ship. Loaded with rifles, rebels, and ammo, the vessel ran aground, then set to sea anyway. Mistake. A fast leak soon flooded the engine room. On deck, hysteria. One sailor fell to his knees before the captain, begging to be thrown overboard. Of our handsome correspondent, the captain would later say, "That man Crane is the spunkiest fellow out.... Many got sick but Crane was like an old sailor.... He was the first to volunteer to help. In the dinghy, he suggested putting up his overcoat for a sail.... He took his turn at the oars ... he's a thoroughbred."

We now know that our narrative guide behaved well; we know he survived events not unlike those he shaped (that first week ashore) into "The Open Boat." But, how did young Stephen Crane transform this anecdotal mishap into a shape so fully mythic? Genius always helps. Crane bypasses the usual glamorous spectacle of a sinking ship; he understands which guys to include, and where to start his tale (40 percent of the way in). He riddles the raw experience with all five senses' awe.

"None of them knew the color of the sky." So our story begins, sensually, in living color, but with the horizon's usual twenty-twenty orientation suspended, withheld. We already feel adrift, hungry for news, eager for some fable's shoreline of hard-earned wisdom. Crane presents his voyage in prose as brisk and water-clear as superb journalism. And yet, the language of this preacher's kid (all those Sundays, he was listening to Dad) grows rhythmically fulfilling and stained-glass pure as the King James Bible. Crane renders his waterlogged survivors as Everymen, while providing just enough identity to make each fellow count.

A favorite nineteenth-century theme pitted brutal Nature against innocent Mankind. Sir Edwin Landseer, the period's best-loved animal painter, depicted polar bears patrolling icy shipwrecks, seeking tasty human victims. What makes Crane's account so everlastingly contemporary? His natural world is not personified—not moralistically adjudged "red in tooth and claw" as Tennyson, Queen Victoria's favorite poet, quaintly described nature's simple ruthlessness. Instead, Crane's ocean seems amoral, as terrifyingly cool and neutral as cyberspace itself. His castaways might be unmoored shuttle astronauts—spun past voice range of any Mission Control—strangers adrift in some nebula unmapped. Their only true relation now is to themselves and to each other. The whole harsh universe seems abruptly masterminded as a great single theological test.

(Hemingway's telegraphic style and man-of-action stance is so prefigured in Crane, it looks cribbed. Hemingway's entire technique and subject matter might be summarized in one sentence written two years before his birth: "A night on the sea in an open boat is a long night.")

Crane's narrative, set down three years before 1900, prophesied and helped found the twentieth century's great theme: how the human psyche, having conquered so much of nature, finally settles into cannibalizing itself. How can sharks ever really scare a species that invented the Holocaust?

As if to predict twentieth-century powerlessness by eliminating the nineteenth century's pride in capacity, Stephen Crane deletes from the record his actual personal heroism.

When the real dinghy, sweeping ashore off Daytona, Florida, capsized, it crushed the first mate. Crane, trying to swim and save this man, sacrificed to the Atlantic his own heavy money belt; it had been laden with gold enough to see him through a long stay in Cuba. Despite his efforts, the other sailor drowned. Next day's newspaper, bearing all the vainglory of its age, read, "YOUNG NEW YORK WRITER ASTONISHED THE SEA DOGS BY HIS COURAGE IN THE FACE OF DEATH." This headline sounds as dated and comically old-fashioned as Crane's fiction still feels briney and immediate, as adaptable and oddly futuristic as the Bible itself.

What twenty-six-year-old man could bear—in his own tale of high-sea adventure—to hide his singular and noble acts? Answer: A great artist.

Crane neutralizes his own crazy physical courage to make room in his open boat for the rest of us sensible cowards. He admits mainly to his solidarity with others and his own quiet terror. Our narrator finally accepts the "serenity of nature amid the struggle of the individual. . . . She did not seem cruel to him then, nor beneficent, nor treacherous, nor wise. But she was indifferent, flatly indifferent."

How to lend heroism to an undifferentiated, carpooling weekday ashore? And how to render as natural, psychological, almost routine, some event harrowing and extreme as a shipwreck?

For all writers and readers, these constitute literature's twin capitals. What percentage of the mundane, how much of the heroic, can we honorably cargo from one into the other, and back and forth all day? Great works of art make peril at sea feel familiar as flossing; they can reveal one mom's carpooling to be headline worthy, brave, and pirate fierce.

Between these harbors, Port Heroic and Bay Mundane, we all commute. Scared to death ourselves, we still guard and reassure each another. Like Crane, we make a mainsail of our overcoat. And somehow—in our art and our acts—we briefly outwit the depths' indifference. Through almost any setback, we somehow tell, tell, tell ourselves to go ahead and row, row, row our little boat.

BARRY HANNAH

Joseph Conrad's Heart of Darkness

There were plenty of nineteenth-century authors to study but just a handful of real writers, among whom Joseph Conrad stood tallest, to my mind. High adventure, high art, high wisdom. In fact, he belongs to the Modernists of our times, with their tentative connection to this earth and its events. The narrator of Modernist fiction is characteristically sick, diminished, or shocked, barely able to express the special grief and ecstasies of our century, which Milan Kundera has aptly described as one of "massacres and optimism." He might have been speaking directly of "Heart of Darkness," which sounds often like an organ played by a malaria victim—fulsome, shrill, then muffled, then suddenly lucid. Marlow's conclusions on Kurtz seem fevered and strange, very. For he calls Kurtz's final insight "a victory." Would we speak of Hitler, Stalin, or Pol Pot as *victorious* had they uttered "the horror, the horror"—at last seeing it all clear—at the end of their lives? How happy for them as they move on in their growth.

T. S. Eliot, the High Modernist, might enlist "Mistah Kurtz—he dead" as a rubric for the Hollow Man, but the horror was that Kurtz was *not* hollow. He was cultured (he painted), efficient, a man of "ideas." Conrad tells us all Europe had gone into his making. And he becomes a genocidal, homicidal maniac, once threatening to kill even his young ragtag Russian sycophant but settling for merely driving him mad—"He showed me love!" (cf. the Hale-Bopp comet cult in San Diego at the end of the twentieth century).

The best of Modernism's tales seem fuller than rational linear discourse. Conrad's best forms proceed from the gut and head, as all good experimental writing does (see Samuel Beckett, who told Harold Pinter that the only form in his work was that of a *scream*). They are not brain work merely, as post-Modernists might have it. Conrad hardly ever told a tale that didn't seem urgent and necessary. In this he ranks with Twain and Dostoevsky, two other great natural writers of the nineteenth century. His themes were honor, sacrifice, grace, duty, shame, greed, and redemption. A Pole, he was a ship's captain who began writing at age thirty-two, in his third language, English. His parents perished in revolutionary action for Poland when he was a child, and he experienced dark depressions all his life. In his early twenties he had a brush with suicide. We might think of him finding family on the seas. The sea is solid and sweet: "The voice of the surf heard now and then was a positive pleasure, like the speech of a brother." But the riverside Congo is vicious and grim: "The air was warm, thick, heavy, sluggish. There was no joy in the brilliance of sunshine." He reports from a trip that almost killed him, a journey into the heart of the land the Belgians "settled" at a cost of three million native lives. He, like Marlow, changed from a young adventurer to the Ancient Mariner, unable to quit his tale, even though—ever the gentleman—Marlow lies about its end to the heartbroken fiancée of Kurtz. Women, Marlow says, "can't handle the truth." The deeper fact is Marlow is not certain yet what his tale means either. He himself is stricken with contagious moral sickness, and behaves like a fever patient wandering the halls of London. Elliptical, oblique, nearly opaque often, his measured raving reveals only glances of the truth, which is what the Modernist claims is all we ever get.

Rimbaud, the proto-Modernist, surrendered his talent to posterity and quit poetry at age twenty-one, then plunged into North Africa, a money belt constantly around his ribs, and sank into vilest commerce, dying early of fever. A bundle of poems of Rimbaud, "Heart of Darkness," *The Sound and the Fury, The Stranger*—one could claim a pocket education in Modernism with knowledge of these four works. It is significant, though probably not deeply important, that Africa figures as a source in all of the prose. (Dilsey in Faulkner's work, transported from Africa to no paradise in Oxford, Mississippi, is the Christian ballast for the degenerate white Compsons.) Marlow may have found Rimbaud in the person of the raving harlequin who is the acolyte of Kurtz. Conrad disliked Russians, but this young man has Marlow's sympathy. He worshiped England and English, lucky for us. But better for the world, his Africa, almost silent, always dark, was revealed as a holocaust brought in by Europe, the results of which continue in modern Rwanda at century's end. Conrad may not be the fullest humanitarian required by contemporary black intellectuals, but he was the best artist of his day to even glance at the Heart of Darkness that lurked in Western Colonial powers.

We recall the little French ship lobbing shells into the continent of Africa, as Marlow reports early on in the adventure. A silly and ridiculous and puny exercise for the viewer—say we on the television side of the "conflict"—but not to the target of the shells in, and for whom they are all the Armageddon ever predicted. As we get in close to the country, down the sick regions and past the bodies, Conrad gives us one of the most memorable hells of our era.

EDWARD P. JONES

Frank O'Connor's "Guests of the Nation"

I discovered "Guests of the Nation" some twenty-five years ago at a time when I was—in a creative and just about every other way—young and naive enough to hope that Frank O'Connor would manage some literary sleight of hand to prevent what even the first pages of the story conveyed to me was inevitable. I was never so naive, however, as not to understand that I had come upon a treasure, a small guide of five pages or so to the way I wanted eventually to begin crafting things.

Stories, that me-of-twenty-five-years-ago was beginning to learn, should strive to illuminate that moment or those moments, however grand, however seemingly insignificant, in a character's life when the earth shifts and the world is forever different: Humpty Dumpty falls off the wall reaching for a butterfly and the inconsolable king forsakes his queen and ultimately exhausts all his power in a hopeless effort to put his best friend back together again. . . . I had read very good stories before "Guests of the Nation," but nothing had for a while—and few stories since have—showed what I was coming to believe stories should be.

I go back to the story at least once each year to rediscover the wonders I was able to appreciate after that first, breathless reading: the way, for example, O'Connor seems to dash through the events in the first three sections, then slows down in the last section—which is about twice as long as each of the previous sections—to a nearly minute-by-minute telling of the last hours in the Englishmen's lives.

There is, as well, an appreciation of the things it was almost too easy to overlook with the thunder of the ending: the way O'Connor, in a few strokes, aims to humanize Jeremiah Donovan, who undeservedly lives in some readers' minds as the villain. "He reddened when you talked to him, . . . looking down at his big farmer's feet. Noble and me used to make fun of his broad accent, because we were from the town." The narrator is pulled down just a bit here. And Bonaparte, doing his "duty," falls even farther when he puts the second bullet in his friend's head.

But perhaps the most important reason I am compelled to reread "Guests of the Nation" is that sense of being a witness as the earth shifts for Bonaparte and he is being re-created, even as his friends, in Noble's words, are "stiffening" in that "little patch of bog." Even twenty-five years later, the story continues to unfold for me with a monstrous inevitability that begins with the coziness of the first paragraph when Belcher "shifts his long legs out of the ashes." Even twenty-five years and dozens of readings later, the story continues to amaze and move me, perhaps because, given the world I grew into, it is so inevitable.

C. C. LOOMIS JR.

Structure and Sympathy in Joyce's "The Dead"[5]

James Joyce's "The Dead" culminates in Gabriel Conroy's timeless moment of almost supreme vision. The fragments of his life's experience, of the epito-mizing experiences of one evening in particular, are fused together into a whole: "self-bounded and self-contained upon the immeasurable background of space and time."[6] Initiated by a moment of deep, if localized, sympathy, his vision and his sympathy expand together to include not only himself, Gretta, and his aunts, but all Ireland, and, with the words "all the living and the dead," all humanity.

Gabriel's epiphany manifests Joyce's fundamental belief that true, objec-tive perception will lead to true, objective sympathy; such perception and such sympathy, however, ultimately defy intellectual analysis. Joyce carefully avoids abstract definition of Gabriel's vision by embodying it within the story's central symbol: the snow, which becomes paradoxically warm in the moment of vision, through which Gabriel at long last feels the deeply unifying bond of common mortality.

Gabriel's experience is intellectual only at that level on which intellect and emotional intuition blend, and the full power of the story can be appre-hended by the reader only if he sympathetically shares the experience with Gabriel. As understanding of himself, then of his world, then of humanity floods Gabriel, so understanding of Gabriel, his world, and humanity in terms of the story floods the reader. The understanding in both cases is largely emotional and intuitive; intellectual analysis of the snow symbol, however successful, leaves a large surplus of emotion unexplained.

Therefore, Joyce had to generate increasing reader-sympathy as he approached the vision, but this sympathy could not be generated by complete reader-identification with Gabriel. If the reader identifies himself unreserv-edly with Gabriel in the first ninety per cent of the story, he will lose that criti-cal insight into him which is necessary for full apprehension of his vision. It

---

5. From *PMLA*, March 1960.   **6.** James Joyce, *A Portrait of the Artist as a Young Man* (New York: Modern Library, 1928), p. 249. See also Irene Hendry, "Joyce's Epiphanies" in *Critiques and Essays on Modern Fiction*, ed. John W. Aldridge (New York: Ronald Press, 1952), p. 129.

is, after all, Gabriel's vision, and there is no little irony in this fact. The vision is in sharp contrast with his previous view of the world: in fact, it literally opens a new world to him. If the reader identifies himself uncritically with Gabriel at any point in the story, he is liable to miss those very shortcomings which make the vision meaningful. Yet, in the actual moments of vision, the reader must share Gabriel's view; in a real sense, he must identify himself with Gabriel: "feel with" him.

Joyce, therefore, had to create sympathy without encouraging the reader to a blind, uncritical identification. One aspect of his solution to this problem is a monument to his genius. In the main body of the story, while he is constantly dropping meaningful, often semi-symbolic details which deepen the gulf between the reader and Gabriel, he is also generating what can best be called "aesthetic sympathy"; by the very structure of the story, he increasingly pulls the reader into the story.

"The Dead" can be divided, not arbitrarily, into five sections: the *musicale*, the dinner, the farewells and the drive to the hotel, the scene between Gabriel and Gretta in their room, and, finally, the vision itself. A few of these sections are separated by a time lapse, a few flow smoothly into one another; in all cases, however, the reader is aware of a slight "shifting of gears" between sections.

These sections become shorter as the story progresses. The effect of this constant shortening of scenes, together with a constant speeding up in the narrative line, is an almost constant increase of pace. Within each of the sections, Joyce carefully builds up to a climax, then slackens the pace slightly at the beginning of the next section as he begins to build up to a new climax. The pace in the sections is progressively more rapid, however, partially because of the cumulative effect of the narrative. As the story progresses, more things happen in less time.

The effect of increasing pace is complemented and strengthened by another structural aspect of the story. As the pace increases, the focus narrows. The constantly narrowing focus and the constantly increasing pace complement one another and act to pull the reader into the story. He is caught up in a whirlpool movement, ever-narrowing, ever-faster.

There is much activity in the first part of "The Dead," but the activity is diffuse and the effect is not of great pace. We are given a slightly confused, overall picture of activity: dancing, drinking, singing, chatter. Characters are introduced one after another: Lily, Gabriel, Gretta, the Misses Morkan, Mary Jane, Mr. Browne, Freddy Malins and his mother, Miss Ivors, and so on. Our scope is broad and general. Increasingly, Gabriel becomes our mode of consciousness, but he himself cannot assimilate all the activity. He retreats, isolates himself within his deep but insecure egotism. Rationalizing that "their grade of culture differed from his," he bides his time until dinner, when he knows he will be the center of all eyes.

In this first section, it is interesting to note how Joyce gives us Gabriel's point of view without compromising his own fundamental objectivity; even though we see largely through Gabriel's "delicate and restless" eyes, we nevertheless become increasingly aware of his character, of his defensive feelings of intellectual and social superiority in particular. His eyes are offended by the glittering, waxed floors, his ears by the "indelicate clattering" of the dancers, his intellect by all those present, particularly Miss Ivors, who "has a crow to pluck" with him, and constitutes a threat to his shaky feelings of superiority. His attitude can best be summed up by his reflection, ironic and revealing in view of the toast to come, that his aunts are "only two ignorant old women." Such comments are introduced quietly, but they serve to keep the reader from identifying himself too wholeheartedly with Gabriel. We feel with him to a degree even in these early sections of the story, but our sympathy is seriously reserved and qualified.[7]

In the second section, our focus narrows to the dinner table, and to a few characters at it; the others are blurred in the background. Tension about Gabriel's toast has been built up in the first section; now the pace increases as this particular tension is relieved. The toast, hypocritical and condescending, makes us further aware of Gabriel's isolation from those around him.

The pace in this scene is considerably more rapid than in the first. It builds up to the climax, the toast, in a few brief pages; then there is a slackening with the applause and singing.

There is a time-lapse between the conclusion of the toast and the next section; Joyce seems to shift to a higher range. From this point to the moment of vision, the pace increases and the focus narrows almost geometrically.

The shouts and laughter of the departure signal the end of the party, but are counter-balanced by the fine, almost silent tableau of Gabriel watching Gretta on the staircase. Our focus is beginning to narrow down to these two main characters. Gretta has been deliberately held in the background until this moment; now she emerges.

The repeated goodnights and the noisy trip through silent, snow-blanketed Dublin are given increased pace through Gabriel's increasing lust; the pace becomes the pace of "the blood bounding along his veins" and the "thoughts rioting through his brain." The fires of this lust begin to thaw the almost life-deep frost of his self-consciousness. The superiority and self-delusion are still dominant: there is much irony in his remembering "their moments of ecstasy," for his lust is far from ecstatic love. It is, however, the first step toward the moment of objective vision.

We are now approaching the still center of the increasingly rapid, increasingly narrow whirlpool. The scene in the hotel room between Gabriel and Gretta takes up only a few brief minutes, but in these minutes much happens. Gabriel "discovers" Gretta: suddenly she becomes more than a mere appendage to his ego. He discovers himself, in a mirror. His lust turns to anger, then his anger to humility. Gretta, caught up in her memories of the "boy in the gasworks," Michael Furey, is not even aware of his presence. "A shameful consciousness of his own person assailed him. He saw himself as a ludicrous figure, acting as a pennyboy for his aunts, a nervous well-meaning sentimentalist, orating to vulgarians and idealising his own clownish lusts, the pitiable fatuous fellow he had caught a glimpse of in the mirror."

The peak of intensity is reached with Gretta's "O, the day I heard that, that he was dead." She collapses on the bed, sobbing, and Gabriel, quietly, shyly, retires to the window. At this moment, Joyce creates another time-lapse to lead into the vision itself.

---

7. For an enlightening discussion of the problem of reader-identification and "extraordinary perspective" in 19th- and 20th-century literature, see R. W. Langbaum, *The Poetry of Experience* (New York: Random House, 1957).

Until this moment, the pace has increased and the focus has narrowed almost constantly. Now Joyce does something remarkable and effective: he reverses the process. In doing so, he makes the structure of the story not only useful as a means of generating an "aesthetic sympathy" (perhaps "empathy" with its impersonal connotations would be a more accurate word), but also makes it reinforce the ultimate emotional-intellectual meaning of the vision itself.[8]

Pace simply ceases to exist in the vision, and, of course, this is fitting. We are in an essentially timeless world at this point; true, the vision involves time and mortality, but it is timeless time and eternal mortality, man's endless fate as man. The snow "falling faintly through the universe" measures absolute, not relative time. The impact of this sudden cessation of pace on the reader is great; in fact, it parallels the impact on Gabriel himself. With this sudden structural change, we share Gabriel's vision; we do not merely analyze it.

Gabriel's vision begins with Gretta; it is narrow in focus. The whole story has led us down to this narrow focus. Now, as he does with pace, Joyce reverses the process. As the vision progresses toward the ultimate image of the snow falling through the universe, the focus broadens, from Gretta, to his aunts, to himself, to Ireland, to "the universe." Time and space are telescoped in the final words of the story: The snow falls on "all the living and the dead."

"The Dead" follows a logical pattern; we move from the general to the particular, then to a final universal. We see Gabriel's world generally; then we focus down to the particular, and from the combination of the general and particular we are given a universal symbol in the vision itself.

The logic of "The Dead," however, is not the logic of mere intellect; it is the logic which exists on a plane where intellectual perception and emotional intuition, form and content, blend.

LEO MARX

Melville's Parable of the Walls[9]

> *Dead,*
> 25. Of a wall . . . : Unbroken, unrelieved by breaks or
> interruptions; absolutely uniform and continuous.
> —*New English Dictionary*

In the spring of 1851, while still at work on *Moby Dick*, Herman Melville wrote his celebrated "dollars damn me" letter to Hawthorne:

> In a week or so, I go to New York, to bury myself in a third-story room, and work and slave on my "Whale" while it is driving through the press. *That* is the

---

8. William T. Noon, S.J., in *Joyce and Aquinas* (New Haven: Yale University Press, 1957), pp. 84–85, places Gabriel's epiphany at "the moment when the full impact of Gretta's disclosure of her secret strikes him": before the snow image of the closing paragraphs. Father Noon separates Gabriel's moment of vision from the reader's, and seems to state that the snow image is for the reader's enlightenment, not Gabriel's. I agree with Father Noon that the reader cannot possibly apprehend the depth of Gabriel's sudden sympathy with Gretta until Joyce gives him the closing image, but I do not believe that Gabriel's own vision is complete until this final image; the epiphany begins with his sympathy for Gretta, but is not complete, because not universal, until he "heard the snow falling faintly through the universe." **9.** First published in the *Sewanee Review* 61.4 (Autumn 1953).

only way I can finish it now—I am so pulled hither and thither by circumstances. The calm, the coolness, the silent grass-growing mood in which a man
ought always to compose,—that, I fear, can seldom be mine. Dollars damn
me.... My dear Sir, a presentiment is on me,—I shall at last be worn out and
perish.... What I feel most moved to write, that is banned,—it will not pay. Yet,
altogether, write the *other* way I cannot.

He went on and wrote the "Whale" as he felt moved to write it; the public was
apathetic and most critics were cool. Nevertheless Melville stubbornly refused
to return to the *other* way, to his more successful earlier modes, the South Sea
romance and the travel narrative. In 1852 he published *Pierre*, a novel even
more certain not to be popular. And this time the critics were vehemently
hostile. Then, the following year, Melville turned to shorter fiction. "Bartleby,
the Scrivener," the first of his stories, dealt with a problem unmistakably like
the one Melville had described to Hawthorne.

There are excellent reasons for reading "Bartleby" as a parable having to do
with Melville's own fate as a writer. To begin with, the story *is* about a kind of
writer, a "copyist" in a Wall Street lawyer's office. Furthermore, the copyist is a
man who obstinately refuses to go on doing the sort of writing demanded of
him. Under the circumstances there can be little doubt about the connection
between Bartleby's dilemma and Melville's own. Although some critics have
noted the autobiographical relevance of this facet of the story, a close examination of the parable reveals a more detailed parallel with Melville's situation
than has been suggested.[1] In fact the theme itself can be described in a way
which at once establishes a more precise relation. "Bartleby" is not only about
a writer who refuses to conform to the demands of society, but it is, more rel-
evantly, about a writer who foresakes conventional modes because of an irresistible preoccupation with the most baffling philosophical questions. This
shift of Bartleby's attention is the symbolic equivalent of Melville's own shift
of interest between *Typee* and *Moby Dick*. And it is significant that Melville's
story, read in this light, does not by any means proclaim the desirability of the
change. It was written in a time of deep hopelessness, and as I shall attempt to
show, it reflects Melville's doubts about the value of his recent work.

Indeed, if I am correct about what this parable means, it has immense
importance, for it provides the most explicit and mercilessly self-critical
statement of his own dilemma that Melville has left us. Perhaps it is because
"Bartleby" reveals so much of his situation that Melville took such extraordinary pains to mask its meaning. This may explain why he chose to rely upon
symbols which derive from his earlier work, and to handle them with so light
a touch that only the reader who comes to the story after an immersion in the
other novels can be expected to see how much is being said here. Whatever
Melville's motive may have been, I believe it may legitimately be accounted a
grave defect of the parable that we must go back to *Typee* and *Moby Dick* and

---

1. The most interesting interpretations of the story are those of Richard Chase and Newton Arvin. Chase
stresses the social implications of the parable in his *Herman Melville, A Critical Study* (New York, 1949),
pp. 143–149. Arvin describes "Bartleby" as a "wonderfully intuitive study in what would now be called
schizophrenia..." in his *Herman Melville* (New York, 1950), pp. 240–242. Neither Chase nor Arvin makes
a detailed analysis of the symbolism of the walls. E. S. Oliver has written of the tale as embodying
Thoreau's political ideas in "A Second Look at 'Bartleby'," *College English* (May, 1945), 431–439.

Pierre for the clues to its meaning. It is as if Melville had decided that the only adequate test of a reader's qualifications for sharing so damaging a self-revelation was a thorough reading of his own work.

• • •

Among the countless imaginative statements of the artist's problems in modern literature, "Bartleby" is exceptional in its sympathy and hope for the average man, and in the severity of its treatment of the artist. This is particularly remarkable when we consider the seriousness of the rebuffs Melville had so recently been given by his contemporaries. But nothing, he is saying, may be allowed to relieve the writer of his obligations to mankind. If he forgets humanity, as Bartleby did, his art will die, and so will he. The lawyer, realizing this, at the last moment couples Bartleby's name with that of humanity itself. The fate of the artist is inseparable from that of all men. The eerie story of Bartleby is a compassionate rebuke to the self-absorption of the artist, and so a plea that he devote himself to keeping strong his bonds with the rest of mankind.

• • •

"Bartleby the Scrivener" is a counter-statement to the large and ever-growing canon of "ordealist" interpretations of the situation of the modern writer.

GARY SAUL MORSON

The Reader as Voyeur: Tolstoi and the Poetics of Didactic Fiction[2]

> Of course, I myself have made up just now all the things
> you say . . . can you really be so credulous as to think that I
> will print all this and give it to you to read, too? . . . I shall
> never have readers.
>
> *Notes from Underground*

Readers of Russian fiction accede with special haste to Stendhal's dictum that "politics in a work of literature is like a pistol shot in the middle of a concert, something loud and vulgar, and yet a thing to which it is not possible to refuse one's attention."[3] There are countless histories of Russian literature that divide its authors and critics into two irreconcilable camps, those who judge art "in its own terms" and those who insist on a moralistic or political framework external to art. The nihilist's assertion that boots are more important than Shakespeare, Maiakovskii's self-destructive pledge to step on the throat of his song, Turgenev's plea to Tolstoi to remain a belles-lettrist and leave religion to the church—these are the usual landmarks in the history of Russian literature. Attempts to save radical critics like Belinskii from opprobrium usually take the form of arguing that he was not so Stalinist as the Stalinists say; when we praise the late Tolstoi we marvel at the great art he was able to produce *in spite of* his moralistic strictures.

---

2. From *Canadian-American Slavic Studies*, 12. No. 4 (Winter 1978), 465–480.   **3.** I am not so much citing Stendhal as Irving Howe citing Stendhal, in *Politics and the Novel* (New York: Avon, 1970), p. 17. Howe asks shrewdly: "Once the pistol is fired, what happens to the music? Can the noise of the interruption ever become part of the performance? When is the interruption welcome and when is it resented?"

It is an account on which the new critics and the Soviets can agree, although their values are reversed. And yet it is possible that both sides misstate the question. It is simply inappropriate to ask whether great art *can be* didactic; the fact is, that it often is. I do not know many scholars, whether formalists or new critics, who would deny *The Possessed* and *The Death of Ivan Il'ich* the status of "great literature"; and to argue that they are such despite their didacticism is simply to force reality into a theoretical mold. I simply cannot imagine what would be left of *The Death of Ivan Il'ich* or *The Kreutzer Sonata* without their moralism: perhaps something like the *War and Peace* Percy Lubbock wished Tolstoi had written—without the lectures on history and the polemical story of Napoleon. The right question, however, should not be *whether* great art can be didactic, but *how* it can be didactic; what we need (and what formalism and new criticism have prevented us from finding) is a poetics of instruction. Only then can we begin to appreciate Russian literature on its own terms.

EDGAR ALLAN POE
Review of Hawthorne's Twice-Told Tales[4]

Were we called upon however to designate that class of composition which, next to a poem [of moderate length], should best fulfil the demands of high genius—should offer it the most advantageous field of exertion—we should unhesitatingly speak of the prose tale, as Mr. Hawthorne has here exemplified it. We allude to the short prose narrative, requiring from a half-hour to one or two hours in its perusal. The ordinary novel is objectionable, from its length, for reasons already stated in substance. As it cannot be read at one sitting, it deprives itself, of course, of the immense force derivable from *totality*. Worldly interests intervening during the pauses of perusal, modify, annul, or counteract, in a greater or less degree, the impressions of the book. But simple cessation in reading would, of itself, be sufficient to destroy the true unity. In the brief tale, however, the author is enabled to carry out the fulness of his intention, be it what it may. During the hour of perusal the soul of the reader is at the writer's control. There are no external or extrinsic influences—resulting from weariness or interruption.

A skilful literary artist has constructed a tale. If wise, he has not fashioned his thoughts to accommodate his incidents; but having conceived, with deliberate care, a certain unique or single *effect* to be wrought out, he then invents such incidents—he then combines such events as may best aid him in establishing this preconceived effect. If his very initial sentence tend not to be outbringing of this effect, then he has failed in his first step. In the whole composition there should be no word written, of which the tendency, direct or indirect, is not to the one pre-established design. And by such means, with such care and skill, a picture is at length painted which leaves the mind of him who contemplates it with a kindred art, a sense of the fullest satisfaction. The idea of the tale has been presented unblemished, because undisturbed; and this is an end unattainable by the novel. Undue brevity is

4. Originally appeared in *Graham's Magazine* (May 1842): 298–300.

just as exceptionable here as in the poem; but undue length is yet more to be avoided.

We have said that the tale has a point of superiority even over the poem. In fact, while the *rhythm* of this latter is an essential aid in the development of the poem's highest idea—the idea of the Beautiful—the artificialities of this rhythm are an inseparable bar to the development of all points of thought or expression which have their basis in *Truth*. But Truth is often, and in very great degree, the aim of the tale. Some of the finest tales are tales of ratiocination. Thus the field of this species of composition, if not in so elevated a region on the mountain of Mind, is a table-land of far vaster extent than the domain of the mere poem. Its products are never so rich, but infinitely more numerous, and more appreciable by the mass of mankind. The writer of the prose tale, in short, may bring to his theme a vast variety of modes or inflections of thought and expression—(the ratiocinative, for example, the sarcastic or the humorous) which are not only antagonistical to the nature of the poem, but absolutely forbidden by one of its most peculiar and indispensable adjuncts; we allude of course, to rhythm. It may be added, here, *par parenthèse,*[5] that the author who aims at the purely beautiful in a prose tale is laboring at great disadvantage. For Beauty can be better treated in the poem. Not so with terror, or passion, or horror, or a multitude of such other points. And here it will be seen how full of prejudice are the usual animadversions against those *tales of effect* many fine examples of which were found in the earlier numbers of Blackwood. The impressions produced were wrought in a legitimate sphere of action, and constituted a legitimate although sometimes an exaggerated interest. They were relished by every man of genius: although there were found many men of genius who condemned them without just ground. The true critic will but demand that the design intended be accomplished, to the fullest extent, by the means most advantageously applicable.

We have very few American tales of real merit—we may say, indeed, none with the exception of "The Tales of a Traveller" of Washington Irving, and these "Twice-Told Tales" of Mr. Hawthorne. Some of the pieces of Mr. John Neal abound in vigor and originality; but in general, his compositions of this class are excessively diffuse, extravagant, and indicative of an imperfect sentiment of Art. Articles at random are, now and then, met with in our periodicals which might be advantageously compared with the best effusions of the British Magazines; but, upon the whole, we are far behind our progenitors in this department of literature.

Of Mr. Hawthorne's Tales we would say, emphatically, that they belong to the highest region of Art—an Art subservient to genius of a very lofty order. We had supposed, with good reason for so supposing, that he had been thrust into his present position by one of the impudent *cliques* which beset our literature, and whose pretensions it is our full purpose to expose at the earliest opportunity; but we have been most agreeably mistaken. We know of few compositions which the critic can more honestly commend [than] these "Twice-Told Tales." As Americans, we feel proud of the book.

Mr. Hawthorne's distinctive trait is invention, creation, imagination, originality—a trait which, in the literature of fiction, is positively worth all the

5. Parenthetically (French).

rest. But the nature of originality, so far as regards its manifestation in letters, is but imperfectly understood. The inventive or original mind as frequently displays itself in novelty of *tone* as in novelty of matter. Mr. Hawthorne is original at *all* points.

In the way of objection we have scarcely a word to say of these tales. There is, perhaps, a somewhat too general or prevalent *tone*—a tone of melancholy and mysticism. The subjects are insufficiently varied. There is not so much of *versatility* evinced as we might well be warranted in expecting from the high powers of Mr. Hawthorne. But beyond these trivial exceptions we have really none to make. The style is purity itself. Force abounds. High imagination gleams from every page. Mr. Hawthorne is a man of the truest genius. We only regret that the limits of our Magazine will not permit us to pay him that full tribute of commendation, which, under other circumstances, we should be so eager to pay.

C. P. SARVAN

Racism and the Heart of Darkness[6]

As I have shown elsewhere,[7] Conrad's setting, themes, and his triumph in writing major literature in his third language, have won him a special admiration in the non-European world. "The African writer and Joseph Conrad share the same world and that is why Conrad's world is so familiar. Both have lived in a world dominated by capitalism, imperialism, colonialism."[8] But African readers are also checked by, and disconcerted at, works such as *The Nigger of the "Narcissus"* and *Heart of Darkness*. The case against the latter was most strongly made by Chinua Achebe in the course of a lecture titled "An Image of Africa," delivered at the University of Massachusetts on the 18th of February 1975.[9] He argued that Conrad sets up Africa "as a foil to Europe, a place of negations . . . in comparison with which Europe's own state of spiritual grace will be manifest." Africa is "the other world," "the antithesis of Europe and therefore of civilization, a place where man's vaunted intelligence and refinement are finally mocked by triumphant bestiality." Achebe commented on Conrad's comparison of the Congo and the Thames, and also alleged that the contrast made between the two women who loved Kurtz, one African, the other European, is highly prejudiced. Any sympathy expressed for the sufferings of the black African under colonialism, argued Achebe, is a sympathy born of a kind of liberalism which, whilst acknowledging distant kinship, repudiates equality. Conrad, continued Achebe, is a "racist"—and great art can only be "on the side of man's deliverance and not his enslave-

---

6. From *The International Fiction Review* 7 (1980): 6–10.   **7.** "Under African Eyes," *Conradiana*, 8 (1976), 233–239.   **8.** Ngũgĩ wa Thiong'o, "Writers in Politics," *Busara*, 8, No. 1 (1976), 5. Previously known as James Ngugi, he is the author of four novels (*Weep Not, Child*, 1964; *The River Between*, 1965; *A Grain of Wheat*, 1967; *Petals of Blood*, 1977), a play (*The Black Hermit*, 1968) and a collection of essays (*Homecoming*, 1972).   **9.** *The Chancellor's Lecture Series: 1974–75*, University of Massachusetts at Amherst, pp. 31–43. Chancellor Bromery in introducing Achebe said *inter alia*, "The Scottish Arts Council has this year awarded him their second annual Neil Gunn International Fellowship. The Modern Language Association of America has voted Professor Achebe an honourary fellowship in their Association. . . . His first novel, *Things Fall Apart*, brought him to world-wide attention and acclaim. . . . His works have now been translated into twenty languages and his literary reputation is secure" (p. 29). I am grateful to Professor Achebe for sending me a copy of his lecture.

ment; for the brotherhood and unity of all mankind and not for the doctrines of Hitler's master races or Conrad's 'rudimentary souls.'" Achebe concluded his attack on *Heart of Darkness* by describing it as "a book which parades in the most vulgar fashion prejudices and insults from which a section of mankind has suffered untold agonies and atrocities in the past and continues to do so in many ways and many places today. I am talking about a story in which the very humanity of black people is called in question. It seems to me totally inconceivable that great art or even good art could possibly reside in such unwholesome surroundings."

I shall in the following pages attempt to narrowly limit myself to an examination of the charge of racism brought against Conrad's *Heart of Darkness*. Let us begin with the fictional Marlow, whose story was once heard and is now related by a fictional narrator. "It might be contended . . . that the attitude to the African. . . . is not Conrad's but that of his fictional narrator, Marlow. . . . [But] Marlow seems to me to enjoy Conrad's complete confidence." Marlow's portrait is drawn with quiet irony and, at times, a mocking humor which denotes "distance" between creator and character. For example, he is described as resembling an idol and he sits like a European Buddha without the lotus. Marlow claims to be deeply, almost pathologically averse to telling lies but we find that he prevaricates at least twice within this tale. He condemns the Roman conquest and contrasts it with the "superior" European colonialism:

> What saves us is efficiency—the devotion to efficiency. But these chaps were not much account really. They were no colonists, their administration was merely a squeeze. . . . They were conquerors, and for that you only want brute force— nothing to boast of, when you have it, since your strength is just an accident arising from the weakness of others. They grabbed what they could. . . . It was just robbery with violence, aggravated murder on a great scale. . . . The conquest of the earth, which mostly means the taking it away from those who have a different complexion or slightly flatter noses than ourselves, is not a pretty thing when you look into it too much. What redeems it is the idea only. An idea at the back of it, not a sentimental pretence but an idea; and an unselfish belief in the idea. . . .

A long quotation but necessary in that it again separates author from character. Significantly, this "idea" is presented in ambiguous "pagan" terms as "something you can set up, and bow down before, and offer a sacrifice to." What is more, the rest of the story shows that the European colonial conquest, contrary to Marlow's claims, was much worse than that of the Romans. One remembers that harrowing description of men waiting to die: "Black shapes crouched, lay, sat between the trees, leaning against the trunks, clinging to the earth, half coming out . . . in all the attitudes of pain, abandonment, and despair. . . . They were not enemies, they were not criminals. . . ." Immediately after this description, Marlow meets the elegant, perfumed, "hairdresser's dummy" and confesses that he "respected his collars," the collars of a man who comes out "to get a breath of fresh air," indifferent to the despair and death by which he is surrounded. It may be argued that Marlow is here speaking with irony and the description "hairdresser's dummy" may appear to make Marlow's attitude to the dummy as clear and unequivocal. But Marlow continues with unmistakable admiration that "in the great demoralisation of the land he kept up his appearance. That's backbone." He kept up *appearances*, and that points to one of the important thematic significances of this work, namely, the discrepancy between appearance and reality; between assumption and fact; between illusion and truth. Thus it is not correct to say that Marlow has Conrad's complete confidence, and even more incorrect to say that Conrad believed Europe to be in a state of grace. The glorious sailors proudly cited by Marlow were pirates and plunderers. This ironic distance between Marlow and Conrad should not be overlooked, though the narrative method makes it all too easy. Nor can Conrad's very forceful criticisms of colonialism be lightly passed over as weak liberalism. What ships unload in Africa are soldiers and customhouse clerks: the one to conquer and the other to administer and efficiently exploit. The cannon pounds a continent and "the merry dance of death and trade goes on." This "rapacious and pitiless folly" attempts to pass itself off as philanthropy, and to hypocritically hide its true nature under words such as *enemies, criminals,* and *rebels.* The counterparts of enemies, criminals, and rebels are the emissaries of light, such as Kurtz!

As a critic has pointed out, "Africa *per se* is not the theme of *Heart of Darkness,* but is used as a locale symbol for the very core of an 'accursed inheritance'."[1] At the risk of oversimplification, the story may be seen as an allegory, the journey ending with the sombre realization of the darkness of man's heart. But it may prove emotionally difficult for some to follow the allegory when it is thought that Conrad, casting about for an external parallel, for a physical setting to match the inner darkness, chose Africa. An argument may be constructed as follows: to the Romans, the people of Britain were barbarians; now when the Europeans come to Africa, the Africans in comparison seem savage, but deep down in the European breast there still lurks the old savagery. "It is not the differentness that worries Conrad but the lurking hint of kinship, of common ancestry . . . if [the Thames] were to visit its primordial relative, the Congo, it would run the terrible risk of hearing grotesque, suggestive echoes of its own forgotten darkness, and falling victim to an avenging recrudescence of the mindless frenzy of the first beginnings." When the Romans looked down upon the people of Britain, and the Europeans upon "natives," it was because they felt they had achieved a much higher civilization than the people they were confronting and conquering. The contempt was not on grounds of race itself, and Conrad suggests that Europe's claim to be civilized and therefore superior, needs earnest reexamination. The reference in *Heart of Darkness* is not to a place (Africa), but to the condition of European man; not to a black people, but to colonialism. The crucial question is whether European "barbarism" is merely a thing of the historical past. Surely the contrast between savage African and "civilized" European, in the light of that greedy and inhuman colonialism, is shown to be "appearance" rather than reality. The emphasis, the present writer would suggest, is on continuity, on persistence through time and peoples, and therefore on the fundamental oneness of man and his nature. If a judgment has to be made, then uncomplicated "savagery" is better than the "subtle hor-

---

1. Robert Lee, *Conrad's Colonialism* (The Hague: Mouton, 1969), p. 49.

rors" manifested by almost all the Europeans Marlow met on that ironic voyage of discovery. When Marlow speaks of the African in European service as one of the "reclaimed," it is grim irony for he has been reclaimed to a worse state of barbarism. Left to itself, Africa has a "greatness" that went "home to one's very heart." As Marlow begins his story, the light changes as though "stricken to death by the touch of that gloom brooding over a crowd of men": yet the gloom is very much over the Thames as well. The Thames as "a waterway leading to the uttermost ends of the earth" is connected with and therefore a part of those uttermost ends. The river signifies what is abiding in nature, in man, and in the nature of man, even as "the sea is always the same" and foreign shores and foreign faces are veiled not by mystery but by ignorance.

The immaculately dressed, fastidious, and sensitive hairdresser's dummy, a representative of civilized Europe and a part of the colonial machinery, is totally insensitive to the suffering he helps to cause and by which he is surrounded. (His extreme cleanliness is perhaps to be seen as compulsive, an attempt to keep clean in the midst of that moral dirt.) Even in the case of Kurtz, one must remember that all Europe had "contributed" to his making. As for pagan rites and savage dances, the Europeans with "imbecile rapacity" were "praying" to ivory, that is, to materialism, and one red-haired man "positively danced," bloodthirsty at the thought that he and the others "must have made a glorious slaughter" of the Africans in the bush.[2] The alleged primitiveness of the boilerman only serves to show the similarity between his *appearance* and the *actions* of the "civilized."

Achebe also noted that Kurtz's African mistress is the "savage counterpart to the refined, European woman." But the European woman is pale and rather anemic whilst the former, to use Conrad's words, is gorgeous, proud, superb, magnificent, tragic, fierce, and filled with sorrow. She is an impressive figure and, importantly, her human feelings are not denied. The contrast, however, is not simply between these two, but between Kurtz's African mistress on the one hand, and Marlow's aunt and Kurtz's "Intended" on the other. The aunt glibly believes that he who goes to the Congo is "a lower sort of apostle": "She talked about 'weaning those ignorant millions from their horrid ways.'" The hairdresser's dummy, we recall, was first taken to be "a sort of vision." The same ignorance and the same illusions are found at the end, in Kurtz's Intended. After all, he was also one of those apostles. The darkness which is often mentioned refers not only to the darkness within man, to the mysterious and the unpredictable, but also to ignorance and illusions: it is significant that as Marlow talks with Kurtz's Intended, the "darkness deepened." The African woman faces the truth and endures the pain of her dereliction, whilst the illusions of the two European women are also the fond illusions of European society.

This is not to claim that Conrad was free of all prejudice, nor to deny that he has wholly resisted the temptation to use physical appearance and setting as indicators of nonphysical qualities.[3] Conrad reflects to some degree the

---

2. Compare Mark Twain, *More Tramps Abroad,* London, 1897, pp. 137–138: "There are many humorous things in the world; among them, the white man's notion that he is less savage than the other savages." **3.** Compare Shiva Naipaul, "Zambia's Compromise with the West," *Spectator,* 11 June 1977, p. 11: "Now and then, in a clearing in the bush, there is the fleeting apparition of a village of mud huts. Women, squatting in the shade, look up expressionlessly from their labours; squads of naked children, shouting, arms flailing, come rushing over the beaten brown earth to wave.... The wilderness closes in again.... Nothing indicates that you have made any progress."

attitudes of his age, and his description of the fireman as a dog in a parody of breeches, is cruel. On the one hand, in terms of technological progress, the gap between London and the Congo was immense; on the other, though it is extreme to say that Conrad called into question the very humanity of the African, one's perspective and evaluation of this work need alteration.

In a conversation with me,[4] Ngũgĩ wa Thiong'o accepted some of Achebe's criticisms but felt he had overlooked the positive aspect, namely, Conrad's attack on colonialism. The skulls stuck on poles outside Kurtz's house, wa Thiong'o said, was the most powerful indictment of colonialism. No African writer, he continued, had created so ironic, apt, and powerful an image: ironic when one considers that Kurtz and many others like him had come to "civilize" the non-European world; apt when one recalls what they really did. But wa Thiong'o also observed that though Conrad (having experienced the evils of Czarist imperialism) castigates Belgian atrocities, he is much milder in his criticisms of British imperialism. This ambivalence, concluded Professor wa Thiong'o, compromised Conrad's otherwise admirable stand. Leonard Kibera (Kenyan novelist, short story writer, critic, and teacher) wrote informally to me as follows: "I study *Heart of Darkness* as an examination of the West itself and not as a comment on Africa. Many Africans do get turned off Conrad because they feel he used the Third World so totally as a background against which he examined Western values and conduct that the people in Africa and Asia are no more than caricatures. I do not object to this and appreciate the fact that in Conrad there is not that Joyce Cary, Graham Greene pretension of understanding the Third World."[5] Nadine Gordimer writing on another famous European in Africa states that Livingstone, reassessed, emerges as a fallible human being.[6] Conrad too was not entirely immune to the infection of the beliefs and attitudes of his age, but he was ahead of most in trying to break free.

JOHN UPDIKE

From *Three* New Yorker *Stalwarts*[7] *[William Maxwell]*

I met William Maxwell in August of 1954, shortly before taking a boat to England, for my first venture out of the United States. I had graduated from college that summer, and had had a poem or two and a short story taken by *The New Yorker,* and hence was invited, before I embarked for the Old World, inside the offices of the magazine that had been the object of my fantasies and aspirations since I was thirteen. The décor was scrupulously unspectacular. The waiting room, if I recall, had nothing in it but some chairs and a big copper platter and in the center of it, like some exquisitely thin and flaky Arabian pastry, a copy of the latest *New Yorker.* Ross and the first generation of editors had tended to be newspaper men, and the premises were furnished in a matter-of-fact masculine style, with steel desks and square wastebaskets and yellowing stacks of old telephone directories. The *New Yorker* of the Fifties managed to combine great literary prestige with impressive advertising

---

4. University of Nairobi, 19 July 1977.   **5.** Letter dated 7 April 1977.   **6.** *Contrast* 30(1973): 82.   **7.** From *More Matter: Essays and Criticism* (New York: Knopf, 1999), pp. 779–787.

revenue, but the decades still ruling the corridors were the no-frills Thirties and Forties. Maxwell, who emerged to shake my hand and usher me through the linoleum-floored maze to his own sunny office, conveyed a murmurous, restrained nervous energy and an infallible grace; I was reminded of Fred Astaire. And my sense of his being incapable of putting a foot wrong remained with me for the coming decades of editorial association. More I think than anyone I have ever met, he could be said not to waste words: not that he was stingy of words, he could talk quite generously, but every word was pertinent and *chosen.* There was none of that backing and filling with which most of us, like a computer looping through an algorithm, approach saying what we mean. Bill, if the right words did not instantly come to him, had a delightful and commanding way of waiting for them to come, a poise I connected with his Midwestern birth and upbringing, a kind of waiting for the corn to ripen. The only thing I can remember from that first encounter, in which he was so deftly, patiently courteous and friendly and I was so bedazzled, was to say, apropos of an expressed fear of mine, that—and I more or less quote—"People imagine that losing your luggage is like death, but it isn't."

At first, my fiction editor was Katharine White, but within a very few years she retired to Maine with her husband and Bill became my editor until he retired in 1976. Those who are innocent of the literary process have a possibly melodramatic view of the editor-writer relationship. The writer, in the end, must live his life and extract from it what poetry and fiction he can; the editor can accept it for print or reject it, but the amount of consultation possible while the work is in progress is limited. This is especially true of *New Yorker* short stories, where so much lies in the writing. Once, at a lunch, I did tell Bill a story about my elementary-school days and he said, "That's a short story" and so I wrote it up, much as I had spoken it, and sent it in, and saw it make it into print, under the title "The Alligators." Of another early story, "Flight," Bill suggested that, while it was acceptable as it was, the beginning seemed too tightly pulled from the narrator; and so I supplied perhaps a thousand more words about the family and background of the adolescent hero, Allan Dow. Bill liked it all, and found it all relevant; he said it was like a beam of light. To show how variable reader reaction can be, however, I will report that rather recently some critic complained, of that same story, "Why is Allan Dow telling us all this?" Not that Bill or I were wrong in our amplification, but it shows that some tiny disproportion, some old seam where the original rhythm was patched, tends to remain after an extensive alteration.

An editor more often suggests trimming than adding, and there was one story, bearing the merry title "Who Made Yellow Roses Yellow?," in which I had ignored his delicate hints that the prose was excessive and strained. I was visiting my parents' home in Pennsylvania and had brought with me the final *New Yorker* proof—the so-called page proof, in which the columns of text were arranged with the cartoons in place. My mother read it and made some frowning remark that threw a sudden revelatory light upon Bill's reservations; in a kind of revisory panic, I phoned in a number of cuts which caused the *New Yorker* make-up department a lot of trouble but did, at the last minute, improve the story. No amount of trouble, Bill's editorial demeanor conveyed, was too much trouble for even a slight improvement. Once we were locked on the telephone, well into dinnertime, over a long story called "The Wait," going through small last-minute changes; he told me afterwards it was like a long climb in which he kept repeating to himself, "Truth and beauty." A short story that has enjoyed a vigorous anthology life which no one would have predicted for it, "A&P," originally ran on for some more pages; Bill suggested that the story ended earlier than I had realized, and I was happy to take his suggestion, which fit my own intimations. With another story, however, called "Eros Rampant," *The New Yorker* was willing to publish only the first half, and here I thought they were, for once, wrong, willing to settle for half of the truth, and I withdrew the story and sold it elsewhere. Yet another story, with the epic title "The Beloved," was actually accepted and set in proof when the magazine's head editor, William Shawn, expressed such qualms about the theatrical background I had concocted for my hero's amorous evolution that we agreed to kill the story, though I, along with the typesetter, had been already paid. I was troubled at this outcome, and offered to return the money, but Bill on his own initiative extracted from the story's thirty or so pages six or seven that he felt would make a *New Yorker* story, and they were duly published—the one instance where I felt his contribution was so major that he should have co-signed the piece.

Generally, however, the verdict was yes or no, and our editorial collaboration was a matter of making the O.K. a little bit better, of getting the prose to something like the absolute polish of poetry. He was endlessly, beautifully patient and responsive in this interpersonal exercise. Many the hour we spent over the phone, looking for the perfect, invisibly precise expression. He and I do not write alike—his prose tends to be plain, a speaking prose, startlingly relaxed and idiomatic at times, and mine at least in my youth aspired toward baroque, high-modernist effects, as were admired in college in the Fifties. Sometimes, as I labored over the phone to refine some locution or other into an impossible richness of connotation, he would cut the Gordian knot by suggesting a phrase so direct and simple it had never occurred to me. But I never felt he was trying to deprive me of my style; like any good editor, he was helping the writer to become his best self. What was above all important was our sharing a hope of perfection, and his communicating to me a sense of basically boundless gratitude when I had done good work— when I had delivered the goods. So that pleasing Bill became, while not the only hope I had when I sat down to write a short story, a concrete objective to spur me on. He gave the ideal reader a living face. He made writing well seem infinitely worthwhile, and yet tangible—all too palpably distinct from not writing well.

Understand that he did not have to shoulder, in his relations with me, the full onus of acceptance and rejection. The magazine worked, as best I understood it, this way: a story was read by a number of editors, whose remarks accumulated on a so-called "opinion sheet"; this sheet was passed on, with the manuscript, to Mr. Shawn, who read fiction over the weekend and decided whether or not to accept a story for the magazine. Monday, then, was the day when I, who had recklessly left a salaried post with the magazine and set myself up as a free-lance writer in New England, would hear if the verdict was yes or no. The very tone in which Bill pronounced the one word "John?" into the telephone would often tell the tale; the message was commonly expressed, "Shawn says yes" or "Shawn says no." Elaboration was needed only in a case where a salvage operation was proposed. This delivery, year after year, of momentous news to a young householder and father of four, multiplied by the dozens of writers under Bill Maxwell's care, adds up to a human task that must take its own toll. Without ever betraying the editorial decorum, he sometimes softened a negative verdict with hints of his own approbation, or of the magazine's incorrigible prejudices. But whatever the verdict, Bill continued to feel like my friend, and a friend to excellence in literature. We loved our work, and our work was words. His own prose, and his own manner, evince a light touch, a cheering reasonableness, and those many years when he was, in effect, the caretaker of my livelihood, figure in my memory now as cheerful; just as losing your luggage wasn't the end of existence, neither were the ups and downs of an ongoing literary career.

We had a curious additional bond; though he was twenty-five years my senior, we became fathers at about the same time, of girl babies. So we had parenthood to discuss. Our second children were born in rough parallel also, though his was another girl and mine a boy. When I expressed to him the fear that my girl might now develop penis envy, he said, very quickly, "Well, having a penis doesn't solve everything"—a piece of wisdom that I will carry to my grave. It is perhaps not an entirely good idea to have a friend for an editor; the relationship is to some inevitable extent adversarial, and once I found myself enough vexed by some recent rejections so that my first wife had to step in with the comment, "Don't personalize it. Maxwell is part of a machine for getting out a certain kind of magazine." It was a helpful remark. In reading the fascinating correspondence between Bill and the Irish writer Frank O'Connor that was published last year, I was struck by how often he speaks to O'Connor of something not being a *New Yorker* short story, or of making something into a *New Yorker* story. Catholic as the magazine's taste was— more adventurous and experimental than it got credit for—there was a border where publishability stopped, a boundary as distinct in Bill's mind as the boundaries of Illinois. He once confided to me, if I understood him right, that he had never had a wholehearted recommendation of his turned down by Shawn.

He came to the magazine in 1936. He was an assistant to Katharine White; she, who had done so much to refine and broaden the magazine's collective taste, would have been one to recognize Bill's superb qualities. In an interview he gave *The Paris Review* he recalls his apprentice days outside her office, of which let me quote one anecdote:

> On Mondays and Fridays I had nothing whatever to do but stare at a Thurber drawing above my desk—until Mrs. White suggested that I get the scrapbooks from the office library and read them. She also gave me a pile of rejected manuscripts and asked me to write letters to go with those that showed any promise. After she had gone over my letters she called me into her office and said, "Mr. Maxwell, have you ever taught school?" It was a fact that I had kept from her in our interview: instinct told me that it was not something you were supposed to have done. Anyway, from her I learned that it is not the work of an editor to teach writers how to write.

It was Wolcott Gibbs, he goes on to say, who asked him to try editing; Maxwell took to it, and tells us,

> In time I came to feel that real editing means changing as little as possible. Various editors and proofreaders would put their oar in, and sometimes I had to change hats and protect the writer from his own agreeableness, or fear, or whatever it was that made him say yes when he ought to have said no. What you hope is that if the writer reads the story ten years after it is published he will not be aware that anybody has ever touched it.

The adjective that I keep coming back to, in thinking of William Maxwell, is *rare*—it is rare to encounter such extreme sensitivity housed in so cogent, unassuming, and matter-of-fact a frame. He is alive, one feels, like certain insects and birds, to colors of the rainbow invisible to the merely human eye. *The New Yorker* was a rarer, more rarefied magazine for having him on the staff, though he made his role in it sound simple: once, when I asked him what it was like being in Ross's art meetings, he said, "It was the easiest thing in the world. You sat there looking at a lot of unfunny roughs, and when a funny one came up, everybody laughed." Valuable as he was to the magazine, he did not exalt *The New Yorker* into a mystical and untouchable entity; when Brendan Gill's *Here at The New Yorker* came out, ruffling the easily ruffled feathers of some veteran staffers, Bill told me cheerfully, "I guess it takes an Irishman to tell the truth."

By the time he was my editor, he had worked out a part-time arrangement— three days a week at the office—that enabled him to write at home on his own work for the other four. I marvelled that he was able then to bring to my work, among that of many others, such an intensity of care and even affection, while carrying in his mind the lineaments of his own luminous, wry, keenly felt short stories, and the novel *The Château,* and the book of personal history called *Ancestors.* All of his published novels but the first were written after 1936, when his association with *The New Yorker* began. I do not know all the other authors whose submissions he dealt with: John Cheever, certainly, and John O'Hara, when after an eleven years' sulk he began again to write short stories for the magazine. Vladimir Nabokov was in Bill's care for a number of English translations of his Russian short stories—an entire novel, *The Luzhin Defense,* was run in two installments. Eudora Welty and Frank O'Connor and Sylvia Townsend Warner were affectionate favorites, and I believe Mavis Gallant and the half-forgotten but ineffable Daniel Fuchs. L. E. Woiwode, now known as Larry, and Bill's own secretary, Elizabeth Cullinan, were among his younger writers. Bill enjoyed people with talent; people without talent, possibly, he enjoyed less. He could be witheringly dismissive of writers who didn't make his grade. And a striking feature of his fictional imagination is his loyalty, after over sixty years away, and an immense subsequent acquaintance, to the people who fondly loomed to him in the Lincoln of his boyhood.

I am in danger of straying from my topic, my experience of Maxwell as an editor. He made me feel cherished and yet held to a certain standard. He radiated the certainty that there *were* standards, that the good could be distinguished from the less good. His own quality, of being rare, rubbed off to a degree—an emboldening, exhilarating, powdery sparkle filled his vicinity, and a writer in his editorial charge was the lucky victim of a kind of ethereal contagion.

CHARLES C. WALCUTT

[Stephen Crane: Naturalist][8]

The works of Stephen Crane (1871–1900) are an early and unique flowering of pure naturalism. It is naturalism in a restricted and special sense, and it contains many non-naturalistic elements, but it is nevertheless entirely consistent and coherent. It marks the first entry, in America, of a deterministic philosophy not confused with ethical motivation into the structure of the novel. Ethical judgment there is, in plenty. To define Crane's naturalism is to understand one of the few perfect and successful embodiments of the theory in the American novel. It illustrates the old truth that literary trends often achieve their finest expressions very early in their histories. *Mutatis mutandis,*[9] Crane is the Christopher Marlowe of American naturalism—and we have had no Shakespeare.

Crane's naturalism is to be found, first, in his attitude toward received values, which he continually assails through his naturalistic method of showing that the traditional concepts of our social morality are shams and the motivations presumably controlled by them are pretenses; second, in his impressionism, which fractures experiences into disordered sensation in a way that shatters the old moral "order" along with the old orderly processes of reward and punishment; third, in his obvious interest in a scientific or deterministic accounting for events, although he does not pretend or attempt to be scientific in either the tone or the management of his fables. Crane's naturalism does not suffer from the problem of the divided stream because each of his works is so concretely developed that it does not have a meaning apart from what happens in it. The meaning is always the action; there is no wandering into theory that runs counter to what happens in the action; and nowhere does a character operate as a genuinely free ethical agent in defiance of the author's intentions. Crane's success is a triumph of style: manner and meaning are one.

• • •

Crane's naturalism is descriptive: he does not pretend to set forth a proof, like a chemical demonstration, that what happened must have happened, inevitably. This is what Zola was forever saying he did, and it is for these pretensions of scientific demonstration and proof that he has been chided by later critics. Crane simply shows how a sequence of events takes place quite independently of the wills and judgments of the people involved. The reader is convinced that it happened that way, and he sees that the ordinary moral sentiments do not adequately judge or account for these happenings. The writer does not have to argue that he has proved anything about causation or determinism: he has absolutely shown that men's wills do not control their destinies.

---

8. From *American Literary Naturalism, A Divided Stream* (Minneapolis: University of Minnesota Press, 1956), pp. vii–viii, 66–67, 74–82.   **9.** Duly noting the differences between them (Latin).

RICHARD WILBUR

The House of Poe[1]

A few weeks ago, in the *New York Times Book Review,* Mr. Saul Bellow expressed impatience with the current critical habit of finding symbols in everything. No self-respecting modern professor, Mr. Bellow observed, would dare to explain Achilles' dragging of Hector around the walls of Troy by the mere assertion that Achilles was in a bad temper. That would be too drearily obvious. No, the professor must say that the circular path of Achilles and Hector relates to the theme of circularity which pervades *The Iliad.*

In the following week's *Book Review,* a pedantic correspondent corrected Mr. Bellow, pointing out that Achilles did not, in Homer's *Iliad,* drag Hector's body around the walls of Troy; this perhaps invalidates the Homeric example, but Mr. Bellow's complaint remains, nevertheless, a very sensible one. We are all getting a bit tired, I think, of that laboriously clever criticism which discovers mandalas in Mark Twain, rebirth archetypes in Edwin Arlington Robinson, and fertility myths in everybody.

Still, we must not be carried away by our impatience, to the point of demanding that no more symbols be reported. The business of the critic, after all, is to divine the intention of the work, and to interpret the work in the light of that intention; and since some writers are intentionally symbolic, there is nothing for it but to talk about their symbols. If we speak of Melville, we must speak of symbols. If we speak of Hawthorne, we must speak of symbols. And as for Edgar Allan Poe, whose sesquicentennial year we are met to observe, I think we can make no sense about him until we consider his work—and in particular his prose fiction—as deliberate and often brilliant allegory.

Not everyone will agree with me that Poe's work has an accessible allegorical meaning. Some critics, in fact, have refused to see any substance, allegorical or otherwise, in Poe's fiction, and have regarded his tales as nothing more than complicated machines for saying "boo." Others have intuited undiscoverable meanings in Poe, generally of an unpleasant kind: I recall one Freudian critic declaring that if we find Poe unintelligible we should congratulate ourselves, since if we *could* understand him it would be proof of our abnormality.

It is not really surprising that some critics should think Poe meaningless, or that others should suppose his meaning intelligible only to monsters. Poe was not a wide-open and perspicuous writer; indeed, he was a secretive writer both by temperament and by conviction. He sprinkled his stories with sly references to himself and to his personal history. He gave his own birthday of January 19 to his character William Wilson; he bestowed his own height and color of eye on the captain of the phantom ship in "Ms. Found in a Bottle"; and the name of one of his heroes, Arthur Gordon Pym, is patently a version of his own. He was a maker and solver of puzzles, fascinated by codes, ciphers, anagrams, acrostics, hieroglyphics, and the Kabbala. He

1. Originally presented as a lecture at the Library of Congress under the auspices of the Gertrude Clarke Whittall Poetry and Literature Fund in 1959.

invented the detective story. He was fond of aliases; he delighted in accounts of swindles; he perpetrated the famous Balloon Hoax of 1844; and one of his most characteristic stories is entitled "Mystification." A man so devoted to concealment and deception and unraveling and detection might be expected to have in his work what Poe himself called "undercurrents of meaning."

And that is where Poe, as a critic, said that meaning belongs: not on the surface of the poem or tale, but below the surface as a dark undercurrent. If the meaning of a work is made overly clear—as Poe said in his "Philosophy of Composition"—if the meaning is brought to the surface and made the upper current of the poem or tale, then the work becomes bald and prosaic and ceases to be art. Poe conceived of art, you see, not as a means of giving imaginative order to earthly experience, but as a stimulus to unearthly visions. The work of literary art does not, in Poe's view, present the reader with a provisional arrangement of reality; instead, it seeks to disengage the reader's mind from reality and propel it toward the ideal. Now, since Poe thought the function of art was to set the mind soaring upward in what he called "a wild effort to reach the Beauty above," it was important to him that the poem or tale should not have such definiteness and completeness of meaning as might contain the reader's mind within the work. Therefore Poe's criticism places a positive value on the obscuration of meaning, on a dark suggestiveness, on a deliberate vagueness by means of which the reader's mind may be set adrift toward the beyond.

Poe's criticism, then, assures us that his work does have meaning. And Poe also assures us that this meaning is not on the surface but in the depths. If we accept Poe's invitation to play detective, and commence to read him with an eye for submerged meaning, it is not long before we sense that there *are* meanings to be found, and that in fact many of Poe's stories, though superficially dissimilar, tell the same tale. We begin to have this sense as we notice Poe's repeated use of certain narrative patterns; his repetition of certain words and phrases; his use, in story after story, of certain scenes and properties. We notice, for instance, the recurrence of the *spiral* or *vortex*. In "Ms. Found in a Bottle," the story ends with a plunge into a whirlpool; the "Descent into the Maelström" also concludes in a watery vortex; the house of Usher, just before it plunges into the tarn, is swaddled in a whirlwind; the hero of "Metzengerstein," Poe's first published story, perishes in "a whirlwind of chaotic fire"; and at the close of "King Pest," Hugh Tarpaulin is cast into a puncheon of ale and disappears "amid a whirlpool of foam." That Poe offers us so many spirals or vortices in his fiction, and that they should always appear at the same terminal point in their respective narratives, is a strong indication that the spiral had some symbolic value for Poe. And it did: What the spiral invariably represents in any tale of Poe's is the loss of consciousness, and the descent of the mind into sleep.

I hope you will grant, before I am through, that to find spirals in Poe is not so silly as finding circles in Homer. The professor who finds circles in Homer does so to the neglect of more important and more provable meanings. But the spiral or vortex is a part of that symbolic language in which Poe said his say, and unless we understand it we cannot understand Poe.

TOBIAS WOLFF

Isak Dinesen's "Sorrow-Acre"

"Sorrow-Acre" is one of those stories, like the parable of the Prodigal Son, that scalds us to attention by insulting our sense of justice. Why should the wastrel be feasted, while the good brother's faithfulness is taken for granted? How can the feudal lord, with all his wealth and power, justify refusing to pardon a poor old woman's son, and release her from the crushing task he has set her to win back the boy's life?

The biblical parable finally soothes us with the promise of mercy when we ourselves have need of it. "Sorrow-Acre" does not soothe; no, it takes its outrageous premise even further by suggesting that mercy itself can be a form of evil and that the ideas of justice that prompt our indignation are sentimental, unnatural, and fatal to human dignity. Those are the ideas expressed by the landowner; and the story itself, with its sensuous evocation of the natural order and the tragic condition of man within that order, seems to confirm his view. Not for nothing is the protagonist named Adam, and his uncle referred to as "the old lord"; but the temptation this Adam must resist is the modern idea that power should always be used to prevent human struggle and suffering. The old lord, who knows plenty about both power and suffering, proposes a different, perhaps longer view of the question: he suggests that effort and pain give meaning to life and that power has no business interfering, that to take desperation out of human existence is to render it a hollow farce.

These ideas are an affront to our customary assumptions; that doesn't mean they're not true. It doesn't mean they *are* true, either; but the force of their expression in this story makes us look again at the ground where we stand, which no longer seems quite so firm. That which before seemed natural appears, in this new light, peculiar, and that which seemed peculiar appears natural. We see the world in a new way. Only the greatest of stories can do this.

Author in Depth: Anton Chekhov

Critics and fellow writers often praise Chekhov for his "realness"—his ability to capture true-to-life details on the page, and his astute observations of human character—an ability Chekhov credited to his training as a doctor. Chekhov's editor and the famous nineteenth-century Russian author D. V. Grigorovich noticed this element in Chekhov's early work, and it is a sentiment that grew not just through the course of his life, but also in the appreciations of his work that have developed in the century since his death. The following documents offer a sense of his evolution as an author, from his shift to more serious fiction and drama, the beliefs and experiences that helped guide his thoughtful delineation of character and setting (consider his advice to his brother when reading "Anna on the Neck," or his voyage to the Siberian penal colony of Sakhalin when reading "Gusev"), as well as appreciations of his work by fellow authors influenced by the innovations he presented in his fiction.

RICHARD FORD

From *Why We Like Chekhov*[1]

As is true of many American readers who encountered Chekhov first in college, my experience with his stories was both abrupt and brief, and came too early. When I read him at age twenty, I had no idea of his prestige and importance or why I should be reading him—one of those gaps of ignorance for which a liberal education tries to be a bridge. But typical of my attentiveness then, I remember no one telling me anything more than that Chekhov was great, and that he was Russian.

And for all of their surface plainness, their apparent accessibility and clarity, Chekhov's stories—especially the greatest ones—still do not seem so easily penetrable by the unexceptional young. Rather, Chekhov seems to me a writer for adults, his work becoming useful and also beautiful by attracting attention to mature feelings, to complicated human responses and small issues of moral choice within large, overarching dilemmas, any part of which, were we to encounter them in our complex, headlong life with others, might evade even sophisticated notice. Chekhov's wish is to complicate and compromise our view of characters we might mistakenly suppose we could understand with only a glance. He almost always approaches us with a great deal of focussed seriousness which he means to make irreducible and accessible, and by this concentration to insist that we take life to heart. Such instruction, of course, is not always easy to comply with when one is young.

• • •

Exquisite beauty's perturbing consequence in everyday life: Loss. Pain. Regret. A rather unpromising view. But who hasn't glimpsed it among beauty's brighter allures, only to force it brusquely out of sight?

---

1. From *The Essential Tales of Chekhov*, ed. Richard Ford (1998).

Not that these stories overflow with pithy observation. Chekhov is *not* famously aphoristic, and seems mostly to prefer stressing the way life struggles unheroically toward normalcy rather than serving up moments in which it is exceptional or by canny observation caused to seem so. And as absolutely full of life's experience as the stories are, Chekhov also seems to proportion and blend the *amount* of complexity they contain, as though there were limits to the literary significance we can accommodate. His stories rarely resolve in highly dramatic, epiphanic endings. And by largely eschewing this strategy they seem to refer us back to their own often unsensational, interior details. There, we are to reconsider moments of overlooked decisiveness and issue and possibly see mankind more clearly. Consequently, we are not only moved that poor Nikolay the waiter goes home to die and *does* die rather undramatically (not at the end), but we are also affected as we re-view the story that Chekhov, master of fine human distinctions, has elected exactly these people, these unlikely peasants to elevate to the condition of human exemplars.

One can say with some assurance that in settling upon the short story as his chosen narrative form, Chekhov elected in essence not to represent *all* of life, not to make a big splash, but to fashion discrete parts of life and focus our attentions and sharpest sensibilities there as a form of indispensable moral instruction; to *not* attempt what Walter Benjamin says the novel *always* attempts: "to carry the incommensurable to extremes in the representation of human life." Chekhov made his stories precisely *commensurate* with life and with a view of it we can accept in an almost homely way. He almost never suggests that life isn't worth living, or makes us feel at a loss or even feel over-indebted to his genius. But rather he measures his genius alongside our own and according to what we can understand as an act of empathy whose message is that life is much as we know it to be in our efforts to accept and go on.

• • •

All this may just be a way of saying that the reason we like Chekhov so much, now at our century's end, is because his stories from the last century's end feel so modern to us, are so much of our own time and mind. His meticulous anatomies of complicated human impulse and response, his view of what's funny and poignant, his clear-eyed observance of life as lived—all somehow matches our experience. His stories could, we feel, be written today, appear in *The New Yorker*, and be read for their insight with avidity and delight—no alterations or footnotes to account for periodicity or foreign provenance. To us, such fresh aptness confirms not only the continuity and saving vitality of the literary impulse, but it also assures us that we ourselves are part of a continuum and are sustainable. How we feel today about a dying wife, our married lover, our unsuitable suitor, our loyalties to our forsaken family, about the overmastering way in which life is too dense with subjectivity and too poor in objectifiable truth—all this was exactly how Russians felt far away in time, and when just as now a story was judged to be a saving response. Chekhov makes us feel corroborated, indemnified inside our human frailty, even smally hopeful of our ability to cope, to order and find clarity.

With Chekhov, we share the frankness of life's inalienable thereness; we share the conviction of how much we would profit if more of human sensation could be elevated into clear, expressive language; we share a view that life (particularly life with others) is a surface beneath which we must strive to construct a convincing subtext in order that more can be clung to less desperately; and we share a hopeful intuition that more of ourselves—especially those parts we feel only *we* know about—can be made susceptible to clear, useful exposition.

ANTON CHEKHOV

Letter to Nikolai Chekhov[2]

Moscow, March, 1886

My Little Zabelin,[3]

. . .

As your brother and intimate, I assure you that I understand you and sympathize with you from the bottom of my heart. I know all your good qualities like the back of my hand. I value them highly and have only the greatest of respect for them. If you like, I can even prove how well I understand you by enumerating them. In my opinion you are kind to the point of fault, magnanimous, unselfish, you'd share your last penny, and you're sincere. Hate and envy are foreign to you, you are open-hearted, you are compassionate with man and beast, you are not greedy, you do not bear grudges, and you are trusting. You are gifted from above with something others lack: you have talent. This talent places you above millions of people, for there is only one artist for every two million people on earth. It places you in a very special position: you could be a toad or a tarantula and you would still be respected, because talent is its own excuse.

You have only one failing, the cause of the lie you've been living, your troubles, and your intestinal catarrh. It's your extreme ill breeding. Please forgive me, but *veritas magis amicitiae.*[4] The thing is, life lays down certain conditions. If you want to feel at home among intellectuals, to fit in and not find their presence burdensome, you have to have a certain amount of breeding. Your talent has brought you into their midst. You belong there, but . . . you seem to yearn to escape and feel compelled to waver between the cultured set and your next-door neighbors. It's the bourgeois side of you coming out, the side raised on birch thrashings beside the wine cellar and handouts, and it's hard to overcome, terribly hard.

To my mind, well-bred people ought to satisfy the following conditions:

1. They respect the individual and are therefore always indulgent, gentle, polite and compliant. They do not throw a tantrum over a hammer or a lost eraser. When they move in with somebody, they do not act as if they were doing him a favor, and when they move out, they do not say, "How can anyone live with you!" They excuse noise and cold and overdone meat and witticisms and the presence of others in their homes.

2. Their compassion extends beyond beggars and cats. They are hurt even by things the naked eye can't see. If for instance, Pyotr knows that his father and mother are turning gray and losing sleep over seeing their Pyotr so rarely (and seeing him drunk when he does turn up), then he rushes home to them and sends his vodka to the devil. They do not sleep nights the better to help the Polevayevs help pay their brothers' tuition, and keep their mother decently dressed.

2. From *Anton Chekhov's Life and Thought: Selected Letters and Commentary*, ed. Simon Karlinsky (1973).   **3.** *Zabelin* was the name of the Zvenigorod town drunk [Karlinsky's note].   **4.** The truth is more than a friend (Latin).

3. They respect the property of others and therefore pay their debts.

4. They are candid and fear lies like the plague. They do not lie even about the most trivial matters. A lie insults the listener and debases him in the liar's eyes. They don't put on airs, they behave in the street as they do at home, and they do not try to dazzle their inferiors. They know how to keep their mouths shut and they do not force uninvited confidences on people. Out of respect for the ears of others they are more often silent than not.

5. They do not belittle themselves merely to arouse sympathy. They do not play on people's heartstrings to get them to sigh and fuss over them. They do not say, "No one understands me!" or "I've squandered my talent on trifles! I am (...)" because this smacks of a cheap effect and is vulgar, false and out-of-date.

6. They are not preoccupied with vain things. They are not taken in by such false jewels as friendships with celebrities, handshakes with drunken Plevako,[5] ecstasy over the first person they happen to meet at the Salon de Variétés,[6] popularity among the tavern crowd. They laugh when they hear, "I represent the press," a phrase befitting only Rodzeviches and Levenbergs.[7] When they have done a penny's worth of work, they don't try to make a hundred rubles out of it, and they don't boast over being admitted to places closed to others. True talents always seek obscurity. They try to merge with the crowd and shun all ostentation. Krylov himself said that an empty barrel has more chance of being heard than a full one.

7. If they have talent, they respect it. They sacrifice comfort, women, wine and vanity to it. They are proud of their talent, and so they do not go out carousing with trade-school employees or Skvortsov's[8] guests, realizing that their calling lies in exerting an uplifting influence on them, not in living with them. What is more, they are fastidious.

8. They cultivate their aesthetic sensibilities. They cannot stand to fall asleep fully dressed, see a slit in the wall teeming with bedbugs, breathe rotten air, walk on a spittle-laden floor or eat off a kerosene stove. They try their best to tame and ennoble their sexual instinct...[...] to endure her logic and never stray from her. What's the point of it all? People with good breeding are not as coarse as that. What they look for in a woman is not a bed partner or horse sweat, [...] not the kind of intelligence that expresses itself in the ability to stage a fake pregnancy and tirelessly reel off lies. They—and especially the artists among them—require spontaneity, elegance, compassion, a woman who will be a mother, not a [...]. They don't guzzle vodka on any old occasion, nor do they go around sniffing cupboards, for they know they are not swine. They drink only when they are free, if the opportunity happens to present itself. For they require a *mens sana in corpore sano*.[9]

And so on. That's how well-bred people act. If you want to be well-bred and not fall below the level of the milieu you belong to, it is not enough to read *The Pickwick Papers* and memorize a soliloquy from *Faust*. It is not enough to hail a cab and drive off to Yakimanka Street if all you're going to do is bolt out again a week later.

---

5. Fyodor Plevako was a celebrated trial lawyer of the period [Karlinsky's note]. **6.** A Moscow nightclub, which also functioned as a pickup point for ladies of the night [Karlinsky's note]. **7.** Two minor Moscow journalists [Karlinsky's note]. **8.** The name of one of Nikolai's trade-school employee friends [Karlinsky's note]. **9.** A healthy mind in a healthy body (Latin).

You must work at it constantly, day and night. You most never stop reading, studying in depth, exercising your will. Every hour is precious.

Trips back and forth to Yakimanka Street won't help. You've got to drop your old way of life and make a clean break. Come home. Smash your vodka bottle, lie down on the couch and pick up a book. You might even give Turgenev a try. You've never read him.

You must swallow your . . . pride. You're no longer a child. You'll be thirty soon. It's high time!

I'm waiting. . . . We're all waiting. . . .

Yours,
A. Chekhov

ANTON CHEKHOV

Letter to D. V. Grigorovich,[1] *March 28, 1886*

. . . If I do have a gift that should be respected, I confess before your pure heart that up to now I haven't respected it. I felt that I had it, but got used to considering it insignificant. There are plenty of purely external reasons to make an individual unfair, extremely suspicious, and distrustful of himself, and I reflect now that there have been plenty of such reasons in my case. All my friends and relatives were always condescending toward my writing and constantly advised me in a friendly way not to give up real work for scribbling. I have hundreds of friends in Moscow, a score of whom write, and I cannot recall a single one who read my work or considered me an artist. There is a so-called "literary circle" in Moscow: talents and mediocrities of all shapes and sizes gather once a week in a restaurant and exercise their tongues. If I were to go there and read them a mere snippet of your letter, they would laugh in my face. During the five years I have been roaming around editorial offices I managed to succumb to the general view of my literary insignificance, quickly got used to looking at my work condescendingly, and—kept plugging away! That's the first reason. The second is that I am a doctor and am up to my ears in medical work, so that the proverb about chasing two hares has cost me more sleep than anyone else.

I write all this merely to justify myself to you in the smallest way for my deep sin. Up to now I have treated my literary work extremely lightly, carelessly, haphazardly. I do not remember working more than a day on *any single* story of mine, and I wrote *The Huntsman*, which you liked, when I went swimming! I wrote my stories as reporters write their news about fires: mechanically, half-consciously, without worrying about either the reader or themselves. I wrote and constantly tried not to waste images and scenes which I valued on these stories, and I tried to save them and carefully hide them, God only knows why.

Suvorin's[2] very friendly and, so far as I can see, sincere letter, was the first thing to impel me to look at my work critically. I began to get ready to write something significant, but I still have no faith in my own literary significance. Then suddenly, completely unexpectedly, your letter came. Forgive

1. From *Anton Chekhov's Short Stories: A Norton Critical Edition*, edited by Ralph E. Matlaw (1979); Grigorovich was an important writer in the 1840s and the later part of the century (1882–1899), who had written to Chekhov on March 25, 1886, praising his outstanding talent and urging him to write more seriously.   2. A. S. Suvorin (1833–1911), influential publisher of the conservative paper *New Times*, became Chekhov's closest friend.

the comparison, but it acted on me like an order "to leave town within twenty-four hours!" that is, I suddenly felt an absolute necessity to hurry, to get out of the place I was stuck in as quickly as possible. . . .

I will liberate myself from deadlines, but not at once. There is no possibility of getting out of the rut into which I have fallen. I don't mind starving as I have already done, but there are others involved too. I give my leisure to writing, two or three hours a day and a little bit of the night, that is, time that is suitable only for trifling work. This summer, when I will have more leisure and will have to earn less, I will undertake something serious. . . .

ANTON CHEKHOV

Letter to A. S. Suvorin, October 27, 1888

. . . I sometimes preach heresy, but I have never yet gone so far as to deny a place in art to topical questions altogether. In conversations with the writing fraternity I always insist that the artist's function is not to solve narrowly specialized questions. It is bad for the artist to undertake something he doesn't understand. We have specialists for specialized questions; it is their function to discuss the peasant commune, the fate of capitalism, the evil of drink, shoes, women's diseases. The artist, however, must treat only what he understands; his sphere is as limited as that of any other specialist's, I repeat that and always insist on it. Only somebody who has never written or had anything to do with images could say that there are no questions in his realm, that there is nothing but answers. The artist observes, chooses, guesses, compounds—these actions in themselves already presuppose a question at the origin; if the artist did not pose a question to himself at the beginning then there was nothing to guess or to choose. To be as brief as possible, I'll end with psychiatry: if you deny questions and intentions in creative work you must acknowledge that the artist creates unintentionally, without purpose, under the influence of a temporary aberration; therefore, if an author were to brag to me that he wrote a tale purely by inspiration, without previously having pondered his intentions, I would call him insane.

You are right in demanding that an artist approach his work consciously, but you are confusing two concepts: *the solution of a problem and the correct formulation of a problem.* Only the second is required of the artist. Not a single problem is resolved in *Anna Karenina* or *Onegin,* but they satisfy you completely only because all the problems in them are formulated correctly. The judge is required to formulate the questions correctly, but the decision is left to the jurors, each according to his own taste. . . .

You write that the main character of my *Name-Day Party* is a figure who should be developed. Good God, I am not a brute without feelings, I understand that. I understand that I cut up my characters and ruin them, that I ruin good material for nothing. Honestly speaking, I would gladly have spent half a year on the *Name-Day Party.* I like leisure and find no attraction in hasty publication. I would gladly, with pleasure, with feeling, and in detail have described *all* of my main character, his soul while his wife was in labor, his trial, his nasty feeling after the acquittal, I would have described how the midwife and the doctor drink tea at night, I would have described the rain.

That would only have given me pleasure, because I like to delve into things and putter around. But what can I do? I begin a story September 10th with the knowledge that I must finish it by October 5th at the latest. If I delay it I break my promise and I remain without money. I start the beginning calmly, I don't restrain myself, but toward the middle I become uneasy and begin to fear that my story will turn out too long: I have to remember that the *Northern Herald* has little money and that I am one of their expensive collaborators. Therefore my openings always promise a great deal, as if I had started a novel; the middle is crumpled up and timid; and the ending is like fireworks, as though in a short story. When you fashion a story you necessarily concern yourself with its limits: out of a slew of main and secondary characters you choose only one—the wife or the husband—place him against the background and describe him alone and therefore also emphasize him, while you scatter the others in the background like small change, and you get something like the night sky: a single large moon and a slew of very small stars. But the moon doesn't turn out right because you can see it only when the other stars are visible too, but the stars aren't set off. So I turn out a sort of patchwork quilt rather than literature. What can I do? I simply don't know. I will simply depend on all-healing time. . . .

RICHARD BAUSCH

Anton Chekhov's "Gusev"

The unusual thing about this story—even as a story of Chekhov's—is its point of view: the radical way it shifts in the last paragraphs, from the limited omniscience of Gusev's consciousness, to a kind of omniscience that includes even the sea and the sky. The way it leaves the province of human thought and action, as Gusev is dropped into the ocean, and enters the animal kingdom. The pilot fish are "in ecstacy," and the shark "languidly opens its jaws with two rows of teeth." The sailcloth that contains Gusev is torn open, the gridiron that was to carry him to the bottom of the sea falls out, and "frightens" the pilot fish. All of this after we have been privy to Gusev's dreams of home, his frustrations with his fellow passengers, his delirium.

Those dreams, his present life as a sick man returning with other sick men to the motherland, a passenger among other passengers, who argue and contend with each other and express strong opinions and speculations about the fate of all of them—this is all delivered with such acute specificity, such fidelity to objects and shapes, personalities and appearances, that we are drawn into it completely: real things in a real world, the palpable world, Gusev's personal life as he sees it in memory and fever:

> Gusev . . . pictures an immense pond covered with drifts. On one side of the pond is the brick-colored building of the pottery with a tall chimney and clouds of black smoke; on the other side is a village. His brother Alexey drives out of the fifth yard from the end in a sleigh; behind him sits his little son Vanka in big felt boots, and his little girl Akulka also wearing felt boots. Alexey has had a drop, Vanka is laughing, Akulka can't be seen, she is muffled up. . . . Gusev's thoughts abruptly break off and suddenly without rhyme or reason the pond is replaced by a huge bull's head without eyes, and the horse and sleigh

are no longer going straight ahead but are whirling round and round, wrapped
in black smoke.

We are deceived into thinking the story is about Gusev, because most of the
world's good stories—indeed, most of its great ones, too—when they make
such gestures, follow them out. Chekhov is using the particulars of this character to lead us into a perception we do not want: the enormity of the world
and the universe, and our puny place in it. Yet the seeds of what he is about
are in the very first line of the story: "It is already dark, it will soon be night."
And there are things the men say to each other that carry the story toward its
fantastic shift from the reasonable world of men in the hold of a ship to the
unreasonable world itself, the unhuman world of matter:

> "One minute a vessel bumps into a fish, the next the wind breaks loose from its
> chain . . . Is the wind a beast that it breaks loose from its chain? . . . One must
> have one's head on one's shoulders and reason it out. You have no sense."

When Gusev dies, Chekhov doesn't even mention it. We are told that he sleeps
for two days and that at noon on the third day two sailors come and carry
him up on deck, where he is wrapped in sailcloth, with two gridirons for
weight; they pray over him, and he is dropped over-board, "plop!" into the sea.
And the point of view continues to move from him, like a movie camera backing away to an enormous distance. As he performs this feat, Chekhov ends up
using an antique literary device, *personification*, which modern writers discarded long ago, and which one of the characters in this very story has questioned ("Is the wind a beast that breaks loose from its chain?") in that
astonishing last paragraph, the ocean *looks* at the sky, it actually *frowns*. "But
soon it, too, takes on tender, joyous, passionate colors for which it is hard to
find a name in the language of man." A modern reader, coming upon this last
line, might feel as if an amateur had written it, were it not for the power and
richness of detail that precedes it and the turn it makes on what has been,
after all, the story of one humble man's death.

There is no more audacious or shocking short story in the world, and it is
very great writing indeed, for although it does express, with what is the equivalent of a jolt to the nervous system, the frailty of human life and hope, it also
lends this one man's death a strange dignity, even a majesty, in the middle of
the tremendous indignity of dying in the hold of a steamer, at sea, among
strangers.

DONALD RAYFIELD

From *Sakhalin*[3]

June–December 1890[4]

Anton's reading had ill prepared him for the island. Six hundred miles long,
but with a land area of Scotland, Sakhalin is a hilly sliver of Arctic tundra,

---

3. From *Anton Chekhov* (New York: Henry Holt & Company), 1997.   **4.** Chekhov visited the Siberian penal
colony of Sakhalin, an island off Russia's eastern coast, north of Japan.

thinly covered with coniferous scrub. For half the year the temperature is below 0°C; for the other half chilly fog and rain alternate. The island barely supported a few thousand aborigines, Gilyals and Ainu, who lived off berries, seeds and fish. A little coal was mined to supply passing ships, but Sakhalin's only use to Russia was as a penal colony that hardened criminals would fear. Nothing could convey the awfulness of Sakhalin; its bogs rendered impassable by tree-roots, its cold, rain, fog and murderous insects.

• • •

The 10,000 prisoners, the 10,000 men and their families who guarded them, the few thousand released prisoners and exiles who tried to farm the intractable Sakhalin bogs, the few hundred aborigines, Gilyaks and Ainu, who had survived the diseases brought by the Japanese (who had territorial claims to Sakhalin) and Russians and the savage plunder by escaped convicts and renegade guards, lived in hell. Until 1888 exile to Sakhalin was for life; even in 1890 exiles were allowed to resettle only in eastern Siberia. The guards, too, were likely to succumb to disease or violence on the island. In late July Kononovich let Chekhov print 10,000 questionnaires in the island's print shop and interview prisoners and exiles. All August Anton surveyed the west coast around Aleksandrovsk and the Tym river valley that runs north from the centre of the island to the Sea of Okhotsk. In mid September he took a boat to Korsakovsk in Aniva Bay on the south side. At Korsakovsk Anton found hospitality with the Feldmans, a family of policemen and prison officials. Despite their notorious brutality, they showed their best side to Chekhov. Aniva Bay was cosmopolitan: Anton picnicked with the Japanese consul, and met shipwrecked American whalers.

The cards that Chekhov distributed to prisoners and exiles recorded name, address, married state, age, religion, place of birth, year of arrival, trade, literacy, source of income, diseases. They provided statistics that the Russian authorities lacked. In poor health, in two regions, each of 10,000 square miles, travelling on foot over treacherous paths, Anton collected data for 10,000 individuals in one short Arctic summer. In August and September 1890 the sun shone exceptionally often on Sakhalin, but Anton's achievement, nevertheless, was Herculean. He recorded hundreds of conversations with men, women and children of every status and nationality (though he met few aborigines); he inspected farms, mines, hospitals; he watched floggings. If he had the wherewithal, he treated the sick. He arrived too late to witness a mass hanging; the death penalty for murder had been abolished in Russia, but on Sakhalin murderers were hanged.

Chekhov's indignation focused on the plight not of the prisoners or guards, but of the children. The schools were closed for the summer, but, even when they were open, they were clearly as fictitious as the hospitals, where there were no scalpels or medicines and the doctors spent the money on brandy for themselves. Chekhov remonstrated with Kononovich: he made his officials order textbooks from Suvorin and telegraphed Vania to send school programmes and books.

• • •

Chekhov enjoyed the *Petersburg*, a sturdy 300-foot steamer built in Scotland twenty years before. It was lightly loaded — no prisoners ever came back from Sakhalin. Leaving Vladivostok on 19 October 1890, the ship held a mere 364 sailors, soldiers and guards, relieved from service in the Far East. The American whalers were to be dropped at Hong Kong. A few passengers occupied the cabins. One was Father Irakli, a Buriat Mongol who had been given a free passage to Russia to report in Moscow on his missionary work with the Gilyaks and Ainu. The Captain appeared only during a storm in the China Sea and told passengers who had revolvers to keep them loaded, since death by shooting was preferable to death by drowning. A midshipman Glinka struck up an acquaintance with Anton: he was the son of a Baroness Ikskul who in Petersburg had given (and broken) a promise to use her power to smooth Anton's passage.

Sakhalin was the evil face of colonialism; Hong Kong impressed Chekhov as the opposite. The ship stayed there eighty hours. Anton told Suvorin, on his return:

> A wonderful bay, such movement on the sea as I have never seen even in pictures; nine roads, horse-trams, a railway up the mountain, museums, botanical gardens; wherever you look you see the Englishmen's most tender concern for their employees, there is even a sailors' club. I . . . was annoyed to hear my Russian companions cursing the English for exploiting the natives. I thought: yes, the English exploit the Chinese, the Sepoys, the Indians, but they do give them roads, piped water, museums, Christianity, you [*Russians*] exploit them and what do you give them?

As they crossed the China Sea, the storms died away. On 20 October, just one day into the voyage home, one soldier died of 'acute pneumonia' in the ship's hospital: his body was thrown overboard in a sailcloth shroud. As they left Hong Kong, on 29 October, another soldier died and was buried at sea. Anton's mood plunged. He barely remembered Singapore for the tears that he was holding back (although in his few hours on shore he ordered a Javanese pony as a present for Suvorin).

Burial at sea inspired Chekhov to write the first fiction he had composed for a year, 'Gusev', an awesome portrayal of nature's indifference to death.

STEPHEN L. BAEHR

From *The Locomotive and the Giant: Power in Chekhov's "Anna on the Neck"*[5]

> "Power tends to corrupt, and absolute power corrupts absolutely."
>
> —*Lord Acton*

Like many of Chekhov's late works, "Anna na shee" ("Anna on the Neck," 1895) can be read as a tale about power. The story depicts a battle between the sexes, opposing the power of money and rank of the 52-year-old bureaucrat-bridegroom, Modest Alekseich, to the power of sexual attraction of his eighteen-year-old bride Anna, who discovers at a ball that beauty empowers. In effect, the two-part tale depicts an agon between nineteenth-century conceptions of "male" and "female" power. *Part I* portrays the patriarchal domination and oppression of Anna by Modest Alekseich, stressing that "she did everything

5. *SEEJ*, Vol. 39. No. 1 (1995): p. 29–37.

that her husband wanted and . . . was afraid of her husband and trembled before him" (8:17–18). *Part II* depicts Anna's "conquest" of her husband (and the male sex in general), culminating in her oft-quoted statement to Modest Alekseich: "Go away, blockhead" (8:24). Several dominant metaphors reinforce this theme of power, especially those of a locomotive and a giant; both at first threaten Anna, but are ultimately defeated by her.

The story is structured on the reversal of power and is divided into two symmetrical parts that are, in effect, reversals of each other. It is thus fitting that *Part I* takes place in summer and *Part II* in winter, and that the *peripeteia* begins when Anna discovers herself in a "huge mirror" at a ball. The reversal of power begins while the newlyweds are heading by train towards the monastery where they will spend their honeymoon. The train stops at a "junction" (*raz"ezd:* a section of double track on a single-line railway), where the lively music of a military orchestra can be heard from an evening of dance at neighboring dachas. This *"raz"ezd"* (etymologically a "movement in different directions") is symbolic, reflecting the changing direction that Anna will give to her life. Until this "junction," Anna has been regretting the situation that led to her wedding, which she implicitly compares to a funeral.

• • •

Within the story, power is described through four central metaphors of strength or force (*sila*—one of the central words in this story): a locomotive that crushes everything in its path; a brewing storm; a huge white bear; and a chthonic giant. The adjective "huge" (*gromadnyi*) is associated with two of these four metaphors (the huge white bear, the huge officer), it is used in only one additional instance in the story—to describe the "huge mirror" at the entrance to the ballroom, where Anna joins the ranks of the powerful.

• • •

Among Anna's other conquests is Artynov, "that famous Don Juan and rake ("balovnik")" (8:15), the rich owner of a colony of dachas near the junction where the train had stopped on the way to the monastery. After Artynov becomes her lover, *his* servitude is stressed when, at the end of the story, he comes to take her for rides in a carriage, sitting *not* inside with her but "on the coachbox instead of the coachman" ("na kozlakh vmesto kuchera") (8:24). After he is conquered, the imagery of virility originally used to describe him is replaced by imagery of infirmity: where he had originally been portrayed as a "Don Juan and rake" whose face is "like that of an Armenian" and who is accompanied by "two borzoi dogs with keen snouts pointed towards the ground" (suggesting, perhaps, that he is a hunter of women), he is portrayed at the ball as having a "shortness of breath" and "suffering from asthma" (8:15, 22).

The reversal of power relationships at the ball is accentuated by the fact that many of the people who had previously frightened Anna with their power appear there and are conquered by her, including His Excellency and her father's fellow teachers. Anna's conquest of His Excellency is marked by his smiling a saccharine smile and "chewing his lips, as he always did when he saw beautiful women;" he even asks permission to call on her again, saying that she is "a treasure" and that she should be awarded "a prize for beauty . . . as in America" (8:22). Through her conquest of His Excellency, Anna reverses the power that Modest Alekseich had exerted over her.

• • •

Perhaps the ultimate parody in Chekhov's story is found in its ironic reversal of Tolstoy's *Anna Karenina*. The marriage of a cold bureaucrat who lives "by rules" (always a bad sign in Russian literature) to a beautiful younger woman recalls the plot of *Anna Karenina*, as does the fact that both women after whom the stories are named are "Anna" and that the patronymic of Chekhov's bureaucrat who plays by the rules is "Alekseich" (making him on one level a "son" of Aleksei Karenin, as Thomas Winner has noted). Given the important role of the locomotive that crushes Tolstoy's Anna Karenina, the initial fear by Chekhov's Anna of a locomotive that crushes everything in its path is significant. But this fear, like Anna's fate, is reversed in Chekhov. Chekhov's Anna is a vulgar variant of Tolstoy's. Where Tolstoy's sensitive, suffering Anna is snubbed by society, disenfranchised, and ultimately destroyed as a result of her honest and open affair, Chekhov's calculating, unfeeling, predatory Anna achieves power precisely because she plays by society's rules. Tolstoy's tragedy becomes Chekhov's *poshlost'*. This opposition reflects a broader distinction between the worlds of Tolstoy and Chekhov. In Chekhov, there is no external moral Force repaying "immorality" through "vengeance." Instead, Chekhov depicts (through a seemingly-objective narrator) a Darwinian universe controlled by manipulative human beings in their everyday struggle for power.

VLADIMIR NABOKOV

From *Chekhov's Prose*[6]

His quiet and subtle humor pervades the grayness of the lives he creates. For the Russian philosophical or social-minded critic he was the unique exponent of a unique Russian type of character. It is rather difficult for me to explain what that type was or is, because it is all so linked up with the general psychological and social history of the Russian nineteenth century. It is not quite exact to say that Chekhov dealt in charming and ineffectual people. It is a little more true to say that his men and women are charming because they are ineffectual. But what really attracted the Russian reader was that in Chekhov's heroes he recognized the type of the Russian intellectual, the Russian idealist, a queer and pathetic creature that is little known abroad and cannot exist in the Russia of the Soviets. Chekhov's intellectual was a man who combined the deepest human decency of which man is capable with an almost ridiculous inability to put his ideals and principles into action; a man devoted to moral beauty, the welfare of his people, the welfare of the universe, but unable in his private life to do anything useful; frittering away his provincial existence in a haze of utopian dreams; knowing exactly what is good, what is worth while living for, but at the same time sinking lower and lower in the mud of a humdrum existence, unhappy in love, hopelessly inefficient in everything—a good man who cannot make good. This is the character that passes—in the guise of a doctor, a student, a village teacher, many other professional people—all through Chekhov's stories.

What rather irritated his politically minded critics was that nowhere does the author assign this type to any definite party or give him any definite politi-

6. From *Critical Essays on Anton Chekhov* (1989).

cal program. But that is the whole point. Chekhov's inefficient idealists were neither terrorists, nor Social Democrats, nor budding Bolsheviks, nor any of the numberless members of numberless revolutionary parties in Russia. What mattered was that this typical Chekhovian hero was the unfortunate bearer of a vague but beautiful human truth, a burden which he could neither get rid of nor carry. What we see is a continuous stumble through all Chekhov's stories, but it is the stumble of a man who stumbles because he is staring at the stars. He is unhappy, that man, and he makes others unhappy; he loves not his brethren, not those nearest to him, but the remotest. The plight of a negro in a distant land, of a Chinese coolie, of a workman in the remote Urals, affects him with a keener pang of moral pain than the misfortunes of his neighbor or the troubles of his wife. Chekhov took a special artistic pleasure in fixing all the delicate varieties of that pre-war, pre-revolution type of Russian intellectual. Those men could dream; they could not rule. They broke their own lives and the lives of others, they were silly, weak, futile, hysterical; but Chekhov suggests, blessed be the country that could produce that particular type of man. They missed opportunities, they shunned action, they spent sleepless nights in planning worlds they could not build; but the mere fact of such men, full of such fervor, fire of abnegation, pureness of spirit, moral elevation, this mere fact of such men having lived and probably still living somewhere somehow in the ruthless and sordid Russia of to-day is a promise of better things to come for the world at large—for perhaps the most admirable among the admirable laws of Nature is the survival of the weakest.

It is from this point of view that those who were equally interested in the misery of the Russian people and in the glory of Russian literature, it is from this point of view that they appreciated Chekhov. Though never concerned with providing a social or ethical message, Chekhov's genius almost involuntarily disclosed more of the blackest realities of hungry, puzzled, servile, angry peasant Russia than a multitude of other writers, such as Gorky for instance, who flaunted their social ideas in a procession of painted dummies. I shall go further and say that the person who prefers Dostoevsky or Gorky to Chekhov will never be able to grasp the essentials of Russian literature and Russian life, and, which is far more important, the essentials of universal literary art. It was quite a game among Russians to divide their acquaintances into those who liked Chekhov and those who did not. Those who did not were not the right sort.

I heartily recommend taking as often as possible Chekhov's books (even in the translations they have suffered) and dreaming through them as they are intended to be dreamed through. In an age of ruddy Goliaths it is very useful to read about delicate Davids. Those bleak landscapes, the withered sallows along dismally muddy roads, the gray crows flapping across gray sides, the sudden whiff of some amazing recollection at a most ordinary corner—all this pathetic dimness, all this lovely weakness, all this Chekhovian dove-gray world is worth treasuring in the glare of those strong, self-sufficient worlds that are promised us by the worshippers of totalitarian states.

Author in Depth: William Faulkner

Faulkner's fiction touched on a wide range of concerns, but a strong current running through much of his work was a mediation of the Old South's influence on an emerging New South. In the stories collected in this anthology, we see the powerful influence of days gone by on the living, but equally so, the flow of fundamental concerns across generations and classes, "the old verities and truths of the heart," as he put it in his Nobel Address.

Collected here are remarks by Faulkner on the ways he went about his work and his ambitions for it; Sherwood Anderson's provocative analysis of the grotesque—useful for understanding not just Faulkner's fiction, but that of O'Connor, Hemingway, Poe, and others; as well as scholarly critiques of the intersection of past, present, and eternal in the two stories collected in this anthology: "Barn Burning" and "A Rose for Emily."

WILLIAM FAULKNER

An Interview[1]

Q. Mr. Faulkner, could I ask you how important you think a college education is to a writer?

A. Well that's—is too much like trying to decide how important is a warm room to a writer. To some writers, some people, the college education might be of great importance, just like some of us couldn't work in a cold room. So that's a question I just wouldn't attempt to answer, and then I'm more or less out of bounds because I didn't have one myself.

Q. I was reading a book . . . yesterday which said that English teachers had gotten a body of American literature and stored it away in musty basements and had sort of stifled the creative impulse in America . . . Do you think that's true?

A. No sir, I do not. I do not. I think that people read into the true meaning of college lots of things that are not there. I think that there's an importance in college that is—adumbrates a specialty like—of being a writer, that is, the college is to produce first a human being, a humanitarian, and no man can write who is not first a humanitarian, and if the college can supply that to him, then the college is of infinite importance. If he has managed to acquire that outside of college, then he doesn't need the college. But you can't—I don't think you can say that the college makes or mars an artist.

Q. If he has it in him, it'll come out.

A. Yes. I would say that the college would help anyone, but it wouldn't make a writer that wouldn't have made himself—that is, I've never held with the mute inglorious Milton.

---

1. From *Faulkner in the University, Class Conferences at the University of Virginia, 1957–58*, ed. by Frederick L. Gwynn and Joseph L. Blotner.

• • •

... Q. I thought I might ask you, Mr. Faulkner, because somebody was speaking of it the other day to me, how you went about writing, how stories came to you. I have a friend, a writer, who has told me sometimes that she will think about her stories for quite a long time and then suddenly they'll be there, and they can be written down without perhaps a great deal of revision or fumbling, that they are there in the mind and they get down on paper that way. Do you have experience of that sort when you write or do you have different things happen?

A. That's sometimes true. I don't think you can make a hard and fast statement about the method of writing, of the conception of a story. It—of course the first thing, the writer's got to be demon-driven. He's got to have to write, he don't know why, and sometimes he will wish that he didn't have to, but he does. The story can come from an anecdote, it can come from a character. With me it never comes from an idea because I don't know too much about ideas and ain't really interested in ideas, I'm interested in people, so what I speak from my experience is probably a limited experience. But I'm interested primarily in people, in man in conflict with himself, with his fellow man, or with his time and place, his environment. So I think there's really no rule for how to begin to write.

. . . . Q. Mr. Faulkner, do you think that a writer can teach young writers?

A. I don't think anybody can teach anybody anything. I think that you learn it, but the young writer that is as I say demon-driven and wants to learn and has got to write he don't know why, he will learn from almost any source that he finds. He will learn from older people who are not writers, he will learn from writers, but he learns it—you can't teach it. Then I think too that the writer who's actually hot to say something hasn't got time to be taught. He's too busy learning—he knows what he wants—his instinct says to take this from this man or that from that man. That he's not—he hasn't got time to sit under a mentor and listen to try to learn.

• • •

Q. . . . Do you feel a necessity to . . . tell all the truth about that character that you feel needs to be told regardless . . . ?

A. No, I think that after about ten books, I had learned enough of judgment to where I could pick and choose the facet of the character which I needed at that particular time to move the story I was telling, so that I can take a facet of one character in one story and another facet of that character in another story. To me it's the same character, though sometimes to the reader it may seem as though the character had changed or had developed more—to me he hasn't. That I used my editorial prerogative of choosing what I needed from that particular character at that particular time.

... Q. Mr. Faulkner, how much do you feel that the writer's being involved with people in his writings is dependent upon his being actively involved with real people in the real world?

A. I think that that has nothing to do with the writing. That he can be involved with people, he can be involved with alcohol, or with gambling or anything and it's not going to affect the writer. Now, I have no patience and I don't hold with the mute inglorious Miltons. I think that if he's demon-driven, with something to be said, then he's going to write it, he can blame his—the fact that he's not turning out the work on lots of things. I've heard lots of people say, Well, if I were not married and had children I would be a writer. I've heard people say, If I could just stop doing this I would be a writer. I don't agree with that. I think if you're going to write, you're going to write and nothing will stop you. If you can be involved, and probably the more you're involved, it may be better for you. That maybe it's bad to crawl off into the ivory tower and stay there—maybe you do need to be involved, to get the edges beaten off of you a little every day—may be good for the writer.

• • •

Q. Sir, in your novels, you said in one of the other classes that you begin with a character in mind or more than one character. In your short stories, do they—do you conceive of them the same way? Do you start with a person or do you—?

A. Sometimes with a person, sometimes with an anecdote, but the short story is conceived in the same terms that the book is. The first job the craftsman faces is to tell this as quickly and as simply as I can, and if he's good, if he's of the first water, like Chekhov, he can do it every time in two or three thousand words, but if he's not that good, sometimes it takes him eighty thousand words. But they are similar, and he is simply trying to tell something which was true and moving in the shortest time he can, and then if he has sense enough stop. That is, I don't believe the man or the woman sits down and says, Now I'm going to write a short story, or Now I'm going to write a novel. It's an idea that begins with the thought, the image of a character, or with an anecdote, and even in the same breath, almost like lightning, it begins to take a shape that he can see whether it's going to be a short story or a novel. Sometimes, not always. Sometimes he thinks it'll be a short story and finds that he can't. Sometimes it looks like it's to be a novel and then after he works on it, he sees that it's not, that he can tell it in two thousand or five thousand words. No rule to it.

• • •

Q. Mr. Faulkner, do you think an author has his prerogative to create his own language? In other words, to go against what the people create, vernacular? Do you think an author has the right to create his own—I believe Joyce and Eliot have done it—have tried to create, they found that language was not—did not suit their purposes, so they had to go beyond and make a—

A. He has the right to do that provided he don't insist on anyone understanding it. That is—what I'm trying to say is—that I believe I'm paraphrasing Whitman, didn't he say, "To have good poets we must have good readers, too," something like that? Who knows?

Q. Whitman, "great audiences."

A. Well, the writer, actually, that's an obligation that he assumes with his vocation, that he's going to write it in a way that people can understand it. He doesn't have to write it in the way that every idiot can understand it—every imbecile in the third grade can understand it, but he's got to use a language which is accepted and in which the words have specific meanings that everybody agrees on. I think that *Finnegans Wake* and *Ulysses* were justified, but then it's hard to say on what terms they were justified. That was a case of a genius who was electrocuted by the divine fire.

Q. Mr. Faulkner, it's often been said about great novels or great short stories that they wouldn't pass muster in a freshman English composition course. Now I was wondering, since this is your first stay at a university, if you had any comments on the traditional or the apparently traditional conflict between the creative writer and the schoolman.

A. Well, as an old veteran sixth-grader, that question is I think outside of my province, because I never got to freshman English. I don't know how much it would conflict. Maybe before I've left the University I will be able to pass freshman English.

. . .

Q. Sir, I think you said that you haven't yet achieved your own personal goal as a writer. What is that goal and is it likely that you will succeed in achieving it?

A. That's difficult to say. It's when I have done something that, to use Hemingway's phrase, makes me feel good, that is completely satisfactory, maybe that will be the goal, and I hope just a little that I'll never quite do that because if I do there won't be any reason to go on writing, and I'm too old to take up another hobby. It's—I think that a writer wants to make something that he knows that a hundred or two hundred or five hundred, a thousand years later will make people feel what they feel when they read Homer, or read Dickens or Balzac, Tolstoy, that that's probably his goal. I don't think that he bothers until he gets old like this and has a right to spend a lot of time talking about it to put that into actual words. But probably that's what he wants, that really the writer doesn't want success, that he knows he has a short span of life, that the day will come when he must pass through the wall of oblivion, and he wants to leave a scratch on that wall—Kilroy was here—that somebody a hundred, a thousand years later will see.

. . .

Q. Sir, a few minutes ago you mentioned that people in your home town were looking into your books for familiar characters. Realizing that you've got a rich legacy in your experiences, but it seems to me that nowadays the modern novelist is writing merely thinly disguised autobiography. Which do you think is really more valuable from the sense of the artist, the disguised autobiography, or making it up from whole cloth, as it were?

A. I would say that the writer has three sources, imagination, observation, and experience. He himself doesn't know how much of which he uses at any given moment because each of the sources themselves are not too important to him. That he is writing about people, and he uses his material from the three sources as the carpenter reaches into his lumber room and finds a board that fits the particular corner he's building. Of course, any writer, to begin with, is writing his own biography because he has discovered the world and then suddenly discovered that the world is important enough or moving enough or tragic enough to put down on paper or in music or on canvas, and at that time all he knows is what has happened to him because he has not developed his capacity to perceive, to draw conclusions, to have an insight into people. His only insight in it is into himself, and it's a biography because that's the only gauge he has to measure—is what he has experienced himself. As he gets older and works more, imagination is like any muscle, it improves with use. Imagination develops, his observation gets shrewder as he gets older, as he writes, so that when he reaches his peak, his best years, when his work is best, he himself doesn't know and doesn't have time to bother and doesn't really care how much of what comes from each of these sources, that then he is writing about people, writing about the aspirations, the troubles, the anguishes, the courage, and the cowardice, the baseness and the splendor of man, of the human heart.

· · ·

Q. Mr. Faulkner, you may have touched on this previously, but could you give some advice to young writers? What advice would you give to young writers?

A. At one time I thought the most important thing was talent. I think now that the young man or the young woman must possess or teach himself, train himself, in infinite patience, which is to try and to try and to try until it comes right. He must train himself in ruthless intolerance—that is, to throw away anything that is false no matter how much he might love that page or that paragraph. The most important thing is insight, that is, to be—curiosity—to wonder, to mull, and to muse why it is that man does what he does, and if you have that, then I don't think the talent makes much difference, whether you've got that or not.

Q. How would you suggest that he get this insight? Through experience?

A. Yes, and then the greatest part of experience is in the books, to read. To read and to read and to read and to read. To watch people, to have—to never judge people. To watch people, what they do, without intolerance. Simply to learn why it is they did what they did. . . .

· · ·

Q. I have heard you use the word "fun" several times, and I'd like to know your idea of fun.

A. Well—fun—let's see if I can define that. In my own case it is to accomplish something which makes me feel good, which may make somebody else feel good, which won't hurt anybody. Fun is to accomplish something which I thought that perhaps I couldn't. That I might not be brave enough or strong enough, and then I do it and I'm successful. I suppose that everyone has a different notion of what "fun" means, so I can tell you only what it means to me, and when I say that, to write for fun, it's to take man's dilemma, the old familiar things in which there's nothing new and can't be anything new, and by the light of my own experience and imagination and a great deal of hard work, to make something which was a little different, which wasn't here yesterday. People write about the same stories because there're so few to write about, but to take one—human beings in the old familiar dilemma and predicament—and by the imagination and the hard work to show them in some new, interesting, tragic, or comical instance of the struggle within the dilemma, that to me is fun. But then so is getting a horse over a fence that I wasn't too sure he could get over or that I would still be on him is fun.

WILLIAM FAULKNER

Nobel Prize Address[2]

I feel that this award was not made to me as a man, but to my work—a life's work in the agony and sweat of the human spirit, not for glory and least of all for profit, but to create out of the materials of the human spirit something which did not exist before. So this award is only mine in trust. It will not be difficult to find a dedication for the money part of it commensurate with the purpose and significance of its origin. But I would like to do the same with the acclaim too, by using this moment as a pinnacle from which I might be listened to by the young men and women already dedicated to the same anguish and travail, among whom is already that one who will some day stand here where I am standing.

Our tragedy today is a general and universal physical fear so long sustained by now that we can even bear it. There are no longer problems of the spirit. There is only the question: When will I be blown up? Because of this, the young man or woman writing today has forgotten the problems of the human heart in conflict with itself which alone can make good writing because only that is worth writing about, worth the agony and the sweat.

He must learn them again. He must teach himself that the basest of all things is to be afraid; and, teaching himself that, forget it forever, leaving no room in his workshop for anything but the old verities and truths of the heart, the old universal truths lacking which any story is ephemeral and doomed—love and honor and pity and pride and compassion and sacrifice. Until he does so, he labors under a curse. He writes not of love but of lust, of defeats in which nobody loses anything of value, of victories without hope and, worst of all, without pity or compassion. His griefs grieve on no universal bones, leaving no scars. He writes not of the heart but of the glands.

Until he relearns these things, he will write as though he stood among and watched the end of man. I decline to accept the end of man. It is easy enough to say that man is immortal simply because he will endure: that when the last dingdong of doom has clanged and faded from the last worthless rock hanging tideless in the last red and dying evening, that even then there will still be one more sound: that of his puny inexhaustible voice, still talking.

I refuse to accept this. I believe that man will not merely endure: he will prevail. He is immortal, not because he alone among creatures has an inexhaustible voice, but because he has a soul, a spirit capable of compassion and sacrifice and endurance. The poet's, the writer's, duty is to write about these things. It is his privilege to help man endure by lifting his heart, by reminding him of the courage and honor and hope and pride and compassion and pity and sacrifice which have been the glory of his past. The poet's voice need

2. From *Nobel Lectures, Literature 1901–1967*, ed. Horst Frenz, Elsevier Publishing Company, Amsterdam, 1969.

not merely be the record of man, it can be one of the props, the pillars to help him endure and prevail.

EDMOND L. VOLPE

"A Rose for Emily"[3]

One of Faulkner's greatest stories, "A Rose for Emily" is a brilliantly wrought, emotionally charged, haunting portrait of the Southern psyche—a psyche tormented by conflicting feelings, impulses, and needs. It is the first story to deal with the village of Jefferson and its community. Publication in *Forum* in 1930 distinguishes it as the first story Faulkner was able to market. Written sometime toward the end of the 1920s, it also dramatically indicates the writer's mastery of the short story form. Faulkner's own ambivalent feelings of love and hate for the South inform every aspect of this story, from its narrative technique to its title. The community's sense of a past, which no winter touches, is countered by the images of death with which Faulkner enshrouds the past. The morbid atmosphere of decay that prepares for the story's macabre ending—revelation of Emily Grierson's necrophilia—is offset by the affectionate tribute of the story's title. The title does not derive from any incident or even image in the story; it is superimposed, Faulkner's expression of affection for what he hates.

What he hates is not so much the South's morbid, pathological attachment to the dead glory of the past but the ghoulish power of the past on the consciousness of the South. And what he loves is the tragic figure of the Southerner, trapped by his pride in his heritage and tormented by conflicting needs to conform and to defy, struggling vainly and helplessly to escape from the past and exist in the present.

"A Rose for Emily" has two major characters: Emily Grierson and the community. They are complementary rather than antagonistic characters; Emily's personal history mirrors the community's collective history. Faulkner provides us three dominant images of Emily, each reflecting a different stage in her history. We catch a brief glimpse of her as a young woman in the tableau the community remembers: Emily's "slender figure in white in the background . . . his [her father's] back to her and clutching a horsewhip, the two of them framed by the back-flung front door" (*CS*, 123). After her father's death, Emily, over thirty, her hair cut short, rides around town in Homer Barron's rented yellow-wheeled buggy to an increasing chorus of disapproval by the community. And after the disappearance of Homer, she becomes the "idol in a niche" (*CS* 128), the small obese figure, looking "bloated, like a body long submerged in motionless water, and of that pallid hue" (*CS*, 121). These three images trace Emily's tragic history: the fearful hold of the past upon her during her youth, her vain attempt to defy "that which had robbed her" of her chance for life, and finally her defeat and regression until she becomes the embodiment of the dead past (*CS*, 124). Faulkner portrays Emily with sufficient: psychological realism to make her a unique, vivid character, but "A Rose for Emily" has two protagonists, and Emily's sick attachment for her father, her affair with Homer Barron, her motivation for murdering her

3. From *A Reader's Guide to William Faulkner: The Short Stories* (2004).

lover, and her necrophilia are meaningful only in the contact in which Faulkner presents them: the context of the community's relationship with Emily.

Faulkner, ingeniously, makes the community a living entity, a character with a past, a personality, a memory, and feelings by means of the ubiquitous narrator who refers to the community as "we" and who spans the several generations of Emily's lifetime. This narrative voice ranges freely through time. The entire story is narrated in the past tense, but present action occurs after the death of Emily. The story opens with the announcement of her death and the attendance of "our whole town" at her funeral (*CS*, 119). It ends with the town's examination, after her burial, of that room that "we knew . . . no one had seen in forty years, and which would have to be forced" (*CS*, 129). Between the opening paragraph and the short closing scene, the narrator presents historical data about Emily and the town, focusing upon various episodes covering some fifty years of Emily's seventy-four years, without regard to chronology. Scenes separated by thirty years are juxtaposed. The narrator moves from scene to scene by association of thought. The narrative technique and the narrative structure convey a sense of temporal continuity, a sense of the past, to use Faulkner's own image, not as "a diminishing road but, instead, a huge meadow which no winter ever quite touches," in the collective consciousness of the community (*CS*, 129). "Alive," the narrator says, "Miss Emily had been a tradition, a duty, and a care; a sort of hereditary obligation upon the town" (*CS*, 119).

"Miss Emily," however, is only a symbol of the community's sense of "hereditary obligation" (*CS*, 119). Emily dies sometime in the second decade of the twentieth century, but the old men come to her funeral dressed in Confederate uniforms. The values of antebellum society continue to exert a very powerful influence upon the community in spite of Appomattox, governing its attitudes toward blacks and toward women. In this story, which is centered upon a woman, the past is appropriately evoked by the tradition of Southern chivalry. There are three paternal figures in the story: Colonel Sartoris, Judge Stevens, and Mr. Grierson. Sartoris and Stevens function in the consciousness of the community in the same way that Mr. Grierson functions in the consciousness of Emily. The episodes in which Sartoris and Stevens figure are two of the major scenes in the narrative, and they establish a link between the community's involvement with the past and with Emily's involvement.

Colonel Sartoris, the narrator informs us parenthetically, fathered an edict that no Negro woman should appear on the streets without an apron. It is this representative of the continuing power of the antebellum world who, in 1894, remits Emily Grierson's taxes with a tale that only a "man of Colonel Sartoris' generation and thought could have invented . . . and only a woman could have believed" (*CS*, 120).

The next generation "with its more modern ideas," refuses to accept this dicturn from the past, and it decides to collect the taxes (*CS*, 120). The new generation has the power to enforce its will, but the past has too strong a hold upon it. The delegation that calls upon Miss Emily and confronts her in that dust-filled, mausoleum-like front parlor where Mr. Grierson is enshrined, retreats into inactivity and silence when Miss Emily tells them to see Colonel Sartoris, ten years dead.

And just as this generation's attempt to defy the dead falls, so their fathers had been "vanquished . . . thirty years before about the smell" (*CS,* 121). The eighty-year-old Judge Stevens is mayor when complaints about the smell from the Grierson house begin to come in. The whole town knows, of course, that the druggist had sold, with much trepidation, arsenic to Miss Emily, just as it knows that Homer Barron entered Emily's kitchen door one evening and disappeared from sight. At first, Judge Stevens tries to fend off the complaints, but finally he calls a meeting of the board of alderman, which consists of "three graybeards and one younger man, a member of the rising generation" (*CS,* 122). This younger man insists that all they need do is order Miss Emily to clean up her place, " 'and if she don't. . . .' 'Dammit, sir,' Judge Stevens said, 'will you accuse a lady to her face of smelling bad?' "(*CS,* 122). That evocation of the old code of Southern chivalry is apparently too much for the member of the rising generation, and the following night all four slink around Miss Emily's yard sprinkling lime.

SHERWOOD ANDERSON

The Book of the Grotesque [4]

The writer, an old man with a white mustache, had some difficulty in getting into bed. The windows of the house in which he lived were high and he wanted to look at the trees when he awoke in the morning. A carpenter came to fix the bed so that it would be on a level with the window.

Quite a fuss was made about the matter. The carpenter, who had been a soldier in the Civil War, came into the writer's room and sat down to talk of building a platform for the purpose of raising the bed. The writer had cigars lying about and the carpenter smoked.

For a time the two men talked of the raising of the bed and then they talked of other things. The soldier got on the subject of the war. The writer, in fact, led him to that subject. The carpenter had once been a prisoner in Andersonville prison and had lost a brother. The brother had died of starvation, and whenever the carpenter got upon that subject he cried. He, like the old writer, had a white mustache, and when he cried he puckered up his lips and the mustache bobbed up and down. The weeping old man with the cigar in his mouth was ludicrous. The plan the writer had for the raising of his bed was forgotten and later the carpenter did it in his own way and the writer, who was past sixty, had to help himself with a chair when he went to bed at night.

In his bed the writer rolled over on his side and lay quite still. For years he had been beset with notions concerning his heart. He was a hard smoker and his heart fluttered. The idea had got into his mind that he would some time die unexpectedly and always when he got into bed he thought of that. It did not alarm him. The effect in fact was quite a special thing and not easily explained. It made him more alive, there in bed, than at any other time. Perfectly still he lay and his body was old and not of much use any more, but something inside him was altogether young. He was like a pregnant woman, only that the thing inside him was not a baby but a youth. No, it wasn't a

4. From *Winesburg, Ohio* (1919).

youth. It was a woman, young, and wearing a coat of mail like a knight. It is absurd, you see to try to tell what was inside the old writer as he lay on his high bed and listened to the fluttering of his heart. The thing to get at is what the writer, or the young thing within the writer, was thinking about.

The old writer, like all of the people in the world, had got, during his long life, a great many notions in his head. He had once been quite handsome and a number of women had been in love with him. And then, of course, he had known people, many people, known them in a peculiarly intimate way that was different from the way in which you and I know people. At least that is what the writer thought and the thought pleased him. Why quarrel with an old man concerning his thoughts?

In the bed the writer had a dream that was not a dream. As he grew somewhat sleepy but was still conscious, figures began to appear before his eyes. He imagined the young indescribable thing within himself was driving a long procession of figures before his eyes.

You see the interest in all this lies in the figures that went before the eyes of the writer. They were all grotesques. All of the men and women the writer had ever known had become grotesques.

The grotesques were not all horrible. Some were amusing, some almost beautiful, and one, a woman all drawn out of shape, hurt the old man by her grotesqueness. When she passed he made a noise like a small dog whimpering. Had you come into the room you might have supposed the old man had unpleasant dreams or perhaps indigestion.

For an hour the procession of grotesques passed before the eyes of the old man, and then, although it was a painful thing to do, he crept out of bed and began to write. Some one of the grotesques had made a deep impression on his mind and he wanted to describe it.

At his desk the writer worked for an hour. In the end he wrote a book which he called "The Book of the Grotesque." It was never published, but I saw it once and it made an indelible impression on my mind. The book had one central thought that is very strange and has always remained with me. By remembering it I have been able to understand many people and things that I was never able to understand before. The thought was involved but a simple statement of it would be something like this:

> That in the beginning when the world was young there were a great many thoughts but no such thing as a truth. Man made the truths himself and each truth was a composite of a great many vague thoughts. All about in the world were the truths and they were all beautiful.

> The old man had listed hundreds of the truths in his book. I will not try to tell you of all of them. There was the truth of virginity and the truth of passion, the truth of wealth and of poverty, of thrift and of profligacy, of carelessness and abandon. Hundreds and hundreds were the truths and they were all beautiful. And then the people came along. Each as he appeared snatched up one of the truths and some who were quite strong snatched up a dozen of them.

> It was the truths that made the people grotesques. The old man had quite an elaborate theory concerning the matter. It was his notion that the moment one of the people took one of the truths to himself, called it his truth, and tried to

live his life by it, he became a grotesque and the truth he embraced became a falsehood.

You can see for yourself how the old man, who had spent all of his life writing and was filled with words, would write hundreds of pages concerning this matter. The subject would become so big in his mind that he himself would be in danger of becoming a grotesque. He didn't, I suppose, for the same reason that he never published the book. It was the young thing inside him that saved the old man.

Concerning the old carpenter who fixed the bed for the writer, I only mentioned him because he, like many of what are called very common people, became the nearest thing to what is understandable and lovable of all the grotesques in the writer's book.

JOEL WILLIAMSON

From *William Faulkner and Southern History*[5]

Beat Two was notorious in Lafayette County for the fierce independence of its white farmers. They were a proud, hard-working, common-sensical, usually poor, and sometimes violent people who frequently came into conflict with the town-dwelling authorities. In 1938 and 1939, Faulkner fell in love with his role as a working farmer, and he came to identify deeply with these "plain folk" of the South. "These are my kind of people," he said to his mother. The people out in Beat Two were very much in his mind as he got into writing the first volume of the Snopes trilogy in those years. It was then that he created his beloved V.K. Radliff, a man squarely out of the plain farmer tradition, a person of high intelligence, deep morality, and great wisdom who had capacities both for seeing the world as it is and for working effectively toward making it what it ought to be. He also elaborated his depiction of the hardy peasantry as represented by Varners, McCallums, Armstids, Bookrights, and Tulls. And, finally, he began to evolve the story of the Snopeses, first conceived a dozen years before.

The Snopeses were people who had begun somewhere in the middling range of the Southern social order before the Civil War. By the turn of the century, however, they were being ground down from farm owning to farm tenanting for a share of the crop, heading toward farm laboring, working sporadically for whatever they could get, drifting, and wintering on sufferance in outbuildings. In the case of Ab Snopes, Flem's father, it was a powerlessness that he countered with a tactic that slaves had favored—the threat to burn the master's barn under the cover of darkness. Arson, it seems, has always been a favored form of retaliation by the powerless of the world. One might begin with the master's barn, and end with the master's house—in extreme cases, at night with the master and his family sleeping in the house. A wise owner would never push his laborers over the edge.

In reality, the people in Beat Two that Faulkner so loved were the direct descendents of what Vanderbilt University historian Frank W. Owsley described as "the plain folk of the Old South." During the last generation of slavery, they

---

5. Joel Williamson, *William Faulkner and Southern History* (1993).

had shared generally in the prosperity of the cotton economy. During the war they had supplied, either willingly or by draft, the great majority of the soldiers in the rank and file of the Confederate armies. In the decades after the war, however, they found it increasingly difficult to maintain their middling status in the economy. While the whole of the white South was reduced considerably in the decades after the war, a minority of these yeoman folk lost out altogether, first by losing their farms, then by losing out as tenants for good farms, then by losing out in the competition to tenant any farms at all and becoming day laborers (the worst case scenario), as such to be used to advantage cheaply when needed and discarded when not. In all of this, after 1865, they faced effective competition from black farmers, who at least had the advantage of seeing themselves as rising up from slavery rather than heading down toward it.

Historically, two things were happening to produce this sad state. First, the South had lost power politically by attempting a rebellion and losing. Economic reduction was one of the prices it had to pay as a result of its miscalculation. Secondly, the Industrial Revolution was in full swing, and it fell to the lot of the South to produce raw materials cheaply, especially cotton, for that system while paying dearly to consume its finished products. In the new order, industrial and commercial elements were several steps ahead of farmers everywhere in controlling production and prices. In the turn-of-the-century years, large combinations such as U.S. Steel, Standard Oil, American Tobacco, and several large railroad corporations were able to balance out supply and demand to promote their own interests while farmers perennially produced all that soil, climate, and unrelenting labor could yield regardless of price. In the 1880s, they attempted to organize Farmers Alliances to gain some control over their economic lives both as to production and consumption. These failed dismally and in 1892 they formed the so-called Populist Party in an effort to achieve by political action what they could not do by economic means. That, too, foundered after the elections of 1896, but there were politicians like James K. Vardaman who carried forward the Populist purpose under the Democratic name. At last, in an American prosperity derived from World War I, 1914–1918, they achieved a modicum of success.

By the time Faulkner was a young man in the 1920s, these plain folk had moved into the third postwar generation. The early twenties brought economic reversal and a deep and dispiriting agricultural depression, well before the general depression ushered in by the crash of 1929. The result of this was a wave of migration by Southern whites to the towns and cities, a forced dislocation that still reverberates through Southern culture. When the Great Depression came to the South in the 1930s, it was not news; it was simply more of the same and deeper. Apparently, Faulkner never used the term "depression" in his fiction, and properly so. Nor did he call the New Deal by name, probably because he so hated it for undermining, as he saw it, the individuality and the freedom of his plain folk by its various "doles."

Author in Depth: Alice Munro

Though Alice Munro often writes that she resists simple one-to-one connections between her biography and her short stories, the interplay between fact and her fiction is irresistible to many readers and critics. The interesting part to Munro herself isn't that her work is rooted in experience, but how her art transforms the experience into something else, something bigger. In the following documents, we catch a glimpse of the method by which Munro crafts her stories out of the details of her upbringing in the small town of Windsor, Ontario, as well as appreciations of the Nobel laureate's work by Margaret Atwood, Russell Banks, and critic Brad Hooper, who argues Munro has permanently expanded the possibilities of the short story.

ALICE MUNRO

What Is Real?[1]

Whenever people get an opportunity to ask me questions about my writing, I can be sure that some of the questions asked will be these:

"Do you write about real people?"

"Did those things really happen?"

"When you write about a small town are you really writing about Wingham?" (Wingham is the small town in Ontario where I was born and grew up, and it has often been assumed, by people who should know better, that I have simply "fictionalized" this place in my work. Indeed, the local newspaper has taken me to task for making it the "butt of a soured and cruel introspection.")

The usual thing, for writers, is to regard these either as very naïve questions, asked by people who really don't understand the difference between autobiography and fiction, who can't recognize the device of the first-person narrator, or else as catch-you-out questions posed by journalists who hope to stir up exactly the sort of dreary (and to outsiders, slightly comic) indignation voiced by my home-town paper. Writers answer such questions patiently or crossly according to temperament and the mood they're in. They say, no, you must understand, my characters are composites; no, those things didn't happen the way I wrote about them; no, of course not, that isn't Wingham (or whatever other place it may be that has had the queer unsought-after distinction of hatching a writer). Or the writer may, riskily, ask the questioners what is real, anyway? None of this seems to be very satisfactory. People go on asking these same questions because the subject really does interest and bewilder them. It would seem to be quite true that they don't actually know what fiction is.

And how could they know, when what it is, is changing all the time, and we differ among ourselves, and we don't really try to explain because it is too difficult?

---

1. From *Making It New: Contemporary Canadian Stories,* ed. John Metcalf (1982).

What I would like to do here is what I can't do in two or three sentences at the end of a reading. I won't try to explain what fiction is, and what short stories are (assuming, which we can't, that there is any fixed thing that it is and they are), but what short stories are to me, and how I write them, and how I use things that are "real." I will start by explaining how I read stories written by other people. For one thing, I can start reading them anywhere; from beginning to end, from end to beginning, from any point in between in either direction. So obviously I don't take up a story and follow it as if it were a road, taking me somewhere, with views and neat diversions along the way. I go into it, and move back and forth and settle here and there, and stay in it for a while. It's more like a house. Everybody knows what a house does, how it encloses space and makes connections between one enclosed space and another and presents what is outside in a new way. This is the nearest I can come to explaining what a story does for me, and what I want my stories to do for other people.

So when I write a story I want to make a certain kind of structure, and I know the feeling I want to get from being inside that structure. This is the hard part of the explanation, where I have to use a word like "feeling," which is not very precise, because if I attempt to be more intellectually respectable I will have to be dishonest. "Feeling" will have to do.

There is no blueprint for the structure. It's not a question of, "I'll make this kind of house because if I do it right it will have this effect." I've got to make, I've got to build up, a house, a story, to fit around the indescribable "feeling" that is like the soul of the story, and which I must insist upon in a dogged, embarrassed way, as being no more definable than that. And I don't know where it comes from. It seems to be already there, and some unlikely clue, such as a shop window or a bit of conversation, makes me aware of it. Then I start accumulating the material and putting it together. Some of the material I may have lying around already, in memories and observations, and some I invent, and some I have to go diligently looking for (factual details), while some is dumped in my lap (anecdotes, bits of speech). I see how this material might go together to make the shape I need, and I try it. I keep trying and seeing where I went wrong and trying again.

I suppose this is the place where I should talk about technical problems and how I solve them. The main reason I can't is that I'm never sure I do solve anything. Even when I say that I see where I went wrong, I'm being misleading. I never figure out how I'm going to change things, I never say to myself, "That page is heavy going, that paragraph's clumsy, I need some dialogue and shorter sentences." I feel a part that's wrong, like a soggy weight; then I pay attention to the story, as if it were really happening somewhere, not just in my head, and in its own way, not mine. As a result, the sentences may indeed get shorter, there may be more dialogue, and so on. But though I've tried to pay attention to the story, I may not have got it right; those shorter sentences may be an evasion, a mistake. Every final draft, every published story, is still only an attempt, an approach, to the story.

I did promise to talk about using reality. "Why, if Jubilee isn't Wingham, has it got Shuter Street in it?" people want to know. Why have I described somebody's real ceramic elephant sitting on the mantelpiece? I could say I get momentum from doing things like this. The fictional room, town, world, needs a bit of starter dough from the real world. It's a device to help the writer—at least it helps me—but it arouses a certain baulked fury in the people who really do live on Shuter Street and the lady who owns the ceramic elephant. "Why do you put in something true and then go and tell lies?" they say, and anybody who has been on the receiving end of this kind of thing knows how they feel.

"I do it for the sake of my art and to make this structure that encloses the soul of my story, which I've been telling you about," says the writer. "That is more important than anything."

Not to everybody, it isn't.

So I can see there might be a case, once you've written the story and got the momentum, for going back and changing the elephant to a camel (though there's always a chance the lady might complain that you made a nasty camel out of a beautiful elephant), and changing Shuter Street to Blank Street. But what about the big chunks of reality, without which your story can't exist? In the story "Royal Beatings," I use a big chunk of reality: the story of the butcher, and of the young men who may have been egged on to "get" him. This is a story out of an old newspaper; it really did happen in a town I know. There is no legal difficulty about using it because it has been printed in a newspaper, and besides, the people who figure in it are all long dead. But there is a difficulty about offending people in that town who would feel that use of this story is a deliberate exposure, taunt, and insult. Other people who have no connection with the real happening would say, "Why write about anything so hideous?" And lest you think that such an objection could only be raised by simple folk who read nothing but Harlequin Romances, let me tell you that one of the questions most frequently asked at universities is, "Why do you write about things that are so depressing?" People can accept almost any amount of ugliness if it is contained in a familiar formula, as it is on television, but when they come closer to their own place, their own lives, they are much offended by a lack of editing.

There are ways I can defend myself against such objections. I can say, "I do it in the interests of historical reality. That is what the old days were really like." Or, "I do it to show the dark side of human nature, the beast let loose, the evil we can run up against in communities and families." In certain countries I could say, "I do it to show how bad things were under the old system when there were prosperous butchers and young fellows hanging around livery stables and nobody thought about building a new society." But the fact is, the minute I say *to show* I am telling a lie. I don't do it to show anything. I put this story at the heart of my story because I need it there and it belongs there. It is the black room at the centre of the house with all other rooms leading to and away from it. That is all. A strange defence. Who told me to write this story? Who feels any need of it before it is written? I do. I do, so that I might grab off this piece of horrid reality and install it where I see fit, even if Hat Nettleton and his friends were still around to make me sorry.

The answer seems to be as confusing as ever. Lots of true answers are. Yes and no. Yes, I use bits of what is real, in the sense of being really there and really happening, in the world, as most people see it, and I transform it into something that is really there and really happening, in my story. No, I am not concerned with using what is real to make any sort of record or prove any sort of point, and I am not concerned with any methods of selection but my own, which I can't fully explain. This is quite presumptuous, and if writers are not allowed to be so—and quite often, in many places, they are not—I see no point in the writing of fiction.

ALICE MUNRO

Introduction[2]

Like many writers, I get letters from people who would like some brass-tacks information. Should I consider writing as my career? some ask. How much yearly income can I expect as a writer? How much education should a writer have? Is it necessary to work on a computer? Have an agent? Associate with other writers?

Some clarifying statements about my work are requested by others. What do you consider to be your basic themes? Your major strengths/weaknesses? Why do you choose to write short stories instead of novels? Do you write from a feminist perspective, and if not, why not? How do yon feel that you contribute to the view of Canada held by a reader inside/outside the country? How has your fiction grown or progressed during your career? Do you prefer to write about relationships between people rather than important events, and if so, why? Do you prefer to write about rural and small-town people rather than sophisticated people, and if so, why? Are you a regional writer?

All this is rather flattering because it assumes that I am a person of brisk intelligence, exercising steady control on a number of fronts. I make advantageous judgments concerning computers and themes, I chart a course which is called a career and expect to make progress in it. I know what I am up to. Short stories, yes. Novels, no. I accept that rural folk are never sophisticated and sophisticates are never rural, and I make my choice. Also I keep an eye on feminism and Canada and try to figure out my duty to both.

This isn't exactly the kind of writer I'd like to be, but I wouldn't mind being a little more that way. In control, and pretty certain about what is going on, when I sit down with a pen and scribbler to do a first draft. Of course, if I was that kind of writer I might not know what a scribbler was, and I would pick up a pen only to write checks and autographs.

I am forced, in writing this introduction, to give the whole matter some thought, and I might as well start by answering a question.

I did not "choose" to write short stories. I hoped to write novels. When you are responsible for running a house and taking care of small children, particularly in the days before disposable diapers or ubiquitous automatic washing machines, it's hard to arrange for large chunks of time. A child's illness, relatives coming to stay, a pileup of unavoidable household jobs, can swallow

---

2. From "Introduction to the Vintage Edition," *Selected Stories* (1997).

a work-in-progress as surely as a power failure used to destroy a piece of work in the computer. You're better to stick with something you can keep in mind and hope to do in a few weeks, or a couple of months at most. I know that there are lots of women who have written novels in the midst of domestic challenges, just as there are men (and women) who have written them after coming home at night from exhausting jobs. That's why I thought I could do it too, but I couldn't. I took to writing in frantic spurts, juggling my life around until I could get a story done, then catching up on other responsibilities. So I got into the habit of writing short stories.

In later years my short stories haven't been so short. They've grown longer, and in a way more disjointed and demanding and peculiar. I didn't choose for that to happen, either. The only choice I make is to write about what interests me in a way that interests me, that gives me pleasure. It may not look like pleasure, because the difficulties can make me morose and distracted, but that's what it is—the pleasure of telling the story I mean to tell as wholly as I can tell it, of finding out in fact what that story is, by working around the different ways of telling it.

· · ·

In "Miles City, Montana" and "The Moons of Jupiter" I have used, with some alteration, incidents and emotions from my own family life.

· · ·

In "Royal Beatings" I turned to unacknowledged history again. Not exactly unofficial history, because the anecdote of father and daughter, the vigilante punishment handed out for suspected incest, comes right out of a nineteenth-century newspaper. But the town in which this happened, and where I grew up, now claims that no untoward incidents ever took place within its boundaries, and that prostitutes, bootleggers, and unhappy families were pretty much unknown—all being, according to an editorial in the local paper, products of my own "soured introspection."

This is all about beginnings. But that, in fact, is the easy part. Endings are another matter. When I've shaped the story in my head, before starting to put it on paper, it has, of course, an ending. Often this ending will stay in place right through the first draft. Sometimes it stays in place for good. Sometimes not. The story, in the first draft, has put on rough but adequate clothes, it is "finished" and might be thought to need no more than a lot of technical adjustments, some tightening here and expanding there, and the slipping in of some telling dialogue and chopping away of flabby modifiers. It's then, in fact, that the story is in the greatest danger of losing its life, of appearing so hopelessly misbegotten that my only relief comes from abandoning it. It doesn't do enough. It does what I intended, but it turns out that my intention was all wrong. Quite often I decide to give up on it. (This was the point at which, in my early days as a writer, I did just chuck everything out and get started on something absolutely new.) And now that the story is free from my controlling hand a change in direction may occur. I can't ever be sure this will happen, and there are bad times, though I should be used to them. I'm no good at letting go, I am thrifty and tenacious now, no spendthrift and addict of fresh starts as in my youth. I go around glum and preoccupied, trying to think of ways to fix the problem. Usually the right way pops up in the middle of this.

A big relief, then. Renewed energy. Resurrection.

Except that it isn't the right way. Maybe a way *to* the right way. Now I write pages and pages I'll have to discard. New angles are introduced, minor characters brought center stage, lively and satisfying scenes are written, and it's all a mistake. Out they go. But by this time I'm on the track, there's no backing out. I know so much more than I did, I know what I want to happen and where I want to end up and I just have to keep trying till I find the best way of getting there.

SHEILA MUNRO

From *Lives of Mothers & Daughters*[3]

As she got older, young Alice felt constantly that she was being judged as bad, that she was always in conflict with her mother. At least once a month, she got into serious trouble of some kind. And it wasn't just with her mother. "I didn't know an adult who wasn't critical of me all the time." At school she was getting in trouble for being "inept, stupid, and terribly messy." Her handwriting was so bad that one teacher called her "Uncle Wiggly." Remember how Del is shaking so badly she starts the treadle sewing machine accidentally and is exempted from sewing? That was my mother. Of course neatness and skill at needlework were more important in a girl than almost anything else in those days, though the letters from my great-grandmother do refer to my mother's triumphs at school, so it couldn't have been all bad.

At home she kept getting in trouble for those things and for everything else, for being sarcastic, for being nasty. "I always talked back. I wasn't a nice child, at that time lots of girls were nice, but being nice meant such a terrible abdication of self." (I don't want her to say this. Surely she *was* nice. I was nice. I wanted to please her. Did I abdicate *my* self?) Her earliest strategy in life was one of protecting herself, thinking her survival depended on it. She often lied and hoped not to be found out, though of course lying was considered a terrible sin.

At the time when Anne[4] was starting to get sick, overtaken by mysterious attacks of lethargy, but before she had any inkling that she was in the early stages of Parkinson's disease, she and her daughter had terrible rows, which culminated in my mother being beaten by her father, in much the same way Rose is punished in "Royal Beatings" in *Who Do You Think You Are?* The arguments between mother and daughter would escalate. My mother would refuse to back down, daring to "talk back" rather than capitulate. Finally her father would be called in from the barn, and Anne would tell her version of events. What my mother found most painful was her perception that "a story was being told on me that wasn't true" and that she was never allowed to tell her side of the story. When things got really bad, which happened two or three times a year, her father would go get his leather belt and beat her with it, exactly the way Rose's father does after Flo calls him in from the barn when she has had enough of Rose's flippancy. "'All right,' says Flo. 'You've done it this time. All right'... Rose tries to butt in, to say it isn't true." But by then it

---

3. Sheila Munro, *Lives of Mothers & Daughters: Growing Up with Alice Munro* (2001).   **4.** Anne Laidlaw, Alice's mother.

is too late. She could not write that story, another of her "breakthrough" stories, until after her father had died.

I was surprised when my mother told me about how very puritanical her family life was, and how puritanical she was herself; surprised because that isn't how I have ever seen my mother, and that is not at all what it was like in our household when I was growing up. In her home, any mention of sex was taboo, of course, and so was swearing. Alcohol was "a badge of sin." When my mother saw a bottle of whisky sitting on the kitchen counter in someone's house, she was shocked. Anyone who drank was a "scoundrel" and a "wastrel."

She was also quite a "churchmouse" who attended the Anglican Church with a friend, and found it aesthetically much more appealing than her own United Church (as Del does in *Lives*). She lost her faith when she was about twelve; every time she asked for a "sign" from God and no sign was forthcoming her faith "went down a notch." It didn't matter much because at about this time "art took over." Art became her religion.

According to my mother, Anne "was a very controlling person but her control was not just a personal control, it was the control of a moral order she believed in and projected on to others. She was full of self-assertion; she had no self-doubt and naturally she would clash with a daughter who questioned everything, who resisted any form of control." Anne's values were based on a model of gentility that came from the Victorian period. My mother considers that rural, small-town Ontario was essentially Victorian up until the Second World War, and that she grew up in the last remnants of that age.

ROBERT THACKER

From *Alice Munro: Writing Her Lives*[5]

Both "Miles City, Montana" and "Progress of Love," each drafted in the same notebook and finished about this same time, are stories close to Munro's own life. The near-drowning incident at the centre of the first is virtually memoir, the four family members who were there remembering it as narrated. Munro and her father rescuing turkeys from drowning is a memory too, but Steve Gauley, his drowning, and his funeral were imagined, though Munro recalls knowing boys who later drowned. "The Progress of Love" draws on the lives of her great-grandmother, her grandmother, and her mother while Phemie (or Fame), its narrator, includes elements of Munro herself. She is given some of Munro's own memories, certainly, but Fame is also a character offering what might have become of Munro herself had she never got away from Wingham. The narrator's perspective, like Munro's, is that of a middle-aged native. All this admitted, Munro is nevertheless right about these two stories: "not one is as close [to her life] as people seem to think." This is so because of Munro's "energy and devotion and secret pains" — they transform whatever had been remembered, whatever is "real," into the different reality that is the story's world. The story, an artifice, is able to affect its readers on its own terms by way of the words she arranges, those words that she thinks never serve her well enough.

5. Robert Thacker, *Alice Munro: Writing Her Lives* (2005).

"Miles City, Montana" and "The Progress of Love" demonstrate just how Munro's writing during this time began in actual experiences but then, through her art, became something considerably more than experience transcribed. "Miles City" seems to have begun when Munro was working on "The Beggar Maid" during 1976–77; a draft of the Miles City incident includes a courtship for the narrator and her husband Hugh similar to Rose and Patrick's. About this time too there was also the draft story, "Shoebox Babies," which Munro worked on during the late 1970s but never published and which drew from the circumstances of Catherine Munro's birth and death in July 1955. It moved into a notebook draft called just "Miles City," which contains a fairly complete rendering of the near-drowning episode and the family's trip; but rather than just the recollected dead deer the family saw when playing "I Spy" in the finished story, the older daughter recalls Elizabeth, the baby who died. This draft also includes the image of the drowned Steve Gauley being carried by the narrator's father, although it appears just at the story's end where it is connected to the narrator's misgivings about their vulnerability. Its narrator is explicitly Munro herself in 1961: "During those years I was trying to be a writer. I could say that I was trying to write — short stories, and, once, a novel — but it would be more accurate to say that I was trying to be a writer, because I felt as if I had to assemble distant parts of myself and hold them together, before I could start the actual writing. This was my job – this assembling — and it was a tricky business." Neither version includes the narrator and her father saving turkeys from drowning, an experience in the finished story that confirms the narrator's role as daughter and allows her to appreciate his hard-working way of life.

Munro's own "assembling" of "Miles City, Montana" was indeed a tricky business. It takes her memoir — the near-drowning and its circumstances — and marries it to the imagined drowning and funeral of Steve Gauley. Human helplessness in the face of death, and her parents' attitudes toward it, are felt as the narrator and Andrew talk in the aftermath. It is then she imagines what it would have been like if Meg had not been saved. "Who is ready to be a father, a mother, who is fit?" the narrator asks in the draft, just before she shifts back to Steve Gauley's drowning and his funeral, asking the central unanswerable question of "Miles City, Montana." And though Munro omitted any direct reference to Catherine Munro's death in the final version, it is felt on the page, created there in Munro's sensed and mediated human vulnerability.

So while it is possible to see Jenny Munro's near-drowning in 1961 in Miles City, Montana, at the centre of the story, to insist on that incident's recounting as the story's core misses the point of any fiction, and of Munro's in particular. What she creates on the page is the feeling of being, the feeling of authentic experience captured through words. This writing has a kind of purity when it works — as it most certainly does in "Miles City, Montana" and in "The Progress of Love." Yet any created purity is not just in the story's details, since those may be grafted on from anywhere (the swimming pool in Miles City, Montana, for example, was not a swimming pool but a man-made body called Scanlon Lake). Their connection to Munro's own life, while real, is secondary to anyone reading a story that emerges from such connections. For Munro, and for her readers too, the significance of any autobiographical connection comes back to the image of Cynthia and Meg, still in their back seat, still headed to Ontario, still expecting to return home to Vancouver: "So we went on, with the two in the back seat trusting us, because of no choice, and we ourselves trusting to be forgiven, in time, for everything that had first to be seen and condemned by those children: whatever was flippant, arbitrary, careless, callous — all our natural, and particular, mistakes."

MARGARET ATWOOD

An Appreciation[6]

The fifties were a very male period of writing in the United States. America didn't have a tradition of women writers. Who, among women, were admired? Eudora Welty, Katherine Anne Porter. Among poets? Emily Dickinson. How many others? In Canada, you didn't get points off for being a woman. The challenge wasn't so much being female as it was being Canadian. Embroidery, oil painting, writing, it was all considered a hobby. Writing wasn't important. There was hardly a market for new novels. The writing community up here was so small at that time. Because of readings and little magazines, poets knew one another's work, but it was different for prose writers in Canada.

When we were growing up the idea of being a writer was so alien. Just to think you could do it was an act of major hubris. Talent was discouraged. Yet as a child, Alice had read L. M. Montgomery's *Anne of Green Gables* and *Emily of New Moon*, about a young girl growing up on Prince Edward Island who wants to be a writer. Alice has written an afterword for the latter book.

Two other early influences on her were *Wuthering Heights* and *Pride and Prejudice*. In *Wuthering Heights* you never hear the story directly from the most powerful people in it. You hear it from the observers: a gentleman named Lockwood, who rents Thrushcross Grange, and Nelly, the housekeeper. This is a very interesting way of putting a book together. Also, there are the two houses. There are the Lintons, who are genteel—not forceful and not sexy. And then there's Heathcliff. *Pride and Prejudice* is another very well put together book that draws on the emotions we love so much, and there's Mr. Darcy, another rude man with lots of money underneath. And economics is such a big factor in Alice's work. Who's got money, who hasn't, who needs money, who's making it, and who's paying for things.

Her other influences were writers of stories set in small towns. Alice read Sherwood Anderson—who made her feel that maybe she could do this kind of thing—as well as Eudora Welty, Flannery O'Connor, and Carson McCullers. Having grown up in a small town herself, Alice knows them well—specifically, small towns in southwestern Ontario. Why are there so many crazy, demented people in a small town? It's just that everyone knows everyone and one another's background. Like a big, dysfunctional family. It's that way in cities, too, but you don't necessarily know about all of it, because you may not know the people across the street, or even next door. In small towns people are con-

6. From "Appreciations of Alice Munro," *Virginia Quarterly Review*, Summer 2006.

scious of gossip, rumor, the keeping up of pretenses, and the varying gradations of social level. It can be confining.

That's why Alice's stories are so place- and time-specific. What people eat,
what they wear, what appliances they are using, are all important to her. She
is interested in questions of authenticity; she looks at her characters' fronts
and pretensions, at what effect they are trying to achieve, and then she examines what lies underneath. Maybe the characters see through each other, and
so they have social lies, such as, "You look terrific." Sometimes they mean it
benignly; sometimes they don't.

She writes about the difficulties faced by people who are bigger or smaller
than they are expected to be. When her protagonists look back, from later
points of view, the older people they have become possess within them all of
the people that they have been. She's very good on what people expect, and
then on the letdown.

One of the many things Alice does so well is to contrast how people thought
something would be, compared to how it turned out. We depend on a certain
amount of fulfilled expectation. The sun will rise in the morning. Mr. Brown
will be at the corner store at 8 A.M. and sell milk. In Alice Munro stories, people
go into a house and find out that someone has been murdered. Every expectation is met; and then, there is an event, a surprise—and that's the story.

RUSSELL BANKS

An Appreciation[7]

There is nothing exotic or off-putting in the opening paragraph or two of an
Alice Munro story. The author puts her hand on your shoulder and invites
you into her fictional world. She is friendly, and there is a neighborly quality
to her narrative prose. She starts in a small place and universalizes characters
and lives that we might otherwise overlook. It is as if you are sitting at a table,
and she's going to tell you a story of what happened a while back, down the
street. Her intimate tone is interesting and immediate, and she is relaxed,
calm, even inactive, almost seductive. Then, once you are in this fictional world,
it becomes more threatening.

You realize there are issues of life and death going on, and Munro's fiction
takes hard swerves abruptly. She is able to break off narrative then start it up
later, and it's still connected. We can travel through time and space and point
of view, shifting our relation to time and space, so we're closer in, or further
away. Most contemporary short fiction writers capture moments in time, but
Munro telescopes backward and forward. Usually this is only seen in novels.

What this does for us is to stretch the range of the dramatic possibility
of the short story, which in the hands of US writers has gone minimalist,
become reductive and compressed. Munro's fiction expands outward, and it
shows us that while the short story form can be as compressed and hard as a
diamond, it can also be as expansive as a novel.

She is almost a cubist. That's the way memory works and storytelling
goes. It's not mathematics, it's not logic. It's remembering and recounting
through memory what happened. This is also the way dreams work. Often

7. From "Appreciations of Alice Munro," *Virginia Quarterly Review*, Summer 2006.

good fiction corresponds closely to the structure of dreams, but it is aesthetically and morally purposeful. Munro has the great moral force and intelligence to refuse to judge or idealize her characters, which would be easy to do, and she won't allow her readers to do so either. Alice Munro's writing casts her as someone who dares to speak the truth about the world, to say the things that we are ashamed or afraid to tell.

BRAD HOOPER

An Appreciation[8]

Munro has modified the short story to suit her own interests, needs, and capabilities, and the short-story genre will remain modified from her efforts. There will always be, now, the Munro-type of short story; and it will be referred to as such. And I do not mean a brand of short story that is simply idiosyncratic to her, which was exercised by her alone. No, I mean a permanent opening of the genre to possibilities—expansion possibilities, primarily—that authors after her can explore for their own purposes.

Munro has not simply taken care of the short story; it has not been up to her, nor has she been inclined to shoulder the responsibility, to maintain its conventions, set them down again intact, after her use of them is done, and send the short story on its way in a healthy condition but still in a traditional form. She has broadened the scope of what defines a short story but by following only the strictest procedures in opening the story form while *keeping* it the short-story form, not calling her product short stories when they are in fact underdeveloped novels. I insist upon this: she writes short stories, not short novels.

It is the resonance of what is on the page that gives her stories the experience of a novel; there is nothing condensed in her stories, only expanded by the universalities she touches upon in the particulars of her stories. That is the essence of a Munro short story, the fundamental process of her technique and the gist of her reader's appeal.

Many instances have been cited in the course of my analysis of her work of her use of first-person narrative; one finds, particularly in the first half of her oeuvre, this is almost exclusively her narrative technique. It is a choice for a reason; it makes no difference whether the narrator proves prejudiced, naive, uninformed, or one-sided, for the point of this narrative technique is to eliminate detachment, to make her stories as personal as possible, to bring her characters to the reader as real as they can be. But not only has Munro claimed the first-person narrative voice as her own, but she has also, as she has adapted the short-story structure to her own needs and interests, adapted it well to suit her purposes. She often uses the technique of first-person narrator narrating from the perspective of many years after the events being recalled as her way of having the narrator reconcile his or her (most often the latter, of course) past to his or her present: not only to see it through the clarifying lens of many years standing between the past and present, but also to help read the past as meaningful provenance of the present.

---

8. From *The Fiction of Alice Munro: An Appreciation* (2008).

Of course, no adequately comprehensive discussion of Munro's fiction can fail to bring into the light her use of, her abiding interest in, the past: not so much the historical past, although that occasionally does play a role, at least as a backdrop to her characters' *personal* past. To be specific—to be accurate— her stories are not so much set in the past as they are remembrance pieces "about" the past, glances backward functioning to explore the present. Conversely, very little in a Munro story is about *just* the present; the past is always present in her stories, which, of course is a main reason for the depths to which her fiction goes in exploration of character. The result is her fiction's intense resonance, the profound analysis of a character that at once defines the character as an individual, yet binds that character to the general human condition with whom all readers can connect.

A corollary theme to the theme of the influence of the past on the present, around which many of her stories are constructed, is the "outsider" consciousness. As observed on numerous occasions, Munro's stories, protagonists frequently feel, are outside the mainstream in socioeconomic and, in the case of schoolgirls, "coolness" terms. The outsider theme is often played out in gender situations: girls and women who don't want to practice/perform traditional female roles. They are not so much in rebellion against accepted practices as simply uninterested. They stand outside, looking in, but not willing to be part of the accepted "crowd." A sub theme, a logical extension of it, or even a refinement of it, is the functioning of the adolescent female narrator as a bridge between the traditional male and female spheres of interest and endeavor; these situations—these that spring from this particular sub theme—offer some of the most intriguing, resonant, reader-appealing stories in all her oeuvre, for who cannot identify with an adolescent lack of desire to fit into neat and tidy boxes? Or, better stated: who, even if they did not experience such lack of interest in resisting the traces of tradition when they were adolescents, cannot understand Munro's characters going through such a psychological process? That is a strong testament to her ability to create characters perfectly comprehensible even to readers with whom they share not much in terms of gender, background, or life pursuits.

That brings us to the major conclusion that must be drawn—given the course that this critical survey has taken—about Munro as a fiction writer. She has moved the boundaries, the dimensions, the techniques in composing the short story beyond traditional methods and expectations, yes. But as I stated in the Introduction, all of that was in service to a higher, more personal objective for her: to achieve a deeper understanding of her characters. Her "invention," if you will, of the Munro short story was not intentional as a goal unto itself; it simply was the by-product of her magnificently achieved goal of building a character within the parameters of the short-story form.

Author in Depth: Joyce Carol Oates

It has become a cliché to talk about Joyce Carol Oates's prolific career, but her astounding oeuvre offers a continuous document of the writer working, reacting, and searching through the events and concerns of seemingly every year, month, and perhaps day of the last fifty years: a constant work in progress, a continual search for meaning. Oates's enviable output extends not just to her fiction, but is also manifest in her criticism and remarks on craft. Collected here is a snapshot of her critical work: essays and reflections on her writing process, the concerns of her work and of fiction broadly, as well as two scholarly criticisms of her work, including one of the pieces featured in this anthology, "How I Contemplated the World . . ."

JOYCE CAROL OATES

The Art and the Craft of Revision[1]

> The last thing one settles in writing . . . is what one should
> put in first.
>
> —*Blaise Pascal*

The advantage of writing over living is self-evident: writing can be revised, living cannot. For the serious writer, writing *is* revising. The writer who is impatient with revision, for all his or her natural gifts, will be disadvantaged; for, however good the work, it isn't so good as it might have been. Any artist who is impatient with revision is probably doomed to be forever an amateur: "promising" through a lifetime.

Writers are fascinated by early drafts and revisions of others' work. Unless one is Mozart or Shakespeare, gifted with a quicksilver ability to create art of surpassing genius without, evidently, toiling over it, one will have to revise, rework, reconsider—sometimes rewrite completely. And sometimes discard that which one has been working on with such hope and diligence.

We write in order to read what we've written in order to have the experience of reading: a mystery. Yet we're immersed in the mystery of why, out of the world's teeming billions, only each one of us, only the individual, could have created this singular work of art. We don't know what we've written until we read it through as a reader, expelled from the process of the work, and no longer as a writer enthralled by its creation. Sometimes it startles us—it reads so much more swiftly and smoothly than we'd dare to imagine. Sometimes it shocks us—it isn't what we'd meant to write at all but leaden, misconceived, *wrong*.

But only until we've read what we've been working to create do we understand, as Pascal says, what we should put in first. Sometimes we learn that the entire effort might be better discarded. This is a hurtful revelation, and some

---

1. From *Telling Stories: An Anthology for Writers*, 1998.

might wish valiantly to deny it; but like all genuine revelations, it is likely to be illuminating, and cleansing.

Students quickly learn, in workshops, that fiction writing is a process. The process may result in a product, or products; but it's the process in which one lives, and thinks, hour following hour, day following day. This process is not in any way alienated from or even detached from "life": it *is* life, as integral to life as eating, dreaming, breathing. Similarly, a work of art is not separate from or in opposition to or a mere "metaphor" for life: it *is* life, as rightfully in existence as any object, person, event.

Fiction and poetry workshops, like all courses in composition, music, art, dance, and theater, are for works-in-progress, works-in-process. The young (or not-young) writer who imagines that his work is already perfect has no need of a workshop, nor would anyone want this individual in one. In matters of art-in-process, in workshop situations in which criticism (of a constructive kind solely) is offered, it is wisest to leave one's ego at the door. The writer who imagines she hasn't any ego, or can easily control her ego, will soon discover otherwise. The more urgent the admonition, then: *leave one's ego at the door.*

JOYCE CAROL OATES

From *The Nature of Short Fiction; or, The Nature of My Short Fiction*[2]

We write in order to give a more coherent, abbreviated form to the world, which is often confusing and terrifying and stupid as it unfolds about us. How to manage this blizzard of days, of moments, of years? The world has no meaning; I am sadly resigned to this fact. But the world has meanings, many individual and alarming and graspable meanings, and the adventure of being human consists in seeking out these meanings. We want to figure out as much of life as we can. We are not very different from scientists, our notorious enemies, who want also to figure things out, to make life more coherent, to set something in order and then go on to something else, erasing mysteries. We write in order to single out meanings from the great confusion of the time, or of our lives: we write because we are convinced that meaning exists and we want to fix it in place.

• • •

Why do you write? To seek out the meanings of life, which are hidden. This is a possible answer, a pleasing, optimistic answer, though perhaps Faustian. I always take my materials from ordinary life. I am greatly interested in the newspapers and in the Ann Landers' columns and in *True Confessions* and in the anecdotes told under the guise of "gossip." Amazing revelations! The world is filled with revelations, with tragedies—go at once to the newspaper and look at page five or page nineteen and let your eye become drawn to a headline, any headline; here is a story. I can't begin to count the stories I have written that are based on the barest newspaper accounts . . . it is the very skeletal nature of the newspaper, I think, that attracts me to it, the need it inspires in me to give flesh to such neatly and thinly-told tales, to resurrect this event which has already become history and will never be understood unless it is

---

2. From *Joyce Carol Oates: A Study of the Short Fiction*, ed. Greg Johnson (1994).

re-lived, re-dramatized. From the fragment of someone's life that is represented in a newspaper story the writer is drawn to reconstruct the entire object. It is like finding a single piece of a jigsaw puzzle on the floor . . . with a little effort you can reconstruct the whole, why not? Or perhaps you will imagine a better whole than the "real" one. Why not?

Therefore, art "dreams" or hallucinates, broods, upon what is given in reality. An overheard remark, a sudden stabbing emotion, a sense of dismay, a sense of anger, a story in *True Confessions* that reads exactly like a nightmare: these are our materials. I don't want to write anything that couldn't have been written, first, for *True Confessions*. I don't want to write anything that couldn't have been sung, in some form, as a ballad, that barest and most dramatic of art forms, a dream hardly made into art. Critical writing intrigues me just as intellectual men intrigue me, perhaps to folly, and I can't resist matching my wits with those of other writers, analyzing and exploring their works, trying to make sense of them—but the gravest and most sacred task is not criticism, but art, and art may be easier to achieve.

• • •

All art is meaningful. Its meaning may be in the violent, rather vicious *process* by which it is created—let us say the paintings of Pollock or de Kooning—or it may be in the more traditional texture of the work itself, spelled out, so that a student may underline *Live all you can; it's a mistake not to* (in James' *The Ambassadors*) and feel that he is getting the "meaning" of the work, without double-talk. The "meaning" of *Moby Dick* is located not just in the famous chapter on the White Whale, but in all the chapters—the tedious ones as well as the dramatic ones—the entire work adding up to its meaning, which is the exploration of reality by Melville.

And so, *Why do you write?* To answer this distinguished question once again: we write because we are ordained to a noble task, that of making clear mysteries, or pointing out mysteries where a numbing and inaccurate simplicity has held power. We write to be truthful to certain facts, certain emotions. We write to "explain" apparently crazy actions . . . why does an intelligent young man go beserk and kill, why does a happy woman ruin her life by running away with someone, why does a well-adjusted person commit suicide? I confess that I am old-fashioned, conventional. I look and behave in a conventional manner and the stimulus behind my writing is conventional, not weird. I am fascinated by weird structures and points of view, and if I could I would tell a story hanging upside-down, or in three columns at once, but really behind all my meek extravaganza is a simple desire to make sense . . . I want to know the *why* behind human emotions, even if I can only say again and again that human emotions are our deepest mystery and there is no understanding them. I am less interested in technical gimmicks that explore the flat surface of the page, emphasizing its unreality (the works of Beckett, for instance, which mock the very process of writing), though certainly cubist and abstract artists have made beautiful things out of the canvas as canvas instead of the canvas as mirror. But mere intellect to me, as a woman, is quickly tiring; if a story is only intelligent, might it not be better as an essay or a letter to the editor? I am preoccupied with verbs that go nowhere except to suggest the fluid nature of the world we inhabit.

• • • •

As to the nature of short fiction? There is no nature to it, but only natures. Different natures. Just as we all have different personalities, so the dreams of our personalities will be different. There are no rules to help us. There used to be a rule—"Don't be boring!"—but that has been by-passed; today writers like Beckett and Albee and Pinter are deliberately boring (though perhaps they succeed more than they know) and anything goes. Outrageous exaggeration. Outrageous understatement. Very short scenes, very long scenes . . . cinematic flashes and impressions, long introspective passages in the manner of Thomas Mann: anything. There is no particular length, certainly, to the short story or to the novel. I believe that any short story can become a novel, and any novel can be converted back into a short story or into a poem. Reality is fluid and monstrous; let us package it in as many shapes as possible, put names on it, publish it in hard-cover. Let us make films of it. Let us declare that everything is sacred and therefore material for art—or, perhaps, nothing is sacred, nothing can be left alone.

The amateur writer wants to write of great things, serious themes. Perhaps he has a social conscience! But there are no "great" things but only great treatments. All themes are serious, or foolish. There are no rules. We are free. Miracles are in the wings, in the ink of unopened typewriter ribbons, craving release. I tell my students to write of their true subjects. How will they know when they are writing of their true subjects? By the ease with which they write. By their reluctance to stop writing. By the headachy, even guilty, joyous sensation of having done something that must be done, having confessed emotions thought unconfessable, having said what had seemed should remain unsaid. If writing is difficult, stop writing. Begin with another subject. The true subject writes itself, it cannot be silenced. Give shape to your dreams, your day-dreams, cultivate your day-dreams and their secret meanings will come out. If you feel that sitting blankly and staring out the window is sinful, then you will never write, and why write anyway? If you feel that sitting in a daze, staring at the sky or at the river, is somehow a sacred event, that your deepest self is pleased by it, then perhaps you are a writer or a poet and in time you will try to communicate your feelings.

Writers write, eventually; but first they feel.

A marvelous life.

JOYCE CAROL OATES

From *Fiction, Dreams, Revelations*[3]

All art is autobiographical. It is the record of an artist's psychic experience, his attempt to explain something to himself: and in the process of explaining it to himself, he explains it to others. When a work of art pleases us it is often because it recounts for us an experience close to our own, something we can recognize. And so we "like" the artist, because he is so human.

But there are works of art that explain nothing, that dispel order and sanity; works of art that contradict our experience and are therefore deeply offensive to us; works of art that refuse to make sense, that are perhaps dangerous because they are unforgettable. Picasso tells us that "Art is a lie that

---

3. From *Joyce Carol Oates: A Study of the Short Fiction*, ed. Greg Johnson (1994).

leads to the truth," and we understand by this paradox that a lie can make us see the truth, a lie can illuminate the truth for us, a lie—especially an extravagant, gorgeous lie—can make us sympathize with a part of the truth that we had always successfully avoided. Instinctively, we want either lies that we can know as lies, or truth that we can know as truth. A newspaper in the mid-South declares bluntly: "We Print Only the Truth—No Fiction." But the two are hopeless mixed together, mysteriously confused. Nothing human is simple.

Every person dreams, and every dreamer is a kind of artist. The formal artist is one who arranges his dreams into a shape that can be experienced by other people. There is no guarantee that art will be understood, not even by the artist; it is not meant to be understood but to be experienced. Emotions flow from one personality to another, altering someone's conception of the world: this is the moment of art, the magical experience of art. It is a revelation. This impact of another personality upon us—our terrible, reluctant, unavoidable acknowledgment of another person, other people, all the consciousness outside ourselves that we cannot control and cannot possess, despite our deepest wishes—all that is humanly sacred is present in this exchange, which is art.

JOYCE CAROL OATES

Why Is Your Writing So Violent?[4]

It was on a chill but sunny May morning in 1980 in an antiquated auditorium of steeply tiered seats at the University of Warsaw that the question was asked of me by an earnest young man of about 25, who, like most of the Poles we met, spoke excellent English: Why was my writing so violent? Might it be that my "personal experience," "perhaps my childhood" and, in any case, my "unique temperament" had so "distorted" my vision of mankind and of history that the fiction of "Joyce Carol Oates" represented only an "extreme attitude," unfortunately prevalent in contemporary American literature?

That this familiar question was asked of me in Warsaw, where in September of 1944 the insurrection against the Germans by the Polish underground had begun, with the eventual consequence that 200,000 Poles were slaughtered; that this question was asked of me in a city blown up by the departing German Army (the Red Army having discreetly paused on the banks of the Vistula to allow five weeks of destruction before crossing to "liberate" what remained of Warsaw); that it was asked of me with a hint of reproach that clearly resonated throughout the crowded gathering struck me as so painful and so ironic and so dispiriting and, in a sad way, so amusing that I could only offer some judiciously chosen and diplomatic words in response.

"Why do you focus on the violent?" The question was asked in Oslo, in Helsinki, in Brussels, in Budapest and in that dramatically "Western" city in Eastern Europe known for its encircling wall. Text: In West Berlin the question was asked with great courtesy and tact, not many miles from where Adolf Hitler proclaimed the Second World War and Dr. Goebbels advanced the notion of "total war." This time the question came with the thoughtful addendum that perhaps my "vision" as a "novelist" had been much influenced by the fact that I had lived for many years in Detroit, Mich (which

---

4. From "An Author's Answer: Why Is Your Writing So Violent?," *The New York Times*, March 29, 1981.

appears to have the reputation throughout the world of being a "violent city").

"You had an unhappy childhood, Miss Oates?"—asked with quizzical smiles, some measure of pity, sympathy. "You were often frightened by life?"

What are we to make of the stubborn bitter truth that one's legitimacy is judged by whether one appears to be "happy" or "unhappy"; that one's work is somehow assessed in terms of the spiritual uplift it offers? "Happiness" is predicated as a cultural norm, so that any deviation from it, however justified, however inescapable, arouses not only pity but reproach. As true as this might be for male writers, it is all the more true for female writers, since there is a violation of some unspoken rule in the very fact that a woman writes— that is, thinks.

It was once put to me directly, and no doubt has often been suggested by indirection, that I should focus my writing on "domestic" and "subjective" material, in the manner (for instance) of Jane Austen or Virginia Woolf, that I should leave large social-philosophical issues to men. The implication is that if Jane Austen and Virginia Woolf had lived in Detroit, they might have been successful in "transcending" their environment and writing novels in which not a hint of "violence" could be detected. Woolf might have been tremulous, quivering with sensitive insights, and not distracted by the vicissitudes of the world around her; Austen might have been arch and amusing and "delight-ful," and fit to be read by virtually anyone. If they successfully resisted writing about large "social issues" in their own times, it is implied, surely they would not have failed in this new and challenging context, and "femininity" would not have to be despoiled.

The question is always insulting. The question is always ignorant. The question is always sexist. We seem to have inherited, along with its two or three blessings, the manifold curse of psychoanalysis: the assumption that the grounds of discontent, anger, rage, despair—"unhappiness" in general— reside within the sufferer rather than outside of him. Psychoanalysis maintains that if the Oedipal aggressions of the male are a function merely of the domestic triangle, arising ineluctably out of the "family romance," so too are the female emotions—with the added embarrassment that the female is doomed to the greater imperfection of being both non-male and presumably resentful as a consequence of this condition. Aggression, discontent, rebellious urges, a sense of injustice—these have nothing to do with the outer world, but only with the sufferer; and if the sufferer is a woman, by definition a creature characterized by envy, how is it possible to take her seriously? The territory of the female artist should be the subjective, the domestic. She is allowed to be "charming," "amusing," "delightful." Her models should not be Shakespeare or Dostoyevsky but one or another woman writer. Her skills should be those of a conscientious seamstress.

"Why is your writing so violent?" Since it is commonly understood that serious writers, as distinct from entertainers or propagandists, take for their natural subjects the complexity of the world, its evils as well as its goods, it is always an insulting question; and it is always sexist.

The serious writer, after all, bears witness. The serious writer restructures "reality" in the service of his or her art, and surely hopes for a unique esthetic vision and some felicity of language; but reality is always the foundation, just as the alphabet, in whatever motley splendor, is the foundation of "Finnegans Wake." (The claustrophobic nature of self-referential art is, perhaps, a paradigm of the infant's world: Nothing objective is grasped as real, everything refers inward, words appear to be created, enhanced with private meanings. Hence such an artist's contempt for "real" worlds and the sentimental hope for a forcible remaking of the universe—as if there were not a universe in existence beyond the artist's control.) So the serious male writer is allowed his vision and takes as his rightful subject a world as vast as Dostoyevsky's Russia, or Melville's oceans or Faulkner's "postage stamp of earth" in Mississippi. One does not inquire of them, "Why is your writing so violent?"

If the lot of womankind has not yet widely diverged from that romantically envisioned by our Moral Majority and by the late Adolf Hitler ("Kirche, Kinder, Küchen"), the lot of the woman writer has been just as severely circumscribed. War, rape, murder and the more colorful minor crimes evidently fall within the exclusive province of the male writer, just as, generally, they fall within the exclusive province of male action.

Occasionally, however, a woman writer is told gravely, "You write like a man." Since this is the highest accolade, presented as a judgment from above and closed to any further discussion, it would be impolite to ask, "Which man? Any man? You?"

"Why is your writing so violent?" The question was asked in Liege, in Hamburg, in London, in Detroit, in New York City. It would be asked in China if I went to China. It would be asked in Moscow. In Hiroshima.

When I point out that, in fact, my writing isn't usually explicitly violent, but deals, most of the time, with the phenomenon of violence and its aftermath, in ways not unlike those of the Greek dramatists; when I point out that, in any case, writing is language and, in a very important sense, is more "about" language than "about" a subject—the interviewer will nod, and take notes, and inquire about my childhood: "Was it tragic? Have you been frightened by life?"

In recent years a variant has been added: How do I defend myself against "critical charges" that my writing is "violent"? How can I "justify" myself?

"Would you ask that question of a male writer," I responded, the last time it was put to me, not very long ago. After some hesitation, the answer came: "No." "Why not?" I asked. Herewith, a long pause ensued. My interrogator knew the answer to the question but declined to answer it. Or perhaps he was thinking. I hope he still is.

JOYCE CAROL OATES

From *American Literary Culture: A Personal Perspective*[5]

For fiction writers who began publishing or who came of literary age in the 1960s (a wonderfully variegated generation-and-a-half that includes E. L. Doctorow. Toni Morrison, Robert Stone, Thomas Pynchon, Robert Coover, Joan Didion, John Gregory Dunne, John Updike, Philip Roth, Russell Banks, Don DeLillo. Ishmael Reed, Jerome Charyn, Alice Walker, Charles Johnson, Joy Williams, T. Coraghessan Boyle, Marge Piercy, Paul Theroux, the late

---

5. From *Openings: Original Essays by Contemporary Soviet and American Writers* (1990).

John Gardner and Raymond Carver, and many others) the seething richness of American society provided us with irresistibly dramatic "historical" material; and individual dissension within society provided numberless aesthetic strategies for expressing that material.

To live, for example, as I did, in Detroit, Michigan, in the 1960s—Detroit, a city billed as both "Automotive Capital of the World" and "Murder City, USA," and the setting of the 1968 riots—was to find myself not only provided with but hardly able to ignore the immediacy of drama, social conflict, tragedy, tragi-comedy . . . the opportunity of realizing firsthand a virtual allegory of American experience. The city of Detroit in its myriad aspects became for me a region of symbolic luminosities: it was itself, of course, uniquely and irreducibly so, but it was also far more—an emblem of American ambition. American delusion. American strife. American hopes, American violence. American dreams-gone-wrong.

Though I was writing and publishing before I came to live in Detroit in 1962, it was only in this city that I conceived of a personal body of literature in which the unique and the emblematic might be conjoined; and the private, the domestic, the idiosyncratic yoked to larger social and political concerns (in such Detroit-set novels as *them* and *Do With Me What You Will*, and such historically focused novels as *Angel of Light*, *Wonderland*, and *You Must Remember This*). So, too, have such writers as E. L. Doctorow. Robert Coover, Robert Stone, and Russell Banks, among others, realized the complexity of their "political" material by way of individual participatory experience.

For instance, E. L. Doctorow took for his subject the divisive domestic politics of the 1960s, culminating in the persecution and execution of the Rosenbergs, in the novel many readers consider his finest, *The Book of Daniel*; Robert Coover surrealistically reimagined the moral chaos of that era in *The Public Burning*—in which Julius and Ethel Rosenberg are publicly executed, with a narration by Richard Nixon; Don DeLillo in his recent *Libra* reimagined, by way of the Warren Report, the events leading up to and surrounding the assassination of President John F. Kennedy; Robert Stone, Joan Didion, Russell Banks, and others, were analyzing American involvement in Central, Latin, and Carribean American politics years before these politics erupted into tragic headlines.

• • •

Ours is recognized as a violent society; or, at the very least, a society that openly airs, discusses, and analyzes its violence. A number of American writers of the generation I have been discussing have been charged with "excessive" violence in their work and with a presumably un-American pessimism. The woman writer who ventures into the political or social sphere is often a special target, for [women] writers are perceived as doubly intrusive: as writers, and as women. (I choose to bracket [woman] writer because the writer who is a woman, while perceiving herself as a writer, foremost, and not gender-determined in her art, is nonetheless perceived by others as a woman primarily, and a writer secondarily: thus, [woman] writer. An ontological paradox, for of course there are no [men] writers, only writers—who are men.)

Yet to be possessed by what might be called a tragic sense of life does not mean that one is indifferent to other interpretations, even the comic; there are, in life, happy endings—as often as not. But from a historical perspective it seems more realistic to view the manifold strivings of civilization as essentially tragic in outline, because so frequently bellicose, self-serving, and self-defeating. Within this context one is likely to be more impressed with the fortitude, resilience, and occasional nobility of human beings when, as individuals, they are put to the test; when by accident or design they are in a position to grow into what they are in embryo. Consequently, in tragic art the focus is upon moments of crisis, not harmony; it is in the fissures of happiness that strength of character asserts itself. From this perspective, the tragic view of life may in fact be the most idealistic. And, as Flannery O'Connor once observed, no writer is a pessimist. The very act of writing is an act of hope.

Postwar American generations differ from previous generations in that we are constantly aware of—indeed, some of our ranks are obsessed by—the possibility of an end: of The End. A generation of children, of which I was one, was baptized into a collective, thus involuntary, sense of mortality in the early 1950s, when atomic bomb drills were routine schoolday exercises under the aegis of the Civil Defense Bureau in Washington, D.C. How like a child's game, the name of this drill: "duck-and-cover"! Like fires, for which fire drills were logical preparations, atomic bomb attacks on America were perceived as not only likely but highly probable. The question was, when? And, who would survive?

Thus, an entire subcategory of mid- and late twentieth-century American literature can be titled the Literature of Paranoia, some of it immensely ambitious, reticulated, and blackly comic.

SUE SIMPSON PARK

From *A Study in Counterpoint*[6]

The title itself, with its seventeen words, suggests a departure from the conventional practice of relatively short titles. The headnote for the story provides a further hint as to the experimental quality of what is to follow: "Notes for an essay for an English class at Baldwin Country Day School; poking around in debris; disgust and curiosity; a revelation of the meaning of life; a happy ending. . . ." A prefiguration of the contrapuntal nature of the story is evident in these preliminaries: on the one hand, the abstractions of contemplation, revelation, the meaning of life, beginning life over again; on the other, the tangibility of the Detroit House of Correction and an English class at Baldwin Country Day School.

When the events of the story are arranged chronologically, what emerges is this: A fifteen-year-old girl from a wealthy family steals a pair of gloves from a department store, even though she has money—"bills, she doesn't know how many bills" in her purse. The store detective stops her, someone notifies her parents, her physician father talks to the owner of the store, and no charges are filed. The girl's mother takes her shopping in an attempt to understand the actions; the girl is apathetic, thinking but not saying aloud, "I wanted to steal but not to buy." Weeks later, the girl leaves school in midafternoon and takes a bus to downtown Detroit. There she is taken in by a prostitute, lives

6. Sue Simpson Park, "A Study in Counterpoint: Joyce Carol Oates's 'How I Contemplated the World from the Detroit House of Correction and Began My Life Over Again.'" *Modern Fiction Studies* 22, no. 2 (Summer 1976) 213–224.

with her and her lover Simon, participates in sexual relations with Simon and with men Simon brings in. Someone, she thinks Simon, turns her in to the authorities as a minor and she is taken to the Detroit House of Correction, where she is most uncooperative and refuses to give any information as to her past or her identity, vowing she will never return home. Then, one night, two girls beat her severely, she is hospitalized, and her father takes her home— back to school, with twice-weekly appointments with a female psychiatrist. Now sixteen, she sits in her pink room on Sioux Drive in Bloomfield Hills and makes notes for an essay for her English class.

The "notes for an essay" are presented in twelve divisions marked with Roman numerals. At first glance, one surmises from the form that this is the work of a careful student, arranging material in an orderly fashion (twelve sections, reminiscent of *The Aeneid, Paradise Lost,* and such novels as James's *The Ambassadors,* a year's installments) for the purpose of organizing experience into a coherent system. Such an assumption, however, is erroneous, for the divisions do not constitute a topical outline; neither are they chronological. Instead, they are repetitive, disjointed, and dispersive—in other words, indicative of the state of mind of the sixteen-year-old protagonist, confused, questioning, attempting to make sense of the senseless to impose order upon chaos.

The major divisions are these:

I	Events
II	Characters
III	World Events
IV	People & Circumstances Contributing to This Delinquency
V	Sioux Drive
VI	Detroit
VII	Events
VIII	Characters
IX	That Night
X	Detroit
XI	Characters We Are Forever Entwined With
XII	Events

Three divisions are labeled "Events"—the first, the seventh, and the twelfth. Hence the story begins, centers, and ends in recollected action; and action at least is relatively unequivocal, however ambiguous the motives behind the action. Two other sections are linked to events—section III, "World Events," the total content of which is the single word "Nothing," and section IX, "That Night," a brief description (five sentences, two of which are short questions) of the beating which sent the girl to the hospital.

Three divisions are labeled "characters." Sections II and VIII follow immediately "event" divisions, and XI, with the amplified heading, "Characters We Are Forever Entwined With," immediately precedes the final "event" division. Section IV seems to link together the idea of characters ("people") and events ("circumstances"), but again the entire section consists of one word, "Nothing."

The remaining three divisions are basically descriptive: V, a picture of Sioux Drive, and VI and X, brief delineations of Detroit. Thus it appears that the girl is trying to organize her material around three points, possibly suggested by her English teacher. Events, Characters, and Places are the local points of her outline, but there is no intrinsic order to the arrangement of points; it is random, apparently unpurposeful. What knits the scraps of information together into a movingly effective totality is not the protagonist's pathetic effort to establish meaningful continuity, but the artist's skillful interweaving of motifs and verbal echoes.

Basic to the ultimate unity of the story is a pattern of contrasts. The title and the headnote suggest this contrapuntal interplay; the story elaborates upon the suggestion. Bloomfield Hills is contrasted with inner-city Detroit, the girl's mother with the prostitute Clarita, the girl's father with the procurer-addict Simon. The differences are vast—and yet in each case the contrast is intensified by a curious and significant identity. But most important is the duality of the girl herself.

The pattern of contrasts is established by unlike settings. Bloomfield Hills is an exclusive suburb with "monumental houses" located on curving lanes with such names as Sioux Drive and Burning Bush Way and Du Maurier Drive and Lois Lane. There are no prosaic "streets" in Bloomfield Hills. The houses are Georgian and Colonial and French-Normandy, imitations of other cultures and other times, with columns and baywindows and "fireplaces in living room, library, recreation room, paneled walls wet bar five bathrooms five bedrooms two lavatories central air conditioning automatic sprinkler automatic garage door . . . a breakfast room a patio a large fenced lot fourteen trees a front door with a brass knocker never knocked". Detroit, on the other hand, is a world that is "falling out the bottom". In Detroit there are streets and avenues, 12th Street, Fourteenth Street, Woodward Avenue, Livernois Avenue. Instead of the "heartbreaking sidewalks, so clean" of Bloomfield Hills, there is filthy pavement from which "scraps of paper flutter in the air like pigeons, dirt flies up and hits you right in the eye, oh Detroit is breaking up into dangerous bits of newspaper and dirt, watch out". While the Bloomfield Hills police are "quiet private police, in unmarked cars. Cruising on Saturday evenings with paternal smiles for the residents", the Detroit city police are hated "cops" who are not paternal: "It took three of them to get me in the police cruiser . . . and they put more than their hands on my arm".

• • •

The story has made clear that Sioux Drive has not in the past provided a sense of security and self-worth for the girl, and it seems unlikely that it will begin to do so now. The "beginning again" of the title, as well as the "happy ending" of the headnote, is really a return to a place that before had failed her miserably. The house to which the girl returns is "a doll's house, so lovely in the sunlight", sunlight which "breaks in movieland patches" on the roof. This is not reality, but a make-believe world of games and movies; for the present, though, it offers at least a pretense of safety. Repeatedly the girl acknowledges her retreat into security, however tenuous it may prove. Nine times in the closing section of the story she uses "never" in connection with her intention never to leave home again; her insistence suggests that this is not a conscious decision to remain, but a desperate attempt to convince herself that this is her home, a place of safety where inner conflict ends.

This incredibly concentrated story, then, is developed in such a way that structure, imagery, motifs, verbal echoes work together to create for the reader the actual experience of the experiencing mind of the protagonist. The author's experiment can only be judged a success.

ALFRED KAZIN

From *Two Cassandras: Joan Didion and Joyce Carol Oates*[7]

Joyce Carol Oates seemed, more than most women writers, entirely open to social turmoil, to the frighteningly undirected and misapplied force of the American powerhouse. She plainly had an instinct for the social menace packed up in Detroit, waiting to explode, that at the end of the nineteenth century Dreiser felt about Chicago and Stephen Crane about New York. The sheer rich chaos of American life, to say nothing of its staggering armies of poor, outraged, by no means peaceful, people, pressed upon her. It is rare to find a woman writer so externally unconcerned with form. After teaching at the University of Detroit from 1962 to 1967, she remarked that Detroit is a city "so transparent, you can hear it ticking." What one woman critic in a general attack on Oates called "Violence in the Head," could also be taken as her inability to blink social violence as the language in which a great many "lower-class" Americans naturally deal with each other.

Joyce Carol Oates is, however, a "social novelist" of a peculiar kind. She is concerned not with demonstrating power relationships but with the struggle of people nowadays to express their fate in terms that are cruelly changeable. Reading her, one sees the real tragedy of so many Americans today, unable to find a language for what is happening to them. The drama of society was once seen by American social novelists as the shifting line between the individual and the mass into which he was helplessly falling. It has now become the free-floating mythology about "them" which each person carries around with him, an idea of causation unconnected to cause. There is no longer a fixed point within people's thinking. In the American social novels earlier in the century, the novelist was a pathfinder and the characters were betrayed as blind, helpless victims of their fate, like Hurstwood in *Sister Carrie* or virtually everybody in Dos Passos's *U.S.A.* Joyce Carol Oates is not particularly ahead of the people she writes about. Since her prime concern is to see people in the terms they present to themselves, she is able to present consciousness as a person, a crazily unaccountable thing. The human mind, as she says in the title of a recent novel, is simply "wonderland." And the significance of that "wonderland" to the social melodrama that is America today is that they collide but do not connect.

Praising Harriette Arnow's strong, little-known novel about southern mountain folk, *The Dollmaker*, Joyce Oates said:

> It seems to me that the greatest works of literature deal with the human soul caught in the stampede of time, unable to gauge the profundity of what passes over it, like the characters of Yeats who live through terrifying events but who cannot understand them; in this way history passes over most of us. Society is caught in a convulsion, whether of growth or of death, and ordinary people are destroyed. They do not, however, understand that they are "destroyed."

7. *Alfred Kazin's America: Critical and Personal Writings*, ed. Ted Solotaroff (2003).

This view of literature as silent tragedy is a central description of what interests Joyce Oates in the writing of fiction. Her own characters move through a world that seems to be wholly physical and even full of global eruption, yet the violence, as Elizabeth Dalton said, is in their own heads—and is no less real for that. They touch us by frightening us, like disembodied souls calling to us from the other world. They live through terrifying events but cannot understand them. This is what makes Oates a new element in our fiction, involuntarily disturbing.

· · ·

The details in Oates's fiction follow each other with a humble truthfulness that make you wonder where she is taking you; this is sometimes disorienting, for she is all attention to the unconscious reactions of her characters. She needs a lot of space, which is why her short stories tend to read like scenarios for novels. The amount of *listening* this involves is certainly singular. My deepest feeling about her is that her mind is unbelievably crowded with psychic existences, with such a mass of stories that she lives by being wholly submissive to "them." She is too attentive to their mysterious clamor to *want* to be an artist, to make the right and well-fitting structure. Much of her fiction seems written to relieve her mind of the people who haunt it, not to create something that will live.

So many inroads on the suddenly frightening American situation is indeed a problem in our fiction just now; the age of high and proud art has yielded to the climate of crisis. Joyce Oates's many stories resemble a card index of situations; they are not the deeply plotted stories that we return to as perfect little dramas; her novels, though they involve the reader through the author's intense connection with her material, tend as incident to fade out of our minds. Too much happens. Indeed, hers are altogether strange books, haunting rather than "successful," because the mind behind them is primarily concerned with a kind of Darwinian struggle for existence between minds, with the truth of some limitless human struggle. We miss the perfectly suggestive shapes that modern art and fiction have taught us to venerate. Oates is another Cassandra bewitched by her private oracle. But it is not disaster that is most on her mind; it is the recognition of each person as the center of the coming disturbance. And this disturbance, as Pascal said of his God, has its center everywhere and its circumference nowhere.

So her characters are opaque, ungiving, uncharming; they have the taciturn qualities that come with the kind of people they are—heavy, hallucinated, outside the chatty middle class. Society speaks in them, but *they* are not articulate. They do not yet feel themselves to be emancipated persons. They are caught up in the social convulsion and move unheedingly, compulsively, blindly, through the paces assigned to them by the power god.

That is exactly what Oates's work expresses just now: a sense that American life is taking some of us by the throat. "Too much" is happening; many will disappear. Above all, and most ominously, hers is a world in which our own people, and not just peasants in Vietnam, get "wasted." There is a constant sense of drift, deterioration, the end of things, that contrasts violently with the era of "high art" and the once-fond belief in immortality through art. Oates is someone plainly caught up in this "avalanche" of time.

[1973]

Flannery O'Connor wrote that the "writer's business is to contemplate experience, not to be merged with it." Lupus, the painful autoimmune disease that
cut short her life, circumscribed her movements—O'Connor spent most of her
writing life on her mother's farm in Milledgeville, Georgia—but it did not stop
the hard work of contemplation, a process she explained in several essays on
her approach to writing fiction, excerpted below. The documents included
here also explore the influence of certain experiences in O'Connor's life, as
well as her perspective as a Southern writer, and her deeply held religious
beliefs, with commentaries by Alice Walker, Lee Smith, and Thomas Merton,
among others. The section ends with moving excerpts from O'Connor's prayer
journal.

FLANNERY O'CONNOR

The Nature and Aim of Fiction[1]

If you go to a school where there are classes in writing, these classes should
not be to teach you how to write, but to teach you the limits and possibilities
of words and the respect due them. One thing that is always with the
writer—no matter how long he has written or how good he is—is the continuing process of learning how to write. As soon as the writer "learns to write," as
soon as he knows what he is going to find, and discovers a way to say what he
knew all along, or worse still, a way to say nothing, he is finished. If a writer is
any good, what he makes will have its source in a realm much larger than
that which his conscious mind can encompass and will always be a greater
surprise to him than it can ever be to his reader.

I don't know which is worse—to have a bad teacher or no teacher at all. In
any case, I believe the teacher's work should be largely negative. He can't put
the gift into you, but if he finds it there, he can try to keep it from going in an
obviously wrong direction. We can learn how not to write, but this is a discipline that does not simply concern writing itself but concerns the whole
intellectual life. A mind cleared of false emotion and false sentiment and
egocentricity is going to have at least those roadblocks removed from its path.
If you don't think cheaply, then there at least won't be the quality of cheap-
ness in your writing, even though you may not be able to write well. The
teacher can try to weed out what is positively bad, and this should be the aim
of the whole college. Any discipline can help your writing: logic, mathematics, theology, and of course and particularly drawing. Anything that helps
you to see, anything that makes you look. The writer should never be ashamed
of staring. There is nothing that doesn't require his attention.

We hear a great deal of lamentation these days about writers having all
taken themselves to the colleges and universities where they live decorously

---

1. From *Mystery and Manners: Occasional Prose,* ed. Robert and Sally Fitzgerald (1969).

instead of going out and getting firsthand information about life. The fact is that anybody who has survived his childhood has enough information about life to last him the rest of his days. If you can't make something out of a little experience, you probably won't be able to make it out of a lot. The writer's business is to contemplate experience, not to be merged in it.

Everywhere I go I'm asked if I think the universities stifle writers. My opinion is that they don't stifle enough of them. There's many a best-seller that could have been prevented by a good teacher. The idea of being a writer attracts a good many shiftless people, those who are merely burdened with poetic feelings or afflicted with sensibility. Granville Hicks, in a recent review of James Jones' novel, quoted Jones as saying, "I was stationed at Hickham Field in Hawaii when I stumbled upon the works of Thomas Wolfe, and his home life seemed so similar to my own, his feelings about himself so similar to mine about myself, that I realized I had been a writer all my life without knowing it or having written." Mr. Hicks goes on to say that Wolfe did a great deal of damage of this sort but that Jones is a particularly appalling example.

Now in every writing class you find people who care nothing about writing, because they think they are already writers by virtue of some experience they've had. It is a fact that if, either by nature or training, these people can learn to write badly enough, they can make a great deal of money, and in a way it seems a shame to deny them this opportunity; but then, unless the college is a trade school, it still has its responsibility to truth, and I believe myself that these people should be stifled with all deliberate speed.

Presuming that the people left have some degree of talent, the question is what can be done for them in a writing class. I believe the teacher's work is largely negative, that it is largely a matter of saying "This doesn't work because . . ." or "This does work because . . ." The *because* is very important. The teacher can help you understand the nature of your medium, and he can guide you in your reading. I don't believe in classes where students criticize each other's manuscripts. Such criticism is generally composed in equal parts of ignorance, flattery, and spite. It's the blind leading the blind, and it can be dangerous. A teacher who tries to impose a way of writing on you can be dangerous too. Fortunately, most teachers I've known were too lazy to do this. In any case, you should beware of those who appear overenergetic.

In the last twenty years the colleges have been emphasizing creative writing to such an extent that you almost feel that any idiot with a nickel's worth of talent can emerge from a writing class able to write a competent story. In fact, so many people can now write competent stories that the short story as a medium is in danger of dying of competence. We want competence, but competence by itself is deadly. What is needed is the vision to go with it, and you do not get this from a writing class.

FLANNERY O'CONNOR

The Grotesque in Southern Fiction[2]

In nineteenth-century American writing, there was a good deal of grotesque literature which came from the frontier and was supposed to be funny; but

---

2. From *Mystery and Manners* (1969).

our present grotesque characters, comic though they may be, are at least not primarily so. They seem to carry an invisible burden; their fanaticism is a reproach, not merely an eccentricity. I believe that they come about from the prophetic vision peculiar to any novelist whose concerns I have been describing. In the novelist's case, prophecy is a matter of seeing near things with their extensions of meaning and thus of seeing far things close up. The prophet is a realist of distances, and it is this kind of realism that you find in the best modern instances of the grotesque.

Whenever I'm asked why Southern writers particularly have a penchant for writing about freaks, I say it is because we are still able to recognize one. To be able to recognize a freak, you have to have some conception of the whole man, and in the South the general conception of man is still, in the main, theological. That is a large statement, and it is dangerous to make it, for almost anything you say about Southern belief can be denied in the next breath with equal propriety. But approaching the subject from the standpoint of the writer, I think it is safe to say that while the South is hardly Christ-centered, it is most certainly Christ-haunted. The Southerner, who isn't convinced of it, is very much afraid that he may have been formed in the image and likeness of God. Ghosts can be very fierce and instructive. They cast strange shadows, particularly in our literature. In any case, it is when the freak can be sensed as a figure for our essential displacement that he attains some depth in literature.

There is another reason in the Southern situation that makes for a tendency toward the grotesque and this is the prevalence of good Southern writers. I think the writer is initially set going by literature more than by life. When there are many writers all employing the same idiom, all looking out on more or less the same social scene, the individual writer will have to be more than ever careful that he isn't just doing badly what has already been done to completion. The presence alone of Faulkner in our midst makes a great difference in what the writer can and cannot permit himself to do. Nobody wants his mule and wagon stalled on the same track the Dixie Limited is roaring down.

The Southern writer is forced from all sides to make his gaze extend beyond the surface, beyond mere problems, until it touches that realm which is the concern of prophets and poets.

FLANNERY O'CONNOR

From *Writing Short Stories* [3]

In good fiction, certain of the details will tend to accumulate meaning from the action of the story itself, and when this happens they become symbolic in the way they work. I once wrote a story called "Good Country People," in which a lady Ph.D. has her wooden leg stolen by a Bible salesman whom she has tried to seduce. Now I'll admit that, paraphrased in this way, the situation is simply a low joke. The average reader is pleased to observe anybody's wooden leg being stolen. But without ceasing to appeal to him and without making any statements of high intention, this story does manage to operate at another level of experience, by letting the wooden leg accumulate meaning.

---

3. From *Mystery and Manners* (1969).

Early in the story, we're presented with the fact that the Ph.D. is spiritually as well as physically crippled. She believes in nothing but her own belief in nothing, and we perceive that there is a wooden part of her soul that corresponds to her wooden leg. Now of course this is never stated. The fiction writer states as little as possible. The reader makes this connection from things he is shown. He may not even know that he makes the connection, but the connection is there nevertheless and it has its effect on him. As the story goes on, the wooden leg continues to accumulate meaning. The reader learns how the girl feels about her leg, how her mother feels about it, and how the country woman on the place feels about it; and finally, by the time the Bible salesman comes along, the leg has accumulated so much meaning that it is, as the saying goes, loaded. And when the Bible salesman steals it, the reader realizes that he has taken away part of the girl's personality and has revealed her deeper affliction to her for the first time.

If you want to say that the wooden leg is a symbol, you can say that. But it is a wooden leg first, and as a wooden leg it is absolutely necessary to the story. It has its place on the literal level of the story, but it operates in depth as well as on the surface. It increases the story in every direction, and this is essentially the way a story escapes being short.

Now a little might be said about the way in which this happens. I wouldn't want you to think that in that story I sat down and said, "I am now going to write a story about a Ph.D. with a wooden leg, using the wooden leg as a symbol for another kind of affliction." I doubt myself if many writers know what they are going to do when they start out. When I started writing that story, I didn't know there was going to be a Ph.D. with a wooden leg in it. I merely found myself one morning writing a description of two women that I knew something about, and before I realized it, I had equipped one of them with a daughter with a wooden leg. As the story progressed, I brought in the Bible salesman, but I had no idea what I was going to do with him. I didn't know he was going to steal that wooden leg until ten or twelve lines before he did it, but when I found out that this was what was going to happen, I realized that it was inevitable. This is a story that produces a shock for the reader, and I think one reason for this is that it produced a shock for the writer.

Now despite the fact that this story came about in this seemingly mindless fashion, it is a story that almost no rewriting was done on. It is a story that was under control throughout the writing of it, and it might be asked how this kind of control comes about, since it is not entirely conscious.

I think the answer to this is what Maritain calls "the habit of art." It is a fact that fiction writing is something in which the whole personality takes part—the conscious as well as the unconscious mind. Art is the habit of the artist; and habits have to be rooted deep in the whole personality. They have to be cultivated like any other habit, over a long period of time, by experience; and teaching any kind of writing is largely a matter of helping the student develop the habit of art. I think this is more than just a discipline, although it is that; I think it is a way of looking at the created world and of using the senses so as to make them find as much meaning as possible in things.

• • •

There are two qualities that make fiction. One is the sense of mystery and the other is the sense of manners. You get the manners from the texture of existence that surrounds you. The great advantage of being a Southern writer is that we don't have to go anywhere to look for manners; bad or good, we've got them in abundance. We in the South live in a society that is rich in contradiction, rich in irony, rich in contrast, and particularly rich in its speech. And yet here are six stories by Southerners in which almost no use is made of the gifts of the region.

Of course the reason for this may be that you have seen these gifts abused so often that you have become self-conscious about using them. There is nothing worse than the writer who doesn't *use* the gifts of the region, but wallows in them. Everything becomes so Southern that it's sickening, so local that it is unintelligible, so literally reproduced that it conveys nothing. The general gets lost in the particular instead of being shown through it.

However, when the life that actually surrounds us is totally ignored, when our patterns of speech are absolutely overlooked, then something is out of kilter. The writer should then ask himself if he is not reaching out for a kind of life that is artificial to him.

An idiom characterizes a society, and when you ignore the idiom, you are very likely ignoring the whole social fabric that could make a meaningful character. You can't cut characters off from their society and say much about them as individuals. You can't say anything meaningful about the mystery of a personality unless you put that personality in a believable and significant social context. And the best way to do this is through the character's own language.

BRAD GOOCH

From *The Bible Salesman*[4]

One spring afternoon in late April 1953, a striking-looking young man appeared at the front door. Tall and blond, described by Caroline Gordon as "a Dane with eyes like blue marbles," Erik Langkjaer was a twenty-six-year-old college textbook salesman for Harcourt Brace, Flannery's publisher. As his recently assigned territory was the entire South east of the Mississippi, he had been visiting with professors at Georgia State College for Women. Among them was Helen Greene, whose English history textbook was published by Harcourt. "After checking out his current offerings in that field, I asked him if he would like to meet one of his company's published authors," Greene has written. As she was his last appointment of the day, the history professor was pleased to take him "out to Andalusia to meet Mary Flannery and Miss Regina."

While Helen Greene remembered Erik's response as an enthusiastic "Of course!" he felt, in truth, puzzled. "She was sure that Flannery would be interested in meeting me," says Langkjaer, "and I must say I couldn't imagine why, because I hadn't read the novel, and I hadn't even been told that she was living in Milledgeville, and why would anyone want to meet a perfect stranger on such a flimsy pretext. But the professor said that she doesn't see too many people, living as she does with her mother. I went along with that idea. Some time in the afternoon, we rang the doorbell of Andalusia." Helen Greene judged the intro-

---

4. From *Flannery: A Life of Flannery O'Connor* (2009).   **5.** Dorothy Day, founder of the Catholic Worker movement.

duction a success: "He and Mary Flannery liked each other a great deal, and, as I recall, she guided him on a tour of Baldwin County in his car. . . . He was happily surprised to find such interesting and attractive people in the area."

• • •

They discussed more on this first visit than Day's[5] social activism, or the ecumenical mission of his "aunt" in reuniting the Russian Orthodox Church with Rome. Erik was quite open about his life situation, "that I had come to the U.S., that I was now traveling somewhat rootlessly in the South, and that I had all these religious concerns and problems." Flannery was tickled by a traveling salesman carrying "The Bible," a joke term in publishing for his standard loose-leaf binder of promotional materials and tables. "It amused her very much that something that was not a bible should have been called a bible," says Langkjaer. And she responded with tenderness to his rootless search. Writing to Erik two years later, Flannery recalled a first rush of empathy with his homelessness: "You wonder how anybody can be happy in his home as long as there is one person without one. I never thought of this so much until I began to know you and your situation and I will never quite have a home again on acct. of it."

• • •

That first afternoon, Mrs. O'Connor served Erik and Flannery tea and then withdrew to take care of various business matters. Erik immediately picked up on the wide gap in sensibility between Flannery and her mother. Not "the saint everyone thinks she was, she was rather rebellious," says Langkjaer of the young woman who struck him as still far from reconciled to her fate. "I did sense that Flannery had a tense relationship with her mother. I got the impression that she was quite dependent on her mother now that she had come down with this disease, but that she was not an easy person for Flannery to talk to. I mean they were really not of one mind, to put it mildly.

• • •

Erik had not read a word by the writer with whom he established such sudden intimacy, but she soon gave him *Wise Blood*, with the inscription "For Erik who has wise blood too," and "A Good Man Is Hard to Find," which she was completing when they met. Holding on to his impression of Mrs. O'Connor as "pleasant," yet "rather restrictive, very much focused on the practical aspects of running the farm," he continued later in life to interpret the grandmother of the story—wearing her white cotton gloves and blue navy straw hat so that "anyone seeing her dead on the highway would know at once that she was a lady"—as a version of Regina, or others of Flannery's female relatives. "This woman represented perhaps the essence of members of Flannery's own family that she distilled into this one character," says Langkjaer. "Here was a very, very limited person. . . . The grandmother is a completely banal, superficial woman."

Erik was stimulated enough by the remarkable new friendship to schedule regular visits to Milledgeville on weekends, often needing to rearrange his itinerary and travel a hundred miles or more out of his way. As Regina made clear to Flannery that she considered his staying overnight improper, he rented a room in a local motel, and then made his "calls" to Andalusia. Textbook orders were placed seasonally, clustered over the next fall and spring, so there were ten or twelve such visits. Erik and Flannery would take long walks, go for rides, or have lunch at Sanford House, talking all the while. "Was he ever handsome," recalls Mary Jo Thompson. "Flannery reserved the table on the porch to have lunch with Erik. It was perfect for a couple." Flannery was invested enough that when Betty Hester mentioned Helene Iswolsky a few years later, she confided, with unusual candor and spunk, "I used to go with her nephew."

TONY MAGISTRALE

From *"I'm Alien to a Great Deal": Flannery O'Connor and the Modernist Ethic*[6]

O'Connor's particular brand of Roman Catholicism is rooted in the church's pre-Vatican II siege mentality; its strict adherence to doctrine, ecclesiastical government, and an apocalyptic cosmology make it a modern illustration of direct medieval influence. Christianity's flame has always burned brightest for purists, and it was the unadulterated traditionalism of the Catholic church before its liberalization in Pope John XXIII's ecumenical movement of the 1960s that is most similar to Flannery O'Connor's fiction.

• • •

Many readers of O'Connor's fiction claim that her tales are too bleak and despairing, that her conclusions are not filled with the light of transcendence, but rather the darkness of loss. Indeed, her Southerners attain moral development and self-knowledge only through experiencing the devastating realities of human tragedy: widows losing sons through a misplaced sense of charity, grandmothers who uncover the true nature of spirituality at the end of a rifle, fanatics who must kill themselves to atone for their failure to recognize Christ, and intelligent rationalists who discover the inadequacies of their guiding philosophies only after it is too late to save the lives of mothers and sons. Perhaps what is most difficult for modern readers to accept is O'Connor's refusal to equate physical suffering and death with evil. True "rising" is possible in her world only at a severe price, and that expense bears little in common with what we have typically come to regard as a sense of improvement.

I am afraid that those who bemoan the violent and tragic circumstances of O'Connor's fiction tend to confuse her absolute lack of sentimentality with callousness. O'Connor is too intelligent to be sentimental; she is romantic, in the very best sense of the word, which is one of the indulgences of the intelligence. To see something romantically is to "assume the full range of its possibilities that it deserves all its implications, its analogies, its symbolism, its metaphysics." If she is hard on her characters, introducing them to tragic situations, it is because she wanted them to be both recognizable and inspirational in an age of cynicism and disbelief. As a writer in what she labelled the "romance tradition," O'Connor was always:

> interested in what we don't understand rather than what we do . . . interested in possibility rather than probability . . . interested in characters who are forced

---

6. "'I'm Alien to a Great Deal': Flannery O'Connor and the Modernist Ethic." *Journal of American Studies*, Vol. 24, No. 1 (April 1990).

to meet evil and grace and who act on a trust beyond themselves—whether they know very clearly what it is they are upon or not. To the modern mind, this kind of character, and his creator are typical Don Quixotes, tilting at what is not there.

O'Connor's stories are about people struggling with one another, trying to wrest victories from the recalcitrance of love and fate. They are about the triumph and failure of the will, the divine and the human, and about the tragic consequences of our flawed perceptivity, which quietly stalk us all, like age and death. In spite of the brutal fates that so often befall her characters, O'Connor possesses a genuine sympathy for them, even as she modelled the majority after the secular humanists and materialists she so vehemently decried. This sympathy is born from a common humanity, the awareness on O'Connor's part that all of us share in concert the fundamental condition of sin and the possibility for spiritual advancement once we recognize the devil's hand within our own.

Flannery O'Connor remains one of the most difficult writers of the modern period, not because her tales are necessarily more complex than another's, but because her sensibilities and values are so foreign to her era. O'Connor's literary vision comes burning out of a distant time and place; it slashes like a demon's talon, repudiating modernity's complacent conviction that God had died a Victorian. To appreciate fully O'Connor's art, we must accept it in the religious context from which it was written.

LEE SMITH

Flannery O'Connor's "A Good Man Is Hard to Find"

"A Good Man Is Hard to Find" first hit me like a revelation. I was a college student trying to learn to write fiction myself; somehow I had got the idea that a short story should follow a kind of recipe, like a Lady Baltimore cake. Conflict, suspense, resolution; a clear theme; an ending that tied it all up in a neat little bow. Yet when I read that famous line of "A Good Man Is Hard to Find," I realized that *nothing* was wrapped up here—instead, a whole world opened out before my astonished eyes, a world as wild and scary as life itself. I turned back to the beginning and read it straight through again. I felt like the grandmother in the story, clinging desperately to her outworn beliefs: "I know you're a good man . . . You're not a bit common . . . I know you wouldn't shoot a lady . . . I know you come from nice people!" The gun went off in my own head as surely as it went off in those Georgia pines, and a number of my own ideas died instantly along with the grandmother. A story does *not* have to be resolved in the end, I realized. It is enough to glimpse something, momentarily, before it slips back into the dark woods.

Furthermore, a story can be both very funny and deadly serious at the same time. Though she drew a steady bead on salvation and kept it always in her sights, Flannery O'Connor had time for the gross world, too, and for people with all their comic posturing and blundering. The mix of menace and hilarity is evident early on in "A Good Man Is Hard to Find"; the ominous foreshadowing in the line "this fellow that calls himself The Misfit is aloose from the Federal pen and headed toward Florida and you read here what it says he did to these people" is immediately undercut by the humorous description of the children's mother, "whose face was as broad and innocent as a cabbage and was tied around with a green headkerchief that had two points on top like rabbit's ears." This kind of juxtaposition continues throughout the story—in the image of Bobby Lee and Hiram ambling back from the woods, for instance, dragging Bailey's ridiculous yellow shirt with blue parrots on it, just after killing him, or in those children screaming, "We've had an ACCI-DENT!" in a frenzy of delight. The world has always struck me as both funny and awful, too, and reading "A Good Man Is Hard to Find" for the first time, I realized that I didn't have to *pick*. What a relief!

The older I get, the more profound this story seems to me. Perhaps the constant presence of death in Flannery O'Connor's life allowed her to see beyond her own years. I never read it now without that deep shock of recognition at the bone, and wonder, and pity for us all.

ALICE WALKER

From *Beyond the Peacock: The Reconstruction of Flannery O'Connor*[7]

It was after a poetry reading I gave at a recently desegregated college in Georgia that someone mentioned that in 1952 Flannery O'Connor and I had lived within minutes of each other on the same Eatonton-to-Milledgeville road. I was eight years old in 1952 (she would have been 28) and we moved away from Milledgeville after less than a year. Still, since I have loved her work for many years, the coincidence of our having lived near each other intrigued me, and started me thinking of her again.

As a college student in the sixties I read her books endlessly, scarcely conscious of the difference between her racial and economic background and my own, but put them away in anger when I discovered that, while I was reading O'Connor—Southern, Catholic, and white—there were other women writers—some Southern, some religious, all black—I had not been allowed to know. For several years, while I searched for, found, and studied black women writers, I deliberately shut O'Connor out, feeling almost ashamed that she had reached me first. And yet, even when I no longer read her, I missed her, and realized that though the rest of America might not mind, having endured it so long, I would never be satisfied with a segregated literature.

• • •

I discovered O'Connor when I was in college in the North and took a course in Southern writers and the South. The perfection of her writing was so dazzling I never noticed that no black Southern writers were taught. The other writers we studied—Faulkner, McCullers, Welty—seemed obsessed with a racial past that would not let them go. They seemed to beg the question of their characters' humanity on every page. O'Connor's characters—whose humanity if not their sanity is taken for granted, and who are miserable, ugly, narrow-minded, atheistic, and of intense racial smugness and arrogance, with not a graceful, pretty one anywhere who is not, at the same time, a joke—shocked and delighted me.

7. From *Critical Essays on Flannery O'Connor* (1985).

It was for her description of Southern white women that I appreciated her work at first, because when she set her pen to them not a whiff of magnolia hovered in the air (and the tree itself might never have been planted), and yes, I could say, yes, these white folks without the magnolia (who are indifferent to the tree's existence), and these black folks without melons and superior racial patience, these are like Southerners that I know.

She was for me the first great modern writer from the South, and was, in any case, the only one I had read who wrote such sly, demythifying sentences about white women as: "The woman would be more or less pretty—yellow hair, fat ankles, muddy-colored eyes."

Her white male characters do not fare any better—all of them misfits, thieves, deformed madmen, idiot children, illiterates, and murderers, and her black characters, male and female, appear equally shallow, demented, and absurd. That she retained a certain distance (only, however, in her later, mature work) from the inner workings of her black characters seems to me all to her credit, since, by deliberately limiting her treatment of them to cover their observable demeanor and actions, she leaves them free, in the reader's imagination, to inhabit another landscape, another life, than the one she creates for them. This is a kind of grace many writers do not have when dealing with representatives of an oppressed people within a story, and their insistence on knowing everything, on being God, in fact, has burdened us with more stereotypes than we can ever hope to shed.

In her life, O'Connor was more casual. In a letter to her friend Robert Fitzgerald in the mid-fifties she wrote, "as the niggers say, I have the misery." He found nothing offensive, apparently, in including this unflattering (to O'Connor) statement in his Introduction to one of her books. O'Connor was then certain she was dying, and was in pain; one assumes she made this comment in an attempt at levity. Even so, I do not find it funny. In another letter she wrote shortly before she died she said: "Justice is justice and should not be appealed to along racial lines. The problem is not abstract for the Southerner, it's concrete: he sees it in terms of persons, not races—which way of seeing does away with easy answers." Of course this observation, though grand, does not apply to the racist treatment of blacks by whites in the South, and O'Connor should have added that she spoke only for herself.

But *essential* O'Connor is not about race at all, which is why it is so refreshing, coming, as it does, out of such a *racial* culture. If it can be said to be "about" anything, then it is "about" prophets and prophecy, "about" revelation, and "about" the impact of supernatural grace on human beings who don't have a chance of spiritual growth without it.

．　．　．

She was an artist who thought she might die young, and who then knew for certain she would. Her view of her characters pierces right through to the skull. Whatever her characters' color or social position she saw them as she saw herself, in the light of imminent mortality.

．　．　．

It mattered to her that she was a Catholic. This comes as a surprise to those who first read her work as that of an atheist. She believed in all the mysteries of her faith. And yet, she was incapable of writing dogmatic or formulaic stories. No religious tracts, nothing haloed softly in celestial light, not even any happy endings. It has puzzled some of her readers and annoyed the Catholic church that in her stories not only does good not triumph, it is not usually present. Seldom are there choices, and God never intervenes to help anyone win. To O'Connor, in fact, Jesus was God, and he won only by losing. She perceived that not much has been learned by his death by crucifixion, and that it is only by his continual, repeated dying—touching one's own life in a direct, searing way—that the meaning of that original loss is pressed into the heart of the individual.

THOMAS MERTON

Flannery O'Connor: A Prose Elegy[8]

Now Flannery is dead and I will write her name with honor, with love for the great slashing innocence of that dry-eyed irony that could keep looking the South in the face without bleeding or even sobbing. Her South was deeper than mine, crazier than Kentucky, but wild with no other madness than the crafty paranoia that is all over the place, including the North! Only madder, craftier, hung up in wilder and more absurd legends, more inventive of more outrageous lies! And solemn! Taking seriously the need to be respectable when one is an obsolescent and very agile fury.

The key word to Flannery's stories probably is "respect." She never gave up examining its ambiguities and its decay. In this bitter dialectic of half-truths that have become endemic to our system, she probed our very life—its conflicts, its falsities, its obsessions, its vanities. Have we become an enormous complex organization of spurious reverences? Respect is continually advertised, and we are still convinced that we respect "everything good"—when we know too well that we have lost the most elementary respect even for ourselves. Flannery saw this and saw, better than others, what it implied.

She wrote in and out of the anatomy of a word that became genteel, then self-conscious, then obsessive, finally dying of contempt, but kept calling itself "respect." Contempt for the child, for the stranger, for the woman, for the Negro, for the animal, for the white man, for the farmer, for the country, for the preacher, for the city, for the world, for reality itself. Contempt, contempt, so that in the end the gestures of respect they kept making to themselves and to each other and to God became desperately obscene.

But respect had to be maintained. Flannery maintained it ironically and relentlessly with a kind of innocent passion long after it had died of contempt—as if she were the only one left who took this thing seriously. One would think (if one put a Catholic chip on his shoulder and decided to make a problem of her) that she could not look so steadily, so drily and so long at so much false respect without herself dying of despair. She never made any funny faces. She never said: "Here is a terrible thing!" She just looked and said what they said and how they said it. It was not she that invented their despair, and perhaps her only way out of despair herself was to respect the way they announced the gospel of contempt. She patiently recorded all they had got themselves into. Their world was a big, fantastic, crawling, exploding junk pile of despair. I will write her name with honor for seeing it so clearly and

---

8. From *Critical Essays on Flannery O'Connor* (1985).

looking straight at it without remorse. Perhaps her way of irony was the only possible catharsis for a madness so cruel and so endemic. Perhaps a dry honesty like hers can save the South more simply than the North can ever be saved.

Flannery's people were two kinds of very advanced primitives: the city kind, exhausted, disillusioned, tired of imagining, perhaps still given to a grim willfulness in the service of doubt, still driving on in fury and ill will, or scientifically expert in nastiness; and the rural kind: furious, slow, cunning, inexhaustible, living sweetly on the verge of the unbelievable, more inclined to prefer the abyss to solid ground, but keeping contact with the world of contempt by raw insensate poetry and religious mirth: the mirth of a god who himself, they suspected, was the craftiest and most powerful deceiver of all. Flannery saw the contempt of primitives who admitted that they would hate to be saved, and the greater contempt of those other primitives whose salvation was an elaborately contrived possibility, always being brought back into question. Take the sweet idiot deceit of the fury grandmother in "A Good Man Is Hard to Find" whose respectable and catastrophic fantasy easily destroyed her urban son with all his plans, his last shred of trust in reason, and his insolent children.

The way Flannery O'Connor made a story: she would put together all these elements of unreason and let them fly slowly and inexorably at one another. Then sometimes the urban madness, less powerful, would fall weakly prey to the rural madness and be inexorably devoured by a superior and more primitive absurdity. Or the rural madness would fail and fall short of the required malice and urban deceit would compass its destruction, with all possible contempt, cursing, superior violence and fully implemented disbelief. For it would usually be wholesome faith that left the rural primitive unarmed. So you would watch, fascinated, almost in despair, knowing that in the end the very worst thing, the least reasonable, the least desirable, was what would have to happen. Not because Flannery wanted it so, but because it turned out to *be* so in a realm where the advertised satisfaction is compounded of so many lies and of so much contempt for the customer. She had seen too clearly all that is sinister in our commercial paradise, and in its rural roots.

Flannery's people were two kinds of trash, able to mix inanity with poetry, with exuberant nonsense, and with the most profound and systematic contempt for reality. Her people knew how to be trash to the limit, unabashed, on purpose, out of self-contempt that has finally won out over every other feeling and turned into a parody of freedom in the spirit. What spirit? A spirit of ungodly stateliness and parody—the pomp and glee of arbitrary sports, freaks not of nature but of blighted and social willfulness, rich in the creation of respectable and three-eyed monsters. Her beings are always raising the question of *worth*. Who is a good man? Where is he? He is "hard to find." Meanwhile you will have to make out with a bad one who is so respectable that he is horrible, so horrible that he is funny, so funny that he is pathetic, but so pathetic that it would be gruesome to pity him. So funny that you do not dare to laugh too loud for fear of demons.

And that is how Flannery finally solved the problem of respect: having peeled the whole onion of respect layer by layer, having taken it all apart with admirable patience, showing clearly that each layer was only another kind of contempt, she ended up by seeing clearly that it was funny, but not merely funny in a way that you could laugh at. Humorous, yes, but also uncanny, inexplicable, demonic, so you could never laugh at it as if you understood. Because if you pretended to understand, you, too, would find yourself among her demons practicing contempt. She respected all her people by searching for some sense in them, searching for truth, searching to the end and then suspending judgment. To have condemned them on moral grounds would have been to connive with their own crafty arts and their own demonic imagination. It would have meant getting tangled up with them in the same machinery of unreality and of contempt. The only way to be saved was to stay out of it, not to think, not to speak, just to record the slow, sweet, ridiculous verbalizing of Southern furies, working their way through their charming lazy hell.

That is why when I read Flannery I don't think of Hemingway, or Katherine Anne Porter, or Sartre, but rather of someone like Sophocles. What more can be said of a writer? I write her name with honor, for all the truth and all the craft with which she shows man's fall and his dishonor.

FLANNERY O'CONNOR

A Prayer Journal[9]

Dear God, I am so discouraged about my work. I have the feeling of discouragement that is. I realize I don't know what I realize. Please help me dear God to be a good writer and to get something else accepted. That is so far from what I deserve, of course, that I am naturally struck with the nerve of it. Contrition in me is largely imperfect. I don't know if I've ever been sorry for a sin because it hurt You. That kind of contrition is better than none but it is selfish. To have the other kind, it is necessary to have knowledge, faith extraordinary. All boils down to grace, I suppose. Again asking God to help us be sorry for having hurt Him. I am afraid of pain and I suppose that is what we have to have to get grace. Give me the courage to stand the pain to get the grace, Oh Lord. Help me with this life that seems so treacherous, so disappointing.

Dear God, tonight it is not disappointing because you have given me a story. Don't let me ever think, dear God, that I was anything but the instrument for Your story—just like the typewriter was mine. Please let the story, dear God, in its revisions, be made too clear for any false & low interpretation because in it, I am not trying to disparage anybody's religion although when it was coming out, I didn't know exactly what I was trying to do or what it was going to mean. I don't know now if it is consistent. Please don't let me have to scrap the story because it turns out to mean more wrong than right—or any wrong. I want it to mean that the good in man sometimes shows through his commercialism but that it is not the fault of the commercialism that it does.

Perhaps the idea would be that good can show through even something that is cheap. I don't know, but dear God, I wish you would take care of making it a sound story because I don't know how, just like I didn't know how to write it but it came. Anyway it all brings me to thanksgiving, the third thing

---

9. From *A Prayer Journal* (2013).

to include in prayer. When I think of all I have to be thankful for I wonder that You don't just kill me now because You've done so much for me already & I haven't been particularly grateful. My thanksgiving is never in the form of self sacrifice—a few memorized prayers babbled once over lightly. All this disgusts me in myself but does not fill me with the poignant feeling I should have to adore You with, to be sorry with, or to thank You with. Perhaps the feeling I keep asking for, is something again selfish—something to help me to feel that everything with *me* is all right. And yet it seems only natural but maybe being thus natural is being thus selfish. My mind is a most insecure thing, not to be depended on. It gives me scruples at one minute & leaves me lax the next. If I must know all these things thru the mind, dear Lord, please strengthen mine. Thank you, dear God, I believe I do feel thankful for all You've done for me. I want to. I do. And thank my dear Mother whom I do love, Our Lady of Perpetual Help.

Glossary of Critical Terms

action Most simply, what happens to, or what is done by, the characters in a story. A somewhat more technical usage—in which "action" is nearly synonymous with **plot**[1]—makes the term signify a unified sequence of events with a beginning, middle, and end.

allegory A literary work in which the characters and their situations clearly represent general qualities and types—as, in an animal fable, each animal may represent a type of human personality. Often the characters of an allegory represent abstract vices or virtues such as avarice, charity, innocence, or prudery. See **symbol**.

ambiguity Any story or element in a story that can be plausibly interpreted in different ways is said to be ambiguous. Ambiguity can be a fault that obstructs clear communication, but it can also provide enrichment by clustering associated and complementary meanings. See **irony** and **paradox**.

atmosphere The enveloping spirit or mood of a story. Used in the same sense as in actual life, it might describe the feeling that prevails at a family reunion, a funeral, or the beginning of a vacation. See also **mood** and **tone**.

authorial intrusion Explanations or statements that go beyond a rendering of the situation to make an interpretive comment about it. The author seems to address the reader directly, abandoning the illusion of his or her tale, to deliver an opinion.

character 1. One of the people who has a role in the story. 2. The quality or the sum of the qualities of such a person. In most stories we can easily distinguish between central characters—on whom most of the author's attention is focused—and the minor characters—who play some part in the development of the situation. *Round characters* are those presented as having the complex or contradictory qualities that we note in most human beings. *Flat characters* are those who display only a small fraction of normal human complexity. Most good stories will show examples of both flat and round characters according to the requirements of the **focus of interest**.

chronology The timeline or calendar of events presented in a story. Chronology may be straightforward—with the narrative beginning at the earliest and running uninterruptedly to the latest point in time—or complicated—with the narrative opening somewhere in the middle and leapfrogging backward or forward. Faulkner's "A Rose for Emily" provides an excellent example for study of complicated chronology. See **flashback**.

climax The outcome of the main **action** of a story. That point at which the reader can see what the complications were leading to. Often the climax is a decisive encounter between characters who have been in **conflict**.

coherence The consistency of various parts of a story. We expect a character's speech and actions to be consistent with his nature. We expect certain consequences to follow from a particular act, certain feelings to arise from disappointments or rewards. Certain kinds of language will be in keeping with the material described. See **unity** and **style**.

complication The emergence of a problem out of the interaction between char-

---

1. Words in boldface type are defined in this glossary.

acters and the situation that prevails as the story begins. See **exposition** and **resolution**.

concreteness Joseph Conrad wrote: "All art...appeals primarily to the senses....My task...is, by the power of the written word, to make you hear, to make you feel—it is, before all, to make you *see*." Fiction renders those concrete details of sensuous experience from which moral and emotional interpretations can be made. Fiction *shows* an action in progress. See **credibility, illusion, setting**.

conflict The active opposition of characters, ideas, or ways of life. A dynamic test of the capacities of one thing or person to overcome adversity. Conflict is often considered the soul of fiction, because it gives rise to suspense, drama, and the emotional tension that sharpens our intuitions about characters and their values.

convention Any aspect of the literary art that has been established by earlier and repeated usage as part of the way in which language represents experience. Punctuation, syntax, and even the alphabet itself are conventions. So are such things as the use of a narrator, the freedom of the author to substitute his or her language for that of the characters, and the use of paragraphs in dialogue passages.

conventional This term frequently has a pejorative meaning—though it derives directly from **convention**, without which no communication would be possible. When used disparagingly, *conventional* means that the writer has tried to find approval by clinging to familiar narrative types and procedures, and uncontroversial values.

credibility Is the author telling you something that is unbelievable because it is impossible? Even if it is possible, is it probable? There are degrees of credibility in all reports of human events, and we measure the plausibility of what we read in fiction much as we measure it in history or the daily news. Just because a report is credible it need not be interest-

ing, emotionally convincing, or intuitively comprehensible. See **concreteness** and **illusion.**

denouement A synonym for **resolution**.

description Those passages devoted to a presentation of the appearance of characters or the setting. Descriptions may appear in passages of dialogue, but they are usually provided by the author or narrator.

dialogue The speech of characters in a story, usually punctuated with quotation marks. See **illusion** and **immediacy**.

diction The choice and arrangement of words. By disciplining their vocabulary to a degree of conformity with the passions and actions of the story, writers enhance their power to convince. See **illusion** and **unity**.

didactic A story is said to be didactic if it deliberately teaches some lesson about the way people should behave. Such teaching was one of the traditional justifications for fiction. Most modern fiction tends to show humanity as it is rather than as it should be, but even modern stories point to general values and distinguish between admirable and contemptible behavior. See **moral** and **parable.**

distance Like many other valuable terms that are now conventionally used to discuss fiction, this one is both metaphorical and ambiguous. It may mean the distinction authors preserve between themselves and their central characters (also called **objectivity**). It may refer to a use of language that separates the adventure described from the experience of the reader. It may mean a lack of **immediacy.** The author may choose to let crucial events take place offstage. In such a case they seem to be taking place at a greater distance than events presented directly.

dramatic This term is most useful in fictional criticism when it is taken to mean "like something presented on the stage of a theater." The modern writer of fiction tries, most of the time, to *show* us an action rather than simply to *tell* us about it. The writer sets a stage and peoples it. However, the term *dramatic* is also used as a synonym for *exciting* or *suspenseful*. See **concreteness** and **objectivity**.

effaced narrator In third-person narration we frequently find that part of the description and narrative is given in a language attributable to the character whose point of view has been assumed by the author, while other parts are in a language that must be attributed to the author's own understanding and observations. The latter is said to come from the effaced narrator, the speaker standing hidden behind his or her character.

episode A single part, often a scene, in the continuing action of a story.

episodic Usually signifies a loosely constructed or incoherent series of actions. See **coherence**.

exposition That part of a story—frequently at or near the beginning—which gives information about the characters and their situation before the action begins to change them.

first- and third-person narration In first-person narration the story is told by a character who habitually refers to himself or herself with the pronoun *I*. In third-person all characters are referred to by third-person pronouns and the story is told directly by the author.

flashback A break in the chronological sequence of a story to deal with earlier events. See **chronology**.

focus of interest Whatever the author tries to make most prominent in his or her narration. May be **plot, setting, characters,** situation, a social problem, or a moral enigma.

foreshadowing Hints of things to come. A foolish, impulsive judgment on a small matter hints that a character may be similarly susceptible in the great crises of life. Sometimes foreshadowing is accomplished by a prophetic episode, sometimes by the author's language or by the dialogue.

form A term so broad that it sums up all the others in this glossary. The totality of conventions exploited and modified by an author in his or her creative act. See **convention**.

illusion Sensory experiences can only be evoked by language; they cannot be duplicated. Nevertheless, in varying degrees, stories can provide the sense that one is morally and emotionally involved in a situation shared with fictional characters. *They* smell the roses and feel the pain of a stab wound, but the reader appreciates the former experience and sympathizes with the latter, much as he or she would if the experiences were real. See **credibility**.

imagery 1. Figures of speech, such as similes and metaphors. 2. More generally, all descriptions that prompt the reader to visualize characters in their setting. These visualizations, in turn, set off imaginative analogies that extend the implications of the story beyond its literal limits.

immediacy The effect or illusion of sharing the characters' experience. An author may gear all the devices of language, including dialogue and use of the present tense, to promote this effect. It may be enhanced by a deliberate choice of subject matter that will play on the reader's enthusiasms or apprehensions. See **illusion**.

interior monologue Sometimes—more popularly—called **stream of consciousness**.

irony A discrepancy between what is expected and what is revealed. It may be found either in language usage or in the working out of the action of a story. Surprise endings always depend on some sort of irony, often crude. Irony may appear in the difference between a character's understanding of his or her situation and the reader's estimate of it. See **paradox**.

milieu The political, social, cultural, economic, and intellectual aspects of the **setting**. Milieu is to setting as Greek culture is to Greek geography. See **setting**.

mood The prevailing feeling of a story, generated by language, **setting,** and the quality of the action. The term is naturally analogous to the moods of our experience—grim, gay, solemn, remorseful, angry, ecstatic, melancholy, anxious, etc. See **atmosphere.**

moral The instructive point of a story. (See **didactic.**) The lesson to be drawn from the outcome of the action. While modern taste inclines away from the pat and clear morals that once adorned a lot of stories, a shrewd and important moral in fiction will have the same worth as a shrewd and important axiom delivered without fictional illustration. Handsome is as handsome does.

motivation The internal and external forces that compel a **character** to take **action.** Sometimes these forces may be chiefly psychological, sometimes sociological, and sometimes a matter of hostility or opportunity in the physical environment. For **credibility,** motivation should be consistent with **character.**

narration 1. A synonym for storytelling, whether the story is told by literary means, by the cinema, or in pantomime. 2. In fiction, narrative passages are to be distinguished from *descriptions* and *scenes.* In narrative passages the **chronology** is condensed so that relatively few words will encompass the events of an extended period of time. Most writers of short stories use narrative passages to fill in the links between events given a scenic treatment.

narrator In **first-person narration,** the character tells the story in his or her own words. It is not uncommon in third-person narration for one of the characters to tell an extended story. In such a case it is quite proper to refer to him or her as a narrator.

novella (or sometimes **novelette**) Flexible term referring to a piece of fiction intermediate in length between a short story (up to about twelve thousand words) and a novel (thirty thousand words or more). Because some complexities beyond mere length are involved, it is probably best to

think of this class of fiction as being defined by notable examples—as in this text: "Heart of Darkness," "The Death of Ivan Ilych," and "Death in Venice."

objectivity Telling a story without bias; telling a story without the interpretive comment to be expected from a partisan or sympathetic observer.

omniscience A **convention** in which the author speaks directly to the reader about events that will come in the future and other matters beyond the knowledge of the central character or of all the characters. This contrasts with the discipline of adhering to the **point of view** of a single character and is little used in modern practice.

pace The speed at which writers develop any given part of a story. Usually they will hasten over unimportant things, and slow to give a detailed view of what is essential.

parable A story told to convey a **moral** or teach a lesson.

paradox A statement that appears to be contradictory or inconsistent with common sense—though it may be quite true.

parody Mimicry of a work or a style of expression. Sometimes the mimicry is undertaken to make fun of what is parodied; sometimes it is done in a sincere effort to gain the understanding that comes from painstaking imitation. Parody is akin to paraphrase; the translation of a work into your own language to make sure you have grasped it.

pathos The pity roused by the situation or the misfortunes of the characters in a story.

pattern Like **distance,** a metaphorical and ambiguous term. It is generally taken to refer to changes in the relative position of the characters—as if they were pieces on a game board, shifted, developed, and sometimes sacrificed by the progress of the **action.** Thus if Character A is happy and prosperous in the beginning and becomes poor and wretched while Character B moves out of poverty and achieves happiness, there is said to be a *crossing pattern.* The term may also refer to the way the author lays out blocks of material. If the author provides a number of small episodes not linked with transitional passages, he or she has made a *mosaic pattern.*

plot Consists of the phases of action in a story that are linked together by a chain of causal relationships. Event A causes or provides motivation for event B, B causes C, etc. Where this chain of causality is not apparent, the story is said to be **episodic.** A well-made plot leads from the potentialities revealed in the **exposition** directly to the situation left in the wake of the **resolution.** Plot may be subordinated to some other **focus of interest** in many stories, but it is one of the most important aspects of fiction, for we understand things best when we are shown what caused them to be as they are.

point of view The events of a story may be told as they appear to one or more participants or observers. In **first-person narration** the point of view is automatically that of the **narrator.** More variation is possible in third-person narration, by which the author may choose to limit his or her report to what could have been observed or known by one of the characters at any given point in the action—or may choose to report the observations and thoughts of several characters. The author might also choose to intrude his or her own point of view. See **omniscience.**

protagonist Chief **character.**

realism An interest in and emphasis on life as it is. In literature this does not mean that writers copy what they see and hear. (Perhaps that is impossible, anyhow.) It means that they will select from their observations the material suitable for constructing a story that faithfully represents what they have understood.

resolution The point in a story at which the **conflict** is decided one way or another and the struggle concluded. The expectations of the reader and of the characters have, at this point, been confirmed or refuted.

satire The satirist aims to correct, by an exposure to ridicule, deviations from desirable conduct or reasonable opinion. The chief tool of satire is to exaggerate deformities to the point at which their absurdity is unmistakably apparent.

sentimentality An author's attempt to produce an emotional response greater than is warranted by what he or she has to tell. While the student should not be fooled by sentimentality, it is well to remember that the symmetrical and equal fault is hardheartedness, a cold insensitivity to the trouble and joys of the human condition.

setting The physical and cultural environment within which **action** takes place. The stage that serves to demonstrate the qualities of a **protagonist.** An arena suitable for the **conflict.** Weather, urban uproar, the majesty and menace of the ocean can signal moods of human characters. See **concreteness** and **milieu.**

short-short story (also called for convenience simply a "short-short") In recent years there has been a growing interest in stories of a length less than that typical of short stories in general. Writers, critics, and readers at all levels have become more sharply aware of the effects obtained in pieces of minimal length, and they are more and more frequently published in collections. Fables, moral **parables,** epiphanies, prose poems, and thin slices of life may be usefully considered as examples of this general type.

stream of consciousness A fictional device or **convention** in which the author undertakes an imitation of a mind responding to exterior experiences. Frequently it involves a free association of ideas in which normal syntax and logical coherence are suspended. It is usually intended to shortcut the processes of reflection and reconsideration that stand between raw experience and logical statement. See **convention, immediacy, interior monologue.**

style A writer's habitual way of expressing himself or herself is his or her style. Examination of it requires consideration of vocabulary, sentence patterns, and other compositional elements. More generally, the appreciation of an author's style comes with a recognition of the way his or her mind plays with experience and literary form.

symbol An act, a person, a thing, or a spectacle that represents something else, usually something less palpable than the named symbol. The relationship between the symbol and its referent is not often one of simple equivalence. Allegorical symbols usually express a neater equivalence with what they represent than the symbols found in modern realistic fiction. See **allegory.**

tension The emotional and intellectual force generated by disparate potentials within a literary work. In every **ambiguity** there is a tension between the primary meaning and the secondary meanings of a word, phrase, or larger unit of expression. There may be tension between a comic tone and pathetic subject matter. See **ambiguity** and **tone.**

theme The unifying point or meaning of a story. Often the theme is implicit in the outcome of the action. It is rarely directly stated, though often it is closely paraphrased by an author's observation or by a statement made by one of the characters.

tone A wide-ranging, metaphorical term that usually invites analogy to the tone of voice in which a speaker relates an episode. For example, the speaker might be trying to make light of something that frightened him or her. If we conclude he or she is doing so, the fear will seem magnified by the attempt to disguise it. Tone reveals a storyteller's attitude toward the material.

understatement The technique of playing down or underemphasizing a statement. It is a rhetorical trick intended to bring the imagination of the reader into play with a resulting magnification of emotional response. The style of Ernest Hemingway offers some of the best modern examples of this device.

unity The shape and consistency of a story. When all the elements and devices of storytelling have been harmonized and nothing extraneous has been included in the text, we speak of it as unified. See **action, coherence, diction, point of view.**

voice May be the characteristic mode of expression of a first-person narrator. (See **diction.**) Sometimes the term refers to the total, individualistic effect of all the devices a writer habitually employs, the combination of tactics that distinguishes his or her work from other fiction. (See **style** and **tone.**)

Permissions Acknowledgments

TEXT

Lee K. Abbott: "One of *Star Wars*, One of *Doom*" was first published in *The Georgia Review*, Vol. 55, No. 3 (Fall 2001). Copyright © 2001 by Lee K. Abbott. Reprinted by permission of the author.

Conrad Aiken: "Silent Snow, Secret Snow," copyright © 1932, 1960 by Conrad Aiken. Reprinted by permission of Brandt & Hochman Literary Agents, Inc. Used by permission of the author. All rights reserved.

Dorothy Allison: "Jason Who Will Be Famous" first published in *Tin House Magazine*, vol. 10, no. 4, Summer 2009. Copyright © 2009 by Dorothy Allison. Reprinted by permission of The Frances Goldin Literary Agency.

Margaret Atwood: "Death by Landscape" from WILDERNESS TIPS by Margaret Atwood, copyright © 1991 by O.W. Toad Limited. Used by permission of Doubleday, an imprint of the Knopf Doubleday Publishing Group, a division of Random House LLC. All rights reserved. Any third party use of the material, outside of this publication, is prohibited. Interested parties must apply directly to Random House LLC for permission. Rights in Canada by permission of McClelland & Stewart, a division of Random House of Canada Limited, a Penguin Random House Company. "Why Do You Write" from NINE BEGINNINGS by Margaret Atwood. Originally published in *The Writer on Her Work, vol II, 1991*, ed. by Janet Sternburg. © 1990 Margaret Atwood. Reprinted by permission of the Author." "In Appreciation of Alice Munro," copyright © 2006 by O.W. Toad Ltd. included by permission of the Author. Originally appeared in "Appreciations of Alice Munro" from *The Virginia Quarterly Review*, Summer 2006.

Stephen L. Baehr: From "The Locomotive and the Giant: Power in Chekhov's Anna on the Neck" first published in *The Slavic and East European Journal*, vol. 39, no. 1, Spring 1995, pp. 29-37. Reprinted by permission of the publisher.

James Baldwin: "Sonny's Blues" © 1957 by James Baldwin was originally published in *The Partisan Review*. Copyright renewed. Collected in GOING TO MEET THE MAN, published by Vintage Books. Reprinted by arrangement with the James Baldwin Estate.

Toni Cade Bambara: From "What Is It I Think I'm Doing Anyhow?" by Toni Cade Bambara from THE WRITER ON HER WORK, vol. 1 by Janet Sternburg. Copyright © 1980 by Janet Sternburg. Used by permission of W. W. Norton & Co., Inc. "Gorilla, My Love" from GORILLA, MY LOVE, copyright © 1971, by Toni Cade Bambara. Used by permission of Random House, an imprint and division of Random House LLC. All rights reserved. Any third party use of the material, outside of this publication, is prohibited. Interested parties must apply directly to Random House LLC for permission.

Russell Banks: "Appreciation of Alice Munro" from the *Virginia Quarterly Review*, Summer 2006, is reprinted by permission of Russell Banks. Copyright © 2006 by Russell Banks.

Andrea Barrett: "The Littoral Zone" from SHIP FEVER AND OTHER STORIES by Andrea Barrett. Copyright © 1996 by Andrea Barrett. Used by permission of W. W. Norton & Company, Inc.

Donald Barthelme: "Me and Miss Mandible" from SIXTY STORIES by Donald Barthelme, copyright © 1981, 1982 by Donald Barthelme, used by permission of The Wylie Agency LLC.

Richard Bausch: "To a Young Writer" is reprinted by permission of the author. "Letter to the Lady of the House" from THE STORIES OF RICHARD BAUSCH, copyright © 2003 by Richard Bausch. Reprinted by permission of HarperCollins Publishers.

Charles Baxter: "The Disappeared" from A RELATIVE STRANGER by Charles Baxter. Copyright © 1990 by Charles Baxter. Used by permission of W. W. Norton & Company, Inc.

Ann Beattie: "Snow" from WHERE YOU'LL FIND ME by Ann Beattie, copyright © 1991 by Ann Beattie. Reprinted by permission of the author.

Madison Smartt Bell: "Witness" by Madison Smartt Bell. Copyright © 1990, collected in BARKING MAN AND OTHER STORIES. Used by permission of the author. First published in *Harper's* magazine.

Wendell Berry: "A Burden" from A PLACE IN TIME: TWENTY STORIES OF THE PORT WILLIAM MEMBERSHIP. Reprinted by permission of Counterpoint.

Joseph L. Blotner and Frederick L. Gwynn: From FAULKNER IN THE UNIVERSITY, copyright © 1995 by the Rector and Visitors of the University of Virginia. Reprinted by permission of the University of Virginia Press.

Jorges Luis Borges: "Pierre Menard, Author of the *Quixote*" from LABYRINTHS, translated by James E. Irby copyright © 1962, 1964 by New Directions Publishing Corp. Used by permission of New Directions Publishing Corp.

Ray Bradbury: "The Veldt" by Ray Bradbury, first published in *The Saturday Evening Post*, is reprinted by permission of Don Congdon Associates, Inc. Copyright © 1950 by the Curtis Publishing Company, renewed 1977 by Ray Bradbury.

Frederick Busch: "Bread" from THE CHILDREN IN THE WOODS: NEW AND SELECTED STORIES by Frederick Busch. Copyright © 1994 by Frederick Busch. Reprinted by permission of the Elaine Markson Literary Agency.

Truman Capote: "Miriam" copyright 1945, 1946, 1947, 1984, 1949 by Truman Capote, originally published in *Mademoiselle*, from A TREE OF NIGHT AND OTHER STORIES by Truman Capote. Used by permission of Random House, an imprint and division of Random House LLC. All rights reserved. Any third party use of the material, outside of this publication, is prohibited. Interested parties must apply directly to Random House LLC for permission.

Raymond Carver: "Cathedral" from CATHEDRAL by Raymond Carver, copyright © 1981, 1982, 1983 by Raymond Carver. Used by permission of Alfred A. Knopf, an imprint of the Knopf Doubleday Publishing Group, a division of Random House LLC. All rights reserved. Any third party use of the material, outside of this publication, is prohibited. Interested parties must apply directly to Random House LLC for permission. "The Student's Wife," copyright © 1963 by Raymond Carver, used by permission of The Wylie Agency LLC.

R. V. Cassill: "The Rationing of Love" from PATRIMONIES: SHORT STORIES (1987). Reprinted by permission of the author.

John Cheever: "The Enormous Radio" and "The Death of Justina" from THE STORIES OF JOHN CHEEVER by John Cheever, copyright © 1978 by John Cheever. Used by permission of Alfred A. Knopf, an imprint of the Knopf Doubleday Publishing Group, a division of Random House LLC. All rights reserved. Any third party use of the material, outside of this publication, is prohibited. Interested parties must apply directly to Random House LLC for permission.

Anton Chekhov: "Selections from Anton Chekhov's Letters" from ANTON CHEKHOV'S SHORT STORIES: A NORTON CRITICAL EDITION by Ralph E. Matlaw, ed. Copyright © 1979 by W. W. Norton & Company, Inc. Used by permission of W. W. Norton & Company, Inc. "Gusev" from THE PORTABLE CHEKHOV by Anton Chekhov, ed. by Avrahm Yarmolinsky, copyright 1947, © 1968 by Viking Penguin, Inc., renewed © 1975 by Avrahm Yarmolinsky. Used by permission of Viking Penguin, a division of Penguin group (USA) LLC. Letter to Nikolai Chekhov (Moscow, March, 1886) from LETTERS OF ANTON CHEKHOV, trans. by Michael Henry Heim and Simon Karlinsky. Copyright © 1973 by Harper & Row, Publishers, Inc. Reprinted by permission of HarperCollins Publishers.

Stanley Corngold: "Kafka's Metamorphosis" from FRANZ KAFKA: THE NECESSITY OF FORM by Stanley Corngold. Copyright © 1988 by Cornell University. Used by permission of the publisher, Cornell University Press.

Julio Cortázar: "Letter to a Young Lady in Paris" from END OF THE GAME AND OTHER STORIES by Julio Cortázar, tr. by Paul Blackburn, copyright © 1963, 1967 by Random House, Inc. Used by permission of Pantheon Books, a division of the Knopf Doubleday Publishing Group, a division of Random House LLC. All rights reserved. Any third party use of the material, outside of this publication, is prohibited. Interested parties must apply directly to Random House LLC for permission.

Edwidge Danticat: "A Wall of Fire Rising" from KRIK? KRAK! Copyright © 1991, 1995 by Edwidge Danticat. Reprinted by permission of Soho Press, Inc. All rights reserved.

Anita Desai: "Royalty" from DIAMOND DUST. Copyright © 2000 by Anita Desai. Reprinted by permission of Houghton Mifflin Harcourt Publishing Company. All rights reserved. Rights in Canada by permission of the author c/o Rogers, Coleridge & White Ltd., 20 Powis Mews, London W11 1JN.

James Dickey: "The Mill Wheel" from WAYFARER: A VOICE IN THE SOUTHERN MOUNTAINS (Oxmoor House, Inc. 1988) is reprinted by permission of Southern Progress Corporation.

Isak Dinesen: "Sorrow-Acre" from WINTER'S TALES by Isak Dinesen, copyright 1942 by Random House, Inc. Copyright renewed 1970 by Johan Philip Thomas Ingerslev c/o The Rungstedlung Foundation. Used by permission of Random House, an imprint and divison of Random House LLC. All rights reserved. Any third party use of the material, outside of this publication, is prohibited. Interested parties must apply directly to Random House LLC for permission.

Andre Dubus: "The Intruder" from DANCING AFTER HOURS by Andre Dubus. Copyright © 1995 by Andre Dubus. Used by permission of Alfred A. Knopf, an imprint of the Knopf Doubleday Publishing Group, a division of Random House LLC. All rights reserved. Any third party use of the material, outside of this publication, is prohibited. Interested parties must apply directly to Random House LLC for permission.

Stuart Dybek: "We Didn't" first published in *Antaeus*, Spring 1993. Copyright © 1993 by Stuart Dybek. Published in I SAILED WITH MAGELLAN (Farrar Straus & Giroux LLC 2003). Used by permission of International Creative Management. All rights reserved.

Ralph Ellison: "King of the Bingo Game" from FLYING HOME AND OTHER STORIES by Ralph Ellison, copyright © 1996 by Fanny Ellison. Used by permission of Random House. From an interview with Ralph Ellison by Alfred Chester and Vilma Howard reprinted from *The Paris Review* with the permission of The Wylie Agency LLC.

Louise Erdrich: "Winter 1912" from TRACKS first appeared in a slightly different version in the *Atlantic Monthly* entitled "Matchimanito." Copyright © 1988 by Louise Erdrich. Reprinted by permission of Henry Holt and Company, LLC. All Rights Reserved.

Percival Everett: "The Fix" from DAMNED IF I DO: STORIES. Copyright © 2004 by Percival Everett. Reprinted with the permission of The Permissions Company, Inc. on behalf of Graywolf Press, Minneapolis, Minnesota, www.graywolfpress.org.

William Faulkner: "Barn Burning" and "A Rose for Emily" from COLLECTED STORIES OF WILLIAM FAULKNER by William Faulkner. Copyright © 1950 by Random House, Inc., and renewed 1977 by Jill Faulkner Summers. Reprinted by permission of W. W. Norton and Company. "Address Upon Receiving the Nobel Prize for Literature, 1950," copyright © 1950 by William Faulkner. Copyright renewed 1965, 2004 by Random House. From ESSAYS, SPEECHES & PUBLIC LETTERS, edited by James B. Meriwether. Used by permission of Random House, an imprint and division of Random House LLC. All rights reserved. Any third party use of the material, outside of this publication, is prohibited. Interested parties must apply directly to Random House LLC for permission.

F. Scott Fitzgerald: "Babylon Revisited" from THE SHORT STORIES OF F. SCOTT FITZGERALD, edited by Matthew J. Bruccoli, is reprinted with permission of Scribner Publishing Group, a division of Simon & Schuster, Inc. Copyright 1931 by The Curtis Publishing Company. Copyright renewed © 1959 by Frances Scott Fitzgerald Lanahan. All rights reserved.

Richard Ford: "Great Falls" from ROCK SPRINGS by Richard Ford. Copyright © 1987 by Richard Ford. Used by permission of Grove/Atlantic, Inc. Any third party use of this material, outside of this publication, is prohibited. Excerpts from the Introduction to THE ESSENTIAL TALES OF CHEKHOV, edited and with an Introduction by Richard Ford. Introduction copyright © 1998 by Richard Ford. Reprinted by permission of HarperCollins Publishers. "Privacy" from A MULTITUDE OF SINS. Copyright © 2001 by Richard Ford. Used by permission of Alfred A. Knopf, an imprint of the Knopf Doubleday Publishing Group, a division of Random House LLC. All rights reserved. Any third party use of this material, outside of this publication, is prohibited. Interested parties must apply directly to Random House LLC for permission.

Mavis Gallant: "The Ice Wagon Going Down the Street" by Mavis Gallant. Copyright © 1963, 1981 by Mavis Gallant. Originally appeared in *The New Yorker* (Dec. 14, 1963). Reprinted by permission of Georges Borchardt, Inc. on behalf of the Mavis Gallant Estate.

George Garrett: "Feeling Good, Feeling Fine" from EMPTY BED BLUES, copyright © 2006 by the Curators of the University of Missouri. Reprinted by permission of the publisher.

Brad Gooch: From FLANNERY: A LIFE OF FLANNERY O'CONNOR. Copyright © 2009 by Brad Gooch. Used by permission of Little Brown and Company.

Nadine Gordimer: "A Soldier's Embrace" from A SOLDIER'S EMBRACE. Copyright © 1980 by Nadine Gordimer. Reprinted by the permission of Russell & Volkening as agents for the author.

Allan Gurganus: "Nativity Caucasian" from WHITE PEOPLE, copyright © 1990 by Allan Gurganus. Used by permission of Alfred A. Knopf, an imprint of the Knopf Doubleday Publishing Group, a division of Random House LLC. All rights reserved. Any third party use of the material, outside of this publication, is prohibited. Interested parties must apply directly to Random House LLC for permission.

Barry Hannah: "Sick Soldier at Your Door" from LONG, LAST HAPPY: NEW AND SELECTED STORIES. Copyright © 1985, 2010 by Barry Hannah. Used by permission of Grove/Atlantic, Inc. Any third party use of this material, outside of this publication, is prohibited.

Ernest Hemingway: "Hills Like White Elephants" from MEN WITHOUT WOMEN by Ernest Hemingway. Copyright 1927 Charles Scribner's Sons. Copyright renewed 1955 by Ernest Hemingway. Reprinted with permission of Scribner Publishing Group, a division of Simon & Schuster, Inc. All rights reserved. From an interview, with Ernest Hemingway by George A.

Ring Lardner: "Ex Parte" is reprinted with the permission of Scribner Publishing Group, a division of Simon & Schuster, Inc. from THE BEST SHORT STORIES OF RING LARDNER. Copyright © 1928 by Charles Scribner's Sons; renewal copyright © 1958 by Ellis A. Lardner. All rights reserved.

D. H. Lawrence: "The Rocking-Horse Winner" from COMPLETE SHORT STORIES OF D. H. LAWRENCE by D. H. Lawrence. Copyright 1933 by the Estate of D. H. Lawrence, copyright renewed © 1961 by Angelo Ravagli and C. Montague Weekley, Executors of the Estate of Frieda Lawrence Ravagli. Used by permission of Viking Penguin, a division of Penguin Group (USA) LLC.

Ursula K. Le Guin: "The Ones Who Walk Away from Omelas." Copyright © 1973 by Ursula K. Le Guin; first appeared in NEW DIMENSIONS, 3 in 1973 and collected in THE WIND'S TWELVE QUARTERS (HarperCollins 1975). Reprinted by permission of Curtis Brown Ltd.

Doris Lessing: From "An Interview with Doris Lessing," from THE DORIS LESSING READER, (1989). "To Room Nineteen" from A MAN AND A WOMAN by Doris Lessing, copyright © 1963 by Doris Lessing. Reprinted by kind permission of Jonathan Clowes, Ltd., London, on behalf of the Estate of Doris Lessing.

John L'Heureux: "Brief Lives in California" from DESIRES. Copyright © 1990 by John L'Heureux. First published in *Fiction*, Spring 1980 and published in DESIRES (Holt, Rinehart, Winston 1981). Reprinted by permission of the author.

Sandra Tsing Loh: "My Father's Chinese Wives." Copyright © 1994 by Sandra Tsing Loh. First appeared in *Quarterly West*. Reprinted by permission.

C. C. Loomis Jr.: From "Structure and Sympathy in Joyce's 'The Dead'" by C. C. Loomis, first published in *PMLA* (1960): 149-51. Copyright © 1960 by the Modern Language Association of America. Reprinted by permission of the copyright owner, Modern Language Association of America.

Tony Magistrale: From "I'm Alien to a Great Deal" from *Journal of American Studies*, April 1990, vol. 24, no. 1. Copyright © 1993 by Cambridge University Press. Reprinted with the permission of Cambridge University Press.

Bernard Malamud: "Angel Levine" from THE MAGIC BARREL by Bernard Malamud. Copyright © 1950, 1958, renewed 1977, 1986 by Bernard Malamud. Reprinted by permission of Farrar, Straus and Giroux, LLC.

Leo Marx: "Melville's Parable of the Walls" by Leo Marx first published in the *Sewanee Review*, vol. 61, no. 4, Autumn 1953. Copyright 1953, 1981 by the University of the South. Reprinted with the permission of the editor.

Bobbie Ann Mason: "Shiloh" from SHILOH AND OTHER STORIES by Bobbie Ann Mason. Copyright © 1982 by Bobbie Ann Mason. Used by permission. All rights reserved.

William Maxwell: "The Thistles in Sweden" from ALL THE DAYS AND NIGHTS by William Maxwell, copyright © 1965, 1986, 1992, 1994 by William Maxwell. Used by permission of Alfred A. Knopf, an imprint of the Knopf Doubleday Publishing Group, a division of Random House LLC. All rights reserved. Any third party use of the material, outside of this publication, is prohibited. Interested parties must apply directly to Random House LLC for permission.

Jill McCorkle: "Intervention" first published in *Ploughshares* 2003. Copyright © 2003 by Jill McCorkle. Reprinted by permission of the author.

Thomas McGuane: "Cowboy" from GALLATIN CANYON: STORIES, copyright © 2006 by Thomas McGuane. Used by permission of Alfred A. Knopf, an imprint of the Knopf Doubleday Publishing Group, a division of Random House LLC. All rights reserved. Any third party use of the material, outside of this publication, is prohibited. Interested parties must apply directly to Random House LLC for permission.

T. M. McNally: "Bastogne" from THE GATEWAY: STORIES published by Southern Methodist University Press (2007) is reprinted by permission of the author.

James Alan McPherson: "Why I Like Country Music" originally appeared in ELBOW ROOM: STORIES by James Alan McPherson. Copyright © 1977, 1986 by James Alan McPherson. Reprinted with the permission of James Alan McPherson through the Faith Childs Literary Agency, Inc.

Thomas Merton: "Flannery O'Connor: A Prose Elegy" from RAIDS ON THE UNSPEAKABLE, copyright © 1964 by The Abbey of Gethsemani, Inc. Reprinted by permission of New Directions Publishing Corp.

Gary Saul Morson: From "The Reader as Voyeur: Tolstoi and the Poetics of Didactic Fiction" by Gary Saul Morson from *Canadian-American Slavic Studies*, 2, No. 4 (Winter 1978). Reprinted by permission of the author.

THING THAT RISES MUST CONVERGE by Flannery O'Connor. Copyright © 1965 by the Estate of Mary Flannery O'Connor. Copyright renewed 1993 by Regina O'Connor. "The Nature and Aim of Fiction," excerpts from "The Grotesque in Southern Short Fiction" and from "Writing Short Stories" from MYSTERY AND MANNERS by Flannery O'Connor. Copyright © 1969 by the Estate of Mary Flannery O'Connor. Excerpt from A PRAYER JOURNAL. Copyright © 2013 by the Mary Flannery O'Connor Charitable Trust. Reprinted by permission of Farrar, Straus and Giroux, LLC.

Frank O'Connor: "Guests of the Nation" from THE COLLECTED STORIES OF FRANK O'CONNOR by Frank O'Connor, copyright © 1981 by Harriet O'Donovan Sheehy, Executrix of the Estate of Frank O'Connor. Used by permission of Alfred A. Knopf, an imprint of the Knopf Doubleday Publishing Group, a division of Random House LLC. All rights reserved. Any third party use of the material, outside of this publication, is prohibited. Interested parties must apply directly to Random House LLC for permission. Rights in Canada by permission of The Jennifer Lyons Literary Agency as agent for the proprietor.

Tillie Olsen: "O Yes" from TELL ME A RIDDLE, REQUA 1, AND OTHER WORKS by Tillie Olsen is used by permission of the University of Nebraska. Copyright© 2014 by the University of Nebraska Press. Rights outside North America by permission of The Frances Goldin Literary Agency. Copyright © 1961 by Tillie Olsen from TELL ME A RIDDLE.

Grace Paley: "The Used-Boy Raisers" from THE LITTLE DISTURBANCES OF MAN. Copyright © 1956, 1957, 1958, 1959 by Grace Paley. Used by permission of Penguin, a division of Penguin Group (USA) LLC.

Sue Simpson Park: From "A Study in Counterpoint: Joyce Carol Oates's 'How I Contemplated the World and Began My Life Over Again'" from *Modern Fiction Studies*, 22, no. 2(Summer 1976) pp. 213-216, 224. Copyright © 1976 by Purdue Research Foundation. Reprinted with permission of John Hopkins University Press.

Jayne Anne Phillips: "El Paso" from BLACK TICKETS by Jayne Anne Phillips. Copyright © 1975, 1976, 1977, 1978, 1979 by Jayne Anne Phillips. Reprinted by permission of the author.

Katherine Anne Porter: "Flowering Judas" and "The Jilting of Granny Weatherall" from FLOWERING JUDAS AND OTHER STORIES, copyright 1930 and renewed 1958 by Katherine Anne Porter, reprinted by permission of Houghton Mifflin Harcourt Publishing Company. All rights reserved. From an interview with Katherine Anne Porter by Barbara Thompson Davis reprinted from *The Paris Review* with the permission of The Wylie Agency LLC.

V. S. Pritchett: "The Fall" from COMPLETE COLLECTED STORIES by V. S. Pritchett, copyright © 1990 by V. S. Pritchett. Used by permission of Random House, an imprint and division of Random House LLC. All rights reserved. Any third party use of the material, outside of this publication, is prohibited. Interested parties must apply directly to Random House LLC for permission. Rights in Canada by permission of SLL/Sterling Lord Literistic, Inc.

E. Annie Proulx: "What Kind of Furniture Would Jesus Pick?" from BAD DIRT: WYOMING STORIES 2, reprinted with the permission of Scribner Publishing Group, a division of Simon & Schuster, Inc. Copyright © 2004 by Dead Line Ltd. All rights reserved.

Ron Rash: "Their Ancient, Glittering Eyes" from CHEMISTRY AND OTHER STORIES. Copyright © 2007 by Ron Rash. Reprinted by permission of Henry Holt and Company, LLC. All rights reserved.

Donald Rayfield: "Sakhalin" from ANTON CHEKHOV: A LIFE. Copyright © 1997 by Donald Rayfield. Reprinted by permission of Henry Holt and Company, LLC. All rights reserved.

Agnes Rossi: "Morpheus" from THE QUICK by Agnes Rossi, copyright © 1992 by Agnes Rossi. Reprinted by the permission of the author.

Philip Roth: "The Conversion of the Jews" from GOODBYE, COLUMBUS by Philip Roth. Copyright © 1959, renewed 1987 by Philip Roth. Reprinted by permission of Houghton Mifflin Harcourt Publishing Company. All rights reserved.

Charles Ruas: "Eudora Welty" from CONVERSATIONS WITH AMERICAN WRITERS, copyright © 1984 by Charles Ruas. Used by permission of Alfred A. Knopf, an imprint of the Knopf Doubleday Publishing Group, a division of Random House LLC. All rights reserved. Any third party use of the material, outside of this publication, is prohibited. Interested parties must apply directly to Random House LLC for permission.

James Salter: "Five" from COLLECTED STORIES (2013), copyright © 2013 by James Salter. Used by permission. All rights reserved.

C. P. Sarvan: "Racism and the 'Heart of Darkness'" by C. P. Sarvan from *The International Fiction Review*, 7, No. 1 (Winter 1980). Reprinted by permission of the author.

Index of Titles

A&P (Updike), 1566
Admission (Senna), 1339
Adventure in Paris, An (Maupassant), 964
Angel Levine (Malamud), 906
Anna on the Neck (Chekhov), 271
Araby (Joyce), 726

Babylon Revisited (Fitzgerald), 520
Barn Burning (Faulkner), 507
Bartleby, the Scrivener (Melville), 1029
Bastogne (McNally), 1004
Birthmark, The (Hawthorne), 629
Blackberry Winter (Warren), 1593
Blue Hotel, The (Crane), 379
Boule de Suif (Maupassant), 936
Bread (Busch), 175
Brief Lives in California (L'Heureux), 887
Brother Grasshopper (Updike), 1571
Bullet in the Brain (Wolff), 1685
Burden, A (Berry), 141

Cathedral (Carver), 202
Chrysanthemums, The (Steinbeck), 1439
Conscience of the Court, The (Hurston), 663
Convalescing (Oates), 1113
Conversion of the Jews, The (Roth), 1310
Cowboy (McGuane), 996

Dead, The (Joyce), 730
Death by Landscape (Atwood), 44
Death of Ivan Ilyich, The (Tolstoy), 1514
Death of Justina, The (Cheever), 254
Disappeared, The (Baxter), 109

El Paso (Phillips), 1212
Enormous Radio, The (Cheever), 246
Events at Drimaghleen (Trevor), 1554
Everyday Use (Walker), 1586
Ex Parte (Lardner), 826

Fall, The (Pritchett), 1270
Fall of the House of Usher, The (Poe), 1227
Feeling Good, Feeling Fine (Garrett), 576
Fix, The (Everett), 488
Flowering Judas (Porter), 1260

Garden Party, The (Mansfield), 914
Gimpel the Fool (Singer), 1377

Girl (Kincaid), 810
Girls in Their Summer Dresses, The (Shaw), 1355
Give (Salter), 1333
Good Country People (O'Connor, Flannery), 1171
Good Man Is Hard to Find, A (O'Connor, Flannery), 1160
Goose Pond (Williams, Thomas), 1663
Gorilla, My Love (Bambara), 80
Great Falls (Ford), 536
Guests of the Nation (O'Connor, Frank), 1186
Gusev (Chekhov), 262

Heart of Darkness (Conrad), 294
Hell-Heaven (Lahiri), 812
Hills Like White Elephants (Hemingway), 642
Horse Dealer's Daughter, The (Lawrence), 834
How I Contemplated the World from the Detroit House of Correction and Began My Life Over Again (Oates), 1126
How to Tell a True War Story (O'Brien), 1150
Hunger Artist, A (Kafka), 795

I Want to Know Why (Anderson), 37
Ice Wagon Going Down the Street, The (Gallant), 559
In the Cemetery Where Al Jolson Is Buried (Hempel), 647
In the Garden of the North American Martyrs (Wolff), 1677
In the Zoo (Stafford), 1424
Intensive Care (Smith), 1401
Intervention (McCorkle), 984
Intruder, The (Dubus), 449
Invalid's Story, The (Clemens), 288

Jason Who Will Be Famous (Allison), 30
Jilting of Granny Weatherall, The (Porter), 1254

Kew Gardens (Woolf), 1689
King of the Bingo Game (Ellison), 467

Letter to a Young Lady in Paris (Cortázar), 355
Letter to the Lady of the House (Bausch), 102
Life of the Body, The (Smiley), 1388
Littoral Zone, The (Barrett), 85
Lost at C (Shepherd), 1362
Lottery, The (Jackson), 673

Man Who Was Almost a Man, The (Wright), 1695

Management of Grief, The (Mukherjee), 1056

Marine Life (Svendsen), 1484

Matchimanito (Erdrich), 475

Me and Miss Mandible (Barthelme), 93

Metamorphosis, The (Kafka), 761

Miles City, Montana (Munro), 1085

Mill Wheel, The (Dickey), 424

Miriam (Capote), 188

Morpheus (Rossi), 1305

Moths, The (Viramontes), 1581

Moving Pictures (Johnson), 711

My Father's Chinese Wives (Loh), 896

Nativity, Caucasian (Gurganus), 603

New England Nun, A (Freeman), 550

New Man, A (Jones), 716

Not Anything to Do with Love (Kennedy), 805

Notorious Jumping Frog of Calaveras County, The (Clemens), 284

O Yes (Olsen), 1195

Occurrence at Owl Creek Bridge, An (Bierce), 149

One of Star Wars, *One of* Doom (Abbott), 1

Ones Who Walk Away from Omelas, The (Le Guin), 858

Open Boat, The (Crane), 362

Passion (Jhabvala), 698

Paul's Case (Cather), 231

Pharmacy (Strout), 1467

Pierre Menard, Author of the Quixote (Borges), 156

Position (Murray), 1099

Privacy (Ford), 547

Purloined Letter, The (Poe), 1241

Rationing of Love, The (Cassill), 213

Real Thing, The (James), 680

Rocking-Horse Winner, The (Lawrence), 846

Rose for Emily, A (Faulkner), 500

Royal Beatings (Munro), 1069

Royalty (Desai), 411

Rules of the Game (Tan), 1490

Shiloh (Mason), 925

Sick Soldier at Your Door (Hannah), 610

Signs and Symbols (Nabokov), 1108

Silent Snow, Secret Snow (Aiken), 17

Snow (Beattie), 127

Soldier's Embrace, A (Gordimer), 592

Sonny's Blues (Baldwin), 57

Sorrow-Acre (Dinesen), 426

Spinster's Tale, A (Taylor), 1498

Story of an Hour, The (Chopin), 281

Student's Wife, The (Carver), 197

Their Ancient, Glittering Eyes (Rash), 1294

Things They Carried, The (O'Brien), 1138

Thistles in Sweden, The (Maxwell), 969

To Room Nineteen (Lessing), 863

Unassigned Territory (Watts), 1621

Under the Pitons (Stone), 1447

Use of Force, The (Williams, William Carlos), 1673

Used-Boy Raisers, The (Paley), 1207

Veldt, The (Bradbury), 164

Victory Lap (Saunders), 1321

Visitation (Watson), 1609

Wagner Matinée, A (Cather), 226

Wall of Fire Rising, A (Danticat), 399

War (Pirandello), 1223

We Didn't (Dybek), 458

Wedding of Snow and Ice, The (Hoffman), 654

What Kind of Furniture Would Jesus Pick? (Proulx), 1279

White Horse, The (Kawabata), 802

Why I Like Country Music (McPherson), 1017

Why I Live at the P.O. (Welty), 1629

Wisteria (Spencer), 1420

Witness (Bell), 129

Worn Path, A (Welty), 1638

Xingu (Wharton), 1645

Yellow Wallpaper, The (Gilman), 580

Young Goodman Brown (Hawthorne), 620